W9-BRO-441

LEFT
OUT

ALSO BY TIM GREEN

FOOTBALL GENIUS NOVELS

Football Genius

Football Hero

Football Champ

The Big Time

Deep Zone

Perfect Season

BASEBALL GREAT NOVELS

Baseball Great

Rivals

Best of the Best

Home Run

AND DON'T MISS

Pinch Hit

Force Out

Unstoppable

New Kid

First Team

Kid Owner

Lost Boy

LEFT
OUT

TIM GREEN

HARPER

An Imprint of HarperCollins*Publishers*

Left Out

 For information address HarperCollins Children's Books, a division of HarperCollins Publishers, 195 Broadway, New York, NY 10007.
www.harpercollinschildrens.com

Library of Congress Control Number: 2016936327
ISBN 978-0-06-229382-4

Typography by Andrea Vandergrift
17 18 19 20 PC/RRDH 10 9 8 7 6 5 4
❖
First Edition

For my beautiful and amazing wife, Illyssa,
the kindest person I've ever known

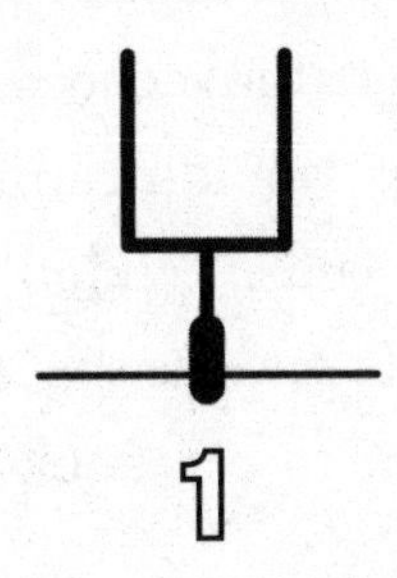

1

The moving van pulled away from the curb, puking a charcoal cloud that spilled down onto the street. The only thing darker than the diesel exhaust was the sky, boiling now with purple clouds and the distant rumble of thunder. Amid shouts of "good-bye" from neighbors and friends, a breeze kicked up, scattering leaves and the exhaust into the yard next door.

Moving was a good thing. Landon's mom had gotten an even bigger job in an even nicer place. At least, that's how she and their dad had tried to sell yet another move to Landon and Genevieve.

Landon glanced over at his little sister, who leaned out the car window taking pictures of her teary-eyed friends on the front lawn. Good at everything, she was like Landon's opposite. Genevieve had so much power over her friends that as they waved they were careful to shout not only, "Good-bye,

Genevieve, we'll miss you!" but also, "Good-bye, Landon! Good-bye!"

Landon could only guess what Genevieve had done to get those good-byes for him. He could easily imagine her threatening that if they didn't think cheering up her brother was important, obviously they wouldn't mind if Genevieve removed them from her list of friends. Landon wouldn't allow himself to enjoy the attention. He saw the show, felt a pang of jealousy, and turned his attention to the book he was reading on his iPad.

Genevieve nudged him. With tears in her eyes, she pointed out the window. "Look, Landon. They're saying good-bye to you, too."

Landon shrugged and went back to his book, feeling a bit guilty, but knowing that if he acknowledged *her* friends it would be too painfully obvious he had none of his own. Kip Meyers, standing there with his mom, didn't count. Landon knew Mrs. Meyers had insisted that Kip make a show of saying good-bye. Her son stood slouched, his hand held up half-heartedly, his beady eyes hidden under long, shaggy hair blown by the wind. Although he had hoodwinked his own mom and Landon's parents into thinking he was nice, Kip was among the worst of Landon's tormentors at school.

"Creep!" "Doofus!" Those were the best of the taunts Landon endured. And he had to admit that with the big earpieces he had to wear along with the thick magnetic discs stuck to the sides of his skull so he could hear some sounds, he often felt alien himself. Like the Wookiee from *Star Wars* or some other weird monster.

Whenever he could, he tried to hide the cochlear implants that were attached to his head by wearing his Cleveland Browns cap. But hats weren't allowed in school, and his mom insisted they not ask for the rules to be bent.

"Rules are made to be followed, Landon." His mother would pucker her lips in a prissy manner. "We don't want anyone to think you need to be treated differently than anyone else. Asking for exceptions suggests 'special needs,' and you're *not* that."

The phrase "special needs" was a red flag in Landon's home, mostly because of his mother's guilt. Because she had refused to have Landon tested for any problem when he was a baby, at age four he was diagnosed as a special needs child. People said he would not do well in school. But Landon's mom insisted he was smart and that the doctors needed to figure out what was really wrong. They finally did, and discovered that Landon couldn't hear—he was deaf in both ears. After months, he was fitted with cochlear implants, devices that helped him to hear. But the training involved in using them forced him to begin school a year late. That's why he and his little sister were in the same class. Even though he got good grades, most people still mistook his trouble with hearing and his slightly garbled speech as a sign of mental slowness that meant he had special needs, so whenever those words came up his mother denied them with great gusts of anger.

The downside to his parents' insistence that he not be different was that Landon couldn't wear his cap in school to cover his implants, but the upside was that he could play off his mom's guilt just like other kids. That age-old strategy of parental manipulation had created a wonderful opportunity when his mother announced that she'd gotten a great new job at SmartChips, which wasn't a high-tech company but one that made organic snacks.

When she told him and Genevieve about their next move, from Cleveland to New York, over a dinner of spaghetti and meatballs, Landon faked distress and sadness, but in that instant he'd decided to make a big change. His mother didn't know that, though.

Over the next few days, he played the role of a victim with heavy sighs and frowns—all with one big goal in mind. And then he made his move, asking for his mom's commitment that when they arrived in Bronxville—where she could take the train in and out of the city to work each day—he would be allowed . . . to play football.

Landon loved football. It was a visual symphony sprinkled with violence that looked like it didn't really hurt because of all that padding. Landon watched religiously: Sunday, Monday, and Thursday nights. His team was the Browns, but he'd watch anyone and visualize himself in the midst of the fray. Being big was one of the most important things about football, and Landon knew he was big—really big. But what attracted him most about football was that its players were heroes, universally beloved by the cities in which they played and sometimes nationwide. Landon craved that same universal acceptance and felt sure his goal of being liked would be achieved by becoming part of his own football team.

As she had every time he'd brought up the idea of playing football in the past, his mom argued again about the dangers of the sport. But Landon insisted that he'd do what she wanted and stop sulking about the move, *if* she would let him do what he wanted when they got to their new home. He tried to reassure her by saying, "Mom, look at me, I'm huge. I'll be great on the line."

"Well," she finally said, "you and your father have tired me out. I don't know if it's even possible with your implants, but if a doctor says it *is*, then I don't see why not."

His mother now sat ramrod straight in the driver's seat, ready for action and adventure. Laura, Genevieve's best friend, kept waving good-bye to Genevieve, and her mother, Mrs. Meyers, leaned in through the window with one arm on the roof of the car. As if on cue, a crack of lightning split the sky and the girls shrieked and headed for the garage overhang. The wind whipped even harder.

"Well, Gina." Mrs. Meyers leaned in for a good-bye hug and then glanced up at the sky. "You and Forrest timed it perfectly, getting out of here in front of this storm."

Landon's mom angled her head to assess the weather up through the windshield.

"Actually," she said, "it looks like we're heading straight into it."

2

As they left the Cleveland suburb with its wide old streets, thick trees, and bright green lawns amid the crack and rumble of thunder, Landon leaned his head against the window and thought about what was to come. He smiled to himself and kept thinking back to his mother's expression when he made his big move to talk about football.

"Football?" Her face had gone from shock to amusement and she'd nodded her head like a bobble-head doll before giving him a knowing look. "Your father never played football, you know?"

Landon had nodded. He knew all about his father, a great big bear of a man who was nearly finished with his third unpublished novel. At six foot ten, Landon's father was a gentle giant, with fists the size of holiday hams, a peaceable man without a violent bone in his body. Landon's mother never tired of comparing him to his father.

"He's so . . . so . . . calm. That's Landon. Calm as a summer day!" his mother would say, beaming at him and then back at whoever she was speaking to.

But Landon knew better. Although he'd never thrown a punch in his life, he fantasized often about getting revenge on his school tormentors on a football field. And what was so pleasant about a summer day? Swimming was the only plus he could see. Give him a pool and a diving board and he became an impressive human cannonball. But because of the extra weight he carried around and the fact that summer heat made his implants more noticeably uncomfortable, he liked fall better. The air was cool and crisp and the surge of football gushed from the TV. Now at his new school, he'd be like one of the NFL stars he'd watched but could never think of being.

He stared at his mother's dark curly hair as she guided their Prius carefully out of town with two hands firmly on the wheel, eyes glued to the road, lips tight. In the passenger seat, his father sat hunched over and squished by the confines of the little car, the back of his head snug against the roof and hands folded in his lap. His father would sit that way for hours on end without a peep of discontent. In fact, he'd be wearing a simple smile as he soaked in the nearness of his family and agreed with Landon's mom on a barrage of ideas.

Landon leaned toward his sister, who was still looking back, saddened by the loss of so many friends.

"It will be okay, Genevieve. You'll make new friends. I know you will." He gave her arm a squeeze. "It will be good. You'll make friends and I'll play football. Yes!" he said with a grin. "That's what I really want to do."

In the mirror he saw his mom's face tense up, and she shot a glance at Landon's father as if the whole thing was his fault. "Are you happy now, Forrest? Landon's looking forward to football. *Foot*ball."

"Right," his dad said. "He's a big boy; he'll be fine, Gina. Watch, it will be good for him."

"I told him *you* never played."

His father laughed. "I told him they couldn't find a helmet big enough for me, and I wasn't all that keen on it anyway, so I played the tuba in the marching band. Talk about good times. . . ."

"A marching band . . ." Landon's mom drifted into a blissful state as she obviously imagined the delights of the marching band.

"Well, I can't play music," Landon reminded them. "But I bet I can block and tackle."

Before his mother could reply, the dark sky opened up with a torrent of raindrops that hit the car like bullets. She redoubled her grip on the wheel and set her body against the storm, leaning into it like a hunter. They were on the highway in the passing lane, and a tractor-trailer raced up behind them blaring its horn.

Landon's mom made it into the right lane, and the ghostly shape of the truck cruised past like a sea monster, its taillights barely visible through the backsplash.

As they crawled along in silence, hazard lights blinking on

and off, Landon grinned to himself about his victory in being able to play football. The idea of beginning practice in just two short weeks gave him goosebumps.

Over an hour later, they finally got clear of the storm and his mother was able to increase their speed. Then she picked up right where they'd left off.

"What do you know about blocking and tackling, Landon?" she asked.

Landon took a breath and surprised everyone. "Keep your head up. Hit 'em hard. Chop your feet!"

Landon started stamping his feet on the floor in a quick staccato rhythm, the way he'd seen it done on YouTube. He got carried away until his mother shouted, "Stop that, Landon! Just stop."

They rode in silence again before his mother reminded Landon of the deal. "All we have to do is make sure the doctor will allow it. Football is okay with me, I said that, but we will have to make sure the doctor is all right with it. We'll see him the week after next."

Then she latched on to a new idea. "And what about a helmet? You might not be able to find one. Your head isn't as big as your father's, but the implants might be a problem, Landon. I didn't even think of that, and I'm sure you didn't either."

Landon nodded and grinned. Without speaking, he stroked his iPad a few times before handing it up to his father, who studied the page in front of him. "Actually, he has thought of it, Gina. Here's an article right here about an Ohio kid named Adam Strecker. They've got helmets for kids with implants. Football helmets. Look . . ."

His father held up the iPad for her to see, but she swatted it away. "I'm driving, Forrest."

Landon took the iPad back. He'd scored points and taken a big lead against his mother, but he knew it wasn't over. She would fight to the end. That was her nature. But Landon knew he could fight too, just as hard.

He tabbed open his book and pretended to read as if he hadn't a care in the world. He did have cares, though. Even though he'd spent his life pretending nothing bothered him, many things did. It bothered him that because of how he talked people thought he was special needs. It bothered him when people snickered at his clumsy size or whispered and pointed at the discs magnetically attached to his head. It bothered him that he had no friends, and it bothered him that there'd been no group outside of his family where he'd ever fit in.

That could all change now. The hope sent a shiver up his spine. He stared at the words on the screen without reading them. In his mind he was dressed in shoulder pads and a helmet, and he was marching out onto the field with his teammates, a band of brothers. They were tall and proud and ready for anything. When they all put their hands in for a common cheer, Landon's would be right there, one of the many.

That's all he wanted: to be, at long last, one of the many.

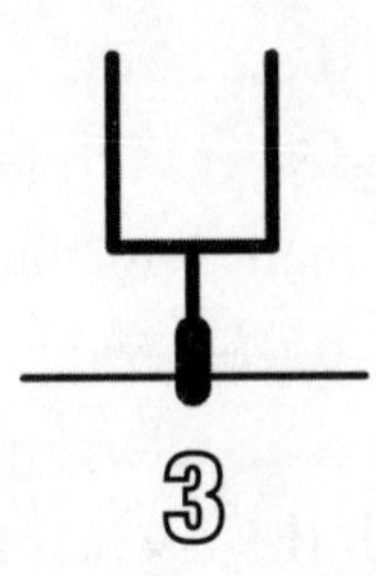

3

They'd stopped halfway to New York to sleep in a motel but were on the road again early the next day. That afternoon they drove through town and pulled up through a pair of gates and along a long driveway past a big front lawn bathed in sunshine. The house, huge and impressive sitting among a host of trees, had thick brown beams, white plaster, and a heavy slate stone roof.

"Wow." Genevieve pushed her face to the glass. "Are we rich?"

"No," their mother said in her fussy way. "We are comfortable. I wouldn't say rich."

"Okay." Genevieve's green eyes were alight as if she didn't believe it. "But we have a pool, right? You said there's a pool."

"It's out back!" Their mother couldn't hide her pride at bringing her family to such a great spot. She stopped the car outside the triple garage door on the side of the house. The moving van was already there, backed up and unloading furniture.

"When you said 'Bronx' I didn't think it would be like this," Landon's sister said. "All these trees."

"It's Bronx*ville*," their father said, slipping out of the car and stretching as he assessed their new home.

"The Bronxville Broncos won the New York State Championship," Landon said, referring to the high school football team. He'd play with them when he was old enough.

"I need to keep an eye on these movers," their mother said. "Forrest, can you take the kids and get some lunch and some groceries?"

"What about you?" Landon's father asked.

"Bring back a salad, spinach if they have it. I'll take care of things here." Their mother walked away, already organizing the movers.

"Well . . ." Their dad looked at the Prius as if it were a dangerous dog, and Landon knew he didn't relish the thought of wedging himself back inside. "Let's take a walk. Good? We're not far from the center of town, and my legs could use it."

Landon tucked his iPad under one arm, tugged on his Cleveland Browns cap, and set off with his father and sister. They lived on Crow's Nest Road, which fed right into Pondfield, the main street of Bronxville. The sun warmed the tree-lined street, but it wasn't too hot. The big houses stood mostly silent. Only an occasional car cruised by. It was as if they had Bronxville mostly to themselves and the pleasant summer day was a greeting to them, a new beginning.

"Library." His dad pointed to a large brick building facing the street, and Landon felt a surge of pleasure because, even though he liked reading on the iPad, he preferred the feel and smell of a real book. The air on the sidewalk in the shadows of the maple trees lining the road was cool and heavy with fresh-cut grass. They only had to cross the street before his father pointed again. "There's the middle school."

That gave Landon the opposite sensation. His hands clenched and his throat went dry. He looked at Genevieve. She had small features and a sharp nose like his mom. She narrowed her green eyes the way a mountain climber might size up Mount Everest.

They continued on toward the center of town before Genevieve pointed out Womrath Book Shop. "A library *and* bookstore, Landon. This place is going to be heaven for you."

"And there's a famous deli across the street, Lange's." Their father consulted his phone "Five stars on TripAdvisor."

They crossed the street and made their way to the deli. Three bikes leaned against a lamppost on the sidewalk outside. They made Landon nervous because with bikes usually came boys. Sure enough, they walked in and Landon saw the three boys sitting near the back in a corner. Two had dark hair. One, with a pug face, wore his hair parted on the side and swept over the top, flopping down so it nearly covered one eye. The other's short hair, pointy stiff with gel, framed the elfin face of a TV character. The third had red hair in a buzz cut. He had freckles and big teeth. When they spotted Landon's father, they immediately began to chatter and point. They were too far for Landon to hear, but he read the pug-faced boy's lips as he laughed and said, "Hey, it's the Giant. Where's Jack?"

Landon knew he should turn away, knew he shouldn't look, shouldn't read their lips and see their words. Nothing good ever came from three boys laughing and gawking, but he felt drawn to it the way he might poke at a bruise to test how much it really hurt. He peeked around the edge of his father, who stood oblivious, looking up at the menu board.

"Dude," the spiky-haired boy said, pointing, "look. It's *got a baby giant from outer space*." The boy made antennae with his fingers and clamped them on his ears. All three of them laughed, and Landon looked away now because they were staring at him. He tugged his cap down, horrified at what they might say if they could see the discs. All they were reacting to now were the battery packs and processors that fit over and behind his ears like giant hearing aids. If they saw the magnetic discs, which looked like fat quarters on the sides of his head, they'd go wild. They wouldn't even have to know that the discs covered implanted discs attached to wires that were tucked beneath his *brain* to get excited. He'd heard it before.

"Hey, Frank!" someone would say.

The first time it happened, Landon shook his head and pointed to himself. "My name is Landon."

"Franken*stein,* dude. Frank-n-stein!" And they'd point to their own heads with fingers in the spots where the moveable magnetic discs connected to the disc implants beneath his scalp. Sometimes they'd stick out their tongues, cross their eyes, or both.

Landon was nervous when a waitress took them to their table near the boys. He sat in the chair with his back to the three boys and focused on the menu. There were lots of choices. His father ordered a tuna melt, and Landon asked for the same. Genevieve got turkey on a croissant with brown mustard and Swiss cheese. She didn't eat like a kid, and it was just another way that she seemed more advanced than Landon, even though she was a year younger.

Landon couldn't understand the chatter behind him now. The sounds he heard with the implants weren't sharp enough for him to understand what was being said without the ability to also see a person's lips. He could read lips fairly well, but the best way for him to understand what was being said was to hear the fuzzy sounds and see the lips at the same time.

Landon tried not to stare at his sister, but he couldn't help feeling concerned each time she glanced past him to where he knew the boys were sitting. Then she put her croissant down without taking a last bite. Her face turned dark. Her eyes moved in a way that told Landon the boys were headed toward their table. Landon tapped Genevieve's arm, trying to get her to look at him. If he could draw her into a conversation, she might not do anything bad, but she swatted his hand away without moving her eyes.

The three boys moved past the table in a tight group. Landon heard one of them say something, but he had no idea what because the diner wasn't quiet and the boy didn't speak loudly. It must have been bad, though, because Genevieve sprang from her chair and darted at the biggest one of them like a terrier on a rat.

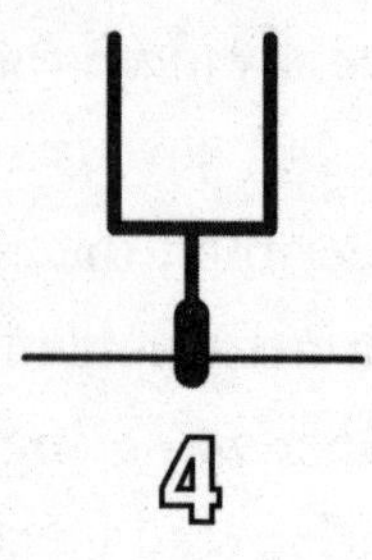

4

Genevieve gave the redhead a shove, pushing him back so that he stumbled into another table, upsetting the drinks of the four ladies who sat there. Landon heard a muffled shriek. Both he and his father jumped up. His father grabbed Genevieve by the shoulders, holding her back.

"What's your problem?" The redhead glared and clenched his fists. He stood nearly as tall as Landon, though half as wide.

"My problem is *you*!" Genevieve struggled to get free. "And you!" She kicked out at the pug-faced boy's shin. Thankfully she missed, but the three boys backed away toward the door.

"Come on, Skip." The spiky-haired one tugged the redhead's arm. He turned to the pug-faced kid with the floppy hair and said, "Xander, let's just go."

The entire diner stared in disbelief as Genevieve's eyes brimmed with tears.

"Genevieve, you can't act like this," their father scolded as he guided her back to her seat. He kept his voice even and calm, though, and then he turned to the ladies at the table of spilled drinks where a waitress was already at work with a towel. He produced his wallet and removed some bills. "I'm very sorry. I'll pay for those drink refills and any cleaning."

Landon took a quick look around. Everyone was staring and whispering. He wanted to disappear. He wanted to die. He shook his head and tapped Genevieve to get her attention. "You know I don't want people staring," he scolded.

"You can't let people disrespect you—here or when you're on the football field, Landon," Genevieve said. "You need to learn that."

"This isn't the football field. This is the diner."

Genevieve gave him a fiery look that quickly melted, and he was afraid she would burst into tears, but she bit her lip and put her hand on top of his and said, "I'm sorry, Landon. I just can't stand . . ."

"Don't worry so much about me, Genevieve," Landon said. "I'm gonna be fine here. This is a football town. When they see me play, no one's gonna laugh. I promise."

"You don't—"

Landon cut her off with his hand. "You have to *ignore* people like that, Genevieve."

Her eyes burned again and her nostrils flared. "Maybe you can ignore them, Landon. You didn't hear what they said, but I *did*."

Landon's mouth turned sour. He glared at his sister, removed his hat, and disconnected his electronic ears, the processors, the magnetic discs, and the wires that connected the two parts. The components dangled in his hand for a moment like small sea creatures, and he showed them to her before he stuffed them into his pockets and put the cap back on his head. Genevieve had humiliated them all. They'd just moved here and Genevieve was already getting in trouble. Whatever those boys had said, she should have ignored it, just like he did.

Removing the external equipment for his implants was the most powerful statement Landon could make. He was cutting off his sister, cutting off the entire world. Now, none of it mattered, and as long as he refused to read their lips, no one could bother him.

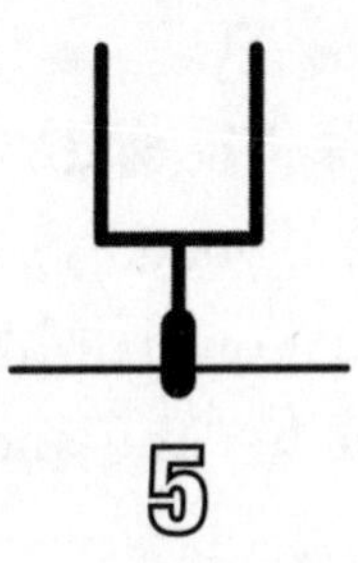

5

They walked home after lunch. Landon's mom was at the kitchen table surrounded by boxes, writing on a notepad and looking busy. She smiled when Landon's father set down her spinach salad. Landon didn't have to hear to know what his sister said as she threw her hands in the air. He snuck a look.

"Landon took off his ears!"

Landon cruised peacefully past them all, headed for the living room and his favorite reading chair, which the movers had positioned near the big window looking out over the pool and lawn. It was a heavenly place dappled with sun shining through the trees, and he took it, iPad already out. The smell of polished wood and the hint of warm dust filled his nose. He knew he'd be spending some serious time in this spot.

His mother usually gave him some space when he pulled the plug on his ears, so he jumped when someone tapped his shoulder. It was her. She motioned for him to reconnect. He stared at her for a moment to make sure she really meant it. She did. Moving slowly, he removed the gear they called his "ears" from his pocket and hooked it all up.

"What happened?" she asked.

"Genevieve is a maniac," he said.

"She's very protective of you."

"She knocked over everyone's drinks and made a big stink." Landon glared at his mom. "You and Dad teach us to walk away."

"It's harder to do that when it's against someone you love," his mother said. "It's easier to walk away when someone is making fun of you than of someone you're close to."

"Why?" Landon tilted his head.

"Because . . ." She threw her hands up. "I don't know, Landon, but it *is.* You just, you need to cut her some slack." She paused for a minute. "Do you want to see your room?"

"I like where they put my chair."

She swatted him playfully. "Who do you think had it put here?"

She sat down on the arm and hugged Landon to her. He hugged her back, but separated when it got too tight. She looked tired and sad.

"Are you okay, Mom?"

"I'm fine, Landon." She sighed. "I want you to be fine."

"I'm always fine, Mom. You know that." He got up. "So, where's my room?"

She studied him for a moment before rising and leading him into the front hall and up a big wooden staircase. Down at the end of a wide hall, they went right and into a long bedroom with its own bathroom. Part of the ceiling slanted at an angle and the whole room was paneled in wood. His desk and bookshelf stood empty on one side, and his bed lay on the other side beneath three rectangular windows. His computer sat on the desk. Boxes were everywhere.

"You like it?" his mom asked.

Landon climbed up on the bed and looked out the windows, smiling. "It's like the inside of a pirate ship."

"There's a park just a few streets away." His mom pointed out his window. "The school—did you see the school?—it's not far either."

"I did." Landon thought about the boys and the school, and then his face brightened. "I can walk to football practice! That'll make things easy for you guys."

"Landon . . ."

"Yes?"

She sat down on his bed and patted the spot beside her. He took it.

"I've been thinking about football."

"It's America's sport, Mom."

She stroked his hair and he made a big effort not to back away. "It's harder than it looks, Landon. You're not a violent person. You don't get angry very often, and when you do, you . . . you . . ." She pointed at his implants. "You unplug."

"Just because I don't push people into other people's tables doesn't mean I don't *want* to. In football, you're *supposed* to push the other guys. It's part of the game." He pulled away from her touch.

His mother stood up and went to one of the boxes. "I'll say this once and only once. Be careful what you wish for, Landon, because you just might get it."

From out of nowhere she produced a razor-blade box cutter and with one quick motion slit open the top of the biggest box. She began taking things out and setting them carefully on the bookshelf. He knew working calmed his mother's nerves. She placed several ceramic animals in a small cluster Landon could see—a lion, a tiger, a bear, an elephant. She stepped back to review them before fussing some more.

While she worked on arranging the cluster, Landon taped a Cleveland Browns poster to the wall.

His mother took a picture from the box, examined it, and smiled before showing him. "Remember this?"

It was a picture of the four of them—Landon, Genevieve, and his mom and dad—plummeting nearly straight down on Splash Mountain, the best ride in Disney World. His sister and his parents had their hands in the air and their mouths open, screaming with joy during that scary final plunge. Landon gripped the seat, ready to endure the fifty-foot drop. It wasn't his idea of fun, but he had wanted to prove to himself he could do it. He'd insisted they get the photo, to record the experience, and whenever he looked at it he was glad he'd taken the ride.

"That was a fun time." Landon glowed with pride.

She smiled warmly and set the picture on the shelf.

Landon removed his football from another box. It was his best present from his dad last Christmas, an official NFL ball, and he placed it next to the Disney World picture. His mom paused to study it.

"You know, I've been thinking . . . ," she said, "you can be part of a football *team* without actually having to be out there with people bashing your noggin where you've already got some sensitive equipment."

He tilted his head at her. "What do you mean?"

"Well . . ." She adjusted the picture. "You can help out the team and be a part of it. Every team has one of these . . . well, it's a manager, a team manager. All the big-time college programs have them, a student manager, and high schools do too. Lots of sports teams have managers, and they're very important, and I think it would be a super way for you to fit in."

She left the picture alone and stared hard at him.

Landon's mouth sagged open as he processed everything she was saying. She had actually devised a plan for him to be on a football team without *playing* football. It was diabolical. He shook his head violently and reached for his ears, ready to pull the plug again because . . . and he had to say this out loud.

"Mom, no. No way!"

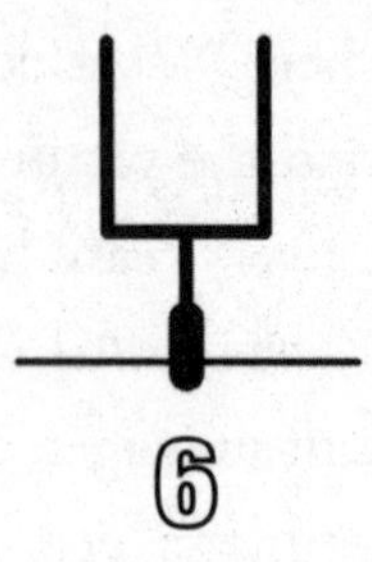

6

Ten days later, Landon was sitting on an exam table in a hospital gown and his boxer shorts while Dr. Davis, a cochlear implant specialist, studied his medical history.

The doctor set the folder down and then took Landon's head in his hands, squeezing like it was a melon in the grocery store. As his long, cool fingers searched around Landon's implants, circling the magnetic discs, he asked how Landon communicated.

Landon watched his mom clear her throat and explain. "His SIR . . . uh, Speech Intelligibility Rating—"

"Of course," said the doctor.

"He's a seven point two," his mom boasted. And Landon was proud of that score. He'd been going to speech therapy every week for years, and as a result, people nearly always understood what he was saying.

The doctor's pale green eyes stared at Landon's face. "What did you have for breakfast, Landon?"

"Uh, eggs and bacon. I had some cinnamon toast too. And juice." Landon knew from a lifetime of wrinkled brows or snickering grins that his speech didn't sound like most people's. "Garbled" was how it was mostly described—off base, not normal.

The doctor pressed his lips, looked at Landon's mom, and then turned back to him and said, "You've worked hard on your speech therapy, haven't you?"

Landon blushed and nodded. He couldn't help feeling proud, because here was a man who knew his business when it came to the way deaf people spoke.

"Yes, your impediment wouldn't keep anyone who's paying attention from understanding you." Dr. Davis looked back at his mom. "How does he understand others?"

"He gets a good deal from sounds, and he's good at lip-reading, but he does best with a combination of sounds and lipreading, unless you shout."

The doctor asked, "No sign language at all?"

Landon's mom's back stiffened. "We made a conscious decision to concentrate on auditory focus and lipreading."

"Also, coaches don't know sign language," Landon blurted. "So it's good to be able to read lips."

"Sports?" The doctor raised an eyebrow. "What do you play?"

"Football." Landon glowed with pride. "That's why I'm here."

"Okay, on your feet." The doctor took out a stethoscope

and began to look Landon all over, from head to toe.

Landon stood there in his boxers, his feet cold against the tile floor. A slight trickle of sweat escaped his armpits.

"But football . . . with the implants, how safe can that be?" Landon's mom seemed to sense the tide going against her.

"Most of that concussion business has to do with the pros, maybe college. And riding a bike can be more dangerous than junior league football. Breathe deep." The doctor speckled Landon's back with the chilly disc, listening to his lungs before he snapped the stethoscope off his neck, folded it, and tucked it away in his long white coat. "And this boy is healthy as an ox."

The doctor put a hand on Landon's shoulder. "He'll need a special helmet, of course, for the ear gear. And you need the skullcap under it."

Landon was ready for that one. He took his iPad off the chair where he'd set his clothes and showed the doctor what he planned to get.

"Yes! That's the best one."

"His . . . the implants?" Landon's mother worked her lips, maybe rehearsing arguments in her mind.

The doctor was a tall man with thick glasses, and authority had been chiseled on his granite face. "There's a risk to any sport, but with the helmets they make today . . ."

The doctor shook his head in amazement at modern technology as he scribbled some notes on Landon's chart. "Clean bill of health and ready to go. Just get that helmet before tackling."

"But . . . ," his mom got ready to protest. "Wouldn't something like soccer be safer?"

The doctor snorted. "Soccer? Mrs. Dorch, look at your son. He's built for football, not soccer. Anyway I'd have my kid in football with all that padding and a helmet any day before I'd have him running around full speed knocking heads or having a ball kicked in his face. Like I said, nothing is without risk, though."

"It's just that you hear so much about football . . ." Landon's mom was losing steam.

The doctor ignored her, stepped back, and surveyed Landon. "One thing's for sure: he could use the exercise."

Landon looked down at his gut and blushed. He was working on it, cutting back on the SmartChips, no matter how healthy they were, and on the second and third servings at meals despite his mother's urgings to eat more.

"Good luck in football, Landon. And remember that helmet!"

That night Landon waited until dinner had been cleaned up and his mom was locked in her home office, busily working away on her laptop, before he tiptoed past the doorway two down from his bedroom and sought out his dad. His father didn't need to lock himself away to do his work. His desk sat downstairs not far from Landon's chair, in the middle of the living room in front of the big window overlooking the backyard. His father kept the surface of the massive claw-foot desk clear except for the iMac he wrote on as well as two leather books held proudly upright by marble busts of William Shakespeare and Charles Dickens.

Landon's father declared that he liked to be in the center

of their home because it let him draw from the lifeblood of their lives for his own work. Landon wasn't exactly sure what lifeblood was, but he presumed it had something to do with the heart. He wondered also at the strategy since it hadn't earned his father anything for the first two books but a box full of rejection letters that he saved as a source of motivation.

He passed Genevieve's room. Ten days in and Genevieve already had friends like Megan Nickell. With a father who was president of the country club and a mother who was a partner at Latham & Watkins, SmartChips's law firm, Megan easily won the approval of Landon's mom. Genevieve was with Megan right now for a sleepover. The house was quiet. He could feel the cool air flowing through the vents—the weather outside had taken a hot turn. Landon's father sat slumped in front of his iMac, fingers on the keyboard, but idle.

"Dad?" Landon tapped him on shoulder to get his attention.

His dad turned and smiled like someone had sprung the lid on a treasure chest. "Hey, buddy. What are you doing? Finish your book?"

"No, but I wanted to talk to you."

"You got it. Want some ice cream?"

"Häagen-Dazs?"

His father wore a look of mock concern. "Is there another kind?"

Landon laughed and followed his dad into the kitchen area, which was separated from the living room only by the rectangular table where they ate. His father yanked open the freezer door and studied the shelves. "Hmm. When you don't know which one, choose both."

He removed a quart of butter pecan as well as one of vanilla, tucked them under his arm, and then grabbed two large spoons from the drawer. "I'd say let's sit out by the pool, but this stuff would be nothing but drool in five minutes flat."

They sat at the kitchen table, scooping out large hunks of ice cream and passing the quart containers back and forth in an easy rhythm until Landon held up both hands.

"Gotta go easy," he said. "Football."

"Ah, yes. The discipline of the Spartan." His father held up a giant scoop of butter pecan and inserted it into his mouth.

"What's that mean?" Landon asked.

"Well . . ." His father worked the ice cream around in his mouth and swallowed. "Discipline is you sacrificing—giving up something—for a greater cause. The Spartans were Greek warriors known for their harsh training. They were even crazy enough, I believe, to forgo butter pecan."

"I know Spartans."

"And now you've become one." His father bowed his head toward Landon.

"That's what I wanted to talk to you about." Landon glanced toward the hall, nervous that his mother might interrupt them. "Everything is going good. I passed my physical. The doctor said I could play. My implants are fine. Heck, he even told Mom playing football would be *good* for me." Landon patted his gut.

"Wonderful." His father took another big bite.

"But I need that helmet, and the special cap that goes under it," Landon said. "Football starts next Wednesday. The first five days it's just conditioning and running through plays, but helmets go on next week, and then the week after that we start to hit. But I need the helmet before so I can get used to it."

His father's eyes widened.

"I told Mom we gotta get my helmet and she keeps saying she'll work on it and how expensive it is, but next Wednesday will be here before you know it, and you can't just snap your fingers and have a helmet fall out of the sky. It's like she's trying to sabotage the whole thing by delaying, making it so I won't have enough practices to play in the first game and then I *will* end up as the manager."

His father put the spoon down and looked at it. "Yes, that's a problem, and I've seen this kind of strategy before. I wanted to see *Carmina Burana*. It was playing at the Cleveland Opera Theater, and your mom said she'd be happy to go and that she'd get the tickets through her office because they were sponsors. Well, I thought that sounded good because we could be in the pit or maybe even a box. Then the day before, when I asked, she snapped her fingers and said she was on it, but that night at dinner she announced that it had been sold out." Landon's father blinked at him. "Your mother hates the opera."

"Just like football." Landon looked down and rapped his knuckles on the table before looking back up. "Can you help me, Dad?"

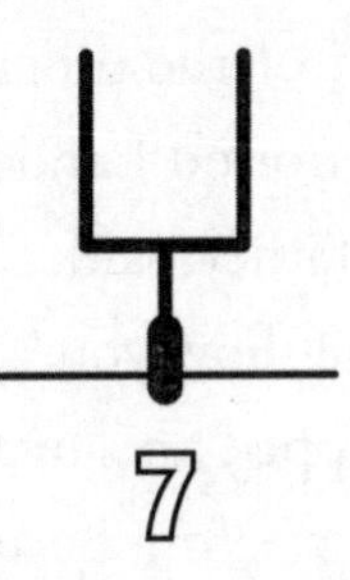

7

Landon peered over his father's shoulder. They were back at his desk, with the spoons rinsed and tucked away in the dishwasher. His father typed and then clicked, bringing up the website for Xenith Helmets, a company that made specialty sports helmets of every kind. They got to the football section and his father scanned the material quickly, his lips moving fast and silently, before he tapped the screen and leaned back.

"It's ingenious, really," he said. "There's a diaphragm in the lining, like a couple of mini beach rafts you can inflate. It says you can play football with the processors right behind your ears. I thought you'd have to take them out for sure, like you do for swimming."

Landon nodded because he already knew all this, but he didn't want to dampen his father's excitement. "That's awesome."

"Let's see . . ." His father tilted his head back for a better look. "We measure your head . . ."

"I can get the tape measure from the garage." Landon was already up and going. When he returned he was thrilled to see that his father had most of the order form already filled out. They wrapped the tape around Landon's head.

"Twenty-four," his father said. "I'm a twenty-*nine.* You believe that? Here, let me show you."

Landon's father wrapped the metal tape around his own head as proof, chuckling before he turned his attention back to the screen. "You know, I believe in this whole team thing. I mean, a marching band is like a team. An orchestra? How about that for working together, right? And those things . . ." Landon's father sat back in his chair and got a faraway look. "Those things are what I remember most. You're part of something."

Landon's dad looked at him and Landon let their eyes stay connected over the empty space. It wasn't something he and his father did very much, just look at each other, but it was as if this moment was one they'd both remember, and for some reason it didn't feel weird. His dad had dark brown eyes and a big forehead. His nose was slightly flattened and his mouth a bit too small for everything else. Looking at him, Landon felt like he was looking into a mirror, seeing himself in the future.

"There's real team spirit," his father said. "I want you to have that." Landon's dad turned back to the iMac and moved through to the purchase screen. He clicked the rush delivery icon, but the earliest delivery for the helmet and skullcap was

Saturday, a few days after the start of Landon's football career.

"Monday we'll get you football shoes—cleats," his dad said. They slapped a high five.

Neither of them had seen his mother creep up on them, so it startled them both when she barked, "What's going on here?"

8

Landon's father jumped out of his seat, and the contrast between Landon's parents was staggering. His father towered, a giant of a man, but his body was soft and slouching like he was made of pillows. He blocked Landon's mom from the iMac. She glared up at him. Standing straight, her chin barely cleared his father's belt line, but her eyes fixed on his like a bird of prey.

"I was uh . . . helping." His father's fingers fluttered in front of him.

Landon sat and watched her peer around him and examine the iMac with growling hostility. Her lips curled away from her teeth. "I see." She took a deep breath and let it out. "Yes, I see."

She turned and marched away. Landon looked at his dad, who smiled, saying, "She'll come around. She's just worried about you."

• • •

By Tuesday night she had come around. Landon knew when his mom called his dad from the kitchen. "Forrest? I could use some help here. It turns out this football business is a family affair in Bronxville. I ran into Landon's coach's wife, Claire Furster, on the train into work this morning and found out that the mothers are expected to supply something for some sort of bake sale, so I was thinking oatmeal cookies with honey instead of white sugar—something partially healthy at least."

Landon looked at his dad.

"Of course." Landon's dad hurried off toward the kitchen.

"And Landon?" His mother pointed at him. "You better get some sleep. Tomorrow's a big day."

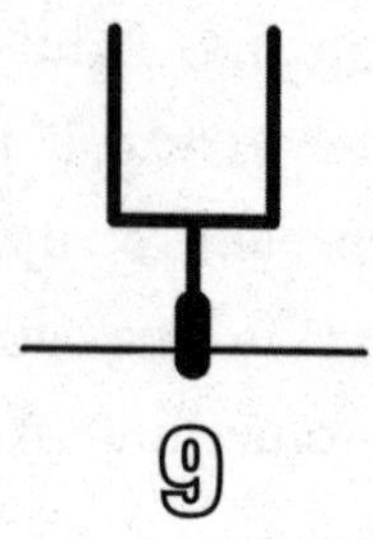

9

On Wednesday morning Landon's mother left for work on an early train. Her cookies rested in a Tupperware container with the doctor's clearance and a note taped to the cover for Landon's father in case she had to work late and couldn't talk to the football people herself. Genevieve was holed up in her room working at her online French class. She told Landon she wanted him to walk into town with her for lunch at the diner with two of her new friends. Later, she said, they'd all swim at the house.

Even though school was still over a week away from starting, football practice wasn't until the evening because the coaches had real jobs, and Landon was up for any distraction that would keep the voices of doubt at bay.

After Genevieve got acquainted with Megan Nickell, she had used Instagram and Snapchat to make friends with the other seventh-grade Bronxville girls as well. But Landon still wondered how she really did it, how she just barged into people's lives like a long-lost relative and found them happy to see her.

Landon tried to read a book, but he kept thinking about football. He put on his new cleats and took them off several times, worrying that they might give him blisters if they weren't broken in.

The morning was dragging on. He knew he shouldn't—because he could see his dad working feverishly—but he couldn't help it. He grabbed the football off his shelf, wandered into his father's space, and tapped his shoulder.

His father jumped. "Whaaa?"

Landon stepped back. He was used to startling people; it was just part of who he was. He needed to *see* them to know what they were saying. "Dad?"

"Landon. Son. I was far away."

"Sorry, Dad. Would you throw the football with me?" Landon turned the ball in his hands. "I feel like I need some practice. Even though I'm a lineman, I mean, everybody throws the ball around."

"Me? Throw? Uh . . ." His father gave the computer a sad look like it was a friend he'd hate to leave, but then he brightened. "Sure!" Standing and stretching he said, "I can throw you the football and you can help me with a problem."

"Okay." Landon followed his father through the kitchen and out the French doors to the pool area. They went through the gate and stood facing each other on the lawn. Overhead the sun shone brightly between fat white clouds and the tall trees that seemed to whisper. Landon tilted his head up at them and wondered how what he heard sounded different than what his father heard. He fluttered his fingers and pointed up at them.

His father smiled and fluttered his own fingers. "Yes, that's right. They're swishing." Seeing Landon's puzzlement, he added, "They sound like waves hitting the shore, but softer swishing."

Landon echoed, "Swishing," trying to fix the sound he heard and the word in his mind. Then he signaled his father to stay put. "You stand here."

Landon backed up, cocked his arm, and fired a wobbling pass. As the ball approached, his father brought his two hands together in a clapping motion, winced, and turned his head. The ball punched him in the gut and dropped to the grass. His father stared at it as if it were a bomb that might go off.

Then his father nodded and scooped it up. "Okay. I can get this," he shouted.

Landon thought about the band and the big tuba his father played. That must have taken some skill. Just a different kind of skill.

Landon jiggled his hands to create a target, and his father reared back with the ball. It flew sideways like a dizzy spaceship. Landon snatched at it, nearly catching hold before it plopped down in front of him.

His father shrugged. "We'll get it," he yelled. "This is why you practice, right? We're doing good."

They heaved the ball back and forth, sometimes getting hold of it, most times not.

"So," his father said after a halfway decent pass, "here's my big problem. Ready?"

Landon caught the ball, smiled, and nodded that he was ready.

10

His father's large face was flushed and he nodded merrily at Landon. "Okay, so—and this is really exciting, Landon—I was doing some research on names because my main character has an uncle on the planet Zovan and I wanted a name that also meant 'powerful,' and I dig and I dig and I find 'Bretwalda,' which is what they called the most powerful Saxon kings."

His father gave him a questioning look to see if he was following.

"Uh, okay, I get that." Landon heaved the ball, happy that his throw wasn't quite so wobbly. He wasn't sure where his dad was going with all this, but he was glad they were throwing around the football.

His father kind of swatted at the ball and ducked at the same time, and then he bent down to retrieve it from the grass. "So, I'm a writer—my mind wanders." His father waved his hands like magic wands, the football almost small in his huge grip. "And my creative curiosity asks a question: 'Forrest, what about Dorch? Where did *that* name come from?'"

Landon's dad paused with the ball cocked back. Landon could feel his father's excitement, and he had to admit that it made him curious too, a name like Dorch. He assumed it wasn't just a variation on "dork," which is what several kids in his Ohio school had called him.

His father threw the ball, a wayward lob, but Landon was able to get his hands on it and pull it proudly to his chest.

"Dorchester." His father stood up straight and saluted. "Yes, Dorchester. *And*, not just Dorchester, but the *guards* of Dorchester castle, the sons of the sons of the sons and so on . . . bred for what?"

Landon held the ball and waited.

His father flung his hands high in the air. "Stature."

Landon wrinkled his brow. "Stature? You mean a statue?"

"No: stature, size. Height." His father held a hand level with the top of his head. "Girth too." He patted the beach-ball bulge of his stomach and its impressive girth with both hands.

Landon looked down at his own hefty gut. In football his weight would be an advantage.

His father waved a hand to get his attention. His face grew serious and he said, "Enter the problem which I'd like you to help me solve."

"What's the problem?"

"*Return to Zovan* is nearly seven hundred pages long, probably halfway finished."

"Halfway?" Landon couldn't imagine anyone reading a

fourteen-hundred-page book. That would be like the Bible, or the dictionary, or . . . something.

"Yes," his father said. "A very good start with *tremendous* momentum. As I said, my main character is about to reach Zovan and meet his uncle, who we shall now name Bretwalda. *But*, a writer has to be *inspired*, and a writer has to be honest about whether he is truly inspired and . . . well, Dorch inspires me. Don't you get it?"

Landon didn't know what to say. He bought some time by turning the ball over in his hands, searching for just the right grip on the laces, like he'd seen Peyton Manning do on YouTube videos.

"I want to write a historical novel about Dorchester Castle. I can *see* it. I can *taste* it." His father paced the grass before he turned his attention back to Landon. "I am inspired, Landon, but will it sell? You read as much as anyone . . ."

"I read kids' stuff, Dad," Landon said, begging off and throwing the ball.

His father nodded excitedly as he muffed the catch, but he didn't bend down for the ball. "And that's what this would *be*—it's middle grade historical fiction based on our forefathers. Can you imagine the excitement of the librarians? You see, people love the past, but they love it when you can bring it into the future. It's like Percy Jackson. It's mythology, only *today*. Brilliant." His father paused and then asked, "So, yes or no?"

Landon looked pointedly at the ball. "Well, how would you bring the story about Dorchester into today?"

"Time travel, of course. You remember the Magic Tree House

books, right?" His father picked up the ball and cocked his arm.

"Sure," Landon said.

"More brilliance." His father didn't throw the ball but instead looked up at the clouds, contemplating the genius of a tree house for time travel.

When his father's eyes remained cast toward the sky, Landon looked up too, expecting to see a cloud in the shape of a dragon or a magic tree house or a castle.

Then he thought he heard something. A word?

Was it "catch"?

Landon looked toward his father the instant before the football hit him in the head and he collapsed on the grass.

11

Landon's father was a ghost above him, a blurry and sobbing figure coming into focus. Landon read his lips. "Landon? Landon? Oh, God . . ."

His father's fingers scampered over his face and the right earpiece and the magnetic disc that had been knocked loose. "Landon? I'm sorry. I'm so sorry . . ."

Landon opened his mouth to say he was just fine. Nothing came out, or maybe it did. His father's panic and the bad sound and being on the grass disoriented him. One ear wasn't working, but otherwise, he was more embarrassed than hurt. He tried to get up.

His father's hands now pressed him down. "Are you okay? I don't know if you should move."

Landon shook his head and kept trying to sit up. "Dad, let me up. I'm *fine*."

"Okay. Okay." His father nodded, and with his knees buried in the grass, he gently helped Landon into a sitting position.

Landon felt for the apparatus on the right side of his head. The cochlear was crooked behind his ear. His father gently removed everything, checked it over with a frown, and then dangled the equipment in front of him. "It looks okay. Just unseated it."

Landon took it and put it back on.

"Is it okay?" His father's eyes were wet, his lips pulled into the frown of a sad clown.

Landon got everything reconnected and listened. "Say something."

His father looked confused. "Uh . . . one, two, three, four, five, six, seven—"

Landon cut off his counting with a nod and a smile. "Got it. All good, Dad."

His father scooped him up like a hundred-and-seventy-pound doll. He hugged him and spun him around before placing him down. "Oh, thank God. I thought I'd hurt you."

Landon laughed. "I'm okay. You threw it and I wasn't looking."

"I know. I know. Stupid, stupid, stupid." His father shook his head. "I wasn't thinking. I mean, I was thinking—about the book—I mean, I can't use time travel, right? And then I remembered I was supposed to be throwing to you and my arm just launched it and . . ."

"I'm okay. I'm okay." Landon couldn't stand when his parents fussed over him.

"Really okay?" his father asked.

"Good thing you don't have a very good throwing arm." Landon smiled and his father mussed his hair.

"And . . ." His father looked around. ". . . I don't see any reason why we need to say anything to . . . Well, this is one of those little things you just forget about because they're so unimportant."

"Absolutely." Landon didn't want to give his mother another reason to freak out about football. He hadn't even gotten the pads on yet. When his father's eyes widened, he turned to see Genevieve staring at them with her hands on her hips. Her frizzy red hair was gathered in a kind of crazed ponytail.

"What happened?"

"Playing football," Landon said.

"Are you okay?" Genevieve eyed them suspiciously.

"Great," his father said. Then his eyes narrowed and he pointed at Genevieve's hand. "And what is that, young lady?"

Genevieve didn't try to hide her nails; instead she splayed the fingers on her free hand to show off the purple paint. "Polish."

"I don't think so." Their father shook his head. "You do something like that and *I'll* catch the blame."

Genevieve pointed to her face. "No lipstick. No eyeliner. That's what you can tell Mom. I will too."

Genevieve had the strong-minded look of their mother, and she jutted out her chin. "I can get by without makeup, but you don't show up at the deli or the park without nail polish. Not in this town anyway."

"What do you mean, 'this town'?" their father asked.

"Bronxville." Genevieve tightened her jaw. "This isn't like Cleveland."

Landon looked back and forth between them like it was a Ping-Pong match.

"Meaning?"

"Certain things are expected here, Dad."

"Like what?"

"Like nail polish. Tevas instead of Crocs." Genevieve wiggled her toes at them. "Nothing too crazy, but it's different. Oh, and Tuckahoe are our mortal enemies."

"Tuckahoe?" Their father wrinkled his brow.

"Arch rivals in all sports, especially football." Genevieve handed Landon the shirt she'd been holding. "Here, put this on."

"I have a shirt on." Landon pointed to his dark gray *Minecraft Eye of Ender* T-shirt.

"Izod. Put it on," Genevieve said. It was an order.

Landon looked at his father and shrugged. "She's good at this stuff."

Genevieve looked away as he tugged the blue collared shirt with its little alligator patch down over his jiggling belly.

"Good." Genevieve turned from Landon to their father. "Now we're off to lunch."

"What do you mean, 'off to lunch'?" he asked.

Genevieve sighed. "It's what kids do here, Dad. They meet at the diner or the club or the pizza place."

"And how do kids *pay* for that lunch?" He scratched his jaw.

"Mom gave me a credit card," Genevieve said. "She said if you had a problem to say it's this or join the country club. Lots of kids eat there."

"I don't golf." Their father blinked.

"I know," Genevieve said.

"Guess I'll make a sandwich and get back to work." He gave Landon a knowing look. "I think I had a breakthrough."

Landon retrieved his Cleveland Browns cap and followed his sister.

"Don't walk behind me, Landon." She waved her hand. "Walk beside me."

Landon hustled up. "Well, you walk so fast. It's always like a death march or something with you. You and Mom."

"We have places to go," she said.

They were passing the library when she tapped him and asked, "What's Dad's breakthrough?"

Landon explained as best he could. Genevieve shook her head. "He's something."

"*I* like it." Landon didn't want to trample his father. In fact, he wanted to look up to him, but sometimes it was hard. Whenever anyone asked what his father did and Landon told them he was a writer, the next question always hurt. He tapped Genevieve's shoulder. "Do you have to have a book *published* to be a writer? Technically, I mean?"

Genevieve frowned. "Of course not. Did you ever hear of *A Confederacy of Dunces?*"

"You saying Dad's stupid?"

"No." Genevieve swatted him. "It was a book no one wanted. Dad told me about it. The author was John Kennedy Toole, and he never published anything. He died . . . actually, he killed himself."

Landon's stomach clenched. "Geez, Genevieve."

"Yeah, but then his mom *forces* some writing professor

to read her son's manuscript and *bam*, it not only gets published, it wins the Pulitzer Prize."

"Gosh." Landon thought about that all the way to the diner.

When they arrived, there were no bikes outside, and that relaxed Landon a bit. They went inside, and Genevieve waved to a table where two girls sat holding two empty places.

"Guys, this is my brother, Landon." Genevieve presented him with a flourish. "Landon, this is Katy Buford and this is Megan Nickell. We'll all be in seventh grade together."

Katy's short hair was straight with bangs and so blond it was nearly white. Megan had dark, wavy hair pulled back by a band across the top of her head. They both wore shorts and colorful Polo shirts with Tevas on their feet. Landon blushed and said hello. As he shook hands he noticed that they not only had painted nails, but also a touch of lipstick and maybe something on their eyelashes.

They all sat down. Katy launched into an excited discussion with Genevieve and Megan about the new middle school girls' soccer coach.

Katy rolled her eyes. "Wait till you see how cute he is! But my mother said he grew up in New Haven, so he's probably poor as a church mouse. Can you believe people *live* in places like New Haven? I bet there are some pretty bad places in Cleveland, huh?"

When Landon looked over, Megan was staring at him with large, pale blue eyes. He was afraid she'd ask about his ears, but she smiled. There was a gap between her front teeth, and they were all strapped together with bright orange braces.

He looked back at her eyes. She was beautiful.

They ordered Cokes and iced tea. While the girls looked at the menu and Katy babbled on about boys and clothes and makeup and money, Landon stole glimpses of Megan. He couldn't take his eyes off her. When the waitress returned with their drinks, Landon reached for his soda too fast and knocked it over, and some spilled on Megan's white shorts. She gave a little shriek and jumped up, her face reddening at the attention from everyone around them. Landon struggled up out of his seat and dabbed at her shorts with his napkin.

"Sorry, sorry, sorry," he said.

Megan laughed nervously and gently pushed him away. "No, I'm okay. Please, Landon. Stop."

Landon stood, his shoulders slouched, a tower of shame. "I . . . I am just so sorry."

"It's okay. It's no big deal." Genevieve patted his shoulder and they all sat down.

Landon could see Megan was still embarrassed by the incident and blotting her shorts with water under the table. He suspected Katy's now-deadpan face was her way of showing contempt. Landon felt his own face burning. To rebuild their image of him, he forced a chuckle and blurted out, "I'm good at knocking things over. That's why I'm going to play football."

"What?" Katy's face morphed into disbelief. "How?"

"Well, he's getting—" Genevieve started to explain.

Megan's face brightened, though. "That's *great,* Landon."

"Is it?" Landon thought so, but her enthusiasm puzzled him.

"Yes." She nodded, smiling.

He had to ask. "Why?"

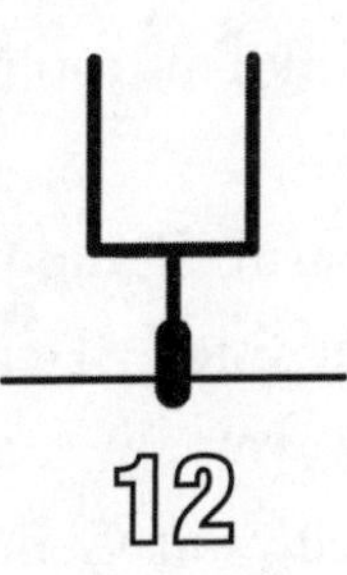

12

Landon leaned toward Megan's face, intent on her lips. The diner around them created a buzzing hum that made hearing even more difficult for him. Crowded places were always a nightmare.

"Well," she said, still bright, "my boyfriend is the quarterback."

"Your . . . wait, what?"

"My boyfriend."

Landon didn't think things could get worse. Then they did.

"His name is Skip," Megan said.

Landon knew of only one Skip, the redheaded boy from their first lunch at the deli, and something told him that was exactly who Megan was talking about.

"He's super nice." Megan spoke very directly to Landon, and he now noticed that her voice was funny, loud and slow, like he was four years old instead of twelve. "He's tall and he's cute and he can help you fit in." Megan reached out and patted Landon's arm and then sat back, proud of her ability to communicate with him.

"You talk like you think I'm stupid." Landon's mood plummeted.

Genevieve poked his arm. "Landon, be nice."

Landon glared at his sister. "I can hear, you know." He pointed to his cochlears.

The waitress appeared, and Genevieve took advantage of the opportunity to change the subject. "Let's order! I'll have prosciutto on toast with a side salad and balsamic vinaigrette, please. Landon, how about you?"

"Pastrami." Landon folded his arms across his chest and slumped in his chair. His brain felt like mud, wet and gooey, a real mess. Katy looked at him like he was some kind of toad. When he felt a tap on his arm, he turned to see Megan, not sulking back or mad or babying him, but with a bright smile.

"I'm sorry, Landon," she said. "I never knew a deaf person before. I'll get it right. Just be patient with me, okay?"

Landon's mouth fell open. He wanted to cry, but knew he had to choke back his emotions. He hadn't really known how he wanted people to treat him before, only that they all either treated him with syrupy kindness that felt fake or, worse, with cruelty for being so big and clumsy and hard to understand and deaf.

Now, here was this beautiful girl who made his heart whirr, and she'd done what he wanted everyone to do: be honest and understanding, offering kindness without pity.

"Yes," he said, "I can be patient. Thank you."

"My pleasure," she said to him before turning to the waitress. "I'll have a grilled cheese with fries, extra pickles, and can you bring my friend another Coke, please?"

Megan nodded at Landon's nearly empty drink, and it was only then he realized she was talking about *him.*

Landon took a breath and held it, savoring the fizz and the flavor, not of the Coke, but of maybe, finally, having a friend.

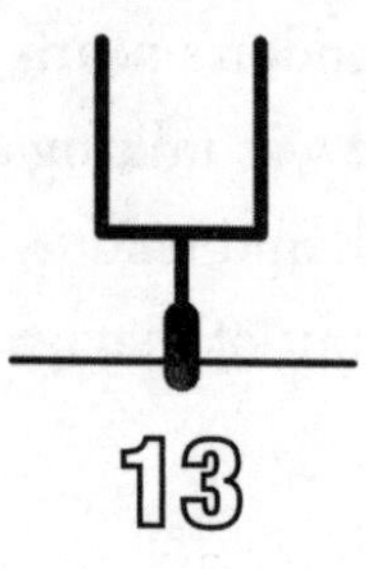

13

Landon stayed busy with his sandwich and then explained to Megan that he could hear, just not like most people. He pointed to the metal disc attached to the back of the right side of his head. “I had surgery. There’s an implant under here. A wire goes from the implant into my inner ear, where they put a computer chip. The disc transmits sound impulses to my inner ear.”

Landon pointed behind his ear. “You might think this is a big hearing aid. Actually, it’s the processor and also the battery, and it picks up sound waves and sends them to the metal disc, which sends them to my inner ear. I’ve got the same things on the left side. My mom just calls the whole setup my ‘ears.’”

Megan nodded, clearly interested. But Katy just looked on, more in bewilderment than anything, like she couldn’t believe Megan was bothering with him.

"So, I hear," Landon explained to Megan, "but it's not like what you hear. Nothing is ever really clear, and I need to see people's faces."

"Like lipreading?" Megan asked.

"Yeah, but really the whole face is important," Landon said. "I put it all together, what I hear and what I see, and I guess I can understand people pretty well, but . . ."

Megan tilted her head. "What?"

"With my family, I tap them to get them to look at me so I can see them. It's a habit," he said.

"So?"

Landon shrugged. "Other people don't always like it."

Megan shrugged back. "Too bad for them." She popped the last of her fries into her mouth. "Hey, are we going swimming or what?"

Genevieve paid with the credit card, and when the other girls tried to give her money she told them they could take her out next time. Landon just watched and felt like a goof, but that didn't stop him from feeling proud of her and mystified at this new world they lived in: his little sister buying lunches on a credit card, ordering iced tea and prosciutto like grownups. On their way out of the diner, Landon tapped Genevieve on the shoulder and spoke low. "You're awesome, you know that?"

"You are, too." She hugged his middle and stood on her tippy toes to kiss his cheek.

Landon walked behind Genevieve and Katy, right alongside Megan.

Landon learned that Katy's father was the richest man in Bronxville, and he supposed that was why Genevieve tolerated her eye-rolling and rude attitude. Megan was confident. She described her father, the president of the country club, as a "climber"—which made Landon think of his mother, although he didn't say so.

Megan was careful to look at him when she spoke, and they talked about *Bridge to Terabithia*, which was her favorite book. Landon mostly listened and felt a little foolish when he told her it was too sad for his taste.

Megan looked disappointed. "Lots of the best books are sad."

Landon wiped the beads of sweat from his upper lip, aware that his bulk was making him feel hotter still. "I know. But life is sad. Why should books be sad, too? I want books to be happy. I like heroes, and adventures."

She brightened. "Do you like *Ella Enchanted*?" Then she scowled. "Did you read *Ella Enchanted*?"

"I did." Landon nodded hard and fast.

Katy laughed, and it seemed to Landon from the flick of her eyes that she was laughing *at* him, but he ignored her and continued. "See? That's a happy ending. How about the Chronicles of Narnia? Have you read those?"

Megan shook her head. "No."

"Oh, well, you have to." Landon trudged on, feeling the solid sidewalk beneath his feet and standing tall so that he easily looked over the top of his sister's head as they walked past the gate posts into their driveway. Now that he saw the house through the eyes of the richest girl in town, it seemed more like a cottage than a mansion, and Landon was sharply aware of the untrimmed hedges and a shutter that needed fixing on one of the upper windows.

As they reached the side door, he wondered if he should have even admitted to reading *Ella Enchanted,* because he doubted that was the kind of book a real football player would read. He felt certain Megan's boyfriend, Skip, wouldn't read such a thing. In a storm of self-doubt and discomfort, he went upstairs to his room to get changed into his bathing suit.

When he arrived at the pool, the girls had already put out their towels on the lounge chairs. Landon claimed a chair, and then he pulled Genevieve aside. "Should I wear my shirt or take it off?"

Genevieve studied his face. "Why would you leave it on?"

Landon lifted his shirt and pointed to the pale roll of blubber spilling over the band of his red bathing suit. "This."

Genevieve frowned and swatted the air. "No one cares, Landon. You're not posing for a magazine." She said louder, "How about a cannonball contest?"

Landon raised his eyebrows.

Katy frowned.

Megan studied Landon's face and seemed to read his mind. "That's a great idea. I love cannonballs."

Landon grinned and disconnected his "ears" without hesitation, wrapping them in his towel and setting them on the table next to his chair beneath a wide green umbrella. He was bursting with pride as he stepped up to the board. He remembered his manners and invited the girls to go first. When they said no, he dove right in, showering them in a geyser of water. They all declared him the clear winner. After that, he sprang off the end of the diving board—time after time—sending up fountains of spray that reached for the sky and waves that had the girls giddy, laughing and rocking like ships in a storm on inflatable rafts.

He didn't have to hear to know they were bubbling with joy, even Katy. It was one of those summer days that were never meant to end. He'd even forgotten about football, until his father called them in for an early dinner. Landon saw the joy drain from everyone's faces. He dried his head and then reattached his ears, nerves already back on edge.

"Your friends are welcome to stay, Genevieve." Their father stood in the kitchen doorway with an apron on and a spatula in his hand.

The girls seemed shaken by his presence. They toweled off and said they had to get home.

"But thank you, Mr. Dorch." Megan gave a happy wave as she and Katy made a fast exit through the gate that led to a path through the bushes to the driveway.

Dripping on the red brick terrace surrounding the pool, Landon said, "That was fun, Genevieve."

"You were great." Genevieve reached up and put a hand on his shoulder. "Landon, they really like you."

Landon blushed. "Well, I think it's you they like and they were just being nice."

She shook her head. "No, Landon, they liked *you*. Especially Megan."

Landon felt a jolt of pleasure at the sound of her name, and he stared at the gate through which she'd departed. "But she has a boyfriend. It's gotta be that Skip kid you shoved."

Genevieve bit her lip. "It is him, but sometimes people make mistakes. Maybe he'll turn out all right. Maybe when she tells him we're all friends, he'll be nice to you. Heck, you're going to be teammates. That counts for a lot, right?"

Landon studied her face. He wanted her to be right, but when he remembered the shove she'd given Skip, knocking him back into that table full of women and spilling their drinks and embarrassing him in front of everyone, he said, "I don't know, Genevieve. Does it?"

They both knew that as soon as dinner was over, he was going to find out.

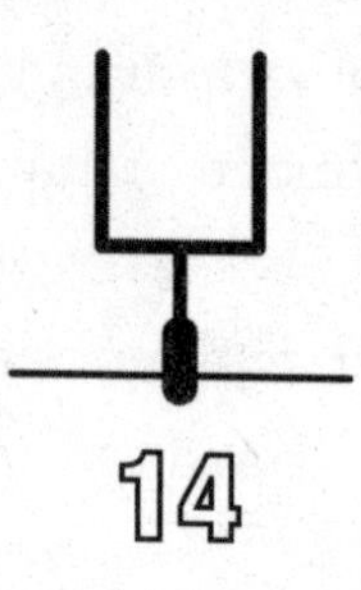

14

A handful of signs taped to broomsticks and stuck into orange highway cones directed Landon and his father to the Westchester Youth Football League weigh-ins. They could have just as easily followed the crowd of parents and their sons ranging in age from four to fourteen.

People were putting baked goods on the check-in table as if they were making an offering to the gods of football. Landon's mom had had to work late, so his father set the oatmeal cookies made with honey down beside a plate of brownies. Landon's father also had the list of things she wanted him to tell the officials, including the doctor's clearance. Under an overhang outside the middle school gym, they got in line in front of the seventh-grade team check-in table. Landon mostly kept his eyes ahead, but stole secret glances all around and tugged his Browns cap down snug on his head. The man behind the desk wore stylish metal-framed glasses. When he saw Landon he reared back. "Whoa! Heh, heh. Guys, this is the seventh-grade line. Eighth is over there."

"No," Landon's dad said, getting out his checkbook. "He's in seventh grade."

The man with glasses turned and nudged the tall man sitting next to him. "Bob, we got a bison here, for sure a Double X."

"What's your name?" the man with glasses asked.

"He's Landon Dorch," Landon's father answered for him. "What's that mean? Double X?"

"Dorch, I got it." The man with the glasses drew a line through Landon's name on his list of registrants from the league's website. "Uh, it means he can only play right tackle on offense and left end on defense. No big deal. A kid his size is a hog anyway, right?"

Landon's father frowned and he straightened his back. "Hog?"

The man with the glasses laughed in a friendly way. "A lineman. A hog. It's a good thing. A football term. We love a kid as big as yours. Coach Bell was a hog, right, Coach?" He turned to the man standing at the scale with a clipboard. Beside him was a boy nearly as big as Landon, but harder looking, like a big sack of rocks.

"Yes, and so is my boy." Coach Bell clapped the big bruiser on the shoulder. "You and Brett will be on the line together."

"Hi, I'm Brett." Brett Bell stepped forward without hesitation and gave Landon a firm handshake and a smile. "See you out there."

Landon watched Brett march off toward the exit before turning toward the coach. Coach Bell was about six feet tall and easily three hundred pounds. He wore a bright green T-shirt, a Bronxville Football cap, and a whistle around his neck.

"Coach Bell was a Division III All-American at Union, and his wife's little brother plays for the Giants. You know, Jonathan Wagner? He's the right tackle." The man with glasses gazed at Coach Bell with respect. "Here, let's get Landon on that scale, and Mr. Dorch, you'll need to sign up for at least two volunteer jobs with Bob, but we'd be happy if you took three or four, depending on your work schedule."

"Let's get Landon weighed," Coach Bell said.

"Should I take off my shoes?" Landon asked Coach Bell, awed by the coach's All-American status and relationship to a real NFL player.

At the sound of Landon's garbled voice, all three men from the league looked at each other with alarm. The man with the glasses turned to Landon's dad and spoke in a low voice so that it was hard for Landon to make out what he was saying. But if Landon read his lips right, he said, "Uh, Mr. Dorch. Is your son . . . uh, does he have a problem we should know about?"

Landon's dad gave Landon a nervous glance, then shook his head at the man with glasses. "Landon has a slight difficulty speaking, but he's a B-plus student. He has cochlear implants to help him hear, so we've got a special helmet on order and a doctor's clearance for him to play."

"Wait a minute," the man said. "I need more than that."

Standing by the scale, Landon swallowed hard and bit his lip. This wasn't how he wanted to begin his football career.

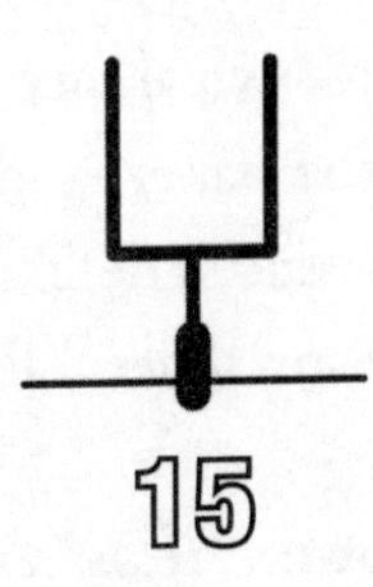

15

Landon's dad went into his speech. "Landon is deaf. When he was four he got cochlear implants, so he hears sound and he can read lips. But to really understand speech it's best if he hears and sees what's said."

"He reads lips?" The man shot what looked like a nervous glance at Landon.

"He uses a combination of sight and sound to understand," Landon's dad said.

"But he can't wear those things with a football helmet," the man said.

Landon's dad nodded. "Yes, he can. There's actually a company that makes custom helmets. Landon isn't the first, either, and we have a doctor's note."

"Okay, okay. That's great. Really." The man with glasses threw his hands up in the air in total surrender. "I'm sorry. I didn't mean any offense at all, and if he has special needs we can work with that, but we just have to know."

Landon's father gritted his teeth and shook his head. "No, he isn't special needs. He just needs to see you speak." He showed them all the doctor's clearance.

The men looked at the paper, and then Coach Bell said, "Super. Okay, let's go. On the scale, Landon. Here we go."

"So, should I take off my shoes?" It seemed like years since Landon first asked this.

Coach Bell looked down. "Yeah, it's the rules."

Landon bent down and took his shoes off. He tugged his T-shirt over his gut before he stepped onto the scale.

"I knew it!" Coach Bell craned his neck to read the digital number. "Yup. Double X. You'll be great on the line."

Landon's father said, "But he can only play certain positions?"

"Yes," Coach Bell explained. "For safety these really big boys—the Double X's—can only play right tackle on offense and left end on defense."

Landon didn't know whether to feel proud or humiliated. The man with glasses gave him a mouth guard in a plastic bag and instructed him to go out on the football field and look for the coaches with the bright green T-shirts. Landon's dad put a hand on his shoulder and guided him toward the field.

When they got there, Landon's dad pointed to one end where two fathers wore bright green T-shirts with matching caps and whistles around their necks, just the same as Coach Bell at the weigh-in. There were blocking dummies and small, bright orange cones set out in some kind of order Landon didn't recognize from his YouTube study of the game. Some of the dummies, big yellow cylinders standing tall, were for blocking and tackling. Others, blue rectangles lying flat in the grass, were used for soft boundary markers. Beyond the end zone was a metal sled with five football-player-shaped pads whose single purpose he knew: blocking.

"Okay." His father stopped at the sideline and pointed. "There's your group—your team. Good luck, son."

Landon looked up at his father, who studied the team from beneath the shade of his hand. When he realized Landon wasn't moving, he gave him a little push. "Go ahead. You can do this, Landon. Everything new is always a little scary."

16

He nodded. "Okay, Dad." Landon put one foot in front of the other and headed toward the growing group of kids wearing shorts and T-shirts and cleats who milled around the coaches in green. Skip was throwing a ball to his spiky-haired friend, and when he saw Landon he called out, "Hey, Mike, the baby giant came back." Landon moved toward the other side of the field where two other boys huddled together on a tipped-over blocking dummy, whispering. Landon sat down on the dummy directly across from them. He looked intently at them until they suddenly stopped talking.

The two boys looked at Landon like he was crazy, then at each other, and simply got up and walked away without a word.

Landon scanned the area and picked some grass. He knew he should have just said hello, but he wasn't comfortable doing it. He knew his speech sounded off. The other kids were fooling around, pushing each other with foam shields or tossing footballs.

That outsider feeling he'd lived with his whole life tightened its grip on Landon's heart, threatening to turn him into a mound of jelly. It felt like the drop at Splash Mountain all over again, so Landon clenched his teeth and dug deep. This was his chance to be a football player, and if he did what he thought he could do, they'd all respect him—and maybe outright *like* him. One coach noticed him and headed his way with a bright white smile that made him feel much, much better.

The coach smelled of citrus cologne, but he looked like a triathlete. His cabled muscles were tan and his close-set, dark eyes intense without effort. Up close, Landon could see a dusting of gray at the edges of his dark, short hair. The coach stopped in front of Landon and extended a hand weighed down by some kind of championship ring. "Hey, buddy, I'm Coach Furster, the head coach. Look, you don't want to sit on the bags like that."

Landon popped right up. "Sorry, Coach. I . . . the other guys . . ." Landon stopped because he didn't want to seem like a rat.

"And lose the hat, buddy." Coach Furster glowered so that his eyes almost appeared to have crossed, and Landon wondered if he had some deep-seated hatred of the Cleveland Browns. "You see anybody else wearing a *hat*?"

"Oh, um," he started, but with Coach glaring at him, Landon reluctantly tugged off his hat. Coach Furster's jaw fell. "What? Whoa. Hey, what the . . ."

"It's . . . it's just my hearing stuff, Coach. My mom calls them my 'ears.' They help me hear."

Coach Furster waved a hand. "No worries, buddy. Hey, you're okay with the hat. That's fine. I had no idea. I know you're new and I was just thinking you'd want to fit in. That's always what you want, but you're fine with the hat."

Landon replaced the hat and studied the coach intently. Coach Furster stood straight and wiped his mouth like there was food on it. "What? What are you looking at?"

"Just . . . your face, Coach."

"Why?" Coach Furster wrinkled his thick brow so that his eyebrows sank and his eyes nearly crossed again.

"Just"—Landon pointed in the general direction of his ears—"so I can hear what you're saying, or know what you're saying."

Coach Furster only blinked at him.

"It's easier to understand when I can see your lips," Landon explained.

"Well, you're apt to miss a lot that way." Coach Furster twirled his whistle and the tattoo on the side of his biceps—some Chinese symbol—jumped and quivered. "But don't worry. We can bring you along slow. Was Coach Bell at your check-in?"

"Yes," Landon said. "He told me I was a Double X player."

"Coach West and I will have to talk to him," Coach Furster said. "Meanwhile, you just watch how we do things and then we can see how you do."

"I'll watch everything, Coach." Landon nodded vigorously. "For sure. I watch drills on YouTube all the time."

"Great." Coach Furster put a hand on Landon's shoulder and escorted him over to the sideline in a cloud of that citrus cologne. "You know what? Heck, who cares?" Coach Furster knocked over a blocking dummy and dragged it ten feet off the field. "You can sit right there. That's fine. You sit and watch and you'll pick up a lot, right? You're a careful observer, I bet." Coach Furster pointed at him and winked.

"For sure, Coach." Landon took a seat and beamed up at his new coach.

"That's great, Landon." Coach Furster patted his shoulder. "This is gonna work out just great. Glad to have you on the team."

Landon followed the coach with his eyes, the smell fading into the grass. Coach Furster returned to the other coach—Coach West—a tall, thin man who made Landon think of an undertaker. They were soon joined by big Coach Bell. They had a short, animated discussion. Landon couldn't make it all out, but he knew by the way they kept looking at him that he—or really his ears—was the topic.

Then he caught a full view of Coach Bell's red face and could clearly see what he was saying. "—not mentally challenged. He talks funny because he's *deaf.* He's huge, and he's got a doctor's clearance and a custom helmet and his dad says he can read lips."

At that, all three coaches looked his way and Landon quickly averted his eyes, studying the grass. The blast of whistles got his attention and he saw that the coaches had moved on. The team fell into five lines, creating a rigid order where before it had been mayhem. Skip and his two friends, floppy-haired Xander and spiky-haired Mike, headed up three of the five lines. Another was headed by Coach Bell's son, Brett.

Whistles tooted and players took off from their lines, running with high knees from the goal line to the thirty-yard line and then stopping and reforming the lines, only to return some other way. They went back and forth with a backward run, a sideways shuffle, cross-over steps, butt kickers, and some runs Landon couldn't even describe.

After about ten minutes of that, everyone spread out and they did some more stretching. Five minutes later they were broken into three equal groups and running through agility drills overseen by the coaches. On the whistle, the players would sprint from one station to the next, with the coaches issuing an occasional bark—it seemed to Landon a mixture of criticism and praise.

After that they worked on form tackling drills, just going through the precise movements of a tackle in slow motion since no one had pads on. Then the team split up into skill players—mostly the smaller guys like Skip and Mike and a kid named Layne Guerrero—who went with Coach Bell, and the lineman, or hogs, like Brett Bell, who went with Coach Furster and Coach West.

When the lineman began getting into stances and firing out into the blocking dummies held by their teammates, Landon stood up.

He felt silly just sitting and was pretty certain he could do what they were doing. There was one guy without a partner, a kid not as big as Landon but with even more girth around the belly and big Band-Aids on each knee. Landon grabbed the dummy he'd been sitting on and dragged it over to him.

"Hey," Landon said cheerfully. The kid looked at him like he was nuts, but Landon pressed on. "I can be your partner. Here, you go first."

Landon hefted the bag between the two of them, grabbed the handles on both sides, and leaned into it just the way the others were doing. The kid got down, and on the coach's cadence, he fired out into the dummy, jarring Landon, who fought to keep his feet.

"Hey! Hey!" Coach West was shouting, and he flew over to Landon's new partner and got right in his face. "Did anyone tell you to pair off with this kid, Timmy?"

The boy named Timmy shook his head with a terrified look.

A whistle shrieked and all motions stopped. Coach Furster marched over in a cloud of cologne. "Whoa, whoa, whoa. Landon, what are you doing, buddy?"

"I just . . ." Landon hefted the bag. "I can do this, Coach. It's easy."

The word "easy" set Coach Furster off. He was suddenly furious. "Easy, Landon? Glad you think it's easy. Okay, let's give you a shot and see how *easy* it is. Ready?"

Coach Furster jammed the whistle in the corner of his mouth and snatched the dummy from Landon, spinning it around without any regard for the fine gold watch on his wrist. "Down!"

Landon looked all around. The kids were all smirking, and some were giggling.

"I said, 'Down!' Come on, you been watching." Coach

Furster's face was turning red. "You know what to do. Down!"

A light went off in Landon's head and he put his hand down in the grass, just one, palm flat in a three-point stance.

"Set . . . Hut!"

Landon stumbled into the dummy with his shoulder and started pumping his feet up and down the way he'd seen the others do, pushing with all his might. Coach Furster dragged the dummy backward and Landon felt it slipping away. He churned his feet, grabbed for the handles on the bag but missed, caught the coach's fine watch, let go with a gasp, tripped, and fell flat on his face. Landon could taste the grass and feel the vibration of laughter all around him. He didn't have to see it.

He didn't have to hear it.

In his ears rang his mother's words: "Be careful what you wish for, Landon, because you just might get it."

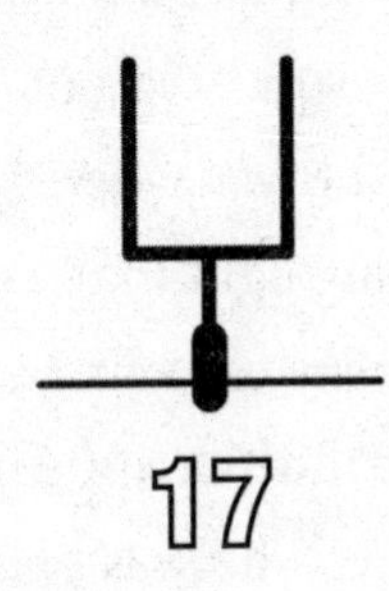

17

“How was practice?” Landon’s mom looked up from her cup of tea as he and his dad walked in through the garage door. Her eyes were red-rimmed and drooping with exhaustion. She had her shoes off and her feet up on an ottoman, stretching her toes. Beside her, a briefcase bulged with papers, and her dress was wrinkled.

Landon didn’t want to alarm her, or anyone. “Fine.”

“Just fine?” She arched an eyebrow and studied his face.

His father stepped into the scene from the kitchen. “He has lots to learn, is all. They don’t give the babies rattles in this town; they give them footballs.”

Landon shook his head. “We had to run about a million sprints at the end of practice. I’m tired.”

He thought she might have said, “Me too,” as he walked on past, heading for the stairs and a shower.

It was under the safety of the pounding water, without his ears and in the silence of his own world, that he let himself sob. Football practice was nothing like he had expected. Instead of being glorious and uplifting, it had confused and belittled him. He felt like an orange with all its juice squeezed out. When he got out of the shower his eyes were so red that he decided to get in bed with his book and the clip-on reading light that wouldn't let his parents get a good look at him when they came in to kiss him good-night.

After a short time, his mother appeared. She gave him a kiss and a hug, and he could tell she was exhausted because it was a rare thing to see her shoulders slump.

His father came in a few minutes later, sat on the edge of the bed, and patted his leg to get his attention.

Landon sighed and looked up. "Tired."

His father looked at the ears Landon had placed on the nightstand beside his bed, and then he made a fist with his thumb sticking out. Even though they didn't use sign language, there were a few signs they all knew, and when his father kept his fist tight, put the thumb into the right side of his stomach, and drew a straight line up toward his face, Landon knew what it meant.

Proud.

Landon bit the inside of his lip and hugged his dad. He tried not to cry again, but it hit him like a tidal wave.

"I don't want to be deaf, Dad," he cried out, painfully aware that he couldn't hear his own words. "I don't want to be different." His whole body lurched and shook, and he squeezed his father tight.

His dad simply hugged him tighter as they sat together in the dim light.

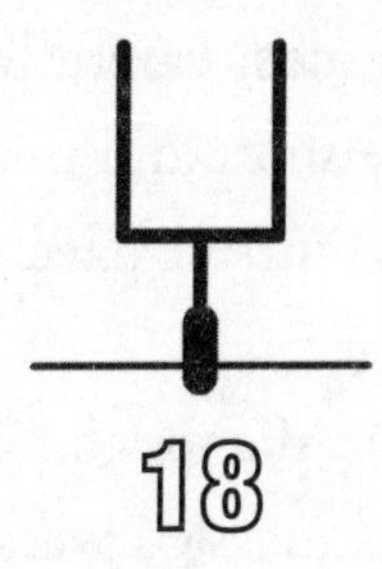

18

Landon spent the next day studying football drills and stances on YouTube. And that evening at practice, he refused to sit out and just watch. Instead, he joined everyone and fell into a line for stretching. The coaches had to have noticed him but didn't say anything, and Landon's apprehension began to fade as he jogged around with the other big guys, running through agility drills. He had watched closely the day before, so he knew what to do in the drills, even though his feet weren't as nimble as his brain. He wasn't expected to look as graceful as the quarterbacks, Skip Dreyfus and his backup, Bryce Rinehart, but he hoped he could match a fireplug like Travis Tinnin or Timmy Nichols. It wasn't pretty, though. Landon stumbled regularly on the bags as he wove in and out or high-stepped over them. He got through it, though, sweating and huffing but proud.

When they began hitting bags, Landon stood back to

watch. He didn't want a repeat of the night before when he'd made a fool out of himself, falling on his face. His plan was to watch until he was confident about exactly what to do. Gunner Miller was the right tackle, the only position Landon could play, so he watched him most carefully. Still, Brett Bell stood out, as did the center, the short and thick Travis Tinnin.

After a while Coach Furster gave his whistle a blast and shouted, "Sled time, boys!"

They all jogged over to the rough patch of grass beyond the end zone where the blocking sled waited with its thick metal skeleton and five firmly padded blocking dummies in a row. Landon thought he might be able to do this drill, but he hesitated and stood back as five players jumped in front of the pads, blasting them on the sound of Coach Furster's whistle. The next group replaced them immediately, striking the bags on the whistle and driving their feet like they were pushing a boulder up a hill.

It didn't look easy. The sled lurched reluctantly across the grass on the thick metal skids. If one of the players on either end didn't do his part, the entire sled would rotate like the spoke of a wheel, with the deficient player stuck in one spot, exposed for all to see.

"We're only as strong as our weakest link," Coach Furster—who rode atop the sled like a rodeo cowboy—growled. Two out of three times that happened, the offender was Timmy Nichols. "Come on, Nichols! Is that all you got? My grandmother could do better than that!"

Landon felt like he could do at least as good as Coach Furster's grandmother, but it was time for the next drill before he had a chance to try.

Sprints at the end were awful. Landon quickly lost his breath. Sweat poured from his skin. He was slick and hurting as he stumbled across the finish line, dead last every time. No one was in as bad a shape as Landon, not even Timmy Nichols, but Landon knew that football was a game of getting up. You had to keep going, again and again. That's how you got better, and that's what he meant to do.

The next day at practice, Landon spotted Timmy Nichols off by himself before the start. Apparently, Timmy arrived early to improve his sled skills by firing out low and hard against his nemesis time after time before practice began. Landon knew what Timmy was trying to do—he'd studied over a dozen YouTube videos on sled work earlier that day. Landon reached the sled without Timmy's notice. He watched the chunky player line up in his three-point stance, fire his shoulder into the sled, chop his feet up and down like engine pistons, and then stop and do it all over again. Landon stood watching several times before he stepped forward and spoke. "Hey, want some help?"

Timmy looked up in disgust. "Get away from me. I don't need any help. I'm not some moron."

Landon scowled and shook his head. "I'm not either. And I watched—"

Timmy let his hands hang uselessly in praying mantis form and turned his toes inward like a pigeon. His mouth hung open and his tongue slid sideways as he mocked Landon. *"I'm not a moron."*

"I'm not." Landon swallowed. He felt like he was falling through space. "I've got a B-plus average."

But Timmy wasn't listening. He'd already turned away, back toward the blocking sled, and Landon didn't catch what he'd said. Determined to get Timmy's attention, Landon moved close and tapped his shoulder. Timmy spun violently and glared up at Landon with the hatred of a small, trapped animal. "Don't touch me!"

Startled by Timmy's poisonous look, Landon only wanted to explain. "I didn't mean to scare you. I just didn't know what you said. I need to see."

"Get out of here!" Timmy gave Landon a shove that barely moved him.

Landon stood still as fury engulfed him. In his mind, he saw himself grabbing Timmy and slamming him into the dirt. "What is your problem? I said I'd help you!"

"Oh?" Timmy acted like he could read Landon's mind. "You think you're tough? Go ahead, if you're so tough; hit me!"

Timmy stuck his chin out and pointed to the sweet spot, jabbing his finger, just off center to the right where his small chin made a dimple in the rolls of neck fat.

Landon's fists balled into tight hammers of war and he reared back, ready to throw the punch of a lifetime.

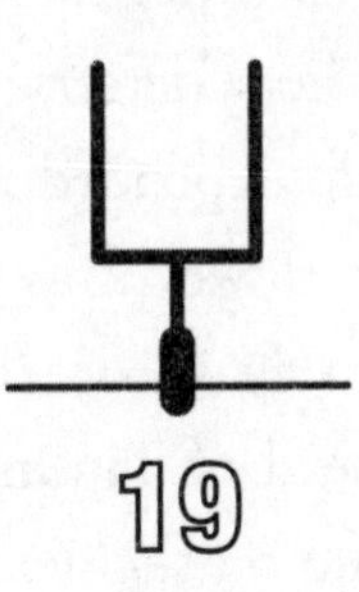
19

The shriek of a whistle shocked Landon like a wet wire.

Timmy jumped and took off.

Landon dropped his fists to his side. He stood, shoulders slumped, as he watched Timmy disappear into the swirling throng of football players who quickly assembled with the precision of a well-trained army.

Still enraged, Landon folded his arms tightly across his chest and marched defiantly to the end of a line. He had to force himself to do the warm-ups correctly, and when the blocking drills began, instead of sitting on a dummy off to the side, he stood scowling and trying to work up his nerve to try. He shadowed the linemen, following them closely so the coaches would know he was watching carefully, even though he never could quite bring himself to enter the drills. He wore an unending frown and muttered to himself, wanting everyone to see how angry he was.

But practice went on as normal, and no one seemed to notice him. When it was time to run, Landon set himself up on the line along with the others, determined to show them something. He ran like his life depended upon it, beating Timmy and several of the other slower kids on the first sprint, and then turned, ready to go again on the whistle. For the first ten sprints, he stayed ahead of Timmy, but then his stomach clenched. Timmy tied him on the next sprint. After that, even Timmy began to pull away. Still Landon labored on. He was going to do better. He wasn't going to let them mock him.

He chased the sluggish Timmy and kept at his heels. On the last sprint, when the rest of the team turned to cheer him over the finish line, he could only hear Timmy's insult crackle in his head over and over. The jolts made his legs pump just a bit faster and just a bit more true. With hatred fueling him, Landon pushed past the pain. Halfway across the width of the field, Landon caught up to Timmy. The rest of the team went wild, cheering now for sure, delighted by the contest between two chubby boys for last place.

Landon felt like if he could only beat Timmy, he'd stop being the biggest loser on the team. He'd have someone beneath him. With an agonizing groan, he flung his arms and legs forward. That's when Timmy made the mistake of looking back. When he turned his head, his tired legs tangled. He tripped and fell and Landon slogged past, pumping his arms and legs for all he was worth, the team now going wild.

"Lan-don! Lan-don! Lan-don!" they all chanted.

When Landon crossed the line, he staggered and collapsed. He rolled to his side and wretched, vomiting the remains of his father's tuna and string bean casserole onto the grass. The entire team roared with laughter, and as Landon lay there, doubled in pain, he was suddenly not so sure that he'd made things any better for himself at all.

Laughter swirled around him like smoke, and his vision was blurred by sweat and maybe a tear, but he tried to think not. Someone was saying something to him. He could hear it amid the other noise. He wasn't sure what they were saying. He thought it was, "Come on, Landon, get up."

Then he felt a hand grip his arm, and he turned his head to see who had reached down to help him. When he saw who it was, Landon got so emotional that he almost lost it.

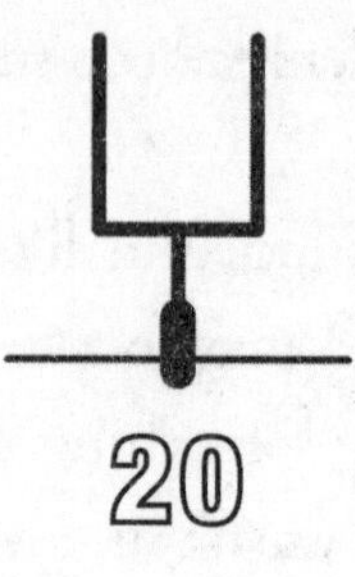

20

Landon didn't break down. He fought his twisted face back into a mask of toughness and let Skip Dreyfus help him up. Everyone else was still laughing, but Dreyfus was all business.

"Let's go!" Coach Furster hollered. "Bring it in on me!"

Everyone reached his hand in toward Coach Furster's fist, carefully avoiding contact with the watch Landon had learned was a Cartier Panther. Landon concentrated on the coach's face.

"You gonna be ready to beat Tuckahoe?" Coach Furster bellowed.

"Yes!" the team answered.

"You sure?" Coach Furster's face turned red and his eyes turned dangerously close to his nose.

"Yes!" they screamed.

"All right, 'Hit, Hustle, Win' on three," the coach barked. "One, two, three . . ."

"HIT, HUSTLE, WIN!" The whole team shouted, raising their hands straight into the air before breaking apart like a wave on the beach.

Landon found himself next to Timmy, with Skip's spiky-haired friend, Mike, who was Coach Furster's son, on the other side. Landon thought he heard Mike Furster talking to him, so he looked, but Mike was talking to Timmy.

". . . careful or he'll take your position."

"My position?" Timmy wrinkled his face.

"Yeah, left out." Mike busted out laughing like a maniac at his own joke. Landon looked away and kept going. He was aware of the joke. Some people played right tackle or left guard or right end, but if someone wasn't even worth being on the field, their position was left out.

Landon trudged uphill toward the parking lot where his dad stood just like the other dads, looking down onto the field.

"Are you okay?" His father kept his voice down, but Landon could see what he'd said and also the alarm on his face.

"I'm fine."

"Fine? It looked like you collapsed. Did you get *sick*?" His father spoke in a hushed tone and he looked around.

"I'm fine." Landon waved his hand dismissively, feeling a bit proud. "It happens, Dad. That's football. You gotta get up. You gotta keep going."

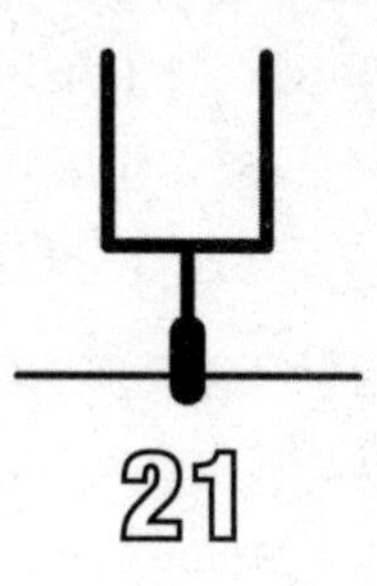

21

Saturday, the FedEx man delivered Landon's helmet. Landon and his father unwrapped it together, and his father helped him put on the skullcap and adjust the chin strap according to the instructions. As promised, the helmet went nicely around his cochlear, and with a rubber bulb pump, his father inflated the inner bladder, making everything good and snug for a safe fit. Landon attached the mouthpiece to the face mask cage and wore the helmet around the house for the rest of the morning.

After lunch, Landon's dad reminded him he had to cut the lawn. Landon got that job done—riding around on their John Deere and sweating beneath the helmet in the hot sun. After a splash in the pool to cool down, he changed into shorts and cleats for football practice. He swapped out the new helmet for his Browns cap, leaving the helmet on his bedpost.

"You don't have to drive me," he said to his father as they

backed out of the driveway. "I could walk to the school—it's close enough."

His dad angled his mouth toward him while keeping his eyes in the mirror as he maneuvered the Prius. "Don't want you wearing out your cleats on the sidewalk. Besides, everyone else gets dropped off."

"Well, thanks." Landon's mind quickly turned to practice—which drills he'd participate in and those he knew he wasn't ready for.

Landon felt the thrill of being on a team as he ran onto the field and looked around from his spot in the back of a line. Stretching was a breeze, even though no one spoke to him, and doing bag drills was easier, but he still hesitated when it came to blocking the sled. He stood close, hoping maybe Coach Furster might invite him to join, but the coach was intent on the players in front of him and his whistle, and sweat flew from his face and arms like insects taking flight. Landon told himself that not this practice, but the next would be the day he would participate fully.

After the first three drills, the whistle blew for their lone water break. The team had water bottles that Coach West seemed to be in charge of, and Landon stayed far away from them. There were two metal-framed carriers that held six bottles each, and Landon didn't want someone asking him to give them one even once, afraid that it could set a pattern for him to be the water boy.

Each plastic bottle had a screw-on cap with a nozzle that looked like a bent straw, and the players would grab them and squirt water into their mouths. This way, Coach Furster explained to the team, they could constantly re-hydrate without having to waste precious practice time on multiple water breaks.

"I'm greedy." Coach Furster looked around at his players with a crooked smile. "The league says we can only practice two hours a day, and I don't want to waste a second of it. It's like an Ironman, boys. When I do one, they run alongside you and squirt fluids into your mouth. You don't even break stride."

At the end of practice, after the first few sprints, Landon lost his steam. By the time they reached the twentieth sprint across the field, he could barely make it. The whole team cheered—or jeered, Landon wasn't exactly sure of the sound—as he dragged himself, gasping, in an agonizing shuffle across the final finish line.

Coach Furster looked at him with something between amazement and disgust and said, "Well, kid, you don't quit. I'll give you that."

Landon blushed and tugged his Cleveland Browns cap low on his head as he fought back the urge to puke up the churning liquid in his stomach.

He didn't know how the other linemen did it. Travis looked so blocky. Gunner and Brett Bell were both big guys too, but they ran right alongside the team's running back, Guerrero, and Rinehart, the backup quarterback. Skip Dreyfus, the starting quarterback, was in a league of his own. He led the team in every sprint, from start to finish. If Skip ever got tired, he never showed it.

Even though he was kind of scary with his burning green

eyes, red hair, and angry freckles, Landon couldn't help but admire Skip. First in everything, he snapped from one place to another like a gear in some kind of machine. As quarterback, he barked out the cadence with command, executed handoffs with precision, and delivered whistling passes that sometimes left the receivers wiggling their fingers to ease the sting. Everyone admired Skip, even the coaches.

Landon wondered if he'd ever get respect like that. Or any respect at all.

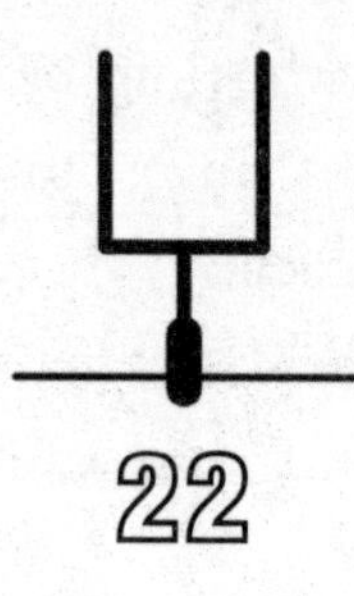

22

After practice he climbed into the Prius without speaking. And even though the drive wasn't more than a few blocks, Landon left a puddle of sweat in the front seat when he got out.

"Landon." His father pointed to the puddle. "Get a towel, please."

"Sorry. We ran super hard." Landon grabbed a rag from the bucket in the garage that his father used when he washed the car, and he mopped up the sweat.

"I know." His father watched him closely and gave a nod of approval before they headed into the house. "I saw you. You worked really hard, and you'll get there someday."

His father's words somehow made Landon feel worse.

Inside, Landon headed upstairs to take a shower. Minutes later, from his bedroom window, dripping and wrapped in a towel, he saw his sister and her two new best friends splashing about in the pool in the evening shadows. Already there was a star in the sky, but he could still make out Megan's skinny figure as she bounced high and did a flip off the diving board. Katy and Genevieve shrieked and clapped from the shallow end. Landon turned away from the window. It felt wrong to spy on them.

When he came back down in clean shorts and a T-shirt, his father was busy in the dusky shadows of the living room, writing feverishly at his desk. Landon wandered over and stood until his father looked up.

"Where's Mom?" Landon asked.

"Oh." His father scratched his neck. "This is a big job she's got now, Landon. Really big. So it's hard for her not to work, even on a Saturday. I think it'll be a while before she gets settled into more regular hours."

"Like days?" Landon asked.

"Maybe weeks. Maybe months." His father glanced at the glowing computer screen, the bluish light spilling over his face. "I'm not sure, really, but my book is coming along well. I'm calling it *Dragon Hunt.* Um . . . my main character is kind of modeled after you."

"Me?" Landon looked suspiciously at the screen. "Why?"

"Well, a good main character has to overcome obstacles, and you want him to be a nice person, and that sounds like you to me." Landon's father smiled and pointed at him before glancing toward the screen. "I thought I'd maybe name him 'Landon' too."

Landon felt a chill. If his father *did* ever get his book published, the last thing Landon needed was another thing people could make fun of—Landon, the oversized guard of Dorchester. "No, that's okay. I don't think so."

"What do you mean?" Landon's dad laughed and offered a puzzled smile. "Why wouldn't you want a character named after you?"

"I just . . . I don't know, Dad. Do I have to have a reason?" Landon backed away toward the kitchen. "Can I get something to eat?"

"Sure, there's plenty of casserole left." His father looked at him but remained seated in front of the computer. "Or you could make yourself a cheese sandwich. There are tomatoes in the crisper."

The thought of the casserole he'd spilled onto the football field the day before turned his empty stomach. "I'll make a sandwich."

Landon had everything out and had just finished construction of his sandwich, with thick wedges of cheddar and juicy, ripe tomato slices on fresh-cut Italian bread, when his father wandered into the kitchen. "What about the name Nodnal?"

"Nodnal?" Landon stopped with the sandwich halfway to his mouth. "Is that even a name?"

"Well, we're talking about the Middle Ages, so . . ." His father's face went from thoughtful to happy. "It's 'Landon' spelled backward."

Landon set the cheese sandwich down in front of him on the kitchen table. "Dad, no. Please."

"Oh, okay. I'm just trying to be creative here."

Landon rolled his eyes and felt a tap on his shoulder. Genevieve and her friends had come in behind him.

"Creative about what?" Genevieve asked.

Landon glanced at Megan and blushed, horrified. "Nothing. Dad's just writing his new book."

"Hi, Landon." Megan stood wrapped in a towel, her long hair dark and damp, her pale blue eyes aglow.

Landon looked down at his sandwich before looking back at them with a wave. "Hi."

"Yeah, hi," said Katy, also waving, but all business.

"Do you guys want a sandwich?" he asked, unable to think of anything else. He pointed at the supplies on the table.

Katy laughed, but Megan shook her head and said, "No, thanks."

"C'mon guys." Genevieve headed for her room.

"How was football, Landon?" Megan hung back and looked at him like she really cared. "What position are you gonna play?"

Landon thought of Mike Furster's words, "Left out."

He cleared his throat. "I won a race yesterday."

"Really? Wow," Megan said. "That's great."

"Yeah, then I, like, collapsed and Skip helped me up."

Megan pinched her lips together but couldn't hold back a smile. "Good. I'm glad he did. I told him we were friends. He already texted Genevieve that he was sorry for what happened at the diner."

"He did?"

"She didn't tell you?" Megan frowned. "I wonder why."

Landon just stared at Megan, unable to take his eyes off her face.

Finally, she shrugged and said, "Okay, well . . . gotta change."

Then she was gone. Landon hadn't even realized that his father had returned to his writing desk, but he found himself alone in the kitchen with his big, thick cheese sandwich. He picked up the sandwich and looked down. He poked at his bulging stomach and then got up and dumped his snack in the trash. It was only one sandwich, but it was a start.

He'd seen Coach Furster tell the team that's how he'd built his half-billion-dollar equity fund—one investor at a time, one deal at a time. He told them one mile at a time was how he qualified for the Ironman in Hawaii. Coach Furster then said you built a champion the same way, one practice at a time. And that's what Landon intended to be.

A champion.

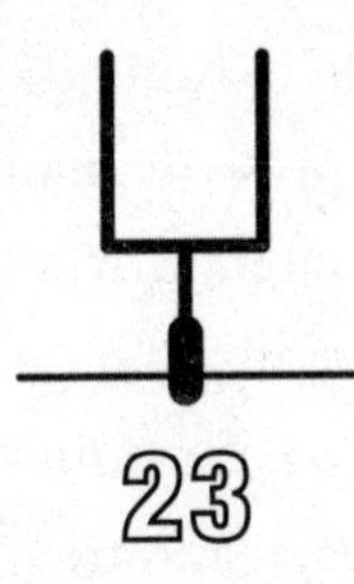

23

Sunday was a day off from football, but Landon's mom had plenty for them all to do around the house.

"Okay, guys. We've got to get settled in for real," she said.

Evidently that meant a lot of cleaning and moving and straightening and throwing things away followed by a mess of yard work that continued for Landon into Monday afternoon. By the time football practice came around that evening, Landon was already exhausted, but he was determined to get more involved. This time, after stretching and agilities and bag work, he got in the back of the line for blocking drills. Watching carefully and visualizing himself doing exactly what Brett Bell did, Landon heard a whistle blast signaling his turn before he knew it. He stepped up, got in his three-point stance, faintly heard the cadence barked out by Coach Furster, and fired into the bag.

It felt more like shoving someone in the aisle of a crowded bus than the blocking he'd seen the others do, but Landon chugged his feet and the bag moved a bit before the blast of a whistle told him to stop. He dashed back to the end of the line, out of breath and beaming to himself. Everything went on as it had before. He hadn't impressed anyone, but he hadn't made a laughingstock of himself either. It was a victory.

Twice more he did the blocking drill on a bag held up by Coach West, and then it was time for the sled.

Landon fretted to himself and tried to get in one of the lines on the inside of the sled, but when he stepped up at the center position, Coach Furster stopped everything.

"Landon! Landon?"

"Yes, Coach?"

"You're a Double X player. You play right tackle on offense, left end on defense, son. You're not a center. Travis is a center. Jones is a center. Not you."

Landon nodded and followed the direction of Coach Furster's finger. Timmy, wearing an impish grin, stepped back to allow Landon a turn.

Landon got in place and hunkered down into his stance, knowing all eyes were on him. On the count, he fired out into the sled. The rigid pad was on a spring-loaded arm, and it bounced him right back. The other linemen were already moving the sled. Landon panicked and hugged the dummy, leaning and pushing, determined not to let it spin on him. With a great roar, he got his end of the sled going. He knew he looked like a dancing bear and his technique wasn't close to the other guys, but the sled didn't spin, even though it wasn't exactly straight.

Finally the whistle blew, and he realized Coach Furster had paused to stare at him.

"Well, that's one way to do it." Coach Furster shook his head and then got back to business. "Okay! Let's go! This isn't a puppet show! Get me that next group up here!"

The next two times on the sled, Landon took his turn and did his thing without comment or reaction from Coach Furster. When it came time to work on plays, Landon took a deep breath and jogged into the huddle with a handful of reserve players, who were a mixture of third- and fourth-stringers, when he felt a tap on his shoulder.

It was Coach Furster. "Let's get a little better at the individual stuff before you jump into running plays, okay, Landon? Just so you don't mess up the timing."

Landon nodded. Happy to be talked to, happy to obey the orders of his coach, he stepped to the back to watch until it came time for sprints.

Sprints went a bit better for him. He beat Timmy for the first seven and then dropped behind before he got a second wind. Landon finished the final sprint second to last and joined the team that was already gathered around a glowering Coach Furster.

"Everything changes tomorrow night," Coach Furster snarled at them, looking all around. "Tomorrow night, it's live. The pads go on and you better remember that football is not a contact sport. Football is a *collision* sport, so you better be ready to *hit*."

The team roared its approval, and even Landon found himself growling, excited for tomorrow.

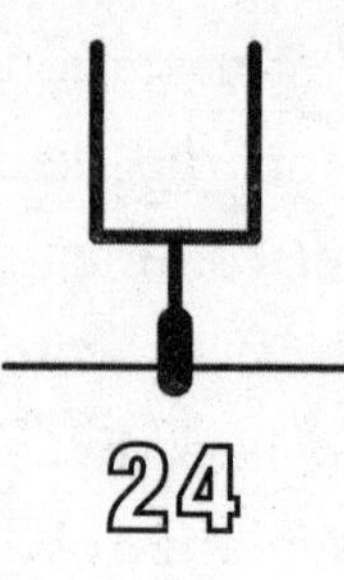

24

The next afternoon Landon attacked the bag of equipment the league had given to all the players. He pulled it out onto the living room floor and began stuffing his pants and the girdle with pads. It was like a puzzle, figuring out which pad went in which pocket and then getting into everything, since the uniform also included rib pads, shoulder pads, elbow pads, and hand pads for the hogs.

"I think the rib pads are supposed to go on first." Genevieve was paying more attention to her phone than him, but after struggling a bit, Landon knew she was right.

Landon figured it all out with Genevieve looking on while their dad flooded the house with the smell of roasting lamb chops and sautéed spinach. He was boiling potatoes that he'd mash to become delicious volcanoes filled with meat gravy.

Genevieve stuck out her tongue, tilted her head, and snapped a selfie with Landon in the background.

"Don't post that!" Landon scolded her.

"Why?" she said. "You look cute."

"I'm not supposed to be *cute*, Genevieve. It's *football*." Landon gritted his teeth.

Genevieve laughed and put her phone down. "Okay, already. Grumpy."

In truth, Landon wasn't grumpy. He was excited because if what the coaches and players had been saying for the last few days was true, then today everything changed. When the pads went on, the real players were supposed to rise to the top like cream.

"Football is not a contact sport. Football is a collision *sport, so you better be ready to* hit."

Landon heard the coach's words in his mind on a closed loop as he stood in front of the full-length hallway mirror, dressed in full uniform, with Genevieve beside him. He bent down in a sort of frog-like, upright three-point stance so she could reach him but he could still see her face. "Go ahead. Hit my shoulders."

Genevieve slapped the pad on his right shoulder.

"Ha-ha. Harder than that," he said.

She made a fist and bopped him.

"Harder!" Landon was feeling bold and unbreakable. "Seriously, hit me with everything you've got."

Genevieve tightened her lips, reared back with a fist, and slammed his shoulder.

POP.

Landon smiled wide. "This is so cool. I can't even *feel* that."

With the pads and helmet and his huge size, Landon felt certain that everything—not just with the football team, but his whole life—was about to change.

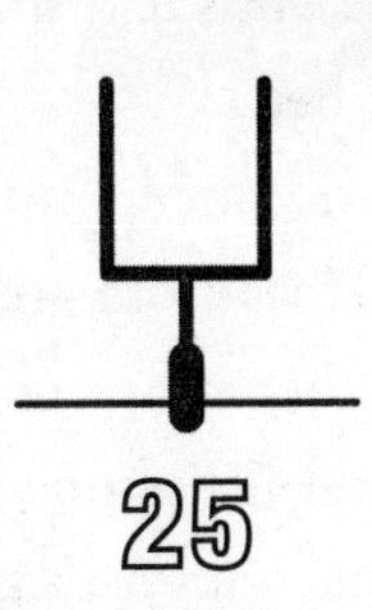

25

Sunshine had grilled the grass, trees, rooftops, and pavement all day long. Even fresh from its shaded harbor in the garage, the Prius felt like a sauna. Landon's palms and feet burst into sweat, and a bead of it scampered down his cheek like a roach. He swiped at it with a padded hand and glanced at his father, hunched over the wheel like a big kid on his little brother's tricycle.

As his father pulled into the school parking lot that overlooked the football field, he glanced Landon's way. "You'll be okay. Your whole team is nervous, I'm sure."

They pulled up to the end of the lot, and Landon craned his neck to look down on the field. Only a handful of guys were there, including Coach Bell and Brett. Skip was rifling footballs to Xander and Mike.

"Skip Dreyfus isn't nervous," Landon declared. "Neither is Brett Bell."

"Well, they're the best two players on the team, and Brett's uncle plays for the *Giants*." His dad stopped the car. "Everyone else is sweating bullets, I bet."

Landon wasn't so sure, but he opened the door and said good-bye to his father. Heat from the parking lot swallowed him, and he wondered if there was a chance that practice might be canceled. He'd seen on his phone app that the heat index was up over ninety. People with asthma were being advised to stay indoors, but Landon didn't have asthma. He took several deep breaths, almost eager for a sudden attack of that ailment, but the air swept in and out of his lungs, filling his nose with the harsh scent of bubbling tar and plastic football pads.

The grass crackled beneath his feet and he could smell the cooked dirt as he slogged down the hillside. Timmy Nichols appeared and went straight for the sled. Landon was sweating from every available pore by the time he reached the sideline, but when he looked around he saw the rest of the team—which was arriving quickly now—frolicking like they were at a pool party. Could such a disregard of the elements be part of this football mania? From his living room couch, he'd never considered the Cleveland Browns baking like potatoes when they had to play down in Houston or Jacksonville early in the season.

Someone smacked his shoulder pad and he turned, smelling the cologne at the same time so that he wasn't surprised to see Coach Furster's black eyes and white smile. "Landon? You've got your pads on."

"I'm supposed to have 'em on, right, Coach?" Panic flashed across Landon's brain like the shadow of a hawk.

"Oh, sure. You'll look good gettin' off the bus. Scare the heck out of Tuckahoe when they see you. Ha-ha. You'll be like our El Cid." Coach chucked Landon's shoulder pad again.

"What do you mean?" Landon shifted the shoulder pads, which now felt too tight.

"El Cid? Famous Spanish knight." Coach Furster's eyes grew close enough to make Landon uncomfortable. "Just the sight of him terrified the enemy. Made them turn and run."

Coach Furster grinned like he owned the memory. "When he died, they sewed open his eyes and let his horse carry him into battle. The enemy fled. He couldn't fight a lick—being dead and all—but he scared the heck out of people."

"Oh." Landon had no idea what else to say.

"Yup. El Cid." Coach Furster shucked a piece of gum, gobbled it up, and marched away, trailing an invisible cloud of citrus cologne toward his son, Mike, and Skip. "Ready to hit, boys?"

The football equipment made Landon feel like he was wrapped in bubble paper. There was comfort in the protection it would provide, but it made him feel even more awkward than normal. He wished he'd had time to practice wearing it, like he'd done with the helmet. Most of the other players had been wearing football pads since they were eight or nine, so for them it was almost second nature. Twice he tripped and fell during agility drills, but no one stopped to laugh. Such was the intensity of the boys around him. Everyone seemed to be in a trance, moving with quick concentration. They alternated between high-knee running, darting around cones placed a few feet apart, and jumping around the rungs of rope ladders stretched out on the practice field. It was organized chaos that almost everyone but Landon and Timmy seemed to ace.

When the last agility drill was complete, Coach Furster gave his whistle three blasts and they all crowded around him. Landon glanced at his teammates' faces, wondering if anyone else's stomach was twisting under the sour smell of their coach's cologne.

"All right." Coach Furster crossed his arms. His Chinese calligraphy tattoo bulged. He stared all around. "You all know what comes now. Tackling drills. Live!"

Everyone let out a roar. Landon joined in.

"Two lines!" Coach Furster broke free and sprinted toward the end zone, where Coach Bell and Coach West had created a narrow column of grass bordered by tipped-over blocking dummies. The team split like geese in a November sky, some breaking to one end of the bags, some breaking the other way, without rhyme or reason. Landon found himself in the line of tacklers in back of Timmy, a loose string of players in the end zone. The runners were at the other end of the dummies, on the ten-yard line. The grass stretched between them was their battlefield.

The first tackler was Skip. The first runner was Brett Bell, looking like a rhinoceros with a football.

Coach Furster howled, "Here we go, boys!"

Then he blasted his whistle. Brett and Skip went at each other like locomotives racing toward a collision on the same track. The crack of pads was thrilling. When they collided, the smaller player, Skip, was able to stop Brett in his tracks, standing him upright with the ball cradled in his arms. Nonetheless, Brett's churning legs carried Skip backward two yards before they went down in a heap.

Both players bounced up unscathed, screaming with excitement, and slapping each other's shoulder pads and helmets with respect.

"Good hit! Good hit!" Coach Furster bellowed as they swapped lines. "Next two!"

Miller, playing defense, and Rinehart, as the runner, fired off like mortal enemies, blasting each other with all the bone-crunching intensity of Brett and Skip. Miller dropped Rinehart like a bag of groceries before they popped up too, howling at the white-hot sun like it was a new moon before they swapped lines, Miller heading to the end of the runner's line while Rinehart fell in the tackler's line behind Landon and Brett.

Players cheered. The coaches laughed and yelled, "Next up!"

And so it went, with Landon's line melting away in front of him. Counting bodies in the opposite line, he saw that his line had an odd number, which would leave him matched up with Skip.

Landon's stomach flipped at the sight of their starting quarterback. His mouth got sticky and then went desert dry. He had no idea what to do, really. He'd seen NFL highlights of the Browns' middle linebacker, Karlos Dansby, on YouTube. He saw right in front of him how his teammates did it—the tacklers lowering their shoulders into the runners' midriffs, exploding, wrapping them up with their arms, and then driving them back if possible. But he didn't see how he could even hope to complete the first step, let alone the last three.

Timmy Nichols was up, and he was blasted apart by the runner like a puff of smoke in a stiff breeze. Nichols rolled over and hopped up, though, jogging to join the runners. When Landon stepped to the goal line, Skip accepted the football from Coach Bell, snorting like a maniac. His feet pawed the earth like a bloodthirsty bull's.

He crouched into a stance and leveled his eyes at Landon, who stood stiff as a tree trunk.

Every fiber in Landon's body begged him to just run far away.

And then the whistle shrieked.

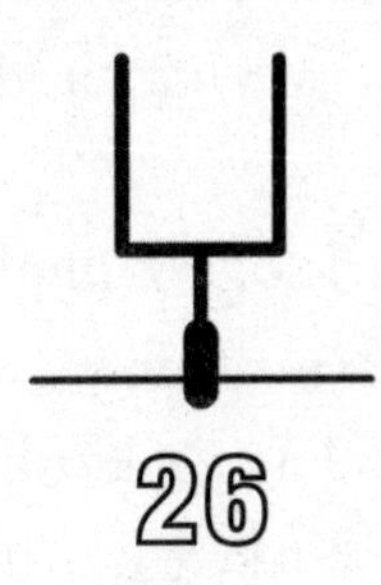

26

Skip paused and stood up.

"Coach?" Skip's killer expression faded and he angled his head at Landon.

Bent over with his hands on his knees to watch the action, Coach Furster looked like a man awakened from a pleasant dream. His mouth tilted open in confusion, and it looked like the whistle might slip loose from his lips as he considered Landon. "Yeah. No."

Coach Furster looked around for someone else, his lips dragged down by a frown and the whistle dropping to the end of the lanyard around his neck before he pointed to the back of Skip's line. "Nichols! You're the runner!"

"Coach?" Landon said. "What's wrong?

Coach Furster ignored him as Nichols looked confused and said, "Huh?"

"Nichols! You jump to the front of the line. Now!"

Nichols shrugged, waddled up to the front of the line, and accepted the football from Skip. Before Landon could think, Nichols crouched in a much less ferocious manner than Skip, Coach Furster blasted his whistle, and Nichols barreled right toward Landon.

Landon's feet did a little dance in place. He took half a step forward and opened his arms before Nichols punched a shoulder pad into his midriff. The air left his body in a great gust. He staggered sideways, shocked by the impact, but aware of Nichols slipping past him. Landon couldn't let that happen. He grabbed for anything to hold. His hands locked onto Nichols's jersey. Like a great felled tree, Landon tipped and went down, dragging Nichols with him.

Nichols collapsed without a fight in the end zone. Landon lay on the grass, looking up at the blazing hot sun. A beam of light cut through the cage of his face mask like a gleaming sword. Coach Furster appeared standing over him in a nauseating funk of cologne and baked dirt.

"Okay, Landon." Coach Furster seemed like he was talking to a kindergartner. "You did it. You got him down. Your first tackle."

Coach Furster turned away, his face cast into darkness by the shadow of the sun, and returned to normal. "Next! Let's go, ladies! This isn't a fashion show! This isn't a candy store!"

Landon scrabbled to his feet and Nichols bumped him with a shoulder that seemed intentional before Landon jogged to the end of the line of runners. No one looked at him. No one celebrated his tackle, and as he watched the backs of his teammates' helmets queuing up in front of him, he realized it wasn't much of a tackle, if it was a tackle at all, because Nichols had made it into the end zone.

Landon stood still at the back of the line, his teammates jumping in front of him without so much as a glance. He was frozen with disappointment. The glorious tackles he had imagined himself making, blowing people up like Karlos Danby did, now seemed utterly impossible. He had barely brought down Timmy. What would Guerrero do to him? Or Brett Bell? It wasn't fear that froze him, but bewilderment. He felt like he was suddenly walking on the moon without gravity.

Because he stood still, people moved in front of him to get their turn to run the ball. Soon a pattern was established, and although no one said anything to him, he found himself standing at the end of the line and watching the tackling drill, big and hot and sweaty and forlorn.

It made him sick to just stand there, but the idea of taking the ball and having someone blast into him full speed suddenly seemed ridiculous. He'd never be a running back anyway. He was too timid to cross the open grass and go back to the line of tacklers in the end zone, so he stood there, and no one said a word, including the coaches. They must have been thinking the same thing he was thinking. Everyone on the same page. A-okay.

Landon grew slowly more comfortable, and he began to entertain the idea that when they got to the blocking drills, that's where he'd prove himself. That's where he belonged.

"I'm a hog," he whispered to himself, and straightened his spine. "Hogs are made for blocking."

Everything seemed just fine, until Coach West looked around as if he'd dropped his keys. When he spotted what he was looking for, it was halfway across the field. Coach West pointed to the water bottle carrier and looked toward Landon from behind a pair of mirrored aviator sunglasses. "Hey, Dorch! Don't just stand there. Make yourself useful and go get me that water, will you?"

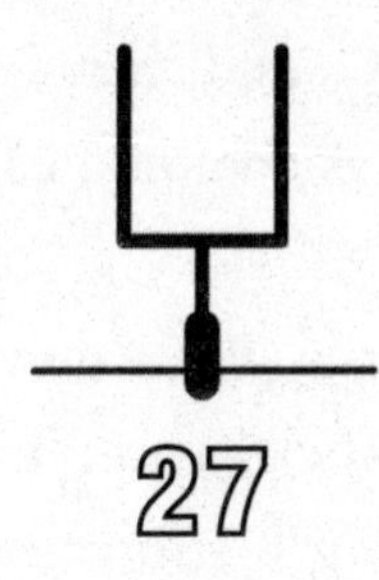

27

Coach Bell stepped up beside Coach West, and Landon could tell by the expression on his face that he understood the situation instantly. Even though Coach Bell coached the skill players, he was an old hog himself, an All-American, so he'd instinctively understand the value of a big guy like Landon. He'd know that Landon wasn't just some water boy, and Coach Bell was the gentlest coach they had. He spoke so softly Landon barely made out what he was saying, but when he did, he saw nothing but words of praise and encouragement. He saw smiles of appreciation and concern. So when Coach Bell opened his mouth to speak, Landon was filled with hope.

"Get the other one too, will you, Landon?" Coach Bell pointed a sausage finger beyond the first water bottle carrier to a second resting alone on the bench. "Please."

When Landon saw the word "please" coming from the kind

face of Coach Bell, a man whose own brother-in-law was an NFL player, he went into action without thinking. He knew about manners and he knew about the order of things: obeying parents and teachers and coaches. He jogged toward the bench, got the water there, and then scooped up the carrier in the grass, trying to look as cool and casual as one could when retrieving water.

Before he could set the water down, he was swarmed by teammates like bees on sticky fruit. They grabbed at the bottles, their sweat sprinkling his forearms, and sucked greedily at their contents. Then they replaced the bottles back in the carriers. Landon set one carrier down and went to work with the second, passing out water.

"Thanks, Landon."

"Thanks."

"Yeah, thanks."

His teammates' words showered down all around him, cooling the boil in his brain in a way he hadn't thought possible. He remembered his mom's words, about being part of a team without actually playing and how the manager was an important role.

"My pleasure," he said. "Sure, Skip."

"Here you go Brett, here's one."

"I'll take that."

"Yup, right here."

He remembered the peanut seller at an Indians baseball game his father had taken him to in Cleveland, the vendor's hands working like an octopus, slinging bags and accepting money in an economy of motion—a circus juggler of sorts.

Finally, Coach Furster blew his whistle three times and shouted, "Hogs with me and Coach West! Skill guys with Coach Bell! On the hop!"

As everyone scattered, Coach Furster stepped up to Landon and nodded at the carrier. Landon hesitated before he understood and handed a bottle to Coach Furster. Coach held the bottle up high and squirted a sparkling silver stream into his mouth, his Adam's apple bobbing like a cork, before he lowered it, smacked and wiped his lips, and released a sigh of pure pleasure.

"Good." He handed the bottle back to Landon. "You know, you don't *have* to help out with the water, Landon."

Landon studied Coach Furster's sweat-drenched face and knew with the confidence of someone who read faces every hour of every day that what Coach really meant was the exact opposite of what he said. Helping with the water was *exactly* what Coach Furster wanted him to do. For a brief moment Landon doubted himself. Maybe that wasn't his coach's intention. Maybe it was just mixed signals . . . but then he figured the coach knew exactly what he was doing.

"I can help out." The words escaped him like doves from a magician's sleeve.

Coach Furster put on a full display of porcelain-white teeth. "Nice, Landon. That's real nice."

And just like that, Landon Dorch got the starting job at a position he'd sworn he'd never play.

Left out.

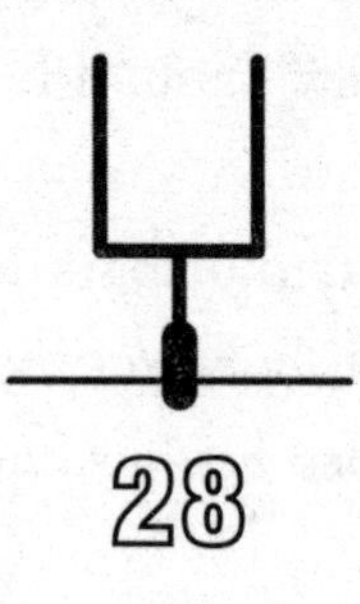

28

At home, Landon showered and changed into his pajamas.

He peeked down through the stair railing at his father, a hulking form aglow in the blue light of the computer, fingers skipping across the keyboard.

All was well, so he retreated to his room. He sighed and flipped open the hardback copy of *The Three Musketeers* his father had found for him at a garage sale in Cleveland. The scratch of his fingers on the pages made no sound. He'd removed his ears when he got back from practice and put them in their dryer case. But even in the total silence, he had a memory of the sound of turning pages, dull and faint, and he flipped through several random pages to feel their snap before settling back into the pillows to read.

In his own mind, Landon was, of course, d'Artagnan, the outsider who must prove his worth as a musketeer. As he read, a part of his mind danced with the idea that d'Artagnan had to serve the musketeers before he could become one. Hadn't d'Artagnan been left out too before becoming the most famous musketeer of all? Landon pursed his lips and set the book in his lap, nodding to himself before he continued. Halfway through the next chapter, when d'Artagnan was about to fight a duel, the overhead light in Landon's bedroom flickered.

He looked up, expecting his mother. She'd yet to return from her office and it was already past nine. Instead, Genevieve gave him a wave and sat on the edge of his bed. She pointed to his ears in their drier on the nightstand and then motioned for him to put them on.

He huffed and mouthed a word he could only sense through the movement of his lips. "Really?"

She nodded yes and motioned again.

Landon sighed, set down his book, and put on his ears. Genevieve waited patiently and didn't speak until he had them on and asked her, "What?"

She gripped his leg through the covers and leaned toward him. "I don't want you to quit."

Landon jerked his head back and lowered his chin. "You mean football? Who said I quit? I didn't quit."

Genevieve held up her iPhone as evidence. "Megan said you did one tackling drill and carried the water bottles around for the rest of practice. Landon, you can't quit. I know you can do this!"

Landon stuttered, the words piling up in his mind, unable to get them out through his mouth fast enough to explain everything. It wasn't as easy as it looked. A manager was a valuable part of a team. Coach Furster *wanted* him to do it. He'd felt joy hearing and seeing people *thank* him. And d'Artagnan! D'Artagnan had served the other musketeers before he could become one.

It all got garbled.

Genevieve scowled and shook her head, showing him her phone. "Look, Skip texted Megan that you're a big powder puff. I want you to *smash* that jerk, and I know you *can*."

Landon looked at the whole text. "Yeah, but see? He says, 'Landon is a great kid.' He says that first, before anything about being a powder puff, so . . ." He looked at her weakly. "Skip's my friend."

Genevieve grabbed the front of Landon's pajamas and yanked him close. Her creamy face was blotched with red and her eyes burned like gas flames. "He's not your *friend*, Landon."

"He's not mean," Landon shot back.

"That's not a *friend.* A friend isn't someone who's just *not mean*. A friend is someone who's *nice. 'Hey, Landon. How you doing, Landon? Come hang out with us, Landon.'* When are you gonna get that?"

She released him, jumped up, and paced the floor. "You are not a powder puff. I know you're not. Now you have to show people you're not. Landon, you're a *giant* and you're strong."

Genevieve stood in the middle of his room, hunched over, and smacked a fist into her open hand. "You have to smash them and *smash* them, over and over, until they *respect* you!"

Landon's head got warm and his stomach complained. He reached for his ears before Genevieve saw him and shrieked, "*Don't* you unplug! You *listen* to me!"

She threw her eyes and her hands toward the ceiling and started to move around the room like a wild thing in a cage. Then she turned on him, glaring. "If I could be you for a *week*, for a *day*, for an *hour*! I'd *crush* them! If I had what you have they'd *run* from me! They'd *whimper*! They'd hide."

He thought she was going to come at him again, but she stopped at the edge of his bed, her face mottled and contorted with pain. Tears coursed down her cheeks, glittering in the yellow light that seeped through the shade from his nightstand lamp. They dropped onto his blanket, and he knew that if he weren't deaf, they would make a sound he could hear.

And then Genevieve held up something from when they were little.

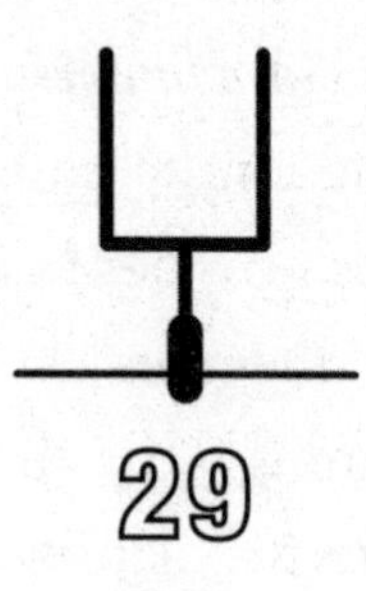

From her shorts pocket, Genevieve removed a gold medallion strung from a red, white, and blue ribbon. She sniffed and let the medal dangle from the ribbon so that it wobbled back and forth, and even in the yellow light of his reading lamp, it flashed brightly. "Remember this?"

Landon turned his head away. "Yeah. I remember."

She tapped his arm. "Here, I want you to have this, Landon."

"Why would I want your gold medal for gymnastics?" he said.

"Oh, come on. You were obsessed with this thing when I first won it." She dangled it in front of his face.

"I was like nine years old, Genevieve."

"I know, but it's special. It means something."

"To *you*." Landon tried to sound grouchy.

"And you," she said. "Remember how hard you rooted for

me to get this medal? People all around were pointing at you. You were losing your mind, you cheered so loud."

Landon felt his face overheating.

"But see, football can be your thing, Landon. You can win a prize that matters. You could get a college scholarship. Who knows? Maybe the NFL one day."

Landon shook his head.

"I'm serious, Landon. You've got a gift. People don't see it, but you have it. I know you do."

Now Landon felt like crying. He reached over and pulled his little sister into him. "I love you, Genevieve."

She laughed and squeezed even harder before stepping back. "So, you'll take it?"

Landon lowered his head and she draped the medal around his neck. "I'm the luckiest sister in the world to have a big brother like you. You have to believe in yourself, Landon. If you don't, no one else but me will believe in you."

"I'll try, Genevieve. I really will." It was all he could say.

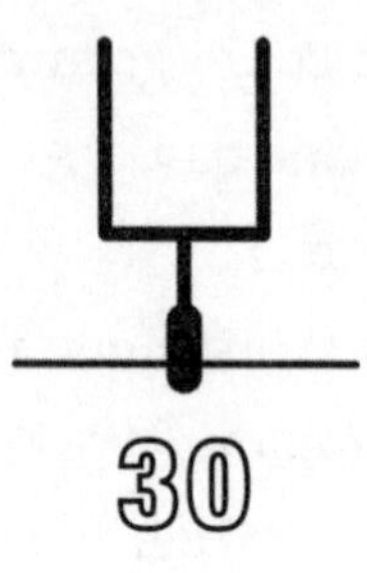

30

Landon intended to try, but helping others came so naturally to him that he couldn't help himself the next evening at practice.

He dropped a water carrier off with the skill players and then jogged over to where the hogs were stretching out in two lines facing each other across the goal line. He took up his spot out of the way in the back of the end zone. Timmy broke loose, grabbed a water bottle from Landon, gulped down a heavy stream, and then put it back without acknowledging Landon in any way. The other linemen were paired off now, two by two, so Timmy took up his spot as a third wheel along with Brett and one of the bigger linemen on the near end of the line for the "fit" drill. The drill was slow and mechanical: each hog simply stepped out of his stance, took one short power step, then a second step, and then "fit" their hands and forehead beneath the armpits and chin of the player opposite them. Coach Furster said it was the ABCs of line play.

"Right guard, left tackle, center; I don't care what position you're at," Coach would say. "Every successful play for a hog starts with a perfect 'fit.'"

Landon felt suddenly like the doors of a bus that was supposed to take him on an excellent journey were rumbling shut. He heard Genevieve's voice insisting that he had to believe in himself. He panicked and dropped the water carrier, his brain hot again because he couldn't miss this chance, not now, not with the pads on. He stepped into the fit drill across from Timmy, capping off the drill with perfectly even numbers.

Just because he was helping the coaches didn't mean he had to be left out. Why couldn't he help the team one way during some drills—as a manager—and yet in another way—as a player—during others? Even in the games, he could help with water or keeping stats when his team was on defense (if he couldn't do a simple tackling drill, he couldn't be expected to play defense) but then switch to a full-fledged hog when his team was on offense, out there rutting around in the dirt, pushing players around like a big bulldozer. It was like his father changing the plot seven hundred pages into a book. Just because other people didn't do something, or even because something had never been done before, didn't mean there was automatically a rule against it. Landon could skip the defensive drills but participate in the offensive blocking drills.

Timmy didn't seem to think so, though.

"Down!" Coach Furster barked. Timmy just stood.

"Get down." Landon tried to infuse his voice with urgency. "Your side is on offense."

Timmy shook his head while everyone else on his side of the line got into a three-point stance.

"One . . ." Everyone on Timmy's side took a power step on Coach Furster's cue.

"Come on, Timmy!" Landon patted his chest where Timmy should be getting ready to deliver a blow with both hands.

Timmy shook his head.

"Two . . ." Everyone took his second step.

"Fit!" Pads popped in unison. Landon patted his chest, desperately wanting to blend in smoothly.

"Get that fit lower, Torin. Come on, hands *inside*. Miller, that's it!" Coach Furster was working his way down the line, adjusting players who needed it, praising those who had the correct position.

Landon saw Brett in a perfect fit position, his eye cranked over to one side, watching Landon through his face mask.

"Perfect, Bell!" Coach Furster was so intent on his work that he came upon an upright Timmy in complete surprise. "Nichols! This isn't a candy—"

Nichols just shook his head and pointed at Landon, who stood shifting from foot to foot and tugging at the shoulder pad strap beneath his arm.

"I got it, Coach." Brett grabbed Nichols by the collar and slung him aside before shoving him into the exact place he himself had vacated. "I'll pair up with Landon."

"You'll . . ." Coach Furster's tongue jammed up behind his lower lip, giving him a crazy look. "Okay, Bell. Good. Nichols, you happy now? Would you like a written invitation next time?"

Timmy wasn't fazed by Coach Furster's gruff treatment, and he seemed perfectly content to be yelled at so long as he wasn't paired up with Landon in the drill.

"Okay, switch sides!" Coach Furster barked.

"Come on, Landon." Brett chucked him on the shoulder. "You can do this. Just stay low."

"DOWN!" Coach Furster hollered, and Landon dropped down into a three-point stance, palm flat.

"Set . . . ," the coach screamed, "one . . . two . . . fit!"

Landon took two awkward steps, stood up, grabbed the jersey beneath Brett's armpits, and banged face masks. Landon knew it wasn't right, but Coach Furster said nothing. He stepped past Landon and Brett. "Nichols! Get your arms *inside*, Nichols. Inside! I can't do it for you, son."

And on the coach went down the line.

Landon felt a tap and he looked at Brett.

"I said, look, would you?" Brett said irritably.

"Sorry," Landon said. "I didn't see you."

"Yeah, well, listen, will you? Here's how you get into a stance." Brett got down and extended his fingers like the legs of a table, before putting them into the grass. While he was down there, Landon heard him saying something, but the words weren't clear.

Landon shook his head and tapped Brett's helmet. When Brett looked up, Landon said, "I can understand better if I *see* what you say. I hear and see together."

Brett gave him a strange look, but shook his head and said, "You don't want to have your hand flat down in the grass. Use your fingers. Make them stiff or you'll be too low and you can't fire out. That's why you popped up like toast."

The face mask made lipreading harder, but Landon could do it.

"Okay. Okay." Landon nodded furiously, eager to please and flooded with gratefulness. He got down in his stance, using his fingertips to support his weight, even though it felt extremely awkward. He heard Bell speaking again and popped up to see what he was saying.

"What?"

Bell shook his head, frustrated. "Just stay low. Keep your helmet below mine. Here, it's my turn. Watch what I do and do that."

Landon nodded, and Brett got down and executed the fit drill on Coach Furster's orders. The coach came down the line. "Good. Good. Head up. Good. Better. Head up, Nichols! Bell, perfect. Okay, last time, then we go live!"

Landon would have one chance only to get it right. He got down in his stance, but he couldn't see Brett in front of him, so he sank his butt, angling his torso more upright. His fingers were in the right position, but on the count he stepped forward, got too high, tripped, and belly-bumped into Brett, grabbing for his jersey. Landon ended up in a position that wouldn't be good for much of anything besides dancing.

Coach Furster blinked and then moved on without a word.

Landon watched him go and then felt a tap on his shoulder.

"It's okay, Landon." Brett reached into his face mask and

wiped some sweat from his eyes. "You'll get it. It takes time, is all."

Landon wanted to hug the kid.

Coach Furster got to the other end of the two lines and gave his whistle a sharp little blast. "Okay, ladies, like I said . . . now it is *live*! So you better be ready!"

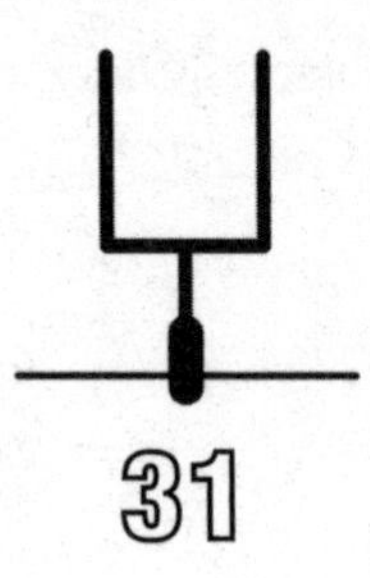

31

"Offense on my side!" Coach Furster was marching up and down behind the boys facing Landon's way like they were troops he was sending into war. "Defense on that side. Offense, you drive block their butts into tomorrow. Defensive guys, you hold your ground and shed them like a disease. Get them off you! Okay, everyone together now, and I want to see some vicious, violent hitting! Down! Set!"

Landon got in a three-point stance. Brett was hunkered down in front of him, legs quivering, face twisted with a rage Landon just didn't get.

Coach Furster gave his whistle a blast.

Landon came out of his stance in a slow rise and got a mouthful of helmet. Brett's two hands gripped the flesh in the crease of his armpits like giant crab pincers. Landon yelped. He was being lifted and driven back at the same time. His feet tangled together, and he crashed flat on his back with Brett coming down full force, pounding out whatever air remained in his lungs.

Landon choked, gagging for air. His hands and feet waddled in space, as if they could somehow suck oxygen back into his body. This was not fun. No way. No how. "Vicious and violent hitting" took on a whole new meaning when you were on the receiving end of things, and Landon was beginning to have serious doubts about his love affair with football.

The big lineman was climbing up off him, and he wasn't being gentle. Brett put a hand in the middle of Landon's soft stomach to steady himself, and he barked Landon's shin with one of his cleats as he got to his feet. Landon looked up in astonishment, expecting a sympathetic expression from the boy who'd just been so kind to him.

Instead, he saw teeth buried deep into a rubber mouthpiece and cold, cruel eyes.

Landon waited for a hand to help him up or a friendly smile, but Brett only turned and walked away.

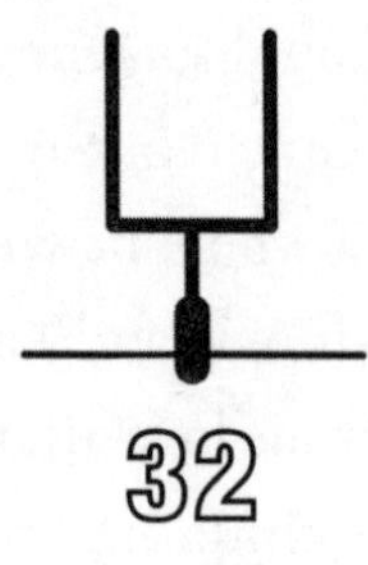

32

That was enough for Landon.

Despite what mean kids sometimes said about him, despite what he may have sounded like because of what people called "slightly garbled" speech, Landon was no dummy. He kept his helmet on, and sweat trickled down his forehead as he did his job as manager. He kept the water bottles handy for anyone who needed one, and he tried to avoid Brett Bell. No one said anything, but he sensed that everyone approved. Midway through practice, Coach West gave him a pat on the back and showed him how he could refill the bottles on a hot night from a cold tap jutting out of the bricks in the school's wall near the rear entrance.

Coach West screwed on the top of a bottle he had filled and then handed Landon an empty one and spoke slowly and loudly. "Okay, Landon. Do you want to try that?"

Landon gave him a funny look, but he nodded and refilled one of the other bottles before replacing it in the carrier.

"Good!" Coach West clapped his hands. "Good job."

"Coach, it's not that hard." Landon bent down and continued to fill the bottles.

Coach West stood watching. When Landon finished, Coach West waved both hands at Landon to get his attention, and he kept speaking in a slow and loud voice. "Landon, if you're going to be helping out like this, like kind of a manager—"

"Not the water boy," Landon interrupted.

"No, not at all. A manager for sure." Coach West seemed amused. "But if you're manager, you do not have to wear your helmet, Landon."

Landon shook his head. "Coach Furster said helmets stay on all practice."

Coach West looked even more amused. "Yes, but . . ."

Landon huffed and scooped up the water carriers. "Let's get back, Coach."

Coach West laughed. "Sure, Landon. That's great." Coach West put a hand on Landon's shoulder pad like some kind of guardian as they trudged back toward practice.

Landon wanted to shrug him off, but he also didn't want to be impolite.

When they got back into the thick of things, teammates came at Landon from all directions. As he worked like the peanut man in the Indians' stadium, his mind kept busy too. The bad thing was that he guessed he'd have to admit to Genevieve that he'd quit. The good news was that everyone seemed to like him as the manager.

It wasn't until the team was doing a drill called "Inside Run" that Landon felt a tap on his shoulder and turned to see Brett standing there. He had somehow snuck up on Landon.

"Hey," Brett said, and he seemed to be happy that Landon knew his role. He didn't look mad at all. He just accepted a bottle and squirted his mouth full of water, gulping it down without pause so that the stream sprayed his face when his mouth briefly closed. When he finished, the big lineman reached in through his face mask and wiped the water from his eyes.

"Thanks, Landon," Brett said, and then dove back into the drill, tapping out a boy who had temporarily replaced him, because that's how it worked for Brett Bell. He went where he wanted, when he wanted. He was the best lineman they had by far. It was almost like Brett and Skip could run the team on their own, without any coaches at all.

Landon ached to be like one of them. He assumed everyone did, but he wasn't even close. He watched Brett line up and destroy the guy in front of him, blasting that kid the way he'd done to Landon and turning away with the same coldhearted look in his eyes. Landon wished more than anything that he could be a star player, but he couldn't make up happy endings the way his father did. Landon was stuck with who he was, and now, *what* he was.

He tried to take comfort in the fact that he'd be the best manager ever. He'd wear his equipment, just like the rest of the team. He'd never take his helmet off, no matter how hot things got, because he was still part of the team, and Coach Furster said being a Bronxville football player wasn't for just anyone.

He'd be there for the guys when they needed him and he'd be part of a team.

He watched Timmy get flattened and felt giddy not to be in the drill. That made him sigh. If he was a powder puff because he didn't like getting pummeled, then he guessed he should be okay with that. It didn't make a lot of sense, really. Someone who enjoyed that—getting blasted around like a paper bag in a windstorm—*that* person would be the real dummy.

When practice was almost over and Coach Furster blew his whistle and told them all to line up for sprints, Landon hustled over to the bench, dumped his water bottle carriers, and stepped up with everyone else. He could do the running. It wasn't pleasant, but it didn't scare him. No one was going to knock his block off running sprints.

He felt a spark of pride as he took off on the first sprint. He'd be a part of the team in almost every way. It didn't matter to him whether he beat Timmy anymore. All Landon had to do was finish, not win. There was no fire in his gut. Timmy outran him in the last half of the sprints, and the team chanted *"Lan-don, Lan-don, Lan-don"* as he slogged through the hot air and over the finish line on the final sprint of the night.

Coach Furster was in a good mood and laughing to himself and he called them in. "All right guys, good work tonight. Good hitting. I saw some toughness from a lot of you."

Coach Furster's face suddenly clouded over. "You other guys? And you know who you are. You need to get it going. I don't want to embarrass anyone, but when you wonder what you should be doing and how you should be doing it, look at Bell and Dreyfus."

Coach pointed at his two top players. "You two guys are old-school, and I love it."

Landon looked from Coach Furster to the coach's son, Mike, and thought that having your dad praise others above you had to hurt. Mike's face went blank. Only his eyes seemed to boil, but Landon was pretty sure no one else noticed.

"All right, in on me!" Coach Furster shouted, holding his hand out for everyone to reach for and cover. "Hit, Hustle, Win. On three! One, two, three . . ."

Landon shouted with the rest of them, and the team broke apart and filtered toward the parking lot. Landon dragged his feet across the dry grass. He was exhausted from the running and in no hurry to get home and face Genevieve. He knew, despite the very good arguments he had perfected in his head over the last hour or so, that Genevieve was not going to be happy with him. That bothered him because he loved Genevieve with all his heart.

She felt the same way, and he knew it. He thought about the medal she'd given him and nearly choked. Disappointing her would be hard. Behind most of the other players, he marched uphill toward the parking lot, head pounding, hot and exhausted, feeling like his insides were swamp water. He didn't think he could feel any worse than he did at that moment, but unfortunately . . . he was wrong.

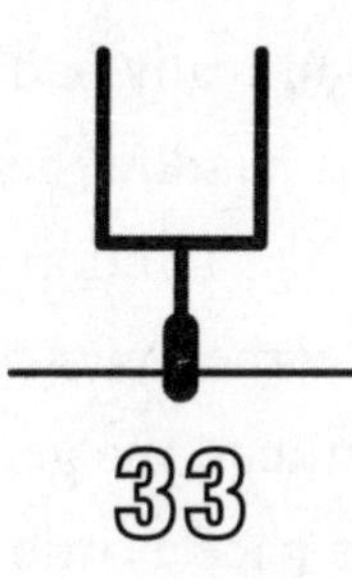

33

A woman with bleach-blond hair stood at the top of the hill. Her lips were pink and thick, reminding Landon of chewed bubble gum. Her eyes hid behind big dark sunglasses, and she was dressed like one of Genevieve's friends in a pale yellow dress dotted with little daisies, and sandals on her feet. When Xander reached her, she gave him a hug and pointed him to the car. Landon guessed she was his mom.

In one hand she held a large striped bag, like something for the beach. She was taking big blue envelopes the color of a robin's egg from the bag and handing them out to each player as he reached her. Landon slowed his pace even more to watch. Xander's mom's pink painted nails flashed along with a gleaming smile as she worked.

Landon moved close and focused hard to read her thick lips as Brett accepted one of the festive envelopes from her.

"We're doing laser tag for Xander's birthday, Saturday," she said. "I hope you can make it, Brett. Everyone's invited."

Landon gulped down his excitement. Laser tag was something he'd done with Scouts in Cleveland once. He was actually good at it because what you really had to do was *see* things well in the dark. The flit of a shadow here or there made all the difference, and it didn't take Landon long to learn that if you just hunkered down in a corner, you could pick people off with deadly certainty and dominate the game.

Landon picked up his pace a little because Timmy Nichols was getting his invitation and Landon didn't want Xander's mom to think Timmy was the last of the players. He took a quick glance over his shoulder and relaxed when he saw that Skip had stopped to help Mike and Coach Furster put the bags into the equipment shed. Landon was certain that Xander's mom would wait for Skip. Everyone wanted a piece of Skip.

Landon huffed and waddled and wished his padded pants weren't suddenly sagging and slowing him down. He reached back and tugged at the droopy girdle. As he crested the top of the hill, he seemed to make eye contact with Xander's mom. He couldn't be exactly sure because of her dark glasses. He was out of breath, but he wrestled his face into an enormous smile as she reached into her bag and pulled out another big, beautiful blue invitation. It was a prize worth having.

Landon was so close that Xander's mom had to be looking right at him. He grinned and he held out his hand. Then her smile suddenly dropped. She stepped aside and then actually walked down the hill to meet Skip and Mike halfway up.

Landon thought he could hear her chirping like a bird as she presented Skip his invitation.

Before Landon saw Skip take it, he turned toward his father's Prius. The heat squeezed him in its fist. Landon staggered a bit as he tried to hurry. When he reached the car he put his hand on the hot corner of the Prius's hood to keep himself from falling over. The metal burned his hand, but he couldn't think about that as he bent over and puked up the swamp water.

His father was suddenly there, tapping his shoulder and bending over in concern until his face filled the space outside Landon's puke-stained metal cage. "Hey, hey, big guy. You okay? I saw that running. Man, it's not easy being a football player, is it? And I used to gripe when I had to carry the *tuba*."

Landon stood up and stared at his father. From the corner of his eye he saw that Brett had stopped to look at him with his blue envelope pinched between a thumb and forefinger, frowning like he knew Landon was a super powder puff.

"Landon? Are you okay?" His father tilted his head.

Landon only nodded and pulled away. "Yes. I'm fine. Let's go."

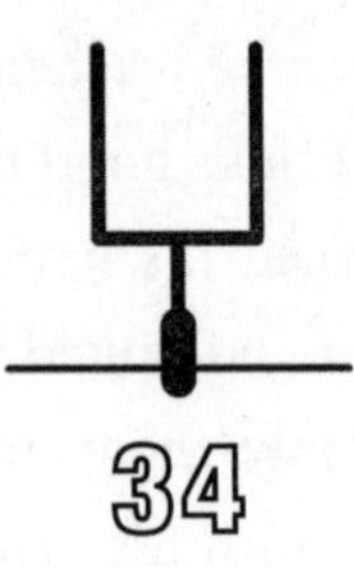

34

"Can we stop for ice cream?" Landon wasn't hungry, but his father didn't know that.

"Hey, sure. Probably hungry after losing your dinner there, huh?" His father gave Landon a cheerful look and started the car. They rolled out of the parking lot. Landon kept his eyes straight ahead and bumped up the AC as high as it would go.

His father found a place to park on the street in the center of town. Landon put his helmet and shoulder pads in the back-seat and wore just his sopping wet T-shirt and football pants into the Häagen-Dazs store, where they sat at the corner table. Landon's dad accepted two menus from a waitress and watched her walk away before he spoke. "Amazing, right? I mean, look at all this. When I was a kid a banana split was a big deal, but now you got, what?" His father began to read off the menu. "Paradise with Whipped Cream? Waffle Dream? The Eiffel

Tower? Wow, Landon, you have no idea how lucky you are."

His father dipped his head into the menu, shaking his head with wonder. When the waitress returned, Landon asked for a glass of water and said he still hadn't made up his mind about his order.

"So, what's Genevieve doing tonight?" he asked when they were alone.

His father lowered the menu and raised an eyebrow. "No idea. On her computer? Texting? I was in a real writing zone and all of a sudden I saw the time. Didn't want to be late picking you up. Why?"

"No reason." Landon dipped his head. "How about this Banana Caramel Crepe?"

"Oh, didn't see that." His father got back to business.

The waitress returned with their water and Landon asked for the Seventh Heaven. His father went for the Banana Caramel Crepe. They sipped their water and watched people walk past on the sidewalk, some of them entering Häagen-Dazs to sit down, others lining up for cones at the counter. His father tapped Landon's hand, and Landon looked up.

"I gotta tell you, Landon, this book is really going good," his father said. "Nodnal is some character."

"Wait," Landon said. "I thought you weren't going to name him Nodnal."

"Well, right. It's a working name. I'll change it at the end, but for now it's really helping me. I see him as Nodnal."

Landon saw the glow of excitement on his father's face and couldn't bring himself to protest, even though he hated the idea.

"I mean, right now." His father leaned toward Landon and motioned with his hands. "He's in the dungeon. He was wrongly accused of conspiring against the king, but he's made a friend, a knight. I'm about to have them escape."

Landon tried his best to look interested, but his own life was such a mess, he just couldn't find room to care about a fictional character.

"Sounds good," he managed to say.

His father sat back, then glanced around at the other tables, but Landon could tell he was trying to decide whether or not to ask him something.

"So, football going good?" Landon's dad folded his arms on the table and leaned in again. "I mean, you like all that hitting and stuff?"

Landon shrugged. "It's not easy."

His father shook his head vigorously. "No way. It's pretty crazy if you ask me, and I don't want you to feel like you have to keep doing it if it's not for you, Landon."

Landon scowled. "Why? Did Genevieve say something to you?"

"Not at all," his father said.

"'Cause I'm not her, you know. Things come easy to her."

"Sometimes it seems that way," his father said, "but she works pretty hard, I gotta say."

The ice cream arrived. Landon dug in, truly hungry because his stomach was completely empty, and facing Genevieve now seemed far off. If she was busy on the computer or texting with her friends, he could sneak right into his bedroom and lock the door. He took a big bite, and mango exploded in his mouth.

He cut that flavor with a dash of raspberry and whipped cream.

"Mmm." He got serious about his dish and didn't look up until he paused before the final scoop.

"You beat me," he said to his dad.

His father scraped some melted goo from the bottom of his dish. "Well, it's not a contest, but wow, was that crepe good. I'm glad we stopped here."

Landon noticed a splotch of caramel on his father's shirt, and that made him think of his mom and what she'd say if she were here. "Dad?"

"Yeah?"

"If I don't get a lot of playing time—in the games—you won't care, right?"

His father's mouth turned down. "Nah. Who cares about that? It's your first time ever trying this thing. Everyone else's been doing it forever, and what's the rush? I told you, it's about being a part of something. That's what a team is. Gosh, my high school buddy Dale Higgens had no rhythm whatsoever, but there he was with that triangle—sometimes the bongos—right there, marching along with the rest of us with his chin high, all the way to Orlando one year for the Nationals. Did I ever tell you we went to the Nationals one year?"

Landon nodded. "Pretty sure you did."

"Yeah, well, we were a *band*, which is the exact same thing as a team. Like a band of brothers. A unit. A squad. Man, did we have some times. Band camp?" His father raised an eyebrow again, twirled his spoon and sighed happily before he let it drop into the bowl. "You ready?"

"Almost." Landon ate his last spoonful, and then he asked

the question that had been on his mind all along. "So, with the band, did anyone ever have some get-together, like a party, and not invite the whole band? I mean, that had to be normal because of how many people you have in a band."

His dad reached across the table and put his hand on Landon's. "Hey, buddy, we got plenty of room. I can fire up the grill. Burgers. Chicken kabobs. We can fit that whole dog-gone football team of yours right around the pool if that's what you're wondering. I like the idea. Mom won't mind."

Landon fought to control himself.

He had no idea what to say.

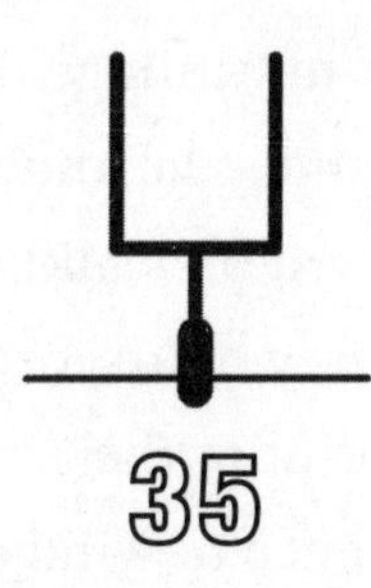

35

Landon sputtered. "No, that's okay. I was just thinking about how big a group you have with a band. I was just wondering."

"Well, yeah. I mean if you're in the band, you're in the band. Everyone just knew everyone was invited. That's what I'm talking about. That's how things work, see?" His father sat up, straight and wise. "A Cub Scout den is a different bird. I think because of all the focus on the individual skills and merit badges and stuff. I think all you did with your den was that laser tag once. Scouts isn't as much about camaraderie as a team or a band is. You sure you don't want to ask the guys over? Even after practice one night? Everybody for a dip?"

Landon shook his head and wiped his mouth. "I don't think so. Maybe some other time."

His father's hands went up in surrender. They paid the bill and headed home.

The sun was well down, and Landon's dad put the head-lights on. They were nearly at the turnoff when they saw a small figure marching down the sidewalk, arms and legs flying high.

"Well, how about this for timing?" His father nodded at the furious display of limbs, and as he pulled over, Landon saw that it was his mom. She insisted on walking to and from the train each day, even with her crazy hours, because she said it not only lowered the carbon footprint of their family but also gave her a bit of exercise and the chance to wind down.

His father rolled down Landon's window. "Hey there, pretty woman. Going my way?"

Landon rolled his eyes, but looked to see how his mom would respond. She shifted her briefcase's strap on her shoulder and put her hands on her hips, smiling. "Forrest, what are you teaching our son?"

"That pretty women are hard to find and if you do find one, you pick her up! That's a lesson worth learning, I'd say."

"Oh, you would?" she teased.

"Definitely."

Landon's mom climbed into the backseat beside the foot-ball gear and then tapped Landon on the shoulder. "And my lesson is that being bold is the only way to win the prize."

Landon's dad tapped his arm. "And what a prize I am."

They went straight home, happy, without speaking. Landon digested the words his parents had spoken, sifting the lessons from the laughs. He knew Megan Nickell would be like that, joking around and happy and appreciative. He could just tell, but thinking of her made him think of Genevieve and the blowout he knew they were going to have as soon as she caught wind of him bailing out of the contact drills in exchange for carrying the water bottles.

He realized his mom was tapping his shoulder, and as they pulled into their driveway, he turned around.

"I said, how is football going?" His mom's sharp look seemed to see right into his head, like his eyes were windows without curtains.

Landon nodded. "Fine. Good."

"Isn't that great to hear?" She patted his shoulder, and they all got out. Landon heard his parents talking but didn't bother to pay attention. He got his football gear from the backseat and laid it out to dry in the garage before following them into the house. He dumped his cleats in the mud room before entering the kitchen.

"Well, we just had some pretty serious ice cream at that Häagen-Dazs store," his father said to his mom, "but I can cook something up for you if you're hungry. I made lobster ravioli. Sound good? Or, I could whip up an omelet, a little sage and white cheddar?"

Landon's mom sat on a bar stool at the granite-topped island in the middle of the kitchen. She wore a tired look. Her shoes were off and her feet were already up on the next stool. "Just some salad if you have it, Forrest."

"I always have salad," Landon's father said. He looked at Landon and winked. "I was a rabbit in another life. I ever tell you that?"

Landon gave his father the grin he was waiting for and then said, "I'm gonna shower."

On his way up the stairs Landon considered his mom. He couldn't remember a time when she'd been gone more or seemed so tired, and he began to wonder if she or his dad regretted coming to Bronxville. It certainly wasn't treating Landon very nicely so far. Before he crossed in front of the open hallway that led to Genevieve's room, he stopped and peeked around the corner and strained for a hint of noise. He heard nothing and tiptoed across, making it safely to his own room, where he put his ears in their drier and took a nice cool shower.

When he got out, he wrapped a towel around his waist, walked into his bedroom, and yelped with fright.

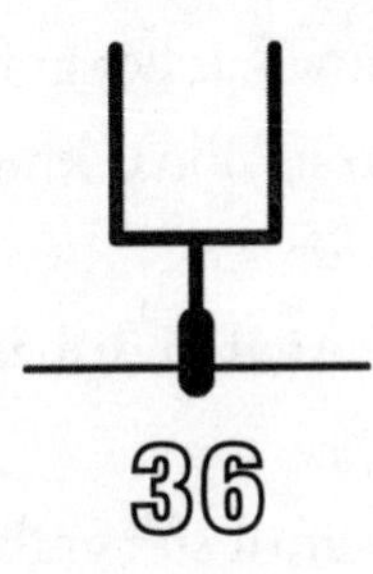
36

Genevieve jumped up off the bed, and it looked like she yelped too.

Everything was silent to Landon. He had an idea of what Genevieve was saying, though. He didn't have to read lips to know she was raving mad. Landon told himself to stay calm. He knew he just had to weather the storm. It would pass. And, a storm was always a lot less frightening when you couldn't hear the thunder.

Genevieve started pacing and flashing her phone in his face. He didn't read the text messages or the Instagram posts. He didn't have to. He knew from the pain and anger on her face that they were about him. He didn't have to read about people calling him a powder puff. He knew what they thought.

"I can't even hear you, Genevieve." Landon stood in the

same spot, folded his arms, and pointed to the ears in their drier.

"Look at me." She mouthed the words slowly. The look in her eyes was so white-hot that he couldn't look away.

She shook her head violently. "You cannot quit!"

Landon just looked down at her and shook his head. "Leave me alone, Genevieve. You don't know what you're talking about. Everything's easy for you."

"For me?" Her face twisted in disbelief. "Do you know what I've done for you?"

Landon looked away until she grabbed his arm and gave it a yank.

He could tell she'd lowered her voice as she leaned close and said, "Don't you look away. You look at me! I know you understand. I've made nice with one of the meanest girls I've ever met in my life because of you. Do you know why? So she won't *torture* you."

Landon was confused. "Not Megan."

"No, not Megan. Katy! She looks at you like a spider looks at a fly. She'd love to wrap you up and suck out every ounce of blood and leave you shriveled up like a mummy, but she won't because she wants to be my friend." Genevieve jabbed her own chest with a thumb. "Do you know how much I hate that? You think that isn't hard?

"No, you don't." Genevieve shook her head violently again, and then she grabbed him by both arms and looked up into his eyes, slowly mouthing the words, "Pain is temporary, Landon, but quitting? Quitting is *forever*."

She turned and left him alone, wrapped in his towel, still dripping.

Landon felt like she'd stabbed him in the stomach and twisted the knife. It hurt and it made him furious. He wanted to strike back, and when he saw the medal she'd given him, he snatched it off the bedpost and marched after her. She'd already disappeared into her bedroom.

He knew he should knock, but he was too mad for manners. With the medal in his hand, he cocked his arm back, ready to throw it onto her floor. He didn't need her medals and he didn't need any of his own.

He grabbed the door handle with his other hand and flung it open.

Landon couldn't hear the screams, but he knew there was screaming.

In a flash of skin and underwear and towels, he realized he'd barged in on Genevieve and her friends changing to take a night swim.

The medal slipped from Landon's hand and fell silently to the floor.

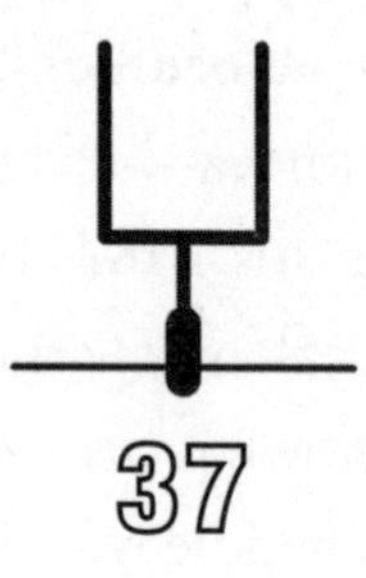

37

Landon squeezed his eyes shut and bolted back to his room.

He lay facedown on his bed with a pillow over the back of his head. His breath got hot and short, and he wondered if a person could suffocate himself. He threw the pillow off and rolled over, gasping for air, and lay there huffing for a long while. Finally, he swung his legs off the bed and sat there with the towel still wrapped tightly around his flabby waist.

He got up and dressed himself.

His hands trembled, and he dropped his ears twice before he had them on and in place. He cracked open the door and listened hard for any sounds, but the house was still. He tiptoed out and peered down Genevieve's hall. Her bedroom door stood ajar, but no light spilled from it. Quietly, he made his way down the stairs. His father's computer was on, but the chair stood crooked and empty. He rounded the corner and saw his parents sitting with Genevieve at the kitchen table. They talked in a low murmur that he hadn't a prayer of understanding. His mother held Genevieve's hand across the corner of the table. Genevieve's head hung low and her back was to him.

Landon touched her shoulder. "I didn't see anything."

Genevieve looked up in horror. "You just had to shove that medal in my face, didn't you?"

Landon's mouth fell open. He'd never seen Genevieve this mad at him. He wanted to tell her about Xander's birthday party. He wanted her to feel bad for him and comfort him, but nothing came out.

"And don't even say you didn't see anything!" Genevieve threw her hands in the air, her eyes as wild as her hair. "They totally freaked and Katy said they had to leave and she's already blabbed about it. It's *out* there."

Genevieve held up her phone as proof and then turned the phone her way, looked at it, and groaned before putting her head down onto her arm to cry.

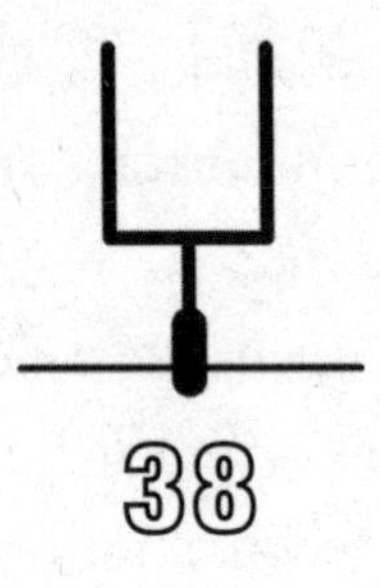

38

Landon's father looked ill. His face was pasty and he twiddled his fingers with his eyes rolled toward Landon's mom, awaiting her response.

Landon's mom stared at the tabletop, searching the rich wood grain for some kind of inspiration or truth. Finally, she sighed and looked up at Landon's dad. "Well, Landon is a normal boy, and normal boys are curious about these things."

Landon's father seemed to have swallowed his tongue. He shook his head uncertainly and gurgled.

Landon's mom looked at Landon now.

Landon shook his head. "No. I'm not curious."

"Landon? It's all right," his mom said. "It's perfectly natural for boys your age; your father will tell you that. Forrest?"

"Uh . . . of course," his father said.

"Mom! I did not see them on *purpose*!" Landon clenched his fists. "I was giving her back her stupid medal."

"Now my medal's stupid?" Genevieve raised her head. Her eyes were red, and she was livid.

Landon kept going. "That's the only reason I went to her room, and I didn't have my ears on and I didn't hear anything or anyone and I had no idea they were even *there*."

His mom removed her glasses and rubbed her eyes before looking up. "Oh . . . well . . . a misunderstanding. All of it. I'll call the girls' mothers and get it worked out."

"Good luck with that." Genevieve looked bitter, but Landon's mom was undaunted.

"I don't need luck," she said. "Just persistence."

"It's already *out* there, Mom." Genevieve groaned and lifted her phone off the table. "Katy called Landon a 'Peeping Tom,' and people are going wild with it. It's a hashtag. #PeepingPowderPuff."

"Well, every sensible person knows the internet is no place for reliable facts," their mom said.

"Like saying President Obama wasn't born in America." Landon's dad raised a finger.

Landon's mom scowled at her husband. "Well, fools are fools, and I can't help that. What I can help with, though, is this Katy Buford. We'll see how long she keeps this up after I call her mother. I'll give *her* a hashtag."

Landon stood there, lost and crushed and wanting to go back to Cleveland. Kip Meyers and his friends calling him a big, fat dummy was a piece of birthday cake compared to this.

Suddenly, the phone rang. They all just stared at it.

Landon's mom sighed. "Maybe she's saving me the trouble of looking up her number."

She got up slowly from her chair to answer. "Hello? Yes, this is Landon's mother."

His mom paused, and then her face turned angry. *"What?"*

Landon wondered how he could continue to sink when he'd already hit the bottom. He grabbed his cochlears and stood there, ready to pull the plug.

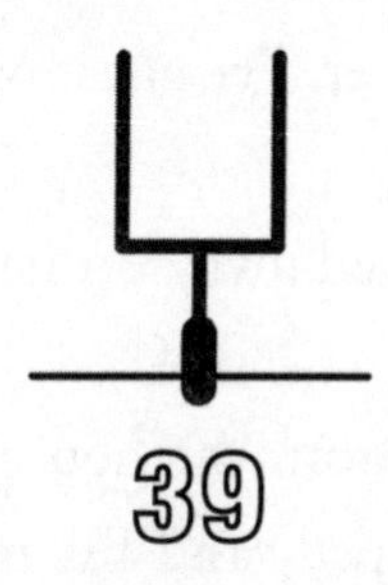

39

Landon's mom looked at him, fuming, but it wasn't him she was mad at. He could tell.

"I hate to say it," his mom said into the phone, "but I've seen things like this before. This isn't the first time Landon's been excluded from a birthday party . . . Uh-huh . . . Uh-huh . . . yes."

Landon's dad bit into his lower lip and began twiddling his fingers again.

"Wait, I'm sorry." Landon's mom's face softened. "What did you say your name was?"

She listened, nodding her head. "Courtney Wagner. Got it. Thank you, Courtney. But your son is Brett? Brett Bell? Yes, I thought about keeping my name too, but my husband is a bit old-fashioned. Ha-ha."

Confusion racked Landon.

His mom held his attention with commanding eyes. "Yes, I think Landon would be happy to talk to Brett, but it would be much easier on Skype, or we can FaceTime. Do you have an account? You do? Super. I've got it on my cell phone and I'll bring it right up. . . ."

Landon's mom tapped away on her phone. "Got it. Calling now."

His mom switched from the house phone to her cell. The Skype blurted and bleeped, and his mom came back toward the table. "Hi, Courtney. It worked! This is so nice. Let me put Landon on, and *thank you.* Thank you so much."

His mom handed Landon the phone and there was Brett, not scowling, not mean-faced, but wearing an easy smile as if he wasn't the one-man wrecking machine he had been earlier on the field.

"Hi, Brett," Landon said.

"Hey, Landon. Can you understand me okay like this? Can you see me good?" Brett asked, pointing to his own face.

"Yes." Landon felt wildly shy, aware that everyone was watching him, and having no idea what was going on. He remembered Brett's anger in the drill. Landon searched for a trick, some kind of falseness, but Brett appeared to be genuine.

"So, Saturday . . . ," Brett began.

Landon just stared.

Brett smiled crookedly, maybe from nerves. "Saturday, we're going down to New Jersey to visit my uncle. He plays for the Giants and they have the day off. He's gonna have a bunch of players over at his house—he's got a pretty big house—for a cookout at the pool. I think Rashad Jennings will be there. Eli Manning, too. Anyway, I thought maybe you'd want to come with us."

A surge of excitement and joy rocketed through Landon's entire body. "I . . . sure. But . . ."

"What's the matter?" Brett asked.

Landon couldn't help being suspicious. This sounded too good to be true. "Don't you have that birthday party, with Xander and the whole team?"

Brett gave him a funny look. "Well, if you're not going, then it can't really be a team party, right? Besides, nothing would stop me from being with my uncle and his friends."

Landon couldn't even speak. He glanced at his mom, who was beaming and nodding and mouthing for him to say yes.

"Uh," Landon said, "yes. Sure. A cookout would be awesome. Rashad Jennings is amazing. He ran for over a hundred yards last year when they played the Browns. I'm a Browns fan, but I won't say that to them."

Off-screen, his mom waved her hands frantically and mouthed for him to say thank you.

"Thanks, Brett. Thanks very much."

"Hey, no problem, Landon. And don't worry about the Browns. Everyone gets it. You're from Cleveland, right? You're supposed to be a Browns fan."

"But I can be a Giants fan too," Landon said. "You know, unless they face off in the Super Bowl."

Brett laughed and then looked at someone off of his screen

and then back. "My mom says we'll pick you up about eleven, if that's okay."

"That's . . . sure. Eleven would be great. Thank you again."

"Here, I'll give you my mom's cell number." Brett told him the number. "Text your address, okay?"

"Sure."

"Okay. See you at practice tomorrow, then."

"See you," Landon said. The phone bleeped and Brett disappeared. Landon looked up to see if the whole thing had really happened.

Genevieve still looked destroyed, but his father beamed and nodded like he'd won the lottery, and his mom reached out and touched his cheek. "See, Landon? See how quickly things can turn around?"

Landon handed her back her phone. "Thanks, Mom."

He didn't want to say anything more. He didn't want to talk. He didn't want to be angry about Xander's party, or sad or afraid. He practically tiptoed back to his room, removed his ears, got into his pajamas, climbed into bed, and lay there with his eyes open and the lights off. His parents came in and kissed him good night, looking at him fondly but sensing that he needed to be left alone.

He felt like he was on the top floor of a house of cards. Any misstep could bring the whole thing down, but for now, for this night, he had a friend—and not just any friend. He had Brett. And if Brett was friends with him, Megan might also be forgiving and understand when she heard his side of the story about barging in on them. She might even help him by telling people he'd done nothing wrong and that it was only a mistake and that Katy Buford was a mean, obnoxious twit.

Landon sighed.

Maybe not. But then again, maybe she would.

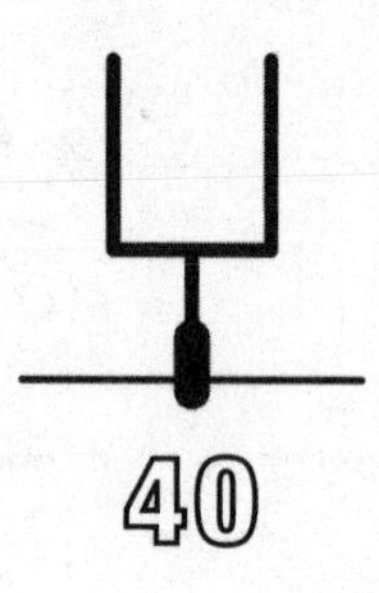

40

Friday afternoon it rained. Landon watched football technique drills and blocking highlights on YouTube while his father pecked away at the computer. Genevieve ignored him, leaving the house with nothing more than a wave. When Landon asked his father where she'd gone, his father said that she was going to the mall with Megan to shop and then see a movie.

"So that's a good sign, right?" Landon said, wishing beyond hope that the Peeping Powder Puff thing had died a quick death and everyone had gotten over it.

His father only shrugged. "Maybe. We'll see. Sometimes people surprise you, and I know your mother is on the case, so . . ."

His mom "working on it" made Landon worry more, but he chose to push it from his mind and instead dwell on the weekend invitation. He wanted to call Brett to make sure it was real, feel him out for signs that it was something his mother had put him up to, but decided that might damage what was a good thing. He needed to be patient and let it all unfold.

He closed his iPad and picked up his book.

It was nearly time for practice and still raining when Landon, sitting in his favorite chair, looked up from reading and, out of the blue, spoke across the room to his father. "Genevieve didn't seem too mad when she left?"

His father looked up from his typing and over at Landon. "The thing about your sister is that she's a lot like your mom. You never have to worry whose side she's on."

Landon waited for his father to go on, but he'd stopped talking. Landon filled the silence, saying, "My side, right?"

His father dipped his chin. "Your side times ten. She might be mad, but she'll fight for you, Landon."

Landon thought for a moment. "But who wants to have a little sister fighting for him? I mean, that looks kind of bad."

His father scratched his chin and pointed. "You seem to really like that book."

"Huh?" Landon wasn't sure if he'd heard his father correctly so he held up the book, and his father nodded. "Yeah, it's awesome."

"But look at it," his father said. "A worn-out green cover with the title and the author's name, both faded. No fireballs or dashing heroes or swords or brilliant, eye-catching colors. But inside? Wow. What could pack a bigger punch than *The Three Musketeers*? It's unforgettable."

"So, don't judge a book by its cover," Landon said.

"I never do." His father smiled and turned back to the screen and his story.

Later, at football practice, Landon watched the other kids warily. The rain hadn't stopped. Maybe that was keeping the fires of rumors under control. The temperature had dipped into the low seventies, so there wasn't as much need for water bottles. Landon found himself shifting from foot to foot, drenched from head to toe, watching the other boys battle in the muddy grass. There was a lot of hooting and hollering. Landon couldn't figure out why. Large drops swelled on his face mask, growing fat until they broke free and splattered his jersey.

No one said anything to him. The one time Landon found himself face-to-face with Skip—before practice on the sideline where Skip was retrieving a football from the ball bag—the quarterback simply walked around Landon like he was a lamppost. He took that as a good sign, but he had a sinking feeling that something might have changed with Brett. It was like their Skype the night before had never happened. He wasn't able to bring himself to tap Brett on the shoulder until after wind sprints.

Brett looked exhausted, which was no surprise. The big lineman had hustled and hit his way through practice like it was a fifty-round boxing match, if there even was such a thing. Even in the cool rain, Brett's face was beaded with sweat and his eyes sagged wearily. "Hey, Landon."

"Everything good?" It was the only question Landon could ask.

"Oh, you mean guys calling you 3P?" Brett shot a glare around at the other players slogging up toward the parking lot. "Don't worry about that junk. People are stupid."

"Wait, what?" Landon had no idea what he was talking about.

Brett waved a padded hand toward the heavy gray sky. "Forget it. Just jerks. You're good for tomorrow, right? My uncle's place?"

"Yeah." Landon nodded. "I'm great for tomorrow, but what's 3P?"

Brett studied him. "Landon, it's okay. Junk happens. People blow things out of proportion. The girls you walked in on? I already told Skip to keep his hands off you."

"You did?" Landon felt a surge of gratitude. "Thanks, but why would Skip . . ."

"Well, you know he and Megan are, like, this thing." Brett wrinkled his face. "Stupid, really. I think they hold hands at the movies or something. Everyone was pushing him to bust you in the mouth, but I got that covered."

"But, 3P?"

Brett tilted his head. "You really don't know? It's not nice. I don't want to even say. It's stupid."

"Wait . . ." Landon lowered his voice. "Peeping Powder Puff?"

Brett looked disgusted. "Don't worry about it. It'll die down, and no one's laying a hand on you." Brett made a fist and tapped his own chest. "They know better."

Pressure built up inside Landon because he felt like he should let Brett go. The two of them were just standing there alone now. Brett's dad was huddled up with the other coaches as they sometimes did after practice, but Landon had to ask, "Why are you doing this?"

"Doing what?"

"Being my friend. What's in it for you?"

Brett shrugged. "Nothing. You're my teammate. My dad says a real leader treats everyone on the team the same. The best player or the . . . the not-best player."

"You mean the worst player." Landon wondered if, despite the drills, he even qualified as a player. "The guy who plays left out."

"It doesn't matter, Landon." Brett set his jaw. "Some people just don't get it, but in my house, that's how we do things. You help people who really need it."

Landon swallowed. "And . . . because of all this stuff, I really need it?"

Brett had that hard look on his face again. "Yeah. You do."

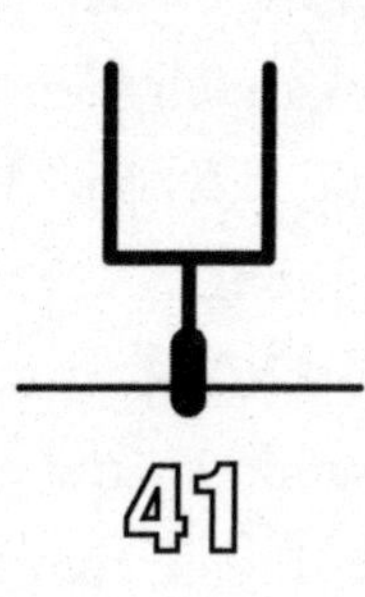

41

Landon woke early the next morning. He packed and repacked his Nike duffel bag with a fresh change of clothes, bathing suit, goggles, and towel, wanting everything to be just right, to look just right. He modeled three different bathing suits in his bathroom mirror and ended up going with the black knee-length one that had a narrow orange stripe down the side. The others, he decided, made his gut look too big.

He was ready to go by eight. His dad had pancakes going before his mom wandered down in her robe, bleary-eyed and feeling her way around the kitchen for a cup of coffee.

Genevieve appeared in a soccer uniform with her wild hair pulled back in a tight ponytail and a headband.

"You got a game?" Landon asked.

"Yup." Genevieve scanned her phone with a blank face. "That's how it works."

Their mom set her coffee cup down with a sharp sound. "What's that supposed to mean, young lady?"

Landon stabbed a pancake but dragged it back and forth across the puddle of syrup instead of shoveling it into his mouth. He wondered how much Genevieve was going to say.

"Just getting my game face on," Genevieve said with the same blank stare at their mom.

Landon stuffed the forkful of pancake into his mouth.

"Hmm." Their mom sat down and raised the coffee with both hands, closing her eyes to inhale the steam, before turning her head toward the stove. "Well, Forrest, we should go to the game."

"Right." Their dad raised a spatula without turning around. "Should be on the family calendar."

"I was hoping I wouldn't have to look at any calendar today," she said with a sigh.

Their father brought another plate of pancakes to the table and sat down beside their mom. "You don't. Just leave everything to me."

Their mom smiled and then turned her attention back to Genevieve. "How's the social media looking?"

Genevieve put her phone down on the placemat and picked up her knife. "Not too bad, actually. Looks like you did your magic."

Their mom fought back a smile. "Good."

"I just hope it's not like the French aristocracy." His sister busied herself with the syrup.

"Meaning?" their mom asked.

"We all know how that ended." Genevieve looked at their mom with a false smile. "The guillotine."

The knife dropped with a clank, and the top of her banana skittered into the puddle of syrup.

"That's an entirely different story." Their mom took a swig of coffee and set it down hard again.

Genevieve only shrugged and dove into her pancakes.

Landon tried not to think about it, but as he waited for eleven o'clock to roll around, he found himself touching his own neck as he sat in his favorite chair to read. At quarter till the hour, Landon gave up his book and positioned himself in the front window.

Finally, at 11:04, Brett and his family pulled into the driveway. Landon grabbed his bag and scrambled toward the garage. "I'm going."

His mom cut him off and straightened the collar of his bright blue polo shirt. "Mind your manners."

"I will." Landon felt his mom right behind him and he turned to see what was up.

"I'm coming out, to say hello to Courtney," she said. Before they got through the garage, she tapped his shoulder again. "Make sure you keep your ears dry—remember, wrap them good in a towel someplace out of the way, and tell everyone you won't be able to hear when you're swimming."

He was too excited to care what she said, and he just kept going.

Brett's mom got out of the big Suburban and circled around to say hello. She stood nearly a foot taller than Landon's mom, and Landon was surprised to see that she had no hair on her head, not even any eyebrows. If Landon's mom noticed, she didn't show it. The two women shook hands before Landon's mom pulled Brett's mom into a hug. "Courtney Wagner, you're my type of gal."

Brett's mom blushed down at Landon's mom, but she seemed pleased. "Well, Brett says Landon is a very nice boy, and we like nice boys."

"He is." Landon's mom gave Brett's mom's hand a squeeze.

Brett's mom pointed to her hairless scalp. "With all my treatments, we've been going through a lot, so we know what it is to look a little different, and it's always nice when people don't care."

Landon's mom beamed. "You're wonderful. Thank you again."

Landon had stopped before getting into the SUV to keep an eye on his mom because he was afraid she was going to start giving Brett's mom instructions on his ears, but she didn't. He gave her a final wave and climbed in next to Brett. In the third row of seats, two twin girls who looked to be kindergarten age wore fluffy, blue bunny ears and were focused on the iPad on the seat between them. Kiddie music jangled and the two of them looked at each other and laughed before staring down again.

"My sisters," Brett said. "Don't worry about them. One's Susie, the other's Sally, and even I have a hard time telling them apart."

"Hi, Landon." Coach Bell reached around from the front seat to shake Landon's hand as Brett's mom got in.

"Hi, Coach," Landon said. "Thank you for bringing me."

Brett's mom turned around in the passenger seat and looked directly at him. He liked what she'd said about looking different, and he was careful not to stare at her missing eyebrows or hair and to look her in the eyes when she spoke.

"It's our pleasure to have you, Landon."

Landon gave her a nod and then watched his mom wave as they pulled out of the driveway. He breathed a sigh of relief when she finally disappeared from sight.

Brett tapped Landon's chest. "Know who's gonna be there?"

"Well, you said Eli and Rashad . . ."

Brett trembled with delight. "Yup, them too, but can you guess who *else*?"

Landon shook his head. "Who?"

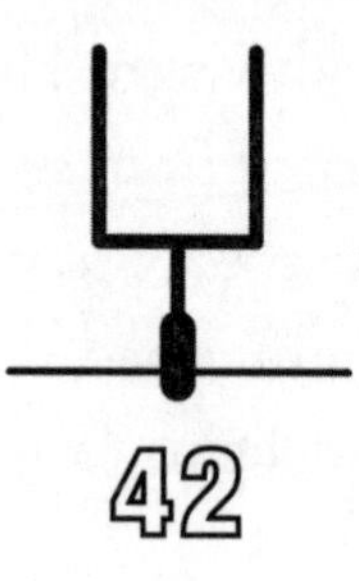

42

"Michael Bamiro." Brett spread his arms as wide as the inside of the SUV would allow him. "Biggest guy on the team and one of the top five big guys in the *whole* NFL."

"Wow," Landon said. "How big?"

Brett nodded, evidently glad to see Landon's enthusiasm. "Six foot eight. Three hundred and forty-five pounds. How about that?"

"Man . . ." Landon shook his head and then raised his eyebrows. "Did I tell you my dad is six-ten?"

"I've seen him." Brett's eyes sparkled. He directed his voice toward the front. "Dad, did you know Landon's dad is six-ten?"

Landon could see Coach Bell shaking his head, but he wasn't sure what he said in response. Landon thought it was, "That's tall." But he couldn't be sure.

"Hey," Brett said, nodding at the duffel bag on Landon's lap. "You bring your phone?"

"Yes." Landon got it out and showed him.

"You do *Clash of Clans*?"

"No."

"You want to? You should. You can be in my clan. Here, I'll set it up. It's free!" Brett took the phone from Landon and got to work.

Landon felt like he was floating as Brett leaned toward him, showing him how to get things set up and then showing him his own phone. "I've got a Town Hall 8, but I've been doing it for over a year. It takes time, but you can be in a clan and still get matched up to battle guys your own strength level."

They spent the rest of the trip with Brett schooling him on *Clash of Clans.* A couple of times, with all the talk of castles and dragons and archers, Landon felt like he had an opening to tell Brett about his father's book, but he kept quiet because he didn't want to ruin anything. And, as they pulled up the long, curving driveway and into the circle in front of Brett's uncle's gigantic house, Landon told himself to keep as quiet as he could about everything. He needed to just get through the day without botching things up. Building a friendship with Brett would be even more spectacular than creating a clan war base, but he sensed it was similar in that he'd have to do it one block at a time, with great care and patience.

They parked among a parade of glittering automobiles and walked through the house out to the backyard without even knocking. Each of Brett's parents held the hand of a twin. Brett and Landon followed behind out onto the sunlit terrace, where two large tents stood on either side of the pool to protect the colorful buffet tables laid out there. The party was already in full swing with people in shorts and bathing suits everywhere in and around the big pool. Landon not only heard but felt the thumping of music from the outdoor sound system. Several men—players, by the look of their muscles—welcomed the Bell family like old friends.

They kissed Brett's mom on the cheek, smiling at her as if she wasn't sick at all.

Then one of the players who had a beer bottle in his hand turned suddenly on Landon, laughed, and asked cheerfully, "Hey, my man? What the heck are those things?"

It seemed like the whole party suddenly stopped so everyone could stare at Landon. Just like that, his plan of keeping a low profile was destroyed.

Brett's mom gave the player an angry look and said, "Jonathan *Wagner*, what's wrong with you?"

Landon realized that the player standing in front of him was Brett's uncle. He couldn't break out in tears. He couldn't hide his face.

He had to say something.

He just had no idea what.

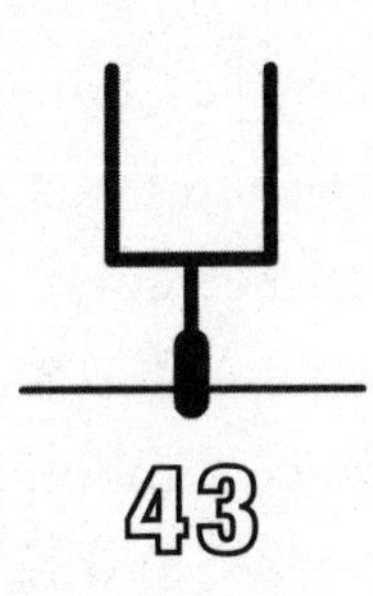

43

"I'm . . ." Landon's mind went blank.

Brett and the others looked stunned.

Landon suddenly turned and dashed back into the house without knowing what he was doing or where he was going. He passed through a great room with a TV the size of a wall and down a hallway that he thought led to the front entrance. He found himself in a huge library, reversed his course, saw a staircase, reversed again, and ducked into a marble-floored bathroom, shutting the door behind him.

He was huffing to catch his breath, and he looked at the pain on his face in the mirror. His fingers crept over his ears, caressed the battery packs, and slid along the wires to the discs magnetically stuck to the implants beneath his scalp. He should have worn his cap. He had been planning to, but the thought of walking into a New York Giants players' cookout with a

Cleveland Browns cap didn't seem right. He wanted to remove his ears—just stash the equipment in his bag and look like a normal kid—but he knew he couldn't. He'd be too cut off if he did.

He stood there for a while. Time seemed to have frozen. He jumped at the sudden sound of a knock on the bathroom door and turned the water faucet on to make it sound like he actually needed to be in there. "Just a minute."

"Landon?" It was a voice Landon didn't recognize, but he was shouting through the door and Landon thought he understood. "Hey, my man, it's Jonathan, Brett's uncle. You all right?"

Landon gathered himself and opened the door. "I just had to use the . . ."

"Hey, my man." Jonathan wore a sad face. Behind him stood Brett's dad.

Jonathan Wagner put his hands on Landon's shoulders. "I am way sorry. Listen, I did *not* mean to insult you or upset you. No way, my man. You gotta believe me."

"It's okay." Landon wanted to melt.

Coach Bell stepped forward and asked, "Landon, are you all right to stay?"

Landon nodded. "Yes."

"For sure," Jonathan said. "Come on, my man. I'm personally dressing up a couple dogs for you. What do you like? Ketchup? Mustard? Chili? How about a chili dog?"

"It's okay." Landon looked down at his sneakers. "I'm fine. Really. I just had to wash my hands."

"Landon, my sister told me your gear there is so you can *hear*," Jonathan said. "I had no idea they could do something like that, implants and all. So, think about it, you're, like, bionic. In a good way. Hey, I am too. I got this plate in my arm here."

Jonathan presented a tattooed forearm split down the middle with a shiny scar and laughed. "Sets off metal detectors in the airport. I know about hardware, my man. It's all good, right? Are you sure you're okay?"

Landon could only nod. He appreciated Jonathan feeling bad and letting Landon know that he meant no harm. He could hear his father's voice. "Forgive and forget, Landon. Forgive and forget."

But in truth, he was horrified that there had been a scene, and he didn't want to go back into the crowd.

"Hey, you gotta come on out because you know who I'm going to introduce you to?" Jonathan said.

Landon shook his head.

"You like Eli Manning?"

Landon nodded vigorously. "Yes!"

"Hey," Coach Bell said. "That's a great idea."

"Sure, everyone likes Eli. Come on." Jonathan turned, saw Landon hesitate, and took hold of his arm. "My man, you're not just gonna meet him. I'm taking a pic you can post on whatever you're into and all the kids at your school are gonna freak. Come on, now. You don't want to hurt Eli's feelings by not wanting to meet him."

Landon let himself be led because how could he resist? Jonathan was built like a battleship, with bulging biceps pushing the sleeves of his polo shirt against cannonball shoulders. Tattoos covered his arms—green, black, and orange, with all kinds of designs and pictures. It reminded Landon of a graffiti-covered brick wall. As he was hauled back out into the crowd, all Landon saw were smiles.

"We worked it out, Courtney." Jonathan motioned for his sister to follow them and then turned to Landon. "My sister's a tough cookie."

Landon laughed. "So is Brett. He's the best player on our team."

Brett and his mom gave Landon thumbs-up and followed with Brett's little sisters in tow.

The crowd parted by the diving board next to the second tent, and there he was: Eli Manning. Landon felt his heart double-clutch. Manning had a can of grape soda in his hand and was talking to a player who could only be Michael Bamiro. The Giants lineman was nearly as tall as Landon's dad, only his chest was twice as wide and his legs were like tree trunks. Stylish black-framed glasses and a shaved head gave him a studious look.

Both men turned their dark brown eyes on Landon and both smiled like he was some long-lost friend.

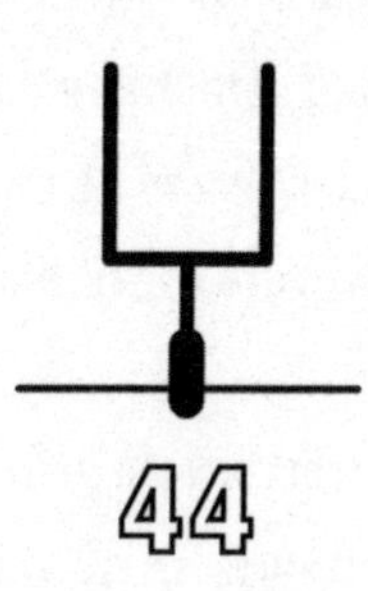

44

“Guys, this is Landon.” Jonathan gave Landon a pat on the back. “I have no idea why he wanted to meet you, Eli, but I told him that if he asked for a picture with you, it would make your day.”

Eli held out a hand and Landon shook it. “It’s a pleasure to meet you, Mr. Manning.”

“Hey, Landon.” Eli spoke quietly, but Landon understood. “You know who Michael Bamiro is, right?”

“Hi, Mr. Bamiro.” Landon shook the giant man’s hand. “I play football too. I want to be a lineman like you and Mr. Wagner.”

“Yeah,” Jonathan said. “He’s on my nephew’s team.”

“Very nice,” Bamiro said. “What high school you guys play for, Landon?”

Landon blinked and stuttered. "I, uh . . . we play for a seventh-grade youth team, sir."

"Seventh?" Bamiro was surprised.

"Yes," Landon said quickly. "I'm twelve."

"You?" Bamiro laughed, flashing a set of bright white teeth. "I think you're bigger than I was at twelve. You hear that, Eli? Maybe you can last long enough for Landon here to block for you."

Eli grinned and pointed at Bamiro and Jonathan Wagner. "With you two knuckleheads in front of me, I'll be lucky to make it through next season."

The three players laughed at that together, and Landon blushed even harder when Brett stepped into their little circle. Landon had to wonder—as nice as Brett had been—if he wouldn't expose Landon for being more of a water boy than a lineman, but Brett only smiled and asked if he could get a picture with Eli too.

Rashad Jennings, the Giants' running back, suddenly appeared and threw his hands up in the air. "Manning, Bamiro, Wagner. Come on, guys. Let's get this lovefest over with. Eli won't be able to fit his head into that new Corvette he's driving."

"Well, it's a convertible," Eli said.

Rashad snapped his fingers. "Of course. Now we know why. You *already* can't fit your head in, so you gotta keep the top down."

The players all laughed again, and so did Landon and Brett.

They got a bunch of pictures with the players individually and all as one big group.

"Okay," Jonathan Wagner said. "We good? 'Cause if we are, I say let's eat. I promised my man some chili dogs."

They all piled plates with food and sat down at one of the long tables on a brick terrace under some enormous shade trees. Landon's eyes were busy, darting back and forth, trying to follow the banter between the players, who seemed to genuinely enjoy each other's company despite the constant kidding.

With winks and slaps on the back, they made him feel part of it all.

Their plates were pretty much empty when Rashad Jennings pointed at the diving board and said, "I'm fixing to light that thing up now, boys."

"Light it up?" Jonathan slapped Rashad on the back. "With a pencil dive or something?"

Everyone laughed.

Rashad kept his chin up. "How about a backflip?"

The players all hooted.

"Yeah!"

"Let's see that!"

Jonathan Wagner held up both his arms. "Who needs something fancy like that when you have the world champion cannonballer right here?"

Landon bit his lip to keep from laughing, and he couldn't help himself from shouting, "I bet I can beat you!"

"What?" Wagner tilted his head and knotted up his face. "Boy, you're gonna be big one day, but I hit that water like a twenty-ton *bomb*."

Landon shrugged. "I think I can beat you."

The players went wild, hooting and laughing, pointing at Wagner and saying Landon called him out.

Wagner stood up and pretended to be angry, throwing his napkin down on the table and pointing at Landon, but he was unable to keep from smiling. "It's on, my man. You and me. Cannonball championship of the *world*!"

Landon's spirit soared.

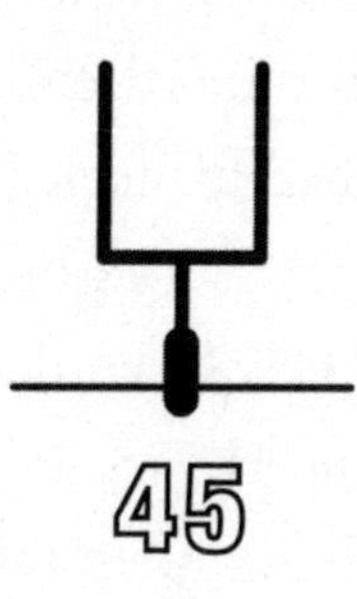
45

Landon changed in the same bathroom he'd tried hiding in. He looked at himself in the mirror, removed his ears, patted his belly, and grinned. He knew he could cannonball. He marched outside, and everyone was lined up around the pool. When they saw him, they cheered, waving their hands and grinning. He wished he could have heard it, but in a way, the silence helped him not to get nervous.

Jonathan Wagner stood on the end of the diving board, and it bowed beneath his tremendous weight. Landon gulped as the big man began bouncing up and down on the end of the board. After half a dozen jumps, he launched himself quite high, dipped, tucked, and plummeted into the water.

A geyser exploded. The column of water shot at a sideways angle, though, drenching a good dozen people, who scattered. Landon laughed at the sight of their happy screaming. When the crowd recovered, everyone began to clap and chant. Landon read their lips.

"Lan-don, Lan-don, Lan-don."

He was briefly reminded of wind sprints, but pushed that ugly thought from his mind and climbed up onto the board. The sandy surface scratched his feet. He strode out to the end, where he curled his toes over the lip and felt the flex of the board beneath him. He knew he couldn't get as high as Wagner and he knew he wasn't nearly as big, but technique was very important when cannonballing, and that he had.

With all eyes on him and the chant of his name on their lips, Landon got into a rhythm, up and down, flexing his legs, getting more height. When he was ready, he took one last jump for balance, launched himself, and tucked like a true human cannonball. When he hit the water, he fought to keep his form and felt the water explode beneath him. Then the suction drew his body into the void with tremendous force.

He let his momentum carry him down until his knees scraped the bottom of the pool, and there he floated, suspended in water and joy until his breath ran out and he sprang off the bottom, breaking the surface to a new round of silent cheers.

He knew by everyone's reaction that he'd won.

Even Jonathan Wagner slapped him on the back, giving him a big thumbs-up. Then Bamiro raised Landon's arm high in the air and said something while people cheered even more.

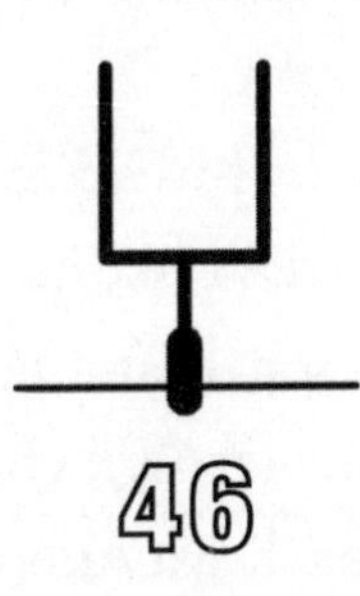

46

Landon and Brett swam the rest of the afternoon, and by the time they had to go, they were exhausted. Landon changed into dry clothes and put his ears back on, so he could hear when Jonathan Wagner stopped Brett as they were getting into the Suburban.

"Hey, Brett," the Giants' right tackle said, "you got one heck of a friend. You'll have to bring him around again."

Landon buckled his seat belt and closed his eyes, concentrating hard, because he was determined to remember the sound of those words for as long as he lived. When he opened his eyes, Jonathan Wagner was at the window and motioning for him to roll it down. Landon did and said, "Thanks for having me. It was a great time."

"Hey, my man, you are more than welcome." Jonathan reached through and shook his hand. "And thanks for bouncing back on me after my off-sides penalty with the implants there. I appreciate you not holding a grudge. It sure wasn't a smart thing to say, that's all. And I just want you to know I'm sorry. Anyway, you'll be seeing me again real soon."

"Really?"

"Yeah, well, we got a bye week coming up, and my sister, Courtney, makes this meatloaf like our mom used to make that keeps me coming back." Jonathan's face looked a bit sad for a second, but then it brightened. "I'll check you guys out at your practice. This is all *if* Coach McAdoo gives us some time off. He should, so . . ."

Jonathan held out a fist and Landon knew to give it a bump, even though his head was spinning.

"I'll get to see you and Brett in action."

And suddenly, even after the magic of the day, Landon's nerves were on edge.

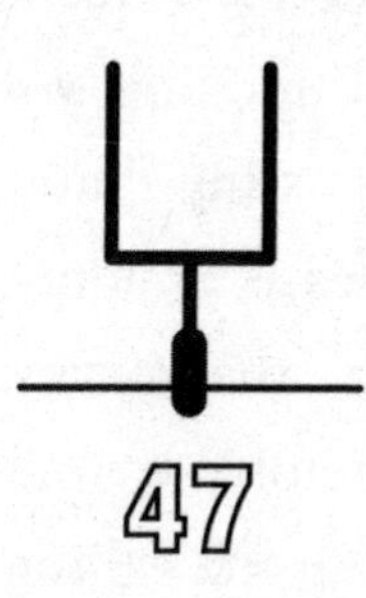

47

"I want to kiss Brett Bell."

Landon's mouth sagged open. "What did you say?" He blinked, unsure of what he'd just seen and heard, because it sounded like his sister had just said she wanted to *kiss* Brett Bell. Landon and Genevieve were out in the yard in the dying light of the day with glass jars, catching fireflies. The damp grass tickled his bare feet. In the twilight beneath the trees he easily could have mistaken what she said.

Genevieve staved him off with a hand as she crouched and then pounced with her jar, scooping it into the grass and clapping the top on in one expert motion. She held the jar up and frowned, searching in the gloom. When the bug lit up, it burned so bright Landon could make out the smile on her face and read her lips clearly when she looked at him. "I said I want to kiss him."

"That's gross."

"Oh, Landon." She rolled her eyes. "In a sister sort of way, or the way the French kiss when they meet."

"A *French* kiss?" Landon scowled at her. "Geez, Genevieve. That's even more gross, sticking your tongue in someone's mouth. What's more disgusting than *that*?"

Genevieve sighed. "Please, Landon. Nothing gross. Nothing romantic. 'Kiss' as in, he's the greatest kid in the world. That post with the split picture of you and Jonathan Wagner doing cannonballs? Michael Bamiro calling you the world champ? It's all over Instagram. That peeping thing is practically *gone*."

Landon caught a glint of light in the corner of his eye, and he spun and flailed after it, missing the fly completely. He watched it blip as it floated up into the trees, and then he turned back to Genevieve. "What about Megan?"

Genevieve nodded. "She's fine, Landon. She felt bad for you with all this."

"But she didn't come over." Landon fit the top onto his empty jar, practicing his scoop, and then hustled across the lawn when he spotted a firefly winking from a blade of grass. He pounced and held the jar up for Genevieve to see the bug blinking away.

"I got it!"

Genevieve came over and patted his shoulder. "Nice work."

Landon studied the insect as it crawled around on the inside of the jar with a wing askew and its bottom glowing, a miniature version of the sticks they carried with them on Halloween. He looked up when his sister tapped his arm.

"She's coming tomorrow to swim."

Landon's face got hot. "Tell her I'll be locked in the closet of my room when you guys are changing. Um . . . what about Katy?"

Genevieve swatted the air. "Forget Katy. She's dead to me."

"You shouldn't talk like that."

"Trust me, Landon." Even in the dim light Genevieve's eyes sparkled with anger. "What I'd like to do to her? Being dead *is* nice."

"Dad always says, 'Forgive and forget.'" Landon angled his head toward the house. In the light of the great room through the big window overlooking the backyard, they could see their father at his desk, working away.

"Forgiveness is for people who ask," Genevieve said.

"It's easier to let things go."

Genevieve shook her head violently. "You've got to fight sometimes, Landon. Fight people like Katy. Fight on the football field."

"That again?" Landon turned away.

Genevieve caught him. "You said Jonathan Wagner's going to be at practice sometime soon. What are you gonna do? Offer him water?"

"Maybe I'm just happy being on the team. Ever think of that?"

"No, Landon. Not the way you love football. No way."

Landon shook himself free from her. "We're catching fireflies, Genevieve. Let's just do that."

He turned his back on her, searching the yard, until he sensed her movement. Genevieve went into high gear. She might have been doing a dance routine, darting here and there, scooping, snatching, spinning, filling her jar. Landon watched her for a minute. Three, four, now five fireflies blinked inside their glass prison.

"Like it's so easy," he said to himself.

The solitary lightning bug flashed in his jar, but not as brightly as before.

Landon unscrewed the lid and let it go.

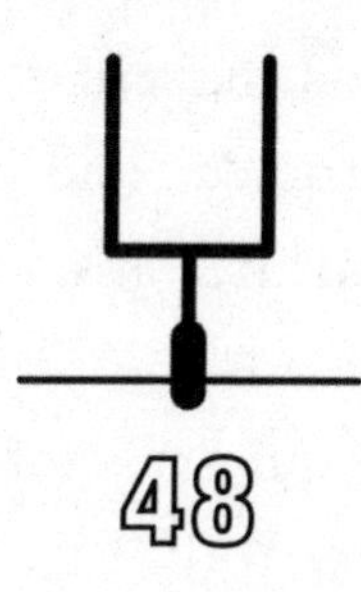

48

Sunday morning, Landon's mother was back to herself.

Gone were the bags under her eyes and the weary frown. She stood straight and moved about the stove like she had springs in her joints.

Bacon snapped beneath her spatula, filling the kitchen with a delicious smell. She was chattering at Landon's father, who presided over the toaster, waiting and watching patiently, butter knife in hand. Landon didn't know what she was saying, but when she realized he was there, she turned with the spatula in hand and beamed at him. "Good morning, sunshine."

"Hi, Mom." Landon sat down at the table at a place where someone had laid out placemats, plates, juice glasses, and silverware wrapped in checkered cloth napkins.

"Ready for a big day?" she asked.

Landon had had a big day yesterday, and this morning he'd

woken with excitement. His joy melted instantly, however, at the thought of Jonathan Wagner visiting practice only to see that his "man" was a powder puff. Landon's mind was stuck on that, and he wasn't thinking about today.

"What are we doing?" he asked.

"Well, school starts Tuesday and you and Genevieve both have games every weekend after this, so I thought we should do something special."

His mom turned to quickly shuffle the bacon and then looked back at him. "New York City. We're taking in the city. Uptown. Downtown. Soho. The Statue of Liberty. Empire State Building. A carriage ride in Central Park, maybe the zoo. Dinner at the Jekyll and Hyde Club."

"The *what?*" Landon unrolled the silverware and put the napkin in his lap.

"It's a haunted restaurant." Landon's mom made a scary face and turned her free hand into a claw. "Ghouls and mummies and such waiting on tables. Talking gargoyles."

Landon's father waved at him from the toaster. "Death by Chocolate. That's for dessert."

Genevieve appeared. "What dessert?"

"We're going to New York City to see *everything*," Landon said, teasing his mom.

"What?" Genevieve stared. "I've got Megan coming over to swim."

"Genevieve," their mom said, "it's Labor Day weekend. We're having a little family getaway, spending the night in New York. I've got us hotel rooms. There are fireworks on the Brooklyn Bridge after dinner."

Genevieve threw her arms in the air. "You don't just announce a family getaway on the morning of the getaway, Mom."

Their mom shrugged. "Well, I didn't know about it until now. I got up this morning at five and thought, yes, a family getaway to the greatest city in the world."

"Mom, this is important." Genevieve looked like she was begging.

"What's important?" their mom snorted. "Taking a swim?"

Genevieve gave Landon a knowing look. "Yes, Mom. It is."

"Not on my watch, young lady. Family first." Landon's mom pointed the spatula at his sister, and he saw that look on his mother's face, the one that said everyone better be careful. His father literally ducked down before buttering another slice of toast.

Landon's eyes went to his sister. He knew she could bite back, and he hoped she wouldn't now.

Genevieve's lips had a little wrestling match, good and bad fighting for control. Finally, she exhaled. "Fine."

The tension melted away, and Landon took a breath.

"The last couple weeks have been hard for everyone." Their mother's face softened. She turned and lifted the bacon out onto a bed of paper towels covering a platter. Beside the bacon rested another platter heaped with steaming scrambled eggs. She turned off the burner, slid a hand under each platter, and headed for the table. "This is a chance for us to reconnect as a total family. *And* do something fun. People come from all over the world to see the sights in New York City. We'd be fools not to take them in when they're right here under our noses."

Landon's dad delivered his platter of toast, and everyone

joined Landon, sitting at the table. Landon piled eggs and bacon onto his plate, got a piece of toast to help shovel, and dug in. He couldn't help focusing on his food, until he realized his mom was talking to Genevieve about the trip and he thought he heard Megan's name.

"I think it would be fun," his mom was saying.

Landon looked at Genevieve, who went for her phone on the table and began to text. "I'll ask her. I don't know if she can, but asking her makes canceling not so bad."

"Ask who what?" Landon took a swig of orange juice from his glass.

"Megan." Genevieve hit the Send button. "Mom said she can come with us."

Landon choked on his juice.

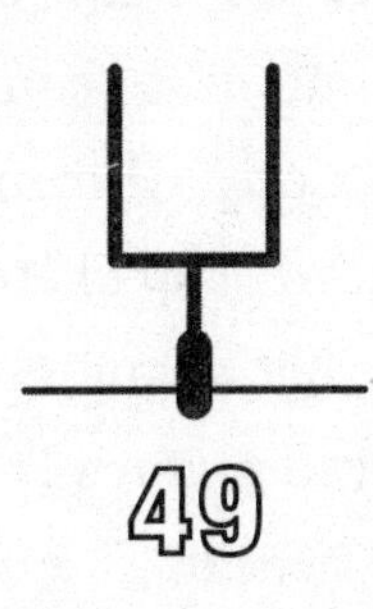

49

The trip to the city was fun. Landon had no idea something so simple and nice could cause yet another problem for him, but it did. A picture was taken after their dinner at Jekyll and Hyde by a man with a tightly trimmed beard on the Bow Bridge in Central Park. It was the five of them—Landon's family plus Megan—all crowded together, arms around one another, smiling, with the water and the incredible Central Park West skyline behind them. Genevieve had posted it on Instagram, a quaint family portrait plus a friend. #CentralPark.

By Monday evening, someone—and everyone seemed to know it was Katy Buford—had taken the image, cropped it so that Landon and Megan were standing together without anyone else in the picture, and added the caption, *Beauty and the Beast #Truelove?*

They couldn't pin it on Katy directly because the post was

on a site called ChitChat Bronxville, a horrid little cesspool on the internet where people in the small town could spew nasty rumors about one another without having to leave their fingerprints behind. It was a site where the posts were anonymous.

The picture and ensuing nasty comments had also revived Landon's 3P nickname, along with lots of other speculation about what he and Megan were up to and how she really mustn't have minded him seeing her changing after all. Landon read over Genevieve's shoulder in a state of shock until their mother took the phone to see for herself.

Landon's mother sat at the head of the kitchen table. With the look of a person about to jump out of an airplane, she started to read. Her lips moved and a frown dragged the corners of her mouth down. She began to tremble with rage. "It's vicious. It should be illegal."

Landon's father shrugged and made the mistake of observing, "It's free speech."

His mother's eyes cut Landon's father to the quick.

"But it shouldn't be," he added, hardly missing a beat.

"Well," his mom said, snapping the phone off, "we won't read it and we won't think about it. We're not going to validate this disgusting site by acknowledging that it's even there. That's what everyone should do. Would you read some nasty comment on the inside of a bathroom stall and then post it to discuss with people? That's all this is."

Landon had never seen Genevieve so defeated. She raised her head and spoke in a low voice Landon could barely make out. "Everyone else is seeing it and talking about it too. Everyone's saying to check out ChitChat Bronxville."

"Was there a site like this in Cleveland?" their mother asked. "A ChitChat Cleveland?"

"Things always start in New York or LA and bleed toward the middle of the country," Genevieve said. "So, no. I'd never heard of ChitChat until now, but Megan told me everyone here knows about it."

"And how is *she*?" Their mom puckered her lips for a moment. "Megan?"

Genevieve shrugged. "Upset, Mom. No good deed goes unpunished."

"What does that mean?" Their mom's back stiffened. "What good deed? Enjoying a getaway with us in the city? How is that a good deed?"

"Just . . ." Genevieve took a quick glance at Landon and then looked down at the kitchen table in front of her. She made a small, tight fist and banged it down. "Nothing."

Like the poison of a snakebite, the realization that Megan being nice to him was nothing more than charity seeped deeper and deeper into Landon's bloodstream, filling his body, and paralyzing it with pain. He sat for a minute, and then he staggered up from his chair and headed for the stairs. He heard his mother call to him gently, but he kept going.

As he climbed, each step brought with it the shred of a memory from the past two days: the cinnamon smell of Megan's hair next to him in the carriage ride through Central Park, the touch of her warm fingertips on the back of his hand to draw his attention to the sunset from atop the Empire State Building, the sound of her shriek when a ghoul popped up behind her chair at the Jekyll and Hyde Club, the sparkle of fireworks in those glassy blue eyes, the feel of her shoulder bones beneath his arm as he wrapped it around her for the picture that was causing all the problems.

And tomorrow?

Landon kicked his bedroom door shut and lay down.

Tomorrow was school, a disaster in and of itself. He'd asked himself before how anything could be worse than the first day of school at Bronxville. He knew now that it could be worse.

It would be so much worse.

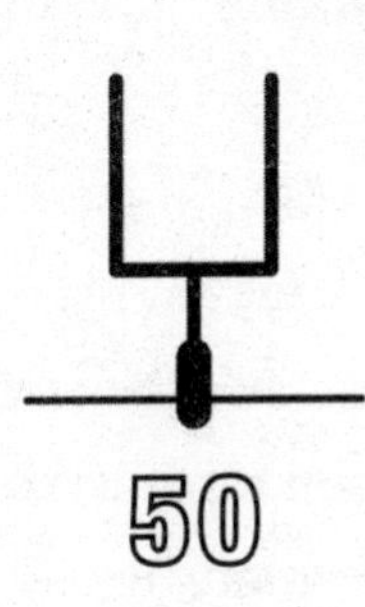
50

Landon woke with a headache and butterflies in his stomach, but knew that with his mom, if there wasn't any vomit or temperature, you were going to school. His mom was a fanatic about school attendance.

"Ninety percent of success is just showing up," she'd say.

So he did his thing in the bathroom, tugged on the khaki shorts and new strawberry-colored Izod shirt his mom had laid out for him, and clomped down the stairs. His dad sat bent over his computer in the great room. Landon waved as he passed into the kitchen, but his father was lost in his writing. Landon's mom was speaking to him, but he didn't hear a thing. He read her lips.

"Where are your ears, Landon?"

He shook his head, thought he might actually throw up from nerves, and returned to his bedroom for the ears. When he got back, Genevieve was at the table, halfway through her pancakes, and looking worried herself.

"Hey," he said.

"Hey." She put her fork down and cleared her plate. "Let's do this, okay?"

Landon forced a chuckle. "That's a little dramatic. We're not going into battle, Genevieve."

She narrowed her eyes. "Maybe *you're* not."

Landon picked at his own pancakes, cleared his plate from the table, and went to say good-bye to his dad. Landon had to tap his father three times before his fingers stopped dancing on the keyboard. He looked up, blinking. "Oh, hey, buddy. Wow. In a zone. Ready for school?"

"I guess so."

"Hey." His dad put his hands on Landon's shoulders. He nodded toward his computer before looking deep into Landon's eyes. "Nodnal is fighting the dragon right now. That's the scene I'm on. His hair and eyebrows have been roasted off his head. He's bleeding from his nose and his sword is broken. The dragon is crashing down on top of him, and do you know what's gonna happen?"

Landon watched his father's eyebrow creep up into an arch on his forehead.

"He's gonna be crushed?" Landon didn't see how it could go any other way.

His father's lips quivered into a small smile. "No, Landon. Nodnal dives to the ground with his sword like this."

Landon's dad gripped the handle of his pretend sword, one hand on top of the other like a baseball bat. "The broken sword is straight up, like a post. The dragon comes down with all his weight and impales his heart, just a nick, on the jagged tip. On reflexes alone, the dragon jumps up and away, trips, falls flat on his back . . . and dies."

Landon simply stared. After a few moments, he said, "This is real life, Dad."

"I know it is." His father mussed Landon's hair. "But happy endings abound. Where do you think happy endings came from, buddy? Real life. Go get yourself one."

Landon's dad turned back toward his screen and went to work.

Landon walked out the door. Genevieve was waiting for him in the driveway. She wore a short Abercrombie dress with a matching dark blue ribbon to hold back her thick hair from her face.

Landon took a deep breath and let it loose. "Ready?"

"Not yet." Genevieve shook her head. "Mom said for us to wait. She's going with us before she goes to the train station."

"Oh, boy."

Genevieve bit her lip. "Yup. She better not do anything crazy."

Their mom came out of the garage, heading their way with her briefcase strap over her shoulder. Her mouth was stretched as thin as a paper cut. "Okay, kids. First day of school in Bronxville. Thought I'd have a little *chat* with the principal. Ready?"

The word "chat" told them that their mom was ready for a fight. Landon and Genevieve exchanged a look.

She was already past them, headed directly for the middle school.

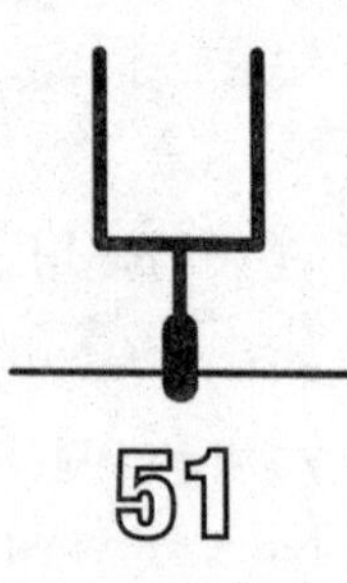

51

Landon and Genevieve sat reluctantly with their mom, staring at Mr. Sanders, who sprouted hair from his head like weeds in a garden. As if to compensate for the hair, his suit was shiny-new, his black-and-blue-striped tie crisply knotted. The principal greeted Landon's mother like an old friend. He said that after all the calls and emails, he felt he knew her.

"Mrs. Dorch, at our last teachers' meeting we discussed Landon's hearing. I emphasized that he needs to read lips to fully understand, and everyone is on board. We want Landon to feel welcome." The principal grinned widely and raised his eyebrows.

Landon's mother said, "Thank you, Mr. Sanders, but we're not here about that."

Then she proceeded to explain the situation.

Now Mr. Sanders wore a look of serious concern. "I told

you on the phone, we have a no-tolerance bullying policy, Mrs. Dorch, and I meant it."

His mom seemed to accept that just fine. "I run fifty offices across the globe. Trust me, I know that even the best leader cannot be responsible for every move her team makes. And I know there are outside forces . . . the internet. Social media."

Mr. Sanders winced at the words. "But we try and educate our students. I assure you."

"Right. But I'm here because this internet bullying is *real.* It's anonymous, but it's not imagined. It's not hypothetical. All you have to do is check out ChitChat Bronxville if you don't believe me. If you do believe me, don't check it out, because looking at those things validates them, don't you think?"

"I see what you're saying." Mr. Sanders started clicking his pen.

"We can't prove any direct accusation because it is all anonymous, but we can bet this came from a student in their grade." She looked at Landon and Genevieve. The smoldering anger in her eyes made Landon's mouth dry.

"Be alert, is all I'm asking, Mr. Sanders," Landon's mom said. "Talk to my kids' teachers. Make them aware. Landon will never say a word, but Genevieve is apt to go ballistic."

Mr. Sanders stopped clicking his pen. He glanced at Genevieve, who gave him a wan smile.

"Get what I'm saying?" Landon's mom asked.

Mr. Sanders cleared his throat and said, "We have another teacher meeting this afternoon. I promise we'll discuss this."

"Great!" Landon's mom popped up. "I'm off to work. Thanks so much for your time, Mr. Sanders."

Their mom gave them each a kiss on the cheek and then gave Mr. Sanders's hand a feisty little shake before disappearing out the door. Genevieve wasn't waiting around. She was in a different homeroom than Landon, one that was on the other side of the school. She was halfway out the door when Landon turned to the principal. "Sorry, Mr. Sanders."

Mr. Sanders circled his desk and put a hand on Landon's shoulder. "Don't be sorry. I wish every mom cared that much about her kids. You can't begin to imagine . . ."

Landon nodded, even though he wasn't quite sure he understood. "See you."

"See you, Landon. And Landon, don't worry about any of this."

Landon nodded again and turned and left the office, plunging into the sea of hostility, hoping for even a scrap of something that could help him stay afloat.

Landon walked into Room 114, and there it was.

A life jacket.

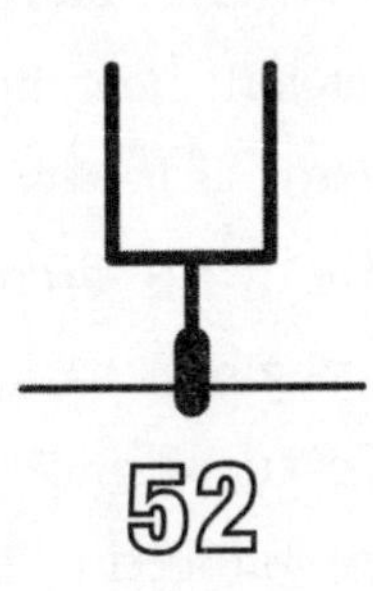

52

Brett jumped out of his chair, slapped his hand into Landon's and pulled him into a teammate hug, thumping him on the back. "Landon, come sit here." He motioned to the seat next to him. "I saved you a seat."

Landon didn't need anything else. He didn't scan the room from the corners of his eyes. He didn't worry about people dipping their heads together to whisper. He was saved.

His friend was wearing a Rashad Jennings Giants jersey and matching gym shorts.

"Dude, put your stuff down and get your schedule." Brett pointed at the desk where Landon rested his backpack. "Let's see how many classes we have together. Schedules are on Mrs. Rigling's desk."

Landon retrieved his schedule and got a smiling wink from Mrs. Rigling. Things were looking up. He returned to his desk and sat down. Brett grabbed the schedule from his hand and placed it down next to his own.

"Let's see. First, I got English. You got math. . . ."

Landon dared to look around. Half the kids were busy with their schedules. The other half he caught gawking at him like a zoo animal. He wasn't sure if it was because of Brett's warm welcome, the internet site, or his cochlear implants, but their eyes scattered when they saw him looking at them.

". . . Fourth, you got earth science. I got . . . social studies. Darn." Brett frowned and glanced at Landon. "Lunch? Nope. Hey, wait, we got gym together! That's a good thing."

Landon felt a ray of thankfulness. Gym was always a nightmare: being picked last, no one wanting to be his partner, getting beaned as the easiest target the game of dodgeball had ever known.

"No for eight. No nine either." Brett frowned and looked up. "Well, it's homeroom and gym, but you'll have some of the other guys on the team in your classes. You'll be okay."

Both of them knew that wasn't true, but Landon kept up appearances, even when Mrs. Rigling arrived at his desk to deliver printed announcements with a secret smile. He knew this came from his mother. She'd made calls and emails to Mr. Sanders because he hadn't a prayer of understanding most of what was said on a loudspeaker. Still, he hated being singled out like that. When the announcements were over, Mrs. Rigling rapped a ruler lightly on her desk, stood, and went through the disciplinary code and the policy on late arrivals to homeroom, often looking straight at Landon.

"Also," she said, "I'll have some of you for math class, and any of you—whether you're in my math class or Mr. Mazella's—are welcome to ask me questions during homeroom period. I love math, and helping you learn it is why I'm here."

When Mrs. Rigling sat down, Landon leaned close to Brett. "See you in gym."

"You got it, my man."

They bumped fists. The bell rang, and Landon took a deep breath as the day began.

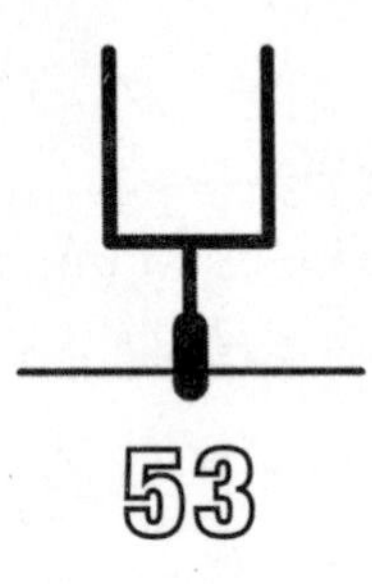
53

The seat that was most helpful for Landon to sit in—front row, middle—was empty. He kept his eyes on the teacher, Mr. Mazella, from the moment he sat down. Math was his favorite class. Numbers were always straightforward. There wouldn't be hidden meanings in a comment made offhandedly. But once Mr. Mazella got started, he often spoke with his back to the class, making it hard for Landon to keep up.

When the bell rang, Landon thought of saying something, but there was no time. Instead, he went directly to his second-period class, English, which was on the opposite end of the school. The halls were crowded, but Landon just kept his head down and plowed along. He focused on people's feet. He liked the shocking orange, blue, and strawberry-colored sneakers with fluorescent green or yellow laces. His own sneakers were electric blue with laces that were school bus yellow.

If anyone did say anything to him, it was lost in the noise. Hearing in a crowd was nearly impossible unless he was looking hard and closely at a person's lips.

When he entered the classroom for English, he froze.

Megan Nickell was in the front row, head hung down and hands folded in her lap. Her face hid behind a curtain of hair, and she seemed to be shaking. Landon walked up to her and tapped her shoulder. She looked up with wet, red eyes and sniffed. "Oh. Landon."

"Are you . . . can I sit here?" Landon pointed to the desk next to hers.

She shrugged. "Sure. Okay."

Landon sat down and took out his things. He was about to say something when he saw the teacher, Mr. Edwards, at his desk with an open book, making notes. Landon wanted to look at Megan. He wanted to do something—anything—to make her feel better. Still, all he could do was stare straight ahead feeling embarrassed.

The bell rang and Mr. Edwards climbed up onto his desk, looking down at them all with an impish smile from his corner of the room. His bright blue eyes flashed from behind gold wire-rimmed glasses. In his hand was a book.

"*The Count of Monte Cristo.* Who's read it?" Mr. Edwards raised a single eyebrow, reminding Landon of his father. "What? No one? Ladies and gentlemen, you're in for a treat. Alexandre Dumas is famous for this book, as well as *The Man in the Iron Mask.*"

Landon's hand shot up, but he spoke without waiting to be called on. "And *The Three Musketeers.*"

The classroom erupted with laughter. Landon looked around. Megan looked embarrassed for him, and Landon realized they were laughing at him, either because of the garbled sound of his voice or the enthusiasm of his words for something most of them couldn't give a hoot about. Landon didn't mind, though, because he felt like he had a connection with Mr. Edwards, and that was all that mattered to him. His heart was racing at the thought of learning more about books like the one he already loved.

Mr. Edwards's blue eyes sparkled. "Yes, that too; and can you tell me why Alexandre Dumas was such a successful writer?"

"He makes you care?" The words simply escaped from Landon's mouth.

"Yes!"

Mr. Edwards looked around at the class with a wild expression. Landon took a glance and soaked up the empty stares and the smirks held back by bitten lips.

Mr. Edwards either didn't see them or chose not to notice. He plunged ahead, taking Landon with him. He told them all about Dumas's life and then read quotes from the book about vengeance. Halfway through the period, he thumped a box down on his desk and began passing out paperback copies. He was waving his arms and talking about General Dumas (the writer's father) being betrayed by Napoleon when the bell rang, and everyone but Landon popped out of the seats.

"Chapters one through five for tomorrow!" Mr. Edwards shouted. "You will be quizzed."

A collective groan went up from the departing students.

Landon couldn't wait to read it, though. He checked his

schedule to see where he had to go next and then tucked the book away in his backpack. The room had nearly emptied out, and he fell in behind Megan at the door.

"Good stuff, huh?"

She turned and gave him a worried look. "Yes. Everyone talks about Mr. Edwards. Whether they love him or hate him, everyone talks about him."

"Hate him?" Landon said as they entered the fray of the hallway. "Why would anyone hate him?" He was intent on Megan's face, so he knew by her expression that something was wrong. Before he could learn what, he was suddenly shoved backward into the lockers. His head slammed against the metal with a crash.

Megan shrieked.

Landon regained his senses, and the hateful face in front of him came into focus.

"Skip?"

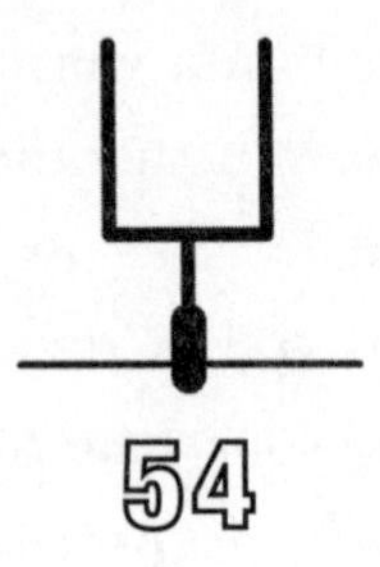

54

The freckles seemed to jump off Skip's burning, snarling face.

Landon wanted to say that they were teammates.

He wanted to say that he hadn't done anything wrong.

But he couldn't get a single word out before Skip hammered him again. Landon covered his head with both arms, and the blows struck his chest and shoulders before Mr. Edwards yelled, "Stop! Immediately!" He yelled at another teacher to get Mr. Sanders.

Megan had dropped her books, and she stood crying as Landon slid his spine down the lockers and took a seat on the floor, covering his head again with his arms and resting it between his knees. One of his battery packs hung loose, and he slipped it back behind his ear.

He glanced up to see Skip scowling as the principal raced toward them.

Megan touched his arm. "Are you okay, Landon?"

Landon almost smiled to see her. "Yes. I'm fine. I don't know why . . ."

Megan looked over at Skip, who was now being marched down the hall by Mr. Sanders. "We . . . I . . . broke up. I told him, and everyone, to leave you alone."

Landon's heart swelled.

Mr. Edwards leaned down. "Are you okay?"

"I'm fine," Landon said, hoping Genevieve wasn't among the hundred-or-so gawking students.

"Come on." Mr. Edwards helped Landon to his feet. "Let's get you to the nurse."

Landon felt a bolt of panic. He wanted this to end, and he shook himself free. "No, I'm fine, Mr. Edwards. Please. Nothing happened."

"You were taking a beating when I got out here." Mr. Edwards took hold of Landon's arm again. "Come on. Nurse. Then Mr. Sanders. This isn't the Wild West. We need to fix this thing."

As Landon marched through the open-mouthed crowd toward the nurse's office, he knew that no matter how good Mr. Edwards's intentions were, some things just couldn't be fixed.

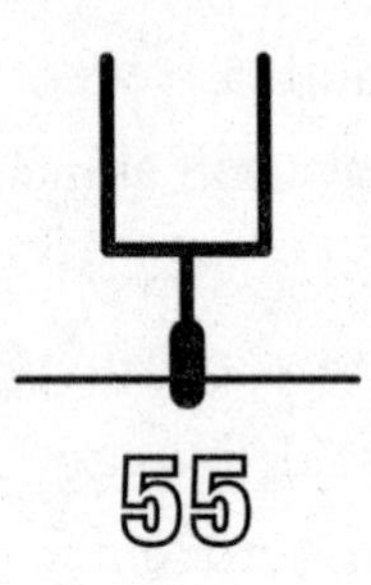

55

Landon blushed, humiliated to be slumped there on the exam table without his shirt, rolls of blubber quivering like Jell-O. He hugged himself to cover up as much as he could while the nurse probed Landon's bruised shoulders and chest. Speaking in a loud voice, she told Mr. Edwards, "Students today are trouble, and the parents can be worse. Mr. Sanders isn't going to want the Dreyfuses on his case."

"How could *they* complain? It's their son who gave Landon these bruises." Mr. Edwards's mouth fell open in disbelief.

"You said the boys were teammates, Dalton. Football?"

"They are."

Landon looked back and forth between them, thinking that it was strange to hear Mr. Edwards called by his first name, Dalton.

"Right." She gave a nod and whisked her hands together

with some Purell before turning to make some notes at her desk. "Football. Bruises. That's consistent, Dalton."

"Skip Dreyfus was using him as a punching bag," Mr. Edwards said.

"I believe you, but the Dreyfuses are apt to suggest these came from football." The nurse clucked her tongue. "Luckily these bruises aren't serious, but I know Mr. Sanders is going to have to deal with this. You can put your shirt on, Landon."

Landon wiggled into his shirt and followed Mr. Edwards to the principal's office. "I'm really okay, sir." His mom would go ballistic if she heard he'd been attacked. "The nurse is right, I might have gotten these bruises in football, or jumping in the pool. We had a cannonball contest Saturday."

Mr. Edwards looked at Landon and sighed. He seemed both disappointed and flustered. "I get it, Landon. You don't want more trouble. But sometimes trouble's what it takes."

They reached the office. "Okay, wait here."

Landon took the seat outside the principal's office and sat for quite a while before Mr. Sanders's door opened and the principal signaled him to come in.

To Landon's complete surprise, Skip was still there, shoulders hunched, head angled down, looking angry. Mr. Sanders pointed at the chair next to Skip. Landon hesitated, but Mr. Sanders gave him an impatient nod, so he sat down.

Mr. Sanders laced his fingers together and laid his locked-up hands on the desk in front of him. "Boys . . . things happen, and sometimes the best thing is to resolve them quietly and move on."

Landon nodded because he was on board with whatever. If

there was a way to avoid bringing his mother in on all this, he was game.

"I don't know how things worked in . . ."—Mr. Sanders searched an open file before him on the desk—". . . Cleveland, Landon, but in Bronxville we like to resolve our differences and move on. Now, I know you two got into a kind of shoving match in the hall. . . ."

Mr. Sanders looked closely at Landon. Landon was briefly confused because a shoving match wasn't anything like what had happened.

"I . . . uh, yes." Landon nodded and looked at Skip, who still appeared furious behind his clenched teeth.

"Right!" Mr. Sanders banged his hands to bring home the point. "And when shoving matches occur, we talk to the offenders and give them a stern warning and send them on their way. But . . ."

Mr. Sanders now raised a single finger and looked back and forth between them. "This *cannot* happen again."

Landon shook his head no. Skip tightened his grip on the armrests of his chair.

"Mr. Dreyfus? Are we clear on this?"

Skip didn't move his mouth when he spoke, but Landon was pretty sure he said, "Yes."

"Mr. Dorch?"

Although Landon was confused, since he'd done nothing wrong, he knew he had to agree and make all this go away. So he said, "Yes, sir." With a nod of his head, Landon prepared to rise.

"Because next time there will be detention and possibly *suspension,* for you *both.*"

Landon kept nodding and rising, and Mr. Sanders said, "Now shake hands before you go."

Landon searched Skip's face and saw a flicker of relief before he smiled a phony smile and stretched out his hand for the shake.

Mr. Sanders said, "Good. Now go."

Landon left without bothering to look back at Skip. He could only assume the redheaded quarterback was right behind him, and with the halls empty now halfway through fourth period, Landon hustled along at nearly a jog because he was seriously unsure whether or not Skip would obey the principal. Landon didn't stop until he reached Room 117 and his earth science class with Mrs. Lewis. He looked in through the window and saw everyone staring at the short, round teacher. Landon turned the knob slowly, trying to be quiet, but when he looked over his shoulder and saw Skip trudging toward him, he fumbled with the knob, sprung it open, and spilled inside, tripping and dumping himself and his backpack onto the floor.

The whole class burst into laughter.

Horrified, Landon looked up to see what Mrs. Lewis was saying to him because he could hear the drone of the teacher's voice.

"What?" Landon asked as he gathered himself and his backpack.

"What?" Mrs. Lewis said. "Are you making fun of me with that tone of voice?"

"No." Landon shook his head fiercely. "I didn't hear what you said. I was just asking what you said."

She studied Landon for a moment before relaxing the smallest bit. "I said, 'Fighting and clowning around is no way to begin your career as a Bronxville student,' Mr. Dorch. And you, Mr. Dreyfus, don't think you fool me with that smile. Take a seat."

Landon wedged himself into an empty seat, front row, middle, and the teacher looked past him. "Magma from deep in the earth's core . . ."

Landon tried to take his things out as quietly and smoothly as possible. By the time he had a blank notebook page and a pencil in his hand, he'd missed at least one, if not three, important points. He glanced around and saw the others writing furiously.

Landon knew he should raise his hand and ask the teacher to explain again. He knew that's what his mother would urge him—demand him, even—to do.

She'd said it a thousand times if she'd said it once. "The squeaky wheel gets the grease, Landon, and no child of mine is going to worry about making a little noise. Bang the drums! Crash the cymbals, Landon!"

Landon heard her words, and his brain steamed like a teakettle.

Several times his hand crept up the front of his shirt, fingers extended, ready to rise up, but he just couldn't do it. So, he sat and spiraled down into an ever-greater state of confusion.

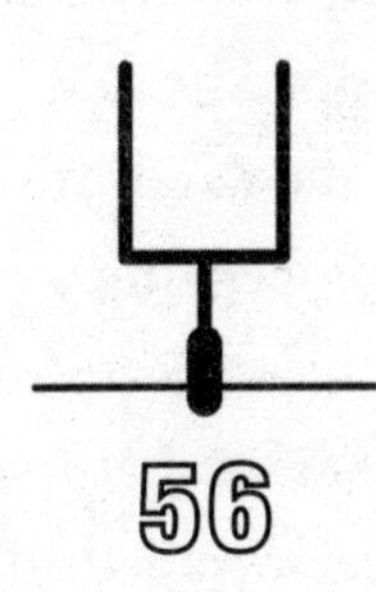

56

Earth science finally ended, and Landon headed for lunch.

It didn't surprise him that Genevieve appeared from nowhere and blocked his path.

"What *happened*?" Her face was red with fury.

"Nothing. Leave it alone." Landon looked around, grabbed his sister, and pulled her into an alcove outside the auditorium so that they could talk up close and personal. He grabbed both of her arms. "Stop it, Genevieve."

She swiped his hands away. "What *happened*?"

"Lower your voice." Landon felt desperate. "Just . . . just listen. It's all going to be fine. Megan broke up with Skip, did you know that?"

"Yes, of course I knew that." She glowered.

"So, he's upset, but Mr. Sanders said everything was going to be fine, not a big deal, but we cannot fight again." Landon made a cutting motion with one hand. "If it happens we'll be suspended, and I'm sure Skip Dreyfus doesn't want to be suspended any more than I do. So, it's over."

"Landon, seriously? How can you be okay with this? Skip is a jerk. I can't just let this go," she said.

"Right now this is off the radar. It's over. Can't we just keep it that way?" Landon was begging now, because he knew it went against everything Genevieve was about. "I don't want people on the football team mad at me because Skip gets suspended and misses a game or something . . ."

"Those jerks? Why do you care? They don't even respect you!"

"People appreciate me, Genevieve." Landon clasped his hands. "They do. Not all of them, but a lot. They say thanks to me for what I do. I'm on the team. That's all that matters. After lunch I've got study hall, then gym class with Brett and he's so cool, and I've got Megan in my English class and . . . I mean, we could even end up doing some projects together. Things are not *that* bad. I'm begging you, Genevieve."

"Landon." She sighed. "What period do you have lunch?"

"Now."

"Shoot. Let me see your schedule."

"Genevieve, you're not supposed to swear." Landon fished the schedule out of his backpack and handed it over.

"I've got lunch next period. I won't be with you."

"That's okay." Landon gave her shoulder a light punch.

"Well, we have social studies and Spanish together for the last two classes of the day, and Megan's with us too."

"Nice. She's great," Landon said.

"What do you mean?" Genevieve wore a stunned look.

Landon shrugged. "Just that she's great."

"Yeah, but you said it like . . ." Genevieve shook her head. "No, Landon. Not like that. She likes you as a friend, so do not ruin it, okay?"

"I have no idea what you're talking about."

The first bell rang.

"Yeah, Landon. I think you do know what I'm talking about." Genevieve bore her eyes into his. "Don't. That's all I can say, just don't."

"I gotta get to class. You too." Landon turned and walked away.

57

At lunch, Landon bought four cartons of milk before he entered the throng. He saw some faces he recognized from football: West and Furster presiding over a tableful of teammates, Nichols at the edge. He quickly turned away, knowing better than to sit with them, and found a table in the far corner where an odd-looking girl with pink-and-blue hair sat with two undersize boys, one with a glaring birthmark on his cheek, the other with glasses as thick as bulletproof glass. They stared at him, warning him away from their territory with dirty looks, so Landon sat at the far end of that table and began unpacking his brown bag. He'd only removed two of his four meatloaf-and-ketchup sandwiches before he detected movement from the other three kids.

Without a sound or a signal, they got up and left the table.

Landon bit down hard on his sandwich and forced himself

to chew and swallow, chew and swallow, until everything was gone. In the dull roar around him, he neither looked nor tried to listen. He was just wadding up his last ball of cellophane when the bell rang and people began to scramble.

The hallways gave Landon a kind of relief because he could move in and out of people without giving them much of a chance to stare or poke fun at his ears or the way he spoke. He set his eyes on the floor, sat through a study hall, struggling with his math homework, and then practically skipped to gym class because he knew Brett would be waiting for him. After that, for the final two periods of the day, he'd have Genevieve and Megan to keep him company. And, as long as Skip wasn't there, his first day of school might not be a total disaster. He didn't even want to think about football practice.

That, he knew, would not be good.

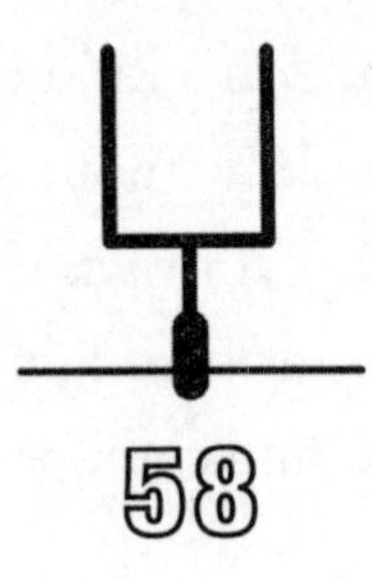

58

The school day ended on an upswing. In the last two class periods, he sat happily between Megan and his sister in the front row. When the final bell rang, Brett was waiting for Landon and the girls at Landon's locker.

"Hey," Brett said, "where we going? Diner for some pie?"

Megan shrugged. "Everyone goes to the diner. Let's do something else."

"Häagen-Dazs?" Landon nearly burst with pride when they all agreed it was a great idea.

On their way outside, it didn't seem to matter that Katy Buford sat on the steps with three heavily made-up girls trying their best to copy her by casting vicious looks their way.

"Hi, Katy." Genevieve sounded as pleasant as the first day she arrived. "We're going to Häagen-Dazs; want to join us?"

Katy was caught so far off guard, she could only snort and

sputter. They'd reached the bottom of the steps, where the trees cast their shade, before Katy got a word out. "You wish!"

Genevieve spun on a dime, still smiling. "No, not really. Enjoy your little cat club. Who's that? Lucinda Rayes? Isn't she the girl you said you'd never invite to another sleepover because she destroyed your bathroom? Probably hard for you to tell one bad smell from another, though, right, Katy?"

Megan looked like she was trying not to laugh, but Brett guffawed, slapping his leg and growing bright with joy. "Classic crush!"

Katy took out her phone and pretended to be busy, but Landon could see that her back had stiffened and her face burned beneath the skin.

They kept on going down the sidewalk and took a right toward the center of town, with Brett on one end and Landon on the other. They talked about the teachers they liked best and worst—Edwards best and Mazella worst for Landon, Edwards and others for the rest.

"I think Mr. Mazella is a good teacher," Genevieve said. "You should just ask him. I bet he'd help you, Landon. He just loves math is all. He gets excited."

Landon was looking ahead to the Häagen-Dazs when Brett stopped in his tracks.

"Uh-oh," Brett said with a weary sigh. "Here comes real trouble."

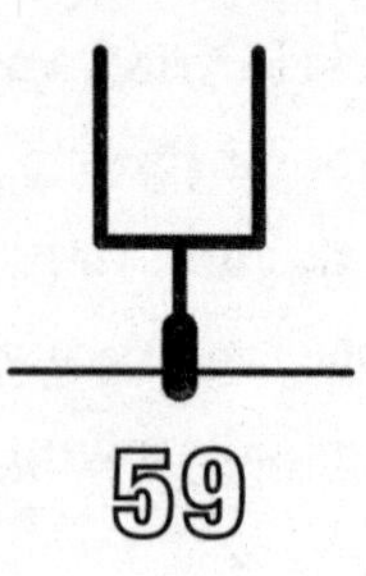

59

Skip was sandwiched between Mike and Xander. They all wore tough-guy looks.

"Going for a little ice cream, kids?" Skip said it like ice cream was for babies.

"Hey, Skip. What's up?" Brett stepped forward.

"Just get out of here, Brett," Skip said. "This has got nothing to do with you. This is me and the dummy." He nodded toward Landon.

"Mr. Sanders said no more fighting, Skip. Neither of us wants to get suspended." Landon tried not to sound afraid, even though he was.

Skip made a show of looking around. "Yeah, which is why we're standing on Pondfield Road instead of in the cafeteria. Sanders can't touch me here, and you're twice my size, so I can do whatever I have to do to protect myself."

"Who's gonna believe that?" Genevieve fired out.

Mike decided to get into the fray. "How about Xander's dad? Chief of police."

Brett shook his head. "Look, you guys don't want to do this. Do you know how stupid you're gonna look wearing your butts as hats?"

"What hats?" Skip narrowed his eyes at Brett. "What are you even talking about, Bell?"

Brett clenched his hands and took another step forward. "If you don't get the heck out of here, I'm gonna kick your butts so hard, you'll be wearing them for hats. Those hats."

"There's three of us." Mike spat his words, but he wasn't moving closer.

Brett snorted. "I only see about two. One for Skip and about a half each for you two clowns."

Furster and West looked at Skip to see how he'd respond.

"Look, Brett, we're teammates. This isn't about you."

"You're right. *We're* teammates," Brett said. "All of us."

"Not *him*." Xander pointed at Landon.

"Yes, him," Brett growled. "Last time I checked, he was on our team. And besides, he's not the one who took your girlfriend, Skip."

"I know he didn't *take* my girlfriend. He's like her big pet Wookiee." Skip laughed with his friends. "That big dork isn't gonna *take* my girlfriend."

"Yeah," Brett said quietly but with a hard edge, "'cause *I* did that."

Skip's eyes went from Brett to Megan, back and forth several times, before settling on Brett. With a blood-curdling yell, Skip launched himself.

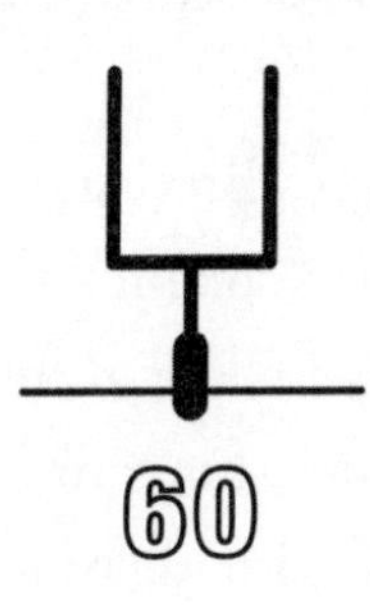
60

Xander and Mike went for Landon.

Landon never found out how serious they were about it because neither of them got their hands on him. Genevieve stepped up and kicked them, hard and directly, right in their shins, just like that, one-two. They cried out and went down like bowling pins.

Brett was amazing.

When Skip got close, Brett hooked an arm under Skip's, lifted, and flipped him to the side. Skip went down with a thud on the grass and then rolled into a tree, but he hopped up and came after Brett again. Every time he got close, Brett just sidestepped him, or tripped him, or spun him around and threw him to the ground. Before too long, Skip was out of breath and hunched over with a bloody nose.

When Genevieve went to give him a bonus kick, Brett

scooped her up and spun her around. "Oh, no you don't. None of that. He's had enough, haven't you, Skip?"

Skip only glared up at him and smeared the back of his hand with a bright swatch of blood from his nose as it dripped steadily into the grass.

"Yeah, he's had enough." Brett started to walk away. "Come on, guys. Let's get some ice cream."

Brett paused and they looked at him. "Come on."

He turned again, and this time they followed. Landon made sure the girls were with them and the bad guys weren't following before he relaxed enough to say, "Brett, what was that? Like, jujitsu?"

"Nah." Brett waved a hand through the air. "Just wrestling."

Landon shook his head. "How can you be so calm about it?"

"I'm not afraid of them, Landon. You were right. I could crush them." Brett held the door for them all. "You could too. You just don't know it."

Genevieve chimed in, "That's what I keep saying to him."

"Yeah, we gotta work on that, Landon." They all sat down at a table in the corner before Brett turned to Megan. The way he looked at her, and she at him, gave Landon a jolt. He'd assumed Brett was kidding when he said *he'd* taken Megan from Skip.

"You okay?" Brett asked her.

"Yes. Thank you," she said.

Then she put her head on Brett's shoulder, breaking Landon's heart.

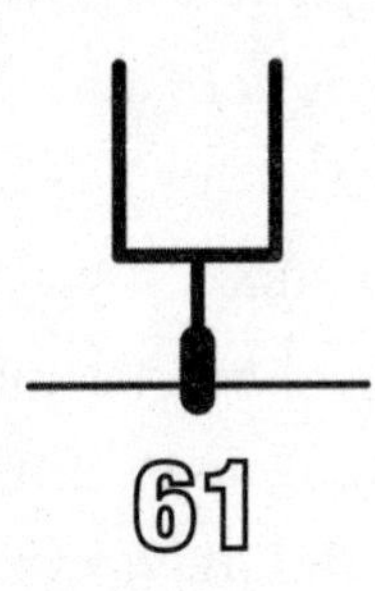

61

Later, after their friends had gone home, it was just Landon and Genevieve by the pool.

"I *told* you not to go there, Landon." Genevieve threw her hands in the air and did a can opener into the pool.

Landon sat at the table beneath the wide, green umbrella with his math homework spread out. Genevieve surfaced and he shouted at her, "I didn't *go there.* I didn't go anywhere!"

"Then why are you sulking like that? You haven't said a word since they left." Genevieve popped up out of the pool and stood dripping on terrace stones until she swiped a towel off the chair next to Landon.

"Because multiplying fractions stinks!" He realized he was shouting.

Genevieve's face turned sad, and she put a hand on his

cheek, which he shrugged away. "I get it, Landon. She's beautiful and she's so nice."

"I don't care about all that." Landon tried to focus on the problem in front of him. "Brett is my friend. My only friend. Even if I liked Megan, I'm not going to do anything stupid if my only friends likes her too."

"I tried to warn you, Landon. I saw that look on your face. I saw you thinking about her like that and I told you, don't do it." Genevieve tossed that grenade at him, and then she bounced off the end of the board and did a swan dive, slipping into the water with barely a splash.

Landon tried to ignore her and instead focus on the fractions in front of him. Genevieve climbed out of the pool, wrapped herself in the towel, and sat down across the table from him. Sunshine poked pinpricks through the wide, green umbrella above. A slight breeze carried with it the ripe promise of fall.

Landon looked up and saw her staring at him. "I'm doing my homework."

"You can't blame anyone," she said. "With people like Megan and Brett, it just happens. They're together with a common cause and they realize they like each other. And their common cause is you, so you can't feel that bad."

"I. Am. Fine." Landon banged a fist down on the glass tabletop, snapping the pencil in his hand. "Now see what you made me do?" He didn't take it back, but he said, "How the heck can you multiply something and it gets smaller, huh? What'd Mom call that? An oxymoron? I'm an oxymoron. No, I'm a just plain moron."

Genevieve stared at him for a moment. "You can't blame yourself, either. I shouldn't have said, 'I warned you.' Everyone's in love with Megan. She's gorgeous. She sweet. She's smart. She and I are probably going to be co-captains of the soccer team. She's got it all."

Landon checked his answer against the key in the back of the book. He had 3/16; the book said the answer was 1/8. He scribbled and scratched at his answer, blotting it out until nothing remained but a horrible mess and a small hole in the homework sheet.

Genevieve got up and peeked over his shoulder. She tapped him. "You added the numerators. One plus two equals three, but you were supposed to multiply them. One times two equals two. Then two over sixteen reduces to one over eight. You're close."

Landon made an arrow on his paper and wrote in the correct number above sixteen: two. "Yup, just like me and Brett and Megan. There's no room for three, just two."

"That's not true. There's room for all of us: four friends."

"You know what I mean."

"Hey." Genevieve grabbed his cheeks. "I know that I'm the luckiest sister in the world. You've got so much, Landon. You're just a late bloomer. When you come into your own, all kinds of things are going to happen."

Landon wanted to cry. "I don't know if that's even true, but in the meantime, I feel like I need to make myself as small as I possibly can, and that's not easy, Genevieve. It's not easy at all. Look at me."

"Well, stop making yourself small," she said. "Stand up for yourself. Don't worry if people notice you."

He wanted to agree with her. Instead, he hugged his little sister, wishing he was half as strong as she was. "I gotta go get my stuff ready for practice."

"I'll help Dad with dinner," she said. "I'm sure he needs it. He doesn't get off that computer, you know? I wonder if Mom will make it home."

Landon hesitated. "Do you think Brett was right? Do you think everything will be like . . . normal with Skip and everyone at practice tonight?"

"I think he gave them a lot to think about," Genevieve said. "I think if Brett wants things to be like nothing happened, they'll count themselves pretty darn lucky. Also, I think he and Megan being an item takes a lot of the pressure off of you."

A spark of hope glowed in Landon's heart. "Do you think that's all it is? Him and her helping me?"

"No, Landon." She shook her head sadly. "I think they're just both nice and they like each other. Just enjoy being friends. They like you. We don't need other friends if we've got Brett and Megan, and we can just be ourselves around them."

"And who are *we?*" Landon made a crazy face and wiggled his fingers.

They laughed and went inside together.

After dinner, Landon's dad dropped him at football practice. Landon did his thing with the water and the running, never taking his helmet off, and Brett was right. It was like nothing had happened. It made the whole first day of school seem like some dream, or a TV show that Landon had seen and not been a part of.

Landon got to math class early the second day of school, and before class started he politely explained to Mr. Mazella that he needed to see what he was saying to fully understand. Mr. Mazella not only told him it wasn't a problem, he also instructed Landon to remind him if he forgot, by simply rapping on his desk. So Genevieve had been right about him.

When he saw Skip or his buddies in the hallway, even though his stomach knotted up waiting for something to happen, nothing did. That didn't mean Landon could shake the sense that they were planning something, because he couldn't. His instincts told him the feud was far from over, but he also had to admit that he might just be paranoid after a lifetime of problems with other kids.

At lunch, he ate alone again. He could handle that, though. It took him nearly the entire period to finish everything anyway, and Landon didn't need a ton of friends. He just needed people *not* to be mean.

After day two ended without a hitch, he dared to hope that life in Bronxville—with Genevieve, Brett, and Megan to rely on—might shape into something that he'd never experienced before.

But the very next day, he came out of the bathroom right before gym class to find Mike leaning against a locker, watching him. Landon looked around. There were only a dozen or so students in the hall because the first bell for the next period had already rung, so it wasn't hard to pick out Xander loitering outside a classroom also, pretending to be tying his shoe. Landon stiffened, immediately sensing trouble.

He started down the hall away from Xander, hugging the lockers on the opposite side of the hallway from Mike. The coach's son didn't move, but his eye, peering out from beneath his dark flopping hair, locked on Landon, and he wore an evil smile. Landon glanced back. Xander was on the move now, heading his way. Landon picked up his pace, glancing back and forth between the two of them and expecting Skip Dreyfus to pop out up ahead of him at any moment to cut him off. The other kids in the hall seemed to sense trouble too. Landon was aware of their nervous looks and their rush to get out of the area.

As Landon passed the spot where Mike leaned with his arms folded like a tough guy, he hurried his pace and glanced nervously ahead. Two more steps and he'd reach open hallway. He could run if he had to.

He had nearly made it past when Mike lunged.

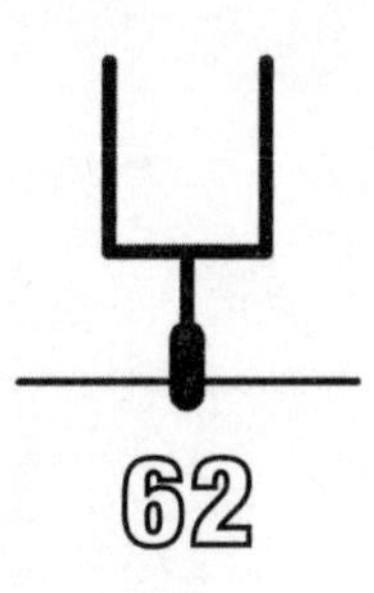

62

Landon bolted.

His arms flailed. He looked back and saw Skip, Mike, and Xander together now, snarling. He surged ahead, tripped, and spilled himself and his backpack onto the floor.

He twisted around in a panic, face burning with shame, and saw them not upon him but howling with laughter, slapping one another on the back as they backed away down the hall.

It was just a joke to them, scaring him. Landon's face burned as he clambered to his feet. Skip and Xander dipped into a classroom and Mike hurried down the hall. The second bell rang.

Late for gym, Landon got a stern warning from the teacher before he could even explain.

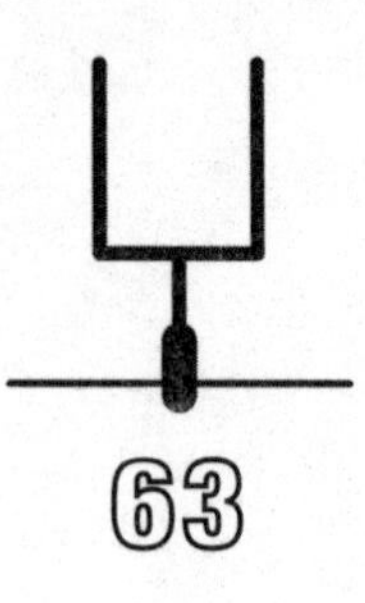

63

Friday evening's pregame practice was a dress rehearsal for their opening game on Sunday. Landon wore his game uniform with pride. The black pants glistened like wet tar and the orange-and-black jersey was bold as a Bengal tiger. Practice wasn't really much of anything. They didn't run and they didn't hit. The only thing they did was line up in positions on the various squads and team units they'd be using in the game.

There were punt teams and kickoff teams and other special teams Landon had nothing to do with. Then there were different squads for offense and defense—first string, second, and third. Landon lined up at right tackle on offense and left end on defense, both third string, which was actually a ragtag bunch of leftovers from the second string squad and the most inept players on the team, guys like Timmy Nichols. Still,

Landon felt proud to be included. It was like he *did* have a position, like he was a real player.

But the third string was whisked on and off the field like an annoying afterthought. Landon watched the first team replace them and walk through a series of important plays. As each starter strove to show the coaches he'd mastered his job, Landon couldn't help feeling left out. That's what third string was, basically. Left out.

He paid close attention anyway. He'd seen Coach Furster chew guys out for not paying attention, and he'd always say, "You never know when someone might get hurt and we need you to step in."

Then Coach would glare all around and say, "Guys, if your number gets called, you'd better be ready."

Gunner Miller was the starting right tackle on offense, and Landon studied his every move, even the way he'd turn his mouthpiece sideways and chew on its ragged end between plays. He watched Gunner's feet and mimicked their motions on every play—a forty-five degree angle to the right on one play or a straight ahead power step on the next. After doing his little silent dance, Landon would look around to see if anyone might be watching him, but no one ever was.

Practice was short. Coach Furster blasted his whistle and gathered his flock. Landon looked around in surprise because it seemed there'd be no sprints in this pregame practice.

"Take a knee," Coach Furster said. "Helmets off."

Landon looked around to make sure he understood correctly, and when everyone else shed his helmet, Landon did the same. He adjusted his skullcap and his ears, patting them gently into place.

"Guys, tomorrow I need every one of you to stay off your feet. Get plenty of rest and plenty of water. Sunday is D-Day, the beginning of a championship season, and it starts with Scarsdale. Now, I know a lot of you—and I have to admit I do this too—are looking ahead to the Tuckahoe game next week because it's a rivalry that goes back to the beginning of youth football in this town. But first we need to focus on Scarsdale." Coach Furster curled his lips like he'd eaten Skittles Sours.

"Coach West had one of his deputies film their scrimmage against Tarrytown, and we've broken them down." Coach Furster and Coach West exchanged a cunning chuckle before Coach Furster frowned. "They are good. But . . . we are better. We just have to play that way, boys." Coach Furster suddenly smiled. "So, rest up and hydrate, go over your assignments. I want you to visualize blocking and tackling, hitting, and winning. Can you do that?"

"Yes!" they all shouted.

"CAN YOU DO THAT!"

"YES!"

"Ha-ha! I like it." Coach Furster grinned. "Be here at eleven sharp Sunday morning, boys. We are gonna whip Scarsdale's butts!"

Landon looked around, chuckling and expecting others to be snickering as well because Coach had said "butts," but all he saw were serious faces, so he quickly coughed to cover his glee and put his hand in for their "Hit, Hustle, Win!" chant before he marched up the hill, heading for the parking lot.

He felt a pang of envy when he saw Brett talking to Gunner Miller about the pass protection they planned to use against Scarsdale's blitzing linebackers. He wanted to stop and talk too, but felt foolish because it seemed impossible that he'd get into the game for even a single play. As he trudged up the hill, though, he couldn't help wondering if, despite everything, tomorrow might be the day he became a true football player.

Hadn't Coach Furster told everyone to be ready?

It made him tremble from head to toe to think of going into a real game, even if it was a blowout and no one cared. And in that moment, he felt determined that if he got the chance, he would be ready.

Landon Dorch would answer the call.

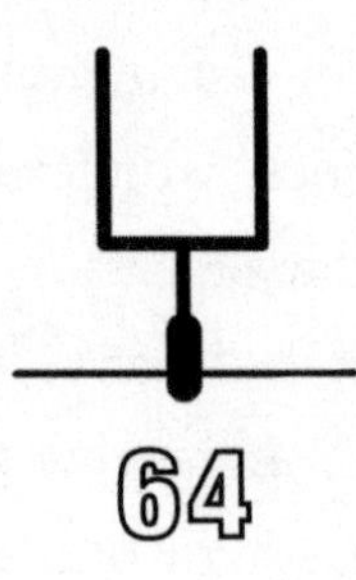

Saturday at the breakfast table, Landon insisted he couldn't do any yard work.

"Because?" Landon's mom asked, not looking happy.

Landon glanced at his dad, who shrugged and looked away, suddenly interested in the clock on the wall.

"Coach said to stay off our feet, Mom. I gotta rest up. I gotta go over things in my mind, visualize blocking and stuff." He studied his mom's face and knew she wasn't impressed. "Winning, Mom. You gotta visualize it to do it."

She huffed and rolled her eyes. "Forrest, do you buy this malarkey?"

Landon's dad pointed to himself and blinked. "Me? Oh, well, you know . . . I never played football, Gina. I've heard of that, though."

"Well, the lawn and the garage are your domain, Forrest. If you're willing to go without help today for your long list of things to do, then I'm not going to stop you." Landon's mom produced the list and slapped it onto the table.

"Well . . ." Landon's dad reached across the table and picked up the list. "I don't see why I can't. Some of this we can do tomorrow after the game, right?"

"As long as it's done by the end of the weekend—and I'd like to have a cookout tomorrow evening before it starts snowing around here." Landon's mom sniffed, and it was settled.

From his bedroom window, Landon looked down at his dad waving the hedge trimmer like a magic wand, shaping shrubs and bushes with no one to pick up the leavings. That inspired him to search the web for some videos of lineman drills, and he watched them all morning long, visualizing himself doing the things he saw big, beefy college players and coaches demonstrating in clinics across the country. He imagined himself as them, big and strong and, most importantly, fearless.

One thing that kept popping up was his hands. Landon knew he was supposed to deliver a blow out of his stance. He knew he was supposed to strike the defensive lineman across from him on either side of his chest, but as he watched clinic after clinic on YouTube, he knew he hadn't been keeping his thumbs up, but rather pointing in, like a traffic cop signaling to stop. After a while of worrying, he peeked out the window. His dad was raking up the last bit of trimmings and dumping them into the wagon hitched to the riding mower.

Landon hustled downstairs and out into the back yard.

"Hey!" His dad smiled warmly and wiped some sweat from his brow with the back of his hand. "Thought you were resting up?"

"Dad, can you help me?"

His father looked around like it was a trick question. "Well . . . sure. What do you need?"

"You gotta be my dummy."

"Now I'm a dummy?"

"No." Landon shook his head. "Just, like, stand there in a preset position," he said.

"I have no idea what that is." His dad laughed and shook his head.

Landon showed him how to stand, crouched over with his hands on his knees. "Now, I'm gonna fire out at you and you just stand there."

"Ah! Just like a dummy," his dad said. "Don't worry. I got it."

"See, I've got to deliver a blow with my hands, but my thumbs have to be up and I just need to do it, in case I get in the game tomorrow."

"Okay—go for it."

Landon got down in his stance. Since they had no quarterback and his dad knew nothing about football, he called the cadence aloud himself. On "hike," he fired out and struck his dad with both hands.

"Oof!" His dad staggered back. "Wow. Good hit."

"Yeah, but my hands still aren't right." Landon studied the position of his thumbs. They were still sideways instead of straight up and down the way he'd intended them to be.

"How about you just do the hand part?" his dad said. "You know, save the stance and all that jumping out at me until you've got the hands just the way you want."

"Dad, that's genius!" Landon beamed, and his father grinned back.

Over and over he shot his hands into his father's chest, and after a dozen tries, he had it down pretty good.

"Now put it all together," his dad said.

"Dad, did you play football and you're just not telling me?" Landon was suspicious because his father seemed to be speaking with authority.

"No, but this is just like band. You work on a piece one line at a time to get it right, and then you put it all together." His dad patted his chest and got down in the preset position. "Come get me."

Landon did, and it worked out pretty well. They kept going until his mom rounded the corner with a floppy hat, gardening gloves, and her pruning shears. She stopped abruptly in front of them. "What?"

Landon and his dad stood and blinked.

"What's going on? I thought you had to rest?" His mom narrowed her eyes.

"Sometimes you gotta realize what you visualize, Gina." Landon's dad put a hand on his shoulder. "That's all. Just fine tuning. And don't worry, I got the yard covered. Look . . ."

Landon's mom pinched her lips and looked around. "You missed that dead limb on the sugar maple, Forrest."

"My next stop." Landon's dad winked and motioned for him to skedaddle.

Landon laughed and started to trundle off, before turning and hugging his dad. "Thanks, Dad. You're the best."

That evening his dad made spaghetti, and they all went out to a movie as a family. Everyone was in good spirits, but Landon passed on a bucket of popcorn. Tomorrow was Sunday and his first football game, and suddenly, he wasn't so hungry anymore.

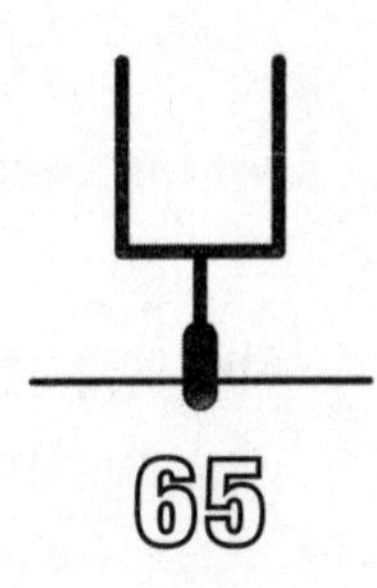

65

Landon woke early, nervous, though he couldn't really say why. Words about Scarsdale's toughness rang in his brain, but he really didn't expect to get into the game unless they were way far ahead. Even then, he couldn't be sure Coach Furster would play him. Because of his size, he knew the only position he could play on offense was right tackle. If Landon had to go against someone as big as himself (or even someone close), it was likely to end in Landon getting creamed.

He turned over the framed picture sitting on his dresser and saw himself with his family plummeting downward on the ride at Disney World. It stiffened his resolve. He knew he had to get out onto the field during a game, just to say he'd done it. It would make him feel like a real team member and not something less, which is what he couldn't help feeling like now, no matter what Brett or Landon's dad said.

At breakfast Landon could only stare at the stack of pancakes in front of him. He took two swigs of orange juice and nearly lost it.

His mom peered at him over a steaming mug of coffee. "Nervous?"

"It's game day, Mom." Landon excused himself and began getting his gear on.

Genevieve had practice, and they dropped her at the soccer field before circling the school and pulling into the parking lot above the football field. A concession trailer churned out smoke, and the smell of hot dogs was in the air, even though it wasn't yet eleven o'clock. The stands were already half full of people. The sun shone and the baking grass smelled freshly cut.

"Go get 'em, big guy." Landon's dad slapped his shoulder pad.

"Good luck," said his mother.

"Okay. See you." Landon strapped on his helmet and took off at a jog down the hillside. He fell in with the rest of his team, full of doubt and uncertainty, but also a sliver of hope.

For the first time in Landon's life, it was game day.

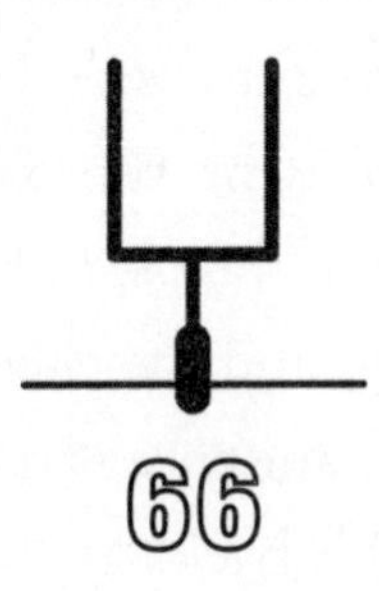

66

The Scarsdale Knights wore red helmets and jerseys, with white pants. They looked big and fast and mean. Their chants about hitting and hustling and winning that rang out over the field sounded more like a threat than a team motto. Landon looked around at his teammates as they stretched and warmed up. None of them seemed troubled by Scarsdale's battle cries, not even Nichols, but Landon fought the urge to feel thankful that he probably wouldn't get into the game.

Before he knew it, Landon found himself on the sideline watching Skip and Brett march to the center of the field with the referees and captains of the Scarsdale team. Landon turned and began to fidget with the water carriers, making sure the bottle tops were on tight and wondering if he'd been remiss in not getting to the game earlier to make sure Coach West didn't need help filling them. Either way, they won the toss, and after the kickoff Bronxville's offense swarmed out onto the field behind their quarterback.

Landon looked up into the stands, saw his parents, and gave them a small wave he trusted no one else would see. Passing the ball and running around the end on naked bootleg plays and sweeps, Skip marched the Bronxville offense right down the field for a touchdown. The stands behind Landon shook with the stomping of feet, and the cheers washed over all other sounds, so much so that Landon was startled when Coach West thumped the middle of his back.

"Huh?"

"Come on, Landon. Let's get water into these guys. A lot of them play both ways and don't have much time." Coach West had a carrier in one hand and gave the other to Landon.

Landon did his best, handing out bottles of water to the guys who needed it most, but when he presented one to Skip, the quarterback turned away and got one from Coach West instead. Landon shrugged it off and made sure Brett got a good drink.

"Hey, thanks, my man." Brett sprayed a thick stream of water into his mouth, and Landon smiled at the way Brett called him "my man," the same way Jonathan Wagner had done.

The Bronxville kickoff team did its job, pinning Scarsdale down deep, and then the defense—led by Brett with two tackles behind the line—did the same. During the next break on the sideline for Brett, Landon handed him a water bottle and said, "They're not as tough as they look, right?"

Brett cast a look across the field. "Don't say that yet. Football's a funny deal. Things can change quick."

As if Brett had a crystal ball, Skip fumbled on the first play of the next series. Scarsdale used the sudden change to throw a long pass and tie the score. Scarsdale kicked off, and Furster muffed the kickoff, giving Scarsdale the ball again. Five plays later they scored another touchdown. When Bronxville was back on offense and Skip fumbled again, Coach Furster called a time-out and marched out onto the field. Even though Skip had recovered his own fumble, everyone could see that Coach Furster was steaming mad.

Landon watched from the sideline, eager for Skip to get dressed down. He heard the yelling all around him, but didn't get that his teammates and coaches were shouting at him until Coach West grabbed his shoulder pad and spun him around.

"Come on, Landon! Get this out there!" Coach West shoved a water bottle carrier into Landon's gut.

Landon got hold of it, but then he paused in confusion.

"Go!" Coach West stabbed a finger at the Bronxville huddle out on the field, where Coach Furster was gesturing wildly to his team. "Get the water out there!"

"Oh, uh, okay, Coach." Landon felt stupid, not having realized that the time-out meant someone could take water out to the team. He turned and dashed toward the huddle. Someone tripped him, and he went down like a collapsing building. The water bottles exploded up out of the carrier, and Landon lay facedown in the grass. It sounded like some people were laughing and like others were shouting angrily. He wasn't sure which was which or how much of any of it was meant for him, but he scrambled with the water bottles, reloading the carrier and then stumbling out to the huddle.

By the time he got there, the ref was blowing his whistle to end the time-out.

Landon held a water bottle out to Brett, who only grimaced and shook his head. "Thanks, my man. No time."

"Let's go, Landon." Coach Furster grabbed the upper sleeve of Landon's jersey and yanked him out of the huddle like he was the one who had fumbled. Landon knew his coach was talking, and he zeroed in on his face. ". . . can't even hang onto the football. Heck, we can't even get the stupid water bottles right."

When he got back to the bench, Landon tried to hand out some water bottles to the guys who were mostly just watching. Some of them took water, but most shook their heads and declined. Xander gave Landon a shove and said, "Get away from me, 3P, you doofus."

It stung to hear "3P," because Landon had thought that issue was dead and gone.

He didn't take any more chances. He kept the water carrier in his hand and stood on the fringe of the players and coaches crowding the sideline, ready at a moment's notice to run out to the huddle if there was another time-out. The game went on, and at halftime the score was 20–7 with Scarsdale in the lead.

Coach Furster led the team beneath the goalpost on one end of the field, where they sat in a circle. "Landon, get that water around to everyone, will you?"

"You got it, Coach." Landon tried to sound somber since they were behind and everyone looked angry. He walked around handing out water while Coach West passed around two buckets with quartered oranges for the players to eat for energy. No one said thanks to him now. Everyone was angry about getting beat, and the coaches seemed to be keyed up and ready to explode.

After ten minutes of telling every kid who played what he'd done wrong and how he needed to be better, Coach Furster blew his whistle and told everyone to line up to get stretched out again. Landon fell into the back of the line, but Coach West tapped him and asked if he wouldn't mind helping pick up the orange peels that some players had left scattered around in the grass. Landon glanced down at the garbage, and a complaint perched on his lips because picking up after everyone else seemed to be taking the water-boy thing a bit too far. And, wasn't he supposed to be warming up? The words got stuck though. He watched the team as it began to jog out onto the field without him, and then he saw the frown on Coach West's face and said, "Sure, Coach. I can get warmed up on my own on the sideline."

Coach West gave him a funny look, and then they began scooping up peels and dumping them into the bucket. They ended up meeting the rest of the guys on the sideline, and the whistle blew beginning the second half. Reaching into the bucket of mostly peels, Landon retrieved an uneaten quarter of orange. He was undoing his chinstrap to get the juicy fruit up under his mask so he could take a bite when someone snatched it from him.

"You don't need to eat anything," Xander snarled. "You haven't done a doggone thing. Give me a break."

Landon watched Xander chomp down on the fruit and then toss the peel at Landon's feet before putting his helmet on and jogging out onto the field. Landon looked around. No one seemed to be looking, so he walked away from the garbage, refusing to add it to the bucket.

By midway through the fourth quarter, the score was 34–13, and Landon's legs ached from standing. Still, Coach Furster's words rang out in his mind. "If your number gets called, you better be ready." Landon thought maybe he should rest his legs so that he *would* be ready, if he got called upon, so he took a seat on the bench. He glanced up in the stands and saw Genevieve sitting there with his parents in her soccer uniform. Megan sat beside her, and Landon wavered between pride and embarrassment. With just two minutes to go, Scarsdale scored yet another touchdown.

It was a blowout.

Coach Furster began substituting players, and Landon started to tremble with excitement. He didn't want to get too excited, so he stuck his hands under his legs to stay calm. Just because the coach was putting people in didn't mean *he'd* get any action, but when Coach Furster slapped Timmy on the shoulder, sending him in, Landon stood up.

He knew he was next.

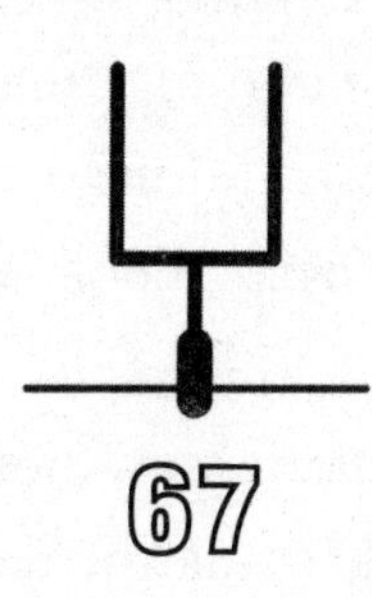

67

The clock wound down.

Scarsdale was running the ball right up the middle to keep the clock winding down. Landon kept his eyes on Coach Furster and saw Brett's dad, who for some reason had a cell phone in one hand, say something to Coach Furster. The two of them argued, but Landon got distracted by the action on the field.

He watched Timmy stand straight up on the snap of the ball and get driven nearly ten yards back before falling in a heap. Landon could do better than that. He knew he could, and he moved closer to where the coaches stood on the sideline. Brett's dad had disappeared somewhere. Landon looked around and thought that Coach Furster had said something to him.

He looked up, but the coach had his eyes glued to the field.

Landon looked at the clock, which said 00:27 and was winding down.

Landon turned and scuffed his cleats all the way to the bench. When he got there, he spun around and slumped down. Coach Furster was staring at him through the crowd of kids on the sideline, as if Landon had done something wrong. Landon could only shrug. The coach shook his head and spit in the grass.

The last play of the game was another run up the middle. Someone from Bronxville made the tackle and got up excited, even though his team had just embarrassed itself. The players and coaches lined up and shook hands, Landon among them. Then the team gathered in the end zone for a post-game speech. Coach Furster kept shaking his head and spitting as if he couldn't get the bad taste out of his mouth.

"That was just pathetic." He glared around at the players, his voice sounding like it might be hoarse from shouting. "Well, next week we've got Tuckahoe, the biggest rivalry in downstate football and our chance to regain the Pondfield Road Cup. You all know that it's practically a holiday when we play them, and the game is on Saturday, so it's a short week. I'll say this: you play like you did today, men, and we may not win a game all season, so you better come to practice Tuesday night ready to work, and be ready to *run* until you *puke.* That's all. Go. Get out of my sight."

The team broke apart, but when Landon turned, his eyes widened at a sight that horrified him much more than the thought of running till he puked.

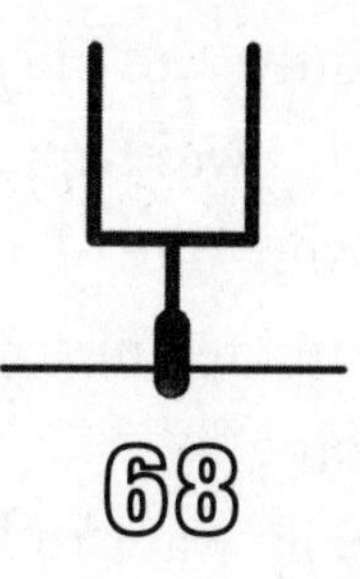

68

Landon's mom had fire in her eyes.

She grabbed him by the arm and blasted through the crowd of football players, heading straight for Coach Furster. Landon was aware that his father was sort of with her, if you could count hanging back a good twenty feet as being with her.

Coach Furster was huddled up with Coach West and Coach Bell.

Landon's mom apparently didn't care. She went straight for Coach Furster, stabbing a finger at his chest without actually poking him. "Coach, you and I need to talk. *Right now.* In private."

There was no room for anything else. The two other coaches melted away fast. Coach Bell had his face in one hand as he went, shaking his head. Landon wished he could go with them, and he actually tried to tug loose, but his mother held his arm with an iron grip. He couldn't help himself from watching.

Landon could see the anger in his mother's face. "You played every single kid on this team except *my* son, and I want to know why. Not one single play."

Coach Furster's lips quivered. He snorted and looked away as if he couldn't believe this was happening.

"Don't look away from me," Landon's mother steamed. "You look me in the eye and tell me who you think you are and what you think you're doing."

"Really, lady? You really want to have this discussion with me?" Coach Furster tugged the bill of his cap down tighter on his head.

"You bet I do."

"Really?" Coach Furster looked both angry and surprised at the same time. "Okay, here it is, lady. Your kid . . . he's fine, a little slow maybe; he's a good enough kid, but he's *soft.* You know what that means?"

"He's the biggest kid on your team, and it's *football.*" Landon's mom spit her words at the coach.

"Yeah, the biggest and the *softest*, and part of my job, believe it or not, is to make sure these kids are safe." Coach Furster folded his arms and leaned down toward Landon's mom so their noses nearly touched. "And I *asked* him if he wanted to go in for the last play of the game, and you know what he did?"

Coach Furster clenched his hands and put them rigidly against his sides. "He *sat down on the bench.* That's right, turned and walked away from me when I asked him. So you just take your attitude and redirect it at your son, lady, and ask yourself what he's even *doing* out here."

Landon's mom took a step back.

"Yeah, that's right. He doesn't want to hit anyone." Coach Furster wore a mean smile, and it looked like he was suddenly enjoying himself. "He got a taste of hitting and that was enough. Since then, he drops out of every contact drill we do, but I'm a nice guy, right? So I let him hang around and wear his uniform and help out. So you huddle up with your kid and figure out what you want to do here, because I'm a volunteer and I'm not paid to take guff from some helicopter mommy with a kid who's obviously got special needs."

Coach Furster gave a final snort, turned, and walked away.

Landon's mom had nowhere else to look but at him. "Landon? Is this *true*?"

Landon looked over at his dad, who had stopped a good ten feet away in order not to catch any wrath.

"Don't look at your father; look at me!" Landon's mom glared up at him, and he didn't even think what to do. He just did it.

Landon turned and ran.

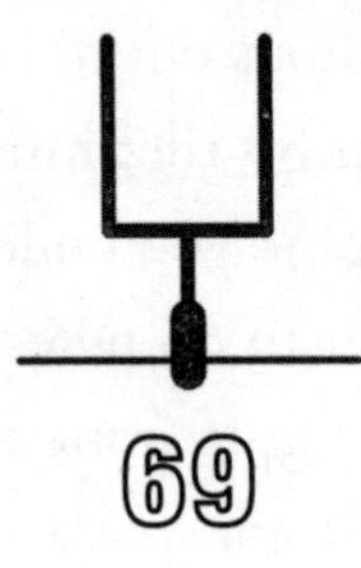

69

Landon ran all the way home.

He dashed up the stairs and threw the football helmet down on his bedroom floor. He whipped off his ears and let them clatter without a sound onto the night table before throwing off every bit of his football gear. He stood panting in the middle of his bedroom wearing nothing but a big yellow pair of boxers spotted with little blue anchors. He paced the floor until he felt the slam of a door beneath him.

Landon slipped on his ears and listened.

Feet stamped up the stairs, and a door down the wide hallway, probably his parents' bedroom door, crashed shut. Landon froze.

He heard more stomping, but lighter feet—his mom's. She pounded on the bedroom door and even Landon could tell what she was saying, she shouted so loudly. "Forrest! Forrest, open this door!"

Landon heard a muffled response. It sounded like "no."

"You get out here! This is on *you*, Forrest! Were you not paying *attention*?"

His mother paused, but if Landon's dad answered, he didn't hear it.

"You just let some moron turn your son into a water boy?" His mother was shrieking. "Really? Do I have to do everything?"

Landon heard the door crash open and now his father was shouting.

"No! You don't have to do *everything*, Gina! But you have to do *something*! Something besides that awful job! You think this is fun for any of us? You think *I* wanted to come here? No! I did not! But I came here for you, and all you can do is work, work, work! Since when did that job become more important than *us*?"

Landon didn't want to hear any more. His hands crept for the wires connected to his head, but he didn't pull the plug. Something wouldn't let him do it.

"This is not my fault!" his mother screamed.

"And it's not my fault either!" his father screamed right back.

"Yes it is!" his mother shouted.

"Then I'll just *leave*!"

Landon heard his father's feet crashing down the stairs. He felt the front door shudder, and then everything went quiet.

He stood for a long while before slowly opening his door and creeping down the hall.

When he got to the open door of his parents' bedroom, he saw his mother curled up on top of the bed, holding herself and crying so hard that she shook.

"Don't do this, Mom." Landon had never seen his mother cry. "Please don't do this. It's not your fault. It's not Dad's fault. It's my fault, and I know how to fix it."

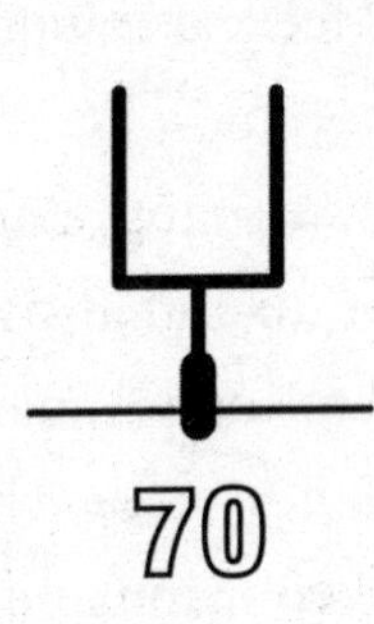

70

Landon told his mom the plan at the kitchen table, just the two of them. His mother had insisted that Landon have a glass of milk along with some Fig Newtons.

She listened to his idea, but when he was finished, she shook her head. "No, Landon, you can't quit. You can't let someone like Coach Furster break you. Once you let that happen, it never ends."

Landon's stomach, already tight, now turned. "I hate it. I don't want to do it."

"This has been your dream, Landon."

"Now it's a nightmare."

She shook her head with short little movements. "No. You don't give up like that. You muscle through it, or you'll look back for the rest of your life and kick yourself and wonder. You'll finish the season. I don't care if you never play a minute—well, I care, but you'll finish, Landon."

Landon sulked for a moment before he looked up.

He bit into a cookie, feeling trapped. He still didn't think he should return to the team. There was just no sense in it. When the phone on the wall rang, Landon's mom gave him a curious look and then got up and answered it.

"Hello, Coach Bell. I'm sorry I made a scene." His mother listened for a several minutes before she spoke again. "Thank you. Thank you. You and your son and wife have been so kind. I'll tell Landon and I'm sure he'll feel much better . . . Yes, I'm sure Landon would love to watch the Giants game with you. I can drop him off after we have some lunch. Just text me the address. Thank you again."

She hung up the phone and turned to Landon. Pointing to the phone, she said, "See? We're not the only ones who believe in you." As she spoke, his father came in through the garage door in the mudroom like nothing was wrong.

His parents gave each other a look and then smiled before his mom said, "Landon got invited to the Bells' to watch the Giants game at four. Coach Bell said I was right and wanted us all to know that he argued with Coach Furster to put Landon in with the other backup players."

Landon's mom turned her sharp eyes on him. "He says he thinks that if you just get used to the whole thing, you'll be fine. He said it might take time, but that's okay. He said Brett started out slow too. He just started much earlier, when he was eight."

Landon had to admit that made him feel better, and his

heart swelled at the notion of having anything in common with Brett at all. Still, he had a hard time believing football was for him anymore.

Landon's dad made grilled cheese sandwiches and tomato soup. Genevieve ate lunch with them, but she was quiet on the subject of football. Landon could only assume she'd been embarrassed by their mother's outburst. Maybe she even blamed him for their parents' fight. Either way, she was impossible to read. When she finished her lunch, she asked if she could go to the country club to play tennis with Megan.

"Yes, of course," their mother answered. "Landon is going to the Bells' to watch the Giants game, but let's all plan on being back for a family dinner by seven thirty."

Landon's parents dropped Genevieve off at the country club first.

"Tell Megan I said hi," Landon said.

"Sure," Genevieve said, but her face told a different story. It was clear that she was still upset. He wanted to stop her, to say he was sorry for all the drama and give her a hug, but before he could act, she was gone.

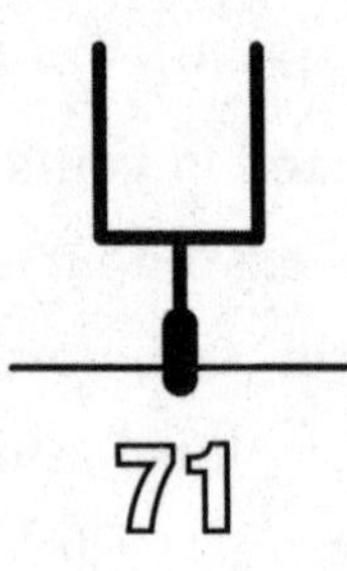

71

They rode to the Bells' house in silence, and Landon was glad to get out of the car.

Brett's mom greeted Landon at the door with a smile. "Hi, Landon. They're down in the man cave. I'll show you."

"Thanks, Mrs. Bell." He followed her through a small living room and down the stairs. At the bottom, a big, hairy dog lay sprawled out, sleeping.

"Just step over her, okay?" Brett's mom said.

Landon turned a corner and went down another small set of stairs, entering the man cave. It was a shrine to the New York Giants. Everything was red and blue. Signed pictures and jerseys covered the walls. A big, blue sectional couch surrounded the enormous flat-screen TV festooned on its edges by Giants pom-poms. Brett and his dad sat side by side on the edge of their seats, and the action hadn't even begun.

"Brett . . . Brett!"

"Huh, what, Mom?" Brett turned his head. "Oh, hi, Landon! Come sit down. Dad, Landon's here."

"Hi, Landon." Coach Bell sprang up. "Rashad's got a bum ankle and they're talking about what it means. . . . Come on over. Sit down. Right here between us. Want some chips?"

"Sure, that'd be great." Landon sat and took a handful from the bag they placed in front of him on the coffee table. Brett offered him an orange soda, and he accepted gratefully. "I guess I should have worn something blue."

"Oh, don't worry." Brett swatted the air and then pointed to the Jonathan Wagner jersey he wore. "I wear this for luck, and I keep this in my hands the whole game." Brett showed him a football that had been signed by the entire team.

"Wow. Nice," Landon said.

"Yeah. Hey, at least you didn't wear brown and orange for Cleveland. Ha-ha." Brett chucked Landon lightly on the shoulder and turned his attention to the screen.

Landon started watching and felt a little jolt of pleasure when he realized they had the closed-captioning feature turned on. Landon had thought about that on his way over, but he had decided he wouldn't mention it. Most people didn't use the closed-captioning feature, even though most new TVs had it. He looked back and forth between Brett and his dad, but their attention was on the screen.

Landon sat back and breathed easy. It choked him up a little bit to be there, just hanging out with such nice people who took his limitations in stride.

On the wall Landon saw Eli's jersey, and Rashad's, and also

older Giants like Michael Strahan and someone named Gifford. There were footballs everywhere, as well as pictures of a much-younger Coach Bell. One shelf held nearly a dozen wrestling trophies, some with gold medals slung over them, confirming that Landon was in the presence of athletic royalty.

The Giants fell behind early in the game, and Landon worried along with his hosts. After two turnovers, though, and a stunning block by Brett's uncle on a sweep, the Giants got right back into it. Once they had the lead in the fourth quarter, it was all a ground game for the Giants. They made no secret of running the ball behind big Jonathan Wagner. Several times the TV announcers ran close-up replays of the huge lineman plowing people down.

"Awesome!" Brett turned to Landon, and the two of them slapped high five.

"We should run the ball like that, Dad." Brett spoke across Landon to his father, so Landon caught every word. "Layne Guerrero is as good a runner as any in our league. We'd be better pounding the ball than all that passing garbage we did today."

Landon thought of Layne as just a quiet kid who never did anything to Landon but smile pleasantly. He hadn't known he was supposed to be a star runner. Like most of the team, Layne hadn't done much of anything in their game earlier.

Landon turned his attention to Brett's dad, who scratched his chin. "Well, I hear you, but Skip's a good quarterback, and Coach Furster likes to air it out."

Landon turned to look at Brett.

"Yeah, 'cause his mopey son is a receiver." Brett slapped the football he'd kept in his lap throughout the game.

"Okay, Brett." Brett's dad rumbled when he spoke. "Let's talk nice, okay?"

"*You* should coach the team." Brett muttered the comment under his breath, but even Landon knew what he said.

Landon wondered if that was even possible. It would be a dream come true for him, having a head coach who was actually nice to him, who *liked* him.

Landon held his breath, waiting to see what Brett's dad would say.

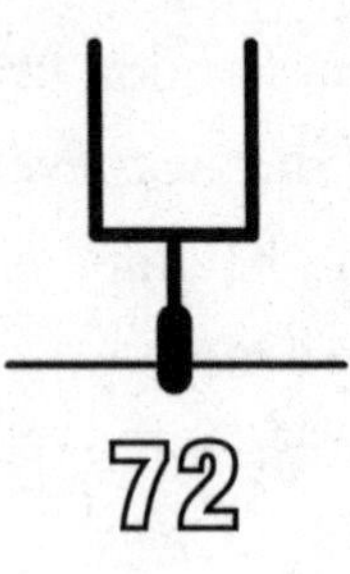

72

"Anyone want some dip for those chips?" Brett's dad pointed at them, and they both nodded before he left the TV room headed for the kitchen.

It was as if Brett had never made the suggestion.

"Why *doesn't* he coach the team?" Landon asked when Brett's father had disappeared.

"He says it's their show. They started coaching when Xander's and Mike's older brothers played. They've been doing it with Coach Furster as head coach ever since." Brett unexpectedly tossed Landon the ball.

Landon surprised himself by catching it.

"Hey, maybe you'll play tight end in high school." Brett looked serious. "Less blocking, more catching. You'd be a big target."

"I don't know if I'll end up playing anything but left out."

Landon's face tightened. "I can't believe my mom did that. Plus the coaches seem to like me handing out water more than being on the field."

"Hey," Brett said, glancing over his shoulder to make sure his dad hadn't returned. "My dad said she was right. They should've played you."

"I'm still not that good."

"Yeah, but you're there. You can line up and take a play. You need to get in the game. See what it feels like. Did you see Nichols?"

"I know I could do better than that." Landon tried to sound confident.

"Yeah." Brett nodded. "You can't do worse than that. But still . . . he got some action. You'll do it. You'll get in there. My dad will make it happen. They were just crabby because we lost. Coach Furster wants to blame everyone but himself. I'm telling you, we could run the ball like the Giants."

"I wish your dad was the head coach," Landon said. "At least the line coach. Why doesn't he coach the line, anyway? He played line."

Brett shrugged. "My dad's the best coach, period, any position. Furster *said* it was because he thinks dads shouldn't be the position coach of their own kids—which I guess makes sense—but I think it's because Furster wanted his kid to have the best coach. I don't know. You know how grown-ups are. Everything's a riddle."

They both turned to the TV set and watched the Giants offense take the field to kneel down on the ball and run out the remaining seconds.

"Giants, 1–0," Landon said.

"Yup." Brett beamed proudly. "And Coach McAdoo will be in a good mood, so the team will get off later this week and my uncle will be at practice. Wait till you see what that does to Coach Furster and Coach West. They'll pee their pants."

Landon snickered. "At the same time?"

"Oh, for sure." Brett grinned at him. "Two yellow puddles. Side by side."

Brett's dad returned with a bowl of dip. "What are you two so giddy about?"

"Giants won, Dad."

"Yeah," Brett's dad said, cracking open a can of iced tea and taking a sip. "Now let's see if *we* can get the Bronxville junior football team a win, huh?"

"*And* get Landon in the game, right?" Brett said.

Brett's dad eyed Landon. "Would you like that, Landon?"

Landon wanted to be honest. He was still just flat afraid of getting smashed around. On the other hand, it would feel so darn good to be out there, on the field, in a real game. Wouldn't that make him a football player, no matter what the rest of them said?

"Landon?" Brett's dad spoke loudly and slowly. "Would you like that? Getting in a game?"

"Yes, sir! I've got to get in the game," Landon said.

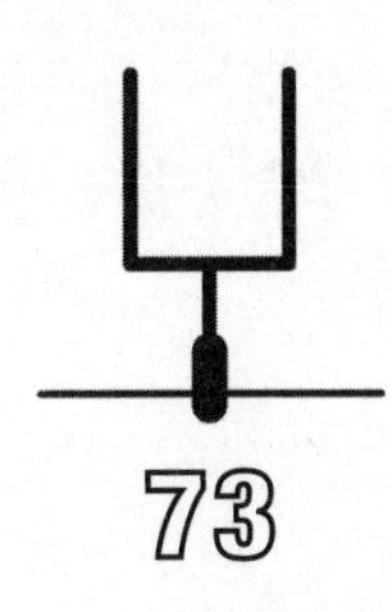

73

Monday in school, no one bothered Landon. In English class it felt like a three-way discussion about *The Count of Monte Cristo* between him, Megan, and Mr. Edwards. Landon loved it and couldn't have cared less if the other kids in the class were bored or annoyed.

Toward the end Mr. Edwards jumped off the top of the desk where he sat and wrote in big block letters on the board: DISAPPOINTMENT!

"This is what you need to know: Dumas was *disappointed*," the teacher turned to them and said. "Disappointed with friends, society, with France itself. So, what will the author do with that disappointment? What will become of Mercedes, eh? Read on. *Read on*, all of you."

The bell rang.

"And I want you each to find a partner by tomorrow!" Mr.

Edwards yelled over the hubbub. "You'll be doing a research paper on Dumas's life with a partner. Pick wisely, my friends. Pick wisely!"

As soon as they spilled out into the hallway, Megan tapped Landon's arm.

He looked into those eyes feeling dizzy.

Would she say it?

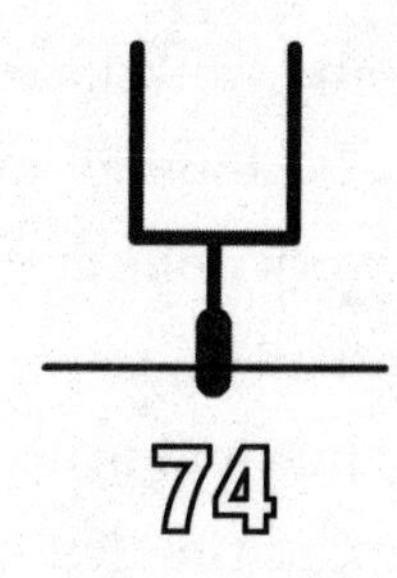

74

Megan smiled. "Partners?"

Landon felt his soul float to the ceiling. "Sure."

Lunch was lonely, but Megan's invitation carried him through the rest of the day. In gym class they played badminton. Landon was pretty bad, but it didn't matter one bit. Brett picked him for a partner. They won every game. Landon couldn't help chuckling when Mike slammed his racket on the gym floor and got detention.

After school Brett and Landon watched Genevieve's and Megan's soccer practice. When the girls were finished, the four friends walked to the diner. They were halfway up the block when Skip and his goons came out and saw them coming down the sidewalk. The three boys did an about-face and went the other way.

"Now that's what I call respect," Genevieve said.

Everyone but Landon grinned. "I don't trust him," he said. He knew Skip and his cronies weren't done with him. Then again, Landon couldn't imagine anyone wanting to tangle with Brett.

They ate french fries and milkshakes at the diner and then headed home. There was no football practice on Mondays, so Landon got all his homework done and still had time to watch some Monday Night Football.

Tuesday, Landon's stomach churned all day. Football practice was looming. The more the day wore on, the tighter his stomach twisted. He could only finish two of his four sandwiches at lunch, and he hurried home at the end of the day to sit in the bathroom for a while before trying to read in his favorite chair. When Landon's dad came up for air from his computer and asked Landon if he wanted a snack before practice, Landon took a pass.

"Ah, building up that intensity, are you?" Landon's dad looked like he hadn't taken a shower since the night before. His hair went in crazy directions atop his head, and he wore only one slipper on his feet, pajama bottoms, and a dress shirt buttoned in the wrong holes.

"Just nervous." Landon tried not to stare at the crooked shirt.

"Well, it'll all work out." His father beamed, rubbing the scruff on his chin and pointing at the computer across the room. "Your alter ego slayed the dragon today. What do you think of that?"

"Nodnal?" Landon raised an eyebrow, the wild hair and crazy clothes making sense now. "You're at the end? Dad, it's only been a couple weeks. . . ."

"Yes, Nodnal and I are close to the end, but it's not quite the end yet. I've been writing like mad. Lots left to happen still, *but* he's got people's attention. The first dragon is always the hardest." Landon's dad stopped talking, but Landon kept looking at him, waiting for him to go on.

His father scratched his belly under the cockeyed shirt. "You get that, right?"

Landon sighed. "I get it. Everything's not a story, though, Dad."

His father scowled. "No, no. That's not true, Landon. Everything *is* a story, and we are the authors of our own lives."

Landon looked out the window at the trees swaying in a stiff wind. Random leaves had gone from green to yellow.

"I don't know, Dad. I don't know if we're writing it, or someone else."

"Why would you say that?" his father asked with a sad face.

Landon stared at him and swallowed. "Sometimes . . . most of the time, I feel like I'm in a crowded room with my hands tied behind my back. I start one way and someone pushes me back. Then another person spins me around and I trip and fall. I get up and start going again and someone else gives me a shove.

"If I was writing my own story . . . it wouldn't go like this."

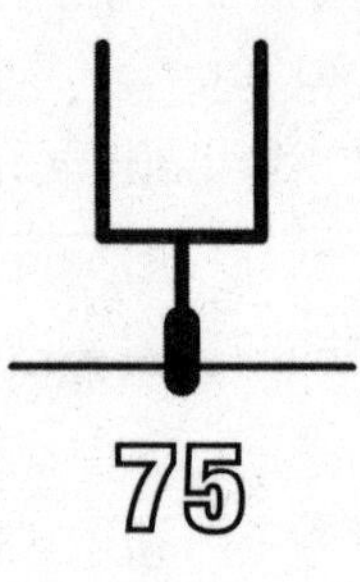

75

During Tuesday's practice Landon kept expecting something to happen, like maybe Brett or his dad would stop things and insist Landon join the contact drills. He just didn't know. Everything was the same, though. Gunner Miller growled and snarled and drove Nichols on his back three plays in a row. Brett hammered Travis in a one-on-one drill, causing the blocky center to kick the grass. Torin and Jones, who appeared to be friends off the field, mixed it up like mortal enemies.

Landon shied away from the contact drills, and the coaches let him. Landon kept watching Brett's dad as he instructed Skip or the backup, Bryce Rinehart, on a pass play or Mike and Xander on how to run a pass route. He expected Coach Bell to do or say something about Landon's situation. On the couch on Sunday, it had seemed like Landon was almost part of the Bell family, and if that was the case, wouldn't Coach Bell take him under his wing?

But the coaches were putting in a bunch of new pass plays—plays Coach Furster said he had devised to get the team a needed win—so there was a lot of teaching the coaches, especially Brett's dad, had to do. Landon reasoned that Coach Bell didn't have time to stop practice and interfere with the linemen. He didn't know what he thought Brett could do either; he just hadn't expected everything to be the same.

Wednesday's football practice was like déjà vu all over again. Landon stretched and went through agility drills and then migrated to the sideline when the hitting started. Nichols shot him a nasty look before asking the question others also seemed to have on the tip of their tongues: "Where's the water, Landon?"

He couldn't help himself. If he wasn't going to dive into the drills, and if no one was going to encourage him, he wanted to do *something*. Without answering, he went for the carrier and began supplying his teammates with bursts of cool liquid, which, pitiful as he knew it was, made him feel like he was contributing to the effort of defeating Tuckahoe. Brett, Gunner, Timmy, and the other linemen hunkered down in their stances and blasted each other with grunts and groans and flying sweat, and Landon told himself that maybe when Brett's uncle showed up on Thursday, he'd give it a try. What reason was there for him to get into the fray now?

"Landon?" Brett took a water bottle from him and spoke so gently that Landon barely heard a sound through the whistle blasts and shouting. "Come on. You should get in there."

"I . . . uh . . ." Landon thought about the hand drills he'd done with his dad. Maybe he was ready, but he glanced at his water carrier and held up an empty bottle. "Let me refill these and then maybe . . ."

Brett nodded his head. Landon thought he said, "Okay," before diving back into the drill.

Landon felt like a tug-of-war rope, stretched and straining, first going one way then the other. The discomfort of disappointing Brett pulled against the discomfort of being smashed into and knocked around like some giant kitten. Paralyzed by indecision, Landon kept the water bottles circulating around and cheerfully refilled them a second time at the spigot outside the back entrance to the school.

Practice was halfway over and they were running through plays as an entire team when Landon saw some of the other backup players nudging each other and pointing up at the parking lot. Skip Dreyfus, who wouldn't even look at Landon, shoved an empty water bottle at him, and Landon replaced it in the carrier before he looked to see whatever was distracting his teammates.

Up on the hill was a gleaming, midnight blue F-350 pickup. The enormous grille and chrome rims the size of manhole covers sparkled in the last rays of sunshine. It was the biggest, nicest truck Landon had ever seen. The door swung open and Jonathan Wagner, the Giants' starting right tackle, got out, hitched up his pants, and marched right for the junior football team's practice.

Everything stopped.

The whistle Coach Furster kept clamped between his teeth dropped from his mouth to the end of its lanyard like a prisoner on the gallows.

Jonathan Wagner wore mirrored sunglasses and a silky black T-shirt. Cowboy boots poked out from the hem of jeans that clung to his telephone-pole legs. His face was set in a concrete scowl. He *looked* like an NFL player—until he stopped and his face turned merry and he spoke in the excited voice of a kid at Christmas. "Hey, Coach Bell. How you guys all doing?"

Brett's dad hugged the Giants player and they clapped each other on the back with thundering strokes. Brett's dad turned to the other coaches. "Guys, you know my wife's brother, Jonathan Wagner?"

Coach Furster stepped right up to shake hands like they were long-lost friends. "Jonathan, heck of a way to start out the season. I've been a Giants fan since before I was born."

"Me too." Coach West got in on a handshake and puffed his skinny chest. "I'm the police chief here in town, so you just let me know if you need anything."

Landon glanced at Brett, who snickered and mouthed, "I told you so."

Coach Furster had his hand on the enormous player's back like they were buddies as he turned to address his team. "Guys, this is Jonathan Wagner. We all know him. He's Brett's uncle and the two-time Pro Bowl tackle for the New York Giants."

Jonathan looked around, nodding and smiling. "Brett, come here, you."

Brett went to him and Jonathan gave him a one-armed hug before his eyes roved over the rest of the team. Landon slowly set the water carrier down in the grass. He didn't want Brett's uncle to see what he really was.

"Where is he?" Jonathan looked around until his eyes locked on Landon. "Hey, *my man*! How you doing, Landon?"

Landon saw the entire team look his way with utter disbelief swirling in their eyes.

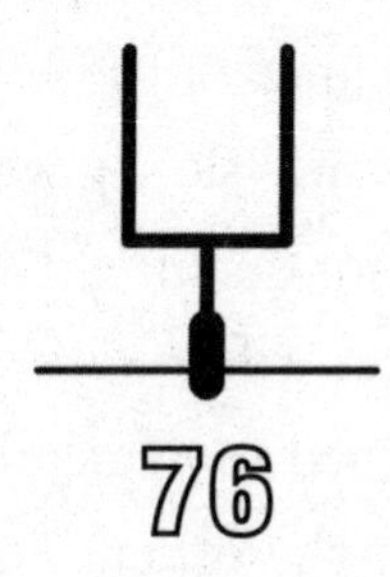

76

Jonathan Wagner pumped Landon's hand once and turned to Coach Furster. "Okay, Coach, don't let me disrupt practice. You guys get back to it and I'll just hang here. Coach McAdoo would have a fit if he saw a football practice stop in its tracks. Seriously, you guys get to it. I'm just here to watch."

Coach Furster's face fell in confusion and maybe disappointment, but he recovered his wits and his whistle and gave it a blast. "Let's go! First team offense, second team defense!"

The players scrambled back to their respective huddles. Coach West held up a card with a diagram that told the defensive players where to line up, mimicking the Tuckahoe team they'd face on Sunday. Coach Furster didn't even check his practice script. He signaled a pass play that had the quarterback throwing a long bomb to his son, Mike, who easily outpaced the second-string cornerback and sailed untouched into the end zone.

"Money!" Coach Furster shouted and pumped a fist before taking a glance at Jonathan Wagner to see if he too appreciated Mike's skill and the brilliance of the coaching.

All Jonathan did was nod slowly without comment.

Practice continued for a time before the second-string offense was put in to get a few reps running the new plays Coach Furster had designed for Tuckahoe. Landon shifted his weight from one foot to the other. The NFL superstar stood next to Brett's dad. Both big men had their arms crossed and both stared intently at the action.

Landon felt equal parts relief and disappointment. The tug-of-war in his brain continued, and he had started to wonder if this was what it was like to go crazy when he saw Jonathan Wagner turn to Coach Furster after a broken running play up the middle. With his thumb, the Giants player pointed at Landon. "Coach? Why don't you get Landon in there? I bet he could've made that inside trap really go. What position does he play?"

Coach Furster's face did a dance, and then he sputtered, "Well . . . he's . . . big, yeah, but . . . he's . . ."

Coach Furster ran out of ideas, and then he gave a short laugh and said, "The kids call him 3P, something about a powder puff. He pretty much plays left out. Heh heh."

Jonathan Wagner simply looked at Furster. No one knew what his eyes were saying behind the sunglasses, but Landon sensed his anger. "He's bigger than Brett, Coach. Kid as big as that? I mean, the kid's a truck. Even for short yardage plays.

What do you think? Maybe I can whip him into some kind of usable shape."

"Whip?" Coach Furster's face colored a bit and he laughed a nervous little laugh. "What do you mean? *Work* with him?"

"Yeah," Jonathan Wagner said, unamused. "Has anyone gone through the fundamentals with him? Flat back, power step, head up, stay low?"

Coach Furster's face turned a deeper shade. He lowered his voice, but Landon read his lips. "Well, he's deaf, right? And he has trouble with things and . . . well, he's got two left feet and he doesn't really *want* to hit, but if you can get something out of him—wow, great. By all means."

"Nice." The Giants' tackle turned toward Landon. "I'll take him to the sled."

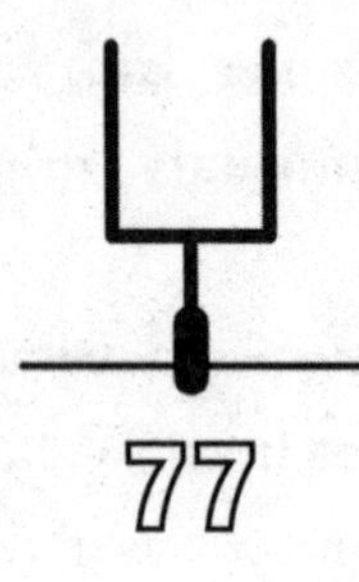

77

Landon was nearly dizzy from the mixture of pride and worry as he tramped along behind Jonathan Wagner. The big NFL lineman swung his hips as he walked atop great bowed legs. His hands hung low like tremendous meat hooks from their long arms. When they got to the blocking sled, Jonathan removed his sunglasses, slapped the top of the dummy on the end, and turned to face Landon with a big smile. "Okay, let me see what you got."

Landon shook his head. "I got nothing."

"Well, you've seen the other guys, right?"

Landon nodded. "And about a million YouTube videos."

"Well, just give me the best stance you can and fire out on my count and block this bad boy, and I'll see where you're at and we can go from there." The NFL player studied Landon's face. "If you could do it perfect already, you wouldn't need me."

"Did you help Brett get so good?" Landon asked.

"Me and his dad." Jonathan nodded. "Brett's a natural. Maybe you are too. Let me see."

"I'm not a natural." Landon got down in his frog-like stance, looking up at Jonathan. "Okay, ready."

"Whoa. No. Not ready." Jonathan grabbed Landon's shoulder pads and raised him up like a sack of beans, and then he pushed him back a bit so they stood facing each other. "Okay, get your feet shoulder-width apart, like this. Keep your feet straight, like you're on skis."

Landon did as he was told.

"Good. Now bend your knees just a bit and slide your right foot back so it's even with the heel of your left foot so you're staggered, like this."

Landon watched Jonathan slide his foot straight back and did the same.

"Not that far," Jonathan said. "That's it, so your toe is even with the heel of your other foot. Good. Now, rest your forearms on your thighs like this. This is your preset stance, and you have to have a good preset stance to have a good stance because we're gonna drop right down into our stance."

Landon watched the enormous player drop down into a three-point stance. A thrill shot through him. Jonathan was the real deal. An NFL player was right in front of him, showing him how it was done. Landon dropped his hand down and got into the stance, proudly remembering to use his fingers as a bridge the way Brett had showed him.

Jonathan stood up and assessed him. "Hmm. Better, but get that hump out of your back. Look, watch me. See how my back is flat. You should be able to have a picnic on the back of a good lineman in his stance."

Landon tried, but it was hard.

"Move your hand out a little. You don't want to be too far forward, but get a little bit longer. That'll help with your back." Jonathan moved Landon's hand and ran a finger down his spine. "That's much better. See? Everything starts with the stance, Landon. You keep flat and you turn that big body into a battering ram that can destroy people. Now you're ready to fire out and hit that dummy."

Landon fired out and struck the dummy.

"Hey, good work with your hands, thumbs up and everything. I like that placement. See? You got this, Landon," Jonathan's voice rumbled. "Okay, again."

On and on it went. For half an hour Jonathan Wagner tutored Landon on blocking before he stood tall and said, "Okay, you're ready."

"I'm ready?" Landon blinked at him.

Jonathan laughed. "Oh, yeah. You come out of that stance like I have you doing? Keep your head tilted up but low? Deliver a blow with your hands and chop your feet the way you've been doing on this dummy? You'll be a beast. You gotta do it with heart, though. Get a little mad about it. Punish people."

Landon thought. "Brett always seems like he's mad when he's blocking. He knocked me over and was like . . . snarling."

"Brett *is* mad when he's blocking. That's a good thing if you've got it."

"I don't think I have it like him," Landon said.

"But you really don't know, do you?" Jonathan said. "You

can't know until you've got the right technique. You've been flopping around like a fish in the bottom of a boat. Now you're gonna swim, and we'll see what happens. I know one thing. . . ."

"What?" Landon asked.

"You're determined."

"I am?" Landon thought about all those YouTube videos he studied. Maybe that counted?

"I watched you in that cannonball contest. You held your form even when you tilted too far and smacked your bare back on the water. That had to hurt, but you held it anyway. Because why?" Jonathan looked at Landon, waiting for the answer.

"Because I wanted to win?" Landon wasn't sure it was the right answer, but it was the truth.

"Yup. That's determination. Bring it to your game on the line. With your size, it'll be enough to dominate these guys. Well, everyone but my nephew." Jonathan put his big hands on his hips. "And if you've got any nasty in you at all, you'll be in the starting lineup."

"Nasty?" Confusion washed over Landon.

"There's this part of you where, like, you see red or you hear the whoosh of a train in your brain and you just lose it." Jonathan twirled his finger beside his head. "You go batty and . . . people better watch out."

Landon snorted at the joke.

"I'm serious, Landon," the NFL player said. "Not a lot of people walking around as big as you who can tuck and hold a cannonball. You learn how to use what you got? You bring a little nasty to the dance?" Jonathan shook his head and broke into a small smile. "My man, I'll be your agent."

The big lineman turned and marched toward the rest of the team and Landon followed. When they reached Coach Furster, he signaled a play to Skip and then turned to face the Giants player.

"Well, Coach," Jonathan said, putting a hand on Landon's shoulder pad, "he's ready."

Coach Furster laughed, but his grin faded when he saw that Jonathan meant it. "You want me to put him in there?"

"Why not?" Jonathan shrugged and looked at Brett's dad, who also shrugged.

"Uh, well. He has no idea what the plays are," Coach Furster said. "He really won't know what to do."

"What's the next play on your script?" Jonathan pointed to Coach Furster's clipboard.

Coach Furster glanced down. "Uh, pro right forty-four veer."

"Great!" Jonathan clapped his hands once. "A run play. Landon, you know what to do on the forty-four veer, or do you need me to tell you?"

"I know." Landon nodded his head. He'd seen that play so many times he could run it in his sleep. He knew the blocking assignments. He knew what the running backs did, and the quarterback too. It was no big deal to Landon, but judging by the look on the coaches' faces, it was a surprise that he had any idea at all what was going on.

"Yeah," Jonathan said. "No more left out. Get him in there at right tackle and let's see how good of a job I did."

"Well, we're running the first team right now." Coach Furster looked like someone had told him the stock market crashed.

"Yeah, that's okay. He can do it." Jonathan Wagner gave Coach Furster a stone-cold stare he probably saved for the Philadelphia Eagles.

Coach Furster bit into his lower lip, but then he wagged his head and shouted, "Miller, go to left end on defense!"

"Coach?" Gunner Miller gave Coach Furster a puzzled look.

"Just do what I say!" Coach Furster barked at the dejected-looking player before he turned to Landon and forced a smile.

"Go ahead, Landon. Get in there."

78

Landon marched to the line of scrimmage.

As he lined up in his spot at right tackle, Landon looked at the defender across from him. Gunner Miller was no Brett Bell, but he was the team's starting left defensive end *and* the starting right tackle on offense and a hitter for sure. Gunner did not look happy about Landon taking his spot. Landon turned to look behind him. Jonathan Wagner stood next to Coach Bell with his arms folded across his chest and his biceps bulging like water balloons. He wore the face of a lion on a high rock, separated from other life forms, but he offered Landon a thumbs-up.

Landon turned back to the line and realized Skip had already begun his cadence. Landon got down into his stance a second behind the other linemen. The defense was ready too, with Gunner hunkered down and trembling with rage right in front of Landon. He could barely hear Skip's voice, and in that instant he was struck by the thought that Skip was being quieter on purpose, because Landon couldn't hear as well as the others by a long shot. Landon pushed the thought away. He checked himself quickly to make sure his stance was correct, looking down through his face mask at his feet.

Just as he glanced up, action exploded all around him and Gunner fired out, cracking Landon's pads. Landon winced, but he took his power step. His hands blasted up into Gunner's chest and Landon stayed low like he'd been told. They were neutral for a moment, and then Landon began to chug his feet, up and down, up and down, plowing forward, and almost in slow motion Gunner began to go backward. Landon kept chugging. Layne Guerrero flashed past in a blur with the football tucked under his arm.

Landon kept blocking, driving Gunner down the field. Gunner tried to separate, but Landon had his hands clamped up under the breastplate edges of his shoulder pads. Gunner turned and squirmed and desperately began swatting Landon's helmet. Landon heard the distant sound of what might have been the whistle, but he wasn't sure, so he kept doing what Jonathan had told him to do, and he did feel a little mad at Gunner for swatting him in the earhole.

Finally, Landon saw that he was alone with Gunner in the middle of the field. No one was around, and he figured it was time to stop because the whistle was really shrieking now.

Landon turned to see Coach Furster's boiling face, teeth

clamped tight on the whistle, marching straight for him.

The coach whipped Landon around by the shoulder pad and gave him a shove. "Are you . . . just . . . stupid?"

Landon saw that everyone had stopped to stare. He shook his head. "No."

"Well, you just got us a fifteen-yard penalty for unnecessary roughness, did you know that?"

"No." Landon felt his insides quiver, but he also felt . . . mad.

There was a flash of movement as Jonathan Wagner dashed up and put a friendly hand on Coach Furster's shoulder. "My bad, Coach. This is on me totally." Jonathan laughed. "I *told* him to keep driving his man until he heard the whistle. Landon asked me what to do if he didn't hear it, and I told him I'd rather see him get a penalty than not finish his block. It's a lineman's code of conduct type of thing. My bad. I'm sorry."

Coach Furster's face softened, but not entirely.

"Did you see that block my man made, though?" Jonathan's eyebrows jumped. "Wow, my grandmother could've run through that hole."

"Yes, it was a . . ." Coach Furster seemed to be choking on a fish bone. "It was a good one. A good block. True, but we can't have a fifteen-yard penalty on every play. You can't have *that*."

Landon knew what was happening. It had happened to him all his life. Just when someone gave him a chance, just when things looked like they were going his way, someone like Coach Furster stepped on him like a bug.

The only difference here was that Landon's savior was a six-foot-six, three-hundred-and thirty-pound All-Pro lineman for the New York Giants.

If the cruel cycle of Landon's life was ever going to be broken, it was now.

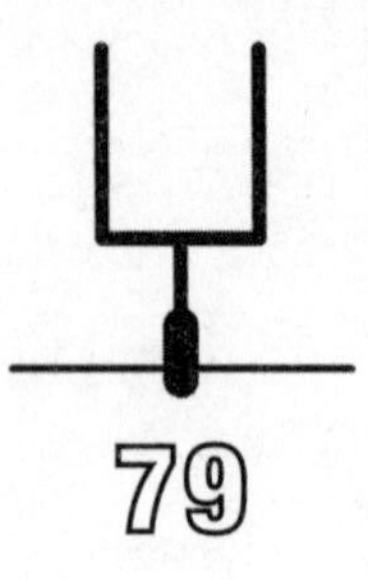

79

"So, Landon." Jonathan turned to face him. "Forget what I said before. You block for five seconds and then stop. That's the length of an average play. Can you count that in your mind? Just one, two, three, four, five; then you get off the block. That'll fix it. Can you?"

"Sure," Landon said.

Coach Furster opened his mouth to protest, but nothing came out except, "He . . . uh . . . uh . . ."

"Coach, you line my man and Brett up next to each other?" Jonathan shook his head with the slow wag of a dog. It looked—and kind of sounded to Landon—like he whistled. "Man oh man. You got yourself a juggernaut. Yes sir, one of them unstoppable, rolling battering ram things that just crushes everything in its way. You tuck your runner up behind 'em? My man!"

"It's an idea." Coach Furster seemed to slowly be regaining

his control of the situation. "Let's see how he does, though. Let's see about this five-second thing."

Jonathan clapped his meaty hands. "I like it, Coach. That's just what Coach McAdoo would've said."

Coach Furster lost his fight not to smile at the comparison, and the toot of his whistle was a little less strong than usual before he barked, "Okay, let's get it back in the huddle. Forty-eight sweep! Let me see it!"

Jonathan winked at Landon and shooed him toward the huddle.

It all happened so fast. Skip called the play in a mutter. Brett pointed at him and smiled from the other side of the huddle. They stepped to the line. Gunner Miller hunkered down in his stance with trembling legs, ready to explode, ready to take revenge. Part of Landon was scared. Part of him wanted to explain to Gunner that he only wanted a true place on the team, not to actually take his job. But part of Landon got mad, and he asked himself, why should he go through life being picked on and being left out? Why shouldn't *he* win the day? Win the battle? Win the war? Landon saw the other linemen drop, so he did too, more ready this time for action.

And in that instant, he felt it.

He went batty with anger.

Nasty.

Even though he couldn't really hear the cadence, Landon exploded at the first sign of movement, low and hard. This time there was no neutral, momentary stand-off. This time Landon plowed through Gunner so fast and hard he fell down. Landon went over him like a lawnmower, let go, and pitilessly grabbed the next body he came upon, Timmy Nichols. Landon manhandled him, driving him three yards back before tossing him to the dirt.

He was huffing and puffing and he stopped and stood up straight, fearful that he might have gone over a five-second count. In truth, he hadn't counted at all. All he knew was that Layne Guerrero was wiggling his butt in the end zone. Landon turned.

Coach Furster looked amazed, but when Landon detected the small smile in the left corner of Jonathan Wagner's mouth, it filled him with joy and pride. Brett was slapping him on the back. Landon turned.

"Dude! You crushed them. Two pancakes in the same play? Ha-ha! I never had *two* pancakes!" Landon's cheeks burned. He shrugged and headed back toward where he knew the huddle would be, unable to keep a huge grin from blooming around his mouthpiece.

Practice went on just like that.

Get the play. Line up. Five seconds of nastiness. Do it again.

Landon kept expecting something bad to happen, some problem to pop up and ruin everything, but by the end of the evening Jonathan Wagner had taught them all four new running plays from an unbalanced line that put Landon and Brett right next to each other to open massive holes in the defense to run through. Landon could see that Coach Furster didn't really like the whole thing, until Jonathan showed them a counter-play that had the quarterback handing the ball off to the wide receiver on an end around to the weak side.

That was a play where Mike would shine.

"See?" Jonathan explained excitedly. "The defense is going to *have* to shift to this unbalanced line, and when they start getting chewed up by your two monster hogs, they'll *over*-shift. Then you come back at them with this wide receiver end around, and they may just lay down on you and quit."

They ran the play, and the grin on Coach Furster's face when his son scampered into the end zone could have lit a Christmas tree.

"We really are a passing team, though." Coach Furster scratched his head.

Jonathan shook his head and frowned. "There's no such thing, Coach. You can ask Coach McAdoo or Eli Manning. You can ask Peyton Manning or Aaron Rodgers or Tom Brady. Even the so-called 'passing' teams know you gotta run the ball to set up the pass. No one ever won a championship any other way."

Landon looked back to Coach Furster to see his reaction.

What he saw, he never expected.

80

Surrender.

That was the best word Landon could think of, and he never thought he'd see it on Coach Furster's face. He never imagined Coach Furster was even capable of it, but in the presence of a man as big and powerful and immovable as Jonathan Wagner, Coach Furster was reduced to a regular dad, chewing on his knuckle.

As the team gathered around, no one could hear them talking, but Landon read the NFL player's and his coach's lips.

Coach Furster said, "I was thinking to myself that we needed to get back to basics. I mean, losing to Scarsdale?"

"It's a funny-shaped ball," Jonathan said. "It doesn't always bounce your way, but you're right about basics. I think you've got something here, Coach. Something that could really give people headaches."

Coach Furster held out a hand. "This has been an honor."

"And a pleasure for me." Jonathan shook the coach's hand.

"Hey, would you mind saying a few words to the team?" Coach Furster asked.

"Sure." Jonathan Wagner turned to the team. He didn't speak until everyone was standing totally still. Only then did he look around like that ferocious lion again. "Guys, you've heard it before. There's no 'I' in 'team.' And that means if you want to be a champion, you have to realize it's about everyone around you. Look around."

He waited until they really did look before he continued. "From the best player to the worst, you're a team, so act like one. Treat each other well and you won't just win, you'll *be winners*."

Coach Furster waited to make sure Jonathan Wagner was finished before he turned to the players, who now stood waiting in anticipation for wind sprints, and shouted, "All right, men. It's not every day you get an NFL player showing up at your practice, so I'm gonna let Jonathan Wagner decide just how many sprints you guys will run. Let's go! On the line!"

Coach Furster blasted his whistle and everyone lined up shoulder-to-shoulder on the sideline.

Jonathan stepped forward and raised his voice. "I like what you guys are doing. I like the way you worked, and when the New York Giants work really hard and have a really good practice, sometimes, *sometimes*, Coach McAdoo says, 'You did your running during practice men, *see you tomorrow*!'"

Everyone around Landon cheered. He looked to make sure that's what it was before joining in.

"You heard him!" Coach Furster shouted, waving them off the field. *"See you tomorrow!"*

More cheering, and the team moved in a wave up the hill toward the parking lot. Landon saw Mike Furster and Skip Dreyfus without their helmets, each with a hand on the shoulder pads of a crestfallen Gunner Miller. Xander West walked backward, talking to them all. Landon was breathless at the sight, and he hesitated. He wanted to thank Jonathan Wagner, but he didn't want to be a pest and Coach Furster was now having his picture taken with the Giants player, so Landon turned and slogged up the hill.

When he got into the car, his father looked at him from his hunched-over position and asked, "What's everyone so excited about, buddy?"

Landon carefully removed his helmet and the skullcap and adjusted the hearing apparatus clinging to his head. He dumped the helmet into the backseat and sat looking down at his hands. Tears rushed into his eyes. He couldn't speak, but only shake his head.

"Hey, hey." Landon's dad gave him a gentle shake until he looked up. "What's wrong, buddy? Hey, what happened? You can tell me."

Landon sniffed and spoke in a choking voice. "*I* happened, Dad. I did it. I did it."

Landon looked through the kaleidoscope of tears. "I'm a football player."

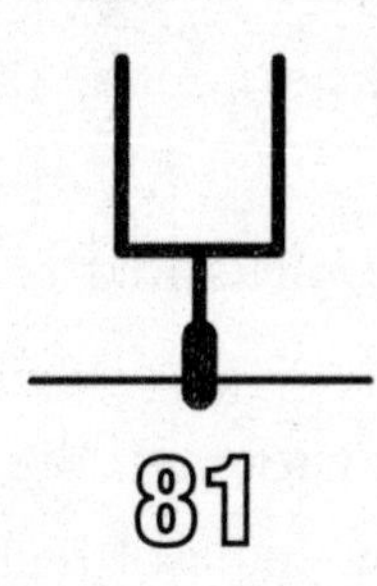

81

That night at home and the next morning before school, Landon didn't boast about it. He didn't even tell Genevieve, not because she didn't deserve to know but because Landon wanted to caress the idea of who he now was in the privacy of his own thoughts.

As Landon dug into his oatmeal, Genevieve pounded her hand on the table between them to get his attention. "Are you okay?"

"Yeah, great." Landon did his best to look normal.

"Something's going on." She stared at him.

Suddenly he could hold it no longer. Landon burst into a smile. "I did it, Genevieve, I showed them all I can play. Really play."

The feel of her arms wrapped around him in a tight hug stayed with Landon all the way to school. Nothing around him seemed to have changed, but he felt somehow taller, and it didn't bother him that he stood out.

Landon got to English class early. Mr. Edwards was making some final notes for his lesson when Megan arrived, and she got right in Landon's face. "I hear you're the new big thing on the football team."

Megan looked to be as delighted as Landon felt. He offered a shy nod.

"Landon, I'm so happy for you. Brett couldn't stop raving." Her laugh was a pleasant jingle of bells. "We were texting all night and then he had to meet me before homeroom to tell me again in person."

Landon felt a mixture of pride and envy. He couldn't help wishing it was him Megan was texting far into the night and him she'd met up with in the hallway before homeroom.

"Seems good so far," he replied.

"I'll say." With a nod she sat down and took out her copy of *The Count of Monte Cristo.*

Landon had a hard time focusing in English—and in all his classes. As he pushed through the hallways from one class to another, he stole glances at the kids around him in a way he never had before. It had always been safer and easier to ignore the looks people gave him because they'd rarely been anything but unkind. Now though, he could only imagine it was a matter of time before news of his new prowess spread, and instead of disgust, he'd be seeing admiration in the faces of his fellow students.

At lunch he half expected someone or other to sit down at his empty table. When no one did, he assured himself it was just a matter of time. He recalled the way heads and eyes magnetically turned toward Jonathan Wagner when he pulled up in his big truck. In time, and of course to a lesser degree, that would happen for Landon. He just knew it.

He hustled right out of study hall so he could make his usual pit stop on the way to gym and realized as he went that he really was standing taller and straighter and that his height allowed him to look down on everyone from his own private rooftop.

He slipped into his usual stall, the last one in a row of five. The chipped gray paint on the inside walls and door of the stall were marked with messages and insults, old and new. As they had every day since he'd found this private spot, two round Ping-Pong-ball eyes drawn in Sharpie stared at him with pupils no bigger than dots. Their heavy lids seemed bored with his business, and he wondered if the crooked line below was an accident or a twisted smile.

Suddenly he stiffened at the sight of a shadow flickering through the thin crack between the door and its frame. He cleared his throat to let the intruder know the end stall was taken, but instead of a departing shadow, Landon saw the tips of two running sneakers.

He strained for even the hint of a sound and then proclaimed, "This one's taken."

The sneakers shifted. He sensed more movement outside the stall before an iPhone appeared beneath the door, attached to a selfie stick and directed at him.

He could see himself on the screen as he stared in horror, and then it blinked.

His mouth fell open in disbelief, and by the time he realized what had really happened—that someone had taken a picture of him sitting on the toilet with his pants down around his ankles—the phone was gone. There was a flurry of shadows in the crack of the stall door and more on the floor as the feet scrambled for the exit.

Landon yanked up his pants and fumbled with his zipper and the stall door at the same time. He heard what sounded like a crazed cackle of laughter and the slam of the bathroom door. Bursting from the stall, he grazed his head against the door, dislodging his cochlear, and saw only the flash of a backpack disappearing into the hall.

"Help!" Landon shouted at the top of his lungs. "Stop!"

He knew it was useless.

He stopped in front of the mirror and looked at the reflection of a huge boy with his pants unbuttoned and his shirt crumpled above the white of his belly. The battery pack from one ear dangled from the wire connecting it to the disc on his skull. His insides trembled with anger and dread.

A moan escaped him because he knew that this would now ruin everything.

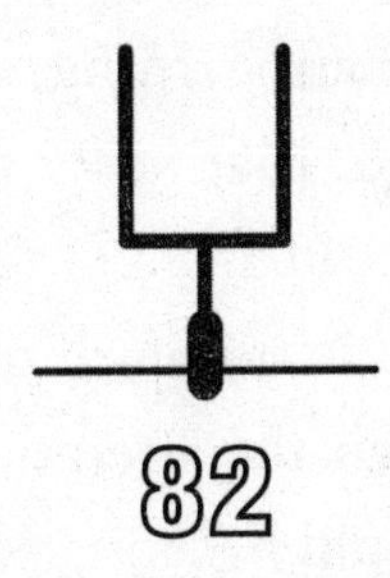
82

The sounds of a commotion out in the hall hurried Landon's fingers. He fastened his pants, tugged his shirt into place, and slipped the battery pack back behind his ear. After hoisting his backpack, Landon took a deep breath and swung open the scarred wooden door.

He blinked and gasped at what he saw.

Mike Furster lay sprawled out on the floor. His backpack and its contents had been flung about. Genevieve had a knee planted in his back, a handful of his spiked hair in one hand and his iPhone in the other. Xander hadn't gotten far, and he now turned back to rescue his friend, closing in fast on Genevieve.

Landon stepped forward to help Genevieve, but he was spun around by Skip.

"Stay out of it, you big slob." Skip yanked Landon's arm,

causing him to stumble into the lockers with a bang.

Landon's eyes darted toward his shrieking sister.

Xander had her in a headlock and he was grabbing for the phone. Skip was moving in.

Landon felt it. Without warning, at the sight of his little sister being manhandled, that nasty blew right through his brain.

Landon got hold of Skip from behind, lifted, and flung him with one motion, through the air and into the lockers with a cymbal crash Landon could *feel*.

Landon grabbed Xander by the neck and tore him free from Genevieve, raising him and tossing him to the floor. Landon roared. Looking at Mike, his head shook with fury. Mike had flipped himself over. With terror in every muscle, he scrabbled backward on the floor like a crab. Landon roared again and Mike took off, without his phone.

Xander started to follow, but Landon grabbed him by the neck again.

That's when Mr. Edwards appeared with his own look of shock and terror. His eyes went up toward Xander, squeezed in Landon's grip.

Mr. Edwards held up both hands the way you'd fend off a monster. "No, Landon. Put him down! You're hurting him!"

Landon dropped Xander to the floor, where he fell in a heap. Genevieve had ahold of Landon's arm, and he looked down.

"What'd they do?" Genevieve's face was aflame. "Take a picture of you in the bathroom?"

Landon nodded.

Genevieve gritted her teeth. “Well, too bad for them.”

Even as the principal rounded the corner flanked by two teachers, Genevieve dropped the phone to the floor and stomped the life out of it.

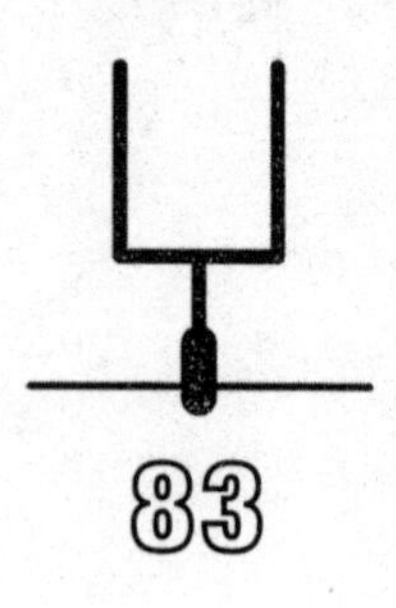
83

Megan was the one who had told Genevieve what was going on. She'd overheard Skip bragging about their plan to Katy after lunch. It embarrassed Landon that Megan knew what had happened, but he couldn't help also feeling grateful that she had helped save him from what would have been a disastrous new assault. Those were Landon's thoughts as he and Genevieve sat in the principal's office waiting for their father.

It took over forty minutes for him to finally arrive, ducking through the door and clicking his tongue. His first words were worried. "Oh, kids. Are you okay?"

Mr. Sanders popped through the door, all business. "Mr. Dorch? Somehow I was expecting your wife."

Landon's dad bit a lip and his cheeks reddened. "Oh, she's on her way. I told her it was an emergency. She'll walk through that door at any minute."

Landon's dad turned a hopeful face toward the door.

Mr. Sanders considered Landon and Genevieve. "I'm not sure it's an *emergency*, but a suspension does go on their disciplinary record."

"Suspension?" Landon's dad looked shocked.

"Your son was *warned*," the principal said, and then he nearly gagged on his next words. "Landon was *choking* another student, Mr. Dorch."

Landon wanted to look down, but then he'd never know what they were saying. When people were angry or serious, their tones always dropped, rendering his cochlear implants nearly useless on their own. So, he watched his father react with shock, sadness, and worry, until he realized that Genevieve was spouting off.

". . . picture of Landon using the bathroom, which is totally *illegal*!" Genevieve's face was on fire.

"You're not a lawyer here, miss." The principal shifted his scowl from Landon to his sister. "You're a young lady in a lot of hot water. Assaulting a fellow student? Destruction of property?"

"I didn't assault him." Genevieve glared right back at the principal. "I *tackled* him because he took a picture of my brother using the *toilet* and he was going to *post* it. Is that okay with you?"

Landon kept his eyes moving to see who would speak first.

It was a standoff.

Then the door flung open and their mother burst into the room.

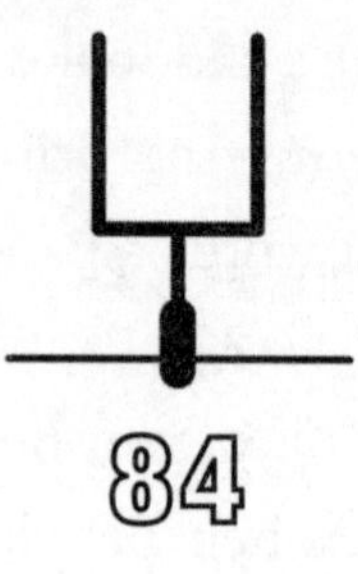

84

Landon had never seen his mother's hair so out of place.

"Why are those other boys not in here?" Landon's mom demanded.

"Those boys were the *victims* of this assault, Mrs. Dorch." The principal stood up to show just how outraged he really was. "And the discipline of children besides your own isn't any of your business, madam."

"Justice is my business." Their mom slapped her iPad down on the principal's desk. The page read: CODE OF CONDUCT AND DISCIPLINE. Beneath that was a seal and then: BRONXVILLE SCHOOL DISTRICT. "Take a look at your own handbook, Mr. Sanders. Those 'victims' were not victims. They're bullies who've tormented my son since before school began, and you will *not* continue to turn a blind eye to that. Being inept is no excuse for a middle school principal paid by my tax dollars."

"You're not going to tell *me* how to do my job, madam. This meeting is over. You can head right out that door, or I'll call security and have you removed." Mr. Sanders trembled and then snatched up the handset of the phone on his desk.

"Good." Their mom held up her cell phone. "I'm calling the newspaper."

"Wait! What?"

"That's right." Landon's mother continued to tap the screen of her phone. "And then I'm calling the superintendent, but first, the newspaper. Bullying is a big issue these days."

"Mrs. Dorch, put the phone down." Mr. Sanders's eyes sputtered like wet candles. "Please."

Landon's mom didn't put it down, but she stopped tapping. "Do you know what that handbook says?"

"Which part?" Mr. Sanders asked.

"The part on page forty-two about aggravated harassment, followed by internet harassment on page forty-three, and especially possession of indecent material on page sixty-seven. I'm not sure about disseminating indecent material because I'm not sure if the perpetrator sent the picture to anyone before he was stopped by this brave young lady who happens to be my daughter." Their mom nodded toward Genevieve.

Everyone in the room stared at Landon's mom with open mouths, none more astounded than Mr. Sanders. "You . . . you . . . but, the camera—the phone, I mean—was broken."

"That's what the cloud is for." Landon's mom folded her

arms across her chest. "If my husband and I want to push this, I think we need to involve the district attorney, don't you? I'm sure you remember the presentation that the DA's office made to the kids last year warning them about crimes like these? It's on your website, Mr. Sanders. It's part of why I chose to move into Bronxville. According to the website, the DA said that disseminating a picture that reveals a private part of a person's anatomy is a Class D felony. You should know that." Their mom wore a look of disgust.

"Of course I know that." Mr. Sanders stood upright in a futile attempt to regain his authority. The principal looked at Landon's dad and then at his mom. "Mrs. Dorch? I think we can settle all this quietly and to everyone's satisfaction, don't you?"

"First you'll admit you've got the wrong kids sitting in your office." Their mom didn't blink.

Mr. Sanders looked like he'd been hung by his thumbs.

Landon's dad glanced at their mom. "I know my wife, Mr. Sanders. I know how she thinks and how she feels, and I have an idea that just might satisfy her, but it won't be easy to pull off. Maybe, just maybe, if you're willing to work with us, my wife and I might find a way to let you resolve this *without* involving the DA."

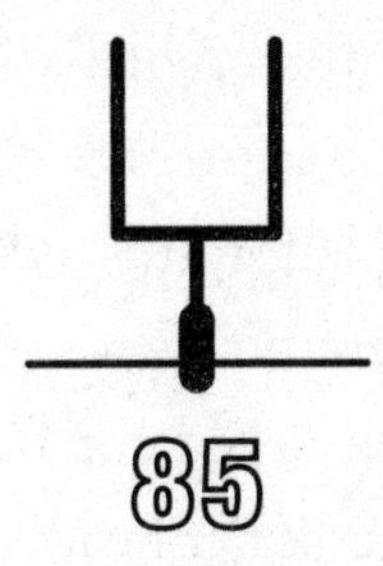

85

Landon's mom didn't say yes, but she didn't say no either. What she said was that she wanted to think about it with the family—at home.

Landon sat with his family around the kitchen table, trying to decide what to do. His dad tried to persuade his mom that an apology from the boys would do.

"See, the thing is, Gina," Landon's dad said, "Saturday's the big game against Tuckahoe. It's a huge tradition. The whole town goes out to watch."

Landon's mom narrowed her eyes. "What does that *mean*, Forrest?"

Landon's dad sputtered. "Well . . ."

"Not to them. What does it mean to *me*? What do you think?" his mother asked.

"Well . . . if we get the DA involved, they may cancel the

game. The whole thing would blow up, and our kids would be in the middle of it." Landon could tell his dad felt like he was on dangerous ground, because he was scratching his neck and blinking a lot.

His mother thumped a small fist onto the table. "What those boys did is a crime. Crimes are meant to be punished."

"But sometimes people forgive and forget?" his father suggested quietly after a pause.

"Has anyone involved asked for forgiveness?" His mother tightened her lips and shook her head.

"Not yet," their dad said.

Their mom's eyes blazed. "Sometimes people cross a line they shouldn't, and if you want them to know you mean business—so it won't happen again, Forrest—then you take action."

Landon's dad hung his head, and Landon knew how he felt, that desire to just have it all go away. Landon knew things did go away too. He'd experienced it. If you just kept your head down and kept going? People would generally leave you alone. But for the first time he could remember, Landon had experienced something better than just being left alone. He had friends. He had people who believed in him. Maybe he even had a gift that people would *admire,* and admiration? It was quite a prize.

His dad came up with another idea. "Listen, I know you say their fathers encourage this kind of bullying, the way they act as coaches. What if they agreed to quietly resign?"

"Coach Bell would bring the right spirit to the team," Landon's mother agreed.

"Look, they don't want this going to the courts any more than Mr. Sanders does. I bet they'll agree."

"And Coach Bell can be the head coach." Landon tried not to sound too excited, because he knew his parents' mood was somber.

"Will they even do that?" Genevieve asked. "I mean, Mr. West is the chief of police."

Landon's dad grinned. "Well, we're just gonna have to find out."

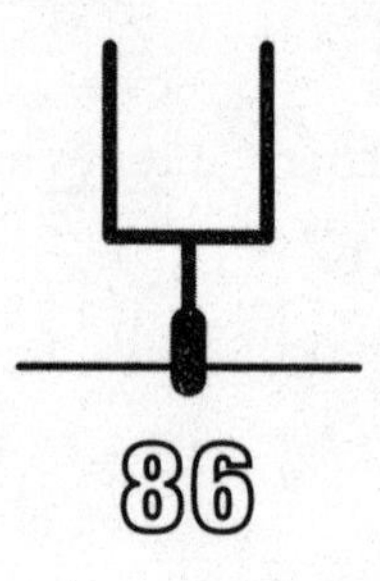

86

The next day, school spirit was soaring. Signs praising Bronxville football plastered the hallways in black and orange. From a distance, Landon saw Mike Furster walking and talking intently to Skip Dreyfus. Landon slowed down so as not to catch up to them. As soon as they disappeared around the corner, he hurried to homeroom, excited.

Brett grinned and jumped up, slapping a piece of paper down in front of Landon. "Here, check this out. My dad drew these up for short yardage. Just what my uncle was talking about. You and me like a *steamroller.*"

Landon looked up from the diagrams of Xs, Os, and arrows. "Really? But we didn't practice them."

"Ahh, in the NFL they put plays in on the sideline." Brett swished a hand. "Everyone knows what to do. How awesome is it that my dad is running things?"

Genevieve had filled Megan and Brett in on what had happened.

Now, Landon looked into Brett's eyes for some sign, a flicker of doubt maybe. Brett stared right back at him, stone-cold serious.

"How many players will we even have Saturday?" Landon asked.

Brett shrugged. "You and me. Guerrero, Miller, Rinehart will be there. There will be others. Lots. Skip, Mike, and Xander will apologize. You'll see. And if they don't? They only have themselves to blame, not you."

Landon looked around the homeroom. No one was watching him, but he leaned close to Brett anyway. "Are they really not going to show up? Coach Furster and Coach West, I mean?"

"I heard your mom scared the heck out of them. I heard they apologized and agreed to resign if your parents didn't press charges against their kids." Brett frowned, but then he smiled brightly. "My uncle said *he'd* help, so who needs them?"

That spark of news lit a small fire in Landon's heart. "If your uncle's there, I think everyone will want to play. I mean, who gets to play for an NFL player? Even if it's just for one game?"

87

In English class, Megan threw Landon several worried glances.

He just couldn't get into the discussion. All he could think about was the game and what would happen. It was the Megan and Mr. Edwards Show, but neither of them could be discouraged. They went back and forth about revenge, its different forms, and the similarities between Dumas and Edmond Dantès, now the Count of Monte Cristo. After the bell, Mr. Edwards took Landon by the arm and steered him toward his desk. "I heard about everything that's going on. You stay strong, Landon."

"I am," Landon said. "Thanks."

Megan was waiting for him outside the class. "You okay?"

He nodded. "Really. I'm fine. I'd be better if everyone wasn't so worried for me."

Megan gave him a crooked smile, and her blue eyes blazed

with kindness. She reached around his middle and pressed the side of her face into the bottom of his rib cage, hugging him tight. "I know what you mean, Landon."

He could feel her fingers sinking into the flesh of his back and was so flustered he couldn't speak. A scent like flowers and honey drifted up from her glossy hair. He wrapped his arms around her too, and her compact frame reminded him of Genevieve and his mom. His nose dipped toward the wonderful smell so that it brushed the top of her head.

"Come on, we'll be late for third period." Megan released him, smiled up, and turned to go. Landon followed.

As they navigated the crowded hallways, Landon felt himself standing a little taller again, and he noticed that the glances people gave him weren't full of loathing but of respect, maybe even fear. He wondered if that had anything to do with him overpowering the kids who'd tormented him, or if it was because his mother had those same kids' parents pinned to the mat and wasn't letting up. Either way, Landon thought he liked it and that it might lead to other things, other friends, someday.

Megan paused outside Mr. Mazella's math class. "See you later, Landon."

Landon's cheek still burned from the hug, and he said a quick thanks before ducking into class.

Buoyed by the image of Megan looking up at him, the smell of her shampoo, and the touch of her hair, which Landon's mind replayed over and over in every spare moment, the day flew by. Once he nearly bumped into Xander in the hallway.

"Hey." Xander's face was frozen. "I'm supposed to apologize to you, so that's what I'm doing. Sorry."

"Uh . . . okay."

And that was it. Xander coasted right on past, leaving Landon's heart at a gallop.

By the end of the school day, Mike Furster had also apologized, but the only thing Landon got from Skip was a hateful stare from the other side of health class. When the last bell rang, it felt to Landon like a prison break. He burst out the front doors of the school and breathed deeply.

Outside, the rain had stopped and the sky had rolled back its clouds. The sun sparkled on the wet grass and dying leaves of the trees. Brett and Landon sat with Landon's dad in the bleachers to watch the girls' soccer game. They too played Tuckahoe, as did every other fall sport, and the crowd was bigger than normal for a middle school girls' soccer game. Genevieve scored twice to defeat the big rival 2–1, and Megan was a force on defense. After the final whistle, the Bronxville girls bounced up and down in a giant group hug, screaming so loud that even Landon heard them.

Landon's dad walked Landon and his sister and Brett and Megan home, distracted and muttering to himself as he sometimes did at his desk when he was writing. The four of them had pizza at the kitchen table. Landon could tell everyone was trying to keep him distracted from what would happen tomorrow, but worry hung like a heavy chain around his neck and his smiles were forced.

When their friends had gone home and Landon's mom arrived from work, the Dorch family assembled at the kitchen table.

"Well?" Landon's dad asked. "Where are we at, Gina?"

Landon's mom had a slice of pizza on a paper plate along with a diet soda for her late dinner. She chewed well, swallowed, and washed her bite down with soda before looking hard at Landon. "Did those boys apologize?"

Landon nodded. "Yup."

"Really apologize?" she asked.

"Mom, they said they were sorry." He didn't tell her about Skip.

"Three apologies?" his mom asked.

Landon looked down. "No, but I didn't see Skip, so maybe he's waiting until tomorrow."

"Well, that's a good start. Now let's see what tomorrow brings," she said before taking another bite.

"I just hope they'll play if their dads aren't coaching," Genevieve said. "Everyone really wants us to win. The whole school's gone crazy about the game."

Landon's mom finished her bite and washed it down before answering. "I spoke to Courtney Wagner on the phone this afternoon, and you know what she said?"

Genevieve just shook her head.

Landon's mom looked at him, and her emerald green eyes sparkled. "She said we don't even need those bullies. She said her brother thinks we can beat the pants off Tuckahoe with our run game."

88

Sometime during the night, in a snarl of bedsheets, exhaustion finally overtook Landon, and he woke the next morning with a buzz in his brain that had nothing to do with his cochlear implants. He went through the motions of getting ready with jittery hands and stomach, passed on breakfast, and strapped himself into his football gear as if he were getting ready for a moonwalk. He even buckled up his helmet because he wanted his ears to be perfectly positioned inside the padding, and then stood staring at his father, who flipped French toast on the griddle until he realized Landon was there.

"Oh, hey." His father held the spatula upright and with pride, like a scepter, and then touched each shoulder pad. "I dub thee Landon the Great."

Landon shook his head. "This is serious, Dad."

His father's face lost its smile. "I know, son. And you're going to do great. Want me to drive you over?"

"Think I'm gonna walk, Dad."

"This early?" His father checked his watch.

"Yeah. I want to be there early. I want to hit the sled a little. Make sure I'm ready."

"What about wearing down your cleats?"

"One time won't hurt. I'll try and walk on the grass."

"Well, we will be there and cheering you on," his dad said.

"If I don't get blown up."

"You're not going to get blown up, Landon. You're going to shine." His dad shrugged. "It's just the way this story has to end."

"End?"

His father laughed and scratched at his chin. "Well, for one story to start, another story always has to end. Today is going to be a new beginning for you. It's like the sequel to *Dragon Hunt*."

"Sequel? Wait, you finished?" Landon forgot about football for a minute.

His father's cheeks colored. "You haven't seen me do much else, have you? It's two hundred and thirty pages, and it kind of wrote itself."

Landon's mind snapped back to reality. "This isn't a novel, dad. Today is real life."

His father shrugged again. "I know, but I keep telling you, you're the author of your life."

Landon sighed. "Okay, gotta go."

Before he got out the door, he felt a tap on his shoulder and turned to see that his father had followed him and stood like a fairy-tale giant blocking out the light. “I’m proud of you, Landon. However the story ends.”

Landon peered at his father. In the gloom of the mudroom it looked like his eyes were glinting with moisture. His father pulled him into a hug, and then he turned him around and sent him on his way like a wind-up toy soldier.

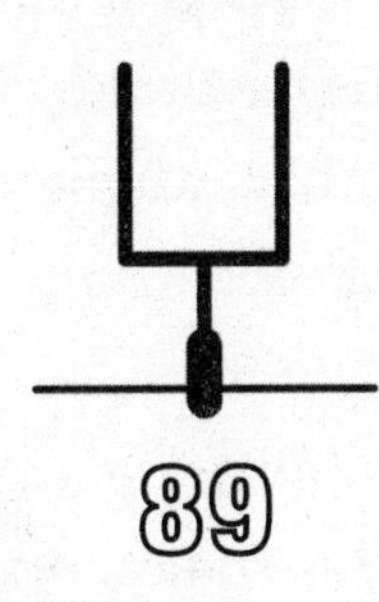

89

The clouds above crowded in on one another, piling up high and leaving almost no room for the blue to peek through. The air was brisk and a small breeze found its way through the cracks in Landon's pads. Still, he felt little, steamy swamps building up in the pits of his arms and the palms of his shaking hands. As he approached the field, cut grass sweetened the swirl of warm blacktop. There wasn't a soul to be seen. Not even a dog.

Landon tramped down the hillside and put a hand on the blue-padded blocking dummy fixed to the single sled they rarely used. The piston behind let loose a rusty squeal as he jiggled it back and forth. Landon looked around and saw only swaying trees and the lifeless windows of the houses bordering the school grounds. A yellow jacket searched the metal tube of the sled for a home and buzzed right for Landon. He jumped and swatted, filled with panic and anticipating a sting, but the bee ticked off the side of his helmet and sailed away into the breeze.

Landon laughed at himself and looked around. He imagined the stands filled with fans and the sidelines crowded with players. Still caught in the daydream, he hunkered down into his stance and heard Jonathan Wagner in his mind.

"Shoulder-width apart."

"Flat back."

"Power step. Head up. Hands inside. Feet chopping."

Landon fired out of his stance, and the dummy squealed the high-pitched cry of a little girl on a swing. He chugged his feet, driving and driving with the clock going in his head.

One, two, three, four, five. He stopped, looked around, lined up, and did it again.

Again and again he drove the sled, zigzagging this way and that, all across the grassy field beyond the end zone until he heard the faint sound of a shout. Landon turned to see Timmy.

"What are you doing here?"

Landon shrugged. "We got a game."

Timmy looked around. "Fat chance. Not much of a game without your quarterback. Thanks to you. I doubt the rest of the team's even gonna show."

Landon stuttered and then said, "It's Tuckahoe. People aren't gonna miss that. You're here."

Timmy scowled. "My mom dumps me off so she can do the *Times* crossword puzzle at the coffee shop. I'm not dumb enough to think I can make myself better the day of a game just by hitting that stupid thing."

Landon shrugged again, saying, "It never hurts to practice."

He turned away and attacked the dummy again. When he finished driving, Timmy was right behind him. He pointed at the sled. "That's pretty good, actually."

Landon studied Timmy's pudgy, angry face through the cage of his face mask for signs of contempt, but saw none. "Thanks."

"Not that it matters. Tuckahoe's gonna crush us even *if* we have enough guys to play." Timmy looked around, expecting an empty field. "Hey, Guerrero's here." His jaw dropped. "And there's Mike and Xander."

Landon followed the direction of Timmy's finger and saw that their first-team running back was jogging down the hill, and his parents weren't far behind, dressed in Bronxville colors with two pom-poms and traveling mugs of coffee. Mike and Xander were at their heels. Another vehicle pulled into the lot. It was the Bells' Suburban, and out hopped not only Brett but Travis and a fullback named Stewy Stewart, as well as Brett's dad.

"Looks like you're the only one who thinks we're gonna get crushed." Landon couldn't help jabbing Timmy. He wanted to knock that smug look off his face.

"We'll see." Timmy wasn't backing down, but for some reason he stayed close to Landon as he pushed the sled around.

Coach Bell dumped a bag of balls on the sideline and began tossing one back and forth with Layne and Stewy Stewart. Xander and Mike took a ball and started their own game of catch. The other linemen huddled up in the end zone and Brett waved Landon over. Timmy followed.

"Hey, guys," Brett said. "Let's line up and run through

those new plays. We got five linemen already. That's all we need to get started. Timmy, you play left tackle, 'cause I'm right guard next to Landon today. Travis at center and Gunner at left guard."

"I'm right tackle." Gunner stood tall.

Tension sucked the wind out of Landon and he forgot to breathe.

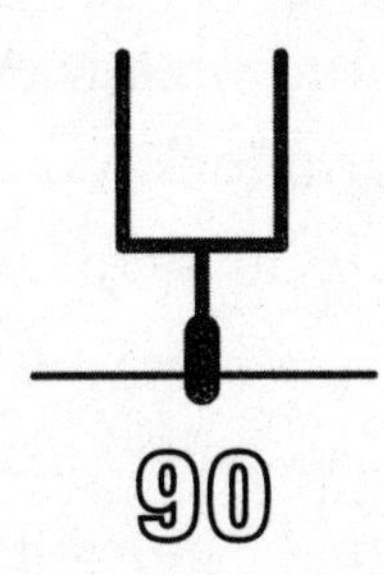

90

Brett shook his head. “Landon has to play there. He’s Double X. It’s in the rules. Play guard, Gunner. What’s the big deal?”

Gunner gave Landon an impatient look and grumbled that it was a stupid rule, but he lined up at left guard all the same. Brett’s dad marched over to the end zone with Guerrero and Stewart and flipped the ball to the center. “I’ll take the snaps and hand off to Layne. Good idea to get some extra reps, guys.”

With seven players and one coach, they began to run some plays. As more players arrived, they filled in at the tight end and receiver positions. Soon they had a full squad and a scout defense to run against. When Torin Bennett, the normal starting left guard, arrived, Gunner and Torin looked at Coach Bell.

“Yeah . . . okay, Torin, you’re starting on defense today, but not offense. Gunner’s got left guard. We’re running a new offense because I don't think we're gonna have Skip to pass it today."

A couple of guys gave Landon dirty looks, but both Mike and Xander stared straight ahead, and the frowns from other guys didn't last. They got to work with Bryce Rinehart under center. Their backup quarterback was excited to be the starter, and handing the ball off to Guerrero instead of throwing passes was fine with him.

When the Tuckahoe bus pulled into the parking lot above, Landon began to worry that Timmy had been right. Skip, one of their best players and the starting quarterback, was obviously boycotting the game instead of offering his apology to Landon. An army of Tuckahoe players filed off the bus and marched in two perfect columns down the hill and through the far goalposts.

The Tuckahoe team snaked around the field on a silent jog, swishing past Landon and his teammates without a single glance before coming out through the far goalposts again and filing into seven columns of seven for warm-ups. Landon couldn't keep from watching. When they were all assembled, the Tuckahoe captain, a boy nearly as large as Landon, barked once, and the entire team roared something Landon didn't understand. Just as suddenly, they broke into jumping jacks, counting them out with sharp sounds that ended in a cascade of clapping.

Landon turned to Brett, who waved a dismissive hand in the air. "Their bark is worse than their bite. If this was a cheerleading competition, we wouldn't stand a chance, but when we start smacking them in the mouth, it won't be about cheering anymore."

Landon wished he could feel some of Brett's swagger, but as they ran through more plays, he couldn't help being slightly disheartened by the loud and disciplined nature of the Tuckahoe team.

The lot was swelling with cars and trucks, and the stands began to fill up too. Landon's family arrived, and he watched his mom with her head held high as she stamped up the center aisle of the stands and took a seat right in the middle of everything like she owned the place. The Tuckahoe stands began to overflow, and their green-and-black-clad fans started to line the fence on their side of the field.

Bronxville's high school marching band suddenly spilled from the school with blasting brass instruments and clanging drums to take up position not far from where Landon and his teammates stretched out. The air vibrated with the sounds of a military march, which ended abruptly. The Bronxville stands were packed. Landon guessed there were close to a thousand people. Coach Bell kept the pregame going as if he'd been their head coach all along. Brett ran the lineman drills efficiently, as if he were Coach Furster's ghost.

During warm-ups, Brett's mom set up a table behind the bench and unpacked a couple dozen bottles of Gatorade for the team to drink. Coach West usually brought the water bottles and carriers, but Landon didn't think anyone would mind Gatorade instead. He knew he didn't, and no one would have to worry about refilling them.

On the next practice play they ran, Landon fired out at the defensive end in front of him when he heard a shriek behind him. He spun and saw everything had stopped. Bryce was lying in a heap behind the line. Guerrero stood over him with the ball, saying he was sorry.

Coach Bell jumped forward.

Bryce rolled and clutched his ankle, howling. As Landon watched the scene unfold, he realized that Guerrero had stepped on Bryce's foot and wrenched his ankle. Bryce's dad was there now, helping his son off the field along with another parent.

Now, they had no quarterback at all.

Landon turned to Brett. "So . . . what are we gonna do?"

Brett turned and looked toward his dad. Landon turned too, and saw Coach Bell out at midfield talking with the referees and the Tuckahoe head coach. The whole group of men checked their watches together. The head ref said something, and Coach Bell nodded and walked back toward the Bronxville bench with his face in a knot.

The Bronxville players huddled around Coach Bell. "Well, guys, we've got no quarterback. They said they'll give us ten extra minutes to figure something out, but we've got to be ready. So . . ."

Everyone held his breath, waiting to see what possible solution Coach Bell might have.

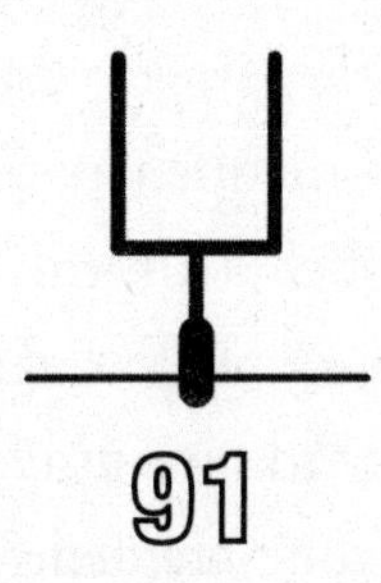
91

Brett's dad exhaled loudly and looked at his son. "Brett, let's have you take a few snaps and see what you can do."

"What?" Brett went rigid. "You want *me* to play quarterback?"

Brett's father squeezed his lips together. "You know the plays and you know the game as well as anyone. You got a better idea?"

"I . . ." Brett looked around at them. "Okay."

Gunner eyed Nichols and raised his hand. "But, Coach, if we don't have Brett on the line, won't these guys bury us?"

"You've got Landon," Coach Bell said. "Torin, you're back at left guard, and Gunner, you go to right guard. Come on. Have some confidence."

"I know, Coach, but it's Tuckahoe." Gunner sounded like they'd lost already.

As if on cue, the band struck up a marching tune from the end zone.

"It's a funny-shaped ball, guys." Coach Bell looked around at his team. "Lots of things can happen. Brett, take some snaps and let's get some handoffs going to Layne."

Brett teamed up in an open patch of grass with Travis to snap, and Layne got behind him to go through the basic mechanics of their running plays. Even Landon had to admit that it looked kind of silly to see a player as big as Brett line up at quarterback, but everyone seemed to be willing to give the whole thing a try.

Landon looked up into the stands. Megan had joined his family along with Brett's mom in a carnival of black and orange. Landon thought about his father's words, about writing your own story, but this just wasn't fair. The whole notion of the team running the ball down Tuckahoe's throat behind him and Brett just wouldn't happen if Brett was being wasted at quarterback.

A rumble like thunder from the parking lot made Landon turn his head. Jonathan Wagner's enormous, gleaming pickup pulled into the parking lot and out onto the grass, the lineman making up his own spot before he hopped out of the truck and hurried down the hill swinging his big bowed legs like backhoe buckets. He arrived out of breath while people in the stands pointed, whispered, and stared. "Sorry, guys, but I made it!"

Jonathan looked around. "Brett at QB? Okay, that'll work. I'll handle the line, Coach Bell."

The presence of the Giants' star lineman raised everyone's spirits, but it also seemed to somehow add to the mayhem.

The good thing about all the confusion was that Landon didn't have the chance to worry. When Bronxville lost the toss, they kicked off, and Jonathan Wagner switched Gunner to defensive tackle before shoving Landon out onto the field with the starting defense to play end. "Go get 'em, Landon. Use your size."

Landon didn't have a chance to even think as he found himself lining up at left end on defense; he had to just play.

"Just stay low, Landon!" Jonathan Wagner bellowed from the sideline. "Use your hands and get rid of the guy and go get the ball!"

Landon lined up, determined to stay low. On the snap, the Tuckahoe lineman fired out low and hard. Still unsure of himself, Landon caught the block rather than attacking his opponent. He got driven back two yards before he could cast the lineman aside, but by then the runner had crossed the line and was into the defensive secondary before he was tackled.

"Lower!" Jonathan hollered, waving his hands, and Landon knew who he was talking to.

On the next play Landon did stay low, and his foe didn't move him an inch. The ball went the other way, though, and Landon didn't get close before Brett tackled the runner for a small gain. The play after that, Landon did even better, driving his opponent back, which tripped the runner and allowed Gunner Miller to catch him from behind and strip the ball. The fumble landed right at Landon's feet, and he simply flopped down on top of it in a moment of burning excitement, buried beneath a pile of bodies.

When the ref peeled everyone away and Landon stood holding the ball up in one hand, the crowd cheered. They *cheered* for *him*!

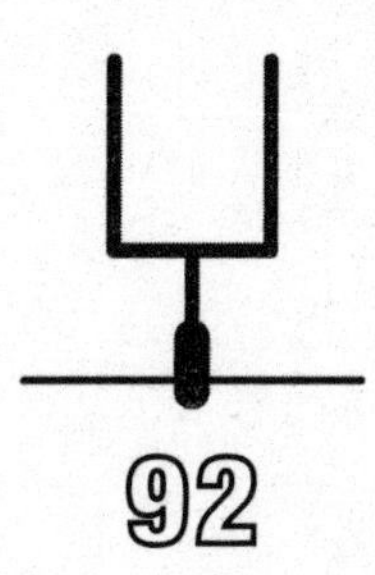
92

Breathless with joy, Landon ran off the field before he realized Coach Bell and Jonathan were waving him to go back. Landon stopped in his tracks, realized he needed to play offense now, and turned back toward the huddle. He heard a noise from the crowd and wondered if it was laughter. For once, he didn't care if people were laughing at him, because only moments before they were *cheering*, and that felt like it had been tattooed onto his heart, where it would remain the rest of his life.

In the offensive huddle, teammates kept congratulating him, and he was miffed when Brett stepped into the huddle and told them to shut up. "It was a good play," Brett said, staring around, "but we've got a long way to go, guys. A long way."

Brett couldn't have spoken a bigger truth.

The Tuckahoe defense was on fire, and by the end of the first half, Bronxville was losing 14–0.

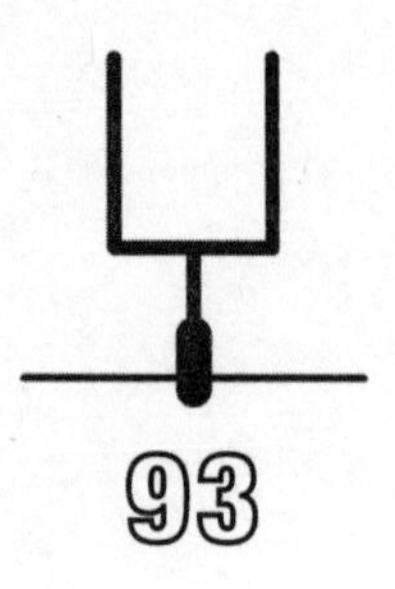

93

Down in the corner of their end zone, the Bronxville team sat flopped down in a small cluster around their coach and his brother-in-law, wheezing to catch their breaths between mouthfuls of orange slices.

"You guys can *do* this!" Jonathan Wagner pounded a fist into his hand and paced like a caged panther.

"Catch your breaths, guys," Coach Bell said. "Get some Gatorade and let's talk about what's going on. Linemen, you've gotta cut those guys on the back side. You don't have to block them, but you've gotta cut their legs out to keep 'em from busting clean into our backfield. Can you do that?"

The offensive line nodded fiercely. Coach Bell and Jonathan Wagner huddled up, just the two of them while the players gasped for breath. The coaches exchanged heated ideas before they nodded together and turned to the team.

The high school band finished their halftime show and filed past, grinning and snickering like fools at the sight of the exhausted kids.

"Okay, listen up!" Coach Bell barked. "We gotta have someone else play quarterback. We gotta try. Anyone, Gunner, Torin, I don't care, but we gotta get Brett back on the line or we don't stand a chance. Someone *has* to be able to take a snap and hand it off to Layne. Someone . . ."

Coach Bell and Jonathan Wagner looked around, expecting a reply.

Behind them, someone jostled the line of band members and finally pushed through to say, "I've got a quarterback for you, Coach."

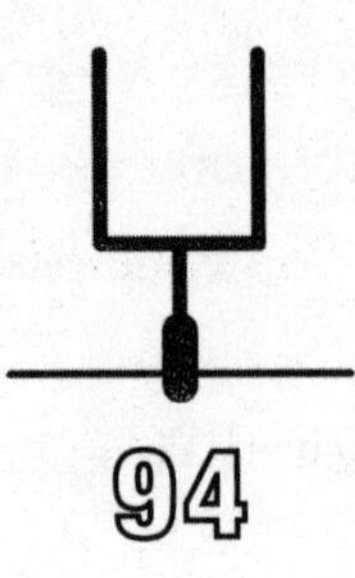

94

Everyone stared at the man in the brown tweed sports coat and expensive-looking dress shoes. Gold cuff links and a watch that looked a lot like Coach Furster's glinted from his wrists. This man was thin and taller than Coach Furster, though, with freckles on his somber face that crept up and over his shiny bald head. He reached around behind himself and produced a Bronxville football player, dressed and ready to go, but with eyes cast toward the ground.

It was Skip Dreyfus.

Mr. Dreyfus took his son by the neck and steered him toward the team. "Is Landon Dorch here?"

All eyes were on Landon, and he felt his face burst into flame.

"Landon, my son has something to say to you." Mr. Dreyfus looked from Landon to the coaches. "Sorry for being late to the party, guys. I just flew in from Hong Kong and got an update from his mother on the drive home from the airport. Skip and I talked, and he's eager to apologize to Landon and move forward with no bad feelings. Aren't you, Skip?"

"Yes, sir." Skip kept his eyes down. "I am."

"You are, what?" Skip's father asked.

"I am sorry, sir."

"Good, now say it to Landon."

Skip stepped forward, and Landon felt sick.

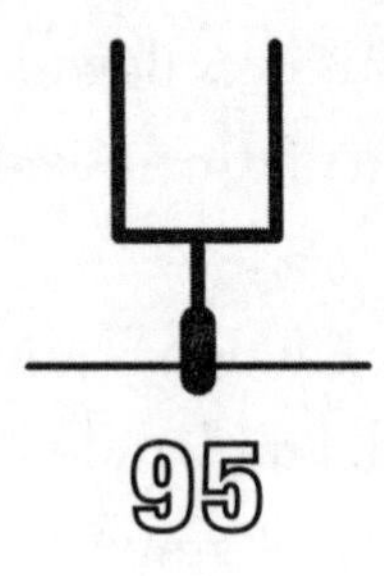

When Skip held out his hand, Landon shook it.

"I'm sorry, Landon." Skip didn't raise his eyes.

"Okay," Landon said.

"And nothing like it will happen again," Mr. Dreyfus said. "Isn't that right, Skip?"

"Yes, sir."

"There you go." Skip's dad gave Coach Bell a salute and disappeared as suddenly as he had arrived.

Jonathan Wagner's grin lit up the world and he slapped Skip heartily on the back. "Nice."

Skip only nodded, looking wildly embarrassed.

"Okay, bring it in." Coach Bell held a fist in the middle of them all, and everyone put his hand in. "Now we can really do this, guys! Here we go! HIT, HUSTLE, WIN, on three . . ."

"HIT! HUSTLE! WIN!"

It was a roar even Landon could clearly hear.

They jogged to the sideline, where Coach Bell pulled Landon and Brett aside. “Guys, it’s bulldozer time. We are gonna line up and cram this ball right down their throats behind the two of you. Once we establish that they can’t stop us, it’ll open up the counter and the naked bootleg with Skip. Wow, wait till Tuckahoe gets a mouthful of this.”

Brett’s dad brandished his fist, and his uncle grinned and hovered beside Brett, nodding like a fool.

Bronxville had the ball. Landon studied Skip’s face in the huddle. Skip wouldn’t meet his eye, but he didn’t offer Landon a sneer either. He was just neutral, and it made Landon wonder at the power of the quarterback’s father.

“Okay,” Skip said. “Heavy right, twenty-six dive on one.”

“And say the count *loud*.” Landon glared at Skip, who looked up at him in total surprise.

They stared at each other for a moment before Skip smiled and blushed and said, “Okay, Landon. I’ll make sure it’s loud.”

Everyone looked at Landon with disbelief.

“Thank you,” Landon said, and they broke the huddle.

Brett bounced up to the line, jittery and muttering to himself. Suddenly, he turned and grabbed Landon’s face mask, pulling him close. “We’re gonna *do* this, Landon. We are gonna *do* this, my man!”

Landon caught the thrill. “Let’s go.”

At the line, a Tuckahoe defender sneered at them, laughed, and mocked Landon in a garbled voice, crooking his arms and waving his hands like there was something wrong with him. “*Let’s go. Let’s go.* What are you gonna do, you big, fat dummy?”

Brett nearly jumped out of his cleats. "You're gonna see what he's gonna do, 'cause you just lost your free ride into our backfield. Time to pay up, wimp."

"Pay this." The defender slapped his own butt.

Brett just growled.

They lined up. The cadence rang out loud and clear. On "one," Landon and Brett fired out together like the double blade of a monster snowplow, lifting and ripping and grinding, driving the two players in front of them back until they crumbled and went down, and then they plowed right over them looking for more defenders.

It was a scrum, but Guerrero picked up eight yards. They lined up and did it again for six, then again for four, before Guerrero hit a crease on the next play and picked up seventeen. They ran the same play over and over, twenty-six dive. It was almost unthinkable, but Bronxville marched down the field. Tuckahoe's head coach was pulling at his hair, throwing his hat, and screaming at his defense from the sideline like a madman. They stacked up linebackers and blitzed the gaps, but with Landon and Brett foot to foot, there was just no stopping them from pushing defenders back or down to the dirt.

When they punched it in from the three-yard line, Landon turned and hugged Brett and Guerrero at the same time, howling to the sky.

Brett yelled, "We are gonna win this thing, Landon. We're gonna win it!"

When things settled down, there was Skip, blocking Landon's path back to the bench.

"Hey." Skip showed no emotion, but he wasn't letting Landon by.

"Hey, what?" Landon asked.

Skip stared hard at him with his lips pursed tight and his eyes swirling with emotion. "I want to tell you something."

"O-kay." Landon let the word drag out of his mouth and still he waited for Skip to speak.

Skip took a deep breath. His eyes skittered around the field before settling on Landon's face and locking in. "Landon, I really am sorry. I'm not just saying it."

Landon studied Skip's face, and a lifetime of reading expressions told him it was true. Skip *was* sorry.

Landon smiled widely and put a heavy paw on the quarterback's shoulder. "That's okay, Skip. Forgive and forget. That's what my dad says . . . and it's true."

"That's . . . nice. Thank you."

"I like right tackle," Landon said.

"Right tackle likes you too." Skip laughed.

"No more left out." Landon felt like he *was* writing his own ending, and he knew it when Skip shook his head, put a hand on his arm, and answered him loud and clear.

"No way. Right tackle only. . . . No more left out."

AUTHOR'S NOTE

It was during a book tour that I first met two deaf boys who were fans of my stories and, like me, avid readers and football players. Anyone who's heard me speak to students at a school knows the thrust of my message is that reading not only makes us better students, but most important, better, kinder people. Kindness begins by understanding and believing that each person is just like you on the inside and disregarding the differences on the outside. When someone is sick or disabled, those differences can be profound. I wanted to write a story about a character we could all identify with, one who dreams of success and acceptance but who was also profoundly different.

While the two deaf boys I met, Brett Bell and Layne Guerrero, appear as characters in this book, it is the main character, Landon Dorch, who more closely resembles them and, more important, their experiences. I want to thank Brett and Layne for sharing their stories, their dreams, and their hardships with me. I hope the result is that you, the reader, will develop the same bond with Landon as I have. And, most important, that when you see someone who is deaf or has cochlear implants, that you reach out to let them know that YOU know it doesn't matter.

Finally, I want to thank Kristi Bell, Brett's mom, who gave me so much time and shared so many personal anecdotes, which I know breathed life into this story.

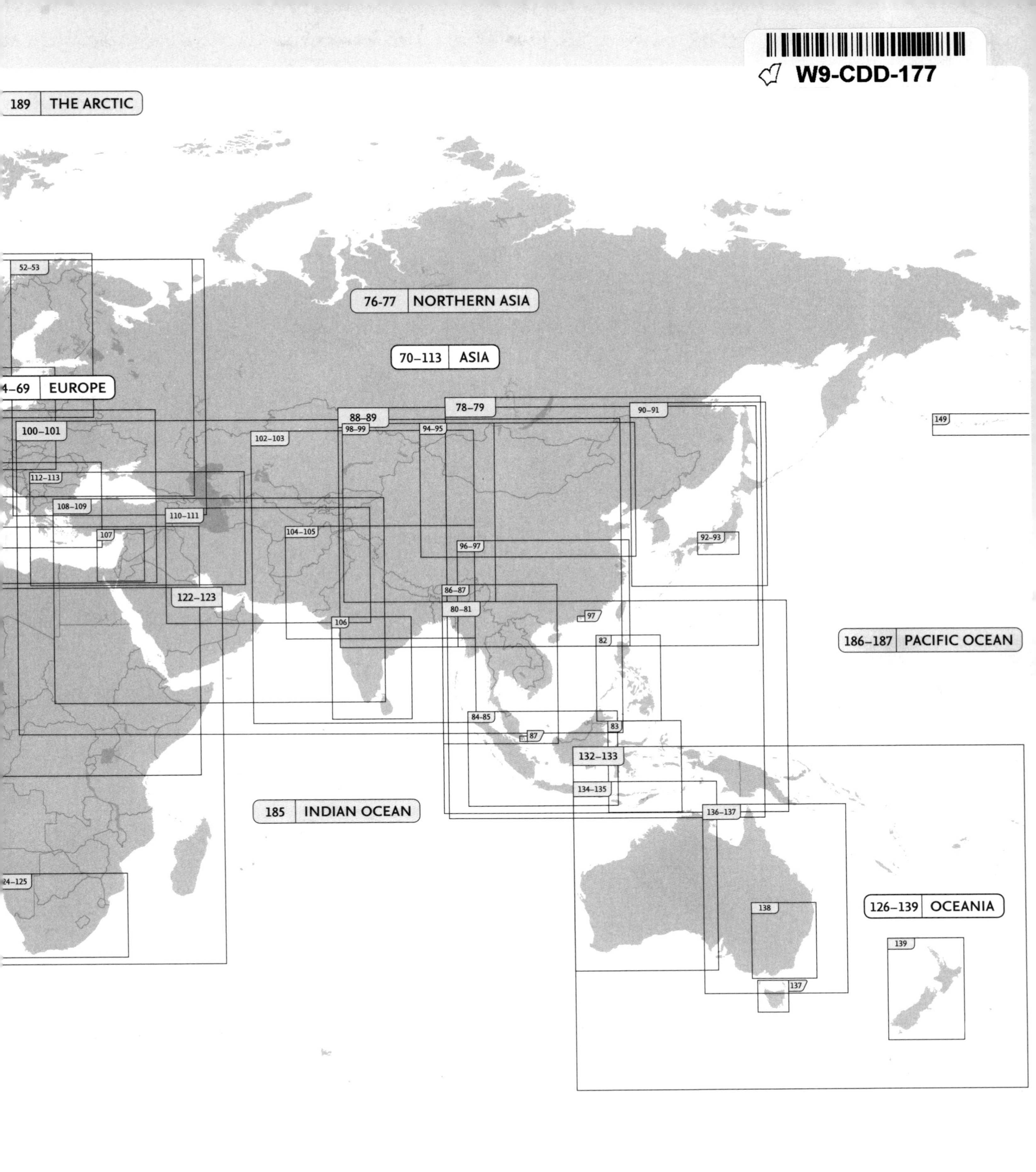
189 THE ARCTIC
76-77 NORTHERN ASIA
70–113 ASIA
4–69 EUROPE
52–53
100–101
112–113
108–109
107
110–111
102–103
88–89
98–99
94–95
78–79
90–91
104–105
96–97
92–93
122–123
106
86–87
80–81
97
82
149
186–187 PACIFIC OCEAN
84–85
87
83
132–133
134–135
136–137
185 INDIAN OCEAN
24–125
138
126–139 OCEANIA
139
137
188 ANTARCTICA

Find your map

COLLINS WORLD ATLAS

REFERENCE EDITION

Collins
An imprint of HarperCollins Publishers
77–85 Fulham Palace Road
London
W6 8JB

First Published 2010

Printed in Thailand by Imago

British Library Cataloguing in Publication Data.
A catalogue record for this book is available from the British Library.

ISBN 978-0-00-734718-6

Imp 001

All mapping in this atlas is generated from Collins Bartholomew™ digital databases. Collins Bartholomew™, the UK's leading independent geographical information supplier, can provide a digital, custom, and premium mapping service to a variety of markets.
For further information:
Tel: +44 (0) 141 306 3752
e-mail: collinsbartholomew@harpercollins.co.uk

Visit our website at: www.collinsbartholomew.com

Cover image: Planetary Visions
www.planetaryvisions.com

More mapping online at
www.collinsmaps.com

Collins World Atlas

Collins

Contents

Title	Scale	Page
Map Symbols		4
World		**5–41**
Time Zones and International Organizations		5
Landscapes		6–7
Countries		8–9
Earthquakes and Volcanoes		10–11
Climate and Weather		12–13
Land Cover		14–15
Population		16–17
Urbanization and Cities		18–19
Communications		20–21
Social Indicators		22–23
Economy and Wealth		24–25
Conflict		26–27
Global Issues		28–29
Environmental Threats		30–31
Change		32–33
Satellite images		34–41
Italy		34
Rome		35
Soufrière Hills Volcano, Montserrat		36
Sarychev Peak, Matua Island		37
Taylor Valley, Antarctica		38–39
Grand Coulee Dam, Washington State, U.S.A.		40–41
Europe		**42–69**
UNESCO World Heritage Sites		42–45
Landscapes		46–47
Countries		48–49
Northern Europe	1:10 000 000	50–51
Western Russian Federation	1:7 500 000	52–53
Scandinavia and the Baltic States	1:5 000 000	54–55
Inset: Iceland	1:6 000 000	
Inset: Faroe Islands	1:5 000 000	
Northwest Europe	1:5 000 000	56–57
England and Wales	1:2 000 000	58–59
Scotland	1:2 000 000	60
Inset: Shetland Islands	1:2 000 000	
Ireland	1:2 000 000	61
Belgium, Netherlands, Luxembourg and Northwest Germany	1:2 000 000	62–63
Southern Europe and the Mediterranean	1:10 000 000	64–65
France	1:5 000 000	66
Spain and Portugal	1:5 000 000	67
Italy and the Balkans	1:5 000 000	68–69
Asia		**70–113**
UNESCO World Heritage Sites		70–71
Landscapes		72–73
Countries		74–75
Northern Asia	1:20 000 000	76–77
Eastern and Southeast Asia	1:20 000 000	78–79
Southeast Asia	1:15 000 000	80–81
Philippines	1:6 500 000	82
Inset: Palau	1:1 145 000	
Central Indonesia	1:6 500 000	83
West Indonesia and Malaysia	1:6 250 000	84–85
Myanmar, Thailand, Peninsular Malaysia and Indo-China	1:7 000 000	86–87
Inset: Singapore	1:550 000	
Eastern Asia	1:15 000 000	88–89
Japan, North Korea and South Korea	1:7 000 000	90–91
Japan – Central Honshū	1:1 250 000	92–93
Northern China and Mongolia	1:7 000 000	94–95
Southeast China	1:7 000 000	96–97
Inset: Hong Kong	1:700 000	
West China	1:7 000 000	98–99
Central and Southern Asia	1:20 000 000	100–101

Contents

Asia (cont)		70–113
Southern Asia	1:13 000 000	102–103
Northern India, Nepal, Bhutan and Bangladesh	1:7 000 000	104–105
Southern India and Sri Lanka	1:7 000 000	106
Middle East	1:3 000 000	107
Southwest Asia	1:13 000 000	108-109
The Gulf, Iran, Afghanistan and Pakistan	1:7 000 000	110–111
Eastern Mediterranean, the Caucasus and Iraq	1:7 000 000	112–113

Africa		114–125
UNESCO World Heritage Sites		114–115
Landscapes		116–117
Countries		118–119
Northern Africa	1:16 000 000	120–121
Inset: Cape Verde	1:16 000 000	
Central and Southern Africa	1:16 000 000	122–123
Republic of South Africa	1:5 000 000	124–125

Oceania		126–139
UNESCO World Heritage Sites		126–127
Landscapes		128–129
Countries		130–131
Australia, New Zealand and Southwest Pacific	1:20 000 000	132–133
Western Australia	1:8 000 000	134–135
Eastern Australia	1:8 000 000	136-137
Inset: Tasmania	1:8 000 000	
Southeast Australia	1:5 000 000	138
New Zealand	1:5 250 000	139

North America		140–169
UNESCO World Heritage Sites		140–141
Landscapes		142–143
Countries		144–145
Canada	1:16 000 000	146–147
Alaska	1:7 000 000	148–149
Western Canada	1:7 000 000	150–151
Eastern Canada	1:7 000 000	152–153
United States of America	1:12 000 000	154–155
Western United States	1:7 000 000	156–157
Inset: Hawaiian Islands	1:7 000 000	
Southwest United States	1:3 500 000	158–159
Central United States	1:7 000 000	160–161
Eastern United States	1:7 000 000	162–163
Northeast United States	1:3 500 000	164–165
Mexico and Central America	1:7 200 000	166–167
Central America and the Caribbean	1:14 000 000	168–169

South America		170–179
UNESCO World Heritage Sites		170–171
Landscapes		172–173
Countries		174–175
Northern South America	1:14 000 000	176–177
Inset: Galapagos Islands	1:14 000 000	
Southern South America	1:14 000 000	178
Southeast Brazil	1:7 000 000	179

Oceans and Poles		180–189
Antarctica Satellite image		180–181
Features	1:50 000 000	182–183
Atlantic Ocean and Indian Ocean	1:50 000 000	184–185
Pacific Ocean	1:26 000 000	186–87
Antarctica	1:26 000 000	188
The Arctic		189

States and Territories	190–213
Index	214–311
Acknowledgements	312

Map Symbols

Southern Europe

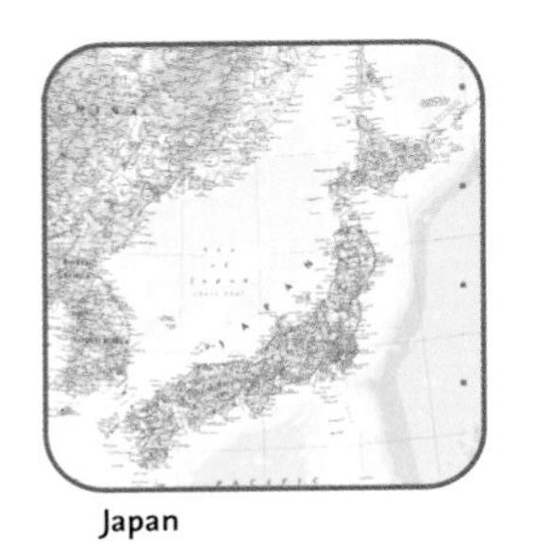
Japan

Antarctica

Settlements

Population	National capital	Administrative capital	Other city or town
over 10 million	BEIJING	Karachi	New York
5 million to 10 million	JAKARTA	Tianjin	Nova Iguaçu
1 million to 5 million	KĀBUL	Sydney	Kaohsiung
500 000 to 1 million	BANGUI	Trujillo	Jeddah
100 000 to 500 000	WELLINGTON	Mansa	Apucarana
50 000 to 100 000	PORT OF SPAIN	Potenza	Arecibo
10 000 to 50 000	MALABO	Chinhoyi	Ceres
under 10 000	VALLETTA	Ati	Venta

Built-up area

Relief

Contour intervals and layer colours

Height metres	feet
5000	16404
3000	9843
2000	6562
1000	3281
500	1640
200	656
0	0
below sea level	
0	0
200	656
2000	6562
4000	13124
6000	19686
Depth	

1234 Summit
height in metres

123 Spot height
height in metres

123 Ocean deep
depth in metres

Boundaries

International boundary

Disputed international boundary or alignment unconfirmed

Administrative boundary

Ceasefire line

Land and sea features

Desert

Oasis

Lava field

Marsh

1234 Volcano
height in metres

Ice cap or Glacier

Escarpment

Coral reef

1234 Pass
height in metres

Lakes and rivers

Lake

Impermanent lake

Salt lake or lagoon

Impermanent salt lake

Dry salt lake or salt pan

123 Lake height
surface height above sea level, in metres

River

Impermanent river or watercourse

Waterfall

Dam

Barrage

Miscellaneous

National park

Reserve or Regional park

Site of specific interest

Wall

Transport

Motorway (tunnel; under construction)

Main road (tunnel; under construction)

Secondary road (tunnel; under construction)

Track

Main railway (tunnel; under construction)

Secondary railway (tunnel; under construction)

Other railway (tunnel; under construction)

Canal

Main airport

Regional airport

Satellite imagery - The thematic pages in the atlas contain a wide variety of photographs and images. These are a mixture of terrestrial and aerial photographs and satellite imagery. All are used to illustrate specific themes and to give an indication of the variety of imagery available today. The main types of imagery used in the atlas are described in the table below. The sensor for each satellite image is detailed on the acknowledgements page.

Main satellites/sensors

Satellite/sensor name	Launch dates	Owner	Aims and applications	Internet links	Additional internet links
Landsat 1, 2, 3, 4, 5, 7	July 1972–April 1999	National Aeronautics and Space Administration (NASA), USA	The first satellite to be designed specifically for observing the Earth's surface. Originally set up to produce images of use for agriculture and geology. Today is of use for numerous environmental and scientific applications.	landsat.gsfc.nasa.gov	asterweb.jpl.nasa.gov earth.jsc.nasa.gov earthnet.esrin.esa.it
SPOT 1, 2, 3, 4, 5 (Satellite Pour l'Observation de la Terre)	February 1986–March 1998	Centre National d'Etudes Spatiales (CNES) and Spot Image, France	Particularly useful for monitoring land use, water resources research, coastal studies and cartography.	www.spotimage.fr	earthobservatory.nasa.gov gs.mdacorporation.com
Space Shuttle	Regular launches from 1981	NASA, USA	Each shuttle mission has separate aims. Astronauts take photographs with high specification hand held cameras. The Shuttle Radar Topography Mission (SRTM) in 2000 obtained the most complete near-global high-resolution database of the earth's topography.	nasascience.nasa.gov www.jpl.nasa.gov/srtm	modis.gsfc.nasa.gov seawifs.gsfc.nasa.gov topex-www.jpl.nasa.gov
IKONOS	September 1999	GeoEye	First commercial high-resolution satellite. Useful for a variety of applications mainly Cartography, Defence, Urban Planning, Agriculture, Forestry and Insurance.	www.geoeye.com	visibleearth.nasa.gov www.usgs.gov
GeoEye-1	September 2008	GeoEye	Another commercial high-resolution satellite which is of use for numerous environmental, scientific, economic and national defense applications.	www.geoeye.com	

Time Zones

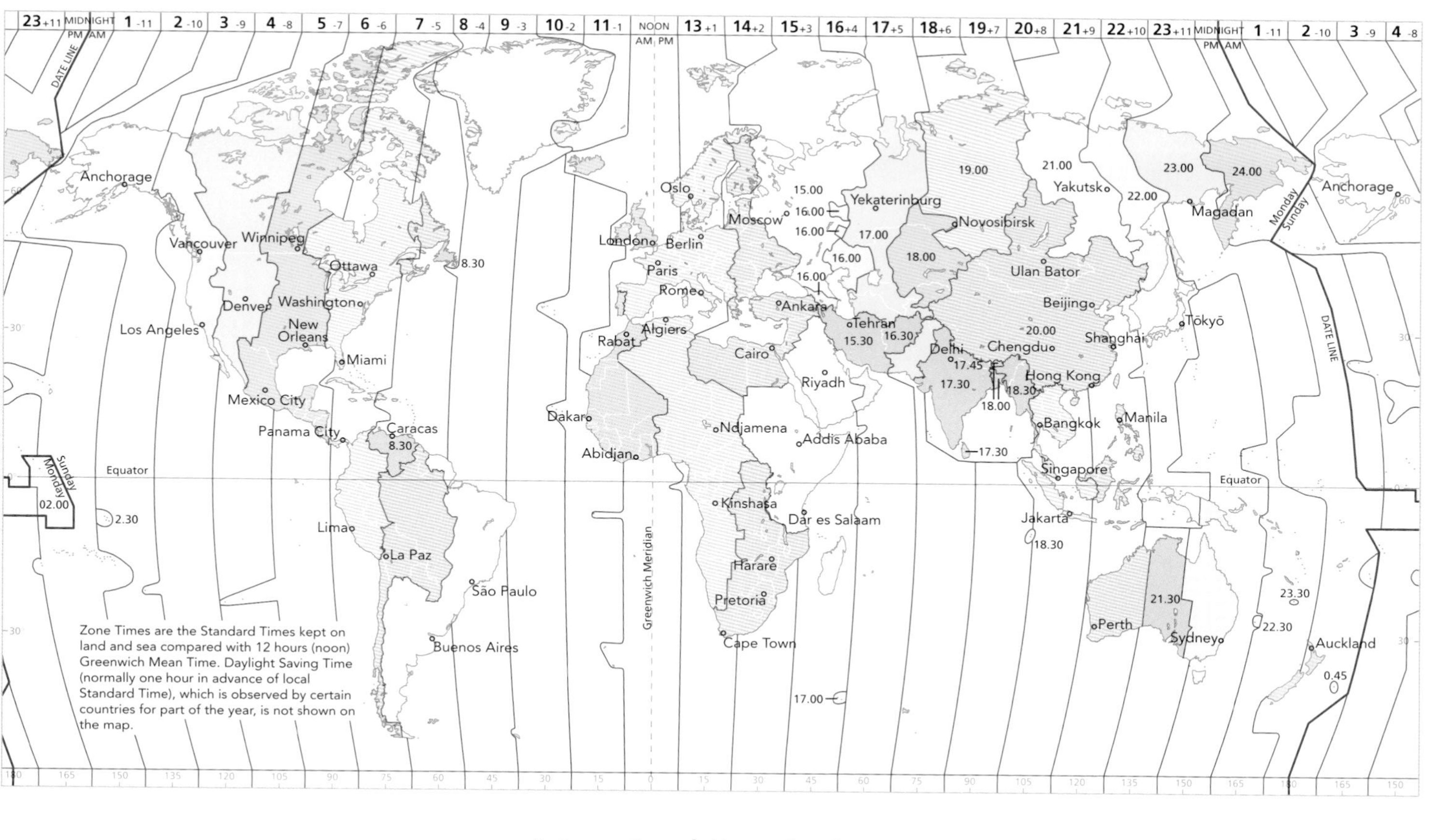
23 +11 MIDNIGHT PM AM
1 -11
2 -10
3 -9
4 -8
5 -7
6 -6
7 -5
8 -4
9 -3
10 -2
11 -1
NOON AM PM
13 +1
14 +2
15 +3
16 +4
17 +5
18 +6
19 +7
20 +8
21 +9
22 +10
23 +11
DATE LINE
Anchorage
Vancouver
Winnipeg
Ottawa
Denver
Washington
Los Angeles
New Orleans
Miami
Mexico City
Panama City
Caracas
8.30
Lima
La Paz
São Paulo
Buenos Aires
Equator
Sunday
Monday
02.00
2.30
Greenwich Meridian
London
Berlin
Oslo
Paris
Rome
Moscow
Rabat
Algiers
Cairo
Dakar
Abidjan
Ndjamena
Kinshasa
Harare
Pretoria
Cape Town
Riyadh
Addis Ababa
Dar es Salaam
Ankara
Tehran
15.30
16.30
15.00
16.00
17.00
Yekaterinburg
Novosibirsk
18.00
19.00
21.00
Yakutsk
22.00
23.00
24.00
Magadan
Ulan Bator
Beijing
20.00
Chengdu
Shanghai
Tōkyō
Delhi
17.45
17.30
18.30
Hong Kong
Bangkok
Manila
Singapore
Jakarta
Perth
21.30
Sydney
23.30
22.30
Auckland
0.45
Zone Times are the Standard Times kept on land and sea compared with 12 hours (noon) Greenwich Mean Time. Daylight Saving Time (normally one hour in advance of local Standard Time), which is observed by certain countries for part of the year, is not shown on the map.

International Organizations

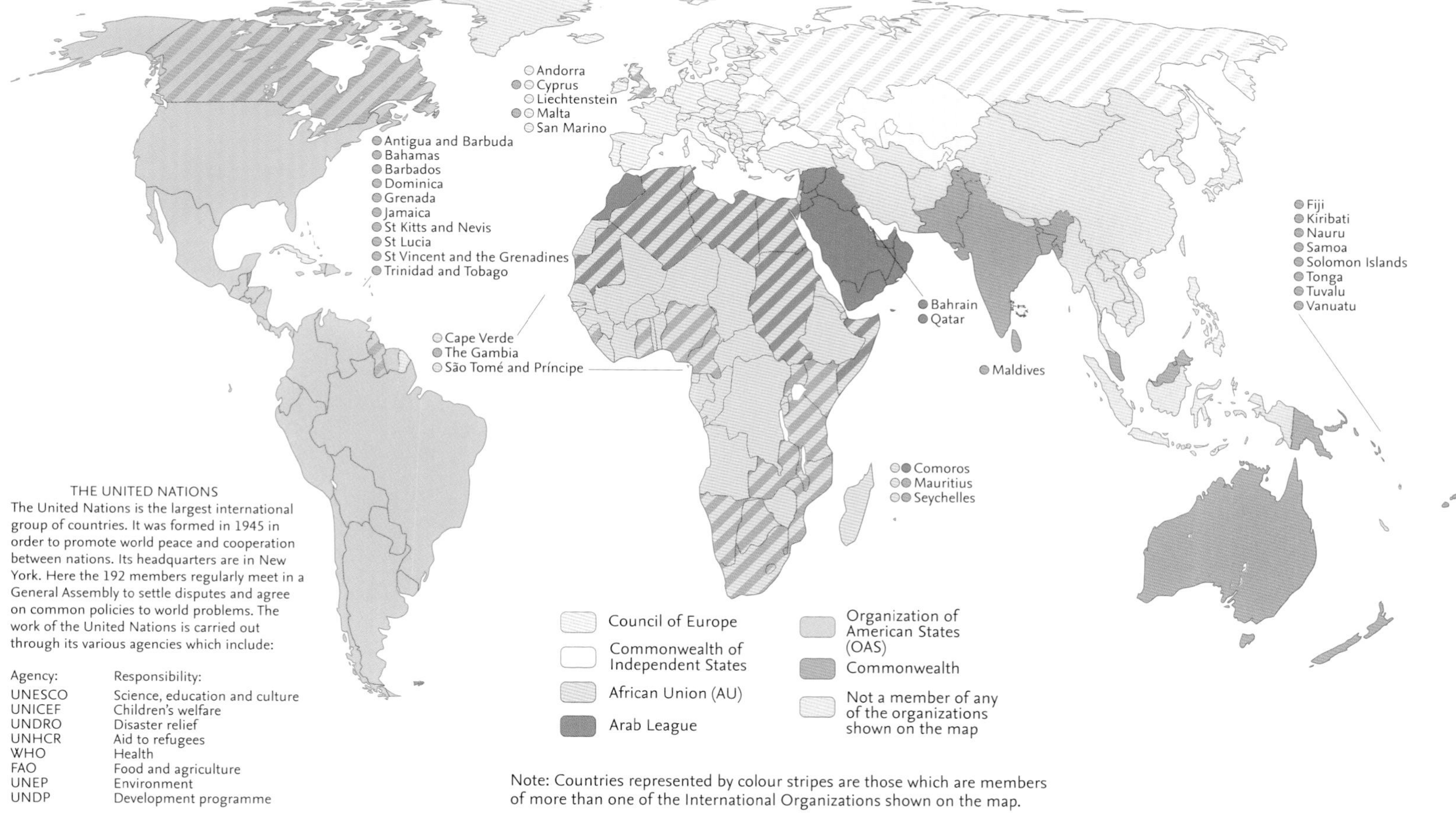
Andorra
Cyprus
Liechtenstein
Malta
San Marino
Antigua and Barbuda
Bahamas
Barbados
Dominica
Grenada
Jamaica
St Kitts and Nevis
St Lucia
St Vincent and the Grenadines
Trinidad and Tobago
Cape Verde
The Gambia
São Tomé and Príncipe
Bahrain
Qatar
Maldives
Comoros
Mauritius
Seychelles
Fiji
Kiribati
Nauru
Samoa
Solomon Islands
Tonga
Tuvalu
Vanuatu
Council of Europe
Commonwealth of Independent States
African Union (AU)
Arab League
Organization of American States (OAS)
Commonwealth
Not a member of any of the organizations shown on the map

THE UNITED NATIONS

The United Nations is the largest international group of countries. It was formed in 1945 in order to promote world peace and cooperation between nations. Its headquarters are in New York. Here the 192 members regularly meet in a General Assembly to settle disputes and agree on common policies to world problems. The work of the United Nations is carried out through its various agencies which include:

Agency:	Responsibility:
UNESCO	Science, education and culture
UNICEF	Children's welfare
UNDRO	Disaster relief
UNHCR	Aid to refugees
WHO	Health
FAO	Food and agriculture
UNEP	Environment
UNDP	Development programme

Note: Countries represented by colour stripes are those which are members of more than one of the International Organizations shown on the map.

World
Landscapes

The Earth's physical features, both on land and on the sea bed, closely reflect its geological structure. The current shapes of the continents and oceans have evolved over millions of years. Movements of the tectonic plates which make up the Earth's crust have created some of the best-known and most spectacular features. The processes which have shaped the Earth continue today with earthquakes, volcanoes, erosion, climatic variations and man's activities all affecting the Earth's landscapes.

The total topographic range of the Earth's surface is nearly 20 000 metres, from the highest point Mount Everest, to the lowest point in the Mariana Trench. Major mountain ranges include the Himalaya, the Andes and the Rocky Mountains, each of which give rise to some of the world's greatest rivers. In contrast, the deserts of the Sahara, Australia, the Arabian Peninsula and the Gobi cover vast areas and each provide unique landscapes.

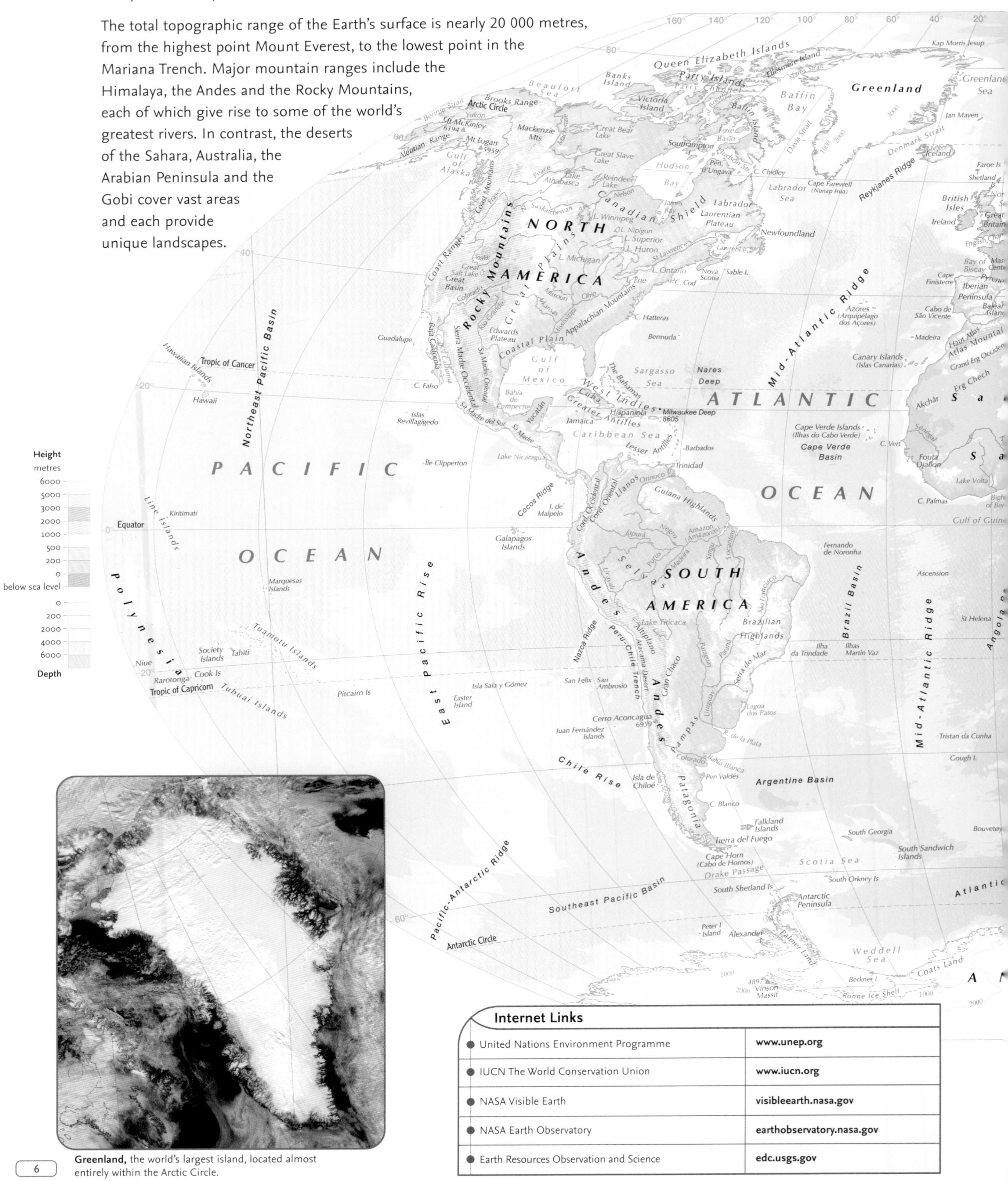
Height
metres
6000
5000
3000
2000
1000
500
200
0
below sea level
0
200
2000
4000
6000
Depth
NORTH AMERICA
SOUTH AMERICA
PACIFIC OCEAN
ATLANTIC OCEAN
Greenland
Queen Elizabeth Islands
Baffin Bay
Hudson Bay
Labrador Sea
Beaufort Sea
Gulf of Alaska
Rocky Mountains
Canadian Shield
Great Plains
Appalachian Mountains
Gulf of Mexico
Caribbean Sea
Sargasso Sea
West Indies
Mid-Atlantic Ridge
Reykjanes Ridge
Northeast Pacific Basin
East Pacific Rise
Polynesia
Andes
Amazon
Brazilian Highlands
Argentine Basin
Scotia Sea
Drake Passage
Weddell Sea
Southeast Pacific Basin
Pacific-Antarctic Ridge
Chile Rise
Tropic of Cancer
Equator
Tropic of Capricorn
Arctic Circle
Antarctic Circle
Mt McKinley 6194
Cerro Aconcagua 6959
Milwaukee Deep 8605

Greenland, the world's largest island, located almost entirely within the Arctic Circle.

Internet Links

United Nations Environment Programme	www.unep.org
IUCN The World Conservation Union	www.iucn.org
NASA Visible Earth	visibleearth.nasa.gov
NASA Earth Observatory	earthobservatory.nasa.gov
Earth Resources Observation and Science	edc.usgs.gov

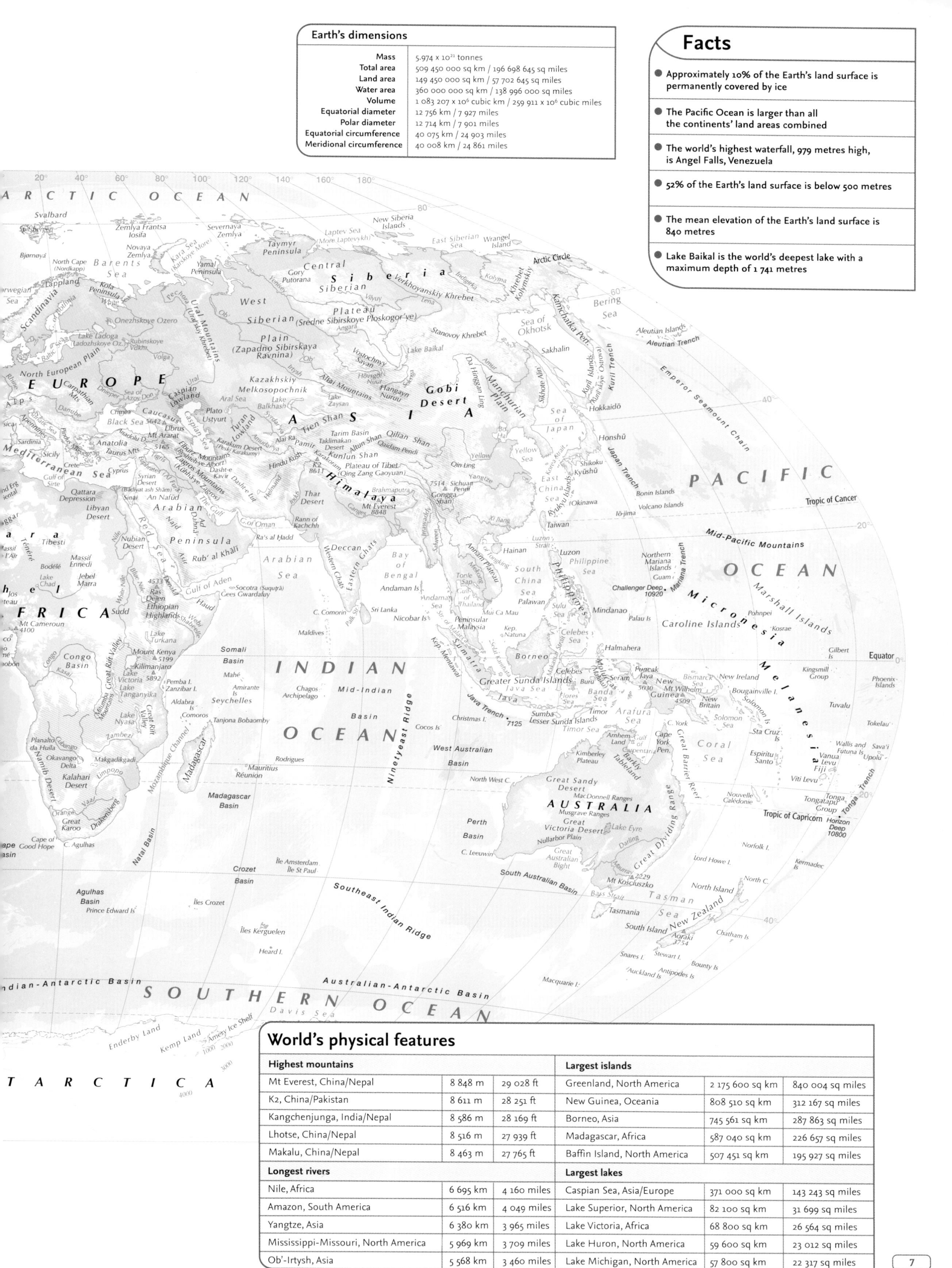
ARCTIC OCEAN
Svalbard
Zemlya Frantsa Iosifa
Severnaya Zemlya
New Siberia Islands
Laptev Sea
East Siberian Sea
Wrangel Island
Taymyr Peninsula
Barents Sea
Kara Sea
Central Siberian Plateau
Siberia
West Siberian Plain
Arctic Circle
Bering Sea
Sea of Okhotsk
Aleutian Islands
Aleutian Trench
Kamchatka Pen.
Sakhalin
Lake Baikal
Ural Mountains
EUROPE
North European Plain
Caspian Lowland
Black Sea
Caucasus
Aral Sea
Kazakhskiy Melkosopochnik
Gobi Desert
ASIA
Manchurian Plain
Sea of Japan
Hokkaidō
Honshū
Emperor Seamount Chain
Mediterranean Sea
Anatolia
Tien Shan
Tarim Basin
Plateau of Tibet
Himalaya
Mt Everest 8848
K2 8611
Arabian Peninsula
Libyan Desert
Thar Desert
Deccan
Bay of Bengal
Arabian Sea
Yellow Sea
East China Sea
South China Sea
Philippine Sea
Philippines
Japan Trench
PACIFIC OCEAN
Tropic of Cancer
Mid-Pacific Mountains
Mariana Trench
Challenger Deep 10920
Micronesia
Marshall Islands
Caroline Islands
Melanesia
Equator
AFRICA
Sahara
Tibesti
Lake Chad
Ethiopian Highlands
Congo Basin
Lake Victoria
Lake Tanganyika
Kilimanjaro 5892
Madagascar
Kalahari Desert
Namib Desert
Cape of Good Hope
INDIAN OCEAN
Mid-Indian Basin
Ninetyeast Ridge
Somali Basin
Seychelles
Mauritius
Réunion
Madagascar Basin
Crozet Basin
Southeast Indian Ridge
Sumatra
Borneo
Java
Java Trench
Celebes
New Guinea
Mt Wilhelm 4509
Arafura Sea
Coral Sea
Great Barrier Reef
AUSTRALIA
Great Sandy Desert
Great Victoria Desert
Great Dividing Range
Lake Eyre
Mt Kosciuszko 2229
Tasmania
Tasman Sea
New Zealand
North Island
South Island
Aoraki 3754
Tropic of Capricorn
Tonga Trench
Horizon Deep 10800
Fiji
West Australian Basin
Perth Basin
South Australian Basin
Australian-Antarctic Basin
Indian-Antarctic Basin
SOUTHERN OCEAN
ANTARCTICA

Earth's dimensions

Mass	5.974 x 10^{21} tonnes
Total area	509 450 000 sq km / 196 698 645 sq miles
Land area	149 450 000 sq km / 57 702 645 sq miles
Water area	360 000 000 sq km / 138 996 000 sq miles
Volume	1 083 207 x 10^{6} cubic km / 259 911 x 10^{6} cubic miles
Equatorial diameter	12 756 km / 7 927 miles
Polar diameter	12 714 km / 7 901 miles
Equatorial circumference	40 075 km / 24 903 miles
Meridional circumference	40 008 km / 24 861 miles

Facts

- Approximately 10% of the Earth's land surface is permanently covered by ice
- The Pacific Ocean is larger than all the continents' land areas combined
- The world's highest waterfall, 979 metres high, is Angel Falls, Venezuela
- 52% of the Earth's land surface is below 500 metres
- The mean elevation of the Earth's land surface is 840 metres
- Lake Baikal is the world's deepest lake with a maximum depth of 1 741 metres

World's physical features

Highest mountains			Largest islands		
Mt Everest, China/Nepal	8 848 m	29 028 ft	Greenland, North America	2 175 600 sq km	840 004 sq miles
K2, China/Pakistan	8 611 m	28 251 ft	New Guinea, Oceania	808 510 sq km	312 167 sq miles
Kangchenjunga, India/Nepal	8 586 m	28 169 ft	Borneo, Asia	745 561 sq km	287 863 sq miles
Lhotse, China/Nepal	8 516 m	27 939 ft	Madagascar, Africa	587 040 sq km	226 657 sq miles
Makalu, China/Nepal	8 463 m	27 765 ft	Baffin Island, North America	507 451 sq km	195 927 sq miles
Longest rivers			**Largest lakes**		
Nile, Africa	6 695 km	4 160 miles	Caspian Sea, Asia/Europe	371 000 sq km	143 243 sq miles
Amazon, South America	6 516 km	4 049 miles	Lake Superior, North America	82 100 sq km	31 699 sq miles
Yangtze, Asia	6 380 km	3 965 miles	Lake Victoria, Africa	68 800 sq km	26 564 sq miles
Mississippi-Missouri, North America	5 969 km	3 709 miles	Lake Huron, North America	59 600 sq km	23 012 sq miles
Ob'-Irtysh, Asia	5 568 km	3 460 miles	Lake Michigan, North America	57 800 sq km	22 317 sq miles

World
Countries

The current pattern of the world's countries and territories is a result of a long history of exploration, colonialism, conflict and politics. The fact that there are currently 195 independent countries in the world – the most recent, Kosovo, only being created in February 2008 – illustrates the significant political changes which have occurred since 1950 when there were only eighty-two. There has been a steady progression away from colonial influences over the last fifty years, although many dependent overseas territories remain.

The shapes of countries and the pattern of international boundaries reflect both physical and political processes. Some borders follow natural features – rivers, mountain ranges, etc – others are defined according to political agreement or as a result of war. Some are still subject to dispute between two or more countries, and many remain undefined on the ground.

ARCTIC
Greenland
(Denmark)
Ellesmere Island
Baffin Bay
Baffin Island
Beaufort Sea
Victoria Island
Point Hope
U.S.A.
Anchorage
Aleutian Islands
Inuvik
Great Bear Lake
Great Slave Lake
Whitehorse
Iqaluit
Nuuk
Hudson Bay
CANADA
Edmonton
Calgary
Vancouver
Winnipeg
Seattle
Portland
Newfoundland
St John's
St Pierre and Miquelon
(France)
Ottawa
Toronto
Montreal
Boise
UNITED STATES OF AMERICA
Chicago
Milwaukee
Detroit
Cleveland
Boston
New York
Philadelphia
Washington D.C.
Denver
St Louis
Indianapolis
San Francisco
Los Angeles
San Diego
Phoenix
Dallas
Memphis
Atlanta
El Paso
San Antonio
Houston
New Orleans
Jacksonville
Miami
Bermuda
(U.K.)
Guadalupe
(Mexico)
Gulf of Mexico
Monterrey
MEXICO
Tropic of Cancer
Hawaiian Islands
(U.S.A.)
Nassau
THE BAHAMAS
Havana
CUBA
Guadalajara
Mexico City
Kingston
HAITI
DOMINICAN REP.
Puerto Rico
(U.S.A.)
Santo Domingo
JAMAICA
ANTIGUA
Guadeloupe (France)
Martinique (France)
BELIZE
Belmopan
GUATEMALA
Guatemala City
HONDURAS
Tegucigalpa
San Salvador
EL SALVADOR
NICARAGUA
Managua
San José
COSTA RICA
PANAMA
Panama City
Caribbean Sea
DOMINICA
ST VINCENT
ST LUCIA
GRENADA
BARBADOS
TRINIDAD AND TOBAGO
Barranquilla
Maracaibo
Caracas
VENEZUELA
Islas Revillagigedo
(Mexico)
Île Clipperton
(France)
PACIFIC OCEAN
ATLANTIC OCEAN
Azores
(Portugal)
Madeira
(Portugal)
Canary Islands
(Spain)
Georgetown
GUYANA
Paramaribo
SUR.
Cayenne
French Guiana
Medellín
Bogotá
Cali
COLOMBIA
Quito
ECUADOR
Guayaquil
Galapagos Islands
(Ecuador)
Equator
KIRIBATI
Line Islands
INTERNATIONAL DATE LINE
Marquesas Islands
Tuamotu Islands
Tahiti
Society Islands
French Polynesia
American Samoa
Cook Islands
(N.Z.)
Niue
(N.Z.)
Rarotonga
Tropic of Capricorn
Tubuai Islands
Pitcairn Is
(U.K.)
Easter Island
(Chile)
Isla Sala y Gómez
(Chile)
Manaus
Amazon
Belém
Teresina
Fortaleza
Natal
Recife
Fernando de Noronha
(Brazil)
BRAZIL
Trujillo
PERU
Lima
La Paz
BOLIVIA
Santa Cruz
Sucre
Arequipa
Brasília
Goiânia
Salvador
Belo Horizonte
Trindade
(Brazil)
Ilhas Martin Vaz
(Brazil)
São Paulo
Rio de Janeiro
PARAGUAY
Asunción
San Miguel de Tucumán
Curitiba
Porto Alegre
CHILE
ARGENTINA
Córdoba
Santiago
Archipiélago Juan Fernández
(Chile)
URUGUAY
Montevideo
Buenos Aires
Mar del Plata
Stanley
Falkland Islands
(U.K.)
Punta Arenas
Cape Horn
South Georgia and South Sandwich Islands
(U.K.)
South Shetland Islands
(U.K.)
South Orkney Islands
(U.K.)
Antarctic Peninsula
Weddell Sea
SOUTH
Ascension
(U.K.)
St Helena and Dependencies
(U.K.)
Tristan da Cunha
(U.K.)
Gough Island
(U.K.)
Bouvetøya
(Norway)
Jan Mayen
(Norway)
ICELAND
Reykjavík
Faroe Islands
(Denmark)
Shetland Islands
UNITED KINGDOM
Edinburgh
Belfast
Dublin
IRELAND
London
North Sea
Amsterdam
The Hague
Brussels
Paris
FRANCE
Marseille
PORTUGAL
Lisbon
Madrid
SPAIN
Seville
Valencia
RABAT
Casablanca
MOROCCO
Oran
Algiers
ALGERIA
Laâyoune
Western Sahara
MAURITANIA
Nouakchott
MALI
CAPE VERDE
Praia
SENEGAL
Dakar
THE GAMBIA
Banjul
GUINEA-BISSAU
Bissau
Bamako
GUINEA
Conakry
BURKINA
Ouagadougou
Niamey
Freetown
SIERRA LEONE
Monrovia
LIBERIA
Yamoussoukro
Abidjan
CÔTE D'IVOIRE
GHANA
Accra
Lomé
Porto-Novo
SÃO TOMÉ AND PRÍNCIPE
160°
140°
120°
100°
80°
60°
40°
20°
0°
80°
60°
40°
20°

Facts

- The longest single continuous land border stretches for 6 416 kilometres between Canada and the USA
- Both China and the Russian Federation have land borders with 14 different countries
- Vatican City, the smallest independent country, was created in 1929 as an enclave within Rome, the capital of Italy
- All countries of the world are members of the United Nations except Kosovo, Taiwan and Vatican City

Internet Links	
United Nations	www.un.org
Foreign and Commonwealth Office	www.fco.gov.uk
International Boundaries Research Unit	www.dur.ac.uk/ibru
Permanent Committee on Geographical Names	www.pcgn.org.uk
U.S. Board on Geographic Names	geonames.usgs.gov

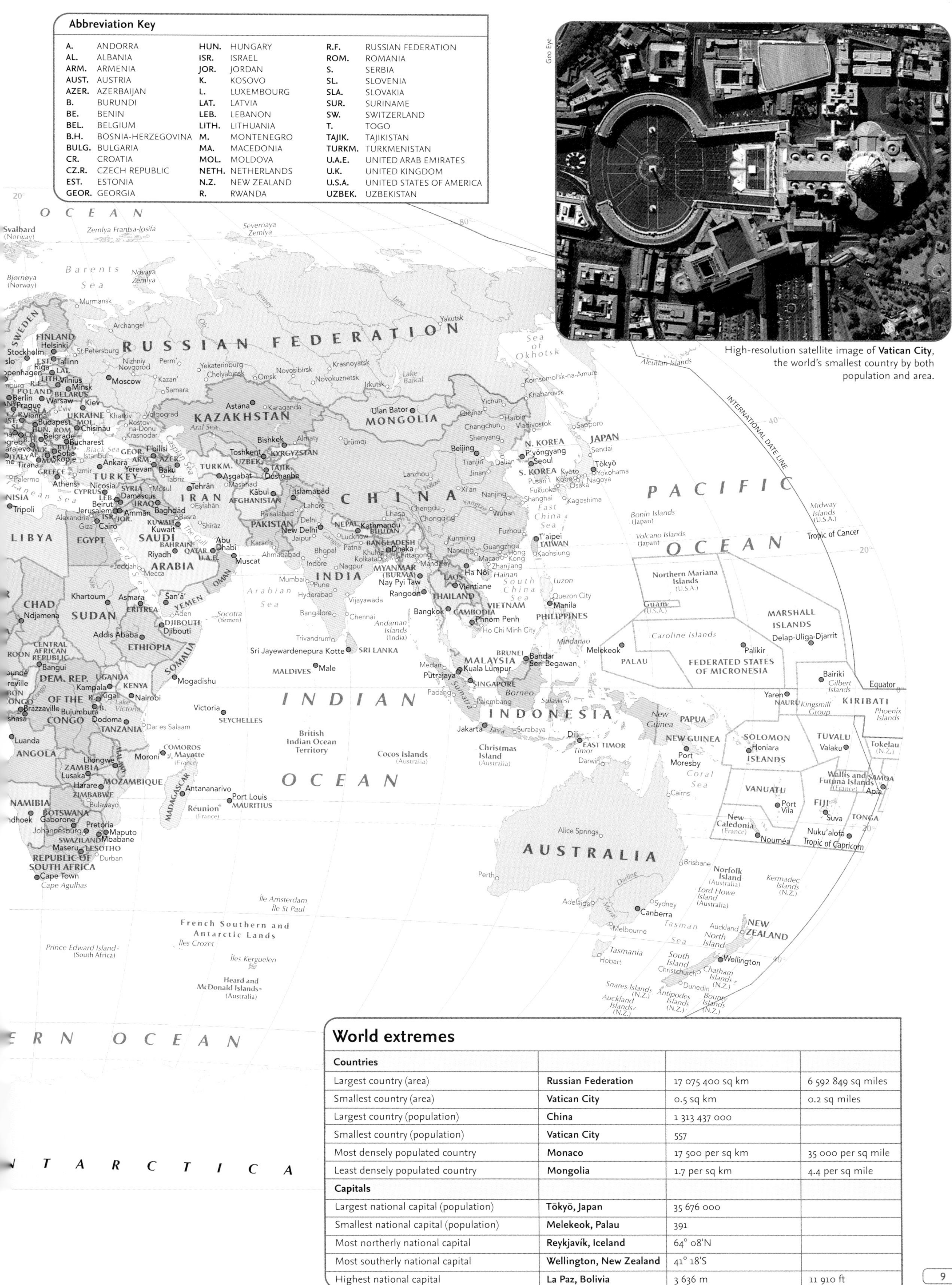

OCEAN
Svalbard (Norway)
Zemlya Frantsa-Iosifa
Severnaya Zemlya
Barents Sea
Novaya Zemlya
Bjørnøya (Norway)
Murmansk
Archangel
RUSSIAN FEDERATION
Yakutsk
Sea of Okhotsk
FINLAND
Helsinki
Stockholm
St Petersburg
Tallinn
Riga
Moscow
Vilnius
Minsk
Warsaw
Kiev
Prague
Vienna
Budapest
Chişinău
Belgrade
Bucharest
Sofia
Skopje
Tirana
Athens
Ankara
T'bilisi
Yerevan
Baku
TURKEY
Nicosia
Beirut
Damascus
Jerusalem
'Ammān
Baghdād
Cairo
LIBYA
EGYPT
Tripoli
Tehrān
IRAN
Kābul
AFGHANISTAN
Islamabad
PAKISTAN
New Delhi
Kathmandu
Dhaka
INDIA
Kuwait
Riyadh
SAUDI ARABIA
Abu Dhabi
Muscat
Astana
KAZAKHSTAN
Bishkek
Toshkent
Dushanbe
Aşgabat
Ulan Bator
MONGOLIA
Beijing
CHINA
P'yŏngyang
Seoul
N. KOREA
S. KOREA
Tōkyō
JAPAN
T'aipei
TAIWAN
Ha Nôi
Vientiane
MYANMAR (BURMA)
Nay Pyi Taw
Rangoon
Bangkok
THAILAND
Phnom Penh
VIETNAM
Manila
PHILIPPINES
Kuala Lumpur
MALAYSIA
SINGAPORE
Bandar Seri Begawan
INDONESIA
Jakarta
Dili
EAST TIMOR
Khartoum
SUDAN
CHAD
Ndjamena
Asmara
ERITREA
San'ā'
YEMEN
DJIBOUTI
Addis Ababa
ETHIOPIA
SOMALIA
Mogadishu
Nairobi
KENYA
Kampala
UGANDA
DEM. REP. OF THE CONGO
Kinshasa
Brazzaville
Luanda
ANGOLA
Dodoma
TANZANIA
Lusaka
ZAMBIA
Lilongwe
Harare
ZIMBABWE
MOZAMBIQUE
Maputo
NAMIBIA
BOTSWANA
Gaborone
Pretoria
REPUBLIC OF SOUTH AFRICA
Cape Town
Antananarivo
MADAGASCAR
Port Louis
MAURITIUS
Victoria
SEYCHELLES
Male
MALDIVES
Sri Jayewardenepura Kotte
SRI LANKA
INDIAN OCEAN
Arabian Sea
PACIFIC OCEAN
Tropic of Cancer
Equator
Tropic of Capricorn
INTERNATIONAL DATE LINE
Melekeok
PALAU
Palikir
FEDERATED STATES OF MICRONESIA
MARSHALL ISLANDS
Delap-Uliga-Djarrit
KIRIBATI
Bairiki
NAURU
Yaren
PAPUA NEW GUINEA
Port Moresby
SOLOMON ISLANDS
Honiara
TUVALU
Vaiaku
VANUATU
Port Vila
FIJI
Suva
TONGA
Nuku'alofa
SAMOA
Apia
AUSTRALIA
Canberra
NEW ZEALAND
Wellington
SOUTHERN OCEAN
ANTARCTICA

Abbreviation Key

A.	ANDORRA	HUN.	HUNGARY	R.F.	RUSSIAN FEDERATION
AL.	ALBANIA	ISR.	ISRAEL	ROM.	ROMANIA
ARM.	ARMENIA	JOR.	JORDAN	S.	SERBIA
AUST.	AUSTRIA	K.	KOSOVO	SL.	SLOVENIA
AZER.	AZERBAIJAN	L.	LUXEMBOURG	SLA.	SLOVAKIA
B.	BURUNDI	LAT.	LATVIA	SUR.	SURINAME
BE.	BENIN	LEB.	LEBANON	SW.	SWITZERLAND
BEL.	BELGIUM	LITH.	LITHUANIA	T.	TOGO
B.H.	BOSNIA-HERZEGOVINA	M.	MONTENEGRO	TAJIK.	TAJIKISTAN
BULG.	BULGARIA	MA.	MACEDONIA	TURKM.	TURKMENISTAN
CR.	CROATIA	MOL.	MOLDOVA	U.A.E.	UNITED ARAB EMIRATES
CZ.R.	CZECH REPUBLIC	NETH.	NETHERLANDS	U.K.	UNITED KINGDOM
EST.	ESTONIA	N.Z.	NEW ZEALAND	U.S.A.	UNITED STATES OF AMERICA
GEOR.	GEORGIA	R.	RWANDA	UZBEK.	UZBEKISTAN

Geo Eye

High-resolution satellite image of **Vatican City**, the world's smallest country by both population and area.

World extremes

Countries			
Largest country (area)	**Russian Federation**	17 075 400 sq km	6 592 849 sq miles
Smallest country (area)	**Vatican City**	0.5 sq km	0.2 sq miles
Largest country (population)	**China**	1 313 437 000	
Smallest country (population)	**Vatican City**	557	
Most densely populated country	**Monaco**	17 500 per sq km	35 000 per sq mile
Least densely populated country	**Mongolia**	1.7 per sq km	4.4 per sq mile
Capitals			
Largest national capital (population)	**Tōkyō, Japan**	35 676 000	
Smallest national capital (population)	**Melekeok, Palau**	391	
Most northerly national capital	**Reykjavík, Iceland**	64° 08'N	
Most southerly national capital	**Wellington, New Zealand**	41° 18'S	
Highest national capital	**La Paz, Bolivia**	3 636 m	11 910 ft

World

Earthquakes and Volcanoes

Earthquakes and volcanoes hold a constant fascination because of their power, their beauty, and the fact that they cannot be controlled or accurately predicted. Our understanding of these phenomena relies mainly on the theory of plate tectonics. This defines the Earth's surface as a series of 'plates' which are constantly moving relative to each other, at rates of a few centimetres per year. As plates move against each other enormous pressure builds up and when the rocks can no longer bear this pressure they fracture, and energy is released as an earthquake. The pressures involved can also melt the rock to form magma which then rises to the Earth's surface to form a volcano. The distribution of earthquakes and volcanoes therefore relates closely to plate boundaries. In particular, most active volcanoes and much of the Earth's seismic activity are centred on the 'Ring of Fire' around the Pacific Ocean.

Facts

- **Over 900 earthquakes of magnitude 5.0 or greater occur every year**
- **An earthquake of magnitude 8.0 releases energy equivalent to 1 billion tons of TNT explosive**
- **Ground shaking during an earthquake in Alaska in 1964 lasted for 3 minutes**
- **Indonesia has more than 120 volcanoes and over 30% of the world's active volcanoes**
- **Volcanoes can produce very fertile soil and important industrial materials and chemicals**

Mt St Helens
NORTH AMERICAN PLATE
Kilauea
El Chichónal
Guatemala
Soufrière Hills
Nevado del Ruiz
CARIBBEAN PLATE
COCOS PLATE
Volcán Galeras
SOUTH AMERICAN PLATE
Huánuco
NAZCA PLATE
Chillán
Volcán Llaima
SCOTIA PLATE
Chlef
SOUTH AMERICAN PLATE

Earthquakes

Earthquakes are caused by movement along fractures or 'faults' in the Earth's crust, particularly along plate boundaries. There are three types of plate boundary: constructive boundaries where plates are moving apart; destructive boundaries where two or more plates collide; conservative boundaries where plates slide past each other. Destructive and conservative boundaries are the main sources of earthquake activity.

The epicentre of an earthquake is the point on the Earth's surface directly above its source. If this is near to large centres of population, and the earthquake is powerful, major devastation can result. The size, or magnitude, of an earthquake is generally measured on the Richter Scale.

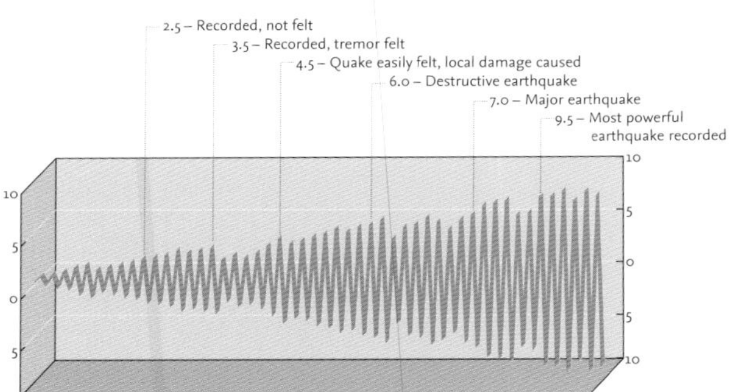

2.5 – Recorded, not felt
3.5 – Recorded, tremor felt
4.5 – Quake easily felt, local damage caused
6.0 – Destructive earthquake
7.0 – Major earthquake
9.5 – Most powerful earthquake recorded
10
5
0
5
10

Earthquake magnitude – the Richter Scale
The scale measures the energy released by an earthquake. It is a logarithmic scale: an earthquake measuring 5 is thirty times more powerful than one measuring 4.

Plate boundaries

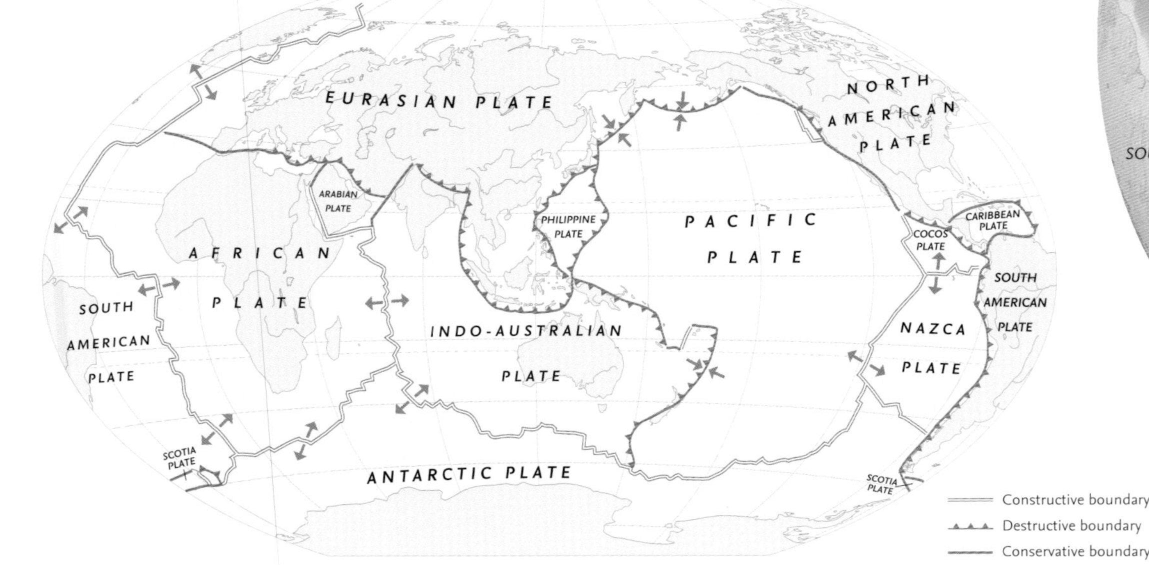

EURASIAN PLATE
NORTH AMERICAN PLATE
ARABIAN PLATE
PHILIPPINE PLATE
PACIFIC PLATE
AFRICAN PLATE
COCOS PLATE
CARIBBEAN PLATE
SOUTH AMERICAN PLATE
INDO-AUSTRALIAN PLATE
NAZCA PLATE
SCOTIA PLATE
ANTARCTIC PLATE
Constructive boundary
Destructive boundary
Conservative boundary

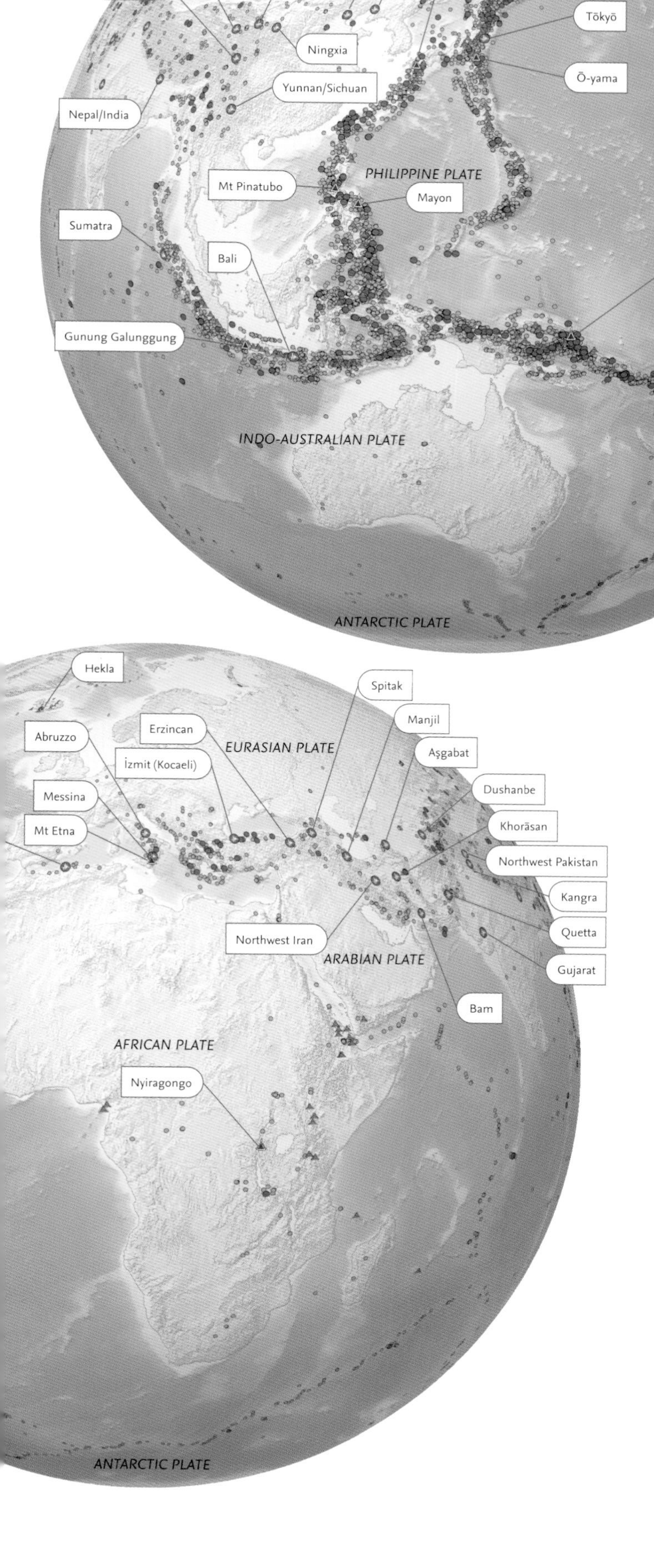
Deadliest earthquake
Earthquake of magnitude 7.5 or greater
Earthquake of magnitude 5.5 – 7.4
Major volcano
Other volcano
Tangshan
Liaoning
Unzen-dake
Qinghai
EURASIAN PLATE
Gansu
Sichuan
Ningxia
Tōkyō
Ō-yama
Yunnan/Sichuan
Nepal/India
PHILIPPINE PLATE
Mt Pinatubo
Mayon
PACIFIC PLATE
Sumatra
Bali
Rabaul
Gunung Galunggung
INDO-AUSTRALIAN PLATE
ANTARCTIC PLATE
Hekla
Spitak
Manjil
Abruzzo
Erzincan
EURASIAN PLATE
Aşgabat
İzmit (Kocaeli)
Dushanbe
Messina
Khorāsan
Mt Etna
Northwest Pakistan
Kangra
Quetta
Northwest Iran
ARABIAN PLATE
Gujarat
Bam
AFRICAN PLATE
Nyiragongo
ANTARCTIC PLATE

Volcanoes

The majority of volcanoes occur along destructive plate boundaries in the 'subduction zone' where one plate passes under another. The friction and pressure causes the rock to melt and to form magma which is forced upwards to the Earth's surface where it erupts as molten rock (lava) or as particles of ash or cinder. This process created the numerous volcanoes in the Andes, where the Nazca Plate is passing under the South American Plate. Volcanoes can be defined by the nature of the material they emit. 'Shield' volcanoes have extensive, gentle slopes formed from free-flowing lava, while steep-sided 'continental' volcanoes are created from thicker, slow-flowing lava and ash.

Major volcanic eruptions since 1980

Volcano	Country	Date
Mt St Helens	USA	1980
El Chichónal	Mexico	1982
Gunung Galunggung	Indonesia	1982
Kilauea	Hawaii, USA	1983
Ō-yama	Japan	1983
Nevado del Ruiz	Colombia	1985
Mt Pinatubo	Philippines	1991
Unzen-dake	Japan	1991
Mayon	Philippines	1993
Volcán Galeras	Colombia	1993
Volcán Llaima	Chile	1994
Rabaul	Papua New Guinea	1994
Soufrière Hills	Montserrat	1997
Hekla	Iceland	2000
Mt Etna	Italy	2001
Nyiragongo	Democratic Republic of the Congo	2002

Deadliest earthquakes since 1900

Year	Location	Deaths
1905	**Kangra,** India	19 000
1907	west of **Dushanbe,** Tajikistan	12 000
1908	**Messina,** Italy	110 000
1915	**Abruzzo,** Italy	35 000
1917	**Bali,** Indonesia	15 000
1920	**Ningxia Province,** China	200 000
1923	**Tōkyō,** Japan	142 807
1927	**Qinghai Province,** China	200 000
1932	**Gansu Province,** China	70 000
1933	**Sichuan Province,** China	10 000
1934	**Nepal/India**	10 700
1935	**Quetta,** Pakistan	30 000
1939	**Chillán,** Chile	28 000
1939	**Erzincan,** Turkey	32 700
1948	**Aşgabat,** Turkmenistan	19 800
1962	northwest **Iran**	12 225
1970	**Huánuco Province,** Peru	66 794
1974	**Yunnan** and **Sichuan Provinces,** China	20 000
1975	**Liaoning Province,** China	10 000
1976	central **Guatemala**	22 778
1976	**Tangshan,** Hebei Province, China	255 000
1978	**Khorāsan Province,** Iran	20 000
1980	**Chlef,** Algeria	11 000
1988	**Spitak,** Armenia	25 000
1990	**Manjil,** Iran	50 000
1999	**İzmit (Kocaeli),** Turkey	17 000
2001	**Gujarat,** India	20 000
2003	**Bam,** Iran	26 271
2004	off **Sumatra,** Indian Ocean	225 000
2005	northwest **Pakistan**	74 648
2008	**Sichuan Province,** China	> 60 000
2009	**Abruzzo** region, Italy	308
2009	**Sumatra,** Indonesia	> 1 100

Internet Links

USGS National Earthquake Hazards Program	**earthquake.usgs.gov/regional/neic**
USGS Volcano Hazards Program	**volcanoes.usgs.gov**
British Geological Survey	**www.bgs.ac.uk**
NASA Natural Hazards	**earthobservatory.nasa.gov/NaturalHazards**
Volcano World	**volcano.oregonstate.edu**

World

Climate and Weather

The climate of a region is defined by its long-term prevailing weather conditions. Classification of Climate Types is based on the relationship between temperature and humidity and how these factors are affected by latitude, altitude, ocean currents and winds. Weather is the specific short term condition which occurs locally and consists of events such as thunderstorms, hurricanes, blizzards and heat waves. Temperature and rainfall data recorded at weather stations can be plotted graphically and the graphs shown here, typical of each climate region, illustrate the various combinations of temperature and rainfall which exist worldwide for each month of the year. Data used for climate graphs are based on average monthly figures recorded over a minimum period of thirty years.

Major climate regions, ocean currents and sea surface temperatures

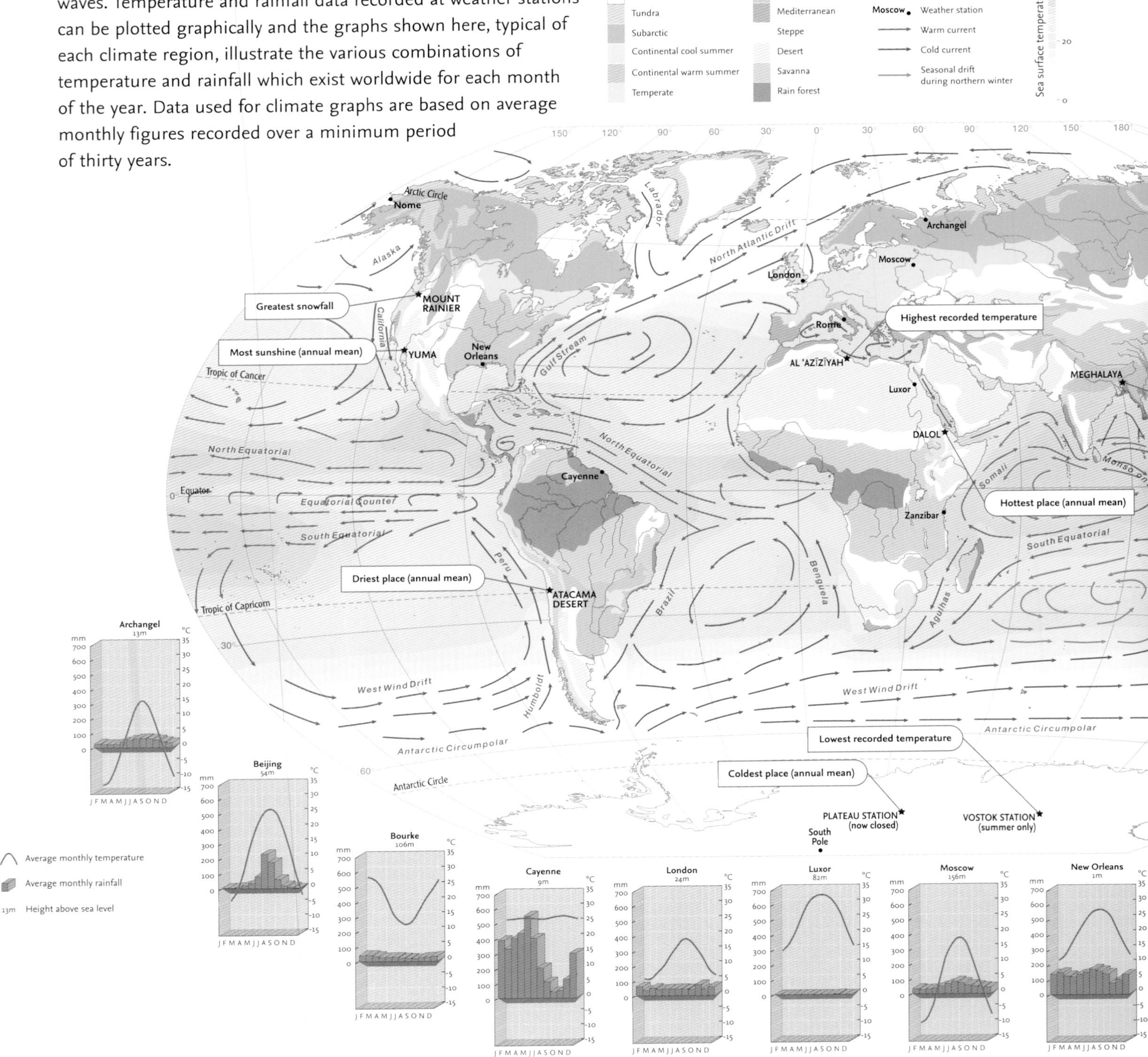

Ice cap
Tundra
Subarctic
Continental cool summer
Continental warm summer
Temperate
Humid subtropical
Mediterranean
Steppe
Desert
Savanna
Rain forest
YUMA ★ Weather extreme location
Moscow • Weather station
Warm current
Cold current
Seasonal drift during northern winter
Sea surface temperature
30°C
20
0
Arctic Circle
Nome
Alaska
Labrador
North Atlantic Drift
Archangel
Moscow
London
Greatest snowfall
MOUNT RAINIER
California
Most sunshine (annual mean)
YUMA
New Orleans
Gulf Stream
Rome
Highest recorded temperature
AL 'AZĪZĪYAH
Tropic of Cancer
Luxor
MEGHALAYA
DALOL
North Equatorial
Cayenne
Equator
Equatorial Counter
South Equatorial
Zanzibar
Somali
Hottest place (annual mean)
Peru
Driest place (annual mean)
ATACAMA DESERT
Brazil
Benguela
Agulhas
Tropic of Capricorn
West Wind Drift
Humboldt
Antarctic Circumpolar
Lowest recorded temperature
Coldest place (annual mean)
Antarctic Circle
PLATEAU STATION (now closed)
South Pole
VOSTOK STATION (summer only)
Archangel 13m
Beijing 54m
Bourke 106m
Cayenne 9m
London 24m
Luxor 82m
Moscow 156m
New Orleans 1m
mm
°C
J F M A M J J A S O N D
Average monthly temperature
Average monthly rainfall
13m Height above sea level

Climate change

In 2008 the global mean temperature was over 0.7°C higher than that at the end of the nineteenth century. Most of this warming is caused by human activities which result in a build-up of greenhouse gases, mainly carbon dioxide, allowing heat to be trapped within the atmosphere. Carbon dioxide emissions have increased since the beginning of the industrial revolution due to burning of fossil fuels, increased urbanization, population growth, deforestation and industrial pollution.

Annual climate indicators such as number of frost-free days, length of growing season, heat wave frequency, number of wet days, length of dry spells and frequency of weather extremes are used to monitor climate change. The map opposite shows how future changes in temperature will not be spread evenly around the world. Some regions will warm faster than the global average, while others will warm more slowly.

Facts

- Arctic Sea ice thickness has declined 40% in the last 40 years
- El Niño and La Niña episodes occur at irregular intervals of 2–7 years
- Sea levels are rising by one centimetre per decade
- Precipitation in the northern hemisphere is increasing
- Droughts have increased in frequency and intensity in parts of Asia and Africa

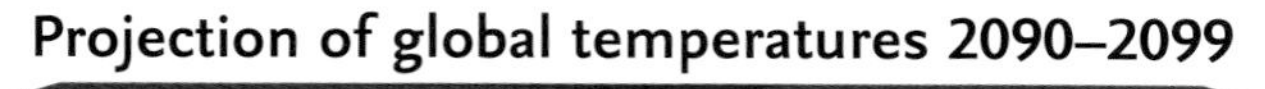

Projection of global temperatures 2090–2099

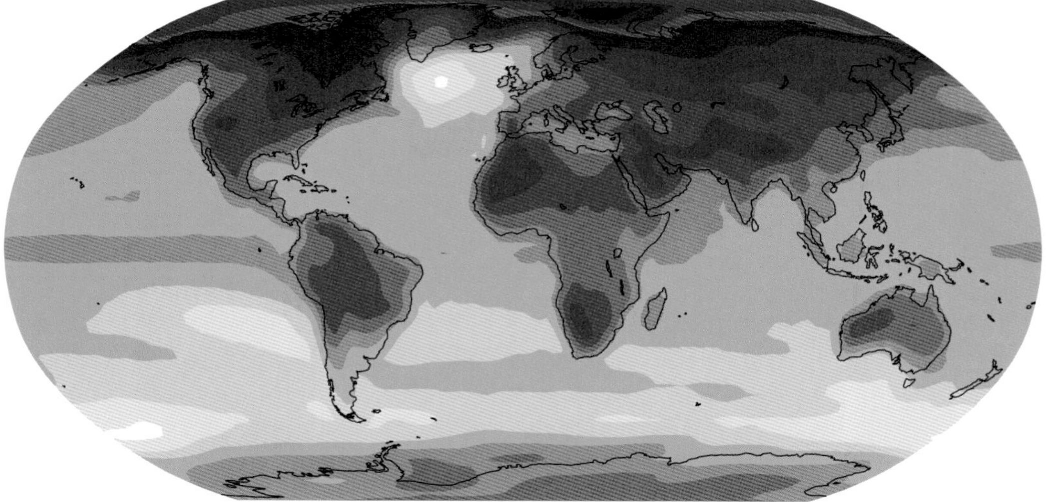
0.5 1 1.5 2 2.5 3 3.5 4 4.5 5 5.5 6 6.5 7 7.5
Change in average surface temperature (°C)

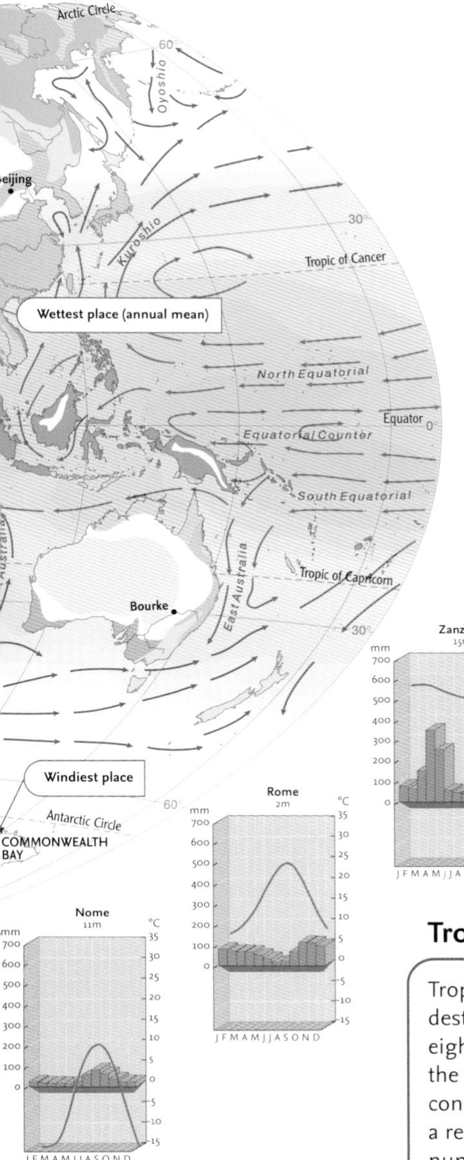
Arctic Circle
Oyoshio
Beijing
Kuroshio
Tropic of Cancer
Wettest place (annual mean)
North Equatorial
Equator
Equatorial Counter
South Equatorial
East Australia
Tropic of Capricorn
Bourke
Windiest place
Antarctic Circle
COMMONWEALTH BAY
Zanzibar 15m
Rome 2m
Nome 11m
mm
°C
J F M A M J J A S O N D

Tracks of tropical storms

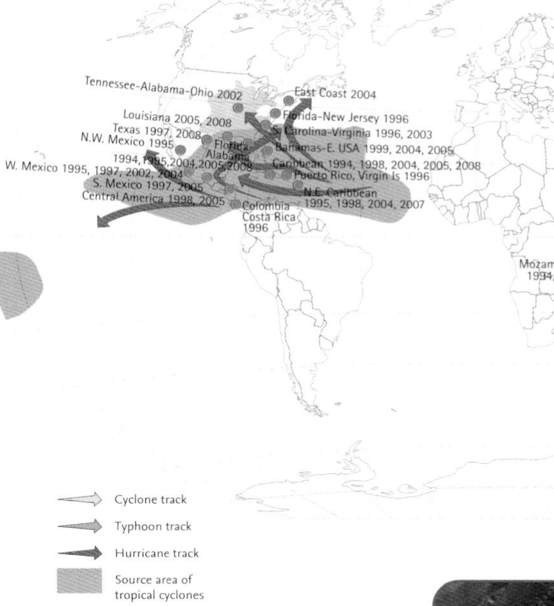
Tennessee-Alabama-Ohio 2002
East Coast 2004
Louisiana 2005, 2008
Florida-New Jersey 1996
Texas 1997, 2008
N.W. Mexico 1995
S. Carolina-Virginia 1996, 2003
Bahamas-E. USA 1999, 2004, 2005
Caribbean 1994, 1998, 2004, 2005, 2008
Puerto Rico, Virgin Is 1996
W. Mexico 1995, 1997, 2002, 2004
S. Mexico 1997, 2005
Central America 1998, 2005
N.E. Caribbean 1995, 1998, 2004, 2007
Colombia Costa Rica 1996
West India 1996, 1998
Andhra Pradesh 1996
Tamil Nadu 1996
Bangladesh 1994, 1997, 2007
Orissa 1999
Myanmar 2008
Zhejiang 1994, 1997
South Korea 1995, 1999
Kyushu 1994, 2005
Taiwan 1994, 1996, 1997, 2005, 2006, 2009
Philippines 1994, 1995, 1998, 2004, 2006
S. Vietnam, Cambodia 1997
Sabah 1996
Papua New Guinea 2007
Mozambique 1994, 2000
Madagascar 1997, 2000
2005
N. Coast 2005
Queensland 2006
N.W. Coast 2005, 2007
Cyclone track
Typhoon track
Hurricane track
Source area of tropical cyclones
Major tropical storm (1994–2009)
Tornado high risk areas

Tropical storms

Tropical storms are among the most powerful and destructive weather systems on Earth. Of the eighty to one hundred which develop annually over the tropical oceans, many make landfall and cause considerable damage to property and loss of life as a result of high winds and heavy rain. Although the number of tropical storms is projected to decrease, their intensity, and therefore their destructive power, is likely to increase.

Tropical storm Gustav, August 2008.

Weather extremes

Highest recorded temperature	**57.8°C/136°F** Al'Azīzīyah, Libya (September 1922)
Hottest place - annual mean	**34.4°C/93.9°F** Dalol, Ethiopia
Driest place - annual mean	**0.1mm/0.004 inches** Atacama Desert, Chile
Most sunshine - annual mean	**90%** Yuma, Arizona, USA (over 4000 hours)
Lowest recorded temperature	**-89.2°C/-128.6°F** Vostok Station, Antarctica (July 1983)
Coldest place - annual mean	**-56.6°C/-69.9°F** Plateau Station, Antarctica
Wettest place annual mean	**11 873 mm/467.4 inches** Meghalaya, India
Greatest snowfall	**31 102 mm/1 224.5 inches** Mount Rainier, Washington, USA (February 1971 – February 1972)
Windiest place	**322 km per hour/200 miles per hour** (in gales) Commonwealth Bay, Antarctica

Internet Links

Met Office	**www.metoffice.gov.uk**
BBC Weather Centre	**www.bbc.co.uk/weather**
National Oceanic and Atmospheric Administration	**www.noaa.gov**
National Climatic Data Center	**www.ncdc.noaa.gov**
United Nations World Meteorological Organization	**www.wmo.ch**

World

Land Cover

The oxygen- and water-rich environment of the Earth has helped create a wide range of habitats. Forest and woodland ecosystems form the predominant natural land cover over most of the Earth's surface. Tropical rainforests are part of an intricate land-atmosphere relationship that is disturbed by land cover changes. Forests in the tropics are believed to hold most of the world's bird, animal, and plant species. Grassland, shrubland and deserts collectively cover most of the unwooded land surface, with tundra on frozen subsoil at high northern latitudes. These areas tend to have lower species diversity than most forests, with the notable exception of Mediterranean shrublands, which support some of the most diverse floras on the Earth. Humans have extensively altered most grassland and shrubland areas, usually through conversion to agriculture, burning and introduction of domestic livestock. They have had less immediate impact on tundra and true desert regions, although these remain vulnerable to global climate change.

World land cover

- Evergreen needleleaf forest
- Evergreen broadleaf forest
- Deciduous needleleaf forest
- Deciduous broadleaf forest
- Mixed forest
- Closed shrublands
- Open shrublands
- Woody savannas
- Savannas
- Grasslands
- Permanent wetlands
- Croplands
- Urban and built-up
- Cropland/Natural vegetation mosaic
- Snow and Ice
- Barren or sparsely vegetated
- Water bodies

Arctic Circle

Tropic of Cancer

Tropic of Capricorn

Antarctic Circle

Land cover

The land cover map shown here was developed at Boston University in Boston, M.A., U.S.A. using data from the Moderate-resolution Imaging-Spectroradiometer (MODIS) instrument aboard NASA's Terra satellite. The high resolution (ground resolution of 1km) of the imagery used to compile the data set and map allows detailed interpretation of land cover patterns across the world. Important uses include managing forest resources, improving estimates of the Earth's water and energy cycles, and modelling climate change.

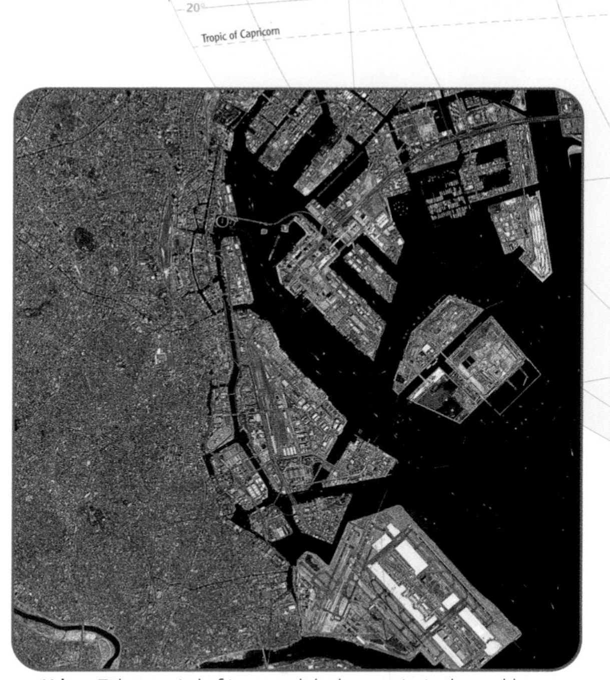

Urban, Tōkyō, capital of Japan and the largest city in the world.

Internet Links

World Resources Institute	**www.wri.org**
World Conservation Monitoring Centre	**www.unep-wcmc.org**
United Nations Environment Programme (UNEP)	**www.unep.org**
IUCN, International Union for Conservation of Nature	**www.iucn.org**
MODIS Land Cover Group at Boston University	**www-modis.bu.edu/landcover/index.html**

Cropland, near Consuegra, Spain.

Barren/Shrubland, Mojave Desert, California, United States of America.

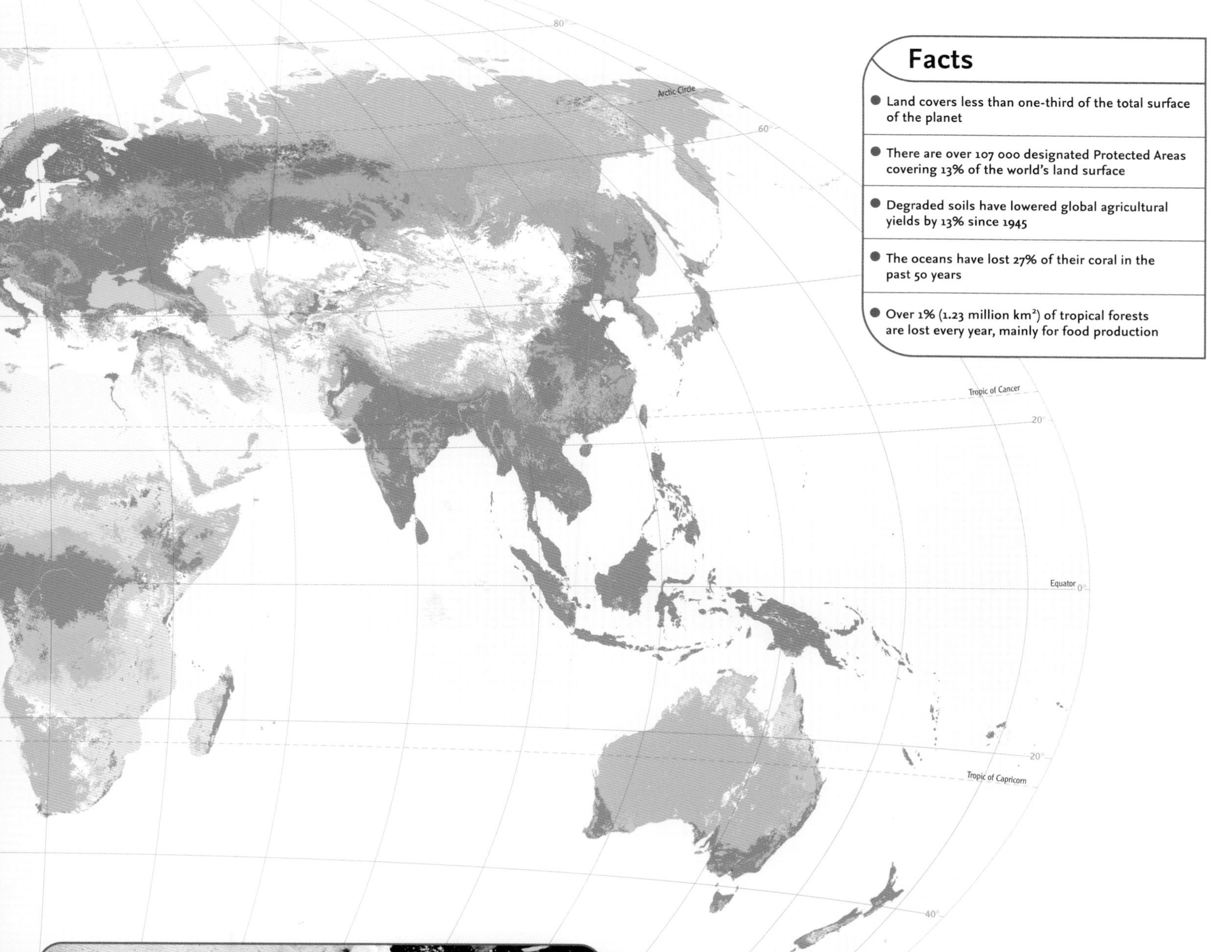

Arctic Circle
Tropic of Cancer
Equator
Tropic of Capricorn
Antarctic Circle

Facts

- Land covers less than one-third of the total surface of the planet
- There are over 107 000 designated Protected Areas covering 13% of the world's land surface
- Degraded soils have lowered global agricultural yields by 13% since 1945
- The oceans have lost 27% of their coral in the past 50 years
- Over 1% (1.23 million km²) of tropical forests are lost every year, mainly for food production

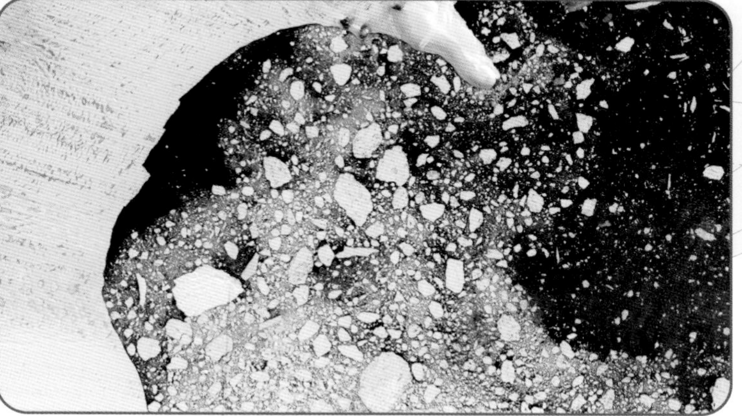
Snow and ice, Larsen Ice Shelf, Antarctica.

Land cover composition and change

The continents all have different characteristics. There are extensive croplands in North America and eastern Europe, while south of the Sahara are belts of grass/shrubland which are at risk from desertification. Tropical forests are not pristine areas either as they show signs of human activity in deforestation of land for crops or grazing.

World

Population

After increasing very slowly for most of human history, world population more than doubled in the last half century. Whereas world population did not pass the one billion mark until 1804 and took another 123 years to reach two billion in 1927, it then added the third billion in 33 years, the fourth in 14 years and the fifth in 13 years. Just twelve years later on October 12, 1999 the United Nations announced that the global population had reached the six billion mark. It is expected that another 2.5 billion people will have been added to the world's population by 2050.

World population distribution

Population density, continental populations (2005) and continental population change (2000–2005)

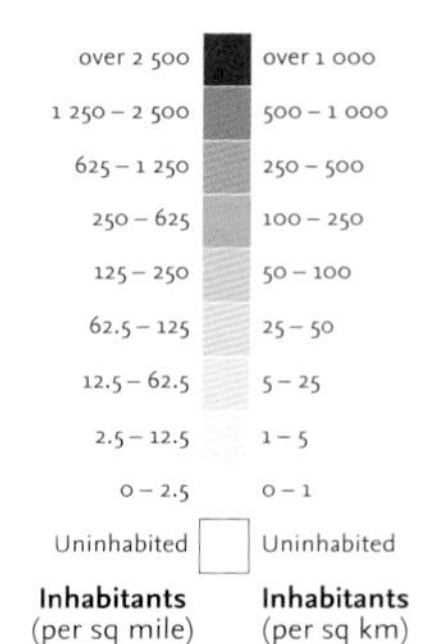
over 2 500
1 250 – 2 500
625 – 1 250
250 – 625
125 – 250
62.5 – 125
12.5 – 62.5
2.5 – 12.5
0 – 2.5
Uninhabited
Inhabitants (per sq mile)
over 1 000
500 – 1 000
250 – 500
100 – 250
50 – 100
25 – 50
5 – 25
1 – 5
0 – 1
Uninhabited
Inhabitants (per sq km)

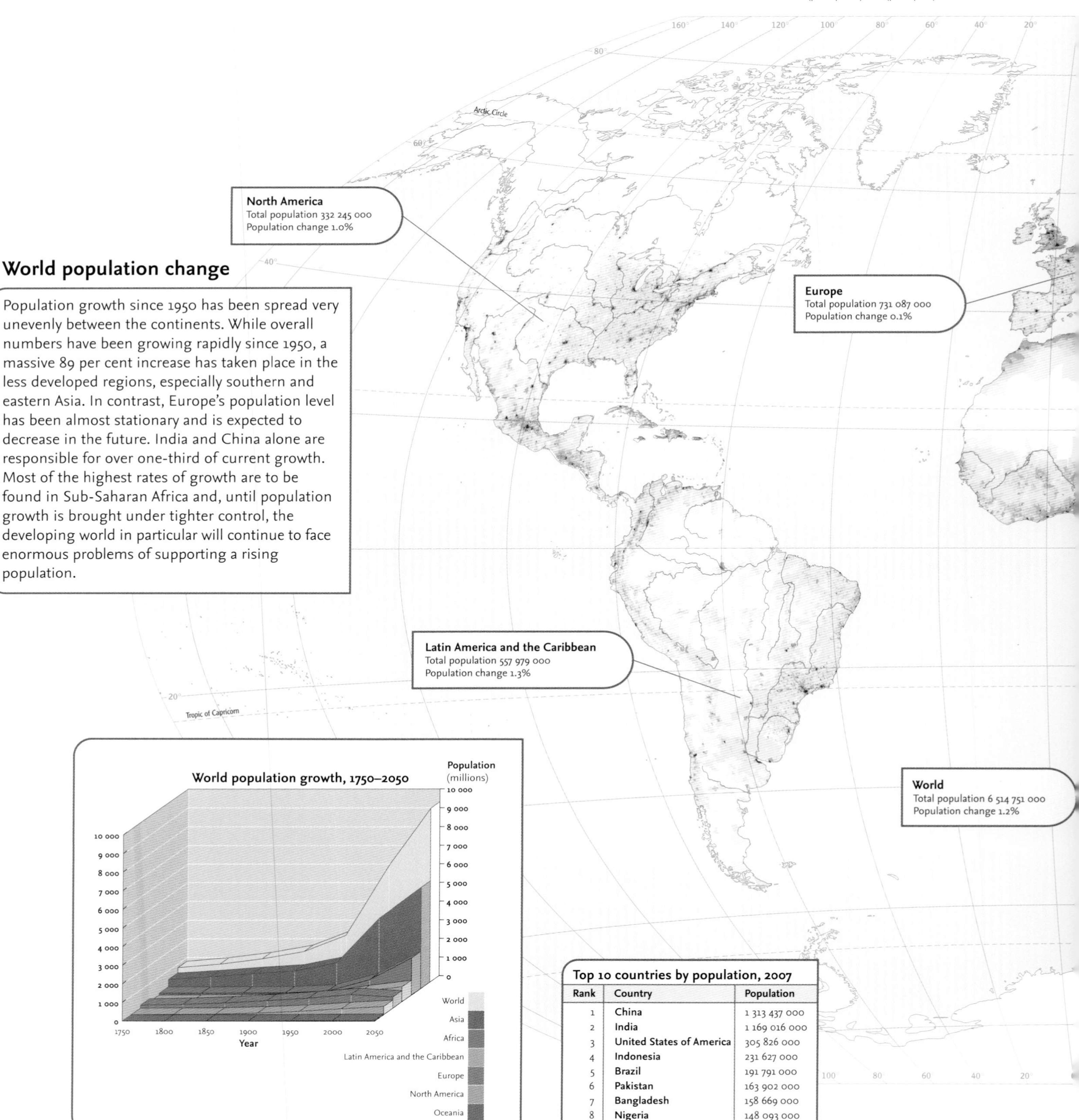
160° 140° 120° 100° 80° 60° 40° 20°
80°
Arctic Circle
60°
40°
20°
Tropic of Capricorn
North America
Total population 332 245 000
Population change 1.0%
Europe
Total population 731 087 000
Population change 0.1%
Latin America and the Caribbean
Total population 557 979 000
Population change 1.3%
World
Total population 6 514 751 000
Population change 1.2%
World population growth, 1750–2050
Population (millions)
10 000
9 000
8 000
7 000
6 000
5 000
4 000
3 000
2 000
1 000
0
1750 1800 1850 1900 1950 2000 2050
Year
World
Asia
Africa
Latin America and the Caribbean
Europe
North America
Oceania
100 80 60 40 20

World population change

Population growth since 1950 has been spread very unevenly between the continents. While overall numbers have been growing rapidly since 1950, a massive 89 per cent increase has taken place in the less developed regions, especially southern and eastern Asia. In contrast, Europe's population level has been almost stationary and is expected to decrease in the future. India and China alone are responsible for over one-third of current growth. Most of the highest rates of growth are to be found in Sub-Saharan Africa and, until population growth is brought under tighter control, the developing world in particular will continue to face enormous problems of supporting a rising population.

Top 10 countries by population, 2007

Rank	Country	Population
1	China	1 313 437 000
2	India	1 169 016 000
3	United States of America	305 826 000
4	Indonesia	231 627 000
5	Brazil	191 791 000
6	Pakistan	163 902 000
7	Bangladesh	158 669 000
8	Nigeria	148 093 000
9	Russian Federation	142 499 000
10	Japan	127 967 000

The island nation of **Singapore,** the world's second most densely populated country.

Kuna Indians inhabit this congested island off the north coast of Panama.

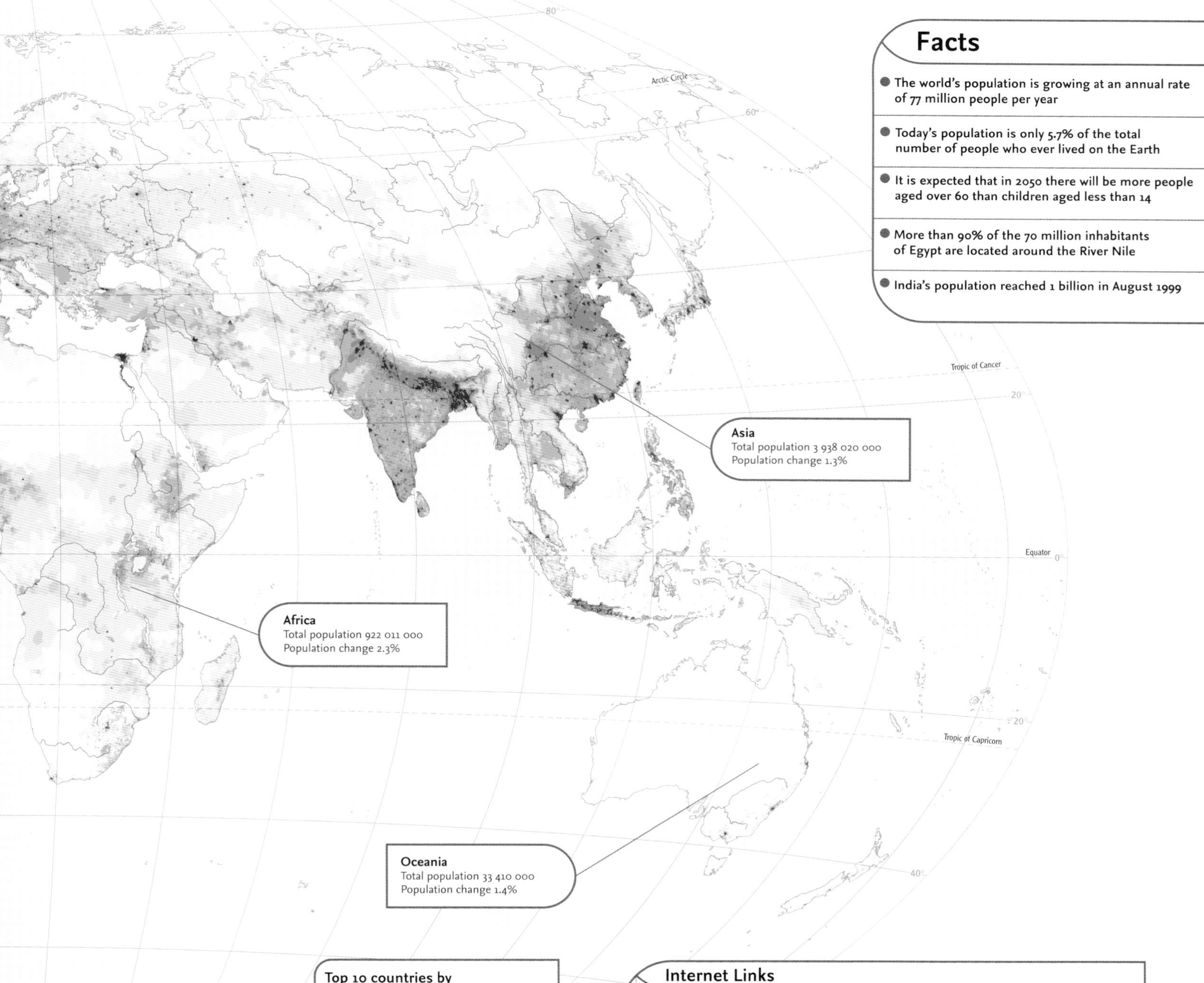

Arctic Circle
Tropic of Cancer
Equator
Tropic of Capricorn
Asia
Total population 3 938 020 000
Population change 1.3%
Africa
Total population 922 011 000
Population change 2.3%
Oceania
Total population 33 410 000
Population change 1.4%

Facts

- The world's population is growing at an annual rate of 77 million people per year
- Today's population is only 5.7% of the total number of people who ever lived on the Earth
- It is expected that in 2050 there will be more people aged over 60 than children aged less than 14
- More than 90% of the 70 million inhabitants of Egypt are located around the River Nile
- India's population reached 1 billion in August 1999

Top 10 countries by population density, 2007
(persons per square kilometre)

Rank	Country*	Population density
1	Bangladesh	1 102
2	Taiwan	632
3	South Korea	486
4	Netherlands	395
5	India	381
6	Belgium	343
7	Japan	339
8	Sri Lanka	294
9	Philippines	293
10	Vietnam	265

*Only countries with a population of over 10 million are considered

Internet Links

United Nations Population Information Network	**www.un.org/popin**
US Census Bureau	**www.census.gov**
Office for National Statistics	**www.statistics.gov.uk/census2001**
Population Reference Bureau	**www.prb.org**
Socioeconomic Data and Applications Center	**sedac.ciesin.columbia.edu**

World
Urbanization and Cities

The world is becoming increasingly urban but the level of urbanization varies greatly between and within continents. At the beginning of the twentieth century only fourteen per cent of the world's population was urban and by 1950 this had increased to thirty per cent. In the more developed regions and in Latin America and the Caribbean over seventy per cent of the population is urban while in Africa and Asia the figure is forty per cent. In recent decades urban growth has increased rapidly to fifty per cent and there are now nearly 400 cities with over 1 000 000 inhabitants. It is in the developing regions that the most rapid increases are taking place and it is expected that by 2030 over half of urban dwellers worldwide will live in Asia. Migration from the countryside to the city in the search for better job opportunities is the main factor in urban growth.

Characteristic high-rise urban development **Hong Kong,** China.

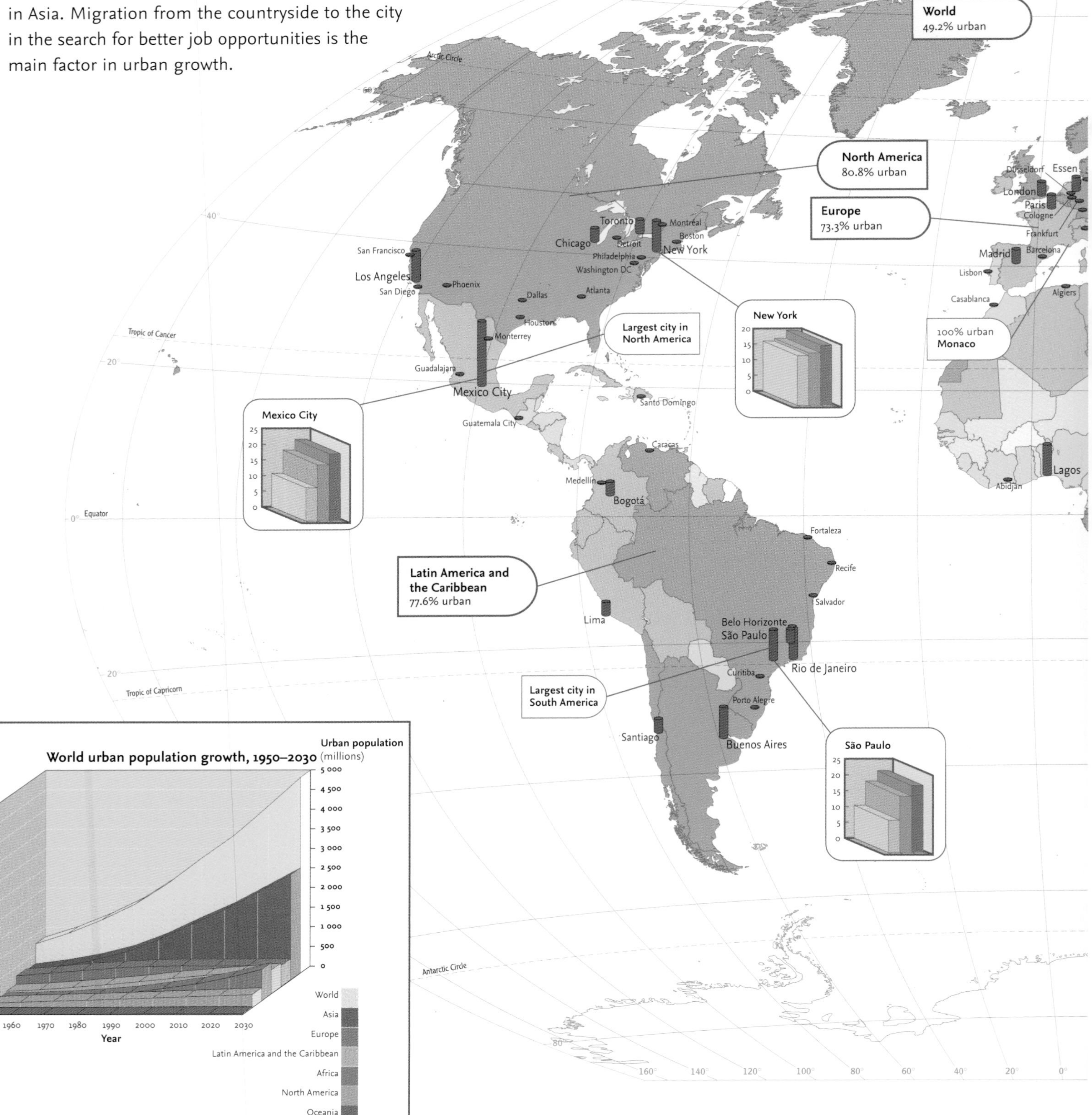

World
49.2% urban
North America
80.8% urban
Europe
73.3% urban
Latin America and the Caribbean
77.6% urban
100% urban
Monaco
Largest city in North America
Largest city in South America
New York
Mexico City
São Paulo
Arctic Circle
Tropic of Cancer
Equator
Tropic of Capricorn
Antarctic Circle
San Francisco
Los Angeles
San Diego
Phoenix
Dallas
Houston
Atlanta
Chicago
Toronto
Detroit
Montréal
Boston
Philadelphia
Washington DC
Monterrey
Guadalajara
Guatemala City
Santo Domingo
Caracas
Medellín
Bogotá
Fortaleza
Recife
Salvador
Lima
Belo Horizonte
Rio de Janeiro
Curitiba
Porto Alegre
Santiago
Buenos Aires
Düsseldorf
Essen
London
Paris
Cologne
Frankfurt
Madrid
Barcelona
Lisbon
Casablanca
Algiers
Lagos
Abidjan
World urban population growth, 1950–2030
Urban population (millions)
Year
World
Asia
Europe
Latin America and the Caribbean
Africa
North America
Oceania

Megacities

There are currently forty-nine cities in the world with over 5 000 000 inhabitants. Nineteen of these, often referred to as megacities, have over 10 000 000 inhabitants and one has over 30 000 000. Tōkyō, with 35 467 000 inhabitants, has remained the world's largest city since 1970 and is likely to remain so for the next decade. Other cities expected to grow to over 20 000 000 by 2015 are Mumbai, São Paulo, Delhi and Mexico City. Eleven of the world's megacities are in Asia, all of them having over 10 000 000 inhabitants.

Level of urbanization and the world's largest cities

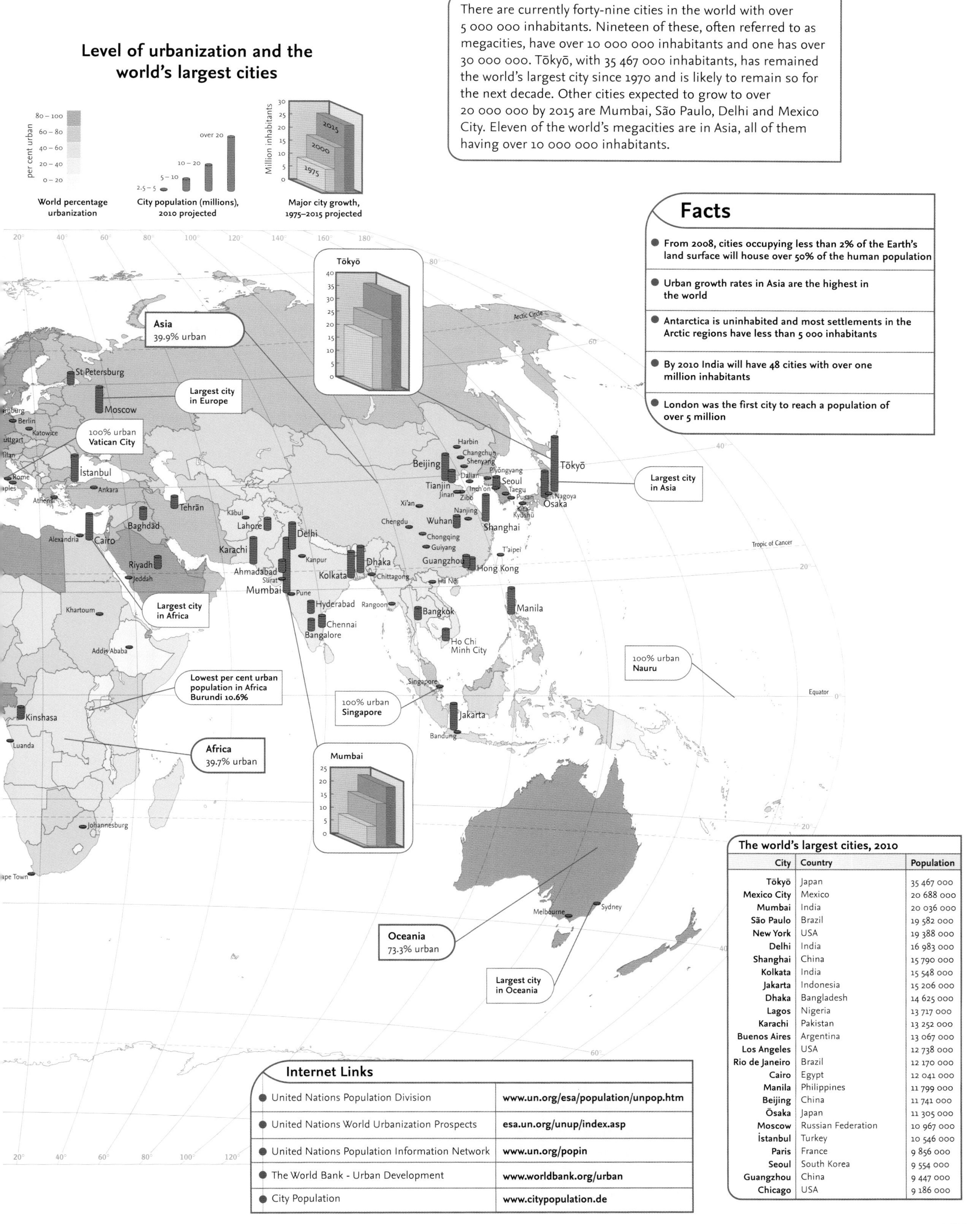

per cent urban
80 – 100
60 – 80
40 – 60
20 – 40
0 – 20
World percentage urbanization
2.5 – 5
5 – 10
10 – 20
over 20
City population (millions), 2010 projected
Million inhabitants
1975
2000
2015
Major city growth, 1975–2015 projected
Tōkyō
Mumbai
Asia 39.9% urban
Africa 39.7% urban
Oceania 73.3% urban
Largest city in Europe
Largest city in Asia
Largest city in Africa
Largest city in Oceania
100% urban Vatican City
100% urban Singapore
100% urban Nauru
Lowest per cent urban population in Africa Burundi 10.6%
Arctic Circle
Tropic of Cancer
Equator
St Petersburg
Moscow
Berlin
Katowice
Rome
Athens
İstanbul
Ankara
Tehrān
Baghdād
Kābul
Lahore
Karachi
Delhi
Kanpur
Ahmadabad
Surat
Mumbai
Pune
Hyderabad
Chennai
Bangalore
Kolkata
Dhaka
Chittagong
Rangoon
Bangkok
Ho Chi Minh City
Hà Nôi
Singapore
Jakarta
Bandung
Manila
Hong Kong
T'aipei
Guangzhou
Guiyang
Chongqing
Chengdu
Wuhan
Nanjing
Shanghai
Xi'an
Jinan
Zibo
Tianjin
Beijing
Dalian
Shenyang
Changchun
Harbin
P'yŏngyang
Seoul
Inch'ŏn
Taegu
Pusan
Kita-Kyūshū
Ōsaka
Nagoya
Tōkyō
Alexandria
Cairo
Riyadh
Jeddah
Khartoum
Addis Ababa
Kinshasa
Luanda
Johannesburg
Cape Town
Melbourne
Sydney

Facts

- From 2008, cities occupying less than 2% of the Earth's land surface will house over 50% of the human population
- Urban growth rates in Asia are the highest in the world
- Antarctica is uninhabited and most settlements in the Arctic regions have less than 5 000 inhabitants
- By 2010 India will have 48 cities with over one million inhabitants
- London was the first city to reach a population of over 5 million

The world's largest cities, 2010

City	Country	Population
Tōkyō	Japan	35 467 000
Mexico City	Mexico	20 688 000
Mumbai	India	20 036 000
São Paulo	Brazil	19 582 000
New York	USA	19 388 000
Delhi	India	16 983 000
Shanghai	China	15 790 000
Kolkata	India	15 548 000
Jakarta	Indonesia	15 206 000
Dhaka	Bangladesh	14 625 000
Lagos	Nigeria	13 717 000
Karachi	Pakistan	13 252 000
Buenos Aires	Argentina	13 067 000
Los Angeles	USA	12 738 000
Rio de Janeiro	Brazil	12 170 000
Cairo	Egypt	12 041 000
Manila	Philippines	11 799 000
Beijing	China	11 741 000
Ōsaka	Japan	11 305 000
Moscow	Russian Federation	10 967 000
İstanbul	Turkey	10 546 000
Paris	France	9 856 000
Seoul	South Korea	9 554 000
Guangzhou	China	9 447 000
Chicago	USA	9 186 000

Internet Links

United Nations Population Division	www.un.org/esa/population/unpop.htm
United Nations World Urbanization Prospects	esa.un.org/unup/index.asp
United Nations Population Information Network	www.un.org/popin
The World Bank - Urban Development	www.worldbank.org/urban
City Population	www.citypopulation.de

World
Communications

Increased availability and ownership of telecommunications equipment since the beginning of the 1970s has aided the globalization of the world economy. Over half of the world's fixed telephone lines have been installed since the mid-1980s and the majority of the world's Internet hosts have come on line since 1997. There are now over one billion fixed telephone lines in the world. The number of mobile cellular subscribers has grown dramatically from sixteen million in 1991 to well over one billion today.

The Internet is the fastest growing communications network of all time. It is relatively cheap and now links over 140 million host computers globally. Its growth has resulted in the emergence of hundreds of Internet Service Providers (ISPs) and Internet traffic is now doubling every six months. In 1993 the number of Internet users was estimated to be just under ten million, there are now over half a billion.

Facts

- The first transatlantic telegraph cable came into operation in 1858
- Fibre-optic cables can now carry approximately 20 million simultaneous telephone calls
- The internet is the fastest growing communications network of all time and now has over 267 million host computers
- Bermuda has the world's highest density of internet and broadband subscribers
- Sputnik, the world's first artificial satellite, was launched in 1957

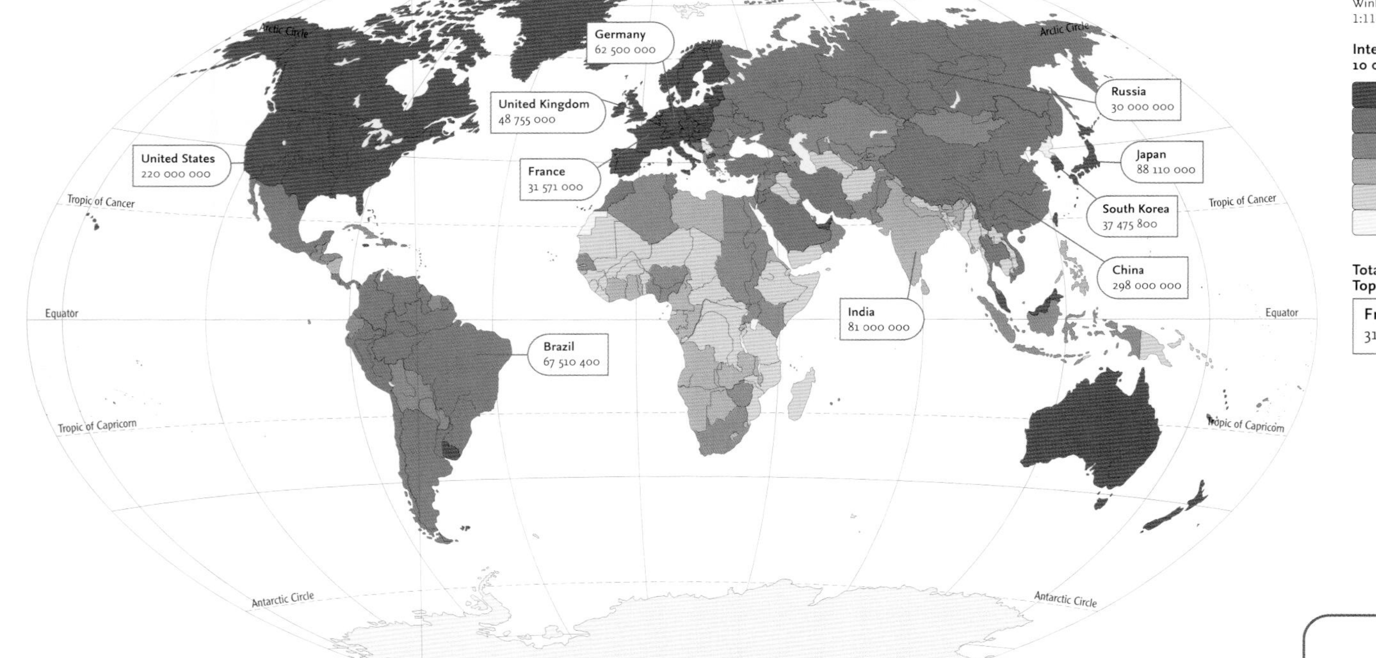

Arctic Circle
Germany
62 500 000
United Kingdom
48 755 000
United States
220 000 000
France
31 571 000
Russia
30 000 000
Japan
88 110 000
South Korea
37 475 800
China
298 000 000
India
81 000 000
Brazil
67 510 400
Tropic of Cancer
Equator
Tropic of Capricorn
Antarctic Circle

Internet Users 2008

Winkel Tripel Projection
1:116 200 000

Internet users per 10 000 inhabitants 2008

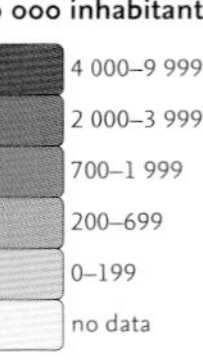

4 000–9 999
2 000–3 999
700–1 999
200–699
0–199
no data

Total internet users 2008
Top ten countries

France
31 571 000

The Internet

The Internet is a global network of millions of computers around the world, all capable of being connected to each other. Internet Service Providers (ISPs) provide access via 'host' computers, of which there are now over 267 million. It has become a vital means of communication and data transfer for businesses, governments and financial and academic institutions, with a steadily increasing proportion of business transactions being carried out on-line. Personal use of the Internet – particularly for access to the World Wide Web information network, and for e-mail communication – has increased enormously and there are now estimated to be over half a billion users worldwide.

Top Broadband Economies 2008

Countries with the highest broadband penetration rate – subscribers per 100 inhabitants

	Top Economies	Rate
1	Sweden	37.3
2	Denmark	36.8
3	Netherlands	35.0
4	Norway	34.0
5	Switzerland	33.0
6	Iceland	32.9
7	South Korea	32.0
8	Finland	30.6
9	Luxembourg	30.3
10	Canada	29.0
11	France	28.6
12	United Kingdom	28.3
13	Belgium	28.3
14	Germany	27.4
15	Hong Kong, China	26.8
16	USA	25.6
17	Macao, China	25.1
18	Australia	24.5
19	Malta	24.2
20	Estonia	23.9

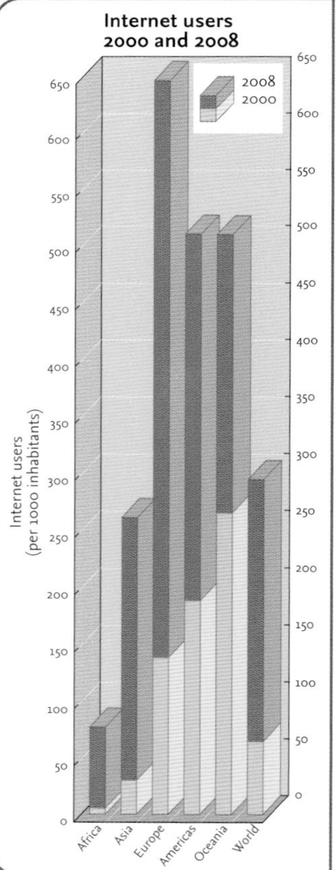

Internet users
2000 and 2008
2008
2000
Internet users
(per 1000 inhabitants)
650
600
550
500
450
400
350
300
250
200
150
100
50
0
Africa
Asia
Europe
Americas
Oceania
World

Internet Links

OECD Organisation for Economic Co-operation and Development	www.oecd.org
TeleGeography	www.telegeography.com
International Telecommunication Union	www.itu.int

Satellite communications

International telecommunications use either fibre-optic cables or satellites as transmission media. Although cables carry the vast majority of traffic around the world, communications satellites are important for person-to-person communication, including cellular telephones, and for broadcasting. The positions of communications satellites are critical to their use, and reflect the demand for such communications in each part of the world. Such satellites are placed in 'geostationary' orbit 36 000 km above the equator. This means that they move at the same speed as the Earth and remain fixed above a single point on the Earth's surface.

Mobile phone subscribers and communications satellites

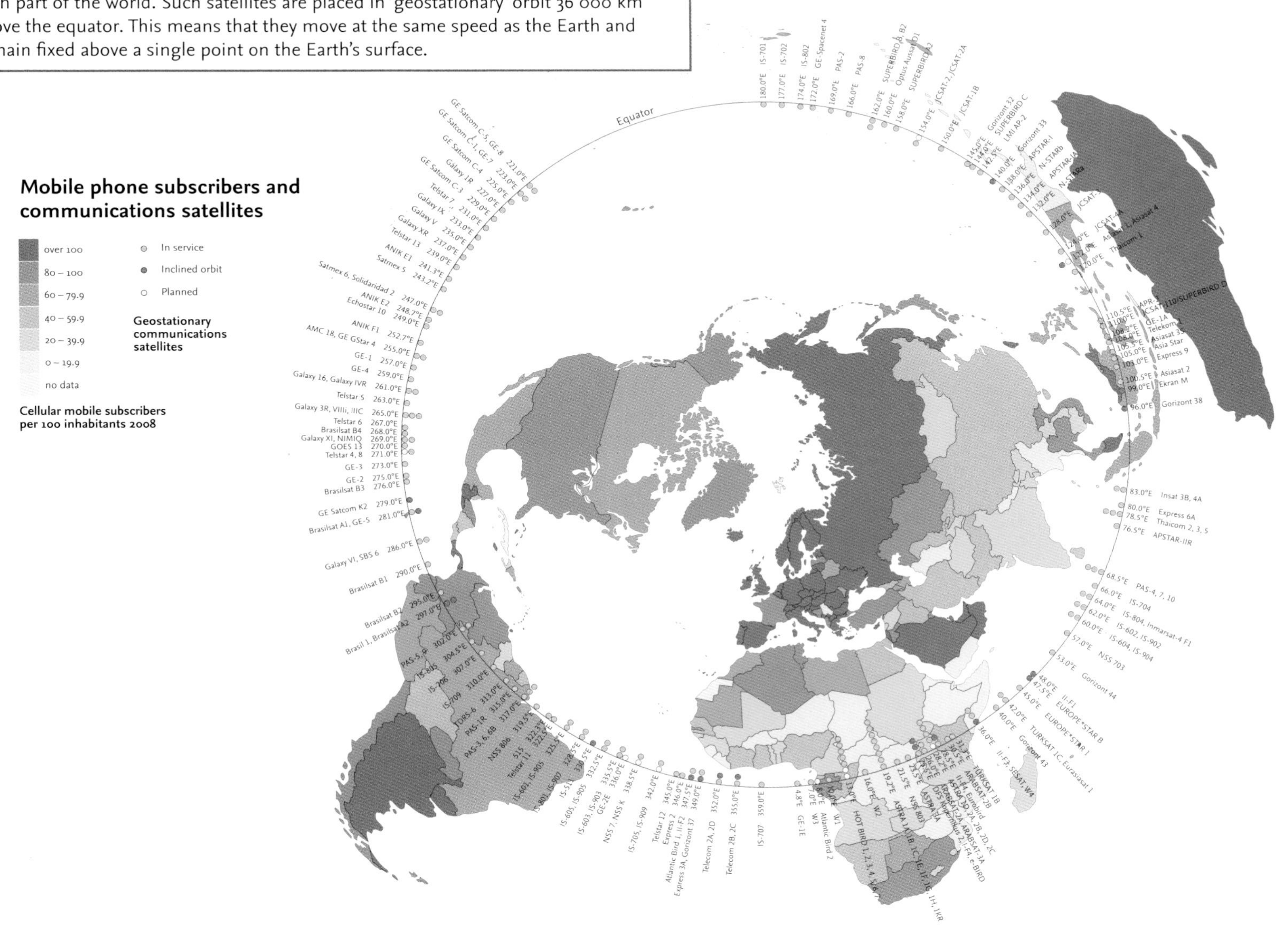

over 100
80 – 100
60 – 79.9
40 – 59.9
20 – 39.9
0 – 19.9
no data
Cellular mobile subscribers per 100 inhabitants 2008
In service
Inclined orbit
Planned
Geostationary communications satellites
Equator

International telecommunications traffic

Winkel Tripel Projection
1:116 000 000

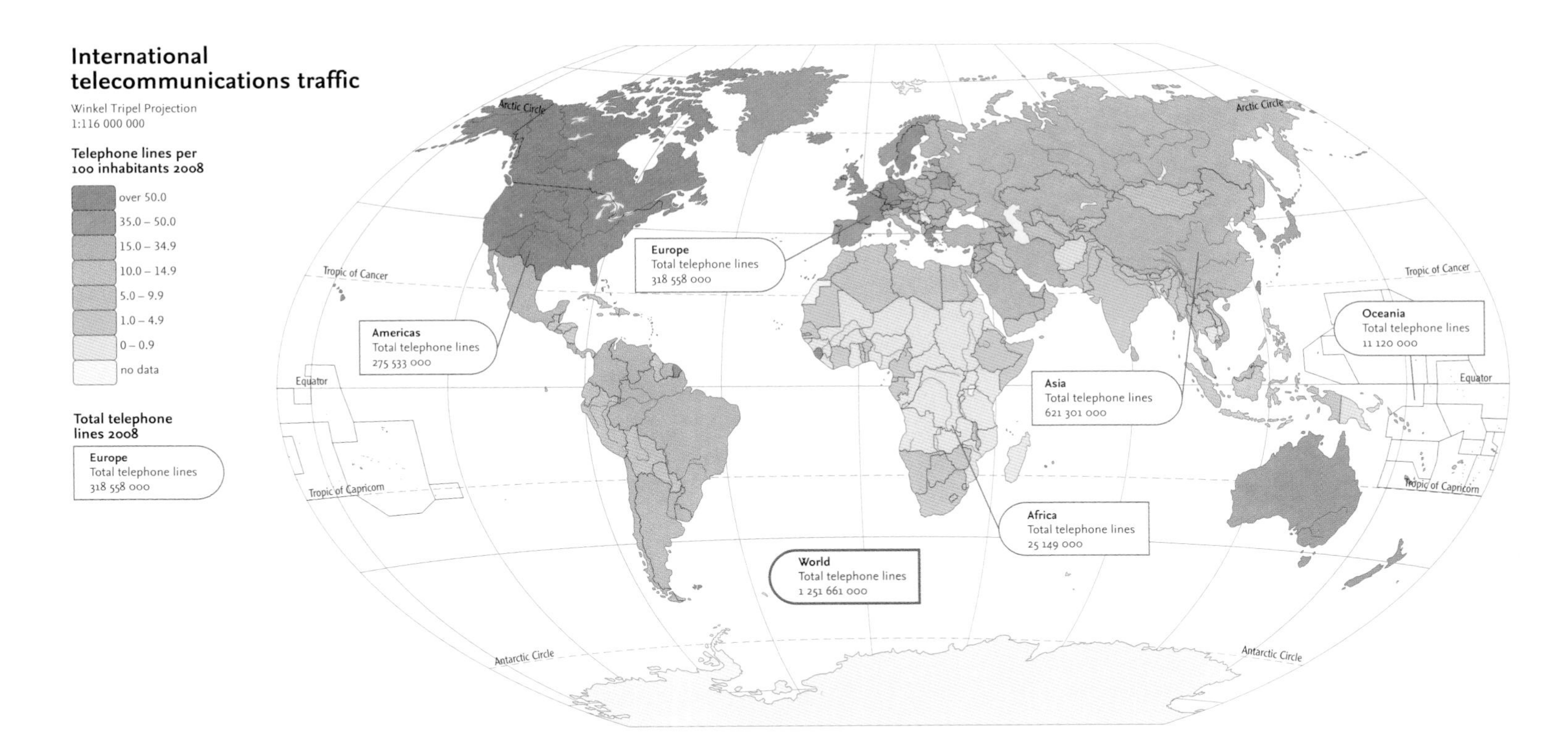

Telephone lines per 100 inhabitants 2008
over 50.0
35.0 – 50.0
15.0 – 34.9
10.0 – 14.9
5.0 – 9.9
1.0 – 4.9
0 – 0.9
no data
Total telephone lines 2008
Europe
Total telephone lines
318 558 000
Arctic Circle
Tropic of Cancer
Equator
Tropic of Capricorn
Antarctic Circle
Europe
Total telephone lines
318 558 000
Americas
Total telephone lines
275 533 000
Asia
Total telephone lines
621 301 000
Oceania
Total telephone lines
11 120 000
Africa
Total telephone lines
25 149 000
World
Total telephone lines
1 251 661 000

World
Social Indicators

Countries are often judged on their level of economic development, but national and personal wealth are not the only measures of a country's status. Numerous other indicators can give a better picture of the overall level of development and standard of living achieved by a country. The availability and standard of health services, levels of educational provision and attainment, levels of nutrition, water supply, life expectancy and mortality rates are just some of the factors which can be measured to assess and compare countries.

While nations strive to improve their economies, and hopefully also to improve the standard of living of their citizens, the measurement of such indicators often exposes great discrepancies between the countries of the 'developed' world and those of the 'less developed' world. They also show great variations within continents and regions and at the same time can hide great inequalities within countries.

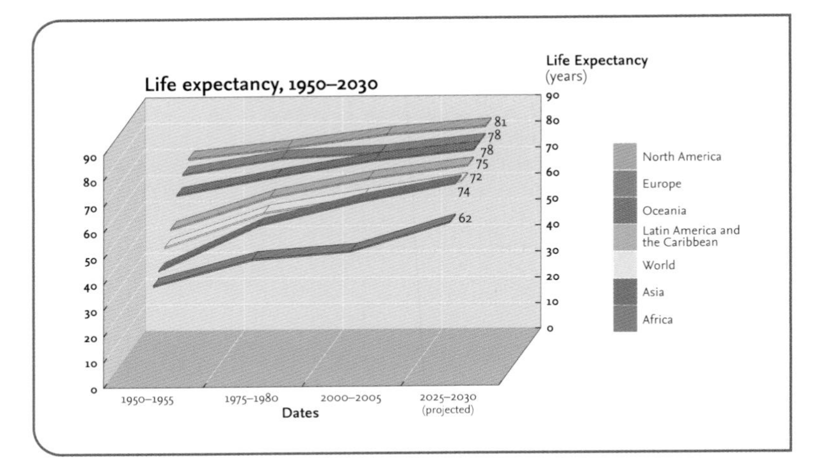

Life expectancy, 1950–2030
Life Expectancy (years)
North America
Europe
Oceania
Latin America and the Caribbean
World
Asia
Africa
81
78
78
75
72
74
62
1950–1955
1975–1980
2000–2005
2025–2030 (projected)
Dates

Under-five mortality rate, 2006 and life expectancy by continent, 2005–2010

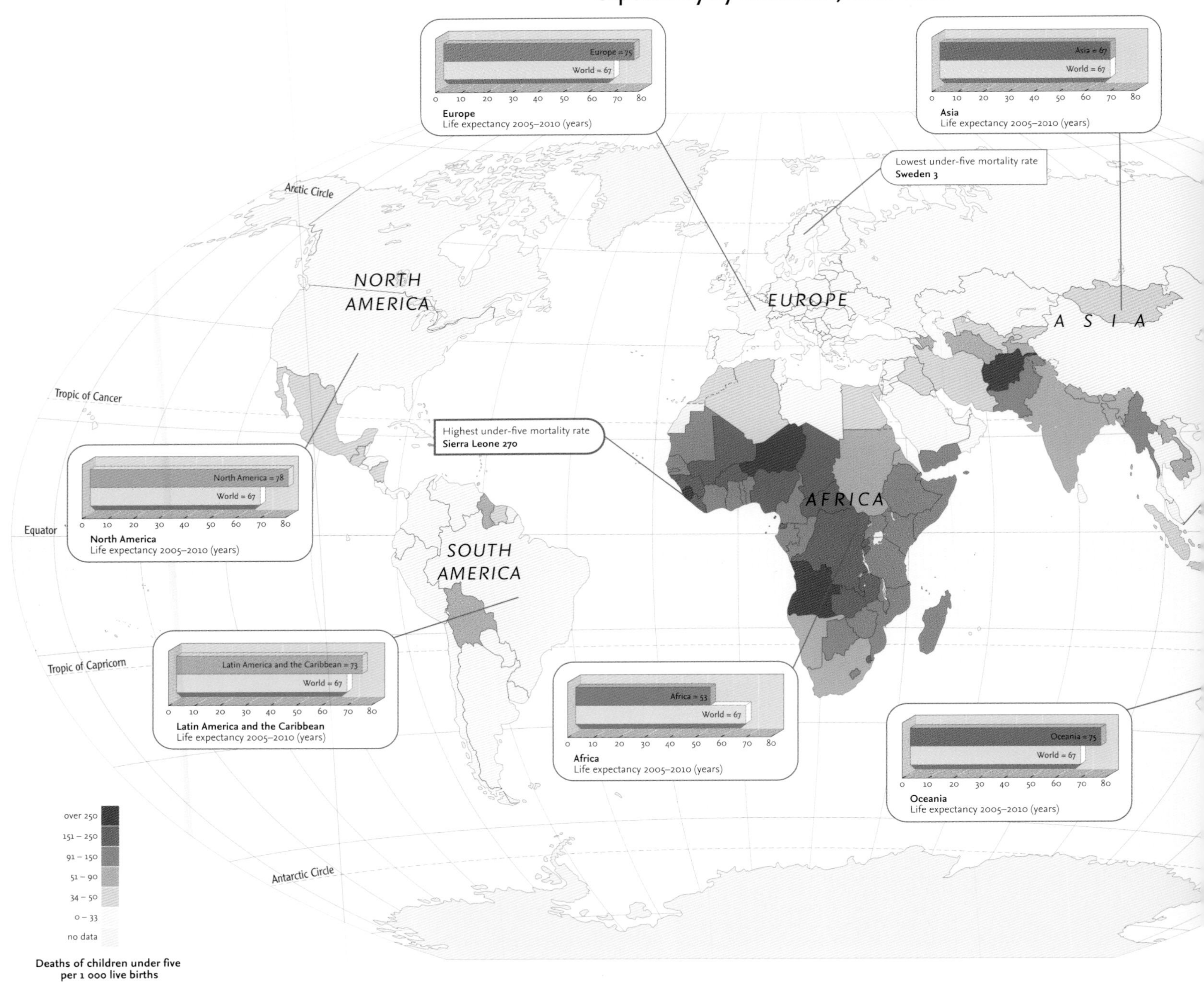

Europe = 75
World = 67
Europe
Life expectancy 2005–2010 (years)
Asia = 67
World = 67
Asia
Life expectancy 2005–2010 (years)
Lowest under-five mortality rate
Sweden 3
Highest under-five mortality rate
Sierra Leone 270
North America = 78
World = 67
North America
Life expectancy 2005–2010 (years)
Latin America and the Caribbean = 73
World = 67
Latin America and the Caribbean
Life expectancy 2005–2010 (years)
Africa = 53
World = 67
Africa
Life expectancy 2005–2010 (years)
Oceania = 75
World = 67
Oceania
Life expectancy 2005–2010 (years)
Arctic Circle
Tropic of Cancer
Equator
Tropic of Capricorn
Antarctic Circle
NORTH AMERICA
SOUTH AMERICA
EUROPE
AFRICA
ASIA
over 250
151 – 250
91 – 150
51 – 90
34 – 50
0 – 33
no data
Deaths of children under five per 1 000 live births

Facts

- Of the 11 countries with under-5 mortality rates of more than 200 per 1000 live births, 10 are in Africa
- Many western countries believe they have achieved satisfactory levels of education and no longer closely monitor levels of literacy
- Children born in Nepal have only a 12% chance of their birth being attended by trained health personnel; for most European countries the figure is 100%
- The illiteracy rate among young women in the Middle East and north Africa is almost twice the rate for young men

Health and education

Perhaps the most important indicators used for measuring the level of national development are those relating to health and education. Both of these key areas are vital to the future development of a country, and if there are concerns in standards attained in either (or worse, in both) of these, then they may indicate fundamental problems within the country concerned. The ability to read and write (literacy) is seen as vital in educating people and encouraging development, while easy access to appropriate health services and specialists is an important requirement in maintaining satisfactory levels of basic health.

Literacy rate

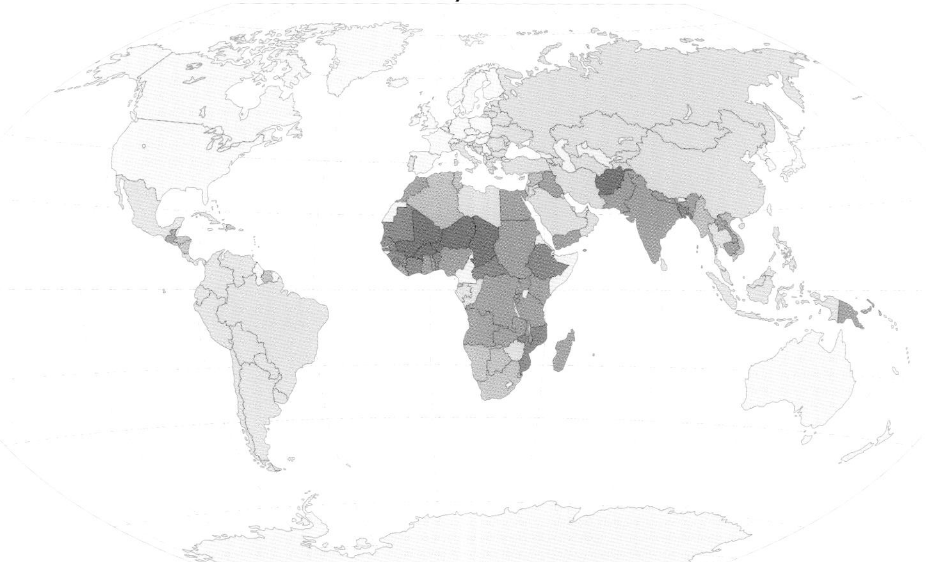

Percentage of population aged 15-24 with at least a basic ability to read and write

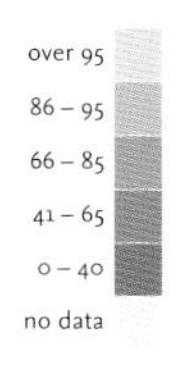
over 95
86 – 95
66 – 85
41 – 65
0 – 40
no data

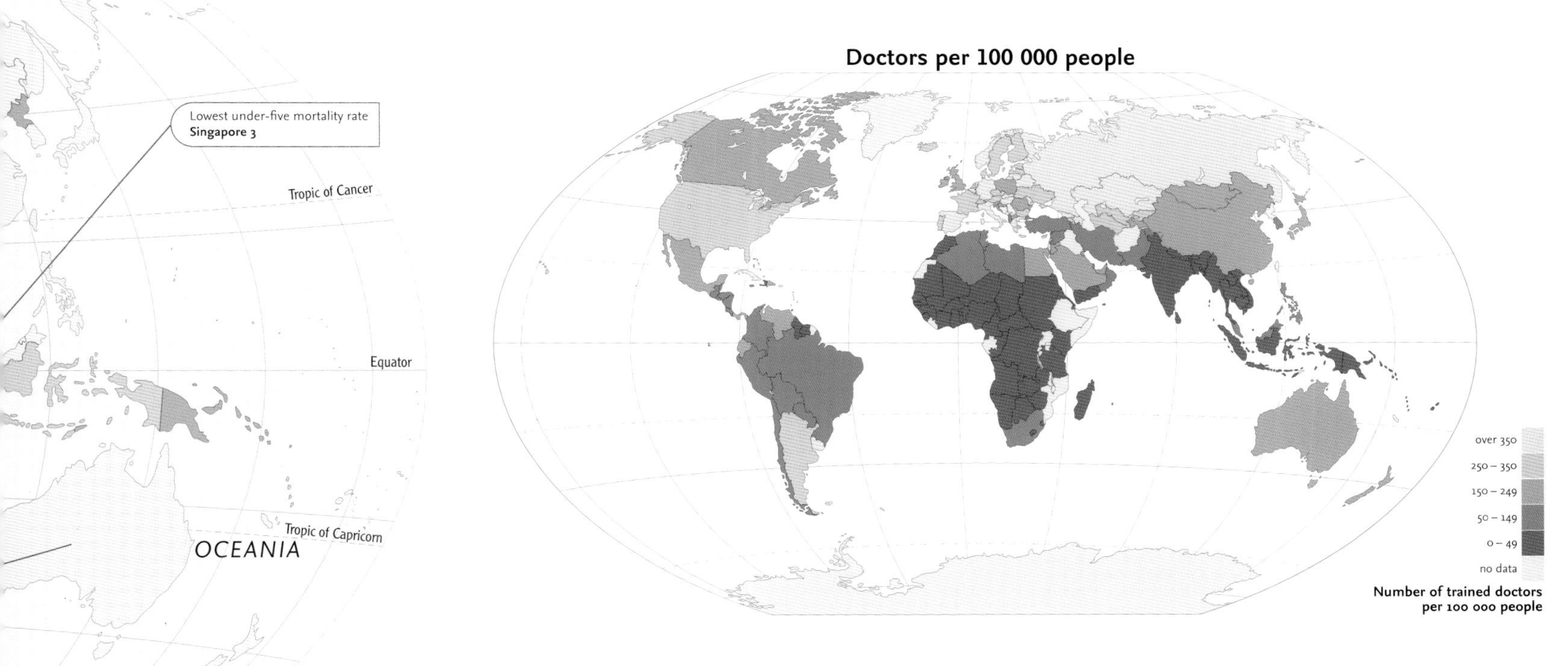
Arctic Circle
Lowest under-five mortality rate
Singapore 3
Tropic of Cancer
Equator
Tropic of Capricorn
OCEANIA
Doctors per 100 000 people
over 350
250 – 350
150 – 249
50 – 149
0 – 49
no data
Number of trained doctors per 100 000 people

Antarctic Circle

UN Millennium Development Goals From the Millennium Declaration, 2000	
Goal 1	Eradicate extreme poverty and hunger
Goal 2	Achieve universal primary education
Goal 3	Promote gender equality and empower women
Goal 4	Reduce child mortality
Goal 5	Improve maternal health
Goal 6	Combat HIV/AIDS, malaria and other diseases
Goal 7	Ensure environmental sustainability
Goal 8	Develop a global partnership for development

Internet Links

United Nations Development Programme	**www.undp.org**
World Health Organization	**www.who.int**
United Nations Statistics Division	**unstats.un.org**
United Nations Millennium Development Goals Indicators	**www.un.org/millenniumgoals**

World
Economy and Wealth

The globalization of the economy is making the world appear a smaller place. However, this shrinkage is an uneven process. Countries are being included in and excluded from the global economy to differing degrees. The wealthy countries of the developed world, with their market-led economies, access to productive new technologies and international markets, dominate the world economic system. Great inequalities exist between and within countries. There may also be discrepancies between social groups within countries due to gender and ethnic divisions. Differences between countries are evident by looking at overall wealth on a national and individual level.

Facts

- The City, one of 33 London boroughs, is the world's largest financial centre and contains Europe's biggest stock market
- Half the world's population earns only 5% of the world's wealth
- During the second half of the 20th century rich countries gave over US$1 trillion in aid
- For every £1 in grant aid to developing countries, more than £13 comes back in debt repayments
- On average, The World Bank distributes US$30 billion each year between 100 countries

Personal wealth

A poverty line set at $1 a day has been accepted as the working definition of extreme poverty in low-income countries. It is estimated that a total of 1.2 billion people live below that poverty line. This indicator has also been adopted by the United Nations in relation to their Millennium Development Goals. The United Nations goal is to halve the proportion of people living on less than $1 a day in 1990 to 14.5 per cent by 2015. Today, over 80 per cent of the total population of Ethiopia, Uganda and Nicaragua live on less than this amount.

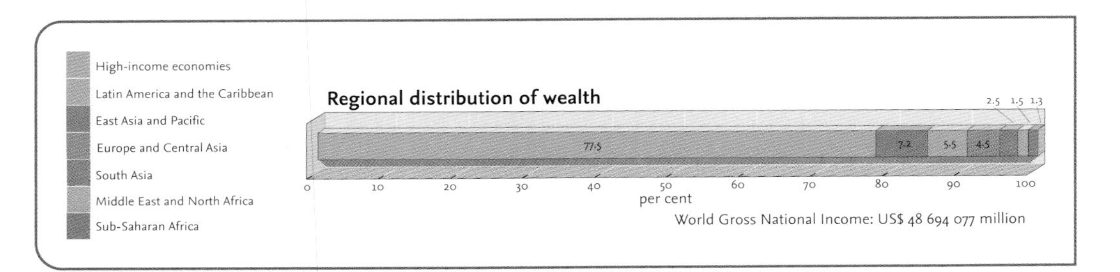

High-income economies
Latin America and the Caribbean
East Asia and Pacific
Europe and Central Asia
South Asia
Middle East and North Africa
Sub-Saharan Africa
Regional distribution of wealth
77.5
7.2
5.5
4.5
2.5
1.5
1.3
0
10
20
30
40
50
60
70
80
90
100
per cent
World Gross National Income: US$ 48 694 077 million

Percentage of population living on less than $1 a day

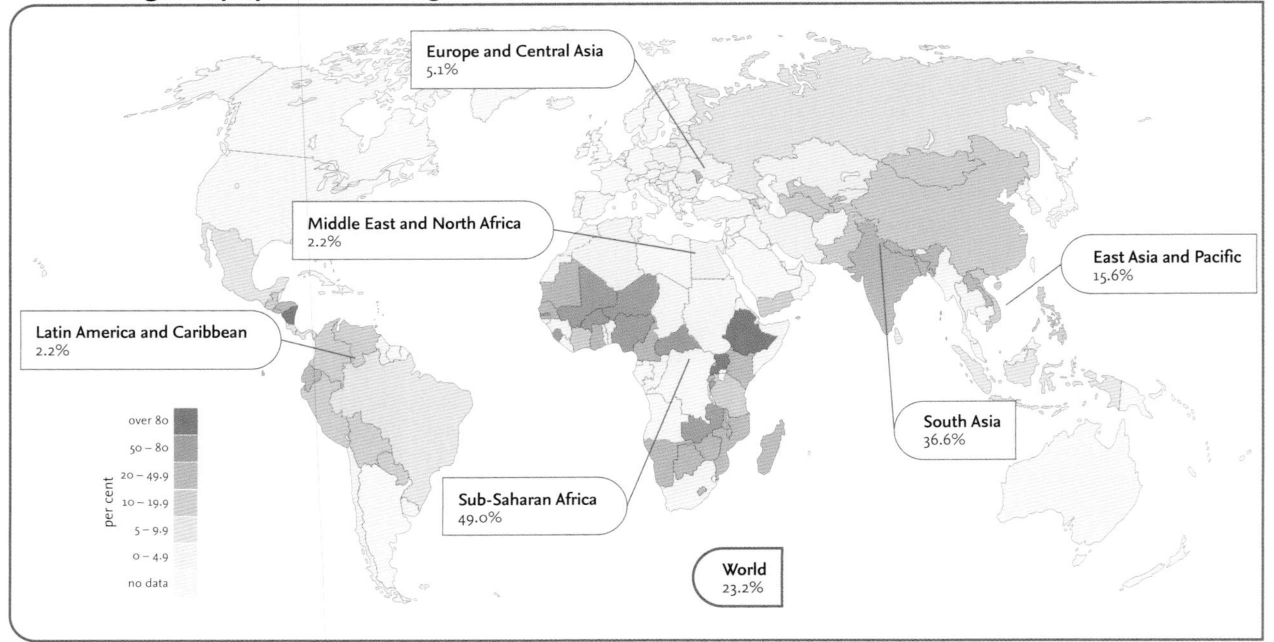

Europe and Central Asia
5.1%
Middle East and North Africa
2.2%
East Asia and Pacific
15.6%
Latin America and Caribbean
2.2%
South Asia
36.6%
Sub-Saharan Africa
49.0%
World
23.2%
per cent
over 80
50 – 80
20 – 49.9
10 – 19.9
5 – 9.9
0 – 4.9
no data

Tropic of Cancer
Equator
KIRIBATI
Tropic of Capricorn

The world's biggest companies, 2009		
Rank	Name	Sales (US$ billions)
1	Royal Dutch/Shell Group	458.36
2	ExxonMobil	425.70
3	Wal-Mart Stores	405.61
4	BP	361.14
5	Toyota Motor	263.42
6	Chevron	255.11
7	ConocoPhillips	225.42
8	Total	223.15
9	ING Group	213.99
10	General Electric	182.52

Rural village, **Malawi** – most of the world's poorest countries are in Africa.

Gross National Income per capita

Highest Gross National Income per capita
Luxembourg US$ 71 240

Highest Gross National Income
United States US$ 13 386 875 million

Lowest Gross National Income
São Tomé and Príncipe US$ 124 million

Lowest Gross National Income per capita
Burundi US$ 100

US$
28 001 – 72 000
16 001 – 28 000
9 001 – 16 000
1 751 – 9 000
751 – 1 750
0 – 750
no data

A.	ANDORRA	LEB.	LEBANON
AL.	ALBANIA	LITH.	LITHUANIA
ARM.	ARMENIA	M.	MACEDONIA
AUST.	AUSTRIA	MO.	MONTENEGRO
AZER.	AZERBAIJAN	MOL.	MOLDOVA
B.	BURUNDI	NETH.	NETHERLANDS
BEL.	BELGIUM	R.	RWANDA
B.H.	BOSNIA-HERZEGOVINA	R.F.	RUSSIAN FEDERATION
BULG.	BULGARIA	ROM.	ROMANIA
CR.	CROATIA	S.	SERBIA
CZ.R.	CZECH REPUBLIC	SL.	SLOVENIA
EST.	ESTONIA	SLA.	SLOVAKIA
GEOR.	GEORGIA	SUR.	SURINAME
HUN.	HUNGARY	SW.	SWITZERLAND
ISR.	ISRAEL	TAJIK.	TAJIKISTAN
JOR.	JORDAN	TURKM.	TURKMENISTAN
K.	KOSOVO	U.A.E.	UNITED ARAB EMIRATES
L.	LUXEMBOURG	U.S.A.	UNITED STATES OF AMERICA
LAT.	LATVIA	UZBEK.	UZBEKISTAN

Measuring wealth

One of the indicators used to determine a country's wealth is its Gross National Income (GNI). This gives a broad measure of an economy's performance. This is the value of the final output of goods and services produced by a country plus net income from non-resident sources. The total GNI is divided by the country's population to give an average figure of the GNI per capita. From this it is evident that the developed countries dominate the world economy with the United States having the highest GNI. China is a growing world economic player with the fourth highest GNI figure and a relatively high GNI per capita (US$2 000) in proportion to its huge population.

Internet Links

United Nations Statistics Division	unstats.un.org
The World Bank	www.worldbank.org
International Monetary Fund	www.imf.org
OECD Organisation for Economic Co-operation and Development	www.oecd.org

Gross National Income per capita		
Highest		
Rank	Country	US$
1	Luxembourg	71 240
2	Norway	68 440
3	Switzerland	58 050
4	Denmark	52 110
5	Iceland	49 960
6	San Marino	45 130
7	Ireland	44 830
8	United States	44 710
9	Sweden	43 530
10	Netherlands	43 050
Lowest		
Rank	Country	US$
156	Niger	270
157	Rwanda	250
158	Sierra Leone	240
159	Malawi	230
160=	Eritrea	190
160=	Guinea-Bissau	190
161	Ethiopia	170
162=	Dem. Rep. Congo	130
162=	Liberia	130
163	Burundi	100

World
Conflict

Geo-political issues shape the countries of the world and the current political situation in many parts of the world reflects a long history of armed conflict. Since the Second World War conflicts have been fairly localized, but there are numerous 'flash points' where factors such as territorial claims, ideology, religion, ethnicity and access to resources can cause friction between two or more countries. Such factors also lie behind the recent growth in global terrorism.

Military expenditure can take up a disproportionate amount of a country's wealth – Eritrea, with a Gross National Income (GNI) per capita of only US$190 spends twenty-four per cent of its total GDP on military activity. There is an encouraging trend towards wider international cooperation, mainly through the United Nations (UN) and the North Atlantic Treaty Organization (NATO), to prevent escalation of conflicts and on peacekeeping missions.

Military spending, 2006 and conflicts, 1946–2003

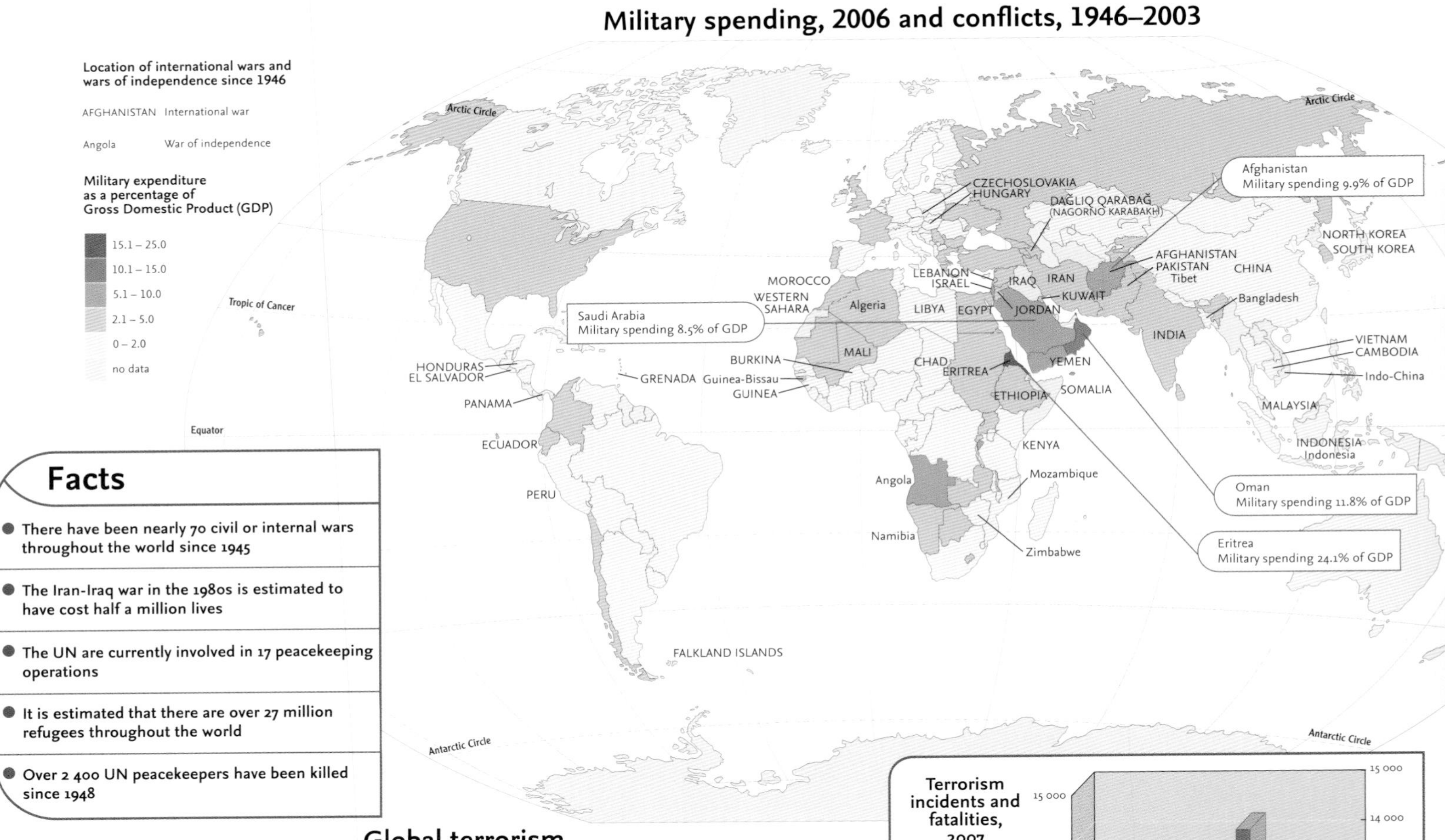

Location of international wars and wars of independence since 1946
AFGHANISTAN International war
Angola War of independence
Military expenditure as a percentage of Gross Domestic Product (GDP)
15.1 – 25.0
10.1 – 15.0
5.1 – 10.0
2.1 – 5.0
0 – 2.0
no data
Arctic Circle
Tropic of Cancer
Equator
Antarctic Circle
Afghanistan Military spending 9.9% of GDP
Saudi Arabia Military spending 8.5% of GDP
Oman Military spending 11.8% of GDP
Eritrea Military spending 24.1% of GDP
CZECHOSLOVAKIA
HUNGARY
DAGLIQ QARABAG (NAGORNO KARABAKH)
NORTH KOREA
SOUTH KOREA
AFGHANISTAN
PAKISTAN
Tibet
CHINA
LEBANON
ISRAEL
IRAQ
IRAN
KUWAIT
JORDAN
EGYPT
LIBYA
MOROCCO
WESTERN SAHARA
Algeria
Bangladesh
INDIA
MALI
CHAD
ERITREA
YEMEN
BURKINA
GRENADA
Guinea-Bissau
GUINEA
HONDURAS
EL SALVADOR
PANAMA
ECUADOR
PERU
ETHIOPIA
SOMALIA
KENYA
VIETNAM
CAMBODIA
Indo-China
MALAYSIA
INDONESIA
Indonesia
Angola
Mozambique
Namibia
Zimbabwe
FALKLAND ISLANDS

Facts

- There have been nearly 70 civil or internal wars throughout the world since 1945
- The Iran-Iraq war in the 1980s is estimated to have cost half a million lives
- The UN are currently involved in 17 peacekeeping operations
- It is estimated that there are over 27 million refugees throughout the world
- Over 2 400 UN peacekeepers have been killed since 1948

Global terrorism

Terrorism is defined by the United Nations as "All criminal acts directed against a State and intended or calculated to create a state of terror in the minds of particular persons or a group of persons or the general public". The world has become increasingly concerned about terrorism and the possibility that terrorists could acquire and use nuclear, chemical and biological weapons. One common form of terrorist attack is suicide bombing. Pioneered by Tamil secessionists in Sri Lanka, it has been widely used by Palestinian groups fighting against Israeli occupation of the West Bank and Gaza. In recent years it has also been used by the Al Qaida network in its attacks on the western world.

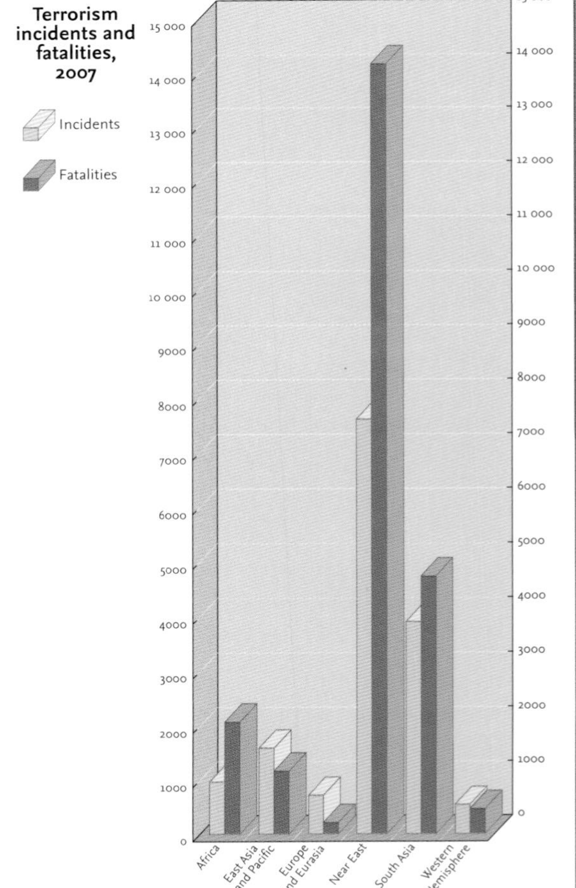

Terrorism incidents and fatalities, 2007
Incidents
Fatalities
0
1000
2000
3000
4000
5000
6000
7000
8000
9000
10 000
11 000
12 000
13 000
14 000
15 000
Africa
East Asia and Pacific
Europe and Eurasia
Near East
South Asia
Western Hemisphere

Internet Links

United Nations Peace and Security	www.un.org/peace
United Nations Refugee Agency	www.unhcr.org
NATO	www.nato.int
BBC News	news.bbc.co.uk
International Boundaries Research Unit	www.dur.ac.uk/ibru
International Peace Research Institute	www.prio.no

United Nations peacekeeping

United Nations peacekeeping was developed by the Organization as a way to help countries torn by conflict create the conditions for lasting peace. The first UN peacekeeping mission was established in 1948, when the Security Council authorized the deployment of UN military observers to the Middle East to monitor the Armistice Agreement between Israel and its Arab neighbours. Since then, there have been a total of 63 UN peacekeeping operations around the world.

UN peacekeeping goals were primarily limited to maintaining ceasefires and stabilizing situations on the ground, so that efforts could be made at the political level to resolve the conflict by peaceful means. Today's peacekeepers undertake a wide variety of complex tasks, from helping to build sustainable institutions of governance, to human rights monitoring, to security sector reform, to the disarmament, demobilization and reintegration of former combatants.

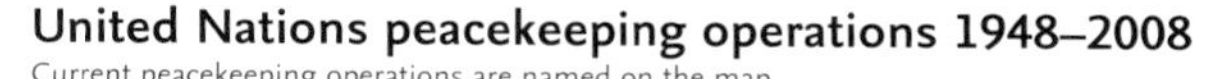

United Nations peacekeeping operations 1948–2008

Current peacekeeping operations are named on the map

KOSOVO
GEORGIA
CYPRUS
LEBANON
INDIA/PAKISTAN
WESTERN SAHARA
MIDDLE EAST
HAITI
DARFUR
SUDAN
LIBERIA
CÔTE D'IVOIRE
CENTRAL AFRICAN REPUBLIC/CHAD
CONGO
ETHIOPIA/ERITREA
EAST TIMOR
Tropic of Cancer
Equator
Tropic of Capricorn

Refugees from **Darfur** in Iridmi refugee camp, Sudan.

Major terrorist incidents

Date	Location	Summary	Killed	Injured
December 1988	Lockerbie, Scotland	Airline bombing	270	5
March 1995	Tōkyō, Japan	Sarin gas attack on subway	12	5 510
April 1995	Oklahoma City, USA	Bomb in the Federal building	168	over 800
August 1998	Nairobi, Kenya and Dar es Salaam, Tanzania	US Embassy bombings	225	over 4 000
August 1998	Omagh, Northern Ireland	Town centre bombing	29	220
September 2001	New York and Washington D.C., USA	Airline hijacking and crashing	3 018	over 6 200
October 2002	Bali, Indonesia	Car bomb outside nightclub	202	over 200
October 2002	Moscow, Russian Federation	Theatre siege	170	over 600
March 2004	Baghdad and Karbalā', Iraq	Suicide bombing of pilgrims	181	over 400
March 2004	Madrid, Spain	Train bombings	191	1 800
September 2004	Beslan, Russian Federation	School siege	385	over 700
July 2005	London, UK	Underground and bus bombings	56	700
July 2005	Sharm ash Shaykh, Egypt	Bombs at tourist sites	88	200
July 2006	Mumbai, India	Train bombings	209	700
August 2007	Qahtaniya, Iraq	Suicide bombing in town centres	796	over 1 500
September 2008	Islamabad, Pakistan	Car bomb at the Marriott Hotel	62	270
November 2008	Mumbai, India	Coordinated shootings at eight sites	183	over 300

Terrorist incidents

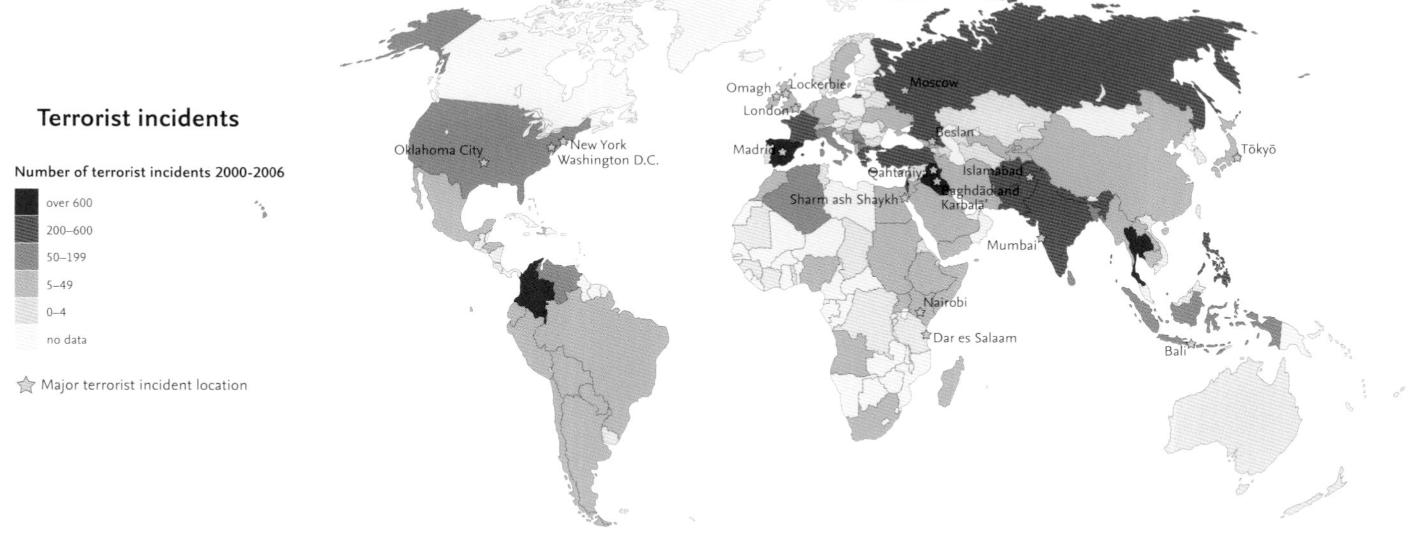
Number of terrorist incidents 2000-2006
over 600
200–600
50–199
5–49
0–4
no data
Major terrorist incident location
Oklahoma City
New York
Washington D.C.
Omagh
Lockerbie
London
Madrid
Moscow
Beslan
Qahtaniya
Islamabad
Sharm ash Shaykh
Baghdad and Karbalā'
Mumbai
Tōkyō
Nairobi
Dar es Salaam
Bali

With the process of globalization has come an increased awareness of, and direct interest in, issues which have global implications. Social issues can now affect large parts of the world and can impact on large sections of society. Perhaps the current issues of greatest concern are those of national security, including the problem of international terrorism, health, crime and natural resources. The three issues highlighted here reflect this and are of immediate concern.

The international drugs trade, and the crimes commonly associated with it, can impact on society and individuals in devastating ways; scarcity of water resources and lack of access to safe drinking water can have major economic implications and cause severe health problems; and the AIDS epidemic is having disastrous consequences in large parts of the world, particularly in sub-Saharan Africa.

The drugs trade

The international trade in illegal drugs is estimated to be worth over US$400 billion. While it may be a lucrative business for the criminals involved, the effects of the drugs on individual users and on society in general can be devastating. Patterns of drug production and abuse vary, but there are clear centres for the production of the most harmful drugs – the opiates (opium, morphine and heroin) and cocaine. The 'Golden Triangle' of Laos, Myanmar and Thailand, and western South America respectively are the main producing areas for these drugs. Significant efforts are expended to counter the drugs trade, and there have been signs recently of downward trends in the production of heroin and cocaine.

Soldiers in **Colombia**, a major producer of cocaine, destroy an illegal drug processing laboratory.

The international drugs trade

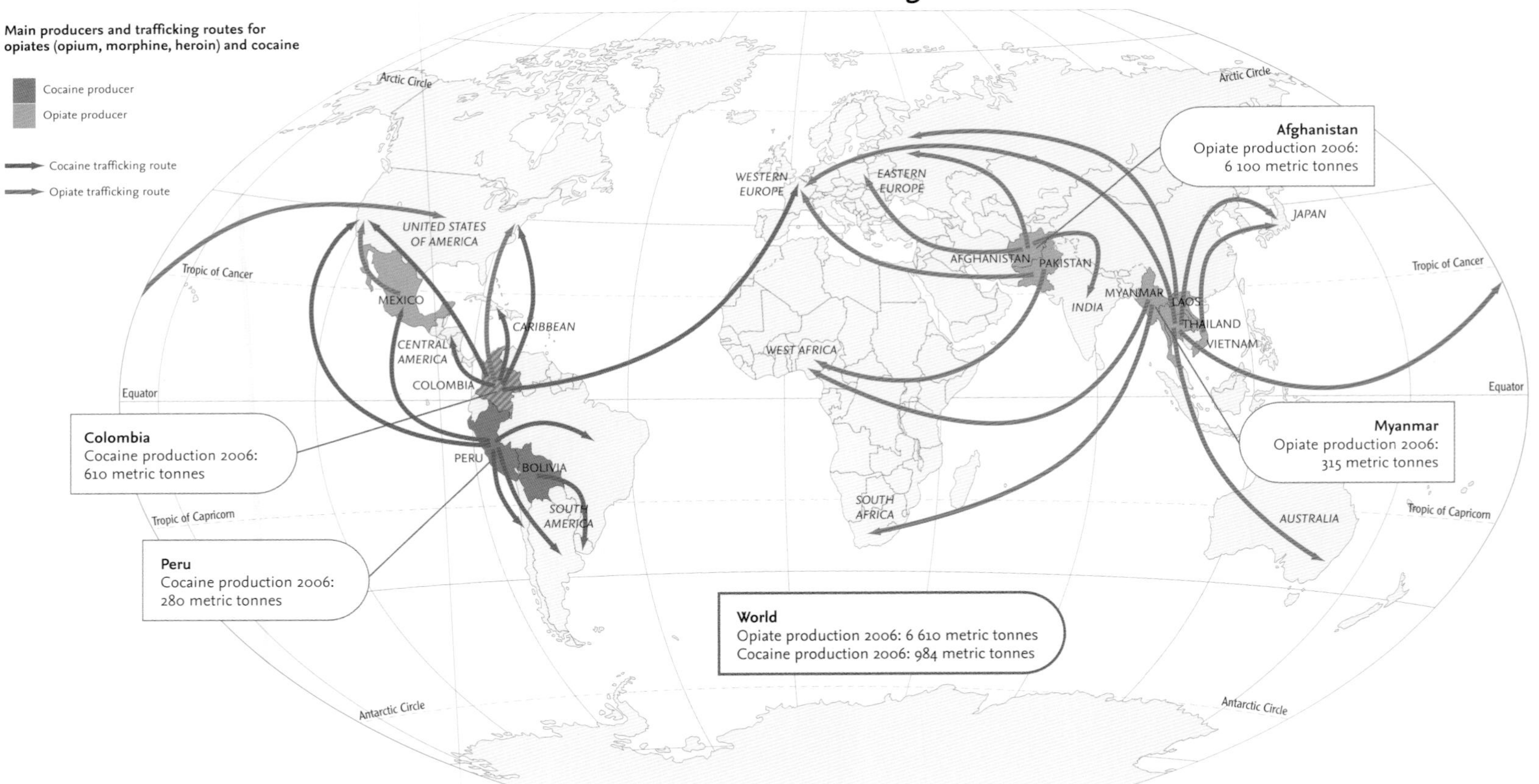

Main producers and trafficking routes for opiates (opium, morphine, heroin) and cocaine
Cocaine producer
Opiate producer
Cocaine trafficking route
Opiate trafficking route
Arctic Circle
Tropic of Cancer
Equator
Tropic of Capricorn
Antarctic Circle
UNITED STATES OF AMERICA
MEXICO
CARIBBEAN
CENTRAL AMERICA
COLOMBIA
PERU
BOLIVIA
SOUTH AMERICA
WESTERN EUROPE
EASTERN EUROPE
AFGHANISTAN
PAKISTAN
INDIA
MYANMAR
LAOS
THAILAND
VIETNAM
JAPAN
WEST AFRICA
SOUTH AFRICA
AUSTRALIA
Afghanistan
Opiate production 2006: 6 100 metric tonnes
Myanmar
Opiate production 2006: 315 metric tonnes
Colombia
Cocaine production 2006: 610 metric tonnes
Peru
Cocaine production 2006: 280 metric tonnes
World
Opiate production 2006: 6 610 metric tonnes
Cocaine production 2006: 984 metric tonnes

AIDS epidemic

With over 33 million people living with HIV/AIDS (Human Immunodeficiency Virus/Acquired Immune Deficiency Syndrome) and more than 20 million deaths from the disease, the AIDS epidemic poses one of the biggest threats to public health. The UNAIDS project estimated that 2.7 million people were newly infected in 2007 and that 2 million AIDS sufferers died. Estimates into the future look bleak, especially for poorer developing countries where an additional 45 million people are likely to become infected by 2010. The human cost is huge. As well as the death count itself, more than 11 million African children, half of whom are between the ages of 10 and 14, have been orphaned as a result of the disease.

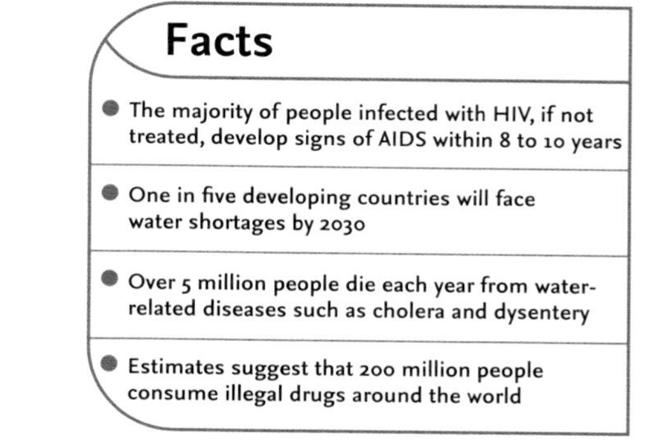

Facts

- The majority of people infected with HIV, if not treated, develop signs of AIDS within 8 to 10 years
- One in five developing countries will face water shortages by 2030
- Over 5 million people die each year from water-related diseases such as cholera and dysentery
- Estimates suggest that 200 million people consume illegal drugs around the world

Population living with HIV/AIDS, 2005

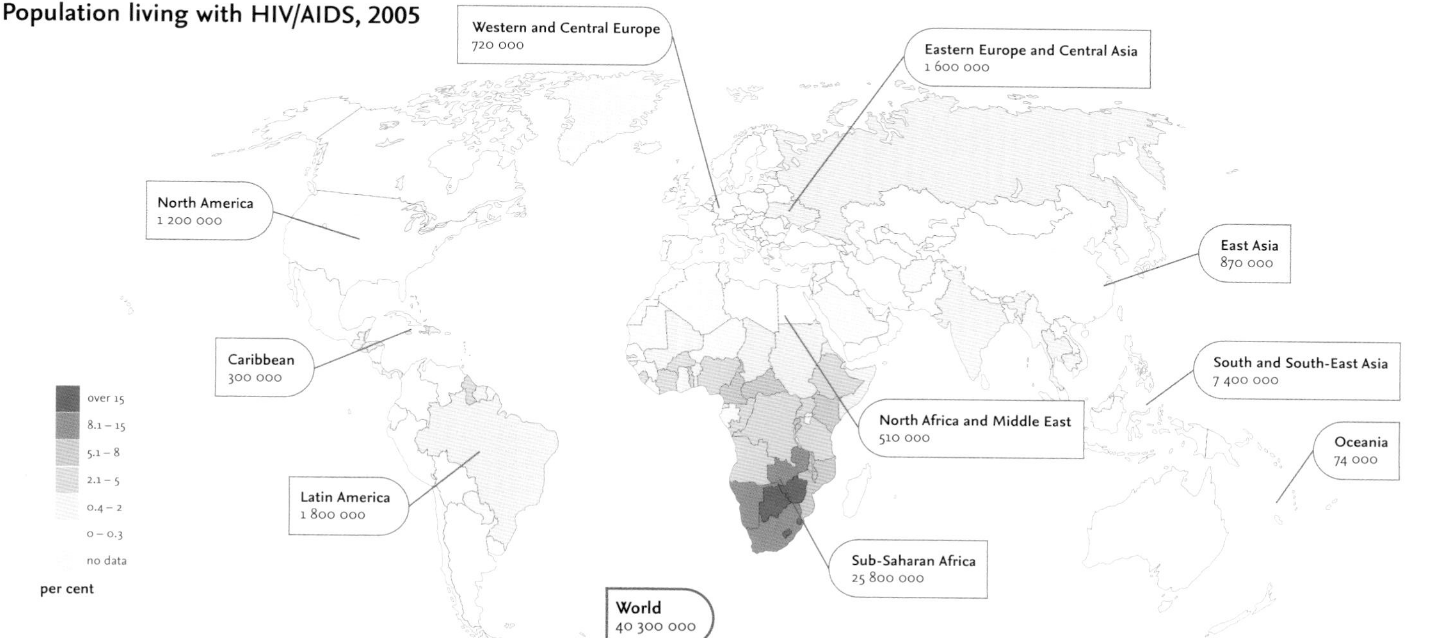
Western and Central Europe
720 000
Eastern Europe and Central Asia
1 600 000
North America
1 200 000
East Asia
870 000
Caribbean
300 000
South and South-East Asia
7 400 000
North Africa and Middle East
510 000
Oceania
74 000
Latin America
1 800 000
Sub-Saharan Africa
25 800 000
World
40 300 000
over 15
8.1 – 15
5.1 – 8
2.1 – 5
0.4 – 2
0 – 0.3
no data
per cent

Water resources

Water is one of the fundamental requirements of life, and yet in some countries it is becoming more scarce due to increasing population and climate change. Safe drinking water, basic hygiene, health education and sanitation facilities are often virtually nonexistent for impoverished people in developing countries throughout the world. WHO/UNICEF estimate that the combination of these conditions results in 6 000 deaths every day, most of these being children. Currently over 1.2 billion people drink untreated water and expose themselves to serious health risks, while political struggles over diminishing water resources are increasingly likely to be the cause of international conflict.

Domestic use of **untreated water** in Varanasi, India

Access to safe water, 2004

Percentage of population with access to improved drinking water

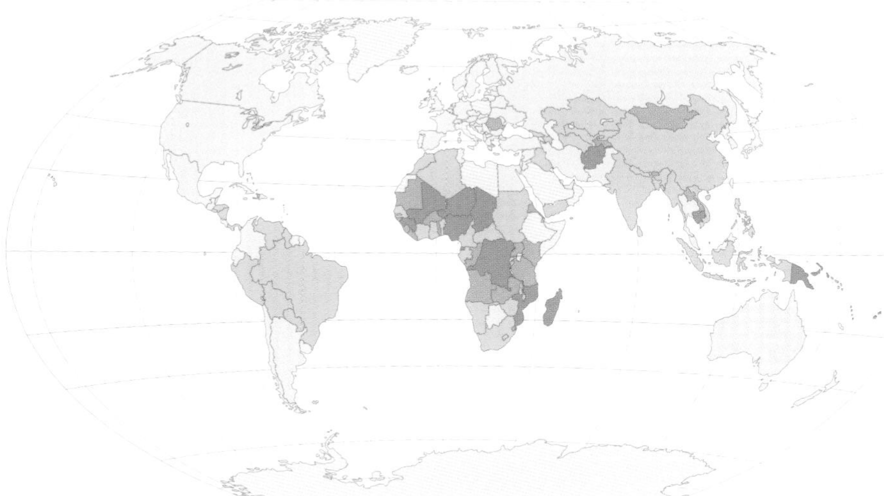
91 – 100
66 – 90
51 – 65
31 – 50
0 – 30
no data
per cent

Internet Links

UNESCO	**www.unesco.org**
UNAIDS	**www.unaids.org**
WaterAid	**www.wateraid.org.uk**
World Health Organization	**www.who.int**
UNODC United Nations Office on Drugs and Crime	**www.unodc.org**

World
Environmental Threats

The Earth has a rich and diverse environment which is under threat from both natural and man-induced forces. Forests and woodland form the predominant natural land cover with tropical rain forests – currently disappearing at alarming rates – believed to be home to the majority of animal and plant species. Grassland and scrub tend to have a lower natural species diversity but have suffered the most impact from man's intervention through conversion to agriculture, burning and the introduction of livestock. Wherever man interferes with existing biological and environmental processes degradation of that environment occurs to varying degrees. This interference also affects inland water and oceans where pollution, over-exploitation of marine resources and the need for fresh water has had major consequences on land and sea environments.

Facts

- The Sundarbans stretching across the Ganges delta is the largest area of mangrove forest in the world, covering 10 000 square kilometres (3 861 square miles) and forming an important ecological area, home to 260 species of birds, the Bengal tiger and other threatened species
- Over 90 000 square kilometres of precious tropical forest and wetland habitats are lost each year
- The surface level of the Dead Sea has fallen by more than 25 metres over the last 50 years
- Climate change and mismanagement of land areas can lead to soils becoming degraded and semi-arid grasslands becoming deserts – a process known as desertification

Environmental change

Whenever natural resources are exploited by man, the environment is changed. Approximately half the area of post-glacial forest has been cleared or degraded, and the amount of old-growth forest continues to decline. Desertification caused by climate change and the impact of man can turn semi-arid grasslands into arid desert. Regions bordering tropical deserts, such as the Sahel region south of the Sahara and regions around the Thar Desert in India, are most vulnerable to this process. Coral reefs are equally fragile environments, and many are under threat from coastal development, pollution and over-exploitation of marine resources.

Water resources in certain parts of the world are becoming increasingly scarce and competition for water is likely to become a common cause of conflict. The Aral Sea in central Asia was once the world's fourth largest lake but it now ranks only sixteenth after shrinking by almost 40 000 square kilometres. This shrinkage has been due to climatic change and to the diversion, for farming purposes, of the major rivers which feed the lake. The change has had a devastating effect on the local fishing industry and the exposure of chemicals on the lake bed has caused health problems for the local population.

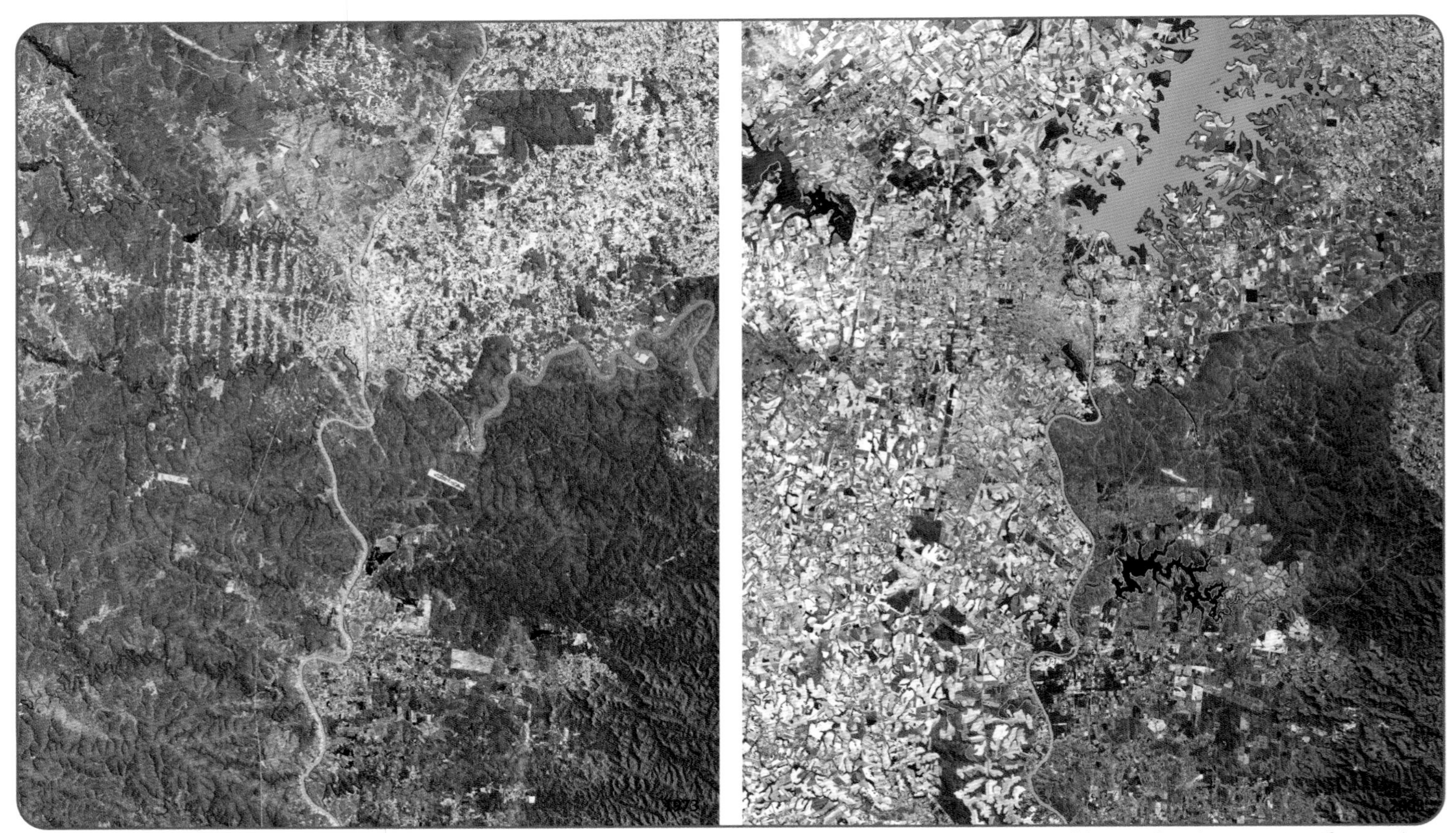

Deforestation and the creation of the **Itaipu Dam** on the Paraná river in Brazil have had a dramatic effect on the landscape and ecosystems of this part of South America. Some forest on the right of the images lies within Iguaçu National Park and has been protected from destruction.

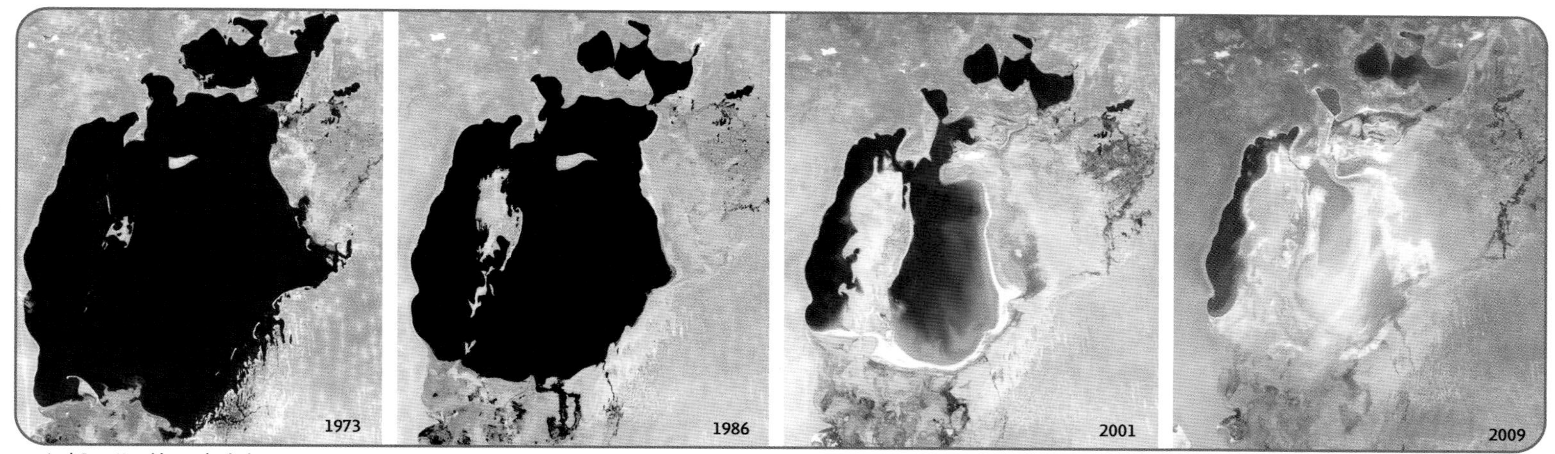
1973
1986
2001
2009

Aral Sea, Kazakhstan/Uzbekistan 1973-2009 Climate change and the diversion of rivers have caused its dramatic shrinkage.

Environmental Impacts

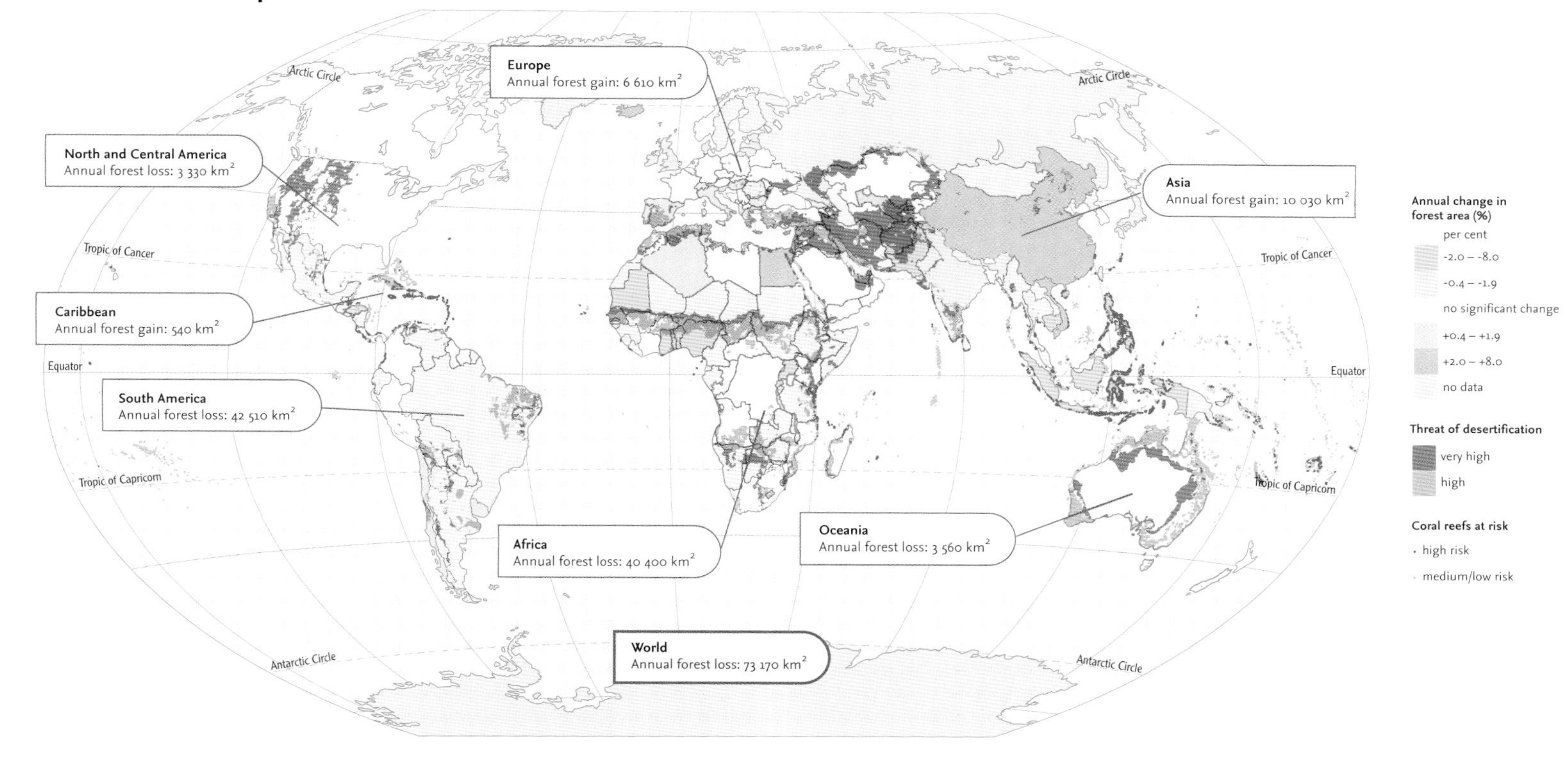
Arctic Circle
Tropic of Cancer
Equator
Tropic of Capricorn
Antarctic Circle
Europe
Annual forest gain: 6 610 km²
North and Central America
Annual forest loss: 3 330 km²
Asia
Annual forest gain: 10 030 km²
Caribbean
Annual forest gain: 540 km²
South America
Annual forest loss: 42 510 km²
Africa
Annual forest loss: 40 400 km²
Oceania
Annual forest loss: 3 560 km²
World
Annual forest loss: 73 170 km²
Annual change in forest area (%)
per cent
-2.0 – -8.0
-0.4 – -1.9
no significant change
+0.4 – +1.9
+2.0 – +8.0
no data
Threat of desertification
very high
high
Coral reefs at risk
high risk
medium/low risk

Internet links

United Nations Environment Programme (UNEP)	**www.unep.org**
IUCN International Union for Conservation of Nature	**www.iucn.org**
UNESCO World Heritage	**whc.unesco.org**

Environmental protection

Top 10 protected areas by size

Rank	Protected area	Country	Size (sq km)	Designation
1	**Northeast Greenland**	Greenland	972 000	National Park
2	**Rub' al-Khālī**	Saudi Arabia	640 000	Wildlife Management Area
3	**Phoenix Islands**	Kiribati	410 500	Marine Protected Area
4	**Great Barrier Reef**	Australia	344 400	Marine Park
5	**Papahānaumokuākea Marine National Monument**	United States	341 362	Coral Reef Ecosystem Reserve
6	**Qiangtang**	China	298 000	Nature Reserve
7	**Macquarie Island**	Australia	162 060	Marine Park
8	**Sanjiangyuan**	China	152 300	Nature Reserve
9	**Galápagos**	Ecuador	133 000	Marine Reserve
10	**Northern Wildlife Management Zone**	Saudi Arabia	100 875	Wildlife Management Area

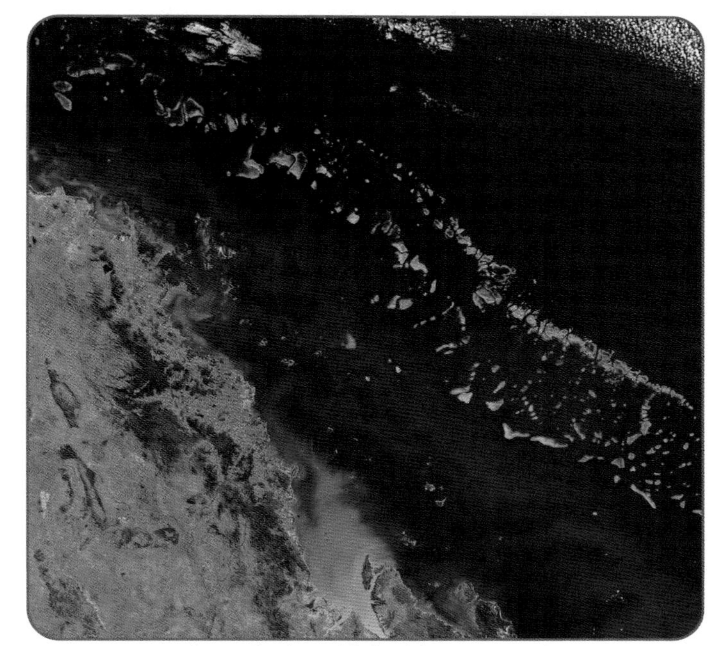

Great Barrier Reef, Australia, the world's fourth largest protected area.

Many parts of the world are undergoing significant changes which can have widespread and long-lasting effects. The principal causes of change are environmental factors – particularly climatic – and the influence of man. However, it is often difficult to separate these causes as man's activities can influence and exaggerate environmental change. Changes, whatever their cause, can have significant effects on the local population, on the wider region and even on a global scale. Major social, economic and environmental impacts can result from often irreversible changes – deforestation can affect a region's biodiversity, land reclamation can destroy fragile marine ecosystems, major dams and drainage schemes can affect whole drainage basins, and local communities can be changed beyond recognition through such projects.

Facts

- Earth-observing satellites can now detect land detail, and therefore changes in land use, of less than 1 metre extent
- Hong Kong International Airport, opened in 1998 and covering an area of over 12 square kilometres, was built almost entirely on reclaimed land
- The UN have estimated that 7 billion people could be short of water by the year 2050
- Approximately 35% of cropland in Asia is irrigated

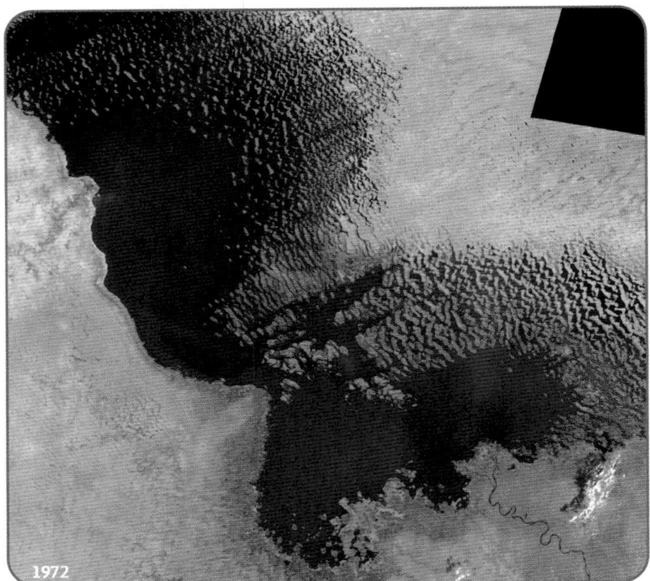

1972

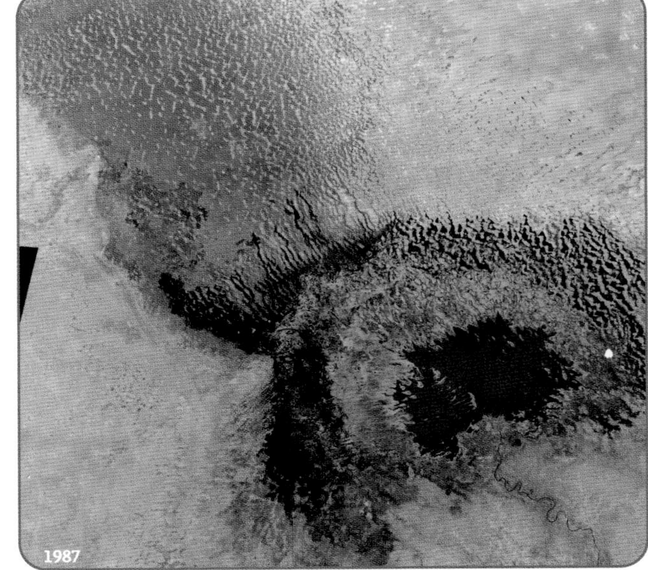

1987

Diversion of water for irrigation and a drier climate have led to the shrinkage of **Lake Chad** in Africa.

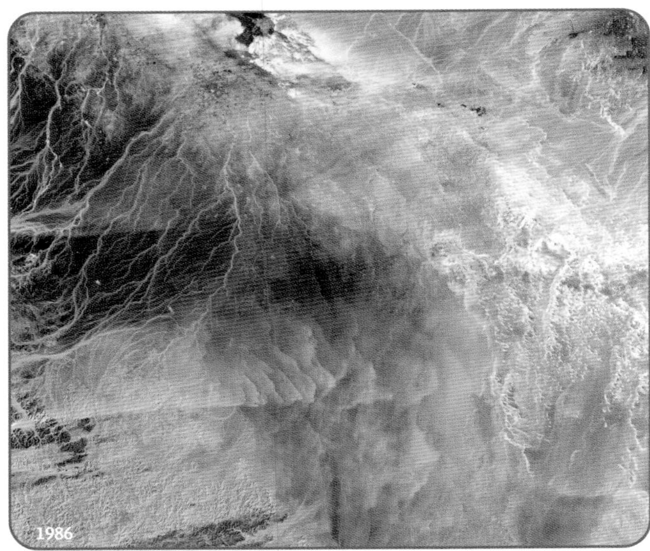

1986

2004

'Centre-pivot' irrigation has transformed the **Arabian Desert** near Tubarjal.

Effects of change

Both natural forces and human activity have irreversibly changed the environment in many parts of the world. Satellite images of the same area taken at different times are a powerful tool for identifying and monitoring such change. Climate change and an increasing demand for water can combine to bring about dramatic changes to lakes and rivers, while major engineering projects, reclamation of land from the sea and the expansion of towns and cities, create completely new environments. Use of water for the generation of hydro-electric power or for irrigation of otherwise infertile land leads to dramatic changes in the landscape and can also be a cause of conflict between countries. All such changes can have major social and economic impacts on the local population.

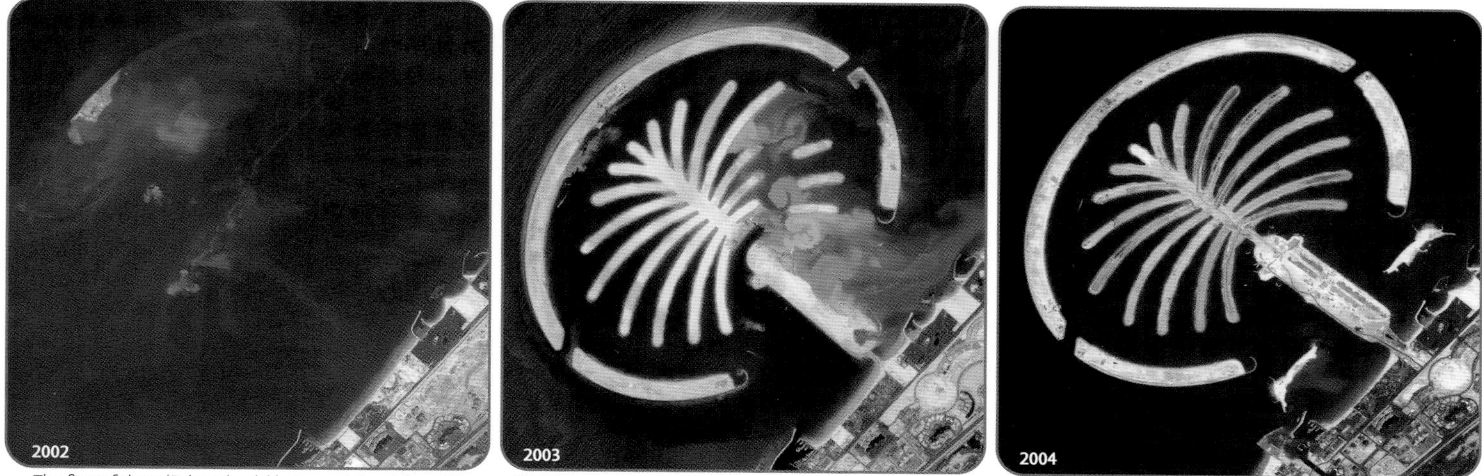
2002
2003
2004
The first of three 'Palm Islands' being reclaimed from the sea off **Dubai**.

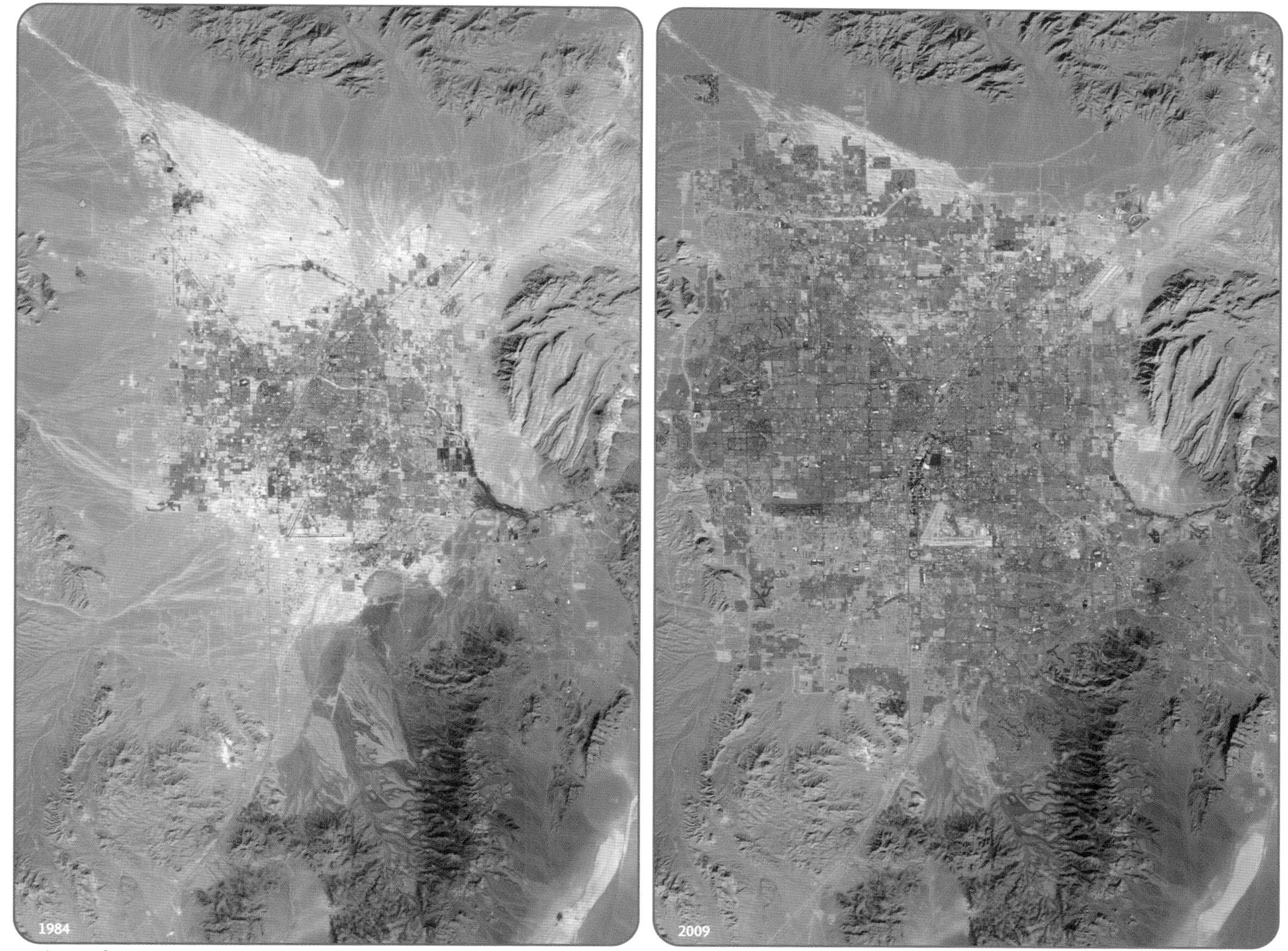
1984
2009
The city of **Las Vegas,** USA has grown dramatically over the last twenty-five years.

Internet Links

NASA Visible Earth	**visibleearth.nasa.gov**
NASA Earth Observatory	**earthobservatory.nasa.gov**
USGS Earthshots: Satellite Images of Environmental Change	**earthshots.usgs.gov**

Rome

This is a true-colour satellite image of Italy, a peninsula in southern Europe. In this image the snow-covered Alps and, just below them, the long Po Valley can be clearly seen. The islands of Corsica and Sardinia are visible on the left hand side of the image, and the island of Sicily appears at the bottom of the image. The light blue colour along Italy's eastern coast is a result of the mixing of sediment from the rivers and phytoplankton blooms.

Rome is the capital of, and largest city in Italy. It is located on the river Tiber and contains many historic monuments, including the Colosseum and the Roman Forum, both of which can be seen at the top right of this satellite image. The Colosseum is the largest amphitheatre ever built in the Roman Empire and was used for gladiatorial contests. The nineteenth-century white-marble Monument of Victor Emmanuel II is also visible in the centre of this image.

World

Soufrière Hills Volcano, Montserrat

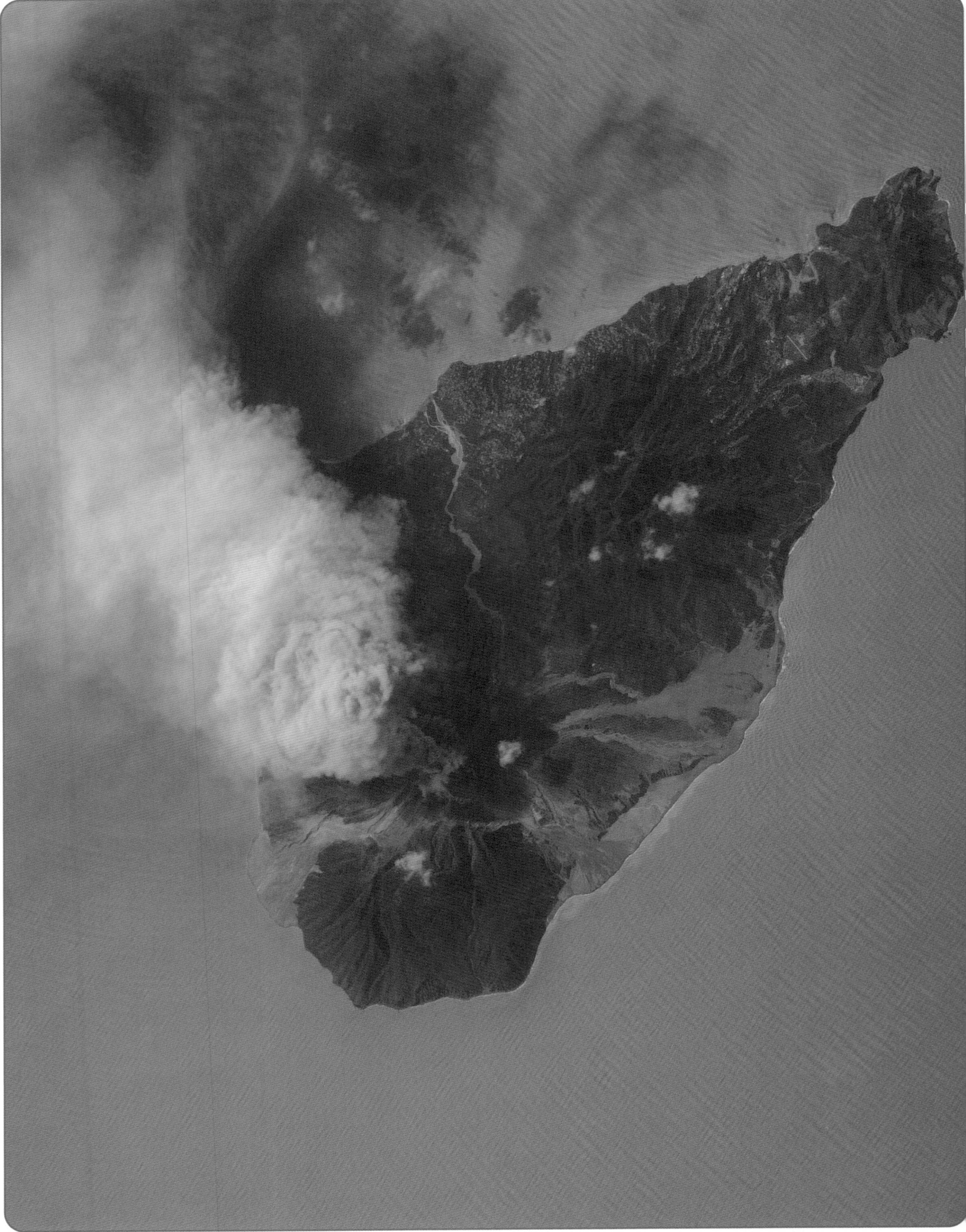

The Soufrière Hills volcano is located on the island of Montserrat in the Lesser Antilles Islands chain in the Caribbean Sea. In 1995 the strato-volcano became active again, and one of its subsequent eruptions destroyed the former capital of Plymouth along with a large section of the southern part of the island. This image shows a further eruption in October 2009. Large plumes of ash and steam can be seen, along with the grey-brown trails of pyroclastic flows and mudflows on the volcano's sides

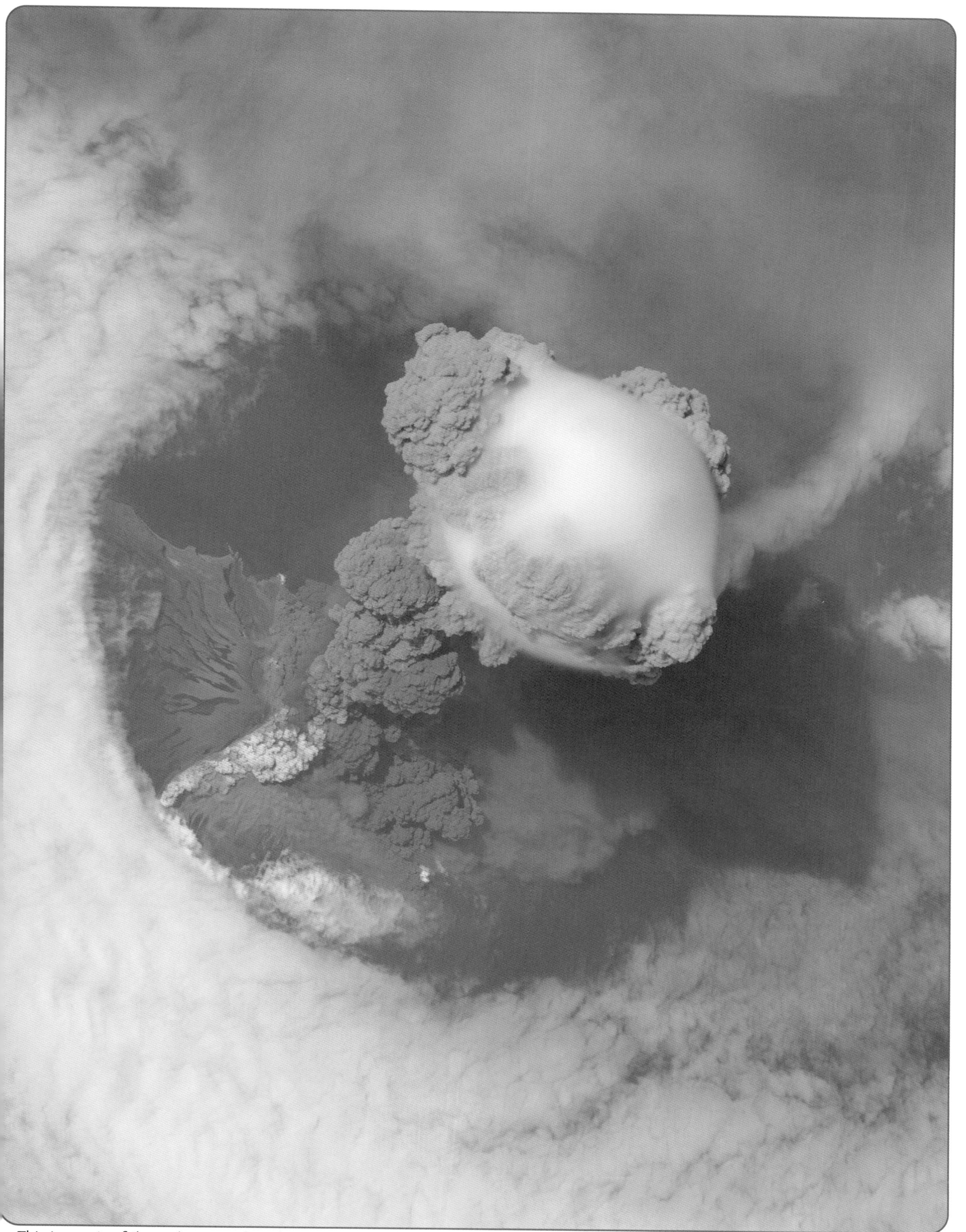

This image is of the early stage of a volcanic eruption of Sarychev Peak in June 2009. Sarychev Peak is located on Matua Island, which forms part of the Kuril Island chain northeast of Japan. In recent years it has been an extremely active volcano. Brown ash and white steam can be seen erupting from the volcano in a great plume, and dark grey pyroclastic flows are also descending from its summit.

The majority of the continent of Antarctica is covered in snow and ice, however, parts of it are kept snow free by strong, cold dry winds. In this image an area known as the Dry Valleys can be seen. They are located between the Ross Sea and the East Antarctica

Ice Sheet. Taylor Valley with its ice-covered lakes and many glaciers flowing into it runs from the bottom left of the image and part of the Ferrar Glacier can also be seen at the bottom right.

Grand Coulee Dam, Washington State, U.S.A.

The Grand Coulee Dam in Washington State U.S.A. took nine years to build and was completed in 1942. A major hydroelectric gravity dam, it is located at the change of the Columbia River's course and created the Franklin D. Roosevelt Lake. The lake covers the top right part of the image and to its south an extensive patchwork of cultivated land including pivot-point irrigation circles

can be seen. The modern channel of the Columbia river snakes off to the north and west while the historic channel in the Grand Coulee canyon to the south west can now be seen where Banks Lake has been created.

Europe
UNESCO World Heritage Sites

In 1959, the government of Egypt decided to build the Aswan High Dam, an event that would flood a valley containing treasures of an ancient civilization such as the Abu Simbel temples. The United Nations Educational, Scientific and Cultural Organization (UNESCO) then launched an international safeguarding campaign and, as a result, Abu Simbel was moved to higher ground where it remains one of Egypt's heritage treasures. This successful project led to the creation of the World Heritage convention and formation of the List of World Heritage sites.

● Cultural site ● Natural site ● Mixed site

Belarus
1. Architectural, Residential and Cultural Complex of the Radziwill Family at Nesvizh
2. Belovezhskaya Pushcha/Białowieża Forest
3. Mir Castle Complex
4. Struve Geodetic Arc

Denmark
5. Jelling Mounds, Runic Stones and Church
6. Kronborg Castle
7. Roskilde Cathedral
Ilulissat Icefjord (see map on p141)

Estonia
8. Historic Centre (Old Town) of Tallinn
4. Struve Geodetic Arc

Finland
9. Bronze Age Burial Site of Sammallahdenmäki
10. Fortress of Suomenlinna
11. High Coast/Kvarken Archipelago
12. Old Rauma
13. Petäjävesi Old Church
4. Struve Geodetic Arc
14. Verla Groundwood and Board Mill

Germany
15. Aachen Cathedral
16. Abbey and Altenmünster of Lorsch
17. Bauhaus and its Sites in Weimar and Dessau
18. Berlin Modernism Housing Estates
19. Castles of Augustusburg and Falkenlust at Brühl
20. Classical Weimar
21. Collegiate Church, Castle and Old Town of Quedlinburg
22. Cologne Cathedral
23. Frontiers of the Roman Empire: Upper German-Raetian Limes
24. Garden Kingdom of Dessau-Wörlitz
25. Hanseatic City of Lübeck
26. Historic Centres of Stralsund and Wismar
27. Luther Memorials in Eisleben and Wittenberg
28. Maulbronn Monastery Complex
29. Messel Pit Fossil Site
30. Mines of Rammelsberg and Historic Town of Goslar
31. Monastic Island of Reichenau
32. Museumsinsel (Museum Island), Berlin
33. Muskauer Park/Park Muzakowski
34. Old town of Regensburg with Stadtamhof
35. Palaces and Parks of Potsdam and Berlin
36. Pilgrimage Church of Wies
37. Roman Monuments, Cathedral of St Peter and Church of Our Lady in Trier
38. Speyer Cathedral
39. St Mary's Cathedral and St Michael's Church at Hildesheim
40. The Wadden Sea
41. Town Hall and Roland on the Marketplace of Bremen
42. Town of Bamberg
43. Upper Middle Rhine Valley
44. Völklingen Ironworks
45. Wartburg Castle
46. Würzburg Residence with the Court Gardens and Residence Square
47. Zollverein Coal Mine Industrial Complex in Essen

Iceland
48. Surtsey
49. Þingvellir National Park

Ireland
50. Archaeological Ensemble of the Bend of the Boyne
51. Skellig Michael

Latvia
52. Historic Centre of Riga
4. Struve Geodetic Arc

Lithuania
53. Curonian Spit
54. Kernavė Archaeological Site (Cultural Reserve of Kernavė)
4. Struve Geodetic Arc
55. Vilnius Historic Centre

Netherlands
56. Defence Line of Amsterdam
57. Droogmakerij de Beemster (Beemster Polder)
58. Ir. D.F. Woudagemaal (D.F. Wouda Steam Pumping Station)
59. Mill Network at Kinderdijk-Elshout
60. Rietveld Schröderhuis (Rietveld Schröder House)
61. Schokland and Surroundings
40. The Wadden Sea
Historic Area of Willemstad, Inner City and Harbour, Netherlands Antilles (see map on p171)

Norway
62. Bryggen
63. Rock Art of Alta
64. Røros Mining Town
4. Struve Geodetic Arc
65. Urnes Stave Church
66. Vegaøyan – the Vega Archipelago
67. West Norwegian Fjords – Geirangerfjord and Nærøyfjord

Poland
68. Auschwitz Birkenau German Nazi Concentration and Extermination Camp (1940–1945)
69. Castle of the Teutonic Order in Malbork
70. Centennial Hall in Wroclaw
2. Belovezhskaya Pushcha/Białowieża Forest
71. Churches of Peace in Jawor and Swidnica
72. Cracow's Historic Centre
73. Historic Centre of Warsaw
74. Kalwaria Zebrzydowska: the Mannerist Architectural and Park Landscape Complex and Pilgrimage Park
75. Medieval Town of Toruń
33. Muskauer Park/Park Muzakowski
76. Old City of Zamość
77. Wieliczka Salt Mine
78. Wooden Churches of Southern Little Poland

Portugal
79. Alto Douro Wine Region
80. Central Zone of the Town of Angra do Heroismo in the Azores
81. Convent of Christ in Tomar
82. Cultural Landscape of Sintra
83. Historic Centre of Évora
84. Historic Centre of Guimarães
85. Historic Centre of Oporto
86. Landscape of the Pico Island Vineyard Culture
87. Laurisilva of Madeira
88. Monastery of Alcobaça
89. Monastery of Batalha
90. Monastery of the Hieronymites and Tower of Belém in Lisbon
91. Prehistoric Rock-Art Sites in the Côa Valley

Russian Federation (see also p70)
92. Architectural Ensemble of the Trinity Sergius Lavra in Sergiev Posad
93. Church of the Ascension, Kolomenskoye
94. Cultural and Historic Ensemble of the Solovetsky Islands
53. Curonian Spit
95. Ensemble of the Ferrapontov Monastery
96. Ensemble of the Novodevichy Convent
97. Historic and Architectural Complex of the Kazan Kremlin
98. Historic Centre of Saint Petersburg and Related Groups of Monuments
99. Historic Monuments of Novgorod and Surroundings
100. Historical Centre of the City of Yaroslavl
101. Kizhi Pogost
102. Kremlin and Red Square, Moscow
4. Struve Geodetic Arc
103. Virgin Komi Forests
104. White Monuments of Vladimir and Suzdal

Spain
105. Alhambra, Generalife and Albayzín, Granada
106. Aranjuez Cultural Landscape
107. Archaeological Ensemble of Mérida
108. Archaeological Ensemble of Tárraco
109. Archaeological Site of Atapuerca
110. Burgos Cathedral
111. Catalan Romanesque Churches of the Vall de Boí
112. Cathedral, Alcázar and Archivo de Indias in Seville
113. Cave of Altamira and Paleolithic Cave Art of Northern Spain
114. Doñana National Park
115. Garajonay National Park
116. Historic Centre of Cordoba
117. Historic City of Toledo
118. Historic Walled Town of Cuenca
119. Ibiza, Biodiversity and Culture
120. La Lonja de la Seda de Valencia
121. Las Médulas
122. Monastery and Site of the Escurial, Madrid
123. Monuments of Oviedo and the Kingdom of the Asturias
124. Mudéjar Architecture of Aragon
125. Old City of Salamanca
126. Old Town of Ávila with its Extra-Muros Churches
127. Old Town of Cáceres
128. Old Town of Segovia and its Aqueduct
129. Palau de la Música Catalana and Hospital de Sant Pau, Barcelona
130. Palmeral of Elche
131. Poblet Monastery
132. Pyrénées - Mont Perdu
133. Renaissance Monumental Ensembles of Úbeda and Baeza
134. Rock Art of the Mediterranean Basin on the Iberian Peninsula
135. Roman Walls of Lugo
136. Route of Santiago de Compostela
137. Royal Monastery of Santa María de Guadalupe
138. San Cristóbal de La Laguna
139. San Millán Yuso and Suso Monasteries
140. Santiago de Compostela (Old Town)
141. Teide National Park
142. University and Historic Precinct of Alcalá de Henares
143. Tower of Hercules
144. Vizcaya Bridge
145. Works of Antoni Gaudí

ICE
49
48
IRELAN
51
ATLANTIC
OCEAN
86
80
Azores
(Portugal)
Bay o
Bisca
PORTUGAL
SPAIN
87
Madeira
(Portugal)
138
115
141
Canary Islands
(Spain)
AF

Sweden
146. Agricultural Landscape of Southern Öland
147. Birka and Hovgården
148. Church Village of Gammelstad, Luleå
149. Engelsberg Ironworks
150. Hanseatic Town of Visby
11. High Coast/Kvarken Archipelago
151. Laponian Area
152. Mining Area of the Great Copper Mountain in Falun
153. Naval Port of Karlskrona
154. Rock Carvings in Tanum
155. Royal Domain of Drottningholm
156. Skogskyrkogården
4. Struve Geodetic Arc
157. Varberg Radio Station

Ukraine
158. Kiev: Saint-Sophia Cathedral and Related Monastic Buildings, Kiev-Pechersk Lavra
159. L'viv – the Ensemble of the Historic Centre
160. Primeval Beech Forests of the Carpathians
4. Struve Geodetic Arc

United Kingdom
161. Blaenavon Industrial Landscape
162. Blenheim Palace
163. Canterbury Cathedral, St Augustine's Abbey and St Martin's Church
164. Castles and Town Walls of King Edward in Gwynedd
165. City of Bath
166. Cornwall and West Devon Mining Landscape
167. Derwent Valley Mills
168. Dorset and East Devon Coast
169. Durham Castle and Cathedral
170. Frontiers of the Roman Empire: Antonine Wall and Hadrian's Wall
171. Giant's Causeway and Causeway Coast
172. Heart of Neolithic Orkney
173. Ironbridge Gorge
174. Liverpool – Maritime Mercantile City
175. Maritime Greenwich
176. New Lanark
177. Old and New Towns of Edinburgh
178. Pontcysyllte Aqueduct and Canal
179. Royal Botanic Gardens, Kew
180. Saltaire
181. St Kilda
182. Stonehenge, Avebury and Associated Sites
183. Studley Royal Park including the Ruins of Fountains Abbey
184. Tower of London
185. Westminster Palace, Westminster Abbey and Saint Margaret's Church
Gough and Inaccessible Islands (see map on p115)
Henderson Island (see map p127)
Historic Town of St George and Related Fortifications, Bermuda (see map on p141)

Bjørnøya (Norway)
Jan Mayen (Norway)
Barents Sea
LAND
Norwegian Sea
Faroe Islands (Denmark)
White Sea
SWEDEN
Gulf of Bothnia
FINLAND
Shetland Islands
Orkney Islands
NORWAY
RUSSIAN FEDERATION
Gulf of Finland
UNITED KINGDOM
ESTONIA
North Sea
LATVIA
DENMARK
Baltic Sea
LITHUANIA
NETHERLANDS
RUS. FED.
GERMANY
BELARUS
POLAND
UKRAINE
see large-scale map on pages 44–45
Black Sea
Caspian Sea
Mediterranean Sea
ASIA
ICA

Europe

UNESCO World Heritage Sites

World Heritage sites in Europe are found across the continent, from the far north of Scandinavia to the extreme south of Sicily. They span the whole of Earth's human history – from Neolithic Orkney and Stonehenge, through the Acropolis and Pompeii, to twentieth century Auschwitz and the Works of Gaudi.

● Cultural site ● Natural site ● Mixed site

Albania
1. Butrint
2. Historic Centres of Berat and Gjirokastra

Andorra
3. Madriu-Perafita-Claror Valley

Austria
4. City of Graz – Historic Centre
5. Fertö/Neusiedlersee Cultural Landscape
6. Hallstatt-Dachstein/Salzkammergut Cultural Landscape
7. Historic Centre of the City of Salzburg
8. Historic Centre of Vienna
9. Palace and Gardens of Schönbrunn
10. Semmering Railway
11. Wachau Cultural Landscape

Belgium
12. Belfries of Belgium and France
13. Flemish Béguinages
14. Historic Centre of Brugge
15. La Grand-Place, Brussels
16. Major Town Houses of the Architect Victor Horta (Brussels)
17. Neolithic Flint Mines at Spiennes (Mons)
18. Notre-Dame Cathedral in Tournai
19. Plantin-Moretus House-Workshops-Museum Complex
20. Stoclet House
21. The Four Lifts on the Canal du Centre and their Environs, La Louvière and Le Roeulx (Hainault)

Bosnia-Herzegovina
22. Mehmed Paša Sokolović Bridge in Višegrad
23. Old Bridge Area of the Old City of Mostar

Bulgaria
24. Ancient City of Nessebar
25. Boyana Church
26. Madara Rider
27. Pirin National Park
28. Rila Monastery
29. Rock-Hewn Churches of Ivanovo
30. Srebarna Nature Reserve
31. Thracian Tomb of Kazanlak
32. Thracian Tomb of Sveshtari

Croatia
33. Cathedral of St James in Šibenik
34. Episcopal Complex of the Euphrasian Basilica in the Historic Centre of Poreč
35. Historic City of Trogir
36. Historical Complex of Split with the Palace of Diocletian
37. Old City of Dubrovnik
38. Plitvice Lakes National Park
39. Stari Grad Plain

Czech Republic
40. Gardens and Castle at Kroměříž
41. Historic Centre of Český Krumlov
42. Historic Centre of Prague
43. Historic Centre of Telč
44. Holašovice Historical Village Reservation
45. Holy Trinity Column in Olomouc
46. Jewish Quarter and St Procopius' Basilica in Třebíč
47. Kutná Hora: Historical Town Centre with the Church of St Barbara and the Cathedral of Our Lady at Sedlec
48. Lednice-Valtice Cultural Landscape
49. Litomyšl Castle
50. Pilgrimage Church of St John of Nepomuk at Zelená Hora
51. Tugendhat Villa in Brno

France
52. Abbey Church of Saint-Savin sur Gartempe
53. Amiens Cathedral
54. Arles, Roman and Romanesque Monuments
12. Belfries of Belgium and France
55. Bordeaux, Port of the Moon
56. Bourges Cathedral
57. Canal du Midi
58. Cathedral of Notre-Dame, Former Abbey of Saint-Rémi and Palace of Tau, Reims
59. Chartres Cathedral
60. Cistercian Abbey of Fontenay
61. Fortifications of Vauban
62. From the Great Saltworks of Salins-les-Bains to the Royal Saltworks of Arc-et-Senans, the production of open-pan salt
63. Gulf of Porto: Calanche of Piana, Gulf of Girolata, Scandola Reserve
64. Historic Centre of Avignon: Papal Palace, Episcopal Ensemble and Avignon Bridge
65. Historic Fortified City of Carcassonne
66. Historic Site of Lyons
67. Jurisdiction of Saint-Emilion
68. Le Havre, the city rebuilt by Auguste Perret
69. Mont-Saint-Michel and its Bay
70. Palace and Park of Fontainebleau
71. Palace and Park of Versailles
72. Paris, Banks of the Seine
73. Place Stanislas, Place de la Carrière and Place d'Alliance in Nancy
74. Pont du Gard (Roman Aqueduct)
75. Prehistoric Sites and Decorated Caves of the Vézère Valley
76. Provins, Town of Medieval Fairs
77. Pyrénées – Mont Perdu
78. Roman Theatre and its Surroundings and the 'Triumphal Arch' of Orange
79. Routes of Santiago de Compostela in France
80. Strasbourg – Grande Île
81. The Loire Valley between Sully-sur-Loire and Chalonnes
82. Vézelay, Church and Hill Lagoons of New Caledonia: Reef Diversity and Associated Ecosystems (see map on page 126)

Greece
83. Acropolis, Athens
84. Archaeological Site of Aigai (modern name Vergina)
85. Archaeological Site of Delphi
86. Archaeological Site of Mystras
87. Archaeological Site of Olympia
88. Archaeological Sites of Mycenae and Tiryns
89. Delos
90. Historic Centre (Chorá) with the Monastery of Saint John, the Theologian, and the Cave of the Apocalypse on the Island of Pátmos
91. Medieval City of Rhodes
92. Meteora
93. Monasteries of Daphni, Hosios Loukas and Nea Moni of Chios
94. Mount Athos
95. Old Town of Corfu
96. Paleochristian and Byzantine Monuments of Thessalonika
97. Pythagoreion and Heraion of Samos
98. Sanctuary of Asklepios at Epidaurus
99. Temple of Apollo Epicurius at Bassae

North Sea
BELGIUM
LUXEMBOURG
FRANCE
SWITZERLA
ANDORRA
MONACO
Corsica (France)
Sardinia (Italy)
Mediterranean
AFRICA

Hungary
100. Budapest, including the Banks of the Danube, the Buda Castle Quarter and Andrássy Avenue
101. Caves of Aggtelek Karst and Slovak Karst
102. Early Christian Necropolis of Pécs (Sopianae)
5. Fertö/Neusiedlersee Cultural Landscape
103. Hortobágy National Park – the Puszta
104. Millenary Benedictine Abbey of Pannonhalma and its Natural Environment
105. Old Village of Hollókő and its Surroundings
106. Tokaj Wine Region Historic Cultural Landscape

Italy
107. Archaeological Area and the Patriarchal Basilica of Aquileia
108. Archaeological Area of Agrigento
109. Archaeological Areas of Pompei, Herculaneum and Torre Annunziata
110. Assisi, the Basilica of San Francesco and Other Franciscan Sites
111. Botanical Garden (Orto Botanico), Padua
112. Castel del Monte
113. Cathedral, Torre Civica and Piazza Grande, Modena
114. Church and Dominican Convent of Santa Maria delle Grazie with 'The Last Supper' by Leonardo da Vinci
115. Cilento and Vallo di Diano National Park with the Archeological sites of Paestum and Velia, and the Certosa di Padula
116. City of Verona
117 City of Vicenza and the Palladian Villas of the Veneto
118. Costiera Amalfitana
119. Crespi d'Adda
120. Early Christian Monuments of Ravenna
121. Eighteenth-Century Royal Palace at Caserta with the Park, the Aqueduct of Vanvitelli, and the San Leucio Complex
122. Etruscan Necropolises of Cerveteri and Tarquinia
123. Ferrara, City of the Renaissance, and its Po Delta
124. Genoa: Le Strade Nuove and the system of the Palazzi dei Rolli
125. Historic Centre of Florence
126. Historic Centre of Naples
127. Historic Centre of Rome, the Properties of the Holy See in that City Enjoying Extraterritorial Rights and San Paolo Fuori le Mura
128. Historic Centre of San Gimignano
129. Historic Centre of Siena
130. Historic Centre of the City of Pienza
131. Historic Centre of Urbino
132. Isole Eolie (Aeolian Islands)
133. Late Baroque Towns of the Val di Noto (South-Eastern Sicily)
134. Mantua and Sabbioneta
135. Piazza del Duomo, Pisa
136. Portovenere, Cinque Terre, and the Islands (Palmaria, Tino and Tinetto)
137. Residences of the Royal House of Savoy
138. Rhaetian Railway in the Albula/Bernina Landscapes
139. Rock Drawings in Valcamonica
140. Sacri Monti of Piedmont and Lombardy
141. Su Nuraxi di Barumini
142. Syracuse and the Rocky Necropolis of Pantalica
143. The Dolomites
144. The Sassi and the park of the Rupestrian Churches of Matera
145. The Trulli of Alberobello
146. Val d'Orcia
147. Venice and its Lagoon
148. Villa Adriana (Tivoli)
149. Villa d'Este, Tivoli
150. Villa Romana del Casale

Kosovo
151. Medieval Monuments in Kosovo

Luxembourg
152. City of Luxembourg: its Old Quarters and Fortifications

Macedonia (F.Y.R.O.M.)
153. Natural and Cultural Heritage of the Ohrid Region

Malta
154. City of Valletta
155. Hal Saflieni Hypogeum
156. Megalithic Temples of Malta

Moldova
157. Struve Geodetic Arc

Montenegro
158. Durmitor National Park
159. Natural and Culturo-Historical Region of Kotor

Romania
160. Churches of Moldavia
161. Dacian Fortresses of the Orastie Mountains
162. Danube Delta
163. Historic Centre of Sighişoara
164. Monastery of Horezu
165. Villages with Fortified Churches in Transylvania
166. Wooden Churches of Maramureş

San Marino
167. San Marino Historic Centre and Mount Titano

Serbia
168. Gamzigrad-Romuliana, Palace of Galerius
169. Stari Ras and Sopoćani
170. Studenica Monastery

Slovakia
171. Bardejov Town Conservation Reserve
101. Caves of Aggtelek Karst and Slovak Karst
172. Historic Town of Banská Štiavnica and the Technical Monuments in its Vicinity
173. Levoča, Spišský Hrad and the Associated Cultural Monuments
174. Primeval Beech Forests of the Carpathians
175. Vlkolínec
176. Wooden Churches of the Slovak part of the Carpathian Mountain Area

Slovenia
177. Škocjan Caves

Switzerland
178. Benedictine Convent of St John at Müstair
179. Convent of St Gall
180. La Chaux-de-Fonds/Le Locle, watchmaking town planning
181. Lavaux, Vineyard Terraces
182. Monte San Giorgio
183. Old City of Berne
138. Rhaetian Railway in the Albula/Bernina Landscapes
184. Swiss Alps Jungfrau-Aletsch
185. Swiss Tectonic Arena Sardona
186. Three Castles, Defensive Wall and Ramparts of the Market-Town of Bellinzone

Vatican City
127. Historic Centre of Rome, the Properties of the Holy See in that City Enjoying Extraterritorial Rights and San Paolo Fuori le Mura
187. Vatican City

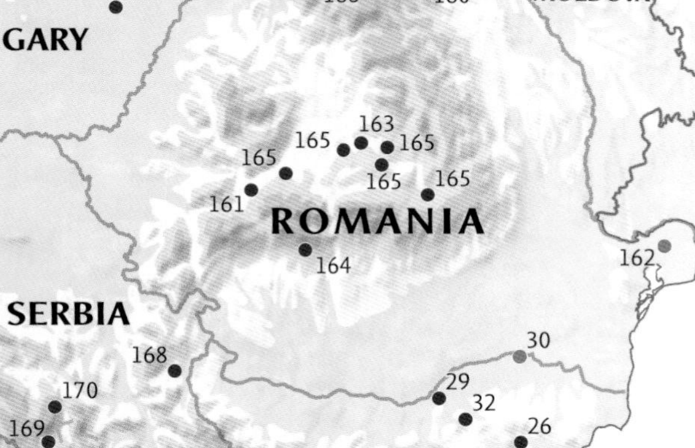
ROMANIA
BOSNIA-
HERZEGOVINA
SERBIA
MONTENEGRO
KOSOVO
BULGARIA

Europe
Landscapes

Europe, the westward extension of the Asian continent and the second smallest of the world's continents, has a remarkable variety of physical features and landscapes. The continent is bounded by mountain ranges of varying character – the highlands of Scandinavia and northwest Britain, the Pyrenees, the Alps, the Carpathian Mountains, the Caucasus and the Ural Mountains. Two of these, the Caucasus and Ural Mountains, define the eastern limits of Europe, with the Black Sea and the Bosporus defining its southeastern boundary with Asia.

Across the centre of the continent stretches the North European Plain, broken by some of Europe's greatest rivers, including the Volga and the Dnieper and containing some of its largest lakes. To the south, the Mediterranean Sea divides Europe from Africa. The Mediterranean region itself has a very distinct climate and landscape.

Facts

- **The Danube flows through 7 countries and has 7 different name forms**
- **Lakes cover almost 10% of the total land area of Finland**
- **The Strait of Gibraltar, separating the Atlantic Ocean from the Mediterranean Sea and Europe from Africa, is only 13 kilometres wide at its narrowest point**
- **The highest mountain in the Alps is Mont Blanc, 4 808 metres, on the France/Italy border**

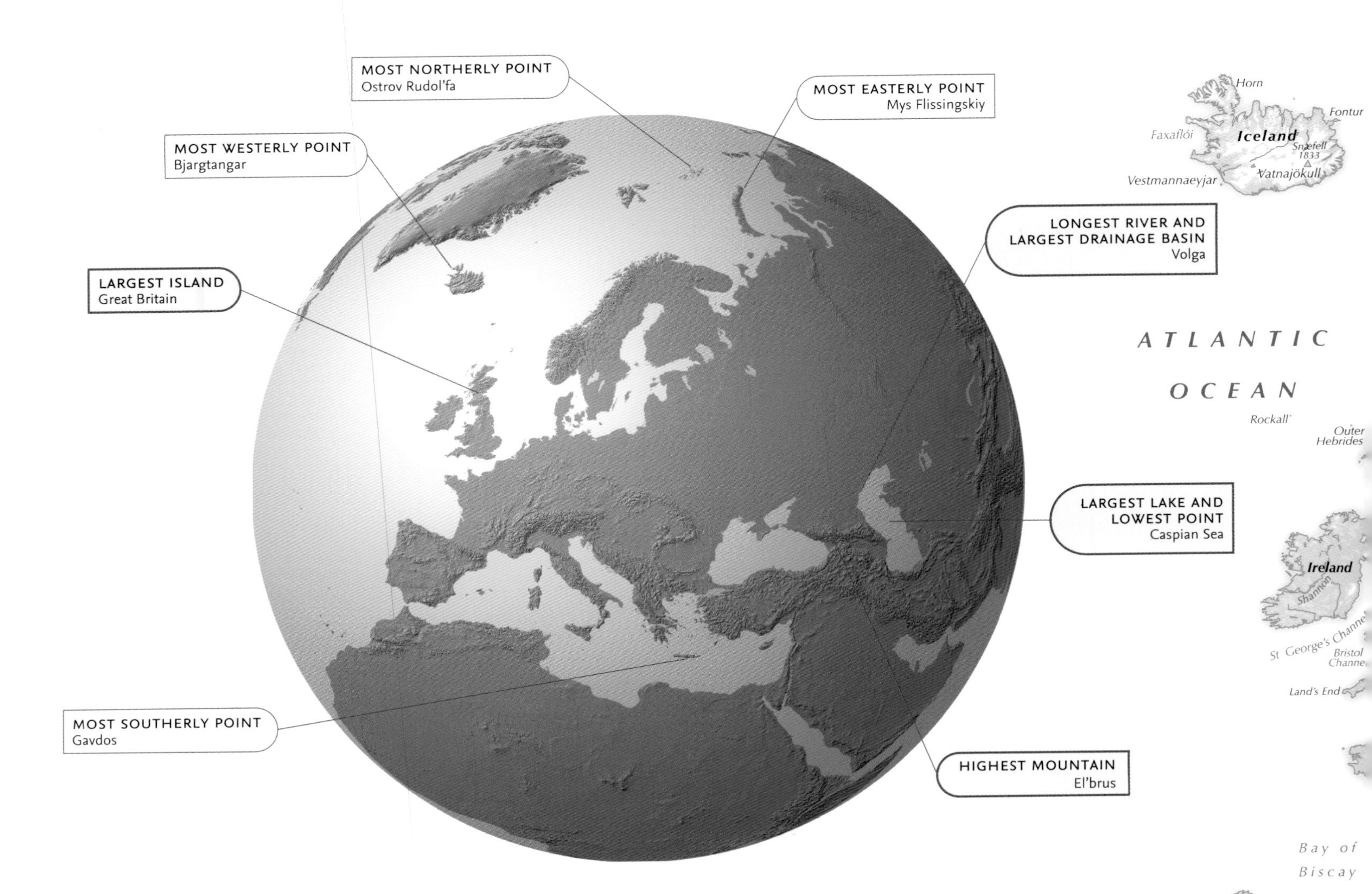

MOST NORTHERLY POINT
Ostrov Rudol'fa
MOST EASTERLY POINT
Mys Flissingskiy
MOST WESTERLY POINT
Bjargtangar
LONGEST RIVER AND LARGEST DRAINAGE BASIN
Volga
LARGEST ISLAND
Great Britain
LARGEST LAKE AND LOWEST POINT
Caspian Sea
MOST SOUTHERLY POINT
Gavdos
HIGHEST MOUNTAIN
El'brus
Horn
Fontur
Faxaflói
Iceland
Snæfell
1833
Vatnajökull
Vestmannaeyjar
ATLANTIC
OCEAN
Rockall
Outer Hebrides
Ireland
Shannon
St George's Channel
Bristol Channel
Land's End
Bay of Biscay
Cape Finisterre
Cordillera Cantábrica
Douro
Iberian
Peninsula
Tagus
Sierra Morena
Guadalquivir
Cabo de São Vicente
Mulhacén
3482
Sierra Nevada
Strait of Gibraltar
AFR

Europe's greatest physical features

Highest mountain	El'brus, Russian Federation	5 642 metres	18 510 feet
Longest river	Volga, Russian Federation	3 688 km	2 292 miles
Largest lake	Caspian Sea	371 000 sq km	143 243 sq miles
Largest island	Great Britain, United Kingdom	218 476 sq km	84 354 sq miles
Largest drainage basin	Volga, Russian Federation	1 380 000 sq km	532 818 sq miles

Europe's extent

TOTAL LAND AREA	9 908 599 sq km / 3 825 710 sq miles
Most northerly point	Ostrov Rudol'fa, Russian Federation
Most southerly point	Gavdos, Crete, Greece
Most westerly point	Bjargtangar, Iceland
Most easterly point	Mys Flissingskiy, Russian Federation

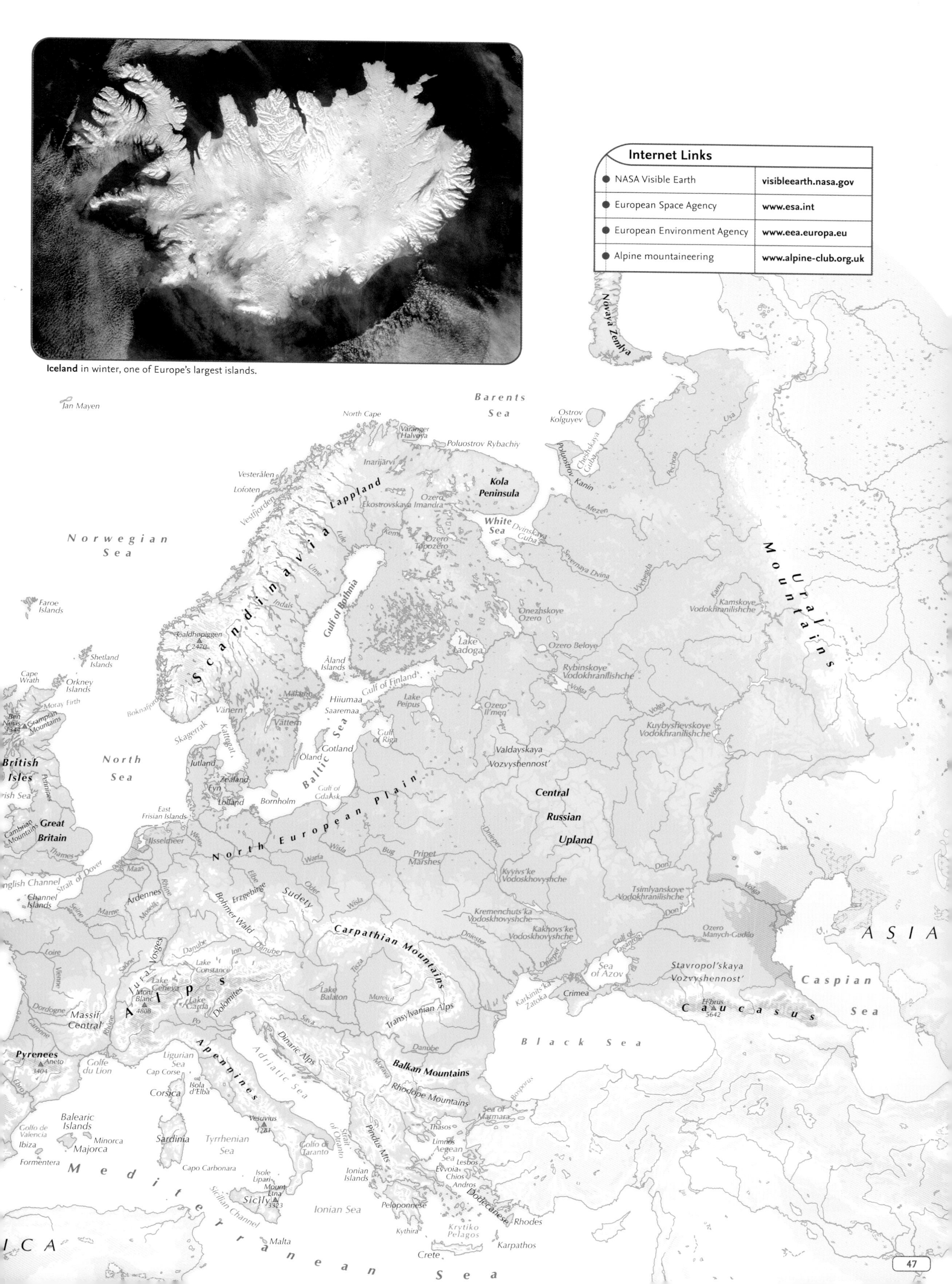

Jan Mayen
Barents Sea
North Cape
Varanger Halvøya
Poluostrov Rybachiy
Ostrov Kolguyev
Poluostrov Kanin
Cheshskaya Guba
Novaya Zemlya
Usa
Pechora
Vesterålen
Lofoten
Vestfjorden
Inarijärvi
Lappland
Kola Peninsula
Ozero Imandra
Ekostrovskaya
Mezen
White Sea
Dvinskaya Guba
Kem
Ozero Topozero
Norwegian Sea
Scandinavia
Lule
Ume
Gulf of Bothnia
Severnaya Dvina
Vychegda
Ural Mountains
Kama
Kamskoye Vodokhranilishche
Faroe Islands
Indals
Onezhskoye Ozero
Galdhøpiggen 2470
Lake Ladoga
Ozero Beloye
Shetland Islands
Åland Islands
Rybinskoye Vodokhranilishche
Cape Wrath
Orkney Islands
Gulf of Finland
Volga
Moray Firth
Mälaren
Hiiumaa
Saaremaa
Lake Peipus
Ben Nevis 1343
Grampian Mountains
Boknafjorden
Vänern
Vättern
Ozero Il'men'
Kuybyshevskoye Vodokhranilishche
Skagerrak
Kattegat
Baltic Sea
Gulf of Riga
British Isles
North Sea
Gotland
Öland
Valdayskaya Vozvyshennost'
Jutland
Zealand
Fyn
Lolland
Bornholm
Gulf of Gdańsk
Central Russian Upland
Irish Sea
Pennines
North European Plain
East Frisian Islands
Cambrian Mountains
Great Britain
IJsselmeer
Weser
Wisła
Bug
Pripet Marshes
Dnieper
Thames
Maas
Warta
Don
English Channel
Strait of Dover
Rhine
Elbe
Oder
Kyyivs'ke Vodoskhovyshche
Tsimlyanskoye Vodokhranilishche
Channel Islands
Ardennes
Erzgebirge
Sudety
Seine
Marne
Moselle
Böhmer Wald
Kremenchuts'ka Vodoskhovyshche
Dniester
Kakhovs'ke Vodoskhovyshche
Ozero Manych-Gudilo
Carpathian Mountains
Gulf of Taganrog
ASIA
Loire
Vosges
Danube
Inn
Lake Constance
Tisza
Sea of Azov
Stavropol'skaya Vozvyshennost'
Saône
Jura
Lake Geneva
Mont Blanc 4808
Alps
Lake Garda
Dolomites
Lake Balaton
Mureş
Karkinits'ka Zatoka
Crimea
Caspian Sea
Vienne
Dordogne
Massif Central
Garonne
Rhône
Po
Sava
Transylvanian Alps
El'brus 5642
Caucasus
Danube
Black Sea
Pyrenees
Aneto 3404
Golfe du Lion
Ligurian Sea
Apennines
Adriatic Sea
Dinaric Alps
Morava
Balkan Mountains
Ebro
Cap Corse
Corsica
Isola d'Elba
Rhodope Mountains
Bosporus
Sea of Marmara
Balearic Islands
Golfo de Valencia
Ibiza
Formentera
Minorca
Majorca
Vesuvius 1281
Sardinia
Tyrrhenian Sea
Strait of Otranto
Golfo di Taranto
Pindus Mts
Thasos
Limnos
Aegean Sea
Lesbos
Evvoia
Chios
Andros
Mediterranean Sea
Capo Carbonara
Isole Lipari
Mount Etna 3323
Sicily
Sicilian Channel
Ionian Islands
Ionian Sea
Peloponnese
Dodecanese
Rhodes
Kythira
Krytiko Pelagos
Karpathos
AFRICA
Malta
Crete

Iceland in winter, one of Europe's largest islands.

Internet Links

NASA Visible Earth	**visibleearth.nasa.gov**
European Space Agency	**www.esa.int**
European Environment Agency	**www.eea.europa.eu**
Alpine mountaineering	**www.alpine-club.org.uk**

Europe
Countries

The predominantly temperate climate of Europe has led to it becoming the most densely populated of the continents. It is highly industrialized, and has exploited its great wealth of natural resources and agricultural land to become one of the most powerful economic regions in the world.

The current pattern of countries within Europe is a result of numerous and complicated changes throughout its history. Ethnic, religious and linguistic differences have often been the cause of conflict, particularly in the Balkan region which has a very complex ethnic pattern. Current boundaries reflect, to some extent, these divisions which continue to be a source of tension. The historic distinction between 'Eastern' and 'Western' Europe is no longer made, following the collapse of Communism and the break up of the Soviet Union in 1991.

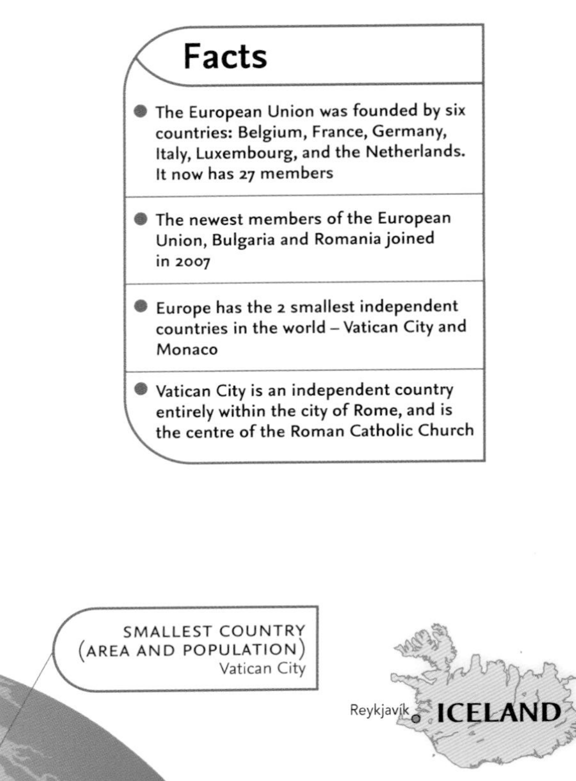

Facts

- The European Union was founded by six countries: Belgium, France, Germany, Italy, Luxembourg, and the Netherlands. It now has 27 members
- The newest members of the European Union, Bulgaria and Romania joined in 2007
- Europe has the 2 smallest independent countries in the world – Vatican City and Monaco
- Vatican City is an independent country entirely within the city of Rome, and is the centre of the Roman Catholic Church

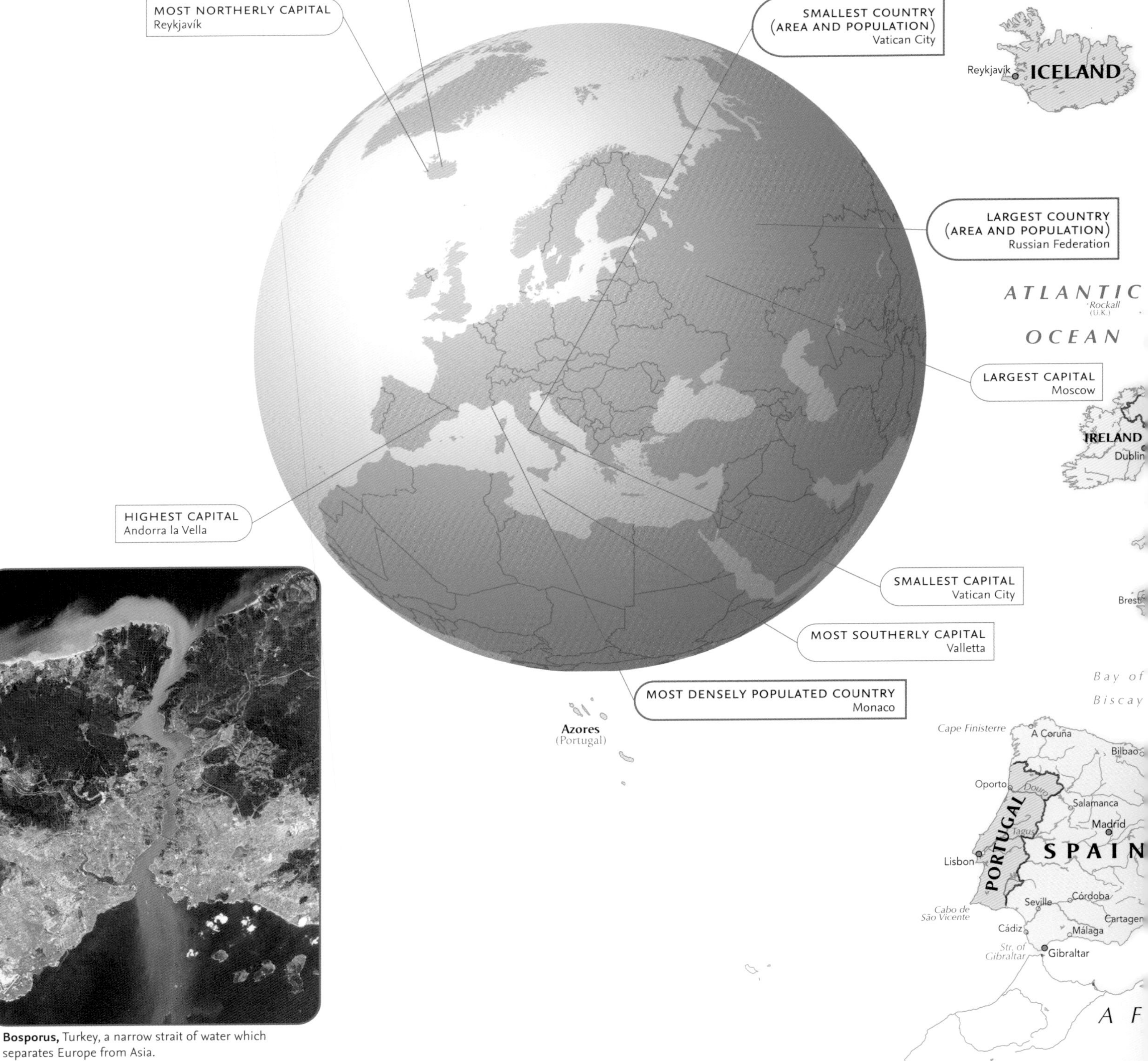
LEAST DENSELY POPULATED COUNTRY
Iceland
MOST NORTHERLY CAPITAL
Reykjavík
SMALLEST COUNTRY (AREA AND POPULATION)
Vatican City
LARGEST COUNTRY (AREA AND POPULATION)
Russian Federation
LARGEST CAPITAL
Moscow
HIGHEST CAPITAL
Andorra la Vella
SMALLEST CAPITAL
Vatican City
MOST SOUTHERLY CAPITAL
Valletta
MOST DENSELY POPULATED COUNTRY
Monaco
Reykjavík
ICELAND
ATLANTIC
Rockall
(U.K.)
OCEAN
IRELAND
Dublin
Brest
Bay of
Biscay
Azores
(Portugal)
Cape Finisterre
A Coruña
Bilbao
Oporto
Douro
Salamanca
Madrid
PORTUGAL
Tagus
SPAIN
Lisbon
Cabo de São Vicente
Seville
Córdoba
Cádiz
Málaga
Cartagena
Str. of Gibraltar
Gibraltar
A F

Bosporus, Turkey, a narrow strait of water which separates Europe from Asia.

Europe's capitals

Largest capital (population)	Moscow, Russian Federation	10 452 000
Smallest capital (population)	Vatican City	557
Most northerly capital	Reykjavík, Iceland	64° 39'N
Most southerly capital	Valletta, Malta	35° 54'N
Highest capital	Andorra la Vella, Andorra	1 029 metres 3 376 feet

Europe's countries

Largest country (area)	Russian Federation	17 075 400 sq km	6 592 849 sq miles
Smallest country (area)	Vatican City	0.5 sq km	0.2 sq miles
Largest country (population)	Russian Federation	143 202 000	
Smallest country (population)	Vatican City	557	
Most densely populated country	Monaco	17 000 per sq km	34 000 per sq mile
Least densely populated country	Iceland	3 per sq km	7 per sq mile

Bjørnøya
(Norway)
Jan Mayen
(Norway)
Barents Sea
North Cape
Ostrov Kolguyev
Vorkuta
Murmansk
Kola Peninsula
White Sea
Lappland
Norwegian Sea
SWEDEN
FINLAND
Gulf of Bothnia
Archangel
RUSSIAN FEDERATION
Syktyvkar
Faroe Islands
(Denmark)
Trondheim
Petrozavodsk
Onezhskoye Ozero
Perm'
Lake Ladoga
Kirov
NORWAY
Shetland Islands
Orkney Islands
Bergen
Oslo
Åland Islands
Turku
Helsinki
Gulf of Finland
Tallinn
St Petersburg
Vologda
Izhevsk
Naberezhnyye Chelny
Ufa
Kazan'
Stockholm
Lake Peipus
Yaroslavl'
ESTONIA
Vänern
Vättern
Skagerrak
Kattegat
Gotland
Gulf of Riga
Nizhniy Novgorod
Ul'yanovsk
Moscow
Riga
LATVIA
Aalborg
Edinburgh
North Sea
Öland
Baltic Sea
Samara
Orenburg
DENMARK
Malmö
Copenhagen
LITHUANIA
Vitsyebsk
Smolensk
Tula
Penza
UNITED KINGDOM
Irish Sea
Leeds
Manchester
Bornholm
RUS. FED.
Kaliningrad
Vilnius
Minsk
Mahilyow
Saratov
Gdańsk
Hrodna
Hamburg
BELARUS
Voronezh
NETHERLANDS
Bremen
Birmingham
The Hague
Amsterdam
Rotterdam
Berlin
Bydgoszcz
Białystok
Homyel'
Poznań
Warsaw
Brest
Chernihiv
Belgorod
London
Essen
Łódź
Volgograd
English Channel
Brussels
Leipzig
Wrocław
POLAND
Kiev
Kharkiv
Rivne
Guernsey
Jersey
Channel Islands
BELGIUM
GERMANY
LUXEMBOURG
Luxembourg
CZECH REPUBLIC
Prague
Katowice
Kraków
UKRAINE
Donets'k
Astrakhan'
ASIA
Frankfurt am Main
L'viv
Kirovohrad
Dnipropetrovs'k
Rennes
Paris
Stuttgart
Brno
SLOVAKIA
Rostov-na-Donu
Orléans
Strasbourg
Chernivtsi
Vienna
Bratislava
Košice
Nantes
Munich
LIECHTENSTEIN
Vaduz
Salzburg
AUSTRIA
Budapest
Mykolayiv
Chişinău
Odessa
Sea of Azov
Stavropol'
Dijon
Zurich
Bern
SWITZERLAND
HUNGARY
Iaşi
MOLDOVA
Caspian Sea
FRANCE
Geneva
Szeged
ROMANIA
Crimea
Krasnodar
Grozny
Lyon
SLOVENIA
Ljubljana
Zagreb
Timişoara
Braşov
Simferopol'
Novorossiysk
El'brus
Caucasus
Bordeaux
Milan
Venice
Trieste
CROATIA
Belgrade
Bucharest
Constanța
Turin
Genoa
Bologna
BOSNIA HERZEGOVINA
SERBIA
Craiova
Black Sea
Toulouse
Florence
Sarajevo
Danube
Pleven
Varna
MONACO
Marseille
SAN MARINO
Adriatic Sea
Split
Niš
BULGARIA
Andorra la Vella
ANDORRA
MONTENEGRO
Prishtinë
Sofia
Burgas
Zaragoza
Podgorica
KOSOVO
Skopje
Plovdiv
Edirne
TURKEY
Corsica
Vatican City
Rome
ITALY
MACEDONIA (F.Y.R.O.M.)
Bosporus
Barcelona
Bari
Tirana
İstanbul
Balearic Islands
ALBANIA
Valencia
Minorca
Palma de Mallorca
Sardinia
Naples
Thessaloniki
Majorca
Ibiza
Larisa
Aegean Sea
Cosenza
GREECE
Mediterranean Sea
Palermo
Messina
Athens
Sicily
Syracuse
Ionian Sea
Dodecanese
Rhodes
MALTA
Valletta
AFRICA
Crete

Internet Links

European Union	europa.eu/
UK Foreign and Commonwealth Office	www.fco.gov.uk
CIA World Factbook	www.cia.gov/library/publications/the-world-factbook/index.html

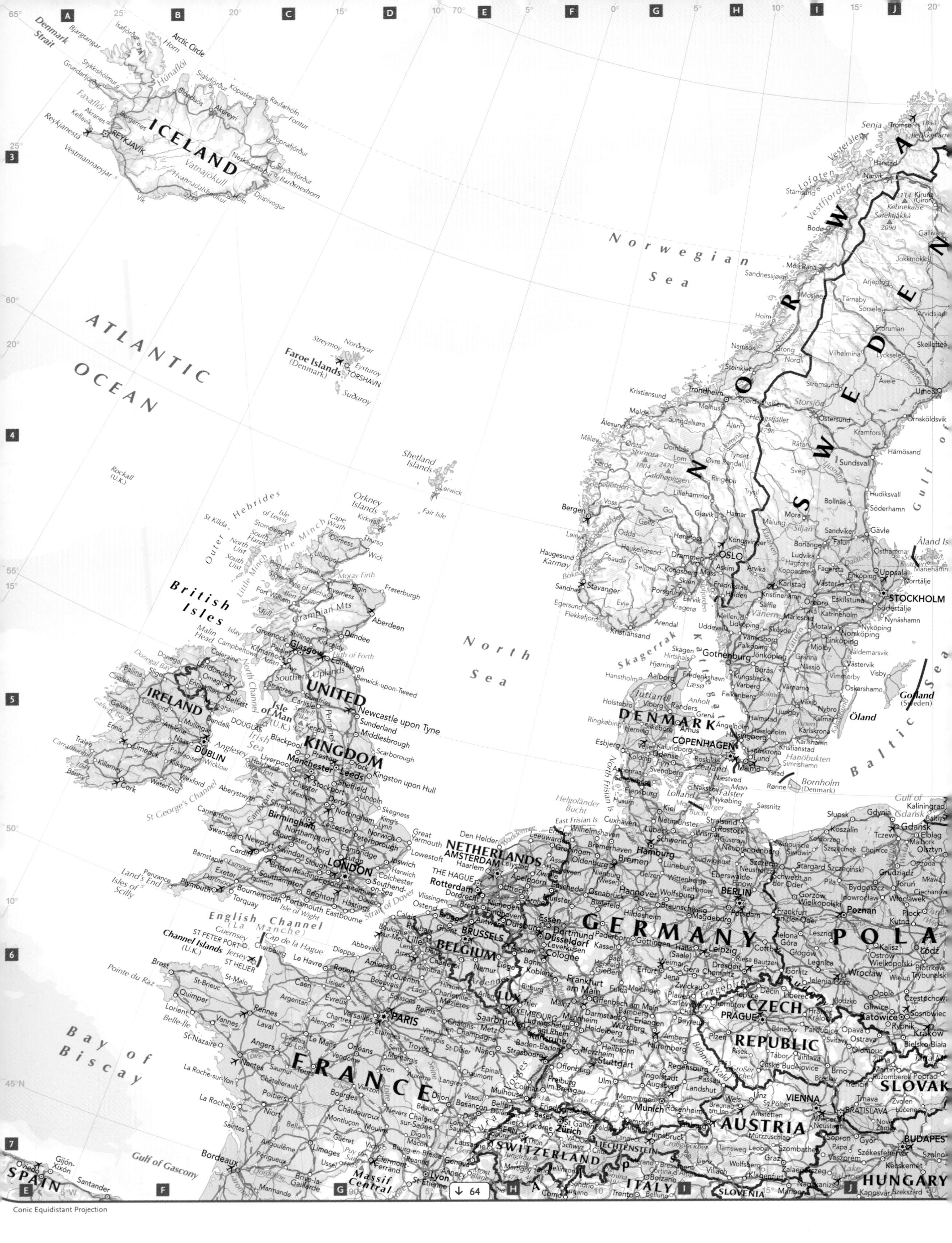

ICELAND
REYKJAVIK
Vatnajökull
Denmark Strait
Arctic Circle
ATLANTIC OCEAN
Faroe Islands (Denmark)
TORSHAVN
Norwegian Sea
NORWAY
SWEDEN
OSLO
STOCKHOLM
Shetland Islands
Orkney Islands
British Isles
North Sea
Skagerrak
DENMARK
COPENHAGEN
IRELAND
DUBLIN
UNITED KINGDOM
LONDON
Irish Sea
English Channel (La Manche)
Channel Islands (U.K.)
NETHERLANDS
AMSTERDAM
BELGIUM
BRUSSELS
LUX.
GERMANY
BERLIN
POLAND
CZECH REPUBLIC
PRAGUE
FRANCE
PARIS
Bay of Biscay
Gulf of Gascony
SWITZERLAND
LIECHTENSTEIN
AUSTRIA
VIENNA
SLOVAKIA
HUNGARY
BUDAPEST
SLOVENIA
ITALY
SPAIN
Baltic Sea
Gotland (Sweden)
Öland
Bornholm (Denmark)

↓ 64

Conic Equidistant Projection

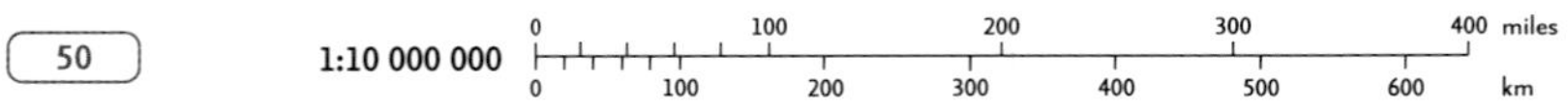

1:10 000 000
0 100 200 300 400 miles
0 100 200 300 400 500 600 km

Barents Sea
White Sea
Kola Peninsula (Kol'skiy Poluostrov)
Murmansk
Arkhangel
FINLAND
HELSINKI
Gulf of Finland
St Petersburg
Lake Ladoga (Ladozhskoye Ozero)
Onezhskoye Ozero
ESTONIA
TALLINN
Gulf of Riga
LATVIA
RĪGA
LITHUANIA
VILNIUS
RUSSIAN FEDERATION
BELARUS
MINSK
MOSCOW
UKRAINE
KIEV
Kharkiv
Odessa (Odesa)
MOLDOVA
CHIŞINĂU
ROMANIA
Carpathian Mountains
KAZAKHSTAN
Volgograd
Samara
Kazan'
Nizhniy Novgorod
Perm'
Ufa
Ural Mountains
Astrakhan'
Caspian Sea
Sea of Azov
Rostov-na-Donu
Central Russian Upland
Caspian Lowland
Timanskiy Kryazh
Yaroslavl'
Voronezh
Saratov
Penza
Tula
Ryazan'
Kirov
Syktyvkar
Ukhta
Vologda
Petrozavodsk
Pskov
Novgorod
Smolensk
Bryansk
Kursk
Belgorod
Lipetsk
Tambov
Izhevsk
Ul'yanovsk
WARSAW
Lviv
Krasnodar
↓ 65
→ 76

Europe
Northern Europe

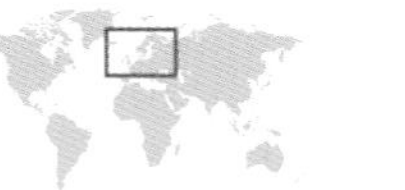

Conic Equidistant Projection

1:7 500 000 — 0, 100, 200, 300 miles; 0, 100, 200, 300, 400, 500 km

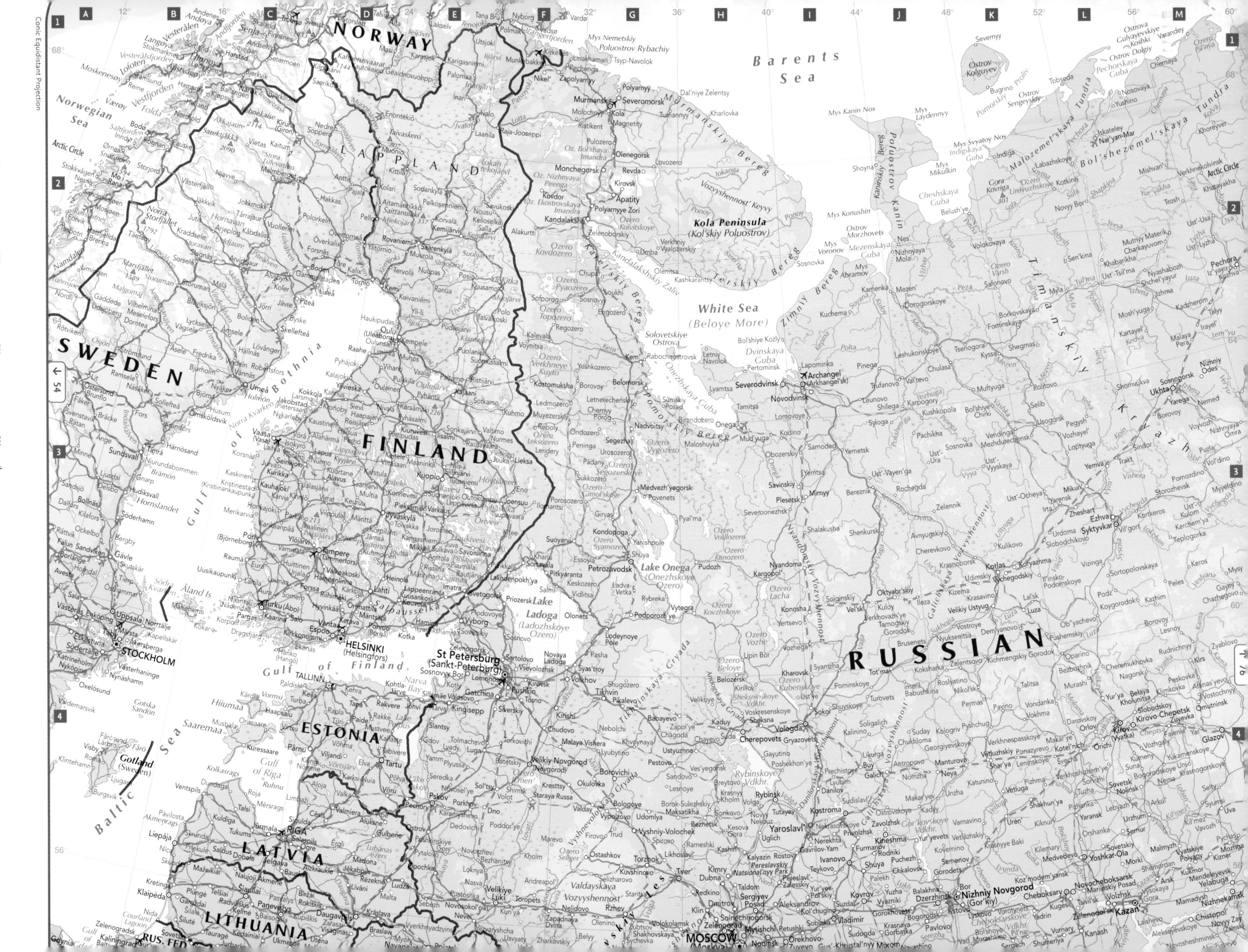

NORWAY
SWEDEN
FINLAND
RUSSIAN
ESTONIA
LATVIA
LITHUANIA
RUS. FED.
LAPPLAND
Barents Sea
White Sea (Beloye More)
Norwegian Sea
Gulf of Bothnia
Gulf of Finland
Baltic Sea
Gulf of Riga
Kola Peninsula (Kol'skiy Poluostrov)
Poluostrov Kanin
Ostrov Kolguyev
Timanskiy Kryazh
Lake Ladoga (Ladozhskoye Ozero)
Lake Onega (Onezhskoye Ozero)
MOSCOW (Moskva)
St Petersburg (Sankt-Peterburg)
HELSINKI (Helsingfors)
STOCKHOLM
TALLINN
RIGA
Archangel (Arkhangel'sk)
Murmansk
Nizhniy Novgorod (Gor'kiy)
Kazan'
Gotland (Sweden)
Åland Is
Arctic Circle

↑ 76
↓ 54

FEDERATION
KAZAKHSTAN
ZAPADNYY KAZAKHSTAN
ATYRAUSKAYA OBLAST'
BELARUS
UKRAINE
POLAND
SLOVAKIA
HUNGARY
ROMANIA
MOLDOVA
BULGARIA
GREECE
TURKEY
GEORGIA
ARMENIA
AZER.
Black Sea
Sea of Azov
Caspian Sea
Crimea
Carpathian Mountains
Central Russian Upland
KIEV (Kyiv)
MINSK
WARSAW (Warszawa)
VILNIUS
BUCHAREST (București)
SOFIA (Sofiya)
CHIȘINĂU (Kishinev)
T'BILISI
← 57
← 69
↑ 113
112 ↓

Europe

Western Russian Federation

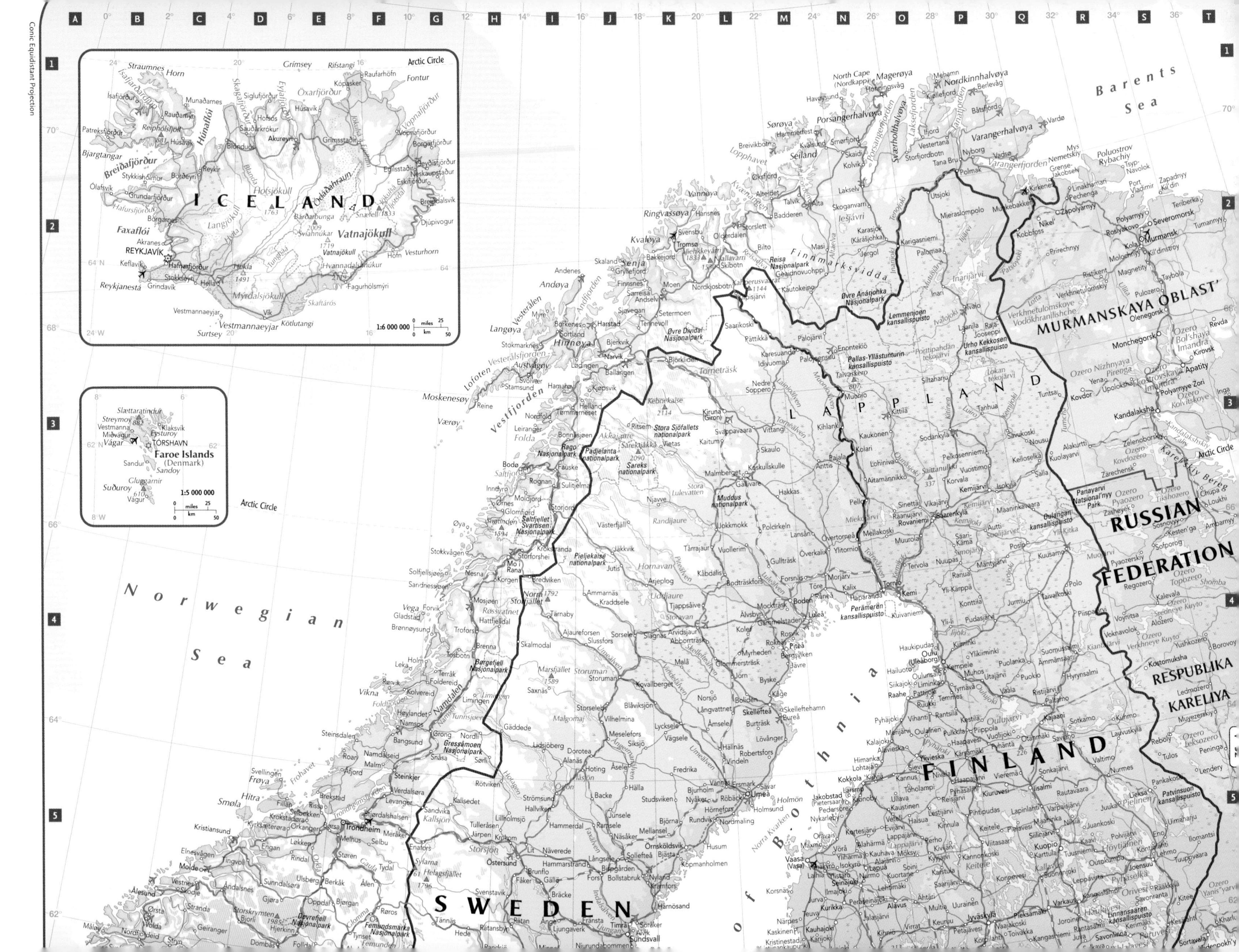

Barents Sea
MURMANSKAYA OBLAST'
RUSSIAN FEDERATION
RESPUBLIKA KARELIYA
LAPPLAND
FINLAND
SWEDEN
Norwegian Sea
Gulf of Bothnia
ICELAND
Vatnajökull
REYKJAVÍK
Faroe Islands
(Denmark)
TÓRSHAVN
Arctic Circle
1:6 000 000
1:5 000 000

Conic Equidistant Projection

1:5 000 000 — 0 50 100 150 miles; 0 50 100 150 200 250 km

NORWAY
SWEDEN
FINLAND
ESTONIA
LATVIA
LITHUANIA
BELARUS
RUSSIAN FEDERATION
PSKOVSKAYA OBLAST'
LENINGRADSKAYA OBLAST'
POLAND
GERMANY
DENMARK
Jutland
OSLO
STOCKHOLM
HELSINKI (Helsingfors)
TALLINN
RIGA
VILNIUS
MINSK
WARSAW (Warszawa)
BERLIN
COPENHAGEN (København)
St Petersburg (Sankt-Peterburg)
Gulf of Finland
Gulf of Riga
Gulf of Gdańsk
Baltic Sea
Skagerrak
Kattegat
Gotland (Sweden)
Öland
Saaremaa
Hiiumaa
Åland Islands
Bornholm (Denmark)
Zealand
Fyn
Lolland
Falster
Møn
Rügen
Lake Peipus
Lake Ladoga
Vänern
Vättern
Hanöbukten
Pomeranian Bay
North Frisian Islands
East Frisian Islands
German Bight
Gothenburg (Göteborg)
Gdańsk
Kaliningrad
Hamburg
Bremen
Hannover
Bergen
Stavanger
Kristiansand
Tampere (Tammerfors)
Turku (Åbo)
Malmö
Poznań
Bydgoszcz
Klaipėda
Kaunas
Daugavpils
Tartu
Pärnu
Liepāja
Ventspils
Örebro
Uppsala
Västerås
Norrköping
Linköping
Jönköping
Karlstad
Kiel
Rostock
Szczecin
Białystok
Aalborg
Århus
57

Europe

Scandinavia and the Baltic States

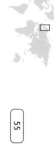

ATLANTIC OCEAN
North Sea
British Isles
UNITED KINGDOM
IRELAND
Great Britain
FRANCE
BELGIUM
Celtic Sea
Irish Sea
English Channel (La Manche)
Outer Hebrides
Orkney Islands
Grampian Mountains
Southern Uplands
ULSTER
CONNAUGHT
LEINSTER
MUNSTER
DUBLIN (Baile Átha Cliath)
LONDON
Glasgow
Edinburgh
Aberdeen
Dundee
Newcastle upon Tyne
Leeds
Manchester
Liverpool
Birmingham
Bristol
Cardiff
Belfast
Cork (Corcaigh)
Isle of Man (U.K.)
DOUGLAS
Bristol Channel
St George's Channel
Cardigan Bay
Channel Islands (Îles Normandes)
Guernsey (U.K.)
Jersey (U.K.)
Golfe de St-Malo
Baie de Seine
NORMANDY
BRITTANY
PICARDY
ARTOIS
ANJOU
POITOU
BRIE
BURGUNDY
PARIS
BRUSSELS
AMSTERDAM
Rotterdam
THE HAGUE ('s-Gravenhage) (Den Haag)
Conic Equidistant Projection

1:5 000 000

0	50	100	150	miles
0	50	100	150	200	250 km

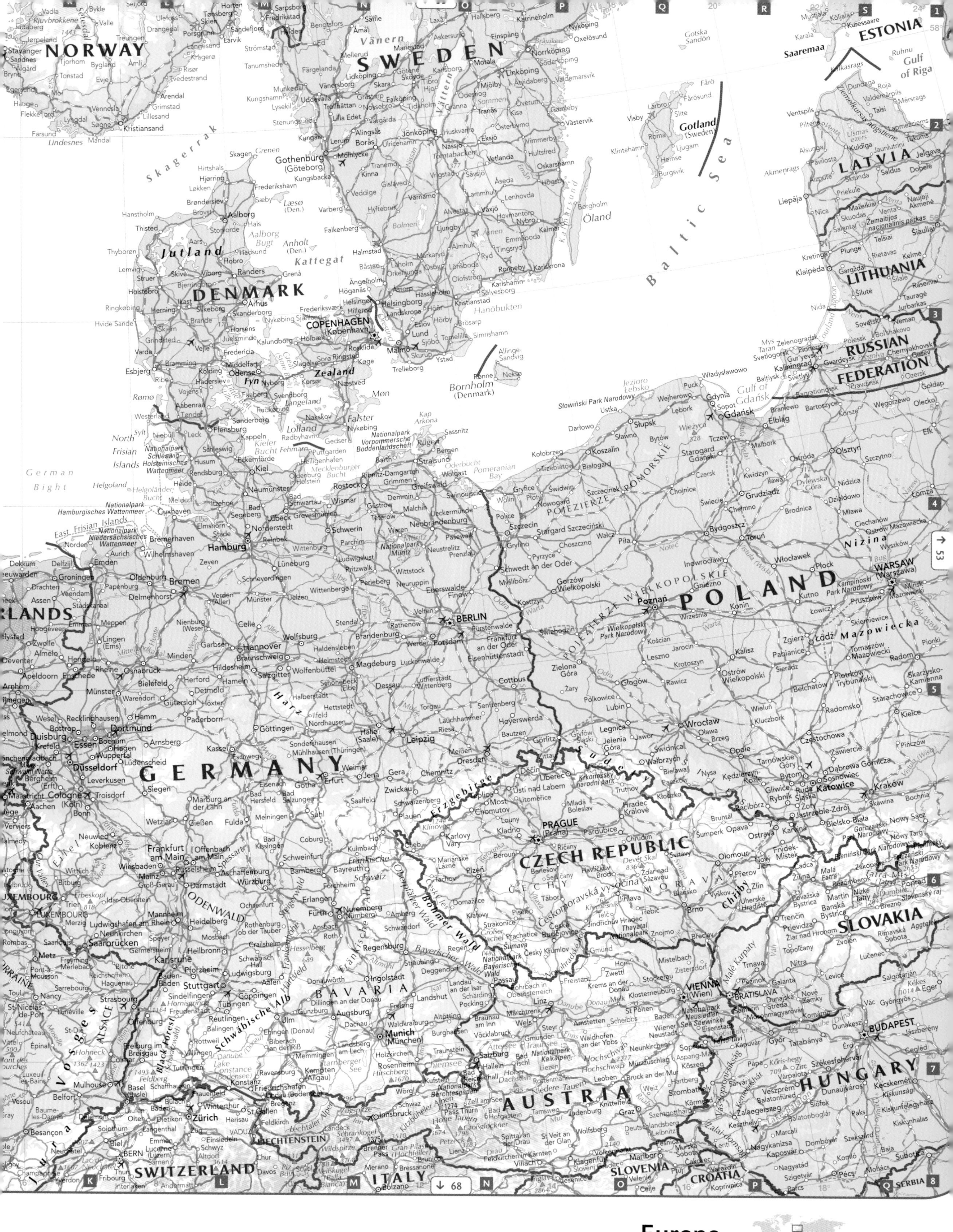
NORWAY
SWEDEN
ESTONIA
LATVIA
LITHUANIA
RUSSIAN FEDERATION
DENMARK
POLAND
GERMANY
CZECH REPUBLIC
SLOVAKIA
HUNGARY
AUSTRIA
SWITZERLAND
LIECHTENSTEIN
SLOVENIA
CROATIA
ITALY
SERBIA
Skagerrak
Kattegat
Baltic Sea
Gulf of Riga
Gulf of Gdańsk
German Bight
Jutland
Zealand
Fyn
Gotland (Sweden)
Öland
Bornholm (Denmark)
Saaremaa
COPENHAGEN (København)
BERLIN
WARSAW (Warszawa)
PRAGUE (Praha)
VIENNA (Wien)
BRATISLAVA
BUDAPEST
BERN
Gothenburg (Göteborg)
Hamburg
Bremen
Hannover
Munich (München)
Frankfurt am Main
Cologne (Köln)
Düsseldorf
Leipzig
Dresden
Nuremberg (Nürnberg)
Stuttgart
Zürich
Salzburg
Linz
Graz
Poznań
Wrocław
Kraków
Katowice
Łódź
Gdańsk
Szczecin
Malmö
Harz
Black Forest
BAVARIA
Böhmer Wald
Erzgebirge
Sudety

→ 53
↓ 68

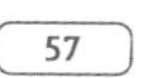

North Sea
UNITED KINGDOM
SCOTLAND
Grampian Mountains
Southern Uplands
Cheviot Hills
Pennines
North York Moors
Yorkshire Wolds
Lincolnshire Wolds
Irish Sea
Isle of Man (U.K.)
DOUGLAS
NORTHERN IRELAND
IRELAND
DUBLIN (Baile Atha Cliath)
Belfast
Glasgow
Edinburgh
Newcastle upon Tyne
Leeds
Manchester
Liverpool
Dundee
Firth of Forth
Firth of Clyde
Firth of Lorn
Solway Firth
North Channel
Anglesey (Ynys Môn)
Arran
Islay
Jura
Mull
Lough Neagh
Lake District National Park
Yorkshire Dales National Park
Northumberland National Park
North York Moors National Park
Loch Lomond & the Trossachs National Park
Cairngorms National Park
↑ 60
← 61

Conic Equidistant Projection

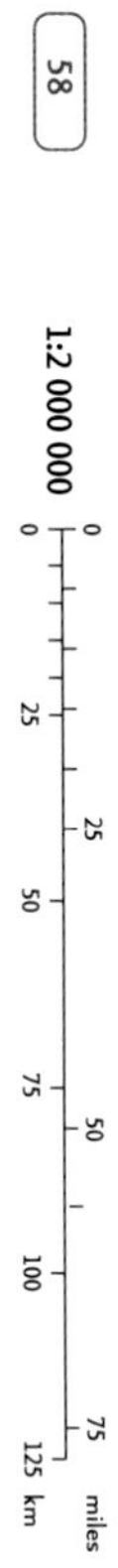
1:2 000 000
0 25 50 75 miles
0 25 50 75 100 125 km

Europe
England and Wales

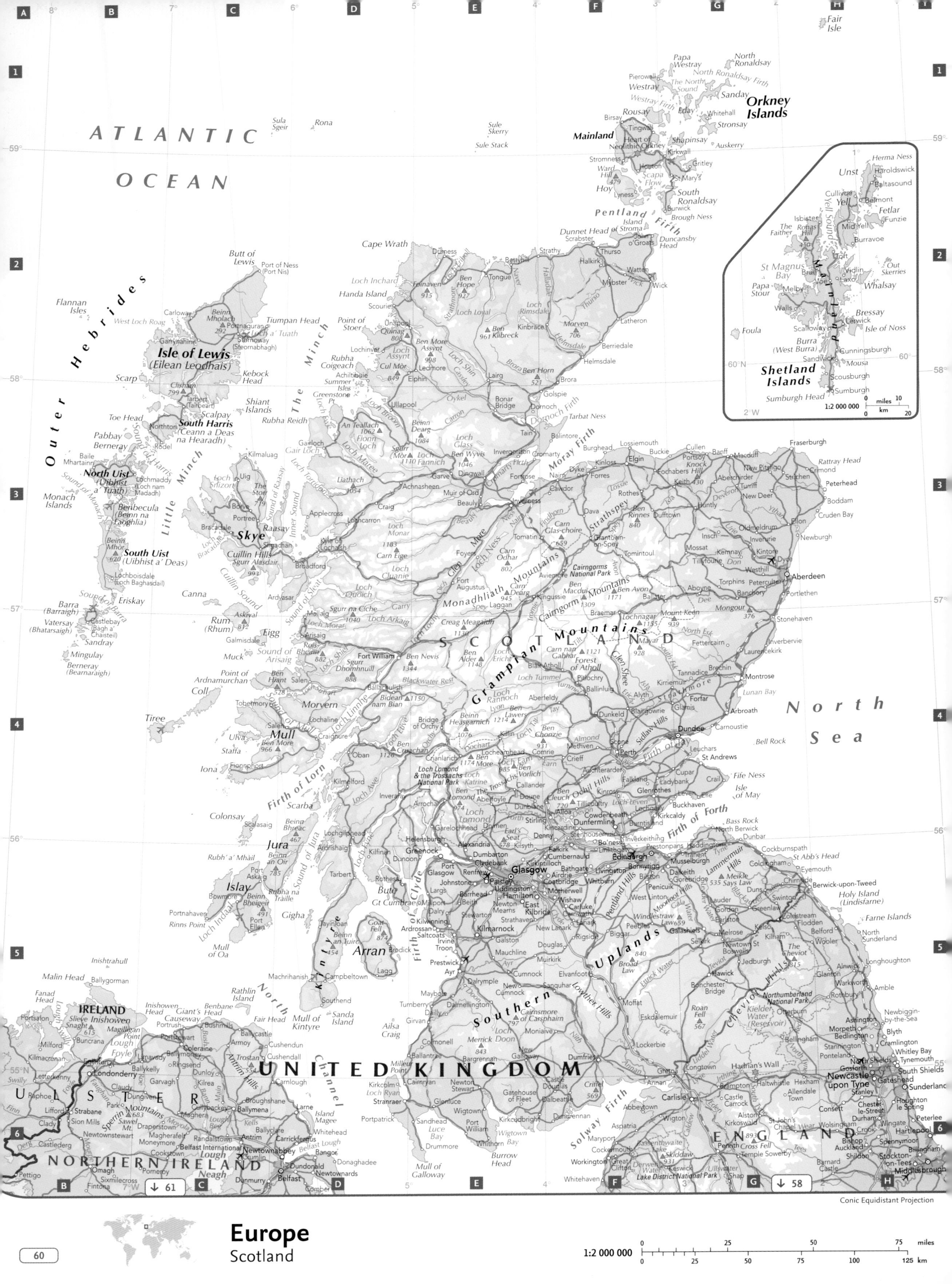

ATLANTIC OCEAN
North Sea
Outer Hebrides
The Minch
Little Minch
SCOTLAND
UNITED KINGDOM
ENGLAND
NORTHERN IRELAND
IRELAND
ULSTER
Orkney Islands
Shetland Islands
Mainland
Fair Isle
North Ronaldsay
Papa Westray
Westray
Sanday
Stronsay
Shapinsay
Hoy
South Ronaldsay
Pentland Firth
Stroma
Dunnet Head
Duncansby Head
John o'Groats
Thurso
Wick
Cape Wrath
Butt of Lewis
Isle of Lewis (Eilean Leodhais)
Stornoway (Steornabhagh)
Flannan Isles
Sula Sgeir
Rona
Sule Skerry
Sule Stack
South Harris (Ceann a Deas na Hearadh)
North Uist (Uibhist a' Tuath)
Benbecula (Beinn na Faoghla)
South Uist (Uibhist a' Deas)
Barra (Barraigh)
Monach Islands
Skye
Cuillin Hills
Raasay
Canna
Rum (Rhum)
Eigg
Coll
Tiree
Mull
Iona
Colonsay
Jura
Islay
Gigha
Kintyre
Arran
Bute
Firth of Lorn
Firth of Clyde
Firth of Forth
Moray Firth
Dornoch Firth
Firth of Tay
Solway Firth
North Channel
Inverness
Aberdeen
Dundee
Perth
Stirling
Edinburgh
Glasgow
Fort William
Oban
Ullapool
Ben Nevis 1344
Ben Macdui 1309
Grampian Mountains
Cairngorm Mountains
Cairngorms National Park
Monadhliath Mountains
Loch Lomond & the Trossachs National Park
Loch Ness
Loch Lomond
Southern Uplands
Cheviot Hills
The Cheviot 815
Northumberland National Park
Lake District National Park
Hadrian's Wall
Carlisle
Newcastle upon Tyne
Sunderland
Middlesbrough
Belfast
Londonderry
Lough Neagh
Fraserburgh
Peterhead
Montrose
Arbroath
St Andrews
Berwick-upon-Tweed
Dumfries
Stranraer
Ayr
Kilmarnock
Mull of Galloway
Mull of Kintyre
Lerwick
Sumburgh Head
Unst
Yell
Fetlar
Whalsay
Foula
Conic Equidistant Projection
1:2 000 000
Europe
Scotland
60
↓ 61
↓ 58

ATLANTIC OCEAN
UNITED KINGDOM
SCOTLAND
NORTHERN IRELAND
IRELAND
ULSTER
CONNAUGHT
LEINSTER
MUNSTER
WALES
Irish Sea
North Channel
St George's Channel
Isle of Man (U.K.)
Colonsay
Jura
Islay
Gigha
Kintyre
Arran
Malin Head
Inishtrahull
Tory Island
Fanad Head
Inishowen
Londonderry
Strabane
Letterkenny
Donegal
Donegal Bay
Sligo
Sligo Bay
Ballyshannon
Enniskillen
Omagh
Coleraine
Ballymena
Antrim
Lough Neagh
Belfast
Belfast International
Newtownabbey
Bangor
Lisburn
Craigavon
Armagh
Newry
Portadown
Dungannon
Downpatrick
Newcastle
Mourne Mts
Sperrin Mountains
Upper Lough Erne
Lower Lough Erne
Monaghan
Cavan
Dundalk
Dundalk Bay
Drogheda
Navan (An Uaimh)
Swords
DUBLIN (Baile Átha Cliath)
Dún Laoghaire
Bray
Howth
Wicklow
Wicklow Head
Wicklow Mts National Park
Lugnaquilla 926
Arklow
Wexford
Rosslare
Carnsore Point
Waterford (Port Láirge)
Tramore
Hook Head
Saltee Islands
Kilkenny (Cill Chainnigh)
Carlow (Ceatharlach)
Clonmel (Cluain Meala)
Knockmealdown Mts
Comeragh Mountains
Galtee Mountains
Cahir
Tipperary
Thurles
Nenagh
Limerick (Luimneach)
Shannon
Ennis (Inis)
Kilrush
Kilkee
Loop Head
Mouth of the Shannon
Cliffs of Moher
Hag's Head
Burren
Aran Islands
Inishmore
Inishmaan
Inisheer
Galway Bay
Galway (Gaillimh)
Athenry
Lough Corrib
Lough Mask
Connemara
Connemara National Park
Clifden
Slyne Head
Westport
Clew Bay
Croagh Patrick 765
Achill Island
Castlebar
Ballina
Nephin
Erris Head
Benwee Head
Blacksod Bay
Inishkea North
Inishkea South
Clare Island
Inishturk
Inishbofin
Inishark
Athlone
Lough Ree
Lough Derg
Mullingar
Longford
Roscommon
Tullamore
Portlaoise
Bog of Allen
Slieve Bloom Mts
Arderin 529
Naas (An Nás)
Newbridge
Kildare
Kerry Head
Tralee
Tralee Bay
Brandon Mountain 953
Dingle Bay
Slieve Mish Mts
Killarney (Cill Airne)
Killarney National Park
Macgillycuddy's Reeks
Carrantuohill 1041
Great Blasket Island (An Blascaod Mór)
Valencia Island
The Skelligs (Na Scealaga)
Kenmare
Bantry
Bantry Bay
Bere Island
Dursey Island
Mizen Head
Cape Clear
Clear Island
Skibbereen
Kinsale
Old Head of Kinsale
Cork (Corcaigh)
Cobh
Youghal
Mallow
Dungarvan
Mine Head
Conic Equidistant Projection
1:2 000 000
miles
km
Europe
Ireland

North Sea
West Frisian Islands
Waddenzee
IJsselmeer
Markermeer
UNITED KINGDOM
ENGLAND
NETHERLANDS
BELGIUM
LUXEMBOURG
FRANCE
AMSTERDAM
THE HAGUE
('s-Gravenhage)
(Den Haag)
Rotterdam
Utrecht
Eindhoven
Groningen
Leeuwarden
Antwerp
BRUSSELS
(Bruxelles)
Ghent
Bruges
Liège
Namur
Charleroi
Lille
Amiens
Reims
PARIS
LUXEMBOURG
Metz
Nancy
Düsseldorf
Cologne
(Köln)
Aachen
Duisburg
Saarbrücken
Norwich
Ipswich
Canterbury
Dover
Calais
Strait of Dover
(Pas de Calais)
FLANDRE
ARTOIS
NORD-PAS-DE-CALAIS
HAINAUT
PICARDY
PICARDIE
THIÉRACHE
HAUTE-NORMANDIE
CHAMPAGNE-ARDENNE
LORRAINE
ÎLE-DE-FRANCE
Ardennes
SAARLAND
Eifel
HUNSRUG
Nationalpark Niedersächsisches Wattenmeer
Conic Equidistant Projection
← 59

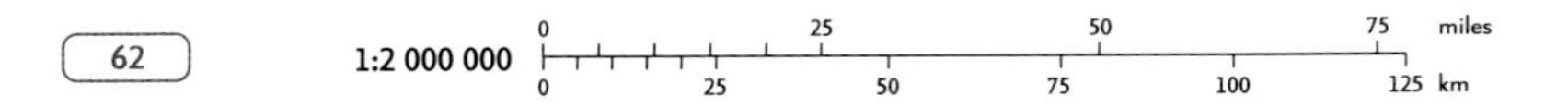
1:2 000 000
0 25 50 75 miles
0 25 50 75 100 125 km

GERMANY
NIEDERSACHSEN
NORDRHEIN-WESTFALEN
HESSEN
THÜRINGEN
SACHSEN
SACHSEN ANHALT
BRANDENBURG
MECKLENBURG-VORPOMMERN
SCHLESWIG-HOLSTEIN
BAVARIA
BAYERN
BADEN-WÜRTTEMBERG
RHEINLAND-PFALZ
ALSACE
CZECH REPUBLIC
ALTMARK
PRIGNITZ
UCKERMARK
ZAUCHE
Fläming
LÜNEBURGER HEIDE
MÜNSTER LAND
TECKLENBURGER LAND
OBERWALDER LAND
BERGISCHES LAND
NORDPFALZER BERGLAND
GOLDENE AUE
AMMERLAND
OSTFRIESLAND
LAND WURSTEN
Harz
Thüringer Wald
Erzgebirge
Krušné hory
Oberpfälzer Wald
Böhmer Wald
Bayerischer Wald
Fränkische Alb
Fichtelgebirge
Frankenwald
Hohe Rhön
Vogelsberg
Spessart
ODENWALD
Taunus
Westerwald
Rothaargebirge
Teutoburger Wald
Wiehengebirge
Weserbergland
Eggegebirge
Haarstrang
Steigerwald
Haßberge
Solling
Ith Hils
Hainleite
Finne
Hamburg
Bremen
Hannover
Berlin
Magdeburg
Leipzig
Erfurt
Kassel
Frankfurt am Main
Mainz
Wiesbaden
Mannheim
Heidelberg
Karlsruhe
Stuttgart
Würzburg
Nuremberg (Nürnberg)
Regensburg
Ingolstadt
Dortmund
Bochum
Münster
Osnabrück
Bielefeld
Braunschweig
Wolfsburg
Göttingen
Halle (Saale)
Dessau
Potsdam
Schwerin
Lübeck
Lüneburg
Oldenburg
Wilhelmshaven
Bremerhaven
Jena
Gera
Chemnitz
Zwickau
Plauen
Hof
Bayreuth
Bamberg
Fürth
Erlangen
Heilbronn
Darmstadt
Fulda
Gießen
Marburg an der Lahn
Siegen
Koblenz
Kaiserslautern
Ludwigshafen am Rhein
Hildesheim
Salzgitter
Celle
Paderborn
Detmold
Hamm
Nationalpark Niedersächsisches Wattenmeer
Nationalpark Müritz
↑ 55
↑ 57
66

ATLANTIC OCEAN
IRELAND
DUBLIN
Galway
Athlone
Limerick
Kilkenny
Waterford
Wexford
Cork
Tralee
Irish Sea
UNITED KINGDOM
LONDON
Birmingham
Manchester
Leeds
Liverpool
Sheffield
Nottingham
Leicester
Bristol
Cardiff
Swansea
Southampton
Portsmouth
Brighton
Plymouth
Exeter
Norwich
Cambridge
Oxford
York
Kingston upon Hull
St George's Channel
English Channel
(La Manche)
Channel Islands
(U.K.)
Jersey
Guernsey
Isles of Scilly
Land's End
NETHERLANDS
AMSTERDAM
THE HAGUE
Rotterdam
Utrecht
Groningen
Eindhoven
BELGIUM
BRUSSELS
Antwerp
Ghent
Brugge
Liège
LUXEMBOURG
GERMANY
BERLIN
Hamburg
Bremen
Hannover
Düsseldorf
Dortmund
Essen
Cologne
Bonn
Frankfurt am Main
Stuttgart
Munich
Nuremberg
Leipzig
Dresden
Kiel
Rostock
Helgoländer Bucht
FRANCE
PARIS
Lyon
Marseille
Toulouse
Bordeaux
Nantes
Rennes
Brest
Lille
Strasbourg
Dijon
Limoges
Clermont-Ferrand
Montpellier
Nice
Le Havre
Rouen
Orléans
Tours
Poitiers
La Rochelle
Massif Central
Bay of Biscay
Gulf of Gascony
(Golfe de Gascogne)
Golfe du Lion
MONACO
SWITZERLAND
BERN
Zürich
Basel
Lausanne
Geneva
LIECHTENSTEIN
ITALY
ROME
Milan
Turin
Genoa
Venice
Verona
Bologna
Florence
Pisa
Dolomites
Ligurian Sea
Gulf of Genoa
Tyrrhenian Sea
Corsica
(Corse)
(France)
Ajaccio
Bastia
Strait of Bonifacio
Sardinia
(Sardegna)
(Italy)
Cagliari
Sassari
Sicily
(Sicilia)
Sicilian Channel
Trapani
Marsala
SAN MARINO
ANDORRA
ANDORRA LA VELLA
Pyrenees
SPAIN
MADRID
Barcelona
Valencia
Seville
Zaragoza
Málaga
Murcia
Alicante
(Alacant)
Córdoba
Granada
Bilbao
Santander
Oviedo
A Coruña
Vigo
Valladolid
Salamanca
Toledo
Cartagena
Almería
Cádiz
Jerez de la Frontera
Cordillera Cantábrica
Sierra Morena
Sierra Nevada
Mar Cantábrico
Balearic Islands
(Islas Baleares)
Majorca
(Mallorca)
Minorca
(Menorca)
Palma de Mallorca
Ibiza
(Eivissa)
Formentera
PORTUGAL
LISBON
Oporto
Coimbra
Faro
Cabo de São Vicente
Cape Finisterre
(Cabo Fisterra)
Gibraltar
(U.K.)
Strait of Gibraltar
Golfo de Cádiz
Mediterranean
MOROCCO
RABAT
Casablanca
Fès
Meknès
Marrakech
Tangier
(Tanger)
Tétouan
Ceuta
(Spain)
Melilla
(Spain)
Oujda
Agadir
Ouarzazate
Atlas Mountains
Anti Atlas
Haut Atlas
Moyen Atlas
Jbel Bani
Hamada du Drâa
ALGERIA
ALGIERS
(Alger)
Oran
Constantine
Annaba
Sétif
Tlemcen
Béchar
Ghardaïa
Ouargla
Biskra
Laghouat
El Goléa
Atlas Tellien
Atlas Saharien
Hauts Plateaux
Grand Erg Occidental
Grand Erg Oriental
Plateau du Tademaït
TUNISIA
TUNIS
Bizerte
Sousse
Sfax
Kairouan
Gabès
Golfe de Gabès
Golfe de Hammamet
Chott el Jerid
Île de Jerba
Isola di Pantelleria
(Italy)
TRIPOLI
(Ṭarābulus)
Jabal Nafūsah
Al Ḥamādah al Ḥamrā'

Conic Equidistant Projection

1:10 000 000

0 100 200 300 400 miles

0 100 200 300 400 500 600 km

POLAND
BELARUS
UKRAINE
RUSSIAN FEDERATION
MOLDOVA
ROMANIA
HUNGARY
SLOVAKIA
CZECH REP.
CROATIA
BOSNIA-HERZEGOVINA
SERBIA
MONTENEGRO
KOSOVO
BULGARIA
MACEDONIA
ALBANIA
GREECE
TURKEY
CYPRUS
SYRIA
LEBANON
ISRAEL
JORDAN
SAUDI ARABIA
EGYPT
LIBYA
MALTA
WARSAW
MINSK
KIEV
BUDAPEST
BUCHAREST
BELGRADE
SOFIA
SARAJEVO
SKOPJE
TIRANA
PRISHTINE
PODGORICA
ZAGREB
LJUBLJANA
BRATISLAVA
VIENNA
CHIȘINĂU
ATHENS
ANKARA
NICOSIA
BEIRUT
DAMASCUS
JERUSALEM
'AMMAN
CAIRO
(Al Qahirah)
VALLETTA
İstanbul
Black Sea
Sea of Azov
Aegean Sea
Ionian Sea
Mediterranean Sea
Red Sea
Gulf of Sirte
(Khalīj Surt)
Carpathian Mountains
Transylvanian Alps
Balkan Mts
Rhodope Mts
Dinaric Alps
Taurus Mountains
Anadolu Dağlari
Caucasus
(Bol'shoy Kavkaz)
Crimea
Crete
(Kriti)
Rhodes
(Rodos)
Cyclades
(Kyklades)
Dodecanese
(Dodekanisa)
Ionian Islands
Sinai
Eastern Desert
Libyan Plateau
Qattara Depression
↑ 51
↓ 121
→ 108

Europe

Southern Europe and the Mediterranean

↑ 56
↑ 57
↑ 68
UNITED KINGDOM
BELGIUM
BRUSSELS
LUXEMBOURG
G E R M A N Y
F R A N C E
SWITZERLAND
AUSTRIA
LIECHTENSTEIN
I T A L Y
MONACO
ANDORRA
S P A I N
English Channel
(La Manche)
Bay of Biscay
Gulf of Gascony
(Golfe de Gascogne)
Mar Cantábrico
Mediterranean Sea
Ligurian Sea
Gulf of Genoa
Golfe du Lion
Channel Islands
(Îles Normandes)
Corsica
(Corse)
(France)
PARIS
Lyon
Marseille
Bordeaux
Toulouse
Nantes
Rennes
Barcelona
Zaragoza
Bilbao
Turin
Milan
Genoa
BERN
Zürich
Strasbourg
NORMANDY
BRITTANY
PICARDY
ARTOIS
LORRAINE
ALSACE
BURGUNDY
CHAMPAGNE
SAVOY
DAUPHINÉ
PROVENCE
LANGUEDOC
AQUITAINE
GASCONY
GUYENNE
LIMOUSIN
AUVERGNE
BOURBONNAIS
POITOU
SAINTONGE
ANJOU
MARCHE
CAMARGUE
MÉDOC
NAVARRA
LA RIOJA
CATALUÑA
CASTILLA Y LEÓN
Massif Central
Pyrenees
Vosges
Jura
Apennines
Ardennes

Conic Equidistant Projection

Europe
France

1:5 000 000

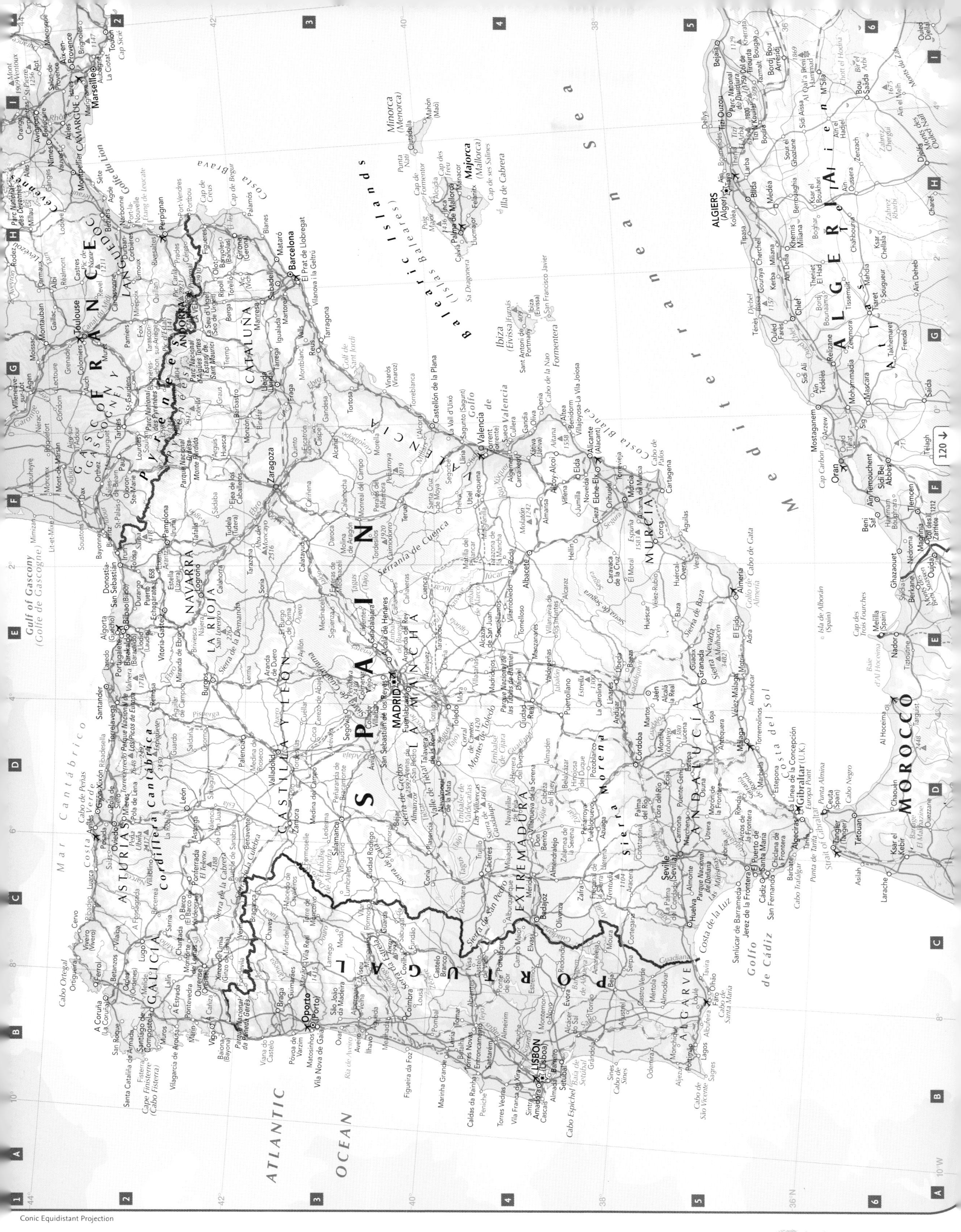

ATLANTIC OCEAN
Gulf of Gascony (Golfe de Gascogne)
Mar Cantábrico
Mediterranean Sea
Balearic Islands (Islas Baleares)
SPAIN
PORTUGAL
FRANCE
ALGERIA
MOROCCO
MADRID
LISBON (Lisboa)
Barcelona
Valencia
Seville (Sevilla)
Zaragoza
Oporto (Porto)
ALGIERS (Alger)
Gibraltar (U.K.)
Majorca (Mallorca)
Minorca (Menorca)
Ibiza (Eivissa)
Formentera
ANDORRA

Conic Equidistant Projection

1:5 000 000

miles	0	50	100	150

km	0	50	100	150	200	250

Europe
Spain and Portugal

↑ 57
↑ 66
↓ 120
AUSTRIA
SWITZERLAND
LIECHTENSTEIN
SLOVENIA
CROATIA
BOSNIA-
HERZEGOVINA
HUN
FRANCE
ITALY
MONACO
SAN MARINO
VATICAN CITY
TUNISIA
ALGERIA
MALTA
ROME (Roma)
Naples (Napoli)
Milan (Milano)
Turin (Torino)
Genoa (Genova)
Venice (Venezia)
Florence (Firenze)
Bologna
Palermo
Cagliari
TUNIS
BERN
LJUBLJANA
ZAGREB
SARAJEVO
VALLETTA
Corsica (Corse) (France)
Sardinia (Sardegna) (Italy)
Sicily (Sicilia)
Ligurian Sea
Tyrrhenian Sea
Adriatic Sea
Ionian Sea
Mediterranean
Gulf of Venice
Gulf of Genoa
Golfo di Taranto
Malta Channel
Sicilian Channel
Strait of Bonifacio
Strait of Messina
Isole Lipari
Isole Egadi
Isole Pelagie (Italy)
Pantelleria
Isola di Pantelleria (Italy)
Alps
Dolomites
Apennines
Marseille
Lyon
Nice
Trieste
Split
Bari
Brindisi
Taranto
Catania
Messina
Syracuse (Siracusa)
Reggio di Calabria
Ancona
Pescara
Livorno
Pisa
Verona
Padua (Padova)
Sfax
Sousse
Bizerte
Annaba

Conic Equidistant Projection

1:5 000 000

0 50 100 150 miles

0 50 100 150 200 250 km

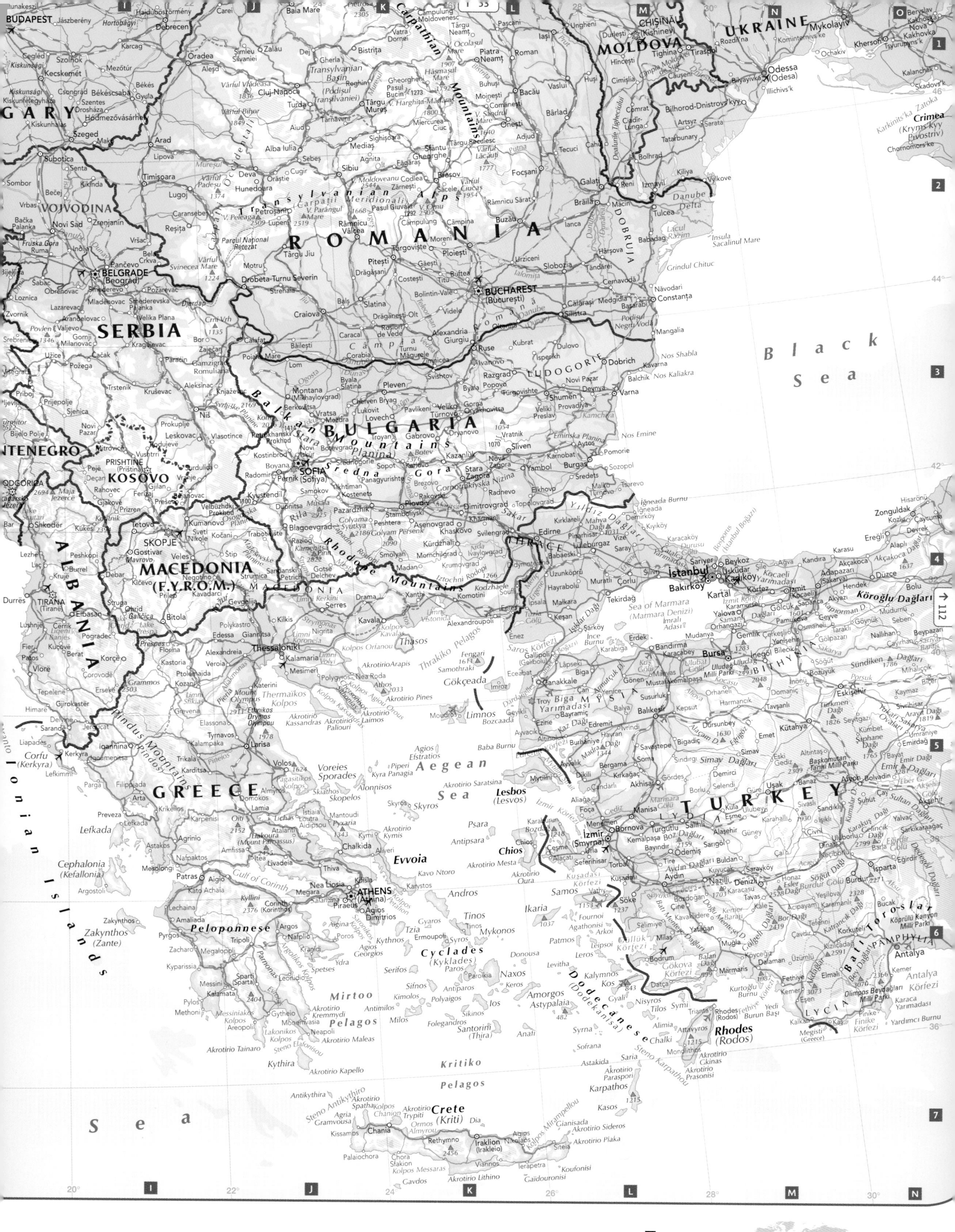

BUDAPEST
UKRAINE
MOLDOVA
CHIȘINĂU (Kishinev)
Odessa (Odesa)
Crimea
ROMANIA
Transylvanian Alps
Carpathian Mountains
BUCHAREST (București)
Constanța
Danube Delta
SERBIA
BELGRADE (Beograd)
VOJVODINA
KOSOVO
PRISHTINE (Priština)
MONTENEGRO
BULGARIA
SOFIA (Sofiya)
Balkan Mountains (Stara Planina)
Rhodope Mountains
Sredna Gora
Varna
Burgas
Plovdiv
Black Sea
MACEDONIA (F.Y.R.O.M.)
SKOPJE
ALBANIA
TIRANA (Tirane)
Durrës
GREECE
ATHENS (Athina)
Thessaloniki
Pindus Mountains (Pindos)
Peloponnese
Cyclades (Kyklades)
Dodecanese (Dodekanisa)
Crete (Kriti)
Rhodes (Rodos)
Lesbos (Lesvos)
Chios
Samos
Evvoia
Ionian Islands
Corfu (Kerkyra)
Cephalonia (Kefallonia)
Zakynthos (Zante)
Aegean Sea
Kritiko Pelagos
Mirtoo Pelagos
Thasos
Limnos
THRACE
MACEDONIA
TURKEY
İstanbul
Sea of Marmara (Marmara Denizi)
Bursa
İzmir (Smyrna)
Antalya
Gökçeada

Asia

UNESCO World Heritage Sites

This vast continent contains some of the world's most spectacular sites. The Great Wall of China, the terracotta warriors in the Tomb of the First Qin Emperor, the temple of Angkor and the Taj Mahal are all well known, but smaller yet equally important sites are also on the World Heritage List.

● Cultural site ● Natural site ● Mixed site

Afghanistan
1. Cultural Landscape and Archaeological Remains of the Bamiyan Valley
2. Minaret and Archaeological Remains of Jam

Armenia
3. Cathedral and Churches of Echmiatsin and the Archaeological Site of Zvartnots
4. Monasteries of Haghpat and Sanahin
5. Monastery of Geghard and the Upper Azat Valley

Azerbaijan
6. Gobustan Rock Art Cultural Landscape
7. Walled City of Baku with the Shirvanshah's Palace and Maiden Tower

Bahrain
8. Qal'at al-Bahrain – Ancient Harbour and Capital of Dilmun

EUROPE
RUSSIAN FEDERATION
Black Sea
TURKEY
GEORGIA
ARMENIA
AZERBAIJAN
Caspian Sea
KAZAKHSTAN
UZBEKISTAN
TURKMENISTAN
KYRGYZSTAN
TAJIKISTAN
MONGOLIA
NORTH KOREA
SOUTH KOREA
CHINA
IRAQ
IRAN
KUWAIT
AFGHANISTAN
SAUDI ARABIA
BAHRAIN
QATAR
PAKISTAN
NEPAL
BHUTAN
U.A.E.
OMAN
YEMEN
Socotra (Yemen)
INDIA
BANGLADESH
MYANMAR (BURMA)
LAOS
VIETNAM
THAILAND
CAMBODIA
TAIWAN
SRI LANKA
MALDIVES
MALAYSIA
BRUNEI
SINGAPORE
INDONE
INDIAN OCEAN
CYPRUS
SYRIA
LEBANON
ISRAEL
JORDAN

Bangladesh
9. Historic Mosque City of Bagerhat
10. Ruins of the Buddhist Vihara at Paharpur
11. The Sundarbans

Cambodia
12. Angkor
13. Temple of Preah Vihear

China
14. Ancient Building Complex in the Wudang Mountains
15. Ancient City of Ping Yao
16. Ancient Villages in Southern Anhui – Xidi and Hongcun
17. Capital Cities and Tombs of the Ancient Koguryo Kingdom
18. Classical Gardens of Suzhou
19. Dazu Rock Carvings
20. Fujian Tulou
21. Historic Centre of Macao
22. Historic Ensemble of the Potala Palace, Lhasa
23. Huanglong Scenic and Historic Interest Area
24. Imperial Palaces of the Ming and Qing Dynasties in Beijing and Shenyang
25. Imperial Tombs of the Ming and Qing Dynasties
26. Jiuzhaigou Valley Scenic and Historic Interest Area
27. Kaiping Diaolou and Villages
28. Longmen Grottoes
29. Lushan National Park
30. Mausoleum of the First Qin Emperor
31. Mogao Caves
32. Mount Emei Scenic Area, including Leshan Giant Buddha Scenic Area
33. Mount Huangshan
34. Mount Qingcheng and the Dujiangyan Irrigation System
35. Mount Sanqingshan National Park
36. Mount Taishan
37. Mount Wutai
38. Mount Wuyi
39. Mountain Resort and its Outlying Temples, Chengde
40. Old Town of Lijiang
41. Peking Man Site at Zhoukoudian
42. Sichuan Giant Panda Sanctuaries – Wolong, Mt Siguniang and Jiajin Mountains
43. South China Karst
44. Summer Palace and Imperial Garden in Beijing
45. Temple and Cemetery of Confucius and the Kong Family Mansion in Qufu
46. Temple of Heaven: an Imperial Sacrificial Altar in Beijing
47. The Great Wall
48. Three Parallel Rivers of Yunnan Protected Areas
49. Wulingyuan Scenic and Historic Interest Area
50. Yin Xu
51. Yungang Grottoes

Cyprus
52. Choirokoitia
53. Painted Churches in the Troodos Region
54. Paphos

Georgia
55. Bagrati Cathedral and Gelati Monastery
56. Historical Monuments of Mtskheta
57. Upper Svaneti

India
58. Agra Fort
59. Ajanta Caves
60. Buddhist Monuments at Sanchi
61. Champaner-Pavagadh Archaeological Park
62. Chhatrapati Shivaji Terminus (formerly Victoria Terminus)
63. Churches and Convents of Goa
64. Elephanta Caves
65. Ellora Caves
66. Fatehpur Sikri
67. Great Living Chola Temples
68. Group of Monuments at Hampi
69. Group of Monuments at Mahabalipuram
70. Group of Monuments at Pattadakal
71. Humayun's Tomb, Delhi
72. Kaziranga National Park
73. Keoladeo National Park
74. Khajuraho Group of Monuments
75. Mahabodhi Temple Complex at Bodh Gaya
76. Manas Wildlife Sanctuary
77. Mountain Railways of India
78. Nanda Devi and Valley of Flowers National Parks
79. Qutb Minar and its Monuments, Delhi
80. Red Fort Complex
81. Rock Shelters of Bhimbetka
82. Sun Temple, Konârak
83. Sundarbans National Park
84. Taj Mahal

Indonesia
85. Borobudur Temple Compounds
86. Komodo National Park
87. Lorentz National Park
88. Prambanan Temple Compounds
89. Sangiran Early Man Site
90. Tropical Rainforest Heritage of Sumatra
91. Ujung Kulon National Park

Iran
92. Armenian Monastic Ensembles of Iran
93. Bam and its Cultural Landscape
94. Bisotun
95. Meidan Emam, Esfahan
96. Pasargadae
97. Persepolis
98. Shushtar Historical Hydraulic System
99. Soltaniyeh
100. Takht-e Soleyman
101. Tchogha Zanbil

Iraq
102. Ashur (Qal'at Sherqat)
103. Hatra
104. Samarra Archaeological City

Israel
105. Bahá'í Holy Places in Haifa and the Western Galilee
106. Biblical Tels – Megiddo, Hazor, Beer Sheba
107. Incense Route – Desert Cities in the Negev
108. Masada
109. Old City of Acre
110. The White City of Tel-Aviv – The Modern Movement

Japan
111. Buddhist Monuments in the Horyu-ji Area
112. Gusuku Sites and Related Properties of the Kingdom of Ryukyu
113. Himeji-jo
114. Hiroshima Peace Memorial (Genbaku Dome)
115. Historic Monuments of Ancient Kyoto (Kyoto, Uji and Otsu Cities)
116. Historic Monuments of Ancient Nara
117. Historic Villages of Shirakawa-go and Gokayama
118. Itsukushima Shinto Shrine
119. Iwami Ginzan Silver Mine and its Cultural Landscape
120. Sacred Sites and Pilgrimage Routes in the Kii Mountain Range
121. Shirakami-Sanchi
122. Shiretoko
123. Shrines and Temples of Nikko
124. Yakushima

Jerusalem (Site proposed by Jordan)
125. Old City of Jerusalem and its Walls

Jordan
126. Petra
127. Quseir Amra
128. Um er-Rasas (Kastrom Mefa'a)

Kazakhstan
129. Mausoleum of Khoja Ahmed Yasawi
130. Petroglyphs within the Archaeological Landscape of Tamgaly
131. Saryarka – Steppe and Lakes of Northern Kazakhstan

Kyrgyzstan
132. Sulaiman-Too Sacred Mountain

Laos
133. Town of Luang Prabang
134. Vat Phou and Associated Ancient Settlements within the Champasak Cultural Landscape

Lebanon
135. Anjar
136. Baalbek
137. Byblos
138. Ouadi Qadisha (the Holy Valley) and the Forest of the Cedars of God (Horsh Arz el-Rab)
139. Tyre

Malaysia
140. Gunung Mulu National Park
141. Kinabalu Park
142. Melaka and George Town, Historic Cities of the Straits of Malacca

Mongolia
143. Orkhon Valley Cultural Landscape
144. Uvs Nuur Basin

Nepal
145. Kathmandu Valley
146. Lumbini, the Birthplace of the Lord Buddha
147. Royal Chitwan National Park
148. Sagarmatha National Park

North Korea
149. Complex of Koguryo Tombs

Oman
150. Aflaj Irrigation Systems of Oman
151. Archaeological sites of Bat, Al-Khutm and Al-Ayn
152. Bahla Fort
153. Land of Frankincense

Pakistan
154. Archaeological Ruins at Moenjodaro
155. Buddhist Ruins of Takht-i-Bahi and Neighbouring City Remains at Sahr-i-Bahlol
156. Fort and Shalamar Gardens in Lahore
157. Historical Monuments at Makli, Thatta
158. Rohtas Fort
159. Taxila

Philippines
160. Baroque Churches of the Philippines
161. Historic Town of Vigan
162. Puerto-Princesa Subterranean River National Park
163. Rice Terraces of the Philippine Cordilleras
164. Tubbataha Reefs Natural Park

Russian Federation (see also pp42–43)
165. Central Sikhote-Alin
166. Citadel, Ancient City and Fortress Buildings of Derbent
167. Golden Mountains of Altai
168. Lake Baikal
169. Natural System of Wrangel Island Reserve
144. Uvs Nuur Basin
170. Volcanoes of Kamchatka
171. Western Caucasus

Saudi Arabia
172. Al-Hijr Archaeological Site (Madâin Sâlih)

South Korea
173. Changdeokgung Palace Complex
174. Gochang, Hwasun and Ganghwa Dolmen Sites
175. Gyeongju Historic Areas
176. Haeinsa Temple Janggyeong Panjeon, the Depositories for the Tripitaka Koreana Woodblocks
177. Hwaseong Fortress
178. Jeju Volcanic Island and Lava Tubes
179. Jongmyo Shrine
180. Royal Tombs of the Joseon Dynasty
181. Seokguram Grotto and Bulguksa Temple

Sri Lanka
182. Ancient City of Polonnaruwa
183. Ancient City of Sigiriya
184. Golden Temple of Dambulla
185. Old Town of Galle and its Fortifications
186. Sacred City of Anuradhapura
187. Sacred City of Kandy
188. Sinharaja Forest Reserve

Syria
189. Ancient City of Aleppo
190. Ancient City of Bosra
191. Ancient City of Damascus
192. Crac des Chevaliers and Qal'at Salah El-Din
193. Site of Palmyra

Thailand
194. Ban Chiang Archaeological Site
195. Dong Phayayen-Khao Yai Forest Complex
196. Historic City of Ayutthaya
197. Historic Town of Sukhothai and Associated Historic Towns
198 Thungyai-Huai Kha Khaeng Wildlife Sanctuaries

Turkey
199. Archaeological Site of Troy
200. City of Safranbolu
201. Göreme National Park and the Rock Sites of Cappadocia
202. Great Mosque and Hospital of Divriği
203. Hattusha: the Hittite Capital
204. Hierapolis-Pamukkale
205. Historic Areas of Istanbul
206. Nemrut Dağ
207. Xanthos-Letoon

Turkmenistan
208. Kunya-Urgench
209. Parthian Fortresses of Nisa
210. State Historical and Cultural Park 'Ancient Merv'

Uzbekistan
211. Historic Centre of Bukhara
212. Historic Centre of Shakhrisyabz
213. Itchan Kala
214. Samarkand – Crossroads of Cultures

Vietnam
215. Complex of Hué Monuments
216. Ha Long Bay
217. Hoi An Ancient Town
218. My Son Sanctuary
219. Phong Nha-Ke Bang National Park

Yemen
220. Historic Town of Zabid
221. Old City of Sana'a
222. Old Walled City of Shibam
223. Socotra Archipelago

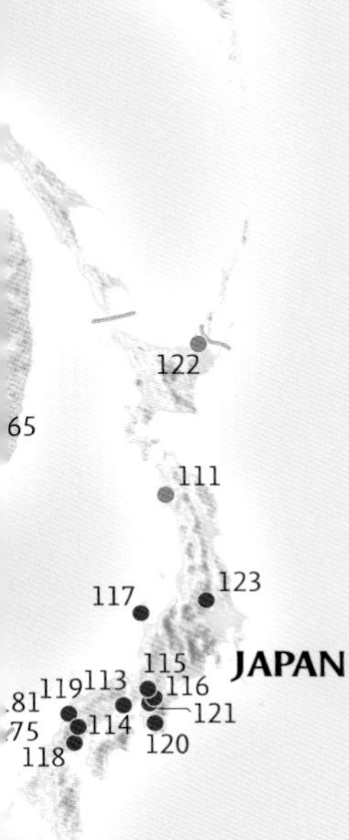

170
122
65
111
117
123
JAPAN
115
119
113
116
121
114
120
118
124

PACIFIC OCEAN

PHILIPPINES

PALAU

S I A

EAST TIMOR

Asia
Landscapes

Asia is the world's largest continent and occupies almost one-third of the world's total land area. Stretching across approximately 165° of longitude from the Mediterranean Sea to the easternmost point of the Russian Federation on the Bering Strait, it contains the world's highest and lowest points and some of the world's greatest physical features. Its mountain ranges include the Himalaya, Hindu Kush, Karakoram and the Ural Mountains and its major rivers – including the Yangtze, Tigris-Euphrates, Indus, Ganges and Mekong – are equally well-known and evocative.

Asia's deserts include the Gobi, the Taklimakan, and those on the Arabian Peninsula, and significant areas of volcanic and tectonic activity are present on the Kamchatka Peninsula, in Japan, and on Indonesia's numerous islands. The continent's landscapes are greatly influenced by climatic variations, with great contrasts between the islands of the Arctic Ocean and the vast Siberian plains in the north, and the tropical islands of Indonesia.

The **Yangtze,** China, Asia's longest river, flowing into the East China Sea near Shanghai.

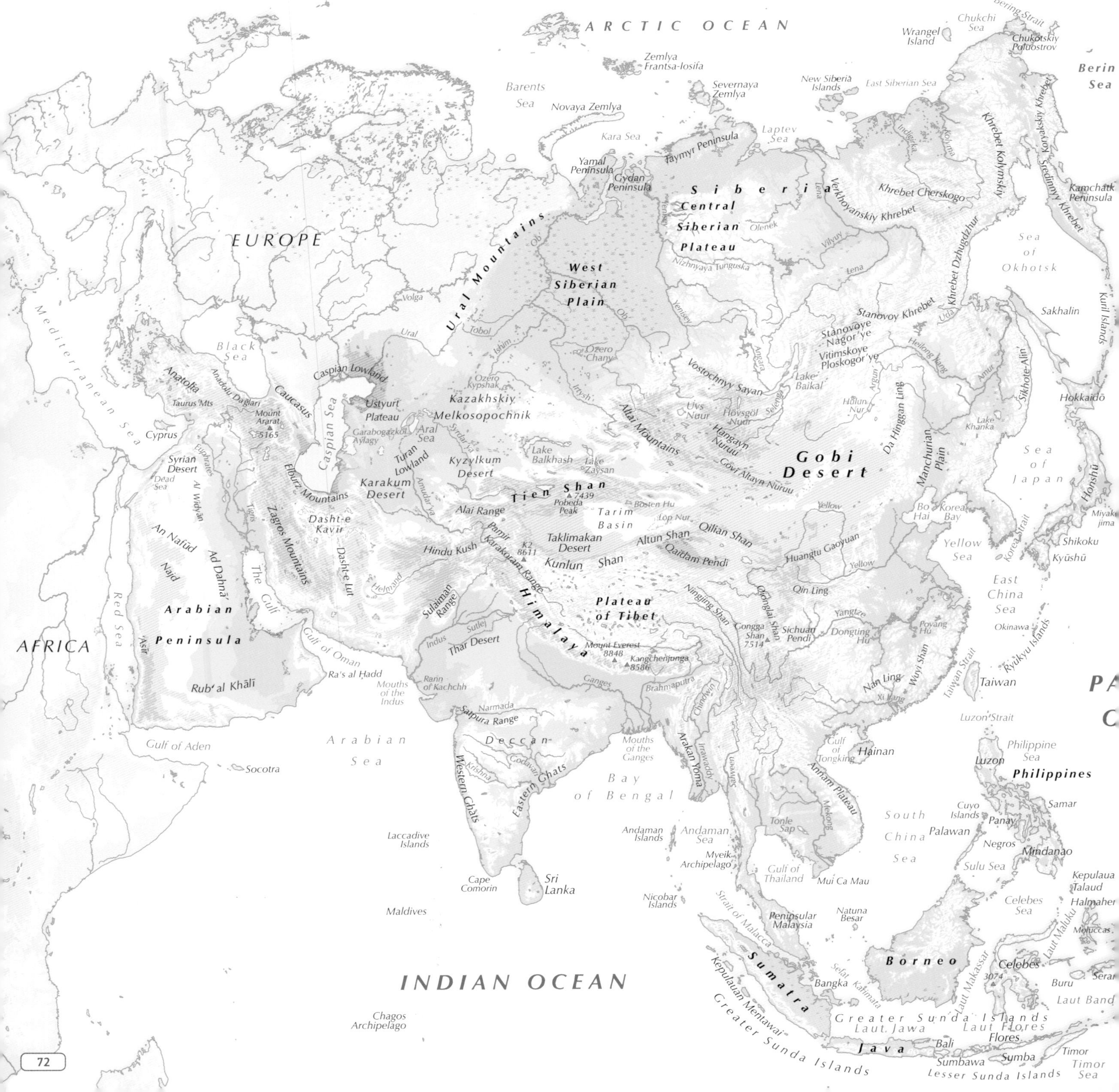

ARCTIC OCEAN
Zemlya Frantsa-Iosifa
Barents Sea
Novaya Zemlya
Severnaya Zemlya
New Siberia Islands
East Siberian Sea
Wrangel Island
Chukchi Sea
Bering Strait
Chukotskiy Poluostrov
Bering Sea
Kara Sea
Laptev Sea
Taymyr Peninsula
Yamal Peninsula
Gydan Peninsula
Siberia
Central Siberian Plateau
Olenek
Lena
Verkhoyanskiy Khrebet
Khrebet Cherskogo
Khrebet Kolymskiy
Koryakskiy Khrebet
Sredinnyy Khrebet
Kamchatka Peninsula
Sea of Okhotsk
Khrebet Dzhugdzhur
Vilyuy
Nizhnyaya Tunguska
EUROPE
Ural Mountains
Ob
West Siberian Plain
Yenisey
Stanovoy Khrebet
Stanovoye Nagor'ye
Vitimskoye Ploskogor'ye
Heilong Jiang
Amur
Uda
Sakhalin
Kuril Islands
Volga
Ural
Tobol
Ishim
Ozero Chany
Angara
Lake Baikal
Vostochnyy Sayan
Sikhote-Alin'
Hokkaidō
Mediterranean Sea
Black Sea
Anatolia
Anadolu Dağlari
Taurus Mts
Caucasus
Mount Ararat 5165
Caspian Lowland
Caspian Sea
Ustyurt Plateau
Kazakhskiy Melkosopochnik
Ozero Kypshak
Irtysh
Altai Mountains
Uvs Nuur
Hövsgöl Nuur
Selenga
Hangayn Nuruu
Hulun Nur
Da Hinggan Ling
Lake Khanka
Cyprus
Garabogazköl Aylagy
Aral Sea
Syrdar'ya
Lake Balkhash
Lake Zaysan
Govi Altayn Nuruu
Gobi Desert
Manchurian Plain
Sea of Japan
Honshū
Syrian Desert
Dead Sea
Euphrates
Al Widyan
Turan Lowland
Kyzylkum Desert
Karakum Desert
Amudar'ya
Elburz Mountains
Tien Shan
7439 Pobeda Peak
Bosten Hu
Tarim Basin
Lop Nur
Yellow
Bo Hai
Korea Bay
Korea Strait
Miyakejima
Tigris
Zagros Mountains
Dasht-e Kavir
Alai Range
Pamir
K2 8611
Taklimakan Desert
Altun Shan
Qilian Shan
Qaidam Pendi
Huangtu Gaoyuan
Yellow Sea
Shikoku
Kyūshū
An Nafūd
Ad Dahnā'
Najd
The Gulf
Dasht-e Lut
Hindu Kush
Karakoram Range
Kunlun Shan
Helmand
Qin Ling
East China Sea
Red Sea
Arabian Peninsula
Asīr
Sulaiman Range
Himalaya
Plateau of Tibet
Ningjing Shan
Qionglai Shan
Gongga Shan 7514
Sichuan Pendi
Yangtze
Dongting Hu
Poyang Hu
Okinawa
Ryukyu Islands
AFRICA
Gulf of Oman
Indus
Sutlej
Thar Desert
Mount Everest 8848
Kangchenjunga 8586
Wuyi Shan
Taiwan Strait
Taiwan
Rub' al Khālī
Ra's al Hadd
Mouths of the Indus
Rann of Kachchh
Ganges
Brahmaputra
Chindwin
Nan Ling
Xi Jiang
Luzon Strait
Narmada
Satpura Range
Gulf of Aden
Arabian Sea
Deccan
Mouths of the Ganges
Arakan Yoma
Irrawaddy
Salween
Gulf of Tongking
Hainan
Philippine Sea
Luzon
Philippines
Socotra
Western Ghats
Krishna
Godavari
Eastern Ghats
Bay of Bengal
Annam Plateau
Mekong
Samar
Tonle Sap
South China Sea
Cuyo Islands
Panay
Palawan
Negros
Laccadive Islands
Andaman Islands
Andaman Sea
Myeik Archipelago
Mindanao
Sulu Sea
Cape Comorin
Sri Lanka
Gulf of Thailand
Mui Ca Mau
Kepulauan Talaud
Halmahera
Nicobar Islands
Maldives
Strait of Malacca
Peninsular Malaysia
Natuna Besar
Celebes Sea
Laut Maluku
Moluccas
Borneo
Sumatra
Celebes
3074
Selat Makassar
INDIAN OCEAN
Kepulauan Mentawai
Bangka
Selat Karimata
Buru
Seram
Laut Banda
Greater Sunda Islands
Laut Jawa
Laut Flores
Flores
Chagos Archipelago
Java
Bali
Sumbawa
Sumba
Timor
Timor Sea
Greater Sunda Islands
Lesser Sunda Islands
PA
C

Internet Links

NASA Visible Earth	visibleearth.nasa.gov
NASA Earth Observatory	earthobservatory.nasa.gov
Peakware World Mountain Encyclopedia	www.peakware.com
The Himalaya	www.alpine-club.org.uk

Asia's physical features

Highest mountain	Mt Everest, China/Nepal	8 848 metres	29 028 feet
Longest river	Yangtze, China	6 380 km	3 965 miles
Largest lake	Caspian Sea	371 000 sq km	143 243 sq miles
Largest island	Borneo	745 561 sq km	287 861 sq miles
Largest drainage basin	Ob'-Irtysh, Kazakhstan/Russian Federation	2 990 000 sq km	1 154 439 sq miles
Lowest point	Dead Sea	-421 metres	-1 381 feet

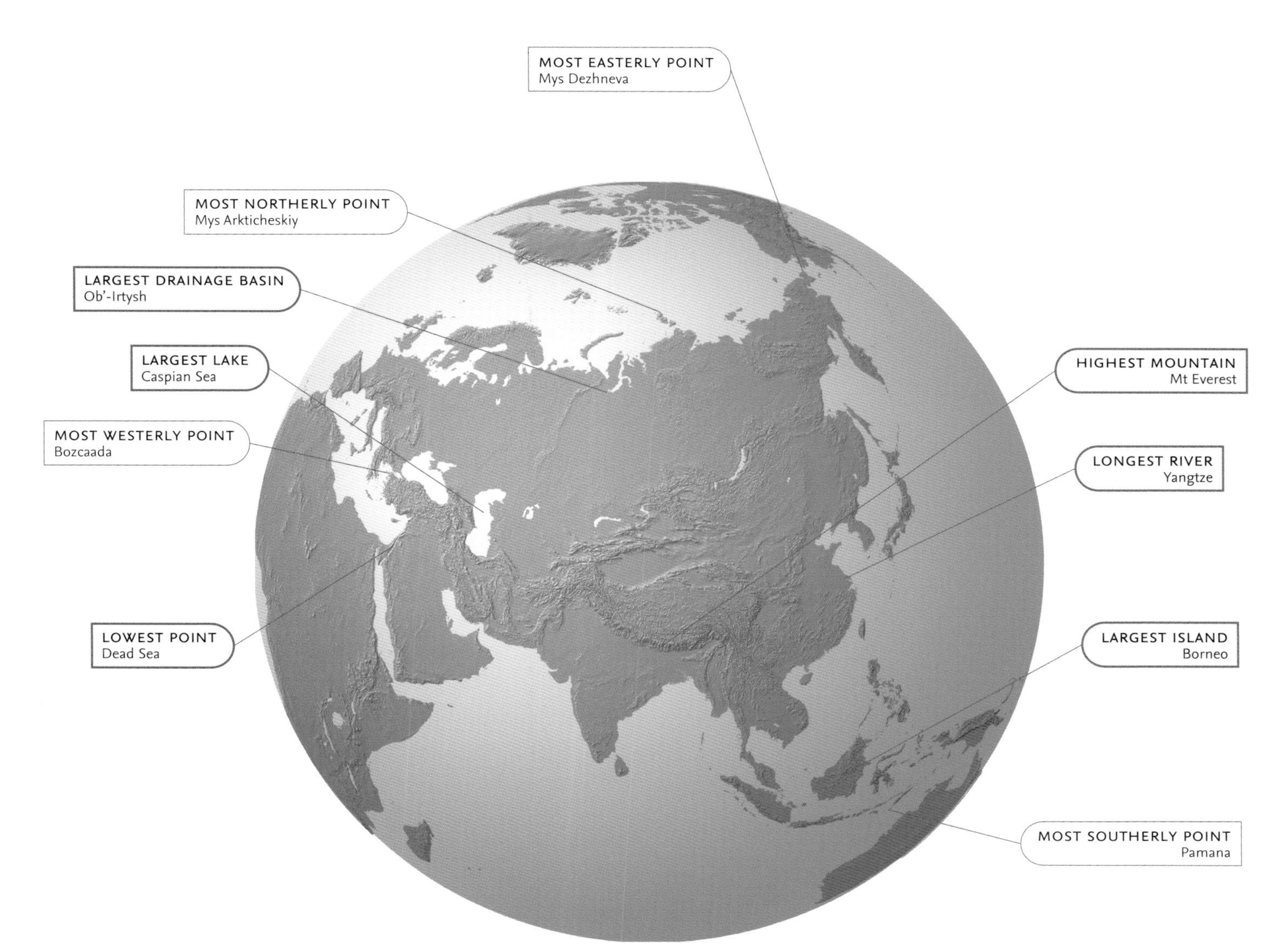

MOST EASTERLY POINT
Mys Dezhneva
MOST NORTHERLY POINT
Mys Arkticheskiy
LARGEST DRAINAGE BASIN
Ob'-Irtysh
LARGEST LAKE
Caspian Sea
MOST WESTERLY POINT
Bozcaada
LOWEST POINT
Dead Sea
HIGHEST MOUNTAIN
Mt Everest
LONGEST RIVER
Yangtze
LARGEST ISLAND
Borneo
MOST SOUTHERLY POINT
Pamana

Asia's extent

TOTAL LAND AREA	45 036 492 sq km / 17 388 686 sq miles
Most northerly point	Mys Arkticheskiy, Russian Federation
Most southerly point	Pamana, Indonesia
Most westerly point	Bozcaada, Turkey
Most easterly point	Mys Dezhneva, Russian Federation

Facts

- **90 of the world's 100 highest mountains are in Asia**
- **The Indonesian archipelago is made up of over 13 500 islands**
- **The height of the land in Nepal ranges from 60 metres to 8 848 metres**
- **The deepest lake in the world is Lake Baikal, Russian Federation, with a maximum depth of 1 741 metres**

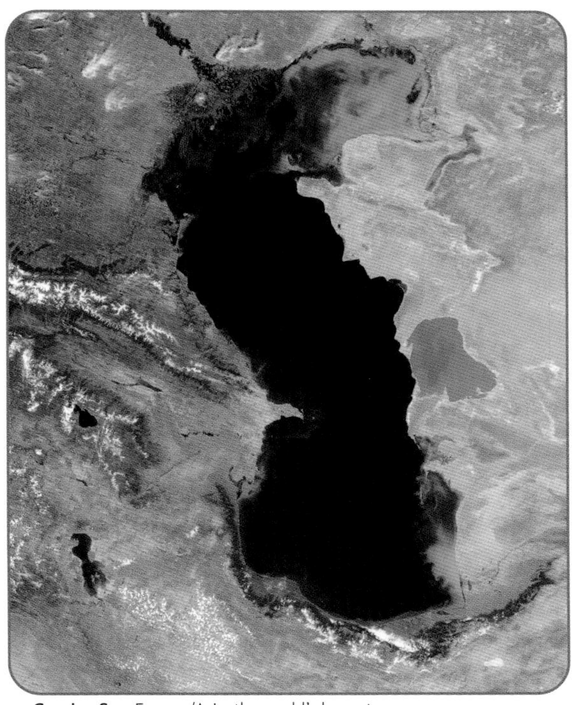

Caspian Sea, Europe/Asia, the world's largest expanse of inland water.

Asia
Countries

With approximately sixty per cent of the world's population, Asia is home to numerous cultures, people groups and lifestyles. Several of the world's earliest civilizations were established in Asia, including those of Sumeria, Babylonia and Assyria. Cultural and historical differences have led to a complex political pattern, and the continent has been, and continues to be, subject to numerous territorial and political conflicts – including the current disputes in the Middle East and in Jammu and Kashmir.

Separate regions within Asia can be defined by the cultural, economic and political systems they support. The major regions are: the arid, oil-rich, mainly Islamic southwest; southern Asia with its distinct cultures, isolated from the rest of Asia by major mountain ranges; the Indian- and Chinese-influenced monsoon region of southeast Asia; the mainly Chinese-influenced industrialized areas of eastern Asia; and Soviet Asia, made up of most of the former Soviet Union.

Timor island in southeast Asia, on which East Timor, Asia's newest independent state, is located.

ARCTIC OCEAN
Barents Sea
Laptev Sea
Bering Sea
Ugol'nyye Kopi
Tiksi
EUROPE
St Petersburg
Noril'sk
Lena
Magadan
Petropavlovsk-Kamchatskiy
Sea of Okhotsk
Urengoy
Ural Mountains
Moscow
Nizhniy Novgorod
Yakutsk
RUSSIAN FEDERATION
Kazan'
Perm'
Surgut
Aldan
Yekaterinburg
Ufa
Saratov
Tobol'sk
Bodaybo
Samara
Chelyabinsk
Tynda
Volgograd
Ural'sk
Orenburg
Omsk
Tomsk
Bratsk
Ust'-Kut
Komsomol'sk-na-Amure
Mediterranean Sea
Bursa
Black Sea
Krasnodar
Novosibirsk
Krasnoyarsk
Lake Baikal
Khabarovsk
Yuzhno-Sakhalinsk
İzmir
Ankara
Samsun
Aktobe
Astrakhan
Barnaul
Novokuznetsk
Irkutsk
Chita
Blagoveshchensk
TURKEY
Atyrau
Astana
Antalya
Konya
Sivas
GEORGIA
Karaganda
Semipalatinsk
Ust'-Kamenogorsk
Kyzyl
Ulan-Ude
Hulun Buir
Qiqihar
Sapporo
Tbilisi
Aktau
Aral'sk
Adana
Caspian Sea
KAZAKHSTAN
Ulaangom
Darhan
Ulan Bator
Harbin
Hakodate
CYPRUS
ARMENIA
Yerevan
Nicosia
Gaziantep
AZERBAIJAN
Aral Sea
Jargalant
Vladivostok
Beirut
Aleppo
Baku
UZBEKISTAN
Lake Balkhash
Altay
MONGOLIA
Changchun
Jilin
Akita
LEBANON
Tabriz
Türkmenbasy
Chongjin
Sea of Japan
Damascus
SYRIA
Mosul
Gobi Desert
JAPAN
Amman
Shymkent
Bishkek
Almaty
Yining
Ürümqi
NORTH KOREA
ISRAEL
Jerusalem
Kirkuk
TURKMENISTAN
Toshkent
Dalandzadgad
Shenyang
Tōkyō
JORDAN
IRAQ
Kermānshāh
Aşgabat
KYRGYZSTAN
Tien Shan
P'yongyang
Kanazawa
Baghdād
Tehrān
Gorgān
Samarqand
Korla
Jining
Beijing
Dalian
Seoul
Kyōto
An Najaf
Mashhad
Dushanbe
TAJIKISTAN
Baotou
Yantai
SOUTH KOREA
Kobe
Osaka
Basra
Ahvāz
Esfahān
Kashi
Yumen
Wuhai
Yinchuan
Taiyuan
Jinan
Zibo
Pusan
Hiroshima
Kuwait
KUWAIT
Ābādān
IRAN
Hotan
Qingdao
Yellow Sea
Herāt
Kābul
Xining
Nagasaki
Kagoshima
Medina
Shīrāz
Birjand
AFGHANISTAN
Peshawar
Golmud
Lanzhou
Zhengzhou
SAUDI ARABIA
Būshehr
Islamabad
Xi'an
Nanjing
Shanghai
East China Sea
BAHRAIN
Dammam
Kandahār
Jeddah
Riyadh
Manama
Zāhedān
Huainan
Wuhu
Mecca
Red Sea
The Gulf
QATAR
Bandar-e 'Abbās
Quetta
Faisalabad
Lahore
Plateau of Tibet
CHINA
Wuhan
Ningbo
Doha
Dubai
Chandigarh
Himalaya
Nanchong
Yangtze
AFRICA
U.A.E.
Abu Dhabi
Gulf of Oman
PAKISTAN
Delhi
Mount Everest 8848
Lhasa
Chengdu
Changde
Nanchang
Wenzhou
Muscat
Pasni
New Delhi
NEPAL
Yibin
Chongqing
Changsha
Fuzhou
Şūr
Hyderabad
Jaipur
Agra
Thimphu
Hengyang
PACIFIC OCEAN
Karachi
Jodhpur
Lucknow
Kathmandu
BHUTAN
Dibrugarh
Panzhihua
Guiyang
Xiamen
T'aipei
TAIWAN
Kota
Varanasi
Ganges
Darjiling
Guwahati
Kunming
Liuzhou
Kaohsiung
San'ā'
Ahmadabad
Bhopal
Patna
BANGLADESH
Myitkyina
Guangzhou
Shantou
Hodeidah
YEMEN
OMAN
Jabalpur
Dhaka
Nanning
Hong Kong
Ta'izz
Jamshedpur
MYANMAR (BURMA)
Macao
Luzon Strait
Aden
Mukalla
Şalālah
Surat
Nagpur
Kolkata
Chittagong
Mandalay
Ha Nôi
Hai Phong
Haikou
Aparri
Gulf of Aden
Arabian Sea
Mumbai
INDIA
Cuttack
Nay Pyi Taw
LAOS
PHILIPPINES
Socotra (Yemen)
Pune
Vishakhapatnam
Sittwe
Louangphabang
VIETNAM
Hyderabad
Bay of Bengal
Ryè
Vientiane
Quezon City
Dharwad
Kurnool
Rangoon
THAILAND
Đa Nẵng
Manila
Mawlamyaing
Mangalore
Bangalore
Chennai
Bangkok
Nha Trang
South China Sea
Laccadive Islands (India)
Calicut
Tiruchchirappalli
Andaman Islands (India)
Andaman Sea
CAMBODIA
Phnom Penh
Dapitan
Surigao
Madurai
Jaffna
Myeik
Davao
Trincomalee
Shanoukville
Ho Chi Minh City
Trivandrum
Nakhon Si Thammarat
Gulf of Thailand
Zamboanga
Kota Kinabalu
Colombo
SRI LANKA
Sri Jayewardenepura Kotte
Nicobar Islands (India)
Sandakan
Strait of Malacca
George Town
Kota Bharu
Bandar Seri Begawan
BRUNEI
Celebes Sea
Male
Banda Aceh
Ipoh
MALAYSIA
MALDIVES
Manado
Kuala Lumpur
Sibu
Medan
Putrajaya
Kuching
Singapore
SINGAPORE
Borneo
Palu
Sumatra
Ketapang
Balikpapan
INDIAN OCEAN
Padang
Parepare
Laut Banda
Palembang
INDONESIA
Bengkulu
Laut Jawa
Dili
Jakarta
Surabaya
Java
Raba
EAST TIMOR
British Indian Ocean Territory
Christmas Island (Australia)
Kupang

Internet Links

UK Foreign and Commonwealth Office	www.fco.gov.uk
CIA World Factbook	www.cia.gov/library/publicaions/the-world-factbook/index.html
Asian Development Bank	www.adb.org
Association of Southeast Asian Nations (ASEAN)	www.aseansec.org
Asia-Pacific Economic Cooperation	www.apec.org

Asia's countries

Largest country (area)	Russian Federation	17 075 400 sq km	6 592 849 sq miles
Smallest country (area)	Maldives	298 sq km	115 sq miles
Largest country (population)	China	1 313 437 000	
Smallest country (population)	Palau	20 000	
Most densely populated country	Singapore	6 770 per sq km	17 534 per sq mile
Least densely populated country	Mongolia	2 per sq km	5 per sq mile

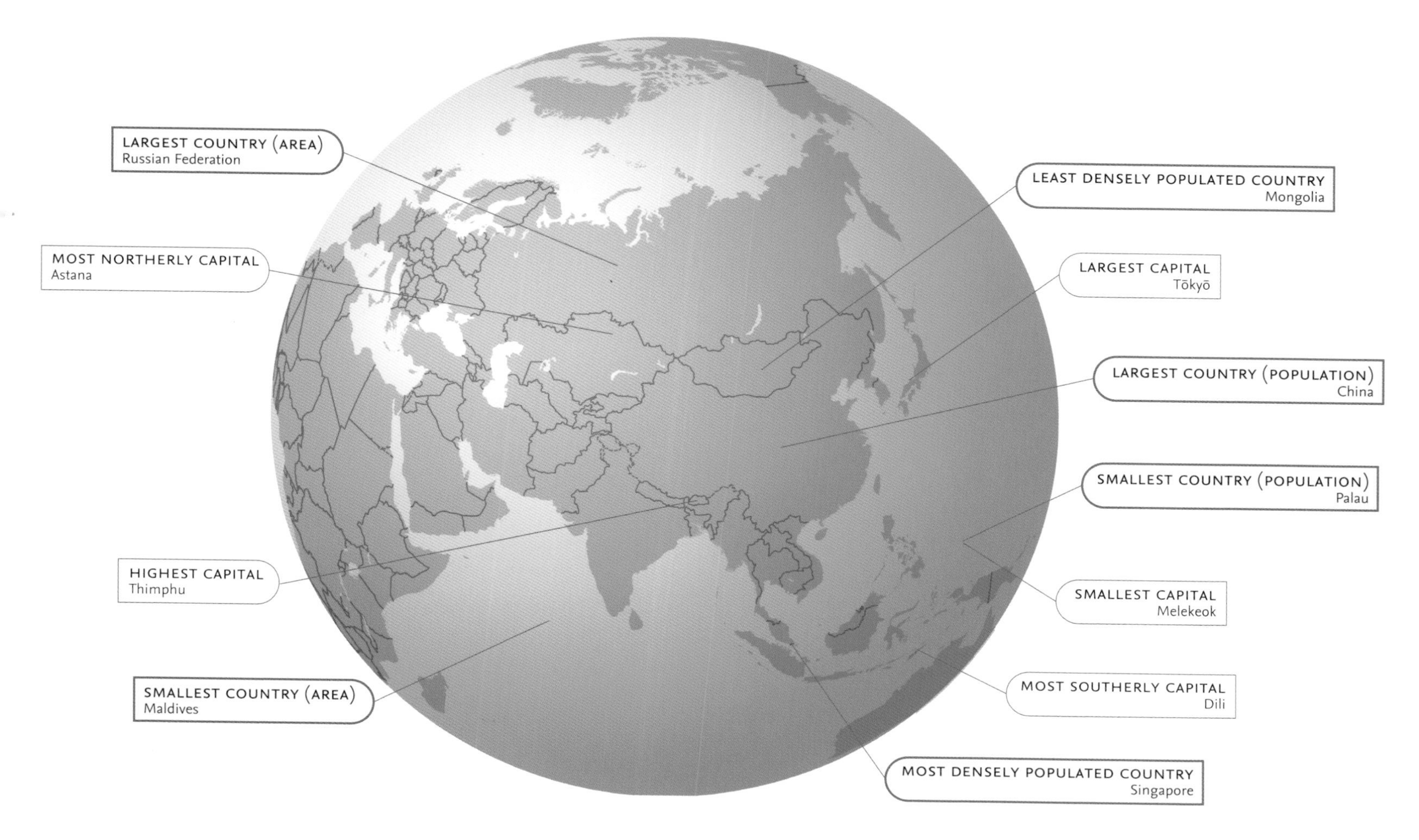

LARGEST COUNTRY (AREA)
Russian Federation
MOST NORTHERLY CAPITAL
Astana
HIGHEST CAPITAL
Thimphu
SMALLEST COUNTRY (AREA)
Maldives
LEAST DENSELY POPULATED COUNTRY
Mongolia
LARGEST CAPITAL
Tōkyō
LARGEST COUNTRY (POPULATION)
China
SMALLEST COUNTRY (POPULATION)
Palau
SMALLEST CAPITAL
Melekeok
MOST SOUTHERLY CAPITAL
Dili
MOST DENSELY POPULATED COUNTRY
Singapore

Asia's capitals

Largest capital (population)	Tōkyō, Japan	35 676 000	
Smallest capital (population)	Melekeok, Palau	391	
Most northerly capital	Astana, Kazakhstan	51° 10'N	
Most southerly capital	Dili, East Timor	8° 35'S	
Highest capital	Thimphu, Bhutan	2 423 metres	7 949 feet

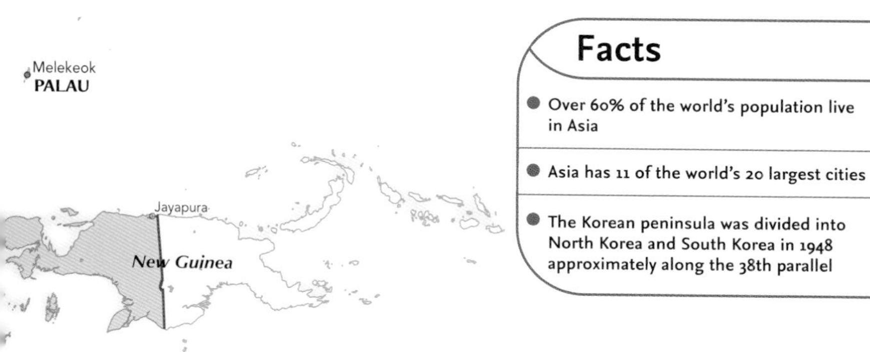

Bonin Islands (Japan)
Volcano Islands (Japan)
Melekeok
PALAU
Jayapura
New Guinea

Facts

- Over 60% of the world's population live in Asia
- Asia has 11 of the world's 20 largest cities
- The Korean peninsula was divided into North Korea and South Korea in 1948 approximately along the 38th parallel

GeoEye

Beijing, capital of China, the most populous country in the world.

UNITED KINGDOM
Faroe Islands (Denmark)
Norwegian Sea
Greenland Sea
ARCTIC
Barents Sea
Svalbard (Norway)
Zemlya Frantsa-Iosifa
Novaya Zemlya
Kara Sea (Karskoye More)
North Sea
NORWAY
SWEDEN
FINLAND
DENMARK
COPENHAGEN
STOCKHOLM
OSLO
HELSINKI
ESTONIA
LATVIA
LITHUANIA
RIGA
VILNIUS
MINSK
BELARUS
POLAND
WARSAW
BERLIN
GERMANY
UKRAINE
KIEV
MOSCOW (Moskva)
St Petersburg
White Sea (Beloye More)
Baltic Sea
Black Sea
Sea of Azov
Caspian Sea
Caspian Lowland
Central Russian Upland
Timanskiy Kryazh
Ural Mountains
West Siberian Plain (Zapadno-Sibirskaya Ravnina)
RUSS FEDER
Yamal Peninsula (Poluostrov Yamal)
Gydan Peninsula (Gydanskiy Poluostrov)
North Siber
Kola Peninsula (Kol'skiy Poluostrov)
Nizhniy Novgorod (Gor'kiy)
Yekaterinburg (Sverdlovsk)
Chelyabinsk
Omsk
Novosibirsk
Krasnoyarsk
Kemerovo
Novokuznetsk
Barnaul
Tomsk
Samara (Kuybyshev)
Volgograd (Stalingrad)
Rostov-na-Donu
Kazan'
Perm'
Ufa
Saratov
Voronezh
Astrakhan'
GEORGIA
TBILISI
ARMENIA
YEREVAN
AZERBAIJAN
BAKU
TURKEY
IRAQ
IRAN
TEHRAN
Mashhad
KAZAKHSTAN
ASTANA (Akmola)
Kazakhskiy Melkosopochnik
Betpak-Dala
Lake Balkhash (Ozero Balkhash)
Almaty (Alma-Ata)
UZBEKISTAN
TOSHKENT (Tashkent)
Kyzylkum Desert
TURKMENISTAN
ASGABAT (Ashkhabad)
Karakum Desert (Garagum)
Ustyurt Plateau
Aral Sea
KYRGYZSTAN
BISHKEK (Frunze)
TAJIKISTAN
DUSHANBE
AFGHANISTAN
Tien Shan
Tarim Basin (Tarim Pendi)
XINJIANG
Altai Mountains
Ürümqi
Dasht-e Kavir
The Gulf

Conic Equidistant Projection

1:20 000 000 — 0, 200, 400, 600 miles; 0, 200, 400, 600, 800, 1000 km

OCEAN
Severnaya Zemlya
New Siberia Islands (Novosibirskiye Ostrova)
East Siberian Sea (Vostochno-Sibirskoye More)
Laptev Sea (More Laptevykh)
Chukchi Sea
Wrangel Island (Ostrov Vrangelya)
Arctic Circle
Seward Peninsula
U.S.A.
Bering Strait
Bering Sea
Aleutian Islands
Koryakskoye Nagor'ye
Kamchatka Peninsula (Poluostrov Kamchatka)
Petropavlovsk-Kamchatskiy
Khrebet Kolymskiy
Khrebet Cherskogo
Verkhoyanskiy Khrebet
Central Siberian Plateau (Sredne-Sibirskoye Ploskogor'ye)
SIBERIA (SIBIR')
Sea of Okhotsk (Okhotskoye More)
Magadan
Yakutsk
Sakhalin
Kuril Islands (Kuril'skiye Ostrova)
ADMINISTERED BY RUSSIAN FEDERATION, CLAIMED BY JAPAN
Stanovoy Khrebet
Khabarovsk
Vladivostok
Irkutsk
Ulan-Ude
Chita
MANCHURIA
Harbin
Hokkaido
Sapporo
PACIFIC OCEAN
JAPAN
Sea of Japan (East Sea)
TOKYO
Yokohama
Nagoya
Osaka
Kyoto
Kobe
Hiroshima
Fukuoka
NORTH KOREA
P'YONGYANG
SOUTH KOREA
SEOUL
Pusan
Yellow Sea (Huang Hai)
Bo Hai
BEIJING (Peking)
Tianjin
INNER MONGOLIA
MONGOLIA
ULAN BATOR (Ulaanbaatar)
Gobi Desert
Da Hinggan Ling
Lake Baikal
Vostochnyy Sayan
CHINA
RUSSIAN FEDERATION
↑ 146
↓ 78

Asia

Northern Asia

RUSSIAN FEDERATION
MONGOLIA
CHINA
INNER MONGOLIA
MANCHURIA
NORTH KOREA
SOUTH KOREA
JAPAN
TAIWAN
MYANMAR (BURMA)
INDIA
BHUTAN
KAZAKHSTAN
TIBET
XINJIANG
Sea of Okhotsk (Okhotskoye More)
Sea of Japan (East Sea)
Yellow Sea (Huang Hai)
East China Sea (Dong Hai)
Bo Hai
Gobi Desert
Kamchatka Peninsula (Poluostrov Kamchatka)
Sakhalin
Hokkaidō
Kuril Islands (Kuril'skiye Ostrova)
Ryukyu Islands (Nansei-shotō) (Japan)
BEIJING (Peking)
ULAN BATOR (Ulaanbaatar)
SEOUL (Sŏul)
P'YONGYANG
TŌKYŌ
T'AIPEI
HA NÔI
NAY PYI TAW
DHAKA (Dacca)
Shanghai
Hong Kong
Tropic of Cancer
Altai Mountains
Qaidam Pendi
Da Hinggan Ling
Sikhote-Alin'
Stanovoy Khrebet
Bonin Islands (Ogasawara-shotō) (Japan)
Volcano Islands (Kazan-rettō) (Japan)
The People's Republic of China claims Taiwan as its 23rd province
ADMINISTERED BY RUSSIAN FEDERATION, CLAIMED BY JAPAN
← 101

Albers Conic Equal Area Projection

1:20 000 000 — 0, 200, 400, 600 miles; 0, 200, 400, 600, 800, 1000 km

PACIFIC OCEAN
PHILIPPINES
MALAYSIA
INDONESIA
AUSTRALIA
THAILAND
CAMBODIA
VIETNAM
LAOS
BRUNEI
SINGAPORE
EAST TIMOR
PAPUA NEW GUINEA
PALAU
FEDERATED STATES OF MICRONESIA
INDIAN OCEAN
South China Sea
Celebes Sea
Sulu Sea
Laut Jawa (Java Sea)
Laut Banda (Banda Sea)
Arafura Sea
Timor Sea
Philippine Sea
Andaman Sea
Gulf of Thailand
Gulf of Tonkin
Gulf of Carpentaria
Strait of Malacca
Borneo
Sumatra (Sumatera)
Java (Jawa)
Celebes (Sulawesi)
New Guinea
Mindanao
Luzon
Hainan
Moluccas (Maluku)
Greater Sunda Islands
Lesser Sunda Islands
NORTHERN TERRITORY
QUEENSLAND
WESTERN AUSTRALIA
MANILA
JAKARTA
KUALA LUMPUR
BANGKOK (Krung Thep)
PHNOM PENH
VIENTIANE (Viangchan)
RANGOON (Yangon)
BANDAR SERI BEGAWAN
Ho Chi Minh City (Saigon)
Equator
Tropic of Capricorn
↑ 132
↓ 132

Asia

Eastern and Southeast Asia

↑ 88
↑ 101
CHINA
YUNNAN
GUANGXI ZHUANGZU ZIZHIQU
GUANGDONG
FUJIAN
INDIA
DHAKA (Dacca)
BANGLADESH
Chittagong
Mouths of the Ganges
MYANMAR (BURMA)
NAY PYI TAW
Mandalay
RANGOON (Yangon)
Bay of Bengal
LAOS
VIENTIANE (Viangchan)
HA NOI
Hai Phong
Kunming
Guangzhou
Shenzhen (Bao'an)
Hong Kong
Macao (Aomen)
Nanning
Zhanjiang (Xiashan)
Gulf of Tongking
HAINAN
Hainan
Haikou
Sanya
THAILAND
BANGKOK (Krung Thep)
Chiang Mai
Gulf of Thailand
CAMBODIA
PHNOM PENH
VIETNAM
INDO-CHINA
Ho Chi Minh City (Saigon)
Da Nang
Hue
Paracel Islands (Xisha Qundao)
Spratly Islands
South China Sea
Andaman Islands (India)
Andaman Sea
Port Blair
Mergui Archipelago
Nicobar Islands (India)
Ten Degree Channel
MALAYSIA
KUALA LUMPUR
PUTRAJAYA
Peninsular Malaysia
Strait of Malacca
SINGAPORE
BANDAR SERI BEGAWAN
BRUNEI
Kota Kinabalu
Kuching
Borneo
KALIMANTAN
Palawan
Sulu
INDONESIA
Sumatra
Medan
Padang
Palembang
Bangka
Selat Karimata
JAKARTA
Bandung
Semarang
Surabaya
Java (Jawa)
Laut Jawa (Java Sea)
Bali
Lombok
Sumbawa
Laut Bali (Bali Sea)
Makassar (Ujung Pandang)
Selat Makassar (Macassar Strait)
Lesser Sunda Islands
Greater Sunda Islands
INDIAN OCEAN
Christmas Island (Australia)
THE SETTLEMENT
Cocos Islands (Aus.)
Equator
95°E
100°
105°
110°
115°
20°
15°
10°
5°
0°
5°
10°S
A
B
C
D
E
F
1
2
3
4
5
6
7
8
9
Mercator Projection

1:15 000 000

0 200 400 miles

0 200 400 600 800 km

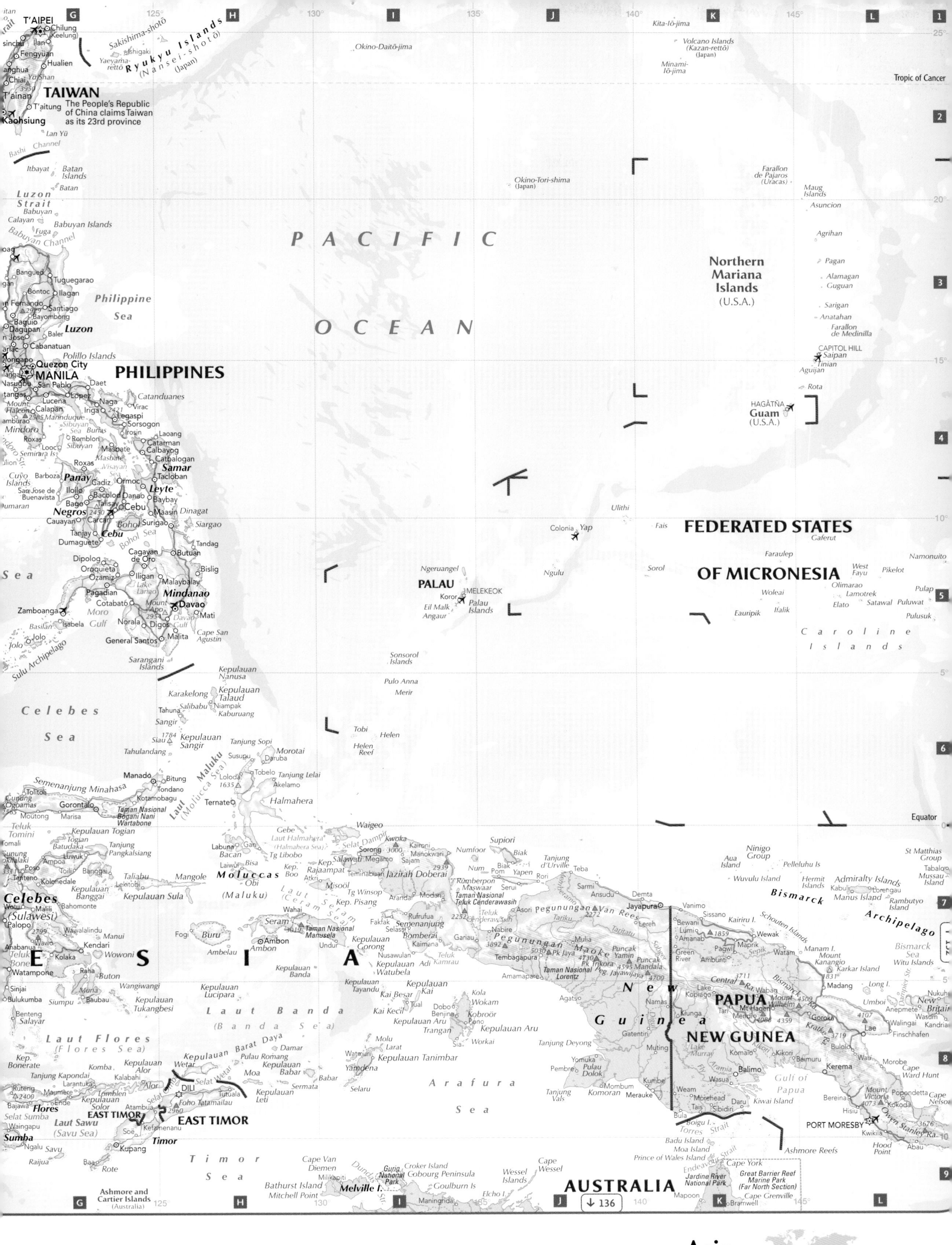

PACIFIC OCEAN
TAIWAN
The People's Republic of China claims Taiwan as its 23rd province
T'AIPEI
Chilung (Keelung)
Hualien
T'aitung
Kaohsiung
Lan Yü
Bashi Channel
Ryukyu Islands (Nansei-shotō) (Japan)
Sakishima-shotō
Yaeyama-rettō
Ishigaki
Okino-Daitō-jima
Kita-Iō-jima
Volcano Islands (Kazan-rettō) (Japan)
Minami-Iō-jima
Tropic of Cancer
Okino-Tori-shima (Japan)
Farallon de Pajaros (Uracas)
Maug Islands
Asuncion
Agrihan
Pagan
Alamagan
Guguan
Sarigan
Anatahan
Farallon de Medinilla
Northern Mariana Islands (U.S.A.)
CAPITOL HILL
Saipan
Tinian
Aguijan
Rota
HAGÅTÑA
Guam (U.S.A.)
Itbayat
Batan Islands
Batan
Luzon Strait
Babuyan
Calayan
Babuyan Islands
Fuga
Babuyan Channel
Philippine Sea
Luzon
Bangued
Tuguegarao
Ilagan
Bontoc
Santiago
San Fernando
Baguio
Bayombong
Dagupan
Baler
Cabanatuan
Polillo Islands
Quezon City
MANILA
PHILIPPINES
San Pablo
Daet
Lucena
Lopez
Calapan
Naga
Iriga
Catanduanes
Virac
Legaspi
Sorsogon
Mindoro
Marinduque
Sibuyan Sea
Romblon
Sibuyan
Masbate
Irosin
Laoang
Catarman
Calbayog
Catbalogan
Samar
Tacloban
Leyte
Baybay
Roxas
Panay
Iloilo
Bacolod
Negros
Cebu
Bohol
Bohol Sea
Maasin
Dinagat
Surigao
Siargao
Tandag
Cuyo Islands
Tanjay
Dumaguete
Dipolog
Cagayan de Oro
Butuan
Iligan
Oroquieta
Ozamiz
Malaybalay
Bislig
Pagadian
Mindanao
Davao
Zamboanga
Cotabato
Moro Gulf
Mati
Basilan
Isabela
Jolo
Sulu Archipelago
Norala
Digos
Davao Gulf
Mount Apo 2954
Malita
General Santos
Cape San Agustin
Sarangani Islands
Celebes Sea
Kepulauan Nanusa
Karakelong
Kepulauan Talaud
Salibabu
Sangir
Kepulauan Sangir
Tahulandang
Tanjung Sopi
Morotai
Manado
Bitung
Tondano
Semenanjung Minahasa
Gorontalo
Ternate
Halmahera
Laut Maluku (Molucca Sea)
Tobelo
Celebes (Sulawesi)
Kepulauan Togian
Teluk Tomini
Kepulauan Banggai
Kepulauan Sula
Taliabu
Mangole
Moluccas (Maluku)
Obi
Bacan
Buru
Seram
Ambon
Laut Seram (Ceram Sea)
Misoöl
Waigeo
Sorong
Salawati
Manokwari
Jazirah Doberai
Supiori
Biak
Numfoor
Yapen
Teluk Cenderawasih
Jayapura
Sarmi
Pegunungan Van Rees
Pegunungan Maoke
Puncak Jaya 5030
Taman Nasional Lorentz
Timika
Agats
Laut Banda (Banda Sea)
Kepulauan Banda
Kepulauan Kai
Kepulauan Aru
Kepulauan Tanimbar
Yamdena
Arafura Sea
Kepulauan Tukangbesi
Buton
Muna
Kendari
Watampone
Wowoni
ASIA
Laut Flores (Flores Sea)
Flores
Sumba
Laut Sawu (Savu Sea)
Timor
Kupang
DILI
EAST TIMOR
Kepulauan Alor
Wetar
Kepulauan Barat Daya
Damar
Kepulauan Babar
Kepulauan Leti
Timor Sea
Ashmore and Cartier Islands (Australia)
AUSTRALIA
Bathurst Island
Melville I.
Cape Van Diemen
Coburg Peninsula
Croker Island
Wessel Islands
Cape Wessel
Goulburn Is
Cape York
Great Barrier Reef Marine Park (Far North Section)
Torres Strait
Prince of Wales Island
Moa Island
Badu Island
Merauke
New Guinea
PAPUA NEW GUINEA
Vanimo
Wewak
Madang
Lae
Mount Hagen
Mount Wilhelm 4509
Goroka
Kerema
Balimo
Daru
Gulf of Papua
Kiwai Island
PORT MORESBY
Owen Stanley Ra.
Hood Point
Ashmore Reefs
Bismarck Archipelago
Bismarck Sea
Admiralty Islands
Manus Island
Schouten Islands
Ninigo Group
Aua Island
Wuvulu Island
Hermit Islands
St Matthias Group
FEDERATED STATES OF MICRONESIA
Caroline Islands
Ulithi
Yap
Colonia
Fais
Ngulu
Sorol
Gaferut
Faraulep
Woleai
Ifalik
Eauripik
West Fayu
Pikelot
Olimarao
Lamotrek
Elato
Satawal
Puluwat
Pulap
Pulusuk
Namonuito
PALAU
MELEKEOK
Koror
Palau Islands
Ngeruangel
Eil Malk
Angaur
Sonsorol Islands
Pulo Anna
Merir
Tobi
Helen
Helen Reef
Equator
↓ 136

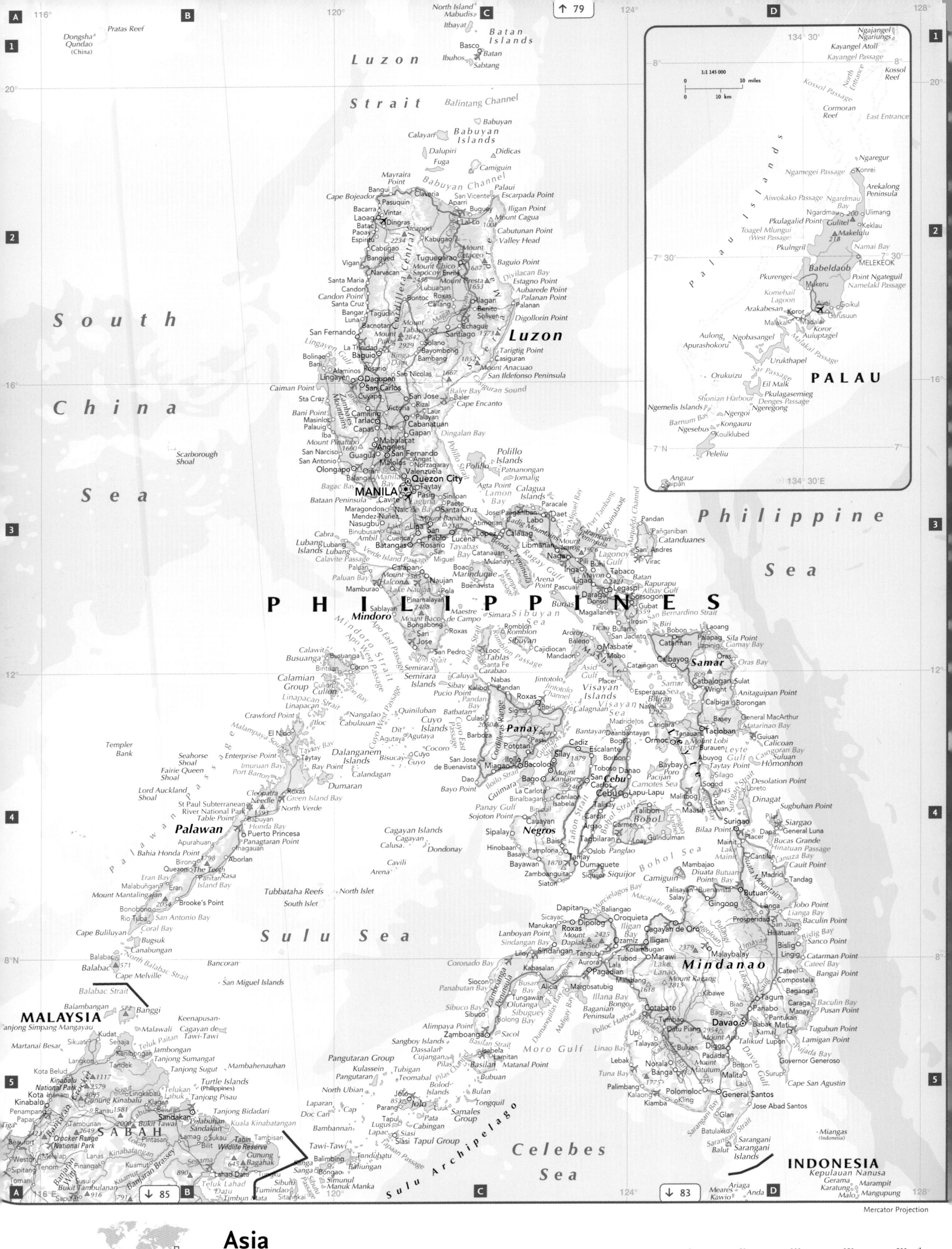

↑ 79
↓ 85
↓ 83
Luzon Strait
Batan Islands
Babuyan Islands
Babuyan Channel
Balintang Channel
South China Sea
Philippine Sea
Sulu Sea
Celebes Sea
Bohol Sea
Sibuyan Sea
Visayan Sea
Sulu Archipelago
PHILIPPINES
MALAYSIA
INDONESIA
SABAH
Luzon
Mindoro
Palawan
Panay
Negros
Cebu
Bohol
Samar
Leyte
Mindanao
MANILA
Quezon City
Dongsha Qundao (China)
Pratas Reef
Scarborough Shoal
Templer Bank
Seahorse Shoal
Fairie Queen Shoal
Lord Auckland Shoal
Tubbataha Reefs
Cagayan Islands
Calamian Group
Cuyo Islands
Dalanganem Islands
Turtle Islands (Philippines)
Pangutaran Group
Tawi-Tawi
Sarangani Islands
Kepulauan Nanusa
Miangas (Indonesia)
Cordillera Central
Sierra Madre
Zambales Mountains
Diuata Mountains
Mount Apo
Baguio
Dagupan
San Fernando
Laoag
Vigan
Tuguegarao
Cabanatuan
Angeles
Olongapo
Batangas
Lucena
Naga
Legaspi
Puerto Princesa
Iloilo
Bacolod
Roxas
Tacloban
Ormoc
Cebu
Lapu-Lapu
Dumaguete
Surigao
Butuan
Cagayan de Oro
Iligan
Zamboanga
Cotabato
Davao
General Santos
Kota Kinabalu
Sandakan
Mount Kinabalu
PALAU
Palau Islands
Babeldaob
Koror
Melekeok
Peleliu
Angaur
Kayangel Atoll
Kossol Reef
Mercator Projection
1:6 500 000

Asia
Philippines

PHILIPPINES
Celebes Sea
Sulu Archipelago
Kepulauan Sangir
Kepulauan Talaud
Semenanjung Minahasa
Manado
GORONTALO
Gorontalo
SULAWESI UTARA
Teluk Tomini
Kepulauan Togian
SULAWESI TENGAH
Palu
Celebes (Sulawesi)
SULAWESI BARAT
SULAWESI TENGGARA
Kendari
SULAWESI SELATAN
Makassar (Ujung Pandang)
Teluk Bone
Kepulauan Banggai
Selat Makassar (Macassar Strait)
Laut Maluku (Molucca Sea)
Halmahera
Morotai
Ternate
MALUKU UTARA
Laut Halmahera
Moluccas (Maluku)
Bacan
Obi
Kepulauan Obi
Kepulauan Sula
Taliabu
Mangole
Sulabesi
PAPUA (IRIAN JAYA)
Waigeo
Misoöl
Equator
INDONESIA
MALUKU
Buru
Seram
Ambon
Laut Seram (Ceram Sea)
Laut Banda (Banda Sea)
Kepulauan Banda
Buton
Muna
Kabaena
Wowoni
Salayar
Kepulauan Barat Daya
Wetar
Kisar
Kepulauan Leti
Kepulauan Babar
Laut Flores (Flores Sea)
Flores
Sumbawa
Komodo
Rinca
Alor
Lomblen
Kepulauan Solor
Kepulauan Alor
NUSA TENGGARA TIMUR
EAST TIMOR
DILI
Ocussi
Timor
Kupang
Rote
Savu
Sumba
Laut Sawu (Savu Sea)
Timor Sea
AUSTRALIA
Cape Van Diemen

Mercator Projection

1:6 500 000

0 50 100 150 200 miles

0 50 100 150 200 250 300 km

Asia

Central Indonesia

Andaman Sea
South
INDIAN OCEAN
THAILAND
MALAYSIA
Peninsular Malaysia
SINGAPORE
Sumatera
Greater Sunda Islands
Kepulauan Mentawai
Strait of Malacca
Selat Sunda
Selat Berhala
Singapore Strait
KEDAH
PERAK
KELANTAN
TERENGGANU
PAHANG
SELANGOR
NEGERI SEMBILAN
MELAKA
JOHOR
ACEH
SUMATERA UTARA
RIAU
KEPULAUAN RIAU
SUMATERA BARAT
JAMBI
BENGKULU
SUMATERA SELATAN
LAMPUNG
BANTEN
BANGKA
KUALA LUMPUR
PUTRAJAYA
JAKARTA
Banda Aceh
Medan
Padang
Palembang
Pekanbaru
Jambi
Bengkulu
Bandar Lampung
Pangkalpinang
Tanjungpinang
Kuantan
Kota Bharu
Kuala Terengganu
George Town
Ipoh
Seremban
Johor Bahru
Hat Yai
Alor Setar
Simeulue
Nias
Siberut
Pagai Utara
Pagai Selatan
Enggano
Bangka
Kepulauan Lingga
Kepulauan Anambas
Equator
Mercator Projection
1:6 250 000
0 50 100 150 200 miles
0 50 100 150 200 250 300 km

China Sea
Sulu Sea
PHILIPPINES
Celebes Sea
BRUNEI
BANDAR SERI BEGAWAN
LABUAN
MALAYSIA
SABAH
SARAWAK
Kota Kinabalu
Sandakan
Tawau
Kuching
Sibu
Bintulu
Miri
Borneo
KALIMANTAN
KALIMANTAN BARAT
KALIMANTAN TENGAH
KALIMANTAN TIMUR
KALIMANTAN SELATAN
Pontianak
Samarinda
Balikpapan
Banjarmasin
Tarakan
Natuna Besar
Belitung
Selat Karimata
Selat Makasar (Makassar Strait)
Celebes (Sulawesi)
SULAWESI BARAT
SULAWESI TENGAH
SULAWESI SELATAN
Makassar (Ujung Pandang)
Laut Jawa (Java Sea)
Madura
Laut Bali (Bali Sea)
Laut Flores (Flores Sea)
JAWA TENGAH
JAWA TIMUR
YOGYAKARTA
Semarang
Surabaya
Surakarta
Malang
Bandung
BALI
Denpasar
Lombok
Sumbawa
NUSA TENGGARA BARAT
Jawa (Java)

C H I N A
YUNNAN
SICHUAN
GUIZHOU
HUNAN
GUANGXI ZHUANGZU ZIZHIQU
HAINAN
MYANMAR
(BURMA)
LAOS
THAILAND
VIETNAM
INDIA
BANGLADESH
BHUTAN
ASSAM
MANIPUR
MIZORAM
NAGALAND
MEGHALAYA
TRIPURA
ARUNACHAL PRADESH
TONKIN
XISHUANGBANNA
Shan Plateau
Gulf of Tongking
Bay of Bengal
Gulf of Mottama (Gulf of Martaban)
Kunming
Nanning
Guiyang
HA NOI
Hai Phong
VIENTIANE (Viangchan)
NAY PYI TAW
RANGOON (Yangon)
Mandalay
Chiang Mai
Louangphabang
Chittagong
Imphal
Guwahati
Đa Nẵng
Huế
Sittwe (Akyab)
Bassein (Pathein)
Mawlamyaing
Beihai
Liuzhou
Zunyi
Zhaotong
Dali (Xiaguan)
↑ 96
↑ 97
105 ↓

Mercator Projection

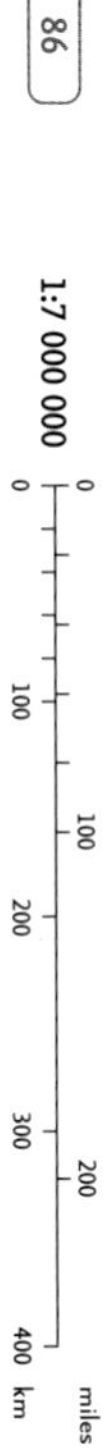

1:7 000 000
0 100 200 miles
0 100 200 300 400 km

CAMBODIA
CHINA
MALAYSIA
INDONESIA
SINGAPORE
South China Sea
Gulf of Thailand
Andaman Sea
INDIAN OCEAN
Strait of Malacca
Peninsular Malaysia
Borneo
Sumatera
BANGKOK (Krung Thep)
PHNOM PENH
KUALA LUMPUR
Ho Chi Minh City (Saigon)
Mergui Archipelago
Andaman Islands (India)
Nicobar Islands (India)
Kepulauan Natuna
1:550 000
↓ 80

Asia

Myanmar, Thailand, Peninsular Malaysia and Indo-China

RUSSIAN FED
KAZAKHSTAN
KYRGYZSTAN
TAJIKISTAN
AFGHANISTAN
UZBEKISTAN
PAKISTAN
INDIA
NEPAL
BHUTAN
BANGLADESH
MYANMAR (BURMA)
THAILAND
LAOS
VIETNAM
MONGOL
CHINA
XINJIANG UYGUR ZIZHIQU (SINKIANG)
XIZANG ZIZHIQU (TIBET)
QINGHAI
GANSU
SICHUAN
YUNNAN
Tarim Basin (Tarim Pendi)
Taklimakan Desert (Taklimakan Shamo)
Plateau of Tibet (Qingzang Gaoyuan)
Kunlun Shan
Tien Shan
Altun Shan
Hindu Kush
Himalaya
Bay of Bengal
ASTANA
ALMATY
BISHKEK
TOSHKENT
DUSHANBE
ISLAMABAD
NEW DELHI
KATHMANDU
THIMPHU
DHAKA (Dacca)
NAY PYI TAW
HA NOI
ULAN BATOR (Ulaanbaatar)
Ürümqi
Lhasa
Kolkata (Calcutta)
Chengdu
Chongqing
Lanzhou
Kunming
Mandalay
Irkutsk
Novokuznetsk
Barnaul

Albers Conic Equal Area Projection

1:15 000 000

0 200 400 miles

0 200 400 600 800 km

↑ 77
RATION
MONGOLIA
INNER MONGOLIA
NEI MONGOL ZIZHIQU
MANCHURIA
HEILONGJIANG
JILIN
LIAONING
HEBEI
SHANXI
SHANDONG
HENAN
HAANXI
HUBEI
ANHUI
JIANGSU
SHANGHAI
ZHEJIANG
HUNAN
JIANGXI
FUJIAN
GUANGDONG
GUANGXI ZHUANGZU ZIZHIQU
HAINAN
NORTH KOREA
SOUTH KOREA
JAPAN
TAIWAN
The People's Republic of China claims Taiwan as its 23rd province
PHILIPPINES
ADMINISTERED BY RUSSIAN FEDERATION. CLAIMED BY JAPAN
BEIJING (Peking)
P'YŎNGYANG
SEOUL (Sŏul)
TŌKYŌ
T'AIPEI
Shanghai
Hong Kong
Macao (Aomen)
Tianjin
Harbin
Shenyang
Dalian (Lüda)
Qingdao (Tsingtao)
Nanjing
Wuhan
Guangzhou
Shenzhen (Bao'an)
Vladivostok
Khabarovsk
Sapporo
Sendai
Yokohama
Nagoya
Kyoto
Ōsaka
Kōbe
Hiroshima
Fukuoka
Kagoshima
Pusan
Sakhalin
Hokkaidō
Honshu
Shikoku
Kyūshū
Sea of Okhotsk (Okhotskoye More)
Sea of Japan (East Sea)
Bo Hai
Korea Bay
Yellow Sea (Huang Hai)
East China Sea (Dong Hai)
South China Sea
PACIFIC OCEAN
Tropic of Cancer
Ryukyu Islands (Nansei-shotō) (Japan)
Kuril Islands (Kuril'skiye Ostrova)
Bonin Islands (Ogasawara-shotō) (Japan)
Volcano Islands (Kazan-rettō) (Japan)
Luzon Strait
Bashi Channel
Babuyan Islands
Batan Islands
Korea Strait
La Pérouse Strait

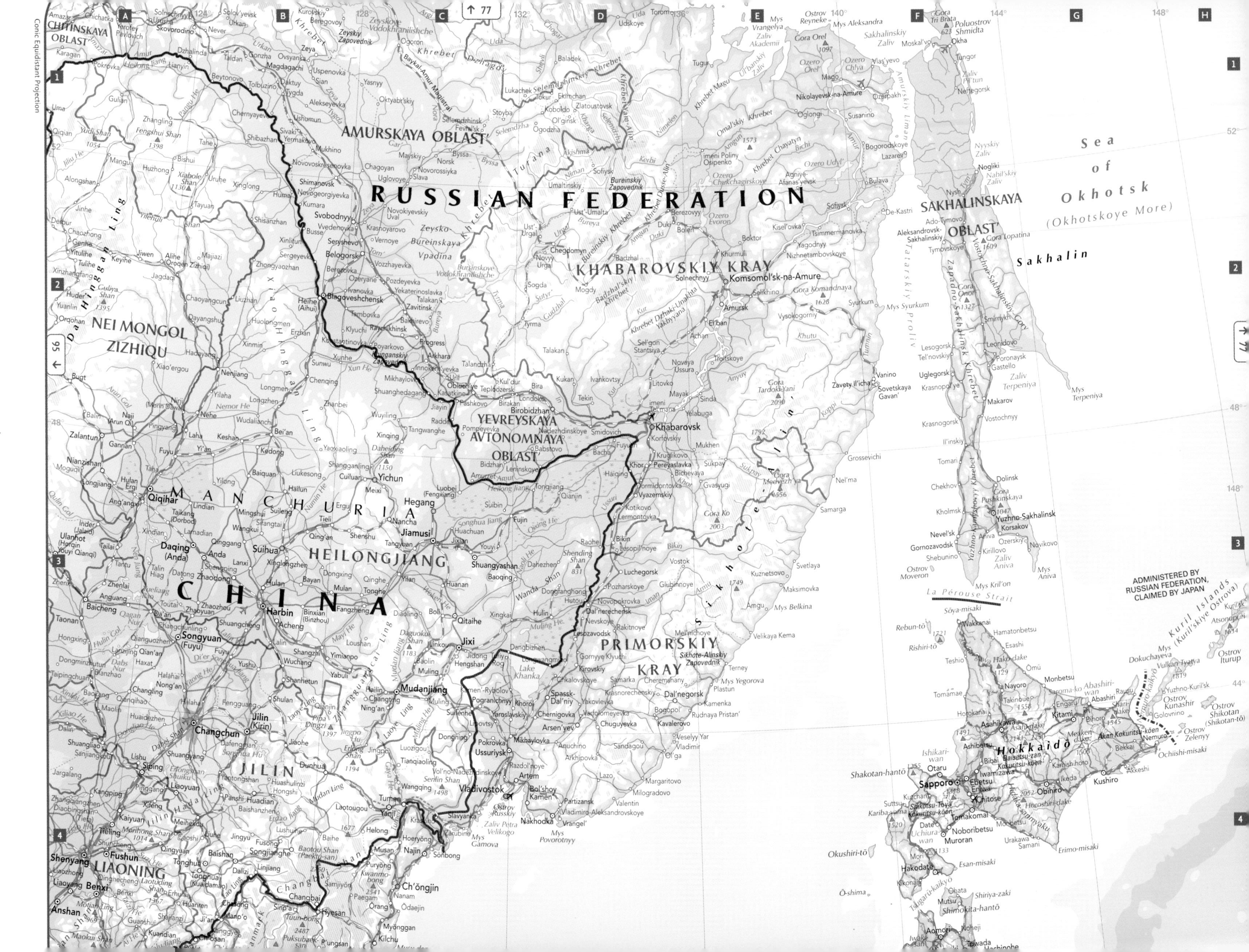

RUSSIAN FEDERATION
CHINA
AMURSKAYA OBLAST'
KHABAROVSKIY KRAY
PRIMORSKIY KRAY
YEVREYSKAYA AVTONOMNAYA OBLAST'
SAKHALINSKAYA OBLAST'
CHITINSKAYA OBLAST'
HEILONGJIANG
JILIN
LIAONING
NEI MONGOL ZIZHIQU
MANCHURIA
Sea of Okhotsk (Okhotskoye More)
Sakhalin
Hokkaidō
Tatarskiy Proliv
La Pérouse Strait
Kuril Islands (Kuril'skiye Ostrova)
ADMINISTERED BY RUSSIAN FEDERATION, CLAIMED BY JAPAN
Lake Khanka
Harbin
Changchun
Jilin (Kirin)
Qiqihar
Daqing (Anda)
Shenyang
Fushun
Anshan
Mudanjiang
Jiamusi
Hegang
Yichun
Jixi
Khabarovsk
Vladivostok
Ussuriysk
Nakhodka
Blagoveshchensk
Komsomol'sk-na-Amure
Yuzhno-Sakhalinsk
Sapporo
Asahikawa
Kushiro
Hakodate

↑ 77
95 ↓

Conic Equidistant Projection

1:7 000 000 — 0, 100, 200 miles; 0, 100, 200, 300, 400 km

Sea of Japan
(East Sea)
JAPAN
Honshū
NORTH KOREA
SOUTH KOREA
Korea Bay
Yellow Sea
(Huang Hai)
East China Sea
(Dong Hai)
PACIFIC OCEAN
Shikoku
Kyūshū
Ryukyu Islands
(Nansei-shotō)
(Japan)
Bonin Islands
(Ogasawara-shotō)
(Japan)
Izu-shotō
Tokara-rettō
Amami-shotō
Ōsumi-shotō
Okinawa
Amami-Ō-shima
TŌKYŌ
Yokohama
Kawasaki
Chiba
Sendai
Nagoya
Kyōto
Kōbe
Ōsaka
Hiroshima
Fukuoka
Kita-Kyūshū
Kumamoto
Kagoshima
Niigata
SEOUL (Sŏul)
Inch'ŏn
Suwŏn
Taejŏn
Taegu
Ulsan
Pusan
Kwangju
P'YŎNGYANG
Namp'o
Hamhŭng
Cheju-do
Ullŭng-do
(South Korea)
Liancourt Rocks
Claimed and administered
by South Korea as Tok-to;
claimed by Japan as Take-shima
Oki-shotō
Tsushima
Korea Strait
97
89

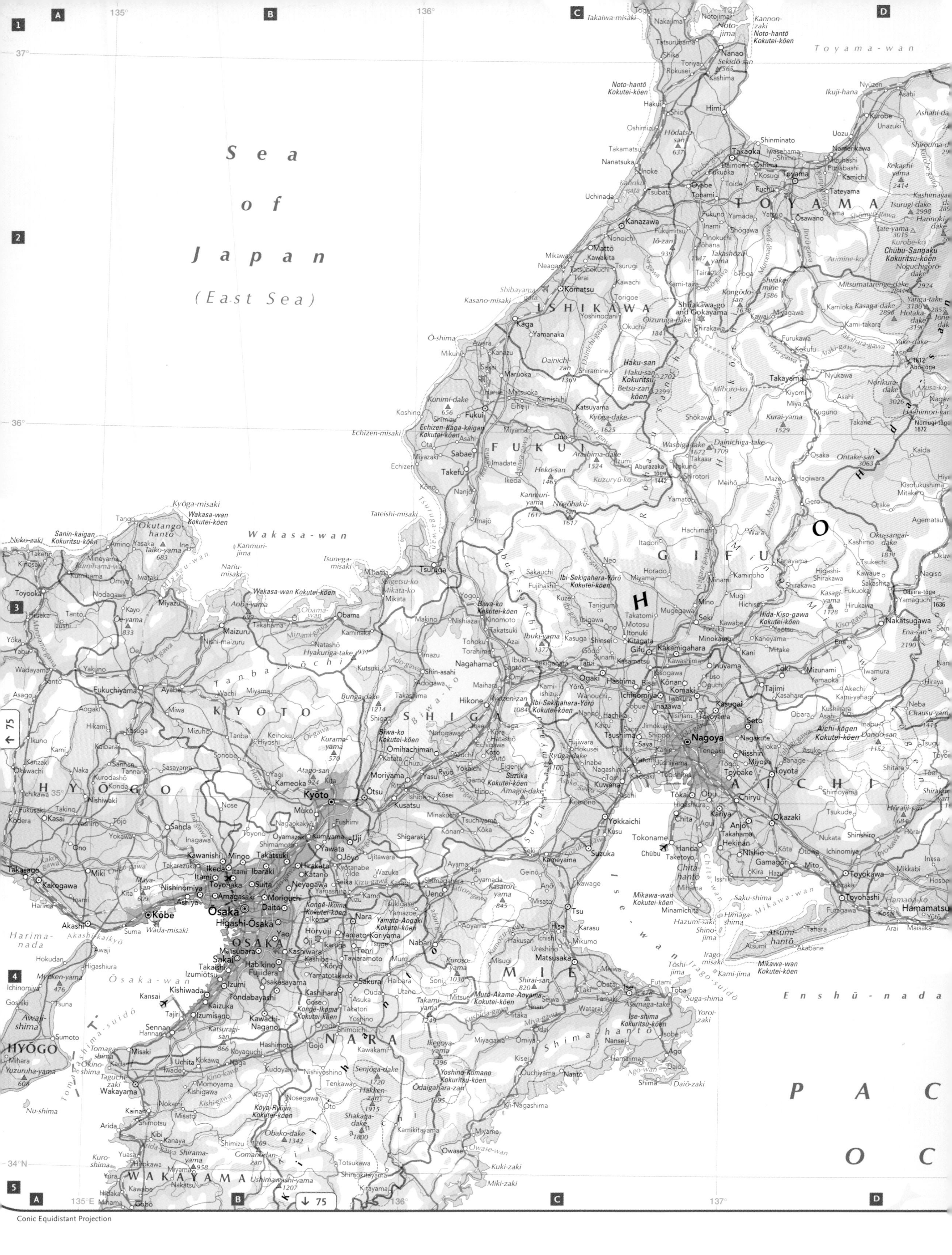
Sea of Japan
(East Sea)
Toyama-wan
Wakasa-wan
Ōsaka-wan
Harima-nada
Ise-wan
Mikawa-wan
Enshū-nada
PACIFIC OCEAN
ISHIKAWA
TOYAMA
FUKUI
GIFU
KYŌTO
SHIGA
HYŌGO
ŌSAKA
NARA
MIE
AICHI
WAKAYAMA
Biwa-ko
Noto-hantō
Kanazawa
Toyama
Takaoka
Fukui
Tsuruga
Kyōto
Ōsaka
Kōbe
Nara
Nagoya
Gifu
Ōtsu
Yokkaichi
Tsu
Wakayama
Takayama
Hamamatsu
Toyohashi
Okazaki
Maizuru
Himeji
Sakai
Conic Equidistant Projection

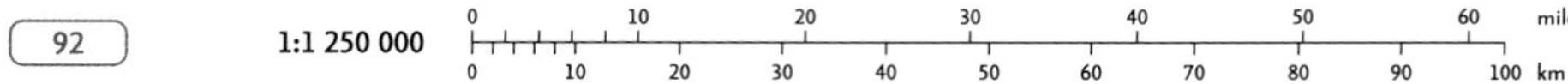
1:1 250 000
0 10 20 30 40 50 60 miles
0 10 20 30 40 50 60 70 80 90 100 km

↑ 75

NIIGATA
GUNMA
TOCHIGI
IBARAKI
SAITAMA
TŌKYŌ
KANAGAWA
YAMANASHI
NAGANO
SHIZUOKA
CHIBA
Mikuni-sanmyaku
Kantō-heiya
Kantō-sanchi
Akaishi-sanmyaku
TŌKYŌ
Yokohama
Kawasaki
Chiba
Saitama
Utsunomiya
Maebashi
Takasaki
Mito
Kōfu
Shizuoka
Nagano
Matsumoto
Hachiōji
Sagamihara
Funabashi
Yokosuka
Tōkyō-wan
Sagami-wan
Sagami-nada
Suruga-wan
Kashima-nada
Kujūkuri-hama
Bōsō-hantō
Izu-hantō
Izu-shotō
Ō-shima
Tō-shima
Udone-jima
Nii-jima
Shikine-jima
Kōzu-shima
Miyake-jima
Ōnohara-jima
Omae-zaki
Irō-zaki
Nojima-zaki
Chikura
Tateyama
Shimoda
Atami
Odawara
Fuji
Numazu
Mishima
Gotenba
Fujinomiya
Shimizu
Hamamatsu
Kakegawa
Fujieda
Yaizu
Hitachi
Kashima
Narita
Kisarazu
Kamogawa
Mobara
Choshi
Kumagaya
Kawagoe
Koshigaya
Tokorozawa
Tachikawa
Machida
Fujisawa
Hiratsuka
Kamakura
Chigasaki
Atsugi
Yamato
Ebina
Hadano
Ashikaga
Kiryū
Ōta
Isesaki
Oyama
Tochigi
Kanuma
Ueda
Suwa
Chino
Okaya
Shiojiri
Ina
Komoro
Saku
Nikkō
I F I C
E A N
138°
139°
140°
35°
36°
34°
E
F
G
1
2
3
4
5

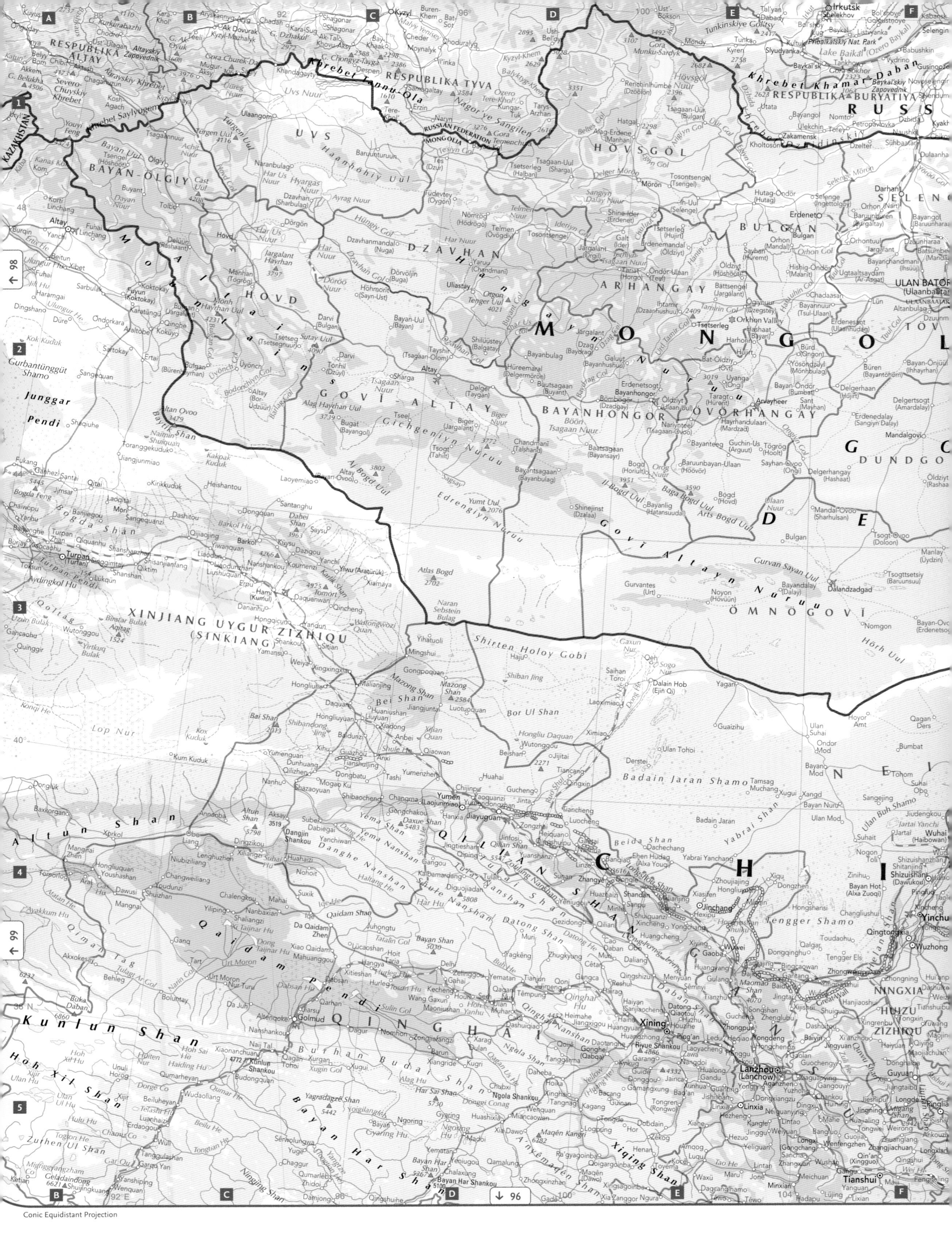
RESPUBLIKA ALTAY
RESPUBLIKA TYVA
RESPUBLIKA BURYATIYA
RUSSIAN FEDERATION
MONGOLIA
KAZAKHSTAN
UVS
BAYAN-ÖLGIY
HOVD
DZAVHAN
HÖVSGÖL
BULGAN
ARHANGAY
GOVĬ-ALTAY
BAYANHONGOR
ÖVÖRHANGAY
ÖMNÖGOVĬ
DUNDGOVĬ
SELENGE
TÖV
MONGOL
XINJIANG UYGUR ZIZHIQU (SINKIANG)
QINGHAI
NINGXIA HUIZU ZIZHIQU
CHINA
Junggar Pendi
Gurbantünggüt Shamo
Bogda Shan
Turpan Pendi
Qoltag
Lop Nur
Altun Shan
Kunlun Shan
Hoh Xil Shan
Qaidam Pendi
Qilian Shan
Badain Jaran Shamo
Tengger Shamo
Bayan Har Shan
Burhan Budai Shan
Shirten Holoy Gobi
Gobi Altayn Nuruu
Hangayn Nuruu
Mongol Altain Nuruu
Khrebet Tannu-Ola
Khrebet Saylyugem
Uvs Nuur
Hövsgöl Nuur
Lake Baikal
Irkutsk
Ulan Bator (Ulaanbaatar)
Ulaangom
Hovd
Uliastay
Altay
Erdenet
Bulgan
Arvayheer
Dalandzadgad
Mandalgovi
Hami (Kumul)
Turpan
Yumen
Jiayuguan
Zhangye
Jinchang
Wuwei
Xining
Lanzhou (Lanchow)
Linxia
Tianshui
Golmud
Yinchuan
Wuzhong
Zhongwei
Guyuan
Dunhuang
Conic Equidistant Projection

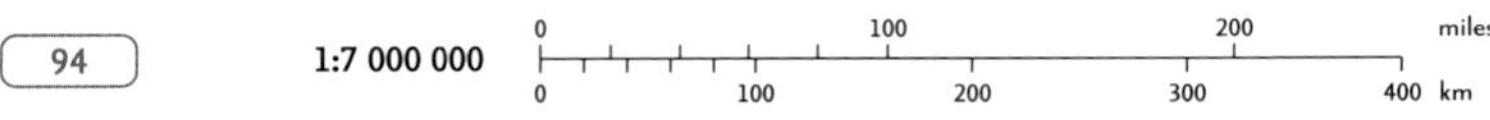
1:7 000 000
0 100 200 miles
0 100 200 300 400 km

↑ 77
↓ 97
→ 90
→ 91
G
H
I
J
K
1
2
3
4
5
RUSSIAN FEDERATION
Yablonovyy Khrebet
Khrebet Cherskogo
AGINSKIY BURYATSKIY AVT. OKRUG
CHITINSKAYA OBLAST'
Chita
Ulan-Ude
Nerchinsk
Shilka
Borzya
Krasnokamensk
Zabaykal'sk
Manzhouli
Hulun Buir (Hailar)
Yakeshi
Blagoveshchensk
Heihe (Aihui)
Xiao Hinggan Ling
Da Hinggan Ling
HEILONGJIANG
Qiqihar
Daqing (Anda)
Harbin
Suihua
Ulanhot
Baicheng
Songyuan
JILIN
Changchun
Siping
Tongliao
Liaoyuan
Shenyang
Fushun
LIAONING
Benxi
Anshan
Dandong (Andong)
Liaodong Bandao
Dalian (Lüda)
Jinzhou
Huludao
Fuxin
Chifeng (Ulanhad)
Chengde
Qinhuangdao
Tangshan
Tianjin
BEIJING (Peking)
Zhangjiakou (Kalgan)
Datong
Hohhot
Baotou
Jining (Tsining)
Xilinhot
MONGOLIA
DORNOD
HENTIY
SÜHBAATAR
DORNOGOVĬ
Choybalsan
Baruun-Urt
Öndörhaan
Erenhot
INNER MONGOLIA (NEI MONGOL ZIZHIQU)
BO HAI
Bohai Wan
Liaodong Wan
Laizhou Wan
Korea Bay
YELLOW SEA (HUANG HAI)
NORTH KOREA
HEBEI
Shijiazhuang
Baoding
Cangzhou
Taiyuan
SHANXI
SHANDONG
Jinan
Zibo
Weifang
Yantai
Weihai
Qingdao (Tsingtao)
Linyi
Zaozhuang
Dongying
Binzhou
Dezhou
Liaocheng
Tai'an
Jining
Heze (Mudan)
Xuzhou
JIANGSU
Lianyungang
Handan
Xingtai
Anyang
Hebi
Xinxiang
Jiaozuo
Kaifeng
Zhengzhou
Luoyang
Shangqiu
Xianyang
Xi'an
Weinan
Yan'an
Linfen
Yuncheng
Ordos
Mu Us Shamo
Huangtu Gaoyuan
Great Wall
Rampart of Genghis Khan

Asia

Northern China and Mongolia

QINGHAI
GANSU
SICHUAN
XIZANG ZIZHIQU
(TIBET)
ARUNACHAL PRADESH
INDIA
ASSAM
NAGALAND
MANIPUR
MIZORAM
YUNNAN
GUIZHOU
CHONGQING
GUANGX
CH
MYANMAR
(BURMA)
THAILAND
LAOS
VIETNAM
TONKIN
XISHUANGBANNA
Bayan Har Shan
Tanggula Shan
Hengduan Shan
Shan Plateau
Sichuan Pendi
Yungui Gaoyuan
Daxue Shan
Annam Highlands
Gulf of Tongking
Bay of Bengal
Chengdu
Chongqing
Kunming
Guiyang
Lanzhou
Linxia
Tianshui
Hanzhong
Mianyang
Deyang
Nanchong
Suining
Leshan
Zigong
Neijiang
Yibin
Luzhou
Xichang
Zhaotong
Panzhihua
(Dukou)
Lupanshui
(Zhongshan)
Qujing
Dali
Yuxi
Gejiu
Mandalay
Sagaing
Monywa
Meiktila
Taunggyi
NAY PYI TAW
Myitkyina
Bhamo
Chiang Mai
Chiang Rai
Louangphabang
VIENTIANE
HA NOI
Hai Phong
Imphal
Kohima
Dimapur
Dibrugarh
Tinsukia
Aizawl
Silchar
Nong Khai

Conic Equidistant Projection

1:7 000 000

0 100 200 miles

0 100 200 300 400 km

↑ 89
↓ 81
SHANXI
SHANDONG
HENAN
JIANGSU
ANHUI
HUBEI
ZHEJIANG
JIANGXI
HUNAN
FUJIAN
GUANGDONG
HAINAN
TAIWAN
ZHUANGZU ZIZHIQU
HONG KONG
MACAO
Yellow Sea
(Huang Hai)
East China Sea
(Dong Hai)
South China Sea
Taiwan Strait
Tropic of Cancer
The People's Republic of China claims Taiwan as its 23rd province
Shanghai
Pudong
Nanjing
Hangzhou
Wuhan
Changsha
Nanchang
Fuzhou
Xiamen
(Amoy)
Guangzhou
Shenzhen
(Bao'an)
Hong Kong
Zhuhai
Macao
(Aomen)
T'AIPEI
Kaohsiung
Haikou
Hefei
Zhengzhou
Xi'an
Guilin
Ningbo
(Yinxian)
Wenzhou
Shantou
Hainan
SHANGHAI DONGHAI BRIDGE
GUANGDONG
SHENZHEN SPECIAL ECONOMIC ZONE
Deep Bay
(Shenzhen Wan)
Kowloon
Lantau Island
(Tai Yue Shan)
Lamma Island
(Pok Liu Chau)
Hong Kong International
miles
km

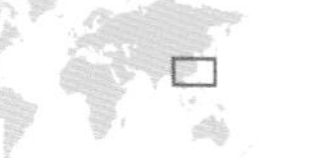

↑ 77
↑ 94
← 102
RUSSIAN FEDERATION
RESPUBLIKA ALTAY
ALTAYSKIY KRAY
RESPUBLIKA TYVA
RESPUBLIKA KHAKASIYA
KRASNOYARSKIY KRAY
KAZAKHSTAN
PAVLODARSKAYA OBLAST'
VOSTOCHNYY KAZAKHSTAN
KARAGANDINSKAYA OBLAST
ALMATINSKAYA OBLAST
ZHAMBYLSKAYA OBLAST
KYRGYZSTAN
CHUY
NARYN
YSYK-KÖL
MONGOLIA
UVS
HOVD
BAYAN-ÖLGIY
DZAVHAN
GOVĬ-ALTAY
HÖVSGÖL
CHINA
XINJIANG UYGUR ZIZHIQU
(SINKIANG)
GANSU
Junggar Pendi
(Dzungarian Basin)
Tarim Basin
(Tarim Pendi)
Taklimakan Desert
(Taklimakan Shamo)
Gurbantünggüt Shamo
Altai Mountains
Semipalatinsk
Ust'-Kamenogorsk
Rubtsovsk
Karaganda
Almaty
(Alma-Ata)
BISHKEK
(Frunze)
Ürümqi
Karamay
Shihezi
Korla
Aksu
Hami
(Kumul)
Turpan
Tacheng
(Qoqek)
Yining
(Gulja)
Taldykorgan
Lop Nur
Lake Zaysan
Ozero Alakol'
Lake Balkhash
Conic Equidistant Projection

1:7 000 000

0 100 200 miles

0 100 200 300 400 km

Plateau of Tibet
QINGHAI
XIZANG ZIZHIQU
(TIBET)
Kunlun Shan
Tanggula Shan
AKSAI CHIN
CLAIMED BY INDIA UNDER CHINESE ADMINISTRATION
JAMMU AND KASHMIR
HIMACHAL PRADESH
UTTARAKHAND
NEPAL
KATHMANDU
BHUTAN
SIKKIM
ARUNACHAL PRADESH
ASSAM
MEGHALAYA
BANGLADESH
INDIA
UTTAR PRADESH
BIHAR
NEW DELHI
Lhasa
96 →
← 109
104 ↓
105 ↓

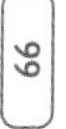

RUSSIAN FEDERATION
UKRAINE
ROMANIA
HUNGARY
SLOVAKIA
AUSTRIA
POLAND
BELARUS
MOLDOVA
CROATIA
SLOVENIA
BOSNIA-HERZEGOVINA
SERBIA
BULGARIA
MACEDONIA
ALBANIA
GREECE
ITALY
TURKEY
GEORGIA
ARMENIA
AZERBAIJAN
KAZAKH
UZBEKISTAN
TURKMENISTAN
AFGHANISTAN
IRAN
IRAQ
SYRIA
LEBANON
ISRAEL
JORDAN
CYPRUS
KUWAIT
BAHRAIN
QATAR
UNITED ARAB EMIRATES
OMAN
SAUDI ARABIA
YEMEN
EGYPT
LIBYA
SUDAN
ERITREA
DJIBOUTI
ETHIOPIA
SOMALIA
KENYA
UGANDA
VIENNA
BRATISLAVA
BUDAPEST
ZAGREB
LJUBLJANA
SARAJEVO
BELGRADE
PODGORICA
PRISHTINE
SOFIA
SKOPJE
TIRANA
BUCHAREST
CHIŞINĂU
KIEV
ATHENS
ANKARA
NICOSIA
BEIRUT
DAMASCUS
JERUSALEM
AMMAN
CAIRO
(Al Qāhirah)
BAGHDĀD
TEHRĀN
T'BILISI
YEREVAN
BAKU
AŞGABAT
DUSHANBE
TOSHKENT
KUWAIT
MANAMA
DOHA
ABU DHABI
MUSCAT
RIYADH
(Ar Riyāḑ)
ṢAN'Ā'
ASMARA
KHARTOUM
ADDIS ABABA
DJIBOUTI
KAMPALA
Istanbul
Odesa
Sevastopol'
Simferopol'
Kharkiv
Dnipropetrovs'k
Zaporizhzhya
Donets'k
Mariupol'
Rostov-na-Donu
Volgograd
(Stalingrad)
Saratov
Samara
(Kuybyshev)
Ufa
Chelyabinsk
Orenburg
Astrakhan'
Mashhad
Eşfahān
Shīrāz
Tabrīz
Ahvāz
Basra
Mosul
Arbīl
Kirkūk
Aleppo
(Ḩalab)
Homs
Adana
Gaziantep
Alexandria
(Al Iskandarīyah)
Tel Aviv-Yafo
Haifa
Giza
Port Said
Suez
Aswān
Luxor
Medina
(Al Madīnah)
Mecca
(Makkah)
Jeddah
(Jiddah)
Dammam
(Ad Dammām)
Dubai
(Dubayy)
Karachi
Hyderabad
Omdurman
Port Sudan
Aden
('Adan)
Hodeidah
Mukalla
Socotra
(Suquṭrā)
(Yemen)
Benghazi
Black Sea
Sea of Azov
Caspian Sea
Aral Sea
Mediterranean Sea
Red Sea
The Gulf
Gulf of Oman
Gulf of Aden
Arabian Sea
INDIAN OCEAN
Ionian Sea
Aegean Sea
Adriatic Sea
Caspian Lowland
Caucasus
Zagros Mountains
Taurus Mts
Elburz Mountains
Karakum Desert
Kyzylkum Desert
Ustyurt Plateau
Dasht-e Kavīr
Dasht-e Lut
Syrian Desert
An Nafūd
Arabian Peninsula
Rub' al Khālī
(Empty Quarter)
Libyan Desert
Western Desert
Eastern Desert
Nubian Desert
Great Sand Sea
Qattara Depression
Tropic of Cancer
Great Rift Valley
Lake Victoria
Lake Turkana
OGADEN
Haud
ILEMI TRIANGLE
UNDER KENYAN
ADMINISTRATION
HALAIB
TRIANGLE
UNDER SUDANESE
ADMINISTRATION
Arabian Sea

Albers Conic Equal Area Projection

1:20 000 000

0 200 400 600 miles

0 200 400 600 800 1000 km

RUSSIAN FEDERATION
MONGOLIA
CHINA
KYRGYZSTAN
NEPAL
BHUTAN
BANGLADESH
INDIA
MYANMAR (BURMA)
LAOS
THAILAND
VIETNAM
CAMBODIA
MALAYSIA
INDONESIA
SRI LANKA
MALDIVES
SINGAPORE
INNER MONGOLIA
XINJIANG
TIBET
JAMMU AND KASHMIR
AKSAI CHIN CLAIMED BY INDIA, UNDER CHINESE ADMIN.
Gobi Desert
Altai Mountains
Tien Shan
Tarim Basin
(Tarim Pendi)
Taklimakan Desert
(Taklimakan Shamo)
Altun Shan
Kunlun Shan
Qaidam Pendi
Qilian Shan
Plateau of Tibet
(Qingzang Gaoyuan)
Tanggula Shan
Himalaya
Gangdisê Shan
Deccan
Western Ghats
Eastern Ghats
Coromandel Coast
Malabar Coast
Bay of Bengal
Andaman Sea
South China Sea
Gulf of Thailand
Gulf of Tonkin
Strait of Malacca
Andaman Islands (India)
Nicobar Islands (India)
Laccadive Islands (India)
Ten Degree Channel
Nine Degree Channel
Eight Degree Channel
Mouths of the Ganges
Mouths of the Irrawaddy
Mouths of the Mekong
Hainan
ULAN BATOR (Ulaanbaatar)
BEIJING (Peking)
ASTANA (Akmola)
BISHKEK (Frunze)
ISLAMABAD
NEW DELHI
Delhi
KATHMANDU
THIMPHU
DHAKA (Dacca)
NAY PYI TAW
RANGOON (Yangon)
VIENTIANE
HA NOI
BANGKOK (Krung Thep)
PHNOM PENH
Ho Chi Minh City (Saigon)
KUALA LUMPUR
PUTRAJAYA
SRI JAYEWARDENEPURA KOTTE
Colombo
Mumbai (Bombay)
Kolkata (Calcutta)
Chennai (Madras)
Bangalore
Hyderabad
Ahmadabad
Karachi
Lahore
Rawalpindi
Peshawar
Novosibirsk
Omsk
Barnaul
Almaty (Alma-Ata)
Ürümqi
Lhasa
Chengdu
Chongqing
Kunming
Wuhan
Xi'an
Lanzhou
Xining
Guangzhou
Hong Kong
Macao
Tianjin
Mandalay
Chittagong
↑ 77
↑ 78
↑ 79
↓ 103

Asia

Central and Southern Asia

RUSSIAN FEDERATION
MONGOLIA
KAZAKHSTAN
UZBEKISTAN
TURKMENISTAN
KYRGYZSTAN
TAJIKISTAN
AFGHANISTAN
PAKISTAN
IRAN
CHINA
NEPAL
BHUTAN
JAMMU AND KASHMIR
AKSAI CHIN
XINJIANG UYGUR ZIZHIQU (SINKIANG)
XIZANG ZIZHIQU (TIBET)
QINGHAI
GANSU
NEI MONGOL ZIZHIQU (INNER MONGOLIA)
Plateau of Tibet (Qingzang Gaoyuan)
Taklimakan Desert (Taklimakan Shamo)
Tarim Basin (Tarim Pendi)
Tien Shan
Kunlun Shan
Himalaya
Hindu Kush
↑ 76
→ 88
← 109

Albers Equal Area Conic Projection

1:13 000 000

INDIA
BANGLADESH
MYANMAR (BURMA)
SRI LANKA
MALDIVES
INDONESIA
Arabian Sea
Bay of Bengal
INDIAN OCEAN
Andaman Sea
Andaman Islands (India)
Nicobar Islands (India)
Laccadive Islands (India)
Mumbai (Bombay)
Kolkata (Calcutta)
Chennai (Madras)
Bangalore
Hyderabad
DHAKA (Dacca)
RANGOON (Yangon)
NAY PYI TAW
Karachi
SRI JAYEWARDENEPURA KOTTE
Colombo
MALE
Tropic of Cancer
Equator
Malabar Coast
Coromandel Coast
Nine Degree Channel
Eight Degree Channel
Ten Degree Channel

Asia
Southern Asia

AFGHANISTAN
PAKISTAN
INDIA
TAJIKISTAN
XINJIANG
AKSAI CHIN
CLAIMED BY INDIA
UNDER CHINESE
ADMINISTRATION
NORTH WEST
FRONTIER
NORTHERN
AREAS
BALTISTAN
JAMMU
AND KASHMIR
LADAKH
ZANSKAR
RUPSHU
LINE OF CONTROL
TRIBAL AREAS
PUNJAB
HIMACHAL
PRADESH
UTTARAKHAND
HARYANA
UTTAR PRA
RAJASTHAN
GUJARAT
MADHYA PRADESH
MAHARASHTRA
BALOCHISTAN
SINDH
Thar Desert
Hindu Kush
Karakoram Range
Himalaya
Ladakh Range
Zanskar Mountains
Salt Range
Sulaiman Range
Kirthar Range
Vindhya Range
Satpura Range
Western Ghats
Rann of Kachchh
Little Rann of Kachchh
Gulf of Kachchh
Gulf of Khambhat
Mouths of the Indus
Arabian Sea
Tropic of Cancer
KABUL
ISLAMABAD
Rawalpindi
Peshawar
Lahore
Faisalabad
Multan
Quetta
Karachi
Hyderabad
Sukkur
Bahawalpur
Gujranwala
Sialkot
Srinagar
Jammu
Amritsar
Ludhiana
Chandigarh
Delhi
NEW DELHI
Faridabad
Meerut
Moradabad
Bareilly
Aligarh
Agra
Jaipur
Jodhpur
Bikaner
Ajmer
Kota
Gwalior
Jhansi
Kanpur
Lucknow
Bhopal
Indore
Ujjain
Jabalpur
Nagpur
Amravati
Akola
Aurangabad
Nashik
Malegaon
Surat
Vadodara
Ahmadabad
Rajkot
Jamnagar
Bhavnagar
Udaipur
Kandahar
Mazar-e Sharif
Administrative divisions in India
numbered on the map:
1. DADRA AND NAGAR HAVELI (C5)
2. DAMAN AND DIU (B5, C5)
Conic Equidistant Projection

1:7 000 000

0 100 200 miles

0 100 200 300 400 km

CHINA
XIZANG ZIZHIQU
(TIBET)
QINGHAI
Plateau of Tibet
(Qingzang Gaoyuan)
Kunlun Shan
Tanggula Shan
Nyainqêntanglha Shan
Gangdisê Shan
Qaidam Pendi
NEPAL
KATHMANDU
BHUTAN
THIMPHU
SIKKIM
ARUNACHAL PRADESH
ASSAM
MEGHALAYA
NAGALAND
MANIPUR
MIZORAM
TRIPURA
BANGLADESH
DHAKA (Dacca)
BIHAR
JHARKHAND
WEST BENGAL
CHHATTISGARH
ORISSA
MYANMAR (BURMA)
NAY PYI TAW
Mandalay
Lhasa
Golmud
Patna
Varanasi
Kolkata (Calcutta)
Chittagong
Guwahati
Shillong
Ranchi
Bhubaneshwar
Cuttack
Raipur
Bay of Bengal
Mouths of the Ganges
Brahmaputra
Mount Everest (Qomolangma Feng) 8848

INDIA
MADHYA PRADESH
GUJARAT
MAHARASHTRA
CHHATTISGARH
JHARKHAND
ORISSA
ANDHRA PRADESH
KARNATAKA
TAMIL NADU
KERALA
GOA
LAKSHADWEEP (India)
SRI LANKA
MALDIVES
Arabian Sea
Bay of Bengal
Gulf of Mannar
Palk Strait
Palk Bay
Gulf of Khambhat
Nine Degree Channel
Eight Degree Channel
Deccan
Western Ghats
Eastern Ghats
Satpura Range
Malabar Coast
Coromandel Coast
Laccadive Islands
Amindivi Islands
Cannanore Islands
Mumbai (Bombay)
Pune (Poona)
Ahmadabad
Vadodara (Baroda)
Surat
Bhopal
Indore
Jabalpur
Nagpur
Raipur
Ranchi
Hyderabad
Secunderabad
Vishakhapatnam
Vijayawada
Bangalore
Chennai (Madras)
Mysore
Mangalore
Calicut (Kozhikode)
Cochin (Kochi)
Coimbatore
Madurai
Tiruchchirappalli
Trivandrum (Thiruvananthapuram)
Puducherry (Pondicherry)
Colombo
SRI JAYEWARDENEPURA KOTTE
Kandy
Jaffna
Galle
Cape Comorin
Minicoy
↑ 104
↓ 103
Administrative divisions in India numbered on the map:
1. DADRA AND NAGAR HAVELI (B1)
2. DAMAN AND DIU (A1, B1)
3. PUDUCHERRY (C4)
Conic Equidistant Projection

Asia

Southern India and Sri Lanka

1:7 000 000

0 100 200 miles

0 100 200 300 400 km

TURKEY
ADANA
MERSİN
KARAMAN
HATAY
KİLİS
GAZİANTEP
ŞANLIURFA
Aleppo (Ḩalab)
Ar Raqqah
Latakia (Al Lādhiqīyah)
SYRIA
Ḩamāh
Homs
Tartūs
Tripoli (Trâblous)
LEBANON
BEIRUT (Beyrouth)
DAMASCUS (Dimashq)
CYPRUS
NICOSIA (Lefkosia)
Limassol (Lemesos)
Larnaca
Famagusta (Ammochostos)
Mediterranean
Sea
IRAQ
Syrian Desert (Bādiyat ash Shām)
Haifa (Hefa)
Tel Aviv-Yafo
WEST BANK
JERUSALEM (Yerushalayim) (El Quds)
AMMĀN
GAZA
ISRAEL
JORDAN
Beersheba
Dead Sea
Negev
EGYPT
Sinai (Shibh Jazīrat Sīnā')
SHAMĀL SĪNĀ'
JANŪB SĪNĀ'
Suez (As Suways)
Elat
Al 'Aqabah
Ma'ān
SAUDI ARABIA

Conic Equidistant Projection

1:3 000 000

0 25 50 75 100 miles

0 25 50 75 100 125 150 175 km

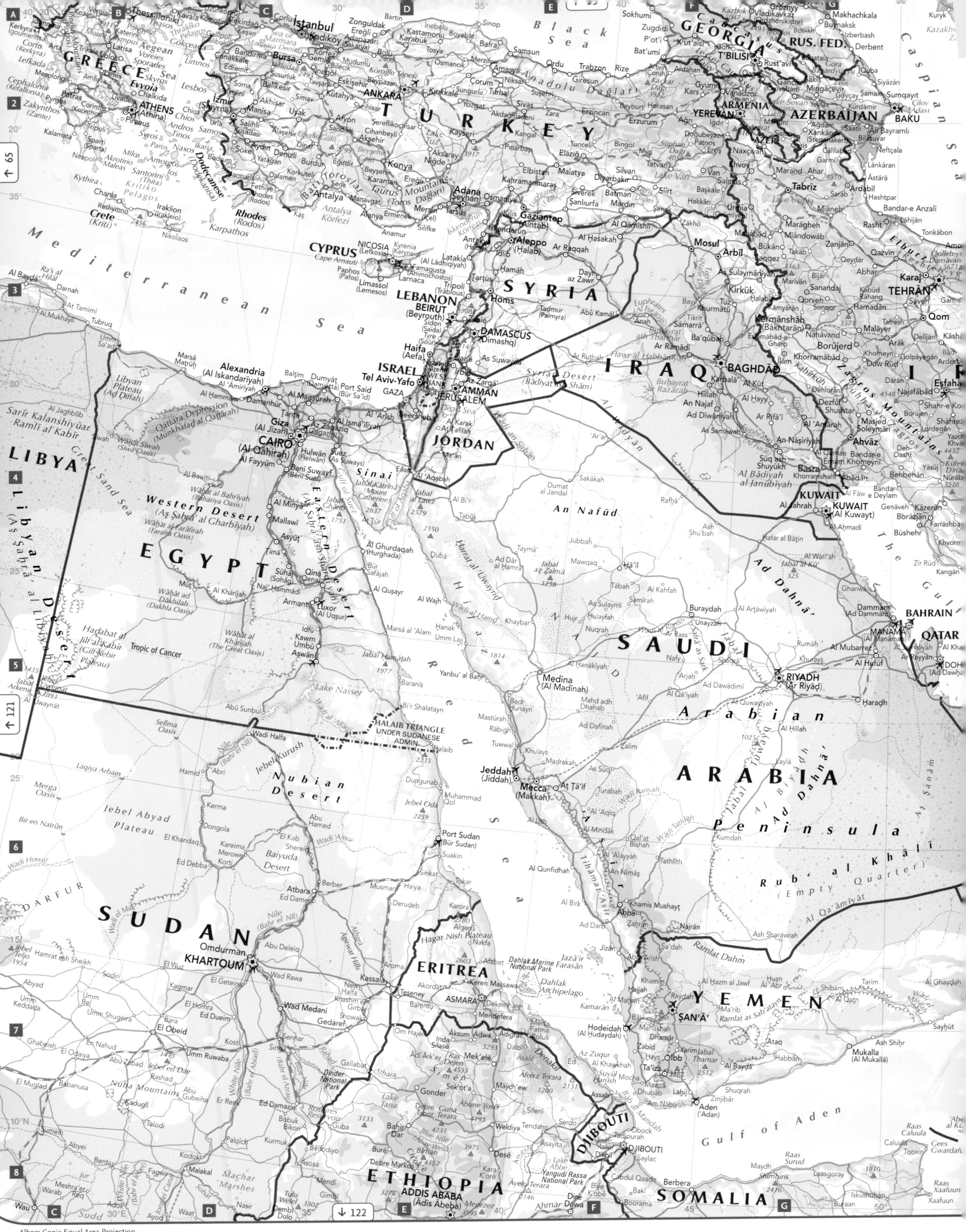
GREECE
ATHENS
(Athina)
Aegean Sea
TURKEY
ANKARA
İstanbul
Black Sea
GEORGIA
T'BILISI
RUS. FED.
ARMENIA
YEREVAN
AZERBAIJAN
BAKU
Caspian Sea
Mediterranean Sea
CYPRUS
NICOSIA
LEBANON
BEIRUT
SYRIA
DAMASCUS
ISRAEL
JERUSALEM
AMMAN
JORDAN
IRAQ
BAGHDAD
TEHRAN
KUWAIT
BAHRAIN
QATAR
RIYADH
SAUDI ARABIA
Arabian Peninsula
LIBYA
EGYPT
CAIRO
Western Desert
Eastern Desert
Sinai
Tropic of Cancer
Lake Nasser
HALAIB TRIANGLE UNDER SUDANESE ADMIN.
Nubian Desert
SUDAN
KHARTOUM
Red Sea
ERITREA
ASMARA
YEMEN
SAN'A'
DJIBOUTI
ETHIOPIA
ADDIS ABABA
SOMALIA
Gulf of Aden
An Nafūd
Rub' al Khālī
(Empty Quarter)
Zagros Mountains
The Gulf

Albers Conic Equal Area Projection

1:13 000 000 — 0 100 200 300 400 500 miles; 0 100 200 300 400 500 600 700 800 km

KAZAKHSTAN
KYRGYZSTAN
UZBEKISTAN
TURKMENISTAN
TAJIKISTAN
AFGHANISTAN
PAKISTAN
CHINA
XINJIANG UYGUR ZIZHIQU (SINKIANG)
XIZANG ZIZHIQU (TIBET)
JAMMU AND KASHMIR
AKSAI CHIN CLAIMED BY INDIA UNDER CHINESE ADMINISTRATION
LINE OF CONTROL
NEPAL
INDIA
OMAN
UNITED ARAB EMIRATES
Taklimakan Desert (Taklimakan Shamo)
Tarim Basin (Tarim Pendi)
Kunlun Shan
Hindu Kush
Himalaya
Karakum Desert (Peski Karakumy)
Thar Desert
Gulf of Oman
Arabian Sea
Gulf of Kachchh
Gulf of Khambhat
Laccadive Islands (India)
Nine Degree Channel
Socotra (Suquṭrá) (Yemen)
TOSHKENT (Tashkent)
DUSHANBE
ASGABAT (Ashkhabad)
KABUL
ISLAMABAD
NEW DELHI
MUSCAT (Masqat)
ABU DHABI (Abū Ẓabī)
Karachi
Lahore
Delhi
Mumbai (Bombay)
Ahmadabad
Hyderabad
Bangalore
Chennai
Mashhad
Kandahār
Herāt
Quetta
Peshawar
Rawalpindi
Multan
Faisalabad
Jaipur
Agra
Lucknow
Kanpur
Bhopal
Nagpur
Pune (Poona)
Surat
Vadodara (Baroda)
Indore
Calicut (Kozhikode)
Cochin (Kochi)
Coimbatore
Trivandrum (Thiruvananthapuram)
Mangalore
Dubai (Dubayy)
Sharjah (Ash Shāriqah)
Tropic of Cancer
↑ 102
↑ 103

TURKEY
ARMENIA
AZER.
AZERBAIJAN
TURKM
IRAQ
MESOPOTAMIA
IRAN
KUWAIT
BAHRAIN
QATAR
SAUDI ARABIA
UNITED ARAB EMIRATES
OMAN
Caspian Sea
Lake Van
Lake Urmia
The Gulf
Gulf of Oman
Strait of Hormuz
Elburz Mountains
Zagros Mountains
Dasht-e Kavir
Dasht-e Lut
KHAMSEH
KHALAJESTAN
LORESTAN
BAKHTIARI COUNTRY
LARISTAN
TEHRĀN
BAGHDĀD
KUWAIT (Al Kuwayt)
RIYADH (Ar Riyāḍ)
DOHA (Ad Dawḥah)
MANAMA (Al Manāmah)
ABU DHABI (Abū Ẓabī)
MUSCAT (Masqaṭ)
ASGABAT (Ashkhabad)
Tropic of Cancer
Conic Equidistant Projection

↑ 113
↑ 113
↓ 108
↑ 108

1:7 000 000

UZBEKISTAN
KYRGYZSTAN
TAJIKISTAN
CHINA
XINJIANG UYGUR ZIZHIQU
AFGHANISTAN
PAKISTAN
INDIA
NORTHERN AREAS
NORTH WEST FRONTIER
TRIBAL AREAS
JAMMU AND KASHMIR
LINE OF CONTROL
PUNJAB
BALOCHISTAN
SINDH
RAJASTHAN
GUJARAT
HARYANA
Arabian Sea
Gulf of Kachchh
Rann of Kachchh
Mouths of the Indus
DUSHANBE
KĀBUL
ISLAMABAD
Rawalpindi
Peshawar
Lahore
Faisalabad
Multan
Quetta
Karachi
Hyderabad
Kandahār
Herāt
Mazār-e Sharīf
Zāhedān
Srinagar
Jammu
Amritsar
Ahmadabad
Jodhpur
Bikaner
Samarqand
Türkmenabat (Chardzhev)
Dasht-e Margow
REGISTĀN
Hindu Kush
Sulaiman Range
Toba and Kakar Ranges
Central Makran Range
Makran Coast Range
Karakoram Range
Thar Desert
Salt Range
Hazarajat
Kirthar Range
F
G
H
I
J
60°
64°
68°
↑ 102
↑ 104

Asia

The Gulf, Iran, Afghanistan and Pakistan

ROMANIA
BUCHAREST (Bucureşti)
SERBIA
KOSOVO
PRISHTINE (Priština)
SKOPJE
MACEDONIA (F.Y.R.O.M.)
BULGARIA
SOFIA (Sofiya)
Balkan Mountains
Rhodope Mountains
THRACE
GREECE
ATHENS (Athína)
Thessaloniki
Aegean Sea
Lesbos (Lesvos)
Evvoia
Cyclades (Kyklades)
Dodecanese (Dodekanisa)
Myrtoo Pelagos
Kritiko Pelagos
Crete (Kriti)
Rhodes (Rodos)
Black Sea
UKRAINE
Crimea
Sevastopol'
Simferopol'
Yalta
Administrative divisions in Russian Federation numbered on the map:
1. RESPUBLIKA KALMYKIYA - KHALM'G-TANGCH (G1)
2. RESPUBLIKA DAGESTAN (G2)
3. CHECHENSKAYA RESPUBLIKA (G2)
4. RESPUBLIKA INGUSHETIYA (G2)
5. RESPUBLIKA SEVERNAYA OSETIYA - ALANIYA (G2)
6. KABARDINO-BALKARSKAYA RESPUBLIKA (F2)
7. KARACHAYEVO-CHERKESSKAYA RESPUBLIKA (F2)
8. RESPUBLIKA ADYGEYA (F1)
TURKEY
ANADOLU (ANATOLIA)
ANKARA
İstanbul
İzmir (Smyrna)
Bursa
Konya
Antalya
Adana (Seyhan)
Gaziantep (Aintab)
Sea of Marmara (Marmara Denizi)
Köroğlu Dağları
Taurus Mountains (Toros Dağları)
PISIDIA
Lake Tuz (Tuz Gölü)
Aleppo (Halab)
Homs
SYR
CYPRUS
NICOSIA (Lefkosia)
Limassol (Lemesos)
Larnaca
Famagusta (Ammochostos)
Paphos (Pafos)
Mediterranean Sea
LEBANON
BEIRUT (Beyrouth)
Tripoli (Trâblous)
DAMASCUS (Dimashq)
Haifa (Hefa)
Tel Aviv-Yafo
JERUSALEM
WEST BANK
GAZA
ISRAEL
JORDAN
'AMMAN
LIBYA
EGYPT
CAIRO (Al Qāhirah)
Alexandria (Al Iskandarīyah)
Giza (Al Jīzah)
Port Said (Būr Sa'īd)
Suez (As Suways)
Qattara Depression (Munkhafaḑ al Qaţţārah)
Great Sand Sea
Western Desert (Aş Şaḩrā' al Gharbīyah)
Eastern Desert (Aş Şaḩrā' ash Sharqīyah)
Sinai (Shibh Jazīrat Sīnā')
Gulf of Suez
Gulf of Aqaba
Red Sea
Nile
SAU
53
69
121
Conic Equidistant Projection

1:7 000 000

0 100 200 miles

0 100 200 300 400 km

RUSSIAN FEDERATION
STAVROPOL'SKIY KRAY
KAZAKHSTAN
MANGISTAUSKAYA OBLAST'
UZBEKISTAN
Ustyurt Plateau
GEORGIA
T'BILISI
ARMENIA
YEREVAN
AZERBAIJAN
BAKU
TURKMENISTAN
Caspian Sea
Elburz Mountains
TEHRĀN
IRAN
Dasht-e Kavīr
Zagros Mountains
IRAQ
BAGHDĀD
MESOPOTAMIA
KUWAIT
KUWAIT (Al Kuwayt)
SAUDI ARABIA
The Gulf
Tabrīz
Mosul
Arbīl
Kirkūk
Esfahān (Isfahan)
Shīrāz
Basra
Ahvāz
Qom
Rasht
Derbent
Makhachkala
Yazd
Hamadān
Kermānshāh (Bākhtarān)
Karbalā'
An Najaf
Al Kūt
Lake Urmia
Lake Van (Van Gölü)
Garabogazköl

↑ 64
↓ 108

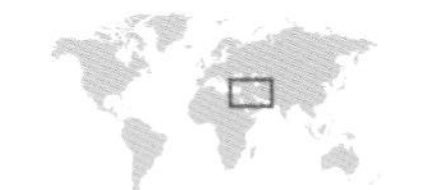

Asia

Eastern Mediterranean, the Caucasus and Iraq

Africa

UNESCO World Heritage Sites

Famous archaeological sites such as the Pyramids of Giza and Abu Simbel, Egypt and the wildlife reserves of the Serengeti and Selous in Tanzania have been on the World Heritage List for a number of years. However more recently Robben Island, where Nelson Mandela was imprisoned, and the rainforests of Madagascar, their biodiversity under threat from development, have been included as representative of Africa's culture and environment.

● Cultural site ● Natural site ● Mixed site

Algeria
1. Al Qal'a of Beni Hammad
2. Djémila
3. Kasbah of Algiers
4. M'Zab Valley
5. Tassili n'Ajjer
6. Timgad
7. Tipasa

Benin
8. Royal Palaces of Abomey

Botswana
9. Tsodilo

Burkina
10. The Ruins of Loropéni

Cameroon
11. Dja Faunal Reserve

Cape Verde
12. Cidade Velha, Historic Centre of Ribeira Grande

Central African Republic
13. Manovo-Gounda St Floris National Park

Congo, Democratic Republic of the
14. Garamba National Park
15. Kahuzi-Biega National Park
16. Okapi Wildlife Reserve
17. Salonga National Park
18. Virunga National Park

Côte d'Ivoire
19. Comoé National Park
20. Mount Nimba Strict Nature Reserve
21. Taï National Park

Egypt
22. Abu Mena
23. Ancient Thebes with its Necropolis
24. Historic Cairo
25. Memphis and its Necropolis – the Pyramid Fields from Giza to Dahshur
26. Nubian Monuments from Abu Simbel to Philae
27. Saint Catherine Area
28. Wadi Al-Hitan (Whale Valley)

Ethiopia
29. Aksum
30. Fasil Ghebbi, Gondar Region
31. Harar Jugol, the Fortified Historic Town
32. Lower Valley of the Awash
33. Lower Valley of the Omo
34. Rock-Hewn Churches, Lalibela
35. Simien National Park
36. Tiya

Gabon
37. Ecosystem and Relict Cultural Landscape of Lopé-Okanda

Gambia, The
38. James Island and Related Sites
39. Stone Circles of Senegambia

Ghana
40. Asante Traditional Buildings
41. Forts and Castles, Volta, Greater Accra, Central and Western Regions

Gough Island
42. Gough and Inaccessible Islands (U.K.)

Guinea
20. Mount Nimba Strict Nature Reserve

Kenya
43. Lake Turkana National Parks
44. Lamu Old Town
45. Mount Kenya National Park/ Natural Forest
46. Sacred Mijikenda Kaya Forests

Libya
47. Archaeological Site of Cyrene
48. Archaeological Site of Leptis Magna
49. Archaeological Site of Sabratha
50. Old Town of Ghadamès
51. Rock-Art Sites of Tadrart Acacus

Madagascar
52. Rainforests of the Atsinanana
53. The Royal Hill of Ambohimanga
54. Tsingy de Bemaraha Strict Nature Reserve

Malawi
55. Chongoni Rock-Art Area
56. Lake Malawi National Park

Mali
57. Cliff of Bandiagara (Land of the Dogons)
58. Old Towns of Djenné
59. Timbuktu
60. Tomb of Askia

Mauritania
61. Ancient Ksour of Ouadane, Chinguetti, Tichitt and Oualata
62. Banc d'Arguin National Park

Mauritius
63. Aapravasi Ghat
64. Le Morne Cultural Landscape

Morocco
65. Archaeological Site of Volubilis
66. Historic City of Meknes
67. Ksar of Ait-Ben-Haddou
68. Medina of Essaouira (formerly Mogador)
69. Medina of Fez
70. Medina of Marrakesh
71. Medina of Tétouan (formerly known as Titawin)
72. Portuguese City of Mazagan (El Jadida)

Mozambique
73. Island of Mozambique

Namibia
74. Twyfelfontein or /Ui-//aes

Niger
75. Aïr and Ténéré Natural Reserves
76. W National Park of Niger

Nigeria
77. Osun-Osogbo Sacred Grove
78. Sukur Cultural Landscape

Senegal
79. Djoudj National Bird Sanctuary
80. Island of Gorée
81. Island of Saint-Louis
82. Niokolo-Koba National Park
39. Stone Circles of Senegambia

Seychelles
83. Aldabra Atoll
84. Vallée de Mai Nature Reserve

South Africa, Republic of
85. Cape Floral Region Protected Areas
86. Fossil Hominid Sites of Sterkfontein, Swartkrans, Kromdraai, and Environs
87. iSimangaliso Wetland Park
88. Mapungubwe Cultural Landscape
89. Richtersveld Cultural and Botanical Landscape
90. Robben Island
91. uKhahlamba/Drakensberg Park
92. Vredefort Dome

Sudan
93. Gebel Barkal and the Sites of the Napatan Region

Tanzania
94. Kilimanjaro National Park
95. Kondoa Rock-Art Sites
96. Ngorongoro Conservation Area
97. Ruins of Kilwa Kisiwani and Ruins of Songo Mnara
98. Selous Game Reserve
99. Serengeti National Park
100. Stone Town of Zanzibar

Togo
101. Koutammakou, the Land of the Batammariba

Tunisia
102. Amphitheatre of El Jem
103. Dougga/Thugga
104. Ichkeul National Park
105. Kairouan
106. Medina of Sousse
107. Medina of Tunis
108. Punic Town of Kerkuane and its Necropolis
109. Site of Carthage

Uganda
110. Bwindi Impenetrable National Park
111. Rwenzori Mountains National Park
112. Tombs of Buganda Kings at Kasubi

Zambia
113. Mosi-oa-Tunya/Victoria Falls

Zimbabwe
114. Great Zimbabwe National Monument
115. Khami Ruins National Monument
116. Mana Pools National Park, Sapi and Chewore Safari Areas
113. Mosi-oa-Tunya/Victoria Falls
117. Matobo Hills

WESTERN SAHARA
62
CAPE VERDE
12
79
81
SENEGAL
80
39
38
THE GAMBIA
39
GUINEA-BISSAU

EUROPE
ASIA
Mediterranean Sea
Red Sea
ATLANTIC OCEAN
INDIAN OCEAN
MOROCCO
ALGERIA
TUNISIA
LIBYA
EGYPT
MAURITANIA
MALI
NIGER
CHAD
SUDAN
ERITREA
DJIBOUTI
ETHIOPIA
SOMALIA
GUINEA
SIERRA LEONE
LIBERIA
CÔTE D'IVOIRE
BURKINA
GHANA
TOGO
BENIN
NIGERIA
CAMEROON
CENTRAL AFRICAN REPUBLIC
EQUATORIAL GUINEA
SÃO TOMÉ AND PRÍNCIPE
GABON
CONGO
CABINDA (Angola)
DEMOCRATIC REPUBLIC OF THE CONGO
UGANDA
KENYA
RWANDA
BURUNDI
TANZANIA
SEYCHELLES
COMOROS
ANGOLA
ZAMBIA
MALAWI
MOZAMBIQUE
ZIMBABWE
NAMIBIA
BOTSWANA
MADAGASCAR
MAURITIUS
Réunion (France)
SWAZILAND
LESOTHO
REPUBLIC OF SOUTH AFRICA
Gough Island (U.K.)

Africa
Landscapes

Some of the world's greatest physical features are in Africa, the world's second largest continent. Variations in climate and elevation give rise to the continent's great variety of landscapes. The Sahara, the world's largest desert, extends across the whole continent from west to east, and covers an area of over nine million square kilometres. Other significant African deserts are the Kalahari and the Namib. In contrast, some of the world's greatest rivers flow in Africa, including the Nile, the world's longest, and the Congo.

The Great Rift Valley is perhaps Africa's most notable geological feature. It stretches for nearly 3 000 kilometres from Jordan, through the Red Sea and south to Mozambique, and contains many of Africa's largest lakes. Significant mountain ranges on the continent are the Atlas Mountains and the Ethiopian Highlands in the north, the Ruwenzori in east central Africa, and the Drakensberg in the far southeast.

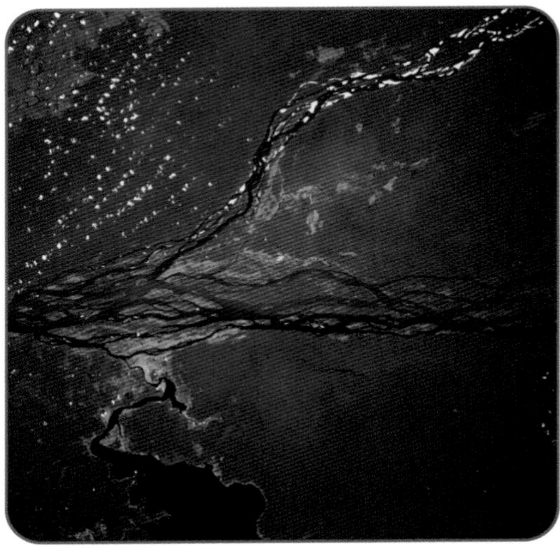

The confluence of the Ubangi and Africa's second longest river, the **Congo**.

Madeira
Canary Islands
Tenerife
Gran Canaria
Cape Verde
Santo Antão
Boa Vista
Ilhas do Cabo Verde
Fogo
Santiago
Cap Vert
Akchâr
Aoukâr
Sénégal
Gambia
Fouta Djallon
Ascension

Africa's extent

TOTAL LAND AREA	30 343 578 sq km / 11 715 655 sq miles
Most northerly point	La Galite, Tunisia
Most southerly point	Cape Agulhas, South Africa
Most westerly point	Santo Antão, Cape Verde
Most easterly point	Raas Xaafuun, Somalia

Internet Links

NASA Visible Earth	**visibleearth.nasa.gov**
NASA Astronaut Photography	**eol.jsc.nasa.gov**
Peace Parks Foundation	**www.peaceparks.org**

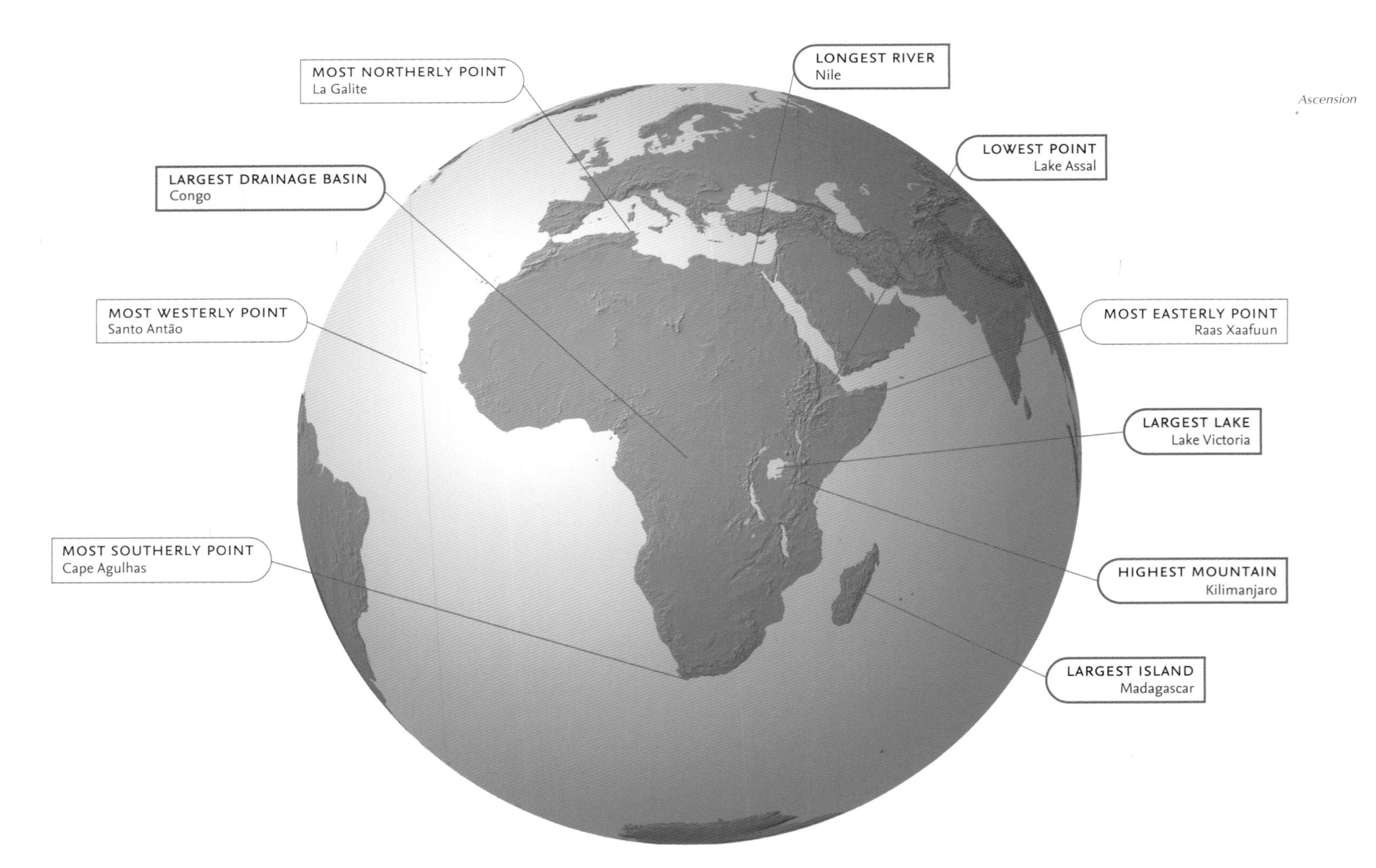
MOST NORTHERLY POINT
La Galite
LONGEST RIVER
Nile
LOWEST POINT
Lake Assal
LARGEST DRAINAGE BASIN
Congo
MOST WESTERLY POINT
Santo Antão
MOST EASTERLY POINT
Raas Xaafuun
LARGEST LAKE
Lake Victoria
MOST SOUTHERLY POINT
Cape Agulhas
HIGHEST MOUNTAIN
Kilimanjaro
LARGEST ISLAND
Madagascar

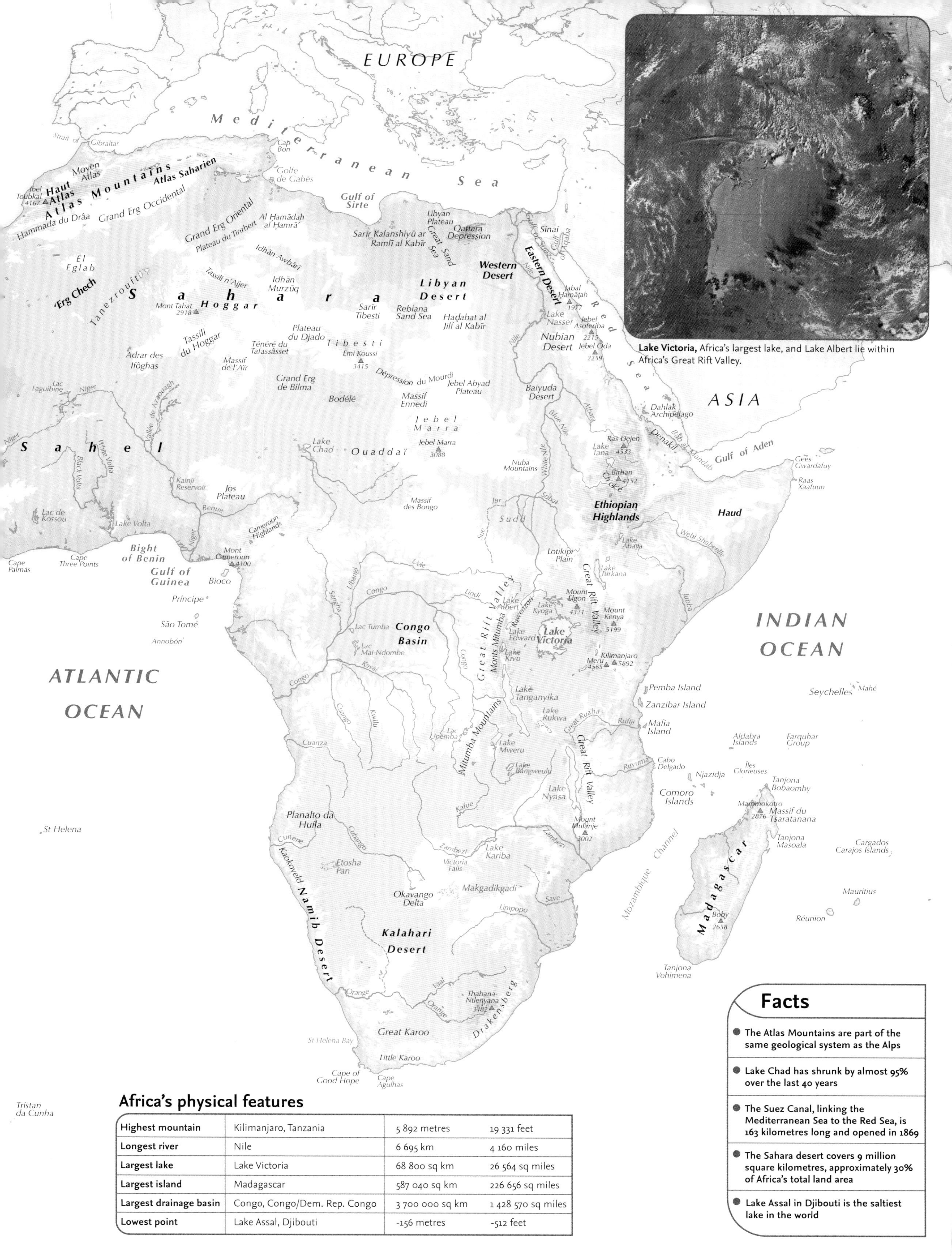
EUROPE
Mediterranean Sea
Strait of Gibraltar
Cap Bon
Golfe de Gabès
Gulf of Sirte
Jbel Toubkal 4167
Haut Atlas
Moyen Atlas
Atlas Mountains
Atlas Saharien
Hammada du Drâa
Grand Erg Occidental
Grand Erg Oriental
Plateau du Tinrhert
Al Hamādah al Ḩamrā'
Idhān Awbārī
Sarīr Kalanshiyū ar Ramlī al Kabīr
Libyan Plateau
Qattara Depression
Great Sand Sea
Sinai
Gulf of Suez
Gulf of Aqaba
Western Desert
Eastern Desert
Nile
El Eglab
'Erg Chech
Tanezrouft
Sahara
Tassili n'Ajjer
Idhān Murzūq
Libyan Desert
Mont Tahat 2918
Hoggar
Sarīr Tibesti
Rebiana Sand Sea
Hadabat al Jilf al Kabīr
Jabal Hamāțah 1977
Lake Nasser
Jebel Asoteriba 2217
Nubian Desert
Jebel Oda 2259
Red Sea
Tassili du Hoggar
Plateau du Djado
Ténéré du Tafassâsset
Tibesti
Emi Koussi 3415
Adrar des Ifôghas
Massif de l'Aïr
Grand Erg de Bilma
Dépression du Mourdi
Jebel Abyad Plateau
Baiyuda Desert
Lac Faguibine
Niger
Bodélé
Massif Ennedi
Jebel Marra
Jebel Marra 3088
Lake Chad
Ouaddaï
Vallée de Azaouagh
Sahel
White Volta
Black Volta
Kainji Reservoir
Jos Plateau
Benue
Nuba Mountains
White Nile
Blue Nile
Atbara
Dahlak Archipelago
ASIA
Danakil
Bab al Mandab
Gulf of Aden
Ras Dejen 4533
Lake Tana
Birhan 4152
Ch'ok'e
Gees Gwardafuy
Raas Xaafuun
Lac de Kossou
Lake Volta
Cameroon Highlands
Massif des Bongo
Jur
Sudd
Sobat
Ethiopian Highlands
Haud
Bight of Benin
Mont Cameroun 4100
Cape Palmas
Cape Three Points
Gulf of Guinea
Bioco
Príncipe
São Tomé
Annobón
Uele
Ubangi
Sangha
Congo
Lindi
Sue
Lotikipi Plain
Lake Turkana
Lake Abaya
Webi Shabeelle
Great Rift Valley
Lake Albert
Lake Kyoga
Mount Elgon 4321
Mount Kenya 5199
Juba
Lac Tumba
Congo Basin
Lac Mai-Ndombe
Monts Mitumba
Ruwenzori
Lake Edward
Lake Victoria
Lake Kivu
Meru 4565
Kilimanjaro 5892
INDIAN OCEAN
ATLANTIC OCEAN
Kasai
Lake Tanganyika
Pemba Island
Zanzibar Island
Seychelles
Mahé
Cuango
Kwilu
Lake Rukwa
Great Ruaha
Rufiji
Mafia Island
Lac Upemba
Mitumba Mountains
Cuanza
Lake Mweru
Aldabra Islands
Farquhar Group
Lake Bangweulu
Ruvuma
Cabo Delgado
Njazidja
Îles Glorieuses
Tanjona Bobaomby
Comoro Islands
Lake Nyasa
Kafue
Maromokotro 2876
Massif du Tsaratanana
Planalto da Huíla
St Helena
Mount Mulanje 3002
Cunene
Cubango
Zambezi
Lake Kariba
Victoria Falls
Tanjona Masoala
Cargados Carajos Islands
Mozambique Channel
Madagascar
Etosha Pan
Kaokoveld
Okavango Delta
Makgadikgadi
Mauritius
Save
Limpopo
Namib Desert
Kalahari Desert
Boby 2658
Réunion
Tanjona Vohimena
Orange
Vaal
Thabana-Ntlenyana 3482
Drakensberg
Great Karoo
St Helena Bay
Little Karoo
Cape of Good Hope
Cape Agulhas
Tristan da Cunha

Lake Victoria, Africa's largest lake, and Lake Albert lie within Africa's Great Rift Valley.

Africa's physical features

Highest mountain	Kilimanjaro, Tanzania	5 892 metres	19 331 feet
Longest river	Nile	6 695 km	4 160 miles
Largest lake	Lake Victoria	68 800 sq km	26 564 sq miles
Largest island	Madagascar	587 040 sq km	226 656 sq miles
Largest drainage basin	Congo, Congo/Dem. Rep. Congo	3 700 000 sq km	1 428 570 sq miles
Lowest point	Lake Assal, Djibouti	-156 metres	-512 feet

Facts

- **The Atlas Mountains are part of the same geological system as the Alps**
- **Lake Chad has shrunk by almost 95% over the last 40 years**
- **The Suez Canal, linking the Mediterranean Sea to the Red Sea, is 163 kilometres long and opened in 1869**
- **The Sahara desert covers 9 million square kilometres, approximately 30% of Africa's total land area**
- **Lake Assal in Djibouti is the saltiest lake in the world**

Africa
Countries

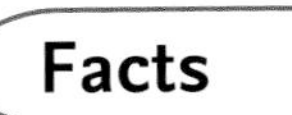

Africa is a complex continent, with over fifty independent countries and a long history of political change. It supports a great variety of ethnic groups, with the Sahara creating the major divide between Arab and Berber groups in the north and a diverse range of groups, including the Yoruba and Masai, in the south.

The current pattern of countries in Africa is a product of a long and complex history, including the colonial period, which saw European control of the vast majority of the continent from the fifteenth century until widespread moves to independence began in the 1950s. Despite its great wealth of natural resources, Africa is by far the world's poorest continent. Many of its countries are heavily dependent upon foreign aid and many are also subject to serious political instability.

Facts

- Africa has over 1 000 linguistic and cultural groups
- Only Liberia and Ethiopia have remained free from colonial rule throughout their history
- Over 30% of the world's minerals, and over 50% of the world's diamonds, come from Africa
- 9 of the 10 poorest countries in the world are in Africa

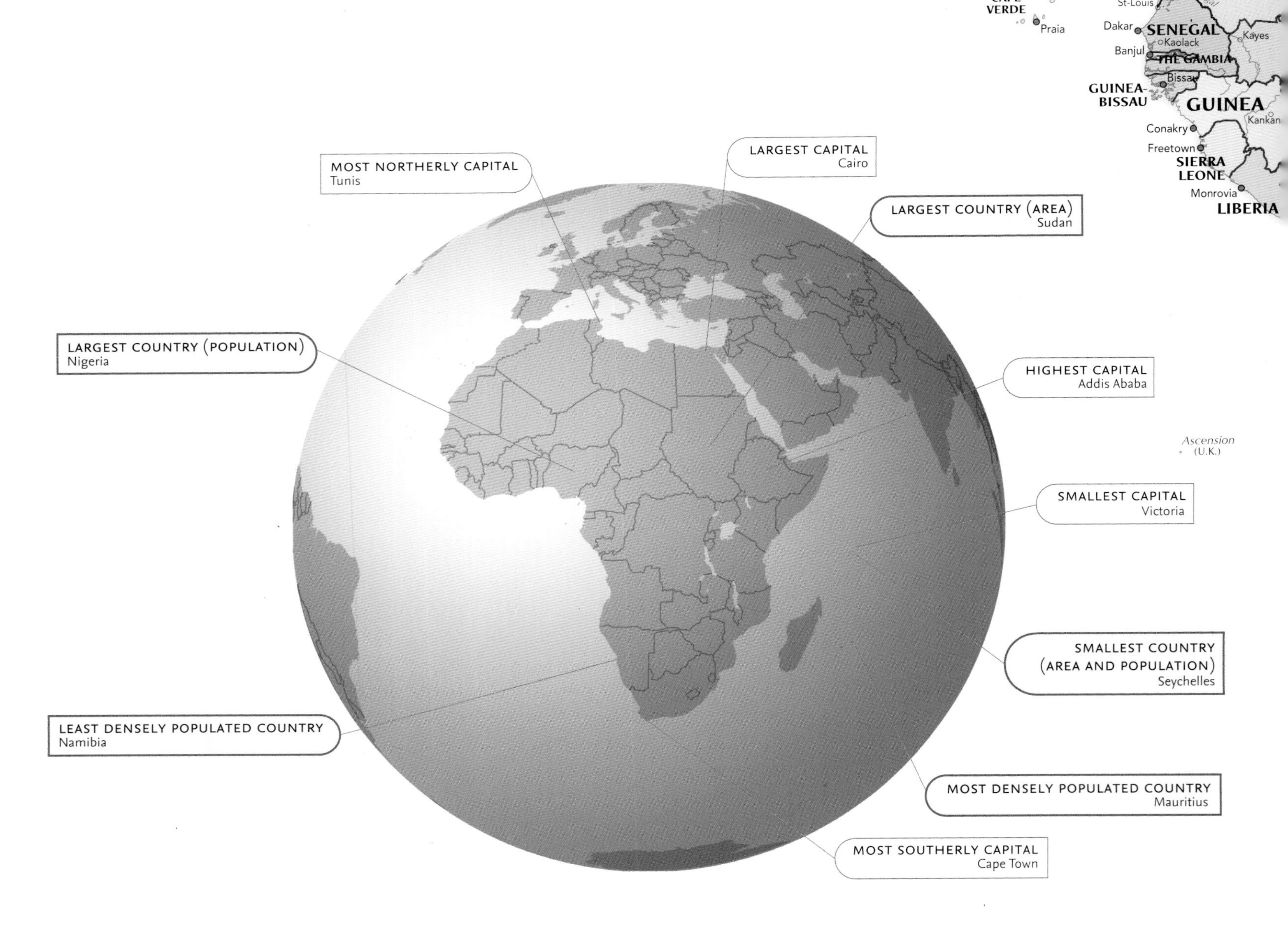
Madeira
(Portugal)
Canary Islands
(Spain)
Laâyoune
WESTERN SAHARA
Nouâdhibou
MAURITANIA
Nouakchott
CAPE VERDE
Praia
St-Louis
Dakar
SENEGAL
Kaolack
Banjul
THE GAMBIA
Kayes
Bissau
GUINEA-BISSAU
GUINEA
Kankan
Conakry
Freetown
SIERRA LEONE
Monrovia
LIBERIA
Ascension
(U.K.)
MOST NORTHERLY CAPITAL
Tunis
LARGEST CAPITAL
Cairo
LARGEST COUNTRY (AREA)
Sudan
LARGEST COUNTRY (POPULATION)
Nigeria
HIGHEST CAPITAL
Addis Ababa
SMALLEST CAPITAL
Victoria
SMALLEST COUNTRY (AREA AND POPULATION)
Seychelles
LEAST DENSELY POPULATED COUNTRY
Namibia
MOST DENSELY POPULATED COUNTRY
Mauritius
MOST SOUTHERLY CAPITAL
Cape Town

Internet Links

UK Foreign and Commonwealth Office	www.fco.gov.uk
CIA World Factbook	www.cia.gov/library/publications/the-world-factbook/index.html
Southern African Development Community	www.sadc.int
GeoEye	www.GeoEye.com

EUROPE
Mediterranean Sea
Strait of Gibraltar
Algiers
Skikda
Annaba
Tunis
Oran
Bejaïa
Constantine
Tangier
Rabat
Casablanca
Fès
Sidi Bel Abbès
Ech Chélif
Sfax
Gabès
Laghouat
Beni Mellal
Atlas Mountains
MOROCCO
TUNISIA
Tripoli
Misrātah
Gulf of Sirte
Al Baydā'
Benghazi
Béchar
Alexandria
Port Said
Tanṭā
Cairo
Giza
Suez
Al Minyā
Asyūṭ
Qinā
Luxor
Aswān
Lake Nasser
ALGERIA
LIBYA
Libyan Desert
EGYPT
Sahara
Red Sea
GeoEye
Port Sudan
ASIA
MALI
NIGER
CHAD
Agadez
Gao
Mopti
Niamey
Zinder
Abéché
Lake Chad
Ndjamena
Omdurman
Khartoum
Wad Medani
Blue Nile
White Nile
SUDAN
El Obeid
ERITREA
Asmara
Gedaref
Mek'ele
DJIBOUTI
Djibouti
Gulf of Aden
Bahir Dar
Dire Dawa
Berbera
Hargeysa
Addis Ababa
ETHIOPIA
SOMALIA
Ouagadougou
Bamako
BURKINA
Sokoto
Kano
Maiduguri
Zaria
Maroua
BENIN
NIGERIA
Kumo
Tamale
TOGO
Parakou
Abuja
Ogbomosho
CÔTE D'IVOIRE
Bouaké
Yamoussoukro
GHANA
Kumasi
Lake Volta
Ibadan
Lagos
Lomé
Porto-Novo
Accra
Abidjan
Cape Coast
Onitsha
Warri
Uyo
Port Harcourt
Douala
CAMEROON
Nkongsamba
Yaoundé
Malabo
Ngaoundéré
Sarh
Moundou
CENTRAL AFRICAN REPUBLIC
Bossangoa
Bouar
Bangui
Wau
Juba
Gulf of Guinea
EQUATORIAL GUINEA
São Tomé
SÃO TOMÉ AND PRÍNCIPE
Libreville
GABON
Port-Gentil
Franceville
CONGO
DEMOCRATIC REPUBLIC OF THE CONGO
Mbandaka
Kisangani
UGANDA
Kampala
Kisumu
Mount Kenya 5199
KENYA
Nakuru
Nairobi
Lake Victoria
Mogadishu
Kismaayo
RWANDA
Kigali
Bukavu
BURUNDI
Bujumbura
Mwanza
Arusha
Kilimanjaro
Bandundu
Brazzaville
Kinshasa
Pointe-Noire
CABINDA (Angola)
Matadi
Kikwit
Kananga
Mbuji-Mayi
Kalemie
Kigoma
Tabora
Lake Tanganyika
Dodoma
Tanga
Mombasa
Zanzibar
Zanzibar Island
Dar es Salaam
TANZANIA
Iringa
Mbeya
INDIAN OCEAN
Victoria
SEYCHELLES
Aldabra Islands
ATLANTIC OCEAN
Luanda
Cuanza
Kamina
ANGOLA
Lobito
Benguela
Huambo
Kasama
Mansa
Likasi
Lubumbashi
Solwezi
Chingola
Ndola
MALAWI
Lake Nyasa
Moroni
COMOROS
Pemba
Antsirañana
Mayotte (France)
Namibe
Lubango
ZAMBIA
Kabwe
Chipata
Lilongwe
Blantyre
Nampula
Nacala
Mahajanga
Mongu
Lusaka
St Helena and Dependencies (U.K.)
Tete
Livingstone
Harare
MOZAMBIQUE
Chitungwiza
Mutare
Quelimane
Mozambique Channel
Etosha Pan
ZIMBABWE
Gweru
Bulawayo
Beira
MADAGASCAR
Toamasina
Antananarivo
NAMIBIA
Okavango Delta
Francistown
Windhoek
Namib Desert
BOTSWANA
Fianarantsoa
Toliara
Port Louis
MAURITIUS
Réunion (France)
Inhambane
Gaborone
Pretoria (Tshwane)
Johannesburg
Xai-Xai
Maputo
Carletonville
Soweto
Mbabane
SWAZILAND
Kimberley
Orange
Bloemfontein
LESOTHO
Maseru
Durban
REPUBLIC OF SOUTH AFRICA
Cape Town
Khayelitsha
East London
Port Elizabeth
Cape of Good Hope
Cape Agulhas
Tristan da Cunha (U.K.)

Cape Town, legislative capital of the Republic of South Africa and the most southerly African capital city.

Africa's capitals

Largest capital (population)	Cairo, Egypt	11 893 000	
Smallest capital (population)	Victoria, Seychelles	25 500	
Most northerly capital	Tunis, Tunisia	36° 46'N	
Most southerly capital	Cape Town, Republic of South Africa	33° 57'S	
Highest capital	Addis Ababa, Ethiopia	2 408 metres	7 900 feet

Africa's countries

Largest country (area)	Sudan	2 505 813 sq km	967 500 sq miles
Smallest country (area)	Seychelles	455 sq km	176 sq miles
Largest country (population)	Nigeria	131 530 000	
Smallest country (population)	Seychelles	81 000	
Most densely populated country	Mauritius	599 per sq km	1 549 per sq mile
Least densely populated country	Namibia	2 per sq km	6 per sq mile

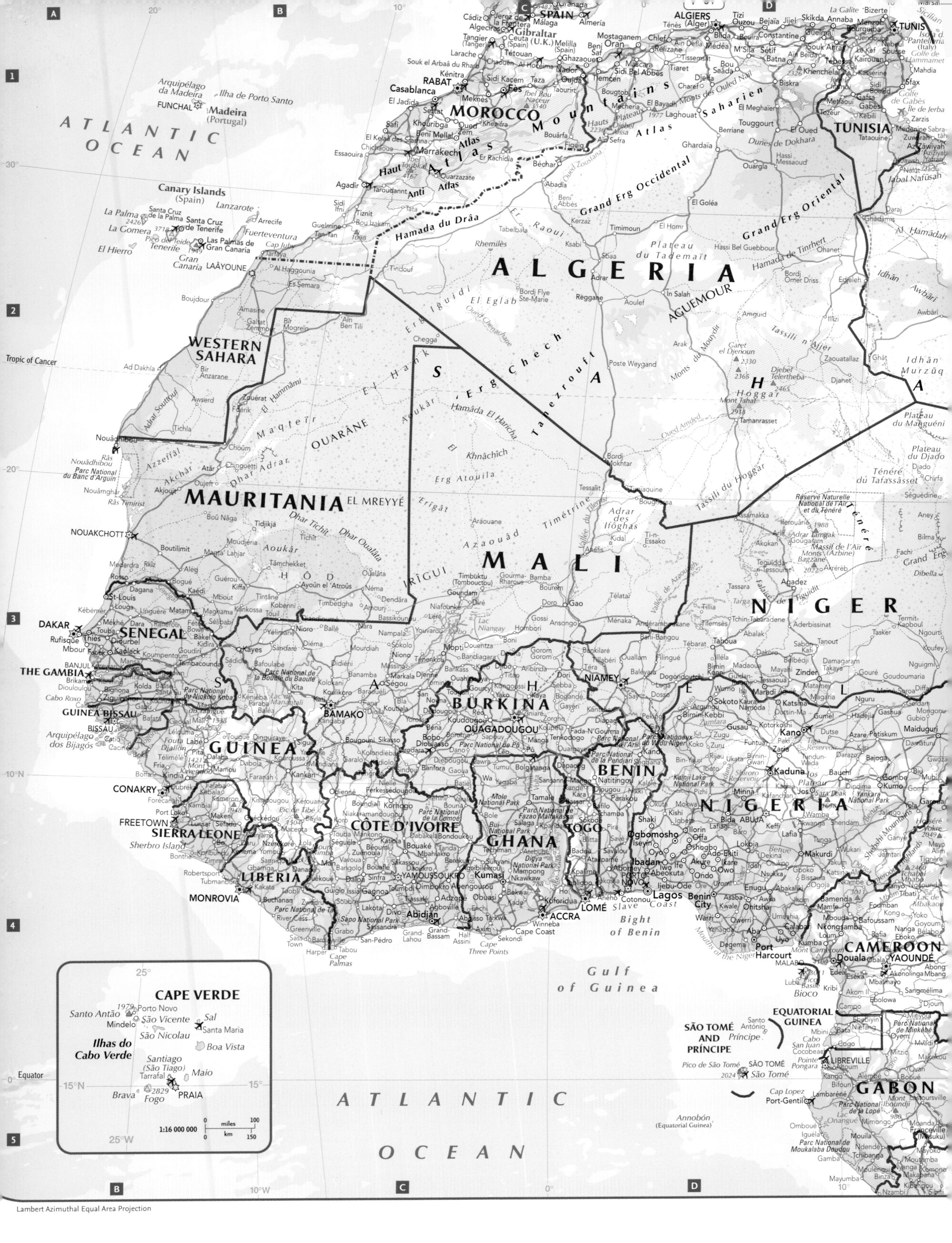
ATLANTIC OCEAN
Arquipélago da Madeira
Ilha de Porto Santo
FUNCHAL
Madeira (Portugal)
Canary Islands (Spain)
La Palma
Santa Cruz de la Palma
Santa Cruz de Tenerife
La Gomera
Tenerife
El Hierro
Gran Canaria
Las Palmas de Gran Canaria
Lanzarote
Fuerteventura
Arrecife
LAÂYOUNE
SPAIN
Cádiz
Algeciras
Gibraltar (U.K.)
Ceuta (Spain)
Melilla (Spain)
Tangier
Málaga
Almería
Granada
RABAT
Casablanca
Fès
Meknès
MOROCCO
Marrakech
Agadir
Essaouira
Safi
El Jadida
Ouarzazate
Haut Atlas
Anti Atlas
Atlas Mountains
Saharien Atlas
Tell Atlas
ALGIERS (Alger)
Oran
Constantine
Annaba
Sétif
Batna
Biskra
Tlemcen
Sidi Bel Abbès
Ghardaïa
Ouargla
Touggourt
El Oued
Béchar
Tindouf
Adrar
Reggane
In Salah
El Goléa
Timimoun
Grand Erg Occidental
Grand Erg Oriental
Hamada du Drâa
Plateau du Tademaït
Hamada de Tinrhert
ALGERIA
AGUEMOUR
Tassili n' Ajjer
Tassili du Hoggar
Hoggar
Tamanrasset
Djanet
Erg Iguidi
Erg Chech
Tanezrouft
TUNIS
TUNISIA
Sfax
Gabès
Kairouan
Golfe de Gabès
Golfe de Hammamet
Île de Jerba
Tropic of Cancer
WESTERN SAHARA
Ad Dakhla
Boujdour
Es Semara
Nouâdhibou
MAURITANIA
NOUAKCHOTT
Atâr
Tidjikja
Zouérat
Rosso
Kiffa
Néma
EL MREYYÉ
OUARÂNE
Adrar Souttouf
Dhar Adrar
Dhar Tichît
Dhar Oualâta
Aoukâr
HÔD
Majâbat al Koubrâ
Tropic of Cancer
MALI
BAMAKO
Timbuktu (Tombouctou)
Gao
Mopti
Ségou
Kayes
Kidal
Tessalit
Adrar des Ifôghas
Timétrine
Azaouâd
Erg Atouila
Hamâda El Haricha
El Khnâchîch
IRÎGUI
Lac Niangay
NIGER
NIAMEY
Agadez
Arlit
Zinder
Maradi
Tahoua
Bilma
Massif de l'Aïr
Ténéré
Réserve Naturelle Nationale de l'Aïr et du Ténéré
Plateau du Djado
Plateau du Manguéni
Idhān Murzūq
SENEGAL
DAKAR
Thiès
Kaolack
Saint-Louis
Ziguinchor
Tambacounda
THE GAMBIA
BANJUL
GUINEA-BISSAU
BISSAU
Arquipélago dos Bijagós
GUINEA
CONAKRY
Kankan
Labé
Kindia
SIERRA LEONE
FREETOWN
Sherbro Island
LIBERIA
MONROVIA
CÔTE D'IVOIRE
YAMOUSSOUKRO
Abidjan
Bouaké
San-Pédro
Cape Palmas
BURKINA
OUAGADOUGOU
Bobo-Dioulasso
GHANA
ACCRA
Kumasi
Tamale
Cape Coast
Cape Three Points
TOGO
LOMÉ
BENIN
PORTO-NOVO
Cotonou
Parakou
NIGERIA
ABUJA
Lagos
Ibadan
Kano
Kaduna
Sokoto
Maiduguri
Jos Plateau
Benin City
Port Harcourt
Enugu
Calabar
Slave Coast
Bight of Benin
Gulf of Guinea
Mouths of the Niger
CAMEROON
YAOUNDÉ
Douala
EQUATORIAL GUINEA
MALABO
Bioco
SÃO TOMÉ AND PRÍNCIPE
SÃO TOMÉ
Príncipe
Pico de São Tomé
Annobón (Equatorial Guinea)
GABON
LIBREVILLE
Port-Gentil
Cap Lopez
Lambaréné
Equator
CAPE VERDE
Ilhas do Cabo Verde
Santo Antão
Mindelo
Porto Novo
São Vicente
São Nicolau
Sal
Santa Maria
Boa Vista
Santiago (São Tiago)
Tarrafal
Maio
Brava
Fogo
PRAIA
1:16 000 000
ATLANTIC OCEAN
Lambert Azimuthal Equal Area Projection

1:16 000 000
0 200 400 miles
0 200 400 600 800 km

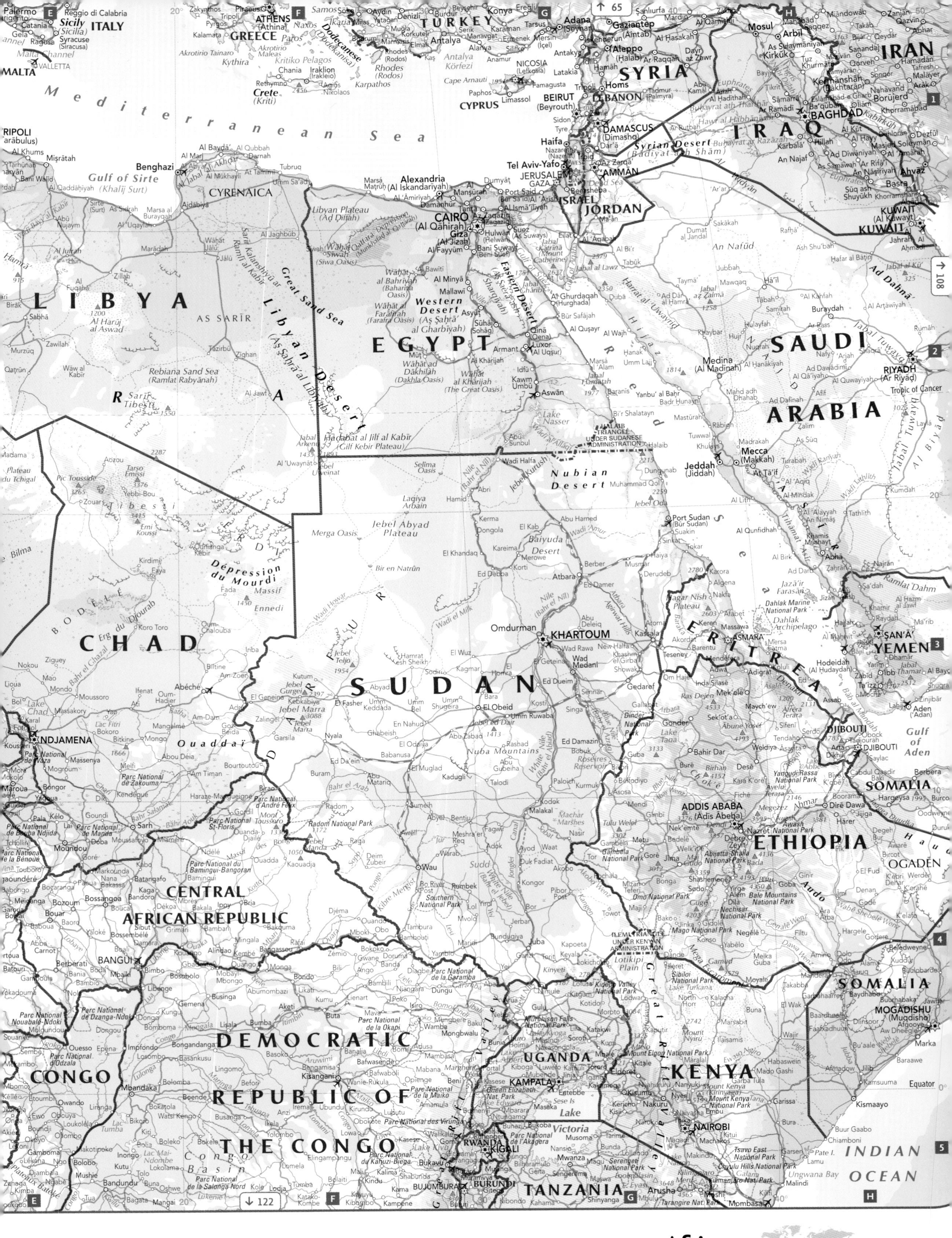

LIBYA
EGYPT
SUDAN
CHAD
CENTRAL AFRICAN REPUBLIC
DEMOCRATIC REPUBLIC OF THE CONGO
CONGO
UGANDA
KENYA
TANZANIA
ETHIOPIA
ERITREA
SOMALIA
DJIBOUTI
YEMEN
SAUDI ARABIA
JORDAN
ISRAEL
SYRIA
IRAQ
IRAN
KUWAIT
TURKEY
GREECE
ITALY
CYPRUS
LEBANON
RWANDA
BURUNDI
MALTA
Mediterranean Sea
Red Sea
Gulf of Aden
INDIAN OCEAN
Gulf of Sirte
Libyan Desert
Western Desert
Eastern Desert
Nubian Desert
Syrian Desert
Lake Victoria
Lake Nasser
CAIRO
KHARTOUM
ADDIS ABABA
NAIROBI
KAMPALA
KIGALI
BUJUMBURA
BANGUI
NDJAMENA
MOGADISHU
ASMARA
DJIBOUTI
ŞAN'Ā'
RIYADH
BAGHDAD
DAMASCUS
BEIRUT
JERUSALEM
'AMMĀN
NICOSIA
ATHENS
VALLETTA
↑ 65
↑ 108
↓ 122
Equator
Tropic of Cancer

Africa
Northern Africa

LIBYA
SAHARA
ALGERIA
Tropic of Cancer
EGYPT
NIGER
CHAD
SUDAN
NIGERIA
CAMEROON
CENTRAL AFRICAN REPUBLIC
DEMOCRATIC REPUBLIC OF THE
CONGO
GABON
EQUATORIAL GUINEA
UGANDA
KENYA
ETHIOPIA
ERITREA
DJIBOUTI
SOMALIA
YEMEN
SAUDI ARABIA
OMAN
QATAR
BAHRAIN
U.A.E.
RWANDA
BURUNDI
Libyan Desert
(Aş Şaḩrā' al Lībīyah)
Great Sand Sea
Western Desert
Eastern Desert
Nubian Desert
Ad Dahnā'
Rub' al Khālī
Red Sea
Gulf of Aden
The Gulf
Lake Victoria
Great Rift Valley
Congo Basin
Darfur
Ogaden
Tibesti
Dépression du Mourdi
Jebel Marra
Nuba Mountains
Equator
KHARTOUM
Omdurman
ADDIS ABABA
(Ādīs Ābeba)
ASMARA
DJIBOUTI
SAN'A'
RIYADH
(Ar Riyāḑ)
DOHA
MANAMA
MOGADISHU
(Muqdisho)
NAIROBI
KAMPALA
KIGALI
BUJUMBURA
BANGUI
NDJAMENA
YAOUNDÉ
LIBREVILLE
Mecca (Makkah)
Medina
(Al Madīnah)
Jeddah
(Jiddah)
Port Sudan
Aswān
Luxor
Wadi Halfa
Juba
Aden ('Adan)
Mukalla
Hodeidah
Berbera
Kismaayo
Douala
Port-Gentil

↑ 121
↑ 108
↓ 120
↑ 108

Lambert Azimuthal Equal Area Projection

1:16 000 000

0 200 400 miles

0 200 400 600 800 km

CONGO
TANZANIA
ANGOLA
ZAMBIA
MALAWI
MOZAMBIQUE
ZIMBABWE
NAMIBIA
BOTSWANA
REPUBLIC OF SOUTH AFRICA
LESOTHO
SWAZILAND
MADAGASCAR
COMOROS
INDIAN OCEAN
ATLANTIC OCEAN
Mozambique Channel
Tropic of Capricorn

Africa

Central and Southern Africa

BOTSWANA
NAMIBIA
REPUBLIC OF SOUTH AFR
ATLANTIC OCEAN
GHANZI
KWENENG
SOUTHERN
KGALAGADI
NORTH
ERONGO
KHOMAS
OMAHEKE
HARDAP
KARAS
GREAT NAMAQUALAND
NAMAQUALAND
NORTHERN CAPE
WESTERN CAPE
GRIQUALAND WEST
Kalahari
Desert
Namib Desert
Great Karoo
Little Karoo
Roggeveld
Nuweveldberge
Langeberg
Central Kalahari Game Reserve
Khutse Game Reserve
Mabuasehube Game Reserve
Gemsbok National Park
Kalahari Gemsbok National Park
Kgalagadi Transfrontier Park
Namib-Naukluft Game Park
National West Coast Tourist Recreation Area
Ai-Ais/Richtersveld Transfrontier Park
Richtersveld National Park
Richtersveld Cultural and Botanical Landscape
Ai-Ais Hot Springs Game Park
Goegap Nature Reserve
Namaqua National Park
Augrabies Falls National Park
Tankwa-Karoo National Park
Karoo National Park
Camdeboo National Park
West Coast National Park
Table Mountain Nature Reserve
Bontebok National Park
De Hoop Nature Reserve
Wilderness National Park
Tsitsikamma Forest and Coastal National Park
Tropic of Capricorn
WINDHOEK
CAPE TOWN
Swakopmund
Walvis Bay
Rehoboth
Mariental
Keetmanshoop
Lüderitz
Oranjemund
Upington
Kimberley
Springbok
Beaufort West
Oudtshoorn
George
Knysna
Mossel Bay
Worcester
Stellenbosch
Paarl
Cape of Good Hope
Cape Agulhas
Orange
Molopo
Nossob
Auob
Fish
Kuruman
Lambert Azimuthal Equal Area Projection
1:5 000 000
0 50 100 150 miles
0 50 100 150 200 250 km

ZIMBABWE
MOZAMBIQUE
SWAZILAND
LESOTHO
LIMPOPO
MPUMALANGA
GAUTENG
KWAZULU-NATAL
FREE STATE
EASTERN CAPE
CENTRAL
KGATLENG
GAZA
INHAMBANE
MAPUTO
GRIQUALAND EAST
INDIAN OCEAN
Drakensberg
PRETORIA (Tshwane)
Johannesburg
Soweto
Vereeniging
GABORONE
MAPUTO
MBABANE
MASERU
Bloemfontein Mangaung
Pietermaritzburg
Durban
Port Elizabeth
East London
Umtata
Richards Bay
Port Shepstone
Kruger National Park
Tropic of Capricorn

Africa

Republic of South Africa

Oceania

UNESCO World Heritage Sites

The sites in this continent cover a huge range in both time and type. In New Zealand the Tongariro site is of great cultural and religious significance to the Maori. There are ancient fossil sites in Australia along with the native peoples' sites such as Uluṟu, associated with the Anangu, one of the ancient Australian Aboriginal peoples. The world famous Great Barrier Reef is a site of great ecological significance and the iconic Sydney Opera House is a landmark feature in the city.

● Cultural site ● Natural site ● Mixed site

PALAU

FEDERATED STATES OF MICRONESIA

A S I A

PAPUA NEW GUINEA

22

Coral Sea

INDIAN OCEAN

A U S T R A L I A

7
16
10
4
1
2
15
12
3
8
17
5
13
1
11
Tasman Sea
14

Heard and McDonald Islands (Australia)

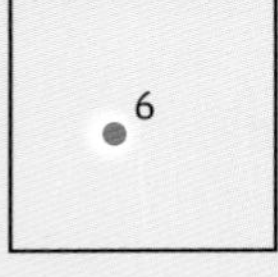

6

9

MARSHALL ISLANDS

NAURU

PACIFIC

KIRIBATI

SOLOMON ISLANDS

TUVALU

VANUATU

SAMOA

25

FIJI

18

New Caledonia (France)

Niue (N.Z.)

TONGA

OCEAN

Cook
Islands
(N.Z.)

NEW ZEALAND
21
20
20
20
20
19
19
19
19

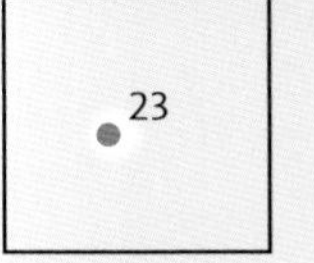

Pitcairn Islands (U.K.)
23

Australia
1. Australian Fossil Mammal Sites (Riversleigh/Naracoorte)
2. Fraser Island
3. Gondwana Rainforests of Australia
4. Great Barrier Reef
5. Greater Blue Mountains Area
6. Heard and McDonald Islands
7. Kakadu National Park
8. Lord Howe Island Group
9. Macquarie Island
10. Purnululu National Park
11. Royal Exhibition Building and Carlton Gardens
12. Shark Bay, Western Australia
13. Sydney Opera House
14. Tasmanian Wilderness
15. Uluṟu-Kata Tjuṯa National Park
16. Wet Tropics of Queensland
17. Willandra Lakes Region

New Caledonia

18. Lagoons of New Caledonia: Reef Diversity and Associated Ecosystems (France)

New Zealand

19. New Zealand Sub-Antarctic Islands
20. Te Wahipounamu – South West New Zealand
21. Tongariro National Park

Papua New Guinea

22. Kuk Early Agricultural Site

Pitcairn Islands

23. Henderson Island (U.K.)

Solomon Islands

24. East Rennell

Vanuatu

25. Chief Roi Mata's Domain

Oceania
Landscapes

Oceania comprises Australia, New Zealand, New Guinea and the islands of the Pacific Ocean. It is the smallest of the world's continents by land area. Its dominating feature is Australia, which is mainly flat and very dry. Australia's western half consists of a low plateau, broken in places by higher mountain ranges, which has very few permanent rivers or lakes. The narrow, fertile coastal plain of the east coast is separated from the interior by the Great Dividing Range, which includes the highest mountain in Australia.

The numerous Pacific islands of Oceania are generally either volcanic in origin or consist of coral. They can be divided into three main regions - Micronesia, north of the equator between Palau and the Gilbert islands; Melanesia, stretching from mountainous New Guinea to Fiji; and Polynesia, covering a vast area of the eastern and central Pacific Ocean.

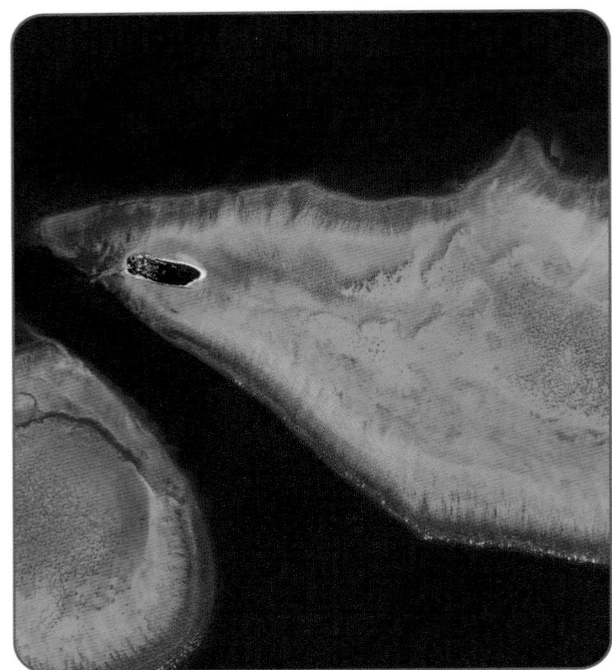

Heron Island, surrounded by coral reefs, lies at the southern end of Australia's Great Barrier Reef.

Facts

- Australia's Great Barrier Reef is the world's largest coral reef and stretches for over 2 000 kilometres
- The highest point of Tuvalu is only 5 metres above sea level
- New Zealand lies directly on the boundary between the Pacific and Indo-Australian tectonic plates
- The Mariana Trench in the Pacific Ocean contains the earth's deepest point – Challenger Deep, 10 920 metres below sea level

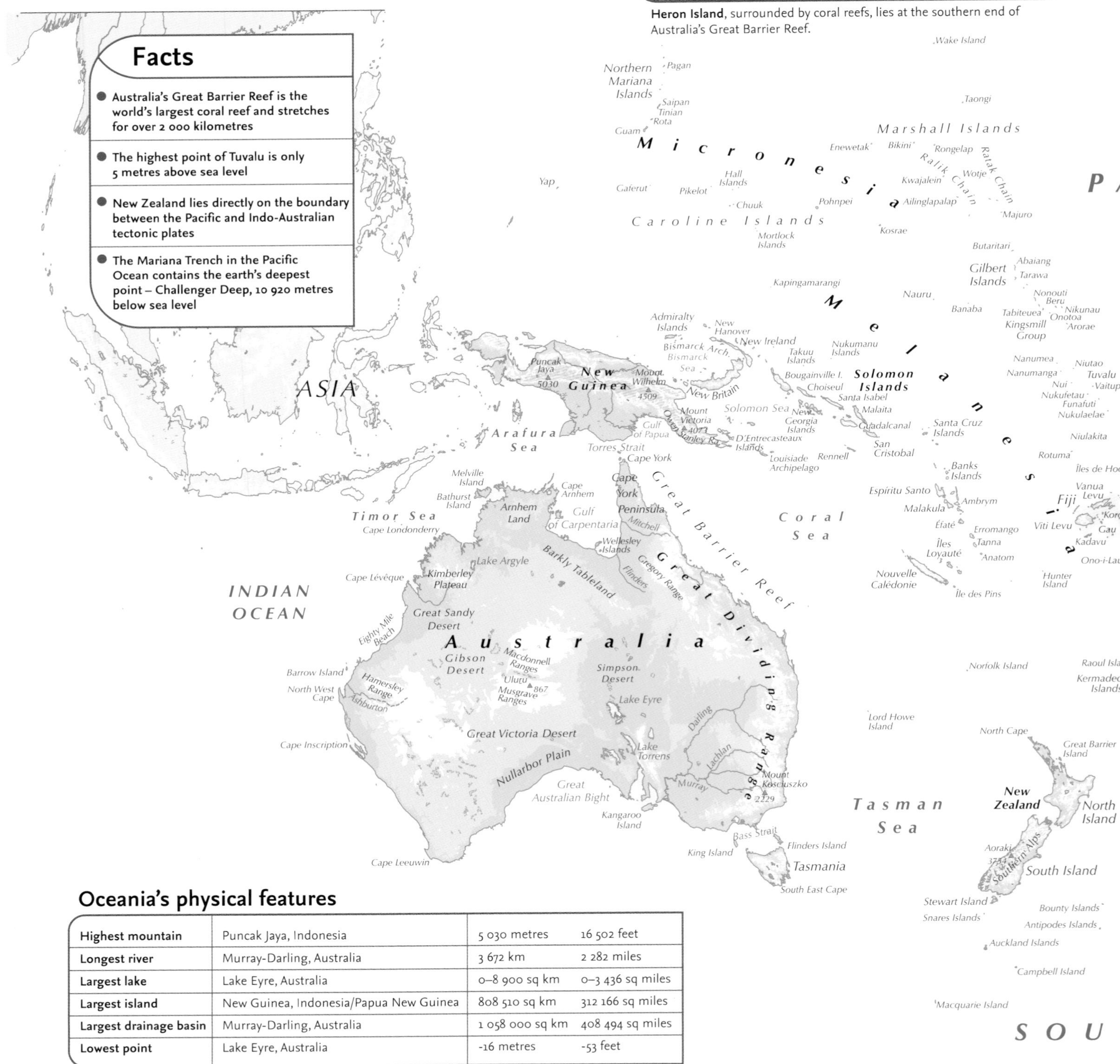

ASIA
INDIAN OCEAN
Micronesia
Melanesia
Northern Mariana Islands
Pagan
Saipan
Tinian
Rota
Guam
Wake Island
Taongi
Marshall Islands
Enewetak
Bikini
Rongelap
Ralik Chain
Ratak Chain
Wotje
Kwajalein
Ailinglapalap
Majuro
Yap
Gaferut
Pikelot
Hall Islands
Chuuk
Pohnpei
Kosrae
Caroline Islands
Mortlock Islands
Butaritari
Abaiang
Tarawa
Gilbert Islands
Kapingamarangi
Nauru
Banaba
Nonouti
Beru
Nikunau
Onotoa
Tabiteuea
Arorae
Kingsmill Group
Admiralty Islands
New Hanover
New Ireland
Bismarck Arch.
Bismarck Sea
Takuu Islands
Nukumanu Islands
Puncak Jaya 5030
New Guinea
Mount Wilhelm 4509
New Britain
Bougainville I.
Choiseul
Solomon Islands
Santa Isabel
Solomon Sea
Malaita
New Georgia Islands
Guadalcanal
Mount Victoria 4073
Owen Stanley Ra.
D'Entrecasteaux Islands
Gulf of Papua
Torres Strait
Cape York
Louisiade Archipelago
Rennell
San Cristobal
Santa Cruz Islands
Nanumea
Nanumanga
Niutao
Tuvalu
Nui
Vaitupu
Nukufetau
Funafuti
Nukulaelae
Niulakita
Rotuma
Arafura Sea
Timor Sea
Cape Londonderry
Melville Island
Bathurst Island
Cape Arnhem
Arnhem Land
Gulf of Carpentaria
Cape York Peninsula
Mitchell
Wellesley Islands
Lake Argyle
Barkly Tableland
Flinders
Gregory Range
Great Barrier Reef
Coral Sea
Banks Islands
Espiritu Santo
Malakula
Ambrym
Éfaté
Erromango
Tanna
Anatom
Îles Loyauté
Nouvelle Calédonie
Île des Pins
Fiji
Viti Levu
Vanua Levu
Kadavu
Ono-i-Lau
Hunter Island
Cape Lévêque
Kimberley Plateau
Great Sandy Desert
Eighty Mile Beach
Australia
Gibson Desert
Macdonnell Ranges
Uluru 867
Musgrave Ranges
Simpson Desert
Lake Eyre
Great Dividing Range
Barrow Island
North West Cape
Hamersley Range
Ashburton
Cape Inscription
Great Victoria Desert
Nullarbor Plain
Great Australian Bight
Lake Torrens
Darling
Lachlan
Murray
Mount Kosciuszko 2229
Kangaroo Island
King Island
Bass Strait
Flinders Island
Tasmania
South East Cape
Cape Leeuwin
Tasman Sea
Norfolk Island
Raoul Isla
Kermadec Islands
Lord Howe Island
North Cape
Great Barrier Island
New Zealand
North Island
South Island
Southern Alps
Aoraki
Stewart Island
Snares Islands
Bounty Islands
Antipodes Islands
Auckland Islands
Campbell Island
Macquarie Island
SOU

Oceania's physical features

Highest mountain	Puncak Jaya, Indonesia	5 030 metres	16 502 feet
Longest river	Murray-Darling, Australia	3 672 km	2 282 miles
Largest lake	Lake Eyre, Australia	0–8 900 sq km	0–3 436 sq miles
Largest island	New Guinea, Indonesia/Papua New Guinea	808 510 sq km	312 166 sq miles
Largest drainage basin	Murray-Darling, Australia	1 058 000 sq km	408 494 sq miles
Lowest point	Lake Eyre, Australia	-16 metres	-53 feet

Internet Links

NASA Visible Earth	**visibleearth.nasa.gov**
NASA Astronaut Photography	**eol.jsc.nasa.gov**
Great Barrier Reef Marine Park Authority	**www.gbrmpa.gov.au**

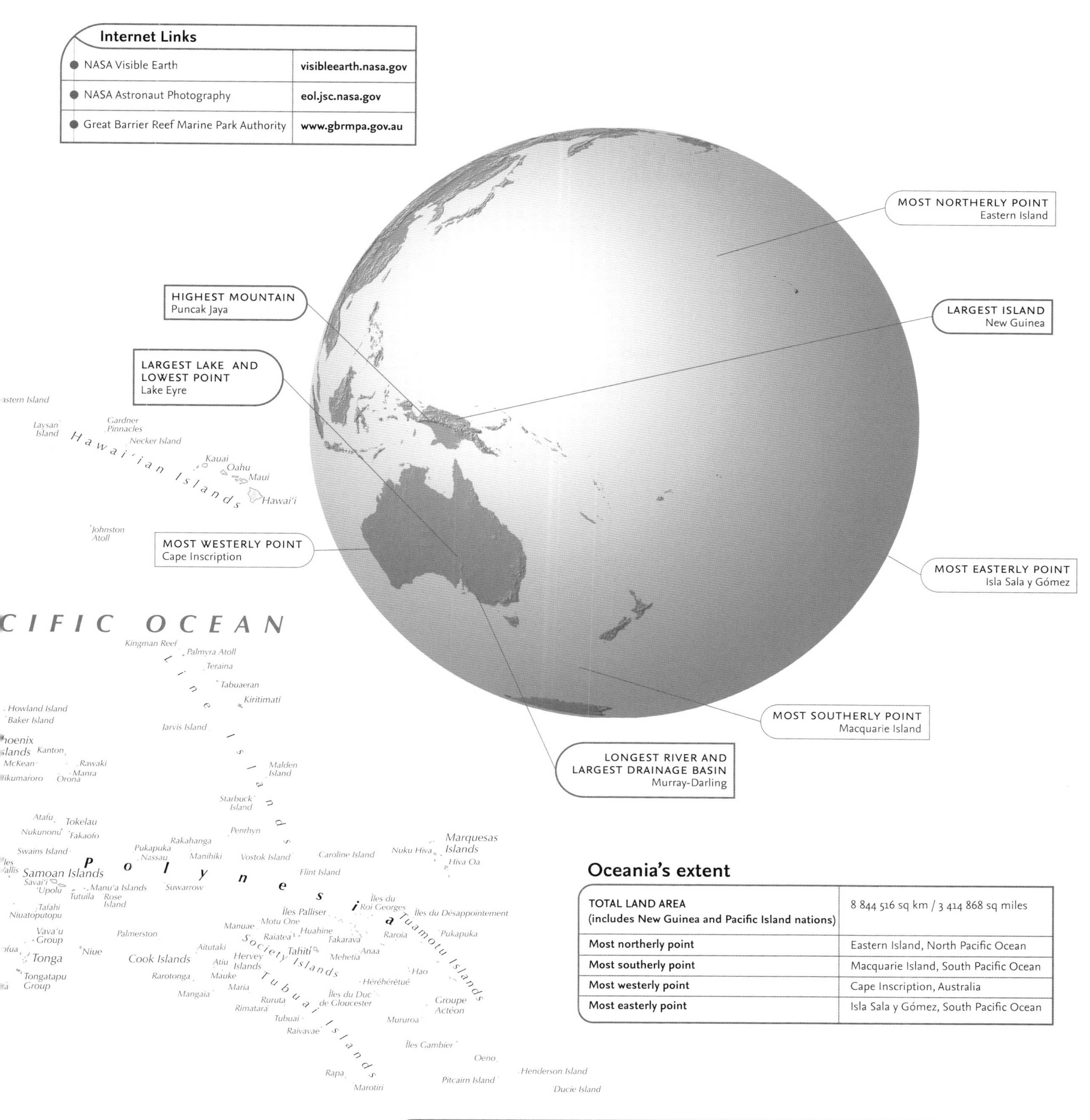

MOST NORTHERLY POINT
Eastern Island
HIGHEST MOUNTAIN
Puncak Jaya
LARGEST ISLAND
New Guinea
LARGEST LAKE AND LOWEST POINT
Lake Eyre
MOST WESTERLY POINT
Cape Inscription
MOST EASTERLY POINT
Isla Sala y Gómez
MOST SOUTHERLY POINT
Macquarie Island
LONGEST RIVER AND LARGEST DRAINAGE BASIN
Murray-Darling
Laysan Island
Gardner Pinnacles
Necker Island
Hawai'ian Islands
Kauai
Oahu
Maui
Hawai'i
Johnston Atoll
CIFIC OCEAN
Kingman Reef
Palmyra Atoll
Teraina
Tabuaeran
Kiritimati
Line Islands
Howland Island
Baker Island
Jarvis Island
Kanton
McKean
Rawaki
Manra
Orona
Malden Island
Starbuck Island
Atafu
Tokelau
Nukunonu
Fakaofo
Penrhyn
Rakahanga
Pukapuka
Nassau
Manihiki
Vostok Island
Caroline Island
Nuku Hiva
Marquesas Islands
Hiva Oa
Swains Island
Samoan Islands
Polynesia
Flint Island
Savai'i
'Upolu
Tutuila
Manu'a Islands
Rose Island
Suwarrow
Îles du Roi Georges
Îles du Désappointement
Îles Palliser
Motu One
Tafahi
Niuatoputapu
Manuae
Huahine
Raiatea
Fakarava
Raroia
Pukapuka
Vava'u Group
Palmerston
Tahiti
Anaa
Tuamotu Islands
Niue
Aitutaki
Society Islands
Mehetia
Tonga
Cook Islands
Atiu
Hervey Islands
Hao
Tongatapu Group
Rarotonga
Mauke
Hereheretue
Mangaia
Maria
Tubuai Islands
Îles du Duc de Gloucester
Groupe Actéon
Rurutu
Rimatara
Tubuai
Mururoa
Raivavae
Îles Gambier
Oeno
Henderson Island
Rapa
Pitcairn Island
Ducie Island
Marotiri

Oceania's extent

TOTAL LAND AREA (includes New Guinea and Pacific Island nations)	8 844 516 sq km / 3 414 868 sq miles
Most northerly point	Eastern Island, North Pacific Ocean
Most southerly point	Macquarie Island, South Pacific Ocean
Most westerly point	Cape Inscription, Australia
Most easterly point	Isla Sala y Gómez, South Pacific Ocean

HERN OCEAN

Banks Peninsula, Canterbury Plains and the **Southern Alps,** South Island, New Zealand.

Oceania

Countries

Stretching across almost the whole width of the Pacific Ocean, Oceania has a great variety of cultures and an enormously diverse range of countries and territories. Australia, by far the largest and most industrialized country in the continent, contrasts with the numerous tiny Pacific island nations which have smaller, and more fragile economies based largely on agriculture, fishing and the exploitation of natural resources.

The division of the Pacific island groups into the main regions of Micronesia, Melanesia and Polynesia – often referred to as the South Sea islands – broadly reflects the ethnological differences across the continent. There is a long history of colonial influence in the region, which still contains dependent territories belonging to Australia, France, New Zealand, the UK and the USA.

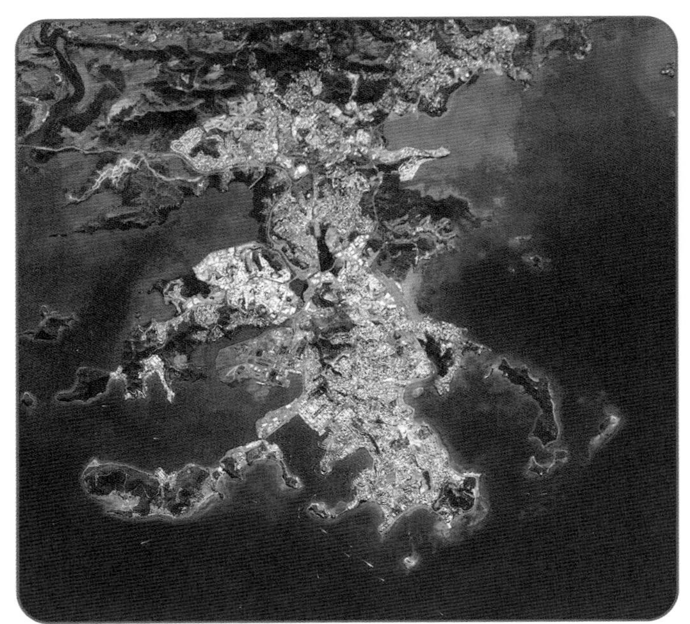

Nouméa, capital of the French dependency of New Caledonia in the southern Pacific Ocean.

ASIA
INDIAN OCEAN
Arafura Sea
Timor Sea
Coral Sea
Tasman Sea
SOUTHERN
PAC
Northern Mariana Islands (U.S.A.)
Pagan
Saipan
Tinian
Rota
Guam (U.S.A.)
Wake Island (U.S.A.)
MARSHALL ISLANDS
Taongi
Enewetak
Bikini
Rongelap
Ratak Chain
Ralik Chain
Wotje
Kwajalein
Ailinglapalap
Delap-Uliga-Djarrit
Majuro
Yap
Gaferut
Pikelot
Hall Islands
Chuuk
Palikir
Pohnpei
Kosrae
Caroline Islands
Mortlock Islands
FEDERATED STATES OF MICRONESIA
Bairiki
Tarawa
Gilbert Islands
Kingsmill Group
Yaren
NAURU
Admiralty Islands
New Ireland
Vanimo
Wewak
Bismarck Sea
Rabaul
New Guinea
Mount Wilhelm 4509
Lae
New Britain
Solomon Sea
Kerema
Balimo
Gulf of Papua
Daru
Torres Strait
Port Moresby
PAPUA NEW GUINEA
Bougainville I.
SOLOMON ISLANDS
Malaita
Honiara
Guadalcanal
Santa Cruz Islands
Nanumea
Niutao
TUVALU
Vaitupu
Nukufetau
Vaiaku
Nukulaelae
Rotuma
Wallis and Futuna Is (France)
VANUATU
Banks Islands
Espiritu Santo
Malakula
Port Vila
Efate
Tanna
New Caledonia (France)
Nouméa
Îles Loyauté
Vanua Levu
FIJI
Viti Levu
Suva
Coral Sea Islands Territory (Australia)
Melville Island
Bathurst Island
Darwin
Gulf of Carpentaria
Cooktown
Cairns
Ashmore and Cartier Islands (Australia)
Wyndham
Normanton
Townsville
Mackay
Cape Lévêque
Halls Creek
NORTHERN TERRITORY
Broome
Cloncurry
Longreach
Rockhampton
QUEENSLAND
Maryborough
Port Hedland
Alice Springs
Charleville
Brisbane
Gold Coast
Barrow Island
North West Cape
Newman
AUSTRALIA
Lake Eyre
Grafton
WESTERN AUSTRALIA
SOUTH AUSTRALIA
Darling
Tamworth
Meekatharra
NEW SOUTH WALES
Broken Hill
Orange
Newcastle
Sydney
Lake Torrens
Port Augusta
Port Pirie
JERVIS BAY TERR.
Canberra
A.C.T.
Geraldton
Kalgoorlie
Great Australian Bight
Adelaide
Murray
Albury
VICTORIA
Geelong
Melbourne
Kangaroo Island
Perth
Fremantle
Esperance
Mount Gambier
Bass Strait
Cape Leeuwin
Albany
Launceston
TASMANIA
Hobart
South East Cape
Norfolk Island (Australia)
Lord Howe Island (Australia)
Kermadec Islands (N.Z.)
North Cape
Whangarei
Auckland
Rotorua
North Island
NEW ZEALAND
Blenheim
Wellington
Greymouth
Christchurch
South Island
Invercargill
Dunedin
Stewart Island
Bounty Islands (N.Z.)
Antipodes Islands (N.Z.)
Auckland Islands (N.Z.)
Campbell Island (N.Z.)
Macquarie Island (Australia)

Facts

- Over 91% of Australia's population live in urban areas
- The Maori name for New Zealand is Aotearoa, meaning 'land of the long white cloud'
- Auckland, New Zealand, has the largest Polynesian population of any city in Oceania
- Over 800 different languages are spoken in Papua New Guinea

Internet Links

UK Foreign and Commonwealth Office	www.fco.gov.uk
CIA World Factbook	www.cia.gov/library/publications/the-world-factbook/index.html
Geoscience Australia	www.ga.gov.au

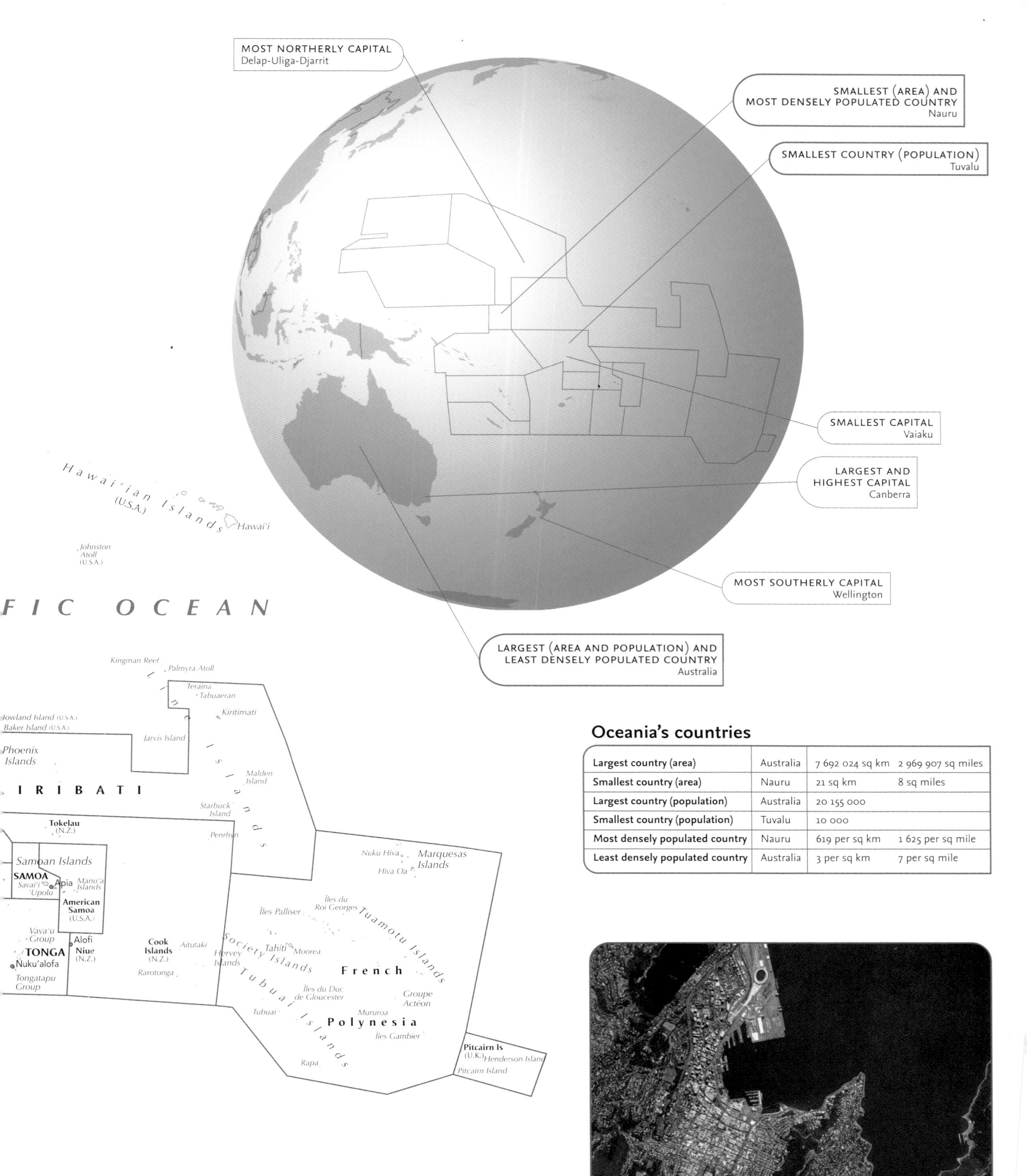
MOST NORTHERLY CAPITAL
Delap-Uliga-Djarrit
SMALLEST (AREA) AND
MOST DENSELY POPULATED COUNTRY
Nauru
SMALLEST COUNTRY (POPULATION)
Tuvalu
SMALLEST CAPITAL
Vaiaku
LARGEST AND
HIGHEST CAPITAL
Canberra
MOST SOUTHERLY CAPITAL
Wellington
LARGEST (AREA AND POPULATION) AND
LEAST DENSELY POPULATED COUNTRY
Australia
Hawai'ian Islands
(U.S.A.)
Hawai'i
Johnston Atoll (U.S.A.)
FIC OCEAN
Kingman Reef
Palmyra Atoll
Teraina
Tabuaeran
Kiritimati
Line Islands
Jarvis Island
Malden Island
Starbuck Island
Penrhyn
Baker Island (U.S.A.)
Phoenix Islands
IRIBATI
Tokelau (N.Z.)
Samoan Islands
SAMOA
Savai'i
'Upolu
Apia
Manu'a Islands
American Samoa (U.S.A.)
Vava'u Group
TONGA
Nuku'alofa
Tongatapu Group
Alofi
Niue (N.Z.)
Cook Islands (N.Z.)
Aitutaki
Rarotonga
Hervey Islands
Nuku Hiva
Hiva Oa
Marquesas Islands
Îles du Roi Georges
Îles Palliser
Tuamotu Islands
Tahiti
Moorea
Society Islands
French Polynesia
Tubuai Islands
Îles du Duc de Gloucester
Groupe Actéon
Tubuai
Mururoa
Îles Gambier
Rapa
Pitcairn Is (U.K.)
Henderson Island
Pitcairn Island

Oceania's countries

Largest country (area)	Australia	7 692 024 sq km	2 969 907 sq miles
Smallest country (area)	Nauru	21 sq km	8 sq miles
Largest country (population)	Australia	20 155 000	
Smallest country (population)	Tuvalu	10 000	
Most densely populated country	Nauru	619 per sq km	1 625 per sq mile
Least densely populated country	Australia	3 per sq km	7 per sq mile

Wellington, capital of New Zealand.

Oceania's capitals

Largest capital (population)	Canberra, Australia	381 000	
Smallest capital (population)	Vaiaku, Tuvalu	516	
Most northerly capital	Delap-Uliga-Djarrit, Marshall Islands	7° 7'N	
Most southerly capital	Wellington, New Zealand	41° 18'S	
Highest capital	Canberra, Australia	581 metres	1 906 feet

Wellington, capital of New Zealand.

O C E A N

↑ 79
Celebes Sea
Borneo
Tanjungselor
Tanjungredeb
Sambaliung
Sangkulirang
Equator
Samarinda
Balikpapan
Selat Makassar (Macassar Strait)
Semenanjung Minahasa
Manado
Tolitoli
Gorontalo
Moutong
Kepulauan Togian
Teluk Tomini
Laut Maluku (Molucca Sea)
Tobelo
Morotai
Ternate
Halmahera
Labuha
Bacan
Obi
Maluku (Moluccas)
Waigeo
Selat Dampier
Sorong
Kwoka 3000
Jazirah Doberai
Manokwari
Biak
Numfoor
Yapen
Teluk Cenderawasih
Misoöl
Salawati
Teminabuan
Palu
Poso
Luwuk
Celebes (Sulawesi)
Kolonedale
Banggai
Taliabu
Mangole
Kepulauan Banggai
Kepulauan Sula
Mamuju
Wotu
Malili
Palopo
Makale
Majene
Kotabaru
Anabanua
Parepare
Teluk Bone
Watampone
Sinjai
Baubau
Kendari
Wowoni
Kolaka
Raha
Buton
Manui
Buru
Ambon
Seram
3019
Wahai
Laut Seram (Ceram Sea)
Fakfak
Semenanjung Bomberai
Kaimana
Teluk Arguni
Adi
Laut
Makassar (Ujung Pandang)
Bontosunggu
Bulukumba
Benteng
Salayar
Kepulauan Tukangbesi
Laut Banda (Banda Sea)
Kepulauan Banda
Kepulauan Watubela
Kepulauan Kai
Tual
Kai Besar
Kai Kecil
Dobo
Benjina
Wokam
Kepulauan Aru
Kobroör
Trangan
INDONESIA
Kepulauan Kangean
Kepulauan Bonerate
Laut Flores (Flores Sea)
Kepulauan Alor
Kalabahi
Wetar
Kepulauan Barat Daya
Pulau Romang
Damar
Babar
Yamdena
Larat
Kepulauan Tanimbar
Selaru
Kepulauan Leti
Kepulauan Tengah
Bali
Lombok
Raba
Ruteng
Flores
Ende
Larantuka
Dompu
Mataram
Denpasar
Sumbawa
Selat Sumba
Waikabubak
Waingapu
Sumba
Laut Sawu (Savu Sea)
EAST TIMOR
DILI
Fobo
2960
Tatamailau
Timor
Kefamenanu
Kupang
Rote
Pegunungan Van Rees
Pegunungan Maoke
Tanjung d'Urville
Sarmi
Nabire
Tembagapura
Puncak Jaya 5030
Puncak Trikora 4730
Puncak Mandala 4700
Amamapare
Tanjung Deyong
Pulau Dolok
Tanjung Vals
Merauke
Jayapura
Vanimo
New Guinea
Wewak
Sepik
Central Range
Mt Wilhelm 4509
Mount Hagen
Goroka
Mendi
Lake Murray
Fly
Balimo
Kikori
Morehead
Daru
Gulf of Papua
Torres Strait
Kerema
Bereina
PORT MORESBY
Mount Victoria 4073
Kokoda
Owen Stanley Range
Kwikila
Abau
Wuvulu Island
Hermit Islands
Admiralty Islands
Manus Island
St Matthias Group
Mussau Island
New Hanover
Rambutyo Island
Bismarck Archipelago
Bismarck Sea
Schouten Islands
Manam Island
Karkar Island
Madang
Long Island
Umboi
Witu Islands
PAPUA
NEW GUINEA
New Britain
Kimbe
Lae
New Ireland
Namatanai
Rabaul
Tabar Islands
Lihir Group
Tanga Islands
Feni Islands
Lyra Reef
Sohano
Bougainville Island
Treasury Islands
Solomon
Morobe
Lusancay Islands and Reefs
Trobriand Islands
Goodenough Island
Fergusson I.
Woodlark Island
D'Entrecasteaux Islands
Normanby Island
Louisiade Archipelago
Conflict Group
Tagula Island
Rossel Island
Arafura Sea
Timor Sea
Ashmore and Cartier Islands (Australia)
INDIAN OCEAN
Prince of Wales Island
Cape York
Cape Wessel
Wessel Islands
Melville Island
Cobourg Peninsula
Croker Island
Goulburn Islands
Van Diemen Gulf
Bathurst Island
Darwin
Beagle Gulf
Rum Jungle
Adelaide River
Jabiru
Pine Creek
Arnhem Land
Cape Arnhem
Alyangula
Groote Eylandt
Gulf of Carpentaria
Albatross Bay
Weipa
Cape York Peninsula
Cape Grenville
Princess Charlotte Bay
Coen
Cape Melville
Osprey Reef
Cape Flattery
Cooktown
Laura
Mossman
Cairns
Mount Bartle Frere 1612
Innisfail
Tully
Mitchell
Gilbert
Great Barrier Reef
Great Dividing Range
Cape Londonderry
Joseph Bonaparte Gulf
Bonaparte Archipelago
Daly
Mataranka
Larrimah
Sir Edward Pellew Group
Mornington Island
Wellesley Islands
Borroloola
Normanton
Wyndham
Kununurra
Timber Creek
Victoria River Downs
Daly Waters
Lake Argyle
Drysdale
Kimberley Plateau
Mount Ord 936
Collier Bay
King Sound
King Leopold Ra.
Cape Lévêque
Derby
Halls Creek
Lajamanu
Lake Woods
Barkly Tableland
NORTHERN TERRITORY
Broome
Liveringa
Fitzroy Crossing
Roebuck Bay
Tanami Desert
Tennant Creek
Camooweal
Kajabbi
Forsayth
Gregory Range
Townsville
Ayr
Bowen
Whitsunday Group
Charters Towers
Richmond
Mackay
Sarina
1277
Swain Reefs
Capricorn Channel
Coral Sea Islands Territory (Australia)
Mount Isa
Cloncurry
Selwyn Range
Winton
Dajarra
Boulia
Georgina
QUEENSLAND
Longreach
Barcaldine
Emerald
Clermont
Rockhampton
Yeppoon
Curtis I.
Gladstone
Eighty Mile Beach
Port Hedland
Shay Gap (abandoned)
Great Sandy Desert
Lake White
Lake Wills
Barrow Creek
Yuendumu
Mount Liebig 1524
Mount Zeil 1531
Alice Springs
Macdonnell Ranges
Lake Mackay
Lake Macdonald
Barrow Island
Karratha
Roebourne
Marble Bar
Nullagine
Oakover
Chichester Range
Pannawonica
Onslow
Exmouth Gulf
North West Cape
Hamersley Range
Paraburdoo
Mount Meharry 1250
Newman
Ashburton
Coral Bay
Tropic of Capricorn
WESTERN AUSTRALIA
Lake Disappointment
Gibson Desert
Lake Neale
Lake Amadeus
Lake Hopkins
Uluru (Ayers Rock) 867
Erldunda
AUSTRALIA
Simpson Desert
Bilpa Morea Claypan
Birdsville
Diamantina
Yaraka
Windorah
Blackall
Buckland Tableland
Moura
Biloela
Monto
Sandy Cape
Bundaberg
Fraser I.
Maryborough
Gympie
Tewantin
Nambour
Caboolture
Brisbane
Beenleigh
Gold Coast
Byron Bay
Ballina
Lake Yamma Yamma
Grey Range
Quilpie
Charleville
Mitchell
Roma
Kingaroy
Darling Downs
Toowoomba
Warwick
Casino
St George
Cunnamulla
Dirranbandi
Goondiwindi
Mungindi
Moree
Minilya
Lake Macleod
Mount Augustus 1106
Robinson Range
Warburton
Musgrave Ranges
Mount Woodroffe 1440
Everard Range
Lake Carnegie
Great Victoria Desert
Lake Wells
Oodnadatta
Sturt Stony Desert
Cooper Creek
Strzelecki Desert
Hungerford
Tibooburra
Lake Eyre (North)
Lake Blanche
Bourke
Brewarrina
Barwon
Narrabri
Inverell
Glen Innes
Grafton
Armidale
Coffs Harbour
Macksville
Port Macquarie
Shark Bay
Denham
Dirk Hartog Island
Meekatharra
Murchison
Wiluna
SOUTH AUSTRALIA
Coober Pedy
Lake Maurice
Maralinga
Lake Torrens
Woomera
Flinders Ranges
Lake Frome
Broken Hill
Wilcannia
NEW SOUTH WALES
Cobar
Warren
Muswellbrook
Taree
Kalbarri
Houtman Abrolhos
Geraldton
Dongara
Northampton
Mullewa
Mount Magnet
Laverton
Lake Carey
Leonora
Lake Barlee
Menzies
Lake Ballard
Lake Moore
Nullarbor Plain
Eucla
Fowlers Bay
Ceduna
Penong
Lake Gairdner
Island Lagoon
Lake Mactarlane
Lake Menindee
Ivanhoe
Darling
Lachlan
Parkes
Dubbo
Orange
Lithgow
Forbes
Newcastle
Sydney
Wollongong
Kalgoorlie
Coolgardie
Kambalda
Lake Cowan
Mundrabilla
Bonnie Rock
Southern Cross
Merredin
Norseman
Balladonia
Great Australian Bight
Streaky Bay
Anxious Bay
Eyre Peninsula
Whyalla
Port Augusta
Port Pirie
Jamestown
Burra
Kyancutta
Lake Victoria
Mildura
Garnpung Lake
Griffith
Hay
Wagga Wagga
Tumut
Yass
Goulburn
CANBERRA
A.C.T.
JERVIS BAY TERR.
Narooma
Yanchep
Perth
Fremantle
Rockingham
Mandurah
Darling Range
York
Hyden
Esperance
Katanning
Bunbury
Geographe Bay
Busselton
Margaret River
Cape Leeuwin
Point D'Entrecasteaux
Denmark
Albany
Hood Point
Archipelago of the Recherche
Spencer Gulf
Yorke Pen.
Port Lincoln
Investigator Strait
Adelaide
Murray Bridge
Kangaroo Island
Lake Tyrrell
Nhill
Swan Hill
Murray
Horsham
Shepparton
Bendigo
Wangaratta
Albury
Mount Kosciuszko 2229
Bega
Eden
Cape Howe
Mount William 1167
Ballarat
VICTORIA
Melbourne
Geelong
Moe
Sale
Bairnsdale
Cape Jaffa
Mount Gambier
Discovery Bay
Portland
Warrnambool
Cape Otway
Bass Strait
Wilson's Promontory
Furneaux Group
Flinders Island
King Island
Currie
Hunter Islands
Eddystone Point
Burnie
Devonport
Launceston
Mount Ossa 1617
Great Lake
Queenstown
TASMANIA
Lake Gordon
Hobart
Port Arthur
South East Cape
Tas
110°E
120°
130°
140°
150°
10°
20°
30°
40°S
Lambert Azimuthal Equal Area Projection

1:20 000 000 — 0, 200, 400, 600 miles; 0, 200, 400, 600, 800, 1000 km

NAURU
YAREN
Nauru
Banaba (Ocean Island)
Aranuka
Nonouti
Beru
Nikunau
Tabiteuea
Onotoa
Kingsmill Group
Tamana
Arorae
K I R I B A T I
Howland Island (U.S.A.)
Baker Island (U.S.A.)
Phoenix Islands
Kanton
McKean
Rawaki
Nikumaroro
Orona
Manra
Takuu Islands
Nukumanu Islands
Ontong Java Atoll
Roncador Reef
Choiseul
SOLOMON ISLANDS
Santa Isabel
Buala
Malu'u
Stewart Islands
Malaita
Florida Islands
Maramasike
Ulawa Island
HONIARA
Auvavu
Guadalcanal
Kirakira
Santa Ana
San Cristobal (Makira)
Rennell
New Georgia
New Georgia Islands
Duff Islands
Nupani
Swallow Islands
Ndeni
Santa Cruz Islands (Solomon Islands)
Utupua
Vanikoro Islands
Mitre Island
Cherry Island
Tikopia
Indispensable Reefs
Torres Islands
Uréparapara
Banks Islands
Vanua Lava
Santa María Island
Espíritu Santo
Mount Tabwémasana 1879
Aoba
Maéwo
Pentecost Island
VANUATU
Norsup
Ambrym
Malakula
Epi
Émae
Shepherd Islands
PORT VILA
Éfaté
Récifs d'Entrecasteaux
Îles Chesterfield (France)
Grand Passage
Îles Belep
Grand Récif de Cook
Récif des Français
Erromango
Tanna 361
Futuna
Anatom (Aneityum)
Nouvelle Calédonie
Ouvéa
Îles Loyauté (France)
Koumac
Lifou
Maré
Tadin
New Caledonia (France)
Bourail
Yaté
NOUMÉA
Île des Pins
Grand Récif du Sud
Hunter Island 100
Ceva-i-Ra (Conway Reef)
Nanumea
Nanumanga
Niutao
Nui
Vaitupu
Nukufetau
TUVALU
Funafuti
VAIAKU
Nukulaelae
Niulakita
Tokelau (New Zealand)
Atafu
Nukunonu
Fakaofo
Swains Island
Pukapuka (Danger Islands)
Nassau
Rotuma (Fiji)
Wallis and Futuna Islands (France)
Îles Wallis
MATĀ'UTU
SAMOA
Îles de Hoorn
Savai'i
'Upolu
APIA
Manu'a Islands
American Samoa (U.S.A.)
Tutuila
FAGATOGO
Rose Island
Suwarrow
Niuafo'ou 210
Tafahi
Niuatoputapu
Yasawa Group
Great Sea Reef
Vanua Levu
Bligh Water
Labasa
Tomanivi
Mt. Victoria
Lautoka
Koro
Taveuni
Northern Lau Group
Viti Levu
Koro Sea
SUVA
Gau
FIJI
Kadavu Passage
Kadavu
Moala
Matuku
Lakeba
Kabara
Southern Lau Group
Vava'u Group
Vatoa
Tofua 500
Ha'apai Group
Doi
Ono-i-Lau
TONGA
NUKU'ALOFA
Tongatapu Group
Ata
ALOFI
Niue (New Zealand)
Cook Islands (New Zealand)
Palmerston
Minerva Reefs
Tropic of Capricorn
P A C I F I C   O C E A N
Norfolk Island (Australia)
KINGSTON
Lord Howe Island (Australia)
Raoul Island
Kermadec Islands (New Zealand)
Macauley Island
Curtis Island
Havre Rock
L'Espérance Rock
Three Kings Islands
North Cape
Cape Maria van Diemen
Awanui
Whangarei
North Island
Great Barrier Island
Takapuna
Auckland
Manukau
NEW ZEALAND
Hamilton
Tauranga
East Cape
Tokoroa
Whakatane
Taupo
Gisborne
New Plymouth
Mount Taranaki (Mount Egmont)
Mount Ruapehu
Wairoa
Mahia Peninsula
Hawera
Wanganui
Napier
Hastings
Cape Farewell
Palmerston North
Tasman Bay
Nelson
Picton
Levin
Masterton
Lower Hutt
Blenheim
WELLINGTON
Cook Strait
Westport
South Island
Greymouth
Hokitika
Aoraki (Mount Cook)
Southern Alps
Christchurch
Mount Aspiring 3030
Ashburton
Banks Peninsula
Timaru
Mount Christina 2502
Queenstown
Oamaru
Cape Providence
Gore
Dunedin
Invercargill
Foveaux Strait
Stewart Island
South West Cape
Snares Islands
Chatham Islands (New Zealand)
Chatham Island
Waitangi
Pitt Island
Bounty Islands (New Zealand)
Antipodes Islands (New Zealand)
Auckland Islands (New Zealand)
Tasman Sea
Coral Sea

Oceania

Australia, New Zealand and Southwest Pacific

INDONESIA
Java (Jawa)
Bali
Lombok
Sumbawa
Flores
Sumba
Timor
EAST TIMOR
DILI
Kupang
Laut Bali (Bali Sea)
Laut Flores (Flores Sea)
Laut Sawu (Savu Sea)
Kepulauan Alor
Kepulauan Tanimbar
Kepulauan Aru
Kepulauan Barat Daya
Wetar
Yamdena
Rote
Savu
Arafura Sea
Timor Sea
INDIAN OCEAN
Ashmore and Cartier Islands (Australia)
Hibernia Reef
Ashmore Reef
Cartier Island
Browse Island
Scott Reef
Seringapatam Reef
Sandy Island
Rowley Shoals
Mermaid Reef
Clerke Reef
Imperieuse Reef
Melville Island
Bathurst Island
Cobourg Peninsula
Croker Island
Darwin
Palmerston
Van Diemen Gulf
Arnhem Land
Kakadu National Park
Nitmiluk National Park
Katherine
Joseph Bonaparte Gulf
Cape Londonderry
Bonaparte Archipelago
Buccaneer Archipelago
Kimberley Plateau
Drysdale River National Park
King Leopold Ranges
King Leopold Range National Park
Purnululu National Park
Gregory National Park
Keep River National Park
Wyndham
Kununurra
Derby
Broome
Fitzroy Crossing
Halls Creek
DAMPIER LAND
King Sound
Roebuck Bay
Eighty Mile Beach
Port Hedland
Karratha
Roebourne
Dampier Archipelago
Barrow Island
Montebello Islands
North West Cape
Exmouth
Hamersley Range
Chichester Range
Millstream-Chichester National Park
Rudall River National Park
Great Sandy Desert
Tanami Desert
NORTHERN TERRITORY
Barkly Tableland
Tennant Creek
Daly Waters
Moray Range
Gregory Range
Paterson Range
Throssel Range
Edgar Ranges
St George Range
South Esk Tableland
Stansmore Range
Lewis Range
Lake Mackay
Lake Gregory
AUSTRALIA
↑ 81
↑ 136

Lambert Azimuthal Equal Area Projection

1:8 000 000

0 100 200 300 miles
0 100 200 300 400 500 km

WESTERN AUSTRALIA
SOUTH AUSTRALIA
Great Victoria Desert
Gibson Desert
Simpson Desert
Little Sandy Desert
Nullarbor Plain
Great Australian Bight
Macdonnell Ranges
Musgrave Ranges
Darling Range
Eyre Peninsula
Gawler Ranges
Lake Gairdner
Spencer Gulf
Kangaroo Island
Perth
Fremantle
Kalgoorlie
Esperance
Albany
Geraldton
Carnarvon
Alice Springs
Port Lincoln
Shark Bay
Houtman Abrolhos
Geelvink Channel
Archipelago of the Recherche
Tropic of Capricorn
Nullarbor National Park
Woomera Prohibited Area
Uluru (Ayers Rock)
↑ 137

PAPUA NEW GUINEA
Coral Sea
Coral Sea Islands Territory
(Australia)
Great Barrier Reef
Gulf of Carpentaria
Arafura Sea
Cape York Peninsula
Arnhem Land
QUEENSLAND
NORTHERN TERRITORY
Great Dividing Range
Barkly Tableland
Gregory Range
Simpson Desert
Tropic of Capricorn
↑ 132
← 134

Lambert Azimuthal Equal Area Projection

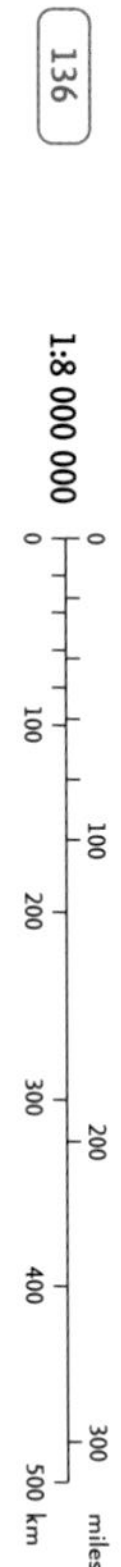
1:8 000 000
0 100 200 300 miles
0 100 200 300 400 500 km

AUSTRALIA
SOUTH AUSTRALIA
NEW SOUTH WALES
VICTORIA
TASMANIA
AUSTRALIAN CAPITAL TERRITORY
JERVIS BAY TERRITORY
Tasman Sea
Bass Strait
Brisbane
Sydney
CANBERRA
Melbourne
Adelaide
Hobart
Newcastle
Wollongong
Geelong
Launceston
Gold Coast
Lake Eyre (North)
Lake Eyre (South)
Lake Torrens
Lake Gairdner
Spencer Gulf
Gulf St Vincent
Kangaroo Island
Eyre Peninsula
Flinders Ranges
Simpson Desert Regional Reserve
Sturt Stony Desert
Strzelecki Desert
Darling Downs
Grey Range
Great Dividing Range
Gippsland
Riverina
Flinders Island
King Island
Wilson's Promontory
Broken Hill
Bendigo
Ballarat
Mildura
Wagga Wagga
Dubbo
Toowoomba
Port Augusta
↓ 135

QUEENSLAND
AUSTRALIA
NEW SOUTH WALES
VICTORIA
AUSTRALIAN CAPITAL TERRITORY
JERVIS BAY TERRITORY
Tasman Sea
Bass Strait
Great Dividing Range
Darling Downs
Liverpool Plains
Riverina
Gippsland
New England Range
Liverpool Range
Nandewar Range
Moonbi Range
Snowy Mts.
Barry Mountains
Brisbane
Gold Coast
Toowoomba
Ipswich
Moreton Island
North Stradbroke Island
Cape Byron
Coffs Harbour
Port Macquarie
Newcastle
Sydney
Parramatta
Penrith
Wollongong
CANBERRA
Melbourne
Geelong
Bendigo
Ballarat
Albury
Wodonga
Wagga Wagga
Dubbo
Tamworth
Orange
Bathurst
Goulburn
Armidale
Moree
Bourke
Broken Bay
Port Jackson
Botany Bay
Port Stephens
Jervis Bay
Port Phillip Bay
Western Port
Wilson's Promontory
Cape Otway
Cape Howe
Gabo Island
Mallacoota Inlet
Lake Eildon
Lake Hume
Hume Reservoir
Lake Burrendong
Lake Eucumbene
Mount Kosciuszko 2228
Royal National Park
Kosciuszko Nat. Park
Murray
Murrumbidgee
Lachlan
Darling
Macquarie
Barwon
Condamine
Balonne
Warrego
144°
146°
148°
150°
152°
154°
28°
30°
32°
34°
36°
38°
A
B
C
D
E
F
G
1
2
3
4
5
6
7
↑ 136
↑ 137
Lambert Azimuthal Equal Area Projection
1:5 000 000
0 50 100 150 miles
0 50 100 150 km

Oceania
Southeast Australia

Tasman Sea
NEW ZEALAND
North Island
South Island
PACIFIC OCEAN
Three Kings Islands
Cape Maria van Diemen
North Cape
Te Paki
Ninety Mile Beach
Cape Karikari
Doubtless Bay
Ahipara Bay
Tauroa Point
Kaitaia
Kerikeri
Bay of Islands
Cape Brett
Russell
Broadwood
Poor Knights Islands
Kawakawa
Whangarei
Donnellys Crossing
Dargaville
Bream Bay
Mokohinau Islands
Little Barrier
Port Fitzroy
Great Barrier Island
Leigh
North Head
Kaipara Harbour
Kawau Island
Colville Channel
Hauraki Gulf
Mercury Islands
East Coast Bays
Takapuna
Waiheke Island
Colville
Auckland
Manukau
Whitianga
Coromandel Peninsula
The Aldermen Islands
Manukau Harbour
Papakura
Pukekohe
Waiuku
Thames
Whangamata
Port Waikato
Mayor Island
Huntly
Matakana Island
Whakaari
Motiti Island
Cape Runaway
Hamilton
Tauranga
Bay of Plenty
Hicks Bay
Te Araroa
East Cape
Kawhia Harbour
Te Awamutu
Cambridge
Otorohanga
Whakatane
Rotorua
Te Kuiti
Tokoroa
Mount Tarawera
Opotiki
Ruatoria
Raukumara Range
Hikurangi
Tokomaru Bay
Mangakino
Urewera National Park
Awakino
Mokau
Tolaga Bay
North Taranaki Bight
Taupo
Lake Taupo
Huiarau Range
New Plymouth
Mount Taranaki (Mount Egmont)
Tongariro National Park
Gisborne
Poverty Bay
Cape Egmont
Whanganui National Park
Egmont National Park
Kaimanawa Mountains
Opunake
Wairoa
Table Cape
Mahia Peninsula
Hawera
Hawke Bay
South Taranaki Bight
Patea
Bay View
Napier
Hastings
Wanganui
Cape Kidnappers
Havelock North
Waimarama
Marton
Feilding
Ruahine Range
Waipukurau
Cape Farewell
Farewell Spit
Collingwood
Golden Bay
Kahurangi Point
Cape Stephens
Cook Strait
Abel Tasman National Park
D'Urville Island
Palmerston North
Dannevirke
Porangahau
Cape Turnagain
Levin
Kapiti Island
Otaki
Tasman Mountains
Tasman Bay
Paraparaumu
Karamea
Karamea Bight
Kahurangi National Park
Riwaka
Motueka
Richmond
Nelson
Havelock
Picton
Porirua
Upper Hutt
Lower Hutt
Masterton
Castlepoint
Seddonville
Wakefield
WELLINGTON
Tararua Range
Martinborough
Featherston
Palliser Bay
Mount Ross
Cape Palliser
Waimangaroa
Westport
Owen River
Hope Saddle
Blenheim
Seddon
Cape Campbell
Charleston
Paparoa National Park
Reefton
Inland Kaikoura Range
Tapuaenuku
Clarence
Greymouth
Ahaura
Springs Junction
Nelson Lakes Nat. Park
Lewis Pass
Manakau
Kaikoura
Hokitika
Lake Brunner
Rotomanu
Hope
Lake Sumner
Oaro
Ross
Otira
Arthur's Pass National Park
Culverden
Parnassus
Cheviot
Abut Head
Harihari
Waikari
Southern Alps
Franz Josef Glacier
Westland National Park
Fox Glacier
Mount Arrowsmith
Waipara
Pegasus Bay
Oxford
Aoraki (Mount Cook)
Lake Paringa
Sheffield
Rangiora
Kaiapoi
Christchurch
Sumner
Canterbury Plains
Aoraki/Mount Cook National Park
Aylesbury
Te Pirita
Tai Tapu
Banks Peninsula
Akaroa
Jackson Head
Cascade Point
Mayfield
Ashburton
Lake Ellesmere
Lake Tekapo
Mount Aspiring National Park
Awarua Point
Burkes Pass
Fairlie
Geraldine
Longbeach
Canterbury Bight
Pleasant Point
Temuka
Timaru
Pareora
Milford Sound
Mount Aspiring
Lake Hawea
Wanaka
Lake Wanaka
Otematata
George Sound
Kurow
Studholme Junction
Waimate
Richardson Mts
Dunstan Mts
Hawkdun Range
Duntroon
Fiordland
Secretary Island
Doubtful Sound
Lake Te Anau
Lake Wakatipu
Queenstown
Ranfurly
Oamaru
Pukeuri Junction
Cape Wanbrow
National
Te Anau
Alexandra
Breaksea Sound
Lake Manapouri
Resolution Island
Park
Eyre Mountains
Hyde
Moeraki Point
Shag Point
Palmerston
Waikouaiti
Middlemarch
Lammerlaw Range
Roxburgh
Mossburn
Lumsden
Warrington
Port Chalmers
Otago Peninsula
Dunedin
Caroline Peak
Ohai
Mosgiel
Cape Providence
Puysegur Point
Winton
Gore
Mandeville
Waipahi
Waiwera South
Henley
Milton
Te Waewae Bay
Orepuki
Edendale
Mataura
Balclutha
Riverton
Invercargill
Mount Pye
Kaitangata
Nugget Point
Solander Island
Foveaux Strait
Bluff
Fortrose
Long Point
Chaslands Mistake
Codfish Island
Mason Bay
Ruapuke Island
Stewart Island
Halfmoon Bay
Titi Islands (Muttonbird Islands)
Shelter Point
South West Cape
North Trap
166°E
168°
170°
172°
174°
176°
178°
180°
34°
36°
38°
40°
42°
44°
46°S

Conic Equidistant Projection

1:5 250 000

0 50 100 150 miles

0 50 100 150 200 250 km

Oceania

New Zealand

North America
UNESCO World Heritage Sites

The New World has relatively few sites compared to Europe or Asia. However the sites represent significant stages in Earth's formation and human history. Ancient geological processes are preserved in Gros Morne National Park in Canada, early civilizations are represented in Central America and evidence of the slave trade and plantations is found in the islands of the Caribbean.

● Cultural site ● Natural site ● Mixed site

Belize
1. Belize Barrier Reef Reserve System

Bermuda
2. Historic Town of St George and Related Fortifications (UK)

Canada
3. Canadian Rocky Mountain Parks
4. Dinosaur Provincial Park
5. Gros Morne National Park
6. Head-Smashed-In Buffalo Jump
7. Historic District of Old Québec
8. Joggins Fossil Cliffs
9. Kluane/Wrangell-St Elias/Glacier Bay/Tatshenshini-Alsek
10. L'Anse aux Meadows National Historic Site
11. Miguasha National Park
12. Nahanni National Park
13. Old Town Lunenburg
14. Rideau Canal
15. SG̲ang Gwaay
16. Waterton Glacier International Peace Park
17. Wood Buffalo National Park

Costa Rica
18. Area de Conservación Guanacaste
19. Cocos Island National Park
20. Talamanca Range-La Amistad Reserves/La Amistad National Park

Cuba
21. Alejandro de Humboldt National Park
22. Archaeological Landscape of the First Coffee Plantations in the South-East of Cuba
23. Desembarco del Granma National Park
24. Historic Centre of Camagüey
25. Old Havana and its Fortifications
26. San Pedro de la Roca Castle, Santiago de Cuba
27. Trinidad and the Valley de los Ingenios
28. Urban Historic Centre of Cienfuegos
29. Viñales Valley

Dominica
30. Morne Trois Pitons National Park

Dominican Republic
31. Colonial City of Santo Domingo

El Salvador
32. Joya de Cerén Archaeological Site

Greenland
33. Ilulissat Icefjord (Denmark)

Guatemala
34. Antigua Guatemala
35. Archaeological Park and Ruins of Quirigua
36. Tikal National Park

Honduras
37. Maya Site of Copán
38. Río Plátano Biosphere Reserve

Haiti
39. National History Park – Citadel, Sans Souci, Ramiers

Mexico
40. Agave Landscape and Ancient Industrial Facilities of Tequila
41. Ancient Maya City of Calakmul, Campeche
42. Archaeological Monuments Zone of Xochicalco
43. Archeological Zone of Paquimé, Casas Grandes
44. Central University City Campus of the Universidad Nacional Autónoma de México (UNAM)
45. Earliest 16th-Century Monasteries on the Slopes of Popocatepetl
46. El Tajin, Pre-Hispanic City
47. Franciscan Missions in the Sierra Gorda of Querétaro
48. Historic Centre of Mexico City and Xochimilco
49. Historic Centre of Morelia
50. Historic Centre of Oaxaca and Archaeological Site of Monte Albán
51. Historic Centre of Puebla
52. Historic Centre of Zacatecas
53. Historic Fortified Town of Campeche
54. Historic Monuments Zone of Querétaro
55. Historic Monuments Zone of Tlacotalpan
56. Historic Town of Guanajuato and Adjacent Mines
57. Hospicio Cabañas, Guadalajara
58. Islands and Protected Areas of the Gulf of California
59. Luis Barragán House and Studio
60. Monarch Butterfly Biosphere Reserve
61. Pre-Hispanic City and National Park of Palenque
62. Pre-Hispanic City of Chichen-Itza
63. Pre-Hispanic City of Teotihuacan
64. Pre-Hispanic Town of Uxmal
65. Protective town of San Miguel and the Sanctuary of Jesús Nazareno de Atotonilco
66. Rock Paintings of the Sierra de San Francisco
67. Sian Ka'an
68. Whale Sanctuary of El Vizcaino

Nicaragua
69. Ruins of León Viejo

Panama
70. Archaeological Site of Panamá Viejo and Historic District of Panamá
71. Coiba National Park and its Special Zone of Marine Protection
72. Darien National Park
73. Fortifications on the Caribbean Side of Panama: Portobelo-San Lorenzo
20. Talamanca Range-La Amistad Reserves/La Amistad National Park

Saint Kitts and Nevis
74. Brimstone Hill Fortress National Park

Saint Lucia
75. Pitons Management Area

United States of America
76. Cahokia Mounds State Historic Site
77. Carlsbad Caverns National Park
78. Chaco Culture
79. Everglades National Park
80. Grand Canyon National Park
81. Great Smoky Mountains National Park
82. Hawaii Volcanoes National Park
83. Independence Hall
84. La Fortaleza and San Juan National Historic Site in Puerto Rico
9. Kluane/Wrangell-St Elias/Glacier Bay/Tatshenshini-Alsek
85. Mammoth Cave National Park
86. Mesa Verde National Park
87. Monticello and the University of Virginia in Charlottesville
88. Olympic National Park
89. Pueblo de Taos
90. Redwood National Park
91. Statue of Liberty
16. Waterton Glacier International Peace Park
92. Yellowstone National Park
93. Yosemite National Park

Greenland
(Denmark)
U.S.A.
CANADA
ATLANTIC
OCEAN
UNITED STATES
OF AMERICA
Hawaii
(U.S.A.)
Bermuda
(U.K.)
THE BAHAMAS
Gulf
of Mexico
DOMINICAN
REP.
CUBA
HAITI
Puerto
Rico
(U.S.A.)
ANTIGUA & BARBUDA
ST KITTS & NEVIS
DOMINICA
ST LUCIA
BARBADOS
ST VINCENT &
THE GRENADINES
GRENADA
TRINIDAD
& TOBAGO
JAMAICA
Caribbean Sea
PACIFIC
OCEAN
MEXICO
BELIZE
HONDURAS
GUATEMALA
EL SALVADOR
NICARAGUA
COSTA
RICA
PANAMA
SOUTH
AMERICA
Isla de Coco
(Costa Rica)

North America

Landscapes

North America, the world's third largest continent, supports a wide range of landscapes from the Arctic north to sub-tropical Central America. The main physiographic regions of the continent are the mountains of the west coast, stretching from Alaska in the north to Mexico and Central America in the south; the vast, relatively flat Canadian Shield; the Great Plains which make up the majority of the interior; the Appalachian Mountains in the east; and the Atlantic coastal plain.

These regions contain some significant physical features, including the Rocky Mountains, the Great Lakes – three of which are amongst the five largest lakes in the world – and the Mississippi-Missouri river system which is the world's fourth longest river. The Caribbean Sea contains a complex pattern of islands, many volcanic in origin, and the continent is joined to South America by the narrow Isthmus of Panama.

Internet Links

NASA Visible Earth	visibleearth.nasa.gov
U.S. Geological Survey	www.usgs.gov
Natural Resources Canada	www.nrcan-rncan.gc.ca
SPOT Image satellite imagery	www.spotimage.fr

Chukchi Sea
Bering Strait
Seward Peninsula
Brooks
Norton Sound
Yukon
Pribilof Islands
Nunivak Island
Andreanof Islands
Aleutian Islands
Fox Islands
Unalaska Island
Unimak Island
Bristol Bay
Iliamna Lake
Alaska Range
6194
Mount McKinley
Aleutian Range
Alaska Peninsula
Kodiak Island
Gulf of Alaska
Mount Logan
Alexander Archipelago
Dixon Entrance
Queen Charlotte Islands

MOST NORTHERLY POINT
Kaffeklubben Ø

MOST EASTERLY POINT
Nordøstrundingen

HIGHEST MOUNTAIN
Mt McKinley

LARGEST ISLAND
Greenland

MOST WESTERLY POINT
Attu Island

LARGEST LAKE
Lake Superior

PACIFIC
OCEAN

LOWEST POINT
Death Valley

LONGEST RIVER AND
LARGEST DRAINAGE BASIN
Mississippi-Missouri

Cape Blanco

MOST SOUTHERLY POINT
Punta Mariato

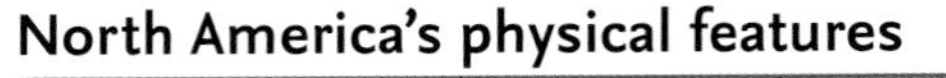

North America's physical features

Highest mountain	Mt McKinley, USA	6 194 metres	20 321 feet
Longest river	Mississippi-Missouri, USA	5 969 km	3 709 miles
Largest lake	Lake Superior, Canada/USA	82 100 sq km	31 699 sq miles
Largest island	Greenland	2 175 600 sq km	839 999 sq miles
Largest drainage basin	Mississippi-Missouri, USA	3 250 000 sq km	1 254 825 sq miles
Lowest point	Death Valley, USA	-86 metres	-282 feet

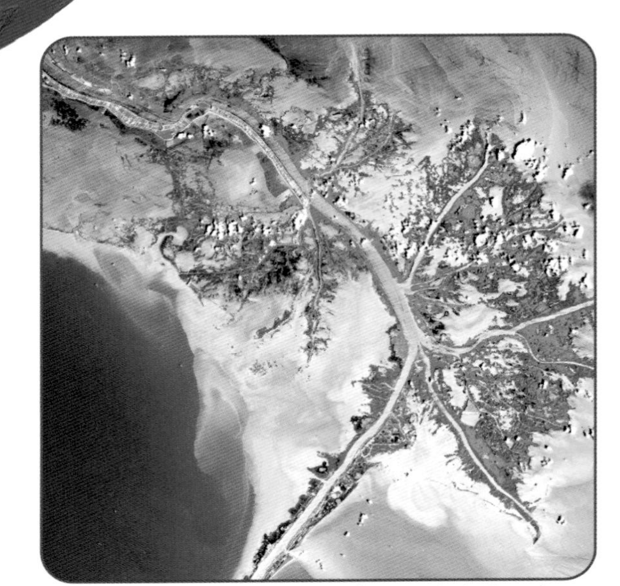

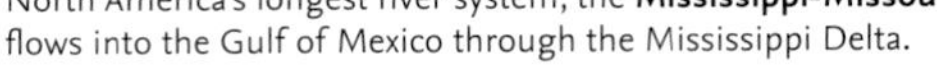

North America's longest river system, the **Mississippi-Missouri,** flows into the Gulf of Mexico through the Mississippi Delta.

North America's extent

TOTAL LAND AREA (including Hawai'ian Islands)	24 680 331 sq km / 9 529 076 sq miles
Most northerly point	Kaffeklubben Ø, Greenland
Most southerly point	Punta Mariato, Panama
Most westerly point	Attu Island, USA
Most easterly point	Nordøstrundingen, Greenland

ARCTIC OCEAN
Kaffeklubben Ø
Greenland Sea
Shannon Ø
Kong Frederik VIII Land
Kong Oscars Fjord
Kangertittivaq
Kong Christian X Land
Kong Christian IX Land
Kong Frederik VI Kyst
Denmark Strait
Greenland
Ellesmere Island
Axel Heiberg Island
Ellef Ringnes Island
Borden Island
Queen Elizabeth Islands
Nares Strait
Prince Patrick Island
Parry Islands
Melville Island
Devon Island
Qimusseriarsuaq
Point Barrow
Beaufort Sea
Banks Island
Parry Channel
Bylot Island
Baffin Bay
Qeqertarsuaq
Somerset Island
Prince of Wales Island
Brodeur Peninsula
Boothia Peninsula
Gulf of Boothia
Baffin Island
Davis Strait
Home Bay
Victoria Island
King William Island
Queen Maud Gulf
Prince Charles Island
Cumberland Peninsula
Cumberland Sound
Nettilling Lake
Melville Peninsula
Foxe Basin
Amadjuak Lake
Cape Farewell
Porcupine
Yukon
Mackenzie Mountains
Selwyn Mountains
Mackenzie
Great Bear Lake
Foxe Pen.
Frobisher Bay
Southampton Island
Hudson Strait
C. Chidley
Labrador Sea
Cassiar Mountains
Liard
Dubawnt Lake
Coats Island
Mansel Island
Péninsule d'Ungava
Ungava Bay
Rocky Mountains
Coast Mountains
Great Slave Lake
Caribou Mountains
Hudson Bay
Labrador
Lake Athabasca
Wollaston Lake
Reindeer Lake
Churchill
Athabasca
Peace
Lac Caniapiscau
Smallwood Reservoir
Belcher Islands
Lac Bienville
Laurentian Plateau
Southern Indian Lake
Nelson
Fraser
Mount Robson 3954
James Bay
Réservoir La Grande
Newfoundland
Cape Race
Severn
Île d'Anticosti
Gulf of St Lawrence
Cabot Strait
North Saskatchewan
Saskatchewan
Albany
Canadian Shield
ATLANTIC OCEAN
Vancouver Island
Lake Winnipeg
South Saskatchewan
Lake Winnipegosis
Cape Breton Island
Lake Nipigon
Sable Island
Mount Rainier 4392
Cascade Range
F. D. Roosevelt Lake
Lake of the Woods
Nova Scotia
Great Lakes
Missouri
Lake Sakakawea
Lake Superior
Ottawa
St Lawrence
Bay of Fundy
Cape Sable
Columbia
Fort Peck Reservoir
Yellowstone
Great Plains
Massachusetts Bay
Coast Ranges
Bitterroot Range
Lake Michigan
Lake Huron
Lake Ontario
Hudson
Cape Cod
Lake Oahe
Mississippi
Snake
Lake Erie
Long Island
Great Salt Lake
Appalachian Mountains
Great Basin
Sangre de Cristo Range
Platte
Allegheny Mts
Sierra Nevada
Illinois
San Joaquin
Chesapeake Bay
Mount Elbert 4398
Lake of the Ozarks
Ohio
Grand Canyon
Colorado
Arkansas
Ozark Plateau
Death Valley
Colorado Plateau
Cape Hatteras
Mount Mitchell 2037
Tennessee
Canadian
Rio Grande
Cape Fear
Alabama
Gila
Llano Estacado
Coastal Plain
Red
Brazos
Pecos
Guadalupe
Baja California
Gulf of California
Edwards Plateau
Yaqui
Conchos
Sierra Madre Occidental
Sierra Madre Oriental
Cape Canaveral
Grand Bahama
The Bahamas
Great Abaco
Mississippi Delta
Padre Island
Andros
West Indies
Straits of Florida
Gulf of Mexico
Acklins Island
Turks and Caicos Islands
Virgin Islands
Anguilla
Great Inagua
Puerto Rico
Guadaloupe
Cabo Falso
Yucatan Channel
Cuba
Hispaniola
Dominica
Martinique
St Lucia
Cayman Islands
Greater Antilles
Barbados
Cabo Corrientes
Yucatán
Jamaica
Lesser Antilles
Islas Revillagigedo
Volcán Popocatépetl 5452
Bahía de Campeche
Islas de la Bahía
Caribbean Sea
Tobago
Trinidad
Sierra Madre del Sur
Aruba
Netherlands Antilles
Gulf of Tehuantepec
Sierra Madre
Golfo de Fonseca
Lake Nicaragua
Panama Canal
Golfo del Darién
SOUTH AMERICA
Île Clipperton
Peninsula de Nicoya
Cordillera Central
Isthmus of Panama
Gulf of Panamá

The **Panama Canal,** Panama, linking the Pacific Ocean to the Atlantic Ocean.

Facts

- Devon Island, Canada, is the world's largest uninhabited island
- Canada has the longest coastline of any country in the world
- Lake Superior is the world's largest freshwater lake
- Over 320 000 square kilometres of the USA is protected for conservation purposes

North America

Countries

North America has been dominated economically and politically by the USA since the nineteenth century. Before that, the continent was subject to colonial influences, particularly of Spain in the south and of Britain and France in the east. The nineteenth century saw the steady development of the western half of the continent. The wealth of natural resources and the generally temperate climate were an excellent basis for settlement, agriculture and industrial development which has led to the USA being the richest nation in the world today.

Although there are twenty-three independent countries and fourteen dependent territories in North America, Canada, Mexico and the USA have approximately eighty-five per cent of the continent's population and eighty-eight per cent of its land area. Large parts of the north remain sparsely populated, while the most densely populated areas are in the northeast USA, and the Caribbean.

North America's capitals

Largest capital (population)	Mexico City, Mexico	19 028 000	
Smallest capital (population)	Belmopan, Belize	13 500	
Most northerly capital	Ottawa, Canada	45° 25'N	
Most southerly capital	Panama City, Panama	8° 56'N	
Highest capital	Mexico City, Mexico	2 300 metres	7 546 feet

Point Hope
Bering Strait
St Lawrence Island
Nome
U.S
Yukon
ALASKA
Fairbank
Mount McKinley
6194
Aleutian Islands
Alaska Peninsula
Anchorage
Valdez
Kodiak Island
Gulf of Alaska
Alexander Archipelago
Queen Charlotte Islands

LARGEST COUNTRY (POPULATION)
United States of America

LARGEST (AREA) AND LEAST DENSELY POPULATED COUNTRY
Canada

MOST NORTHERLY CAPITAL
Ottawa

SMALLEST COUNTRY
(AREA AND POPULATION)
St Kitts and Nevis

MOST DENSELY POPULATED COUNTRY
Barbados

LARGEST AND
HIGHEST CAPITAL
Mexico City

SMALLEST CAPITAL
Belmopan

MOST SOUTHERLY CAPITAL
Panama City

False-colour satellite image of the **Mexico-USA** boundary at Mexicali.

North America's countries

Largest country (area)	Canada	9 984 670 sq km	3 855 103 sq miles
Smallest country (area)	St Kitts and Nevis	261 sq km	101 sq miles
Largest country (population)	United States of America	298 213 000	
Smallest country (population)	St Kitts and Nevis	43 000	
Most densely populated country	Barbados	628 per sq km	1 627 per sq mile
Least densely populated country	Canada	3 per sq km	8 per sq mile

Greenland Sea
Station Nord
Daneborg
Ellesmere Island
Greenland
(Denmark)
Queen Elizabeth Islands
Parry Islands
Melville Island
Devon Island
Nares Strait
Dundas
Nuussuaq
Barrow
Beaufort Sea
Banks Island
Sachs Harbour
Parry Channel
Prince of Wales Island
Somerset Island
Baffin Bay
Ilulissat
Ammassalik
Pond Inlet
Clyde River
Davis Strait
Baffin Island
Nuuk
Nanortalik
Inuvik
Victoria Island
Hall Beach
Prince Charles Island
Cumberland Sound
Dawson
Great Bear Lake
Foxe Basin
Iqaluit
YUKON
Déline
Bathurst Inlet
Repulse Bay
NUNAVUT
Cape Dorset
NORTHWEST TERRITORIES
Whitehorse
Southampton Island
Hudson Strait
Fort Simpson
Yellowknife
Chesterfield Inlet
Ivujivik
Kangirsuk
Ungava Bay
Juneau
Great Slave Lake
Arviat
Hudson Bay
Nain
NEWFOUNDLAND AND LABRADOR
Fort Nelson
Uranium City
CANADA
Lake Athabasca
Churchill
Schefferville
Smallwood Reservoir
Strait of Belle Isle
Prince Rupert
Fort McMurray
Belcher Islands
Grande Prairie
BRITISH COLUMBIA
ALBERTA
La Ronge
Nelson
MANITOBA
Gander
St John's
Newfoundland
Corner Brook
Chisasibi
James Bay
Réservoir La Grande
Île d'Anticosti
Gulf of St Lawrence
Cabot Strait
St Pierre and Miquelon (France)
Jasper
Edmonton
The Pas
Sept-Îles
QUÉBEC
Lloydminster
SASKATCHEWAN
Lake Winnipeg
Moosonee
P.E.I.
Charlottetown
Kamloops
Vancouver Island
Vancouver
Calgary
Saskatoon
ONTARIO
Chicoutimi
NEW BRUNSWICK
Victoria
Lethbridge
Medicine Hat
Regina
Lake Nipigon
Rouyn-Noranda
Québec
Fredericton
Halifax
Sable Island
Olympia
Seattle
Spokane
Winnipeg
Thunder Bay
NOVA SCOTIA
Cape Sable
ATLANTIC OCEAN
WASHINGTON
International Falls
MAINE
Augusta
Montréal
MONTANA
NORTH DAKOTA
Grand Forks
Duluth
Lake Superior
Sault Sainte Marie
Ottawa
VT.
N.H.
Concord
Boston
Portland
Salem
Helena
Billings
Bismarck
MINNESOTA
MICHIGAN
Lake Huron
Montpelier
Albany
MASS.
OREGON
Toronto
Lake Ontario
NEW YORK
Providence
RHODE I.
CONNECTICUT
Hartford
Boise
IDAHO
WYOMING
SOUTH DAKOTA
Pierre
Minneapolis
St Paul
WISCONSIN
Sioux Falls
Milwaukee
Lansing
Detroit
Buffalo
New York
N.J.
Trenton
Philadelphia
Lake Michigan
Madison
Chicago
Casper
IOWA
Des Moines
Lake Erie
Erie
PENNSYLVANIA
Pittsburgh
NEBRASKA
Omaha
Cleveland
OHIO
Dover
DELAWARE
Reno
Great Salt Lake
Salt Lake City
Cheyenne
North Platte
INDIANA
Columbus
Annapolis
MD.
Washington D.C.
Sacramento
Carson City
San Francisco
San Jose
NEVADA
UTAH
UNITED STATES OF AMERICA
Indianapolis
Cincinnati
Charleston
Richmond
Denver
Colorado Springs
KANSAS
Topeka
Kansas City
ILLINOIS
W.V.
VIRGINIA
Jefferson City
St Louis
Frankfort
COLORADO
Wichita
MISSOURI
KENTUCKY
Raleigh
Las Vegas
Nashville
Knoxville
N. CAROLINA
Charlotte
Cape Hatteras
CALIFORNIA
Oklahoma City
TENNESSEE
Los Angeles
Albuquerque
OKLAHOMA
Little Rock
Memphis
Columbia
Atlanta
S. CAROLINA
ARIZONA
Phoenix
San Diego
Mexicali
ARKANSAS
GEORGIA
Ensenada
Tucson
NEW MEXICO
MISS.
Montgomery
ALABAMA
El Paso
Fort Worth
Dallas
Jackson
Jacksonville
TEXAS
Ciudad Juárez
Guadalupe (Mex.)
LOUISIANA
Tallahassee
Baton Rouge
Austin
Houston
New Orleans
Orlando
Hermosillo
San Antonio
Tampa
Baja California
Gulf of California
Chihuahua
FLORIDA
THE BAHAMAS
Miami
Nassau
Corpus Christi
Turks & Caicos Islands (U.K.)
Los Mochis
Nuevo Laredo
Gulf of Mexico
Straits of Florida
Monterrey
Matamoros
Virgin Islands (U.K.)
Virgin Islands (U.S.A.)
Anguilla (U.K.)
ANTIGUA & BARBUDA
Montserrat (U.K.)
La Paz
Durango
Ciudad Victoria
Havana
Santa Clara
San Juan
Puerto Rico (U.S.A.)
Mazatlán
MEXICO
CUBA
Holguín
DOMINICAN REP.
HAITI
Santo Domingo
ST KITTS & NEVIS
Guadeloupe (France)
DOMINICA
San Luis Potosí
Tampico
Yucatan Channel
Cayman Islands (U.K.)
Greater Antilles
Port-au-Prince
Martinique (Fr.)
Tepic
León
Mérida
Yucatán
Montego Bay
ST LUCIA
Guadalajara
Kingston
JAMAICA
BARBADOS
Campeche
Lesser Antilles
ST VINCENT & THE GRENADINES
Islas Revillagigedo (Mex.)
Mexico City
Bahía de Campeche
GRENADA
TRINIDAD & TOBAGO
Volcán Popocatépetl
Veracruz
BELIZE
Belmopan
Caribbean Sea
Port of Spain
Oaxaca
Villahermosa
Aruba (Neths.)
Netherlands Antilles
Acapulco
PACIFIC OCEAN
San Pedro Sula
GUATEMALA
HONDURAS
Tegucigalpa
Gulf of Tehuantepec
San Salvador
EL SALVADOR
NICARAGUA
Managua
Lake Nicaragua
Golfo del Darién
SOUTH AMERICA
COSTA RICA
San José
Colón
Panama City
PANAMA
Gulf of Panama
Île Clipperton (France)

Internet Links

UK Foreign and Commonwealth Office	www.fco.gov.uk
CIA World Factbook	www.cia.gov/library/publications/the-world-factbook/index.html
U.S. Board on Geographic Names	geonames.usgs.gov
NASA Astronaut Photography	eol.jsc.nasa.gov

The Bahamas, a chain of islands in the North Atlantic Ocean, lying southeast of Florida, USA.

Facts

- The Panama Canal, opened in 1914, cut the journey between the Atlantic and the Pacific by over 14 000 km
- Mexico City is the highest city in North America and houses approximately 18% of Mexico's population
- The state of Alaska was bought by the USA from Russia in 1867
- The territory of Nunavut is Canada's newest administrative division, created in 1999 from the eastern part of Northwest Territories

ARCTIC OCEAN
Beaufort Sea
Bering Sea
Aleutian Islands
Gulf of Alaska
PACIFIC OCEAN
U.S.A.
ALASKA
Brooks Range
Alaska Range
YUKON
NORTHWEST TERRITORIES
BRITISH COLUMBIA
ALBERTA
SASKATCHEWAN
CA
UNITED STATES OF
WASHINGTON
OREGON
IDAHO
MONTANA
WYOMING
NORTH DAKOTA
SOUTH DAKOTA
NEBRASKA
NEVADA
UTAH
CALIFORNIA
Rocky Mountains
Coast Mountains
Cascade Range
Sierra Nevada
Great Basin
Vancouver Island
Queen Charlotte Is
Anchorage
Fairbanks
Whitehorse
Yellowknife
Edmonton
Calgary
Vancouver
Victoria
Seattle
Portland
Spokane
Boise
Salt Lake City
Sacramento
San Francisco
San Jose
Great Slave Lake
Great Bear Lake
Victoria Island
Banks Island
↓ 154

Lambert Conformal Conic Projection

1:16 000 000 — 0, 200, 400 miles; 0, 200, 400, 600, 800 km

Greenland (Kalaallit Nunaat) (Denmark)
ICELAND
REYKJAVÍK
Denmark Strait
Baffin Bay
Davis Strait
Labrador Sea
Hudson Bay
James Bay
Hudson Strait
Foxe Basin
Baffin Island
Ellesmere Island
Queen Elizabeth Islands
Devon Island
Southampton Island
NUNAVUT
MANITOBA
ONTARIO
QUÉBEC
NEWFOUNDLAND AND LABRADOR
Newfoundland
NEW BRUNSWICK
NOVA SCOTIA
PRINCE EDWARD I.
CANADA
MINNESOTA
WISCONSIN
MICHIGAN
IOWA
MAINE
NEW YORK
PENNSYLVANIA
AMERICA
Lake Superior
Lake Michigan
Lake Winnipeg
Gulf of St Lawrence
Gulf of Maine
ATLANTIC OCEAN
OTTAWA
Montréal
Québec
Toronto
Winnipeg
Chicago
Detroit
Boston
New York
Halifax
St John's
Nuuk (Godthåb)
↓ 155
States in the U.S.A. numbered on the map:
1. CONNECTICUT (K5)
2. MASSACHUSETTS (K5)
3. NEW HAMPSHIRE (K5)
4. RHODE ISLAND (K5)
5. VERMONT (K5)

RUSSIAN FEDERATION
CHUKOTSKIY AVTONOMNYY OKRUG
Chukotskiy Poluostrov
Anadyrskiy Zaliv
Chukchi Sea
Bering Strait
Diomede Islands
Kotzebue Sound
Seward Peninsula
Norton Sound
St Lawrence Island
Arctic Circle
Brooks Range
Arctic Plains
Lookout Ridge
De Long Mountains
Baird Mountains
Waring Mountains
Kobuk Valley National Park
Gates of the Arctic National Park and Preserve
Selawik National Wildlife Refuge
Bering Land Bridge National Preserve
Cape Krusenstern National Monument
Noatak National Preserve
Alaska Maritime National Wildlife Refuge
Point Hope
Point Barrow
Wainwright
Icy Cape
Point Lay
Cape Lisburne
Kivalina
Kotzebue
Nome
Unalakleet
Yukon Delta
Yukon Delta National Wildlife Refuge
Innoko National Wildlife Refuge
Koyukuk National Wildlife Refuge
Nowitna National Wildlife Refuge
Kuskokwim Mountains
Kilbuck Mountains
Kuskokwim Bay
Togiak National Wildlife Refuge
Ahklun Mountains
Nunivak Island
Etolin Strait
Cape Newenham
St Matthew Island
Hall Island
Bering Sea
Pribilof Islands
St Paul Island
St George Island
Bristol Bay
Lake Clark National Park and Preserve
Katmai National Park and Preserve
Becharof National Wildlife Refuge
Alaska Peninsula
Aniakchak National Monument and Preserve
Kodiak Island
Shelikof Strait
Chirikof Island
Semidi Islands
Shumagin Islands
Izembek National Wildlife Refuge
Unimak Island
Unalaska Island
Fox Islands
Islands of the Four Mountains
ALEUTIAN ISLANDS
Alaska Maritime National Wildlife Refuge
Attu Island
Near Islands
ALASKA
U.
A
B
C
D
E
F
G
H
I
2
3
4
5
6
← 77
60°
56°
52°N
172°W
168°
164°
160°
156°
152°
1:7 000 000
miles
km
Lambert Conformal Conic Projection

1:7 000 000

0	100	200	miles
0 100	200	300	400 km

Beaufort Sea
Gulf of Alaska
CANADA
NORTHWEST TERRITORIES
YUKON
BRITISH COLUMBIA
NUNAVUT
Alexander Archipelago
ALEUTIAN ISLANDS
Alaska Maritime National Wildlife Refuge
Andreanof Islands
Rat Islands
Mackenzie Mountains
Ogilvie Mountains
Selwyn Mountains
Pelly Mountains
Cassiar Mountains
Wrangell Mountains
Chugach Mountains
St Elias Mountains
British Mountains
Richardson Mountains
Franklin Mountains
Backbone Ranges
Stikine Ranges
Skeena Mountains
Dawson Range
Anvil Range
Logan Mountains
Great Bear Lake
Arctic Circle
Fairbanks
Anchorage
Whitehorse
Juneau
Prince Rupert
Kenai Peninsula
Chichagof Island
Baranof Island
Prince of Wales Island
Graham Island
Moresby Island
Queen Charlotte Islands
Dixon Entrance
Hecate Strait
Stikine Plateau
Liard Plateau
Melville Hills
Old Crow Flats
Vuntut National Park
Ivvavik National Park
Kluane National Park
Arctic National Wildlife Refuge
Yukon Flats National Wildlife Refuge
Tetlin National Wildlife Refuge
Wrangell-St Elias National Park and Preserve
Glacier Bay National Park and Preserve
Mackenzie River Delta
Mackenzie Bay
→ 150
↓ 150

ALASKA
YUKON
NORTHWEST TER
U.S.A.
BRITISH COLUMBIA
ALBERTA
CAN
WASHINGTON
IDAHO
PACIFIC OCEAN
Alexander Archipelago
Queen Charlotte Islands
Hecate Strait
Queen Charlotte Sound
Vancouver Island
Mackenzie Mountains
Rocky Mountains
Coast Mountains
Cassiar Mountains
Skeena Mountains
Omineca Mountains
Selkirk Mountains
Purcell Mountains
Monashee Mts
Cariboo Mts
Columbia Mts
Liard Plateau
Fraser Plateau
Stikine Plateau
Great Bear Lake
Great Slave Lake
Whitehorse
Yellowknife
Prince George
Prince Rupert
Kamloops
Kelowna
Vancouver
Victoria
Edmonton
Calgary
Red Deer
Grande Prairie
Dawson Creek
Fort St John
Fort Nelson
Watson Lake
Fort Simpson
Hay River
Juneau
Sitka
Ketchikan
Conic Equidistant Projection
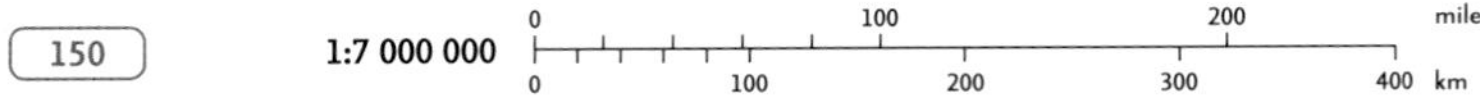
1:7 000 000
0 100 200 miles
0 100 200 300 400 km

NUNAVUT
RITORIES
A D A
SASKATCHEWAN
MANITOBA
ONTARIO
U. MONTANA S. A.
NORTH DAKOTA
MINNESOTA
Hudson Bay
Southampton Island
Coats Island
Lake Athabasca
Lake Winnipeg
Lake Manitoba
Lake Winnipegosis
Reindeer Lake
Wollaston Lake
Southern Indian Lake
Baker Lake
Chesterfield Inlet
Rankin Inlet
Arviat (Eskimo Point)
Churchill
Cape Churchill
Wapusk National Park
Thompson
Flin Flon
The Pas
Prince Albert
Prince Albert Nat. Park
Saskatoon
Regina
Moose Jaw
Swift Current
Medicine Hat
Lloydminster
North Battleford
Yorkton
Brandon
Winnipeg
Portage la Prairie
Riding Mountain National Park
Grasslands National Park
Cypress Hills
Trans Canada Highway
Fort McMurray
Fort Chipewyan
Uranium City
Lake of the Woods
Voyageurs National Park
Grand Forks
Minot
Williston
Bemidji
→ 152
↓ 160

North America
Western Canada

Hudson Bay
James Bay
NUNAVUT
MANITOBA
ONTARIO
CANADA
UNITED STATES OF AMERICA
MINNESOTA
WISCONSIN
MICHIGAN
ILLINOIS
IOWA
NEW YORK
Lake Superior
Lake Michigan
Lake Huron
Lake Erie
Lake Ontario
Georgian Bay
Lake Nipigon
Belcher Islands
Akimiski Island
Wapusk National Park
Pukaskwa National Park
Isle Royale National Park
Voyageurs National Park
Churchill
Thompson
Fort Severn
Moosonee
Thunder Bay
Sault Sainte Marie
Sudbury
Toronto
OTTAWA
Montréal
Chicago
Milwaukee
Detroit
Minneapolis
St Paul
Duluth
Buffalo
Rochester
Cleveland
Grand Rapids
Hamilton
London
Kingston
↑ 147
← 151
↓ 162

Conic Equidistant Projection

1:7 000 000

0 100 200 miles

0 100 200 300 400 km

Labrador Sea
Ungava Bay
Torngat Mountains National Park Reserve
Mount Eliot
Mt Caubvick
Cape Uivak
Hebron
Kaumajet Mts
Cod Island
Okak Islands
Kiglapait Mts
South Aulatsivik Island
Dog Island
Paul Island
Nain
Tunungayualok Island
Nunaksaluk Island
Davis Inlet (abandoned)
Hopedale
Cape Makkovik
Makkovik
Adlavik Islands
Cape Harrison
Postville
Mount Benedict
Indian Harbour
West Bay
Cape Porcupine
Rigolet
Hamilton Inlet
Cartwright
Sandwich Bay
Black Tickle
Labrador
NEWFOUNDLAND AND LABRADOR
Smallwood Reservoir
Churchill Falls
Happy Valley-Goose Bay
North West River
Lake Melville
Mealy Mountains
Port Hope Simpson
Mary's Harbour
Cape Charles
Belle Isle
Red Bay
Cape Bauld
St Anthony
Blanc-Sablon
Strait of Belle Isle
Grey Islands
Englee
Horse Islands
Cape St John
Notre Dame Bay
Fogo Island
Musgrave Harbour
Cape Freels
Wesleyville
Bonavista Bay
Bonavista
Gander
Terra Nova National Park
Trinity Bay
Clarenville
Long Range Mountains
White Bay
Gros Morne National Park
Rocky Harbour
Corner Brook
Lewis Hills
Grand Lake
Red Indian Lake
Newfoundland
Meelpaeg Reservoir
Lark Harbour
Lourdes
Cape St George
St George's Bay
Cape Anguille
Cape Ray
Channel-Port-aux-Basques
Burgeo
Rose Blanche
Hermitage Bay
Fortune Bay
Burin Peninsula
Placentia Bay
Placentia
Avalon Peninsula
St John's
Mount Pearl
Ferryland
Renews
Trepassey
Cape Race
St Mary's Bay
St Pierre and Miquelon (France)
Miquelon
ST-PIERRE
Gulf of St Lawrence
Cabot Strait
QUÉBEC
Îles de la Madeleine
Île Brion
Cap-aux-Meules
Havre Aubert
Cape St Lawrence
Cape North
Cape Breton Highlands National Park
Chéticamp
Cape Breton Island
Ingonish
Sydney
Sydney Mines
Glace Bay
Louisbourg
Bras d'Or Lake
St Peter's
Chedabucto Bay
Canso
Cape Canso
Antigonish
New Glasgow
Pictou
Truro
Guysborough
Sheet Harbour
NOVA SCOTIA
Halifax
Dartmouth
Bedford
Windsor
Wolfville
Middleton
Bridgewater
Chester
Liverpool
Kejimkujik National Park
Digby
Bridgetown
Yarmouth
Argyle
Shelburne
Barrington
Cape Sable
Baccaro Point
Sable Island
ATLANTIC OCEAN
Bay of Fundy
Point Lepreau
Grand Manan I.
Long Island
PRINCE EDWARD ISLAND
Charlottetown
Summerside
Northumberland Strait
NEW BRUNSWICK
Moncton
Riverview
Sackville
Amherst
Springhill
Fredericton
Saint John
St John
Oromocto
Woodstock
Miramichi
Bathurst
Campbellton
Dalhousie
Edmundston
Kouchibouguac National Park
Mt Carleton
Chaleur Bay
Miscou Island
Shippegan Island
Anticosti
Île d'Anticosti
Gaspé
Percé
Péninsule de la Gaspésie
Monts Chic-Chocs
Monts Notre-Dame
Forillon
Matane
Rimouski
Rivière-du-Loup
Baie-Comeau
Sept-Îles
Port-Cartier
Havre-St-Pierre
Natashquan
Réserve du Parc National de l'Archipel de Mingan
Détroit de Jacques-Cartier
Détroit d'Honguedo
St Lawrence
Chicoutimi
Jonquière
La Baie
Alma
Roberval
Tadoussac
Québec
Lévis
Charlesbourg
Trois-Rivières
Shawinigan
La Tuque
Drummondville
Sherbrooke
Thetford Mines
Victoriaville
St-Hyacinthe
Magog
Granby
Réservoir Manicouagan
Fermont
Labrador City
Wabush
Schefferville
Kuujjuaq (Fort Chimo)
Kangiqsualujjuaq (Port-Nouveau-Québec)
Tasiujaq (Leaf Bay)
Aupaluk (Hopes Advance Bay)
Kangirsuk (Payne)
Akpatok Island
Réservoir de Caniapiscau
QUÉBEC
MAINE
VERMONT
NEW HAMPSHIRE
Augusta
Bangor
Portland
Lewiston
Mt Katahdin
Acadia National Park
Mount Desert Island
Gulf of Maine
Casco Bay
Concord
Manchester
Nashua
Portsmouth
Burlington
Montpelier
Mt Washington
White Mts
Lowell
Haverhill
Lawrence
Salem
Pittsfield

North America

Eastern Canada

↑ 146
BRITISH COLUMBIA
ALBERTA
SASKATCHEWAN
WASHINGTON
OREGON
IDAHO
MONTANA
WYOMING
NORTH DAKOTA
SOUTH DAKOTA
NEBRASKA
NEVADA
UTAH
COLORADO
CALIFORNIA
ARIZONA
NEW MEXICO
TEXAS
MEXICO
UNITED STATES OF AMERICA
PACIFIC OCEAN
Vancouver Island
Vancouver
Victoria
Seattle
Tacoma
Spokane
Portland
Salem
Eugene
Boise
Calgary
Edmonton
Regina
Saskatoon
Great Falls
Helena
Billings
Casper
Cheyenne
Salt Lake City
Reno
Sacramento
San Francisco
Oakland
San Jose
Fresno
Bakersfield
Los Angeles
Riverside
San Diego
Tijuana
Mexicali
Las Vegas
Phoenix
Tucson
Albuquerque
Santa Fe
Denver
El Paso
Ciudad Juárez
Chihuahua
Hermosillo
Culiacán
Torreón
Monterrey
Saltillo
San Antonio
Lubbock
Amarillo
Great Basin
Colorado Plateau
Mojave Desert
Sierra Nevada
Cascade Range
Coast Ranges
Rocky Mountains
Great Plains
Sierra Madre Occidental
Sierra Madre Oriental
Gulf of California
Baja California
Tropic of Cancer
Llano Estacado
Edwards Plateau
↓ 168

Lambert Conformal Conic Projection

1:12 000 000

0 100 200 300 400 miles

0 100 200 300 400 500 600 700 km

CANADA
ONTARIO
QUÉBEC
NEW BRUNSWICK
NOVA SCOTIA
PRINCE EDWARD ISLAND
James Bay
Lake Superior
Lake Michigan
Lake Huron
Lake Erie
Lake Ontario
Gulf of St Lawrence
Gulf of Maine
Bay of Fundy
Massachusetts Bay
Cape Cod
UNITED STATES OF AMERICA
MINNESOTA
WISCONSIN
MICHIGAN
IOWA
ILLINOIS
INDIANA
OHIO
PENNSYLVANIA
NEW YORK
VERMONT
NEW HAMPSHIRE
MAINE
MASSACHUSETTS
CONNECTICUT
RHODE ISLAND
NEW JERSEY
DELAWARE
MARYLAND
WEST VIRGINIA
VIRGINIA
KENTUCKY
TENNESSEE
NORTH CAROLINA
SOUTH CAROLINA
GEORGIA
FLORIDA
ALABAMA
MISSISSIPPI
LOUISIANA
ARKANSAS
MISSOURI
WASHINGTON D.C.
Ozark Plateau
Cumberland Plateau
Allegheny Mountains
Appalachian Mountains
Coastal Plain
ATLANTIC OCEAN
Gulf of Mexico
THE BAHAMAS
NASSAU
CUBA
Straits of Florida
Great Bahama Bank
Tropic of Cancer
Winnipeg
Ottawa
Toronto
Montréal
Québec
Minneapolis
Milwaukee
Chicago
Detroit
Cleveland
Pittsburgh
Buffalo
Boston
New York
Philadelphia
Baltimore
Indianapolis
Columbus
Cincinnati
St Louis
Louisville
Nashville
Memphis
Atlanta
Charlotte
Virginia Beach
Jacksonville
Orlando
Tampa
Miami
New Orleans
Houston
Dallas
↑ 147
↓ 169

North America

United States of America

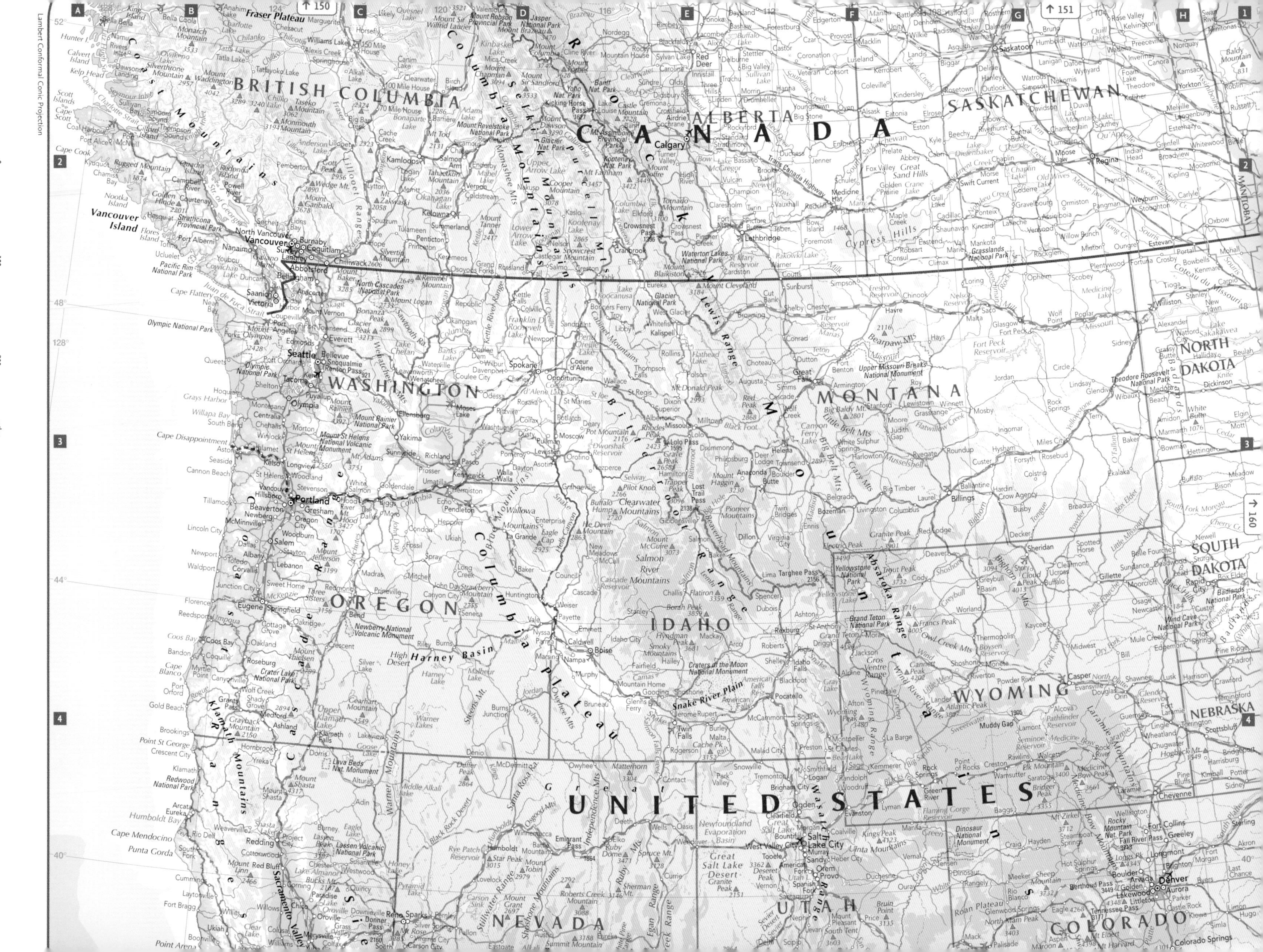

Lambert Conformal Conic Projection

1:7 000 000

0 100 200 miles

0 100 200 300 400 km

PACIFIC OCEAN
OF AMERICA
MEXICO
CALIFORNIA
ARIZONA
NEW MEXICO
TEXAS
SONORA
CHIHUAHUA
BAJA CALIFORNIA
BAJA CALIFORNIA SUR
SINALOA
DURANGO
HAWAII (U.S.A.)
Gulf of California
Sonoran Desert
Sierra Madre Occidental
Colorado Plateau
Sangre de Cristo Range
Sacramento Mts
Sierra Nevada
San Joaquin Valley
Mojave Desert
Death Valley
Los Angeles
San Diego
Tijuana
Mexicali
Phoenix
Tucson
Las Vegas
Albuquerque
El Paso
Ciudad Juárez
Chihuahua
Hermosillo
San Francisco
Sacramento
San Jose
Fresno
Bakersfield
Honolulu
Kaua'i
O'ahu
Maui
Hawai'i
↑ 161
↓ 166

PACIFIC
OCEAN
CALIFORNIA
NEVADA
UNIT
OF
BAJA CA
Coast Ranges
Sacramento Valley
Sierra Nevada
San Joaquin Valley
Diablo Range
Coast Ranges
Santa Lucia Range
Mojave Desert
Death Valley
San Bernardino Mountains
San Gabriel Mountains
Sierra Madre Mountains
San Rafael Mountains
Channel Islands
Santa Barbara Channel
San Pedro Channel
Outer Santa Barbara Channel
Gulf of Santa Catalina
Monterey Bay
San Luis Obispo Bay
Estero Bay
Santa Monica Bay
Drakes Bay
Cape Mendocino
Point Arena
Point Reyes
Point Conception
Point Sur
Point Delgada
Punta Gorda
Bodega Head
Redding
Red Bluff
Chico
Oroville
Marysville
Yuba City
Sacramento
Citrus Heights
Santa Rosa
Napa
Vallejo
Concord
Richmond
Berkeley
Oakland
Alameda
San Francisco
Daly City
South San Francisco
San Mateo
Redwood City
Palo Alto
Sunnyvale
Santa Clara
San Jose
Hayward
Fremont
Milpitas
Livermore
Stockton
Lodi
Modesto
Turlock
Merced
Fresno
Clovis
Visalia
Tulare
Hanford
Bakersfield
Salinas
Monterey
Santa Cruz
San Luis Obispo
Santa Maria
Lompoc
Santa Barbara
Ventura
Oxnard
Thousand Oaks
Lancaster
Palmdale
Santa Clarita
Los Angeles
Glendale
Pasadena
Burbank
Santa Monica
Inglewood
Long Beach
Anaheim
Santa Ana
Irvine
Riverside
San Bernardino
Ontario
Pomona
Oceanside
Escondido
San Diego
Chula Vista
Tijuana
Reno
Sparks
Carson City
South Lake Tahoe
Lake Tahoe
Mono Lake
Yosemite National Park
Sequoia National Park
Kings Canyon National Park
Lassen Volcanic National Park
Pinnacles National Monument
Channel Islands National Park
San Miguel Island
Santa Rosa Island
Santa Cruz Island
Anacapa Island
Santa Barbara Island
Santa Catalina Island
San Nicolas Island
San Clemente Island
Mount Whitney 4418
Mount Diablo 1187
Mount Hamilton 1299
Donner Pass 2160
Tejon Pass 1292
Tehachapi Pass
Walker Pass 1600
Lambert Conformal Conic Projection

1:3 500 000

0 50 100 miles
0 50 100 150 200 km

UTAH
COLORADO
ARIZONA
NEW MEXICO
UNITED STATES OF AMERICA
MEXICO
SONORA
Great Salt Lake Desert
Sevier Desert
Escalante Desert
Colorado Plateau
Sonoran Desert
Painted Desert
Grand Canyon
Mogollon Plateau
Coconino Plateau
Kaibab Plateau
Paria Plateau
Roan Plateau
East Tavaputs Plateau
Uncompahgre Plateau
Black Mesa
Glen Canyon
Monument Valley
Vermilion Cliffs
Book Cliffs
Uinta Mountains
San Juan Mountains
Chuska Mountains
Zuni Mountains
Gallo Mountains
Mogollon Mountains
Black Range
Plains of San Agustin
Virgin Mountains
Black Mountains
Hualapai Peak
Bill Williams Mountain
Humphreys Peak
Great Salt Lake
Lake Powell
Lake Mead
Lake Havasu
Salt Lake City
Provo
Orem
Grand Junction
Durango
Farmington
Gallup
Flagstaff
Prescott
Phoenix
Glendale
Mesa
Tempe
Chandler
Tucson
Yuma
Las Vegas
Henderson
Kingman
St George
Cedar City
Moab
Mexicali
Calexico
El Centro
Grand Canyon National Park
Zion National Park
Bryce Canyon National Park
Capitol Reef National Park
Arches National Park
Canyonlands National Park
Great Basin National Park
Mesa Verde National Park
Petrified Forest National Park
Saguaro National Park
Black Canyon of the Gunnison National Park
Grand Staircase-Escalante National Monument
Canyon de Chelly National Monument
Organ Pipe Cactus National Monument
Chaco Culture National Historical Park
F
G
H
I
J
1
2
3
4
5
6
↑ 157
↓ 157

North America
Southwest United States

CANADA
UNITED STATES
ALBERTA
SASKATCHEWAN
MANITOBA
ONTARIO
MONTANA
NORTH DAKOTA
SOUTH DAKOTA
MINNESOTA
WISCONSIN
MICHIGAN
IOWA
NEBRASKA
WYOMING
COLORADO
KANSAS
MISSOURI
ILLINOIS
INDIANA
KENTUCKY
Lake Superior
Lake Michigan
Lake Winnipeg
Rocky Mountains
Great Plains
↑ 151
↑ 152
↑ 162
↓ 156

Lambert Conformal Conic Projection

1:7 000 000

0 100 200 miles

0 100 200 300 400 km

UNITED STATES OF AMERICA
MEXICO
TENNESSEE
ALABAMA
MISSISSIPPI
ARKANSAS
LOUISIANA
OKLAHOMA
TEXAS
NEW MEXICO
FLORIDA
CHIHUAHUA
COAHUILA
NUEVO LEÓN
TAMAULIPAS
DURANGO
ZACATECAS
Gulf of Mexico
Coastal Plain
Edwards Plateau
Llano Estacado
Sierra Madre Oriental
Desierto de Chihuahua
Ouachita Mountains
Sacramento Mts
Mississippi Delta
Tropic of Cancer
↑ 163
↓ 157
↓ 166

North America
Central United States

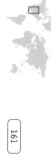

CANADA
QUÉBEC
ONTARIO
NEW BRUNSWICK
MAINE
VERMONT
NEW HAMPSHIRE
NEW YORK
NEW JERSEY
PENNSYLVANIA
MARYLAND
WEST VIRGINIA
VIRGINIA
NORTH CAROLINA
OHIO
MICHIGAN
INDIANA
ILLINOIS
WISCONSIN
MINNESOTA
IOWA
MISSOURI
KENTUCKY
TENNESSEE
UNITED STATES
Lake Superior
Lake Huron
Lake Michigan
Lake Erie
Lake Ontario
Georgian Bay
Gulf of Maine
Chesapeake Bay
Long Island
Cape Cod
Martha's Vineyard
Nantucket Island
Adirondack Mts
Appalachian Mountains
OTTAWA
WASHINGTON D.C.
Montréal
Québec
Toronto
Boston
New York
Philadelphia
Baltimore
Pittsburgh
Buffalo
Cleveland
Detroit
Chicago
Milwaukee
Columbus
Cincinnati
Indianapolis
Louisville
St Louis
Nashville
Knoxville
Richmond
Virginia Beach
Norfolk
Providence
Hartford
States in the U.S.A. numbered on the map:
1. CONNECTICUT (F3)
2. DELAWARE (F4)
3. MASSACHUSETTS (F3)
4. RHODE ISLAND (G3)
Lambert Conformal Conic Projection
1:7 000 000
0 100 200 miles
0 100 200 300 400 km

↑ 152
↑ 153
← 160

ATLANTIC OCEAN
Gulf of Mexico
OF AMERICA
SOUTH CAROLINA
GEORGIA
ALABAMA
MISSISSIPPI
FLORIDA
Coastal Plain
THE BAHAMAS
CUBA
MEXICO
Turks and Caicos Islands (U.K.)
Straits of Florida
Great Bahama Bank
Little Bahama Bank
Tropic of Cancer
HAVANA (La Habana)
NASSAU
Miami
Tampa
Orlando
Jacksonville
Atlanta
Savannah
Charleston
Tallahassee
Montgomery
Mobile
Pensacola
Birmingham
Charlotte
Wilmington
Cape Hatteras
Cape Canaveral
Grand Bahama
Great Abaco
Andros
Eleuthera
Yucatan Channel
Old Bahama Channel
Nicholas Channel
← 161
↓ 169

MICHIGAN
WISCONSIN
ILLINOIS
INDIANA
OHIO
KENTUCKY
WEST VIRGINIA
TENNESSEE
ONTA
UNITED STATES OF AMERICA
Lake Michigan
Lake Huron
Lake Erie
Georgian Bay
Saginaw Bay
Green Bay
CANADA
U.S.A.
Milwaukee
Chicago
Detroit
Toledo
Cleveland
Columbus
Indianapolis
Cincinnati
Louisville
Lexington
Pittsburgh
Dayton
Fort Wayne
Grand Rapids
Lansing
Flint
Windsor
London
Hamilton
Toronto
Charleston
Huntington
Akron
Canton
Youngstown
Cumberland Mountains
Allegheny
Appalachian
Blue Ridge
Sleeping Bear Dunes National Lakeshore
Mammoth Cave National Park
Point Pelee National Park
Big South Fork National River and Recreation Area
Mount Rogers National Recreation Area

↑ 152
↑ 162
↓ 162

Lambert Conformal Conic Projection

1:3 500 000

0 50 100 miles

0 50 100 150 200 km

CANADA
QUEBEC
OTTAWA
Lake Ontario
NEW YORK
VERMONT
NEW HAMPSHIRE
MAINE
MASSACHUSETTS
CONNECTICUT
RHODE ISLAND
PENNSYLVANIA
NEW JERSEY
DELAWARE
MARYLAND
VIRGINIA
WASHINGTON D.C.
Adirondack Mountains
Catskill Mountains
White Mountains
Green Mountains
Appalachian Mountains
Gulf of Maine
Massachusetts Bay
Cape Cod Bay
Nantucket Sound
Long Island Sound
Long Island
Chesapeake Bay
Delaware Bay
ATLANTIC
OCEAN
Boston
Providence
Hartford
New York
Philadelphia
Baltimore
Richmond
Virginia Beach
Buffalo
Rochester
Syracuse
Albany
Springfield
Bridgeport
Chesapeake

North America
Northeast United States

↑ 153

ARIZONA
NEW MEXICO
UNITED
SONORA
CHIHUAHUA
SINALOA
DURANGO
NAYARIT
JALISCO
COLIMA
ZACATECA
BAJA CALIFORNIA
BAJA CALIFORNIA SUR
Golfo de California
Sierra Madre Occidental
Tropic of Cancer
San Diego
Tijuana
Mexicali
Ensenada
Tucson
El Paso
Ciudad Juárez
Hermosillo
Chihuahua
Guaymas
Ciudad Obregón
Los Mochis
Culiacán
La Paz
Mazatlán
Durango
Torreón
Tepic
Guadalajara
Guadalupe
Isla Cedros
Islas Marías
PACIFIC
Gulf of Honduras
HONDURAS
TEGUCIGALPA
EL SALVADOR
NICARAGUA
MANAGUA
Lake Nicaragua
COSTA RICA
SAN JOSÉ
PANAMA
PANAMA CITY
COLOMBIA
Caribbean Sea
PACIFIC OCEAN
Gulf of Panama
BELIZE
GUATEMALA
↑ 157
↓ 176

Lambert Conformal Conic Projection

North America

Mexico and Central America

1:7 200 000

161
163
F
G
H
I
1
2
3
4
5
6
STATES OF AMERICA
TEXAS
LOUISIANA
MISSISSIPPI
ALABAMA
FLORIDA
COASTAL PLAIN
Edwards Plateau
Dallas
Fort Worth
Shreveport
Jackson
Montgomery
Mobile
Pensacola
Austin
San Antonio
Houston
Galveston
Beaumont
Baton Rouge
New Orleans
Mississippi Delta
Corpus Christi
Laredo
Nuevo Laredo
Brownsville
Matamoros
Monterrey
NUEVO LEÓN
TAMAULIPAS
SAN LUIS POTOSÍ
San Luis Potosí
MEXICO
Tampico
Ciudad Madero
VERACRUZ
Veracruz
GUANAJUATO
Querétaro
HIDALGO
MEXICO CITY
Toluca
Puebla
MORELOS
PUEBLA
GUERRERO
Acapulco
OAXACA
Oaxaca
Sierra Madre del Sur
Istmo de Tehuantepec
Gulf of Tehuantepec
TABASCO
Villahermosa
CHIAPAS
Tuxtla Gutiérrez
Sierra Madre de Chiapas
CAMPECHE
Campeche
YUCATÁN
Mérida
QUINTANA ROO
Cancún
BELIZE
GUATEMALA
GUATEMALA CITY
HONDURAS
TEGUCIGALPA
EL SALVADOR
SAN SALVADOR
Gulf of Honduras
Gulf of Mexico
Bahía de Campeche
Yucatan Channel
Arrecife Alacrán
Cayo Nuevo
Cayos Arcas
Padre Island
Laguna Madre
Matagorda Island
Tropic of Cancer
OCEAN
28°
24°
20°
16°
100°
96°
92°
88°

UNITED STATES OF AMERICA
MEXICO
CALIFORNIA
ARIZONA
NEW MEXICO
TEXAS
OKLAHOMA
KANSAS
MISSOURI
ARKANSAS
LOUISIANA
MISSISSIPPI
COLORADO
GUATEMALA
BELIZE
EL SALVADOR
PACIFIC OCEAN
Gulf of Mexico
Gulf of California
Baja California
Bahía de Campeche
Gulf of Tehuantepec
Sierra Madre Occidental
Sierra Madre Oriental
Sierra Madre del Sur
Yucatán
Tropic of Cancer
MEXICO CITY
GUATEMALA CITY
SAN SALVADOR
Los Angeles
San Diego
Tijuana
Phoenix
Tucson
El Paso
Ciudad Juárez
Chihuahua
Hermosillo
Monterrey
Guadalajara
Puebla
Acapulco
Houston
Dallas
San Antonio
Austin
New Orleans
Mérida
Île Clipperton (France)
Islas Revillagigedo (Mexico)
Lambert Conformal Conic Projection

1:14 000 000

0 200 400 miles

0 200 400 600 800 km

↑ 155
ATLANTIC OCEAN
Bermuda (U.K.)
HAMILTON
Tropic of Cancer
THE BAHAMAS
NASSAU
Great Abaco
Eleuthera
Andros
Cat Island
San Salvador
Great Exuma
Crooked Island
Acklins Island
Great Inagua
Turks and Caicos Islands (U.K.)
GRAND TURK (Cockburn Town)
West Indies
Greater Antilles
Lesser Antilles
Leeward Islands
Windward Islands
Caribbean Sea
Straits of Florida
Great Bahama Bank
Yucatan Channel
Windward Passage
HAVANA (La Habana)
CUBA
Isla de la Juventud
Santiago de Cuba
Cayman Islands (U.K.)
GEORGE TOWN
JAMAICA
KINGSTON
Montego Bay
Hispaniola
HAITI
PORT-AU-PRINCE
DOMINICAN REPUBLIC
SANTO DOMINGO
Puerto Rico (U.S.A.)
SAN JUAN
Virgin Islands (U.K.)
Virgin Islands (U.S.A.)
Anguilla (U.K.)
ANTIGUA AND BARBUDA
ST KITTS AND NEVIS
Montserrat (U.K.)
Guadeloupe (France)
DOMINICA
ROSEAU
Martinique (France)
FORT-DE-FRANCE
ST LUCIA
CASTRIES
BARBADOS
BRIDGETOWN
ST VINCENT AND THE GRENADINES
KINGSTOWN
GRENADA
ST GEORGE'S
TRINIDAD AND TOBAGO
PORT OF SPAIN
Aruba (Neth.)
ORANJESTAD
Netherlands Antilles
WILLEMSTAD
Curaçao
Bonaire
VENEZUELA
CARACAS
Maracaibo
Valencia
Barquisimeto
Ciudad Guayana
COLOMBIA
BOGOTÁ
Medellín
Cali
Barranquilla
Cartagena
Bucaramanga
Cúcuta
GUYANA
BRAZIL
Guiana Highlands
Llanos
PANAMA
PANAMA CITY
Gulf of Panama
COSTA RICA
SAN JOSÉ
NICARAGUA
MANAGUA
TEGUCIGALPA
HONDURAS
UNITED STATES
FLORIDA
GEORGIA
SOUTH CAROLINA
NORTH CAROLINA
VIRGINIA
KENTUCKY
TENNESSEE
ALABAMA
Appalachian Mts
Cumberland Plateau
Miami
Orlando
Tampa
Jacksonville
Tallahassee
Atlanta
Charlotte
Raleigh
Richmond
Norfolk
Cape Hatteras
Cape Canaveral
↓ 176

South America
UNESCO World Heritage Sites

The first World Heritage site to be listed in 1978 was the Gálapagos Islands off the coast of South America. Famous for its association with Darwin and its giant tortoises it was followed on to the List by sites representing ancient civilizations, European invaders and the continent's rich and diverse physical and natural environment.

● Cultural site ● Natural site ● Mixed site

Argentina
1. Cueva de las Manos, Río Pinturas
2. Iguazu National Park
3. Ischigualasto/Talampaya Natural Parks
4. Jesuit Block and Estancias of Córdoba
5. Jesuit Missions of the Guaranis: San Ignacio Miní, Santa Ana, Nuestra Señora de Loreto and Santa María Mayor (Argentina), Ruins of Saõ Miguel das Missões (Brazil)
6 Los Glaciares
7 Península Valdés
8. Quebrada de Humahuaca

Bolivia
9. City of Potosí
10. Fuerte de Samaipata
11. Historic City of Sucre
12. Jesuit Missions of the Chiquitos
13. Noel Kempff Mercado National Park
14. Tiwanaku: Spiritual and Political Centre of the Tiwanaku Culture

Brazil
15. Atlantic Forest South-East Reserves
16. Brasilia
17. Brazilian Atlantic Islands: Fernando de Noronha and Atol das Rocas Reserves
18. Central Amazon Conservation Complex
19. Cerrado Protected Areas: Chapada dos Veadeiros and Emas National Parks
20. Discovery Coast Atlantic Forest Reserves
21. Historic Centre of Salvador de Bahia
22. Historic Centre of São Luís
23. Historic Centre of the Town of Diamantina
24. Historic Centre of the Town of Goiás
25. Historic Centre of the Town of Olinda
26. Historic Town of Ouro Preto
27. Iguaçu National Park
5. Jesuit Missions of the Guaranis: San Ignacio Miní, Santa Ana, Nuestra Señora de Loreto and Santa María Mayor (Argentina), Ruins of Saõ Miguel das Missões (Brazil)
28. Pantanal Conservation Area
29. Sanctuary of Bom Jesus do Congonhas
30. Serra da Capivara National Park

Chile
31. Churches of Chiloé
32. Historic Quarter of the Seaport City of Valparaíso
33. Humberstone and Santa Laura Saltpeter Works
34. Rapa Nui National Park
35. Sewell Mining Town

Colombia
36. Historic Centre of Santa Cruz de Mompox
37. Los Katíos National Park
38. Malpelo Fauna and Flora Sanctuary
39. National Archeological Park of Tierradentro
40. Port, Fortresses and Group of Monuments, Cartagena
41. San Agustín Archeological Park

Curaçao
42. Historic Area of Willemstad, Inner City and Harbour, Netherlands Antilles (Netherlands)

Ecuador
43. City of Quito
44. Galápagos Islands
45. Historic Centre of Santa Ana de los Ríos de Cuenca
46. Sangay National Park

Paraguay
47. Jesuit Missions of La Santísima Trinidad de Paraná and Jesús de Tavarangue

Peru
48. Chan Chan Archaeological Zone
49. Chavín (Archaeological site)
50. City of Cuzco
51. Historic Centre of Lima
52. Historic Sanctuary of Machu Picchu
53. Historical Centre of the City of Arequipa
54. Huascarán National Park
55. Lines and Geoglyphs of Nasca and Pampas de Jumana
56. Manú National Park
57. Río Abiseo National Park
58. Sacred City of Caral-Supe

Suriname
59. Central Suriname Nature Reserve
60. Historic Inner City of Paramaribo

Uruguay
61. Historic Quarter of the City of Colonia del Sacramento

Venezuela
62. Canaima National Park
63. Ciudad Universitaria de Caracas
64. Coro and its Port

34
Easter Island (Chile)

Caribbean Sea
NORTH AMERICA
Curaçao (Netherlands)
VENEZUELA
GUYANA
SURINAME
French Guiana
COLOMBIA
ECUADOR
Galápagos Islands (Ecuador)
PERU
BRAZIL
BOLIVIA
PARAGUAY
URUGUAY
ARGENTINA
CHILE
ATLANTIC OCEAN
PACIFIC OCEAN
1
2
3
4
5
6
7
8
9
10
11
12
13
14
15
16
17
18
19
20
21
22
23
24
25
26
27
28
29
30
31
32
33
35
36
37
38
39
40
41
42
43
44
45
46
47
48
49
50
51
52
53
54
55
56
57
58
59
60
61
62
63
64

South America
Landscapes

South America is a continent of great contrasts, with landscapes varying from the tropical rainforests of the Amazon Basin, to the Atacama Desert, the driest place on earth, and the sub-Antarctic regions of southern Chile and Argentina. The dominant physical features are the Andes, stretching along the entire west coast of the continent and containing numerous mountains over 6 000 metres high, and the Amazon, which is the second longest river in the world and has the world's largest drainage basin.

The Altiplano is a high plateau lying between two of the Andes ranges. It contains Lake Titicaca, the world's highest navigable lake. By contrast, large lowland areas dominate the centre of the continent, lying between the Andes and the Guiana and Brazilian Highlands. These vast grasslands stretch from the Llanos of the north through the Selvas and the Gran Chaco to the Pampas of Argentina.

Confluence of the **Amazon** and **Negro** rivers at Manaus, northern Brazil.

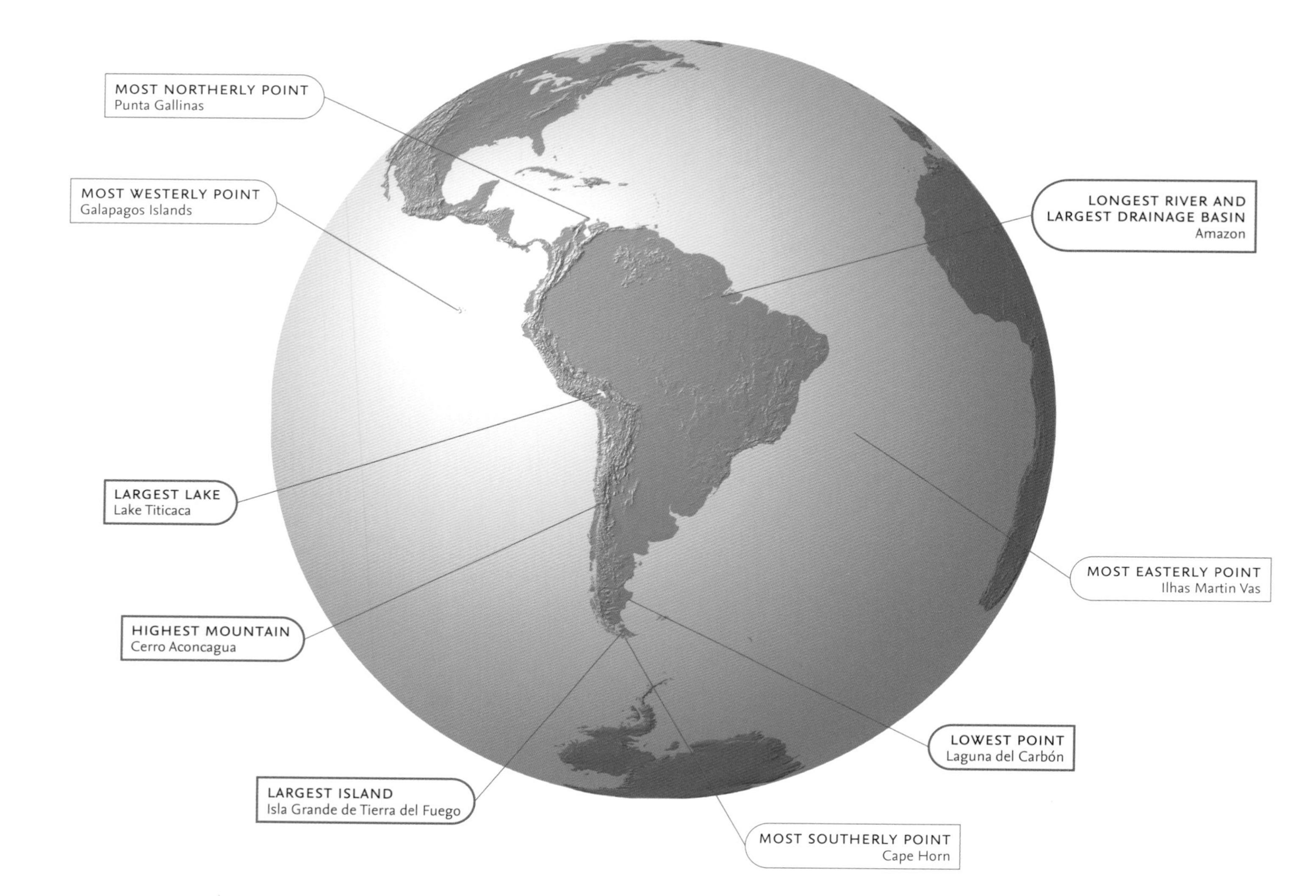
MOST NORTHERLY POINT
Punta Gallinas
MOST WESTERLY POINT
Galapagos Islands
LONGEST RIVER AND LARGEST DRAINAGE BASIN
Amazon
LARGEST LAKE
Lake Titicaca
MOST EASTERLY POINT
Ilhas Martin Vas
HIGHEST MOUNTAIN
Cerro Aconcagua
LOWEST POINT
Laguna del Carbón
LARGEST ISLAND
Isla Grande de Tierra del Fuego
MOST SOUTHERLY POINT
Cape Horn

South America's physical features

Highest mountain	Cerro Aconcagua, Argentina	6 959 metres	22 831 feet
Longest river	Amazon	6 516 km	4 049 miles
Largest lake	Lake Titicaca, Bolivia/Peru	8 340 sq km	3 220 sq miles
Largest island	Isla Grande de Tierra del Fuego, Argentina/Chile	47 000 sq km	18 147 sq miles
Largest drainage basin	Amazon	7 050 000 sq km	2 722 005 sq miles
Lowest point	Laguna del Carbón, Argentina	-105 metres	-345 feet

Internet Links

NASA Visible Earth	**visibleearth.nasa.gov**
NASA Astronaut Photography	**eol.jsc.nasa.gov**
World Rainforest Information Portal	**www.ran.org**
Peakware World Mountain Encyclopedia	**www.peakware.com**

Caribbean Sea
NORTH AMERICA
PACIFIC OCEAN
ATLANTIC OCEAN
Punta Gallinas
Golfo de Venezuela
Isla de Margarita
Golfo del Darién
Lake Maracaibo
Orinoco Delta
Waini Point
Orinoco
Gulf of Panama
Cabo Corrientes
Isla de Malpelo
Cordillera Occidental
Cordillera Central
Magdalena
Cordillera Oriental
Llanos
Meta
Cerro Yavi 2285
Guiana Highlands
La Gran Sabana
Pakaraima Mountains
Point Isère
Maroni
Cabo Orange
Guaviare
Orinoco
Branco
Ilha de Maracá
Mouths of the Amazon
Volcán Cotopaxi 5896
6310 Chimborazo
Caquetá
Japurá
Amazon Basin
Represa de Balbina
Negro
Amazon
Ilha de Marajó
Baía de São Marcos
Galapagos Islands
Punta Santa Elena
Golfo de Guayaquil
Putumayo
Amazon
Xingu
Tocantins
Represa Tucuruí
Marañón
Yavari
Juruá
Purus
Madeira
Tapajós
Selvas
Andes
Cordillera Central
Punta Negra
Ucayali
Iriri
Cabo de São Roque
Nevado de Huascarán 6768
Madeira
Teles Pires
Parnaíba
Barragem de Sobradinho
São Francisco
Juruena
Arinos
Xingu
Araguaia
Tocantins
Jiparaná
Guaporé
Lago de San Luis
Cordillera Oriental
Cordillera Occidental
Beni
Mamoré
Chapada Diamantina
Cabo Santo Antonio
Represa Serra da Mesa
São Francisco
Lake Titicaca
Yungas
San Miguel
Paraguai
Pantanal
Altiplano
Punta de Coles
Bañados del Izozog
Lago de Poopó
Salar de Uyuni
Paranaíba
Velhas
Ponta da Baleia
Brazilian Highlands
Grande
Paraguay
Paranapanema
Cabo de São Tomé
Punta Tetas
Atacama Desert
Gran Chaco
Pilcomayo
Paraná
Teuco
Ilha de São Sebastião
Iguaçu
Iguaçu Falls
Punta Ballena
Nevado Ojos del Salado 6908
Cerro Bonete 6872
Islas Desventuradas
Salado
Salinas Grandes
Uruguay
Serra do Mar
Sierras de Córdoba
Desaguadero
Paraná
Lagoa dos Patos
Pampas
Cerro Aconcagua 6959
Negro
Lagoa Mirim
Salado
Río de la Plata
Punta Norte
Punta Sur
Archipiélago Juan Fernández
Punta Lavapié
Colorado
Negro
Bahía Blanca
Punta Galera
Golfo San Matías
Península Valdés
Isla de Chiloé
Chubut
Patagonia
Archipiélago de los Chonos
Golfo de San Jorge
Cabo Tres Puntas
Golfo de Penas
Lago San Martín
Lago Argentino
Bahía Grande
Falkland Islands
West Falkland
East Falkland
Strait of Magellan
Isla Grande de Tierra del Fuego
Isla de los Estados
Cape Horn
Drake Passage
Scotia Sea
South Georgia

Isla Grande de Tierra del Fuego, South America's largest island, situated at the southernmost tip of the continent.

South America's extent

TOTAL LAND AREA	17 815 420 sq km / 6 878 534 sq miles
Most northerly point	Punta Gallinas, Colombia
Most southerly point	Cape Horn, Chile
Most westerly point	Galagapos Islands, Ecuador
Most easterly point	Ilhas Martin Vas, Atlantic Ocean

Facts

- Water flow along the Amazon is over 1 500 times that of the River Thames
- Cerro Aconcagua, 6 959 metres, is the highest point in the western hemisphere
- The Amazon rainforest supports approximately half of all the world's living species
- The Pantanal in Brazil is the largest area of wetland in the world
- The world's driest desert is the Atacama, where only 1mm of rain may fall as infrequently as once every 5–20 years

South America
Countries

French Guiana, a French Department, is the only remaining territory under overseas control on a continent which has seen a long colonial history. Much of South America was colonized by Spain in the sixteenth century, with Britain, Portugal and the Netherlands each claiming territory in the northeast of the continent. This colonization led to the conquering of ancient civilizations, including the Incas in Peru. Most countries became independent from Spain and Portugal in the early nineteenth century.

The population of the continent reflects its history, being composed primarily of indigenous Indian peoples and mestizos – reflecting the long Hispanic influence. There has been a steady process of urbanization within the continent, with major movements of the population from rural to urban areas. The majority of the population now lives in the major cities and within 300 kilometres of the coast.

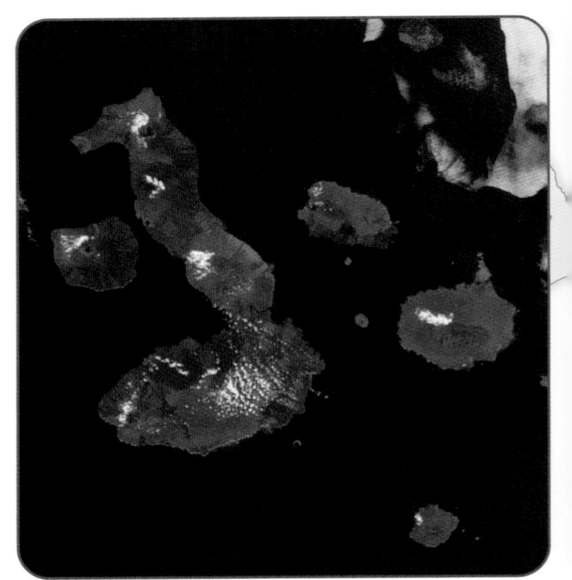

Galapagos Islands, an island territory of Ecuador which lies on the equator in the eastern Pacific Ocean over 900 kilometres west of the coast of Ecuador.

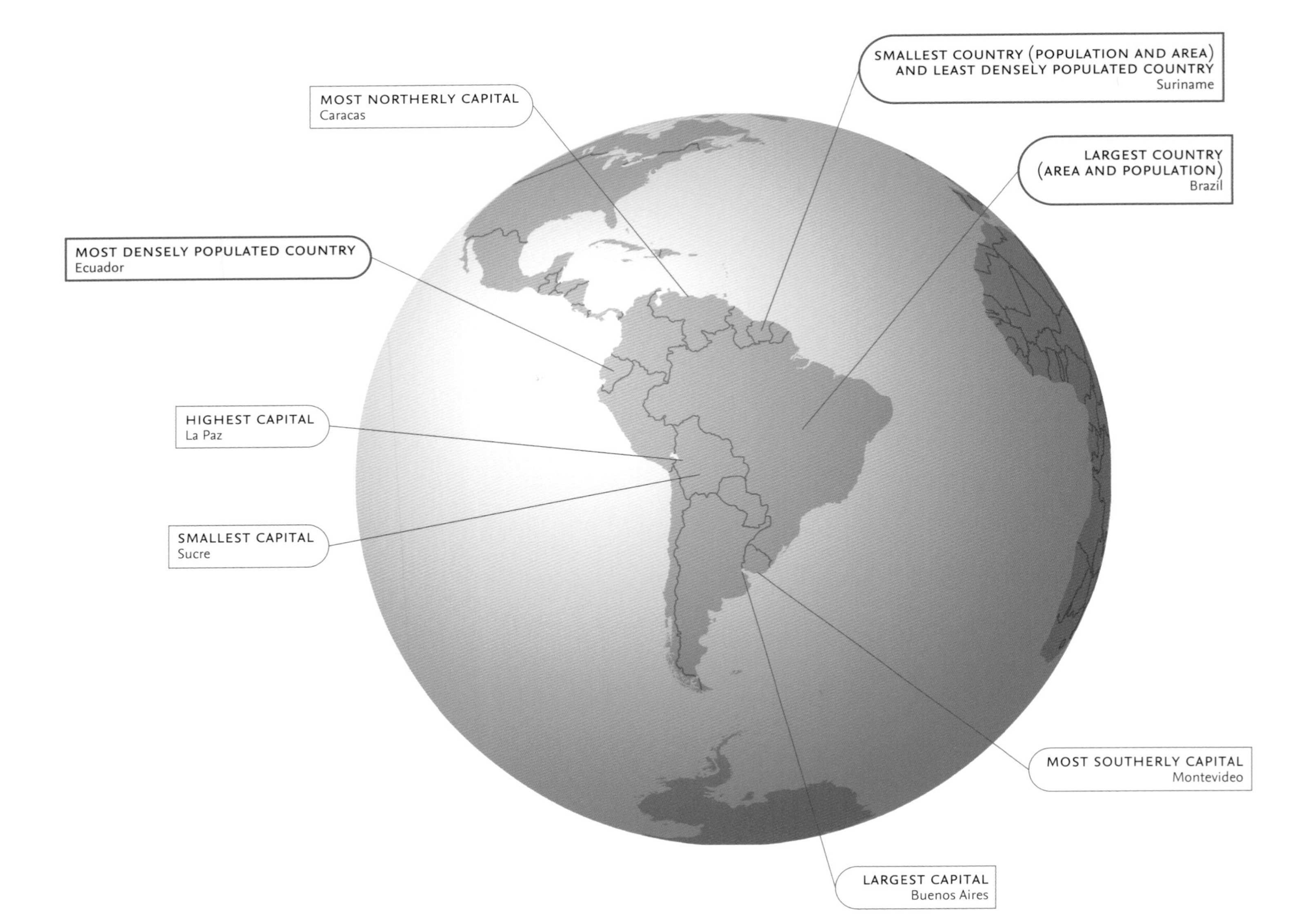
MOST NORTHERLY CAPITAL
Caracas
SMALLEST COUNTRY (POPULATION AND AREA) AND LEAST DENSELY POPULATED COUNTRY
Suriname
LARGEST COUNTRY (AREA AND POPULATION)
Brazil
MOST DENSELY POPULATED COUNTRY
Ecuador
HIGHEST CAPITAL
La Paz
SMALLEST CAPITAL
Sucre
MOST SOUTHERLY CAPITAL
Montevideo
LARGEST CAPITAL
Buenos Aires

South America's countries

Largest country (area)	Brazil	8 514 879 sq km	3 287 613 sq miles
Smallest country (area)	Suriname	163 820 sq km	63 251 sq miles
Largest country (population)	Brazil	186 405 000	
Smallest country (population)	Suriname	449 000	
Most densely populated country	Ecuador	48 per sq km	124 per sq mile
Least densely populated country	Suriname	3 per sq km	7 per sq mile

Internet Links

UK Foreign and Commonwealth Office	**www.fco.gov.uk**
CIA World Factbook	**www.cia.gov/library/publications/the-world-factbook/index.html**
Caribbean Community (Caricom)	**www.caricom.org**
Latin American Network Information Center	**lanic.utexas.edu**

Caribbean Sea
NORTH AMERICA
Punta Gallinas
Barranquilla
Cartagena
Maracaibo
Cabimas
Maracay
Caracas
Barquisimeto
Valencia
Cumaná
Ciudad Bolívar
Orinoco
Montería
San Cristóbal
VENEZUELA
Georgetown
Paramaribo
Cayenne
GUYANA
SURINAME
French Guiana
Meta
Medellín
Puerto Ayacucho
Tunja
Bogotá
Ibagué
Cali
COLOMBIA
Guaviare
Neiva
Isla de Malpelo (Colombia)
Boa Vista
Branco
Pasto
Esmeraldas
Caquetá
Japurá
Mouths of the Amazon
Represa de Balbina
Negro
Amazon
Xingu
Quito
Manta
ECUADOR
Guayaquil
Cuenca
Putumayo
Tonantins
Manaus
Santarém
Belém
São Luís
Parnaíba
Fortaleza
Galapagos Islands (Ecuador)
Iquitos
Marañón
Yavari
Juruá
Carauari
Purus
Madeira
Tapajós
Tocantins
Represa Tucuruí
Marabá
Teresina
Natal
Sullana
Tarapoto
Chiclayo
Trujillo
Ucayali
Pucallpa
Cruzeiro do Sul
Iriri
Teles Pires
Parnaíba
João Pessoa
Recife
Maceió
Aracaju
Porto Velho
B R A Z I L
Araguaia
Tocantins
Xingu
Juruena
Arinos
São Francisco
Juàzeiro
Florestal
PERU
Rio Branco
Jiparaná
Guaporé
Callao
Lima
Huancayo
Puerto Maldonado
Beni
Mamoré
Lago de San Luis
Trinidad
Cuiabá
Salvador
Ilhéus
PACIFIC OCEAN
Ica
Cusco
Juliaca
Lake Titicaca
BOLIVIA
La Paz
Arequipa
Cochabamba
Santa Cruz
Pantanal
Brasília
Goiânia
Teófilo Otôni
Arica
Sucre
Potosí
Patos de Minas
Uberaba
Campo Grande
Iquique
Tarija
PARAGUAY
Pedro Juan Caballero
Araçatuba
Ribeirão Preto
Belo Horizonte
Vitória
Paranapanema
Campinas
Nova Iguaçu
Rio de Janeiro
Antofagasta
San Salvador de Jujuy
Pilcomayo
Maringá
São Paulo
Teuco
Asunción
Foz do Iguaçu
Curitiba
San Miguel de Tucumán
Formosa
Resistencia
Corrientes
Encarnación
Posadas
Joinville
Florianópolis
Copiapó
Islas Desventuradas (Chile)
Catamarca
Salado
La Rioja
Santa Maria
Porto Alegre
Lagoa dos Patos
ATLANTIC OCEAN
San Juan
Córdoba
Santa Fé
Paraná
Concordia
Paysandú
Rio Grande
Cerro Aconcagua 6959
Mendoza
San Luis
Rosario
URUGUAY
Valparaíso
Santiago
Archipiélago Juan Fernández (Chile)
San Rafael
Buenos Aires
La Plata
Montevideo
Río de la Plata
Talca
Chillán
ARGENTINA
Concepción
Colorado
Santa Rosa
Bahía Blanca
Mar del Plata
Neuquén
Valdivia
Negro
Viedma
Puerto Montt
Isla de Chiloé
Patagonia
Trelew
CHILE
Comodoro Rivadavia
Golfo de San Jorge
Archipiélago de los Chonos
Punta Medanosa
Falkland Islands (U.K.)
Stanley
Bahía Grande
Río Gallegos
Puerto Natales
Punta Arenas
Isla Grande de Tierra del Fuego
Ushuaia
Cape Horn
South Georgia (U.K.)

South America's capitals

Largest capital (population)	Buenos Aires, Argentina	13 349 000
Smallest capital (population)	Sucre, Bolivia	231 000
Most northerly capital	Caracas, Venezuela	10° 28'N
Most southerly capital	Montevideo, Uruguay	34° 52'S
Highest capital	La Paz, Bolivia	3 630 metres 11 909 feet

Facts

- South America is often referred to as 'Latin America', reflecting the historic influences of Spain and Portugal
- The largest city in each South American country is the capital, except in Brazil and Ecuador
- South America has only two landlocked countries – Bolivia and Paraguay
- Chile is over 4 000 kilometres long but has an average width of only 177 kilometres

Falkland Islands, an overseas UK territory in the South Atlantic Ocean.

NICARAGUA
MANAGUA
COSTA RICA
SAN JOSE
PANAMA
PANAMA CITY
Gulf of Panama
Isthmus of Panama
COLOMBIA
BOGOTÁ
Medellín
Cali
Cartagena
Barranquilla
Bucaramanga
VENEZUELA
CARACAS
Maracaibo
Valencia
Barquisimeto
Ciudad Guayana
TRINIDAD AND TOBAGO
GRENADA
ST GEORGE'S
Netherlands Antilles
ECUADOR
QUITO
Guayaquil
Equator
PERU
LIMA
Callao
Trujillo
Arequipa
Iquitos
Cusco
BOLIVIA
LA PAZ
SUCRE
Santa Cruz
Cochabamba
CHILE
Arica
Iquique
Antofagasta
ARGENTINA
Manaus
Porto Velho
Rio Branco
Llanos
Guiana Highlands
Selvas
Andes
Lake Titicaca
Tropic of Capricorn
PACIFIC OCEAN
Galapagos Islands (Islas Galápagos) (Ecuador)
Isla Fernandina
Isla Isabela
Isla Santa Cruz
Isla San Salvador
Isla San Cristóbal
Isla Santa María
1:14 000 000

Lambert Azimuthal Equal Area Projection

1:14 000 000 — 0, 200, 400 miles; 0, 200, 400, 600, 800 km

ATLANTIC OCEAN
BRAZIL
GUYANA
SURINAME
French Guiana
PARAGUAY
GEORGETOWN
PARAMARIBO
CAYENNE
BRASÍLIA
Brazilian Highlands
Mouths of the Amazon
Equator
Macapá
Belém
São Luís
Teresina
Fortaleza (Ceará)
Natal
João Pessoa
Recife (Pernambuco)
Maceió
Aracaju
Salvador (Bahia)
Vitória
Belo Horizonte
Rio de Janeiro
São Paulo
Campinas
Goiânia
Campo Grande
Cuiabá
Santarém
Altamira
Marabá
Palmas
Imperatriz
Juazeiro
Petrolina
Feira de Santana
Uberlândia
Ilha de Marajó
Ilhas de São João
Fernando de Noronha (Brazil)
Ilha da Trindade (Brazil)
Cabo de São Roque
Cabo de São Tomé
Cabo Frio
Serra do Espinhaço
Chapada Diamantina
Serra do Cachimbo
Serra dos Carajás
Serra do Gurupi
Serra Tumucumaque
Pantanal
Chaco Boreal
↓ 178

BOLIVIA
PARAGUAY
BRAZIL
URUGUAY
ARGENTINA
CHILE
PATAGONIA
ATLANTIC OCEAN
ASUNCIÓN
SANTIAGO
BUENOS AIRES
MONTEVIDEO
São Paulo
Rio de Janeiro
Belo Horizonte
Curitiba
Porto Alegre
Florianópolis
Córdoba
Rosario
Mendoza
Mar del Plata
Bahía Blanca
Valparaíso
Concepción
Antofagasta
Iquique
Tropic of Capricorn
Río de la Plata
Golfo San Matías
Golfo de San Jorge
Península Valdés
Falkland Islands
(U.K.)
West Falkland
East Falkland
STANLEY
South Georgia
(U.K.)
Isla Grande de Tierra del Fuego
Cape Horn
Islas Wollaston
Isla de los Estados
Estrecho de Le Maire
Isla de Chiloé
Archipiélago de los Chonos
Archipiélago de la Reina Adelaida
Isla Desolación
Lagoa dos Patos
Lambert Azimuthal Equal Area Projection

South America

Southern South America

1:14 000 000

BRAZIL
MATO GROSSO
TOCANTINS
GOIÁS
DISTRITO FEDERAL
BRASÍLIA
BAHIA
MINAS GERAIS
ESPÍRITO SANTO
RIO DE JANEIRO
SÃO PAULO
PARANÁ
SANTA CATARINA
RIO GRANDE DO SUL
ATLANTIC OCEAN
Salvador (Bahia)
Belo Horizonte
Vitória
Rio de Janeiro
São Paulo
Campinas
Curitiba
Florianópolis
Porto Alegre
Goiânia
Tropic of Capricorn
↑ 177
← 178

Lambert Azimuthal Equal Area Projection

1:7 000 000 0 100 200 miles; 0 100 200 300 400 km

South America
Southeast Brazil

Protected from commercial exploitation and from the implementation of territorial claims by the Antarctic Treaty implemented in 1959, Antarctica is perhaps the world's greatest unspoilt, and relatively unexplored, wilderness. This image combines bathymetric data (incomplete in some black areas) with satellite images to show the extent of the continental ice sheet in an austral summer.

Floating sea ice is not shown. The Antarctic Peninsula – home to numerous scientific research stations – in the top left of the image reaching towards South America, the huge Ronne and Ross ice shelves, and the Transantarctic Mountains – dividing the continent into West and East Antarctica – are the dominant physical features.

Oceans and Poles
Features

Between them, the world's oceans and polar regions cover approximately seventy per cent of the Earth's surface. The oceans contain ninety-six per cent of the Earth's water and a vast range of flora and fauna. They are a major influence on the world's climate, particularly through ocean currents. The Arctic and Antarctica are the coldest and most inhospitable places on the Earth. They both have vast amounts of ice which, if global warming continues, could have a major influence on sea level across the globe.

Our understanding of the oceans and polar regions has increased enormously over the last twenty years through the development of new technologies, particularly that of satellite remote sensing, which can generate vast amounts of data relating to, for example, topography (both on land and the seafloor), land cover and sea surface temperature.

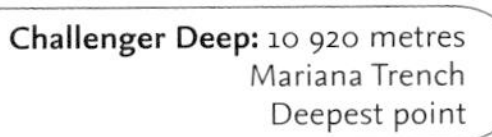

Challenger Deep: 10 920 metres
Mariana Trench
Deepest point

Pacific Ocean
World's largest ocean: 166 241 000 sq km
Average depth: 4 200m
PACIFIC
OCEAN
AUSTRALIA
South Pacific Ocean
Average depth: 3 935 metres

The oceans

The world's major oceans are the Pacific, the Atlantic and the Indian Oceans. The Arctic Ocean is generally considered as part of the Atlantic, and the Southern Ocean, which stretches around the whole of Antarctica is usually treated as an extension of each of the three major oceans.

One of the most important factors affecting the earth's climate is the circulation of water within and between the oceans. Differences in temperature and surface winds create ocean currents which move enormous quantities of water around the globe. These currents re-distribute heat which the oceans have absorbed from the sun, and so have a major effect on the world's climate system. El Niño is one climatic phenomenon directly influenced by these ocean processes.

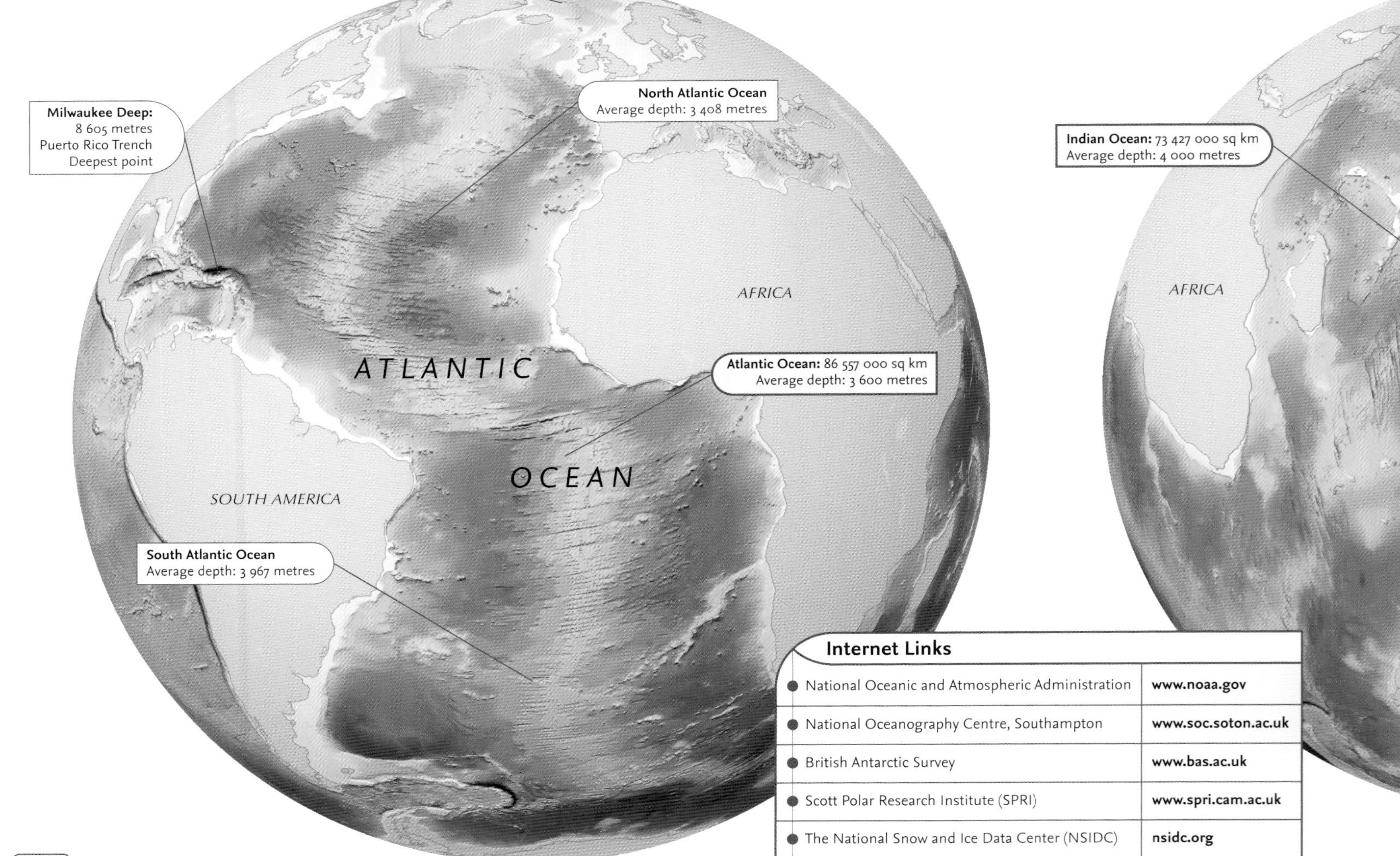

Arctic Ocean: 9 485 000 sq km
Average depth: 2 496 metres
Milwaukee Deep:
8 605 metres
Puerto Rico Trench
Deepest point
North Atlantic Ocean
Average depth: 3 408 metres
AFRICA
ATLANTIC
OCEAN
Atlantic Ocean: 86 557 000 sq km
Average depth: 3 600 metres
SOUTH AMERICA
South Atlantic Ocean
Average depth: 3 967 metres
Indian Ocean: 73 427 000 sq km
Average depth: 4 000 metres
AFRICA

Internet Links

National Oceanic and Atmospheric Administration	**www.noaa.gov**
National Oceanography Centre, Southampton	**www.soc.soton.ac.uk**
British Antarctic Survey	**www.bas.ac.uk**
Scott Polar Research Institute (SPRI)	**www.spri.cam.ac.uk**
The National Snow and Ice Data Center (NSIDC)	**nsidc.org**

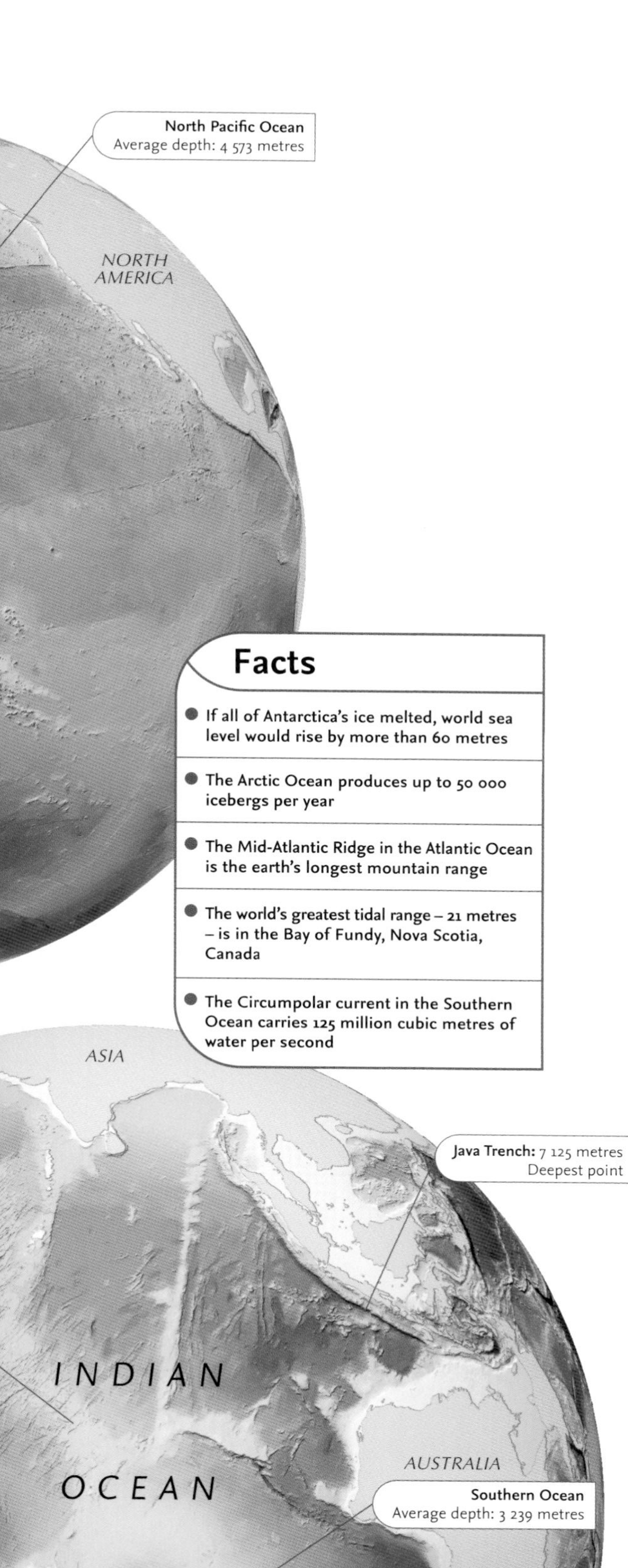
North Pacific Ocean
Average depth: 4 573 metres
NORTH AMERICA
ASIA
Java Trench: 7 125 metres
Deepest point
INDIAN
OCEAN
AUSTRALIA
Southern Ocean
Average depth: 3 239 metres
ANTARCTICA

Facts

- If all of Antarctica's ice melted, world sea level would rise by more than 60 metres
- The Arctic Ocean produces up to 50 000 icebergs per year
- The Mid-Atlantic Ridge in the Atlantic Ocean is the earth's longest mountain range
- The world's greatest tidal range – 21 metres – is in the Bay of Fundy, Nova Scotia, Canada
- The Circumpolar current in the Southern Ocean carries 125 million cubic metres of water per second

Polar regions

Although a harsh climate is common to the two polar regions, there are major differences between the Arctic and Antarctica. The North Pole is surrounded by the Arctic Ocean, much of which is permanently covered by sea ice, while the South Pole lies on the huge land mass of Antarctica. This is covered by a permanent ice cap which reaches a maximum thickness of over four kilometres. Antarctica has no permanent population, but Europe, Asia and North America all stretch into the Arctic region which is populated by numerous ethnic groups. Antarctica is subject to the Antarctic Treaty of 1959 which does not recognize individual land claims and protects the continent in the interests of international scientific cooperation.

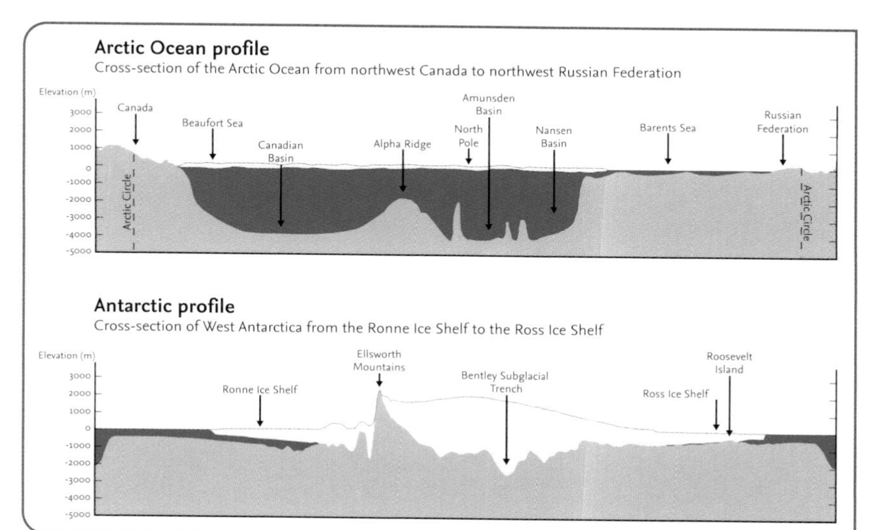
Arctic Ocean profile
Cross-section of the Arctic Ocean from northwest Canada to northwest Russian Federation
Elevation (m)
3000
2000
1000
0
-1000
-2000
-3000
-4000
-5000
Canada
Beaufort Sea
Canadian Basin
Alpha Ridge
Amundsen Basin
North Pole
Nansen Basin
Barents Sea
Russian Federation
Arctic Circle
Arctic Circle
Antarctic profile
Cross-section of West Antarctica from the Ronne Ice Shelf to the Ross Ice Shelf
Elevation (m)
3000
2000
1000
0
-1000
-2000
-3000
-4000
-5000
Ronne Ice Shelf
Ellsworth Mountains
Bentley Subglacial Trench
Ross Ice Shelf
Roosevelt Island

Antarctica's physical features

Highest mountain: Vinson Massif	4 897 m	16 066 ft
Total land area (excluding ice shelves)	12 093 000 sq km	4 669 107 sq miles
Ice shelves	1 559 000 sq km	601 930 sq miles
Exposed rock	49 000 sq km	18 919 sq miles
Lowest bedrock elevation (Bentley Subglacial Trench)	2 496 m below sea level	8 189 ft below sea level
Maximum ice thickness (Astrolabe Subglacial Basin)	4 776 m	15 669 ft
Mean ice thickness (including ice shelves)	1 859 m	6 099 ft
Volume of ice sheet (including ice shelves)	25 400 000 cubic km	6 094 628 cubic miles

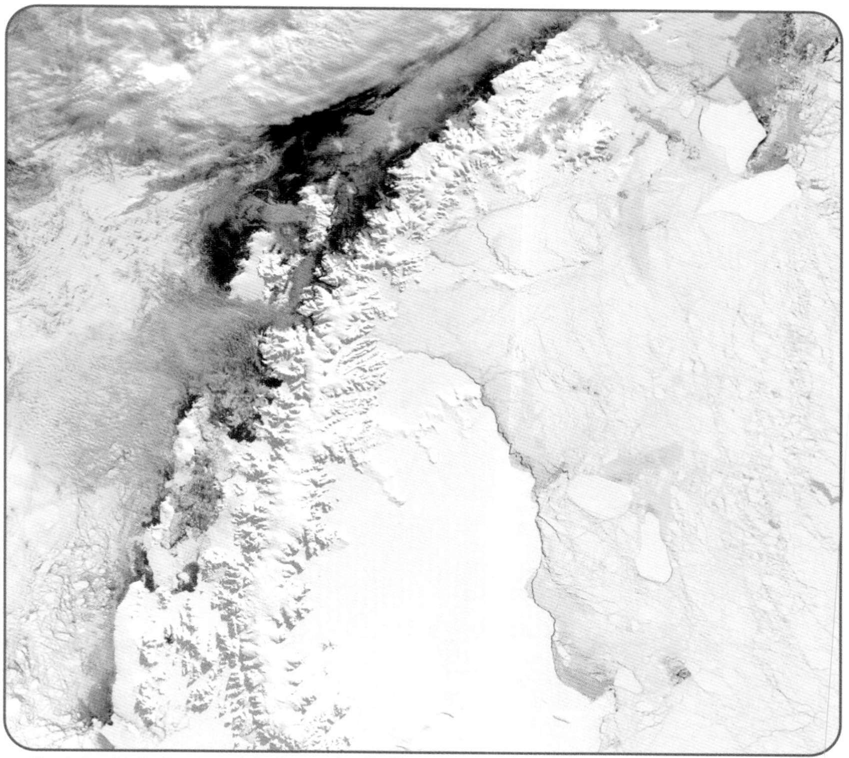

The **Antarctic Peninsula** and the **Larsen Ice Shelf** in western Antarctica.

CANADA
UNITED STATES OF AMERICA
Rocky Mountains
Baja California
Chicago
Milwaukee
Detroit
Toronto
Montreal
OTTAWA
Québec
Indianapolis
St Louis
Nashville
Memphis
Columbus
Cleveland
Pittsburgh
Buffalo
Boston
Providence
New York
Philadelphia
Baltimore
WASHINGTON D.C.
Richmond
Raleigh
Charlotte
Atlanta
Appalachian Mountains
Dallas
Fort Worth
El Paso
Ciudad Juárez
Tucson
Albuquerque
Oklahoma City
Tulsa
Amarillo
Lubbock
Austin
San Antonio
Houston
Corpus Christi
Baton Rouge
New Orleans
Mobile
Montgomery
Tallahassee
Jacksonville
Savannah
Orlando
Tampa
Miami
Cape Hatteras
Cape Cod
Halifax
Cape Sable
Newfoundland
St John's
Gander
Cape Race
St Pierre and Miquelon (France)
Grand Banks of Newfoundland
Gulf of St Lawrence
New England Seamounts
Bermuda (U.K.)
Bermuda Rise
Hatteras Abyssal Plain
Corner Seamounts
Gulf of Mexico
MEXICO
MEXICO CITY
Monterrey
Guadalajara
León
San Luis Potosí
Tampico
Mérida
Puebla
Acapulco
Hermosillo
Mazatlán
Durango
Matamoros
Tropic of Cancer
Islas Revillagigedo (Mexico)
Florida Keys
Straits of Florida
Grand Bahama
THE BAHAMAS
NASSAU
Andros
HAVANA
CUBA
Holguín
Cayman Islands (U.K.)
Cayman Trench
Yucatán Channel
Nares Abyssal Plain
Nares Deep
Sargasso Sea
Turks and Caicos Islands
PORT-AU-PRINCE
HAITI
DOMINICAN REP.
SANTO DOMINGO
JAMAICA
KINGSTON
Puerto Rico
Puerto Rico Trench
Milwaukee Deep
ST KITTS AND NEVIS
ANTIGUA AND BARBUDA
Guadeloupe (France)
DOMINICA
Martinique (France)
ST LUCIA
ST VINCENT AND THE GRENADINES
BARBADOS
GRENADA
PORT OF SPAIN
TRINIDAD AND TOBAGO
Aruba
Netherlands Antilles
Caribbean Sea
Venezuelan Basin
Colombian Basin
GUATEMALA
GUATEMALA CITY
BELIZE
BELMOPAN
HONDURAS
TEGUCIGALPA
SAN SALVADOR
EL SALVADOR
NICARAGUA
MANAGUA
Lake Nicaragua
COSTA RICA
SAN JOSÉ
PANAMA
PANAMA CITY
Gulf of Panama
Middle America Trench
Isla de Coco (Costa Rica)
Cocos Ridge
Isla de Malpelo (Colombia)
Barranquilla
Cartagena
Maracaibo
Barquisimeto
CARACAS
Cumaná
VENEZUELA
Valencia
San Cristóbal
Ciudad Bolívar
Orinoco
Puerto Ayacucho
Llanos
Medellín
Ibagué
Tunja
BOGOTÁ
Cali
Neiva
COLOMBIA
GEORGETOWN
PARAMARIBO
CAYENNE
GUYANA
SURINAME
French Guiana
Boa Vista
Amazon Cone
Demerara Abyssal Plain
Guiana Basin
Ceara Abyssal Plain
Esmeraldas
Pasto
Equator
QUITO
ECUADOR
Guayaquil
Galapagos Islands (Ecuador)
Iquitos
Amazon
Negro
Manaus
Santarém
Belém
São Luís
Parnaíba
Fortaleza
Teresina
Natal
João Pessoa
Recife
Maceió
Aracaju
Salvador
Ilhéus
Floresta
Juazeiro
Marabá
Tocantins
Xingu
Tapajós
Madeira
Selvas
Carauari
Cruzeiro do Sul
Rio Branco
Porto Velho
Pucallpa
BRAZIL
PACIFIC OCEAN
Sullana
Tarapoto
Chiclayo
Trujillo
PERU
Huancayo
LIMA
Cusco
Ica
Juliaca
Arequipa
Arica
LA PAZ
BOLIVIA
Trinidad
SUCRE
Santa Cruz
Potosí
Tarija
Cuiabá
Goiânia
BRASÍLIA
Teófilo Otoni
Belo Horizonte
Vitória
Uberaba
Patos de Minas
Campo Grande
Ribeirão Preto
Araçatuba
Campinas
São Paulo
Rio de Janeiro
Santos Plateau
Curitiba
Florianópolis
PARAGUAY
ASUNCIÓN
Formosa
Resistencia
Corrientes
Posadas
Santa Maria
Porto Alegre
Rio Grande
Iquique
Antofagasta
San Salvador de Jujuy
San Miguel de Tucumán
Catamarca
La Rioja
Córdoba
Paraná
Rosario
Concordia
Paysandú
URUGUAY
BUENOS AIRES
MONTEVIDEO
Río de la Plata
Copiapó
San Juan
Mendoza
San Luis
Cerro Aconcagua
Valparaíso
SANTIAGO
Talca
Chillán
Concepción
Santa Rosa
Mar del Plata
Bahía Blanca
Neuquén
Viedma
Golfo San Matías
Valdivia
Puerto Montt
Isla de Chiloé
Trelew
Comodoro Rivadavia
Golfo de San Jorge
Archipiélago de los Chonos
Golfo de Penas
Río Gallegos
Punta Arenas
Ushuaia
Isla Grande de Tierra del Fuego
Isla de los Estados
Cape Horn
Drake Passage
ARGENTINA
Andes
Argentine Rise
Argentine Basin
Argentine Abyssal Plain
Falkland Escarpment
Falkland Islands (U.K.)
STANLEY
Falkland Plateau
Shag Rocks
South Georgia (U.K.)
Meteor Depth
South Sandwich Trench
South Sandwich Islands (U.K.)
Scotia Ridge
Scotia Sea
South Orkney Islands (U.K.)
Yaghan Basin
Elephant Island
South Shetland Islands (U.K.)
Joinville Island
Bransfield Strait
Antarctic Peninsula
Larsen Ice Shelf
Weddell Sea
Weddell Abyssal Plain
Riiser-Larsen Ice Shelf
Brunt Ice Shelf
Norvegia
Kirwan Escarpment
Queen Maud
Fimbull Ice Shelf
Maud Seamount
Atlantic-Indian Ridge
American-Antarctic Ridge
Bouvetøya (Norway)
Shona Ridge
Agulhas Ridge
Cape Basin
Gough Island (U.K.)
Tristan da Cunha (U.K.)
Vema Seamount
Walvis Ridge
Namibia Abyssal Plain
Angola Basin
St Helena and Dependencies (U.K.)
JAMESTOWN
St Helena
Ascension (U.K.)
Mid-Atlantic Ridge
Brazil Basin
Rio Grande Rise
Ilhas Martin Vas (Brazil)
Ilha da Trindade (Brazil)
Vitória Seamount
Abrolhos Bank
Pernambuco Plain
Fernando de Noronha (Brazil)
Romanche Gap
São Pedro e São Paulo (Brazil)
ATLANTIC OCEAN
Guinea Basin
Sierra Leone Basin
Sierra Leone Rise
Cape Verde Basin
CAPE VERDE
PRAIA
Cape Verde Plateau
Krylov Seamount
Galapagos Rise
Peru Basin
Peru-Chile Trench
Nazca Ridge
(South-West Peru Ridge)
Islas Desventuradas (Chile)
Chile Basin
Chile Rise
Archipiélago Juan Fernández (Chile)
Roggeveen Basin
Isla Sala y Gomez (Chile)
Easter Island (Isla de Pascua) (Chile)
Tropic of Capricorn
Mornington Abyssal Plain
Greenland (Denmark)
Irminger Basin
Eirik Ridge
Reykjanes Ridge
Iceland Basin
ICELAND
REYKJAVIK
Faroe Islands (Denmark)
TÓRSHAVN
Norwegian Basin
Vøring Plateau
Norwegian Sea
Shetland Islands
Orkney Islands
NORWAY
OSLO
Rockall Bank
British Isles
UNITED KINGDOM
IRELAND
DUBLIN
Belfast
Edinburgh
LONDON
North Sea
COPENHAGEN
DENMARK
NETH.
AMSTERDAM
THE HAGUE
BERLIN
GERMANY
BRUSSELS
PARIS
Celtic Shelf
English Channel
Porcupine Abyssal Plain
Rennes
Nantes
Biscay Abyssal Plain
Bay of Biscay
Bordeaux
FRANCE
Toulouse
Marseille
Corsica
ITALY
ROME
Naples
Sardinia
Tyrrhenian Sea
A Coruña
Azores-Biscay Rise
Azores (Portugal)
PONTA DELGADA
São Miguel
Oporto
PORTUGAL
LISBON
MADRID
SPAIN
Seville
Barcelona
Cádiz
Gibraltar (U.K.)
Strait of Gibraltar
Horseshoe Seamounts
Great Meteor Tablemount
Monaco Basin
Madeira (Portugal)
FUNCHAL
RABAT
Casablanca
MOROCCO
Marrakech
Oran
ALGIERS
Bejaïa
TUNIS
TUNISIA
Sfax
Gabès
TRIPOLI
Laghouat
Béchar
Las Palmas de Gran Canaria
LAÂYOUNE
WESTERN SAHARA
ALGERIA
Sahara
Hoggar
Ténéré du Tafassâsset
Nouâdhibou
MAURITANIA
NOUAKCHOTT
MALI
NIGER
Agadez
Zinder
St-Louis
DAKAR
SENEGAL
BANJUL
THE GAMBIA
BISSAU
GUINEA-BISSAU
Kayes
BAMAKO
GUINEA
Mopti
Ségou
Gao
Niger
NIAMEY
BURKINA
Bobo-Dioulasso
OUAGADOUGOU
Kankan
CONAKRY
FREETOWN
SIERRA LEONE
MONROVIA
LIBERIA
CÔTE D'IVOIRE
YAMOUSSOUKRO
Abidjan
GHANA
Kumasi
ACCRA
LOMÉ
BENIN
PORTO-NOVO
Lagos
Ibadan
Ogbomosho
ABUJA
NIGERIA
Sokoto
Kano
Zaria
Maiduguri
Lake Chad
Port Harcourt
CAMEROON
YAOUNDÉ
Douala
MALABO
Bioco
Gulf of Guinea
Niger Cone
Príncipe
SÃO TOMÉ AND PRÍNCIPE
SÃO TOMÉ
Annobón
EQUATORIAL GUINEA
LIBREVILLE
GABON
Port-Gentil
BRAZZAVILLE
Pointe-Noire
Congo Cone
LUANDA
Benguela
Lubango
Namibe
Orange Cone
Mid-Atlantic Ridge
Northwest Atlantic Mid-Ocean Channel
Labrador Sea
Lambert Azimuthal Equal Area Projection
1:50 000 000
0 500 1000 1500 miles
0 500 1000 1500 2000 2500 km

RUSSIAN FEDERATION
West Siberian Plain
FINLAND
HELSINKI
St Petersburg
Moscow
Nizhniy Novgorod
Kazan'
Perm'
Yekaterinburg
Chelyabinsk
Omsk
Novosibirsk
Tomsk
Krasnoyarsk
Barnaul
Ufa
Samara
Orenburg
Volgograd
Saratov
Voronezh
MINSK
BELARUS
WARSAW
KIEV
UKRAINE
Kharkiv
Dnipropetrovs'k
Donets'k
Rostov-na-Donu
Astrakhan'
Krasnodar
MOLDOVA
CHIȘINĂU
BUDAPEST
ROMANIA
BELGRADE
BUCHAREST
BULGARIA
SOFIA
İstanbul
ANKARA
TURKEY
Black Sea
Caspian Sea
Aral Sea
KAZAKHSTAN
ASTANA
Karaganda
UZBEKISTAN
TASHKENT
BISHKEK
Almaty
KYRGYZSTAN
TAJIKISTAN
DUSHANBE
TURKMENISTAN
AŞGABAT
GEORGIA
T'BILISI
YEREVAN
BAKU
Thessaloniki
ATHENS
GREECE
Izmir
Bursa
Adana
Antalya
NICOSIA
CYPRUS
LEBANON
BEIRUT
SYRIA
DAMASCUS
AMMAN
JERUSALEM
ISRAEL
JORDAN
IRAQ
BAGHDAD
TEHRĀN
IRAN
Mashhad
Esfahān
Shīrāz
KUWAIT
Basra
Bandar-e 'Abbās
Riyadh
SAUDI ARABIA
Medina
Jeddah
Mecca
Arabian Peninsula
Rub' al Khālī
QATAR
DOHA
BAHRAIN
MANAMA
ABU DHABI
U.A.E.
Dubai
MUSCAT
OMAN
Gulf of Oman
SAN'A'
YEMEN
Aden
Mukalla
Gulf of Aden
Socotra (Yemen)
Alexandria
CAIRO
Giza
EGYPT
Aswān
Red Sea
Nubian Desert
Libyan Desert
Tibesti
CHAD
Omdurman
KHARTOUM
SUDAN
ERITREA
ASMARA
DJIBOUTI
ADDIS ABABA
ETHIOPIA
Hargeysa
SOMALIA
MOGADISHU
KENYA
NAIROBI
Mombasa
KAMPALA
UGANDA
KIGALI
RWANDA
BURUNDI
BUJUMBURA
DODOMA
TANZANIA
Dar es Salaam
Zanzibar
DEMOCRATIC REPUBLIC OF THE CONGO
KINSHASA
CENTRAL AFRICAN REPUBLIC
BANGUI
Lake Victoria
Great Rift Valley
ANGOLA
ZAMBIA
LUSAKA
Lubumbashi
HARARE
ZIMBABWE
MALAWI
LILONGWE
MOZAMBIQUE
Mozambique Channel
Beira
Bulawayo
BOTSWANA
GABORONE
PRETORIA
Johannesburg
Soweto
MAPUTO
SWAZILAND
MASERU
LESOTHO
REPUBLIC OF SOUTH AFRICA
Durban
East London
Port Elizabeth
CAPE TOWN
Cape Agulhas
Kalahari Desert
COMOROS
MORONI
Mayotte (France)
ANTANANARIVO
MADAGASCAR
Toamasina
Mahajanga
Toliara
MAURITIUS
PORT LOUIS
Réunion (France)
ST-DENIS
SEYCHELLES
VICTORIA
CHINA
BEIJING
Shanghai
Tianjin
Chongqing
Wuhan
Chengdu
Nanjing
Hangzhou
Guangzhou
Hong Kong
Kowloon
Kunming
Lanzhou
Xi'an
Ürümqi
Plateau of Tibet
Himalaya
Kunlun Shan
Tarim Basin
Gobi Desert
MONGOLIA
ULAN BATOR
NORTH KOREA
PYONGYANG
SOUTH KOREA
SEOUL
Busan
JAPAN
TOKYO
Osaka
Hiroshima
Kita-Kyūshū
Fukuoka
Kagoshima
TAIPEI
TAIWAN
AFGHANISTAN
KĀBUL
Herāt
Kandahār
PAKISTAN
ISLAMABAD
Rawalpindi
Lahore
Faisalabad
Multan
Quetta
Hyderabad
Karachi
INDIA
Delhi
NEW DELHI
NEPAL
KATHMANDU
BHUTAN
BANGLADESH
DHAKA
Kolkata
Ahmadabad
Jaipur
Kanpur
Lucknow
Varanasi
Patna
Nagpur
Surat
Vadodara
Mumbai
Pune
Hyderabad
Bangalore
Chennai
Coimbatore
Madurai
Cochin
Trivandrum
Vishakhapatnam
Deccan
SRI LANKA
SRI JAYEWARDENEPURA KOTTE
Colombo
MALE
MALDIVES
Bay of Bengal
Arabian Sea
Arabian Basin
MYANMAR (BURMA)
RANGOON
THAILAND
BANGKOK
LAOS
VIENTIANE
VIETNAM
HA NOI
CAMBODIA
PHNOM PENH
Ho Chi Minh City
Da Nang
South China Sea
PHILIPPINES
MANILA
Luzon
Quezon City
Mindanao
Davao
MALAYSIA
KUALA LUMPUR
SINGAPORE
BRUNEI
INDONESIA
JAKARTA
Bandung
Semarang
Surabaya
Java
Sumatra
Medan
Palembang
Padang
Makassar
Celebes Sea
Java Sea
EAST TIMOR
PALAU
PACIFIC OCEAN
Philippine Trench
Kyushu-Palau Ridge
South Honshu Ridge
Japan Trench
INDIAN OCEAN
Somali Basin
Carlsberg Ridge
Chagos-Laccadive Ridge
Chagos Archipelago
British Indian Ocean Territory
Mid-Indian Basin
Mid-Indian Ridge
Ninetyeast Ridge
Mascarene Basin
Mascarene Ridge
Madagascar Basin
Southwest Indian Ridge
Southeast Indian Ridge
Mozambique Ridge
Madagascar Ridge
Natal Basin
Agulhas Plateau
Agulhas Basin
Crozet Plateau
Crozet Basin
Îles Crozet (France)
Prince Edward Islands (South Africa)
French Southern and Antarctic Lands
Îles Kerguelen (France)
Kerguelen Plateau
Heard and McDonald Islands (Australia)
Île Amsterdam (France)
Île St-Paul (France)
Conrad Rise
Wharton Basin
Cocos Basin
Cocos Islands (Australia)
Christmas Island (Australia)
Investigator Ridge
Java Trench (Sunda Trench)
West Australian Basin
Broken Plateau
East Indiaman Ridge
Perth Basin
Diamantina Deep
South Australian Basin
Australian-Antarctic Basin
Antarctic Basin
AUSTRALIA
Perth
Adelaide
Darwin
Townsville
Cairns
Alice Springs
Kalgoorlie
Great Sandy Desert
Great Victoria Desert
Great Dividing Range
Nullarbor Plain
Great Australian Bight
Gulf of Carpentaria
Cape York Peninsula
Arafura Sea
Timor Sea
North Australian Basin
Exmouth Plateau
Naturaliste Plateau
Enderby Land
Kemp Land
Amundsen Bay
Cape Ann
Lützow-Holm Bay
Davis Sea
West Ice Shelf
East Antarctica
ANTARCTICA

Atlantic Ocean
Indian Ocean

PAKISTAN
MONGOLIA
RUS. FED.
CHINA
NEPAL
KATHMANDU
INDIA
BURMA
THAILAND
BANGKOK
VIETNAM
CAMBODIA
PHNOM PENH
Ho Chi Minh City
MANILA
PHILIPPINES
MALAYSIA
KUALA LUMPUR
SINGAPORE
BANDAR SERI BEGAWAN
BRUNEI
INDONESIA
JAKARTA
EAST TIMOR
DILI
SRI LANKA
Colombo
Mumbai
Pune
Hyderabad
Bangalore
Chennai
Kolkata
DHAKA
RANGOON
NORTH KOREA
P'YONGYANG
SEOUL
SOUTH KOREA
JAPAN
TŌKYŌ
Osaka
Nagoya
Sapporo
BEIJING
Tianjin
Shanghai
Wuhan
Chongqing
Chengdu
Guangzhou
Hong Kong
T'AIPEI
TAIWAN
Kaohsiung
Sea of Okhotsk
Sea of Japan
East China Sea
South China Sea
Bay of Bengal
Andaman Sea
Kamchatka Peninsula
Bering Sea
Aleutian Islands
Aleutian Basin
Aleutian Trench
Kuril Islands
Kuril Trench
Emperor Seamount Chain
Emperor Trough
Chinook Trough
Northwest Pacific Basin
Japan Trench
Izu-Ogasawara Trench
Ramapo Deep
Bonin Islands (Japan)
Volcano Islands (Japan)
Mid-Pacific Mountains
Mapmakers Seamounts
Hawaiian Ridge
Midway Islands
Kure Atoll
Wake Island (U.S.A.)
Johnston Atoll (U.S.A.)
Northern Mariana Islands (U.S.A.)
Saipan
Tinian
Rota
Guam (U.S.A.)
Mariana Trench
Challenger Deep 10920
Magellan Seamounts
East Mariana Basin
West Mariana Basin
Kyushu-Palau Ridge
South Honshu Ridge
Philippine Basin
Philippine Trench
PALAU
MELEKEOK
Yap Trench
West Caroline Basin
East Caroline Basin
Caroline Islands
FEDERATED STATES OF MICRONESIA
PALIKIR
Pohnpei
Chuuk
Kosrae
MICRONESIA
MARSHALL ISLANDS
DELAP-ULIGA-DJARRIT
Majuro
Kwajalein
Enewetak
Bikini
MELANESIA
NAURU
YAREN
Central Pacific Basin
BAIRIKI
Gilbert Islands
KIRIBATI
Phoenix Islands
TUVALU
VAIAKU
Tokelau (N.Z.)
POLYNESIA
PAPUA NEW GUINEA
PORT MORESBY
New Guinea
Bismarck Sea
Solomon Sea
SOLOMON ISLANDS
HONIARA
Coral Sea
Coral Sea Basin
VANUATU
PORT VILA
FIJI
SUVA
Wallis and Futuna Islands (France)
SAMOA
APIA
American Samoa (U.S.A.)
TONGA
Tonga Trench
Niue (N.Z.)
Cook Islands (N.Z.)
New Caledonia (France)
NOUMÉA
New Hebrides Trench
South Fiji Basin
Norfolk Island (Australia)
KINGSTON
Kermadec Islands (N.Z.)
Kermadec Trench
Louisville Ridge
Horizon Deep 10800
Great Barrier Reef
Arafura Sea
Timor Sea
Torres Strait
Gulf of Carpentaria
AUSTRALIA
Great Sandy Desert
Great Victoria Desert
Nullarbor Plain
Great Australian Bight
Darwin
Brisbane
Sydney
CANBERRA
Melbourne
Adelaide
Perth
Alice Springs
Tasmania
Bass Strait
Tasman Sea
Tasman Basin
Lord Howe Rise
NEW ZEALAND
Auckland
WELLINGTON
Christchurch
Dunedin
North Island
South Island
Chatham Rise
Campbell Plateau
Macquarie Ridge
South Australian Basin
South Tasman Rise
Indian-Antarctic Ridge
Southeast Indian Ridge
Australian-Antarctic Basin
INDIAN OCEAN
West Australian Basin
North Australian Basin
Wharton Basin
Java Trench (Sunda Trench)
Christmas Island (Australia)
Cocos Islands (Australia)
Ninetyeast Ridge
Broken Plateau
Mid-Indian Basin
Tropic of Capricorn
Equator
PACIFIC
SOUTHERN
ANTARCTICA
Wilkes Land
Adélie Land
George V Land
Transantarctic Mountains
Ross Ice Shelf
Lambert Azimuthal Equal Area Projection
1:50 000 000
0 500 1000 1500 miles
0 500 1000 1500 2000 2500 km

CANADA
Gulf of Alaska
Kodiak Island
Rocky Mountains
Coast Mountains
Edmonton
Calgary
Saskatoon
Regina
Winnipeg
Lethbridge
Prince George
Prince Rupert
Queen Charlotte Sound
Vancouver
Victoria
Seattle
Olympia
Portland
Salem
Eugene
Boise
Salt Lake City
Tufts Abyssal Plain
UNITED STATES OF AMERICA
Great Basin
Colorado Plateau
Denver
Sacramento
San Francisco
San Jose
Las Vegas
Los Angeles
San Diego
Ensenada
Mexicali
Tucson
Phoenix
Albuquerque
El Paso
Ciudad Juárez
Hermosillo
Chihuahua
Los Mochis
Durango
Guadalupe (Mexico)
Villa Insurgentes
La Paz
Mazatlán
MEXICO
San Luis Potosí
León
Guadalajara
Morelia
MEXICO CITY
Puebla
Oaxaca
Acapulco
Tampico
Monterrey
Matamoros
Veracruz
Mérida
Sigsbee Deep
Gulf of Mexico
Islas Revillagigedo (Mexico)
Minneapolis
Milwaukee
Chicago
Detroit
Toronto
OTTAWA
Montreal
Québec
Boston
Providence
New York
Philadelphia
Baltimore
WASHINGTON D.C.
Richmond
Raleigh
Charlotte
Columbia
Atlanta
Savannah
Jacksonville
Orlando
Tampa
Miami
Pittsburgh
Columbus
Cleveland
Buffalo
Indianapolis
St Louis
Nashville
Memphis
Jackson
Montgomery
Mobile
Tallahassee
New Orleans
Baton Rouge
Houston
San Antonio
Austin
Dallas
Fort Worth
Oklahoma City
Tulsa
Little Rock
Amarillo
Lubbock
Shreveport
Omaha
Lincoln
Topeka
Corpus Christi
Thunder Bay
Timmins
ATLANTIC OCEAN
New England Seamounts
Corner Seamounts
Bermuda (UK)
Bermuda Rise
Hatteras Abyssal Plain
Sargasso Sea
Nares Deep
Mid-Atlantic Ridge
Tropic of Cancer
NASSAU
THE BAHAMAS
HAVANA
CUBA
Cayman Islands (U.K.)
JAMAICA
KINGSTON
PORT-AU-PRINCE
HAITI
DOMINICAN REPUBLIC
SANTO DOMINGO
SAN JUAN
Puerto Rico
Milwaukee Deep
Puerto Rico Trench
ANTIGUA AND BARBUDA
ST KITTS AND NEVIS
Guadeloupe (France)
DOMINICA
Martinique (France)
ST LUCIA
BARBADOS
ST VINCENT AND THE GRENADINES
GRENADA
PORT OF SPAIN
TRINIDAD AND TOBAGO
Caribbean Sea
Venezuelan Basin
Demerara Abyssal Plain
BELIZE
BELMOPAN
GUATEMALA
GUATEMALA CITY
HONDURAS
TEGUCIGALPA
EL SALVADOR
SAN SALVADOR
NICARAGUA
MANAGUA
COSTA RICA
SAN JOSÉ
PANAMA
PANAMA CITY
Colombian Basin
Middle America Trench
Barranquilla
Cartagena
Maracaibo
Barquisimeto
CARACAS
Cumaná
Ciudad Bolívar
VENEZUELA
GEORGETOWN
GUYANA
PARAMARIBO
SURINAME
CAYENNE
French Guiana
Medellín
BOGOTÁ
COLOMBIA
Cali
Neiva
Pasto
Esmeraldas
QUITO
ECUADOR
Guayaquil
Isla de Coco (Costa Rica)
Isla de Malpelo (Colombia)
Cocos Ridge
Galapagos Islands (Ecuador)
Île Clipperton (France)
Equator
Belém
São Luís
Manaus
Santarém
Iquitos
Teresina
BRAZIL
Selvas
PERU
Sullana
Chiclayo
Trujillo
Pucallpa
Cruzeiro do Sul
Rio Branco
Porto Velho
LIMA
Huancayo
Cusco
Ica
Juliaca
Arequipa
Arica
LA PAZ
BOLIVIA
SUCRE
Santa Cruz
Cuiabá
BRASÍLIA
Goiânia
Salvador
Belo Horizonte
Vitória
Abrolhos Bank
Campo Grande
PARAGUAY
ASUNCIÓN
São Paulo
Rio de Janeiro
Curitiba
Florianópolis
Porto Alegre
Santos Plateau
Tropic of Capricorn
Iquique
Antofagasta
Salta
Tucumán
Córdoba
Rosario
Corrientes
Posadas
Santa Fe
Mendoza
Valparaíso
SANTIAGO
Talca
Concepción
Chillán
Valdivia
Puerto Montt
Isla de Chiloé
Archipiélago de los Chonos
BUENOS AIRES
MONTEVIDEO
URUGUAY
Rio Grande
Mar del Plata
Bahía Blanca
ARGENTINA
CHILE
Peru-Chile Trench
Nazca Ridge (Southwest Peru Ridge)
Peru Basin
Chile Basin
Islas Desventuradas (Chile)
Archipiélago Juan Fernández (Chile)
Argentine Rise
Argentine Basin
Argentine Abyssal Plain
Trelew
Comodoro Rivadavia
Puerto Natales
Punta Arenas
Río Gallegos
Ushuaia
Isla Grande de Tierra del Fuego
Cape Horn
Isla de los Estados
Falkland Islands (U.K.)
STANLEY
Falkland Plateau
Yaghan Basin
Scotia Ridge
Scotia Sea
Drake Passage
Honolulu
Maui
Hawai'i
Northeast Pacific Basin
PACIFIC OCEAN
East Pacific Rise
Gallego Rise
Galapagos Rise
Kiritimati
Malden Island
Penrhyn
Vostok Island
Caroline Island (Millennium Island)
Flint Island
Marquesas Islands (Îles Marquises)
Nuku Hiva
Hiva Oa
Îles du Désappointement
Îles du Roi-Georges
Tuamotu Islands (Archipel des Tuamotu)
French Polynesia
PAPEETE
Tahiti
Society Islands (Archipel de la Société)
Raiatea
Manuae
Hervey Islands
Maria
Mangaia
Tubuai
Raivavae
Tubuai Islands (Îles Australes)
Rapa
Îles du Duc de Gloucester
Moruroa
Groupe Actéon
Îles Gambier
Pitcairn Islands (U.K.)
Henderson Island
Ducie Island
ADAMSTOWN
Tiki Basin
Isla Sala y Gómez (Chile)
Easter Island (Isla de Pascua) (Chile)
Roggeveen Basin
Challenger Fracture Zone
Southwest Basin
Pacific-Antarctic Ridge
Mornington Abyssal Plain
Southeast Pacific Basin
Amundsen Abyssal Plain
Amundsen Ridge
Amundsen Sea
Antarctic Circle
Siple Island
Carney Island
Grant Island
Driscoll Island
Marie Byrd Land
Saunders Coast
Rockefeller Plateau
Siple Coast
West Antarctica
Walgreen Coast
Thurston Island
Peter I Island
Bellingshausen Sea
Ronne Entrance
Alexander Island
Hudson Mountains
Antarctic Peninsula
Adelaide Island
Graham Land
Livingston Island
Palmer Land
Vinson Massif
Whitmore Mountains
ANTARCTICA

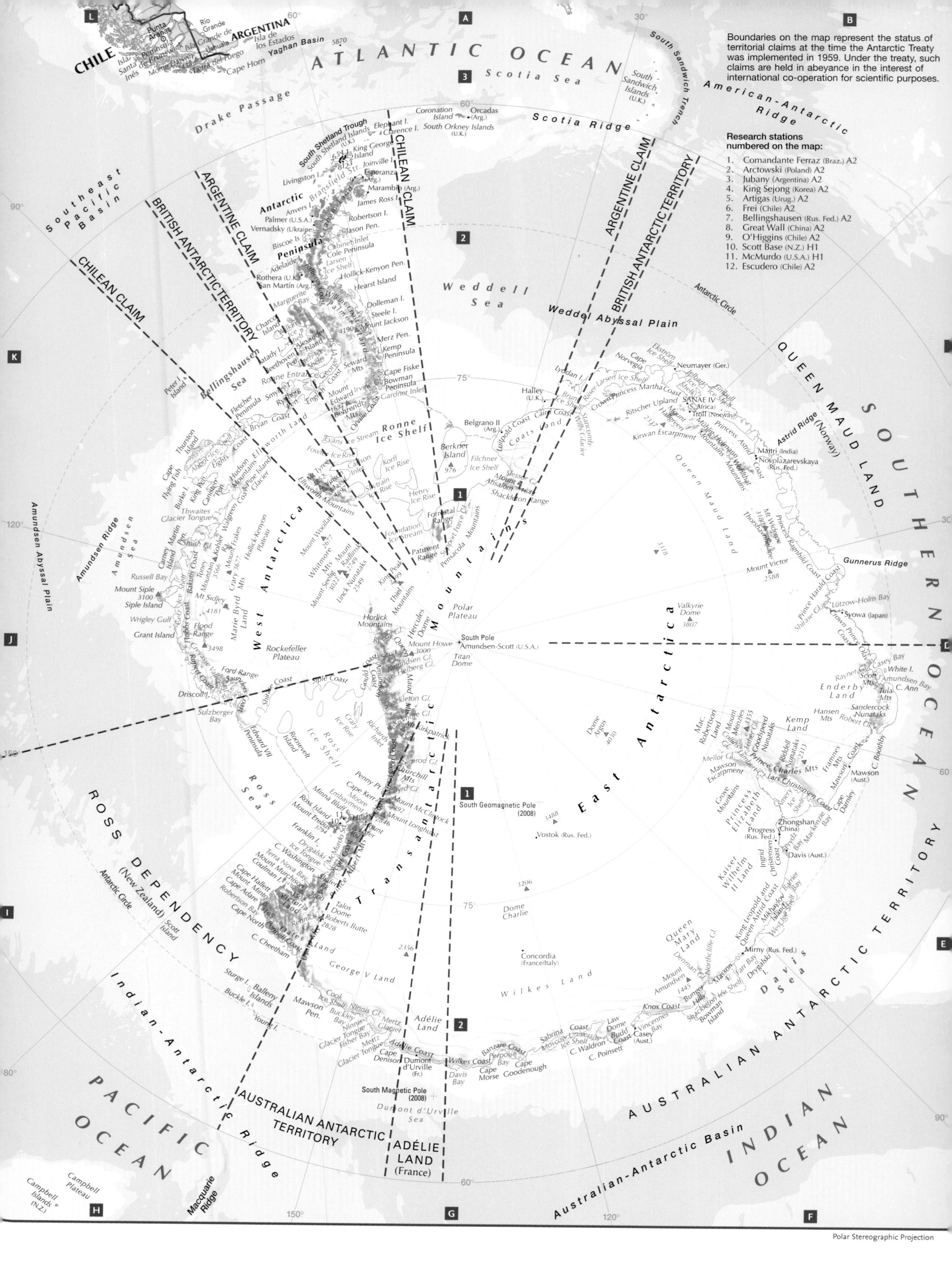
Boundaries on the map represent the status of territorial claims at the time the Antarctic Treaty was implemented in 1959. Under the treaty, such claims are held in abeyance in the interest of international co-operation for scientific purposes.
Research stations numbered on the map:
1. Comandante Ferraz (Braz.) A2
2. Arctowski (Poland) A2
3. Jubany (Argentina) A2
4. King Sejong (Korea) A2
5. Artigas (Urug.) A2
6. Frei (Chile) A2
7. Bellingshausen (Rus. Fed.) A2
8. Great Wall (China) A2
9. O'Higgins (Chile) A2
10. Scott Base (N.Z.) H1
11. McMurdo (U.S.A.) H1
12. Escudero (Chile) A2
ATLANTIC OCEAN
Scotia Sea
Drake Passage
Scotia Ridge
South Sandwich Trench
South Sandwich Islands (U.K.)
American-Antarctic Ridge
CHILE
ARGENTINA
Yaghan Basin
Cape Horn
South Orkney Islands (U.K.)
South Shetland Islands (U.K.)
Antarctic Peninsula
Southeast Pacific Basin
CHILEAN CLAIM
BRITISH ANTARCTIC TERRITORY
ARGENTINE CLAIM
Weddell Sea
Weddel Abyssal Plain
Antarctic Circle
QUEEN MAUD LAND (Norway)
SOUTHERN OCEAN
Bellingshausen Sea
Ronne Ice Shelf
Berkner Island
Filchner Ice Shelf
Queen Maud Land
Ellsworth Land
Ellsworth Mountains
West Antarctica
Amundsen Sea
Amundsen Ridge
Amundsen Abyssal Plain
Marie Byrd Land
Rockefeller Plateau
Polar Plateau
South Pole Amundsen-Scott (U.S.A.)
Transantarctic Mountains
East Antarctica
Enderby Land
Kemp Land
Ross Ice Shelf
Ross Sea
ROSS DEPENDENCY (New Zealand)
South Geomagnetic Pole (2008)
Vostok (Rus. Fed.)
Dome Argus 4030
Dome Charlie
Concordia (France/Italy)
Queen Mary Land
Wilkes Land
George V Land
Adélie Land
South Magnetic Pole (2008)
Dumont d'Urville Sea
AUSTRALIAN ANTARCTIC TERRITORY
ADÉLIE LAND (France)
Indian-Antarctic Ridge
PACIFIC OCEAN
INDIAN OCEAN
Australian-Antarctic Basin
Davis Sea
Macquarie Ridge
Campbell Plateau
Campbell Islands (N.Z.)
Polar Stereographic Projection

1:26 000 000 — 0 200 400 600 800 1000 miles; 0 200 400 600 800 1000 1200 1400 1600 km

ARCTIC OCEAN
CANADA
U.S.A.
RUSSIAN FEDERATION
NORWAY
SWEDEN
FINLAND
ESTONIA
LATVIA
DENMARK
GERMANY
ICELAND
UNITED KINGDOM
PACIFIC OCEAN
Beaufort Sea
Chukchi Sea
East Siberian Sea
Laptev Sea
Kara Sea
Barents Sea
Norwegian Sea
Greenland Sea
Lincoln Sea
Baffin Bay
Hudson Bay
Bering Sea
Gulf of Alaska
White Sea
Baltic Sea
Gulf of Bothnia
North Sea
Denmark Strait
Davis Strait
Bering Strait
Canada Basin
Canadian Abyssal Plain
Northwind Ridge
Chukchi Plateau
Chukchi Abyssal Plain
Mendeleyev Ridge
Alpha Ridge
Makarov Basin
Lomonosov Ridge
North Pole
Amundsen Basin
Arctic Mid-Ocean Ridge
Nansen Basin
Yermak Plateau
Greenland Basin
Greenland Fracture Zone
Boreas Abyssal Plain
Jan Mayen Fracture Zone
Norwegian Basin
Voring Plateau
Icelandic Plateau
Faroe - Iceland Ridge
Baffin Basin
Aleutian Trench
Aleutian Basin
Aleutian Islands
Aleutian Range
North Magnetic Pole (2008)
North Geomagnetic Pole (2008)
Arctic Circle
Greenland (Kalaallit Nunaat) (Denmark)
Ellesmere Island
Queen Elizabeth Islands
Parry Islands
Victoria Island
Banks Island
Baffin Island
Svalbard (Norway)
Zemlya Frantsa-Iosifa
Severnaya Zemlya
Novaya Zemlya
New Siberia Islands
Wrangel Island
Taymyr Peninsula
North Siberian Lowland
West Siberian Plain
Ural Mountains
Brooks Range
Alaska Range
Mackenzie Mountains
Coast Mountains
Khrebet Kolymskiy
Khrebet Verkhoyanskiy
Khr. Cherskogo
Anchorage
Fairbanks
Whitehorse
Yellowknife
Inuvik
Prudhoe Bay
Point Barrow
Murmansk
Archangel
St Petersburg
HELSINKI
STOCKHOLM
OSLO
COPENHAGEN
TALLINN
RIGA
Norilsk
Vorkuta
Salekhard
Tiksi
Omsk
Novosibirsk
Tomsk
Perm'
Vologda
Polar Stereographic Projection
1:26 000 000
0 200 400 600 800 1000 miles
0 200 400 600 800 1000 1200 1400 1600 km

The Arctic

States and Territories

All 195 independent countries and all populated dependent and disputed territories are included in this list of the states and territories of the world; the list is arranged in alphabetical order by the conventional name form. For independent states, the full name is given below the conventional name, if this is different; for territories, the status is given. The capital city name is given in conventional English form with selected alternative, usually local, form in brackets.

Area and population statistics are the latest available and include estimates. The information on languages and religions is based on the latest information on 'de facto' speakers of the language or 'de facto' adherents of the religion. This varies greatly from country to country because some countries include questions in censuses while others do not, in which case best estimates are used. The order of the languages and religions reflects their relative importance within the country; generally, languages or religions are included when more than one per cent of the population are estimated to be speakers or adherents.

ABBREVIATIONS

CURRENCIES

CFA	Communauté Financière Africaine
CFP	Comptoirs Français du Pacifique

Membership of selected international organizations is shown by the abbreviations below; dependent territories do not normally have separate memberships of these organizations.

ORGANIZATIONS

APEC	Asia-Pacific Economic Cooperation
ASEAN	Association of Southeast Asian Nations
CARICOM	Caribbean Community
CIS	Commonwealth of Independent States
Comm.	The Commonwealth
EU	European Union
NATO	North Atlantic Treaty Organization
OECD	Organisation for Economic Co-operation and Development
OPEC	Organization of the Petroleum Exporting Countries
SADC	Southern African Development Community
UN	United Nations

AFGHANISTAN

Islamic State of Afghanistan

Area Sq Km	652 225	Languages	Dari, Pushtu, Uzbek, Turkmen
Area Sq Miles	251 825	Religions	Sunni Muslim, Shi'a Muslim
Population	27 145 000	Currency	Afghani
Capital	Kābul	Organizations	UN

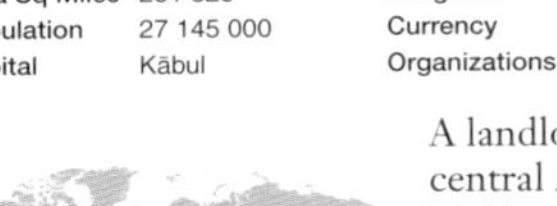

A landlocked country in central Asia with central highlands bordered by plains in the north and southwest, and by the Hindu Kush mountains in the northeast. The climate is dry continental. Over the last twenty-five years war has disrupted the economy, which is highly dependent on farming and livestock rearing. Most trade is with the former USSR, Pakistan and Iran.

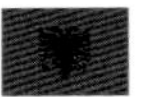

ALBANIA

Republic of Albania

Area Sq Km	28 748	Languages	Albanian, Greek
Area Sq Miles	11 100	Religions	Sunni Muslim, Albanian Orthodox, Roman Catholic
Population	3 190 000	Currency	Lek
Capital	Tirana (Tiranë)	Organizations	NATO, UN

Albania lies in the western Balkan Mountains in southeastern Europe, bordering the Adriatic Sea. It is mountainous, with coastal plains where half the population lives. The economy is based on agriculture and mining. Albania is one of the poorest countries in Europe and relies heavily on foreign aid.

ALGERIA

People's Democratic Republic of Algeria

Area Sq Km	2 381 741	Languages	Arabic, French, Berber
Area Sq Miles	919 595	Religions	Sunni Muslim
Population	33 858 000	Currency	Algerian dinar
Capital	Algiers (Alger)	Organizations	OPEC, UN

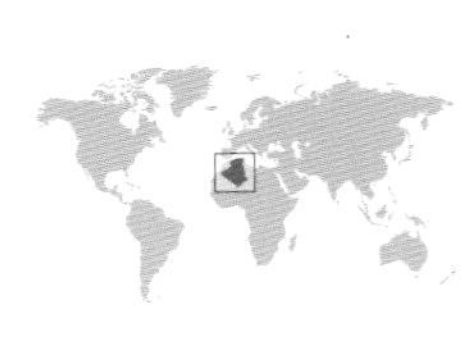

Algeria, the second largest country in Africa, lies on the Mediterranean coast of northwest Africa and extends southwards to the Atlas Mountains and the dry sandstone plateau and desert of the Sahara. The climate ranges from Mediterranean on the coast to semi-arid and arid inland. The most populated areas are the coastal plains and the fertile northern slopes of the Atlas Mountains. Oil, natural gas and related products account for over ninety-five per cent of export earnings. Agriculture employs about a quarter of the workforce, producing mainly food crops. Algeria's main trading partners are Italy, France and the USA.

American Samoa

United States Unincorporated Territory

Area Sq Km	197	Languages	Samoan, English
Area Sq Miles	76	Religions	Protestant, Roman Catholic
Population	67 000	Currency	United States dollar
Capital	Fagatogo		

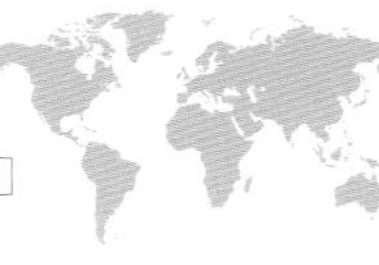

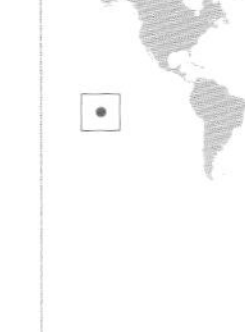

Lying in the south Pacific Ocean, American Samoa consists of five main islands and two coral atolls. The largest island is Tutuila. Tuna and tuna products are the main exports, and the main trading partner is the USA.

ANDORRA

Principality of Andorra

Area Sq Km	465	Languages	Spanish, Catalan, French
Area Sq Miles	180	Religions	Roman Catholic
Population	75 000	Currency	Euro
Capital	Andorra la Vella	Organizations	UN

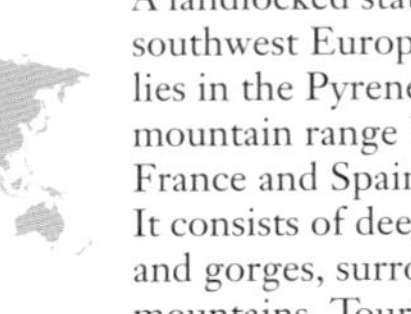

A landlocked state in southwest Europe, Andorra lies in the Pyrenees mountain range between France and Spain. It consists of deep valleys and gorges, surrounded by mountains. Tourism, encouraged by the development of ski resorts, is the mainstay of the economy. Banking is also an important economic activity.

ANGOLA

Republic of Angola

Area Sq Km	1 246 700	Languages	Portuguese, Bantu, local languages
Area Sq Miles	481 354	Religions	Roman Catholic, Protestant, traditional beliefs
Population	17 024 000	Currency	Kwanza
Capital	Luanda	Organizations	OPEC, SADC, UN

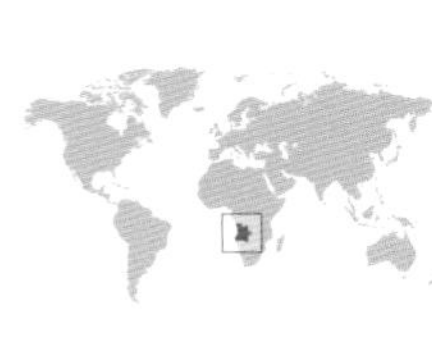

Angola lies on the Atlantic coast of south central Africa. Its small northern province, Cabinda, is separated from the rest of the country by part of the Democratic Republic of the Congo. Much of Angola is high plateau. In the west is a narrow coastal plain and in the southwest is desert. The climate is equatorial in the north but desert in the south. Over eighty per cent of the population relies on subsistence agriculture. Angola is rich in minerals (particularly diamonds), and oil accounts for approximately ninety per cent of export earnings. The USA, South Korea and Portugal are its main trading partners.

Anguilla

United Kingdom Overseas Territory

Area Sq Km	155	Languages	English
Area Sq Miles	60	Religions	Protestant, Roman Catholic
Population	13 000	Currency	East Caribbean dollar
Capital	The Valley		

Anguilla lies at the northern end of the Leeward Islands in the eastern Caribbean. Tourism and fishing form the basis of the economy.

ANTIGUA AND BARBUDA

Area Sq Km	442	Languages	English, Creole
Area Sq Miles	171	Religions	Protestant, Roman Catholic
Population	85 000	Currency	East Caribbean dollar
Capital	St John's	Organizations	CARICOM, Comm., UN

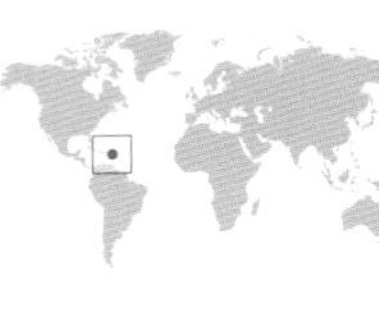

The state comprises the islands of Antigua, Barbuda and the tiny rocky outcrop of Redonda, in the Leeward Islands in the eastern Caribbean. Antigua, the largest and most populous island, is mainly hilly scrubland, with many beaches. The climate is tropical, and the economy relies heavily on tourism. Most trade is with other eastern Caribbean states and the USA.

ARGENTINA

Argentine Republic

Area Sq Km	2 766 889	Languages	Spanish, Italian, Amerindian languages
Area Sq Miles	1 068 302	Religions	Roman Catholic, Protestant
Population	39 531 000	Currency	Argentinian peso
Capital	Buenos Aires	Organizations	UN

Argentina, the second largest state in South America, extends from Bolivia to Cape Horn and from the Andes mountains to the Atlantic Ocean. It has four geographical regions: subtropical forests and swampland in the northeast; temperate fertile plains or Pampas in the centre; the wooded foothills and valleys of the Andes in the west; and the cold, semi-arid plateaus of Patagonia in the south. The highest mountain in South America, Cerro Aconcagua, is in Argentina. Nearly ninety per cent of the population lives in towns and cities. The country is rich in natural resources including petroleum, natural gas, ores and precious metals. Agricultural products dominate exports, which also include motor vehicles and crude oil. Most trade is with Brazil and the USA.

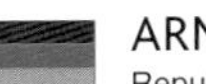

ARMENIA

Republic of Armenia

Area Sq Km	29 800	Languages	Armenian, Azeri
Area Sq Miles	11 506	Religions	Armenian Orthodox
Population	3 002 000	Currency	Dram
Capital	Yerevan (Erevan)	Organizations	CIS, UN

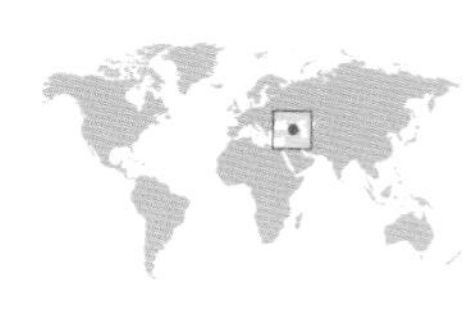

A landlocked state in southwest Asia, Armenia lies in the south of the Lesser Caucasus mountains. It is a mountainous country with a continental climate. One-third of the population lives in the capital, Yerevan. Exports include diamonds, scrap metal and machinery. Many Armenians depend on remittances from abroad.

Aruba

Self-governing Netherlands Territory

Area Sq Km	193	Languages	Papiamento, Dutch, English
Area Sq Miles	75	Religions	Roman Catholic, Protestant
Population	104 000	Currency	Aruban florin
Capital	Oranjestad		

The most southwesterly of the islands in the Lesser Antilles in the Caribbean, Aruba lies just off the coast of Venezuela. Tourism, offshore finance and oil refining are the most important sectors of the economy. The USA is the main trading partner.

AUSTRALIA

Commonwealth of Australia

Area Sq Km	7 692 024	Languages	English, Italian, Greek
Area Sq Miles	2 969 907	Religions	Protestant, Roman Catholic, Orthodox
Population	20 743 000	Currency	Australian dollar
Capital	Canberra	Organizations	APEC, Comm., OECD, UN

Australia, the world's sixth largest country, occupies the smallest, flattest and driest continent. The western half of the continent is mostly arid plateaus, ridges and vast deserts. The central eastern area comprises the lowlands of river systems draining into Lake Eyre, while to the east is the Great Dividing Range, a belt of ridges and plateaus running from Queensland to Tasmania. Climatically, more than two-thirds of the country is arid or semi-arid. The north is tropical monsoon, the east subtropical, and the southwest and southeast temperate. The majority of Australia's highly urbanized population lives along the east, southeast and southwest coasts. Australia has vast mineral deposits and various sources of energy. It is among the world's leading producers of iron ore, bauxite, nickel, copper and uranium. It is a major producer of coal, and oil and natural gas are also being exploited. Although accounting for only five per cent of the workforce, agriculture continues to be an important sector of the economy, with food and agricultural raw materials making up most of Australia's export earnings. Fuel, ores and metals, and manufactured goods, account for the remainder of exports. Japan and the USA are Australia's main trading partners.

Australian Capital Territory (Federal Territory)

Area Sq Km (Sq Miles)	Population	Capital
2 358 (910)	329 500	Canberra

Jervis Bay Territory (Territory)

Area Sq Km (Sq Miles)	Population
73 (28)	611

New South Wales (State)

Area Sq Km (Sq Miles)	Population	Capital
800 642 (309 130)	6 844 200	Sydney

Northern Territory (Territory)

Area Sq Km (Sq Miles)	Population	Capital
1 349 129 (520 902)	207 700	Darwin

Queensland (State)

Area Sq Km (Sq Miles)	Population	Capital
1 730 648 (668 207)	4 070 400	Brisbane

South Australia (State)

Area Sq Km (Sq Miles)	Population	Capital
983 482 (379 725)	1 558 200	Adelaide

Tasmania (State)

Area Sq Km (Sq Miles)	Population	Capital
68 401 (26 410)	489 600	Hobart

Victoria (State)

Area Sq Km (Sq Miles)	Population	Capital
227 416 (87 806)	5 110 500	Melbourne

Western Australia (State)

Area Sq Km (Sq Miles)	Population	Capital
2 529 875 (976 790)	2 061 500	Perth

AUSTRIA

Republic of Austria

Area Sq Km	83 855	Languages	German, Croatian, Turkish
Area Sq Miles	32 377	Religions	Roman Catholic, Protestant
Population	8 361 000	Currency	Euro
Capital	Vienna (Wien)	Organizations	EU, OECD, UN

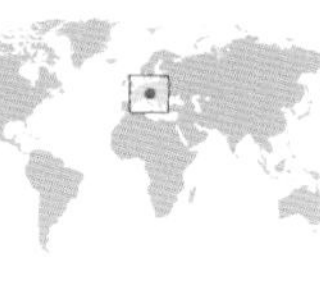

Two-thirds of Austria, a landlocked state in central Europe, lies within the Alps, with lower mountains to the north. The only lowlands are in the east. The Danube river valley in the northeast contains almost all the agricultural land and most of the population. Although the climate varies with altitude, in general summers are warm and winters cold with heavy snowfalls. Manufacturing industry and tourism are the most important sectors of the economy. Exports are dominated by manufactured goods. Germany is Austria's main trading partner.

AZERBAIJAN

Republic of Azerbaijan

Area Sq Km	86 600	Languages	Azeri, Armenian, Russian, Lezgian
Area Sq Miles	33 436	Religions	Shi'a Muslim, Sunni Muslim, Russian and Armenian Orthodox
Population	8 467 000	Currency	Azerbaijani manat
Capital	Baku	Organizations	CIS, UN

Azerbaijan lies to the southeast of the Caucasus mountains, on the Caspian Sea. Its region of Naxçıvan is separated from the rest of the country by part of Armenia. It has mountains in the northeast and west, valleys in the centre, and a low coastal plain. The climate is continental. It is rich in energy and mineral resources. Oil production, onshore and offshore, is the main industry and the basis of heavy industries. Agriculture is important, with cotton and tobacco the main cash crops.

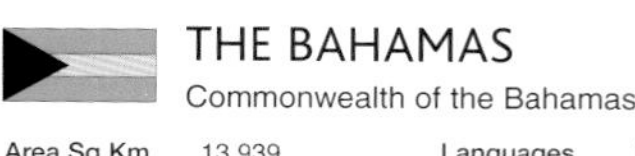

THE BAHAMAS

Commonwealth of the Bahamas

Area Sq Km	13 939	Languages	English, Creole
Area Sq Miles	5 382	Religions	Protestant, Roman Catholic
Population	331 000	Currency	Bahamian dollar
Capital	Nassau	Organizations	CARICOM, Comm., UN

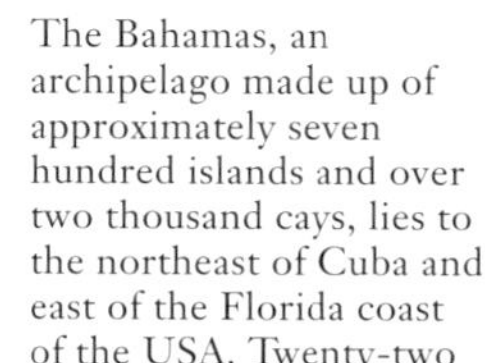

The Bahamas, an archipelago made up of approximately seven hundred islands and over two thousand cays, lies to the northeast of Cuba and east of the Florida coast of the USA. Twenty-two islands are inhabited, and two-thirds of the population lives on the main island of New Providence. The climate is warm for much of the year, with heavy rainfall in the summer. Tourism is the islands' main industry. Offshore banking, insurance and ship registration are also major foreign exchange earners.

BAHRAIN

Kingdom of Bahrain

Area Sq Km	691	Languages	Arabic, English
Area Sq Miles	267	Religions	Shi'a Muslim, Sunni Muslim, Christian
Population	753 000	Currency	Bahraini dinar
Capital	Manama (Al Manāmah)	Organizations	UN

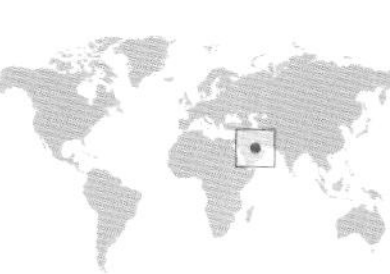

Bahrain consists of more than thirty islands lying in a bay in The Gulf, off the coasts of Saudi Arabia and Qatar. Bahrain Island, the largest island, is connected to other islands and to the mainland of Arabia by causeways. Oil production and processing are the main sectors of the economy.

BANGLADESH

People's Republic of Bangladesh

Area Sq Km	143 998	Languages	Bengali, English
Area Sq Miles	55 598	Religions	Sunni Muslim, Hindu
Population	158 665 000	Currency	Taka
Capital	Dhaka (Dacca)	Organizations	Comm., UN

The south Asian state of Bangladesh is in the northeast of the Indian subcontinent, on the Bay of Bengal. It consists almost entirely of the low-lying alluvial plains and deltas of the Ganges and Brahmaputra rivers. The southwest is swampy, with mangrove forests in the delta area. The north, northeast and southeast have low forested hills. Bangladesh is one of the world's most densely populated and least developed countries. The economy is based on agriculture, though the garment industry is the main export sector. Storms during the summer monsoon season often cause devastating flooding and crop destruction. The country relies on large-scale foreign aid and remittances from workers abroad.

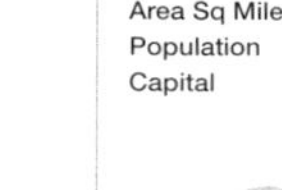

BARBADOS

Area Sq Km	430	Languages	English, Creole
Area Sq Miles	166	Religions	Protestant, Roman Catholic
Population	294 000	Currency	Barbados dollar
Capital	Bridgetown	Organizations	CARICOM, Comm., UN

The most easterly of the Caribbean islands, Barbados is small and densely populated. It has a tropical climate and is subject to hurricanes. The economy is based on tourism, financial services, light industries and sugar production.

BELARUS

Republic of Belarus

Area Sq Km	207 600	Languages	Belorussian, Russian
Area Sq Miles	80 155	Religions	Belorussian Orthodox, Roman Catholic
Population	9 689 000	Currency	Belarus rouble
Capital	Minsk	Organizations	CIS, UN

Belarus, a landlocked state in eastern Europe, consists of low hills and plains, with many lakes, rivers and, in the south, extensive marshes. Forests cover approximately one-third of the country. It has a continental climate. Agriculture contributes one-third of national income, with beef cattle and grains as the major products. Manufacturing industries produce a range of items, from construction equipment to textiles. The Russian Federation and Ukraine are the main trading partners.

BELGIUM

Kingdom of Belgium

Area Sq Km	30 520	Languages	Dutch (Flemish), French (Walloon), German
Area Sq Miles	11 784	Religions	Roman Catholic, Protestant
Population	10 457 000	Currency	Euro
Capital	Brussels (Bruxelles)	Organizations	EU, NATO, OECD, UN

Belgium lies on the North Sea coast of western Europe. Beyond low sand dunes and a narrow belt of reclaimed land, fertile plains extend to the Sambre-Meuse river valley. The land rises to the forested Ardennes plateau in the southeast. Belgium has mild winters and cool summers. It is densely populated and has a highly urbanized population. With few mineral resources, Belgium imports raw materials for processing and manufacture. The agricultural sector is small, but provides for most food needs. A large services sector reflects Belgium's position as the home base for over eight hundred international institutions. The headquarters of the European Union are in the capital, Brussels.

States and Territories

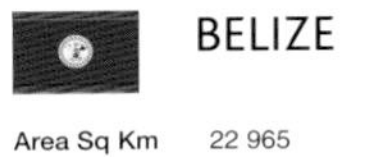

BELIZE

Area Sq Km	22 965	Languages	English, Spanish, Mayan, Creole
Area Sq Miles	8 867	Religions	Roman Catholic, Protestant
Population	288 000	Currency	Belize dollar
Capital	Belmopan	Organizations	CARICOM, Comm., UN

Belize lies on the Caribbean coast of central America and includes numerous cays and a large barrier reef offshore. The coastal areas are flat and swampy. To the southwest are the Maya Mountains. Tropical jungle covers much of the country and the climate is humid tropical, but tempered by sea breezes. A third of the population lives in the capital. The economy is based primarily on agriculture, forestry and fishing, and exports include raw sugar, orange concentrate and bananas.

BENIN

Republic of Benin

Area Sq Km	112 620	Languages	French, Fon, Yoruba, Adja, local languages
Area Sq Miles	43 483	Religions	Traditional beliefs, Roman Catholic, Sunni Muslim
Population	9 033 000	Currency	CFA franc
Capital	Porto-Novo	Organizations	UN

Benin is in west Africa, on the Gulf of Guinea. The climate is tropical in the north, equatorial in the south. The economy is based mainly on agriculture and transit trade. Agricultural products account for two-thirds of export earnings. Oil, produced offshore, is also a major export.

Bermuda

United Kingdom Overseas Territory

Area Sq Km	54	Languages	English
Area Sq Miles	21	Religions	Protestant, Roman Catholic
Population	65 000	Currency	Bermuda dollar
Capital	Hamilton		

In the Atlantic Ocean to the east of the USA, Bermuda comprises a group of small islands with a warm and humid climate. The economy is based on international business and tourism.

BHUTAN

Kingdom of Bhutan

Area Sq Km	46 620	Languages	Dzongkha, Nepali, Assamese
Area Sq Miles	18 000	Religions	Buddhist, Hindu
Population	658 000	Currency	Ngultrum, Indian rupee
Capital	Thimphu	Organizations	UN

Bhutan lies in the eastern Himalaya mountains, between China and India. It is mountainous in the north, with fertile valleys. The climate ranges between permanently cold in the far north and subtropical in the south. Most of the population is involved in livestock rearing and subsistence farming. Bhutan is the world's largest producer of cardamom. Tourism is an increasingly important foreign currency earner.

BOLIVIA

Republic of Bolivia

Area Sq Km	1 098 581	Languages	Spanish, Quechua, Aymara
Area Sq Miles	424 164	Religions	Roman Catholic, Protestant, Baha'i
Population	9 525 000	Currency	Boliviano
Capital	La Paz/Sucre	Organizations	UN

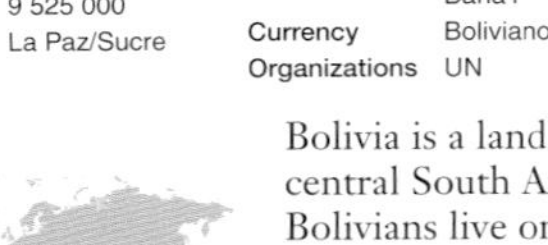

Bolivia is a landlocked state in central South America. Most Bolivians live on the high plateau within the Andes mountains. The lowlands range between dense rainforest in the northeast and semi-arid grasslands in the southeast. Bolivia is rich in minerals (zinc, tin and gold), and sales generate approximately half of export income. Natural gas, timber and soya beans are also exported. The USA is the main trading partner.

BOSNIA-HERZEGOVINA

Republic of Bosnia and Herzegovina

Area Sq Km	51 130	Languages	Bosnian, Serbian, Croatian
Area Sq Miles	19 741	Religions	Sunni Muslim, Serbian Orthodox, Roman Catholic, Protestant
Population	3 935 000	Currency	Marka
Capital	Sarajevo	Organizations	UN

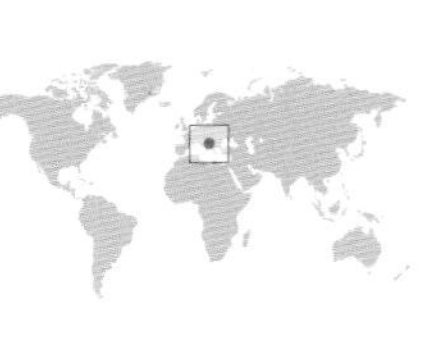

Bosnia-Herzegovina lies in the western Balkan Mountains of southern Europe, on the Adriatic Sea. It is mountainous, with ridges running northwest-southeast. The main lowlands are around the Sava valley in the north. Summers are warm, but winters can be very cold. The economy relies heavily on overseas aid.

BOTSWANA

Republic of Botswana

Area Sq Km	581 370	Languages	English, Setswana, Shona, local languages
Area Sq Miles	224 468	Religions	Traditional beliefs, Protestant, Roman Catholic
Population	1 882 000	Currency	Pula
Capital	Gaborone	Organizations	Comm., SADC, UN

Botswana is a landlocked state in southern Africa. Over half of the country lies within the Kalahari Desert, with swamps to the north and salt-pans to the northeast. Most of the population lives near the eastern border. The climate is subtropical, but drought-prone. The economy was founded on cattle rearing, and although beef remains an important export, the economy is now based on mining. Diamonds account for seventy per cent of export earnings. Copper-nickel matte is also exported. Most trade is with other members of the Southern African Customs Union.

BRAZIL

Federative Republic of Brazil

Area Sq Km	8 514 879	Languages	Portuguese
Area Sq Miles	3 287 613	Religions	Roman Catholic, Protestant
Population	191 791 000	Currency	Real
Capital	Brasília	Organizations	UN

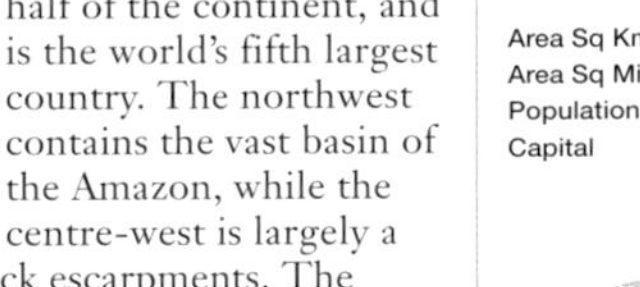

Brazil, in eastern South America, covers almost half of the continent, and is the world's fifth largest country. The northwest contains the vast basin of the Amazon, while the centre-west is largely a vast plateau of savanna and rock escarpments. The northeast is mostly semi-arid plateaus, while to the east and south are rugged mountains, fertile valleys and narrow, fertile coastal plains. The Amazon basin is hot, humid and wet; the rest of the country is cooler and drier, with seasonal variations. The northeast is drought-prone. Most Brazilians live in urban areas along the coast and on the central plateau. Brazil has well-developed agricultural, mining and service sectors, and the economy is larger than that of all other South American countries combined. Brazil is the world's biggest producer of coffee, and other agricultural crops include grains and sugar cane. Mineral production includes iron, aluminium and gold. Manufactured goods include food products, transport equipment, machinery and industrial chemicals. The main trading partners are the USA and Argentina. Despite its natural wealth, Brazil has a large external debt and a growing poverty gap.

BRUNEI

State of Brunei Darussalam

Area Sq Km	5 765	Languages	Malay, English, Chinese
Area Sq Miles	2 226	Religions	Sunni Muslim, Buddhist, Christian
Population	390 000	Currency	Brunei dollar
Capital	Bandar Seri Begawan	Organizations	APEC, ASEAN, Comm., UN

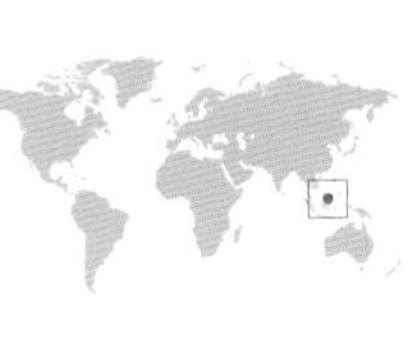

The southeast Asian oil-rich state of Brunei lies on the northwest coast of the island of Borneo, on the South China Sea. Its two enclaves are surrounded by the Malaysian state of Sarawak. Tropical rainforest covers over two-thirds of the country. The economy is dominated by the oil and gas industries.

BULGARIA

Republic of Bulgaria

Area Sq Km	110 994	Languages	Bulgarian, Turkish, Romany, Macedonian
Area Sq Miles	42 855	Religions	Bulgarian Orthodox, Sunni Muslim
Population	7 639 000	Currency	Lev
Capital	Sofia (Sofiya)	Organizations	EU, NATO, UN

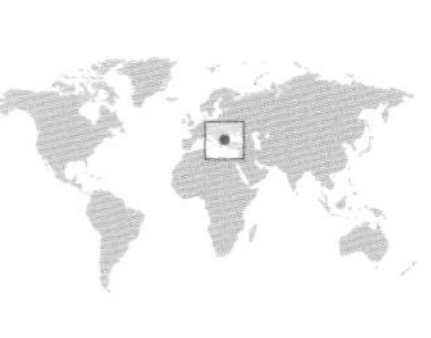

Bulgaria, in southern Europe, borders the western shore of the Black Sea. The Balkan Mountains separate the Danube plains in the north from the Rhodope Mountains and the lowlands in the south. The economy has a strong agricultural base. Manufacturing industries include machinery, consumer goods, chemicals and metals. Most trade is with the Russian Federation, Italy and Germany.

BURKINA

Democratic Republic of Burkina Faso

Area Sq Km	274 200	Languages	French, Moore (Mossi), Fulani, local languages
Area Sq Miles	105 869	Religions	Sunni Muslim, traditional beliefs, Roman Catholic
Population	14 784 000	Currency	CFA franc
Capital	Ouagadougou	Organizations	UN

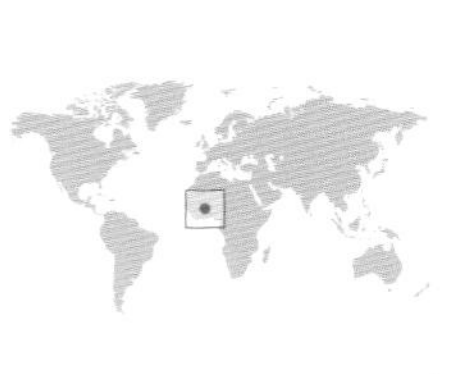

Burkina, a landlocked country in west Africa, lies within the Sahara desert to the north and semi-arid savanna to the south. Rainfall is erratic, and droughts are common. Livestock rearing and farming are the main activities, and cotton, livestock, groundnuts and some minerals are exported. Burkina relies heavily on foreign aid, and is one of the poorest and least developed countries in the world.

BURUNDI

Republic of Burundi

Area Sq Km	27 835	Languages	Kirundi (Hutu, Tutsi), French
Area Sq Miles	10 747	Religions	Roman Catholic, traditional beliefs, Protestant
Population	8 508 000	Currency	Burundian franc
Capital	Bujumbura	Organizations	UN

The densely populated east African state of Burundi consists of high plateaus rising from the shores of Lake Tanganyika in the southwest. It has a tropical climate and depends on subsistence farming. Coffee is its main export, and its main trading partners are Germany and Belgium. The country has been badly affected by internal conflict since the early 1990s.

CAMBODIA

Kingdom of Cambodia

Area Sq Km	181 000	Languages	Khmer, Vietnamese
Area Sq Miles	69 884	Religions	Buddhist, Roman Catholic, Sunni Muslim
Population	14 444 000	Currency	Riel
Capital	Phnom Penh (Phnum Pénh)	Organizations	ASEAN, UN

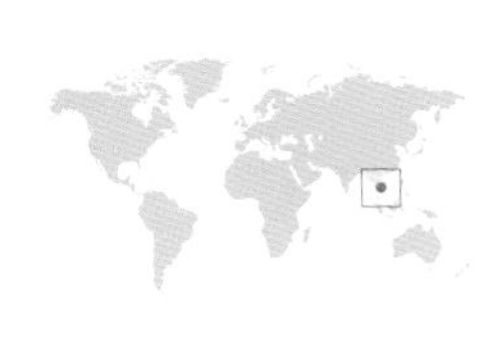

Cambodia lies in southeast Asia on the Gulf of Thailand, and occupies the Mekong river basin, with the Tônlé Sap (Great Lake) at its centre. The climate is tropical monsoon. Forests cover half the country. Most of the population lives on the plains and is engaged in farming (chiefly rice growing), fishing and forestry. The economy is recovering slowly following the devastation of civil war in the 1970s.

CAMEROON

Republic of Cameroon

Area Sq Km	475 442	Languages	French, English, Fang, Bamileke, local languages
Area Sq Miles	183 569	Religions	Roman Catholic, traditional beliefs, Sunni Muslim, Protestant
Population	18 549 000	Currency	CFA franc
Capital	Yaoundé	Organizations	Comm., UN

Cameroon is in west Africa, on the Gulf of Guinea. The coastal plains and southern and central plateaus are covered with tropical forest. Despite oil resources and favourable agricultural conditions Cameroon still faces problems of underdevelopment. Oil, timber and cocoa are the main exports. France is the main trading partner.

CANADA

Area Sq Km	9 984 670	Languages	English, French
Area Sq Miles	3 855 103	Religions	Roman Catholic, Protestant, Eastern Orthodox, Jewish
Population	32 876 000	Currency	Canadian dollar
Capital	Ottawa	Organizations	APEC, Comm., NATO, OECD, UN

The world's second largest country, Canada covers the northern two-fifths of North America and has coastlines on the Atlantic, Arctic and Pacific Oceans. In the west are the Coast Mountains, the Rocky Mountains and interior plateaus. In the centre lie the fertile Prairies. Further east, covering about half the total land area, is the Canadian Shield, a relatively flat area of infertile lowlands around Hudson Bay, extending to Labrador on the east coast. The Shield is bordered to the south by the fertile Great Lakes-St Lawrence lowlands. In the far north climatic conditions are polar, while the rest has a continental climate. Most Canadians live in the urban areas of the Great Lakes-St Lawrence basin. Canada is rich in mineral and energy resources. Only five per cent of land is arable. Canada is among the world's leading producers of wheat, of wood from its vast coniferous forests, and of fish and seafood from its Atlantic and Pacific fishing grounds. It is a major producer of nickel, uranium, copper, iron ore, zinc and other minerals, as well as oil and natural gas. Its abundant raw materials are the basis for many manufacturing industries. Main exports are machinery, motor vehicles, oil, timber, newsprint and paper, wood pulp and wheat. Since the 1989 free trade agreement with the USA and the 1994 North America Free Trade Agreement, trade with the USA has grown and now accounts for around seventy-five per cent of imports and around eighty-five per cent of exports.

	Area Sq Km (Sq Miles)	Population	Capital
Alberta (Province)	661 848 (255 541)	3 435 511	Edmonton
British Columbia (Province)	944 735 (364 764)	4 338 106	Victoria
Manitoba (Province)	647 797 (250 116)	1 180 004	Winnipeg
New Brunswick (Province)	72 908 (28 150)	748 582	Fredericton
Newfoundland and Labrador (Province)	405 212 (156 453)	508 548	St John's
Northwest Territories (Territory)	1 346 106 (519 734)	41 777	Yellowknife
Nova Scotia (Province)	55 284 (21 345)	933 793	Halifax
Nunavut (Territory)	2 093 190 (808 185)	30 947	Iqaluit
Ontario (Province)	1 076 395 (415 598)	12 726 336	Toronto
Prince Edward Island (Province)	5 660 (2 185)	138 632	Charlottetown
Québec (Province)	1 542 056 (595 391)	7 676 097	Québec
Saskatchewan (Province)	651 036 (251 366)	987 939	Regina
Yukon (Territory)	482 443 (186 272)	31 032	Whitehorse

CAPE VERDE

Republic of Cape Verde

Area Sq Km	4 033	Languages	Portuguese, Creole
Area Sq Miles	1 557	Religions	Roman Catholic, Protestant
Population	530 000	Currency	Cape Verde escudo
Capital	Praia	Organizations	UN

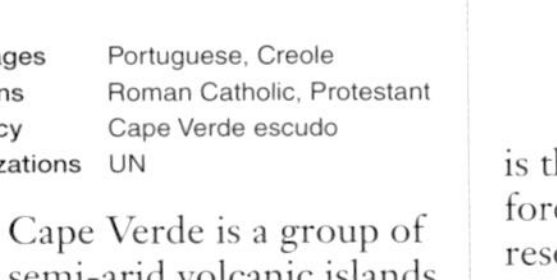

Cape Verde is a group of semi-arid volcanic islands lying off the coast of west Africa. The economy is based on fishing and subsistence farming but relies on emigrant workers' remittances and foreign aid.

Cayman Islands

United Kingdom Overseas Territory

Area Sq Km	259	Languages	English
Area Sq Miles	100	Religions	Protestant, Roman Catholic
Population	47 000	Currency	Cayman Islands dollar
Capital	George Town		

A group of islands in the Caribbean, northwest of Jamaica. There are three main islands: Grand Cayman, Little Cayman and Cayman Brac. The Cayman Islands are one of the world's major offshore financial centres. Tourism is also important to the economy.

CENTRAL AFRICAN REPUBLIC

Area Sq Km	622 436	Languages	French, Sango, Banda, Baya, local languages
Area Sq Miles	240 324	Religions	Protestant, Roman Catholic, traditional beliefs, Sunni Muslim
Population	4 343 000	Currency	CFA franc
Capital	Bangui	Organizations	UN

A landlocked country in central Africa, the Central African Republic is mainly savanna plateau, drained by the Ubangi and Chari river systems, with mountains to the east and west. The climate is tropical, with high rainfall. Most of the population lives in the south and west, and a majority of the workforce is involved in subsistence farming. Some cotton, coffee, tobacco and timber are exported, but diamonds account for around half of export earnings.

CHAD

Republic of Chad

Area Sq Km	1 284 000	Languages	Arabic, French, Sara, local languages
Area Sq Miles	495 755	Religions	Sunni Muslim, Roman Catholic, Protestant, traditional beliefs
Population	10 781 000	Currency	CFA franc
Capital	Ndjamena	Organizations	UN

Chad is a landlocked state of north-central Africa. It consists of plateaus, the Tibesti mountains in the north and the Lake Chad basin in the west. Climatic conditions range between desert in the north and tropical forest in the southwest. With few natural resources, Chad relies on subsistence farming, exports of raw cotton, and foreign aid. The main trading partners are France, Portugal and Cameroon.

CHILE

Republic of Chile

Area Sq Km	756 945	Languages	Spanish, Amerindian languages
Area Sq Miles	292 258	Religions	Roman Catholic, Protestant
Population	16 635 000	Currency	Chilean peso
Capital	Santiago	Organizations	APEC, UN

Chile lies along the Pacific coast of the southern half of South America. Between the Andes in the east and the lower coastal ranges is a central valley, with a mild climate, where most Chileans live. To the north is the arid Atacama Desert and to the south is cold, wet forested grassland. Chile has considerable mineral resources and is the world's leading exporter of copper. Nitrates, molybdenum, gold and iron ore are also mined. Agriculture (particularly viticulture), forestry and fishing are also important to the economy.

CHINA

People's Republic of China

Area Sq Km	9 584 492	Languages	Mandarin, Wu, Cantonese, Hsiang, regional languages
Area Sq Miles	3 700 593	Religions	Confucian, Taoist, Buddhist, Christian, Sunni Muslim
Population	1 313 437 000	Currency	Yuan, Hong Kong dollar, Macao pataca
Capital	Beijing (Peking)	Organizations	APEC, UN

China, the world's most populous and fourth largest country, occupies a large part of east Asia, borders fourteen states and has coastlines on the Yellow, East China and South China Seas. It has a huge variety of landscapes. The southwest contains the high Plateau of Tibet, flanked by the Himalaya and Kunlun Shan mountains. The north is mountainous with arid basins and extends from the Tien Shan and Altai Mountains and the vast Taklimakan Desert in the west to the plateau and Gobi Desert in the centre-east. Eastern China is predominantly lowland and is divided broadly into the basins of the Yellow River (Huang He) in the north, the Yangtze (Chang Jiang) in the centre and the Pearl River (Xi Jiang) in the southeast. Climatic conditions and vegetation are as diverse as the topography: much of the country experiences temperate conditions, while the southwest has an extreme mountain climate and the southeast enjoys a moist, warm subtropical climate. Nearly seventy per cent of China's huge population lives in rural areas, and agriculture employs around half of the working population. The main crops are rice, wheat, soya beans, peanuts, cotton, tobacco and hemp. China is rich in coal, oil and natural gas and has the world's largest potential in hydroelectric power. It is a major world producer of iron ore, molybdenum, copper, asbestos and gold. Economic reforms from the early 1980's led to an explosion in manufacturing development concentrated on the 'coastal economic open region'. The main exports are machinery, textiles, footwear, toys and sports goods. Japan and the USA are China's main trading partners.

Anhui (Province)
Area Sq Km (Sq Miles)	Population	Capital
139 000 (53 668)	61 140 000	Hefei

Beijing (Municipality)
Area Sq Km (Sq Miles)	Population	Capital
16 800 (6 487)	15 360 000	Beijing (Peking)

Chongqing (Municipality)
Area Sq Km (Sq Miles)	Population	Capital
23 000 (8 880)	27 970 000	Chongqing

Fujian (Province)
Area Sq Km (Sq Miles)	Population	Capital
121 400 (46 873)	35 320 000	Fuzhou

Gansu (Province)
Area Sq Km (Sq Miles)	Population	Capital
453 700 (175 175)	25 920 000	Lanzhou

Guangdong (Province)
Area Sq Km (Sq Miles)	Population	Capital
178 000 (68 726)	91 850 000	Guangzhou (Canton)

Guangxi Zhuangzu Zizhiqu (Autonomous Region)
Area Sq Km (Sq Miles)	Population	Capital
236 000 (91 120)	46 550 000	Nanning

Guizhou (Province)
Area Sq Km (Sq Miles)	Population	Capital
176 000 (67 954)	37 250 000	Guiyang

Hainan (Province)
Area Sq Km (Sq Miles)	Population	Capital
34 000 (13 127)	8 260 000	Haikou

Hebei (Province)
Area Sq Km (Sq Miles)	Population	Capital
187 700 (72 471)	68 440 000	Shijiazhuang

Heilongjiang (Province)
Area Sq Km (Sq Miles)	Population	Capital
454 600 (175 522)	38 180 000	Harbin

Henan (Province)
Area Sq Km (Sq Miles)	Population	Capital
167 000 (64 479)	93 710 000	Zhengzhou

Hong Kong (Special Administrative Region)
Area Sq Km (Sq Miles)	Population	Capital
1 075 (415)	6 936 000	Hong Kong

Hubei (Province)
Area Sq Km (Sq Miles)	Population	Capital
185 900 (71 776)	57 070 000	Wuhan

Hunan (Province)
Area Sq Km (Sq Miles)	Population	Capital
210 000 (81 081)	63 200 000	Changsha

Jiangsu (Province)
Area Sq Km (Sq Miles)	Population	Capital
102 600 (39 614)	74 680 000	Nanjing

Jiangxi (Province)
Area Sq Km (Sq Miles)	Population	Capital
166 900 (64 440)	43 070 000	Nanchang

Jilin (Province)
Area Sq Km (Sq Miles)	Population	Capital
187 000 (72 201)	27 150 000	Changchun

Liaoning (Province)
Area Sq Km (Sq Miles)	Population	Capital
147 400 (56 911)	42 200 000	Shenyang

Macao (Special Administrative Region)
Area Sq Km (Sq Miles)	Population	Capital
17 (7)	477 000	Macao

Nei Mongol Zizhiqu Inner Mongolia (Autonomous Region)
Area Sq Km (Sq Miles)	Population	Capital
1 183 000 (456 759)	23 860 000	Hohhot

Ningxia Huizu Zizhiqu (Autonomous Region)
Area Sq Km (Sq Miles)	Population	Capital
66 400 (25 637)	5 950 000	Yinchuan

Qinghai (Province)
Area Sq Km (Sq Miles)	Population	Capital
721 000 (278 380)	5 430 000	Xining

Shaanxi (Province)
Area Sq Km (Sq Miles)	Population	Capital
205 600 (79 383)	37 180 000	Xi'an

Shandong (Province)
Area Sq Km (Sq Miles)	Population	Capital
153 300 (59 189)	92 390 000	Jinan

Shanghai (Municipality)
Area Sq Km (Sq Miles)	Population	Capital
6 300 (2 432)	17 780 000	Shanghai

Shanxi (Province)
Area Sq Km (Sq Miles)	Population	Capital
156 300 (60 348)	33 520 000	Taiyuan

Sichuan (Province)
Area Sq Km (Sq Miles)	Population	Capital
569 000 (219 692)	82 080 000	Chengdu

Tianjin (Municipality)
Area Sq Km (Sq Miles)	Population	Capital
11 300 (4 363)	10 430 000	Tianjin

Xinjiang Uygur Zizhiqu Sinkiang (Autonomous Region)
Area Sq Km (Sq Miles)	Population	Capital
1 600 000 (617 763)	20 080 000	Ürümqi

Xizang Zizhiqu Tibet (Autonomous Region)
Area Sq Km (Sq Miles)	Population	Capital
1 228 400 (474 288)	2 760 000	Lhasa

Yunnan (Province)
Area Sq Km (Sq Miles)	Population	Capital
394 000 (152 124)	44 420 000	Kunming

Zhejiang (Province)
Area Sq Km (Sq Miles)	Population	Capital
101 800 (39 305)	48 940 000	Hangzhou

Taiwan: The People's Republic of China claims Taiwan as its 23rd Province

Christmas Island
Australian External Territory

Area Sq Km	135	Languages	English
Area Sq Miles	52	Religions	Buddhist, Sunni Muslim, Protestant, Roman Catholic
Population	1 508		
Capital	The Settlement (Flying Fish Cove)	Currency	Australian dollar

The island is situated in the east of the Indian Ocean, to the south of Indonesia. The economy was formerly based on phosphate extraction, although reserves are now nearly depleted. Tourism is developing and is a major employer.

Cocos Islands (Keeling Islands)
Australian External Territory

Area Sq Km	14	Languages	English
Area Sq Miles	5	Religions	Sunni Muslim, Christian
Population	621	Currency	Australian dollar
Capital	West Island		

The Cocos Islands consist of numerous islands on two coral atolls in the eastern Indian Ocean between Sri Lanka and Australia. Most of the population lives on West Island or Home Island. Coconuts are the only cash crop, and the main export.

COLOMBIA
Republic of Colombia

Area Sq Km	1 141 748	Languages	Spanish, Amerindian languages
Area Sq Miles	440 831	Religions	Roman Catholic, Protestant
Population	46 156 000	Currency	Colombian peso
Capital	Bogotá	Organizations	UN

A state in northwest South America, Colombia has coastlines on the Pacific Ocean and the Caribbean Sea. Behind coastal plains lie three ranges of the Andes mountains, separated by high valleys and plateaus where most Colombians live. To the southeast are grasslands and the forests of the Amazon. The climate is tropical, although temperatures vary with altitude. Only five per cent of land is cultivable. Coffee (Colombia is the world's second largest producer), sugar, bananas, cotton and flowers are exported. Coal, nickel, gold, silver, platinum and emeralds (Colombia is the world's largest producer) are mined. Oil and its products are the main export. Industries include the processing of minerals and crops. The main trade partner is the USA. Internal violence – both politically motivated and relating to Colombia's leading role in the international trade in illegal drugs – continues to hinder development.

COMOROS
Union of the Comoros

Area Sq Km	1 862	Languages	Comorian, French, Arabic
Area Sq Miles	719	Religions	Sunni Muslim, Roman Catholic
Population	839 000	Currency	Comoros franc
Capital	Moroni	Organizations	UN

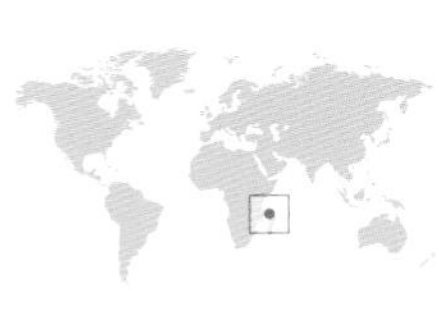

This state, in the Indian Ocean off the east African coast, comprises three volcanic islands of Njazidja (Grande Comore), Nzwani (Anjouan) and Mwali (Mohéli), and some coral atolls. These tropical islands are mountainous, with poor soil and few natural resources. Subsistence farming predominates. Vanilla, cloves and ylang-ylang (an essential oil) are exported, and the economy relies heavily on workers' remittances from abroad.

CONGO
Republic of the Congo

Area Sq Km	342 000	Languages	French, Kongo, Monokutuba, local languages
Area Sq Miles	132 047	Religions	Roman Catholic, Protestant, traditional beliefs, Sunni Muslim
Population	3 768 000	Currency	CFA franc
Capital	Brazzaville	Organizations	UN

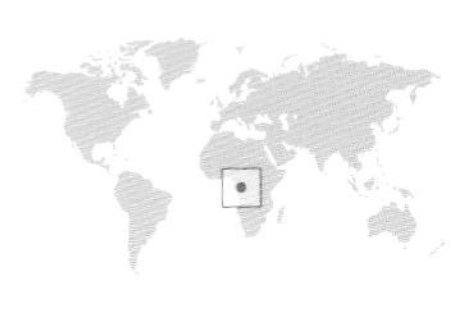

Congo, in central Africa, is mostly a forest or savanna-covered plateau drained by the Ubangi-Congo river systems. Sand dunes and lagoons line the short Atlantic coast. The climate is hot and tropical. Most Congolese live in the southern third of the country. Half of the workforce are farmers, growing food and cash crops including sugar, coffee, cocoa and oil palms. Oil and timber are the mainstays of the economy, and oil generates over fifty per cent of the country's export revenues.

CONGO, DEMOCRATIC REPUBLIC OF THE

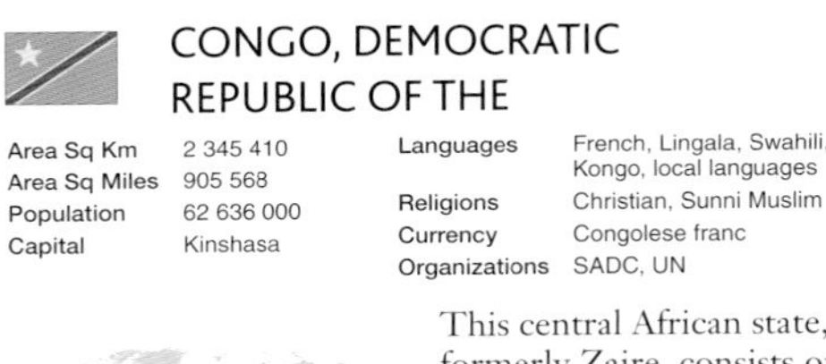

Area Sq Km	2 345 410	Languages	French, Lingala, Swahili, Kongo, local languages
Area Sq Miles	905 568	Religions	Christian, Sunni Muslim
Population	62 636 000	Currency	Congolese franc
Capital	Kinshasa	Organizations	SADC, UN

This central African state, formerly Zaire, consists of the basin of the Congo river flanked by plateaus, with high mountain ranges to the east and a short Atlantic coastline to the west. The climate is tropical, with rainforest close to the Equator and savanna to the north and south. Fertile land allows a range of food and cash crops to be grown, chiefly coffee. The country has vast mineral resources, with copper, cobalt and diamonds being the most important.

Cook Islands
New Zealand Overseas Territory

Area Sq Km	293	Languages	English, Maori
Area Sq Miles	113	Religions	Protestant, Roman Catholic
Population	13 000	Currency	New Zealand dollar
Capital	Avarua		

These consist of groups of coral atolls and volcanic islands in the southwest Pacific Ocean. The main island is Rarotonga. Distance from foreign markets and restricted natural resources hinder development.

COSTA RICA
Republic of Costa Rica

Area Sq Km	51 100	Languages	Spanish
Area Sq Miles	19 730	Religions	Roman Catholic, Protestant
Population	4 468 000	Currency	Costa Rican colón
Capital	San José	Organizations	UN

Costa Rica, in central America, has coastlines on the Caribbean Sea and Pacific Ocean. From tropical coastal plains, the land rises to mountains and a temperate central plateau, where most of the population lives.
The economy depends on agriculture and tourism, with ecotourism becoming increasingly important. Main exports are textiles, coffee and bananas, and almost half of all trade is with the USA.

CÔTE D'IVOIRE (Ivory Coast)

Republic of Côte d'Ivoire

Area Sq Km	322 463	Languages	French, Creole, Akan, local languages
Area Sq Miles	124 504	Religions	Sunni Muslim, Roman Catholic, traditional beliefs, Protestant
Population	19 262 000	Currency	CFA franc
Capital	Yamoussoukro	Organizations	UN

Côte d'Ivoire (Ivory Coast) is in west Africa, on the Gulf of Guinea. In the north are plateaus and savanna; in the south are low undulating plains and rainforest, with sand-bars and lagoons on the coast. Temperatures are warm, and rainfall is heavier in the south. Most of the workforce is engaged in farming. Côte d'Ivoire is a major producer of cocoa and coffee, and agricultural products (also including cotton and timber) are the main exports. Oil and gas have begun to be exploited.

CROATIA

Republic of Croatia

Area Sq Km	56 538	Languages	Croatian, Serbian
Area Sq Miles	21 829	Religions	Roman Catholic, Serbian Orthodox, Sunni Muslim
Population	4 555 000	Currency	Kuna
Capital	Zagreb	Organizations	NATO, UN

The southern European state of Croatia has a long coastline on the Adriatic Sea, with many offshore islands. Coastal areas have a Mediterranean climate; inland is cooler and wetter. Croatia was once strong agriculturally and industrially, but conflict in the early 1990s, and associated loss of markets and a fall in tourist revenue, caused economic difficulties from which recovery has been slow.

CUBA

Republic of Cuba

Area Sq Km	110 860	Languages	Spanish
Area Sq Miles	42 803	Religions	Roman Catholic, Protestant
Population	11 268 000	Currency	Cuban peso
Capital	Havana (La Habana)	Organizations	UN

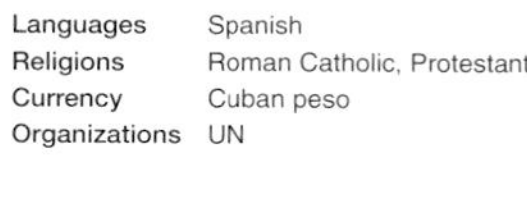

The country comprises the island of Cuba (the largest island in the Caribbean), and many islets and cays. A fifth of Cubans live in and around Havana. Cuba is slowly recovering from the withdrawal of aid and subsidies from the former USSR. Sugar remains the basis of the economy, although tourism is developing and is, together with remittances from workers abroad, an important source of revenue.

CYPRUS

Republic of Cyprus

Area Sq Km	9 251	Languages	Greek, Turkish, English
Area Sq Miles	3 572	Religions	Greek Orthodox, Sunni Muslim
Population	855 000	Currency	Euro
Capital	Nicosia (Lefkosia)	Organizations	Comm., EU, UN

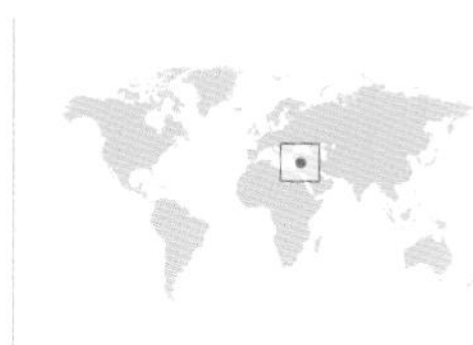

The eastern Mediterranean island of Cyprus has effectively been divided into two since 1974. The economy of the Greek-speaking south is based mainly on specialist agriculture and tourism, with shipping and offshore banking. The ethnically Turkish north depends on agriculture, tourism and aid from Turkey. The island has hot dry summers and mild winters. Cyprus joined the European Union in May 2004.

CZECH REPUBLIC

Area Sq Km	78 864	Languages	Czech, Moravian, Slovakian
Area Sq Miles	30 450	Religions	Roman Catholic, Protestant
Population	10 186 000	Currency	Koruna
Capital	Prague (Praha)	Organizations	EU, NATO, OECD, UN

The landlocked Czech Republic in central Europe consists of rolling countryside, wooded hills and fertile valleys. The climate is continental. The country has substantial reserves of coal and lignite, timber and some minerals, chiefly iron ore. It is highly industrialized, and major manufactured goods include industrial machinery, consumer goods, cars, iron and steel, chemicals and glass. Germany is the main trading partner. The Czech Republic joined the European Union in May 2004.

DENMARK

Kingdom of Denmark

Area Sq Km	43 075	Languages	Danish
Area Sq Miles	16 631	Religions	Protestant
Population	5 442 000	Currency	Danish krone
Capital	Copenhagen (København)	Organizations	EU, NATO, OECD, UN

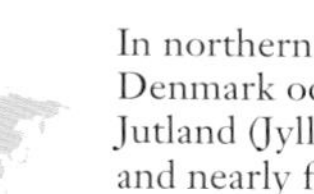

In northern Europe, Denmark occupies the Jutland (Jylland) peninsula and nearly five hundred islands in and between the North and Baltic Seas. The country is low-lying, with long, indented coastlines. The climate is cool and temperate, with rainfall throughout the year. A fifth of the population lives in and around the capital, Copenhagen (København), on the largest of the islands, Zealand (Sjælland).
The country's main natural resource is its agricultural potential: two-thirds of the total area is fertile farmland or pasture. Agriculture is high-tech, and with forestry and fishing employs only around six per cent of the workforce. Denmark is self-sufficient in oil and natural gas, produced from fields in the North Sea. Manufacturing, largely based on imported raw materials, accounts for over half of all exports, which include machinery, food, furniture and pharmaceuticals. The main trading partners are Germany and Sweden.

DJIBOUTI

Republic of Djibouti

Area Sq Km	23 200	Languages	Somali, Afar, French, Arabic
Area Sq Miles	8 958	Religions	Sunni Muslim, Christian
Population	833 000	Currency	Djibouti franc
Capital	Djibouti	Organizations	UN

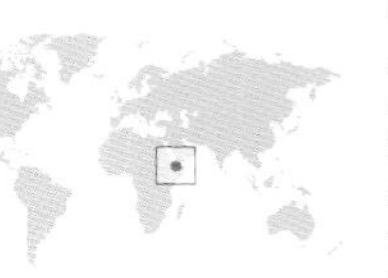

Djibouti lies in northeast Africa, on the Gulf of Aden at the entrance to the Red Sea. Most of the country is semi-arid desert with high temperatures and low rainfall. More than two-thirds of the population live in the capital. There is some camel, sheep and goat herding, but with few natural resources the economy is based on services and trade. Djibouti serves as a free trade zone for northern Africa, and the capital's port is a major transhipment and refuelling destination.
It is linked by rail to Addis Ababa in Ethiopia.

DOMINICA

Commonwealth of Dominica

Area Sq Km	750	Languages	English, Creole
Area Sq Miles	290	Religions	Roman Catholic, Protestant
Population	67 000	Currency	East Caribbean dollar
Capital	Roseau	Organizations	CARICOM, Comm., UN

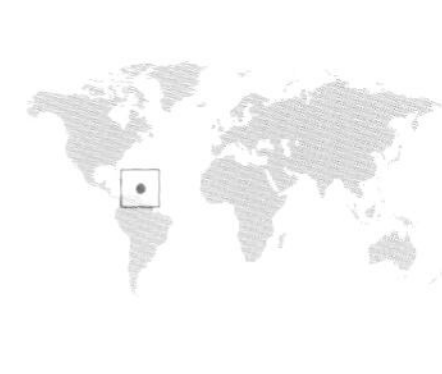

Dominica is the most northerly of the Windward Islands, in the eastern Caribbean. It is very mountainous and forested, with a coastline of steep cliffs. The climate is tropical and rainfall is abundant. Approximately a quarter of Dominicans live in the capital. The economy is based on agriculture, with bananas (the major export), coconuts and citrus fruits the most important crops. Tourism is a developing industry.

DOMINICAN REPUBLIC

Area Sq Km	48 442	Languages	Spanish, Creole
Area Sq Miles	18 704	Religions	Roman Catholic, Protestant
Population	9 760 000	Currency	Dominican peso
Capital	Santo Domingo	Organizations	UN

The state occupies the eastern two-thirds of the Caribbean island of Hispaniola (the western third is Haiti). It has a series of mountain ranges, fertile valleys and a large coastal plain in the east. The climate is hot tropical, with heavy rainfall. Sugar, coffee and cocoa are the main cash crops. Nickel (the main export), and gold are mined, and there is some light industry. The USA is the main trading partner. Tourism is the main foreign exchange earner.

EAST TIMOR

Democratic Republic of Timor-Leste

Area Sq Km	14 874	Languages	Portuguese, Tetun, English
Area Sq Miles	5 743	Religions	Roman Catholic
Population	1 155 000	Currency	United States dollar
Capital	Dili	Organizations	UN

The island of Timor is part of the Indonesian archipelago, to the north of western Australia. East Timor occupies the eastern section of the island, and a small coastal enclave (Ocussi) to the west. A referendum in 1999 ended Indonesia's occupation, after which the country was under UN transitional administration until full independence was achieved in 2002. The economy is in a poor state and East Timor is heavily dependent on foreign aid.

ECUADOR

Republic of Ecuador

Area Sq Km	272 045	Languages	Spanish, Quechua, and other Amerindian languages
Area Sq Miles	105 037	Religions	Roman Catholic
Population	13 341 000	Currency	United States dollar
Capital	Quito	Organizations	OPEC, UN

Ecuador is in northwest South America, on the Pacific coast. It consists of a broad coastal plain, high mountain ranges in the Andes, and part of the forested upper Amazon basin to the east. The climate is tropical, moderated by altitude. Most people live on the coast or in the mountain valleys. Ecuador is one of South America's main oil producers, and mineral reserves include gold. Most of the workforce depends on agriculture. Petroleum, bananas, shrimps, coffee and cocoa are exported. The USA is the main trading partner.

States and Territories

EGYPT
Arab Republic of Egypt

Area Sq Km	1 000 250	Languages	Arabic
Area Sq Miles	386 199	Religions	Sunni Muslim, Coptic Christian
Population	75 498 000	Currency	Egyptian pound
Capital	Cairo (Al Qāhirah)	Organizations	UN

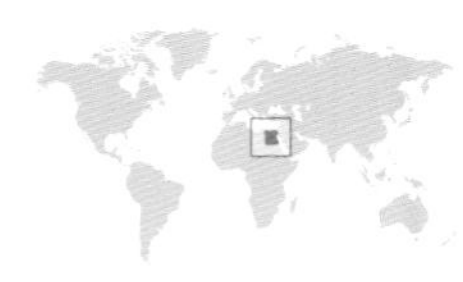

Egypt, on the eastern Mediterranean coast of north Africa, is low-lying, with areas below sea level in the Qattara depression. It is a land of desert and semi-desert, except for the Nile valley, where ninety-nine per cent of Egyptians live. The Sinai peninsula in the northeast of the country forms the only land bridge between Africa and Asia. The summers are hot, the winters mild and rainfall is negligible. Less than four per cent of land (chiefly around the Nile floodplain and delta) is cultivated. Farming employs about one-third of the workforce; cotton is the main cash crop. Egypt imports over half its food needs. There are oil and natural gas reserves, although nearly a quarter of electricity comes from hydroelectric power. Main exports are oil and oil products, cotton, textiles and clothing.

EL SALVADOR
Republic of El Salvador

Area Sq Km	21 041	Languages	Spanish
Area Sq Miles	8 124	Religions	Roman Catholic, Protestant
Population	6 857 000	Currency	El Salvador colón, United States dollar
Capital	San Salvador	Organizations	UN

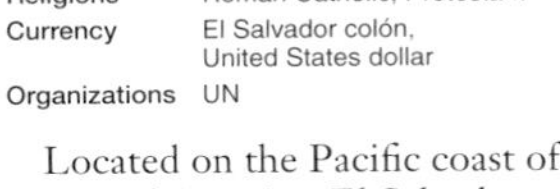

Located on the Pacific coast of central America, El Salvador consists of a coastal plain and volcanic mountain ranges which enclose a densely populated plateau area. The coast is hot, with heavy summer rainfall; the highlands are cooler. Coffee (the chief export), sugar and cotton are the main cash crops. The main trading partners are the USA and Guatemala.

EQUATORIAL GUINEA
Republic of Equatorial Guinea

Area Sq Km	28 051	Languages	Spanish, French, Fang
Area Sq Miles	10 831	Religions	Roman Catholic, traditional beliefs
Population	507 000	Currency	CFA franc
Capital	Malabo	Organizations	UN

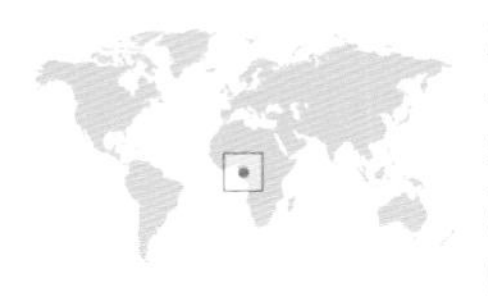

The state consists of Río Muni, an enclave on the Atlantic coast of central Africa, and the islands of Bioco, Annobón and the Corisco group. Most of the population lives on the coastal plain and upland plateau of Río Muni. The capital city, Malabo, is on the fertile volcanic island of Bioco. The climate is hot, humid and wet. Oil production started in 1992, and oil is now the main export, along with timber. The economy depends heavily on foreign aid.

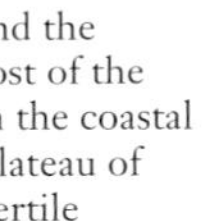

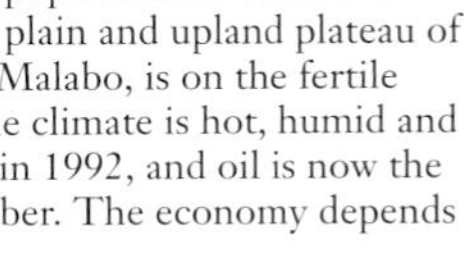

ERITREA
State of Eritrea

Area Sq Km	117 400	Languages	Tigrinya, Tigre
Area Sq Miles	45 328	Religions	Sunni Muslim, Coptic Christian
Population	4 851 000	Currency	Nakfa
Capital	Asmara	Organizations	UN

Eritrea, on the Red Sea coast of northeast Africa, consists of a high plateau in the north with a coastal plain which widens to the south. The coast is hot; inland is cooler. Rainfall is unreliable. The agriculture-based economy has suffered from over thirty years of war and occasional poor rains. Eritrea is one of the least developed countries in the world.

ESTONIA
Republic of Estonia

Area Sq Km	45 200	Languages	Estonian, Russian
Area Sq Miles	17 452	Religions	Protestant, Estonian and Russian Orthodox
Population	1 335 000	Currency	Kroon
Capital	Tallinn	Organizations	EU, NATO, UN

Estonia is in northern Europe, on the Gulf of Finland and the Baltic Sea. The land, over one-third of which is forested, is generally low-lying with many lakes. Approximately one-third of Estonians live in the capital, Tallinn. Exported goods include machinery, wood products, textiles and food products. The main trading partners are the Russian Federation, Finland and Sweden. Estonia joined the European Union in May 2004.

ETHIOPIA
Federal Democratic Republic of Ethiopia

Area Sq Km	1 133 880	Languages	Oromo, Amharic, Tigrinya, local languages
Area Sq Miles	437 794	Religions	Ethiopian Orthodox, Sunni Muslim, traditional beliefs
Population	83 099 000	Currency	Birr
Capital	Addis Ababa (Ādīs Ābeba)	Organizations	UN

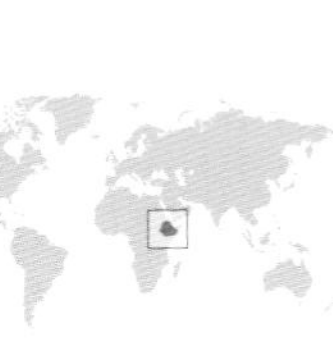

A landlocked country in northeast Africa, Ethiopia comprises a mountainous region in the west which is traversed by the Great Rift Valley. The east is mostly arid plateau land. The highlands are warm with summer rainfall. Most people live in the central–northern area. In recent years civil war, conflict with Eritrea and poor infrastructure have hampered economic development. Subsistence farming is the main activity, although droughts have led to frequent famines. Coffee is the main export and there is some light industry. Ethiopia is one of the least developed countries in the world.

Falkland Islands
United Kingdom Overseas Territory

Area Sq Km	12 170	Languages	English
Area Sq Miles	4 699	Religions	Protestant, Roman Catholic
Population	3 000	Currency	Falkland Islands pound
Capital	Stanley		

Lying in the southwest Atlantic Ocean, northeast of Cape Horn, two main islands, West Falkland and East Falkland and many smaller islands, form the territory of the Falkland Islands. The economy is based on sheep farming and the sale of fishing licences.

Faroe Islands
Self-governing Danish Territory

Area Sq Km	1 399	Languages	Faroese, Danish
Area Sq Miles	540	Religions	Protestant
Population	49 000	Currency	Danish krone
Capital	Thorshavn (Tórshavn)		

A self-governing territory, the Faroe Islands lie in the north Atlantic Ocean between the UK and Iceland. The islands benefit from the North Atlantic Drift ocean current, which has a moderating effect on the climate. The economy is based on deep-sea fishing.

FIJI
Republic of the Fiji Islands

Area Sq Km	18 330	Languages	English, Fijian, Hindi
Area Sq Miles	7 077	Religions	Christian, Hindu, Sunni Muslim
Population	839 000	Currency	Fiji dollar
Capital	Suva	Organizations	Comm., UN

The southwest Pacific republic of Fiji comprises two mountainous and volcanic islands, Vanua Levu and Viti Levu, and over three hundred smaller islands. The climate is tropical and the economy is based on agriculture (chiefly sugar, the main export), fishing, forestry, gold mining and tourism.

FINLAND
Republic of Finland

Area Sq Km	338 145	Languages	Finnish, Swedish
Area Sq Miles	130 559	Religions	Protestant, Greek Orthodox
Population	5 277 000	Currency	Euro
Capital	Helsinki (Helsingfors)	Organizations	EU, OECD, UN

Finland is in northern Europe, and nearly one-third of the country lies north of the Arctic Circle. Forests cover over seventy per cent of the land area, and ten per cent is covered by lakes. Summers are short and warm, and winters are long and severe, particularly in the north. Most of the population lives in the southern third of the country, along the coast or near the lakes. Timber is a major resource and there are important minerals, chiefly chromium. Main industries include metal working, electronics, paper and paper products, and chemicals. The main trading partners are Germany, Sweden and the UK.

FRANCE
French Republic

Area Sq Km	543 965	Languages	French, Arabic
Area Sq Miles	210 026	Religions	Roman Catholic, Protestant, Sunni Muslim
Population	61 647 000	Currency	Euro
Capital	Paris	Organizations	EU, NATO, OECD, UN

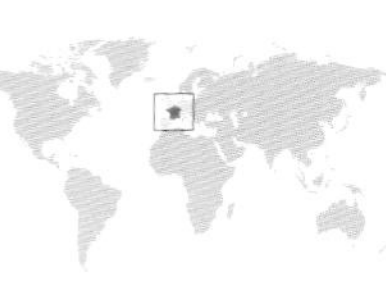

France lies in western Europe and has coastlines on the Atlantic Ocean and the Mediterranean Sea. It includes the Mediterranean island of Corsica. Northern and western regions consist mostly of flat or rolling countryside, and include the major lowlands of the Paris basin, the Loire valley and the Aquitaine basin, drained by the Seine, Loire and Garonne river systems respectively. The centre-south is dominated by the hill region of the Massif Central. To the east are the Vosges and Jura mountains and the Alps. In the southwest, the Pyrenees form a natural border with Spain. The climate is temperate with warm summers and cool winters, although the Mediterranean coast has hot, dry summers and mild winters. Over seventy per cent of the population lives in towns, with almost a sixth of the population living in the Paris area. The French economy has a substantial and varied agricultural base. It is a major producer of both fresh and processed food. There are relatively few mineral resources; it has coal reserves, and some oil and natural gas, but it relies heavily on nuclear and hydroelectric power and imported fuels. France is one of the world's major industrial countries. Main industries include food processing, iron, steel and aluminium production, chemicals, cars, electronics and oil refining. The main exports are transport equipment, plastics and chemicals. Tourism is a major source of revenue and employment. Trade is predominantly with other European Union countries.

French Guiana
French Overseas Department

Area Sq Km	90 000	Languages	French, Creole
Area Sq Miles	34 749	Religions	Roman Catholic
Population	202 000	Currency	Euro
Capital	Cayenne		

French Guiana, on the north coast of South America, is densely forested. The climate is tropical, with high rainfall. Most people live in the coastal strip, and agriculture is mostly subsistence farming. Forestry and fishing are important, but mineral resources are largely unexploited and industry is limited. French Guiana depends on French aid. The main trading partners are France and the USA.

French Polynesia

French Overseas Country

Area Sq Km	3 265	Languages	French, Tahitian, Polynesian languages
Area Sq Miles	1 261	Religions	Protestant, Roman Catholic
Population	263 000	Currency	CFP franc
Capital	Papeete		

Extending over a vast area of the southeast Pacific Ocean, French Polynesia comprises more than one hundred and thirty islands and coral atolls. The main island groups are the Marquesas Islands, the Tuamotu Archipelago and the Society Islands. The capital, Papeete, is on Tahiti in the Society Islands. The climate is subtropical, and the economy is based on tourism. The main export is cultured pearls.

GABON

Gabonese Republic

Area Sq Km	267 667	Languages	French, Fang, local languages
Area Sq Miles	103 347	Religions	Roman Catholic, Protestant, traditional beliefs
Population	1 331 000	Currency	CFA franc
Capital	Libreville	Organizations	UN

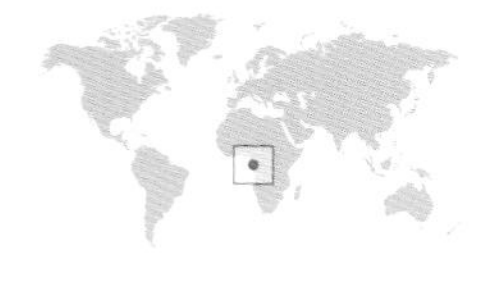

Gabon, on the Atlantic coast of central Africa, consists of low plateaus and a coastal plain lined by lagoons and mangrove swamps. The climate is tropical and rainforests cover over three-quarters of the land area. Over seventy per cent of the population lives in towns. The economy is heavily dependent on oil, which accounts for around seventy-five per cent of exports; manganese, uranium and timber are the other main exports. Agriculture is mainly at subsistence level.

THE GAMBIA

Republic of the Gambia

Area Sq Km	11 295	Languages	English, Malinke, Fulani, Wolof
Area Sq Miles	4 361	Religions	Sunni Muslim, Protestant
Population	1 709 000	Currency	Dalasi
Capital	Banjul	Organizations	Comm., UN

The Gambia, on the coast of west Africa, occupies a strip of land along the lower Gambia river. Sandy beaches are backed by mangrove swamps, beyond which is savanna. The climate is tropical, with most rainfall in the summer. Over seventy per cent of Gambians are farmers, growing chiefly groundnuts (the main export), cotton, oil palms and food crops. Livestock rearing and fishing are important, while manufacturing is limited. Re-exports, mainly from Senegal, and tourism are major sources of income.

Gaza

Semi-autonomous region

Area Sq Km	363	Languages	Arabic
Area Sq Miles	140	Religions	Sunni Muslim, Shi'a Muslim
Population	1 586 008	Currency	Israeli shekel
Capital	Gaza		

Gaza is a narrow strip of land on the southeast corner of the Mediterranean Sea, between Egypt and Israel. This Palestinian territory has limited autonomy from Israel, but hostilities between Israel and the indigenous Arab population continue to restrict its economic development.

GEORGIA

Republic of Georgia

Area Sq Km	69 700	Languages	Georgian, Russian, Armenian, Azeri, Ossetian, Abkhaz
Area Sq Miles	26 911	Religions	Georgian Orthodox, Russian Orthodox, Sunni Muslim
Population	4 395 000	Currency	Lari
Capital	T'bilisi	Organizations	CIS, UN

Georgia is in the northwest Caucasus area of southwest Asia, on the eastern coast of the Black Sea. Mountain ranges in the north and south flank the Kura and Rioni valleys. The climate is generally mild, and along the coast it is subtropical. Agriculture is important, with tea, grapes, and citrus fruits the main crops. Mineral resources include manganese ore and oil, and the main industries are steel, oil refining and machine building. The main trading partners are the Russian Federation and Turkey.

GERMANY

Federal Republic of Germany

Area Sq Km	357 022	Languages	German, Turkish
Area Sq Miles	137 847	Religions	Protestant, Roman Catholic
Population	82 599 000	Currency	Euro
Capital	Berlin	Organizations	EU, NATO, OECD, UN

The central European state of Germany borders nine countries and has coastlines on the North and Baltic Seas. Behind the indented coastline, and covering about one-third of the country, is the north German plain, a region of fertile farmland and sandy heaths drained by the country's major rivers. The central highlands are a belt of forested hills and plateaus which stretch from the Eifel region in the west to the Erzgebirge mountains along the border with the Czech Republic. Farther south the land rises to the Swabian Alps (Schwäbische Alb), with the high rugged and forested Black Forest (Schwarzwald) in the southwest. In the far south the Bavarian Alps form the border with Austria. The climate is temperate, with continental conditions in eastern areas. The population is highly urbanized, with over eighty-five per cent living in cities and towns. With the exception of coal, lignite, potash and baryte, Germany lacks minerals and other industrial raw materials. It has a small agricultural base, although a few products (chiefly wines and beers) enjoy an international reputation. Germany is the world's third ranking economy after the USA and Japan. Its industries are amongst the world's most technologically advanced. Exports include machinery, vehicles and chemicals. The majority of trade is with other countries in the European Union, the USA and Japan.

Baden-Württemberg (State)

Area Sq Km (Sq Miles)	Population	Capital
35 752 (13 804)	10 736 000	Stuttgart

Bayern (State)

Area Sq Km (Sq Miles)	Population	Capital
70 550 (27 240)	12 469 000	Munich (München)

Berlin (State)

Area Sq Km (Sq Miles)	Population	Capital
892 (344)	3 395 000	Berlin

Brandenburg (State)

Area Sq Km (Sq Miles)	Population	Capital
29 476 (11 381)	2 559 000	Potsdan

Bremen

Area Sq Km (Sq Miles)	Population	Capital
404 (156)	663 000	Bremen

Hamburg (State)

Area Sq Km (Sq Miles)	Population	Capital
755 (292)	1 744 000	Hamburg

Hessen (State)

Area Sq Km (Sq Miles)	Population	Capital
21 114 (8 152)	6 092 000	Wiesbaden

Mecklenburg-Vorpommern (State)

Area Sq Km (Sq Miles)	Population	Capital
23 173 (8 947)	1 707 000	Schwerin

Niedersachsen (State)

Area Sq Km (Sq Miles)	Population	Capital
47 616 (18 385)	7 994 000	Hannover

Nordrhein-Westfalen (State)

Area Sq Km (Sq Miles)	Population	Capital
34 082 (13 159)	18 058 000	Düsseldorf

Rheinland-Pfalz (State)

Area Sq Km (Sq Miles)	Population	Capital
19 847 (7 663)	4 059 000	Mainz

Saarland (State)

Area Sq Km (Sq Miles)	Population	Capital
2 568 (992)	1 050 000	Saarbrücken

Sachsen (State)

Area Sq Km (Sq Miles)	Population	Capital
18 413 (7 109)	4 274 000	Dresden

Sachsen-Anhalt (State)

Area Sq Km (Sq Miles)	Population	Capital
20 447 (7 895)	2 470 000	Magdeburg

Schleswig-Holstein (State)

Area Sq Km (Sq Miles)	Population	Capital
15 761 (6 085)	2 833 000	Kiel

Thüringen (State)

Area Sq Km (Sq Miles)	Population	Capital
16 172 (6 244)	2 335 000	Erfurt

GHANA

Republic of Ghana

Area Sq Km	238 537	Languages	English, Hausa, Akan, local languages
Area Sq Miles	92 100	Religions	Christian, Sunni Muslim, traditional beliefs
Population	23 478 000	Currency	Cedi
Capital	Accra	Organizations	Comm., UN

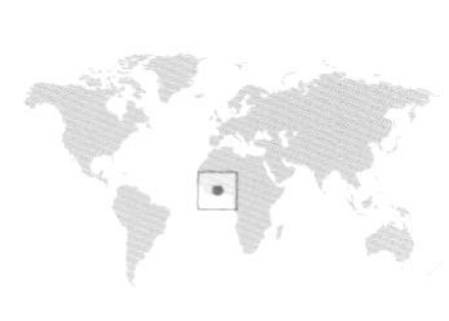

A west African state on the Gulf of Guinea, Ghana is a land of plains and low plateaus covered with savanna and rainforest. In the east is the Volta basin and Lake Volta. The climate is tropical, with the highest rainfall in the south, where most of the population lives. Agriculture employs around sixty per cent of the workforce. Main exports are gold, timber, cocoa, bauxite and manganese ore.

Gibraltar

United Kingdom Overseas Territory

Area Sq Km	7	Languages	English, Spanish
Area Sq Miles	3	Religions	Roman Catholic, Protestant, Sunni Muslim
Population	29 000	Currency	Gibraltar pound
Capital	Gibraltar		

Gibraltar lies on the south coast of Spain at the western entrance to the Mediterranean Sea. The economy depends on tourism, offshore banking and shipping services.

GREECE

Hellenic Republic

Area Sq Km	131 957	Languages	Greek
Area Sq Miles	50 949	Religions	Greek Orthodox, Sunni Muslim
Population	11 147 000	Currency	Euro
Capital	Athens (Athina)	Organizations	EU, NATO, OECD, UN

Greece comprises a mountainous peninsula in the Balkan region of southeastern Europe and many islands in the Ionian, Aegean and Mediterranean Seas. The islands make up over one-fifth of its area. Mountains and hills cover much of the country. The main lowland areas are the plains of Thessaly in the centre and around Thessaloniki in the northeast. Summers are hot and dry while winters are mild and wet, but colder in the north with heavy snowfalls in the mountains. One-third of Greeks live in the Athens area. Employment in agriculture accounts for approximately twenty per cent of the workforce, and exports include citrus fruits, raisins, wine, olives and olive oil. Aluminium and nickel are mined and a wide range of manufactures are produced, including food products and tobacco, textiles, clothing, and chemicals. Tourism is an important industry and there is a large services sector. Most trade is with other European Union countries.

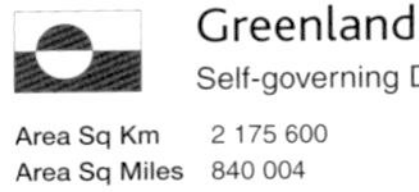

Greenland

Self-governing Danish Territory

Area Sq Km	2 175 600	Languages	Greenlandic, Danish
Area Sq Miles	840 004	Religions	Protestant
Population	58 000	Currency	Danish krone
Capital	Nuuk (Godthåb)		

Situated to the northeast of North America between the Atlantic and Arctic Oceans, Greenland is the largest island in the world. It has a polar climate and over eighty per cent of the land area is covered by permanent ice cap. The economy is based on fishing and fish processing.

GRENADA

Area Sq Km	378	Languages	English, Creole
Area Sq Miles	146	Religions	Roman Catholic, Protestant
Population	106 000	Currency	East Caribbean dollar
Capital	St George's	Organizations	CARICOM, Comm., UN

The Caribbean state comprises Grenada, the most southerly of the Windward Islands, and the southern islands of the Grenadines. Grenada has wooded hills, with beaches in the southwest. The climate is warm and wet. Agriculture is the main activity, with bananas, nutmeg and cocoa the main exports. Tourism is the main foreign exchange earner.

Guadeloupe

French Overseas Department

Area Sq Km	1 780	Languages	French, Creole
Area Sq Miles	687	Religions	Roman Catholic
Population	445 000	Currency	Euro
Capital	Basse-Terre		

Guadeloupe, in the Leeward Islands in the Caribbean, consists of two main islands (Basse-Terre and Grande-Terre, connected by a bridge), Marie-Galante, and a few outer islands. The climate is tropical, but moderated by trade winds. Bananas, sugar and rum are the main exports and tourism is a major source of income.

Guam

United States Unincorporated Territory

Area Sq Km	541	Languages	Chamorro, English, Tagalog
Area Sq Miles	209	Religions	Roman Catholic
Population	173 000	Currency	United States dollar
Capital	Hagåtña		

Lying at the south end of the Northern Mariana Islands in the western Pacific Ocean, Guam has a humid tropical climate. The island has a large US military base and the economy relies on that and on tourism.

GUATEMALA

Republic of Guatemala

Area Sq Km	108 890	Languages	Spanish, Mayan languages
Area Sq Miles	42 043	Religions	Roman Catholic, Protestant
Population	13 354 000	Currency	Quetzal, United States dollar
Capital	Guatemala City (Guatemala)	Organizations	UN

The most populous country in Central America after Mexico, Guatemala has long Pacific and short Caribbean coasts separated by a mountain chain which includes several active volcanoes. The climate is hot tropical in the lowlands and cooler in the highlands, where most of the population lives. Farming is the main activity and coffee, sugar and bananas are the main exports. There is some manufacturing of clothing and textiles. The main trading partner is the USA.

Guernsey

United Kingdom Crown Dependency

Area Sq Km	78	Languages	English, French
Area Sq Miles	30	Religions	Protestant, Roman Catholic
Population	63 923	Currency	Pound sterling
Capital	St Peter Port		

Guernsey is one of the Channel Islands, lying off northern France. The dependency also includes the nearby islands of Alderney, Sark and Herm. Financial services are an important part of the island's economy.

GUINEA

Republic of Guinea

Area Sq Km	245 857	Languages	French, Fulani, Malinke, local languages
Area Sq Miles	94 926	Religions	Sunni Muslim, traditional beliefs, Christian
Population	9 370 000	Currency	Guinea franc
Capital	Conakry	Organizations	UN

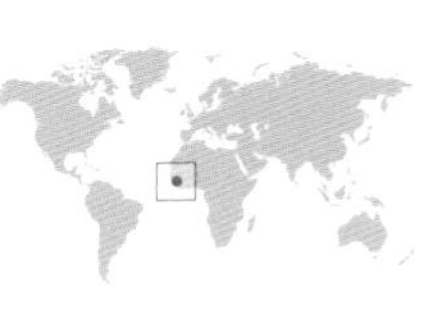

Guinea is in west Africa, on the Atlantic Ocean. There are mangrove swamps along the coast, while inland are lowlands and the Fouta Djallon mountains and plateaus. To the east are savanna plains drained by the upper Niger river system. The southeast is hilly. The climate is tropical, with high coastal rainfall. Agriculture is the main activity, employing nearly eighty per cent of the workforce, with coffee, bananas and pineapples the chief cash crops. There are huge reserves of bauxite, which accounts for more than seventy per cent of exports. Other exports include aluminium oxide, gold, coffee and diamonds.

GUINEA-BISSAU

Republic of Guinea-Bissau

Area Sq Km	36 125	Languages	Portuguese, Crioulo, local languages
Area Sq Miles	13 948	Religions	Traditional beliefs, Sunni Muslim, Christian
Population	1 695 000	Currency	CFA franc
Capital	Bissau	Organizations	UN

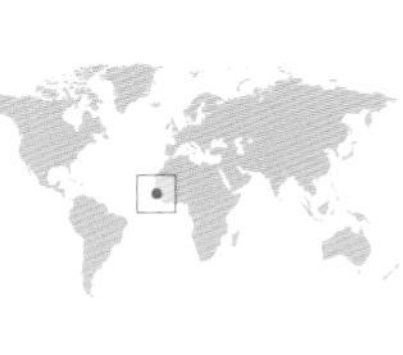

Guinea-Bissau is on the Atlantic coast of west Africa. The mainland coast is swampy and contains many estuaries. Inland are forested plains, and to the east are savanna plateaus. The climate is tropical. The economy is based mainly on subsistence farming. There is little industry, and timber and mineral resources are largely unexploited. Cashews account for seventy per cent of exports. Guinea-Bissau is one of the least developed countries in the world.

GUYANA

Co-operative Republic of Guyana

Area Sq Km	214 969	Languages	English, Creole, Amerindian languages
Area Sq Miles	83 000	Religions	Protestant, Hindu, Roman Catholic, Sunni Muslim
Population	738 000	Currency	Guyana dollar
Capital	Georgetown	Organizations	CARICOM, Comm., UN

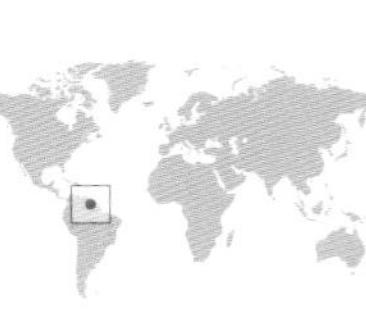

Guyana, on the northeast coast of South America, consists of highlands in the west and savanna uplands in the southwest. Most of the country is densely forested. A lowland coastal belt supports crops and most of the population. The generally hot, humid and wet conditions are modified along the coast by sea breezes. The economy is based on agriculture, bauxite, and forestry. Sugar, bauxite, gold, rice and timber are the main exports.

HAITI

Republic of Haiti

Area Sq Km	27 750	Languages	French, Creole
Area Sq Miles	10 714	Religions	Roman Catholic, Protestant, Voodoo
Population	9 598 000	Currency	Gourde
Capital	Port-au-Prince	Organizations	CARICOM, UN

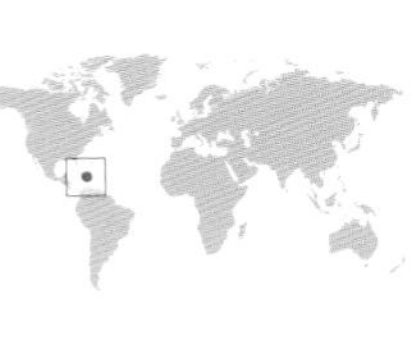

Haiti, occupying the western third of the Caribbean island of Hispaniola, is a mountainous state with small coastal plains and a central valley. The Dominican Republic occupies the rest of the island. The climate is tropical, and is hottest in coastal areas. Haiti has few natural resources, is densely populated and relies on exports of local crafts and coffee, and remittances from workers abroad.

HONDURAS

Republic of Honduras

Area Sq Km	112 088	Languages	Spanish, Amerindian languages
Area Sq Miles	43 277	Religions	Roman Catholic, Protestant
Population	7 106 000	Currency	Lempira
Capital	Tegucigalpa	Organizations	UN

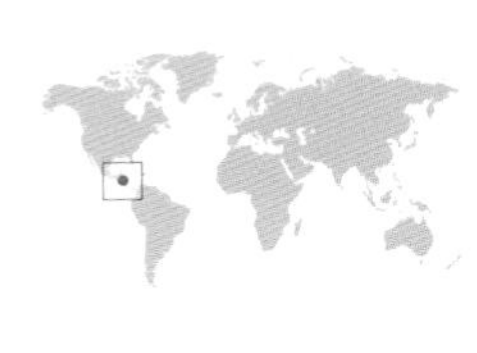

Honduras, in central America, is a mountainous and forested country with lowland areas along its long Caribbean and short Pacific coasts. Coastal areas are hot and humid with heavy summer rainfall; inland is cooler and drier. Most of the population lives in the central valleys. Coffee and bananas are the main exports, along with shellfish and zinc. Industry involves mainly agricultural processing.

HUNGARY

Republic of Hungary

Area Sq Km	93 030	Languages	Hungarian
Area Sq Miles	35 919	Religions	Roman Catholic, Protestant
Population	10 030 000	Currency	Forint
Capital	Budapest	Organizations	EU, NATO, OECD, UN

The Danube river flows north-south through central Hungary, a landlocked country in eastern Europe. In the east lies a great plain, flanked by highlands in the north. In the west low mountains and Lake Balaton separate a smaller plain and southern uplands. The climate is continental. Sixty per cent of the population lives in urban areas, and one-fifth lives in the capital, Budapest. Some minerals and energy resources are exploited, chiefly bauxite, coal and natural gas. Hungary has an industrial economy based on metals, machinery, transport equipment, chemicals and food products. The main trading partners are Germany and Austria. Hungary joined the European Union in May 2004.

ICELAND

Republic of Iceland

Area Sq Km	102 820	Languages	Icelandic
Area Sq Miles	39 699	Religions	Protestant
Population	301 000	Currency	Icelandic króna
Capital	Reykjavík	Organizations	NATO, OECD, UN

Iceland lies in the north Atlantic Ocean near the Arctic Circle, to the northwest of Scandinavia. The landscape is volcanic, with numerous hot springs, geysers, and approximately two hundred volcanoes. One-tenth of the country is covered by ice caps. Only coastal lowlands are cultivated and settled, and over half the population lives in the Reykjavik area. The climate is mild, moderated by the North Atlantic Drift ocean current and by southwesterly winds. The mainstays of the economy are fishing and fish processing, which account for seventy per cent of exports. Agriculture involves mainly sheep and dairy farming. Hydroelectric and geothermal energy resources are considerable. The main industries produce aluminium, ferro-silicon and fertilizers. Tourism, including ecotourism, is growing in importance.

INDIA

Republic of India

Area Sq Km	3 064 898	Languages	Hindi, English, many regional languages
Area Sq Miles	1 183 364	Religions	Hindu, Sunni Muslim, Shi'a Muslim, Sikh, Christian
Population	1 169 016 000	Currency	Indian rupee
Capital	New Delhi	Organizations	Comm., UN

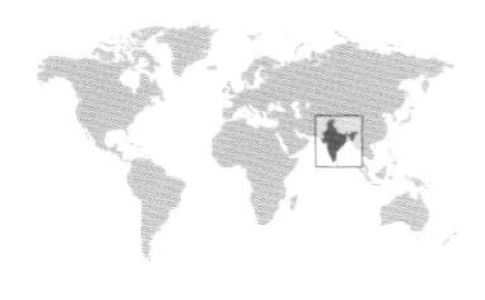

The south Asian country of India occupies a peninsula that juts out into the Indian Ocean between the Arabian Sea and Bay of Bengal. The heart of the peninsula is the Deccan plateau, bordered on either side by ranges of hills, the western Ghats and the lower eastern Ghats, which fall away to narrow coastal plains. To the north is a broad plain, drained by the Indus, Ganges and Brahmaputra rivers and their tributaries. The plain is intensively farmed and is the most populous region. In the west is the Thar Desert. The mountains of the Himalaya form India's northern border, together with parts of the Karakoram and Hindu Kush ranges in the northwest. The climate shows marked seasonal variation: a hot season from March to June; a monsoon season from June to October; and a cold season from November to February. Rainfall ranges between very high in the northeast Assam region to negligible in the Thar Desert. Temperatures range from very cold in the Himalaya to tropical heat over much of the south. Over seventy per cent of the huge population – the second largest in the world – is rural, although Delhi, Mumbai (Bombay) and Kolkata (Calcutta) all rank among the ten largest cities in the world. Agriculture, forestry and fishing account for a quarter of national output and two-thirds of employment. Much of the farming is on a subsistence basis and involves mainly rice and wheat. India is a major world producer of tea, sugar, jute, cotton and tobacco. Livestock is reared mainly for dairy products and hides. There are major reserves of coal, reserves of oil and natural gas, and many minerals, including iron, manganese, bauxite, diamonds and gold. The manufacturing sector is large and diverse – mainly chemicals and chemical products, textiles, iron and steel, food products, electrical goods and transport equipment; software and pharmaceuticals are also important. All the main manufactured products are exported, together with diamonds and jewellery. The USA, Germany, Japan and the UK are the main trading partners.

INDONESIA

Republic of Indonesia

Area Sq Km	1 919 445	Languages	Indonesian, local languages
Area Sq Miles	741 102	Religions	Sunni Muslim, Protestant, Roman Catholic, Hindu, Buddhist
Population	231 627 000	Currency	Rupiah
Capital	Jakarta	Organizations	APEC, ASEAN, OPEC, UN

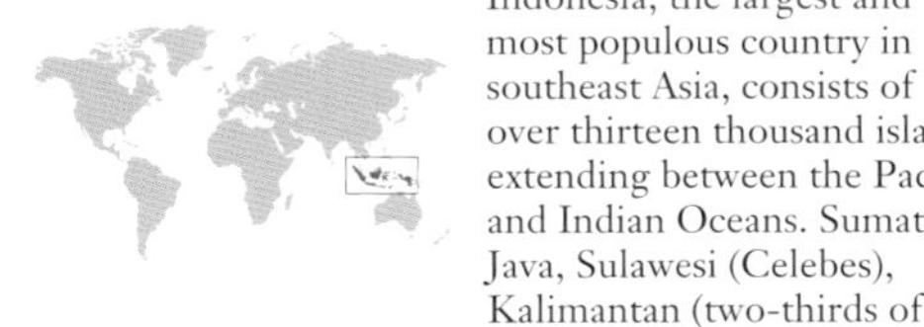

Indonesia, the largest and most populous country in southeast Asia, consists of over thirteen thousand islands extending between the Pacific and Indian Oceans. Sumatra, Java, Sulawesi (Celebes), Kalimantan (two-thirds of Borneo) and Papua (formerly Irian Jaya, western New Guinea) make up ninety per cent of the land area. Most of Indonesia is mountainous and covered with rainforest or mangrove swamps, and there are over three hundred volcanoes, many active. Two-thirds of the population lives in the lowland areas of the islands of Java and Madura. The climate is tropical monsoon. Agriculture is the largest sector of the economy and Indonesia is among the world's top producers of rice, palm oil, tea, coffee, rubber and tobacco. Many goods are produced, including textiles, clothing, cement, tin, fertilizers and vehicles. Main exports are oil, natural gas, timber products and clothing. Main trading partners are Japan, the USA and Singapore. Indonesia is a relatively poor country, and ethnic tensions and civil unrest often hinder economic development.

IRAN

Islamic Republic of Iran

Area Sq Km	1 648 000	Languages	Farsi, Azeri, Kurdish, regional languages
Area Sq Miles	636 296	Religions	Shi'a Muslim, Sunni Muslim
Population	71 208 000	Currency	Iranian rial
Capital	Tehrān	Organizations	OPEC, UN

Iran is in southwest Asia, and has coasts on The Gulf, the Caspian Sea and the Gulf of Oman. In the east is a high plateau, with large salt pans and a vast sand desert. In the west the Zagros Mountains form a series of ridges, and to the north lie the Elburz Mountains. Most farming and settlement is on the narrow plain along the Caspian Sea and in the foothills of the north and west. The climate is one of extremes, with hot summers and very cold winters. Most of the light rainfall is in the winter months. Agriculture involves approximately one-third of the workforce. Wheat is the main crop, but fruit (especially dates) and pistachio nuts are grown for export. Petroleum (the main export) and natural gas are Iran's leading natural resources. Manufactured goods include carpets, clothing, food products and construction materials.

IRAQ

Republic of Iraq

Area Sq Km	438 317	Languages	Arabic, Kurdish, Turkmen
Area Sq Miles	169 235	Religions	Shi'a Muslim, Sunni Muslim, Christian
Population	28 993 000	Currency	Iraqi dinar
Capital	Baghdād	Organizations	OPEC, UN

Iraq, in southwest Asia, has at its heart the lowland valley of the Tigris and Euphrates rivers. In the southeast, where the two rivers join, are the Mesopotamian marshes and the Shaṭṭ al 'Arab waterway leading to The Gulf. The north is hilly, while the west is mostly desert. Summers are hot and dry, and winters are mild with light, unreliable rainfall. The Tigris-Euphrates valley contains most of the country's arable land. One in five of the population lives in the capital, Baghdad. The economy has suffered following the 1991 Gulf War and the invasion of US-led coalition forces in 2005. The latter resulted in the overthrow of the dictator Saddam Hussein, but there is continuing internal instability. Oil is normally the main export.

IRELAND

Republic of Ireland

Area Sq Km	70 282	Languages	English, Irish
Area Sq Miles	27 136	Religions	Roman Catholic, Protestant
Population	4 301 000	Currency	Euro
Capital	Dublin (Baile Átha Cliath)	Organizations	EU, OECD, UN

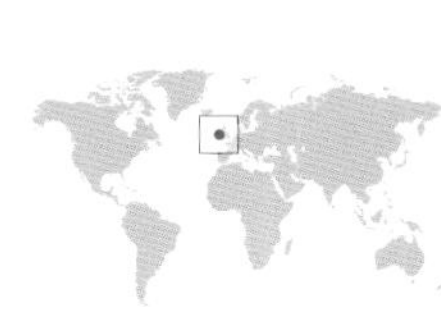

The Irish Republic occupies some eighty per cent of the island of Ireland, in northwest Europe. It is a lowland country of wide valleys, lakes and peat bogs, with isolated mountain ranges around the coast. The west coast is rugged and indented with many bays. The climate is mild due to the modifying effect of the North Atlantic Drift ocean current and rainfall is plentiful, although highest in the west. Nearly sixty per cent of the population lives in urban areas, Dublin and Cork being the main cities. Resources include natural gas, peat, lead and zinc. Agriculture, the traditional mainstay, now employs less than ten per cent of the workforce, while industry employs nearly thirty per cent. The main industries are electronics, pharmaceuticals and engineering as well as food processing, brewing and textiles. Service industries are expanding, with tourism a major earner. The UK is the main trading partner.

Isle of Man

United Kingdom Crown Dependency

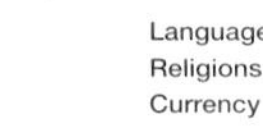

Area Sq Km	572	Languages	English
Area Sq Miles	221	Religions	Protestant, Roman Catholic
Population	79 000	Currency	Pound sterling
Capital	Douglas		

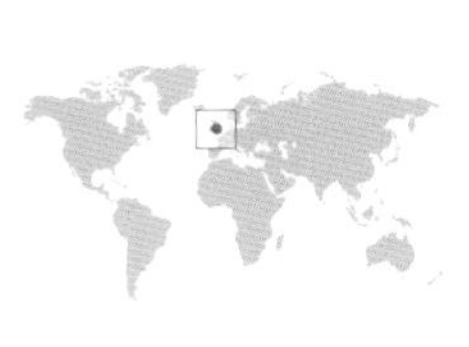

The Isle of Man lies in the Irish Sea between England and Northern Ireland. The island is self-governing, although the UK is responsible for its defence and foreign affairs. It is not part of the European Union, but has a special relationship with the EU which allows for free trade. Eighty per cent of the economy is based on the service sector, particularly financial services.

ISRAEL

State of Israel

Area Sq Km	20 770	Languages	Hebrew, Arabic
Area Sq Miles	8 019	Religions	Jewish, Sunni Muslim, Christian, Druze
Population	6 928 000	Currency	Shekel
Capital	Jerusalem (Yerushalayim) (El Quds) De facto capital. Disputed.	Organizations	UN

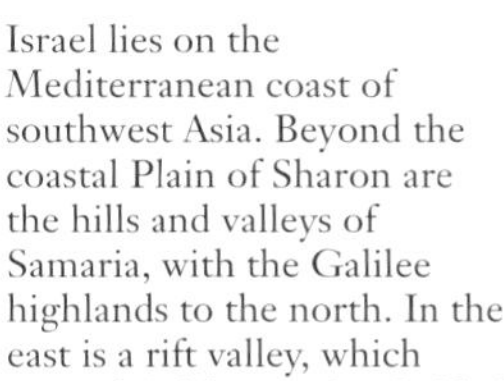

Israel lies on the Mediterranean coast of southwest Asia. Beyond the coastal Plain of Sharon are the hills and valleys of Samaria, with the Galilee highlands to the north. In the east is a rift valley, which extends from Lake Tiberias (Sea of Galilee) to the Gulf of Aqaba and contains the Jordan river and the Dead Sea. In the south is the Negev, a triangular semi-desert plateau. Most of the population lives on the coastal plain or in northern and central areas. Much of Israel has warm summers and mild, wet winters. The south is hot and dry. Agricultural production was boosted by the occupation of the West Bank in 1967. Manufacturing makes the largest contribution to the economy, and tourism is also important. Israel's main exports are machinery and transport equipment, software, diamonds, clothing, fruit and vegetables. The country relies heavily on foreign aid. Security issues relating to territorial disputes over the West Bank and Gaza have still to be resolved.

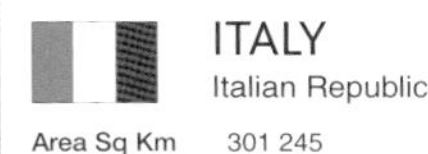

ITALY

Italian Republic

Area Sq Km	301 245	Languages	Italian
Area Sq Miles	116 311	Religions	Roman Catholic
Population	58 877 000	Currency	Euro
Capital	Rome (Roma)	Organizations	EU, NATO, OECD, UN

Most of the southern European state of Italy occupies a peninsula that juts out into the Mediterranean Sea. It includes the islands of Sicily and Sardinia and approximately seventy much smaller islands in the surrounding seas. Italy is mountainous, dominated by the Alps, which form its northern border, and the various ranges of the Apennines, which run almost the full length of the peninsula. Many of Italy's mountains are of volcanic origin, and its active volcanoes are Vesuvius, near Naples, Etna and Stromboli. The main lowland area, the Po river valley in the northeast, is the main agricultural and industrial area and is the most populous region. Italy has a Mediterranean climate, although the north experiences colder, wetter winters, with heavy snow in the Alps. Natural resources are limited, and only about twenty per cent of the land is suitable for cultivation. The economy is fairly diversified. Some oil, natural gas and coal are produced, but most fuels and minerals used by industry are imported. Agriculture is important, with cereals, vines, fruit and vegetables the main crops. Italy is the world's largest wine producer. The north is the centre of Italian industry, especially around Turin, Milan and Genoa. Leading manufactures include industrial and office equipment, domestic

appliances, cars, textiles, clothing, leather goods, chemicals and metal products. There is a strong service sector, and with over twenty-five million visitors a year, tourism is a major employer and accounts for five per cent of the national income. Finance and banking are also important. Most trade is with other European Union countries.

JAMAICA

Area Sq Km	10 991	Languages	English, Creole
Area Sq Miles	4 244	Religions	Protestant, Roman Catholic
Population	2 714 000	Currency	Jamaican dollar
Capital	Kingston	Organizations	CARICOM, Comm., UN

Jamaica, the third largest Caribbean island, has beaches and densely populated coastal plains traversed by hills and plateaus rising to the forested Blue Mountains in the east. The climate is tropical, but cooler and wetter on high ground. The economy is based on tourism, agriculture, mining and light manufacturing. Bauxite, aluminium oxide, sugar and bananas are the main exports. The USA is the main trading partner. Foreign aid is also significant.

Jammu and Kashmir

Disputed territory (India/Pakistan/China)

Area Sq Km	222 236	Population	13 000 000
Area Sq Miles	85 806	Capital	Srinagar

A disputed region in the north of the Indian subcontinent, to the west of the Karakoram and Himalaya mountains. The 'Line of Control' separates the northwestern, Pakistani-controlled area and the southeastern, Indian-controlled area. China occupies the Himalayan section known as the Aksai Chin, which is also claimed by India.

JAPAN

Area Sq Km	377 727	Languages	Japanese
Area Sq Miles	145 841	Religions	Shintoist, Buddhist, Christian
Population	127 967 000	Currency	Yen
Capital	Tōkyō	Organizations	APEC, OECD, UN

Japan lies in the Pacific Ocean off the coast of eastern Asia and consists of four main islands – Hokkaidō, Honshū, Shikoku and Kyūshū – and more than three thousand smaller islands in the surrounding Sea of Japan, East China Sea and Pacific Ocean. The central island of Honshū accounts for sixty per cent of the total land area and contains eighty per cent of the population. Behind the long and deeply indented coastline, nearly three-quarters of the country is mountainous and heavily forested. Japan has over sixty active volcanoes, and is subject to frequent earthquakes and typhoons. The climate is generally temperate maritime, with warm summers and mild winters, except in western Hokkaidō and northwest Honshū, where the winters are very cold with heavy snow. Only fourteen per cent of the land area is suitable for cultivation, and its few raw materials (coal, oil, natural gas, lead, zinc and copper) are insufficient for its industry. Most materials must be imported, including about ninety per cent of energy requirements. Yet Japan has the world's second largest industrial economy, with a range of modern heavy and light industries centred mainly around the major ports of Yokohama, Ōsaka and Tōkyō. It is the world's largest manufacturer of cars, motorcycles and merchant ships, and a major producer of steel, textiles, chemicals and cement. It is also a leading producer of many consumer durables, such as washing machines, and electronic equipment, chiefly office equipment and computers. Japan has a strong service sector, banking and finance being particularly important, and Tōkyō has one of the world's major stock exchanges. Owing to intensive agricultural production, Japan is seventy per cent self-sufficient in food. The main food crops are rice, barley, fruit, wheat and soya beans. Livestock rearing (chiefly cattle, pigs and chickens) and fishing are also important, and Japan has one of the largest fishing fleets in the world. A major trading nation, Japan has trade links with many countries in southeast Asia and in Europe, although its main trading partner is the USA.

Jersey

United Kingdom Crown Dependency

Area Sq Km	116	Languages	English, French
Area Sq Miles	45	Religions	Protestant, Roman Catholic
Population	88 200	Currency	Pound sterling
Capital	St Helier		

One of the Channel Islands lying off the west coast of the Cherbourg peninsula in northern France. Financial services are the most important part of the economy.

JORDAN

Hashemite Kingdom of Jordan

Area Sq Km	89 206	Languages	Arabic
Area Sq Miles	34 443	Religions	Sunni Muslim, Christian
Population	5 924 000	Currency	Jordanian dinar
Capital	'Ammān	Organizations	UN

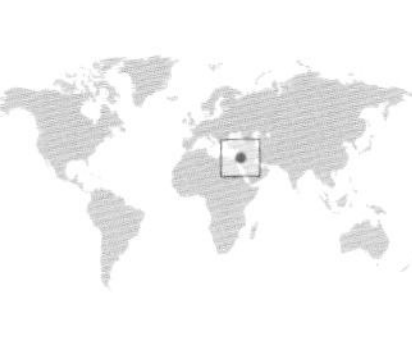

Jordan, in southwest Asia, is landlocked apart from a short coastline on the Gulf of Aqaba. Much of the country is rocky desert plateau. To the west of the mountains, the land falls below sea level to the Dead Sea and the Jordan river. The climate is hot and dry. Most people live in the northwest. Phosphates, potash, pharmaceuticals, fruit and vegetables are the main exports. The tourist industry is important, and the economy relies on workers' remittances from abroad and foreign aid.

KAZAKHSTAN

Republic of Kazakhstan

Area Sq Km	2 717 300	Languages	Kazakh, Russian, Ukrainian, German, Uzbek, Tatar
Area Sq Miles	1 049 155	Religions	Sunni Muslim, Russian Orthodox, Protestant
Population	15 422 000	Currency	Tenge
Capital	Astana (Akmola)	Organizations	CIS, UN

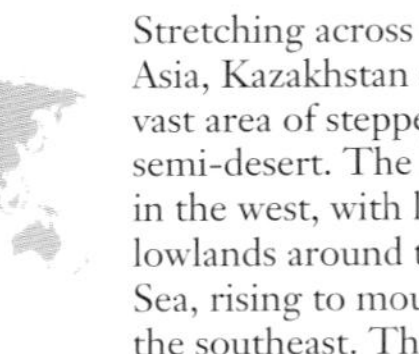

Stretching across central Asia, Kazakhstan covers a vast area of steppe land and semi-desert. The land is flat in the west, with large lowlands around the Caspian Sea, rising to mountains in the southeast. The climate is continental. Agriculture and livestock rearing are important, and cotton and tobacco are the main cash crops. Kazakhstan is very rich in minerals, including coal, chromium, gold, molybdenum, lead and zinc, and has substantial reserves of oil and gas. Mining, metallurgy, machine building and food processing are major industries. Oil, gas and minerals are the main exports, and the Russian Federation is the dominant trading partner.

KENYA

Republic of Kenya

Area Sq Km	582 646	Languages	Swahili, English, local languages
Area Sq Miles	224 961	Religions	Christian, traditional beliefs
Population	37 538 000	Currency	Kenyan shilling
Capital	Nairobi	Organizations	Comm., UN

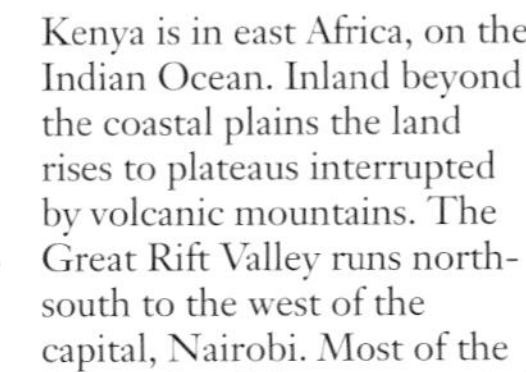

Kenya is in east Africa, on the Indian Ocean. Inland beyond the coastal plains the land rises to plateaus interrupted by volcanic mountains. The Great Rift Valley runs north-south to the west of the capital, Nairobi. Most of the population lives in the central area. Conditions are tropical on the coast, semi-desert in the north and savanna in the south. Hydroelectric power from the Upper Tana river provides most of the country's electricity. Agricultural products, mainly tea, coffee, fruit and vegetables, are the main exports. Light industry is important, and tourism, oil refining and re-exports for landlocked neighbours are major foreign exchange earners.

KIRIBATI

Republic of Kiribati

Area Sq Km	717	Languages	Gilbertese, English
Area Sq Miles	277	Religions	Roman Catholic, Protestant
Population	95 000	Currency	Australian dollar
Capital	Bairiki	Organizations	Comm., UN

Kiribati, in the Pacific Ocean, straddles the Equator and comprises coral islands in the Gilbert, Phoenix and Line Island groups and the volcanic island of Banaba. Most people live on the Gilbert Islands, and the capital, Bairiki, is on Tarawa island in this group. The climate is hot, and wetter in the north. Copra and fish are exported. Kiribati relies on remittances from workers abroad and foreign aid.

KOSOVO

Republic of Kosovo

Area Sq Km	10 908	Languages	Albanian, Serbian
Area Sq Miles	4 212	Religions	Sunni Muslim, Serbian Orthodox
Population	2 069 989	Currency	Euro
Capital	Prishtinë (Priština)		

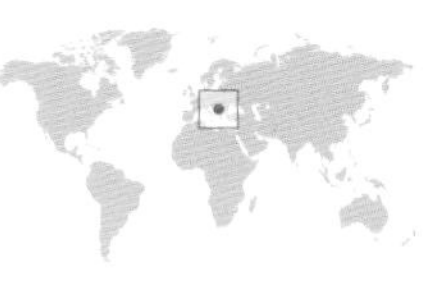

Kosovo, traditionally an autonomous southern province of Serbia, was the focus of ethnic conflict between Serbs and the majority ethnic Albanians in the 1990s until international intervention in 1999, after which it was administered by the UN. Kosovo declared its independence from Serbia in February 2008. The landscape is largely hilly or mountainous, especially along the southern and western borders.

KUWAIT

State of Kuwait

Area Sq Km	17 818	Languages	Arabic
Area Sq Miles	6 880	Religions	Sunni Muslim, Shi'a Muslim, Christian, Hindu
Population	2 851 000	Currency	Kuwaiti dinar
Capital	Kuwait (Al Kuwayt)	Organizations	OPEC, UN

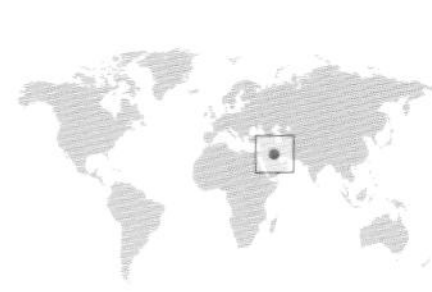

Kuwait lies on the northwest shores of The Gulf in southwest Asia. It is mainly low-lying desert, with irrigated areas along the bay, Kuwait Jun, where most people live. Summers are hot and dry, and winters are cool with some rainfall. The oil industry, which accounts for eighty per cent of exports, has largely recovered from the damage caused by the Gulf War in 1991. Income is also derived from extensive overseas investments. Japan and the USA are the main trading partners.

KYRGYZSTAN

Kyrgyz Republic

Area Sq Km	198 500	Languages	Kyrgyz, Russian, Uzbek
Area Sq Miles	76 641	Religions	Sunni Muslim, Russian Orthodox
Population	5 317 000	Currency	Kyrgyz som
Capital	Bishkek (Frunze)	Organizations	CIS, UN

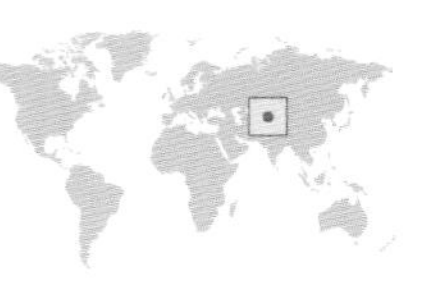

A landlocked central Asian state, Kyrgyzstan is rugged and mountainous, lying to the west of the Tien Shan mountain range. Most of the population lives in the valleys of the north and west. Summers are hot and winters cold. Agriculture (chiefly livestock farming) is the main activity. Some oil and gas, coal, gold, antimony and mercury are produced. Manufactured goods include machinery, metals and metal products, which are the main exports. Most trade is with Germany, the Russian Federation, Kazakhstan and Uzbekistan.

LAOS
Lao People's Democratic Republic

Area Sq Km	236 800	**Languages**	Lao, local languages
Area Sq Miles	91 429	**Religions**	Buddhist, traditional beliefs
Population	5 859 000	**Currency**	Kip
Capital	Vientiane (Viangchan)	**Organizations**	ASEAN, UN

A landlocked country in southeast Asia, Laos is a land of mostly forested mountains and plateaus. The climate is tropical monsoon. Most of the population lives in the Mekong valley and the low plateau in the south, where food crops, chiefly rice, are grown. Hydroelectricity from a plant on the Mekong river, timber, coffee and tin are exported. Laos relies heavily on foreign aid.

LATVIA
Republic of Latvia

Area Sq Km	64 589	**Languages**	Latvian, Russian
Area Sq Miles	24 938	**Religions**	Protestant, Roman Catholic, Russian Orthodox
Population	2 277 000	**Currency**	Lats
Capital	Rīga	**Organizations**	EU, NATO, UN

Latvia is in northern Europe, on the Baltic Sea and the Gulf of Riga. The land is flat near the coast but hilly with woods and lakes inland. The country has a modified continental climate. One-third of the people live in the capital, Rīga. Crop and livestock farming are important. There are few natural resources. Industries and main exports include food products, transport equipment, wood and wood products and textiles. The main trading partners are the Russian Federation and Germany. Latvia joined the European Union in May 2004.

LEBANON
Republic of Lebanon

Area Sq Km	10 452	**Languages**	Arabic, Armenian, French
Area Sq Miles	4 036	**Religions**	Shi'a Muslim, Sunni Muslim, Christian
Population	4 099 000	**Currency**	Lebanese pound
Capital	Beirut (Beyrouth)	**Organizations**	UN

Lebanon lies on the Mediterranean coast of southwest Asia. Beyond the coastal strip, where most of the population lives, are two parallel mountain ranges, separated by the Bekaa Valley (El Beq'a). The economy and infrastructure have been recovering since the 1975–1991 civil war crippled the traditional sectors of financial services and tourism. Italy, France and the UAE are the main trading partners.

LESOTHO
Kingdom of Lesotho

Area Sq Km	30 355	**Languages**	Sesotho, English, Zulu
Area Sq Miles	11 720	**Religions**	Christian, traditional beliefs
Population	2 008 000	**Currency**	Loti, South African rand
Capital	Maseru	**Organizations**	Comm., SADC, UN

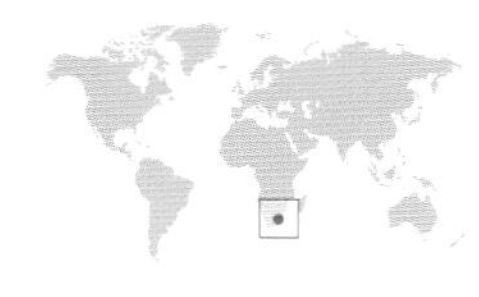

Lesotho is a landlocked state surrounded by the Republic of South Africa. It is a mountainous country lying within the Drakensberg mountain range. Farming and herding are the main activities. The economy depends heavily on South Africa for transport links and employment. A major hydroelectric plant completed in 1998 allows the sale of water to South Africa. Exports include manufactured goods (mainly clothing and road vehicles), food, live animals, wool and mohair.

LIBERIA
Republic of Liberia

Area Sq Km	111 369	**Languages**	English, Creole, local languages
Area Sq Miles	43 000	**Religions**	Traditional beliefs, Christian, Sunni Muslim
Population	3 750 000	**Currency**	Liberian dollar
Capital	Monrovia	**Organizations**	UN

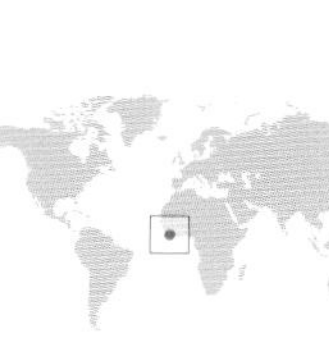

Liberia is on the Atlantic coast of west Africa. Beyond the coastal belt of sandy beaches and mangrove swamps the land rises to a forested plateau and highlands along the Guinea border. A quarter of the population lives along the coast. The climate is hot with heavy rainfall. Liberia is rich in mineral resources and forests. The economy is based on the production and export of basic products. Exports include diamonds, iron ore, rubber and timber. Liberia has a huge international debt and relies heavily on foreign aid.

LIBYA
Great Socialist People's Libyan Arab Jamahiriya

Area Sq Km	1 759 540	**Languages**	Arabic, Berber
Area Sq Miles	679 362	**Religions**	Sunni Muslim
Population	6 160 000	**Currency**	Libyan dinar
Capital	Tripoli (Ṭarābulus)	**Organizations**	OPEC, UN

Libya lies on the Mediterranean coast of north Africa. The desert plains and hills of the Sahara dominate the landscape and the climate is hot and dry. Most of the population lives in cities near the coast, where the climate is cooler with moderate rainfall. Farming and herding, chiefly in the northwest, are important but the main industry is oil. Libya is a major producer, and oil accounts for virtually all of its export earnings. Italy and Germany are the main trading partners.

LIECHTENSTEIN
Principality of Liechtenstein

Area Sq Km	160	**Languages**	German
Area Sq Miles	62	**Religions**	Roman Catholic, Protestant
Population	35 000	**Currency**	Swiss franc
Capital	Vaduz	**Organizations**	UN

A landlocked state between Switzerland and Austria, Liechtenstein has an industrialized, free-enterprise economy. Low business taxes have attracted companies to establish offices which provide approximately one-third of state revenues. Banking is also important. Major products include precision instruments, ceramics and textiles.

LITHUANIA
Republic of Lithuania

Area Sq Km	65 200	**Languages**	Lithuanian, Russian, Polish
Area Sq Miles	25 174	**Religions**	Roman Catholic, Protestant, Russian Orthodox
Population	3 390 000	**Currency**	Litas
Capital	Vilnius	**Organizations**	EU, NATO, UN

Lithuania is in northern Europe on the eastern shores of the Baltic Sea. It is mainly lowland with many lakes, rivers and marshes. Agriculture, fishing and forestry are important, but manufacturing dominates the economy. The main exports are machinery, mineral products and chemicals. The Russian Federation and Germany are the main trading partners. Lithuania joined the European Union in May 2004.

LUXEMBOURG
Grand Duchy of Luxembourg

Area Sq Km	2 586	**Languages**	Letzeburgish, German, French
Area Sq Miles	998	**Religions**	Roman Catholic
Population	467 000	**Currency**	Euro
Capital	Luxembourg	**Organizations**	EU, NATO, OECD, UN

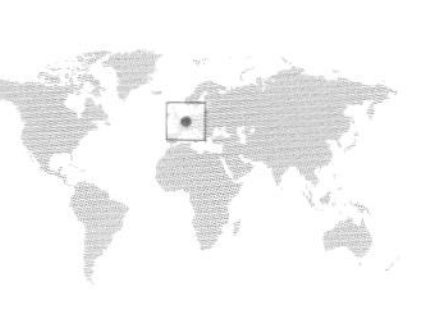

Luxembourg, a small landlocked country in western Europe, borders Belgium, France and Germany. The hills and forests of the Ardennes dominate the north, with rolling pasture to the south, where the main towns, farms and industries are found. The iron and steel industry is still important, but light industries (including textiles, chemicals and food products) are growing. Luxembourg is a major banking centre. Main trading partners are Belgium, Germany and France.

MACEDONIA (F.Y.R.O.M.)
Republic of Macedonia

Area Sq Km	25 713	**Languages**	Macedonian, Albanian, Turkish
Area Sq Miles	9 928	**Religions**	Macedonian Orthodox, Sunni Muslim
Population	2 038 000	**Currency**	Macedonian denar
Capital	Skopje	**Organizations**	NATO, UN

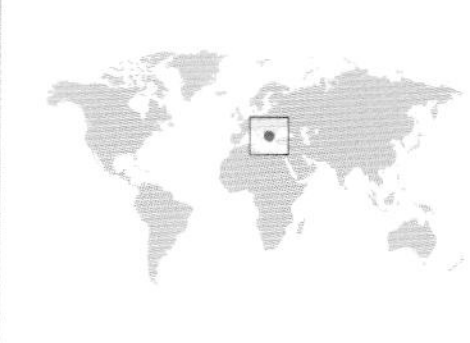

The Former Yugoslav Republic of Macedonia is a landlocked state in southern Europe. Lying within the southern Balkan Mountains, it is traversed northwest-southeast by the Vardar valley. The climate is continental. The economy is based on industry, mining and agriculture, but conflicts in the region have reduced trade and caused economic difficulties. Foreign aid and loans are now assisting in modernization and development of the country.

MADAGASCAR
Republic of Madagascar

Area Sq Km	587 041	**Languages**	Malagasy, French
Area Sq Miles	226 658	**Religions**	Traditional beliefs, Christian, Sunni Muslim
Population	19 683 000	**Currency**	Malagasy franc
Capital	Antananarivo	**Organizations**	SADC, UN

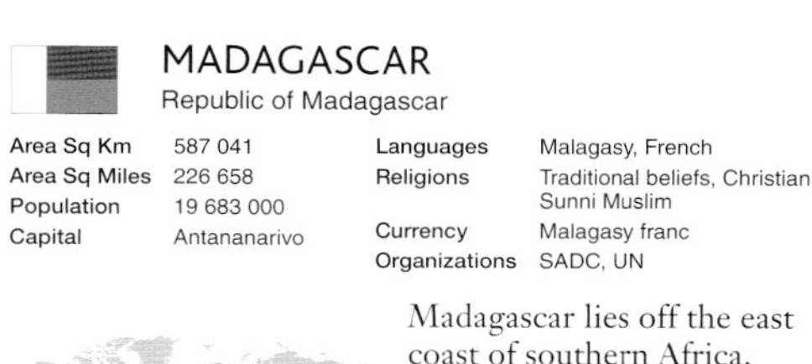

Madagascar lies off the east coast of southern Africa. The world's fourth largest island, it is mainly a high plateau, with a coastal strip to the east and scrubby plain to the west. The climate is tropical, with heavy rainfall in the north and east. Most of the population lives on the plateau. Although the amount of arable land is limited, the economy is based on agriculture. The main industries are agricultural processing, textile manufacturing and oil refining. Foreign aid is important. Exports include coffee, vanilla, cotton cloth, sugar and shrimps. France is the main trading partner.

MALAWI
Republic of Malawi

Area Sq Km	118 484	**Languages**	Chichewa, English, local languages
Area Sq Miles	45 747	**Religions**	Christian, traditional beliefs, Sunni Muslim
Population	13 925 000	**Currency**	Malawian kwacha
Capital	Lilongwe	**Organizations**	Comm., SADC, UN

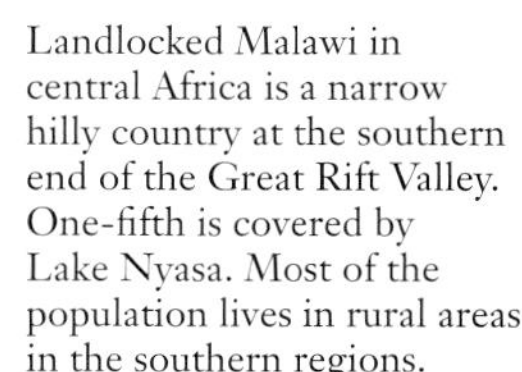

Landlocked Malawi in central Africa is a narrow hilly country at the southern end of the Great Rift Valley. One-fifth is covered by Lake Nyasa. Most of the population lives in rural areas in the southern regions. The climate is mainly subtropical, with varying rainfall. The economy is predominantly agricultural, with tobacco, tea and sugar the main exports. Malawi is one of the world's least developed countries and relies heavily on foreign aid. South Africa is the main trading partner.

States and Territories

MALAYSIA

Federation of Malaysia

Area Sq Km	332 965	Languages	Malay, English, Chinese, Tamil, local languages
Area Sq Miles	128 559	Religions	Sunni Muslim, Buddhist, Hindu, Christian, traditional beliefs
Population	26 572 000	Currency	Ringgit
Capital	Kuala Lumpur/ Putrajaya	Organizations	APEC, ASEAN, Comm., UN

Malaysia, in southeast Asia, comprises two regions, separated by the South China Sea. The western region occupies the southern Malay Peninsula, which has a chain of mountains dividing the eastern coastal strip from wider plains to the west. East Malaysia, consisting of the states of Sabah and Sarawak in the north of the island of Borneo, is mainly rainforest-covered hills and mountains with mangrove swamps along the coast. Both regions have a tropical climate with heavy rainfall. About eighty per cent of the population lives in Peninsular Malaysia. The country is rich in natural resources and has reserves of minerals and fuels. It is an important producer of tin, oil, natural gas and tropical hardwoods. Agriculture remains a substantial part of the economy, but industry is the most important sector. The main exports are transport and electronic equipment, oil, chemicals, palm oil, wood and rubber. The main trading partners are Japan, the USA and Singapore.

MALDIVES

Republic of the Maldives

Area Sq Km	298	Languages	Divehi (Maldivian)
Area Sq Miles	115	Religions	Sunni Muslim
Population	306 000	Currency	Rufiyaa
Capital	Male	Organizations	Comm., UN

The Maldive archipelago comprises over a thousand coral atolls (around two hundred of which are inhabited), in the Indian Ocean, southwest of India. Over eighty per cent of the land area is less than one metre above sea level. The main atolls are North and South Male and Addu. The climate is hot, humid and monsoonal. There is little cultivation and almost all food is imported. Tourism has expanded rapidly and is the most important sector of the economy.

MALI

Republic of Mali

Area Sq Km	1 240 140	Languages	French, Bambara, local languages
Area Sq Miles	478 821	Religions	Sunni Muslim, traditional beliefs, Christian
Population	12 337 000	Currency	CFA franc
Capital	Bamako	Organizations	UN

A landlocked state in west Africa, Mali is low-lying, with a few rugged hills in the northeast. Northern regions lie within the Sahara desert. To the south, around the Niger river, are marshes and savanna grassland. Rainfall is unreliable. Most of the population lives along the Niger and Falémé rivers. Exports include cotton, livestock and gold. Mali is one of the least developed countries in the world and relies heavily on foreign aid.

MALTA

Republic of Malta

Area Sq Km	316	Languages	Maltese, English
Area Sq Miles	122	Religions	Roman Catholic
Population	407 000	Currency	Euro
Capital	Valletta	Organizations	Comm., EU, UN

The islands of Malta and Gozo lie in the Mediterranean Sea, off the coast of southern Italy. The islands have hot, dry summers and mild winters. The economy depends on foreign trade, tourism and the manufacture of electronics and textiles. Main trading partners are the USA, France and Italy. Malta joined the European Union in May 2004.

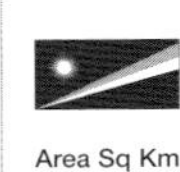

MARSHALL ISLANDS

Republic of the Marshall Islands

Area Sq Km	181	Languages	English, Marshallese
Area Sq Miles	70	Religions	Protestant, Roman Catholic
Population	59 000	Currency	United States dollar
Capital	Delap-Uliga-Djarrit	Organizations	UN

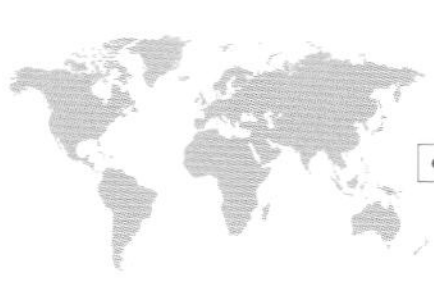

The Marshall Islands consist of over a thousand atolls, islands and islets, within two chains in the north Pacific Ocean. The main atolls are Majuro (home to half the population), Kwajalein, Jaluit, Enewetak and Bikini. The climate is tropical, with heavy autumn rainfall. About half the workforce is employed in farming or fishing. Tourism is a small source of foreign exchange and the islands depend heavily on aid from the USA.

Martinique

French Overseas Department

Area Sq Km	1 079	Languages	French, Creole
Area Sq Miles	417	Religions	Roman Catholic, traditional beliefs
Population	399 000		
Capital	Fort-de-France	Currency	Euro

Martinique, one of the Caribbean Windward Islands, has volcanic peaks in the north, a populous central plain, and hills and beaches in the south. Tourism is a major source of foreign exchange, and substantial aid is received from France. The main trading partners are France and Guadeloupe.

MAURITANIA

Islamic Arab and African Republic of Mauritania

Area Sq Km	1 030 700	Languages	Arabic, French, local languages
Area Sq Miles	397 955	Religions	Sunni Muslim
Population	3 124 000	Currency	Ouguiya
Capital	Nouakchott	Organizations	UN

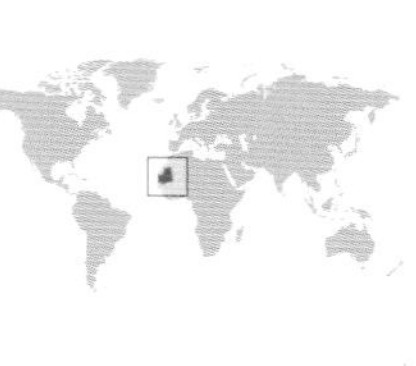

Mauritania is on the Atlantic coast of northwest Africa and lies almost entirely within the Sahara desert. Oases and a fertile strip along the Senegal river to the south are the only areas suitable for cultivation. The climate is generally hot and dry. About a quarter of Mauritanians live in the capital, Nouakchott. Most of the workforce depends on livestock rearing and subsistence farming. There are large deposits of iron ore which account for more than half of total exports. Mauritania's coastal waters are among the richest fishing grounds in the world. The main trading partners are France, Japan and Italy.

MAURITIUS

Republic of Mauritius

Area Sq Km	2 040	Languages	English, Creole, Hindi, Bhojpuri, French
Area Sq Miles	788	Religions	Hindu, Roman Catholic, Sunni Muslim
Population	1 262 000	Currency	Mauritius rupee
Capital	Port Louis	Organizations	Comm., SADC, UN

The state comprises Mauritius, Rodrigues and some twenty small islands in the Indian Ocean, east of Madagascar. The main island of Mauritius is volcanic in origin and has a coral coast, rising to a central plateau. Most of the population lives on the north and west sides of the island. The climate is warm and humid. The economy is based on sugar production, light manufacturing (chiefly clothing) and tourism.

Mayotte

French Departmental Collectivity

Area Sq Km	373	Languages	French, Mahorian
Area Sq Miles	144	Religions	Sunni Muslim, Christian
Population	186 026	Currency	Euro
Capital	Dzaoudzi		

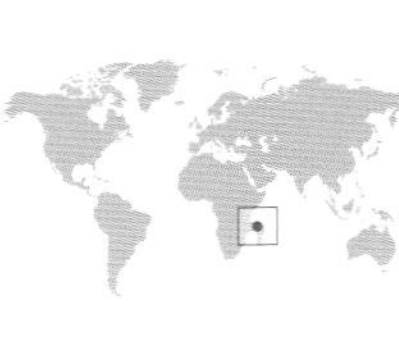

Lying in the Indian Ocean off the east coast of central Africa, Mayotte is geographically part of the Comoro archipelago. The economy is based on agriculture, but Mayotte depends heavily on aid from France.

MEXICO

United Mexican States

Area Sq Km	1 972 545	Languages	Spanish, Amerindian languages
Area Sq Miles	761 604	Religions	Roman Catholic, Protestant
Population	106 535 000	Currency	Mexican peso
Capital	México City (Mexico)	Organizations	APEC, OECD, UN

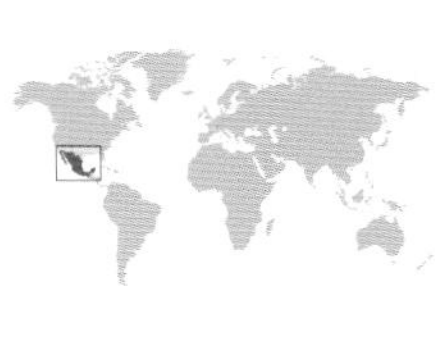

The largest country in Central America, Mexico extends south from the USA to Guatemala and Belize, and from the Pacific Ocean to the Gulf of Mexico. The greater part of the country is high plateau flanked by the western and eastern ranges of the Sierra Madre mountains. The principal lowland is the Yucatán peninsula in the southeast. The climate varies with latitude and altitude: hot and humid in the lowlands, warm on the plateau and cool with cold winters in the mountains. The north is arid, while the far south has heavy rainfall. Mexico City is the second largest conurbation in the world and the country's centre of trade and industry. Agriculture involves a fifth of the workforce; crops include grains, coffee, cotton and vegetables. Mexico is rich in minerals, including copper, zinc, lead, tin, sulphur, and silver. It is one of the world's largest producers of oil, from vast reserves in the Gulf of Mexico. The oil and petrochemical industries still dominate the economy, but a variety of manufactured goods are produced, including iron and steel, motor vehicles, textiles, chemicals and food and tobacco products. Tourism is growing in importance. Over three-quarters of all trade is with the USA.

MICRONESIA, FEDERATED STATES OF

Area Sq Km	701	Languages	English, Chuukese, Pohnpeian, local languages
Area Sq Miles	271	Religions	Roman Catholic, Protestant
Population	111 000	Currency	United States dollar
Capital	Palikir	Organizations	UN

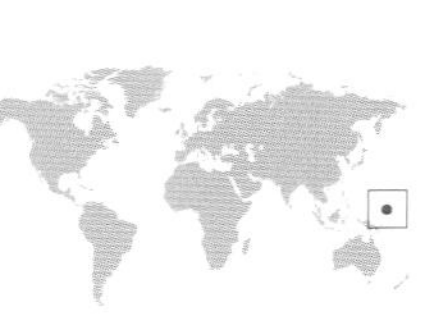

Micronesia comprises over six hundred atolls and islands of the Caroline Islands in the north Pacific Ocean. A third of the population lives on Pohnpei. The climate is tropical, with heavy rainfall. Fishing and subsistence farming are the main activities. Fish, garments and bananas are the main exports. Income is also derived from tourism and the licensing of foreign fishing fleets. The islands depend heavily on aid from the USA.

MOLDOVA

Republic of Moldova

Area Sq Km	33 700	Languages	Romanian, Ukrainian, Gagauz, Russian
Area Sq Miles	13 012	Religions	Romanian Orthodox, Russian Orthodox
Population	3 794 000	Currency	Moldovan leu
Capital	Chişinău (Kishinev)	Organizations	CIS, UN

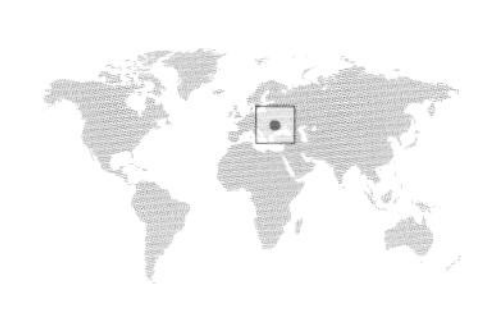

Moldova lies between Romania and Ukraine in eastern Europe. It consists of hilly steppe land, drained by the Prut and Dniester rivers. Moldova has no mineral resources, and the economy is mainly agricultural, with sugar beet, tobacco, wine and fruit the chief products. Food processing, machinery and textiles are the main industries. The Russian Federation is the main trading partner.

MONACO

Principality of Monaco

Area Sq Km	2	Languages	French, Monégasque, Italian
Area Sq Miles	1	Religions	Roman Catholic
Population	33 000	Currency	Euro
Capital	Monaco-Ville	Organizations	UN

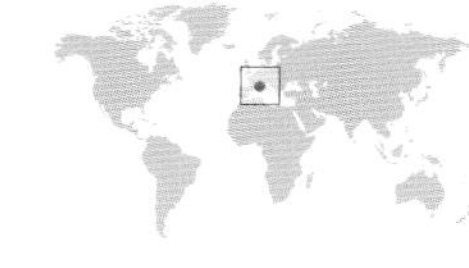

The principality occupies a rocky peninsula and a strip of land on France's Mediterranean coast. Monaco's economy depends on service industries (chiefly tourism, banking and finance) and light industry.

MONGOLIA

Area Sq Km	1 565 000	Languages	Khalka (Mongolian), Kazakh, local languages
Area Sq Miles	604 250	Religions	Buddhist, Sunni Muslim
Population	2 629 000	Currency	Tugrik (tögrög)
Capital	Ulan Bator (Ulaanbaatar)	Organizations	UN

Mongolia is a landlocked country in eastern Asia between the Russian Federation and China. Much of it is high steppe land, with mountains and lakes in the west and north. In the south is the Gobi desert. Mongolia has long, cold winters and short, mild summers. A quarter of the population lives in the capital, Ulaanbaatar. Livestock breeding and agricultural processing are important. There are substantial mineral resources. Copper and textiles are the main exports. China and the Russian Federation are the main trading partners.

MONTENEGRO

Area Sq Km	13 812	Languages	Serbian (Montenegrin), Albanian
Area Sq Miles	5 333	Religions	Montenegrin Orthodox, Sunni Muslim
Population	598 000	Currency	Euro
Capital	Podgorica	Organizations	UN

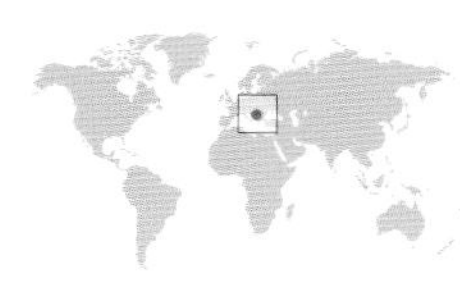

Montenegro, previously a constituent republic of the former Yugoslavia, became an independent nation in June 2006 when it opted to split from the state union of Serbia and Montenegro. Montenegro separates the much larger Serbia from the Adriatic coast. The landscape is rugged and mountainous, and the climate Mediterranean.

Montserrat

United Kingdom Overseas Territory

Area Sq Km	100	Languages	English
Area Sq Miles	39	Religions	Protestant, Roman Catholic
Population	6 000	Currency	East Caribbean dollar
Capital	Brades (Temporary Capital)	Organizations	CARICOM

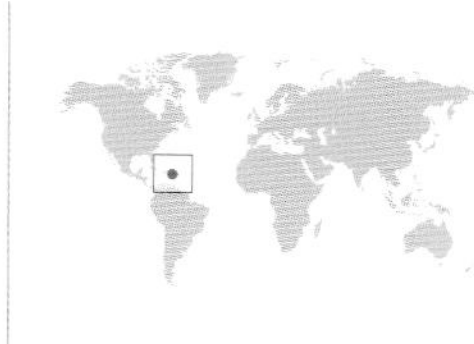

An island in the Leeward Islands group in the Lesser Antilles, in the Caribbean. From 1995 to 1997 the volcanoes in the Soufrière Hills erupted for the first time since 1630. Over sixty per cent of the island was covered in volcanic ash and Plymouth, the capital, was virtually destroyed. Many people emigrated, and the remaining population moved to the north of the island. Brades has replaced Plymouth as the temporary capital. Reconstruction is being funded by aid from the UK.

MOROCCO

Kingdom of Morocco

Area Sq Km	446 550	Languages	Arabic, Berber, French
Area Sq Miles	172 414	Religions	Sunni Muslim
Population	31 224 000	Currency	Moroccan dirham
Capital	Rabat	Organizations	UN

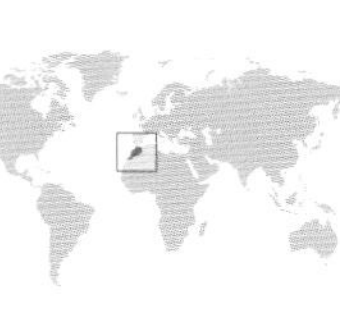

Lying in the northwest of Africa, Morocco has both Atlantic and Mediterranean coasts. The Atlas Mountains separate the arid south and disputed region of western Sahara from the fertile west and north, which have a milder climate. Most Moroccans live on the Atlantic coastal plain. The economy is based on agriculture, phosphate mining and tourism; the most important industries are food processing, textiles and chemicals.

MOZAMBIQUE

Republic of Mozambique

Area Sq Km	799 380	Languages	Portuguese, Makua, Tsonga, local languages
Area Sq Miles	308 642	Religions	Traditional beliefs, Roman Catholic, Sunni Muslim
Population	21 397 000	Currency	Metical
Capital	Maputo	Organizations	Comm., SADC, UN

Mozambique lies on the east coast of southern Africa. The land is mainly a savanna plateau drained by the Zambezi and Limpopo rivers, with highlands to the north. Most of the population lives on the coast or in the river valleys. In general the climate is tropical with winter rainfall, but droughts occur. The economy is based on subsistence agriculture. Exports include shrimps, cashews, cotton and sugar, but Mozambique relies heavily on aid, and remains one of the least developed countries in the world.

MYANMAR (Burma)

Union of Myanmar

Area Sq Km	676 577	Languages	Burmese, Shan, Karen, local languages
Area Sq Miles	261 228	Religions	Buddhist, Christian, Sunni Muslim
Population	48 798 000	Currency	Kyat
Capital	Nay Pyi Taw/ Rangoon (Yangôn)	Organizations	ASEAN, UN

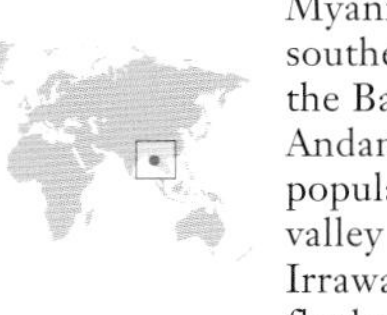

Myanmar (Burma) is in southeast Asia, bordering the Bay of Bengal and the Andaman Sea. Most of the population lives in the valley and delta of the Irrawaddy river, which is flanked by mountains and high plateaus. The climate is hot and monsoonal, and rainforest covers much of the land. Most of the workforce is employed in agriculture. Myanmar is rich in minerals, including zinc, lead, copper and silver. Political and social unrest and lack of foreign investment have affected economic development.

NAMIBIA

Republic of Namibia

Area Sq Km	824 292	Languages	English, Afrikaans, German, Ovambo, local languages
Area Sq Miles	318 261	Religions	Protestant, Roman Catholic
Population	2 074 000	Currency	Namibian dollar
Capital	Windhoek	Organizations	Comm., SADC, UN

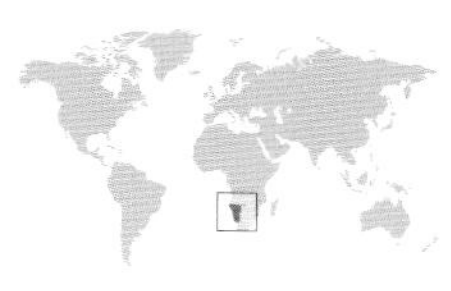

Namibia lies on the southern Atlantic coast of Africa. Mountain ranges separate the coastal Namib Desert from the interior plateau, bordered to the south and east by the Kalahari Desert. The country is hot and dry, but some summer rain in the north supports crops and livestock. Employment is in agriculture and fishing, although the economy is based on mineral extraction – diamonds, uranium, lead, zinc and silver. The economy is closely linked to the Republic of South Africa.

NAURU

Republic of Nauru

Area Sq Km	21	Languages	Nauruan, English
Area Sq Miles	8	Religions	Protestant, Roman Catholic
Population	10 000	Currency	Australian dollar
Capital	Yaren	Organizations	Comm., UN

Nauru is a coral island near the Equator in the Pacific Ocean. It has a fertile coastal strip and a barren central plateau. The climate is tropical. The economy was based on phosphate mining, but reserves are exhausted and replacement of this income is a serious long-term problem.

NEPAL

Federal Democratic Republic of Nepal

Area Sq Km	147 181	Languages	Nepali, Maithili, Bhojpuri, English, local languages
Area Sq Miles	56 827	Religions	Hindu, Buddhist, Sunni Muslim
Population	28 196 000	Currency	Nepalese rupee
Capital	Kathmandu	Organizations	UN

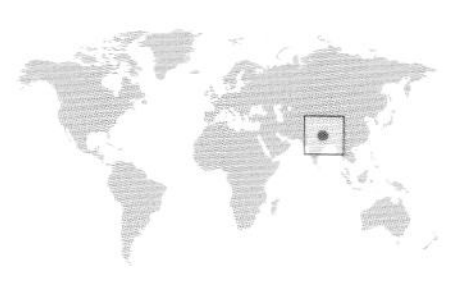

Nepal lies in the eastern Himalaya mountains between India and China. High mountains (including Everest) dominate the north. Most people live in the temperate central valleys and subtropical southern plains. The economy is based largely on agriculture and forestry. There is some manufacturing, chiefly of textiles and carpets, and tourism is important. Nepal relies heavily on foreign aid.

NETHERLANDS

Kingdom of the Netherlands

Area Sq Km	41 526	Languages	Dutch, Frisian
Area Sq Miles	16 033	Religions	Roman Catholic, Protestant, Sunni Muslim
Population	16 419 000	Currency	Euro
Capital	Amsterdam/ 's-Gravenhage (The Hague)	Organizations	EU, NATO, OECD, UN

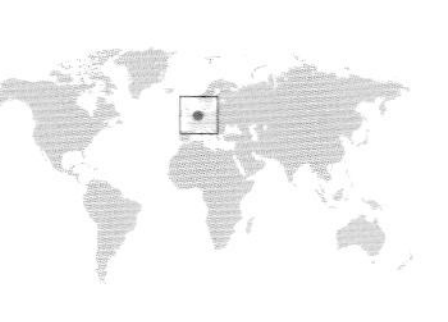

The Netherlands lies on the North Sea coast of western Europe. Apart from low hills in the far southeast, the land is flat and low-lying, much of it below sea level. The coastal region includes the delta of five rivers and polders (reclaimed land), protected by sand dunes, dykes and canals. The climate is temperate, with cool summers and mild winters. Rainfall is spread evenly throughout the year. The Netherlands is a densely populated and highly urbanized country, with the majority of the population living in the cities of Amsterdam, Rotterdam and The Hague. Horticulture and dairy farming are important activities, although they employ less than four per cent of the workforce. The Netherlands ranks as the world's third agricultural exporter, and is a leading producer and exporter of natural gas from reserves in the North Sea. The economy is based mainly on international trade and manufacturing industry. The main industries produce food products, chemicals, machinery, electrical and electronic goods and transport equipment. Germany is the main trading partner, followed by other European Union countries.

Netherlands Antilles

Self-governing Netherlands Territory

Area Sq Km	800	Languages	Dutch, Papiamento, English
Area Sq Miles	309	Religions	Roman Catholic, Protestant
Population	192 000	Currency	Netherlands Antilles guilder
Capital	Willemstad		

The territory comprises two island groups: Curaçao and Bonaire off the coast of Venezuela, and Saba, Sint Eustatius and Sint Maarten in the Lesser Antilles. Tourism, oil refining and offshore finance are the mainstays of the economy. The main trading partners are the USA, Venezuela and Mexico. Plans are in place for the dissolution of the territory in 2010. Under these plans, Curaçao and Sint Maarten will become Self-governing Netherlands Territories, and Bonaire, Saba and Sint Eustatius will be governed directly from the Netherlands.

New Caledonia

French Overseas Collectivity

Area Sq Km	19 058	Languages	French, local languages
Area Sq Miles	7 358	Religions	Roman Catholic, Protestant, Sunni Muslim
Population	242 000		
Capital	Nouméa	Currency	CFP franc

An island group lying in the southwest Pacific, with a sub-tropical climate. New Caledonia has over one-fifth of the world's nickel reserves, and the main economic activity is metal mining. Tourism is also important. New Caledonia relies on aid from France.

NEW ZEALAND

Area Sq Km	270 534	Languages	English, Maori
Area Sq Miles	104 454	Religions	Protestant, Roman Catholic
Population	4 179 000	Currency	New Zealand dollar
Capital	Wellington	Organizations	APEC, Comm., OECD, UN

New Zealand comprises two main islands separated by the narrow Cook Strait, and a number of smaller islands. North Island, where three-quarters of the population lives, has mountain ranges, broad fertile valleys and a central plateau with hot springs and active volcanoes. South Island is also mountainous, with the Southern Alps running its entire length. The only major lowland area is the Canterbury Plains in the centre-east. The climate is generally temperate, although South Island has colder winters. Farming is the mainstay of the economy. New Zealand is one of the world's leading producers of meat (beef, lamb and mutton), wool and dairy products; fruit and fish are also important. Hydroelectric and geothermal power provide much of the country's energy needs. Other industries produce timber, wood pulp, iron, aluminium, machinery and chemicals. Tourism is the fastest growing sector of the economy. The main trading partners are Australia, the USA and Japan.

NICARAGUA

Republic of Nicaragua

Area Sq Km	130 000	Languages	Spanish, Amerindian languages
Area Sq Miles	50 193		
Population	5 603 000	Religions	Roman Catholic, Protestant
Capital	Managua	Currency	Córdoba
		Organizations	UN

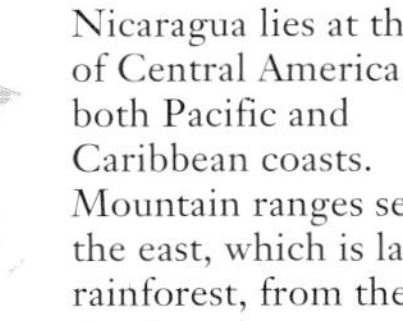

Nicaragua lies at the heart of Central America, with both Pacific and Caribbean coasts. Mountain ranges separate the east, which is largely rainforest, from the more developed western regions, which include Lake Nicaragua and some active volcanoes. The highest land is in the north. The climate is tropical. Nicaragua is one of the western hemisphere's poorest countries, and the economy is largely agricultural. Exports include coffee, seafood, cotton and bananas. The USA is the main trading partner. Nicaragua has a huge national debt, and relies heavily on foreign aid.

NIGER

Republic of Niger

Area Sq Km	1 267 000	Languages	French, Hausa, Fulani, local languages
Area Sq Miles	489 191		
Population	14 226 000	Religions	Sunni Muslim, traditional beliefs
Capital	Niamey		
		Currency	CFA franc
		Organizations	UN

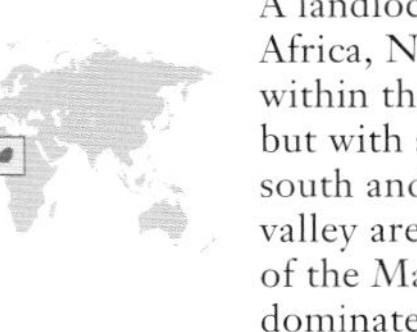

A landlocked state of west Africa, Niger lies mostly within the Sahara desert, but with savanna in the south and in the Niger valley area. The mountains of the Massif de l'Aïr dominate central regions. Much of the country is hot and dry. The south has some summer rainfall, although droughts occur. The economy depends on subsistence farming and herding, and uranium exports, but Niger is one of the world's least developed countries and relies heavily on foreign aid. France is the main trading partner.

NIGERIA

Federal Republic of Nigeria

Area Sq Km	923 768	Languages	English, Hausa, Yoruba, Ibo, Fulani, local languages
Area Sq Miles	356 669		
Population	148 093 000	Religions	Sunni Muslim, Christian, traditional beliefs
Capital	Abuja		
		Currency	Naira
		Organizations	Comm., OPEC, UN

Nigeria is in west Africa, on the Gulf of Guinea, and is the most populous country in Africa. The Niger delta dominates coastal areas, fringed with sandy beaches, mangrove swamps and lagoons. Inland is a belt of rainforest which gives way to woodland or savanna on high plateaus. The far north is the semi-desert edge of the Sahara. The climate is tropical, with heavy summer rainfall in the south but low rainfall in the north. Most of the population lives in the coastal lowlands or in the west. About half the workforce is involved in agriculture, mainly growing subsistence crops. Agricultural production, however, has failed to keep up with demand, and Nigeria is now a net importer of food. Cocoa and rubber are the only significant export crops. The economy is heavily dependent on vast oil resources in the Niger delta and in shallow offshore waters, and oil accounts for over ninety per cent of export earnings. Nigeria also has natural gas reserves and some mineral deposits, but these are largely undeveloped. Industry involves mainly oil refining, chemicals (chiefly fertilizers), agricultural processing, textiles, steel manufacture and vehicle assembly. Political instability in the past has left Nigeria with heavy debts, poverty and unemployment.

Niue

Self-governing New Zealand Territory

Area Sq Km	258	Languages	English, Nivean
Area Sq Miles	100	Religions	Christian
Population	2 000	Currency	New Zealand dollar
Capital	Alofi		

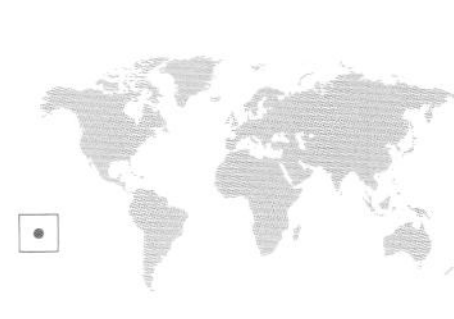

Niue, one of the largest coral islands in the world, lies in the south Pacific Ocean about 500 kilometres (300 miles) east of Tonga. The economy depends on aid and remittances from New Zealand. The population is declining because of migration to New Zealand.

Norfolk Island

Australian External Territory

Area Sq Km	35	Languages	English
Area Sq Miles	14	Religions	Protestant, Roman Catholic
Population	2 523	Currency	Australian dollar
Capital	Kingston		

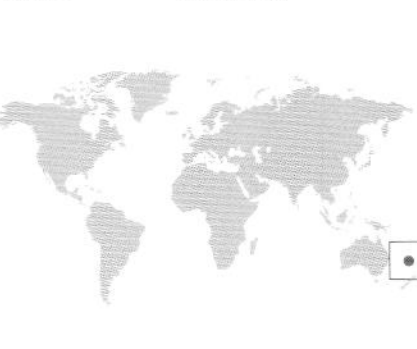

In the south Pacific Ocean, Norfolk Island lies between Vanuatu and New Zealand. Tourism has increased steadily and is the mainstay of the economy and provides revenues for agricultural development.

Northern Mariana Islands

United States Commonwealth

Area Sq Km	477	Languages	English, Chamorro, local languages
Area Sq Miles	184		
Population	84 000	Religions	Roman Catholic
Capital	Capitol Hill	Currency	United States dollar

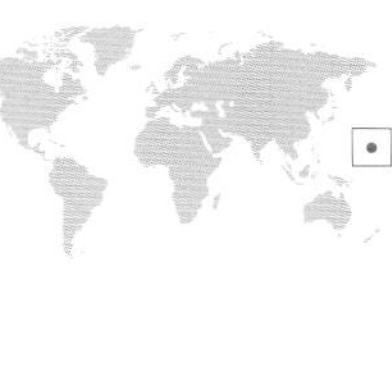

A chain of islands in the northwest Pacific Ocean, extending over 550 kilometres (350 miles) north to south. The main island is Saipan. Tourism is a major industry, employing approximately half the workforce.

NORTH KOREA

Democratic People's Republic of Korea

Area Sq Km	120 538	Languages	Korean
Area Sq Miles	46 540	Religions	Traditional beliefs, Chondoist, Buddhist
Population	23 790 000		
Capital	P'yŏngyang	Currency	North Korean won
		Organizations	UN

Occupying the northern half of the Korean peninsula in eastern Asia, North Korea is a rugged and mountainous country. The principal lowlands and the main agricultural areas are the plains in the southwest. More than half the population lives in urban areas, mainly on the coastal plains. North Korea has a continental climate, with cold, dry winters and hot, wet summers. Approximately one-third of the workforce is involved in agriculture, mainly growing food crops on cooperative farms. Various minerals, notably iron ore, are mined and are the basis of the country's heavy industries. Exports include minerals (lead, magnesite and zinc) and metal products (chiefly iron and steel). The economy declined after 1991, when ties to the former USSR and eastern bloc collapsed, and there have been serious food shortages.

NORWAY
Kingdom of Norway

Area Sq Km	323 878	Languages	Norwegian
Area Sq Miles	125 050	Religions	Protestant, Roman Catholic
Population	4 698 000	Currency	Norwegian krone
Capital	Oslo	Organizations	NATO, OECD, UN

Norway stretches along the north and west coasts of Scandinavia, from the Arctic Ocean to the North Sea. Its extensive coastline is indented with fjords and fringed with many islands. Inland, the terrain is mountainous, with coniferous forests and lakes in the south. The only major lowland areas are along the southern North Sea and Skagerrak coasts, where most of the population lives. The climate is modified by the effect of the North Atlantic Drift ocean current. Norway has vast petroleum and natural gas resources in the North Sea. It is one of western Europe's leading producers of oil and gas, and exports of oil account for approximately half of total export earnings. Related industries include engineering (oil and gas platforms) and petrochemicals. More traditional industries process local raw materials, particularly fish, timber and minerals. Agriculture is limited, but fishing and fish farming are important. Norway is the world's leading exporter of farmed salmon. Merchant shipping and tourism are major sources of foreign exchange.

OMAN
Sultanate of Oman

Area Sq Km	309 500	Languages	Arabic, Baluchi, Indian languages
Area Sq Miles	119 499	Religions	Ibadhi Muslim, Sunni Muslim
Population	2 595 000	Currency	Omani riyal
Capital	Muscat (Masqaṭ)	Organizations	UN

In southwest Asia, Oman occupies the east and southeast coasts of the Arabian Peninsula and an enclave north of the United Arab Emirates. Most of the land is desert, with mountains in the north and south. The climate is hot and mainly dry. Most of the population lives on the coastal strip on the Gulf of Oman. The majority depend on farming and fishing, but the oil and gas industries dominate the economy with around eighty per cent of export revenues coming from oil.

PAKISTAN
Islamic Republic of Pakistan

Area Sq Km	803 940	Languages	Urdu, Punjabi, Sindhi, Pushtu, English
Area Sq Miles	310 403	Religions	Sunni Muslim, Shi'a Muslim, Christian, Hindu
Population	163 902 000	Currency	Pakistani rupee
Capital	Islamabad	Organizations	Comm., UN

Pakistan is in the northwest part of the Indian subcontinent in south Asia, on the Arabian Sea. The east and south are dominated by the great basin of the Indus river system. This is the main agricultural area and contains most of the predominantly rural population. To the north the land rises to the mountains of the Karakoram, Hindu Kush and Himalaya mountains. The west is semi-desert plateaus and mountain ranges. The climate ranges between dry desert, and arctic tundra on the mountain tops. Temperatures are generally warm and rainfall is monsoonal. Agriculture is the main sector of the economy, employing approximately half of the workforce, and is based on extensive irrigation schemes. Pakistan is one of the world's leading producers of cotton and a major exporter of rice. Pakistan produces natural gas and has a variety of mineral deposits including coal and gold, but they are little developed. The main industries are textiles and clothing manufacture and food processing, with fabrics and ready-made clothing the leading exports. Pakistan also produces leather goods, fertilizers, chemicals, paper and precision instruments. The country depends heavily on foreign aid and remittances from workers abroad.

PALAU
Republic of Palau

Area Sq Km	497	Languages	Palauan, English
Area Sq Miles	192	Religions	Roman Catholic, Protestant, traditional beliefs
Population	20 000	Currency	United States dollar
Capital	Melekeok	Organizations	UN

Palau comprises over three hundred islands in the western Caroline Islands, in the west Pacific Ocean. The climate is tropical. The economy is based on farming, fishing and tourism, but Palau is heavily dependent on aid from the USA.

PANAMA
Republic of Panama

Area Sq Km	77 082	Languages	Spanish, English, Amerindian languages
Area Sq Miles	29 762	Religions	Roman Catholic, Protestant, Sunni Muslim
Population	3 343 000	Currency	Balboa
Capital	Panama City (Panamá)	Organizations	UN

Panama is the most southerly state in central America and has Pacific and Caribbean coasts. It is hilly, with mountains in the west and jungle near the Colombian border. The climate is tropical. Most of the population lives on the drier Pacific side. The economy is based mainly on services related to the Panama Canal: shipping, banking and tourism. Exports include bananas, shrimps, coffee, clothing and fish products. The USA is the main trading partner.

PAPUA NEW GUINEA
Independent State of Papua New Guinea

Area Sq Km	462 840	Languages	English, Tok Pisin (Creole), local languages
Area Sq Miles	178 704	Religions	Protestant, Roman Catholic, traditional beliefs
Population	6 331 000	Currency	Kina
Capital	Port Moresby	Organizations	APEC, Comm., UN

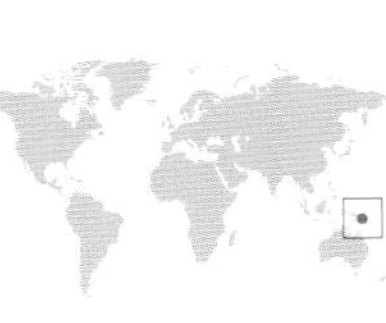

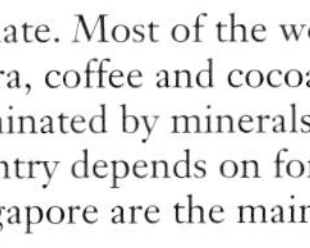

Papua New Guinea occupies the eastern half of the island of New Guinea and includes many island groups. It has a forested and mountainous interior, bordered by swampy plains, and a tropical monsoon climate. Most of the workforce are farmers. Timber, copra, coffee and cocoa are important, but exports are dominated by minerals, chiefly gold and copper. The country depends on foreign aid. Australia, Japan and Singapore are the main trading partners.

PARAGUAY
Republic of Paraguay

Area Sq Km	406 752	Languages	Spanish, Guaraní
Area Sq Miles	157 048	Religions	Roman Catholic, Protestant
Population	6 127 000	Currency	Guaraní
Capital	Asunción	Organizations	UN

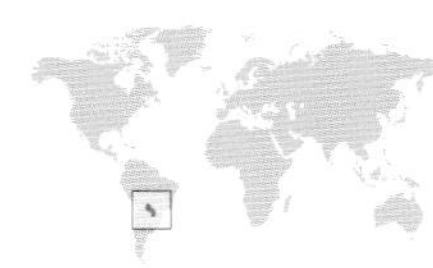

Paraguay is a landlocked country in central South America, bordering Bolivia, Brazil and Argentina. The Paraguay river separates a sparsely populated western zone of marsh and flat alluvial plains from a more developed, hilly and forested region to the east and south. The climate is subtropical. Virtually all electricity is produced by hydroelectric plants, and surplus power is exported to Brazil and Argentina. The hydroelectric dam at Itaipú is one of the largest in the world. The mainstay of the economy is agriculture and related industries. Exports include cotton, soya bean and edible oil products, timber and meat. Brazil and Argentina are the main trading partners.

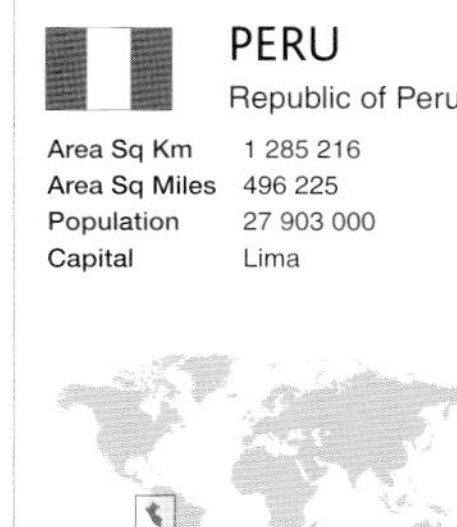

PERU
Republic of Peru

Area Sq Km	1 285 216	Languages	Spanish, Quechua, Aymara
Area Sq Miles	496 225	Religions	Roman Catholic, Protestant
Population	27 903 000	Currency	Sol
Capital	Lima	Organizations	APEC, UN

Peru lies on the Pacific coast of South America. Most Peruvians live on the coastal strip and on the plateaus of the high Andes mountains. East of the Andes is the Amazon rainforest. The coast is temperate with low rainfall while the east is hot, humid and wet. Agriculture involves one-third of the workforce and fishing is also important. Agriculture and fishing have both been disrupted by the El Niño climatic effect in recent years. Sugar, cotton, coffee and, illegally, coca are the main cash crops. Copper and copper products, fishmeal, zinc products, coffee, petroleum and its products, and textiles are the main exports. The USA and the European Union are the main trading partners.

PHILIPPINES
Republic of the Philippines

Area Sq Km	300 000	Languages	English, Filipino, Tagalog, Cebuano, local languages
Area Sq Miles	115 831	Religions	Roman Catholic, Protestant, Sunni Muslim, Aglipayan
Population	87 960 000	Currency	Philippine peso
Capital	Manila	Organizations	APEC, ASEAN, UN

The Philippines, in southeast Asia, consists of over seven thousand islands and atolls lying between the South China Sea and the Pacific Ocean. The islands of Luzon and Mindanao account for two-thirds of the land area. They and nine other fairly large islands are mountainous and forested. There are active volcanoes, and earthquakes and tropical storms are common. Most of the population lives in the plains on the larger islands or on the coastal strips. The climate is hot and humid with heavy monsoonal rainfall. Rice, coconuts, sugar cane, pineapples and bananas are the main agricultural crops, and fishing is also important. Main exports are electronic equipment, machinery and transport equipment, garments and coconut products. Foreign aid and remittances from workers abroad are important to the economy, which faces problems of high population growth rate and high unemployment. The USA and Japan are the main trading partners.

Pitcairn Islands
United Kingdom Overseas Territory

Area Sq Km	45	Languages	English
Area Sq Miles	17	Religions	Protestant
Population	48	Currency	New Zealand dollar
Capital	Adamstown		

An island group in the southeast Pacific Ocean consisting of Pitcairn Island and three uninhabited islands. It was originally settled by mutineers from HMS *Bounty* in 1790.

POLAND
Polish Republic

Area Sq Km	312 683	Languages	Polish, German
Area Sq Miles	120 728	Religions	Roman Catholic, Polish Orthodox
Population	38 082 000	Currency	Złoty
Capital	Warsaw (Warszawa)	Organizations	EU, NATO, OECD, UN

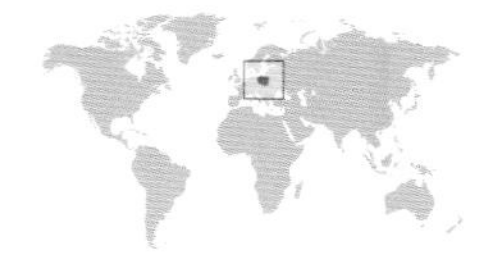

Poland lies on the Baltic coast of eastern Europe. The Oder (Odra) and Vistula (Wisła) river deltas dominate the coast. Inland, much of the country is low-lying, with woods and lakes. In the south the land rises to the Sudeten Mountains and the western part of the Carpathian Mountains, which form the borders with the Czech Republic and Slovakia respectively. The climate is continental. Around a quarter of the workforce is involved in agriculture, and exports include livestock products and sugar. The economy is heavily industrialized, with mining and manufacturing accounting for forty per cent of national income. Poland is one of the world's major producers of coal, and also produces copper, zinc, lead, sulphur and natural gas. The main industries are machinery and transport equipment, shipbuilding, and metal and chemical production. Exports include machinery and transport equipment, manufactured goods, food and live animals. Germany is the main trading partner. Poland joined the European Union in May 2004.

PORTUGAL
Portuguese Republic

Area Sq Km	88 940	Languages	Portuguese
Area Sq Miles	34 340	Religions	Roman Catholic, Protestant
Population	10 623 000	Currency	Euro
Capital	Lisbon (Lisboa)	Organizations	EU, NATO, OECD, UN

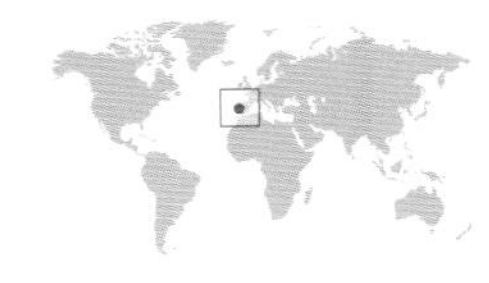

Portugal lies in the western part of the Iberian peninsula in southwest Europe, has an Atlantic coastline and is bordered by Spain to the north and east. The island groups of the Azores and Madeira are parts of Portugal. On the mainland, the land north of the river Tagus (Tejo) is mostly highland, with extensive forests of pine and cork. South of the river is undulating lowland. The climate in the north is cool and moist; the south is warmer, with dry, mild winters. Most Portuguese live near the coast, and more than one-third of the total population lives around the capital, Lisbon (Lisboa). Agriculture, fishing and forestry involve approximately ten per cent of the workforce. Mining and manufacturing are the main sectors of the economy. Portugal produces kaolin, copper, tin, zinc, tungsten and salt. Exports include textiles, clothing and footwear, electrical machinery and transport equipment, cork and wood products, and chemicals. Service industries, chiefly tourism and banking, are important to the economy, as are remittances from workers abroad. Most trade is with other European Union countries.

Puerto Rico
United States Commonwealth

Area Sq Km	9 104	Languages	Spanish, English
Area Sq Miles	3 515	Religions	Roman Catholic, Protestant
Population	3 991 000	Currency	United States dollar
Capital	San Juan		

The Caribbean island of Puerto Rico has a forested, hilly interior, coastal plains and a tropical climate. Half of the population lives in the San Juan area. The economy is based on manufacturing (chiefly chemicals, electronics and food), tourism and agriculture. The USA is the main trading partner.

QATAR
State of Qatar

Area Sq Km	11 437	Languages	Arabic
Area Sq Miles	4 416	Religions	Sunni Muslim
Population	841 000	Currency	Qatari riyal
Capital	Doha (Ad Dawḩah)	Organizations	OPEC, UN

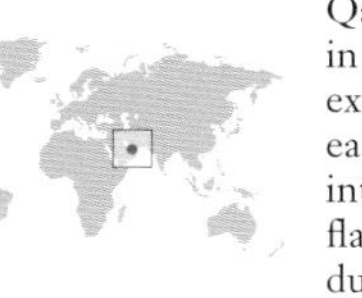

Qatar occupies a peninsula in southwest Asia that extends northwards from east-central Saudi Arabia into The Gulf. The land is flat and barren with sand dunes and salt pans. The climate is hot and mainly dry. Most people live in the area of the capital, Doha. The economy is heavily dependent on oil and natural gas production and the oil-refining industry. Income also comes from overseas investment. Japan is the largest trading partner.

Réunion
French Overseas Department

Area Sq Km	2 551	Languages	French, Creole
Area Sq Miles	985	Religions	Roman Catholic
Population	807 000	Currency	Euro
Capital	St-Denis		

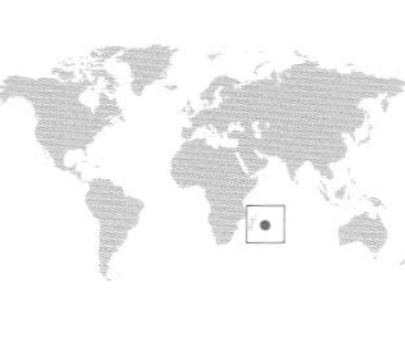

The Indian Ocean island of Réunion is mountainous, with coastal lowlands and a warm climate. The economy depends on tourism, French aid, and exports of sugar. In 2005 France transferred the administration of various small uninhabited islands in the seas around Madagascar from Réunion to the French Southern and Antarctic Lands.

ROMANIA

Area Sq Km	237 500	Languages	Romanian, Hungarian
Area Sq Miles	91 699	Religions	Romanian Orthodox, Protestant, Roman Catholic
Population	21 438 000	Currency	Romanian leu
Capital	Bucharest (București)	Organizations	EU, NATO, UN

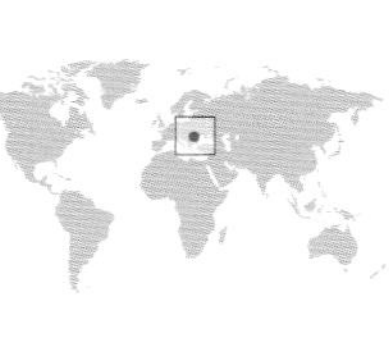

Romania lies in eastern Europe, on the northwest coast of the Black Sea. Mountains separate the Transylvanian Basin in the centre of the country from the populous plains of the east and south and from the Danube delta. The climate is continental. Romania has mineral resources (zinc, lead, silver and gold) and oil and natural gas reserves. Economic development has been slow and sporadic, but measures to accelerate change were introduced in 1999. Agriculture employs over one-third of the workforce. The main exports are textiles, mineral products, chemicals, machinery and footwear. The main trading partners are Germany and Italy.

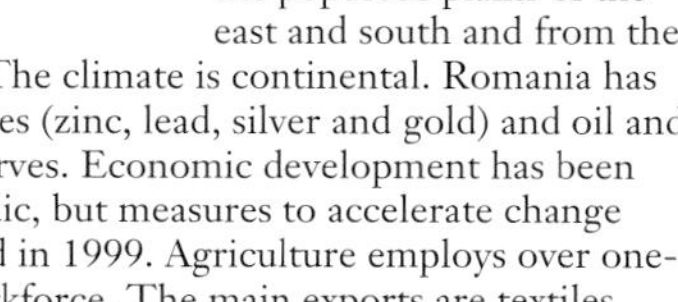

RUSSIAN FEDERATION

Area Sq Km	17 075 400	Languages	Russian, Tatar, Ukrainian, local languages
Area Sq Miles	6 592 849	Religions	Russian Orthodox, Sunni Muslim, Protestant
Population	142 499 000	Currency	Russian rouble
Capital	Moscow (Moskva)	Organizations	APEC, CIS, UN

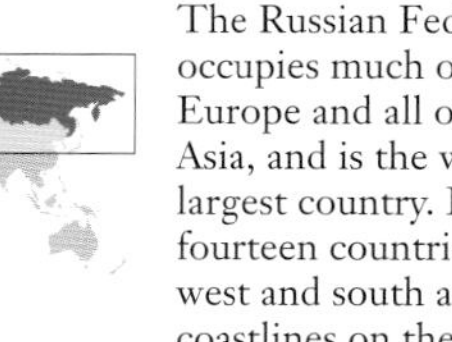

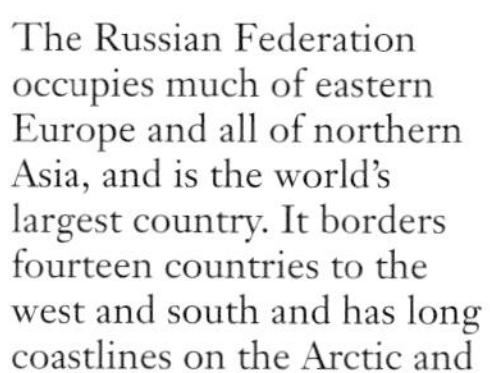

The Russian Federation occupies much of eastern Europe and all of northern Asia, and is the world's largest country. It borders fourteen countries to the west and south and has long coastlines on the Arctic and Pacific Oceans to the north and east. European Russia lies west of the Ural Mountains. To the south the land rises to uplands and the Caucasus mountains on the border with Georgia and Azerbaijan. East of the Urals lies the flat West Siberian Plain and the Central Siberian Plateau. In the south-east is Lake Baikal, the world's deepest lake, and the Sayan ranges on the border with Kazakhstan and Mongolia. Eastern Siberia is rugged and mountainous, with many active volcanoes in the Kamchatka Peninsula. The country's major rivers are the Volga in the west and the Ob', Irtysh, Yenisey, Lena and Amur in Siberia. The climate and vegetation range between arctic tundra in the north and semi-arid steppe towards the Black and Caspian Sea coasts in the south. In general, the climate is continental with extreme temperatures. The majority of the population (the eighth largest in the world), and industry and agriculture are concentrated in European Russia. The economy is dependent on exploitation of raw materials and on heavy industry. Russia has a wealth of mineral resources, although they are often difficult to exploit because of climate and remote locations. It is one of the world's leading producers of petroleum, natural gas and coal as well as iron ore, nickel, copper, bauxite, and many precious and rare metals. Forests cover over forty per cent of the land area and supply an important timber, paper and pulp industry. Approximately eight per cent of the land is suitable for cultivation, but farming is generally inefficient and food, especially grains, must be imported. Fishing is important and Russia has a large fleet operating around the world. The transition to a market economy has been slow and difficult, with considerable underemployment. As well as mining and extractive industries there is a wide range of manufacturing industry, from steel mills to aircraft and space vehicles, shipbuilding, synthetic fabrics, plastics, cotton fabrics, consumer durables, chemicals and fertilizers. Exports include fuels, metals, machinery, chemicals and forest products. The most important trading partners include Germany, the USA and Belarus.

RWANDA
Republic of Rwanda

Area Sq Km	26 338	Languages	Kinyarwanda, French, English
Area Sq Miles	10 169	Religions	Roman Catholic, traditional beliefs, Protestant
Population	9 725 000	Currency	Rwandan franc
Capital	Kigali	Organizations	Comm., UN

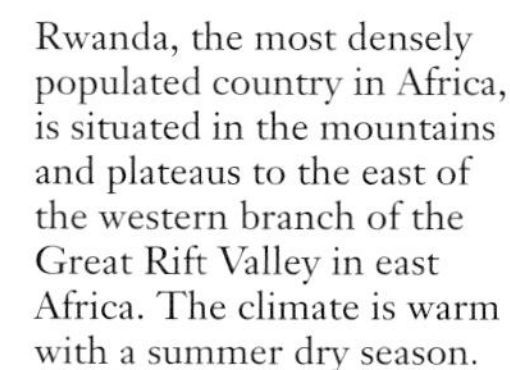

Rwanda, the most densely populated country in Africa, is situated in the mountains and plateaus to the east of the western branch of the Great Rift Valley in east Africa. The climate is warm with a summer dry season. Rwanda depends on subsistence farming, coffee and tea exports, light industry and foreign aid. The country is slowly recovering from serious internal conflict which caused devastation in the early 1990s.

St-Barthélemy
French Overseas Collectivity

Area Sq Km	21	Languages	French
Area Sq Miles	8	Religions	Roman Catholic
Population	6 852	Currency	Euro
Capital	Gustavia		

An island in the Leeward Islands in the Lesser Antilles, in the Caribbean south of St-Martin. It was separated from Guadeloupe politically in 2007. Tourism is the main economic activity.

St Helena and Dependencies
United Kingdom Overseas Territory

Area Sq Km	307	Languages	English
Area Sq Miles	119	Religions	Protestant, Roman Catholic
Population	7 000	Currency	St Helena pound, Pound sterling
Capital	Jamestown		

St Helena and its dependencies Ascension and Tristan da Cunha are isolated island groups lying in the south Atlantic Ocean. St Helena is a rugged island of volcanic origin. The main activity is fishing, but the economy relies on financial aid from the UK. Main trading partners are the UK and South Africa.

ST KITTS AND NEVIS

Federation of St Kitts and Nevis

Area Sq Km	261	Languages	English, Creole
Area Sq Miles	101	Religions	Protestant, Roman Catholic
Population	50 000	Currency	East Caribbean dollar
Capital	Basseterre	Organizations	CARICOM, Comm., UN

St Kitts and Nevis are in the Leeward Islands, in the Caribbean. Both volcanic islands are mountainous and forested, with sandy beaches and a warm, wet climate. About three-quarters of the population lives on St Kitts. Agriculture is the main activity, with sugar the main product. Tourism and manufacturing (chiefly garments and electronic components) and offshore banking are important activities.

ST LUCIA

Area Sq Km	616	Languages	English, Creole
Area Sq Miles	238	Religions	Roman Catholic, Protestant
Population	165 000	Currency	East Caribbean dollar
Capital	Castries	Organizations	CARICOM, Comm., UN

St Lucia, one of the Windward Islands in the Caribbean Sea, is a volcanic island with forested mountains, hot springs, sandy beaches and a wet tropical climate. Agriculture is the main activity, with bananas accounting for approximately forty per cent of export earnings. Tourism, agricultural processing and light manufacturing are increasingly important.

St-Martin

French Overseas Collectivity

Area Sq Km	54	Languages	French
Area Sq Miles	21	Religions	Roman Catholic
Population	33 102	Currency	Euro
Capital	Marigot		

The northern part of St-Martin, one of the Leeward Islands, in the Caribbean. The other part of the island is part of the Netherlands Antilles (Sint Maarten). It was separated from Guadeloupe politically in 2007. Tourism is the main source of income.

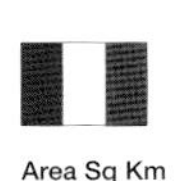

St Pierre and Miquelon

French Territorial Collectivity

Area Sq Km	242	Languages	French
Area Sq Miles	93	Religions	Roman Catholic
Population	6 000	Currency	Euro
Capital	St-Pierre		

A group of islands off the south coast of Newfoundland in eastern Canada. The islands are largely unsuitable for agriculture, and fishing and fish processing are the most important activities. The islands rely heavily on financial assistance from France.

ST VINCENT AND THE GRENADINES

Area Sq Km	389	Languages	English, Creole
Area Sq Miles	150	Religions	Protestant, Roman Catholic
Population	120 000	Currency	East Caribbean dollar
Capital	Kingstown	Organizations	CARICOM, Comm., UN

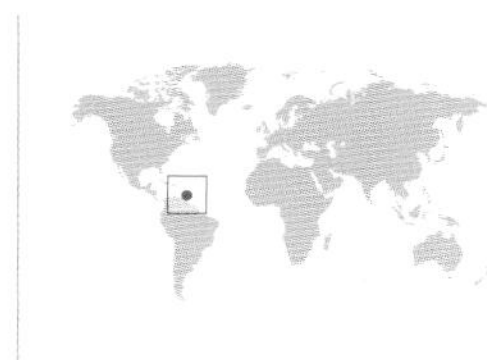

St Vincent, whose territory includes islets and cays in the Grenadines, is in the Windward Islands, in the Caribbean. St Vincent itself is forested and mountainous, with an active volcano, Soufrière. The climate is tropical and wet. The economy is based mainly on agriculture and tourism. Bananas account for approximately one-third of export earnings and arrowroot is also important. Most trade is with the USA and other CARICOM countries.

SAMOA

Independent State of Samoa

Area Sq Km	2 831	Languages	Samoan, English
Area Sq Miles	1 093	Religions	Protestant, Roman Catholic
Population	187 000	Currency	Tala
Capital	Apia	Organizations	Comm., UN

Samoa consists of two larger mountainous and forested islands, Savai'i and Upolu, and seven smaller islands, in the south Pacific Ocean. Over half the population lives on Upolu. The climate is tropical. The economy is based on agriculture, with some fishing and light manufacturing. Traditional exports are coconut products, fish and beer. Tourism is increasing, but the islands depend on workers' remittances and foreign aid.

SAN MARINO

Republic of San Marino

Area Sq Km	61	Languages	Italian
Area Sq Miles	24	Religions	Roman Catholic
Population	31 000	Currency	Euro
Capital	San Marino	Organizations	UN

Landlocked San Marino lies in northeast Italy. A third of the people live in the capital. There is some agriculture and light industry, but most income comes from tourism. Italy is the main trading partner.

SÃO TOMÉ AND PRÍNCIPE

Democratic Republic of São Tomé and Príncipe

Area Sq Km	964	Languages	Portuguese, Creole
Area Sq Miles	372	Religions	Roman Catholic, Protestant
Population	158 000	Currency	Dobra
Capital	São Tomé	Organizations	UN

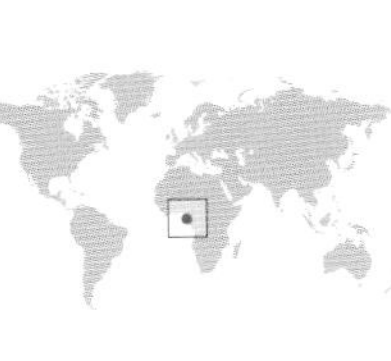

The two main islands and adjacent islets lie off the coast of west Africa in the Gulf of Guinea. São Tomé is the larger island, with over ninety per cent of the population. Both São Tomé and Príncipe are mountainous and tree-covered, and have a hot and humid climate. The economy is heavily dependent on cocoa, which accounts for around ninety per cent of export earnings.

SAUDI ARABIA

Kingdom of Saudi Arabia

Area Sq Km	2 200 000	Languages	Arabic
Area Sq Miles	849 425	Religions	Sunni Muslim, Shi'a Muslim
Population	24 735 000	Currency	Saudi Arabian riyal
Capital	Riyadh (Ar Riyāḍ)	Organizations	OPEC, UN

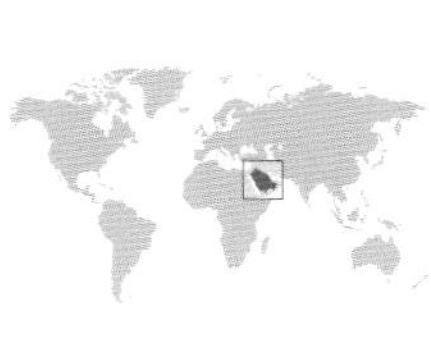

Saudi Arabia occupies most of the Arabian Peninsula in southwest Asia. The terrain is desert or semi-desert plateaus, which rise to mountains running parallel to the Red Sea in the west and slope down to plains in the southeast and along The Gulf in the east. Over eighty per cent of the population lives in urban areas. There are around four million foreign workers in Saudi Arabia, employed mainly in the oil and service industries. Summers are hot, winters are warm and rainfall is low. Saudi Arabia has the world's largest reserves of oil and significant natural gas reserves, both onshore and in The Gulf. Crude oil and refined products account for over ninety per cent of export earnings. Other industries and irrigated agriculture are being encouraged, but most food and raw materials are imported. Saudi Arabia has important banking and commercial interests. Japan and the USA are the main trading partners.

SENEGAL

Republic of Senegal

Area Sq Km	196 720	Languages	French, Wolof, Fulani, local languages
Area Sq Miles	75 954	Religions	Sunni Muslim, Roman Catholic, traditional beliefs
Population	12 379 000	Currency	CFA franc
Capital	Dakar	Organizations	UN

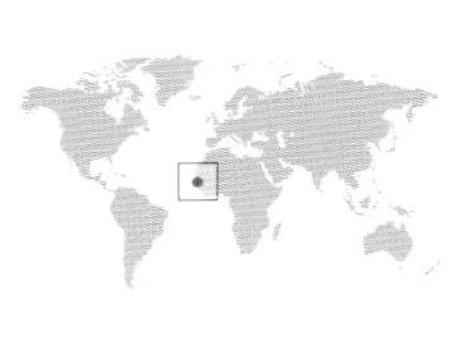

Senegal lies on the Atlantic coast of west Africa. The north is arid semi-desert, while the south is mainly fertile savanna bushland. The climate is tropical with summer rains, although droughts occur. One-fifth of the population lives in and around Dakar, the capital and main port. Fish, groundnuts and phosphates are the main exports. France is the main trading partner.

SERBIA

Republic of Serbia

Area Sq Km	77 453	Languages	Serbian, Hungarian
Area Sq Miles	29 904	Religions	Serbian Orthodox, Roman Catholic, Sunni Muslim
Population	7 788 448	Currency	Serbian dinar
Capital	Belgrade (Beograd)	Organizations	UN

Following ethnic conflict and the break-up of Yugoslavia through the 1990s, the state union of Serbia and Montenegro retained the name Yugoslavia until 2003. The two then became separate independent countries in 2006. The southern Serbian province of Kosovo declared its independence from Serbia in February 2008. The landscape is rugged, mountainous and forested in the south, while the north is low-lying and drained by the Danube river system.

SEYCHELLES

Republic of Seychelles

Area Sq Km	455	Languages	English, French, Creole
Area Sq Miles	176	Religions	Roman Catholic, Protestant
Population	87 000	Currency	Seychelles rupee
Capital	Victoria	Organizations	Comm., SADC, UN

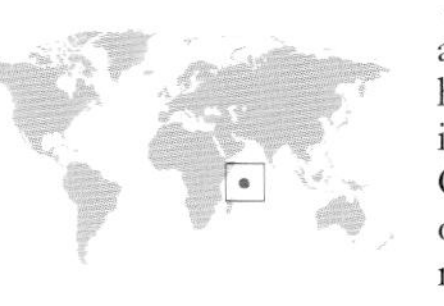

The Seychelles comprises an archipelago of over one hundred granitic and coral islands in the western Indian Ocean. Over ninety per cent of the population lives on the main island, Mahé. The climate is hot and humid with heavy rainfall. The economy is based mainly on tourism, fishing and light manufacturing.

SIERRA LEONE

Republic of Sierra Leone

Area Sq Km	71 740	Languages	English, Creole, Mende, Temne, local languages
Area Sq Miles	27 699	Religions	Sunni Muslim, traditional beliefs
Population	5 866 000	Currency	Leone
Capital	Freetown	Organizations	Comm., UN

Sierra Leone lies on the Atlantic coast of west Africa. Its coastline is heavily indented and is lined with mangrove swamps. Inland is a forested area rising to savanna plateaus, with mountains to the northeast. The climate is tropical and rainfall is heavy. Most of the workforce is involved in subsistence farming. Cocoa and coffee are the main cash crops. Diamonds and rutile (titanium ore) are the main exports. Sierra Leone is one of the world's poorest countries, and the economy relies on substantial foreign aid.

SINGAPORE

Republic of Singapore

Area Sq Km	639	Languages	Chinese, English, Malay, Tamil
Area Sq Miles	247	Religions	Buddhist, Taoist, Sunni Muslim, Christian, Hindu
Population	4 436 000	Currency	Singapore dollar
Capital	Singapore	Organizations	APEC, ASEAN, Comm., UN

The state comprises the main island of Singapore and over fifty other islands, lying off the southern tip of the Malay Peninsula in southeast Asia. Singapore is generally low-lying and includes land reclaimed from swamps and the sea. It is hot and humid, with heavy rainfall throughout the year. There are fish farms and vegetable gardens in the north and east of the island, but most food is imported. Singapore also lacks mineral and energy resources. Manufacturing industries and services are the main sectors of the economy. Their rapid development has fuelled the nation's impressive economic growth during recent decades. Main industries include electronics, oil refining, chemicals, pharmaceuticals, ship repair, food processing and textiles. Singapore is also a major financial centre. Its port is one of the world's largest and busiest and acts as an entrepôt for neighbouring states. Tourism is also important. Japan, the USA and Malaysia are the main trading partners.

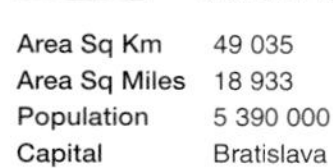

SLOVAKIA

Slovak Republic

Area Sq Km	49 035	Languages	Slovak, Hungarian, Czech
Area Sq Miles	18 933	Religions	Roman Catholic, Protestant, Orthodox
Population	5 390 000	Currency	Euro
Capital	Bratislava	Organizations	EU, NATO, OECD, UN

A landlocked country in central Europe, Slovakia is mountainous in the north, but low-lying in the southwest. The climate is continental. There is a range of manufacturing industries, and the main exports are machinery and transport equipment, but in recent years there have been economic difficulties and growth has been slow. Slovakia joined the European Union in May 2004. Most trade is with other EU countries, especially the Czech Republic.

SLOVENIA

Republic of Slovenia

Area Sq Km	20 251	Languages	Slovene, Croatian, Serbian
Area Sq Miles	7 819	Religions	Roman Catholic, Protestant
Population	2 002 000	Currency	Euro
Capital	Ljubljana	Organizations	EU, NATO, UN

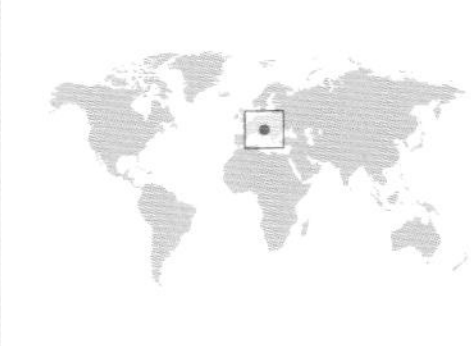

Slovenia lies in the northwest Balkan Mountains of southern Europe and has a short coastline on the Adriatic Sea. It is mountainous and hilly, with lowlands on the coast and in the Sava and Drava river valleys. The climate is generally continental inland and Mediterranean nearer the coast. The main agricultural products are potatoes, grain and sugar beet; the main industries include metal processing, electronics and consumer goods. Trade has been re-orientated towards western markets and the main trading partners are Germany and Italy. Slovenia joined the European Union in May 2004.

SOLOMON ISLANDS

Area Sq Km	28 370	Languages	English, Creole, local languages
Area Sq Miles	10 954	Religions	Protestant, Roman Catholic
Population	496 000	Currency	Solomon Islands dollar
Capital	Honiara	Organizations	Comm., UN

The state consists of the Solomon, Santa Cruz and Shortland Islands in the southwest Pacific Ocean. The six main islands are volcanic, mountainous and forested, although Guadalcanal, the most populous, has a large lowland area. The climate is generally hot and humid. Subsistence farming, forestry and fishing predominate. Exports include timber products, fish, copra and palm oil. The islands depend on foreign aid.

SOMALIA

Somali Republic

Area Sq Km	637 657	Languages	Somali, Arabic
Area Sq Miles	246 201	Religions	Sunni Muslim
Population	8 699 000	Currency	Somali shilling
Capital	Mogadishu (Muqdisho)	Organizations	UN

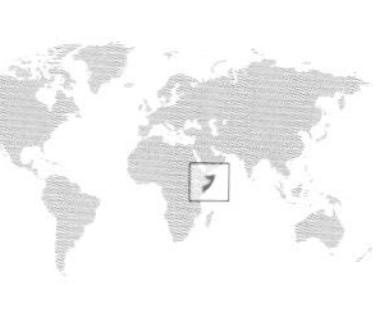

Somalia is in northeast Africa, on the Gulf of Aden and Indian Ocean. It consists of a dry scrubby plateau, rising to highlands in the north. The climate is hot and dry, but coastal areas and the Jubba and Webi Shabeelle river valleys support crops and most of the population. Subsistence farming and livestock rearing are the main activities. Exports include livestock and bananas. Frequent drought and civil war have prevented economic development. Somalia is one of the poorest, most unstable and least developed countries in the world.

SOUTH AFRICA, REPUBLIC OF

Area Sq Km	1 219 090	Languages	Afrikaans, English, nine other official languages
Area Sq Miles	470 693	Religions	Protestant, Roman Catholic, Sunni Muslim, Hindu
Population	48 577 000	Currency	Rand
Capital	Pretoria (Tshwane)/ Cape Town	Organizations	Comm., SADC, UN

The Republic of South Africa occupies most of the southern part of Africa. It surrounds Lesotho and has a long coastline on the Atlantic and Indian Oceans. Much of the land is a vast plateau, covered with grassland or bush and drained by the Orange and Limpopo river systems. A fertile coastal plain rises to mountain ridges in the south and east, including Table Mountain near Cape Town and the Drakensberg range in the east. Gauteng is the most populous province, with Johannesburg and Pretoria its main cities. South Africa has warm summers and mild winters. Most of the country has the majority of its rainfall in summer, but the coast around Cape Town has winter rains. South Africa has the largest economy in Africa, although wealth is unevenly distributed and unemployment is very high. Agriculture employs approximately one-third of the workforce, and produce includes fruit, wine, wool and maize. The country is the world's leading producer of gold and chromium and an important producer of diamonds. Many other minerals are also mined. The main industries are mineral and food processing, chemicals, electrical equipment, textiles and motor vehicles. Financial services are also important.

SOUTH KOREA

Republic of Korea

Area Sq Km	99 274	Languages	Korean
Area Sq Miles	38 330	Religions	Buddhist, Protestant, Roman Catholic
Population	48 224 000	Currency	South Korean won
Capital	Seoul (Sŏul)	Organizations	APEC, OECD, UN

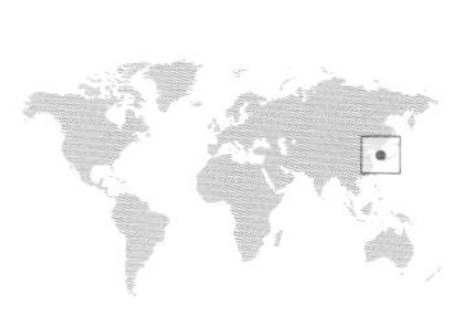

The state consists of the southern half of the Korean Peninsula in eastern Asia and many islands lying off the western and southern coasts in the Yellow Sea. The terrain is mountainous, although less rugged than that of North Korea. Population density is high and the country is highly urbanized; most of the population lives on the western coastal plains and in the river basins of the Han-gang in the northwest and the Naktong-gang in the southeast. The climate is continental, with hot, wet summers and dry, cold winters. Arable land is limited by the mountainous terrain, but because of intensive farming South Korea is nearly self-sufficient in food. Sericulture (silk) is important, as is fishing, which contributes to exports. South Korea has few mineral resources, except for coal and tungsten. It has achieved high economic growth based mainly on export manufacturing. The main manufactured goods are cars, electronic and electrical goods, ships, steel, chemicals and toys, as well as textiles, clothing, footwear and food products. The USA and Japan are the main trading partners.

SPAIN

Kingdom of Spain

Area Sq Km	504 782	Languages	Spanish, Castilian, Catalan, Galician, Basque
Area Sq Miles	194 897	Religions	Roman Catholic
Population	44 279 000	Currency	Euro
Capital	Madrid	Organizations	EU, NATO, OECD, UN

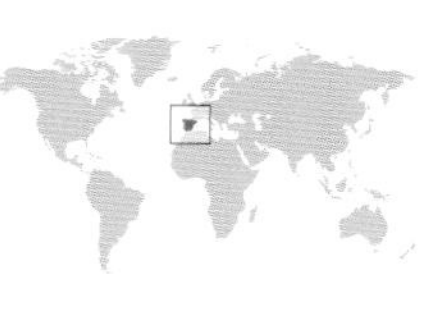

Spain occupies the greater part of the Iberian peninsula in southwest Europe, with coastlines on the Atlantic Ocean and Mediterranean Sea. It includes the Balearic Islands in the Mediterranean, the Canary Islands in the Atlantic, and two enclaves in north Africa (Ceuta and Melilla). Much of the mainland is a high plateau drained by the Douro (Duero), Tagus (Tajo) and Guadiana rivers. The plateau is interrupted by a low mountain range and bounded to the east and north also by mountains, including the Pyrenees, which form the border with France and Andorra. The main lowland areas are the Ebro basin in the northeast, the eastern coastal plains and the Guadalquivir basin in the southwest. Over three-quarters of the population lives in urban areas. The plateau experiences hot summers and cold winters. Conditions are cooler and wetter to the north, and warmer and drier to the south. Agriculture involves about ten per cent of the workforce, and fruit, vegetables and wine are exported. Fishing is an important industry, and Spain has a large fishing fleet. Mineral resources include lead, copper, mercury and fluorspar. Some oil is produced, but Spain has to import most energy needs.

The economy is based mainly on manufacturing and services. The principal products are machinery, transport equipment, motor vehicles and food products, with a wide variety of other manufactured goods. With approximately fifty million visitors a year, tourism is a major industry. Banking and commerce are also important. Approximately seventy per cent of trade is with other European Union countries.

SRI LANKA

Democratic Socialist Republic of Sri Lanka

Area Sq Km	65 610	Languages	Sinhalese, Tamil, English
Area Sq Miles	25 332	Religions	Buddhist, Hindu, Sunni Muslim, Roman Catholic
Population	19 299 000	Currency	Sri Lankan rupee
Capital	Sri Jayewardenepura Kotte	Organizations	Comm., UN

Sri Lanka lies in the Indian Ocean off the southeast coast of India in south Asia. It has rolling coastal plains, with mountains in the centre-south. The climate is hot and monsoonal. Most people live on the west coast. Manufactures (chiefly textiles and clothing), tea, rubber, copra and gems are exported. The economy relies on foreign aid and workers' remittances. The USA and the UK are the main trading partners.

SUDAN

Republic of the Sudan

Area Sq Km	2 505 813	Languages	Arabic, Dinka, Nubian, Beja, Nuer, local languages
Area Sq Miles	967 500	Religions	Sunni Muslim, traditional beliefs, Christian
Population	38 560 000	Currency	Sudanese pound (Sudani)
Capital	Khartoum	Organizations	UN

Africa's largest country, the Sudan is in the northeast of the continent, on the Red Sea. It lies within the upper Nile basin, much of which is arid plain but with swamps to the south. Mountains lie to the northeast, west and south. The climate is hot and arid with light summer rainfall, and droughts occur. Most people live along the Nile and are farmers and herders. Cotton, gum arabic, livestock and other agricultural products are exported. The government is working with foreign investors to develop oil resources, but civil war in the south and ethnic cleansing in Darfur continue to restrict the growth of the economy. Main trading partners are Saudi Arabia, China and Libya.

SURINAME

Republic of Suriname

Area Sq Km	163 820	Languages	Dutch, Surinamese, English, Hindi
Area Sq Miles	63 251	Religions	Hindu, Roman Catholic, Protestant, Sunni Muslim
Population	458 000	Currency	Suriname guilder
Capital	Paramaribo	Organizations	CARICOM, UN

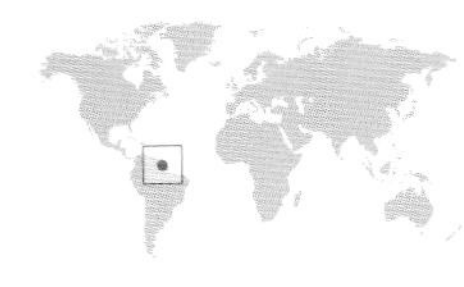

Suriname, on the Atlantic coast of northern South America, consists of a swampy coastal plain (where most of the population lives), central plateaus, and highlands in the south. The climate is tropical, and rainforest covers much of the land. Bauxite mining is the main industry, and alumina and aluminium are the chief exports, with shrimps, rice, bananas and timber also exported. The main trading partners are the Netherlands, Norway and the USA.

SWAZILAND

Kingdom of Swaziland

Area Sq Km	17 364	Languages	Swazi, English
Area Sq Miles	6 704	Religions	Christian, traditional beliefs
Population	1 141 000	Currency	Emalangeni, South African rand
Capital	Mbabane	Organizations	Comm., SADC, UN

Landlocked Swaziland in southern Africa lies between Mozambique and the Republic of South Africa. Savanna plateaus descend from mountains in the west towards hill country in the east. The climate is subtropical, but temperate in the mountains. Subsistence farming predominates. Asbestos and diamonds are mined. Exports include sugar, fruit and wood pulp. Tourism and workers' remittances are important to the economy. Most trade is with South Africa.

SWEDEN

Kingdom of Sweden

Area Sq Km	449 964	Languages	Swedish
Area Sq Miles	173 732	Religions	Protestant, Roman Catholic
Population	9 119 000	Currency	Swedish krona
Capital	Stockholm	Organizations	EU, OECD, UN

Sweden occupies the eastern part of the Scandinavian peninsula in northern Europe and borders the Baltic Sea, the Gulf of Bothnia, and the Kattegat and Skagerrak, connecting with the North Sea. Forested mountains cover the northern half, part of which lies within the Arctic Circle. The southern part of the country is a lowland lake region where most of the population lives. Sweden has warm summers and cold winters, which are more severe in the north. Natural resources include coniferous forests, mineral deposits and water resources. Some dairy products, meat, cereals and vegetables are produced in the south. The forests supply timber for export and for the important pulp, paper and furniture industries. Sweden is an important producer of iron ore and copper. Zinc, lead, silver and gold are also mined. Machinery and transport equipment, chemicals, pulp and wood, and telecommunications equipment are the main exports. The majority of trade is with other European Union countries.

SWITZERLAND

Swiss Confederation

Area Sq Km	41 293	Languages	German, French, Italian, Romansch
Area Sq Miles	15 943	Religions	Roman Catholic, Protestant
Population	7 484 000	Currency	Swiss franc
Capital	Bern	Organizations	OECD, UN

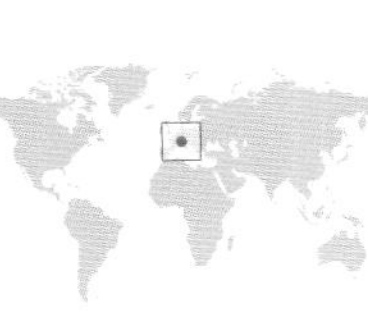

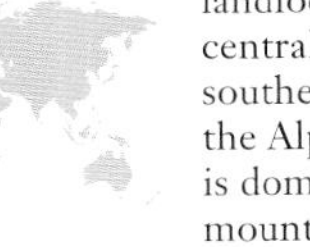

Switzerland is a mountainous landlocked country in west central Europe. The southern regions lie within the Alps, while the northwest is dominated by the Jura mountains. The rest of the land is a high plateau, where most of the population lives. The climate varies greatly, depending on altitude and relief, but in general summers are mild and winters are cold with heavy snowfalls. Switzerland has one of the highest standards of living in the world, yet it has few mineral resources, and most food and industrial raw materials are imported. Manufacturing makes the largest contribution to the economy. Engineering is the most important industry, producing precision instruments and heavy machinery. Other important industries are chemicals and pharmaceuticals. Banking and financial services are very important, and Zürich is one of the world's leading banking cities. Tourism, and international organizations based in Switzerland, are also major foreign currency earners. Germany is the main trading partner.

SYRIA

Syrian Arab Republic

Area Sq Km	185 180	Languages	Arabic, Kurdish, Armenian
Area Sq Miles	71 498	Religions	Sunni Muslim, Shi'a Muslim, Christian
Population	19 929 000	Currency	Syrian pound
Capital	Damascus (Dimashq)	Organizations	UN

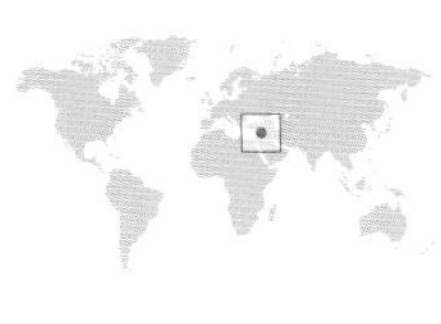

Syria is in southwest Asia, has a short coastline on the Mediterranean Sea, and stretches inland to a plateau traversed northwest-southeast by the Euphrates river. Mountains flank the southwest borders with Lebanon and Israel. The climate is Mediterranean in coastal regions, hotter and drier inland. Most Syrians live on the coast or in the river valleys. Cotton, cereals and fruit are important products, but the main exports are petroleum and related products, and textiles.

TAIWAN

Republic of China

Area Sq Km	36 179	Languages	Mandarin, Min, Hakka, local languages
Area Sq Miles	13 969	Religions	Buddhist, Taoist, Confucian, Christian
Population	22 880 009	Currency	Taiwan dollar
Capital	T'aipei	Organizations	APEC

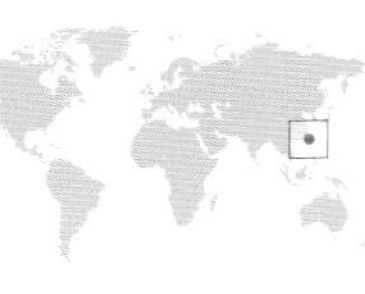

The east Asian state consists of the island of Taiwan, separated from mainland China by the Taiwan Strait, and several much smaller islands. Much of Taiwan is mountainous and forested. Densely populated coastal plains in the west contain the bulk of the population and most economic activity. Taiwan has a tropical monsoon climate, with warm, wet summers and mild winters. Agriculture is highly productive. The country is virtually self-sufficient in food and exports some products. Coal, oil and natural gas are produced and a few minerals are mined, but none of them are of great significance to the economy. Taiwan depends heavily on imports of raw materials and exports of manufactured goods. The main manufactures are electrical and electronic goods, including television sets, personal computers and calculators, textiles, fertilizers, clothing, footwear and toys. The main trading partners are the USA, Japan and Germany. The People's Republic of China claims Taiwan as its 23rd Province.

TAJIKISTAN

Republic of Tajikistan

Area Sq Km	143 100	Languages	Tajik, Uzbek, Russian
Area Sq Miles	55 251	Religions	Sunni Muslim
Population	6 736 000	Currency	Somoni
Capital	Dushanbe	Organizations	CIS, UN

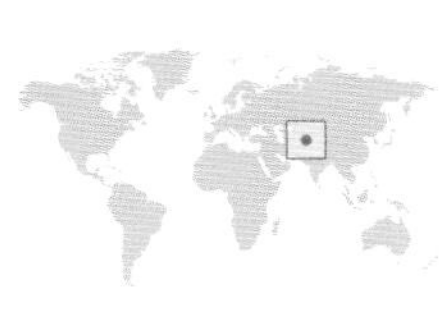

Landlocked Tajikistan in central Asia is a mountainous country, dominated by the mountains of the Alai Range and the Pamir. In the less mountainous western areas summers are warm, although winters are cold. Agriculture is the main sector of the economy, chiefly cotton growing and cattle breeding. Mineral deposits include lead, zinc, and uranium. Processed metals, textiles and clothing are the main manufactured goods; the main exports are aluminium and cotton. Uzbekistan, Kazakhstan and the Russian Federation are the main trading partners.

TANZANIA

United Republic of Tanzania

Area Sq Km	945 087	Languages	Swahili, English, Nyamwezi, local languages
Area Sq Miles	364 900	Religions	Shi'a Muslim, Sunni Muslim, traditional beliefs, Christian
Population	40 454 000	Currency	Tanzanian shilling
Capital	Dodoma	Organizations	Comm., SADC, UN

States and Territories

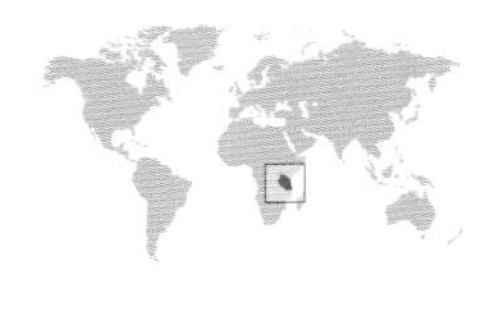

Tanzania lies on the coast of east Africa and includes the island of Zanzibar in the Indian Ocean. Most of the mainland is a savanna plateau lying east of the Great Rift Valley. In the north, near the border with Kenya, is Kilimanjaro, the highest mountain in Africa. The climate is tropical. The economy is predominantly based on agriculture, which employs an estimated ninety per cent of the workforce. Agricultural processing and gold and diamond mining are the main industries, although tourism is growing. Coffee, cotton, cashew nuts and tobacco are the main exports, with cloves from Zanzibar. Most export trade is with India and the UK. Tanzania depends heavily on foreign aid.

THAILAND

Kingdom of Thailand

Area Sq Km	513 115	Languages	Thai, Lao, Chinese, Malay, Mon-Khmer languages
Area Sq Miles	198 115	Religions	Buddhist, Sunni Muslim
Population	63 884 000	Currency	Baht
Capital	Bangkok (Krung Thep)	Organizations	APEC, ASEAN, UN

The largest country in the Indo-China peninsula, Thailand has coastlines on the Gulf of Thailand and Andaman Sea. Central Thailand is dominated by the Chao Phraya river basin, which contains Bangkok, the capital city and centre of most economic activity. To the east is a dry plateau drained by tributaries of the Mekong river, while to the north, west and south, extending down most of the Malay peninsula, are forested hills and mountains. Many small islands line the coast. The climate is hot, humid and monsoonal. About half the workforce is involved in agriculture. Fishing and fish processing are important. Thailand produces natural gas, some oil and lignite, minerals (chiefly tin, tungsten and baryte) and gemstones. Manufacturing is the largest contributor to national income, with electronics, textiles, clothing and footwear, and food processing the main industries. With around seven million visitors a year, tourism is the major source of foreign exchange. Thailand is one of the world's leading exporters of rice and rubber, and a major exporter of maize and tapioca. Japan and the USA are the main trading partners.

TOGO

Republic of Togo

Area Sq Km	56 785	Languages	French, Ewe, Kabre, local languages
Area Sq Miles	21 925	Religions	Traditional beliefs, Christian, Sunni Muslim
Population	6 585 000	Currency	CFA franc
Capital	Lomé	Organizations	UN

Togo is a long narrow country in west Africa with a short coastline on the Gulf of Guinea. The interior consists of plateaus rising to mountainous areas. The climate is tropical, and is drier inland. Agriculture is the mainstay of the economy. Phosphate mining and food processing are the main industries. Cotton, phosphates, coffee and cocoa are the main exports. Lomé, the capital, is an entrepôt trade centre.

Tokelau

New Zealand Overseas Territory

Area Sq Km	10	Languages	English, Tokelauan
Area Sq Miles	4	Religions	Christian
Population	1 000	Currency	New Zealand dollar

Tokelau consists of three atolls, Atafu, Nukunonu and Fakaofa, lying in the Pacific Ocean north of Samoa. Subsistence agriculture is the main activity, and the islands rely on aid from New Zealand and remittances from workers overseas.

TONGA

Kingdom of Tonga

Area Sq Km	748	Languages	Tongan, English
Area Sq Miles	289	Religions	Protestant, Roman Catholic
Population	100 000	Currency	Pa'anga
Capital	Nuku'alofa	Organizations	Comm., UN

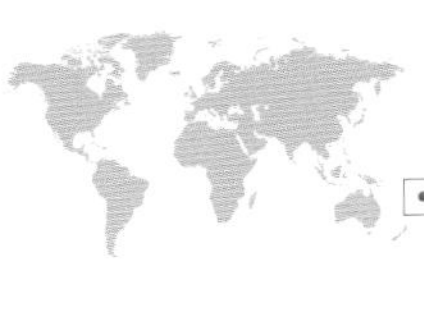

Tonga comprises some one hundred and seventy islands in the south Pacific Ocean, northeast of New Zealand. The three main groups are Tongatapu (where sixty per cent of Tongans live), Ha'apai and Vava'u. The climate is warm and wet, and the economy relies heavily on agriculture. Tourism and light industry are also important to the economy. Exports include squash, fish, vanilla beans and root crops. Most trade is with New Zealand, Japan and Australia.

TRINIDAD AND TOBAGO

Republic of Trinidad and Tobago

Area Sq Km	5 130	Languages	English, Creole, Hindi
Area Sq Miles	1 981	Religions	Roman Catholic, Hindu, Protestant, Sunni Muslim
Population	1 333 000	Currency	Trinidad and Tobago dollar
Capital	Port of Spain	Organizations	CARICOM, Comm., UN

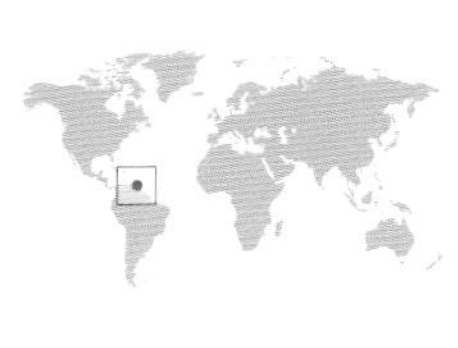

Trinidad, the most southerly Caribbean island, lies off the Venezuelan coast. It is hilly in the north, with a central plain. Tobago, to the northeast, is smaller, more mountainous and less developed. The climate is tropical. The main crops are cocoa, sugar cane, coffee, fruit and vegetables. Oil and petrochemical industries dominate the economy. Tourism is also important. The USA is the main trading partner.

TUNISIA

Republic Tunisian

Area Sq Km	164 150	Languages	Arabic, French
Area Sq Miles	63 379	Religions	Sunni Muslim
Population	10 327 000	Currency	Tunisian dinar
Capital	Tunis	Organizations	UN

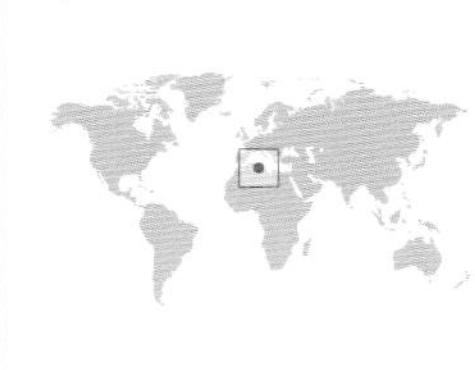

Tunisia is on the Mediterranean coast of north Africa. The north is mountainous with valleys and coastal plains, has a Mediterranean climate and is the most populous area. The south is hot and arid. Oil and phosphates are the main resources, and the main crops are olives and citrus fruit. Tourism is an important industry. Exports include petroleum products, textiles, fruit and phosphorus. Most trade is with European Union countries.

TURKEY

Republic of Turkey

Area Sq Km	779 452	Languages	Turkish, Kurdish
Area Sq Miles	300 948	Religions	Sunni Muslim, Shi'a Muslim
Population	74 877 000	Currency	Lira
Capital	Ankara	Organizations	NATO, OECD, UN

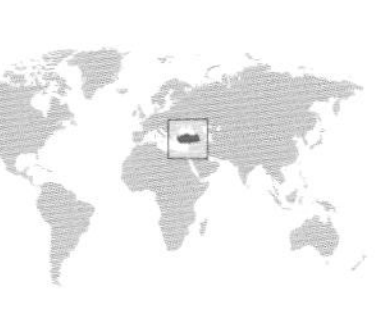
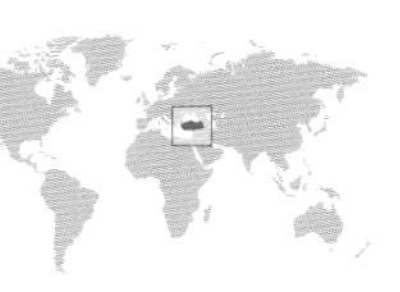

Turkey occupies a large peninsula of southwest Asia and has coastlines on the Black, Mediterranean and Aegean Seas. It includes eastern Thrace, which is in southeastern Europe and is separated from the rest of the country by the Bosporus, the Sea of Marmara and the Dardanelles. The Asian mainland consists of the semi-arid Anatolian plateau, flanked to the north, south and east by mountains. Over forty per cent of Turks live in central Anatolia and on the Marmara and Aegean coastal plains. The coast has a Mediterranean climate, but inland conditions are more extreme with hot, dry summers and cold, snowy winters. Agriculture involves about forty per cent of the workforce, and products include cotton, grain, tobacco, fruit, nuts and livestock. Turkey is a leading producer of chromium, iron ore, lead, tin, borate, and baryte while coal is also mined. The main manufactured goods are clothing, textiles, food products, steel and vehicles. Tourism is a major industry, with nine million visitors a year. Germany and the USA are the main trading partners. Remittances from workers abroad are important to the economy.

TURKMENISTAN

Republic of Turkmenistan

Area Sq Km	488 100	Languages	Turkmen, Uzbek, Russian
Area Sq Miles	188 456	Religions	Sunni Muslim, Russian Orthodox
Population	4 965 000	Currency	Turkmen manat
Capital	Aşgabat (Ashkhabad)	Organizations	UN

Turkmenistan, in central Asia, comprises the plains of the Karakum Desert, the foothills of the Kopet Dag mountains in the south, the Amudar'ya valley in the north and the Caspian Sea plains in the west. The climate is dry, with extreme temperatures. The economy is based mainly on irrigated agriculture (chiefly cotton growing), and natural gas and oil. Main exports are natural gas, oil and cotton fibre. Ukraine, Iran, Turkey and the Russian Federation are the main trading partners.

Turks and Caicos Islands

United Kingdom Overseas Territory

Area Sq Km	430	Languages	English
Area Sq Miles	166	Religions	Protestant
Population	26 000	Currency	United States dollar
Capital	Grand Turk (Cockburn Town)		

The state consists of over forty low-lying islands and cays in the northern Caribbean. Only eight islands are inhabited, and two-fifths of the people live on Grand Turk and Salt Cay. The climate is tropical, and the economy is based on tourism, fishing and offshore banking.

TUVALU

Area Sq Km	25	Languages	Tuvaluan, English
Area Sq Miles	10	Religions	Protestant
Population	11 000	Currency	Australian dollar
Capital	Vaiaku	Organizations	Comm., UN

Tuvalu comprises nine low-lying coral atolls in the south Pacific Ocean. One-third of the population lives on Funafuti, and most people depend on subsistence farming and fishing. The islands export copra, stamps and clothing, but rely heavily on foreign aid. Most trade is with Fiji, Australia and New Zealand.

UGANDA

Republic of Uganda

Area Sq Km	241 038	Languages	English, Swahili, Luganda, local languages
Area Sq Miles	93 065	Religions	Roman Catholic, Protestant, Sunni Muslim, traditional beliefs
Population	30 884 000	Currency	Ugandan shilling
Capital	Kampala	Organizations	Comm., UN

A landlocked country in east Africa, Uganda consists of a savanna plateau with mountains and lakes. The climate is warm and wet. Most people live in the southern half of the country. Agriculture employs around eighty per cent of the workforce and dominates the economy. Coffee, tea, fish and fish products are the main exports. Uganda relies heavily on aid.

UKRAINE

Area Sq Km	603 700	Languages	Ukrainian, Russian
Area Sq Miles	233 090	Religions	Ukrainian Orthodox, Ukrainian Catholic, Roman Catholic
Population	46 205 000	Currency	Hryvnia
Capital	Kiev (Kyiv)	Organizations	CIS, UN

The country lies on the Black Sea coast of eastern Europe. Much of the land is steppe, generally flat and treeless, but with rich black soil, and it is drained by the river Dnieper. Along the border with Belarus are forested, marshy plains. The only uplands are the Carpathian Mountains in the west and smaller ranges on the Crimean peninsula. Summers are warm and winters are cold, with milder conditions in the Crimea. About a quarter of the population lives in the mainly industrial areas around Donets'k, Kiev and Dnipropetrovs'k. The Ukraine is rich in natural resources: fertile soil, substantial mineral and natural gas deposits, and forests. Agriculture and livestock rearing are important, but mining and manufacturing are the dominant sectors of the economy. Coal, iron and manganese mining, steel and metal production, machinery, chemicals and food processing are the main industries. The Russian Federation is the main trading partner.

UNITED ARAB EMIRATES

Federation of Emirates

Area Sq Km	77 700	Languages	Arabic, English
Area Sq Miles	30 000	Religions	Sunni Muslim, Shi'a Muslim
Population	4 380 000	Currency	United Arab Emirates dirham
Capital	Abu Dhabi (Abū Ẓabī)	Organizations	OPEC, UN

The UAE lies on the Gulf coast of the Arabian Peninsula. Six emirates are on The Gulf, while the seventh, Fujairah, is on the Gulf of Oman. Most of the land is flat desert with sand dunes and salt pans. The only hilly area is in the northeast. Over eighty per cent of the population lives in three of the emirates - Abu Dhabi, Dubai and Sharjah. Summers are hot and winters are mild, with occasional rainfall in coastal areas. Fruit and vegetables are grown in oases and irrigated areas, but the Emirates' wealth is based on hydrocarbons found in Abu Dhabi, Dubai, Sharjah and Ras al Khaimah. The UAE is one of the major oil producers in the Middle East. Dubai is an important entrepôt trade centre The main trading partner is Japan.

Abu Dhabi (Emirate)

Area Sq Km (Sq Miles)	Population	Capital
67 340 (26 000)	1 292 119	Abu Dhabi (Abū Ẓabī)

Ajman (Emirate)

Area Sq Km (Sq Miles)	Population	Capital
259 (100)	189 849	Ajman

Dubai (Emirate)

Area Sq Km (Sq Miles)	Population	Capital
3 885 (1 500)	1 200 309	Dubai

Fujairah (Emirate)

Area Sq Km (Sq Miles)	Population	Capital
1 165 (450)	118 617	Fujairah

Ra's al Khaymah (Emirate)

Area Sq Km (Sq Miles)	Population	Capital
1 684 (650)	197 571	Ra's al Khaymah

Sharjah (Emirate)

Area Sq Km (Sq Miles)	Population	Capital
2 590 (1 000)	724 859	Sharjah

Umm al Qaywayn (Emirate)

Area Sq Km (Sq Miles)	Population	Capital
777 (300)	45 756	Umm al Qaywayn

UNITED KINGDOM

United Kingdom of Great Britain and Northern Ireland

Area Sq Km	243 609	Languages	English, Welsh, Gaelic
Area Sq Miles	94 058	Religions	Protestant, Roman Catholic, Muslim
Population	60 769 000	Currency	Pound sterling
Capital	London	Organizations	Comm., EU, NATO, OECD, UN

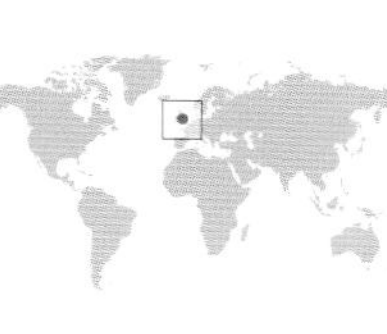

The United Kingdom, in northwest Europe, occupies the island of Great Britain, part of Ireland, and many small adjacent islands. Great Britain comprises England, Scotland and Wales. England covers over half the land area and supports over four-fifths of the population, at its densest in the southeast. The English landscape is flat or rolling with some uplands, notably the Cheviot Hills on the Scottish border, the Pennines in the centre-north, and the hills of the Lake District in the northwest. Scotland consists of southern uplands, central lowlands, the Highlands (which include the UK's highest peak) and many islands. Wales is a land of hills, mountains and river valleys. Northern Ireland contains uplands, plains and the UK's largest lake, Lough Neagh. The climate of the UK is mild, wet and variable. There are few mineral deposits, but important energy resources. Agricultural activities involve sheep and cattle rearing, dairy farming, and crop and fruit growing in the east and southeast. Productivity is high, but approximately one-third of food is imported. The UK produces petroleum and natural gas from reserves in the North Sea and is self-sufficient in energy in net terms. Major manufactures are food and drinks, motor vehicles and parts, aerospace equipment, machinery, electronic and electrical equipment, and chemicals and chemical products. However, the economy is dominated by service industries, including banking, insurance, finance and business services. London, the capital, is one of the world's major financial centres. Tourism is also a major industry, with approximately twenty-five million visitors a year. International trade is also important, equivalent to one-third of national income. Over half of the UK's trade is with other European Union countries.

England (Constituent country)

Area Sq Km (Sq Miles)	Population	Capital
130 433 (50 360)	50 431 700	London

Northern Ireland (Province)

Area Sq Km (Sq Miles)	Population	Capital
13 576 (5 242)	1 724 400	Belfast

Scotland (Constituent country)

Area Sq Km (Sq Miles)	Population	Capital
78 822 (30 433)	5 094 800	Edinburgh

Wales (Principality)

Area Sq Km (Sq Miles)	Population	Capital
20 778 (8 022)	2 958 600	Cardiff

UNITED STATES OF AMERICA

Area Sq Km	9 826 635	Languages	English, Spanish
Area Sq Miles	3 794 085	Religions	Protestant, Roman Catholic, Sunni Muslim, Jewish
Population	305 826 000	Currency	United States dollar
Capital	Washington D.C.	Organizations	APEC, NATO, OECD, UN

The USA comprises forty-eight contiguous states in North America, bounded by Canada and Mexico, plus the states of Alaska, to the northwest of Canada, and Hawaii, in the north Pacific Ocean. The populous eastern states cover the Atlantic coastal plain (which includes the Florida peninsula and the Gulf of Mexico coast) and the Appalachian Mountains. The central states occupy a vast interior plain drained by the Mississippi-Missouri river system. To the west lie the Rocky Mountains, separated from the Pacific coastal ranges by intermontane plateaus. The Pacific coastal zone is also mountainous, and prone to earthquakes. Hawaii is a group of some twenty volcanic islands. Climatic conditions range between arctic in Alaska to desert in the intermontane plateaus. Most of the USA has a temperate climate, although the interior has continental conditions. There are abundant natural resources, including major reserves of minerals and energy resources. The USA has the largest and most technologically advanced economy in the world, based on manufacturing and services. Although agriculture accounts for approximately two per cent of national income, productivity is high and the USA is a net exporter of food, chiefly grains and fruit. Cotton is the major industrial crop. The USA produces iron ore, copper, lead, zinc, and many other minerals. It is a major producer of coal, petroleum and natural gas, although being the world's biggest energy user it imports significant quantities of petroleum and its products. Manufacturing is diverse. The main industries are petroleum, steel, motor vehicles, aerospace, telecommunications, electronics, food processing, chemicals and consumer goods. Tourism is a major foreign currency earner, with approximately forty-five million visitors a year. Other important service industries are banking and finance, Wall Street in New York being one of the world's major stock exchanges. Canada and Mexico are the main trading partners.

Alabama (State)

Area Sq Km (Sq Miles)	Population	Capital
135 765 (52 419)	4 599 030	Montgomery

Alaska (State)

Area Sq Km (Sq Miles)	Population	Capital
1 717 854 (663 267)	670 053	Juneau

Arizona (State)

Area Sq Km (Sq Miles)	Population	Capital
295 253 (113 998)	6 166 318	Phoenix

Arkansas (State)

Area Sq Km (Sq Miles)	Population	Capital
137 733 (53 179)	2 810 872	Little Rock

California (State)

Area Sq Km (Sq Miles)	Population	Capital
423 971 (163 696)	36 457 549	Sacramento

Colorado (State)

Area Sq Km (Sq Miles)	Population	Capital
269 602 (104 094)	4 753 377	Denver

Connecticut (State)

Area Sq Km (Sq Miles)	Population	Capital
14 356 (5 543)	3 504 809	Hartford

Delaware (State)

Area Sq Km (Sq Miles)	Population	Capital
6 446 (2 489)	853 476	Dover

District of Columbia (District)

Area Sq Km (Sq Miles)	Population	Capital
176 (68)	581 530	Washington

Florida (State)

Area Sq Km (Sq Miles)	Population	Capital
170 305 (65 755)	18 089 888	Tallahassee

Georgia (State)

Area Sq Km (Sq Miles)	Population	Capital
153 910 (59 425)	9 363 941	Atlanta

Hawaii (State)

Area Sq Km (Sq Miles)	Population	Capital
28 311 (10 931)	1 285 498	Honolulu

Idaho (State)

Area Sq Km (Sq Miles)	Population	Capital
216 445 (83 570)	1 466 465	Boise

Illinois (State)

Area Sq Km (Sq Miles)	Population	Capital
149 997 (57 914)	12 831 970	Springfield

States and Territories

Indiana (State)

Area Sq Km (Sq Miles)	Population	Capital
94 322 (36 418)	6 313 520	Indianapolis

Iowa (State)

Area Sq Km (Sq Miles)	Population	Capital
145 744 (56 272)	2 982 085	Des Moines

Kansas (State)

Area Sq Km (Sq Miles)	Population	Capital
213 096 (82 277)	2 764 075	Topeka

Kentucky (State)

Area Sq Km (Sq Miles)	Population	Capital
104 659 (40 409)	4 206 074	Frankfort

Louisiana (State)

Area Sq Km (Sq Miles)	Population	Capital
134 265 (51 840)	4 287 768	Baton Rouge

Maine (State)

Area Sq Km (Sq Miles)	Population	Capital
91 647 (35 385)	1 321 574	Augusta

Maryland (State)

Area Sq Km (Sq Miles)	Population	Capital
32 134 (12 407)	5 615 727	Annapolis

Massachusetts (State)

Area Sq Km (Sq Miles)	Population	Capital
27 337 (10 555)	6 437 193	Boston

Michigan (State)

Area Sq Km (Sq Miles)	Population	Capital
250 493 (96 716)	10 095 643	Lansing

Minnesota (State)

Area Sq Km (Sq Miles)	Population	Capital
225 171 (86 939)	5 167 101	St Paul

Mississippi (State)

Area Sq Km (Sq Miles)	Population	Capital
125 433 (48 430)	2 910 540	Jackson

Missouri (State)

Area Sq Km (Sq Miles)	Population	Capital
180 533 (69 704)	5 842 713	Jefferson City

Montana (State)

Area Sq Km (Sq Miles)	Population	Capital
380 837 (147 042)	944 632	Helena

Nebraska (State)

Area Sq Km (Sq Miles)	Population	Capital
200 346 (77 354)	1 768 331	Lincoln

Nevada (State)

Area Sq Km (Sq Miles)	Population	Capital
286 352 (110 561)	2 495 529	Carson City

New Hampshire (State)

Area Sq Km (Sq Miles)	Population	Capital
24 216 (9 350)	1 314 895	Concord

New Jersey (State)

Area Sq Km (Sq Miles)	Population	Capital
22 587 (8 721)	8 724 560	Trenton

New Mexico (State)

Area Sq Km (Sq Miles)	Population	Capital
314 914 (121 589)	1 954 599	Santa Fe

New York (State)

Area Sq Km (Sq Miles)	Population	Capital
141 299 (54 556)	19 306 183	Albany

North Carolina (State)

Area Sq Km (Sq Miles)	Population	Capital
139 391 (53 819)	8 856 505	Raleigh

North Dakota (State)

Area Sq Km (Sq Miles)	Population	Capital
183 112 (70 700)	635 867	Bismarck

Ohio (State)

Area Sq Km (Sq Miles)	Population	Capital
116 096 (44 825)	11 478 006	Columbus

Oklahoma (State)

Area Sq Km (Sq Miles)	Population	Capital
181 035 (69 898)	3 579 212	Oklahoma City

Oregon (State)

Area Sq Km (Sq Miles)	Population	Capital
254 806 (98 381)	3 700 758	Salem

Pennsylvania (State)

Area Sq Km (Sq Miles)	Population	Capital
119 282 (46 055)	12 440 621	Harrisburg

Rhode Island (State)

Area Sq Km (Sq Miles)	Population	Capital
4 002 (1 545)	1 067 610	Providence

South Carolina (State)

Area Sq Km (Sq Miles)	Population	Capital
82 931 (32 020)	4 321 249	Columbia

South Dakota (State)

Area Sq Km (Sq Miles)	Population	Capital
199 730 (77 116)	781 919	Pierre

Tennessee (State)

Area Sq Km (Sq Miles)	Population	Capital
109 150 (42 143)	6 038 803	Nashville

Texas (State)

Area Sq Km (Sq Miles)	Population	Capital
695 622 (268 581)	23 507 783	Austin

Utah (State)

Area Sq Km (Sq Miles)	Population	Capital
219 887 (84 899)	2 550 063	Salt Lake City

Vermont (State)

Area Sq Km (Sq Miles)	Population	Capital
24 900 (9 614)	623 908	Montpelier

Virginia (State)

Area Sq Km (Sq Miles)	Population	Capital
110 784 (42 774)	7 642 884	Richmond

Washington (State)

Area Sq Km (Sq Miles)	Population	Capital
184 666 (71 300)	6 395 798	Olympia

West Virginia (State)

Area Sq Km (Sq Miles)	Population	Capital
62 755 (24 230)	1 818 470	Charleston

Wisconsin (State)

Area Sq Km (Sq Miles)	Population	Capital
169 639 (65 498)	5 556 506	Madison

Wyoming (State)

Area Sq Km (Sq Miles)	Population	Capital
253 337 (97 814)	515 004	Cheyenne

URUGUAY

Oriental Republic of Uruguay

Area Sq Km	176 215	Languages	Spanish
Area Sq Miles	68 037	Religions	Roman Catholic, Protestant, Jewish
Population	3 340 000	Currency	Uruguayan peso
Capital	Montevideo	Organizations	UN

Uruguay, on the Atlantic coast of central South America, is a low-lying land of prairies. The coast and the River Plate estuary in the south are fringed with lagoons and sand dunes. Almost half the population lives in the capital, Montevideo. Uruguay has warm summers and mild winters. The economy is based on cattle and sheep ranching, and the main industries produce food products, textiles, and petroleum products. Meat, wool, hides, textiles and agricultural products are the main exports. Brazil and Argentina are the main trading partners.

UZBEKISTAN

Republic of Uzbekistan

Area Sq Km	447 400	Languages	Uzbek, Russian, Tajik, Kazakh
Area Sq Miles	172 742	Religions	Sunni Muslim, Russian Orthodox
Population	27 372 000	Currency	Uzbek som
Capital	Toshkent (Tashkent)	Organizations	CIS, UN

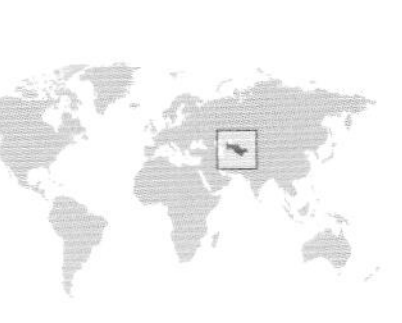

A landlocked country of central Asia, Uzbekistan consists mainly of the flat Kyzylkum Desert. High mountains and valleys are found towards the southeast borders with Kyrgyzstan and Tajikistan. Most settlement is in the Fergana basin. The climate is hot and dry. The economy is based mainly on irrigated agriculture, chiefly cotton production. Uzbekistan is rich in minerals, including gold, copper, lead, zinc and uranium, and it has one of the largest gold mines in the world. Industry specializes in fertilizers and machinery for cotton harvesting and textile manufacture. The Russian Federation is the main trading partner.

VANUATU

Republic of Vanuatu

Area Sq Km	12 190	Languages	English, Bislama (Creole), French
Area Sq Miles	4 707	Religions	Protestant, Roman Catholic, traditional beliefs
Population	226 000	Currency	Vatu
Capital	Port Vila	Organizations	Comm., UN

Vanuatu occupies an archipelago of approximately eighty islands in the southwest Pacific. Many of the islands are mountainous, of volcanic origin and densely forested. The climate is tropical, with heavy rainfall. Half of the population lives on the main islands of Éfaté and Espíritu Santo, and the majority of people are employed in agriculture. Copra, beef, timber, vegetables, and cocoa are the main exports. Tourism is becoming important to the economy. Australia, Japan and Germany are the main trading partners.

VATICAN CITY

Vatican City State or Holy See

Area Sq Km	0.5	Languages	Italian
Area Sq Miles	0.2	Religions	Roman Catholic
Population	557	Currency	Euro
Capital	Vatican City		

The world's smallest sovereign state, the Vatican City occupies a hill to the west of the river Tiber within the Italian capital, Rome. It is the headquarters of the Roman Catholic church, and income comes from investments, voluntary contributions and tourism.

VENEZUELA

Bolivarian Republic of Venezuela

Area Sq Km	912 050	Languages	Spanish, Amerindian languages
Area Sq Miles	352 144	Religions	Roman Catholic, Protestant
Population	27 657 000	Currency	Bolívar fuerte
Capital	Caracas	Organizations	OPEC, UN

Venezuela is in northern South America, on the Caribbean. Its coast is much indented, with the oil-rich area of Lake Maracaibo at the western end, and the swampy Orinoco Delta to the east. Mountain ranges run parallel to the coast, and turn southwestwards to form a northern extension of the Andes. Central Venezuela is an area of lowland grasslands drained by the Orinoco river system. To the south are the Guiana Highlands, which contain the Angel Falls, the world's highest waterfall. Almost ninety per cent of the population lives in towns, mostly in the coastal mountain areas. The climate is tropical, with most rainfall in summer. Farming is important, particularly cattle ranching and dairy farming; coffee, maize, rice and sugar cane are the main crops. Venezuela is a major oil producer, and oil accounts for about seventy-five per cent of export earnings. Aluminium, iron ore, copper and gold are also mined, and manufactures include petrochemicals, aluminium, steel, textiles and food products. The USA and Puerto Rico are the main trading partners.

VIETNAM
Socialist Republic of Vietnam

Area Sq Km	329 565	Languages	Vietnamese, Thai, Khmer, Chinese, local languages
Area Sq Miles	127 246	Religions	Buddhist, Taoist, Roman Catholic, Cao Dai, Hoa Hao
Population	87 375 000	Currency	Dong
Capital	Ha Nôi (Hanoi)	Organizations	APEC, ASEAN, UN

Vietnam lies in southeast Asia on the west coast of the South China Sea. The Red River delta lowlands in the north are separated from the huge Mekong delta in the south by long, narrow coastal plains backed by the mountainous and forested terrain of the Annam Highlands. Most of the population lives in the river deltas. The climate is tropical, with summer monsoon rains. Over three-quarters of the workforce is involved in agriculture, forestry and fishing. Coffee, tea and rubber are important cash crops, but Vietnam is the world's second largest rice exporter. Oil, coal and copper are produced, and other main industries are food processing, clothing and footwear, cement and fertilizers. Exports include oil, coffee, rice, clothing, fish and fish products. Japan and Singapore are the main trading partners.

Virgin Islands (U.K.)
United Kingdom Overseas Territory

Area Sq Km	153	Languages	English
Area Sq Miles	59	Religions	Protestant, Roman Catholic
Population	23 000	Currency	United States dollar
Capital	Road Town		

The Caribbean territory comprises four main islands and over thirty islets at the eastern end of the Virgin Islands group. Apart from the flat coral atoll of Anegada, the islands are volcanic in origin and hilly. The climate is subtropical, and tourism is the main industry.

Virgin Islands (U.S.A.)
United States Unincorporated Territory

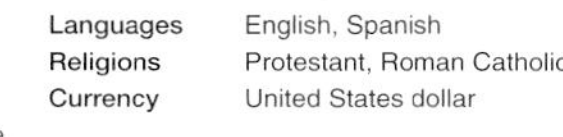

Area Sq Km	352	Languages	English, Spanish
Area Sq Miles	136	Religions	Protestant, Roman Catholic
Population	111 000	Currency	United States dollar
Capital	Charlotte Amalie		

The territory consists of three main islands and over fifty islets in the Caribbean's western Virgin Islands. The islands are hilly, of volcanic origin, and the climate is subtropical. The economy is based on tourism, with some manufacturing, including a major oil refinery on St Croix.

Wallis and Futuna Islands
French Overseas Collectivity

Area Sq Km	274	Languages	French, Wallisian, Futunian
Area Sq Miles	106	Religions	Roman Catholic
Population	15 000	Currency	CFP franc
Capital	Matā'utu		

The south Pacific territory comprises the volcanic islands of the Wallis archipelago and the Hoorn Islands. The climate is tropical. The islands depend on subsistence farming, the sale of licences to foreign fishing fleets, workers' remittances from abroad and French aid.

West Bank
Disputed territory

Area Sq Km	5 860	Languages	Arabic, Hebrew
Area Sq Miles	2 263	Religions	Sunni Muslim, Jewish, Shi'a Muslim, Christian
Population	2 676 284	Currency	Jordanian dinar, Israeli shekel

The territory consists of the west bank of the river Jordan and parts of Judea and Samaria. The land was annexed by Israel in 1967, but some areas have been granted autonomy under agreements between Israel and the Palestinian Authority. Conflict between the Israelis and the Palestinians continues to restrict economic development.

Western Sahara
Disputed territory (Morocco)

Area Sq Km	266 000	Languages	Arabic
Area Sq Miles	102 703	Religions	Sunni Muslim
Population	480 000	Currency	Moroccan dirham
Capital	Laâyoune		

Situated on the northwest coast of Africa, the territory of the Western Sahara is now effectively controlled by Morocco. The land is low, flat desert with higher land in the northeast. There is little cultivation and only about twenty per cent of the land is pasture. Livestock herding, fishing and phosphate mining are the main activities. All trade is controlled by Morocco.

YEMEN
Republic of Yemen

Area Sq Km	527 968	Languages	Arabic
Area Sq Miles	203 850	Religions	Sunni Muslim, Shi'a Muslim
Population	22 389 000	Currency	Yemeni riyal
Capital	Şan'ā'	Organizations	UN

Yemen occupies the southwestern part of the Arabian Peninsula, on the Red Sea and the Gulf of Aden. Beyond the Red Sea coastal plain the land rises to a mountain range and then descends to desert plateaus. Much of the country is hot and arid, but there is more rainfall in the west, where most of the population lives. Farming and fishing are the main activities, with cotton the main cash crop. The main exports are crude oil, fish, coffee and dried fruit. Despite some oil resources Yemen is one of the poorest countries in the Arab world. Main trading partners are Thailand, China, South Korea and Saudi Arabia.

ZAMBIA
Republic of Zambia

Area Sq Km	752 614	Languages	English, Bemba, Nyanja, Tonga, local languages
Area Sq Miles	290 586	Religions	Christian, traditional beliefs
Population	11 922 000	Currency	Zambian kwacha
Capital	Lusaka	Organizations	Comm., SADC, UN

A landlocked state in south central Africa, Zambia consists principally of high savanna plateaus and is bordered by the Zambezi river in the south. Most people live in the Copperbelt area in the centre-north. The climate is tropical, with a rainy season from November to May. Agriculture employs approximately eighty per cent of the workforce, but is mainly at subsistence level. Copper mining is the mainstay of the economy, although reserves are declining. Copper and cobalt are the main exports. Most trade is with South Africa.

ZIMBABWE
Republic of Zimbabwe

Area Sq Km	390 759	Languages	English, Shona, Ndebele
Area Sq Miles	150 873	Religions	Christian, traditional beliefs
Population	13 349 000	Currency	Zimbabwean dollar
Capital	Harare	Organizations	SADC, UN

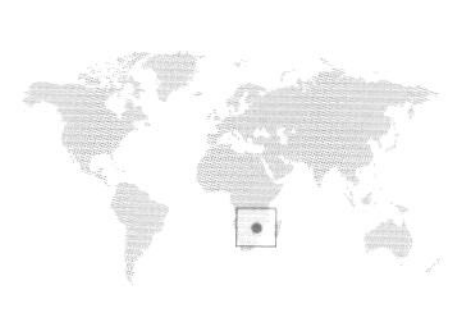

Zimbabwe, a landlocked state in south-central Africa, consists of high plateaus flanked by the Zambezi river valley and Lake Kariba in the north and the Limpopo river in the south. Most of the population lives in the centre of the country. There are significant mineral resources, including gold, nickel, copper, asbestos, platinum and chromium. Agriculture is a major sector of the economy, with crops including tobacco, maize, sugar cane and cotton. Beef cattle are also important. Exports include tobacco, gold, ferroalloys, nickel and cotton. South Africa is the main trading partner. The economy has suffered recently through significant political unrest and instability.

Index

Introduction to the index

The index includes all names shown on the reference maps in the atlas. Each entry includes the country or geographical area in which the feature is located, a page number and an alphanumeric reference. Additional entry details and aspects of the index are explained below.

Name forms

The names policy in this atlas is generally to use local name forms which are officially recognized by the governments of the countries concerned. Rules established by the Permanent Committee on Geographical Names for British Official Use (PCGN) are applied to the conversion of non-roman alphabet names, for example in the Russian Federation, into the roman alphabet used in English.

However, English conventional name forms are used for the most well-known places for which such a form is in common use. In these cases, the local form is included in brackets on the map and appears as a cross-reference in the index. Other alternative names, such as well-known historical names or those in other languages, may also be included in brackets on the map and as cross-references in the index. All country names and those for international physical features appear in their English forms. Names appear in full in the index, although they may appear in abbreviated form on the maps.

Referencing

Names are referenced by page number and by grid reference. The grid reference relates to the alphanumeric values which appear on the edges of each map. These reflect the graticule on the map – the letter relates to longitude divisions, the number to latitude divisions. Names are generally referenced to the largest scale map page on which they appear. For large geographical features, including countries, the reference is to the largest scale map on which the feature appears in its entirety, or on which the majority of it appears.

Rivers are referenced to their lowest downstream point – either their mouth or their confluence with another river. The river name will generally be positioned as close to this point as possible.

Alternative names

Alternative names appear as cross-references and refer the user to the index entry for the form of the name used on the map.

For rivers with multiple names - for example those which flow through several countries - all alternative name forms are included within the main index entries, with details of the countries in which each form applies.

Administrative qualifiers

Administrative divisions are included in entries to differentiate duplicate names - entries of exactly the same name and feature type within the one country - where these division names are shown on the maps. In such cases, duplicate names are alphabetized in the order of the administrative division names.

Additional qualifiers are included for names within selected geographical areas, to indicate more clearly their location.

Descriptors

Entries, other than those for towns and cities, include a descriptor indicating the type of geographical feature. Descriptors are not included where the type of feature is implicit in the name itself, unless there is a town or city of exactly the same name.

Insets

Where relevant, the index clearly indicates [inset] if a feature appears on an inset map.

Alphabetical order

The Icelandic characters Þ and þ are transliterated and alphabetized as 'Th' and 'th'. The German character ß is alphabetized as 'ss'. Names beginning with Mac or Mc are alphabetized exactly as they appear. The terms Saint, Sainte, etc, are abbreviated to St, Ste, etc, but alphabetized as if in the full form.

Numerical entries

Entries beginning with numerals appear at the beginning of the index, in numerical order. Elsewhere, numerals are alphabetized before 'a'.

Permuted terms

Names beginning with generic geographical terms are permuted - the descriptive term is placed after, and the index alphabetized by, the main part of the name. For example, Mount Everest is indexed as Everest, Mount; Lake Superior as Superior, Lake. This policy is applied to all languages. Permuting has not been applied to names of towns, cities or administrative divisions beginning with such geographical terms. These remain in their full form, for example, Lake Isabella, USA.

Gazetteer entries

Selected entries have been extended to include gazetteer-style information. Important geographical facts which relate specifically to the entry are included within the entry.

Abbreviations

admin. dist.	administrative district	IL	Illinois	plat.	plateau
admin. div.	administrative division	imp. l.	impermanent lake	P.N.G.	Papua New Guinea
admin. reg.	administrative region	IN	Indiana	Port.	Portugal
Afgh.	Afghanistan	Indon.	Indonesia	pref.	prefecture
AK	Alaska	Kazakh.	Kazakhstan	prov.	province
AL	Alabama	KS	Kansas	pt	point
Alg.	Algeria	KY	Kentucky	Qld	Queensland
AR	Arkansas	Kyrg.	Kyrgyzstan	Que.	Québec
Arg.	Argentina	l.	lake	r.	river
aut. comm.	autonomous community	LA	Louisiana	reg.	region
aut. reg.	autonomous region	lag.	lagoon	res.	reserve
aut. rep.	autonomous republic	Lith.	Lithuania	resr	reservoir
AZ	Arizona	Lux.	Luxembourg	RI	Rhode Island
Azer.	Azerbaijan	MA	Massachusetts	Rus. Fed.	Russian Federation
b.	bay	Madag.	Madagascar	S.	South, Southern
Bangl.	Bangladesh	Man.	Manitoba	S.A.	South Australia
B.C.	British Columbia	MD	Maryland	salt l.	salt lake
Bol.	Bolivia	ME	Maine	Sask.	Saskatchewan
Bos.-Herz.	Bosnia-Herzegovina	Mex.	Mexico	SC	South Carolina
Bulg.	Bulgaria	MI	Michigan	SD	South Dakota
c.	cape	MN	Minnesota	sea chan.	sea channel
CA	California	MO	Missouri	Sing.	Singapore
Cent. Afr. Rep.	Central African Republic	Moz.	Mozambique	Switz.	Switzerland
CO	Colorado	MS	Mississippi	Tajik.	Tajikistan
Col.	Colombia	MT	Montana	Tanz.	Tanzania
CT	Connecticut	mt.	mountain	Tas.	Tasmania
Czech Rep.	Czech Republic	mts	mountains	terr.	territory
DC	District of Columbia	N.	North, Northern	Thai.	Thailand
DE	Delaware	nat. park	national park	TN	Tennessee
Dem. Rep. Congo	Democratic Republic of the Congo	N.B.	New Brunswick	Trin. and Tob.	Trinidad and Tobago
depr.	depression	NC	North Carolina	Turkm.	Turkmenistan
des.	desert	ND	North Dakota	TX	Texas
Dom. Rep.	Dominican Republic	NE	Nebraska	U.A.E.	United Arab Emirates
E.	East, Eastern	Neth.	Netherlands	U.K.	United Kingdom
Equat. Guinea	Equatorial Guinea	NH	New Hampshire	Ukr.	Ukraine
esc.	escarpment	NJ	New Jersey	U.S.A.	United States of America
est.	estuary	NM	New Mexico	UT	Utah
Eth.	Ethiopia	N.S.	Nova Scotia	Uzbek.	Uzbekistan
Fin.	Finland	N.S.W.	New South Wales	VA	Virginia
FL	Florida	N.T.	Northern Territory	Venez.	Venezuela
for.	forest	NV	Nevada	Vic.	Victoria
Fr. Guiana	French Guiana	N.W.T.	Northwest Territories	vol.	volcano
F.Y.R.O.M.	Former Yugoslav Republic of Macedonia	NY	New York	vol. crater	volcanic crater
g.	gulf	N.Z.	New Zealand	VT	Vermont
GA	Georgia	OH	Ohio	W.	West, Western
Guat.	Guatemala	OK	Oklahoma	WA	Washington
HI	Hawaii	OR	Oregon	W.A.	Western Australia
H.K.	Hong Kong	PA	Pennsylvania	WI	Wisconsin
Hond.	Honduras	Para.	Paraguay	WV	West Virginia
i.	island	P.E.I.	Prince Edward Island	WY	Wyoming
IA	Iowa	pen.	peninsula	Y.T.	Yukon
ID	Idaho	Phil.	Philippines		

1

1st Three Mile Opening sea chan. Australia 136 D2
2nd Three Mile Opening sea chan. Australia 136 C2
3-y Severnyy Rus. Fed. 51 S3
5 de Outubro Angola see Xá-Muteba
9 de Julio Arg. 178 D5
25 de Mayo Buenos Aires Arg. 178 D5
25 de Mayo La Pampa Arg. 178 C5
70 Mile House Canada 150 F5
100 Mile House Canada 150 F5
150 Mile House Canada 150 F4

A

Aabenraa Denmark 55 F9
Aachen Germany 62 G4
Aalborg Denmark 55 F8
Aalborg Bugt b. Denmark 55 G8
Aalen Germany 63 K6
Aalesund Norway see Ålesund
Aaley Lebanon see Aley
Aalst Belgium 62 E4
Aanaar Fin. see Inari
Aarhus Denmark see Århus
Aarlen Belgium see Arlon
Aars Denmark 55 F8
Aarschot Belgium 62 E4
Aasiaat Greenland 147 M3
Aath Belgium see Ath
Aba China 96 D1
Aba Dem. Rep. Congo 122 D3
Aba Nigeria 120 D4
Abacaxis r. Brazil 177 G4
Ābādān Iran 110 C4
Abadan Turkm. 110 E2
Ābādeh Iran 110 D4
Ābādeh Ţashk Iran 110 D4
Abadla Alg. 64 D5
Abaeté Brazil 179 B2
Abaetetuba Brazil 177 I4
Abagaytuy Rus. Fed. 95 I1
Abagnar Qi Nei Mongol China see Xilinhot
Abag Qi Nei Mongol China see Xin Hot
Abaiang atoll Kiribati 186 H5
Abajo Peak U.S.A. 159 I3
Abakaliki Nigeria 120 D4
Abakan Rus. Fed. 88 G2
Abakanskiy Khrebet mts Rus. Fed. 88 F2
Abalak Niger 120 D3
Abana Turkey 112 D2
Abancay Peru 176 D6
Abariringa atoll Kiribati see Kanton
Abarkūh, Kavīr-e des. Iran 110 D4
Abarqū Iran 110 D4
Abarshahr Iran see Neyshābūr
Abashiri Japan 90 G3
Abashiri-wan b. Japan 90 G3
Abasolo Mex. 161 D7
Abau P.N.G. 136 E1
Abaya, Lake Eth. 122 D3
Ābaya Hāyk' l. Eth. see Abaya, Lake
Ābay Wenz r. Eth. 122 D2 see Blue Nile
Abaza Rus. Fed. 88 G2
Abba Cent. Afr. Rep. 122 B3
'Abbāsābād Iran 110 D3
'Abbāsābād Iran 110 E2
Abbasanta Sardinia Italy 68 C4
Abbatis Villa France see Abbeville
Abbe, Lake Djibouti/Eth. 108 F7
Abbeville France 62 B4
Abbeville AL U.S.A. 163 C6
Abbeville GA U.S.A. 163 D6
Abbeville LA U.S.A. 161 E6
Abbeville SC U.S.A. 163 D5
Abbey Canada 151 I5
Abbeyfeale Ireland 61 C5
Abbeytown U.K. 58 D4
Abborrträsk Sweden 54 K4
Abbot, Mount Australia 136 D4
Abbot Ice Shelf Antarctica 188 K2
Abbotsford Canada 150 F5
Abbott NM U.S.A. 157 G5
Abbott VA U.S.A. 164 E5
Abbottabad Pak. 111 I3
'Abd al 'Azīz, Jabal hill Syria 113 F3
'Abd al Kūrī i. Yemen 108 H7
'Abd Allah, Khawr sea chan. Iraq/Kuwait 110 C4
Abd al Ma'asīr well Saudi Arabia 107 D4
Ābdānān Iran 110 B3
'Abdollāhābād Iran 110 D3
Abdulino Rus. Fed. 51 Q5
Abéché Chad 121 F3
Abe-gawa r. Japan 93 E4
Abellinum Italy see Avellino
Abel Tasman National Park N.Z. 139 D5
Abengourou Côte d'Ivoire 120 C4
Åbenrå Denmark see Aabenraa
Abensberg Germany 63 L6
Abeokuta Nigeria 120 D4
Aberaeron U.K. 59 C6
Aberchirder U.K. 60 G3
Abercorn Zambia see Mbala
Abercrombie r. Australia 138 D4
Aberdare U.K. 59 D7
Aberdaron U.K. 59 C6
Aberdaugleddau U.K. see Milford Haven
Aberdeen Australia 138 E4
Aberdeen H.K. China 97 [inset]
Aberdeen S. Africa 124 G7
Aberdeen U.K. 60 G3
Aberdeen U.S.A. 160 D2
Aberdeen Lake Canada 151 L1
Aberdovey U.K. 59 C6
Aberdyfi Wales U.K. see Aberdovey
Aberfeldy U.K. 60 F4
Aberford U.K. 58 F5
Aberfoyle U.K. 60 E4
Abergavenny U.K. 59 D7
Abergwaun U.K. see Fishguard
Aberhonddu U.K. see Brecon
Abermaw U.K. see Barmouth
Abernathy U.S.A. 161 C5
Aberporth U.K. 59 C6
Abersoch U.K. 59 C6
Abertawe U.K. see Swansea
Aberteifi U.K. see Cardigan
Aberystwyth U.K. 59 C6
Abeshr Chad see Abéché
Abez' Rus. Fed. 51 S2
Āb Gāh Iran 111 E5
Abhā Saudi Arabia 108 F6
Abhar Iran 110 C2
Abiad, Bahr el r. Sudan/Uganda 108 D6 see White Nile

▶Abidjan Côte d'Ivoire 120 C4
Former capital of Côte d'Ivoire.

Abijatta-Shalla National Park Eth. 122 D3
Ab-i-Kavīr salt flat Iran 110 E3
Abiko Japan 93 G3
Abilene KS U.S.A. 160 D4
Abilene TX U.S.A. 161 D5
Abingdon U.K. 59 F7
Abingdon U.S.A. 164 D5
Abington Reef Australia 136 E3
Abinsk Rus. Fed. 112 E1
Abitau Lake Canada 151 J2
Abitibi, Lake Canada 152 E4
Ab Khūr Iran 110 E3
Abminga Australia 135 F6
Abnūb Egypt 112 C6
Åbo Fin. see Turku
Abohar India 104 C3
Aboisso Côte d'Ivoire 120 C4
Aboite U.S.A. 164 C3
Abomey Benin 120 D4
Abongabong, Gunung mt. Indon. 84 B1
Abong Mbang Cameroon 120 E4
Aborlan Palawan Phil. 82 B4
Abō-tōge pass Japan 92 D2
Abou Déia Chad 121 E3
Abovyan Armenia 113 G2
Aboyne U.K. 60 G3
Abqaiq Saudi Arabia 110 C5
Abraham's Bay Bahamas 163 F8
Abramov, Mys pt Rus. Fed. 52 I2
Abrantes Port. 67 B4
Abra Pampa Arg. 178 C2
Abreojos, Punta pt Mex. 166 B3
'Abri Sudan 108 D5
Abrolhos Bank sea feature S. Atlantic Ocean 184 F7
Abruzzo, Parco Nazionale d' nat. park Italy 68 E4
Absalom, Mount Antarctica 188 B1
Absaroka Range mts U.S.A. 156 F3
Abtar, Jabal al hills Syria 107 C2
Abtsgmünd Germany 63 J6
Abū aḍ Ḍuhūr Syria 107 C2
Abū al Abyaḍ i. U.A.E. 110 D5
Abū al Ḩusayn, Qā' imp. l. Jordan 107 D3
Abū 'Alī i. Saudi Arabia 110 C5
Abū 'Āmūd, Wādī watercourse Jordan 107 C4
Abū 'Arīsh Saudi Arabia 108 F6
Abu 'Aweigīla well Egypt see Abū 'Uwayqilah
Abu Deleiq Sudan 108 D6

▶Abu Dhabi U.A.E. 110 D5
Capital of the United Arab Emirates.

Abū Du'ān Syria 107 D1
Abu Gubeiha Sudan 108 D7
Abū Ḩafnah, Wādī watercourse Jordan 107 D3
Abu Haggag Egypt see Ra's al Ḩikmah
Abū Ḩallūfah, Jabal hill Jordan 107 C4
Abu Hamed Sudan 108 D6

▶Abuja Nigeria 120 D4
Capital of Nigeria.

Abū Jifān well Saudi Arabia 110 B5
Abū Jurdhān Jordan 107 B4
Abū Kamāl Syria 113 F4
Abukuma-gawa r. Japan 93 G1
Abukuma-kōchi plat. Japan 93 G2
Abu Matariq Sudan 121 F3
Abū Mīnā tourist site Egypt 112 C5
Abumombazi Dem. Rep. Congo 122 C3
Abu Musa i. The Gulf 110 D5
Abū Mūsá, Jazīreh-ye i. The Gulf see Abu Musa
Abunã r. Bol. 176 E5
Abunã Brazil 176 E5
Ābune Yosēf mt. Eth. 108 E7
Abū Nujaym Libya 121 E1
Abū Qa'ṭūr Syria 107 C2
Abū Rawthah, Jabal mt. Egypt 107 B5
Aburazaka-tōge pass Japan 92 C3
Aburo mt. Dem. Rep. Congo 122 D3
Abu Road India 101 G4
Abū Rujmayn, Jabal mts Syria 107 D2
Abu Rûtha, Gebel mt. Egypt see Abū Rawthah, Jabal
Abū Sawādah well Saudi Arabia 110 C5
Abu Simbil Egypt see Abū Sunbul
Abū Sunbul Egypt 108 D5
Abū Ṭarfā', Wādī watercourse Egypt 107 A5
Abut Head hd N.Z. 139 C6
Abū 'Uwayqilah well Egypt 107 B4
Abuyog Leyte Phil. 82 D4
Abu Zabad Sudan 108 C7
Abū Ẓabī U.A.E. see Abu Dhabi
Abūzam Iran 110 C4
Abū Zanīmah Egypt 112 D5
Abu Zenīma Egypt see Abū Zanīmah
Abyad Sudan 108 C7
Abyaḍ, Jabal al mts Syria 107 C2
Abyār al Hakīm well Libya 112 A5
Abydos Australia 134 B5
Abyei Sudan 108 C8
Abyssinia country Africa see Ethiopia
Academician Vernadskiy research station Antarctica see Vernadsky
Academy Bay Rus. Fed. see Akademii, Zaliv
Acadia prov. Canada see Nova Scotia
Acadia National Park U.S.A. 162 G2
Açailândia Brazil 177 I5
Acajutla El Salvador 167 H6
Acamarachi mt. Chile see Pili, Cerro
Acambaro Mex. 167 E4
Acampamento de Caça do Mucusso Angola 123 C5
Acancéh Mex. 167 H4
Acandí Col. 176 C2
A Cañiza Spain 67 B2
Acaponeta Mex. 168 C4
Acapulco Mex. 168 E5
Acapulco de Juárez Mex. see Acapulco
Acará Brazil 177 I4
Acarai Mountains hills Brazil/Guyana 177 G3
Acaraú Brazil 177 J4
Acaray, Represa de resr Para. 178 E3
Acarigua Venez. 176 E2
Acatlán Mex. 168 E5
Acatzingo Mex. 167 F5
Acayucán Mex. 167 G5
Accho Israel see 'Akko
Accomac U.S.A. 165 H5
Accomack U.S.A. see Accomac

▶Accra Ghana 120 C4
Capital of Ghana.

Accrington U.K. 58 E5
Aceh admin. dist. Indon. 84 B1
Ach r. Germany 63 L6
Achacachi Bol. 176 E7
Achaguas Venez. 176 E2
Achalpur India 104 D5
Achampet India 106 C2
Achan Rus. Fed. 90 E2
Achayvayam Rus. Fed. 77 S3
Achchen Rus. Fed. 148 D2
Acheh admin. dist. Indon. see Aceh
Acheng China 90 B3
Achhota India 106 D1
Achi Japan 92 D3
Achicourt France 62 C4
Achill Ireland 61 C4
Achillbeg Island Ireland 61 C4
Achill Island Ireland 61 B4
Achiltibuie U.K. 60 D2
Achim Germany 63 J1
Achin admin. dist. Indon. see Aceh
Achinsk Rus. Fed. 76 K4
Achit Rus. Fed. 51 R4
Achit Nuur l. Mongolia 94 B1
Achkhoy-Martan Rus. Fed. 113 G2
Achna Cyprus 107 A2
Achnasheen U.K. 60 D3
Acıgöl l. Turkey 69 M6
Acıpayam Turkey 69 M6
Acireale Sicily Italy 68 F6
Ackerman U.S.A. 161 F5
Ackley U.S.A. 160 E3
Acklins Island Bahamas 163 F8
Acle U.K. 59 I6

▶Aconcagua, Cerro mt. Arg. 178 B4
Highest mountain in South America.

Acopiara Brazil 177 K5
A Coruña Spain 67 B2
Acoyapa Nicaragua 166 [inset] I7
Acqui Terme Italy 68 C2
Acra U.S.A. 165 H2
Acragas Sicily Italy see Agrigento
Acraman, Lake salt flat Australia 137 A7
Acre r. Brazil 176 E6
Acre Israel see 'Akko
Acre, Bay of Israel see Haifa, Bay of
Acri Italy 68 G5
Ács Hungary 57 Q7
Actaeon Group is Fr. Polynesia see Actéon, Groupe
Actéon, Groupe is Fr. Polynesia 187 K7
Acton Canada 164 E2
Acton U.S.A. 158 D4
Actopán Mex. 167 F4
Acungui Brazil 179 A4
Acunum Acusio France see Montélimar
Ada MN U.S.A. 160 D2
Ada OH U.S.A. 164 D3
Ada OK U.S.A. 161 D5
Ada WI U.S.A. 164 B2
Adabazar Sakarya Turkey see Adapazarı
Adaja r. Spain 67 D3
Adak AK U.S.A. 149 [inset]
Adak Island AK U.S.A. 149 [inset]
Adalia Turkey see Antalya
Adam Oman 109 I5
Adam, Mount hill Falkland Is 178 E8
Adamantina Brazil 179 A3
Adams IN U.S.A. 164 C4
Adams KY U.S.A. 164 D4
Adams MA U.S.A. 165 I2
Adams NY U.S.A. 165 G2
Adams, Mount U.S.A. 156 C3
Adams Center U.S.A. 165 G2
Adams Lake Canada 150 G5
Adams Mountain AK U.S.A. 149 O5
Adam's Peak Sri Lanka 106 D5
Adams Peak U.S.A. 158 C2
Adamstown Pitcairn Is 187 L7
'Adan Yemen see Aden
Adana Turkey 107 B1
Adana prov. Turkey 107 B1
Adana Yemen see Aden
Adang, Teluk b. Indon. 85 G3
Adapazarı Turkey 69 N4
Adare Ireland 61 D5
Adare, Cape Antarctica 188 H2
Adavale Australia 137 D5
Adban Afgh. 111 H2
Ad Dabbah Sudan see Ed Debba
Ad Ḑabbīyah well Saudi Arabia 110 C5
Ad Dafinah Saudi Arabia 108 F5
Ad Dahnā' des. Saudi Arabia 108 G5
Ad Dakhla W. Sahara 120 B2
Ad Damir Sudan see Ed Damer
Ad Dammām Saudi Arabia see Dammam
Addanki India 106 C3
Ad Dār al Ḩamrā' Saudi Arabia 108 E4
Ad Darb Saudi Arabia 108 F6
Ad Dawādimī Saudi Arabia 108 F5
Ad Dawḩah Qatar see Doha
Ad Dawr Iraq 113 F4
Ad Daww plain Syria 107 C2
Ad Dayr Iraq 113 G5
Ad Dibdibah plain Saudi Arabia 110 B5
Aḑ Ḑiffah plat. Egypt see Libyan Plateau

▶Addis Ababa Eth. 122 D3
Capital of Ethiopia.

Addison U.S.A. 165 G2
Ad Dīwānīyah Iraq 113 G5
Addlestone U.K. 59 G7
Addo Elephant National Park S. Africa 125 G7
Addoo Atoll Maldives see Addu Atoll
Addu Atoll Maldives 103 D12
Ad Duwayd well Saudi Arabia 113 F5
Ad Duwaym Sudan see Ed Dueim
Ad Duwayris well Saudi Arabia 110 C6
Adegaon India 104 D5
Adel GA U.S.A. 163 D6
Adel IA U.S.A. 160 E3

▶Adelaide Australia 137 B7
Capital of South Australia.

Adelaide r. Australia 134 E3
Adelaide Bahamas 163 E7
Adelaide Island Antarctica 188 L2
Adelaide River Australia 134 E3
Adele Island Australia 134 C3
Adélie Coast Antarctica 188 G2
Adélie Coast reg. Antarctica see Adélie Land
Adélie Land reg. Antarctica 188 G2
Adelong Australia 138 D5
Aden Yemen 108 F7
Aden, Gulf of Somalia/Yemen 108 G7
Adena U.S.A. 164 E3
Adenau Germany 62 G4
Adendorf Germany 63 K1
Aderbissinat Niger 120 D3
Aderno Sicily Italy see Adrano
Adesar India 104 B5
Adhan, Jabal mt. U.A.E. 110 E5
Adh Dhāyūf well Saudi Arabia 113 G6
'Adhfā' well Saudi Arabia 113 F5
'Āḑhiriyāt, Jibāl al mts Jordan 107 C4
Adi i. Indon. 81 I7
Ādī Ārk'ay Eth. 108 E7
Adige r. Italy 68 E2
Ādīgrat Eth. 122 D2
Adilabad India 106 C2
Adilcevaz Turkey 113 F3
Adin U.S.A. 156 C4
Adīrī Libya 121 E2
Adirondack Mountains U.S.A. 165 H1
Ādīs Ābeba Eth. see Addis Ababa
Adi Ugri Eritrea see Mendefera
Adıyaman Turkey 112 E3
Adjud Romania 69 L1
Adlavik Islands Canada 153 K3
Admiralty Island Canada 147 H3
Admiralty Island AK U.S.A. 149 N4
Admiralty Island National Monument-Kootznoowoo Wilderness nat. park U.S.A. 146 E4
Admiralty Islands P.N.G. 81 L7
Ado-Ekiti Nigeria 120 D4
Adogawa Japan 92 C3
Ado-gawa r. Japan 92 C3
Adok Sudan 108 D8
Adolfo L. Mateos Mex. 157 E8
Adolphus U.S.A. 164 B5
Adonara i. Indon. 83 B5
Adoni India 106 C3
Adorf Germany 63 M4
Adorf (Diemelsee) Germany 63 I3
Ado-Tymovo Rus. Fed. 90 F2
Adour r. France 66 D5
Adra Spain 67 E5
Adramyttium Turkey see Edremit
Adramyttium, Gulf of Turkey see Edremit Körfezi
Adrano Sicily Italy 68 F6
Adrar Alg. 120 C2
Adrar hills Mali see Ifôghas, Adrar des
Adraskand r. Afgh. 111 F3
Adré Chad 121 F3
Adrian MI U.S.A. 164 C3
Adrian TX U.S.A. 161 C5
Adrianople Turkey see Edirne
Adrianopolis Turkey see Edirne
Adriatic Sea Europe 68 E2
Adua Eth. see Ādwa
Adunara i. Indon. see Adonara
Adusa Dem. Rep. Congo 122 C3
Aduwa Eth. see Ādwa
Adverse Well Australia 134 C5
Ādwa Eth. 122 D2
Adycha r. Rus. Fed. 77 O3
Adyk Rus. Fed. 53 J7
Adzopé Côte d'Ivoire 120 C4
Aegean Sea Greece/Turkey 69 K5
Aegina i. Greece see Aigina
Aegyptus country Africa see Egypt
Aela Jordan see Al 'Aqabah
Aelana Jordan see Al 'Aqabah
Aelia Capitolina Israel/West Bank see Jerusalem
Aelōnlaplap atoll Marshall Is see Ailinglaplap
Aenus Turkey see Enez
Aerzen Germany 63 J2
Aesernia Italy see Isernia
A Estrada Spain 67 B2
Afabet Eritrea 108 E6
Afanas'yevo Rus. Fed. 52 L4
Affreville Alg. see Khemis Miliana
Afghānestān country Asia see Afghanistan
Afghanistan country Asia 111 G3
Afgooye Somalia 122 E3
'Afīf Saudi Arabia 108 F5
Afiun Karahissar Turkey see Afyon
Åfjord Norway 54 G5
Aflou Alg. 64 E5
Afmadow Somalia 122 E3
Afogados da Ingazoira Brazil 177 K5
Afognak AK U.S.A. 148 I4
Afognak Island AK U.S.A. 148 I4
A Fonsagrada Spain 67 C2
Afonso Cláudio Brazil 179 C3
Āfrēra Terara vol. Eth. 108 F7
Africa Nova country Africa see Tunisia
'Afrīn Syria 107 C1
'Afrīn, Nahr r. Syria/Turkey 107 C1
Afşin Turkey 112 E3
Afsluitdijk barrage Neth. 62 F2
Afton U.S.A. 156 F4
Afuá Brazil 177 H4
'Afula Israel 107 B3
Afyon Turkey 69 N5
Afyonkarahisar Turkey see Afyon
Aga Germany 63 M4
Aga Rus. Fed. 95 H1
Aga r. Rus. Fed. 95 H1
Aga-Buryat Autonomous Okrug admin. div. Rus. Fed. see Aginskiy Buryatskiy Avtonomnyy Okrug
Agadès Niger see Agadez
Agadez Niger 120 D3
Agadir Morocco 120 C1
Agadyr' Kazakh. 102 D2
Agalega Islands Mauritius 185 L6
Agalta nat. park Hond. 166 [inset] I6
Agalta, Sierra de mts Hond. 166 [inset] I6
Agana Guam see Hagåtña
Aganzhen Gansu China 94 E5
Agara Georgia 113 F2
Agartala India 105 G5
Agashi India 106 B2
Agate Canada 152 E4
Agathe France see Agde
Agathonisi i. Greece 69 L6
Agats Indon. 81 J8
Agatsuma Japan 93 E2
Agatsuma-gawa r. Japan 93 F2
Agatti i. India 106 B4
Agattu Island AK U.S.A. 148 [inset]
Agattu Strait AK U.S.A. 148 [inset]
Agboville Côte d'Ivoire 120 C4
Ağcabädi Azer. 113 G2
Ağdam Azer. 113 G3
Ağdaş Azer. 113 G2
Agdash Azer. see Ağdaş
Agde France 66 F5
Agdzhabedi Azer. see Ağcabädi
Agedabia Libya see Ajdābiyā
Agematsu Japan 92 D3
Agen France 66 E4
Ageo Japan 93 F3
Aggeneys S. Africa 124 D5
Aggteleki nat. park Hungary 57 R6
Aghil Pass China 104 D1
Agiabampo Mex. 166 C3
Agiguan i. N. Mariana Is see Aguijan
Ağın Turkey 112 E3
Aginskiy Buryatskiy Avtonomnyy Okrug admin. div. Rus. Fed. 95 H1
Aginskoye Rus. Fed. 95 H1
Aginskoye Rus. Fed. 88 G1
Aginum France see Agen
Agios Dimitrios Greece 69 J6
Agios Efstratios i. Greece 69 K5
Agios Georgios i. Greece 69 J6
Agios Nikolaos Greece 69 K7
Agios Theodoros Cyprus 107 B2
Agiou Orous, Kolpos b. Greece 69 J4
Agirwat Hills Sudan 108 E6
Agisanang S. Africa 125 G4
Agnes, Mount hill Australia 135 E6
Agnew Australia 135 C6
Agnibilékrou Côte d'Ivoire 120 C4
Agnita Romania 69 K2
Agniye-Afanas'yevsk Rus. Fed. 90 E2
Ago Japan 92 C4
Agose Japan 93 F3
Ago-wan b. Japan 92 C4
Agra India 104 D4
Agrakhanskiy Poluostrov pen. Rus. Fed. 113 G2
Agram Croatia see Zagreb
Ağrı Turkey 113 F3
Agria Gramvousa i. Greece 69 J7
Agrigan i. N. Mariana Is see Agrihan
Agrigento Sicily Italy 68 E6
Agrigentum Sicily Italy see Agrigento
Agrihan i. N. Mariana Is 81 L3
Agrinio Greece 69 I5
Agropoli Italy 68 F4
Agryz Rus. Fed. 51 Q4
Ağsu Azer. 113 H2
Agta Point Phil. 82 C3
Agua, Volcán de vol. Guat. 168 F6
Agua Brava, Laguna lag. Mex. 166 D4
Água Clara Brazil 178 F2
Aguada Mex. 167 H5
Agua de Correra Mex. 167 E5
Aguadilla Puerto Rico 169 K5
Aguadulce Panama 166 [inset] J7
Agua Escondida Arg. 178 C5
Agua Fria r. U.S.A. 159 G5
Agua Fria National Monument nat. park U.S.A. 159 G4
Aguamilpa, Presa l. Mex. 166 D4
Aguanaval r. Mex. 161 C7
Aguanga U.S.A. 158 E5
Aguanish r. Canada 153 J4
Aguanqueterique Hond. 166 [inset] I6
Agua Nueva Mex. 166 D3
Aguapeí r. Brazil 179 A3
Agua Prieta Mex. 166 C2
Aguaro-Guariquito, Parque Nacional nat. park Venez. 176 E2
Aguaruto Mex. 166 D3
Aguascalientes Mex. 168 D4
Aguascalientes state Mex. 166 E4
Agudos Brazil 179 A3
Águeda Port. 67 B3
Aguemour reg. Alg. 120 D2
Agui Japan 92 C4
Aguié Niger 120 D3
Aguijan i. N. Mariana Is 81 L4
Aguilar U.S.A. 157 G5
Aguilar de Campóo Spain 67 D2
Águilas Spain 67 F5
Aguililla Mex. 166 E5

▶Agulhas, Cape S. Africa 124 E8
Most southerly point of Africa.

Agulhas Basin sea feature Southern Ocean 185 J9
Agulhas Negras mt. Brazil 179 B3
Agulhas Plateau sea feature Southern Ocean 185 J8
Agulhas Ridge sea feature S. Atlantic Ocean 184 I8
Agusan r. Mindanao Phil. 82 D4
Agutaya Phil. 82 C4
Agutaya i. Phil. 82 C4
Ağva Turkey 69 M4
Agvali Rus. Fed. 113 G2
Ahaggar plat. Alg. see Hoggar
Āhangarān Iran 111 F3
Ahar Iran 110 B2
Ahaura N.Z. 139 C6
Ahaus Germany 62 H2
Ahipara Bay N.Z. 139 D2
Ahiri India 106 D2
Ahklun Mountains AK U.S.A. 148 G4
Ahlen Germany 63 H3
Ahmadabad India 104 C5
Aḩmadābād Iran 111 E3
Aḩmad al Bāqir, Jabal mt. Jordan 107 B5
Ahmadī Iran 110 E5
Ahmadnagar India 106 B2
Ahmadpur East Pak. 111 H4
Ahmar mts Eth. 122 E3
Ahmar Mountains Eth. see Ahmar
Ahmedabad India see Ahmadabad
Ahmednagar India see Ahmadnagar
Ahome Mex. 166 C3
Ahorn Germany 63 K4
Ahr r. Germany 62 H4
Ahram Iran 110 C4
Ahrensburg Germany 63 K1
Āhtāri Fin. 54 N5
Ahtme Estonia 55 O7
Ahu China 97 H1
Āhū Iran 110 C4
Ahuacatlán Mex. 166 D4
Ahuachapán El Salvador 167 H6
Ahualulco Jalisco Mex. 166 E4
Ahualulco San Luis Potosí Mex. 167 E4
Ahun France 66 F3
Ahuzhen China see Ahu
Ahvāz Iran 110 C4
Ahwa India 106 B1
Ahwāz Iran see Ahvāz
Ai i. Maluku Indon. 83 D4
Ai-Ais Namibia 124 C4
Ai-Ais Hot Springs and Fish River Canyon Park nature res. Namibia see Ai-Ais Hot Springs Game Park
Ai-Ais Hot Springs Game Park nature res. Namibia 124 C4
Ai-Ais/Richtersveld Transfrontier Park Namibia/S. Africa 124 C5
Aibag Gol r. China 95 G3
Aichi pref. Japan 92 D4
Aichi-kōgen Kokutei-kōen park Japan 92 D3
Aichilik r. AK U.S.A. 149 L1
Aichwara India 104 D4
Aid U.S.A. 164 D4
Aigialousa Cyprus 107 B2
Aigina i. Greece 69 J6
Aigio Greece 69 J5
Aigle de Chambeyron mt. France 66 H4
Aigües Tortes i Estany de Sant Maurici, Parc Nacional d' nat. park Spain 67 G2
Ai He r. China 90 B4
Aihua China see Yunxian
Aihui China see Heihe
Aijal India see Aizawl
Aikawa Kanagawa Japan 93 F3
Aikawa Japan 91 E5
Aiken U.S.A. 163 D5
Ailao Shan mts China 96 D3
Aileron Australia 134 F5
Aileu East Timor 83 C5
Ailigandi Panama 166 [inset] K7
Ailinglabelab atoll Marshall Is see Ailinglaplap
Ailinglaplap atoll Marshall Is 186 H5

Ailly-sur-Noye France 62 C5
Ailsa Craig Canada 164 E2
Ailsa Craig i. U.K. 60 D5
Ailt an Chorráin Ireland 61 D3
Aimangala India 106 C3
Aimere Flores Indon. 83 B5
Aimorés, Serra dos hills Brazil 179 C2
Aïn Beïda Alg. 68 B7
'Aïn Ben Tili Mauritania 120 C2
'Aïn Dâlla spring Egypt see 'Ayn Dāllah
Aïn Defla Alg. 67 H5
Aïn Deheb Alg. 67 G6
Aïn el Hadjel Alg. 67 H6
'Aïn el Maqfi spring Egypt see 'Ayn al Maqfī
Aïn el Melh Alg. 67 I6
Aïn Mdila well Alg. 68 B7
Aïn-M'Lila Alg. 64 F4
Aïn Oussera Alg. 67 H6
Ain Salah Alg. see In Salah
Aïn Sefra Alg. 64 D5
Ainsworth U.S.A. 160 D3
Aintab Turkey see Gaziantep
Aïn Taya Alg. 67 H5
Aïn Tédélès Alg. 67 G6
Aïn Temouchent Alg. 67 F6
'Ain Tibaghbagh spring Egypt see 'Ayn Tabaghbugh
'Ain Timeira spring Egypt see 'Ayn Tumayrah
'Ain Zeitûn Egypt see 'Ayn Zaytūn
Aiquile Bol. 176 E7
Air i. Indon. 84 D2
Airai Palau 82 [inset]
Airaines France 62 B5
Airbangis Sumatera Indon. 84 B2
Airdrie Canada 150 H5
Airdrie U.K. 60 F5
Aire r. France 62 E5
Aire, Canal d' France 62 C4
Aire-sur-l'Adour France 66 D5
Aïr et du Ténéré, Réserve Naturelle Nationale de l' Niger 122 A2
Air Force Island Canada 147 K3
Airgin Sum Nei Mongol China 95 G3
Airhitam r. Indon. 85 E3
Airhitam, Teluk b. Indon. 85 E3
Air Muda, Tasik l. Malaysia 84 C1
Airpanas Maluku Indon. 83 C4
Air Pedu, Tasik l. Malaysia 84 C1
Aisatung Mountain Myanmar 86 A2
Aisch r. Germany 63 L5
Ai Shan hill Shandong China 95 J4
Aishihik Y.T. Canada 149 M3
Aishihik Lake Y.T. Canada 149 M3
Aisne r. France 62 C5
Aïssa, Djebel mt. Alg. 64 D5
Aitamännikkö Fin. 54 N3
Aitana mt. Spain 67 F4
Aït Benhaddou tourist site Morocco 64 C5
Aiterach r. Germany 63 M6
Aitkin U.S.A. 160 E2
Aitō Japan 92 C3
Aiud Romania 69 J1
Aiwokako Passage Palau 82 [inset]
Aix France see Aix-en-Provence
Aix-en-Provence France 66 G5
Aix-la-Chapelle Germany see Aachen
Aix-les-Bains France 66 G4
Aíyina i. Greece see Aigina
Aíyion Greece see Aigio
Aizawl India 105 H5
Aizkraukle Latvia 55 N8
Aizpute Latvia 55 L8
Aizu-Wakamatsu Japan 91 E5
Ajaccio Corsica France 66 I6
Ajalpán Mex. 167 F5
Ajanta India 106 B1
Ajanta Range hills India see Sahyadriparvat Range
Ajaureforsen Sweden 54 I4
Ajax Canada 164 F2
Ajayameru India see Ajmer
Ajban U.A.E. 110 D5
Aj Bogd Uul mt. Mongolia 102 I3
Aj Bogd Uul mts Mongolia 94 C2
Ajdābiyā Libya 121 F1
a-Jiddét des. Oman see Ḥarāsīs, Jiddat al
Ajiro Japan 93 F3
'Ajlūn Jordan 107 B3
'Ajman U.A.E. 110 D5
Ajmer India 104 C4
Ajmer-Merwara India see Ajmer
Ajnala India 104 C3
Ajo U.S.A. 159 G5
Ajo, Mount U.S.A. 159 G5
Ajrestan Afgh. 111 G3
Ajuchitlán Mex. 167 E5
Ajuy Panay Phil. 82 C4
Ajyyap Turkm. 110 D2
Akabane Japan 92 D4
Akabori Japan 93 F2
Akademii, Zaliv b. Rus. Fed. 90 E1
Akademii Nauk, Khrebet mt. Tajik. see Akademiyai Fanho, Qatorkŭhi
Akademiyai Fanho, Qatorkŭhi mt. Tajik. 111 H2
Akagera National Park Rwanda 122 D4
Akagi Gunma Japan 93 F2
Akagi-yama vol. Japan 93 F2
Akaishi-dake mt. Japan 93 E3
Akaishi-sanmyaku mts Japan 93 D4
Akalkot India 106 C2
Akama, Akra c. Cyprus see Arnauti, Cape
Akamagaseki Japan see Shimonoseki
Akan Kokuritsu-kōen Japan 90 G4
Akaroa N.Z. 139 D6
Akas reg. India 96 B3
Akāshat Iraq 113 E4
Akashi Japan 92 A4
Akashi-kaikyō str. Japan 92 A4
Akashina Japan 93 D2
Akbalyk Kazakh. 98 B3
Akbarābād Iran 113 I5
Akbarpur Uttar Prad. India 104 E4
Akbarpur Uttar Prad. India 105 E4
Akbaur Kazakh. 98 A2
Akbaytal, Pereval pass Tajik. 111 I2
Akbaytal Pass Tajik. see Akbaytal, Pereval
Akbez Turkey 107 C1
Akbulak Kazakh. 98 B2
Akbulak Kazakh. 98 D2
Akçadağ Turkey 112 E3
Akçakale Turkey 107 D1
Akçakoca Turkey 69 N4
Akçakoca Dağları mts Turkey 69 N4
Akçakoyunlu Turkey 107 C1
Akçalı Dağları mts Turkey 107 A1
Akchâr reg. Mauritania 120 B3
Akchatau Kazakh. 98 A3
Akchi Kazakh. see Akshiy
Akdağlar mts Turkey 69 M6
Akdağmadeni Turkey 112 D3
Akdere Turkey 107 A1
Akechi Japan 92 D3
Akelamo Halmahera Indon. 83 C3
Akelamo Halmahera Indon. 83 D2
Akeno Ibaraki Japan 93 G2
Akeno Yamanashi Japan 93 E3
Åkersberga Sweden 55 K7
Akersloot Neth. 62 E2
Aketi Dem. Rep. Congo 122 C3
Akgyr Erezi hills Turkm. 110 D1
Akhali-Afoni Georgia see Akhali Ap'oni
Akhali Ap'oni Georgia 113 F2
Akhḍar, Al Jabal al mts Libya 121 F1
Akhḍar, Jabal mts Oman 110 E6
Akhiok AK U.S.A. 148 I4
Akhisar Turkey 69 L5
Akhnoor India 104 C2
Akhsu Azer. see Ağsu
Akhta Armenia see Hrazdan
Akhtarīn Syria 107 C1
Akhtubinsk Rus. Fed. 53 J6
Akhty Rus. Fed. 113 G2
Akhtyrka Ukr. see Okhtyrka
Aki Japan 91 D6
Akiachak AK U.S.A. 148 G3
Akiéni Gabon 122 B4
Akimiski Island Canada 152 E3
Akiruno Japan 93 F3
Akishma r. Rus. Fed. 90 D1
Akita Japan 91 F5
Akiyama-gawa r. Japan 93 F2
Akjoujt Mauritania 120 B3
Akkajaure l. Sweden 54 J3
Akkani Rus. Fed. 148 E2
Akkem Rus. Fed. 98 D2
Akkerman Ukr. see Bilhorod-Dnistrovs'kyy
Akkeshi Japan 90 G4
'Akko Israel 107 B3
Akkol' Akmolinskaya Oblast' Kazakh. 102 D1
Akkol' Almatinskaya Oblast' Kazakh. 98 A3
Akkol' Atyrauskaya Oblast' Kazakh. 53 K7
Akku Kazakh. 102 E1
Akkul' Kazakh. see Akkol'
Akkuş Turkey 112 E2
Akkyr, Gory hills Turkm. see Akgyr Erezi
Aklavik N.W.T. Canada 149 N1
Aklera India 104 D4
Ak-Mechet Kazakh. see Kyzylorda
Akmeņrags pt Latvia 55 L8
Akmeqit Xinjiang China 99 B5
Akmola Kazakh. see Astana
Akmolinsk Kazakh. see Astana
Ak-Moyun Kyrg. 98 B4
Akobo Sudan 121 G4
Akobo Wenz r. Eth./Sudan 122 D3
Akokan Niger 120 D3
Akola India 106 C1
Akom II Cameroon 120 E4
Akongkür Xinjiang China 98 B4
Akonolinga Cameroon 120 E4
Akordat Eritrea 108 E6
Akören Turkey 112 D3
Akot India 104 D5
Akpatok Island Canada 153 I1
Akqi Xinjiang China 98 B4
Akra, Jabal mt. Syria/Turkey see Aqra', Jabal al
Akranes Iceland 54 [inset]
Åkrehamn Norway 55 D7
Akréréb Niger 120 D3
Akron CO U.S.A. 160 C3
Akron IN U.S.A. 164 B3
Akron OH U.S.A. 164 E3
Akrotiri Bay Cyprus 107 A2
Akrotirion Bay Cyprus see Akrotiri Bay
Akrotiriou, Kolpos b. Cyprus see Akrotiri Bay
Akrotiri Sovereign Base Area military base Cyprus 107 A2

▶Aksai Chin terr. Asia 104 D2
Disputed territory (China/India).

Aksaray Turkey 112 D3
Aksay Gansu China 98 F5
Aksay Kazakh. 51 Q5
Ak-Say r. Kyrg. 109 M1
Aksay Rus. Fed. 53 H7
Aksayqin Hu l. Aksai Chin 99 B6
Akşehir Turkey 69 N5
Akşehir Gölü l. Turkey 69 N5
Akseki Turkey 112 C3
Aksha Rus. Fed. 95 H1
Akshiganak Kazakh. 102 B2
Akshiy Kazakh. 102 E3
Akshukur Kazakh. 113 H2
Aksu Xinjiang China 98 C4
Aksu Xinjiang China 98 C4
Aksu Almatinskaya Oblast' Kazakh. 98 B3
Aksu Kazakh. 102 E1
Aksu r. Kazakh. 98 B3
Aksu r. Tajik. see Oqsu
Aksu r. Turkey 69 N6
Aksuat Kazakh. 102 F2
Aksu-Ayuly Kazakh. 102 D2
Aksubayevo Rus. Fed. 53 K5
Aksu He r. China 98 C4
Āksum Eth. 108 E7
Aksüme Xinjiang China 98 C3
Aksuyek Kazakh. 98 A3
Aktag mt. Xinjiang China 99 D5
Aktam Xinjiang China 98 B5
Aktas Dağı mt. Turkey 113 G3
Aktash Rus. Fed. 98 D2
Aktau Karagandinskaya Oblast' Kazakh. 98 A2
Aktau Kazakh. 100 E2
Akto Xinjiang China 98 B5
Aktobe Kazakh. 100 E1
Aktogay Karagandinskaya Oblast' Kazakh. 102 E2
Aktogay Vostochnyy Kazakhstan Kazakh. 102 E2
Aktsyabrski Belarus 53 F5
Ak-Tüz Kyrg. 98 A4
Aktyubinsk Kazakh. see Aktobe
Akulivik Canada 147 K3
Akune Japan 91 C6
Akun Island AK U.S.A. 148 F5
Akure Nigeria 120 D4
Akuressa Sri Lanka 106 D5
Akureyri Iceland 54 [inset]
Akusha Rus. Fed. 53 J8
Akutan AK U.S.A. 148 F5
Akutan Island AK U.S.A. 148 F5
Akutan Pass sea channel AK U.S.A. 148 F5
Akwanga Nigeria 120 D4
Akxokesay Qinghai China 99 E5
Akyab Myanmar see Sittwe
Akyatan Gölü salt l. Turkey 107 B1
Akyazı Turkey 69 N4
Akzhal Karagandinskaya Oblast' Kazakh. 98 A3
Akzhal Vostochnyy Kazakhstan Kazakh. 98 C2
Akzhar Vostochnyy Kazakhstan Kazakh. 98 C3
Akzhartas Kazakh. 98 A3
Akzhaykyn, Ozero salt l. Kazakh. 102 C3
Ål Norway 55 F6
'Alā, Jabal al hills Syria 107 C2
Alabama r. U.S.A. 163 C6
Alabama state U.S.A. 163 C5
Alabaster AL U.S.A. 163 C5
Alabaster MI U.S.A. 164 D1
Al 'Abṭīyah well Iraq 113 G5
Al Abyār Libya 120 F1
Alaca Turkey 112 D2
Alacahan Turkey 112 E3
Alaçam Turkey 112 D2
Alaçam Dağları mts Turkey 69 M5
Alacant Valencia Spain see Alicante
Alaçatı Turkey 69 L5
Alacrán, Arrecife rf Mex. 167 H4
Aladağ Turkey 112 D3
Ala Dağlar mts Turkey 113 F3
Ala Dağları mts Turkey 112 D3
Al 'Adam Libya 112 A5
Ala'er Xinjiang China 98 C4
Al Aflāj reg. Saudi Arabia 110 B6
Alaganik AK U.S.A. 149 K3
Alag-Erdene Hövsgöl Mongolia 94 D1
Alag Hayrhan Uul mt. Mongolia 94 C2
Alag Hu l. Qinghai China 94 D5
Alagir Rus. Fed. 113 G2
Alagnak r. AK U.S.A. 148 H4
Alagoinhas Brazil 179 D1
Ala Gou r. China 98 E4
Alah r. Mindanao Phil. 82 D5
Alahanpanjang Sumatera Indon. 84 C3
Alahärmä Fin. 54 M5
Al Aḥmadī Kuwait 110 C4
Alai Range mts Asia 111 H2
Älaivān Iran 110 D3
Alājah Syria 107 B2
Alajärvi Fin. 54 M5
Al 'Ajrūd well Egypt 107 B4
Alajuela Costa Rica 166 [inset] I7
Alakanuk AK U.S.A. 148 F3
Al Akhḍar Saudi Arabia 112 E5
Alakol', Ozero salt l. Kazakh. 102 F2
Alaktak AK U.S.A. 148 I1
Ala Kul salt l. Kazakh. see Alakol', Ozero
Alakurtti Rus. Fed. 54 Q3
Al 'Alamayn Egypt 112 C5
Al 'Alayyah Saudi Arabia 108 F6
Alama Somalia 122 E3
Al 'Amādīyah Iraq 113 F3
Alamagan i. N. Mariana Is 81 L3
Alamaguan i. N. Mariana Is see Alamagan
Al 'Amārah Iraq 113 G5
'Alam ar Rūm, Ra's pt Egypt 112 B5
'Alāmarvdasht watercourse Iran 110 D4
Alameda U.S.A. 158 B3
'Alam el Rûm, Râs pt Egypt see 'Alam ar Rūm, Ra's
Al Amghar waterhole Iraq 113 G5
Alamícamba Nicaragua 166 [inset] I6
Alaminos Luzon Phil. 82 B2
Al 'Āmirīyah Egypt 112 C5
Alamítos, Sierra de los mt. Mex. 166 E3
Alamo GA U.S.A. 163 D5
Alamo NV U.S.A. 159 F3
Alamo Dam U.S.A. 159 G4
Alamogordo U.S.A. 157 G6
Alamo Heights U.S.A. 161 D6
Alamos Sonora Mex. 166 C2
Alamos Sonora Mex. 166 C3
Alamos r. Mex. 167 E3
Alamos, Sierra mts Mex. 166 C3
Alamosa U.S.A. 157 G5
Alamos de Peña Mex. 166 D2
Alampur India 106 C3
Alan Myanmar see Aunglan
Alanäs Sweden 54 I4
Åland is Fin. see Åland Islands
Aland r. Germany 63 L1
Aland India 106 C2
Al Andarīn Syria 107 C2
Åland Islands Fin. 55 K6
Alando Xizang China 99 F7
Alandur India 106 D3
Alang Kalimantan Indon. 85 G1
Alangalang, Tanjung pt Indon. 85 G3
Alang Besar i. Indon. 84 C2
Alanggantang i. Indon. 84 D3
Alanson U.S.A. 164 C1
Alanya Turkey 112 D3
Alaplı Turkey 69 N4
Alappuzha India see Alleppey
Alapuzha India see Alleppey
Al 'Aqabah Jordan 107 B5
Al 'Aqīq Saudi Arabia 108 F5
Al 'Arabīyah as Sa'ūdīyah country Asia see Saudi Arabia
Alarcón, Embalse de resr Spain 67 E4
Al 'Arīsh Egypt 107 A4
Al Arṭāwīyah Saudi Arabia 108 G4
Alas Sumbawa Indon. 85 G5
Alas, Selat sea chan. Indon. 85 G5
Alaşehir Turkey 69 M5
Alashiya country Asia see Cyprus
Al Ashmūnayn Egypt 112 C6
Alaska state U.S.A. 149 L3
Alaska, Gulf of AK U.S.A. 149 K4
Alaska Highway Canada/U.S.A. 149 L3
Alaska Maritime National Wildlife Refuge nature res. AK U.S.A. 149 [inset]
Alaska Peninsula AK U.S.A. 148 G5
Alaska Peninsula National Wildlife Refuge nature res. AK U.S.A. 148 H4
Alaska Range mts AK U.S.A. 149 J3
Alas Purwo, Taman Nasional nat. park Indon. 85 F5
Älät Azer. 113 H3
Alat Uzbek. see Olot
Alataw Shankou pass China/Kazakh. see Dzungarian Gate
Alatna AK U.S.A. 148 I2
Alatna r. AK U.S.A. 148 I2
Al Atwā' well Saudi Arabia 113 F5
Alatyr' Rus. Fed. 53 J5
Alatyr' r. Rus. Fed. 53 J5
Alausí Ecuador 176 C4
Alaverdi Armenia 113 G2
'Alavī Iran 110 C3
Alavieska Fin. 54 N4
Alavus Fin. 54 M5
Alawbum Myanmar 86 B1
Alawoona Australia 137 C7
Alay Kyrka Toosu mts Asia see Alai Range
Al 'Ayn Oman 110 E6
Al 'Ayn U.A.E. 110 D5
Alayskiy Khrebet mts Asia see Alai Range
Al 'Azīzīyah Iraq 113 G4

▶Al 'Azīzīyah Libya 120 E1
Highest recorded shade temperature in the world.

Al Azraq al Janūbī Jordan 107 C4
Alba Italy 68 C2
Alba U.S.A. 164 C1
Al Bāb Syria 107 C1
Albacete Spain 67 F4
Al Badī' Saudi Arabia 110 B6
Al Bādiyah al Janūbīyah hill Iraq 113 G5
Al Bahrayn country Asia see Bahrain
Alba Iulia Romania 69 J1
Al Bajā' well U.A.E. 110 C5
Albājī Iran 110 C4
Al Bakhrā well Saudi Arabia 110 B5
Albanel, Lac l. Canada 153 G4
Albania country Europe 69 H4
Albany Australia 135 B8
Albany r. Canada 152 E3
Albany GA U.S.A. 163 C6
Albany IN U.S.A. 164 C3
Albany KY U.S.A. 164 C5
Albany MO U.S.A. 160 E3

▶Albany NY U.S.A. 165 I2
Capital of New York state.

Albany OH U.S.A. 164 D4
Albany OR U.S.A. 156 C3
Albany TX U.S.A. 161 D5
Albany Downs Australia 138 D1
Albardão do João Maria coastal area Brazil 178 F4
Al Bardī Libya 112 B5
Al Bāridah hills Saudi Arabia 107 D5
Al Başrah Iraq see Basra
Al Baṭḥa' marsh Iraq 113 G5
Al Bāṭinah reg. Oman 110 E5
Albatross Bay Australia 136 C2
Albatross Island Australia 137 [inset]
Al Bawīṭī Egypt 112 C5
Al Bayḍā' Libya 108 B3
Al Bayḍā' Yemen 108 G7
Albay Gulf Luzon Phil. 82 C3
Albemarle U.S.A. 163 D5
Albemarle Island Galápagos Ecuador see Isabela, Isla
Albemarle Sound sea chan. U.S.A. 162 E5
Albenga Italy 68 C2
Alberche r. Spain 67 D4
Alberga Australia 137 A5
Alberga watercourse Australia 137 A5
Albergaria-a-Velha Port. 67 B3
Albert Australia 138 C4
Albert France 62 C5
Albert, Lake Dem. Rep. Congo/Uganda 122 D3
Albert, Parc National nat. park Dem. Rep. Congo see Virunga, Parc National des
Alberta prov. Canada 150 H4
Alberta U.S.A. 165 G5
Albert Kanaal canal Belgium 62 F4
Albert Lea U.S.A. 160 E3
Albert Nile r. Sudan/Uganda 121 G4
Alberto de Agostini, Parque Nacional nat. park Chile 178 B8
Alberton S. Africa 125 I4
Alberton U.S.A. 156 E3
Albert Town Bahamas 163 F8
Albertville Dem. Rep. Congo see Kalemie
Albertville France 66 H4
Albertville U.S.A. 163 C5
Albestroff France 62 G6
Albi France 66 F5
Albia U.S.A. 160 E3
Al Biḍah des. Saudi Arabia 110 C5
Albina Suriname 177 H2
Albino Italy 68 C2
Albion CA U.S.A. 158 B2
Albion IL U.S.A. 160 F4
Albion IN U.S.A. 164 C3
Albion MI U.S.A. 164 C2
Albion NE U.S.A. 160 D3
Albion NY U.S.A. 165 F2
Albion PA U.S.A. 164 E3
Al Biqā' valley Lebanon see El Béqaa
Al Bi'r Saudi Arabia 112 E5
Al Birk Saudi Arabia 108 F6
Al Biyāḍh reg. Saudi Arabia 108 G5
Alborán, Isla de i. Spain 67 E6
Ålborg Denmark see Aalborg
Ålborg Bugt b. Denmark see Aalborg Bugt
Albro Australia 136 D4
Al Budayyi' Bahrain 110 C5
Albufeira Port. 67 B5
Al Buḥayrāt al Murrah lakes Egypt see Bitter Lakes
Albuquerque U.S.A. 157 G6
Albuquerque, Cayos de is Caribbean Sea 166 [inset] J6
Al Burayj Syria 107 C2
Al Buraymī Oman 110 D5
Al Burj Jordan 107 B5
Alburquerque Spain 67 C4
Albury Australia 138 C6
Al Buşayrah Syria 113 F4
Al Busayṭā' plain Saudi Arabia 107 D4
Al Bushūk well Saudi Arabia 110 B4
Alcácer do Sal Port. 67 B4
Alcalá de Henares Spain 67 E3
Alcalá la Real Spain 67 E5
Alcamo Sicily Italy 68 E6
Alcañiz Spain 67 F3
Alcántara Spain 67 C4
Alcantara Lake Canada 151 I2
Alcaraz Spain 67 E4
Alcázar de San Juan Spain 67 E4
Alcazarquivir Morocco see Ksar el Kebir
Alchevs'k Ukr. 53 H6
Alcobaça Brazil 179 D2
Alcoi Spain see Alcoy-Alcoi
Alcoota Australia 134 F5
Alcova U.S.A. 156 G4
Alcoy Spain see Alcoy-Alcoi
Alcoy-Alcoi Spain 67 F4
Alcúdia Spain 67 H4
Aldabra Islands Seychelles 123 E4
Aldama Chihuahua Mex. 166 D2
Aldama Tamaulipas Mex. 167 F4
Aldan Rus. Fed. 77 N4
Aldan r. Rus. Fed. 77 N3
Alde r. U.K. 59 I6
Aldeboarn Neth. 62 F1
Aldeburgh U.K. 59 I6
Alder Creek U.S.A. 165 H2
Alderney i. Channel Is 59 E9
Alder Peak U.S.A. 158 C4
Aldershot U.K. 59 G7
Al Dhafrah reg. U.A.E. 110 D6
Aldingham U.K. 58 D4
Aldridge U.K. 59 F6
Aleg Mauritania 120 B3
Alegre Espírito Santo Brazil 179 C3
Alegre Minas Gerais Brazil 179 B2
Alegrete Brazil 178 E3
Alegros Mountain U.S.A. 159 I4
Aleknagik AK U.S.A. 148 H4
Aleknagik, Lake AK U.S.A. 148 H4
Aleksandra, Mys hd Rus. Fed. 90 E1
Aleksandriya Ukr. see Oleksandriya
Aleksandro-Nevskiy Rus. Fed. 53 I5
Aleksandropol Armenia see Gyumri
Aleksandrov Rus. Fed. 52 H4
Aleksandrov Gay Rus. Fed. 53 K6
Aleksandrovsk Rus. Fed. 51 R4
Aleksandrovsk Ukr. see Zaporizhzhya
Aleksandrovskiy Rus. Fed. see Aleksandrovsk
Aleksandrovskoye Rus. Fed. 113 F1
Aleksandrovsk-Sakhalinskiy Rus. Fed. 90 F2
Aleksandry, Zemlya i. Rus. Fed. 76 F1
Alekseyevka Akmolinskaya Oblast' Kazakh. see Akkol'
Alekseyevka Pavlodarskaya Oblast' Kazakh. 98 A2
Alekseyevka Vostochnyy Kazakhstan Kazakh. see Terekty
Alekseyevka Amurskaya Oblast' Rus. Fed. 90 B1
Alekseyevka Belgorodskaya Oblast' Rus. Fed. 53 H6
Alekseyevka Belgorodskaya Oblast' Rus. Fed. 53 H6
Alekseyevskaya Rus. Fed. 53 I6
Alekseyevskoye Rus. Fed. 52 K5
Aleksin Rus. Fed. 53 H5
Aleksinac Serbia 69 I3
Alèmbé Gabon 122 B4
Ålen Norway 54 G5
Alençon France 66 E2
Alenquer Brazil 177 H4
'Alenuihāhā Channel U.S.A. 157 [inset]
Alep Syria see Aleppo
Aleppo Syria 107 C1
Alert Canada 147 L1
Alerta Peru 176 D6
Alès France 66 G4
Aleşd Romania 69 J1
Aleshki Ukr. see Tsyurupyns'k
Aleşkirt Turkey see Eleşkirt
Alessandria Italy 68 C2
Alessio Albania see Lezhë
Ålesund Norway 54 E5
Aleutian Basin sea feature Bering Sea 186 H2
Aleutian Islands U.S.A. 146 A4
Aleutian Range mts AK U.S.A. 148 H4
Aleutian Trench sea feature N. Pacific Ocean 186 I2
Alevina, Mys c. Rus. Fed. 77 Q4
Alevişik Turkey see Samandağı
Alexander U.S.A. 160 C2
Alexander, Kap c. Greenland see Ullersuaq
Alexander, Mount hill Australia 136 B2
Alexander Archipelago is AK U.S.A. 149 M4
Alexander Bay b. Namibia/S. Africa 124 C5
Alexander Bay S. Africa 124 C5
Alexander City U.S.A. 163 C5
Alexander Island Antarctica 188 L2
Alexandra Australia 138 B6
Alexandra N.Z. 139 B7
Alexandra, Cape S. Georgia 178 I8
Alexandra Channel India 87 A4
Alexandra Land i. Rus. Fed. see Aleksandry, Zemlya
Alexandreia Greece 69 J4
Alexandretta Turkey see İskenderun
Alexandria Afgh. see Ghaznī
Alexandria Canada 165 H1

▶Alexandria Egypt 112 C5
5th most populous city in Africa.

Alexandria Romania 69 K3
Alexandria S. Africa 125 H7
Alexandria Turkm. see Mary
Alexandria U.K. 60 E5
Alexandria IN U.S.A. 164 C3
Alexandria KY U.S.A. 164 C4
Alexandria LA U.S.A. 161 E6
Alexandria VA U.S.A. 165 G4
Alexandria Arachoton Afgh. see Kandahār
Alexandria Areion Afgh. see Herāt
Alexandria Bay U.S.A. 165 H1
Alexandria Prophthasia Afgh. see Farāh
Alexandrina, Lake Australia 137 B7
Alexandroupoli Greece 69 K4
Alexis r. Canada 153 K3
Alexis Creek Canada 150 F4
Aley Lebanon 107 B3
Aleyak Iran 110 E2
Aleysk Rus. Fed. 88 E2
Alf Germany 62 H4
Al Farwānīyah Kuwait 110 B4
Al Fas Morocco see Fès
Al Fatḥah Iraq 113 F4
Al Fāw Iraq 113 H5
Al Fayyūm Egypt 112 C5
Alfeld (Leine) Germany 63 J3
Alfenas Brazil 179 B3
Alford U.K. 58 H5
Alfred ME U.S.A. 165 J2
Alfred NY U.S.A. 165 G2
Alfred and Marie Range hills Australia 135 D6
Alfred M. Terrazas Mex. 167 F4
Al Fujayrah U.A.E. see Fujairah
Al Fuqahā' Libya 121 E2
Al Furāt r. Iraq/Syria 107 D2 see Euphrates
Alga Kazakh. 102 A2
Ålgård Norway 55 D7
Algarrobo del Aguilla Arg. 178 C5
Algarve reg. Port. 67 B5
Algeciras Spain 67 D5
Algemesí Spain 67 F4
Algena Eritrea 108 E6
Alger Alg. see Algiers
Alger U.S.A. 164 C1

▶Algeria country Africa 120 C2
2nd largest country in Africa.

Algérie country Africa see Algeria
Algermissen Germany 63 J2
Algha Kazakh. see Alga
Al Ghāfāt Oman 110 E6
Al Ghammās Iraq 113 G5
Al Ghardaqah Egypt see Al Ghurdaqah
Al Ghawr plain Jordan/West Bank 107 B4
Al Ghayḍah Yemen 108 H6
Alghero Sardinia Italy 68 C4
Al Ghurdaqah Egypt 108 D4
Al Ghuwayr well Qatar 110 C5

▶Algiers Alg. 67 H5
Capital of Algeria.

Algoa Bay S. Africa 125 G7
Algoma U.S.A. 164 B1
Algona U.S.A. 160 E3
Algonac U.S.A. 164 D2
Algonquin Park Canada 165 F1
Algonquin Provincial Park Canada 165 F1
Algorta Spain 67 E2

Algueirao Moz. see Hacufera
Al Habakah well Saudi Arabia 113 F5
Al Ḩabbānīyah Iraq 113 F4
Al Ḩadaqah well Saudi Arabia 110 B4
Al Ḩadd Bahrain 110 C5
Al Hadhālīl plat. Saudi Arabia 113 F5
Al Ḩadīdīyah Syria 107 C2
Al Ḩadīthah Iraq 113 F4
Al Ḩadīthah Saudi Arabia 107 C4
Al Ḩaḍr Iraq see Hatra
Al Ḩafār well Saudi Arabia 113 F5
Al Ḩaffah Syria 107 C2
Al Haggounia W. Sahara 120 B2
Al Ḩajar al Gharbī mts Oman 110 E5
Al Ḩajar ash Sharqī mts Oman 110 E6
Al Ḩamād plain Asia 112 E5
Al Ḩamādah al Ḩamrā' plat. Libya 120 E2
Alhama de Murcia Spain 67 F5
Al Ḩamar Saudi Arabia 110 B6
Al Ḩamīdīyah Syria 107 B2
Al Ḩammām Egypt 112 C5
Al Ḩanākīyah Saudi Arabia 108 F5
Al Haniyah esc. Iraq 113 G5
Al Hariq Saudi Arabia 110 B6
Al Ḩarrah Egypt 112 C5
Al Harūj al Aswad hills Libya 121 E2
Al Hasa reg. Saudi Arabia 110 C5
Al Ḩasakah Syria 113 F3
Al Hawi salt pan Saudi Arabia 107 D5
Al Hawjā' Saudi Arabia 112 E5
Al Ḩawṭah reg. Saudi Arabia 110 B6
Al Ḩayy Iraq 113 G4
Al Ḩayz Egypt 112 C5
Al Hazīm Jordan 107 C4
Al Ḩazm Saudi Arabia 112 E5
Al Ḩazm al Jawf Yemen 108 F6
Al Ḩibāk des. Saudi Arabia 109 H6
Al Hījānah Syria 107 C3
Al Ḩillah Iraq see Hillah
Al Ḩillah Saudi Arabia 108 G5
Al Ḩinnāh Saudi Arabia 122 E1
Al Ḩinw mt. Saudi Arabia 107 D4
Al Hirrah well Saudi Arabia 110 C6
Al Hīshah Syria 107 D1
Al Ḩismā plain Saudi Arabia 112 D5
Al Ḩiṣn Jordan 107 B3
Al Hoceima Morocco 67 E6
Al Ḩudaydah Yemen see Hodeidah
Al Ḩufrah reg. Saudi Arabia 112 E5
Al Hufūf Saudi Arabia see Hofūf
Al Hūj hills Saudi Arabia 112 E5
Al Husayfīn Oman 110 E5
Al Huwwah Saudi Arabia 110 B6
Ali Xizang China 99 B6
'Alīābād Afgh. 111 H2
'Alīābād Golestān Iran 110 D2
'Alīābād Hormozgan Iran 110 D4
'Alīābād Khorāsān Iran 111 F4
'Alīābād Kordestān Iran 110 B2
'Alīābād, Kūh-e mt. Iran 110 C3
Aliağa Turkey 69 L5
Aliakmonas r. Greece 69 J4
Aliambata East Timor 83 C5
Alibag India 106 B2
Äli Bayramlı Azer. 113 H3
Alicante Spain 67 F4
Alice r. Australia 136 C2
Alice watercourse Australia 136 D5
Alice U.S.A. 161 D7
Alice, Punta pt Italy 68 G5
Alice Arm B.C. Canada 149 O5
Alice Springs Australia 135 F5
Alice Town Bahamas 163 E7
Aliceville U.S.A. 161 F5
Alichur Tajik. 111 I2
Alichur r. Tajik. 111 I2
Alicia Mindanao Phil. 82 C5
Alick Creek r. Australia 136 C4
Alifu Atoll Maldives see Ari Atoll
Al Ifzi'iyyah i. U.A.E. 110 C5
Aliganj India 104 D4
Aligarh Rajasthan India 104 D4
Aligarh Uttar Prad. India 104 D4
Alīgūdarz Iran 110 C3
Alihe Nei Mongol China 95 J1
Alījūq, Kūh-e mt. Iran 110 C4
'Alī Kheyl Afgh. 111 H3
Al Imārāt al 'Arabīyah at Muttaḩidah country Asia see United Arab Emirates
Alimia i. Greece 69 L6
Alimpaya Point Mindanao Phil. 82 C5
Alindao Cent. Afr. Rep. 122 C3
Alindau Sulawesi Indon. 83 A3
Alingsås Sweden 55 H8
Aliova r. Turkey 69 M5
Alipura India 104 D4
Alipur Duar India 105 G4
Alirajpur India 104 C5
Al 'Irāq country Asia see Iraq
Al 'Īsāwīyah Saudi Arabia 107 C4
Al Iskandarīyah Egypt see Alexandria
Al Iskandarīyah Iraq 113 G4
Al Ismā'īlīyah Egypt 112 D5
Al Ismā'īlīyah governorate Egypt 107 A4
Alitak Bay AK U.S.A. 148 I4
Aliveri Greece 69 K5
Aliwal North S. Africa 125 H6
Alix Canada 150 H4
Al Jafr Jordan 107 C4
Al Jāfūrah des. Saudi Arabia 110 C5
Al Jaghbūb Libya 112 B5
Al Jahrah Kuwait 110 B4
Al Jamalīyah Qatar 110 C5
Al Jarāwī well Saudi Arabia 107 D4
Al Jauf Saudi Arabia see Dumat al Jandal
Al Jawb reg. Saudi Arabia 110 C6
Al Jawf Libya 121 F2
Al Jawsh Libya 120 E1
Al Jaza'ir country Africa see Algeria
Al Jaza'ir Alg. see Algiers
Aljezur Port. 67 B5
Al Jībān reg. Saudi Arabia 110 C5
Al Jil well Iraq 113 F5
Al Jilh esc. Saudi Arabia 110 B5
Al Jithāmīyah Saudi Arabia 113 F6
Al Jīzah Egypt see Giza
Al Jīzah Jordan 107 B4
Al Jubayl hills Saudi Arabia 110 B5
Al Jubaylah Saudi Arabia 110 B5
Al Jufrah Libya 121 E2
Al Julayqah well Saudi Arabia 110 C5
Aljustrel Port. 67 B5
Al Juwayf depr. Syria 107 C3
Al Kahfah Al Qaṣīm Saudi Arabia 108 F4
Al Kahfah Ash Sharqīyah Saudi Arabia 110 C5
Alkali Lake Canada 150 F5
Al Karak Jordan 107 B4
Al'katvaam Rus. Fed. 148 B3
Al Kāẓimīyah Iraq see Kādhimain
Al Khābūrah Oman 110 E6
Al Khalīl West Bank see Hebron
Al Khāliṣ Iraq 113 G4
Al Khārijah Egypt 108 D4
Al Kharj reg. Saudi Arabia 110 B6
Al Kharrārah Qatar 110 C5
Al Kharrūbah Egypt 107 A4
Al Khaṣab Oman 110 E5
Al Khatam reg. U.A.E. 110 D5
Al Khawkhah Yemen 108 F7
Al Khawr Qatar 110 C5
Al Khizāmī well Saudi Arabia 110 C5
Al Khums Libya 121 E1
Al Khunfah sand area Saudi Arabia 112 E5
Al Khunn Saudi Arabia 122 E1
Al Kifl Iraq 113 G4
Al Kir'ānah Qatar 110 C5
Al Kiswah Syria 107 C3
Alkmaar Neth. 62 E2
Al Kūbrī Egypt 107 A4
Al Kūfah Iraq see Kūfah
Al Kumayt Iraq 113 G4
Al Kuntillah Egypt 107 B5
Al Kusūr hills Saudi Arabia 107 D4
Al Kūt Iraq 113 G4
Al Kuwayt country Asia see Kuwait
Al Kuwayt Kuwait see Kuwait
Al Labbah plain Saudi Arabia 113 F5
Al Lādhiqīyah Syria see Latakia
Allagadda India 106 C3
Allahabad India 105 E4
Al Lajā lava field Syria 107 C3
Allakaket AK U.S.A. 148 I2
Allakh-Yun' Rus. Fed. 77 O3
Allanmyo Myanmar see Aunglan
Allanridge S. Africa 125 H4
Allapalli India 106 D2
'Allāqī, Wādī al watercourse Egypt 108 D5
'Allâqi, Wâdi el watercourse Egypt see 'Allāqī, Wādī al
Allardville Canada 153 I5
Alldays S. Africa 125 I2
Allegan U.S.A. 164 C2
Allegheny r. U.S.A. 164 F3
Allegheny Mountains U.S.A. 164 D5
Allegheny Reservoir U.S.A. 165 F3
Allen, Lough l. Ireland 61 D3
Allen, Mount AK U.S.A. 149 L3
Allendale U.S.A. 163 D5
Allendale Town U.K. 58 E4
Allende Coahuila Mex. 167 E2
Allende Nuevo León Mex. 167 E3
Allendorf (Lumda) Germany 63 I4
Allenford Canada 164 E1
Allenstein Poland see Olsztyn
Allensville U.S.A. 164 B5
Allentown U.S.A. 165 H3
Alleppey India 106 C4
Aller r. Germany 63 J2
Alliance NE U.S.A. 160 C3
Alliance OH U.S.A. 164 E3
Al Lībīyah country Africa see Libya
Allier r. France 66 F3
Al Lihābah well Saudi Arabia 110 B5
Allinge-Sandvig Denmark 55 I9
Al Liṣāfah well Saudi Arabia 110 B5
Al Lisān pen. Jordan 107 B4
Alliston Canada 164 F1
Al Līth Saudi Arabia 108 F5
Al Liwā' oasis U.A.E. 110 D6
Alloa U.K. 60 F4
Allons U.S.A. 164 C5
Allora Australia 138 F2
Allu Sulawesi Indon. 83 A4
Allur India 106 D3
Alluru Kottapatnam India 106 D3
Al Lussuf well Iraq 113 F5
Alma Canada 153 H4
Alma MI U.S.A. 164 C2
Alma NE U.S.A. 160 D3
Alma WI U.S.A. 160 F2
Al Ma'ānīyah Iraq 113 F5
Alma-Ata Kazakh. see Almaty
Almada Port. 67 B4
Al Madāfi' plat. Saudi Arabia 112 E5
Al Ma'danīyāt well Iraq 113 G5
Almaden Australia 136 D3
Almadén Spain 67 D4
Al Madīnah Saudi Arabia see Medina
Al Mafraq Jordan 107 C3
Al Maghrib country Africa see Morocco
Al Maghrib reg. U.A.E. 110 D6
Al Mahākik reg. Saudi Arabia 110 C6
Al Mahdum Syria 107 C1
Al Maḩīā depr. Saudi Arabia 112 E6
Al Maḩwīt Yemen 108 F6
Al Malsūnīyah reg. Saudi Arabia 110 C5
Almalyk Uzbek. see Olmaliq
Al Manadir reg. Oman 110 D6
Al Manāmah Bahrain see Manama
Al Manjūr well Saudi Arabia 110 B6
Almanor, Lake U.S.A. 158 C1
Almansa Spain 67 F4
Al Manṣūrah Egypt 112 C5
Almanzor mt. Spain 67 D3
Al Mariyyah U.A.E. 110 D6
Al Marj Libya 121 F1
Almas, Rio das r. Brazil 179 A1
Al Maṭarīyah Egypt 112 D5
Almatinskaya Oblast' admin. div. Kazakh. 98 B3
▶Almaty Kazakh. 102 E3
Former capital of Kazakhstan.
Al Mawṣil Iraq see Mosul
Al Mayādīn Syria 113 F4
Al Mazār Egypt 107 A4
Almaznyy Rus. Fed. 77 M3
Almeirim Brazil 177 H4
Almeirim Port. 67 B4
Almelo Neth. 62 G2
Almenara Brazil 179 C2
Almendra, Embalse de resr Spain 67 C3
Almendralejo Spain 67 C4
Almere Neth. 62 F2
Almería Spain 67 E5
Almería, Golfo de b. Spain 67 E5
Al'metievsk Rus. Fed. see Al'met'yevsk
Al'met'yevsk Rus. Fed. 51 Q5
Älmhult Sweden 55 I8
Almina, Punta pt Spain 67 D6
Al Mindak Saudi Arabia 108 F5
Al Minyā Egypt 112 C5
Almirós Greece see Almyros
Al Mish'āb Saudi Arabia 110 C4
Almodôvar Port. 67 B5
Almoloya Mex. 167 E5
Almond r. U.K. 60 F4
Almont U.S.A. 164 D2
Almonte Spain 67 C5
Almora India 104 D3
Al Mu'ayzīlah hill Saudi Arabia 107 D5
Al Mubarrez Saudi Arabia 108 G4
Al Muḍaibī Oman 109 I5
Al Muḍairib Oman 110 E6
Al Muḩarraq Bahrain 110 C5
Al Mukallā Yemen see Mukalla
Al Mukhā Yemen see Mocha
Al Mukhaylī Libya 108 B3
Al Munbaṭiḩ des. Saudi Arabia 110 C6
Almuñécar Spain 67 E5
Al Muqdādīyah Iraq 113 G4
Al Mūrītānīyah country Africa see Mauritania
Al Murūt well Saudi Arabia 113 E5
Almus Turkey 112 E2
Al Musannāh ridge Saudi Arabia 110 B4
Al Musayyib Iraq 110 B3
Al Muwaqqar Jordan 107 C4
Almyros Greece 69 J5
Almyrou, Ormos b. Greece 69 K7
Alnwick U.K. 58 F3
▶Alofi Niue 133 J3
Capital of Niue.
Aloja Latvia 55 N8
Alon Myanmar 86 A2
Along India 105 H3
Alongshan China 90 A2
Alonnisos i. Greece 69 J5
Alor i. Indon. 83 C5
Alor, Kepulauan is Indon. 83 C5
Alor, Selat sea chan. Indon. 83 B5
Alor Setar Malaysia 84 C1
Alor Star Malaysia see Alor Setar
Alost Belgium see Aalst
Aloysius, Mount Australia 135 E6
Alozero Rus. Fed. 54 Q4
Alpen Germany 62 G3
Alpena U.S.A. 164 D1
Alpercatas, Serra das hills Brazil 177 J5
Alpha Australia 136 D4
Alpha Ridge sea feature Arctic Ocean 189 A1
Alpine AZ U.S.A. 159 I5
Alpine NY U.S.A. 165 G2
Alpine TX U.S.A. 161 C6
Alpine WY U.S.A. 156 F4
Alpine National Park Australia 138 C6
Alps mts Europe 66 H4
Al Qa'āmīyāt reg. Saudi Arabia 108 G6
Al Qaddāḩīyah Libya 121 E1
Al Qadmūs Syria 107 C2
Al Qaffāy i. U.A.E. 110 D5
Al Qāhirah Egypt see Cairo
Al Qā'īyah Saudi Arabia 108 F5
Al Qā'īyah well Saudi Arabia 110 B5
Al Qal'a Beni Hammad tourist site Alg. 67 I6
Al Qalībah Saudi Arabia 112 E5
Al Qāmishlī Syria 113 F3
Al Qar'ah Libya 112 B5
Al Qar'ah well Saudi Arabia 110 B5
Al Qar'ah lava field Syria 107 C3
Al Qardāḩah Syria 107 C2
Al Qarqar Saudi Arabia 107 C4
Al Qaryatayn Syria 107 C2
Al Qaṣab Ar Riyāḍ Saudi Arabia 110 B5
Al Qaṣab Ash Sharqīyah Saudi Arabia 110 C6
Al Qaṭīf Saudi Arabia 110 C5
Al Qaṭn Yemen 108 G6
Al Qaṭrānah Jordan 107 C4
Al Qaṭrūn Libya 121 E2
Al Qayṣūmah well Saudi Arabia 113 F5
Al Qubbah Libya 121 F1
Alqueva, Barragem de resr Port. 67 C4
Al Qumur country Africa see Comoros
Al Qunayṭirah Syria 107 B3
Al Qunfidhah Saudi Arabia 108 F6
Al Qurayyāt Saudi Arabia 107 C4
Al Qurnah Iraq 113 G5
Al Quṣaymah Egypt 107 B4
Al Quṣayr Egypt 108 D4
Al Quṣayr Syria 107 C2
Al Qūṣīyah Egypt 112 C6
Al Qūṣūrīyah Saudi Arabia 110 B6
Al Quṭayfah Syria 107 C3
Al Quwayi' Saudi Arabia 110 B6
Al Quwayīyah Saudi Arabia 108 G5
Al Quwayrah Jordan 107 B5
Al Rabbād reg. U.A.E. 110 D6
Alroy Downs Australia 136 B3
Alsace admin. reg. France 63 H6
Alsace reg. France 66 H2
Alsager U.K. 59 E5
Al Samīt well Iraq 113 F5
Alsask Canada 151 I5
Alsatia reg. France see Alsace
Alsek r. AK U.S.A. 149 M4
Alsfeld Germany 63 J4
Alsleben (Saale) Germany 63 L3
Alston U.K. 58 E4
Alstonville Australia 138 F2
Alsunga Latvia 55 L8
Alta Norway 54 M2
Alta, Mount N.Z. 139 B7
Altaelva r. Norway 54 M2
Altafjorden sea chan. Norway 54 M1
Alta Floresta Brazil 177 G5
Alta Gracia Nicaragua 166 [inset] I7
Altai Mountains Asia 88 F3
Altamaha r. U.S.A. 163 D6
Altamira Brazil 177 H4
Altamira Costa Rica 166 [inset] I7
Altamíra Mex. 167 F4
Altamirano Chiapas Mex. 167 G5
Altamura Italy 68 G4
Altan Chitinskaya Oblast' Rus. Fed. 95 G1
Altan Chitinskaya Oblast' Rus. Fed. 95 G1
Altanbulag Mongolia 94 F2
Altan Emel Nei Mongol China 95 I1
Altan Ovoo mt. China/Mongolia 94 B2
Altan Shiret Nei Mongol China 95 G4
Altan Xiret Nei Mongol China see Altan Shiret
Alta Paraiso de Goiás Brazil 179 B1
Altar Mex. 166 C2
Altar r. Mex. 157 F7
Altar, Desierto de des. Mex. 166 B1
Altata Mex. 166 D3
Altavista U.S.A. 164 F5
Altay Xinjiang China 98 E3
Altay Govĭ-Altay Mongolia 94 C2
Altay Mongolia 94 D2
Altay Mongolia 94 C2
Altay, Respublika aut. rep. Rus. Fed. 94 A1
Altayskiy Rus. Fed. 102 G1
Altayskiy Khrebet mts Asia see Altai Mountains
Altayskiy Zapovednik nature res. Rus. Fed. 94 B1
Altdorf Switz. 66 I3
Altea Spain 67 F4
Alteidet Norway 54 M1
Altenahr Germany 62 G4
Altenberge Germany 63 H2
Altenburg Germany 63 M4
Altenkirchen (Westerwald) Germany 63 H4
Altenqoke Qinghai China 94 C4
Altin Köprü Iraq 113 G4
Altınoluk Turkey 69 L5
Altınözü Turkey 107 C1
Altıntaş Turkey 69 N5
Altiplano plain Bol. 176 E7
Altmark reg. Germany 63 L2
Altmühl r. Germany 63 L6
Alto, Monte hill Italy 68 D2
Alto Chicapa Angola 123 B5
Alto Cuchumatanes mts Guat. 167 H6
Alto del Moncayo mt. Spain 67 F3
Alto de Pencoso hills Arg. 178 C4
Alto Garças Brazil 177 H7
Alto Madidi, Parque Nacional nat. park Bol. 176 E6
Alton CA U.S.A. 158 A1
Alton IL U.S.A. 160 F4
Alton MO U.S.A. 161 F4
Alton NH U.S.A. 165 J2
Altona Canada 150 F3
Altoona U.S.A. 165 F3
Alto Parnaíba Brazil 177 I5
Alto Taquarí Mato Grosso Brazil 177 H7
Altotonga Mex. 167 F5
Altötting Germany 57 N6
Altrincham U.K. 58 E5
Alt Schwerin Germany 63 M1
Altūn Kūbrī Iraq see Altin Köprü
Altun Shan mt. Qinghai China 98 F5
Altun Shan mts China 99 D5
Alturas U.S.A. 156 C4
Altus U.S.A. 161 D5
Al 'Ubaylah Saudi Arabia 122 F1
Alucra Turkey 112 E2
Alūksne Latvia 55 O8
Alūm Iran 110 C3
Alum Bridge U.S.A. 164 E4
Al 'Uqaylah Libya 121 E1
Al 'Uqaylah Saudi Arabia see An Nabk
Al Uqṣur Egypt see Luxor
Alur India 106 C3
Al 'Urayq des. Saudi Arabia 112 E5
Al 'Urdun country Asia see Jordan
Alur Setar Malaysia see Alor Setar
'Ālūt Iran 110 B3
Aluva India see Alwaye
Al 'Uwayjā' well Saudi Arabia 110 C6
Al 'Uwaynāt Libya 108 B5
Al 'Uwayqīlah Saudi Arabia 113 F5
Al 'Uzayr Iraq 113 G5
Alva U.S.A. 161 D4
Alvand, Kūh-e mt. Iran 110 C3
Alvarado Mex. 167 G5
Alvarado TX U.S.A. 167 F1
Alvarães Brazil 176 F4
Alvaton U.S.A. 164 B5
Ålvdal Norway 54 G5
Älvdalen Sweden 55 I6
Alvesta Sweden 55 I8
Ålvik Norway 55 E6
Alvik Sweden 54 J5
Alvin U.S.A. 161 E6
Alvorada do Norte Brazil 179 B1
Älvsbyn Sweden 54 L4
Al Wafrah Kuwait 110 B4
Al Wajh Saudi Arabia 108 E4
Al Wakrah Qatar 110 C5
Al Waqbá well Saudi Arabia 110 B4
Alwar India 104 D4
Al Wari'ah Saudi Arabia 108 G4
Al Wāṭiyah well Egypt 112 B5
Alwaye India 106 C4
Al Widyān plat. Iraq/Saudi Arabia 113 F4
Al Wusayṭ well Saudi Arabia 110 B4
Alxa Youqi Nei Mongol China see Ehen Hudag
Alxa Zuoqi Nei Mongol China see Bayan Hot
Al Yamāmah Saudi Arabia 110 B5
Al Yaman country Asia see Yemen
Alyangula Australia 136 B2
Al Yāsāt i. U.A.E. 110 C5
Alyth U.K. 60 F4
Alytus Lith. 55 N9
Alzette r. Lux. 62 G5
Alzey Germany 63 I5
Amacayacu, Parque Nacional nat. park Col. 176 D4
Amadeus, Lake salt flat Australia 135 E6
Amadjuak Lake Canada 147 K3
Amadora Port. 67 B4
Amaga-dake mt. Japan 93 E3
Amagasaki Japan 92 B4
Amagi-san vol. Japan 93 E4
Amagi-tōge pass Japan 93 E4
Amagiyugashima Japan 93 E4
Amagoi-dake mt. Japan 92 C3
Amahai Seram Indon. 83 D3
Amakazari-yama mt. Japan 93 D2
Amakusa-nada b. Japan 91 C6
Åmål Sweden 55 H7
Amalia S. Africa 125 G4
Amaliada Greece 69 I6
Amalner India 104 C5
Amamapare Indon. 81 J7
Amambaí Brazil 178 E2
Amambaí, Serra de hills Brazil/Para. 178 E2
Amami-Ō-shima i. Japan 91 C7
Amami-shotō is Japan 91 C8
Amamula Dem. Rep. Congo 122 C4
Amanab P.N.G. 81 K7
Amangel'dy Kazakh. 102 C1
Amankeldi Kazakh. see Amangel'dy
Amantea Italy 68 G5
Amanzimtoti S. Africa 125 J6
Amapá Brazil 177 H3
Amapala Hond. 166 [inset] I6
Amara Iraq see Al 'Amārah
Amarante Brazil 177 J5
Amarapura Myanmar 86 B2
Amardalay Mongolia see Delgertsogt
Amareleja Port. 67 C4
Amargosa Brazil 179 D1
Amargosa watercourse U.S.A. 158 E3
Amargosa Desert U.S.A. 158 E3
Amargosa Range mts U.S.A. 158 E3
Amargosa Valley U.S.A. 158 E3
Amarillo U.S.A. 161 C5
Amarillo, Cerro mt. Arg. 178 C4
Amarkantak India 105 E5
Amarpur Madh. Prad. India 104 E5
Amasia Turkey see Amasya
Amasine W. Sahara 120 B2
Amasra Turkey 112 D2
Amasya Turkey 112 D2
Amata Australia 135 E6
Amatenango Mex. 167 G5
Amatique, Bahía de b. Guat. 166 [inset] H6
Amatitán Mex. 166 E4
Amatlán de Cañas Mex. 166 D4
Amatsu-Kominato Japan 93 G3
Amatulla India 105 H4
Amau P.N.G. 136 E1
Amay Belgium 62 F4
Amazar Rus. Fed. 90 A1
Amazar r. Rus. Fed. 90 A1
▶Amazon r. S. America 176 F4
Longest river and largest drainage basin in South America and 2nd longest river in the world.
Also known as Amazonas or Solimões
Amazon, Mouths of the Brazil 177 I3
Amazonas r. S. America 176 F4 see Amazon
Amazon Cone sea feature S. Atlantic Ocean 184 E5
Amazonía, Parque Nacional nat. park Brazil 177 G4
Ambajogai India 106 C2
Ambala India 104 D3
Ambalangoda Sri Lanka 106 D5
Ambalavao Madag. 123 E6
Ambam Cameroon 122 B3
Ambar Iran 110 E4
Ambarnyy Rus. Fed. 54 R4
Ambasa India see Ambassa
Ambasamudram India 106 C4
Ambassa India 105 G5
Ambathala Australia 137 D5
Ambato Ecuador 176 C4
Ambato Boeny Madag. 123 E5
Ambato Finandrahana Madag. 123 E6
Ambatolampy Madag. 123 E5
Ambatomainty Madag. 123 E5
Ambatondrazaka Madag. 123 E5
Ambejogai India see Ambajogai
Ambelau i. Maluku Indon. 83 C3
Amberg Germany 63 L5
Ambergris Cay i. Belize 167 I5
Ambérieu-en-Bugey France 66 G4
Amberley Canada 164 E1
Ambgaon India 106 D1
Ambianum France see Amiens
Ambikapur India 105 E5
Ambil i. Phil. 82 C3
Ambilobe Madag. 123 E5
Ambition, Mount B.C. Canada 149 O4
Amble U.K. 58 F3
Ambler AK U.S.A. 148 H2
Ambler r. AK U.S.A. 148 H2
Ambleside U.K. 58 E4
Amblève r. Belgium 62 F4
Ambo India 105 F5
Amboasary Madag. 123 E6
Ambodifotatra Madag. 123 E5
Ambohimahasoa Madag. 123 E6
Ambohitra mt. Madag. 123 E5
Amboina Maluku Indon. see Ambon
Ambon Maluku Indon. 83 D3
Ambon i. Maluku Indon. 83 C3
Amboró, Parque Nacional nat. park Bol. 176 F7
Ambositra Madag. 123 E6
Ambovombe Madag. 123 E6
Amboy U.S.A. 159 F4
Ambre, Cap d' c. Madag. see Bobaomby, Tanjona
Ambrim i. Vanuatu see Ambrym
Ambriz Angola 123 B4
Ambrizete Angola see N'zeto
Ambrosia Lake U.S.A. 159 J4
Ambrym i. Vanuatu 133 G3
Ambunten Jawa Indon. 85 F4
Ambunti P.N.G. 81 K7
Ambur India 106 C3
Amchitka Island AK U.S.A. 149 [inset]
Amchitka Pass sea channel AK U.S.A. 149 [inset]
Am-Dam Chad 121 F3
Amded, Oued watercourse Alg. 120 D2
Amdo Xizang China 99 E6
Ameca Jalisco Mex. 166 D4
Amecameca Mex. 167 F5
Ameland i. Neth. 62 F1
Amelia Court House U.S.A. 165 G5
Amellu Uttar Prad. India 99 C8
Amenia U.S.A. 165 I3
Amer, Erg d' des. Alg. 122 A1
Amereli India see Amreli
American, North Fork r. U.S.A. 158 C2
Americana Brazil 179 B3
American-Antarctic Ridge sea feature S. Atlantic Ocean 184 G9
American Falls U.S.A. 156 E4
American Falls Reservoir U.S.A. 156 E4
American Fork U.S.A. 159 H1
▶American Samoa terr. S. Pacific Ocean 133 J3
United States Unincorporated Territory.
Americus U.S.A. 163 C5
Amersfoort Neth. 62 F2
Amersfoort S. Africa 125 I4
Amersham U.K. 59 G7
Amery Canada 151 M3
Amery Ice Shelf Antarctica 188 E2
Ames U.S.A. 160 E3
Amesbury U.K. 59 F7
Amesbury U.S.A. 165 J2
Amet India 104 C4
Amethi India 105 E4
Amfissa Greece 69 J5
Amga Rus. Fed. 77 O3
Amgalang Nei Mongol China 95 I1
Amgu Rus. Fed. 90 E3
Amguema Rus. Fed. 148 C2
Amguema r. Rus. Fed. 148 C1
Amguid Alg. 120 D2
Amgun' r. Rus. Fed. 90 E1
Amherst Canada 153 I5
Amherst Myanmar see Kyaikkami
Amherst MA U.S.A. 165 I2
Amherst OH U.S.A. 164 D3
Amherst VA U.S.A. 164 F5
Amherstburg Canada 164 D2
Amherst Island Canada 165 G1
Ami Japan 93 G2
Amiata, Monte mt. Italy 68 D3
Amida Turkey see Diyarbakır
Amidon U.S.A. 160 C2
Amiens France 62 C5
'Amīj, Wādī watercourse Iraq 113 F4
Amik Ovası marsh Turkey 107 C1
'Amīnābād Iran 110 D4
Amindivi atoll India see Amini
Amindivi Islands India 106 B4
Amini atoll India 106 B4
Amino Eth. 122 E3
Amino Japan 92 B3
Aminuis Namibia 124 D2
Amīrābād Iran 110 B3
Amirante Islands Seychelles 185 L6
Amirante Trench sea feature Indian Ocean 185 L6
Amisk Lake Canada 151 K4
Amistad, Represa de resr Mex./U.S.A. see Amistad Reservoir
Amistad Reservoir Mex./U.S.A. 167 E2
Amisus Turkey see Samsun
Amite U.S.A. 161 F6
Amity Point Australia 138 F1
Amla India 104 D5
Amlash Iran 110 C2
Amlekhganj Nepal 105 F4
Åmli Norway 55 F7
Amlia Island AK U.S.A. 149 [inset]
Amlwch U.K. 58 C5
▶'Ammān Jordan 107 B4
Capital of Jordan.
Ammanazar Turkm. 110 D2
Ammanford U.K. 59 D7

Ämmänsaari Fin. 54 P4
'Ammār, Tall hill Syria 107 C3
Ammarnäs Sweden 54 J4
Ammaroo Australia 136 A4
Ammassalik Greenland 189 J2
Ammerland reg. Germany 63 H1
Ammern Germany 63 K3
Ammochostos Cyprus see Famagusta
Ammochostos Bay Cyprus 107 B2
Am Nābiyah Yemen 108 F7
Amne Machin Range mts China see A'nyêmaqên Shan
Amnok-kang r. China/N. Korea see Yalu Jiang
Amo Jiang r. China 96 D4
Amol Iran 110 D2
Amorbach Germany 63 J5
Amorgos i. Greece 69 K6
Amory U.S.A. 161 F5
Amos Canada 152 F4
Amourj Mauritania 120 C3
Amoy China see Xiamen
Ampah Kalimantan Indon. 85 F3
Ampana Sulawesi Indon. 83 B3
Ampani India 106 D2
Ampanihy Madag. 123 E6
Amparai Sri Lanka 106 D5
Amparo Brazil 179 B3
Ampasimanolotra Madag. 123 E5
Ampenan Lombok Indon. 85 G5
Amphitheatre Australia 138 A6
Amphitrite Group is Paracel Is 80 E3
Ampibaku Sulawesi Indon. 83 B3
Ampoa Sulawesi Indon. 83 B3
Amqog Gansu China 94 E5
Amraoti India see Amravati
Amravati India 106 C1
Amrawad India 104 D5
Amreli India 104 B5
Amri Pak. 111 H5
Amring India 105 H4
'Amrīt Syria 107 B2
Amritsar India 104 C3
Amroha India 104 D3
Amsden U.S.A. 164 D3
Åmsele Sweden 54 K4
Amstelveen Neth. 62 E2

▶Amsterdam Neth. 62 E2
Official capital of the Netherlands.

Amsterdam S. Africa 125 J4
Amsterdam U.S.A. 165 H2
Amsterdam, Île i. Indian Ocean 185 N8
Amstetten Austria 57 O6
Am Timan Chad 121 F3
Amu Co l. Xizang China 99 E6
Amudar'ya r. Asia 111 F2
Amudaryo r. Asia see Amudar'ya
Amukta Island AK U.S.A. 148 E5
Amukta Pass sea channel AK U.S.A. 148 D5
Amund Ringnes Island Canada 147 I2
Amundsen, Mount Antarctica 188 F2
Amundsen Abyssal Plain sea feature Southern Ocean 188 J2
Amundsen Basin sea feature Arctic Ocean 189 H1
Amundsen Bay Antarctica 188 D2
Amundsen Coast Antarctica 188 J1
Amundsen Glacier Antarctica 188 I1
Amundsen Gulf Canada 146 F2
Amundsen Ridges sea feature Southern Ocean 188 J2
Amundsen-Scott research station Antarctica 188 C1
Amundsen Sea Antarctica 188 K2
Amuntai Kalimantan Indon. 85 F3
Amur r. China/Rus Fed 90 D2
also known as Heilong Jiang (China)
Amur r. Rus. Fed. 90 F1
'Amur, Wadi watercourse Sudan 108 D6
Amurang Sulawesi Indon. 83 C2
Amur Oblast admin. div. Rus. Fed. see Amurskaya Oblast'
Amursk Rus. Fed. 90 E2
Amurskaya Oblast' admin. div. Rus. Fed. 90 C1
Amurskiy Liman strait Rus. Fed. 90 F1
Amurzet Rus. Fed. 90 C3
Amvrosiyivka Ukr. 53 H7
Amyderya r. Asia see Amudar'ya
Am-Zoer Chad 121 F3
An Myanmar 86 A3
Anaa atoll Fr. Polynesia 187 K7
Anabanua Sulawesi Indon. 83 B3
Anabar r. Rus. Fed. 77 M2
Anacapa Islands U.S.A. 158 D4
Anaconda U.S.A. 156 E3
Anacortes U.S.A. 156 C2
Anacuao, Mount Phil. 82 C2
Anadarko U.S.A. 161 D5
Anadolu reg. Turkey 112 D3
Anadolu Dağları mts Turkey 112 E2
Anadyr' Rus. Fed. 148 B2
Anadyrskaya Nizmennost' lowland Rus. Fed. 148 B2
Anadyrskiy Liman b. Rus. Fed. 148 B2
Anadyrskiy Zaliv b. Rus. Fed. 148 C3
Anafi i. Greece 69 K6
Anagé Brazil 179 C1
'Ānah Iraq 113 F4
Anaheim U.S.A. 158 E5
Anahim Lake Canada 150 E4
Anáhuac Nuevo León Mex. 167 E3
Anahuac U.S.A. 161 E6
Anaimalai Hills India 106 C4
Anaiteum i. Vanuatu see Anatom
Anajás Brazil 177 I4
Anakapalle India 106 D2
Anakie Australia 136 D4
Anaktuvuk r. AK U.S.A. 149 J1
Anaktuvuk Pass AK U.S.A. 149 J1
Analalava Madag. 123 E5
Anamã Brazil 176 F4
Anambas, Kepulauan is Indon. 84 D2
Anamosa U.S.A. 160 F3
Anamur Turkey 107 A1
Anan Nagano Japan 93 D3
Anan Japan 91 D6
Anand India 104 C5
Anandapur India 105 F5
Anan'ev Kyrg. 98 B4
Anano i. Indon. 83 C4
Anantapur India 106 C3
Ananthapur India see Anantapur
Anantnag India 104 C2
Anant Peth India 104 D4
Anantpur India see Anantapur
Ananyev Ukr. see Anan'yiv
Anan'yiv Ukr. 53 F7
Anapa Rus. Fed. 112 E1
Anápolis Brazil 179 A2
Anár Fin. see Inari
Anār Iran 110 D4
Anardara Afgh. 111 F3
Anatahan i. N. Mariana Is 81 L3
Anatajan i. N. Mariana Is see Anatahan
Anatolia reg. Turkey see Anadolu
Anatom i. Vanuatu 133 G4
Añatuya Arg. 178 D3
Anaypazari Turkey see Gülnar
An Baile Breac Ireland 61 B6
Anbei Gansu China 94 D3
An Blascaod Mór Ireland see Great Blasket Island
An Bun Beag Ireland 61 D2
Anbūr-e Kālārī Iran 110 D5
Anbyon N. Korea 91 B5
Ancenis France 66 D3
Anchorage AK U.S.A. 149 J3
Anchorage Island atoll Cook Is see Suwarrow
Anchor Bay U.S.A. 164 D2
Anchor Point AK U.S.A. 149 J4
Anchuthengu India see Anjengo
Anci Hebei China see Langfang
An Clochán Liath Ireland 61 D3
An Cóbh Ireland see Cobh
Ancona Italy 68 E3
Ancud, Golfo de g. Chile 178 B6
Ancyra Turkey see Ankara
Anda Heilong. China see Daqing
Anda Heilong. China 90 B3
Anda i. Indon. 83 C1
Andacollo Chile 178 B4
Andado Australia 136 A5
Andahuaylas Peru 176 D6
An Daingean Ireland 61 B5
Andal India 105 F5
Åndalsnes Norway 54 E5
Andalucía aut. comm. Spain 67 D5
Andalusia aut. comm. Spain see Andalucía
Andalusia U.S.A. 163 C6
Andaman Basin sea feature Indian Ocean 185 O5
Andaman Islands India 87 A4
Andaman Sea Indian Ocean 87 A5
Andaman Strait India 87 A4
Andamooka Australia 137 B6
Andapa Madag. 123 E5
Andarāb reg. Afgh. 111 H3
Ande China 96 E4
Andegavum France see Angers
Andelle r. France 62 B5
Andenes Norway 54 J2
Andenne Belgium 62 F4
Andéramboukane Mali 120 D3
Anderlecht Belgium 62 E4
Andermatt Switz. 66 I3
Andernos-les-Bains France 66 D4
Anderson r. N.W.T. Canada 149 O1
Anderson AK U.S.A. 149 J2
Anderson IN U.S.A. 164 C3
Anderson SC U.S.A. 163 D5
Anderson TX U.S.A. 161 E6
Anderson Bay Australia 137 [inset]
Anderson Lake Canada 150 F5
Andes mts S. America 178 C4
Andfjorden sea chan. Norway 54 J2
Andhíparos i. Greece see Antiparos
Andhra Lake India 106 B2
Andhra Pradesh state India 106 C2
Andijon Uzbek. 102 D3
Andikíthira i. Greece see Antikythira
Andilamena Madag. 123 E5
Andilanatoby Madag. 123 E5
Andīmeshk Iran 110 C3
Andímilos i. Greece see Antimilos
Andípsara i. Greece see Antipsara
Andir He r. China 99 C5
Andırın Turkey 112 E3
Andirlangar Xinjiang China 99 C5
Andizhan Uzbek. see Andijon
Andkhvoy Afgh. 111 G2
Andoany Madag. 123 E5
Andoas Peru 176 C4
Andogskaya Gryada hills Rus. Fed. 52 H4
Andol India 106 C2
Andong China see Dandong
Andong S. Korea 91 C5
Andongwei Shandong China 95 I5
Andoom Australia 136 C2
Andorra country Europe 67 G2

▶Andorra la Vella Andorra 67 G2
Capital of Andorra.

Andorra la Vieja Andorra see Andorra la Vella
Andover U.K. 59 F7
Andover NY U.S.A. 165 G2
Andover OH U.S.A. 164 E3
Andøya i. Norway 54 I2
Andrade U.S.A. 159 F5
Andradina Brazil 179 A3
Andranomavo Madag. 123 E5
Andranopasy Madag. 123 E6
Andreafsky r. AK U.S.A. 148 G3
Andreafsky, East Fork r. AK U.S.A. 148 G3
Andreanof Islands U.S.A. 186 I2
Andreapol' Rus. Fed. 52 G4
Andreas Isle of Man 58 C4
André Félix, Parc National d' nat. park Cent. Afr. Rep. 122 C3
Andrelândia Brazil 179 B3
Andrew Canada 151 H4
Andrew Bay Myanmar 86 A3
Andrews SC U.S.A. 163 E5
Andrews TX U.S.A. 161 C5
Andria Italy 68 G4
Androka Madag. 123 E6
Andropov Rus. Fed. see Rybinsk
Andros i. Bahamas 163 E7
Andros i. Greece 69 K6
Androscoggin r. U.S.A. 165 K2
Andros Town Bahamas 163 E7
Andrott i. India 106 B4
Andselv Norway 54 K2
Andújar Spain 67 D4
Andulo Angola 123 B5
Anec, Lake salt flat Australia 135 E5
Äneen-Kio terr. N. Pacific Ocean see Wake Island
Anéfis Mali 120 D3
Anegada, Bahía b. Arg. 178 D6
Anegada Passage Virgin Is (U.K.) 169 L5
Aného Togo 120 D4
Aneityum i. Vanuatu see Anatom
'Aneiza, Jabal hill Iraq see 'Unayzah, Jabal
Anemourion tourist site Turkey 107 A1
Anepmete P.N.G. 81 L8
Anet France 62 B6
Anetchom, Île i. Vanuatu see Anatom
Aneto mt. Spain 67 G2
Änewetak atoll Marshall Is see Enewetak
Aney Niger 120 E3
Aneytioum, Île i. Vanuatu see Anatom
Anfu China 97 G3
Angalarri r. Australia 134 E3
Angamos, Punta pt Chile 178 B2
Ang'angxi Heilong. China 95 J2

▶Angara r. Rus. Fed. 88 G1
Part of the Yenisey-Angara-Selenga, 3rd longest river in Asia.

Angarsk Rus. Fed. 88 I2
Angas Downs Australia 135 F6
Angat Luzon Phil. 82 C3
Angatuba Brazil 179 A3
Angaur i. Palau 82 [inset]
Ånge Sweden 54 I5
Angel, Salto waterfall Venez. see Angel Falls
Ángel de la Guarda, Isla i. Mex. 166 B2
Angeles Luzon Phil. 82 C3

▶Angel Falls waterfall Venez. 176 F2
Highest waterfall in the world.

Ängelholm Sweden 55 H8
Angellala Creek r. Australia 138 C1
Angels Camp U.S.A. 158 C2
Ångermanälven r. Sweden 54 J5
Angers France 66 D3
Anggana Kalimantan Indon. 85 G3
Angikuni Lake Canada 151 L2
Angiola U.S.A. 158 D4
Angkor tourist site Cambodia 87 C4
Anglesea Australia 138 B7
Anglesey i. U.K. 58 C5
Angleton U.S.A. 161 E6
Anglo-Egyptian Sudan country Africa see Sudan
Angmagssalik Greenland see Ammassalik
Ang Mo Kio Sing. 87 [inset]
Ango Dem. Rep. Congo 122 C3
Angoche Moz. 123 D5
Angohrān Iran 110 E5
Angol Chile 178 B5
Angola country Africa 123 B5
Angola IN U.S.A. 164 C3
Angola NY U.S.A. 164 F2
Angola Basin sea feature S. Atlantic Ocean 184 H7
Angora Turkey see Ankara
Angostura Mex. 157 F8
Angoulême France 66 E4
Angra dos Reis Brazil 179 B3
Angren Uzbek. 102 D3
Ang Thong Thai. 87 C4
Anguang Jilin China 95 J2

▶Anguilla terr. West Indies 169 L5
United Kingdom Overseas Territory.

Anguilla Cays is Bahamas 163 E8
Anguille, Cape Canada 153 K5
Angul India 106 E1
Anguli Nur l. China 95 H3
Anguo Hebei China 95 H4
Angus Canada 164 F1
Angutia Char i. Bangl. 105 G5
Angutikada Peak AK U.S.A. 148 H2
Anholt i. Denmark 55 G8
Anhua China 97 F2
Anhui prov. China 97 H1
Anhumas Brazil 177 H7
Anhwei prov. China see Anhui
Aniak AK U.S.A. 148 H3
Aniak r. AK U.S.A. 148 H3
Aniakchak National Monument and Preserve nat. park U.S.A. 146 C4
Animaki-san hill Japan 93 G2
Anin Myanmar 86 B4
Anini Arun. Prad. India 99 F7
Anitaguipan Point Samar Phil. 82 D4
Anitápolis Brazil 179 A4
Anıtlı Turkey 107 A1
Aniva Rus. Fed. 90 F3
Aniva, Mys c. Rus. Fed. 90 F3
Aniva, Zaliv b. Rus. Fed. 90 F3
Anizy-le-Château France 62 D5
Anjadip i. India 106 B3
Anjalankoski Fin. 55 O6
Anjengo India 106 C4
Anji China 97 H2
Anjihai Xinjiang China 98 D3
Anjir Avand Iran 110 D3
Anjō Japan 92 D4
Anjoman Iran 110 E3
Anjou reg. France 66 D3
Anjouan i. Comoros see Nzwani
Anjozorobe Madag. 123 E5
Anjuman reg. Afgh. 111 H3
Anjuthengu India see Anjengo
Ankang China 97 F1

▶Ankara Turkey 112 D3
Capital of Turkey.

Ankaratra mt. Madag. 123 E5
Ankazoabo Madag. 123 E6
Ankeny U.S.A. 160 E3
An Khê Vietnam 87 E4
Ankleshwar India 104 C5
Anklesvar India see Ankleshwar
Ankola India 106 B3
Ankouzhen Gansu China 94 F5
Anling Henan China see Yanling
An Lôc Vietnam 87 D5
Anlong China 96 E3
Anlu China 97 G2
Anmoore U.S.A. 164 E4
An Muileann gCearr Ireland see Mullingar
Anmyŏn-do i. S. Korea 91 B5
Ann, Cape Antarctica 188 D2
Ann, Cape U.S.A. 165 J2
Anna Rus. Fed. 53 I6
Anna, Lake U.S.A. 165 G4
Annaba Alg. 68 B6
Annaberg-Buchholtz Germany 63 N4
An Nabk Saudi Arabia 107 C4
An Nabk Syria 107 C2
An Nafūd des. Saudi Arabia 113 F5
An Najaf Iraq see Najaf
Annaka Japan 93 E2
Annalee r. Ireland 61 E3
Annalong U.K. 61 G3
Annam reg. Vietnam 80 D3
Annam Highlands mts Laos/Vietnam 86 D3
Annan U.K. 60 F6
Annan r. U.K. 60 F6
'Annān, Wādī al watercourse Syria 107 D2
Annanba Gansu China 94 C4
Annandale U.S.A. 165 G4
Anna Plains Australia 134 C4

▶Annapolis U.S.A. 165 G4
Capital of Maryland.

Annapurna Conservation Area nature res. Nepal 105 F3

▶Annapurna I mt. Nepal 105 E3
10th highest mountain in the world and in Asia.

Ann Arbor U.S.A. 164 D2
Anna Regina Guyana 177 G2
An Nás Ireland see Naas
An Nāṣirīyah Iraq see Nāṣirīyah
An Naṣrānī, Jabal mts Syria 107 C3
Annean, Lake salt flat Australia 135 B6
Anne Arundel Town U.S.A. see Annapolis
Annecy France 66 H4
Anne Marie Lake Canada 153 J3
Annen Neth. 62 G1
Annette Island AK U.S.A. 149 O5
An Nimārah Syria 107 C3
An Nimāṣ Saudi Arabia 108 F6
Anning China 96 D3
Anniston U.S.A. 163 C5
Annobón i. Equat. Guinea 120 D5
Annonay France 66 G4
An Nu'mānīyah Iraq 113 G4
An Nuṣayrīyah, Jabal mts Syria 107 C2
Anō Japan 92 C4
Anonima atoll Micronesia see Namonuito
Anoón de Sardinas, Bahía de b. Col. 176 C3
Anorontany, Tanjona hd Madag. 123 E5
Ano Viannos Kriti Greece see Viannos
Anpu Gang b. China 97 F4
Anqing China 97 H2
Anqiu Shandong China 95 I4
An Ráth Ireland see Charleville
Anren China 97 G3
Ans Belgium 62 F4
Ansai Shaanxi China 95 G4
Ansbach Germany 63 K5
Anser Group is Australia 138 C7
Anshan Liaoning China 95 J3
Anshun China 96 E3
Anshunchang China 96 D2
An Sirḥān, Wādī watercourse Saudi Arabia 112 E5
Ansley U.S.A. 160 D3
Anson U.S.A. 161 D5
Anson Bay Australia 134 E3
Ansongo Mali 120 D3
Ansonville Canada 152 E4
Ansted U.S.A. 164 E4
Ansu Hebei China see Xushui
Ansudu Indon. 81 J7
Antabamba Peru 176 D6
Antakya Turkey 107 C1
Antalaha Madag. 123 F5
Antalya Turkey 69 N6
Antalya prov. Turkey 107 A1
Antalya Körfezi g. Turkey 69 N6

▶Antananarivo Madag. 123 E5
Capital of Madagascar.

An tAonach Ireland see Nenagh

▶Antarctica 188
Most southerly and coldest continent, and the continent with the highest average elevation.

Antarctic Peninsula Antarctica 188 L2
Antas r. Brazil 179 A5
An Teallach mt. U.K. 60 D3
Antelope Island U.S.A. 159 G1
Antelope Range mts U.S.A. 158 E2
Antequera Spain 67 D5
Anthony NM U.S.A. 166 D1
Anthony Lagoon Australia 136 A3
Anti Atlas mts Morocco 64 C6
Antibes France 66 H5
Anticosti, Île d' i. Canada 153 J4
Anticosti Island Canada see Anticosti, Île d'
Antifer, Cap d' c. France 59 H9
Antigo U.S.A. 160 F2
Antigonish Canada 153 J5
Antigua i. Antigua and Barbuda 169 L5
Antigua Guat. see Antigua Guatemala
Antigua country West Indies see Antigua and Barbuda
Antigua and Barbuda country West Indies 169 L5
Antigua Guatemala Guat. 167 H6
Antiguo-Morelos Mex. 167 F4
Antikythira i. Greece 69 J7
Antikythiro, Steno sea chan. Greece 69 J7
Anti Lebanon mts Lebanon/Syria see Sharqī, Jabal ash
Antimilos i. Greece 69 K6
Antimony U.S.A. 159 H2
An tInbhear Mór Ireland see Arklow
Antioch Turkey see Antakya
Antioch U.S.A. 158 C2
Antiocheia ad Cragum tourist site Turkey 107 A1
Antiochia Turkey see Antakya
Antiparos i. Greece 69 K6
Antipodes Islands N.Z. 133 H6
Antipsara i. Greece 69 K5
Antium Italy see Anzio
Antlers U.S.A. 161 E5
Antofagasta Chile 178 B2
Antofagasta de la Sierra Arg. 178 C3
Antofalla, Volcán vol. Arg. 178 C3
Antoing Belgium 62 D4
António Enes Moz. see Angoche
Antri India 104 D4
Antrim U.K. 61 F3
Antrim Hills U.K. 61 F2
Antrim Plateau Australia 134 E4
Antropovo Rus. Fed. 52 I4
Antsalova Madag. 123 E5
Antseranana Madag. see Antsirañana
Antsirabe Madag. 123 E5
Antsirañana Madag. 123 E5
Antsla Estonia 55 O8
Antsohihy Madag. 123 E5
Anttis Sweden 54 M3
Anttola Fin. 55 O6
An Tuc Vietnam see An Khê
Antwerp Belgium 62 E3
Antwerp U.S.A. 165 H1
Antwerpen Belgium see Antwerp
An Uaimh Ireland see Navan
Anuc, Lac l. Canada 152 G2
Anuchino Rus. Fed. 90 D4
Anugul India see Angul
Anupgarh India 104 C3
Anuradhapura Sri Lanka 106 D4
Anveh Iran 110 D5
Anvers Island Antarctica 188 L2
Anvik AK U.S.A. 148 G3
Anvik r. AK U.S.A. 148 G3
Anvil Range mts Y.T. Canada 149 N3
Anxi Fujian China 97 H3
Anxi Gansu China 94 C3
Anxiang China 97 G2
Anxin Hebei China 95 H4
Anxious Bay Australia 135 F8
Anyang Guangxi China see Du'an
Anyang Henan China 95 H4
Anyang S. Korea 91 B5
Anyar Jawa Indon. 84 D4
A'nyêmaqên Shan mts China 94 D5
Anyuan Jiangxi China 97 G3
Anyuan Jiangxi China 97 G3
Anyue China 96 E2
Anyuy r. Rus. Fed. 90 E2
Anyuysk Rus. Fed. 77 R3
Anzac Alta Canada 151 I3
Anzac B.C. Canada 150 F4
Anze Shanxi China 95 H4
Anzhero-Sudzhensk Rus. Fed. 76 J4
Anzi Dem. Rep. Congo 122 C4
Anzio Italy 68 E4
Aoba Japan 93 F3
Aoba i. Vanuatu 133 G3
Aoba-yama hill Japan 92 B3
Aogaki Japan 92 B3
Aoga-shima i. Japan 91 E6
Aohan Qi Nei Mongol China see Xinhui
Ao Kham, Laem pt Thai. 87 B5
Aoki Japan 93 E2
Aomen China see Macao
Aomen Tebie Xingzhengqu aut. reg. China see Macao
Aomori Japan 90 F4
A'ong Co l. Xizang China 99 C6
Ao Phang Nga National Park Thai. 87 B5

▶Aoraki mt. N.Z. 139 C6
Highest mountain in New Zealand.

Aoraki/Mount Cook National Park N.Z. 139 C6
Aôral, Phnum mt. Cambodia 87 D4
Aorangi mt. N.Z. see Aoraki
Aosta Italy 68 B2
Aotearoa country Oceania see New Zealand
Aouk, Bahr r. Cent. Afr. Rep./Chad 121 E4
Aoukâr reg. Mali/Mauritania 120 C2
Aoulef Alg. 120 D2
Aoyama Japan 92 C4
Aozou Chad 121 E2
Apa r. Brazil 178 E2
Apache Creek U.S.A. 159 I5
Apache Junction U.S.A. 159 H5
Apaiang atoll Kiribati see Abaiang
Apalachee Bay U.S.A. 163 C6
Apalachicola U.S.A. 163 C6
Apalachicola r. U.S.A. 163 C6
Apalachin U.S.A. 165 G2
Apamea Turkey see Dinar
Apan Mex. 167 F5
Apaporis r. Col. 176 E4
Apar, Teluk b. Indon. 85 G3
Aparecida do Tabuado Brazil 179 A3
Aparima N.Z. see Riverton
Aparri Luzon Phil. 82 C2
Apatity Rus. Fed. 54 R3
Apatzingán Mex. 168 D5
Apavawook Cape AK U.S.A. 148 E3
Ape Latvia 55 O8
Apeldoorn Neth. 62 F2
Apelern Germany 63 J2
Apennines mts Italy 68 C2
Apensen Germany 63 J1
Apex Mountain Y.T. Canada 149 M3
Aphrewn r. AK U.S.A. 148 F3
Api mt. Nepal 104 E3
Api i. Vanuatu see Epi
Api, Tanjung pt Indon. 83 B3
Apia atoll Kiribati see Abaiang

▶Apia Samoa 133 I3
Capital of Samoa.

Apiacas, Serra dos hills Brazil 177 G6
Apiaí Brazil 179 A4
Apipilulco Mex. 167 F5
Apishapa r. U.S.A. 160 C4
Apiti N.Z. 139 E4
Apizaco Mex. 167 F5
Apizolaya Mex. 166 E3
Aplao Peru 176 D7
Apo, Mount vol. Mindanao Phil. 82 D5
Apo East Passage Phil. 82 C3
Apoera Suriname 177 G2
Apolda Germany 63 L3
Apollo Bay Australia 138 A7
Apollonia Bulg. see Sozopol
Apolo Bol. 176 E6
Aporé Brazil 179 A2
Aporé r. Brazil 179 A2
Apostle Islands U.S.A. 160 F2
Apostolens Tommelfinger mt. Greenland 147 N3
Apostolos Andreas, Cape Cyprus 107 B2
Apoteri Guyana 177 G3
Apo West Passage Phil. 82 C3
Apozai Pak. 111 H4
Appalachian Mountains U.S.A. 164 D5
Appalla i. Fiji see Kabara
Appennines mts Italy 68 D2
Appennino mts Italy see Apennines
Appennino Abruzzese mts Italy 68 E3
Appennino Tosco-Emiliano mts Italy 68 D3
Appennino Umbro-Marchigiano mts Italy 68 E3
Appingedam Neth. 62 G1
Applecross U.K. 60 D3
Appleton MN U.S.A. 160 D2
Appleton WI U.S.A. 164 A1
Apple Valley U.S.A. 158 E4
Appomattox U.S.A. 165 F5
Aprilia Italy 68 E4
Aprunyi India 96 B2
Apsheronsk Rus. Fed. 113 E1
Apsheronskaya Rus. Fed. see Apsheronsk
Apsley Canada 165 F1
Apt France 66 G5
Apucarana Brazil 179 A3
Apucarana, Serra da hills Brazil 179 A3
Apulum Romania see Alba Iulia
Apurahuan Palawan Phil. 82 B4
Apurashokoru i. Palau 82 [inset]
Aq"a Georgia see Sokhumi
'Aqaba Jordan see Al 'Aqabah
Aqaba, Gulf of Asia 112 D5
'Aqaba, Wâdi el watercourse Egypt see 'Aqabah, Wādī al
'Aqabah, Birkat al well Iraq 110 A4
'Aqabah, Wādī al watercourse Egypt 107 A4
Aqadyr Kazakh. see Agadyr'
Aqal Xinjiang China 98 B4
Aqdoghmish r. Iran 110 B2
Aqitag mt. Xinjiang China 94 B3
Aqköl Akmolinskaya Oblast' Kazakh. see Akkol'
Aqköl Atyrauskaya Oblast' Kazakh. see Akkol'
Aqmola Kazakh. see Astana
Aqqan Xinjiang China 99 C5
Aqqan Xinjiang China 99 D5
Aqqikkol Hu salt l. China 99 E5
Aqra', Jabal al mt. Syria/Turkey 107 B2
'Aqran hill Saudi Arabia 107 D4
Aqsay Kazakh. see Aksay

Aqsayqin Hit terr. Asia see Aksai Chin
Aqshī Kazakh. see Akshiy
Aqshuqyr Kazakh. see Akshukur
Aqsū Kazakh. see Aksu
Aqsūat Kazakh. see Aksuat
Aqsū-Ayuly Kazakh. see Aksu-Ayuly
Aqtaū Kazakh. see Aktau
Aqtōbe Kazakh. see Aktobe
Aqtoghay Kazakh. see Aktogay
Aquae Grani Germany see Aachen
Aquae Gratianae France see Aix-les-Bains
Aquae Sextiae France see Aix-en-Provence
Aquae Statiellae Italy see Acqui Terme
Aquarius Mountains U.S.A. 159 G4
Aquarius Plateau U.S.A. 159 H3
Aquaviva delle Fonti Italy 68 G4
Aquidauana Brazil 178 E2
Aquila Mex. 166 E5
Aquiles Mex. 166 D2
Aquincum Hungary see Budapest
Aquiry r. Brazil see Acre
Aquisgranum Germany see Aachen
Aquitaine reg. France 66 D5
Aquitania reg. France see Aquitaine
Aqzhayqyn Kōli salt l. Kazakh. see Akzhaykyn, Ozero
Ara India 105 F4
Āra Ārba Eth. 122 E3
Arab Afgh. 111 G4
Arab, Bahr el watercourse Sudan 121 F4
'Arab, Khalîg el b. Egypt see 'Arab, Khalīj al
'Arab, Khalīj al b. Egypt 112 C5
'Arabah, Wādī al watercourse Israel/Jordan 107 B5
Arabian Basin sea feature Indian Ocean 185 M5
Arabian Gulf Asia see The Gulf
Arabian Peninsula Asia 108 G5
Arabian Sea Indian Ocean 109 K6
Araç Turkey 112 D2
Araça r. Brazil 176 F4
Aracaju Brazil 177 K6
Aracati Brazil 177 K4
Aracatu Brazil 179 C1
Araçatuba Brazil 179 A3
Aracena Spain 67 C5
Aracruz Brazil 179 C2
Araçuaí Brazil 179 C2
Araçuaí r. Brazil 179 C2
'Arad Israel 107 B4
Arad Romania 69 I1
'Arādah U.A.E. 110 D6
Arafune-yama mt. Japan 93 E2
Arafura Sea Australia/Indon. 132 D2
Arafura Shelf sea feature Australia/Indon. 186 E6
Aragarças Brazil 177 H7
Ara-gawa r. Japan 93 E1
Ara-gawa r. Japan 93 F3
Aragón r. Spain 67 F2
Araguaçu Brazil 179 A1
Araguaia r. Brazil 179 A1
Araguaia, Parque Indígena res. Brazil 177 H6
Araguaia, Parque Nacional do nat. park Brazil 177 H6
Araguaiana Brazil 179 A1
Araguaína Brazil 177 I5
Araguari Brazil 179 A2
Araguari r. Brazil 177 H3
Araguatins Brazil 177 I5
Arai Brazil 179 B1
Arai Niigata Japan 93 E2
Arai Shizuoka Japan 92 D4
'Arâif el Naga, Gebel hill Egypt see 'Urayf an Nāqah, Jabal
Árainn Mhór i. Ireland see Arranmore Island
Araiosos Brazil 177 J4
Arak Alg. 120 D2
Arāk Iran 110 C3
Arak Syria 107 D2
Arakai-yama mt. Japan 93 F1
Arakamchechen, Ostrov i. Rus. Fed. 148 D2
Arakan reg. Myanmar 86 A2
Arakan Yoma mts Myanmar 86 A2
Araki-gawa r. Japan 92 D2
Arakkonam India 106 C3
Araks r. Armenia see Araz
Araku India 106 D2
Aral Qinghai China 99 E5
Aral Kazakh. see Aral'sk
Aral Tajik. see Vose

▶Aral Sea salt l. Kazakh./Uzbek. 102 B2
4th largest lake in Asia.

Aral'sk Kazakh. 102 B2
Aral'skoye More salt l. Kazakh./Uzbek. see Aral Sea
Aralsor, Ozero l. Kazakh. 53 K6
Aral Tengizi salt l. Kazakh./Uzbek. see Aral Sea
Araltobe Xinjiang China 94 B2
Aramac Australia 136 D4
Aramac Creek watercourse Australia 136 D4
Aramah plat. Saudi Arabia 110 B5
Aramberri Mex. 167 E4
Aramia r. P.N.G. 81 K8
Aran r. India 106 C2
Aranda de Duero Spain 67 E3
Arandai Indon. 81 I7
Aranđelovac Serbia 69 I2
Arandis Namibia 124 B2
Arang India 105 E5
Arani India 106 C3
Aran Islands Ireland 61 C4
Aranjuez Spain 67 E3
Aranos Namibia 124 D3
Aransas Pass U.S.A. 161 D7
Arantangi India 106 C4
Aranuka atoll Kiribati 133 H1
Aranyaprathet Thai. 87 C4
Arao Japan 91 C6
Araouane Mali 120 C3
Arapaho U.S.A. 161 D5
Arapgir Turkey 112 E3
Arapiraca Brazil 177 K5
Arapis, Akra pt Greece see Arapis, Akrotirio
Arapis, Akrotirio pt Greece 69 K4
Arapkir Turkey see Arapgir
Arapongas Brazil 179 A3
Araquari Brazil 179 A4
'Ar'ar Saudi Arabia 113 F5
Araracuara Col. 176 D4
Araraj Bihar India 99 D8
Araranguá Brazil 179 A5
Araraquara Brazil 179 A3
Araras Brazil 177 H5
Ararat Armenia 113 G3
Ararat Australia 138 A6
Ararat, Mount Turkey 113 G3
Araria India 105 F4
Araripina Brazil 177 J5
Aras Turkey 113 F3
Aras r. Turkey see Araz
Ar-Asgat Mongolia see Ugtaaltsaydam
Arashima-dake mt. Japan 92 C3
Arataca Brazil 179 D1
Aratürük Xinjiang China see Yiwu
Arauca Col. 176 D2
Arauca r. Venez. 176 E2
Aravalli Range mts India 104 C4
Aravete Estonia 55 N7
Arawa P.N.G. 132 F2
Araxá Brazil 179 B2
Araxes r. Asia see Araz
Arayıt Dağı mt. Turkey 69 N5
Araz r. Azer. 113 H2
also spelt Araks (Armenia), Aras (Turkey), formerly known as Araxes
Arbailu Iraq see Arbīl
Arbat Iraq 113 G4
Arbela Iraq see Arbīl
Arberth U.K. see Narberth
Arbīl Iraq 113 G3
Arboga Sweden 55 I7
Arborfield Canada 151 K4
Arborg Canada 151 L5
Arbroath U.K. 60 G4
Arbuckle U.S.A. 158 B2
Arbu Lut, Dasht-e des. Afgh. 111 F4
Arcachon France 66 D4
Arcade U.S.A. 165 F2
Arcadia FL U.S.A. 163 D7
Arcadia LA U.S.A. 161 E5
Arcadia MI U.S.A. 164 B1
Arcanum U.S.A. 164 C4
Arcas, Cayos is Mex. 167 H4
Arcata U.S.A. 156 B4
Arc Dome mt. U.S.A. 158 E2
Arcelia Mex. 168 D5
Archangel Rus. Fed. 52 I2
Archer r. Australia 79 G9
Archer Bend National Park Australia 136 C2
Archer City U.S.A. 161 D5
Arches National Park U.S.A. 159 I2
Archipiélago Los Roques nat. park Venez. 176 E1
Ärçivan Azer. 113 H3
Arckaringa watercourse Australia 137 A6
Arco U.S.A. 156 E4
Arcos Brazil 179 B3
Arcos de la Frontera Spain 67 D5
Arctic Bay Canada 147 J2
Arctic Institute Islands Rus. Fed. see Arkticheskogo Instituta, Ostrova
Arctic Lagoon AK U.S.A. 148 F2
Arctic Mid-Ocean Ridge sea feature Arctic Ocean 189 H1
Arctic National Wildlife Refuge nature res. AK U.S.A. 149 K1
Arctic Ocean 189 B1
Arctic Red r. N.W.T. Canada 149 N2
Arctic Red River N.W.T. Canada see Tsiigehtchic
Arctic Village AK U.S.A. 149 K1
Arctowski research station Antarctica 188 A2
Arda r. Bulg. 69 L4
also known as Ardas (Greece)
Ardabīl Iran 110 C2
Ardahan Turkey 113 F2
Ardakān Iran 110 D3
Årdalstangen Norway 55 E6
Ardara Ireland 61 D3
Ardas r. Bulg. see Arda
Ard aş Şawwān plain Jordan 107 C4
Ardatov Nizhegorodskaya Oblast' Rus. Fed. 53 I5
Ardatov Respublika Mordoviya Rus. Fed. 53 J5
Ardee Ireland 61 F4
Ardennes plat. Belgium 62 E5
Ardennes, Canal des France 62 E5
Arden Town U.S.A. 158 C2
Arderin hill Ireland 61 E4
Ardestān Iran 110 D3
Ardglass U.K. 61 G3
Ardila r. Port. 67 C4
Ardlethan Australia 138 C5
Ardmore U.S.A. 161 D5
Ardnamurchan, Point of U.K. 60 C4
Ardon Rus. Fed. 113 G2
Ardrishaig U.K. 60 D4
Ardrossan U.K. 60 E5
Ardvasar U.K. 60 D3
Areia Branca Brazil 177 K4
Arekalong Peninsula Palau 82 [inset]
Arel Belgium see Arlon
Arelas France see Arles
Arelate France see Arles
Aremberg hill Germany 62 G4
Arena rf Phil. 82 C4
Arena, Point U.S.A. 158 B2
Arena, Punta pt Mex. 166 C4
Arena de la Ventana, Punta pt Mex. 166 C3
Arenal, Volcán vol. Costa Rica 166 [inset] I7
Arena Point Luzon Phil. 82 C3
Arenas de San Pedro Spain 67 D3
Arendal Norway 55 F7
Arendsee (Altmark) Germany 63 L2
Areopoli Greece 69 J6
Areponapuchi Mex. 166 D3
Arequipa Peru 176 D7
Arere Brazil 177 H4
Arévalo Spain 67 D3
Arezzo Italy 68 D3
'Arfajah well Saudi Arabia 107 D4
Argadargada Australia 136 B4
Argalant Mongolia 95 G2
Argan Xinjiang China 98 E4
Arganda del Rey Spain 67 E3
Argao Cebu Phil. 82 C4
Argatay Mongolia see Bayanjargalan
Argel Alg. see Algiers
Argentan France 66 D2
Argentario, Monte hill Italy 68 D3
Argentera, Cima dell' mt. Italy 68 B2
Argenthal Germany 63 H5

▶Argentina country S. America 178 C5
2nd largest and 3rd most populous country in South America, and 8th largest in the world.

Argentine Abyssal Plain sea feature S. Atlantic Ocean 184 E9
Argentine Basin sea feature S. Atlantic Ocean 184 F8
Argentine Republic country S. America see Argentina
Argentine Rise sea feature S. Atlantic Ocean 184 E8
Argentino, Lago l. Arg. 178 B8
Argenton-sur-Creuse France 66 E3
Argentoratum France see Strasbourg
Argeș r. Romania 69 L2
Arghandab r. Afgh. 111 G4
Argi r. Rus. Fed. 90 C1
Argolikos Kolpos b. Greece 69 J6
Argos Greece 69 J6
Argos U.S.A. 164 B3
Argostoli Greece 69 I5
Arguís Spain 67 F2
Argun' r. China/Rus. Fed. 89 M2
Argun Rus. Fed. 113 G2
Argungu Nigeria 120 D3
Argunskiy Khrebet mts Rus. Fed. 95 I1
Argus Range mts U.S.A. 158 E4
Arguut Mongolia see Guchin-Us
Argyle Canada 153 I6
Argyle, Lake Australia 134 E4
Argyrokastron Albania see Gjirokastër
Arhangay prov. Mongolia 94 E2
Ar Horqin Qi Nei Mongol China see Tianshan
Århus Denmark 55 G8
Arhymot Lake AK U.S.A. 148 G3
Ariaga i. Indon. 83 C1
Ariah Park Australia 138 C5
Ariamsvlei Namibia 124 D5
Ariana Tunisia see L'Ariana
Ariano Irpino Italy 68 F4
Ari Atoll Maldives 103 D11
Aribinda Burkina 120 C3
Arica Chile 176 D7
Arid, Cape Australia 135 C8
Arida Japan 92 B4
Arida-gawa r. Japan 92 B4
Arigiyn Gol r. Mongolia 94 E1
Arigza China 96 C1
Arīḩā Syria 107 C2
Arīḩā West Bank see Jericho
Arikaree r. U.S.A. 160 C3
Arima Trin. and Tob. 169 L6
Arimine-ko resr Japan 92 D2
Ariminum Italy see Rimini
Arinos Brazil 179 B1
Ario de Rosáles Mex. 167 E5
Aripuanã Brazil 177 G6
Aripuanã r. Brazil 176 F5
Aripuanã, Parque Indígena res. Brazil 176 F6
Ariquemes Brazil 176 F5
Aris Namibia 124 C2
Arisaig U.K. 60 D4
Arisaig, Sound of sea chan. U.K. 60 D4
'Arīsh, Wādī al watercourse Egypt 107 A4
Aristazabal Island Canada 150 D4
Arixang Xinjiang China see Wenquan
Ariyalur India 106 C4
Arizaro, Salar de salt flat Arg. 178 C2
Arizona Arg. 178 C5
Arizona state U.S.A. 157 F6
Arizpe Mex. 166 C2
'Arjah Saudi Arabia 108 F5
Arjasa Jawa Indon. 85 F4
Arjeplog Sweden 54 J3
Arjuni Chhattisgarh India 106 D1
Arjuni India 104 E5
Arkadak Rus. Fed. 53 I6
Arkadelphia U.S.A. 161 E5
Arkaig, Loch l. U.K. 60 D4
Arkalyk Kazakh. 102 C1
Arkansas r. U.S.A. 161 F5
Arkansas state U.S.A. 161 E5
Arkansas City AR U.S.A. 161 F5
Arkansas City KS U.S.A. 161 D4
Arkatag Shan mts China 99 E5
Arkell, Mount Y.T. Canada 149 N3
Arkenu, Jabal mt. Libya 108 B5
Arkhangel'sk Rus. Fed. see Archangel
Arkhara Rus. Fed. 90 C2
Arkhipovka Rus. Fed. 90 D4
Árki i. Greece see Arkoi
Arklow Ireland 61 F5
Arkoi i. Greece 69 L6
Arkona Canada 164 E2
Arkona, Kap c. Germany 57 N3
Arkonam India see Arakkonam
Arkport U.S.A. 165 G2

▶Arkticheskiy, Mys c. Rus. Fed. 189 E1
Most northerly point of Asia.

Arkticheskogo Instituta, Ostrova is Rus. Fed. 76 J2
Arkul' Rus. Fed. 52 K4
Arlandag mt. Turkm. 110 D2
Arles France 66 G5
Arlington S. Africa 125 H5
Arlington NY U.S.A. 165 I3
Arlington OH U.S.A. 164 D3
Arlington SD U.S.A. 160 D2
Arlington VA U.S.A. 165 G4
Arlington Heights U.S.A. 164 A2
Arlit Niger 120 D3
Arlon Belgium 62 F5
Arm r. Canada 151 J5
Armadale Australia 135 A8
Armadores i. Indon. 83 C1
Armagh U.K. 61 F3
Armant Egypt 108 D4
Armavir Armenia 113 G2
Armavir Rus. Fed. 113 F1
Armenia country Asia 113 G2
Armenia Col. 176 C3
Armenopolis Romania see Gherla
Armeria Mex. 168 D5
Armidale Australia 138 E3
Armington U.S.A. 156 F3
Armit Lake Canada 151 N1
Armori India 106 D1
Armour U.S.A. 160 D3
Armoy U.K. 61 F2
Armstrong r. Australia 134 E4
Armstrong Canada 152 C4
Armstrong, Mount Y.T. Canada 149 N3
Armstrong Island Cook Is see Rarotonga
Armu r. Rus. Fed. 90 E3
Armur India 106 C2
Armutçuk Dağı mts Turkey 69 L5
Armyanskaya S.S.R. country Asia see Armenia
Arnaoutis, Cape Cyprus see Arnauti, Cape
Arnaud r. Canada 153 H2
Arnauti, Cape Cyprus 107 A2
Årnes Norway 55 G6
Arnett U.S.A. 161 D4
Arnhem Neth. 62 F3
Arnhem, Cape Australia 136 B2
Arnhem Land reg. Australia 134 F3
Arno r. Italy 68 D3
Arno Bay Australia 137 B7
Arnold U.K. 59 F5
Arnold's Cove Canada 153 L5
Arnon r. Jordan see Mawjib, Wādī al
Arnprior Canada 165 G1
Arnsberg Germany 63 I3
Arnstadt Germany 63 K4
Arnstein Germany 63 J5
Arnstorf Germany 63 M6
Aroab Namibia 124 D4
Aroland Canada 152 D4
Arolsen Germany 63 J3
Aroma Sudan 108 E6
Arona Italy 68 C2
Aropuk Lake AK U.S.A. 148 G3
Arorae i. Kiribati 133 H2
Arore i. Kiribati see Arorae
Aroroy Masbate Phil. 82 C3
Aros r. Mex. 166 C2
Arossi i. Solomon Is see San Cristobal
Arpa Kyrg. 98 A4
Arqalyq Kazakh. see Arkalyk
Arquipélago da Madeira aut. reg. Port. 120 B1
Arrabury Australia 137 C5
Arrah India see Ara
Arraias Brazil 179 B1
Arraias, Serra de hills Brazil 179 B1
Ar Ramādī Iraq see Ramādī
Ar Ramlah Jordan 107 B5
Ar Ramthā Jordan 107 C3
Arran i. U.K. 60 D5
Arranmore Island Ireland 61 D3
Ar Raqqah Syria 107 D2
Arras France 62 C4
Ar Rass Saudi Arabia 108 F4
Ar Rastān Syria 107 C2
Ar Rayyān Qatar 110 C5
Arrecife Canary Is 120 B2
Arretium Italy see Arezzo
Arriagá Mex. 168 F5
Arriaga Mex. 167 E4
Ar Rifā'ī Iraq 113 G5
Ar Riḩāb salt flat Iraq 113 G5
Ar Rimāl reg. Saudi Arabia 122 F1
Arrington U.S.A. 165 F5
Ar Riyāḑ Saudi Arabia see Riyadh
Arrochar U.K. 60 E4
Arrojado r. Brazil 179 B1
Arrow, Lough l. Ireland 61 D3
Arrowsmith, Mount N.Z. 139 C6
Arroyo Grande U.S.A. 158 C4
Arroyo Seco Querétaro Mex. 167 F4
Ar Rubay'iyah Saudi Arabia 110 B5
Ar Rummān Jordan 107 B3
Ar Ruq'ī well Saudi Arabia 110 B4
Ar Ruşāfah Syria 107 D2
Ar Ruşayfah Jordan 107 C3
Ar Rustāq Oman 110 E6
Ar Ruţbah Iraq 113 F4
Ar Ruwaydah Saudi Arabia 110 B5
Ar Ruwaydah Saudi Arabia 110 B6
Ar Ruwaydah Syria 107 C2
Års Denmark see Aars
Ars Iran 110 B2
Arseno Lake Canada 150 H1
Arsen'yev Rus. Fed. 90 D3
Arshaly Kazakh. 98 C2
Arsk Rus. Fed. 52 K4
Arta Djibouti 122 E2
Arta Greece 69 I5
Arteaga Coahuila Mex. 167 E3
Arteaga Michoacán Mex. 166 E5
Artem Rus. Fed. 90 D4
Artemisa Cuba 163 D8
Artemivs'k Ukr. 53 H6
Artemovsk Ukr. see Artemivs'k
Artenay France 66 E2
Artesia AZ U.S.A. 159 I5
Artesia NM U.S.A. 157 G6
Arthur Canada 164 E2
Arthur NE U.S.A. 160 C3
Arthur TN U.S.A. 164 D5
Arthur, Lake U.S.A. 164 E3
Arthur's Pass National Park N.Z. 139 C6
Arthur's Town Bahamas 163 F7
Arti Rus. Fed. 51 R4
Artigas research station Antarctica 188 A2
Artigas Uruguay 178 E4
Art'ik Armenia 113 F2
Artillery Lake Canada 151 I2
Artisia Botswana 125 H3
Artois reg. France 62 B4
Artois, Collines d' hills France 62 B4
Artos Dağı mt. Turkey 113 F3
Artova Turkey 112 E2
Artsakh aut. reg. Azer. see Dağlıq Qarabağ
Arts Bogd Uul mts Mongolia 94 E2
Artsiz Ukr. see Artsyz
Artsyz Ukr. 69 M2
Artur de Paiva Angola see Kuvango
Artux Xinjiang China 98 B5
Artvin Turkey 113 F2
Artyk Turkm. 110 E2
Aru, Kepulauan is Indon. 134 F1
Arua Uganda 122 D3
Aruanã Brazil 179 A1

▶Aruba terr. West Indies 169 K6
Self-governing Netherlands territory.

Arumã Brazil 176 F4
Arunachal Pradesh state India 105 H4
Arundel U.K. 59 G8
Arun Gol r. China 95 K2
Arun Qi Nei Mongol China see Naji
Aruppukkottai India 106 C4
Arus, Tanjung pt Indon. 83 B2
Arusha Tanz. 122 D4
Arut r. Indon. 85 E3
Aruwimi r. Dem. Rep. Congo 122 C3
Arvada U.S.A. 156 G5
Arvagh Ireland 61 E4
Arvayheer Mongolia 94 E2
Arviat Canada 151 M2
Arvidsjaur Sweden 54 K4
Arvika Sweden 55 H7
Arvonia U.S.A. 165 F5
Arwā' Saudi Arabia 110 B6
Arwād i. Syria 107 B2
Arwala Maluku Indon. 83 C4
Arxan Nei Mongol China 95 I2
Arxan Xinjiang China 98 D4
Aryanah Tunisia see L'Ariana
Arys' Kazakh. 102 C3
Arzamas Rus. Fed. 53 I5
Arzanah i. U.A.E. 110 D5
Arzberg Germany 63 M4
Arzew Alg. 67 F6
Arzgir Rus. Fed. 113 G1
Arzila Morocco see Asilah
Aš Czech Rep. 63 M4
Asaba Japan 93 D4
Asaba Nigeria 120 D4
Asad, Buḩayrat al resr Syria 107 D1
Asadābād Afgh. 111 H3
Asadābād Iran 110 C3
Asago Japan 92 A3
Asahan r. Indon. 84 B2
Asahi Aichi Japan 92 D3
Asahi Chiba Japan 93 G3
Asahi Fukui Japan 92 C3
Asahi Gifu Japan 92 D2
Asahi Ibaraki Japan 93 G2
Asahi Kanagawa Japan 93 F3
Asahi Mie Japan 92 C3
Asahi Nagano Japan 93 D2
Asahi Toyama Japan 92 D2
Asahi-dake vol. Japan 90 F4
Asahikawa Japan 90 F4
Asaka Japan 93 F3
Asakawa Japan 93 G1
Asake-gawa r. Japan 92 C3
'Asal Egypt 107 A5
Āsalē l. Eth. 122 E2
Asālem Iran 110 C2
'Asalūyeh Iran 110 D5
Asamaga-take hill Japan 92 C4
Asama-yama vol. Japan 93 E2
Asan-man b. S. Korea 91 B5
Asansol India 105 F5
Asao Japan 93 F3
Asar Nei Mongol China 95 I2
Asashina Japan 93 E2
Āsayita Eth. 122 E2
Asbach Germany 63 H4
Asbestos Mountains S. Africa 124 F5
Asbury Park U.S.A. 165 H3
Ascalon Israel see Ashqelon
Ascea Italy 68 F4
Ascensión Bol. 176 F7
Ascensión Chihuahua Mex. 166 D2
Ascensión Nuevo León Mex. 167 F3
Ascension atoll Micronesia see Pohnpei

▶Ascension i. S. Atlantic Ocean 184 H6
Dependency of St Helena.

Aschaffenburg Germany 63 J5
Ascheberg Germany 63 H3
Aschersleben Germany 63 L3
Ascoli Piceno Italy 68 E3
Asculum Italy see Ascoli Piceno
Asculum Picenum Italy see Ascoli Piceno
Ascutney U.S.A. 165 I2
Āseb Eritrea see Assab
Åseda Sweden 55 I8
Åsele Sweden 54 J4
Asenovgrad Bulg. 69 K3
Aşfar, Jabal al mt. Jordan 107 C3
Aşfar, Tall al hill Syria 107 C3

▶Aşgabat Turkm. 110 E2
Capital of Turkmenistan.

Asha Rus. Fed. 51 R5
Ashahi-dake mt. Japan 92 D2
Ashburn U.S.A. 163 D6
Ashburton watercourse Australia 134 A5
Ashburton N.Z. 139 C6
Ashburton Range hills Australia 134 F4
Ashdod Israel 107 B4
Ashdown U.S.A. 161 E5
Asheboro U.S.A. 162 E5
Asher U.S.A. 161 D5
Ashern Canada 151 L5
Asheville U.S.A. 162 D5
Asheweig r. Canada 152 D3
Ashford Australia 138 E2
Ashford U.K. 59 H7
Ash Fork U.S.A. 159 G4
Ashgabat Turkm. see Aşgabat
Ashibetsu Japan 90 F4
Ashigawa Japan 93 E3
Ashikaga Japan 93 F2
Ashington U.K. 58 F3
Ashino-ko l. Japan 93 F3
Ashio Japan 93 F2
Ashio-sanchi mts Japan 93 F2
Ashiwada Japan 93 E3
Ashiya Japan 92 B4
Ashizuri-misaki pt Japan 91 D6
Ashkelon Israel see Ashqelon
Ashkhabad Turkm. see Aşgabat
Ashkum U.S.A. 164 B3
Ashkun reg. Afgh. 111 H3
Ashland AL U.S.A. 163 C5
Ashland ME U.S.A. 162 G2
Ashland NH U.S.A. 165 J2
Ashland OH U.S.A. 164 D3
Ashland OR U.S.A. 156 C4
Ashland VA U.S.A. 165 G5
Ashland WI U.S.A. 160 F2
Ashland City U.S.A. 164 B5
Ashley Australia 138 D2
Ashley MI U.S.A. 164 C2
Ashley ND U.S.A. 160 D2

▶Ashmore and Cartier Islands terr. Australia 134 C3
Australian External Territory.

Ashmore Reef Australia 134 C3
Ashmore Reefs Australia 136 D1
Ashmyany Belarus 55 N9
Ashqelon Israel 107 B4
Ash Shabakah Iraq 113 F5
Ash Shaddādah Syria 113 F3
Ash Shallūfah Egypt 107 A4
Ash Sham Syria see Damascus
Ash Shanāfiyah Iraq 113 G5
Ash Shaqīq well Saudi Arabia 113 F5
Ash Sharāh mts Jordan 107 B4
Ash Sharawrah Saudi Arabia 108 G6
Ash Shāriqah U.A.E. see Sharjah
Ash Sharqāţ Iraq 113 F4
Ash Shaţrah Iraq 113 G5
Ash Shaţţ Egypt 107 A5
Ash Shawbak Jordan 107 B4
Ash Shaybānī well Saudi Arabia 113 F5
Ash Shaykh Ibrāhīm Syria 107 D2
Ash Shiblīyāt hill Saudi Arabia 107 C5
Ash Shiḩr Yemen 108 G7
Ash Shu'āybah Saudi Arabia 113 F6
Ash Shu'bah Saudi Arabia 108 F4
Ash Shurayf Saudi Arabia see Khaybar
Ashta India 104 D5
Ashtabula U.S.A. 164 E3
Ashtarak Armenia 113 G2
Ashti Mahar. India 104 D5
Ashti Mahar. India 106 B2
Ashti Mahar. India 106 C2
Āshtiān Iran 110 C3
Ashton S. Africa 124 E7
Ashton U.S.A. 156 F3
Ashton-under-Lyne U.K. 58 E5
Ashuanipi r. Canada 153 I3
Ashuanipi Lake Canada 153 I3
Ashur Iraq see Ash Sharqāţ
Ashville U.S.A. 163 C5
Ashwaubenon U.S.A. 164 A1
Asi r. Asia 112 E3 see 'Āşī, Nahr al
'Āşī r. Lebanon/Syria see Orontes
'Āşī, Nahr al r. Asia 112 E3
also known as Asi or Orontes
Āsīā Bak Iran 110 C3
Asid Gulf Masbate Phil. 82 C3
Asientos Mex. 166 E4
Āsīfābād India 106 C2
Asika India 106 E2
Asilah Morocco 67 C6
Asinara, Golfo dell' b. Sardinia Italy 68 C4
Asino Rus. Fed. 76 J4
Asipovichy Belarus 53 F5
Asīr Iran 110 D5
'Asīr reg. Saudi Arabia 108 F5

Asisium Italy see Assisi
Askale Pak. 104 C2
Aşkale Turkey 113 F3
Asker Norway 55 G7
Askersund Sweden 55 I7
Askim Norway 55 G7
Askī Mawşil Iraq 113 F3
Askino Rus. Fed. 51 R4
Askival hill U.K. 60 C4
Asl Egypt see 'Asal
Aslanköy r. Turkey 107 B1
Asmar reg. Afgh. 111 H3
▶Asmara Eritrea 108 E6
Capital of Eritrea.
Āsmera Eritrea see Asmara
Åsnen l. Sweden 55 I8
Asō Japan 93 G3
Aso-Kuju Kokuritsu-kōen Japan 91 C6
Asom state India see Assam
Asonli India 96 B2
Asop India 104 C4
Asori Indon. 81 J7
Āsosa Eth. 122 D2
Asotin U.S.A. 156 D3
Aspang-Markt Austria 57 P7
Aspara Kazakh. 98 A4
Aspatria U.K. 58 D4
Aspen U.S.A. 156 G5
Asperg Germany 63 J6
Aspermont U.S.A. 161 C5
Aspiring, Mount N.Z. 139 B7
Aspro, Cape Cyprus 107 A2
Aspromonte, Parco Nazionale dell' nat. park Italy 68 F5
Aspron, Cape Cyprus see Aspro, Cape
Aspur India 111 I6
Asquith Canada 151 J4
As Sa'an Syria 107 C2
Assab Eritrea 108 F7
As Sabsab well Saudi Arabia 110 C5
Assad, Lake resr Syria see Asad, Buḩayrat al
Aş Şadr U.A.E. 110 D5
Aş Şafā lava field Syria 107 C3
Aş Şafāqis Tunisia see Sfax
Aş Şaff Egypt 112 C5
As Safīrah Syria 107 C1
Aş Şaḩrā' al Gharbīyah des. Egypt see Western Desert
Aş Şaḩrā' ash Sharqīyah des. Egypt see Eastern Desert
Assake-Audan, Vpadina depr. Kazakh./Uzbek. 113 J2
'Assal, Lac l. Djibouti see Assal, Lake
Assal, Lake Djibouti 108 F7
Aş Şāliḩīyah Syria 113 F4
As Sallūm Egypt 112 B5
As Salmān Iraq 113 G5
As Salṭ Jordan 107 B3
Assam state India 105 G4
Assamakka Niger 120 D3
As Samāwah Iraq 113 G5
As Samrā' Jordan 107 C3
Aş Şanām reg. Saudi Arabia 108 H5
As Sarīr reg. Libya 121 F2
Assateague Island U.S.A. 165 H4
As Sawādah reg. Saudi Arabia 110 B6
Assayeta Eth. see Āsayita
As Sayḩ Saudi Arabia 110 B6
Assen Neth. 62 G1
Assenede Belgium 62 D3
Assesse Belgium 62 F4
As Sidrah Libya 121 E1
As Sīfah Oman 110 E6
Assigny, Lac l. Canada 153 I3
As Sikak Saudi Arabia 110 C5
Assiniboia Canada 151 J5
Assiniboine r. Canada 151 L5
Assiniboine, Mount Canada 150 H5
Assis Brazil 179 A3
Assisi Italy 68 E3
Aßlar Germany 63 I4
Aş Şubayḩīyah Kuwait 110 B4
Aş Şufayrī well Saudi Arabia 110 B4
As Sukhnah Syria 107 D2
As Sulaymānīyah Iraq see Sulaymānīyah
As Sulaymī Saudi Arabia 108 F4
Aş Şulb reg. Saudi Arabia 110 C5
Aş Şummān plat. Saudi Arabia 110 B5
Aş Şummān plat. Saudi Arabia 110 C6
As Sūq Saudi Arabia 108 F5
As Sūrīyah country Asia see Syria
Aş Şuwar Syria 113 F4
As Suwaydā' Syria 107 C3
As Suways Egypt see Suez
As Suways governorate Egypt 107 A4
Assynt, Loch l. U.K. 60 D2
Astacus Kocaeli Turkey see İzmit
Astakida i. Greece 69 L7
Astakos Greece 69 I5
Astalu Island Pak. see Astola Island
▶Astana Kazakh. 102 D1
Capital of Kazakhstan.
Astaneh Iran 110 C2
Astara Azer. 113 H3
Āstārā Iran 108 G2
Asterabad Iran see Gorgān
Asti Italy 68 C2
Astillero Peru 176 E6
Astin Tag mts China see Altun Shan
Astipálaia i. Greece see Astypalaia
Astola Island Pak. 111 F5
Astor Pak. 99 A6
Astor r. Pak. 111 I3
Astorga Spain 67 C2
Astoria U.S.A. 156 C3
Åstorp Sweden 55 H8
Astrabad Iran see Gorgān
Astrakhan' Rus. Fed. 53 K7
Astrakhan' Bazar Azer. see Cälilabad
Astravyets Belarus 55 N9
Astrida Rwanda see Butare
Astrid Ridge sea feature Antarctica 188 C2
Asturias aut. comm. Spain 67 C2
Asturias, Principado de aut. comm. Spain see Asturias
Asturica Augusta Spain see Astorga
Astypalaia i. Greece 69 L6
Asubulak Kazakh. 98 C2
Asuka Japan 92 B4
Asuke Japan 92 D3
Asuncion i. N. Mariana Is 81 L3
▶Asunción Para. 178 E3
Capital of Paraguay.
Asuwa-gawa r. Japan 92 C2
Aswad Oman 110 E5
Aswān Egypt 108 D5
Aswân Egypt see Aswān
Asyūţ Egypt 112 C6
Asyûţ Egypt see Asyūţ
Ata i. Tonga 133 I4
Atacama, Desierto de des. Chile see Atacama Desert
Atacama, Salar de salt flat Chile 178 C2
▶Atacama Desert Chile 178 C3
Driest place in the world.
Atafu atoll Tokelau 133 I2
Atafu i. Tokelau 186 I6
Atago-san hill Japan 92 B3
Atago-yama hill Japan 93 F3
'Aţā'iţah, Jabal al mt. Jordan 107 B4
Atakent Turkey 107 B1
Atakpamé Togo 120 D4
Atalándi Greece see Atalanti
Atalanti Greece 69 J5
Atalaya Panama 166 [inset] J7
Atalaya Peru 176 D6
Ataléia Brazil 179 C2
Atambua Indon. 134 D2
Atami Japan 93 F3
Atamyrat Turkm. 111 G2
Ataniya Turkey see Adana
Atapupu Timor Indon. 83 C5
'Ataq Yemen 108 G7
Atâr Mauritania 120 B2
Atari Pak. 111 I4
Atascadero U.S.A. 158 C4
Atasu Kazakh. 102 D2
Atatan He r. China 99 E5
Ataúro, Ilha de i. East Timor 83 C5
Atáviros mt. Greece see Attavyros
Atayurt Turkey 107 A1
Atbara Sudan 108 D6
Atbara r. Sudan 108 D6
Atbasar Kazakh. 102 C1
At-Bashy Kyrg. 98 A4
Atchafalaya Bay LA U.S.A. 167 H2
Atchison U.S.A. 160 E4
Atchueelinguk r. AK U.S.A. 148 G3
Atebubu Ghana 120 C4
Atema-yama mt. Japan 93 E1
Ateransk Kazakh. see Atyrau
Āteshān Iran 110 D3
Āteshkhāneh, Kūh-e hill Afgh. 111 F3
Atessa Italy 68 F3
Ath Belgium 62 D4
Athabasca r. Canada 151 I3
Athabasca, Lake Canada 151 I3
Athalia U.S.A. 164 D4
'Athāmīn, Birkat al well Iraq 110 A4
Atharan Hazari Pak. 111 I4
Athboy Ireland 61 F4
Athenae Greece see Athens
Athenry Ireland 61 D4
Athens Canada 165 H1
▶Athens Greece 69 J6
Capital of Greece.
Athens AL U.S.A. 163 C5
Athens GA U.S.A. 163 D5
Athens MI U.S.A. 164 C2
Athens OH U.S.A. 164 D4
Athens PA U.S.A. 165 G3
Athens TN U.S.A. 162 C5
Athens TX U.S.A. 161 E5
Atherstone U.K. 59 F6
Atherton Australia 136 D3
Athies France 62 C5
Athina Greece see Athens
Athínai Greece see Athens
Athleague Ireland 61 D4
Athlone Ireland 61 E4
Athnā', Wādī al watercourse Jordan 107 D3
Athni India 106 B2
Athol N.Z. 139 B7
Athol U.S.A. 165 I2
Atholl, Forest of reg. U.K. 60 E4
Athos mt. Greece 69 K4
Ath Thamad Egypt 107 B5
Ath Thāyat mt. Saudi Arabia 107 C5
Ath Thumāmī well Saudi Arabia 110 B5
Athy Ireland 61 F5
Ati Chad 121 E3
Aţīābād Iran 110 E3
Atico Peru 176 D7
Atigun Pass AK U.S.A. 149 J1
Atikameg Canada 150 H4
Atikameg r. Canada 152 E3
Atik Lake Canada 151 M4
Atikokan Canada 147 I5
Atikonak Lake Canada 153 I3
Atimonan Luzon Phil. 82 C3
Atiquizaya El Salvador 167 H6
Atitlán Guat. 167 H6
Atitlán, Parque Nacional nat. park Guat. 167 H6
Atjeh admin. dist. Indon. see Aceh
Atka Rus. Fed. 77 Q3
Atka AK U.S.A. 149 [inset]
Atka Island AK U.S.A. 149 [inset]
Atkarsk Rus. Fed. 53 J6
Atkinson Point pt N.W.T. Canada 149 O1
Atkri Papua Indon. 83 D3
▶Atlanta GA U.S.A. 163 C5
Capital of Georgia.
Atlanta IN U.S.A. 164 B3
Atlanta MI U.S.A. 164 C1
Atlantic IA U.S.A. 160 E3
Atlantic NC U.S.A. 163 E5
Atlantic City U.S.A. 165 H4
Atlantic-Indian-Antarctic Basin sea feature S. Atlantic Ocean 184 H10
Atlantic-Indian Ridge sea feature Southern Ocean 184 H9
▶Atlantic Ocean 184
2nd largest ocean in the world.
Atlantic Peak U.S.A. 156 F4
Atlantis S. Africa 124 D7
Atlas Bogd mt. Mongolia 94 D3
Atlas Méditerranéen mts Alg. see Atlas Tellien
Atlas Mountains Africa 64 C5
Atlas Saharien mts Alg. 64 E5
Atlas Tellien mts Alg. 67 H6
Atlin Lake B.C./Y.T. Canada 149 N4
Atlixco Mex. 167 F5
Atmakur India 106 C3
Atmautluak AK U.S.A. 148 G3
Atmore U.S.A. 163 C6
Atnur India 106 C2
Atocha Bol. 176 E8
Atoka U.S.A. 161 D5
Atotonilco el Alto Mex. 166 E4
Atouat mt. Laos 86 D3
Atouila, Erg des. Mali 120 C2
Atoyac de Álvarez Mex. 167 E5
Atqan Xinjiang China see Aqqan
Atqasuk AK U.S.A. 148 H1
Atrato r. Col. 176 C2
Atrek r. Iran/Turkm. 110 D2
also known as Etrek
Atropatene country Asia see Azerbaijan
Atsonupuri vol. Rus. Fed. 90 G3
Atsugi Japan 93 F3
Atsumi Aichi Japan 92 D4
Atsumi-hantō pen. Japan 92 D4
Aţ Ţafīlah Jordan 107 B4
Aţ Ţā'if Saudi Arabia 108 F5
Attalea Turkey see Antalya
Attalia Turkey see Antalya
At Tamīmī Libya 112 A4
Attapu Laos 86 D4
Attavyros mt. Greece 69 L6
Attawapiskat Canada 152 E3
Attawapiskat r. Canada 152 E3
Attawapiskat Lake Canada 152 D3
Aţ Ţawīl mts Saudi Arabia 113 E5
At Taysīyah plat. Saudi Arabia 113 F5
Attendorn Germany 63 H3
Attersee l. Austria 57 N7
Attica IN U.S.A. 164 B3
Attica NY U.S.A. 165 F2
Attica OH U.S.A. 164 D3
Attigny France 62 E5
Attikamagen Lake Canada 153 I3
Attila Line Cyprus 107 A2
Attleborough U.K. 59 I6
Attopeu Laos see Attapu
Attu Greenland 147 M3
Attu AK U.S.A. 148 [inset]
Aţ Ţubayq reg. Saudi Arabia 107 C5
▶Attu Island AK U.S.A. 148 [inset]
Most westerly point of North America.
At Tūnisīyah country Africa see Tunisia
Aţ Ţūr Egypt 112 D5
Attur India 106 C4
Aţ Ţuwayyah well Saudi Arabia 113 F6
Atuk Mountain hill AK U.S.A. 148 E3
Åtvidaberg Sweden 55 I7
Atwari Bangl. 99 E8
Atwater U.S.A. 158 C3
Atwood U.S.A. 160 C4
Atwood Lake U.S.A. 164 E3
Atyashevo Rus. Fed. 53 J5
Atyrau Kazakh. 100 E2
Atyraū admin. div. Kazakh. see Atyrauskaya Oblast'
Atyrau Oblast admin. div. Kazakh. see Atyrauskaya Oblast'
Atyrauskaya Oblast' admin. div. Kazakh. 51 Q6
Aua Island P.N.G. 81 K7
Aub Germany 63 K5
Aubagne France 66 G5
Aubange Belgium 62 F5
Aubarede Point Luzon Phil. 82 C2
Aubenas France 66 G4
Aubergenville France 62 B6
Auboué France 62 F5
Aubrey Cliffs mts U.S.A. 159 G4
Aubry Lake N.W.T. Canada 149 P2
Auburn r. Australia 137 E5
Auburn Canada 164 E2
Auburn AL U.S.A. 163 C5
Auburn CA U.S.A. 158 C2
Auburn IN U.S.A. 164 C3
Auburn KY U.S.A. 164 B5
Auburn ME U.S.A. 165 J1
Auburn NE U.S.A. 160 E3
Auburn NY U.S.A. 165 G2
Auburn Range hills Australia 136 E5
Aubusson France 66 F4
Auch France 66 E5
Auche Myanmar 86 B1
Auchterarder U.K. 60 F4
▶Auckland N.Z. 139 E3
5th most populous city in Oceania.
Auckland Islands N.Z. 133 G7
Auden Canada 152 D4
Audenarde Belgium see Oudenaarde
Audo mts Eth. 122 E3
Audo Range mts Eth. see Audo
Audruicq France 62 C4
Audubon U.S.A. 160 E3
Aue Germany 63 M4
Auerbach Germany 63 M4
Auerbach in der Oberpfalz Germany 63 L5
Auersberg mt. Germany 63 M4
Auezov Kazakh. 98 C2
Augathella Australia 137 D5
Augher U.K. 61 E3
Aughnacloy U.K. 61 F3
Aughrim Ireland 61 F5
Augrabies S. Africa 124 E5
Augrabies Falls S. Africa 124 E5
Augrabies Falls National Park S. Africa 124 E5
Au Gres U.S.A. 164 D1
Augsburg Germany 57 M6
Augusta Australia 135 A8
Augusta Sicily Italy 68 F6
Augusta AR U.S.A. 161 F5
Augusta GA U.S.A. 163 D5
Augusta KY U.S.A. 164 C4
▶Augusta ME U.S.A. 165 K1
Capital of Maine.
Augusta MT U.S.A. 156 E3
Augusta Auscorum France see Auch
Augusta Taurinorum Italy see Turin
Augusta Treverorum Germany see Trier
Augusta Vindelicorum Germany see Augsburg
Augustine Island AK U.S.A. 148 I4
Augusto de Lima Brazil 179 B2
Augustus, Mount Australia 135 B6
Auke Bay AK U.S.A. 149 N4
Aukštaitijos nacionalinis parkas nat. park Lith. 55 O9
Aulavik National Park Canada 146 G2
Auld, Lake salt flat Australia 134 C5
Auliye Ata Kazakh. see Taraz
Aulnoye-Aymeries France 62 D4
Aulon Albania see Vlorë
Aulong i. Palau 82 [inset]
Ault France 62 B4
Auluptagel i. Palau 82 [inset]
Aumale Alg. see Sour el Ghozlane
Aumale France 62 B5
Aundh India 106 B2
Aundhi India 106 D1
Aunglan Myanmar 86 A3
Auob watercourse Namibia/S. Africa 124 E4
Aupaluk Canada 153 H2
Auponhia Maluku Indon. 83 C3
Aur i. Malaysia 84 D2
Aura Fin. 55 M6
Auraiya India 104 D4
Aurangabad Bihar India 105 F4
Aurangabad Mahar. India 106 B2
Aure r. France 59 F9
Aurich Germany 63 H1
Aurigny i. Channel Is see Alderney
Aurilândia Brazil 179 A2
Aurillac France 66 F4
Aurkuning Kalimantan Indon. 85 E3
Aurora Mindanao Phil. 82 C5
Aurora CO U.S.A. 156 G5
Aurora IL U.S.A. 164 A3
Aurora MO U.S.A. 161 E4
Aurora NE U.S.A. 160 D3
Aurora UT U.S.A. 159 H2
Aurora Island Vanuatu see Maéwo
Aurukun Australia 136 C2
Aus Namibia 124 C4
Au Sable U.S.A. 164 D1
Au Sable Point U.S.A. 164 D1
Auskerry i. U.K. 60 G1
Austin IN U.S.A. 164 C4
Austin MN U.S.A. 160 E3
Austin NV U.S.A. 158 E2
▶Austin TX U.S.A. 161 D6
Capital of Texas.
Austin, Lake salt flat Australia 135 B6
Austintown U.S.A. 164 E3
Austral Downs Australia 136 B4
Australes, Îles is Fr. Polynesia see Tubuai Islands
▶Australia country Oceania 132 C4
Largest and most populous country in Oceania, and 6th largest in the world.
Australian-Antarctic Basin sea feature S. Atlantic Ocean 186 C9
Australian Antarctic Territory reg. Antarctica 188 G2
Australian Capital Territory admin. div. Australia 138 D5
Austria country Europe 57 N7
Austvågøy i. Norway 54 I2
Autazes Brazil 177 G4
Autesiodorum France see Auxerre
Authie r. France 62 B4
Autlán Mex. 166 D5
Autti Fin. 54 O3
Auvergne reg. France 66 F4
Auvergne, Monts d' mts France 66 F4
Auxerre France 66 F3
Auxi-le-Château France 62 C4
Auxonne France 66 G3
Auyuittuq National Park Canada 147 L3
Auzangate, Nevado mt. Peru 176 D6
Ava MO U.S.A. 161 E4
Ava NY U.S.A. 165 H2
Avalik r. AK U.S.A. 148 H1
Avallon France 66 F3
Avalon U.S.A. 158 D5
Avalon Peninsula Canada 153 L5
Ávalos Mex. 167 E3
Avān Iran 113 G3
Avarau atoll Cook Is see Palmerston
Avaré Brazil 179 A3
Avaricum France see Bourges
▶Avarua Cook Is 187 J7
Capital of the Cook Islands, on Rarotonga.
Avawam U.S.A. 164 D5
Avaz Iran 111 F3
Aveiro Port. 67 B3
Aveiro, Ria de est. Port. 67 B3
Āvej Iran 110 C3
Avellino Italy 68 F4
Avenal U.S.A. 158 C3
Avenhorn Neth. 62 E2
Avenio France see Avignon
Aversa Italy 68 F4
Avesnes-sur-Helpe France 62 D4
Avesta Sweden 55 J6
Aveyron r. France 66 E4
Avezzano Italy 68 E3
Aviemore U.K. 60 F3
Avignon France 66 G5
Ávila Spain 67 D3
Avilés Spain 67 D2
Avion France 62 C4
Avis U.S.A. 165 G3
Avlama Dağı mt. Turkey 107 A1
Avlama Dağı mts Turkey 107 A1
Avlona Albania see Vlorë
Avnyugskiy Rus. Fed. 52 J3
Avoca Australia 138 A6
Avoca r. Australia 138 A5
Avoca Ireland 61 F5
Avoca IA U.S.A. 160 E3
Avoca NY U.S.A. 165 G2
Avola Sicily Italy 68 F6
Avon r. England U.K. 59 E6
Avon r. England U.K. 59 E7
Avon r. England U.K. 59 F8
Avon r. Scotland U.K. 60 F3
Avon U.S.A. 165 G2
Avondale U.S.A. 159 G5
Avonmore r. Ireland 61 F5
Avonmore U.S.A. 164 F3
Avonmouth U.K. 59 E7
Avranches France 66 D2
Avre r. France 62 C5
Avsuyu Turkey 107 C1
Avuavu Solomon Is 133 G2
Avveel Fin. see Ivalo
Avvil Fin. see Ivalo
A'waj r. Syria 107 B3
Awaji Japan 92 B4
Awaji-shima i. Japan 92 A4
Awakino N.Z. 139 E4
'Awālī Bahrain 110 C5
Awang Lombok Indon. 85 G5
Awano Japan 93 F2
Awanui N.Z. 139 D2
Awara Japan 92 C2
Awarawar, Tanjung pt Indon. 85 F4
Āwarē Eth. 122 E3
'Awāriḑ, Wādī al watercourse Syria 107 D2
Awarua Point N.Z. 139 B7
Āwash Eth. 122 E3
Āwash r. Eth. 122 E2
Awa-shima i. Japan 91 E5
Āwash National Park Eth. 122 D3
Awasib Mountains Namibia 124 B3
Awat Xinjiang China 98 C4
Awatere r. N.Z. 139 E5
Awbārī Libya 120 E2
Awbeg r. Ireland 61 D5
'Awdah well Saudi Arabia 110 C6
'Awdah, Hawr al imp. l. Iraq 113 G5
Aw Dheegle Somalia 121 H4
Awe, Loch l. U.K. 60 D4
Aweil Sudan 121 F4
Awka Nigeria 120 D4
Awo r. Indon. 83 B3
Awserd W. Sahara 120 B2
Awu vol. Indon. 83 C2
Awuna r. AK U.S.A. 148 I1
Axe r. England U.K. 59 D8
Axe r. England U.K. 59 E7
Axedale Australia 138 B6
Axel Heiberg Glacier Antarctica 188 I1
Axel Heiberg Island Canada 147 I2
Axim Ghana 120 C4
Axminster U.K. 59 E8
Axum Eth. see Āksum
Ay France 62 E5
Ay Kazakh. 98 C3
Ayabe Japan 92 B3
Ayachi, Jbel mt. Morocco 64 D5
Ayacucho Arg. 178 E5
Ayacucho Peru 176 D6
Ayadaw Myanmar 86 A2
Ayagoz Kazakh. 102 F2
Ayagoz watercourse Kazakh. 98 B3
Ayaguz Kazakh. see Ayagoz
Ayakkum Hu salt l. China 99 E5
Ayaköz Kazakh. see Ayagoz
Ayakulik AK U.S.A. 148 I4
Ayama Japan 92 C4
Ayan Rus. Fed. 77 O4
Ayancık Turkey 112 D2
Ayang N. Korea 91 B5
Ayaş Turkey 112 D2
Ayase Japan 93 F3
Āybak Afgh. 111 H2
Aybas Kazakh. 53 K7
Aydar r. Ukr. 53 H6
Aydarko'l ko'li l. Uzbek. 102 C3
Aydere Turkm. 110 E2
Aydın Turkey 69 L6
Aydıncık Turkey 107 A1
Aydın Dağları mts Turkey 69 L5
Aydingkol Hu marsh China 98 E4
Aýdyň Turkm. 110 D2
Āyelu Terara vol. Eth. 108 F7
Ayer U.S.A. 165 J2
Ayers Rock hill Australia see Uluṟu
Ayeyarwady r. Myanmar see Irrawaddy
Aygulakskiy Khrebet mts Rus. Fed. 98 D2
Aygyrzhal Kazakh. 98 C2
Ayila Ri'gyü mts Xizang China 99 B6
Áyios Dhimítrios Greece see Agios Dimitrios
Áyios Evstrátios i. Greece see Agios Efstratios
Áyios Nikólaos Greece see Agios Nikolaos
Áyios Yeóryios i. Greece see Agios Georgios
Aykol Xinjiang China 98 C4
Aylesbury N.Z. 139 D6
Aylesbury U.K. 59 G7
Aylett U.S.A. 165 G5
Ayllón Spain 67 E3
Aylmer Ont. Canada 164 E2
Aylmer Que. Canada 165 H1
Aylmer Lake Canada 151 I1
Aynabulak Kazakh. 98 B3
'Ayn al 'Abd well Saudi Arabia 110 C4
'Ayn al Baidā' Saudi Arabia 107 C4
'Ayn al Bayḑā' well Syria 107 C2
'Ayn al Ghazalah well Libya 112 A4
'Ayn al Maqfī spring Egypt 112 C6
'Ayn Dāllah spring Egypt 112 B6
Ayní Tajik. 111 H2
'Ayn 'Īsá Syria 107 D1
'Ayn Tabaghbugh spring Egypt 112 B5
'Ayn Tumayrah spring Egypt 112 B5
'Ayn Zaytūn Egypt 112 B5
Ayod Sudan 108 D8
Ayon, Ostrov i. Rus. Fed. 77 R3
'Ayoûn el 'Atroûs Mauritania 120 C3
Ayr Australia 136 D3
Ayr Canada 164 E2
Ayr U.K. 60 E5
Ayr r. U.K. 60 E5
Ayr, Point of U.K. 58 D5
Ayrag Nuur salt l. Mongolia 94 C1
Ayrancı Turkey 112 D3
Ayre, Point of Isle of Man 58 C4
Aytos Bulg. 69 L3
Ayu i. Papua Indon. 83 D2
Ayu, Kepulauan atoll Papua Indon. 83 D2
A Yun Pa Vietnam 87 E4
Ayuthia Thai. see Ayutthaya
Ayutla Guerrero Mex. 167 F5
Ayutla Jalisco Mex. 166 D4
Ayutthaya Thai. 87 C4
Ayvacık Turkey 69 L5
Ayvalı Turkey 112 E3
Ayvalık Turkey 69 L5
Azai Japan 92 C3
Azak Rus. Fed. see Azov
Azalia U.S.A. 164 C4
Azamgarh India 105 E4
Azaouâd reg. Mali 120 C3
Azaouagh, Vallée de watercourse Mali/Niger 120 D3
Azaran Iran see Hashtrud
Azärbaycan country Asia see Azerbaijan
Azärbayjan country Asia see Azerbaijan
Azare Nigeria 120 E3
A'zāz Syria 107 C1
Azbine mts Niger see L'Aïr, Massif de
Azdavay Turkey 112 D2
Azerbaijan country Asia 113 G2
Azerbaydzhanskaya S.S.R. country Asia see Azerbaijan
Azhikal India 106 B4
Aziscohos Lake U.S.A. 165 J1
'Azīzābād Iran 110 E4
Aziziye Turkey see Pınarbaşı
Azogues Ecuador 176 C4
Azores terr. N. Atlantic Ocean 184 G3
Azores-Biscay Rise sea feature N. Atlantic Ocean 184 G3
Azotus Israel see Ashdod
Azov Rus. Fed. 53 H7
Azov, Sea of Rus. Fed./Ukr. 53 H7
Azovs'ke More sea Rus. Fed./Ukr. see Azov, Sea of
Azovskoye More sea Rus. Fed./Ukr. see Azov, Sea of
Azraq, Bahr el r. Sudan 108 D6 see Blue Nile
Azraq ash Shīshān Jordan 107 C4
Azrou Morocco 64 C5
Aztec U.S.A. 159 I3
Azuaga Spain 67 D4
Azuchi Japan 92 C3
Azuero, Península de pen. Panama 166 [inset] J8
Azul r. Mex. 167 H5
Azul, Cordillera mts Peru 176 C5
Azul Meambar, Parque Nacional nat. park Hond. 166 [inset] I6
Azuma Gunma Japan 93 F2
Azuma Gunma Japan 93 F2
Azuma Ibaraki Japan 93 G3
Azuma-san vol. Japan 91 F5
Azumaya-san mt. Japan 93 E2
Azumi Japan 93 D2
Azusa-ko resr Japan 92 D2
'Azza Gaza see Gaza
Azzaba Alg. 68 B6
Az Zahrān Saudi Arabia see Dhahran
Az Zaqāzīq Egypt 112 C5
Az Zarbah Syria 107 C1
Az Zarqā' Jordan 107 C3
Az Zāwiyah Libya 121 E1
Az Zawr, Ra's pt Saudi Arabia 113 H6
Azzeffāl hills Mauritania/W. Sahara 120 B2

Az Zubayr Iraq 113 G5
Az Zuqur i. Yemen 108 F7

B

Ba, Sông r. Vietnam 87 E4
Baa Indon. 83 B5
Baabda Lebanon 107 B3
Baai r. Indon. 85 G2
Ba'albek Lebanon 107 C2
Ba'al Hazor mt. West Bank 107 B4
Baan Baa Australia 138 D3
Baardheere Somalia 122 E3
Baatsagaan Mongolia 94 D2
Bab India 104 D4
Bābā, Kūh-e mts Afgh. 111 H3
Baba Burnu pt Turkey 69 L5
Babadağ mt. Azer. 113 H2
Babadag Romania 69 M2
Babadurmaz Turkm. 110 E2
Babaeski Turkey 69 L4
Babahoyo Ecuador 176 C4
Babai India 104 D5
Babai r. Nepal 105 E3
Babak Phil. 82 D5
Bābā Kalān Iran 110 C4
Bab al Mandab strait Africa/Asia 108 F7
Babana Sulawesi Barat Indon. 83 A3
Babanusa Sudan 108 C7
Babao Qinghai China see Qilian
Babao Yunnan China 96 E4
Babar i. Maluku Indon. 83 D4
Babar, Kepulauan is Maluku Indon. 83 D4
Babati Tanz. 123 D4
Babau Timor Indon. 83 B5
Babayevo Rus. Fed. 52 G4
Babayurt Rus. Fed. 113 G2
Babbage r. Y.T. Canada 149 M1
B'abdā Lebanon see Baabda
Babeldaob i. Palau 82 [inset]
Bab el Mandeb, Straits of Africa/Asia see Bāb al Mandab
Babelthuap i. Palau see Babeldaob
Babi, Pulau i. Indon. 84 B2
Babian Jiang r. China 96 D4
Babine r. Canada 150 E4
Babine Lake Canada 150 E4
Babine Range mts Canada 150 E4
Bābol Iran 110 D2
Bābol Sar Iran 110 D2
Babongo Cameroon 121 E4
Baboon Point S. Africa 124 D7
Baboua Cent. Afr. Rep. 122 B3
Babruysk Belarus 53 F5
Babstovo Rus. Fed. 90 D2
Babu China see Hezhou
Babuhri India 104 B4
Babusar Pass Pak. 111 I3
Babuyan Palawan Phil. 82 B4
Babuyan i. Phil. 82 C2
Babuyan Channel Phil. 82 C2
Babuyan Islands Phil. 82 C2
Bacaadweyn Somalia 122 E3
Bacabáchi Mex. 166 C3
Bacabal Brazil 177 J4
Bacalar Mex. 167 H5
Bacalar Chico, Boca sea chan. Mex. 167 I5
Bacan i. Maluku Indon. 83 C3
Bacang Qinghai China 94 E5
Bacanora Mex. 166 C2
Bacarra Luzon Phil. 82 C2
Bacău Romania 69 L1
Baccaro Point Canada 153 I6
Băc Giang Vietnam 86 D2
Bacha China 90 D2
Bach Ice Shelf Antarctica 188 L2
Bach Long Vi, Đao i. Vietnam 86 D2
Bachu Xinjiang China 98 B5
Bachuan China see Tongliang
Back r. Australia 136 C3
Back r. Canada 151 M1
Bačka Palanka Serbia 69 H2
Backbone Mountain U.S.A. 164 F4
Backbone Ranges mts N.W.T. Canada 149 O3
Backe Sweden 54 J5
Backstairs Passage Australia 137 B7
Băc Liêu Vietnam 87 D5
Băc Ninh Vietnam 86 D2
Bacnotan Luzon Phil. 82 C2
Baco, Mount Mindoro Phil. 82 C3
Bacoachi Mex. 166 C2
Bacoachi watercourse Mex. 157 F7
Bacobampo Mex. 166 C3
Bacolod Negros Phil. 82 C4
Bacqueville, Lac l. Canada 152 G2
Bacqueville-en-Caux France 59 H9
Bacubirito Mex. 166 D3
Baculin Bay Mindanao Phil. 82 D5
Baculin Point Mindanao Phil. 82 D4
Bād Iran 110 D3
Bada China see Xilin
Bada mt. Eth. 122 D3
Bada i. Myanmar 87 B5
Badabayhan Turkm. 111 F2
Bad Abbach Germany 63 M6
Badagara India 106 B4
Badain Jaran Nei Mongol China 94 E4
Badain Jaran Shamo des. Nei Mongol China 94 E3
Badajoz Spain 67 C4
Badami India 106 B3
Badampaharh India 105 F5
Badanah Saudi Arabia 113 F5
Badaojiang China see Baishan
Badarpur India 105 H4
Badas Brunei 85 F1
Badas, Kepulauan is Indon. 84 D2
Badaun India see Budaun
Bad Axe U.S.A. 164 D2
Bad Bederkesa Germany 63 I1
Bad Bergzabern Germany 63 H5
Bad Berleburg Germany 63 I3
Bad Bevensen Germany 63 K1
Bad Blankenburg Germany 63 L4
Bad Camberg Germany 63 I4
Badderen Norway 54 M2
Bad Driburg Germany 63 J3
Bad Düben Germany 63 M3
Bad Dürkheim Germany 63 I5
Bad Dürrenberg Germany 63 M3
Bademli Turkey see Aladağ
Bademli Geçidi pass Turkey 112 C3
Bad Ems Germany 63 H4
Baden Austria 57 P6
Baden Switz. 66 I3
Baden-Baden Germany 63 I6
Baden-Württemberg land Germany 63 I6
Bad Essen Germany 63 I2
Bad Grund (Harz) Germany 63 K3
Bad Harzburg Germany 63 K3
Bad Hersfeld Germany 63 J4
Bad Hofgastein Austria 57 N7
Bad Homburg vor der Höhe Germany 63 I4
Badia Polesine Italy 68 D2
Badin Pak. 111 H5
Bad Ischl Austria 57 N7
Bādiyat ash Shām des. Asia see Syrian Desert
Bad Kissingen Germany 63 K4
Bad Königsdorff Poland see Jastrzębie-Zdrój
Bad Kösen Germany 63 L3
Bad Kreuznach Germany 63 H5
Bad Laasphe Germany 63 I4
Badlands reg. ND U.S.A. 160 C2
Badlands reg. SD U.S.A. 160 C3
Badlands National Park U.S.A. 160 C3
Bad Langensalza Germany 63 K3
Bad Lauterberg im Harz Germany 63 K3
Bad Liebenwerda Germany 63 N3
Bad Lippspringe Germany 63 I3
Bad Marienberg (Westerwald) Germany 63 H4
Bad Mergentheim Germany 63 J5
Bad Nauheim Germany 63 I4
Badnawar India 104 C5
Badnera India 106 C1
Bad Neuenahr-Ahrweiler Germany 62 H4
Bad Neustadt an der Saale Germany 63 K4
Badnor India 104 C4
Badong China 97 F2
Ba Đông Vietnam 87 D5
Badou Shandong China 95 I4
Badou Togo 120 D4
Bad Pyrmont Germany 63 J3
Badrah Iraq 113 G4
Bad Reichenhall Germany 57 N7
Badr Hunayn Saudi Arabia 108 E5
Bad Sachsa Germany 63 K3
Bad Salzdetfurth Germany 63 K2
Bad Salzuflen Germany 63 I2
Bad Salzungen Germany 63 K4
Bad Schwalbach Germany 63 I4
Bad Schwartau Germany 57 M4
Bad Segeberg Germany 57 M4
Bad Sobernheim Germany 63 H5
Badu Island Australia 136 C1
Badulla Sri Lanka 106 D5
Bad Vilbel Germany 63 I4
Bad Wilsnack Germany 63 L2
Bad Windsheim Germany 63 K5
Badzhal Rus. Fed. 90 D2
Badzhal'skiy Khrebet mts Rus. Fed. 90 D2
Bad Zwischenahn Germany 63 I1
Bae Colwyn U.K. see Colwyn Bay
Baesweiler Germany 62 G4
Baeza Spain 67 E5
Bafatá Guinea-Bissau 120 B3
Baffa Pak. 111 I3
Baffin Basin sea feature Arctic Ocean 189 K2
Baffin Bay sea Canada/Greenland 147 L2
Baffin Island Canada 147 L3
2nd largest island in North America, and 5th in the world.
Bafia Cameroon 120 E4
Bafilo Togo 120 D4
Bafing r. Africa 120 B3
Bafoulabé Mali 120 B3
Bafoussam Cameroon 120 E4
Bāfq Iran 110 D4
Bafra Turkey 112 D2
Bafra Burnu pt Turkey 112 D2
Bāft Iran 110 E4
Bafwaboli Dem. Rep. Congo 122 C3
Bafwasende Dem. Rep. Congo 122 C3
Baga Bogd Uul mts Mongolia 94 E2
Bagac Bay Luzon Phil. 82 C3
Bagaha India 105 F4
Bagahak, Gunung hill Malaysia 85 G1
Bagalkot India 106 B2
Bagalkote India see Bagalkot
Bagamoyo Tanz. 123 D4
Bagan China 96 C1
Bagan Datoh Malaysia see Bagan Datuk
Bagan Datuk Malaysia 84 C2
Baganga Mindanao Phil. 82 D5
Baganian Peninsula Mindanao Phil. 82 C5
Bagan Serai Malaysia 84 C1
Bagansiapiapi Sumatera Indon. 84 C2
Baganuur Mongolia 95 G2
Bagar Xizang China 99 F7
Bagata Dem. Rep. Congo 122 B4
Bagdad U.S.A. 159 G4
Bagdarin Rus. Fed. 89 K2
Bagé Brazil 178 F4
Bagenalstown Ireland 61 F5
Bagerhat Bangl. 105 G5
Bageshwar India 104 D3
Baggs U.S.A. 156 G4
Baggy Point U.K. 59 C7
Bagh India 104 C5
Bàgh a' Chaisteil U.K. see Castlebay
Baghak Pak. 111 G4
Baghbaghū Iran 111 F2
Baghdād Iraq 113 G4
Capital of Iraq.
Bāgh-e Malek Iran 110 C4
Bagherhat Bangl. see Bagerhat
Bāghīn Iran 110 E4
Baghlān Afgh. 111 H2
Baghrān Afgh. 111 G3
Baginda, Tanjung pt Indon. 84 D3
Bağırsak r. Turkey 107 C1
Bağırsak Deresi r. Syria/Turkey see Sājūr, Nahr
Bagley U.S.A. 160 E2
Bagley Icefield AK U.S.A. 149 J4
Baglung Nepal 105 E3
Bagnères-de-Luchon France 66 E5
Bagnuiti r. Nepal 99 D8
Bago Myanmar see Pegu
Bago Negros Phil. 82 C4
Bagong China see Sansui
Bagor India 111 I5
Bagrationovsk Rus. Fed. 55 L9
Bagrax Xinjiang China see Bohu
Bagrax Hu l. China see Bosten Hu
Baguio Luzon Phil. 82 C2
Baguio Mindanao Phil. 82 D5
Baguio Point Luzon Phil. 82 C2
Bagur, Cabo c. Spain see Begur, Cap de
Bagzane, Monts mts Niger 120 D3
Bahādorābād-e Bālā Iran 110 E4
Bahadurganj Nepal 99 C8
Bahalda India 105 F5
Bahāmabād Iran see Rafsanjān
Bahamas, The country West Indies 163 E7
Bahara Pak. 111 G5
Baharampur India 105 G4
Bahardipur Pak. 111 H5
Bahariya Oasis oasis Egypt see Bahrīyah, Wāḥāt al
Bahau r. Indon. 85 G2
Bahau Malaysia 84 C2
Bahaur Kalimantan Indon. 85 F3
Bahawalnagar Pak. 111 I4
Bahawalpur Pak. 111 H4
Bahçe Adana Turkey 107 B1
Bahçe Osmaniye Turkey 112 E3
Baher Dar Eth. see Bahir Dar
Baheri India 104 D3
Bahia Brazil see Salvador
Bahia state Brazil 179 C1
Bahía, Islas de la is Hond. 166 [inset] I5
Bahía Asunción Mex. 157 E8
Bahía Blanca Arg. 178 D5
Bahia Honda Point Palawan Phil. 82 B4
Bahía Kino Mex. 166 C2
Bahía Laura Arg. 178 C7
Bahía Negra Para. 178 E2
Bahía Tortugas Mex. 166 B3
Bahir Dar Eth. 122 D2
Bahl India 104 C3
Bahlā Oman 110 E6
Bahomonte Sulawesi Indon. 83 B3
Bahraich India 105 E4
Bahrain country Asia 110 C5
Bahrain, Gulf of Asia 110 C5
Bahrām Beyg Iran 110 C2
Bahrāmjerd Iran 110 E4
Bahrīyah, Wāḥāt al oasis Egypt 112 C6
Bahuaja-Sonene, Parque Nacional nat. park Peru 176 E6
Bahubulu i. Indon. 83 B3
Baia Mare Romania 69 J1
Baiazeh Iran 110 D3
Baicang China 105 G3
Baicheng Henan China see Xiping
Baicheng Jilin China 95 J2
Baicheng Xinjiang China 98 C4
Baidoa Somalia see Baydhabo
Baidoi Co l. Xizang China 99 D6
Baidu China 97 H3
Baidunzi Gansu China 94 F4
Baidunzi Gansu China 98 F4
Baie-aux-Feuilles Canada see Tasiujaq
Baie-Comeau Canada 153 H4
Baie-du-Poste Canada see Mistissini
Baie-St-Paul Canada 153 H5
Baie-Trinité Canada 153 I4
Baie Verte Canada 153 K4
Baigou He r. China 95 I4
Baiguan China see Shangyu
Baiguo Hubei China 97 G2
Baiguo Hunan China 97 G3
Baihanchang China 96 C3
Baihar India 104 E5
Baihe Jilin China 90 C4
Baihe Shaanxi China 97 F1
Bai He r. China 95 I3
Baiji Iraq see Bayjī
Baijiantan Xinjiang China 98 D3
Baikal, Lake l. Rus. Fed. 94 F1
Deepest and 2nd largest lake in Asia, and 8th largest in the world.
Baikouquan Xinjiang China 98 D3
Baikunthpur India 105 E5
Bailang Nei Mongol China 95 J2
Baile an Bhuinneánaigh Ireland see Ballybunion
Baile an Chinnéidigh Ireland see Newtown Mount Kennedy
Baile Átha Cliath Ireland see Dublin
Baile Átha Luain Ireland see Athlone
Baile Mhartainn U.K. 60 B3
Baile na Finne Ireland 61 D3
Băileşti Romania 69 J2
Bailey Range hills Australia 135 C7
Bailianhe Shuiku resr China 97 G2
Bailieborough Ireland 61 F4
Bailingmiao Nei Mongol China 95 G3
Bailleul France 62 C4
Baillie r. Canada 151 J1
Baillie Islands N.W.T. Canada 149 O1
Bailong Gansu China see Hadapu
Bailong Jiang r. China 96 E1
Baima Qinghai China 96 D1
Baima Xizang China see Baxoi
Baima Jian mt. China 97 H2
Baimuru P.N.G. 81 K8
Bain r. U.K. 58 G5
Bainang Xizang China see Norkyung
Bainbridge GA U.S.A. 163 C6
Bainbridge IN U.S.A. 164 B4
Bainbridge NY U.S.A. 165 H2
Bainduru India 106 B3
Baingoin Xizang China 99 E7
Baini China see Yuqing
Baiona Spain 67 B2
Baiqên China 96 D1
Baiquan China 90 B3
Bā'ir Jordan 107 C4
Bā'ir, Wādī watercourse Jordan/Saudi Arabia 107 C4
Bairab Co l. China 99 C6
Bairat India 104 D4
Baird U.S.A. 161 D5
Baird, Mount Y.T. Canada 149 N2
Baird Inlet AK U.S.A. 148 F3
Baird Mountains AK U.S.A. 148 H2
Bairiki Kiribati 186 H5
Capital of Kiribati, on Tarawa atoll.
Bairin Qiao Nei Mongol China 95 I3
Bairin Youqi Nei Mongol China see Daban
Bairin Zuoqi Nei Mongol China see Lindong
Bairnsdale Australia 138 C6
Bais Negros Phil. 82 C4
Baisha Chongqing China 96 E2
Baisha Hainan China 97 F5
Baisha Sichuan China 97 F2
Baishan Guangxi China see Mashan
Baishan Jilin China 90 B4
Baishan Jilin China see Baishanzhen
Bai Shan mt. Gansu China 98 F4
Baishanzhen China 90 B4
Baishi Shuiku resr Liaoning China 95 J3
Baishui Shaanxi China 95 G5
Baishui Sichuan China 96 E1
Baishui Jiang r. China 96 E1
Baisogala Lith. 55 M9
Baitadi Nepal 104 E3
Baitang China 96 C1
Bai Thường Vietnam 86 D3
Baixi China see Yibin
Baixiang Hebei China 95 H4
Baixingt Nei Mongol China 95 J3
Baiyanghe Xinjiang China 98 E4
Baiyashi China see Dong'an
Baiyin Gansu China 94 F4
Baiyü China 96 C2
Baiyuda Desert Sudan 108 D6
Baiyu Shan mts China 95 F4
Baja Hungary 68 H1
Baja, Punta pt Mex. 166 B2
Baja California pen. Mex. 166 B2
Baja California state Mex. 166 B2
Baja California Sur state Mex. 166 B3
Bajan Mex. 167 E3
Bajau i. Indon. 84 D2
Bajaur reg. Pak. 111 H3
Bajawa Flores Indon. 83 B5
Baj Baj India 105 G5
Bājgīrān Iran 110 E2
Bājil Yemen 108 F7
Bajo Boquete Panama 166 [inset] J7
Bajo Caracoles Arg. 178 B7
Bajoga Nigeria 120 E3
Bajoi China 96 D2
Bajrakot India 105 F5
Baka, Bukit mt. Indon. 85 F3
Bakala Cent. Afr. Rep. 121 F4
Bakanas Kazakh. 102 E3
Bakanas watercourse Kazakh. 98 B3
Bakar Pak. 111 H5
Bakaucengal Kalimantan Indon. 85 G3
Bakayan, Gunung mt. Indon. 85 G2
Bakel Senegal 120 B3
Baker CA U.S.A. 158 E4
Baker ID U.S.A. 156 E3
Baker LA U.S.A. 161 F6
Baker MT U.S.A. 156 G3
Baker NV U.S.A. 159 F2
Baker OR U.S.A. 156 D3
Baker WV U.S.A. 165 F4
Baker, Mount vol. U.S.A. 156 C2
Baker Butte mt. U.S.A. 159 H4
Baker Island terr. N. Pacific Ocean 133 I1
United States Unincorporated Territory.
Baker Island AK U.S.A. 149 N5
Baker Lake salt flat Australia 135 D6
Baker Lake Canada 151 M1
Baker Lake l. Canada 151 M1
Baker's Dozen Islands Canada 152 F2
Bakersfield U.S.A. 158 D4
Bakersville U.S.A. 162 D4
Bâ Kêv Cambodia 87 D4
Bakhardok Turkm. see Bokurdak
Bākharz mts Iran 111 F3
Bakhasar India 104 B4
Bakhirevo Rus. Fed. 90 C2
Bakhmach Ukr. 53 G6
Bakhma Dam Iraq see Bēkma, Sadd
Bakhmut Ukr. see Artemivs'k
Bākhtarān Iran see Kermānshāh
Bakhtegan, Daryācheh-ye l. Iran 110 D4
Bakhtiari Country reg. Iran 110 C3
Bakhty Kazakh. 98 C3
Bakı Azer. see Baku
Baki 122 E2
Bakırköy Turkey 69 M4
Bakkejord Norway 54 K2
Bakloh India 104 C2
Bako Eth. 122 D3
Bako National Park Malaysia 85 E2
Bakongan Sumatera Indon. 84 B2
Bakouma Cent. Afr. Rep. 122 C3
Baksan Rus. Fed. 113 F2
Baku Azer. 113 H2
Capital of Azerbaijan.
Baku Dem. Rep. Congo 122 D3
Bakung i. Indon. 84 D2
Bakutis Coast Antarctica 188 J2
Baky Azer. see Baku
Balâ Turkey 112 D3
Bala U.K. 59 D6
Bala, Cerros de mts Bol. 176 E6
Balabac Phil. 82 B4
Balabac i. Phil. 82 B5
Balabac Strait Malaysia/Phil. 85 G1
Balabalangan, Kepulauan atolls Indon. 85 G3
Baladeh Māzandarān Iran 110 C2
Baladeh Māzandarān Iran 110 C2
Baladek Rus. Fed. 90 D1
Balaghat India 104 E5
Balaghat Range hills India 106 B2
Bālā Howz Iran 110 E4
Balaiberkuak Kalimantan Indon. 85 E3
Balaikarangan Kalimantan Indon. 85 E2
Balaipungut Sumatera Indon. 84 C2
Balairiam Kalimantan Indon. 85 E3
Balaka Malawi 123 D5
Balakān Azer. 113 G2
Balakhna Rus. Fed. 52 I4
Balakhta Rus. Fed. 88 G1
Balaklava Australia 137 B7
Balaklava Ukr. 112 D1
Balakleya Ukr. see Balakliya
Balakliya Ukr. 53 H6
Balakovo Rus. Fed. 53 J5
Bala Lake l. U.K. 59 D6
Balaman India 104 E4
Balan India 104 B4
Balancán Mex. 167 H5
Balanda Rus. Fed. see Kalininsk
Balanda r. Rus. Fed. 53 J6
Balan Dağı hill Turkey 69 M6
Balanga Luzon Phil. 82 C3
Balangir India see Bolangir
Balantak Sulawesi Indon. 83 B3
Balaözen r. Kazakh./Rus. Fed. see Malyy Uzen'
Balarampur India see Balrampur
Balase r. Indon. 83 B3
Balashov Rus. Fed. 53 I6
Balasore India see Baleshwar
Balaton, Lake Hungary 68 G1
Balatonboglár Hungary 68 G1
Balatonfüred Hungary 68 G1
Balauring Indon. 83 B5
Balbina Brazil 177 G4
Balbina, Represa de resr Brazil 177 G4
Balbriggan Ireland 61 F4
Balchik Bulg. 69 M3
Balclutha N.Z. 139 B8
Balcones Escarpment U.S.A. 161 C6
Bald Knob U.S.A. 164 E5
Bald Mountain U.S.A. 159 F3
Baldock Lake Canada 151 L3
Baldwin Canada 164 F1
Baldwin FL U.S.A. 163 D6
Baldwin MI U.S.A. 164 C2
Baldwin PA U.S.A. 164 F3
Baldwin Peninsula AK U.S.A. 148 G2
Baldy Mount Canada 156 D2
Baldy Mountain hill Canada 151 K5
Baldy Peak U.S.A. 159 I5
Bal'dzhikan Rus. Fed. 95 G1
Bale Indon. 84 C3
Bâle Switz. see Basel
Baléa Mali 120 B3
Baleares is Spain see Balearic Islands
Baleares, Islas is Spain see Balearic Islands
Baleares Insulae is Spain see Balearic Islands
Balearic Islands is Spain 67 G4
Balears is Spain see Balearic Islands
Balears, Illes is Spain see Balearic Islands
Baleh r. Malaysia 85 F2
Baleia, Ponta da pt Brazil 179 D2
Bale Mountains National Park Eth. 122 D3
Baleno Masbate Phil. 82 C3
Baler Luzon Phil. 82 C3
Baler Bay Luzon Phil. 82 C3
Baleshwar India 105 F5
Balestrand Norway 55 E6
Baléyara Niger 120 D3
Balezino Rus. Fed. 51 Q4
Balfate Hond. 166 [inset] I6
Balfe's Creek Australia 136 D4
Balfour Downs Australia 134 C5
Balgatay Mongolia see Shilüüstey
Balgo Australia 134 D5
Balguntay Xinjiang China 98 D4
Bali India 104 C4
Bali i. Indon. 85 F5
Bali prov. Indon. 85 F5
Bali, Laut sea Indon. 85 F4
Bali, Selat sea chan. Indon. 85 F5
Balia India see Ballia
Baliangao Mindanao Phil. 82 C4
Baliapal India 105 F5
Bali Barat, Taman Nasional nat. park Bali Indon. 85 F5
Balige Sumatera Indon. 84 B2
Baliguda India 106 D1
Balihan Nei Mongol China 95 I3
Balıkesir Turkey 69 L5
Balīkh r. Syria/Turkey 107 D2
Balikpapan Kalimantan Indon. 85 G3
Balikpapan, Teluk b. Indon. 85 G3
Balimbing Phil. 82 B5
Balimila Reservoir India 106 D2
Balimo P.N.G. 81 K8
Balin Nei Mongol China 95 J1
Baling Malaysia 84 C1
Balingen Germany 57 L6
Balingian Sarawak Malaysia 85 F2
Balingian r. Malaysia 85 F2
Balinqiao Nei Mongol China see Bairin Qiao
Balintang Channel Phil. 82 C2
Balintore U.K. 60 F3
Bali Sea Indon. see Bali, Laut
Baliungan i. Phil. 82 C5
Balk Neth. 62 F2
Balkanabat Turkm. 110 D2
Balkan Mountains Bulg./Serbia 69 J3
Balkassar Pak. 111 I3
Balkhash Kazakh. 102 D2
Balkhash, Lake Kazakh. 102 D2
3rd largest lake in Asia.
Balkhash, Ozero l. Kazakh. see Balkhash, Lake
Balkuduk Kazakh. 53 J7
Ballachulish U.K. 60 D4
Balladonia Australia 135 C8
Balladoran Australia 138 D3
Ballaghaderreen Ireland 61 D4
Ballan Australia 138 B6
Ballangen Norway 54 J2
Ballantine U.S.A. 156 F3
Ballantrae U.K. 60 E5
Ballarat Australia 138 A6
Ballard, Lake salt flat Australia 135 C7
Ballarpur India 106 C2
Ballater U.K. 60 F3
Ballé Mali 120 C3
Ballena, Punta pt Chile 178 B3
Balleny Islands Antarctica 188 H2
Ballia India 105 F4
Ballina Australia 138 F2
Ballina Ireland 61 C3
Ballinafad Ireland 61 D3
Ballinalack Ireland 61 E4
Ballinamore Ireland 61 E3
Ballinasloe Ireland 61 D4
Ballindine Ireland 61 D4
Ballinger U.S.A. 161 D6
Ballinluig U.K. 60 F4
Ballinrobe Ireland 61 C4
Ballston Spa U.S.A. 165 I2
Ballybay Ireland 61 F3
Ballybrack Ireland see An Baile Breac
Ballybunion Ireland 61 C5
Ballycanew Ireland 61 F5
Ballycastle Ireland 61 C3
Ballycastle U.K. 61 F2
Ballyclare U.K. 61 G3
Ballyconnell Ireland 61 E3
Ballygar Ireland 61 D4
Ballygawley U.K. 61 E3
Ballygorman Ireland 61 E2
Ballyhaunis Ireland 61 D4
Ballyheigue Ireland 61 C5
Ballykelly U.K. 61 E2
Ballylynan Ireland 61 E5
Ballymacmague Ireland 61 E5
Ballymahon Ireland 61 E4
Ballymena U.K. 61 F3
Ballymoney U.K. 61 F2
Ballymote Ireland 61 D3
Ballynahinch U.K. 61 G3
Ballyshannon Ireland 61 D3
Ballyteige Bay Ireland 61 F5
Ballyvaughan Ireland 61 C4
Ballyward U.K. 61 F3
Balmartin U.K. see Baile Mhartainn
Balmer India see Barmer
Balmertown Canada 151 M5
Balmorhea U.S.A. 161 C6
Baloa Sulawesi Indon. 83 B3
Balochistan prov. Pak. 111 G4
Balok, Teluk b. Indon. 85 D3
Balombo Angola 123 B5
Balonne r. Australia 138 D2
Balontohe i. Indon. 83 C2
Balotra India 104 C4
Balpyk Bi Kazakh. 98 B3
Balqash Kazakh. see Balkhash
Balqash Köli l. Kazakh. see Balkhash, Lake
Balrampur India 105 E4
Balranald Australia 138 A5
Balş Romania 69 K2
Balsam Lake Canada 165 F1
Balsas Brazil 177 I5
Balsas Mex. 167 F5
Balsas r. Mex. 166 E5
Balta Ukr. 53 F7
Baltasound U.K. 60 [inset]
Baltay Rus. Fed. 53 J5
Bălţi Moldova 53 E7
Baltic U.S.A. 164 E3
Baltic Sea g. Europe 55 J9
Balṭīm Egypt 112 C5
Balṭīm Egypt see Balṭīm
Baltimore S. Africa 125 I2
Baltimore MD U.S.A. 165 G4
Baltimore OH U.S.A. 164 D4
Baltinglass Ireland 61 F5
Baltistan reg. Pak. 104 C2
Baltiysk Rus. Fed. 55 K9
Balu India 96 B3

Baluarte, Arroyo *watercourse* U.S.A. 161 D7
Baluch Ab *well* Iran 110 E4
Balui *r.* Malaysia 85 F2
Balumundam *Sumatera* Indon. 84 B2
Baluran, Gunung *mt.* Indon. 85 F3
Baluran, Taman Nasional *nat. park* Indon. 85 F4
Balurghat India 105 G4
Balut *i.* Phil. 82 D5
Balve Germany 63 H3
Balvi Latvia 55 O8
Balya Turkey 69 L5
Balyaga Rus. Fed. 95 G1
Balykchy Kyrg. 102 E3
Balykshi Kazakh. 100 E2
Balyktyg-Khem *r.* Rus. Fed. 94 D1
Balyqshy Kazakh. *see* Balykshi
Bam Iran 110 E4
Bām Iran 110 E2
Bama China 96 E3

▶Bamako Mali 120 C3
Capital of Mali.

Bamba Mali 120 C3
Bambang *Luzon* Phil. 82 C2
Bambannan *i.* Phil. 82 C5
Bambari Cent. Afr. Rep. 122 C3
Bambel *Sumatera* Indon. 84 B2
Bamberg Germany 63 K5
Bamberg U.S.A. 163 D5
Bambili Dem. Rep. Congo 122 C3
Bambio Cent. Afr. Rep. 122 B3
Bamboesberg *mts* S. Africa 125 H6
Bamboo Creek Australia 134 C5
Bambouti Cent. Afr. Rep. 122 C3
Bambuí Brazil 179 B3
Bambulung *Kalimantan* Indon. 85 F3
Bamda China 96 C2
Bamenda Cameroon 120 E4
Bāmīān Afgh. 111 G3
Bamiancheng *Liaoning* China 95 K3
Bamiantong China *see* Muling
Bamingui Cent. Afr. Rep. 122 C3
Bamingui-Bangoran, Parc National du *nat. park* Cent. Afr. Rep. 122 B3
Bamkeri *Papua* Indon. 83 D3
Bâmnak Cambodia 87 D4
Bamnet Narong Thai. 86 C4
Bamoa Mex. 166 C3
Bamor India 104 D4
Bamori India 106 C1
Bam Posht *reg.* Iran 111 F5
Bam Posht, Kūh-e *mts* Iran 111 F5
Bampton U.K. 59 D8
Bampūr Iran 111 F5
Bampūr *watercourse* Iran 111 E5
Bamrūd Iran 111 F3
Bam Tso *l.* China 105 G3
Bamyili Australia 134 F3
Banaba *i.* Kiribati 133 G2
Banabuiu, Açude *resr* Brazil 177 K5
Bañados del Izozog *swamp* Bol. 176 F7
Banagher Ireland 61 E4
Banahao, Mount *vol. Luzon* Phil. 82 C3
Banalia Dem. Rep. Congo 122 C3
Banamana, Lagoa *l.* Moz. 125 K2
Banamba Mali 120 C3
Banámichi Mex. 166 C2
Banana Australia 136 E5
Bananal, Ilha do *i.* Brazil 177 H6
Bananga India 87 A6
Banapur India 106 E2
Banas *r.* India 104 D4
Banawaya *i.* Indon. 83 A4
Banaz Turkey 69 M5
Ban Ban Laos 86 C3
Banbar *Xizang* China 99 F7
Ban Bo Laos 86 C3
Banbridge U.K. 61 F3
Ban Bua Chum Thai. 86 C4
Ban Bua Yai Thai. 86 C4
Ban Bungxai Laos 86 D4
Banbury U.K. 59 F6
Ban Cang Vietnam 86 C2
Banc d'Arguin, Parc National du *nat. park* Mauritania 120 B2
Ban Channabot Thai. 86 C3
Banchory U.K. 60 G3
Bancoran *i.* Phil. 82 B5
Bancroft Canada 165 G1
Bancroft Zambia *see* Chililabombwe
Banda Dem. Rep. Congo 122 C3
Banda India 104 E4
Banda, Kepulauan *is Maluku* Indon. 83 D4
Banda, Laut *sea* Indon. 83 D4
Banda Aceh *Sumatera* Indon. 84 A1
Banda Banda, Mount Australia 138 F3
Banda Daud Shah Pak. 111 H3
Bandahara, Gunung *mt.* Indon. 84 B2
Bandama *r.* Côte d'Ivoire 120 C4
Bandaneira *Maluku* Indon. 83 D4
Bandān Kūh *mts* Iran 111 F4
Bandar India *see* Machilipatnam
Bandar Moz. 123 D5
Bandar Abbas Iran *see* Bandar-e 'Abbās
Bandaragung *Sumatera* Indon. 84 D4
Bandarban Bangl. 105 H5
Bandar-e 'Abbās Iran 110 E5
Bandar-e Anzalī Iran 110 C2
Bandar-e Deylam Iran 110 C4
Bandar-e Emām Khomeynī Iran 110 C4
Bandar-e Lengeh Iran 110 D5
Bandar-e Ma'shur Iran 110 C4
Bandar-e Nakhīlū Iran 110 D5
Bandar-e Pahlavī Iran *see* Bandar-e Anzalī
Bandar-e Shāh Iran *see* Bandar-e Torkeman
Bandar-e Shāhpūr Iran *see* Bandar-e Emām Khomeynī
Bandar-e Shīū' Iran 110 D5
Bandar-e Torkeman Iran 110 D2
Bandar Lampung *Sumatera* Indon. 84 D4
Bandarpunch *mt.* India 104 D3

▶Bandar Seri Begawan Brunei 85 F1
Capital of Brunei.

Banda Sea Indon. *see* Banda, Laut
Band-e Amīr *l.* Afgh. 111 G3
Band-e Amīr, Daryā-ye *r.* Afgh. 111 G2
Band-e Bābā *mts* Afgh. 111 F3
Bandeira Brazil 179 C1
Bandeirante Brazil 179 A1
Bandeiras, Pico de *mt.* Brazil 179 C3
Bandelierkop S. Africa 125 I2
Banderas Mex. 166 D2
Banderas, Bahía de *b.* Mex. 168 C4
Band-e Sar Qom Iran 110 D3
Band-e Torkestān *mts* Afgh. 111 F3
Bandhi Pak. 111 H5
Bandhogarh India 104 E5
Bandi *r.* India 104 C4
Bandiagara Mali 120 C3
Bandikui India 104 D4
Bandipur National Park India 106 C4
Bandırma Turkey 69 L4
Bandjarmasin *Kalimantan* Indon. *see* Banjarmasin
Bandon Ireland 61 D6
Bandon *r.* Ireland 61 D6
Ban Don Thai. *see* Surat Thani
Bandon U.S.A. 156 B4
Band Qīr Iran 110 C4
Bandra India 106 B2
Bandundu Dem. Rep. Congo 122 B4
Bandung *Jawa* Indon. 85 D4
Bandya Australia 135 C6
Bāneh Iran 110 B3
Banemo *Halmahera* Indon. 83 D2
Banera India 104 C4
Banes Cuba 169 I4
Banff Canada 150 H5
Banff U.K. 60 G3
Banff National Park Canada 150 G5
Banfora Burkina 120 C3
Bang, Gunung *mt.* Indon. 85 F2
Banga Dem. Rep. Congo 123 C4
Banga *Mindanao* Phil. 82 D5
Banga *r. Mindanao* Phil. 82 D5
Bangai Point *Mindanao* Phil. 82 D5
Bangalore India 106 C3
Bangalow Australia 138 F2
Banganga *r.* India 99 B8
Bangaon India 105 G5
Bangar Brunei 85 F1
Bangar *Luzon* Phil. 82 C2
Bangassou Cent. Afr. Rep. 122 C3
Bangdag Co *salt l.* China 99 C6
Banggai *Sulawesi* Indon. 83 B3
Banggai, Kepulauan *is* Indon. 81 G7
Banggai, Kepulauan *is* Indon. 83 B3
Banggi *i.* Malaysia 85 G1
Banghāzī Libya *see* Benghazi
Banghiang, Xé *r.* Laos 86 D3
Bangil *Jawa* Indon. 85 F4
Bangka *i.* Indon. 83 C2
Bangka *i.* Indon. 84 D3
Bangka, Selat *sea chan.* Indon. 83 C2
Bangka, Selat *sea chan.* Indon. 84 D3
Bangka-Belitung *prov.* Indon. 84 D3
Bangkal *Kalimantan* Indon. 85 F3
Bangkala, Teluk *b.* Indon. 83 A4
Bangkalan *Jawa* Indon. 85 F4
Bangkalan *i.* Indon. 83 B3
Bangkaru *i.* Indon. 84 B2
Bangkinang *Sumatera* Indon. 84 C2
Bangkir *Sulawesi* Indon. 83 B2
Bangko *Sumatera* Indon. 84 C3
Bangkog Co *salt l.* China 99 E7

▶Bangkok Thai. 87 C4
Capital of Thailand.

Bangkok, Bight of *b.* Thai. 87 C4
Bangkor *Xizang* China 99 D7
Bangkuang *Kalimantan* Indon. 85 F3
Bangkulu *i.* Indon. 83 B3
Bangkulua *Sumbawa* Indon. 85 G5
Bangla *state* India *see* West Bengal

▶Bangladesh *country* Asia 105 G4
7th most populous country in the world.

Bang Lang, Ang Kep Nam Thai. 84 C1
Bangluo *Gansu* China 94 F5
Bangma Shan *mts* China 96 C4
Bang Mun Nak Thai. 86 C3
Ba Ngoi Vietnam 87 E5
Bangolo Côte d'Ivoire 120 C4
Bangong Co *salt l.* China/India 104 D2
Bangor Ireland 61 C3
Bangor *Northern Ireland* U.K. 61 G3
Bangor *Wales* U.K. 58 C5
Bangor *ME* U.S.A. 162 G2
Bangor *MI* U.S.A. 164 B2
Bangor *PA* U.S.A. 165 H3
Bangs, Mount U.S.A. 159 G3
Bangsalsepulun *Kalimantan* Indon. 85 G3
Bang Saphan Yai Thai. 87 B5
Bangsund Norway 54 G4
Bangued *Luzon* Phil. 82 C2

▶Bangui Cent. Afr. Rep. 122 B3
Capital of the Central African Republic.

Bangui *Luzon* Phil. 82 C2
Bangunpurba *Sumatera* Indon. 84 B2
Bangweulu, Lake Zambia 123 C5
Banhā Egypt 112 C5
Banhine, Parque Nacional de *nat. park* Moz. 125 K2
Ban Hin Heup Laos 86 C3
Ban Houei Sai Laos *see* Huayxay
Ban Huai Khon Thai. 86 C3
Ban Huai Yang Thai. 87 B5
Bani *Luzon* Phil. 82 B2
Bani, Jbel *ridge* Morocco 64 C6
Bania Cent. Afr. Rep. 122 B3
Bani-Bangou Niger 120 D3
Banifing *r.* Mali 120 C3
Banī Forūr, Jazīreh-ye *i.* Iran 110 D5
Banihal Pass and Tunnel India 104 C2
Bani Point *Luzon* Phil. 82 B3
Banister *r.* U.S.A. 164 F5
Banī Suwayf Egypt 112 C5
Banī Walīd Libya 121 E1
Banī Wuṭayfān *well* Saudi Arabia 110 C5
Bāniyās *Al Qunayṭirah* Syria 107 B3
Bāniyās *Ṭarṭūs* Syria 107 B2
Bani Yas *reg.* U.A.E. 110 D6
Banja Luka Bos.-Herz. 68 G2
Banjarmasin *Kalimantan* Indon. 85 F3
Banjes, Liqeni i *resr* Albania 69 I4
Banjiegou *Xinjiang* China 98 E4
Banjieta *Hebei* China 95 I3

▶Banjul Gambia 120 B3
Capital of The Gambia.

Banka India 105 F4
Banka Banka Australia 134 F4
Bankapur India 106 B3
Bankass Mali 120 C3
Ban Kengkabao Laos 86 D3
Ban Khao Yoi Thai. 87 B4
Ban Khok Kloi Thai. 87 B5
Bankilaré Niger 120 D3
Bankobankoang *i.* Indon. 85 G4
Banks Island *B.C.* Canada 149 O5
Banks Island *N.W.T.* Canada 146 F2
Banks Islands Vanuatu 133 G3
Banks Lake Canada 151 M2
Banks Lake U.S.A. 156 D3
Banks Peninsula N.Z. 139 D6
Banks Strait Australia 137 [inset]
Bankura India 105 F5
Ban Lamduan Thai. 87 C4
Banlan China 97 F3
Ban Mae La Luang Thai. 86 B3
Banmaw Myanmar *see* Bhamo
Banmo Myanmar *see* Bhamo
Bann *r.* Ireland 61 F5
Bann *r.* U.K. 61 F2
Ban Nakham Laos 86 D3
Bannerman Town Bahamas 163 E7
Banning U.S.A. 158 E5
Banningville Dem. Rep. Congo *see* Bandundu
Ban Noi Myanmar 86 B3
Ban Nong Kung Thai. 86 D3
Bannu Pak. 111 H3
Bano India 105 F5
Bañolas Spain *see* Banyoles
Ban Phai Thai. 86 C3
Ban Phôn Laos *see* Lamam
Ban Phôn-Hông Laos 86 C3
Banqiao *Gansu* China 94 E4
Banqiao *Yunnan* China 96 C3
Banqiao *Yunnan* China 96 E3
Ban Sanam Chai Thai. 84 C1
Bansgaon *Uttar Prad.* India 99 C8
Bansi *Bihar* India 105 F4
Bansi *Rajasthan* India 104 C4
Bansi *Uttar Prad.* India 104 D4
Bansi *Uttar Prad.* India 105 E4
Bansihari India 105 G4
Banská Bystrica Slovakia 57 Q6
Banspani India 105 F5
Bansur India 104 D4
Ban Sut Ta Thai. 86 B3
Ban Suwan Wari Thai. 86 D4
Banswara India 104 C5
Banta *i.* Indon. 83 A5
Bantaeng *Sulawesi* Indon. 83 A4
Bantayan *i.* Phil. 82 C4
Banteer Ireland 61 D5
Banten *prov.* Indon. 84 D4
Ban Tha Song Yang Thai. 86 B3
Banthat *mts* Cambodia/Thai. *see* Cardamom Range
Ban Tha Tum Thai. 86 C4
Ban Thepha Thai. 84 C1
Ban Tôp Laos 86 D3
Bantry Ireland 61 C6
Bantry Bay Ireland 61 C6
Bantul Indon. 85 E4
Bantval India 106 B3
Ban Wang Chao Thai. 86 B3
Ban Woen Laos 86 C3
Ban Xepian Laos 86 D4
Banyak, Pulau-pulau *is* Indon. 84 B2
Ban Yang Yong Thai. 87 B4
Banyo Cameroon 120 E4
Banyoles Spain 67 H2
Banyuasin *r.* Indon. 84 D3
Banyuwangi *Jawa* Indon. 85 F5
Banzare Coast Antarctica 188 G2
Banzare Seamount *sea feature* Indian Ocean 185 N9
Banzart Tunisia *see* Bizerte
Banzkow Germany 63 L1
Banzyville Dem. Rep. Congo *see* Mobayi-Mbongo
Bao'an China *see* Shenzhen
Bao'an *Qinghai* China 94 E5
Bao'an *Shaanxi* China *see* Zhidan
Baochang *Nei Mongol* China 95 H3
Baocheng China 96 E1
Baodi *Tianjin* China 95 I4
Baoding *Hebei* China 95 H4
Baofeng China 97 G1
Baohe China *see* Weixi
Baoji *Shaanxi* China 95 F5
Baoji *Shaanxi* China 95 F5
Baokang *Hubei* China 97 F2
Baokang *Nei Mongol* China 95 J2
Bao Lac Vietnam 86 D2
Baolin China 90 C3
Bao Lôc Vietnam 87 D5
Baoqing China 90 D3
Baoro Cent. Afr. Rep. 122 B3
Baoshan China 96 C3
Baotou *Nei Mongol* China 95 G3
Baotou Shan *mt.* China/N. Korea 90 C4
Baoulé *r.* Mali 120 C3
Baoxing China 96 D2
Baoying China 97 H1
Baoyou China *see* Ledong
Bap India 104 C4
Bapatla India 106 D3
Bapaume France 62 C4
Baptiste Lake Canada 165 F1
Bapu China *see* Meigu
Baq'ā' *oasis* Saudi Arabia 113 F6
Baqbaq Egypt *see* Buqbuq
Baqên *Xizang* China 99 F6
Baqên *Xizang* China 99 F7
Baqiu China 97 G3
Ba'qūbah Iraq 113 G4
Bar Montenegro 69 H3
Bar Rus. Fed. 95 F1
Bara *Buru* Indon. 83 C3
Bara Sudan 108 D7
Baraawe Somalia 122 E3
Barabai *Kalimantan* Indon. 85 F3
Barabanki India 104 E4
Bara Banki India *see* Barabanki
Baraboo U.S.A. 160 F3
Baracaju *r.* Brazil 179 A1
Baracaldo Spain *see* Barakaldo
Baracoa Cuba 169 J4
Baradá, Nahr *r.* Syria 107 C3
Baradine Australia 138 D3
Baradine *r.* Australia 138 D3
Baragarh India *see* Bargarh
Barahona Dom. Rep. 169 J5
Barahoti *Uttaranchal* India 99 B7
Barail Range *mts* India 105 H4
Baraka *watercourse* Eritrea/Sudan 121 G3
Barakaldo Spain 67 E2
Barakī Barak Afgh. 111 H3
Baralaba Australia 136 E5
Bara Lacha Pass India 104 D2
Baralzon Lake Canada 151 L3
Baram India 105 F5
Baram *r.* Malaysia 85 F1
Baram, Tanjung *pt* Malaysia 85 F1
Baramati India 106 B2
Baramula India *see* Baramulla
Baramulla India 104 C2
Baran India 104 D4
Baran *r.* Pak. 111 H5
Bārān, Kūh-e *mts* Iran 111 F3
Baranavichy Belarus 55 O10
Barang, Dasht-i *des.* Afgh. 111 F3
Baranikha Rus. Fed. 77 R3
Baranīs Egypt 108 E5
Baranîs Egypt *see* Baranīs
Barannda India 104 E4
Baranof *AK* U.S.A. 149 N4
Baranof Island *AK* U.S.A. 149 N4
Baranovichi Belarus *see* Baranavichy
Baranowicze Belarus *see* Baranavichy
Baraouéli Mali 120 C3
Baraque de Fraiture *hill* Belgium 62 F4
Barasat India 105 G5
Barat Daya, Kepulauan *is Maluku* Indon. 83 C4
Barati *Timor* Indon. 83 B5
Baraut India 104 D3
Barbacena Brazil 179 C3
Barbados *country* West Indies 169 M6
Barbar, Gebel el *mt.* Egypt *see* Barbar, Jabal
Barbar, Jabal *mt.* Egypt 107 A5
Barbara Lake Canada 152 D4
Barbastro Spain 67 G2
Barbate Spain 67 D5
Barbechitos Mex. 166 D3
Barberton S. Africa 125 J3
Barberton U.S.A. 164 E3
Barbezieux-St-Hilaire France 66 D4
Barbour Bay Canada 151 M2
Barbourville U.S.A. 164 D5
Barboza *Panay* Phil. 82 C4
Barbuda *i.* Antigua and Barbuda 169 L5
Barby (Elbe) Germany 63 L3
Barcaldine Australia 136 D4
Barce Libya *see* Al Marj
Barcelona Spain 67 H3
Barcelona Venez. 176 F1
Barcelonnette France 66 H4
Barcelos Brazil 176 F4
Barchfeld Germany 63 K4
Barcino Spain *see* Barcelona
Barclay de Tolly *atoll* Fr. Polynesia *see* Raroia
Barclayville Liberia 120 C4
Barcoo *watercourse* Australia 136 C5
Barcoo Creek *watercourse* Australia *see* Cooper Creek
Barcoo National Park Australia *see* Welford National Park
Barcs Hungary 68 G2
Bärdä Azer. 113 G2
Bárðarbunga *mt.* Iceland 54 [inset]
Bardaskan Iran 110 E3
Bardawīl, Khabrat al *salt pan* Saudi Arabia 107 D4
Bardawīl, Sabkhat al *lag.* Egypt 107 A4
Barddhaman India 105 F5
Bardejov Slovakia 53 D6
Bardera Somalia *see* Baardheere
Bardhaman India *see* Barddhaman
Bardsey Island U.K. 59 C6
Bardsīr Iran 110 E4
Barðsneshorn *pt* Iceland 50 D2
Bardstown U.S.A. 164 C5
Barduli Italy *see* Barletta
Bardwell U.S.A. 161 F4
Bareilly India 104 D3
Barellan Australia 138 C5
Barentin France 59 H9
Barentsburg Svalbard 76 C2
Barents Sea Arctic Ocean 52 I1
Barentu Eritrea 108 E6
Bareo *Sarawak* Malaysia 85 F2
Barfleur, Pointe de *pt* France 59 F9
Barga *Xizang* China 99 C7
Bārgāh Iran 110 E5
Bargarh India 105 E5
Barghamad Iran 110 E2
Bargrennan U.K. 60 E5
Bargteheide Germany 63 K1
Barguna Bangl. 105 G5
Barhaj India 105 E4
Barham Australia 138 B5
Bari Italy 68 G4
Bari Doab *lowland* Pak. 111 I4
Barika Alg. 64 F4
Barinas Venez. 176 D2
Baripada India 105 F5
Bariri Brazil 179 A3
Bari Sadri India 104 C4
Barisal Bangl. 105 G5
Barisan, Pegunungan *mts* Indon. 84 C3
Barito *r.* Indon. 85 F3
Barium Italy *see* Bari
Barkal Bangl. 105 H5
Barkam China 96 D2
Barkan, Ra's-e *pt* Iran 110 C4
Barkava Latvia 55 O8
Bark Lake Canada 165 G1
Barkly East S. Africa 125 H6
Barkly Homestead Australia 136 A3
Barkly-Oos S. Africa *see* Barkly East
Barkly Tableland *reg.* Australia 136 A3
Barkly-Wes S. Africa *see* Barkly West
Barkly West S. Africa 124 G5
Barkol *Xinjiang* China 94 C3
Barkol Hu *salt l. Xinjiang* China 94 C3
Barla Turkey 69 N5
Bârlad Romania 69 L1
Barlag Gol *watercourse* Mongolia 94 C2
Bar-le-Duc France 62 F6
Barlee, Lake *salt flat* Australia 135 B7
Barlee Range *hills* Australia 135 A5
Barletta Italy 68 G4
Barlow *Y.T.* Canada 149 M3
Barlow Lake Canada 151 K2
Barmah Forest Australia 138 B5
Barmedman Australia 138 C5
Barmen-Elberfeld Germany *see* Wuppertal
Barmer India 104 B4
Barm Fīrūz, Kūh-e *mt.* Iran 110 C4
Barmouth U.K. 59 C6
Barnala India 104 C3
Barnard, Mount Canada/U.S.A. 149 M4
Barnard Castle U.K. 58 F4
Barnato Australia 138 B3
Barnaul Rus. Fed. 88 E2
Barnegat Bay U.S.A. 165 H4
Barnes Icecap Canada 147 K2
Barnesville *GA* U.S.A. 163 D5
Barnesville *MN* U.S.A. 160 D2
Barneveld Neth. 62 F2
Barneville-Carteret France 59 F9
Barneys Lake *imp. l.* Australia 138 B4
Barney Top *mt.* U.S.A. 159 H3
Barnhart *TX* U.S.A. 167 E2
Barnsley U.K. 58 F5
Barnstable U.S.A. 165 J3
Barnstaple U.K. 59 C7
Barnstaple Bay U.K. 59 C7
Barnstorf Germany 63 I2
Barnum Bay Palau 82 [inset]
Baro Nigeria 120 D4
Baroda *Gujarat* India *see* Vadodara
Baroda *Madh. Prad.* India 104 D4
Barong China 96 C2
Barons Range *hills* Australia 135 D6
Barowghīl, Kowtal-e Afgh. 111 I2
Barpathar India 96 B3
Barpeta India 105 G4
Bar Pla Soi Thai. *see* Chon Buri
Barques, Point Aux U.S.A. 164 D1
Barquisimeto Venez. 176 E1
Barra Brazil 177 J6
Barra *i.* U.K. 60 B4
Barra, Ponta da *pt* Moz. 125 L2
Barra, Sound of *sea chan.* U.K. 60 B3
Barraba Australia 138 E3
Barra Bonita Brazil 179 A3
Barracão do Barreto Brazil 177 G5
Barra de Navidad Mex. 166 D5
Barra do Bugres Brazil 177 G7
Barra do Corda Brazil 177 I5
Barra do Cuieté Brazil 179 C2
Barra do Garças Brazil 177 H7
Barra do Piraí Brazil 179 C3
Barra do São Manuel Brazil 177 G5
Barra do Turvo Brazil 179 A4
Barra Falsa, Ponta da *pt* Moz. 125 L2
Barraigh *i.* U.K. *see* Barra
Barra Kruta Hond. 166 [inset] J6
Barra Mansa Brazil 179 B3
Barrana Pak. 111 I4
Barranca Peru 176 C4
Barranca del Cobre, Parque Natural *nature res.* Mex. 166 D3
Barranqueras Arg. 178 E3
Barranquilla Col. 176 D1
Barre *MA* U.S.A. 165 I2
Barre *VT* U.S.A. 165 I1
Barre des Écrins *mt.* France 66 H4
Barreiras Brazil 177 J6
Barreirinha Brazil 177 G4
Barreirinhas Brazil 177 J4
Barreiro Port. 67 B4
Barreiros Brazil 177 K5
Barren Island India 87 A4
Barren Island Kiribati *see* Starbuck Island
Barren Islands *AK* U.S.A. 148 I4
Barren River Lake U.S.A. 164 B5
Barretos Brazil 179 A3
Barrett, Mount *hill* Australia 134 D4
Barrhead Canada 150 H4
Barrhead U.K. 60 E5
Barrie Canada 164 F1
Barrier Bay Antarctica 188 E2
Barrière Canada 150 F5
Barrier Range *hills* Australia 137 C6
Barrier Reef Belize 167 H5
Barrington Canada 153 I6
Barrington, Mount Australia 138 E4
Barrington Tops National Park Australia 138 E4
Barringun Australia 138 B2
Barro Alto Brazil 179 A1
Barrocão Brazil 179 C2
Barron U.S.A. 160 F2
Barroterán Mex. 167 E3
Barrow *r.* Ireland 61 F5
Barrow *AK* U.S.A. 148 H1
Barrow, Point *pt AK* U.S.A. 148 H1
Barrow Creek Australia 134 F5
Barrow-in-Furness U.K. 58 D4
Barrow Island Australia 134 A5
Barrow Range *hills* Australia 135 D6
Barrow Strait Canada 147 I2
Barr Smith Range *hills* Australia 135 C6
Barry U.K. 59 D7
Barrydale S. Africa 124 E7
Barry Mountains Australia 138 C6
Barrys Bay Canada 165 G1
Barryville U.S.A. 165 H3
Barsalpur India 104 C3
Barshatas Kazakh. 102 E2
Barshi India *see* Barsi
Barsi India 106 B2
Barsinghausen Germany 63 J2
Barstow U.S.A. 158 E4
Barsur India 106 D2
Bar-sur-Aube France 66 G2
Bartang Tajik. 111 H2
Barter Island *AK* U.S.A. 149 L1
Barth Germany 57 N3
Bartica Guyana 177 G2
Bartın Turkey 112 D2
Bartle Frere, Mount Australia 136 D3
Bartlett U.S.A. 160 D3
Bartlett Reservoir U.S.A. 159 H5
Barton U.S.A. 165 I1
Barton-upon-Humber U.K. 58 G5
Bartoszyce Poland 57 R3
Bartow U.S.A. 163 D7
Barú, Volcán *vol.* Panama 169 H7
Barumun *r.* Indon. 84 C2
Barun *Qinghai* China 94 D4
Barung *i.* Indon. 85 F5
Barunga Australia *see* Bamyili
Barun-Torey, Ozero *l.* Rus. Fed. 95 H1
Barus *Sumatera* Indon. 84 B2
Baruunbayan-Ulaan Mongolia 94 E2
Baruunbüren Mongolia 94 F1
Baruunharaa Mongolia *see* Bayangol
Baruunsuu Mongolia *see* Tsogttsetsiy
Baruunturuun Mongolia 94 C1
Baruun-Urt Mongolia 95 H2
Baruva India 106 E2
Barwani India 104 C5
Barwéli Mali *see* Baraouéli
Barwon *r.* Australia 138 C3
Barygaza India *see* Bharuch
Barykova, Mys *hd* Rus. Fed. 148 B3
Barysaw Belarus 55 P9
Barysh Rus. Fed. 53 J5
Basaga Turkm. 111 G2
Basăk, Tônlé *r.* Cambodia 87 D5
Basalt *r.* Australia 136 D3
Basalt Island *H.K.* China 97 [inset]
Basankusu Dem. Rep. Congo 122 B3
Basar India 106 C2
Basarabi Romania 69 M2
Basargechar Armenia *see* Vardenis
Basay *Negros* Phil. 82 C4
Basco Phil. 82 C1
Bascuñán, Cabo *c.* Chile 178 B3
Basel Switz. 66 H3
Basey *Samar* Phil. 82 D4
Bashākerd, Kūhhā-ye *mts* Iran 110 E5
Bashanta Rus. Fed. *see* Gorodovikovsk
Bashaw Canada 150 H4
Bashee *r.* S. Africa 125 I7
Bāshī Iran 110 C4
Bashi Channel *sea chan.* Phil./Taiwan 97 I4
Bashkaus *r.* Rus. Fed. 98 D2
Bashmakovo Rus. Fed. 53 I5
Bāsht Iran 110 C4
Bashtanka Ukr. 53 G7
Basi *Punjab* India 104 D3
Basi *Rajasthan* India 104 D4
Basia India 105 F5
Basilan *i.* Phil. 82 C5
Basilan Strait Phil. 82 C5
Basildon U.K. 59 H7
Basile, Pico *mt.* Equat. Guinea 120 D4
Basin U.S.A. 156 F3
Basingstoke U.K. 59 F7
Basin Lake Canada 151 J4
Basirhat India 105 G5
Basīṭ, Ra's al *pt* Syria 107 B2
Başkale Turkey 113 G3
Baskatong, Réservoir *resr* Canada 152 G5
Baskerville, Cape Australia 134 C4
Başkomutan Tarıhı Milli Parkı *nat. park* Turkey 69 N5
Başköy Turkey 107 A1
Baskunchak, Ozero *l.* Rus. Fed. 53 J6
Basle Switz. *see* Basel
Basmat India 106 C2
Baso *i.* Indon. 84 C3
Basoko Dem. Rep. Congo 122 C3

Basra Iraq 113 G5
Bassano Canada 151 H5
Bassano del Grappa Italy 68 D2
Bassar Togo 120 D4
Bassas da India reef Indian Ocean 123 D6
Bassas de Pedro Padua Bank sea feature India 106 B3
Bassein Myanmar 86 A3
Bassein r. Myanmar 86 A3
Basse-Normandie admin. reg. France 59 F9
Bassenthwaite Lake U.K. 58 D4
Basse Santa Su Gambia 120 B3

▶Basse-Terre Guadeloupe 169 L5
Capital of Guadeloupe.

▶Basseterre St Kitts and Nevis 169 L5
Capital of St Kitts and Nevis.

Bassett NE U.S.A. 160 D3
Bassett VA U.S.A. 164 F5
Bassikounou Mauritania 120 C3
Bass Rock i. U.K. 60 G4
Bass Strait Australia 137 D8
Bassum Germany 63 I2
Basswood Lake Canada 152 C4
Båstad Sweden 55 H8
Bāstānābād Iran 110 B2
Bastheim Germany 63 K4
Basti India 105 E4
Bastia Corsica France 66 I5
Bastioes r. Brazil 177 K5
Bastogne Belgium 62 F4
Bastrop LA U.S.A. 161 F5
Bastrop TX U.S.A. 161 D6
Basu, Tanjung pt Indon. 84 C3
Basul r. Pak. 111 G5
Basuo China see Dongfang
Basutoland country Africa see Lesotho
Başyayla Turkey 107 A1
Bata Equat. Guinea 120 D4
Bataan Peninsula Luzon Phil. 82 C3
Batabanó, Golfo de b. Cuba 169 H4
Batac Luzon Phil. 82 C2
Batagay Rus. Fed. 77 O3
Batakan Kalimantan Indon. 85 F4
Batala India 104 C3
Batalha Port. 67 B4
Batam i. Indon. 84 D2
Batamay Rus. Fed. 77 N3
Batamshinskiy Kazakh. 102 A1
Batamshy Kazakh. see Batamshinskiy
Batan Jiangsu China 97 I1
Batan Qinghai China 96 D1
Batan i. Phil. 82 C1
Batan i. Phil. 82 D3
Batan is Phil. 82 C1
Batang China 96 C2
Batang Jawa Indon. 85 E4
Batangafo Cent. Afr. Rep. 122 B3
Batang Ai National Park Malaysia 85 F2
Batangas Luzon Phil. 82 C3
Batanghari r. Indon. 84 D3
Batangpele i. Papua Indon. 83 D3
Batangtarang Kalimantan Indon. 85 E2
Batangtoru Sumatera Indon. 84 B2
Batan Islands Phil. 82 C1
Batanta i. Papua Indon. 83 D3
Batavia Jawa Indon. see Jakarta
Batavia NY U.S.A. 165 F2
Batavia OH U.S.A. 164 C4
Bataysk Rus. Fed. 53 H7
Batbatan i. Phil. 82 C4
Batchawana Mountain hill Canada 152 D5
Bătdâmbâng Cambodia 87 C4
Bateemeucica, Gunung mt. Indon. 84 A1
Batéké, Plateaux Congo 122 B4
Batemans Bay Australia 138 E5
Bates Range hills Australia 135 C6
Batesville AR U.S.A. 161 F5
Batesville IN U.S.A. 164 C4
Batesville MS U.S.A. 161 F5
Batetskiy Rus. Fed. 52 F4
Bath N.B. Canada 153 I5
Bath Ont. Canada 165 G1
Bath U.K. 59 E7
Bath ME U.S.A. 165 K2
Bath NY U.S.A. 165 G2
Bath PA U.S.A. 165 H3
Batha watercourse Chad 121 E3
Bathgate U.K. 60 F5
Bathinda India 104 C3
Bathurst Australia 138 D4
Bathurst Canada 153 I5
Bathurst Gambia see Banjul
Bathurst S. Africa 125 H7
Bathurst, Cape N.W.T. Canada 149 P1
Bathurst, Lake Australia 138 D5
Bathurst Inlet inlet Canada 146 H3
Bathurst Inlet (abandoned) Canada 146 H3
Bathurst Island Australia 134 E2
Bathurst Island Canada 147 I2
Bathyz Döwlet Gorugy nature res. Turkm. 111 F3
Batié Burkina 120 C4
Batikala, Tanjung pt Indon. 83 B3
Batı Menteşe Dağları mts Turkey 69 L6
Batı Toroslar mts Turkey 69 N6
Batken Kyrg. 102 D4
Batkes Indon. 134 E1
Bāṭlāq-e Gavkhūnī marsh Iran 110 D3
Batley U.K. 58 F5
Batlow Australia 138 D5
Batman Turkey 113 F3
Batna Alg. 64 F4
Batnorov Mongolia 95 G2
Batō Japan 93 G2
Batok, Bukit hill Sing. 87 [inset]
Bat-Öldziy Mongolia 94 E2
Batong, Ko i. Thai. 84 B1

▶Baton Rouge U.S.A. 161 F6
Capital of Louisiana.

Batopilas Mex. 166 D3
Batouri Cameroon 121 E4
Batrā' tourist site Jordan see Petra
Batrā', Jabal al mt. Jordan 107 B5
Batroûn Lebanon 107 B2
Båtsfjord Norway 54 P1
Batshireet Mongolia 95 G1
Batsümber Töv Mongolia 94 F1
Battambang Cambodia see Bătdâmbâng
Batticaloa Sri Lanka 106 D5
Batti Malv i. India 87 A5
Battipaglia Italy 68 F4
Battle r. Canada 151 I4
Battle Creek U.S.A. 164 C2
Battleford Canada 151 I4
Battle Mountain U.S.A. 158 E1
Battle Mountain mt. U.S.A. 158 E1
Battsengel Arhangay Mongolia 94 E2
Battura Glacier Pak. 104 C1
Batu mt. Eth. 122 D3
Batu, Bukit mt. Malaysia 85 F2
Batu, Pulau-pulau is Indon. 84 B3
Batu, Tanjung pt Indon. 85 G2
Batuata i. Indon. 83 B4
Batubetumbang Indon. 84 D3
Batu Bora, Bukit mt. Malaysia 85 F2
Batudaka i. Indon. 83 B3
Batu Gajah Malaysia 84 C1
Batuhitam, Tanjung pt Indon. 83 B3
Batui Sulawesi Indon. 83 B3
Batulaki Mindanao Phil. 82 D5
Batulicin Kalimantan Indon. 85 G3
Batulilangmebang, Gunung mt. Indon. 85 F2
Batum Georgia see Bat'umi
Bat'umi Georgia 113 F2
Batumonga Indon. 84 C3
Batu Pahat Malaysia 84 C2
Batu Putih, Gunung mt. Malaysia 84 C1
Baturaja Sumatera Indon. 84 D4
Baturetno Jawa Indon. 85 E5
Baturité Brazil 177 K4
Batusangkar Sumatera Indon. 84 C3
Batyrevo Rus. Fed. 53 J5
Batys Qazaqstan admin. div. Kazakh. see Zapadnyy Kazakhstan
Bau Sarawak Malaysia 85 E2
Baubau Sulawesi Indon. 83 B4
Baucau East Timor 83 C5
Bauchi Nigeria 120 D3
Bauda India see Boudh
Baudette U.S.A. 160 E1
Baudh India see Boudh
Baugé France 66 D3
Bauhinia Australia 136 E5
Baukau East Timor see Baucau
Baula Sulawesi Indon. 83 B4
Bauld, Cape Canada 153 L4
Baume-les-Dames France 66 H3
Baunach r. Germany 63 K5
Baundal India 104 C2
Baura Bangl. 105 G4
Bauru Brazil 179 A3
Bausendorf Germany 62 G4
Bauska Latvia 55 N8
Bautino Kazakh. 113 H1
Bautzen Germany 57 O5
Bavānāt Iran 110 D4
Bavaria land Germany see Bayern
Bavaria reg. Germany 63 L6
Bavda India 106 B2
Baviaanskloofberge mts S. Africa 124 F7
Bavispe Mex. 166 C2
Bavispe r. Mex. 166 C2
Bavla India 104 C5
Bavly Rus. Fed. 51 Q5
Baw Myanmar 86 A2
Bawal India 104 D3
Bawal i. Indon. 85 E3
Bawan Kalimantan Indon. 85 F3
Bawang, Tanjung pt Indon. 85 E3
Baw Baw National Park Australia 138 C6
Bawdeswell U.K. 59 I6
Bawdwin Myanmar 86 B2
Bawean i. Indon. 85 F4
Bawinkel Germany 63 H2
Bawlake Myanmar 86 B3
Bawolung China 96 D2
Baxi China 96 D1
Baxian Hebei China see Bazhou
Baxkorgan Xinjiang China 98 E5
Baxley U.S.A. 163 D6
Baxoi China 96 C2
Baxter Mountain U.S.A. 159 J2
Bay Xinjiang China see Baicheng
Bay, Laguna de lag. Luzon Phil. 82 C3
Bayamo Cuba 169 I4
Bayan Heilong. China 90 B3
Bayan Qinghai China 94 D5
Bayan Qinghai China see Hualong
Bayan Lombok Indon. 85 G5
Bayan Arhangay Mongolia see Hashaat
Bayan Govĭ-Altay Mongolia see Bayan-Uul
Bayan Töv Mongolia 95 F2
Bayana India 104 D4
Bayan-Adraga Hentiy Mongolia 95 G1
Bayanaul Kazakh. 102 E1
Bayanbulag Bayanhongor Mongolia 94 D2
Bayanbulag Bayanhongor Mongolia see Bayantsagaan
Bayanbulag Hentiy Mongolia see Ömnödelger
Bayanbulak Xinjiang China 98 D3
Bayanbulak Xinjiang China 98 D4
Bayanchandmanĭ Mongolia 94 F1
Bayandalay Mongolia 94 E3
Bayanday Rus. Fed. 88 J2
Bayandelger Mongolia 95 H2
Bayandelger Mongolia 95 G2
Bayandun Dornod Mongolia 95 H1
Bayang, Pegunungan mts Indon. 85 E2
Bayan Gol Nei Mongol China see Dengkou
Bayangol Mongolia see Bugat
Bayangol Mongolia 94 F1
Bayangol Rus. Fed. 94 E1
Bayan Har Shan mts China 94 C5
Bayan Har Shankou pass Qinghai China 94 D5
Bayanhongor Mongolia 94 E2
Bayanhongor prov. Mongolia 94 D2
Bayan Hot Nei Mongol China 94 F4
Bayanhushuu Mongolia see Galuut
Bayanjargalan Mongolia 95 F2
Bayanlig Mongolia 94 E2
Bayan Mod Nei Mongol China 94 F3
Bayanmönh Mongolia 95 G2
Bayan Nuru Nei Mongol China 94 F3
Bayannuur Mongolia 94 F2
Bayan Obo Nei Mongol China 95 G3
Bayan-Ölgiy prov. Mongolia 94 B1
Bayan-Öndör Mongolia 94 F2
Bayan-Önjüül Mongolia 94 F2
Bayan-Ovoo Govĭ-Altay Mongolia see Altay
Bayan-Ovoo Hentiy Mongolia see Dadal
Bayan-Ovoo Hentiy Mongolia 95 H2
Bayan-Ovoo Ömnögovĭ Mongolia 94 F3
Bayan Qagan Nei Mongol China 95 H3
Bayan Qagan Nei Mongol China 95 J2
Bayansayr Mongolia see Baatsagaan
Bayan Shan mt. China 94 D4
Bayansumküre Xinjiang China 98 D4
Bayan Tal Nei Mongol China 95 I1
Bayanteeg Mongolia 94 E2
Bayan Tohoi Nei Mongol China 95 I1
Bayantöhöm Mongolia see Büren
Bayantsagaan Bayanhongor Mongolia 94 D2
Bayantsagaan Mongolia 95 F2
Bayan Ul Hot Nei Mongol China 95 I2
Bayan Us Nei Mongol China 95 G3
Bayan-Uul Mongolia 95 H1
Bayan-Uul Govĭ-Altay Mongolia 94 C2
Bayan Uul mts Mongolia 94 B1
Bayard U.S.A. 159 I5
Bayasgalant Mongolia see Mönhaan
Bayat Turkey 69 N5
Bayawan Negros Phil. 82 C4
Bayāz Iran 110 E4
Baybay Leyte Phil. 82 D4
Bayboro U.S.A. 163 E5
Bayburt Turkey 113 F2
Bay Canh, Hon i. Vietnam 87 D5
Bay City MI U.S.A. 164 D2
Bay City TX U.S.A. 161 D6
Baydaratskaya Guba Rus. Fed. 76 H3
Baydhabo Somalia 122 E3
Baydrag Mongolia see Dzag
Baydrag Gol r. Mongolia 94 D2
Bayerischer Wald mts Germany 63 M5
Bayerischer Wald, Nationalpark nat. park Germany 57 N6
Bayern land Germany 63 L6
Bayeux France 59 G9
Bayfield Canada 164 E2
Bayiji Jiangsu China 95 I5
Bayındır Turkey 69 L5
Bay Islands is Hond. see Bahía, Islas de la
Bayizhen Xizang China 99 F7
Bayjī Iraq 113 F4
Baykal, Ozero Rus. Fed. see Baikal, Lake
Baykal-Amur Magistral Rus. Fed. 90 C1
Baykal Range mts Rus. Fed. see Baykal'skiy Khrebet
Baykal'sk Rus. Fed. 94 F1
Baykal'skiy Khrebet mts Rus. Fed. 89 J2
Baykal'skiy Zapovednik nature res. Rus. Fed. 94 F1
Baykan Turkey 113 F3
Bay-Khaak Rus. Fed. 102 H1
Baykibashevo Rus. Fed. 51 R4
Baykonur Kazakh. see Baykonyr
Baykonyr Kazakh. 102 B2
Baymak Rus. Fed. 76 G4
Bay Minette U.S.A. 163 C6
Baynūna'h reg. U.A.E. 110 D6
Bayombong Luzon Phil. 82 C2
Bayona Spain see Baiona
Bayonne France 66 D5
Bayonne U.S.A. 165 H3
Bayo Point Panay Phil. 82 C4
Bay Point Phil. 82 B4
Bay Port U.S.A. 164 D2
Bayqongyr Kazakh. see Baykonyr
Bayram-Ali Turkm. see Bayramaly
Baýramaly Turkm. 111 F2
Bayramiç Turkey 69 L5
Bayreuth Germany 63 L5
Bayrūt Lebanon see Beirut
Bays, Lake of Canada 164 F1
Bayshore U.S.A. 164 C1
Bay Shore U.S.A. 165 I3
Bay Springs U.S.A. 161 F6
Bayston Hill U.K. 59 E6
Baysun Uzbek. see Boysun
Baytik Shan mts China 94 B2
Bayt Lahm West Bank see Bethlehem
Baytown U.S.A. 161 E6
Bayu Sulawesi Indon. 83 B3
Bayunglincir Sumatera Indon. 84 C3
Bay View N.Z. 139 F4
Bayy al Kabīr, Wādī watercourse Libya 121 E1
Baza Spain 67 E5
Baza, Sierra de mts Spain 67 E5
Bazar watercourse Kazakh. 98 C2
Bāzārak Afgh. 111 G3
Bazardüzü Dağı mt. Azer./Rus. Fed. see Bazardyuzyu, Gora
Bazardyuzyu, Gora mt. Azer./Rus. Fed. 113 G2
Bāzār-e Māsāl Iran 110 C2
Bazarnyy Karabulak Rus. Fed. 53 J5
Bazaruto, Ilha do i. Moz. 123 D6
Bazdar Pak. 111 G5
Bazhong China 96 E2
Bazhou Hebei China 95 I4
Bazhou China see Bazhong
Bazin r. Canada 152 G5
Bazmān Iran 111 F5
Bazmān, Kūh-e mt. Iran 111 F4
Bcharré Lebanon 107 C2
Be, Sông r. Vietnam 87 D5
Beach U.S.A. 160 C2
Beachy Head hd U.K. 59 H8
Beacon U.S.A. 165 I3
Beacon Bay S. Africa 125 H7
Beaconsfield U.K. 59 G7
Beagle, Canal sea chan. Arg. 178 C8
Beagle Bank reef Australia 134 C3
Beagle Bay Australia 134 C4
Beagle Gulf Australia 134 E3
Bealanana Madag. 123 E5
Béal an Átha Ireland see Ballina
Béal an Mhuirthead Ireland 61 C3
Béal Átha na Sluaighe Ireland see Ballinasloe
Beale, Lake India 106 B2
Beaminster U.K. 59 E8
Bear r. U.S.A. 156 E4
Bearalváhki Norway see Berlevåg
Bear Cove Point Canada 151 O2
Beardmore Canada 152 D4
Beardmore Glacier Antarctica 188 H1
Bear Island Arctic Ocean see Bjørnøya
Bear Island Canada 152 E3
Bear Lake l. Canada 152 A3
Bear Lake U.S.A. 164 B1
Bear Lake l. U.S.A. 156 F4
Bearma r. India 104 D4
Bear Mountain U.S.A. 160 C3
Bearnaraigh i. U.K. see Berneray
Bear Paw Mountain U.S.A. 156 F2
Bearpaw Mountains U.S.A. 156 F2
Bearskin Lake Canada 151 N4
Beas Dam India 104 C3
Beata, Cabo c. Dom. Rep. 169 J5
Beatrice U.S.A. 160 D3
Beatrice, Cape Australia 136 B2
Beatton r. Canada 150 F3
Beatton River Canada 150 F3
Beatty U.S.A. 158 E3
Beattyville Canada 152 F4
Beattyville U.S.A. 164 D5
Beaucaire France 66 G5
Beauchene Island Falkland Is 178 E8
Beaufort Australia 138 A6
Beaufort Sabah Malaysia 85 F1
Beaufort NC U.S.A. 163 E5
Beaufort SC U.S.A. 163 D5
Beaufort Island H.K. China 97 [inset]
Beaufort Lagoon AK U.S.A. 149 L1
Beaufort Sea Canada/U.S.A. 146 D2
Beaufort West S. Africa 124 F7
Beaulieu r. Canada 151 H2
Beauly U.K. 60 E3
Beauly r. U.K. 60 E3
Beaumaris U.K. 58 C5
Beaumont Belgium 62 E4
Beaumont N.Z. 139 B7
Beaumont MS U.S.A. 161 F6
Beaumont TX U.S.A. 161 E6
Beaune France 66 G3
Beaupréau France 66 D3
Beauquesne France 62 C4
Beauraing Belgium 62 E4
Beauséjour Canada 151 L5
Beauvais France 62 C5
Beauval France 62 C4
Beaver r. Alberta/Saskatchewan Canada 151 J4
Beaver r. Ont. Canada 152 D3
Beaver r. Y.T. Canada 150 E3
Beaver r. Y.T. Canada 149 N3
Beaver AK U.S.A. 149 K2
Beaver OK U.S.A. 161 C4
Beaver PA U.S.A. 164 E3
Beaver UT U.S.A. 159 G2
Beaver r. U.S.A. 159 G2
Beaver Creek Y.T. Canada 149 L3
Beavercreek U.S.A. 164 C4
Beaver Creek r. AK U.S.A. 149 K2
Beaver Creek r. MT U.S.A. 160 B1
Beaver Creek r. ND U.S.A. 160 C2
Beaver Dam KY U.S.A. 164 B5
Beaver Dam WI U.S.A. 160 F3
Beaver Falls U.S.A. 164 E3
Beaverhead Mountains U.S.A. 156 E3
Beaverhill Lake Alta Canada 151 H4
Beaver Hill Lake Canada 151 M4
Beaverhill Lake N.W.T. Canada 151 J2
Beaver Island U.S.A. 162 C2
Beaverlodge Canada 150 G4
Beaver Mountains AK U.S.A. 148 H3
Beaverton Canada 164 F1
Beaverton MI U.S.A. 164 C2
Beaverton OR U.S.A. 156 C3
Beawar India 104 C4
Beazley Arg. 178 C4
Bebedouro Brazil 179 A3
Bebington U.K. 58 D5
Bebra Germany 63 J4
Bêca China 96 C2
Bécard, Lac l. Canada 153 G1
Beccles U.K. 59 I6
Bečej Serbia 69 I2
Becerreá Spain 67 C2
Béchar Alg. 64 D5
Becharof Lake AK U.S.A. 148 H4
Becharof National Wildlife Refuge nature res. AK U.S.A. 148 H4
Bechevin Bay AK U.S.A. 148 G5
Bechhofen Germany 63 K5
Bechuanaland country Africa see Botswana
Beckley U.S.A. 164 E5
Beckum Germany 63 I3
Becky Peak U.S.A. 159 F2
Beco East Timor 83 C5
Bečov nad Teplou Czech Rep. 63 M4
Bedale U.K. 58 F4
Bedburg Germany 62 G4
Bedel', Pereval pass China/Kyrg. see Bedel Pass
Bedelē Eth. 122 D3
Bedel Pass China/Kyrg. 98 B4
Bedford N.S. Canada 153 J5
Bedford Que. Canada 165 I1
Bedford E. Cape S. Africa 125 H7
Bedford Kwazulu-Natal S. Africa 125 J5
Bedford U.K. 59 G6
Bedford IN U.S.A. 164 B4
Bedford KY U.S.A. 164 C4
Bedford PA U.S.A. 165 F3
Bedford VA U.S.A. 164 F5
Bedford, Cape Australia 136 D2
Bedford Downs Australia 134 D4
Bedgerebong Australia 138 C4
Bedi India 104 B5
Bedinggong Indon. 84 D3
Bedla India 104 C4
Bedlington U.K. 58 F3
Bedok Sing. 87 [inset]
Bedok Jetty Sing. 87 [inset]
Bedok Reservoir Sing. 87 [inset]
Bedou China 97 F3
Bedourie Australia 136 B5
Bedum Neth. 62 G1
Bedworth U.K. 59 F6
Beechworth Australia 138 C6
Beechy Canada 151 J5
Beecroft Peninsula Australia 138 E5
Beed India see Bid
Beelitz Germany 63 M2
Beenleigh Australia 138 F1
Beernem Belgium 62 D3
Beersheba Israel 107 B4
Be'ér Sheva' Israel see Beersheba
Be'ér Sheva' watercourse Israel 107 B4
Beervlei Dam S. Africa 124 F7
Beerwah Australia 138 F1
Beetaloo Australia 134 F4
Beethoven Peninsula Antarctica 188 L2
Beeville U.S.A. 161 D6
Befori Dem. Rep. Congo 122 C3
Beg, Lough l. U.K. 61 F3
Bega Australia 138 D6
Bega Maluku Indon. 83 C3
Begari r. Pak. 111 H4
Begicheva, Ostrov i. Rus. Fed. see Bol'shoy Begichev, Ostrov
Begur, Cap de c. Spain 67 H3
Begusarai India 105 F4
Béhague, Pointe pt Fr. Guiana 177 H3
Behbehān Iran 110 C4
Behchokô N.W.T. Canada 149 R3
Behleg Qinghai China 99 E5
Behrendt Mountains Antarctica 188 L2
Behrūsī Iran 110 D4
Behshahr Iran 110 D2
Behsūd Afgh. 111 G3
Bei'an China 90 B2
Bei'ao China see Dongtou
Beibei China 96 E2
Beichuan China 96 E2
Beida Libya see Al Bayḍā'
Beida Shan mts Nei Mongol China 94 E4
Beigang Taiwan see Peikang
Beihai China 97 F4
Bei Hulsan Hu salt l. Qinghai China 99 F5

▶Beijing Beijing China 95 I4
Capital of China.

Beijing mun. China 95 I3
Beik Myanmar see Myeik
Beilen Neth. 62 G2
Beiliu China 97 F4
Beilngries Germany 63 L5
Beilu He r. Qinghai China 99 F6
Beiluheyan Qinghai China 94 C5
Beining Liaoning China 95 J3
Beinn an Oir hill U.K. 60 D5
Beinn an Tuirc hill U.K. 60 D5
Beinn Bheigeir hill U.K. 60 C5
Beinn Bhreac hill U.K. 60 D4
Beinn Dearg mt. U.K. 60 E3
Beinn Heasgarnich mt. U.K. 60 E4
Beinn Mholach hill U.K. 60 C2
Beinn Mhòr hill U.K. 60 B3
Beinn na Faoghlia i. U.K. see Benbecula
Beipan Jiang r. China 96 E3
Beipiao Liaoning China 95 J3
Beira Moz. 123 D5
Beiru He r. China 95 H5

▶Beirut Lebanon 107 B3
Capital of Lebanon.

Beishan Nei Mongol China 94 D3
Bei Shan mts China 94 C3
Beitai Ding mt. China 95 H4
Beitbridge Zimbabwe 123 C6
Beith U.K. 60 E5
Beit Jālā West Bank 107 B4
Beitun Xinjiang China 98 D3
Beizhen Liaoning China see Beining
Beja Port. 67 C4
Béja Tunisia 68 C6
Bejaïa Alg. 67 I5
Béjar Spain 67 D3
Beji r. Pak. 102 C6
Bejucos Mex. 167 E5
Bekaa valley Lebanon see El Béqaa
Bekasi Jawa Indon. 84 D4
Békés Hungary 69 I1
Békéscsaba Hungary 69 I1
Bekily Madag. 123 E6
Bekkai Japan 90 G4
Bēkma, Sadd dam Iraq 113 G3
Bekovo Rus. Fed. 53 I5
Bekwai Ghana 120 C4
Bela India 105 E4
Bela Pak. 111 G5
Belab r. Pak. 111 H4
Bela-Bela S. Africa 125 I3
Bélabo Cameroon 120 E4
Bela Crkva Serbia 69 I2
Belaga Sarawak Malaysia 85 F2
Bel'agash Kazakh. 98 C2
Bel Air U.S.A. 165 G4
Belalcázar Spain 67 D4
Bělá nad Radbuzou Czech Rep. 63 M5
Belang Sulawesi Indon. 83 C2
Belangbelang i. Maluku Indon. 83 C3
Belapur India 106 B2
Belarus country Europe 53 E5
Belau country N. Pacific Ocean see Palau
Bela Vista Brazil 178 E2
Bela Vista Moz. 125 K4
Bela Vista de Goiás Brazil 179 A2
Belawan Sumatera Indon. 84 B2
Belaya r. Rus. Fed. 77 S3
also known as Bilo
Belaya, Gora mt. Rus. Fed. 148 A2
Belaya Glina Rus. Fed. 53 I7
Belaya Kalitva Rus. Fed. 53 I6
Belaya Kholunitsa Rus. Fed. 52 K4
Belayan r. Indon. 85 G3
Belayan, Gunung mt. Indon. 85 F2
Belaya Tserkva Ukr. see Bila Tserkva
Belbédji Niger 120 D3
Bełchatów Poland 57 Q5
Belcher U.S.A. 164 D5
Belcher Islands Canada 152 F2
Belchiragh Afgh. 111 G3
Belcoo U.K. 61 E3
Belden U.S.A. 158 C1
Belding U.S.A. 164 C2
Beleapani reef India see Cherbaniani Reef
Belebey Rus. Fed. 51 Q5
Beledweyne Somalia 122 E3
Belém Brazil 177 I4
Belém Novo Brazil 179 A5
Belén Arg. 178 C3
Belen Antalya Turkey 107 A1
Belen Hatay Turkey 107 C1
Belen U.S.A. 157 G6
Belep, Îles is New Caledonia 133 G3
Belev Rus. Fed. 53 H5
Belfast S. Africa 125 J3

▶Belfast U.K. 61 G3
Capital of Northern Ireland.

Belfast U.S.A. 162 G2
Belfast Lough inlet U.K. 61 G3
Bēlfodiyo Eth. 122 D2
Belford U.K. 58 F3
Belfort France 66 H3
Belgaum India 106 B3
Belgern Germany 63 N3
Belgian Congo country Africa see Congo, Democratic Republic of the
België country Europe see Belgium
Belgique country Europe see Belgium
Belgium country Europe 62 E4
Belgorod Rus. Fed. 53 H6
Belgorod-Dnestrovskyy Ukr. see Bilhorod-Dnistrovs'kyy

▶Belgrade Serbia 69 I2
Capital of Serbia.

Belgrade ME U.S.A. 165 K1
Belgrade MT U.S.A. 156 F3
Belgrano II research station Antarctica 188 A1
Belice r. Sicily Italy 68 E6
Beliliou i. Palau see Peleliu
Belimbing Sumatera Indon. 84 D4
Belinskiy Rus. Fed. 53 I5
Belinyu Indon. 84 D3
Belitung i. Indon. 85 E3
Belize Angola 123 B4

▶Belize Belize 167 H5
Former capital of Belize.

Belize country Central America 167 H5
Beljak Austria see Villach
Belkina, Mys pt Rus. Fed. 90 E3
Belkofski AK U.S.A. 148 G5
Bel'kovskiy, Ostrov i. Rus. Fed. 77 O2
Bell Australia 138 E1
Bell r. Australia 138 D4
Bell r. Canada 152 F4
Bell r. Y.T. Canada 149 M2
Bella Bella Canada 150 D4
Bellac France 66 E3
Bella Coola Canada 150 E4
Bellaire U.S.A. 164 C1
Bellaire TX U.S.A. 167 G2
Bellary India 106 C3
Bellata Australia 138 D2
Bella Unión Uruguay 178 E4
Bella Vista U.S.A. 158 B1
Bellbrook Australia 138 F3
Bell Cay reef Australia 136 E4
Belledonne mts France 66 G4
Bellefontaine U.S.A. 164 D3
Bellefonte U.S.A. 165 G3
Belle Fourche U.S.A. 160 C2

Belle Fourche r. U.S.A. 160 C2
Belle Glade U.S.A. 163 D7
Belle-Île i. France 66 C3
Belle Isle i. Canada 153 L4
Belle Isle, Strait of Canada 153 K4
Belleville Canada 165 G1
Belleville IL U.S.A. 160 F4
Belleville KS U.S.A. 160 D4
Bellevue IA U.S.A. 160 F3
Bellevue MI U.S.A. 164 C2
Bellevue OH U.S.A. 164 D3
Bellevue WA U.S.A. 156 C3
Bellin Canada see **Kangirsuk**
Bellingham U.K. 58 E3
Bellingham U.S.A. 156 C2
Bellingshausen research station Antarctica 188 A2
Bellingshausen Sea Antarctica 188 L2
Bellinzona Switz. 66 I3
Bellows Falls U.S.A. 165 I2
Bellpat Pak. 111 H4
Belluno Italy 68 E1
Belluru India 106 C3
Bell Ville Arg. 178 D4
Bellville S. Africa 124 D7
Belm Germany 63 I2
Belmont Australia 138 E4
Belmont U.K. 60 [inset]
Belmont U.S.A. 165 F2
Belmonte Brazil 179 D1

▶**Belmopan** Belize 167 H5
Capital of Belize.

Belmore, Mount hill Australia 138 F2
Belmullet Ireland see **Béal an Mhuirthead**
Belo Madag. 123 E6
Belo Campo Brazil 179 C1
Belœil Belgium 62 D4
Belogorsk Rus. Fed. 90 C2
Belogorsk Ukr. see **Bilohirs'k**
Beloha Madag. 123 E6
Belo Horizonte Brazil 179 C2
Beloit KS U.S.A. 160 D4
Beloit WI U.S.A. 160 F3
Belokurikha Rus. Fed. 102 F1
Belo Monte Brazil 177 H4
Belomorsk Rus. Fed. 52 G2
Belonia India 105 G5
Belopa Sulawesi Indon. 83 B3
Belorechensk Rus. Fed. 113 E1
Belorechenskaya Rus. Fed. see **Belorechensk**
Belören Turkey 112 D3
Beloretsk Rus. Fed. 76 G4
Belorussia country Europe see **Belarus**
Belorusskaya S.S.R. country Europe see **Belarus**
Belostok Poland see **Białystok**
Belot, Lac l. N.W.T. Canada 149 P2
Belo Tsiribihina Madag. 123 E5
Belousovka Kazakh. 98 C2
Belovo Rus. Fed. 88 F2
Beloyarskiy Rus. Fed. 51 T3
Beloye, Ozero l. Rus. Fed. 52 H3
Beloye More sea Rus. Fed. see **White Sea**
Belozersk Rus. Fed. 52 H3
Belpre U.S.A. 164 E4
Beltana Australia 137 B6
Belted Range mts U.S.A. 158 E3
Beltes Gol r. Mongolia 94 D1
Belton U.S.A. 161 D6
Bel'ts' Moldova see **Bălți**
Bel'tsy Moldova see **Bălți**
Beluga Lake AK U.S.A. 149 J3
Belukha, Gora mt. Kazakh./Rus. Fed. 102 G2
Beluran Sabah Malaysia 85 G1
Belush'ye Rus. Fed. 52 J2
Belvidere IL U.S.A. 160 F3
Belvidere NJ U.S.A. 165 H3
Belyaka, Kosa spit Rus. Fed. 148 D2
Belyando r. Australia 136 D4
Belyayevka Ukr. see **Bilyayivka**
Belyy Rus. Fed. 52 G5
Belyy, Ostrov i. Rus. Fed. 76 I2
Belyy Bom Rus. Fed. 98 D2
Belzig Germany 63 M2
Belzoni U.S.A. 161 F5
Bemaraha, Plateau du Madag. 123 E5
Bembe Angola 123 B4
Bemidji U.S.A. 160 E2
Béna Burkina 120 C3
Bena Dibele Dem. Rep. Congo 122 C4
Benagin Kalimantan Indon. 85 F3
Ben Alder mt. U.K. 60 E4
Benalla Australia 138 B6
Benares India see **Varanasi**
Ben Arous Tunisia 68 D6
Benavente Spain 67 D2
Ben Avon mt. U.K. 60 F3
Benbane Head hd U.K. 61 F2
Benbecula i. U.K. 60 B3
Ben Boyd National Park Australia 138 E6
Benburb U.K. 61 F3
Bencha China 97 I1
Bencheng Hebei China see **Luannan**
Ben Chonzie hill U.K. 60 F4
Ben Cleuch hill U.K. 60 F4
Ben Cruachan mt. U.K. 60 D4
Bend U.S.A. 156 C3
Bendearg mt. S. Africa 125 H6
Bendeleben, Mount AK U.S.A. 148 F2
Bendeleben Mountains AK U.S.A. 148 F2
Bender Moldova see **Tighina**
Bender-Bayla Somalia 122 F3
Bendery Moldova see **Tighina**
Bendigo Australia 138 B6
Bendoc Australia 138 D6
Bene Moz. 123 D5
Benedict, Mount hill Canada 153 K3
Benenitra Madag. 123 E6
Benešov Czech Rep. 57 O6
Bénestroff France 62 G6
Benevento Italy 68 F4
Beneventum Italy see **Benevento**
Benezette U.S.A. 165 F3
Beng, Nam r. Laos 86 C3
Bengal, Bay of sea Indian Ocean 103 G8
Bengamisa Dem. Rep. Congo 122 C3
Bengbu China 97 H1
Benghazi Libya 121 F1
Beng He r. China 95 I5
Bengkalis Sumatera Indon. 84 C2
Bengkalis i. Indon. 84 C2
Bengkayang Kalimantan Indon. 85 E2
Bengkulu Sumatera Indon. 84 C3
Bengkulu prov. Indon. 84 C3
Bengkung Kalimantan Indon. 85 G3
Bengoi Seram Indon. 83 D3
Bengtsfors Sweden 55 H7
Benguela Angola 123 B5
Benha Egypt see **Banhā**
Ben Hiant hill U.K. 60 C4
Ben Hope hill U.K. 60 E2
Ben Horn hill U.K. 60 E2
Beni r. Bol. 176 E6
Beni Dem. Rep. Congo 122 C3
Beni Nepal 105 E3
Beni Abbès Alg. 64 D5
Beniah Lake Canada 151 H2
Benidorm Spain 67 F4
Beni Mellal Morocco 64 C5
Benin country Africa 120 D4
Benin, Bight of g. Africa 120 D4
Benin City Nigeria 120 D4
Beni Saf Alg. 67 F6
Beni Snassen, Monts des mts Morocco 67 E6
Beni Suef Egypt see **Banī Suwayf**
Benito, Islas is Mex. 166 B2
Benito Juárez Arg. 178 E5
Benito Juárez Mex. 159 F5
Benito Soliven Luzon Phil. 82 C2
Benjamin Constant Brazil 176 E4
Benjamin U.S.A. 161 D5
Benjamín Hill Mex. 166 C2
Benjina Indon. 81 I8
Benkelman U.S.A. 160 C3
Ben Klibreck hill U.K. 60 E2
Ben Lavin Nature Reserve S. Africa 125 I2
Ben Lawers mt. U.K. 60 E4
Ben Lomond mt. Australia 138 E3
Ben Lomond hill U.K. 60 E4
Ben Lomond National Park Australia 137 [inset]
Ben Macdui mt. U.K. 60 F3
Benmara Australia 136 B3
Ben More hill U.K. 60 C4
Ben More mt. U.K. 60 E4
Benmore, Lake N.Z. 139 C7
Ben More Assynt hill U.K. 60 E2
Bennetta, Ostrov i. Rus. Fed. 77 P2
Bennett Island Rus. Fed. see **Bennetta, Ostrov**
Bennett Lake B.C. Canada 149 N4
Bennettsville U.S.A. 163 E5
Ben Nevis mt. U.K. 60 D4
Bennington NH U.S.A. 165 J2
Bennington VT U.S.A. 165 I2
Benoni S. Africa 125 I4
Ben Rinnes hill U.K. 60 F3
Bensheim Germany 63 I5
Benson AZ U.S.A. 159 H6
Benson MN U.S.A. 160 E2
Benta Seberang Malaysia 84 C1
Benteng Sulawesi Indon. 83 B4
Bentinck Island Myanmar 87 B5
Bentiu Sudan 108 C8
Bent Jbaïl Lebanon 107 B3
Bentley U.K. 58 F5
Bento Gonçalves Brazil 179 A5
Benton AR U.S.A. 161 E5
Benton CA U.S.A. 158 D3
Benton IL U.S.A. 160 F4
Benton KY U.S.A. 161 F4
Benton LA U.S.A. 161 E5
Benton MO U.S.A. 161 F4
Benton PA U.S.A. 165 G3
Bentong Malaysia see **Bentung**
Benton Harbor U.S.A. 164 B2
Bentonville U.S.A. 161 E4
Bên Tre Vietnam 87 D5
Bentung Malaysia 84 C2
Benua Sulawesi Indon. 83 B4
Benua i. Indon. 84 D2
Benuamartinus Kalimantan Indon. 85 F2
Benue r. Nigeria 120 D4
Benum, Gunung mt. Malaysia 84 C2
Ben Vorlich hill U.K. 60 E4
Benwee Head hd Ireland 61 C3
Benwood U.S.A. 164 E3
Ben Wyvis mt. U.K. 60 E3
Benxi Liaoning China 90 B4
Benxi Liaoning China 95 J3
Beo Sulawesi Indon. 83 C1
Beograd Serbia see **Belgrade**
Béoumi Côte d'Ivoire 120 C4
Bepagut, Gunung mt. Indon. 84 C4
Beppu Japan 91 C6
Béqaa valley Lebanon see **El Béqaa**
Bera, Tasik l. Malaysia 84 C2
Berach r. India 104 C4
Beraketa Madag. 123 E6
Berangas Kalimantan Indon. 85 G3
Bérard, Lac l. Canada 153 H2
Berasia India 104 D5
Berastagi Sumatera Indon. 84 B2
Berat Albania 69 H4
Beratus, Gunung mt. Indon. 85 G3
Berau r. Indon. 85 G2
Beravina Madag. 123 E5
Berbak, Taman Nasional nat. park Indon. 84 D3
Berber Sudan 108 D6
Berbera Somalia 122 E2
Berbérati Cent. Afr. Rep. 122 B3
Berchtesgaden, Nationalpark nat. park Germany 57 N7
Berck France 62 B4
Berdichev Ukr. see **Berdychiv**
Berdigestyakh Rus. Fed. 77 N3
Berdyans'k Ukr. 53 H7
Berdychiv Ukr. 53 F6
Berea KY U.S.A. 164 C5
Berea OH U.S.A. 164 E3
Berebere Maluku Indon. 83 D2
Beregovo Ukr. see **Berehove**
Beregovoy Rus. Fed. 90 B1
Berehove Ukr. 53 D6
Bereina P.N.G. 81 L8
Bere Island Ireland 61 C6
Bereket Turkm. 110 D2
Berekum Ghana 120 C4
Berel' Kazakh. 98 D2
Berenice Egypt see **Baranīs**
Berenice Libya see **Benghazi**
Berens r. Canada 151 L4
Berens Island Canada 151 L4
Berens River Canada 151 L4
Beresford U.S.A. 160 D3
Bereza Belarus see **Byaroza**
Berezino Belarus see **Byerazino**
Berezivka Ukr. 53 F7
Berezne Ukr. 53 E6
Bereznik Rus. Fed. 52 I3
Berezniki Rus. Fed. 51 R4
Berezov Rus. Fed. see **Berezovo**
Berezovka Rus. Fed. 90 B2
Berezovka Ukr. see **Berezivka**
Berezovo Rus. Fed. 51 T3
Berezovyy Rus. Fed. 90 D2
Berga Germany 63 L3
Berga Spain 67 G2
Bergama Turkey 69 L5
Bergamo Italy 68 C2
Bergby Sweden 55 J6
Bergen Mecklenburg-Vorpommern Germany 57 N3
Bergen Niedersachsen Germany 63 J2
Bergen Norway 55 D6
Bergen U.S.A. 165 G2
Bergen op Zoom Neth. 62 E3
Bergerac France 66 E4
Bergères-lès-Vertus France 62 E6
Bergheim (Erft) Germany 62 G4
Bergisches Land reg. Germany 63 H4
Bergisch Gladbach Germany 62 H4
Bergland Namibia 124 C2
Bergomum Italy see **Bergamo**
Bergoo U.S.A. 164 E4
Bergsjö Sweden 55 J6
Bergsviken Sweden 54 L4
Bergtheim Germany 63 K5
Bergues France 62 C4
Bergum Neth. see **Burgum**
Bergville S. Africa 125 I5
Berh Mongolia 95 G2
Berhala, Selat sea chan. Indon. 84 C3
Berhampur India see **Baharampur**
Berikat, Tanjung pt Indon. 84 D3
Beringa, Ostrov i. Rus. Fed. 77 R4
Beringen Belgium 62 F3
Bering Glacier AK U.S.A. 148 H4
Bering Glacier AK U.S.A. 149 L3
Bering Lake AK U.S.A. 149 K3
Bering Land Bridge National Preserve nature res. AK U.S.A. 148 F2
Beringovskiy Rus. Fed. 77 S3
Bering Sea N. Pacific Ocean 77 S4
Bering Strait Rus. Fed./U.S.A. 148 E2
Berīs, Ra's pt Iran 111 F5
Berislav Ukr. see **Beryslav**
Berkåk Norway 54 G5
Berkane Morocco 67 E6
Berkel r. Neth. 62 G2
Berkeley U.S.A. 158 B3
Berkeley Springs U.S.A. 165 F4
Berkhout Neth. 62 F2
Berkner Island Antarctica 188 A1
Berkovitsa Bulg. 69 J3
Berkshire Downs hills U.K. 59 F7
Berkshire Hills U.S.A. 165 I2
Berland r. Canada 150 G4
Berlare Belgium 62 E3
Berlevåg Norway 54 P1

▶**Berlin** Germany 63 N2
Capital of Germany.

Berlin land Germany 63 N2
Berlin MD U.S.A. 165 H4
Berlin NH U.S.A. 165 J1
Berlin PA U.S.A. 165 F4
Berlin Lake U.S.A. 164 E3
Bermagui Australia 138 E6
Bermejillo Mex. 166 E3
Bermejo r. Arg./Bol. 178 E3
Bermejo Bol. 176 F8
Bermen, Lac l. Canada 153 H3

▶**Bermuda** terr. N. Atlantic Ocean 169 L2
United Kingdom Overseas Territory.

Bermuda Rise sea feature N. Atlantic Ocean 184 D4

▶**Bern** Switz. 66 H3
Capital of Switzerland.

Bernalillo U.S.A. 157 G6
Bernardino de Campos Brazil 179 A3
Bernardo O'Higgins, Parque Nacional nat. park Chile 178 B7
Bernasconi Arg. 178 D5
Bernau Germany 63 N2
Bernburg (Saale) Germany 63 L3
Berne Germany 63 I1
Berne Switz. see **Bern**
Berne U.S.A. 164 C3
Berner Alpen mts Switz. 66 H3
Berneray i. Scotland U.K. 60 B3
Berneray i. Scotland U.K. 60 B4
Bernier Island Australia 135 A6
Bernina Pass Switz. 66 J3
Bernkastel-Kues Germany 62 H5
Beroea Greece see **Veroia**
Beroea Syria see **Aleppo**
Beroroha Madag. 123 E6
Beroun Czech Rep. 57 O6
Berounka r. Czech Rep. 57 O6
Berovina Madag. see **Beravina**
Berri Australia 137 C7
Berriane Alg. 64 E5
Berridale Australia 138 D6
Berriedale U.K. 60 F2
Berrigan Australia 138 B5
Berrima Australia 138 E5
Berrouaghia Alg. 67 H5
Berry Australia 138 E5
Berry U.S.A. 164 C4
Berryessa, Lake U.S.A. 158 B2
Berry Head hd U.K. 59 D8
Berry Islands Bahamas 163 E7
Berryville U.S.A. 165 G4
Berseba Namibia 124 C4
Bersenbrück Germany 63 H2
Bertam Malaysia 84 C1
Berté, Lac l. Canada 153 H4
Berthoud Pass U.S.A. 156 G5
Bertolinía Brazil 177 J5
Bertoua Cameroon 120 E4
Bertraghboy Bay Ireland 61 C4
Beru atoll Kiribati 133 H2
Beruri Brazil 176 F4
Beruwala Sri Lanka 106 C5
Berwick Australia 138 B7
Berwick U.S.A. 165 G3
Berwick-upon-Tweed U.K. 58 E3
Berwyn hills U.K. 59 D6
Beryslav Ukr. 69 O1
Berytus Lebanon see **Beirut**
Besah Kalimantan Indon. 85 G2
Besalampy Madag. 123 E5
Besançon France 66 H3
Besar i. Indon. 83 B5
Besar, Gunung mt. Indon. 85 F3
Besar, Gunung mt. Malaysia 87 C7
Besbay Kazakh. 102 A2
Besboro Island AK U.S.A. 148 G2
Beserah Malaysia 84 C2
Beshkent Uzbek. 111 G2
Beshneh Iran 110 D4
Besikama Timor Indon. 83 C5
Besitang Sumatera Indon. 84 B1
Beskra Alg. see **Biskra**
Beslan Rus. Fed. 113 G2
Besnard Lake Canada 151 J4
Besni Turkey 112 E3
Besoba Kazakh. 98 A2
Besor watercourse Israel 107 B4
Beşparmak Dağları mts Cyprus see **Pentadaktylos Range**
Bessbrook U.K. 61 F3
Bessemer U.S.A. 163 C5
Besshoky, Gora hill Kazakh. 113 I1
Besskorbnaya Rus. Fed. 53 I7
Bessonovka Rus. Fed. 53 J5
Bestamak Vostochnyy Kazakhstan Kazakh. 98 B2
Betanzos Spain 67 B2
Betet i. Indon. 84 D3
Bethal S. Africa 125 I4
Bethanie Namibia 124 C4
Bethany U.S.A. 160 E3
Bethari Nepal 99 C8
Bethel AK U.S.A. 148 G3
Bethel U.S.A. 153 H5
Bethel Park U.S.A. 164 E3
Bethesda U.K. 58 C5
Bethesda MD U.S.A. 165 G4
Bethesda OH U.S.A. 164 E3
Bethlehem S. Africa 125 I5
Bethlehem U.S.A. 165 H3
Bethlehem West Bank 107 B4
Bethulie S. Africa 125 G6
Béthune France 62 C4
Beti Pak. 111 H4
Betim Brazil 179 B2
Betiri, Gunung mt. Indon. 85 F5
Bet Lehem West Bank see **Bethlehem**
Betma India 104 C5
Betong Sarawak Malaysia 85 E2
Betong Thai. 87 C6
Betoota Australia 136 C5
Betpak-Dala plain Kazakh. 102 D2
Betroka Madag. 123 E6
Bet She'an Israel 107 B3
Betsiamites Canada 153 H4
Betsiamites r. Canada 153 H4
Betsu-zan mt. Japan 92 C2
Bettiah India 105 F4
Bettles AK U.S.A. 149 J2
Bettyhill U.K. 60 E2
Bettystown Ireland 61 F4
Betul India 104 D5
Betun Timor Indon. 83 C5
Betung Kerihun, Taman Nasional Indon. 85 F2
Betwa r. India 104 D4
Betws-y-coed U.K. 59 D5
Betzdorf Germany 63 H4
Beulah Australia 137 C7
Beulah MI U.S.A. 164 B1
Beulah ND U.S.A. 160 C2
Beult r. U.K. 59 H7
Beuthen Poland see **Bytom**
Bever r. Germany 63 H2
Beverley U.K. 58 G5
Beverley, Lake AK U.S.A. 148 H4
Beverly MA U.S.A. 165 J2
Beverly OH U.S.A. 164 E4
Beverly Hills U.S.A. 158 D4
Beverly Lake Canada 151 K1
Beverstedt Germany 63 I1
Beverungen Germany 63 J3
Beverwijk Neth. 62 E2
Bewani P.N.G. 81 K7
Bexbach Germany 63 H5
Bexhill U.K. 59 H8
Bexley, Cape Canada 146 G3
Beyānlū Iran 110 B3
Beyce Turkey see **Orhaneli**
Bey Dağları mts Turkey 69 N6
Beykoz Turkey 69 M4
Beyla Guinea 120 C4
Beylagan Azer. see **Beyläqan**
Beyläqan Azer. 113 G3
Beyneu Kazakh. 100 E2
Beypazarı Turkey 69 N4
Beypınarı Turkey 112 E3
Beypore India 106 B4
Beyrouth Lebanon see **Beirut**
Beyşehir Turkey 112 C3
Beyşehir Gölü l. Turkey 112 C3
Beytonovo Rus. Fed. 90 B1
Beytüşşebap Turkey 113 F3
Bezameh Iran 110 E3
Bezbozhnik Rus. Fed. 52 K4
Bezhanitsy Rus. Fed. 52 F4
Bezhetsk Rus. Fed. 52 H4
Béziers France 66 F5
Bezmein Turkm. see **Abadan**
Bezwada India see **Vijayawada**
Bhabha India see **Bhabhua**
Bhabhar India 104 B4
Bhabhua India 105 E4
Bhabua India see **Bhabhua**
Bhachau India 104 B5
Bhachbhar India 104 B4
Bhadarwah India 99 A6
Bhadgaon Nepal see **Bhaktapur**
Bhadohi India 105 E4
Bhadra India 104 C3
Bhadrachalam Road Station India see **Kottagudem**
Bhadrak India 105 F5
Bhadrakh India see **Bhadrak**
Bhadravati India 106 B3
Bhag Pak. 111 G4
Bhaga r. India 99 B6
Bhagalpur India 105 F4
Bhainsa India 106 C2
Bhainsdehi India 104 D5
Bhairab Bazar Bangl. 105 G4
Bhairi Hol mt. Pak. 111 G5
Bhaktapur Nepal 105 F4
Bhalki India 106 C2
Bhamo Myanmar 86 B1
Bhamragarh India 106 D2
Bhandara India 104 D5
Bhanjanagar India 106 E2
Bhanrer Range hills India 104 D5
Bhaptiahi India 105 F4
Bharat country Asia see **India**
Bharatpur India 104 D4
Bhareli r. India 105 H4
Bharuch India 104 C5
Bhatapara India 105 E5
Bhatarsaigh i. U.K. see **Vatersay**
Bhatghar Lake India 106 B2
Bhatinda India see **Bathinda**
Bhatnair India see **Hanumangarh**
Bhatpara India 105 G5
Bhaunagar India see **Bhavnagar**
Bhavani r. India 106 C4
Bhavani Sagar l. India 106 C4
Bhavnagar India 104 C5
Bhawana Pak. 111 I4
Bhawanipatna India 106 D2
Bhearnaraigh, Eilean i. U.K. see **Berneray**
Bheemavaram India see **Bhimavaram**
Bhekuzulu S. Africa 125 J4
Bhera Pak. 111 I3
Bheri r. Nepal 99 C7
Bhigvan India 106 B2
Bhikhna Thori Nepal 105 F4
Bhilai India 104 E5
Bhildi India 104 C4
Bhilwara India 104 C4
Bhima r. India 106 C2
Bhimar India 104 B4
Bhimavaram India 106 D2
Bhimlath India 104 E5
Bhimphedi Nepal 99 D8
Bhind India 104 D4
Bhinga India 105 E4
Bhisho S. Africa 125 H7
Bhiwandi India 106 B2
Bhiwani India 104 D3
Bhogaipur India 104 D4
Bhojpur Nepal 105 F4
Bhola Bangl. 105 G5
Bhongweni S. Africa 125 I6
Bhopal India 104 D5
Bhopalpatnam India 106 D2
Bhrigukaccha India see **Bharuch**
Bhuban India 106 E1
Bhubaneshwar India 106 E1
Bhubaneswar India see **Bhubaneshwar**
Bhuj India 104 B5
Bhusawal India 104 C5
Bhutan country Asia 105 G4
Bhuttewala India 104 B4
Bia r. Ghana 120 C4
Bia, Phou mt. Laos 86 C3
Bīabān mts Iran 110 E5
Biafo Glacier Pak. 104 C2
Biafra, Bight of g. Africa see **Benin, Bight of**
Biak Indon. 81 J7
Biak Sulawesi Indon. 83 B3
Biak i. Indon. 81 J7
Biała Podlaska Poland 53 D5
Białogard Poland 57 O4
Białystok Poland 53 D5
Bianco, Monte mt. France/Italy see **Blanc, Mont**
Biandangang Kou r. mouth China 95 J5
Bianzhao Jilin China 95 J2
Bianzhuang Shandong China see **Cangshan**
Biao Mindanao Phil. 82 D5
Biaora India 104 D5
Biaro i. Indon. 83 C2
Biarritz France 66 D5
Bi'ār Tabrāk well Saudi Arabia 110 B5
Bibai Japan 90 F4
Bibbenluke Australia 138 D6
Bibbiena Italy 68 D3
Bibby Island Canada 151 M2
Biberach an der Riß Germany 57 L6
Bibile Sri Lanka 106 D5
Biblis Germany 63 I5
Biblos Lebanon see **Jbail**
Bicas Brazil 179 C3
Biçer Turkey 69 N5
Bicester U.K. 59 F7
Bichabhera India 104 C4
Bicheng China see **Bishan**
Bichevaya Rus. Fed. 90 D3
Bichi r. Rus. Fed. 90 E1
Bichraltar Nepal 99 D8
Bichura Rus. Fed. 95 F1
Bickerton Island Australia 136 B2
Bickleigh U.K. 59 D8
Bicknell U.S.A. 164 B4
Bicoli Halmahera Indon. 83 D2
Bicuari, Parque Nacional do nat. park Angola 123 B5
Bid India 106 B2
Bida Nigeria 120 D4
Bidadari, Tanjung pt Malaysia 85 G1
Bidar India 106 C2
Biddeford U.S.A. 165 J2
Biddinghuizen Neth. 62 F2
Bidean nam Bian mt. U.K. 60 D4
Bideford U.K. 59 C7
Bideford Bay U.K. see **Barnstaple Bay**
Bidokht Iran 110 E3
Bidzhan Rus. Fed. 90 C3
Bié Angola see **Kuito**
Bié, Planalto do Angola 123 B5
Biebrzański Park Narodowy nat. park Poland 55 M10
Biedenkopf Germany 63 I4
Biel Switz. 66 H3
Bielawa Poland 57 P5
Bielefeld Germany 63 I2
Bielitz Poland see **Bielsko-Biała**
Biella Italy 68 C2
Bielsko-Biała Poland 57 Q6
Bielstein hill Germany 63 J3
Bienenbüttel Germany 63 K1
Biên Hoa Vietnam 87 D5
Bienne Switz. see **Biel**
Bienville, Lac l. Canada 153 G3
Bierbank Australia 138 B1
Biesiesvlei S. Africa 125 G4
Bietigheim-Bissingen Germany 63 J6
Bièvre Belgium 62 F5
Bifoun Gabon 122 B4
Big r. Canada 153 K3
Big r. AK U.S.A. 148 I3
Biga Turkey 69 L4
Bigadiç Turkey 69 M5
Biga Yarımadası pen. Turkey 69 L5
Big Baldy Mountain U.S.A. 156 F3
Big Bar Creek Canada 150 F5
Big Bear Lake U.S.A. 158 E4
Big Belt Mountains U.S.A. 156 F3
Big Bend Swaziland 125 J4
Big Bend National Park U.S.A. 161 C6
Big Black r. MS U.S.A. 167 H1
Bigbury-on-Sea U.K. 59 D8
Big Canyon watercourse U.S.A. 161 C6
Big Delta AK U.S.A. 149 K2
Biger Govĭ-Altay Mongolia 94 D2
Biger Nuur salt l. Mongolia 94 D2
Big Falls U.S.A. 160 E1
Big Fork r. U.S.A. 160 E1
Biggar Canada 151 J4
Biggar U.K. 60 F5
Biggar, Lac l. Canada 152 G4
Bigge Island Australia 134 D3
Biggenden Australia 137 F5
Bigger, Mount B.C. Canada 149 M4
Biggesee l. Germany 63 H3
Biggleswade U.K. 59 G6
Biggs CA U.S.A. 158 C2
Biggs OR U.S.A. 156 C3
Big Hole r. U.S.A. 156 E3
Bighorn r. U.S.A. 156 G3
Bighorn Mountains U.S.A. 156 G3
Big Island Nunavut Canada 147 K3
Big Island N.W.T. Canada 150 G2
Big Island Ont. Canada 151 M5
Big Kalzas Lake Y.T. Canada 149 N3
Big Koniuji Island AK U.S.A. 148 H5
Big Lake l. Canada 151 H1
Big Lake AK U.S.A. 149 J3
Big Lake U.S.A. 161 C6
Bignona Senegal 120 B3
Big Pine U.S.A. 158 D3
Big Pine Peak U.S.A. 158 D4
Big Raccoon r. U.S.A. 164 B4
Big Rapids U.S.A. 164 C2
Big River Canada 151 J4
Big Sable Point U.S.A. 164 B1
Big Salmon r. Y.T. Canada 149 N3
Big Salmon (abandoned) Y.T. Canada 149 N3
Big Sand Lake Canada 151 L3
Big Sandy r. U.S.A. 156 F4
Big Sandy Lake Canada 151 J4
Big Smokey Valley U.S.A. 158 E2
Big South Fork National River and Recreation Area park U.S.A. 164 C5
Big Spring U.S.A. 161 C5
Big Stone Canada 151 I5
Big Stone Gap U.S.A. 164 D5
Bigstone Lake Canada 151 M4
Big Timber U.S.A. 156 F3
Big Trout Lake Canada 151 N4
Big Trout Lake l. Canada 151 N4
Big Valley Canada 151 H4

Big Water U.S.A. 159 H3
Bihać Bos.-Herz. 68 F2
Bihar state India 105 F4
Bihariganj India 105 F4
Bihar Sharif India 105 F4
Bihor, Vârful mt. Romania 69 J1
Bihoro Japan 90 G4
Bijagós, Arquipélago dos is Guinea-Bissau 120 B3
Bijaipur India 104 D4
Bijapur India 106 B2
Bījār Iran 110 B3
Bijbehara India 104 C2
Bijeljina Bos.-Herz. 69 H2
Bijelo Polje Montenegro 69 H3
Bijeraghogarh India 104 E5
Bijiang China see Zhiziluo
Bijie China 96 E3
Bijji India 106 D2
Bijnor India 104 D3
Bijnore India see Bijnor
Bijnot Pak. 111 H4
Bijrān well Saudi Arabia 110 C5
Bijrān, Khashm hill Saudi Arabia 110 C5
Bikampur India 104 C4
Bikaner India 104 C3
Bīkhūyeh Iran 110 D5
Bikin Rus. Fed. 90 D3
Bikin r. Rus. Fed. 90 D3
Bikini atoll Marshall Is 186 H5
Bikori Sudan 108 D7
Bikoro Dem. Rep. Congo 122 B4
Bikou China 96 E1
Bikramganj India 105 F4
Bilaa Point Mindanao Phil. 82 D4
Bilād Banī Bū 'Alī Oman 109 I5
Bilaigarh India 106 D1
Bilangbilangan i. Indon. 85 G2
Bilara India 104 C4
Bilaspur Chhattisgarh India 105 E5
Bilaspur Hima. Prad. India 104 D3
Biläsuvar Azer. 113 H3
Bila Tserkva Ukr. 53 F6
Bilauktaung Range mts Myanmar/Thai. 87 B4
Bilbao Spain 67 E2
Bilbays Egypt 112 C5
Bilbeis Egypt see Bilbays
Bilbo Spain see Bilbao
Bil'chir Rus. Fed. 95 G1
Bilecik Turkey 69 M4
Biłgoraj Poland 53 D6
Bilharamulo Tanz. 122 D4
Bilhaur India 104 E4
Bilhorod-Dnistrovs'kyy Ukr. 69 N1
Bili Dem. Rep. Congo 122 C3
Bilibino Rus. Fed. 77 R3
Bilin Myanmar 86 B3
Biliran i. Phil. 82 D4
Bilit Sabah Malaysia 85 G1
Bill U.S.A. 156 G4
Billabalong Australia 135 A6
Billabong Creek r. Australia see Moulamein Creek
Billericay U.K. 59 H7
Billiluna Australia 134 D4
Billingham U.K. 58 F4
Billings U.S.A. 156 F3
Billiton i. Indon. see Belitung
Bill Moores AK U.S.A. 148 G3
Bill of Portland hd U.K. 59 E8
Bill Williams r. U.S.A. 159 F4
Bill Williams Mountain U.S.A. 159 G4
Bilma Niger 120 E3
Bilo r. Rus. Fed. see Belaya
Biloela Australia 136 E5
Bilohirs'k Ukr. 112 D1
Bilohir"ya Ukr. 53 E6
Biloku Guyana 177 G3
Biloli India 106 C2
Bilovods'k Ukr. 53 H6
Biloxi U.S.A. 161 F6
Bilpa Morea Claypan salt flat Australia 136 B5
Bilston U.K. 60 F5
Biltine Chad 121 F3
Bilto Norway 54 L2
Bilugyun Island Myanmar 86 B3
Bilungala Sulawesi Indon. 83 B2
Bilwascarma Nicaragua 166 [inset] J6
Bilyayivka Ukr. 69 N1
Bilzen Belgium 62 F4
Bima Sumbawa Indon. 85 G5
Bima, Teluk b. Sumbawa Indon. 85 G5
Bimberi, Mount Australia 138 D5
Bimbo Cent. Afr. Rep. 121 E4
Bimini Islands Bahamas 163 E7
Bimlipatam India 106 D2
Bināb Iran 110 C2
Bina-Etawa India 104 D4
Binaija, Gunung mt. Seram Indon. 83 D3
Binalbagan Negros Phil. 82 C4
Bīnālūd, Kūh-e mts Iran 110 E2
Binatang Sarawak Malaysia 85 E2
Binboğa Daği mt. Turkey 112 E3
Bincheng Shandong China see Binzhou
Bincheng Shandong China 95 I4
Binchuan China 96 D3
Bindebango Australia 138 C1
Binder Mongolia 95 G1
Bindle Australia 138 D1
Bindu Dem. Rep. Congo 123 B4
Bindura Zimbabwe 123 D5
Binefar Spain 67 G3
Binga Zimbabwe 123 C5
Binga, Monte mt. Moz. 123 D5
Bingara Australia 138 E2
Bingaram i. India 106 B4
Bing Bong Australia 136 B2
Bingcaowan Gansu China 94 E4
Bingen am Rhein Germany 63 H5
Bingham U.S.A. 165 K1
Binghamton U.S.A. 165 H2
Bingmei China see Congjiang
Bingöl Turkey 113 F3
Bingol Daği mt. Turkey 113 F3
Bingxi China see Yushan
Bingzhongluo China 96 C2
Binh Gia Vietnam 86 D2
Binicuil Negros Phil. 82 C4
Binika India 105 E5
Binjai Sumatera Indon. 84 B2
Bin Mürkhan well U.A.E. 110 D5
Binnaway Australia 138 D3
Binongko i. Indon. 83 C4
Binpur India 105 F5
Bintan i. Indon. 84 D2
Bintang, Bukit mts Malaysia 84 C1
Bint Jbeil Lebanon see Bent Jbaïl
Bintuan Phil. 82 C3
Bintuhan Sumatera Indon. 84 C4
Bintulu Sarawak Malaysia 85 F2
Binubusan Luzon Phil. 82 C3
Binxian Heilong. China 90 B3
Binxian Shaanxi China 95 G5
Binxian Shandong China see Bincheng
Binya Australia 138 C5
Binyang China 97 F4
Bin-Yauri Nigeria 120 D3
Binzhou Guangxi China see Binyang
Binzhou Heilong. China see Binxian
Binzhou Shandong China 95 I4
Bioco i. Equat. Guinea 120 D4
Biograd na Moru Croatia 68 F3
Bioko i. Equat. Guinea see Bioco
Biokovo mts Croatia 68 G3
Bi Qu r. Qinghai China 99 F6
Biquinhas Brazil 179 B2
Bir India see Bid
Bira Rus. Fed. 90 D2
Bi'r Abū Jady oasis Syria 107 D1
Bīrag, Kūh-e mts Iran 111 F5
Birāk Libya 121 E2
Birakan Rus. Fed. 90 C2
Bi'r al 'Abd Egypt 107 A4
Bi'r al Ḥalbā well Syria 107 D2
Bi'r al Jifjāfah well Egypt 107 A4
Bi'r al Khamsah well Egypt 112 B5
Bi'r al Māliḥah well Egypt 107 A5
Bi'r al Mulūsi Iraq 113 F4
Bi'r al Munbaṭiḥ well Syria 107 D2
Bi'r al Qaṭrānī well Egypt 112 B5
Bi'r al Ubbayiḍ well Egypt 112 B6
Birandozero Rus. Fed. 52 H3
Bi'r an Nuṣf well Egypt see Bi'r an Nuṣṣ
Bi'r an Nuṣṣ well Egypt 112 B5
Bir Anzarane W. Sahara 120 B2
Birao Cent. Afr. Rep. 122 C2
Bi'r ar Rābiyah well Egypt 112 B5
Birata Turkm. 111 F1
Biratar Bulak spring China 98 E4
Biratnagar Nepal 105 F4
Bi'r aṭ Ṭarfāwī well Libya 112 B5
Bi'r Başīrī well Syria 107 C2
Bi'r Bayḍā' well Egypt 107 B4
Bi'r Baylī well Egypt 112 B5
Bîr Beiḍa well Egypt see Bi'r Bayḍā'
Bi'r Buṭaymān Syria 113 E3
Birch r. Canada 151 H3
Birch Creek AK U.S.A. 149 K2
Birch Creek r. AK U.S.A. 149 K2
Birches AK U.S.A. 148 I2
Birch Hills Canada 151 J4
Birch Island Canada 150 G5
Birch Lake N.W.T. Canada 150 G2
Birch Lake Ont. Canada 151 M5
Birch Lake Sask. Canada 151 I4
Birch Mountains Canada 150 H3
Birch River U.S.A. 164 E4
Birch Run U.S.A. 164 D2
Bircot Eth. 122 E3
Birdaard Neth. see Burdaard
Bîr Dignâsh well Egypt see Bi'r Diqnāsh
Bi'r Diqnāsh well Egypt 112 B5
Bird Island N. Mariana Is see Farallon de Medinilla
Birdseye U.S.A. 159 H2
Birdsville Australia 137 B5
Birecik Turkey 112 E3
Bîr el 'Abd Egypt see Bi'r al 'Abd
Bir el Arbi well Alg. 67 I6
Bîr el Istabl well Egypt see Bi'r Iṣṭabl
Bîr el Khamsa well Egypt see Bi'r al Khamsah
Bîr el Nuṣṣ well Egypt see Bi'r an Nuṣṣ
Bîr el Obeiyiḍ well Egypt see Bi'r al Ubbayiḍ
Bîr el Qatrâni well Egypt see Bi'r al Qaṭrānī
Bîr el Râbia well Egypt see Bi'r ar Rābiyah
Birendranagar Nepal see Surkhet
Bir en Natrûn well Sudan 108 C6
Bireun Sumatera Indon. 84 B1
Bi'r Fāḍil well Saudi Arabia 110 C6
Bi'r Fajr well Saudi Arabia 112 E5
Bi'r Fu'ād well Egypt 112 B5
Bîr Gifgâfa well Egypt see Bi'r al Jifjāfah
Bi'r Ḥajal well Syria 107 D2
Birhan mt. Eth. 122 D2
Bi'r Ḥasanah well Egypt 107 A4
Bi'r Ḥayzān well Saudi Arabia 112 E6
Biri i. Phil. 82 D3
Bi'r Ibn Hirmās Saudi Arabia see Al Bi'r
Bir Ibn Juhayyim Saudi Arabia 110 C6
Birigüi Brazil 179 A3
Bīrīn Syria 107 C2
Bi'r Iṣṭabl well Egypt 112 B5
Bīrjand Iran 110 E3
Bi'r Jubnī well Libya 112 B5
Birkát Hamad well Iraq 113 G5
Birkenfeld Germany 63 H5
Birkenhead U.K. 58 D5
Birkirkara Malta 68 F7
Birksgate Range hills Australia 135 E6
Bîrlad Romania see Bârlad
Bi'r Lahfān well Egypt 107 A4
Birlik Kazakh. 102 D3
Birlik Zhambylskaya Oblast' Kazakh. 98 A3
Birmal reg. Afgh. 111 H3
Birmingham U.K. 59 F6
Birmingham U.S.A. 163 C5
Bîr Mogreïn Mauritania 120 B2
Bi'r Muḥaymid al Wazwaz well Syria 107 D2
Bi'r Nāḥid oasis Egypt 112 C5
Birnin-Gwari Nigeria 120 D3
Birnin-Kebbi Nigeria 120 D3
Birnin Konni Niger 120 D3
Birobidzhan Rus. Fed. 90 D2
Birong Palawan Phil. 82 B4
Bi'r Qaṣīr as Sirr well Egypt 112 B5
Birr Ireland 61 E4
Bi'r Rawḍ Sālim well Egypt 107 A4
Birrie r. Australia 138 C2
Birrindudu Australia 134 E4
Bîr Rôḍ Sâlim well Egypt see Bi'r Rawḍ Sālim
Birsay U.K. 60 F1
Bi'r Shalatayn Egypt 108 E5
Bîr Shalatein Egypt see Bi'r Shalatayn
Birsk Rus. Fed. 51 R4
Birstall U.K. 59 F6
Birstein Germany 63 J4
Bir Ṭalḥah well Saudi Arabia 110 B6
Birthday Mountain hill Australia 136 C2
Birtle Canada 151 K5
Biru Xizang China 99 F7
Birur India 106 B3
Bi'r Usaylīlah well Saudi Arabia 110 B6
Biržai Lith. 55 N8
Bisa India 86 A1
Bisa i. Maluku Indon. 83 C3
Bisai Japan 92 C3
Bisalpur India 104 D3
Bisau India 104 C3
Bisbee U.S.A. 157 F7
Biscay, Bay of sea France/Spain 66 B4
Biscay Abyssal Plain sea feature N. Atlantic Ocean 184 H3
Biscayne National Park U.S.A. 163 D7
Biscoe Islands Antarctica 188 L2
Biscotasi Lake Canada 152 E5
Biscotasing Canada 152 E5
Bisezhai China 96 D4
Bishan China 96 E2
Bishbek Kyrg. see Bishkek
Bishenpur India see Bishnupur

▶Bishkek Kyrg. 102 D3
Capital of Kyrgyzstan.

Bishnath India 96 B3
Bishnupur Manipur India 105 H4
Bishnupur W. Bengal India 105 F5
Bishop U.S.A. 158 D3
Bishop Auckland U.K. 58 F4
Bishop Lake Canada 150 G1
Bishop's Stortford U.K. 59 H7
Bishopville U.S.A. 163 D5
Bishrī, Jabal hills Syria 107 D2
Bishui Heilong. China 90 A1
Bishui Henan China see Biyang
Biskra Alg. 64 F5
Bislig Mindanao Phil. 82 D4
Bislig Bay Mindanao Phil. 82 D4

▶Bismarck U.S.A. 160 C2
Capital of North Dakota.

Bismarck Archipelago is P.N.G. 81 L7
Bismarck Range mts P.N.G. 81 K7
Bismarck Sea P.N.G. 81 L7
Bismark (Altmark) Germany 63 L2
Bismil Turkey 113 F3
Bismo Norway 54 F6
Bison U.S.A. 160 C2
Bīsotūn Iran 110 B3
Bispgården Sweden 54 J5
Bispingen Germany 63 K1
Bissa, Djebel mt. Alg. 67 G5
Bissamcuttak India 106 D2

▶Bissau Guinea-Bissau 120 B3
Capital of Guinea-Bissau.

Bissaula Nigeria 120 E4
Bissett Canada 151 M5
Bistcho Lake Canada 150 G3
Bistrița Romania 69 K1
Bistrița r. Romania 69 L1
Bisucay i. Phil. 82 C4
Bitburg Germany 62 G5
Bitche France 63 H5
Bithur India 104 E4
Bithynia reg. Turkey 69 M4
Bitkine Chad 121 E3
Bitlis Turkey 113 F3
Bitola Macedonia 69 I4
Bitolj Macedonia see Bitola
Bitonto Italy 68 G4
Bitrān, Jabal hill Saudi Arabia 110 B6
Bitra Par reef India 106 B4
Bitter Creek r. U.S.A. 159 I2
Bitterfeld Germany 63 M3
Bitterfontein S. Africa 124 D6
Bitter Lakes Egypt 112 D5
Bitterroot r. U.S.A. 156 E3
Bitterroot Range mts U.S.A. 156 E3
Bitterwater U.S.A. 158 C3
Bittkau Germany 63 L2
Bitung Sulawesi Indon. 83 C2
Biu Nigeria 120 E3
Biwa-ko l. Japan 92 B3
Biwa-ko Kokutei-kōen park Japan 92 C3
Biwmaris U.K. see Beaumaris
Biyang China 97 G1
Biye K'obē Eth. 122 E2
Biysk Rus. Fed. 88 F2
Bizana S. Africa 125 I6
Bizerta Tunisia see Bizerte
Bizerte Tunisia 68 C6
Bīzhanābād Iran 110 E5

▶Bjargtangar hd Iceland 54 [inset]
Most westerly point of Europe.

Bjästa Sweden 54 K5
Bjelovar Croatia 68 G2
Bjerkvik Norway 54 J2
Bjerringbro Denmark 55 F8
Bjørgan Norway 54 G5
Björkliden Sweden 54 K2
Björklinge Sweden 55 J6
Bjorli Norway 54 F5
Björna Sweden 54 K5
Björneborg Fin. see Pori

▶Bjørnøya i. Arctic Ocean 76 C2
Part of Norway.

Bjurholm Sweden 54 K5
Bla Mali 120 C3
Black r. Man. Canada 151 L5
Black r. Ont. Canada 152 E4
Black r. Canada/U.S.A. 149 K2
Black AK U.S.A. 148 F3
Black r. AR U.S.A. 161 F5
Black r. AR U.S.A. 161 F5
Black r. AZ U.S.A. 159 H5
Black r. Vietnam 86 D2
Blackadder Water r. U.K. 60 G5
Blackall Australia 136 D5
Blackbear r. Canada 151 N4
Black Birch Lake Canada 151 J3
Black Bourton U.K. 59 F7
Blackbull Australia 136 C3
Blackburn U.K. 58 E5
Blackburn, Mount AK U.S.A. 149 L3
Blackbutt Australia 138 F1
Black Butte mt. U.S.A. 158 B2
Black Butte Lake U.S.A. 158 B2
Black Canyon gorge U.S.A. 159 F4
Black Canyon of the Gunnison National Park U.S.A. 159 J2
Black Combe hill U.K. 58 D4
Black Creek watercourse U.S.A. 159 I4
Black Donald Lake Canada 165 G1
Blackdown Tableland National Park Australia 136 E4
Blackduck U.S.A. 160 E2
Blackfalds Canada 150 H4
Blackfoot U.S.A. 156 E4
Black Foot r. U.S.A. 156 E3
Black Forest mts Germany 57 L7
Black Hill hill U.K. 58 F5
Black Hills SD U.S.A. 154 G3
Black Hills SD U.S.A. 156 G3
Black Island Canada 151 L5
Black Lake Canada 151 J3
Black Lake l. Canada 151 J3
Black Lake l. U.S.A. 164 C1
Black Mesa mt. U.S.A. 159 I5
Black Mesa ridge U.S.A. 159 H3
Black Mountain Pak. 111 I3
Black Mountain hill U.K. 59 D7
Black Mountain AK U.S.A. 148 G1
Black Mountain CA U.S.A. 158 E4
Black Mountain KY U.S.A. 164 D5
Black Mountain NM U.S.A. 159 I5
Black Mountains hills U.K. 59 D7
Black Mountains U.S.A. 159 F4
Black Nossob watercourse Namibia 124 D2
Black Pagoda India see Konarka
Blackpool U.K. 58 D5
Black Range mts U.S.A. 159 I5
Black Rapids AK U.S.A. 149 K3
Black River MI U.S.A. 164 D1
Black River NY U.S.A. 165 H1
Black River Falls U.S.A. 160 F2
Black Rock hill Jordan see 'Unāb, Jabal al
Black Rock Desert U.S.A. 156 D4
Blacksburg U.S.A. 164 E5
Black Sea Asia/Europe 53 H8
Blacks Fork r. U.S.A. 156 F4
Blackshear U.S.A. 163 D6
Blacksod Bay Ireland 61 B3
Black Springs U.S.A. 158 D2
Blackstairs Mountains hills Ireland 61 F5
Blackstone r. Y.T. Canada 149 M2
Blackstone U.S.A. 165 F5
Black Sugarloaf mt. Australia 138 E3
Black Tickle Canada 153 L3
Blackville Australia 138 E3
Blackwater Australia 136 E4
Blackwater Ireland 61 F5
Blackwater r. Ireland 61 E5
Blackwater r. Ireland/U.K. 61 F3
Blackwater watercourse U.S.A. 161 C5
Blackwater Lake N.W.T. Canada 149 Q3
Blackwater Reservoir U.K. 60 E4
Blackwood r. Australia 135 A8
Blackwood National Park Australia 136 D4
Bladensburg National Park Australia 136 C4
Blaenavon U.K. 59 D7
Blagodarnoye Kazakh. 98 C3
Blagodarnyy Rus. Fed. 113 F1
Blagoevgrad Bulg. 69 J3
Blagoveshchensk Amurskaya Oblast' Rus. Fed. 90 B2
Blagoveshchensk Respublika Bashkortostan Rus. Fed. 51 R4
Blaikiston, Mount Canada 150 H5
Blaine Lake Canada 151 J4
Blair U.S.A. 160 D3
Blair Athol Australia 136 D4
Blair Atholl U.K. 60 F4
Blairgowrie U.K. 60 F4
Blairsden U.S.A. 158 C2
Blairsville U.S.A. 163 D5
Blakang Mati, Pulau i. Sing. see Sentosa
Blakely U.S.A. 163 C6
Blakeney U.K. 59 I6
Blambangan, Semenanjung pen. Indon. 85 F5

▶Blanc, Mont mt. France/Italy 66 H4
5th highest mountain in Europe.

Blanca, Bahía b. Arg. 178 D5
Blanca, Sierra mt. U.S.A. 157 G6
Blanca Peak U.S.A. 157 G5
Blanche, Lake salt flat S.A. Australia 137 B6
Blanche, Lake salt flat W.A. Australia 134 C5
Blanchester U.S.A. 164 D4
Blanc Nez, Cap c. France 62 B4
Blanco r. Bol. 176 F6
Blanco U.S.A. 159 J3
Blanco, Cabo c. Costa Rica 166 [inset] I7
Blanco, Cape U.S.A. 156 B4
Blanc-Sablon Canada 153 K4
Bland r. Australia 138 C4
Bland U.S.A. 164 E5
Blanda r. Iceland 54 [inset]
Blandford Forum U.K. 59 E8
Blanding U.S.A. 159 I3
Blanes Spain 67 H3
Blangah, Telok Sing. 87 [inset]
Blangkejeren Sumatera Indon. 84 B2
Blangpidie Sumatera Indon. 84 B2
Blankenberge Belgium 62 D3
Blankenheim Germany 62 G4
Blanquilla, Isla i. Venez. 176 F1
Blansko Czech Rep. 57 P6
Blantyre Malawi 123 D5
Blarney Ireland 61 D6
Blau Sulawesi Indon. 83 B2
Blaufelden Germany 63 J5
Blåviksjön Sweden 54 K4
Blaye France 66 D4
Blayney Australia 138 D4
Blaze, Point Australia 134 E3
Bleckede Germany 63 K1
Blega Jawa Indon. 85 F4
Bleilochtalsperre resr Germany 63 L4
Blenheim Canada 164 E2
Blenheim N.Z. 139 D5
Blenheim Palace tourist site U.K. 59 F7
Blerick Neth. 62 G3
Blessington Lakes Ireland 61 F4
Bletchley U.K. 59 G6
Blida Alg. 67 H5
Blies r. Germany 63 H5
Bligh Water b. Fiji 133 H3
Blind River Canada 152 E5
Bliss U.S.A. 156 E4
Blissfield U.S.A. 164 D3
Blitar Jawa Indon. 85 F5
Blitta Togo 120 D4
Blocher U.S.A. 164 C4
Block Island U.S.A. 165 J3
Block Island Sound sea chan. U.S.A. 165 J3
Bloemfontein S. Africa 125 H5
Bloemhof S. Africa 125 G4
Bloemhof Dam S. Africa 125 G4
Bloemhof Dam Nature Reserve S. Africa 125 G4
Blomberg Germany 63 J3
Blönduós Iceland 54 [inset]
Blongas Lombok Indon. 85 G5
Bloods Range mts Australia 135 E6
Bloodsworth Island U.S.A. 165 G4
Bloodvein r. Canada 151 L5
Bloody r. N.W.T. Canada 149 Q2
Bloody Foreland pt Ireland 61 D2
Bloomer U.S.A. 160 F2
Bloomfield Canada 165 G2
Bloomfield IA U.S.A. 160 E3
Bloomfield IN U.S.A. 164 B4
Bloomfield MO U.S.A. 161 F4
Bloomfield NM U.S.A. 159 J3
Blooming Prairie U.S.A. 160 E3
Bloomington IL U.S.A. 160 F3
Bloomington IN U.S.A. 164 B4
Bloomington MN U.S.A. 160 E2
Bloomsburg U.S.A. 165 G3
Blora Jawa Indon. 85 E4
Blossburg U.S.A. 165 G3
Blosseville Kyst coastal area Greenland 147 P3
Blouberg S. Africa 125 I2
Blouberg Nature Reserve S. Africa 125 I2
Blountstown U.S.A. 163 C6
Blountville U.S.A. 164 D5
Blow r. Y.T. Canada 149 M1
Bloxham U.K. 59 F6
Blue r. B.C. Canada 149 O4
Blue watercourse U.S.A. 159 I5
Blue Bell Knoll mt. U.S.A. 159 H2
Blueberry r. Canada 150 F3
Blue Creek r. Mex. see Azul
Blue Diamond U.S.A. 159 F3
Blue Earth U.S.A. 160 E3
Bluefield VA U.S.A. 162 D4
Bluefield WV U.S.A. 164 E5
Bluefields Nicaragua 166 [inset] J6
Blue Hills Turks and Caicos Is 163 F8
Blue Knob hill U.S.A. 165 F3
Blue Mesa Reservoir U.S.A. 159 J2
Blue Mountain hill Canada 153 K4
Blue Mountain India 105 H5
Blue Mountain Lake U.S.A. 165 H2
Blue Mountain Pass Lesotho 125 H5
Blue Mountains Australia 138 D4
Blue Mountains U.S.A. 156 D3
Blue Mountains National Park Australia 138 E4
Blue Nile r. Eth./Sudan 108 D6
also known as Abay Wenz (Ethiopia), Bahr el Azraq (Sudan)
Bluenose Lake Nunavut Canada 149 R1
Blue Ridge GA U.S.A. 163 C5
Blue Ridge VA U.S.A. 164 F5
Blue Ridge mts U.S.A. 164 E5
Blue Stack hill Ireland 61 D3
Blue Stack Mts hills Ireland 61 D3
Bluestone Lake U.S.A. 164 E5
Bluewater U.S.A. 159 J4
Bluff N.Z. 139 B8
Bluff U.S.A. 159 I3
Bluffdale U.S.A. 159 H1
Bluff Island H.K. China 97 [inset]
Bluff Knoll mt. Australia 135 B8
Bluffton IN U.S.A. 164 C3
Bluffton OH U.S.A. 164 D3
Blumenau Brazil 179 A4
Blustry Mountain Canada 156 C2
Blyde River Canyon Nature Reserve S. Africa 125 J3
Blying Sound sea channel AK U.S.A. 149 J4
Blyth Canada 164 E2
Blyth England U.K. 58 F3
Blyth England U.K. 58 F5
Blythe U.S.A. 159 F5
Blytheville U.S.A. 161 F5
Bø Norway 55 F7
Bo Sierra Leone 120 B4
Boac Phil. 82 C3
Boaco Nicaragua 166 [inset] I6
Boa Esperança Brazil 179 B3
Bo'ai Henan China 95 H5
Bo'ai Yunnan China 96 E4
Boali Cent. Afr. Rep. 122 B3
Boalsert Neth. see Bolsward
Boane Moz. 125 K4
Boano i. Maluku Indon. 83 C3
Boano, Selat sea chan. Maluku Indon. 83 C3
Boa Nova Brazil 179 C1
Boardman U.S.A. 164 E3
Boatlaname Botswana 125 G2
Boa Viagem Brazil 177 K5
Boa Vista Brazil 176 F3
Boa Vista i. Cape Verde 120 [inset]
Bobadah Australia 138 C4
Bobai China 97 F4
Bobaomby, Tanjona c. Madag. 123 E5
Bobbili India 106 D2
Bobcaygeon Canada 165 F1
Bobo-Dioulasso Burkina 120 C3
Bobon Samar Phil. 82 D3
Bobotov Kuk mt. Montenegro see Durmitor
Bobriki Rus. Fed. see Novomoskovsk
Bobrinets Ukr. see Bobrynets'
Bobrov Rus. Fed. 53 I6
Bobrovitsa Ukr. see Bobrovytsya
Bobrovytsya Ukr. 53 F6
Bobruysk Belarus see Babruysk
Bobrynets' Ukr. 53 G6
Bobs Lake Canada 165 G1
Bobuk Sudan 108 D7
Bobures Venez. 176 D2
Boby mt. Madag. 123 E6
Boca del Río Mex. 167 F5
Boca de Macareo Venez. 176 F2
Boca do Acre Brazil 176 E5
Boca do Jari Brazil 177 H4
Bocaiúva Brazil 179 C2
Bocaranga Cent. Afr. Rep. 122 B3
Boca Raton U.S.A. 163 D7
Bocas del Toro Panama 166 [inset] J7
Bocas del Toro, Archipiélago de is Panama 166 [inset] J7
Bochnia Poland 57 R6
Bocholt Germany 62 G3
Bochum Germany 63 H3
Bochum S. Africa see Senwabarwana
Bockenem Germany 63 K2
Bocoio Angola 123 B5
Bocoyna Mex. 166 D3
Boda Cent. Afr. Rep. 122 B3
Bodalla Australia 138 E6
Bodallin Australia 135 B7
Bodaybo Rus. Fed. 77 M4
Boddam U.K. 60 H3
Bode r. Germany 63 L3
Bodega Head hd U.S.A. 158 B2
Bodélé reg. Chad 121 E3
Boden Sweden 54 L4
Bodenham U.K. 59 E6
Bodensee l. Germany/Switz. see Constance, Lake
Bodenteich Germany 63 K2
Bodenwerder Germany 63 J3
Bodie (abandoned) U.S.A. 158 D2
Bodinayakkanur India 106 C4
Bodmin U.K. 59 C8
Bodmin Moor moorland U.K. 59 C8
Bodø Norway 54 I3
Bodonchiyn Gol watercourse Mongolia 94 C2
Bodoquena Brazil 177 G7
Bodoquena, Serra da hills Brazil 178 E2
Bodrum Turkey 69 L6
Bodträskfors Sweden 54 L3
Boechout Belgium 62 E3
Boende Dem. Rep. Congo 121 F5
Bo Epinang Sulawesi Indon. 83 B4
Boerne U.S.A. 161 D6
Boeuf r. U.S.A. 161 F6
Boffa Guinea 120 B3
Bogalay Myanmar see Bogale
Bogale Myanmar 86 A3
Bogale r. Myanmar 86 A4
Bogalusa U.S.A. 161 F6
Bogan r. Australia 138 C2
Bogandé Burkina 120 C3
Bogan Gate Australia 138 C4
Bogani Nani Wartabone, Taman Nasional nat. park Indon. 83 B2
Boğazlıyan Turkey 112 D3

Bogcang Zangbo *r. Xizang* China 99 D7
Bogd Mongolia **94** E2
Bogd *Övörhangay* Mongolia **94** E2
Bogda Feng *mt. Xinjiang* China 98 E4
Bogda Shan *mts* China **94** B3
Boggabilla Australia **138** E2
Boggabri Australia **138** E3
Boggeragh Mts *hills* Ireland **61** C5
Boghar Alg. **67** H6
Boghari Alg. *see* **Ksar el Boukhari**
Bognor Regis U.K. **59** G8
Bogo *Cebu* Phil. **82** D4
Bogodukhov Ukr. *see* **Bohodukhiv**
Bog of Allen *reg.* Ireland **61** E4
Bogong, Mount Australia **138** C6
Bogopol' Rus. Fed. **90** D3
Bogor *Jawa* Indon. **84** D4
Bogoroditsk Rus. Fed. **53** H5
Bogorodsk Rus. Fed. **52** I4
Bogorodskoye *Khabarovskiy Kray* Rus. Fed. **90** F1
Bogorodskoye *Kirovskaya Oblast'* Rus. Fed. **52** K4
Bogoslof Island *AK* U.S.A. **148** E5

▶**Bogotá** Col. **176** D3
Capital of Colombia. 4th most populous city in South America.

Bogotol Rus. Fed. **76** J4
Bogoyavlenskoye Rus. Fed. *see* **Pervomayskiy**
Bogra Bangl. **105** G4
Boguchany Rus. Fed. **77** K4
Boguchar Rus. Fed. **53** I6
Bogué Mauritania **120** B3
Boh *r.* Indon. **85** F2
Bo Hai *g.* China **95** I4
Bohai Haixia *sea chan.* China **95** J4
Bohain-en-Vermandois France **62** D5
Bohai Wan *b.* China **78** D4
Bohemian Forest *mts* Germany *see* **Böhmer Wald**
Böhlen Germany **63** M3
Bohlokong S. Africa **125** I5
Böhme *r.* Germany **63** J2
Böhmer Wald *mts* Germany **63** M5
Bohmte Germany **63** I2
Bohodukhiv Ukr. **53** G6
Bohol *i.* Phil. **82** D4
Bohol Sea Phil. **82** D4
Bohol Strait Phil. **82** C4
Bohu *Xinjiang* China **98** D4
Boiaçu Brazil **176** F4
Boichoko S. Africa **124** F5
Boigu Island Australia **81** K8
Boikhutso S. Africa **125** H4
Boileau, Cape Australia **134** C4
Boim Brazil **177** G4
Boipeba, Ilha *i.* Brazil **179** D1
Bois *r.* Brazil **179** A2
Bois, Lac des *l.* N.W.T. Canada **149** P2
Bois Blanc Island U.S.A. **162** C2

▶**Boise** U.S.A. **156** D4
Capital of Idaho.

Boise City U.S.A. **161** C4
Boissevain Canada **151** K5
Boitumelong S. Africa **125** G4
Boizenburg Germany **63** K1
Bojd Iran **110** E3
Bojeador, Cape *Luzon* Phil. **82** C2
Bojnūrd Iran **110** E2
Bojonegoro *Jawa* Indon. **85** E4
Bojong *Jawa* Indon. **84** D4
Bokaak *atoll* Marshall Is *see* **Taongi**
Bokajan India **105** H4
Bokaro India **105** F5
Bokaro Reservoir India **105** F5
Bokat *Sulawesi* Indon. **83** B2
Bokatola Dem. Rep. Congo **122** B4
Boké Guinea **120** B3
Boke Kazakh. **98** C2
Bokele Dem. Rep. Congo **122** C4
Bokhara *r.* Australia **138** C2
Bo Kheo Cambodia *see* **Bå Kêv**
Boknafjorden *sea chan.* Norway **55** D7
Bokoko Dem. Rep. Congo **122** C3
Bökönbaev Kyrg. **98** B4
Bokoro Chad **121** E3
Bokovskaya Rus. Fed. **53** I6
Bokspits S. Africa **124** E4
Boktor Rus. Fed. **90** E2
Bokurdak Turkm. **110** E2
Bol Chad **121** E3
Bolaang *Sulawesi* Indon. **83** B3
Bolaiti Dem. Rep. Congo **121** F5
Bolama Guinea-Bissau **120** B3
Bolangir India **106** D1
Bolan Pass Pak. **111** G4
Bolavén, Phouphiang *plat.* Laos **86** D4
Bolbec France **66** E2
Bole *Xinjiang* China **98** C3
Bole Ghana **120** C4
Boleko Dem. Rep. Congo **122** B4
Bolen Rus. Fed. **90** D2
Bolgar Rus. Fed. **53** K5
Bolgatanga Ghana **120** C3
Bolgrad Ukr. *see* **Bolhrad**
Bolhrad Ukr. **69** M2
Boli China **90** C3
Bolia Dem. Rep. Congo **122** B4
Boliden Sweden **54** L4
Bolinao *Luzon* Phil. **82** B2
Bolingbrook U.S.A. **164** A3
Bolintin-Vale Romania **69** K2
Bolívar Peru **176** C5
Bolivar *NY* U.S.A. **165** F2
Bolivar *TN* U.S.A. **161** F5
Bolívar, Pico *mt.* Venez. **176** D2
Bolivia Cuba **163** E8

▶**Bolivia** *country* S. America **176** E7
5th largest country in South America.

Bolkhov Rus. Fed. **53** H5
Bollène France **66** G4
Bollnäs Sweden **55** J6
Bollon Australia **138** C2
Bollstabruk Sweden **54** J5
Bolmen *l.* Sweden **55** H8
Bolo *Panay* Phil. **82** C4
Bolobo Dem. Rep. Congo **122** B4
Bolod Islands Phil. **82** C5
Bologna Italy **68** D2
Bolognesi Peru **176** D5
Bologoye Rus. Fed. **52** G4
Bolokanang S. Africa **125** G5
Bolomba Dem. Rep. Congo **122** B3
Bolon' Rus. Fed. *see* **Achan**
Bolong *Mindanao* Phil. **82** C5
Bolpur India **105** F5
Bolsena, Lago di *l.* Italy **68** D3
Bol'shakovo Rus. Fed. **55** L9
Bol'shaya Chernigovka Rus. Fed. **51** Q5
Bol'shaya Glushitsa Rus. Fed. **53** K5
Bol'shaya Imandra, Ozero *l.* Rus. Fed. **54** R3
Bol'shaya Martinovka Rus. Fed. **53** I7
Bol'shaya Osinovaya *r.* Rus. Fed. **148** A2
Bol'shaya Tsarevshchina Rus. Fed. *see* **Volzhskiy**
Bol'shaya Vladimirovka Kazakh. **98** B2
Bol'shenarymskoye Kazakh. **102** F2
Bol'shevik, Ostrov *i.* Rus. Fed. **77** L2
Bol'shezemel'skaya Tundra *lowland* Rus. Fed. **52** L2
Bol'shiye Barsuki, Peski *des.* Kazakh. **102** A2
Bol'shiye Chirki Rus. Fed. **52** J3
Bol'shiye Kozly Rus. Fed. **52** H2
Bol'shoy Aksu Kazakh. **98** B4
Bol'shoy Begichev, Ostrov *i.* Rus. Fed. **189** E2
Bol'shoy Bukon' Kazakh. **98** C2
Bol'shoye Murashkino Rus. Fed. **52** J5
Bol'shoy Irgiz *r.* Rus. Fed. **53** J6
Bol'shoy Kamen' Rus. Fed. **90** D4
Bol'shoy Kavkaz *mts* Asia/Europe *see* **Caucasus**
Bol'shoy Kundysh *r.* Rus. Fed. **52** J4
Bol'shoy Lyakhovskiy, Ostrov *i.* Rus. Fed. **77** P2
Bol'shoy Tokmak Kyrg. *see* **Tokmok**
Bol'shoy Tokmak Ukr. *see* **Tokmak**
Bolsón de Mapimí *des.* Mex. **166** D3
Bolsward Neth. **62** F1
Bolton Canada **164** F2
Bolton *Mindanao* Phil. **82** D5
Bolton U.K. **58** E5
Bolu Turkey **69** N4
Boluntay *Qinghai* China **99** F5
Boluo China **97** G4
Bolus Head *hd* Ireland **61** B6
Bolvadin Turkey **69** N5
Bolzano Italy **68** D1
Boma Dem. Rep. Congo **123** B4
Bomaderry Australia **138** E5
Bombala Australia **138** D6
Bombay India *see* **Mumbai**
Bombay Beach U.S.A. **159** F5
Bomberai, Semenanjung *pen.* Indon. **81** I7
Bömbögör Mongolia **94** D2
Bomboma Dem. Rep. Congo **122** B3
Bom Comércio Brazil **176** E5
Bomdila India **105** H4
Bomi *Xizang* China **99** F7
Bomili Dem. Rep. Congo **122** C3
Bom Jardim Brazil **179** D1
Bom Jardim de Goiás Brazil **179** A2
Bom Jesus Brazil **179** A5
Bom Jesus da Gurgueia, Serra do *hills* Brazil **177** J5
Bom Jesus da Lapa Brazil **179** C1
Bom Jesus do Norte Brazil **179** C3
Bømlo *i.* Norway **55** D7
Bomokandi *r.* Dem. Rep. Congo **122** C3
Bom Retiro Brazil **179** A4
Bom Sucesso Brazil **179** B3
Bon, Cap *c.* Tunisia **68** D6
Bon, Ko *i.* Thai. **87** B5
Bona Alg. *see* **Annaba**
Bona, Mount *AK* U.S.A. **149** L3
Bonāb Iran **110** B2
Bon Air U.S.A. **165** G5
Bonaire *i.* Neth. Antilles **169** K6
Bonandolok *Sumatera* Indon. **84** B2
Bonanza Nicaragua **166** [inset] I6
Bonanza Peak U.S.A. **156** C2
Bonaparte Archipelago *is* Australia **134** D3
Bonaparte Lake Canada **150** F5
Bonar Bridge U.K. **60** E3
Bonasila Dome *hill AK* U.S.A. **148** G3
Bonavista Canada **153** L4
Bonavista Bay Canada **153** L4
Bonchester Bridge U.K. **60** G5
Bondo Dem. Rep. Congo **122** C3
Bondoc Peninsula *Luzon* Phil. **82** C3
Bondokodi *Sumba* Indon. **83** A5
Bondoukou Côte d'Ivoire **120** C4
Bondowoso *Jawa* Indon. **85** F4
Bonduel U.S.A. **164** A1
Bondyuzhskiy Rus. Fed. *see* **Mendeleyevsk**
Bône Alg. *see* **Annaba**
Bone *Sulawesi* Indon. **83** B4
Bone, Teluk *b.* Indon. **83** B4
Bonelipu *Sulawesi* Indon. **83** B4
Bönen Germany **63** H3
Bonerate *Sulawesi* Indon. **83** B4
Bonerate *i.* Indon. **83** B4
Bonerate, Kepulauan *is* Indon. **83** B4
Bo'ness U.K. **60** F4
Bonete, Cerro *mt.* Arg. **178** C3
Bonga Eth. **122** D3
Bongabong *Mindoro* Phil. **82** C3
Bongaigaon India **105** G4
Bongandanga Dem. Rep. Congo **122** C3
Bongani S. Africa **124** F5
Bongao Phil. **82** B5
Bongba *Xizang* China **99** C6
Bong Co *l.* China **99** E7
Bongka *r.* Indon. **83** B3
Bongo *i.* Phil. **82** D5
Bongo, Massif des *mts* Cent. Afr. Rep. **122** C3
Bongo, Serra do *mts* Angola **123** B4
Bongolava *mts* Madag. **123** E5
Bongor Chad **121** E3
Bông Sơn Vietnam **87** E4
Bonham U.S.A. **161** D5
Bonheiden Belgium **62** E3
Boni Mali **120** C3
Bonifacio *Corsica* France **66** I6
Bonifacio, Bocche di *strait* France/Italy *see* **Bonifacio, Strait of**
Bonifacio, Bouches de *strait* France/Italy *see* **Bonifacio, Strait of**
Bonifacio, Strait of France/Italy **66** I6

▶**Bonin Islands** Japan **91** F8
Part of Japan.

Bonjol *Sumatera* Indon. **84** C2

▶**Bonn** Germany **62** H4
Former capital of Germany.

Bonna Germany *see* **Bonn**
Bonnåsjøen Norway **54** I3
Bonners Ferry U.S.A. **156** D2
Bonnet, Lac du *resr* Canada **151** M5
Bonnet Plume *r. Y.T.* Canada **149** N2
Bonneville France **66** H3
Bonneville Salt Flats U.S.A. **159** G1
Bonnières-sur-Seine France **62** B5
Bonnie Rock Australia **135** B7
Bonnieville U.S.A. **164** C5
Bonnyrigg U.K. **60** F5
Bonnyville Canada **151** I4
Bonobono *Palawan* Phil. **82** B4
Bononia Italy *see* **Bologna**
Bonorva *Sardinia* Italy **68** C4
Bonshaw Australia **138** E2
Bontang *Kalimantan* Indon. **85** G2
Bontebok National Park S. Africa **124** E8
Bonthe Sierra Leone **120** B4
Bontoc *Luzon* Phil. **82** C2
Bontomatane *Sulawesi* Indon. **83** B4
Bontosunggu *Sulawesi* Indon. **83** A4
Bontrug S. Africa **125** G7
Bonvouloir Islands P.N.G. **136** E1
Bonwapitse Botswana **125** H2
Boo, Kepulauan *is Papua* Indon. **83** D3
Book Cliffs *ridge* U.S.A. **159** I2
Booker U.S.A. **161** C4
Boolba Australia **138** D2
Booligal Australia **138** B4
Boomer U.S.A. **164** E4
Boomi Australia **138** D2
Boon U.S.A. **164** C1
Boonah Australia **138** F1
Boone *CO* U.S.A. **157** G5
Boone *IA* U.S.A. **160** E3
Boone *NC* U.S.A. **162** D4
Boone Lake U.S.A. **164** D5
Boones Mill U.S.A. **164** F5
Booneville *AR* U.S.A. **161** E5
Booneville *KY* U.S.A. **164** D5
Booneville *MS* U.S.A. **161** F5
Bööntsagaan Nuur *salt l.* Mongolia **94** D2
Boonville *CA* U.S.A. **158** B2
Boonville *IN* U.S.A. **164** B4
Boonville *MO* U.S.A. **160** E4
Boonville *NY* U.S.A. **165** H2
Boorabin National Park Australia **135** C7
Booroma Somalia **122** E3
Booroorban Australia **138** B5
Boorowa Australia **138** D5
Boort Australia **138** A6
Boothby, Cape Antarctica **188** D2
Boothia, Gulf of Canada **147** J3
Boothia Peninsula Canada **147** I2
Bootle U.K. **58** E5
Booué Gabon **122** B4
Boppard Germany **63** H4
Boqê *Xizang* China **99** E7
Boqueirão, Serra do *hills* Brazil **177** J6
Boquilla, Presa de la *resr* Mex. **166** D3
Boquillas del Carmen Mex. **166** E2
Bor Czech Rep. **63** M5
Bor Rus. Fed. **52** J4
Bor Serbia **69** J2
Bor Sudan **121** G4
Bor Turkey **112** D3
Boraha, Nosy *i.* Madag. **123** F5
Borah Peak U.S.A. **156** E3
Borai India **106** D1
Borakalalo Nature Reserve S. Africa **125** H3
Boran Kazakh. *see* **Buran**
Boraphet, Bung *l.* Thai. **86** C4
Boraphet, Nong *l.* Thai. *see* **Boraphet, Bung**
Borås Sweden **55** H8
Borasambar India **106** D1
Borāzjān Iran **110** C4
Borba Brazil **177** G4
Borba China **96** C1
Borbon *Cebu* Phil. **82** D4
Borborema, Planalto da *plat.* Brazil **177** K5
Borchen Germany **63** I3
Borçka Turkey **113** F2
Bor Dağı *mt.* Turkey **69** M6
Bordeaux France **66** D4
Borden Island Canada **147** G2
Borden Peninsula Canada **147** J2
Border Ranges National Park Australia **138** F2
Borðeyri Iceland **54** [inset]
Bordj Bou Arréridj Alg. **67** I5
Bordj Bounaama Alg. **67** G6
Bordj Flye Ste-Marie Alg. **120** C2
Bordj Messaouda Alg. **64** F5
Bordj Mokhtar Alg. **120** D2
Bordj Omar Driss Alg. *see* **Bordj Omer Driss**
Bordj Omer Driss Alg. **120** D2
Bordu Kyrg. **98** A4
Boreas Abyssal Plain *sea feature* Arctic Ocean **189** H1
Borel *r.* Canada **153** H2
Borgå Fin. *see* **Porvoo**
Borgarfjörður Iceland **54** [inset]
Borgarnes Iceland **54** [inset]
Børgefjell Nasjonalpark *nat. park* Norway **54** H4
Borger U.S.A. **161** C5
Borgholm Sweden **55** J8
Borgne, Lake *b.* U.S.A. **161** F6
Borgo San Lorenzo Italy **68** D3
Bori India **106** C1
Bori *r.* India **104** C5
Borikhan Laos **86** C3
Borislav Ukr. *see* **Boryslav**
Borisoglebsk Rus. Fed. **53** I6
Borisov Belarus *see* **Barysaw**
Borisovka Rus. Fed. **53** H6
Borispol' Ukr. *see* **Boryspil'**
Bo River Post Sudan **121** F4
Borja Peru **176** C4
Borken Germany **62** G3
Borkenes Norway **54** J2
Borkovskaya Rus. Fed. **52** K2
Borkum Germany **62** G1
Borkum *i.* Germany **62** G1
Borlänge Sweden **55** I6
Borlaug Norway **55** E6
Borlu Turkey **69** M5
Borna Germany **63** M3
Born-Berge *hill* Germany **63** K3
Borndiep *sea chan.* Neth. **62** F1
Borne Neth. **62** G2

▶**Borneo** *i.* Asia **80** E6
Largest island in Asia, and 3rd in the world.

Bornholm *county* Denmark **189** H3
Bornholm *i.* Denmark **55** I9
Bornova Turkey **69** L5
Borobudur *tourist site* Indon. **85** E4
Borodino Rus. Fed. **76** J3
Borodinskoye Rus. Fed. **55** P6
Borogontsy Rus. Fed. **77** O3
Borohoro Shan *mts* China **98** C3
Boroko *Sulawesi* Indon. **83** B2
Borok-Sulezhskiy Rus. Fed. **52** H4
Boromo Burkina **120** C3
Boron U.S.A. **158** E4
Borondi India **106** D2
Borongan *Samar* Phil. **82** D4
Boroughbridge U.K. **58** F4
Borovichi Rus. Fed. **52** G4
Borovoy *Kirovskaya Oblast'* Rus. Fed. **52** K4
Borovoy *Respublika Kareliya* Rus. Fed. **54** R4
Borovoy *Respublika Komi* Rus. Fed. **52** L3
Borpeta India *see* **Barpeta**
Borrisokane Ireland **61** D5
Borroloola Australia **136** B3
Børsa Norway **54** G5
Borşa Romania **53** E7
Borsakelmas sho'rxogi *salt marsh* Uzbek. **113** J2
Borshchiv Ukr. **53** E6
Borshchovochnyy Khrebet *mts* Rus. Fed. **95** G1
Bortala *Xinjiang* China *see* **Bole**
Bortala He *r.* China **98** C3
Borton U.S.A. **164** B4
Bor-Üdzüür Mongolia *see* **Altay**
Borūjen Iran **110** C4
Borūjerd Iran **110** C3
Bor Ul Shan *mts* China **94** D3
Borun Iran **110** E3
Borve U.K. **60** C3
Boryslav Ukr. **53** D6
Boryspil' Ukr. **53** F6
Borzna Ukr. **53** G6
Borzya Rus. Fed. **95** I1
Borzya *r.* Rus. Fed. **95** H1
Bosaga Kazakh. **98** A3
Bosanska Dubica Bos.-Herz. **68** G2
Bosanska Gradiška Bos.-Herz. **68** G2
Bosanska Krupa Bos.-Herz. **68** G2
Bosanski Novi Bos.-Herz. **68** G2
Bosansko Grahovo Bos.-Herz. **68** G2
Boscawen Island Tonga *see* **Niuatoputopu**
Bose China **96** E4
Bosencheve, Parque Nacional *nat. park* Mex. **167** E5
Boshof S. Africa **125** G5
Boshruyeh Iran **110** E3
Bosna i Hercegovina *country* Europe *see* **Bosnia-Herzegovina**
Bosna Saray Bos.-Herz. *see* **Sarajevo**
Bosnia-Herzegovina *country* Europe **68** G2
Bosobogolo Pan *salt pan* Botswana **124** F3
Bosobolo Dem. Rep. Congo **122** B3
Bōsō-hantō *pen.* Japan **93** G3
Bosporus *strait* Turkey **69** M4
Bossaga Turkm. *see* **Basaga**
Bossangoa Cent. Afr. Rep. **122** B3
Bossembélé Cent. Afr. Rep. **122** B3
Bossier City U.S.A. **161** E5
Bossiesvlei Namibia **124** C3
Bossut, Cape Australia **134** C4
Bostan *Xinjiang* China **99** D5
Bostān Iran **110** B4
Bostan Pak. **111** G4
Bostāneh, Ra's-e *pt* Iran **110** D5
Bosten Hu *l.* China **98** D4
Boston U.K. **59** G6

▶**Boston** U.S.A. **165** J2
Capital of Massachusetts.

Boston Mountains U.S.A. **161** E5
Boston Spa U.K. **58** F5
Boswell U.S.A. **164** B3
Botad India **104** B5
Botany Bay Australia **138** E4
Botev *mt.* Bulg. **69** K3
Botevgrad Bulg. **69** J3
Bothaville S. Africa **125** H4
Bothnia, Gulf of Fin./Sweden **55** K6
Bothwell Canada **164** E2
Botkins U.S.A. **164** C3
Botlikh Rus. Fed. **113** G2
Botoşani Romania **53** E7
Botou *Hebei* China **95** I4
Botshabelo S. Africa **125** H5
Botswana *country* Africa **123** C6
Botte Donato, Monte *mt.* Italy **68** G5
Bottesford U.K. **58** G5
Bottrop Germany **62** G3
Botucatu Brazil **179** A3
Botuporã Brazil **179** C1
Botwood Canada **153** L4
Bouaflé Côte d'Ivoire **120** C4
Bouaké Côte d'Ivoire **120** C4
Bouar Cent. Afr. Rep. **122** B3
Bouârfa Morocco **64** D5
Bouba Ndjida, Parc National de *nat. park* Cameroon **121** E4
Bouca Cent. Afr. Rep. **122** B3
Boucaut Bay Australia **134** F3
Bouchain France **62** D4
Bouctouche Canada **153** I5
Boudh India **106** E1
Bougaa Alg. **67** I5
Bougainville, Cape Australia **134** D3
Bougainville, Selat *sea chan. Papua* Indon. **83** D3
Bougainville Island P.N.G. **132** F2
Bougainville Reef Australia **136** D2
Boughessa Mali **120** D3
Bougie Alg. *see* **Bejaïa**
Bougouni Mali **120** C3
Bougtob Alg. **64** E5
Bouillon Belgium **62** F5
Bouira Alg. **67** H5
Bou Izakarn Morocco **120** C2
Boujdour W. Sahara **120** B2
Boulder Australia **135** C7
Boulder *CO* U.S.A. **156** G4
Boulder *MT* U.S.A. **156** E3
Boulder *UT* U.S.A. **159** H3
Boulder Canyon *gorge* U.S.A. **159** F3
Boulder City U.S.A. **159** F4
Boulevard U.S.A. **158** E5
Boulia Australia **136** B4
Boulogne France *see* **Boulogne-sur-Mer**
Boulogne-Billancourt France **62** C6
Boulogne-sur-Mer France **62** B4
Boumerdes Alg. **67** H5
Bouna Côte d'Ivoire **120** C4
Bou Naceur, Jbel *mt.* Morocco **64** D5
Boû Nâga Mauritania **120** B3
Boundary *AK* U.S.A. **149** L2
Boundary Mountains U.S.A. **165** J1
Boundary Peak U.S.A. **158** D3
Boundiali Côte d'Ivoire **120** C4
Boundji Congo **122** B4
Boun Nua Laos **86** C2
Bountiful U.S.A. **159** H1
Bounty Islands N.Z. **133** H6
Bounty Trough *sea feature* S. Pacific Ocean **186** H9
Bourail New Caledonia **133** G4
Bourbon *reg.* France *see* **Bourbonnais**
Bourbon *terr.* Indian Ocean *see* **Réunion**
Bourbon U.S.A. **164** B3
Bourbonnais *reg.* France **66** F3
Bourem Mali **120** C3
Bouressa Mali *see* **Boughessa**
Bourg-Achard France **59** H9
Bourganeuf France **66** E4
Bourg-en-Bresse France **66** G3
Bourges France **66** F3
Bourget Canada **165** H1
Bourgogne *reg.* France *see* **Burgundy**
Bourgogne, Canal de France **66** G3
Bourke Australia **138** B3
Bourne U.K. **59** G6
Bournemouth U.K. **59** F8
Bourtoutou Chad **121** F3
Bou Saâda Alg. **67** I6
Bou Salem Tunisia **68** C6
Bouse U.S.A. **159** F5
Bouse Wash *watercourse* U.S.A. **159** F4
Boussu Belgium **62** D4
Boutilimit Mauritania **120** B3
Bouvet Island *terr.* S. Atlantic Ocean *see* **Bouvetøya**

▶**Bouvetøya** *terr.* S. Atlantic Ocean **184** I9
Dependency of Norway.

Bouy France **62** E5
Bova Marina Italy **68** F6
Bovenden Germany **63** J3
Boven Kapuas Mountains Indon./Malaysia *see* **Kapuas Hulu, Pegunungan**
Bow *r. Alta* Canada **151** I5
Bow *r. Alta* Canada **156** F2
Bowa China *see* **Muli**
Bowbells U.S.A. **160** C1
Bowden U.S.A. **164** F4
Bowditch *atoll* Tokelau *see* **Fakaofo**
Bowen Australia **136** E4
Bowen, Mount Australia **138** D6
Bowenville Australia **138** E1
Bowers Ridge *sea feature* Bering Sea **186** H2
Bowie Australia **136** D4
Bowie *AZ* U.S.A. **159** I5
Bowie *TX* U.S.A. **161** D5
Bow Island Canada **151** I5
Bowling Green *KY* U.S.A. **164** B5
Bowling Green *MO* U.S.A. **160** F4
Bowling Green *OH* U.S.A. **164** D3
Bowling Green *VA* U.S.A. **165** G4
Bowling Green Bay National Park Australia **136** D3
Bowman U.S.A. **160** C2
Bowman, Mount Canada **156** C2
Bowman Island Antarctica **188** F2
Bowman Peninsula Antarctica **188** L2
Bowmore U.K. **60** C5
Bowo *Xizang* China *see* **Bomi**
Bowral Australia **138** E5
Bowser Lake *B.C.* Canada **149** O4
Boxberg Germany **63** J5
Box Elder U.S.A. **160** C2
Box Elder *r.* U.S.A. **160** C2
Boxing *Shandong* China **95** I4
Boxtel Neth. **62** F3
Boyabat Turkey **112** D2
Boyana *tourist site* Bulg. **69** J3
Boyang China **97** H2
Boyd *r.* Australia **138** F2
Boyd Lagoon *salt flat* Australia **135** D6
Boyd Lake Canada **151** K2
Boydton U.S.A. **165** F5
Boyers U.S.A. **164** F3
Boykins U.S.A. **165** G5
Boyle Canada **151** H4
Boyle Ireland **61** D4
Boyne *r.* Ireland **61** F4
Boyne City U.S.A. **164** C1
Boysen Reservoir U.S.A. **156** F4
Boysun Uzbek. **111** G2
Boyuibe Bol. **176** F8
Böyük Qafqaz *mts* Asia/Europe *see* **Caucasus**
Bozanbay Kazakh. **98** C2

▶**Bozcaada** *i.* Turkey **69** L5
Most westerly point of Asia.

Bozdağ *mt.* Turkey **69** L5
Bozdağ *mt.* Turkey **107** C1
Boz Dağları *mts* Turkey **69** L5
Bozdoğan Turkey **69** M6
Bozeat U.K. **59** G6
Bozeman U.S.A. **156** F3
Bozen Italy *see* **Bolzano**
Bozhou China **97** G1
Bozoum Cent. Afr. Rep. **122** B3
Bozova Turkey **112** E3
Bozqūsh, Kūh-e *mts* Iran **110** B2
Bozüyük Turkey **69** N5
Bozyazı Turkey **107** A1
Bra Italy **68** B2
Brač *i.* Croatia **68** G3
Bracadale U.K. **60** C3
Bracadale, Loch *b.* U.K. **60** C3
Bracara Port. *see* **Braga**
Bracciano, Lago di *l.* Italy **68** E3
Bracebridge Canada **164** F1
Bräcke Sweden **54** I5
Brackenheim Germany **63** J5
Brackettville U.S.A. **161** C6
Bracknell U.K. **59** G7
Bradano *r.* Italy **68** G4
Bradenton U.S.A. **163** D7

▶**Brades** Montserrat **169** L5
Temporary capital of Montserrat. Plymouth was abandoned in 1997 owing to volcanic activity.

Bradford Canada **164** F1
Bradford U.K. **58** F5
Bradford *OH* U.S.A. **164** C3
Bradford *PA* U.S.A. **165** F3
Bradley U.S.A. **164** B3
Brady U.S.A. **161** D6
Brady Glacier U.S.A. **150** B3
Brae U.K. **60** [inset]
Braemar U.K. **60** F3
Braga Port. **67** B3
Bragado Arg. **178** D5
Bragança Brazil **177** I4
Bragança Port. **67** C3
Bragança Paulista Brazil **179** B3
Brahin Belarus **53** F6
Brahlstorf Germany **63** K1
Brahmanbaria Bangl. **105** G5
Brahmapur India **106** E2
Brahmaputra *r.* Asia **105** H4
also known as Dihang (India), Siang (India) or Yarlung Zangbo (China)
Brahmaur India **104** D2
Brăila Romania **69** L2
Braine France **62** D5
Braine-le-Comte Belgium **62** E4
Brainerd U.S.A. **160** E2
Braintree U.K. **59** H7
Braithwaite Point Australia **134** F2
Brak *r.* S. Africa **125** I2
Brake (Unterweser) Germany **63** I1
Brakel Belgium **62** D4
Brakel Germany **63** J3
Brakwater Namibia **124** C2
Bramfield Australia **135** F8
Bramming Denmark **55** F9
Brämön *i.* Sweden **54** J5
Brampton Canada **164** F2
Brampton *England* U.K. **58** E4

Brampton *England* U.K. 59 I6
Bramsche Germany 63 I2
Bramwell Australia 136 C2
Brancaster U.K. 59 H6
Branch Canada 153 L5
Branco *r.* Brazil 176 F4
Brandberg *mt.* Namibia 123 B6
Brandbu Norway 55 G6
Brande Denmark 55 F9
Brandenburg Germany 63 M2
Brandenburg *land* Germany 63 N2
Brandenburg U.S.A. 164 B5
Brandfort S. Africa 125 H5
Brandis Germany 63 N3
Brandon Canada 151 L5
Brandon U.K. 59 H6
Brandon *MS* U.S.A. 161 F5
Brandon *VT* U.S.A. 165 I2
Brandon Head *hd* Ireland 61 B5
Brandon Mountain *hill* Ireland 61 B5
Brandvlei S. Africa 124 E6
Braniewo Poland 57 Q3
Bransfield Strait Antarctica 188 L2
Branson U.S.A. 161 C4
Brantas *r.* Indon. 85 F4
Brantford Canada 164 E2
Branxton Australia 138 E4
Bras d'Or Lake Canada 153 J5
Brasil *country* S. America *see* **Brazil**
Brasil, Planalto do *plat.* Brazil *see* **Brazilian Highlands**
Brasileia Brazil 176 E6

▶**Brasília** Brazil 179 B1
Capital of Brazil.

Brasília de Minas Brazil 179 B2
Braslav Belarus *see* **Braslaw**
Braslaw Belarus 55 O9
Brașov Romania 69 K2
Brassey, Banjaran *mts* Malaysia 85 G1
Brassey, Mount Australia 135 F5
Brassey Range *hills* Australia 135 C6
Brasstown Bald *mt.* U.S.A. 163 D5

▶**Bratislava** Slovakia 57 P6
Capital of Slovakia.

Bratsk Rus. Fed. 88 I1
Bratskoye Vodokhranilishche *resr* Rus. Fed. 88 I1
Brattleboro U.S.A. 165 I2
Braulio Carrillo, Parque Nacional *nat. park* Costa Rica 166 [inset] J7
Braunau am Inn Austria 57 N6
Braunfels Germany 63 I4
Braunlage Germany 63 K3
Braunsbedra Germany 63 L3
Braunschweig Germany 63 K2
Brava *i.* Cape Verde 120 [inset]
Brave U.S.A. 164 E4
Bråviken *inlet* Sweden 55 J7
Bravo, Cerro *mt.* Bol. 176 F7
Bravo del Norte, Río *r.* Mex./U.S.A. *see* **Rio Grande**
Brawley U.S.A. 159 F5
Bray Ireland 61 F4
Bray Island Canada 147 K3
Brazeau *r.* Canada 150 H4
Brazeau, Mount Canada 150 G4

▶**Brazil** *country* S. America 177 G5
Largest and most populous country in South America, and 5th largest and 5th most populous in the world.

Brazil U.S.A. 164 B4
Brazil Basin *sea feature* S. Atlantic Ocean 184 G7
Brazilian Highlands *plat.* Brazil 179 B2
Brazos *r.* U.S.A. 161 E6

▶**Brazzaville** Congo 123 B4
Capital of Congo.

Brčko Bos.-Herz. 68 H2
Bré Ireland *see* **Bray**
Breadalbane Australia 136 B4
Breaksea Sound *inlet* N.Z. 139 A7
Bream Bay N.Z. 139 E2
Brebes *Jawa* Indon. 85 E4
Brebes, Tanjung *pt* Indon. 85 E4
Brechfa U.K. 59 C7
Brechin U.K. 60 G4
Brecht Belgium 62 E3
Breckenridge *MI* U.S.A. 164 C2
Breckenridge *MN* U.S.A. 160 D2
Breckenridge *TX* U.S.A. 161 D5
Břeclav Czech Rep. 57 P6
Brecon U.K. 59 D7
Brecon Beacons *reg.* U.K. 59 D7
Brecon Beacons National Park U.K. 59 D7
Breda Neth. 62 E3
Bredasdorp S. Africa 124 E8
Bredbo Australia 138 D5
Breddin Germany 63 M2
Bredevoort Neth. 62 G3
Bredviken Sweden 54 I3
Bree Belgium 62 F3
Breed U.S.A. 164 A1
Bregenz Austria 57 L7
Breiðafjörður *b.* Iceland 54 [inset]
Breiðdalsvík Iceland 54 [inset]
Breidenbach Germany 63 I4
Breien U.S.A. 160 C2
Breitenfelde Germany 63 K1
Breitengüßbach Germany 63 K5
Breiter Luzinsee *l.* Germany 63 N1
Breivikbotn Norway 54 M1
Breizh *reg.* France *see* **Brittany**
Brejo Velho Brazil 179 C1
Brekstad Norway 54 F5
Bremen Germany 63 I1
Bremen *land* Germany 63 I1
Bremen *IN* U.S.A. 164 B3
Bremen *OH* U.S.A. 164 D4
Bremer Bay Australia 135 B8
Bremerhaven Germany 63 I1
Bremer Range *hills* Australia 135 C8
Bremersdorp Swaziland *see* **Manzini**
Bremervörde Germany 63 J1
Bremm Germany 62 H4
Bremner *r. AK* U.S.A. 149 K3
Brenham U.S.A. 161 D6
Brenna Norway 54 H4
Brennero, Passo di *pass* Austria/Italy *see* **Brenner Pass**
Brenner Pass Austria/Italy 68 D1
Brennerpaß *pass* Austria/Italy *see* **Brenner Pass**
Brentwood U.K. 59 H7
Brescia Italy 68 D2
Breslau Poland *see* **Wrocław**
Bresle *r.* France 62 B4
Brésolles, Lac *l.* Canada 153 H3
Bressanone Italy 68 D1
Bressay *i.* U.K. 60 [inset]
Bressuire France 66 D3
Brest Belarus 55 M10
Brest France 66 B2
Brest-Litovsk Belarus *see* **Brest**
Bretagne *reg.* France *see* **Brittany**
Breteuil France 62 C5
Brétigny-sur-Orge France 62 C6
Breton Canada 150 H4
Breton Sound *b.* U.S.A. 161 F6
Brett, Cape N.Z. 139 E2
Bretten Germany 63 I5
Bretton U.K. 58 E5
Breueh, Pulau *i.* Indon. 84 A1
Brevard U.S.A. 163 D5
Breves Brazil 177 H4
Brevig Mission *AK* U.S.A. 148 F2
Brewarrina Australia 138 C2
Brewer U.S.A. 162 G2
Brewster *NE* U.S.A. 160 D3
Brewster *OH* U.S.A. 164 E3
Brewster, Kap *c.* Greenland *see* **Kangikajik**
Brewster, Lake *imp. l.* Australia 138 B4
Brewton U.S.A. 163 C6
Breyten S. Africa 125 I4
Breytovo Rus. Fed. 52 H4
Brezhnev Rus. Fed. *see* **Naberezhnyye Chelny**
Brezno Slovakia 57 Q6
Brezovo Bulg. 69 K3
Brezovo Polje *hill* Croatia 68 G2
Bria Cent. Afr. Rep. 122 C3
Briançon France 66 H4
Brian Head *mt.* U.S.A. 159 G3
Bribbaree Australia 138 C5
Bribie Island Australia 138 F1
Briceni Moldova 53 E6
Brichany Moldova *see* **Briceni**
Brichen' Moldova *see* **Briceni**
Bridgend U.K. 59 D7
Bridge of Orchy U.K. 60 E4
Bridgeport *CA* U.S.A. 158 D2
Bridgeport *CT* U.S.A. 165 I3
Bridgeport *IL* U.S.A. 164 B4
Bridgeport *NE* U.S.A. 160 C3
Bridgeport *TX* U.S.A. 167 F1
Bridger Peak U.S.A. 156 G4
Bridgeton U.S.A. 165 H4
Bridgetown Australia 135 B8

▶**Bridgetown** Barbados 169 M6
Capital of Barbados.

Bridgetown Canada 153 I5
Bridgeville U.S.A. 165 H4
Bridgewater Canada 153 I5
Bridgewater U.S.A. 165 H2
Bridgnorth U.K. 59 E6
Bridgton U.S.A. 165 J1
Bridgwater U.K. 59 D7
Bridgwater Bay U.K. 59 D7
Bridlington U.K. 58 G4
Bridlington Bay U.K. 58 G4
Bridport Australia 137 [inset]
Bridport U.K. 59 E8
Brie *reg.* France 66 F2
Brie-Comte-Robert France 62 C6
Brieg Poland *see* **Brzeg**
Briery Knob *mt.* U.S.A. 164 E4
Brig Switz. 66 H3
Brigg U.K. 58 G5
Brigham City U.S.A. 156 E4
Brightlingsea U.K. 59 I7
Brighton Canada 165 G1
Brighton U.K. 59 G8
Brighton *CO* U.S.A. 156 G5
Brighton *MI* U.S.A. 164 D2
Brighton *NY* U.S.A. 165 G2
Brighton *WV* U.S.A. 164 D4
Brignoles France 66 H5
Brikama Gambia 120 B3
Brillion U.S.A. 164 A1
Brilon Germany 63 I3
Brindisi Italy 68 G4
Brinkley U.S.A. 161 F5
Brion, Île *i.* Canada 153 J5
Brioude France 66 F4
Brisay Canada 153 H3

▶**Brisbane** Australia 138 F1
Capital of Queensland. 3rd most populous city in Oceania.

Brisbane Ranges National Park Australia 138 B6
Bristol U.K. 59 E7
Bristol *CT* U.S.A. 165 I3
Bristol *FL* U.S.A. 163 C6
Bristol *NH* U.S.A. 165 J2
Bristol *RI* U.S.A. 165 J3
Bristol *TN* U.S.A. 164 D5
Bristol *VT* U.S.A. 165 I1
Bristol Bay *AK* U.S.A. 148 G4
Bristol Channel *est.* U.K. 59 C7
Bristol Lake U.S.A. 159 F4
Britannia Island New Caledonia *see* **Maré**
British Antarctic Territory *reg.* Antarctica 188 L2
British Columbia *prov.* Canada 150 F5
British Empire Range *mts* Canada 147 J1
British Guiana *country* S. America *see* **Guyana**

▶**British Indian Ocean Territory** *terr.* Indian Ocean 185 M6
United Kingdom Overseas Territory.

British Isles Europe 56 D3
British Mountains Canada/U.S.A. 149 L1
British Solomon Islands *country* S. Pacific Ocean *see* **Solomon Islands**
Brito Godins Angola *see* **Kiwaba N'zogi**
Brits S. Africa 125 H3
Britstown S. Africa 124 F6
Brittany *reg.* France 66 C2
Britton U.S.A. 160 D2
Brive-la-Gaillarde France 66 E4
Briviesca Spain 67 E2
Brixham U.K. 59 D8
Brixia Italy *see* **Brescia**
Brlik Kazakh. *see* **Birlik**
Brno Czech Rep. 57 P6
Broach India *see* **Bharuch**
Broad *r.* U.S.A. 163 D5
Broadalbin U.S.A. 165 H2
Broad Arrow Australia 135 C7
Broadback *r.* Canada 152 F4
Broad Bay U.K. *see* **Tuath, Loch a'**
Broadford Australia 138 B6
Broadford Ireland 61 D5
Broadford U.K. 60 D3
Broad Law *hill* U.K. 60 F5
Broadmere Australia 136 A3
Broad Pass *AK* U.S.A. 149 J3
Broad Peak China/Pak. 111 J3
Broad Sound *sea chan.* Australia 136 E4
Broadstairs U.K. 59 I7
Broadus U.S.A. 156 G3
Broadview Canada 151 K5
Broadway U.S.A. 165 F4
Broadwood N.Z. 139 D2
Brochet Canada 151 K3
Brochet, Lac *l.* Canada 151 K3
Brochet, Lac au *l.* Canada 153 H4
Brock *r. N.W.T.* Canada 149 Q1
Brocken *mt.* Germany 63 K3
Brockman, Mount Australia 134 B5
Brockport *NY* U.S.A. 165 G2
Brockport *PA* U.S.A. 165 F3
Brockton U.S.A. 165 J2
Brockville Canada 165 H1
Brockway U.S.A. 165 F3
Brodeur Peninsula Canada 147 J2
Brodhead U.S.A. 164 C5
Brodick U.K. 60 D5
Brodnica Poland 57 Q4
Brody Ukr. 53 E6
Broken Arrow U.S.A. 161 E4
Broken Bay Australia 138 E4
Broken Bow *NE* U.S.A. 160 D3
Broken Bow *OK* U.S.A. 161 E5
Brokenhead *r.* Canada 151 L5
Broken Hill Australia 137 C6
Broken Hill Zambia *see* **Kabwe**
Broken Plateau *sea feature* Indian Ocean 185 O8
Brokopondo Suriname 177 G2
Brokopondo Stuwmeer *resr* Suriname *see* **Professor van Blommestein Meer**
Bromberg Poland *see* **Bydgoszcz**
Brome Germany 63 K2
Bromo Tengger Semeru, Taman Nasional *nat. park* Indon. 85 F4
Bromsgrove U.K. 59 E6
Brønderslev Denmark 55 F8
Brønnøysund Norway 54 H4
Bronson *FL* U.S.A. 163 D6
Bronson *MI* U.S.A. 164 C3
Brooke U.K. 59 I6
Brooke's Point *Palawan* Phil. 82 B4
Brookfield U.S.A. 164 A2
Brookhaven U.S.A. 161 F6
Brookings *OR* U.S.A. 156 B4
Brookings *SD* U.S.A. 160 D2
Brookline U.S.A. 165 J2
Brooklyn U.S.A. 164 C2
Brooklyn Park U.S.A. 160 E2
Brookneal U.S.A. 165 F5
Brooks Canada 151 I5
Brooks Brook *Y.T.* Canada 149 N3
Brooks Mountain *hill AK* U.S.A. 148 F2
Brooks Range *mts AK* U.S.A. 149 K1
Brookston U.S.A. 164 B3
Brooksville *FL* U.S.A. 163 D6
Brooksville *KY* U.S.A. 164 C4
Brookton Australia 135 B8
Brookville *IN* U.S.A. 164 C4
Brookville *PA* U.S.A. 164 F3
Brookville Lake U.S.A. 164 C4
Broom, Loch *inlet* U.K. 60 D3
Broome Australia 134 C4
Brora U.K. 60 F2
Brora *r.* U.K. 60 F2
Brösarp Sweden 55 I9
Brosna *r.* Ireland 61 E4
Brosville U.S.A. 164 F5
Brothers *is* India 87 A5
Brough U.K. 58 E4
Brough Ness *pt* U.K. 60 G2
Broughshane U.K. 61 F3
Broughton Island Canada *see* **Qikiqtarjuaq**
Broughton Islands Australia 138 F4
Brovary Ukr. 53 F6
Brovinia Australia 137 E5
Brovst Denmark 55 F8
Brown City U.S.A. 164 D2
Brown Deer U.S.A. 164 B2
Browne Range *hills* Australia 135 D6
Brownfield U.S.A. 161 C5
Browning U.S.A. 156 E2
Brown Mountain U.S.A. 158 E4
Brownstown U.S.A. 164 B4
Brownsville *KY* U.S.A. 164 B5
Brownsville *PA* U.S.A. 164 F3
Brownsville *TN* U.S.A. 161 F5
Brownsville *TX* U.S.A. 161 D7
Brownwood U.S.A. 161 D6
Brownwood, Lake *TX* U.S.A. 167 F2
Browse Island Australia 134 C3
Bruay-la-Bussière France 62 C4
Bruce Peninsula Canada 164 E1
Bruce Peninsula National Park Canada 164 E1
Bruce Rock Australia 135 B7
Bruchsal Germany 63 I5
Brück Germany 63 M2
Bruck an der Mur Austria 57 O7
Brue *r.* U.K. 59 E7
Bruges Belgium *see* **Brugge**
Brugge Belgium 62 D3
Brühl *Baden-Württemberg* Germany 63 I5
Brühl *Nordrhein-Westfalen* Germany 62 G4
Bruin *KY* U.S.A. 164 D4
Bruin *PA* U.S.A. 164 F3
Bruin Point *mt.* U.S.A. 159 H2
Bruint India 105 I3
Brûk, Wâdi el *watercourse* Egypt *see* **Burūk, Wādī al**
Brukkaros Namibia 124 D3
Brûlé Canada 150 G4
Brûlé, Lac *l.* Canada 153 J3
Brûly Belgium 62 E5
Brumado Brazil 179 C1
Brumath France 63 H6
Brumunddal Norway 55 G6
Brunau Germany 63 L2
Brundisium Italy *see* **Brindisi**
Bruneau U.S.A. 156 E4
Brunei *country* Asia 85 F1
Brunei Brunei *see* **Bandar Seri Begawan**
Brunei Bay Malaysia 85 F1
Brunette Downs Australia 136 A3
Brunflo Sweden 54 I5
Brunico Italy 68 D1
Brünn Czech Rep. *see* **Brno**
Brunner, Lake N.Z. 139 C6
Bruno Canada 151 J4
Brunswick Germany *see* **Braunschweig**
Brunswick *GA* U.S.A. 163 D6
Brunswick *MD* U.S.A. 165 G4
Brunswick *ME* U.S.A. 165 K2
Brunswick, Península de *pen.* Chile 178 B8
Brunswick Bay Australia 134 D3
Brunswick Lake Canada 152 E4
Bruntál Czech Rep. 57 P6
Brunt Ice Shelf Antarctica 188 B2
Bruntville S. Africa 125 J5
Bruny Island Australia 137 [inset]
Brusa Turkey *see* **Bursa**
Brusenets Rus. Fed. 52 I3
Brushton U.S.A. 165 H1
Brusque Brazil 179 A4
Brussel Belgium *see* **Brussels**

▶**Brussels** Belgium 62 E4
Capital of Belgium.

Bruthen Australia 138 C6
Bruxelles Belgium *see* **Brussels**
Bruzual Venez. 176 E2
Bryan *OH* U.S.A. 164 C3
Bryan *TX* U.S.A. 161 D6
Bryan, Mount *hill* Australia 137 B7
Bryan Coast Antarctica 188 L2
Bryansk Rus. Fed. 53 G5
Bryanskoye Rus. Fed. 113 G1
Bryant Pond U.S.A. 165 J1
Bryantsburg U.S.A. 164 C4
Bryce Canyon National Park U.S.A. 159 G3
Bryce Mountain U.S.A. 159 I5
Brynbuga U.K. *see* **Usk**
Bryne Norway 55 D7
Bryukhovetskaya Rus. Fed. 53 H7
Brzeg Poland 57 P5
Brześć nad Bugiem Belarus *see* **Brest**
Bua *r.* Malawi 123 D5
Bu'aale Somalia 122 E3
Buala Solomon Is 133 F2
Buang *i.* Indon. 83 C2
Buatan *Sumatera* Indon. 84 C2
Bu'ayj *well* Saudi Arabia 110 C5
Būbiyān, Jazīrat Kuwait 110 C4
Bubuan *i.* Phil. 82 C5
Bucak Turkey 69 N6
Bucaramanga Col. 176 D2
Bucas Grande *i.* Phil. 82 D4
Buccaneer Archipelago *is* Australia 134 C4
Buchanan Liberia 120 B4
Buchanan *MI* U.S.A. 164 B3
Buchanan *VA* U.S.A. 164 F5
Buchanan, Lake *salt flat* Australia 136 D4
Buchanan, Lake *TX* U.S.A. 167 F2
Buchan Gulf Canada 147 K2

▶**Bucharest** Romania 69 L2
Capital of Romania.

Büchen Germany 63 K1
Buchen (Odenwald) Germany 63 J5
Buchholz Germany 63 M1
Bucholz in der Nordheide Germany 63 J1
Buchon, Point U.S.A. 158 C4
Buchy France 62 B5
Bucin, Pasul *pass* Romania 69 K1
Buckambool Mountain *hill* Australia 138 B3
Bückeburg Germany 63 J2
Bücken Germany 63 J2
Buckeye U.S.A. 159 G5
Buckhannon U.S.A. 164 E4
Buckhaven U.K. 60 F4
Buckhorn Lake Canada 165 F1
Buckie U.K. 60 G3
Buckingham U.K. 59 G6
Buckingham U.S.A. 165 F5
Buckingham Bay Australia 79 F9
Buckland *AK* U.S.A. 148 G2
Buckland *r. AK* U.S.A. 148 G2
Buckland Tableland *reg.* Australia 136 E5
Buckleboo Australia 135 G8
Buckle Island Antarctica 188 H2
Buckley *watercourse* Australia 136 B4
Buckley Bay Antarctica 188 G2
Bucklin U.S.A. 160 D4
Buckskin Mountains U.S.A. 159 G4
Bucks Mountain U.S.A. 158 C2
Bucksport U.S.A. 153 H5
Bückwitz Germany 63 M2
București Romania *see* **Bucharest**
Bucyrus U.S.A. 164 D3
Buda-Kashalyova Belarus 53 F5
Budalin Myanmar 86 A2

▶**Budapest** Hungary 69 H1
Capital of Hungary.

Budaun India 104 D3
Budawang National Park Australia 138 E5
Budda Australia 138 B3
Budd Coast Antarctica 188 F2
Buddusò *Sardinia* Italy 68 C4
Bude U.K. 59 C8
Bude U.S.A. 161 F6
Budennovsk Rus. Fed. 113 G1
Buderim Australia 138 F1
Būding Iran 110 E5
Büdingen Germany 63 J4
Budīyah, Jabal *hills* Egypt 107 A5
Budongquan *Qinghai* China 94 C5
Budoni *Sardinia* Italy 68 C4
Budū, Ḥadabat al *plain* Saudi Arabia 110 C6
Budū', Sabkhat al *salt pan* Saudi Arabia 110 C6
Budweis Czech Rep. *see* **České Budějovice**
Buenaventura Col. 176 C3
Buenaventura Mex. 166 D2
Buena Vista *i.* N. Mariana Is *see* **Tinian**
Buenavista *Mindanao* Phil. 82 D4
Buenavista Phil. 82 C3
Buena Vista *CO* U.S.A. 156 G5
Buena Vista *VA* U.S.A. 164 F5
Buendia, Embalse de *resr* Spain 67 E3

▶**Buenos Aires** Arg. 178 E4
Capital of Argentina. 2nd most populous city in South America.

Buenos Aires Costa Rica 166 [inset] J7
Buenos Aires, Lago *l.* Arg./Chile 178 B7
Buenos Aires National Wildlife Refuge *nature res. AZ* U.S.A. 166 C2
Buerarema Brazil 179 D1
Buet *r.* Canada 153 H1
Búfalo Mex. 166 D3
Buffalo *r.* Canada 150 H2
Buffalo *KY* U.S.A. 164 C5
Buffalo *MO* U.S.A. 160 E4
Buffalo *NY* U.S.A. 165 F2
Buffalo *OK* U.S.A. 161 D4
Buffalo *SD* U.S.A. 160 C2
Buffalo *TX* U.S.A. 161 D6
Buffalo *WY* U.S.A. 156 G3
Buffalo Head Hills Canada 150 G3
Buffalo Head Prairie Canada 150 G3
Buffalo Hump *mt.* U.S.A. 156 E3
Buffalo Lake *Alta* Canada 151 H4
Buffalo Lake *N.W.T.* Canada 150 H2
Buffalo Narrows Canada 151 I4
Buffels *watercourse* S. Africa 124 C5
Buffels Drift S. Africa 125 H2
Buftea Romania 69 K2
Bug *r.* Poland 57 S5
Buga Col. 176 C3
Buga Mongolia *see* **Dörvöljin**
Bugaldie Australia 138 D3
Bugant Mongolia 95 F1
Bugat Mongolia 94 C2
Bugdaýly Turkm. 110 D2
Bugel, Tanjung *pt* Indon. 85 E4
Buggenhout Belgium 62 E3
Bugojno Bos.-Herz. 68 G2
Bugrino Rus. Fed. 52 K1
Bugsuk *i.* Phil. 82 B4
Bugt *Nei Mongol* China 95 J1
Buguey *Luzon* Phil. 82 C2
Bugul'ma Rus. Fed. 51 Q5
Bugun' Kazakh. 102 B2
Bügür *Xinjiang* China *see* **Luntai**
Buguruslan Rus. Fed. 51 Q5
Bühābād Iran 110 D4
Buḥayrat Dahūk *resr.* Iraq 113 F3
Buhera Zimbabwe 123 D5
Buh He *r.* China 94 D4
Buhi *Luzon* Phil. 82 C3
Bühl Germany 63 I6
Buhuși Romania 69 L1
Buick Canada 150 F3
Builth Wells U.K. 59 D6
Bui National Park Ghana 120 C4
Buinsk Rus. Fed. 53 K5
Bu'in Zahrā Iran 110 C3
Buir Nur *l.* Mongolia 95 I2
Buitepos Namibia 124 D2
Bujanovac Serbia 69 I3

▶**Bujumbura** Burundi 122 C4
Capital of Burundi.

Bukachacha Rus. Fed. 89 L2
Buka Daban *mt. Qinghai/Xinjiang* China 99 E5
Buka Island P.N.G. 132 F2
Būkān Iran 110 B2
Būkand Iran 110 D4
Bukavu Dem. Rep. Congo 122 C4
Bukhara *Buxoro* Uzbek. *see* **Buxoro**
Bukhoro Uzbek. *see* **Buxoro**
Bukhtarminskoye Vodokhranilishche *resr* Kazakh. 98 D2
Bukide *i.* Indon. 83 C2
Bukit Baka-Bukit Raya, Taman Nasional *nat. park* Indon. 85 F3
Bukitlidi *Kalimantan* Indon. 85 F3
Bukit Timah Sing. 87 [inset]
Bukittinggi *Sumatera* Indon. 84 C3
Bukkapatnam India 106 C3
Bukoba Tanz. 122 D4
Bükreș Romania *see* **Bucharest**
Buku, Tanjung *pt* Indon. 84 D3
Bukukun Rus. Fed. 95 G1
Būl, Kūh-e *mt.* Iran 110 D4
Bula *Seram* Indon. 83 D3
Bula P.N.G. 81 K8
Bülach Switz. 66 I3
Bulag Mongolia *see* **Möngönmorīt**
Bulagtay Mongolia *see* **Hüder**
Bulan *i.* Indon. 84 C2
Bulan *Luzon* Phil. 82 C3
Bulan *i.* Phil. 82 C5
Bulancak Turkey 112 E2
Bulandshahr India 104 D3
Bulanık Turkey 113 F3
Bulava Rus. Fed. 90 F2
Bulawa, Gunung *mt.* Indon. 83 B2
Bulawayo Zimbabwe 123 C6
Buldan Turkey 69 M5
Buldana India *see* **Buldhana**
Buldhana India 106 C1
Buldir Island *AK* U.S.A. 149 [inset]
Buldur *Hima. Prad.* India 99 B7
Buleda *reg.* Pak. 111 F5
Bulembu Swaziland 125 J3
Bulgan *Bayan-Ölgiy* Mongolia 94 B2
Bulgan *Bulgan* Mongolia 94 E1
Bulgan Mongolia 95 H1
Bulgan Mongolia 94 B2
Bulgan *Hovd* Mongolia *see* **Darvi**
Bulgan *Hövsgöl* Mongolia *see* **Tsagaan-Üür**
Bulgan *Ömnögovĭ* Mongolia 94 E2
Bulgan *prov.* Mongolia 94 E1
Bulgan Gol *r.* Mongolia 94 B2
Bulgar Rus. Fed. *see* **Bolgar**
Bulgaria *country* Europe 69 K3
Bŭlgariya *country* Europe *see* **Bulgaria**
Buli *Halmahera* Indon. 83 D2
Buli, Teluk *b. Halmahera* Indon. 83 D2
Bulilyan, Cape *Palawan* Phil. 82 B4
Bulkley Ranges *mts B.C.* Canada 149 O5
Bullawarra, Lake *salt flat* Australia 138 A1
Bullen *r.* Canada 151 K1
Bullen *AK* U.S.A. 149 K1
Buller *r.* N.Z. 139 C5
Buller, Mount Australia 138 C6
Bulleringa National Park Australia 136 C3
Bullfinch Australia 135 B7
Bullhead City U.S.A. 159 F4
Bulli Australia 138 E5
Bullion Mountains U.S.A. 158 E4
Bullo *r.* Australia 134 E3
Bulloo Downs Australia 137 C6
Bulloo Lake *salt flat* Australia 137 C6
Büllsport Namibia 124 C3
Bully Choop Mountain U.S.A. 158 B1
Bulman Australia 134 F3
Bulman Gorge Australia 134 F3
Bulmer Lake Canada 150 F2
Buloh, Pulau *i.* Sing. 87 [inset]
Buloke, Lake *dry lake* Australia 138 A6
Bulolo P.N.G. 81 L8
Bulsar India *see* **Valsad**
Bultfontein S. Africa 125 H5
Bulu, Gunung *mt.* Indon. 85 G2
Buluan *Mindanao* Phil. 82 D5
Bulubulu *Sulawesi* Indon. 83 B4
Bulukumba *Sulawesi* Indon. 83 B4
Bulun Rus. Fed. 77 N2
Bulungu Dem. Rep. Congo 123 C4
Bulung'ur Uzbek. 111 G2
Bumba Dem. Rep. Congo 122 C3
Bümbah Libya 112 A4
Bumbah, Khalīj *b.* Libya 112 A4
Bumbat *Nei Mongol* China 94 F3
Bumbat Mongolia *see* **Bayan-Öndör**
Bumhkang Myanmar 86 B1
Bumpha Bum *mt.* Myanmar 86 B1
Buna Dem. Rep. Congo 122 B4
Buna Kenya 122 D3
Bunayyān *well* Saudi Arabia 110 C6
Bunazi Tanz. 122 D4
Bunbeg Ireland *see* **An Bun Beag**
Bunbury Australia 135 A8
Bunclody Ireland 61 F5
Buncrana Ireland 61 E2
Bunda Tanz. 122 D4
Bundaberg Australia 136 F5
Bundaleer Australia 138 C2
Bundarra Australia 138 E3
Bundi India 104 C4
Bundjalung National Park Australia 138 F2
Bundoran Ireland 61 D3
Bunduqiya Sudan 121 G4
Buner *reg.* Pak. 111 I3
Bunga-dake *mt.* Japan 92 B3

Bungalaut, Selat sea chan. Indon. 84 B3
Bungay U.K. 59 I6
Bungendore Australia 138 D5
Bunger Hills Antarctica 188 F2
Bungi Sulawesi Indon. 83 B4
Bungku Sulawesi Indon. 83 B3
Bungle Bungle National Park Australia see **Purnululu National Park**
Bungona'og Xizang China 99 E6
Bungo-suidō sea chan. Japan 91 D6
Bunguran, Kepulauan is Indon. see **Natuna, Kepulauan**
Bunguran, Pulau i. Indon. see **Natuna Besar**
Buni, Ci r. Indon. 84 D4
Bunia Dem. Rep. Congo 122 D3
Bunianga Dem. Rep. Congo 122 C4
Buningonia well Australia 135 C7
Bunji Pak. 104 C2
Bunker Group atolls Australia 136 F4
Bunker Hill AK U.S.A. 148 F2
Bunkeya Dem. Rep. Congo 123 C5
Bunkie LA U.S.A. 167 G2
Bunnell U.S.A. 163 D6
Bünsum Xizang China 99 C7
Buntok Kalimantan Indon. 85 F3
Buntokecil Kalimantan Indon. 85 F3
Bunya Mountains National Park Australia 138 E1
Bünyan Turkey 112 D3
Bunyu i. Indon. 85 G2
Buôn Đôn Vietnam 87 D4
Buôn Ma Thuôt Vietnam 87 E4
Buorkhaya, Guba b. Rus. Fed. 77 O2
Bup r. China 99 D7
Buqayq Saudi Arabia see **Abqaiq**
Buqbuq Egypt 112 B5
Bura Kenya 122 D4
Buraan Somalia 122 E2
Buram Sudan 121 F3
Buran Kazakh. 102 G2
Burang Xizang China 99 C7
Buranhaém Brazil 179 C2
Buranhaém r. Brazil 179 D2
Burāq Syria 107 C3
Burauen Leyte Phil. 82 D4
Buray r. India 104 C5
Buraydah Saudi Arabia 108 F4
Burbach Germany 63 I4
Burbank U.S.A. 158 D4
Burcher Australia 138 C4
Burco Somalia 122 E3
Bürd Mongolia 94 E2
Burdaard Neth. 62 F1
Burdalyk Turkm. 111 G2
Burdigala France see **Bordeaux**
Burdur Turkey 69 N6
Burdur Gölü l. Turkey 69 N6
Burdwan India see **Barddhaman**
Burē Eth. 122 D2
Bure r. U.K. 59 I6
Bureå Sweden 54 L4
Bureinskiy Khrebet mts Rus. Fed. 90 D2
Bureinskiy Zapovednik nature res. Rus. Fed. 90 D2
Büren Mongolia 94 F2
Bürentsogt Mongolia 95 G2
Bureya r. Rus. Fed. 90 C2
Bureya Range mts Rus. Fed. see **Bureinskiy Khrebet**
Burford Canada 164 E2
Burgaltay Mongolia see **Baruunbüren**
Burgas Bulg. 69 L3
Burgaw U.S.A. 163 E5
Burg bei Magdeburg Germany 63 L2
Burgbernheim Germany 63 K5
Burgdorf Germany 63 K2
Burgeo Canada 153 K5
Burgersdorp S. Africa 125 H6
Burgersfort S. Africa 125 J3
Burges, Mount hill Australia 135 C7
Burgess, Mount Y.T. Canada 149 M2
Burgess Hill U.K. 59 G8
Burghaun Germany 63 J4
Burghausen Germany 57 N6
Burghead U.K. 60 F3
Burgh-Haamstede Neth. 62 D3
Burgio, Serra di hill Sicily Italy 68 F6
Burglengenfeld Germany 63 M5
Burgos Mex. 167 F3
Burgos Spain 67 E2
Burgstädt Germany 63 M4
Burgsvik Sweden 55 K8
Burgum Neth. 62 G1
Burgundy reg. France 66 G3
Burhan Budai Shan mts China 94 C5
Burhaniye Turkey 69 L5
Burhanpur India 104 D5
Burhar-Dhanpuri India 105 E5
Burhi Gandak r. India 99 D8
Buri Brazil 179 A3
Buriai Indon. 84 C3
Burias i. Phil. 82 C3
Buriat-Mongol Republic aut. rep. Rus. Fed. see **Buryatiya, Respublika**
Burica, Punta pt Costa Rica 166 [inset] J7
Buri Gandak r. Nepal 99 C8
Burin Canada 153 L5
Burin Peninsula Canada 153 L5
Buriram Thai. 86 C4
Buritama Brazil 179 A3
Buriti Alegre Brazil 179 A2
Buriti Bravo Brazil 177 J5
Buritirama Brazil 177 J6
Buritis Brazil 179 B1
Burjay Xinjiang China 98 E4
Burj Aziz Khan Pak. 111 G4
Burkan-Suu r. Kyrg. 98 B4
Burke U.S.A. 160 D3
Burke Island Antarctica 188 K2
Burke Pass N.Z. see **Burkes Pass**
Burkes Pass N.Z. 139 C7
Burkesville U.S.A. 164 C5
Burketown Australia 136 B3
Burkeville U.S.A. 165 F5
Burkina country Africa 120 C3
Burkina Faso country Africa see **Burkina**
Burk's Falls Canada 152 F5
Burkutty Kazakh. 98 B2
Burley U.S.A. 156 E4
Burlington Canada 164 F2
Burlington CO U.S.A. 160 C4
Burlington IA U.S.A. 160 F3
Burlington KS U.S.A. 160 E4
Burlington KY U.S.A. 164 C4
Burlington VT U.S.A. 165 I1
Burlington WI U.S.A. 164 A2
Burmantovo Rus. Fed. 51 S3
Burnaby Canada 150 F5
Burnet U.S.A. 161 D6
Burney U.S.A. 158 C1
Burney, Monte vol. Chile 178 B8
Burnham U.S.A. 165 G3
Burnie Australia 137 [inset]
Burniston U.K. 58 G4
Burnley U.K. 58 E5
Burns U.S.A. 156 D4
Burnside r. Canada 146 H3
Burnside U.S.A. 164 C5
Burnside, Lake salt flat Australia 135 C6
Burns Junction U.S.A. 156 D4
Burns Lake Canada 150 E4
Burntisland U.K. 60 F4
Burnt Lake Canada see **Brûlé, Lac**
Burntwood r. Canada 151 L4
Burog Co l. Xizang China 99 D6
Buron r. Canada 153 H2
Burovoy Uzbek. 111 F1
Burqin Xinjiang China 98 D3
Burqin He r. China 98 D3
Burqu' Jordan 107 D3
Burra Australia 137 B7
Burra i. U.K. 60 [inset]
Burravoe U.K. 60 [inset]
Burrel Albania 69 I4
Burrel U.S.A. 158 D3
Burren reg. Ireland 61 C4
Burrendong, Lake Australia 138 D4
Burren Junction Australia 138 D3
Burrewarra Point Australia 138 E5
Burrinjuck Australia 138 D5
Burrinjuck Reservoir Australia 138 D5
Burro, Serranías del mts Mex. 167 E2
Burr Oak Reservoir U.S.A. 164 D4
Burro Creek watercourse U.S.A. 159 G4
Burro Peak U.S.A. 159 I5
Burrowa Pine Mountain National Park Australia 138 C6
Burrow Head hd U.K. 60 E6
Burrows U.S.A. 164 B3
Burrundie Australia 134 E3
Bursa Turkey 69 M4
Būr Safāga Egypt see **Būr Safājah**
Būr Safājah Egypt 108 D4
Būr Sa'īd Egypt see **Port Said**
Būr Sa'īd Egypt see **Port Said**
Būr Sa'īd governorate Egypt 107 A4
Būr Sa'īd governorate Egypt see **Būr Sa'īd**
Bursinskoye Vodokhranilishche resr Rus. Fed. 90 C2
Bürstadt Germany 63 I5
Būr Sudan Sudan see **Port Sudan**
Burt Lake U.S.A. 162 C2
Burton U.S.A. 164 D2
Burton, Lac l. Canada 152 F3
Burtonport Ireland see **Ailt an Chorráin**
Burton upon Trent U.K. 59 F6
Burträsk Sweden 54 L4
Burt Well Australia 135 F5
Buru i. Maluku Indon. 83 C3
Burubaytal Kazakh. 98 A3
Burūk, Wādī al watercourse Egypt 107 A4
Burullus, Baḥra el lag. Egypt see **Burullus, Lake**
Burullus, Buḥayrat al lag. Egypt see **Burullus, Lake**
Burullus, Lake lag. Egypt 112 C5
Burultokay Xinjiang China see **Fuhai**
Burūn, Ra's pt Egypt 107 A4
Burundi country Africa 122 C4
Burunniy Rus. Fed. see **Tsagan Aman**
Bururi Burundi 122 C4
Burwash Landing Y.T. Canada 149 M3
Burwick U.K. 60 G2
Buryatiya aut. rep. Rus. Fed. see **Buryatiya, Respublika**
Buryatiya, Respublika aut. rep. Rus. Fed. 94 E1
Buryatskaya Mongolskaya A.S.S.R. aut. rep. Rus. Fed. see **Buryatiya, Respublika**
Buryn' Ukr. 53 G6
Bury St Edmunds U.K. 59 H6
Burzil Pass Pak. 104 C2
Busan S. Korea see **Pusan**
Busan Bay Mindanao Phil. 82 C5
Busanga Dem. Rep. Congo 122 C4
Busby U.S.A. 156 G3
Buseire Syria see **Al Buşayrah**
Bush r. U.K. 61 F2
Būshehr Iran 110 C4
Bushêngcaka China 105 E2
Bushenyi Uganda 122 D4
Bushire Iran see **Būshehr**
Bushmills U.K. 61 F2
Bushnell U.S.A. 163 D6
Businga Dem. Rep. Congo 122 C3
Busobuso Maluku Indon. 83 D2
Buşrá ash Shām Syria 107 C3
Busse Rus. Fed. 90 B2
Busselton Australia 135 A8
Bussum Neth. 62 F2
Bustamante Nuevo León Mex. 167 E3
Bustillos, Lago l. Mex. 166 D2
Busto Arsizio Italy 68 C2
Busuanga Phil. 82 B3
Busuanga i. Phil. 82 B3
Buta Dem. Rep. Congo 122 C3
Butare Rwanda 122 C4
Butaritari atoll Kiribati 186 H5
Bute Australia 137 B7
Bute i. U.K. 60 D5
Butedale Canada 150 D4
Butha Buthe Lesotho 125 I5
Butha Qi Nei Mongol China see **Zalantun**
Buthidaung Myanmar 86 A2
Butler AL U.S.A. 161 F5
Butler GA U.S.A. 163 C5
Butler IN U.S.A. 164 C3
Butler KY U.S.A. 164 C4
Butler MO U.S.A. 160 E4
Butler PA U.S.A. 164 F3
Butlers Bridge Ireland 61 E3
Buton i. Indon. 83 B4
Buton, Selat sea chan. Indon. 83 B4
Bütow Germany 63 M1
Butte MT U.S.A. 156 E3
Butte NE U.S.A. 160 D3
Buttelstedt Germany 63 L3
Butterworth Malaysia 84 C1
Butterworth S. Africa 125 I7
Buttes, Sierra mt. U.S.A. 158 C2
Buttevant Ireland 61 D5
Butt of Lewis hd U.K. 60 C2
Button Bay Canada 151 M3
Butuan Mindanao Phil. 82 D4
Butuan Bay Mindanao Phil. 82 D4
Butuo China 96 D3
Buturlinovka Rus. Fed. 53 I6
Butwal Nepal 105 E4
Butzbach Germany 63 I4
Buulobarde Somalia 122 E3
Buur Gaabo Somalia 122 E4
Buurhabaka Somalia 122 E3
Buutsagaan Bayanhongor Mongolia 94 D2
Buxar India 105 F4
Buxoro Uzbek. 111 G2
Buxtehude Germany 63 J1
Buxton U.K. 58 F5
Buy Rus. Fed. 52 I4
Buyant Bayanhongor Mongolia see **Buutsagaan**
Buyant Bayan-Ölgiy Mongolia 94 B1
Buyant Hentiy Mongolia see **Galshar**
Buyant Gol r. Mongolia 94 D2
Buyant Gol r. Mongolia 98 E2
Buyant-Ovoo Mongolia 95 F2
Buyant-Uhaa Mongolia 95 G2
Buynaksk Rus. Fed. 113 G2
Büyükçekmece Turkey 112 C2
Büyük Egri Dağ mt. Turkey 107 A1
Büyükmenderes r. Turkey 69 L6
Buyun Shan mt. Liaoning China 95 J3
Buzancy France 62 E5
Buzău Romania 69 L2
Buzdyak Rus. Fed. 51 Q5
Búzi Moz. 123 D5
Büzmeýin Turkm. see **Abadan**
Buzuluk Rus. Fed. 51 Q5
Buzuluk r. Rus. Fed. 53 I6
Buzzards Bay U.S.A. 165 J3
Byakar Bhutan see **Jakar**
Byala Bulg. 69 K3
Byala Slatina Bulg. 69 J3
Byalynichy Belarus 53 F5
Byarezina r. Belarus 53 F5
Byaroza Belarus 55 N10
Byblos tourist site Lebanon 107 B2
Bydgoszcz Poland 57 Q4
Byelorussia country Europe see **Belarus**
Byerazino Belarus 53 F5
Byers U.S.A. 156 G5
Byeshankovichy Belarus 53 F5
Byesville U.S.A. 164 E4
Bygland Norway 55 E7
Bykhaw Belarus 53 F5
Bykhov Belarus see **Bykhaw**
Bykle Norway 55 E7
Bykovo Rus. Fed. 53 J6
Bylas U.S.A. 159 H5
Bylkyldak Kazakh. 98 A2
Bylot Island Canada 147 K2
Byramgore Reef India 106 A4
Byrd Glacier Antarctica 188 H1
Byrdstown U.S.A. 164 C5
Byrka Rus. Fed. 95 I1
Byrkjelo Norway 55 E6
Byrock Australia 138 C3
Byron U.S.A. 165 J1
Byron, Cape Australia 138 F2
Byron Bay Australia 138 F2
Byron Island Kiribati see **Nikunau**
Byrranga, Gory mts Rus. Fed. 77 K2
Byske Sweden 54 L4
Byssa Rus. Fed. 90 C1
Byssa r. Rus. Fed. 90 C1
Bystrinskiy Golets, Gora mt. Rus. Fed. 95 G1
Bytom Poland 57 Q5
Bytów Poland 57 P3
Byurgyutli Turkm. 110 D2
Byzantium Turkey see **İstanbul**

C

Ca, Sông r. Vietnam 86 D3
Caacupé Para. 178 E3
Caatinga Brazil 179 B2
Caazapá Para. 178 E3
Cabaiguán Cuba 163 E8
Caballas Peru 176 C6
Caballococha Peru 176 D4
Caballo Reservoir NM U.S.A. 166 D1
Caballos Mesteños, Llano de los plain Mex. 166 D2
Cabanaconde Peru 176 D7
Cabanatuan Luzon Phil. 82 C3
Cabano Canada 153 H5
Cabdul Qaadir Somalia 122 E2
Cabeceira Rio Manso Brazil 177 G7
Cabeceiras Brazil 179 B1
Cabeza del Buey Spain 67 D4
Cabeza Prieta National Wildlife Refuge nature res. AZ U.S.A. 166 B1
Cabezas Bol. 176 F7
Cabimas Venez. 176 D1
Cabinda Angola 123 B4
Cabinda prov. Angola 123 B5
Cabinet Inlet Antarctica 188 L2
Cabinet Mountains U.S.A. 156 E2
Cabingan i. Phil. 82 C5
Cabistra Turkey see **Ereğli**
Cabo Frio Brazil 179 C3
Cabo Frio, Ilha do i. Brazil 179 C3
Cabonga, Réservoir resr Canada 152 F5
Cabool U.S.A. 161 E4
Caboolture Australia 138 F1
Cabo Orange, Parque Nacional de nat. park Brazil 177 H3
Cabo Pantoja Peru 176 C4
Cabora Bassa, Lake resr Moz. 123 D5
Cabo Raso Arg. 178 C6
Caborca Mex. 166 B2
Cabot Head hd Canada 164 E1
Cabot Strait Canada 153 J5
Cabourg France 59 G9
Cabo Verde country N. Atlantic Ocean see **Cape Verde**
Cabo Verde, Ilhas do is N. Atlantic Ocean 120 [inset]
Cabo Yubi Morocco see **Tarfaya**
Cabra i. Phil. 82 C3
Cabral, Serra do mts Brazil 179 B2
Cäbrayıl Azer. 113 G3
Cabrera, Illa de i. Spain 67 H4
Cabri Canada 151 I5
Cabugao Luzon Phil. 82 C2
Cabulauan i. Phil. 82 C4
Cabullona Mex. 166 C2
Cabutunan Point Luzon Phil. 82 C2
Caçador Brazil 179 A4
Cacagoin China see **Qagca**
Cacahuatepec Mex. 167 F5
Čačak Serbia 69 I3
Caccia, Capo c. Sardinia Italy 68 C4
Çäçe Turkm. 111 F2
Cacequi Brazil 178 F3
Cáceres Brazil 177 G7
Cáceres Spain 67 C4
Cache Creek Canada 150 F5
Cache Peak U.S.A. 156 E4
Cacheu Guinea-Bissau 120 B3
Cachi, Nevados de mts Arg. 178 C2
Cachimbo, Serra do hills Brazil 177 H5
Cachoeira Brazil 179 D1
Cachoeira Alta Brazil 179 A2
Cachoeira de Goiás Brazil 179 A2
Cachoeira do Arari Brazil 177 I4
Cachoeiro de Itapemirim Brazil 179 C3
Cacine Guinea-Bissau 120 B3
Caciporé, Cabo c. Brazil 177 H3
Cacolo Angola 123 B5
Caconda Angola 123 B4
Cactus U.S.A. 161 C4
Caçu Brazil 179 A2
Caculé Brazil 179 C1
Čadca Slovakia 57 Q6
Caddo Lake TX U.S.A. 167 G1
Cadereyta Nuevo León Mex. 167 E3
Cadibarrawirracanna, Lake salt flat Australia 137 A6
Cadig Mountains Luzon Phil. 82 C3
Cadillac Canada 151 J5
Cadillac U.S.A. 164 C1
Cadiz Negros Phil. 82 C4
Cádiz Spain 67 C5
Cadiz IN U.S.A. 164 C4
Cadiz KY U.S.A. 162 C4
Cadiz OH U.S.A. 164 E3
Cádiz, Golfo de g. Spain 67 C5
Cadiz Lake U.S.A. 159 F4
Cadomin Canada 150 G4
Cadotte r. Canada 150 G3
Cadotte Lake Canada 150 G3
Caen France 66 D2
Caerdydd U.K. see **Cardiff**
Caerffili U.K. see **Caerphilly**
Caerfyrddin U.K. see **Carmarthen**
Caergybi U.K. see **Holyhead**
Caernarfon U.K. 59 C5
Caernarfon Bay U.K. 59 C5
Caernarvon U.K. see **Caernarfon**
Caerphilly U.K. 59 D7
Caesaraugusta Spain see **Zaragoza**
Caesarea Alg. see **Cherchell**
Caesarea Cappadociae Turkey see **Kayseri**
Caesarea Philippi Syria see **Bāniyās**
Caesarodunum France see **Tours**
Caesaromagus U.K. see **Chelmsford**
Caetité Brazil 179 C1
Cafayate Arg. 178 C3
Cafelândia Brazil 179 A3
Caffa Ukr. see **Feodosiya**
Cagayan i. Phil. 82 C4
Cagayan r. Luzon Phil. 82 C2
Cagayan de Oro Mindanao Phil. 82 D4
Cagayan de Tawi-Tawi i. Phil. 82 B5
Cagayan Islands Phil. 82 C4
Cagles Mill Lake U.S.A. 164 B4
Cagli Italy 68 E3
Cagliari Sardinia Italy 68 C5
Cagliari, Golfo di b. Sardinia Italy 68 C5
Cagua, Mount vol. Phil. 82 C2
Çagyl Turkm. 113 I2
Cahama Angola 123 B5
Caha Mts hills Ireland 61 C6
Cahermore Ireland 61 B6
Cahir Ireland 61 E5
Cahirsiveen Ireland 61 B6
Cahora Bassa, Lago de resr Moz. see **Cabora Bassa, Lake**
Cahore Point Ireland 61 F5
Cahors France 66 E4
Cahuapanas Peru 176 C5
Cahuita, Punta pt Costa Rica 166 [inset] J7
Cahul Moldova 69 M2
Caia Moz. 123 D5
Caiabis, Serra dos hills Brazil 177 G6
Caianda Angola 123 C5
Caiapó r. Brazil 179 A1
Caiapó, Serra do mts Brazil 179 A2
Caiapônia Brazil 179 A2
Caibarién Cuba 163 E8
Cai Bâu, Đao i. Vietnam 86 D2
Caicara Venez. 176 E2
Caicos Islands Turks and Caicos Is 169 J4
Caicos Passage Bahamas/Turks and Caicos Is 163 F8
Caidian China 97 G2
Caiguna Australia 135 D8
Caimanero, Laguna del lag. Mex. 166 D4
Caiman Point Luzon Phil. 82 B3
Caimodorro mt. Spain 67 F3
Cainnyigoin China 96 D1
Cains Store U.S.A. 164 C5
Caipe Arg. 178 C2
Caird Coast Antarctica 188 B1
Cairngorm Mountains U.K. 60 F3
Cairngorms National Park 60 F3
Cairn Mountain AK U.S.A. 148 I3
Cairnryan U.K. 60 D6
Cairns Australia 136 D3
Cairnsmore of Carsphairn hill U.K. 60 E5

▶**Cairo** Egypt 112 C5
Capital of Egypt. 2nd most populous city in Africa.

Cairo U.S.A. 163 C6
Caisleán an Bharraigh Ireland see **Castlebar**
Caiundo Angola 123 B5
Caiwarro (abandoned) Australia 138 B2
Caiyuanzhen China see **Shengsi**
Caizi Hu l. China 97 H2
Cajamarca Peru 176 C5
Cajati Brazil 179 A4
Cajidiocan Phil. 82 C3
Cajuru Brazil 179 B3
Caka Qinghai China 94 D4
Caka'lho China see **Yanjing**
Čakovec Croatia 68 G1
Çal Denizli Turkey 69 M5
Çal Hakkâri Turkey see **Çukurca**
Cala S. Africa 125 H6
Calabar Nigeria 120 D4
Calabogie Canada 165 G1
Calabria, Parco Nazionale della nat. park Italy 68 G5
Calafat Romania 69 J3
Calagnaan i. Phil. 82 C4
Calagua Mex. 166 C3
Calagua Islands Phil. 82 C3
Calagurris Spain see **Calahorra**
Calahorra Spain 67 F2
Calai Angola 123 B5
Calais France 62 B4
Calais U.S.A. 153 I5
Calakmus tourist site Mex. 167 H5
Calalasteo, Sierra de mts Arg. 178 C3
Calama Brazil 176 F5
Calama Chile 178 C2
Calamajué Mex. 157 E7
Calamar Col. 176 D1
Calamian Group is Phil. 82 B4
Calamocha Spain 67 F3
Calandagan i. Phil. 82 C4
Calandula Angola 123 B4
Calang Sumatera Indon. 84 A1
Calapan Mindoro Phil. 82 C3
Călărași Romania 69 L2
Calatayud Spain 67 F3
Calauag Luzon Phil. 82 C3
Calavite Passage Phil. 82 C3
Calawit i. Phil. 82 B3
Calayan i. Phil. 82 C2
Calbayog Samar Phil. 82 D3
Calbe (Saale) Germany 63 L3
Calbiga Samar Phil. 82 D4
Calcasieu r. LA U.S.A. 167 G2
Calcasieu Lake LA U.S.A. 167 G2
Calçoene Brazil 177 H3
Calcutta India see **Kolkata**
Caldas da Rainha Port. 67 B4
Caldas Novas Brazil 177 I7
Calden Germany 63 J3
Calder r. Canada 150 G1
Caldera Chile 178 B3
Calderitas Mex. 167 H5
Caldervale Australia 136 D5
Caldew r. U.K. 58 E4
Caldwell ID U.S.A. 156 D4
Caldwell KS U.S.A. 161 D4
Caldwell OH U.S.A. 164 E4
Caldwell TX U.S.A. 161 D6
Caledon r. Lesotho/S. Africa 125 H6
Caledon S. Africa 124 D8
Caledon Bay Australia 136 B2
Caledonia Canada 164 F2
Caledonia admin. div. U.K. see **Scotland**
Caledonia U.S.A. 165 G2
Caleta el Cobre Chile 178 B2
Calexico U.S.A. 159 F5
Calf of Man i. Isle of Man 58 C4
Calgary Canada 150 H5
Calhoun U.S.A. 164 B5
Cali Col. 176 C3
Calicoan i. Phil. 82 D4
Calicut India 106 B4
Caliente U.S.A. 159 F3
California U.S.A. 164 F3
California state U.S.A. 157 C4
California, Golfo de g. Mex. 166 B2
California Aqueduct canal U.S.A. 158 C3
Cälilabad Azer. 113 H3
Calingasta Arg. 178 C4
Calipatria U.S.A. 159 F5
Calistoga U.S.A. 158 B2
Calkiní Mex. 167 H4
Callabonna, Lake salt flat Australia 137 C6
Callaghan, Mount U.S.A. 158 E2
Callan Ireland 61 E5
Callan r. U.K. 61 F3
Callander Canada 152 F5
Callander U.K. 60 E4
Callang Luzon Phil. 82 C2
Callao Peru 176 C6
Callao U.S.A. 159 G2
Calles Mex. 167 F4
Callicoon U.S.A. 165 H3
Calling Lake Canada 150 H4
Callington U.K. 59 C8
Calliope Australia 136 E5
Callipolis Turkey see **Gallipoli**
Calmar U.S.A. 160 F3
Calobre Panama 166 [inset] J7
Caloosahatchee r. U.S.A. 163 D7
Calotmul Mex. 167 H4
Caloundra Australia 138 F1
Calpulálpan Mex. 167 F5
Caltagirone Sicily Italy 68 F6
Caltanissetta Sicily Italy 68 F6
Calucinga Angola 123 B5
Calulo Angola 123 B4
Calunga Angola 123 B5
Caluquembe Angola 123 B5
Calusa i. Phil. 82 C4
Caluula Somalia 122 F2
Caluula, Raas pt Somalia 122 F2
Caluya i. Phil. 82 C4
Calvert Hills Australia 136 B3
Calvert Island Canada 150 D5
Calvi Corsica France 66 I5
Calvià Spain 67 H4
Calvinia S. Africa 124 D6
Calvo, Monte mt. Italy 68 F4
Cam r. U.K. 59 H6
Camaçari Brazil 179 D1
Camache Reservoir U.S.A. 158 C2
Camachigama r. Canada 152 F5
Camacho Mex. 161 C7
Camacuio Angola 123 B5
Camacupa Angola 123 B5
Camagüey Cuba 169 I4
Camagüey, Archipiélago de is Cuba 169 I4
Camamu Brazil 179 D1
Camana Peru 176 D7
Camanongue Angola 123 C5
Camapuã Brazil 177 H7
Camaquã Brazil 178 F4
Çamardı Turkey 112 D3
Camargo Bol. 176 E8
Camargo Mex. 167 F3
Camargo, Parque Natural nature res. Mex. 167 F3
Camargue reg. France 66 G5
Camarillo U.S.A. 158 D4
Camarón, Cabo c. Hond. 166 [inset] I6
Camarones Arg. 178 C6
Camarones, Bahía b. Arg. 178 C6
Camas r. U.S.A. 156 E4
Ca Mau Vietnam 87 D5
Cambay India see **Khambhat**
Cambay, Gulf of India see **Khambhat, Gulf of**
Camberley U.K. 59 G7
Cambodia country Asia 87 D4
Camboriú Brazil 179 A4
Camborne U.K. 59 B8
Cambrai France 62 D4
Cambria admin. div. U.K. see **Wales**
Cambrian Mountains hills U.K. 59 D6
Cambridge Canada 164 E2
Cambridge N.Z. 139 E3
Cambridge U.K. 59 H6
Cambridge MA U.S.A. 165 J2
Cambridge MD U.S.A. 165 G4
Cambridge MN U.S.A. 160 E2
Cambridge NY U.S.A. 165 I2
Cambridge OH U.S.A. 164 E3
Cambridge Bay Canada 147 H3
Cambridge City U.S.A. 164 C4
Cambridge Springs U.S.A. 164 E3
Cambrien, Lac l. Canada 153 H2
Cambulo Angola 123 C4
Cambundi-Catembo Angola 123 B5
Cambuquira Brazil 179 B3
Cam Co l. Xizang China 99 C6
Camdeboo National Park S. Africa 124 G7
Camden AL U.S.A. 163 C5
Camden AR U.S.A. 161 E5
Camden NJ U.S.A. 165 H4
Camden NY U.S.A. 165 H2
Camden SC U.S.A. 163 D5
Camden Bay AK U.S.A. 149 K1
Camdenton U.S.A. 160 E4
Cameia Angola 123 C5
Cameia, Parque Nacional da nat. park Angola 123 C5
Cameron AZ U.S.A. 159 H4
Cameron LA U.S.A. 161 E6
Cameron MO U.S.A. 160 E4
Cameron TX U.S.A. 161 D6
Cameron Highlands mts Malaysia 84 C1
Cameron Hills Canada 150 G3
Cameron Island Canada 147 H2
Cameron Park U.S.A. 158 C2
Cameroon country Africa 120 E4
Cameroon, Mount vol. Cameroon see **Cameroun, Mont**

Cameroon Highlands slope Cameroon/Nigeria 120 E4
Cameroun country Africa see Cameroon
Cameroun, Mont vol. Cameroon 120 D4
Cametá Brazil 177 I4
Camiguin i. Phil. 82 C2
Camiguin i. Phil. 82 D4
Camiling Luzon Phil. 82 C3
Camiña Chile 176 E7
Camiri Bol. 176 F8
Camisea Peru 176 D6
Camocim Brazil 177 J4
Camooweal Australia 136 B3
Camooweal Caves National Park Australia 136 B4
Camorta i. India 103 H10
Camotes Sea g. Phil. 82 D4
Campamento Hond. 166 [inset] I6
Campana Mex. 166 E3
Campana, Isla i. Chile 178 A7
Campania Island Canada 150 D4
Campbell S. Africa 124 F5
Campbell, Cape N.Z. 139 E5
Campbell, Mount hill Australia 134 E5
Campbellford Canada 165 G1
Campbell Hill hill U.S.A. 164 D3
Campbell Island N.Z. 186 H9
Campbell Lake Canada 151 J2
Campbell Lake N.W.T. Canada 149 N1
Campbell Plateau sea feature S. Pacific Ocean 186 H9
Campbell Range hills Australia 134 D3
Campbell River Canada 150 E5
Campbellsville U.S.A. 164 C5
Campbellton Canada 153 I5
Campbelltown Australia 138 E5
Campbeltown U.K. 60 D5
Campeche Mex. 167 H5
Campeche state Mex. 167 H5
Campeche, Bahía de g. Mex. 168 F5
Camperdown Australia 138 A7
Câmpina Romania 69 K2
Campina Grande Brazil 177 K5
Campinas Brazil 179 B3
Campina Verde Brazil 179 A2
Camplong Timor Indon. 83 B5
Campo Cameroon 120 D4
Campobasso Italy 68 F4
Campo Belo Brazil 179 B3
Campo Belo do Sul Brazil 179 A4
Campo de Diauarum Brazil 177 H6
Campo Florido Brazil 179 A2
Campo Gallo Arg. 178 D3
Campo Grande Brazil 178 F2
Campo Largo Brazil 179 A4
Campo Maior Brazil 177 J4
Campo Maior Port. 67 C4
Campo Mourão Brazil 178 F2
Campos Brazil 179 C3
Campos Altos Brazil 179 B2
Campos Novos Brazil 179 A4
Campos Sales Brazil 177 J5
Campton U.S.A. 164 D5
Câmpulung Romania 69 K2
Câmpulung Moldovenesc Romania 69 K1
Camp Verde U.S.A. 159 H4
Camrose Canada 151 H4
Camrose U.K. 59 B7
Camsell Lake Canada 151 I2
Camsell Portage Canada 151 I3
Camsell Range mts Canada 150 F2
Camulodunum U.K. see Colchester
Çan Turkey 69 L4
Ca Na, Mui hd Vietnam 87 E5
Canaan r. Canada 153 I5
Canaan U.S.A. 165 I2
Canaan Peak U.S.A. 159 H3
Canabrava Brazil 179 B2
Canabungan i. Phil. 82 B4
Canacona India 106 B3

▶Canada country N. America 146 H4
Largest country in North America and 2nd in the world. 3rd most populous country in North America.

Canada Basin sea feature Arctic Ocean 189 A1
Canadian U.S.A. 161 C5
Canadian r. U.S.A. 161 C5
Canadian Abyssal Plain sea feature Arctic Ocean 189 A1
Cañadon Grande, Sierra mts Arg. 178 C7
Canaima, Parque Nacional nat. park Venez. 176 F2
Çanakkale Turkey 69 L4
Çanakkale Boğazı strait Turkey see Dardanelles
Canalejas Arg. 178 C5
Cañamares Spain 67 E3
Canandaigua U.S.A. 165 G2
Cananea Mex. 166 C2
Cananéia Brazil 179 B4
Canápolis Brazil 179 A2
Cañar Ecuador 176 C4
Canarias terr. N. Atlantic Ocean see Canary Islands
Canárias, Ilha das i. Brazil 177 J4
Canarias, Islas terr. N. Atlantic Ocean see Canary Islands

▶Canary Islands terr. N. Atlantic Ocean 120 B2
Autonomous Community of Spain.

Canasayab Mex. 167 H5
Canaseraga U.S.A. 165 G2
Canastota U.S.A. 165 H2
Canastra, Serra da mts Brazil 179 B2
Canastra, Serra da mts Brazil 179 A1
Canatiba Brazil 179 C1
Canatlán Mex. 161 B7
Canaveral, Cape U.S.A. 163 D6
Cañaveras Spain 67 E3
Canavieiras Brazil 179 D1
Cañazas Panama 166 [inset] J7
Canbelego Australia 138 C3

▶Canberra Australia 138 D5
Capital of Australia and Australian Capital Territory.

Cancún Mex. 167 I4
Çandar Turkey see Kastamonu
Çandarlı Turkey 69 L5
Candela Mex. 167 E3
Candela r. Mex. 161 C7
Candelaria Campeche Mex. 167 H5
Candelaria Chihuahua Mex. 166 D2
Candia Greece see Iraklion
Cândido de Abreu Brazil 179 A4
Çandır Turkey 112 D2
Candle AK U.S.A. 148 G2
Candle Lake Canada 151 J4
Candlewood, Lake U.S.A. 165 I3
Cando U.S.A. 160 D1
Candon Luzon Phil. 82 C2
Candon Point Luzon Phil. 82 C2
Cane r. Australia 134 A5
Canea Greece see Chania
Canela Brazil 179 A5
Canelones Uruguay 178 E4
Cane Valley U.S.A. 164 C5
Cangallo Peru 176 D6
Cangamba Angola 123 B5
Cangandala, Parque Nacional de nat. park Angola 123 B4
Canglun Malaysia see Changlun
Cango Caves S. Africa 124 F7
Cangola Angola 123 B4
Cangshan Shandong China 95 I5
Canguaretama Brazil 177 K5
Canguçu Brazil 178 F4
Canguçu, Serra do hills Brazil 178 F4
Cangwu China 97 F4
Cangzhou Hebei China 95 I4
Caniapiscau Canada 153 H3
Caniapiscau r. Canada 153 H2
Caniapiscau, Réservoir de l. Canada 153 H3
Caniçado Moz. see Guija
Canicattì Sicily Italy 68 E6
Canigao Channel Phil. 82 D4
Canim Lake Canada 150 F5
Canindé Brazil 177 K4
Canisteo U.S.A. 165 G2
Canisteo r. U.S.A. 165 G2
Canisteo Peninsula Antarctica 188 K2
Cañitas de Felipe Pescador Mex. 161 C8
Çankırı Turkey 112 D2
Canlaon Negros Phil. 82 C4
Canna Australia 135 A7
Canna i. U.K. 60 C3
Cannanore India 106 B4
Cannanore Islands India 106 B4
Cannelton U.S.A. 164 B5
Cannes France 66 H5
Canning r. AK U.S.A. 149 K1
Cannock U.K. 59 E6
Cannon Beach U.S.A. 156 C3
Cann River Australia 138 D6
Canoas Brazil 179 A5
Canõas, Rio das r. Brazil 179 A4
Canoeiros Brazil 179 B2
Canoe Lake Canada 151 I4
Canoe Lake l. Canada 151 I4
Canoinhas Brazil 179 A4
Canon City U.S.A. 157 G5
Cañón del Sumidero, Parque Nacional nat. park Mex. 167 G5
Cañon Largo watercourse U.S.A. 159 J3
Canoona Australia 136 E4
Canora Canada 151 K5
Canowindra Australia 138 D4
Canso Canada 153 J5
Canso, Cape Canada 153 J5
Cantabrian Mountains Spain see Cantábrica, Cordillera
Cantábrica, Cordillera mts Spain 67 D2
Cantábrico, Mar sea Spain 67 C2
Canterbury U.K. 59 I7
Canterbury Bight b. N.Z. 139 C7
Canterbury Plains N.Z. 139 C6
Cân Thơ Vietnam 87 D5
Cantil U.S.A. 158 E4
Cantilan Mindanao Phil. 82 D4
Canton GA U.S.A. 163 C5
Canton IL U.S.A. 160 F3
Canton MO U.S.A. 160 F3
Canton MS U.S.A. 161 F5
Canton NY U.S.A. 165 H1
Canton OH U.S.A. 164 E3
Canton PA U.S.A. 165 G3
Canton SD U.S.A. 160 D3
Canton TX U.S.A. 161 E5
Canton Island atoll Kiribati see Kanton
Cantuaria U.K. see Canterbury
Cantwell AK U.S.A. 149 J3
Canunda National Park Australia 137 C8
Canutama Brazil 176 F5
Canutillo Mex. 157 G8
Canvey Island U.K. 59 H7
Canwood Canada 151 J4
Cany-Barville France 59 H9
Canyon U.S.A. 161 C5
Canyon (abandoned) Y.T. Canada 149 M3
Canyon City U.S.A. 156 D3
Canyondam U.S.A. 158 C1
Canyon de Chelly National Monument nat. park U.S.A. 159 I3
Canyon Ferry Lake U.S.A. 156 F3
Canyon Lake U.S.A. 159 H5
Canyonlands National Park U.S.A. 159 I2
Canyon Ranges mts N.W.T. Canada 149 P3
Canyons of the Ancients National Monument nat. park U.S.A. 159 I3
Canyonville U.S.A. 156 C4
Cao Bằng Vietnam 86 D2
Caocheng Shandong China see Caoxian
Cao Daban Qinghai China 94 E4
Caohai China see Weining
Caohe China see Qichun
Caohu Xinjiang China 98 D4
Caohu Xinjiang China 98 D4
Caojiahe China see Qichun
Caojian China 96 C3
Caoshi China 90 B4
Caoxian Shandong China 95 H5
Caozhou Shandong China see Heze
Cap i. Phil. 82 C5
Capac U.S.A. 164 D2
Çapakçur Turkey see Bingöl
Capalulu, Selat sea chan. Indon. 83 C3
Capanaparo r. Venez. 176 E2
Capanema Brazil 177 I4
Capão Bonito Brazil 179 A4
Caparaó, Serra do mts Brazil 179 C3
Capas Luzon Phil. 82 C3
Cap-aux-Meules Canada 153 J5
Cap-de-la-Madeleine Canada 153 G5
Cape r. Australia 136 D4
Cape Arid National Park Australia 135 C8
Cape Barren Island Australia 137 [inset]
Cape Basin sea feature S. Atlantic Ocean 184 I8
Cape Breton Highlands National Park Canada 153 J5
Cape Breton Island Canada 153 J5
Cape Charles Canada 153 L3
Cape Charles U.S.A. 165 G5
Cape Coast Ghana 120 C4
Cape Coast Castle Ghana see Cape Coast
Cape Cod Bay U.S.A. 165 J3
Cape Cod National Seashore nature res. U.S.A. 165 K3
Cape Coral U.S.A. 163 D7
Cape Crawford Australia 136 A3
Cape Dorset Canada 147 K3
Cape Fanshaw AK U.S.A. 149 N4
Cape Fear r. U.S.A. 163 E5
Cape George Canada 153 J5
Cape Girardeau U.S.A. 161 F4
Cape Johnson Depth sea feature N. Pacific Ocean 186 E5
Cape Juby Morocco see Tarfaya
Cape Krusenstern National Monument nat. park AK U.S.A. 148 G2
Capel Australia 135 A8
Cape Le Grand National Park Australia 135 C8
Capelinha Brazil 179 C2
Capella Australia 136 E4
Capelle aan de IJssel Neth. 62 E3
Capelongo Angola see Kuvango
Cape May U.S.A. 165 H4
Cape May Court House U.S.A. 165 H4
Cape May Point U.S.A. 165 H4
Cape Melville National Park Australia 136 D2
Capenda-Camulemba Angola 123 B4
Cape of Good Hope Nature Reserve S. Africa 124 D8
Cape Palmerston National Park Australia 136 E4
Cape Range National Park Australia 134 A5
Cape St George Canada 153 K4

▶Cape Town S. Africa 124 D7
Legislative capital of South Africa.

Cape Tribulation National Park Australia 136 D2
Cape Upstart National Park Australia 136 D3
Cape Verde country N. Atlantic Ocean 120 [inset]
Cape Verde Basin sea feature N. Atlantic Ocean 184 F5
Cape Verde Plateau sea feature N. Atlantic Ocean 184 F4
Cape Vincent U.S.A. 165 G1
Cape Yakataga AK U.S.A. 149 L3
Cape York Peninsula Australia 136 C2
Cap-Haïtien Haiti 169 J5
Capim r. Brazil 177 I4
Capitán Arturo Prat research station Antarctica 188 A2

▶Capitol Hill N. Mariana Is 81 L3
Capital of the Northern Mariana Islands, on Saipan.

Capitol Reef National Park U.S.A. 159 H2
Capivara, Represa resr Brazil 179 A3
Čapljina Bos.-Herz. 68 G3
Cappoquin Ireland 61 E5
Capraia, Isola di i. Italy 68 C3
Caprara, Punta pt Sardinia Italy 68 C4
Capri, Isola di i. Italy 68 F4
Capricorn Channel Australia 136 E4
Capricorn Group atolls Australia 136 F4
Caprivi Strip reg. Namibia 123 C5
Cap Rock Escarpment U.S.A. 161 C5
Capsa Tunisia see Gafsa
Captain Cook U.S.A. 157 [inset]
Captina r. U.S.A. 164 E4
Capuava Brazil 179 B4
Caquetá r. Col. 176 E4
Carabao i. Phil. 82 C3
Caracal Romania 69 K2

▶Caracas Venez. 176 E1
Capital of Venezuela.

Caraga Mindanao Phil. 82 D5
Caraguatatuba Brazil 179 B3
Caraí Brazil 179 C2
Carajás Brazil 177 H5
Carajás, Serra dos hills Brazil 177 H5
Carales Sardinia Italy see Cagliari
Caralis Sardinia Italy see Cagliari
Caramoan Peninsula Luzon Phil. 82 C3
Carandaí Brazil 179 C3
Caransebeş Romania 69 J2
Caraquet Canada 153 I5
Carat, Tanjung pt Indon. 84 D3
Caratasca Hond. 166 [inset] J6
Caratasca, Laguna de lag. Hond. 166 [inset] J6
Caratinga Brazil 179 C2
Carauari Brazil 176 E4
Caravaca de la Cruz Spain 67 F4
Caravelas Brazil 179 D2
Carberry Canada 151 L5
Carbó Mex. 166 C2
Carbon, Cap hd Alg. 67 F6

▶Carbón, Laguna del l. Arg. 178 C7
Lowest point in South America.

Carbonara, Capo c. Sardinia Italy 68 C5
Carbondale CO U.S.A. 159 J2
Carbondale PA U.S.A. 165 H3
Carboneras Mex. 161 D7
Carbonia Sardinia Italy 68 C5
Carbonita Brazil 179 C2
Carcaixent Spain 67 F4
Carcajou Canada 150 G3
Carcajou r. N.W.T. Canada 149 O2
Carcar Cebu Phil. 82 C4
Carcassonne France 66 F5
Carcross Y.T. Canada 149 N3
Cardamomes, Chaîne des mts Cambodia/Thai. see Cardamom Range
Cardamom Hills India 106 C4
Cardamom Range mts Cambodia/Thai. 87 C4
Cárdenas Cuba 169 H4
Cárdenas Mex. 168 E4
Cárdenas Tabasco Mex. 167 G5
Cardenyabba watercourse Australia 138 A2
Çardi Turkey see Harmancık
Cardiel, Lago l. Arg. 178 B7

▶Cardiff U.K. 59 D7
Capital of Wales.

Cardiff U.S.A. 165 G4
Cardigan U.K. 59 C6
Cardigan Bay U.K. 59 C6
Cardinal Lake Canada 150 G3
Cardington U.S.A. 164 D3
Cardón, Cerro hill Mex. 166 B3
Cardoso Brazil 179 A3
Cardoso, Ilha do i. Brazil 179 B4
Cardston Canada 150 H5
Careen Lake Canada 151 I3
Carei Romania 69 J1
Carentan France 66 D2
Carey U.S.A. 164 D3
Carey, Lake salt flat Australia 135 C7
Carey Lake Canada 151 K2
Cargados Carajos Islands Mauritius 185 L7
Carhaix-Plouguer France 66 C2
Cariacica Brazil 179 C3
Cariamanga Ecuador 176 C4
Caribbean Sea N. Atlantic Ocean 169 H5
Cariboo Mountains Canada 150 F4
Caribou r. Man. Canada 151 M3
Caribou r. N.W.T. Canada 149 P3
Caribou r. Y.T. Canada 149 N2
Caribou AK U.S.A. 149 K2
Caribou U.S.A. 162 G2
Caribou Lake Canada 147 J4
Caribou Mountains Canada 150 H3
Carichic Mex. 166 D3
Carigara Leyte Phil. 82 D4
Carignan France 62 F5
Carinda Australia 138 C3
Cariñena Spain 67 F3
Carinhanha r. Brazil 179 C1
Carlabhagh U.K. see Carloway
Carleton U.S.A. 164 D2
Carleton, Mount hill Canada 153 I5
Carletonville S. Africa 125 H4
Carlin U.S.A. 158 E1
Carlingford Lough inlet Ireland/U.K. 61 F3
Carlinville U.S.A. 160 F4
Carlisle U.K. 58 E4
Carlisle IN U.S.A. 164 B4
Carlisle KY U.S.A. 164 C4
Carlisle NY U.S.A. 165 H2
Carlisle PA U.S.A. 165 G3
Carlisle Lakes salt flat Australia 135 D7
Carlit, Pic mt. France 66 E5
Carlos Chagas Brazil 179 C2
Carlow Ireland 61 F5
Carloway U.K. 60 C2
Carlsbad Czech Rep. see Karlovy Vary
Carlsbad CA U.S.A. 158 E5
Carlsbad NM U.S.A. 157 G6
Carlsbad TX U.S.A. 167 E2
Carlsbad Caverns National Park U.S.A. 157 G6
Carlsberg Ridge sea feature Indian Ocean 185 L5
Carlson Inlet Antarctica 188 L1
Carlton U.S.A. 160 E2
Carlton Hill Australia 134 E3
Carluke U.K. 60 F5
Carlyle Canada 151 K5
Carmacks Y.T. Canada 149 M3
Carmagnola Italy 68 B2
Carman Canada 151 L5
Carmana Iran see Kermān
Carmarthen U.K. 59 C7
Carmarthen Bay U.K. 59 C7
Carmaux France 66 F4
Carmel IN U.S.A. 164 B4
Carmel NY U.S.A. 165 I3
Carmel, Mount hill Israel 107 B3
Carmel Head hd U.K. 58 C5
Carmelita Guat. 167 H5
Carmel Valley U.S.A. 158 C3
Carmen Mex. 167 E3
Carmen r. Mex. 166 D2
Carmen Bohol Phil. 82 D4
Carmen U.S.A. 157 F7
Carmen, Isla i. Mex. 166 C3
Carmen, Isla del i. Mex. 167 H5
Carmen de Patagones Arg. 178 D6
Carmi U.S.A. 160 F4
Carmichael U.S.A. 158 C2
Carmo da Cachoeira Brazil 179 B3
Carmo do Paranaíba Brazil 179 B2
Carmona Angola see Uíge
Carmona Hond. 166 [inset] I7
Carmona Spain 67 D5
Carnac France 66 C3
Carnamah Australia 135 A7
Carnarvon Australia 135 A6
Carnarvon S. Africa 124 F6
Carnarvon National Park Australia 136 D5
Carnarvon Range hills Australia 135 C6
Carnarvon Range mts Australia 136 E5
Carn Dearg hill U.K. 60 E3
Carndonagh Ireland 61 E2
Carnegie Australia 135 C6
Carnegie, Lake salt flat Australia 135 C6
Carn Eige mt. U.K. 60 D3
Carnes Australia 135 F7
Carney Island Antarctica 188 J2
Carnforth U.K. 58 E4
Carn Glas-choire hill U.K. 60 F3
Car Nicobar i. India 87 A5
Carnlough U.K. 61 G3
Carn nan Gabhar mt. U.K. 60 F4
Carn Odhar hill U.K. 60 E3
Carnot Cent. Afr. Rep. 122 B3
Carnoustie U.K. 60 G4
Carnsore Point Ireland 61 F5
Carnwath r. N.W.T. Canada 149 O1
Carnwath U.K. 60 F5
Caro AK U.S.A. 149 J2
Caro U.S.A. 164 D2
Carola Cay reef Australia 136 F3
Carol City U.S.A. 163 D7
Carolina Brazil 177 I5
Carolina S. Africa 125 J4
Carolina Beach U.S.A. 163 E5
Caroline Canada 150 H4
Caroline Island atoll Kiribati 187 J6
Caroline Islands N. Pacific Ocean 81 K5
Caroline Peak N.Z. 139 A7
Caroline Range hills Australia 134 D4
Caroní r. Venez. 176 F2
Carp Canada 165 G1
Carpathian Mountains Europe 53 C6
Carpații mts Europe see Carpathian Mountains
Carpații Meridionali mts Romania see Transylvanian Alps
Carpații Occidentali mts Romania 69 J2
Carpentaria, Gulf of Australia 136 B2
Carpentras France 66 G4
Carpi Italy 68 D2
Carpinteria U.S.A. 158 D4
Carpio U.S.A. 160 C1
Carra, Lough l. Ireland 61 C4
Carraig na Siuire Ireland see Carrick-on-Suir
Carraig Thuathail Ireland see Carrigtohill
Carrantuohill mt. Ireland 61 C6
Carrara Italy 68 D2
Carrasco, Parque Nacional nat. park Bol. 176 F7
Carrathool Australia 138 B5
Carrhae Turkey see Harran
Carrickfergus U.K. 61 G3
Carrickmacross Ireland 61 F4
Carrick-on-Shannon Ireland 61 D4
Carrick-on-Suir Ireland 61 E5
Carrigallen Ireland 61 E4
Carrigtohill Ireland 61 D6
Carrillo Mex. 166 E3
Carrington U.S.A. 160 D2
Carrizal Mex. 166 D2
Carrizal Bajo Chile 178 B3
Carrizo U.S.A. 159 H4
Carrizo Creek r. U.S.A. 161 C4
Carrizos Mex. 167 F3
Carrizo Springs U.S.A. 161 D6
Carrizo Wash watercourse U.S.A. 159 I4
Carrizozo U.S.A. 157 G6
Carroll U.S.A. 160 E3
Carrollton AL U.S.A. 161 F5
Carrollton GA U.S.A. 163 C5
Carrollton IL U.S.A. 160 F4
Carrollton KY U.S.A. 164 C4
Carrollton MO U.S.A. 160 E4
Carrollton OH U.S.A. 164 E3
Carrolltown U.S.A. 165 F3
Carron r. U.K. 60 E3
Carrot r. Canada 151 K4
Carrothers U.S.A. 164 D3
Carrot River Canada 151 K4
Carrowmore Lake Ireland 61 C3
Carrsville U.S.A. 165 G5
Carruthers Lake Canada 151 K2
Carruthersville U.S.A. 161 F4
Carry Falls Reservoir U.S.A. 165 H1
Çarşamba Turkey 112 E2
Carson r. U.S.A. 158 D2
Carson City MI U.S.A. 164 C2

▶Carson City NV U.S.A. 158 D2
Capital of Nevada.

Carson Escarpment Australia 134 D3
Carson Lake U.S.A. 158 D2
Carson Sink l. U.S.A. 158 D2
Carstensz Pyramid mt. Indon. see Jaya, Puncak
Carstensz-top mt. Indon. see Jaya, Puncak
Carswell Lake Canada 151 I3
Cartagena Col. 176 C1
Cartagena Spain 67 F5
Cartago Costa Rica 166 [inset] J7
Carteret Group is P.N.G. see Kilinailau Islands
Carteret Island Solomon Is see Malaita
Cartersville U.S.A. 163 C5
Carthage tourist site Tunisia 68 D6
Carthage MO U.S.A. 161 E4
Carthage NC U.S.A. 163 E5
Carthage NY U.S.A. 165 H2
Carthage TX U.S.A. 161 E5
Carthago tourist site Tunisia see Carthage
Carthago Nova Spain see Cartagena
Cartier Island Australia 134 C3
Cartmel U.K. 58 E4
Cartwright Man. Canada 151 L5
Cartwright Nfld. and Lab. Canada 153 K3
Caruarú Brazil 177 K5
Carúpano Venez. 176 F1
Carver U.S.A. 164 D5
Carvin France 62 C4
Cary U.S.A. 162 E5
Caryapundy Swamp Australia 137 C6
Casablanca Morocco 64 C5
Casa Branca Brazil 179 B3
Casa de Janos Mex. 166 C2
Casadepaga AK U.S.A. 148 F2
Casa de Piedra, Embalse resr Arg. 178 C5
Casa Grande U.S.A. 159 H5
Casale Monferrato Italy 68 C2
Casalmaggiore Italy 68 D2
Casares Nicaragua 166 [inset] I7
Casas Grandes Mex. 166 D2
Casas Grandes r. Mex. 166 D2
Casca Brazil 179 A5
Cascada de Bassaseachic, Parque Nacional nat. park Mex. 166 C2
Cascade Australia 135 C8
Cascade r. N.Z. 139 B7
Cascade ID U.S.A. 156 D3
Cascade MT U.S.A. 156 F3
Cascade Point N.Z. 139 B7
Cascade Range mts Canada/U.S.A. 156 C4
Cascade Reservoir U.S.A. 156 D3
Cascais Port. 67 B4
Cascal, Paso del pass Nicaragua 166 [inset] I7
Cascavel Brazil 178 F2
Casco Bay U.S.A. 165 K2
Caserta Italy 68 F4
Casey research station Antarctica 188 F2
Casey Bay Antarctica 188 D2
Caseyr, Raas c. Somalia see Gwardafuy, Gees
Cashel Ireland 61 E5
Cashmere Australia 138 D1
Casiguran Luzon Phil. 82 C2
Casiguran Sound sea chan. Luzon Phil. 82 C2
Casino Australia 138 F2
Casiquiare, Canal r. Venez. 176 E3
Casita Mex. 157 F7
Casnewydd U.K. see Newport
Casogoran Bay Phil. 82 D4
Caspe Spain 67 F3
Casper U.S.A. 156 G4
Caspian Lowland Kazakh./Rus. Fed. 100 D2

▶Caspian Sea l. Asia/Europe 113 H1
Largest lake in the world and in Asia/Europe, and lowest point in Europe.

Cass U.S.A. 164 F4
Cass r. U.S.A. 164 D2
Cassacatiza Moz. 123 D5
Cassadaga U.S.A. 164 F2
Cassaigne Alg. see Sidi Ali
Cassamba Angola 123 C5
Cass City U.S.A. 164 D2
Cassel France 62 C4
Casselman Canada 165 H1
Cássia Brazil 179 B3
Cassiar B.C. Canada 149 O4
Cassiar Mountains B.C. Canada 149 O4
Cassilândia Brazil 179 A2
Cassilis Australia 138 D4
Cassino Italy 68 E4
Cassley r. U.K. 60 E3
Cassongue Angola 123 B5
Cassopolis U.S.A. 164 B3
Cassville U.S.A. 161 E4
Castanhal Brazil 177 I4
Castanho Brazil 176 F5
Castaños Mex. 167 E3
Castelfranco Veneto Italy 68 D2
Castell-nedd U.K. see Neath
Castell Newydd Emlyn U.K. see Newcastle Emlyn
Castellón Spain see Castellón de la Plana
Castellón de la Plana Spain 67 F4
Castelo Branco Port. 67 C4
Castelo de Vide Port. 67 C4

Casteltermini Sicily Italy 68 E6
Castelvetrano Sicily Italy 68 E6
Castiglione della Pescaia Italy 68 D3
Castignon, Lac l. Canada 153 H2
Castilla y León reg. Spain 66 B6
Castlebar Ireland 61 C4
Castlebay U.K. 60 B4
Castlebellingham Ireland 61 F4
Castleblayney Ireland 61 F3
Castlebridge Ireland 61 F5
Castle Carrock U.K. 58 E4
Castle Cary U.K. 59 E7
Castle Dale U.S.A. 159 H2
Castlederg U.K. 61 E3
Castledermot Ireland 61 F5
Castle Dome Mountains U.S.A. 159 F5
Castle Donington U.K. 59 F6
Castle Douglas U.K. 60 F6
Castleford U.K. 58 F5
Castlegar Canada 150 G5
Castlegregory Ireland 61 B5
Castle Island Bahamas 163 F8
Castleisland Ireland 61 C5
Castlemaine Australia 138 B6
Castlemaine Ireland 61 C5
Castlemartyr Ireland 61 D6
Castle Mountain Alta Canada 150 H5
Castle Mountain Y.T. Canada 149 N2
Castle Mountain U.S.A. 158 C4
Castle Peak hill H.K. China 97 [inset]
Castle Peak Bay H.K. China 97 [inset]
Castlepoint N.Z. 139 F5
Castlepollard Ireland 61 E4
Castlerea Ireland 61 D4
Castlereagh r. Australia 138 C3
Castle Rock U.S.A. 156 G5
Castletown Ireland 61 E5
Castletown Isle of Man 58 C4
Castor Canada 151 I4
Castor r. U.S.A. 161 F4
Castor, Rivière du r. Canada 152 F3
Castra Regina Germany see Regensburg
Castres France 66 F5
Castricum Neth. 62 E2

▶Castries St Lucia 169 L6
Capital of St Lucia.

Castro Brazil 179 A4
Castro Chile 178 B6
Castro Alves Brazil 179 D1
Castro Verde Port. 67 B5
Castroville U.S.A. 158 C3
Cast Uul mt. Mongolia 94 B1
Caswell AK U.S.A. 149 J3
Çat Turkey 113 F3
Catacamas Hond. 166 [inset] I6
Catacaos Peru 176 B5
Cataguases Brazil 179 C3
Catahoula Lake U.S.A. 161 E6
Catainġan Masbate Phil. 82 C3
Çatak Turkey 113 F3
Catalão Brazil 179 B2
Çatalca Yarımadası pen. Turkey 69 M4
Catalina U.S.A. 159 H5
Catalonia aut. comm. Spain see Cataluña
Cataluña aut. comm. Spain 67 G3
Catalunya aut. comm. Spain see Cataluña
Catamarca Arg. 178 C3
Catana Sicily Italy see Catania
Catanauan Luzon Phil. 82 C3
Catanduanes i. Phil. 82 D3
Catanduva Brazil 179 A3
Catania Sicily Italy 68 F6
Catanzaro Italy 68 G5
Cataract Creek watercourse U.S.A. 159 G3
Catarina U.S.A. 161 D6
Catarino Rodríguez Mex. 167 E3
Catarman Samar Phil. 82 D3
Catarman Point Mindanao Phil. 82 D5
Catastrophe, Cape Australia 137 A7
Catawba r. U.S.A. 163 D5
Cataxa Moz. 123 D5
Cat Ba, Đao i. Vietnam 86 D2
Catbalogan Samar Phil. 82 D4
Cateel Mindanao Phil. 82 D5
Cateel Bay Mindanao Phil. 82 D5
Catemaco Mex. 167 G5
Catembe Moz. 125 K4
Catengue Angola 123 B5
Catete Angola 123 B4
Cathair Dónall Ireland 61 B6
Cathair Saidhbhín Ireland see Cahirsiveen
Cathcart Australia 138 D6
Cathcart S. Africa 125 H7
Cathedral Peak S. Africa 125 I5
Cathedral Rock National Park Australia 138 F3
Catherdaniel Ireland see Cathair Dónall
Catherine, Mount U.S.A. 159 G2
Catheys Valley U.S.A. 158 C3
Cathlamet U.S.A. 156 C3
Catió Guinea-Bissau 120 B3
Catisimiña Venez. 176 F3
Cat Island Bahamas 163 F7
Cat Lake Canada 151 N5
Catlettsburg U.S.A. 164 D4
Catoche, Cabo c. Mex. 167 I4
Cato Island and Bank reef Australia 136 F4
Catorce Mex. 167 E4
Catriló Arg. 178 D5
Cats, Mont des hill France 62 C4
Catskill U.S.A. 165 I2
Catskill Mountains U.S.A. 165 H2
Catuane Moz. 125 K4
Cauayan Negros Phil. 82 C4
Caubvick, Mount Canada 153 J2
Cauca r. Col. 169 J7
Caucaia Brazil 177 K4
Caucasia Col. 176 C2
Caucasus mts Asia/Europe 113 F2
Cauchon Lake Canada 151 L4
Caudry France 62 D4
Câu Giat Vietnam 86 D3
Cauit Point Mindanao Phil. 82 D4
Caulonia Italy 68 G5
Caungula Angola 123 B4
Cauquenes Chile 178 B5
Causapscal Canada 153 I4
Căuşeni Moldova 69 M1
Cavaglià Italy 68 C2
Cavalcante, Serra do hills Brazil 179 B1
Cavalier U.S.A. 160 D1
Cavan Ireland 61 E4
Çavdır Turkey 69 M6
Cave City U.S.A. 164 C5
Cave Creek U.S.A. 159 H5
Caveira r. Brazil 179 C1
Cavern Island Myanmar 87 B5
Cave Run Lake U.S.A. 164 D4
Caviana, Ilha i. Brazil 177 H3
Cavili rf Phil. 82 C4
Cavite Luzon Phil. 82 C3
Cawdor U.K. 60 F3
Cawnpore India see Kanpur
Cawston U.K. 59 I6
Caxias Brazil 177 J4
Caxias do Sul Brazil 179 A5
Caxito Angola 123 B4
Çay Turkey 69 N5
Cayambe, Volcán vol. Ecuador 176 C3
Çaybaşı Turkey see Çayeli
Çaycuma Turkey 69 O4
Çayeli Turkey 113 F2

▶Cayenne Fr. Guiana 177 H3
Capital of French Guiana.

Cayeux-sur-Mer France 62 B4
Çayırhan Turkey 69 N4
Cayman Brac i. Cayman Is 169 I5

▶Cayman Islands terr. West Indies 169 H5
United Kingdom Overseas Territory.

Cayman Trench sea feature Caribbean Sea 184 C4
Caynabo Somalia 122 E3
Cay Sal i. Bahamas 163 D8
Cay Sal Bank sea feature Bahamas 163 D8
Cay Santa Domingo i. Bahamas 163 F8
Cayucos U.S.A. 158 C4
Cayuga Canada 164 F2
Cayuga Lake U.S.A. 165 G2
Cay Verde i. Bahamas 163 F8
Cazê Xizang China 99 D7
Cazenovia U.S.A. 165 H2
Cazombo Angola 123 C5
Ceadâr-Lunga Moldova see Ciadîr-Lunga
Ceanannus Mór Ireland see Kells
Ceann a Deas na Hearadh pen. U.K. see South Harris
Ceará Brazil see Fortaleza
Ceara Abyssal Plain sea feature S. Atlantic Ocean 184 F6
Ceatharlach Ireland see Carlow
Ceballos Mex. 166 D3
Ceboruco, Volcán vol. Mex. 166 D4
Cebu Cebu Phil. 82 C4
Cebu i. Phil. 82 C4
Čechy reg. Czech Rep. 57 N6
Cecil Plains Australia 138 E1
Cecil Rhodes, Mount hill Australia 135 C6
Cecina Italy 68 D3
Cedar r. ND U.S.A. 160 C2
Cedar r. NE U.S.A. 160 D3
Cedar City U.S.A. 159 G3
Cedar Creek Reservoir TX U.S.A. 167 F1
Cedaredge U.S.A. 159 J2
Cedar Falls U.S.A. 160 E3
Cedar Grove U.S.A. 164 B2
Cedar Hill NM U.S.A. 159 J3
Cedar Hill TN U.S.A. 164 B5
Cedar Island U.S.A. 165 H5
Cedar Lake Canada 151 K4
Cedar Point U.S.A. 164 D3
Cedar Rapids U.S.A. 160 F3
Cedar Run U.S.A. 165 H4
Cedar Springs U.S.A. 164 C2
Cedartown U.S.A. 163 C5
Cedarville S. Africa 125 I6
Cedeño Hond. 166 [inset] I6
Cedral Quintana Roo Mex. 167 I4
Cedral San Luis Potosí Mex. 167 E4
Cedros Hond. 166 [inset] I6
Cedros Sonora Mex. 166 C3
Cedros Zacatecas Mex. 167 E3
Cedros, Cerro mt. Mex. 157 E7
Cedros, Isla i. Mex. 166 B2
Ceduna Australia 135 F8
Ceeldheere Somalia 122 E3
Ceerigaabo Somalia 122 E2
Cefalù Sicily Italy 68 F5
Cegléd Hungary 69 H1
Cêgnê Xizang China 99 F6
Ceheng China 96 E3
Çekerek Turkey 112 D2
Çekiçler Turkm. 110 D2
Celah, Gunung mt. Malaysia see Mandi Angin, Gunung
Celaque, Parque Nacional nat. park Hond. 167 H6
Celaya Mex. 168 D4
Celbridge Ireland 61 F4
Celebes i. Indon. 83 B3
Celebes Basin sea feature Pacific Ocean 186 E5
Celebes Sea Indon./Phil. 81 G6
Celestún Mex. 167 H4
Celina OH U.S.A. 164 C3
Celina TN U.S.A. 164 C5
Celje Slovenia 68 F1
Celle Germany 63 K2
Celovec Austria see Klagenfurt
Celtic Sea Ireland/U.K. 56 D5
Celtic Shelf sea feature N. Atlantic Ocean 184 H2
Cemaru, Gunung mt. Indon. 85 F2
Çemenibit Turkm. 111 F3
Cempi, Teluk b. Sumbawa Indon. 85 G5
Cenderawasih, Teluk b. Indon. 81 J7
Çendir r. Turkm. 110 D2
Cenrana Sulawesi Barat Indon. 83 A3
Centane S. Africa see Kentani
Centenary Zimbabwe 123 D5
Center NE U.S.A. 160 D3
Center TX U.S.A. 161 E6
Centereach U.S.A. 165 I3
Center Point U.S.A. 163 C5
Centerville IA U.S.A. 160 E3
Centerville MO U.S.A. 161 F4
Centerville TX U.S.A. 161 E6
Centerville WV U.S.A. 164 E4
Centrafricaine, République country Africa see Central African Republic
Central admin. dist. Botswana 125 H2
Central AK U.S.A. 149 K2
Central U.S.A. 159 I5
Central, Cordillera mts Col. 176 C3
Central, Cordillera mts Panama 166 [inset] J7
Central, Cordillera mts Peru 176 C6
Central, Cordillera mts Luzon Phil. 82 C2
Central African Empire country Africa see Central African Republic
Central African Republic country Africa 122 B3
Central Brahui Range mts Pak. 111 G4
Central Butte Canada 156 G2
Central City U.S.A. 160 D3
Centralia IL U.S.A. 160 F4
Centralia WA U.S.A. 156 C3
Central Kalahari Game Reserve nature res. Botswana 124 F2
Central Kara Rise sea feature Arctic Ocean 189 F1
Central Makran Range mts Pak. 111 G5
Central Mount Stuart hill Australia 134 F5
Central Pacific Basin sea feature Pacific Ocean 186 H5
Central Provinces state India see Madhya Pradesh
Central Range mts P.N.G. 81 K7
Central Russian Upland hills Rus. Fed. 53 H5
Central Siberian Plateau Rus. Fed. 77 M3
Central Square U.S.A. 165 G2
Centre U.S.A. 163 C5
Centreville AL U.S.A. 163 C5
Centreville U.S.A. 165 G4
Cenxi China 97 F4
Cenyang China see Hengfeng
Ceos i. Greece see Tzia
Cephaloedium Sicily Italy see Cefalù
Cephalonia i. Greece 69 I5
Cepu Jawa Indon. 85 E4
Ceram i. Maluku Indon. see Seram
Ceram Sea Indon. see Seram, Laut
Cerbat Mountains U.S.A. 159 F4
Čerchov mt. Czech Rep. 63 M5
Ceres Arg. 178 D3
Ceres Brazil 179 A1
Ceres S. Africa 124 D7
Ceres U.S.A. 158 C3
Céret France 66 F5
Cerezo de Abajo Spain 67 E3
Cêri Xizang China 99 D7
Cerignola Italy 68 F4
Cerigo i. Greece see Kythira
Cêringgolêb Xizang China see Dongco
Çerkeş Turkey 112 D2
Çerkeşli Turkey 69 M4
Çermik Turkey 113 E3
Cernăuţi Ukr. see Chernivtsi
Cernavodă Romania 69 M2
Cerralvo Mex. 167 F3
Cerralvo, Isla i. Mex. 166 C3
Cërrik Albania 69 H4
Cerritos Mex. 168 D4
Cerro Azul Brazil 179 A4
Cerro Azul Mex. 167 F4
Cerro de Pasco Peru 176 C6
Cerro Hoya, Parque Nacional nat. park Panama 166 [inset] J8
Cerro Prieto Mex. 166 D3
Cerros Colorados, Embalse resr Arg. 178 C5
Cervantes, Cerro mt. Arg. 178 B8
Cervati, Monte mt. Italy 68 F4
Cervione Corsica France 66 I5
Cervo Spain 67 C2
Cesena Italy 68 E2
Cēsis Latvia 55 N8
Česká Republika country Europe see Czech Republic
České Budějovice Czech Rep. 57 O6
Českomoravská vysočina hills Czech Rep. 57 O6
Český Krumlov Czech Rep. 57 O6
Český les mts Czech Rep./Germany 63 M5
Çeşme Turkey 69 L5
Cessnock Australia 138 E4
Cetaceo, Mount Phil. 82 C2
Cêtar Qinghai China 94 E4
Cetatea Albă Ukr. see Bilhorod-Dnistrovs'kyy
Cetinje Montenegro 68 H3
Cetraro Italy 68 F5

▶Ceuta N. Africa 67 D6
Autonomous Community of Spain.

Ceva-i-Ra reef Fiji 133 H4
Cévennes mts France 66 F5
Cévennes, Parc National des nat. park France 66 F4
Cevizli Turkey 107 C1
Cevizlik Turkey see Maçka
Ceyhan Turkey 112 D3
Ceyhan r. Turkey 107 B1
Ceyhan Boğazı r. mouth Turkey 107 B1
Ceylanpınar Turkey 113 F3
Ceylon country Asia see Sri Lanka
Chābahār Iran 111 F5
Chablé Mex. 167 H5
Chabrol i. New Caledonia see Lifou
Chabug Xizang China 99 C6
Chabyêr Caka salt l. China 99 D7
Chachapoyas Peru 176 C5
Chacharan Pak. 111 H4
Chäche Turkm. see Çäçe
Chachoengsao Thai. 87 C4
Chachro Pak. 111 H5
Chaco r. U.S.A. 159 I3
Chaco Boreal reg. Para. 178 E2
Chaco Culture National Historical Park U.S.A. 159 J3
Chaco Mesa plat. U.S.A. 159 J4

▶Chad country Africa 121 E3
5th largest country in Africa.

Chad, Lake Africa 121 E3
Chadaasan Mongolia 94 E2
Chadan Rus. Fed. 102 H1
Chadibe Botswana 125 H2
Chadron U.S.A. 160 C3
Chadyr-Lunga Moldova see Ciadîr-Lunga
Chae Hom Thai. 86 B3
Chaek Kyrg. 98 A4
Chaeryŏng N. Korea 91 B5
Chae Son National Park Thai. 86 B3
Chagai Pak. 111 G4
Chagai Hills Afgh./Pak. 111 F4
Chagan Kazakh. 98 B2
Chaganuzun Rus. Fed. 98 E2
Chagdo Kangri mt. China 105 F2
Chaggur Qinghai China 99 F6
Chaghā Khūr mt. Iran 110 C4
Chaghcharān Afgh. 111 G3
Chagny France 66 G3
Chagoda Rus. Fed. 52 G4
Chagos Archipelago is B.I.O.T. 185 M6
Chagos-Laccadive Ridge sea feature Indian Ocean 185 M6
Chagos Trench sea feature Indian Ocean 185 M6
Chagoyan Rus. Fed. 90 C1
Chagrayskoye Plato plat. Kazakh. see Shagyray, Plato
Chagres, Parque Nacional nat. park Panama 166 [inset] K7
Chāh Ākhvor Iran 111 E3
Chāh 'Ali Akbar Iran 110 E3
Chahbounia Alg. 67 H6
Chahchaheh Turkm. 111 F2
Chāh-e Āb Afgh. 111 H2
Chāh-e Bāgh well Iran 110 D4
Chāh-e Bāzargānī Iran 110 D4
Chāh-e Dow Chāhī Iran 110 D3
Chāh-e Gonbad well Iran 110 D3
Chāh-e Kavīr well Iran 110 E3
Chāh-e Khorāsān well Iran 110 D3
Chāh-e Khoshāb Iran 110 E3
Chāh-e Malek well Iran 110 D3
Chāh-e Malek Mīrzā well Iran 110 D4
Chāh-e Mūjān well Iran 110 D3
Chāh-e Qeyşar well Iran 110 D4
Chāh-e Qobād well Iran 110 D3
Chāh-e Rāh Iran 110 D4
Chāh-e Raḩmān well Iran 111 E4
Chāh-e Shūr well Iran 110 D3
Chāh-e Tūnī well Iran 110 E3
Chāh Kūh Iran 110 D4
Chāh Lak Iran 110 E5
Chāh Pās well Iran 110 D3
Chah Sandan Pak. 111 F4
Chahuites Mex. 167 G5
Chaibasa India 105 F5
Chaigneau, Lac l. Canada 153 I3
Chaigoubu Hebei China see Huai'an
Chaihe Nei Mongol China 95 J2
Chainat Thai. 86 C4
Chainjoin Co l. Xizang China 99 D6
Chai Prakan Thai. 86 B3
Chaitén Chile 178 B6
Chai Wan H.K. China 97 [inset]
Chaiwopu Xinjiang China 98 D4
Chaiya Thai. 87 B5
Chaiyaphum Thai. 86 C4
Chajarí Arg. 178 E4
Chakachamna Lake AK U.S.A. 148 I3
Chakai India 105 F4
Chak Amru Pak. 111 I3
Chakar r. Pak. 111 H4
Chakaria Bangl. 105 H5
Chakdarra Pak. 111 I3
Chakku Pak. 111 G5
Chakonipau, Lac l. Canada 153 H2
Chakoria Bangl. see Chakaria
Ch'ak'vi Georgia 113 F2
Chala Peru 176 D7
Chalap Dalan mts Afgh. 111 G3
Chalatenango El Salvador 166 [inset] H6
Chaláua Moz. 123 D5
Chalaxung Qinghai China 94 D5
Chalcedon Turkey see Kadıköy
Chalengkou Qinghai China 99 F5
Chaleur Bay inlet Canada 153 I4
Chaleurs, Baie des inlet Canada see Chaleur Bay
Chali China 96 C2
Chaling China 97 G3
Chalisgaon India 106 B1
Chalki i. Greece 69 L6
Chalkida Greece 69 J5
Chalkyitsik AK U.S.A. 149 L2
Challakere India 106 C3
Challans France 66 D3
Challapata Bol. 176 E7

▶Challenger Deep sea feature N. Pacific Ocean 186 F5
Deepest point in the world (Mariana Trench).

Challenger Fracture Zone sea feature S. Pacific Ocean 186 M8
Challis U.S.A. 156 E3
Chalmette U.S.A. 161 F6
Châlons-en-Champagne France 62 E6
Châlons-sur-Marne France see Châlons-en-Champagne
Chalon-sur-Saône France 66 G3
Chaltan Pass Azer. 113 H2
Chālūs Iran 110 C2
Cham Germany 63 M5
Cham, Kūh-e hill Iran 110 C3
Chamah, Gunung mt. Malaysia 84 C1
Chamaico Arg. 178 D5
Chamais Bay Namibia 124 B4
Chaman Pak. 100 F3
Chaman Bid Iran 110 E2
Chamao, Khao mt. Thai. 87 C4
Chamba India 104 D2
Chamba Tanz. 123 D5
Chambal r. India 104 D4
Chambas Cuba 163 E8
Chambeaux, Lac l. Canada 153 H3
Chamberlain r. Australia 134 D4
Chamberlain Canada 151 J5
Chamberlain U.S.A. 160 D3
Chamberlain Lake U.S.A. 162 G2
Chamberlin, Mount AK U.S.A. 149 K1
Chambers U.S.A. 159 I4
Chambersburg U.S.A. 165 G4
Chambers Island U.S.A. 164 B1
Chambéry France 66 G4
Chambeshi r. Zambia 123 C5
Chambi, Jebel mt. Tunisia 68 C7
Chamda Xizang China 99 E7
Chamdo China see Qamdo
Chame Panama 166 [inset] K7
Chamechaude mt. France 66 G4
Chamela Mex. 166 D5
Chamiss Bay Canada 150 E5
Chamoli India see Gopeshwar
Chamonix-Mont-Blanc France 66 H4
Champa India 105 E5
Champagne Y.T. Canada 149 M3
Champagne-Ardenne admin. reg. France 62 E6
Champagne Castle mt. S. Africa 125 I5
Champagne Humide reg. France 66 G2
Champagne Pouilleuse reg. France 66 F2
Champagnole France 66 G3
Champagny Islands Australia 134 D3
Champaign U.S.A. 160 F3
Champasak Laos 86 D4
Champdoré, Lac l. Canada 153 I3
Champhai India 105 H5
Champion Canada 150 H5
Champlain U.S.A. 165 G4
Champlain, Lake Canada/U.S.A. 165 I1
Champotón Mex. 167 H5
Chamrajnagar India 106 C4
Chamu Co l. Qinghai China 99 E6
Chamzinka Rus. Fed. 53 J5
Chana Thai. 87 C6
Chanak Turkey see Çanakkale
Chanal Mex. 167 G5
Chañaral Chile 178 B3
Chanārān Iran 110 E2
Chanchén Mex. 167 H5
Chanda India see Chandrapur
Chandalar AK U.S.A. 149 J2
Chandalar r. AK U.S.A. 149 K2
Chandalar, East Fork r. AK U.S.A. 149 K2
Chandalar, Middle Fork r. AK U.S.A. 149 J2
Chandalar, North Fork r. AK U.S.A. 149 J2
Chandalar Lake AK U.S.A. 149 J2
Chandausi India 104 D3
Chandbali India 105 F5
Chandeleur Islands U.S.A. 161 F6
Chanderi India 104 D4
Chandigarh India 104 D3
Chandil India 105 F5
Chandir Uzbek. 111 G2
Chandler Canada 153 I4
Chandler AZ U.S.A. 159 H5
Chandler IN U.S.A. 164 B4
Chandler OK U.S.A. 161 D5
Chandler r. AK U.S.A. 149 J1
Chandler Lake AK U.S.A. 148 I1
Chandmanī Mongolia see Yaruu
Chandmanī Mongolia 94 D2
Chandod India 104 C5
Chandos Lake Canada 165 G1
Chandpur Bangl. 105 G5
Chandpur India 104 D3
Chandragiri India 106 C3
Chandrapur India 106 C2
Chandvad India 106 B1
Chang, Ko i. Thai. 87 C4
Chang'an Shaanxi China 95 G5
Changane r. Moz. 125 K3
Changbai China 90 C4
Changbai Shan mts China/N. Korea 90 B4
Chang Cheng research station Antarctica see Great Wall
Changcheng China 97 F5
Changchow Fujian China see Zhangzhou
Changchow Jiangsu China see Changzhou
Changchun China 90 B4
Changchunling China 90 B3
Changdao Shandong China 95 J4
Changde China 97 F2
Changgang China 97 G3
Changge Henan China 95 H5
Changgi-ap pt S. Korea 91 C5
Changgo Xizang China 99 D7
Chang Hu l. China 97 G2
Changhua Taiwan 97 I3
Changhŭng S. Korea 91 B6
Changhwa Taiwan see Changhua
Changi Sing. 87 [inset]
Changji Xinjiang China 98 D4
Changjiang China 97 F5
Chang Jiang r. China 97 I2 see Yangtze
Changjiang Kou China see Mouth of the Yangtze
Changjin-ho resr N. Korea 91 B4
Changkiang China see Zhanjiang
Changlang India 105 H4
Changleng China see Xinjian
Changli Hebei China 95 I4
Changling Jilin China 95 J2
Changliushui Nei Mongol China 94 F4
Changlun Malaysia 84 C1
Changlung India 109 M3
Changma Gansu China 94 D4
Changmar Xizang China 99 C6
Changning Jiangxi China see Xunwu
Changning Sichuan China 96 E2
Changnyŏn N. Korea 91 B5
Ch'ang-pai Shan mts China/N. Korea see Changbai Shan
Changping Beijing China 95 I3
Changpu China see Suining
Changp'yŏng S. Korea 91 C5
Changsan-got pt N. Korea 91 B5
Changsha China 97 G2
Changshan China 97 H2
Changshan Qundao is China 95 J4
Changshi China 96 E3
Changshoujie China 97 G2
Changshu China 97 I2
Changtai China 97 H3
Changteh China see Changde
Changting Fujian China 97 H3
Changting Heilong. China 90 C3
Changuinola Panama 166 [inset] J7
Changweiliang Qinghai China 99 F5
Ch'angwŏn S. Korea 91 C6
Changwu Shaanxi China 95 F5
Changxing China 97 H2
Changxing Dao i. China 95 J4
Changyang China 97 F2
Changyi Shandong China 95 I4
Changyŏn N. Korea 91 B5
Changyuan Henan China 95 H5
Changzhi Shanxi China 95 H4
Changzhi Shanxi China 95 H5
Changzhou China 97 H2
Chañi, Nevado de mt. Arg. 178 C2
Chania Greece 69 K7
Chanion, Kolpos b. Greece 69 J7
Chankou Gansu China 94 F5
Channahon U.S.A. 164 A3
Channapatna India 106 C3
Channel Islands English Chan. 59 E9
Channel Islands U.S.A. 158 D5
Channel Islands National Park U.S.A. 158 D4
Channel-Port-aux-Basques Canada 153 K5
Channel Rock i. Bahamas 163 E8
Channel Tunnel France/U.K. 59 I7
Channing U.S.A. 161 C5
Chantada Spain 67 C2
Chantal'skiy mt. Rus. Fed. 148 B2
Chantal'vergyrgyn r. Rus. Fed. 148 C2
Chanthaburi Thai. 87 C4
Chantilly France 62 C5
Chanumla India 87 A5
Chanute U.S.A. 160 E4
Chanuwala Pak. 111 I3
Chany, Ozero salt l. Rus. Fed. 76 I4
Chaohu China 97 H2
Chao Hu l. China 97 H2
Chaor Nei Mongol China 95 J1
Chaouèn Morocco 67 D6
Chaowula Shan mt. China 96 C1
Chaoyang Guangdong China 97 H4
Chaoyang Heilong. China see Jiayin
Chaoyang Liaoning China 95 J3
Chaoyangcun Nei Mongol China 95 K1
Chaoyang Hu l. Xizang China 99 D6
Chaozhong Nei Mongol China 95 J1
Chaozhou China 97 H4
Chapada Diamantina, Parque Nacional nat. park Brazil 179 C1
Chapada dos Veadeiros, Parque Nacional da nat. park Brazil 179 B1
Chapais Canada 152 G4
Chapak Guzar Afgh. 111 G2
Chapala Mex. 166 E4
Chapala, Laguna de l. Mex. 168 D4
Chāpārī, Kowtal-e Afgh. 111 G3
Chapayevo Kazakh. 100 E1
Chapayevsk Rus. Fed. 53 K5
Chapecó Brazil 178 F3
Chapecó r. Brazil 178 F3
Chapel-en-le-Frith U.K. 58 F5
Chapelle-lez-Herlaimont Belgium 62 E4
Chapeltown U.K. 58 F5
Chapleau Canada 152 E5
Chaplin Canada 151 J5
Chaplin Lake Canada 151 J5
Chaplino Rus. Fed. 148 D2
Chaplygin Rus. Fed. 53 H5
Chapman, Mount Canada 150 G5
Chapmanville U.S.A. 164 D5
Chappell U.S.A. 160 C3

Chappell Islands Australia **137** [inset]
Chapra *Bihar* India *see* **Chhapra**
Chapra *Jharkhand* India *see* **Chatra**
Chaqmaqtīn, Kowl-e Afgh. **111** I2
Charagua Bol. **176** F7
Charay Mex. **166** C3
Charcas Mex. **168** D4
Charcot Island Antarctica **188** L2
Chard Canada **151** I4
Chard U.K. **59** E8
Chardara Kazakh. *see* **Shardara**
Chardara, Step' *plain* Kazakh. **102** C3
Chardon U.S.A. **164** E3
Chardzhev Turkm. *see* **Türkmenabat**
Chardzhou Turkm. *see* **Türkmenabat**
Charef Alg. **67** H6
Charef, Oued *watercourse* Morocco **64** D5
Charente *r.* France **66** D4
Chari *r.* Cameroon/Chad **121** E3
Chārī Iran **110** E4
Chārīkār Afgh. **111** H3
Chariot *AK* U.S.A. **148** F1
Chariton U.S.A. **160** E3
Chärjew Turkm. *see* **Türkmenabat**
Charkayuvom Rus. Fed. **52** L2
Chār Kent Afgh. **111** G2
Charkhlik *Xinjiang* China *see* **Ruoqiang**
Charleroi Belgium **62** E4
Charles, Cape U.S.A. **165** H5
Charlesbourg Canada **153** H5
Charles City *IA* U.S.A. **160** E3
Charles City *VA* U.S.A. **165** G5
Charles Hill Botswana **124** E2
Charles Island *Galápagos* Ecuador *see* **Santa María, Isla**
Charles Lake Canada **151** I3
Charles Point Australia **134** E3
Charleston N.Z. **139** C5
Charleston *IL* U.S.A. **160** F4
Charleston *MO* U.S.A. **161** F4
Charleston *SC* U.S.A. **163** E5
▶**Charleston** *WV* U.S.A. **164** E4
Capital of West Virginia.
Charleston Peak U.S.A. **159** F3
Charlestown Ireland **61** D4
Charlestown *IN* U.S.A. **164** C4
Charlestown *NH* U.S.A. **165** I2
Charlestown *RI* U.S.A. **165** J3
Charles Town U.S.A. **165** G4
Charleville Australia **137** D5
Charleville Ireland **61** D5
Charleville-Mézières France **62** E5
Charlevoix U.S.A. **164** C1
Charley *r. AK* U.S.A. **149** L2
Charlie Lake Canada **150** F3
Charlotte *MI* U.S.A. **164** C2
Charlotte *NC* U.S.A. **163** D5
Charlotte *TN* U.S.A. **164** B5
▶**Charlotte Amalie** Virgin Is (U.S.A.) **169** L5
Capital of the U.S. Virgin Islands.
Charlotte Bank *sea feature* S. China Sea **85** D1
Charlotte Harbor *b.* U.S.A. **163** D7
Charlotte Lake Canada **150** E4
Charlottesville U.S.A. **165** F4
▶**Charlottetown** Canada **153** J5
Capital of Prince Edward Island.
Charlton Australia **138** A6
Charlton Island Canada **152** F3
Charron Lake Canada **151** M4
Charsadda Pak. **111** H3
Charshanga Turkm. *see* **Köýtendag**
Charshangngy Turkm. *see* **Köýtendag**
Charters Towers Australia **136** D4
Chartres France **66** E2
Charyn Kazakh. **98** B4
Charyn *r.* Kazakh. **98** B4
Chas India **105** F5
Chase Canada **150** G5
Chase U.S.A. **164** C2
Chase City U.S.A. **165** F5
Chashmeh Nūrī Iran **110** E3
Chashmeh-ye Ab-e Garm *spring* Iran **110** E3
Chashmeh-ye Magu *well* Iran **110** E3
Chashmeh-ye Mūkīk *spring* Iran **110** E3
Chashmeh-ye Palasi Iran **110** D3
Chashmeh-ye Safid *spring* Iran **110** E3
Chashmeh-ye Shotoran *well* Iran **110** D3
Chashniki Belarus **53** F5
Chaska U.S.A. **160** E2
Chaslands Mistake *c.* N.Z. **139** B8
Chasŏng N. Korea **90** B4
Chasseral *mt.* Switz. **57** K7
Chassiron, Pointe de *pt* France **66** D3
Chastab, Kūh-e *mts* Iran **110** D3
Chāt Iran **110** D2
Chatanika *AK* U.S.A. **149** K2
Chatanika *r. AK* U.S.A. **149** J2
Châteaubriant France **66** D3
Château-du-Loir France **66** E3
Châteaudun France **66** E2
Chateaugay U.S.A. **165** H1
Châteauguay Canada **165** I1
Châteauguay *r.* Canada **153** H2
Châteauguay, Lac *l.* Canada **153** H2
Châteaulin France **66** B2
Châteaumeillant France **66** F3
Châteauneuf-en-Thymerais France **62** B6
Châteauneuf-sur-Loire France **66** F3
Chateau Pond *l.* Canada **153** K3
Châteauroux France **66** E3
Château-Salins France **62** G6
Château-Thierry France **62** D5
Chateh Canada **150** G3
Châtelet Belgium **62** E4
Châtellerault France **66** E3
Chatfield U.S.A. **152** B6
Chatham Canada **164** D2
Chatham U.K. **59** H7
Chatham *AK* U.S.A. **149** N4
Chatham *MA* U.S.A. **165** K3
Chatham *NY* U.S.A. **165** I2
Chatham *PA* U.S.A. **165** H4
Chatham *VA* U.S.A. **164** F5
Chatham, Isla *i.* Chile **178** B8
Chatham Island *Galápagos* Ecuador *see* **San Cristóbal, Isla**
Chatham Island N.Z. **133** I6
Chatham Island Samoa *see* **Savai'i**
Chatham Islands N.Z. **133** I6
Chatham Rise *sea feature* S. Pacific Ocean **186** I8
Chatham Sound *sea channel B.C.* Canada **149** O5
Chatham Strait *AK* U.S.A. **149** N4
Châtillon-sur-Seine France **66** G3
Chatkal Range *mts* Kyrg./Uzbek. **102** D3
Chatom U.S.A. **161** F6
Chatra India **105** F4
Chatra Nepal **105** F4
Chatsworth Canada **164** E1
Chatsworth U.S.A. **165** H4
Chattagam Bangl. *see* **Chittagong**
Chattanooga U.S.A. **163** C5
Chattarpur India *see* **Chhatarpur**
Chatteris U.K. **59** H6
Chattisgarh *state* India *see* **Chhattisgarh**
Chatturat Thai. **86** C4
Chatyr-Köl *l.* Kyrg. **98** A4
Chatyr-Tash Kyrg. **102** E3
Châu Đốc Vietnam **87** D5
Chauhtan India **104** B4
Chauk Myanmar **86** A2
Chauka *r.* India **99** C8
Chaukhamba *mts Uttaranchal* India **99** B7
Chaumont France **66** G2
Chauncey U.S.A. **164** D4
Chaungzon Myanmar **86** B3
Chaunskaya Guba *b.* Rus. Fed. **77** R3
Chauny France **62** D5
Chau Phu Vietnam *see* **Châu Đốc**
Chausu-yama *mt.* Japan **92** D3
Chausy Belarus *see* **Chavusy**
Chautauqua, Lake U.S.A. **164** F2
Chauter Pak. **111** G4
Chauvin Canada **151** I4
Chavakachcheri Sri Lanka **106** D4
Chaves Port. **67** C3
Chavigny, Lac *l.* Canada **152** G2
Chavusy Belarus **53** F5
Chawal *r.* Pak. **111** G4
Chay, Sông *r.* Vietnam **86** D2
Chayatyn, Khrebet *ridge* Rus. Fed. **90** E1
Chayevo Rus. Fed. **52** H4
Chaykovskiy Rus. Fed. **51** Q4
Chäyul *Xizang* China *see* **Qayü**
Chazhegovo Rus. Fed. **52** L3
Chazy U.S.A. **165** I1
Cheadle U.K. **59** F6
Cheaha Mountain *hill* U.S.A. **163** C5
Cheat *r.* U.S.A. **164** F4
Cheatham Lake U.S.A. **164** B5
Cheb Czech Rep. **63** M4
Chebba Tunisia **68** D7
Cheboksarskoye Vodokhranilishche *resr* Rus. Fed. **52** J5
Cheboksary Rus. Fed. **52** J4
Cheboygan U.S.A. **162** C2
Chechen Rus. Fed. **148** D2
Chechen', Ostrov *i.* Rus. Fed. **113** G2
Chech'ŏn S. Korea **91** C5
Chedabucto Bay Canada **153** J5
Chedao *Shandong* China **95** J4
Cheddar U.K. **59** E7
Cheduba Myanmar *see* **Man-aung**
Cheduba Island *i.* Myanmar *see* **Man-aung Kyun**
Chée *r.* France **62** E6
Cheektowaga U.S.A. **165** F2
Cheepie Australia **138** B1
Cheetham, Cape Antarctica **188** H2
Chefoo *Shandong* China *see* **Yantai**
Chefornak *AK* U.S.A. **148** F3
Chefu Moz. **125** K2
Chegdomyn Rus. Fed. **90** D2
Chegga Mauritania **120** C2
Chegitun' Rus. Fed. **148** E2
Chegitun' *r.* Rus. Fed. **148** E2
Chegutu Zimbabwe **123** D5
Chehalis U.S.A. **156** C3
Chehar Burj Iran **110** E2
Chehardeh Iran **110** E3
Chehel Chashmeh, Kūh-e *hill* Iran **110** B3
Chehel Dokhtarān, Kūh-e *mt.* Iran **111** F4
Chehell'āyeh Iran **110** E4
Cheju S. Korea **91** B6
Cheju-do *i.* S. Korea **91** B6
Cheju-haehyŏp *sea chan.* S. Korea **91** B6
Chek Chue *H.K.* China *see* **Stanley**
Chekhov *Moskovskaya Oblast'* Rus. Fed. **53** H5
Chekhov *Sakhalinskaya Oblast'* Rus. Fed. **90** F3
Chekiang *prov.* China *see* **Zhejiang**
Chekichler Turkm. *see* **Çekiçler**
Chek Lap Kok *reg. H.K.* China **97** [inset]
Chek Mun Hoi Hap *H.K.* China *see* **Tolo Channel**
Chekunda Rus. Fed. **90** D2
Chela, Serra da *mts* Angola **123** B5
Chelan, Lake U.S.A. **156** C2
Chelatna Lake *AK* U.S.A. **149** J3
Cheleken Turkm. *see* **Hazar**
Cheline Moz. **125** L2
Chelkar Kazakh. *see* **Shalkar**
Chełm Poland **53** D6
Chelmer *r.* U.K. **59** H7
Chełmno Poland **57** Q4
Chelmsford U.K. **59** H7
Chelsea *MI* U.S.A. **164** C2
Chelsea *VT* U.S.A. **165** I2
Cheltenham U.K. **59** E7
Chelva Spain **67** F4
Chelyabinsk Rus. Fed. **76** H4
Chelyuskin Rus. Fed. **189** E1
Chemax Mex. **167** I4
Chemba Moz. **123** D5
Chêm Co *l.* China **99** B6
Chemnitz Germany **63** M4
Chemulpo S. Korea *see* **Inch'ŏn**
Chemyndy *Naryn* Kyrg. **98** A4
Chena *r. AK* U.S.A. **149** K2
Chenab *r.* India/Pak. **104** B3
Chenachane, Oued *watercourse* Alg. **120** C2
Chena Hot Springs *AK* U.S.A. **149** K2
Chenderoh, Tasik *resr* Malaysia **84** C1
Chendir *r.* Turkm. *see* **Çendir**
Chenega *AK* U.S.A. **149** J3
Cheney U.S.A. **156** D3
Cheney Reservoir U.S.A. **160** D4
Chengalpattu India **106** D3
Cheng'an *Hebei* China **95** H4
Chengbu China **97** F3
Chengcheng *Shaanxi* China **95** G5
Chengchow *Henan* China *see* **Zhengzhou**
Chengde *Hebei* China **95** I3
Chengde *Hebei* China **95** I3
Chengdu China **96** E2
Chengele India **96** C2
Chenggong China **96** D3
Chenghai China **97** H4
Cheng Hai *l.* China **96** D3
Chengjiang China *see* **Taihe**
Chengmai China **97** F5
Chengqian *Shandong* China **95** I5
Chengtu China *see* **Chengdu**
Chengwu *Shandong* China **95** H5
Chengxian China **96** E1
Chengxiang *Chongqing* China *see* **Wuxi**
Chengxiang *Jiangxi* China *see* **Quannan**
Chengyang *Shandong* China *see* **Juxian**
Chengzhong China *see* **Ningming**
Cheniu Shan *i.* China **95** I5
Chenkaladi Sri Lanka **106** D5
Chennai India **106** D3
Chenqian Shan *i.* China **97** I2
Chenqing China **90** B2
Chenqingqiao China *see* **Chenqing**
Chenstokhov Poland *see* **Częstochowa**
Chentejn Nuruu *mts* Mongolia **95** F1
Chenxi China **97** F3
Chenyang China *see* **Chenxi**
Chenying China *see* **Wannian**
Chenzhou China **97** G3
Chenzhuang *Hebei* China **95** H4
Chepén Peru **176** C5
Chepes Arg. **178** C4
Chepo Panama **166** [inset] K7
Chepstow U.K. **59** E7
Cheptsa *r.* Rus. Fed. **52** K4
Chequamegon Bay U.S.A. **160** F2
Cher *r.* France **66** E3
Chera *state* India *see* **Kerala**
Cherán Mex. **167** E5
Cheraw U.S.A. **163** E5
Cherbaniani Reef India **106** A3
Cherbourg France **66** D2
Cherchell Alg. **67** H5
Cherchen *Xinjiang* China *see* **Qiemo**
Cherdakly Rus. Fed. **53** K5
Cherdoyak Kazakh. **98** C2
Cherdyn' Rus. Fed. **51** R3
Chereapani *reef* India *see* **Byramgore Reef**
Cheremkhovo Rus. Fed. **88** I2
Cheremshany Rus. Fed. **90** D3
Cheremukhovka Rus. Fed. **52** K4
Cherepanovo Rus. Fed. **88** E2
Cherepovets Rus. Fed. **52** H4
Cherevkovo Rus. Fed. **52** J3
Chergui, Chott ech *imp. l.* Alg. **64** D5
Chéria Alg. **68** B7
Cheriton U.S.A. **165** H5
Cheriyam *atoll* India **106** B4
Cherkassy Ukr. *see* **Cherkasy**
Cherkasy Ukr. **53** G6
Cherkessk Rus. Fed. **113** F1
Cherla India **106** D2
Chernabura Island *AK* U.S.A. **148** H5
Chernaya Rus. Fed. **52** M1
Chernaya *r.* Rus. Fed. **52** M1
Chernigov Ukr. *see* **Chernihiv**
Chernigovka Rus. Fed. **90** D3
Chernihiv Ukr. **53** F6
Cherninivka Ukr. **53** H7
Chernivtsi Ukr. **53** E6
Chernobyl' Ukr. *see* **Chornobyl'**
Chernogorsk Rus. Fed. **88** G2
Chernovtsy Ukr. *see* **Chernivtsi**
Chernoye More *sea* Asia/Europe *see* **Black Sea**
Chernushka Rus. Fed. **51** R4
Chernyakhiv Ukr. **53** F6
Chernyakhovsk Rus. Fed. **55** L9
Chernyanka Rus. Fed. **53** H6
Chernyayeve Rus. Fed. **90** B1
Chernyshevsk Rus. Fed. **89** L2
Chernyshevskiy Rus. Fed. **77** M3
Chernyshkovskiy Rus. Fed. **53** I6
Chernyye Zemli *reg.* Rus. Fed. **53** J7
Chernyy Irtysh *r.* China/Kazakh. *see* **Ertix He**
Chernyy Porog Rus. Fed. **52** G3
Chernyy Yar Rus. Fed. **53** J6
Cherokee U.S.A. **160** E3
Cherokee Sound Bahamas **163** E7
▶**Cherrapunji** India **105** G4
Highest recorded annual rainfall in the world.
Cherry Creek *r.* U.S.A. **160** C2
Cherry Creek Mountains U.S.A. **159** F1
Cherry Hill U.S.A. **165** H4
Cherry Island Solomon Is **133** G3
Cherry Lake U.S.A. **158** D2
Cherskiy Rus. Fed. **189** C2
Cherskiy Range *mts* Rus. Fed. *see* **Cherskogo, Khrebet**
Cherskogo, Khrebet *mts* Rus. Fed. **77** P3
Cherskogo, Khrebet *mts* Rus. Fed. **95** G1
Chertkov Ukr. *see* **Chortkiv**
Chertkovo Rus. Fed. **53** I6
Cherven Bryag Bulg. **69** K3
Chervonoarmeyskoye Ukr. *see* **Vil'nyans'k**
Chervonoarmiys'k *Donets'ka Oblast'* Ukr. *see* **Krasnoarmiys'k**
Chervonoarmiys'k *Rivnens'ka Oblast'* Ukr. *see* **Radyvyliv**
Chervonograd Ukr. *see* **Chervonohrad**
Chervonohrad Ukr. **53** E6
Chervyen' Belarus **53** F5
Cherwell *r.* U.K. **59** F7
Cherykaw Belarus **53** F5
Chesapeake U.S.A. **165** G5
Chesapeake Bay U.S.A. **165** G4
Chesham U.K. **59** G7
Cheshire Plain U.K. **58** E5
Cheshme Vtoroy Turkm. **111** F2
Cheshskaya Guba *b.* Rus. Fed. **52** J2
Cheshtebe Tajik. **111** I2
Cheshunt U.K. **59** G7
Chesnokovka Rus. Fed. *see* **Novoaltaysk**
Chester Canada **153** I5
Chester U.K. **58** E5
Chester *CA* U.S.A. **158** C1
Chester *IL* U.S.A. **160** F4
Chester *MT* U.S.A. **156** F2
Chester *OH* U.S.A. **164** E4
Chester *SC* U.S.A. **163** D5
Chester *r.* U.S.A. **165** G4
Chesterfield U.K. **58** F5
Chesterfield U.S.A. **165** G5
Chesterfield, Îles *is* New Caledonia **133** F3
Chesterfield Inlet Canada **151** N2
Chesterfield Inlet *inlet* Canada **151** M2
Chester-le-Street U.K. **58** F4
Chestertown *MD* U.S.A. **165** G4
Chestertown *NY* U.S.A. **165** I2
Chesterville Canada **165** H1
Chestnut Ridge U.S.A. **164** F3
Chesuncook Lake U.S.A. **162** G2
Chetaïbi Alg. **68** B6
Chéticamp Canada **153** J5
Chetlat *i.* India **106** B4
Chetumal Mex. **167** H5
Chetwynd Canada **150** F4
Cheung Chau *H.K.* China **97** [inset]
Chevak *AK* U.S.A. **148** F3
Chevelon Creek *r.* U.S.A. **159** H4
Cheviot N.Z. **139** D6
Cheviot Hills U.K. **58** E3
Cheviot Range *hills* Australia **136** C5
Chevreulx *r.* Canada **152** G3
Cheyenne *OK* U.S.A. **161** D5
▶**Cheyenne** *WY* U.S.A. **156** G4
Capital of Wyoming.
Cheyenne *r.* U.S.A. **160** C2
Cheyenne Wells U.S.A. **160** C4
Cheyne Bay Australia **135** B8
Cheyur India **106** D3
Chezacut Canada **150** E4
Chhapra India **105** F4
Chhata India **104** D4
Chhatak Bangl. **105** G4
Chhatarpur *Jharkhand* India **105** F4
Chhatarpur *Madh. Prad.* India **104** D4
Chhatr Pak. **111** H4
Chhatrapur India **106** E2
Chhattisgarh *state* India **105** E5
Chhay Arêng, Stœng *r.* Cambodia **87** C5
Chhindwara India **104** D5
Chhitkul India **104** D3
Chhukha Bhutan **105** G4
Chi, Lam *r.* Thai. **87** C4
Chi, Mae Nam *r.* Thai. **86** D4
Chiai Taiwan **97** I4
Chiamboni Somalia **122** E4
Chiange Angola **123** B5
Chiang Kham Thai. **86** C3
Chiang Khan Thai. **86** C3
Chiang Mai Thai. **86** B3
Chiang Rai Thai. **86** B3
Chiang Saen Thai. **86** C2
Chiapa Mex. **167** G5
Chiapas *state* Mex. **167** G5
Chiapilla Mex. **167** G5
Chiari Italy **68** C2
Chiautla Mex. **168** E5
Chiavenna Italy **68** C1
Chiayi Taiwan *see* **Chiai**
Chiba Japan **93** G3
Chiba *pref.* Japan **93** G3
Chibi China **97** G2
Chibia Angola **123** B5
Chibit Rus. Fed. **98** D2
Chibizovka Rus. Fed. *see* **Zherdevka**
Chiboma Moz. **123** D6
Chibougamau Canada **152** G4
Chibougamau, Lac *l.* Canada **152** G4
Chibuto Moz. **125** K3
Chicacole India *see* **Srikakulam**
▶**Chicago** U.S.A. **164** B3
4th most populous city in North America.
Chic-Chocs, Monts *mts* Canada **153** I4
Chichagof *AK* U.S.A. **149** M4
Chichagof Island *AK* U.S.A. **149** N4
Chichak *r.* Pak. **111** G5
Chichaoua Morocco **64** C5
Chichatka Rus. Fed. **90** A1
Chicheng *Hebei* China **95** H3
Chicheng China *see* **Pengxi**
Chichén Itzá *tourist site* Mex. **167** H4
Chichester U.K. **59** G8
Chichester Range *mts* Australia **134** B5
Chichgarh India **106** D1
Chichibu Japan **93** F3
Chichibu-gawa *r.* Japan **93** F2
Chichibu-Tama Kokuritsu-kōen *nat. park* Japan **93** E3
Chichijima-rettō *is* Japan **91** F8
Chickaloon *AK* U.S.A. **149** J3
Chickasawhay *r. MS* U.S.A. **167** H2
Chickasha U.S.A. **161** D5
Chicken *AK* U.S.A. **149** L2
Chiclana de la Frontera Spain **67** C5
Chiclayo Peru **176** C5
Chico *r.* Arg. **178** C6
Chico U.S.A. **158** C2
Chicomo Moz. **125** L3
Chicomucelo Mex. **167** G6
Chicopee U.S.A. **165** I2
Chico Sapocoy, Mount *Luzon* Phil. **82** C2
Chicoutimi Canada **153** H4
Chicualacuala Moz. **125** J2
Chidambaram India **106** C4
Chidenguele Moz. **125** L3
Chidley, Cape Canada **147** L3
Chido *Xizang* China *see* **Sêndo**
Chido S. Korea **91** B6
Chiducuane Moz. **125** L3
Chiefland U.S.A. **163** D6
Chiemsee *l.* Germany **57** N7
Chiengmai Thai. *see* **Chiang Mai**
Chiers *r.* France **62** F5
Chieti Italy **68** F3
Chifeng *Nei Mongol* China **95** I3
Chifre, Serra do *mts* Brazil **179** C2
Chiganak Kazakh. **102** D2
Chigasaki Japan **93** F3
Chiginagak Volcano, Mount U.S.A. **146** C4
Chigmit Mountains *AK* U.S.A. **148** I3
Chignik *AK* U.S.A. **148** H4
Chignik Bay *AK* U.S.A. **148** H4
Chignik Lagoon *AK* U.S.A. **148** H4
Chignik Lake *AK* U.S.A. **148** H4
Chigu *Xizang* China **99** E7
Chigubo Moz. **125** K2
Chigu Co *l.* China **99** E7
Chihuahua Mex. **166** D2
Chihuahua *state* Mex. **166** D2
Chihuahua, Desierto de *des* Mex. **157** G7
Chiili Kazakh. **102** C3
Chijinpu *Gansu* China **94** D3
Chikalda India **104** D5
Chikan China **97** F4
Chikaskia *r.* U.S.A. **161** D4
Chikhali Kalan Parasia India **104** D5
Chikhli India **106** C1
Chikishlyar Turkm. *see* **Çekiçler**
Chikmagalur India **106** B3
Chikodi India **106** B2
Chikoy Rus. Fed. **94** F1
Chikoy *r.* Rus. Fed. **95** F1
Chikuma-gawa *r.* Japan **93** E1
Chikuminuk Lake *AK* U.S.A. **148** H3
Chikura Japan **93** F4
Chilanko *r.* Canada **150** F4
Chilapa *Guerrero* Mex. **167** F5
Chilas Pak. **104** C2
Chilaw Sri Lanka **106** C5
Chilcotin *r.* Canada **150** F5
Childers Australia **136** F5
Childress U.S.A. **161** C5
Chile *country* S. America **178** B4
Chile Basin *sea feature* S. Pacific Ocean **187** O8
Chile Chico Chile **178** B7
Chile Rise *sea feature* S. Pacific Ocean **187** O8
Chilgir Rus. Fed. **53** J7
Chilhowie U.S.A. **164** E5
Chilia-Nouă Ukr. *see* **Kiliya**
Chilik Kazakh. **102** E3
Chilik *r.* Kazakh. **98** B4
Chilika Lake India **106** E2
Chililabombwe Zambia **123** C5
Chilko *r.* Canada **150** F4
Chilko Lake Canada **150** E5
Chilkoot Pass Canada/U.S.A. **149** N4
Chilkoot Trail National Historic Site *nat. park B.C.* Canada **149** N4
Chillán Chile **178** B5
Chillicothe *MO* U.S.A. **160** E4
Chillicothe *OH* U.S.A. **164** D4
Chilliwack Canada **150** F5
Chilo India **104** C4
Chiloé, Isla de *i.* Chile **178** B6
Chiloé, Isla Grande de *i.* Chile *see* **Chiloé, Isla de**
Chilpancingo Mex. **168** E5
Chilpancingo de los Bravos Mex. *see* **Chilpancingo**
Chilpi Pak. **104** C1
Chiltern Hills U.K. **59** G7
Chilton U.S.A. **164** A1
Chiluage Angola **123** C4
Chilubi Zambia **123** C5
Chilung Taiwan **97** I3
Chilwa, Lake Malawi **123** D5
Chimala Tanz. **123** D4
Chimalapa Mex. **167** G5
Chimaltenango Guat. **167** H6
Chimán Panama **166** [inset] K7
Chi Ma Wan *H.K.* China **97** [inset]
Chimay Belgium **62** E4
Chimbas Arg. **178** C4
Chimbay Uzbek. *see* **Chimboy**
Chimborazo *mt.* Ecuador **176** C4
Chimbote Peru **176** C5
Chimboy Uzbek. **102** A3
Chimian Pak. **111** I4
Chimishliya Moldova *see* **Cimişlia**
Chimkent Kazakh. *see* **Shymkent**
Chimney Rock U.S.A. **159** J3
Chimoio Moz. **123** D5
Chimtargha, Qullai *mt.* Tajik. **111** H2
Chimtorga, Gora *mt.* Tajik. *see* **Chimtargha, Qullai**
▶**China** *country* Asia **88** H5
Most populous country in the world and in Asia. 2nd largest country in Asia and 4th largest in the world.
China Mex. **167** F3
China, Republic of *country* Asia *see* **Taiwan**
China Bakir *r.* Myanmar *see* **To**
Chinacates Mex. **166** D3
Chinajá Guat. **167** H5
China Lake *CA* U.S.A. **158** E4
China Lake *ME* U.S.A. **165** K1
Chinandega Nicaragua **166** [inset] I6
China Point U.S.A. **158** D5
Chinati Peak U.S.A. **161** B6
Chincha Alta Peru **176** C6
Chinchaga *r.* Canada **150** G3
Chinchilla Australia **138** E1
Chincholi India **106** C2
Chinchorro, Banco *sea feature* Mex. **167** I5
Chincoteague Bay U.S.A. **165** H5
Chinde Moz. **123** D5
Chindo S. Korea **91** B6
Chin-do *i.* S. Korea **91** B6
Chindwin *r.* Myanmar **86** A2
Chinese Turkestan *aut. reg.* China *see* **Xinjiang Uygur Zizhiqu**
Chinghai *prov.* China *see* **Qinghai**
Chingiz-Tau, Khrebet *mts* Kazakh. **102** E2
Chingleput India *see* **Chengalpattu**
Chingola Zambia **123** C5
Chinguar Angola **123** B5
Chinguetti Mauritania **120** B2
Chinhae S. Korea **91** C6
Chinhoyi Zimbabwe **123** D5
Chini India *see* **Kalpa**
Chiniak *AK* U.S.A. **148** I4
Chiniak, Cape *AK* U.S.A. **148** I4
Chining *Shandong* China *see* **Jining**
Chiniot Pak. **111** I4
Chinipas Mex. **166** C3
Chinit, Stœng *r.* Cambodia **87** D4
Chinju S. Korea **91** C6
Chinle U.S.A. **159** I3
Chinmen Taiwan **97** H3
Chinmen Tao *i.* Taiwan **97** H3
Chinnamp'o N. Korea *see* **Namp'o**
Chinnur India **106** C2
Chino Japan **93** E3
Chino Creek *watercourse* U.S.A. **159** G4
Chinon France **66** E3
Chinook U.S.A. **156** F2
Chinook Trough *sea feature* N. Pacific Ocean **186** I3
Chino Valley U.S.A. **159** G4
Chin-shan China *see* **Zhujing**
Chintamani India **106** C3
Chioggia Italy **68** E2
Chios Greece **69** L5
Chios *i.* Greece **69** K5
Chipam Guat. **167** H6
Chipata Zambia **123** D5
Chip Chap *r.* China/India **99** B6
Chipchihua, Sierra de *mts* Arg. **178** C6
Chiphu Cambodia **87** D5
Chipindo Angola **123** B5
Chiping *Shandong* China **95** I4
Chipinga Zimbabwe *see* **Chipinge**
Chipinge Zimbabwe **123** D6
Chipley U.S.A. **163** C6
Chipman Canada **153** I5
Chippenham U.K. **59** E7
Chippewa, Lake U.S.A. **160** F2
Chippewa Falls U.S.A. **160** F2
Chipping Norton U.K. **59** F7
Chipping Sodbury U.K. **59** E7
Chipurupalle *Andhra Prad.* India **106** D2
Chipurupalle *Andhra Prad.* India **106** D2
Chiquibul National Park Belize **167** H5
Chiquilá Mex. **167** I4
Chiquimula Guat. **167** H6
Chiquinquira Col. **176** D2
Chir *r.* Rus. Fed. **53** I6
Chirada India **106** D3
Chirala India **106** D3
Chiras Afgh. **111** G3
Chirchiq Uzbek. **102** C3
Chiredzi Zimbabwe **123** D6
Chirfa Niger **120** E2
Chiricahua National Monument *nat. park* U.S.A. **159** I5
Chiricahua Peak U.S.A. **159** I6
Chirikof Island *AK* U.S.A. **148** I5
Chiriquí, Golfo de *b.* Panama **166** [inset] J7
Chiriquí, Laguna de *b.* Panama **166** [inset] J7
Chiriquí, Volcán de *vol.* Panama *see* **Barú, Volcán**
Chiriquí Grande Panama **166** [inset] J7
Chiri-san *mt.* S. Korea **91** B6
Chirk U.K. **59** D6
Chirnside U.K. **60** G5

Chirripó mt. Costa Rica 169 H7
Chirripó, Parque Nacional nat. park Costa Rica 166 [inset] J7
Chiryū Japan 92 D3
Chisamba Zambia 123 C5
Chisana AK U.S.A. 149 L3
Chisana r. AK U.S.A. 149 L3
Chisana Glacier AK U.S.A. 149 J3
Chisasibi Canada 152 F3
Chisec Guat. 167 H6
Chishima-retto is Rus. Fed. see Kuril Islands
Chisholm Canada 150 H4
Chishtian Mandi Pak. 111 I4
Chishui China 96 E2
Chishuihe China 96 E3
Chisimaio Somalia see Kismaayo

▶Chişinău Moldova 69 M1
Capital of Moldova.

Chistochina AK U.S.A. 149 K3
Chistopol' Rus. Fed. 52 K5
Chita Japan 92 C4
Chita Rus. Fed. 89 K2
Chitado Angola 123 B5
Chita-hantō pen. Japan 92 C4
Chitaldrug India see Chitradurga
Chitalwana India 104 B4
Chitambo Zambia 123 D5
Chitanana r. AK U.S.A. 149 J2
Chitanga Rus. Fed. 95 G1
Chita Oblast admin. div. Rus. Fed. see Chitinskaya Oblast'
Chitato Angola 123 C4
Chita-wan b. Japan 92 C4
Chitek Lake Canada 151 J4
Chitek Lake l. Canada 151 L4
Chitembo Angola 123 B5
Chitina AK U.S.A. 149 K3
Chitina r. AK U.S.A. 149 K3
Chitinskaya Oblast' admin. div. Rus. Fed. 90 A1
Chitipa Malawi 123 D4
Chitkul India see Chhitkul
Chitobe Moz. 123 D6
Chitoor India see Chittoor
Chitor India see Chittaurgarh
Chitose Japan 90 F4
Chitradurga India 106 C3
Chitrakoot India 104 E4
Chitrakut India see Chitrakoot
Chitral Pak. 111 H3
Chitral r. Pak. 111 H3
Chitravati r. India 106 C3
Chitré Panama 166 [inset] J8
Chitrod India 104 B5
Chittagong Bangl. 105 G5
Chittaurgarh India 104 C4
Chittoor India 106 C3
Chittor India see Chittoor
Chittorgarh India see Chittaurgarh
Chittur India 106 C4
Chitungwiza Zimbabwe 123 D5
Chiu Lung H.K. China see Kowloon
Chiume Angola 123 C5
Chivasso Italy 68 B2
Chivato, Punta pt Mex. 166 C3
Chivela Mex. 167 G5
Chivhu Zimbabwe 123 D5
Chixi China 97 G4
Chiyoda Gunma Japan 93 F2
Chiyoda Ibaraki Japan 93 G2
Chiyogawa Japan 93 F2
Chizarira National Park Zimbabwe 123 C5
Chizha Vtoraya Kazakh. 53 K6
Chizhou China 97 H2
Chizu Japan 91 D6
Chkalov Rus. Fed. see Orenburg
Chkalovsk Rus. Fed. 52 I4
Chkalovskoye Rus. Fed. 90 D3
Chlef Alg. 67 G5
Chlef, Oued r. Alg. 67 G5
Chloride U.S.A. 159 F4
Chlya, Ozero l. Rus. Fed. 90 F1
Choa Chu Kang Sing. 87 [inset]
Choa Chu Kang hill Sing. 87 [inset]
Chobe National Park Botswana 123 C5
Chodov Czech Rep. 63 M4
Chodro Rus. Fed. 98 E2
Choele Choel Arg. 178 C5
Chōfu Japan 93 F3
Chogar r. Rus. Fed. 90 D1
Chogo Lungma Glacier Pak. 99 A6
Chogori Feng mt. China/Pak. see K2
Chograyskoye Vodokhranilishche resr Rus. Fed. 53 J7
Choiseul i. Solomon Is 133 F2
Choix Mex. 166 C3
Chojnice Poland 57 P4
Chōkai-san vol. Japan 91 F5
Ch'ok'ē mts Eth. 122 D2
Ch'ok'ē Mountains Eth. see Ch'ok'ē
Chokola mt. China 104 E3
Chokpar Kazakh. 98 A4
Choksum China 105 F3
Chok-Tal Kyrg. 98 B4
Chokue Moz. see Chókwè
Chokurdakh Rus. Fed. 77 P2
Chókwè Moz. 125 K3
Cho La pass China 96 C2
Cholame U.S.A. 158 C4
Chola Shan mts China 96 C1
Cholet France 66 D3
Choloma Hond. 166 [inset] I6
Cholpon Kyrg. 98 A4
Cholpon-Ata Kyrg. 102 E3
Cholula Mex. 167 F5
Choluteca Hond. 166 [inset] I6
Choma Zambia 123 C5
Chomo Ganggar mt. Xizang China 99 E7
Chơ Moi Vietnam 86 D2
Chomo Lhari mt. China/Bhutan 105 G4
Chom Thong Thai. 86 B3
Chomun Rajasthan India 99 A8
Chomutov Czech Rep. 57 N5
Chōnan Japan 93 G3
Ch'ŏnan S. Korea 91 B5
Chon Buri Thai. 87 C4
Ch'ŏnch'ŏn N. Korea 90 B4
Chone Ecuador 176 B4
Ch'ŏngch'ŏn-gang r. N. Korea 91 B5
Ch'ongdo S. Korea 91 C6
Chonggye Xizang China see Qonggyai
Ch'ŏngjin N. Korea 90 C4
Ch'ŏngju S. Korea 91 B5
Chŏng Kal Cambodia 87 C4
Chongkü China 96 C2
Chongli Hebei China 95 H3
Chonglong China see Zizhong
Chongming Dao i. China 97 I2
Chongoroi Angola 123 B5
Chŏngp'yŏng N. Korea 91 B5
Chongqing China 96 E2
Chongqing municipality China 96 E2
Chonguene Moz. 125 K3
Chŏngŭp S. Korea 91 B6
Chongyang China 97 G2
Chongyi China 97 G3
Chongzuo China 96 E4
Chŏnju S. Korea 91 B6
Chonogol Mongolia see Erdenetsagaan
Chontalpa Mex. 167 G5

▶Cho Oyu mt. China/Nepal 105 F3
6th highest mountain in the world and in Asia.

Chopda India 104 C5
Chor Pak. 111 H5
Chora Sfakion Greece 69 K7
Chorley U.K. 58 E5
Chornobyl' Ukr. 53 F6
Chornomors'ke Ukr. 69 O2
Chortkiv Ukr. 53 E6
Ch'osan N. Korea 90 B4
Chōshi Japan 93 G3
Chosŏn country Asia see South Korea
Chosŏn-minjujuŭi-inmin-konghwaguk country Asia see North Korea
Choszczno Poland 57 O4
Chota Peru 176 C5
Chota Sinchula hill India 105 G4
Choteau U.S.A. 156 E3
Choti Pak. 111 H4
Choûm Mauritania 120 B2
Chowchilla U.S.A. 158 C3
Chowghat India 106 B4
Chown, Mount Canada 150 G4
Choybalsan Mongolia 95 H2
Choyr Mongolia 95 G2
Chrétiens, Île aux i. Canada see Christian Island
Chřiby hills Czech Rep. 57 P6
Chrisman U.S.A. 164 B4
Chrissiesmeer S. Africa 125 J4
Christchurch N.Z. 139 D6
Christchurch U.K. 59 F8
Christian AK U.S.A. 149 K2
Christian r. AK U.S.A. 149 K2
Christian, Cape Canada 147 L2
Christiana S. Africa 125 G4
Christiania Norway see Oslo
Christian Island Canada 164 E1
Christiansburg U.S.A. 164 E5
Christianshåb Greenland see Qasigiannguit
Christie Bay Canada 151 I2
Christie Island Myanmar 87 B5
Christina r. Canada 151 I3
Christina, Mount N.Z. 139 B7

▶Christmas Island terr. Indian Ocean 80 D9
Australian External Territory.

Christopher, Lake salt flat Australia 135 D6
Chrudim Czech Rep. 57 O6
Chrysi i. Kriti Greece see Gaïdouronisi
Chrysochou Bay Cyprus 107 A2
Chrysochous, Kolpos b. Cyprus see Chrysochou Bay
Chu Kazakh. see Shu
Chu r. Kazakh./Kyrg. 102 C3
Chuadanga Bangl. 105 G5
Chuali, Lago l. Moz. 125 K3
Chuanhui China see Zhoukou
Chuansha China 97 I2
Chuathbaluk AK U.S.A. 148 H3
Chubalung China 96 C2
Chubarovka Ukr. see Polohy
Chubartau Kazakh. see Barshatas
Chūbu airport Aichi Japan 92 C4
Chūbu-Sangaku Kokuritsu-kōen nat. park Japan 92 D2
Chubxi Qinghai China 94 D5
Chu-ching China see Zhujing
Chuchkovo Rus. Fed. 53 I5
Chuckwalla Mountains U.S.A. 159 F5
Chucunaque r. Panama 166 [inset] K7
Chudniv Ukr. 53 F6
Chudovo Rus. Fed. 52 F4
Chudskoye, Ozero l. Estonia/Rus. Fed. see Peipus, Lake
Chugach Mountains AK U.S.A. 149 K3
Chuginadak Island AK U.S.A. 148 E5
Chūgoku-sanchi mts Japan 91 D6
Chugqênsumdo China see Jigzhi
Chuguchak Xinjiang China see Tacheng
Chuguyev Ukr. see Chuhuyiv
Chuguyevka Rus. Fed. 90 D3
Chugwater U.S.A. 156 G4
Chuhai China see Zhuhai
Chuhuyiv Ukr. 53 H6
Chu-Iliyskiye Gory mts Kazakh. 102 D3
Chuimatan Gansu China see Jishishan
Chujiang China see Shimen
Chukai Malaysia see Cukai
Chukchagirskoye, Ozero l. Rus. Fed. 90 E1
Chukchi Abyssal Plain sea feature Arctic Ocean 189 B1
Chukchi Plateau sea feature Arctic Ocean 189 B1
Chukchi Sea Rus. Fed./U.S.A. 148 E1
Chukhloma Rus. Fed. 52 I4
Chukotskiy, Mys c. Rus. Fed. 148 D2
Chukotskiy Khrebet mts Rus. Fed. 148 B2
Chukotskiy Poluostrov pen. Rus. Fed. 148 D2
Chulakkurgan Kazakh. see Sholakkorgan
Chulaktau Kazakh. see Karatau
Chulasa Rus. Fed. 52 J2
Chula Vista U.S.A. 158 E5
Chulitna AK U.S.A. 149 J3
Chuloonawick AK U.S.A. 148 F3
Chulucanas Peru 176 B5
Chulung Pass Pak. 104 D2
Chuluut Gol r. Mongolia 94 E1
Chulym Rus. Fed. 76 J4
Chulyshman r. Rus. Fed. 98 D2
Chumar India 104 D2
Chumbicha Arg. 178 C3
Chumda China 96 C1
Chumek Kazakh. 98 D2
Chumikan Rus. Fed. 77 O4
Chum Phae Thai. 86 C3
Chumphon Thai. 87 B5
Chum Saeng Thai. 86 C4
Chunar India 105 E4
Ch'unch'ŏn S. Korea 91 B5
Chunchura India 105 G5
Chundzha Kazakh. 102 E3
Chunga Zambia 123 C5
Chung-hua Jen-min Kung-ho-kuo country Asia see China
Chung-hua Min-kuo country Asia see Taiwan
Ch'ungju S. Korea 91 B5
Chungking China see Chongqing
Ch'ungmu S. Korea see T'ongyŏng
Chŭngsan N. Korea 91 B5
Chungyang Shanmo mts Taiwan 97 I4
Chunhua Shaanxi China 95 G5
Chunhuhux Mex. 167 H5
Chunskiy Rus. Fed. 88 H1
Chunya r. Rus. Fed. 77 K3
Chuôi, Hon i. Vietnam 87 D5
Chuosijia China see Guanyinqiao
Chupa Rus. Fed. 54 R3
Chūplū Iran 110 B2
Chuquicamata Chile 178 C2
Chur Switz. 66 I3
Churachandpur India 105 H4
Chūrān Iran 110 D4
Churapcha Rus. Fed. 77 O3
Churchill Canada 151 M3
Churchill r. Man. Canada 151 M3
Churchill r. Nfld. and Lab. Canada 153 J3
Churchill, Cape Canada 151 M3
Churchill Falls Canada 153 J3
Churchill Lake Canada 151 I4
Churchill Mountains Antarctica 188 H1
Churchill Sound sea chan. Canada 152 F2
Churchs Ferry U.S.A. 160 D1
Churchville U.S.A. 164 F4
Churek-Dag, Gora mt. Rus. Fed. 94 B1
Churia Ghati Hills Nepal 105 F4
Churu India 104 C3
Churubusco U.S.A. 164 C3
Churumuco Mex. 167 E5
Churún-Merú waterfall Venez. see Angel Falls
Chushul India 104 D2
Chuska Mountains U.S.A. 159 I3
Chusovaya r. Rus. Fed. 51 R4
Chusovoy Rus. Fed. 51 R4
Chust Ukr. see Khust
Chute-des-Passes Canada 153 H4
Chutia Assam India 105 H4
Chutia Jharkhand India 105 F5
Chutung Taiwan 97 I3
Chuuk is Micronesia 186 G5
Chuxiong China 96 D3
Chüy r. Kazakh./Kyrg. see Chu
Chüy admin. div. Kyrg. 98 A4
Chư Yang Sin mt. Vietnam 87 E4
Chūzenji-ko l. Japan 93 F2
Chuzhou Anhui China 97 H1
Chuzhou Jiangsu China 97 H1
Chūzu Japan 92 C3
Chymyshliya Moldova see Cimişlia
Chyulu Hills National Park Kenya 122 D4
Ciadâr-Lunga Moldova see Ciadîr-Lunga
Ciadîr-Lunga Moldova 69 M1
Ciamis Jawa Indon. 85 E4
Cianjur Jawa Indon. 84 D4
Cianorte Brazil 178 F2
Cibadak Jawa Indon. 84 D4
Cibatu Jawa Indon. 85 E4
Cibecue U.S.A. 159 H4
Cibinong Jawa Indon. 84 D4
Cibolo Creek r. U.S.A. 161 D6
Cibuta Mex. 166 C2
Cibuta, Sierra mt. Mex. 166 C2
Čićarija mts Croatia 68 E2
Cicero U.S.A. 164 B3
Cidaun Jawa Indon. 84 D4
Cide Turkey 112 D2
Ciechanów Poland 57 R4
Ciego de Ávila Cuba 169 I4
Ciénaga Col. 176 D1
Ciénega Mex. 167 E3
Ciénega de Flores Mex. 161 C7
Cieneguillas Mex. 166 D3
Cienfuegos Cuba 169 H4
Cieza Spain 67 F4
Çiftlik Turkey see Kelkit
Cifuentes Spain 67 E3
Cigeulis Jawa Indon. 84 D4
Cigüela r. Spain 67 E4
Cihanbeyli Turkey 112 D3
Cihuatlán Mex. 166 D5
Cíjara, Embalse de resr Spain 67 D4
Cikalong Jawa Indon. 85 E4
Cilacap Jawa Indon. 85 E4
Cilangkahan Jawa Indon. 84 D4
Çıldır Turkey 113 F2
Çıldır Gölü l. Turkey 113 F2
Çıldıroba Turkey 107 C1
Ciledug Jawa Indon. 85 E4
Cilento e del Vallo di Diano, Parco Nazionale del nat. park Italy 68 F4
Cili China 97 F2
Cilician Gates pass Turkey see Gülek Boğazı
Cill Airne Ireland see Killarney
Cill Chainnigh Ireland see Kilkenny
Cill Mhantáin Ireland see Wicklow
Çilmämmetgum des. Turkm. 110 D1
Cilo Dağı mt. Turkey 113 G3
Çilov Adası i. Azer. 113 H2
Cimahi Jawa Indon. 84 D4
Cimarron CO U.S.A. 159 J2
Cimarron KS U.S.A. 160 C4
Cimarron NM U.S.A. 157 G5
Cimarron r. U.S.A. 161 D4
Cimişlia Moldova 69 M1
Cimone, Monte mt. Italy 68 D2
Cîmpina Romania see Câmpina
Cîmpulung Romania see Câmpulung
Cîmpulung Moldovenesc Romania see Câmpulung Moldovenesc
Cina, Tanjung c. Indon. 84 D4
Çınar Turkey 113 F3
Cinaruco-Capanaparo, Parque Nacional nat. park Venez. 176 E2
Cinca r. Spain 67 G3
Cincinnati U.S.A. 164 C4
Cinco de Outubro Angola see Xá-Muteba
Cinderford U.K. 59 E7
Çine Turkey 69 M6
Ciney Belgium 62 F4
Cintalapa Mex. 168 F5
Cinto, Monte mt. France 66 I5
Cipatuja Jawa Indon. 85 E4
Ciping China see Jinggangshan
Cirata, Waduk resr Jawa Indon. 84 D4
Circeo, Parco Nazionale del nat. park Italy 68 E4
Circle AK U.S.A. 149 K2
Circle MT U.S.A. 156 G3
Circle Hot Springs AK U.S.A. 149 K2
Circleville OH U.S.A. 164 D4
Circleville UT U.S.A. 159 G2
Cirebon Jawa Indon. 85 E4
Cirencester U.K. 59 F7
Cirenti Sumatera Indon. 84 C3
Cirò Marina Italy 68 G5
Cirta Alg. see Constantine
Cisco U.S.A. 159 I2
Cisne, Islas del is Caribbean Sea 169 H5
Citlaltépetl vol. Mex. see Orizaba, Pico de
Čitluk Bos.-Herz. 68 G3
Citronelle U.S.A. 161 F6
Citrus Heights U.S.A. 158 C2
Città di Castello Italy 68 E3
Ciucaş, Vârful mt. Romania 69 K2
Ciudad Acuña Mex. 167 E2
Ciudad Altamirano Mex. 168 D5
Ciudad Bolívar Venez. 176 F2
Ciudad Camargo Mex. 166 D3
Ciudad Constitución Baja California Sur Mex. 166 C3
Ciudad Cuauhtémoc Mex. 167 H6
Ciudad del Carmen Mex. 167 H5
Ciudad Delicias Mex. 166 D2
Ciudad del Maíz Mex. 167 F4
Ciudad de Valles Mex. 168 E4
Ciudad Guayana Venez. 176 F2
Ciudad Guerrero Mex. 157 G7
Ciudad Guzmán Mex. 168 D5
Ciudad Hidalgo Mex. 167 E5
Ciudad Ixtepec Mex. 167 G5
Ciudad Juárez Mex. 166 D2
Ciudad Lerdo Mex. 166 E3
Ciudad Madero Mex. 167 F4
Ciudad Mante Mex. 168 E4
Ciudad Manuel Doblado Mex. 167 E4
Ciudad Mendoza Mex. 167 F5
Ciudad Mier Mex. 167 F3
Ciudad Obregón Mex. 166 C3
Ciudad Real Spain 67 E4
Ciudad Río Bravo Mex. 167 F3
Ciudad Rodrigo Spain 67 C3
Ciudad Tecún Uman Guat. 167 G6
Ciudad Trujillo Dom. Rep. see Santo Domingo
Ciudad Victoria Mex. 161 D8
Ciutadella Spain 67 H3
Cıva Burnu pt Turkey 112 E2
Cividale del Friuli Italy 68 E1
Civitanova Marche Italy 68 E3
Civitavecchia Italy 68 D3
Çivril Turkey 69 M5
Cixi China 97 I2
Cixian Hebei China 95 H4
Ciyao Shandong China 95 I5
Cizhou Hebei China see Cixian
Cizre Turkey 113 F3
Clacton-on-Sea U.K. 59 I7
Clady U.K. 61 E3
Claire, Lake Canada 151 H3
Clairfontaine Alg. see El Aouinet
Clamecy France 66 F3
Clam Gulch AK U.S.A. 149 J3
Clane Ireland 61 F4
Clanton U.S.A. 163 C5
Clanwilliam Dam S. Africa 124 D7
Clara Ireland 61 E4
Clara Island Myanmar 87 B5
Claraville Australia 136 C3
Clare N.S.W. Australia 138 A4
Clare S.A. Australia 137 B7
Clare r. Ireland 61 C4
Clare U.S.A. 164 C2
Clarecastle Ireland 61 D5
Clare Island Ireland 61 B4
Claremont U.S.A. 165 I2
Claremore U.S.A. 161 E4
Claremorris Ireland 61 D4
Clarence r. Australia 138 F2
Clarence N.Z. 139 D6
Clarence Island Antarctica 188 A2
Clarence Strait Iran see Khūran
Clarence Strait AK U.S.A. 149 N4
Clarence Town Bahamas 163 F8
Clarendon AR U.S.A. 161 F5
Clarendon PA U.S.A. 164 F3
Clarendon TX U.S.A. 161 C5
Clarenville Canada 153 L4
Claresholm Canada 150 H5
Clarie Coast Antarctica see Wilkes Coast
Clarinda U.S.A. 160 E3
Clarington U.S.A. 164 E4
Clarion IA U.S.A. 160 E3
Clarion PA U.S.A. 164 F3
Clarion r. U.S.A. 164 F3
Clarión, Isla i. Mex. 168 B5
Clark U.S.A. 160 D2
Clark, Lake AK U.S.A. 148 I3
Clark, Mount N.W.T. Canada 149 Q2
Clarkdale U.S.A. 159 G4
Clarkebury S. Africa 125 I6
Clarke Range mts Australia 136 D4
Clarke River Australia 136 D3
Clarke's Head Canada 153 L4
Clark Mountain U.S.A. 159 F4
Clark Point Canada 164 E1
Clarksburg U.S.A. 164 E4
Clarksdale U.S.A. 161 F5
Clarks Hill U.S.A. 164 B3
Clarks Point AK U.S.A. 148 H4
Clarksville AR U.S.A. 161 E5
Clarksville TN U.S.A. 164 B5
Clarksville TX U.S.A. 161 E5
Clarksville VA U.S.A. 165 F5
Claro r. Goiás Brazil 179 A2
Claro r. Mato Grosso Brazil 179 A1
Clashmore Ireland 61 E5
Claude U.S.A. 161 C5
Claudy U.K. 61 E3
Claveria Luzon Phil. 82 C2
Clavier Belgium 62 F4
Claxton U.S.A. 163 D5
Clay U.S.A. 164 E4
Clayburg U.S.A. 165 I1
Clay Center KS U.S.A. 160 D4
Clay Center NE U.S.A. 160 D3
Clay City IN U.S.A. 164 B4
Clay City KY U.S.A. 164 D5
Clayhole Wash watercourse U.S.A. 159 G3
Claypool U.S.A. 159 H5
Clay Springs U.S.A. 159 H4
Clayton DE U.S.A. 165 H4
Clayton GA U.S.A. 163 D5
Clayton MI U.S.A. 164 C3
Clayton MO U.S.A. 160 F4
Clayton NM U.S.A. 161 C4
Clayton NY U.S.A. 165 G1
Claytor Lake U.S.A. 164 E5
Clay Village U.S.A. 164 C4
Clear, Cape Ireland 61 C6
Clearco U.S.A. 164 E4
Clear Creek Canada 164 E2
Clear Creek r. U.S.A. 159 H4
Cleare, Cape U.S.A. 146 D4
Clearfield PA U.S.A. 165 F3
Clearfield UT U.S.A. 156 E4
Clear Fork Brazos r. U.S.A. 161 D5
Clear Hills Canada 150 G3
Clear Island Ireland 61 C6
Clear Lake IA U.S.A. 160 E3
Clear Lake SD U.S.A. 160 D2
Clear Lake l. CA U.S.A. 158 B2
Clear Lake l. UT U.S.A. 159 G2
Clearmont U.S.A. 156 G3
Clearwater Canada 150 G5
Clearwater r. Alberta/Saskatchewan Canada 151 I3
Clearwater r. Alberta Canada 150 H4
Clearwater U.S.A. 163 D7
Clearwater Lake Canada 151 K4
Clearwater Mountains U.S.A. 156 E3
Cleaton U.S.A. 164 B5
Cleburne U.S.A. 161 D5
Cleethorpes U.K. 58 G5
Clementi Sing. 87 [inset]
Clendenin U.S.A. 164 E4
Clendening Lake U.S.A. 164 E3
Cleopatra Needle mt. Palawan Phil. 82 B4
Clères France 62 B5
Clerf Lux. see Clervaux
Clerke Reef Australia 134 B4
Clermont Australia 136 D4
Clermont France 62 C5
Clermont-en-Argonne France 62 F5
Clermont-Ferrand France 66 F4
Clervaux Lux. 62 G4
Cles Italy 68 D1
Clevedon U.K. 59 E7
Cleveland MS U.S.A. 161 F5
Cleveland OH U.S.A. 164 E3
Cleveland TN U.S.A. 163 C5
Cleveland TX U.S.A. 167 G2
Cleveland UT U.S.A. 159 H2
Cleveland WI U.S.A. 164 B2
Cleveland, Cape Australia 136 D3
Cleveland, Mount U.S.A. 156 E2
Cleveland Heights U.S.A. 164 E3
Cleveland Hills U.K. 58 F4
Cleveleys U.K. 58 D5
Cleves Germany see Kleve
Clew Bay Ireland 61 C4
Clifden Ireland 61 B4
Cliff U.S.A. 159 I5
Cliffoney Ireland 61 D3
Clifton Australia 138 E1
Clifton U.S.A. 159 I5
Clifton Beach Australia 136 D3
Clifton Forge U.S.A. 164 F5
Clifton Park U.S.A. 165 I2
Climax Canada 151 I5
Climax U.S.A. 164 C2
Clinch Mountain mts U.S.A. 164 D5
Cline River Canada 150 G4
Clinton B.C. Canada 150 F5
Clinton Ont. Canada 164 E2
Clinton IA U.S.A. 160 F3
Clinton IL U.S.A. 160 F3
Clinton IN U.S.A. 164 B4
Clinton KY U.S.A. 161 F4
Clinton MI U.S.A. 164 D2
Clinton MO U.S.A. 160 E4
Clinton MS U.S.A. 161 F5
Clinton NC U.S.A. 163 E5
Clinton OK U.S.A. 161 D5
Clinton-Colden Lake Canada 151 J1
Clinton Creek (abandoned) Y.T. Canada 149 L2
Clintwood U.S.A. 164 D5

▶Clipperton, Île terr. N. Pacific Ocean 187 M5
French Overseas Territory. Most easterly point of Oceania.

Clisham hill U.K. 60 C3
Clitheroe U.K. 58 E5
Clive Lake Canada 150 G2
Cliza Bol. 176 E7
Clocolan S. Africa 125 H5
Cloghan Ireland 61 E4
Clonakilty Ireland 61 D6
Clonbern Ireland 61 D4
Cloncurry Australia 136 C4
Cloncurry r. Australia 136 C3
Clones Ireland 61 E3
Clonmel Ireland 61 E5
Clonygowan Ireland 61 E4
Cloonbannin Ireland 61 C5
Clooneagh Ireland 61 E4
Cloppenburg Germany 63 I2
Cloquet U.S.A. 160 E2
Cloquet r. U.S.A. 160 E2
Cloud Peak WY U.S.A. 154 F3
Cloud Peak WY U.S.A. 156 G3
Clova Canada 152 G4
Clover U.S.A. 159 G1
Cloverdale CA U.S.A. 158 B2
Cloverdale IN U.S.A. 164 B4
Cloverport U.S.A. 164 B5
Clovis CA U.S.A. 158 D3
Clovis NM U.S.A. 161 C5
Cloyne Canada 165 G1
Cluain Meala Ireland see Clonmel
Cluanie, Loch l. U.K. 60 D3
Cluff Lake Mine Canada 151 I3
Cluj-Napoca Romania 69 J1
Clun U.K. 59 D6
Clunes Australia 138 A6
Cluny Australia 136 B5
Cluses France 66 H3
Cluster Springs U.S.A. 165 F5
Clut Lake Canada 150 G1
Clutterbuck Head hd Canada 153 H1
Clutterbuck Hills hill Australia 135 D6
Clwydian Range hills U.K. 58 D5
Clyde Canada 150 H4
Clyde r. U.K. 60 E5
Clyde NY U.S.A. 165 G2
Clyde OH U.S.A. 164 D3
Clyde, Firth of est. U.K. 60 E5
Clydebank U.K. 60 E5
Clyde River Canada 147 L2
Côa r. Port. 67 C3
Coachella U.S.A. 158 E5
Coahuayutla de Guerrero Mex. 167 E5
Coahuila state Mex. 166 E3
Coal r. Y.T. Canada 149 P4
Coal City U.S.A. 164 A3
Coalcomán Mex. 166 E5
Coaldale U.S.A. 158 E2
Coalgate U.S.A. 161 D5
Coal Harbour Canada 150 E5
Coalinga U.S.A. 158 C3
Coalport U.S.A. 165 F3
Coal River B.C. Canada 149 P4
Coal Valley U.S.A. 159 F3
Coalville U.K. 59 F6
Coalville U.S.A. 159 H1
Coari Brazil 176 F4
Coari r. Brazil 176 F4
Coarsegold U.S.A. 158 D3
Coastal Plain U.S.A. 161 E6
Coast Mountains Canada 150 E4
Coast Range hills Australia 137 E5
Coast Ranges mts U.S.A. 158 B1
Coatbridge U.K. 60 E5
Coatepec Mex. 167 F5
Coatepeque Guat. 167 H6
Coatesville U.S.A. 165 H4
Coaticook Canada 165 J1
Coatlán Mex. 167 F5
Coats Island Canada 151 P2
Coats Land reg. Antarctica 188 A1
Coatzacoalcos Mex. 168 F5
Cobán Guat. 167 H6
Cobar Australia 138 B3
Cobargo Australia 138 D6
Cobden Australia 138 A7
Cobh Ireland 61 D6
Cobham r. Canada 151 M4
Cobija Bol. 176 E6
Coblenz Germany see Koblenz
Cobleskill U.S.A. 165 H2
Cobos Mex. 167 F4

Cobourg Peninsula Australia 134 F2
Cobra Australia 135 B6
Cobram Australia 138 B5
Coburg Germany 63 K4
Coburg Island Canada 147 K2
Coca Ecuador 176 C4
Coca Spain 67 D3
Cocalinho Brazil 179 A1
Cocanada India *see* **Kakinada**
Cochabamba Bol. 176 E7
Cochem Germany 63 H4
Cochin India 106 C4
Cochin *reg.* Vietnam 87 D5
Cochinos, Bahía de *b.* Cuba *see* **Pigs, Bay of**
Cochise U.S.A. 159 I5
Cochise Head *mt.* U.S.A. 159 I5
Cochrane *Alta* Canada 150 H5
Cochrane *Ont.* Canada 152 E4
Cochrane *r.* Canada 151 K3
Cockburn Australia 137 C7
Cockburnspath U.K. 60 G5
Cockburn Town Bahamas 163 F7
Cockburn Town Turks and Caicos Is *see* **Grand Turk**
Cockermouth U.K. 58 D4
Cocklebiddy Australia 135 D8
Cockscomb *mt.* S. Africa 124 G7
Coclé del Norte Panama 166 [inset] J7
Coco *r.* Hond./Nicaragua 166 [inset] J6
Coco, Cayo *i.* Cuba 163 E8
Coco, Isla de *i.* N. Pacific Ocean 169 G7
Cocobeach Gabon 122 A3
Coco Channel India 87 A4
Cocomórachic Mex. 166 D2
Coconino Plateau U.S.A. 159 G4
Cocopara National Park Australia 138 C5
Cocoro *i.* Phil. 82 C4
Cocos Brazil 179 B1
Cocos Basin *sea feature* Indian Ocean 185 O5

▶**Cocos Islands** *terr.* Indian Ocean 80 B9
Australian External Territory.

Cocos Ridge *sea feature* N. Pacific Ocean 187 O5
Cocula Mex. 166 E4
Cocuy, Sierra Nevada del *mt.* Col. 176 D2
Cod, Cape U.S.A. 165 J3
Codajás Brazil 176 F4
Coderre Canada 151 J5
Codfish Island N.Z. 139 A8
Codigoro Italy 68 E2
Cod Island Canada 153 J2
Codlea Romania 69 K2
Codó Brazil 177 J4
Codsall U.K. 59 E6
Cod's Head *hd* Ireland 61 B6
Cody U.S.A. 156 F3
Coeburn U.S.A. 164 D5
Coen Australia 136 C2
Coesfeld Germany 63 H3
Coeur d'Alene U.S.A. 156 D3
Coeur d'Alene Lake U.S.A. 156 D3
Coevorden Neth. 62 G2
Coffee Bay S. Africa 125 I6
Coffeyville U.S.A. 161 E4
Coffin Bay Australia 137 A7
Coffin Bay National Park Australia 137 A7
Coffs Harbour Australia 138 F3
Cofimvaba S. Africa 125 H7
Cofradía Hond. 166 [inset] H6
Cofre de Perote, Parque Nacional *nat. park* Mex. 167 F5
Cognac France 66 D4
Cogo Equat. Guinea 120 D4
Coguno Moz. 125 L3
Cohoes U.S.A. 165 I2
Cohuna Australia 138 B5
Coiba, Isla de *i.* Panama 166 [inset] J8
Coigeach, Rubha *pt* U.K. 60 D2
Coihaique Chile 178 B7
Coimbatore India 106 C4
Coimbra Port. 67 B3
Coipasa, Salar de *salt flat* Bol. 176 E7
Coire Switz. *see* **Chur**
Colac Australia 138 A7
Colair Lake India *see* **Kolleru Lake**
Colatina Brazil 179 C2
Colbitz Germany 63 L2
Colborne Canada 165 G2
Colby U.S.A. 160 C4
Colchester U.K. 59 H7
Colchester U.S.A. 165 I3
Cold Bay *AK* U.S.A. 148 G5
Cold Bay *AK* U.S.A. 148 G5
Coldfoot *AK* U.S.A. 149 J2
Coldingham U.K. 60 G5
Colditz Germany 63 M3
Cold Lake Canada 151 I4
Cold Lake *l.* Canada 151 I4
Coldspring U.S.A. 161 E6
Coldstream Canada 150 G5
Coldstream U.K. 60 G5
Coldwater Canada 164 F1
Coldwater *KS* U.S.A. 161 D4
Coldwater *MI* U.S.A. 164 C3
Coldwater *r.* U.S.A. 161 F5
Coleambally Australia 138 B5
Colebrook U.S.A. 165 J1
Coleen *r.* *AK* U.S.A. 149 L2
Coleman *r.* Australia 136 C2
Coleman U.S.A. 161 D6
Çölemerik Turkey *see* **Hakkâri**
Colenso S. Africa 125 I5
Cole Peninsula Antarctica 188 L2
Coleraine Australia 137 C8
Coleraine U.K. 61 F2
Coles, Punta de *pt* Peru 176 D7
Coles Bay Australia 137 [inset]
Colesberg S. Africa 125 G6
Coleville Canada 151 I5
Colfax *CA* U.S.A. 158 C2
Colfax *LA* U.S.A. 161 E6
Colfax *WA* U.S.A. 156 D3
Colhué Huapí, Lago *l.* Arg. 178 C7
Coligny S. Africa 125 H4
Colima Mex. 168 D5
Colima *state* Mex. 166 E5
Colima, Nevado de *vol.* Mex. 168 D5
Coll *i.* U.K. 60 C4
Collado Villalba Spain 67 E3
Collarenebri Australia 138 D2
College *AK* U.S.A. 149 K2
College Station U.S.A. 161 D6
Collerina Australia 138 C2
Collie *N.S.W.* Australia 138 D3
Collie *W.A.* Australia 135 B8
Collier Bay Australia 134 D4
Collier Range National Park Australia 135 B6
Collingwood Canada 164 E1
Collingwood N.Z. 139 D5
Collins U.S.A. 161 F6
Collins Glacier Antarctica 188 E2
Collinson Peninsula Canada 147 H2
Collipulli Chile 178 B5
Collmberg *hill* Germany 63 N3
Collooney Ireland 61 D3
Colmar France 66 H2
Colmenar Viejo Spain 67 E3
Colmonell U.K. 60 E5
Colne *r.* U.K. 59 H7
Cologne Germany 62 G4
Coloma U.S.A. 164 B2
Colomb-Béchar Alg. *see* **Béchar**
Colômbia Brazil 179 A3
Colombia Mex. 167 F3

▶**Colombia** *country* S. America 176 D3
2nd most populous and 4th largest country in South America.

Colombian Basin *sea feature* S. Atlantic Ocean 184 C5

▶**Colombo** Sri Lanka 106 C5
Former capital of Sri Lanka.

Colomiers France 66 E5
Colón *Buenos Aires* Arg. 178 D4
Colón *Entre Ríos* Arg. 178 E4
Colón Cuba 163 D8
Colón Panama 166 [inset] K7
Colon U.S.A. 164 C3
Colón, Archipiélago de *is* Ecuador *see* **Galapagos Islands**
Colón, Isla de *i.* Panama 166 [inset] J7
Colona Australia 135 F7
Colonelganj India 105 E4
Colonel Hill Bahamas 163 F8
Colonet, Cabo *c.* Mex. 166 A2
Colônia *r.* Brazil 179 D1
Colonia Micronesia 81 J5
Colonia Agrippina Germany *see* **Cologne**
Colonia Díaz Mex. 166 C2
Colonia Julia Fenestris Italy *see* **Fano**
Colonia Las Heras Arg. 178 C7
Colonial Heights U.S.A. 165 G5
Colonna, Capo *c.* Italy 68 G5
Colonsay *i.* U.K. 60 C4
Colorado *r.* Arg. 178 D5
Colorado *r.* Mex./U.S.A. 166 B2
Colorado *r.* U.S.A. 161 D6
Colorado *state* U.S.A. 156 G5
Colorado City *AZ* U.S.A. 159 G3
Colorado City *TX* U.S.A. 161 C5
Colorado Desert U.S.A. 158 E5
Colorado National Monument *nat. park* U.S.A. 159 I2
Colorado Plateau U.S.A. 159 I3
Colorado River Aqueduct *canal* U.S.A. 159 F4
Colorado Springs U.S.A. 156 G5
Colossae Turkey *see* **Honaz**
Colotlán Mex. 168 D4
Cölpin Germany 63 N1
Colquiri Bol. 176 E7
Colquitt U.S.A. 163 C6
Colson U.S.A. 164 D5
Colsterworth U.K. 59 G6
Colstrip U.S.A. 156 G3
Coltishall U.K. 59 I6
Colton *CA* U.S.A. 158 E4
Colton *NY* U.S.A. 165 H1
Colton *UT* U.S.A. 159 H2
Columbia *KY* U.S.A. 164 C5
Columbia *LA* U.S.A. 161 E5
Columbia *MD* U.S.A. 165 G4
Columbia *MO* U.S.A. 160 E4
Columbia *MS* U.S.A. 161 F6
Columbia *NC* U.S.A. 162 E5
Columbia *PA* U.S.A. 165 G3

▶**Columbia** *SC* U.S.A. 163 D5
Capital of South Carolina.

Columbia *TN* U.S.A. 162 C5
Columbia *r.* U.S.A. 156 C3
Columbia, District of *admin. dist.* U.S.A. 165 G4
Columbia, Mount Canada 150 G4
Columbia, Sierra *mts* Mex. 166 B2
Columbia City U.S.A. 164 C3
Columbia Lake Canada 150 H5
Columbia Mountains Canada 150 F4
Columbia Plateau U.S.A. 156 D3
Columbine, Cape S. Africa 124 C7
Columbus *GA* U.S.A. 163 C5
Columbus *IN* U.S.A. 164 C4
Columbus *MS* U.S.A. 161 F5
Columbus *MT* U.S.A. 156 F3
Columbus *NC* U.S.A. 163 D5
Columbus *NE* U.S.A. 160 D3
Columbus *NM* U.S.A. 157 G7

▶**Columbus** *OH* U.S.A. 164 D4
Capital of Ohio.

Columbus *TX* U.S.A. 161 D6
Columbus Grove U.S.A. 164 C3
Columbus Salt Marsh U.S.A. 158 D2
Colusa U.S.A. 158 B2
Colville N.Z. 139 E3
Colville U.S.A. 156 D2
Colville *r.* *AK* U.S.A. 149 J1
Colville Channel N.Z. 139 E3
Colville Lake *N.W.T.* Canada 149 P2
Colwyn Bay U.K. 58 D5
Comacchio Italy 68 E2
Comacchio, Valli di *lag.* Italy 68 E2
Comai *Xizang* China 99 E7
Comalcalco Mex. 167 G5
Comanche U.S.A. 161 D6
Comandante Ferraz *research station* Antarctica 188 A2
Comandante Salas Arg. 178 C4
Comănești Romania 69 L1
Comayagua Hond. 166 [inset] I6
Combahee *r.* U.S.A. 163 D5
Combarbalá Chile 178 B4
Comber U.K. 61 G3
Combermere Bay Myanmar 86 A3
Combles France 62 C4
Combol *i.* Indon. 84 C2
Combomune Moz. 125 K2
Comboyne Australia 138 F3
Comencho, Lac *l.* Canada 152 G4
Comendador Dom. Rep. *see* **Elías Piña**
Comendador Gomes Brazil 179 A2
Comeragh Mountains *hills* Ireland 61 E5
Comercinho Brazil 179 C2
Cometela Moz. 125 L1
Comfort U.S.A. 161 D6
Comilla Bangl. 105 G5
Comines Belgium 62 C4
Comino, Capo *c. Sardinia* Italy 68 C4
Comitán de Domínguez Mex. 167 G5
Commack U.S.A. 165 I3
Commentry France 66 F3
Committee Bay Canada 147 J3
Commonwealth Territory *admin. div.* Australia *see* **Jervis Bay Territory**
Como Italy 68 C2
Como, Lago di Italy *see* **Como, Lake**
Como, Lake Italy 68 C2
Como Chamling *l.* China 99 E7
Comodoro Rivadavia Arg. 178 C7
Comonfort Mex. 167 E4
Comores *country* Africa *see* **Comoros**
Comorin, Cape India 106 C4
Comoro Islands *country* Africa *see* **Comoros**
Comoros *country* Africa 123 E5
Compiègne France 62 C5
Compostela Mex. 166 D4
Compostela *Mindanao* Phil. 82 D5
Comprida, Ilha *i.* Brazil 179 B4
Comrat Moldova 69 M1
Comrie U.K. 60 F4
Comstock U.S.A. 161 C6
Cơn, Sông *r.* Vietnam 87 E4
Cona *Xizang* China 99 E8

▶**Conakry** Guinea 120 B4
Capital of Guinea.

Cona Niyeo Arg. 178 C6
Conceição *r.* Brazil 179 B2
Conceição da Barra Brazil 179 D2
Conceição do Araguaia Brazil 177 I5
Conceição do Mato Dentro Brazil 179 C2
Concepción Chile 178 B5
Concepción Mex. 167 C7
Concepción *r.* Mex. 166 B2
Concepción Para. 178 E2
Concepción, Punta *pt* Mex. 166 C3
Concepción de la Vega Dom. Rep. *see* **La Vega**
Conception, Point U.S.A. 158 C4
Conception Island Bahamas 163 F8
Concha Mex. 166 D4
Conchas U.S.A. 157 G6
Conchas Lake U.S.A. 157 G6
Concho Mex. 166 D3
Concho U.S.A. 159 I4
Conchos *r.* *Nuevo León/Tamaulipas* Mex. 167 F3
Conchos *r.* Mex. 166 D2
Concord *CA* U.S.A. 158 B3
Concord *NC* U.S.A. 163 D5

▶**Concord** *NH* U.S.A. 165 J2
Capital of New Hampshire.

Concord *VT* U.S.A. 165 J1
Concordia Arg. 178 E4
Concordia Mex. 161 B8
Concordia Peru 176 D4
Concordia S. Africa 124 C5
Concordia *KS* U.S.A. 160 D4
Concordia *KY* U.S.A. 164 B4
Concordia 188 G2
Concord Peak Afgh. 111 I2
Con Cuông Vietnam 86 D3
Condamine Australia 138 E1
Condamine *r.* Australia 138 D1
Côn Đao Vietnam 87 D5
Condega Nicaragua 166 [inset] I6
Condeúba Brazil 179 C1
Condobolin Australia 138 C4
Condom France 66 E5
Condon U.S.A. 156 C3
Condor, Cordillera del *mts* Ecuador/Peru 176 C4
Condroz *reg.* Belgium 62 E4
Conecuh *r.* U.S.A. 163 C6
Conegliano Italy 68 E2
Conejos Mex. 166 E3
Conejos U.S.A. 157 G5
Conemaugh *r.* U.S.A. 164 F3
Cone Mountain *AK* U.S.A. 148 H2
Conestogo Lake Canada 164 E2
Conesus Lake U.S.A. 165 G2
Conflict Group *is* P.N.G. 136 E1
Confoederatio Helvetica *country* Europe *see* **Switzerland**
Confusion Range *mts* U.S.A. 159 G2
Congdü *Xizang* China 99 D7
Conghua China 97 G4
Congjiang China 97 F3
Congleton U.K. 58 E5
Congo *country* Africa 122 B4

▶**Congo** *r.* Congo/Dem. Rep. Congo 122 B4
2nd longest river in Africa, and 8th in the world. Formerly known as Zaïre.

Congo (Brazzaville) *country* Africa *see* **Congo**
Congo (Kinshasa) *country* Africa *see* **Congo, Democratic Republic of the**

▶**Congo, Democratic Republic of the** *country* Africa 122 C4
3rd largest and 4th most populous country in Africa.

Congo, Republic of *country* Africa *see* **Congo**
Congo Basin Dem. Rep. Congo 122 C4
Congo Cone *sea feature* S. Atlantic Ocean 184 I6
Congo Free State *country* Africa *see* **Congo, Democratic Republic of the**
Congonhas Brazil 179 C3
Congress U.S.A. 159 G4
Conhuas Mex. 167 H5
Conimbla National Park Australia 138 D4
Coningsby U.K. 59 G5
Coniston Canada 152 E5
Coniston U.K. 58 D4
Conjuboy Australia 136 D3
Conkal Mex. 167 H4
Conklin Canada 151 I4
Conn *r.* Canada 152 F3
Conn, Lough *l.* Ireland 61 C3
Connacht *reg.* Ireland *see* **Connaught**
Connaught *reg.* Ireland 61 C4
Conneaut U.S.A. 164 E3
Connecticut *state* U.S.A. 165 I3
Connemara *reg.* Ireland 61 C4
Connemara National Park Ireland 61 C4
Connersville U.S.A. 164 C4
Connolly, Mount *Y.T.* Canada 149 N3
Connors Range *hills* Australia 136 E4
Conoble Australia 138 B4
Conquista Brazil 179 B2
Conrad U.S.A. 156 F2
Conrad Rise *sea feature* Southern Ocean 185 K9
Conroe U.S.A. 161 E6
Conroe, Lake *TX* U.S.A. 167 G2
Consejo Belize 167 H5
Conselheiro Lafaiete Brazil 179 C3
Consett U.K. 58 F4
Consolación del Sur Cuba 163 D8
Côn Sơn, Đao *i.* Vietnam 87 D5
Consort Canada 151 I4
Constance Germany *see* **Konstanz**
Constance, Lake Germany/Switz. 57 L7
Constância dos Baetas Brazil 176 F5
Constanța Romania 69 M2
Constantia *tourist site* Cyprus *see* **Salamis**
Constantia Germany *see* **Konstanz**
Constantina Spain 67 D5
Constantine Alg. 64 F4
Constantine, Cape *AK* U.S.A. 148 H4
Constantine Harbor *AK* U.S.A. 149 [inset]
Constantinople Turkey *see* **İstanbul**
Constitución de 1857, Parque Nacional *nat. park* Mex. 166 B1
Consul Canada 151 I5
Contact U.S.A. 156 E4
Contagalo Brazil 179 C3
Contamana Peru 176 C5
Contas *r.* Brazil 179 D1
Contoy, Isla *i.* Mex. 167 I4
Contria Brazil 179 B2
Contwoyto Lake Canada 151 I1
Convención Col. 176 D2
Convent U.S.A. 161 F6
Conway U.K. *see* **Conwy**
Conway *AR* U.S.A. 161 E5
Conway *ND* U.S.A. 160 D1
Conway *NH* U.S.A. 165 J2
Conway *SC* U.S.A. 163 E5
Conway, Cape Australia 136 E4
Conway, Lake *salt flat* Australia 137 A6
Conway National Park Australia 136 E4
Conway Reef Fiji *see* **Ceva-i-Ra**
Conwy U.K. 58 D5
Conwy *r.* U.K. 59 D5
Coober Pedy Australia 135 F7
Cooch Behar India *see* **Koch Bihar**
Coochbehar India *see* **Koch Bihar**
Cook Australia 135 E7
Cook, Cape Canada 150 E5
Cook, Grand Récif de *reef* New Caledonia 133 G3
Cook, Mount Canada/U.S.A. 149 M3
Cook, Mount N.Z. *see* **Aoraki**
Cookes Peak U.S.A. 157 G6
Cookeville U.S.A. 162 C4
Cookhouse S. Africa 125 G7
Cook Ice Shelf Antarctica 188 H2
Cook Inlet *sea channel* *AK* U.S.A. 148 I3
Cook Islands *terr.* S. Pacific Ocean 186 J7
Cooksburg U.S.A. 165 H2
Cooks Passage Australia 136 D2
Cookstown U.K. 61 F3
Cook Strait N.Z. 139 E5
Cooktown Australia 136 D2
Coolabah Australia 138 C3
Cooladdi Australia 138 B1
Coolah Australia 138 D3
Coolamon Australia 138 C5
Coolgardie Australia 135 C7
Coolibah Australia 134 E3
Coolidge U.S.A. 159 H5
Cooloola National Park Australia 137 F5
Coolum Beach Australia 137 F5
Cooma Australia 138 D6
Coombah Australia 137 C7
Coonabarabran Australia 138 D3
Coonamble Australia 138 D3
Coondambo Australia 137 A6
Coondapoor India *see* **Kundapura**
Coongoola Australia 138 B1
Coon Rapids U.S.A. 160 E2
Cooper Creek *watercourse* Australia 137 B6
Cooper Mountain Canada 150 G5
Coopernook Australia 138 F3
Cooper's Town Bahamas 163 E7
Cooperstown *ND* U.S.A. 160 D2
Cooperstown *NY* U.S.A. 165 H2
Coopracambra National Park Australia 138 D6
Coorabie Australia 135 F7
Coorong National Park Australia 137 B8
Coorow Australia 135 B7
Coosa *r.* U.S.A. 163 C5
Coos Bay U.S.A. 156 B4
Coos Bay *b.* U.S.A. 156 B4
Cootamundra Australia 138 D5
Cootehill Ireland 61 E3
Cooyar Australia 138 E1
Copainalá Mex. 167 G5
Copala Mex. 168 E5
Copán *tourist site* Hond. 166 [inset] H6
Cope U.S.A. 160 C4
Copemish U.S.A. 164 C1

▶**Copenhagen** Denmark 55 H9
Capital of Denmark.

Copenhagen U.S.A. 165 H2
Copertino Italy 68 H4
Copeton Reservoir Australia 138 E2
Cô Pi, Phou *mt.* Laos/Vietnam 86 D3
Copiapó Chile 178 B3
Copley Australia 137 B6
Copparo Italy 68 D2
Copper *r.* *AK* U.S.A. 149 K3
Copper Cliff Canada 152 E5
Copper Harbor U.S.A. 162 C2
Coppermine Canada *see* **Kugluktuk**
Coppermine *r.* Canada 150 H1
Coppermine Point Canada 152 D5
Copperton S. Africa 124 F5
Copp Lake Canada 150 H2
Coqên *Xizang* China 99 D7
Coqên *Xizang* China 99 D7
Coquilhatville Dem. Rep. Congo *see* **Mbandaka**
Coquille *i.* Micronesia *see* **Pikelot**
Coquille U.S.A. 156 B4
Coquimbo Chile 178 B3
Coquitlam Canada 150 F5
Corabia Romania 69 K3
Coração de Jesus Brazil 179 B2
Coracesium Turkey *see* **Alanya**
Coraki Australia 138 F2
Coral Bay Australia 135 A5
Coral Bay *Palawan* Phil. 82 B4
Coral Harbour Canada 147 J3
Coral Sea S. Pacific Ocean 132 F3
Coral Sea Basin S. Pacific Ocean 186 G6

▶**Coral Sea Islands Territory** *terr.* Australia 132 F3
Australian External Territory.

Corangamite, Lake Australia 138 A7
Corat Azer. 113 H2
Corbeny France 62 D5
Corbett Inlet Canada 151 M2
Corbett National Park India 104 D3
Corbie France 62 C5
Corbin U.S.A. 164 C5
Corby U.K. 59 G6
Corcaigh Ireland *see* **Cork**
Corcoran U.S.A. 158 D3
Corcovado, Golfo de *sea chan.* Chile 178 B6
Corcovado, Parque Nacional *nat. park* Costa Rica 166 [inset] J7
Corcyra *i.* Greece *see* **Corfu**
Cordele U.S.A. 163 D6
Cordelia U.S.A. 158 B2
Cordell U.S.A. 161 D5
Cordilheiras, Serra das *hills* Brazil 177 I5
Cordillera Azul, Parque Nacional *nat. park* Peru 176 C5
Cordillera de los Picachos, Parque Nacional *nat. park* Col. 176 D3
Cordilleras Range *mts* *Panay* Phil. 82 C4
Cordillo Downs Australia 137 C5
Cordisburgo Brazil 179 B2
Córdoba Arg. 178 D4
Córdoba *Durango* Mex. 166 E3
Córdoba *Veracruz* Mex. 168 E5
Córdoba Spain 67 D5
Córdoba, Sierras de *mts* Arg. 178 D4
Cordova Spain *see* **Córdoba**
Cordova *AK* U.S.A. 149 K3
Cordova Peak *AK* U.S.A. 149 K3
Corduba Spain *see* **Córdoba**
Corfu *i.* Greece 69 H5
Coria Spain 67 C4
Coribe Brazil 179 B1
Coricudgy *mt.* Australia 138 E4
Corigliano Calabro Italy 68 G5
Coringa Islands Australia 136 E3
Corinium U.K. *see* **Cirencester**
Corinth Greece 69 J6
Corinth *KY* U.S.A. 164 C4
Corinth *MS* U.S.A. 161 F5
Corinth *NY* U.S.A. 165 I2
Corinth, Gulf of *sea chan.* Greece 69 J5
Corinthus Greece *see* **Corinth**
Corinto Brazil 179 B2
Corinto Nicaragua 166 [inset] I6
Cork Ireland 61 D6
Corleone *Sicily* Italy 68 E6
Çorlu Turkey 69 L4
Cormeilles France 59 H9
Cormoran Reef Palau 82 [inset]
Cornelia S. Africa 125 I4
Cornélio Procópio Brazil 179 A3
Cornélios Brazil 179 A5
Cornell U.S.A. 160 F2
Corner Brook Canada 153 K4
Corner Inlet *b.* Australia 138 C7
Corner Seamounts *sea feature* N. Atlantic Ocean 184 E3
Corneto Italy *see* **Tarquinia**
Cornillet, Mont *hill* France 62 E5
Corning *AR* U.S.A. 161 F4
Corning *CA* U.S.A. 158 B2
Corning *NY* U.S.A. 165 G2
Cornish *watercourse* Australia 136 D4
Corn Islands *is* Nicaragua *see* **Maíz, Islas del**
Corno, Monte *mt.* Italy 68 E3
Corno di Campo *mt.* Italy/Switz. 66 J3
Cornwall Canada 165 H1
Cornwallis Island Canada 147 I2
Cornwall Island Canada 147 I2
Coro Venez. 176 E1
Coroaci Brazil 179 C2
Coroatá Brazil 177 J4
Corofin Ireland 61 C5
Coromandel Brazil 179 B2
Coromandel Coast India 106 D4
Coromandel Peninsula N.Z. 139 E3
Coromandel Range *hills* N.Z. 139 E3
Coron Phil. 82 C3
Corona *CA* U.S.A. 158 E5
Corona *NM* U.S.A. 157 G6
Coronado U.S.A. 158 E5
Coronado, Bahía de *b.* Costa Rica 166 [inset] J7
Coronado Bay *Mindanao* Phil. 82 C5
Coronation Canada 151 I4
Coronation Gulf Canada 146 G3
Coronation Island S. Atlantic Ocean 188 A2
Coronation Island *AK* U.S.A. 149 N5
Coron Bay Phil. 82 C4
Coronda Arg. 178 D4
Coronel Fabriciano Brazil 179 C2
Coronel Oviedo Para. 178 E3
Coronel Pringles Arg. 178 D5
Coronel Suárez Arg. 178 D5
Çorovodë Albania 69 I4
Corowa Australia 138 C5
Corozal Belize 167 H5
Corpus Christi U.S.A. 161 D7
Corpus Christi, Lake *TX* U.S.A. 167 F2
Corque Bol. 176 E7
Corral de Cantos *mt.* Spain 67 D4
Corrales Mex. 157 G8
Corralilla Cuba 163 D8
Corrandibby Range *hills* Australia 135 A6
Corrente Brazil 177 I6
Corrente *r.* *Bahia* Brazil 179 C1
Corrente *r.* *Minas Gerais* Brazil 179 A2
Correntes Brazil 177 H7
Correntina Brazil 179 B1
Correntina *r.* Brazil *see* **Éguas**
Corrib, Lough *l.* Ireland 61 C4
Corrientes Arg. 178 E3
Corrientes, Cabo *c.* Col. 176 C2
Corrientes, Cabo *c.* Cuba 163 C8
Corrientes, Cabo *c.* Mex. 168 C4
Corrigan *TX* U.S.A. 167 G2
Corrigin Australia 135 B8
Corris U.K. 59 D6
Corry U.S.A. 164 F3
Corse *i.* France *see* **Corsica**
Corse, Cap *c. Corsica* France 66 I5
Corsham U.K. 59 E7
Corsica *i.* France 66 I5
Corsicana U.S.A. 161 D5
Corte *Corsica* France 66 I5
Cortegana Spain 67 C5
Cortes, Sea of *g.* Mex. *see* **California, Golfo de**
Cortez U.S.A. 159 I3
Cortina d'Ampezzo Italy 68 E1
Cortland U.S.A. 165 G2
Corton U.K. 59 I6
Cortona Italy 68 D3
Coruche Port. 67 B4
Çoruh Turkey *see* **Artvin**
Çoruh *r.* Turkey 113 F2
Çorum Turkey 112 D2
Corumbá Brazil 177 G7
Corumbá *r.* Brazil 179 A2
Corumbá de Goiás Brazil 179 A1
Corumbaíba Brazil 179 A2
Corumbaú, Ponta *pt* Brazil 179 D2
Corunna Spain *see* **A Coruña**
Corunna U.S.A. 164 C2
Corvallis U.S.A. 156 C3
Corwen U.K. 59 D6
Corydon *IA* U.S.A. 160 E3
Corydon *IN* U.S.A. 164 B4
Coryville U.S.A. 165 F3
Cos *i.* Greece *see* **Kos**

Cosalá Mex. 166 D3
Cosamaloapan Mex. 167 G5
Cosentia Italy see Cosenza
Cosenza Italy 68 G5
Coshocton U.S.A. 164 E3
Cosne-Cours-sur-Loire France 66 F3
Costa Blanca coastal area Spain 67 F4
Costa Brava coastal area Spain 67 H3
Costa de la Luz coastal area Spain 67 C5
Costa del Sol coastal area Spain 67 D5
Costa de Mosquitos coastal area Nicaragua 166 [inset] J6
Costa Marques Brazil 176 F6
Costa Rica Brazil 177 H7
Costa Rica country Central America 169 H6
Costa Rica Mex. 166 D3
Costa Verde coastal area Spain 67 C2
Costermansville Dem. Rep. Congo see Bukavu
Costeşti Romania 69 K2
Costigan Lake Canada 151 J3
Coswig Germany 63 M3
Cotabato Mindanao Phil. 82 D5
Cotagaita Bol. 176 E8
Cotahuasi Peru 176 D7
Cote, Mount AK U.S.A. 149 O4
Coteau des Prairies slope U.S.A. 160 D2
Coteau du Missouri slope ND U.S.A. 160 C1
Côte d'Azur coastal area France 66 H5
Côte d'Ivoire country Africa 120 C4
Côte Française de Somalis country Africa see Djibouti
Cotentin pen. France 59 F9
Côtes de Meuse ridge France 62 E5
Cothi r. U.K. 59 C7
Cotiaeum Turkey see Kütahya
Cotiella mt. Spain 67 G2
Cotonou Benin 120 D4
Cotopaxi, Volcán vol. Ecuador 176 C4
Cotswold Hills U.K. 59 E7
Cottage Grove U.S.A. 156 C4
Cottbus Germany 57 O5
Cottenham U.K. 59 H6
Cottian Alps mts France/Italy 66 H4
Cottica Suriname 177 H3
Cottiennes, Alpes mts France/Italy see Cottian Alps
Cottonwood AZ U.S.A. 159 G4
Cottonwood CA U.S.A. 158 B1
Cottonwood r. U.S.A. 160 D4
Cottonwood Falls U.S.A. 160 D4
Cotulla U.S.A. 161 D6
Coudersport U.S.A. 165 F3
Couedic, Cape du Australia 137 B8
Coulee City U.S.A. 156 D3
Coulee Dam U.S.A. 156 D3
Coulman Island Antarctica 188 H2
Coulogne France 62 B4
Coulommiers France 62 D6
Coulonge r. Canada 152 F5
Coulterville U.S.A. 158 C3
Council AK U.S.A. 148 G2
Council U.S.A. 156 D3
Council Bluffs U.S.A. 160 E3
Council Grove U.S.A. 160 D4
Councillor Island Australia 137 [inset]
Counselor U.S.A. 159 J3
Coupeville U.S.A. 156 C2
Courageous Lake Canada 151 I1
Courland Lagoon b. Lith./Rus. Fed. 55 L9
Courtenay Canada 150 E5
Courtland U.S.A. 165 G5
Courtmacsherry Ireland 61 D6
Courtmacsherry Bay Ireland 61 D6
Courtown Ireland 61 F5
Courtrai Belgium see Kortrijk
Coushatta U.S.A. 161 E5
Coutances France 66 D2
Coutts Canada 151 I5
Couture, Lac l. Canada 152 G2
Couvin Belgium 62 E4
Cove Fort U.S.A. 159 G2
Cove Island Canada 164 E1
Cove Mountains hills U.S.A. 165 F4
Coventry U.K. 59 F6
Covered Wells U.S.A. 159 G5
Covesville U.S.A. 165 F5
Covilhã Port. 67 C3
Coville, Lake AK U.S.A. 148 I4
Covington GA U.S.A. 163 D5
Covington IN U.S.A. 164 B3
Covington KY U.S.A. 164 C4
Covington LA U.S.A. 161 F6
Covington MI U.S.A. 160 F2
Covington TN U.S.A. 161 F5
Covington VA U.S.A. 164 E5
Cowal, Lake dry lake Australia 138 C4
Cowan, Lake salt flat Australia 135 C7
Cowansville Canada 165 I1
Cowargarzê China 96 C1
Cowcowing Lakes salt flat Australia 135 B7
Cowdenbeath U.K. 60 F4
Cowell Australia 137 B7
Cowes U.K. 59 F8
Cowichan Lake Canada 150 E5
Cowley Australia 138 B1
Cowper Point Canada 147 G2
Cowra Australia 138 D4
Cox r. Australia 136 A2
Coxá r. Brazil 179 B1
Coxen Hole Hond. see Roatán
Coxilha de Santana hills Brazil/Uruguay 178 E4
Coxilha Grande hills Brazil 178 F3
Coxim Brazil 177 H7
Cox's Bazar Bangl. 105 G5
Coyame Mex. 161 B6
Coyhaique Chile see Coihaique
Coyote, Punta pt Mex. 166 C3
Coyote Lake U.S.A. 158 E4
Coyote Peak hill U.S.A. 159 F5
Coyotitán Mex. 166 D4
Coyuca de Benitez Mex. 167 E5
Cozhê China 105 F2
Cozie, Alpi mts France/Italy see Cottian Alps
Cozumel Mex. 167 I4
Cozumel, Isla de i. Mex. 167 I4
Craboon Australia 138 D4
Cracovia Poland see Kraków
Cracow Australia 136 E5
Cracow Poland see Kraków
Cradle Mountain Lake St Clair National Park Australia 137 [inset]
Cradock S. Africa 125 G7
Craig U.K. 60 D3
Craig AK U.S.A. 149 N5
Craig CO U.S.A. 159 J1
Craigavon U.K. 61 F3
Craigieburn Australia 138 B6
Craig Island Taiwan see Mienhua Yü
Craignure U.K. 60 D4
Craigsville U.S.A. 164 E4
Crail U.K. 60 G4
Crailsheim Germany 63 K5
Craiova Romania 69 J2
Cramlington U.K. 58 F3
Cranberry Junction B.C. Canada 149 O5
Cranberry Lake U.S.A. 165 H1
Cranberry Portage Canada 151 K4
Cranborne Chase for. U.K. 59 E8
Cranbourne Australia 138 B7
Cranbrook Canada 150 H5
Crandon U.S.A. 160 F2
Crane TX U.S.A. 166 E2
Crane Lake Canada 151 I5
Cranston KY U.S.A. 164 D4
Cranston RI U.S.A. 165 J3
Cranz Rus. Fed. see Zelenogradsk
Crary Ice Rise Antarctica 188 I1
Crary Mountains Antarctica 188 J1
Crater Lake National Park U.S.A. 156 C4
Crater Peak U.S.A. 158 C1
Craters of the Moon National Monument nat. park U.S.A. 156 E4
Crateús Brazil 177 J5
Crato Brazil 177 K5
Crawford CO U.S.A. 159 J2
Crawford NE U.S.A. 160 C3
Crawford Point Palawan Phil. 82 B4
Crawfordsville U.S.A. 164 B3
Crawfordville FL U.S.A. 163 C6
Crawfordville GA U.S.A. 163 D5
Crawley U.K. 59 G7
Crazy Mountains AK U.S.A. 149 K2
Crazy Mountains U.S.A. 156 F3
Creag Meagaidh mt. U.K. 60 E4
Crécy-en-Ponthieu France 62 B4
Credenhill U.K. 59 E6
Crediton U.K. 59 D8
Cree r. Canada 151 J3
Creel Mex. 157 G8
Cree Lake Canada 151 J3
Creemore Canada 164 E1
Creighton Canada 151 K4
Creil France 62 C5
Creil Neth. 62 F2
Crema Italy 68 C2
Cremlingen Germany 63 K2
Cremona Canada 150 H5
Cremona Italy 68 D2
Crépy-en-Valois France 62 C5
Cres i. Croatia 68 F2
Crescent U.S.A. 156 C4
Crescent City CA U.S.A. 156 B4
Crescent City FL U.S.A. 163 D6
Crescent Group is Paracel Is 80 E3
Crescent Head Australia 138 F3
Crescent Junction U.S.A. 159 I2
Crescent Valley U.S.A. 158 E1
Cressy Australia 138 A7
Cresta, Mount Phil. 82 C2
Crest Hill hill H.K. China 97 [inset]
Crestline U.S.A. 164 D3
Creston Canada 150 G5
Creston IA U.S.A. 160 E3
Creston WY U.S.A. 156 G4
Crestview U.S.A. 163 C6
Creswick Australia 138 A6
Creta i. Greece see Crete
Crete i. Greece 69 K7
Crete U.S.A. 160 D3
Creus, Cap de c. Spain 67 H2
Creuse r. France 66 E3
Creußen Germany 63 L5
Creutzwald France 62 G5
Creuzburg Germany 63 K3
Crevasse Valley Glacier Antarctica 188 J1
Crewe U.K. 59 E5
Crewe U.S.A. 165 F5
Crewkerne U.K. 59 E8
Crianlarich U.K. 60 E4
Criccieth U.K. 59 C6
Criciúma Brazil 179 A5
Crieff U.K. 60 F4
Criffel hill U.K. 60 F6
Criffell hill U.K. see Criffel
Crikvenica Croatia 68 F2
Crillon, Mount AK U.S.A. 149 M4
Crimea pen. Ukr. 112 D1
Crimmitschau Germany 63 M4
Crimond U.K. 60 H3
Cripple Landing AK U.S.A. 148 H3
Crisfield U.S.A. 165 H5
Cristalândia Brazil 177 I6
Cristalina Brazil 179 B2
Cristalino r. Brazil see Mariembero
Cristóbal Colón, Pico mt. Col. 176 D1
Crixás Brazil 179 A1
Crixás Açu r. Brazil 179 A1
Crixás Mirim r. Brazil 179 A1
Crna Gora country Europe see Montenegro
Crni Vrh mt. Serbia 69 J2
Črnomelj Slovenia 68 F2
Croagh Patrick hill Ireland 61 C4
Croajingolong National Park Australia 138 D6
Croatia country Europe 68 G2
Crocker, Banjaran mts Malaysia 85 F1
Crocker Range National Park Malaysia 85 G1
Crockett U.S.A. 161 E6
Crofton KY U.S.A. 164 B5
Crofton NE U.S.A. 160 D3
Croghan U.S.A. 165 H2
Croisilles France 62 C4
Croker r. Nunavut Canada 149 R1
Croker, Cape Canada 164 E1
Croker Island Australia 134 F2
Cromarty U.K. 60 E3
Cromarty Firth est. U.K. 60 E3
Cromer U.K. 59 I6
Crook U.K. 58 F4
Crooked Creek AK U.S.A. 148 H3
Crooked Creek AK U.S.A. 149 L2
Crooked Harbour b. H.K. China 97 [inset]
Crooked Island Bahamas 163 F8
Crooked Island H.K. China 97 [inset]
Crooked Island Passage Bahamas 163 F8
Crookston U.S.A. 160 D2
Crooksville U.S.A. 164 D4
Crookwell Australia 138 D5
Croom Ireland 61 D5
Croppa Creek Australia 138 E2
Crosby U.K. 58 D5
Crosby MN U.S.A. 160 E2
Crosby ND U.S.A. 160 C1
Crosbyton U.S.A. 161 C5
Cross Bay Canada 151 M2
Cross City U.S.A. 163 D6
Cross Fell hill U.K. 58 E4
Crossfield Canada 150 H5
Crossgar U.K. 61 G3
Crosshaven Ireland 61 D6
Cross Inn U.K. 59 C6
Cross Lake Canada 151 L4
Cross Lake l. Canada 151 L4
Cross Lake l. U.S.A. 165 G2
Crossley Lakes N.W.T. Canada 149 O1
Crossmaglen U.K. 61 F3
Crossman Peak U.S.A. 159 F4
Cross Sound sea channel AK U.S.A. 149 M4
Crossville U.S.A. 162 C5
Crotch Lake Canada 165 G1
Croton Italy see Crotone
Crotone Italy 68 G5
Crouch r. U.K. 59 H7
Crow r. Canada 150 E3
Crow Agency U.S.A. 156 G3
Crowal watercourse Australia 138 C3
Crowborough U.K. 59 H7
Crowdy Bay National Park Australia 138 F3
Crowell U.S.A. 161 D5
Crowland U.K. 59 G6
Crowley U.S.A. 161 E6
Crowley, Lake U.S.A. 158 D3
Crown Point IN U.S.A. 164 B3
Crownpoint U.S.A. 159 I4
Crown Point NY U.S.A. 165 I2
Crown Prince Olav Coast Antarctica 188 D2
Crown Princess Martha Coast Antarctica 188 B1
Crows Nest Australia 138 F1
Crowsnest Pass Canada 150 H5
Crowsnest Pass pass Canada 150 H5
Crow Wing r. U.S.A. 160 E2
Croydon Australia 136 C3
Crozet U.S.A. 165 F4
Crozet, Îles is Indian Ocean 185 L9
Crozet Basin sea feature Indian Ocean 185 M8
Crozet Plateau sea feature Indian Ocean 185 K8
Crozon France 66 B2
Cruces Cuba 163 D8
Cruden Bay U.K. 60 H3
Cruillas Mex. 161 D7
Crum U.S.A. 164 D5
Crumlin U.K. 61 F3
Crusheen Ireland 61 D5
Cruz Alta Brazil 178 F3
Cruz del Eje Arg. 178 D4
Cruzeiro Brazil 179 B3
Cruzeiro do Sul Brazil 176 D5
Cruz Grande Mex. 167 F5
Cry Lake B.C. Canada 149 O4
Crysdale, Mount Canada 150 F4
Crystal U.S.A. 159 I3
Crystal City Canada 151 L5
Crystal City U.S.A. 161 D6
Crystal Falls U.S.A. 160 F2
Crystal Lake U.S.A. 164 A2
Crystal River U.S.A. 163 D6
Csongrád Hungary 69 I1
Cửa Lớn, Sông r. Vietnam 87 D5
Cuamba Moz. 123 D5
Cuando r. Angola/Zambia 123 C5
Cuangar Angola 123 B5
Cuango Angola 123 B4
Cuanza r. Angola 123 B4
Cuatro Ciénegas Mex. 166 E3
Cuauhtémoc Chihuahua Mex. 166 D2
Cuautla Mex. 167 F5
Cuba NM U.S.A. 157 G5
Cuba NY U.S.A. 165 F2

▶Cuba country West Indies 169 H4
5th largest island and 5th most populous country in North America.

Cubal Angola 123 B5
Cubango r. Angola/Namibia 123 C5
Cubatão Brazil 179 B3
Cub Hills Canada 151 J4
Çubuk Turkey 112 D2
Cubulco Guat. 167 H6
Cucapa, Sierra mts Mex. 159 F5
Cuchi Angola 123 B5
Cuchilla Grande hills Uruguay 178 E4
Cucuí Brazil 176 E3
Cucurpe Mex. 166 C2
Cúcuta Col. 176 D2
Cudal Australia 138 D4
Cuddalore India 106 C4
Cuddapah India 106 C3
Cuddeback Lake U.S.A. 158 E4
Cue Australia 135 B6
Cuéllar Spain 67 D3
Cuemba Angola 123 B5
Cuenca Ecuador 176 C4
Cuenca Luzon Phil. 82 C3
Cuenca Spain 67 E3
Cuenca, Serranía de mts Spain 67 E3
Cuencamé Mex. 166 E3
Cuernavaca Mex. 168 E5
Cuero U.S.A. 161 D6
Cuervos Mex. 159 F5
Cugir Romania 69 J2
Cuiabá Amazonas Brazil 177 G5
Cuiabá Mato Grosso Brazil 177 G7
Cuiabá r. Brazil 177 G7
Cuicatlan Mex. 167 F5
Cuihua China see Daguan
Cuijiang China see Ninghua
Cuijk Neth. 62 F3
Cuilapa Guat. 167 H6
Cuilcagh hill Ireland/U.K. 61 E3
Cuillin Hills U.K. 60 C3
Cuillin Sound sea chan. U.K. 60 C3
Cuilo Angola 123 B4
Cuiluan China 90 C3
Cuité r. Brazil 179 C2
Cuitláhuac Mex. 167 F5
Cuito r. Angola 123 C5
Cuito Cuanavale Angola 123 B5
Cuitzeo, Laguna de l. Mex. 167 E5
Cujangan i. Phil. 82 C5
Cukai Malaysia 84 C1
Çukurca Turkey 110 A2
Çukurova plat. Turkey 107 B1
Culai Shan mt. Shandong China 95 I4
Cu Lao Cham i. Vietnam 86 E4
Cu Lao Xanh i. Vietnam 87 E4
Culasi Panay Phil. 82 C4
Culcairn Australia 138 C5
Culfa Azer. 113 G3
Culgoa r. Australia 138 C2
Culiacán Mex. 166 D3
Culion Phil. 82 B4
Culion i. Phil. 82 B4
Cullen U.K. 60 G3
Cullen Point Australia 136 C1
Cullera Spain 67 F4
Cullivoe U.K. 60 [inset]
Cullman U.S.A. 163 C5
Cullybackey U.K. 61 F3
Cul Mòr hill U.K. 60 D2
Culpeper U.S.A. 165 G4
Culuene r. Brazil 177 H6
Culver, Point Australia 135 D8
Culverden N.Z. 139 D6
Cumaná Venez. 176 F1
Cumari Brazil 179 A2
Cumbal, Nevado de vol. Col. 176 C3
Cumberland KY U.S.A. 164 D5
Cumberland MD U.S.A. 165 F4
Cumberland VA U.S.A. 165 F5
Cumberland r. U.S.A. 162 C4
Cumberland, Lake U.S.A. 164 C5
Cumberland Lake Canada 151 K4
Cumberland Mountains U.S.A. 164 D5
Cumberland Peninsula Canada 147 L3
Cumberland Plateau U.S.A. 162 C5
Cumberland Point U.S.A. 160 F2
Cumberland Sound sea chan. Canada 147 L3
Cumbernauld U.K. 60 F5
Cumbres de Majalca, Parque Nacional nat. park Mex. 166 D2
Cumbres de Monterey, Parque Nacional nat. park Mex. 167 E3
Cumbum India 106 C3
Cumlosen Germany 63 L1
Cummings U.S.A. 158 B2
Cummins Australia 137 A7
Cummins Range hills Australia 134 D4
Cumnock Australia 138 D4
Cumnock U.K. 60 E5
Cumpas Mex. 166 C2
Çumra Turkey 112 D3
Cumuripa Mex. 166 C2
Cumuruxatiba Brazil 179 D2
Cunagua Cuba see Bolivia
Cunderdin Australia 135 B7
Cunén Guat. 167 H6
Cunene r. Angola 123 B5
also known as Kunene
Cuneo Italy 68 B2
Cung Sơn Vietnam 87 E4
Cunnamulla Australia 138 B2
Cunningsburgh U.K. 60 [inset]
Cupar U.K. 60 F4
Cupica, Golfo de b. Col. 176 C2
Cupula, Pico mt. Mex. 166 C3
Curaçá Brazil 177 K5
Curaçá r. Brazil 176 D4
Curaçao i. Neth. Antilles 169 K6
Curaray r. Ecuador 176 D4
Curdlawidny Lagoon salt flat Australia 137 B6
Curia Switz. see Chur
Curicó Chile 178 B4
Curitiba Brazil 179 A4
Curitibanos Brazil 179 A4
Curlewis Australia 138 E3
Curlew Lake AK U.S.A. 148 G3
Curnamona Australia 137 B6
Currabubula Australia 138 E3
Currais Novos Brazil 177 K5
Curran U.S.A. 164 D1
Currane, Lough l. Ireland 61 B6
Currant U.S.A. 159 F2
Curranyalpa Australia 138 B3
Currawilla Australia 136 C5
Currawinya National Park Australia 138 B2
Currie Australia 132 E5
Currie U.S.A. 159 F1
Currituck U.S.A. 165 G5
Currockbilly, Mount Australia 138 E5
Curry AK U.S.A. 149 J3
Curtis Channel Australia 136 F5
Curtis Island Australia 136 E4
Curtis Island N.Z. 133 I5
Curuá r. Brazil 177 H5
Curup Sumatera Indon. 84 C3
Curupira, Serra mts Brazil/Venez. 176 F3
Cururupu Brazil 177 J4
Curvelo Brazil 179 B2
Curwood, Mount hill U.S.A. 160 F2
Cusco Peru 176 D6
Cushendall U.K. 61 F2
Cushendun U.K. 61 F2
Cushing U.S.A. 161 D4
Cusseta U.S.A. 163 C5
Custer MT U.S.A. 156 G3
Custer SD U.S.A. 160 C3
Cut Bank U.S.A. 156 E2
Cuthbert U.S.A. 163 C6
Cuthbertson Falls Australia 134 F3
Cut Knife Canada 151 I4
Cutler Ridge U.S.A. 163 D7
Cut Off LA U.S.A. 167 H2
Cuttaburra Creek r. Australia 138 B2
Cuttack India 106 E1
Cuvelai Angola 123 B5
Cuxhaven Germany 57 L4
Cuya Chile 176 D7
Cuyahoga Falls U.S.A. 164 E3
Cuyama U.S.A. 158 D4
Cuyama r. U.S.A. 158 C4
Cuyapo Luzon Phil. 82 C3
Cuyo Phil. 82 C4
Cuyo i. Phil. 82 C4
Cuyo East Passage Phil. 82 C4
Cuyo Islands Phil. 82 C4
Cuyo West Passage Phil. 82 C4
Cuyuni r. Guyana 177 G2
Cuyutingni Nicaragua see Kuyu Tingni
Cuzco Peru see Cusco
Cwmbrân U.K. 59 D7
Cyangugu Rwanda 122 C4
Cyclades is Greece 69 K6
Cydonia Greece see Chania
Cygnet U.S.A. 164 D3
Cymru admin. div. U.K. see Wales
Cynthiana U.S.A. 164 C4
Cypress Hills Canada 151 I5
Cyprus country Asia 107 A2
Cyrenaica reg. Libya 121 F2
Cythera i. Greece see Kythira
Czar Canada 151 I4
Czechia country Europe see Czech Republic
Czech Republic country Europe 57 O6
Czernowitz Ukr. see Chernivtsi
Czersk Poland 57 P4
Częstochowa Poland 57 Q5

D

Đa, Sông r. Vietnam see Black
Da'an Jilin China 95 K2
Daanbantayan Phil. 82 C4
Daba Xizang China 99 B7
Ḍabāb, Jabal aḍ mt. Jordan 107 B4
Dabakala Côte d'Ivoire 120 C4
Daban Nei Mongol China 95 I3
Daban Shan mts China 94 E4
Dabao China 96 D2
Daba Shan mts China 97 F1
Dabba China see Daocheng
Dabein Myanmar 86 B3
Dabhoi India 104 C5
Ḍab'ī, Wādī aḍ watercourse Jordan 107 C4
Dabiegai Gansu China 94 C4
Dabie Shan mts China 97 G2
Dablana India 104 C4
Dabola Guinea 120 B3
Dabqig Nei Mongol China 95 G4
Dąbrowa Górnicza Poland 57 Q5
Dabsan Qinghai China 94 C4
Dabsan Hu salt l. Qinghai China 99 F5
Dabs Nur l. China 90 A3
Dabu Guangdong China 97 H3
Dabu Guangxi China see Liucheng
Dabusu Pao l. China see Dabs Nur
Dacca Bangl. see Dhaka
Dachau Germany 57 M6
Dachechang Nei Mongol China 94 E4
Dachengzi Liaoning China 95 I3
Dachuan China see Dazhou
Dacre Canada 165 G1
Dadal Hentiy Mongolia 95 G1
Daday Turkey 112 D2
Dade City U.S.A. 163 D6
Dadeville U.S.A. 163 C5
Dādkān Iran 111 F5
Dadong China see Donggang
Dadra India see Achalpur
Dadu Pak. 111 G5
Daegu S. Korea see Taegu
Daejŏn S. Korea see Taejŏn
Daet Luzon Phil. 82 C3
Dafang China 96 E3
Dafeng China 97 I1
Dafengman China 90 B4
Dafla Hills India 105 H4
Dafoe Canada 151 J5
Dafoe r. Canada 151 M4
Dagana Senegal 120 B3
Dagasuli i. Maluku Indon. 83 C2
Dagcagoin China see Zoigê
Dagcanglhamo Gansu China 94 E5
Dage Hebei China see Fengning
Dagezhen Hebei China see Fengning
Daghmar Oman 110 E6
Dağlıq Qarabağ aut. reg. Azer. 113 G3
Daglung Xizang China 99 E7
Dagma Xizang China 99 F7
Dagö i. Estonia see Hiiumaa
Dagon Myanmar see Rangoon
Dagrag Zangbo r. Xizang China 99 D7
Dagu Tianjin China 95 I4
Daguan China 96 D3
Daguokui Shan hill China 90 C3
Dagupan Luzon Phil. 82 C2
Dagur Qinghai China 94 C4
Dagxoi Sichuan China see Yidun
Dagxoi Sichuan China see Sowa
Dagzê Xizang China 99 E7
Dagzê Co salt l. China 99 D7
Dagzhuka Xizang China 99 E7
Dahadinni r. N.W.T. Canada 149 P3
Dahalach, Isole is Eritrea see Dahlak Archipelago
Dahana des. Saudi Arabia see Ad Dahnā'
Dahe China see Ziyuan
Daheba Qinghai China 94 D5
Daheiding Shan mt. China 90 C3
Dahei Shan mt. Xinjiang China 94 C3
Dahei Shan mts China 90 B4
Dahej India 104 C5
Daheng China 97 H3
Daheyan Xinjiang China see Turpan Zhan
Dahezhen China 90 D3
Da Hinggan Ling mts China 95 I3
Dahlak Archipelago is Eritrea 108 F6
Dahlak Marine National Park Eritrea 108 F6
Daḥl al Furayy well Saudi Arabia 110 B5
Dahlem Germany 62 G4
Dahlenburg Germany 63 K1
Dahm, Ramlat des. Saudi Arabia/Yemen 108 G6
Dahmani Tunisia 68 C7
Dahme Germany 63 N3
Dahn Germany 63 H5
Dahnā' plain Saudi Arabia 110 B5
Dahod India 104 C5
Dahomey country Africa see Benin
Dahongliutan Aksai Chin 99 B6
Dahra Senegal see Dara
Dähre Germany 63 K2
Dahūk Iraq 113 F3
Dahūk, Buḥayrat resr Iraq 113 F3
Dai i. Maluku Indon. 83 D4
Daibosatsu-rei mt. Japan 93 E3
Daicheng Hebei China 95 I4
Daigo Japan 93 G2
Daik Indon. 84 D3
Daik-U Myanmar 86 B3
Đai Lanh, Mui pt Vietnam 87 E4
Dailekh Nepal 105 E3
Dailly U.K. 60 E5
Daimiel Spain 67 E4
Daimon Japan 92 D2
Daimon-tōge pass Japan 93 E2
Daimugen-zan mt. Japan 93 E3
Dainichiga-take vol. Japan 92 C2
Dainichi-gawa r. Japan 92 C2
Dainichi-zan mt. Japan 92 C2
Dainkog China 96 C1
Dainkognubma China 96 C1
Daintree National Park Australia 136 D3
Daiō Japan 92 C4
Daiō-zaki pt Japan 92 C4
Dair, Jebel ed mt. Sudan 108 D7
Dairen Liaoning China see Dalian
Dai-sen vol. Japan 91 D6
Daisetsu-zan Kokuritsu-kōen Japan 90 F4
Daishan China 97 I2
Daitō Ōsaka Japan 92 B4
Daitō Shizuoka Japan 93 E4
Daiya-gawa r. Japan 93 F2
Daiyue Shanxi China see Shanyin
Daiyun Shan mts China 97 H3
Dajan Japan 92 C3
Dajarra Australia 136 B4
Dajin Chuan r. China 96 D2
Dajing Gansu China 94 E4
Da Juh Qinghai China 94 C4

▶Dakar Senegal 120 B3
Capital of Senegal.

Dākhilah, Wāḥāt ad oasis Egypt 108 C4
Dakhla W. Sahara see Ad Dakhla
Dakhla Oasis oasis Egypt see Dākhilah, Wāḥāt ad
Dakituy Rus. Fed. 95 G1
Đak Lăk, Cao Nguyên plat. Vietnam 87 E4
Dakoank India 87 A6
Dakol'ka r. Belarus 53 F5
Dakor India 104 C5
Dakoro Niger 120 D3
Dakota City IA U.S.A. 160 E3
Dakota City NE U.S.A. 160 D3
Đakovica Kosovo see Gjakovë
Đakovo Croatia 68 H2
Daktuy Rus. Fed. 90 B1
Dala Angola 123 C5
Dalaba Guinea 120 B3
Dalad Qi Nei Mongol China see Shulinzhao
Dalai Jilin China see Da'an
Dalain Hob Nei Mongol China 94 E3
Dalai Nur l. China 95 I3
Dālakī Iran 110 C4
Dalälven r. Sweden 55 J6
Dalamamiao Nei Mongol China 95 H3
Dalaman Turkey 69 M6

Dalandzadgad Mongolia 94 F3
Dalanganem Islands Phil. 82 C4
Dalaoba Xinjiang China 98 C4
Dalap-Uliga-Darrit Marshall Is see Delap-Uliga-Djarrit
Dalat Sarawak Malaysia 85 E2
Đa Lat Vietnam 87 E5
Dalatando Angola see N'dalatando
Dalaud India 104 C5
Dalauda India 104 C5
Dalay Mongolia see Bayandalay
Dalbandin Pak. 111 G4
Dalbeattie U.K. 60 F6
Dalbeg Australia 136 D4
Dalby Australia 138 E1
Dalby Isle of Man 58 C4
Dale Hordaland Norway 55 D6
Dale Sogn og Fjordane Norway 55 D6
Dale City U.S.A. 165 G4
Dale Hollow Lake U.S.A. 164 C5
Dalen Neth. 62 G2
Dalet Myanmar 86 A3
Daletme Myanmar 86 A2
Dalfors Sweden 55 I6
Dalgān Iran 110 E5
Dalgety Australia 138 D6
Dalgety r. Australia 135 A6
Dalhart U.S.A. 161 C4
Dalhousie Canada 153 I4
Dalhousie, Cape N.W.T. Canada 149 O1
Dali Shaanxi China 95 G5
Dali Yunnan China 96 D3
Dalian Liaoning China 95 J4
Daliang China see Shunde
Daliang Qinghai China 94 E4
Daliang Shan mts China 96 D2
Dalian Wan b. China 95 J4
Dali He r. China 95 G4
Daliji China 97 H1
Dalin Nei Mongol China 95 J3
Dalinghe Liaoning China see Linghai
Daling He r. China 95 J3
Dalizi China 90 B4
Dalkeith U.K. 60 F5
Dall, Mount AK U.S.A. 148 I3
Dallas OR U.S.A. 156 C3
Dallas TX U.S.A. 161 D5
Dalles City U.S.A. see The Dalles
Dall Island AK U.S.A. 149 N5
Dall Lake AK U.S.A. 148 G3
Dall Mountain AK U.S.A. 149 J2
Dalmā i. U.A.E. 110 D5
Dalmacija reg. Bos.-Herz./Croatia see Dalmatia
Dalmas, Lac l. Canada 153 H3
Dalmatia reg. Bos.-Herz./Croatia 100 A2
Dalmau India 104 E4
Dalmellington U.K. 60 E5
Dalmeny Canada 151 J4
Dalmi India 105 F5
Dal'negorsk Rus. Fed. 90 D3
Dal'nerechensk Rus. Fed. 90 D3
Dal'niye Zelentsy Rus. Fed. 52 H1
Dalny Liaoning China see Dalian
Daloa Côte d'Ivoire 120 C4
▶Dalol Eth. 108 F7
Highest recorded annual mean temperature in the world.
Daloloia Group is P.N.G. 136 E1
Dalou Shan mts China 96 E3
Dalqān well Saudi Arabia 110 B5
Dalry U.K. 60 E5
Dalrymple U.K. 60 E5
Dalrymple, Lake Australia 136 D4
Daltenganj India 105 F4
Dalton Canada 152 D4
Dalton S. Africa 125 J5
Dalton GA U.S.A. 163 C5
Dalton MA U.S.A. 165 I2
Dalton PA U.S.A. 165 H3
Daltonganj India see Daltenganj
Dalton-in-Furness U.K. 58 D4
Daludalu Sumatera Indon. 84 C2
Daluo China 96 D4
Dalupiri i. Phil. 82 C2
Daly r. Australia 134 E3
Daly City U.S.A. 158 B3
Daly River Australia 134 E3
Daly Waters Australia 134 F4
Damagaram Takaya Niger 120 D3
Daman India 106 B1
Daman and Diu union terr. India 106 A1
Damanhūr Egypt 112 C5
Damanhûr Egypt see Damanhūr
Damant Lake Canada 151 J2
Damão India see Daman
Damaqun Shan mts China 95 H3
Damar Sulawesi Indon. 83 C2
Damar i. Maluku Indon. 83 D3
Damar i. Maluku Indon. 83 D4
Damara Cent. Afr. Rep. 122 B3
Damaraland reg. Namibia 123 B6
Damas Syria see Damascus
▶Damascus Syria 107 C3
Capital of Syria.
Damascus U.S.A. 164 E5
Damaturu Nigeria 120 E3
Damāvand Iran 110 D3
Damāvand, Qolleh-ye mt. Iran 110 D3
Dambulla Sri Lanka 106 D5
Damdy Kazakh. 102 B1
Damghan Iran 110 D2
Damianópolis Brazil 179 B1
Damietta Egypt see Dumyāṭ
Daming Hebei China 95 H4
Daming Shan mt. China 97 F4
Dāmiyā Jordan 107 B3
Damjong China 96 B1
Damlasu Turkey 107 D1
Dammam Saudi Arabia 108 H4
Damme Belgium 62 D3
Damme Germany 63 I2
Damoh India 104 D5
Damour Lebanon 107 B3
Dampar, Tasik l. Malaysia 84 C2
Dampelas, Tanjung pt Indon. 83 A2
Dampier Archipelago is Australia 134 B5
Dampier Island P.N.G. see Karkar Island
Dampier Land reg. Australia 134 C4
Dampier Strait P.N.G. 81 L8
Dampir, Selat sea chan. Papua Indon. 83 D3
Damqoq Zangbo r. Xizang China see Maquan He
Dam Qu r. Qinghai China 99 F6
Dâmrei, Chuŏr Phnum mts Cambodia 87 D5
Damroh India 96 B2
Damwâld Neth. see Damwoude
Damwoude Neth. 62 G1
Damxoi Xizang China see Comai
Damxung Xizang China 99 E7
Dana i. Indon. 83 B5
Ḍānā Jordan 107 B4
Dana Nepal 105 E3
Danakil reg. Africa see Denakil
Danané Côte d'Ivoire 120 C4
Đa Năng Vietnam 86 E3
Đa Năng, Vung b. Vietnam 86 E3
Dananhu Xinjiang China 94 C3
Danao Cebu Phil. 82 D4
Danata Turkm. 110 D2
Danau Sentarum, Taman Nasional nature res. Kalimantan Indon. 85 F2
Danba China 96 D2
Danbazhai Shaanxi China 95 G4
Danbury CT U.S.A. 165 I3
Danbury NC U.S.A. 162 D4
Danby U.S.A. 165 I2
Danby Lake U.S.A. 159 F4
Dancheng Henan China 95 H5
Dandaragan Australia 135 A7
Dande Eth. 122 D3
Dandeldhura Nepal 104 E3
Dandeli India 106 B3
Dandong China 91 B4
Dando-san mt. Japan 92 D3
Dandot Pak. 111 I3
Dandridge U.S.A. 162 D4
Dane r. U.K. 58 E5
Daneborg Greenland 189 I2
Danese U.S.A. 164 E5
Danfeng China see Shizong
Dangan Liedao i. China 97 G4
Dangara Tajik. see Danghara
Dangbizhen Rus. Fed. 90 C3
Dangchang Gansu China 94 F5
Dangchengwan Gansu China see Subei
Danger Islands atoll Cook Is see Pukapuka
Danger Point S. Africa 124 D8
Danghara Tajik. 111 H2
Dang He r. Gansu China 94 C3
Danghe Nanshan mts China 94 C4
Dangjin Shankou pass Gansu/Qinghai China 98 F5
Dangla Shan mts Xizang China see Tanggula Shan
Dangqên Xizang China 99 E7
Dângrêk, Chuŏr Phnum mts Cambodia/Thai. see Phanom Dong Rak, Thiu Khao
Dangriga Belize 167 H5
Dangshan Anhui China 95 I5
Dangtu China 97 H2
Daniel's Harbour Canada 153 K4
Danielskuil S. Africa 124 F5
Danilov Rus. Fed. 52 I4
Danilovka Rus. Fed. 53 J6
Danilovskaya Vozvyshennost' hills Rus. Fed. 52 H4
Daning Shanxi China 95 G4
Danjiang China see Leishan
Danjiangkou China 97 F1
Danjiangkou Shuiku resr China 97 F1
Danjo-guntō is Japan 91 C6
Ḍank Oman 110 E6
Dankhar India 104 D2
Dankov Rus. Fed. 53 H5
Dankova, Pik mt. Kyrg. 98 B4
Danlí Hond. 166 [inset] I6
Danmark country Europe see Denmark
Dannebrog Ø i. Greenland see Qillak
Dannenberg (Elbe) Germany 63 L1
Dannenwalde Germany 63 N1
Dannevirke N.Z. 139 F5
Dannhauser S. Africa 125 J5
Dano Burkina 120 C3
Danshui Taiwan see Tanshui
Dansville U.S.A. 165 G2
Danta India 104 C4
Dantan India 105 F5
Dantevada India see Dantewara
Dantewada India see Dantewara
Dantewara India 106 D2
Dantu China see Zhenjiang
Danube r. Europe 57 P6
Also spelt Donau (Austria/Germany), Duna (Hungary), Dunaj (Slovakia), Dunărea (Romania), Dunav (Bulgaria/Croatia/Serbia) or Dunay (Ukraine).
Danube Delta Romania/Ukr. 69 M2
Danubyu Myanmar 86 A3
Danumparai Kalimantan Indon. 85 F2
Danum Valley Conservation Area nature res. Malaysia 85 G1
Danville IL U.S.A. 164 B3
Danville IN U.S.A. 164 B4
Danville KY U.S.A. 164 C5
Danville OH U.S.A. 164 D3
Danville PA U.S.A. 165 G3
Danville VA U.S.A. 164 F5
Danville VT U.S.A. 165 I1
Danxian China see Danzhou
Danzhai China 96 E3
Danzhou Guangxi China 97 F3
Danzhou Hainan China 97 F5
Danzhou Shaanxi China see Yichuan
Danzig Poland see Gdańsk
Danzig, Gulf of Poland/Rus. Fed. see Gdańsk, Gulf of
Dao Panay Phil. 82 C4
Daocheng China 96 D2
Daokou Henan China see Huaxian
Daotanghe Qinghai China 94 E4
Dao Tay Sa is S. China Sea see Paracel Islands
Daoud Alg. see Aïn Beïda
Daoukro Côte d'Ivoire 120 C4
Daozhen China 96 E2
Dapa Phil. 82 D4
Dapaong Togo 120 D3
Dapeng Wan b. H.K. China see Mirs Bay
Daphabum mt. India 105 I4
Dapiak, Mount Mindanao Phil. 82 C4
Dapitan Mindanao Phil. 82 C4
Daporijo India 105 H4
Dapu China see Liucheng
Da Qaidam Zhen Qinghai China 99 F5
Daqiao China 96 D3
Daqing China 90 B3
Daqinghe Hebei China 95 I4
Daqing Shan mts China 95 G3
Daqin Tal Nei Mongol China 95 J3
Daqiu China 97 H3
Dāq Mashī Iran 110 E3
Daqq-e Patargān salt flat Iran 111 F3
Daqq-e Sorkh, Kavīr-e salt flat Iran 110 D3
Daqq-e Tundi, Dasht-e imp. l. Afgh. 111 F3
Daquan Gansu China 98 F4
Daquanwan Xinjiang China 94 C3
Daqu Shan i. China 97 I2
Dara Senegal 120 B3
Dar'ā Syria 107 C3
Dâra, Gebel mt. Egypt see Dārah, Jabal
Dārāb Iran 110 D4
Daraga Luzon Phil. 82 C3
Darāgāh Iran 110 D4
Dārah, Jabal mt. Egypt 112 D6
Daraj Libya 120 E1
Dārākūyeh Iran 110 D4
Dārān Iran 110 C3
Daraut-Korgon Kyrg. 111 I2
Darazo Nigeria 120 E3
Darband, Kūh-e mt. Iran 110 E4
Darband-e Hajjī Boland Turkm. 111 F2
Darbhanga India 105 F4
Darby, Cape AK U.S.A. 148 G2
Darby Mountains AK U.S.A. 148 G2
Darcang China 96 C1
Dardanelle U.S.A. 161 E5
Dardanelles strait Turkey 69 L4
Dardesheim Germany 63 K3
Dardo China see Kangding
Dar el Beida Morocco see Casablanca
Darende Turkey 112 E3
▶Dar es Salaam Tanz. 123 D4
Former capital of Tanzania.
Darfo Boario Terme Italy 68 D2
Dargai Pak. 111 H3
Dargaville N.Z. 139 D2
Dargo Australia 138 C6
Dargo Zangbo r. China 105 F3
Darhan Mongolia 94 F1
Darhan Muminggan Lianheqi Nei Mongol China see Bailingmiao
Darien U.S.A. 163 D6
Darién, Golfo del g. Col. 176 C2
Darién, Parque Nacional de nat. park Panama 166 [inset] K8
Darién, Serranía del mts Panama 166 [inset] K7
Dariga Pak. 111 G5
Darīganga Mongolia 95 H2
Dar'inskiy Kazakh. 98 A2
Darío Nicaragua 166 [inset] I6
Darjeeling India see Darjiling
Darjiling India 105 G4
Darkhazīneh Iran 110 C4
Darlag China 96 C1
▶Darling r. Australia 138 B3
2nd longest river in Oceania, and a major part of the longest (Murray-Darling)
Darling Downs hills Australia 138 D1
Darling Range hills Australia 135 A8
Darlington U.K. 58 F4
Darlington U.S.A. 160 F3
Darlington Point Australia 138 C5
Darlot, Lake salt flat Australia 135 C6
Darłowo Poland 57 P3
Darma Pass China/India 99 C7
Darmstadt Germany 63 I5
Darnah Libya 112 A4
Darnall S. Africa 125 J5
Darnick Australia 138 A4
Darnley, Cape Antarctica 188 E2
Darnley Bay N.W.T. Canada 149 P1
Daroca Spain 67 F3
Daroot-Korgon Kyrg. see Daraut-Korgon
Darovskoy Rus. Fed. 52 J4
Darr watercourse Australia 136 C4
Darreh Bīd Iran 110 E3
Darreh-ye Bāhābād Iran 110 D4
Darreh-ye Shahr Iran 110 B3
Darsi India 106 C3
Dart r. U.K. 59 D8
Dartang Xizang China see Baqên
Dartford U.K. 59 H7
Dartmoor Australia 137 C8
Dartmoor hills U.K. 59 C8
Dartmoor National Park U.K. 59 D8
Dartmouth Canada 153 J5
Dartmouth U.K. 59 D8
Dartmouth, Lake salt flat Australia 137 D5
Dartmouth Reservoir Australia 138 C6
Darton U.K. 58 F5
Daru P.N.G. 81 K8
Daru Sierra Leone 120 B4
Daruba Maluku Indon. 83 D2
Daruga-mine mt. Japan 92 A3
Darvaza Turkm. see Derweze
Darvi Govĭ-Altay Mongolia 94 C2
Darvi Hovd Mongolia 94 C2
Darvoz, Qatorkŭhi mts Tajik. 111 H2
Darwazgai Afgh. 111 G4
Darwen U.K. 58 E5
Darweshan Afgh. 111 G4
▶Darwin Australia 134 E3
Capital of Northern Territory.
Darwin, Monte mt. Chile 178 C8
Daryācheh-ye Orūmīyeh salt l. Iran see Urmia, Lake
Dar'yalyktakyr, Ravnina plain Kazakh. 102 B2
Dar"yoi Amu r. Asia see Amudar'ya
Darzhuo Xizang China 99 E6
Dārzīn Iran 110 E4
Dās i. U.A.E. 110 D5
Dasada India 104 B5
Dashbalbar Mongolia 95 H1
Dashennongjia mt. China see Shennong Ding
Dashetai Nei Mongol China 95 G3
Dashhowuz Turkm. see Daşoguz
Dashiqiao Liaoning China 95 J3
Dashitou Xinjiang China 94 B3
Dashizhai Nei Mongol China 95 J2
Dashkesan Azer. see Daşkäsän
Dashkhovuz Turkm. see Daşoguz
Dashköpri Turkm. see Daşköpri
Dashoguz Daşoguz Turkm. see Daşoguz
Dasht Iran 110 E2
Dashtiari Iran 111 F5
Dashuikeng Ningxia China 94 F4
Dashuiqiao Qinghai China 94 D4
Dashuitou Gansu China 94 F4
Daska Pak. 111 I3
Daşkäsän Azer. 113 G2
Daşköpri Turkm. 111 F2
Daşoguz Turkm. 109 I1
Dasongshu China 96 E3
Daspar mt. Pak. 111 I2
Dassalan i. Phil. 82 C5
Dassel Germany 63 J3
Dastgardān Iran 110 E3
Datadian Kalimantan Indon. 85 F2
Datça Turkey 69 L6
Date Japan 90 F4
Date Creek watercourse U.S.A. 159 G4
Dateland U.S.A. 159 G5
Datha India 104 C5
Datia India 104 D4
Datian China 97 H3
Datian Ding mt. China 97 F4
Datil U.S.A. 159 J4
Datong Anhui China 97 H2
Datong Heilong. China 90 B3
Datong Qinghai China 94 E4
Datong Shanxi China 95 H3
Datong He r. China 94 E4
Datong Shan mts China 94 D4
Dattapur India 106 C1
Datu i. Indon. 85 E2
Datu, Tanjung c. Indon./Malaysia 85 E2
Datuk, Tanjung pt Indon. 84 C3
Datu Piang Mindanao Phil. 82 D5
Daudkandi Bangl. 105 G5
Daugava r. Latvia 55 N8
Daugavpils Latvia 55 O9
Daulatabad India 106 B2
Daulatabad Iran see Maläyer
Daulatpur Bangl. 105 G5
Daun Germany 62 G4
Daungyu r. Myanmar 86 A2
Dauphin Canada 151 K5
Dauphiné reg. France 66 G4
Dauphiné, Alpes du mts France 66 G4
Dauphin Island AL U.S.A. 167 H2
Dauphin Lake Canada 151 L5
Daurie Creek r. Australia 135 A6
Dauriya Rus. Fed. 95 I1
Daurskiy Khrebet mts Rus. Fed. 95 G1
Dausa India 104 D4
Dâu Tiêng, Hô resr Vietnam 87 D5
Dava U.K. 60 F3
Däväçi Azer. 113 H2
Davanagere India see Davangere
Davangere India 106 B3
Davao Mindanao Phil. 82 D5
Davao Gulf Mindanao Phil. 82 D5
Dāvarī Iran 110 E5
Dāvarzan Iran 110 E2
Davel S. Africa 125 I4
Davenport IA U.S.A. 160 F3
Davenport WA U.S.A. 156 D3
Davenport Downs Australia 136 C5
Davenport Range hills Australia 134 F5
Daventry U.K. 59 F6
Daveyton S. Africa 125 I4
David Panama 166 [inset] J7
David City U.S.A. 160 D3
Davidson Canada 151 J5
Davidson, Mount hill Australia 134 E5
Davidson Mountains AK U.S.A. 149 L1
Davis research station Antarctica 188 E2
Davis r. Australia 134 C5
Davis i. Myanmar see Than Kyun
Davis CA U.S.A. 158 C2
Davis WV U.S.A. 164 F4
Davis, Mount hill U.S.A. 164 F4
Davis Bay Antarctica 188 G2
Davis Dam U.S.A. 159 F4
Davis Inlet (abandoned) Canada 153 J3
Davis Sea Antarctica 188 F2
Davis Strait Canada/Greenland 147 M3
Davlekanovo Rus. Fed. 51 Q5
Davos Switz. 66 I3
Davy Lake Canada 151 I3
Dawa Liaoning China 95 J3
Dawa Co l. Xizang China 99 D7
Dawa Wenz r. Eth. 122 E3
Dawaxung Xizang China 99 D7
Dawê China 96 D2
Dawei Myanmar see Tavoy
Dawei r. mouth Myanmar see Tavoy
Daweloor i. Maluku Indon. 83 D4
Dawera i. Maluku Indon. 83 D4
Dawna Range mts Myanmar/Thai. 86 B3
Dawna Taungdan mts Myanmar/Thai. see Dawna Range
Dawo Qinghai China see Maqên
Dawqah Oman 109 H6
Dawson r. Australia 136 E4
Dawson Y.T. Canada 149 M2
Dawson GA U.S.A. 163 C6
Dawson ND U.S.A. 160 D2
Dawson, Mount Canada 150 G5
Dawson Bay Canada 151 K4
Dawson Creek Canada 150 F4
Dawson Inlet Canada 151 M2
Dawson Range mts Y.T. Canada 149 L3
Dawsons Landing Canada 150 E5
Dawu Hubei China 97 G2
Dawu Taiwan see Tawu
Dawukou Ningxia China see Shizuishan
Dawu Shan hill China 97 G2
Dawusi Qinghai China 99 E5
Dax France 66 D5
Daxian China see Dazhou
Daxiang Ling mts China 96 D2
Daxihaizi Shuiku resr China 98 D4
Daxin China 96 E4
Daxing Yunnan China see Ninglang
Daxing Yunnan China see Lüchun
Daxue Shan mt. China 94 D4
Da Xueshan mts China 96 D2
Dayan China see Lijiang
Dayang r. India 99 F8
Dayangshu Nei Mongol China 95 K1
Dayan Nuur l. Mongolia 94 B1
Dayao China 96 D3
Dayao Shan mts China 97 F4
Daye China 97 G2
Daying China 96 E2
Daying Jiang r. China 96 C3
Dayishan Jiangsu China see Guanyun
Dāykundī Afgh. 111 G3
Daylesford Australia 138 B6
Daylight Pass U.S.A. 158 E3
Dayong China see Zhangjiajie
Dayr Abū Sa'īd Jordan 107 B3
Dayr az Zawr Syria 113 F4
Dayr Ḥāfir Syria 107 C1
Daysland Canada 151 H4
Dayton OH U.S.A. 164 C4
Dayton TN U.S.A. 162 C5
Dayton TX U.S.A. 167 G2
Dayton VA U.S.A. 165 F4
Dayton WA U.S.A. 156 D3
Daytona Beach U.S.A. 163 D6
Dayu Kalimantan Indon. 85 F3
Dayu Ling mts China 97 G3
Da Yunhe canal China 95 I5
Dayyer Iran 110 C5
Dayyīna i. U.A.E. 110 D5
Dazhai Shanxi China 95 H4
Dazhongji China see Dafeng
Dazhou China 96 E2
Dazhou Dao i. China 97 F5
Dazhu China 96 E2
Dazigou Xinjiang China 94 C3
Dazu China 96 E2
Dazu Rock Carvings tourist site China 96 E2
Ddhaw Gro Habitat Protection Area nature res. Y.T. Canada 149 N3
De Aar S. Africa 124 G6
Dead r. Ireland 61 D5
Deadhorse AK U.S.A. 149 J1
Deadman Lake U.S.A. 158 E4
Deadman's Cay Bahamas 163 F8
Dead Mountains U.S.A. 159 F4
▶Dead Sea salt l. Asia 107 B4
Lowest point in the world and in Asia.
Deadwood U.S.A. 160 C2
Deakin Australia 135 E7
Deal U.K. 59 I7
Dealesville S. Africa 125 G5
De'an China 97 G2
Dean, Forest of U.K. 59 E7
Deán Funes Arg. 178 D4
Deanuvuotna inlet Norway see Tanafjorden
Dearborn U.S.A. 164 D2
Dearne r. U.K. 58 F5
Deary U.S.A. 156 D3
Dease r. B.C. Canada 149 O4
Dease Arm b. N.W.T. Canada 149 Q2
Dease Inlet AK U.S.A. 148 I1
Dease Lake B.C. Canada 149 O4
Dease Lake B.C. Canada 149 O4
Dease Strait Canada 146 H3
▶Death Valley depr. U.S.A. 158 E3
Lowest point in the Americas.
Death Valley Junction U.S.A. 158 E3
Death Valley National Park U.S.A. 158 E3
Deauville France 66 E2
Deaver U.S.A. 156 F3
De Baai S. Africa see Port Elizabeth
Debak Sarawak Malaysia 85 E2
Debao China 96 E4
Debar Macedonia 69 I4
Debauch Mountain AK U.S.A. 148 H2
Debden Canada 151 J4
Debenham U.K. 59 I6
De Beque U.S.A. 159 I2
De Biesbosch, Nationaal Park nat. park Neth. 62 E3
Débo, Lac l. Mali 120 C3
Deborah, Mount AK U.S.A. 149 K3
Deborah East, Lake salt flat Australia 135 B7
Deborah West, Lake salt flat Australia 135 B7
Debrecen Hungary 69 I1
Debre Markos Eth. 108 E7
Debre Tabor Eth. 108 E7
Debre Zeyit Eth. 122 D3
Deçan Kosovo 69 I3
Dečani Kosovo see Deçan
Decatur AL U.S.A. 163 C5
Decatur GA U.S.A. 163 C5
Decatur IL U.S.A. 160 F4
Decatur IN U.S.A. 164 C3
Decatur MI U.S.A. 164 C2
Decatur MS U.S.A. 161 F5
Decatur TX U.S.A. 161 D5
▶Deccan plat. India 106 C2
Plateau making up most of southern and central India.
Deception Bay Australia 138 F1
Dechang China 96 D3
Děčín Czech Rep. 57 O5
Decker U.S.A. 156 G3
Decorah U.S.A. 160 F3
Dedap i. Indon. see Penasi, Pulau
Dedaye Myanmar 86 A3
Deddington U.K. 59 F7
Dedegöl Dağları mts Turkey 69 N6
Dedeleben Germany 63 K2
Dedelstorf Germany 63 K2
Dedemsvaart Neth. 62 G2
Dedo de Deus mt. Brazil 179 B4
Dédougou Burkina 120 C3
Dedovichi Rus. Fed. 52 F4
Dedu China see Wudalianchi
Dee r. Ireland 61 F4
Dee est. U.K. 58 D5
Dee r. England/Wales U.K. 59 D5
Dee r. Scotland U.K. 60 G3
Deel r. Ireland 61 D5
Deel r. Ireland 61 F4
Deep Bay H.K. China 97 [inset]
Deep Creek Lake U.S.A. 164 F4
Deep Creek Range mts U.S.A. 159 G2
Deep River Canada 152 F5
Deepwater Australia 138 E2
Deeri Somalia 122 E3
Deering AK U.S.A. 148 G2
Deering, Mount Australia 135 E6
Deer Island AK U.S.A. 148 G5
Deer Lake Canada 151 M4
Deer Lake l. Canada 151 M4
Deer Lodge U.S.A. 156 E3
Deerpass Bay N.W.T. Canada 149 Q2
Deesa India see Disa
Deeth U.S.A. 156 E4
Defeng China see Liping
Defensores del Chaco, Parque Nacional nat. park Para. 178 D2
Defiance U.S.A. 164 C3
Defiance Plateau U.S.A. 159 I4
De Funiak Springs FL U.S.A. 167 I2
Degana India 104 C4
Degeh Bur Eth. 122 E3
Degema Nigeria 120 D4
Deggendorf Germany 63 M6
Degh r. Pak. 111 I4
De Grey r. Australia 134 B5
De Groote Peel, Nationaal Park nat. park Neth. 62 F3
Degtevo Rus. Fed. 53 I6
De Haan Belgium 62 D3
Dehak Iran 111 F4
De Hamert, Nationaal Park nat. park Neth. 62 G3
Deh-Dasht Iran 110 C4
Deheq Iran 110 C3
Dehestān Iran 110 D4
Deh Golān Iran 110 B3
Dehgon Afgh. 111 F3
Dehi Afgh. 111 G3
Dehkūyeh Iran 110 D5
Dehlorān Iran 110 B3
De Hoge Veluwe, Nationaal Park nat. park Neth. 62 F2
De Hoop Nature Reserve S. Africa 124 E8
Dehqonobod Uzbek. 111 G2
Dehra Dun India 104 D3
Dehradun India see Dehra Dun
Dehri India 105 F4
Deh Shū Afgh. 111 F4
Deim Zubeir Sudan 121 F4
Deinze Belgium 62 D4
Deir-ez-Zor Syria see Dayr az Zawr
Dej Romania 69 J1
Deji Xizang China see Rinbung
Dejiang China 97 F2
De Jouwer Neth. see Joure
De Kalb IL U.S.A. 160 F3
De Kalb MS U.S.A. 161 F5
De Kalb TX U.S.A. 161 E5
De Kalb Junction U.S.A. 165 H1
De-Kastri Rus. Fed. 90 F2
Dekemhare Eritrea 108 E6
Dekhkanabad Uzbek. see Dehqonobod
Dekina Nigeria 120 D4
Dékoa Cent. Afr. Rep. 122 B3
De Koog Neth. 62 E1
De Kooy Neth. 62 E2
Delaki Indon. 83 C5

Delamar Lake U.S.A. 159 F3
De Land U.S.A. 163 D6
Delano U.S.A. 158 D4
Delano Peak U.S.A. 159 G2

▶Delap-Uliga-Djarrit Marshall Is 186 H5
Capital of the Marshall Islands, on Majuro atoll.

Delārām Afgh. 111 F3
Delareyville S. Africa 125 G4
Delarof Islands AK U.S.A. 149 [inset]
Delaronde Lake Canada 151 J4
Delavan U.S.A. 152 C6
Delaware U.S.A. 164 D3
Delaware r. U.S.A. 165 H4
Delaware state U.S.A. 165 H4
Delaware, East Branch r. U.S.A. 165 H3
Delaware Bay U.S.A. 165 H4
Delaware Lake U.S.A. 164 D3
Delaware Water Gap National Recreational Area park U.S.A. 165 H3
Delay r. Canada 153 H2
Delbarton U.S.A. 164 D5
Delbrück Germany 63 I3
Delburne Canada 150 H4
Dêlêg Xizang China 99 D7
Delegate Australia 138 D6
De Lemmer Neth. see Lemmer
Delémont Switz. 66 H3
Delevan CA U.S.A. 158 B2
Delevan NY U.S.A. 165 F2
Delfinópolis Brazil 179 B3
Delft Neth. 62 E2
Delfzijl Neth. 62 G1
Delgada, Point U.S.A. 158 A1
Delgado, Cabo c. Moz. 123 E5
Delger Mongolia 94 D2
Delgerhaan Töv Mongolia 94 F2
Delgerhangay Mongolia 94 F2
Delgermörön Mongolia see Hüreemaral
Delger Mörön r. Mongolia 94 E1
Delgertsogt Mongolia 94 F2
Delhi Canada 164 E2
Delhi Qinghai China 94 D4

▶Delhi India 104 D3
3rd most populous city in Asia and 6th in the world.

Delhi admin. div. India 99 B7
Delhi CO U.S.A. 157 G5
Delhi LA U.S.A. 161 F5
Delhi NY U.S.A. 165 H2
Deli i. Indon. 84 D4
Delice Turkey 112 D3
Delice r. Turkey 112 D2
Delījān Iran 110 C3
Déline N.W.T. Canada 149 Q2
Delingha Qinghai China see Delhi
Delisle Canada 151 J5
Delitua Sumatera Indon. 84 B2
Delitzsch Germany 63 M3
Delligsen Germany 63 J3
Dell Rapids U.S.A. 160 D3
Dellys Alg. 67 H5
Del Mar U.S.A. 158 E5
Delmenhorst Germany 63 I1
Delnice Croatia 68 F2
Del Norte U.S.A. 157 G5
Delong China see Ande
De-Longa, Ostrova is Rus. Fed. 77 Q2
De Long Islands Rus. Fed. see De-Longa, Ostrova
De Long Mountains AK U.S.A. 148 G1
De Long Strait Rus. Fed. see Longa, Proliv
Deloraine Canada 151 K5
Delphi U.S.A. 164 B3
Delphos U.S.A. 164 C3
Delportshoop S. Africa 124 G5
Delray Beach U.S.A. 163 D7
Delrey U.S.A. 164 A3
Del Río Mex. 166 C2
Del Rio U.S.A. 161 C6
Delsbo Sweden 55 J6
Delta CO U.S.A. 159 I2
Delta OH U.S.A. 164 C3
Delta UT U.S.A. 159 G2
Delta r. AK U.S.A. 149 K2
Delta Downs Australia 136 C3
Delta Junction AK U.S.A. 149 K2
Deltona U.S.A. 163 D6
Delungra Australia 138 E2
Delüün Bayan-Ölgiy Mongolia 94 B2
Delvin Ireland 61 E4
Delvinë Albania 69 I5
Delwara India 104 C4
Demak Jawa Indon. 85 E4
Demarcation Point pt AK U.S.A. 149 L1
Demavend mt. Iran see Damāvand, Qolleh-ye
Demba Dem. Rep. Congo 123 C4
Dembī Dolo Eth. 108 D8
Demerara Guyana see Georgetown
Demerara Abyssal Plain sea feature S. Atlantic Ocean 184 E5
Demidov Rus. Fed. 53 F5
Deming U.S.A. 157 G6
Demirci Turkey 69 M5
Demirköy Turkey 69 L4
Demirtaş Turkey 107 A1
Demmin Germany 57 N4
Demopolis U.S.A. 163 C5
Demotte U.S.A. 164 B3
Dempo, Gunung vol. Indon. 84 C4
Dempster Highway Canada 149 M2
Dêmqog China 104 D2
Demta Indon. 81 K7
Dem'yanovo Rus. Fed. 52 J3
De Naawte S. Africa 124 E6
Denakil reg. Africa 122 E2
Denali AK U.S.A. 149 K3
Denali AK U.S.A. see McKinley, Mount
Denali Highway AK U.S.A. 149 K3
Denali National Park and Preserve AK U.S.A. 149 J3
Denan Eth. 122 E3
Denbigh Canada 165 G1
Denbigh U.K. 58 D5
Denbigh, Cape AK U.S.A. 148 G2
Den Bosch Neth. see 's-Hertogenbosch
Den Burg Neth. 62 E1
Den Chai Thai. 86 C3
Dendang Indon. 85 D3
Dendâra Mauritania 120 C3
Dendermonde Belgium 62 E3
Dendi mt. Eth. 122 D3
Dendre r. Belgium 62 E3
Dendron S. Africa see Mogwadi
Denezhkin Kamen', Gora mt. Rus. Fed. 51 R3
Denges Passage Palau 82 [inset]
Dengfeng Henan China 95 H5
Dênggar Xizang China 99 D7
Dêngka Gansu China see Têwo
Dêngkagoin Gansu China see Têwo
Dengkou Nei Mongol China 95 F3
Dêngqên Xizang China 99 F7
Dengta China 97 G4
Dengxian China see Dengzhou
Dêngzê Xizang China 99 C6
Dengzhou China 97 G1
Dengzhou Shandong China see Penglai
Den Haag Neth. see The Hague
Denham Australia 135 A6
Denham r. Australia 134 E3
Den Ham Neth. 62 G2
Denham Range mts Australia 136 E4
Den Helder Neth. 62 E2
Denholm Canada 151 I4
Denia Spain 67 G4
Denial Bay Australia 137 A7
Deniliquin Australia 138 B5
Denio U.S.A. 156 D4
Denison IA U.S.A. 160 E3
Denison TX U.S.A. 161 D5
Denison, Cape Antarctica 188 G2
Denison Plains Australia 134 E4
Deniyaya Sri Lanka 106 D5
Denizli Turkey 69 M6
Denman Australia 138 E4
Denman Glacier Antarctica 188 F2
Denmark Australia 132 B5
Denmark country Europe 55 G8
Denmark U.S.A. 164 B1
Denmark Strait Greenland/Iceland 50 A2
Dennis, Lake salt flat Australia 134 E5
Dennison IL U.S.A. 164 B4
Dennison OH U.S.A. 164 E3
Denny U.K. 60 F4
Denov Uzbek. 111 G2
Denow Uzbek. see Denov
Denpasar Bali Indon. 85 F5
Densongi Sulawesi Indon. 83 B3
Denton MD U.S.A. 165 H4
Denton TX U.S.A. 161 D5
D'Entrecasteaux, Point Australia 135 A8
D'Entrecasteaux, Récifs reef New Caledonia 133 G3
D'Entrecasteaux Islands P.N.G. 132 F2
D'Entrecasteaux National Park Australia 135 A8

▶Denver CO U.S.A. 156 G5
Capital of Colorado.

Denver PA U.S.A. 165 G3
Denys r. Canada 152 F3
Deo India 105 F4
Deoband India 104 D3
Deogarh Jharkhand India see Deoghar
Deogarh Orissa India 105 F5
Deogarh Rajasthan India 104 C4
Deogarh Uttar Prad. India 104 D4
Deogarh mt. India 105 E5
Deoghar India 105 F4
Deolali India 106 B2
Deoli India 105 F5
Deori Madh. Prad. India 104 D5
Deoria India 105 E4
Deosai, Plains of Pak. 104 C2
Deosil India 105 E5
Deothang Bhutan 105 G4
De Panne Belgium 62 C3
De Pere U.S.A. 164 A1
Deposit U.S.A. 165 H2
Depsang Point hill Aksai Chin 99 B6
Deputatskiy Rus. Fed. 77 O3
Dêqên Xizang China see Dagzê
Dêqên Xizang China 99 E7
Dêqên Xizang China 99 E7
De Queen U.S.A. 161 E5
De Quincy LA U.S.A. 167 G2
Dera Ghazi Khan Pak. 111 H4
Dera Ismail Khan Pak. 111 H4
Derajat reg. Pak. 111 H4
Derawar Fort Pak. 111 H4
Derbent Rus. Fed. 113 H2
Derbesiye Turkey see Şenyurt
Derbur China 90 A2
Derby Australia 134 C4
Derby U.K. 59 F6
Derby CT U.S.A. 165 I3
Derby KS U.S.A. 161 D4
Derby NY U.S.A. 165 F2
Dereham U.K. 59 H6
Derg r. Ireland/U.K. 61 E3
Derg, Lough l. Ireland 61 D5
Dergachi Rus. Fed. 53 K6
Dergachi Ukr. see Derhachi
Derhachi Ukr. 53 H6
De Ridder U.S.A. 161 E6
Derik Turkey 113 F3
Derm Namibia 124 D2
Derna Libya see Darnah
Dernberg, Cape Namibia 124 B4
Dêrong China 96 C2
Derravaragh, Lough l. Ireland 61 E4
Derry U.K. see Londonderry
Derry U.S.A. 165 J2
Derryveagh Mts hills Ireland 61 D3
Derst Nei Mongol China 95 H3
Derstei Nei Mongol China 94 E3
Dêrub Xizang China 99 B6
Derudeb Sudan 108 E6
De Rust S. Africa 124 F7
Derventa Bos.-Herz. 68 G2
Derwent r. England U.K. 58 F6
Derwent r. England U.K. 58 G5
Derwent Water l. U.K. 58 D4
Derweze Turkm. 110 E1
Derzhavinsk Kazakh. 102 C1
Derzhavinskiy Kazakh. see Derzhavinsk
Desaguadero r. Arg. 178 C4
Désappointement, Îles du is Fr. Polynesia 187 K6
Desatoya Mountains U.S.A. 158 E2
Deschambault Lake Canada 151 K4
Deschutes r. U.S.A. 156 C3
Desē Eth. 122 D2
Deseado Arg. 178 C7
Deseado r. Arg. 178 C7
Desemboque Mex. 166 B2
Desengaño, Punta pt Arg. 178 C7
Deseret U.S.A. 159 G2
Deseret Peak U.S.A. 159 G1
Deseronto Canada 165 G1
Desert Canal Pak. 111 H4
Desert Center U.S.A. 159 F5
Desert Lake U.S.A. 159 F3
Desert View U.S.A. 159 H3
Deshler U.S.A. 164 D3
Desierto Central de Baja California, Parque Natural del nature res. Mex. 166 B2
De Smet U.S.A. 160 D2

▶Des Moines IA U.S.A. 160 E3
Capital of Iowa.

Des Moines NM U.S.A. 161 C4
Des Moines r. U.S.A. 160 F3
Desna r. Rus. Fed./Ukr. 53 F6
Desnogorsk Rus. Fed. 53 G5
Desolación, Isla i. Chile 178 B8
Desolation Point Phil. 82 D4
Despen Rus. Fed. 94 C1
Des Plaines U.S.A. 164 B2
Dessau Germany 63 M3
Dessye Eth. see Desē
Destelbergen Belgium 62 D3
Destruction Bay Canada 189 A2
Desvres France 62 B4
Detah Canada 150 H2
Dete Zimbabwe 123 C5
Detmold Germany 63 I3
Detrital Wash watercourse U.S.A. 159 F3
Detroit U.S.A. 164 D2
Detroit Lakes U.S.A. 160 E2
Dett Zimbabwe see Dete
Deua National Park Australia 138 D5
Deuben Germany 63 M3
Deurne Neth. 62 F3
Deutschland country Europe see Germany
Deutschlandsberg Austria 57 O7
Deutzen Germany 63 M3
Deva Romania 69 J2
Deva U.K. see Chester
Devana U.K. see Aberdeen
Devangere India see Davangere
Devanhalli India 106 C3
Deve Bair pass Bulg./Macedonia see Velbŭzhdki Prokhod
Develi Turkey 112 D3
Deventer Neth. 62 G2
Deveron r. U.K. 60 G3
Devét Skal hill Czech Rep. 57 P6
Devgarh India 106 B2
Devghar India see Deoghar
Devikot India 104 B4
Devil Mountain hill AK U.S.A. 148 F2
Devil's Bridge U.K. 59 D6
Devil's Gate pass U.S.A. 158 D2
Devils Lake U.S.A. 160 D1
Devil's Lake l. TX U.S.A. 167 E2
Devil's Paw mt. AK U.S.A. 149 N4
Devil's Peak U.S.A. 158 D3
Devil's Point Bahamas 163 F7
Devil's Thumb mt. Canada/U.S.A. 149 N4
Devine U.S.A. 161 D6
Devizes U.K. 59 F7
Devli India 104 C4
Devnya Bulg. 69 L3
Devon r. U.K. 60 F4
Devon Island Canada 147 I2
Devonport Australia 137 [inset]
Devrek Turkey 69 N4
Devrukh India 106 B2
Dewa, Tanjung pt Indon. 84 A2
Dewakang Besar i. Indon. 85 G4
Dewas India 104 D5
De Weerribben, Nationaal Park nat. park Neth. 62 G2
Dewetsdorp S. Africa 125 H5
De Witt AR U.S.A. 161 F5
De Witt IA U.S.A. 160 F3
Dewsbury U.K. 58 F5
Dexing Jiangxi China 97 H2
Dêxing Xizang China 99 F7
Dexter ME U.S.A. 165 K1
Dexter MI U.S.A. 164 D2
Dexter MO U.S.A. 161 F4
Dexter NM U.S.A. 157 G6
Dexter NY U.S.A. 165 G1
Deyang China 96 E2
Dey-Dey Lake salt flat Australia 135 E7
Deyhuk Iran 110 E3
Deyong, Tanjung pt Indon. 81 J8
Dez r. Iran 108 G3
Dezadeash Lake Y.T. Canada 149 M3
Dezfūl Iran 110 C3
Dezhneva, Mys c. Rus. Fed. 148 E2
Dezhou Shandong China 95 I4
Dezhou Sichuan China see Dechang
Dezh Shāhpūr Iran see Marīvān
Dhabarau India 105 E4
Dhahab, Wādī adh r. Syria 107 B3
Dhāhiriya West Bank 107 B4
Dhahran Saudi Arabia 110 C5

▶Dhaka Bangl. 105 G5
Capital of Bangladesh. 10th most populous city in the world.

Dhalbhum reg. India 105 F5
Dhalgaon India 106 B2
Dhamār Yemen 108 F7
Dhamoni India 104 D4
Dhamtari India 106 D1
Dhana Pak. 111 H5
Dhana Sar Pak. 111 H4
Dhanbad India 105 F5
Dhanera India 104 C4
Dhang Range mts Nepal 105 E3
Dhankuta Nepal 105 F4
Dhansia India 104 C3
Dhar India 104 C5
Dhar Adrar hills Mauritania 120 B3
Dharampur India 106 B1
Dharan Bazar Nepal 105 F4
Dharashiv India see Osmanabad
Dhari India 104 B5
Dharmapuri India 106 C3
Dharmavaram India 106 C3
Dharmsala Hima. Prad. India see Dharmshala
Dharmsala Orissa India 105 F5
Dharmshala India 104 D2
Dharnaoda India 104 D4
Dhar Oualâta hills Mauritania 120 C3
Dhar Tîchît hills Mauritania 120 C3
Dharug National Park Australia 138 E4
Dharur India 106 C2
Dharwad India 106 B3
Dharwar India see Dharwad
Dharwas India 104 D2
Dhasan r. India 104 D4
Dhāt al Ḥājj Saudi Arabia 112 E5

▶Dhaulagiri mt. Nepal 105 E3
7th highest mountain in the world and in Asia.

Dhaulpur India see Dholpur
Dhaura India 104 D4
Dhaurahra India 104 E4
Dhawlagiri mt. Nepal see Dhaulagiri
Dhebar Lake India see Jaisamand Lake
Dhekelia Sovereign Base Area military base Cyprus 107 A2
Dhemaji India 105 H4
Dhenkanal India 106 E1
Dhībān Jordan 107 B4
Dhidhimótikhon Greece see Didymoteicho
Dhing India 105 H4
Dhirwah, Wādī adh watercourse Jordan 107 C4
Dhodhekánisos is Greece see Dodecanese
Dhola India 104 B5
Dholera India 104 C5
Dholpur India 104 D4
Dhomokós Greece see Domokos
Dhone India 106 C3
Dhoraji India 104 B5
Dhori India 104 B5
Dhrangadhra India 104 B5
Dhubāb Yemen 108 F7
Dhubri India 105 G4
Dhuburi India see Dhubri
Dhudial Pak. 111 I3
Dhule India 106 B1
Dhulia India see Dhule
Dhulian India 105 F4
Dhulian Pak. 111 I3
Dhuma India 104 D5
Dhund r. India 104 D4
Dhurwai India 104 D4
Dhuusa Marreeb Somalia 122 E3
Dia i. Greece 69 K7
Diablo, Mount U.S.A. 158 C3
Diablo, Picacho del mt. Mex. 166 B2
Diablo Range mts U.S.A. 158 C3
Diagbe Dem. Rep. Congo 122 C3
Diamante Arg. 178 D4
Diamantina watercourse Australia 136 B5
Diamantina Brazil 179 C2
Diamantina, Chapada plat. Brazil 179 C1
Diamantina Deep sea feature Indian Ocean 185 O8
Diamantina Gates National Park Australia 136 C4
Diamantino Brazil 177 G6
Diamond Islets Australia 136 E3
Diamond Peak U.S.A. 159 F2
Dianbai China 97 F4
Diancang Shan mt. China 96 D3
Dian Chi l. China 96 D3
Diandioumé Mali 120 C3
Diane Bank sea feature Australia 136 E2
Dianjiang China 96 E2
Dianópolis Brazil 177 I6
Dianyang China see Shidian
Diaobingshan Liaoning China 95 J3
Diaokou Shandong China 95 I4
Diaoling China 90 C3
Diapaga Burkina 120 D3
Diarizos r. Cyprus 107 A2
Diavolo, Mount hill India 87 A4
Diaz Point Namibia 124 B4
Dibaya Dem. Rep. Congo 123 C4
Dibella well Niger 120 E3
Dibeng S. Africa 124 F4
Dibete Botswana 125 H2
Dibrugarh India 105 H4
Dibse Syria see Dibsī
Dibsī Syria 107 D2
Dickens U.S.A. 161 C5
Dickinson U.S.A. 160 C2
Dicle r. Turkey 113 F3 see Tigris
Dīdēsa Wenz r. Eth. 122 D3
Didicas i. Phil. 82 C2
Didiéni Mali 120 C3
Didsbury Canada 150 H5
Didwana India 104 C4
Didymoteicho Greece 69 L4
Die France 66 G4
Dieblich Germany 63 H4
Diébougou Burkina 120 C3
Dieburg Germany 63 I5
Diedenhofen France see Thionville
Diefenbaker, Lake Canada 151 I5
Diego de Almagro, Isla i. Chile 178 A8
Diégo Suarez Madag. see Antsirañana
Diekirch Lux. 62 G5
Diéma Mali 120 C3
Diemel r. Germany 63 J3
Điện Biên Vietnam see Điện Biên Phu
Điện Biên Phu Vietnam 86 C2
Diên Châu Vietnam 86 D3
Diên Khanh Vietnam 87 E4
Diepholz Germany 63 I2
Dieppe France 62 B5
Dierks U.S.A. 161 E5
Di'er Songhua Jiang r. China 90 B3
Diessen Neth. 62 F3
Diest Belgium 62 F4
Dietikon Switz. 66 I3
Dietrich Camp AK U.S.A. 149 J2
Diez Germany 63 I4
Diffa Niger 120 E3
Digby Canada 153 I5
Diggi India 104 C4
Diglur India 106 C2
Digne France see Digne-les-Bains
Digne-les-Bains France 66 H4
Digoin France 66 F3
Digollorin Point Luzon Phil. 82 C2
Digos Mindanao Phil. 82 D5
Digras India 106 C1
Digri Pak. 111 H5
Digul r. Indon. 81 K8
Diguojiadan Qinghai China 94 D4
Digya National Park Ghana 120 C4
Dihang r. India 105 H4 see Brahmaputra
Dihōk Iraq see Dahūk
Dihourse, Lac l. Canada 153 I2
Diinsoor Somalia 122 E3
Dijon France 66 G3
Dik Chad 121 E4
Diken India 104 C4
Dikhil Djibouti 108 F7
Dikho r. India 99 F8
Dikili Turkey 69 L5
Diklosmta mt. Rus. Fed. 53 J8
Diksmuide Belgium 62 C3
Dikson Rus. Fed. 76 J2
Dīla Eth. 122 D3
Dilaram Iran 110 E4

▶Dili East Timor 83 C5
Capital of East Timor.

Di Linh Vietnam 87 E5
Dillenburg Germany 63 I4
Dilley U.S.A. 161 D6
Dillingen (Saar) Germany 62 G5
Dillingen an der Donau Germany 57 M6
Dillingham AK U.S.A. 148 H4
Dillon r. Canada 151 I4
Dillon MT U.S.A. 156 E3
Dillon SC U.S.A. 163 E5
Dillwyn U.S.A. 165 F5
Dilolo Dem. Rep. Congo 123 C5
Dilsen Belgium 62 F3
Dimapur India 105 H4
Dimas Mex. 166 D4
Dimashq Syria see Damascus
Dimbokro Côte d'Ivoire 120 C4
Dimboola Australia 137 C8
Dime Landing AK U.S.A. 148 G2
Dimitrov Ukr. see Dymytrov
Dimitrovgrad Bulg. 69 K3
Dimitrovgrad Rus. Fed. 53 K5
Dimitrovo Bulg. see Pernik
Dimmitt U.S.A. 161 C5
Dīmona Israel 107 B4
Dimpho Pan salt pan Botswana 124 E3
Dinagat i. Phil. 82 D4
Dinajpur Bangl. 105 G4
Dinan France 66 C2
Dinant Belgium 62 E4
Dinapur India 105 F4
Dinar Turkey 69 N5
Dīnār, Kūh-e mt. Iran 110 C4
Dinara Planina mts Bos.-Herz./Croatia see Dinaric Alps
Dinaric Alps mts Bos.-Herz./Croatia 68 G2
Dinbych U.K. see Denbigh
Dinbych-y-pysgod U.K. see Tenby
Dinder National Park Sudan 121 G3
Dindi r. India 106 C2
Dindigul India 106 C4
Dindima Nigeria 120 E3
Dindiza Moz. 125 K2
Dindori India 104 E5
Dingalan Bay Luzon Phil. 82 C3
Dingbian Shaanxi China 95 F4
Dingcheng China see Dingyuan
Dingelstädt Germany 63 K3
Dinggo Xizang China 99 D6
Dingin, Bukit mt. Indon. 84 C3
Dingla Nepal 105 F4
Dingle Ireland see An Daingean
Dingle Bay Ireland 61 B5
Dingnan China 97 G3
Dingo Australia 136 E4
Dingolfing Germany 63 M6
Dingping China see Linshui
Dingras Luzon Phil. 82 C2
Dingshan Xinjiang China 98 D3
Dingtao Shandong China 95 H5
Dinguiraye Guinea 120 B3
Dingwall U.K. 60 E3
Dingxi Gansu China 94 F5
Dingxian Hebei China see Dingzhou
Dingxin Gansu China 94 D3
Dingxing Hebei China 95 H4
Dingyuan China 97 H1
Dingzhou Hebei China 95 H4
Dingzi Gang b. China 95 J4
Dingzikou Qinghai China 98 F5
Dinh Lâp Vietnam 86 D2
Dinkelsbühl Germany 63 K5
Dinngyê Xizang China 99 D7
Dinokwe Botswana 125 H2
Dinosaur U.S.A. 159 I1
Dinosaur National Monument nat. park U.S.A. 159 I1
Dinslaken Germany 62 G3
Dintiteladas Sumatera Indon. 84 D4
Dinwiddie U.S.A. 165 G5
Dioïla Mali 120 C3
Diomede AK U.S.A. 148 E2
Diomede Islands Rus. Fed./U.S.A. 148 E2
Dionísio Cerqueira Brazil 178 F3
Diorama Brazil 179 A2
Dioscurias Georgia see Sokhumi
Diouloulou Senegal 120 B3
Diourbel Senegal 120 B3
Dipayal India 104 E3
Diphu India 105 H4
Dipkarpaz Cyprus see Rizokarpason
Diplo Pak. 111 H5
Dipolog Mindanao Phil. 82 C4
Dipperu National Park Australia 136 E4
Dipu China see Anji
Dir reg. Pak. 111 I3
Dirang India 105 H4
Diré Mali 120 C3
Direction, Cape Australia 136 C2
Dirē Dawa Eth. 122 E3
Diriamba Nicaragua 166 [inset] I7
Dirico Angola 123 C5
Dirk Hartog Island Australia 135 A6
Dirranbandi Australia 138 D2
Ḑirs Saudi Arabia 122 E2
Dirschau Poland see Tczew
Dirty Devil r. U.S.A. 159 H3
Disa India 104 C4
Disang r. India 105 H4
Disappointment, Cape S. Georgia 178 I8
Disappointment, Cape U.S.A. 156 B3
Disappointment, Lake salt flat Australia 135 C5
Disappointment Islands Fr. Polynesia see Désappointement, Îles du
Disappointment Lake Canada 153 J3
Disaster Bay Australia 138 D6
Discovery Bay Australia 137 C8
Dishna r. AK U.S.A. 148 H3
Disko i. Greenland see Qeqertarsuaq
Disko Bugt b. Greenland see Qeqertarsuup Tunua
Dismal Swamp U.S.A. 162 E4
Dispur India 105 G4
Disputanta U.S.A. 165 G5
Disraëli Canada 153 H5
Diss U.K. 59 I6
Distrito Federal admin. dist. Brazil 179 B1
Distrito Federal admin. dist. Mex. 167 F5
Disūq Egypt 112 C5
Dit i. Phil. 82 C4
Ditloung S. Africa 124 F5
Dittaino r. Sicily Italy 68 F6
Diu India 106 A1
Diuata Mountains Mindanao Phil. 82 D4
Diuata Point Mindanao Phil. 82 D4
Dīvān Darreh Iran 110 B3
Divehi country Indian Ocean see Maldives
Divi, Point India 106 D3
Divichi Azer. see Däväçi
Divide Mountain AK U.S.A. 149 L3
Divilacan Bay Luzon Phil. 82 C2
Divinópolis Brazil 179 B3
Divnoye Rus. Fed. 53 I7
Divo Côte d'Ivoire 120 C4
Divriği Turkey 112 E3
Diwana Pak. 111 G5
Diwaniyah Iraq see Ad Dīwānīyah
Dixfield U.S.A. 165 J1
Dixon CA U.S.A. 158 C2
Dixon IL U.S.A. 160 F3
Dixon KY U.S.A. 164 B5
Dixon MT U.S.A. 156 E3
Dixon Entrance sea channel Canada/U.S.A. 149 N5
Dixonville Canada 150 G3
Dixville Canada 165 J1
Diyadin Turkey 113 F3
Diyarbakır Turkey 113 F3
Diz Pak. 111 F5
Diz Chah Iran 110 D3
Dize Turkey see Yüksekova
Dizney U.S.A. 164 D5
Djado Niger 120 E2
Djado, Plateau du Niger 120 E2
Djaja, Puntjak mt. Indon. see Jaya, Puncak

Djakarta *Jawa* Indon. *see* **Jakarta**
Djakovica Kosovo *see* **Gjakovë**
Djakovo Croatia *see* **Đakovo**
Djambala Congo **122** B4
Djanet Alg. **120** D2
Djarrit-Uliga-Dalap Marshall Is *see* **Delap-Uliga-Djarrit**
Djelfa Alg. **67** H6
Djéma Cent. Afr. Rep. **122** C3
Djenné Mali **120** C3
Djerdap *nat. park* Serbia **69** J2
Djibo Burkina **120** C3
Djibouti *country* Africa **108** F7

▶**Djibouti** Djibouti **108** F7
Capital of Djibouti.

Djidjelli Alg. *see* **Jijel**
Djizak Uzbek. *see* **Jizzax**
Djougou Benin **120** D4
Djoum Cameroon **120** E4
Djourab, Erg du *des.* Chad **121** E3
Djúpivogur Iceland **54** [inset]
Djurås Sweden **55** I6
Djurdjura, Parc National du Alg. **67** I5
Dmitriya Lapteva, Proliv *sea chan.* Rus. Fed. **77** P2
Dmitriyev-L'govskiy Rus. Fed. **53** G5
Dmitriyevsk Ukr. *see* **Makiyivka**
Dmitrov Rus. Fed. **52** H4
Dmytriyevs'k Ukr. *see* **Makiyivka**
Dnepr *r.* Rus. Fed. **53** F5 *see* **Dnieper**
Dneprodzerzhinsk Ukr. *see* **Dniprodzerzhyns'k**
Dnepropetrovsk Ukr. *see* **Dnipropetrovs'k**

▶**Dnieper** *r.* Europe **53** G7
3rd longest river in Europe. Also spelt Dnepr (Rus. Fed.), Dnipro (Ukraine) or Dnyapro (Belarus).

Dniester *r.* Ukr. **53** F6
also spelt Dnister (Ukraine) or Nistru (Moldova)
Dnipro *r.* Ukr. **53** G7 *see* **Dnieper**
Dniprodzerzhyns'k Ukr. **53** G6
Dnipropetrovs'k Ukr. **53** G6
Dnister *r.* Ukr. **53** F6 *see* **Dniester**
Dno Rus. Fed. **52** F4
Dnyapro *r.* Belarus **53** F6 *see* **Dnieper**
Doāb Afgh. **111** G3
Doaba Pak. **111** H3
Doangdoangan Besar *i.* Indon. **85** G4
Doangdoangan Kecil *i.* Indon. **85** G4
Doan Hung Vietnam **86** D2
Doba Chad **121** E4
Dobdain *Qinghai* China **94** E5
Dobele Latvia **55** M8
Döbeln Germany **63** N3
Doberai, Jazirah *pen.* Indon. **81** I7
Doberai Peninsula Indon. *see* **Doberai, Jazirah**
Dobo Indon. **81** I8
Doboj Bos.-Herz. **68** H2
Do Borjī Iran **110** D4
Döbraberg *hill* Germany **63** L4
Dobrich Bulg. **69** L3
Dobrinka Rus. Fed. **53** I5
Dobroye Rus. Fed. **53** H5
Dobrudja *reg.* Romania *see* **Dobruja**
Dobruja *reg.* Romania **69** L3
Dobrush Belarus **53** F5
Dobryanka Rus. Fed. **51** R4
Dobzha *Xizang* China **99** E7
Doc Can *rf* Phil. **82** B5
Doce *r.* Brazil **179** D2
Dochart *r.* U.K. **60** E4
Do China Qala Afgh. **111** H4
Docking U.K. **59** H6
Doctor Arroyo Mex. **167** E4
Doctor Belisario Domínguez Mex. **166** D2
Doctor Hicks Range *hills* Australia **135** D7
Doctor Pedro P. Peña Para. **178** D2
Doda India **104** C2
Doda Betta *mt.* India **106** C4
Dod Ballapur India **106** C3
Dodê *Xizang* China **99** E7
Dodecanese *is* Greece **69** L7
Dodekanisa *is* Greece *see* **Dodecanese**
Dodekanisos *is* Greece *see* **Dodecanese**
Dodge City U.S.A. **160** C4
Dodgeville U.S.A. **160** F3
Dodman Point U.K. **59** C8

▶**Dodoma** Tanz. **123** D4
Capital of Tanzania.

Dodsonville U.S.A. **164** D4
Doetinchem Neth. **62** G3
Dofa *Maluku* Indon. **83** C3
Dog *r.* Canada **152** C4
Dogai Coring *salt l.* China **99** E6
Dogaicoring Qangco *salt l.* China **99** E6
Doğanşehir Turkey **112** E3
Dogên Co *l.* *Xizang* China *see* **Bam Tso**
Dogên Co *l.* China **99** E7
Dōgen-ko *l.* Japan **93** F2
Doghārūn Iran **111** F3
Dog Island Canada **153** J2
Dog Lake *Man.* Canada **151** L5
Dog Lake *Ont.* Canada **152** C4
Dog Lake *Ont.* Canada **152** D4
Dōgo *i.* Japan **91** D5
Dogondoutchi Niger **120** D3
Dog Rocks *is* Bahamas **163** E7
Doğubeyazıt Turkey **113** G3
Doğu Menteşe Dağları *mts* Turkey **69** M6
Dogxung Zangbo *r.* *Xizang* China **99** D7
Do'gyaling China **105** G3

▶**Doha** Qatar **110** C5
Capital of Qatar.

Dohad India *see* **Dahod**
Dohazari Bangl. **105** H5
Dohrighat *Uttar Prad.* India **99** C8
Doi *i.* Fiji **133** I4
Doi *i.* *Maluku* Indon. **83** C2
Doi Inthanon National Park Thai. **86** B3
Doijang *Xizang* China **99** E7
Doi Luang National Park Thai. **86** B3
Doire U.K. *see* **Londonderry**
Doi Saket Thai. **86** B3
Dois Irmãos, Serra dos *hills* Brazil **177** J5
Dokan, Sadd Iraq **113** G4
Dok-dō *i.* N. Pacific Ocean *see* **Liancourt Rocks**
Dokhara, Dunes de *des.* Alg. **64** F5
Dokka Norway **55** G6
Dokkum Neth. **62** F1
Dokog He *r.* China **96** D2
Dokri Pak. **111** H5
Dokshukino Rus. Fed. *see* **Nartkala**
Dokshytsy Belarus **55** O9
Dokuchayeva, Mys *c.* Rus. Fed. **90** G3
Dokuchayevka Kazakh. *see* **Karamendy**
Dokuchayevs'k Ukr. **53** H7
Dolbeau-Mistassini Canada **153** G4
Dolbenmaen U.K. **59** C6
Dol-de-Bretagne France **66** D2
Dole France **66** G3
Dolgellau U.K. **59** D6
Dolgen Germany **63** N1
Dolgiy, Ostrov *i.* Rus. Fed. **52** L1
Dolgorukovo Rus. Fed. **53** H5
Dolina Ukr. *see* **Dolyna**
Dolinsk Rus. Fed. **90** F3
Dolisie Congo *see* **Loubomo**
Dolit *Halmahera* Indon. **83** C3
Dolleman Island Antarctica **188** L2
Dollnstein Germany **63** L6
Dolo *Sulawesi* Indon. **83** A3
Dolok, Pulau *i.* Indon. **81** J8
Dolomites *mts* Italy **68** D2
Dolomiti *mts* Italy *see* **Dolomites**
Dolomiti Bellunesi, Parco Nazionale delle *nat. park* Italy **68** D1
Dolomitiche, Alpi *mts* Italy *see* **Dolomites**
Dolon Ashuusu *pass* Kyrg. **98** A4
Dolonnur *Nei Mongol* China **95** I3
Dolo Odo Eth. **122** E3
Doloon Mongolia *see* **Tsogt-Ovoo**
Dolores Arg. **178** E5
Dolores Guat. **167** H5
Dolores Mex. **166** C3
Dolores Uruguay **178** E4
Dolores U.S.A. **159** I3
Dolores Hidalgo Mex. **167** E4
Dolphin and Union Strait Canada **146** G3
Dolphin Head *hd* Namibia **124** B3
Đô Lương Vietnam **86** D3
Dolyna Ukr. **53** D6
Domaila India **104** D3
Domaniç Turkey **69** M5
Domar Bangl. **99** E8
Domar *Xizang* China **99** C6
Domartang *Xizang* China **99** F7
Domažlice Czech Rep. **63** M5
Domba *Qinghai* China **99** F6
Dom Bākh Iran **110** B3
Dombås Norway **54** F5
Dombóvár Hungary **68** H1
Dombrau Poland *see* **Dąbrowa Górnicza**
Dombrovitsa Ukr. *see* **Dubrovytsya**
Dombrowa Poland *see* **Dąbrowa Górnicza**
Domda China *see* **Qingshuihe**
Dome Argus *ice feature* Antarctica **188** E1
Dome Charlie *ice feature* Antarctica **188** F2
Dome Creek Canada **150** F4
Dome Rock Mountains U.S.A. **159** F5
Domeyko Chile **178** B3
Domfront France **66** D2
Dominica *country* West Indies **169** L5
Dominicana, República *country* West Indies *see* **Dominican Republic**
Dominican Republic *country* West Indies **169** J5
Dominion, Cape Canada **147** K3
Dominique *i.* Fr. Polynesia *see* **Hiva Oa**
Dömitz Germany **63** L1
Dom Joaquim Brazil **179** C2
Dommel *r.* Neth. **62** F3
Domo Eth. **122** E3
Domokos Greece **69** J5
Dompu *Sumbawa* Indon. **85** G5
Domuyo, Volcán *vol.* Arg. **178** B5
Domville, Mount *hill* Australia **138** E2
Don Mex. **166** C3

▶**Don** *r.* Rus. Fed. **53** H7
5th longest river in Europe.

Don *r.* U.K. **60** G3
Don, Xé *r.* Laos **86** D4
Donaghadee U.K. **61** G3
Donaghmore U.K. **61** F3
Donald Australia **138** A6
Donaldsonville U.S.A. **161** F6
Donalsonville U.S.A. **163** C6
Doñana, Parque Nacional de *nat. park* Spain **67** C5
Donau *r.* Austria/Germany **57** P6 *see* **Danube**
Donauwörth Germany **63** K6
Don Benito Spain **67** D4
Doncaster U.K. **58** F5
Dondo Angola **123** B4
Dondo Moz. **123** D5
Dondo, Tanjung *pt* Indon. **83** B2
Dondo, Teluk *b.* Indon. **83** B2
Dondonay *i.* Phil. **82** C4
Dondra Head *hd* Sri Lanka **106** D5
Donegal Ireland **61** D3
Donegal Bay Ireland **61** D3
Donets'k Ukr. **53** H7
Donetsko-Amvrosiyevka Ukr. *see* **Amvrosiyivka**
Donets'kyy Kryazh *hills* Rus. Fed./Ukr. **53** H6
Donga *r.* Cameroon/Nigeria **120** D4
Dong'an China **97** F3
Dongane, Lagoa *lag.* Moz. **125** L3
Dongara Australia **135** A7
Dongbatu *Gansu* China **98** F4
Dongbei Pingyuan *plain* China **95** J3
Dongbo *Xizang* China *see* **Mêdog**
Dongchuan *Yunnan* China **96** D3
Dongchuan *Yunnan* China *see* **Yao'an**
Dongco *Xizang* China **99** D6
Dong Co *l.* *Xizang* China **99** D6
Dongcun *Shandong* China *see* **Haiyang**
Dongcun *Shanxi* China *see* **Lanxian**
Dong'e *Shandong* China **95** I4
Dongfang China **97** F5
Dongfanghong China **90** D3
Donggala *Sulawesi* Indon. **83** A3
Donggang China **91** B5
Donggang *Shandong* China **95** I5
Donggi Conag *l.* *Qinghai* China **94** D5
Donggou China *see* **Donggang**
Donggou *Qinghai* China **94** E5
Donggu China **97** G3
Dongguan China **97** G4
Donghai *Jiangsu* China **95** I5
Dong Hai *sea* N. Pacific Ocean *see* **East China Sea**
Donghaiba *Ningxia* China **94** F4
Dong He *watercourse* China **94** E3
Đông Hơi Vietnam **86** D3
Donghuachi *Gansu* China **95** G4
Donghuang China *see* **Xishui**
Dongjiang Shuiku *resr* China **97** G3
Dongjug China **96** B2
Dongkait, Tanjung *pt* Indon. **83** A3
Dongkar *Xizang* China **99** E7
Dongkou China **97** F3
Donglan China **96** E3
Dongle *Gansu* China **94** E4
Dongliao He *r.* China **95** J3
Donglük *Xinjiang* China **98** E5
Dongmen China *see* **Luocheng**
Dongming *Shandong* China **95** H5
Dongminzhutun China **90** A3
Dongning China **90** C3
Dongo Angola **123** B5
Dongo Dem. Rep. Congo **122** B3
Dongola Sudan **108** D6
Dongou Congo **122** B3
Dong Phraya Yen *esc.* Thai. **86** C4
Dongping *Guangdong* China **97** G4
Dongping *Hunan* China *see* **Anhua**
Dongping Hu *l.* China **95** I4
Dongpo China *see* **Meishan**
Dongqiao *Xizang* China **99** E7
Dongqinghu *Nei Mongol* China **94** F4
Dong Qu *r.* *Qinghai* China **99** F6
Dongquan *Xinjiang* China **94** C3
Dongshan *Fujian* China **97** H4
Dongshan *Jiangsu* China **97** I2
Dongshan *Jiangxi* China *see* **Shangyou**
Dongshao China **97** G3
Dongsha Qundao *is* China **80** F2
Dongsheng *Nei Mongol* China *see* **Ordos**
Dongsheng *Sichuan* China *see* **Shuangliu**
Dongshuan China *see* **Tangdan**
Dongtai China **97** I1
Dong Taijnar Hu *l.* *Qinghai* China **99** F5
Dongting Hu *l.* China **97** G2
Dongtou China **97** I3
Đông Triều Vietnam **86** D2
Dong Ujimqin Qi *Nei Mongol* China *see* **Uliastai**
Đông Văn Vietnam **86** D2
Dongxiang China **97** H2
Dongxiangzu *Gansu* China **94** E5
Dongxi Liandao *i.* China **97** H1
Dongxing *Guangxi* China **96** E4
Dongxing *Heilong.* China **90** B3
Dongyang China **97** I2
Dongying *Shandong* China **95** I4
Dongzhen *Gansu* China **94** E4
Dongzhi China **97** H2
Donkerbroek Neth. **62** G1
Donnacona Canada **153** H5
Donnelly *AK* U.S.A. **149** K3
Donnellys Crossing N.Z. **139** D2
Donner Pass U.S.A. **158** C2
Donnersberg *hill* Germany **63** H5
Donostia-San Sebastián Spain **67** F2
Donousa *i.* Greece **69** K6
Donoussa *i.* Greece *see* **Donousa**
Donskoye Rus. Fed. **53** I7
Donsol *Luzon* Phil. **82** C3
Donyztau, Sor *dry lake* Kazakh. **102** A2
Dooagh Ireland **61** B4
Doomadgee Australia **136** B3
Doon *r.* U.K. **60** E5
Doon, Loch *l.* U.K. **60** E5
Doonbeg *r.* Ireland **61** C5
Doonerak, Mount *AK* U.S.A. **149** J2
Doorn Neth. **62** F2
Door Peninsula U.S.A. **164** B1
Doorwerth Neth. **62** F3
Dooxo Nugaaleed *valley* Somalia **122** E3
Doqêmo *Xizang* China **99** F7
Doqoi *Xizang* China **99** E7
Do Qu *r.* *Qinghai* China **94** D5
Dor *watercourse* Afgh. **111** F4
Dor Israel **107** B3
Dora U.S.A. **161** C5
Dora, Lake *salt flat* Australia **134** C5
Dorado Mex. **166** D3
Dorah Pass Pak. **111** H2
Doran Lake Canada **151** I2
Dorbiljin *Xinjiang* China *see* **Emin**
Dorbod *Heilong.* China *see* **Taikang**
Dorbod Qi *Nei Mongol* China *see* **Ulan Hua**
Dorchester U.K. **59** E8
Dordabis Namibia **124** C2
Dordogne *r.* France **66** D4
Dordrecht Neth. **62** E3
Dordrecht S. Africa **125** H6
Doreenville Namibia **124** D2
Doré Lake Canada **151** J4
Doré Lake *l.* Canada **151** J4
Dores do Indaiá Brazil **179** B2
Dorgê Co *l.* *Qinghai* China **94** C5
Dörgön Mongolia **94** C1
Dori *r.* Afgh. **111** G4
Dori Burkina **120** C3
Doring *r.* S. Africa **124** D6
Dorisvale Australia **134** E3
Dorking U.K. **59** G7
Dormagen Germany **62** G3
Dormans France **62** D5
Dormidontovka Rus. Fed. **90** D3
Dornoch U.K. **60** E3
Dornoch Firth *est.* U.K. **60** E3
Dornod *prov.* Mongolia **95** H1
Dornogovĭ *prov.* Mongolia **95** G2
Dornum Germany **63** H1
Doro Mali **120** C3
Dorogobuzh Rus. Fed. **53** G5
Dorogorskoye Rus. Fed. **52** J2
Dorohoi Romania **53** E7
Döröö Nuur *salt l.* Mongolia **94** C2
Dorostol Bulg. *see* **Silistra**
Dorotea Sweden **54** J4
Dorpat Estonia *see* **Tartu**
Dorre Island Australia **135** A6
Dorrigo Australia **138** F3
Dorris U.S.A. **156** C4
Dorset Canada **165** F1
Dorsoidong Co *l.* *Xizang* China **99** E6
Dortmund Germany **63** H3
Dörtyol Turkey **107** C1
Dorum Germany **63** I1
Doruma Dem. Rep. Congo **122** C3
Dorüneh, Kūh-e *mts* Iran **110** E3
Dörverden Germany **63** J2
Dörvöljin Mongolia **94** C2
Dorylaeum Turkey *see* **Eskişehir**
Dos Bahías, Cabo *c.* Arg. **178** C6
Dos de Mayo Peru **176** C5
Doshakh, Koh-i- *mt.* Afgh. *see* **Do Shākh, Kūh-e**
Do Shākh, Kūh-e *mt.* Afgh. **111** F3
Dōshi Japan **93** F3
Dos Lagunos Guat. **167** H5
Đo Sơn Vietnam **86** D2
Dos Palos U.S.A. **158** C3
Dosse *r.* Germany **63** M2
Dosso Niger **120** D3
Dostyk Kazakh. **98** C3
Dothan U.S.A. **163** C6
Dot Lake *AK* U.S.A. **149** K3
Dotsero U.S.A. **159** J2
Douai France **62** D4
Douala Cameroon **120** D4
Douarnenez France **66** B2
Double Headed Shot Cays *is* Bahamas **163** D8
Double Island *H.K.* China **97** [inset]
Double Island Point Australia **137** F5
Double Mountain Fork *r.* U.S.A. **161** C5
Double Peak *AK* U.S.A. **148** I3
Double Peak U.S.A. **158** D4
Double Point Australia **136** D3
Double Springs U.S.A. **163** C5
Doubs *r.* France/Switz. **66** H3
Doubtful Sound *inlet* N.Z. **139** A7
Doubtless Bay N.Z. **139** D2
Doucan *Shaanxi* China *see* **Fuping**
Douentza Mali **120** C3
Dougga *tourist site* Tunisia **68** C6

▶**Douglas** Isle of Man **58** C4
Capital of the Isle of Man.

Douglas S. Africa **124** F5
Douglas U.K. **60** F5
Douglas *AZ* U.S.A. **157** F7
Douglas *GA* U.S.A. **163** D6
Douglas *WY* U.S.A. **156** G4
Douglas, Cape *AK* U.S.A. **148** I4
Douglas Reef *i.* Japan *see* **Okino-Tori-shima**
Douglasville U.S.A. **163** C5
Douhudi China *see* **Gong'an**
Doulatpur Bangl. *see* **Daulatpur**
Douliu Taiwan *see* **Touliu**
Doullens France **62** C4
Douna Mali **120** C3
Doune U.K. **60** E4
Doupovské hory *mts* Czech Rep. **63** N4
Dourada, Serra *hills* Brazil **179** A2
Dourada, Serra *mts* Brazil **179** A1
Dourados Brazil **178** F2
Douro *r.* Port. **67** B3
also known as Duero (Spain)
Doushi China *see* **Gong'an**
Doushui Shuiku *resr* China **97** G3
Douve *r.* France **59** F9
Douzy France **62** F5
Dove *r.* U.K. **59** F6
Dove Brook Canada **153** K3
Dove Creek U.S.A. **159** I3
Dover U.K. **59** I7

▶**Dover** *DE* U.S.A. **165** H4
Capital of Delaware.

Dover *NH* U.S.A. **165** J2
Dover *NJ* U.S.A. **165** H3
Dover *OH* U.S.A. **164** E3
Dover *TN* U.S.A. **162** C4
Dover, Strait of France/U.K. **66** E1
Dover-Foxcroft U.S.A. **165** K1
Dovey *r.* U.K. **59** D6
Dovrefjell Nasjonalpark *nat. park* Norway **54** F5
Dowagiac U.S.A. **164** B3
Dowi, Tanjung *pt* Indon. **84** B2
Dowlaiswaram India **106** D2
Dowlatābād Afgh. **111** F3
Dowlatābād *Fārs* Iran **110** C4
Dowlatābād *Fārs* Iran **110** D4
Dowlatābād *Khorāsān* Iran **110** E2
Dowlatābād *Khorāsān* Iran **111** F2
Dowl at Yār Afgh. **111** G3
Downieville U.S.A. **158** C2
Downpatrick U.K. **61** G3
Downsville U.S.A. **165** H2
Dow Rūd Iran **110** C3
Doxong *Xizang* China **99** F7
Doyle U.S.A. **158** C1
Doylestown U.S.A. **165** H3
Dozdān *r.* Iran **110** E5
Dōzen *is* Japan **91** D5
Dozois, Réservoir *resr* Canada **152** F5
Dozulé France **59** G9
Drâa, Hamada du *plat.* Alg. **64** C6
Dracena Brazil **179** A3
Drachten Neth. **62** G1
Drăgănești-Olt Romania **69** K2
Drăgășani Romania **69** K2
Dragonera, Isla *i.* Spain *see* **Sa Dragonera**
Dragoon U.S.A. **159** H5
Dragsfjärd Fin. **55** M6
Draguignan France **66** H5
Drahichyn Belarus **55** N10
Drake Australia **138** F2
Drake U.S.A. **160** C2
Drakensberg *mts* S. Africa **125** I3
Drake Passage S. Atlantic Ocean **184** D9
Drakes Bay U.S.A. **158** B3
Drama Greece **69** K4
Drammen Norway **55** G7
Drang, Prêk *r.* Cambodia **87** D4
Drangedal Norway **55** F7
Drangme Chhu *r.* Bhutan **99** E8
Dransfeld Germany **63** J3
Draper, Mount *AK* U.S.A. **149** M4
Draperstown U.K. **61** F3
Drapsaca Afgh. *see* **Kunduz**
Dras India **104** C2
Drasan Pak. **111** I2
Drau *r.* Austria **57** O7 *see* **Drava**
Drava *r.* Europe **68** H2
also known as Drau (Austria), Drave or Dráva (Hungary)
Dráva *r.* Hungary *see* **Drava**
Drave *r.* Slovenia/Croatia *see* **Drava**
Drayton Valley Canada **150** H4
Drazinda Pak. **111** H4
Dréan Alg. **68** B6
Dreistelzberge *hill* Germany **63** J4
Drentse Hoofdvaart *canal* Neth. **62** G2
Drepano, Akra *pt* Greece *see* **Laimos, Akrotirio**
Dresden Canada **164** D2
Dresden Germany **57** N5
Dreux France **62** B6
Drevsjø Norway **55** H6
Drewryville U.S.A. **165** G5
Dri China **96** C2
Driffield U.K. **58** G4
Driftwood U.S.A. **165** F3
Driggs U.S.A. **156** F4
Drillham Australia **138** E1
Drimoleague Ireland **61** C6
Drina *r.* Bosnia-Herzegovina/Serbia **69** H2
Driscoll Island Antarctica **188** J1
Drissa Belarus *see* **Vyerkhnyadzvinsk**
Drniš Croatia **68** G3
Drobeta-Turnu Severin Romania **69** J2
Drochtersen Germany **63** J1
Drogheda Ireland **61** F4
Drogichin Belarus *see* **Drahichyn**
Drogobych Ukr. *see* **Drohobych**
Drohobych Ukr. **53** D6
Droichead Átha Ireland *see* **Drogheda**
Droichead Nua Ireland *see* **Newbridge**
Droitwich U.K. *see* **Droitwich Spa**
Droitwich Spa U.K. **59** E6
Dromedary, Cape Australia **138** E6
Dromod Ireland **61** E4
Dromore *Northern Ireland* U.K. **61** E3
Dromore *Northern Ireland* U.K. **61** F3
Dronfield U.K. **58** F5
Dronning Louise Land *reg.* Greenland **189** I1
Dronning Maud Land *reg.* Antarctica *see* **Queen Maud Land**
Dronten Neth. **62** F2
Drovyanaya Rus. Fed. **95** H1
Druk-Yul *country* Asia *see* **Bhutan**
Drumheller Canada **151** H5
Drummond *atoll* Kiribati *see* **Tabiteuea**
Drummond U.S.A. **156** E3
Drummond, Lake U.S.A. **165** G5
Drummond Island Kiribati *see* **McKean**
Drummond Range *hills* Australia **136** D5
Drummondville Canada **153** G5
Drummore U.K. **60** E6
Drury Lake Canada **150** C2
Druskieniki Lith. *see* **Druskininkai**
Druskininkai Lith. **55** N10
Druzhina Rus. Fed. **77** P3
Druzhnaya Gorka Rus. Fed. **55** Q7
Dry *r.* Australia **134** F3
Dryanovo Bulg. **69** K3
Dryberry Lake Canada **151** M5
Dry Creek *AK* U.S.A. **149** K3
Dryden Canada **151** M5
Dryden U.S.A. **165** G2
Dry Fork *r.* U.S.A. **156** G4
Drygalski Ice Tongue Antarctica **188** H1
Drygalski Island Antarctica **188** F2
Dry Lake U.S.A. **159** F3
Dry Lake *l.* U.S.A. **160** D1
Drymen U.K. **60** E4
Dry Ridge U.S.A. **164** C4
Drysdale *r.* Australia **134** D3
Drysdale River National Park Australia **134** D3
Dry Tortugas *is* U.S.A. **163** D7
Du'an China **97** F4
Duancun *Shanxi* China *see* **Wuxiang**
Duaringa Australia **136** E4
Duars *reg.* *Assam* India **99** E8
Duarte, Pico *mt.* Dom. Rep. **169** J5
Duartina Brazil **179** A3
Ḍubā Saudi Arabia **108** E4
Dubai U.A.E. **110** D5
Dubakella Mountain U.S.A. **158** B1
Dubăsari Moldova **53** F7
Dubawnt *r.* Canada **151** L2
Dubawnt Lake Canada **151** K2
Dubayy U.A.E. *see* **Dubai**
Dubbo Australia **138** D4
Dubin Kazakh. **98** C4
Dublán Mex. **166** D2

▶**Dublin** Ireland **61** F4
Capital of Ireland.

Dublin U.S.A. **163** D5
Dubna Rus. Fed. **52** H4
Dubno Ukr. **53** E6
Dubois *ID* U.S.A. **156** E3
Dubois *IN* U.S.A. **164** B4
Du Bois U.S.A. **165** F3
Dubovka Rus. Fed. **53** J6
Dubovskoye Rus. Fed. **53** I7
Dubréka Guinea **120** B4
Dubris U.K. *see* **Dover**
Dubrovnik Croatia **68** H3
Dubrovytsya Ukr. **53** E6
Dubuque U.S.A. **160** F3
Dubysa *r.* Lith. **55** M9
Đưc Bôn Vietnam **87** D5
Duc de Gloucester, Îles du *is* Fr. Polynesia **187** K7
Duchang China **97** H2
Ducheng China *see* **Yunan**
Duchesne U.S.A. **159** H1
Duchesne *r.* U.S.A. **159** I1
Duchess Australia **136** B4
Duchess Canada **151** I5
Ducie Island *atoll* Pitcairn Is **187** L7
Duck Bay Canada **151** K4
Duck Creek *r.* Australia **134** B5
Duck Lake Canada **151** J4
Duckwater Peak U.S.A. **159** F2
Duc Tho Vietnam **86** D3
Ducun *Shaanxi* China *see* **Fuping**
Dudelange Lux. **62** G5
Duderstadt Germany **63** K3
Dudhi India **105** E4
Dudhwa India **104** E3
Dudinka Rus. Fed. **76** J3
Dudley U.K. **59** E6
Dudleyville U.S.A. **159** H5
Dudna *r.* India **106** C2
Dudu India **104** C4
Duékoué Côte d'Ivoire **120** C4
Duen, Bukit *vol.* Indon. **84** C3
Duero *r.* Spain **67** C3
also known as Douro (Portugal)
Duffel Belgium **62** E3
Dufferin, Cape Canada **152** F2
Duffer Peak U.S.A. **156** D4
Duff Islands Solomon Is **133** G2
Duffreboy, Lac *l.* Canada **153** H2
Dufftown U.K. **60** F3
Dufourspitze *mt.* Italy/Switz. **66** H4
Dufrost, Pointe *pt* Canada **152** F1
Dugi Otok *i.* Croatia **68** F2
Dugi Rat Croatia **68** G3
Dugui Qarag *Nei Mongol* China **95** G4
Du He *r.* China **97** F1
Duida-Marahuaca, Parque Nacional *nat. park* Venez. **176** E3
Duisburg Germany **62** G3
Duiwelskloof S. Africa **125** J2
Dujiangyan China **96** D2
Dukathole S. Africa **125** H6
Duke Island *AK* U.S.A. **149** O5
Duke of Clarence *atoll* Tokelau *see* **Nukunonu**
Duke of Gloucester Islands Fr. Polynesia *see* **Duc de Gloucester, Îles du**
Duke of York *atoll* Tokelau *see* **Atafu**
Duk Fadiat Sudan **121** G4
Dukhovnitskoye Rus. Fed. **53** K5
Duki Pak. **111** H4
Duki Rus. Fed. **90** D2
Duki *r.* Rus. Fed. **90** D2
Dukou China *see* **Panzhihua**
Dūkštas Lith. **55** O9
Dulaanhaan Mongolia **94** F1
Dulac U.S.A. **161** F6
Dulan *Qinghai* China **94** D4
Dulawan *Mindanao* Phil. *see* **Datu Piang**
Dulbi *r.* *AK* U.S.A. **148** H2
Dulce *r.* Arg. **178** D4
Dulce U.S.A. **157** G5
Dulce, Golfo *b.* Costa Rica **166** [inset] J7
Dulce Nombre de Culmí Hond. **166** [inset] I6
Dul'durga Rus. Fed. **95** H1
Dulhunty *r.* Australia **136** C1
Dulishi Hu *salt l.* China **99** C6
Dulit, Pegunungan *mts* Malaysia **85** F2
Duliu Jiang *r.* China **97** F3

Dullewala Pak. **111** H4
Dullstroom S. Africa **125** J3
Dülmen Germany **63** H3
Dulmera India **104** C3
Dulovo Bulg. **69** L3
Duluth U.S.A. **160** E2
Dulverton U.K. **59** D7
Dūmā Syria **107** C3
Dumaguete *Negros* Phil. **82** C4
Dumai *Sumatera* Indon. **84** C2
Dumanquilas Bay *Mindanao* Phil. **82** C5
Dumaran *i.* Phil. **82** C4
Dumarchen *i.* Indon. **83** C1
Dumaresq *r.* Australia **138** E2
Dumas U.S.A. **161** C5
Dumat al Jandal Saudi Arabia **113** E5
Ḑumayr Syria **107** C3
Ḑumayr, Jabal *mts* Syria **107** C3
Dumbakh Iran *see* **Dom Bākh**
Dumbarton U.K. **60** E5
Dumbe S. Africa **125** J4
Ďumbier *mt.* Slovakia **57** Q6
Dumchele India **104** D2
Dum-Dum India **105** G5
Dumdum *i.* Indon. **84** D2
Dum Duma India **105** H4
Dumfries U.K. **60** F5
Dumka India **105** F4
Dumoga *Sulawesi* Indon. **83** C2
Dumont d'Urville *research station* Antarctica **188** G2
Dumont d'Urville Sea Antarctica **188** G2
Dümpelfeld Germany **62** G4
Dumyāṭ Egypt **112** C5
Dumyâṭ Egypt *see* **Dumyāṭ**
Duna *r.* Hungary **68** H2 *see* **Danube**
Dünaburg Latvia *see* **Daugavpils**
Dunaj *r.* Slovakia *see* **Danube**
Dunajská Streda Slovakia **57** P7
Dunakeszi Hungary **69** H1
Dunany Point Ireland **61** F4
Dunărea *r.* Romania **69** L2 *see* **Danube**
Dunării, Delta Romania/Ukr. *see* **Danube Delta**
Dunaújváros Hungary **68** H1
Dunav *r.* Bulg./Croatia/Serbia **68** L2 *see* **Danube**
Dunay *r.* Ukr. *see* **Danube**
Dunayivtsi Ukr. **53** E6
Dunbar Australia **136** C3
Dunbar U.K. **60** G4
Dunbar *AK* U.S.A. **149** J2
Dunblane U.K. **60** F4
Dunboyne Ireland **61** F4
Duncan Canada **150** F5
Duncan *AZ* U.S.A. **159** I5
Duncan *OK* U.S.A. **161** D5
Duncan, Cape Canada **152** E3
Duncan, Lac *l.* Canada **152** F3
Duncan Lake Canada **150** H2
Duncan Passage India **87** A5
Duncansby Head *hd* U.K. **60** F2
Duncan Town Bahamas **163** F8
Duncormick Ireland **61** F5
Dundaga Latvia **55** M8
Dundalk Ireland **61** F3
Dundalk U.S.A. **165** G4
Dundalk Bay Ireland **61** F4
Dundas Canada **164** F2
Dundas Greenland **147** L2
Dundas, Lake *salt flat* Australia **135** C8
Dundas Island *B.C.* Canada **149** O5
Dundas Strait Australia **134** E2
Dundbürd Mongolia *see* **Batnorov**
Dún Dealgan Ireland *see* **Dundalk**
Dundee S. Africa **125** J5
Dundee U.K. **60** G4
Dundee *MI* U.S.A. **164** D3
Dundee *NY* U.S.A. **165** G2
Dundgovĭ *prov.* Mongolia **94** F2
Dund Hot *Nei Mongol* China **95** I3
Dundonald U.K. **61** G3
Dundoo Australia **138** B1
Dundrennan U.K. **60** F6
Dundrum U.K. **61** G3
Dundrum Bay U.K. **61** G3
Dundwa Range *mts* India/Nepal **105** E4
Dune, Lac *l.* Canada **152** G2
Dunedin N.Z. **139** C7
Dunedin U.S.A. **163** D6
Dunenbay Kazakh. **98** C2
Dunfermline U.K. **60** F4
Dungannon U.K. **61** F3
Dún Garbhán Ireland *see* **Dungarvan**
Dungarpur India **104** C5
Dungarvan Ireland **61** E5
Dung Co *l. Xizang* China **99** E7
Dungeness *hd* U.K. **59** H8
Dungeness, Punta *pt* Arg. **178** C8
Düngenheim Germany **63** H4
Dungiven U.K. **61** F3
Dungloe Ireland *see* **An Clochán Liath**
Dungog Australia **138** E4
Dungu Dem. Rep. Congo **122** C3
Dungun Malaysia **84** C1
Dungunab Sudan **108** E5
Dunhua China **90** C4
Dunhuang *Gansu* China **98** F4
Dunkeld Australia **138** D1
Dunkeld U.K. **60** F4
Dunkellin *r.* Ireland **61** D4
Dunkerque France *see* **Dunkirk**
Dunkery Hill *hill* U.K. **59** D7
Dunkirk France **62** C3
Dunkirk U.S.A. **164** F2
Dún Laoghaire Ireland **61** F4
Dunlap *IA* U.S.A. **160** E3
Dunlap *TN* U.S.A. **162** C5
Dunlavin Ireland **61** F4
Dunleer Ireland **61** F4
Dunloy U.K. **61** F2
Dunmanway Ireland **61** C6
Dunmarra Australia **134** F4
Dunmor U.S.A. **164** B5
Dunmore Ireland **61** D4
Dunmore U.S.A. **165** H3
Dunmore Town Bahamas **163** E7
Dunmurry U.K. **61** G3
Dunnet Head *hd* U.K. **60** F2
Dunnigan U.S.A. **158** C2
Dunning U.S.A. **160** C3
Dunnville Canada **164** F2
Dunnville U.S.A. **164** C5
Dunolly Australia **138** A6
Dunoon U.K. **60** E5
Dunphy U.S.A. **158** E1
Duns U.K. **60** G5
Dunseith U.S.A. **160** C1
Dunstable U.K. **59** G7
Dunstan Mountains N.Z. **139** B7
Dun-sur-Meuse France **62** F5
Duntroon N.Z. **139** C7
Dunvegan Lake Canada **151** J2
Dunyapur Pak. **111** H4
Duobukur He *r.* China **95** K1
Duolun *Nei Mongol* China *see* **Dolonnur**
Duomula *Xizang* China **99** C6
Dupang Ling *mts* China **97** F3
Duperré Alg. *see* **Aïn Defla**
Dupnitsa Bulg. **69** J3
Dupree U.S.A. **160** C2
Duque de Bragança Angola *see* **Calandula**
Dūrā West Bank **107** B4
Durack *r.* Australia **134** D3
Durack Range *hills* Australia **134** D4
Dura Europos Syria *see* **Aş Şāliḥīyah**
Durağan Turkey **112** D2
Durance *r.* France **66** G5
Durand U.S.A. **160** F2
Durango Mex. **161** B7
Durango *state* Mex. **161** B7
Durango Spain **67** E2
Durango U.S.A. **159** J3
Durani *reg.* Afgh. **111** G4
Durant U.S.A. **161** D5
Durazno Uruguay **178** E4
Durazzo Albania *see* **Durrës**
Durban S. Africa **125** J5
Durban-Corbières France **66** F5
Durbanville S. Africa **124** D7
Durbin U.S.A. **164** F4
Durbun Pak. **111** G4
Durbuy Belgium **62** F4
Düre *Xinjiang* China **98** E3
Düren Germany **62** G4
Düren Iran **110** E3
Duren, Kūh-e *mt.* Iran **110** E3
Durg India **104** E5
Durgapur Bangl. **105** G4
Durgapur India **105** F5
Durham Canada **164** E1
Durham U.K. **58** F4
Durham U.S.A. **162** E5
Durham Downs Australia **137** C5
Duri *Sumatera* Indon. **84** C2
Duriansebatang *Kalimantan* Indon. **85** E3
Durlas Ireland *see* **Thurles**
Durleşti Moldova **69** M1
Durmersheim Germany **63** I6
Durmitor *mt.* Montenegro **69** H3
Durmitor *nat. park* Montenegro **68** H3
Durness U.K. **60** E2
Durocortorum France *see* **Reims**
Durong South Australia **137** E5
Durostorum Bulg. *see* **Silistra**
Durour Island P.N.G. *see* **Aua Island**
Durovernum U.K. *see* **Canterbury**
Durrës Albania **69** H4
Durrie Australia **136** C5
Durrington U.K. **59** F7
Dursey Island Ireland **61** B6
Dursunbey Turkey **69** M5
Duru China *see* **Wuchuan**
Dūruḥ Iran **111** F3
Durukhsi Somalia **122** E3
Durusu Gölü *l.* Turkey **69** M4
Durūz, Jabal ad *mt.* Syria **107** C3
D'Urville, Tanjung *pt* Indon. **81** J7
D'Urville Island N.Z. **139** D5
Durzab Afgh. **111** G3
Duşak Turkm. **111** E2
Dushai Pak. **111** G4
Dushan China **96** E3

▶**Dushanbe** Tajik. **111** H2
Capital of Tajikistan.

Dushanzi *Xinjiang* China **98** D3
Dushet'i Georgia **113** G2
Dushikou *Hebei* China **95** H3
Dushore U.S.A. **165** G3
Dusse-Alin', Khrebet *mts* Rus. Fed. **90** D2
Düsseldorf Germany **62** G3
Dusty *NM* U.S.A. **159** J5
Dusty *WA* U.S.A. **156** D3
Dutch East Indies *country* Asia *see* **Indonesia**
Dutch Guiana *country* S. America *see* **Suriname**
Dutch Mountain U.S.A. **159** G1
Dutch New Guinea *prov.* Indon. *see* **Papua**
Dutch West Indies *terr.* West Indies *see* **Netherlands Antilles**
Dutlwe Botswana **124** F2
Dutse Nigeria **120** D3
Dutsin-Ma Nigeria **120** D3
Dutton *r.* Australia **136** C4
Dutton Canada **164** E2
Dutton U.S.A. **156** F3
Dutton, Lake *salt flat* Australia **137** B6
Dutton, Mount U.S.A. **159** G2
Duval Canada **151** J5
Duvert, Lac *l.* Canada **153** H2
Duvno Bos.-Herz. *see* **Tomislavgrad**
Duwa *Xinjiang* China **99** B5
Duwin Iraq **113** G3
Düxanbibazar *Xinjiang* China **99** C5
Duyun China **96** E3
Duzab Pak. **111** F5
Düzce Turkey **69** N4
Duzdab Iran *see* **Zāhedān**
Dvina *r.* Europe *see* **Zapadnaya Dvina**
Dvina *r.* Rus. Fed. *see* **Severnaya Dvina**
Dvinsk Latvia *see* **Daugavpils**
Dvinskaya Guba *g.* Rus. Fed. **52** H2
Dwarka India **104** B5
Dwarsberg S. Africa **125** H3
Dwingelderveld, Nationaal Park *nat. park* Neth. **62** G2
Dworshak Reservoir U.S.A. **156** E3
Dwyka S. Africa **124** E7
Dyat'kovo Rus. Fed. **53** G5
Dyce U.K. **60** G3
Dyer, Cape Canada **147** L3
Dyer Bay Canada **164** E1
Dyersburg U.S.A. **161** F4
Dyffryn U.K. *see* **Valley**
Dyfi *r.* U.K. *see* **Dovey**
Dyfrdwy *r.* U.K. *see* **Dee**
Dyfrdwy *r. England/Wales* U.K. *see* **Dee**
Dyje *r.* Austria/Czech Rep. **57** P6
Dyke U.K. **60** F3

▶**Dykh-Tau, Gora** *mt.* Rus. Fed. **113** F2
2nd highest mountain in Europe.

Dyle *r.* Belgium **62** E4
Dyleň *hill* Czech Rep. **63** M5
Dylewska Góra *hill* Poland **57** Q4
Dymytrov Ukr. **53** H6
Dynevor Downs Australia **138** B2
Dyoki S. Africa **125** I6
Dyrrhachium Albania *see* **Durrës**
Dysart Australia **136** E4
Dysselsdorp S. Africa **124** F7
Dyurtyuli Rus. Fed. **51** Q4
Dzaanhushuu Mongolia *see* **Ihtamir**
Dzadgay Mongolia *see* **Bömbögör**
Dzag Mongolia **94** D2
Dzag Gol *r.* Mongolia **94** D2
Dzalaa Mongolia *see* **Shinejinst**
Dzamïn Üüd Mongolia **95** G3
Dzanga-Ndoki, Parc National de *nat. park* Cent. Afr. Rep. **122** B3

▶**Dzaoudzi** Mayotte **123** E5
Capital of Mayotte.

Dzaudzhikau Rus. Fed. *see* **Vladikavkaz**
Dzavhan Mongolia **94** C1
Dzavhan *prov.* Mongolia **94** C1
Dzavhan Gol *r.* Mongolia **94** C1
Dzavhanmandal Mongolia **94** C1
Dzegstey Mongolia *see* **Ögiynuur**
Dzelter Mongolia **94** F1
Dzerzhinsk Belarus *see* **Dzyarzhynsk**
Dzerzhinsk Rus. Fed. **52** I4
Dzhagdy, Khrebet *mts* Rus. Fed. **90** C1
Dzhaki-Unakhta Yakbyyana, Khrebet *mts* Rus. Fed. **90** D2
Dzhalalabad Azer. *see* **Cälilabad**
Dzhalal-Abad Kyrg. *see* **Jalal-Abad**
Dzhalil' Rus. Fed. **51** Q4
Dzhalinda Rus. Fed. **90** A1
Dzhaltyr Kazakh. *see* **Zhaltyr**
Dzhambeyty Kazakh. *see* **Zhympity**
Dzhambul Kazakh. *see* **Taraz**
Dzhangala Kazakh. **51** Q6
Dzhankoy Ukr. **53** G7
Dzhansugurov Kazakh. **98** B3
Dzhanybek Kazakh. *see* **Zhanibek**
Dzharkent Kazakh. *see* **Zharkent**
Dzhava Georgia *see* **Java**
Dzhetygara Kazakh. *see* **Zhitikara**
Dzhezkazgan Kazakh. *see* **Zhezkazgan**
Dzhida Rus. Fed. **94** F1
Dzhida *r.* Rus. Fed. **94** F1
Dzhidinskiy, Khrebet *mts* Mongolia/Rus. Fed. **94** E1
Dzhirgatal' Tajik. *see* **Jirgatol**
Dzhizak Uzbek. *see* **Jizzax**
Dzhokhar Ghala Rus. Fed. *see* **Groznyy**
Dzhubga Rus. Fed. **112** E1
Dzhugdzhur, Khrebet *mts* Rus. Fed. **77** O4
Dzhul'fa Azer. *see* **Culfa**
Dzhuma Uzbek. *see* **Juma**
Dzhungarskiy Alatau, Khrebet *mts* China/Kazakh. **102** E3
Dzhungarskiye Vorota *val.* Kazakh. **98** C3
Dzhungarskiye Vorota *val.* Kazakh. **98** C3
Dzhusaly Kazakh. **102** B2
Działdowo Poland **57** R4
Dzibalchén Mex. **167** H5
Dzilam de Bravo Mex. **167** H4
Dzitás Mex. **167** H4
Dzogsool Mongolia *see* **Bayantsagaan**
Dzöölön Mongolia *see* **Renchinlhümbe**
Dzūkija *nat. park* Lith. **55** N9
Dzungarian Basin China *see* **Junggar Pendi**
Dzungarian Gate *pass* China/Kazakh. **102** F2
Dzur Mongolia *see* **Tes**
Dzüünbayan Mongolia **95** G2
Dzüünharaa Mongolia **94** F1
Dzuunmod Mongolia **94** F2
Dzüyl Mongolia *see* **Tonhil**
Dzyanìskavichy Belarus **55** O10
Dzyarzhynsk Belarus **55** O10
Dzyatlavichy Belarus **55** O10

E

Eabamet Lake Canada **152** D4
Eads U.S.A. **160** C4
Eagar U.S.A. **159** I4
Eagle *r.* Canada **153** K3
Eagle *r. Y.T.* Canada **149** M2
Eagle *AK* U.S.A. **146** D3
Eagle *CO* U.S.A. **156** G5
Eagle Cap *mt.* U.S.A. **156** D3
Eagle Crags *mt.* U.S.A. **158** E4
Eagle Creek *r.* Canada **151** J4
Eagle Lake Canada **151** M5
Eagle Lake *CA* U.S.A. **158** C1
Eagle Lake *ME* U.S.A. **162** G2
Eagle Mountain U.S.A. **159** F5
Eagle Mountain *hill* U.S.A. **160** F2
Eagle Mountain Lake *TX* U.S.A. **167** F1
Eagle Pass U.S.A. **161** C6
Eagle Peak U.S.A. **157** G7
Eagle Plain *Y.T.* Canada **149** M2
Eagle Plains *Y.T.* Canada **149** M2
Eagle River *AK* U.S.A. **149** J3
Eagle River U.S.A. **160** F2
Eagle Rock U.S.A. **164** F5
Eaglesham Canada **150** G4
Eagle Summit *pass AK* U.S.A. **149** K2
Eagle Village *AK* U.S.A. **149** L2
Eap *i.* Micronesia *see* **Yap**
Ear Falls Canada **151** M5
Earlimart U.S.A. **158** D4
Earl's Seat *hill* U.K. **60** E4
Earlston U.K. **60** G5
Earn *r.* U.K. **60** F4
Earn, Loch *l.* U.K. **60** E4
Earn Lake *Y.T.* Canada **149** N3
Earp U.S.A. **159** F4
Earth U.S.A. **161** C5
Easington U.K. **58** H5
Easley U.S.A. **163** D5
East Alligator *r.* Australia **134** F3
East Antarctica *reg.* Antarctica **188** F1
East Ararat U.S.A. **165** H3
East Aurora U.S.A. **165** F2
East Bay *LA* U.S.A. **167** H2
East Bay *inlet* U.S.A. **163** C6
East Bengal *country* Asia *see* **Bangladesh**
Eastbourne U.K. **59** H8
East Branch Clarion River Reservoir U.S.A. **165** F3
East Caicos *i.* Turks and Caicos Is **163** G8
East Cape N.Z. **139** G3
East Cape *AK* U.S.A. **149** [inset]
East Carbon City U.S.A. **159** H2
East Caroline Basin *sea feature* N. Pacific Ocean **186** F5
East Channel *watercourse N.W.T.* Canada **149** N1
East China Sea N. Pacific Ocean **89** N6
East Coast Bays N.Z. **139** E3
East Dereham *England* U.K. *see* **Dereham**
Eastend Canada **151** I5
East Entrance *sea chan.* Palau **82** [inset]

▶**Easter Island** S. Pacific Ocean **187** M7
Part of Chile.

Eastern Cape *prov.* S. Africa **125** H6
Eastern Desert Egypt **108** D4
Eastern Fields *reef* Australia **136** D1
Eastern Ghats *mts* India **106** C4

▶**Eastern Island** U.S.A. **186** I4
Most northerly point of Oceania.

Eastern Nara *canal* Pak. **111** H5
Eastern Samoa *terr.* S. Pacific Ocean *see* **American Samoa**
Eastern Sayan Mountains Rus. Fed. *see* **Vostochnyy Sayan**
Eastern Taurus *plat.* Turkey *see* **Güneydoğu Toroslar**
Eastern Transvaal *prov.* S. Africa *see* **Mpumalanga**
Easterville Canada **151** L4
Easterwâlde Neth. *see* **Oosterwolde**
East Falkland *i.* Falkland Is **178** E8
East Falmouth U.S.A. **165** J3
East Frisian Islands Germany **57** K4
Eastgate U.S.A. **158** E2
East Greenwich U.S.A. **165** J3
East Grinstead U.K. **59** G7
Easthampton U.S.A. **165** I2
East Hampton U.S.A. **165** I3
East Hartford U.S.A. **165** I3
East Indiaman Ridge *sea feature* Indian Ocean **185** O7
East Jordan U.S.A. **164** C1
East Kilbride U.K. **60** E5
Eastlake U.S.A. **164** E3
East Lamma Channel *H.K.* China **97** [inset]
Eastland U.S.A. **161** D5
East Lansing U.S.A. **164** C2
Eastleigh U.K. **59** F8
East Liverpool U.S.A. **164** E3
East London S. Africa **125** H7
East Lynn Lake U.S.A. **164** D4
Eastmain Canada **152** F3
Eastmain *r.* Canada **152** F3
Eastman U.S.A. **163** D5
East Mariana Basin *sea feature* N. Pacific Ocean **186** G5
Eastmere Australia **136** D4
East Naples U.S.A. **163** D7
Easton *MD* U.S.A. **165** G4
Easton *PA* U.S.A. **165** H3
East Orange U.S.A. **165** H3
East Pacific Rise *sea feature* N. Pacific Ocean **187** M4
East Pakistan *country* Asia *see* **Bangladesh**
East Palestine U.S.A. **164** E3
East Park Reservoir U.S.A. **158** B2
East Point Canada **153** J5
East Porcupine *r. Y.T.* Canada **149** M2
Eastport U.S.A. **162** H2
East Providence U.S.A. **165** J3
East Range *mts* U.S.A. **158** E1
East Retford U.K. *see* **Retford**
East St Louis U.S.A. **160** F4
East Sea N. Pacific Ocean *see* **Japan, Sea of**
East Shoal Lake Canada **151** L5
East Siberian Sea Rus. Fed. **77** P2
East Side Canal *r.* U.S.A. **158** D4
East Stroudsburg U.S.A. **165** H3
East Tavaputs Plateau U.S.A. **159** I2

▶**East Timor** *country* Asia **83** C5
Former Portuguese territory. Gained independence from Indonesia in 2002.

East Tons *r.* India **99** D8
East Toorale Australia **138** B3
East Troy U.S.A. **164** A2
East Verde *r.* U.S.A. **159** H4
Eastville U.S.A. **165** H5
East-Vlylân Neth. *see* **Oost-Vlieland**
East York Canada **164** F2
Eaton U.S.A. **164** C4
Eatonia Canada **151** I5
Eaton Rapids U.S.A. **164** C2
Eatonton U.S.A. **163** D5
Eau Claire U.S.A. **160** F2
Eauripik *atoll* Micronesia **81** K5
Eauripik Rise-New Guinea Rise *sea feature* N. Pacific Ocean **186** F5
Eaurypyg *atoll* Micronesia *see* **Eauripik**
Ebano Mex. **167** F4
Ebbw Vale U.K. **59** D7
Ebebiyin Equat. Guinea **120** E4
Ebenerde Namibia **124** C3
Ebensburg U.S.A. **165** F3
Eber Gölü *l.* Turkey **69** N5
Ebergötzen Germany **63** K3
Eberswalde-Finow Germany **57** N4
Ebetsu Japan **90** F4
Ebian China **96** D2
Ebina Japan **93** F3
Ebi Nor *salt l.* China *see* **Ebinur Hu**
Ebinur Hu *salt l.* China **98** C3
Eboli Italy **68** F4
Ebolowa Cameroon **120** E4
Ebony Namibia **124** B2
Ebre *r.* Spain *see* **Ebro**
Ebro *r.* Spain **67** G3
Ebstorf Germany **63** K1
Eburacum U.K. *see* **York**
Ebusus *i.* Spain *see* **Ibiza**
Ecbatana Iran *see* **Hamadān**
Eceabat Turkey **69** L4
Echague *Luzon* Phil. **82** C2
Ech Chélif Alg. *see* **Chlef**
Echegárate, Puerto *pass* Spain **67** E2
Echeng China *see* **Ezhou**
Echeverria, Pico *mt.* Mex. **166** B2
Echigawa Japan **92** C3
Echigo-Sanzan-Tadami Kokutei-kōen *park* Japan **93** F1
Echizen Japan **92** C3
Echizen-dake *mt.* Japan **93** E3
Echizen-Kaga-kaigan Kokutei-kōen *park* Japan **92** C2
Echizen-misaki *pt* Japan **92** B3
Echmiadzin Armenia *see* **Ejmiatsin**
Echo U.S.A. **156** D3
Echo Bay *N.W.T.* Canada **150** G1
Echo Bay *Ont.* Canada **152** D5
Echo Cliffs U.S.A. **159** H3
Echoing *r.* Canada **151** M4
Echt Neth. **62** F3
Echternach Lux. **62** G5
Echuca Australia **138** B6
Echzell Germany **63** I4
Écija Spain **67** D5
Eckental Germany **63** L5
Eckernförde Germany **57** L3
Eclipse Sound *sea chan.* Canada **147** J2
Écrins, Parc National des *nat. park* France **66** H4
Ecuador *country* S. America **176** C4
Écueils, Pointe aux *pt* Canada **152** F2
Ed Eritrea **108** F7
Ed Sweden **55** G7
Edam Neth. **62** F2
Eday *i.* U.K. **60** G1
Ed Da'ein Sudan **121** F3
Ed Damazin Sudan **108** D7
Ed Damer Sudan **108** D6
Ed Debba Sudan **108** D6
Eddies Cove Canada **153** K4
Ed Dueim Sudan **108** D7
Eddystone Point Australia **137** [inset]
Eddyville U.S.A. **161** F4
Ede Neth. **62** F2
Edéa Cameroon **120** E4
Edehon Lake Canada **151** L2
Edéia Brazil **179** A2
Eden Australia **138** D6
Eden *r.* U.K. **58** D4
Eden *NC* U.S.A. **164** F5
Eden *TX* U.S.A. **161** D6
Eden, Tanjung *pt Maluku* Indon. **83** C4
Edenburg S. Africa **125** G5
Edendale N.Z. **139** B8
Edenderry Ireland **61** E4
Edenton U.S.A. **162** E4
Edenville S. Africa **125** H4
Eder *r.* Germany **63** J3
Eder-Stausee *resr* Germany **63** I3
Edessa Greece **69** J4
Edessa Turkey *see* **Şanlıurfa**
Edewecht Germany **63** H1
Edfu Egypt *see* **Idfū**
Edgar Ranges *hills* Australia **134** C4
Edgartown U.S.A. **165** J3
Edgecumbe Island Solomon Is *see* **Utupua**
Edgefield U.S.A. **163** D5
Edge Island Svalbard *see* **Edgeøya**
Edgemont U.S.A. **160** C3
Edgeøya *i.* Svalbard **76** D2
Edgerton Canada **151** I4
Edgerton U.S.A. **164** C3
Edgeworthstown Ireland **61** E4
Édhessa Greece *see* **Edessa**
Edina U.S.A. **160** E3
Edinboro U.S.A. **164** E3
Edinburg *TX* U.S.A. **161** D7
Edinburg *VA* U.S.A. **165** F4

▶**Edinburgh** U.K. **60** F5
Capital of Scotland.

Edineţ Moldova **53** F7
Edirne Turkey **69** L4
Edith, Mount U.S.A. **156** F3
Edith Cavell, Mount Canada **150** G4
Edith Ronne Land *ice feature* Antarctica *see* **Ronne Ice Shelf**
Edjeleh Libya **120** D2
Edjudina Australia **135** C7
Edku Egypt *see* **Idkū**
Edmond U.S.A. **161** D5
Edmonds U.S.A. **156** C3

▶**Edmonton** Canada **150** H4
Capital of Alberta.

Edmonton U.S.A. **164** C5
Edmore *MI* U.S.A. **164** C2
Edmore *ND* U.S.A. **160** D1
Edmund Lake Canada **151** M4
Edmundston Canada **153** H5
Edna U.S.A. **161** D6
Edna Bay *AK* U.S.A. **149** N5
Edo Japan *see* **Tōkyō**
Edo-gawa *r.* Japan **93** F3
Edom *reg.* Israel/Jordan **107** B4
Edosaki Japan **93** G3
Édouard, Lac *l.* Dem. Rep. Congo/Uganda *see* **Edward, Lake**
Edremit Turkey **69** L5
Edremit Körfezi *b.* Turkey **69** L5
Edrengiyn Nuruu *mts* Mongolia **94** D2
Edsbyn Sweden **55** I6
Edson Canada **150** G4
Eduni, Mount *N.W.T.* Canada **149** O2
Edward *r. N.S.W.* Australia **138** B5
Edward *r. Qld* Australia **136** C2
Edward, Lake Dem. Rep. Congo/Uganda **122** C4
Edward, Mount Antarctica **188** L1
Edwardesabad Pak. *see* **Bannu**
Edwards U.S.A. **165** H1
Edward's Creek Australia **137** A6
Edwards Plateau U.S.A. **161** C6
Edwardsville U.S.A. **160** F4
Edward VII Peninsula Antarctica **188** I1
Edziza, Mount *B.C.* Canada **149** O4
Eek *AK* U.S.A. **148** G3
Eek *r. AK* U.S.A. **148** G3
Eeklo Belgium **62** D3
Eel *r.* U.S.A. **158** A1
Eel, South Fork *r.* U.S.A. **158** B1
Eem *r.* Neth. **62** F2
Eemshaven *pt* Neth. **62** G1
Eenrum Neth. **62** G1
Eenzamheid Pan *salt pan* S. Africa **124** E4
Eesti *country* Europe *see* **Estonia**
Éfaté *i.* Vanuatu **133** G3
Effingham U.S.A. **160** F4
Efsus Turkey *see* **Afşin**
Eg Mongolia *see* **Batshireet**
Egadi, Isole *is Sicily* Italy **68** D5
Egan Range *mts* U.S.A. **159** F2
Eganville Canada **165** G1
Egavik *AK* U.S.A. **148** G2
Egedesminde Greenland *see* **Aasiaat**
Egegik Bay *AK* U.S.A. **148** H4
Eger *r.* Germany **63** M4
Eger Hungary **57** R7
Egersund Norway **55** E7
Egerton, Mount *hill* Australia **135** B6
Eggegebirge *hills* Germany **63** I3
Egg Island *AK* U.S.A. **148** G3
Egg Lake Canada **151** J4
Eggolsheim Germany **63** L5
Eghezée Belgium **62** E4
Egilsstaðir Iceland **54** [inset]
Eğin Turkey *see* **Kemaliye**
Eğirdir Turkey **69** N6
Eğirdir Gölü *l.* Turkey **69** N6
Egiyn Gol *r.* Mongolia **94** E1
Eglinton U.K. **61** E2
Egmond aan Zee Neth. **62** E2
Egmont, Cape N.Z. **139** D4
Egmont, Mount *vol.* N.Z. *see* **Taranaki, Mount**
Egmont National Park N.Z. **139** E4
eGoli S. Africa *see* **Johannesburg**
Eğrigöz Dağı *mts* Turkey **69** M5
Egton U.K. **58** G4
Éguas *r.* Brazil **179** B1
Egvekinot Rus. Fed. **148** C2

▶**Egypt** *country* Africa **108** C4
3rd most populous country in Africa.

Ehden Lebanon **107** B2
Ehen Hudag *Nei Mongol* China **94** E4
Ehingen (Donau) Germany **57** L6
Ehle *r.* Germany **63** L2
Ehra-Lessien Germany **63** K2
Ehrenberg U.S.A. **159** F5
Ehrenberg Range *hills* Australia **135** E5
Eibelstadt Germany **63** K5
Eibergen Neth. **62** G2
Eichenzell Germany **63** J4
Eichstätt Germany **63** L6
Eidfjord Norway **55** E6
Eidsvold Australia **136** E5
Eidsvoll Norway **55** G6

Eifel hills Germany 62 G4
Eigenji Japan 92 C3
Eigg i. U.K. 60 C4
Eight Degree Channel India/Maldives 106 B5
Eights Coast Antarctica 188 K2
Eighty Mile Beach Australia 134 C4
Eiheiji Japan 92 C2
Eilat Israel 107 B5
Eildon Australia 138 B6
Eildon, Lake Australia 138 C6
Eileen Lake Canada 151 J2
Eilenburg Germany 63 M3
Eil Malk i. Palau 82 [inset]
Eimke Germany 63 K2
Einasleigh Australia 136 D3
Einasleigh r. Australia 136 C3
Einbeck Germany 63 J3
Eindhoven Neth. 62 F3
Einme Myanmar 86 A3
Einsiedeln Switz. 66 I3
Éire country Europe see Ireland
Eirik Ridge sea feature N. Atlantic Ocean 184 F2
Eiriosgaigh i. U.K. see Eriskay
Eirunepé Brazil 176 E5
Eisberg hill Germany 63 J3
Eiseb watercourse Namibia 123 C5
Eisenach Germany 63 K4
Eisenberg Germany 63 L4
Eisenhower, Mount Canada see Castle Mountain
Eisenhüttenstadt Germany 57 O4
Eisenstadt Austria 57 P7
Eisfeld Germany 63 K4
Eisleben Lutherstadt Germany 63 L3
Eite, Loch inlet U.K. see Etive, Loch
Eiterfeld Germany 63 J4
Eivissa Spain see Ibiza
Eivissa i. Spain see Ibiza
Ejea de los Caballeros Spain 67 F2
Ejeda Madag. 123 E6
Ejin Horo Qi Nei Mongol China see Altan Shiret
Ejin Qi Nei Mongol China see Dalain Hob
Ejmiadzin Armenia see Ejmiatsin
Ejmiatsin Armenia 113 G2
Ejutla Mex. 167 F5
Ekalaka U.S.A. 156 G3
Ekenäs Fin. 55 M7
Ekerem Turkm. 110 D2
Ekeren Belgium 62 E3
Eketahuna N.Z. 139 E5
Ekibastuz Kazakh. 102 E1
Ekimchan Rus. Fed. 90 D1
Ekinyazı Turkey 107 D1
Ekityki, Ozero l. Rus. Fed. 148 B2
Ekka Island N.W.T. Canada 149 Q2
Ekonda Rus. Fed. 77 L3
Ekostrovskaya Imandra, Ozero l. Rus. Fed. 54 R3
Ekshärad Sweden 55 H6
Eksjö Sweden 55 I8
Eksteenfontein S. Africa 124 C5
Ekström Ice Shelf Antarctica 188 B2
Ekuk AK U.S.A. 148 H4
Ekwan r. Canada 152 E3
Ekwan Point Canada 152 E3
Ekwok AK U.S.A. 148 H4
Ela Myanmar 86 B3
El Aaiún W. Sahara see Laâyoune
Elafonisou, Steno sea chan. Greece 69 J6
El 'Agrûd well Egypt see Al 'Ajrūd
Elaia, Cape Cyprus 107 B2
El 'Alamein Egypt see Al 'Alamayn
El Alamo Mex. 166 A2
El 'Âmirîya Egypt see Al 'Āmirīyah
Elands r. S. Africa 125 I3
Elandsdoorn S. Africa 125 I3
El Aouinet Alg. 68 B7
Elar Armenia see Abovyan
El Araîche Morocco see Larache
El Arco Mex. 166 B2
El Ariana Tunisia see L'Ariana
El Aricha Alg. 64 D5
El 'Arîsh Egypt see Al 'Arīsh
El Arrouch Alg. 68 B6
El Ashmûnein Egypt see Al Ashmūnayn
El Asnam Alg. see Chlef
Elassona Greece 69 J5
Elat Israel see Eilat
Elato atoll Micronesia 81 L5
Elazığ Turkey 113 E3
Elba U.S.A. 163 C6
Elba, Isola d' i. Italy 68 D3
El'ban Rus. Fed. 90 E2
El Barco de Valdeorras Spain see O Barco
El Barreal salt l. Mex. 166 D2
Elbasan Albania 69 I4
El Batroun Lebanon see Batroûn
El Baúl Venez. 176 E2
El Bawîti Egypt see Al Bawīṭī
El Bayadh Alg. 64 E5
Elbe r. Germany 63 J1
also known as Labe (Czech Republic)
Elbe-Havel-Kanal canal Germany 63 L2
El Béqaa valley Lebanon 107 C2
Elbert, Mount U.S.A. 156 G5
Elberta U.S.A. 159 H2
Elberton U.S.A. 163 D5
Elbeuf France 66 E2
Elbeyli Turkey 107 C1
El Billete, Cerro mt. Mex. 167 E5
Elbing Poland see Elbląg
Elbistan Turkey 112 E3
Elbląg Poland 57 Q3
El Bluff Nicaragua 166 [inset] J6
El Boulaïda Alg. see Blida
Elbow Canada 151 J5
Elbow Lake U.S.A. 160 D2
El Bozal Mex. 161 C8
El Brasil Mex. 167 E3
►El'brus mt. Rus. Fed. 113 F2
Highest mountain in Europe.
Elburg Neth. 62 F2
El Burgo de Osma Spain 67 E3
Elburz Mountains Iran 110 C2
El Cajon U.S.A. 158 E5
El Cajón, Represa dam Hond. 166 [inset] I6
El Callao Venez. 176 F2
El Campo U.S.A. 161 D6
El Capitan Mountain U.S.A. 157 G6
El Capulín r. Mex. 161 C7
El Casco Mex. 166 D3
El Cebú, Cerro mt. Mex. 167 G6
El Centro U.S.A. 159 F5
El Cerro Bol. 176 F7
Elche Spain see Elche-Elx
Elche-Elx Spain 67 F4
El Chichónal vol. Mex. 167 G5
El Chilicote Mex. 166 D2
Elcho Island Australia 136 A1
El Coca Orellana Ecuador see Coca
El Coca Ecuador see Coca
El Cocuy, Parque Nacional nat. park Col. 176 D2
El Cuyo Mex. 167 I4
Elda Spain 67 F4
El Dátil Mex. 166 B2
El Desemboque Mex. 157 E7
El Diamante Mex. 166 E2
El'dikan Rus. Fed. 77 O3
El Djezair country Africa see Algeria
El Djezair Alg. see Algiers
El Doctor Mex. 166 B2
Eldon U.S.A. 160 E4
Eldorado Arg. 178 F3
Eldorado Brazil 179 A4
El Dorado Col. 176 D3
El Dorado Mex. 166 D3
El Dorado AR U.S.A. 161 E5
El Dorado KS U.S.A. 160 D4
Eldorado U.S.A. 161 C6
El Dorado Venez. 176 F2
Eldorado Mountains U.S.A. 159 F4
Eldoret Kenya 122 D3
Eldridge, Mount AK U.S.A. 149 L2
Elea, Cape Cyprus see Elaia, Cape
Eleanor U.S.A. 164 E4
Electric Peak U.S.A. 156 F3
Elefantes r. Moz. see Olifants
El Eglab plat. Alg. 120 C2
El Ejido Spain 67 E5
Elemi Triangle terr. Africa see Ilemi Triangle
El Encanto Col. 176 D4
Elend Germany 63 K3
Elephanta Caves tourist site India 106 B2
Elephant Butte Reservoir U.S.A. 157 G6
Elephant Island Antarctica 188 A2
Elephant Pass Sri Lanka 106 D4
Elephant Point Bangl. 105 H5
Elephant Point AK U.S.A. 148 G2
Eleşkirt Turkey 113 F3
El Estor Guat. 167 H6
El Eulma Alg. 64 F4
Eleuthera i. Bahamas 163 E7
Eleven Point r. U.S.A. 161 F4
El Fahs Tunisia 68 C6
El Faiyûm Egypt see Al Fayyūm
El Fasher Sudan 121 F3
El Ferrol Spain see Ferrol
El Ferrol del Caudillo Spain see Ferrol
Elfershausen Germany 63 J4
El Fud Eth. 122 E3
El Fuerte Mex. 166 C3
El Gara Egypt see Qārah
El Geneina Sudan 121 F3
El Geteina Sudan 108 D7
El Ghardaqa Egypt see Al Ghurdaqah
El Ghor plain Jordan/West Bank see Al Ghawr
Elgin U.K. 60 F3
Elgin IL U.S.A. 160 F3
Elgin ND U.S.A. 160 C2
Elgin NV U.S.A. 159 F3
Elgin TX U.S.A. 161 D6
El'ginskiy Rus. Fed. 77 P3
El Gîza Egypt see Giza
El Goléa Alg. 64 E5
El Golfo de Santa Clara Mex. 166 B2
Elgon, Mount Kenya/Uganda 100 C6
El Grullo Tamaulipas Mex. 167 F3
El Guante Mex. 166 D2
El Hadjar Alg. 68 B6
El Ḥammâm Egypt see Al Ḥammām
El Ḥammâmi reg. Mauritania 120 B2
El Ḥank esc. Mali/Mauritania 120 C2
El Ḥarra Egypt see Al Ḥarrah
El Hazim Jordan see Al Hazīm
El Ḥeiz Egypt see Al Ḥayz
El Hierro i. Canary Is 120 B2
El Higo Mex. 167 F4
El Homr Alg. 64 E6
El Homra Sudan 108 D7
Eliase Maluku Indon. 83 D5
Elías Piña Dom. Rep. 169 J5
Elichpur India see Achalpur
Elida U.S.A. 164 C3
Elie U.K. 60 G4
Elila r. Dem. Rep. Congo 122 C4
Elim AK U.S.A. 148 G2
Elimberrum France see Auch
Eling China see Yinjiang
Elingampangu Dem. Rep. Congo 122 C4
Eliot, Mount Canada 153 J2
Élisabethville Dem. Rep. Congo see Lubumbashi
Eliseu Martins Brazil 177 J5
El Iskandarîya Egypt see Alexandria
Elista Rus. Fed. 53 J7
Elixku Xinjiang China 98 B5
Elizabeth NJ U.S.A. 165 H3
Elizabeth WV U.S.A. 164 E4
Elizabeth, Mount hill Australia 134 D4
Elizabeth Bay Namibia 124 B4
Elizabeth City U.S.A. 162 E4
Elizabeth Island Pitcairn Is see Henderson Island
Elizabeth Point Namibia 124 B4
Elizabethton U.S.A. 162 D4
Elizabethtown IL U.S.A. 160 F4
Elizabethtown KY U.S.A. 164 C5
Elizabethtown NC U.S.A. 163 E5
Elizabethtown NY U.S.A. 165 I1
El Jadida Morocco 64 C5
El Jaralito Mex. 166 D3
El Jem Tunisia 68 D7
El Jicaro Nicaragua 166 [inset] I6
El Juile Mex. 167 G5
Elk r. Canada 150 H5
Ełk Poland 57 S4
Elk r. U.S.A. 165 H4
El Kaa Lebanon see Qaa
El Kab Sudan 108 D6
Elkader U.S.A. 160 F3
El Kala Alg. 68 C6
Elk City U.S.A. 161 D5
Elkedra Australia 136 A4
Elkedra watercourse Australia 136 B4
El Kef Tunisia see Le Kef
El Kelaâ des Srarhna Morocco 64 C5
Elkford Canada 150 H5
Elk Grove U.S.A. 158 C2
El Khalil West Bank see Hebron
El Khandaq Sudan 108 D6
El Khârga Egypt see Al Khārijah
El Kharrûba Egypt see Al Kharrūbah
Elkhart IN U.S.A. 164 C3
Elkhart KS U.S.A. 161 C4
El Khartûm Sudan see Khartoum
El Khenachich esc. Mali see El Khnâchîch
El Khnâchîch esc. Mali 120 C2
Elkhorn U.S.A. 160 F3
Elkhorn City U.S.A. 164 D5
Elkhovo Bulg. 69 L3
Elki Turkey see Beytüşşebap
Elkin U.S.A. 162 D4
Elkins U.S.A. 164 F4
Elk Island National Park Canada 151 H4
Elk Lake Canada 152 E5
Elk Lake l. U.S.A. 164 C1
Elkland U.S.A. 165 G3
Elk Mountain U.S.A. 156 G4
Elk Mountains U.S.A. 159 J2
Elko Canada 150 H5
Elko U.S.A. 159 F1
Elk Point Canada 151 I4
Elk Point U.S.A. 160 D3
Elk Springs U.S.A. 159 I1
Elkton MD U.S.A. 165 H4
Elkton VA U.S.A. 165 F4
El Kûbri Egypt see Al Kūbrī
El Kuntilla Egypt see Al Kuntillah
Elkview U.S.A. 164 E4
Ellas country Europe see Greece
Ellaville U.S.A. 163 C5
Ell Bay Canada 151 O1
Ellef Ringnes Island Canada 147 H2
Ellen, Mount U.S.A. 159 H2
Ellenburg Depot U.S.A. 165 I1
Ellendale U.S.A. 160 D2
Ellensburg U.S.A. 156 C3
Ellenville U.S.A. 165 H3
El León, Cerro mt. Mex. 161 B7
Ellesmere, Lake N.Z. 139 D6
►Ellesmere Island Canada 147 J2
4th largest island in North America, and 10th in the world.
Ellesmere Island National Park Reserve Canada see Quttinirpaaq National Park
Ellesmere Port U.K. 58 E5
Ellettsville U.S.A. 164 B4
Ellice r. Canada 151 K1
Ellice Island N.W.T. Canada 149 N1
Ellice Island atoll Tuvalu see Funafuti
Ellice Islands country S. Pacific Ocean see Tuvalu
Ellicott City U.S.A. 165 G4
Ellijay U.S.A. 163 C5
El Limón Tamaulipas Mex. 167 F4
Ellingen Germany 63 K5
Elliot S. Africa 125 H6
Elliot, Mount Australia 136 D3
Elliotdale S. Africa 125 I6
Elliot Knob mt. U.S.A. 164 F4
Elliot Lake Canada 152 E5
Elliott Australia 134 F4
Elliott Highway AK U.S.A. 149 J2
Elliston U.S.A. 164 E5
Ellon U.K. 60 G3
Ellora Caves tourist site India 106 B1
Ellsworth KS U.S.A. 160 D4
Ellsworth ME U.S.A. 162 G2
Ellsworth NE U.S.A. 160 C3
Ellsworth WI U.S.A. 160 E2
Ellsworth Land reg. Antarctica 188 K1
Ellsworth Mountains Antarctica 188 L1
Ellwangen (Jagst) Germany 63 K6
El Maghreb country Africa see Morocco
Elmakuz Dağı mt. Turkey 107 A1
Elmalı Turkey 69 M6
El Malpais National Monument nat. park U.S.A. 159 J4
El Manşûra Egypt see Al Manşūrah
El Maţarîya Egypt see Al Maţarīyah
El Mazâr Egypt see Al Mazār
El Médano Mex. 166 C3
El Meghaïer Alg. 64 F5
El Milia Alg. 64 F4
El Minya Egypt see Al Minyā
Elmira Ont. Canada 164 E2
Elmira P.E.I. Canada 153 J5
Elmira MI U.S.A. 164 C1
Elmira NY U.S.A. 165 G2
El Mirage U.S.A. 159 G5
El Moral Mex. 167 E2
El Moral Spain 67 E5
Elmore Australia 138 B6
El Mreyyé reg. Mauritania 120 C3
Elmshorn Germany 63 J1
El Muglad Sudan 108 C7
Elmvale Canada 164 F1
Elnesvågen Norway 54 E5
El Nevado, Cerro mt. Col. 176 D3
El Nido Palawan Phil. 82 B4
El Oasis Mex. 159 F5
El Obeid Sudan 108 D7
El Ocote, Parque Natural nature res. Mex. 167 G5
El Odaiya Sudan 108 C7
El Oro Coahuila Mex. 166 E3
Elorza Venez. 176 E2
Elota Mex. 166 D4
El Oued Alg. 64 F5
Eloy U.S.A. 159 H5
El Palmito Mex. 166 D3
Elpaputih, Teluk b. Seram Indon. 83 D3
El Paso IL U.S.A. 160 F3
El Paso KS U.S.A. see Derby
El Paso TX U.S.A. 157 G7
El Peñasco Mex. 167 E4
Elphin U.K. 60 D2
Elphinstone i. Myanmar see Thayawthadangyi Kyun
El Pino, Sierra mts Mex. 166 E2
El Portal U.S.A. 158 D3
El Porvenir Mex. 166 D2
El Porvenir Panama 166 [inset] K7
El Prat de Llobregat Spain 67 H3
El Progreso Guat. see Guastatoya
El Progreso Hond. 166 [inset] I6
El Puente Nicaragua 166 [inset] I6
El Puerto de Santa María Spain 67 C5
El Qâhira Egypt see Cairo
El Qasimiye r. Lebanon 107 B3
El Quds Israel/West Bank see Jerusalem
El Quşeima Egypt see Al Quşaymah
El Quşeir Egypt see Al Quşayr
El Qûşîya Egypt see Al Qūşīyah
El Real Panama 166 [inset] K7
El Regocijo Mex. 161 B8
El Reno U.S.A. 161 D5
El Retorno Mex. 167 E4
Elrose Canada 151 I5
El Rucio Zacatecas Mex. 166 E4
Elsa Y.T. Canada 149 N3
El Sabinal, Parque Nacional nat. park Mex. 167 F3
El Şaff Egypt see Aş Şaff
El Sahuaro Mex. 166 B2
El Salado Mex. 161 C7
El Salto Mex. 161 B8
El Salvador country Central America 167 H6
El Salvador Chile 178 C3
El Salvador Mex. 161 C7
Elsass reg. France see Alsace
El Sauz Chihuahua Mex. 166 D2
Else r. Germany 63 I2
El Sellûm Egypt see As Sallūm
Elsey Australia 134 F3
El Shallûfa Egypt see Ash Shallūfah
El Sharana Australia 134 F3
El Shaţţ Egypt see Ash Shaţţ
Elsie U.S.A. 164 C2
Elsinore Denmark see Helsingør
Elsinore CA U.S.A. 158 E5
Elsinore UT U.S.A. 159 G2
Elsinore Lake U.S.A. 158 E5
El Socorro Mex. 166 E3
Elson Lagoon AK U.S.A. 148 H1
El Sueco Mex. 166 D2
El Suweis Egypt see Suez
El Suweis governorate Egypt see As Suways
El Tajín tourist site Mex. 167 F4
El Tama, Parque Nacional nat. park Venez. 176 D2
El Tarf Alg. 68 C6
El Teleno mt. Spain 67 C2
El Temascal Mex. 161 D7
El Ter r. Spain 67 H2
El Thamad Egypt see Ath Thamad
El Tigre Venez. 176 F2
El Tigre, Parque Nacional nat. park Guat. 167 H5
Eltmann Germany 63 K5
El'ton Rus. Fed. 53 J6
El'ton, Ozero l. Rus. Fed. 53 J6
El Tren Mex. 166 B2
El Triunfo Mex. 166 C4
El Tuparro, Parque Nacional nat. park Col. 176 E2
El Tûr Egypt see Aţ Ţūr
El Turbio Arg. 178 B8
El Uqşur Egypt see Luxor
Eluru India 106 D2
Elva Estonia 55 O7
El Vallecillo Mex. 166 C2
Elvanfoot U.K. 60 F5
Elvas Port. 67 C4
Elverum Norway 55 G6
El Vigía, Cerro mt. Mex. 166 D4
Elvira Brazil 176 D5
El Wak Kenya 122 E3
El Wâtya well Egypt see Al Wāţiyah
Elwood IN U.S.A. 164 C3
Elwood NE U.S.A. 160 D3
El Wuz Sudan 108 D7
Elx Spain see Elche-Elx
Elxleben Germany 63 K3
Ely U.K. 59 H6
Ely MN U.S.A. 160 F2
Ely NV U.S.A. 159 F2
Elyria U.S.A. 164 D3
Elz Germany 63 I4
El Zacatón, Cerro mt. Mex. 167 F5
El Zagâzîg Egypt see Az Zaqāzīq
El Zape Mex. 166 D3
Elze Germany 63 J2
Émaé i. Vanuatu 133 G3
Emāmrūd Iran 110 D2
Emām Şaḩēb Afgh. 111 H2
Emām Taqī Iran 110 E2
Emån r. Sweden 55 J8
E. Martínez Mex. see Emiliano Martínez
Emas, Parque Nacional das nat. park Brazil 177 H7
Emazar Kazakh. 98 C3
Emba Kazakh. 102 A2
Emba r. Kazakh. 102 A2
Embalenhle S. Africa 125 I4
Embarcación Arg. 178 D2
Embarras Portage Canada 151 I3
Embi Kazakh. see Emba
Embira r. Brazil see Envira
Emborcação, Represa de resr Brazil 179 B2
Embrun Canada 165 H1
Embu Kenya 122 D4
Emden Germany 63 H1
Emden Deep sea feature N. Pacific Ocean see Cape Johnson Depth
Emei China see Emeishan
Emeishan China 96 D2
Emei Shan mt. China 96 D2
Emel' r. Kazakh. 98 C3
Emerald Australia 136 E4
Emeril Canada 153 I3
Emerita Augusta Spain see Mérida
Emerson Canada 151 L5
Emerson U.S.A. 164 D4
Emery U.S.A. 159 H2
Emesa Syria see Homs
Emet Turkey 69 M5
eMgwenya S. Africa 125 J3
Emigrant Pass U.S.A. 158 E1
Emigrant Valley U.S.A. 159 F3
Emi Koussi mt. Chad 121 E3
Emile r. Canada 150 G2
Emiliano Martínez Mex. 166 D3
Emiliano Zapata Chiapas Mex. 167 H5
Emin Xinjiang China 98 C3
Emine, Nos pt Bulg. 69 L3
Eminence U.S.A. 164 C4
Emin He r. China 98 C3
Eminska Planina hills Bulg. 69 L3
Emirdağ Turkey 69 N5
Emir Dağı mt. Turkey 69 N5
Emir Dağları mts Turkey 69 N5
eMjindini S. Africa 125 J3
Emmaboda Sweden 55 I8
Emmahaven Sumatera Indon. see Telukbayur
Emmaste Estonia 55 M7
Emmaville Australia 138 E2
Emmeloord Neth. 62 F2
Emmelshausen Germany 63 H4
Emmen Neth. 62 G2
Emmen Switz. 66 I3
Emmerich Germany 62 G3
Emmet Australia 136 D5
Emmetsburg U.S.A. 160 E3
Emmett U.S.A. 156 D4
Emmiganuru India 106 C3
Emmonak AK U.S.A. 148 F3
Emo Canada 151 M5
Emona Slovenia see Ljubljana
Emory Peak U.S.A. 161 C6
Empalme Mex. 166 C3
Empangeni S. Africa 125 J5
Emperor Seamount Chain sea feature N. Pacific Ocean 186 H2
Emperor Trough sea feature N. Pacific Ocean 186 H2
Empingham Reservoir U.K. see Rutland Water
Emplawas Maluku Indon. 83 D5
Empoli Italy 68 D3
Emporia KS U.S.A. 160 D4
Emporia VA U.S.A. 165 G5
Emporium U.S.A. 165 F3
Empress Canada 151 I5
Empty Quarter des. Saudi Arabia see Rub' al Khālī
Ems r. Germany 63 H1
Emsdale Canada 164 F1
Emsdetten Germany 63 H2
Ems-Jade-Kanal canal Germany 63 H1
eMzinoni S. Africa 125 I4
Ena Japan 92 D3
Enafors Sweden 54 H5
Ena-san mt. Japan 92 D3
Enbek Kazakh. 98 B2
Encantadas, Serra das hills Brazil 178 F4
Encanto, Cape Luzon Phil. 82 C3
Encarnación Mex. 166 E4
Encarnación Para. 178 E3
Enchi Ghana 120 C4
Encinal U.S.A. 161 D6
Encinitas U.S.A. 158 E5
Encino U.S.A. 157 G6
Encruzilhada Brazil 179 C1
Endako Canada 150 E4
Endau r. Malaysia 84 C2
Endau-Rompin National Park nat. park Malaysia 87 C7
Ende Flores Indon. 83 B5
Ende i. Indon. 83 B5
Endeavour Strait Australia 136 C1
Enderby Canada 150 G5
Enderby atoll Micronesia see Puluwat
Enderby Land reg. Antarctica 188 D2
Endicott U.S.A. 165 G2
Endicott Mountains AK U.S.A. 148 I2
EnenKio terr. N. Pacific Ocean see Wake Island
Energodar Ukr. see Enerhodar
Enerhodar Ukr. 53 G7
Enewetak atoll Marshall Is 186 G5
Enez Turkey 69 L4
Enfe Lebanon 107 B2
Enfião, Ponta do pt Angola 123 B5
Enfidaville Tunisia 68 D6
Enfield U.S.A. 162 E4
Engan Norway 54 F5
Engaru Japan 90 F3
Engcobo S. Africa 125 H6
En Gedi Israel 107 B4
Engelhard U.S.A. 162 F5
Engel's Rus. Fed. 53 J6
Engelschmangat sea chan. Neth. 62 E1
Enggano i. Indon. 84 C4
Enghien Belgium 62 E4
England admin. div. U.K. 59 E6
Englee Canada 153 L4
Englehart Canada 152 F5
Englewood FL U.S.A. 163 D7
Englewood OH U.S.A. 164 C4
English r. Canada 151 M5
English U.S.A. 164 B4
English Bazar India see Ingraj Bazar
English Channel France/U.K. 59 F9
English Coast Antarctica 188 L2
Engozero Rus. Fed. 52 G2
Enhlalakahle S. Africa 125 J5
Enid U.S.A. 161 D4
Eniwa Japan 90 F4
Eniwetok atoll Marshall Is see Enewetak
Enjiang China see Yongfeng
Enkeldoorn Zimbabwe see Chivhu
Enkhuizen Neth. 62 F2
Enköping Sweden 55 J7
Enmelen Rus. Fed. 148 D2
Enna Sicily Italy 68 F6
Ennadai Lake Canada 151 K2
En Nahud Sudan 108 C7
Ennedi, Massif mts Chad 121 F3
Ennell, Lough l. Ireland 61 E4
Enngonia Australia 138 B2
Enning U.S.A. 160 C2
Ennis Ireland 61 D5
Ennis MT U.S.A. 156 F3
Ennis TX U.S.A. 161 D5
Enniscorthy Ireland 61 F5
Enniskillen U.K. 61 E3
Ennistymon Ireland 61 C5
Enn Nâqoûra Lebanon 107 B3
Enns r. Austria 57 O6
Eno Fin. 54 Q5
Enoch U.S.A. 159 G3
Enok Sumatera Indon. 84 C3
Enontekiö Fin. 54 M2
Enosburg Falls U.S.A. 165 I1
Enosville U.S.A. 164 B4
Enping China 97 G4
Enrekang Sulawesi Indon. 83 A3
Enrile Luzon Phil. 82 C2
Ens Neth. 62 F2
Ensay Australia 138 C6
Enschede Neth. 62 G2
Ense Germany 63 I3
Ensenada Baja California Mex. 166 A2
Ensenada Baja California Sur Mex. 166 C4
Enshi China 97 F2
Enshū-nada g. Japan 92 D4
Ensley U.S.A. 163 C6
Entebbe Uganda 122 D3
Enterprise Canada 150 G2
Enterprise AL U.S.A. 163 C6
Enterprise OR U.S.A. 156 D3
Enterprise UT U.S.A. 159 G3
Enterprise Point Palawan Phil. 82 B4
Entimau, Bukit hill Malaysia 85 F2
Entre Ríos Bol. 176 F8
Entre Rios Brazil 177 H5
Entre Rios de Minas Brazil 179 B3
Entroncamento Port. 67 B4
Enugu Nigeria 120 D4
Enurmino Rus. Fed. 148 E2
Envira Brazil 176 D5
Envira r. Brazil 176 D5
'En Yahav Israel 107 B4
Enyamba Dem. Rep. Congo 122 C4
Enzan Japan 93 E3
Eochaill Ireland see Youghal
Epe Neth. 62 F2
Epéna Congo 122 B3
Épernay France 62 D5
Ephraim U.S.A. 159 H2
Ephrata U.S.A. 165 G3
Epi i. Vanuatu 133 G3
Epidamnus Albania see Durrës
Épinal France 66 H2
Episkopi Bay Cyprus 107 A2
Episkopis, Kolpos b. Cyprus see Episkopi Bay
ePitoli S. Africa see Pretoria
Epomeo, Monte hill Italy 68 E4
Epping U.K. 59 H7
Epping Forest National Park Australia 136 D4
Eppstein Germany 63 I4
Eppynt, Mynydd hills U.K. 59 D6
Epsom U.K. 59 G7
Epte r. France 62 B5
Eqlīd Iran 110 D4
Equatorial Guinea country Africa 120 D4
Équeurdreville-Hainneville France 59 F9
Erac Creek watercourse Australia 138 B1
Eran Palawan Phil. 82 B4
Eran Bay Palawan Phil. 82 B4
Erandol India 106 B1
Erawadi r. Myanmar see Irrawaddy
Erawan National Park Thai. 87 B4
Erbaa Turkey 112 E2
Erbendorf Germany 63 M5
Erbeskopf hill Germany 62 H5
Ercan airport Cyprus 107 A2
Erciş Turkey 113 F3
Erciyes Dağı mt. Turkey 112 D3

Érd Hungary 68 H1
Erdaobaihe China see Baihe
Erdaogou Qinghai China 94 C5
Erdao Jiang r. China 90 B4
Erdek Turkey 69 L4
Erdemli Turkey 107 B1
Erdene Dornogovĭ Mongolia 95 G2
Erdenedalay Mongolia 94 F2
Erdenemandal Arhangay Mongolia 94 E1
Erdenesant Mongolia 94 F2
Erdenet Hövsgöl Mongolia see Shine-Ider
Erdenet Orhon Mongolia 94 F1
Erdenetsagaan Mongolia 95 H2
Erdenetsogt Bayanhongor Mongolia 94 E2
Erdenetsogt Ömnögovĭ Mongolia see Bayan-Ovoo
Erdi reg. Chad 121 F3
Erdniyevskiy Rus. Fed. 53 J7

▶Erebus, Mount vol. Antarctica 188 H1
Highest active volcano in Antarctica.

Erechim Brazil 178 F3
Ereentsav Mongolia 95 H1
Ereğli Konya Turkey 112 D3
Ereğli Zonguldak Turkey 69 N4
Erego Moz. see Errego
Erei, Monti mts Sicily Italy 68 F6
Ereke Sulawesi Indon. 83 B4
Erementaū Kazakh. see Yereymentau
Eréndira Mex. 167 E5
Erenhaberga Shan mts China 98 D4
Erenhot Nei Mongol China 95 H3
Erepucu, Lago de l. Brazil 177 G4
Erevan Armenia see Yerevan
Erfurt Germany 63 L4
Erfurt airport Germany 63 K4
Ergani Turkey 113 E3
'Erg Chech des. Alg./Mali 120 C2
Ergel Mongolia see Hatanbulag
Ergene r. Turkey 69 L4
Ērgļi Latvia 55 N8
Ergu China 90 C3
Ergun Nei Mongol China 95 J1
Ergun He r. China/Rus. Fed. see Argun'
Ergun Youqi Nei Mongol China see Ergun
Ergun Zuoqi China see Genhe
Erguveyem r. Rus. Fed. 148 C2
Er Hai l. China 96 D3
Erhulai China 90 B4
Eriboll, Loch inlet U.K. 60 E2
Ericht r. U.K. 60 F4
Ericht, Loch l. U.K. 60 E4
Erickson Canada 151 L5
Erie KS U.S.A. 161 E4
Erie PA U.S.A. 164 E2
Erie, Lake Canada/U.S.A. 164 E2
'Erîgât des. Mali 120 C3
Erik Eriksenstretet sea chan. Svalbard 76 D2
Eriksdale Canada 151 L5
Erimo-misaki c. Japan 90 F4
Erin Canada 164 E2
Erinpura Road India 104 C4
Eriskay i. U.K. 60 B3
Eritrea country Africa 108 E6
Erlangen Germany 63 L5
Erlangping China 97 F1
Erldunda Australia 135 F6
Erlistoun watercourse Australia 135 C6
Erlong Shan mt. China 90 C4
Erlongshan Shuiku resr China 90 B4
Ermak Kazakh. see Aksu
Ermana, Khrebet mts Rus. Fed. 95 H1
Ermelo Neth. 62 F2
Ermelo S. Africa 125 I4
Ermenek Turkey 107 A1
Ermenek r. Turkey 107 A1
Ermont Egypt see Armant
Ermoupoli Greece 69 K6
Ernakulam India 106 C4
Erne r. Ireland/U.K. 61 D3
Ernest Giles Range hills Australia 135 C6
Erode India 106 C4
Eromanga Australia 137 C5
Erongo admin. reg. Namibia 124 B1
Erp Neth. 62 F3
Erpu Xinjiang China 94 C3
Erqu Shaanxi China see Zhouzhi
Errabiddy Hills Australia 135 A6
Er Rachidia Morocco 64 D5
Er Raoui des. Alg. 64 D6
Errego Moz. 123 D5
Er Remla Tunisia 68 D7
Er Renk Sudan 108 D7
Errigal hill Ireland 61 D2
Errinundra National Park Australia 138 D6
Erris Head hd Ireland 61 B3
Errol U.S.A. 165 J1
Erromango i. Vanuatu 133 G3
Erronan i. Vanuatu see Futuna
Erseka Albania see Ersekë
Ersekë Albania 69 I4
Erskine U.S.A. 160 D2
Ersmark Sweden 54 L5
Ertai Xinjiang China 94 B2
Ertil' Rus. Fed. 53 I6
Ertis r. Kazakh./Rus. Fed. see Irtysh
Ertix He r. China/Kazakh. 102 G2
Ērtra country Africa see Eritrea
Eruh Turkey 113 F3
Erwin U.S.A. 162 D4
Erwitte Germany 63 I3
Erxleben Sachsen-Anhalt Germany 63 L2
Erxleben Sachsen-Anhalt Germany 63 L2
Eryuan China 96 C3
Erzerum Turkey see Erzurum
Erzgebirge mts Czech Rep./Germany 63 N4
Erzhan China 90 B2
Erzin Rus. Fed. 94 C1
Erzin Turkey 107 C1
Erzincan Turkey 113 E3
Erzurum Turkey 113 F3
Esa-ala P.N.G. 136 E1
Esan-misaki pt Japan 90 F4
Esashi Japan 90 F3
Esbjerg Denmark 55 F9
Esbo Fin. see Espoo
Escalante Negros Phil. 82 C4
Escalante U.S.A. 159 H3
Escalante r. U.S.A. 159 H3
Escalante Desert U.S.A. 159 G3
Escalón Mex. 166 D3
Escambia r. U.S.A. 163 C6
Escanaba U.S.A. 162 C2
Escárcega Mex. 167 H5
Escarpada Point Luzon Phil. 82 C2
Escatrón Spain 67 F3
Escaut r. Belgium 62 D4
Esch Neth. 62 F3
Eschede Germany 63 K2
Eschscholtz atoll Marshall Is see Bikini
Eschscholtz Bay AK U.S.A. 148 G2
Esch-sur-Alzette Lux. 62 F5
Eschwege Germany 63 K3
Eschweiler Germany 62 G4
Escondido r. Mex. 161 C6
Escondido r. Nicaragua 166 [inset] J6
Escondido U.S.A. 158 E5
Escudilla mt. U.S.A. 159 I5
Escuinapa Mex. 166 C4
Escuintla Guat. 167 H6
Escuintla Mex. 167 G6
Eséka Cameroon 120 E4
Eşen Turkey 69 M6
Esenguly Turkm. 110 D2
Esenguly Döwlet Gorugy nature res. Turkm. 110 D2
Esens Germany 63 H1
Eşfahān Iran 110 C3
Esfarayen, Reshteh-ye mts Iran 110 E2
Esfideh Iran 111 E3
Eshan China 96 D3
Eshāqābād Iran 110 E3
Eshkamesh Afgh. 111 H2
Eshkanān Iran 110 D5
Eshowe S. Africa 125 J5
Esikhawini S. Africa 125 K5
Esil Kazakh. see Yesil'
Esil r. Kazakh./Rus. Fed. see Ishim
Esk Australia 138 F1
Esk r. Australia 137 [inset]
Esk r. U.K. 58 D4
Eskdalemuir U.K. 60 F5
Esker Canada 153 I3
Eskifjörður Iceland 54 [inset]
Eski Gediz Turkey 69 M5
Eskilstuna Sweden 55 J7
Eskimo Lakes N.W.T. Canada 149 O1
Eskimo Point Canada see Arviat
Eskipazar Turkey 112 D2
Eskişehir Turkey 69 N5
Eski-Yakkabog' Uzbek. 111 G2
Esla r. Spain 67 C3
Eslāmābād-e Gharb Iran 110 B3
Esler Dağı mt. Turkey 69 M6
Eslohe (Sauerland) Germany 63 I3
Eslöv Sweden 55 H9
Esmā'īlī-ye Soflá Iran 110 E4
Eşme Turkey 69 M5
Esmeraldas Ecuador 176 C3
Esmont U.S.A. 165 F5
Esnagami Lake Canada 152 D4
Esnes France 62 D4
Espakeh Iran 111 F5
Espalion France 66 F4
España country Europe see Spain
Espanola Canada 152 E5
Espanola U.S.A. 161 B4
Esparta Hond. 166 [inset] I6
Espe Kazakh. 98 A4
Espelkamp Germany 63 I2
Espenberg, Cape AK U.S.A. 148 G2
Esperance Australia 135 C8
Esperance Bay Australia 135 C8
Esperanza research station Antarctica 188 A2
Esperanza Arg. 178 B8
Esperanza Sonora Mex. 166 C3
Esperanza Masbate Phil. 82 D4
Esperanza, Sierra de la mts Hond. 166 [inset] I6
Espichel, Cabo c. Port. 67 B4
Espigão, Serra do mts Brazil 179 A4
Espigüete mt. Spain 67 D2
Espinazo Mex. 167 E3
Espinhaço, Serra do mts Brazil 179 C2
Espinosa Brazil 179 C1
Espírito Santo Brazil see Vila Velha
Espírito Santo state Brazil 179 C2
Espiritu Luzon Phil. 82 C2
Espíritu Santo i. Vanuatu 133 G3
Espíritu Santo, Isla i. Mex. 166 C3
Espita Mex. 167 H4
Espoo Fin. 55 N6
Espuña mt. Spain 67 F5
Esqueda Mex. 166 C2
Esquel Arg. 178 B6
Esquimalt Canada 150 F5
Essang Sulawesi Indon. 83 C1
Essaouira Morocco 120 C1
Es Semara W. Sahara 120 B2
Essen Belgium 62 E3
Essen Germany 62 H3
Essen (Oldenburg) Germany 63 H2
Essequibo r. Guyana 177 G2
Essex Canada 164 D2
Essex CA U.S.A. 159 F4
Essex MD U.S.A. 165 G4
Essex NY U.S.A. 165 I1
Essexville U.S.A. 164 D2
Esslingen am Neckar Germany 63 J6
Esso Rus. Fed. 77 Q4
Essoyla Rus. Fed. 52 G3
Estagno Point Luzon Phil. 82 C2
Eşṭahbān Iran 110 D4
Estância Brazil 177 K6
Estancia U.S.A. 157 G6
Estand, Kūh-e mt. Iran 111 F4
Estats, Pic d' mt. France/Spain 66 E5
Estcourt S. Africa 125 I5
Este r. Germany 63 J1
Estelí Nicaragua 166 [inset] I6
Estella Spain 67 E2
Estepa Spain 67 D5
Estepona Spain 67 D5
Ester AK U.S.A. 149 K2
Esteras de Medinaceli Spain 67 E3
Esterhazy Canada 151 K5
Estero Bay U.S.A. 158 C4
Esteros Mex. 167 F4
Esteros Para. 178 D2
Este Sudeste, Cayos del is Col. 166 [inset] J6
Estevan Canada 151 K5
Estevan Group is Canada 150 D4
Estherville U.S.A. 160 E3
Estill U.S.A. 163 D5
Eston Canada 151 I5
Estonia country Europe 55 N7
Estonskaya S.S.R. country Europe see Estonia
Estrées-St-Denis France 62 C5
Estrela Brazil 179 A5
Estrela, Serra da mts Port. 67 C3
Estrela do Sul Brazil 179 B2
Estrella mt. Spain 67 E4
Estrella, Punta pt Mex. 166 B2
Estremoz Port. 67 C4
Estrondo, Serra hills Brazil 177 I5
Etadunna Australia 137 B6
Etah India 104 D4
Étain France 62 F5
Étamamiou Canada 153 K4
Étampes France 66 F2
Étaples France 62 B4
Etawah Rajasthan India 104 D4
Etawah Uttar Prad. India 104 D4
Etchojoa Mex. 166 C3
Ethandakukhanya S. Africa 125 J4
Ethelbert Canada 151 K5
Ethel Creek Australia 135 C5
E'Thembini S. Africa 124 F5

▶Ethiopia country Africa 122 D3
2nd most populous country in Africa.

Etimesğut Turkey 112 D3
Etive, Loch inlet U.K. 60 D4
Etivluk r. AK U.S.A. 148 H1

▶Etna, Mount vol. Sicily Italy 68 F6
Highest active volcano in Europe.

Etne Norway 55 D7
Etobicoke Canada 164 F2
Etolin Strait AK U.S.A. 148 F3
Etorofu-tō i. Rus. Fed. see Iturup, Ostrov
Etosha National Park Namibia 123 B5
Etosha Pan salt pan Namibia 123 B5
Etoumbi Congo 122 B3
Etrek r. Iran/Turkm. see Atrek
Etrek Turkm. 110 D2
Étrépagny France 62 B5
Étretat France 59 H9
Ettelbruck Lux. 62 G5
Etten-Leur Neth. 62 E3
Ettlingen Germany 63 I6
Ettrick Water r. U.K. 60 F5
Etzatlán Mex. 166 D4
Euabalong Australia 138 C4
Euboea i. Greece see Evvoia
Eucla Australia 135 E7
Euclid U.S.A. 164 E3
Euclides da Cunha Brazil 177 K6
Eucumbene, Lake Australia 138 D6
Eudistes, Lac des l. Canada 153 I4
Eudora U.S.A. 161 F5
Eudunda Australia 137 B7
Eufaula AL U.S.A. 163 C6
Eufaula OK U.S.A. 161 E5
Eufaula Lake resr U.S.A. 161 E5
Eugene U.S.A. 156 C3
Eugenia, Punta pt Mex. 166 B3
Eugowra Australia 138 D4
Eulo Australia 138 B2
Eumungerie Australia 138 D3
Eungella Australia 136 E4
Eungella National Park Australia 136 E4
Eunice LA U.S.A. 161 E6
Eunice NM U.S.A. 161 C5
Eupen Belgium 62 G4

▶Euphrates r. Asia 113 G5
Longest river in western Asia.
Also known as Al Furāt (Iraq/Syria) or Fırat (Turkey).

Eura Fin. 55 M6
Eure r. France 62 B5
Eureka AK U.S.A. 149 J2
Eureka CA U.S.A. 156 B4
Eureka KS U.S.A. 160 D4
Eureka MT U.S.A. 156 E2
Eureka NV U.S.A. 159 F2
Eureka OH U.S.A. 164 D4
Eureka SD U.S.A. 160 D2
Eureka UT U.S.A. 159 G2
Eureka Roadhouse AK U.S.A. 149 K3
Eureka Sound sea chan. Canada 147 J2
Eureka Springs U.S.A. 161 E4
Eureka Valley U.S.A. 158 E3
Euriowie Australia 137 C6
Euroa Australia 138 B6
Eurombah Australia 137 E5
Eurombah Creek r. Australia 137 E5
Europa, Île i. Indian Ocean 123 E6
Europa, Punta de pt Gibraltar see Europa Point
Europa Point Gibraltar 67 D5
Euskirchen Germany 62 G4
Eutaw U.S.A. 163 C5
Eutsuk Lake Canada 150 E4
Eutzsch Germany 63 M3
Eva Downs Australia 134 F4
Evans, Lac l. Canada 152 F4
Evans, Mount U.S.A. 156 G5
Evansburg Canada 150 H4
Evans City U.S.A. 164 E3
Evans Head Australia 138 F2
Evans Head hd Australia 138 F2
Evans Ice Stream Antarctica 188 L1
Evans Strait Canada 151 P2
Evanston IL U.S.A. 164 B2
Evanston WY U.S.A. 156 F4
Evansville Canada 152 E5
Evansville AK U.S.A. 149 J2
Evansville IN U.S.A. 164 B5
Evansville WY U.S.A. 156 G4
Evant U.S.A. 161 D6
Eva Perón Arg. see La Plata
Evart U.S.A. 164 C2
Evaton S. Africa 125 H4
Evaz Iran 110 D5
Evening Shade U.S.A. 161 F4
Evensk Rus. Fed. 77 Q3
Everard, Cape Australia see Hicks, Point
Everard, Lake salt flat Australia 137 A6
Everard, Mount Australia 135 F5
Everard Range hills Australia 135 F6
Everdingen Neth. 62 F3
Everek Turkey see Develi

▶Everest, Mount China/Nepal 105 F4
Highest mountain in the world and in Asia.

Everett PA U.S.A. 165 F3
Everett WA U.S.A. 156 C3
Evergem Belgium 62 D3
Everglades swamp U.S.A. 163 D7
Everglades National Park U.S.A. 163 D7
Evergreen U.S.A. 163 C6
Evesham Australia 136 C4
Evesham U.K. 59 F6
Evesham, Vale of valley U.K. 59 F6
Evijärvi Fin. 54 M5
Evje Norway 55 E7
Évora Port. 67 C4
Evoron, Ozero l. Rus. Fed. 90 E2
Évreux France 62 B5
Evros r. Greece/Turkey see Maritsa
Evrotas r. Greece 69 J6
Évry France 62 C6
Evrychou Cyprus 107 A2
Evrykhou Cyprus see Evrychou
Evvoia i. Greece 69 K5
Ewan Australia 136 D3
Ewaso Ngiro r. Kenya 122 E3
Ewe, Loch b. U.K. 60 D3
Ewenkizu Zizhiqi Nei Mongol China see Bayan Tohoi
Ewing U.S.A. 164 D5
Ewirgol Xinjiang China 98 D4
Ewo Congo 122 B4
Exaltación Bol. 176 E6
Excelsior S. Africa 125 H5
Excelsior Mountain U.S.A. 158 D2
Excelsior Mountains U.S.A. 158 D2
Exe r. U.K. 59 D8
Exeter Australia 138 E5
Exeter Canada 164 E2
Exeter U.K. 59 D8
Exeter CA U.S.A. 158 D3
Exeter NH U.S.A. 165 J2
Exeter Lake Canada 151 I1
Exloo Neth. 62 G2
Exminster U.K. 59 D8
Exmoor hills U.K. 59 D7
Exmoor National Park U.K. 59 D7
Exmore U.S.A. 165 H5
Exmouth Australia 134 A5
Exmouth U.K. 59 D8
Exmouth, Mount Australia 138 D3
Exmouth Gulf Australia 134 A5
Exmouth Lake Canada 150 H1
Exmouth Plateau sea feature Indian Ocean 185 P7
Expedition National Park Australia 136 E5
Expedition Range mts Australia 136 E5
Exploits r. Canada 153 L4
Exton U.S.A. 165 H3
Extremadura aut. comm. Spain 67 D4
Exuma Cays is Bahamas 163 E7
Exuma Sound sea chan. Bahamas 163 F7
Eyasi, Lake salt l. Tanz. 122 D4
Eyawadi r. Myanmar see Irrawaddy
Eye U.K. 59 I6
Eyeberry Lake Canada 151 J2
Eyelenoborsk Rus. Fed. 51 S3
Eyemouth U.K. 60 G5
Eyjafjörður inlet Iceland 54 [inset]
Eyl Somalia 122 E3
Eylau Rus. Fed. see Bagrationovsk
Eynsham U.K. 59 F7

▶Eyre (North), Lake Australia 137 B6
Largest lake in Oceania, and lowest point.

Eyre (South), Lake Australia 137 B6
Eyre, Lake Australia 137 B6
Eyre Creek watercourse Australia 136 B5
Eyre Mountains N.Z. 139 B7
Eyre Peninsula Australia 137 A7
Eystrup Germany 63 J2
Eysturoy i. Faroe Is 54 [inset]
Ezakheni S. Africa 125 J5
Ezel U.S.A. 164 D5
Ezenzeleni S. Africa 125 I4
Ezequiel Ramos Mexía, Embalse resr Arg. 178 C5
Ezhou China 97 G2
Ezhva Rus. Fed. 52 K3
Ezine Turkey 69 L5
Ezo i. Japan see Hokkaidō
Ezousa r. Cyprus 107 A2

F

Faaborg Denmark 55 G9
Faadhippolhu Atoll Maldives 106 B5
Faafxadhuun Somalia 122 E3
Fabens U.S.A. 157 G7
Faber, Mount hill Sing. 87 [inset]
Faber Lake Canada 150 G2
Fåborg Denmark see Faaborg
Fabriano Italy 68 E3
Faches-Thumesnil France 62 D4
Fachi Niger 120 E3
Fada Chad 121 F3
Fada-N'Gourma Burkina 120 D3
Fadghāmī Syria 113 F4
Fadiffolu Atoll Maldives see Faadhippolhu Atoll
Fadippolu Atoll Maldives see Faadhippolhu Atoll
Faenza Italy 68 D2
Færoerne terr. N. Atlantic Ocean see Faroe Islands
Faeroes terr. N. Atlantic Ocean see Faroe Islands
Fafanlap Papua Indon. 83 D3
Făgăraş Romania 69 K2

▶Fagatogo American Samoa 133 I3
Capital of American Samoa.

Fagersta Sweden 55 I7
Fagita Papua Indon. 83 D3
Fagne reg. Belgium 62 E4
Fagurhólsmýri Iceland 54 [inset]
Fagwir Sudan 108 D8
Fahraj Iran 110 D4
Fā'id Egypt 112 D5
Fairbanks AK U.S.A. 149 K2
Fairborn U.S.A. 164 C4
Fairbury U.S.A. 160 D3
Fairchance U.S.A. 164 F4
Fairfax U.S.A. 165 G4
Fairfield CA U.S.A. 158 B2
Fairfield IA U.S.A. 160 F3
Fairfield ID U.S.A. 156 E4
Fairfield IL U.S.A. 160 F4
Fairfield OH U.S.A. 164 C4
Fairfield TX U.S.A. 161 D6
Fair Haven U.S.A. 165 I2
Fair Head hd U.K. 61 F2
Fairie Queen Shoal sea feature Phil. 82 B4
Fair Isle i. U.K. 60 H1
Fairlee U.S.A. 165 I2
Fairlie 139 C7
Fairmont MN U.S.A. 160 E3
Fairmont WV U.S.A. 164 E4
Fair Oaks U.S.A. 164 B3
Fairplay, Mount AK U.S.A. 149 L3
Fairview Australia 136 D2
Fairview Canada 150 G3
Fairview MI U.S.A. 164 C1
Fairview OK U.S.A. 161 D4
Fairview PA U.S.A. 164 E2
Fairview UT U.S.A. 159 H2
Fairview Park H.K. China 97 [inset]
Fairweather, Cape AK U.S.A. 149 M4
Fairweather, Mount Canada/U.S.A. 149 M4
Fais i. Micronesia 81 K5
Faisalabad Pak. 111 I4
Faissault France 62 E5
Faith U.S.A. 160 C2
Faizabad Afgh. see Feyzābād
Faizabad India 105 E4
Fakaofo atoll Tokelau 133 I2
Fakaofu atoll Tokelau see Fakaofo
Fakenham U.K. 59 H6
Fåker Sweden 54 I5
Fakfak Indon. 81 I7
Fakhrābād Iran 110 D4
Fakiragram India 105 G4
Fako vol. Cameroon see Cameroun, Mont
Faku Liaoning China 95 J3
Fal r. U.K. 59 C8
Falaba Sierra Leone 120 B4
Falaise Lake Canada 150 G2
Falam Myanmar 86 A2
Falavarjan Iran 110 C3
Falcon Lake Canada 151 M5
Falcon Lake l. Mex./U.S.A. 167 F3
Falenki Rus. Fed. 52 K4
Falfurrias U.S.A. 161 D7
Falher Canada 150 G4
Falkenberg Germany 63 N3
Falkenberg Sweden 55 H8
Falkenhagen Germany 63 M1
Falkenhain Germany 63 M3
Falkensee Germany 63 N2
Falkenstein Germany 63 M5
Falkirk U.K. 60 F5
Falkland U.K. 60 F4
Falkland Escarpment sea feature S. Atlantic Ocean 184 E9

▶Falkland Islands terr. S. Atlantic Ocean 178 E8
United Kingdom Overseas Territory.

Falkland Plateau sea feature S. Atlantic Ocean 184 E9
Falkland Sound sea chan. Falkland Is 178 D8
Falköping Sweden 55 H7
Fallbrook U.S.A. 158 E5
Fallieres Coast Antarctica 188 L2
Fallingbostel Germany 63 J2
Fallon U.S.A. 158 D2
Fall River U.S.A. 165 J3
Fall River Pass U.S.A. 156 G4
Falls City U.S.A. 160 E3
Falmouth U.K. 59 B8
Falmouth KY U.S.A. 164 C4
Falmouth VA U.S.A. 165 G4
False r. Canada 153 H2
False Bay S. Africa 124 D8
False Pass AK U.S.A. 148 G5
False Point India 105 F5
Falso, Cabo c. Hond. 166 [inset] J6
Falster i. Denmark 55 G9
Fălticeni Romania 53 E7
Falun Sweden 55 I6
Fam, Kepulauan is Papua Indon. 83 D3
Famagusta Cyprus 107 A2
Famagusta Bay Cyprus see Ammochostos Bay
Fameck France 62 G5
Famenin Iran 110 C3
Fame Range hills Australia 135 C6
Family Lake Canada 151 M5
Family Well Australia 134 D5
Fāmūr, Daryācheh-ye l. Iran 110 C4
Fana Mali 120 C3
Fanad Head hd Ireland 61 E2
Fandriana Madag. 123 E6
Fane r. Ireland 61 F4
Fang Thai. 86 B3
Fangcheng Guangxi China see Fangchenggang
Fangcheng Henan China 97 G1
Fangchenggang China 97 F4
Fangdou Shan mts China 97 F2
Fangliao Taiwan 97 I4
Fangshan Taiwan 97 I4
Fangxian China 97 F1
Fangzheng China 90 C3
Fankuai China 97 F2
Fankuaidian China see Fankuai
Fanling H.K. China 97 [inset]
Fannich, Loch l. U.K. 60 D3
Fannūj Iran 111 E5
Fano Italy 68 E3
Fanshan Anhui China 97 H2
Fanshan Zhejiang China 97 I3
Fanshi Shanxi China 95 H4
Fanum Fortunae Italy see Fano
Faqīh Aḥmadān Iran 110 C4
Farab Turkm. see Farap
Faraba Mali 120 B3
Faradofay Madag. see Tôlañaro
Farafangana Madag. 123 E6
Farāfirah, Wāḥāt al oasis Egypt 108 C4
Farafra Oasis oasis Egypt see Farāfirah, Wāḥāt al
Farāh Afgh. 111 F3
Faraḥābād Iran see Khezerābād
Farallon de Medinilla i. N. Mariana Is 81 L3
Farallon de Pajaros vol. N. Mariana Is 81 K2
Farallones de Cali, Parque Nacional nat. park Col. 176 C3
Faranah Guinea 120 B3
Farap Turkm. 111 F2
Fararah Oman 109 I6
Farasān, Jazā'ir is Saudi Arabia 108 F6
Faraulep atoll Micronesia 81 K5
Fareham U.K. 59 F8
Farewell AK U.S.A. 148 I3
Farewell, Cape Greenland 147 N3
Farewell, Cape N.Z. 139 D5
Farewell Spit N.Z. 139 D5
Färgelanda Sweden 55 H7
Farghona Uzbek. see Farg'ona
Fargo U.S.A. 160 D2
Farg'ona Uzbek. 109 L1
Faribault U.S.A. 160 E2
Faribault, Lac l. Canada 153 H2
Faridabad India 104 D3
Faridkot India 104 C3
Faridpur Bangl. 105 G5
Farīmān Iran 111 E3
Farkhar Afgh. see Farkhato
Farkhato Afgh. 111 H2
Farkhor Tajik. 111 H2
Farmahin Iran 110 C3
Farmer Island Canada 152 E2
Farmerville U.S.A. 161 E5
Farmington Canada 150 F4
Farmington ME U.S.A. 165 J1
Farmington MO U.S.A. 160 F4
Farmington NH U.S.A. 165 J2
Farmington NM U.S.A. 159 I3
Farmington Hills U.S.A. 164 D2
Far Mountain Canada 150 E4
Farmville U.S.A. 165 F5
Farnborough U.K. 59 G7
Farne Islands U.K. 58 F3
Farnham U.K. 59 G7
Farnham, Lake salt flat Australia 135 D6
Farnham, Mount Canada 150 G5
Faro Brazil 177 G4
Faro Y.T. Canada 149 N3
Faro Port. 67 C5
Fårö i. Sweden 55 K8
Faroe - Iceland Ridge sea feature Arctic Ocean 189 I2

▶Faroe Islands terr. N. Atlantic Ocean 54 [inset]
Self-governing Danish territory.

Fårösund Sweden 55 K8
Farquhar Group is Seychelles 123 F5
Farquharson Tableland hills Australia 135 C6

Farrāshband Iran 110 D4
Farr Bay Antarctica 188 F2
Farristown U.S.A. 164 C5
Farrukhabad India see Fatehgarh
Fārsī Afgh. 111 F3
Farsund Norway 55 E7
Fārūj Iran 110 E2
Farwell MI U.S.A. 164 C2
Farwell TX U.S.A. 161 C5
Fasā Iran 110 D4
Fasano Italy 68 G4
Faşikan Geçidi pass Turkey 107 A1
Faßberg Germany 63 K2
Fastiv Ukr. 53 F6
Fastov Ukr. see Fastiv
Fatehabad India 104 C3
Fatehgarh India 104 D4
Fatehpur Rajasthan India 104 C4
Fatehpur Uttar Prad. India 104 E4
Fatick Senegal 120 B3
Fattoilep atoll Micronesia see Faraulep
Faughan r. U.K. 61 E2
Faulkton U.S.A. 160 D2
Faulquemont France 62 G5
Fauresmith S. Africa 125 G5
Fauske Norway 54 I3
Faust Canada 150 H4
Fawcett Canada 150 H4
Fawley U.K. 59 F8
Fawn r. Canada 151 N4
Faxaflói b. Iceland 54 [inset]
Faxälven r. Sweden 54 J5
Faya Chad 121 E3
Fayette AL U.S.A. 163 C5
Fayette MO U.S.A. 160 E4
Fayette MS U.S.A. 161 F6
Fayette OH U.S.A. 164 C3
Fayetteville AR U.S.A. 161 E4
Fayetteville NC U.S.A. 163 E5
Fayetteville TN U.S.A. 163 C5
Fayetteville WV U.S.A. 164 E4
Fâyid Egypt see Fā'id
Faylakah i. Kuwait 110 C4
Fazao Malfakassa, Parc National de nat. park Togo 120 D4
Fazilka India 104 C3
Fazrān, Jabal hill Saudi Arabia 110 C5
Fdérik Mauritania 120 B2
Fead Group is P.N.G. see Nuguria Islands
Feale r. Ireland 61 C5
Fear, Cape U.S.A. 163 E5
Featherston N.Z. 139 E5
Feathertop, Mount Australia 138 C6
Fécamp France 66 E2
Federal District admin. dist. Brazil see Distrito Federal
Federalsburg U.S.A. 165 H4
Fedusar India 104 C4
Fehet Lake Canada 151 M1
Fehmarn i. Germany 57 M3
Fehrbellin Germany 63 M2
Feia, Lagoa lag. Brazil 179 C3
Feicheng Shandong China see Feixian
Feijó Brazil 176 D5
Feilding N.Z. 139 E5
Fei Ngo Shan hill H.K. China see Kowloon Peak
Feio r. Brazil see Aguapeí
Feira de Santana Brazil 179 D1
Feixi China 97 H2
Feixian Shandong China 95 I5
Feixiang Hebei China 95 H4
Fejd el Abiod pass Alg. 68 B6
Feke Turkey 112 D3
Felanitx Spain 67 H4
Feldberg Germany 63 N1
Feldberg mt. Germany 57 L7
Feldkirch Austria 57 L7
Feldkirchen in Kärnten Austria 57 O7
Felidhu Atoll Maldives 103 D11
Felidu Atoll Maldives see Felidhu Atoll
Felipe C. Puerto Mex. 167 H5
Felixlândia Brazil 179 B2
Felixstowe U.K. 59 I7
Felixton S. Africa 125 J5
Fellowsville U.S.A. 164 F4
Felsina Italy see Bologna
Felton U.S.A. 165 H4
Feltre Italy 68 D1
Femunden l. Norway 54 G5
Femundsmarka Nasjonalpark nat. park Norway 54 H5
Fenaio, Punta del pt Italy 68 D3
Fence Lake U.S.A. 159 I4
Fener Burnu hd Turkey 107 B1
Fénérive Madag. see Fenoarivo Atsinanana
Fengari mt. Greece 69 K4
Fengcheng Fujian China see Lianjiang
Fengcheng Fujian China see Yongding
Fengcheng Fujian China see Anxi
Fengcheng Guangdong China see Xinfeng
Fengcheng Guangxi China see Fengshan
Fengcheng Guizhou China see Tianzhu
Fengcheng Jiangxi China 97 G2
Fenggang Fujian China see Shaxian
Fenggang Guizhou China 96 E3
Fenggang Jiangxi China see Yihuang
Fenggeling Gansu China 94 F5
Fengguang China 90 B3
Fenghuang China 97 F3
Fengjiaba China see Wangcang
Fengjie China 97 F2
Fengkai China 97 F4
Fenglin Taiwan 97 I4
Fengming Shaanxi China see Qishan
Fengming Sichuan China see Pengshan
Fengnan Hebei China 95 I4
Fengning Hebei China 95 I3
Fengqi Shaanxi China see Luochuan
Fengqing China 96 C3
Fengqiu Henan China 95 H5
Fengrun Hebei China 95 I4
Fengshan Fujian China see Luoyuan
Fengshan Guangxi China 96 E3
Fengshan Hubei China see Luotian
Fengshan Yunnan China see Fengqing
Fengshuba Shuiku resr China 97 G3
Fengshui Shan mt. China 90 A1
Fengtongzhai Giant Panda Reserve nature res. China 96 D2
Fengxian Jiangsu China 95 I5
Fengxian Shanghai China 96 E1
Fengxiang Heilong. China see Luobei
Fengxiang Yunnan China see Lincang
Fengyang China 97 H1
Fengyuan Shaanxi China 95 G5
Fengyüan Taiwan 97 I3
Fengzhen Nei Mongol China 95 H3
Feni Bangl. 105 G5
Feniak Lake AK U.S.A. 148 H1
Feni Islands P.N.G. 132 F2
Fenimore Pass sea channel AK U.S.A. 149 [inset]
Fennville U.S.A. 164 B2
Feno, Capo di c. Corsica France 66 I6
Fenoarivo Atsinanana Madag. 123 E5
Fenshui Guan pass China 97 H3
Fenton U.S.A. 164 D2
Fenua Ura atoll Fr. Polynesia see Manuae
Fenxiang Shaanxi China 95 F5
Fenyang Shanxi China 95 G4
Fenyi China 97 G3
Feodosiya Ukr. 112 D1
Fer, Cap de c. Alg. 68 B6
Férai Greece see Feres
Ferdows Iran 110 E3
Fère-Champenoise France 62 D6
Feres Greece 69 L4
Fergus Canada 164 E2
Fergus Falls U.S.A. 160 D2
Ferguson Lake Canada 151 L2
Fergusson Island P.N.G. 132 F2
Fériana Tunisia 68 C7
Ferijaz Kosovo 69 I3
Ferkessédougou Côte d'Ivoire 120 C4
Fermo Italy 68 E3
Fermont Canada 153 I3
Fermoselle Spain 67 C3
Fermoy Ireland 61 D5
Fernandina, Isla i. Galápagos Ecuador 176 [inset]
Fernandina Beach U.S.A. 163 D6
Fernando de Magallanes, Parque Nacional nat. park Chile 178 B8
Fernando de Noronha i. Brazil 184 F6
Fernandópolis Brazil 179 A3
Fernando Poó i. Equat. Guinea see Bioco
Fernão Dias Brazil 179 B2
Ferndale U.S.A. 158 A1
Ferndown U.K. 59 F8
Fernlee Australia 138 C2
Fernley U.S.A. 158 D2
Ferns Ireland 61 F5
Ferozepore India see Firozpur
Ferrara Italy 68 D2
Ferreira-Gomes Brazil 177 H3
Ferriday LA U.S.A. 167 H2
Ferro, Capo c. Sardinia Italy 68 C4
Ferrol Spain 67 B2
Ferron U.S.A. 159 H2
Ferros Brazil 179 C2
Ferry AK U.S.A. 149 J2
Ferryland Canada 153 L5
Ferryville Tunisia see Menzel Bourguiba
Fertő-tavi nat. park Hungary 68 G1
Ferwerd Neth. see Ferwert
Ferwert Neth. 62 F1
Fès Morocco 64 D5
Feshi Dem. Rep. Congo 123 B4
Fessenden U.S.A. 160 D2
Festus U.S.A. 160 F4
Fet Dom, Tanjung pt Papua Indon. 83 D3
Fété Bowé Senegal 120 B3
Fethard Ireland 61 E5
Fethiye Malatya Turkey see Yazıhan
Fethiye Muğla Turkey 69 M6
Fethiye Körfezi b. Turkey 69 M6
Fetisovo Kazakh. 113 I2
Fetlar i. U.K. 60 [inset]
Fettercairn U.K. 60 G4
Feucht Germany 63 L5
Feuchtwangen Germany 63 K5
Feuilles, Rivière aux r. Canada 153 H2
Fevral'sk Rus. Fed. 90 C1
Fevzipaşa Turkey 112 E3
Feyzābād Afgh. 111 H2
Feyzābād Kermān Iran 110 D4
Feyzābād Khorāsān Iran 110 E3
Fez Morocco see Fès
Ffestiniog U.K. 59 D6
Fianarantsoa Madag. 123 E6
Fichē Eth. 122 D3
Fichtelgebirge hills Germany 63 M4
Field U.S.A. 164 D5
Fier Albania 69 H4
Fiery Creek r. Australia 136 B3
Fife Lake U.S.A. 164 C1
Fife Ness pt U.K. 60 G4
Fifield Australia 138 C4
Fifth Meridian Canada 150 H3
Figeac France 66 F4
Figueira da Foz Port. 67 B3
Figueras Spain see Figueres
Figueres Spain 67 H2
Figuig Morocco 64 D5
Figuil Cameroon 121 E4

▶Fiji country S. Pacific Ocean 133 H3
4th most populous and 5th largest country in Oceania.

Fīk' Eth. 122 E3
Filadelfia Para. 178 D2
Filchner Ice Shelf Antarctica 188 A1
Filey U.K. 58 G4
Filibe Bulg. see Plovdiv
Filingué Niger 120 D3
Filipinas country Asia see Philippines
Filippiada Greece 69 I5
Filipstad Sweden 55 I7
Fillan Norway 54 F5
Fillmore CA U.S.A. 158 D4
Fillmore UT U.S.A. 159 G2
Fils r. Germany 63 J6
Fīltu Eth. 122 E3
Fimbull Ice Shelf Antarctica 188 C2
Fin Iran 110 C3
Finch Canada 165 H1
Findhorn r. U.K. 60 F3
Fındık Turkey 110 A2
Findlay U.S.A. 164 D3
Fine U.S.A. 165 H1
Finger Lake Canada 151 M4
Finger Lakes U.S.A. 165 G2
Finike Turkey 69 N6
Finike Körfezi b. Turkey 69 N6
Finisterre Spain see Fisterra
Finisterre, Cabo c. Spain see Finisterre, Cape
Finisterre, Cape Spain 67 B2
Fink Creek AK U.S.A. 148 G2
Finke watercourse Australia 136 A5
Finke, Mount hill Australia 135 F7
Finke Bay Australia 134 E3
Finke Gorge National Park Australia 135 F6
Finland country Europe 54 O5
Finland, Gulf of Europe 55 M7

▶Finlay r. Canada 150 E3
Part of the Mackenzie-Peace-Finlay, the 2nd longest river in North America.

Finlay, Mount Canada 150 E3
Finlay Forks Canada 150 F4
Finley U.S.A. 160 D2
Finn r. Ireland 61 E3
Finne ridge Germany 63 L3
Finnigan, Mount Australia 136 D2
Finniss, Cape Australia 135 F8
Finnmarksvidda reg. Norway 54 H2
Finnsnes Norway 54 J2
Fins Oman 110 E6
Finschhafen P.N.G. 81 L8
Finspång Sweden 55 I7
Fintona U.K. 61 E3
Fintown Ireland see Baile na Finne
Finucane Range hills Australia 136 C4
Fionn Loch l. U.K. 60 D3
Fionnphort U.K. 60 C4
Fiordland National Park N.Z. 139 A7
Fir reg. Saudi Arabia 110 B4
Fırat r. Turkey 112 E3 see Euphrates
Firebaugh U.S.A. 158 C3
Firedrake Lake Canada 151 J2
Fire Island AK U.S.A. 149 J3
Firenze Italy see Florence
Fireside B.C. Canada 149 P4
Firk, Sha'īb watercourse Iraq 113 G5
Firmat Arg. 178 D4
Firminy France 66 G4
Firmum Italy see Fermo
Firmum Picenum Italy see Fermo
Firovo Rus. Fed. 52 G4
Firozabad India 104 D4
Firozkoh reg. Afgh. 111 G3
Firozpur Haryana India 99 B8
Firozpur Punjab India 104 C3
Firth r. Y.T. Canada 149 M1
Fīrūzābād Iran 110 D4
Fīrūzkūh Iran 110 D3
Firyuza Turkm. see Pöwrize
Fischbach Germany 63 H5
Fischersbrunn Namibia 124 B3
Fish watercourse Namibia 124 C5
Fisher (abandoned) Australia 135 E7
Fisher Bay Antarctica 188 G2
Fisher Glacier Antarctica 188 E2
Fisher River Canada 151 L5
Fishers U.S.A. 164 B4
Fishers Island U.S.A. 165 J3
Fisher Strait Canada 147 J3
Fishguard U.K. 59 C7
Fishing Branch Wilderness Territorial Park Reserve nature res. Y.T. Canada 149 M2
Fishing Creek U.S.A. 165 G4
Fishing Lake Canada 151 M4
Fish Lake Canada 150 F2
Fish Lake AK U.S.A. 149 J2
Fish Point U.S.A. 164 D2
Fish Ponds H.K. China 97 [inset]
Fiske, Cape Antarctica 188 L2
Fiskenæsset Greenland see Qeqertarsuatsiaat
Fismes France 62 D5
Fisterra Spain 67 B2
Fisterra, Cabo c. Spain see Finisterre, Cape
Fitchburg U.S.A. 160 F3
Fitri, Lac l. Chad 121 E3
Fitton, Mount Y.T. Canada 149 M1
Fitzgerald Canada 151 I3
Fitzgerald U.S.A. 163 D6
Fitzgerald River National Park Australia 135 B8
Fitz Hugh Sound sea chan. Canada 150 D5
Fitz Roy Arg. 178 C7
Fitzroy r. Australia 134 C4
Fitz Roy, Cerro mt. Arg. 178 B7
Fitzroy Crossing Australia 134 D4
Fitzwilliam Island Canada 164 E1
Fiume Croatia see Rijeka
Fivemiletown U.K. 61 E3
Five Points U.S.A. 158 C3
Fizi Dem. Rep. Congo 123 C4
Fizuli Azer. see Füzuli
Flå Norway 55 F6
Flagstaff S. Africa 125 I6
Flagstaff U.S.A. 159 H4
Flagstaff Lake U.S.A. 162 G2
Flaherty Island Canada 152 F2
Flambeau r. U.S.A. 160 F2
Flamborough Head hd U.K. 58 G4
Fläming hills Germany 63 M2
Flaming Gorge Reservoir U.S.A. 156 F4
Flaminksvlei salt pan S. Africa 124 E6
Flanagan r. Canada 151 M4
Flandre reg. France 62 C4
Flannagan Lake U.S.A. 164 D5
Flannan Isles U.K. 60 B2
Flåsjön l. Sweden 54 I4
Flat r. N.W.T. Canada 149 P3
Flat AK U.S.A. 148 H3
Flat r. U.S.A. 164 C2
Flat Creek Y.T. Canada 149 M3
Flathead r. U.S.A. 154 E2
Flathead Lake U.S.A. 156 E3
Flatiron mt. U.S.A. 156 E3
Flat Island S. China Sea 80 F4
Flat Lick U.S.A. 164 D5
Flattery, Cape Australia 136 D2
Flattery, Cape U.S.A. 156 B2
Flat Top mt. Y.T. Canada 149 M3
Flatwillow Creek r. U.S.A. 156 G3
Flatwoods U.S.A. 164 E4
Fleetmark Germany 63 L2
Fleetwood Australia 136 D4
Fleetwood U.K. 58 D5
Fleetwood U.S.A. 165 H3
Flekkefjord Norway 55 E7
Flemingsburg U.S.A. 164 D4
Flemington U.S.A. 165 H3
Flen Sweden 55 J7
Flensburg Germany 57 L3
Flers France 66 D2
Flesherton Canada 164 E1
Flesko, Tanjung pt Indon. 83 C2
Fletcher Lake Canada 151 I2
Fletcher Peninsula Antarctica 188 L2
Fleur de Lys Canada 153 K4
Fleur-de-May, Lac l. Canada 153 I4
Flinders r. Australia 136 C3
Flinders Chase National Park Australia 137 B7
Flinders Group National Park Australia 136 D2
Flinders Island Australia 137 [inset]
Flinders Passage Australia 136 E3
Flinders Ranges mts Australia 137 B7
Flinders Ranges National Park Australia 137 B6
Flinders Reefs Australia 136 E3
Flin Flon Canada 151 K4
Flint U.K. 58 D5
Flint U.S.A. 164 D2
Flint r. U.S.A. 163 C6
Flint Island Kiribati 187 J6
Flinton Australia 138 D1
Flisa Norway 55 H6

▶Flissingskiy, Mys c. Rus. Fed. 76 H2
Most easterly point of Europe.

Flixecourt France 62 C4
Flodden U.K. 58 E3
Flöha Germany 63 N4
Flood Range mts Antarctica 188 J1
Flora r. Australia 134 E3
Flora U.S.A. 164 B3
Florac France 66 F4
Florala U.S.A. 163 C6
Florange France 62 G5
Flora Reef Australia 136 D3
Florence Italy 68 D3
Florence AL U.S.A. 163 C5
Florence AZ U.S.A. 159 H5
Florence CO U.S.A. 157 G5
Florence OR U.S.A. 156 B4
Florence SC U.S.A. 163 E5
Florence WI U.S.A. 160 F2
Florence Junction U.S.A. 159 H5
Florencia Col. 176 C3
Florennes Belgium 62 E4
Florentia Italy see Florence
Florentino Ameghino, Embalse resr Arg. 178 C6
Flores r. Arg. 178 E5
Flores Guat. 167 H5
Flores i. Indon. 83 B5
Flores, Laut sea Indon. 83 A4
Flores Island Canada 150 E5
Flores Sea Indon. see Flores, Laut
Floresta Brazil 177 K5
Floresville U.S.A. 161 D6
Floriano Brazil 177 J5
Florianópolis Brazil 179 A4
Florida Uruguay 178 E4
Florida state U.S.A. 163 D6
Florida, Straits of Bahamas/U.S.A. 163 D8
Florida Bay U.S.A. 163 D7
Florida City U.S.A. 163 D7
Florida Islands Solomon Is 133 G2
Florida Keys is U.S.A. 163 D7
Florin U.S.A. 158 C2
Florina Greece 69 I4
Florissant U.S.A. 160 F4
Florø Norway 55 D6
Flour Lake Canada 153 I3
Floyd U.S.A. 164 E5
Floyd, Mount U.S.A. 159 G4
Floydada U.S.A. 161 C5
Fluessen l. Neth. 62 F2
Fluk Maluku Indon. 83 C3
Flushing Neth. see Vlissingen
Fly r. P.N.G. 81 K8
Flying Fish, Cape Antarctica 188 K2
Flying Mountain U.S.A. 159 I6
Flylân i. Neth. see Vlieland
Foam Lake Canada 151 K5
Foča Bos.-Herz. 68 H3
Foça Turkey 69 L5
Fochabers U.K. 60 F3
Focşani Romania 69 L2
Fogang China 97 G4
Foggia Italy 68 F4
Foggo Buru Indon. 83 C3
Fogo i. Cape Verde 120 [inset]
Fogo Island Canada 153 L4
Foinaven hill U.K. 60 E2
Foix France 66 E5
Folda sea chan. Norway 54 I3
Foldereid Norway 54 H4
Foldfjorden sea chan. Norway 54 G4
Folegandros i. Greece 69 K6
Foleyet Canada 152 E4
Foley Island Canada 147 K3
Folger AK U.S.A. 148 H3
Foligno Italy 68 E3
Folkestone U.K. 59 I7
Folkingham U.K. 59 G6
Folkston U.S.A. 163 D6
Folldal Norway 54 G5
Follonica Italy 68 D3
Folsom Lake U.S.A. 158 C2
Fomboni Comoros 123 E5
Fomento Cuba 163 E8
Fomin Rus. Fed. 53 I7
Fominskaya Rus. Fed. 52 K2
Fominskoye Rus. Fed. 52 I4
Fonda U.S.A. 165 H2
Fond-du-Lac Canada 151 J3
Fond du Lac r. Canada 151 J3
Fond du Lac U.S.A. 164 A2
Fondevila Spain 67 B3
Fondi Italy 68 E4
Fonni Sardinia Italy 68 C4
Fonsagrada Spain see A Fonsagrada
Fonseca, Golfo do b. Central America 166 [inset] H6
Fontaine Lake Canada 151 J3
Fontanges Canada 153 H3
Fontas Canada 150 F3
Fontas r. Canada 150 F3
Fonte Boa Brazil 176 E4
Fonteneau, Lac l. Canada 153 J4
Fontur pt Iceland 54 [inset]
Foochow China see Fuzhou
Foot's Bay Canada 164 F1
Foping China 97 F1
Foraker, Mount AK U.S.A. 149 J3
Foraulep atoll Micronesia see Faraulep
Forbes Australia 138 D4
Forbes, Mount Canada 150 G4
Forchheim Germany 63 L5
Ford r. U.S.A. 162 C2
Ford City U.S.A. 158 D4
Førde Norway 55 D6
Forde Lake Canada 151 L2
Fordham U.K. 59 H6
Fordingbridge U.K. 59 F8
Ford Range mts Antarctica 188 J1
Fords Bridge Australia 138 B2
Fordsville U.S.A. 164 B5
Fordyce U.S.A. 161 E5
Forécariah Guinea 120 B4
Forel, Mont mt. Greenland 147 O3
Foreland hd U.K. 59 F8
Foreland Point U.K. 59 D7
Foremost Canada 156 F2
Foresight Mountain Canada 150 E4
Forest Canada 164 E2
Forest MS U.S.A. 161 F5
Forest OH U.S.A. 164 D3
Forestburg Canada 151 H4
Forest Creek r. Australia 136 C3
Forest Hill Australia 138 C5
Forest Ranch U.S.A. 158 C2
Forestville Canada 153 H4
Forestville CA U.S.A. 158 B2
Forestville MI U.S.A. 164 D2
Forfar U.K. 60 G4
Forgan U.S.A. 161 C4
Forges-les-Eaux France 62 B5
Forillon, Parc National de nat. park Canada 153 I4
Forked River U.S.A. 165 H4
Forks U.S.A. 156 B3
Fork Union U.S.A. 165 F5
Forlì Italy 68 E2
Forman U.S.A. 160 D2
Formby U.K. 58 D5
Formentera i. Spain 67 G4
Formentor, Cap de c. Spain 67 H4
Formerie France 62 B5
Former Yugoslav Republic of Macedonia country Europe see Macedonia
Formiga Brazil 179 B3
Formosa Arg. 178 E3
Formosa country Asia see Taiwan
Formosa Brazil 179 B1
Formosa, Serra hills Brazil 177 G6
Formosa Bay Kenya see Ungwana Bay
Formosa Strait China/Taiwan see Taiwan Strait
Formoso r. Bahia Brazil 179 B1
Formoso r. Tocantins Brazil 179 A1
Fornos Moz. 125 L2
Forres U.K. 60 F3
Forrest Vic. Australia 138 A7
Forrest W.A. Australia 135 E7
Forrestal Range mts Antarctica 188 A1
Forrest City U.S.A. 161 F5
Forrester Island AK U.S.A. 149 N5
Forrest Lake Canada 151 I3
Forrest Lakes salt flat Australia 135 E7
Fors Sweden 54 J5
Forsayth Australia 136 C3
Forsnäs Sweden 54 M3
Forssa Fin. 55 M6
Forster Australia 138 F4
Forsyth GA U.S.A. 163 D5
Forsyth MT U.S.A. 156 G3
Forsyth Range hills Australia 136 C4
Fort Abbas Pak. 111 I4
Fort Albany Canada 152 E3
Fortaleza Brazil 177 K4
Fort Amsterdam U.S.A. see New York
Fort Archambault Chad see Sarh
Fort Ashby U.S.A. 165 F4
Fort Assiniboine Canada 150 H4
Fort Augustus U.K. 60 E3
Fort Beaufort S. Africa 125 H7
Fort Benton U.S.A. 156 F3
Fort Bragg U.S.A. 158 B2
Fort Branch U.S.A. 164 B4
Fort Carillon U.S.A. see Ticonderoga
Fort Charlet Alg. see Djanet
Fort Chimo Canada see Kuujjuaq
Fort Chipewyan Canada 151 I3
Fort Collins U.S.A. 156 G4
Fort-Coulonge Canada 152 F5
Fort Crampel Cent. Afr. Rep. see Kaga Bandoro
Fort-Dauphin Madag. see Tôlañaro
Fort Davis U.S.A. 161 C6

▶Fort-de-France Martinique 169 L6
Capital of Martinique.

Fort de Kock Sumatera Indon. see Bukittinggi
Fort de Polignac Alg. see Illizi
Fort Deposit AL U.S.A. 167 I1
Fort Dodge U.S.A. 160 E3
Fort Duchesne U.S.A. 159 I1
Fort Edward U.S.A. 165 I2
Fortescue r. Australia 134 B5
Forte Veneza Brazil 177 H5
Fort Flatters Alg. see Bordj Omer Driss
Fort Foureau Cameroon see Kousséri
Fort Franklin N.W.T. Canada see Déljne
Fort Gardel Alg. see Zaouatallaz
Fort Gay U.S.A. 164 D4
Fort George Canada see Chisasibi
Fort Glenn AK U.S.A. 148 F5
Fort Good Hope N.W.T. Canada 149 O2
Fort Gouraud Mauritania see Fdérik
Forth r. U.K. 60 F4
Forth, Firth of est. U.K. 60 F4
Fort Hancock TX U.S.A. 166 D2
Fort Hertz Myanmar see Putao
Fortification Range mts U.S.A. 159 F2
Fortín General Mendoza Para. 178 D2
Fortín Leonida Escobar Para. 178 D2
Fortín Madrejón Para. 178 E2
Fortín Pilcomayo Arg. 178 D2
Fortín Ravelo Bol. 176 F7
Fortín Sargento Primero Leyes Arg. 178 E2
Fortín Suárez Arana Bol. 176 F7
Fortín Teniente Juan Echauri López Para. 178 D2
Fort Jameson Zambia see Chipata
Fort Johnston Malawi see Mangochi
Fort Kent U.S.A. 162 G2
Fort Lamy Chad see Ndjamena
Fort Laperrine Alg. see Tamanrasset
Fort Laramie U.S.A. 156 G4
Fort Lauderdale U.S.A. 163 D7
Fort Liard Canada 150 F2
Fort Mackay Canada 151 I3
Fort Macleod Canada 150 H5
Fort Madison U.S.A. 160 F3
Fort Manning Malawi see Mchinji
Fort McMurray Canada 151 I3
Fort McPherson N.W.T. Canada 149 N2
Fort Meyers Beach U.S.A. 163 D7
Fort Morgan U.S.A. 160 C3
Fort Munro Pak. 111 H4
Fort Myers U.S.A. 163 D7
Fort Nelson Canada 150 F3
Fort Nelson r. Canada 150 F3
Fort Norman N.W.T. Canada see Tulita
Fort Orange U.S.A. see Albany
Fort Payne U.S.A. 163 C5
Fort Peck U.S.A. 156 G2
Fort Peck Reservoir U.S.A. 156 G3
Fort Pierce U.S.A. 163 D7
Fort Portal Uganda 122 D3
Fort Providence Canada 150 G2
Fort Resolution Canada 150 H2
Fortrose N.Z. 139 B8
Fortrose U.K. 60 E3
Fort Rosebery Zambia see Mansa
Fort Rousset Congo see Owando
Fort Rupert Canada see Waskaganish
Fort St James Canada 150 E4
Fort St John Canada 150 F3
Fort Sandeman Pak. see Zhob
Fort Saskatchewan Canada 150 H4
Fort Scott U.S.A. 160 E4
Fort Severn Canada 152 D2
Fort-Shevchenko Kazakh. 100 E2
Fort Simpson Canada 150 F2
Fort Smith Canada 151 H2
Fort Smith U.S.A. 161 E5
Fort Stockton U.S.A. 161 C6
Fort Sumner U.S.A. 157 G6
Fort Supply U.S.A. 161 D4
Fort Thomas U.S.A. 159 I5
Fort Trinquet Mauritania see Bîr Mogreïn
Fortuna U.S.A. 160 C1
Fortune Bay Canada 153 L5
Fort Valley U.S.A. 163 D5
Fort Vermilion Canada 150 G3
Fort Victoria Zimbabwe see Masvingo
Fort Walton Beach FL U.S.A. 167 I2
Fort Ware Canada see Ware
Fort Wayne U.S.A. 164 C3
Fort William U.K. 60 D4
Fort Worth U.S.A. 161 D5
Fort Yates U.S.A. 160 C2
Fortymile r. Canada/U.S.A. 149 L2
Fortymile, Middle Fork r. AK U.S.A. 149 L2
Fortymile, West Fork r. AK U.S.A. 149 L2
Fort Yukon AK U.S.A. 149 K2
Forum Iulii France see Fréjus
Forūr, Jazīreh-ye i. Iran 110 D5

Forvik Norway **54** H4
Foshan China **97** G4
Fo Shek Chau *H.K.* China *see* **Basalt Island**
Fossano Italy **68** B2
Fossil U.S.A. **156** C3
Fossil Downs Australia **134** D4
Foster Australia **138** C7
Foster U.S.A. **164** C4
Foster, Mount Canada/U.S.A. **149** N4
Foster Lakes Canada **151** J3
Fostoria U.S.A. **164** D3
Fotadrevo Madag. **123** E6
Fotherby U.K. **58** G5
Fotokol Cameroon **121** E3
Fotuna *i.* Vanuatu *see* **Futuna**
Fougères France **66** D2
Foula *i.* U.K. **60** [inset]
Foul Island Myanmar **86** A3
Foulness Point U.K. **59** H7
Foul Point Sri Lanka **106** D4
Foumban Cameroon **120** E4
Foundation Ice Stream *glacier* Antarctica **188** L1
Fount U.S.A. **164** D5
Fountains Abbey and Royal Water Garden (NT) *tourist site* U.K. **58** F4
Fourches, Mont des *hill* France **66** G2
Four Corners U.S.A. **158** E4
Fouriesburg S. Africa **125** I5
Fourmies France **62** E4
Four Mountains, Islands of the *AK* U.S.A. **148** E5
Fournier, Lac *l.* Canada **153** I4
Fournoi *i.* Greece **69** L6
Fourpeaked Mountain *AK* U.S.A. **148** I4
Fouta Djallon *reg.* Guinea **120** B3
Foveaux Strait N.Z. **139** A8
Fowey *r.* U.K. **59** C8
Fowler *CO* U.S.A. **157** G5
Fowler *IN* U.S.A. **164** B3
Fowler Ice Rise Antarctica **188** L1
Fowlers Bay Australia **132** D5
Fowlers Bay *b.* Australia **135** F8
Fowlerville U.S.A. **164** C2
Fox *r. B.C.* Canada **150** E3
Fox *r. Man.* Canada **151** M3
Fox *r.* U.S.A. **160** F3
Fox Creek Canada **150** G4
Fox Creek U.S.A. **164** C5
Foxdale Isle of Man **58** C4
Foxe Basin *g.* Canada **147** K3
Foxe Channel Canada **147** J3
Foxe Peninsula Canada **147** K3
Fox Glacier N.Z. **139** C6
Fox Islands *AK* U.S.A. **148** E5
Fox Lake Canada **150** H3
Fox Mountain *Y.T.* Canada **149** N3
Fox Valley Canada **151** I5
Foyers U.K. **60** E3
Foyle *r.* Ireland/U.K. **61** E3
Foyle, Lough *b.* Ireland/U.K. **61** E2
Foynes Ireland **61** C5
Foz de Areia, Represa de *resr* Brazil **179** A4
Foz do Cunene Angola **123** B5
Foz do Iguaçu Brazil **178** F3
Fraga Spain **67** G3
Frakes, Mount Antarctica **188** K1
Framingham U.S.A. **165** J2
Framnes Mountains Antarctica **188** E2
Franca Brazil **179** B3
Français, Récif des *reef* New Caledonia **133** G3
Francavilla Fontana Italy **68** G4

▶**France** *country* Europe **66** F3
3rd largest and 3rd most populous country in Europe.

Frances Australia **137** C8
Frances *r. Y.T.* Canada **149** O3
Frances Lake Canada **150** D2
Frances Lake *Y.T.* Canada **149** O3
Franceville Gabon **122** B4
Francis Canada **151** K5
Francis *atoll* Kiribati *see* **Beru**
Francis, Lake U.S.A. **165** J1
Francisco de Orellana Ecuador *see* **Coca**
Francisco I. Madero *Coahuila* Mex. **166** E3
Francisco I. Madero *Durango* Mex. **161** B7
Francisco Zarco Mex. **166** A1
Francistown Botswana **123** C6
Francois Canada **153** K5
François Lake Canada **150** E4
Francois Peron National Park Australia **135** A6
Francs Peak U.S.A. **156** F4
Franeker Neth. **62** F1
Frankenberg Germany **63** N4
Frankenberg (Eder) Germany **63** I3
Frankenhöhe *hills* Germany **57** M6
Frankenmuth U.S.A. **164** D2
Frankenthal (Pfalz) Germany **63** I5
Frankenwald *mts* Germany **63** L4
Frankford Canada **165** G1
Frankfort *IN* U.S.A. **164** B3

▶**Frankfort** *KY* U.S.A. **164** C4
Capital of Kentucky.

Frankfort *MI* U.S.A. **164** B1
Frankfort *OH* U.S.A. **164** D4
Frankfurt Germany *see* **Frankfurt am Main**
Frankfurt am Main Germany **63** I4
Frankfurt an der Oder Germany **57** O4
Frank Hann National Park Australia **135** C8
Frankin Lake U.S.A. **159** F1
Fränkische Alb *hills* Germany **63** K6
Fränkische Schweiz *reg.* Germany **63** L5
Frankland, Cape Australia **137** [inset]
Franklin *AZ* U.S.A. **159** I5
Franklin *GA* U.S.A. **163** C5
Franklin *IN* U.S.A. **164** B4
Franklin *KY* U.S.A. **164** B5
Franklin *LA* U.S.A. **161** F6
Franklin *MA* U.S.A. **165** J2
Franklin *NC* U.S.A. **163** D5
Franklin *NE* U.S.A. **160** D3
Franklin *NH* U.S.A. **165** J2
Franklin *PA* U.S.A. **164** F3
Franklin *TN* U.S.A. **162** C5
Franklin *TX* U.S.A. **161** D6
Franklin *VA* U.S.A. **165** G5
Franklin *WV* U.S.A. **164** F4
Franklin, Point *pt AK* U.S.A. **148** H1
Franklin Bay *N.W.T.* Canada **149** P1
Franklin D. Roosevelt Lake *resr* U.S.A. **156** D2
Franklin Furnace U.S.A. **164** D4
Franklin-Gordon National Park Australia **137** [inset]
Franklin Island Antarctica **188** H1
Franklin Mountains *N.W.T.* Canada **149** Q3
Franklin Mountains *AK* U.S.A. **149** K1
Franklin Strait Canada **147** I2
Franklinton U.S.A. **161** F6
Franklinville U.S.A. **165** F2
Frankston Australia **138** B7
Fränsta Sweden **54** J5
Frantsa-Iosifa, Zemlya *is* Rus. Fed. **76** G2
Franz Canada **152** D4
Franz Josef Glacier N.Z. **139** C6
Frasca, Capo della *c. Sardinia* Italy **68** C5
Frascati Italy **68** E4
Fraser *r.* Australia **134** C4
Fraser *r. B.C.* Canada **150** F5
Fraser *r. Nfld. and Lab.* Canada **153** J2
Fraser, Mount *hill* Australia **135** B6
Fraserburg S. Africa **124** E6
Fraserburgh U.K. **60** G3
Fraserdale Canada **152** E4
Fraser Island Australia **136** F5
Fraser Island National Park Australia **136** F5
Fraser Lake Canada **150** E4
Fraser National Park Australia **138** B6
Fraser Plateau Canada **150** E4
Fraser Range *hills* Australia **135** C8
Frauenfeld Switz. **66** I3
Fray Bentos Uruguay **178** E4
Frazeysburg U.S.A. **164** D3
Frechen Germany **62** G4
Freckleton U.K. **58** E5
Frederic U.S.A. **164** C1
Frederica U.S.A. **165** H4
Fredericia Denmark **55** F9
Frederick *MD* U.S.A. **165** G4
Frederick *OK* U.S.A. **161** D5
Frederick Reef Australia **136** F4
Fredericksburg *TX* U.S.A. **161** D6
Fredericksburg *VA* U.S.A. **165** G4
Frederick Sound *sea channel AK* U.S.A. **149** N4
Fredericktown U.S.A. **160** F4

▶**Fredericton** Canada **153** I5
Capital of New Brunswick.

Frederikshåb Greenland *see* **Paamiut**
Frederikshavn Denmark **55** G8
Frederiksværk Denmark **55** H9
Fredonia *AZ* U.S.A. **159** G3
Fredonia *KS* U.S.A. **161** E4
Fredonia *NY* U.S.A. **164** F2
Fredonia *WI* U.S.A. **164** B2
Fredrika Sweden **54** K4
Fredrikshamn Fin. *see* **Hamina**
Fredrikstad Norway **55** G7
Freedonyer Peak U.S.A. **158** C1
Freehold U.S.A. **165** H3
Freeland U.S.A. **165** H3
Freeling Heights *hill* Australia **137** B6
Freel Peak U.S.A. **158** D2
Freels, Cape Canada **153** L4
Freeman U.S.A. **160** D3
Freeman, Lake U.S.A. **164** B3
Freeport *FL* U.S.A. **163** C6
Freeport *IL* U.S.A. **160** F3
Freeport *TX* U.S.A. **161** E6
Freeport City Bahamas **163** E7
Freer U.S.A. **161** D7
Freesoil U.S.A. **164** B1
Free State *prov.* S. Africa **125** H5

▶**Freetown** Sierra Leone **120** B4
Capital of Sierra Leone.

Fregenal de la Sierra Spain **67** C4
Fregon Australia **135** F6
Fréhel, Cap *c.* France **66** C2
Frei (Chile) *research station* Antarctica **188** A2
Freiberg Germany **63** N4
Freiburg Switz. *see* **Fribourg**
Freiburg im Breisgau Germany **57** K6
Freisen Germany **63** H5
Freising Germany **57** M6
Freistadt Austria **57** O6
Fréjus France **66** H5
Fremantle Australia **135** A8
Fremont *CA* U.S.A. **158** C3
Fremont *IN* U.S.A. **164** C3
Fremont *MI* U.S.A. **164** C2
Fremont *NE* U.S.A. **160** D3
Fremont *OH* U.S.A. **164** D3
Fremont *r.* U.S.A. **159** H2
Fremont Junction U.S.A. **159** H2
Frenchburg U.S.A. **164** D5
French Cay *i.* Turks and Caicos Is **163** F8
French Congo *country* Africa *see* **Congo**

▶**French Guiana** *terr.* S. America **177** H3
French Overseas Department.

French Guinea *country* Africa *see* **Guinea**
French Island Australia **138** B7
French Lick U.S.A. **164** B4
Frenchman *r.* U.S.A. **156** G2
Frenchman Lake *CA* U.S.A. **158** C2
Frenchman Lake *NV* U.S.A. **159** F3
Frenchpark Ireland **61** D4
French Pass N.Z. **139** D5

▶**French Polynesia** *terr.* S. Pacific Ocean **187** K7
French Overseas Country.

French Somaliland *country* Africa *see* **Djibouti**

▶**French Southern and Antarctic Lands** *terr.* Indian Ocean **185** M8
French Overseas Territory.

French Sudan *country* Africa *see* **Mali**
French Territory of the Afars and Issas *country* Africa *see* **Djibouti**
Frenda Alg. **67** G6
Frentsjer Neth. *see* **Franeker**
Freren Germany **63** H2
Fresco *r.* Brazil **177** H5
Freshford Ireland **61** E5
Fresnillo Mex. **168** D4
Fresno U.S.A. **158** D3
Fresno *r.* U.S.A. **158** C3
Fresno Reservoir U.S.A. **156** F2
Fressel, Lac *l.* Canada **152** G3
Freu, Cap des *c.* Spain **67** H4
Freudenberg Germany **63** H4
Freudenstadt Germany **57** L6
Frévent France **62** C4
Frew *watercourse* Australia **136** A4
Frewena Australia **136** A3
Freycinet Estuary *inlet* Australia **135** A6
Freycinet Peninsula Australia **137** [inset]
Freyenstein Germany **63** M1
Freyming-Merlebach France **62** G5
Fria Guinea **120** B3
Fria, Cape Namibia **123** B5
Friant U.S.A. **158** D3
Frias Arg. **178** C3
Fribourg Switz. **66** H3
Friday Harbor U.S.A. **156** C2
Friedeburg Germany **63** H1
Friedens U.S.A. **165** F3
Friedland Rus. Fed. *see* **Pravdinsk**
Friedrichshafen Germany **57** L7
Friedrichskanal *canal* Germany **63** L2
Friend U.S.A. **160** D3
Friendly Islands *country* S. Pacific Ocean *see* **Tonga**
Friendship U.S.A. **160** F3
Friesack Germany **63** M2
Friese Wad *tidal flat* Neth. **62** F1
Friesoythe Germany **63** H1
Frinton-on-Sea U.K. **59** I7
Frio *r.* U.S.A. **161** D6
Frio *watercourse* U.S.A. **161** C5
Frisco Mountain U.S.A. **159** G2
Frissell, Mount *hill* U.S.A. **165** I2
Fritzlar Germany **63** J3
Frjentsjer Neth. *see* **Franeker**
Frobisher Bay Canada *see* **Iqaluit**
Frobisher Bay *b.* Canada **147** L3
Frobisher Lake Canada **151** I3
Frohavet *b.* Norway **54** F5
Frohburg Germany **63** M3
Froissy France **62** C5
Frolovo Rus. Fed. **53** I6
Frome *watercourse* Australia **137** B6
Frome U.K. **59** E7
Frome *r.* U.K. **59** E8
Frome, Lake *salt flat* Australia **137** B6
Frome Downs Australia **137** B6
Fröndenberg Germany **63** H3
Frontera *Coahuila* Mex. **167** E3
Frontera *Tabasco* Mex. **167** G5
Frontera, Punta *pt* Mex. **167** G5
Fronteras Mex. **166** C2
Front Royal U.S.A. **165** F4
Frosinone Italy **68** E4
Frostburg U.S.A. **165** F4
Frøya *i.* Norway **54** F5
Fruges France **62** C4
Fruita U.S.A. **159** I2
Fruitland U.S.A. **159** H1
Fruitvale U.S.A. **159** I2
Frunze Kyrg. *see* **Bishkek**
Frusino Italy *see* **Frosinone**
Fruska Gora *nat. park* Serbia **69** H2
Frýdek-Místek Czech Rep. **57** Q6
Fu'an China **97** H3
Fucheng *Anhui* China *see* **Fengyang**
Fucheng *Shaanxi* China *see* **Fuxian**
Fuchū Japan **93** F3
Fuchū *Toyama* Japan **92** D2
Fuchuan China **97** F3
Fuchun Jiang *r.* China **97** I2
Fude China **97** H3
Fuding China **97** I3
Fudul *reg.* Saudi Arabia **110** B6
Fuenlabrada Spain **67** E3
Fuerte *r.* Mex. **157** F8
Fuerte Olimpo Para. **178** E2
Fuerteventura *i.* Canary Is **120** B2
Fufeng China **96** E1
Fuga *i.* Phil. **82** C2
Fugong China **96** C3
Fugou China **97** G1
Fugu *Shaanxi* China **95** G4
Fuguo *Shandong* China *see* **Zhanhua**
Fuhai *Xinjiang* China **98** D3
Fuhai Linchang *Xinjiang* China **98** E3
Fuḩaymī Iraq **113** F4
Fujairah U.A.E. **110** E5
Fujeira U.A.E. *see* **Fujairah**
Fuji Japan **93** E3
Fujian *prov.* China **97** H3
Fujieda Japan **93** E4
Fuji-Hakone-Izu Kokuritsu-kōen *nat. park* Japan **93** F4
Fujihashi Japan **92** C3
Fujiidera Japan **92** B4
Fujikawa Japan **93** E3
Fuji-kawa *r.* Japan **93** E3
Fujimi *Nagano* Japan **93** E3
Fujimi *Saitama* Japan **93** F3
Fujin China **90** C3
Fujino Japan **93** F3
Fujinomiya Japan **93** E3
Fujioka *Aichi* Japan **92** D3
Fujioka *Gunma* Japan **93** F2
Fujioka *Tochigi* Japan **93** F2
Fuji-san *vol.* Japan **93** E3
Fujisawa Japan **93** F3
Fujishiro Japan **93** G3
Fujiwara *Mie* Japan **92** C3
Fujiwara *Tochigi* Japan **93** F2
Fujiyoshida Japan **93** E3
Fûka Egypt *see* **Fūkah**
Fūkah Egypt **112** B5
Fukang *Xinjiang* China **98** D3
Fukaya Japan **93** F2
Fukiage Japan **93** F2
Fukien *prov.* China *see* **Fujian**
Fukuchiyama Japan **92** B3
Fukude Japan **93** D4
Fukue-jima *i.* Japan **91** C6
Fukui Japan **92** C2
Fukui *pref.* Japan **92** C3
Fukumitsu Japan **92** C2
Fukuno Japan **92** C2
Fukuoka Japan **91** C6
Fukuoka *Gifu* Japan **92** D3
Fukuoka *Toyama* Japan **92** C2
Fukuroi Japan **93** D4
Fukusaki Japan **92** A4
Fukushima Japan **91** F5
Fukuyama Japan **91** C7
Fûl, Gebel *hill* Egypt *see* **Fūl, Jabal**
Fūl, Jabal *hill* Egypt **107** A5
Fulchhari Bangl. **105** G4
Fulda Germany **63** J4
Fulda *r.* Germany **63** J3
Fulham U.K. **59** G7
Fuli China *see* **Jixian**
Fuliji China **97** H1
Fuling China **96** E2
Fulitun China *see* **Jixian**
Fullerton *CA* U.S.A. **158** E5
Fullerton *NE* U.S.A. **160** D3
Fullerton, Cape Canada **151** N2
Fulton *IN* U.S.A. **164** B3
Fulton *MO* U.S.A. **160** F4
Fulton *MS* U.S.A. **161** F5
Fulton *NY* U.S.A. **165** G2
Fumane Moz. **125** K3
Fumay France **62** E5
Fumin China **96** D3
Funabashi *Chiba* Japan **93** F3
Funabashi *Toyama* Japan **92** D2
Funafuti *atoll* Tuvalu **133** H2
Funan China **97** G1

▶**Funchal** Madeira **120** B1
Capital of Madeira.

Fundão Brazil **179** C2
Fundão Port. **67** C3
Fundi Italy *see* **Fondi**
Fundición Mex. **166** C3
Fundy, Bay of *g.* Canada **153** I5
Fundy National Park Canada **153** I5
Fünen *i.* Denmark *see* **Fyn**
Funeral Peak U.S.A. **158** E3
Fünfkirchen Hungary *see* **Pécs**
Fung Wong Shan *hill H.K.* China *see* **Lantau Peak**
Funhalouro Moz. **125** L2
Funing *Jiangsu* China **97** H1
Funing *Yunnan* China **96** E4
Funiu Shan *mts* China **97** F1
Funtua Nigeria **120** D3
Funzie U.K. **60** [inset]
Fuping *Hebei* China **95** H4
Fuping *Shaanxi* China **95** G5
Fuqing China **97** H3
Fūrgun, Kūh-e *mt.* Iran **110** E5
Furmanov Rus. Fed. **52** I4
Furmanovka Kazakh. *see* **Moyynkum**
Furmanovo Kazakh. *see* **Zhalpaktal**
Furnás *hill* Spain **67** G4
Furnas, Represa *resr* Brazil **179** B3
Furneaux Group *is* Australia **137** [inset]
Furnes Belgium *see* **Veurne**
Furong China *see* **Wan'an**
Fürstenau Germany **63** H2
Fürstenberg Germany **63** N1
Fürstenwalde Germany **57** O4
Fürth Germany **63** K5
Furth im Wald Germany **63** M5
Furudono Japan **93** G1
Furukawa *Gifu* Japan **92** D2
Furukawa Japan **91** F5
Fury and Hecla Strait Canada **147** J3
Fusan S. Korea *see* **Pusan**
Fushan *Shandong* China **95** J4
Fushan *Shanxi* China **95** G5
Fushimi Japan **92** B4
Fushun *Liaoning* China **95** J3
Fushuncheng *Liaoning* China *see* **Shuncheng**
Fuso Japan **92** C3
Fusong China **90** B4
Fussa Japan **93** F3
Futaba Japan **93** E3
Futagawa Japan **92** D4
Futago-yama *mt.* Japan **93** E2
Futami Japan **92** C4
Fu Tau Pun Chau *i. H.K.* China **97** [inset]
Futtsu Japan **93** F3
Futtsu-misaki *pt* Japan **93** F3
Futuna *i.* Vanuatu **133** H3
Futuna Islands Wallis and Futuna Is *see* **Hoorn, Îles de**
Fuxian *Liaoning* China *see* **Wafangdian**
Fuxian *Shaanxi* China **95** G5
Fuxian Hu *l.* China **96** D3
Fuxin *Liaoning* China **95** J3
Fuxin *Liaoning* China **95** J3
Fuxing China *see* **Wangmo**
Fuxinzhen *Liaoning* China *see* **Fuxin**
Fuyang *Anhui* China **97** G1
Fuyang *Guangxi* China *see* **Fuchuan**
Fuyang *Zhejiang* China **97** H2
Fuyang He *r.* China **95** I4
Fuying Dao *i.* China **97** I3
Fuyu *Anhui* China *see* **Susong**
Fuyu *Heilong.* China **95** K2
Fuyu *Jilin* China *see* **Songyuan**
Fuyu *Jilin* China **90** B3
Fuyuan *Heilong.* China **90** D2
Fuyuan *Yunnan* China **96** E3
Fuyun *Xinjiang* China **94** B2
Fuzhou *Fujian* China **97** H3
Fuzhou *Jiangxi* China **97** H3
Füzuli Azer. **113** G3
Fyn *i.* Denmark **55** G9
Fyne, Loch *inlet* U.K. **60** D5
F.Y.R.O.M. (Former Yugoslav Republic of Macedonia) *country* Europe *see* **Macedonia**

G

Gaaf Atoll Maldives *see* **Huvadhu Atoll**
Gaâfour Tunisia **68** C6
Gaalkacyo Somalia **122** E3
Gaat *r.* Malaysia **85** F2
Gabakly Turkm. **111** F2
Gabasumdo *Qinghai* China *see* **Tongde**
Gabbs U.S.A. **158** E2
Gabbs Valley Range *mts* U.S.A. **158** D2
Gabd Pak. **111** F5
Gabela Angola **123** B5
Gaberones Botswana *see* **Gaborone**
Gabès Tunisia **64** G5
Gabès, Golfe de *g.* Tunisia **64** G5
Gabo Island Australia **138** D6
Gabon *country* Africa **122** B4

▶**Gaborone** Botswana **125** G3
Capital of Botswana.

Gābrīk Iran **110** E5
Gabrovo Bulg. **69** K3
Gabú Guinea-Bissau **120** B3
Gadag India **106** B3
Gadaisu P.N.G. **136** E1
Gadap Pak. **111** G5
Gadchiroli India **106** D1
Gäddede Sweden **54** I4
Gadê China **96** C1
Gades Spain *see* **Cádiz**
Gadhka India **111** H6
Gadhra India **104** B5
Gadra Pak. **111** H5
Gadsden U.S.A. **163** C5
Gadsden *AZ* U.S.A. **166** B1
Gadwal India **106** C2
Gadyach Ukr. *see* **Hadyach**
Gaer U.K. **59** D7
Găeşti Romania **69** K2
Gaeta Italy **68** E4
Gaeta, Golfo di *g.* Italy **68** E4
Gaferut *i.* Micronesia **81** L5
Gaffney U.S.A. **163** D5
Gafsa Tunisia **68** C7
Gag *i. Papua* Indon. **83** D3
Gagarin Rus. Fed. **53** G5
Gagnoa Côte d'Ivoire **120** C4
Gagnon Canada **153** H4
Gago Coutinho Angola *see* **Lumbala N'guimbo**
Gagra Georgia **53** I8
Gahai *Qinghai* China **94** D4
Gaiab *watercourse* Namibia **124** D5
Gaibanda Bangl. *see* **Gaibandha**
Gaibandha Bangl. **105** G4
Gaïdouronisi *i.* Greece **69** K7
Gaifi, Wâdi el *watercourse* Egypt *see* **Jayfī, Wādī al**
Gail U.S.A. **161** C5
Gaildorf Germany **63** J6
Gaillac France **66** E5
Gaillimh Ireland *see* **Galway**
Gaillon France **62** B5
Gaindainqoinkor *Xizang* China **99** E7
Gainesboro U.S.A. **164** C5
Gainesville *FL* U.S.A. **163** D6
Gainesville *GA* U.S.A. **163** D5
Gainesville *MO* U.S.A. **161** E4
Gainesville *TX* U.S.A. **161** D5
Gainsborough U.K. **58** G5
Gairdner, Lake *salt flat* Australia **137** A6
Gairloch U.K. **60** D3
Gair Loch *b.* U.K. **60** D3
Gaixian *Liaoning* China *see* **Gaizhou**
Gaizhou *Liaoning* China **95** J3
Gajah Hutan, Bukit *hill* Malaysia **84** C1
Gajipur India *see* **Ghazipur**
Gajol India **105** G4
Gakarosa *mt.* S. Africa **124** F4
Gakona *AK* U.S.A. **149** K3
Gala *Xizang* China **99** E7
Galaasiya Uzbek. *see* **Galaosiyo**
Gala Co *l.* China **99** E7
Galâla el Baḥarîya, Gebel el *plat.* Egypt *see* **Jalālah al Baḥrīyah, Jabal**
Galana *r.* Kenya **122** E4
Galang Besar *i.* Indon. **84** D2
Galanta Slovakia **57** P6
Galaosiyo Uzbek. **111** G2

▶**Galapagos Islands** *is* Ecuador **187** O6
Part of Ecuador. Most westerly point of South America.

Galapagos Rise *sea feature* Pacific Ocean **187** N6
Galashiels U.K. **60** G5
Galaţi Romania **69** M2
Galatina Italy **68** H4
Gala Water *r.* U.K. **60** G5
Galax U.S.A. **164** E5
Galaýmor Turkm. **111** F3
Galaymor Turkm. *see* **Galaýmor**
Galbally Ireland **61** D5
Galdhøpiggen *mt.* Norway **55** F6
Galeana *Chihuahua* Mex. **166** D2
Galeana *Nuevo León* Mex. **167** E3
Galela *Halmahera* Indon. **83** C2
Galena *AK* U.S.A. **148** H2
Galena *IL* U.S.A. **160** F3
Galena *MD* U.S.A. **165** H4
Galena *MO* U.S.A. **161** E4
Galera, Punta *pt* Chile **178** B6
Galera, Punta *pt* Mex. **167** F6
Galesburg *IL* U.S.A. **160** F3
Galesburg *MI* U.S.A. **164** C2
Galeshewe S. Africa **124** G5
Galeton U.S.A. **165** G3
Galey *r.* Ireland **61** C5
Galheirão *r.* Brazil **179** B1
Galiano Island Canada **150** F5
Galich Rus. Fed. **52** I4
Galichskaya Vozvyshennost' *hills* Rus. Fed. **52** I4
Galicia *aut. comm.* Spain **67** C2
Galičica *nat. park* Macedonia **69** I4
Galilee, Lake *salt flat* Australia **136** D4
Galilee, Sea of *l.* Israel **107** B3
Galion U.S.A. **164** D3
Galiuro Mountains U.S.A. **159** H5
Galizia *aut. comm.* Spain *see* **Galicia**
Gallabat Sudan **108** E7
G'allaorol Uzbek. **111** G1
Gallatin *MO* U.S.A. **160** E4
Gallatin *TN* U.S.A. **164** B5
Galle Sri Lanka **106** D5
Gallego Rise *sea feature* Pacific Ocean **187** M6
Gallegos *r.* Arg. **178** C8
Gallia *country* Europe *see* **France**

▶**Gallinas, Punta** *pt* Col. **176** D1
Most northerly point of South America.

Gallipoli Italy **68** H4
Gallipoli Turkey **69** L4
Gallipolis U.S.A. **164** D4
Gällivare Sweden **54** L3
Gällö Sweden **54** I5
Gallo Island U.S.A. **165** G2
Gallo Mountains U.S.A. **159** I4
Gallup U.S.A. **159** I4
Galmisdale U.K. **60** C4
Galong Australia **138** D5
Galoya Sri Lanka **106** D4
Gal Oya National Park Sri Lanka **106** D5
Galshar *Hentiy* Mongolia **95** G2
Galston U.K. **60** E5
Galt Mongolia **94** D1
Galt U.S.A. **158** C2
Galtat Zemmour W. Sahara **120** B2
Galtee Mountains *hills* Ireland **61** D5
Galtymore *hill* Ireland **56** C4
Galūgāh, Kūh-e *mts* Iran **110** D4
Galuut Mongolia **94** E2
Galveston *IN* U.S.A. **164** B3
Galveston *TX* U.S.A. **161** E6
Galveston Bay U.S.A. **161** E6
Galwa Nepal **105** E3
Galway Ireland **61** C4
Galway Bay Ireland **61** C4
Gam *i. Papua* Indon. **83** D3
Gam *i. Papua* Indon. **83** D3
Gâm, Sông *r.* Vietnam **86** D2
Gamagōri Japan **92** D4
Gamalakhe S. Africa **125** J6
Gamalama *vol. Maluku* Indon. **83** C2
Gamay Bay *Samar* Phil. **82** D3
Gamba *Xizang* China *see* **Gongbalou**
Gamba Gabon **122** A4
Gambēla Eth. **122** D3
Gambēla National Park Eth. **122** D3
Gambell *AK* U.S.A. **148** E3
Gambella Eth. *see* **Gambēla**
Gambia, The *country* Africa **120** B3
Gambier, Îles *is* Fr. Polynesia **187** L7
Gambier Islands Australia **137** B7
Gambier Islands Fr. Polynesia *see* **Gambier, Îles**
Gambo Canada **153** L4
Gamboma Congo **122** B4
Gamboola Australia **136** C3
Gamboula Cent. Afr. Rep. **122** B3
Gamda China *see* **Zamtang**
Gamêtî *N.W.T.* Canada **149** R2
Gamkunoro, Gunung *vol. Halmahera* Indon. **83** C2
Gamlakarleby Fin. *see* **Kokkola**
Gamleby Sweden **55** J8
Gammelstaden Sweden **54** M4
Gammon Ranges National Park Australia **137** B6
Gamō Japan **92** C3
Gamova, Mys *pt* Rus. Fed. **90** C4
Gamshadzai Kūh *mts* Iran **111** F4
Gamtog China **96** C2
Gamud *mt.* Eth. **122** D3

Gamzigrad-Romuliana tourist site Serbia 69 J3
Gana China 96 D1
Ganado U.S.A. 159 I4
Gananoque Canada 165 G1
Gäncä Azer. 113 G2
Gancaohu Xinjiang China 98 E4
Gancheng China 97 F5
Ganda Angola 123 B5
Ganda Xizang China 99 F7
Gandadiwata, Bukit mt. Indon. 83 A3
Gandaingoin China 105 G3
Gandajika Dem. Rep. Congo 123 C4
Gandak Barrage Nepal 105 E4
Gandari Mountain Pak. 111 H4
Gandava Pak. 111 G4
Gander Canada 153 L4
Ganderkesee Germany 63 I1
Gandesa Spain 67 G3
Gandhidham India 104 B5
Gandhinagar India 104 C5
Gandhi Sagar resr India 104 C4
Gandia Spain 67 F4
Gandu Qinghai China 94 E5
Gandzha Azer. see Gäncä
Ganes Creek AK U.S.A. 148 H3
Ganga r. Bangl./India 105 G5 see Ganges
Ganga Cone sea feature Indian Ocean see Ganges Cone
Gangán Arg. 178 C6
Ganganagar India 104 C3
Gangapur India 104 D4
Ganga Sera India 104 B4
Gangaw Myanmar 86 A2
Gangawati India 106 C3
Gangaw Range mts Myanmar 86 B2
Gangca Qinghai China 94 E4
Gangdisê Shan mts Xizang China 99 C7
Ganges r. Bangl./India 105 G5 also known as Ganga
Ganges France 66 F5
Ganges, Mouths of the Bangl./India 105 G5
Ganges Cone sea feature Indian Ocean 185 N4
Gangou Qinghai China 94 D4
Gangouyi Gansu China 94 F5
Gangra Turkey see Çankırı
Gangtok India 105 G4
Gangu Gansu China 94 F5
Gangziyao Hebei China 95 H4
Gan He r. China 95 K1
Ganhezi Xinjiang China 98 E3
Gani Halmahera Indon. 83 D3
Gan Jiang r. China 97 H2
Ganjig Nei Mongol China 95 J3
Ganjing Shaanxi China 95 G5
Ganjur Sum Nei Mongol China 95 H2
Ganluo China 96 D2
Ganmain Australia 138 C5
Gannan Heilong. China 95 J2
Gannat France 66 F3
Gannett Peak U.S.A. 156 F4
Ganq Qinghai China 99 F5
Ganquan Shaanxi China 95 G4
Ganshui China 96 E2
Gansu prov. China 94 D3
Gantang Nei Mongol China 94 F4
Gantheaume Point Australia 134 C4
Ganting Shaanxi China see Huxian
Gantsevichi Belarus see Hantsavichy
Gantung Indon. 85 E3
Ganxian China 97 G3
Ganye Nigeria 120 E4
Ganyu Jiangsu China 95 I5
Ganyushkino Kazakh. 51 P6
Ganzhou China 97 G3
Ganzi Sudan 121 G4
Gao Mali 120 C3
Gaoba Gansu China 94 E4
Gaocheng Hebei China 95 H4
Gaocheng China see Litang
Gaocun China see Mayang
Gaohe China see Huaining
Gaohebu China see Huaining
Gaolan Gansu China 94 E4
Gaoleshan China see Xianfeng
Gaoliangjian China see Hongze
Gaoling Shaanxi China 95 G5
Gaomi Shandong China 95 I4
Gaomutang China 97 F3
Gaoping Shanxi China 95 H5
Gaoqing Shandong China 95 I4
Gaotai Gansu China 94 D4
Gaotang Shandong China 95 I4
Gaoth Dobhair Ireland 61 D2
Gaoting China see Daishan
Gaotingzhen China see Daishan
Gaotouyao Nei Mongol China 95 G4
Gaoua Burkina 120 C3
Gaoual Guinea 120 B3
Gaoxiong Taiwan see Kaohsiung
Gaoyang Hebei China 95 H4
Gaoyao China see Zhaoqing
Gaoyi Hebei China 95 H4
Gaoyou China 97 H1
Gaoyou Hu l. China 97 H1
Gap France 66 H4
Gapan Luzon Phil. 82 C3
Gapuwiyak Australia 136 A2
Gaqoi Xizang China 99 C7
Gaqung Xizang China 99 D7
Gar China 104 E2
Gar Pak. 111 F5
Gar' r. Rus. Fed. 90 C1
Gara, Lough l. Ireland 61 D4
Garabekevyul Turkm. see Garabekewül
Garabekewül Turkm. 111 G2
Garabil Belentligi hills Turkm. 111 F2
Garabogaz Turkm. 113 I2
Garabogaz Aylagy b. Turkm. see Garabogazköl Aýlagy
Garabogazköl Aýlagy b. Turkm. 113 I2
Garabogazköl Aylagy b. Turkm. see Garabogazköl Aýlagy
Garabogazköl Bogazy sea chan. Turkm. 113 I2
Garachiné Panama 166 [inset] K7
Garachiné, Punta pt Panama 166 [inset] K7
Garägheh Iran 111 F4
Garagum des. Turkm. 110 E2
Garagum des. Turkm. see Karakum Desert
Garagum Kanaly canal Turkm. 111 F2
Garah Australia 138 D2
Garalo Mali 120 C3
Garamätnyýaz Turkm. 111 G2
Garamätnyyaz Turkm. see Garamätnyýaz
Garamba r. Dem. Rep. Congo 122 C3
Garang Qinghai China 94 E4
Garanhuns Brazil 177 K5
Ga-Rankuwa S. Africa 125 H3
Garapuava Brazil 179 B2
Gárasavvon Sweden see Karesuando
Garautha India 104 D4
Garba China see Jiulong
Garbahaarrey Somalia 122 E3
Garba Tula Kenya 122 D3
Garberville U.S.A. 158 B1
Garbsen Germany 63 J2
Garça Brazil 179 A3
Garco China 105 G2
Garda, Lago di Italy see Garda, Lake
Garda, Lake Italy 68 D2
Garde, Cap de c. Alg. 68 B6
Gardelegen Germany 63 L2
Garden City U.S.A. 160 C4
Garden Hill Canada 151 M4
Garden Mountain U.S.A. 164 E5
Gardeyz Afgh. see Gardēz
Gardēz Afgh. 111 H3
Gardinas Belarus see Hrodna
Gardiner U.S.A. 165 K1
Gardiner, Mount Australia 134 F5
Gardiner Range hills Australia 134 E4
Gardiners Island U.S.A. 165 I3
Gardīz Afgh. see Gardēz
Gardner atoll Micronesia see Faraulep
Gardner U.S.A. 165 J2
Gardner Inlet Antarctica 188 L1
Gardner Island atoll Kiribati see Nikumaroro
Gardner Pinnacles is U.S.A. 186 I4
Gáregasnjárga Fin. see Karigasniemi
Garelochhead U.K. 60 E4
Gareloi Island AK U.S.A. 149 [inset]
Garet el Djenoun mt. Alg. 120 D2
Gargano, Parco Nazionale del nat. park Italy 68 F4
Gargantua, Cape Canada 152 D5
Gargunsa China see Gar
Gargždai Lith. 55 L9
Garhchiroli India see Gadchiroli
Garhi Madh. Prad. India 106 C1
Garhi Rajasthan India 104 C5
Garhi Khairo Pak. 111 G4
Garhmuktesar Uttar Prad. India 99 B7
Garhwa India 105 E4
Gari Rus. Fed. 51 S4
Gariau Indon. 81 I7
Garibaldi, Mount Canada 150 F5
Gariep Dam resr S. Africa 125 G6
Garies S. Africa 124 C6
Garigliano r. Italy 68 E4
Garissa Kenya 122 D4
Garkalne Latvia 55 N8
Garkung Caka l. Xizang China 99 D6
Garland U.S.A. 161 D5
Garm Tajik. see Gharm
Garm Āb Iran 111 E3
Garmāb Iran 110 E3
Garm Āb, Chashmeh-ye spring Iran 110 E3
Garmī Iran 110 C2
Garmsar Iran 110 D3
Garmsel reg. Afgh. 111 F4
Garner IA U.S.A. 160 E3
Garner KY U.S.A. 164 D5
Garnett U.S.A. 160 E4
Garnpung Lake imp. l. Australia 138 A4
Garo Hills India 105 G4
Garonne r. France 66 D4
Garoowe Somalia 122 E3
Garopaba Brazil 179 A5
Garoua Cameroon 120 E4
Garoua Boulai Cameroon 121 E4
Gar Qu r. Qinghai China 99 F6
Garqu Yan Qinghai China 99 F6
Garré Arg. 178 D5
Garrett U.S.A. 164 C3
Garrison U.S.A. 160 E2
Garruk Pak. 111 G4
Garry r. U.K. 60 E3
Garrychyrla Turkm. see Garryçyrla
Garryçyrla Turkm. 111 F2
Garry Island N.W.T. Canada 149 N1
Garry Lake Canada 151 K1
Garrynahine U.K. 60 C2
Garsen Kenya 122 E4
Garshy Turkm. see Garşy
Garsila Sudan 121 F3
Garşy Turkm. 113 I2
Gartar China see Qianning
Garth U.K. 59 D6
Gartog China see Markam
Gartok Xizang China see Garyarsa
Gartow Germany 63 L1
Garub Namibia 124 C4
Garusuun Palau 82 [inset]
Garut Jawa Indon. 85 D4
Garvagh U.K. 61 F3
Garve U.K. 60 E3
Garwa India see Garhwa
Garwha India see Garhwa
Gar Xincun Xizang China 99 C6
Gary IN U.S.A. 164 B3
Gary WV U.S.A. 164 E5
Garyarsa Xizang China 99 C7
Garyi China 96 C2
Garyū-zan mt. Japan 91 D6
Garza García Mex. 161 C7
Gar Zangbo r. China 99 B6
Garzê China 96 C2
Gasan-Kuli Turkm. see Esenguly
Gas City U.S.A. 164 C3
Gascogne reg. France see Gascony
Gascogne, Golfe de g. France see Gascony, Gulf of
Gascony reg. France 66 D5
Gascony, Gulf of France 66 C5
Gascoyne r. Australia 135 A6
Gascoyne Junction Australia 135 A6
Gase Xizang China 99 D7
Gasherbrum I mt. China/Pak. 104 D2
Gas Hu salt l. China 99 E5
Gashua Nigeria 120 E3
Gask Iran 111 E3
Gaspar Cuba 163 E8
Gaspar, Selat sea chan. Indon. 84 D3
Gaspé Canada 153 I4
Gaspé, Cap c. Canada 153 I4
Gaspésie, Péninsule de la pen. Canada 153 I4
Gassan vol. Japan 91 F5
Gassaway U.S.A. 164 E4
Gasselte Neth. 62 G2
Gasteiz Spain see Vitoria-Gasteiz
Gastello Rus. Fed. 90 F2
Gaston U.S.A. 165 G5
Gaston, Lake U.S.A. 165 G5
Gastonia U.S.A. 163 D5
Gata, Cabo de c. Spain 67 E5
Gata, Cape Cyprus 107 A2
Gata, Sierra de mts Spain 67 C3
Gataga r. B.C. Canada 149 P4
Gatas, Akra c. Cyprus see Gata, Cape
Gatchina Rus. Fed. 55 Q7
Gate City U.S.A. 164 D5
Gatehouse of Fleet U.K. 60 E6
Gatentiri Indon. 81 K8
Gateshead U.K. 58 F4
Gates of the Arctic National Park and Preserve AK U.S.A. 148 I2
Gatesville U.S.A. 161 D6
Gateway U.S.A. 159 I2
Gatineau Canada 165 H1
Gatineau r. Canada 152 G5
Gatong China see Jomda
Gatooma Zimbabwe see Kadoma
Gatton Australia 138 F1
Gatvand Iran 110 C3
Gatyana S. Africa see Willowvale
Gau i. Fiji 133 H3
Gauer Lake Canada 151 L3
Gauhati India see Guwahati
Gaujas nacionālais parks nat. park Latvia 55 N8
Gaul country Europe see France
Gaula r. Norway 54 G5
Gaume reg. Belgium 62 F5
Gaurama Brazil 179 A4
Gauribidanur India 106 C3
Gauteng prov. S. Africa 125 I4
Gavarr Armenia 113 G2
Gāvbandī Iran 110 D5
Gāvbūs, Kūh-e mts Iran 110 D5

▶Gavdos i. Greece 69 K7
Most southerly point of Europe.

Gavião r. Brazil 179 C1
Gavīleh Iran 110 B3
Gav Khūnī Iran 110 D3
Gävle Sweden 55 J6
Gavrilovka Vtoraya Rus. Fed. 53 I5
Gavrilov-Yam Rus. Fed. 52 H4
Gawachab Namibia 124 C4
Gawai Myanmar 96 C3
Gawan India 105 F4
Gawilgarh Hills India 104 D5
Gawler Australia 137 B7
Gawler Ranges hills Australia 137 A7
Gaxun Nur salt l. Nei Mongol China 94 E3
Gaya India 105 F4
Gaya i. Malaysia 85 G1
Gaya i. Malaysia 85 G1
Gaya Niger 120 D3
Gaya He r. China 90 C4
Gayam Jawa Indon. 85 F4
Gayéri Burkina 120 D3
Gaylord U.S.A. 164 C1
Gayndah Australia 137 E5
Gayny Rus. Fed. 52 L3
Gaysin Ukr. see Haysyn
Gayutino Rus. Fed. 52 H4
Gaz Iran 110 C3

▶Gaza terr. Asia 107 B4
Semi-autonomous region.

▶Gaza Gaza 107 B4
Capital of Gaza.

Gaza prov. Moz. 125 K2
Gazan Pak. 111 G4
Gazandzhyk Turkm. see Bereket
Gazanjyk Turkm. see Bereket
Gaza Strip terr. Asia see Gaza
Gaziantep Turkey 112 E3
Gaziantep prov. Turkey 107 C1
Gazibenli Turkey see Yahyalı
Gazīk Iran 111 F3
Gazimağusa Cyprus see Famagusta
Gazimuro-Ononskiy Khrebet mts Rus. Fed. 95 G1
Gazimurskiy Khrebet mts Rus. Fed. 89 L2
Gazimurskiy Zavod Rus. Fed. 89 L2
Gazipaşa Turkey 107 A1
Gazli Uzbek. 111 F1
Gaz Māhū Iran 110 E5
Gbadolite Dem. Rep. Congo 122 C3
Gbarnga Liberia 120 C4
Gboko Nigeria 120 D4
Gcuwa S. Africa see Butterworth
Gdańsk Poland 57 Q3
Gdańsk, Gulf of Poland/Rus. Fed. 57 Q3
Gdańska, Zatoka g. Poland/Rus. Fed. see Gdańsk, Gulf of
Gdingen Poland see Gdynia
Gdov Rus. Fed. 55 O7
Gdynia Poland 57 Q3
Geaidnovuohppi Norway 54 M2
Gearhart Mountain U.S.A. 156 C4
Gearraidh na h-Aibhne U.K. see Garrynahine
Gebe i. Maluku Indon. 83 D2
Gebesee Germany 63 K3
Geçitkale Cyprus see Lefkonikon
Gedang, Gunung mt. Indon. 84 C3
Gedaref Sudan 108 E7
Gedern Germany 63 J4
Gedinne Belgium 62 E5
Gediz r. Turkey 69 L5
Gedney Drove End U.K. 59 H6
Gedong Sarawak Malaysia 85 E2
Gedong, Tanjong pt Sing. 87 [inset]
Gedser Denmark 55 G9
Gedungpakuan Sumatera Indon. 84 D4
Geel Belgium 62 F3
Geelong Australia 138 B7
Geelvink Channel Australia 135 A7
Geel Vloer salt pan S. Africa 124 E5
Gees Gwardafuy c. Somalia see Gwardafuy, Gees
Geeste Germany 63 H2
Geesthacht Germany 63 K1
Gê'gyai Xizang China 99 C6
Ge Hu l. China 97 H2
Geidam Nigeria 120 E3
Geiersberg hill Germany 63 J5
Geikie r. Canada 151 K3
Geilenkirchen Germany 62 G4
Geilo Norway 55 F6
Geinō Japan 92 C4
Geiranger Norway 54 E5
Geislingen an der Steige Germany 63 J6
Geisûm, Gezâ'ir is Egypt see Qaysūm, Juzur
Geita Tanz. 122 D4
Geithain Germany 63 M3
Gejiu China 96 D4
Geka, Mys hd Rus. Fed. 148 B2
Geka, Mys hd Rus. Fed. 148 B2
Gēkdepe Turkm. 110 E2
Gela Sicily Italy 68 F6
Gēladaindong mt. Qinghai China 99 E6
Geladī Eth. 122 E3
Gelam i. Indon. 85 E3
Gelang, Tanjung pt Malaysia 87 C7
Geldern Germany 62 G3
Gelendzhik Rus. Fed. 112 E1
Gelibolu Turkey see Gallipoli
Gelidonya Burnu pt Turkey see Yardımcı Burnu
Gelincik Dağı mt. Turkey 69 N5
Gelmord Iran 110 E3
Gelnhausen Germany 63 J4
Gelsenkirchen Germany 62 H3
Gelumbang Sumatera Indon. 84 D3
Gemas Malaysia 84 C2
Gemena Dem. Rep. Congo 122 B3
Geminokağı Cyprus see Karavostasi
Gemlik Turkey 69 M4
Gemona del Friuli Italy 68 E1
Gemsa Egypt see Jamsah
Gemsbok National Park Botswana 124 E3
Gemsbokplein well S. Africa 124 E4
Gemuk Mountain AK U.S.A. 148 H3
Genalē Wenz r. Eth. 122 E3
Genappe Belgium 62 E4
Genāveh Iran 110 C4
General Acha Arg. 178 D5
General Alvear Arg. 178 C5
General Belgrano II research station Antarctica see Belgrano II
General Bravo Mex. 161 D7

▶General Carrera, Lago l. Arg./Chile 178 B7
Deepest lake in South America.

General Conesa Arg. 178 D6
General Escobeda Mex. 167 E3
General Freire Angola see Muxaluando
General Juan Madariaga Arg. 178 E5
General La Madrid Arg. 178 D5
General Luna Phil. 82 D4
General MacArthur Samar Phil. 82 D4
General Machado Angola see Camacupa
General Pico Arg. 178 D5
General Pinedo Arg. 178 D3
General Roca Arg. 178 C5
General Salgado Brazil 179 A3
General San Martín research station Antarctica see San Martín
General Santos Mindanao Phil. 82 D5
General Simón Bolívar Mex. 161 C7
General Terán Mex. 167 F3
General Trías Mex. 166 D2
General Villegas Arg. 178 D5
Genesee U.S.A. 165 G3
Geneseo U.S.A. 165 G2
Geneva S. Africa 125 H4
Geneva Switz. 66 H3
Geneva AL U.S.A. 163 C6
Geneva IL U.S.A. 164 A3
Geneva NE U.S.A. 160 D3
Geneva NY U.S.A. 165 G2
Geneva OH U.S.A. 164 E3
Geneva, Lake France/Switz. 66 H3
Genève Switz. see Geneva
Genf Switz. see Geneva
Gengda China see Gana
Gengma China 96 C4
Gengxuan China see Gengma
Genhe China 90 A2
Gen He r. China 95 I1
Genichesk Ukr. see Heniches'k
Genji India 104 C5
Genk Belgium 62 F4
Gennep Neth. 62 F3
Genoa Australia 138 D6
Genoa Italy 68 C2
Genoa, Gulf of Italy 68 C2
Genova Italy see Genoa
Genova, Golfo di Italy see Genoa, Gulf of
Gent Belgium see Ghent
Genteng Jawa Indon. 84 D4
Genteng i. Indon. 85 F4
Genthin Germany 63 M2
Genting Highlands Malaysia 84 C2
Gentioux, Plateau de France 66 F4
Genua Italy see Genoa
Geographe Bay Australia 135 A8
Geographical Society Ø i. Greenland 147 P2
Geok-Tepe Turkm. see Gēkdepe
Georga, Zemlya i. Rus. Fed. 76 F1
George r. Canada 153 I2
George S. Africa 124 F7
George, Lake Australia 138 D5
George, Lake AK U.S.A. 149 K3
George, Lake FL U.S.A. 163 D6
George, Lake NY U.S.A. 165 I2
George Land i. Rus. Fed. see Georga, Zemlya
Georges Mills U.S.A. 165 I2
George Sound inlet N.Z. 139 A7
Georgetown Australia 136 C3

▶George Town Cayman Is 169 H5
Capital of the Cayman Islands.

Georgetown Gambia 120 B3

▶Georgetown Guyana 177 G2
Capital of Guyana.

George Town Malaysia 84 C1
Georgetown AK U.S.A. 148 H3
Georgetown DE U.S.A. 165 H4
Georgetown GA U.S.A. 163 C6
Georgetown IL U.S.A. 164 B4
Georgetown KY U.S.A. 164 C4
Georgetown OH U.S.A. 164 D4
Georgetown SC U.S.A. 163 E5
Georgetown TX U.S.A. 161 D6
George VI Sound sea chan. Antarctica 188 L2
George V Land reg. Antarctica 188 G2
George West U.S.A. 161 D6
Georgia country Asia 113 F2
Georgia state U.S.A. 163 D5
Georgia, Strait of Canada 150 E5
Georgiana U.S.A. 161 G6
Georgian Bay Canada 164 E1
Georgian Bay Islands National Park Canada 164 F1
Georgienne, Baie b. Canada see Georgian Bay
Georgina watercourse Australia 136 B5
Georgiu-Dezh Rus. Fed. see Liski
Georgiyevka Vostochnyy Kazakhstan Kazakh. 102 F2
Georgiyevka Zhambylskaya Oblast' Kazakh. see Korday
Georgiyevsk Rus. Fed. 113 F1
Georgiyevskoye Rus. Fed. 52 J4
Georg von Neumayer research station Antarctica see Neumayer
Gera Germany 63 M4
Geraardsbergen Belgium 62 D4
Geral, Serra mts Brazil 179 A4
Geral de Goiás, Serra hills Brazil 179 B1
Geraldine N.Z. 139 C7
Geral do Paraná, Serra hills Brazil 179 B1
Geraldton Australia 135 A7
Gerama i. Indon. 83 C1
Gerar watercourse Israel 107 B4
Gerber U.S.A. 158 B1
Gercüş Turkey 113 F3
Gerdine, Mount AK U.S.A. 148 I3
Gerede Turkey 112 D2
Gereshk Afgh. 111 G4
Gerik Malaysia 84 C1
Gerlach U.S.A. 158 D1
Gerlachovský Štít mt. Slovakia 57 R6
Germaine, Lac l. Canada 153 I3
German Bight g. Denmark/Germany 57 K3
Germania country Europe see Germany
Germanicea Turkey see Kahramanmaraş
Germansen Landing Canada 150 E4
German South-West Africa country Africa see Namibia
Germantown OH U.S.A. 164 C4
Germantown WI U.S.A. 164 A2

▶Germany country Europe 57 L5
2nd most populous country in Europe.

Germersheim Germany 63 I5
Gernsheim Germany 63 I5
Gero Japan 92 D3
Gerolstein Germany 62 G4
Gerolzhofen Germany 63 K5
Gerona Spain see Girona
Gerrit Denys is P.N.G. see Lihir Group
Gers r. France 66 E4
Gersfeld (Rhön) Germany 63 J4
Gersoppa India 106 B3
Gerstungen Germany 63 K4
Gerwisch Germany 63 L2
Géryville Alg. see El Bayadh
Gêrzê Xizang China 99 D6
Gerze Turkey 112 D2
Gescher Germany 62 H3
Gesoriacum France see Boulogne-sur-Mer
Gessie U.S.A. 164 B3
Getai Shaanxi China 95 G5
Gete r. Belgium 62 F4
Gettysburg PA U.S.A. 165 G4
Gettysburg SD U.S.A. 160 D2
Gettysburg National Military Park nat. park U.S.A. 165 G4
Getz Ice Shelf Antarctica 188 J2
Geumapang r. Indon. 84 B2
Geumpang Sumatera Indon. 84 B1
Geureudong, Gunung vol. Indon. 84 B1
Geurie Australia 138 D4
Gevaş Turkey 113 F3
Gevgelija Macedonia 69 J4
Gexianzhuang Hebei China see Qinghe
Gexto Spain see Algorta
Gey Iran see Nīkshahr
Geyikli Turkey 69 L5
Geylegphug Bhutan 105 G4
Geysdorp S. Africa 125 G4
Geyserville U.S.A. 158 B2
Geyve Turkey 69 N4
Gezidong Qinghai China 94 E4
Gezīr Iran 110 D5
Ghaap Plateau S. Africa 124 F4
Ghāb, Wādī al r. Syria 107 C2
Ghabāghib Syria 107 C3
Ghabeish Sudan 108 C7
Ghadaf, Wādī al watercourse Jordan 107 C4
Ghadamés Libya see Ghadāmis
Ghadāmis Libya 120 D1
Gha'em Shahr Iran 110 D2
Ghaghara r. India 105 F4
Ghaibi Dero Pak. 111 G5
Ghalend Iran 111 F4
Ghallaorol Uzbek. see G'allaorol
Ghana country Africa 120 C4
Ghanādah, Rās pt U.A.E. 110 D5
Ghantila India 104 B5
Ghanwā Saudi Arabia 108 G4
Ghanzi Botswana 123 C6
Ghanzi admin. dist. Botswana 124 F2
Ghap'an Armenia see Kapan
Ghār, Ras al pt Saudi Arabia 110 C5
Ghardaïa Alg. 67 G6
Gharghoda India 106 D1
Ghârib, Gebel mt. Egypt see Ghārib, Jabal
Ghārib, Jabal mt. Egypt 112 D5
Gharm Tajik. 111 H2
Gharq Ābād Iran 110 C3
Gharwa India see Garhwa
Gharyān Libya 121 E1
Ghāt Libya 120 E2
Ghatgan India 105 F5
Ghatol India 104 C5
Ghawdex i. Malta see Gozo
Ghazal, Bahr el watercourse Chad 121 E3
Ghazaouet Alg. 67 F6
Ghaziabad India 104 D3
Ghazi Ghat Pak. 111 H4
Ghazipur India 105 E4
Ghazna Afgh. see Ghaznī
Ghaznī Afgh. 111 H3
Ghaznī r. Afgh. 111 G3
Ghazoor Afgh. 111 G3
Ghazzah Gaza see Gaza
Ghebar Gumbad Iran 110 E3
Ghent Belgium 62 D3
Gheorghe Gheorghiu-Dej Romania see Onești
Gheorgheni Romania 69 K1
Gherla Romania 69 J1
Ghijduwon Uzbek. see G'ijduvon
Ghilzai reg. Afgh. 111 G4
Ghīnah, Wādī al watercourse Saudi Arabia 107 D4
Ghisonaccia Corsica France 66 I5
Ghorak Afgh. 111 G3
Ghost Lake Canada 150 H2
Ghotaru India 104 B4
Ghotki Pak. 111 H5
Ghudamis Libya see Ghadāmis
Ghugri r. India 105 F4
Ghurayfah hill Saudi Arabia 107 C4
Ghūrī Iran 110 D4
Ghurian Afgh. 111 F3
Ghurrab, Jabal hill Saudi Arabia 110 B5
Ghuzor Uzbek. see G'uzor
Ghyvelde France 62 C3
Giaginskaya Rus. Fed. 113 F1
Gialias r. Cyprus 107 A2
Gia Nghia Vietnam 87 D4
Gianisada i. Greece 69 L7
Giannitsa Greece 69 J4
Giant's Castle mt. S. Africa 125 I5
Giant's Causeway lava field U.K. 61 F2
Gianysada i. Kriti Greece see Gianisada
Gia Rai Vietnam 87 D5
Giarre Sicily Italy 68 F6
Gibb r. Australia 134 D3
Gibbonsville U.S.A. 156 E3
Gibeon Namibia 124 C3
Gibraltar terr. Europe 67 D5

▶Gibraltar Gibraltar 184 H3
United Kingdom Overseas Territory.

Gibraltar, Strait of Morocco/Spain 67 C6
Gibraltar Range National Park Australia 138 F2
Gibson Australia 135 C8
Gibson City U.S.A. 164 A3
Gibson Desert Australia 135 C6

Gichgeniyn Nuruu mts Mongolia 94 C2
Gidar Pak. 111 G4
Giddalur India 106 C3
Gîddi, Gebel el hill Egypt see Jiddī, Jabal al
Giddings U.S.A. 161 D6
Gīdolē Eth. 121 G4
Gien France 66 F3
Gießen Germany 63 I4
Gīfan Iran 110 E2
Gifford r. Canada 147 J2
Gifhorn Germany 63 K2
Gift Lake Canada 150 H4
Gifu Japan 92 C3
Gifu pref. Japan 92 C3
Giganta, Cerro mt. Mex. 166 C3
Gigha i. U.K. 60 D5
Gīgīga Eth. see Jijiga
G'ijduvon Uzbek. 111 G1
Gijón Spain see Gijón-Xixón
Gijón-Xixón Spain 67 D2
Gila r. U.S.A. 159 F5
Gila, Tanjung pt Maluku Indon. 83 D2
Gila Bend U.S.A. 159 G5
Gila Bend Mountains U.S.A. 159 G5
Gīlān-e Gharb Iran 110 B3
Gilbert r. Australia 136 C3
Gilbert AZ U.S.A. 159 H5
Gilbert WV U.S.A. 164 E5
Gilbert, Mount AK U.S.A. 149 J3
Gilbert Islands Kiribati 186 H5
Gilbert Islands country Pacific Ocean see Kiribati
Gilbert Peak U.S.A. 159 H1
Gilbert Ridge sea feature Pacific Ocean 186 H6
Gilbert River Australia 136 C3
Gilbués Brazil 177 I5
Gil Chashmeh Iran 110 E3
Gilé Moz. 123 D5
Giles Creek r. Australia 134 E4
Gilford Island Canada 150 E5
Gilgai Australia 138 E2
Gilgandra Australia 138 D3
Gil Gil Creek r. Australia 138 D2
Gilgit Pak. 104 C2
Gilgit r. Pak. 109 L2
Gilgunnia Australia 138 C4
Gili Iyang i. Indon. 85 F4
Gilimanuk Bali Indon. 85 F5
Gılındire Turkey see Aydıncık
Gillam Canada 151 M3
Gillen, Lake salt flat Australia 135 D6
Gilles, Lake salt flat Australia 137 B7
Gillett U.S.A. 165 G3
Gillette U.S.A. 156 G3
Gilliat Australia 136 C4
Gillingham England U.K. 59 E7
Gillingham England U.K. 59 H7
Gilling West U.K. 58 F4
Gillon Point pt AK U.S.A. 148 [inset]
Gilman U.S.A. 164 B3
Gilmer U.S.A. 161 E5
Gilmour Island Canada 152 F2
Gilroy U.S.A. 158 C3
Gīmbī Eth. 122 D3
Gimhae S. Korea see Kimhae
Gimli Canada 151 L5
Gimol'skoye, Ozero l. Rus. Fed. 52 G3
Ginebra, Laguna l. Bol. 176 E6
Gineifa Egypt see Junayfah
Gin Gin Australia 136 E5
Gingin Australia 135 A7
Gingoog Mindanao Phil. 82 D4
Gīnīr Eth. 122 E3
Ginosa Italy 68 G4
Ginzo de Limia Spain see Xinzo de Limia
Gioia del Colle Italy 68 G4
Gipouloux r. Canada 152 G3
Gippsland reg. Australia 138 B7
Girâ, Wâdi watercourse Egypt see Jirā', Wādī
Gīrān Rīg mt. Iran 110 E4
Girard U.S.A. 164 E2
Girardin, Lac l. Canada 153 I2
Girdab Iran 110 E3
Girdwood AK U.S.A. 149 J3
Giresun Turkey 112 E2
Girgenti Sicily Italy see Agrigento
Giridh India see Giridih
Giridih India 105 F4
Girilambone Australia 138 C3
Girna r. India 104 C5
Gir National Park India 104 B5
Girne Cyprus see Kyrenia
Girón Ecuador 176 C4
Giron Sweden see Kiruna
Girona Spain 67 H3
Gironde est. France 66 D4
Girot Pak. 111 I3
Girral Australia 138 C4
Girraween National Park Australia 138 E2
Girvan U.K. 60 E5
Girvas Rus. Fed. 52 G3
Gisasa r. AK U.S.A. 148 H2
Gisborne N.Z. 139 G4
Giscome Canada 150 F4
Gislaved Sweden 55 H8
Gisors France 62 B5
Gissar Tajik. see Hisor
Gissar Range mts Tajik./Uzbek. 111 G2
Gissarskiy Khrebet mts Tajik./Uzbek. see Gissar Range
Gitarama Rwanda 122 C4
Gitega Burundi 122 C4
Giuba r. Somalia see Jubba
Giulianova Italy 68 E3
Giurgiu Romania 69 K3
Giuvala, Pasul pass Romania 69 K2
Givar Iran 110 E2
Givet France 62 E4
Givors France 66 G4
Givry-en-Argonne France 62 E6
Giyani S. Africa 125 J2
Giza Egypt 112 C5
Gizhiga Rus. Fed. 77 R3
Gjakovë Kosovo 69 I3
Gjilan Kosovo 69 I3
Gjirokastër Albania 69 I4
Gjirokastra Albania see Gjirokastër
Gjoa Haven Canada 147 I3
Gjøra Norway 54 F5
Gjøvik Norway 55 G6
Gkinas, Akrotirio pt Greece 69 M6
Glace Bay Canada 153 K5
Glacier Bay AK U.S.A. 149 N4
Glacier Bay National Park and Preserve AK U.S.A. 149 M4
Glacier National Park Canada 150 G5
Glacier National Park U.S.A. 156 E2
Glacier Peak vol. U.S.A. 156 C2
Gladstad Norway 54 G4
Gladstone Australia 136 E4
Gladstone Canada 151 L5
Gladwin U.S.A. 164 C2
Gladys U.S.A. 164 F5
Gladys Lake Canada 150 C3
Glamis U.K. 60 F4
Glamis U.S.A. 159 F5
Glamoč Bos.-Herz. 68 G2
Glan r. Germany 63 H5
Glan Mindanao Phil. 82 D5
Glandorf Germany 63 I2
Glanton U.K. 58 F3
Glasgow U.K. 60 E5
Glasgow KY U.S.A. 164 C5
Glasgow MT U.S.A. 156 G2
Glasgow VA U.S.A. 164 F5
Glaslyn Canada 151 I4
Glass, Loch l. U.K. 60 E3
Glass Mountain U.S.A. 158 D3
Glass Peninsula AK U.S.A. 149 N4
Glastonbury U.K. 59 E7
Glauchau Germany 63 M4
Glazov Rus. Fed. 52 L4
Gleiwitz Poland see Gliwice
Glen U.S.A. 165 J1
Glen Allen U.S.A. 165 G5
Glen Alpine Dam S. Africa 125 I2
Glenamaddy Ireland 61 D4
Glenamoy r. Ireland 61 C3
Glen Arbor U.S.A. 164 C1
Glenbawn, Lake Australia 138 E4
Glenboro Canada 151 L5
Glen Canyon gorge U.S.A. 159 H3
Glen Canyon Dam U.S.A. 159 H3
Glencoe Canada 164 E2
Glencoe S. Africa 125 J5
Glencoe U.S.A. 160 E2
Glendale AZ U.S.A. 159 G5
Glendale CA U.S.A. 158 D4
Glendale UT U.S.A. 159 G3
Glendale Lake U.S.A. 165 F3
Glen Davis Australia 138 E4
Glenden Australia 136 E4
Glendive U.S.A. 156 G3
Glendon Canada 151 I4
Glendo Reservoir U.S.A. 156 G4
Glenfield U.S.A. 165 H2
Glengavlen Ireland 61 E3
Glengyle Australia 136 B5
Glen Innes Australia 138 E2
Glenluce U.K. 60 E6
Glen Lyon U.S.A. 165 G3
Glenlyon Peak Y.T. Canada 149 N3
Glen More valley U.K. 60 E3
Glenmorgan Australia 138 D1
Glenn U.S.A. 158 B2
Glennallen AK U.S.A. 149 K3
Glenn Highway AK U.S.A. 149 K3
Glennie U.S.A. 164 D1
Glenns Ferry U.S.A. 156 E4
Glenora B.C. Canada 149 O4
Glenore Australia 136 C3
Glenormiston Australia 136 B4
Glenreagh Australia 138 F3
Glen Rose U.S.A. 161 D5
Glenrothes U.K. 60 F4
Glens Falls U.S.A. 165 I2
Glen Shee valley U.K. 60 F4
Glenties Ireland 61 D3
Glenveagh National Park Ireland 61 E2
Glenville U.S.A. 164 E4
Glenwood AR U.S.A. 161 E5
Glenwood IA U.S.A. 160 E3
Glenwood MN U.S.A. 160 E2
Glenwood NM U.S.A. 159 I5
Glenwood Springs U.S.A. 159 J2
Glevum U.K. see Gloucester
Glinde Germany 63 K1
Glittertinden mt. Norway 55 F6
Gliwice Poland 57 Q5
Globe U.S.A. 159 H5
Glogau Poland see Głogów
Głogów Poland 57 P5
Glomfjord Norway 54 H3
Glomma r. Norway 54 G7
Glommersträsk Sweden 54 K4
Glorieuses, Îles is Indian Ocean 123 E5
Glorioso Islands Indian Ocean see Glorieuses, Îles
Glory of Russia Cape AK U.S.A. 148 D3
Gloster U.S.A. 161 F6
Gloucester Australia 138 E3
Gloucester U.K. 59 E7
Gloucester MA U.S.A. 165 J2
Gloucester VA U.S.A. 165 G5
Glover Reef Belize 167 I5
Gloversville U.S.A. 165 H2
Glovertown Canada 153 L4
Glöwen Germany 63 M2
Glubinnoye Rus. Fed. 90 D3
Glubokiy Krasnoyarskiy Kray Rus. Fed. 88 H2
Glubokiy Rostovskaya Oblast' Rus. Fed. 53 I6
Glubokoye Belarus see Hlybokaye
Glubokoye Kazakh. 102 F1
Gluggarnir hill Faroe Is 54 [inset]
Glukhov Ukr. see Hlukhiv
Glusburn U.K. 58 F5
Glynebwy U.K. see Ebbw Vale
Gmelinka Rus. Fed. 53 J6
Gmünd Austria 57 O6
Gmunden Austria 57 N7
Gnarp Sweden 55 J5
Gnarrenburg Germany 63 J1
Gnesen Poland see Gniezno
Gniezno Poland 57 P4
Gnjilane Kosovo see Gjilan
Gnowangerup Australia 135 B8
Gnows Nest Range hills Australia 135 B7
Goa India 106 B3
Goa state India 106 B3
Goageb Namibia 124 C4
Goalen Head hd Australia 138 E6
Goalpara India 105 G4
Goang Flores Indon. 83 A5
Goat Fell hill U.K. 60 D5
Goba Eth. 122 E3
Gobabis Namibia 124 D2
Gobannium U.K. see Abergavenny
Gobas Namibia 124 D4
Gobi Desert des. China/Mongolia 88 J4
Gobindpur India 105 F5
Gobles U.S.A. 164 C2
Gobō Japan 92 B5
Goch Germany 62 G3
Gochas Namibia 124 D3
Go Công Vietnam 87 D5
Godalming U.K. 59 G7
Godavari r. India 106 D2
Godavari, Cape India 106 D2
Godda India 105 F4
Godē Eth. 122 E3
Godere Eth. 122 E3
Goderich Canada 164 E2
Goderville France 59 H9
Godhavn Greenland see Qeqertarsuaq
Godhra India 104 C5
Godia Creek b. India 111 H6
Gōdo Japan 92 C3
Godo, Gunung mt. Indon. 83 C3
Gods r. Canada 151 M3
Gods Lake Canada 151 M4
God's Mercy, Bay of Canada 151 O2
Godthåb Greenland see Nuuk
Godwin-Austen, Mount China/Pak. see K2
Goedereede Neth. 62 D3
Goedgegun Swaziland see Nhlangano
Goegap Nature Reserve S. Africa 124 D5
Goélands, Lac aux l. Canada 153 J3
Goes Neth. 62 D3
Gogama Canada 152 E5
Gogebic Range hills U.S.A. 160 F2
Gogra r. India see Ghaghara
Goiana Brazil 177 L5
Goiandira Brazil 179 A2
Goianésia Brazil 179 A1
Goiânia Brazil 179 A2
Goiás Brazil 179 A1
Goiás state Brazil 179 A2
Goicangmai Xizang China 99 C6
Goikul Palau 82 [inset]
Goincang Qinghai China 94 E5
Goinsargoin China 96 C2
Goio-Erê Brazil 178 F2
Gojō Japan 92 B4
Gojra Pak. 111 I4
Goka Japan 93 F2
Gokak India 106 B2
Gokarn India 106 B3
Gök Çay r. Turkey 107 A1
Gökçeada i. Turkey 69 K4
Gökdepe Turkm. see Gëkdepe
Gökdere r. Turkey 107 A1
Goklenkuy, Solonchak salt l. Turkm. 110 E1
Gökova Körfezi b. Turkey 69 L6
Gokprosh Hills Pak. 111 F5
Göksun Turkey 112 E3
Goksu Parkı Turkey 107 A1
Gokteik Myanmar 86 B2
Gokwe Zimbabwe 123 C5
Gol Norway 55 F6
Golaghat India 105 H4
Golbāf Iran 110 E4
Gölbaşı Turkey 112 E3
Golconda U.S.A. 158 E1
Gölcük Turkey 69 M4
Gold U.S.A. 165 G3
Gołdap Poland 57 S3
Gold Beach U.S.A. 156 B4
Goldberg Germany 63 M1
Gold Coast country Africa see Ghana
Gold Coast Australia 138 F2
Gold Creek AK U.S.A. 149 J3
Golden U.S.A. 156 G5
Golden Bay N.Z. 139 D5
Goldendale U.S.A. 156 C3
Goldene Aue reg. Germany 63 K3
Golden Gate Highlands National Park S. Africa 125 I5
Golden Hinde mt. Canada 150 E5
Golden Lake Canada 165 G1
Golden Meadow LA U.S.A. 167 H2
Golden Prairie Canada 151 I5
Goldenstedt Germany 63 I2
Goldfield U.S.A. 158 E3
Goldsand Lake Canada 151 K3
Goldsboro U.S.A. 163 E5
Goldstone Lake U.S.A. 158 E4
Goldsworthy (abandoned) Australia 134 B5
Goldthwaite U.S.A. 161 D6
Goldvein U.S.A. 165 G4
Göle Turkey 113 F2
Golestān Afgh. 111 F3
Goleta U.S.A. 158 D4
Golets-Davydov, Gora mt. Rus. Fed. 89 J2
Golfito Costa Rica 166 [inset] J7
Golfo di Orosei Gennargentu e Asinara, Parco Nazionale del nat. park Sardinia Italy 68 C4
Gölgeli Dağları mts Turkey 69 M6
Goliad U.S.A. 161 D6
Golin Baixing Nei Mongol China 95 J2
Gölköy Turkey 112 E2
Gollel Swaziland see Lavumisa
Golm Germany 63 M2
Golmberg hill Germany 63 N2
Golmud Qinghai China 94 C4
Golmud He r. China 94 C4
Golovin AK U.S.A. 148 G2
Golovin Bay AK U.S.A. 148 G2
Golovnino Rus. Fed. 90 G4
Golpāyegān Iran 110 C3
Gölpazarı Turkey 69 N4
Golsovia AK U.S.A. 148 G3
Golspie U.K. 60 F3
Gol Vardeh Iran 111 F3
Golyama Syutkya mt. Bulg. 69 K4
Golyam Persenk mt. Bulg. 69 K4
Golyshi Rus. Fed. see Vetluzhskiy
Golzow Germany 63 M2
Goma Dem. Rep. Congo 122 C4
Gomang Co salt l. China 99 E7
Gomangxung Qinghai China 94 E5
Gomanodan-zan mt. Japan 92 B4
Gomati r. India 109 N4
Gombak, Bukit hill Sing. 87 [inset]
Gombe Nigeria 120 E3
Gombe r. Tanz. 123 D4
Gombi Nigeria 120 E3
Gombroon Iran see Bandar-e 'Abbās
Gomel' Belarus see Homyel'
Gómez Palacio Mex. 166 E3
Gomīshān Iran 110 D2
Gommern Germany 63 L2
Gomo Xizang China 99 D6
Gomo Co salt l. China 99 D6
Gomumu i. Maluku Indon. 83 C3
Gonābād Iran 110 E2
Gonaïves Haiti 169 J5
Gonarezhou National Park Zimbabwe 123 D6
Gonbad-e Kavus Iran 110 D2
Gonda India 105 E4
Gondal India 104 B5
Gondar Eth. see Gonder
Gonder Eth. 122 D2
Gondia India 104 E5
Gondiya India see Gondia
Gönen Turkey 69 L4
Gonfreville-l'Orcher France 59 H9
Gong'an China 97 G2
Gongbalou Xizang China 99 E7
Gongbo'gyamda Xizang China 99 F7
Gongchakou Gansu China 94 D4
Gongchang Gansu China see Longxi
Gongcheng China 97 F3
Gonggar Xizang China 99 E7
Gongga Shan mt. China 96 D2
Gonghe Qinghai China 94 E4
Gonghe Yunnan China see Mouding
Gonghui Hebei China 95 H3
Gongjiang China see Yudu
Gongliu Xinjiang China 98 C4
Gongogi r. Brazil 179 D1
Gongolgon Australia 138 C3
Gongpoquan Gansu China 94 D3
Gongquan China 96 E2
Gongwang Shan mts China 96 D3
Gongxian Henan China see Gongyi
Gongxian China see Gongquan
Gongyi Henan China 95 H5
Gonjo China see Kasha
Gonzáles Mex. 167 F4
Gonzales CA U.S.A. 158 C3
Gonzales TX U.S.A. 161 D6
Gonzha Rus. Fed. 90 B1
Goochland U.S.A. 165 G5
Goodenough, Cape Antarctica 188 G2
Goodenough, Mount hill N.W.T. Canada 149 N2
Goodenough Island P.N.G. 132 F2
Gooderham Canada 165 F1
Good Hope, Cape of S. Africa 124 D8
Goodhope Bay AK U.S.A. 148 G2
Good Hope Mountain Canada 156 B2
Gooding U.S.A. 156 E4
Goodland IN U.S.A. 164 B3
Goodland KS U.S.A. 160 C4
Goodlettsville U.S.A. 164 B5
Goodnews Bay AK U.S.A. 148 G4
Goodnews Bay b. AK U.S.A. 148 G4
Goodooga Australia 138 C2
Goodpaster r. AK U.S.A. 149 K2
Goodspeed Nunataks Antarctica 188 E2
Goole U.K. 58 G5
Goolgowi Australia 138 B5
Goolma Australia 138 D4
Gooloogong Australia 138 D4
Goomalling Australia 135 B7
Goombalie Australia 138 B2
Goondiwindi Australia 138 E2
Goongarrie, Lake salt flat Australia 135 C7
Goongarrie National Park Australia 135 C7
Goonyella Australia 136 D4
Goorly, Lake salt flat Australia 135 B7
Goose Bay Canada see Happy Valley-Goose Bay
Goose Creek U.S.A. 163 D5
Goose Lake U.S.A. 156 C4
Gooty India 106 C3
Gopalganj Bangl. 105 G5
Gopalganj India 105 F4
Gopeshwar India 104 D3
Göppingen Germany 63 J6
Gorakhpur India 105 E4
Goražde Bos.-Herz. 68 H3
Gorbernador U.S.A. 159 J3
Gorczański Park Narodowy nat. park Poland 57 R6
Gorda, Punta pt Nicaragua 166 [inset] J6
Gorda, Punta pt U.S.A. 158 A1
Gördes Turkey 69 M5
Gordil Cent. Afr. Rep. 122 C3
Gordon r. Canada 151 O1
Gordon U.K. 60 G5
Gordon AK U.S.A. 149 L1
Gordon U.S.A. 160 C3
Gordon, Lake Australia 137 [inset]
Gordon Downs (abandoned) Australia 134 E4
Gordon Lake Canada 151 I3
Gordon Lake U.S.A. 165 F4
Gordonsville U.S.A. 165 F4
Goré Chad 121 E4
Gorē Eth. 122 D3
Gore N.Z. 139 B8
Gore U.S.A. 165 F4
Gorebridge U.K. 60 F5
Gore Point pt AK U.S.A. 149 J4
Gorey Ireland 61 F5
Gorg Iran 111 E4
Gorgān Iran 110 D2
Gorgān, Khalīj-e Iran 110 D2
Gorge Range hills Australia 134 B5
Gorgona, Isla i. Col. 176 C3
Gorham U.S.A. 165 J1
Gori Georgia 108 F1
Gorinchem Neth. 62 E3
Goris Armenia 113 G3
Gorizia Italy 68 E2
Gorki Belarus see Horki
Gor'kiy Rus. Fed. see Nizhniy Novgorod
Gor'kovskoye Vodokhranilishche resr Rus. Fed. 52 I4
Gorlice Poland 53 D6
Görlitz Germany 57 O5
Gorlovka Ukr. see Horlivka
Gorna Dzhumaya Bulg. see Blagoevgrad
Gorna Oryakhovitsa Bulg. 69 K3
Gornji Milanovac Serbia 69 I2
Gornji Vakuf Bos.-Herz. 68 G3
Gorno-Altaysk Rus. Fed. 102 G1
Gorno-Altayskaya Avtonomnaya Oblast' aut. rep. Rus. Fed. see Altay, Respublika
Gornotrakiyska Nizina lowland Bulg. 69 K3
Gornozavodsk Permskaya Oblast' Rus. Fed. 51 R4
Gornozavodsk Sakhalinskaya Oblast' Rus. Fed. 90 F3
Gornyak Altayskiy Kray Rus. Fed. 98 C2
Gornyy Rus. Fed. 53 K6
Gornyy Altay aut. rep. Rus. Fed. see Altay, Respublika
Gornyye Klyuchi Rus. Fed. 90 D3
Goro i. Fiji see Koro
Gorodenka Ukr. see Horodenka
Gorodets Rus. Fed. 52 I4
Gorodishche Penzenskaya Oblast' Rus. Fed. 53 J5
Gorodishche Volgogradskaya Oblast' Rus. Fed. 53 J6
Gorodok Belarus see Haradok
Gorodok Rus. Fed. see Zakamensk
Gorodok Khmel'nyts'ka Oblast' Ukr. see Horodok
Gorodok L'vivs'ka Oblast' Ukr. see Horodok
Gorodovikovsk Rus. Fed. 53 I7
Goroka P.N.G. 81 L8
Gorokhovets Rus. Fed. 52 I4
Gorom Gorom Burkina 120 C3
Gorong, Kepulauan is Indon. 81 I7
Gorongosa mt. Moz. 123 D5
Gorongosa, Parque Nacional de nat. park Moz. 123 D5
Gorontalo Sulawesi Indon. 83 B2
Gorontalo prov. Indon. 83 B2
Gorshechnoye Rus. Fed. 53 H6
Gort Ireland 61 D4
Gortahork Ireland see Gort an Choirce
Gort an Choirce Ireland 61 D2
Gorutuba r. Brazil 179 C1
Gorveh Iran 110 E4
Goryachiy Klyuch Rus. Fed. 113 E1
Görzke Germany 63 M2
Gorzów Wielkopolski Poland 57 O4
Gosainthan mt. Xizang China see Xixabangma Feng
Gose Japan 92 B4
Gosforth U.K. 58 F3
Goshen CA U.S.A. 158 D3
Goshen IN U.S.A. 164 C3
Goshen NH U.S.A. 165 I2
Goshen NY U.S.A. 165 H3
Goshen VA U.S.A. 164 F5
Goshiki Japan 92 A4
Goshoba Turkm. see Goşoba
Goslar Germany 63 K3
Goşoba Turkm. 113 I2
Gospić Croatia 68 F2
Gosport U.K. 59 F8
Gossi Mali 120 C3
Gostivar Macedonia 69 I4
Gosu China 96 C1
Göteborg Sweden see Gothenburg
Gotemba Shizuoka Japan see Gotenba
Gotenba Shizuoka Japan 93 E3
Götene Sweden 55 H7
Gotenhafen Poland see Gdynia
Gotha Germany 63 K4
Gothenburg Sweden 55 G8
Gothenburg U.S.A. 160 C3
Gotland i. Sweden 55 K8
Gotō-rettō is Japan 91 C6
Gotse Delchev Bulg. 69 J4
Gotska Sandön i. Sweden 55 K7
Gōtsu Japan 91 D6
Göttingen Germany 63 J3
Gott Peak Canada 150 F5
Gottwaldow Czech Rep. see Zlín
Gouda Neth. 62 E2
Goudiri Senegal 120 B3
Goudoumaria Niger 120 E3
Goûgaram Niger 120 D3

▶Gough Island S. Atlantic Ocean 184 H8
Dependency of St Helena.

Gouin, Réservoir resr Canada 152 G4
Goulburn Australia 138 D5
Goulburn r. N.S.W. Australia 138 E4
Goulburn r. Vic. Australia 138 B6
Goulburn Islands Australia 134 F2
Goulburn River National Park Australia 138 E4
Gould Coast Antarctica 188 J1
Goulou atoll Micronesia see Ngulu
Goundam Mali 120 C3
Goundi Chad 121 E4
Goupil, Lac l. Canada 153 H3
Gouraya Alg. 67 G5
Gourcy Burkina 120 C3
Gourdon France 66 E4
Gouré Niger 120 E3
Gouripur Bangl. 105 G4
Gourits r. S. Africa 124 E8
Gourma-Rharous Mali 120 C3
Gournay-en-Bray France 62 B5
Goussainville France 62 C5
Gouverneur U.S.A. 165 H1
Governador Valadares Brazil 179 C2
Governor Generoso Mindanao Phil. 82 D5
Governor's Harbour Bahamas 163 E7
Govĭ-Altay prov. Mongolia 94 C2
Govĭ Altayn Nuruu mts Mongolia 94 D2
Govind Ballash Pant Sagar resr India 105 E4
Govind Sagar resr India 99 B7
Govĭ-Ugtaal Mongolia 95 F2
Gowanda U.S.A. 165 F2
Gowan Range hills Australia 136 D5
Gowaqungo Xizang China 99 D7
Gowārān Afgh. 111 G4
Gowd-e Mokh l. Iran 110 D4
Gowd-e Zereh plain Afgh. 111 F4
Gowmal Kalay Afgh. 111 H3
Gowna, Lough l. Ireland 61 E4
Goya Arg. 178 E3
Göyçay Azer. 113 G2
Goyder watercourse Australia 135 F6
Goýmatdag hills Turkm. 110 D1
Goymatdag hills Turkm. see Goýmatdag
Göynük Turkey 69 N4
Goyoum Cameroon 120 E4
Gozareh Afgh. 111 F3
Goz-Beïda Chad 121 F3
Gozen-yama Japan 93 G2
Gozha Co salt l. China 99 C6
Gözkaya Turkey 107 C1
Gozo i. Malta 68 F6
Graaff-Reinet S. Africa 124 G7
Grabfeld plain Germany 63 K4
Grabo Côte d'Ivoire 120 C4
Grabouw S. Africa 124 D8
Grabow Germany 63 L1
Gračac Croatia 68 F2
Gracefield Canada 152 F5
Gracey U.S.A. 164 B5
Grachi Kazakh. 98 B2
Gracias Hond. 166 [inset] H6
Gradaús, Serra dos hills Brazil 177 H5
Gradiška Bos.-Herz. see Bosanska Gradiška
Grady U.S.A. 161 C5
Gräfenhainichen Germany 63 M3
Grafenwöhr Germany 63 L5
Grafton Australia 138 F2
Grafton ND U.S.A. 160 D1
Grafton WI U.S.A. 164 B2
Grafton WV U.S.A. 164 E4
Grafton, Cape Australia 136 D3
Grafton, Mount U.S.A. 159 F2
Grafton Passage Australia 136 D3
Graham NC U.S.A. 162 E4
Graham TX U.S.A. 161 D5
Graham, Mount U.S.A. 159 I5
Graham Bell Island Rus. Fed. see Greem-Bell, Ostrov
Graham Island B.C. Canada 149 N5
Graham Island Nunavut Canada 147 I2
Graham Land reg. Antarctica 188 L2
Grahamstown S. Africa 125 H7
Grahovo Bos.-Herz. see Bosansko Grahovo
Graigue Ireland 61 F5
Grajagan Jawa Indon. 85 F5
Grajaú Brazil 177 I5
Grajaú r. Brazil 177 J4
Grammont Belgium see Geraardsbergen
Grammos mt. Greece 69 I4
Grampian Mountains U.K. 60 E4
Grampians National Park Australia 137 C8
Granada Nicaragua 166 [inset] I7
Granada Spain 67 E5
Granada U.S.A. 160 C4
Granard Ireland 61 E4
Granbury U.S.A. 161 D5
Granby Canada 153 G5
Gran Canaria i. Canary Is 120 B2
Gran Chaco reg. Arg./Para. 178 D3
Grand r. MO U.S.A. 164 B2
Grand r. SD U.S.A. 160 C2
Grand Atlas mts Morocco see Haut Atlas
Grand Bahama i. Bahamas 163 E7
Grand Ballon mt. France 57 K7
Grand Bank Canada 153 L5

Grand Banks of Newfoundland *sea feature* N. Atlantic Ocean **184** E3
Grand-Bassam Côte d'Ivoire **120** C4
Grand Bay-Westfield Canada **153** I5
Grand Bend Canada **164** E2
Grand Blanc U.S.A. **164** D2
Grand Canal Ireland **61** E4
Grand Canary *i.* Canary Is *see* **Gran Canaria**
Grand Canyon U.S.A. **159** G3
Grand Canyon *gorge* U.S.A. **159** G3
Grand Canyon National Park U.S.A. **159** G3
Grand Canyon - Parashant National Monument *nat. park* U.S.A. **159** G3
Grand Cayman *i.* Cayman Is **169** H5
Grand Drumont *mt.* France **57** K7
Grande *r. Bahia* Brazil **179** B1
Grande *r. São Paulo* Brazil **179** A3
Grande *r.* Nicaragua **166** [inset] J6
Grande, Bahía *b.* Arg. **178** C8
Grande, Cerro *mt.* Mex. **167** F5
Grande, Ilha *i.* Brazil **179** B3
Grande Cache Canada **150** G4
Grande Comore *i.* Comoros *see* **Njazidja**
Grande Prairie Canada **150** G4
Grand Erg de Bilma *des.* Niger **120** E3
Grand Erg Occidental *des.* Alg. **64** D5
Grand Erg Oriental *des.* Alg. **64** F6
Grande-Rivière Canada **153** I4
Grandes, Salinas *salt marsh* Arg. **178** C4
Gran Desierto del Pinacate, Parque Natural del *nature res.* Mex. **166** B2
Grande-Vallée Canada **153** I4
Grand Falls *N.B.* Canada **153** I5
Grand Falls-Windsor *Nfld. and Lab.* Canada **153** L4
Grand Forks Canada **150** G5
Grand Forks U.S.A. **160** D2
Grand Gorge U.S.A. **165** H2
Grand Haven U.S.A. **164** B2
Grandin, Lac *l.* Canada **150** G1
Grandioznyy, Pik *mt.* Rus. Fed. **88** H2
Grand Island U.S.A. **160** D3
Grand Isle U.S.A. **161** F6
Grand Junction U.S.A. **159** I2
Grand Lac Germain *l.* Canada **153** I4
Grand-Lahou Côte d'Ivoire **120** C4
Grand Lake *N.B.* Canada **153** I5
Grand Lake *Nfld. and Lab.* Canada **153** J3
Grand Lake *Nfld. and Lab.* Canada **153** K4
Grand Lake *LA* U.S.A. **161** E6
Grand Lake *MI* U.S.A. **164** D1
Grand Lake St Marys U.S.A. **164** C3
Grand Ledge U.S.A. **164** C2
Grand Manan Island Canada **153** I5
Grand Marais *MI* U.S.A. **162** C2
Grand Marais *MN* U.S.A. **160** F2
Grand-Mère Canada **153** G5
Grand Mesa U.S.A. **159** J2
Grândola Port. **67** B4
Grand Passage New Caledonia **133** G3
Grand Rapids Canada **151** L4
Grand Rapids *MI* U.S.A. **164** C2
Grand Rapids *MN* U.S.A. **160** E2
Grand-Sault Canada *see* **Grand Falls**
Grand Staircase-Escalante National Monument *nat. park* U.S.A. **159** H3
Grand St-Bernard, Col du *pass* Italy/Switz. *see* **Great St Bernard Pass**
Grand Teton *mt.* U.S.A. **156** F4
Grand Teton National Park U.S.A. **156** F4
Grand Traverse Bay U.S.A. **164** C1

▶**Grand Turk** Turks and Caicos Is **169** J4
Capital of the Turks and Caicos Islands.

Grandville U.S.A. **164** C2
Grandvilliers France **62** B5
Grand Wash Cliffs *mts* U.S.A. **159** F4
Grange Ireland **61** E6
Grängesberg Sweden **55** I6
Grangeville U.S.A. **156** D3
Granisle Canada **150** E4
Granite Falls U.S.A. **160** E2
Granite Mountain *hill AK* U.S.A. **148** G2
Granite Mountain *hill AK* U.S.A. **148** H3
Granite Mountain U.S.A. **158** E1
Granite Mountains *CA* U.S.A. **159** F4
Granite Mountains *CA* U.S.A. **159** F5
Granite Peak *MT* U.S.A. **156** F3
Granite Peak *UT* U.S.A. **159** G1
Granite Range *mts AK* U.S.A. **149** K4
Granite Range *mts NV* U.S.A. **158** D1
Granitola, Capo *c. Sicily* Italy **68** E6
Granja Brazil **177** J4
Gran Laguna Salada *l.* Arg. **178** C6
Gränna Sweden **55** I7
Gran Paradiso *mt.* Italy **68** B2
Gran Paradiso, Parco Nazionale del *nat. park* Italy **68** B2
Gran Pilastro *mt.* Austria/Italy **57** M7
Gran San Bernardo, Colle del *pass* Italy/Switz. *see* **Great St Bernard Pass**
Gran Sasso e Monti della Laga, Parco Nazionale del *nat. park* Italy **68** E3
Granschütz Germany **63** M3
Gransee Germany **63** N1
Grant U.S.A. **160** C3
Grant, Mount U.S.A. **158** E2
Grant Creek *AK* U.S.A. **148** I2
Grantham U.K. **59** G6
Grant Island Antarctica **188** J2
Grant Lake Canada **150** G1
Grantown-on-Spey U.K. **60** F3
Grant Range *mts* U.S.A. **159** F2
Grants U.S.A. **159** J4
Grants Pass U.S.A. **156** C4
Grantsville *UT* U.S.A. **159** G1
Grantsville *WV* U.S.A. **164** E4
Granville France **66** D2
Granville *AZ* U.S.A. **159** I5
Granville *NY* U.S.A. **165** I2
Granville *TN* U.S.A. **164** C5
Granville (abandoned) *Y.T.* Canada **149** M3
Granville Lake Canada **151** K3
Grão Mogol Brazil **179** C2
Grapevine Mountains U.S.A. **158** E3
Gras, Lac de *l.* Canada **151** I1
Graskop S. Africa **125** J3
Grasplatz Namibia **124** B4
Grass *r.* Canada **151** L3
Grass *r.* U.S.A. **165** H1
Grasse France **66** H5
Grassflat U.S.A. **165** F3
Grassington U.K. **58** F4
Grasslands National Park Canada **151** J5
Grassrange U.S.A. **156** F3
Grass Valley U.S.A. **158** C2
Grassy Butte U.S.A. **160** C2
Grästorp Sweden **55** H7
Gratz U.S.A. **164** C4
Graudenz Poland *see* **Grudziądz**
Graus Spain **67** G2
Gravatai Brazil **179** A5
Grave, Pointe de *pt* France **66** D4
Gravelbourg Canada **151** J5
Gravel Hill Lake Canada **151** K2
Gravelines France **62** C4
Gravelotte S. Africa **125** J2
Gravenhurst Canada **164** F1
Grave Peak U.S.A. **156** E3
Gravesend Australia **138** E2
Gravesend U.K. **59** H7
Gravina in Puglia Italy **68** G4
Grawn U.S.A. **164** C1
Gray France **66** G3
Gray *GA* U.S.A. **163** D5
Gray *KY* U.S.A. **164** C5
Gray *ME* U.S.A. **165** J2
Grayback Mountain U.S.A. **156** C4
Gray Lake Canada **151** I2
Grayling *r.* Canada **150** E3
Grayling *AK* U.S.A. **148** G3
Grayling U.S.A. **164** C1
Grayling Fork *r.* Canada/U.S.A. **149** L2
Grays U.K. **59** H7
Grays Harbor *inlet* U.S.A. **156** B3
Grays Lake U.S.A. **156** F4
Grayson U.S.A. **164** D4
Graz Austria **57** O7
Greasy Lake Canada **150** F2
Great Abaco *i.* Bahamas **163** E7
Great Australian Bight *g.* Australia **135** E8
Great Baddow U.K. **59** H7
Great Bahama Bank *sea feature* Bahamas **163** E7
Great Barrier Island N.Z. **139** E3
Great Barrier Reef Australia **136** D1
Great Barrier Reef Marine Park (Cairns Section) Australia **136** D3
Great Barrier Reef Marine Park (Capricorn Section) Australia **136** E4
Great Barrier Reef Marine Park (Central Section) Australia **136** E3
Great Barrier Reef Marine Park (Far North Section) Australia **136** D2
Great Barrington U.S.A. **165** I2
Great Basalt Wall National Park Australia **136** D3
Great Basin U.S.A. **158** E2
Great Basin National Park U.S.A. **159** F2
Great Bear *r. N.W.T.* Canada **149** P2

▶**Great Bear Lake** Canada **150** G1
4th largest lake in North America, and 7th in the world.

Great Belt *sea chan.* Denmark **55** G9
Great Bend U.S.A. **160** D4
Great Bitter Lake Egypt **107** A4
Great Blasket Island Ireland **61** B5

▶**Great Britain** *i.* U.K. **56** G4
Largest island in Europe, and 8th in the world.

Great Clifton U.K. **58** D4
Great Coco Island Cocos Is **80** A4
Great Cumbrae *i.* U.K. **60** E5
Great Dismal Swamp National Wildlife Refuge *nature res.* U.S.A. **165** G5
Great Dividing Range *mts* Australia **138** B6
Great Eastern Erg *des.* Alg. *see* **Grand Erg Oriental**
Greater Antarctica *reg.* Antarctica *see* **East Antarctica**
Greater Antilles *is* Caribbean Sea **169** H4
Greater Khingan Mountains China *see* **Da Hinggan Ling**
Greater St Lucia Wetland Park *nature res.* S. Africa **125** K4
Greater Sunda Islands Indon. **80** B7
Greater Tunb *i.* The Gulf **110** D5
Great Exuma *i.* Bahamas **163** F8
Great Falls U.S.A. **156** F3
Great Fish *r.* S. Africa **125** H7
Great Fish Point S. Africa **125** H7
Great Fish River Reserve Complex *nature res.* S. Africa **125** H7
Great Gandak *r.* India **105** F4
Great Ganges *atoll* Cook Is *see* **Manihiki**
Great Guana Cay *i.* Bahamas **163** E7
Great Inagua *i.* Bahamas **169** J4
Great Karoo *plat.* S. Africa **124** F7
Great Kei *r.* S. Africa **125** I7
Great Lake Australia **137** [inset]
Great Limpopo Transfrontier Park **125** J2
Great Malvern U.K. **59** E6
Great Meteor Tablemount *sea feature* N. Atlantic Ocean **184** G4
Great Namaqualand *reg.* Namibia **124** C4
Great Nicobar *i.* India **87** A6
Great Ormes Head *hd* U.K. **58** D5
Great Ouse *r.* U.K. **59** H6
Great Oyster Bay Australia **137** [inset]
Great Palm Islands Australia **136** D3
Great Plain of the Koukdjuak Canada **147** K3
Great Plains U.S.A. **160** C3
Great Point U.S.A. **165** J3
Great Rift Valley Africa **122** D4
Great Ruaha *r.* Tanz. **123** D4
Great Sacandaga Lake U.S.A. **165** H2
Great St Bernard Pass Italy/Switz. **68** B2
Great Salt Lake U.S.A. **159** G1
Great Salt Lake Desert U.S.A. **159** G1
Great Sand Dunes National Park U.S.A. **157** G5
Great Sand Hills Canada **151** I5
Great Sand Sea *des.* Egypt/Libya **112** B5
Great Sandy Desert Australia **134** C5
Great Sandy Island Australia *see* **Fraser Island**
Great Sea Reef Fiji **133** H3
Great Sitkin Island *AK* U.S.A. **149** [inset]

▶**Great Slave Lake** Canada **150** H2
Deepest and 5th largest lake in North America and 10th largest in the world.

Great Smoky Mountains U.S.A. **163** C5
Great Smoky Mountains National Park U.S.A. **162** D5
Great Snow Mountain Canada **150** E3
Greatstone-on-Sea U.K. **59** H8
Great Stour *r.* U.K. **59** I7
Great Torrington U.K. **59** C8
Great Victoria Desert Australia **135** E7
Great Wall *research station* Antarctica **188** A2
Great Wall *tourist site* China **95** I3
Great Waltham U.K. **59** H7
Great Western Erg *des.* Alg. *see* **Grand Erg Occidental**
Great West Torres Islands Myanmar **87** B5
Great Whernside *hill* U.K. **58** F4
Great Yarmouth U.K. **59** I6
Grebenkovskiy Ukr. *see* **Hrebinka**
Grebyonka Ukr. *see* **Hrebinka**
Greco, Cape Cyprus *see* **Greko, Cape**
Gredos, Sierra de *mts* Spain **67** D3
Greece *country* Europe **69** I5
Greece U.S.A. **165** G2
Greeley U.S.A. **156** G4
Greely Center U.S.A. **160** D3
Greem-Bell, Ostrov *i.* Rus. Fed. **76** H1
Green *r. KY* U.S.A. **164** B5
Green *r. WY* U.S.A. **159** I2
Green Bay U.S.A. **164** A1
Green Bay *b.* U.S.A. **164** B1
Greenbrier U.S.A. **164** B5
Greenbrier *r.* U.S.A. **164** E5
Green Cape Australia **138** E6
Greencastle Bahamas **163** E7
Greencastle U.K. **61** F3
Greencastle U.S.A. **164** B4
Green Cove Springs U.S.A. **163** D6
Greene *ME* U.S.A. **165** J1
Greene *NY* U.S.A. **165** H2
Greeneville U.S.A. **162** D4
Greenfield *CA* U.S.A. **158** C3
Greenfield *IN* U.S.A. **164** C4
Greenfield *MA* U.S.A. **165** I2
Greenfield *OH* U.S.A. **164** D4
Green Head *hd* Australia **135** A7
Greenhill Island Australia **134** F2
Green Island Taiwan *see* **Lü Tao**
Green Island Bay *Palawan* Phil. **82** B4
Green Lake Canada **151** J4

▶**Greenland** *terr.* N. America **147** N3
Self-governing Danish territory. Largest island in North America and in the world, and 3rd largest political entity in North America.

Greenland Basin *sea feature* Arctic Ocean **189** I2
Greenland Fracture Zone *sea feature* Arctic Ocean **189** I1
Greenland Sea Greenland/Svalbard **76** A2
Greenlaw U.K. **60** G5
Green Mountains U.S.A. **165** I1
Greenock U.K. **60** E5
Greenore Ireland **61** F3
Greenough, Mount *AK* U.S.A. **149** L1
Greenport U.S.A. **165** I3
Green River P.N.G. **81** K7
Green River *UT* U.S.A. **159** H2
Green River *WY* U.S.A. **156** F4
Green River Lake U.S.A. **164** C5
Greensboro U.S.A. **163** D5
Greensburg *IN* U.S.A. **164** C4
Greensburg *KS* U.S.A. **160** D4
Greensburg *KY* U.S.A. **164** C5
Greensburg *LA* U.S.A. **161** F6
Greensburg *PA* U.S.A. **164** F3
Greens Peak U.S.A. **159** I4
Greenstone Point U.K. **60** D3
Green Swamp U.S.A. **163** E5
Greentown U.S.A. **164** C3
Greenup *IL* U.S.A. **160** F4
Greenup *KY* U.S.A. **164** D4
Green Valley Canada **165** H1
Green Valley *AZ* U.S.A. **166** C2
Greenville *B.C.* Canada *see* **Laxgalts'ap**
Greenville Liberia **120** C4
Greenville *AL* U.S.A. **163** C6
Greenville *IL* U.S.A. **160** F4
Greenville *KY* U.S.A. **164** B5
Greenville *ME* U.S.A. **162** G2
Greenville *MI* U.S.A. **164** C2
Greenville *MS* U.S.A. **161** F5
Greenville *NC* U.S.A. **162** E5
Greenville *NH* U.S.A. **165** J2
Greenville *OH* U.S.A. **164** C3
Greenville *PA* U.S.A. **164** E3
Greenville *SC* U.S.A. **163** D5
Greenville *TX* U.S.A. **161** D5
Greenwich *atoll* Micronesia *see* **Kapingamarangi**
Greenwich *CT* U.S.A. **165** I3
Greenwich *OH* U.S.A. **164** D3
Greenwood *AR* U.S.A. **161** E5
Greenwood *IN* U.S.A. **164** B4
Greenwood *MS* U.S.A. **161** F5
Greenwood *SC* U.S.A. **163** D5
Gregory *r.* Australia **136** B3
Gregory, Lake *salt flat S.A.* Australia **137** B6
Gregory, Lake *salt flat W.A.* Australia **134** D5
Gregory, Lake *salt flat W.A.* Australia **135** B6
Gregory Downs Australia **136** B3
Gregory National Park Australia **134** E4
Gregory Range *hills Qld* Australia **136** C3
Gregory Range *hills W.A.* Australia **134** C5
Greifswald Germany **57** N3
Greiz Germany **63** M4
Greko, Cape Cyprus **107** B2
Gremikha Rus. Fed. **189** G2
Gremyachinsk Rus. Fed. **51** R4
Grenå Denmark **55** G8
Grenaa Denmark *see* **Grenå**
Grenada U.S.A. **161** F5
Grenada *country* West Indies **169** L6
Grenade France **66** E5
Grenen *spit* Denmark **55** G8
Grenfell Australia **138** D4
Grenfell Canada **151** K5
Grenoble France **66** G4
Grense-Jakobselv Norway **54** Q2
Grenville, Cape Australia **136** C1
Grenville Island Fiji *see* **Rotuma**
Greshak Pak. **111** G5
Gresham U.S.A. **156** C3
Gresik *Jawa* Indon. **85** F4
Gressåmoen Nasjonalpark *nat. park* Norway **54** H4
Greta *r.* U.K. **58** E4
Gretna U.K. **60** F6
Gretna *LA* U.S.A. **161** F6
Gretna *VA* U.S.A. **164** F5
Greußen Germany **63** K3
Grevelingen *sea chan.* Neth. **62** D3
Greven Germany **63** H2
Grevena Greece **69** I4
Grevenbicht Neth. **62** F3
Grevenbroich Germany **62** G3
Grevenmacher Lux. **62** G5
Grevesmühlen Germany **57** M4
Grey, Cape Australia **136** B2
Greybull U.S.A. **156** F3
Greybull *r.* U.S.A. **156** F3
Grey Hunter Peak *Y.T.* Canada **149** N3
Grey Islands Canada **153** L4
Greylock, Mount U.S.A. **165** I2
Greymouth N.Z. **139** C6
Grey Range *hills* Australia **138** A2
Grey's Plains Australia **135** A6
Greytown S. Africa **125** J5
Grez-Doiceau Belgium **62** E4
Gribanovskiy Rus. Fed. **53** I6
Gridley U.S.A. **158** C2
Griffin U.S.A. **163** C5
Griffin Point *pt AK* U.S.A. **149** L1
Griffith Australia **138** C5
Grigan *i.* N. Mariana Is *see* **Agrihan**
Grik Malaysia *see* **Gerik**
Grim, Cape Australia **137** [inset]
Grimari Cent. Afr. Rep. **122** C3
Grimma Germany **63** M3
Grimmen Germany **57** N3
Grimnitzsee *l.* Germany **63** N2
Grimsby U.K. **58** G5
Grímsey *i.* Iceland **54** [inset]
Grimshaw Canada **150** G3
Grímsstaðir Iceland **54** [inset]
Grimstad Norway **55** F7
Grindavík Iceland **54** [inset]
Grindsted Denmark **55** F9
Grind Stone City U.S.A. **164** D1
Grindul Chituc *spit* Romania **69** M2
Grinnell Peninsula Canada **147** I2
Griqualand East *reg.* S. Africa **125** I6
Griqualand West *reg.* S. Africa **124** F5
Griquatown S. Africa **124** F5
Grise Fiord Canada **147** J2
Grishino Ukr. *see* **Krasnoarmiys'k**
Grisik *Sumatera* Indon. **84** C3
Gris Nez, Cap *c.* France **62** B4
Gritley U.K. **60** G2
Grizzly Bear Mountain *hill* Canada **150** F1
Grmeč *mts* Bos.-Herz. **68** G2
Grobbendonk Belgium **62** E3
Groblersdal S. Africa **125** I3
Groblershoop S. Africa **124** F5
Grodno Belarus *see* **Hrodna**
Groen *watercourse* S. Africa **124** F6
Groen *watercourse* S. Africa **124** C6
Groix, Île de *i.* France **66** C3
Grombalia Tunisia **68** D6
Gronau (Westfalen) Germany **62** H2
Grong Norway **54** H4
Groningen Neth. **62** G1
Groninger Wad *tidal flat* Neth. **62** G1
Grønland *terr.* N. America *see* **Greenland**
Groom Lake U.S.A. **159** F3
Groot-Aar Pan *salt pan* S. Africa **124** E4
Groot Berg *r.* S. Africa **124** D7
Groot Brakrivier S. Africa **124** F8
Grootdraaidam *dam* S. Africa **125** I4
Grootdrink S. Africa **124** E5
Groote Eylandt *i.* Australia **136** B2
Grootfontein Namibia **123** B5
Groot Karas Berg *plat.* Namibia **124** D4
Groot Letaba *r.* S. Africa **125** J2
Groot Marico S. Africa **125** H3
Groot Swartberge *mts* S. Africa **124** E7
Grootvloer *salt pan* S. Africa **124** E5
Groot Winterberg *mt.* S. Africa **125** H7
Gros Morne National Park Canada **153** K4
Gross Barmen Namibia **124** C2
Große Aue *r.* Germany **63** J2
Große Laaber *r.* Germany **63** M6
Großengottern Germany **63** K3
Großenkneten Germany **63** I2
Großenlüder Germany **63** J4
Großer Arber *mt.* Germany **63** N5
Großer Beerberg *hill* Germany **63** K4
Großer Eyberg *hill* Germany **63** H5
Großer Gleichberg *hill* Germany **63** K4
Großer Kornberg *hill* Germany **63** M4
Großer Osser *mt.* Czech Rep./Germany **63** N5
Großer Rachel *mt.* Germany **57** N6
Grosser Speikkogel *mt.* Austria **57** O7
Grosseto Italy **68** D3
Grossevichi Rus. Fed. **90** E3
Groß-Gerau Germany **63** I5
Großglockner *mt.* Austria **57** N7
Groß Oesingen Germany **63** K2
Großrudestedt Germany **63** L3
Groß Schönebeck Germany **63** N2
Gross Ums Namibia **124** D2
Großvenediger *mt.* Austria **57** N7
Gros Ventre Range *mts* U.S.A. **156** F4
Groswater Bay Canada **153** K3
Groton U.S.A. **160** D2
Grottoes U.S.A. **165** F4
Grou Neth. **62** F1
Groundhog *r.* Canada **152** E4
Grouw Neth. *see* **Grou**
Grove U.S.A. **161** E4
Grove City U.S.A. **164** D4
Grove Hill U.S.A. **163** C6
Grove Mountains Antarctica **188** E2
Grover Beach U.S.A. **158** C4
Grovertown U.S.A. **164** B3
Groveton *NH* U.S.A. **165** J1
Groveton *TX* U.S.A. **161** E6
Growler Mountains U.S.A. **159** G5
Groznyy Rus. Fed. **113** G2
Grubišno Polje Croatia **68** G2
Grudovo Bulg. *see* **Sredets**
Grudziądz Poland **57** Q4
Grünau Namibia **124** D4
Grünberg Poland *see* **Zielona Góra**
Grundarfjörður Iceland **54** [inset]
Grundy U.S.A. **164** D5
Gruñidora Mex. **161** C7
Grünstadt Germany **63** I5
Gruver U.S.A. **161** C4
Gruzinskaya S.S.R. *country* Asia *see* **Georgia**
Gryazi Rus. Fed. **53** H5
Gryazovets Rus. Fed. **52** I4
Gryfice Poland **57** O4
Gryfino Poland **57** O4
Gryfów Śląski Poland **57** O5
Gryllefjord Norway **54** J2
Grytviken S. Georgia **178** I8
Gua India **105** F5
Guacanayabo, Golfo de *b.* Cuba **169** I4
Guachochi Mex. **157** G8
Guadajoz *r.* Spain **67** D5
Guadalajara Mex. **168** D4
Guadalajara Spain **67** E3
Guadalcanal *i.* Solomon Is **133** G2
Guadalete *r.* Spain **67** C5
Guadalope *r.* Spain **67** F3
Guadalquivir *r.* Spain **67** C5
Guadalupe *Nuevo León* Mex. **167** E3
Guadalupe *Zacatecas* Mex. **166** E4
Guadalupe *i.* Mex. **166** A2
Guadalupe *watercourse* Mex. **158** E5
Guadalupe U.S.A. **158** C4
Guadalupe *r. TX* U.S.A. **167** F2
Guadalupe, Sierra de *mts* Spain **67** D4
Guadalupe Aguilera Mex. **161** B7
Guadalupe Bravos Mex. **157** G7
Guadalupe Mountains National Park U.S.A. **157** G7
Guadalupe Peak U.S.A. **157** G7
Guadalupe Victoria *Baja California* Mex. **159** F5
Guadalupe Victoria *Durango* Mex. **161** B7
Guadalupe y Calvo Mex. **166** D3
Guadarrama, Sierra de *mts* Spain **67** D3

▶**Guadeloupe** *terr.* West Indies **169** L5
French Overseas Department.

Guadeloupe Passage Caribbean Sea **169** L5
Guadiana *r.* Port./Spain **67** C5
Guadix Spain **67** E5
Guafo, Isla *i.* Chile **178** B6
Guagua *Luzon* Phil. **82** C3
Guaíba Brazil **179** A5
Guaiçuí Brazil **179** B2
Guaíra Brazil **178** F2
Guaizihu *Nei Mongol* China **94** E3
Guajaba, Cayo *i.* Cuba **163** E8
Guaje, Laguna de *l.* Mex. **166** E2
Guaje, Llano de *plain* Mex. **166** E3
Gualala U.S.A. **158** B2
Gualán Guat. **167** H6
Gualeguay Arg. **178** E4
Gualeguaychu Arg. **178** E4
Gualicho, Salina *salt flat* Arg. **178** C6

▶**Guam** *terr.* N. Pacific Ocean **81** K4
United States Unincorporated Territory.

Guamblin, Isla *i.* Chile **178** A6
Guampí, Sierra de *mts* Venez. **176** E2
Guamúchil Mex. **166** C3
Gua Musang Malaysia **84** C1
Gu'an *Hebei* China **95** I4
Guanabacoa Cuba **163** D8
Guanacaste, Cordillera de *mts* Costa Rica **166** [inset] I7
Guanacaste, Parque Nacional *nat. park* Costa Rica **166** [inset] I7
Guanacevi Mex. **166** D3
Guanahacabibes, Península de *pen.* Cuba **163** C8
Guanaja Hond. **166** [inset] I5
Guanajay Cuba **163** D8
Guanajuato Mex. **168** D4
Guanajuato *state* Mex. **167** E4
Guanambi Brazil **179** C1
Guanare Venez. **176** E2
Guandaokou *Henan* China **95** G5
Guandi Shan *mt. Shanxi* China **95** G4
Guandu China **97** G3
Guane Cuba **169** H4
Guang'an China **96** E2
Guangchang China **97** H3
Guangdong *prov.* China **97** [inset]
Guanghai China **97** G4
Guanghan China **96** E2
Guanghua China *see* **Laohekou**
Guangling *Shanxi* China **95** H4
Guangming China *see* **Xide**
Guangming Ding *mt.* China **97** H2
Guangnan China **96** E3
Guangning *Liaoning* China *see* **Beining**
Guangrao *Shandong* China **95** I4
Guangshan China **97** G2
Guangxi *aut. reg.* China *see* **Guangxi Zhuangzu Zizhiqu**
Guangxi Zhuangzu Zizhiqu *aut. reg.* China **96** F4
Guangyuan China **96** E1
Guangze China **97** H3
Guangzhou China **97** G4
Guangzong *Hebei* China **95** H4
Guanhães Brazil **179** C2
Guan He *r.* China **95** I5
Guanhe Kou *r. mouth* China **95** I5
Guanipa *r.* Venez. **176** F2
Guanling China **96** E3
Guanmian Shan *mts* China **97** F2
Guannan China **97** H1
Guanpo China **97** F1
Guanshui China **90** B4
Guansuo China *see* **Guanling**
Guantánamo Cuba **169** I4
Guantao *Hebei* China **95** H4
Guanting *Qinghai* China **94** E5
Guanxian China *see* **Dujiangyan**
Guanyang China **97** F3
Guanyinqiao China **96** D2
Guanyun *Jiangsu* China **95** I5
Guapé Brazil **179** B3
Guapí Col. **176** C3
Guápiles Costa Rica **166** [inset] J7
Guaporé *r.* Bol./Brazil **176** F6
Guaporé Brazil **179** A5
Guaqui Bol. **176** E7
Guará *r.* Brazil **179** B1
Guarabira Brazil **177** K5
Guaranda Ecuador **176** C4
Guarapari Brazil **179** C3
Guarapuava Brazil **179** A4
Guararapes Brazil **179** A3
Guaratinguetá Brazil **179** B3
Guaratuba Brazil **179** A4
Guaratuba, Baía de *b.* Brazil **179** A4
Guarda Port. **67** C3
Guardafui, Cape Somalia *see* **Gwardafuy, Gees**
Guardiagrele Italy **68** F3
Guardo Spain **67** D2
Guárico, del Embalse *resr* Venez. **176** E2
Guarujá Brazil **179** B3
Guasave Mex. **166** C3
Guasdualito Venez. **176** D2
Guastatoya Guat. **167** H6

▶**Guatemala** *country* Central America **167** H6
4th most populous country in North America.

Guatemala Guat. *see* **Guatemala City**

▶**Guatemala City** Guat. **167** H6
Capital of Guatemala.

Guaviare *r.* Col. **176** E3
Guaxupé Brazil **179** B3
Guayaquil Ecuador **176** C4
Guayaquil, Golfo de *g.* Ecuador **176** B4
Guaymas Mex. **166** C3
Guazacapán Guat. **167** H6
Guazhou *Gansu* China **94** C3
Guba Eth. **122** D2
Gubakha Rus. Fed. **51** R4
Gubat *Luzon* Phil. **82** D3
Gubbi India **106** C3
Gubeikou *Beijing* China **95** I3
Gubio Nigeria **120** E3
Gubkin Rus. Fed. **53** H6
Gucheng *Gansu* China **94** D3
Gucheng *Gansu* China **94** E4
Gucheng *Hebei* China **95** H4
Gucheng China **97** F1
Gucheng *Shanxi* China **95** G5

Guchin-Us Mongolia 94 E2
Gudari India 106 D2
Gudbrandsdalen valley Norway 55 F6
Gudermes Rus. Fed. 113 G2
Gudivada India 106 D2
Gudiyattam India 106 C3
Gudur Andhra Prad. India 106 C3
Gudur Andhra Prad. India 106 C3
Gudvangen Norway 55 E6
Gudzhal r. Rus. Fed. 90 D2
Gué, Rivière du r. Canada 153 H2
Guecho Spain see Algorta
Guéckédou Guinea 120 B4
Guelma Alg. 68 B6
Guelmine Morocco 120 B2
Guelph Canada 164 E2
Guémez Mex. 161 D8
Guénange France 62 G5
Guerara Alg. 64 E5
Guérard, Lac l. Canada 153 I2
Guercif Morocco 64 D5
Guéret France 66 E3

▶Guernsey terr. Channel Is 59 E9
United Kingdom Crown Dependency.

Guernsey U.S.A. 156 G4
Guérou Mauritania 120 B3
Guerrah Et-Tarf salt pan Alg. 68 B7
Guerrero Tamaulipas Mex. 167 F3
Guerrero state Mex. 167 E5
Guerrero Negro Mex. 166 B3
Guers, Lac l. Canada 153 I2
Gueugnon France 66 G3
Gufeng China see Pingnan
Gufu China see Xingshan
Gugë mt. Eth. 122 D3
Gūgerd, Kūh-e mts Iran 110 D3
Guguan i. N. Mariana Is 81 L3
Guhakolak, Tanjung pt Indon. 84 D4
Guhe China 97 H2
Gūh Kūh mt. Iran 110 E5
Guhuai China see Pingyu
Guiana Basin sea feature N. Atlantic Ocean 184 E5
Guiana Highlands mts S. America 176 E2
Guichi China see Chizhou
Guichicovi Mex. 167 G5
Guidan-Roumji Niger 120 D3
Guide Qinghai China 94 E5
Guider Cameroon 121 E4
Guiding China 96 E3
Guidong China 97 G3
Guidonia-Montecelio Italy 68 E4
Guigang China 97 F4
Guiglo Côte d'Ivoire 120 C4
Guignicourt France 62 D5
Guija Moz. 125 K3
Guiji Shan mts China 97 I2
Guildford U.K. 59 G7
Guilford U.S.A. 162 G2
Guilherme Capelo Angola see Cacongo
Guilin China 97 F3
Guillaume-Delisle, Lac l. Canada 152 F2
Guimarães Brazil 177 J4
Guimarães Port. 67 B3
Guimaras i. Phil. 82 C4
Guimaras Strait Phil. 82 C4
Guimeng Ding mt. Shandong China 95 I5
Guinan Qinghai China 94 E5
Guindulman Bohol Phil. 82 D4
Guinea country Africa 120 B3
Guinea, Gulf of Africa 120 D4
Guinea Basin sea feature N. Atlantic Ocean 184 H5
Guinea-Bissau country Africa 120 B3
Guinea-Conakry country Africa see Guinea
Guinea Ecuatorial country Africa see Equatorial Guinea
Guiné-Bissau country Africa see Guinea-Bissau
Guinée country Africa see Guinea
Güines Cuba 169 H4
Guînes France 62 B4
Guines, Lac l. Canada 153 J3
Guingamp France 66 C2
Guiones, Punta pt Costa Rica 166 [inset] I7
Guipavas France 66 B2
Guiping China 97 F4
Güira de Melena Cuba 163 D8
Guiratinga Brazil 177 H7
Guiscard France 62 D5
Guise France 62 D5
Guishan China see Xinping
Guishun China 96 E3
Guiuan Samar Phil. 82 D4
Guixi Chongqing China see Dianjiang
Guixi Jiangxi China 97 H2
Guiyang Guizhou China 96 E3
Guiyang Hunan China 97 G3
Guizhou prov. China 96 E3
Guizi China 97 F4
Gujarat state India 104 C5
Gujar Khan Pak. 111 I3
Gujerat state India see Gujarat
Gujiao Shanxi China 95 H4
Gujranwala Pak. 111 I3
Gujrat Pak. 111 I3
Gukovo Rus. Fed. 53 H6
Gulabgarh India 104 D2
Gulang Gansu China 94 E4
Gulbarga India 106 C2
Gulbene Latvia 55 O8
Gul'cha Kyrg. see Gülchö
Gülchö Kyrg. 102 D3
Gülcihan Turkey 107 B1
Gülek Boğazı pass Turkey 112 D3
Gulf, The Asia. 110 C4
Gulf of Chihli China see Bo Hai
Gulfport U.S.A. 161 F6
Gulian China 90 A1
Gulin China 96 E3
Gulistan Uzbek. see Guliston
Guliston Uzbek. 102 C3
Gulitel hill Palau 82 [inset]
Gülitz Germany 63 L1
Guliya Shan mt. Nei Mongol China 95 J1
Gulja Xinjiang China see Yining
Gul Kach Pak. 111 H4
Gulkana AK U.S.A. 149 K3
Gul'kevichi Rus. Fed. 113 F1
Gull Lake Canada 151 I5
Gullrock Lake Canada 151 M5
Gullträsk Sweden 54 L3
Güllük Körfezi b. Turkey 69 L6
Gülnar Turkey 107 A1
Gul'shat Kazakh. 98 A3
Gulü China see Xincai
Gulu Uganda 122 D3
Guluwuru Island Australia 136 B1
Gulyayevskiye Koshki, Ostrova is Rus. Fed. 52 L1
Guma Xinjiang China see Pishan
Gumal r. Pak. 111 H4
Gumare Botswana 123 C5
Gumbaz Pak. 111 H4
Gumbinnen Rus. Fed. see Gusev
Gumdag Turkm. 110 D2
Gumel Nigeria 120 D3
Gümgüm Turkey see Varto
Gumla India 105 F5
Gumma Japan see Gunma
Gumma pref. Japan see Gunma
Gummersbach Germany 63 H3
Gumpang r. Indon. 84 B1
Gümüşhacıköy Turkey 112 D2
Gümüşhane Turkey 113 E2
Guna India 104 D4
Gunan China see Qijiang
Guna Terara mt. Eth. 108 E7
Gunbar Australia 138 B5
Gunbower Australia 138 B5
Güncang China 96 B2
Gund r. Tajik. see Gunt
Gundagai Australia 138 D5
Gundelsheim Germany 63 J5
Güney Turkey 69 M5
Güneydoğu Toroslar plat. Turkey 112 F3
Gunglilap Myanmar 86 B1
Gungu Dem. Rep. Congo 123 B4
Gunib Rus. Fed. 113 G2
Gunisao r. Canada 151 L4
Gunisao Lake Canada 151 L4
Gunma Japan 93 F2
Gunma pref. Japan 93 E2
Gunnaur India 104 D3
Gunnbjørn Fjeld nunatak Greenland 147 P3
Gunnedah Australia 138 E3
Gunnerus Ridge sea feature Antarctica 188 D2
Gunning Australia 138 D5
Gunnison U.S.A. 157 G5
Gunnison r. U.S.A. 159 I2
Gunong Ayer Sarawak Malaysia see Gunung Ayer
Güns Hungary see Kőszeg
Gunt r. Tajik. 111 H2
Guntakal India 106 C3
Güntersberge Germany 63 K3
Guntur India 106 D2
Gunungapi i. Maluku Indon. 83 C4
Gunung Ayer Sarawak Malaysia 85 E2
Gunungbatubesar Kalimantan Indon. 85 G3
Gunung Gading National Park Malaysia 85 E2
Gunung Gede Pangrango, Taman Nasional nat. park Indon. 84 D4
Gunung Halimun, Taman Nasional nat. park Indon. 84 D4
Gunung Leuser, Taman Nasional nat. park Indon. 84 B2
Gunung Mulu National Park Malaysia 85 F1
Gunung Niyut, Suaka Margasatwa nature res. Indon. 85 E2
Gunung Palung, Taman Nasional nat. park Indon. 85 E3
Gunung Rinjani, Taman Nasional nat. park Lombok Indon. 85 G5
Gunungsitoli Indon. 84 B2
Gunungsugih Sumatera Indon. 84 D4
Gunungtua Sumatera Indon. 84 B2
Günyüzü Turkey 112 C3
Gunza Angola see Porto Amboim
Günzburg Germany 57 M6
Gunzenhausen Germany 63 K5
Guochengyi Gansu China 94 F4
Guo He r. China 97 H1
Guo He r. China 95 H5
Guojia Gansu China 94 F5
Guojiatun Hebei China 95 I3
Guoluezhen Henan China see Lingbao
Guovdageaidnu Norway see Kautokeino
Guoyang Anhui China 95 I5
Guozhen Shaanxi China see Baoji
Gupis Pak. 104 C1
Gurban Obo Nei Mongol China 95 H3
Gurbantünggüt Shamo des. China 98 D3
Gurdaspur India 104 C2
Gurdon U.S.A. 161 E5
Gurdzhaani Georgia see Gurjaani
Güre Turkey 69 M5
Gurgan Iran see Gorgān
Gurgaon India 104 D3
Gurgei, Jebel mt. Sudan 121 F3
Gurha India 104 B4
Guri, Embalse de resr Venez. 176 F2
Gurig National Park Australia 134 F2
Gurinhatã Brazil 179 A2
Gurjaani Georgia 113 G2
Gur Khar Iran 111 E4
Guro Moz. 123 D5
Gurşunmagdan Kärhanasy Turkm. 111 G2
Guru China 105 G3
Gürün Turkey 112 E3
Gurupá Brazil 177 H4
Gurupi Brazil 177 I6
Gurupi r. Brazil 177 I4
Gurupi, Serra do hills Brazil 177 I4
Guru Sikhar mt. India 104 C4
Guruzala India 106 C2
Gurvandzagal Mongolia 95 H1
Gurvan Sayan Uul mts Mongolia 94 E3
Gurvansayhan Mongolia 95 F2
Gurvantes Mongolia 94 E3
Gur'yev Kazakh. see Atyrau
Gur'yevsk Rus. Fed. 55 L9
Gur'yevskaya Oblast' admin. div. Kazakh. see Atyrauskaya Oblast'
Gurz Afgh. 111 G3
Gusau Nigeria 120 D3
Güsen Germany 63 L2
Gusev Rus. Fed. 55 M9
Gushan China 91 A5
Gushgy Turkm. see Serhetabat
Gushi China 97 G1
Gusino Rus. Fed. 53 F5
Gusinoozersk Rus. Fed. 94 F1
Gusinoye, Ozero l. Rus. Fed. 94 F1
Gus'-Khrustal'nyy Rus. Fed. 52 I5
Guspini Sardinia Italy 68 C5
Gustav Holm, Kap c. Greenland see Tasiilap Karra
Gustavo Sotelo Mex. 166 B2
Gustavus AK U.S.A. 149 N4
Güsten Germany 63 L3
Gustine U.S.A. 158 C3
Güstrow Germany 57 N4
Gutang Xizang China 99 F7
Güterfelde Germany 63 N2
Gütersloh Germany 63 I3
Guthrie AZ U.S.A. 159 I5
Guthrie KY U.S.A. 164 B5
Guthrie OK U.S.A. 161 D5
Guthrie TX U.S.A. 161 C5
Gutian Fujian China 97 H3
Gutian Fujian China 97 H3
Gutian Shuiku resr China 97 H3
Guting Shandong China see Yutai
Gutsuo China 105 F3
Guwahati India 105 G4
Guwēr Iraq 113 F3
Guwlumaýak Turkm. 110 D1
Guwlumayak Turkm. see Guwlumaýak
Guxhagen Germany 63 J3
Guxian China 97 G3
Guyana country S. America 177 G2
Guyane Française terr. S. America see French Guiana
Guyang Hunan China see Guzhang
Guyang Nei Mongol China 95 G3
Guyenne reg. France 66 D4
Guy Fawkes River National Park Australia 138 F3
Guyi China see Sanjiang
Guymon U.S.A. 161 C4
Guyot Glacier Canada/U.S.A. 149 L3
Guyra Australia 138 E3
Guysborough Canada 153 J5
Guyuan Hebei China 95 H3
Guyuan Ningxia China 94 F5
Güzeloluk Turkey 107 B1
Güzelyurt Cyprus see Morfou
Guzhang China 97 F2
Guzhen China 97 H1
Guzhou China see Rongjiang
Guzmán Mex. 166 D2
Guzmán, Lago de l. Mex. 166 D2
G'uzor Uzbek. 111 G2
Gvardeysk Rus. Fed. 55 L9
Gvasyugi Rus. Fed. 90 E3
Gwa Myanmar 86 A3
Gwabegar Australia 138 D3
Gwadar West Bay Pak. 111 F5
Gwaii Haanas National Park Reserve B.C. Canada 149 O5
Gwaldam Uttaranchal India 99 B7
Gwal Haidarzai Pak. 111 H4
Gwalior India 104 D4
Gwanda Zimbabwe 123 C6
Gwane Dem. Rep. Congo 122 C3
Gwardafuy, Gees c. Somalia 122 F2
Gwash Pak. 111 G4
Gwatar Bay Pak. 111 F5
Gwedaukkon Myanmar 86 A1
Gweebarra Bay Ireland 61 D3
Gweedore Ireland see Gaoth Dobhair
Gwelo Zimbabwe see Gweru
Gweru Zimbabwe 123 C5
Gweta Botswana 123 C6
Gwinner U.S.A. 160 D2
Gwoza Nigeria 120 E3
Gwydir r. Australia 138 D2
Gyablung Xizang China 99 F7
Gyaca Xizang China 99 F7
Gyaco Xizang China 99 C6
Gyagartang China 96 D1
Gyaijêpozhanggê Qinghai China see Zhidoi
Gyai Qu r. Xizang China 99 F7
Gyairong China 96 C1
Gyaisi China see Jiulong
Gyali i. Greece 69 L6
Gyamug Xizang China 99 C6
Gyandzha Azer. see Gäncä
Gyangnyi Caka salt l. China 99 D6
Gyangrang Xizang China 99 D7
Gyangtse Xizang China see Gyangzê
Gyangzê Xizang China 99 E7
Gya'nyima Xizang China 99 C7
Gyaring Qinghai China 94 D5
Gyaring Co l. China 99 E7
Gyaring Hu l. Qinghai China 94 D5
Gyarishing India 96 B2
Gyaros i. Greece 69 K6
Gyarubtang China 96 B2
Gydan, Khrebet mts Rus. Fed. see Kolymskiy, Khrebet
Gydan Peninsula Rus. Fed. 76 I2
Gydanskiy Poluostrov pen. Rus. Fed. see Gydan Peninsula
Gyêgu China see Yushu
Gyêmdong Xizang China 99 F7
Gyêsar Co l. Xizang China 99 D7
Gyêwa Xizang China see Zabqung
Gyigang China 96 C2
Gyimda Xizang China 99 F7
Gyipug Xizang China 99 C6
Gyirong Xizang China 99 D7
Gyirong Xizang China 99 D7
Gyixong Xizang China see Gonggar
Gyiza Qinghai China 99 F6
Gyldenløve Fjord inlet Greenland see Umiiviip Kangertiva
Gympie Australia 137 F5
Gyobingauk Myanmar 86 A3
Gyōda Japan 93 F2
Gyöngyös Hungary 57 Q7
Győr Hungary 68 G1
Gypsum Point Canada 150 H2
Gypsumville Canada 151 L5
Gyrfalcon Islands Canada 153 H2
Gytheio Greece 69 J6
Gyula Hungary 69 I1
Gyulafehérvár Romania see Alba Iulia
Gyümai China see Darlag
Gyumri Armenia 113 F2
Gyungcang Xizang China 99 B6
Gyzylarbat Turkm. see Serdar
Gyzylbaýdak Turkm. 111 F2
Gyzylbaydak Turkm. see Gyzylbaýdak
Gzhatsk Rus. Fed. see Gagarin

H

Ha Bhutan 105 G4
Haa-Alif Atoll Maldives see Ihavandhippolhu Atoll
Haanhöhiy Uul mts Mongolia 94 C1
Ha'apai Group is Tonga 133 I3
Haapajärvi Fin. 54 N5
Haapavesi Fin. 54 N4
Haapsalu Estonia 55 M7
Ha 'Arava watercourse Israel/Jordan see 'Arabah, Wādī al
Ha'Arava, Naḥal watercourse Israel/Jordan see Jayb, Wādī al
Haarlem Neth. 62 E2
Haarlem S. Africa 124 F7
Haarstrang ridge Germany 63 H3
Hab r. Pak. 111 G5
Habahe Xinjiang China 98 D2
Habana Cuba see Havana
Habarane Sri Lanka 106 D4
Habarōn well Saudi Arabia 110 C6
Habaswein Kenya 122 D3
Habay Canada 150 G3
Habbān Yemen 108 G7
Ḥabbānīyah, Hawr al l. Iraq 113 F4
Hab Chauki Pak. 111 G5
Habiganj Bangl. 105 G4
Habikino Japan 92 B4
Habirag Nei Mongol China 95 H3
Habra India 105 G5
Hachibuse-yama mt. Japan 93 E2
Hachijō-jima i. Japan 91 E6
Hachikai Japan 92 C3
Hachiman Japan 92 C3
Hachiman-misaki c. Japan 93 G3
Hachimori-yama mt. Japan 92 D2
Hachinohe Japan 90 F4
Hachiōji Japan 93 F3
Hachita U.S.A. 159 I6
Hacıköy Turkey see Çekerek
Hack, Mount Australia 137 B6
Hackberry U.S.A. 159 G4
Hackensack U.S.A. 165 H3
Hacufera Moz. 123 D6
Ḥaḍabat al Jilf al Kabīr plat. Egypt see Jilf al Kabīr, Haḍabat al
Hadadong Xinjiang China 98 C4
Hadagalli India 106 B3
Hada Mountains Afgh. 111 G4
Hadano Japan 93 F3
Hadapu Gansu China 94 F5
Hadat Nei Mongol China 95 I1
Hadayang Nei Mongol China 95 K1
Ḥadd, Ra's al pt Oman 111 E6
Haddington U.K. 60 G5
Haddumati Atoll Maldives see Hadhdhunmathi Atoll
Haddunmahti Atoll Maldives see Hadhdhunmathi Atoll
Hadejia Nigeria 120 E3
Ḥadera Israel 107 B3
Ḥadera r. Israel 107 B3
Haderslev Denmark 55 F9
Hadhdhunmathi Atoll Maldives 103 D11
Hadhramaut reg. Yemen see Ḥaḍramawt
Hādī, Jabal al mts Jordan 107 C4
Hadilik Xinjiang China 99 D5
Hadım Turkey 112 D3
Hadleigh U.K. 59 H6
Hadong S. Korea 91 B6
Ḥadraj, Wādī watercourse Saudi Arabia 107 C4
Ḥaḍramawt reg. Yemen 122 E2
Hadranum Sicily Italy see Adrano
Hadrian's Wall tourist site U.K. 58 E3
Hadrumetum Tunisia see Sousse
Hadsund Denmark 55 G8
Hadweenzic r. AK U.S.A. 149 K2
Hadyach Ukr. 53 G6
Haeju N. Korea 91 B5
Haeju-man b. N. Korea 91 B5
Haenam S. Korea 91 B6
Haenertsburg S. Africa 125 I2
Ha'erbin China see Harbin
Ḥafar al 'Atk well Saudi Arabia 110 B5
Ḥafar al Bāṭin Saudi Arabia 108 G4
Hafford Canada 151 J4
Hafik Turkey 112 E3
Ḥafirah, Qā' al salt pan Jordan 107 C4
Hafirat Nasah Saudi Arabia 110 B5
Hafizabad Pak. 111 I3
Haflong India 105 H4
Hafnarfjörður Iceland 54 [inset]
Hafren r. U.K. see Severn
Haft Gel Iran 110 C4
Hafursfjörður b. Iceland 54 [inset]
Haga Myanmar see Haka
Hagachi-zaki pt Japan 93 E4
Hagar Nish Plateau Eritrea 108 E6

▶Hagåtña Guam 81 K4
Capital of Guam.

Hagelberg hill Germany 63 M2
Hagemeister Island AK U.S.A. 148 G4
Hagemeister Strait AK U.S.A. 148 G4
Hagen Germany 63 H3
Hagenow Germany 63 L1
Hagerhill U.S.A. 164 D5
Hagerstown U.S.A. 165 G4
Hagfors Sweden 55 H6
Haggin, Mount U.S.A. 156 E3
Hagi Japan 91 C6
Ha Giang Vietnam 86 D2
Hagiwara Japan 92 D3
Hagley U.K. 59 E6
Hag's Head hd Ireland 61 C5
Hague U.S.A. 165 I2
Haguenau France 63 H6
Hahajima-rettō is Japan 91 F8
Hai Tanz. 121 G5
Hai, Ko i. Thai. 84 B1
Hai'an China 97 F4
Haib watercourse Namibia 124 C5
Haibara Nara Japan 92 B4
Haibara Shizuoka Japan 93 E4
Haibowan Nei Mongol China see Wuhai
Haicheng Guangdong China see Haifeng
Haicheng Liaoning China 95 J3
Haicheng Ningxia China see Haiyuan
Haiding Hu salt l. Qinghai China 94 C5
Hai Dương Vietnam 86 D2
Haifa Israel 107 B3
Haifa, Bay of Israel 107 B3
Haifeng China 97 G4
Haig Australia 135 D7
Haiger Germany 63 I4
Haihu Qinghai China 94 E4
Haikakan country Asia see Armenia
Haikang China see Leizhou
Haikou China 97 F4
Ḥā'il Saudi Arabia 113 F6
Ḥā'il, Wādī al watercourse Saudi Arabia 113 F6
Hailar Nei Mongol China see Hulun Buir
Hailey U.S.A. 156 E4
Haileybury Canada 152 F5
Hailin China 90 C3
Hailong China see Meihekou
Hails Nei Mongol China 95 I3
Hailsham U.K. 59 H8
Hailun China 90 B3
Hailuoto Fin. 54 N4
Hainan i. China 97 F5
Hainan prov. China 97 F5
Hai-nang Myanmar 86 B2
Hainan Strait China 97 F5
Hainaut reg. France 62 D4
Haines AK U.S.A. 149 N4
Haines Junction Y.T. Canada 149 M3
Haines Road Canada/U.S.A. 149 M3
Hainichen Germany 63 N4
Hainleite ridge Germany 63 K3
Hai Phong Vietnam 86 D2
Haiphong Vietnam see Hai Phong
Haiqing China 90 D3
Hairag Qinghai China 94 E4
Haitan Dao i. China 97 H3
Haiti country West Indies 169 J5
Haitou China 97 F5
Hai Triều Vietnam 87 E4
Haiwee Reservoir U.S.A. 158 E3
Haiya Sudan 108 E6
Haiyan Qinghai China 94 E4
Haiyan Zhejiang China 97 I2
Haiyang China see Xiuning
Haiyang Shandong China 95 J4
Haiyang Dao i. China 91 A5
Haiyou China see Sanmen
Haiyuan Ningxia China 94 F4
Haizhou Wan b. China 95 I5
Hāj Ali Qoli, Kavīr-e salt l. Iran 110 D3
Hajdúböszörmény Hungary 69 I1
Hajeb El Ayoun Tunisia 68 C7
Ḥajhir mt. Yemen 109 H7
Haji Mahesar Pak. 111 G4
Hajipur India 105 F4
Hajir reg. Saudi Arabia 110 C5
Ḥajjah Yemen 108 F6
Ḥājjīābād Fārs Iran 110 D4
Ḥājjīābād Hormozgan Iran 110 D4
Ḥājjīābād Iran 110 D3
Haju Nei Mongol China 94 D3
Hajuu-Us Mongolia see Govĭ-Ugtaal
Haka Myanmar 86 A2
Hakha Myanmar see Haka
Hakkârı Turkey 113 F3
Hakkas Sweden 54 L3
Hakken-zan mt. Japan 92 B4
Hakkō-san hill Japan 93 E4
Hako-dake mt. Japan 90 F3
Hakodate Japan 90 F4
Hakone Japan 93 F3
Hakone-tōge pass Japan 93 F3
Hakos Mountains Namibia 124 C2
Hakseen Pan salt pan S. Africa 124 E4
Hakuba Japan 93 D2
Hakui Japan 92 C2
Hakusan Japan 92 C4
Haku-san vol. Japan 92 C2
Haku-san Kokuritsu-kōen nat. park Japan 92 C2
Hakushū Japan 93 E3
Hal Belgium see Halle
Hala Pak. 111 H5
Ḥalab Syria see Aleppo
Ḥalabja Iraq 113 G4
Halaç Turkm. 111 G2
Halaç Turkm. see Halaç
Halachó Mex. 167 H4
Halaha China 90 B3
Halahai China 90 B3
Halaib Sudan 108 E5

▶Halaib Triangle terr. Egypt/Sudan 108 E5
Disputed territory (Egypt/Sudan) administered by Sudan.

Halâl, Gebel hill Egypt see Hilāl, Jabal
Ha Lam Vietnam 86 E4
Ḥalāniyāt, Juzur al is Oman 109 I6
Hālawa U.S.A. 157 [inset]
Halba Lebanon 107 C2
Halban Hövsgöl Mongolia see Tsetserleg
Halberstadt Germany 63 L3
Halcon, Mount Mindoro Phil. 82 C3
Haldane r. N.W.T. Canada 149 Q2
Halden Norway 55 G7
Haldensleben Germany 63 L2
Haldwani India 104 D3
Hale watercourse Australia 136 A5
Hale Nei Mongol China 95 G3
Hale U.S.A. 164 D1
Hāleh Iran 110 D5
Haleparki Deresi r. Syria/Turkey see Quwayq, Nahr
Halesowen U.K. 59 E6
Halesworth U.K. 59 I6
Half Assini Ghana 120 C4
Halfmoon Bay N.Z. 139 B8
Halfway r. Canada 150 F3
Halfway Ireland 61 D6
Halfway Mountain hill AK U.S.A. 148 I3
Halfweg Neth. 62 E2
Halhgol Dornod Mongolia 95 I2
Halhgol Dornod Mongolia 95 I2
Halia India 105 E4
Ḥalībīyah Syria 113 E4
Haliburton Canada 165 F1
Haliburton Highlands hills Canada 165 F1
Halicarnassus Turkey see Bodrum

▶Halifax Canada 153 J5
Capital of Nova Scotia.

Halifax U.K. 58 F5
Halifax NC U.S.A. 162 E4
Halifax VA U.S.A. 165 F5
Halifax, Mount Australia 136 D3
Halik Shan mts Xinjiang China 98 C4
Halilulik Timor Indon. 83 C5
Ḥalīmah mt. Lebanon/Syria 107 C2
Haliut Nei Mongol China 95 G3
Halkett, Cape AK U.S.A. 148 I1
Halkirk U.K. 60 F2
Hall U.S.A. 164 C5
Hälla Sweden 54 J5
Halladale r. U.K. 60 F2
Halla-san National Park S. Korea 91 B6
Hall Beach Canada 147 J3
Halle Belgium 62 E4
Halle Neth. 62 G3
Halle (Saale) Germany 63 L3
Halleck U.S.A. 159 F1
Hällefors Sweden 55 I7
Hallein Austria 57 N7
Halle-Neustadt Germany 63 L3
Hallett, Cape Antarctica 188 H2
Hallettsville U.S.A. 161 D6
Halley research station Antarctica 188 B1
Hallgreen, Mount Antarctica 188 B2
Halliday U.S.A. 160 C2
Halliday Lake Canada 151 I2
Hall Island AK U.S.A. 148 D3
Hall Islands Micronesia 186 G5
Hällnäs Sweden 54 K4
Hallock U.S.A. 160 D1
Hall Peninsula Canada 147 L3
Hallsberg Sweden 55 I7
Halls Creek Australia 134 D4
Halls Gap U.S.A. 164 C5
Halls Lake Canada 165 F1
Hallstead U.S.A. 165 H3
Halluin Belgium 62 D4
Hallviken Sweden 54 I5
Halmahera i. Maluku Indon. 83 D2
Halmahera, Laut sea Maluku Indon. 83 D3
Halmahera Sea Maluku Indon. see Halmahera, Laut
Halmstad Sweden 55 H8
Ha Long Vietnam 86 D2
Hals Denmark 55 G8
Hälsingborg Sweden see Helsingborg
Halsua Fin. 54 N5
Haltang He r. China 94 C4
Haltern Germany 63 H3
Haltunchén Mex. 167 H5
Haltwhistle U.K. 58 E4
Ḥālūl i. Qatar 110 D5
Halura i. Indon. 83 B5
Halvān Iran 110 E3
Halver Germany 63 H3
Haly, Mount hill Australia 138 E1
Ham France 62 D5
Hamada Japan 91 D6
Ḥamâda El Ḥaricha des. Mali 120 C2

Hamadān Iran 110 C3
Ḥamādat Murzuq plat. Libya 122 B1
Ḥamāh Syria 107 C2
Hamajima Japan 92 C4
Hamakita Japan 93 D4
Hamam Turkey 107 C1
Hamamatsu Japan 92 D4
Hamana-ko l. Japan 92 D4
Hamaoka Japan 93 E4
Hamar Norway 55 G6
Hamarøy Norway 54 I2
Ḥamâṭa, Gebel mt. Egypt see Ḥamāṭah, Jabal
Ḥamāṭah, Jabal mt. Egypt 108 D5
Hamatonbetsu Japan 90 F3
Hambantota Sri Lanka 106 D5
Hambergen Germany 63 I1
Hambleton Hills U.K. 58 F4
Hamburg Germany 63 J1
Hamburg land Germany 63 J1
Hamburg S. Africa 125 H7
Hamburg AR U.S.A. 161 F5
Hamburg NY U.S.A. 165 F2
Hamburgisches Wattenmeer, Nationalpark nat. park Germany 57 L4
Ḥamḍ, Wādī al watercourse Saudi Arabia 108 E4
Hamden U.S.A. 165 I3
Hämeenlinna Fin. 55 N6
HaMelaḥ, Yam salt l. Asia see Dead Sea
Hamelin Australia 135 A6
Hameln Germany 63 J2
Hamersley Lakes salt flat Australia 135 B7
Hamersley Range mts Australia 134 B5
Hamhŭng N. Korea 91 B5
Hami Xinjiang China 94 C3
Hamid Sudan 108 D5
Hamilton Qld Australia 136 C4
Hamilton S.A. Australia 137 A5
Hamilton Vic. Australia 137 C8
Hamilton watercourse Qld Australia 136 B4
Hamilton watercourse S.A. Australia 137 A5

▶Hamilton Bermuda 169 L2
Capital of Bermuda.

Hamilton Canada 164 F2
Hamilton r. Canada see Churchill
Hamilton N.Z. 139 E3
Hamilton U.K. 60 E5
Hamilton AK U.S.A. 148 G3
Hamilton AL U.S.A. 163 C5
Hamilton CO U.S.A. 159 J1
Hamilton MI U.S.A. 164 B2
Hamilton MT U.S.A. 156 E3
Hamilton NY U.S.A. 165 H2
Hamilton OH U.S.A. 164 C4
Hamilton TX U.S.A. 161 D6
Hamilton, Mount AK U.S.A. 148 H3
Hamilton, Mount CA U.S.A. 158 C3
Hamilton, Mount NV U.S.A. 159 F2
Hamilton City U.S.A. 158 B2
Hamilton Inlet Canada 153 K3
Hamilton Mountain hill U.S.A. 165 H2
Hamīm, Wādī al watercourse Libya 65 I5
Hamina Fin. 55 O6
Hamirpur Hima. Prad. India 104 D3
Hamirpur Uttar Prad. India 104 E4
Hamitabat Turkey see Isparta
Hamju N. Korea 91 B5
Hamlet U.S.A. 163 E5
Hamlin TX U.S.A. 161 C5
Hamlin WV U.S.A. 164 D4
Hamm Germany 63 H3
Ḥammām al 'Alīl Iraq 113 F3
Hammam Boughrara Alg. 67 F6
Hammamet Tunisia 68 D6
Hammamet, Golfe de g. Tunisia 68 D6
Ḥammār, Hawr al imp. l. Iraq 113 G5
Hammarstrand Sweden 54 J5
Hammelburg Germany 63 J4
Hammerdal Sweden 54 I5
Hammerfest Norway 54 M1
Hamminkeln Germany 62 G3
Hammond U.S.A. 164 B3
Hammond LA U.S.A. 167 H2
Hammone, Lac l. Canada 153 K4
Hammonton U.S.A. 165 H4
Ham Ninh Vietnam 87 D5
Hamoir Belgium 62 F4
Hampden Sydney U.S.A. 165 F5
Hampshire Downs hills U.K. 59 F7
Hampton AR U.S.A. 161 E5
Hampton IA U.S.A. 160 E3
Hampton NH U.S.A. 165 J2
Hampton SC U.S.A. 163 D5
Hampton VA U.S.A. 165 G5
Hampton Tableland reg. Australia 135 D8
Ḥamrā, Birkat al well Saudi Arabia 113 F5
Hamra, Vâdii watercourse Syria/Turkey see Ḥimār, Wādī al
Ḥamrā Jūdah plat. Saudi Arabia 110 C5
Hamrat esh Sheikh Sudan 108 C7
Ham Tân Vietnam 87 D5
Hamta Pass India 104 D2
Hāmūn-e Jaz Mūrīān salt marsh Iran 110 E5
Hāmūn-e Lowrah dry lake Afgh./Pak. see Hamun-i-Lora
Hāmūn Helmand salt flat Afgh./Iran 111 F4
Hamun-i-Lora dry lake Afgh./Pak. 111 G4
Hamun-i-Mashkel salt flat Pak. 111 F4
Hamunt Kūh hill Iran 111 F5
Hamur Turkey 113 F3
Hamura Japan 93 F3
Hamwic U.K. see Southampton
Hāna U.S.A. 157 [inset]
Hanábana r. Cuba 163 D8
Hanahai watercourse Botswana/Namibia 124 F2
Ḥanak Saudi Arabia 108 E4
Hanakpınar Turkey see Çınar
Hanalei U.S.A. 157 [inset]
Hanamaki Japan 91 F5
Hanamigawa Japan 93 G3
Hanang mt. Tanz. 123 D4
Hanau Germany 63 I4
Hanawa Japan 93 G2
Hanbin China see Ankang
Hanbogd Mongolia 95 F3
Hanchang China see Pingjiang
Hancheng Shaanxi China 95 G5
Hanchuan China 97 G2
Hancock MD U.S.A. 165 F4
Hancock NY U.S.A. 165 H3
Handa Japan 92 C4
Handa Island U.K. 60 D2
Handan Hebei China 95 H4
Handeni Tanz. 123 D4
Handian Shanxi China see Changzhi
Haneda airport Japan 93 F3
HaNegev des. Israel see Negev
HaNeqarot watercourse Israel 107 B4
Hanfeng China see Kaixian
Hanford U.S.A. 158 D3
Hangan Myanmar 86 B4
Hangayn Nuruu mts Mongolia 94 D1
Hangchow China see Hangzhou
Hangchuan China see Guangze
Hanggin Houqi Nei Mongol China see Xamba
Hanggin Qi Nei Mongol China see Xin
Hangö Fin. see Hanko
Hangu Tianjin China 95 I4
Hanguang China 97 G3
Hangya Qinghai China 94 D4
Hangzhou China 97 I2
Hangzhou Wan b. China 97 I2
Hani Turkey 113 F3
Hanish Kabir i. Yemen see Suyūl Ḥanīsh
Hanji Gansu China see Linxia
Hanjia China see Pengshui
Hanjiaoshui Ningxia China 94 F4
Hankensbüttel Germany 63 K2
Hankey S. Africa 124 G7
Hanko Fin. 55 M7
Hanksville U.S.A. 159 H2
Hanle India 104 D2
Hanley Canada 151 J5
Hann, Mount hill Australia 134 D3
Hanna Canada 151 I5
Hannagan Meadow U.S.A. 159 I5
Hannah Bay Canada 152 E4
Hannibal MO U.S.A. 160 F4
Hannibal NY U.S.A. 165 G2
Hannō Japan 93 F3
Hannover Germany 63 J2
Hannoversch Münden Germany 63 J3
Hann Range mts Australia 135 F5
Hannut Belgium 62 F4
Hanöbukten b. Sweden 55 I9

▶Ha Nôi Vietnam 86 D2
Capital of Vietnam.

Hanoi Vietnam see Ha Nôi
Hanover Canada 164 E1
Hanover Germany see Hannover
Hanover S. Africa 124 G6
Hanover NH U.S.A. 165 I2
Hanover PA U.S.A. 165 G4
Hanover VA U.S.A. 165 G5
Hansen Mountains Antarctica 188 D2
Hanshou China 97 F2
Han Shui r. China 97 G2
Hansi India 104 D3
Hansnes Norway 54 K2
Hanstholm Denmark 55 F8
Han Sum Nei Mongol China 95 I2
Han-sur-Nied France 62 G6
Hantsavichy Belarus 55 O10
Hanumangarh India 104 C3
Hanuy Gol r. Mongolia 94 E1
Hanwood Australia 138 C5
Hanxia Gansu China 94 D4
Hanyang China see Caidian
Hanyang Feng mt. China 97 G2
Hanyin China 97 F1
Hanyū Japan 93 F2
Hanzhong China 96 E1
Hao atoll Fr. Polynesia 187 K7
Haomen Qinghai China see Menyuan
Haora India 105 G5
Haparanda Sweden 54 N4
Happy Jack U.S.A. 159 H4
Happy Valley-Goose Bay Canada 153 J3
Hapur Uttar Prad. India 99 B7
Ḥaql Saudi Arabia 107 B5
Haqshah well Saudi Arabia 110 C6
Hara Japan 93 E3
Ḥaraḍ well Saudi Arabia 110 C5
Ḥarad, Jabal al mt. Jordan 107 B5
Ḥaraḍh Saudi Arabia 108 G5
Haradok Belarus 53 F5
Haramachi Japan 91 F5
Haramgai Xinjiang China 98 D3
Haramukh mt. India 104 C2
Haran Turkey see Harran
Harappa Road Pak. 111 I4
Harar Eth. see Hārer
▶Harare Zimbabwe 123 D5
Capital of Zimbabwe.

Ḥarāsīs, Jiddat al des. Oman 109 I6
Harāt Iran 110 D4
Har-Ayrag Mongolia 95 G2
Haraze-Mangueigne Chad 121 F3
Harb, Jabal mt. Saudi Arabia 112 D6
Harbin China 90 B3
Harboi Hills Pak. 111 G4
Harbor Beach U.S.A. 164 D2
Harchoka India 105 E5
Harda India 104 D5
Harda Khas India see Harda
Hardangerfjorden sea chan. Norway 55 D7
Hardangervidda plat. Norway 55 E6
Hardangervidda Nasjonalpark nat. park Norway 55 E6
Hardap admin. reg. Namibia 124 C3
Hardap nature res. Namibia 124 C3
Hardap Dam Namibia 124 C3
Harden, Bukit mt. Indon. 85 F1
Hardenberg Neth. 62 G2
Harderwijk Neth. 62 F2
Hardeveld mts S. Africa 124 D6
Hardheim Germany 63 J5
Hardin U.S.A. 156 G3
Harding r. Nunavut Canada 149 R1
Harding S. Africa 125 I6
Harding Ice Field AK U.S.A. 149 J3
Harding Range hills Australia 135 B6
Hardinsburg IN U.S.A. 164 B4
Hardinsburg KY U.S.A. 164 B5
Hardoi India 104 E4
Hardwar India see Haridwar
Hardwick U.S.A. 165 I1
Hardy U.S.A. 161 F4
Hardy Reservoir U.S.A. 164 C2
Hare Bay Canada 153 L4
Ḥareidīn, Wâdi watercourse Egypt see Ḥuraydīn, Wādī
Hare Indian r. N.W.T. Canada 149 O2
Harelbeke Belgium 62 D4
Haren Neth. 62 G1
Haren (Ems) Germany 63 H2
Hārer Eth. 122 E3
Harf el Mreffi mt. Lebanon 107 B3
Hargant Nei Mongol China 95 I1
Hargeisa Somalia see Hargeysa
Hargele Eth. 122 E3
Hargeysa Somalia 122 E3
Harghita-Mădăraş, Vârful mt. Romania 69 K1
Harhatan Nei Mongol China 95 F4
Harhorin Mongolia 94 E2
Har Hu l. Qinghai China 94 D4
Haridwar India 104 D3
Ḥarif, Har mt. Israel 107 B4
Harihar India 106 B3
Harihari N.Z. 139 C6
Hariharpur India 106 B3
Ḥārim Syria 107 C1
Harīm, Jabal al mt. Oman 110 E5
Harima Japan 92 A4
Harima-nada b. Japan 92 A4
Haringhat r. Bangl. 105 G5
Haringvliet est. Neth. 62 E3
Harinoki-dake mt. Japan 92 D2
Ḥarīr, Wādī adh r. Syria 107 C3
Hari Rūd r. Afgh./Iran 111 F2
Harjavalta Fin. 55 M6
Harlan IA U.S.A. 160 E3
Harlan KY U.S.A. 164 D5
Harlan County Lake U.S.A. 160 D3
Harlech U.K. 59 C6
Harleston U.K. 59 I6
Harlingen Neth. 62 F1
Harlingen U.S.A. 161 D7
Harlow U.K. 59 H7
Harlowton U.S.A. 156 F3
Harly France 62 D5
Harman U.S.A. 164 F4
Harmancık Turkey 69 M5
Harmony U.S.A. 165 K1
Harmsdorf Germany 63 K1
Harnai India 106 B2
Harnai Pak. 111 G4
Harnes France 62 C4
Harney Basin U.S.A. 156 D4
Harney Lake U.S.A. 156 D4
Härnösand Sweden 54 J5
Harns Neth. see Harlingen
Har Nuden Nei Mongol China 95 I1
Har Nuur l. Mongolia 94 C1
Har Nuur l. Mongolia 94 D1
Haroldswick U.K. 60 [inset]
Harper Liberia 120 C4
Harper U.S.A. 161 D4
Harper, Mount Y.T. Canada 149 M2
Harper, Mount AK U.S.A. 149 L2
Harper Bend reg. AK U.S.A. 149 J2
Harper Creek r. Canada 150 H3
Harper Lake U.S.A. 158 E4
Harp Lake Canada 153 J3
Harpstedt Germany 63 I2
Harqin Qi Nei Mongol China see Jinshan
Harqin Zuoqi Mongolzu Zizhixian Liaoning China see Dachengzi
Harquahala Mountains U.S.A. 157 E6
Harrai India 104 D5
Harran Turkey 107 D1
Harrand Pak. 111 H4
Harricana, Rivière d' r. Canada 152 F4
Harrington Australia 138 F3
Harrington U.S.A. 165 H4
Harris, Lake salt flat Australia 137 A6
Harris, Mount Australia 135 E6
Harris, Sound of sea chan. U.K. 60 B3
Harrisburg AR U.S.A. 161 F5
Harrisburg IL U.S.A. 160 F4
Harrisburg NE U.S.A. 160 C3

▶Harrisburg PA U.S.A. 165 G3
Capital of Pennsylvania.

Harrismith Australia 135 B8
Harrison AR U.S.A. 161 E4
Harrison MI U.S.A. 164 C1
Harrison NE U.S.A. 160 C3
Harrison OH U.S.A. 164 C4
Harrison, Cape Canada 153 K3
Harrison Bay AK U.S.A. 149 J1
Harrisonburg LA U.S.A. 161 F6
Harrisonburg VA U.S.A. 165 F4
Harrisonville U.S.A. 160 E4
Harriston Canada 164 E2
Harrisville MI U.S.A. 164 D1
Harrisville NY U.S.A. 165 H1
Harrisville PA U.S.A. 164 E3
Harrisville WV U.S.A. 164 E4
Harrodsburg IN U.S.A. 164 B4
Harrodsburg KY U.S.A. 164 C5
Harrodsville N.Z. see Otorohanga
Harrogate U.K. 58 F5
Harrowsmith Canada 165 G1
Harry S. Truman Reservoir U.S.A. 160 E4
Har Sai Shan mt. Qinghai China 94 D5
Harsefeld Germany 63 J1
Harsīn Iran 110 B3
Harşit r. Turkey 112 E2
Hârşova Romania 69 L2
Harstad Norway 54 J2
Harsud India 104 D5
Harsum Germany 63 J2
Hart r. Canada 146 E3
Hart U.S.A. 164 B2
Hartao Liaoning China 95 J3
Hartbees watercourse S. Africa 124 E5
Hartberg Austria 57 O7
Harteigan mt. Norway 55 E6
Harter Fell hill U.K. 58 E4

▶Hartford CT U.S.A. 165 I3
Capital of Connecticut.

Hartford KY U.S.A. 164 B5
Hartford MI U.S.A. 164 B2
Hartford City U.S.A. 164 C3
Hartland U.K. 59 C8
Hartland U.S.A. 165 K1
Hartland Point U.K. 59 C7
Hartlepool U.K. 58 F4
Hartley U.S.A. 161 C5
Hartley Zimbabwe see Chegutu
Hartley Bay Canada 150 D4
Hartola Fin. 55 O6
Harts r. S. Africa 125 G5
Härtsfeld hills Germany 63 K6
Harts Range mts Australia 135 F5
Hartsville U.S.A. 164 B5
Hartswater S. Africa 124 G4
Hartville U.S.A. 161 E4
Hartwell U.S.A. 163 D5
Harue Japan 92 C2
Haruku i. Maluku Indon. 83 D3
Haruna Japan 93 E2
Haruno Japan 93 D3
Har Us Nuur l. Mongolia 94 C2
Har Us Nuur salt l. Mongolia 94 C1
Haruuhin Gol r. Mongolia 94 F1
Harūz-e Bālā Iran 110 E4
Harvard, Mount U.S.A. 156 G5
Harvey Australia 135 A8
Harvey U.S.A. 160 C2
Harvey Mountain U.S.A. 158 C1
Harwich U.K. 59 I7
Haryana state India 104 D3
Harz hills Germany 57 M5
Har Zin Israel 107 B4
Ḥaṣāh, Wādī al watercourse Jordan 107 B4
Ḥaṣāh, Wādī al watercourse Jordan/Saudi Arabia 107 C4
Hasalbag Xinjiang China 99 B5
Ḥasanah, Wādī watercourse Egypt 107 A4
Hasan Dağı mts Turkey 112 D3
Hasan Guli Turkm. see Esenguly
Hasankeyf Turkey 113 F3
Hasan Kūleh Afgh. 111 F3
Hasanur India 106 C4
Hasardag mt. Turkm. 110 E2
Hasbaïya Lebanon 107 B3
Hasbaya Lebanon see Hasbaïya
Hase r. Germany 63 H2
Hase Japan 93 E3
Haselünne Germany 63 H2
Hashaat Arhangay Mongolia 94 E2
Hashaat Mongolia see Delgerhangay
Hashak Iran 111 F5
HaSharon plain Israel 107 B3
Hashima Japan 92 C3
Hashimoto Japan 92 B4
Hashtgerd Iran 110 C3
Hashtpar Iran 110 C2
Hashtrud Iran 110 B2
Haskell U.S.A. 161 D5
Haslemere U.K. 59 G7
Hăşmaşul Mare mt. Romania 69 K1
Ḥaṣṣ, Jabal al hills Syria 107 C1
Hassan India 106 C3
Hassayampa watercourse U.S.A. 159 G5
Haßberge hills Germany 63 K4
Hasselt Belgium 62 F4
Hasselt Neth. 62 G2
Hassi Bel Guebbour Alg. 120 D2
Hassi Messaoud Alg. 64 F5
Hässleholm Sweden 55 H8
Hastings Australia 138 B7
Hastings r. Australia 138 F3
Hastings Canada 165 G1
Hastings N.Z. 139 F4
Hastings U.K. 59 H8
Hastings MI U.S.A. 164 C2
Hastings MN U.S.A. 160 E2
Hastings NE U.S.A. 160 D3
Hasuda Japan 93 F3
Hasunuma Japan 93 G3
Hata India 105 E4
Hata Japan 93 D2
Hatanbulag Mongolia 95 G3
Hatansuudal Mongolia see Bayanlig
Hatashō Japan 92 C3
Hatay Turkey see Antakya
Hatay prov. Turkey 107 C1
Hatch U.S.A. 159 G3
Hatches Creek (abandoned) Australia 136 A4
Hatchet Lake Canada 151 K3
Hatfield Australia 138 A4
Hatfield U.K. 58 G5
Hatgal Mongolia 94 E1
Hath India 106 D1
Hat Head National Park Australia 138 F3
Hathras India 104 D4
Ha Tiên Vietnam 87 D5
Ha Tinh Vietnam 86 D3
Hatisar Bhutan see Geylegphug
Hatod India 104 C5
Hato Hud East Timor see Hatudo
Hatra Iraq 113 F4
Hatsu-shima i. Japan 93 F3
Hattah Australia 137 C7
Hattah Kulkyne National Park Australia 137 C7
Hatteras, Cape U.S.A. 163 F5
Hatteras Abyssal Plain sea feature S. Atlantic Ocean 184 D4
Hattfjelldal Norway 54 H4
Hattiesburg U.S.A. 161 F6
Hattingen Germany 63 H3
Hatton, Gunung hill Malaysia 85 G1
Hattori-gawa r. Japan 92 C4
Hattras Passage Myanmar 87 B4
Hatudo East Timor 83 C5
Hat Yai Thai. 87 C6
Hau Bon Vietnam see A Yun Pa
Haubstadt U.S.A. 164 B4
Haud reg. Eth. 122 E3
Hauge Norway 55 E7
Haugesund Norway 55 D7
Haukeligrend Norway 55 E7
Haukipudas Fin. 54 N4
Haukivesi l. Fin. 54 P5
Haultain r. Canada 151 J4
Hauraki Gulf N.Z. 139 E3
Haut Atlas mts Morocco 64 C5
Haute-Normandie admin. reg. France 62 B5
Haute-Volta country Africa see Burkina
Haut-Folin hill France 66 G3
Hauts Plateaux Alg. 64 D5

▶Havana Cuba 169 H4
Capital of Cuba.

Havana U.S.A. 160 F3
Havant U.K. 59 G8
Havasu, Lake U.S.A. 159 F4
Havel r. Germany 63 L2
Havelange Belgium 62 F4
Havelberg Germany 63 M2
Havelock Canada 165 G1
Havelock N.Z. 139 D5
Havelock Swaziland see Bulembu
Havelock U.S.A. 163 E5
Havelock Falls Australia 134 F3
Havelock Island India 87 A5
Havelock North N.Z. 139 F4
Haverfordwest U.K. 59 C7
Haverhill U.S.A. 165 J2
Haveri India 106 B3
Haversin Belgium 62 F4
Havixbeck Germany 63 H3
Havlíčkův Brod Czech Rep. 57 O6
Havøysund Norway 54 N1
Havran Turkey 69 L5
Havre U.S.A. 156 F2
Havre Aubert, Île du i. Canada 153 J5
Havre Rock i. Kermadec Is 133 I5
Havre-St-Pierre Canada 153 J4
Havza Turkey 112 D2
Hawai'i i. U.S.A. 157 [inset]
Hawai'ian Islands N. Pacific Ocean 186 I4
Hawaiian Ridge sea feature N. Pacific Ocean 186 I4
Hawai'i Volcanoes National Park U.S.A. 157 [inset]
Ḥawallī Kuwait 110 C4
Hawar i. Bahrain see Ḥuwār
Hawarden U.K. 58 D5
Hawea, Lake N.Z. 139 B7
Hawera N.Z. 139 E4
Hawes U.K. 58 E4
Hawesville U.S.A. 164 B5
Hāwī U.S.A. 157 [inset]
Hawick U.K. 60 G5
Ḥawīzah, Hawr al imp. l. Iraq 113 G5
Hawkdun Range mts N.Z. 139 B7
Hawke Bay N.Z. 139 F4
Hawkes Bay Canada 153 K4
Hawkins Peak U.S.A. 159 G3
Hawlēr Iraq see Arbīl
Hawley U.S.A. 165 H3
Hawng Luk Myanmar 86 B2
Ḥawrān, Wādī watercourse Iraq 113 F4
Ḥawshah, Jibāl al mts Saudi Arabia 110 B6
Hawston S. Africa 124 D8
Hawthorne U.S.A. 158 D2
Haxat China 90 B3
Haxat Hudag Nei Mongol China 95 H2
Haxby U.K. 58 F4
Hay Australia 138 B5
Hay watercourse Australia 136 B5
Hay r. Canada 150 H2
Haya Seram Indon. 83 D3
Hayachine-san mt. Japan 91 F5
Haya-gawa r. Japan 93 D1
Hayakawa Japan 93 E3
Haya-kawa r. Japan 93 E3
Hayama Japan 93 F3
Hayastan country Asia see Armenia
Haycock AK U.S.A. 148 G2
Haydān, Wādī al r. Jordan 107 B4
Hayden AZ U.S.A. 159 H5
Hayden CO U.S.A. 159 J1
Hayden IN U.S.A. 164 C4
Hayes r. Man. Canada 151 M3
Hayes r. Nunavut Canada 147 I3
Hayes, Mount AK U.S.A. 149 K3
Hayes Halvø pen. Greenland 147 L2
Hayfield Reservoir U.S.A. 159 F5
Hayfork U.S.A. 158 B1
Hayl, Wādī watercourse Syria 107 C3
Hayl, Wādī al watercourse Syria 107 D2
Haylaastay Mongolia see Sühbaatar
Hayle U.K. 59 B8
Haymā' Oman 109 I6
Haymana Turkey 112 D3
Haymarket U.S.A. 165 G4
Hay-on-Wye U.K. 59 D6
Hayrabolu Turkey 69 L4
Hayrhandulaan Mongolia 94 E2
Hay River Canada 146 G3
Hay River Reserve Canada 150 H2
Hays KS U.S.A. 160 D4
Hays MT U.S.A. 156 F2
Ḥays Yemen 108 F7
Haysville U.S.A. 161 D4
Haysyn Ukr. 53 F6
Ḥayṭān, Jabal hill Egypt 107 A4
Hayward CA U.S.A. 158 B3
Hayward WI U.S.A. 160 F2
Haywards Heath U.K. 59 G8
Hazar Turkm. 110 D2
Hazarajat reg. Afgh. 111 G3
Hazard U.S.A. 164 D5
Hazaribag India see Hazaribagh
Hazaribagh India 105 F5
Hazaribagh Range mts India 105 E5
Hazār Masjed, Kūh-e mts Iran 110 E2
Hazebrouck France 62 C4
Hazelton Canada 150 E4
Hazen Bay AK U.S.A. 148 F3
Hazen Strait Canada 147 G2
Hazerswoude-Rijndijk Neth. 62 E2
Hazhdanahr reg. Afgh. 111 G2
Hazlehurst MS U.S.A. 167 H2
Hazleton IN U.S.A. 164 B4
Hazleton PA U.S.A. 165 H3
Hazlett, Lake salt flat Australia 134 E5
Ḥaẓrat-e Solṭān Afgh. 111 G2
Hazu Japan 92 D4
Hazumi-saki pt Japan 92 C4
H. Bouchard Arg. 178 D4
Headford Ireland 61 C4
Headingly Australia 136 B4
Head of Bight b. Australia 135 E7
Healdsburg U.S.A. 158 B2
Healesville Australia 138 B6
Healy AK U.S.A. 149 J3
Healy Lake AK U.S.A. 149 K3
Heanor U.K. 59 F5

▶Heard and McDonald Islands terr. Indian Ocean 185 M9
Australian External Territory.

Heard Island Indian Ocean 185 M9
Hearne U.S.A. 161 D6
Hearne Lake Canada 151 H2
Hearrenfean Neth. see Heerenveen
Hearst Canada 152 E4
Hearst Island Antarctica 188 L2
Heart r. U.S.A. 160 C2
Heart of Neolithic Orkney tourist site U.K. 60 F1
Heathcote Australia 138 B6
Heathfield U.K. 59 H8
Heathsville U.S.A. 165 G5
Hebbardsville U.S.A. 164 B5
Hebbronville U.S.A. 161 D7
Hebei prov. China 95 H4
Hebel Australia 138 C2
Heber U.S.A. 159 H4
Heber City U.S.A. 159 H1
Heber Springs U.S.A. 161 E5
Hebi Henan China 95 H5
Hebian Shanxi China 95 H4
Hebron Canada 153 J2
Hebron U.S.A. 160 D3
Hebron West Bank 107 B4
Hecate Strait B.C. Canada 149 O5
Hecelchakán Mex. 167 H4
Hecheng Jiangxi China see Zixi
Hecheng Zhejiang China see Qingtian
Hechi China 97 F3
Hechuan Chongqing China 96 E2
Hechuan Jiangxi China see Yongxing
Hecla Island Canada 151 L5
Heda Japan 93 E4
Hede China see Sheyang
Hede Sweden 54 H5
Hedemora Sweden 55 I6
He Devil Mountain U.S.A. 156 D3
Hedionda Grande Mex. 167 E3
Hedi Shuiku resr China 97 F4
Heech Neth. see Heeg
Heeg Neth. 62 F2
Heek Germany 62 H2
Heer Belgium 62 E4
Heerde Neth. 62 G2
Heerenveen Neth. 62 F2
Heerhugowaard Neth. 62 E2
Heerlen Neth. 62 F4
Hefa Israel see Haifa
Hefa, Mifraz Israel see Haifa, Bay of
Hefei China 97 H2
Hefeng China 97 F2
Heflin U.S.A. 163 C5
Hegang China 90 C3
Heho Myanmar 86 B2
Heidan r. Jordan see Haydān, Wādī al
Heidberg hill Germany 63 L3
Heide Germany 57 L3
Heide Namibia 124 C2
Heidelberg Germany 63 I5
Heidelberg S. Africa 125 I4
Heidenheim an der Brenz Germany 63 K6
Heihe China 90 B2
Heilbron S. Africa 125 H4
Heilbronn Germany 63 J5
Heiligenhafen Germany 57 M3
Hei Ling Chau i. H.K. China 97 [inset]
Heilongjiang prov. China 95 J2

Heilong Jiang r. China 90 D2
also known as Amur (Rus. Fed.)
Heilong Jiang r. Rus. Fed. see Amur
Heilsbronn Germany 63 K5
Heilungkiang prov. China see Heilongjiang
Heimahe Qinghai China 94 D4
Heinola Fin. 55 O6
Heinze Islands Myanmar 87 B4
Heiquan Gansu China 94 D4
Heirnkut Myanmar 86 A1
Heishan Liaoning China 95 J3
Heishantou Nei Mongol China 95 I1
Heishantou Xinjiang China 94 B2
Heishi Beihu l. Xizang China 99 C6
Heishui China 96 D1
Heisker Islands U.K. see Monach Islands
Heist-op-den-Berg Belgium 62 E3
Heiṭân, Gebel hill Egypt see Ḥayṭān, Jabal
Heituo Shan mt. Shanxi China 95 H4
Hejaz reg. Saudi Arabia see Hijaz
Hejian Hebei China 95 I4
Hejiang China 96 E2
He Jiang r. China 97 F4
Hejiao Nei Mongol China 95 G3
Hejin Shanxi China 95 G5
Hejing Xinjiang China 98 D4
Hekimhan Turkey 112 E3
Hekinan Japan 92 C4
Hekla vol. Iceland 54 [inset]
Heko-san mt. Japan 92 C3
Hekou Gansu China 94 E4
Hekou Hubei China 97 G2
Hekou Jiangxi China see Yanshan
Hekou Sichuan China see Yajiang
Hekou Yunnan China 96 D4
Helagsfjället mt. Sweden 54 H5
Helam India 96 B3
Helan Shan mts China 94 F4
Helbra Germany 63 L3
Helen atoll Palau 81 I6
Helena AR U.S.A. 161 F5

▶Helena MT U.S.A. 156 E3
Capital of Montana.

Helen Reef Palau 81 I6
Helensburgh U.K. 60 E4
Helen Springs Australia 134 F4
Ḥelez Israel 107 B4
Helgoland i. Germany 57 K3
Helgoländer Bucht g. Germany 57 L3
Heligoland i. Germany see Helgoland
Heligoland Bight g. Germany see Helgoländer Bucht
Heliopolis Lebanon see Ba'albek
Helixi China see Ningguo
Hella Iceland 54 [inset]
Helland Norway 54 J2
Hellas country Europe see Greece
Helleh r. Iran 110 C4
Hellespont strait Turkey see Dardanelles
Hellevoetsluis Neth. 62 E3
Hellhole Gorge National Park Australia 136 D5
Hellín Spain 67 F4
Hellinikon tourist site Greece 112 A3
Hells Canyon gorge U.S.A. 156 D3
Hell-Ville Madag. see Andoany
Helmand prov. Afgh. 111 F4
Helmand r. Afgh. 111 F4
Helmantica Spain see Salamanca
Helmbrechts Germany 63 L4
Helme r. Germany 63 L3
Helmeringhausen Namibia 124 C3
Helmet Mountain AK U.S.A. 149 K2
Helmond Neth. 62 F3
Helmsdale U.K. 60 F2
Helmsdale r. U.K. 60 F2
Helmstedt Germany 63 L2
Helong China 90 C4
Helper U.S.A. 159 H2
Helpter Berge hills Germany 63 N1
Helsingborg Sweden 55 H8
Helsingfors Fin. see Helsinki
Helsingør Denmark 55 H8

▶Helsinki Fin. 55 N6
Capital of Finland.

Helston U.K. 59 B8
Helvécia Brazil 179 D2
Helvetic Republic country Europe see Switzerland
Ḥelwân Egypt see Ḥulwān
Hemel Hempstead U.K. 59 G7
Hemet U.S.A. 158 E5
Hemingford U.S.A. 160 C3
Hemlock Lake U.S.A. 165 G2
Hemmingen Germany 63 J2
Hemmingford Canada 165 I1
Hemmoor Germany 63 J1
Hempstead U.S.A. 161 D6
Hemsby U.K. 59 I6
Hemse Sweden 55 K8
Henan Qinghai China 94 E5
Henan prov. China 97 G1
Henares r. Spain 67 E3
Henashi-zaki pt Japan 91 E4
Henbury Australia 135 F6
Hendek Turkey 69 N4
Henderson KY U.S.A. 164 B5
Henderson NC U.S.A. 162 E4
Henderson NV U.S.A. 159 F3
Henderson NY U.S.A. 165 G2
Henderson TN U.S.A. 161 F5
Henderson TX U.S.A. 161 E5
Henderson Island Pitcairn Is 187 L7
Hendersonville NC U.S.A. 163 D5
Hendersonville TN U.S.A. 164 B5
Henderville atoll Kiribati see Aranuka
Hendon U.K. 59 G7
Hendorābī i. Iran 110 D5
Hendy-Gwyn U.K. see Whitland
Hengām Iran 111 E5
Hengduan Shan mts China 96 C2
Hengelo Neth. 62 G2
Hengfeng China 97 H2
Hengnan China see Hengyang
Hengshan China 90 C3
Hengshan Shaanxi China 95 G4
Heng Shan mt. China 97 G3
Heng Shan mts China 95 H4
Hengshui Hebei China 95 H4
Hengshui Jiangxi China see Chongyi
Hengxian China 97 F4
Hengyang Hunan China 97 G3
Hengyang Hunan China 97 G3
Hengzhou China see Hengxian
Heniches'k Ukr. 53 G7
Henley N.Z. 139 C7
Henley-on-Thames U.K. 59 G7
Henlopen, Cape U.S.A. 165 H4
Hennef (Sieg) Germany 63 H4
Hennenman S. Africa 125 H4
Hennepin U.S.A. 160 F3
Hennessey U.S.A. 161 D4
Hennigsdorf Berlin Germany 63 N2
Henniker U.S.A. 165 J2
Henning U.S.A. 164 B3
Henrietta U.S.A. 161 D5
Henrietta Maria, Cape Canada 152 E3
Henrieville U.S.A. 159 H3
Henrique de Carvalho Angola see Saurimo
Henry, Cape U.S.A. 165 G5
Henry Ice Rise Antarctica 188 A1
Henryk Arctowski research station Antarctica see Arctowski
Henry Kater, Cape Canada 147 L3
Henry Mountains U.S.A. 159 H2
Hensall Canada 164 E2
Henshaw, Lake U.S.A. 158 E5
Hentiesbaai Namibia 124 B2
Hentiy prov. Mongolia 95 G2
Henty Australia 138 C5
Henzada Myanmar see Hinthada
Heping Guangdong China 97 G3
Heping Guizhou China see Huishui
Heping Guizhou China see Yanhe
Hepo China see Jiexi
Heppner U.S.A. 156 D3
Heptanesus is Ionia Nisia Greece see Ionian Islands
Heptanesus is Greece see Ionian Islands
Hepu China 97 F4
Heqiao Gansu China 94 E4
Heqing China 96 D3
Hequ Shanxi China 95 G4
Heraclea Turkey see Ereğli
Heraclea Pontica Turkey see Ereğli
Heraklion Greece see Iraklion
Herald Cays atolls Australia 136 E3
Herāt Afgh. 111 F3
Hérault r. France 66 F5
Herbertabad India 87 A5
Herbert Downs Australia 136 B4
Herbert Island AK U.S.A. 148 E5
Herbert River Falls National Park Australia 136 D3
Herbert Wash salt flat Australia 135 D6
Herborn Germany 63 I4
Herbstein Germany 63 J4
Hercules Dome ice feature Antarctica 188 K1
Herdecke Germany 63 H3
Herdorf Germany 63 H4
Heredia Costa Rica 166 [inset] I7
Hereford U.K. 59 E6
Hereford U.S.A. 161 C5
Héréhérétué atoll Fr. Polynesia 187 K7
Herent Belgium 62 E4
Herford Germany 63 I2
Heringen (Werra) Germany 63 K4
Herington U.S.A. 160 D4
Herīs Iran 110 B2
Herisau Switz. 66 I3
Herkimer U.S.A. 165 H2
Herlen Mongolia 95 G2
Herlen Gol r. China/Mongolia 89 L3
Herlen He r. China/Mongolia see Herlen Gol
Herleshausen Germany 63 K3
Herlong U.S.A. 158 C1
Herm i. Channel Is 59 E9
Hermanas Mex. 167 E3
Herma Ness hd U.K. 60 [inset]
Hermann U.S.A. 160 F4
Hermannsburg Germany 63 K2
Hermanus S. Africa 124 D8
Hermel Lebanon 107 C2
Hermes, Cape S. Africa 125 I6
Hermidale Australia 138 C3
Hermiston U.S.A. 156 D3
Hermitage MO U.S.A. 160 E4
Hermitage PA U.S.A. 164 E3
Hermitage Bay Canada 153 K5
Hermite, Islas is Chile 178 C9
Hermit Islands P.N.G. 81 L7
Hermon, Mount Lebanon/Syria 107 B3
Hermonthis Egypt see Armant
Hermopolis Magna Egypt see Al Ashmūnayn
Hermosa U.S.A. 159 J3
Hermosillo Mex. 166 C2
Hernandarias Para. 178 F3
Hernando U.S.A. 161 F5
Herndon CA U.S.A. 158 D3
Herndon PA U.S.A. 165 G3
Herndon WV U.S.A. 164 E5
Herne Germany 63 H3
Herne Bay U.K. 59 I7
Herning Denmark 55 F8
Heroica Nogales Mex. see Nogales
Heroica Puebla de Zaragoza Mex. see Puebla
Hérouville-St-Clair France 59 G9
Herowābād Iran see Khalkhāl
Herradura Mex. 167 E4
Herrera del Duque Spain 67 D4
Herrero, Punta pt Mex. 167 I5
Herrieden Germany 63 K5
Herschel Y.T. Canada 149 M1
Herschel Island Y.T. Canada 149 M1
Hershey U.S.A. 165 G3
Hertford U.K. 59 G7
Hertzogville S. Africa 125 G5
Herve Belgium 62 F4
Hervé, Lac l. Canada 153 H3
Hervey Islands Cook Is 187 J7
Herzberg Brandenburg Germany 63 M2
Herzberg Brandenburg Germany 63 N3
Herzlake Germany 63 H2
Herzliyya Israel 107 B3
Herzogenaurach Germany 63 K5
Herzsprung Germany 63 M1
Ḥeṣār Iran 110 C4
Ḥeṣār Iran 110 E5
Hesdin France 62 C4
Hesel Germany 63 H1
Heshan China 97 F4
Heshengqiao China 97 G2
Heshui Gansu China 95 G5
Heshun Shanxi China 95 H4
Hesperia U.S.A. 158 E4
Hesperus U.S.A. 159 I3
Hesperus, Mount AK U.S.A. 148 I3
Hesperus Peak U.S.A. 159 I3
Hesquiat Canada 150 E5
Hess r. Y.T. Canada 149 N3
Hess Creek r. AK U.S.A. 149 J2
Heßdorf Germany 63 K5
Hesse land Germany see Hessen
Hesselberg hill Germany 63 K5
Hessen land Germany 63 J4
Hessisch Lichtenau Germany 63 J3
Hess Mountains Y.T. Canada 149 N3
Het r. Laos 86 D2
Heteren Neth. 62 F3
Hetou China 97 F4
Hettinger U.S.A. 160 C2
Hetton U.K. 58 E4
Hettstedt Germany 63 L3
Heung Kong Tsai H.K. China see Aberdeen
Ḥevron West Bank see Hebron
Hexham U.K. 58 E4
Hexian Anhui China 97 H2
Hexian Guangxi China see Hezhou
Hexigten Qi Nei Mongol China see Jingpeng
Hexipu Gansu China 94 E4
Heyang Shaanxi China 95 G5
Ḥeydarābād Iran 110 B2
Ḥeydarābād Iran 111 F4
Heydebreck Poland see Kędzierzyn-Koźle
Heyin Qinghai China see Guide
Heysham U.K. 58 E4
Heyshope Dam S. Africa 125 J4
Heyuan China 97 G4
Heywood U.K. 58 E5
Heze Shandong China 95 H5
Hezhang China 96 E3
Hezheng Gansu China 94 E5
Hezhou China 97 F3
Hezuo Gansu China 94 E5
Hialeah U.S.A. 163 D7
Hiawassee U.S.A. 163 D5
Hiawatha U.S.A. 160 E4
Hibbing U.S.A. 160 E2
Hibbs, Point Australia 137 [inset]
Hibernia Reef Australia 134 C3
Hīchān Iran 111 F5
Hichisō Japan 92 D3
Hicks, Point Australia 138 D6
Hicks Bay N.Z. 139 G3
Hicks Cays is Belize 167 H5
Hicks Lake Canada 151 K2
Hicksville U.S.A. 164 C3
Hico U.S.A. 161 D5
Hida-gawa r. Japan 92 D3
Hidaka Hyōgo Japan 92 A3
Hidaka Saitama Japan 93 F3
Hidaka Wakayama Japan 92 B5
Hidaka-gawa r. Japan 92 B5
Hidaka-sanmyaku mts Japan 90 F4
Hida-Kiso-gawa Kokutei-kōen park Japan 92 D3
Hida-kōchi plat. Japan 92 C2
Hidalgo Coahuila Mex. 167 F3
Hidalgo Mex. 161 D7
Hidalgo state Mex. 167 F4
Hidalgo del Parral Mex. 166 D3
Hidalgotitlán Mex. 167 G5
Hida-sanmyaku mts Japan 92 D2
Hidrolândia Brazil 179 A2
Hierosolyma Israel/West Bank see Jerusalem
Higashi Japan 93 G1
Higashiizu Japan 93 F4
Higashi-Matsuyama Japan 93 F2
Higashimurayama Japan 93 F3
Higashi-Ōsaka Japan 92 B4
Higashi-Shirakawa Japan 92 D3
Higashi-suidō sea chan. Japan 91 C6
Higashiura Aichi Japan 92 C4
Higashiura Hyōgo Japan 92 A4
Higashi-yama mt. Japan 93 D2
Higgins U.S.A. 161 C4
Higgins Bay U.S.A. 165 H2
Higgins Lake U.S.A. 164 C1
High Atlas mts Morocco see Haut Atlas
High Desert U.S.A. 156 C4
High Island i. H.K. China 97 [inset]
High Island U.S.A. 161 E6
High Island Reservoir H.K. China 97 [inset]
Highland Peak CA U.S.A. 158 D2
Highland Peak NV U.S.A. 159 F3
Highlands U.S.A. 165 I3
Highland Springs U.S.A. 165 G5
High Level Canada 150 G3
Highmore U.S.A. 160 D2
High Point U.S.A. 162 E5
High Point hill U.S.A. 165 H3
High Prairie Canada 150 G4
High River Canada 150 H5
Highrock Lake Man. Canada 151 K4
Highrock Lake Sask. Canada 151 J3
High Springs U.S.A. 163 D6
High Tatras mts Poland/Slovakia see Tatra Mountains
High Wycombe U.K. 59 G7
Higuera de Abuya Mex. 166 D3
Higuera de Zaragoza Mex. 166 C3
Higüey Dom. Rep. 169 K5
Higuri-gawa r. Japan 93 F3
Hiiumaa i. Estonia 55 M7
Hijānah, Buḥayrat al imp. l. Syria 107 C3
Hijau, Gunung mt. Indon. 84 C3
Hijaz reg. Saudi Arabia 108 E4
Hijiri-dake mt. Japan 93 E3
Hikabo-yama mt. Japan 93 E2
Hikami Japan 92 B3
Hikata Japan 93 G3
Hiki-gawa r. Japan 92 B5
Ḥikmah, Ra's al pt Egypt 112 B5
Hiko U.S.A. 159 F3
Hikone Japan 92 C3
Hikurangi mt. N.Z. 139 G3
Hila Maluku Indon. 83 C4
Hilahila Sulawesi Indon. 83 B4
Hilāl, Jabal hill Egypt 107 A4
Hilāl, Ra's al pt Libya 108 B3
Hilary Coast Antarctica 188 H1
Hildale U.S.A. 159 G3
Hildburghausen Germany 63 K4
Hilders Germany 63 K4
Hildesheim Germany 63 J2
Hillah Iraq 113 G4
Hill Bank Belize 167 H5
Hill City U.S.A. 160 D4
Hillegom Neth. 62 E2
Hill End Australia 138 D4
Hillerød Denmark 55 H9
Hillgrove Australia 136 D3
Hill Island Lake Canada 151 I2
Hillman U.S.A. 164 D1
Hillsboro ND U.S.A. 160 D2
Hillsboro NM U.S.A. 157 G6
Hillsboro OH U.S.A. 164 D4
Hillsboro OR U.S.A. 156 C3
Hillsboro TX U.S.A. 161 D5
Hillsdale IN U.S.A. 164 B4
Hillsdale MI U.S.A. 164 C3
Hillside Australia 134 B5
Hillston Australia 138 B4
Hillsville U.S.A. 164 E5
Hilo U.S.A. 157 [inset]
Hilton Australia 136 B4
Hilton S. Africa 125 J5
Hilton U.S.A. 165 G2
Hilton Head Island U.S.A. 163 D5
Hilvan Turkey 112 E3
Hilversum Neth. 62 F2
Himachal Pradesh state India 104 D3
Himaga-shima i. Japan 92 D4
Himalaya mts Asia 104 D2
Himalchul mt. Nepal 105 F3
Himanka Fin. 54 M4
Ḥimār, Wādī al watercourse Syria/Turkey 107 D1
Himarë Albania 69 H4
Himatnagar India 104 C5
Hime-gawa r. Japan 93 D1
Himeji Japan 92 A4
Himi Japan 92 C2
Ḥimṣ Syria see Homs
Ḥimṣ, Baḥrat resr Syria see Qaṭṭīnah, Buḥayrat
Hinako i. Indon. 84 B2
Hinatuan Mindanao Phil. 82 D4
Hinatuan Passage Phil. 82 D4
Hîncești Moldova 69 M1
Hinchinbrook Entrance sea channel AK U.S.A. 149 K3
Hinchinbrook Island Australia 136 D3
Hinchinbrook Island AK U.S.A. 149 K3
Hinckley U.K. 59 F6
Hinckley MN U.S.A. 160 E2
Hinckley UT U.S.A. 159 G2
Hinckley Reservoir U.S.A. 165 H2
Hindan r. India 99 B7
Hindaun India 104 D4
Hinderwell U.K. 58 G4
Hindley U.K. 58 E5
Hindman U.S.A. 164 D5
Hindmarsh, Lake dry lake Australia 137 C8
Hindu Kush mts Afgh./Pak. 111 G3
Hindupur India 106 C3
Hines Creek Canada 150 G3
Hinesville U.S.A. 163 D6
Hinganghat India 106 C1
Hingoli India 106 C2
Hınıs Turkey 113 F3
Hinnøya i. Norway 54 I2
Hino Shiga Japan 92 C3
Hino Tōkyō Japan 93 F3
Hinobaan Negros Phil. 82 C4
Hinoemata Japan 93 F1
Hino-gawa r. Japan 92 C2
Hino-gawa r. Japan 92 C3
Hinojosa del Duque Spain 67 D4
Hino-misaki pt Japan 92 B5
Hinsdale U.S.A. 165 I2
Hinte Germany 63 H1
Hinthada Myanmar 86 A3
Hinton Canada 150 G4
Hinton U.S.A. 164 E5
Hi-numa l. Japan 93 G2
Hiort i. U.K. see St Kilda
Hippolytushoef Neth. 62 E2
Hipponium Italy see Vibo Valentia
Hippo Regius Alg. see Annaba
Hippo Zarytus Tunisia see Bizerte
Hirabit Dağ mt. Turkey 113 G3
Hiraga-take mt. Japan 93 F1
Hirakata Japan 92 B4
Hirakud Dam India 105 E5
Hirakud Reservoir India 105 E5
Hirapur India 104 D4
Hiratsuka Japan 93 F3
Hiraya Japan 92 D3
Hiriyur India 106 C3
Hirokawa Japan 92 B4
Hirosaki Japan 90 F4
Hiroshima Japan 91 D6
Hirschaid Germany 63 L5
Hirschberg Germany 63 L4
Hirschberg mt. Germany 57 M7
Hirschberg Poland see Jelenia Góra
Hirschenstein mt. Germany 63 M6
Hirson France 62 E5
Hîrșova Romania see Hârșova
Hirta is U.K. see St Kilda
Hirtshals Denmark 55 F8
Hiruga-take mt. Japan 93 F3
Hirukawa Japan 92 D3
Hisai Japan 92 C4
Hisar India 104 C3
Hisar Iran 110 C2
Hisarköy Turkey see Domaniç
Hisarönü Turkey 69 O4
Ḥisb, Sha'īb watercourse Iraq 113 G5
Ḥisbān Jordan 107 B4
Hishig-Öndör Bulgan Mongolia 94 E1
Hisiu P.N.G. 81 L8
Hisor Tajik. 111 H2
Hisor Tizmasi mts Tajik./Uzbek. see Gissar Range
Hispalis Spain see Seville
Hispania country Europe see Spain

▶Hispaniola i. Caribbean Sea 169 J4
Consists of the Dominican Republic and Haiti.

Hispur Glacier Pak. 104 C1
Hissar India see Hisar
Hisua India 105 F4
Ḥisyah Syria 107 C2
Hīt Iraq 113 F4
Hitachi Japan 93 G2
Hitachinaka Japan 93 G2
Hitachi-Ōta Japan 93 G2
Hitra i. Norway 54 F5
Hitzacker Germany 63 L1
Hiuchiga-take vol. Japan 93 F2
Hiva Oa i. Fr. Polynesia 187 K6
Hixon Canada 150 F4
Hixson Cay reef Australia 136 F4
Hiyoshi Kyōto Japan 92 B3
Hiyoshi Nagano Japan 92 D3
Hiyyon watercourse Israel 107 B4
Hizan Turkey 113 F3
Hjälmaren l. Sweden 55 I7
Hjerkinn Norway 54 F5
Hjo Sweden 55 I7
Hjørring Denmark 55 G8
Hkakabo Razi mt. China/Myanmar 96 C2
Hlaingdet Myanmar 86 B2
Hlako Kangri mt. Xizang China see Lhagoi Kangri
Hlane Royal National Park Swaziland 125 J4
Hlatikulu Swaziland 125 J4
Hlegu Myanmar 86 B3
Hlohlowane S. Africa 125 H5
Hlotse Lesotho 125 I5
Hluhluwe-Umfolozi Park nature res. S. Africa 125 J5
Hlukhiv Ukr. 53 G6
Hlung-Tan Myanmar 86 B2
Hlusha Belarus 53 F5
Hlybokaye Belarus 55 O9
Ho Ghana 120 D4
Hoa Binh Vietnam 86 D2
Hoa Binh Vietnam 86 D3
Hoachanas Namibia 124 D2
Hoagland U.S.A. 164 C3
Hoang Liên Sơn mts Vietnam 86 C2
Hoang Sa is S. China Sea see Paracel Islands
Hoan Lao Vietnam 86 D3

▶Hobart Australia 137 [inset]
Capital of Tasmania.

Hobart U.S.A. 161 D5
Hobbs U.S.A. 161 C5
Hobbs Coast Antarctica 188 J1
Hobe Sound U.S.A. 163 D7
Hobiganj Bangl. see Habiganj
Hoboksar Xinjiang China 98 D3
Hobor Nei Mongol China 95 H3
Hobro Denmark 55 F8
Hobyo Somalia 122 E3
Hoceima, Baie d'Al b. Morocco 67 E6
Hochandochtla Mountain hill AK U.S.A. 148 I2
Höchberg Germany 63 J5
Hochfeiler mt. Austria/Italy see Gran Pilastro
Hochfeld Namibia 123 B6
Hochharz nat. park Germany 63 K3
Hô Chi Minh Vietnam see Ho Chi Minh City
Ho Chi Minh City Vietnam 87 D5
Hochschwab mt. Austria 57 O7
Hochschwab mts Austria 57 O7
Hockenheim Germany 63 I5
Ḥôḍ reg. Mauritania 120 C3
Hodal Haryana India 99 B8
Hōdatsu-san hill Japan 92 C2
Hoddesdon U.K. 59 G7
Hodeidah Yemen 108 F7
Hodgenville U.S.A. 164 C5
Hodgson Downs Australia 134 F3
Hódmezővásárhely Hungary 69 I1
Hodna, Chott el salt l. Alg. 67 I6
Hodo-dan pt N. Korea 91 B5
Hödrögö Mongolia see Nömrög
Hodzana r. AK U.S.A. 149 K2
Hoek van Holland Neth. see Hook of Holland
Hoensbroek Neth. 62 F4
Hoeryŏng N. Korea 90 C4
Hof Germany 63 L4
Hoffman Mountain U.S.A. 165 I2
Hofheim in Unterfranken Germany 63 K4
Hofmeyr S. Africa 125 G6
Höfn Iceland 54 [inset]
Hofors Sweden 55 J6
Hofsjökull ice cap Iceland 54 [inset]
Hofsós Iceland 54 [inset]
Hōfu Japan 91 C6
Hofūf Saudi Arabia 108 G4
Höganäs Sweden 55 H8
Hogan Group is Australia 138 C7
Hogansburg U.S.A. 165 H1
Hogatza AK U.S.A. 148 I2
Hogatza r. AK U.S.A. 148 I2
Hogback Mountain U.S.A. 160 C3
Hoge Vaart canal Neth. 62 F2
Hogg, Mount Y.T. Canada 149 N3
Hoggar plat. Alg. 120 D2
Hog Island U.S.A. 165 H5
Högsby Sweden 55 J8
Hohenloher Ebene plain Germany 63 J5
Hohenmölsen Germany 63 M3
Hohennauen Germany 63 M2
Hohensalza Poland see Inowrocław
Hohenwald U.S.A. 162 C5
Hohenwartetalsperre resr Germany 63 L4
Hoher Dachstein mt. Austria 57 N7
Hoh Ereg Nei Mongol China see Wuchuan
Hohe Rhön mts Germany 63 J4
Hohe Tauern mts Austria 57 N7
Hohe Venn moorland Belgium 62 G4
Hohhot Nei Mongol China 95 G3
Höhmorït Mongolia 94 C2
Hohneck mt. France 66 H2
Hoholitna r. AK U.S.A. 148 H3
Hoh Sai Hu l. Qinghai China 94 C5
Hoh Xil Hu salt l. China 99 E6
Hoh Xil Shan mts China 99 E6
Hoh Yanhu salt l. Qinghai China 94 D4
Hôi An Vietnam 86 E4
Hoika Qinghai China 94 D5
Hoima Uganda 122 D3
Hoit Taria Qinghai China 94 D4
Hojagala Turkm. 110 E2
Hojai India 105 H4
Hojambaz Turkm. 111 G2
Højryggen mts Greenland 147 M2
Hōki-gawa r. Japan 93 G2
Hokitika N.Z. 139 C6
Hokkaidō i. Japan 90 F4
Hokksund Norway 55 F7
Hokota Japan 93 G2
Hokudan Japan 92 A4
Hokunō Japan 92 C3
Hokusei Japan 92 C3
Hol Norway 55 F6
Holbæk Denmark 55 G9
Holbeach U.K. 59 H6
Holbrook Australia 138 C5
Holbrook U.S.A. 159 H4
Holden U.S.A. 159 G2
Holdenville U.S.A. 161 D5
Holdrege U.S.A. 160 D3
Holgate U.S.A. 164 C3
Holguín Cuba 169 I4
Holikachuk AK U.S.A. 148 H3
Holitna r. AK U.S.A. 148 H3
Höljes Sweden 55 H6
Holland country Europe see Netherlands
Holland MI U.S.A. 164 B2
Holland NY U.S.A. 165 F2
Hollandia Indon. see Jayapura
Hollick-Kenyon Peninsula Antarctica 188 L2
Hollick-Kenyon Plateau Antarctica 188 K1
Hollidaysburg U.S.A. 165 F3
Hollis AK U.S.A. 149 N5
Hollis OK U.S.A. 161 D5
Hollister U.S.A. 158 C3
Holly U.S.A. 164 D2
Hollyhill U.S.A. 164 C5
Holly Springs U.S.A. 161 F5
Hollywood CA U.S.A. 159 D4
Hollywood FL U.S.A. 163 D7
Holm Norway 54 H4
Holman Canada see Ulukhaktok
Holmes Reef Australia 136 D3
Holmestrand Norway 55 G7
Holmgard Rus. Fed. see Velikiy Novgorod
Holm Ø i. Greenland see Kiatassuaq
Holmön i. Sweden 54 L5
Holmsund Sweden 54 L5
Holokuk Mountain hill AK U.S.A. 148 H3
Ḥolon Israel 107 B3
Holoog Namibia 124 C4
Holothuria Banks reef Australia 134 D3
Holroyd r. Australia 136 C2
Holstebro Denmark 55 F8
Holstein U.S.A. 160 E3
Holsteinsborg Greenland see Sisimiut
Holston r. U.S.A. 162 D4
Holsworthy U.K. 59 C8
Holt U.K. 59 I6
Holt U.S.A. 164 C2
Holton U.S.A. 164 B2
Holwerd Neth. 62 F1
Holwert Neth. see Holwerd
Holycross Ireland 61 E5
Holy Cross AK U.S.A. 148 H3

Holy Cross, Mount of the U.S.A. 156 G5
Holyhead U.K. **58** C5
Holyhead Bay U.K. **58** C5
Holy Island *England* U.K. **58** F3
Holy Island *Wales* U.K. **58** C5
Holyoke U.S.A. **160** C3
Holy See Europe *see* **Vatican City**
Holywell U.K. **58** D5
Holzhausen Germany **63** M3
Holzkirchen Germany **57** M7
Holzminden Germany **63** J3
Homand Iran **111** E3
Homāyūnshahr Iran *see* **Khomeynīshahr**
Homberg (Efze) Germany **63** J3
Hombori Mali **120** C3
Homburg Germany **63** H5
Home Bay Canada **147** L3
Homécourt France **62** F5
Homer *AK* U.S.A. **149** J4
Homer *GA* U.S.A. **163** D5
Homer *LA* U.S.A. **161** E5
Homer *MI* U.S.A. **164** C2
Homer *NY* U.S.A. **165** G2
Homerville U.S.A. **163** D6
Homestead Australia **136** D4
Homnabad India **106** C2
Homoine Moz. **125** L2
Homs Libya *see* **Al Khums**
Homs Syria **107** C2
Homyel' Belarus **53** F5
Honan *prov.* China *see* **Henan**
Honavar India **106** B3
Honaz Turkey **69** M6
Hon Chông Vietnam **87** D5
Honda Bay *Palawan* Phil. **82** B4
Hondeklipbaai S. Africa **124** C6
Hondo *r.* Belize/Mex. **167** H5
Hondo U.S.A. **161** D6
Hondsrug *reg.* Neth. **62** G1
Honduras *country* Central America **169** G6
Honduras, Gulf of Belize/Hond. **166** [inset] I5
Hønefoss Norway **55** G6
Honesdale U.S.A. **165** H3
Honey Mex. **167** F4
Honey Lake *salt l.* U.S.A. **158** C1
Honeyoye Lake U.S.A. **165** G2
Honfleur France **66** E2
Hong, Mouths of the Vietnam *see* **Red River, Mouths of the**
Hông, Sông *r.* Vietnam *see* **Red**
Hongchengzi *Gansu* China **94** E4
Hongchuan China *see* **Hongya**
Hongde *Gansu* China **95** F4
Honggouzi *Qinghai* China **98** E5
Honggu *Gansu* China **94** E4
Hongguo China *see* **Panxian**
Honghai Wan *b.* China **97** G4
Honghe China **96** D4
Hong He *r.* China **97** G1
Honghu China **97** G2
Hongjialou *Shandong* China *see* **Licheng**
Hongjiang *Hunan* China **97** F3
Hongjiang *Sichuan* China *see* **Wangcang**
Hong Kong *H.K.* China **97** [inset]
Hong Kong *aut. reg.* China **97** [inset]
Hong Kong Harbour *sea chan.* H.K. China **97** [inset]
Hong Kong Island *H.K.* China **97** [inset]
Hongliu Daquan *well Nei Mongol* China **94** D3
Hongliuhe *Gansu* China **94** C3
Hongliu He *r.* China **95** G4
Hongliuquan *Qinghai* China **98** E5
Hongliuwan *Gansu* China *see* **Aksay**
Hongliuyuan *Gansu* China **94** E4
Hongliuyuan *Gansu* China **98** F4
Hongor *Nei Mongol* China **95** H2
Hongor Mongolia *see* **Naran**
Hongqiao China *see* **Qidong**
Hongqicun *Xinjiang* China **94** C3
Hongqizhen *Hainan* China *see* **Wuzhishan**
Hongqizhen China *see* **Wuzhishan**
Hongshansi *Nei Mongol* China **94** F4
Hongshi China **90** B4
Hongshui He *r.* China **96** F4
Hongtong *Shanxi* China **95** G4
Honguedo, Détroit d' *sea chan.* Canada **153** I4
Hongwansi *Gansu* China *see* **Sunan**
Hongwŏn N. Korea **91** B4
Hongxing *Jilin* China **95** J2
Hongya China **96** D2
Hongyashan Shuiku *resr Gansu* China **94** E4
Hongyuan China **96** D1
Hongze China **97** H1
Hongze Hu *l.* China **97** H1

▶**Honiara** Solomon Is **133** F2
Capital of the Solomon Islands.

Honiton U.K. **59** D8
Honjō Japan **91** F5
Honjo Japan **93** D2
Honjō *Saitama* Japan **93** F2
Honkajoki Fin. **55** M6
Honkawane Japan **93** E3
Honningsvåg Norway **54** N1
Honoka'a U.S.A. **157** [inset]

▶**Honolulu** U.S.A. **157** [inset]
Capital of Hawaii.

▶**Honshū** *i.* Japan **91** D6
Largest island in Japan, 3rd largest in Asia and 7th in the world.

Honwad India **106** B2
Hood, Mount *vol.* U.S.A. **156** C3
Hood Bay *AK* U.S.A. **149** N4
Hood Point Australia **135** B8
Hood Point P.N.G. **136** D1
Hood River U.S.A. **156** C3
Hoogeveen Neth. **62** G2
Hoogezand-Sappemeer Neth. **62** G1
Hooghly *r. mouth* India *see* **Hugli**
Hooker U.S.A. **161** C4
Hook Head *hd* Ireland **61** F5
Hook of Holland Neth. **62** E3
Hook Reef Australia **136** E3
Hoolt Mongolia *see* **Tögrög**
Hoonah *AK* U.S.A. **149** N4
Hooper Bay *AK* U.S.A. **148** F3
Hooper Bay *AK* U.S.A. **148** F3
Hooper Island U.S.A. **165** G4
Hoopeston U.S.A. **164** B3
Hoopstad S. Africa **125** G4
Höör Sweden **55** H9
Hoorn Neth. **62** F2
Hoorn, Îles de *is* Wallis and Futuna Is **133** I3
Hōō-san *mt.* Japan **93** E3
Hoosick U.S.A. **165** I2
Hoover Dam U.S.A. **159** F3
Hoover Memorial Reservoir U.S.A. **164** D3
Höövör Mongolia *see* **Baruunbayan-Ulaan**
Hopa Turkey **113** F2
Hope Canada **150** F5
Hope *r.* N.Z. **139** D6
Hope *AK* U.S.A. **149** J3
Hope *AR* U.S.A. **161** E5
Hope *IN* U.S.A. **164** C4
Hope, Lake *salt flat* Australia **135** C8
Hope, Point *pt AK* U.S.A. **148** F1
Hopedale Canada **153** J3
Hopefield S. Africa **124** D7
Hopei *prov.* China *see* **Hebei**
Hopelchén Mex. **167** H5
Hope Mountains Canada **153** J3
Hope Saddle *pass* N.Z. **139** D5
Hopes Advance, Baie *b.* Canada **153** H2
Hopes Advance, Cap *c.* Canada **147** L3
Hopes Advance Bay Canada *see* **Aupaluk**
Hopetoun Australia **137** C7
Hopetown S. Africa **124** G5
Hopewell U.S.A. **165** G5
Hopewell Islands Canada **152** F2
Hopin Myanmar **86** B1
Hopkins *r.* Australia **137** C8
Hopkins, Lake *salt flat* Australia **135** E6
Hopkinsville U.S.A. **164** B5
Hopland U.S.A. **158** B2
Hoquiam U.S.A. **156** C3
Hor *Qinghai* China **94** E5
Hor *Xizang* China **99** C7
Horace Mountain *AK* U.S.A. **149** J2
Horado Japan **92** C3
Hōrai Japan **92** D4
Hōraiji-san *hill* Japan **92** D4
Horasan Turkey **113** F2
Hörby Sweden **55** H9
Horcasitas Mex. **166** D2
Horgo Mongolia *see* **Tariat**
Hörh Uul *mts* Mongolia **94** F3
Horigane Japan **93** D2
Horinger *Nei Mongol* China **95** G3
Horiult Mongolia *see* **Bogd**

▶**Horizon Deep** *sea feature* S. Pacific Ocean **186** I7
Deepest point in the Tonga Trench, and 2nd in the world.

Horki Belarus **53** F5
Horlick Mountains Antarctica **188** K1
Horlivka Ukr. **53** H6
Hormoz *i.* Iran **110** E5
Hormoz, Kūh-e *mt.* Iran **110** D5
Hormuz, Strait of Iran/Oman **110** E5
Horn Austria **57** O6
Horn *r.* Canada **150** G2
Horn *c.* Iceland **54** [inset]

▶**Horn, Cape** Chile **178** C9
Most southerly point of South America.

Hornaday *r. N.W.T.* Canada **149** Q1
Hornavan *l.* Sweden **54** J3
Hornbeck *LA* U.S.A. **167** G2
Hornbrook U.S.A. **156** C4
Hornburg Germany **63** K2
Horncastle U.K. **58** G5
Horndal Sweden **55** J6
Horne, Îles de *is* Wallis and Futuna Is *see* **Hoorn, Îles de**
Horneburg Germany **63** J1
Hörnefors Sweden **54** K5
Hornell U.S.A. **165** G2
Hornepayne Canada **152** D4
Hornillos Mex. **166** C3
Hornisgrinde *mt.* Germany **57** L6
Horn Island *MS* U.S.A. **167** H2
Hornkranz Namibia **124** C2
Horn Mountains Canada **150** F2
Horn Mountains *AK* U.S.A. **148** H3
Hornos, Cabo de Chile *see* **Horn, Cape**
Hornoy-le-Bourg France **62** B5
Horn Peak *Y.T.* Canada **149** O3
Hornsby Australia **138** E4
Hornsea U.K. **58** G5
Hornslandet *pen.* Sweden **55** J6
Horodenka Ukr. **53** E6
Horodnya Ukr. **53** F6
Horodok *Khmel'nyts'ka Oblast'* Ukr. **53** E6
Horodok *L'vivs'ka Oblast'* Ukr. **53** D6
Horokanai Japan **90** F3
Horo Shan *mts* China **98** C4
Horoshiri-dake *mt.* Japan **90** F4

Horqin Shadi *reg.* China **95** J3
Horqin Youyi Qianqi *Nei Mongol* China *see* **Ulanhot**
Horqin Zuoyi Houqi *Nei Mongol* China *see* **Ganjig**
Horqin Zuoyi Zhongqi *Nei Mongol* China *see* **Baokang**
Horrabridge U.K. **59** C8
Horrocks Australia **135** A7
Horru *Xizang* China **99** E7
Horse Cave U.S.A. **164** C5
Horsefly Canada **150** F4
Horseheads U.S.A. **165** G2
Horse Islands Canada **153** L4
Horseleap Ireland **61** D4
Horsens Denmark **55** F9
Horseshoe Bend Australia **135** F6
Horseshoe Reservoir U.S.A. **159** H4
Horseshoe Seamounts *sea feature* N. Atlantic Ocean **184** G3
Horsham Australia **137** C8
Horsham U.K. **59** G7
Horšovský Týn Czech Rep. **63** M5
Horst *hill* Germany **63** J4
Hörstel Germany **63** H2
Horten Norway **55** G7
Hortobágyi *nat. park* Hungary **69** I1
Horton *r. N.W.T.* Canada **149** P1
Horwood Lake Canada **152** E4
Hōryūji *tourist site* Japan **92** B4
Hösbach Germany **63** J4
Hose, Pegunungan *mts* Malaysia **85** F2
Ḥoseynābād Iran **110** B3
Ḥoseynīyeh Iran **110** C4
Hoshab Pak. **111** F5
Hoshangabad India **104** D5
Hoshiarpur India **104** C3
Höshööt *Arhangay* Mongolia *see* **Öldziyt**
Höshööt *Bayan-Ölgiy* Mongolia *see* **Tsengel**
Hosoe Japan **92** D4
Hospet India **106** C3
Hospital Ireland **61** D5
Hosséré Vokre *mt.* Cameroon **120** E4
Hosta Butte *mt.* U.S.A. **159** I4
Hotagen *r.* Sweden **54** I5
Hotahudo East Timor *see* **Hatudo**
Hotaka Japan **93** D2
Hotaka-dake *mt.* Japan **92** D2
Hotaka-yama *mt.* Japan **93** F2
Hotan *Xinjiang* China **99** C5
Hotan He *watercourse* China **98** C4
Hotazel S. Africa **124** F4
Hot Creek Range *mts* U.S.A. **158** E2
Hotgi India **106** C2
Hotham *r.* Australia **135** B8
Hotham Inlet *AK* U.S.A. **148** G2
Hoti *Seram* Indon. **83** D3
Hoting Sweden **54** J4
Hot Springs *AR* U.S.A. **161** E5
Hot Springs *NM* U.S.A. *see* **Truth or Consequences**
Hot Springs *SD* U.S.A. **160** C3
Hot Sulphur Springs U.S.A. **156** G4
Hottah Lake Canada **150** G1
Hottentots Bay Namibia **124** B4
Hottentots Point Namibia **124** B4
Houdan France **62** B6
Houffalize Belgium **62** F4
Hougang Sing. **87** [inset]
Houghton *MI* U.S.A. **160** F2
Houghton *NY* U.S.A. **165** F2
Houghton Lake U.S.A. **164** C1
Houghton Lake *l.* U.S.A. **164** C1
Houghton le Spring U.K. **58** F4
Houie Moc, Phou *mt.* Laos **86** C2
Houlton U.S.A. **162** H2
Houma *Shanxi* China **95** G5
Houma U.S.A. **161** F6
Houmen China **97** G4
Houri *Qinghai* China **94** D4
House Range *mts* U.S.A. **159** G2
Houston Canada **150** E4
Houston *AK* U.S.A. **149** J3
Houston *MO* U.S.A. **161** F4
Houston *MS* U.S.A. **161** F5
Houston *TX* U.S.A. **161** E6
Hout *r.* S. Africa **125** I2
Houtman Abrolhos *is* Australia **135** A7
Houton U.K. **60** F2
Houwater S. Africa **124** F6
Houxia *Xinjiang* China **98** D4
Houzihe *Qinghai* China **94** E4
Hovd *Hovd* Mongolia **94** B2
Hovd *Övörhangay* Mongolia *see* **Bogd**
Hovd *prov.* Mongolia **94** C2
Hovd Gol *r.* Mongolia **94** C1
Hove U.K. **59** G8
Hoveton U.K. **59** I6
Hovmantorp Sweden **55** I8
Hövsgöl Mongolia **95** G3
Hövsgöl *prov.* Mongolia **94** E1
Hövsgöl Nuur *l.* Mongolia **94** E1
Hövüün Mongolia *see* **Noyon**
Howar, Wadi *watercourse* Sudan **108** C6
Howard Australia **136** F5
Howard *PA* U.S.A. **165** G3
Howard *SD* U.S.A. **160** D2
Howard *WI* U.S.A. **164** A1
Howard City U.S.A. **164** C2
Howard Lake Canada **151** J2
Howard Pass *AK* U.S.A. **148** H1
Howden U.K. **58** G5
Howe, Cape Australia **138** D6
Howe, Mount Antarctica **188** J1
Howell U.S.A. **164** D2
Howick Canada **165** I1
Howick S. Africa **125** J5
Howland U.S.A. **162** G2

▶**Howland Island** *terr.* N. Pacific Ocean **133** I1
United States Unincorporated Territory.

Howlong Australia **138** C5
Howrah India *see* **Haora**
Howth Ireland **61** F4
Ḥowz *well* Iran **110** E3
Ḥowz-e Khān *well* Iran **110** E3
Ḥowz-e Panj Iran **110** E4
Ḥowz-e Panj *waterhole* Iran **110** D3
Howz i-Mian i-Tak Iran **110** D3
Hô Xa Vietnam **86** D3
Höxter Germany **63** J3
Hoxtolgay *Xinjiang* China **98** D3
Hoxud *Xinjiang* China **98** D4
Hoy *i.* U.K. **60** F2
Hoya Germany **63** J2
Hōya Japan **93** F3
Høyanger Norway **55** E6
Hoyerswerda Germany **57** O5
Høylandet Norway **54** H4
Hoym Germany **63** L3
Hoyor Amt *Nei Mongol* China **94** F3
Höytiäinen *l.* Fin. **54** P5
Hoyt Peak U.S.A. **159** H1
Hozu-gawa *r.* Japan **92** B3
Hpa-an Myanmar **86** B3
Hpapun Myanmar **86** B3
Hradec Králové Czech Rep. **57** O5
Hradiště *hill* Czech Rep. **63** N4
Hrasnica Bos.-Herz. **68** H3
Hrazdan Armenia **113** G2
Hrebinka Ukr. **53** G6
Hrodna Belarus **55** M10
Hrvatska *country* Europe *see* **Croatia**
Hrvatsko Grahovo Bos.-Herz. *see* **Bosansko Grahovo**
Hsenwi Myanmar **86** B2
Hsiang Chang *i. H.K.* China *see* **Hong Kong Island**
Hsiang Kang *H.K.* China *see* **Hong Kong**
Hsi-hseng Myanmar **86** B2
Hsin-chia-p'o *country* Asia *see* **Singapore**
Hsin-chia-p'o Sing. *see* **Singapore**
Hsin-chia-p'o Sing. *see* **Singapore**
Hsinchu Taiwan **97** I3
Hsinking China *see* **Changchun**
Hsinying Taiwan **97** I4
Hsipaw Myanmar **86** B2
Hsi-sha Ch'ün-tao *is* S. China Sea *see* **Paracel Islands**
Hsiyüp'ing Yü *i.* Taiwan **97** H4
Hsüeh Shan *mt.* Taiwan **97** I3
Huab *watercourse* Namibia **123** B6
Huabei Pingyuan *plain* China **95** H4
Huachi *Gansu* China **95** G4
Huachinera Mex. **166** C2
Huacho Peru **176** C6
Huachuan China **90** C3
Huade *Nei Mongol* China **95** H3
Huadian China **90** B4
Huadu China **97** G4
Huahai *Gansu* China **94** D3
Huahaizi *Qinghai* China **98** F5
Hua Hin Thai. **87** B4
Huai'an *Hebei* China **95** H3
Huai'an *Jiangsu* China **97** H1
Huai'an *Jiangsu* China *see* **Chuzhou**
Huaibei China **97** H1
Huaibin China **97** G1
Huaicheng *Guangdong* China *see* **Huaiji**
Huaicheng *Jiangsu* China *see* **Chuzhou**
Huaidezhen China **90** B4
Huaidian China *see* **Shenqiu**
Huai Had National Park Thai. **86** D3
Huaihua China **97** F3
Huaiji China **97** G4
Huai Kha Khaeng Wildlife Reserve *nature res.* Thai. **86** B4
Huailai *Hebei* China **95** H3
Huaillilas *mt.* Peru **176** C5
Huainan China **97** H1
Huaining *Anhui* China **97** H2
Huaining *Anhui* China *see* **Shipai**
Huairen *Shanxi* China **95** H4
Huairou *Beijing* China **95** I3
Huaiyang China **97** G1
Huaiyin *Jiangsu* China **97** H1
Huaiyin *Jiangsu* China *see* **Huai'an**
Huaiyuan China **97** H1
Huajialing *Gansu* China **94** F5
Huajuápan de León Mex. **168** E5
Huaki *Maluku* Indon. **83** C4
Hualahuises Mex. **167** F3
Hualapai Peak U.S.A. **159** G4
Hualian Taiwan *see* **Hualien**
Hualien Taiwan **97** I3
Huallaga *r.* Peru **176** C5
Hualong *Qinghai* China **94** E4
Huambo Angola **123** B5
Huanan China **90** C3
Huancane Peru **176** E7
Huancavelica Peru **176** C6
Huancayo Peru **176** C6
Huancheng *Gansu* China *see* **Huanxian**
Huangbei China **97** G3
Huangcaoba China *see* **Xingyi**
Huangcheng *Gansu* China **94** E4
Huang-chou *Hubei* China *see* **Huanggang**
Huangchuan China **97** G1
Huanggang China **97** G2
Huang Hai *sea* N. Pacific Ocean *see* **Yellow Sea**
Huang He *r.* China *see* **Yellow**
Huanghe Kou *r. mouth* China **95** I4
Huanghua *Hebei* China **95** I4
Huangjiajian China **97** I1
Huang-kang *Hubei* China *see* **Huanggang**
Huangling *Shaanxi* China **95** G5
Huangliu China **97** F5
Huanglong *Shaanxi* China **95** G5
Huanglongsi *Henan* China *see* **Kaifeng**
Huangmao Jian *mt.* China **97** H3
Huangmei China **97** G2

Huangpu China **97** G4
Huangqi China **97** H3
Huangshan China **97** H2
Huangshi China **97** G2
Huangtu Gaoyuan *plat.* China **95** F4
Huangxian *Shandong* China **95** J4
Huangyan China **97** I2
Huangyang *Gansu* China **94** E4
Huangyuan *Qinghai* China **94** E4
Huangzhong *Qinghai* China **94** E4
Huangzhou *Hubei* China *see* **Huanggang**
Huaning China **96** D3
Huaniushan *Gansu* China **94** C3
Huanjiang China **97** F3
Huanren China **90** B4
Huanshan China *see* **Yuhuan**
Huantai *Shandong* China **95** I4
Huánuco Peru **176** C5
Huanxian *Gansu* China **95** F4
Huaping China **96** D3
Huap'ing Yü *i.* Taiwan **97** I3
Huaqiao China **96** E2
Huaqiaozhen China *see* **Huaqiao**
Huaráz Peru **176** C5
Huarmey Peru **176** C6
Huarong China **97** G2
Huascarán, Nevado de *mt.* Peru **176** C5
Huasco Chile **178** B3
Hua Shan *mt. Shaanxi* China **95** G5
Huashaoying *Hebei* China **95** H3
Huashixia *Qinghai* China **94** D5
Huashugou *Gansu* China *see* **Jingtieshan**
Huashulinzi China **90** B4
Huatabampo Mex. **166** C3
Huatong *Liaoning* China **95** J3
Huatusco Mex. **167** F5
Huauchinango Mex. **167** F4
Huaxian *Guangdong* China *see* **Huadu**
Huaxian *Henan* China **95** H5
Huaxian *Shaanxi* China **95** G5
Huayacocotla Mex. **167** F4
Huayang China *see* **Jixi**
Huayin China **97** F1
Huayuan China **97** F2
Huayxay Laos **86** C2
Huazangsi *Gansu* China *see* **Tianzhu**
Huazhaizi *Gansu* China **94** E4
Hubbard, Mount Canada/U.S.A. **149** M3
Hubbard, Pointe *pt* Canada **153** I2
Hubbard Lake U.S.A. **164** D1
Hubbart Point Canada **151** M3
Hubei *prov.* China **97** G2
Hubli India **106** B3
Hückelhoven Germany **62** G3
Hucknall U.K. **59** F5
Huddersfield U.K. **58** F5
Huder *Nei Mongol* China **95** J1
Hüder Mongolia **95** F1
Hudiksvall Sweden **55** J6
Hudson *MA* U.S.A. **165** J2
Hudson *MD* U.S.A. **165** G4
Hudson *MI* U.S.A. **164** C3
Hudson *NH* U.S.A. **165** J2
Hudson *NY* U.S.A. **165** I2
Hudson *r.* U.S.A. **165** I3
Hudson, Baie d' *sea* Canada *see* **Hudson Bay**
Hudson, Détroit d' *strait* Canada *see* **Hudson Strait**
Hudson Bay Canada **151** K4
Hudson Bay *sea* Canada **151** O3
Hudson Falls U.S.A. **165** I2
Hudson Island Tuvalu *see* **Nanumanga**
Hudson Mountains Antarctica **188** K2
Hudson's Hope Canada **150** F3
Hudson Strait Canada **147** K3
Huê Vietnam **86** D3
Huehuetán Mex. **167** G6
Huehuetenango Guat. **167** H6
Huehueto, Cerro *mt.* Mex. **161** B7
Huejuqilla Mex. **166** E4
Huejutla Mex. **167** F4
Huelva Spain **67** C5
Huentelauquén Chile **178** B4
Huépac Mex. **166** C2
Huércal-Overa Spain **67** F5
Huertecillas Mex. **161** C7
Huesca Spain **67** F2
Huéscar Spain **67** E5
Huétamo Mex. **167** E5
Huggins Island *AK* U.S.A. **148** I2
Hughenden Australia **136** D4
Hughes *r.* Canada **151** K3
Hughes *AK* U.S.A. **148** I2
Hughes (abandoned) Australia **135** E7
Hughson U.S.A. **158** C3
Hugli *r. mouth* India **105** F5
Hugo *CO* U.S.A. **160** C4
Hugo *OK* U.S.A. **161** E5
Hugo Lake U.S.A. **161** E5
Hugoton U.S.A. **161** C4
Huhehot *Nei Mongol* China *see* **Hohhot**
Huhhot *Nei Mongol* China *see* **Hohhot**
Huhudi S. Africa **124** G4
Hui'an China **97** H3
Hui'anpu *Ningxia* China **94** F4
Huiarau Range *mts* N.Z. **139** F4
Huib-Hoch Plateau Namibia **124** C4
Huichang China **97** G3
Huicheng *Anhui* China *see* **Shexian**
Huicheng *Guangdong* China *see* **Huilai**
Huicholes, Sierra de los *mts* Mex. **166** D4
Huidong China **96** D3
Huihe *Nei Mongol* China **95** I1
Huijbergen Neth. **62** E3
Huiji He *r.* China **95** H5
Huila, Nevado de *vol.* Col. **176** C3
Huíla, Planalto da Angola **123** B5
Huilai China **97** H4
Huili China **96** D3

Huimanguillo Mex. **167** G5
Huimin *Shandong* China **95** I4
Huinan China *see* **Nanhui**
Huining *Gansu* China **94** F5
Huinong *Ningxia* China **94** F4
Huishi *Gansu* China *see* **Huining**
Huishui China **96** E3
Huiten Nur *l.* China **94** B5
Huitong China **97** F3
Huittinen Fin. **55** M6
Huitupan Mex. **167** G5
Huixian *Gansu* China **96** E1
Huixian *Henan* China **95** H5
Huixtla Mex. **167** G6
Huiyang China *see* **Huizhou**
Huize China **96** D3
Huizhou China **97** G4
Hujirt *Arhangay* Mongolia *see* **Tsetserleg**
Hujirt *Övörhangay* Mongolia **94** E2
Hujirt *Töv* Mongolia *see* **Delgerhaan**
Hujr Saudi Arabia **108** F4
Hukawng Valley Myanmar **86** B1
Hukuntsi Botswana **124** E2
Hulahula *r. AK* U.S.A. **149** K1
Hulan China **90** B3
Hulan Ergi *Heilong.* China **95** J2
Ḩulayfah Saudi Arabia **108** F4
Ḩulayḩilah *well* Syria **107** D2
Huliao China *see* **Dabu**
Hulilan Iran **110** B3
Hulin China **90** D3
Hulingol *Nei Mongol* China **95** J2
Hulin Gol *r.* China **90** B3
Hull Canada **165** H1
Hull U.K. *see* **Kingston upon Hull**
Hull Island *atoll* Kiribati *see* **Orona**
Hultsfred Sweden **55** I8
Huludao *Liaoning* China **95** J3
Hulu Hu *salt l. Qinghai* China **99** E6
Hulun Buir *Nei Mongol* China **95** I1
Hulun Nur *l.* China **95** I1
Ḩulwān Egypt **112** C5
Huma China **90** B2
Humahuaca Arg. **178** C2
Humaitá Brazil **176** F5
Humaya *r.* Mex. **157** G8
Humaym *well* U.A.E. **110** D6
Humayyān, Jabal *hill* Saudi Arabia **110** B5
Humber, Mouth of the U.K. **58** H5
Humboldt Canada **151** J4
Humboldt *AZ* U.S.A. **159** G4
Humboldt *NE* U.S.A. **160** E3
Humboldt *NV* U.S.A. **158** D1
Humboldt *r.* U.S.A. **158** D1
Humboldt Bay U.S.A. **156** B4
Humboldt Range *mts* U.S.A. **158** D1
Humbolt Salt Marsh U.S.A. **158** E2
Hume *r. N.W.T.* Canada **149** O2
Humeburn Australia **138** B1
Hu Men *sea chan.* China **97** G4
Hume Reservoir Australia **138** C5
Humphrey Island *atoll* Cook Is *see* **Manihiki**
Humphreys, Mount U.S.A. **158** D3
Humphreys Peak U.S.A. **159** H4
Hūn Libya **121** E2
Húnaflói *b.* Iceland **54** [inset]
Hunan *prov.* China **97** F3
Hundeluft Germany **63** M3
Hunedoara Romania **69** J2
Hünfeld Germany **63** J4
Hungary *country* Europe **65** H2
Hungerford Australia **138** B2
Hung Fa Leng *hill H.K.* China *see* **Robin's Nest**
Hüngiy Gol *r.* Mongolia **94** C1
Hŭngnam N. Korea **91** B5
Hung Shui Kiu *H.K.* China **97** [inset]
Hưng Yên Vietnam **86** D2
Hun He *r.* China **95** J3
Hunjiang China *see* **Baishan**
Huns Mountains Namibia **124** C4
Hunstanton U.K. **59** H6
Hunte *r.* Germany **63** I1
Hunter *r.* Australia **138** E4
Hunter, Mount *AK* U.S.A. **149** J3
Hunter Island Australia **137** [inset]
Hunter Island Canada **150** D5
Hunter Island S. Pacific Ocean **133** H4
Hunter Islands Australia **137** [inset]
Huntingburg U.S.A. **164** B4
Huntingdon Canada **165** H1
Huntingdon U.K. **59** G6
Huntingdon *PA* U.S.A. **165** G3
Huntingdon *TN* U.S.A. **161** F4
Huntington *IN* U.S.A. **164** C3
Huntington *OR* U.S.A. **156** D3
Huntington *WV* U.S.A. **164** D4
Huntington Beach U.S.A. **158** D5
Huntington Creek *r.* U.S.A. **159** F1
Huntly N.Z. **139** E3
Huntly U.K. **60** G3
Hunt Mountain U.S.A. **156** G3
Huntsville Canada **164** F1
Huntsville *AL* U.S.A. **163** C5
Huntsville *AR* U.S.A. **161** E4
Huntsville *TN* U.S.A. **164** C5
Huntsville *TX* U.S.A. **161** E6
Hunucmá Mex. **167** H4
Hunyuan *Shanxi* China **95** H4
Hunza *reg.* Pak. **104** C1
Hunza *r.* Pak. **99** A6
Huocheng *Xinjiang* China **98** C3
Huoer *Xizang* China *see* **Hor**
Huojia *Henan* China **95** H5
Huolin He *r.* China *see* **Hulin Gol**
Huolongmen China **90** B2
Huolu *Hebei* China *see* **Luquan**
Hương Khê Vietnam **86** D3
Huonville Australia **137** [inset]
Huoqiu China **97** H1
Huoshan China **97** H2
Huo Shan *mt.* China *see* **Baima Jian**
Huoshao Tao *i.* Taiwan *see* **Lü Tao**

Huoxian Shanxi China see Huozhou
Huozhou Shanxi China 95 G4
Hupeh prov. China see Hubei
Hupnik r. Turkey 107 C1
Hupu India 96 B2
Hūr Iran 110 E4
Hurault, Lac l. Canada 153 H3
Ḩurayḑin, Wādī watercourse Egypt 107 A4
Huraysān reg. Saudi Arabia 110 B6
Hurd, Cape Canada 164 E1
Hurd Island Kiribati see Arorae
Hure Nei Mongol China 95 J3
Hüreemaral Mongolia 94 D2
Hüremt Mongolia see Sayhan
Hürent Mongolia see Taragt
Hure Qi Nei Mongol China see Hure
Hurghada Egypt see Al Ghurdaqah
Hurleg Qinghai China 94 D4
Hurleg Hu l. Qinghai China 94 D4
Hurler's Cross Ireland 61 D5
Hurley NM U.S.A. 159 I5
Hurley WI U.S.A. 160 F2
Hurmagai Pak. 111 G4
Huron CA U.S.A. 158 C3
Huron SD U.S.A. 160 D2

▶Huron, Lake Canada/U.S.A. 164 D1
2nd largest lake in North America, and 4th in the world.

Hurricane U.S.A. 159 G3
Hursley U.K. 59 F7
Hurst Green U.K. 59 H7
Hurung, Gunung mt. Indon. 85 F2
Husain Nika Pak. 111 H4
Húsavík Norðurland eystra Iceland 54 [inset]
Húsavík Vestfirðir Iceland 54 [inset]
Huseyinabat Turkey see Alaca
Huseyinli Turkey see Kızılırmak
Hushan Zhejiang China 97 H2
Hushan Zhejiang China see Wuyi
Hushan Zhejiang China see Cixi
Huşi Romania 69 M1
Huskvarna Sweden 55 I8
Huslia AK U.S.A. 148 H2
Huslia r. AK U.S.A. 148 H2
Husn Jordan see Al Ḩişn
Ḩuşn Āl 'Abr Yemen 108 G6
Husnes Norway 55 D7
Husum Germany 57 L3
Husum Sweden 54 K5
Hutag Mongolia see Hutag-Öndör
Hutag-Öndör Mongolia 94 E1
Hutanopan Sumatera Indon. 84 B2
Hutchinson KS U.S.A. 160 D4
Hutchinson MN U.S.A. 160 E2
Hutch Mountain U.S.A. 159 H4
Hutou China 90 D3
Hutsonville U.S.A. 164 B4
Hutton, Mount hill Australia 137 E5
Hutton Range hills Australia 135 C6
Hutubi Xinjiang China 98 D3
Hutubi He r. China 98 D3
Hutuo He r. China 95 I4
Huvadhu Atoll Maldives 103 D11
Hüvek Turkey see Bozova
Hūvīān, Kūh-e mts Iran 111 E5
Ḩuwār i. Bahrain 110 C5
Huwaytat reg. Saudi Arabia 107 C5
Huxi China 97 G3
Huxian Shaanxi China 95 G5
Huzhong China 90 A2
Huzhou China 97 I2
Huzhu Qinghai China 94 E4
Hvannadalshnúkur vol. Iceland 54 [inset]
Hvar i. Croatia 68 G3
Hvide Sande Denmark 55 F8
Hvíta r. Iceland 54 [inset]
Hwange Zimbabwe 123 C5
Hwange National Park Zimbabwe 123 C5
Hwang Ho r. China see Yellow
Hwedza Zimbabwe 123 D5
Hwlffordd U.K. see Haverfordwest
Hyakuriga-take hill Japan 92 B3
Hyannis MA U.S.A. 165 J3
Hyannis NE U.S.A. 160 C3
Hyargas Nuur salt l. Mongolia 94 C1
Hyco Lake U.S.A. 164 F5
Hyde N.Z. 139 C7
Hyden Australia 135 B8
Hyden U.S.A. 164 D5
Hyde Park U.S.A. 165 I1
Hyder AK U.S.A. 149 O5
Hyderabad India 106 C2
Hyderabad Pak. 111 H5
Hydra i. Greece see Ydra
Hyères France 66 H5
Hyères, Îles d' is France 66 H5
Hyesan N. Korea 90 C4
Hyland r. Y.T. Canada 149 O4
Hyland, Mount Australia 138 F3
Hyland Post Canada 150 D3
Hyllestad Norway 55 D6
Hyltebruk Sweden 55 H8
Hyndman Peak U.S.A. 156 E4
Hyōgo pref. Japan 92 A3
Hyōno-sen mt. Japan 91 D6
Hyrcania Iran see Gorgān
Hyrynsalmi Fin. 54 P4
Hysham U.S.A. 156 G3
Hythe Canada 150 G4
Hythe U.K. 59 I7
Hyūga Japan 91 C6
Hyvinkää Fin. 55 N6

I

Iaciara Brazil 179 B1
Iaco r. Brazil 176 E5
Iaçu Brazil 179 C1
Iadera Croatia see Zadar
Iaeger U.S.A. 164 E5
Iakora Madag. 123 E6
Ialomiţa r. Romania 69 L2
Ianca Romania 69 L2
Iaşi Romania 69 L1
Iba Luzon Phil. 82 B3
Ibadan Nigeria 120 D4
Ibagué Col. 176 C3
Ibaiti Brazil 179 A3
Ibapah U.S.A. 159 G1
Ibaraki Ibaraki Japan 93 G2
Ibaraki Ōsaka Japan 92 B4
Ibaraki pref. Japan 93 G2
Ibarra Ecuador 176 C3
Ibb Yemen 108 F7
Ibbenbüren Germany 63 H2
Iberá, Esteros del marsh Arg. 178 E3
Iberia Peru 176 E6

▶Iberian Peninsula Europe 67
Consists of Portugal, Spain and Gibraltar.

Iberville, Lac d' l. Canada 153 G3
Ibeto Nigeria 120 D3
iBhayi S. Africa see Port Elizabeth
Ibi Sumatera Indon. 84 B1
Ibi Nigeria 120 D4
Ibiá Brazil 179 B2
Ibiaí Brazil 179 B2
Ibiapaba, Serra da hills Brazil 177 J4
Ibiassucê Brazil 179 C1
Ibicaraí Brazil 179 D1
Ibigawa Japan 92 C3
Ibi-gawa r. Japan 92 C3
Ibiquera Brazil 179 C1
Ibirama Brazil 179 A4
Ibiranhém Brazil 179 C2
Ibi-Sekigahara-Yōrō Kokutei-kōen park Japan 92 C3
Ibitinga Brazil 179 A3
Ibiza Spain 67 G4
Ibiza i. Spain 67 G4
Iblei, Monti mts Sicily Italy 68 F6
Ibn Buşayyiş well Saudi Arabia 110 B5
Ibotirama Brazil 177 J6
Iboundji, Mont hill Gabon 122 B4
Ibrā' Oman 110 E6
İbradı Turkey 112 C3
Ibrī Oman 110 E6
Ibu Halmahera Indon. 83 C2
Ibuhos i. Phil. 82 C1
Ibuki Japan 92 C3
Ibuki-sanchi mts Japan 92 C3
Ibuki-yama mt. Japan 92 C3
Ica Peru 176 C6
Ica r. Peru see Putumayo
Icaiché Mex. 167 H5
Içana Brazil 176 E3
Içana r. Brazil 176 E3
Icaria i. Greece see Ikaria
Icatu Brazil 177 J4
Iceberg Canyon gorge U.S.A. 159 F3
İçel Mersin Turkey see Mersin

▶Iceland country Europe 54 [inset]
2nd largest island in Europe.

Iceland Basin sea feature N. Atlantic Ocean 184 G2
Icelandic Plateau sea feature N. Atlantic Ocean 189 I2
Ichalkaranji India 106 B2
Ichifusa-yama mt. Japan 91 C6
Ichihara Japan 93 G3
Ichikai Japan 93 G2
Ichikawa Chiba Japan 93 F3
Ichikawa Hyōgo Japan 92 A3
Ichi-kawa r. Japan 92 A4
Ichikawadaimon Japan 93 E3
Ichinomiya Aichi Japan 92 C3
Ichinomiya Aichi Japan 92 D4
Ichinomiya Chiba Japan 93 G3
Ichinomiya Hyōgo Japan 92 A4
Ichinomiya Yamanashi Japan 93 E3
Ichinoseki Japan 91 F5
Ichinskaya Sopka vol. Rus. Fed. 77 Q4
Ichishi Japan 92 C4
Ichkeul, Parc National de l' Tunisia 68 C6
Ichnya Ukr. 53 G6
Ichtegem Belgium 62 D3
Ichtershausen Germany 63 K4
Icó Brazil 177 K5
Iconha Brazil 179 C3
Iconium Turkey see Konya
Icosium Alg. see Algiers
Iculisma France see Angoulême
Icy Bay AK U.S.A. 149 K4
Icy Bay AK U.S.A. 149 L4
Icy Cape AK U.S.A. 148 G1
Icy Strait AK U.S.A. 149 N4
Id Turkey see Narman
Idabel U.S.A. 161 E5
Ida Grove U.S.A. 160 E3
Idah Nigeria 120 D4
Idaho state U.S.A. 156 E3
Idaho City U.S.A. 156 E4
Idaho Falls U.S.A. 156 E4
Idalia National Park Australia 136 D5
Idar India 104 C5
Idar-Oberstein Germany 63 H5
Ide Japan 92 B4
Ider Mongolia see Galt
Ideriyn Gol r. Mongolia 94 E1
Idfū Egypt 108 D5
Idhān Awbārī des. Libya 120 E2
Idhān Murzūq des. Libya 120 E2
Idhra i. Greece see Ydra
Idi Amin Dada, Lake Dem. Rep. Congo/Uganda see Edward, Lake
Idiofa Dem. Rep. Congo 123 B4
Iditarod AK U.S.A. 148 H3
Iditarod r. AK U.S.A. 148 H3
Idivuoma Sweden 54 M2
Idkū Egypt 112 C5
Idle r. U.K. 58 G5
Idlewild airport U.S.A. see John F. Kennedy
Idlib Syria 107 C2
Idra i. Greece see Ydra
Idre Sweden 55 H6
Idstein Germany 63 I4
Idutywa S. Africa 125 I7
Idzhevan Armenia see Ijevan
Iecava Latvia 55 N8
Iepê Brazil 179 A3
Ieper Belgium 62 C4
Ierapetra Greece 69 K7
Ierissou, Kolpos b. Greece 69 J4
Iešjávri l. Norway 54 N2
Ifakara Tanz. 123 D4
Ifalik atoll Micronesia 81 K5
Ifaluk atoll Micronesia see Ifalik
Ifanadiana Madag. 123 E6
Ife Nigeria 120 D4
Ifenat Chad 121 E3
Iferouâne Niger 120 D3
Iffley Australia 136 C3
Ifjord Norway 54 O1
Ifôghas, Adrar des hills Mali 120 D3
Iforas, Adrar des hills Mali see Ifôghas, Adrar des
Iga Japan 92 C4
Igan Sarawak Malaysia 85 E2
Igan r. Malaysia 85 E2
Iganga Uganda 121 G4
Igarapava Brazil 179 B3
Igarka Rus. Fed. 76 J3
Igatpuri India 106 B2
Igbeti Nigeria see Igbetti
Igbetti Nigeria 120 D4
Igdir Iran 110 B2
Iğdır Turkey 113 G3
Igel'veyem r. Rus. Fed. 148 D2
Iggesund Sweden 55 J6
Igikpak, Mount AK U.S.A. 148 I2
Igiugig AK U.S.A. 148 I4
Igizyar China 111 J2
Iglesias Sardinia Italy 68 C5
Iglesiente reg. Sardinia Italy 68 C5
Igloolik Canada 147 J3
Igluligaarjuk Canada see Chesterfield Inlet
Ignace Canada 151 N5
Ignacio Zaragoza Mex. 166 D2
Ignacio Zaragoza Tamaulipas Mex. 167 F4
Ignacio Zaragoza Mex. 161 C8
Ignalina Lith. 55 O9
İğneada Turkey 69 L4
İğneada Burnu pt Turkey 69 M4
Ignoitijala India 87 A5
iGoli S. Africa see Johannesburg
Igom Papua Indon. 83 D3
Igoumenitsa Greece 69 I5
Igra Rus. Fed. 51 Q4
Igrim Rus. Fed. 51 S3
Iguaçu r. Brazil 179 A4
Iguaçu, Saltos do waterfall Arg./Brazil see Iguaçu Falls
Iguaçu Falls Arg./Brazil 178 F3
Iguaí Brazil 179 C1
Iguala Mex. 168 E5
Igualada Spain 67 G3
Iguape Brazil 179 B4
Iguaraçu Brazil 179 A3
Iguatama Brazil 179 B3
Iguatemi Brazil 178 F2
Iguatu Brazil 177 K5
Iguazú, Cataratas do waterfall Arg./Brazil see Iguaçu Falls
Iguéla Gabon 122 A4
Iguidi, Erg des des. Alg./Mauritania 120 C2
Igunga Tanz. 123 D4
Iharaña Madag. 123 E5
Ihavandhippolhu Atoll Maldives 106 B5
Ihavandiffulu Atoll Maldives see Ihavandhippolhu Atoll
Ih Bogd Uul mt. Mongolia 102 J3
Ihbulag Mongolia see Hanbogd
Ihhayrhan Mongolia see Bayan-Önjüül
Ihosy Madag. 123 E6
Ih Tal Nei Mongol China 95 J3
Ihtamir Mongolia 94 E2
Ih-Uul Mongolia 94 E1
Iida Japan 93 D3
Iide-san mt. Japan 91 E5
Iijärvi l. Fin. 54 O2
Iijima Japan 93 D3
Iijoki r. Fin. 54 N4
Iinan Japan 92 C4
Iioka Japan 93 G3
Iisalmi Fin. 54 O5
Iitaka Japan 92 C4
Iiyama Japan 93 E2
Iizuka Japan 91 C6
Ijebu-Ode Nigeria 120 D4
Ijen-Merapi-Maelang, Cagar Alam nature res. Jawa Indon. 85 F5
Ijevan Armenia 113 G2
IJmuiden Neth. 62 E2
IJssel r. Neth. 62 F2
IJsselmeer l. Neth. 62 F2
Ijzer r. Belgium see Yser
Ikaahuk Canada see Sachs Harbour
Ikaalinen Fin. 55 M6
Ikageleng S. Africa 125 H3
Ikageng S. Africa 125 H4
Ikaho Japan 93 E2
iKapa S. Africa see Cape Town
Ikare Nigeria 120 D4
Ikaria i. Greece 69 L6
Ikaruga Japan 92 B4
Ikast Denmark 55 F8
Ikawa Japan 93 E3
Ikeda Fukui Japan 92 C3
Ikeda Japan 90 F4
Ikeda Nagano Japan 93 D2
Ikeda Ōsaka Japan 92 B3
Ikegoya-yama mt. Japan 92 C4
Ikela Dem. Rep. Congo 122 C4
Ikhtiman Bulg. 69 J3
Ikhutseng S. Africa 124 G5
Iki-Burul Rus. Fed. 53 J7
Ikom Nigeria 120 D4
Ikoma Japan 92 B4
Ikpikpuk r. AK U.S.A. 148 I1
Iksan S. Korea 91 B6
Ikuji-hana pt Japan 92 D2
Ikungu Tanz. 123 D4
Ikuno Japan 92 A3
Ikusaka Japan 93 D2
Ilagan Luzon Phil. 82 C2
Ilaisamis Kenya 122 D3
Īlām Iran 110 B3
Ilam Nepal 105 F4
Ilan Taiwan 97 I3
Ilave Peru 176 E7
Iława Poland 57 Q4
Ilazārān, Kūh-e mt. Iran 110 E4
Il Bogd Uul mts Mongolia 94 D2
Île-à-la-Crosse Canada 151 J4
Île-à-la-Crosse, Lac l. Canada 151 J4
Ilebo Dem. Rep. Congo 123 C4
Île-de-France admin. reg. France 62 C6
Île Europa i. Indian Ocean see Europa, Île
Ilek Kazakh. 51 Q5

▶Ilemi Triangle terr. Africa 122 D3
Disputed territory (Ethiopia/Kenya/Sudan) administered by Kenya.

Ilen r. Ireland 61 C6
Ileret Kenya 122 D3
Ileza Rus. Fed. 52 I3
Ilfeld Germany 63 K3
Ilford Canada 151 M3
Ilford U.K. 59 H7
Ilfracombe Australia 136 D4
Ilfracombe U.K. 59 C7
Ilgaz Turkey 112 D2
Ilgın Turkey 112 C3
Ilha Grande, Represa resr Brazil 178 F2
Ilha Solteíra, Represa resr Brazil 179 A3
Ílhavo Port. 67 B3
Ilhéus Brazil 179 D1
Ili Kazakh. see Kapchagay
Iliamna AK U.S.A. 148 I4
Iliamna Lake AK U.S.A. 148 I4
Iliamna Volcano AK U.S.A. 148 I3
İliç Turkey 112 E3
Il'ichevsk Azer. see Şärur
Il'ichevsk Ukr. see Illichivs'k
Ilici Spain see Elche-Elx
Iligan Mindanao Phil. 82 D4
Iligan Bay Mindanao Phil. 82 D4
Iligan Point Luzon Phil. 82 C2
Ilimananngip Nunaa i. Greenland 147 P2
Il'inka Rus. Fed. 53 J7
Il'inka Respublika Tyva Rus. Fed. 94 C1
Il'inskiy Permskaya Oblast' Rus. Fed. 51 R4
Il'inskiy Sakhalinskaya Oblast' Rus. Fed. 90 F3
Il'insko-Podomskoye Rus. Fed. 52 J3
Ilin Strait Phil. 82 C3
Iliomar East Timor 83 C5
Ilion U.S.A. 165 H2
Ilium tourist site Turkey see Troy
Ilivit Mountains AK U.S.A. 148 G3
Iliysk Kazakh. see Kapchagay
Ilkal India 106 C3
Ilkeston U.K. 59 F6
Ilkley U.K. 58 F5
Illana Bay Mindanao Phil. 82 C5
Illapel Chile 178 B4
Illéla Niger 120 D3
Iller r. Germany 57 L6
Illichivs'k Ukr. 69 N1
Illimani, Nevado de mt. Bol. 176 E7
Illinois r. U.S.A. 160 F4
Illinois state U.S.A. 164 A3
Illizi Alg. 120 D2
Illogwa watercourse Australia 136 A5
Ilm r. Germany 63 L3
Ilmajoki Fin. 54 M5
Il'men', Ozero l. Rus. Fed. 52 F4
Ilmenau Germany 63 K4
Ilmenau r. Germany 63 K1
Ilminster U.K. 59 E8
Ilnik AK U.S.A. 148 H4
Ilo Peru 176 D7
Iloc i. Phil. 82 B4
Iloilo Panay Phil. 82 C4
Iloilo Strait Phil. 82 C4
Ilomantsi Fin. 54 Q5
Ilong India 96 B3
Ilorin Nigeria 120 D4
Ilovlya Rus. Fed. 53 I6
Ilsede Germany 63 K2
Iluka Australia 138 F2
Ilulissat Greenland 147 M3
Iluppur India 106 C4
Ilva i. Italy see Elba, Isola d'
Imabari Japan 91 D6
Imadate Japan 92 C3
Imaichi Japan 93 F2
Imajō Japan 92 C3
Imala Moz. 123 D5
Imam-baba Turkm. 111 F2
İmamoğlu Turkey 112 D3
Iman Rus. Fed. see Dal'nerechensk
Iman r. Rus. Fed. 90 D3
Imari Japan 91 C6
Imaruí Brazil 179 A5
Imataca, Serranía de mts Venez. 176 F2
Imatra Fin. 55 P6
Imazu Japan 92 C3
Imba-numa l. Japan see Inba-numa
Imbituva Brazil 179 A4
imeni 26 Bakinskikh Komissarov Azer. see Uzboy
imeni Babushkina Rus. Fed. 52 I4
imeni Chapayevka Turkm. see S. A. Nyýazow Adyndaky
imeni Kalinina Tajik. see Cheshtebe
imeni Kirova Kazakh. see Kopbirlik
imeni Petra Stuchki Latvia see Aizkraukle
imeni Poliny Osipenko Rus. Fed. 90 E1
imeni Tel'mana Rus. Fed. 90 D2
Īmī Eth. 122 E3
Imishli Azer. see İmişli
İmişli Azer. 113 H3
Imit Pak. 104 C1
Imja-do i. S. Korea 91 B6
Imlay U.S.A. 158 D1
Imlay City U.S.A. 164 D2
Imola Italy 68 D2
iMonti S. Africa see East London
Impendle S. Africa 125 I5
Imperatriz Brazil 177 I5
Imperia Italy 68 C3
Imperial CA U.S.A. 159 F5
Imperial NE U.S.A. 160 C3
Imperial Beach U.S.A. 158 E5
Imperial Dam U.S.A. 159 F5
Imperial Valley plain U.S.A. 159 F5
Imperieuse Reef Australia 134 B4
Impfondo Congo 122 B3
Imphal India 105 H4
İmralı Adası i. Turkey 69 M4
İmroz Turkey 69 K4
Imroz i. Turkey see Gökçeada
Imtān Syria 107 C3
Imuris Mex. 166 C2
Imuruan Bay Palawan Phil. 82 B4
Imuruk Basin l. AK U.S.A. 148 F2
Imuruk Lake AK U.S.A. 148 G2
In r. Rus. Fed. 90 D2
Ina Ibaraki Japan 93 G3
Ina Nagano Japan 93 D3
Inabe Japan 92 C3
Inabu Japan 92 D3
Inae Japan 92 C3
Inagauan Palawan Phil. 82 B4
Inagawa Japan 92 B4
Ina-gawa r. Japan 92 B4
Inage Japan 93 G3
Inagi Japan 93 F3
Inalik U.S.A. see Diomede
Inambari r. Peru 176 E6
Inami Hyōgo Japan 92 A4
Inami Toyama Japan 92 C2
Inanam Sabah Malaysia 85 G1
Inanda S. Africa 125 J5
Inanudak Bay AK U.S.A. 148 E5
Inari Fin. 54 O2
Inarijärvi l. Fin. 54 O2
Inarijoki r. Fin./Norway 54 N2
Inasa Japan 92 D4
Inazawa Japan 92 C3
Inba Japan 93 G3
Inba-numa l. Japan 93 G3
Inca Spain 67 H4
İnce Burnu pt Turkey 69 L4
İnce Burun pt Turkey 112 D2
Inch Ireland 61 F5
Inchard, Loch b. U.K. 60 D2
Incheon S. Korea see Inch'ŏn
Inchicronan Lough l. Ireland 61 D5
Inch'ŏn S. Korea 91 B5
Inchoun Rus. Fed. 148 E2
Incirli Turkey see Karasu
Indaal, Loch b. U.K. 60 C5
Indalsälven r. Sweden 54 J5
Indalstø Norway 55 D6
Inda Silasē Eth. 122 D2
Indaw Myanmar 86 A2
Indawgyi, Lake Myanmar 96 C3
Indé Mex. 166 D3
Indefatigable Island Galápagos Ecuador see Santa Cruz, Isla
Independence CA U.S.A. 158 D3
Independence IA U.S.A. 160 F3
Independence KS U.S.A. 161 E4
Independence KY U.S.A. 164 C4
Independence MO U.S.A. 160 E4
Independence VA U.S.A. 164 E5
Independence Mountains U.S.A. 156 D4
Inder Nei Mongol China 95 J2
Inderborskiy Kazakh. 100 E2
Indi India 106 C2

▶India country Asia 103 E7
2nd most populous country in the world and in Asia. 3rd largest country in Asia, and 7th in the world.

Indian r. Y.T. Canada 149 M3
Indiana U.S.A. 164 F3
Indiana state U.S.A. 164 B3
Indian-Antarctic Ridge sea feature Southern Ocean 186 D9

▶Indianapolis U.S.A. 164 B4
Capital of Indiana.

Indian Cabins Canada 150 G3
Indian Desert India/Pak. see Thar Desert
Indian Harbour Canada 153 K3
Indian Head Canada 151 K5
Indian Lake U.S.A. 165 H1
Indian Lake l. NY U.S.A. 165 H2
Indian Lake l. OH U.S.A. 164 D3
Indian Lake l. PA U.S.A. 165 F3
Indian Mountain AK U.S.A. 148 I2

▶Indian Ocean 185
3rd largest ocean in the world.

Indianola IA U.S.A. 160 E3
Indianola MS U.S.A. 161 F5
Indian Peak U.S.A. 159 G2
Indian Springs IN U.S.A. 164 B4
Indian Springs NV U.S.A. 159 F3
Indian Wells U.S.A. 159 H4
Indiga Rus. Fed. 52 K2
Indigirka r. Rus. Fed. 77 P2
Indigskaya Guba b. Rus. Fed. 52 K2
Inđija Serbia 69 I2
Indin Lake Canada 150 H1
Indio r. Nicaragua 166 [inset] J7
Indio U.S.A. 158 E5
Indira Point India see Pygmalion Point
Indira Priyadarshini Pench National Park India 104 D5
Indispensable Reefs Solomon Is 133 G3
Indjija Serbia see Inđija
Indo-China reg. Asia 86 D3

▶Indonesia country Asia 80 E7
4th most populous country in the world and 3rd in Asia.

Indore India 104 C5
Indragiri r. Indon. 84 C3
Indramayu Jawa Indon. 85 E4
Indramayu, Tanjung pt Indon. 85 E4
Indrapura Sumatera Indon. 84 C3
Indrapura, Gunung vol. Indon. see Kerinci, Gunung
Indrapura, Tanjung pt Indon. 84 C3
Indravati r. India 106 D2
Indre r. France 66 E3
Indulkana Australia 135 F6
Indur India see Nizamabad
Indus r. China/Pakistan 111 G6
also known as Sênggê Zangbo (China) or Shiquan He (China)
Indus, Mouths of the Pak. 111 G5
Indus Cone sea feature Indian Ocean 185 M4
Indwe S. Africa 125 H6
Ine Japan 92 B3
İnebolu Turkey 112 D2
İnegöl Turkey 69 M4
Inerie vol. Flores Indon. 83 B5
Inevi Turkey see Cihanbeyli
Inez U.S.A. 164 D5
Infantes Spain see Villanueva de los Infantes
Infiernillo, Presa resr Mex. 168 D5
Ing, Nam Mae r. Thai. 86 C2
Inga Rus. Fed. 54 S3
Ingalls, Mount U.S.A. 158 C2
Ingelmunster Belgium 62 D4
Ingenika r. Canada 150 E3
Ingersoll Canada 164 E2
Ingettolgoy Mongolia see Selenge
Inggelang i. Maluku Indon. 83 D2
Ingham Australia 136 D3
Ingichka Uzbek. 111 G2
Ingleborough hill U.K. 58 E4
Inglefield Land reg. Greenland 147 K2
Ingleton U.K. 58 E4
Inglewood Qld Australia 138 E2
Inglewood Vic. Australia 138 A6
Inglewood U.S.A. 158 D5
Ingoda r. Rus. Fed. 95 H1
Ingoka Pum mt. Myanmar 86 B1
Ingoldmells U.K. 58 H5
Ingolstadt Germany 63 L6
Ingomar Australia 135 F7
Ingomar U.S.A. 156 G3
Ingonish Canada 153 J5
Ingraj Bazar India 105 G4
Ingram U.S.A. 164 F5
Ingray Lake Canada 150 G1
Ingrid Christensen Coast Antarctica 188 E2
Ingwavuma S. Africa 125 K4
Ingwavuma r. S. Africa/Swaziland see Ngwavuma
Ingwiller France 63 H6
Inhaca Moz. 125 K3
Inhaca, Península pen. Moz. 125 K4
Inhambane Moz. 125 L2
Inhambane prov. Moz. 125 L2
Inhaminga Moz. 123 D5
Inharrime Moz. 125 L3
Inhassoro Moz. 123 D6
Inhaúmas Brazil 179 B1
Inhobim Brazil 179 C1
Inhumas Brazil 179 A2
Inielika vol. Flores Indon. 83 B5
Inis Ireland see Ennis
Inis Córthaidh Ireland see Enniscorthy
Inishark i. Ireland 61 B4
Inishbofin i. Ireland 61 B4
Inisheer i. Ireland 61 C4
Inishkea North i. Ireland 61 B3
Inishkea South i. Ireland 61 B3
Inishmaan i. Ireland 61 C4
Inishmore i. Ireland 61 C4
Inishmurray i. Ireland 61 D3
Inishowen pen. Ireland 61 E2
Inishowen Head hd Ireland 61 F2
Inishtrahull i. Ireland 61 E2
Inishturk i. Ireland 61 B4
Injgan Sum Nei Mongol China 95 I2
Injune Australia 137 E5
Inkerman Australia 136 C3
Inklin Canada 150 C3
Inklin r. B.C. Canada 149 N4
Inkylap Turkm. 111 F2
Inland Kaikoura Range mts N.Z. 139 D6
Inland Lake AK U.S.A. 148 H2
Inland Sea Japan see Seto-naikai
Inlet U.S.A. 165 H2
Inman r. Nunavut Canada 149 R1
Inn r. Europe 57 M7
Innaanganeq c. Greenland 147 L2
Innamincka Australia 137 C5
Innamincka Regional Reserve nature res. Australia 137 C5
Inndyr Norway 54 I3

Inner Mongolia *aut. reg.* China *see* **Nei Mongol Zizhiqu**
Inner Sound *sea chan.* U.K. **60** D3
Innes National Park Australia **137** B7
Innisfail Australia **136** D3
Innisfail Canada **150** H4
Innokent'yevka Rus. Fed. **90** C2
Innoko *r.* *AK* U.S.A. **148** H3
Innoko National Wildlife Refuge *nature res.* *AK* U.S.A. **148** H3
Innsbruck Austria **67** M7
Innuksuak *r.* Canada **152** F2
Inny *r.* Ireland **61** E4
Inobonto *Sulawesi* Indon. **83** C2
Inocência Brazil **179** A2
Inokuchi Japan **92** C2
Inongo Dem. Rep. Congo **122** B4
İnönü Turkey **69** N5
Inoucdjouac Canada *see* **Inukjuak**
Inowrocław Poland **57** Q4
In Salah Alg. **120** D2
Insch U.K. **60** G3

▶**Inscription, Cape** Australia **136** B3
Most westerly point of Oceania.

Insein Myanmar **86** B3
Insterburg Rus. Fed. *see* **Chernyakhovsk**
Inta Rus. Fed. **51** S2
Interamna Italy *see* **Teramo**
Interlaken Switz. **66** H3
International Falls U.S.A. **160** E1
Interview Island India **87** A4
Intracoastal Waterway *canal* U.S.A. **161** E6
Intutu Peru **176** D4
Inubō-zaki *pt* Japan **91** F6
Inukjuak Canada **152** F2
Inuvik *N.W.T.* Canada **149** N1
Inuyama Japan **92** C3
Inveraray U.K. **60** D4
Inverbervie U.K. **60** G4
Invercargill N.Z. **139** B8
Inverell Australia **138** E2
Invergordon U.K. **60** E3
Inverkeithing U.K. **60** F4
Inverleigh Australia **136** C3
Invermay Canada **151** K5
Inverness Canada **153** J5
Inverness U.K. **60** E3
Inverness *CA* U.S.A. **158** B2
Inverness *FL* U.S.A. **163** D6
Inverurie U.K. **60** G3
Investigator Channel Myanmar **87** B4
Investigator Group *is* Australia **135** F8
Investigator Ridge *sea feature* Indian Ocean **185** O6
Investigator Strait Australia **137** B7
Inwood U.S.A. **165** F4
Inya Rus. Fed. **98** D2
Inyanga Zimbabwe *see* **Nyanga**
Inyangani *mt.* Zimbabwe **123** D5
Inyokern U.S.A. **158** E4
Inyo Mountains U.S.A. **158** D3
Inyonga Tanz. **123** D4
Inza Rus. Fed. **53** J5
Inzai Japan **93** G3
Inzhavino Rus. Fed. **53** I5
Ioannina Greece **69** I5
Iokanga *r.* Rus. Fed. **52** H2
Iola U.S.A. **160** E4
Iolgo, Khrebet *mts* Rus. Fed. **102** G1
Iolotan' Turkm. *see* **Ýolöten**
Iona Canada **153** J5
Iona *i.* U.K. **60** C4
Iona, Parque Nacional do *nat. park* Angola **123** B5
Ione U.S.A. **158** E2
Iongo Angola **123** B4
Ionia U.S.A. **164** C2
Ionia Nisia *is* Ionia Nisia Greece *see* **Ionian Islands**
Ionian Islands Greece **69** H5
Ionian Sea Greece/Italy **68** H5
Ionioi Nisoi *is* Ionia Nisia Greece *see* **Ionian Islands**
Ionioi Nisoi *is* Greece *see* **Ionian Islands**
Ioniveyem *r.* Rus. Fed. **148** D2
Iōno Japan **93** G2
Ios *i.* Greece **69** K6
Iowa *state* U.S.A. **160** E3
Iowa City U.S.A. **160** F3
Iowa Falls U.S.A. **160** E3
Iō-zan *hill* Japan **92** C2
Ipameri Brazil **179** A2
Ipanema Brazil **179** C2
Iparía Peru **176** D5
Ipatinga Brazil **179** C2
Ipatovo Rus. Fed. **53** I7
Ipelegeng S. Africa **125** G4
Ipewik *r.* *AK* U.S.A. **148** F1
Ipiales Col. **176** C3
Ipiaú Brazil **179** D1
Ipirá Brazil **179** D1
Ipiranga Brazil **179** A4
iPitoli S. Africa *see* **Pretoria**
Ipixuna *r.* Brazil **176** F5
Ipoh Malaysia **84** C1
Iporá Brazil **179** A2
Ippy Cent. Afr. Rep. **122** C3
Ipsala Turkey **69** L4
Ipswich Australia **138** F1
Ipswich U.K. **59** I6
Ipswich U.S.A. **160** D2
Ipu Brazil **177** J4
Ipuh *Sumatera* Indon. **84** C3

▶**Iqaluit** Canada **147** L3
Capital of Nunavut.

Iqe *Qinghai* China **94** C4
Iqe He *r.* China **99** F5
Iquique Chile **178** B2
Iquiri *r.* Brazil *see* **Ituxi**
Iquitos Peru **176** D4
Īrafshān *reg.* Iran **111** F5
Irago-misaki *pt* Japan **92** D4
Irago-suidō *str.* Japan **92** C4
Irai Brazil **178** F3
Irakleio Greece *see* **Iraklion**
Iraklion Greece **69** K7
Iramaia Brazil **179** C1
Iran *country* Asia **110** D3
Iran, Pegunungan *mts* Indon. **85** F2
Īrānshahr Iran **111** F5
Irapuato Mex. **168** D4
Iraq *country* Asia **113** F4
Irara Brazil **179** D1
Irati Brazil **179** A4
Irayel' Rus. Fed. **52** L2
Irazú, Volcán *vol.* Costa Rica **166** [inset] J7
Irbid Jordan **107** B3
Irbil Iraq *see* **Arbīl**
Irbit Rus. Fed. **76** H4
Irecê Brazil **177** J6
Ireland *country* Europe **61** E4

▶**Ireland** *i.* Ireland/U.K. **61**
4th largest island in Europe.

Irema Dem. Rep. Congo **122** C4
Irgiz Kazakh. **102** B2
Irgiz *r.* Kazakh. **102** B2
Iri S. Korea *see* **Iksan**
Irian, Teluk *b.* Indon. *see* **Cenderawasih, Teluk**
Irian Barat *prov.* Indon. *see* **Papua**
Irian Jaya *prov.* Indon. *see* **Papua**
Iriba Chad **121** F3
Īrī Dāgh *mt.* Iran **110** B2
Iriga *Luzon* Phil. **82** C3
Irîgui *reg.* Mali/Mauritania **120** C3
Iringa Tanz. **123** D4
Iriri *r.* Brazil **177** H4
Irish Free State *country* Europe *see* **Ireland**
Irish Sea Ireland/U.K. **61** G4
Irituia Brazil **177** I4
'Irj *well* Saudi Arabia **110** C5
Irkutsk Rus. Fed. **88** I2
Irma Canada **151** I4
Irmak Turkey **112** D3
Irminger Basin *sea feature* N. Atlantic Ocean **184** F2
Iron Baron Australia **137** B7
Iron Creek *AK* U.S.A. **148** F2
Irondequoit U.S.A. **165** G2
Iron Mountain U.S.A. **160** F2
Iron Mountain *mt.* U.S.A. **159** G3
Iron Range National Park Australia **136** C2
Iron River U.S.A. **160** F2
Ironton *MO* U.S.A. **160** F4
Ironton *OH* U.S.A. **164** D4
Ironwood Forest National Monument *nat. park* U.S.A. **159** H5
Iroquois *r.* *N.W.T.* Canada **149** O1
Iroquois *r.* U.S.A. **164** B3
Iroquois Falls Canada **152** E4
Irosin *Luzon* Phil. **82** D3
Irō-zaki *pt* Japan **93** E4
Irpen' Ukr. *see* **Irpin'**
Irpin' Ukr. **53** F6
'Irq al Ḩarūrī *des.* Saudi Arabia **110** B5
'Irq Banbān *des.* Saudi Arabia **110** B5
Irrawaddy *r.* Myanmar **86** A4
Irrawaddy, Mouths of the Myanmar **86** A4
Irshad Pass Afgh./Pak. **111** I2
Irta Rus. Fed. **52** K3
Irthing *r.* U.K. **58** E4

▶**Irtysh** *r.* Kazakh./Rus. Fed. **102** E1
5th longest river in Asia and 10th in the world, and a major part of the 2nd longest in Asia (Ob'-Irtysh).

Iruma Japan **93** F3
Iruma-gawa *r.* Japan **93** F3
Irun Spain **67** F2
Iruña Spain *see* **Pamplona**
Iruñea Spain *see* **Pamplona**
Irvine U.K. **60** E5
Irvine *CA* U.S.A. **158** E5
Irvine *KY* U.S.A. **164** D5
Irvine Glacier Antarctica **188** L2
Irving U.S.A. **161** D5
Irvington U.S.A. **164** B5
Irwin *r.* Australia **135** A7
Irwinton U.S.A. **163** D5
Isa Nigeria **120** D3
Isaac *r.* Australia **136** E4
Isabel U.S.A. **160** C2
Isabela *Negros* Phil. **82** C4
Isabela Phil. **82** C5
Isabela, Isla *i.* *Galápagos* Ecuador **176** [inset]
Isabelia, Cordillera *mts* Nicaragua **166** [inset] I6
Isabella Lake U.S.A. **158** D4
Isachsen, Cape Canada **147** H2
Ísafjarðardjúp *est.* Iceland **54** [inset]
Ísafjörður Iceland **54** [inset]
Isa Khel Pak. **111** H3
Isar *r.* Germany **63** M6
Isarog, Mount Phil. **82** C3
Isawa Japan **93** E3
Isbister U.K. **60** [inset]
Ischia, Isola d' *i.* Italy **68** E4
Ise Japan **92** C4
Isehara Japan **93** F3
Isère *r.* France **66** G4
Isère, Pointe *pt* Fr. Guiana **177** H2
Iserlohn Germany **63** H3
Isernhagen Germany **63** J2
Isernia Italy **68** F4
Isesaki Japan **93** F2
Ise-shima Kokuritsu-kōen *nat. park* Japan **92** C4
Ise-wan *b.* Japan **92** C4
Iseyin Nigeria **120** D4
Isfahan Iran *see* **Eşfahān**
Isfana Kyrg. **111** H2
Isheyevka Rus. Fed. **53** K5
Ishibe Japan **92** C3
Ishigaki Japan **89** M8
Ishige Japan **93** F2
Ishikari-wan *b.* Japan **90** F4
Ishikawa *pref.* Japan **92** C2
Ishim *r.* Kazakh./Rus. Fed. **102** D1
Ishinomaki Japan **91** F5
Ishinomaki-wan *b.* Japan **89** Q5
Ishioka Japan **93** G2
Ishkoshim Tajik. **111** H2
Ishpeming U.S.A. **162** C2
Ishtikhon Uzbek. *see* **Ishtixon**
Ishtixon Uzbek. **111** G2
Ishtragh Afgh. **111** H2
Ishurdi Bangl. **105** G4
Ishwardi Bangl. *see* **Ishurdi**
Isiboro Sécure, Parque Nacional *nat. park* Bol. **176** E7
Isigny-sur-Mer France **59** F9
Işıklar Dağı *mts* Turkey **69** L4
Işıklı Turkey **69** M5
Isil'kul' Rus. Fed. **76** I4
Isipingo S. Africa **125** J5
Isiro Dem. Rep. Congo **122** C3
Isisford Australia **136** D5
Iskateley Rus. Fed. **52** L2
İskenderun Turkey **107** C1
İskenderun Körfezi *b.* Turkey **107** B1
İskilip Turkey **112** D2
Iskitim Rus. Fed. **76** J4
Iskŭr *r.* Bulg. **69** K3
Iskushuban Somalia **122** F2
Iskut *r.* *B.C.* Canada **149** O4
Isla *r.* *Scotland* U.K. **60** F4
Isla *r.* *Scotland* U.K. **60** G3
Isla Gorge National Park Australia **136** E5
İslahiye Turkey **112** E3
Islamabad India *see* **Anantnag**

▶**Islamabad** Pak. **111** I3
Capital of Pakistan.

Islamgarh Pak. **111** H5
Islamkot Pak. **111** H5
Island *r.* Canada **150** F2
Ísland *country* Europe *see* **Iceland**
Island U.S.A. **164** B5
Island Bay *Palawan* Phil. **82** B4
Island Falls U.S.A. **162** G2
Island Lagoon *salt flat* Australia **137** B6
Island Lake Canada **151** M4
Island Lake *l.* Canada **151** M4
Island Magee *pen.* U.K. **61** G3
Island Pond U.S.A. **165** J1
Islands, Bay of N.Z. **139** E2
Islas de Bahá, Parque Nacional *nat. park* Hond. **166** [inset] I5
Islay *i.* U.K. **60** C5
Isle of Man *terr.* Irish Sea **58** C4
Isle of Wight U.S.A. **165** G5
Isle Royale National Park U.S.A. **160** F2
Ismail Ukr. *see* **Izmayil**
Ismâ'ilîya Egypt *see* **Al Ismā'īlīyah**
Ismâ'ilîya *governorate* Egypt *see* **Al Ismā'īlīyah**
Ismailly Azer. *see* **İsmayıllı**
İsmayıllı Azer. **113** H2
Isobe Japan **92** C4
Isogo Japan **93** F3
Isojoki Fin. **54** L5
Isoka Zambia **123** D5
Isokylä Fin. **54** O3
Isokyrö Fin. **54** M5
Isola di Capo Rizzuto Italy **68** G5
Ispahan Iran *see* **Eşfahān**
Isparta Turkey **69** N6
Isperikh Bulg. **69** L3
Ispikan Pak. **111** F5
İspir Turkey **113** F2
Ispisar Tajik. *see* **Khŭjand**
Isplinji Pak. **111** G4
Israel *country* Asia **107** B4
Israelite Bay Australia **135** C8
Isra'īl *country* Asia *see* **Israel**
Isselburg Germany **62** G3
Isshiki Japan **92** D4
Issia Côte d'Ivoire **120** C4
Issimu *Sulawesi* Indon. **83** B2
Issoire France **66** F4
Issyk-Kul' Kyrg. *see* **Balykchy**
Issyk-Kul', Ozero *salt l.* Kyrg. *see* **Ysyk-Köl**
Istalif Afgh. **111** H3

▶**İstanbul** Turkey **69** M4
2nd most populous city in Europe.

İstanbul Boğazı *strait* Turkey *see* **Bosporus**
Īstgāh-e Eznā Iran **110** C3
Istiaia Greece **69** J5
Istik *r.* Tajik. **111** I2
Istočni Drvar Bos.-Herz. **68** G2
Istra *pen.* Croatia *see* **Istria**
Istres France **66** G5
Istria *pen.* Croatia **68** E2
Isumi Japan **93** G3
Isumi-gawa *r.* Japan **93** G3
Isüüj Mongolia *see* **Bayanchandmanī**
Iswardi Bangl. *see* **Ishurdi**
Itabapoana *r.* Brazil **179** C3
Itaberá Brazil **179** A3
Itaberaba Brazil **179** C1
Itaberaí Brazil **179** A2
Itabira Brazil **179** C2
Itabirito Brazil **179** C3
Itabuna Brazil **179** D1
Itacajá Brazil **177** I5
Itacarambi Brazil **179** B1
Itacoatiara Brazil **177** G4
Itadori Japan **92** C3
Itaetê Brazil **179** C1
Itagmatana Iran *see* **Hamadān**
Itaguaçu Brazil **179** C2
Itaí Brazil **179** A3
Itaiópolis Brazil **179** A4
Itäisen Suomenlahden kansallispuisto *nat. park* Fin. **55** O6
Itaituba Brazil **177** G4
Itajaí Brazil **179** A4
Itajubá Brazil **179** B3
Itajuipe Brazil **179** D1
Itako Japan **93** G3
Itakura *Gunma* Japan **93** F2
Itakura *Niigata* Japan **93** E1
Italia *country* Europe *see* **Italy**
Italia, Laguna *l.* Bol. **176** F6

▶**Italy** *country* Europe **68** E3
5th most populous country in Europe.

Itamarandiba Brazil **179** C2
Itambé Brazil **179** C1
Itambé, Pico de *mt.* Brazil **179** C2
It Amelân *i.* Neth. *see* **Ameland**
Itami Japan **92** B4
Itami *airport* Japan **92** B4
Itampolo Madag. **123** E6
Itanagar India **105** H4
Itanguari *r.* Brazil **179** B1
Itanhaém Brazil **179** B4
Itanhém Brazil **179** C2
Itanhém *r.* Brazil **179** D2
Itaobím Brazil **179** C2
Itapaci Brazil **179** A1
Itapajipe Brazil **179** A2
Itapebi Brazil **179** D1
Itapecerica Brazil **179** B3
Itapemirim Brazil **179** C3
Itaperuna Brazil **179** C3
Itapetinga Brazil **179** C1
Itapetininga Brazil **179** A3
Itapeva Brazil **179** A3
Itapeva, Lago *l.* Brazil **179** A5
Itapicuru Brazil **177** J6
Itapicuru, Serra de *hills* Brazil **177** I5
Itapicuru Mirim Brazil **177** J4
Itapipoca Brazil **177** K4
Itapira Brazil **179** B3
Itaporanga Brazil **179** A3
Itapuã Brazil **179** A5
Itaqui Brazil **178** E3
Itararé Brazil **179** A4
Itarsi India **104** D5
Itarumã Brazil **179** A2
Itatiba Brazil **179** B3
Itatuba Brazil **176** F5
Itaúna Brazil **179** B3
Itaúnas Brazil **179** D2
Itbayat *i.* Phil. **82** C1
Itchen Lake Canada **151** H1
Itea Greece **69** J5
Ithaca *MI* U.S.A. **164** C2
Ithaca *NY* U.S.A. **165** G2
It Hearrenfean Neth. *see* **Heerenveen**
iThekweni S. Africa *see* **Durban**
Ith Hils *ridge* Germany **63** J2
Ithrah Saudi Arabia **107** C4
Itilleq Greenland **147** M3
Itimbiri *r.* Dem. Rep. Congo **122** C3
Itinga Brazil **179** C2
Itiquira Brazil **177** H7
Itiruçu Brazil **179** C1
Itiúba, Serra de *hills* Brazil **177** K6
Itkillik *r.* *AK* U.S.A. **149** J1
Itō Japan **93** F4
Itoigawa Japan **93** D1
Itonuki Japan **92** C3
iTswane S. Africa *see* **Pretoria**
Ittiri *Sardinia* Italy **68** C4
Ittoqqortoormiit Greenland **147** P2
Itu Brazil **179** B3
Itu Abu Island Spratly Is **80** E4
Ituaçu Brazil **179** C1
Ituberá Brazil **179** D1
Ituí *r.* Brazil **176** D4
Ituiutaba Brazil **179** A2
Itumbiara Brazil **179** A2
Itumbiara, Barragem *resr* Brazil **179** A2
Ituni Guyana **177** G2
Itupiranga Brazil **177** I5
Ituporanga Brazil **179** A4
Iturama Brazil **179** A2
Iturbide *Campeche* Mex. **167** H5
Iturbide Mex. **161** D7
Ituri *r.* Dem. Rep. Congo **122** C3
Iturup, Ostrov *i.* Rus. Fed. **90** G3
Itutinga Brazil **179** B3
Ituxi *r.* Brazil **176** F5
Ītyop'ia *country* Africa *see* **Ethiopia**
Itz *r.* Germany **63** K5
Itzehoe Germany **57** L4
Iuka U.S.A. **161** F5
Iul'tin Rus. Fed. **148** C2
Ivalo Fin. **54** O2
Ivalojoki *r.* Fin. **54** O2
Ivanava Belarus **55** N10
Ivanhoe Australia **138** B4
Ivanhoe U.S.A. **160** D2
Ivanhoe Lake Canada **151** J2
Ivankiv Ukr. **53** F6
Ivankovtsy Rus. Fed. **90** D2
Ivanof Bay *AK* U.S.A. **148** H5
Ivano-Frankivs'k Ukr. **53** E6
Ivano-Frankovsk Ukr. *see* **Ivano-Frankivs'k**
Ivanovka Rus. Fed. **90** B2
Ivanovo Belarus *see* **Ivanava**
Ivanovo *tourist site* Bulg. **69** K3
Ivanovo Rus. Fed. **52** I4
Ivanovskiy Khrebet *mts* Kazakh. **98** C2
Ivanteyevka Rus. Fed. **53** K5
Ivantsevichi Belarus *see* **Ivatsevichy**
Ivatsevichy Belarus **55** N10
Ivaylovgrad Bulg. **69** L4
Ivdel' Rus. Fed. **51** S3
Ivishak *r.* *AK* U.S.A. **149** J1
Ivittuut Greenland **147** N3
Iviza *i.* Spain *see* **Ibiza**
Ivory Coast *country* Africa *see* **Côte d'Ivoire**
Ivrea Italy **68** B2
İvrindi Turkey **69** L5
Ivris Ugheltekhili *pass* Georgia **113** G2
Ivry-la-Bataille France **62** B6
Ivugivik Canada *see* **Ivujivik**
Ivujivik Canada **147** K3
Ivvavik National Park *Y.T.* Canada **149** M1
Ivyanyets Belarus **55** O10
Ivydale U.S.A. **164** E4
Iwade Japan **92** B4
Iwafune Japan **93** F2
Iwai Japan **93** F2
Iwaki Japan **93** G1
Iwaki-san *vol.* Japan **90** F4
Iwakuni Japan **91** D6
Iwakura Japan **92** C3
Iwama Japan **93** G2
Iwamizawa Japan **90** F4
Iwamura Japan **92** D3
Iwamurada Japan **93** E2
Iwan *r.* Indon. **85** F2
Iwase Japan **93** G2
Iwasehama Japan **92** D2
Iwasuge-yama *vol.* Japan **93** E2
Iwata Japan **93** D4
Iwataki Japan **92** B3
Iwatsuki Japan **93** F3
Iwo Nigeria **120** D4
Iwye Belarus **55** N10
Ixcamilpa Mex. **167** F5
Ixelles Belgium **62** E4
Ixhuatlán *Veracruz* Mex. **167** F4
Ixiamas Bol. **176** E6
Ixmiquilpán Mex. **168** E4
Ixopo S. Africa **125** J6
Ixtacomitán Mex. **167** G5
Ixtapa, Punta *pt* Mex. **167** E5
Ixtlán Mex. **168** D4
Ixtlán *Oaxaca* Mex. **167** F5
Ixworth U.K. **59** H6
Iya *i.* Indon. **83** B5
İyirmi Altı Bakı Komissarı Azer. *see* **Uzboy**
Izabal Guat. **166** [inset] H6
Izabal, Lago de *l.* Guat. **167** H6
Izamal Mex. **167** H4
Izapa *tourist site* Mex. **167** G6
Izberbash Rus. Fed. **113** G2
Izegem Belgium **62** D4
Īzeh Iran **110** C4
Izembek National Wildlife Refuge *nature res.* *AK* U.S.A. **148** G5
Izgal Pak. **111** I3
Izhevsk Rus. Fed. **51** Q4
Izhma *Respublika Komi* Rus. Fed. **52** L2
Izhma *Respublika Komi* Rus. Fed. *see* **Sosnogorsk**
Izhma *r.* Rus. Fed. **52** L2
Izigan, Cape *AK* U.S.A. **148** F5
Izmail Ukr. *see* **Izmayil**
Izmayil Ukr. **69** M2
İzmir Turkey **69** L5
İzmir Körfezi *g.* Turkey **69** L5
İzmit Turkey **69** M4
İzmit Körfezi *b.* Turkey **69** M4
Izozog Bol. **176** F7
Izra' Syria **107** C3
Iztochni Rodopi *mts* Bulg. **69** K4
Izúcar de Matamoros Mex. **167** F5
Izu-hantō *pen.* Japan **93** E4
Izuhara Japan **91** C6
Izumi *Fukui* Japan **92** C3
Izumi *Fukushima* Japan **93** G2
Izumi *Kanagawa* Japan **93** F3
Izumi *Ōsaka* Japan **92** B4
Izumiōtsu Japan **92** B4
Izumisano Japan **92** B4
Izumo Japan **91** D6
Izunagaoka Japan **93** E3

▶**Izu-Ogasawara Trench** *sea feature* N. Pacific Ocean **186** F3
5th deepest trench in the world.

Izushi Japan **92** A3
Izu-shotō *is* Japan **93** F4
Izyaslav Ukr. **53** E6
Iz"yayu Rus. Fed. **52** M2
Izyum Ukr. **53** H6

J

Jabal Dab Saudi Arabia **110** C6
Jabalón *r.* Spain **67** D4
Jabalpur India **104** D5
Jabbūl, Sabkhat al *salt flat* Syria **107** C2
Jabir *reg.* Oman **110** E6
Jabiru Australia **134** F3
Jablah Syria **107** B2
Jablanica Bos.-Herz. **68** G3
Jaboatão Brazil **177** L5
Jaboticabal Brazil **179** A3
Jabung, Tanjung *pt* Indon. **84** D3
Jacala Mex. **167** F4
Jacaltenango Guat. **167** H6
Jacaraci Brazil **179** C1
Jacareacanga Brazil **177** G5
Jacareí Brazil **179** B3
Jacarézinho Brazil **179** A3
Jáchymov Czech Rep. **63** M4
Jacinto Brazil **179** C2
Jack *r.* Australia **136** D2
Jack Lake Canada **165** F1
Jackman U.S.A. **162** G2
Jacksboro U.S.A. **161** D5
Jackson Australia **138** D1
Jackson *AL* U.S.A. **163** C6
Jackson *CA* U.S.A. **158** C2
Jackson *GA* U.S.A. **163** D5
Jackson *KY* U.S.A. **164** D5
Jackson *MI* U.S.A. **164** C2
Jackson *MN* U.S.A. **160** E3

▶**Jackson** *MS* U.S.A. **161** F5
Capital of Mississippi.

Jackson *NC* U.S.A. **162** E4
Jackson *OH* U.S.A. **164** D4
Jackson *TN* U.S.A. **161** F5
Jackson *WY* U.S.A. **156** F4
Jackson, Mount Antarctica **188** L2
Jackson Head *hd* N.Z. **139** B6
Jacksonville *AR* U.S.A. **161** E5
Jacksonville *FL* U.S.A. **163** D6
Jacksonville *IL* U.S.A. **160** F4
Jacksonville *NC* U.S.A. **163** E5
Jacksonville *OH* U.S.A. **164** D4
Jacksonville *TX* U.S.A. **161** E6
Jacksonville Beach U.S.A. **163** D6
Jack Wade U.S.A. **146** D3
Jacmel Haiti **169** J5
Jaco *i.* East Timor **83** C5
Jacobabad Pak. **111** H4
Jacobina Brazil **177** J6
Jacob Lake U.S.A. **159** G3
Jacobsdal S. Africa **124** G5
Jacques-Cartier, Détroit de *sea chan.* Canada **153** I4
Jacques-Cartier, Mont *mt.* Canada **153** I4
Jacques Cartier Passage Canada *see* **Jacques-Cartier, Détroit de**
Jacuí Brazil **179** B3
Jacuípe *r.* Brazil **177** K6
Jacunda Brazil **177** I4
Jaddangi India **106** D2
Jaddi, Ras *pt* Pak. **111** F5
Jadebusen *b.* Germany **63** I1
J. A. D. Jensen Nunatakker *nunataks* Greenland **147** N3
Jadotville Dem. Rep. Congo *see* **Likasi**
Jādū Libya **120** E1
Jaen *Luzon* Phil. **82** C3
Jaén Spain **67** E5
Ja'farābād Iran **110** E2
Jaffa, Cape Australia **137** B8
Jaffna Sri Lanka **106** C4
Jafr, Qā' al *imp. l.* Jordan **107** C4
Jagadhri India **104** D3
Jagalur India **106** C3
Jagatsinghapur India *see* **Jagatsinghpur**
Jagatsinghpur India **105** F5
Jagdalpur India **106** D2
Jagdaqi *Nei Mongol* China **95** K1
Jagersfontein S. Africa **125** G5
Jaggang *Xizang* China **99** B6
Jaggayyapeta India **106** D2
Jaghīn Iran **110** E5
Jagok Tso *salt l.* China *see* **Urru Co**
Jagsamka *Sichuan* China *see* **Luding**
Jagst *r.* Germany **63** J5
Jagtial India **106** C2
Jaguariaíva Brazil **179** A4
Jaguaripe Brazil **179** D1
Jagüey Grande Cuba **163** D8
Jahām, 'Irq *des.* Saudi Arabia **110** B5
Jahanabad India *see* **Jehanabad**
Jahmah *well* Iraq **113** G5
Jahrom Iran **110** D4
Jaicós Brazil **177** J5
Jaigarh India **106** B2
Jailolo *Halmahera* Indon. **83** C2
Jailolo, Selat *sea chan.* *Maluku* Indon. **83** D3
Jailolo Gilolo *i.* *Maluku* Indon. *see* **Halmahera**
Jainca *Qinghai* China **94** E5
Jainpur India **105** E4
Jaintapur Bangl. *see* **Jaintiapur**
Jaintiapur Bangl. **105** H4
Jainzhug *Xizang* China *see* **Gutang**
Jaipur India **104** C4
Jaipurhat Bangl. *see* **Joypurhat**
Jais India **105** E4
Jaisalmer India **104** B4
Jaisamand Lake India **104** C4
Jaitaran India **104** C4
Jaitgarh *hill* India **106** C1
Jajapur India *see* **Jajpur**
Jajarkot Nepal **109** N4
Jajce Bos.-Herz. **68** G2
Jajnagar *state* India *see* **Orissa**
Jajpur India **105** F5
Jakar Bhutan **105** G4

▶**Jakarta** *Jawa* Indon. **84** D4
Capital of Indonesia. 9th most populous city in the world.

Jakes Corner *Y.T.* Canada **149** N3
Jakhau India **104** B5
Jakin *mt.* Afgh. **111** G4
Jakkī Kowr Iran **111** F5
Jäkkvik Sweden **54** J3
Jakliat India **104** C3
Jako *i.* East Timor *see* **Jaco**
Jakobshavn Greenland *see* **Ilulissat**
Jakobstad Fin. **54** M5
Jal U.S.A. **161** C5
Jalaid *Nei Mongol* China *see* **Inder**
Jalājil Saudi Arabia **110** B5
Jalālābād Afgh. **111** H3
Jalalabad *Uttar Prad.* India **99** B8
Jalal-Abad Kyrg. **102** D3
Jalal-Abad *admin. div.* Kyrg. **98** A4
Jalālah al Baḩrīyah, Jabal *plat.* Egypt **112** C5
Jalalpur Pirwala Pak. **111** H4
Jalāmid, Ḩazm al *ridge* Saudi Arabia **113** E5
Jalandhar India **104** C3
Jalapa Guat. **167** H6

Jalapa Mex. 167 G5
Jalapa Mex. 168 E5
Jalapa Nicaragua 166 [inset] I6
Jalapa Enríquez Mex. see Jalapa
Jalasjärvi Fin. 54 M5
Jalaun India 104 D4
Jalawlā' Iraq 113 G4
Jaldak Afgh. 111 G4
Jaldhaka r. Bangl. 99 E8
Jaldrug India 106 C2
Jales Brazil 179 A3
Jalesar India 104 D4
Jalgaon India 104 C5
Jalībah Iraq 113 G5
Jalingo Nigeria 120 E4
Jalisco state Mex. 166 D5
Jallābī Iran 110 E5
Jalna India 106 B2
Jālo Iran 111 F5
Jalón r. Spain 67 F3
Jalor India see Jalore
Jalore India 104 C4
Jalostotitlán Mex. 166 E4
Jalpa Guanajuato Mex. 167 E4
Jalpa Mex. 168 D4
Jalpaiguri India 105 G4
Jalpan Mex. 167 F4
Jālū Libya 121 F2
Jalūlā Iraq see Jalawlā'
Jām reg. Iran 111 F3
Jamaica country West Indies 169 I5
Jamaica Channel Haiti/Jamaica 169 I5
Jamalpur Bangl. 105 G4
Jamalpur India 105 F4
Jamanxim r. Brazil 177 G4
Jamati Xinjiang China 98 C3
Jambi Sumatera Indon. 84 C3
Jambi prov. Indon. 84 C3
Jambin Australia 136 E5
Jambo India 104 C4
Jamboaye r. Indon. 84 B1
Jambongan i. Malaysia 85 G1
Jambu Kalimantan Indon. 85 G3
Jambuair, Tanjung pt Indon. 84 B1
Jamda India 105 F5
Jamekunte India 106 C2
James r. N. Dakota/S. Dakota U.S.A. 160 D3
James r. VA U.S.A. 165 G5
James, Baie b. Canada see James Bay
Jamesabad Pak. 111 H5
James Bay Canada 152 E3
Jamesburg U.S.A. 165 H3
James Island Galápagos Ecuador see San Salvador, Isla
Jameson Land reg. Greenland 147 P2
James Peak N.Z. 139 B7
James Ranges mts Australia 135 F6
James Ross Island Antarctica 188 A2
James Ross Strait Canada 147 I3
Jamestown Australia 137 B7
Jamestown Canada see Wawa
Jamestown S. Africa 125 H6

▶Jamestown St Helena 184 H7
Capital of St Helena.

Jamestown ND U.S.A. 160 D2
Jamestown NY U.S.A. 164 F2
Jamestown TN U.S.A. 164 C5
Jamkhed India 106 B2
Jammu India 104 C2

▶Jammu and Kashmir terr. Asia 104 D2
Disputed territory (India/Pakistan).

Jamnagar India 104 B5
Jampang Kulon Jawa Indon. 84 D4
Jampur Pak. 111 H4
Jamrud Pak. 111 H3
Jämsä Fin. 55 N6
Jamsah Egypt 112 D6
Jämsänkoski Fin. 54 N6
Jamshedpur India 105 F5
Jamtai Xinjiang China 98 C4
Jamtari Nigeria 120 E4
Jamui India 105 F4
Jamuk, Gunung mt. Indon. 85 G2
Jamuna r. Bangl. see Raimangal
Jamuna r. India see Yamuna
Jamuna r. India 99 F8
Janā i. Saudi Arabia 110 C5
Janāb, Wādī al watercourse Jordan 107 C4
Janakpur India 105 E5
Janaúba Brazil 179 C1
Jand Pak. 111 I3
Jandaia Brazil 179 A2
Jandaq Iran 110 D3
Jandola Pak. 111 H3
Jandowae Australia 138 E1
Janesville CA U.S.A. 158 C1
Janesville WI U.S.A. 160 F3
Jang, Tanjung pt Indon. 84 D3
Jangada Brazil 179 A4
Jangal Iran 110 E3
Jangamo Moz. 125 L3
Jangaon India 106 C2
Jangco Xizang China 99 E7
Jangipur India 105 G4
Jangnga Turkm. see Jaňňa
Jangngai Ri mts Xizang China 99 D6
Jangngai Zangbo r. Xizang China 99 D6
Jänickendorf Germany 63 N2
Jani Khel Pak. 111 H3

▶Jan Mayen terr. Arctic Ocean 189 I2
Part of Norway.

Jan Mayen Fracture Zone sea feature Arctic Ocean 189 I2
Jaňňa Turkm. 110 D1
Janos Mex. 166 C2
Jans Bay Canada 151 I4
Jansenville S. Africa 124 G7
Januária Brazil 179 B1
Janūb Sīnā' governorate Egypt 107 A5
Janûb Sînâ' governorate Egypt see Janūb Sīnā'
Janzar mt. Pak. 111 F5
Jaodar Pak. 111 F5

▶Japan country Asia 91 D5
10th most populous country in the world.

Japan, Sea of N. Pacific Ocean 91 D5
Japan Alps National Park Japan see Chūbu-Sangaku Kokuritsu-kōen
Japan Trench sea feature N. Pacific Ocean 186 F3
Japiim Brazil 176 D5
Japón Hond. 166 [inset] I6
Japurá r. Brazil 176 F4
Japvo Mount India 105 H4
Jaqué Panama 166 [inset] K8
Jarābulus Syria 107 D1
Jaraguá Brazil 179 A1
Jaraguá, Serra mts Brazil 179 A4
Jaraguá do Sul Brazil 179 A4
Jarash Jordan 107 B3
Jarboesville U.S.A. see Lexington Park
Jardine River National Park Australia 136 C1
Jardinésia Brazil 179 A2
Jardinópolis Brazil 179 B3
Jargalang China 90 A4
Jargalant Arhangay Mongolia see Battsengel
Jargalant Bayanhongor Mongolia 94 D2
Jargalant Bayan-Ölgiy Mongolia see Bulgan
Jargalant Dornod Mongolia see Matad
Jargalant Govĭ-Altay Mongolia see Biger
Jargalant Hovd Mongolia see Hovd
Jargalant Mongolia 94 D1
Jargalant Töv Mongolia 94 F1
Jargalant Hayrhan mt. Mongolia 94 C2
Jargalthaan Mongolia 95 G2
Jari r. Brazil 177 H4
Järna Sweden 55 J7
Jarocin Poland 57 P5
Jarosław Poland 53 D6
Järpen Sweden 54 H5
Jarqo'rg'on Uzbek. 111 G2
Jarqŭrghon Uzbek. see Jarqo'rg'on
Jarrettsville U.S.A. 165 G4
Jartai Nei Mongol China 94 F4
Jartai Yanchi salt l. Nei Mongol China 94 F4
Jarú Brazil 176 F6
Jarud Nei Mongol China see Lubei
Järvakandi Estonia 55 N7
Järvenpää Fin. 55 N6

▶Jarvis Island terr. S. Pacific Ocean 186 J6
United States Unincorporated Territory.

Jarwa India 105 E4
Jashpurnagar India 105 F5
Jāsk Iran 110 E5
Jāsk-e Kohneh Iran 110 E5
Jasliq Uzbek. 113 J2
Jasło Poland 53 D6
Jasol India 104 C4
Jason Islands Falkland Is 178 D8
Jason Peninsula Antarctica 188 L2
Jasonville U.S.A. 164 B4
Jasper Canada 150 G4
Jasper AL U.S.A. 163 C5
Jasper FL U.S.A. 163 D6
Jasper GA U.S.A. 163 C5
Jasper IN U.S.A. 164 B4
Jasper NY U.S.A. 165 G2
Jasper TN U.S.A. 163 C5
Jasper TX U.S.A. 161 E6
Jasper National Park Canada 150 G4
Jasrasar India 104 C4
Jaşşān Iraq 113 G4
Jassy Romania see Iaşi
Jastrzębie-Zdrój Poland 57 Q6
Jaswantpura India 104 C4
Jászberény Hungary 69 H1
Jataí Brazil 179 A2
Jatapu r. Brazil 177 G4
Jath India 106 B2
Jati Pak. 111 H5
Jatibarang Jawa Indon. 85 E4
Jatibonico Cuba 163 E8
Jatiluhur, Waduk resr Jawa Indon. 84 D4
Játiva Spain see Xàtiva
Jatiwangi Jawa Indon. 85 E4
Jatoi Pak. 111 H4
Jat Poti Afgh. 111 G4
Jaú Brazil 179 A3
Jaú r. Brazil 176 F4
Jaú, Parque Nacional do nat. park Brazil 176 F4
Jaua Sarisariñama, Parque Nacional nat. park Venez. 176 F3
Jauja Peru 176 C6
Jaumave Mex. 167 F4
Jaunlutriņi Latvia 55 M8
Jaunpiebalga Latvia 55 O8
Jaunpur India 105 E4
Jauri Iran 111 F4
Java Georgia 113 F2

▶Java i. Indon. 85 E4
5th largest island in Asia.

Javaés r. Brazil see Formoso
Javand Afgh. 111 G3
Javari r. Brazil/Peru see Yavari
Java Ridge sea feature Indian Ocean 185 P6
Javarthushuu Mongolia see Bayan-Uul
Java Sea Indon. see Jawa, Laut

▶Java Trench sea feature Indian Ocean 186 C6
Deepest point in the Indian Ocean.

Jävenitz Germany 63 L2
Jävre Sweden 54 L4
Jawa i. Indon. see Java
Jawa, Laut sea Indon. 85 E4
Jawa Barat prov. Indon. 84 D4
Jawa Tengah prov. Indon. 85 E4
Jawa Timur prov. Indon. 85 F4
Jawhar India 106 B2
Jawhar Somalia 122 E3
Jawor Poland 57 P5
Jay U.S.A. 161 E4

▶Jaya, Puncak mt. Indon. 81 J7
Highest mountain in Oceania.

Jayakusumu mt. Indon. see Jaya, Puncak
Jayakwadi Sagar l. India 106 B2
Jayantiapur Bangl. see Jaintiapur
Jayapura Indon. 81 K7
Jayawijaya, Pegunungan mts Indon. 81 J7
Jayb, Wādī al watercourse Israel/Jordan 107 B4
Jayfī, Wādī al watercourse Egypt 107 B4
Jaypur India 106 D2
Jayrūd Syria 107 C3
Jayton U.S.A. 161 C5
Jazīreh-ye Shīf Iran 110 C4
Jazminal Mex. 167 E3
Jbail Lebanon 107 B2
J. C. Murphey Lake U.S.A. 164 B3
Jean U.S.A. 159 F4
Jean Marie River Canada 150 F2
Jeannin, Lac l. Canada 153 I2
Jebāl Bārez, Kūh-e mts Iran 110 E4
Jebel, Bahr el r. Sudan/Uganda see White Nile
Jebel Abyad Plateau Sudan 108 C6
Jebus Indon. 84 D3
Jech Doab lowland Pak. 111 I4
Jedburgh U.K. 60 G5
Jeddah Saudi Arabia 108 E5
Jedeida Tunisia 68 C6
Jeetze r. Germany 63 L1
Jefferson IA U.S.A. 160 E3
Jefferson NC U.S.A. 162 D4
Jefferson OH U.S.A. 164 E3
Jefferson TX U.S.A. 161 E5
Jefferson, Mount U.S.A. 158 E2
Jefferson, Mount vol. U.S.A. 156 C3

▶Jefferson City U.S.A. 160 E4
Capital of Missouri.

Jeffersonville GA U.S.A. 163 D5
Jeffersonville IN U.S.A. 164 C4
Jeffersonville OH U.S.A. 164 D4
Jeffreys Bay S. Africa 124 G8
Jehanabad India 105 F4
Jeju S. Korea see Cheju
Jejuí Guazú r. Para. 178 E2
Jēkabpils Latvia 55 N8
Jelbart Ice Shelf Antarctica 188 B2
Jelenia Góra Poland 57 O5
Jelep La pass China/India 99 E8
Jelgava Latvia 55 M8
Jellico U.S.A. 164 C5
Jellicoe Canada 152 D4
Jelloway U.S.A. 164 D3
Jemaja i. Indon. 84 D2
Jember Jawa Indon. 85 F5
Jeminay Xinjiang China 98 D3
Jeminay Kazakh. 98 D3
Jempang, Danau l. Indon. 85 G3
Jena Germany 63 L4
Jena U.S.A. 161 E6
Jendouba Tunisia 68 C6
Jengish Chokusu mt. China/Kyrg. see Pobeda Peak
Jenīn West Bank 107 B3
Jenkins U.S.A. 164 D5
Jênlung Xizang China 99 D7
Jenne Mali see Djenné
Jenner Canada 151 I5
Jennings r. B.C. Canada 149 N4
Jennings U.S.A. 161 E6
Jenolan Caves Australia 138 E4
Jenpeg Canada 151 L4
Jensen U.S.A. 159 I1
Jens Munk Island Canada 147 K3
Jepara Jawa Indon. 85 E4
Jeparit Australia 137 C8
Jequié Brazil 179 C1
Jequitaí r. Brazil 179 B2
Jequitinhonha Brazil 179 C2
Jequitinhonha r. Brazil 179 D1
Jerantut Malaysia 84 C2
Jerba, Île de i. Tunisia 64 G5
Jerbar Sudan 121 G4
Jereh Iran 110 C4
Jérémie Haiti 169 J5
Jerez Mex. 168 D4
Jerez de la Frontera Spain 67 C5
Jergol Norway 54 N2
Jergucat Albania 69 I5
Jericho Australia 136 D4
Jericho West Bank 107 B4
Jerichow Germany 63 M2
Jerid, Chott el salt l. Tunisia 64 F5
Jerijeh, Tanjung pt Malaysia 85 E2
Jerilderie Australia 138 B5
Jerimoth Hill hill U.S.A. 165 J3
Jeroaquara Brazil 179 A1
Jerome U.S.A. 156 E4
Jerruck Pak. 111 H5

▶Jersey terr. Channel Is 59 E9
United Kingdom Crown Dependency.

Jersey City U.S.A. 165 H3
Jersey Shore U.S.A. 165 G3
Jerseyville U.S.A. 160 F4
Jerumenha Brazil 177 J5

▶Jerusalem Israel/West Bank 107 B4
De facto capital of Israel, disputed.

Jervis Bay Australia 138 E5
Jervis Bay b. Australia 138 E5
Jervis Bay Territory admin. div. Australia 138 E5
Jesenice Slovenia 68 F1
Jesenice, Vodní nádrž resr Czech Rep. 63 M4
Jesi Italy 68 E3
Jesselton Sabah Malaysia see Kota Kinabalu
Jessen Germany 63 M3
Jessheim Norway 55 G6
Jessore Bangl. 105 G5
Jesteburg Germany 63 J1
Jesu Maria Island P.N.G. see Rambutyo Island
Jesup U.S.A. 163 D6
Jesús Carranza Mex. 167 G5
Jesús María, Barra spit Mex. 161 D7
Jeti-Ögüz Kyrg. 98 B4
Jetmore U.S.A. 160 D4
Jetpur India 104 B5
Jever Germany 63 H1
Jewell Ridge U.S.A. 164 E5
Jewish Autonomous Oblast admin. div. Rus. Fed. see Yevreyskaya Avtonomnaya Oblast'
Jeypur India see Jaypur
Jezzine Lebanon 107 B3
Jhabua India 104 C5
Jhajhar India see Jhajjar
Jhajjar India 104 D3
Jhal Pak. 111 G4
Jhalawar India 104 D4
Jhal Jhao Pak. 111 G5
Jhang Pak. 111 I4
Jhansi India 104 D4
Jhanzi r. India 86 A1
Jhapa Nepal 105 F4
Jharia India 105 F5
Jharkhand state India 105 F5
Jharsuguda India 105 F5
Jhawani Nepal 105 F4
Jhelum r. India/Pak. 111 I4
Jhelum Pak. 111 I3
Jhenaidah Bangl. 105 G5
Jhenaidaha Bangl. see Jhenaidah
Jhenida Bangl. see Jhenaidah
Jhimpir Pak. 111 H5
Jhudo Pak. 111 H5
Jhumritilaiya India 105 F4
Jhund India 104 B5
Jhunjhunun India 104 C3
Jiachuan China 96 E1
Jiachuanzhen China see Jiachuan
Jiading Jiangxi China see Xinfeng
Jiading Shanghai China 97 I2
Jiahe China 97 G3
Jiajiang China 96 D2
Jialing Jiang r. Sichuan China 94 F6
Jialu Shaanxi China see Jiaxian
Jialu He r. China 95 H5
Jiamusi China 90 C3
Ji'an Jiangxi China 97 G3
Ji'an Jilin China 90 B4
Jianchang Liaoning China 95 I3
Jianchuan China 96 C3
Jiande China 97 H2
Jiangbei China see Yubei
Jiangbiancun China 97 G3
Jiangcheng China 96 D4
Jiangcun China 97 F3
Jiangdu China 97 H1
Jiange China see Pu'an
Jianghong China 97 F4
Jiangjiapo Shandong China 95 I4
Jiangjin China 96 E2
Jiangjunmiao Xinjiang China 94 B2
Jiangjunmu Hebei China 95 H4
Jiangjuntai Gansu China 94 D3
Jiangkou Guangdong China see Fengkai
Jiangkou Guizhou China 97 F3
Jiangkou Shaanxi China 96 E1
Jiangling China see Jingzhou
Jiangluozhen China 96 E1
Jiangmen China 97 G4
Jiangna China see Yanshan
Jiangshan China 97 H2
Jiangsi China see Dejiang
Jiangsu prov. China 97 H1
Jiangtaibu Ningxia China 94 F5
Jiangxi prov. China 97 G3
Jiangxia China 97 G2
Jiangxian Shanxi China 95 G5
Jiangxigou Qinghai China 94 E4
Jiangyan China 97 I1
Jiangyin China 97 I2
Jiangyou China 96 E2
Jiangyu Shandong China 95 I4
Jiangzhesongrong Xizang China 99 D7
Jianhu Jiangsu China 95 I5
Jianjun Shaanxi China see Yongshou
Jiankang China 96 D3
Jianli China 97 G2
Jian'ou China 97 H3
Jianping China see Langxi
Jianping Liaoning China 95 I3
Jianping Liaoning China 95 I3
Jianqiao Hebei China 95 I4
Jianshe Qinghai China 94 D5
Jianshi China 97 F2
Jianshui China 96 D4
Jianshui Hu l. Xizang China 99 C6
Jianxing China 96 E2
Jianyang Fujian China 97 H3
Jianyang Sichuan China 96 E2
Jiaochang China 96 D1
Jiaochangba China see Jiaochang
Jiaocheng China see Jiaoling
Jiaocheng Shanxi China 95 H4
Jiaohe Hebei China 95 I4
Jiaohe China 90 B4
Jiaojiang China see Taizhou
Jiaokou Shanxi China 95 G4
Jiaokui China see Yiliang
Jiaolai He r. China 95 J3
Jiaoling China 97 H3
Jiaonan Shandong China 95 I5
Jiaopingdu China 96 D3
Jiaowei China 97 H3
Jiaozhou Shandong China 95 J4
Jiaozuo Henan China 95 H5
Jiarsu Qinghai China 94 C4
Jiasa China 96 D3
Jiashan China see Mingguang
Jiashi Xinjiang China 98 B5
Jia Tsuo La pass Xizang China 99 D7
Jiawang China 97 H1
Jiaxian China 97 G1
Jiaxian Shaanxi China 95 G4
Jiaxing China 97 I2
Jiayi Taiwan see Chiai
Jiayin China 90 C2
Jiayuguan Gansu China 94 D4
Jiazi China 97 H4
Jībūtī country Africa see Djibouti
Jibuti Djibouti see Djibouti
Jiddah Saudi Arabia see Jeddah
Jiddī, Jabal al hill Egypt 107 A4
Jidong China 90 C3
Jiehkkevárri mt. Norway 54 K2
Jiehu Shandong China see Yinan
Jieshi China 97 G4
Jieshipu Gansu China 94 F5
Jieshi Wan b. China 97 G4
Jiexi China 97 G4
Jiexiu Shanxi China 95 G4
Jieyang China 97 H4
Jieznas Lith. 55 N9
Jigzhi China 96 D1
Jiḥār, Wādī al watercourse Syria 107 C2
Jihlava Czech Rep. 57 O6
Jija Sarai Afgh. 111 F3
Jijel Alg. 64 F4
Jijiga Eth. 122 E3
Jījīrud Iran 110 C3
Jijitai Gansu China 94 D3
Jijü China 96 D2
Jil'ād reg. Jordan 107 B3
Jilf al Kabīr, Haḍabat al plat. Egypt 108 C5
Jilh al 'Ishār plain Saudi Arabia 110 B5
Jilib Somalia 122 E3
Jili Hu l. China 98 D3
Jilin China 90 B4
Jilin prov. China 95 K3
Jiling Gansu China 94 E4
Jilin Hada Ling mts China 90 B4
Jiliu He r. China 90 A2
Jilo India 104 C4
Jilong Taiwan see Chilung
Jīma Eth. 122 D3
Jimda China see Zindo
Jiménez Chihuahua Mex. 166 D3
Jiménez Coahuila Mex. 167 E2
Jiménez Tamaulipas Mex. 161 D7
Jimeng Qinghai China 94 D4
Jimía, Cerro mt. Hond. 168 G5
Jimo Shandong China 95 J4
Jimokuji Japan 92 C3
Jimsar Xinjiang China 98 E4
Jim Thorpe U.S.A. 165 H3
Jinan Shandong China 95 I4
Jin'an China see Songpan
Jinbi China see Dayao
Jinchang Gansu China 94 E4
Jincheng Shanxi China 95 H5
Jincheng Sichuan China see Yilong
Jincheng Yunnan China see Wuding
Jinchengjiang China see Hechi
Jinchuan Gansu China see Jinchang
Jinchuan Jiangxi China see Xingan
Jind India 104 D3
Jinding China see Lanping
Jindřichův Hradec Czech Rep. 57 O6
Jin'e China see Longchang
Jinfosi Gansu China 94 D4
Jing Xinjiang China see Jinghe
Jingbian Shaanxi China 95 G4
Jingchuan Gansu China 95 F5
Jingde China 97 H2
Jingdezhen China 97 H2
Jingellic Australia 138 C5
Jinggangshan China 97 G3
Jinggang Shan hill China 97 G3
Jinggongqiao China 97 H2
Jinggu Gansu China 94 E5
Jinggu China 96 D4
Jinghai Tianjin China 95 I4
Jinghe Xinjiang China 98 C3
Jing He r. China 95 G5
Jinghong China 96 D4
Jingle Shanxi China 95 H4
Jingmen China 97 G2
Jingning Gansu China 94 F5
Jingpeng Nei Mongol China 95 I3
Jingpo China 90 C4
Jingpo Hu resr China 90 C4
Jingsha China see Jingzhou
Jingtai Gansu China 94 E4
Jingtieshan Gansu China 94 D4
Jingxi China 96 E4
Jingxian Anhui China 97 H2
Jingxian Hunan China see Jingzhou
Jingyang China see Jingde
Jingyu China 90 B4
Jingyuan Gansu China 94 F4
Jingzhou Hubei China 97 G2
Jingzhou Hubei China 97 G2
Jingzhou Hunan China 97 F3
Jinhe Nei Mongol China 90 A2
Jinhe Yunnan China see Jinping
Jinhu China 97 H1
Jinhua Yunnan China see Jianchuan
Jinhua Zhejiang China 97 H2
Jining Nei Mongol China 95 H3
Jining Shandong China 95 I5
Jinja Uganda 122 D3
Jinjiang Hainan China see Chengmai
Jinjiang Yunnan China 96 D3
Jin Jiang r. China 97 G2
Jinka Eth. 122 D3
Jinmen Taiwan see Chinmen
Jinmen Dao i. Taiwan see Chinmen Tao
Jinmu Jiao pt China 97 F5
Jinning China 96 D3
Jinotega Nicaragua 166 [inset] I6
Jinotepe Nicaragua 166 [inset] I7
Jinping Guizhou China 97 F3
Jinping Yunnan China 96 D4
Jinping Yunnan China see Qiubei
Jinping Shan mts China 96 D3
Jinsen S. Korea see Inch'ŏn
Jinsha China 96 E3
Jinsha Jiang r. China 96 E2 see Yangtze
Jinshan Nei Mongol China see Guyang
Jinshan Nei Mongol China 95 I3
Jinshan China see Zhujing
Jinshan Yunnan China see Lufeng
Jinshi Hunan China 97 F2
Jinshi Hunan China see Xinning
Jinta Gansu China 94 D4
Jintotolo i. Phil. 82 C4
Jintotolo Channel Phil. 82 C4
Jintur India 106 C2
Jinxi Anhui China see Taihu
Jinxi Jiangxi China 97 H3
Jinxi Liaoning China see Lianshan
Jin Xi r. China 97 H3
Jinxian China 97 H2
Jinxian Liaoning China see Linghai
Jinxiang Shandong China 95 I5
Jinyun China 97 I2
Jinz, Qā' al salt flat Jordan 107 C4
Jinzhai China 97 G2
Jinzhong Shanxi China 95 H4
Jinzhou Liaoning China 95 J3
Jinzhou Liaoning China 95 J4
Jinzhou Wan b. China 95 J4
Jinzhu China see Daocheng
Jinzū-gawa r. Japan 92 D2
Ji-Paraná Brazil 176 F6
Jipijapa Ecuador 176 B4
Ji Qu r. Qinghai China 99 G7
Jiquilisco El Salvador 166 [inset] H6
Jiquiricá Brazil 179 D1
Jiquitaia Brazil 179 D2
Jirā', Wādī watercourse Egypt 107 A5
Jirānīyāt, Shi'bān al watercourse Saudi Arabia 107 D4
Jirgatol Tajik. 111 H2
Jiri r. India 86 A1
Jirin Gol Nei Mongol China 95 I2
Jīroft Iran 110 E4
Jirriiban Somalia 122 E3
Jirwān Saudi Arabia 110 C6
Jirwan well Saudi Arabia 110 C6
Jishan Shanxi China 95 G5
Jishi Qinghai China see Xunhua
Jishishan Gansu China 94 E5
Jishou China 97 F2
Jisr ash Shughūr Syria 107 C2
Jitian China see Lianshan
Jitotol Mex. 167 G5
Jitra Malaysia 84 C1
Jiu r. Romania 69 J3
Jiuchenggong Shaanxi China see Linyou
Jiudengkou Nei Mongol China 94 F4
Jiuding Shan mt. China 96 D2
Jiujiang Jiangxi China 97 G2
Jiujiang Jiangxi China 97 H2
Jiulian China see Mojiang
Jiuling Shan mts China 97 G2
Jiulong H.K. China see Kowloon
Jiulong Sichuan China 96 D2
Jiumiao Liaoning China 95 J3
Jiuqian China 97 F3
Jiuquan Gansu China 94 D4
Jiurongcheng Shandong China 95 J4
Jiuxian Shanxi China 95 G4
Jiuxu China 96 E3
Jiuzhou Jiang r. China 97 F4
Jiwani Pak. 111 F5
Jiwen Nei Mongol China 95 J1
Jixi Anhui China 97 H2
Jixi Heilong. China 90 C3
Jixian Hebei China see Jizhou
Jixian China 90 C3
Jixian Henan China see Weihui
Jixian Shanxi China 95 G4
Jiyuan Henan China 95 H5
Jīzah, Ahrāmāt al tourist site Egypt see Pyramids of Giza
Jīzān Saudi Arabia 108 F6
Jizhou Hebei China 95 H4
Jizō-dake mt. Japan 93 F2
Jizzakh Uzbek. see Jizzax
Jizzax Uzbek. 111 G1
Joaçaba Brazil 179 A4
Joaíma Brazil 179 C2
João Belo Moz. see Xai-Xai
João de Almeida Angola see Chibia
João Pessoa Brazil 177 L5
João Pinheiro Brazil 179 B2
Joaquin V. González Arg. 178 D3
Jōban Japan 93 G2
Jobo Point Mindanao Phil. 82 D4
Job Peak U.S.A. 158 D2
Jocketa Germany 63 M4
Jocotán Guat. 167 H6
Joda India 105 F5
Jodhpur India 104 C4
Jodiya India 104 B5
Joensuu Fin. 54 P5
Jōetsu Japan 93 E1
Jofane Moz. 123 D6
Joffre, Mount Canada 150 H5
Jōganji-gawa r. Japan 92 D2

Jōga-shima *i.* Japan **93** F3
Jogbura Nepal **104** E3
Jõgeva Estonia **55** O7
Jogjakarta Indon. *see* **Yogyakarta**
Jōhana Japan **92** C2
Johannesburg S. Africa **125** H4
Johannesburg U.S.A. **158** E4
Johan Peninsula Canada **147** K2
Johi Pak. **111** G5
John *r. AK* U.S.A. **149** J2
John Day U.S.A. **156** D3
John Day *r.* U.S.A. **156** C3
John D'Or Prairie Canada **150** H3
John F. Kennedy *airport* U.S.A. **165** I3
John H. Kerr Reservoir U.S.A. **165** F5
John Jay, Mount Canada/U.S.A. **149** O4
John o'Groats U.K. **60** F2
Johnson U.S.A. **160** C4
Johnsonburg U.S.A. **165** F3
Johnson City *NY* U.S.A. **165** H2
Johnson City *TN* U.S.A. **162** D4
Johnson City *TX* U.S.A. **161** D6
Johnsondale U.S.A. **158** D4
Johnson Draw *watercourse* U.S.A. **161** C6
Johnson's Crossing *Y.T.* Canada **149** N3
Johnston, Lake *salt flat* Australia **135** C8
Johnston and Sand Islands *terr.* N. Pacific Ocean *see* **Johnston Atoll**

▶**Johnston Atoll** *terr.* N. Pacific Ocean **186** I4
United States Unincorporated Territory.

Johnstone U.K. **60** E5
Johnstone Lake Canada *see* **Old Wives Lake**
Johnston Range *hills* Australia **135** B7
Johnstown Ireland **61** E5
Johnstown *NY* U.S.A. **165** H2
Johnstown *PA* U.S.A. **165** F3
Jōhoku Japan **93** G2
Johor *state* Malaysia **84** C2
Johor, Selat *strait* Malaysia/Sing. **87** [inset]
Johor, Sungai *r.* Malaysia **87** [inset]
Johor Bahru Malaysia **84** C2
Jõhvi Estonia **55** O7
Joinville Brazil **179** A4
Joinville France **66** G2
Joinville Island Antarctica **188** A2
Jojutla Mex. **167** F5
Jokkmokk Sweden **54** K3
Jökulsá *r.* Iceland **54** [inset]
Jökulsá á Fjöllum *r.* Iceland **54** [inset]
Jökulsá í Fljótsdal *r.* Iceland **54** [inset]
Jolfa Iran **110** B2
Joliet U.S.A. **164** A3
Joliet, Lac *l.* Canada **152** F4
Joliette Canada **153** G5
Jolly Lake Canada **151** H1
Jolo Phil. **82** C5
Jolo *i.* Phil. **82** C5
Jomalig *i.* Phil. **82** C3
Jombang *Jawa* Indon. **85** F4
Jomda China **96** C2
Jōmine-san *mt.* Japan **93** F2
Jonancy U.S.A. **164** D5
Jonathan Point Belize **167** H5
Jonava Lith. **55** N9
Jonê *Gansu* China **94** E5
Jōnen-dake *mt.* Japan **92** D2
Jonesboro *AR* U.S.A. **161** F5
Jonesboro *LA* U.S.A. **161** E5
Jones Islands *AK* U.S.A. **149** J1
Jones Sound *sea chan.* Canada **147** J2
Jonesville *MI* U.S.A. **164** C3
Jonesville *VA* U.S.A. **164** D5
Jonglei Canal Sudan **108** D8
Jönköping Sweden **55** I8
Jonquière Canada **153** H4
Jonuta Mex. **167** G5
Joplin U.S.A. **161** E4
Joppa Israel *see* **Tel Aviv-Yafo**
Jora India **104** D4
Jordan *country* Asia **107** C4
Jordan *r.* Asia **107** B4
Jordan U.S.A. **156** G3
Jordan *r.* U.S.A. **156** D4
Jordânia Brazil **179** C1
Jordet Norway **55** H6
Jorhat India **105** H4
Jor Hu *l.* China **98** B5
Jork Germany **63** J1
Jorm Afgh. **111** H2
Jörn Sweden **54** L4
Joroinen Fin. **54** O5
Jorong *Kalimantan* Indon. **85** F3
Jørpeland Norway **55** E7
Jos Nigeria **120** D4
Jose Abad Santos *Mindanao* Phil. **82** D5
José Cardel Mex. **167** F5
José de San Martín Arg. **178** B6
Jose Pañganiban *Luzon* Phil. **82** C3
Joseph, Lac *l.* Canada **153** I3
Joseph Bonaparte Gulf Australia **134** E3
Joseph City U.S.A. **159** H4
Joshimath India **104** D3
Jōshinetsu-kōgen Kokuritsu-kōen *nat. park* Japan **93** E2
Joshipur India **106** E1
Joshua Tree National Park U.S.A. **159** F5
Jos Plateau Nigeria **120** D4
Jostedalsbreen Nasjonalpark *nat. park* Norway **55** E6
Jotunheimen Nasjonalpark *nat. park* Norway **55** F6
Jouaiya Lebanon **107** B3
Joubertina S. Africa **124** F7
Jouberton S. Africa **125** H4
Jõuga Estonia **55** O7
Joûnié Lebanon **107** B3
Joure Neth. **62** F2
Joutsa Fin. **55** O6
Joutseno Fin. **55** P6
Jouy-aux-Arches France **62** G5
Jovellanos Cuba **163** D8
Jowai India **105** H4
Jowr Deh Iran **110** C2
Jowzak Iran **111** F4
Joy, Mount *Y.T.* Canada **149** N3
Joya de Cerén *tourist site* El Salvador **167** H6
Joyce's Country *reg.* Ireland **61** C4
Jōyō Japan **92** B4
Joypurhat Bangl. **105** G4
Juan Aldama Mex. **161** C7
Juancheng *Shandong* China **95** H5
Juan de Fuca Strait Canada/U.S.A. **154** C2
Juan Escutia Mex. **166** D4
Juan Fernández, Archipiélago *is* S. Pacific Ocean **187** O8
Juan Fernández Islands S. Pacific Ocean *see* **Juan Fernández, Archipiélago**
Juanjuí Peru **176** C5
Juankoski Fin. **54** P5
Juan Mata Ortíz Mex. **166** C2
Juaréz Mex. **167** E3
Juárez, Sierra de *mts* Mex. **166** A1
Juàzeiro Brazil **177** J5
Juàzeiro do Norte Brazil **177** K5
Juba *r.* Somalia *see* **Jubba**
Juba Sudan **121** G4
Jubany *research station* Antarctica **188** A2
Jubba *r.* Somalia **122** E4
Jubbah Saudi Arabia **113** F5
Jubbulpore India *see* **Jabalpur**
Jubilee Lake *salt flat* Australia **135** D7
Juby, Cap *c.* Morocco **120** B2
Juchatengo Mex. **167** F5
Juchitán Mex. **168** E5
Jucuruçu Brazil **179** D2
Jucuruçu *r.* Brazil **179** D2
Judaberg Norway **55** D7
Judaidat al Hamir Iraq **113** F5
Judayyidat 'Ar'ar *well* Iraq **113** F5
Judenburg Austria **57** O7
Judian China **96** C3
Judith Gap U.S.A. **156** F3
Juegang China *see* **Rudong**
Juelsminde Denmark **55** G9
Juerana Brazil **179** D2
Jugar China *see* **Sêrxü**
Juh *Nei Mongol* China **95** G4
Juhongtu *Qinghai* China **94** D4
Juigalpa Nicaragua **166** [inset] I6
Juillet, Lac *l.* Canada **153** J3
Juína Brazil **177** G6
Juist *i.* Germany **62** H1
Juiz de Fora Brazil **179** C3
Jujuhan *r.* Indon. **84** C3
Ju Ju Klu Turkm. **111** F2
Jukkoku-tōge *pass* Japan **93** E2
Julaca Bol. **176** E8
Julesburg U.S.A. **160** C3
Julia Brazil **176** E4
Juliaca Peru **176** D7
Julia Creek Australia **136** C4
Julian U.S.A. **158** E5
Julian, Lac *l.* Canada **152** F3
Julianadorp Neth. **62** E2
Julian Alps *mts* Slovenia *see* **Julijske Alpe**
Julianatop *mt.* Indon. *see* **Mandala, Puncak**
Juliana Top *mt.* Suriname **177** G3
Julianehåb Greenland *see* **Qaqortoq**
Jülich Germany **62** G4
Julijske Alpe *mts* Slovenia **68** E1
Julimes Mex. **166** D2
Juliomagus France *see* **Angers**
Julius, Lake Australia **136** B4
Jullundur India *see* **Jalandhar**
Juma Uzbek. **111** G2
Jumbilla Peru **176** C5
Jumilla Spain **67** F4
Jumla Nepal **105** E3
Jümme *r.* Germany **63** H1
Jumna *r.* India *see* **Yamuna**
Jump *r.* U.S.A. **160** F2
Junagadh India **104** B5
Junagarh India **106** D2
Junan *Shandong* China **95** I5
Junayfah Egypt **107** A4
Junbuk Iran **110** E3
Jun Bulen *Nei Mongol* China **95** I2
Junction *TX* U.S.A. **161** D6
Junction *UT* U.S.A. **159** G2
Junction City *KS* U.S.A. **160** D4
Junction City *KY* U.S.A. **164** C5
Junction City *OR* U.S.A. **156** C3
Jundiaí Brazil **179** B3
Junding China **97** F1

▶**Juneau** *AK* U.S.A. **149** N4
Capital of Alaska.

Juneau *WI* U.S.A. **160** F3
Juneau Icefield *B.C.* Canada **149** N4
Junee Australia **138** C5
Jûn el Khudr *b.* Lebanon **107** B3
Jungar Qi *Nei Mongol* China *see* **Xuejiawan**
Jungfrau *mt.* Switz. **66** H3
Junggar Pendi *basin* China **102** G2
Jungsi *Xizang* China **99** E6
Juniata *r.* U.S.A. **165** G3
Junín Arg. **178** D4
Junín Peru **176** C6
Junior U.S.A. **164** F4
Juniper Mountain U.S.A. **159** I1
Juniper Mountains U.S.A. **159** G4
Junipero Serro Peak U.S.A. **158** C3
Junlian China **96** E2
Junmenling China **97** G3
Juno U.S.A. **161** C6
Junsele Sweden **54** J5
Junshan Hu *l.* China **97** H2
Junxi China *see* **Datian**
Junxian China *see* **Danjiangkou**
Ju'nyung China **96** C1
Ju'nyunggoin China *see* **Ju'nyung**
Jūō Japan **93** G2
Juodupė Lith. **55** N8
Jupiá Brazil **179** A3
Jupía, Represa *resr* Brazil **179** A3
Jupiter U.S.A. **163** D7
Juquiá *r.* Brazil **179** B4
Jur *r.* Sudan **108** C8
Jura *mts* France/Switz. **66** G4
Jura *i.* U.K. **60** D4
Jura, Sound of *sea chan.* U.K. **60** D5
Juraci Brazil **179** C1
Juradó Col. **166** [inset] K8
Jurbarkas Lith. **55** M9
Jurf ad Darāwīsh Jordan **107** B4
Jürgenstorf Germany **63** M1
Jurh *Nei Mongol* China **95** J2
Jurh *Nei Mongol* China **95** J2
Jūrmala Latvia **55** M8
Jurmu Fin. **54** O4
Jurong Sing. **87** [inset]
Jurong, Sungai *r.* Sing. **87** [inset]
Jurong Island *reg.* Sing. **87** [inset]
Juruá *r.* Brazil **176** E4
Juruena *r.* Brazil **177** G5
Juruena, Parque Nacional do *nat. park* Brazil **177** G5
Juruti Brazil **177** G4
Jurva Fin. **54** L5
Jūshiyama Japan **92** C3
Jūshqān Iran **110** E2
Jūsīyah Syria **107** C2
Jussara Brazil **179** A1
Justice U.S.A. **164** E5
Jutaí Brazil **176** E5
Jutaí *r.* Brazil **176** E4
Jüterbog Germany **63** N3
Jutiapa Guat. **167** H6
Jutiapa Hond. **166** [inset] I6
Juticalpa Hond. **166** [inset] I6
Jutis Sweden **54** J3
Jutland *pen.* Denmark **55** F8
Juuka Fin. **54** P5
Juva Fin. **54** O6
Juwain Afgh. **111** F4
Juwana *Jawa* Indon. **85** E4
Juxian *Shandong* China **95** I5
Juye *Shandong* China **95** I5
Jūyom Iran **110** D4
Južnoukrajinsk Ukr. *see* **Yuzhnoukrayinsk**
Jwaneng Botswana **124** G3
Jylland *pen.* Denmark *see* **Jutland**
Jyrgalang Kyrg. **98** B4
Jyväskylä Fin. **54** N5

K

▶**K2** *mt.* China/Pak. **104** D2
2nd highest mountain in Asia and in the world.

Ka *r.* Nigeria **120** D3
Kaafu Atoll Maldives *see* **Male Atoll**
Kaa-Iya del Gran Chaco, Parque Nacional *nat. park* Bol. **176** F7
Kaakhka Turkm. *see* **Kaka**
Ka'ala *mt.* U.S.A. **157** [inset]
Kaapstad S. Africa *see* **Cape Town**
Kaarina Fin. **55** M6
Kaarßen Germany **63** L1
Kaarst Germany **62** G3
Kaavi Fin. **54** P5
Kaba *Xinjiang* China *see* **Habahe**
Kaba *r.* China/Kazakh. **98** D3
Kabaena *i.* Indon. **83** B4
Kabakly Turkm. *see* **Gabakly**
Kabala Sierra Leone **120** B4
Kabale Uganda **122** C4
Kabalega Falls National Park Uganda *see* **Murchison Falls National Park**
Kabalo Dem. Rep. Congo **123** C4
Kabambare Dem. Rep. Congo **123** C4
Kabanbay Kazakh. **102** F2
Kabangu Dem. Rep. Congo **123** C5
Kabanjahe *Sumatera* Indon. **84** B2
Kabara *i.* Fiji **133** I3
Kabarai *Papua* Indon. **83** D3
Kabarega National Park Uganda *see* **Murchison Falls National Park**
Kabasalan *Mindanao* Phil. **82** C5
Kaba-san *hill* Japan **93** G2
Kabaw Valley Myanmar **86** A2
Kabbani *r.* India **106** C3
Kåbdalis Sweden **54** L3
Kabetan *i.* Indon. **83** B2
Kabinakagami *r.* Canada **152** D4
Kabinakagami Lake Canada **152** D4
Kabinda Dem. Rep. Congo **123** C4
Kabir Indon. **83** C5
Kabīr *r.* Syria **107** B2
Kabīrkūh *mts* Iran **110** B3
Kabo Cent. Afr. Rep. **122** B3
Kābol Afgh. *see* **Kābul**
Kabompo *r.* Zambia **123** C5
Kabong *Sarawak* Malaysia **85** E2
Kabongo Dem. Rep. Congo **123** C4
Kabūdeh Iran **111** F3
Kabūd Gonbad Iran **111** E2
Kabūd Rāhang Iran **110** C3
Kabugao *Luzon* Phil. **82** C2

▶**Kābul** Afgh. **111** H3
Capital of Afghanistan.

Kābul *r.* Afgh. **111** I3
Kabuli P.N.G. **81** L7
Kabunda Dem. Rep. Congo **123** C5
Kabunduk *Sumba* Indon. **83** A5
Kabura-gawa *r.* Japan **93** F2
Kaburuang *i.* Indon. **83** C2
Kabūtar Khān Iran **110** E4
Kabwe Zambia **123** C5
Kacepi *Maluku* Indon. **83** D3
Kacha Kuh *mts* Iran/Pak. **111** F4
Kachalinskaya Rus. Fed. **53** J6
Kachchh, Great Rann of *marsh* India *see* **Kachchh, Rann of**
Kachchh, Gulf of India **104** B5
Kachchh, Little Rann of *marsh* India **104** B5
Kachchh, Rann of *marsh* India **104** B4
Kachemak Bay *AK* U.S.A. **149** J4
Kachia Nigeria **120** D4
Kachiry Kazakh. **88** D2
Kachkanar Rus. Fed. **51** R4
Kachret'i Georgia **113** G2
Kachug Rus. Fed. **88** J2
Kaçkar Dağı *mt.* Turkey **113** F2
Kada Japan **92** B4
Kadaingti Myanmar **86** B3
Kadaiyanallur India **106** C4
Kadanai *r.* Afgh./Pak. **111** G4
Kadan Kyun *i.* Myanmar **87** B4
Kadapongan *i.* Indon. **85** F4
Kadatuang *i.* Indon. **83** B4
Kadavu *i.* Fiji **133** H3
Kadavu Passage Fiji **133** H3
Kadaya Rus. Fed. **95** I1
Kaddam *l.* India **106** C2
Kade Ghana **120** C4
Kādhimain Iraq **113** G4
Kadi India **104** C5
Kadıköy Turkey **69** M4
Kadınhanı Turkey **112** D3
Kadiolo Mali **120** C3
Kadiri India **106** C3
Kadirli Turkey **112** E3
Kadirpur Pak. **111** I4
Kadiyevka Ukr. *see* **Stakhanov**
Kadmat *atoll* India **106** B4
Ka-do *i.* N. Korea **91** B5
Kadok Malaysia **84** C1
Kadoka U.S.A. **160** C3
Kadoma Zimbabwe **123** C5
Kadonkani Myanmar **86** A4
Kadu Myanmar **86** B1
Kadugli Sudan **108** C7
Kaduna Nigeria **120** D3
Kaduna *r.* Nigeria **120** D4
Kadusam *mt.* China/India **105** I3
Kaduy Rus. Fed. **52** H4
Kadyy Rus. Fed. **52** I4
Kadzherom Rus. Fed. **52** L2
Kaédi Mauritania **120** B3
Kaélé Cameroon **121** E3
Kaeng Krachan National Park Thai. **87** B4
Kaesŏng N. Korea **91** B5
Kāf Saudi Arabia **107** C4
Kafa Ukr. *see* **Feodosiya**
Kafakumba Dem. Rep. Congo **123** C4
Kafan Armenia *see* **Kapan**
Kafanchan Nigeria **120** D4

▶**Kaffeklubben Ø** *i.* Greenland **189** I1
Most northerly point of North America.

Kafiau *i. Papua* Indon. **83** D3
Kafireas, Akra *pt* Greece *see* **Ntoro, Kavo**
Kafiristan *reg.* Pak. **111** H3
Kafr ash Shaykh Egypt **112** C5
Kafr el Sheikh Egypt *see* **Kafr ash Shaykh**
Kafue Zambia **123** C5
Kafue *r.* Zambia **123** C5
Kafue National Park Zambia **123** C5
Kaga Japan **92** C2
Kaga Bandoro Cent. Afr. Rep. **122** B3
Kagan Pak. **111** I3
Kagan Uzbek. *see* **Kogon**
Kagang *Qinghai* China **94** E5
Kaganovichabad Tajik. *see* **Kolkhozobod**
Kaganovichi Pervyye Ukr. *see* **Polis'ke**
Kagarlyk Ukr. *see* **Kaharlyk**
Kåge Sweden **54** L4
Kağızman Turkey **113** F2
Kaglik Lake *N.W.T.* Canada **149** O1
Kagmar Sudan **108** D7
Kagologolo Indon. **84** B3
Kagosaka-tōge *pass* Japan **93** E3
Kagoshima Japan **91** C7
Kagoshima *pref.* Japan **91** C7
Kagul Moldova *see* **Cahul**
Kaguyak *AK* U.S.A. **148** I4
Kahama Tanz. **122** D4
Kaharlyk Ukr. **53** F6
Kahatola *i. Maluku* Indon. **83** C2
Kahayan *r.* Indon. **85** F3
Kaherekoau Mountains N.Z. **139** A7
Kahla Germany **63** L4
Kahnūj Iran **110** E4
Kahoka U.S.A. **160** F3
Kahoku-gata *l.* Japan **92** C2
Kaho'olawe *i.* U.S.A. **157** [inset]
Kahperusvaarat *mts* Fin. **54** L2
Kahramanmaraş Turkey **112** E3
Kahror Pak. Pak. **111** H4
Kâhta Turkey **112** E3
Kahuku U.S.A. **157** [inset]
Kahuku Point U.S.A. **157** [inset]
Kahulaui *i.* U.S.A. *see* **Kaho'olawe**
Kahurangi National Park N.Z. **139** D5
Kahurangi Point N.Z. **139** D5
Kahuta Pak. **111** I3
Kahuzi-Biega, Parc National du *nat. park* Dem. Rep. Congo **122** C4
Kai, Kepulauan *is* Indon. **81** I8
Kaiapoi N.Z. **139** D6
Kaibab U.S.A. **159** G3
Kaibab Plateau U.S.A. **159** G3
Kaibamardang *Qinghai* China **94** D4
Kaibara Japan **92** B3
Kai Besar *i.* Indon. **81** I8
Kaibito Plateau U.S.A. **159** H3
Kaida Japan **92** D3
Kaidu He *r.* China **98** D4
Kaifeng *Henan* China **95** H5
Kaifeng *Henan* China **95** H5
Kaihua *Yunnan* China *see* **Wenshan**
Kaihua *Zhejiang* China **97** H2
Kaiingveld *reg.* S. Africa **124** E5
Kaijiang China **96** E2
Kai Kecil *i.* Indon. **81** I8
Kai Keung Leng *H.K.* China **97** [inset]
Kaikoura N.Z. **139** D6
Kailas *mt. Xizang* China *see* **Kangrinboqê Feng**
Kailasahar India *see* **Kailashahar**
Kailashahar India **105** H4
Kailas Range *mts Xizang* China *see* **Gangdisê Shan**
Kaili China **96** E3
Kailu *Nei Mongol* China **95** J3
Kailua U.S.A. **157** [inset]
Kailua-Kona U.S.A. **157** [inset]
Kaimana Indon. **81** I7
Kaimanawa Mountains N.Z. **139** E4
Kaimar China **96** B1
Kaimganj *Uttar Prad.* India **99** B8
Kaimur Range *hills* India **104** E4
Käina Estonia **55** M7
Kainan *Wakayama* Japan **92** B4
Kainda Kyrg. *see* **Kayyngdy**
Kaindy Kyrg. *see* **Kayyngdy**
Kainji Lake National Park Nigeria **120** D4
Kaipara Harbour N.Z. **139** E3
Kaiparowits Plateau U.S.A. **159** H3
Kaiping China **97** G4
Kaipokok Bay Canada **153** K3
Kairana India **104** D3
Kairatu *Seram* Indon. **83** D3
Kairiru Island P.N.G. **81** K7
Kaironi Indon. **81** I7
Kairouan Tunisia **68** D7
Kaiserslautern Germany **63** H5
Kaiser Wilhelm II Land *reg.* Antarctica **188** E2
Kait, Tanjung *pt* Indon. **84** D3
Kaitaia N.Z. **139** D2
Kaitangata N.Z. **139** B8
Kaitawa N.Z. **139** F4
Kaithal India **104** D3
Kaitong *Jilin* China *see* **Tongyu**
Kaitum Sweden **54** L3
Kaiwatu *Maluku* Indon. **83** C5
Kaiwi Channel U.S.A. **157** [inset]
Kaixian China **97** F2
Kaiyang China **96** E3
Kaiyuan *Liaoning* China **95** K3
Kaiyuan *Yunnan* China **96** D4
Kaiyuh Mountains *AK* U.S.A. **148** H3
Kaizu Japan **92** C3
Kaizuka Japan **92** B4
Kajaani Fin. **54** O4
Kajabbi Australia **136** C4
Kajaki Afgh. **111** G3
Kajang Malaysia **84** C2
Kajarabie, Lake Australia **138** D1
Kajikazawa Japan **93** E3
Kajrān Afgh. **111** G3
Kajy-Say Kyrg. **98** B4
Kaka Turkm. **111** E2
Kakaban *i.* Indon. **85** G2
Kakabeka Falls Canada **152** C4
Kakabia *i.* Indon. **83** B4
Kakadu National Park Australia **134** F3
Kakagi Lake Canada **151** M5
Kakal *r. Mindanao* Phil. **82** D5
Kakali *Sulawesi Barat* Indon. **83** A3
Kakamas S. Africa **124** E5
Kakamega Kenya **122** D3
Kakamigahara Japan **92** C3
Kakana India **87** A5
Kakar Pak. **111** G5
Kakata Liberia **120** B4
Kake *AK* U.S.A. **149** N4
Kakegawa Japan **93** E4
Kakenge Dem. Rep. Congo **123** C4
Kakerbeck Germany **63** L2
Kakhi Azer. *see* **Qax**
Kakhonak *AK* U.S.A. **148** I4
Kakhovka Ukr. **69** O1
Kakhovs'ke Vodoskhovyshche *resr* Ukr. **53** G7
Kakhul Moldova *see* **Cahul**
Kākī Iran **110** C4
Kakinada India **106** D2
Kakisa Canada **150** G2
Kakisa *r.* Canada **150** G2
Kakisa Lake Canada **150** G2
Kakogawa Japan **92** A4
Kako-gawa *r.* Japan **92** A4
Kakori India **104** E4
Kakpak Kuduk *well Xinjiang* China **94** B2
Kakshaal-Too *mts* China/Kyrg. **102** E3
Kaktovik *AK* U.S.A. **149** L1
Kakul Pak. **111** I3
Kakus *r.* Malaysia **85** F2
Kakwa *r.* Canada **150** G4
Kala Pak. **111** H4
Kala Tanz. **123** D4
Kalaâ Kebira Tunisia **68** D7
Kalaallit Nunaat *terr.* N. America *see* **Greenland**
Kalabahi Indon. **83** C5
Kalabáka Greece *see* **Kalampaka**
Kalabakan *Sabah* Malaysia **85** G1
Kalabgur India **106** C2
Kalabo Zambia **123** C5
Kalach Rus. Fed. **53** I6
Kalacha Dida Kenya **122** D3
Kalach-na-Donu Rus. Fed. **53** I6
Kaladan *r.* India/Myanmar **86** A2
Kaladar Canada **165** G1
Ka Lae *pt* U.S.A. **157** [inset]
Kalaena *r.* Indon. **83** B3
Kalagwe Myanmar **86** B2
Kalahari Desert Africa **124** F2
Kalahari Gemsbok National Park S. Africa **124** E3
Kalaikhum Tajik. *see* **Qal'aikhum**
Kalai-Khumb Tajik. *see* **Qal'aikhum**
Kalajoki Fin. **54** M4
Kalalé Benin **120** D3
Kalaliok *Sulawesi* Indon. **83** B3
Kalalusu *i.* Indon. **83** C1
Kalam India **106** C1
Kalam Pak. **111** I3
Kalámai Greece *see* **Kalamata**
Kalamare Botswana **125** H2
Kalamaria Greece **69** J4
Kalamata Greece **69** J6
Kalamazoo U.S.A. **164** C2
Kalambau *i.* Indon. **85** F4
Kalampaka Greece **69** I5
Kalanchak Ukr. **69** O1
Kalandi Pak. **111** F4
Kalandula Angola *see* **Calandula**
Kalanguy Rus. Fed. **95** I1
Kalannie Australia **135** B7
Kalanshiyū ar Ramlī al Kabīr, Sarīr *des.* Libya **108** B3
Kālān Zīād Iran **111** E5
Kalao *i.* Indon. **83** B4
Kalaong *Mindanao* Phil. **82** D5
Kalaotoa *i.* Indon. **83** B4
Kalapa Indon. **84** D3
Kalapana (abandoned) U.S.A. **157** [inset]
Kalār Iraq **113** G4
Kalasin Thai. **86** C3
Kalāt Afgh. **111** G3
Kalāt *Khorāsān* Iran *see* **Kabūd Gonbad**
Kalāt *Sīstān va Balūchestān* Iran **111** E5
Kalat *Balochistan* Pak. **111** G4
Kalat *Balochistan* Pak. **111** G5
Kalat, Kūh-e *mt.* Iran **110** E3
Kalaupapa U.S.A. **157** [inset]
Kalaus *r.* Rus. Fed. **53** J7
Kalaw Myanmar **86** B2
Kälbäcär Azer. **113** G2
Kalbarri Australia **135** A6
Kalbarri National Park Australia **135** A6
Kalbe (Milde) Germany **63** L2
Kalbinskiy Khrebet *mts* Kazakh. **98** C2
Kale Turkey **69** M6
Kalecik Turkey **112** D2
Kaledupa *i.* Indon. **83** B4
Kalefeld Germany **63** K3
Kaleindaung *inlet* Myanmar **86** A3
Kalemie Dem. Rep. Congo **123** C4
Kalemyo Myanmar **86** A2
Kāl-e Namak Iran **110** D3
Kalevala Rus. Fed. **54** Q4
Kalewa Myanmar **86** A2
Kaleybar Iran **110** B2
Kalga Rus. Fed. **95** I1
Kalgan *Hebei* China *see* **Zhangjiakou**
Kalghatgi India **106** B3
Kalgoorlie Australia **135** C7
Kāl Gūsheh Iran **110** E4
Kali Croatia **68** F2
Kali *r.* India/Nepal **104** E3
Kaliakra, Nos *pt* Bulg. **69** M3
Kalianda *Sumatera* Indon. **84** D4
Kalibo *Panay* Phil. **82** C4
Kaliet Indon. **84** B3
Kali Gandaki *r.* Nepal **105** F4
Kaligiri India **106** C3
Kalikata India *see* **Kolkata**
Kalima Dem. Rep. Congo **122** C4
Kalimantan *reg.* Indon. **85** E3
Kalimantan Barat *prov.* Indon. **85** E2
Kalimantan Selatan *prov.* Indon. **85** F3
Kalimantan Tengah *prov.* Indon. **85** F3
Kalimantan Timur *prov.* Indon. **85** G2
Kálimnos *i.* Greece *see* **Kalymnos**
Kali Nadi *r.* India **99** C8
Kalinin Rus. Fed. *see* **Tver'**
Kalinin Adyndaky Tajik. *see* **Cheshtebe**
Kaliningrad Rus. Fed. **55** L9
Kalinino Armenia *see* **Tashir**
Kalinino Rus. Fed. **52** I4
Kalininsk Rus. Fed. **53** J6
Kalininskaya Rus. Fed. **53** H7
Kalinjara India **104** C5
Kalinkavichy Belarus **53** F5
Kalinkovichi Belarus *see* **Kalinkavichy**
Kalisat *Jawa* Indon. **85** F5
Kalisch Poland *see* **Kalisz**
Kalispell U.S.A. **156** E2
Kalisz Poland **57** Q5
Kalitva *r.* Rus. Fed. **53** I6
Kaliua Tanz. **123** D4
Kaliujar India **104** E4
Kalix Sweden **54** M4
Kalkalighat India **105** H4
Kalkalpen, Nationalpark *nat. park* Austria **57** O7
Kalkan Turkey **69** M6
Kalkaska U.S.A. **164** C1
Kalkfeld Namibia **123** B6
Kalkfonteindam *dam* S. Africa **125** G5
Kalkudah Sri Lanka **106** D5
Kall Germany **62** G4
Kallang *r.* Sing. **87** [inset]
Kallaste Estonia **55** O7
Kallavesi *l.* Fin. **54** O5
Kallsedet Sweden **54** H5
Kallsjön *l.* Sweden **54** H5
Kallur India **106** C2
Kalmar Sweden **55** J8
Kalmarsund *sea chan.* Sweden **55** J8
Kalmit *hill* Germany **63** I5
Kalmūkh Qal'eh Iran **110** E2
Kalmunai Sri Lanka **106** D5
Kalmykia *aut. rep.* Rus. Fed. *see* **Kalmykiya-Khalm'g-Tangch, Respublika**

Kalmykiya-Khalm'g-Tangch, Respublika *aut. rep.* Rus. Fed. **113** G1
Kalmykovo Kazakh. *see* **Taypak**
Kalmytskaya Avtonomnaya Oblast' *aut. rep.* Rus. Fed. *see* **Kalmykiya-Khalm'g-Tangch, Respublika**
Kalnai India **105** E5
Kalodnaye Belarus **55** O11
Kalol India **104** C5
Kaloma *i.* Indon. **83** C2
Kalomo Zambia **123** C5
Kalone Peak Canada **150** E4
Kalongan *Sulawesi* Indon. **83** C1
Kalpa India **104** D3
Kalpeni *atoll* India **106** B4
Kalpetta India **106** C4
Kalpi India **104** D4
Kalpin *Xinjiang* China **98** B4
Kalsi *Uttaranchal* India **99** B7
Kaltag *AK* U.S.A. **148** H2
Kaltensundheim Germany **63** K4
Kaltukatjara Australia **135** E6
Kalu India **111** I4
Kaluga Rus. Fed. **53** H5
Kalukalukuang *i.* Indon. **85** G4
Kaluku *Sulawesi Barat* Indon. **83** A3
Kalulong, Bukit *mt.* Malaysia **85** F2
Kalundborg Denmark **55** G9
Kalupis Falls Malaysia **85** G1
Kalush Ukr. **53** E6
Kalvakol India **106** C2
Kälviä Fin. **54** M5
Kal'ya Rus. Fed. **51** R3
Kalyan India **106** B2
Kalyandurg India **109** M7
Kalyansingapuram India **106** D2
Kalyazin Rus. Fed. **52** H4
Kalymnos *i.* Greece **69** L6
Kama Dem. Rep. Congo **122** C4
Kama Myanmar **86** A3

▶**Kama** *r.* Rus. Fed. **52** L4
4th longest river in Europe.

Kamagaya Japan **93** F3
Kamaishi Japan **91** F5
Kamakura Japan **93** F3
Kamalia Pak. **111** I4
Kaman *Rajasthan* India **99** B8
Kaman Turkey **112** D3
Kamanashi-gawa *r.* Japan **93** E3
Kamanashi-yama *mt.* Japan **93** E3
Kamaniskeg Lake Canada **165** G1
Kamanjab Namibia **123** B5
Kamarān *i.* Yemen **108** F6
Kamaran Island Yemen *see* **Kamarān**
Kamard *reg.* Afgh. **111** G3
Kamarod Pak. **111** F5
Kamaron Sierra Leone **120** B4
Kamashi Uzbek. *see* **Qamashi**
Kamasin India **104** E4
Kambaiti Myanmar **86** B1
Kambalda Australia **135** C7
Kambam India **106** C4
Kambang *Sumatera* Indon. **84** C3
Kambangan *i.* Indon. **85** E5
Kambara *i.* Fiji *see* **Kabara**
Kambara Japan *see* **Kanbara**
Kambardi *Xinjiang* China **98** C4
Kambia Sierra Leone **120** B4
Kambing, Pulau *i.* East Timor *see* **Ataúro, Ilha de**
Kambo-san *mt.* N. Korea *see* **Kwanmo-bong**
Kambove Dem. Rep. Congo **123** C5
Kambuno, Bukit *mt.* Indon. **83** B3
Kambūt Libya **112** B5
Kamchatka, Poluostrov *pen.* Rus. Fed. *see* **Kamchatka Peninsula**
Kamchatka Basin *sea feature* Bering Sea **186** H2
Kamchatka Peninsula Rus. Fed. **77** Q4
Kamchiya *r.* Bulg. **69** L3
Kameia, Parque Nacional de *nat. park* Angola *see* **Cameia, Parque Nacional da**
Kamelik *r.* Rus. Fed. **53** K5
Kamen Germany **63** H3
Kamen', Gory *mt.* Rus. Fed. **76** K3
Kamenets-Podol'skiy Ukr. *see* **Kam"yanets'-Podil's'kyy**
Kamenitsa *mt.* Bulg. **69** J4
Kamenjak, Rt *pt* Croatia **68** E2
Kamenka Kazakh. **51** Q5
Kamenka *Arkhangel'skaya Oblast'* Rus. Fed. **52** J2
Kamenka *Penzenskaya Oblast'* Rus. Fed. **53** J5
Kamenka *Primorskiy Kray* Rus. Fed. **90** E3
Kamenka-Bugskaya Ukr. *see* **Kam"yanka-Buz'ka**
Kamenka-Strumilovskaya Ukr. *see* **Kam"yanka-Buz'ka**
Kamen'-na-Obi Rus. Fed. **88** E2
Kamennogorsk Rus. Fed. **55** P6
Kamennomostskiy Rus. Fed. **113** F1
Kamenolomni Rus. Fed. **53** I7
Kamenongue Angola *see* **Camanongue**
Kamen'-Rybolov Rus. Fed. **90** D3
Kamenskoye Rus. Fed. **77** R3
Kamenskoye Ukr. *see* **Dniprodzerzhyns'k**
Kamensk-Shakhtinskiy Rus. Fed. **53** I6
Kamensk-Ural'skiy Rus. Fed. **76** H4
Kameoka Japan **92** B3
Kamet *mt. Xizang* China **99** B7
Kameyama Japan **92** C4
Kami *Hyōgo* Japan **92** A3
Kami *Nagano* Japan **93** D3
Kamichi Japan **92** D2
Kamiesberge *mts* S. Africa **124** D6
Kamieskroon S. Africa **124** C6
Kamifukuoka Japan **93** F3
Kami-ishizu Japan **92** C3
Kami-jima *i.* Japan **92** C4
Kamikawa *Saitama* Japan **93** F2
Kamikawachi Japan **93** F2
Kamikitayama Japan **92** B4
Kamikuishiki Japan **93** E3
Kamileroi Australia **136** C3
Kamilukuak Lake Canada **151** K2
Kamina Dem. Rep. Congo **123** C4
Kaminaka Japan **92** B3
Kaminak Lake Canada **151** M2
Kaminoho Japan **92** D3
Kaminokawa Japan **93** F2
Kaminuriak Lake Canada *see* **Qamanirjuaq Lake**
Kamioka Japan **92** D2
Kamishak Bay *AK* U.S.A. **148** I4
Kamishihi Japan **92** C2
Kamishihoro Japan **90** F4
Kamisu Japan **93** G3
Kami-taira Japan **92** C2
Kami-takara Japan **92** D2
Kami-yahagi Japan **92** D3
Kamiyamada Japan **93** E2
Kamla *r.* India **99** F8
Kamloops Canada **150** F5
Kammuri-jima *i.* Japan *see* **Kanmuri-jima**
Kammuri-yama *mt.* Japan *see* **Kanmuri-yama**
Kamo Armenia *see* **Gavarr**
Kamo *Kyōto* Japan **92** B4
Kamo *Yamanashi* Japan **93** E4
Kamogawa Japan **93** G3
Kamoke Pak. **111** I4
Kamonia Dem. Rep. Congo **123** C4
Kampa Indon. **84** D3

▶**Kampala** Uganda **122** D3
Capital of Uganda.

Kampar *r.* Indon. **84** C2
Kampar Malaysia **84** C1
Kampara India **106** D1
Kamparkiri *r.* Indon. **84** C2
Kampen Neth. **62** F2
Kampene Dem. Rep. Congo **122** C4
Kamphaeng Phet Thai. **86** B3
Kampinoski Park Narodowy *nat. park* Poland **57** R4
Kâmpóng Cham Cambodia **87** D5
Kâmpóng Chhnăng Cambodia **87** D4
Kâmpóng Khleăng Cambodia **87** D4
Kâmpóng Saôm Cambodia *see* **Sihanoukville**
Kâmpóng Spœ Cambodia **87** D5
Kâmpóng Thum Cambodia **87** D4
Kâmpóng Trâbêk Cambodia **87** D5
Kâmpôt Cambodia **87** D5
Kamptee India *see* **Kamthi**
Kampuchea *country* Asia *see* **Cambodia**
Kamrau, Teluk *b.* Indon. **81** I7
Kamsack Canada **151** K5
Kamskoye Vodokhranilishche *resr* Rus. Fed. **51** R4
Kamsuuma Somalia **122** E3
Kamthi India **104** D5
Kamuchawie Lake Canada **151** K3
Kamuli Uganda **122** D3
Kam"yanets'-Podil's'kyy Ukr. **53** E6
Kam"yanka-Buz'ka Ukr. **53** E6
Kamyanyets Belarus **55** M10
Kāmyārān Iran **110** B3
Kamyshin Rus. Fed. **53** J6
Kamystybas, Ozero *l.* Kazakh. **102** B2
Kamyzyak Rus. Fed. **53** K7
Kamzar Oman **110** E5
Kanaaupscow *r.* Canada **152** F3
Kanab U.S.A. **159** G3
Kanab Creek *r.* U.S.A. **159** G3
Kanae Japan **93** D3
Kanaga Island *AK* U.S.A. **149** [inset]
Kanagawa *pref.* Japan **93** F3
Kanairiktok *r.* Canada **153** K3
Kanak Pak. **111** G4
Kanakanak *AK* U.S.A. **148** H4
Kananga Dem. Rep. Congo **123** C4
Kanangio, Mount *vol.* P.N.G. **81** L7
Kanangra-Boyd National Park Australia **138** E4
Kanarak India *see* **Konarka**
Kanarraville U.S.A. **159** G3
Kanas *watercourse* Namibia **124** C4
Kanasagō Japan **93** G2
Kanash Rus. Fed. **52** J5
Kanas Köl *l.* China **98** D2
Kanatak *AK* U.S.A. **148** H4
Kanauj India *see* **Kannauj**
Kanaya *Shizuoka* Japan **93** E4
Kanaya *Wakayama* Japan **92** B4
Kanayama Japan **92** D3
Kanayka Kazakh. **98** C2
Kanazawa *Ishikawa* Japan **92** C2
Kanazawa *Kanagawa* Japan **93** F3
Kanazu Japan **92** C2
Kanbalu Myanmar **86** A2
Kanbara Japan **93** E3
Kanchalan Rus. Fed. **148** B2
Kanchalan *r.* Rus. Fed. **148** B2
Kanchanaburi Thai. **87** B4
Kanchanjanga *mt.* India/Nepal *see* **Kangchenjunga**
Kanchipuram India **106** C3
Kand *mt.* Pak. **111** G4
Kanda Pak. **111** G4
Kandahār Afgh. **111** G4
Kandalaksha Rus. Fed. **54** R3
Kandalakshskiy Zaliv *g.* Rus. Fed. **54** R3
Kandang *Sumatera* Indon. **84** B2
Kandangan *Kalimantan* Indon. **85** F3
Kandar Indon. **134** E2
Kandavu *i.* Fiji *see* **Kadavu**
Kandavu Passage Fiji *see* **Kadavu Passage**
Kandé Togo **120** D4
Kandh Kot Pak. **111** H4
Kandi Benin **120** D3
Kandi India **106** C2
Kandi, Tanjung *pt* Indon. **83** B2
Kandiaro Pak. **111** H5
Kandik *r.* Canada/U.S.A. **149** L2
Kandıra Turkey **69** N4
Kandos Australia **138** D4
Kandreho Madag. **123** E5
Kandrian P.N.G. **81** L8
Kandukur India **106** C3
Kandy Sri Lanka **106** D5
Kandyagash Kazakh. **102** A2
Kane U.S.A. **165** F3
Kane Bassin *b.* Greenland **189** K1
Kaneh *watercourse* Iran **110** D5
Kanektok *r. AK* U.S.A. **148** G4
Kāne'ohe U.S.A. **157** [inset]
Kaneti Pak. **111** G4
Kanevskaya Rus. Fed. **53** H7
Kaneyama *Gifu* Japan **92** D3
Kang Afgh. **111** F4
Kang Botswana **124** F2
Kangaamiut Greenland **147** M3
Kangaarsussuaq *c.* Greenland **147** K2
Kangaba Mali **120** C3
Kangal Turkey **112** E3
Kangān *Būshehr* Iran **110** D5
Kangān *Hormozgan* Iran **110** E5
Kangandala, Parque Nacional de *nat. park* Angola *see* **Cangandala, Parque Nacional de**
Kangar Malaysia **84** C1
Kangaroo Island Australia **137** B7
Kangaroo Point Australia **136** B3
Kangaslampi Fin. **54** P5
Kangasniemi Fin. **54** O6
Kangāvar Iran **110** B3
Kangbao *Hebei* China **95** H3

▶**Kangchenjunga** *mt.* India/Nepal **105** G4
3rd highest mountain in Asia and in the world.

Kangding China **96** D2
Kangean, Kepulauan *is* Indon. **85** F4
Kangen *r.* Sudan **121** G4
Kangerlussuaq Greenland **147** M3
Kangerlussuaq *inlet* Greenland **147** M3
Kangerlussuaq *inlet* Greenland **189** J2
Kangersuatsiaq Greenland **147** M2
Kangertittivaq *sea chan.* Greenland **147** P2
Kanggye N. Korea **90** B4
Kanghwa S. Korea **91** B5
Kangikajik *c.* Greenland **147** P2
Kangiqsualujjuaq Canada **153** I2
Kangirsuk Canada **153** H1
Kang Krung National Park Thai. **87** B5
Kangle *Gansu* China **94** E5
Kangle *Jiangxi* China *see* **Wanzai**
Kanglong China **96** C1
Kangmar *Xizang* China **105** F3
Kangmar *Xizang* China **99** E7
Kangnŭng S. Korea **91** C5
Kango Gabon **122** B3
Kangping *Liaoning* China **95** J3
Kangri Karpo Pass China/India **105** I3
Kangrinboqê Feng *mt. Xizang* China **99** C7
Kangro *Xizang* China **99** D6
Kangsangdobdê *Xizang* China *see* **Xainza**
Kang Tipayan Dakula *i.* Phil. **85** H1
Kangto *mt.* China/India **99** F8
Kangtog *Xizang* China **99** D6
Kangxian China **96** E1
Kangxiwar *Xinjiang* China **99** B5
Kani Japan **92** D3
Kanibongan *Sabah* Malaysia **85** G1
Kanie Japan **92** C3
Kanifing Gambia **120** B3
Kanigiri India **106** C3
Kanin, Poluostrov *pen.* Rus. Fed. **52** J2
Kanin Nos Rus. Fed. **189** G2
Kanin Nos, Mys *c.* Rus. Fed. **52** I1
Kaninskiy Bereg *coastal area* Rus. Fed. **52** I2
Kanjiroba *mt.* Nepal **105** E3
Kankaanpää Fin. **55** M6
Kankakee U.S.A. **164** B3
Kankan Guinea **120** C3
Kanker India **106** D1
Kankesanturai Sri Lanka **106** D4
Kankossa Mauritania **120** B3
Kanlaon, Mount *vol.* Phil. **82** C4
Kanmaw Kyun *i.* Myanmar **87** B5
Kanmuri-jima *i.* Japan **92** B3
Kanmuri-yama *mt.* Japan **92** C3
Kanna-gawa *r.* Japan **93** F2
Kannami Japan **93** E3
Kannauj India **104** D4
Kanniya Kumari *c.* India *see* **Comorin, Cape**
Kannonkoski Fin. **54** N5
Kannon-zaki *pt* Japan **92** D1
Kannur India *see* **Cannanore**
Kannus Fin. **54** M5
Kano *i.* Indon. **83** C3
Kano Nigeria **120** D3
Kano-gawa *r.* Japan **93** E3
Kanonerka Kazakh. **98** B2
Kanonpunt *pt* S. Africa **124** E8
Kanosh U.S.A. **159** G2
Kanovlei Namibia **123** B5
Kanowit *Sarawak* Malaysia **85** F2
Kanoya Japan **91** C7
Kanpur *Orissa* India **106** E1
Kanpur *Uttar Prad.* India **104** E4
Kanra Japan **93** F2
Kanrach *reg.* Pak. **111** G5
Kansai *airport* Japan **92** B4
Kansas U.S.A. **164** B4
Kansas *r.* U.S.A. **160** E4
Kansas *state* U.S.A. **160** D4
Kansas City *KS* U.S.A. **160** E4
Kansas City *MO* U.S.A. **160** E4
Kansk Rus. Fed. **77** K4
Kansu *Xinjiang* China **98** A5
Kansu *prov.* China *see* **Gansu**
Kantang Thai. **87** B6
Kantara *hill* Cyprus **107** A2
Kantaralak Thai. **87** D4
Kantavu *i.* Fiji *see* **Kadavu**
Kantchari Burkina **120** D3
Kantemirovka Rus. Fed. **53** H6
Kanthi India **105** F5
Kantishna *AK* U.S.A. **149** J3
Kantishna *r. AK* U.S.A. **149** J2
Kantli *r.* India **99** A7
Kantō-heiya *plain* Japan **93** F3
Kanton *atoll* Kiribati **133** I2
Kanto-sanchi *mts* Japan **93** E3
Kantulong Myanmar **86** B3
Kanturk Ireland **61** D5
Kanuku Mountains Guyana **177** G3
Kanuma Japan **93** F2
Kanur India **106** C3
Kanus Namibia **124** D4
Kanuti *r. AK* U.S.A. **148** I2
Kanuti National Wildlife Refuge *nature res. AK* U.S.A. **149** J2
Kanyakubja India *see* **Kannauj**
Kanyamazane S. Africa **125** J3
Kanye Botswana **125** G3
Kanzaki Japan **92** A3
Kao *Halmahera* Indon. **83** C2
Kao, Teluk *b. Halmahera* Indon. **83** C2
Kaôh Pring *i.* Cambodia **87** C5
Kaohsiung Taiwan **97** I4
Kaôh Smăch *i.* Cambodia **87** C5
Kaôh Tang *i.* Cambodia **87** C5
Kaokoveld *plat.* Namibia **123** B5
Kaolack Senegal **120** B3
Kaoma Zambia **123** C5
Kaouadja Cent. Afr. Rep. **122** C3
Kapa S. Africa *see* **Cape Town**
Kapa'a U.S.A. **157** [inset]
Kapa'au U.S.A. **157** [inset]
Kapal Kazakh. **98** B3
Kapalabuaya *Maluku* Indon. **83** C3
Kapan Armenia **113** G3
Kapanga Dem. Rep. Congo **123** C4
Kaparhā Iran **110** C4
Kapatu Zambia **123** D4
Kapchagay Kazakh. **102** E3
Kapchagayskoye Vodokhranilishche *resr* Kazakh. **102** E3
Kap Dan Greenland *see* **Kulusuk**
Kapellen Belgium **62** E3
Kapello, Akra *pt Attiki* Greece *see* **Kapello, Akrotirio**
Kapello, Akrotirio *pt* Greece **69** J6
Kapellskär Sweden **55** K7
Kapelskär Sweden *see* **Kapellskär**
Kapili *r.* India **105** G4
Kapingamarangi *atoll* Micronesia **186** G5
Kapingamarangi Rise *sea feature* N. Pacific Ocean **186** G5
Kapıorman Dağları *mts* Turkey **69** N4
Kapip Pak. **111** H4
Kapiri Mposhi Zambia **123** C5
Kapisillit Greenland **147** M3
Kapiskau *r.* Canada **152** E3
Kapit *Sarawak* Malaysia **85** F2
Kapiti Island N.Z. **139** E5
Kaplamada, Gunung *mt. Buru* Indon. **83** C3
Kaplankyr, Chink *hills* Asia **113** I2
Kaplankyr Döwlet Gorugy *nature res.* Turkm. **110** E1
Kapoeta Sudan **121** G4
Kapondai, Tanjung *pt Flores* Indon. **83** B5
Kaposvár Hungary **68** G1
Kappel Germany **63** H5
Kappeln Germany **57** L3
Kapsukas Lith. *see* **Marijampolė**
Kaptai Bangl. **105** H5
Kaptsegaytuy Rus. Fed. **95** I1
Kapuas *r.* Indon. **85** E3
Kapuas *r.* Indon. **85** F3
Kapuas Hulu, Pegunungan *mts* Indon./Malaysia **85** F2
Kapuriya India **104** C4
Kapurthala India **104** C3
Kapuskasing Canada **152** E4
Kapustin Yar Rus. Fed. **53** J6
Kaputar *mt.* Australia **138** E3
Kaputir Kenya **122** D3
Kapuvár Hungary **68** G1
Kapydzhik, Gora *mt.* Armenia/Azer. *see* **Qazangödağ**
Kapyl' Belarus **55** O10
Ka Qu *r. Xizang* China **99** F7
Kaqung China **111** J2
Kara India **104** E4
Kara Togo **120** D4
Kara *r.* Turkey **113** F3
Kara Art Pass *Xinjiang* China **98** A5
Kara-Balta Kyrg. **102** D3
Karabalyk Kazakh. **100** F1
Karabas Kazakh. **98** A2
Karabekaul' Turkm. *see* **Garabekewül**
Karabiga Turkey **69** L4
Karabil', Vozvyshennost' *hills* Turkm. *see* **Garabil Belentligi**
Kara-Bogaz-Gol, Proliv *sea chan.* Turkm. *see* **Garabogazköl Bogazy**
Kara-Bogaz-Gol'skiy Zaliv *b.* Turkm. *see* **Garabogazköl Aýlagy**
Karabük Turkey **112** D2
Karabulak *Almatinskaya Oblast'* Kazakh. **98** B3
Karabulak *Vostochnyy Kazakhstan* Kazakh. **98** D3
Karabulakskaya Kazakh. **98** A2
Karabura *Xinjiang* China *see* **Yumin**
Karaburun Turkey **69** L5
Karabutak Kazakh. **102** B2
Karacabey Turkey **69** M4
Karacaköy Turkey **69** M4
Karacalı Dağ *mt.* Turkey **113** E3
Karaçal Tepe *mt.* Turkey **107** A1
Karacasu Turkey **69** M6
Karaca Yarımadası *pen.* Turkey **69** N6
Karachayevsk Rus. Fed. **113** F2
Karachev Rus. Fed. **53** G5
Karachi Pak. **111** G5
Karacurun Turkey *see* **Hilvan**
Karad India **106** B2
Kara Dağ *hill* Turkey **107** D1
Kara Dağ *mt.* Turkey **112** D3
Kara-Dar'ya Uzbek. *see* **Payshanba**
Kara Deniz *sea* Asia/Europe *see* **Black Sea**
Karagan Rus. Fed. **90** A1
Karaganda Kazakh. **102** D2
Karagandinskaya Oblast' *admin. div.* Kazakh. **98** A2
Karagash Kazakh. **98** B3
Karagayly Kazakh. **102** E2
Karagaylybulak Kazakh. **98** D2
Karaginskiy Zaliv *b.* Rus. Fed. **77** R4
Karagiye, Vpadina *depr.* Kazakh. **113** H2
Karagola India **105** F4
Karaguzhikha Kazakh. **98** C2
Karahallı Turkey **69** M5
Karahasanlı Turkey **112** D3
Karaikal India **106** C4
Karaikkudi India **106** C4
Kara Irtysh *r.* Kazakh. **98** D3
Karaisalı Turkey **112** D3
Karaitan *Kalimantan* Indon. **85** G2
Karaj Iran **110** C3
Karak Jordan *see* **Al Karak**
Karakalli Turkey *see* **Özalp**
Karakax *Xinjiang* China *see* **Moyu**
Karakax He *r.* China **99** C5
Karakax Shan *mts Xinjiang* China **99** C6
Karakelong *i.* Indon. **83** C1
Karaki *Xinjiang* China **99** C5
Karakitang *i.* Indon. **83** C2
Karaklis Armenia *see* **Vanadzor**
Karakoçan Turkey **113** F3
Kara-Köl Kyrg. **101** G2
Karakol Kyrg. **102** E3
Karakol *Ysyk-Köl* Kyrg. **98** B4
Karakoram Pass China/India **104** D2
Karakoram Range *mts* Asia **101** G3
Karakoram Range *mts* Asia **111** I2
Kara K'orē Eth. **122** D2
Karakorum Range *mts* Asia *see* **Karakoram Range**
Karakorum Range *mts* Asia *see* **Karakoram Range**
Karaköse Turkey *see* **Ağrı**
Kara Kul' Kyrg. *see* **Kara-Köl**
Karakul', Ozero *l.* Tajik. *see* **Qarokŭl**
Karakum Kazakh. **98** B3
Kara Kum *des.* Turkm. *see* **Garagum**
Kara Kum *des.* Turkm. *see* **Karakum Desert**
Karakum, Peski Kazakh. *see* **Karakum Desert**
Karakum Desert Kazakh. **100** E2
Karakum Desert Turkm. *see* **Garagum**
Karakum Desert Turkm. **110** F2
Karakumskiy Kanal *canal* Turkm. *see* **Garagum Kanaly**
Kara Kumy *des.* Turkm. *see* **Garagum**
Karakurt Turkey **113** F2
Karakuş Dağı *ridge* Turkey **69** N5
Karal Chad **121** E3
Karala Estonia **55** L7
Karalundi Australia **135** B6
Karama *r.* Indon. **83** A3
Karamagay *Xinjiang* China *see* **Haramgai**
Karaman Turkey **112** D3
Karaman *prov.* Turkey **107** A1
Karamanlı Turkey **69** M6
Karamay *Xinjiang* China **98** D3
Karambar Pass Afgh./Pak. **111** I2
Karambu *Kalimantan* Indon. **85** G3
Karamea N.Z. **139** D5
Karamea Bight *b.* N.Z. **139** C5
Karamendy Kazakh. **102** B1
Karamian *i.* Indon. **85** F4
Karamiran *Xinjiang* China **99** D5
Karamiran He *r.* China **99** D5
Karamiran Shankou *pass Xinjiang* China **99** D5
Karamürsel Turkey **69** M4
Karamyshevo Rus. Fed. **55** P8
Karān *i.* Saudi Arabia **110** C5
Karang, Tanjung *pt* Indon. **83** A3
Karangagung *Sumatera* Indon. **84** D3
Karangan *Sumatera* Indon. **84** D4
Karangasem *Bali* Indon. **85** F5
Karangbolong, Tanjung *pt* Indon. **85** E5
Karangetang *vol.* Indon. **83** C2
Karanja India **106** C1
Karanjia India **104** E5
Karaoy *Almatinskaya Oblast'* Kazakh. **98** A3
Karaoy *Almatinskaya Oblast'* Kazakh. **98** A3
Karapınar *Gaziantep* Turkey **107** C1
Karapınar *Konya* Turkey **112** D3
Karaqi *Xinjiang* China **98** B4
Karas *admin. reg.* Namibia **124** C4
Karasay *Xinjiang* China **99** C5
Kara-Say Kyrg. **98** B4
Karasburg Namibia **124** D5
Kara Sea Rus. Fed. **76** I2
Kárášjohka *Finnmark* Norway *see* **Karasjok**
Karasjok Norway **54** N2
Karasor, Ozero *salt l.* Kazakh. **98** A2
Kara Strait Rus. Fed. *see* **Karskiye Vorota, Proliv**
Karasu Japan **92** C4
Karasu *Karagandinskaya Oblast'* Kazakh. **98** A3
Karasu *r.* Syria/Turkey **107** C1
Karasu *Bitlis* Turkey *see* **Hizan**
Karasu *Sakarya* Turkey **69** N4
Karasu *r.* Turkey **113** F3
Karasubazar Ukr. *see* **Bilohirs'k**
Karasu-gawa *r.* Japan **93** F2
Karasuk Rus. Fed. **76** I4
Karasuyama Japan **93** G2
Karāt Iran **111** F3
Karatal Kazakh. **98** D3
Karataş Turkey **107** B1
Karataş Burnu *hd* Turkey *see* **Fener Burnu**
Karatau Kazakh. **102** D3
Karatau, Khrebet *mts* Kazakh. **102** C3
Karatepe Turkey **107** A1
Karathuri Myanmar **87** B5
Karativu *i.* Sri Lanka **106** C4
Karatol *r.* Kazakh. **98** B3
Karatsu Japan **91** C6
Karatung *i.* Indon. **83** C1
Karatüngü *Xinjiang* China **94** B2
Karaudanawa Guyana **177** G3
Karaul Kazakh. **98** B2
Karauli India **104** D4
Karavan Kyrg. *see* **Kerben**
Karavostasi Cyprus **107** A2
Karawang *Jawa* Indon. **84** D4
Karaxahar *r.* China *see* **Kaidu He**
Karayılan Turkey **107** C1
Karayulgan *Xinjiang* China **98** C4
Karazhal Kazakh. **102** D2
Karazhingil Kazakh. **98** A3
Karbalā' Iraq **113** G4
Karben Germany **63** I4
Karbushevka Kazakh. **98** A2
Karcag Hungary **69** I1
Karden Germany **63** H4
Kardhítsa Greece *see* **Karditsa**
Karditsa Greece **69** I5
Kärdla Estonia **55** M7
Karee S. Africa **125** H5
Kareeberge *mts* S. Africa **124** E6
Kareima Sudan **108** D6
Kareli India **104** D5
Karelia *aut. rep.* Rus. Fed. *see* **Kareliya, Respublika**
Kareliya, Respublika *aut. rep.* Rus. Fed. **54** R5
Karel'skaya A.S.S.R. *aut. rep.* Rus. Fed. *see* **Kareliya, Respublika**
Karel'skiy Bereg *coastal area* Rus. Fed. **54** R3
Karema Tanz. **123** D4
Karera India **104** D4
Karesuando Sweden **54** M2
Kārevāndar Iran **111** F5
Kargalinskaya Rus. Fed. **113** G2
Kargalinski Rus. Fed. *see* **Kargalinskaya**
Kargaly Kazakh. **98** A2
Kargapazarı Dağları *mts* Turkey **113** F3
Karghalik *Xinjiang* China *see* **Yecheng**
Kargı Turkey **112** D2
Kargil India **104** D2
Kargilik *Xinjiang* China *see* **Yecheng**
Kargıpınarı Turkey **107** B1
Kargopol' Rus. Fed. **52** H3
Kari Nigeria **120** E3
Karīān Iran **110** E5
Kariba Zimbabwe **123** C5
Kariba, Lake *resr* Zambia/Zimbabwe **123** C5
Kariba Dam Zambia/Zimbabwe **123** C5
Kariba-yama *vol.* Japan **90** E4
Karibib Namibia **124** B1
Karigasniemi Fin. **54** N2
Karijini National Park Australia **135** B5
Karijoki Fin. **54** L5
Karikachi-tōge *pass* Japan **90** F4
Karikari, Cape N.Z. **139** D2
Karimata *i.* Indon. **85** E3
Karimata, Pulau-pulau *is* Indon. **85** E3
Karimata, Selat *str.* Indon. **85** E3
Karimganj India **105** H4
Karimnagar India **106** C2
Karimun Besar *i.* Indon. **84** C2
Karimunjawa *i.* Indon. **85** E4
Karimunjawa, Pulau-pulau *is* Indon. **85** E4
Káristos Greece *see* **Karystos**
Kariya Japan **92** C4
Karjat *Mahar.* India **106** B2
Karjat *Mahar.* India **106** B2
Karkaralinsk Kazakh. **102** E2
Karkaralong, Kepulauan *is* Indon. **82** D5
Karkar Island P.N.G. **81** L7
Karkh Pak. **111** G5
Karkinits'ka Zatoka *g.* Ukr. **69** O2
Kärkölä Fin. **55** N6
Karkonoski Park Narodowy *nat. park* Czech Rep./Poland *see* **Krkonošský narodní park**
Karksi-Nuia Estonia **55** N7
Karkük Iraq *see* **Kirkük**
Karlachi Pak. **111** H3
Karlholmsbruk Sweden **55** J6
Karlik Shan *mts Xinjiang* China **94** C3
Karlıova Turkey **113** F3
Karlivka Ukr. **53** G6
Karl Marks, Qullai *mt.* Tajik. **111** I2
Karl-Marx-Stadt Germany *see* **Chemnitz**
Karlovac Croatia **68** F2
Karlovka Ukr. *see* **Karlivka**
Karlovo Bulg. **69** K3
Karlovy Vary Czech Rep. **63** M4
Karlsbad Germany **63** I6
Karlsborg Sweden **55** I7
Karlsburg Romania *see* **Alba Iulia**
Karlshamn Sweden **55** I8
Karlskoga Sweden **55** I7
Karlskrona Sweden **55** I8
Karlsruhe Germany **63** I5

Karlstad Sweden 55 H7
Karlstad U.S.A. 160 D1
Karlstadt Germany 63 J5
Karluk AK U.S.A. 148 I4
Karlyk Turkm. 111 G2
Karmala India 106 B2
Karmel, Har hill Israel see Carmel, Mount
Karmona Spain see Córdoba
Karmøy i. Norway 55 D7
Karmpur Pak. 111 I4
Karnafuli Reservoir Bangl. 105 H5
Karnal India 104 D3
Karnali r. Nepal 99 C7
Karnataka state India 106 B3
Karnavati India see Ahmadabad
Karnes City U.S.A. 161 D6
Karnobat Bulg. 69 L3
Karodi Pak. 111 G5
Karoi Zimbabwe 123 C5
Karokpi Myanmar 86 B4
Karo La pass Xizang China 99 E7
Karompalompo i. Indon. 83 B4
Karong India 105 H4
Karonga Malawi 123 D4
Karonie Australia 135 C7
Karool-Döbö Kyrg. 98 B4
Karoo National Park S. Africa 124 F7
Karoo Nature Reserve S. Africa see Camdeboo National Park
Karoonda Australia 137 B7
Karora Eritrea 108 E6
Káros i. Greece see Keros
Karossa Sulawesi Barat Indon. 83 A3
Karossa, Tanjung pt Sumba Indon. 85 G5
Karow Germany 63 M1
Karpasia pen. Cyprus 107 B2
Karpas Peninsula Cyprus see Karpasia
Karpathos i. Greece 69 L7
Karpathou, Steno sea chan. Greece 69 L6
Karpaty mts Europe see Carpathian Mountains
Karpenisi Greece 69 I5
Karpilovka Belarus see Aktsyabrski
Karpinsk Rus. Fed. 51 S4
Karpogory Rus. Fed. 52 J2
Karpuz r. Turkey 107 A1
Karratha Australia 134 B5
Karroo plat. S. Africa see Great Karoo
Karrychirla Turkm. see Garryçyrla
Kars Turkey 113 F2
Kärsämäki Fin. 54 N5
Kārsava Latvia 55 O8
Karshi Qashqadaryo Uzbek. see Qarshi
Karskiye Vorota, Proliv strait Rus. Fed. 76 G3
Karskoye More sea Rus. Fed. see Kara Sea
Karstädt Germany 63 L1
Karstula Fin. 54 N5
Karsu Turkey 107 C1
Karsun Rus. Fed. 53 J5
Kartal Turkey 69 M4
Kartaly Rus. Fed. 76 H4
Kartayel' Rus. Fed. 52 L2
Karttula Fin. 54 O5
Karuizawa Japan 93 E2
Karumba Australia 136 C3
Karumbhar Island India 104 B5
Karun, Kūh-e hill Iran 110 C4
Kārūn, Rūd-e r. Iran 110 C4
Karuni Sumba Indon. 83 A5
Karur India 106 C4
Karvia Fin. 54 M5
Karviná Czech Rep. 57 Q6
Karwar India 106 B3
Karyagino Azer. see Füzuli
Karymskoye Rus. Fed. 89 K2
Karynzharyk, Peski des. Kazakh. 113 I2
Karystos Greece 69 K5
Kaş Turkey 69 M6
Kasa India 106 B2
Kasaba Turkey see Turgutlu
Kasabonika Canada 152 C3
Kasabonika Lake Canada 152 C3
Kasaga-dake mt. Japan 92 D2
Kasagi Japan 92 B4
Kasagi-yama mt. Japan 92 D3
Kasahara Japan 92 D3
Kasaï r. Dem. Rep. Congo 122 B4 also known as Kwa
Kasai Japan 92 A4
Kasaï, Plateau du Dem. Rep. Congo 123 C4
Kasaji Dem. Rep. Congo 123 C5
Kasama Japan 93 G2
Kasama Zambia 123 D5
Kasamatsu Japan 92 C3
Kasan Uzbek. see Koson
Kasane Botswana 123 C5
Kasano-misaki pt Japan 92 C2
Kasaragod India 106 B3
Kasargod India see Kasaragod
Kasargode India see Kasaragod
Kasatkino Rus. Fed. 90 C2
Kasatori-yama hill Japan 92 C4
Kasba Lake Canada 151 K2
Kasba Tadla Morocco 64 C5
Kasegaluk Lagoon AK U.S.A. 148 G1
Kasenga Dem. Rep. Congo 123 C5
Kasengu Dem. Rep. Congo 123 C4
Kasese Dem. Rep. Congo 122 C4
Kasese Uganda 122 D3
Kasevo Rus. Fed. see Neftekamsk
Kasganj India 104 D4
Kasha China 96 C2
Kashabowie Canada 152 C4
Kāshān Iran 110 C3
Kashary Rus. Fed. 53 I6
Kashechewan Canada 152 E3
Kashega AK U.S.A. 148 F5
Kashegelok AK U.S.A. 148 H3
Kashgar Xinjiang China see Kashi
Kashi Xinjiang China 98 B5
Kashiba Japan 92 B4
Kashihara Japan 92 B4
Kashima Ibaraki Japan 93 G3
Kashima Ishikawa Japan 92 C2
Kashima-nada b. Japan 93 G2
Kashimayaria-dake mt. Japan 92 D2
Kashimo Japan 92 D3
Kashin Rus. Fed. 52 H4
Kashipur India 104 D3
Kashira Rus. Fed. 53 H5
Kashiwa Japan 93 F3
Kashiwara Japan 92 B4
Kashiwazaki Japan 91 E5
Kashkanteniz Kazakh. 98 A3
Kashkarantsy Rus. Fed. 52 H2
Kashku'iyeh Iran 110 D4
Kāshmar Iran 110 E3
Kashmir terr. Asia see Jammu and Kashmir
Kashmir, Vale of reg. India 104 C2
Kashunuk r. AK U.S.A. 148 F3
Kashyukulu Dem. Rep. Congo 123 C4
Kasi India see Varanasi
Kasigar Afgh. 111 H3
Kasigluk AK U.S.A. 148 G3
Kasimbar Sulawesi Indon. 83 A3
Kasimov Rus. Fed. 53 I5
Kasiruta i. Maluku Indon. 83 C3
Kaskattama r. Canada 151 N3
Kaskelen Kazakh. 98 B4
Kaskinen Fin. 54 L5
Kas Klong i. Cambodia see Kŏng, Kaôh
Kaskö Fin. see Kaskinen
Kaslo Canada 150 G5
Kasmere Lake Canada 151 K3
Kasongan Kalimantan Indon. 85 F3
Kasongo Dem. Rep. Congo 123 C4
Kasongo-Lunda Dem. Rep. Congo 123 B4
Kasos i. Greece 69 L7
Kaspīy Mangy Oypaty lowland Kazakh./Rus. Fed. see Caspian Lowland
Kaspiysk Rus. Fed. 113 G2
Kaspiyskiy Rus. Fed. see Lagan'
Kaspiyskoye More l. Asia/Europe see Caspian Sea
Kassa Slovakia see Košice
Kassala Sudan 108 E6
Kassandras, Akra pt Greece see Kassandras, Akrotirio
Kassandras, Akrotirio pt Greece 69 J5
Kassandras, Kolpos b. Greece 69 J4
Kassel Germany 63 J3
Kasserine Tunisia 68 C7
Kastag Pak. 111 F5
Kastamonu Turkey 112 D2
Kastellaun Germany 63 H4
Kastelli Kriti Greece see Kissamos
Kastéllion Greece see Kissamos
Kastéllion Kriti Greece see Kissamos
Kastellorizon i. Greece see Megisti
Kasterlee Belgium 62 E3
Kastoria Greece 69 I4
Kastornoye Rus. Fed. 53 H6
Kastsyukovichy Belarus 53 G5
Kasuga Gifu Japan 92 C3
Kasuga Hyōgo Japan 92 B3
Kasugai Japan 92 C3
Kasukabe Japan 93 F3
Kasukawa Japan 93 F2
Kasulu Tanz. 123 D4
Kasumigaura Japan 93 G2
Kasumiga-ura l. Japan 93 G2
Kasumkent Rus. Fed. 113 H2
Kasungu Malawi 123 D5
Kasungu National Park Malawi 123 D5
Kasur Pak. 111 I4
Katâdtlit Nunât terr. N. America see Greenland
Katahdin, Mount U.S.A. 162 G2
Kataklik India 104 D2
Katako-Kombe Dem. Rep. Congo 122 C4
Katakwi Uganda 122 D3
Katalla AK U.S.A. 149 K3
Katana India 104 C5
Katangi India 104 D5
Katanning Australia 135 B8
Katano Japan 92 B4
Katashina Japan 93 F2
Katashina-gawa r. Japan 93 F2
Katata Japan 92 B3
Katavi National Park Tanz. 123 D4
Katawaz reg. Afgh. 111 G3
Katchall i. India 87 A6
Katea Dem. Rep. Congo 123 C4
Kateel r. AK U.S.A. 148 H2
Katerini Greece 69 J4
Katesh Tanz. 123 D4
Kate's Needle mt. Canada/U.S.A. 149 N4
Katete Zambia 123 D5
Katherîna, Gebel mt. Egypt see Kātrīnā, Jabal
Katherine Australia 134 F3
Katherine Gorge National Park Australia see Nitmiluk National Park
Kathi India 111 I6
Kathiawar pen. India 104 B5
Kathihar India see Katihar
Kathiraveli Sri Lanka 106 D4
Kathiwara India 104 C5
Kathleen Falls Australia 134 E3

▶Kathmandu Nepal 105 F4
Capital of Nepal.

Kathu S. Africa 124 F4
Kathua India 104 C2
Kati Mali 120 C3
Katibas r. Malaysia 85 F2
Katihar India 105 F4
Katikati S. Africa 125 H7
Katima Mulilo Namibia 123 C5
Katimik Lake Canada 151 L4
Katiola Côte d'Ivoire 120 C4
Kā Tiritiri o te Moana mts N.Z. see Southern Alps
Katkop Hills S. Africa 124 E6
Katlehong S. Africa 125 I4
Katma Xinjiang China 99 D5
Katmai National Park and Preserve U.S.A. 146 C4
Katmandu Nepal see Kathmandu
Kato Achaïa Greece 69 I5
Kat O Chau H.K. China see Crooked Island
Kat O Hoi b. H.K. China see Crooked Harbour
Katon-Karagay Kazakh. 98 D2
Katoomba Australia 138 E4
Katoposa, Gunung mt. Indon. 83 B3
Katowice Poland 57 Q5
Katoya India 105 G5
Katrancık Dağı mts Turkey 69 M6
Kātrīnā, Jabal mt. Egypt 112 D5
Katrine, Loch l. U.K. 60 E4
Katrineholm Sweden 55 J7
Katse Dam Lesotho 125 I5
Katsina Nigeria 120 D3
Katsina-Ala Nigeria 120 D4
Katsunuma Japan 93 E3
Katsura-gawa r. Japan 93 F3
Katsuragi-san hill Japan 92 B4
Katsuura Japan 93 G3
Katsuyama Fukui Japan 92 C2
Kattaktoc, Cap c. Canada 153 I2
Kattamudda Well Australia 134 D5
Kattaqo'rg'on Uzbek. 111 G2
Kattaqŭrghon Uzbek. see Kattaqo'rg'on
Kattasang Hills Afgh. 111 G3
Kattegat strait Denmark/Sweden 55 G8
Kattowitz Poland see Katowice
Katumbar India 104 D4
Katun' r. Rus. Fed. 98 D1
Katunino Rus. Fed. 52 J4
Katunskiy Khrebet mts Rus. Fed. 98 D2
Katuri Pak. 111 H4
Katwa India see Katoya
Katwijk aan Zee Neth. 62 E2
Katzenbuckel hill Germany 63 J5
Kaua'i i. U.S.A. 157 [inset]
Kaua'i Channel U.S.A. 157 [inset]
Kaub Germany 63 H4
Kaufungen Germany 63 J3
Kauhajoki Fin. 54 M5
Kauhava Fin. 54 M5
Kaukauna U.S.A. 164 A1
Kaukkwè Hills Myanmar 86 B1
Kaukonen Fin. 54 N3
Ka'ula i. U.S.A. 157 [inset]
Kaulakahi Channel U.S.A. 157 [inset]
Kaumajet Mountains Canada 153 J2
Kaunakakai U.S.A. 157 [inset]
Kaunas Lith. 55 M9
Kaunata Latvia 55 O8
Kaundy, Vpadina depr. Kazakh. 113 I2
Kaunia Bangl. 105 G4
Kaura-Namoda Nigeria 120 D3
Kau Sai Chau i. H.K. China 97 [inset]
Kaustinen Fin. 54 M5
Kautokeino Norway 54 M2
Kau-ye Kyun i. Myanmar 87 B5
Kavadarci Macedonia 69 J4
Kavak Turkey 112 E2
Kavaklıdere Turkey 69 M6
Kavala Greece 69 K4
Kavalas, Kolpos b. Greece 69 K4
Kavalerovo Rus. Fed. 90 D3
Kavali India 106 D3
Kavār Iran 110 D4
Kavaratti India 106 B4
Kavaratti atoll India 106 B4
Kavarna Bulg. 69 M3
Kavendou, Mont mt. Guinea 120 B3
Kaveri r. India 106 C4
Kavīr Iran 110 C3
Kavīr, Dasht-e des. Iran 110 D3
Kavīr Kūshk well Iran 110 E3
Kavkasioni mts Asia/Europe see Caucasus
Kawa Seram Indon. 83 D3
Kawa Myanmar 86 B3
Kawabe Gifu Japan 92 D3
Kawabe Wakayama Japan 92 B5
Kawachi Ibaraki Japan 93 G3
Kawachi Ishikawa Japan 92 C2
Kawachi Tochigi Japan 93 F2
Kawachi-Nagano Japan 92 B4
Kawagama Lake Canada 165 F1
Kawage Japan 92 C4
Kawagoe Japan 93 F3
Kawaguchi Saitama Japan 93 F3
Kawaguchiko Japan 93 E3
Kawaguchi-ko l. Japan 93 E3
Kawai Gifu Japan 92 D2
Kawaihae U.S.A. 157 [inset]
Kawaikini U.S.A. 157 [inset]
Kawakami Nagano Japan 93 E3
Kawakami Nara Japan 92 B4
Kawakawa N.Z. 139 E2
Kawakita Japan 92 C2
Kawambwa Zambia 123 C4
Kawamoto Japan 93 F2
Kawana Zambia 123 C5
Kawanakajima Japan 93 E2
Kawana-zaki pt Japan 93 F4
Kawane Japan 93 E4
Kawangkoan Sulawesi Indon. 83 C2
Kawanishi Japan 92 B3
Kawarazawa-gawa r. Japan 93 F2
Kawardha India 104 E5
Kawartha Lakes Canada 165 F1
Kawasaki Japan 93 F3
Kawashima Japan 92 C3
Kawato Sulawesi Indon. 83 B3
Kawaue Japan 92 D3
Kawau Island N.Z. 139 E3
Kawawachikamach Canada 153 I3
Kawazu Japan 93 E4
Kawdut Myanmar 86 B4
Kawe i. Papua Indon. 83 D2
Kawerau N.Z. 139 F4
Kawhia N.Z. 139 E4
Kawhia Harbour N.Z. 139 E4
Kawich Peak U.S.A. 158 E3
Kawich Range mts U.S.A. 158 E3
Kawinaw Lake Canada 151 L4
Kawinda Sumbawa Indon. 85 G5
Kawio i. Indon. 83 C1
Kaw Lake U.S.A. 161 D4
Kawlin Myanmar 86 A2
Kawm Umbū Egypt 108 D5
Kawngmeum Myanmar 86 B2
Kawthaung Myanmar 87 B5
Kaxgar Xinjiang China see Kashi
Kaxgar He r. China 98 B5
Kax He r. China 98 C4
Kaxtax Shan mts China 99 C5
Kaya Burkina 120 C3
Kayadibi Turkey 112 E3
Kayaga-take mt. Japan 93 E3
Kayak Island AK U.S.A. 149 K4
Kayan r. Indon. 85 E3
Kayan r. Indon. 85 G2
Kayangel Atoll Palau 82 [inset]
Kayangel Passage Palau 82 [inset]
Kayankulam India 106 C4
Kayan Mentarang, Taman Nasional nat. park Indon. 85 F2
Kayar India 106 C2
Kayasa Halmahera Indon. 83 C2
Kaycee U.S.A. 156 G4
Kaydak, Sor dry lake Kazakh. 113 I1
Kaydanovo Belarus see Dzyarzhynsk
Kayembe-Mukulu Dem. Rep. Congo 123 C4
Kayenta U.S.A. 159 H3
Kayes Mali 120 B3
Kayigyalik Lake AK U.S.A. 148 G3
Kaymaz Turkey 69 N5
Kaynar Kazakh. 102 E2
Kaynar Zhambylskaya Oblast' Kazakh. 98 A4
Kaynar Turkey 112 E3
Kaynupil'gyn, Laguna lag. Rus. Fed. 148 B3
Kayo Japan 92 B3
Kayoa i. Maluku Indon. 83 C2
Kay Point pt Y.T. Canada 149 M1
Kayseri Turkey 112 D3
Kayuadi i. Indon. 83 B4
Kayuagung Sumatera Indon. 84 D3
Kayuyu Dem. Rep. Congo 122 C4
Kayyngdy Kyrg. 102 D3
Kazach'ye Rus. Fed. 77 O2
Kazakh Azer. see Qazax
Kazakhskaya S.S.R. country Asia see Kazakhstan
Kazakhskiy Melkosopochnik plain Kazakh. 102 D1
Kazakhskiy Zaliv b. Kazakh. 113 I2

▶Kazakhstan country Asia 100 F2
4th largest country in Asia, and 9th in the world.

Kazakhstan Kazakh. see Aksay
Kazakstan country Asia see Kazakhstan
Kazan r. Canada 151 M2
Kazan' Rus. Fed. 52 K5
Kazanchunkur Kazakh. 98 C2
Kazandzhik Turkm. see Bereket
Kazanka r. Rus. Fed. 52 K5
Kazanlı Turkey 107 B1
Kazanlŭk Bulg. 69 K3
Kazan-rettō is Japan see Volcano Islands
Kazatin Ukr. see Kozyatyn

▶Kazbek mt. Georgia/Rus. Fed. 53 J8
4th highest mountain in Europe.

Kaz Dağı mts Turkey 69 L5
Kāzerūn Iran 110 C4
Kazhim Rus. Fed. 52 K3
Kazidi Tajik. see Qozideh
Kazi Magomed Azer. see Qazımämmäd
Kazincbarcika Hungary 53 D6
Kaziranga National Park India 105 H4
Kazo Japan 93 F2
Kazret'i Georgia 113 G2
Kaztalovka Kazakh. 51 P6
Kazusa Japan 93 G3
Kazy Turkm. 110 E2
Kazym r. Rus. Fed. 51 T3
Kazymskiy Mys Rus. Fed. 51 T3
Keady U.K. 61 F3
Keams Canyon U.S.A. 159 H4
Kéamu i. Vanuatu see Anatom
Kearney U.S.A. 160 D3
Kearny U.S.A. 159 H5
Keban Turkey 112 E3
Keban Barajı resr Turkey 112 E3
Kebatu i. Indon. 85 E3
Kébémèr Senegal 120 B3
Kebili Tunisia 64 F5
Kebīr, Nahr al r. Lebanon/Syria 107 B2
Kebkabiya Sudan 121 F3
Kebnekaise mt. Sweden 54 K3
Kebock Head hd U.K. 60 C2
K'ebrī Dehar Eth. 122 E3
Kebumen Jawa Indon. 85 E4
Kebur Sumatera Indon. 84 C3
Kech reg. Pak. 111 F5
Kecheng Qinghai China 94 D4
Kechika r. B.C. Canada 149 P4
Keçiborlu Turkey 69 N6
Kecskemét Hungary 69 H1
K'eda Georgia 113 F2
Kedah state Malaysia 84 C1
Kėdainiai Lith. 55 M9
Kedairu Passage Fiji see Kadavu Passage
Kedarnath Peak Uttaranchal India 99 B7
Kedgwick Canada 153 I5
Kedian China 97 G2
Kediri Jawa Indon. 85 F4
Kedong China 90 B3
Kedva r. Rus. Fed. 52 L2
Kędzierzyn-Koźle Poland 57 Q5
Keele r. Y.T. Canada 149 P2
Keele Peak Y.T. Canada 149 O3
Keeler U.S.A. 158 E3
Keeley Lake Canada 151 I4
Keeling Islands terr. Indian Ocean see Cocos Islands
Keen, Mount hill U.K. 60 G4
Keenapusan i. Phil. 82 B5
Keene CA U.S.A. 158 D4
Keene KY U.S.A. 164 C5
Keene NH U.S.A. 165 I2
Keene OH U.S.A. 164 E3
Keeper Hill hill Ireland 61 D5
Keepit, Lake resr Australia 138 E3
Keep River National Park Australia 134 E3
Keerbergen Belgium 62 E3
Keer-weer, Cape Australia 136 C2
Keetmanshoop Namibia 124 D4
Keewatin Canada 151 M5
Kefallinía i. Greece see Cephalonia
Kefallonia i. Greece see Cephalonia
Kefamenanu Timor Indon. 83 C5
Kefe Ukr. see Feodosiya
Keffi Nigeria 120 D4
Keflavík Iceland 54 [inset]
Kê Ga, Mui pt Vietnam 87 E5
Kegalla Sri Lanka 106 D5
Kegen Kazakh. 102 E3
Kegeti Kyrg. 98 A4
Keglo, Baie de b. Canada 153 I2
Keg River Canada 150 G3
Kegul'ta Rus. Fed. 53 J7
Kehra Estonia 55 N7
Kehsi Mansam Myanmar 86 B2
Keighley U.K. 58 F5
Keihoku Japan 92 B3
Keila Estonia 55 N7
Keimoes S. Africa 124 E5
Keitele Fin. 54 O5
Keitele l. Fin. 54 O5
Keith Australia 137 C8
Keith U.K. 60 G3
Keith Arm b. N.W.T. Canada 149 Q2
Kejimkujik National Park Canada 153 I5
Kekachi-yama mt. Japan 92 D2
Kekaha U.S.A. 157 [inset]
Kékes mt. Hungary 57 R7
Kekik i. Maluku Indon. 83 D3
Keklau Palau 82 [inset]
Kekri India 104 C4
K'elafo Eth. 122 E3
Kelai i. Maldives 106 B5
Kelan Shanxi China 95 G4
Kelang i. Maluku Indon. 83 C3
Kelang Malaysia see Klang
Kelantan r. Malaysia 84 C1
Kelantan state Malaysia 84 C1
Kelapa i. Maluku Indon. 83 D5
Kelara r. Indon. 83 A4
Kelawar i. Indon. 85 E3
Kelberg Germany 62 G4
Kelheim Germany 63 L6
Kelibia Tunisia 68 D6
Kelif Uzboýy marsh Turkm. 111 F2
Kelīrī Iran 110 E5
Kelkheim (Taunus) Germany 63 I4
Kelkit Turkey 113 E2
Kelkit r. Turkey 112 E2
Kéllé Congo 122 B4
Keller Lake Canada 150 F2
Kellett, Cape Canada 146 F2
Kelleys Island U.S.A. 164 D3
Kelliher Canada 151 K5
Kelloselkä Fin. 54 P3
Kells Ireland 61 F4
Kells r. U.K. 61 F3
Kelly U.S.A. 164 B5
Kelly r. AK U.S.A. 148 G2
Kelly, Mount hill AK U.S.A. 148 G1
Kelly Lake N.W.T. Canada 149 P2
Kelly Range hills Australia 135 C6
Kelmė Lith. 55 M9
Kelmis Belgium 62 G4
Kélo Chad 121 E4
Kelowna Canada 150 G5
Kelp Head hd Canada 150 E5
Kelseyville U.S.A. 158 B2
Kelso U.K. 60 G5
Kelso CA U.S.A. 159 F4
Kelso WA U.S.A. 156 C3
Keluang Malaysia 84 C2
Kelvington Canada 151 K4
Kem' Rus. Fed. 52 G2
Kem' r. Rus. Fed. 52 G2
Kemabung Sabah Malaysia 85 F1
Ke Macina Mali see Massina
Kemah Turkey 112 E3
Kemaliye Turkey 112 E3
Kemalpaşa Turkey 69 L5
Kemano (abandoned) Canada 150 E4
Kemasik Malaysia 84 C1
Kembayan Kalimantan Indon. 85 E2
Kembé Cent. Afr. Rep. 122 C3
Kemeneshát hills Hungary 68 G1
Kemer Antalya Turkey 69 N6
Kemer Muğla Turkey 69 M6
Kemer Barajı resr Turkey 69 M6
Kemerovo Rus. Fed. 76 J4
Kemi Fin. 54 N4
Kemijärvi Fin. 54 O3
Kemijärvi l. Fin. 54 O3
Kemijoki r. Fin. 54 N4
Kemin Kyrg. 98 A4
Kemiö Fin. see Kimito
Kemir Turkm. see Keymir
Kemmerer U.S.A. 156 F4
Kemnath Germany 63 L5
Kemnay U.K. 60 G3
Kemp Coast reg. Antarctica see Kemp Land
Kempele Fin. 54 N4
Kempen Germany 62 G3
Kempisch Kanaal canal Belgium 62 F3
Kemp Land reg. Antarctica 188 D2
Kemp Peninsula Antarctica 188 A2
Kemp's Bay Bahamas 163 E7
Kempsey Australia 138 F3
Kempt, Lac l. Canada 152 G5
Kempten (Allgäu) Germany 57 M7
Kempton U.S.A. 164 B3
Kempton Park S. Africa 125 I4
Kemptville Canada 165 H1
Kemujan i. Indon. 85 E4
Ken r. India 104 E4
Kenai AK U.S.A. 149 J3
Kenai Fiords National Park AK U.S.A. 149 J4
Kenai Lake AK U.S.A. 149 J3
Kenai Mountains AK U.S.A. 149 J4
Kenai National Wildlife Refuge nature res. AK U.S.A. 149 J3
Kenai Peninsula AK U.S.A. 149 J3
Kenam, Tanjung pt Indon. 84 D4
Kenamu r. Canada 153 K3
Kenansville U.S.A. 163 E5
Kenâyis, Râs el pt Egypt see Ḥikmah, Ra's al
Kenbridge U.S.A. 165 F5
Kencong Jawa Indon. 85 F5
Kendal Jawa Indon. 85 E4
Kendal U.K. 58 E4
Kendall Australia 138 F3
Kendall, Cape Canada 147 J3
Kendall Island Bird Sanctuary nature res. N.W.T. Canada 149 N1
Kendallville U.S.A. 164 C3
Kendari Sulawesi Indon. 83 B3
Kendawangan Kalimantan Indon. 85 E3
Kendawangan r. Indon. 85 E3
Kendégué Chad 121 E3
Kendrapara India 105 F5
Kendraparha India see Kendrapara
Kendrick Peak U.S.A. 159 H4
Kendujhar India see Keonjhar
Kendujhargarh India see Keonjhar
Kendyktas mts Kazakh. 98 A4
Kendyrli-Kayasanskoye, Plato plat. Kazakh. 113 I2
Kendyrlisor, Solonchak salt l. Kazakh. 113 I2
Kenebri Australia 138 D3
Kenedy U.S.A. 161 D6
Kenema Sierra Leone 120 B4
Kenepai, Gunung mt. Indon. 85 E2
Kenge Dem. Rep. Congo 123 B4
Keng Lap Myanmar 86 C2
Kengtung Myanmar 86 B2
Kenhardt S. Africa 124 E5
Kéniéba Mali 120 B3
Kénitra Morocco 64 C5
Kenli Shandong China 95 I4
Kenmare Ireland 61 C6
Kenmare U.S.A. 160 C1
Kenmare River inlet Ireland 61 B6
Kenmore U.S.A. 165 F2
Kenn Germany 62 G5
Kenna U.S.A. 161 C5
Kennebec U.S.A. 160 D3
Kennebec r. U.S.A. 162 G2
Kennebunkport U.S.A. 165 J2
Kennedy, Cape U.S.A. see Canaveral, Cape
Kennedy Entrance sea channel AK U.S.A. 148 I4
Kennedy Range National Park Australia 135 A6
Kennedy Town H.K. China 97 [inset]
Kenner U.S.A. 161 F6
Kennet r. U.K. 59 G7
Kenneth Range hills Australia 135 B5
Kennett U.S.A. 161 F4
Kennewick U.S.A. 156 D3
Kennicott AK U.S.A. 149 L3
Kenn Reef Australia 136 F4
Kenny Lake AK U.S.A. 149 K3
Kenogami r. Canada 152 D4
Keno Hill Y.T. Canada 149 N3
Kenora Canada 151 M5
Kenosha U.S.A. 164 B2
Kenozero, Ozero l. Rus. Fed. 52 H3
Kent r. U.K. 58 E4
Kent OH U.S.A. 164 E3
Kent TX U.S.A. 161 B6
Kent VA U.S.A. 164 E5
Kent WA U.S.A. 156 C3
Kentani S. Africa 125 I7
Kent Group is Australia 137 [inset]
Kentland U.S.A. 164 B3
Kenton U.S.A. 164 D3
Kent Peninsula Canada 146 H3
Kentucky state U.S.A. 164 C5
Kentucky Lake U.S.A. 161 F4
Kentwood LA U.S.A. 167 H2
Kenya country Africa 122 D3

▶Kenya, Mount Kenya 122 D4
2nd highest mountain in Africa.

Kenyir, Tasik resr Malaysia 84 C1
Ken-zaki pt Japan 93 F3
Keokuk U.S.A. 160 F3
Keoladeo National Park India 104 D4
Keonjhar India 105 F5
Keonjhargarh India see Keonjhar
Keosauqua U.S.A. 160 F3
Keowee, Lake resr U.S.A. 163 D5
Kepahiang Sumatera Indon. 84 C3
Kepina r. Rus. Fed. 52 I2
Keppel Bay Australia 136 E4
Kepsut Turkey 69 M5

Kepulauan Bangka-Belitung prov. Indon. see Bangka-Belitung
Kera India 105 F5
Kerāh Iran 110 E4
Kerala state India 106 B4
Kerang Australia 138 A5
Kerava Fin. 55 N6
Kerba Alg. 67 G5
Kerbau, Tanjung pt Indon. 84 C3
Kerbela Iraq see Karbalā'
Kerben Kyrg. 102 D3
Kerbi r. Rus. Fed. 90 E1
Kerbodot, Lac l. Canada 153 I3
Kerch Ukr. 112 E1
Kerchem'ya Rus. Fed. 52 L3
Kerema P.N.G. 81 L8
Keremeos Canada 150 G5
Kerempe Burun pt Turkey 112 D2
Keren Eritrea 108 E6
Kerewan Gambia 120 B3
Kergeli Turkm. 110 E2
Kerguélen, Îles is Indian Ocean 185 M9
Kerguelen Islands Indian Ocean see Kerguélen, Îles
Kerguelen Plateau sea feature Indian Ocean 185 M9
Kericho Kenya 122 D4
Kerihun mt. Indon. 85 F2
Kerikeri N.Z. 139 D2
Kerimäki Fin. 54 P6
Kerinci, Danau l. Indon. 84 C3
Kerinci, Gunung vol. Indon. 84 C3
Kerinci Seblat, Taman Nasional nat. park Indon. 84 C3
Kerintji vol. Indon. see Kerinci, Gunung
Keriya Xinjiang China see Yutian
Keriya He watercourse China 99 C5
Keriya Shankou pass Xinjiang China 99 C6
Kerken Germany 62 G3
Kerkennah, Îles is Tunisia 68 D7
Kerkiçi Turkm. 111 G2
Kerkini, Limni l. Greece 69 J4
Kerkinitis, Limni l. Greece see Kerkini, Limni
Kérkira i. Greece see Corfu
Kerkouane tourist site Tunisia 68 D6
Kerkyra Greece 69 H5
Kerkyra i. Greece see Corfu
Kerma Sudan 108 D6
Kermadec Islands S. Pacific Ocean 133 I5

▶Kermadec Trench sea feature S. Pacific Ocean 186 I8
4th deepest trench in the world.

Kermān Iran 110 E4
Kerman U.S.A. 158 C3
Kermān, Bīābān-e Iran 110 E4
Kermānshāh Iran 110 B3
Kermānshāhān Iran 110 D4
Kermine Uzbek. see Navoiy
Kermit U.S.A. 161 C6
Kern r. U.S.A. 158 D4
Kernertut, Cap c. Canada 153 I2
Keroh Malaysia see Pengkalan Hulu
Keros i. Greece 69 K6
Keros Rus. Fed. 52 L3
Kérouané Guinea 120 C4
Kerpen Germany 62 G4
Kerr, Cape Antarctica 188 H1
Kerrobert Canada 151 I5
Kerrville U.S.A. 161 D6
Kerry Head hd Ireland 61 C5
Kerteh Malaysia 84 C1
Kerteminde Denmark 55 G9
Kertosono Jawa Indon. 85 F4
Keruak Lombok Indon. 85 G5
Kerulen r. China/Mongolia see Herlen Gol
Kerumutan, Suaka Margasatwa nature res. Indon. 84 C3
Kerur India 106 B2
Keryneia Cyprus see Kyrenia
Kerzaz Alg. 120 C2
Kerzhenets r. Rus. Fed. 52 J4
Kesagami Lake Canada 152 E4
Kesälahti Fin. 54 P6
Keşan Turkey 69 L4
Keşap Turkey 53 H8
Kesariya India 105 F4
Kesennuma Japan 91 F5
Keshan China 90 B2
Keshem Afgh. 111 H2
Keshena U.S.A. 164 A1
Keshendeh-ye Bala Afgh. 111 G2
Keshod India 104 B5
Keshvar Iran 110 C3
Keskin Turkey 112 D3
Keskozero Rus. Fed. 52 G3
Kesova Gora Rus. Fed. 52 H4
Kessel Neth. 62 G3
Kestell S. Africa 125 I5
Kesten'ga Rus. Fed. 54 Q4
Kestilä Fin. 54 O4
Keswick Canada 164 F1
Keswick U.K. 58 D4
Keszthely Hungary 68 G1
Ketahun Sumatera Indon. 84 C3
Ketapang Jawa Indon. 85 F4
Ketapang Kalimantan Indon. 85 E3
Ketchikan AK U.S.A. 149 O5
Ketian Qinghai China 99 E6
Keti Bandar Pak. 111 G5
Ketik r. AK U.S.A. 148 H1
Ketlkede Mountain hill AK U.S.A. 148 H2
Ketmen', Khrebet mts China/Kazakh. 102 F3
Kettering U.K. 59 G6
Kettering U.S.A. 164 C4
Kettle r. Canada 150 G5
Kettle Creek r. U.S.A. 165 G3
Kettle Falls U.S.A. 156 D2
Kettleman City U.S.A. 158 D3
Kettle River Range mts U.S.A. 156 D2
Ketungau r. Indon. 85 E2
Keuka U.S.A. 165 G2
Keuka Lake U.S.A. 165 G2
Keumgang, Mount N. Korea see Kumgang-san
Keumsang, Mount N. Korea see Kumgang-san
Keuruu Fin. 54 N5
Kew Turks and Caicos Is 163 F8
Kewanee U.S.A. 160 F3
Kewapante Flores Indon. 83 B5
Kewaunee U.S.A. 164 B1
Keweenaw Bay U.S.A. 160 F2
Keweenaw Peninsula U.S.A. 160 F2
Keweenaw Point U.S.A. 162 C2
Key, Lough l. Ireland 61 D3
Keyala Sudan 121 G4
Keyano Canada 153 G3
Keya Paha r. U.S.A. 160 D3
Key Harbour Canada 152 E5
Keyi Xinjiang China 98 C4
Keyihe Nei Mongol China 95 J1
Key Largo U.S.A. 163 D7
Keymir Turkm. 110 D2
Keynsham U.K. 59 E7
Keyser U.S.A. 165 F4
Keystone Lake U.S.A. 161 D4
Keystone Peak U.S.A. 159 H6
Keysville U.S.A. 165 F5
Keytesville U.S.A. 160 E4
Keyvy, Vozvyshennost' hills Rus. Fed. 52 H2
Key West U.S.A. 163 D7
Kez Rus. Fed. 51 Q4
Kezi Zimbabwe 123 C6
Kgalagadi admin. dist. Botswana 124 E3
Kgalagadi Transfrontier National Park 125 D2
Kgalazadi admin. dist. Botswana see Kgalagadi
Kgatlen admin. dist. Botswana see Kgatleng
Kgatleng admin. dist. Botswana 125 H3
Kgomofatshe Pan salt pan Botswana 124 E2
Kgoro Pan salt pan Botswana 124 G3
Kgotsong S. Africa 125 H4
Kgun Lake AK U.S.A. 148 G3
Khabab Syria 107 C3
Khabar Iran 110 D4
Khabarikha Rus. Fed. 52 L2
Khabarovsk Rus. Fed. 90 D2
Khabarovskiy Kray admin. div. Rus. Fed. 90 D2
Khabarovsk Kray admin. div. Rus. Fed. see Khabarovskiy Kray
Khabary Rus. Fed. 88 D2
Khabis Iran see Shahdād
Khabody Pass Afgh. 111 F3
Khachmas Azer. see Xaçmaz
Khadar, Jabal mt. Oman 110 E6
Khadro Pak. 111 H5
Khadzhiolen Turkm. 110 E2
Khafs Banbān well Saudi Arabia 110 B5
Khagaria India 105 F4
Khagrachari Bangl. 105 G5
Khagrachhari Bangl. see Khagrachari
Khairgarh Pak. 111 H4
Khairpur Punjab Pak. 111 I4
Khairpur Sindh Pak. 111 H5
Khāīz, Kūh-e mt. Iran 110 C4
Khaja Du Koh hill Afgh. 111 G2
Khajuha India 104 E4
Khāk-e Jabbar Afgh. 111 H3
Khakhea Botswana 124 F3
Khak-rēz Afgh. 111 G4
Khakriz reg. Afgh. 111 G4
Khalajestan reg. Iran 110 C3
Khalatse India 104 D2
Khalifat mt. Pak. 111 G4
Khalīj Surt g. Libya see Sirte, Gulf of
Khalilabad India 105 E4
Khalīlī Iran 110 D5
Khalkabad Turkm. 111 F1
Khalkhāl Iran 110 C2
Khálki i. Greece see Chalki
Khalkís Greece see Chalkida
Khallikot India 106 E2
Khalturin Rus. Fed. see Orlov
Khamar-Daban, Khrebet mts Rus. Fed. 94 E1
Khamaria India 106 D1
Khambhat India 104 C5
Khambhat, Gulf of India 106 A2
Khamgaon India 106 C1
Khamir Yemen 108 F6
Khamis Mushayṭ Saudi Arabia 108 F6
Khamkkeut Laos 86 D3
Khamma well Saudi Arabia 110 B5
Khammam India 106 D2
Khammouan Laos see Thakèk
Khamra Rus. Fed. 77 M3
Khamseh reg. Iran 110 C3
Khan Afgh. 111 H3
Khan, Nam r. Laos 86 C3
Khānābād Afgh. 111 H2
Khān al Baghdādī Iraq 113 F4
Khān al Mashāhidah Iraq 113 G4
Khān al Muşallá Iraq 113 G4
Khanapur India 106 B2
Khān ar Raḥbah Iraq 113 G5
Khanasur Pass Iran/Turkey 113 G3
Khanbalik Beijing China see Beijing
Khānch Iran 110 B2
Khandagayty Rus. Fed. 94 C1
Khandu India 111 I6
Khandwa India 104 D5
Khandyga Rus. Fed. 77 O3
Khanewal Pak. 111 H4
Khan Hung Vietnam see Soc Trăng
Khaniá Greece see Chania
Khānī Yek Iran 110 D4
Khanka, Lake China/Rus. Fed. 90 D3
Khanka, Ozero l. China/Rus. Fed. see Khanka, Lake
Khankendi Azer. see Xankändi
Khanna India 104 D3
Khannā, Qā' salt pan Jordan 107 C3
Khanpur Pak. 111 H5
Khanpur Pak. 111 H4
Khān Ruḥābah Iraq see Khān ar Raḥbah
Khansar Pak. 111 H4
Khān Shaykhūn Syria 107 C2
Khantau Kazakh. 98 A3
Khantayskoye, Ozero l. Rus. Fed. 76 K3
Khan-Tengri, Pik mt. Kazakh./Kyrg. 98 C4
Khanthabouli Laos see Savannakhét
Khanty-Mansiysk Rus. Fed. 76 H3
Khān Yūnis Gaza 107 B4
Khanzi admin. dist. Botswana see Ghanzi
Khao Ang Rua Nai Wildlife Reserve nature res. Thai. 87 C4
Khao Banthat Wildlife Reserve nature res. Thai. 87 B6
Khao Chum Thong Thai. 87 B5
Khaoen Si Nakarin National Park Thai. 87 B4
Khao Laem, Ang Kep Nam Thai. 86 B4
Khao Laem National Park Thai. 86 B4
Khao Luang National Park Thai. 87 B5
Khao Pu-Khao Ya National Park Thai. 87 B6
Khao Soi Dao Wildlife Reserve nature res. Thai. 87 C4
Khao Sok National Park Thai. 87 B5
Khao Yai National Park Thai. 87 C4
Khapcheranga Rus. Fed. 95 H1
Khaplu Pak. 102 E4
Khaptad National Park Nepal 104 E3
Kharabali Rus. Fed. 53 J7
Kharagpur Bihar India 105 F4
Kharagpur W. Bengal India 105 F5
Khārān r. Iran 109 I4
Kharanor Rus. Fed. 95 I1
Kharari India see Abu Road
Kharda India 106 B2
Khardi India 106 C6
Khardong La pass India see Khardung La
Khardung La pass India 104 D2
Kharez Ilias Afgh. 111 F3
Kharfiyah Iraq 113 G5
Kharga Egypt see Al Khārijah
Kharga r. Rus. Fed. 90 D1
Khârga, El Wâhât el oasis Egypt see Khārijah, Wāḥāt al
Kharga Oasis Egypt see Khārijah, Wāḥāt al
Kharg Islands Iran 110 C4
Khargon India 104 C5
Khari r. Rajasthan India 104 C4
Khari r. Rajasthan India 104 C4
Kharian Pak. 111 I3
Khariar India 106 D1
Khārijah, Wāḥāt al oasis Egypt 108 D5
Kharīm, Gebel hill Egypt see Kharīm, Jabal
Kharīm, Jabal hill Egypt 107 A4
Kharkhara r. India 104 E5
Kharkhauda Haryana India 99 B7
Kharkiv Ukr. 53 H6
Khar'kov Ukr. see Kharkiv
Khār Kūh mt. Iran 110 D4
Kharlovka Rus. Fed. 52 H1
Kharlu Rus. Fed. 54 Q6
Kharmanli Bulg. 69 K4
Kharoti reg. Afgh. 111 H3
Kharovsk Rus. Fed. 52 I4
Kharsia India 105 E5

▶Khartoum Sudan 108 D6
Capital of Sudan. 4th most populous city in Africa.

Kharwar reg. Afgh. 111 H3
Khasavyurt Rus. Fed. 113 G2
Khash Afgh. 111 F4
Khāsh Iran 111 F4
Khāsh, Dasht-e Afgh. 111 F4
Khashgort Rus. Fed. 51 T2
Khashm el Girba Sudan 108 E7
Khashm Şana' Saudi Arabia 112 E6
Khash Rūd r. Afgh. 111 F4
Khashuri Georgia 113 F2
Khasi Hills India 105 G4
Khaskovo Bulg. 69 K4
Khatanga Rus. Fed. 77 L2
Khatanga, Gulf of Rus. Fed. see Khatangskiy Zaliv
Khatangskiy Zaliv b. Rus. Fed. 77 L2
Khatayakha Rus. Fed. 52 M2
Khatinza Pass Pak. 111 H2
Khatmat al Malāha Oman 110 E5
Khatyrka Rus. Fed. 77 S3
Khāvāk, Khowtal-e Afgh. 111 H3
Khavda India 104 B5
Khayamnandi S. Africa 125 G6
Khaybar Saudi Arabia 108 E4
Khayelitsha S. Africa 124 D8
Khayrān, Ra's al pt Oman 110 E6
Khedrī Iran 110 E3
Khefa Israel see Haifa
Khehuene, Ponta pt Moz. 125 L2
Khemis Miliana Alg. 67 H5
Khemmarat Thai. 86 D3
Khenchela Alg. 68 B7
Khenifra Morocco 64 C5
Kherāmeh Iran 110 D4
Kherrata Alg. 67 I5
Kherreh Iran 110 D5
Khersan r. Iran 110 C4
Kherson Ukr. 69 O1
Kheta r. Rus. Fed. 77 L2
Kheyrābād Iran 110 D4
Khezerābād Iran 110 D2
Khiching India 105 F5
Khilok Rus. Fed. 95 G1
Khilok r. Rus. Fed. 95 F1
Khinganskiy Zapovednik nature res. Rus. Fed. 90 C2
Khinsar Pak. 111 H5
Khíos i. Greece see Chios
Khipro Pak. 111 H5
Khirbat Isrīyah Syria 107 C2
Khitai Dawan pass Aksai Chin 99 B6
Khīyāv Iran 110 B2
Khiytola Rus. Fed. 55 P6
Khlevnoye Rus. Fed. 53 H5
Khlong, Mae r. Thai. 87 C4
Khlong Saeng Wildlife Reserve nature res. Thai. 87 B5
Khlong Wang Chao National Park Thai. 86 B3
Khlung Thai. 87 C4
Khmel'nik Ukr. see Khmil'nyk
Khmel'nitskiy Ukr. see Khmel'nyts'kyy
Khmel'nyts'kyy Ukr. 53 E6
Khmer Republic country Asia see Cambodia
Khmil'nyk Ukr. 53 E6
Khoai, Hon i. Vietnam 87 D5
Khobda Kazakh. 102 A1
Khobi Georgia 113 F2
Khodā Āfarīd spring Iran 110 E3
Khodzha-Kala Turkm. see Hojagala
Khodzhambaz Turkm. see Hojambaz
Khodzhent Tajik. see Khŭjand
Khodzheyli Qoraqalpog'iston Respublikasi Uzbek. see Xo'jayli
Khojand Tajik. see Khŭjand
Khokhowe Pan salt pan Botswana 124 E3
Khokhropar Pak. 111 H5
Khoksar India 104 D2
Kholm Afgh. 111 G2
Kholm Poland see Chełm
Kholm Rus. Fed. 52 F4
Kholmsk Rus. Fed. 90 F3
Kholon Israel see Holon
Kholtoson Rus. Fed. 94 E1
Kholzun, Khrebet mts Kazakh./Rus. Fed. 98 D2
Khomas admin. reg. Namibia 124 C2
Khomas Highland hills Namibia 124 B2
Khomeyn Iran 110 C3
Khomeynīshahr Iran 110 C3
Khong, Ménam r. Laos/Thai. 86 D4 see Mekong
Khonj Iran 110 D5
Khonj, Kūh-e mts Iran 110 D5
Khon Kaen Thai. 86 C3
Khon Kriel Cambodia see Phumī Kon Kriel
Khonsa India 105 H4
Khonuu Rus. Fed. 77 P3
Khoper r. Rus. Fed. 53 I6
Khor Rus. Fed. 90 D3
Khor r. Rus. Fed. 90 D3
Khorat Plateau Thai. 86 C3
Khorda India see Khurda
Khordha India see Khurda
Khoreyver Rus. Fed. 52 M2
Khorinsk Rus. Fed. 89 J2
Khorixas Namibia 123 B6
Khormūj, Kūh-e mt. Iran 110 C4
Khorog Tajik. see Khorugh
Khorol Rus. Fed. 90 D3
Khorol Ukr. 53 G6
Khoroslū Dāgh hills Iran 110 B2
Khorramābād Iran 110 C3
Khorramshahr Iran 110 C4
Khorugh Tajik. 111 H2
Khosheutovo Rus. Fed. 53 J7
Khōst reg. Afgh./Pak. 111 H3
Khōst 111 H3
Khosūyeh Iran 110 D4
Khotan Xinjiang China see Hotan
Khotang Nepal 99 D8
Khotol Mountain hill AK U.S.A. 148 H2
Khouribga Morocco 64 C5
Khovaling Tajik. 111 H2
Khowrjān Iran 110 D4
Khowrnag, Kūh-e mt. Iran 110 D3
Khreum Myanmar 86 A2
Khri r. India 99 E8
Khroma r. Rus. Fed. 77 P2
Khromtau Kazakh. 102 A1
Khru r. India 99 F8
Khrushchev Ukr. see Svitlovods'k
Khrysokhou Bay Cyprus see Chrysochou Bay
Khrystynivka Ukr. 53 F6
Khuar Pak. 111 I3
Khudumelapye Botswana 124 G2
Khudzhand Tajik. see Khŭjand
Khufaysah, Khashm al hill Saudi Arabia 110 B6
Khugiana Afgh. see Pirzada
Khuis Botswana 124 E4
Khŭjand Tajik. 102 C3
Khŭjayli Qoraqalpog'iston Respublikasi Uzbek. see Xo'jayli
Khŭjayli Uzbek. see Xo'jayli
Khu Khan Thai. 87 D4
Khulays Saudi Arabia 108 E5
Khulkhuta Rus. Fed. 53 J7
Khulm r. Afgh. 111 G2
Khulna Bangl. 105 G5
Khulo Georgia 113 F2
Khuma S. Africa 125 H4
Khŭm Batheay Cambodia 87 D5
Khunayzīr, Jabal al mts Syria 107 C2
Khūnīk Bālā Iran 110 E3
Khūnīnshahr Iran see Khorramshahr
Khunjerab Pass China/Pak. 104 C1
Khunsar Iran 110 C3
Khun Yuam Thai. 86 B3
Khūr Iran 110 E3
Khūran sea chan. Iran 110 D5
Khurayş Saudi Arabia 108 G4
Khurd, Koh-i- mt. Afgh. 111 G3
Khurda India 106 E1
Khurdha India see Khurda
Khurja India 104 D3
Khurmalik Afgh. 111 F3
Khurmuli Rus. Fed. 90 E2
Khūrrāb Iran 110 D4
Khurz Iran 110 D3
Khushab Pak. 111 I3
Khushalgarh Pak. 111 H3
Khushshah, Wādī al watercourse Jordan/Saudi Arabia 107 C5
Khust Ukr. 53 D6
Khutse Game Reserve nature res. Botswana 124 G2
Khutsong S. Africa 125 H4
Khutu r. Rus. Fed. 90 E2
Khuzdar Pak. 111 G5
Khvāf Iran 111 F3
Khvāf reg. Iran 111 F3
Khvājeh Iran 110 B2
Khvalynsk Rus. Fed. 53 K5
Khvodrān Iran 110 D4
Khvord Nārvan Iran 110 E3
Khvormūj Iran 110 C4
Khvoy Iran 110 B2
Khvoynaya Rus. Fed. 52 G4
Khwaja Amran mt. Pak. 111 G4
Khwaja Muhammad Range mts Afgh. 111 H2
Khyber Pass Afgh./Pak. 111 H3
Kiama Australia 138 E5
Kiamba Mindanao Phil. 82 D5
Kiamichi r. U.S.A. 161 E5
Kiana AK U.S.A. 148 G2
Kiangsi prov. China see Jiangxi
Kiangsu prov. China see Jiangsu
Kiantajärvi l. Fin. 54 P4
Kiari India 99 B6
Kīāseh Iran 110 D2
Kiatassuaq i. Greenland 147 M2
Kibaha Tanz. 123 D4
Kibali r. Dem. Rep. Congo 122 C3
Kibangou Congo 122 B4
Kibawe Mindanao Phil. 82 D5
Kibaya Tanz. 123 D4
Kibi Japan 92 B4
Kiboga Uganda 122 D3
Kibombo Dem. Rep. Congo 122 C4
Kibondo Tanz. 122 D4
Kibre Mengist Eth. 121 G4
Kibris country Asia see Cyprus
Kibungo Rwanda 122 D4
Kičevo Macedonia 69 I4
Kichmengskiy Gorodok Rus. Fed. 52 J4
Kiçik Qafqaz mts Asia see Lesser Caucasus
Kicking Horse Pass Canada 150 G5
Kidal Mali 120 D3
Kidderminster U.K. 59 E6
Kidepo Valley National Park Uganda 122 D3
Kidira Senegal 120 B3
Kidmang India 104 D2
Kidnappers, Cape N.Z. 139 F4
Kidsgrove U.K. 59 E5
Kidurong, Tanjung pt Malaysia 85 F2
Kiel Germany 57 M3
Kiel U.S.A. 164 A2
Kiel Canal Germany 57 L3
Kielce Poland 57 R5
Kielder Water resr U.K. 58 E3
Kieler Bucht b. Germany 57 M3
Kienge Dem. Rep. Congo 123 C5
Kierspe Germany 63 H3

▶Kiev Ukr. 53 F6
Capital of Ukraine.

Kiffa Mauritania 120 B3
Kifisia Greece 69 J5
Kifrī Iraq 113 G4

▶Kigali Rwanda 122 D4
Capital of Rwanda.

Kigalik r. AK U.S.A. 148 I1
Kiğı Turkey 113 F3
Kiglapait Mountains Canada 153 J2
Kigluaik Mountains AK U.S.A. 148 F2
Kigoma Tanz. 123 C4
Kihambatang Kalimantan Indon. 85 F3
Kihlanki Fin. 54 M3
Kihniö Fin. 54 M5
Kiholo U.S.A. 157 [inset]
Kii-hantō pen. Japan 92 B5
Kiik Kazakh. 98 A3
Kiiminki Fin. 54 N4
Kii-Nagashima Japan 92 C4
Kii-sanchi mts Japan 92 B5
Kii-suidō sea chan. Japan 89 O6
Kijimadaira Japan 93 E2
Kikerino Rus. Fed. 55 P7
Kikiakrorak r. AK U.S.A. 149 J1
Kikinda Serbia 69 I2
Kikki Pak. 111 F5
Kikládhes is Greece see Cyclades
Kikmiktalikamiut AK U.S.A. 148 F3
Kiknur Rus. Fed. 52 J4
Kikonai Japan 90 F4
Kikori P.N.G. 81 K8
Kikori r. P.N.G. 81 K8
Kikugawa Japan 93 E4
Kikwit Dem. Rep. Congo 123 B4
Kilafors Sweden 55 J6
Kilar India 104 D2
Kilauea U.S.A. 157 [inset]
Kilauea Crater U.S.A. 157 [inset]
Kilbon Seram Indon. 83 D3
Kilbuck Mountains AK U.S.A. 148 H3
Kilchu N. Korea 90 C4
Kilcoole Ireland 61 F4
Kilcormac Ireland 61 E4
Kilcoy Australia 138 F1
Kildare Ireland 61 F4
Kil'dinstroy Rus. Fed. 54 R2
Kilekale Lake N.W.T. Canada 149 Q2
Kilemary Rus. Fed. 52 J4
Kilembe Dem. Rep. Congo 123 B4
Kilfinan U.K. 60 D5
Kilgore U.S.A. 161 E5
Kilham U.K. 58 E3
Kilia Ukr. see Kiliya
Kılıç Dağı mt. Syria/Turkey see Aqra', Jabal al
Kilifi Kenya 122 D4
Kilik Pass Xinjiang China 99 A5

▶Kilimanjaro vol. Tanz. 122 D4
Highest mountain in Africa.

Kilimanjaro National Park Tanz. 122 D4
Kilinailau Islands P.N.G. 132 F2
Kilindoni Tanz. 123 D4
Kilingi-Nõmme Estonia 55 N7
Kilis Turkey 107 C1
Kilis prov. Turkey 107 C1
Kiliuda Bay AK U.S.A. 148 I4
Kiliya Ukr. 69 M2
Kilkee Ireland 61 C5
Kilkeel U.K. 61 G3
Kilkenny Ireland 61 E5
Kilkhampton U.K. 59 C8
Kilkis Greece 69 J4
Killala Ireland 61 C3
Killala Bay Ireland 61 C3
Killaloe Ireland 61 D5
Killam Canada 151 I4
Killarney N.T. Australia 134 E4
Killarney Qld Australia 138 F2
Killarney Canada 152 E5
Killarney Ireland 61 C5
Killarney National Park Ireland 61 C6
Killary Harbour b. Ireland 61 C4
Killbuck U.S.A. 164 E3
Killeen U.S.A. 161 D6
Killenaule Ireland 61 E5
Killik r. AK U.S.A. 148 I1
Killimor Ireland 61 D4
Killin U.K. 60 E4
Killinchy U.K. 61 G3
Killíni mt. Greece see Kyllini
Killinick Ireland 61 F5
Killorglin Ireland 61 C5
Killurin Ireland 61 F5
Killybegs Ireland 61 D3
Kilmacrenan Ireland 61 E2
Kilmaine Ireland 61 C4
Kilmallock Ireland 61 D5
Kilmaluag U.K. 60 C3
Kilmarnock U.K. 60 E5
Kilmelford U.K. 60 D4
Kil'mez' Rus. Fed. 52 K4
Kil'mez' r. Rus. Fed. 52 K4
Kilmona Ireland 61 D6
Kilmore Australia 138 B6
Kilmore Quay Ireland 61 F5
Kilosa Tanz. 123 D4
Kilpisjärvi Fin. 54 L2
Kilrea U.K. 61 F3
Kilrush Ireland 61 C5
Kilsyth U.K. 60 E5
Kiltan atoll India 106 B4
Kiltullagh Ireland 61 D4
Kilwa Masoko Tanz. 123 D4
Kilwinning U.K. 60 E5
Kim U.S.A. 161 C4
Kimanis, Teluk b. Malaysia 85 F1
Kimba Australia 135 G8
Kimba Congo 122 B4
Kimball U.S.A. 160 C3
Kimball, Mount AK U.S.A. 149 K3
Kimbe P.N.G. 132 F2
Kimberley S. Africa 124 G5
Kimberley Plateau Australia 134 D4
Kimberley Range hills Australia 135 B6
Kimch'aek N. Korea 91 C4
Kimch'ŏn S. Korea 91 C5
Kimhae S. Korea 91 C6
Kimhandu mt. Tanz. 123 D4
Kimhwa S. Korea 91 B5
Kími Greece see Kymi
Kimito Fin. 55 M6
Kimitsu Japan 93 F3
Kimmirut Canada 147 L3
Kimolos i. Greece 69 K6
Kimovsk Rus. Fed. 53 H5
Kimpese Dem. Rep. Congo 123 B4
Kimpoku-san mt. Japan see Kinpoku-san
Kimry Rus. Fed. 52 H4
Kimsquit Canada 150 E4
Kimvula Dem. Rep. Congo 123 B4
Kinabalu, Gunung mt. Sabah Malaysia 85 G1
Kinabalu National Park Malaysia 85 G1
Kinabatangan r. Malaysia 85 G1
Kinabatangan, Kuala r. mouth Malaysia 85 G1
Kinango Kenya 123 D4
Kinasa Japan 93 E2
Kinaskan Lake B.C. Canada 149 O4
Kinbasket Lake Canada 150 G4
Kinbrace U.K. 60 F2
Kincaid Canada 151 J5
Kincardine Canada 164 E1
Kincardine U.K. 60 F4
Kinchega National Park Australia 137 C7
Kincolith B.C. Canada 149 O5
Kinda Dem. Rep. Congo 123 C4
Kindat Myanmar 86 A2
Kinde U.S.A. 164 D2
Kinder LA U.S.A. 167 G2
Kinder Scout hill U.K. 58 F5
Kindersley Canada 151 I5
Kindia Guinea 120 B3
Kindu Dem. Rep. Congo 122 C4

Kinegnak AK U.S.A. 148 G4
Kinel' Rus. Fed. 53 K5
Kineshma Rus. Fed. 52 I4
Kingaroy Australia 138 E1
King Christian Island Canada 147 H2
King City U.S.A. 158 C3
King Cove AK U.S.A. 148 G5
King Edward VII Land pen. Antarctica see Edward VII Peninsula
Kingfield U.S.A. 165 J1
Kingfisher U.S.A. 161 D5
King George U.S.A. 165 G4
King George, Mount Canada 156 E2
King George Island Antarctica 188 A2
King George Islands Canada 152 F2
King George Islands Fr. Polynesia see Roi Georges, Îles du
King Hill hill Australia 134 C5
Kingisepp Rus. Fed. 55 P7
King Island Australia 137 [inset]
King Island Canada 150 E4
King Island Myanmar see Kadan Kyun
King Island AK U.S.A. 148 E2
Kingisseppa Estonia see Kuressaare
Kinglake National Park Australia 138 B6
King Leopold and Queen Astrid Coast Antarctica 188 E2
King Leopold Range National Park Australia 134 D4
King Leopold Ranges hills Australia 134 D4
Kingman U.S.A. 159 F4

▶Kingman Reef terr. N. Pacific Ocean 186 J5
United States Unincorporated Territory.

King Mountain B.C. Canada 149 O4
King Mountain hill U.S.A. 161 C6
Kingoonya Australia 137 A6
King Peak Antarctica 188 L1
King Peninsula Antarctica 188 K2
Kingri Pak. 111 H4
Kings r. Ireland 61 E5
Kings r. CA U.S.A. 158 C3
Kings r. NV U.S.A. 156 D4
King Salmon AK U.S.A. 148 H4
King Salmon r. AK U.S.A. 148 H4
Kingsbridge U.K. 59 D8
Kingsburg U.S.A. 158 D3
Kings Canyon National Park U.S.A. 158 D3
Kingscliff Australia 138 F2
Kingscote Australia 137 B7
Kingscourt Ireland 61 F4
King Sejong research station Antarctica 188 A2
King's Lynn U.K. 59 H6
Kingsmill Group is Kiribati 133 H2
Kingsnorth U.K. 59 H7
King Sound b. Australia 134 C4
Kings Peak U.S.A. 159 H1
Kingsport U.S.A. 162 D4
Kingston Australia 137 [inset]
Kingston Canada 165 G1

▶Kingston Jamaica 169 I5
Capital of Jamaica.

▶Kingston Norfolk I. 133 G4
Capital of Norfolk Island.

Kingston MO U.S.A. 160 E4
Kingston NY U.S.A. 165 H3
Kingston OH U.S.A. 164 D4
Kingston PA U.S.A. 165 H3
Kingston Peak U.S.A. 159 F4
Kingston South East Australia 137 B8
Kingston upon Hull U.K. 58 G5

▶Kingstown St Vincent 169 L6
Capital of St Vincent.

Kingstree U.S.A. 163 E5
Kingsville U.S.A. 161 D7
Kingswood U.K. 59 E7
Kington U.K. 59 D6
Kingungi Dem. Rep. Congo 123 B4
Kingurutik r. Canada 153 J2
Kingussie U.K. 60 E3
King William U.S.A. 165 G5
King William Island Canada 147 I3
King William's Town S. Africa 125 H7
Kingwood TX U.S.A. 161 E6
Kingwood WV U.S.A. 164 F4
Kinloch N.Z. 139 B7
Kinloss U.K. 60 F3
Kinmen Taiwan see Chinmen
Kinmen i. Taiwan see Chinmen Tao
Kinmount Canada 165 F1
Kinna Sweden 55 H8
Kinnegad Ireland 61 E4
Kinneret, Yam l. Israel see Galilee, Sea of
Kinniyai Sri Lanka 106 D4
Kinnula Fin. 54 N5
Kinoje r. Canada 152 E3
Kino-kawa r. Japan 92 B4
Kinomoto Japan 92 C3
Kinoosao Canada 151 K3
Kinosaki Japan 92 A3
Kinpoku-san mt. Japan 91 E5
Kinross U.K. 60 F4
Kinsale Ireland 61 D6
Kinsale U.S.A. 165 G4

▶Kinshasa Dem. Rep. Congo 123 B4
Capital of the Democratic Republic of the Congo. 3rd most populous city in Africa.

Kinsley U.S.A. 160 D4
Kinsman U.S.A. 164 E3
Kinston U.S.A. 163 E5
Kintom Sulawesi Indon. 83 B3
Kintop Kalimantan Indon. 85 F3
Kintore U.K. 60 G3
Kintyre pen. U.K. 60 D5
Kin-U Myanmar 86 A2
Kinu-gawa r. Japan 93 G3
Kinunuma-yama mt. Japan 93 F2
Kinushseo r. Canada 152 E3
Kinyeti mt. Sudan 121 G4
Kinzig r. Germany 63 I4
Kiowa CO U.S.A. 156 G5
Kiowa KS U.S.A. 161 D4
Kipahigan Lake Canada 151 K4
Kiparissia Greece see Kyparissia
Kipawa, Lac l. Canada 152 F5
Kipchak Pass Xinjiang China 98 B4
Kipling Canada 151 K5
Kipling Station Canada see Kipling
Kipnuk AK U.S.A. 148 F4
Kiptopeke U.S.A. 165 H5
Kipungo Angola see Quipungo
Kipushi Dem. Rep. Congo 123 C5
Kira Japan 92 D4
Kirakira Solomon Is 133 G3
Kirandul India 106 D2
Kirchdorf Germany 63 I2
Kirchheim-Bolanden Germany 63 I5
Kirchheim unter Teck Germany 63 J6
Kircubbin U.K. 61 G3
Kirdimi Chad 121 E3
Kirenga r. Rus. Fed. 89 J1
Kirensk Rus. Fed. 77 L4
Kireyevsk Rus. Fed. 53 H5
Kirghizia country Asia see Kyrgyzstan
Kirghiz Range mts Kazakh./Kyrg. 102 D3
Kirgizskaya S.S.R. country Asia see Kyrgyzstan
Kirgizskiy Khrebet mts Kazakh./Kyrg. see Kirghiz Range
Kirgizstan country Asia see Kyrgyzstan
Kiri Dem. Rep. Congo 122 B4
Kiribati country Pacific Ocean 186 I6
Kiriga-mine mt. Japan 93 E2
Kırıkhan Turkey 107 C1
Kırıkkale Turkey 112 D3
Kirikkuduk Xinjiang China 94 B2
Kirillov Rus. Fed. 52 H4
Kirillovo Rus. Fed. 90 F3
Kirin China see Jilin
Kirin prov. China see Jilin
Kirinda Sri Lanka 106 D5
Kirinyaga mt. Kenya see Kenya, Mount
Kirishi Rus. Fed. 52 G4
Kirishima-Yaku Kokuritsu-kōen Japan 91 C7
Kirishima-yama vol. Japan 91 C7
Kiritimati atoll Kiribati 187 J5
Kiriwina Islands P.N.G. see Trobriand Islands
Kırkağaç Turkey 69 L5
Kirk Bulāg Dāgi mt. Iran 110 B2
Kirkby U.K. 58 E5
Kirkby in Ashfield U.K. 59 F5
Kirkby Lonsdale U.K. 58 E4
Kirkby Stephen U.K. 58 E4
Kirkcaldy U.K. 60 F4
Kirkcolm U.K. 60 D6
Kirkcudbright U.K. 60 E6
Kirkenær Norway 55 H6
Kirkenes Norway 54 Q2
Kirkfield Canada 165 F1
Kirkintilloch U.K. 60 E5
Kirkkonummi Fin. 55 N6
Kirkland U.S.A. 159 G4
Kirkland Lake Canada 152 E4
Kırklareli Turkey 69 L4
Kirklin U.S.A. 164 B3
Kirk Michael Isle of Man 58 C4
Kirkoswald U.K. 58 E4
Kirkpatrick, Mount Antarctica 188 H1
Kirksville U.S.A. 160 E3
Kirkūk Iraq 113 G4
Kirkwall U.K. 60 G2
Kirkwood S. Africa 125 G7
Kirman Iran see Kermān
Kirn Germany 63 H5
Kirov Kaluzhskaya Oblast' Rus. Fed. 53 G5
Kirov Kirovskaya Oblast' Rus. Fed. 52 K4
Kirova, Zaliv b. Azer. see Qızılağac Körfäzi
Kirovabad Azer. see Gäncä
Kirovabad Tajik. see Panj
Kirovakan Armenia see Vanadzor
Kirovo Ukr. see Kirovohrad
Kirovo-Chepetsk Rus. Fed. 52 K4
Kirovo-Chepetskiy Rus. Fed. see Kirovo-Chepetsk
Kirovograd Ukr. see Kirovohrad
Kirovohrad Ukr. 53 G6
Kirovsk Leningradskaya Oblast' Rus. Fed. 52 F4
Kirovsk Murmanskaya Oblast' Rus. Fed. 54 R3
Kirovsk Turkm. see Badabaýhan
Kirovs'ke Ukr. 112 D1
Kirovskiy Rus. Fed. 90 D3
Kirovskoye Ukr. see Kirovs'ke
Kırpaşa pen. Cyprus see Karpasia
Kirpili Turkm. 110 E2
Kirriemuir U.K. 60 F4
Kirs Rus. Fed. 52 L4
Kirsanov Rus. Fed. 53 I5
Kırşehir Turkey 112 D3
Kirthar National Park Pak. 111 G5
Kirthar Range mts Pak. 111 G5
Kirtland U.S.A. 159 I3
Kirtorf Germany 63 J4
Kiruna Sweden 54 L3
Kirundu Dem. Rep. Congo 122 C4
Kirwan Escarpment Antarctica 188 B2
Kiryū Japan 93 F2
Kisa Sweden 55 I8
Kisama, Parque Nacional de nat. park Angola see Quiçama, Parque Nacional do
Kisandji Dem. Rep. Congo 123 B4
Kisangani Dem. Rep. Congo 122 C3
Kisantu Dem. Rep. Congo 123 B4
Kisar i. Maluku Indon. 83 C5
Kisaralik r. AK U.S.A. 148 G3
Kisaran Sumatera Indon. 84 B2
Kisarazu Japan 93 F3
Kisei Japan 92 C4
Kiselevsk Rus. Fed. 88 F2
Kisel'ovka Rus. Fed. 90 E2
Kish i. Iran 110 D5
Kishanganj India 105 F4
Kishangarh Madh. Prad. India 104 D4
Kishangarh Rajasthan India 104 B4
Kishangarh Rajasthan India 104 C4
Kishangarh Rajasthan India 104 D4
Kishi Nigeria 120 D4
Kishigawa Japan 92 B4
Kishi-gawa r. Japan 92 B4
Kishinev Moldova see Chişinău
Kishiwada Japan 92 B4
Kishkenekol' Kazakh. 101 G1
Kishoreganj Bangl. 105 G4
Kishorganj Bangl. see Kishoreganj
Kisi Nigeria see Kishi
Kisii Kenya 122 D4
Kiska Island AK U.S.A. 149 [inset]
Kiskittogisu Lake Canada 151 L4
Kiskitto Lake Canada 151 L4
Kiskunfélegyháza Hungary 69 H1
Kiskunhalas Hungary 69 H1
Kiskunsági nat. park Hungary 69 H1
Kislovodsk Rus. Fed. 113 F2
Kismaayo Somalia 122 E4
Kismayu Somalia see Kismaayo
Kiso Japan 93 D3
Kisofukushima Japan 92 D3
Kisogawa Japan 92 C3
Kiso-gawa r. Japan 92 C3
Kiso-gawa r. Japan 93 E3
Kisoro Uganda 121 F5
Kisosaki Japan 92 C3
Kiso-sanmyaku mts Japan 93 D3
Kispiox Canada 150 E4
Kispiox r. Canada 150 E4
Kissamos Greece 69 J7
Kisseraing Island Myanmar see Kanmaw Kyun
Kissidougou Guinea 120 B4
Kissimmee U.S.A. 163 D6
Kissimmee, Lake U.S.A. 163 D7
Kississing Lake Canada 151 K4
Kistendey Rus. Fed. 53 I5
Kistigan Lake Canada 151 M4
Kistna r. India see Krishna
Kisumu Kenya 122 D4
Kisykkamys Kazakh. see Dzhangala
Kita Hyōgo Japan 92 B4
Kita Kyōto Japan 92 B3
Kita Mali 120 C3
Kitab Uzbek. see Kitob
Kita-Daitō-jima i. Japan 89 O7
Kitagata Japan 92 C3
Kitaibaraki Japan 93 G2
Kita-Iō-jima vol. Japan 81 K1
Kitakami Japan 91 F5
Kita-Kyūshū Japan 91 C6
Kitale Kenya 122 D3
Kitami Japan 90 F4
Kitamimaki Japan 93 E2
Kitamoto Japan 93 F2
Kitatachibana Japan 93 F2
Kitaura Ibaraki Japan 93 G2
Kita-ura l. Japan 93 G3
Kitayama Japan 92 B5
Kit Carson U.S.A. 160 C4
Kitchener Canada 164 E2
Kitchigama r. Canada 152 F4
Kitee Fin. 54 Q5
Kitgum Uganda 122 D3
Kíthira i. Greece see Kythira
Kíthnos i. Greece see Kythnos
Kiti, Cape Cyprus see Kition, Cape
Kitimat Canada 150 D4
Kitinen r. Fin. 54 O3
Kition, Cape Cyprus 107 A2
Kitiou, Akra c. Cyprus see Kition, Cape
Kitkatla B.C. Canada 149 O5
Kitob Uzbek. 111 G2
Kitsault B.C. Canada 149 O5
Kitsuregawa Japan 93 G2
Kittanning U.S.A. 164 F3
Kittatinny Mountains hills U.S.A. 165 H3
Kittery U.S.A. 165 J2
Kittilä Fin. 54 N3
Kittur India 106 B3
Kitty Hawk U.S.A. 162 F4
Kitui Kenya 122 D4
Kitwanga Canada 150 D4
Kitwe Zambia 123 C5
Kitzbüheler Alpen mts Austria 57 N7
Kitzingen Germany 63 K5
Kitzscher Germany 63 M3
Kiukpalik Island AK U.S.A. 148 I4
Kiu Lom, Ang Kep Nam Thai. 86 B3
Kiunga P.N.G. 81 K8
Kiuruvesi Fin. 54 O5
Kivak Rus. Fed. 148 D2
Kivalina AK U.S.A. 148 F2
Kividlo AK U.S.A. 148 F2
Kivijärvi Fin. 54 N5
Kiviõli Estonia 55 O7
Kivu, Lake Dem. Rep. Congo/Rwanda 122 C4
Kiwaba N'zogi Angola 123 B4
Kiwai Island P.N.G. 81 K8
Kiwalik AK U.S.A. 148 G2
Kiwalik r. AK U.S.A. 148 G2
Kiyev Ukr. see Kiev
Kiyevskoye Vodokhranilishche resr Ukr. see Kyyivs'ke Vodoskhovyshche
Kıyıköy Turkey 69 M4
Kiyomi Japan 92 D2
Kiyosumi-yama hill Japan 93 G3
Kiyotsu-gawa r. Japan 93 E1
Kizel Rus. Fed. 51 R4
Kizema Rus. Fed. 52 J3
Kizha Rus. Fed. 95 G1
Kizil Xinjiang China 98 C4
Kizilawat Xinjiang China 98 B5
Kızılcadağ Turkey 69 M6
Kızılca Dağ mt. Turkey 112 C3
Kızılcahamam Turkey 112 D2
Kızıldağ mt. Turkey 107 A1
Kızıldağ mt. Turkey 107 B1
Kızıl Dağı mt. Turkey 112 E3
Kızılırmak Turkey 112 D2
Kızılırmak r. Turkey 112 D2
Kiziltepe Turkey 113 F3
Kizilyurt Rus. Fed. 113 G2
Kızkalesi Turkey 107 B1
Kizlyar Rus. Fed. 113 G2
Kizlyarskiy Zaliv b. Rus. Fed. 113 G1
Kizner Rus. Fed. 52 K4
Kizu Japan 92 B4
Kizu-gawa r. Japan 92 B4
Kizyl-Arbat Turkm. see Serdar
Kizyl-Atrek Turkm. see Etrek
Kizyl Jilga Aksai Chin 99 B6
Kjøllefjord Norway 54 O1
Kjøpsvik Norway 54 J2
Kladno Czech Rep. 57 O5
Klagan Sabah Malaysia 85 G1
Klagenfurt Austria 57 O7
Klagetoh U.S.A. 159 I4
Klaipėda Lith. 55 L9
Klaksvík Faroe Is 54 [inset]
Klamath U.S.A. 156 B4
Klamath r. U.S.A. 146 F5
Klamath Falls U.S.A. 156 C4
Klamath Mountains U.S.A. 156 C4
Klampo Kalimantan Indon. 85 G2
Klang Malaysia 84 C2
Klappan r. B.C. Canada 149 O4
Klarälven r. Sweden 55 H7
Klaten Jawa Indon. 85 E4
Klatovy Czech Rep. 57 N6
Klawer S. Africa 124 D6
Klawock AK U.S.A. 149 N5
Klazienaveen Neth. 62 G2
Kleides Islands Cyprus 107 B2
Kleinbegin S. Africa 124 E5
Klein Karas Namibia 124 D4
Klein Nama Land reg. S. Africa see Namaqualand
Klein Roggeveldberge mts S. Africa 124 E7
Kleinsee S. Africa 124 C5
Klemtu Canada 150 D4
Klerksdorp S. Africa 125 H4
Klery Creek AK U.S.A. 148 G2
Kletnya Rus. Fed. 53 G5
Kletsk Belarus see Klyetsk
Kletskaya Rus. Fed. 53 I6
Kletskiy Rus. Fed. see Kletskaya
Kleve Germany 62 G3
Klichka Rus. Fed. 95 I1
Klidhes Islands Cyprus see Kleides Islands
Klimkovka Rus. Fed. 52 K4
Klimovo Rus. Fed. 53 G5
Klin Rus. Fed. 52 H4
Kling Mindanao Phil. 82 D5
Klingenberg am Main Germany 63 J5
Klingenthal Germany 63 M4
Klingkang, Banjaran mts Indon./Malaysia 85 E2
Klink Germany 63 M1
Klínovec mt. Czech Rep. 63 N4
Klintehamn Sweden 55 K8
Klintsy Rus. Fed. 53 G5
Ključ Bos.-Herz. 68 G2
Kłodzko Poland 57 P5
Klondike r. Y.T. Canada 149 M2
Klondike Gold Rush National Historical Park nat. park AK U.S.A. 149 N4
Kloosterhaar Neth. 62 G2
Klosterneuburg Austria 57 P6
Klotz, Mount Y.T. Canada 149 L2
Klötze (Altmark) Germany 63 L2
Kluane Game Sanctuary nature res. Y.T. Canada 149 L3
Kluane Lake Y.T. Canada 149 M3
Kluane National Park Y.T. Canada 149 M3
Kluang Malaysia see Keluang
Kluang, Tanjung pt Indon. 85 E3
Kluczbork Poland 57 Q5
Klukhori Rus. Fed. see Karachayevsk
Klukhorskiy, Pereval Georgia/Rus. Fed. 113 F2
Klukwan AK U.S.A. 149 N4
Klumpang, Teluk b. Indon. 85 G3
Klungkung Bali Indon. 85 F5
Klutina Lake AK U.S.A. 149 K3
Klyetsk Belarus 55 O10
Klyosato Japan 93 E1
Klyuchevskaya, Sopka vol. Rus. Fed. 77 R4
Klyuchi Rus. Fed. 90 B2
Knåda Sweden 55 I6
Knaresborough U.K. 58 F4
Knee Lake Man. Canada 151 M4
Knee Lake Sask. Canada 151 J4
Knetzgau Germany 63 K5
Knife r. U.S.A. 160 C2
Knight Inlet Canada 150 E5
Knighton U.K. 59 D6
Knights Landing U.S.A. 158 C2
Knightstown U.S.A. 164 C4
Knin Croatia 68 G2
Knittelfeld Austria 57 O7
Knjaževac Serbia 69 J3
Knob Lake Canada see Schefferville
Knob Lick U.S.A. 164 C5
Knob Peak hill Australia 134 E3
Knock Ireland 61 D4
Knockalongy hill Ireland 61 D3
Knockalough Ireland 61 C5
Knockanaffrin hill Ireland 61 E5
Knockboy hill Ireland 61 C6
Knock Hill hill U.K. 60 G3
Knockmealdown Mts hills Ireland 61 D5
Knocknaskagh hill Ireland 61 D5
Knokke-Heist Belgium 62 D3
Knorrendorf Germany 63 N1
Knowle U.K. 59 F6
Knowlton Canada 165 I1
Knox IN U.S.A. 164 B3
Knox PA U.S.A. 164 F3
Knox, Cape B.C. Canada 149 N5
Knox Coast Antarctica 188 F2
Knoxville GA U.S.A. 163 D5
Knoxville TN U.S.A. 162 D5
Knud Rasmussen Land reg. Greenland 147 L2
Knysna S. Africa 124 F8
Ko, Gora mt. Rus. Fed. 90 E3
Koartac Canada see Quaqtaq
Koba Indon. 84 D3
Kobbfoss Norway 54 P2
Kobe Halmahera Indon. 83 C2
Kōbe Japan 92 B4
København Denmark see Copenhagen
Kobenni Mauritania 120 C3
Kobi Seram Indon. 83 D3
Koblenz Germany 63 H4
Koboldo Rus. Fed. 90 D1
Kobrin Belarus see Kobryn
Kobroör i. Indon. 81 I8
Kobryn Belarus 55 N10
Kobuchizawa Japan 93 E3
Kobuk AK U.S.A. 148 H2
Kobuk r. AK U.S.A. 148 G2
Kobuk Valley National Park AK U.S.A. 148 H2
K'obulet'i Georgia 113 F2
Kobushiga-take mt. Japan 93 E3
Kocaeli Turkey see İzmit
Kocaeli Yarımadası pen. Turkey 69 M4
Kočani Macedonia 69 J4
Kocasu r. Turkey 69 M4
Kocê Gansu China 94 E5
Kočevje Slovenia 68 F2
Koch Bihar India 105 G4
Kocher r. Germany 63 J5
Kochevo Rus. Fed. 51 Q4
Kochi India see Cochin
Kōchi Japan 91 D6
Koçhisar Turkey see Kızıltepe
Koch Island Canada 147 K3
Kochkor Kyrg. 102 E3
Kochkorka Kyrg. see Kochkor
Kochkurovo Rus. Fed. 53 J5
Kochubeyevskoye Rus. Fed. 113 F1
Kod India 106 B3
Kodaira Japan 93 F3
Kodala India 106 E2
Kodama Japan 93 F2
Kodarma India 105 F4
Kōdera Japan 92 A4
Koderma India see Kodarma
Kodiak AK U.S.A. 148 I4
Kodiak Island AK U.S.A. 148 I4
Kodiak National Wildlife Refuge nature res. AK U.S.A. 148 I4
Kodibeleng Botswana 125 H2
Kodino Rus. Fed. 52 H3
Kodiyakkarai India 106 C4
Kodok Sudan 108 D8
Kodyma Ukr. 53 F6
Kodzhaele mt. Bulg./Greece 69 K4
Koedoesberg mts S. Africa 124 E7
Koegrabie S. Africa 124 E5
Koekenaap S. Africa 124 D6
Koersel Belgium 62 F3
Koës Namibia 124 D3
Kofa Mountains U.S.A. 159 G5
Koffiefontein S. Africa 124 G5
Koforidua Ghana 120 C4
Kōfu Yamanashi Japan 93 E3
Koga Japan 93 F2
Kogaluc r. Canada 152 F2
Kogaluc, Baie de b. Canada 152 F2
Kogaluk r. Canada 153 J2
Kogan Australia 138 E1
Køge Denmark 55 H9
Kogon r. Guinea 120 B3
Kogon Uzbek. 111 G2
Kohan Pak. 111 G5
Kohat Pak. 111 H3
Kohestānāt Afgh. 111 G3
Kohila Estonia 55 N7
Kohima India 105 H4
Kohistan reg. Afgh. 111 H3
Kohistan reg. Pak. 111 I3
Kohler Range mts Antarctica 188 K2
Kohlu Pak. 111 H4
Kohsan Afgh. 111 F3
Kohtla-Järve Estonia 55 O7
Kohŭng S. Korea 91 B6
Koidern Y.T. Canada 149 L3
Koidern Mountain Y.T. Canada 149 L3
Koidu Sierra Leone see Sefadu
Koihoa India 87 A5
Koikyim Qu r. Qinghai China 99 F6
Koilkonda India 106 C2
Koin N. Korea 91 B4
Koin r. Rus. Fed. 52 K3
Koi Sanjaq Iraq 113 G3
Koito-gawa r. Japan 93 F3
Kōje-do i. S. Korea 91 C6
Kojonup Australia 135 B8
Kōka Japan 92 C4
Kokai-gawa r. Japan 93 G3
Kokand Farg'ona Uzbek. see Qo'qon
Kökar Fin. 55 L7
Kök-Art Osh Kyrg. 98 A4
Kokawa Japan 92 B4
Kök-Aygyr Kyrg. 98 A4
Kokchetav Kazakh. see Kokshetau
Kokemäenjoki r. Fin. 55 L6
Kokerboom Namibia 124 D5
Ko Kha Thai. 86 B3
Kokkilai Sri Lanka 106 D4
Kokkola Fin. 54 M5
Kok Kuduk well Xinjiang China 98 D3
Koko Nigeria 120 D3
Kokoda P.N.G. 81 L8
Kokolik r. AK U.S.A. 148 G1
Kokomo U.S.A. 164 B3
Kokong Botswana 124 F3
Kokos i. Indon. 87 A7
Kokosi S. Africa 125 H4
Kokpekti Kazakh. 102 F2
Kokrines AK U.S.A. 148 I2
Kokrines Hills AK U.S.A. 148 I2
Kokruagarok AK U.S.A. 148 I1
Koksan N. Korea 91 B5
Kokshaal-Tau, Khrebet mts China/Kyrg. see Kakshaal-Too
Koksharka Rus. Fed. 52 J4
Kokshetau Kazakh. 101 F1
Koksoak r. Canada 153 H2
Kokstad S. Africa 125 I6
Koksu Almatinskaya Oblast' Kazakh. 98 B3
Koksu Kazakh. 98 B3
Koktal Kazakh. 102 E3
Kokterek Almatinskaya Oblast' Kazakh. 98 B3
Kokterek Kazakh. 53 K6
Koktokay Xinjiang China see Fuyun
Koktokay Xinjiang China 94 B2
Koktuma Kazakh. 98 C3
Koku, Tanjung pt Indon. 83 B4
Kokubunji Japan 93 F2
Kokufu Japan 92 D2
Kokushiga-take mt. Japan 93 E3
Koküy Xinjiang China 94 B2
Kokyar Xinjiang China 99 B5
Kokzhayyk Kazakh. 98 C2
Kola i. Indon. 81 I8
Kola Rus. Fed. 54 R2
Kolachi r. Pak. 111 G5
Kolahoi mt. India 104 C2
Kolaka Sulawesi Indon. 83 B4
Kolambugan Mindanao Phil. 82 C4
Kolana Indon. 83 C5
Ko Lanta Thai. 87 B6
Kola Peninsula Rus. Fed. 52 H2
Kolar Chhattisgarh India 106 D2
Kolar Karnataka India 106 C3
Kolaras India 104 D4
Kolar Gold Fields India 106 C3
Kolari Fin. 54 M3
Kolarovgrad Bulg. see Shumen
Kolasib India 105 H4
Kolayat India 104 C4
Kolbano Timor Indon. 83 C5
Kolberg Poland see Kołobrzeg
Kol'chugino Rus. Fed. 52 H4
Kolda Senegal 120 B3
Kolding Denmark 55 F9
Kole Kasaï-Oriental Dem. Rep. Congo 122 C4
Kole Orientale Dem. Rep. Congo 122 C3
Koléa Alg. 67 H5
Kolekole mt. U.S.A. 157 [inset]
Koler Sweden 54 L4
Kolguyev, Ostrov i. Rus. Fed. 52 K1
Kolhan reg. India 105 F5
Kolhapur India 106 B2
Kolhumadulu Atoll Maldives 103 D11
Koliganek AK U.S.A. 148 H4
Kolikata India see Kolkata
Kõljala Estonia 55 M7
Kolkasrags pt Latvia 55 M8

▶Kolkata India 105 G5
5th most populous city in Asia and 8th in the world.

Kolkhozabad Khatlon Tajik. see Vose
Kolkhozabad Khatlon Tajik. see Kolkhozobod
Kolkhozobod Tajik. 111 H2
Kollam India see Quilon
Kolleru Lake India 106 D2
Kollum Neth. 62 G1
Kolmanskop (abandoned) Namibia 124 B4
Köln Germany see Cologne
Köln-Bonn airport Germany 63 H4
Kołobrzeg Poland 57 O3
Kologriv Rus. Fed. 52 J4
Kolokani Mali 120 C3
Kolombangara i. Solomon Is 133 F2
Kolomea Ukr. see Kolomyya
Kolomna Rus. Fed. 53 H5
Kolomyja Ukr. see Kolomyya
Kolomyya Ukr. 53 E6
Kolondiéba Mali 120 C3
Kolonedale Sulawesi Indon. 83 B3
Koloni Cyprus 107 A2
Kolonkwaneng Botswana 124 E4
Kolono Sulawesi Indon. 83 B4
Kolowana Watobo, Teluk b. Indon. 83 B4
Kolozsvár Romania see Cluj-Napoca
Kolpashevo Rus. Fed. 76 J4
Kolpos Messaras b. Greece 69 K7
Kol'skiy Poluostrov pen. Rus. Fed. see Kola Peninsula
Kölük Turkey see Kâhta
Koluli Eritrea 108 F7
Kolumadulu Atoll Maldives see Kolhumadulu Atoll
Kolva r. Rus. Fed. 52 M2
Kolvan India 106 B2
Kolvereid Norway 54 G4
Kolvik Norway 54 N1
Kolvitskoye, Ozero l. Rus. Fed. 54 R3
Kolwa reg. Pak. 111 G5
Kolwezi Dem. Rep. Congo 123 C5
Kolyma r. Rus. Fed. 77 R3

Kolyma Lowland Rus. Fed. see Kolymskaya Nizmennost'
Kolyma Range mts Rus. Fed. see Kolymskiy, Khrebet
Kolymskaya Nizmennost' lowland Rus. Fed. 77 Q3
Kolymskiy, Khrebet mts Rus. Fed. 77 R3
Kolyshley Rus. Fed. 53 J5
Kolyuchaya, Gora mt. Rus. Fed. 148 A2
Kolyuchin, Ostrov i. Rus. Fed. 148 D2
Kolyuchinskaya Guba b. Rus. Fed. 148 D2
Kol'zhat Kazakh. 98 C4
Kom mt. Bulg. 69 J3
Kom Xinjiang China 98 D2
Komadugu-gana watercourse Nigeria 120 E3
Komae Japan 93 F3
Komaga-dake mt. Japan 93 D3
Komagane Japan 93 D3
Komaga-take mt. Japan 93 F1
Komaggas S. Africa 124 C5
Komaio P.N.G. 81 K8
Komaki Japan 92 C3
Komandnaya, Gora mt. Rus. Fed. 90 E2
Komandorskiye Ostrova is Rus. Fed. 77 R4
Komárno Slovakia 57 Q7
Komati r. Swaziland 125 J3
Komatipoort S. Africa 125 J3
Komatsu Japan 92 C2
Komba i. Indon. 83 B4
Kombakomba Sulawesi Indon. 83 B3
Komebail Lagoon Palau 82 [inset]
Komering r. Indon. 84 D3
Komga S. Africa 125 H7
Komintern Ukr. see Marhanets'
Kominternivs'ke Ukr. 69 N1
Komiža Croatia 68 G3
Komló Hungary 68 H1
Kommunarsk Ukr. see Alchevs'k
Komodo i. Indon. 83 A5
Komodo, Taman Nasional nat. park Indon. 83 A5
Kôm Ombo Egypt see Kawm Umbū
Komono Congo 122 B4
Komono Japan 92 C3
Komoran i. Indon. 81 J8
Komoro Japan 93 E2
Komotini Greece 69 K4
Kompong Cham Cambodia see Kâmpóng Cham
Kompong Chhnang Cambodia see Kâmpóng Chhnăng
Kompong Kleang Cambodia see Kâmpóng Khleăng
Kompong Som Cambodia see Sihanoukville
Kompong Speu Cambodia see Kâmpóng Spœ
Kompong Thom Cambodia see Kâmpóng Thum
Komrat Moldova see Comrat
Komsberg mts S. Africa 124 E7
Komsomol Kazakh. see Karabalyk
Komsomolabad Tajik. see Komsomolobod
Komsomolets Kazakh. see Karabalyk
Komsomolets, Ostrov i. Rus. Fed. 76 K1
Komsomolobod Tajik. 111 H2
Komsomol's'k Ukr. 53 G6
Komsomol'skiy Chukotskiy Avtonomnyy Okrug Rus. Fed. 189 C2
Komsomol'skiy Khanty-Mansiyskiy Avtonomnyy Okrug Rus. Fed. see Yugorsk
Komsomol'skiy Respublika Kalmykiya - Khalm'g-Tangch Rus. Fed. 53 J7
Komsomol'sk-na-Amure Rus. Fed. 90 E2
Komsomol'skoye Kazakh. 102 B1
Komsomol'skoye Rus. Fed. 53 J6
Kömürlü Turkey 113 F2
Kon India 105 E4
Konacık Turkey 107 B1
Konada India 106 D2
Kōnan Aichi Japan 92 C3
Kōnan Shiga Japan 92 C4
Konarak India see Konarka
Konarka India 105 F6
Konch India 104 D4
Konda Japan 92 B3
Kondagaon India 106 D2
Kondinin Australia 135 B8
Kondinskoye Rus. Fed. see Oktyabr'skoye
Kondoa Tanz. 123 D4
Kondol' Rus. Fed. 53 J5
Kondopoga Rus. Fed. 52 G3
Kondoz Afgh. see Kunduz
Kondrovo Rus. Fed. 53 G5
Konergino Rus. Fed. 148 C2
Köneürgenç Turkm. 109 I1
Köneürgenç Turkm. see Köneürgenç
Kong Cameroon 120 E4
Kông, Kaôh i. Cambodia 87 C5
Kông, Tônlé r. Cambodia 87 D4
Kong, Xé r. Laos 86 D4
Kongakut r. AK U.S.A. 149 L1
Kongauru i. Palau 82 [inset]
Kong Christian IX Land reg. Greenland 147 O3
Kong Christian X Land reg. Greenland 147 P2
Kongelab atoll Marshall Is see Rongelap
Kong Frederik IX Land reg. Greenland 147 M3
Kong Frederik VI Kyst coastal area Greenland 147 N3
Kongiganak AK U.S.A. 148 G4
Kong Kat hill Indon. 85 G2
Kongkemul mt. Indon. 85 G2
Kongōdo-san mt. Japan 92 D2
Kongō-Ikoma Kokutei-kōen park Japan 92 B4
Kongolo Dem. Rep. Congo 123 C4
Kongor Sudan 121 G4
Kong Oscars Fjord inlet Greenland 147 P2
Kongoussi Burkina 120 C3
Kongsberg Norway 55 F7
Kongsvinger Norway 55 H6
Kongur Shan mt. Xinjiang China 98 A5
Königsberg Rus. Fed. see Kaliningrad
Königsee Germany 63 L4
Königswinter Germany 63 H4
Königs Wusterhausen Germany 63 N2
Konimekh Uzbek. see Konimex
Konimex Uzbek. 111 G1
Konin Poland 57 Q4
Konjic Bos.-Herz. 68 G3
Konkiep watercourse Namibia 124 C5
Könnern Germany 63 L3
Konnevesi Fin. 54 O5
Kōno Japan 92 C3
Konosha Rus. Fed. 52 I3
Kōnosu Japan 93 F2
Konotop Ukr. 53 G6
Konpara India 105 E5
Kon Plông Vietnam 87 E4
Konqi He r. China 98 E4
Konrei Palau 82 [inset]
Konsei-tōge pass Japan 93 F2
Konso Eth. 122 D3
Konstantinograd Ukr. see Krasnohrad
Konstantinovka Rus. Fed. 90 B2
Konstantinovka Ukr. see Kostyantynivka
Konstantinovy Lázně Czech Rep. 63 M5
Konstanz Germany 57 L7
Kontha Myanmar 86 B2
Kontiolahti Fin. 54 P5
Konttila Fin. 54 O4
Kon Tum Vietnam 87 D4
Kon Tum, Cao Nguyên Vietnam 87 E4
Könugard Ukr. see Kiev
Konus mt. Rus. Fed. 148 B2
Konushin, Mys pt Rus. Fed. 52 I2
Konya Turkey 112 D3
Konyrat Kazakh. 98 A3
Konyrolen Kazakh. 98 B3
Konz Germany 62 G5
Konzhakovskiy Kamen', Gora mt. Rus. Fed. 51 R4
Koocanusa, Lake resr Canada/U.S.A. 150 H5
Kooch Bihar India see Koch Bihar
Kookynie Australia 135 C7
Koolyanobbing Australia 135 B7
Koondrook Australia 138 B5
Koorawatha Australia 138 D5
Koordarrie Australia 134 A5
Kootenay r. Canada 150 G5
Kootenay Lake Canada 150 G5
Kootenay National Park Canada 150 G5
Kootjieskolk S. Africa 124 E6
Koozata Lagoon AK U.S.A. 148 E3
Kopa Almatinskaya Oblast' Kazakh. 98 A4
Kopa Vostochnyy Kazakhstan Kazakh. 98 B3
Kópasker Iceland 54 [inset]
Kopbirlik Kazakh. 102 E2
Koper Slovenia 68 E2
Kopet Dag mts Iran/Turkm. 110 E2
Kopet-Dag, Khrebet mts Iran/Turkm. see Kopet Dag
Köpetdag Gershi mts Iran/Turkm. see Kopet Dag
Köping Sweden 55 J7
Köpmanholmen Sweden 54 K5
Kopong Botswana 125 G3
Koppal India 106 C3
Koppang Norway 55 G6
Kopparberg Sweden 55 I7
Koppeh Dāgh mts Iran/Turkm. see Kopet Dag
Köppel hill Germany 63 H4
Koppi r. Rus. Fed. 90 F2
Koppies S. Africa 125 H4
Koppieskraal Pan salt pan S. Africa 124 E4
Koprivnica Croatia 68 G1
Köprülü Turkey 107 A1
Köprülü Kanyon Milli Parkı nat. park Turkey 69 N6
Kopyl' Belarus see Kapyl'
Kora India 104 E4
Kōra Japan 92 C3
Korablino Rus. Fed. 53 I5
K'orahē Eth. 122 E3
Korak Pak. 111 G5
Koramlik Xinjiang China 99 D5
Korangal India 106 C2
Korangi Pak. 111 G5
Korān va Monjan Afgh. 111 H2
Koraput India 106 D2
Korat Thai. see Nakhon Ratchasima
Koratla India 106 C2
Korba India 105 E5
Korbach Germany 63 I3
Korbu, Gunung mt. Malaysia 84 C1
Korçë Albania 69 I4
Korčula Croatia 68 G3
Korčula i. Croatia 68 G3
Korčulanski Kanal sea chan. Croatia 68 G3
Korday Kazakh. 102 D3
Kord Küv Iran 110 D2
Kords reg. Iran 111 F5
Korea, North country Asia 91 B5
Korea, South country Asia 91 B5
Korea Bay g. China/N. Korea 91 B5
Korea Strait Japan/S. Korea 91 C6
Koregaon India 106 B2
Korenovsk Rus. Fed. 113 E1
Korenovskaya Rus. Fed. see Korenovsk
Korepino Rus. Fed. 51 R3
Korets' Ukr. 53 E6
Körfez Turkey 69 M4
Korff Ice Rise Antarctica 188 L1
Korfovskiy Rus. Fed. 90 D2
Korgalzhyn Kazakh. 102 D1
Korgas Xinjiang China 98 C3
Korgen Norway 54 H3
Korhogo Côte d'Ivoire 120 C4
Koribundu Sierra Leone 120 B4
Kori Creek inlet India 104 B5
Korinthiakos Kolpos sea chan. Greece see Corinth, Gulf of
Korinthos Greece see Corinth
Kōris-hegy hill Hungary 68 G1
Koritnik mt. Albania 69 I3
Koritsa Albania see Korçë
Kōriyama Japan 91 F5
Korkuteli Turkey 69 N6
Korla Xinjiang China 98 D4
Kormakitis, Cape Cyprus 107 A2
Körmend Hungary 68 G1
Kornat nat. park Croatia 68 F3
Korneyevka Karagandinskaya Oblast' Kazakh. 98 A2
Korneyevka Rus. Fed. 53 K6
Koro Côte d'Ivoire 120 C4
Koro i. Fiji 133 H3
Koro r. Indon. 83 B3
Koro Mali 120 C3
Koroc r. Canada 153 I2
Köroğlu Dağları mts Turkey 69 O4
Köroğlu Tepesi mt. Turkey 112 D2
Korogwe Tanz. 123 D4
Koroneia, Limni l. Greece 69 J4
Korong Vale Australia 138 A6
Koronia, Limni l. Greece see Koroneia, Limni

▶Koror Palau 82 [inset]
Former capital of Palau.

Koror i. Palau 82 [inset]
Koro Sea b. Fiji 133 H3
Korosten' Ukr. 53 F6
Korostyshiv Ukr. 53 F6
Koro Toro Chad 121 E3
Korovin Bay AK U.S.A. 149 [inset]
Korovin Volcano AK U.S.A. 149 [inset]
Korpilahti Fin. 54 N5
Korpo Fin. 55 L6
Korppoo Fin. see Korpo
Korsakov Rus. Fed. 90 F3
Korsnäs Fin. 54 L5
Korsør Denmark 55 G9
Korsun'-Shevchenkivs'kyy Ukr. 53 F6
Korsun'-Shevchenkovskiy Ukr. see Korsun'-Shevchenkivs'kyy
Korsze Poland 57 R3
Kortesjärvi Fin. 54 M5
Korti Sudan 108 D6
Kortkeros Rus. Fed. 52 K3
Kortrijk Belgium 62 D4
Korvala Fin. 54 O3
Koryakskaya, Sopka vol. Rus. Fed. 77 Q4
Koryakskoye Nagor'ye mts Rus. Fed. 77 S3
Koryazhma Rus. Fed. 52 J3
Koryō Japan 92 B4
Koryŏng S. Korea 91 C6
Kos i. Greece 69 L6
Kosa Rus. Fed. 51 Q4
Kosai Japan 92 D4
Kosam India 104 E4
Kosan N. Korea 91 B5
Kościan Poland 57 P4
Kosciusko, Mount Australia see Kosciuszko, Mount
Kosciuszko, Mount Australia 138 D6
Kosciuszko National Park Australia 138 D6
Köse Turkey 113 E2
Köseçobanlı Turkey 107 A1
Kōsei Japan 92 C3
Kosgi India 106 C2
Kosh-Agach Rus. Fed. 94 B1
Kosh-Döbö Kyrg. 98 A4
Koshigaya Japan 93 F3
Koshikijima-rettō is Japan 91 C7
Koshino Japan 92 C2
Koshk Afgh. 111 F3
Koshkarkol', Ozero l. Kazakh. 98 C3
Koshk-e Kohneh Afgh. 111 F3
Koshki Rus. Fed. 53 K5
Kōshoku Japan 93 E2
Kosi r. India 99 B7
Kosi Bay S. Africa 125 K4
Košice Slovakia 53 D6
Kosigi India 106 C3
Kosi Reservoir Nepal 99 D8
Koskuduk Kazakh. 98 B3
Koskullskulle Sweden 54 L3
Köslin Poland see Koszalin
Kosma r. Rus. Fed. 52 K2
Koson Uzbek. 111 G2
Kosŏng N. Korea 91 C5
Kosova country Europe see Kosovo

▶Kosovo country Europe 69 I3
World's newest independent country. Gained independence from Serbia in February 2008.

Kosovska Mitrovica Kosovo see Mitrovicë
Kosrae atoll Micronesia 186 G5
Kosrap Xinjiang China 99 B5
Kösseine hill Germany 63 L5
Kossol Passage Palau 82 [inset]
Kossol Reef Palau 82 [inset]
Kosta-Khetagurovo Rus. Fed. see Nazran'
Kostanay Kazakh. 100 F1
Kostenets Bulg. 69 J3
Kosti Sudan 108 D7
Kostinbrod Bulg. 69 J3
Kostino Rus. Fed. 76 J3
Kostomuksha Rus. Fed. 54 Q4
Kostopil' Ukr. 53 E6
Kostopol' Ukr. see Kostopil'
Kostroma Rus. Fed. 52 I4
Kostrzyn Poland 57 O4
Kostyantynivka Ukr. 53 H6
Kostyukovichi Belarus see Kastsyukovichy
Kosuge Japan 93 E3
Kosugi Japan 92 D2
Kos'yu Rus. Fed. 51 R2
Koszalin Poland 57 P3
Kőszeg Hungary 68 G1
Kota Andhra Prad. India 106 D3
Kota Chhattisgarh India 105 E5
Kota Rajasthan India 104 C4
Kōta Japan 92 D4
Kotaagung Sumatera Indon. 84 D4
Kota Baharu Malaysia see Kota Bharu
Kotabaru Kalimantan Indon. 85 E3
Kotabaru Kalimantan Indon. 85 G3
Kotabaru Sumatera Indon. 84 B2
Kota Belud Sabah Malaysia 85 G1
Kotabesi Kalimantan Indon. 85 F3
Kota Bharu Malaysia 84 C1
Kotabumi Sumatera Indon. 84 D4
Kotabunan Sulawesi Indon. 83 C2
Kot Addu Pak. 111 H4
Kota Kinabalu Sabah Malaysia 85 G1
Kotamobagu Sulawesi Indon. 83 C2
Kotaneelee Range mts Canada 150 E2
Kotanemel', Gora mt. Kazakh. 98 B3
Kotaparh India 106 D2
Kotapinang Sumatera Indon. 84 C2
Kota Samarahan Sarawak Malaysia 85 E2
Kotatengah Sumatera Indon. 84 C2
Kota Tinggi Malaysia 84 C2
Kotawaringin Kalimantan Indon. 85 E3
Kotcho r. Canada 150 F3
Kotcho Lake Canada 150 F3
Kot Diji Pak. 111 H5
Kotdwara Uttaranchal India 99 B7
Kotel'nich Rus. Fed. 52 K4
Kotel'nikovo Rus. Fed. 53 I7
Kotel'nyy, Ostrov i. Rus. Fed. 77 O2
Kotgar India 106 D2
Kotgarh India 104 D3
Kothagudem India see Kottagudem
Köthen (Anhalt) Germany 63 L3
Kotido Uganda 121 G4
Kotikovo Rus. Fed. 90 D3
Kot Imamgarh Pak. 111 H5
Kotka Fin. 55 O6
Kot Kapura India 104 C3
Kotkino Rus. Fed. 52 K2
Kotlas Rus. Fed. 52 J3
Kotli Pak. 111 I3
Kotlik AK U.S.A. 148 G3
Kötlutangi pt Iceland 54 [inset]
Kotly Rus. Fed. 55 P7
Kotō Japan 92 C3
Kotorkoshi Nigeria 120 D3
Kotovo Rus. Fed. 53 J6
Kotovsk Rus. Fed. 53 I5
Kotra India 104 C4
Kotra Pak. 111 G4
Kotri r. India 106 D2
Kot Sarae Pak. 111 G6
Kottagudem India 106 D2
Kottarakara India 106 C4
Kottayam India 106 C4
Kotte Sri Lanka see Sri Jayewardenepura Kotte
Kotto r. Cent. Afr. Rep. 122 C3
Kotturu India 106 C3
Kotuy r. Rus. Fed. 77 L2
Kotzebue AK U.S.A. 148 G2
Kotzebue Sound sea channel AK U.S.A. 148 G2
Kötzting Germany 63 M5
Kouango Cent. Afr. Rep. 122 C3
Koubia Guinea 120 B3
Kouchibouguac National Park Canada 153 I5
Koudougou Burkina 120 C3
Kouebokkeveld mts S. Africa 124 D7
Koufey Niger 120 E3
Koufonisi i. Greece 69 L7
Kougaberge mts S. Africa 124 F7
Koukourou r. Cent. Afr. Rep. 122 B3
Koulen Cambodia see Kulen
Koulikoro Mali 120 C3
Koumac New Caledonia 133 G4
Koumenzi Xinjiang China 94 C3
Koumi Japan 93 E2
Koumpentoum Senegal 120 B3
Koundâra Guinea 120 B3
Kounradskiy Karagandinskaya Oblast' Kazakh. 98 A3
Kountze U.S.A. 161 E6
Koupéla Burkina 120 C3
Kourou Fr. Guiana 177 H2
Kouroussa Guinea 120 C3
Kousséri Cameroon 121 E3
Koutiala Mali 120 C3
Kouvola Fin. 55 O6
Kovallberget Sweden 54 J4
Kovdor Rus. Fed. 54 Q3
Kovdozero, Ozero l. Rus. Fed. 54 R3
Kovel' Ukr. 53 E6
Kovernino Rus. Fed. 52 I4
Kovilpatti India 106 C4
Kovno Lith. see Kaunas
Kovriga, Gora hill Rus. Fed. 52 K2
Kovrov Rus. Fed. 52 I4
Kovylkino Rus. Fed. 53 I5
Kovzhskoye, Ozero l. Rus. Fed. 52 H3
Kowangge Sumbawa Indon. 85 G5
Kowanyama Australia 136 C2
Kowloon H.K. China 97 [inset]
Kowloon Peak hill H.K. China 97 [inset]
Kowloon Peninsula H.K. China 97 [inset]
Kowŏn N. Korea 91 B5
Kox Kuduk well Xinjiang China 94 C3
Koxlax Xinjiang China 99 C5
Koxtag Xinjiang China 99 B5
Kōya Japan 92 B4
Kōyaguchi Japan 92 B4
Kōyama-misaki pt Japan 91 C6
Kōya-Ryūjin Kokutei-kōen park Japan 92 B4
Köyceğiz Turkey 69 M6
Koyginveyem r. Rus. Fed. 148 A2
Koygorodok Rus. Fed. 52 K3
Koyna Reservoir India 106 B2
Köytendag Turkm. 111 G2
Koyuk AK U.S.A. 148 G2
Koyuk r. AK U.S.A. 148 G2
Koyukuk AK U.S.A. 148 H2
Koyukuk r. AK U.S.A. 148 H2
Koyukuk, Middle Fork r. AK U.S.A. 149 J2
Koyukuk, North Fork r. AK U.S.A. 149 J2
Koyukuk, South Fork r. AK U.S.A. 149 J2
Koyukuk Island AK U.S.A. 148 H2
Koyukuk National Wildlife Refuge nature res. AK U.S.A. 148 H2
Koyulhisar Turkey 112 E2
Kozağacı Turkey see Günyüzü
Kozakai Japan 92 D4
Kōzaki Japan 93 G3
Kō-zaki pt Japan 91 C6
Kozan Turkey 112 D3
Kozani Greece 69 I4
Kozara mts Bos.-Herz. 68 G2
Kozara nat. park Bos.-Herz. 68 G2
Kozarska Dubica Bos.-Herz. see Bosanska Dubica
Kozelets' Ukr. 53 F6
Kozel'sk Rus. Fed. 53 G5
Kozhikode India see Calicut
Kozhva Rus. Fed. 52 M2
Kozlu Turkey 69 N4
Koz'modem'yansk Rus. Fed. 52 J4
Kožuf mts Greece/Macedonia 69 J4
Kōzu-shima i. Japan 93 F4
Kozyatyn Ukr. 53 F6
Kpalimé Togo 120 D4
Kpandae Ghana 120 C4
Kpungan Pass India/Myanmar 86 B1
Kra, Isthmus of Thai. 87 B5
Krabi Thai. 87 B5
Kra Buri Thai. 87 B5
Krâchéh Cambodia 87 D4
Kraddsele Sweden 54 J4
Kragan Jawa Indon. 85 E4
Kragerø Norway 55 F7
Kraggenburg Neth. 62 F2
Kragujevac Serbia 69 I2

▶Krakatau i. Indon. 84 D4
2nd deadliest recorded volcanic eruption (1883).

Krakatau vol. Indon. 80 D8
Krakatau, Taman Nasional nat. park Indon. 84 D4
Krakau Poland see Kraków
Kraków Poland 57 Q5
Krakower See l. Germany 63 M1
Krâlănh Cambodia 87 C4
Kralendijk Neth. Antilles 169 K6
Kramators'k Ukr. 53 H6
Kramfors Sweden 54 J5
Krammer est. Neth. 62 E3
Kranidi Greece 69 J6
Kranj Slovenia 68 F1
Kranji Reservoir Sing. 87 [inset]
Kranskop S. Africa 125 J5
Krasavino Rus. Fed. 52 J3
Krasilov Ukr. see Krasyliv
Krasino Rus. Fed. 76 G2
Kraskino Rus. Fed. 90 C4
Krāslava Latvia 55 O9
Kraslice Czech Rep. 63 M4
Krasnaya Gorbatka Rus. Fed. 52 I5
Krasnaya Polyana Kazakh. 98 A2
Krasnaya Yaranga Rus. Fed. 148 D2
Krasnaya Zarya Rus. Fed. 53 H5
Krasnoarmeysk Rus. Fed. 53 J6
Krasnoarmeysk Ukr. see Krasnoarmiys'k
Krasnoarmiys'k Ukr. 53 H6
Krasnoborsk Rus. Fed. 52 J3
Krasnodar Rus. Fed. 112 E1
Krasnodar Kray admin. div. Rus. Fed. see Krasnodarskiy Kray
Krasnodarskiy Kray admin. div. Rus. Fed. 112 E1
Krasnodon Ukr. 53 H6
Krasnogorodskoye Rus. Fed. 55 P8
Krasnogorsk Rus. Fed. 90 F2
Krasnogorskoye Rus. Fed. 52 L4
Krasnograd Ukr. see Krasnohrad
Krasnogvardeysk Uzbek. see Bulung'ur
Krasnogvardeyskoye Rus. Fed. 53 I7
Krasnohrad Ukr. 53 G6
Krasnohvardiys'ke Ukr. 53 G7
Krasnokamensk Rus. Fed. 95 I1
Krasnokamsk Rus. Fed. 51 R4
Krasnoperekops'k Ukr. 53 G7
Krasnopol'ye Rus. Fed. 90 F2
Krasnorechenskiy Rus. Fed. 90 D3
Krasnoslobodsk Rus. Fed. 53 I5
Krasnotur'insk Rus. Fed. 51 S4
Krasnoufimsk Rus. Fed. 51 R4
Krasnovishersk Rus. Fed. 51 R3
Krasnovodsk Turkm. see Türkmenbaşy
Krasnovodsk, Mys pt Turkm. 110 D2
Krasnovodskoye Plato plat. Turkm. 113 I2
Krasnowodsk Aylagy b. Turkm. see Türkmenbaşy Aýlagy
Krasnoyarovo Rus. Fed. 90 C2
Krasnoyarsk Rus. Fed. 76 K4
Krasnoyarskoye Vodokhranilishche resr Rus. Fed. 88 G2
Krasnoye Lipetskaya Oblast' Rus. Fed. 53 H5
Krasnoye Respublika Kalmykiya - Khalm'g-Tangch Rus. Fed. see Ulan Erge
Krasnoznamenskiy Kazakh. see Yegindykol'
Krasnoznamenskoye Kazakh. see Yegindykol'
Krasnyy Rus. Fed. 53 F5
Krasnyy Chikoy Rus. Fed. 95 G1
Krasnyye Baki Rus. Fed. 52 J4
Krasnyy Kamyshanik Rus. Fed. see Komsomol'skiy
Krasnyy Kholm Rus. Fed. 52 H4
Krasnyy Kut Rus. Fed. 53 J6
Krasnyy Luch Ukr. 53 H6
Krasnyy Lyman Ukr. 53 H6
Krasnyy Oktyabr' Kazakh. 98 B3
Krasnyy Yar Rus. Fed. 53 K7
Krasyliv Ukr. 53 E6
Kratie Cambodia see Krâchéh
Kratke Range mts P.N.G. 81 L8
Kraulshavn Greenland see Nuussuaq
Krâvanh, Chuŏr Phnum mts Cambodia/Thai. see Cardamom Range
Kraynovka Rus. Fed. 113 G2
Krefeld Germany 62 G3
Krekatok Island AK U.S.A. 148 F3
Kremenchug Ukr. see Kremenchuk
Kremenchugskoye Vodokhranilishche resr Ukr. see Kremenchuts'ke Vodoskhovyshche
Kremenchuk Ukr. 53 G6
Kremenchuts'ka Vodoskhovyshche resr Ukr. 53 G6
Křemešník hill Czech Rep. 57 O6
Kremges Ukr. see Svitlovods'k
Kremmidi, Akra pt Greece see Kremmydi, Akrotirio
Kremmydi, Akrotirio pt Greece 69 J6
Krems Austria see Krems an der Donau
Krems an der Donau Austria 57 O6
Krenitzin Islands AK U.S.A. 148 F5
Kresta, Zaliv g. Rus. Fed. 148 C2
Kresttsy Rus. Fed. 52 G4
Kretinga Lith. 55 L9
Kreuzau Germany 62 G4
Kreuztal Germany 63 H4
Kreva Belarus 55 O9
Kribi Cameroon 120 D4
Krichev Belarus see Krychaw
Kriel S. Africa 125 I4
Krikellos Greece 69 I5
Kril'on, Mys c. Rus. Fed. 90 F3
Krishna India 106 C2
Krishna r. India 106 D2
Krishnanagar India 105 G5
Krishnaraja Sagara l. India 106 C3
Kristiania Norway see Oslo
Kristiansand Norway 55 E7
Kristianstad Sweden 55 I8
Kristiansund Norway 54 E5
Kristiinankaupunki Fin. see Kristinestad
Kristinehamn Sweden 55 I7
Kristinestad Fin. 54 L5
Kristinopol' Ukr. see Chervonohrad
Kriti i. Greece see Crete
Kritiko Pelagos sea Greece 69 K6
Krivoy Rog Ukr. see Kryvyy Rih
Križevci Croatia 68 G1
Krk i. Croatia 68 F2
Krkonošský narodní park nat. park Czech Rep./Poland 57 O5
Krokom Sweden 54 I5
Krokstadøra Norway 54 F5
Krokstranda Norway 54 I3
Krolevets' Ukr. 53 G6
Kronach Germany 63 L4
Krŏng Kaôh Kŏng Cambodia 87 C5
Kronoby Fin. 54 M5
Kronprins Christian Land reg. Greenland 189 I1
Kronprins Frederik Bjerge nunataks Greenland 147 O3
Kronshtadt Rus. Fed. 55 P7
Kronstadt Romania see Braşov
Kronstadt Rus. Fed. see Kronshtadt
Kronwa Myanmar 86 B4
Kroonstad S. Africa 125 H4
Kropotkin Rus. Fed. 113 F1
Kropstädt Germany 63 M3
Krosno Poland 53 D6
Krotoszyn Poland 57 P5
Kroya Jawa Indon. 85 E4
Kruger National Park S. Africa 125 J2
Kruglikovo Rus. Fed. 90 D2
Krugloi Point pt AK U.S.A. 148 [inset]
Kruglyakov Rus. Fed. see Oktyabr'skiy
Krui Sumatera Indon. 84 C4
Kruisfontein S. Africa 124 G8
Kruja Albania see Krujë
Krujë Albania 69 H4
Krumovgrad Bulg. 69 K4
Krungkao Thai. see Ayutthaya
Krung Thep Thai. see Bangkok
Krupa Bos.-Herz. see Bosanska Krupa
Krupa na Uni Bos.-Herz. see Bosanska Krupa
Krupki Belarus 53 F5
Krusenstern, Cape AK U.S.A. 148 G2
Kruševac Serbia 69 I3
Krušné hory mts Czech Rep. 63 M4
Kruzof Island AK U.S.A. 149 N4
Krychaw Belarus 53 F5
Krylov Seamount sea feature N. Atlantic Ocean 184 G4
Krym' pen. Ukr. see Crimea
Krymsk Rus. Fed. 112 E1
Krymskaya Rus. Fed. see Krymsk

Kryms'kyy Pivostriv *pen.* Ukr. *see* **Crimea**
Krypsalo Kazakh. **98** A3
Krystynopol Ukr. *see* **Chervonohrad**
Krytiko Pelagos *sea* Greece *see* **Kritiko Pelagos**
Kryvyy Rih Ukr. **53** G7
Ksabi Alg. **64** D6
Ksar Chellala Alg. **67** H6
Ksar el Boukhari Alg. **67** H6
Ksar el Kebir Morocco **67** D6
Ksar-es-Souk Morocco *see* **Er Rachidia**
Ksenofontova Rus. Fed. **51** R3
Kshirpai India **105** F5
Ksour Essaf Tunisia **68** D7
Kstovo Rus. Fed. **52** J4
Kū', Jabal al *hill* Saudi Arabia **108** G4
Kuah Malaysia **84** B1
Kuaidamao China *see* **Tonghua**
Kuala Belait Brunei **85** F1
Kuala Dungun Malaysia *see* **Dungun**
Kualajelai *Kalimantan* Indon. **85** E3
Kuala Kangsar Malaysia **84** C1
Kualakapuas *Kalimantan* Indon. **85** F3
Kuala Kerai Malaysia **84** C1
Kualakuayan *Kalimantan* Indon. **85** F3
Kuala Kubu Baharu Malaysia **84** C2
Kualakurun *Kalimantan* Indon. **85** F3
Kualalangsa *Sumatera* Indon. **84** B1
Kuala Lipis Malaysia **84** C1

▶**Kuala Lumpur** Malaysia **84** C2
Joint capital (with Putrajaya) of Malaysia.

Kuala Nerang Malaysia **84** C1
Kualapembuang *Kalimantan* Indon. **85** F3
Kuala Penyu *Sabah* Malaysia **85** F1
Kuala Pilah Malaysia **84** C2
Kuala Rompin Malaysia **84** C2
Kualasampit Indon. **85** F3
Kuala Selangor Malaysia **84** C2
Kualasimpang *Sumatera* Indon. **84** B1
Kuala Terengganu Malaysia **84** C1
Kualatungal *Sumatera* Indon. **84** C3
Kuamut *Sabah* Malaysia **85** G1
Kuamut *r.* Malaysia **85** G1
Kuancheng *Hebei* China **95** I3
Kuandian China **90** B4
Kuantan Malaysia **84** C2
Kuba Azer. *see* **Quba**
Kuban' *r.* Rus. Fed. **53** H7
Kubār Syria **113** E4
Kubaybāt Syria **107** C2
Kubaysah Iraq **113** F4
Kubenskoye, Ozero *l.* Rus. Fed. **52** H4
Kubrat Bulg. **69** L3
Kubu *Bali* Indon. **85** F5
Kubu *Kalimantan* Indon. **85** E3
Kubuang *Kalimantan* Indon. **85** F2
Kubukhay Rus. Fed. **95** H1
Kubumesaäi *Kalimantan* Indon. **85** F2
Kuchaman Road India **111** I5
Kuchema Rus. Fed. **52** I2
Kuching *Sarawak* Malaysia **85** E2
Kuchino-Erabu-shima *i.* Japan **91** C7
Kucing *Sarawak* Malaysia *see* **Kuching**
Kuçovë Albania **69** H4
Kuda India **104** B5
Kudal India **106** B3
Kudangan *Kalimantan* Indon. **85** E3
Kudap *Sumatera* Indon. **84** C2
Kudara-Somon Rus. Fed. **95** F1
Kudat *Sabah* Malaysia **85** G1
Kudiakof Islands *AK* U.S.A. **148** G5
Kudligi India **106** C3
Kudobin Islands *AK* U.S.A. **148** G4
Kudoyama Japan **92** B4
Kudremukh *mt.* India **106** B3
Kudus *Jawa* Indon. **85** E4
Kudymkar Rus. Fed. **51** Q4
Kueishan Tao *i.* Taiwan **97** I3
Kūfah Iraq **112** G4
Kufar *Seram* Indon. **83** D3
Kufstein Austria **57** N7
Kugaaruk Canada **147** J3
Kugaluk *r. N.W.T.* Canada **149** O1
Kugaly Kazakh. **98** B3
Kugesi Rus. Fed. **52** J4
Kugka Lhai *Xizang* China **99** E7
Kugluktuk Canada **189** L2
Kugmallit Bay *N.W.T.* Canada **149** N1
Kugri *Qinghai* China **94** D5
Kuguno Japan **92** D2
Kūh, Ra's-al- *pt* Iran **110** E5
Kūhak Iran **111** F5
Kuhanbokano *mt.* China **105** E3
Kuhbier Germany **63** M1
Kūhdasht Iran **110** B3
Kūhīn Iran **110** C2
Kūhīrī Iran **111** F5
Kuhmo Fin. **54** P4
Kuhmoinen Fin. **55** N6
Kūhpāyeh *mt.* Iran **110** E4
Kūhrān, Kūh-e *mt.* Iran **110** E5
Kühren Germany **63** M3
Kui Buri Thai. **87** B4
Kuile He *r.* China **95** K1
Kuis Namibia **124** C3
Kuiseb *watercourse* Namibia **124** B2
Kuitan China **97** G4
Kuito Angola **123** B5
Kuitun *Xinjiang* China *see* **Kuytun**
Kuiu Island *AK* U.S.A. **149** N4
Kuivaniemi Fin. **54** N4
Kujang N. Korea **91** B5
Kuji Japan **91** F4
Kuji-gawa *r.* Japan **93** G2
Kujikuri Japan **93** G3
Kujūkuri-hama *coastal area* Japan **93** G3
Kujū-san *vol.* Japan **91** C6
Kuk *r. AK* U.S.A. **148** G1
Kukaklek Lake *AK* U.S.A. **148** I4
Kukālār, Kūh-e *hill* Iran **110** C4
Kukan Rus. Fed. **90** D2
Kukës Albania **69** I3
Kukesi Albania *see* **Kukës**
Kuki Japan **93** F2
Kukizaki Japan **93** G3
Kuki-zaki *pt* Japan **92** C4
Kukmor Rus. Fed. **52** K4
Kukpowruk *r. AK* U.S.A. **148** G1
Kukpuk *r. AK* U.S.A. **148** F1
Kukshi India **104** C5
Kukunuru India **106** D2
Kukup Malaysia **84** C2
Kükürtli Turkm. **110** E2
Kukusan, Gunung *hill* Indon. **85** F3
Kūl *r.* Iran **110** D5
Kula Turkey **69** M5
Kulabu, Gunung *mt.* Indon. **84** B2
Kulaisila India **105** F5
Kula Kangri *mt.* China/Bhutan **105** G3
Kulanak Kyrg. **98** A4
Kulandy Kazakh. **102** A2
Kulaneh *reg.* Pak. **111** F5
Kular Rus. Fed. **77** O2
Kulassein *i.* Phil. **82** C5
Kulat, Gunung *mt.* Indon. **85** G2
Kulawi *Sulawesi* Indon. **83** A3
Kuldīga Latvia **55** L8
Kuldja *Xinjiang* China *see* **Yining**
Kul'dur Rus. Fed. **90** C2
Kule Botswana **124** E2
Kulebaki Rus. Fed. **53** I5
Kulen Cambodia **87** D4
Kulgera Australia **135** F6
Kulikovka Kazakh. **98** B4
Kulikovo Rus. Fed. **52** J3
Kulim Malaysia **84** C1
Kulin Australia **135** B8
Kulja Australia **135** B7
Kulkyne *watercourse* Australia **138** B3
Kullu India **104** D3
Kulmbach Germany **63** L4
Kŭlob Tajik. **111** H2
Kuloy Rus. Fed. **52** I3
Kuloy *r.* Rus. Fed. **52** I2
Kulp Turkey **113** F3
Kul'sary Kazakh. **100** E2
Külsheim Germany **63** J5
Kulu India *see* **Kullu**
Kulu Turkey **112** D3
Kulunda Rus. Fed. **88** D2
Kulundinskaya Step' *plain* Kazakh./Rus. Fed. **88** D2
Kulundinskoye, Ozero *salt l.* Rus. Fed. **88** D2
Kulusuk Greenland **147** O3
Kulusutay Rus. Fed. **95** H1
Kulwin Australia **137** C7
Kulyab Tajik. *see* **Kŭlob**
Kuma *r.* Rus. Fed. **53** J7
Kumagaya Japan **93** F2
Kumai *Kalimantan* Indon. **85** E3
Kumai, Teluk *b.* Indon. **85** E3
Kumakhta Rus. Fed. **95** H1
Kumalar Dağı *mts* Turkey **69** N5
Kumamoto Japan **91** C6
Kumano Japan **91** E6
Kumanovo Macedonia **69** I3
Kumara Rus. Fed. **90** B2
Kumasi Ghana **120** C4
Kumayri Armenia *see* **Gyumri**
Kumba Cameroon **120** D4
Kumbakonam India **106** C4
Kumbe Indon. **81** K8
Kümbet Turkey **69** N5
Kumbharli Ghat *mt.* India **106** B2
Kumbher Nepal **99** C7
Kumbla India **106** B3
Kumchuru Botswana **124** F2
Kum-Dag Turkm. *see* **Gumdag**
Kumdah Saudi Arabia **108** G5
Kumel *well* Iran **110** D3
Kumeny Rus. Fed. **52** K4
Kumertau Rus. Fed. **76** G4
Kumgang-san *mt.* N. Korea **91** C5
Kumguri India **105** G4
Kumi S. Korea **91** C5
Kumi Uganda **121** G4
Kumihama Japan **92** A3
Kumihama-wan *l.* Japan **92** A3
Kumiyama Japan **92** B4
Kum Kuduk *well Xinjiang* China **98** E4
Kumla Sweden **55** I7
Kumlu Turkey **107** C1
Kummersdorf-Alexanderdorf Germany **63** N2
Kumo Nigeria **120** E3
Kŭmŏ-do *i.* S. Korea **91** B6
Kumon Range *mts* Myanmar **86** B1
Kumotori-yama *mt.* Japan **93** E3
Kumozu-gawa *r.* Japan **92** C4
Kumphawapi Thai. **86** C3
Kums Namibia **124** D5
Kumta India **106** B3
Kumu Dem. Rep. Congo **122** C3
Kumukh Rus. Fed. **113** G2
Kumul *Xinjiang* China *see* **Hami**
Kumund India **106** D1
Kümüx *Xinjiang* China **98** E4
Kumylzhenskaya Rus. Fed. *see* **Kumylzhenskiy**
Kumylzhenskiy Rus. Fed. **53** I6
Kun *r.* Myanmar **86** B3
Kuna *r. AK* U.S.A. **148** H1
Kunar *r.* Afgh. **111** H3
Kunashir, Ostrov *i.* Rus. Fed. **90** G3
Kunashirskiy Proliv *sea chan.* Japan/Rus. Fed. *see* **Nemuro-kaikyō**
Kunchaung Myanmar **86** B2
Kunchuk Tso *salt l.* China **105** E2
Kunda Estonia **55** O7
Kunda India **105** E4
Kundapura India **106** B3
Kundelungu, Parc National de *nat. park* Dem. Rep. Congo **123** C5
Kundelungu Ouest, Parc National de *nat. park* Dem. Rep. Congo **123** C5
Kundia India **104** C4
Kundur *i.* Indon. **84** C2
Kunduz Afgh. **111** H2
Kunene *r.* Angola *see* **Cunene**
Kuneneng *admin. dist.* Botswana *see* **Kweneng**
Künes *Xinjiang* China *see* **Xinyuan**
Künes Chang *Xinjiang* China **98** C4
Künes He *r.* China **98** C4
Künes Linchang *Xinjiang* China **98** D4
Kungälv Sweden **55** G8
Kungar-Tuk Rus. Fed. **94** D1
Kungei Alatau *mts* Kazakh./Kyrg. **98** B4
Kunggar *Xizang* China *see* **Maizhokunggar**
Kunghit Island *B.C.* Canada **149** O5
Kungsbacka Sweden **55** H8
Kungshamn Sweden **55** G7
Kungu Dem. Rep. Congo **122** B3
Kungur *mt. Xinjiang* China *see* **Kongur Shan**
Kungur Rus. Fed. **51** R4
Kunhing Myanmar **86** B2
Kuni *r.* India **106** C2
Kuni Japan **93** E2
Kūnīch Iran **110** E5
Kunié *i.* New Caledonia *see* **Pins, Île des**
Kunigai India **106** C3
Kunimi-dake *hill* Japan **92** C2
Kunimi-dake *mt.* Japan **91** C6
Kuningan *Jawa* Indon. **85** E4
Kunkavav India **104** B5
Kunlong Myanmar **86** B2
Kunlui *r.* India/Nepal **99** E8

▶**Kunlun Shan** *mts* China **94** B5
Location of highest active volcano in Asia.

Kunlun Shankou *pass Qinghai* China **94** C5
Kunming China **96** D3
Kuno *r.* India **99** B8
Kunsan S. Korea **91** B6
Kunshan China **97** I2
Kununurra Australia **134** E3
Kunwak *r.* Canada **151** L2
Kunwari *r.* India **99** B8
Kun'ya Rus. Fed. **52** F4
Kunyang *Yunnan* China *see* **Jinning**
Kunyang *Zhejiang* China *see* **Pingyang**
Kunya-Urgench Turkm. *see* **Köneürgenç**
Kunyu Shan *mts* China **95** J4
Künzelsau Germany **63** J5
Künzels-Berg *hill* Germany **63** L3
Kuocang Shan *mts* China **97** I2
Kuohijärvi *l.* Fin. **55** N6
Kuolayarvi Rus. Fed. **54** P3
Kuopio Fin. **54** O5
Kuortane Fin. **54** M5
Kupa *r.* Croatia/Slovenia **68** G2
Kupang *Timor* Indon. **83** B5
Kupang, Teluk *b. Timor* Indon. **83** B5
Kupari India **105** F5
Kuparuk *r. AK* U.S.A. **149** J1
Kupiškis Lith. **55** N9
Kupreanof Island *AK* U.S.A. **149** N4
Kupreanof Point *pt AK* U.S.A. **148** H5
Kupreanof Strait *AK* U.S.A. **148** I4
Kupwara India **104** C2
Kup''yans'k Ukr. **53** H6
Kuqa *Xinjiang* China **98** C4
Kur *r.* Rus. Fed. **90** D2
also known as Kür (Georgia), Kura
Kura *r.* Georgia **113** G2
also known as Kur (Russian Federation), Kura
Kuragino Rus. Fed. **88** G2
Kurai-yama *mt.* Japan **92** D2
Kurakh Rus. Fed. **53** J8
Kurama Range *mts* Asia **109** K1
Kurama-yama *hill* Japan **92** B3
Kuraminskiy Khrebet *mts* Asia *see* **Kurama Range**
Kūrān Dap Iran **111** E5
Kurashiki Japan **91** D6
Kurasia India **105** E5
Kurayn *i.* Saudi Arabia **110** C5
Kurayoshi Japan **91** D6
Kurayskiy Khrebet *mts* Rus. Fed. **94** B1
Kurchatov Rus. Fed. **53** G6
Kurchum Kazakh. **102** F2
Kurchum *r.* Kazakh. **98** C2
Kürdämir Azer. **113** H2
Kurday Kazakh. **98** A4
Kŭrdzhali Bulg. **69** K4
Kure Japan **91** D6
Küre Turkey **112** D2
Kure Atoll U.S.A. **186** I4
Kuressaare Estonia **55** M7
Kurgal'dzhino Kazakh. *see* **Korgalzhyn**
Kurgal'dzhinskiy Kazakh. *see* **Korgalzhyn**
Kurgan Rus. Fed. **76** H4
Kurganinsk Rus. Fed. **113** F1
Kurgannaya Rus. Fed. *see* **Kurganinsk**
Kurgantyube Tajik. *see* **Qŭrghonteppa**
Kuri Afgh. **111** H2
Kuri India **104** B4
Kuria Muria Islands Oman *see* **Ḥalāniyāt, Juzur al**
Kuridala Australia **136** C4
Kurigram Bangl. **105** G4
Kurihama Japan **93** F3
Kurihashi Japan **93** F2
Kurikka Fin. **54** M5
Kuril Basin *sea feature* Sea of Okhotsk **186** F2
Kuril Islands Rus. Fed. **90** H3
Kurilovka Rus. Fed. **53** K6
Kuril'sk Rus. Fed. **90** G3
Kuril'skiye Ostrova *is* Rus. Fed. *see* **Kuril Islands**
Kuril Trench *sea feature* N. Pacific Ocean **186** F3
Kurimoto Japan **93** G3
Kuriyama *Tochigi* Japan **93** F2
Kurkino Rus. Fed. **53** H5
Kurmashkino Kazakh. *see* **Kurchum**
Kurmuk Sudan **108** D7
Kurnool India **106** C3
Kurobane Japan **93** G2
Kurobe Japan **92** D2
Kurobe-gawa *r.* Japan **92** D2
Kurobe-ko *resr* Japan **92** D2
Kurodashō Japan **92** B3
Kurohime-yama *mt.* Japan **93** D2
Kurohone Japan **93** F2
Kuroiso Japan **93** G2
Kurort Schmalkalden Germany **63** K4
Kuro-shima *i.* Japan **92** B4
Kuroso-yama *mt.* Japan **92** C4
Kurovskiy Rus. Fed. **90** B1
Kurow N.Z. **139** C7
Kurram Pak. **111** H3
Kurri Kurri Australia **138** E4
Kursavka Rus. Fed. **113** F1
Kürshim Kazakh. *see* **Kurchum**
Kurshskiy Zaliv *b.* Lith./Rus. Fed. *see* **Courland Lagoon**
Kuršių marios *b.* Lith./Rus. Fed. *see* **Courland Lagoon**
Kursk Rus. Fed. **53** H6
Kurskaya Rus. Fed. **113** G1
Kurskiy Zaliv *b.* Lith./Rus. Fed. *see* **Courland Lagoon**
Kurşunlu Turkey **112** D2
Kurtalan Turkey **113** F3
Kurtoğlu Burnu *pt* Turkey **69** M6
Kurtpınar Turkey **107** B1
Kurtty *r.* Kazakh. **98** B3
Kurucaşile Turkey **112** D2
Kuruçay Turkey **112** E3
Kurukshetra India **104** D3
Kuruktag *mts* China **98** D4
Kuruman S. Africa **124** F4
Kuruman *watercourse* S. Africa **124** E4
Kurume Japan **91** C6
Kurumkan Rus. Fed. **89** K2
Kurunegala Sri Lanka **106** D5
Kurunzulay Rus. Fed. **95** I1
Kurupa *r. AK* U.S.A. **148** I1
Kurupam India **106** D2
Kurupkan Rus. Fed. **148** D2
Kurush, Jebel *hills* Sudan **108** D5
Kur'ya Rus. Fed. **51** R3
Kuryk Kazakh. **113** H2
Kuşadası Turkey **69** L6
Kuşadası Körfezi *b.* Turkey **69** L6
Kusaie *atoll* Micronesia *see* **Kosrae**
Kusary Azer. *see* **Qusar**
Kusatsu *Gunma* Japan **93** E2
Kusatsu *Shiga* Japan **92** B3
Kuşcenneti *nature res.* Turkey **107** B1
Kuschke Nature Reserve S. Africa **125** I3
Kusel Germany **63** H5
Kuş Gölü *l.* Turkey **69** L4
Kushalgarh India **104** C5
Kushchevskaya Rus. Fed. **53** H7
Kushida-gawa *r.* Japan **92** C4
Kushigata Japan **93** E3
Kushihara Japan **92** D3
Kushimoto Japan **91** D6
Kushiro Japan **90** G4
Kushka Turkm. *see* **Serhetabat**
Kushkopola Rus. Fed. **52** J3
Kushmurun Kazakh. **100** F1
Kushtagi India **106** C3
Kushtia Bangl. **105** G5
Kushtih Iran **111** E4
Kuskan Turkey **107** A1
Kuskokwim *r. AK* U.S.A. **148** G3
Kuskokwim, North Fork *r. AK* U.S.A. **148** I3
Kuskokwim, South Fork *r. AK* U.S.A. **148** I3
Kuskokwim Bay *AK* U.S.A. **148** F4
Kuskokwim Mountains *AK* U.S.A. **148** I2
Kuşluyan Turkey *see* **Gölköy**
Kusŏng N. Korea **91** B5
Kustanay Kazakh. *see* **Kostanay**
Kustatan *AK* U.S.A. **149** J3
Küstence Romania *see* **Constanța**
Küstenkanal *canal* Germany **63** H1
Kustia Bangl. *see* **Kushtia**
Kusu *Halmahera* Indon. **83** C2
Kusu Japan **92** C4
Kut Iran **110** C4
Kut, Ko *i.* Thai. **87** C5
Kuta *Bali* Indon. **85**
Kutabagok *Sumatera* Indon. **84** B1
Kūt 'Abdollāh Iran **110** C4
Kutacane *Sumatera* Indon. **84** B2
Kütahya Turkey **69** M5
Kutai, Taman Nasional *nat. park* Indon. **85** G2
K'ut'aisi Georgia **113** F2
Kut-al-Imara Iraq *see* **Al Kūt**
Kutan Rus. Fed. **113** G1
Kutanibong Indon. **87** B7
Kutaraja *Sumatera* Indon. *see* **Banda Aceh**
Kutayfat Ţurayf *vol.* Saudi Arabia **107** D4
Kutch, Gulf of India *see* **Kachchh, Gulf of**
Kutch, Rann of *marsh* India *see* **Kachchh, Rann of**
Kutchan Japan **90** F4
Kutina Croatia **68** G2
Kutjevo Croatia **68** G2
Kutkai Myanmar **86** B2
Kutno Poland **57** Q4
Kutru India **106** D2
Kutsuki Japan **92** B3
Kutu Dem. Rep. Congo **122** B4
Kutubdia Island Bangl. **105** G5
Kutum Sudan **121** F3
Kutztown U.S.A. **165** H3
Kuujjua *r.* Canada **146** G2
Kuujjuaq Canada **153** H2
Kuujjuarapik Canada **152** F3
Kuusamo Fin. **54** P4
Kuusankoski Fin. **55** O6
Kuvango Angola **123** B5
Kuvshinovo Rus. Fed. **52** G4
Kuwait *country* Asia **110** B4

▶**Kuwait** Kuwait **110** B4
Capital of Kuwait.

Kuwajleen *atoll* Marshall Is *see* **Kwajalein**
Kuwana Japan **92** C3
Kuybyshev *Novosibirskaya Oblast'* Rus. Fed. **76** I4
Kuybyshev *Respublika Tatarstan* Rus. Fed. *see* **Bolgar**
Kuybyshev *Samarskaya Oblast'* Rus. Fed. *see* **Samara**
Kuybysheve Ukr. **53** H7
Kuybyshevka-Vostochnaya Rus. Fed. *see* **Belogorsk**
Kuybyshevskoye Vodokhranilishche *resr* Rus. Fed. **53** K5
Kuyeda Rus. Fed. **51** R4
Kuye He *r.* China **95** G4
Kuygan Kazakh. **102** D2
Küysu *Xinjiang* China **94** C3
Kuytun *Xinjiang* China **98** D3
Kuytun Rus. Fed. **88** I2
Kuytun He *r.* China **98** C3
Kuyucak Turkey **69** M6
Kuyus Rus. Fed. **98** D2
Kuyu Tingni Nicaragua **166** [inset] J6
Kuze Japan **92** C3
Kuzino Rus. Fed. **51** R4
Kuzitrin *r. AK* U.S.A. **148** F2
Kuznechnoye Rus. Fed. **55** P6
Kuznetsk Rus. Fed. **53** J5
Kuznetsovo Rus. Fed. **90** E3
Kuznetsovs'k Ukr. **53** E6
Kuzovatovo Rus. Fed. **53** J5
Kuzuryū-gawa *r.* Japan **92** C3
Kuzuryū-ko *resr* Japan **92** C3
Kuzuu Japan **93** F2
Kværangen *sea chan.* Norway **54** L1
Kvaløya *i.* Norway **54** K2
Kvalsund Norway **54** M1
Kvarnerić *sea chan.* Croatia **68** F2
Kvichak *AK* U.S.A. **148** H4
Kvichak *r. AK* U.S.A. **148** H4
Kvichak Bay *AK* U.S.A. **148** H4
Kvitøya *ice feature* Svalbard **76** E2
Kwa *r.* Dem. Rep. Congo *see* **Kasaï**
Kwabhaca S. Africa *see* **Mount Frere**
Kwadelen *atoll* Marshall Is *see* **Kwajalein**
Kwajalein *atoll* Marshall Is **186** H5
Kwala *Sumatera* Indon. **84** B2
Kwale Nigeria **120** D4
KwaMashu S. Africa **125** J5
KwaMhlanga S. Africa **125** I3
Kwa Mtoro Tanz. **123** D4
Kwandang *Sulawesi* Indon. **83** B2
Kwangch'ŏn S. Korea **91** B5
Kwangchow China *see* **Guangzhou**
Kwangju S. Korea **91** B6
Kwangsi Chuang Autonomous Region *aut. reg.* China *see* **Guangxi Zhuangzu Zizhiqu**
Kwangtung *prov.* China *see* **Guangdong**
Kwanmo-bong *mt.* N. Korea **90** C4
Kwanobuhle S. Africa **125** G7
KwaNojoli S. Africa **125** G7
Kwanonqubela S. Africa **125** H7
KwaNonzame S. Africa **124** G6
Kwanza *r.* Angola *see* **Cuanza**
Kwatinidubu S. Africa **125** H7
KwaZamokuhle S. Africa **125** I4
KwaZamukucinga S. Africa **124** G7
Kwazamuxolo S. Africa **124** G6
KwaZanele S. Africa **125** I4
KwaZulu-Natal *prov.* S. Africa **125** J5
Kweichow *prov.* China *see* **Guizhou**
Kweiyang China *see* **Guiyang**
Kwekwe Zimbabwe **123** C5
Kweneng *admin. dist.* Botswana **124** G2
Kwenge *r.* Dem. Rep. Congo **123** B4
Kwetabohigan *r.* Canada **152** E4
Kwethluk *AK* U.S.A. **148** G3
Kwethluk *r. AK* U.S.A. **148** G3
Kwezi-Naledi S. Africa **125** H6
Kwidzyn Poland **57** Q4
Kwigillingok *AK* U.S.A. **148** G4
Kwiguk *AK* U.S.A. **148** F3
Kwikila P.N.G. **81** L8
Kwilu *r.* Angola/Dem. Rep. Congo **123** B4
Kwo Chau Kwan To *is H.K.* China *see* **Ninepin Group**
Kwoka *mt.* Indon. **81** I7
Kyabra Australia **137** C5
Kyabram Australia **138** B6
Kyadet Myanmar **86** A2
Kyaikkami Myanmar **86** B3
Kyaiklat Myanmar **86** A3
Kyaikto Myanmar **86** B3
Kyakhta Rus. Fed. **94** F1
Kyalite Australia **138** A5
Kyancutta Australia **135** F8
Kyangin Myanmar **86** B3
Kyangngoin *Xizang* China **99** F7
Kyaukhnyat Myanmar **86** B3
Kyaukkyi Myanmar **86** B3
Kyaukme Myanmar **86** B2
Kyaukpadaung Myanmar **86** A2
Kyaukpyu Myanmar **86** A3
Kyaukse Myanmar **86** B2
Kyauktaw Myanmar **86** A2
Kyaunggon Myanmar **86** A3
Kybartai Lith. **55** M9
Kyebogyi Myanmar **86** B3
Kyêbxang Co *l.* China **105** G2
Kyeikdon Myanmar **86** B3
Kyeikywa Myanmar **86** B3
Kyeintali Myanmar **86** A3
Kyela Tanz. **123** D4
Kyelang India **104** D2
Kyidaunggan Myanmar **86** B3
Kyikug *Qinghai* China **94** E4
Kyiv Ukr. *see* **Kiev**
Kyklades *is* Greece *see* **Cyclades**
Kyle Canada **151** I5
Kyle of Lochalsh U.K. **60** D3
Kyll *r.* Germany **62** G5
Kyllini *mt.* Greece **69** J6
Kymi Greece **69** K5
Kymis, Akra *pt* Greece *see* **Kymis, Akrotirio**
Kymis, Akrotirio *pt* Greece **69** K5
Kyneton Australia **138** B6
Kynuna Australia **136** C4
Kyoga, Lake Uganda **122** D3
Kyōga-dake *mt.* Japan **92** C2
Kyōga-dake *mt.* Japan **93** D3
Kyōga-misaki *pt* Japan **92** B3
Kyogle Australia **138** F2
Kyonan Japan **93** F3
Kyong Myanmar **86** B2
Kyŏngju S. Korea **91** C6
Kyonpyaw Myanmar **86** A3
Kyōtanabe Japan **92** B4
Kyōto Japan **92** B4
Kyōto *pref.* Japan **92** B3
Kyōwa *Ibaraki* Japan **93** G2
Kyparissia Greece **69** I6
Kypros *country* Asia *see* **Cyprus**
Kypshak, Ozero *salt l.* Kazakh. **101** F1
Kyra Rus. Fed. **95** H1
Kyra Panagia *i.* Greece **69** K5
Kyrenia Cyprus **107** A2
Kyrenia Mountains Cyprus *see* **Pentadaktylos Range**
Kyrgyz Ala-Too *mts* Kazakh./Kyrg. *see* **Kirghiz Range**
Kyrgyzstan *country* Asia **102** D3
Kyritz Germany **63** M2
Kyrksæterøra Norway **54** F5
Kyrta Rus. Fed. **51** R3
Kyssa Rus. Fed. **52** J2
Kytalyktakh Rus. Fed. **77** O3
Kythira *i.* Greece **69** J6
Kythnos *i.* Greece **69** K6
Kyunglung *Xizang* China **99** C7
Kyunhla Myanmar **86** A2
Kyun Pila *i.* Myanmar **87** B5
Kyuquot Canada **150** E5
Kyurdamir Azer. *see* **Kürdämir**
Kyūshū *i.* Japan **91** C7
Kyushu-Palau Ridge *sea feature* N. Pacific Ocean **186** F4
Kyustendil Bulg. **69** J3
Kywebwe Myanmar **86** B3
Kywong Australia **138** C5
Kyyev Ukr. *see* **Kiev**
Kyyiv Ukr. *see* **Kiev**
Kyyivs'ke Vodoskhovyshche *resr* Ukr. **53** F6
Kyyjärvi Fin. **54** N5
Kyzyl Rus. Fed. **102** H1
Kyzylagash Kazakh. **98** B3
Kyzyl-Art, Pereval *pass* Kyrg./Tajik. *see* **Kyzylart Pass**
Kyzylart Pass Kyrg./Tajik. **111** I2
Kyzyl-Burun Azer. *see* **Siyäzän**
Kyzylkesek Kazakh. **98** C3
Kyzyl-Khaya Rus. Fed. **94** B1
Kyzyl-Kiya Kyrg. *see* **Kyzyl-Kyya**
Kyzylkum, Peski *des.* Kazakh./Uzbek. *see* **Kyzylkum Desert**
Kyzylkum Desert Kazakh./Uzbek. **102** B3
Kyzyl-Kyya Kyrg. **102** D3
Kyzyl-Mazhalyk Rus. Fed. **102** H1
Kyzylorda Kazakh. **102** C3
Kyzylrabot Tajik. *see* **Qizilrabot**
Kyzylsay Kazakh. **113** I2
Kyzyl-Suu Kyrg. **98** B4
Kyzylysor Kazakh. **113** H1
Kyzylzhar Kazakh. **102** C2
Kzyl-Dzhar Kazakh. *see* **Kyzylzhar**
Kzyl-Orda Kazakh. *see* **Kyzylorda**
Kzyltu Kazakh. *see* **Kishkenekol'**

L

Laagri Estonia **55** N7
La Aguja Mex. **166** C4
Laam Atoll Maldives *see* **Hadhdhunmathi Atoll**
La Amistad, Parque Internacional *nat. park* Costa Rica/Panama **166** [inset] J7
La Angostura, Presa de *resr* Mex. **167** G6
Laanila Fin. **54** O2
La Ardilla, Cerro *mt.* Mex. **166** E4
Laascaanood Somalia **122** E3
La Ascensión, Bahía de *b.* Mex. **169** G5
Laasgoray Somalia **122** E2

▶**Laâyoune** W. Sahara **120** B2
Capital of Western Sahara.

La Babia Mex. **166** E2
La Baie Canada **153** H4
Labala Indon. **83** B5
La Baleine, Grande Rivière de *r.* Canada **152** F3
La Baleine, Petite Rivière de *r.* Canada **152** F3
La Baleine, Rivière à *r.* Canada **153** I2
La Banda Arg. **178** D3
Labang *Sarawak* Malaysia **85** F2

La Barge U.S.A. 156 F4
Labasa Fiji 133 H3
La Baule-Escoublac France 66 C3
Labazhskoye Rus. Fed. 52 L2
Labe r. Czech Rep. see Elbe
Labé Guinea 120 B3
La Belle U.S.A. 163 D7
Labengke i. Indon. 83 B3
La Bénoué, Parc National de nat. park Cameroon 121 E4
Laberge, Lake Y.T. Canada 149 N3
Labi Brunei 85 F1
Labian, Tanjung pt Malaysia 85 G1
La Biche, Lac l. Canada 151 H4
Labinsk Rus. Fed. 113 F1
Labis Malaysia 84 C2
La Biznaga Mex. 166 C2
Labo Luzon Phil. 82 C3
Labobo i. Indon. 83 B3
La Boquilla Mex. 166 D3
La Boucle du Baoulé, Parc National de nat. park Mali 120 C3
Labouheyre France 66 D4
Laboulaye Arg. 178 D4
Labrador reg. Canada 153 J3
Labrador City Canada 153 I3
Labrador Sea Canada/Greenland 147 M3
Labrang Gansu China see Xiahe
Lábrea Brazil 176 F5
Labuan Malaysia 85 F1
Labuan i. Malaysia 85 F1
Labuan state Malaysia 85 F1
Labuanbajo Sulawesi Indon. 83 B3
Labudalin Nei Mongol China see Ergun
La Bufa, Cerro mt. Mex. 166 E5
Labuhan Jawa Indon. 84 D4
Labuhanbajo Flores Indon. 83 A5
Labuhanbilik Sumatera Indon. 84 C2
Labuhanhaji Sumatera Indon. 84 B2
Labuhanmeringgai Sumatera Indon. 84 D4
Labuhanruku Sumatera Indon. 84 B2
Labuk r. Malaysia 85 G1
Labuk, Teluk b. Malaysia 85 G1
Labuna Maluku Indon. 83 C3
Labutta Myanmar 86 A3
Labyrinth, Lake salt flat Australia 137 A6
Labytnangi Rus. Fed. 76 H3
Laç Albania 69 H4
La Cabrera, Sierra de mts Spain 67 C2
La Cadena Mex. 166 D3
Lac-Allard Canada 153 J4
La Calle Alg. see El Kala
Lacandón, Parque Nacional nat. park Guat. 167 H5
La Cañiza Spain see A Cañiza
Lacantún r. Mex. 167 H5
La Capelle France 62 D5
La Carlota Arg. 178 D4
La Carlota Negros Phil. 82 C4
La Carolina Spain 67 E4
Lăcăuţi, Vârful mt. Romania 69 L2
Laccadive, Minicoy and Amindivi Islands union terr. India see Lakshadweep
Laccadive Islands India 106 B4
Lac du Bonnet Canada 151 L5
Lacedaemon Greece see Sparti
La Ceiba Hond. 166 [inset] I6
Lacepede Bay Australia 137 B8
Lacepede Islands Australia 134 C4
Lacha, Ozero l. Rus. Fed. 52 H3
Lachendorf Germany 63 K2
Lachine U.S.A. 164 D1

▶Lachlan r. Australia 138 A5
5th longest river in Oceania.

La Chorrera Panama 166 [inset] K7
Lachute Canada 152 G5
Laçın Azer. 113 G3
La Ciotat France 66 G5
La Ciudad Mex. 166 D4
Lac La Biche Canada 151 I4
Lac la Martre N.W.T. Canada see Whatî
Lacolle Canada 165 I1
La Colorada Sonora Mex. 166 C2
La Colorada Zacatecas Mex. 161 C8
Lacombe Canada 150 H4
La Comoé, Parc National de nat. park Côte d'Ivoire 120 C4
La Concepción Panama 166 [inset] J7
La Concordia Mex. 167 G5
Laconi Sardinia Italy 68 C5
Laconia U.S.A. 165 J2
La Corey Canada 151 I4
La Coruña Spain see A Coruña
La Corvette, Lac de l. Canada 152 G3
La Coubre, Pointe de pt France 66 D4
La Crete Canada 150 G3
La Crosse KS U.S.A. 160 D4
La Crosse VA U.S.A. 165 F5
La Crosse WI U.S.A. 160 F3
La Cruz Costa Rica 166 [inset] I7
La Cruz Chihuahua Mex. 166 D3
La Cruz Sinaloa Mex. 166 D4
La Cruz Tamaulipas Mex. 167 F3
La Cruz Nicaragua 166 [inset] I6
La Cruz, Cerro mt. Mex. 167 E5
La Cuesta Coahuila Mex. 166 E2
La Culebra, Sierra de mts Spain 67 C3
La Cygne U.S.A. 160 E4
Lada, Teluk b. Indon. 84 D4
Ladainha Brazil 179 C2
Ladakh reg. India/Pak. 104 D2
Ladakh Range mts India 104 D2
Ladang, Ko i. Thai. 87 B6
La Demajagua Cuba 163 D8
La Demanda, Sierra de mts Spain 67 E2
La Democracia Guat. 167 H6
La Déroute, Passage de strait Channel Is/France 59 E9
Ladik Turkey 112 D2
Lādīz Iran 111 F4
Ladnun India 104 C4

▶Ladoga, Lake Rus. Fed. 52 F3
2nd largest lake in Europe.

Ladong China 97 F3
Ladozhskoye Ozero l. Rus. Fed. see Ladoga, Lake
Ladrones terr. N. Pacific Ocean see Northern Mariana Islands
Ladrones, Islas is Panama 166 [inset] J8
Ladu mt. India 105 H4
Ladue r. Canada/U.S.A. 149 L3
La Dura Mex. 166 C2
Ladva-Vetka Rus. Fed. 52 G3
Ladybank U.K. 60 F4
Ladybrand S. Africa 125 H5
Lady Frere S. Africa 125 H6
Lady Grey S. Africa 125 H6
Ladysmith S. Africa 125 I5
Ladysmith U.S.A. 160 F2
Ladzhanurges Georgia see Lajanurpekhi
Lae P.N.G. 81 L8
Laem Ngop Thai. 87 C4
Lærdalsøyri Norway 55 E6
La Esmeralda Bol. 176 F8
Læsø i. Denmark 55 G8
La Esperanza Hond. 166 [inset] H6
Lafayette Alg. see Bougaa
La Fayette AL U.S.A. 163 C5
Lafayette IN U.S.A. 164 B3
Lafayette LA U.S.A. 161 E6
Lafayette TN U.S.A. 164 B5
Lafé Cuba 163 C8
La Fère France 62 D5
Laferte r. Canada 150 G2
La Ferté-Gaucher France 62 D6
La-Ferté-Milon France 62 D5
La Ferté-sous-Jouarre France 62 D6
Lafia Nigeria 120 D4
Lafiagi Nigeria 120 D4
Laflamme r. Canada 152 F4
Lafleche Canada 151 J5
La Flèche France 66 D3
La Follette U.S.A. 164 C5
La Forest, Lac l. Canada 153 H3
Laforge Canada 153 G3
Laforge r. Canada 153 G3
La Frégate, Lac de l. Canada 152 G3
Lāft Iran 110 D5
Laful India 87 A6
La Galissonnière, Lac l. Canada 153 J4

▶La Galite i. Tunisia 68 C6
Most northerly point of Africa.

La Galite, Canal de sea chan. Tunisia 68 C6
La Gallega Mex. 166 D3
Lagan' Rus. Fed. 53 J7
Lagan r. U.K. 61 G3
La Garamba, Parc National de nat. park Dem. Rep. Congo 122 C3
Lagarto Brazil 177 K6
Lage Germany 63 I3
Lågen r. Norway 55 G7
Lage Vaart canal Neth. 62 F2
Lagg U.K. 60 D5
Laggan U.K. 60 E3
Lagh Bor watercourse Kenya/Somalia 122 E3
Laghouat Alg. 64 E5
Lagkor Co salt l. China 99 D6
La Gloria Mex. 161 D7
Lago Agrio Ecuador 176 C3
Lagoa Santa Brazil 179 C2
Lagoa Vermelha Brazil 179 A5
Lagodekhi Georgia 113 G2
Lagolândia Brazil 179 A1
La Gomera i. Canary Is 120 B2
La Gomera Guat. 167 H6
La Gonâve, Île de i. Haiti 169 J5
Lagong i. Indon. 85 E2
Lagonoy Gulf Luzon Phil. 82 C3

▶Lagos Nigeria 120 D4
Former capital of Nigeria. Most populous city in Africa.

Lagos Port. 67 B5
Lagosa Tanz. 123 C4
Lagos de Moreno Mex. 167 E4
La Grande r. Canada 152 F3
La Grande U.S.A. 156 D3
La Grande 3, Réservoir resr Canada 152 G3
La Grande 4, Réservoir resr Que. Canada 147 K4
La Grande 4, Réservoir resr Que. Canada 153 G3
La Grange Australia 134 C4
La Grange CA U.S.A. 158 C3
La Grange GA U.S.A. 163 C5
Lagrange U.S.A. 164 C3
La Grange KY U.S.A. 162 C4
La Grange TX U.S.A. 161 D6
La Gran Sabana plat. Venez. 176 F2
La Grita Venez. 176 D2
La Guajira, Península de pen. Col. 176 D1
Laguna Brazil 179 A5
Laguna, Picacho de la mt. Mex. 166 C4
Laguna Dam U.S.A. 159 F5
Laguna de Perlas Nicaragua 166 [inset] J6
Laguna de Temascal, Parque Natural nature res. Mex. 167 F5
Laguna Lachua, Parque Nacional nat. park Guat. 167 H6
Laguna Mountains U.S.A. 158 E5
Laguna Ojo de Liebre, Parque Natural de la nature res. Mex. 166 B3
Lagunas Chile 178 C2
Laguna San Rafael, Parque Nacional nat. park Chile 178 B7
Lagunas de Catemaco, Parque Natural nature res. Mex. 167 G5
Lagunas de Chacahua, Parque Nacional nat. park Mex. 167 F6
Lagunas de Montebello, Parque Nacional nat. park Mex. 167 H5
Laha Heilong. China 95 K1
La Habana Cuba see Havana
La Habra U.S.A. 158 E5
Lahad Datu Sabah Malaysia 85 G1
Lahad Datu, Teluk b. Malaysia 85 G1
La Hague, Cap de c. France 66 D2
Lahar Madh. Prad. India 99 B8
Laharpur India 104 E4
Lahat Sumatera Indon. 84 C3
Lahe Myanmar 86 A1
Lahemaa rahvuspark nat. park Estonia 55 N7
La Hève, Cap de c. France 59 H9
Lahewa Indon. 84 B2
Laḩij Yemen 108 F7
Lāhījān Iran 110 C2
Lahn r. Germany 63 H4
Lahnstein Germany 63 H4
Laholm Sweden 55 H8
Lahontan Reservoir U.S.A. 158 D2
Lahore Pak. 111 I4
Lahri Pak. 111 H4
Lahti Fin. 55 N6
La Huerta Mex. 166 D5
Laï Chad 121 E4
Lai'an China 97 H1
Laibach Slovenia see Ljubljana
Laibin China 97 F4
Laidley Australia 138 F1
Laifeng China 97 F2
L'Aigle France 66 E2
Laihia Fin. 54 M5
Lai-hka Myanmar 86 B2
Lai-Hsak Myanmar 86 B2
Laimakuri India 105 H4
Laimos, Akrotirio pt Greece 69 J5
Laingsburg S. Africa 124 E7
Laingsburg U.S.A. 164 C2
Lainioälven r. Sweden 54 M3
Lair U.S.A. 164 C4
L'Aïr, Massif de mts Niger 120 D3
Lairg U.K. 60 E2
Lais Sumatera Indon. 84 C3
Lais Mindanao Phil. 82 D5
La Isabela Cuba 163 D8
Laishevo Rus. Fed. 52 K5
Laishui Hebei China 95 H4
Laitila Fin. 55 L6
Laives Italy 68 D1
Laiwu Shandong China 95 I4
Laiwui Maluku Indon. 83 C3
Laixi Shandong China 95 J4
Laiyang Shandong China 95 J4
Laiyuan Hebei China 95 H4
Laizhou Shandong China 95 I4
Laizhou Wan b. China 95 I4
Lajamanu Australia 134 E4
Lajanurpekhi Georgia 113 F2
Lajeado Brazil 179 A5
Lajes Rio Grande do Norte Brazil 177 K5
Lajes Santa Catarina Brazil 179 A4
La Joya Chihuahua Mex. 166 D3
La Junta Mex. 166 D2
La Junta U.S.A. 160 C4
La Juventud, Isla de i. Cuba 169 H4
Lakadiya India 104 B5
La Kagera, Parc National de nat. park Rwanda see Akagera National Park
L'Akagera, Parc National de nat. park Rwanda see Akagera National Park
Lake U.S.A. 164 D5
Lake Andes U.S.A. 160 D3
Lakeba i. Fiji 133 I3
Lake Bardawil Reserve nature res. Egypt 107 A4
Lake Bolac Australia 138 A6
Lake Butler U.S.A. 163 D6
Lake Cargelligo Australia 138 C4
Lake Cathie Australia 138 F3
Lake Charles U.S.A. 161 E6
Lake City CO U.S.A. 159 J3
Lake City FL U.S.A. 163 D6
Lake City MI U.S.A. 164 C1
Lake Clark National Park and Preserve AK U.S.A. 148 I3
Lake Clear U.S.A. 165 H1
Lake District National Park U.K. 58 D4
Lake Eyre National Park Australia 137 B6
Lakefield Australia 136 D2
Lakefield Canada 165 F1
Lakefield National Park Australia 136 D2
Lake Forest U.S.A. 164 B2
Lake Gairdner National Park Australia 137 B7
Lake Geneva U.S.A. 160 F3
Lake George MI U.S.A. 164 C2
Lake George NY U.S.A. 165 I2
Lake Grace Australia 135 B8
Lake Harbour Canada see Kimmirut
Lake Havasu City U.S.A. 159 F4
Lakehurst U.S.A. 165 H3
Lake Isabella U.S.A. 158 D4
Lake Jackson U.S.A. 161 E6
Lake King Australia 135 B8
Lake Kopiago P.N.G. 81 K8
Lakeland FL U.S.A. 163 D7
Lakeland GA U.S.A. 163 D6
Lake Louise Canada 150 G5
Lakemba i. Fiji see Lakeba
Lake Mills U.S.A. 160 E3
Lake Minchumina AK U.S.A. 148 I3
Lake Nash Australia 136 B4
Lake Odessa U.S.A. 164 C2
Lake Paringa N.Z. 139 B6
Lake Placid FL U.S.A. 163 D7
Lake Placid NY U.S.A. 165 I1
Lake Pleasant U.S.A. 165 H2
Lakeport CA U.S.A. 158 B2
Lakeport MI U.S.A. 164 D2
Lake Providence U.S.A. 161 F5
Lake Range mts U.S.A. 158 D1
Lake River Canada 152 E3
Lakes Entrance Australia 138 D6
Lakeside AZ U.S.A. 159 I4
Lakeside VA U.S.A. 165 G5
Lake Tabourie Australia 138 E5
Lake Tekapo N.Z. 139 C7
Lake Torrens National Park Australia 137 B6
Lakeview MI U.S.A. 164 C2
Lakeview OH U.S.A. 164 D3
Lakeview OR U.S.A. 156 C4
Lake Village U.S.A. 161 F5
Lake Wales U.S.A. 163 D7
Lakewood CO U.S.A. 156 G5
Lakewood NJ U.S.A. 165 H3
Lakewood NY U.S.A. 164 F2
Lakewood OH U.S.A. 164 E3
Lake Worth U.S.A. 163 D7
Lakha India 104 B4
Lakhdenpokh'ya Rus. Fed. 54 Q6
Lakhimpur Assam India see North Lakhimpur
Lakhimpur Uttar Prad. India 104 E4
Lakhisarai India 105 F4
Lakhish r. Israel 107 B4
Lakhnadon India 104 D5
Lakhpat India 104 B5
Lakhtar India 104 B5
Lakin U.S.A. 160 C4
Lakitusaki r. Canada 152 E3
Lakki Marwat Pak. 111 H3
Lakohembi Sumba Indon. 83 B5
Lakonikos Kolpos b. Greece 69 J6
Lakor i. Maluku Indon. 83 D5
Lakota Côte d'Ivoire 120 C4
Lakota U.S.A. 160 D1
Laksefjorden sea chan. Norway 54 O1
Lakselv Norway 54 N1
Lakshadweep is India see Laccadive Islands
Lakshadweep union terr. India 106 B4
Lakshettipet India 106 C2
Lakshmipur Bangl. 105 G5
Laksmipur Bangl. see Lakshmipur
Lala Mindanao Phil. 82 C5
Lalaghat India 105 H4
Lalbara India 106 D1
L'Alcora Spain 67 F3
Lāleh Zār, Kūh-e mt. Iran 110 E4
Lalganj India 105 F4
Lālī Iran 110 C3
La Libertad El Salvador 167 H6
La Libertad Guat. 167 H5
La Libertad Nicaragua 166 [inset] I6
La Ligua Chile 178 B4
Laliki Maluku Indon. 83 C4
Lalimboee Sulawesi Indon. 83 B3
Lalin China 90 B3
Lalín Spain 67 B2
La Línea de la Concepción Spain 67 D5
Lalin He r. China 90 B3
Lalitpur India 104 D4
Lalitpur Nepal see Patan
Lal-Lo Luzon Phil. 82 C2
Lalmanirhat Bangl. see Lalmonirhat
Lalmonirhat Bangl. 105 G4
Laloa Sulawesi Indon. 83 B4
La Loche Canada 151 I3
La Loche, Lac l. Canada 151 I3
La Louvière Belgium 62 E4
Lal'sk Rus. Fed. 52 J3
Laluin i. Maluku Indon. 83 C3
Lalung La pass Xizang China 99 D7
Lama Bangl. 105 H5
La Macarena, Parque Nacional nat. park Col. 176 D3
La Maddalena Sardinia Italy 68 C4
La Madeleine, Îles de is Canada 153 J5
La Madeleine, Monts de mts France 66 F3
Lamadian Heilong. China 95 K2
Lamadianzi Heilong. China see Lamadian
Lamag Sabah Malaysia 85 G1
La Maiko, Parc National de nat. park Dem. Rep. Congo 122 C4
Lamakera Indon. 83 B5
La Malbaie Canada 153 H5
La Malinche, Parque Nacional nat. park Mex. 167 F5
Lamam Laos 86 D4
La Mancha Mex. 166 E3
La Mancha reg. Spain 67 E4
La Manche strait France/U.K. see English Channel
La Máquina Mex. 166 D2
Lamar CO U.S.A. 160 C4
Lamar MO U.S.A. 161 E4
Lamard Iran 110 D5
La Margeride, Monts de mts France 66 F4
La Marmora, Punta mt. Sardinia Italy 68 C5
La Marne au Rhin, Canal de France 62 G6
La Marque U.S.A. 161 E6
La Martre, Lac l. Canada 150 G2
Lamas r. Turkey 107 B1
La Masica Hond. 166 [inset] I6
La Mauricie, Parc National de nat. park Canada 153 G5
Lamawan Nei Mongol China 95 G3
Lambaréné Gabon 122 B4
Lambasa Fiji see Labasa
Lambasina i. Indon. 83 B4
Lambayeque Peru 176 C5
Lambay Island Ireland 61 G4
Lambeng Kalimantan Indon. 85 F3
Lambert atoll Marshall Is see Ailinglaplap

▶Lambert Glacier Antarctica 188 E2
Largest series of glaciers in the world.

Lambert's Bay S. Africa 124 D7
Lambeth Canada 164 E2
Lambi India 104 C3
Lambourn Downs hills U.K. 59 F7
Lame Sumatera Indon. 84 B2
La Medjerda, Monts de mts Alg. 68 B6
Lamego Port. 67 C3
Lamèque, Île i. Canada 153 I5
La Merced Arg. 178 C3
La Merced Peru 176 C6
Lameroo Australia 137 C7
La Mesa U.S.A. 158 E5
Lamesa U.S.A. 161 C5
Lamia Greece 69 J5
Lamigan Point Mindanao Phil. 82 D5
Lamington National Park Australia 138 F2
La Misa Mex. 166 C2
La Misión Mex. 158 E5
Lamitan Phil. 82 C5
Lamlam Papua Indon. 83 D3
Lamma Island H.K. China 97 [inset]
Lammerlaw Range mts N.Z. 139 B7
Lammermuir Hills U.K. 60 G5
Lammhult Sweden 55 I8
Lammi Fin. 55 N6
Lamon Bay Phil. 82 C3
Lamongan Jawa Indon. 85 F4
Lamont CA U.S.A. 158 D4
Lamont WY U.S.A. 156 G4
La Montagne d'Ambre, Parc National de nat. park Madag. 123 E5
La Montaña de Covadonga, Parque Nacional de nat. park Spain see Los Picos de Europa, Parque Nacional de
La Mora Mex. 166 E3
La Morita Chihuahua Mex. 166 D2
La Morita Coahuila Mex. 161 C6
Lamotrek atoll Micronesia 81 L5
La Moure U.S.A. 160 D2
Lampang Thai. 86 B3
Lam Pao, Ang Kep Nam Thai. 86 C3
Lampasas U.S.A. 161 D6
Lampazos Mex. 167 E3
Lampedusa, Isola di i. Sicily Italy 68 E7
Lampeter U.K. 59 C6
Lamphun Thai. 86 B3
Lampsacus Turkey see Lâpseki
Lampung prov. Indon. 84 D4
Lampung, Teluk b. Indon. 84 D4
Lam Tin H.K. China 97 [inset]
Lamu Kenya 122 E4
Lamu Myanmar 86 A3
Lāna'i i. U.S.A. 157 [inset]
Lāna'i City U.S.A. 157 [inset]
La Nao, Cabo de c. Spain 67 G4
Lanao, Lake Mindanao Phil. 82 D5
Lanark Canada 165 G1
Lanark U.K. 60 F5
Lanas Sabah Malaysia 85 G1
Lanbi Kyun i. Myanmar 87 B5
Lanboyan Point Mindanao Phil. 82 C4
Lancang China 96 C4
Lancang Jiang r. China 96 C2
Lancaster Canada 165 H1
Lancaster U.K. 58 E4
Lancaster CA U.S.A. 158 D4
Lancaster KY U.S.A. 164 C5
Lancaster MO U.S.A. 160 E3
Lancaster NH U.S.A. 165 J1
Lancaster OH U.S.A. 164 D4
Lancaster PA U.S.A. 165 G3
Lancaster SC U.S.A. 163 D5
Lancaster VA U.S.A. 165 G5
Lancaster WI U.S.A. 160 F3
Lancaster Canal U.K. 58 E5
Lancaster Sound strait Canada 147 J2
Lancun Shandong China 95 J4
Landak r. Indon. 85 E3
Landana Angola see Cacongo
Landau an der Isar Germany 63 M6
Landau in der Pfalz Germany 63 I5
Landeck Austria 57 M7
Lander watercourse Australia 134 E5
Lander U.S.A. 156 F4
Landesbergen Germany 63 J2
Landfall Island India 87 A4
Landhi Pak. 111 G5
Landik, Gunung mt. Indon. 84 C3
Landis Canada 151 I4
Landor Australia 135 B6
Landsberg Poland see Gorzów Wielkopolski
Landsberg am Lech Germany 57 M6
Land's End pt U.K. 59 B8
Landshut Germany 63 M6
Landskrona Sweden 55 H9
Landstuhl Germany 63 H5
Land Wursten reg. Germany 63 I1
Lanesborough Ireland 61 E4
Lanfeng Henan China see Lankao
La'nga Co l. China 99 C7
Langao China 97 F1
Langar Afgh. 111 H3
Langara Sulawesi Indon. 83 B4
Langberg mts S. Africa 124 F5
Langdon U.S.A. 160 D1
Langeac France 66 F4
Langeberg mts S. Africa 124 D7
Langeland i. Denmark 55 G9
Längelmäki Fin. 55 N6
Langelsheim Germany 63 K3
Langen Germany 63 I1
Langenburg Canada 151 K5
Langenhagen Germany 63 J2
Langenhahn Germany 63 H4
Langenlonsheim Germany 63 H5
Langenthal Switz. 66 H3
Langenweddingen Germany 63 L2
Langeoog Germany 63 H1
Langesund Norway 55 F7
Langfang Hebei China 95 I4
Langgam Sumatera Indon. 84 C2
Langgapayung Sumatera Indon. 84 C2
Langgar Xizang China 99 F7
Langgöns Germany 63 I4
Langjan Nature Reserve S. Africa 125 I2
Langjökull ice cap Iceland 54 [inset]
Langka Sumatera Indon. 84 B1
Langkawi i. Malaysia 84 B1
Langkesi, Kepulauan is Indon. 83 C4
Lang Kha Toek, Khao mt. Thai. 87 B5
Langklip S. Africa 124 E5
Langkon Sabah Malaysia 85 G1
Langley Canada 150 F5
Langley U.S.A. 164 D5
Langlo Crossing Australia 137 D5
Langmusi Gansu China see Dagcanglhamo
Langong, Xé r. Laos 86 D3
Langøya i. Norway 54 I2
Langphu mt. China 105 F3
Langport U.K. 59 E7
Langqên Zangbo r. China 99 B7
Langqi China 97 H3
Langres France 66 G3
Langres, Plateau de France 66 G3
Langru Xinjiang China 99 B5
Langsa Sumatera Indon. 84 B1
Langsa, Teluk b. Indon. 84 B1
Långsele Sweden 54 J5
Langshan Nei Mongol China 95 F3
Lang Shan mts China 95 F3
Lang Sơn Vietnam 86 D2
Langtang National Park Nepal 105 F3
Langtao Myanmar 86 B1
Langting India 105 H4
Langtoft U.K. 58 G4
Langtoutun Nei Mongol China 95 J2
Langtry U.S.A. 161 C6
Languan Shaanxi China see Lantian
Languedoc reg. France 66 E5
Langundu, Tanjung pt Sumbawa Indon. 85 G5
Långvattnet Sweden 54 L4
Langwedel Germany 63 J2
Langxi China 97 H2
Langya Shan mt. Hebei China 95 H4
Langzhong China 96 E2
Lanigan Canada 151 J5
Lanín, Parque Nacional nat. park Arg. 178 B5
Lanín, Volcán vol. Arg./Chile 178 B5
Lanjak, Bukit mt. Malaysia 85 E2
Lanji India 104 E5
Lanka country Asia see Sri Lanka
Lankao Henan China 95 H5
Länkäran Azer. 113 H3
Lannion France 66 C2
La Noria Mex. 166 D4
Lanping China 96 C3
Lansån Sweden 54 M3
L'Anse U.S.A. 160 F2
Lanshan China 97 G3

▶Lansing U.S.A. 164 C2
Capital of Michigan.

Lanta, Ko i. Thai. 87 B6
Lantau Island H.K. China 97 [inset]
Lantau Peak hill H.K. China 97 [inset]
Lantian Shaanxi China 95 G5
Lanuza Bay Mindanao Phil. 82 D4
Lanxi Heilong. China 90 B3
Lanxi Zhejiang China 97 H2
Lanxian Shanxi China 95 G4
Lan Yü i. Taiwan 97 I4
Lanzarote i. Canary Is 120 B2
Lanzhou Gansu China 94 E4
Lanzijing Jilin China 95 J2
Laoag Luzon Phil. 82 C2
Laoang Phil. 82 D3
Laobie Shan mts China 96 C4
Laobukou China 97 F3
Lao Cai Vietnam 86 C2
Laodicea Syria see Latakia
Laodicea Turkey see Denizli
Laodicea ad Lycum Turkey see Denizli
Laodicea ad Mare Syria see Latakia
Laofengkou Xinjiang China 98 C3
Laoha He r. China 95 J3
Laohekou China 97 F1
Laohutun Liaoning China 95 J4
Laojie China see Yongping
Laojunmiao Gansu China see Yumen
La Okapi, Parc National de nat. park Dem. Rep. Congo 122 C3
Lao Ling mts China 90 B4
Laon France 62 D5
Laoqitai Xinjiang China 94 B3
La Oroya Peru 176 C6
Laos country Asia 86 C3
Laoshan Shandong China 95 J4
Laoshawan Xinjiang China 98 D3
Laotieshan Shuidao sea chan. China see Bohai Haixia
Laotougou China 90 C4
Laotuding Shan hill China 90 B4
Laowohi pass India see Khardung La
Laoximiao Nei Mongol China 94 E3
Laoyacheng Qinghai China 94 E4
Laoye Ling mts Heilongjiang/Jilin China 90 B4
Laoye Ling mts Heilongjiang/Jilin China 90 C4
Laoyemiao Xinjiang China 94 C2
Lapa Brazil 179 A4
Lapac i. Phil. 82 C5
La Palma i. Canary Is 120 B2
La Palma Guat. 167 H5
La Palma Panama 166 [inset] K7
La Palma U.S.A. 159 H5
La Palma del Condado Spain 67 C5
La Panza Range mts U.S.A. 158 C4

La Paragua Venez. 176 F2
Laparan i. Phil. 82 B5
La Parilla Mex. 161 B8
La Paya, Parque Nacional nat. park Col. 176 D3
La Paz Arg. 178 E4

▶La Paz Bol. 176 E7
Official capital of Bolivia.

La Paz Hond. 166 [inset] I6
La Paz Mex. 166 C3
La Paz Nicaragua 166 [inset] I6
La Paz, Bahía b. Mex. 166 C3
La Pedrera Col. 176 E4
Lapeer U.S.A. 164 D2
La Pendjari, Parc National de nat. park Benin 120 D3
La Perla Mex. 166 D2
La Pérouse Strait Japan/Rus. Fed. 90 F3
La Pesca Mex. 161 D8
La Piedad Mex. 166 E4
Lapinig Samar Phil. 82 D3
Lapinlahti Fin. 54 O5
La Pintada Panama 166 [inset] J7
Lapithos Cyprus 107 A2
Laplace LA U.S.A. 167 H2
Lap Lae Thai. 86 C3
La Plant U.S.A. 160 C2
La Plata Arg. 178 E4
La Plata MD U.S.A. 165 G4
La Plata MO U.S.A. 160 E3
La Plata, Isla i. Ecuador 176 B4

▶La Plata, Río de sea chan. Arg./Uruguay 178 E4
Part of the Río de la Plata - Paraná, 2nd longest river in South America, and 9th in the world.

La Plonge, Lac l. Canada 151 J4
Lapmežciems Latvia 55 M8
Lapominka Rus. Fed. 52 I2
La Porte U.S.A. 164 B3
Laporte U.S.A. 165 G3
Laporte, Mount Y.T. Canada 149 P3
Laposo, Bukit mt. Indon. 83 A4
La Potherie, Lac l. Canada 153 G2
La Poza Grande Mex. 166 B3
Lappajärvi Fin. 54 M5
Lappajärvi l. Fin. 54 M5
Lappeenranta Fin. 55 P6
Lappersdorf Germany 63 M5
Lappi Fin. 55 L6
Lappland reg. Europe 54 K3
La Pryor U.S.A. 161 D6
Lâpseki Turkey 69 L4
Laptevo Rus. Fed. see Yasnogorsk
Laptev Sea Rus. Fed. 77 N2
Lapua Fin. 54 M5
Lapuko Sulawesi Indon. 83 B4
Lapu-Lapu Phil. 82 C4
Lapurdum France see Bayonne
La Purísima Mex. 166 B3
Laqiya Arbain well Sudan 108 C5
La Quiaca Arg. 178 C2
L'Aquila Italy 68 E3
La Quinta U.S.A. 158 E5
Lār Iran 110 D5
Larache Morocco 67 C6
Lārak i. Iran 110 E5
Laramie U.S.A. 156 G4
Laramie r. U.S.A. 156 G4
Laramie Mountains U.S.A. 156 G4
Laranda Turkey see Karaman
Laranjal Paulista Brazil 179 B3
Laranjeiras do Sul Brazil 178 F3
Laranjinha r. Brazil 179 A3
Larantuka Flores Indon. 83 B5
Larat Indon. 134 E1
Larat i. Indon. 134 E1
Larba Alg. 67 H5
Lärbro Sweden 55 K8
L'Archipélago de Mingan, Réserve du Parc National de nat. park Canada 153 J4
L'Ardenne, Plateau de plat. Belgium see Ardennes
Laredo Spain 67 E2
Laredo U.S.A. 161 D7
La Reforma Veracruz Mex. 167 F4
La Reina Adelaida, Archipiélago de is Chile 178 B8
Largeau Chad see Faya
Largo U.S.A. 163 D7
Largs U.K. 60 E5
Lārī Iran 110 B2
L'Ariana Tunisia 68 D6
Lariang Sulawesi Barat Indon. 83 A3
Lariang r. Indon. 83 A3
Larimore U.S.A. 160 D2
La Rioja Arg. 178 C3
La Rioja aut. comm. Spain 67 E2
Larisa Greece 69 J5
Larissa Greece see Larisa
Laristan reg. Iran 110 E5
Larkana Pak. 111 H5
Lark Harbour Canada 153 K4
Lar Koh mt. Afgh. 111 F3
Lark Passage Australia 136 D2
L'Arli, Parc National de nat. park Burkina 120 D3
Larnaca Cyprus 107 A2
Larnaka Cyprus see Larnaca
Larnaka Bay Cyprus 107 A2
Larnakos, Kolpos b. Cyprus see Larnaka Bay
Larne U.K. 61 G3
Larned U.S.A. 160 D4
La Robe Noire, Lac de l. Canada 153 J4
La Robla Spain 67 D2
La Roche-en-Ardenne Belgium 62 F4
La Rochelle France 66 D3
La Roche-sur-Yon France 66 D3
La Roda Spain 67 E4
La Romana Dom. Rep. 169 K5
La Ronge Canada 151 J4
La Ronge, Lac l. Canada 151 J4
La Rosa Mex. 167 E3
La Rosita Mex. 167 E2
Larrey Point Australia 134 B4
Larrimah Australia 134 F3
Lars Christensen Coast Antarctica 188 E2
Larsen Bay AK U.S.A. 148 I4
Larsen Ice Shelf Antarctica 188 L2
Larsmo Fin. 54 M5
Larvik Norway 55 G7
Las Adjuntas, Presa de resr Mex. 161 D8
Lasahau Sulawesi Indon. 83 B4
La Sal U.S.A. 159 I2
LaSalle Canada 165 I1
La Salle U.S.A. 152 C6
La Salonga Nord, Parc National de nat. park Dem. Rep. Congo 122 C4
La Sambre à l'Oise, Canal de France 62 D5
Lasan Kalimantan Indon. 85 F2
Las Animas U.S.A. 160 C4
Las Ánimas, Punta pt Mex. 166 B2
Las Anod Somalia see Laascaanood
La Sarre Canada 152 F4
Las Avispas Mex. 166 C2
La Savonnière, Lac l. Canada 153 G3
La Scie Canada 153 L4
Las Cruces Mex. 166 D2
Las Cruces CA U.S.A. 158 C4
Las Cruces NM U.S.A. 157 G6
La Selle, Pic mt. Haiti 169 J5
La Serena Chile 178 B3
Las Esperanças Mex. 167 E3
La Seu d'Urgell Spain 67 G2
Las Flores Arg. 178 E5
Las Guacamatas, Cerro mt. Mex. 157 F7
Lāshār r. Iran 111 F5
Lashburn Canada 151 I4
Las Heras Arg. 178 C4
Las Herreras Mex. 166 D3
Lashio Myanmar 86 B2
Lashkar India 104 D4
Lashkar Gāh Afgh. 111 G4
Las Juntas Chile 178 C3
Las Lavaderos Mex. 167 F4
Las Lomitas Arg. 178 D2
Las Marismas marsh Spain 67 C5
Las Martinetas Arg. 178 C7
Las Mesteñas Mex. 166 D2
Las Minas, Cerro de mt. Hond. 167 H6
Las Mulatas is Panama see San Blas, Archipiélago de
Las Nieves Mex. 166 D3
Las Nopaleras, Cerro mt. Mex. 166 E3
La Société, Archipel de is Fr. Polynesia see Society Islands
Lasolo, Teluk b. Indon. 83 B3
La Somme, Canal de France 62 C5
Las Palmas watercourse Mex. 158 E5
Las Palmas Panama 166 [inset] J7
Las Palmas de Gran Canaria Canary Is 120 B2
Las Petas Bol. 177 G7
La Spezia Italy 68 C2
Las Piedras, Río de r. Peru 176 E6
Las Planchas Hond. 166 [inset] I6
Las Plumas Arg. 178 C6
Laspur Pak. 111 I2
Lassance Brazil 179 B2
Lassen Peak vol. U.S.A. 158 C1
Lassen Volcanic National Park U.S.A. 158 C1
Las Tablas Mex. 167 F4
Las Tablas Panama 166 [inset] J8
Las Tablas de Daimiel, Parque Nacional de nat. park Spain 67 E4
Last Chance U.S.A. 160 C4
Las Termas Arg. 178 D3
Last Mountain Lake Canada 151 J5
Las Tórtolas, Cerro mt. Chile 178 C3
Lastoursville Gabon 122 B4
Lastovo i. Croatia 68 G3
Las Tres Vírgenes, Volcán vol. Mex. 166 B3
Lastrup Germany 63 H2
Las Tunas Cuba 169 I4
Las Varas Chihuahua Mex. 166 D2
Las Varas Nayarit Mex. 168 C4
Las Varillas Arg. 178 D4
Las Vegas NM U.S.A. 157 G6
Las Vegas NV U.S.A. 159 F3
Las Viajas, Isla de i. Peru 176 C6
Las Villuercas mt. Spain 67 D4
La Tabatière Canada 153 K4
Latacunga Ecuador 176 C4
Latady Island Antarctica 188 L2
Latakia Syria 107 B2
Latalata i. Maluku Indon. 83 C3
La Teste-de-Buch France 66 D4
La Tetilla, Cerro mt. Mex. 166 D4
Latham Australia 135 B7
Lathen Germany 63 H2
Latheron U.K. 60 F2
Lathi India 104 B4
Latho India 104 D2
Lathrop U.S.A. 158 C3
Latina Italy 68 E4
La Tortuga, Isla i. Venez. 176 E1
Latouche AK U.S.A. 149 K3
Latouche Island AK U.S.A. 149 K3
La Trinidad Nicaragua 166 [inset] I6
La Trinidad Luzon Phil. 82 C2
La Trinitaria Mex. 167 G5
Latrobe U.S.A. 164 F3
Latrun West Bank 107 B4
Lattaquié Syria see Latakia
Lattrop Neth. 62 G2
La Tuque Canada 153 G5
Latur India 106 C2
Latvia country Europe 55 N8
Latvija country Europe see Latvia
Latviyskaya S.S.R. country Europe see Latvia
Lauca, Parque Nacional nat. park Chile 176 E7
Lauchhammer Germany 57 N5
Lauder U.K. 60 G5
Laudio Spain see Llodio
Lauenbrück Germany 63 J1
Lauenburg (Elbe) Germany 63 K1
Lauf an der Pegnitz Germany 63 L5
Laufen Switz. 66 H3
Lauge Koch Kyst reg. Greenland 147 L2
Laughlen, Mount Australia 135 F5
Laughlin Peak U.S.A. 157 G5
Lauka Estonia 55 M7
Launceston Australia 137 [inset]
Launceston U.K. 59 C8
Laune r. Ireland 61 C5
Launggyaung Myanmar 86 B1
Launglon Myanmar 87 B4
Launglon Bok Islands Myanmar 87 B4
La Unidad Mex. 167 G6
La Unión Bol. 176 F7
La Unión El Salvador 166 [inset] I6
La Unión Hond. 166 [inset] I6
La Unión Mex. 167 E5
Laur Luzon Phil. 82 C3
Laura Australia 136 D2
Laurel DE U.S.A. 165 H4
Laurel MS U.S.A. 161 F6
Laurel MT U.S.A. 156 F3
Laureldale U.S.A. 165 H3
Laurel Hill hills U.S.A. 164 F4
Laurencekirk U.K. 60 G4
Laurieton Australia 138 F3
Laurinburg U.S.A. 163 E5
Lauru i. Solomon Is see Choiseul
Lausanne Switz. 66 H3
Laut i. Indon. 85 E1
Laut i. Indon. 85 E3
Laut i. Indon. 85 G3
Laut, Selat sea chan. Indon. 85 F3
Lautem East Timor 83 C5
Lautersbach (Hessen) Germany 63 J4
Laut Kecil, Kepulauan is Indon. 85 F4
Lautoka Fiji 133 H3
Lauttawar, Danau l. Indon. 84 B1
Lauvuskylä Fin. 54 P5
Lauwersmeer l. Neth. 62 G1
Lava Beds National Monument nat. park U.S.A. 156 C4
Laval Canada 152 G5
Laval France 66 D2
La Vall d'Uixó Spain 67 F4
Lāvān i. Iran 110 D5
La Vanoise, Massif de mts France 66 H4
La Vanoise, Parc National de nat. park France 66 H4
Lavapié, Punta pt Chile 178 B5
Lāvar Iran 110 C4
Laveaga Peak U.S.A. 158 C3
La Vega Dom. Rep. 169 J5
La Venta Hond. 166 [inset] I6
Laverne U.S.A. 161 D4
Laverton Australia 135 C7
La Víbora Mex. 166 E3
La Vila Joíosa Spain see Villajoyosa-La Vila Joíosa
La Viña Peru 176 C5
Lavongai i. P.N.G. see New Hanover
Lavras Brazil 179 B3
Lavrentiya Rus. Fed. 148 E2
Lavumisa Swaziland 125 J4
Lavushi-Manda National Park Zambia 123 D5
Lawa India 104 C4
Lawa Myanmar 86 B1
Lawa Pak. 111 H3
Lawang i. Indon. 85 G5
Lawas Sarawak Malaysia 85 F1
Lawashi r. Canada 152 E3
Law Dome ice feature Antarctica 188 F2
Lawele Sulawesi Indon. 83 B4
Lawin i. Maluku Indon. 83 D3
Lawit, Gunung mt. Indon./Malaysia 85 F2
Lawit, Gunung mt. Malaysia 84 C1
Lawksawk Myanmar 86 B2
Lawn Hill National Park Australia 136 B3
La Woëvre, Plaine de plain France 62 F5
Lawra Ghana 120 C3
Lawrence IN U.S.A. 164 B4
Lawrence KS U.S.A. 160 E4
Lawrence MA U.S.A. 165 J2
Lawrenceburg IN U.S.A. 164 C4
Lawrenceburg KY U.S.A. 164 C4
Lawrenceburg TN U.S.A. 162 C5
Lawrenceville GA U.S.A. 163 D5
Lawrenceville IL U.S.A. 164 B4
Lawrenceville VA U.S.A. 165 G5
Lawrence Wells, Mount hill Australia 135 C6
Lawton U.S.A. 161 D5
Lawu, Gunung vol. Indon. 85 E4
Lawz, Jabal al mt. Saudi Arabia 112 D5
Laxå Sweden 55 I7
Laxey Isle of Man 58 C4
Laxgalts'ap B.C. Canada 149 O5
Lax Kw'alaams B.C. Canada 149 O5
Laxo U.K. 60 [inset]
Laxong Co l. Xizang China 99 D6
Laya r. Rus. Fed. 52 M2
Layar, Tanjung pt Indon. 85 G4
Laydennyy, Mys c. Rus. Fed. 52 J1
Layeni Maluku Indon. 83 D4
Laylá Saudi Arabia 108 G5
Layla salt pan Saudi Arabia 107 D4
Laysan Island U.S.A. 186 I4
Laysu Xinjiang China 98 C4
Laytonville U.S.A. 158 B2
Layyah Pak. 111 H4
Laza Myanmar 86 B1
La Zacatosa, Picacho mt. Mex. 166 C4
Lazarev Rus. Fed. 90 F1
Lazarevac Serbia 69 I2
Lázaro Cárdenas Baja California Mex. 166 B2
Lázaro Cárdenas Baja California Mex. 166 B2
Lázaro Cárdenas Mex. 168 D5
Lazcano Uruguay 178 F4
Lazdijai Lith. 55 M9
Lazhuglung Xizang China 99 C6
Lazikou China 96 D1
Lazo Primorskiy Kray Rus. Fed. 90 D4
Lazo Respublika Sakha (Yakutiya) Rus. Fed. 77 O3
Lead U.S.A. 160 C2
Leader Water r. U.K. 60 G5
Leadville Australia 138 D4
Leaf r. U.S.A. 161 F6
Leaf Bay Canada see Tasiujaq
Leaf Rapids Canada 151 K3
Leakey U.S.A. 161 D6
Leaksville U.S.A. see Eden
Leamington Canada 164 D2
Leamington Spa, Royal U.K. 59 F6
Leane, Lough l. Ireland 61 C5
Leap Ireland 61 C6
Leatherhead U.K. 59 G7
L'Eau Claire, Lac à l. Canada 152 G2
L'Eau Claire, Rivière à r. Canada 152 G2
L'Eau d'Heure l. Belgium 62 E4
Leavenworth IN U.S.A. 164 B4
Leavenworth KS U.S.A. 160 E4
Leavenworth WA U.S.A. 156 C3
Leavitt Peak U.S.A. 158 D2
Lebach Germany 62 G5
Lebak Mindanao Phil. 82 D5
Lebanon country Asia 107 B2
Lebanon IN U.S.A. 164 B3
Lebanon KY U.S.A. 164 C5
Lebanon MO U.S.A. 160 E4
Lebanon NH U.S.A. 165 I2
Lebanon OH U.S.A. 164 C4
Lebanon OR U.S.A. 156 C3
Lebanon PA U.S.A. 165 G3
Lebanon TN U.S.A. 162 C4
Lebanon VA U.S.A. 164 D5
Lebanon Junction U.S.A. 164 C5
Lebanon Mountains Lebanon see Liban, Jebel
Lebbeke Belgium 62 E3
Lebec U.S.A. 158 D4
Lebedyan' Rus. Fed. 53 H5
Lebel-sur-Quévillon Canada 152 F4
Le Blanc France 66 E3
Lebo Sulawesi Indon. 83 B4
Lębork Poland 57 P3
Lebowakgomo S. Africa 125 I3
Lebrija Spain 67 C5
Łebsko, Jezioro lag. Poland 57 P3
Lebu Chile 178 B5
Lebyazh'ye Kazakh. see Akku
Lebyazh'ye Rus. Fed. 52 K4
Le Caire Egypt see Cairo
Le Cateau-Cambrésis France 62 D4
Le Catelet France 62 D4
Lecce Italy 68 H4
Lecco Italy 68 C2
Lech r. Austria/Germany 57 M7
Lechaina Greece 69 I6
Lechang China 97 G3
Le Chasseron mt. Switz. 66 H3
Le Chesne France 62 E5
Lechtaler Alpen mts Austria 57 M7
Leck Germany 57 L3
Lecompte U.S.A. 161 E6
Le Creusot France 66 G3
Le Crotoy France 62 B4
Lectoure France 66 E5
Ledang, Gunung mt. Malaysia 84 C2
Ledbury U.K. 59 E6
Ledesma Spain 67 D3
Ledmore U.K. 60 E2
Ledmozero Rus. Fed. 54 R4
Ledo Kalimantan Indon. 85 E2
Ledong Hainan China 86 E3
Ledong Hainan China 97 F5
Le Dorat France 66 E3
Ledu Qinghai China 94 E4
Leduc Canada 150 H4
Lee r. Ireland 61 D6
Lee IN U.S.A. 164 B3
Lee MA U.S.A. 165 I2
Leech Lake U.S.A. 160 E2
Leeds U.K. 58 F5
Leedstown U.K. 59 B8
Leek Neth. 62 G1
Leek U.K. 59 E5
Leende Neth. 62 F3
Leer (Ostfriesland) Germany 63 H1
Leesburg FL U.S.A. 163 D6
Leesburg GA U.S.A. 163 C6
Leesburg OH U.S.A. 164 D4
Leesburg VA U.S.A. 165 G4
Leese Germany 63 J2
Lee Steere Range hills Australia 135 C6
Leesville U.S.A. 161 E6
Leesville Lake OH U.S.A. 164 E3
Leesville Lake VA U.S.A. 164 F5
Leeton Australia 138 C5
Leeu-Gamka S. Africa 124 E7
Leeuwarden Neth. 62 F1
Leeuwin, Cape Australia 135 A8
Leeuwin-Naturaliste National Park Australia 135 A8
Lee Vining U.S.A. 158 D3
Leeward Islands Caribbean Sea 169 L5
Lefka Cyprus 107 A2
Lefkada Greece 69 I5
Lefkada i. Greece 69 I5
Lefkás Greece see Lefkada
Lefke Cyprus see Lefka
Lefkimmi Greece 69 I5
Lefkoniko Cyprus see Lefkonikon
Lefkonikon Cyprus 107 A2
Lefkoşa Cyprus see Nicosia
Lefkosia Cyprus see Nicosia
Lefroy r. Canada 153 H2
Lefroy, Lake salt flat Australia 135 C7
Legarde r. Canada 152 D4
Legaspi Luzon Phil. 82 C3
Legden Germany 62 H2
Legges Tor mt. Australia 137 [inset]
Leghorn Italy see Livorno
Legnago Italy 68 D2
Legnica Poland 57 P5
Legohli N.W.T. Canada see Norman Wells
Le Grand U.S.A. 158 C3
Legune Australia 134 E3
Leh India 104 D2
Le Havre France 66 E2
Lehi U.S.A. 159 H1
Lehighton U.S.A. 165 H3
Lehmo Fin. 54 P5
Lehre Germany 63 K2
Lehrte Germany 63 J2
Lehtimäki Fin. 54 M5
Lehututu Botswana 124 E2
Leibnitz Austria 57 O7
Leicester U.K. 59 F6
Leichhardt r. Australia 132 B3
Leichhardt Falls Australia 136 B3
Leichhardt Range mts Australia 136 D4
Leiden Neth. 62 E2
Leie r. Belgium 62 D3
Leigh N.Z. 139 E3
Leigh U.K. 58 E5
Leighton Buzzard U.K. 59 G7
Leiktho Myanmar 86 B3
Leimen Germany 63 I5
Leine r. Germany 63 J2
Leinefelde Germany 63 K3
Leinster Australia 135 C6
Leinster reg. Ireland 61 F4
Leinster, Mount hill Ireland 61 F5
Leipsic U.S.A. 164 D3
Leipsoi i. Greece 69 L6
Leipzig Germany 63 M3
Leipzig-Halle airport Germany 63 M3
Leiranger Norway 54 I3
Leiria Port. 67 B4
Leirvik Norway 55 D7
Leishan China 97 F3
Leisler, Mount hill Australia 135 E5
Leisnig Germany 63 M3
Leitchfield U.S.A. 164 B5
Leith Hill hill U.K. 59 G7
Leiva, Cerro mt. Col. 176 D3
Leixlip Ireland 61 F4
Leiyang China 97 G3
Leizhou China 97 F4
Leizhou Bandao pen. China 97 F4
Leizhou Wan b. China 97 F4
Lek r. Neth. 62 E3
Leka Norway 54 G4
Lékana Congo 122 B4
Le Kef Tunisia 68 C6
Lekhainá Greece see Lechaina
Lekitobi Maluku Indon. 83 C3
Lekkersing S. Africa 124 C5
Lékoni Gabon 122 B4
Leksand Sweden 55 I6
Leksozero, Ozero l. Rus. Fed. 54 Q5
Leksula Buru Indon. 83 C3
Lelai, Tanjung pt Halmahera Indon. 83 D2
Leland U.S.A. 164 C1
Leli China see Tianlin
Leling Shandong China 95 I4
Lelinta Papua Indon. 83 D3
Lelogama Timor Indon. 83 B5
Lélouma Guinea 120 B3
Lelystad Neth. 62 F2
Le Maire, Estrecho de sea chan. Arg. 178 C9
Léman, Lac l. France/Switz. see Geneva, Lake
Le Mans France 66 E2
Le Mars U.S.A. 160 D3
Lembeh i. Indon. 83 C2
Lemberg France 63 H5
Lemberg Ukr. see L'viv
Lembruch Germany 63 I2
Lembu Kalimantan Indon. 85 G2
Lembu, Gunung mt. Indon. 84 B1
Lembubut Kalimantan Indon. 85 G1
Lemdiyya Alg. see Médéa
Leme Brazil 179 B3
Lemele Neth. 62 G2
Lemesos Cyprus see Limassol
Lemgo Germany 63 I2
Lemhi Range mts U.S.A. 156 E3
Lemi Fin. 55 O6
Lemieux Islands Canada 147 L3
Lemmenjoen kansallispuisto nat. park Fin. 54 N2
Lemmer Neth. 62 F2
Lemmon U.S.A. 160 C2
Lemmon, Mount U.S.A. 159 H5
Lemnos i. Greece see Limnos
Lemoncove U.S.A. 158 D3
Lemoore U.S.A. 158 D3
Le Moyne, Lac l. Canada 153 H2
Lemro r. Myanmar 86 A2
Lemtybozh Rus. Fed. 51 R3
Lemukutan i. Indon. 85 E2
Le Murge hills Italy 68 G4
Lemvig Denmark 55 F8
Lem"yu r. Rus. Fed. 52 M3
Lena r. Rus. Fed. 88 J1
Lena U.S.A. 164 A1
Lena, Mount U.S.A. 159 I1
Lenadoon Point Ireland 61 C3
Lenangguar Sumbawa Indon. 85 G5
Lenchung Tso salt l. China 105 E2
Lencóis Brazil 179 C1
Lençóis Maranhenses, Parque Nacional dos nat. park Brazil 177 J4
Lendeh Iran 110 C4
Lendery Rus. Fed. 54 Q5
Le Neubourg France 59 H9
Lengerich Germany 63 H2
Lenghuzhen Qinghai China 98 F5
Lenglong Ling mts China 94 E4
Lengshuijiang China 97 F3
Lengshuitan China 97 F3
Lenham U.K. 59 H7
Lenhovda Sweden 55 I8
Lenin Tajik. 111 H2
Lenin, Qullai mt. Kyrg./Tajik. see Lenin Peak
Lenina, Pik mt. Kyrg./Tajik. see Lenin Peak
Leninabad Tajik. see Khŭjand
Leninakan Armenia see Gyumri
Lenin Atyndagy Choku mt. Kyrg./Tajik. see Lenin Peak
Lenine Ukr. 112 D1
Leningrad Rus. Fed. see St Petersburg
Leningrad Tajik. 111 H2
Leningrad Oblast admin. div. Rus. Fed. see Leningradskaya Oblast'
Leningradskaya Rus. Fed. 53 H7
Leningradskaya Oblast' admin. div. Rus. Fed. 55 R7
Leningradskiy Rus. Fed. 77 S3
Leningradskiy Tajik. see Leningrad
Lenino Ukr. see Lenine
Leninobod Tajik. see Khŭjand
Lenin Peak Kyrg./Tajik. 111 I2
Leninsk Kazakh. see Baykonyr
Leninsk Rus. Fed. 53 J6
Leninskiy Rus. Fed. 53 H5
Leninsk-Kuznetskiy Rus. Fed. 76 J4
Leninskoye Kazakh. 53 K6
Leninskoye Kirovskaya Oblast' Rus. Fed. 52 J4
Leninskoye Yevreyskaya Avtonomnaya Oblast' Rus. Fed. 90 D3
Lenkoran' Azer. see Länkäran
Lenne r. Germany 63 H3
Lennoxville Canada 165 J1
Lenoir U.S.A. 162 D5
Lenore U.S.A. 164 D5
Lenore Lake Canada 151 J4
Lenox U.S.A. 165 I2
Lens France 62 C4
Lensk Rus. Fed. 77 M3
Lenti Hungary 68 G1
Lentini Sicily Italy 68 F6
Lenya Myanmar 87 B5
Lenzen Germany 63 L1
Léo Burkina 120 C3
Leoben Austria 57 O7
Leodhais, Eilean i. U.K. see Lewis, Isle of
Leok Sulawesi Indon. 83 B2
Leominster U.K. 59 E6
Leominster U.S.A. 165 J2
León Mex. 168 D4
León Nicaragua 166 [inset] I6
León Spain 67 D2
Leon r. U.S.A. 161 D6
Leonardtown U.S.A. 165 G4
Leonardville Namibia 124 D2
Leona Vicario Mex. 167 I4
Leongatha Australia 138 B7
Leonidi Peloponnisos Greece see Leonidio
Leonidio Greece 69 J6
Leonidovo Rus. Fed. 90 F2
Leonora Australia 135 C7
Leontovich, Cape AK U.S.A. 148 G5
Leopold U.S.A. 164 E4
Leopold and Astrid Coast Antarctica see King Leopold and Queen Astrid Coast
Léopold II, Lac l. Dem. Rep. Congo see Mai-Ndombe, Lac
Leopoldina Brazil 179 C3
Leopoldo de Bulhões Brazil 179 A2
Léopoldville Dem. Rep. Congo see Kinshasa
Leoti U.S.A. 160 C4
Leoville Canada 151 J4
Lepalale S. Africa see Lephalale
Lepar i. Indon. 84 D3
Lepaya Latvia see Liepāja
Lepel' Belarus see Lyepyel'
Lepellé r. Canada 153 H1
Lephalala r. S. Africa 125 H2
Lephalale S. Africa 125 H2
Lephephe Botswana 125 G2
Lephoi S. Africa 125 G6
Leping China 97 H2
Lepontine, Alpi mts Italy/Switz. 68 C1
Leppävirta Fin. 54 O5
Lepreau, Point Canada 153 I5
Lepsa Kazakh. see Lepsy
Lepsinsk Kazakh. 98 C3
Lepsy Kazakh. 102 E2
Lepsy r. Kazakh. 98 B3
Le Puy France see Le Puy-en-Velay
Le Puy-en-Velay France 66 F4
Le Quesnoy France 62 D4
Lerala Botswana 125 H2
Leratswana S. Africa 125 H5
Léré Mali 120 C3
Lereh Indon. 81 J7
Lereh, Tanjung pt Indon. 83 A3
Leribe Lesotho see Hlotse
Lérida Col. 176 D4
Lérida Spain see Lleida
Lerik Azer. 113 H3
Lerma Mex. 167 H5
Lerma Spain 67 E2
Lermontov Rus. Fed. 113 F1
Lermontovka Rus. Fed. 90 D3
Lermontovskiy Rus. Fed. see Lermontovo
Leros i. Greece 69 L6
Le Roy U.S.A. 165 G2

Le Roy, Lac *l.* Canada **152** G2
Lerum Sweden **55** H8
Lerwick U.K. **60** [inset]
Les Amirantes *is* Seychelles *see* **Amirante Islands**
Lesbos *i.* Greece **69** K5
Les Cayes Haiti **169** J5
Leshan China **96** D2
Leshou *Hebei* China *see* **Xianxian**
Leshukonskoye Rus. Fed. **52** J2
Lesi *watercourse* Sudan **121** F4
Leskhimstroy Ukr. *see* **Syeverodonets'k**
Leskovac Serbia **69** I3
Leslie U.S.A. **164** C2
Lesneven France **66** B2
Lesnoy *Kirovskaya Oblast'* Rus. Fed. **52** L4
Lesnoy *Murmanskaya Oblast'* Rus. Fed. *see* **Umba**
Lesnoye Rus. Fed. **52** G4
Lesogorsk Rus. Fed. **90** F2
Lesopil'noye Rus. Fed. **90** D3
Lesosibirsk Rus. Fed. **76** K4
Lesotho *country* Africa **125** I5
Lesozavodsk Rus. Fed. **90** D3
L'Espérance Rock *i.* Kermadec Is **133** I5
Les Pieux France **59** F9
Les Sables-d'Olonne France **66** D3
Lesse *r.* Belgium **62** E4
Lesser Antarctica *reg.* Antarctica *see* **West Antarctica**
Lesser Antilles *is* Caribbean Sea **169** K6
Lesser Caucasus *mts* Asia **113** F2
Lesser Himalaya *mts* India/Nepal **104** D3
Lesser Khingan Mountains China *see* **Xiao Hinggan Ling**
Lesser Slave Lake Canada **150** H4
Lesser Sunda Islands Indon. **80** F8
Lesser Tunb *i.* The Gulf **110** D5
Lessines Belgium **62** D4
L'Est, Canal de France **62** G6
L'Est, Île de *i.* Canada **153** J5
L'Est, Pointe de *pt* Canada **153** J4
Lester U.S.A. **164** E5
Lestijärvi Fin. **54** N5
Lesung, Bukit *mt.* Indon. **85** F2
Les Vans France **66** G4
Lesvos *i.* Greece *see* **Lesbos**
Leszno Poland **57** P5
Letaba S. Africa **125** J2
Letchworth Garden City U.K. **59** G7
Le Télégraphe *hill* France **66** G3
Leteri India **104** D4
Letha Range *mts* Myanmar **86** A2
Lethbridge *Alta* Canada **151** H5
Lethbridge *Nfld. and Lab.* Canada **153** L4
Leti *i. Maluku* Indon. **83** C5
Leti, Kepulauan *is Maluku* Indon. **83** C5
Leticia Col. **176** E4
Leting *Hebei* China **95** I4
Letlhakeng Botswana **125** G3
Letnerechenskiy Rus. Fed. **52** G2
Letniy Navolok Rus. Fed. **52** H2
Letoda *Maluku* Indon. **83** D5
Le Touquet-Paris-Plage France **62** B4
Letpadan Myanmar **86** A3
Le Tréport France **62** B4
Letsitele S. Africa **125** J2
Letsopa S. Africa **125** G4
Letterkenny Ireland **61** E3
Letung Indon. **84** D2
Letwurung *Maluku* Indon. **83** D4
Lëtzebuerg *country* Europe *see* **Luxembourg**
Letzlingen Germany **63** L2
Léua Angola **123** C5
Leucas Greece *see* **Lefkada**
Leucate, Étang de *l.* France **66** F5
Leuchars U.K. **60** G4
Leukas Greece *see* **Lefkada**
Leung Shuen Wan Chau *i. H.K.* China *see* **High Island**
Leunovo Rus. Fed. **52** I2
Leupp U.S.A. **159** H4
Leupung Indon. **87** A6
Leura Australia **136** E4
Leusden Neth. **62** F2
Leuser, Gunung *mt.* Indon. **84** B2
Leutershausen Germany **63** K5
Leuven Belgium **62** E4
Levadeia *Sterea Ellada* Greece *see* **Livadeia**
Levan U.S.A. **159** H2
Levanger Norway **54** G5
Levante, Riviera di *coastal area* Italy **68** C2
Levanto Italy **68** C2
Levashi Rus. Fed. **113** G2
Levelland U.S.A. **161** C5
Levelock *AK* U.S.A. **148** H4
Leven *England* U.K. **58** G5
Leven *Scotland* U.K. **60** G4
Leven, Loch *l.* U.K. **60** F4
Lévêque, Cape Australia **134** C4
Leverkusen Germany **62** G3
Lévézou *mts* France **66** F4
Levice Slovakia **57** Q6
Levin N.Z. **139** E5
Lévis Canada **153** H5
Levitha *i.* Greece **69** L6
Levittown *NY* U.S.A. **165** I3
Levittown *PA* U.S.A. **165** H3
Levkás *i.* Greece *see* **Lefkada**
Levkímmi Greece *see* **Lefkimmi**
Levskigrad Bulg. *see* **Karlovo**
Lev Tolstoy Rus. Fed. **53** H5
Lévy, Cap *c.* France **59** F9
Lewa *Sumba* Indon. **83** A5
Lewe Myanmar **86** B3
Lewerberg *mt.* S. Africa **124** C5
Lewes U.K. **59** H8
Lewes U.S.A. **165** H4
Lewis *CO* U.S.A. **159** I3
Lewis *IN* U.S.A. **164** B4
Lewis *KS* U.S.A. **160** D4
Lewis, Isle of *i.* U.K. **60** C2
Lewis, Lake *salt flat* Australia **134** F5
Lewisburg *KY* U.S.A. **164** B5
Lewisburg *PA* U.S.A. **165** G3
Lewisburg *WV* U.S.A. **164** E5
Lewis Cass, Mount Canada/U.S.A. **149** O4
Lewis Hills *hill* Canada **153** K4
Lewis Pass N.Z. **139** D6
Lewis Range *hills* Australia **134** E5
Lewis Range *mts* U.S.A. **156** E2
Lewis Smith, Lake U.S.A. **163** C5
Lewiston *ID* U.S.A. **156** D3
Lewiston *ME* U.S.A. **165** J1
Lewistown *IL* U.S.A. **160** F3
Lewistown *MT* U.S.A. **156** F3
Lewistown *PA* U.S.A. **165** G3
Lewisville U.S.A. **161** E5
Lewoleba Indon. **83** B5
Lewotobi, Gunung *vol. Flores* Indon. **83** B5
Lexington *KY* U.S.A. **164** C4
Lexington *MI* U.S.A. **164** D2
Lexington *NC* U.S.A. **162** D5
Lexington *NE* U.S.A. **160** D3
Lexington *TN* U.S.A. **161** F5
Lexington *VA* U.S.A. **164** F5
Lexington Park U.S.A. **165** G4
Leyden Neth. *see* **Leiden**
Leye China **96** E3
Leyla Dāgh *mt.* Iran **110** B2
Leyte *i.* Phil. **82** D4
Leyte Gulf Phil. **82** D4
Lezha Albania *see* **Lezhë**
Lezhë Albania **69** H4
Lezhi China **96** E2
Lezhu China **97** G4
L'gov Rus. Fed. **53** G6
Lhagoi Kangri *mt. Xizang* China **99** D7
Lhari *Xizang* China *see* **Si'erdingka**
Lhari *Xizang* China **99** F7
Lharigarbo *Xizang* China **99** E6
Lhasa *Xizang* China **99** E7
Lhasa He *r.* China **99** E7
Lhasoi *Xizang* China **99** F7
Lhatog China **96** C2
Lhaviyani Atoll Maldives *see* **Faadhippolhu Atoll**
Lhazê *Xizang* China **99** D7
Lhazê *Xizang* China **99** F7
Lhazhong China **105** F3
Lhokkruet *Sumatera* Indon. **84** A1
Lhokseumawe *Sumatera* Indon. **84** B1
Lhoksukon *Sumatera* Indon. **84** B1
Lhomar *Xizang* China **99** E7
Lhorong *Xizang* China **99** F7

▶**Lhotse** *mt.* China/Nepal **105** F4
4th highest mountain in the world and in Asia.

Lhozhag *Xizang* China **99** E7
Lhuntshi Bhutan **105** G4
Lhünzê *Xizang* China *see* **Xingba**
Lhünzê *Xizang* China **99** F7
Liakoura *mt.* Greece **69** J5
Liancheng China *see* **Guangnan**
Liancourt France **62** C5
Liancourt Rocks *i.* N. Pacific Ocean **91** C5
Liandu China *see* **Lishui**
Liang *Sulawesi* Indon. **83** B3
Lianga *Mindanao* Phil. **82** D4
Lianga Bay *Mindanao* Phil. **82** D4
Liangcheng *Nei Mongol* China **95** H3
Liangdang China **96** E1
Liangdaohe *Xizang* China **99** E7
Lianghe *Chongqing* China **97** F2
Lianghe *Yunnan* China **96** C3
Lianghekou *Chongqing* China *see* **Lianghe**
Lianghekou *Gansu* China **96** E1
Lianghekou *Sichuan* China **96** D2
Liangping China **96** E2
Liangpran, Bukit *mt.* Indon. **85** F2
Liangshan China *see* **Liangping**
Liang Shan *mt.* Myanmar **86** B1
Liangshi China *see* **Shaodong**
Liangtian China **97** F4
Liang Timur, Gunung *mt.* Malaysia **84** C2
Liangzhen *Shaanxi* China **95** G4
Liangzhou *Gansu* China *see* **Wuwei**
Liangzi Hu *l.* China **97** G2
Lianhe China *see* **Qianjiang**
Lianhua China **97** G3
Lianhua Shan *mts* China **97** G4
Lianjiang *Fujian* China **97** H3
Lianjiang *Jiangxi* China *see* **Xingguo**
Liannan China **97** G3
Lianping China **97** G3
Lianran China *see* **Anning**
Lianshan *Guangdong* China **97** G3
Lianshan *Liaoning* China **95** J3
Lianshui China **97** H1
Liant, Cape *i.* Thai. *see* **Samae San, Ko**
Liantang China *see* **Nanchang**
Lianxian China *see* **Lianzhou**
Lianyin China **90** A1
Lianyungang *Jiangsu* China **95** I5
Lianzhou *Guangdong* China **97** G3
Lianzhou *Guangxi* China *see* **Hepu**
Liaocheng *Shandong* China **95** H4
Liaodong Bandao *pen.* China **95** J3
Liaodong Wan *b.* China **95** J3
Liaodun *Xinjiang* China **94** C3
Liaodunzhan *Xinjiang* China **94** C3
Liaogao China *see* **Songtao**
Liao He *r.* China **95** J3
Liaoning *prov.* China **95** J3
Liaoyang *Liaoning* China **95** J3
Liaoyuan China **90** B4
Liaozhong *Liaoning* China **95** J3
Liapades Greece **69** H5
Liard *r.* Canada **150** F2
Liard Highway Canada **150** F2
Liard Plateau *B.C./Y.T.* Canada **149** P3
Liard River *B.C.* Canada **149** P4
Liari Pak. **111** G5
Liat *i.* Indon. **84** D3
Liathach *mt.* U.K. **60** D3
Liban *country* Asia *see* **Lebanon**
Liban, Jebel *mts* Lebanon **107** C2
Libau Latvia *see* **Liepāja**
Libby U.S.A. **156** E2
Libenge Dem. Rep. Congo **122** B3
Liberal U.S.A. **161** C4
Liberdade Brazil **179** B3
Liberec Czech Rep. **57** O5
Liberia *country* Africa **120** C4
Liberia Costa Rica **166** [inset] I7
Liberty *AK* U.S.A. **149** L2
Liberty *IN* U.S.A. **164** C4
Liberty *KY* U.S.A. **164** C5
Liberty *ME* U.S.A. **165** K1
Liberty *MO* U.S.A. **160** E4
Liberty *MS* U.S.A. **161** F6
Liberty *NY* U.S.A. **165** H3
Liberty *TX* U.S.A. **161** E6
Liberty Lake U.S.A. **165** G4
Libin Belgium **62** F5
Libmanan *Luzon* Phil. **82** C3
Libni, Gebel *hill* Egypt *see* **Libnī, Jabal**
Libnī, Jabal *hill* Egypt **107** A4
Libo China **96** E3
Libobo, Tanjung *pt Halmahera* Indon. **83** D3
Libode S. Africa **125** I6
Libong, Ko *i.* Thai. **87** B6
Libourne France **66** D4
Libral Well Australia **134** D5
Libre, Sierra *mts* Mex. **166** C2

▶**Libreville** Gabon **122** A3
Capital of Gabon.

Libuganon *r. Mindanao* Phil. **82** D5

▶**Libya** *country* Africa **121** E2
4th largest country in Africa.

Libyan Desert Egypt/Libya **108** C5
Libyan Plateau Egypt **112** B5
Licantén Chile **178** B4
Licata *Sicily* Italy **68** E6
Lice Turkey **113** F3
Lich Germany **63** I4
Lichas *pen.* Greece **69** J5
Licheng *Guangxi* China *see* **Lipu**
Licheng *Jiangsu* China *see* **Jinhu**
Licheng *Shandong* China **95** I4
Licheng *Shanxi* China **95** H4
Lichfield U.K. **59** F6
Lichinga Moz. **123** D5
Lichte Germany **63** L4
Lichtenau Germany **63** I3
Lichtenburg S. Africa **125** H4
Lichtenfels Germany **63** L4
Lichtenvoorde Neth. **62** G3
Lichuan *Hubei* China **97** F2
Lichuan *Jiangxi* China **97** H3
Licun *Shandong* China *see* **Laoshan**
Lida Belarus **55** N10
Liddel Water *r.* U.K. **60** G5
Lidfontein Namibia **124** D3
Lidköping Sweden **55** H7
Lidsjöberg Sweden **54** I4
Liebenau Germany **63** J2
Liebenburg Germany **63** K2
Liebenwalde Germany **63** N2
Liebig, Mount Australia **135** E5
Liechtenstein *country* Europe **66** I3
Liège Belgium **62** F4
Liegnitz Poland *see* **Legnica**
Lieksa Fin. **54** Q5
Lielupe *r.* Latvia **55** N8
Lielvārde Latvia **55** N8
Lienart Dem. Rep. Congo **122** C3
Lienchung *i.* Taiwan *see* **Matsu Tao**
Liên Nghia Vietnam **87** E5
Liên Sơn Vietnam **87** E4
Lienz Austria **57** N7
Liepāja Latvia **55** L8
Liepaya Latvia *see* **Liepāja**
Lier Belgium **62** E3
Lierre Belgium *see* **Lier**
Lieshout Neth. **62** F3
Lietuva *country* Europe *see* **Lithuania**
Liévin France **62** C4
Lièvre, Rivière du *r.* Canada **152** G5
Liezen Austria **57** O7
Lifamatola *i.* Indon. **83** C3
Liffey *r.* Ireland **61** F4
Lifford Ireland **61** E3
Lifi Mahuida *mt.* Arg. **178** C6
Lifou *i.* New Caledonia **133** G4
Lifu *i.* New Caledonia *see* **Lifou**
Ligao *Luzon* Phil. **82** C3
Līgatne Latvia **55** N8
Lighthouse Reef Belize **167** I5
Lightning Ridge Australia **138** C2
Ligny-en-Barrois France **62** F6
Ligonha *r.* Moz. **123** D5
Ligonier U.S.A. **164** C3
Ligui Mex. **166** C3
Ligure, Mar *sea* France/Italy *see* **Ligurian Sea**
Ligurian Sea France/Italy **68** C3
Ligurienne, Mer *sea* France/Italy *see* **Ligurian Sea**
Ligurta U.S.A. **159** F5
Lihir Group *is* P.N.G. **132** F2
Lihou Reef and Cays Australia **136** E3
Liivi laht *b.* Estonia/Latvia *see* **Riga, Gulf of**
Lijiang *Yunnan* China **96** D3
Lijiang *Yunnan* China *see* **Yuanjiang**
Lijiazhai China **97** G2
Lika *reg.* Croatia **68** F2
Likasi Dem. Rep. Congo **123** C5
Likati Dem. Rep. Congo **122** C3
Likely Canada **150** F4
Likhachevo Ukr. *see* **Pervomays'kyy**
Likhachyovo Ukr. *see* **Pervomays'kyy**
Likhapani India **105** H4
Likhás *pen.* Greece *see* **Lichas**
Likhoslavl' Rus. Fed. **52** G4
Likisia East Timor *see* **Liquiçá**
Liku *Kalimantan* Indon. **85** E2
Liku *Sarawak* Malaysia **85** F1
Likupang *Sulawesi* Indon. **83** C2
Likurga Rus. Fed. **52** I4
L'Île-Rousse *Corsica* France **66** I5
Lilienthal Germany **63** I1
Liling China **97** G3
Lilla Pak. **111** I3
Lilla Edet Sweden **55** H7
Lille Belgium **62** E3
Lille France **62** D4
Lille (Lesquin) *airport* France **62** D4
Lille Bælt *sea chan.* Denmark *see* **Little Belt**
Lillebonne France **59** H9
Lillehammer Norway **55** G6
Lillers France **62** C4
Lillesand Norway **55** F7
Lillestrøm Norway **55** G7
Lilley U.S.A. **164** C2
Lillholmsjö Sweden **54** I5
Lillian, Point *hill* Australia **135** D6
Lillington U.S.A. **163** E5
Lillooet Canada **150** F5
Lillooet *r.* Canada **150** F5
Lillooet Range *mts* Canada **150** F5

▶**Lilongwe** Malawi **123** D5
Capital of Malawi.

Liloy *Mindanao* Phil. **82** C4
Lilydale Australia **137** B7

▶**Lima** Peru **176** C6
Capital of Peru. 5th most populous city in South America.

Lima *MT* U.S.A. **156** E3
Lima *NY* U.S.A. **165** G2
Lima *OH* U.S.A. **164** C3
Lima Duarte Brazil **179** C3
Lima Islands China *see* **Wanshan Qundao**
Liman Rus. Fed. **53** J7
Limar *Maluku* Indon. **83** C4
Limas Indon. **84** D2
Limassol Cyprus **107** A2
Limavady U.K. **61** F2
Limay *r.* Arg. **178** C5
Limbang *Sarawak* Malaysia **85** F1
Limbaži Latvia **55** N8
Limboto *Sulawesi* Indon. **83** B2
Limboto, Danau *l.* Indon. **83** B2
Limbung *Sulawesi* Indon. **83** A4
Limbungan *Kalimantan* Indon. **85** F3
Limbunya Australia **134** E4
Limburg an der Lahn Germany **63** I4
Lim Chu Kang *hill* Sing. **87** [inset]
Lime Acres S. Africa **124** F5
Lime Hills *AK* U.S.A. **148** I3
Limeira Brazil **179** B3
Limerick Ireland **61** D5
Limestone Point Canada **151** L4
Lime Village *AK* U.S.A. **148** I3
Limingen Norway **54** H4
Limingen *l.* Norway **54** H4
Limington U.S.A. **165** J2
Liminka Fin. **54** N4
Limmen Bight *b.* Australia **136** B2
Limnos *i.* Greece **69** K5
Limoeiro Brazil **177** K5
Limoges Canada **165** H1
Limoges France **66** E4
Limón Hond. **166** [inset] I6
Limon U.S.A. **160** C4
Limonlu Turkey **107** B1
Limonum France *see* **Poitiers**
Limousin *reg.* France **66** E4
Limoux France **66** F5
Limpopo *prov.* S. Africa **125** I2
Limpopo *r.* S. Africa/Zimbabwe **125** K3
Limpopo National Park **125** J2
Limu China **97** F3
Līnah *well* Saudi Arabia **113** F5
Linakhamari Rus. Fed. **54** Q2
Lin'an China *see* **Jianshui**
Linao Bay *Mindanao* Phil. **82** D5
Linapacan *i.* Phil. **82** B4
Linapacan Strait Phil. **82** B4
Linares Chile **178** B5
Linares Mex. **167** F3
Linares Spain **67** E4
Linau Balui *plat.* Malaysia **85** F2
Lincang China **96** D4
Lincheng *Hainan* China *see* **Lingao**
Lincheng *Hunan* China *see* **Huitong**
Linchuan China *see* **Fuzhou**
Linck Nunataks *nunataks* Antarctica **188** K1
Lincoln Arg. **178** D4
Lincoln U.K. **58** G5
Lincoln *CA* U.S.A. **158** C2
Lincoln *IL* U.S.A. **160** F3
Lincoln *MI* U.S.A. **164** D1

▶**Lincoln** *NE* U.S.A. **160** D3
Capital of Nebraska.

Lincoln City *IN* U.S.A. **164** B4
Lincoln City *OR* U.S.A. **156** B3
Lincoln Island Paracel Is **80** E3
Lincoln National Park Australia **137** A7
Lincoln Sea Canada/Greenland **189** J1
Lincolnshire Wolds *hills* U.K. **58** G5
Lincolnton U.S.A. **163** D5
Linda, Serra *hills* Brazil **179** C1
Linda Creek *watercourse* Australia **136** B4
Lindau Germany **63** M2
Lindau (Bodensee) Germany **57** L7
Lindeman Group *is* Australia **136** E4
Linden Canada **150** H5
Linden Germany **63** I4
Linden Guyana **177** G2
Linden *AL* U.S.A. **163** C5
Linden *MI* U.S.A. **164** D2
Linden *TN* U.S.A. **162** C5
Linden *TX* U.S.A. **161** E5
Linden Grove U.S.A. **160** E2
Lindern (Oldenburg) Germany **63** H2
Lindesnes *c.* Norway **55** E7
Líndhos Greece *see* **Lindos**
Lindi *r.* Dem. Rep. Congo **122** C3
Lindi Tanz. **123** D4
Lindian *Heilong.* China **95** K2
Lindisfarne *i.* U.K. *see* **Holy Island**
Lindley S. Africa **125** H4
Lindong *Nei Mongol* China **95** I3
Lindos Greece **65** J4
Lindos, Akra *pt Notio Aigaio* Greece *see* **Gkinas, Akrotirio**
Lindsay Canada **165** F1
Lindsay *CA* U.S.A. **158** D3
Lindsay *MT* U.S.A. **156** G3
Lindsborg U.S.A. **160** D4
Lindside U.S.A. **164** E5
Lindum U.K. *see* **Lincoln**
Line Islands Kiribati **187** J5
Linesville U.S.A. **164** E3
Linfen *Shanxi* China **95** G4
Lingampet India **106** C2
Linganamakki Reservoir India **106** B3
Lingao China **97** F5
Lingayen *Luzon* Phil. **82** C2
Lingayen Gulf *Luzon* Phil. **82** C2
Lingbao *Henan* China **95** G5
Lingbi China **97** H1
Lingcheng *Anhui* China *see* **Lingbi**
Lingcheng *Guangxi* China *see* **Lingshan**
Lingcheng *Hainan* China *see* **Lingshui**
Lingcheng *Shandong* China *see* **Lingxian**
Lingchuan *Guangxi* China **97** F3
Lingchuan *Shanxi* China **95** H5
Lingelethu S. Africa **125** H7
Lingen (Ems) Germany **63** H2
Lingga *i.* Indon. **84** D3
Lingga *Sarawak* Malaysia **85** E2
Lingga, Kepulauan *is* Indon. **84** D3
Linggo Co *l. Xizang* China **99** E6
Linghai *Liaoning* China **95** J3
Lingig *Mindanao* Phil. **82** D5
Lingkabau *Sabah* Malaysia **85** G1
Lingkas *Kalimantan* Indon. **85** G2
Lingle U.S.A. **156** G4
Lingomo Dem. Rep. Congo **122** C3
Lingqiu *Shanxi* China **95** H4
Lingshan China **97** F4
Lingshan Wan *b.* China **95** J5
Lingshi *Shanxi* China **95** G4
Lingshui China **97** F5
Lingshui Wan *b.* China **97** F5
Lingsugur India **106** C2
Lingtai *Gansu* China **95** F5
Linguère Senegal **120** B3
Lingui China **97** F3
Lingxi China *see* **Yongshun**
Lingxian China *see* **Yanling**
Lingxian *Shandong* China **95** I4
Lingxiang China **97** G2
Lingyang China *see* **Cili**
Lingyuan *Liaoning* China **95** I3
Lingyun China **96** E3
Lingzi Tang *reg.* Aksai Chin **99** B6
Linhai China **97** I2
Linhares Brazil **179** C2
Linhe *Nei Mongol* China **95** F3
Linhpa Myanmar **86** A1
Linjiang China **90** B4
Linjin China **97** F1
Linköping Sweden **55** I7
Linkou China **90** C3
Linli China **97** F2
Linlithgow U.K. **60** F5
Linlü Shan *mt. Henan* China **95** H4
Linmingguan *Hebei* China *see* **Yongnian**
Linn *MO* U.S.A. **160** F4
Linn *TX* U.S.A. **161** D7
Linn, Mount U.S.A. **158** B1
Linnansaaren kansallispuisto *nat. park* Fin. **54** P5
Linnhe, Loch *inlet* U.K. **60** D4
Linnich Germany **62** G4
Linosa, Isola di *i. Sicily* Italy **68** E7
Linpo Myanmar **86** B2
Linqing *Shandong* China **95** H4
Linquan China **97** G1
Linru *Henan* China *see* **Ruzhou**
Linruzhen *Henan* China **95** H5
Lins Brazil **179** A3
Linshu China **97** H1
Linshui China **96** E2
Lintah, Selat *sea chan.* Indon. **83** A5
Lintan *Gansu* China **94** E5
Lintao *Gansu* China **94** E5
Linton *IN* U.S.A. **164** B4
Linton *ND* U.S.A. **160** C2
Lintong *Shaanxi* China **95** G5
Linwu China **97** G3
Linxi *Nei Mongol* China **95** I3
Linxia *Gansu* China **94** E5
Linxia *Gansu* China **94** E5
Linxian *Henan* China *see* **Linzhou**
Linxian *Shanxi* China **95** G4
Linxiang China **97** G2
Linyi *Shandong* China **95** I4
Linyi *Shandong* China **95** I5
Linyi *Shanxi* China **95** G5
Linying China **97** G1
Linyou *Shaanxi* China **95** F5
Linz Austria **57** O6
Linze *Gansu* China **94** E4
Linzhou *Henan* China **95** H4
Lio Matoh *Sarawak* Malaysia **85** F2
Lion, Golfe du *g.* France **66** F5
Lions, Gulf of France *see* **Lion, Golfe du**
Lions Bay Canada **150** F5
Lioppa *Maluku* Indon. **83** C4
Lioua Chad **121** E3
Lipa *Luzon* Phil. **82** C3
Lipang *i.* Indon. **83** C2
Lipari *Sicily* Italy **68** F5
Lipari, Isole *is* Italy **68** F5
Lipatkain *Sumatera* Indon. **84** C2
Lipetsk Rus. Fed. **53** H5
Lipin Bor Rus. Fed. **52** H3
Liping China **97** F3
Lipova Romania **69** I1
Lipovtsy Rus. Fed. **90** C3
Lippe *r.* Germany **63** G3
Lippstadt Germany **63** I3
Lipsoí *i.* Greece *see* **Leipsoi**
Lipti Lekh *pass* Nepal **104** E3
Liptrap, Cape Australia **138** B7
Lipu China **97** F3
Liquiçá East Timor **83** C5
Liquissa East Timor *see* **Liquiçá**
Lira Uganda **122** D3
Liran *i. Maluku* Indon. **83** C4
Liranga Congo **122** B4
Lircay Peru **176** D6
Lirung *Sulawesi* Indon. **83** C2
Lisala Dem. Rep. Congo **122** C3
L'Isalo, Massif de *mts* Madag. **123** E6
L'Isalo, Parc National de *nat. park* Madag. **123** E6
Lisbellaw U.K. **61** E3
Lisboa Port. *see* **Lisbon**

▶**Lisbon** Port. **67** B4
Capital of Portugal.

Lisbon *ME* U.S.A. **165** J1
Lisbon *NH* U.S.A. **165** J1
Lisbon *OH* U.S.A. **164** E3
Lisburn U.K. **61** F3
Lisburne, Cape *AK* U.S.A. **148** F1
Liscannor Bay Ireland **61** C5
Lisdoonvarna Ireland **61** C4
Lishan *Shaanxi* China *see* **Lintong**
Lishan Taiwan **97** I3
Lishe Jiang *r.* China **96** D3
Lishi *Jiangxi* China *see* **Dingnan**
Lishi *Shanxi* China **95** G4
Lishu China **90** B4
Lishui China **97** H2
Li Shui *r.* China **97** F2
Lisichansk Ukr. *see* **Lysychans'k**
Lisieux France **66** E2
Liskeard U.K. **59** C8
Liski Rus. Fed. **53** H6
L'Isle-Adam France **62** C5
Lismore Australia **138** F2
Lismore Ireland **61** E5
Lisnarrick U.K. **61** E3
Lisnaskea U.K. **61** E3
Liss *mt.* Saudi Arabia **107** D4
Lissa Poland *see* **Leszno**
Lister, Mount Antarctica **188** H1
Listowel Canada **164** E2
Listowel Ireland **61** C5
Listvyaga, Khrebet *mts* Kazakh./Rus. Fed. **98** D2
Lit Sweden **54** I5
Litang *Guangxi* China **97** F4
Litang *Sichuan* China **96** D2
Līṭānī, Nahr el *r.* Lebanon **107** B3
Litchfield *CA* U.S.A. **158** C1
Litchfield *CT* U.S.A. **165** I3
Litchfield *IL* U.S.A. **160** F4
Litchfield *MI* U.S.A. **164** C2
Litchfield *MN* U.S.A. **160** E2
Lit-et-Mixe France **66** D4
Lithgow Australia **138** E4
Lithino, Akra *pt Kriti* Greece *see* **Lithino, Akrotirio**
Lithino, Akrotirio *pt* Greece **69** K7
Lithuania *country* Europe **55** M9
Lititz U.S.A. **165** G3
Litoměřice Czech Rep. **57** O5
Litovko Rus. Fed. **90** D2
Litovskaya S.S.R. *country* Europe *see* **Lithuania**
Little *r.* U.S.A. **161** E6
Little Abaco *i.* Bahamas **163** E7
Little Abitibi *r.* Canada **152** E4
Little Abitibi Lake Canada **152** E4
Little Andaman *i.* India **87** A5
Little Bahama Bank *sea feature* Bahamas **163** E7
Little Barrier *i.* N.Z. **139** E3
Little Belt *sea chan.* Denmark **55** F9
Little Belt Mountains U.S.A. **156** F3
Little Bitter Lake Egypt **107** A4
Little Black *r. AK* U.S.A. **149** K2
Little Cayman *i.* Cayman Is **169** H5
Little Churchill *r.* Canada **151** M3
Little Chute U.S.A. **164** A1
Little Coco Island Cocos Is **87** A4
Little Colorado *r.* U.S.A. **159** H3
Little Creek Peak U.S.A. **159** G3
Little Current Canada **152** E5
Little Current *r.* Canada **152** D4
Little Desert National Park Australia **137** C8
Little Diomede *i. AK* U.S.A. **148** E2
Little Egg Harbor *inlet* U.S.A. **165** H4
Little Exuma *i.* Bahamas **163** F8
Little Falls U.S.A. **160** E2
Littlefield *AZ* U.S.A. **159** G3
Littlefield *TX* U.S.A. **161** C5
Little Fork *r.* U.S.A. **160** E1
Little Grand Rapids Canada **151** M4
Littlehampton U.K. **59** G8
Little Inagua Island Bahamas **163** F8

Little Karas Berg *plat.* Namibia **124** D4
Little Karoo *plat.* S. Africa **124** E7
Little Lake U.S.A. **158** E4
Little Mecatina Island Canada *see* **Petit Mécatina, Île du**
Little Minch *sea chan.* U.K. **60** B3
Little Missouri *r.* U.S.A. **160** C2
Little Namaqualand *reg.* S. Africa *see* **Namaqualand**
Little Nicobar *i.* India **87** A6
Little Ouse *r.* U.K. **59** H6
Little Pamir *mts* Asia **111** I2
Little Rancheria *r.* Canada **150** D2
Little Red River Canada **150** H3

▶**Little Rock** U.S.A. **161** E5
Capital of Arkansas.

Littlerock U.S.A. **158** E4
Little Sable Point U.S.A. **164** B2
Little Salmon Lake *Y.T.* Canada **149** N3
Little Salt Lake U.S.A. **159** G3
Little Sandy Desert Australia **135** B5
Little San Salvador *i.* Bahamas **163** F7
Little Sitkin Island *AK* U.S.A. **149** [inset]
Little Smoky Canada **150** G4
Little Tibet *reg.* India/Pak. *see* **Ladakh**
Littleton U.S.A. **156** G5
Little Valley U.S.A. **165** F2
Little Wind *r.* U.S.A. **156** F4
Litunde Moz. **123** D5
Liu'an China *see* **Lu'an**
Liuba China **96** E1
Liucheng China **97** F3
Liuchiu Yü *i.* Taiwan **97** I4
Liuchong He *r.* China **96** E3
Liuchow China *see* **Liuzhou**
Liugong Dao *i.* China **95** J4
Liuhe China **90** B4
Liuheng Dao *i.* China **97** I2
Liujiachang China **97** F2
Liujiaxia *Gansu* China *see* **Yongjing**
Liujiaxia Shuiku *resr* China **96** D1
Liukesong China **90** B3
Liulin *Gansu* China *see* **Jonê**
Liulin *Shanxi* China **95** G4
Liupan Shan *mts* China **94** F5
Liupanshui China *see* **Lupanshui**
Liuquan *Jiangsu* China **95** I5
Liure Hond. **166** [inset] I6
Liushuquan *Xinjiang* China **94** C3
Liuwa Plain National Park Zambia **123** C5
Liuyang China **97** G2
Liuyuan *Gansu* China **98** F4
Liuzhan *Heilong.* China **95** K1
Liuzhangzhen *Shanxi* China *see* **Yuanqu**
Liuzhou China **97** F3
Livadeia Greece **69** J5
Līvāni Latvia **55** O8
Livengood *AK* U.S.A. **149** J2
Live Oak U.S.A. **163** D6
Liveringa Australia **132** C3
Livermore *CA* U.S.A. **158** C3
Livermore *KY* U.S.A. **164** B5
Livermore, Mount U.S.A. **161** B6
Livermore Falls U.S.A. **165** J1
Liverpool Australia **138** E4
Liverpool Canada **153** I5
Liverpool U.K. **58** E5
Liverpool Bay *N.W.T.* Canada **149** O1
Liverpool Plains Australia **138** E3
Liverpool Range *mts* Australia **138** D3
Livia U.S.A. **164** B5
Livingston Guat. **167** H6
Livingston U.K. **60** F5
Livingston *AL* U.S.A. **161** F5
Livingston *KY* U.S.A. **164** C5
Livingston *MT* U.S.A. **156** F3
Livingston *TN* U.S.A. **164** C5
Livingston *TX* U.S.A. **161** E6
Livingston, Lake U.S.A. **161** E6
Livingstone Zambia **123** C5
Livingston Island Antarctica **188** L2
Livingston Manor U.S.A. **165** H3
Livno Bos.-Herz. **68** G3
Livny Rus. Fed. **53** H5
Livojoki *r.* Fin. **54** O4
Livonia *MI* U.S.A. **164** D2
Livonia *NY* U.S.A. **165** G2
Livorno Italy **68** D3
Livramento do Brumado Brazil **179** C1
Liwā Oman **110** E5
Liwā', Wādī al *watercourse* Syria **107** C3
Liwale Tanz. **123** D4
Liwu *Hebei* China *see* **Lixian**
Lixian *Gansu* China **94** F5
Lixian *Hebei* China **95** H4
Lixian *Sichuan* China **96** D2
Lixus Morocco *see* **Larache**
Liyang China *see* **Hexian**
Liyuan China *see* **Sangzhi**
Lizard U.K. **59** B9
Lizarda Brazil **177** I5
Lizard Point U.K. **59** B9
Lizarra Spain *see* **Estella**
Lizemores U.S.A. **164** E4
Liziping China **96** D2
Lizy-sur-Ourcq France **62** D5
Ljouwert Neth. *see* **Leeuwarden**

▶**Ljubljana** Slovenia **68** F1
Capital of Slovenia.

Ljugarn Sweden **55** K8
Ljungan *r.* Sweden **54** J5
Ljungaverk Sweden **54** J5
Ljungby Sweden **55** H8
Ljusdal Sweden **55** J6
Ljusnan *r.* Sweden **55** J6
Ljusne Sweden **55** J6
Llaima, Volcán *vol.* Chile **178** B5
Llanandras U.K. *see* **Presteigne**
Llanbadarn Fawr U.K. **59** C6
Llanbedr Pont Steffan U.K. *see* **Lampeter**
Llanbister U.K. **59** D6
Llandeilo U.K. **59** D7
Llandissilio U.K. **59** C7
Llandovery U.K. **59** D7
Llandrindod Wells U.K. **59** D6
Llandudno U.K. **58** D5
Llandysul U.K. **59** C6
Llanegwad U.K. **59** C7
Llanelli U.K. **59** C7
Llanfair Caereinion U.K. **59** D6
Llanfair-ym-Muallt U.K. *see* **Builth Wells**
Llangefni U.K. **58** C5
Llangollen U.K. **59** D6
Llangurig U.K. **59** D6
Llanllyfni U.K. **59** C5
Llannerch-y-medd U.K. **58** C5
Llannor U.K. **59** C6
Llano Mex. **166** C2
Llano U.S.A. **161** D6
Llano *r.* U.S.A. **161** D6
Llano Estacado *plain* U.S.A. **161** C5
Llano Grande *Durango* Mex. **166** D4
Llanos *plain* Col./Venez. **176** E2
Llanquihue, Lago *l.* Chile **178** B6
Llanrhystud U.K. **59** C6
Llantrisant U.K. **59** D7
Llanuwchllyn U.K. **59** D6
Llanwnog U.K. **59** D6
Llanymddyfri U.K. *see* **Llandovery**
Llay U.K. **59** D5
Lleida Spain **67** G3
Llerena Spain **67** C4
Llíria Spain **67** F4
Llodio Spain **67** E2
Lloyd George, Mount Canada **150** E3
Lloyd Lake Canada **151** I3
Lloydminster Canada **151** I4
Lluchmayor Spain *see* **Llucmajor**
Llucmajor Spain **67** H4

▶**Llullaillaco, Volcán** *vol.* Chile **178** C2
Highest active volcano in the world and South America.

Lô, Sông *r.* China/Vietnam **86** D2
Loa *r.* Chile **178** B2
Loa U.S.A. **159** H2
Loagan Bunut National Park Malaysia **85** F2
Loakulu *Kalimantan* Indon. **85** G3
Loay *Bohol* Phil. **82** D4
Loban' *r.* Rus. Fed. **52** K4
Lobata *Sulawesi* Indon. **83** B3
Lobatejo *mt.* Spain **67** D5
Lobatse Botswana **125** G3
Lobaye *r.* Cent. Afr. Rep. **122** B3
Löbejün Germany **63** L3
Löbenberg *hill* Germany **63** M3
Loberia Arg. **178** E5
Lobi, Mount *vol.* Phil. **82** D4
Lobito Angola **123** B5
Lobos Arg. **178** E5
Lobos, Cabo *c.* Mex. **166** B2
Lobos, Isla *i.* Mex. **166** C3
Lobos, Isla de *i.* Mex. **167** F4
Lobos de Tierra, Isla *i.* Peru **176** B5
Loburg Germany **63** M2
Lôc Binh Vietnam **86** D2
Lochaline U.K. **60** D4
Lo Chau *H.K.* China *see* **Beaufort Island**
Loch Baghasdail U.K. *see* **Lochboisdale**
Lochboisdale U.K. **60** B3
Lochcarron U.K. **60** D3
Lochearnhead U.K. **60** E4
Lochem Neth. **62** G2
Lochern National Park Australia **136** C5
Loches France **66** E3
Loch Garman Ireland *see* **Wexford**
Lochgelly U.K. **60** F4
Lochgilphead U.K. **60** D4
Lochinver U.K. **60** D2
Loch Lomond and Trossachs National Park U.K. **60** E4
Lochmaddy U.K. **60** B3
Lochnagar *mt.* U.K. **60** F4
Loch nam Madadh U.K. *see* **Lochmaddy**
Loch Raven Reservoir U.S.A. **165** G4
Lochy, Loch *l.* U.K. **60** E4
Lock Australia **137** A7
Lockerbie U.K. **60** F5
Lockhart Australia **138** C5
Lockhart U.S.A. **161** D6
Lock Haven U.S.A. **165** G3
Löcknitz *r.* Germany **63** L1
Lockport U.S.A. **165** F2
Lockwood Hills *AK* U.S.A. **148** H2
Lôc Ninh Vietnam **87** D5
Lod Israel **107** B4
Loddon *r.* Australia **138** A5
Lodève France **66** F5
Lodeynoye Pole Rus. Fed. **52** G3
Lodge, Mount Canada/U.S.A. **149** M4
Lodhikheda India **104** D5
Lodhran Pak. **111** H4
Lodi Italy **68** C2
Lodi *CA* U.S.A. **158** C2
Lodi *OH* U.S.A. **164** D3
Lødingen Norway **54** I2
Lodja Dem. Rep. Congo **122** C4
Lodomeria Rus. Fed. *see* **Vladimir**
Lodrani India **104** B5
Lodwar Kenya **122** D3
Łódź Poland **57** Q5
Loei Thai. **86** C3
Loeriesfontein S. Africa **124** D6
Lofoten *is* Norway **54** H2
Lofusa Sudan **121** G4
Log Rus. Fed. **53** I6
Loga Niger **120** D3
Logan *IA* U.S.A. **160** E3
Logan *OH* U.S.A. **164** D4
Logan *UT* U.S.A. **156** F4
Logan *WV* U.S.A. **164** E5

▶**Logan, Mount** *Y.T.* Canada **149** L3
2nd highest mountain in North America.

Logan, Mount U.S.A. **156** C2
Logan Creek *r.* Australia **136** D4
Logan Lake Canada **150** F5
Logan Mountains *N.W.T./Y.T.* Canada **149** O3
Logansport *IN* U.S.A. **164** B3
Logansport *LA* U.S.A. **161** E6
Logatec Slovenia **68** F2
Logpung *Qinghai* China **94** E5
Logroño Spain **67** E2
Logtak Lake India **105** H4
Lohardaga India **105** F5
Loharu India **104** C3
Lohatlha S. Africa **124** F5
Lohawat India **104** C4
Lohfelden Germany **63** J3
Lohil *r.* China/India *see* **Zayü Qu**
Lohiniva Fin. **54** N3
Lohjanjärvi *l.* Fin. **55** M6
Löhne Germany **63** I2
Lohne (Oldenburg) Germany **63** I2
Lohtaja Fin. **54** M4
Loi, Nam *r.* Myanmar **86** C2
Loikaw Myanmar **86** B3
Loi Lan *mt.* Myanmar/Thai. **86** B3
Loi-lem Myanmar **86** B2
Loi Lun Myanmar **86** B2
Loimaa Fin. **55** M6
Loipyet Hills Myanmar **86** B1
Loire *r.* France **66** C3
Loi Sang *mt.* Myanmar **86** B2
L'Oise à l'Aisne, Canal de France **62** D5
Loi Song *mt.* Myanmar **86** B2
Loja Ecuador **176** C4
Loja Spain **67** D5
Lokan *r.* Malaysia **85** G1
Lokan tekojärvi *l.* Fin. **54** O3
Lokchim *r.* Rus. Fed. **52** K3
Lokeren Belgium **62** E3
Lokgwabe Botswana **124** E3
Lokichar Kenya **100** C6
Lokichokio Kenya **122** D3
Lokilalaki, Gunung *mt.* Indon. **83** B3
Løkken Denmark **55** F8
Løkken Norway **54** F5
Loknya Rus. Fed. **52** F4
Lokoja Nigeria **120** D4
Lokolama Dem. Rep. Congo **122** B4
Lokossa Benin **120** D4
Lokot' Rus. Fed. **53** G5
Lol Sudan **121** F4
Lola Guinea **120** C4
Lola, Mount U.S.A. **158** C2
Loleta U.S.A. **158** A1
Lolland *i.* Denmark **55** G9
Lollondo Tanz. **122** D4
Lolo U.S.A. **156** E3
Lolobata *Halmahera* Indon. **83** D2
Loloda *Halmahera* Indon. **83** C2
Loloda Utara, Kepulauan *is Maluku* Indon. **83** C2
Lolo Pass U.S.A. **156** E3
Lolotoi East Timor **83** C5
Lolowau Indon. **84** B2
Lolwane S. Africa **124** F4
Lom Bulg. **69** J3
Lom Norway **55** F6
Loma U.S.A. **159** I2
Lomami *r.* Dem. Rep. Congo **122** C3
Lomar Pass Afgh. **111** G3
Lomas, Bahía de *b.* Chile **178** C8
Lomas de Zamora Arg. **178** E4
Lombarda, Serra *hills* Brazil **177** H3
Lomblen *i.* Indon. **83** B5
Lombok *Lombok* Indon. **85** G5
Lombok *i.* Indon. **85** G5
Lombok, Selat *sea chan.* Indon. **85** F5

▶**Lomé** Togo **120** D4
Capital of Togo.

Lomela Dem. Rep. Congo **122** C4
Lomela *r.* Dem. Rep. Congo **121** F5
Lomira U.S.A. **164** A2
Lomme France **62** C4
Lommel Belgium **62** F3
Lomond Canada **153** K4
Lomond, Loch *l.* U.K. **60** E4
Lomonosov Rus. Fed. **55** P7
Lomonosov Ridge *sea feature* Arctic Ocean **189** B1
Lomovoye Rus. Fed. **52** I2
Lomphat Cambodia *see* **Lumphăt**
Lompobatang, Hutan Lindung *nature res. Sulawesi* Indon. **85** G4
Lompobattang, Gunung *mt.* Indon. **83** A4
Lompoc U.S.A. **158** C4
Lom Sak Thai. **86** C3
Łomża Poland **57** S4
Lơn, Hon *i.* Vietnam **87** E4
Lonar India **106** C2
Londa Bangl. **105** G5
Londa India **106** B3
Londinières France **62** B5
Londinium U.K. *see* **London**
Londoko Rus. Fed. **90** D2
London Canada **164** E2

▶**London** U.K. **59** G7
Capital of the United Kingdom and of England. 4th most populous city in Europe.

London *KY* U.S.A. **164** C5
London *OH* U.S.A. **164** D4
Londonderry U.K. **61** E3
Londonderry *OH* U.S.A. **164** D4
Londonderry *VT* U.S.A. **165** I2
Londonderry, Cape Australia **134** D3
Londrina Brazil **179** A3
Lone Pine U.S.A. **158** D3
Long Thai. **86** B3
Long *AK* U.S.A. **148** I2
Longa Angola **123** B5
Longa, Proliv *sea chan.* Rus. Fed. **77** S2
Longagung *Kalimantan* Indon. **85** F2
Long Akah *Sarawak* Malaysia **85** F2
Long'an China **96** E4
Long'anqiao *Heilong.* China **95** K2
Long Ashton U.K. **59** E7
Longbawan *Kalimantan* Indon. **85** F2
Long Bay U.S.A. **163** E5
Longbeach N.Z. **139** C7
Long Beach U.S.A. **158** D5
Longberini *Kalimantan* Indon. **85** F2
Longbia *Kalimantan* Indon. **85** G2
Longbo China *see* **Shuangpai**
Longboh *Kalimantan* Indon. **85** F2
Long Branch U.S.A. **165** I3
Longchang China **96** E2
Longcheng *Anhui* China *see* **Xiaoxian**
Longcheng *Guangdong* China *see* **Longmen**
Longcheng *Yunnan* China *see* **Chenggong**
Longchuan China *see* **Nanhua**
Longchuan Jiang *r.* China **96** C4
Long Creek *r.* Canada **151** K5
Long Creek U.S.A. **156** D3
Longde *Ningxia* China **94** F5
Long Eaton U.K. **59** F6
Longford Ireland **61** E4
Longgang *Chongqing* China *see* **Dazu**
Longgang *Guangdong* China **97** G4
Longgi *r.* Indon. **85** G2
Longhoughton U.K. **58** F3
Longhua *Hebei* China **95** I3
Longhui China **97** F3
Longhurst, Mount Antarctica **188** H1
Longibau *Kalimantan* Indon. **85** G2
Longikis *Kalimantan* Indon. **85** G3
Longiram *Kalimantan* Indon. **85** F3
Long Island Bahamas **163** F8
Long Island *N.S.* Canada **153** I5
Long Island *Nunavut* Canada **152** F3
Long Island India **87** A4
Long Island P.N.G. **81** L8
Long Island U.S.A. **165** I3
Long Island Sound *sea chan.* U.S.A. **165** I3
Longjiang *Heilong.* China **95** J2
Longjin China *see* **Qingliu**
Longju China **96** B2
Longkou *Shandong* China **95** J4
Longlac Canada **152** D4
Long Lake *l.* Canada **152** D4
Long Lake U.S.A. **165** H2
Long Lake *l.* *ME* U.S.A. **162** G2
Long Lake *l.* *MI* U.S.A. **164** D1
Long Lake *l.* *ND* U.S.A. **160** C2
Long Lake *l.* *NY* U.S.A. **165** H1
Long Lama *Sarawak* Malaysia **85** F2
Longli China **96** E3
Longlin China **96** E3
Longling China **96** C3
Longmeadow U.S.A. **165** I2
Long Melford U.K. **59** H6
Longmen *Guangdong* China **97** G4
Longmen *Heilong.* China **90** B2
Longmen Shan *hill* China **97** F1
Longmen Shan *mts* China **96** E1
Longming China **96** E4
Longmont U.S.A. **156** G4
Long Murum *Sarawak* Malaysia **85** F2
Longnan China **96** E1
Longnan China **97** G3
Longnawan *Kalimantan* Indon. **85** F2
Longpahangai *Kalimantan* Indon. **85** F2
Long Phu Vietnam **87** D5
Longping China *see* **Luodian**
Long Point *Ont.* Canada **164** E2
Long Point *Man.* Canada **151** L4
Long Point *Ont.* Canada **164** E2
Long Point N.Z. **139** B8
Long Point Bay Canada **164** E2
Long Prairie U.S.A. **160** E2
Long Preston U.K. **58** E4
Longpujungan *Kalimantan* Indon. **85** F2
Longquan *Guizhou* China *see* **Danzhai**
Longquan *Guizhou* China *see* **Fenggang**
Longquan *Hunan* China *see* **Xintian**
Longquan Xi *r.* China **97** I2
Long Range Mountains *Nfld. and Lab.* Canada **153** K4
Long Range Mountains *Nfld. and Lab.* Canada **153** K5
Longreach Australia **136** D4
Longriba China **96** D1
Longshan *Guizhou* China *see* **Longli**
Longshan *Hunan* China **97** F2
Longshan *Yunnan* China *see* **Longling**
Long Shan *mts* China **94** F5
Longsheng China **97** F3
Longshou Shan *mts* China **94** E4
Longs Peak U.S.A. **156** G4
Long Stratton U.K. **59** I6
Long Teru *Sarawak* Malaysia **85** F2
Longtom Lake Canada **150** G1
Longtou *Nei Mongol* China **95** J1
Longtown U.K. **58** E3
Longue-Pointe-de-Mingan Canada **153** I4
Longueuil Canada **152** G5
Longuyon France **62** F5
Longvale U.S.A. **158** B2
Longview *TX* U.S.A. **161** E5
Longview *WA* U.S.A. **156** C3
Longwai *Kalimantan* Indon. **85** G2
Longwangmiao China **90** D3
Longwei Co *l.* *Xizang* China **99** E6
Longxi *Gansu* China **94** F5
Longxian *Guangdong* China *see* **Wengyuan**
Longxian *Shaanxi* China **94** F5
Longxingchang *Nei Mongol* China *see* **Wuyuan**
Longxi Shan *mt.* China **97** H3
Longxu China *see* **Cangwu**
Long Xuyên Vietnam **87** D5
Longyan China **97** H3
Longyao *Hebei* China **95** H4

▶**Longyearbyen** Svalbard **76** C2
Capital of Svalbard.

Longzhen China **90** B2
Longzhou China **96** E4
Longzhouping China *see* **Changyang**
Löningen Germany **63** H2
Lonoke U.S.A. **161** F5
Lönsboda Sweden **55** I8
Lons-le-Saunier France **66** G3
Lontar *i. Maluku* Indon. **83** D4
Lonton Myanmar **86** B1
Looc Phil. **82** C3
Loochoo Islands Japan *see* **Ryukyu Islands**
Loogootee U.S.A. **164** B4
Lookout, Cape Canada **152** E3
Lookout, Cape U.S.A. **163** E5
Lookout, Point Australia **138** F1
Lookout, Point U.S.A. **164** D1
Lookout Mountain U.S.A. **159** I4
Lookout Point Australia **135** B8
Lookout Ridge *AK* U.S.A. **148** H1
Loolmalasin *vol. crater* Tanz. **122** D4
Loon Canada **152** C4
Loon *r.* Canada **150** H3
Loongana Australia **135** D7
Loon Lake Canada **151** I4
Loop Head *hd* Ireland **61** C5
Lop *Xinjiang* China **99** C5
Lopasnya Rus. Fed. *see* **Chekhov**
Lopatina, Gora *mt.* Rus. Fed. **90** F2
Lop Buri Thai. **86** C4
Lopé, Parc National de la *nat. park* Gabon **122** B4
Lopez *Luzon* Phil. **82** C3
Lopez, Cap *c.* Gabon **122** A4
Lopnur *Xinjiang* China *see* **Yuli**
Lop Nur *salt flat* China **98** E4
Lopphavet *b.* Norway **54** L1
Loptyuga Rus. Fed. **52** K3
Lora Pak. **111** G5
Lora *r.* Venez. **176** D2
Lora del Río Spain **67** D5
Lorain U.S.A. **164** D3
Loralai Pak. **111** H4
Loralai *r.* Pak. **111** H4
Loramie, Lake U.S.A. **164** C3
Lorana *Sulawesi* Indon. **83** B3
Lorca Spain **67** F5
Lorch Germany **63** H4
Lord Auckland Shoal *sea feature* Phil. **82** B4
Lordegān Iran **110** C4
Lord Howe Atoll Solomon Is *see* **Ontong Java Atoll**
Lord Howe Island Australia **133** F5
Lord Howe Rise *sea feature* S. Pacific Ocean **186** G7
Lord Loughborough Island Myanmar **87** B5
Lordsburg U.S.A. **159** I5
Lore East Timor **83** C5
Lore Lindu, Taman Nasional *nat. park* Indon. **83** B3
Lorena Brazil **179** B3
Lorengau P.N.G. **81** L7
Lorentz, Taman Nasional Indon. **81** J7
Lorenzo del Real Mex. **167** F4
Loreto Brazil **177** I5
Loreto *Baja California Sur* Mex. **166** C3
Loreto Phil. **82** D4
Lorient France **66** C3
Lorillard *r.* Canada **151** N1
Loring U.S.A. **156** G2
Lorino Rus. Fed. **148** E2
Lorn, Firth of *est.* U.K. **60** D4
Lorne Australia **136** D5
Lorne *watercourse* Australia **136** B3
Loro *r.* China **99** F7
Lorrain, Plateau France **63** G6
Lorraine Australia **136** B3
Lorraine *admin. reg.* France **62** G6
Lorraine *reg.* France **62** F5
Lorsch Germany **63** I5
Lorup Germany **63** H2
Losal India **104** C4
Los Alamos *CA* U.S.A. **158** C4
Los Alamos *NM* U.S.A. **157** G6
Los Aldamas Mex. **167** F3
Los Alerces, Parque Nacional *nat. park* Arg. **178** B6
Los Ángeles Chile **178** B5

▶**Los Angeles** U.S.A. **158** D4
3rd most populous city in North America.

Los Angeles Aqueduct *canal* U.S.A. **158** D4
Los Arabos Cuba **163** D8
Los Baños Mex. **166** D3
Los Banos U.S.A. **158** C3
Los Blancos Arg. **178** D2
Los Canarreos, Archipiélago de *is* Cuba **169** H4
Los Cerritos *watercourse* Mex. **157** F8
Los Chiles Costa Rica **166** [inset] I7
Los Chonos, Archipiélago de *is* Chile **178** A6
Los Coronados, Islas *is* Mex. **158** E5
Los Desventurados, Islas de *is* S. Pacific Ocean **187** O7
Los Estados, Isla de *i.* Arg. **178** D8
Los Gigantes, Llanos de *plain* Mex. **161** B6
Los Glaciares, Parque Nacional *nat. park* Arg. **178** B8
Losheim Germany **62** G5
Los Hoyos Mex. **166** C2
Lošinj *i.* Croatia **68** F2
Los Jardines de la Reina, Archipiélago de *is* Cuba **169** I4
Los Juríes Arg. **178** D3
Los Katios, Parque Nacional *nat. park* Col. **169** I7
Loskop Dam S. Africa **125** I3
Los Leones Mex. **166** D2
Los Lunas U.S.A. **157** G6
Los Mármoles, Parque Nacional *nat. park* Mex. **167** F4
Los Menucos Arg. **178** C6
Los Mochis Mex. **166** C3
Los Molinos U.S.A. **158** B1
Losombo Dem. Rep. Congo **122** B3
Los Palacios Cuba **163** D8
Lospatos East Timor **83** C5
Los Picos de Europa, Parque Nacional de *nat. park* Spain **67** D2
Los Remedios *r.* Mex. **161** B7
Los Reyes Mex. **166** E5
Los Roques, Islas *is* Venez. **176** E1
Losser Neth. **62** G2
Lossie *r.* U.K. **60** F3
Lossiemouth U.K. **60** F3
Lößnitz Germany **63** M4
Lost Creek *KY* U.S.A. **164** D5
Lost Creek *WV* U.S.A. **164** E4
Los Teques Venez. **176** E1
Los Testigos *is* Venez. **176** F1
Lost Hills U.S.A. **158** D4
Lost Trail Pass U.S.A. **156** E3
Lostwithiel U.K. **59** C8
Los Vidrios Mex. **159** G6
Los Vilos Chile **178** B4
Lot *r.* France **66** E4
Lota Chile **178** B5
Lotfābād Turkm. **110** E2
Lothringen *reg.* France *see* **Lorraine**
Lotikipi Plain Kenya/Sudan **122** D3
Loto Dem. Rep. Congo **122** C4
Lotsane *r.* Botswana **125** I2
Lot's Wife *i.* Japan *see* **Sōfu-gan**
Lotta *r.* Fin./Rus. Fed. **54** Q2
also known as Lutto
Lotte Germany **63** H2
Louangnamtha Laos **86** C2
Louangphabang Laos **86** C3
Loubomo Congo **123** B4
Loudéac France **66** C2
Loudi China **97** F3
L'Ouest, Pointe de *pt* Canada **153** I4
Loufan *Shanxi* China **95** G4
Louga Senegal **120** B3
Loughborough U.K. **59** F6
Lougheed Island Canada **147** H2
Loughor *r.* U.K. **59** C7
Loughrea Ireland **61** D4
Loughton U.K. **59** H7
Louhans France **66** G3
Louisa *KY* U.S.A. **164** D4
Louisa *VA* U.S.A. **165** G4
Louisbourg Canada **153** K5
Louisburg Canada *see* **Louisbourg**
Louisburgh Ireland **61** C4
Louise, Lake *AK* U.S.A. **149** K3
Louise Falls Canada **150** G2
Louis-Gentil Morocco *see* **Youssoufia**
Louisiade Archipelago *is* P.N.G. **136** F1
Louisiana U.S.A. **160** F4
Louisiana *state* U.S.A. **161** F6
Louis Trichardt S. Africa *see* **Makhado**
Louisville *GA* U.S.A. **163** D5
Louisville *IL* U.S.A. **160** F4
Louisville *KY* U.S.A. **164** C4
Louisville *MS* U.S.A. **161** F5
Louisville Ridge *sea feature* S. Pacific Ocean **186** I8
Louis-XIV, Pointe *pt* Canada **152** F3
Loukhi Rus. Fed. **54** R3
Loukoléla Congo **122** B4
Loukouo Congo **121** E5
Loulé Port. **67** B5
Loum Cameroon **120** D4
Louny Czech Rep. **57** N5
Loup *r.* U.S.A. **160** D3
Loups Marins, Lacs des *lakes* Canada **152** G2
Loups Marins, Petit lac des *l.* Canada **153** G2
Lourdes Canada **153** K4
Lourdes France **66** D5
Lourenço Marques Moz. *see* **Maputo**
Lousã Port. **67** B3
Loushan China **90** C3
Loushanguan China *see* **Tongzi**
Louth Australia **138** B3
Louth U.K. **58** G5
Loutra Aidipsou Greece **69** J5
Louvain Belgium *see* **Leuven**
Louviers France **62** B5
Louwater-Suid Namibia **124** C2
Louwsburg S. Africa **125** J4
Lövånger Sweden **54** L4
Lovat' *r.* Rus. Fed. **52** F4
Lovech Bulg. **69** K3
Lovell U.S.A. **165** J1
Lovelock U.S.A. **158** D1
Lovendegem Belgium **62** D3
Lovers' Leap *mt.* U.S.A. **164** E5
Loviisa Fin. **55** O6
Lovington U.S.A. **161** C5
Lovozero Rus. Fed. **52** G1
Lóvua Angola **123** C4
Lóvua Angola **123** C5
Low, Cape Canada **147** J3
Lowa Dem. Rep. Congo **122** C4
Lowa *r.* Dem. Rep. Congo **122** C4
Lowarai Pass Pak. **111** H3

Lowell IN U.S.A. 164 B3
Lowell MA U.S.A. 165 J2
Lower Arrow Lake Canada 150 G5
Lower California pen. Mex. see **Baja California**
Lower Glenelg National Park Australia 137 C8
Lower Granite Gorge U.S.A. 159 G4
Lower Hutt N.Z. 139 E5
Lower Laberge Y.T. Canada 149 N3
Lower Lake U.S.A. 158 B2
Lower Lough Erne l. U.K. 61 E3
Lower Post B.C. Canada 149 O4
Lower Red Lake U.S.A. 160 E2
Lower Saxony land Germany see **Niedersachsen**
Lower Tunguska r. Rus. Fed. see **Nizhnyaya Tunguska**
Lower Zambezi National Park Zambia 123 C5
Lowestoft U.K. 59 I6
Łowicz Poland 57 Q4
Low Island Kiribati see **Starbuck Island**
Lowkhi Afgh. 111 F4
Lowther Hills U.K. 60 F5
Lowville U.S.A. 165 H2
Loxicha Mex. 167 F5
Loxstedt Germany 63 I1
Loxton Australia 137 C7
Loyal, Loch l. U.K. 60 E2
Loyalsock Creek r. U.S.A. 165 G3
Loyalton U.S.A. 158 C2
Loyalty Islands New Caledonia see **Loyauté, Îles**
Loyang Henan China see **Luoyang**
Loyauté, Îles is New Caledonia 133 G4
Loyev Belarus see **Loyew**
Loyew Belarus 53 F6
Lozère, Mont mt. France 66 F4
Loznica Serbia 69 H2
Lozova Ukr. 53 H6
Lozovaya Ukr. see **Lozova**
Lua r. Dem. Rep. Congo 122 B3
Luacano Angola 123 C5
Lu'an China 97 H2
Luân Châu Vietnam 86 C2
Luanchuan China 97 F1

▶**Luanda** Angola 123 B4
Capital of Angola.

Luang i. Maluku Indon. 83 D5
Luang, Khao mt. Thai. 87 B5
Luang, Thale lag. Thai. 87 C6
Luang Namtha Laos see **Louangnamtha**
Luang Phrabang, Thiu Khao mts Laos/Thai. 86 C3
Luang Prabang Laos see **Louangphabang**
Luanhaizi Qinghai China 94 C5
Luan He r. China 95 I4
Luannan Hebei China 95 I4
Luanping Hebei China 95 I3
Luanshya Zambia 123 C5
Luanxian Hebei China 95 I4
Luanza Dem. Rep. Congo 123 C4
Luanzhou Hebei China see **Luanxian**
Luao Angola see **Luau**
Luar, Danau l. Indon. 85 F2
Luarca Spain 67 C2
Luashi Dem. Rep. Congo 123 C5
Luau Angola 123 C5
Luba Equat. Guinea 120 D4
Lubaczów Poland 53 D6
Lubalo Angola 123 B4
Lubānas ezers l. Latvia 55 O8
Lubang Phil. 82 C3
Lubang i. Phil. 82 C3
Lubang Islands Phil. 82 B3
Lubango Angola 123 B5
Lubao Dem. Rep. Congo 123 C4
Lubartów Poland 53 D6
Lübbecke Germany 63 I2
Lubbeskolk salt pan S. Africa 124 D5
Lubbock U.S.A. 161 C5
Lübbow Germany 63 L2
Lübeck Germany 57 M4
Lubeck U.S.A. 164 E4
Lubefu Dem. Rep. Congo 123 C4
Lubei Nei Mongol China 95 J2
Lüben Poland see **Lubin**
Lubersac France 66 E4
Lubin Poland 57 P5
Lublin Poland 53 D6
Lubnān country Asia see **Lebanon**
Lubnān, Jabal mts Lebanon see **Liban, Jebel**
Lubny Ukr. 53 G6
Lubok Antu Sarawak Malaysia 85 E2
Lübtheen Germany 63 L1
Lubuagan Luzon Phil. 82 C2
Lubudi Dem. Rep. Congo 123 C4
Lubukbalang Sumatera Indon. 84 D3
Lubuklinggau Sumatera Indon. 84 C3
Lubukpakam Sumatera Indon. 84 B2
Lubuksikaping Sumatera Indon. 84 C2
Lubumbashi Dem. Rep. Congo 123 C5
Lubutu Dem. Rep. Congo 122 C4
Lübz Germany 63 M1
Lucala Angola 123 B4
Lucan Canada 164 E2
Lucan Ireland 61 F4
Lucania, Mount Y.T. Canada 149 L3
Lücaoshan Qinghai China 99 F5
Lucapa Angola 123 C4
Lucas U.S.A. 164 B5
Lucasville U.S.A. 164 D4
Lucca Italy 68 D3
Luce Bay U.K. 60 E6
Lucedale U.S.A. 161 F6
Lucélia Brazil 179 A3
Lucena Luzon Phil. 82 C3
Lucena Spain 67 D5
Lučenec Slovakia 57 Q6
Lucera Italy 68 F4
Lucerne Switz. 66 I3
Lucerne Valley U.S.A. 158 E4
Lucero Mex. 166 D2
Luchegorsk Rus. Fed. 90 D3
Lucheng Guangxi China see **Luchuan**
Lucheng Shanxi China 95 H4
Lucheng Sichuan China see **Kangding**
Luchuan China 97 F4
Lüchun China 96 D4
Lucipara, Kepulauan is Maluku Indon. 83 C4
Łuck Ukr. see **Luts'k**
Luckeesarai India see **Lakhisarai**
Luckenwalde Germany 63 N2
Luckhoff S. Africa 124 G5
Lucknow Canada 164 E2
Lucknow India 104 E4
Lücongpo China 97 F2
Lucrecia, Cabo c. Cuba 169 I4
Lucusse Angola 123 C5
Lucy Creek Australia 136 B4
Lüda Liaoning China see **Dalian**
Lüdenscheid Germany 63 H3
Lüderitz Namibia 124 B4
Ludewa Tanz. 123 D5
Ludhiana India 104 C3
Ludian China 96 D3
Luding China 96 D2
Ludington U.S.A. 164 B2
Ludlow U.K. 59 E6
Ludlow U.S.A. 158 E4
Ludogorie reg. Bulg. 69 L3
Ludowici U.S.A. 163 D6
Ludvika Sweden 55 I6
Ludwigsburg Germany 63 J6
Ludwigsfelde Germany 63 N2
Ludwigshafen am Rhein Germany 63 I5
Ludwigslust Germany 63 L1
Ludza Latvia 55 O8
Luebo Dem. Rep. Congo 123 C4
Luena Angola 123 B5
Luena Flats plain Zambia 123 C5
Lüeyang China 96 E1
Lufeng Guangdong China 97 G4
Lufeng Yunnan China 96 D3
Lufkin U.S.A. 161 E6
Lufu China see **Shilin**
Luga Rus. Fed. 55 P7
Luga r. Rus. Fed. 55 P7
Lugano Switz. 66 I3
Lugansk Ukr. see **Luhans'k**
Lugau Germany 63 M4
Lügde Germany 63 J3
Lugdunum France see **Lyon**
Lugg r. U.K. 59 E6
Luggudontsen mt. Xizang China 99 E7
Lugnaquilla hill Ireland 61 F5
Lugo Italy 68 D2
Lugo Spain 67 C2
Lugoj Romania 69 I2
Lugu Xizang China 99 D6
Lugus i. Phil. 82 C5
Luhans'k Ukr. 53 H6
Luhe China 97 H1
Lu He r. China 95 G4
Luhe r. Germany 63 K1
Luḥfī, Wādī watercourse Jordan 107 C3
Luhin Sum Nei Mongol China 95 I2
Luhit r. China/India see **Zayü Qu**
Luhit r. India 105 H4
Luhua China see **Heishui**
Luhuo China 96 D2
Luhyny Ukr. 53 F6
Luia Angola 123 C4
Luiana Angola 123 C5
Luichow Peninsula China see **Leizhou Bandao**
Luik Belgium see **Liège**
Luimneach Ireland see **Limerick**
Luiro r. Fin. 54 O3
Luis Echeverría Álvarez Mex. 158 E5
Luis L. León, Presa resr Mex. 166 D2
Luis Moya Zacatecas Mex. 166 E4
Luitpold Coast Antarctica 188 A1
Luiza Dem. Rep. Congo 123 C4
Lujiang China 97 H2
Lüjing Gansu China 94 F5
Lukachek Rus. Fed. 90 D1
Lukapa Angola see **Lucapa**
Lukavac Bos.-Herz. 68 H2
Lukenga, Lac l. Dem. Rep. Congo 123 C4
Lukenie r. Dem. Rep. Congo 122 B4
Lukeville AZ U.S.A. 166 B2
Lukh r. Rus. Fed. 52 I4
Lukhovitsy Rus. Fed. 53 H5
Luk Keng H.K. China 97 [inset]
Lukou China see **Zhuzhou**
Lukovit Bulg. 69 K3
Łuków Poland 53 D6
Lukoyanov Rus. Fed. 53 J5
Lükqün Xinjiang China 98 E4
Luksagu Sulawesi Indon. 83 B3
Lukusuzi National Park Zambia 123 D5
Luleå Sweden 54 M4
Luleälven r. Sweden 54 M4
Lüleburgaz Turkey 69 L4
Luliang China 96 D3
Lüliang Shan mts China 95 G4
Lulimba Dem. Rep. Congo 123 C4
Luling U.S.A. 161 D6
Lulong Hebei China 95 I4
Lulonga r. Dem. Rep. Congo 122 B3
Luluabourg Dem. Rep. Congo see **Kananga**
Lülung Xizang China 99 D7
Lumachomo Xizang China 99 D7
Lumajang Jawa Indon. 85 F5
Lumajangdong Co salt l. China 99 C6
Lumbala Moxico Angola see **Lumbala Kaquengue**
Lumbala Moxico Angola see **Lumbala N'guimbo**
Lumbala Kaquengue Angola 123 C5
Lumbala N'guimbo Angola 123 C5
Lumberton U.S.A. 163 E5
Lumbini Nepal 105 E4
Lumbis Kalimantan Indon. 85 G1
Lumbrales Spain 67 C3
Lumezzane Italy 68 D2
Lumi P.N.G. 81 K7
Lumphăt Cambodia 87 D4
Lumpkin U.S.A. 163 C5
Lumsden Canada 151 J5
Lumsden N.Z. 139 B7
Lumut Malaysia 84 C1
Lumut, Gunung mt. Indon. 85 F3
Lumut, Tanjung pt Indon. 84 D3
Lün Mongolia 94 F2
Luna Luzon Phil. 82 C2
Luna U.S.A. 159 I5
Lunan China see **Shilin**
Lunan Bay U.K. 60 G4
Lunan Lake Canada 151 M1
Lunan Shan mts China 96 D3
Luna Pier U.S.A. 164 D3
Lund Pak. 111 H5
Lund Sweden 55 H9
Lund NV U.S.A. 159 F2
Lund UT U.S.A. 159 G2
Lundar Canada 151 L5
Lundu Sarawak Malaysia 85 E2
Lundy U.K. 59 C7
Lune r. Germany 63 I1
Lune r. U.K. 58 E4
Lüneburg Germany 63 K1
Lüneburger Heide reg. Germany 63 K1
Lünen Germany 63 H3
Lunenburg U.S.A. 165 F5
Lunéville France 66 H2
Lunga r. Zambia 123 C5
Lungdo China 105 E2
Lunggar Xizang China 99 C7
Lunggar Shan mts Xizang China 99 C7
Lung Kwu Chau i. H.K. China 97 [inset]
Lungleh India see **Lunglei**
Lunglei India 105 H5
Lungmari mt. Xizang China 99 D7
Lungmu Co salt l. China 99 C6
Lungwebungu r. Zambia 123 C5
Lunh Nepal 105 E3
Luni India 104 C4
Luni r. India 104 B4
Luni r. Pak. 111 H4
Luninets Belarus see **Luninyets**
Luning U.S.A. 158 D2
Luninyets Belarus 55 O10
Lunkaransar India 104 C3
Lunkha India 104 C3
Lünne Germany 63 H2
Lunsar Sierra Leone 120 B4
Lunsklip S. Africa 125 I3
Luntai Xinjiang China 98 D4
Lunyuk Sumbawa Indon. 85 G5
Luobei China 90 C3
Luobuzhuang Xinjiang China 98 E5
Luocheng Fujian China see **Hui'an**
Luocheng Gansu China 94 D4
Luocheng Guangxi China 97 F3
Luochuan Shaanxi China 95 G5
Luodian China 96 E3
Luoding China 97 F4
Luodou Sha i. China 97 F4
Luohe China 97 G1
Luo He r. Henan China 95 H5
Luo He r. Shaanxi China 95 G5
Luoma Hu l. China 95 I5
Luonan Shaanxi China 95 G5
Luoning Henan China 95 G5
Luoping China 96 E3
Luotian China 97 G2
Luoto Fin. see **Larsmo**
Luotuoquan Gansu China 94 D3
Luoxiao Shan mts China 97 G3
Luoxiong China see **Luoping**
Luoyang Guangdong China see **Boluo**
Luoyang Henan China 95 H5
Luoyang Zhejiang China see **Taishun**
Luoyuan China 97 H3
Luozigou China 90 C4
Lupane Zimbabwe 123 C5
Lupanshui China 96 E3
Lupar r. Malaysia 85 E2
L'Upemba, Parc National de nat. park Dem. Rep. Congo 123 C4
Lupeni Romania 69 J2
Lupilichi Moz. 123 D5
Lupon Mindanao Phil. 82 D5
Lupton U.S.A. 159 I4
Luqiao China see **Luding**
Luqu Gansu China 94 E5
Lu Qu r. China see **Tao He**
Luquan Hebei China 95 H4
Luquan China 86 C1
Luray U.S.A. 165 F4
Luremo Angola 123 B4
Lurgan U.K. 61 F3
Lúrio Moz. 123 E5
Lurio r. Moz. 123 E5

▶**Lusaka** Zambia 123 C5
Capital of Zambia.

Lusambo Dem. Rep. Congo 123 C4
Lusancay Islands and Reefs P.N.G. 132 F2
Lusangi Dem. Rep. Congo 123 C4
Luseland Canada 151 I4
Lush, Mount hill Australia 134 D4
Lushar Qinghai China see **Huangzhong**
Lushi Henan China 95 G5
Lushnja Albania see **Lushnjë**
Lushnjë Albania 69 H4
Lushui China see **Luzhang**
Lushuihe China 90 B4
Lüshun Liaoning China 95 J4
Lüsi China 97 I1
Lusi r. Indon. 85 E4
Lusikisiki S. Africa 125 I6
Lusk U.S.A. 156 G4
Luso Angola see **Luena**
Lussvale Australia 138 C1
Lut, Bahrat salt l. Asia see **Dead Sea**
Lut, Dasht-e des. Iran 110 E4
Lutai Tianjin China see **Ninghe**
Lü Tao i. Taiwan 97 I4
Lutetia France see **Paris**
Lūt-e Zangī Aḥmad des. Iran 110 E4
Luther U.S.A. 164 C1
Luther Lake Canada 164 E2
Lutherstadt Wittenberg Germany 63 M3
Luton U.K. 59 G7
Lutong Sarawak Malaysia 85 F1
Łutselk'e Canada 151 I2
Luts'k Ukr. 53 E6
Luttelgeest Neth. 62 F2
Luttenberg Neth. 62 G2
Lutto r. Fin./Rus. Fed. see **Lotta**
Lutz U.S.A. 163 D6
Lützelbach Germany 63 J5
Lützow-Holm Bay Antarctica 188 D2
Lutzputs S. Africa 124 E5
Lutzville S. Africa 124 D6
Luuk Phil. 82 C5
Luumäki Fin. 55 O6
Luuq Somalia 122 E3
Luverne AL U.S.A. 163 C6
Luverne MN U.S.A. 160 D3
Luvuei Angola 123 C5
Luvuvhu r. S. Africa 125 J2
Luwero Uganda 122 D3
Luwingu Zambia 123 C5
Luwuhuyu Kalimantan Indon. 85 E3
Luwuk Sulawesi Indon. 83 B3
Luxembourg country Europe 62 G5

▶**Luxembourg** Lux. 62 G5
Capital of Luxembourg.

Luxemburg country Europe see **Luxembourg**
Luxeuil-les-Bains France 66 H3
Luxi Hunan China see **Wuxi**
Luxi Yunnan China 96 C3
Luxi Yunnan China 96 D3
Luxolweni S. Africa 125 G6
Luxor Egypt 108 D4
Luya Shan mts China 95 G4
Luyi China 97 G1
Luyksgestel Neth. 62 F3
Luyuan Shaanxi China see **Gaoling**
Luza Rus. Fed. 52 J3
Luza r. Rus. Fed. 52 J3
Luza r. Rus. Fed. 52 M2
Luzern Switz. see **Lucerne**
Luzhai China 97 F3
Luzhang China 96 C3
Luzhi China 96 E3
Luzhou China 96 E2
Luziânia Brazil 179 B2
Luzon i. Phil. 82 C3
Luzon Strait Phil. 82 C1
Luzy France 66 F3
L'viv Ukr. 53 E6
L'vov Ukr. see **L'viv**
Lwów Ukr. see **L'viv**
Lyady Rus. Fed. 55 P7
Lyakhavichy Belarus 55 O10
Lyakhovichi Belarus see **Lyakhavichy**
Lyallpur Pak. see **Faisalabad**
Lyamtsa Rus. Fed. 52 H2
Lycia reg. Turkey 69 M6
Lyck Poland see **Ełk**
Lycksele Sweden 54 K4
Lycopolis Egypt see **Asyūṭ**
Lydd U.K. 59 H8
Lydda Israel see **Lod**
Lyddan Island Antarctica 188 B2
Lydenburg S. Africa see **Mashishing**
Lydia reg. Turkey 69 L5
Lydney U.K. 59 E7
Lyel'chytsy Belarus 53 F6
Lyell, Mount U.S.A. 158 D3
Lyell Brown, Mount hill Australia 135 E5
Lyell Island B.C. Canada 149 O5
Lyepyel' Belarus 55 P9
Lykens U.S.A. 165 G3
Lyman U.S.A. 156 F4
Lyme Bay U.K. 59 E8
Lyme Regis U.K. 59 E8
Lymington U.K. 59 F8
Lynchburg OH U.S.A. 164 D4
Lynchburg TN U.S.A. 162 C5
Lynchburg VA U.S.A. 164 F5
Lynchville U.S.A. 165 J1
Lyndhurst N.S.W. Australia 138 D4
Lyndhurst Qld Australia 136 D3
Lyndhurst S.A. Australia 137 B6
Lyndon Australia 135 A5
Lyndon r. Australia 135 A5
Lyndonville U.S.A. 165 I1
Lyne r. U.K. 58 D4
Lyness U.K. 60 F2
Lyngdal Norway 55 E7
Lynn U.K. see **King's Lynn**
Lynn IN U.S.A. 164 C3
Lynn MA U.S.A. 165 J2
Lynndyl U.S.A. 159 G2
Lynn Lake Canada 151 K3
Lynton U.K. 59 D7
Lynx Lake Canada 151 J2
Lyon France 66 G4
Lyon r. U.K. 60 F4
Lyon Mountain U.S.A. 165 I1
Lyons Australia 135 F7
Lyons France see **Lyon**
Lyons GA U.S.A. 163 D5
Lyons NY U.S.A. 165 G2
Lyons Falls U.S.A. 165 H2
Lyozna Belarus 53 F5
Lyra Reef P.N.G. 132 F2
Lys r. France 62 D4
Lysekil Sweden 55 G7
Lyskovo Rus. Fed. 52 J4
Ly Sơn, Đao i. Vietnam 86 E4
Lys'va Rus. Fed. 51 R4
Lysychans'k Ukr. 53 H6
Lysyye Gory Rus. Fed. 53 J6
Lytham St Anne's U.K. 58 D5
Lytton Canada 150 F5
Lyuban' Belarus 55 P10
Lyubertsy Rus. Fed. 51 N4
Lyubeshiv Ukr. 53 E6
Lyubim Rus. Fed. 52 I4
Lyubytino Rus. Fed. 52 G4
Lyudinovo Rus. Fed. 53 G5
Lyunda r. Rus. Fed. 52 J4
Lyzha r. Rus. Fed. 52 M2

M

Ma r. Myanmar 86 B2
Ma, Nam r. Laos 86 C2
Ma'agan Israel 107 B3
Maale Maldives see **Male**
Maale Atholhu atoll Maldives see **Male Atoll**
Maalhosmadulu Atholhu Uthuruburi atoll Maldives see **North Maalhosmadulu Atoll**
Maalhosmadulu Atoll Maldives 106 B5
Ma'ān Jordan 107 B4
Maan Turkey see **Nusratiye**
Maaninka Fin. 54 O5
Maaninkavaara Fin. 54 P3
Maanĭt Bulgan Mongolia see **Hishig-Öndör**
Maanĭt Töv Mongolia see **Bayan**
Ma'anshan China 97 H2
Maardu Estonia 55 N7
Maarianhamina Fin. see **Mariehamn**
Ma'arrat an Nu'mān Syria 107 C2
Maarssen Neth. 62 F2
Maas r. Neth. 62 E3
also known as Meuse (Belgium/France)
Maaseik Belgium 62 F3
Maasin Leyte Phil. 82 D4
Maasmechelen Belgium 62 F4
Maas-Schwalm-Nette nat. park Germany/Neth. 62 F3
Maastricht Neth. 62 F4
Maaza Plateau Egypt 112 C6
Maba Guangdong China see **Qujiang**
Maba Jiangsu China 97 H1
Maba Halmahera Indon. 83 D2
Mabai China see **Maguan**
Mabalacat Luzon Phil. 82 C3
Mabalane Moz. 125 K2
Mabana Dem. Rep. Congo 122 C3
Mabaruma Guyana 176 G2
Mabein Myanmar 86 B2
Mabel Creek Australia 135 F7
Mabel Downs Australia 134 D4
Mabella Canada 152 C4
Mabel Lake Canada 150 G5
Maberly Canada 165 G1
Mabian China 96 D2
Mabja Xizang China 99 D7
Mablethorpe U.K. 58 H5
Mabopane S. Africa 125 I3
Mabote Moz. 125 L2
Mabou Canada 153 J5
Mabrak, Jabal mt. Jordan 107 B4
Mabuasehube Game Reserve nature res. Botswana 124 F3
Mabudis i. Phil. 82 C1
Mabule Botswana 124 G3
Mabutsane Botswana 124 F3
Macá, Monte mt. Chile 178 B7
Macadam Plains Australia 135 B6
Macaé Brazil 179 C3
Macajalar Bay Mindanao Phil. 82 D4
Macajuba Brazil 179 C1
Macaloge Moz. 123 D5
MacAlpine Lake Canada 147 H3
Macamic Canada 152 F4
Macan, Kepulauan atolls Indon. see **Taka'Bonerate, Kepulauan**
Macandze Moz. 125 K2
Macao China 97 G4
Macao Special Administrative Region. China 97 G4
Macapá Brazil 177 H3
Macará Ecuador 176 C4
Macaracas Panama 166 [inset] J8
Macarani Brazil 179 C1
Macas Ecuador 176 C4
Macassar Sulawesi Indon. see **Makassar**
Macassar Strait Indon. see **Makassar, Selat**
Macau Brazil 177 K5
Macau aut. reg. China see **Macao**
Macaúba Brazil 177 H6
Macauley Island N.Z. 133 I5
Macau aut. reg. China see **Macao**
Maccaretane Moz. 125 K3
Macclenny U.S.A. 163 D6
Macclesfield U.K. 58 E5
Macdiarmid Canada 152 C4
Macdonald, Lake salt flat Australia 135 E5
Macdonald Range hills Australia 134 D3
Macdonnell Ranges mts Australia 135 E5
MacDowell Lake Canada 151 M4
Macduff U.K. 60 G3
Macedo de Cavaleiros Port. 67 C3
Macedon mt. Australia 138 B6
Macedon country Europe see **Macedonia**
Macedonia country Europe 69 I4
Macedonia reg. Greece/Macedonia 69 J4
Maceió Brazil 177 K5
Macenta Guinea 120 C4
Macerata Italy 68 E3
Macfarlane, Lake salt flat Australia 137 B7
Macgillycuddy's Reeks mts Ireland 61 C6
Machachi Ecuador 176 C4
Machaila Moz. 125 K2
Machakos Kenya 122 D4
Machala Ecuador 176 C4
Machali Qinghai China see **Madoi**
Machan Sarawak Malaysia 85 F2
Machanga Moz. 123 D6
Machar Marshes Sudan 108 D8
Machattie, Lake salt flat Australia 136 B5
Machatuine Moz. 125 K3
Machault France 62 E5
Machaze Moz. see **Chitobe**
Macheng China 97 G2
Macherla India 106 C2
Machhagan India 105 F5
Machhakund Reservoir India 106 D2
Machias ME U.S.A. 162 H2
Machias NY U.S.A. 165 F2
Machida Japan 93 F3
Machilipatnam India 106 D2
Machiques Venez. 176 D1
Māch Kowr Iran 111 F5
Machrihanish U.K. 60 D5
Machu Picchu tourist site Peru 176 D6
Machynlleth U.K. 59 D6
Macia Moz. 125 K3
Macias Nguema i. Equat. Guinea see **Bioco**
Măcin Romania 69 M2
Macintyre r. Australia 138 E2
Macintyre Brook r. Australia 138 E2
Mack U.S.A. 159 I2
Maçka Turkey 113 E2
Mackay Australia 136 E4
MacKay r. Canada 151 I3
Mackay U.S.A. 156 E3
Mackay, Lake salt flat Australia 134 E5
MacKay Lake Canada 151 I2
Mackenzie r. Australia 136 E4
Mackenzie Canada 150 F4

▶**Mackenzie** r. N.W.T. Canada 149 N1
Part of the Mackenzie-Peace-Finlay, the 2nd longest river in North America.

Mackenzie Guyana see **Linden**
Mackenzie atoll Micronesia see **Ulithi**
Mackenzie Bay Antarctica 188 E2
Mackenzie Bay N.W.T./Y.T. Canada 149 M1
Mackenzie Highway Canada 150 G2
Mackenzie King Island Canada 147 G2
Mackenzie Mountains N.W.T./Y.T. Canada 149 N2

▶**Mackenzie-Peace-Finlay** r. Canada 146 E3
2nd longest river in North America

Mackillop, Lake salt flat Australia see **Yamma Yamma, Lake**
Mackintosh Range hills Australia 135 D6
Macklin Canada 151 I4
Macksville Australia 138 F3
Maclean Australia 138 F2
Maclear S. Africa 125 I6
MacLeod Canada see **Fort Macleod**
MacLeod, Lake imp. l. Australia 135 A6
Macmillan r. Y.T. Canada 149 N3
Macmillan Pass Y.T. Canada 149 O3
Macomb U.S.A. 160 F3
Macomer Sardinia Italy 68 C4
Mâcon France 66 G3
Macon GA U.S.A. 163 D5
Macon MO U.S.A. 160 E4
Macon MS U.S.A. 161 F5
Macon OH U.S.A. 164 D4
Macondo Angola 123 C5
Macoun Lake Canada 151 K3
Macpherson Robertson Land reg. Antarctica see **Mac. Robertson Land**
Macpherson's Strait India 87 A5
Macquarie r. Australia 138 C3
Macquarie, Lake b. Australia 138 E4

▶**Macquarie Island** S. Pacific Ocean 186 G9
Part of Australia. Most southerly point of Oceania.

Macquarie Marshes Australia 138 C3
Macquarie Mountain Australia 138 D4
Macquarie Ridge sea feature S. Pacific Ocean 186 G9
MacRitchie Reservoir Sing. 87 [inset]
Mac. Robertson Land reg. Antarctica 188 E2
Macroom Ireland 61 D6
Mactún Mex. 167 H5
Macumba Australia 137 A5
Macumba watercourse Australia 137 B5
Macuspana Mex. 167 G5
Macuzari, Presa resr Mex. 166 C3
Mādabā Jordan 107 B4
Madadeni S. Africa 125 J4

Madagascar country Africa 123 E6
Largest island in Africa and 4th in the world.

Madagascar Basin sea feature Indian Ocean 185 L7
Madagascar Ridge sea feature Indian Ocean 185 K8
Madagasikara country Africa see **Madagascar**
Madakasira India 106 C3
Madalai Palau 82 [inset]
Madama Niger 121 E2
Madan Bulg. 69 K4

Madanapalle India 106 C3
Madang P.N.G. 81 L8
Madaoua Niger 120 D3
Madaripur Bangl. 105 G5
Madau Turkm. see Madaw
Madaw Turkm. 110 D2
Madawaska Canada 165 G1
Madawaska r. Canada 165 G1
Madaya Myanmar 86 B2
Madded India 106 D2

▶Madeira r. Brazil 176 G4
4th longest river in South America.

▶Madeira terr. N. Atlantic Ocean 120 B1
Autonomous Region of Portugal.

Madeira, Arquipélago da terr. N. Atlantic Ocean see Madeira
Maden Turkey 113 E3
Madeniyet Kazakh. 98 B3
Madera Mex. 166 C2
Madera U.S.A. 158 C3
Madgaon India 106 B3
Madha India 106 B2
Madhavpur India 104 B5
Madhepura India 105 F4
Madhipura India see Madhepura
Madhubani India 105 F4
Madhya Pradesh state India 104 D5
Madi, Dataran Tinggi plat. Indon. 85 F2
Madibogo S. Africa 125 G4
Madidi r. Bol. 176 E6
Madikeri India 106 B3
Madikwe Game Reserve nature res. S. Africa 125 H3
Madill U.S.A. 161 D5
Madīnat ath Thawrah Syria 107 D2
Madingo-Kayes Congo 123 B4
Madingou Congo 123 B4
Madison FL U.S.A. 163 D6
Madison GA U.S.A. 163 D5
Madison IN U.S.A. 164 C4
Madison ME U.S.A. 165 K1
Madison NE U.S.A. 160 D3
Madison SD U.S.A. 160 D2
Madison VA U.S.A. 165 F4

▶Madison WI U.S.A. 160 F3
Capital of Wisconsin.

Madison WV U.S.A. 164 E4
Madison r. U.S.A. 156 F3
Madison Heights U.S.A. 164 F5
Madisonville KY U.S.A. 164 B5
Madisonville TX U.S.A. 161 E6
Madita Sumba Indon. 83 B5
Madiun Jawa Indon. 85 E4
Madley, Mount hill Australia 135 C6
Madoc Canada 165 G1
Mado Gashi Kenya 122 D3
Madoi Qinghai China 94 D5
Madona Latvia 55 O8
Madpura India 104 B4
Madra Dağı mts Turkey 69 L5
Madrakah Saudi Arabia 108 E5
Madrakah, Ra's c. Oman 109 I6
Madras India see Chennai
Madras state India see Tamil Nadu
Madras U.S.A. 156 C3
Madre, Laguna lag. Mex. 161 D7
Madre, Laguna lag. U.S.A. 161 D7
Madre, Sierra mt. Luzon Phil. 82 C2
Madre de Chiapas, Sierra mts Mex. 167 G5
Madre de Dios r. Peru 176 E6
Madre de Dios, Isla i. Chile 178 A8
Madre del Sur, Sierra mts Mex. 168 D5
Madre Mountain U.S.A. 159 J4
Madre Occidental, Sierra mts Mex. 157 F7
Madre Oriental, Sierra mts Mex. 161 C7
Madrid Mindanao Phil. 82 D4

▶Madrid Spain 67 E3
Capital of Spain. 5th most populous city in Europe.

Madridejos Phil. 82 C4
Madridejos Spain 67 E4
Madruga Cuba 163 D8
Madu i. Indon. 83 B4
Madugula India 106 D2
Madura i. Indon. 85 F4
Madura, Selat sea chan. Indon. 85 F4
Madurai India 106 C4
Madurantakam India 106 C3
Madvār, Kūh-e mt. Iran 110 D4
Madwas India 105 E4
Maé i. Vanuatu see Émaé
Maebashi Japan 93 F2
Mae Hong Son Thai. 86 B3
Maelang Sulawesi Indon. 83 B2
Mae Ping National Park Thai. 86 B3
Mae Ramat Thai. 86 B3
Mae Sai Thai. 86 B2
Mae Sariang Thai. 86 B3
Mae Sot Thai. 86 B3
Maestre de Campo i. Phil. 82 C3
Mae Suai Thai. 86 B3
Mae Tuen Wildlife Reserve nature res. Thai. 86 B3
Maevatanana Madag. 123 E5
Maéwo i. Vanuatu 133 G3
Mae Wong National Park Thai. 86 B4
Mae Yom National Park Thai. 86 C3
Mafa Halmahera Indon. 83 C2
Mafeking Canada 151 K4
Mafeking S. Africa see Mafikeng
Mafeteng Lesotho 125 H5
Maffra Australia 138 C6
Mafia Island Tanz. 123 D4
Mafikeng S. Africa 125 G3
Mafinga Tanz. 123 D4
Mafra Brazil 179 A4
Mafraq Jordan see Al Mafraq
Magabeni S. Africa 125 J6
Magadan Rus. Fed. 77 Q4
Magadi Kenya 122 D4
Magaiza Moz. 125 K2
Magallanes Chile see Punta Arenas
Magallanes Luzon Phil. 82 C3
Magallanes, Estrecho de Chile see Magellan, Strait of
Magangue Col. 176 D2
Mağara Dağı mt. Turkey 107 A1
Magaramkent Rus. Fed. 113 H2
Magaria Niger 120 D3
Magarida P.N.G. 136 E1
Magas Rus. Fed. 113 G2
Magat r. Luzon Phil. 82 C2
Magazine Mountain hill U.S.A. 161 E5
Magdagachi Rus. Fed. 90 B1
Magdalena Bol. 176 F6
Magdalena r. Col. 176 D1
Magdalena Baja California Sur Mex. 166 B3
Magdalena Sonora Mex. 166 C2
Magdalena r. Mex. 166 C2
Magdalena, Bahía b. Mex. 166 C3
Magdalena, Isla i. Chile 178 B6
Magdalena, Isla i. Mex. 166 B3
Magdaline, Gunung mt. Malaysia 85 G1
Magdeburg Germany 63 L2
Magdelaine Cays atoll Australia 136 E3
Magelang Jawa Indon. 85 E4
Magellan, Strait of Chile 178 B8
Magellan Seamounts sea feature N. Pacific Ocean 186 F4
Magenta, Lake salt flat Australia 135 B8
Magerøya i. Norway 54 N1
Maggiorasca, Monte mt. Italy 68 C2
Maggiore, Lago Italy see Maggiore, Lake
Maggiore, Lake Italy 68 C2
Maghâgha Egypt see Maghāghah
Maghāghah Egypt 112 C5
Maghama Mauritania 120 B3
Maghâra, Gebel hill Egypt see Maghārah, Jabal
Maghārah, Jabal hill Egypt 107 A4
Maghera U.K. 61 F3
Magherafelt U.K. 61 F3
Maghnia Alg. 67 F6
Maghor Afgh. 111 F3
Maghull U.K. 58 E5
Magilligan Point U.K. 61 F2
Magiscatzín Mex. 167 F4
Magitang Qinghai China see Jainca
Magma U.S.A. 159 H5
Magna Grande mt. Sicily Italy 68 F6
Magnetic Island Australia 136 D3
Magnetic Passage Australia 136 D3
Magnetity Rus. Fed. 54 R2
Magnitogorsk Rus. Fed. 76 G4
Magnolia AR U.S.A. 161 E5
Magnolia MS U.S.A. 161 F6
Magny-en-Vexin France 62 B5
Mago Rus. Fed. 90 F1
Màgoé Moz. 123 D5
Magog Canada 165 I1
Mago National Park Eth. 122 D3
Magosa Cyprus see Famagusta
Magozal Mex. 167 F4
Magpie r. Canada 153 I4
Magpie, Lac l. Canada 153 I4
Magta' Lahjar Mauritania 120 B3
Magu Tanz. 122 D4
Magu, Khrebet mts Rus. Fed. 90 E1
Maguan China 96 E4
Magude Moz. 125 K3
Magueyal Mex. 166 E3
Magura Bangl. 105 G5
Maguse Lake Canada 151 M2
Magway Myanmar see Magwe
Magwe Myanmar 86 A2
Magyar Köztársaság country Europe see Hungary
Magyichaung Myanmar 86 A2
Mahābād Iran 110 B2
Mahabharat Range mts Nepal 105 F4
Mahaboobnagar India see Mahbubnagar
Mahad India 106 B2
Mahadeo Hills India 104 D5
Mahaffey U.S.A. 165 F3
Mahai Qinghai China 99 F5
Mahajamba r. Madag. 123 E5
Mahajan India 104 C3
Mahajanga Madag. 123 E5
Mahakam r. Indon. 85 G3
Mahalapye Botswana 125 H2
Mahale Mountains National Park Tanz. 123 C4
Mahalevona Madag. 123 E5
Mahallāt Iran 110 C3
Māhān Iran 110 E4
Mahanadi r. India 106 E1
Mahanoro Madag. 123 E5
Maha Oya Sri Lanka 106 D5
Maharajganj Bihar India 99 D8
Maharajganj Uttar Prad. India 99 C8
Maharashtra state India 106 B2
Maha Sarakham Thai. 86 C3
Mahasham, Wâdi el watercourse Egypt see Muhashsham, Wādī al
Mahaxai Laos 86 D3
Mahbubabad India 106 D2
Mahbubnagar India 106 C2
Mahd adh Dhahab Saudi Arabia 108 F5
Mahdia Alg. 67 G6
Mahdia Guyana 177 G2
Mahdia Tunisia 68 D7
Mahe Gansu China 94 F5
Mahé i. Seychelles 185 L6
Mahendragiri mt. India 106 E2
Mahenge Tanz. 123 D4
Mahesana India 104 C5
Mahgawan Madh. Prad. India 99 B8
Mahi r. India 104 C5
Mahia Peninsula N.Z. 139 F4
Mahilyow Belarus 53 F5
Mahim India 106 B2
Mah Jān Iran 110 D4
Mahlabatini S. Africa 125 J5
Mahlsdorf Germany 63 L2
Maḩmūdābād Iran 110 D2
Maḩmūd-e 'Erāqī Afgh. see Maḩmūd-e Rāqī
Maḩmūd-e Rāqī Afgh. 111 H3
Mahnomen U.S.A. 160 D2
Maho Sri Lanka 106 D5
Mahoba India 104 D4
Maholi India 104 E4
Mahón Spain 67 I4
Mahony Lake N.W.T. Canada 149 P2
Mahrauni India 104 D4
Mahrès Tunisia 68 D7
Māhrūd Iran 111 F3
Mahsana India see Mahesana
Mahuanggou Qinghai China 99 F5
Mahudaung mts Myanmar 86 A2
Māhukona U.S.A. 157 [inset]
Mahur India 106 C2
Mahuva India 104 B5
Mahwa India 104 D4
Mahya Dağı mt. Turkey 69 L4
Mai i. Maluku Indon. 83 C4
Mai i. Vanuatu see Émaé
Maiaia Moz. see Nacala
Maibang India 86 A1
Maicao Col. 176 D1
Maicasagi r. Canada 152 F4
Maicasagi, Lac l. Canada 152 F4
Maichen China 97 F4
Maidenhead U.K. 59 G7
Maidi Halmahera Indon. 83 C2
Maidstone Canada 151 I4
Maidstone U.K. 59 H7
Maiduguri Nigeria 120 E3
Maiella, Parco Nazionale della nat. park Italy 68 F3
Mai Gudo mt. Eth. 122 D3
Maigue r. Ireland 61 D5
Maihar India 104 E4
Maihara Japan 92 C3
Maiji Gansu China 94 F5
Maiji Shan mt. China 96 E1
Maikala Range hills India 104 E5
Maiko r. Dem. Rep. Congo 122 C3
Mailan Hill mt. India 105 E5
Mailani Uttar Prad. India 99 C7
Maileppe Indon. 84 B3
Mailly-le-Camp France 62 E6
Mailsi Pak. 111 I4
Main r. Germany 63 I4
Main r. U.K. 61 F3
Main Brook Canada 153 L4
Mainburg Germany 63 L6
Main Channel lake channel Canada 164 E1
Maindargi India 106 C2
Mai-Ndombe, Lac l. Dem. Rep. Congo 122 B4
Main-Donau-Kanal canal Germany 63 K5
Main Duck Island Canada 165 G2
Maine state U.S.A. 165 K1
Maine, Gulf of Canada/U.S.A. 165 K2
Mainé Hanari, Cerro hill Col. 176 D4
Maïné-Soroa Niger 120 E3
Maingkaing Myanmar 86 A1
Maingkwan Myanmar 86 B1
Maingy Island Myanmar 87 B4
Mainhardt Germany 63 J5
Mainit Mindanao Phil. 82 D4
Mainit, Lake Mindanao Phil. 82 D4
Mainkung China 96 C2
Mainland i. Scotland U.K. 60 F1
Mainland i. Scotland U.K. 60 [inset]
Mainleus Germany 63 L4
Mainling Xizang China 99 F7
Mainoru Australia 134 F3
Mainpat reg. India 105 E5
Mainpuri India 104 D4
Main Range National Park Australia 138 F2
Maintenon France 62 B6
Maintirano Madag. 123 E5
Mainz Germany 63 I4
Maio i. Cape Verde 120 [inset]
Maipú Arg. 178 E5
Maisaka Japan 92 D4
Maiskhal Island Bangl. 105 G5
Maisons-Laffitte France 62 C6
Maitengwe Botswana 123 C6
Maitland N.S.W. Australia 138 E4
Maitland S.A. Australia 137 B7
Maitland r. Australia 134 B5
Maitland, Banjaran mts Malaysia 85 G1
Maitland Point pt N.W.T. Canada 149 O1
Maitri research station Antarctica 188 C2
Maiwo i. Vanuatu see Maéwo
Maiyu, Mount hill Australia 134 E4
Maíz, Islas del is Nicaragua 166 [inset] J6
Maizar Pak. 111 H3
Maizhokunggar Xizang China 99 E7
Maizuru Japan 92 B3
Maja Jezercë mt. Albania 69 H3
Majdel Aanjar tourist site Lebanon 107 B3
Majene Sulawesi Barat Indon. 83 A3
Majestic U.S.A. 164 D5
Majḩūd well Saudi Arabia 110 C6
Majī Eth. 122 D3
Majia He r. China 95 I4
Majiang Guangxi China 97 F4
Majiang Guizhou China 96 E3
Majiawan Ningxia China see Huinong
Majiazi China 90 B2
Majōl country N. Pacific Ocean see Marshall Islands
Major, Puig mt. Spain 67 H4
Majorca i. Spain 67 H4
Mājro atoll Marshall Is see Majuro
Majuli Island India 99 F8
Majunga Madag. see Mahajanga
Majuro atoll Marshall Is 186 H5
Majwemasweu S. Africa 125 H5
Makabana Congo 122 B4
Makabe Japan 93 G2
Makale Sulawesi Indon. 83 A3
Makalehi i. Indon. 83 C2

▶Makalu mt. China/Nepal 105 F4
5th highest mountain in the world and in Asia.

Makalu Barun National Park Nepal 105 F4
Makanchi Kazakh. 102 F2
Makanpur India 104 E4
Makari Mountain National Park Tanz. see Mahale Mountains National Park
Makarov Rus. Fed. 90 F2
Makarov Basin sea feature Arctic Ocean 189 B1
Makarska Croatia 68 G3
Makarwal Pak. 111 H3
Makar'ye Rus. Fed. 52 K4
Makar'yev Rus. Fed. 52 I4
Makassar Sulawesi Indon. 83 A4
Makassar, Selat str. Indon. 83 A3
Makat Kazakh. 100 E2
Makatini Flats lowland S. Africa 125 K4
Makedonija country Europe see Macedonia
Makelulu hill Palau 82 [inset]
Makeni Sierra Leone 120 B4
Makete Tanz. 123 D4
Makeyevka Ukr. see Makiyivka
Makgadikgadi depr. Botswana 123 C6
Makgadikgadi Pans National Park Botswana 123 C6
Makhachkala Rus. Fed. 113 G2
Makhad Pak. 111 H3
Makhado S. Africa 125 I2
Makhāzin, Kathīb al des. Egypt 107 A4
Makhâzin, Kathîb el des. Egypt see Makhāzin, Kathīb al
Makhazine, Barrage El dam Morocco 67 D6
Makhmūr Iraq 113 F4
Makhtal India 106 C2
Maki Japan 93 E1
Makian vol. Maluku Indon. 83 C2
Makihata-yama mt. Japan 93 E2
Makin atoll Kiribati see Butaritari
Makindu Kenya 122 D4
Makino Japan 92 C3
Makinsk Kazakh. 101 G1
Makioka Japan 93 E3
Makira i. Solomon Is see San Cristobal
Makiyivka Ukr. 53 H6
Makkah Saudi Arabia see Mecca
Makkovik Canada 153 K3
Makkovik, Cape Canada 153 K3
Makkum Neth. 62 F1
Makó Hungary 69 I1
Makokou Gabon 122 B3
Makopong Botswana 124 F3
Makotipoko Congo 121 E5
Makran reg. Iran/Pak. 111 F5
Makrana India 104 C4
Makran Coast Range mts Pak. 111 F5
Makri India 106 D2
Maksatikha Rus. Fed. 52 G4
Maksi India 104 D5
Maksimovka Rus. Fed. 90 E3
Maksotag Iran 111 F4
Maksudangarh India 104 D5
Mākū Iran 110 B2
Makunguwiro Tanz. 123 D5
Makurdi Nigeria 120 D4
Makushin Bay AK U.S.A. 148 F5
Makwassie S. Africa 125 G4
Mal India 105 G4
Mala Ireland see Mallow
Mala i. Solomon Is see Malaita
Malå Sweden 54 K4
Mala, Punta pt Panama 166 [inset] J8
Malabang Mindanao Phil. 82 D5
Malabar Coast India 106 B3

▶Malabo Equat. Guinea 120 D4
Capital of Equatorial Guinea.

Malabuñgan Palawan Phil. 82 B4
Malaca Spain see Málaga
Malacca Malaysia see Melaka
Malacca state Malaysia see Melaka
Malacca, Strait of Indon./Malaysia 84 B1
Malad City U.S.A. 156 E4
Maladzyechna Belarus 55 O9
Malá Fatra nat. park Slovakia 57 Q6
Málaga Spain 67 D5
Malaga U.S.A. 161 B5
Malagasy Republic country Africa see Madagascar
Malahar Sumba Indon. 83 B5
Málainn Mhóir Ireland 61 D3
Malaita i. Solomon Is 133 G2
Malaka mt. Sumbawa Indon. 85 G5
Malakal Palau 82 [inset]
Malakal Sudan 108 D8
Malakal Passage Palau 82 [inset]
Malakanagiri India see Malkangiri
Malakheti Nepal 104 E3
Malakula i. Vanuatu 133 G3
Malamala Sulawesi Indon. 83 B3
Malampaya Sound sea chan. Palawan Phil. 82 B4
Malan, Ras pt Pak. 111 G5
Malang Jawa Indon. 85 F4
Malangana Nepal see Malangwa
Malange Angola see Malanje
Malangwa Nepal 105 F4
Malanje Angola 123 B4
Malappuram India 106 C4
Mälaren l. Sweden 55 J7
Malargüe Arg. 178 C5
Malartic Canada 152 F4
Malasoro, Teluk b. Indon. 83 A4
Malaspina Glacier AK U.S.A. 149 L4
Malatayur, Tanjung pt Indon. 85 F3
Malatya Turkey 112 E3
Malavalli India 106 C3
Malawali i. Malaysia 85 G1
Malawi country Africa 123 D5
Malawi, Lake Africa see Nyasa, Lake
Malawi National Park Zambia see Nyika National Park
Malaya pen. Malaysia see Malaysia, Semenanjung
Malaya Pera Rus. Fed. 52 L2
Malaya Vishera Rus. Fed. 52 G4
Malaybalay Mindanao Phil. 82 D4
Malāyer Iran 110 C3
Malay Peninsula Asia 87 B4
Malay Reef Australia 136 E3
Malay Sary Kazakh. 98 B3
Malaysia country Asia 84 F2
Malaysia, Semenanjung pen. Malaysia see Peninsular Malaysia
Malazgirt Turkey 113 F3
Malbon Australia 136 C4
Malbork Poland 57 Q3
Malborn Germany 62 G5
Malchin Germany 57 N4
Malcolm Australia 135 C7
Malcolm, Point Australia 135 C8
Malcolm Island Myanmar 87 B5
Maldegem Belgium 62 D3
Malden U.S.A. 161 F4
Malden Island Kiribati 187 J6
Maldives country Indian Ocean 103 D10
Maldon Australia 138 B6
Maldon U.K. 59 H7
Maldonado Uruguay 178 F4
Maldonado, Punta pt Mex. 167 F5

▶Male Maldives 103 D11
Capital of the Maldives.

Maleas, Akra pt Peloponnisos Greece see Maleas, Akrotirio
Maleas, Akrotirio pt Greece 69 J6
Male Atoll Maldives 103 D11
Malebogo S. Africa 125 G5
Malegaon Mahar. India 106 B1
Malegaon Mahar. India 106 C2
Malé Karpaty hills Slovakia 57 P6
Malek Sīāh, Kūh-e mt. Afgh. 111 F4
Malele Dem. Rep. Congo 123 B4
Maler Kotla India 104 C3
Maleševske Planine mts Bulg./Macedonia 69 J4
Maleta Rus. Fed. 95 G1
Malgobek Rus. Fed. 113 G2
Malgomaj l. Sweden 54 J4
Malḩa, Naqb mt. Egypt see Māliḩah, Naqb
Malhada Brazil 179 C1
Malheur r. U.S.A. 156 D3
Malheur Lake U.S.A. 156 D4
Mali country Africa 120 C3
Mali Dem. Rep. Congo 122 C4
Mali Guinea 120 B3
Maliana East Timor 83 C5
Malianjing Gansu China 94 C3
Malianjing Gansu China 94 E4
Maligay Bay Mindanao Phil. 82 C5
Malihabad Uttar Prad. India 99 C8
Māliḩah, Naqb mt. Egypt 107 A5
Malik Naro mt. Pak. 111 F4
Maliku Sulawesi Indon. 83 B3
Mali Kyun i. Myanmar 87 B4
Malili Sulawesi Indon. 83 B3
Malin Ukr. see Malyn
Malindi Kenya 122 E4
Malines Belgium see Mechelen
Maling Gansu China 95 F4
Malin Head hd Ireland 61 E2
Malin More Ireland see Málainn Mhóir
Malino Sulawesi Indon. 83 B2
Malino, Gunung mt. Indon. 83 B2
Malipo China 96 E4
Mali Raginac mt. Croatia 68 F2
Malita Mindanao Phil. 82 D5
Malitbog Leyte Phil. 82 D4
Malka r. Rus. Fed. 113 G2
Malkangiri India 106 D2
Malkapur India 106 B2
Malkara Turkey 69 L4
Mal'kavichy Belarus 55 O10
Malkhanskiy Khrebet mts Rus. Fed. 95 G1
Malko Tŭrnovo Bulg. 69 L4
Mallacoota Australia 138 D6
Mallacoota Inlet b. Australia 138 D6
Mallaig U.K. 60 D4
Mallani reg. India 111 H5
Mallawī Egypt 112 C6
Mallee Cliffs National Park Australia 137 C7
Mallery Lake Canada 151 L1
Mallét Brazil 179 A4
Mallorca i. Spain see Majorca
Mallow Ireland 61 D5
Mallowa Well Australia 134 D5
Mallwyd U.K. 59 D6
Malm Norway 54 G4
Malmberget Sweden 54 L3
Malmédy Belgium 62 G4
Malmesbury S. Africa 124 D7
Malmesbury U.K. 59 E7
Malmö Sweden 55 H9
Malmyzh Rus. Fed. 52 K4
Malo i. Indon. 83 C1
Maloca Brazil 177 G3
Malolos Luzon Phil. 82 C3
Malone U.S.A. 165 H1
Malonje mt. Tanz. 123 D4
Maloshuyka Rus. Fed. 52 H3
Malosmadulu Atoll Maldives see Maalhosmadulu Atoll
Måløy Norway 54 D6
Maloyaroslavets Rus. Fed. 53 H5
Malozemel'skaya Tundra lowland Rus. Fed. 52 K2
Malpaso Mex. 166 E4
Malpelo, Isla de i. N. Pacific Ocean 169 H8
Malprabha r. India 106 C2
Malta country Europe 68 F7
Malta Latvia 55 O8
Malta ID U.S.A. 156 E4
Malta MT U.S.A. 156 G2
Malta Channel Italy/Malta 68 F6
Maltahöhe Namibia 124 C3
Maltby U.K. 58 F5
Maltby le Marsh U.K. 58 H5
Malton U.K. 58 G4
Maluku is Indon. see Moluccas
Maluku prov. Indon. 83 D3
Maluku, Laut sea Indon. 83 C3
Maluku Utara prov. Indon. 83 C3
Ma'lūlā, Jabal mts Syria 107 C3
Malung Sweden 55 H6
Maluti Mountains Lesotho 125 I5
Malu'u Solomon Is 133 G2
Malvan India 106 B2
Malvasia Greece see Monemvasia
Malvern U.K. see Great Malvern
Malvern U.S.A. 161 E5
Malvérnia Moz. see Chicualacuala
Malvinas, Islas terr. S. Atlantic Ocean see Falkland Islands
Malyn Ukr. 53 F6
Malyy Anyuy r. Rus. Fed. 77 R3
Malyye Derbety Rus. Fed. 53 J7
Malyy Kavkaz mts Asia see Lesser Caucasus
Malyy Kunaley Rus. Fed. 95 F1
Malyy Lyakhovskiy, Ostrov i. Rus. Fed. 77 P2
Malyy Uzen' r. Kazakh./Rus. Fed. 53 K6
Mamadysh Rus. Fed. 52 K5
Mamafubedu S. Africa 125 I4
Mamasa Sulawesi Barat Indon. 83 A3
Mamatān Nāvar l. Afgh. 111 G4
Mamba Xizang China 99 F7
Mamba Japan see Manba
Mambahenauhan i. Phil. 82 B5
Mambai Brazil 179 B1
Mambajao Phil. 82 D4
Mambasa Dem. Rep. Congo 122 C3
Mambi Sulawesi Barat Indon. 83 A3
Mamburao Mindoro Phil. 82 C3
Mamelodi S. Africa 125 I3
Mamfe Cameroon 120 D4
Mamit India 105 H5
Mammoth U.S.A. 159 H5
Mammoth Cave National Park U.S.A. 164 B5
Mammoth Reservoir U.S.A. 158 D3
Mamonas Brazil 179 C1
Mamoré r. Bol./Brazil 176 E6
Mamou Guinea 120 B3
Mampikony Madag. 123 E5
Mampong Ghana 120 C4
Mamuju Sulawesi Barat Indon. 83 A3
Mamuno Botswana 124 E2
Man Côte d'Ivoire 120 C4
Man India 106 B2
Man r. India 106 B2
Man U.S.A. 164 E5
Man, Isle of terr. Irish Sea 58 C4
Manacapuru Brazil 176 F4
Manacor Spain 67 H4
Manado Sulawesi Indon. 83 C2
Manadotua i. Indon. 83 C2

▶Managua Nicaragua 166 [inset] I6
Capital of Nicaragua.

Managua, Lago de l. Nicaragua 166 [inset] I6
Manakara Madag. 123 E6
Manakau mt. N.Z. 139 D6
Manākhah Yemen 108 F6

▶Manama Bahrain 110 C5
Capital of Bahrain.

Manamadurai India 106 C4
Mana Maroka National Park S. Africa 125 H5
Manamelkudi India 106 C4
Manam Island P.N.G. 81 L7
Mananara Avaratra Madag. 123 E5
Manangoora Australia 136 B3
Mananjary Madag. 123 E6
Manantali, Lac de l. Mali 120 B3
Manantenina Madag. 123 E6
Mana Pass China/India 99 B7
Mana Pools National Park Zimbabwe 123 C5

▶Manapouri, Lake N.Z. 139 A7
Deepest lake in Oceania.

Manas Xinjiang China 98 D3
Manasa India 104 C4
Manas He r. China 98 D3
Manas Hu l. China 98 D3
Manāşīr reg. U.A.E. 110 D6

▶Manaslu mt. Nepal 105 F3
8th highest mountain in the world and in Asia.

Manassas U.S.A. 165 G4

Manastir Macedonia *see* **Bitola**
Manas Wildlife Sanctuary *nature res.* Bhutan **105** G4
Manatang Indon. **83** C5
Manatsuru Japan **93** F3
Manatuto East Timor **83** C5
Man-aung Myanmar **86** A3
Man-aung Kyun Myanmar **86** A3
Manaus Brazil **176** F4
Manavgat Turkey **112** C3
Manay *Mindanao* Phil. **82** D5
Manazuru-misaki *pt* Japan **93** F3
Manba Japan **93** E2
Manbazar India **105** F5
Manbij Syria **107** C1
Manby U.K. **58** H5
Mancelona U.S.A. **164** C1
Manchar India **106** B2
Manchester U.K. **58** E5
Manchester *CT* U.S.A. **165** I3
Manchester *IA* U.S.A. **160** F3
Manchester *KY* U.S.A. **164** D5
Manchester *MD* U.S.A. **165** G4
Manchester *MI* U.S.A. **164** C2
Manchester *NH* U.S.A. **165** J2
Manchester *OH* U.S.A. **164** D4
Manchester *TN* U.S.A. **162** C5
Manchester *VT* U.S.A. **165** I2
Mancılık Turkey **112** E3
Mand Pak. **111** F5
Mand, Rūd-e *r.* Iran **110** C4
Manda Tanz. **123** D4
Manda, Jebel *mt.* Sudan **121** F4
Manda, Parc National de *nat. park* Chad **121** E4
Mandabe Madag. **123** E6
Mandah *Sumatera* Indon. **84** C3
Mandah Mongolia **95** G2
Mandai Sing. **87** [inset]
Mandal *Bulgan* Mongolia *see* **Orhon**
Mandal *Töv* Mongolia *see* **Batsümber**
Mandal Norway **55** E7

▶**Mandala, Puncak** *mt.* Indon. **81** K7
3rd highest mountain in Oceania.

Mandalay Myanmar **86** B2
Mandale Myanmar *see* **Mandalay**
Mandalgovĭ Mongolia **94** F2
Mandalī Iraq **113** G4
Mandal-Ovoo Mongolia **94** F2
Mandalt *Nei Mongol* China **95** H3
Mandalt Sum *Nei Mongol* China **95** H2
Mandan U.S.A. **160** C2
Mandaon *Masbate* Phil. **82** C3
Mandar, Teluk *b.* Indon. **83** A3
Mandas *Sardinia* Italy **68** C5
Mandasa India **106** E2
Mandasor India *see* **Mandsaur**
Mandav Hills India **104** B5
Mandel Afgh. **111** F3
Mandera Kenya **122** E3
Manderfield U.S.A. **159** G2
Manderscheid Germany **62** G4
Mandeville Jamaica **169** I5
Mandeville N.Z. **139** B7
Mandha India **104** B4
Mandhoúdhíon Greece *see* **Mantoudi**
Mandi India **104** D3
Mandiana Guinea **120** C3
Mandi Angin, Gunung *mt.* Malaysia **84** C1
Mandi Burewala Pak. **111** I4
Mandié Moz. **123** D5
Mandini S. Africa **125** J5
Mandioli *i. Maluku* Indon. **83** C3
Mandira Dam India **105** F5
Mandla India **104** E5
Mandleshwar India **104** C5
Mandor *Kalimantan* Indon. **85** E2
Mandor, Cagar Alam *nature res.* Indon. **85** E2
Mandrael India **104** D4
Mandritsara Madag. **123** E5
Mandsaur India **104** C4
Mandul *i.* Indon. **85** G2
Mandurah Australia **135** A8
Manduria Italy **68** G4
Mandvi India **104** B5
Mandya India **106** C3
Manerbio Italy **68** D2
Manevychi Ukr. **53** E6
Manfalūţ Egypt **112** C6
Manfredonia Italy **68** F4
Manfredonia, Golfo di *g.* Italy **68** G4
Manga Brazil **179** C1
Manga Burkina **120** C3
Mangabeiras, Serra das *hills* Brazil **177** I6
Mangai Dem. Rep. Congo **122** B4
Mangaia *i.* Cook Is **187** J7
Mangakino N.Z. **139** E4
Mangalagiri India **106** D2
Mangaldai India **86** A1
Mangaldoi India *see* **Mangaldai**
Mangalia Romania **69** M3
Mangalmé Chad **121** E3
Mangalore India **106** B3
Mangaon India **106** B2
Mangareva Islands Fr. Polynesia *see* **Gambier, Îles**
Mangaung *Free State* S. Africa **125** H5
Mangaung *Free State* S. Africa *see* **Bloemfontein**
Mangawan India **105** E4
Ma'ngê *Gansu* China *see* **Luqu**
Mangea *i.* Cook Is *see* **Mangaia**
Manggar Indon. **85** E3
Mangghyshlaq Kazakh. *see* **Mangystau**
Mangghystaū Kazakh. *see* **Mangystau**
Mangghystaū *admin. div.* Kazakh. *see* **Mangistauskaya Oblast'**
Mangghyt Uzbek. *see* **Mang'it**
Manghit Uzbek. *see* **Mang'it**
Mangin Range *mts* Myanmar *see* **Mingin Range**
Mangistau Kazakh. *see* **Mangystau**
Mangistauskaya Oblast' *admin. div.* Kazakh. **113** I2
Mang'it Uzbek. **102** B3
Mangkalihat, Tanjung *pt* Indon. **85** G2
Mangkutup *r.* Indon. **85** F3
Mangla Bangl. *see* **Mongla**
Mangla Pak. **111** I3
Mangnai *Qinghai* China **99** E5
Mangnai Zhen *Qinghai* China **99** E5
Mangochi Malawi **123** D5
Mangoky *r.* Madag. **123** E6
Mangole *i.* Indon. **83** C3
Mangole, Selat *sea chan.* Indon. **83** C3
Mangoli India **106** B2
Mangotsfield U.K. **59** E7
Mangqystaū Shyghanaghy *b.* Kazakh. *see* **Mangyshlakskiy Zaliv**
Mangra *Qinghai* China *see* **Guinan**
Mangrol India **104** B5
Mangrul India **106** C1
Mangshi China *see* **Luxi**
Mangualde Port. **67** C3
Manguéni, Plateau du Niger **120** E2
Mangui China **90** A2
Mangula Zimbabwe *see* **Mhangura**
Mangulile Hond. **166** [inset] I6
Mangum U.S.A. **161** D5
Mangupung *i.* Indon. **83** C1
Mangut Rus. Fed. **95** H1
Mangyshlak Kazakh. *see* **Mangystau**
Mangyshlak, Poluostrov *pen.* Kazakh. **113** H1
Mangyshlak Oblast *admin. div.* Kazakh. *see* **Mangistauskaya Oblast'**
Mangyshlakskaya Oblast' *admin. div.* Kazakh. *see* **Mangistauskaya Oblast'**
Mangyshlakskiy Zaliv *b.* Kazakh. **113** H1
Mangystau Kazakh. **113** H2
Manhã Brazil **179** B1
Manhan Mongolia **94** C2
Manhan *Hövsgöl* Mongolia *see* **Alag-Erdene**
Manhattan U.S.A. **160** D4
Manhica Moz. **125** K3
Manhoca Moz. **125** K4
Manhuaçu Brazil **179** C3
Manhuaçu *r.* Brazil **179** C2
Mani *Xizang* China **99** D6
Mania *r.* Madag. **123** E5
Maniago Italy **68** E1
Manicouagan Canada **153** H4
Manicouagan *r.* Canada **153** H4
Manicouagan, Réservoir *resr* Canada **153** H4
Manic Trois, Réservoir *resr* Canada **153** H4
Manīfah Saudi Arabia **110** C5
Maniganggo China **96** C2
Manigotagan Canada **151** L5
Manihiki *atoll* Cook Is **186** J6
Maniitsoq Greenland **147** M3
Manikchhari Bangl. **105** H5
Manikgarh India *see* **Rajura**

▶**Manila** *Luzon* Phil. **82** C3
Capital of the Philippines.

Manila U.S.A. **156** F4
Manila Bay *Luzon* Phil. **82** C3
Manildra Australia **138** D4
Manilla Australia **138** E3
Manimbaya, Tanjung *pt* Indon. **83** A3
Maningrida Australia **134** F3
Maninjau, Danau *l.* Indon. **84** C3
Manipa *i. Maluku* Indon. **83** C3
Manipa, Selat *sea chan. Maluku* Indon. **83** C3
Manipur India *see* **Imphal**
Manipur *state* India **105** H4
Manisa Turkey **69** L5
Manismata *Kalimantan* Indon. **85** E3
Manistee U.S.A. **164** B1
Manistee *r.* U.S.A. **164** B1
Manistique U.S.A. **162** C2
Manitoba *prov.* Canada **151** L4
Manitoba, Lake Canada **151** L5
Manito Lake Canada **151** I4
Manitou Canada **151** L5
Manitou, Lake U.S.A. **164** B3
Manitou Beach U.S.A. **165** G2
Manitou Falls Canada **151** M5
Manitou Islands U.S.A. **164** B1
Manitoulin Island Canada **152** E5
Manitouwadge Canada **152** D4
Manitowoc U.S.A. **164** B1
Maniwaki Canada **152** G5
Manizales Col. **176** C2
Manja Madag. **123** E6
Manjarabad India **106** B3
Manjeri India **106** C4
Manjhand Pak. **111** H5
Manjhi India **105** F4
Manjra *r.* India **106** C2
Man Kabat Myanmar **86** B1
Mankaiana Swaziland *see* **Mankayane**
Mankato *KS* U.S.A. **160** D4
Mankato *MN* U.S.A. **160** E2
Mankayane Swaziland **125** J4
Mankera Pak. **111** H4
Mankono Côte d'Ivoire **120** C4
Mankota Canada **151** J5
Manlay Mongolia **94** F2
Manley Hot Springs *AK* U.S.A. **149** J2
Manmad India **106** B1
Mann *r.* Australia **134** F3
Mann, Mount Australia **135** E6
Manna *Sumatera* Indon. **84** C4
Man Na Myanmar **86** B2
Mannahill Australia **137** B7
Mannar Sri Lanka **106** C4
Mannar, Gulf of India/Sri Lanka **106** C4
Manneru *r.* India **106** D3
Mannessier, Lac *l.* Canada **153** H3
Mannheim Germany **63** I5
Mannicolo Islands Solomon Is *see* **Vanikoro Islands**
Manning *r.* Australia **138** F3
Manning Canada **150** G3
Manning U.S.A. **163** D5
Mannington U.S.A. **164** E4
Manningtree U.K. **59** I7
Mann Ranges *mts* Australia **135** E6
Mannsville *KY* U.S.A. **164** C5
Mannsville *NY* U.S.A. **165** G2
Mannu, Capo *c. Sardinia* Italy **68** C4
Mannville Canada **151** I4
Man-of-War Rocks *is* U.S.A. *see* **Gardner Pinnacles**
Manoharpur *Rajasthan* India **99** B8
Manohar Thana India **104** D4
Manokotak *AK* U.S.A. **148** H4
Manokwari Indon. **81** I7
Manoron Myanmar **87** B5
Manosque France **66** G5
Manouane *r.* Canada **153** H4
Manouane, Lac *l.* Canada **153** H4
Man Pan Myanmar **86** B2
Manp'o N. Korea **90** B4
Manra *i.* Kiribati **133** I2
Manresa Spain **67** G3
Mansa *Gujarat* India **104** C5
Mansa *Punjab* India **104** C3
Mansa Zambia **123** C5
Mansa Konko Gambia **120** B3
Mansalean *Sulawesi* Indon. **83** B3
Man Sam Myanmar **86** B2
Mansehra Pak. **109** L3
Mansel Island Canada **147** K3
Mansfield Australia **138** C6
Mansfield U.K. **59** F5
Mansfield *LA* U.S.A. **161** E5
Mansfield *OH* U.S.A. **164** D3
Mansfield *PA* U.S.A. **165** G3
Mansfield, Mount U.S.A. **165** I1
Man Si Myanmar **86** B1
Mansi Myanmar **86** A1
Manso *r.* Brazil *see* **Mortes, Rio das**
Mansuela *Seram* Indon. **83** D3
Manta Ecuador **176** B4
Mantalingajan, Mount *Palawan* Phil. **82** B4
Mantarara *Maluku* Indon. **83** C3
Mantaro *r.* Peru **176** D6
Manteca U.S.A. **158** C3
Mantehage *i.* Indon. **83** C2
Mantena Brazil **179** C2
Manteo U.S.A. **162** F5
Mantes-la-Jolie France **62** B6
Mantiqueira, Serra da *mts* Brazil **179** B3
Manto Hond. **166** [inset] I6
Manton U.S.A. **164** C1
Mantoudi Greece **69** J5
Mantova Italy *see* **Mantua**
Mäntsälä Fin. **55** N6
Mänttä Fin. **54** N5
Mantua Cuba **163** C8
Mantua Italy **68** D2
Mantuan Downs Australia **136** D5
Manturovo Rus. Fed. **52** J4
Mäntyharju Fin. **55** O6
Mäntyjärvi Fin. **54** O3
Manú Peru **176** D6
Manu, Parque Nacional *nat. park* Peru **176** D6
Manuae *atoll* Fr. Polynesia **187** J7
Manu'a Islands American Samoa **133** I3
Manuel Ribas Brazil **179** A4
Manuel Vitorino Brazil **179** C1
Manuelzinho Brazil **177** H5
Manui *i.* Indon. **83** B3
Manuk *i. Maluku* Indon. **83** D4
Manukan *Mindanao* Phil. **82** C4
Manukau N.Z. **139** E3
Manukau Harbour N.Z. **139** E3
Manuk Manka *i.* Phil. **82** B5
Manunda *watercourse* Australia **137** B7
Manusela, Taman Nasional *nat. park Seram* Indon. **83** D3
Manus Island P.N.G. **81** L7
Manvi India **106** C3
Many U.S.A. **161** E6
Manyana Botswana **125** G3
Manyas Turkey **69** L4
Manyas Gölü *l.* Turkey *see* **Kuş Gölü**
Manych-Gudilo, Ozero *l.* Rus. Fed. **53** I7
Many Island Lake Canada **151** I5
Manyoni Tanz. **123** D4
Manzai Pak. **111** H3
Manzanares Spain **67** E4
Manzanillo Cuba **169** I4
Manzanillo Mex. **168** D5
Manzanillo, Punta *pt* Panama **166** [inset] K7
Manzhouli *Nei Mongol* China **95** I1
Manzini Swaziland **125** J4
Mao Chad **121** E3
Maó Spain *see* **Mahón**
Maoba *Guizhou* China **96** E3
Maoba *Hubei* China **97** F2
Maocifan China **97** G2
Mao'ergai China **96** D1
Maojiachuan *Gansu* China **94** F4
Maojing *Gansu* China **94** F4
Maoke, Pegunungan *mts* Indon. **81** J7
Maokeng S. Africa **125** H4
Maokui Shan *mt.* China **90** A4
Maolin *Jilin* China **95** J3
Maomao Shan *mt. Gansu* China **94** E4
Maoming China **97** F4
Maoniupo *Xizang* China **99** D6
Maoniushan *Qinghai* China **94** D4
Ma On Shan *hill* H.K. China **97** [inset]
Maopi T'ou *c.* Taiwan **97** I4
Maopora *i. Maluku* Indon. **83** C4
Maotou Shan *mt.* China **96** D3
Mapai Moz. **125** J2
Mapam Yumco *l.* China **99** C7
Mapane *Sulawesi* Indon. **83** B3
Mapanza Zambia **123** C5
Mapastepec Mex. **167** G6
Maphodi S. Africa **125** G6
Mapimí Mex. **166** E3
Mapinhane Moz. **125** L2
Mapiri Bol. **176** E7
Maple *r. MI* U.S.A. **164** C2
Maple *r. ND* U.S.A. **160** D2
Maple Creek Canada **151** I5
Maple Heights U.S.A. **164** E3
Maple Peak U.S.A. **159** I5
Mapmakers Seamounts *sea feature* N. Pacific Ocean **186** H4
Mapoon Australia **136** C1
Mapor *i.* Indon. **84** D2
Mapoteng Lesotho **125** H5
Maprik P.N.G. **81** K7
Mapuera *r.* Brazil **177** G4
Mapulanguene Moz. **125** K3
Mapungubwe National Park S. Africa **125** I2

▶**Maputo** Moz. **125** K3
Capital of Mozambique.

Maputo *prov.* Moz. **125** K3
Maputo *r.* Moz./S. Africa **125** K4
Maputo, Baía de *b.* Moz. **125** K4
Maputsoe Lesotho **125** H5
Maqanshy Kazakh. *see* **Makanchi**
Maqar an Na'am *well* Iraq **113** F5
Maqat Kazakh. *see* **Makat**
Maqên *Qinghai* China **94** E5
Maqên *Xizang* China **99** E7
Maqên Kangri *mt. Qinghai* China **94** D5
Maqiao *Xinjiang* China **98** D3
Maqnā Saudi Arabia **112** D5
Maqteïr *reg.* Mauritania **120** B2
Maqu China **96** D1
Ma Qu *r.* China *see* **Huang He**
Maquan He *r. Xizang* China **99** D7
Maqueda Channel Phil. **82** C3
Maquela do Zombo Angola **123** B4
Maquinchao Arg. **178** C6
Mar *r.* Pak. **111** G5
Mar, Serra do *mts Rio de Janeiro/São Paulo* Brazil **179** B3
Mar, Serra do *mts Rio Grande do Sul/Santa Catarina* Brazil **179** A5
Mara *r.* Canada **151** I1
Mara India **105** E5
Mara S. Africa **125** I2
Maraã Brazil **176** E4
Marabá Brazil **177** I5
Marabahan *Kalimantan* Indon. **85** F3
Marabatua *i.* Indon. **85** F4
Maraboon, Lake *resr* Australia **136** E4
Maracá, Ilha de *i.* Brazil **177** H3
Maracaibo Venez. **176** D1
Maracaibo, Lago de Venez. *see* **Maracaibo, Lake**
Maracaibo, Lake Venez. **176** D2
Maracaju Brazil **178** E2
Maracaju, Serra de *hills* Brazil **178** E2
Maracanda Uzbek. *see* **Samarqand**
Maracás Brazil **179** C1
Maracás, Chapada de *hills* Brazil **179** C1
Maracay Venez. **176** E1
Marādah Libya **121** E2
Maradi Niger **120** D3
Marāgheh Iran **110** B2
Maragondon *Luzon* Phil. **82** C3
Marahuaca, Cerro *mt.* Venez. **176** E3
Marajó, Baía de *est.* Brazil **177** I4
Marajó, Ilha de *i.* Brazil **177** H4
Marakele National Park S. Africa **125** H3
Maralal Kenya **122** D3
Maralbashi *Xinjiang* China *see* **Bachu**
Maralinga Australia **135** E7
Maralwexi *Xinjiang* China *see* **Bachu**
Maramasike *i.* Solomon Is **133** G2
Maramba Zambia *see* **Livingstone**
Marambio *research station* Antarctica **188** A2
Marampit *i.* Indon. **83** C1
Maran Malaysia **84** C2
Maran *mt.* Pak. **111** G4
Marana U.S.A. **159** H5
Marand Iran **110** B2
Marandellas Zimbabwe *see* **Marondera**
Marang Malaysia **84** C1
Marang Myanmar **87** B5
Maranhão *r.* Brazil **179** A1
Maranoa *r.* Australia **138** D1
Marañón *r.* Peru **176** D4
Marão Moz. **125** L3
Marão *mt.* Port. **67** C3
Marapi, Gunung *vol. Sumatera* Indon. **84** C3
Mara Rosa Brazil **179** A1
Maraş Turkey *see* **Kahramanmaraş**
Marasende *i.* Indon. **85** G4
Marathon Canada **152** D4
Marathon *FL* U.S.A. **163** D7
Marathon *NY* U.S.A. **165** G2
Marathon *TX* U.S.A. **161** C6
Maratua *i.* Indon. **85** G2
Maraú Brazil **179** D1
Marau *Kalimantan* Indon. **85** E3
Maravillas Creek *watercourse* U.S.A. **161** C6
Marawi *Mindanao* Phil. **82** D4
Märäzä Azer. **113** H2
Marbella Spain **67** D5
Marble Bar Australia **134** B5
Marble Canyon U.S.A. **159** H3
Marble Canyon *gorge* U.S.A. **159** H3
Marble Hall S. Africa **125** I3
Marble Hill U.S.A. **161** F4
Marble Island Canada **151** N2
Marbul Pass India **104** C2
Marburg S. Africa **125** J6
Marburg Slovenia *see* **Maribor**
Marburg an der Lahn Germany **63** I4
Marca, Ponta do *pt* Angola **123** B5
Marcala Hond. **166** [inset] H6
Marcali Hungary **68** G1
Marcelino Ramos Brazil **179** A4
March U.K. **59** H6
Marche *reg.* France **66** E3
Marche-en-Famenne Belgium **62** F4
Marchena Spain **67** D5
Marchinbar Island Australia **136** B1
Mar Chiquita, Laguna *l.* Arg. **178** D4
Marchtrenk Austria **57** O6
Marco U.S.A. **163** D7
Marcoing France **62** D4
Marcona Peru **176** C7
Marcopeet Islands Canada **152** F2
Marcus Baker, Mount *AK* U.S.A. **149** K3
Marcy, Mount U.S.A. **165** I1
Mardan Pak. **111** I3
Mar del Plata Arg. **178** E5
Mardīan Afgh. **111** G2
Mardin Turkey **113** F3
Mardzad Mongolia *see* **Hayrhandulaan**
Maré *i.* New Caledonia **133** G4
Maree, Loch *l.* U.K. **60** D3
Mareh Iran **111** E5
Marengo *IA* U.S.A. **160** E3
Marengo *IN* U.S.A. **164** B4
Marevo Rus. Fed. **52** G4
Marfa U.S.A. **161** B6
Margai Caka *l. Xizang* China **99** D6
Margam Ri *mts Xizang* China **99** D6
Marganets Ukr. *see* **Marhanets'**
Margao India *see* **Madgaon**
Margaret *r.* Australia **134** D4
Margaret *watercourse* Australia **137** B6
Margaret, Mount *hill* Australia **134** B5
Margaret Lake *Alta* Canada **150** H3
Margaret Lake *N.W.T.* Canada **150** G1
Margaret River Australia **135** A8
Margaretville U.S.A. **165** H2
Margarita, Isla de *i.* Venez. **176** F1
Margaritovo Rus. Fed. **90** D4
Margate U.K. **59** I7
Margherita, Lake Eth. *see* **Abaya, Lake**

▶**Margherita Peak** Dem. Rep. Congo/Uganda **122** C3
3rd highest mountain in Africa.

Marghilon Uzbek. *see* **Marg'ilon**
Marg'ilon Uzbek. **102** D3
Mārgo, Dasht-i *des.* Afgh. *see* **Mārgow, Dasht-e**
Margog Caka *l. Xizang* China **99** D6
Margosatubig *Mindanao* Phil. **82** C5
Mārgow, Dasht-e *des.* Afgh. **111** F4
Margraten Neth. **62** F4
Marguerite Canada **150** F4
Marguerite, Pic *mt.* Dem. Rep. Congo/Uganda *see* **Margherita Peak**
Marguerite Bay Antarctica **188** L2
Margyang *Xizang* China **99** E7
Marhaj Khalīl Iraq **113** G4
Marhanets' Ukr. **53** G7
Marhoum Alg. **64** D5
Mari Myanmar **86** B1
Maria *atoll* Fr. Polynesia **187** J7
María Cleofas, Isla *i.* Mex. **166** D4
María Elena Chile **178** C2
Maria Island Australia **136** A2
Maria Island Myanmar **87** B5
Maria Island National Park Australia **137** [inset]
Mariala National Park Australia **137** D5
María Madre, Isla *i.* Mex. **166** D4
María Magdelena, Isla *i.* Mex. **166** D4
Mariana Brazil **179** C3
Marianao Cuba **163** D8
Mariana Ridge *sea feature* N. Pacific Ocean **186** F4

▶**Mariana Trench** *sea feature* N. Pacific Ocean **186** F5
Deepest trench in the world.

Mariani India **105** H4
Mariánica, Cordillera *mts* Spain *see* **Morena, Sierra**
Marian Lake Canada **150** G2
Marianna *AR* U.S.A. **161** F5
Marianna *FL* U.S.A. **163** C6
Mariano Machado Angola *see* **Ganda**
Mariánské Lázně Czech Rep. **63** M5
Marias *r.* U.S.A. **156** F3
Marías, Islas *is* Mex. **168** C4

▶**Mariato, Punta** *pt* Panama **166** [inset] J8
Most southerly point of North America.

Maria van Diemen, Cape N.Z. **139** D2
Ma'rib Yemen **108** G6
Maribor Slovenia **68** F1
Marica *r.* Bulg. *see* **Maritsa**
Maricopa *AZ* U.S.A. **159** G5
Maricopa *CA* U.S.A. **158** D4
Maricopa Mountains U.S.A. **159** G5
Maridi Sudan **121** F4
Marie Byrd Land *reg.* Antarctica **188** J1
Marie-Galante *i.* Guadeloupe **169** L5
Mariehamn Fin. **55** K6
Mariembero *r.* Brazil **179** A1
Marienbad Czech Rep. *see* **Mariánské Lázně**
Marienberg Germany **63** N4
Marienburg Poland *see* **Malbork**
Marienhafe Germany **63** H1
Mariental Namibia **124** C3
Marienwerder Poland *see* **Kwidzyn**
Mariestad Sweden **55** H7
Mariet *r.* Canada **152** F2
Marietta *GA* U.S.A. **163** C5
Marietta *OH* U.S.A. **164** E4
Marietta *OK* U.S.A. **161** D5
Marignane France **66** G5
Marii, Mys *pt* Rus. Fed. **78** G2
Mariinsk Rus. Fed. **76** J4
Mariinskiy Posad Rus. Fed. **52** J4
Marijampolė Lith. **55** M9
Marília Brazil **179** A3
Marillana Australia **134** B5
Marimba Angola **123** B4
Marimun *Kalimantan* Indon. **85** F3
Marín Mex. **167** E3
Marín Spain **67** B2
Marina U.S.A. **158** C3
Marina di Gioiosa Ionica Italy **68** G5
Mar'ina Gorka Belarus *see* **Mar"ina Horka**
Mar"ina Horka Belarus **55** P10
Marinduque *i.* Phil. **82** C3
Marinette U.S.A. **164** B1
Maringá Brazil **179** A3
Maringa *r.* Dem. Rep. Congo **122** B3
Maringo U.S.A. **164** D3
Marinha Grande Port. **67** B4
Marion *AL* U.S.A. **163** C5
Marion *AR* U.S.A. **161** F5
Marion *IL* U.S.A. **160** F4
Marion *IN* U.S.A. **164** C3
Marion *KS* U.S.A. **160** D4
Marion *MI* U.S.A. **164** C1
Marion *NY* U.S.A. **165** G2
Marion *OH* U.S.A. **164** D3
Marion *SC* U.S.A. **163** E5
Marion *VA* U.S.A. **164** E5
Marion, Lake U.S.A. **163** D5
Marion Reef Australia **136** F3
Maripa Venez. **176** E2
Mariposa U.S.A. **158** D3
Marisa *Sulawesi* Indon. **83** B2
Mariscala Mex. **167** F5
Mariscal José Félix Estigarribia Para. **178** D2
Maritime Alps *mts* France/Italy **66** H4
Maritime Kray *admin. div.* Rus. Fed. *see* **Primorskiy Kray**
Maritimes, Alpes *mts* France/Italy *see* **Maritime Alps**
Maritsa *r.* Bulg. **69** L4
also known as Euros (Greece/Turkey), Marica (Bulgaria), Meriç (Turkey)
Marittime, Alpi *mts* France/Italy *see* **Maritime Alps**
Mariupol' Ukr. **53** H7
Mariusa *nat. park* Venez. **176** F2
Marīvān Iran **110** B3
Marjan Afgh. *see* **Wazi Khwa**
Marjayoûn Lebanon **107** B3
Marka Somalia **122** E3
Markakol', Ozero *l.* Kazakh. **98** D2
Markala Mali **120** C3
Markam China **96** C2
Markaryd Sweden **55** H8
Markdale Canada **164** E1
Marken S. Africa **125** I2
Markermeer *l.* Neth. **62** F2
Market Deeping U.K. **59** G6
Market Drayton U.K. **59** E6
Market Harborough U.K. **59** G6
Markethill U.K. **61** F3
Market Weighton U.K. **58** G5
Markha *r.* Rus. Fed. **77** M3
Markham Canada **164** F2
Markit *Xinjiang* China **98** B5
Markkleeberg Germany **63** M3
Markleeville U.S.A. **158** D2
Marklohe Germany **63** J2
Markog Qu *r.* China **96** D1
Markounda Cent. Afr. Rep. **122** B3
Markovo Rus. Fed. **189** C2
Markranstädt Germany **63** M3
Marks Rus. Fed. **53** J6
Marks U.S.A. **161** F5
Marksville U.S.A. **161** E6
Marktheidenfeld Germany **63** J5
Marktredwitz Germany **63** M4
Marl Germany **62** H3
Marla Australia **135** F6
Marlborough Downs *hills* U.K. **59** F7
Marle France **62** D5
Marlette U.S.A. **164** D2
Marlin U.S.A. **161** D6
Marlinton U.S.A. **164** E4
Marlo Australia **138** D6
Marmagao India **106** B3
Marmande France **66** E4
Marmara, Sea of *g.* Turkey **69** M4
Marmara Denizi *g.* Turkey *see* **Marmara, Sea of**
Marmara Gölü *l.* Turkey **69** M5
Marmarica *reg.* Libya **112** B5
Marmaris Turkey **69** M6
Marmarth U.S.A. **160** C2
Marmê *Xizang* China **99** C6
Marmet U.S.A. **164** E4
Marmion, Lake *salt l.* Australia **135** C7
Marmion Lake Canada **151** N5
Marmolada *mt.* Italy **68** D1
Marmot Bay *AK* U.S.A. **148** I4
Marmot Island *AK* U.S.A. **149** J4
Marne *r.* France **62** C6
Marne-la-Vallée France **62** C6
Marnitz Germany **63** L1
Maroantsetra Madag. **123** E5
Maroc *country* Africa *see* **Morocco**
Marol Pak. **104** D2
Marol Pak. **111** I4
Maroldsweisach Germany **63** K4
Maromokotro *mt.* Madag. **123** E5
Marondera Zimbabwe **123** D5
Maroochydore Australia **138** F1
Maroonah Australia **135** A5
Maroon Peak U.S.A. **156** G5
Maros *Sulawesi* Indon. **83** A4
Maros *r.* Indon. **83** A4

Marosvásárhely Romania see Târgu Mureș
Maroua Cameroon 121 E3
Marovoay Madag. 123 E5
Marowali Sulawesi Indon. 83 B3
Marqādah Syria 113 F4
Mar Qu r. China see Markog Qu
Marquard S. Africa 125 H5
Marquesas Islands Fr. Polynesia 187 K6
Marquesas Keys is U.S.A. 163 D7
Marquês de Valença Brazil 179 C3
Marquette U.S.A. 162 C2
Marquez U.S.A. 161 D6
Marquion France 62 D4
Marquise France 62 B4
Marquises, Îles is Fr. Polynesia see Marquesas Islands
Marra Australia 138 A3
Marra r. Australia 138 C3
Marra, Jebel mt. Sudan 121 F3
Marra, Jebel Sudan 121 F3
Marracuene Moz. 125 K3
Marrakech Morocco 64 C5
Marrakesh Morocco see Marrakech
Marrangua, Lagoa l. Moz. 125 L3
Marrar Australia 138 C5
Marrawah Australia 137 [inset]
Marree Australia 137 B6
Marrowbone U.S.A. 164 C5
Marruecos country Africa see Morocco
Marrupa Moz. 123 D5
Marryat Australia 135 F6
Marsá al 'Alam Egypt 108 D4
Marsa 'Alam Egypt see Marsá al 'Alam
Marsa al Burayqah Libya 121 E1
Marsabit Kenya 122 D3
Marsala Sicily Italy 68 E6
Marsá Maṭrūḥ Egypt 112 B5
Marsberg Germany 63 I3
Marsciano Italy 68 E3
Marsden Australia 138 C4
Marsden Canada 151 I4
Marsdiep sea chan. Neth. 62 E2
Marseille France 66 G5
Marseilles France see Marseille
Marsfjället mt. Sweden 54 I4
Marshall watercourse Australia 136 B4
Marshall AK U.S.A. 148 G3
Marshall AR U.S.A. 161 E5
Marshall IL U.S.A. 164 B4
Marshall MI U.S.A. 164 C2
Marshall MN U.S.A. 160 E2
Marshall MO U.S.A. 160 E4
Marshall TX U.S.A. 161 E5
Marshall Islands country N. Pacific Ocean 186 H5
Marshalltown U.S.A. 160 E3
Marshfield MO U.S.A. 161 E4
Marshfield WI U.S.A. 160 F2
Marsh Harbour Bahamas 163 E7
Mars Hill U.S.A. 162 H2
Marsh Island U.S.A. 161 F6
Marsh Lake Y.T. Canada 149 N3
Marsh Lake l. Y.T. Canada 149 N3
Marsh Peak U.S.A. 159 I1
Marsh Point Canada 151 M3
Marsing U.S.A. 156 D4
Märsta Sweden 55 J7
Marsyaty Rus. Fed. 51 S3
Martaban, Gulf of g. Myanmar see Mottama, Gulf of
Martanai Besar i. Malaysia 85 G1
Martapura Kalimantan Indon. 85 F3
Martapura Sumatera Indon. 84 D4
Marten River Canada 152 F5
Marte R. Gómez, Presa resr Mex. 167 F3
Martha's Vineyard i. U.S.A. 165 J3
Martigny Switz. 66 H3
Martim Vaz, Ilhas is S. Atlantic Ocean see Martin Vas, Ilhas
Martin r. Canada 150 F2
Martin Slovakia 57 Q6
Martin MI U.S.A. 164 C2
Martin SD U.S.A. 160 C3
Martínez Mex. 167 F4
Martinez Lake U.S.A. 159 F5
Martinho Campos Brazil 179 B2
▶Martinique terr. West Indies 169 L6
French Overseas Department.
Martinique Passage Dominica/Martinique 169 L5
Martin Peninsula Antarctica 188 K2
Martin Point pt AK U.S.A. 149 L1
Martinsburg U.S.A. 165 G4
Martins Ferry U.S.A. 164 E3
Martinsville IL U.S.A. 164 B4
Martinsville IN U.S.A. 164 B4
Martinsville VA U.S.A. 164 F5
▶Martin Vas, Ilhas is S. Atlantic Ocean 184 G7
Most easterly point of South America.
Martin Vaz Islands S. Atlantic Ocean see Martin Vas, Ilhas
Martök Kazakh. see Martuk
Marton N.Z. 139 E5
Martorell Spain 67 G3
Martos Spain 67 E5
Martuk Kazakh. 100 E1
Martuni Armenia 113 G2
Maru Gansu China 94 E5
Marudi Sarawak Malaysia 85 F1
Marudu, Teluk b. Malaysia 85 G1
Maruf Afgh. 111 G4
Maruim Brazil 177 K6
Marukhis Ugheltekhili pass Georgia/Rus. Fed. 113 F2
Maruko Japan 93 E2
Marulan Australia 138 D5
Maruoka Japan 92 C2
Marusthali reg. India 111 H5
Maruyama Japan 93 F3
Maruyama-gawa r. Japan 92 A3
Marvast Iran 110 D4
Marv Dasht Iran 110 D4
Marvejols France 66 F4
Marvine, Mount U.S.A. 159 H2
Marwayne Canada 151 I4
Mary r. Australia 134 E3
Mary Turkm. 111 F2
Maryborough Qld Australia 137 F5
Maryborough Vic. Australia 138 A6
Marydale S. Africa 124 F5
Mary Frances Lake Canada 151 J2
Mary Lake Canada 151 K2
Maryland state U.S.A. 165 G4
Maryport U.K. 58 D4
Mary's Harbour Canada 153 L3
Marys Igloo AK U.S.A. 148 F2
Marysvale U.S.A. 159 G2
Marysville CA U.S.A. 158 C2
Marysville KS U.S.A. 160 D4
Marysville OH U.S.A. 164 D3
Maryvale N.T. Australia 135 F6
Maryvale Qld Australia 136 D3
Maryville MO U.S.A. 160 E3
Maryville TN U.S.A. 162 D5
Marzagão Brazil 179 A2
Marzahna Germany 63 M2
Masachapa Nicaragua 166 [inset] I7
Masada tourist site Israel 107 B4
Masagua Guat. 167 H6
Masāhūn, Kūh-e mt. Iran 110 D4
Masai Steppe plain Tanz. 123 D4
Masaka Uganda 122 D4
Masakhane S. Africa 125 H6
Masalembu Besar i. Indon. 85 F4
Masalembu Kecil i. Indon. 85 F4
Masallı Azer. 113 H3
Masamba Sulawesi Indon. 83 B3
Masamba mt. Indon. 83 B3
Masan S. Korea 91 C6
Masapun Maluku Indon. 83 C4
Masasi Tanz. 123 D5
Masavi Bol. 176 F7
Masaya Nicaragua 166 [inset] I7
Masaya, Volcán vol. Nicaragua 166 [inset] I7
Masbate Masbate Phil. 82 C3
Masbate i. Phil. 82 C3
Mascara Alg. 67 G6
Mascarene Basin sea feature Indian Ocean 185 L7
Mascarene Plain sea feature Indian Ocean 185 L7
Mascarene Ridge sea feature Indian Ocean 185 L6
Mascota Mex. 166 D4
Mascote Brazil 179 D1
Masein Myanmar 86 A2
Ma Sekatok b. Indon. 85 G2
Masela Maluku Indon. 83 D5
Masela i. Maluku Indon. 83 D5
Masepe i. Indon. 83 B3
▶Maseru Lesotho 125 H5
Capital of Lesotho.
Mashai Lesotho 125 I5
Mashan China 97 F4
Masherbrum mt. Pak. 104 D2
Mashhad Iran 111 E2
Mashiko Japan 93 G2
Mashishing S. Africa 125 J3
Mashket r. Pak. 111 F5
Mashki Chah Pak. 111 F4
Masi Norway 54 M2
Masiáca Mex. 166 C3
Masibambane S. Africa 125 H6
Masīlah, Wādī al watercourse Yemen 108 H6
Masilo S. Africa 125 H5
Masi-Manimba Dem. Rep. Congo 123 B4
Masimbu Sulawesi Barat Indon. 83 A3
Masindi Uganda 122 D3
Masinloc Luzon Phil. 82 B3
Masinyusane S. Africa 124 F6
Masira, Gulf of Oman see Maşīrah, Khalīj
Maşīrah, Jazīrat i. Oman 109 I5
Maşīrah, Khalīj b. Oman 109 I6
Masira Island Oman see Maşīrah, Jazīrat
Masiwang r. Seram Indon. 83 D3
Masjed Soleymān Iran 110 C4
Mask, Lough l. Ireland 61 C4
Maskūtān Iran 111 E5
Maslovo Rus. Fed. 51 S3
Masoala, Tanjona c. Madag. 123 F5
Masohi Seram Indon. 83 D3
Mason MI U.S.A. 164 C2
Mason OH U.S.A. 164 C4
Mason TX U.S.A. 161 D6
Mason, Lake salt flat Australia 135 B6
Mason Bay N.Z. 139 A8
Mason City U.S.A. 160 E3
Masoni i. Indon. 83 C3
Masontown U.S.A. 164 F4
Masqaṭ Oman see Muscat
Masqaṭ reg. Oman see Muscat
'Masrūg well Oman 110 D6
Massa Italy 68 D2
Massachusetts state U.S.A. 165 I2
Massachusetts Bay U.S.A. 165 J2
Massadona U.S.A. 159 I1
Massafra Italy 68 G4
Massakory Chad 121 E3
Massa Marittimo Italy 68 D3
Massangena Moz. 123 D6
Massango Angola 123 B4
Massawa Eritrea 108 E6
Massawippi, Lac l. Canada 165 I1
Massena U.S.A. 165 H1
Massenya Chad 121 E3
Masset B.C. Canada 149 N5
Massieville U.S.A. 164 D4
Massif Central mts France 66 F4
Massilia France see Marseille
Massillon U.S.A. 164 E3
Massina Mali 120 C3
Massinga Moz. 125 L2
Massingir Moz. 125 K2
Massingir, Barragem de resr Moz. 125 K2
Masson Island Antarctica 188 F2
Mastchoh Tajik. 111 H2
Masterton N.Z. 139 E5
Masticho, Akra pt Voreio Aigaio Greece see Oura, Akrotirio
Mastung Pak. 100 F4
Mastūrah Saudi Arabia 108 E5
Masty Belarus 55 N10
Masuda Japan 91 C6
Masuho Japan 93 E3
Masuku Gabon see Franceville
Masulipatam India see Machilipatnam
Masulipatnam India see Machilipatnam
Masuna i. American Samoa see Tutuila
Masurai, Bukit mt. Indon. 84 C3
Masvingo Zimbabwe 123 D6
Masvingo prov. Zimbabwe 125 J1
Maswa Tanz. 122 D4
Maswaar i. Indon. 81 I7
Maşyāf Syria 107 C2
Mat, Nam r. Laos 86 D3
Mata Myanmar 86 B1
Matabeleland South prov. Zimbabwe 125 I1
Matachewan Canada 152 E5
Matachic Mex. 166 D2
Matad Dornod Mongolia 95 H2
Matadi Dem. Rep. Congo 123 B4
Matador U.S.A. 161 C5
Matagalpa Nicaragua 166 [inset] I6
Matagami Canada 152 F4
Matagami, Lac l. Canada 152 F4
Matagorda TX U.S.A. 167 F2
Matagorda Island U.S.A. 161 D6
Mataigou Ningxia China see Taole
Matak i. Indon. 84 D2
Matak Kazakh. 98 A2
Matakana Island N.Z. 139 F3
Matala Angola 123 B5
Maṭāli', Jabal hill Saudi Arabia 113 F6
Matam Senegal 120 B3
Matamey Niger 120 D3
Matamoras U.S.A. 165 H3
Matamoros Coahuila Mex. 166 E3
Matamoros Tamaulipas Mex. 167 F3
Matana, Danau l. Indon. 83 B3
Matanal Point Phil. 82 C5
Matandu r. Tanz. 123 D4
Matane Canada 153 I4
Matanuska AK U.S.A. 149 J3
Matanzas Cuba 169 H4
Matapalo, Cabo c. Costa Rica 166 [inset] J7
Matapan, Cape pt Greece see Tainaro, Akrotirio
Matapédia, Lac l. Canada 153 I4
Maţār well Saudi Arabia 110 B5
Matara Sri Lanka 106 D5
Mataram Lombok Indon. 85 G5
Matarani Peru 176 D7
Mataranka Australia 134 F3
Matarape, Teluk b. Indon. 83 B3
Matarinao Bay Samar Phil. 82 D4
Mataripe Brazil 179 D1
Mataró Spain 67 H3
Matarombea r. Indon. 83 B3
Matasiri i. Indon. 85 F4
Matatiele S. Africa 125 I6
Matatila Reservoir India 104 D4
Mataura N.Z. 139 B8
▶Matā'utu Wallis and Futuna Is 133 I3
Capital of Wallis and Futuna Islands.
Mata-Utu Wallis and Futuna Is see Matā'utu
Matawai N.Z. 139 F4
Matay Kazakh. 102 E2
Matcha Tajik. see Mastchoh
Mat Con, Hon i. Vietnam 86 D3
Mategua Bol. 176 F6
Matehuala Mex. 161 C8
Matemanga Tanz. 123 D5
Matera Italy 68 G4
Mateur Tunisia 68 C6
Mathaji India 104 B4
Matheson Canada 152 E4
Mathews U.S.A. 165 G5
Mathis U.S.A. 161 D6
Mathoura Australia 138 B5
Mathura India 104 D4
Mati Mindanao Phil. 82 D5
Matiali India 105 G4
Matias Cardoso Brazil 179 C1
Matías Romero Mex. 168 E5
Matimekosh Canada 153 I3
Matin India 105 E5
Matina Costa Rica 166 [inset] J7
Matinenda Lake Canada 152 E5
Matizi China 96 D1
Matla r. India 105 G5
Matlabas r. S. Africa 125 H2
Matli Pak. 111 H5
Matlock U.K. 59 F5
Mato, Cerro mt. Venez. 176 E2
Matobo Hills Zimbabwe 123 C6
Mato Grosso Brazil 176 G7
Mato Grosso state Brazil 179 A1
Matopo Hills Zimbabwe see Matobo Hills
Matos Costa Brazil 179 A4
Matosinhos Port. 67 B3
Mato Verde Brazil 179 C1
Maţraḥ Oman 110 E6
Matroosberg mt. S. Africa 124 D7
Matsesta Rus. Fed. 113 E2
Matsubara Japan 92 B4
Matsuda Japan 93 F3
Matsudai Japan 93 E1
Matsudo Japan 93 F3
Matsue Japan 91 D6
Matsuida Japan 93 E2
Matsukawa Nagano Japan 93 D2
Matsukawa Nagano Japan 93 D3
Matsumoto Japan 93 D2
Matsunoyama Japan 93 E1
Matsuo Japan 93 G3
Matsuoka Japan 92 C2
Matsusaka Japan 92 C4
Matsushiro Japan 93 E2
Matsu Tao i. Taiwan 97 I3
Matsuyama Japan 91 D6
Matsuzaki Japan 93 E4
Mattagami r. Canada 152 E4
Mattamuskeet, Lake U.S.A. 162 E5
Mattawa Canada 152 F5
Matterhorn mt. Italy/Switz. 68 B2
Matterhorn mt. U.S.A. 156 E4
Matthew Town Bahamas 169 J4
Maţţī, Sabkhat salt pan Saudi Arabia 110 D6
Mattō Japan 92 C2
Mattoon U.S.A. 160 F4
Matturai Sri Lanka see Matara
Matu Sarawak Malaysia 85 E2
Matuku i. Fiji 133 H3
Matumbo Angola 123 B5
Maturín Venez. 176 F2
Matusadona National Park Zimbabwe 123 C5
Matutuang i. Indon. 83 C1
Matutum, Mount vol. Phil. 82 D5
Matwabeng S. Africa 125 H5
Maty Island P.N.G. see Wuvulu Island
Mau India see Maunath Bhanjan
Maúa Moz. 123 D5
Maubeuge France 62 D4
Maubin Myanmar 86 A3
Ma-ubin Myanmar 86 B1
Maubourguet France 66 E5
Mauchline U.K. 60 E5
Maudaha India 104 E4
Maude Australia 137 D7
Maud Seamount sea feature S. Atlantic Ocean 184 I10
Mau-é-ele Moz. see Marão
Maués Brazil 177 G4
Maughold Head hd Isle of Man 58 C4
Maug Islands N. Mariana Is 81 L2
Maui i. U.S.A. 157 [inset]
Maukkadaw Myanmar 86 A2
Maulbronn Germany 63 I6
Maule r. Chile 178 B5
Maulvi Bazar Bangl. see Moulvibazar
Maumee U.S.A. 164 D3
Maumee Bay U.S.A. 164 D3
Maumere Flores Indon. 83 B5
Maumturk Mts hills Ireland 61 C4
Maun Botswana 123 C5
Mauna Kea vol. U.S.A. 157 [inset]
Mauna Loa vol. U.S.A. 157 [inset]
Maunath Bhanjan India 105 E4
Maunatlala Botswana 125 H2
Mauneluk r. AK U.S.A. 148 H2
Maungaturoto N.Z. 139 E3
Maungdaw Myanmar 86 A2
Maungmagan Islands Myanmar 87 B4
Maunoir, Lac l. N.W.T. Canada 149 P2
Maurepas, Lake U.S.A. 161 F6
Mauriac France 66 F4
Maurice country Indian Ocean see Mauritius
Maurice, Lake salt flat Australia 135 E7
Maurik Neth. 62 F3
Mauritania country Africa 120 B3
Mauritanie country Africa see Mauritania
Mauritius country Indian Ocean 185 L7
Maurs France 66 F4
Mauston U.S.A. 160 F3
Mava Dem. Rep. Congo 122 C3
Mavago Moz. 123 D5
Mavan, Kūh-e hill Iran 110 E3
Mavanza Moz. 125 L2
Mavinga Angola 123 C5
Mavrovo nat. park Macedonia 69 I4
Mavume Moz. 125 L2
Mavuya S. Africa 125 H6
Mawa, Bukit mt. Indon. 85 F2
Ma Wan i. H.K. China 97 [inset]
Māwān, Khashm hill Saudi Arabia 110 B6
Mawana India 104 D3
Mawanga Dem. Rep. Congo 123 B4
Ma Wang Dui tourist site China 97 G2
Mawasangka Sulawesi Indon. 83 B4
Mawei China 97 H3
Mawjib, Wādī al r. Jordan 107 B4
Mawkmai Myanmar 86 B2
Mawlaik Myanmar 86 A2
Mawlamyaing Myanmar 86 B3
Mawlamyine Myanmar see Mawlamyaing
Mawqaq Saudi Arabia 113 F6
Mawson research station Antarctica 188 E2
Mawson Coast Antarctica 188 E2
Mawson Escarpment Antarctica 188 E2
Mawson Peninsula Antarctica 188 H2
Maw Taung mt. Myanmar 87 B5
Mawza Yemen 108 F7
Maxán Arg. 178 C3
Maxcanú Mex. 167 H4
Maxhamish Lake Canada 150 F3
Maxia, Punta mt. Sardinia Italy 68 C5
Maxixe Moz. 125 L2
Maxmo Fin. 54 M5
May, Isle of i. U.K. 60 G4
Maya i. Indon. 85 E3
Maya r. Rus. Fed. 77 O3
Mayaguana i. Bahamas 163 F8
Mayaguana Passage Bahamas 163 F8
Mayagüez Puerto Rico 169 K5
Mayahi Niger 120 D3
Mayak Rus. Fed. 90 E2
Mayakovskiy, Qullai mt. Tajik. 111 H2
Mayakovskogo, Pik mt. Tajik. see Mayakovskiy, Qullai
Mayalibit, Teluk b. Papua Indon. 83 D3
Mayama Congo 122 B4
Maya Mountains Belize/Guat. 167 H5
Mayan Gansu China see Mayanhe
Mayang China 97 F3
Mayanhe Gansu China 94 F5
Mayar hill U.K. 60 F4
Maya-san hill Japan 92 B4
Maybeury U.S.A. 164 E5
Maybole U.K. 60 E5
Maych'ew Eth. 122 D2
Maydān Shahr Afgh. see Meydān Shahr
Maydh Somalia 108 G7
Maydos Turkey see Eceabat
Mayen Germany 63 H4
Mayenne France 66 D2
Mayenne r. France 66 D3
Mayer U.S.A. 159 G4
Mayêr Kangri mt. Xizang China 99 D6
Mayersville U.S.A. 161 F5
Mayerthorpe Canada 150 H4
Mayfield N.Z. 139 C6
Mayhan Mongolia see Sant
Mayhill NM U.S.A. 166 D1
Mayi He r. China 90 C3
Maykamys Kazakh. 98 B3
Maykop Rus. Fed. 113 F1
Maymanah Afgh. 111 G3
Mayna Respublika Khakasiya Rus. Fed. 76 K4
Mayna Ul'yanovskaya Oblast' Rus. Fed. 53 J5
Mayni India 106 B2
Maynooth Canada 165 G1
Mayo Y.T. Canada 149 N3
Mayo r. Mex. 166 C3
Mayo U.S.A. 163 D6
Mayo Alim Cameroon 120 E4
Mayoko Congo 122 B4
Mayo Lake Y.T. Canada 149 N3
Mayon vol. Luzon Phil. 82 C3
Mayor, Puig mt. Spain see Major, Puig
Mayor Island N.Z. 139 F3
Mayor Pablo Lagerenza Para. 178 D1
▶Mayotte terr. Africa 123 E5
French Departmental Collectivity.
Mayraira Point Luzon Phil. 82 C2
Mayskiy Amurskaya Oblast' Rus. Fed. 90 C1
Mayskiy Kabardino-Balkarskaya Respublika Rus. Fed. 113 G2
Mays Landing U.S.A. 165 H4
Mayson Lake Canada 151 J3
Maysville U.S.A. 164 D4
Maytag Xinjiang China see Dushanzi
Mayu i. Maluku Indon. 83 C2
Mayumba Gabon 122 B4
Mayum La pass Xizang China 99 C7
Mayuram India 106 C4
Mayville MI U.S.A. 164 D2
Mayville ND U.S.A. 160 D2
Mayville NY U.S.A. 164 F2
Mayville WI U.S.A. 164 A2
Mazabuka Zambia 123 C5
Mazaca Turkey see Kayseri
Mazagan Morocco see El Jadida
Mazapil Mex. 167 E3
Mazar Xinjiang China 99 B5
Mazar, Koh-i- mt. Afgh. 111 G3
Mazara, Val di valley Sicily Italy 68 E6
Mazara del Vallo Sicily Italy 68 E6
Mazār-e Sharīf Afgh. 111 G2
Mazārī' reg. U.A.E. 110 D6
Mazartag Xinjiang China 98 C5
Mazartag mt. Xinjiang China 98 B5
Mazatán Mex. 166 C2
Mazatenango Guat. 167 H6
Mazatlán Mex. 168 C4
Mazatzal Peak U.S.A. 159 H4
Mazdaj Iran 113 H4
Maze Japan 92 D3
Maze-gawa r. Japan 92 D3
Mažeikiai Lith. 55 M8
Maẓhūr, 'Irq al des. Saudi Arabia 110 A5
Mazīm Oman 110 E6
Mazocahui Mex. 166 C2
Mazocruz Peru 176 E7
Mazomora Tanz. 123 D4
Mazong Shan mt. Gansu China 94 D3
Mazong Shan mts China 94 C3
Mazu Dao i. Taiwan see Matsu Tao
Mazunga Zimbabwe 123 C6
Mazyr Belarus 53 F5
Mazzouna Tunisia 68 C7
▶Mbabane Swaziland 125 J4
Capital of Swaziland.
Mbahiakro Côte d'Ivoire 120 C4
Mbaïki Cent. Afr. Rep. 122 B3
Mbakaou, Lac de l. Cameroon 120 E4
Mbala Zambia 123 D4
Mbale Uganda 122 D3
Mbalmayo Cameroon 120 E4
Mbam r. Cameroon 120 E4
Mbandaka Dem. Rep. Congo 122 B4
M'banza Congo Angola 123 B4
Mbarara Uganda 121 G5
Mbari r. Cent. Afr. Rep. 122 C3
Mbaswana S. Africa 125 K4
Mbemkuru r. Tanz. 123 D4
Mbeya Tanz. 123 D4
Mbinga Tanz. 123 D5
Mbini Equat. Guinea 120 D4
Mbizi Zimbabwe 123 D6
Mboki Cent. Afr. Rep. 122 C3
Mbomo Congo 122 B3
Mbouda Cameroon 120 E4
Mbour Senegal 120 B3
Mbout Mauritania 120 B3
Mbozi Tanz. 123 D4
Mbrès Cent. Afr. Rep. 122 B3
Mbuji-Mayi Dem. Rep. Congo 123 C4
Mbulu Tanz. 122 D4
Mburucuyá Arg. 178 E3
McAdam Canada 153 I5
McAlester U.S.A. 161 E5
McAlister mt. Australia 138 D5
McAllen U.S.A. 161 D7
McArthur r. Australia 136 B2
McArthur U.S.A. 164 D4
McArthur Mills Canada 165 G1
McBain U.S.A. 164 C1
McBride Canada 150 F4
McCall U.S.A. 156 D3
McCamey U.S.A. 161 C6
McCammon U.S.A. 156 E4
McCarthy AK U.S.A. 149 L3
McCauley Island B.C. Canada 149 O5
McClintock, Mount Antarctica 188 H1
McClintock Channel Canada 147 H2
McClintock Range hills Australia 134 D4
McClure, Lake U.S.A. 158 C3
McClure Strait Canada 146 G2
McClusky U.S.A. 160 C2
McComb U.S.A. 161 F6
McConaughy, Lake U.S.A. 160 C3
McConnell Range mts N.W.T. Canada 149 P2
McConnellsburg U.S.A. 165 G4
McConnelsville U.S.A. 164 E4
McCook U.S.A. 160 C3
McCormick U.S.A. 163 D5
McCrea r. Canada 150 H2
McCreary Canada 151 L5
McCullum, Mount Y.T. Canada 149 M2
McDame Canada 150 D3
McDermitt U.S.A. 156 D4
McDonald Islands Indian Ocean 185 M9
McDonald Peak U.S.A. 156 E3
McDonough U.S.A. 163 C5
McDougall AK U.S.A. 149 J3
McDougall's Bay S. Africa 124 C5
McDowell Peak U.S.A. 159 H5
McFarland U.S.A. 158 D4
McGill U.S.A. 159 F2
McGivney Canada 153 I5
McGrath AK U.S.A. 148 I3
McGrath MN U.S.A. 160 E2
McGraw U.S.A. 165 G2
McGregor r. Canada 150 F4
McGregor S. Africa 124 D7
McGregor, Lake Canada 150 H5
McGregor Range hills Australia 137 C5
McGuire, Mount U.S.A. 156 E3
Mchinga Tanz. 123 D4
Mchinji Malawi 123 D5
McIlwraith Range hills Australia 136 C2
McInnes Lake Canada 151 M4
McIntosh U.S.A. 160 C2
McKay Range hills Australia 134 C5
McKean i. Kiribati 133 I2
McKee U.S.A. 164 C5
McKenzie r. U.S.A. 156 C3
McKinlay r. Australia 136 C4
▶McKinley, Mount AK U.S.A. 149 J3
Highest mountain in North America.
McKinley Park AK U.S.A. 149 J3
McKinney U.S.A. 161 D5
McKittrick U.S.A. 158 D4
McLaughlin U.S.A. 160 C2
McLeansboro U.S.A. 160 F4
McLennan Canada 150 G4
McLeod r. Canada 150 H4
McLeod Bay Canada 151 I2
McLeod Lake Canada 150 F4
McLoughlin, Mount U.S.A. 156 C4
McMillan, Lake U.S.A. 161 B5
McMinnville OR U.S.A. 156 C3
McMinnville TN U.S.A. 162 C5
McMurdo research station Antarctica 188 H1
McMurdo Sound b. Antarctica 188 H1
McNary U.S.A. 159 I4
McNaughton Lake Canada see Kinbasket Lake
McPherson U.S.A. 160 D4
McQuesten r. Y.T. Canada 149 M3
McRae U.S.A. 163 D5
McTavish Arm b. Canada 150 G1
McVeytown U.S.A. 165 G3
McVicar Arm b. Canada 150 F1
Mdantsane S. Africa 125 H7
M'Daourouch Alg. 68 B6
M'Đrak Vietnam 87 E4
Mê, Hon i. Vietnam 86 D3
Mead, Lake resr U.S.A. 159 F3
Meade U.S.A. 161 C4
Meade r. U.S.A. 146 C2
Meade r. AK U.S.A. 148 H1
Meade r. AK U.S.A. 148 H1
Meadow Australia 135 A6
Meadow SD U.S.A. 160 C2
Meadow UT U.S.A. 159 G2
Meadow Lake Canada 151 I4
Meadville MS U.S.A. 161 F6
Meadville PA U.S.A. 164 E3
Meaford Canada 164 E1
Meaken-dake vol. Japan 90 G4
Mealhada Port. 67 B3
Mealy Mountains Canada 153 K3
Meandarra Australia 138 D1
Meander River Canada 150 G3
Meares i. Indon. 83 C1
Meaux France 62 C6
Mebulu, Tanjung pt Indon. 85 F5

Mecca Saudi Arabia **108** E5
Mecca CA U.S.A. **158** E5
Mecca OH U.S.A. **164** E3
Mechanic Falls U.S.A. **165** J1
Mechanicsville U.S.A. **165** G5
Mechelen Belgium **62** E3
Mechelen Neth. **62** F4
Mecherchar i. Palau see **Eil Malk**
Mecheria Alg. **64** D5
Mechernich Germany **62** G4
Mechigmen Rus. Fed. **148** D2
Mecitözü Turkey **112** D2
Meckenheim Germany **62** H4
Mecklenburger Bucht b. Germany **57** M3
Mecklenburg-Vorpommern land Germany **63** M1
Mecklenburg - West Pomerania land Germany see **Mecklenburg-Vorpommern**
Meda r. Australia **134** C4
Meda Port. **67** C3
Medak India **106** C2
Medan Sumatera Indon. **84** B2
Medang i. Indon. **85** G5
Medanosa, Punta pt Arg. **178** C7
Médanos de Coro, Parque Nacional nat. park Venez. **176** E1
Medawachchiya Sri Lanka **106** D4
Médéa Alg. **67** H5
Medebach Germany **63** I3
Medellín Col. **176** C2
Meden r. U.K. **58** G5
Medenine Tunisia **68** C7
Mederdra Mauritania **120** B3
Medford NY U.S.A. **165** I3
Medford OK U.S.A. **161** D4
Medford OR U.S.A. **156** C4
Medford WI U.S.A. **160** F2
Medfra AK U.S.A. **148** I3
Medgidia Romania **69** M2
Media U.S.A. **165** H4
Mediaş Romania **69** K1
Medicine Bow r. U.S.A. **156** G4
Medicine Bow Mountains U.S.A. **156** G4
Medicine Bow Peak U.S.A. **156** G4
Medicine Hat Canada **151** I5
Medicine Lake U.S.A. **156** G2
Medicine Lodge U.S.A. **161** D4
Medina Brazil **179** C2
Medina Saudi Arabia **108** E5
Medina ND U.S.A. **160** D2
Medina NY U.S.A. **165** F2
Medina OH U.S.A. **164** E3
Medinaceli Spain **67** E3
Medina del Campo Spain **67** D3
Medina de Rioseco Spain **67** D3
Medina Lake U.S.A. **161** D6
Medinipur India **105** F5
Mediolanum Italy see **Milan**
Mediterranean Sea **64** K5
Mednyy, Ostrov i. Rus. Fed. **186** H2
Médoc reg. France **66** D4
Mêdog Xizang China **99** F7
Medora U.S.A. **160** C2
Medstead Canada **151** I4
Medu Kongkar Xizang China see **Maizhokunggar**
Meduro atoll Marshall Is see **Majuro**
Medvedevo Rus. Fed. **52** J4
Medveditsa r. Rus. Fed. **53** I6
Medvednica mts Croatia **68** F2
Medvezh'i, Ostrova is Rus. Fed. **77** R2
Medvezh'ya vol. Rus. Fed. **90** H3
Medvezh'ya, Gora mt. Rus. Fed. **90** E3
Medvezh'yegorsk Rus. Fed. **52** G3
Medway r. U.K. **59** H7
Meekatharra Australia **135** B6
Meeker CO U.S.A. **159** J1
Meeker OH U.S.A. **164** D3
Meelpaeg Reservoir Canada **153** K4
Meemu Atoll Maldives see **Mulaku Atoll**
Meerane Germany **63** M4
Meerlo Neth. **62** G3
Meerut India **104** D3
Mega i. Indon. **84** C3
Mega Escarpment Eth./Kenya **122** D3
Megalopoli Greece **69** J6
Megamo Indon. **81** I7
Mégantic, Lac l. Canada **153** H5
Megara Greece **69** J5
Megezez mt. Eth. **122** D3

▶**Meghalaya** state India **105** G4
Highest mean annual rainfall in the world.

Meghasani mt. India **105** F5
Meghri Armenia **113** G3
Megin Turkm. **110** E2
Megisti i. Greece **69** M6
Megri Armenia see **Meghri**
Mehamn Norway **54** O1
Mehar Pak. **111** G5
Meharry, Mount Australia **135** B5
Mehbubnagar India see **Mahbubnagar**
Mehdia Tunisia see **Mahdia**
Meherpur Bangl. **105** G5
Meherrin U.S.A. **165** F5
Meherrin r. U.S.A. **165** G5
Mehlville U.S.A. **160** F4
Mehrakān salt marsh Iran **110** D5
Mehrān Hormozgan Iran **110** D5
Mehrān Īlām Iran **110** B3
Mehren Germany **62** G4
Mehriz Iran **110** D4
Mehsana India see **Mahesana**
Mehtar Lām Afgh. **111** H3
Meia Ponte r. Brazil **179** A2
Meicheng China see **Minqing**
Meichuan Gansu China **94** F5
Meiganga Cameroon **121** E4
Meighen Island Canada **147** I2
Meigu China **96** D2
Meihekou China **90** B4
Meihō Japan **92** D3
Meikeng China **97** G3
Meikle r. Canada **150** G3
Meikle Says Law hill U.K. **60** G5
Meiktila Myanmar **86** A2
Meilin China see **Ganxian**
Meilleur r. Canada **150** E2
Meilu China **97** F4
Meine Germany **63** K2
Meinersen Germany **63** K2
Meiningen Germany **63** K4
Meishan Anhui China see **Jinzhai**
Meishan Sichuan China **96** D2
Meishan Shuiku resr China **97** G2
Meißen Germany **57** N5
Meister r. Y.T. Canada **149** O3
Meitan China **96** E3
Meiwa Gunma Japan **93** F2
Meiwa Mie Japan **92** C4
Meixi China **90** C3
Meixian China see **Meizhou**
Meixian Shaanxi China **95** F5
Meixing China see **Xiaojin**
Meizhou China **97** H3
Mej r. India **104** D4
Mejicana mt. Arg. **178** C3
Mejillones Chile **178** B2
Mékambo Gabon **122** B3
Mek'elē Eth. **122** D2
Mekelle Eth. see **Mek'elē**
Mékhé Senegal **120** B3
Mekhtar Pak. **111** H4
Meknassy Tunisia **68** C7
Meknès Morocco **64** C5
Mekong r. Asia **86** D4
also known as Ménam Khong (Laos/Thailand)
Mekong, Mouths of the Vietnam **87** D5
Mekoryuk AK U.S.A. **148** F3
Melaka Malaysia **84** C2
Melaka state Malaysia **84** C2
Melalap Sabah Malaysia **85** F1
Melalo, Tanjung pt Indon. **84** D3
Melanau, Gunung hill Indon. **87** E7
Melanesia is Pacific Ocean **186** G6
Melanesian Basin sea feature Pacific Ocean **186** G5
Melawi r. Indon. **85** E2

▶**Melbourne** Australia **138** B6
Capital of Victoria. 2nd most populous city in Oceania.

Melbourne U.S.A. **163** D6
Melby U.K. **60** [inset]
Melchor de Mencos Guat. **167** H5
Melchor Ocampo Mex. **167** E3
Meldorf Germany **57** L3

▶**Melekeok** Palau **82** [inset]
Capital of Palau.

Melekess Rus. Fed. see **Dimitrovgrad**
Melenki Rus. Fed. **53** I5
Melet Turkey see **Mesudiye**
Mélèzes, Rivière aux r. Canada **153** H2
Melfa U.S.A. **165** H5
Melfi Chad **121** E3
Melfi Italy **68** F4
Melfort Canada **151** J4
Melhus Norway **54** G5
Meliadine Lake Canada **151** M2
Meliau Kalimantan Indon. **85** E3
Melide Spain **67** C2
Melilis i. Indon. **83** B3

▶**Melilla** N. Africa **67** E6
Autonomous Community of Spain.

Melimoyu, Monte mt. Chile **178** B6
Melintang, Danau l. Indon. **85** G3
Meliskerke Neth. **62** D3
Melita Canada **151** K5
Melitene Turkey see **Malatya**
Melitopol' Ukr. **53** G7
Melk Austria **57** O6
Melka Guba Eth. **122** D3
Melksham U.K. **59** E7
Mellakoski Fin. **54** N3
Mellansel Sweden **54** K5
Melle Germany **63** I2
Mellerud Sweden **55** H7
Mellette U.S.A. **160** D2
Mellid Spain see **Melide**
Mellilia N. Africa see **Melilla**
Mellor Glacier Antarctica **188** E2
Mellrichstadt Germany **63** K4
Mellum i. Germany **63** I1
Melmoth S. Africa **125** J5
Mel'nichoye Rus. Fed. **90** D3
Melo Uruguay **178** F4
Meloco Moz. **123** D5
Melolo Sumba Indon. **83** B5
Melozitna r. AK U.S.A. **148** I2
Melrhir, Chott salt l. Alg. **64** F5
Melrose Australia **135** C6
Melrose U.K. **60** G5
Melrose U.S.A. **160** E2
Melsungen Germany **63** J3
Melta, Mount Malaysia see **Tawai, Bukit**
Melton Australia **138** B6
Melton Mowbray U.K. **59** G6
Meluan Sarawak Malaysia **85** E2
Melun France **66** F2
Melville Canada **151** K5
Melville, Cape Australia **136** D2
Melville, Cape Phil. **82** B5
Melville, Lake Canada **153** K3
Melville Bugt b. Greenland see **Qimusseriarsuaq**
Melville Hills Nunavut Canada **149** Q1
Melville Island Australia **134** E2
Melville Island Canada **147** H2
Melville Peninsula Canada **147** J3
Melvin U.S.A. **164** A3
Melvin, Lough l. Ireland/U.K. **61** D3
Mêmar Co salt l. China **99** C6
Memba Moz. **123** E5
Memberamo r. Indon. **81** J7
Memboro Sumba Indon. **83** A5
Memel Lith. see **Klaipėda**
Memel S. Africa **125** I4
Memmelsdorf Germany **63** K5
Memmingen Germany **57** M7
Mempawah Kalimantan Indon. **85** E2
Memphis tourist site Egypt **112** C5
Memphis MI U.S.A. **164** D2
Memphis TN U.S.A. **161** F5
Memphis TX U.S.A. **161** C5
Memphrémagog, Lac l. Canada **165** I1
Mena Timor Indon. **83** C5
Mena Ukr. **53** G6
Mena U.S.A. **161** E5
Ménaka Mali **120** D3
Menanga Maluku Indon. **83** C3
Menard U.S.A. **161** D6
Menasha U.S.A. **164** A1
Mendanau i. Indon. **84** D3
Mendanha Brazil **179** C2
Mendarik i. Indon. **84** D2
Mendawai Kalimantan Indon. **85** F3
Mendawai r. Indon. **85** F3
Mende France **66** F4
Mendefera Eritrea **108** E7
Mendeleyev Ridge sea feature Arctic Ocean **189** B1
Mendeleyevsk Rus. Fed. **52** L5
Mendenhall U.S.A. **161** F6
Mendenhall, Cape AK U.S.A. **148** F4
Mendenhall Glacier AK U.S.A. **149** N4
Méndez Tamaulipas Mex. **167** F3
Mendez-Nuñez Luzon Phil. **82** C3
Mendī Eth. **122** D3
Mendi P.N.G. **81** K8
Mendip Hills U.K. **59** E7
Mendocino U.S.A. **158** B2
Mendocino, Cape U.S.A. **158** A1
Mendocino, Lake U.S.A. **158** B2
Mendooran Australia **138** D3
Mendota CA U.S.A. **158** C3
Mendota IL U.S.A. **160** F3
Mendoza Arg. **178** C4
Menemen Turkey **69** L5
Ménerville Alg. see **Thenia**
Mengalum i. Malaysia **85** F1
Mengba Gansu China **95** F5
Mengban China **96** D4
Mengcheng China **97** H1
Menggala Sumatera Indon. **84** D4
Menghai China **96** D4
Mengjin China **97** G1
Mengkatip Kalimantan Indon. **85** F3
Mengkiang r. Indon. **85** E2
Mengkoka, Gunung mt. Indon. **83** B3
Mengla China **96** D4
Menglang China see **Lancang**
Menglie China see **Jiangcheng**
Mengxian Henan China see **Mengzhou**
Mengyang China see **Mingshan**
Mengyin Shandong China **95** I5
Mengzhou Henan China **95** H5
Mengzi China **96** D4
Menihek Canada **153** I3
Menihek Lakes Canada **153** I3
Menindee Australia **137** C7
Menindee, Lake Australia **137** C7
Ménistouc, Lac l. Canada **153** I3
Menkere Rus. Fed. **77** N3
Mennecy France **62** C6
Menominee U.S.A. **164** B1
Menomonee Falls U.S.A. **164** A2
Menomonie U.S.A. **160** F2
Menongue Angola **123** B5
Menorca i. Spain see **Minorca**
Mensalong Kalimantan Indon. **85** G2
Mentakab Malaysia **84** C2
Mentarang r. Indon. **85** G2
Mentasta Lake AK U.S.A. **149** L3
Mentasta Mountains AK U.S.A. **149** K3
Mentawai, Kepulauan is Indon. **84** B3
Mentawai, Selat sea chan. Indon. **84** C3
Mentaya r. Indon. **85** F3
Menteroda Germany **63** K3
Mentmore U.S.A. **159** I4
Mentok Indon. **84** D3
Menton France **66** H5
Mentone U.S.A. **161** C6
Mentuba r. Indon. **85** F3
Menuf Egypt see **Minūf**
Menukung Kalimantan Indon. **85** F3
Menuma Japan **93** F2
Menunu Sulawesi Indon. **83** B2
Menyapa, Gunung mt. Indon. **85** G2
Menyuan Qinghai China **94** E4
Menza Rus. Fed. **95** G1
Menza r. Rus. Fed. **95** G1
Menzel Bourguiba Tunisia **68** C6
Menzelet Barajı resr Turkey **112** E3
Menzelinsk Rus. Fed. **51** Q4
Menzel Temime Tunisia **68** D6
Menzies Australia **135** C7
Menzies, Mount Antarctica **188** E2
Meobbaai b. Namibia **124** B3
Meoqui Mex. **166** D2
Meppel Neth. **62** G2
Meppen Germany **63** H2
Mepuze Moz. **125** K2
Meqheleng S. Africa **125** H5
Mequon U.S.A. **164** B2
Merah Kalimantan Indon. **85** G2
Merak Jawa Indon. **84** D4
Meråker Norway **54** G5
Merano Italy **68** D1
Merapi, Gunung vol. Jawa Indon. **85** E4
Meratswe r. Botswana **124** G2
Meratus, Pegunungan mts Indon. **85** F3
Merauke Indon. **81** K8
Merbau Sumatera Indon. **84** C2
Merca Somalia see **Marka**
Mercantour, Parc National du nat. park France **66** H4
Merced U.S.A. **158** C3
Merced r. U.S.A. **158** C3
Mercedes Arg. **178** E3
Mercedes Uruguay **178** E4
Mercer ME U.S.A. **165** K1
Mercer PA U.S.A. **164** E3
Mercer WI U.S.A. **160** F2
Mercês Brazil **179** C3
Mercury Islands N.Z. **139** E3
Mercy, Cape Canada **147** L3
Merdenik Turkey see **Göle**
Mere Belgium **62** D4
Mere U.K. **59** E7
Meredith U.S.A. **165** J2
Meredith, Lake U.S.A. **161** C5
Merefa Ukr. **53** H6
Merga Oasis Sudan **108** C6
Mergui Myanmar see **Myeik**
Mergui Archipelago is Myanmar **87** B5
Meriç r. Turkey **69** L4
also known as Evros (Greece/Turkey), Marica (Bulgaria), Maritsa (Bulgaria)
Mérida Mex. **167** H4
Mérida Spain **67** C4
Mérida Venez. **176** D2
Mérida, Cordillera de mts Venez. **176** D2
Meriden U.S.A. **165** I3
Meridian MS U.S.A. **161** F5
Meridian TX U.S.A. **161** D6
Mérignac France **66** D4
Merijärvi Fin. **54** N4
Merikarvia Fin. **55** L6
Merimbula Australia **138** D6
Merín, Laguna l. Brazil/Uruguay see **Mirim, Lagoa**
Meringur Australia **137** C7
Merir i. Palau **81** I6
Merit Sarawak Malaysia **85** F2
Merjayoun Lebanon see **Marjayoûn**
Merkel U.S.A. **161** C5
Merluna Australia **136** C2
Mermaid Reef Australia **134** B4
Meron, Har mt. Israel **107** B3
Merowe Sudan **108** D6
Mêrqung Co l. China **105** F3
Merredin Australia **135** B7
Merrick hill U.K. **60** E5
Merrickville Canada **165** H1
Merrill MI U.S.A. **164** C2
Merrill WI U.S.A. **160** F2
Merrill, Mount Canada **150** E2
Merrillville U.S.A. **164** B3
Merriman U.S.A. **160** C3
Merritt Canada **150** F5
Merritt Island U.S.A. **163** D6
Merriwa Australia **138** E4
Merrygoen Australia **138** D3
Mersa Fatma Eritrea **108** F7
Mersa Maṭrûḥ Egypt see **Marsá Maṭrūḥ**
Mersch Lux. **62** G5
Merseburg (Saale) Germany **63** L3
Mersey est. U.K. **58** E5
Mersin Turkey **107** B1
Mersin prov. Turkey **107** A1
Mersing Malaysia **84** C2
Mersing, Bukit mt. Malaysia **85** F2
Mērsrags Latvia **55** M8
Merta India **104** C4
Merthyr Tydfil U.K. **59** D7
Mértola Port. **67** C5
Mertz Glacier Antarctica **188** G2
Mertz Glacier Tongue Antarctica **188** G2
Mertzon U.S.A. **161** C6
Méru France **62** C5

▶**Meru** vol. Tanz. **122** D4
4th highest mountain, and highest active volcano, in Africa.

Meru Betiri, Taman Nasional nat. park Indon. **85** F5
Merui Pak. **111** F4
Merutai Sabah Malaysia **85** G1
Merv Turkm. see **Mary**
Merweville S. Africa **124** E7
Merzifon Turkey **112** D2
Merzig Germany **62** G5
Merz Peninsula Antarctica **188** L2
Mesa Halmahera Indon. **83** D2
Mesa AZ U.S.A. **159** H5
Mesa NM U.S.A. **157** G6
Mesabi Range hills U.S.A. **160** E2
Mesagne Italy **68** G4
Mesa Mountain hill AK U.S.A. **148** I3
Mesanak i. Indon. **84** D2
Mesa Negra mt. U.S.A. **159** J4
Mesara, Ormos b. Kriti Greece see **Kolpos Messaras**
Mesara, Ormos b. Kriti Greece see **Kolpos Messaras**
Mesa Verde National Park U.S.A. **159** I3
Mescalero Apache Indian Reservation res. NM U.S.A. **166** D1
Meschede Germany **63** I3
Mese Myanmar **86** B3
Meselefors Sweden **54** J4
Mesgouez, Lac Canada **152** G4
Meshed Iran see **Mashhad**
Meshkān Iran **110** E2
Meshra'er Req Sudan **108** C8
Mesick U.S.A. **164** C1
Mesimeri Greece **69** J4
Mesolongi Greece **69** I5
Mesolóngion Greece see **Mesolongi**
Mesopotamia reg. Iraq **113** F4
Mesquita Brazil **179** C2
Mesquite NV U.S.A. **159** F3
Mesquite TX U.S.A. **161** D5
Mesquite Lake U.S.A. **159** F4
Messaad Alg. **64** E5
Messana Sicily Italy see **Messina**
Messina Sicily Italy **68** F5
Messina, Strait of Italy **68** F5
Messina, Stretta di Italy see **Messina, Strait of**
Messini Greece **69** J6
Messiniakos Kolpos b. Greece **69** J6
Mesta r. Bulg. **69** K4
Mesta r. Greece see **Nestos**
Mesta, Akrotirio pt Greece **69** K5
Mestghanem Alg. see **Mostaganem**
Mestlin Germany **63** L1
Meston, Akra pt Voreio Aigaio Greece see **Mesta, Akrotirio**
Mestre Italy **68** E2
Mesudiye Turkey **112** E2
Mesuji r. Indon. **84** D4
Meta r. Col./Venez. **176** E2
Métabetchouan Canada **153** H4
Meta Incognita Peninsula Canada **147** L3
Metairie U.S.A. **161** F6
Metallifere, Colline mts Italy **68** D3
Metán Arg. **178** C3
Metangai Kalimantan Indon. **85** F3
Metapán El Salvador **167** H6
Meteghan Canada **153** I5
Meteor Depth sea feature S. Atlantic Ocean **184** G9
Methoni Greece **69** I6
Methuen U.S.A. **165** J2
Methven U.K. **60** F4
Metionga Lake Canada **152** C4
Metković Croatia **68** G3
Metlaoui Tunisia **64** F5
Metoro Moz. **123** D5
Metro Sumatera Indon. **84** D4
Metropolis U.S.A. **161** F4
Metsada tourist site Israel see **Masada**
Metter U.S.A. **163** D5
Mettet Belgium **62** E4
Mettingen Germany **63** H2
Mettler U.S.A. **158** D4
Mettur India **106** C4
Metu Eth. **122** D3
Metz France **62** G5
Metz U.S.A. **164** C3
Meulaboh Sumatera Indon. **84** B1
Meureudu Sumatera Indon. **84** B1
Meuse r. Belgium/France **62** F3
also known as Maas (Netherlands)
Meuselwitz Germany **63** M3
Mevagissey U.K. **59** C8
Mêwa China **96** D1
Mexcala Mex. **167** F5
Mexia U.S.A. **161** D6
Mexiana, Ilha i. Brazil **177** I3
Mexicali Mex. **166** B1
Mexican Hat U.S.A. **159** I3
Mexicanos, Lago de los l. Mex. **166** D2
Mexican Water U.S.A. **159** I3

▶**Mexico** country Central America **166** B2
2nd most populous and 3rd largest country in North America.

México Mex. see **Mexico City**
México state Mex. **167** F5
Mexico ME U.S.A. **165** J1
Mexico MO U.S.A. **160** F4
Mexico NY U.S.A. **165** G2
Mexico, Gulf of Mex./U.S.A. **155** H6

▶**Mexico City** Mex. **168** E5
Capital of Mexico. Most populous city in North America, and 2nd in the world.

Meybod Iran **110** D3
Meydanī, Ra's-e pt Iran **110** E5
Meydān Shahr Afgh. **111** H3
Meyenburg Germany **63** M1
Meyersdale U.S.A. **164** F4
Meymeh Iran **110** C3
Meynypil'gyno Rus. Fed. **189** C2
Mezada tourist site Israel see **Masada**
Mezcalapa Mex. **167** G5
Mezcalapa r. Mex. **167** G5
Mezdra Bulg. **69** J3
Mezen' Rus. Fed. **52** J2
Mezen' r. Rus. Fed. **52** J2
Mézenc, Mont mt. France **66** G4
Mezenskaya Guba b. Rus. Fed. **52** I2
Mezhdurechensk Kemerovskaya Oblast' Rus. Fed. **88** F2
Mezhdurechensk Respublika Komi Rus. Fed. **52** K3
Mezhdurechye Rus. Fed. see **Shali**
Mezhdusharskiy, Ostrov i. Rus. Fed. **76** G2
Mezitli Turkey **107** B1
Mezőtúr Hungary **69** I1
Mezquital Mex. **166** D4
Mezquital r. Mex. **166** D4
Mezquitic Mex. **166** E4
Mežvidi Latvia **55** O8
Mhàil, Rubh' a' pt U.K. **60** C5
Mhangura Zimbabwe **123** D5
Mhlume Swaziland **125** J4
Mhow India **104** C5
Mi r. Myanmar **105** H5
Miahuatlán Mex. **168** E5
Miajadas Spain **67** D4
Miaméré Cent. Afr. Rep. **122** B3
Miami AZ U.S.A. **159** H5

▶**Miami** FL U.S.A. **163** D7
5th most populous city in North America.

Miami OK U.S.A. **161** E4
Miami Beach U.S.A. **163** D7
Miancaowan Qinghai China **94** D5
Mianchi Henan China **95** G5
Mīāndehī Iran **110** E3
Mīāndowāb Iran **110** B2
Miandrivazo Madag. **123** E5
Mianduhe Nei Mongol China **95** J1
Mīāneh Iran **110** B2
Miang, Phu mt. Thai. **86** C3
Miangas i. Phil. **82** D5
Miani India **111** I4
Miani Hor b. Pak. **111** G5
Mianjoi Afgh. **111** G3
Mianning China **96** D2
Mianwali Pak. **111** H3
Mianxian China **96** E1
Mianyang Hubei China see **Xiantao**
Mianyang Shaanxi China see **Mianxian**
Mianyang Sichuan China **96** E2
Mianzhu China **96** E2
Miaodao Liedao is China **95** J4
Miao'ergou Xinjiang China **98** C3
Miaoli Taiwan **97** I3
Miarinarivo Madag. **123** E5
Miarritze France see **Biarritz**
Miasa Japan **93** D2
Miass Rus. Fed. **76** H4
Miboro-ko l. Japan **92** C2
Mibu Japan **93** F2
Mibu-gawa r. Japan **93** D3
Mica Creek Canada **150** G4
Mica Mountain U.S.A. **159** H5
Micang Shan mts China **96** E1
Michalovce Slovakia **53** D6
Michel Canada **151** I4
Michelau in Oberfranken Germany **63** L4
Michelson, Mount AK U.S.A. **149** K1
Michelstadt Germany **63** J5
Michendorf Germany **63** N2
Micheng China see **Midu**
Michigan state U.S.A. **164** C2

▶**Michigan, Lake** U.S.A. **164** B2
3rd largest lake in North America, and 5th in the world.

Michigan City U.S.A. **164** B3
Michinberi India **106** D2
Michipicoten Bay Canada **152** D5
Michipicoten Island Canada **152** D5
Michipicoten River Canada **152** D5
Michoacán state Mex. **167** E5
Michurin Bulg. see **Tsarevo**
Michurinsk Rus. Fed. **53** I5
Mico r. Nicaragua **166** [inset] I6
Micronesia country N. Pacific Ocean see **Micronesia, Federated States of**
Micronesia is Pacific Ocean **186** F5
Micronesia, Federated States of country N. Pacific Ocean **186** G5
Midai i. Indon. **85** D2
Mid-Atlantic Ridge sea feature Atlantic Ocean **184** E4
Mid-Atlantic Ridge sea feature Atlantic Ocean **184** G8
Middelburg Neth. **62** D3
Middelburg E. Cape S. Africa **125** G6
Middelburg Mpumalanga S. Africa **125** I3
Middelfart Denmark **55** F9
Middelharnis Neth. **62** E3
Middelwit S. Africa **125** H3
Middle Alkali Lake U.S.A. **156** C4
Middle America Trench sea feature N. Pacific Ocean **187** N5
Middle Andaman i. India **87** A4
Middle Atlas mts Morocco see **Moyen Atlas**
Middle Bay Canada **153** K4
Middlebourne U.S.A. **164** E4
Middleburg U.S.A. **165** G3
Middleburgh U.S.A. **165** H2
Middlebury IN U.S.A. **164** C3
Middlebury VT U.S.A. **165** I1
Middle Caicos i. Turks and Caicos Is **163** G8
Middle Channel watercourse N.W.T. Canada **149** N1
Middle Concho r. U.S.A. **161** C6
Middle Congo country Africa see **Congo**
Middle Island Thai. see **Tasai, Ko**
Middle Loup r. U.S.A. **160** D3
Middlemarch N.Z. **139** C7
Middlemount Australia **136** E4
Middle River U.S.A. **165** G4
Middlesbrough U.K. **58** F4
Middle Strait India see **Andaman Strait**
Middleton Australia **136** C4
Middleton Canada **153** I5
Middleton Island atoll American Samoa see **Rose Island**
Middleton Island AK U.S.A. **149** K4
Middletown CA U.S.A. **158** B2
Middletown CT U.S.A. **165** I3
Middletown NY U.S.A. **165** H3
Middletown VA U.S.A. **165** F4
Midelt Morocco **64** D5
Midhurst U.K. **59** G8
Midi, Canal du France **66** F5
Mid-Indian Basin sea feature Indian Ocean **185** N6
Mid-Indian Ridge sea feature Indian Ocean **185** M7
Midland Canada **165** F1
Midland CA U.S.A. **159** F5
Midland IN U.S.A. **164** B4
Midland MI U.S.A. **164** C2
Midland SD U.S.A. **160** C2
Midland TX U.S.A. **161** C5
Midleton Ireland **61** D6
Midnapore India see **Medinipur**
Midnapur India see **Medinipur**
Midongy Atsimo Madag. **123** E6
Midori Japan **93** F3
Mid-Pacific Mountains sea feature N. Pacific Ocean **186** G4

Midu China 96 D3
Miðvágur Faroe Is 54 [inset]
Midway Oman see Thamarīt

▶Midway Islands terr.
N. Pacific Ocean 186 I4
United States Unincorporated Territory.

Midway Islands AK U.S.A. 149 J1
Midway Well Australia 135 C5
Midwest U.S.A. 156 G4
Midwest City U.S.A. 161 D5
Midwoud Neth. 62 F2
Midyat Turkey 113 F3
Midye Turkey see Kıyıköy
Mid Yell U.K. 60 [inset]
Midzhur mt. Bulg./Serbia 112 A2
Mie pref. Japan 92 C4
Miehikkälä Fin. 55 O6
Miekojärvi l. Fin. 54 N3
Mielec Poland 53 D6
Mienhua Yü i. Taiwan 97 I3
Mieraslompolo Fin. 54 O2
Mierašluoppal Fin. see Mieraslompolo
Miercurea-Ciuc Romania 69 K1
Mieres Spain 67 D2
Mieres del Camín Spain see Mieres
Mī'ēso Eth. 122 E3
Mieste Germany 63 L2
Mifflinburg U.S.A. 165 G3
Mifflintown U.S.A. 165 G3
Migang Shan mt. Gansu/Ningxia China 94 F5
Migdol S. Africa 125 G4
Miging India 96 B2
Migriggyangzham Co l. Qinghai China 99 E6
Miguel Alemán, Presa resr Mex. 167 F5
Miguel Auza Mex. 161 C7
Miguel de la Borda Panama 166 [inset] J7
Miguel Hidalgo, Presa resr Mex. 166 C3
Mihalıççık Turkey 69 N5
Mihama Aichi Japan 92 C4
Mihama Fukui Japan 92 B3
Mihama Wakayama Japan 92 B5
Mihara Japan 91 D6
Mihara Hyōgo Japan 92 A4
Mihara-yama vol. Japan 93 F4
Mihintale Sri Lanka 106 D4
Mihmandar Turkey 107 B1
Mihō Japan 93 G3
Mijares r. Spain see Millárs
Mijdrecht Neth. 62 E2
Mikata Japan 92 B3
Mikata-ko l. Japan 92 B3
Mikawa Japan 92 C2
Mikawa-wan b. Japan 92 D4
Mikawa-wan Kokutei-kōen park Japan 92 D4
Mikhalkino Rus. Fed. 77 R3
Mikhaylov Rus. Fed. 53 H5
Mikhaylovgrad Bulg. see Montana
Mikhaylov Island Antarctica 188 E2
Mikhaylovka Amurskaya Oblast' Rus. Fed. 90 C2
Mikhaylovka Primorskiy Kray Rus. Fed. 90 D4
Mikhaylovka Tul'skaya Oblast' Rus. Fed. see Kimovsk
Mikhaylovka Volgogradskaya Oblast' Rus. Fed. 53 I6
Mikhaylovskiy Rus. Fed. 102 E1
Mikhaylovskoye Rus. Fed. see Shpakovskoye
Mikhrot Timna Israel 107 B5
Miki Japan 92 A4
Mikir Hills India 105 H4
Miki-zaki pt Japan 92 C5
Mikkabi Japan 92 D4
Mikkeli Fin. 55 O6
Mikkelin mlk Fin. 55 O6
Mikkwa r. Canada 150 H3
Míkonos i. Greece see Mykonos
Mikoyan Armenia see Yeghegnadzor
Mikulkin, Mys c. Rus. Fed. 52 J2
Mikumi National Park Tanz. 123 D4
Mikumo Japan 92 C4
Mikun' Rus. Fed. 52 K3
Mikuni Japan 92 C2
Mikuni-sanmyaku mts Japan 93 E2
Mikuni-yama mt. Japan 93 E3
Mikura-jima i. Japan 91 E6
Milaca U.S.A. 160 E2
Miladhunmadulu Atoll Maldives 106 B5
Miladummadulu Atoll Maldives see Miladhunmadulu Atoll
Milan Italy 68 C2
Milan MI U.S.A. 164 D2
Milan MO U.S.A. 160 E3
Milan OH U.S.A. 164 D3
Milange Moz. 123 D5
Milano Italy see Milan
Milas Turkey 69 L6
Milazzo Sicily Italy 68 F5
Milazzo, Capo di c. Sicily Italy 68 F5
Milbank U.S.A. 160 D2
Milbridge U.S.A. 162 H2
Milde r. Germany 63 L2
Mildenhall U.K. 59 H6
Mildura Australia 137 C7
Mile China 96 D3
Mileiz, Wâdi el watercourse Egypt see Mulayz, Wādī al
Miles Australia 138 E1
Miles City U.S.A. 156 G3
Milestone Ireland 61 D5
Miletto, Monte mt. Italy 68 F4
Mileura Australia 135 B6
Milford Ireland 61 E2
Milford DE U.S.A. 165 H4
Milford IL U.S.A. 164 B3
Milford MA U.S.A. 165 J2
Milford MI U.S.A. 164 D2
Milford NE U.S.A. 160 D3
Milford NH U.S.A. 165 J2
Milford PA U.S.A. 165 H3
Milford UT U.S.A. 159 G2
Milford VA U.S.A. 165 G4
Milford Haven U.K. 59 B7
Milford Sound N.Z. 139 A7
Milford Sound inlet N.Z. 139 A7
Milgarra Australia 136 C3
Milḩ, Baḩr al l. Iraq see Razāzah, Buḩayrat ar Miliana Alg. 67 H5
Milid Turkey see Malatya
Milikapiti Australia 134 E2
Miling Australia 135 B7
Milk r. U.S.A. 156 G2
Milk, Wadi el watercourse Sudan 108 D6
Mil'kovo Rus. Fed. 77 Q4
Millaa Millaa Australia 136 D3
Millárs r. Spain 67 F4
Millau France 66 F4
Millbrook Canada 165 F1
Mill Creek r. U.S.A. 158 B1
Milledgeville U.S.A. 163 D5
Mille Lacs lakes U.S.A. 160 E2
Mille Lacs, Lac des l. Canada 147 I5
Millen U.S.A. 163 D5
Millennium Island atoll Kiribati see Caroline Island
Miller U.S.A. 160 D2
Miller, Mount AK U.S.A. 149 L3
Miller Lake Canada 164 E1
Millerovo Rus. Fed. 53 I6
Millersburg OH U.S.A. 164 E3
Millersburg PA U.S.A. 165 G3
Millers Creek U.S.A. 164 D5
Millersville U.S.A. 165 G4
Millerton Lake U.S.A. 158 D3
Millet Canada 150 H4
Milleur Point U.K. 60 D5
Mill Hall U.S.A. 165 G3
Millicent Australia 137 C8
Millington MI U.S.A. 164 D2
Millington TN U.S.A. 161 F5
Millinocket U.S.A. 162 G2
Mill Island Canada 147 K3
Millmerran Australia 138 E1
Millom U.K. 58 D4
Millport U.K. 60 E5
Millsboro U.S.A. 165 H4
Mills Creek watercourse Australia 136 C4
Mills Lake Canada 150 G2
Millstone KY U.S.A. 164 D5
Millstone WV U.S.A. 164 E4
Millstream-Chichester National Park Australia 134 B5
Millthorpe Australia 138 D4
Milltown Canada 153 I5
Milltown U.S.A. 156 E3
Milltown Malbay Ireland 61 C5
Millungera Australia 136 C3
Millville U.S.A. 165 H4
Millwood U.S.A. 164 B5
Millwood Lake U.S.A. 161 E5
Milly Milly Australia 135 B6
Milne Land i. Greenland see Ilimananngip Nunaa
Milner U.S.A. 159 J1
Milo r. Guinea 120 C3
Milogradovo Rus. Fed. 90 D4
Milolii U.S.A. 157 [inset]
Milos i. Greece 69 K6
Milparinka Australia 137 C6
Milpitas U.S.A. 158 C3
Milroy U.S.A. 165 G3
Milton N.Z. 139 B8
Milton DE U.S.A. 165 H4
Milton FL U.S.A. 167 I2
Milton NH U.S.A. 165 J2
Milton WV U.S.A. 164 D4
Milton Keynes U.K. 59 G6
Miluo China 97 G2
Milverton Canada 164 E2
Milwaukee U.S.A. 164 B2

▶Milwaukee Deep sea feature
Caribbean Sea 184 D4
Deepest point in the Puerto Rico Trench and in the Atlantic.

Milybulabk Kazakh. 98 A2
Mimbres watercourse U.S.A. 159 J5
Mimili Australia 135 F6
Mimisal India 106 C4
Mimizan France 66 D4
Mimongo Gabon 122 B4
Mimosa Rocks National Park Australia 138 E6
Mina Mex. 167 E3
Mina U.S.A. 158 D2
Mīnāb Iran 110 E5
Minaçu Brazil 179 A1
Minahasa, Semenanjung pen. Indon. 83 B2
Minahassa Peninsula Indon. see Minahasa, Semenanjung
Minakami Japan 93 E2
Minaker Canada see Prophet River
Mīnakh Syria 107 C1
Minaki Canada 151 M5
Minakuchi Japan 92 C4
Minami Japan 92 C3
Minamia Australia 134 F3
Minami-arupusu Kokuritsu-kōen nat. park Japan 93 E3
Minamiashigara Japan 93 F3
Minami-Bōsō Kokutei-kōen park Japan 93 F4
Minamichita Japan 92 C4
Minami-Daitō-jima i. Japan 89 O7
Minami-gawa r. Japan 92 B3
Minami-Iō-jima vol. Japan 81 K2
Minamiizu Japan 93 E4
Minami-kawara Japan 93 F2
Minamimaki Japan 93 E2
Minamiminowa Japan 93 D3
Minaminasu Japan 93 G2
Minamishinano Japan 93 D3
Min'an China see Longshan
Minano Japan 93 F2
Minaret of Jam tourist site Afgh. 111 G3
Minas Sumatera Indon. 84 C2
Minas Uruguay 178 E4
Minas, Sierra de las mts Guat. 167 H6
Minas de Matahambre Cuba 163 D8
Minas Gerais state Brazil 179 B2
Minas Novas Brazil 179 C2
Minatitlán Mex. 168 F5
Minbu Myanmar 86 A2
Minbya Myanmar 86 A2
Minchinmávida vol. Chile 178 B6
Minchumina, Lake AK U.S.A. 148 I3
Mindanao i. Phil. 82 D5
Mindanao r. Mindanao Phil. 82 D5
Mindanao Trench sea feature N. Pacific Ocean see Philippine Trench
Mindelo Cape Verde 120 [inset]
Minden Canada 165 F1
Minden Germany 63 I2
Minden LA U.S.A. 161 E5
Minden NE U.S.A. 154 H3
Minden NV U.S.A. 158 D2
Mindon Myanmar 86 A3
Mindoro i. Phil. 82 C3
Mindoro Strait Phil. 82 B3
Mindouli Congo 122 B4
Mine Head hd Ireland 61 E6
Minehead U.K. 59 D7
Mineola U.S.A. 165 I3
Mineola TX U.S.A. 167 G1
Miner r. N.W.T. Canada 149 O1
Miner r. Y.T. Canada 149 M2
Mineral U.S.A. 165 G4
Mineral'nyye Vody Rus. Fed. 113 F1
Mineral Wells U.S.A. 161 D5
Mineralwells U.S.A. 164 E4
Minersville PA U.S.A. 165 G3
Minersville UT U.S.A. 159 G2
Minerva U.S.A. 164 E3
Minerva Reefs Fiji 133 I4
Mineyama Japan 92 B3
Minfeng Xinjiang China 99 C5
Minga Dem. Rep. Congo 123 C5
Mingäçevir Azer. 113 G2
Mingäçevir Su Anbarı resr Azer. 113 G2
Mingala Cent. Afr. Rep. 122 C3
Mingan, Îles de is Canada 153 J4
Mingan Archipelago National Park Reserve Canada see L'Archipélago de Mingan,Réserve du Parc National de
Mingbuloq Uzbek. 102 B3
Mingechaur Azer. see Mingäçevir
Mingechaurskoye Vodokhranilishche resr Azer. see Mingäçevir Su Anbarı
Mingenew Australia 135 A7
Mingfeng China see Yuan'an
Minggang China 97 G1
Mingguang China 97 H1
Mingin Range mts Myanmar 86 A2
Ming-Kush Kyrg. 98 A4
Minglanilla Spain 67 F4
Mingoyo Tanz. 123 D5
Mingshan China 96 D2
Mingshui Gansu China 94 D3
Mingshui Heilong. China 90 B3
Mingteke Xinjiang China 99 A5
Mingulay i. U.K. 60 B4
Mingxi China 97 H3
Mingzhou Hebei China see Weixian
Mingzhou Shaanxi China see Suide
Minhe China see Jinxian
Minhla Magwe Myanmar 86 A3
Minhla Pegu Myanmar 86 A3
Minho r. Port./Spain see Miño
Minicoy atoll India 106 B4
Minigwal, Lake salt flat Australia 135 C7
Minilya Australia 135 A5
Minilya r. Australia 135 A5
Minipi Lake Canada 153 J3
Miniss Lake Canada 151 N5
Minitonas Canada 151 K4
Minjian China see Mabian
Min Jiang r. Sichuan China 96 E2
Min Jiang r. China 97 H3
Minkébé, Parc National de nat. park Gabon 122 B3
Minle Gansu China 94 E4
Minna Nigeria 120 D4
Minna Bluff pt Antarctica 188 H1
Minne Sweden 54 I5
Minneapolis KS U.S.A. 160 D4
Minneapolis MN U.S.A. 160 E2
Minnedosa Canada 151 L5
Minnehaha Springs U.S.A. 164 F4
Minneola U.S.A. 161 C4
Minnesota r. U.S.A. 160 E2
Minnesota state U.S.A. 160 E2
Minnewaukan U.S.A. 160 D1
Minnitaki Lake Canada 151 N5
Mino Japan 92 C3
Miño r. Port./Spain 67 B3
also known as Minho
Minobu Japan 93 E3
Minobu-san mt. Japan 93 E3
Minobu-sanchi mts Japan 93 E4
Minokamo Japan 92 D3
Mino-Mikawa-kōgen reg. Japan 92 D3
Minoo Japan 92 B4
Minorca i. Spain 67 H3
Minori Japan 93 G2
Minot U.S.A. 160 C1
Minowa Japan 93 D3
Minqār, Ghadīr imp. l. Syria 107 C3
Minqin Gansu China 94 E4
Minqing China 97 H3
Minquan Henan China 95 H5
Min Shan mts China 96 D1
Minsin Myanmar 86 A1

▶Minsk Belarus 55 O10
Capital of Belarus.

Mińsk Mazowiecki Poland 57 R4
Minsterley U.K. 59 E6
Mintaka Pass China/Pak. 104 C1
Mintang Qinghai China 94 E5
Minto AK U.S.A. 149 J2
Minto, Lac l. Canada 152 G2
Minto, Mount Antarctica 188 H2
Minto Inlet Canada 146 G2
Minton Canada 151 J5
Mīnudasht Iran 110 D2
Minūf Egypt 112 C5
Minusinsk Rus. Fed. 88 G2
Minvoul Gabon 122 B3
Minxian Gansu China 94 F5
Minya Konka mt. China see Gongga Shan
Minywa Myanmar 86 A2
Minzong India 105 I4
Mio U.S.A. 164 C1
Miquan Xinjiang China 98 D4
Miquelon Canada 152 F4
Miquelon i. St Pierre and Miquelon 153 K5
Mirabad Afgh. 111 F4
Mirabela Brazil 179 B2
Mirador-Dos Lagunos-Río Azul, Parque Nacional nat. park Guat. 167 H5
Miraflores Mex. 166 C4
Mīrah, Wādī al watercourse Iraq/Saudi Arabia 113 F4
Miraí Brazil 179 C3
Miraj India 106 B2
Miramar Arg. 178 E5
Miramar, Lago l. Mex. 167 H5
Miramichi Canada 153 I5
Miramichi Bay Canada 153 I5
Mirampellou, Kolpos b. Greece 69 K7
Mirampelou, Kolpos b. Kriti Greece see Mirampellou, Kolpos
Miran Xinjiang China 98 E5
Miranda Brazil 178 E2
Miranda Moz. see Macaloge
Miranda U.S.A. 158 B1
Miranda, Lake salt flat Australia 135 C6
Miranda de Ebro Spain 67 E2
Mirandela Port. 67 C3
Mirandola Italy 68 D2
Mirante Brazil 179 C1
Mirante, Serra do hills Brazil 179 A3
Mirassol Brazil 179 A3
Mir-Bashir Azer. see Tärtär
Mirbāţ Oman 109 H6
Mirboo North Australia 138 C7
Mirepoix France 66 E5
Mirgarh Pak. 111 I4
Mirgorod Ukr. see Myrhorod
Miri Sarawak Malaysia 85 F1
Miri mt. Pak. 111 F4
Mirialguda India 106 C2
Miri Hills India 105 H4
Mirim, Lagoa l. Brazil/Uruguay 178 F4
Mirim, Lagoa do l. Brazil 179 A5
Mirintu watercourse Australia 138 A2
Mirjan India 106 B3
Mirny research station Antarctica 188 F2
Mirnyy Arkhangel'skaya Oblast' Rus. Fed. 52 I3
Mirnyy Respublika Sakha (Yakutiya) Rus. Fed. 77 M3
Mirond Lake Canada 151 K4
Mironovka Ukr. see Myronivka
Mirow Germany 63 M1
Mirpur Khas Pak. 111 H5
Mirpur Sakro Pak. 111 G5
Mirsali Xinjiang China 98 D4
Mirs Bay H.K. China 97 [inset]
Mirtoan Sea Greece see Myrtoo Pelagos
Mirtoö Pelagos sea Greece see Myrtoo Pelagos
Miryalaguda India see Mirialguda
Miryang S. Korea 91 C6
Mirzachirla Turkm. see Murzechirla
Mirzachul Uzbek. see Guliston
Mirzapur India 105 E4
Mirzawal India 104 C3
Misaka Japan 93 E3
Misaki Chiba Japan 93 G3
Misaki Ōsaka Japan 92 B4
Misakubo Japan 93 D3
Misalay Xinjiang China 99 C5
Misantla Mex. 167 F5
Misato Gunma Japan 93 E2
Misato Mie Japan 92 C4
Misato Nagano Japan 93 D2
Misato Saitama Japan 93 F2
Misato Saitama Japan 93 F3
Misato Wakayama Japan 92 B4
Misaw Lake Canada 151 K3
Miscou Island Canada 153 I5
Misehkow r. Canada 152 C4
Mīsh, Kūh-e hill Iran 110 E3
Misha India 87 A6
Mishāsh al Ashāwī well Saudi Arabia 110 C5
Mishāsh az Ẓuayyinī well Saudi Arabia 110 C5
Mishawaka U.S.A. 164 B3
Misheguk Mountain AK U.S.A. 148 G1
Mishicot U.S.A. 164 B1
Mishima Japan 93 E3
Mi-shima i. Japan 91 C6
Mishmi Hills India 105 H3
Mishvan' Rus. Fed. 52 L2
Misima Island P.N.G. 136 F1
Misis Dağ hills Turkey 107 B1
Miskin Oman 110 E6
Miskitos, Cayos is Nicaragua 166 [inset] J6
Miskitos, Costa de coastal area Nicaragua see Costa de Mosquitos
Miskolc Hungary 53 D6
Mismā, Tall al hill Jordan 107 C3
Misoöl i. Papua Indon. 83 D3
Misquah Hills U.S.A. 160 F2
Misr country Africa see Egypt
Misraç Turkey see Kurtalan
Miṣrātah Libya 121 E1
Missinaibi r. Canada 152 E4
Mission TX U.S.A. 167 F3
Mission Beach Australia 136 D3
Mission Viejo U.S.A. 158 E5
Missisa r. Canada 152 D3
Missisa Lake Canada 152 D3
Missisicabi r. Canada 152 F4
Mississauga Canada 164 F2
Mississinewa Lake U.S.A. 164 C3

▶Mississippi r. U.S.A. 161 F6
4th longest river in North America, and a major part of the longest (Mississippi-Missouri).

Mississippi state U.S.A. 161 F5
Mississippi Delta U.S.A. 161 F6
Mississippi Lake Canada 165 G1

▶Mississippi-Missouri r. U.S.A. 155 I4
Longest river in North America, and 4th in the world.

Mississippi Sound sea chan. U.S.A. 161 F6
Missolonghi Greece see Mesolongi
Missoula U.S.A. 156 E3

▶Missouri r. U.S.A. 160 F4
3rd longest river in North America, and a major part of the longest (Mississippi-Missouri).

Missouri state U.S.A. 160 E4
Mistanipisipou r. Canada 153 J4
Mistassibi r. Canada 147 K5
Mistassini r. Canada 153 G4
Mistassini, Lac l. Canada 152 G4
Mistastin Lake Canada 153 J3
Mistelbach Austria 57 P6
Mistinibi, Lac l. Canada 153 J2
Mistissini Canada 152 G4
Misty Fiords National Monument Wilderness nat. park U.S.A. 149 O5
Misugi Japan 92 C4
Misumba Dem. Rep. Congo 123 C4
Misuratah Libya see Miṣrātah
Mita, Punta de pt Mex. 166 D4
Mitaka Japan 93 F3
Mitake Gifu Japan 92 D3
Mitake Nagano Japan 92 D3
Mitchell Australia 137 D5
Mitchell r. N.S.W. Australia 138 F2
Mitchell r. Qld Australia 136 C2
Mitchell r. Vic. Australia 138 C6
Mitchell Canada 164 E2
Mitchell IN U.S.A. 164 B4
Mitchell OR U.S.A. 156 C3
Mitchell SD U.S.A. 160 D3
Mitchell, Lake Australia 136 D3
Mitchell, Mount U.S.A. 162 D5
Mitchell and Alice Rivers National Park Australia 136 C2
Mitchell Island Cook Is see Nassau
Mitchell Island atoll Tuvalu see Nukulaelae
Mitchell Point Australia 134 E2
Mitchelstown Ireland 61 D5
Mīt Ghamr Egypt 112 C5
Mīt Ghamr Egypt see Mīt Ghamr
Mithi Pak. 111 H5
Mithrau Pak. 111 H5
Mithri Pak. 111 G4
Miti i. Maluku Indon. 83 D2
Mitilíni Greece see Mytilini
Mitkof Island AK U.S.A. 149 N4
Mito Aichi Japan 92 D4
Mito Ibaraki Japan 93 G2
Mitole Tanz. 123 D4
Mitomi Japan 93 E3
Mitre mt. N.Z. 139 E5
Mitre Island Solomon Is 133 H3
Mitrofania Island AK U.S.A. 148 H5
Mitrofanovka Rus. Fed. 53 H6
Mitrovica Kosovo see Mitrovicë
Mitrovicë Kosovo 69 I3
Mitsinjo Madag. 123 E5
Mits'iwa Eritrea see Massawa
Mitsue Japan 92 C4
Mitsukaidō Japan 93 F2
Mitsumatarenge-dake mt. Japan 92 D2
Mitsutōge-yama mt. Japan 93 E3
Mitta Mitta Australia 138 C6
Mittellandkanal canal Germany 63 I2
Mitterteich Germany 63 M5
Mittimatalik Canada see Pond Inlet
Mittweida Germany 63 M4
Mitú Col. 176 D3
Mitumba, Chaîne des mts Dem. Rep. Congo 123 C5
Mitzic Gabon 122 B3
Miughalaigh i. U.K. see Mingulay
Miura Japan 93 F3
Miura-hantō pen. Japan 93 F3
Miwa Fukushima Japan 93 G1
Miwa Ibaraki Japan 93 G2
Miwa Kyōto Japan 92 B3
Mixian Henan China see Xinmi
Miya Japan 92 D2
Miyada Japan 93 D3
Miyagase-ko resr Japan 93 F3
Miyagawa Gifu Japan 92 D2
Miyagawa Mie Japan 92 C4
Miya-gawa r. Japan 92 C4
Miya-gawa r. Japan 92 D2
Miyake-jima i. Japan 93 F4
Miyako Japan 91 F5
Miyakonojō Japan 91 C7
Miyama Fukui Japan 92 C2
Miyama Gifu Japan 92 C3
Miyama Kyōto Japan 92 B3
Miyama Mie Japan 92 C4
Miyama Wakayama Japan 92 B5
Miyamae Japan 93 F3
Miyang China see Mile
Miyani India 104 B5
Miyazaki Fukui Japan 92 C3
Miyazaki Japan 91 C7
Miyazu Japan 92 B3
Miyazu-wan b. Japan 92 B3
Miyi China 96 D3
Miyoshi Aichi Japan 92 D3
Miyoshi Chiba Japan 93 F3
Miyoshi Japan 91 D6
Miyota Japan 93 E2
Miyun Beijing China 95 I3
Miyun Shuiku resr China 95 I3
Mīzānī Afgh. 111 G3
Mīzan Teferī Eth. 122 D3
Mizdah Libya 121 E1
Mizen Head hd Ireland 61 C6
Mizhhir"ya Ukr. 53 D6
Mizhi Shaanxi China 95 G4
Mizo Hills state India see Mizoram
Mizoram state India 105 H5
Mizpé Ramon Israel 107 B4
Mizugaki-yama mt. Japan 93 E3
Mizuhashi Japan 92 D2
Mizuho Kyōto Japan 92 B3
Mizuho Tōkyō Japan 93 F3
Mizunami Japan 92 D3
Mizuno-gawa r. Japan 93 F2
Mizusawa Japan 91 F5
Mjölby Sweden 55 I7
Mkata Tanz. 123 D4
Mkushi Zambia 123 C5
Mladá Boleslav Czech Rep. 57 O5
Mladenovac Serbia 69 I2
Mława Poland 57 R4
Mlilwane Nature Reserve Swaziland 125 J4
Mljet i. Croatia 68 G3
Mlungisi S. Africa 125 H6
Mmabatho S. Africa 125 G3
Mmamabula Botswana 125 H2
Mmathethe Botswana 125 G3
Mo Norway 55 D6
Moa i. Maluku Indon. 83 D5
Moab reg. Jordan 107 B4
Moab U.S.A. 159 I2
Moa Island Australia 136 C1
Moala i. Fiji 133 H3
Mo'alla Iran 110 D3
Moamba Moz. 125 K3
Moanda Gabon 122 B4
Moapa U.S.A. 159 F3
Moate Ireland 61 E4
Mobara Japan 93 G3
Mobārakeh Iran 110 C3
Mobayembongo Dem. Rep. Congo see Mobayi-Mbongo
Mobayi-Mbongo Dem. Rep. Congo 122 C3
Moberly U.S.A. 160 E4
Moberly Lake Canada 150 F4
Mobha India 104 C5
Mobile AL U.S.A. 161 F6
Mobile AZ U.S.A. 159 G5
Mobile Bay U.S.A. 161 F6
Mobile Point AL U.S.A. 167 I2
Moble watercourse Australia 138 B1
Mobo Masbate Phil. 82 C3
Mobridge U.S.A. 160 C2
Mobutu, Lake Dem. Rep. Congo/Uganda see Albert, Lake
Mobutu Sese Seko, Lake Dem. Rep. Congo/Uganda see Albert, Lake
Moca Geçidi pass Turkey 107 A1
Moçambique country Africa see Mozambique
Moçambique Moz. 123 E5
Moçâmedes Angola see Namibe
Môc Châu Vietnam 86 D2
Mocha Yemen 108 F7
Mocha, Isla i. Chile 178 B5
Mochicahui Mex. 166 C3
Mochirma, Parque Nacional nat. park Venez. 176 F1
Mochudi Botswana 125 H3
Mochudi admin. dist. Botswana see Kgatleng
Mocimboa da Praia Moz. 123 E5
Möckern Germany 63 L2
Möckmühl Germany 63 J5
Mockträsk Sweden 54 L4
Mocoa Col. 176 C3
Mococa Brazil 179 B3
Mocoduene Moz. 125 L2
Mocorito Mex. 166 D3
Moctezuma Chihuahua Mex. 166 D2
Moctezuma San Luis Potosí Mex. 168 D4
Moctezuma Sonora Mex. 166 C2
Mocuba Moz. 123 D5
Mocun China 97 G4
Modan Indon. 81 I7
Modane France 66 H4
Modder r. S. Africa 125 G5
Modena Italy 68 D2
Modena U.S.A. 159 G3
Modesto U.S.A. 158 C3
Modesto Lake U.S.A. 158 C3
Modimolle S. Africa 125 I3
Modot Mongolia see Tsenhermandal
Modung China 96 C2
Moe Australia 138 C7
Moel Sych hill U.K. 59 D6

Moelv Norway 55 G6
Moen Norway 54 K2
Moenkopi U.S.A. 159 H3
Moenkopi Wash r. U.S.A. 159 H4
Moeraki Point N.Z. 139 C7
Moero, Lake Dem. Rep. Congo/Zambia see Mweru, Lake
Moers Germany 62 G3
Moffat U.K. 60 F5
Moga India 104 C3

▶Mogadishu Somalia 122 E3
Capital of Somalia.

Mogador Morocco see Essaouira
Mogadore Reservoir U.S.A. 164 E3
Moganyaka S. Africa 125 I3
Mogao Ku Gansu China 98 F5
Mogaung Myanmar 86 B1
Mogdy Rus. Fed. 90 D2
Mögelin Germany 63 M2
Mogilev Belarus see Mahilyow
Mogilev Podol'skiy Ukr. see Mohyliv Podil's'kyy
Mogi-Mirim Brazil 179 B3
Mogiquiçaba Brazil 179 D2
Mogocha Rus. Fed. 89 L2
Mogod mts Tunisia 68 C6
Mogoditshane Botswana 125 G3
Mogollon Mountains U.S.A. 159 I5
Mogollon Plateau U.S.A. 159 H4
Mogontiacum Germany see Mainz
Mogoytuy Rus. Fed. 95 H1
Mogroum Chad 121 E3
Moguqi Nei Mongol China 95 J2
Mogwadi S. Africa 125 I2
Mogwase S. Africa 125 H3
Mogzon Rus. Fed. 89 K2
Mohács Hungary 68 H2
Mohaka r. N.Z. 139 F4
Mohala India 106 D1
Mohale Dam Lesotho 125 I5
Mohale's Hoek Lesotho 125 H6
Mohall U.S.A. 160 C1
Mohammad Iran 110 E3
Mohammadia Alg. 67 G6
Mohan r. India/Nepal 104 E3
Mohana India 104 D4
Mohave, Lake U.S.A. 159 F4
Mohawk r. U.S.A. 165 I2
Mohawk Mountains U.S.A. 159 G5
Mohenjo Daro tourist site Pak. 111 H5
Moher, Cliffs of Ireland 61 C5
Mohican, Cape AK U.S.A. 148 F3
Mohill Ireland 61 E4
Möhne r. Germany 63 H3
Möhnetalsperre resr Germany 63 I3
Mohon Peak U.S.A. 159 G4
Mohoro Tanz. 123 D4
Mohyliv Podil's'kyy Ukr. 53 E6
Moi Norway 55 E7
Moijabana Botswana 125 H2
Moincêr Xizang China 99 C7
Moinda Xizang China 99 E7
Moindawang Arun. Prad. India 99 E8
Moine Moz. 125 K3
Moinești Romania 69 L1
Mointy Kazakh. see Moyynty
Mo i Rana Norway 54 I3
Moirang India 96 B3
Mõisaküla Estonia 55 N7
Moisie Canada 153 I4
Moisie r. Canada 153 I4
Moissac France 66 E4
Mojave U.S.A. 158 D4
Mojave r. U.S.A. 158 E4
Mojave Desert U.S.A. 158 E4
Mojiang China 96 D4
Moji das Cruzes Brazil 179 B3
Mojokerto Jawa Indon. 85 F4
Mojos, Llanos de plain Bol. 176 E6
Moju r. Brazil 177 I4
Mōka Japan 93 G2
Mokama India 105 F4
Mokau N.Z. 139 E4
Mokau r. N.Z. 139 E4
Mokelumne r. U.S.A. 158 C2
Mokelumne Aqueduct canal U.S.A. 158 C2
Mokhoabong Pass Lesotho 125 I5
Mokhotlong Lesotho 125 I5
Mokhtārān Iran 110 E3
Moknine Tunisia 68 D7
Mokohinau Islands N.Z. 139 E2
Mokokchung India 105 H4
Mokolo Cameroon 121 E3
Mokolo r. S. Africa 125 H2
Mokopane S. Africa 125 I3
Mokp'o S. Korea 91 B6
Mokrous Rus. Fed. 53 J6
Moksha r. Rus. Fed. 53 I5
Mokshan Rus. Fed. 53 J5
Möksy Fin. 54 N5
Môktama Myanmar see Mottama
Môktama, Gulf of Myanmar see Mottama, Gulf of
Mokundurra India see Mukandwara
Mokwa Nigeria 120 D4
Molango Mex. 167 F4
Molatón mt. Spain 67 F4
Moldary Kazakh. 98 B2
Moldavia country Europe see Moldova
Moldavskaya S.S.R. country Europe see Moldova
Molde Norway 54 E5
Moldjord Norway 54 I3
Moldova country Europe 53 F7
Moldoveanu, Vârful mt. Romania 69 K2
Moldovei de Sud, Câmpia plain Moldova 69 M1
Molega Lake Canada 153 I5
Molen r. S. Africa 125 I4
Mole National Park Ghana 120 C4
Molepolole Botswana 125 G3
Molėtai Lith. 55 N9
Molfetta Italy 68 G4
Molière Alg. see Bordj Bounaama
Molihong Shan mt. China see Morihong Shan
Molina de Aragón Spain 67 F3
Moline U.S.A. 161 D4
Molkom Sweden 55 H7
Mollagara Turkm. 110 D2
Mollakara Turkm. see Mollagara
Mol Len mt. India 105 H4
Möllenbeck Germany 63 N1
Mollendo Peru 176 D7
Mölln Germany 63 K1
Mölnlycke Sweden 55 H8
Molochnyy Rus. Fed. 54 R2
Molodechno Belarus see Maladzyechna
Molodezhnaya research station Antarctica 188 D2
Moloka'i i. U.S.A. 157 [inset]
Moloma r. Rus. Fed. 52 K4
Molong Australia 138 D4
Molopo watercourse Botswana/S. Africa 124 E5
Molotov Rus. Fed. see Perm'
Molotovsk Kyrg. see Kayyngdy
Molotovsk Arkhangel'skaya Oblast' Rus. Fed. see Severodvinsk
Molotovsk Kirovskaya Oblast' Rus. Fed. see Nolinsk
Moloundou Cameroon 121 E4
Molson Lake Canada 151 L4
Molu i. Indon. 81 I8
Moluccas is Indon. 83 C3
Molucca Sea Indon. see Maluku, Laut
Moma Moz. 123 D5
Moma r. Rus. Fed. 77 P3
Momba Australia 138 A3
Mombaça Brazil 177 K5
Mombasa Kenya 122 D4
Mombetsu Hokkaidō Japan see Monbetsu
Mombetsu Hokkaidō Japan see Monbetsu
Mombi New India 105 H4
Mombum Indon. 81 J8
Momchilgrad Bulg. 69 K4
Momence U.S.A. 164 B3
Momi, Ra's pt Yemen 109 H7
Momotombo, Volcán vol. Nicaragua 166 [inset] I6
Momoyama Japan 92 B4
Mompog Passage Phil. 82 C3
Mompós Col. 176 D2
Møn i. Denmark 55 H9
Mon India 105 H4
Mona terr. Irish Sea see Isle of Man
Mona U.S.A. 159 H2
Monaca U.S.A. 164 E3
Monach, Sound of sea chan. U.K. 60 B3
Monach Islands U.K. 60 B3
Monaco country Europe 66 H5
Monaco Basin sea feature N. Atlantic Ocean 184 G4
Monadhliath Mountains U.K. 60 E3
Monaghan Ireland 61 F3
Monahans U.S.A. 161 C6
Mona Passage Dom. Rep./Puerto Rico 169 K5
Monapo Moz. 123 E5
Monar, Loch l. U.K. 60 D3
Monarch Mountain Canada 150 E5
Monarch Pass U.S.A. 157 G5
Mona Reservoir U.S.A. 159 H2
Monashee Mountains Canada 150 G5
Monastir Macedonia see Bitola
Monastir Tunisia 68 D7
Monastyrishche Ukr. see Monastyryshche
Monastyryshche Ukr. 53 F6
Monbetsu Hokkaidō Japan 90 F3
Monbetsu Hokkaidō Japan 90 F4
Moncalieri Italy 68 B2
Monchegorsk Rus. Fed. 54 R3
Mönchengladbach Germany 62 G3
Monchique Port. 67 B5
Moncks Corner U.S.A. 163 D5
Monclova Mex. 167 E3
Moncouche, Lac l. Canada 153 H4
Moncton Canada 153 I5
Mondego r. Port. 67 B3
Mondlo S. Africa 125 J4
Mondo Chad 121 E3
Mondovì Italy 68 B2
Mondragone Italy 68 E4
Mondy Rus. Fed. 88 I2
Monemvasia Greece 69 J6
Monessen U.S.A. 164 F3
Moneta U.S.A. 156 G4
Moneygall Ireland 61 E5
Moneymore U.K. 61 F3
Monfalcone Italy 68 E2
Monfalut Egypt see Manfalūṭ
Monforte de Lemos Spain 67 C2
Monga Dem. Rep. Congo 122 C3
Mongala r. Dem. Rep. Congo 122 B3
Mongar Bhutan 105 G4
Mongbwalu Dem. Rep. Congo 122 D3
Mông Cai Vietnam 86 D2
Mongers Lake salt flat Australia 135 B7
Monggon Qulu Nei Mongol China 95 I1
Mong Hang Myanmar 86 B2
Mong Hkan Myanmar 86 C2
Mong Hpayak Myanmar 86 B2
Mong Hsat Myanmar 86 B2
Mong Hsawk Myanmar 86 B2
Mong Hsu Myanmar 86 B2
Monghyr India see Munger
Mong Kung Myanmar 86 B2
Mong Kyawt Myanmar 86 B3
Mongla Bangl. 105 G5
Mong Lin Myanmar 86 C2
Mong Loi Myanmar 86 C2
Mong Long Myanmar 86 B2
Mong Nai Myanmar 86 B2
Mong Nawng Myanmar 86 B2
Mongo Chad 121 E3
Mongolia country Asia 88 I3
Mongolküre Xinjiang China see Zhaosu
Mongol Uls country Asia see Mongolia
Möngönmorīt Mongolia 95 G1
Mongonu Nigeria 120 E3
Mongora Pak. 111 I3
Mongour hill U.K. 60 G4
Mong Pan Myanmar 86 B2
Mong Ping Myanmar 86 B2
Mong Pu Myanmar 86 B2
Mong Pu-awn Myanmar 86 B2
Mongrove, Punta pt Mex. 166 E5
Mong Si Myanmar 86 B2
Mongu Zambia 123 C5
Mong Un Myanmar 86 C2
Mong Yai Myanmar 86 B2
Mong Yang Myanmar 86 B2
Mong Yawn Myanmar 86 B2
Mong Yawng Myanmar 86 C2
Mönhaan Mongolia 95 H2
Mönhbulag Mongolia see Yösöndzüyl
Mönh Hayrhan Uul mt. Mongolia 94 B2
Moniaive U.K. 60 F5
Monitor Mountain U.S.A. 158 E2
Monitor Range mts U.S.A. 158 E2
Monivea Ireland 61 D4
Monkey Bay Malawi 123 D5
Monkira Australia 136 C5
Monkton Canada 164 E2
Monmouth U.K. 59 E7
Monmouth U.S.A. 160 F3
Monmouth Mountain Canada 150 F5
Monnow r. U.K. 59 E7
Mono, Punta del pt Nicaragua 166 [inset] J7
Mono Lake U.S.A. 158 D2
Monolithos Greece 69 L6
Monomoy Point U.S.A. 165 J3
Monon U.S.A. 164 B3
Monopoli Italy 68 G4
Monreal del Campo Spain 67 F3
Monreale Sicily Italy 68 E5
Monroe IN U.S.A. 164 C3
Monroe LA U.S.A. 161 E5
Monroe MI U.S.A. 164 D3
Monroe NC U.S.A. 163 D5
Monroe WI U.S.A. 160 F3
Monroe Center U.S.A. 160 F2
Monroe Lake U.S.A. 164 B4
Monroeton U.S.A. 165 G3
Monroeville AL U.S.A. 167 I2

▶Monrovia Liberia 120 B4
Capital of Liberia.

Mons Belgium 62 D4
Monschau Germany 62 G4
Monselice Italy 68 D2
Montabaur Germany 63 H4
Montagu S. Africa 124 E7
Montague Canada 153 J5
Montague MI U.S.A. 164 B2
Montague TX U.S.A. 161 D5
Montague Island AK U.S.A. 149 K3
Montague Range hills Australia 135 B6
Montague Strait AK U.S.A. 149 J4
Montalat r. Indon. 85 F3
Montalto mt. Italy 68 F5
Montalto Uffugo Italy 68 G5
Montana Bulg. 69 J3
Montana AK U.S.A. 149 J3
Montana state U.S.A. 156 F3
Montaña de Comayagua, Parque Nacional nat. park Hond. 166 [inset] I6
Montaña de Cusuco, Parque Nacional nat. park Hond. 167 H6
Montaña de Yoro nat. park Hond. 166 [inset] I6
Montañas de Colón mts Hond. 166 [inset] I6
Montanhas do Tumucumaque, Parque Nacional 177 H3
Montargis France 66 F3
Montauban France 66 E4
Montauk U.S.A. 165 J3
Montauk Point U.S.A. 165 J3
Mont-aux-Sources mt. Lesotho 125 I5
Montbard France 66 G3
Mont Blanc mt. France/Italy 66 H4
Montblanc Spain 67 G3
Montblanch Spain see Montblanc
Montbrison France 66 G4
Montceau-les-Mines France 66 G3
Montcornet France 62 E5
Mont-de-Marsan France 66 D5
Montdidier France 62 C5
Monte Alban tourist site Mex. 167 F5
Monte Alegre Brazil 177 H4
Monte Alegre de Goiás Brazil 179 B1
Monte Alegre de Minas Brazil 179 A2
Monte Azul Brazil 179 C1
Monte Azul Paulista Brazil 179 A3
Montebello Canada 152 G5
Montebello Islands Australia 134 A5
Montebelluna Italy 68 E2
Monte-Carlo Monaco 66 H5
Monte Cristi Dom. Rep. 169 J5
Monte Cristo S. Africa 125 H2
Monte Dourado Brazil 177 H4
Monte Escobedo Mex. 166 E4
Monte Falterona, Campigna e delle Foreste Casentinesi, Parco Nazionale del nat. park Italy 68 D3
Montego Bay Jamaica 169 I5
Montélimar France 66 G4
Monte Lindo r. Para. 178 E2
Montello U.S.A. 160 F3
Montemorelos Mex. 167 F3
Montemor-o-Novo Port. 67 B4
Montenegro country Europe 68 H2
Montepulciano Italy 68 D3
Monte Quemado Arg. 178 D3
Montereau-Fault-Yonne France 66 F2
Monterey Mex. see Monterrey
Monterey CA U.S.A. 158 C3
Monterey VA U.S.A. 164 F4
Monterey Bay U.S.A. 158 B3
Montería Col. 176 C2
Monteros Arg. 178 C3
Monterrey Baja California Mex. 159 F5
Monterrey Nuevo León Mex. 167 E3
Montesano U.S.A. 156 C3
Montesano sulla Marcellana Italy 68 F4
Monte Santo Brazil 177 K6
Monte Santu, Capo di c. Sardinia Italy 68 C4
Montes Claros Brazil 179 C2
Montesilvano Italy 68 F3
Montevarchi Italy 68 D3

▶Montevideo Uruguay 178 E4
Capital of Uruguay.

Montevideo U.S.A. 160 E2
Montezuma U.S.A. 160 E3
Montezuma Creek U.S.A. 159 I3
Montezuma Peak U.S.A. 158 E3
Montfort Neth. 62 F3
Montgomery U.K. 59 D6

▶Montgomery AL U.S.A. 163 C5
Capital of Alabama.

Montgomery WV U.S.A. 164 E4
Montgomery Islands Australia 134 C3
Monthey Switz. 66 H3
Monticello AR U.S.A. 161 F5
Monticello FL U.S.A. 163 D6
Monticello IN U.S.A. 164 B3
Monticello KY U.S.A. 164 C5
Monticello MO U.S.A. 160 F3
Monticello NY U.S.A. 165 H3
Monticello UT U.S.A. 159 I3
Montignac France 66 E4
Montignies-le-Tilleul Belgium 62 E4
Montigny-lès-Metz France 62 G5
Montilla Spain 67 D5
Monti Sibillini, Parco Nazionale dei nat. park Italy 68 E3
Montividiu Brazil 179 A2
Montivilliers France 59 H9
Mont-Joli Canada 153 H4
Mont-Laurier Canada 152 G5
Montluçon France 66 F3
Montmagny Canada 153 H5
Montmédy France 62 F5
Montmirail France 62 D6
Montmorillon France 66 E3
Montmort-Lucy France 62 D6
Monto Australia 136 E5
Montour Falls U.S.A. 165 G2
Montoursville U.S.A. 165 G3
Montpelier ID U.S.A. 156 F4

▶Montpelier VT U.S.A. 165 I1
Capital of Vermont.

Montpellier France 66 F5
Montréal Canada 152 G5
Montreal r. Ont. Canada 152 D5
Montreal r. Ont. Canada 152 F5
Montreal Lake Canada 151 J4
Montreal Lake l. Canada 151 J4
Montréal-Mirabel airport Canada 152 G5
Montreal River Canada 152 D5
Montréal-Trudeau airport Canada 152 G5
Montreuil France 62 B4
Montreux Switz. 66 H3
Montrose well S. Africa 124 E4
Montrose U.K. 60 G4
Montrose CO U.S.A. 159 J2
Montrose PA U.S.A. 165 H3
Montross U.S.A. 165 G4
Monts, Pointe des pt Canada 153 I4
Mont-St-Aignan France 59 I9

▶Montserrat terr. West Indies 169 L5
United Kingdom Overseas Territory.

Montuosa, Isla i. Panama 166 [inset] J8
Montviel, Lac l. Canada 153 H3
Monument Mountain hill AK U.S.A. 148 G2
Monument Valley reg. U.S.A. 159 H3
Monywa Myanmar 86 A2
Monza Italy 68 C2
Monze, Cape pt Pak. see Muari, Ras
Monzón Spain 67 G3
Mooi r. S. Africa 125 J5
Mooifontein Namibia 124 C4
Mookane Botswana 125 H2
Mookgopong S. Africa see Naboomspruit
Moolawatana Australia 137 B6
Moomba Australia 137 C6
Moomin Creek r. Australia 138 D2
Moonaree Australia 137 A6
Moonbi Range mts Australia 138 E3
Moonda Lake salt flat Australia 137 C5
Moonie Australia 138 E1
Moonie r. Australia 138 D2
Moora Australia 135 B7
Mooraberree Australia 136 C5
Moorcroft U.S.A. 156 G3
Moore r. Australia 135 A7
Moore U.S.A. 156 F3
Moore, Lake salt flat Australia 135 B7
Moore Creek AK U.S.A. 148 H3
Moore Embayment b. Antarctica 188 H1
Moorefield U.S.A. 165 F4
Moore Haven U.S.A. 163 D7
Moore Reef Australia 136 E3
Moore Reservoir U.S.A. 165 J1
Moore River National Park Australia 135 A7
Moores Island Bahamas 163 E7
Moorfoot Hills U.K. 60 F5
Moorhead U.S.A. 160 D2
Moorman U.S.A. 164 B5
Moornanyah Lake imp. l. Australia 138 A4
Mooroopna Australia 138 B6
Moorreesburg S. Africa 124 D7
Moorrinya National Park Australia 136 D4
Moose r. Canada 152 E4
Moose Creek AK U.S.A. 149 K2
Moose Factory Canada 152 E4
Moosehead Lake U.S.A. 162 G2
Moose Jaw Canada 151 J5
Moose Jaw r. Canada 151 J5
Moose Lake U.S.A. 160 E2
Mooselookmeguntic Lake U.S.A. 165 J1
Moose Mountain Creek r. Canada 151 K5
Moose Pass AK U.S.A. 149 J3
Moosilauke, Mount U.S.A. 165 J1
Moosomin Canada 151 K5
Moosonee Canada 152 E4
Mootwingee National Park Australia 137 C6
Mopane S. Africa 125 I2
Mopeia Moz. 123 D5
Mopipi Botswana 123 C6
Mopti Mali 120 C3
Moqor Afgh. 111 G3
Moquegua Peru 176 D7
Mora Cameroon 121 E3
Mora Spain 67 E4
Mora Sweden 55 I6
Mora MN U.S.A. 160 E2
Mora NM U.S.A. 157 G6
Mora r. U.S.A. 157 G6
Moradabad India 104 D3
Morada Nova Brazil 177 K5
Moraine Lake Canada 151 J1
Moraleda, Canal sea chan. Chile 178 B6
Morales Guat. 166 [inset] H6
Moram India 106 C2
Moramanga Madag. 123 E5
Moran U.S.A. 156 F4
Moranbah Australia 136 E4
Morang Nepal see Biratnagar
Morar, Loch l. U.K. 60 D4
Morari, Tso l. India 104 D2
Moratuwa Sri Lanka 106 C5
Morava reg. Czech Rep. 57 P6
Moravia U.S.A. 165 G2
Morawa Australia 135 A7
Moray Firth b. U.K. 60 E3
Moray Range hills Australia 134 E3
Morbach Germany 62 H5
Morbeng S. Africa see Soekmekaar
Morbi India 104 B5
Morcenx France 66 D4
Morcillo Mex. 161 B7
Mordaga China 89 M2
Mor Dağı mt. Turkey 113 G3
Morden Canada 151 L5
Mordovo Rus. Fed. 53 I5
Mordvinof, Cape AK U.S.A. 148 F5
Moreau r. U.S.A. 160 C2
Moreau, South Fork r. U.S.A. 160 C2
Morecambe U.K. 58 E4
Morecambe Bay U.K. 58 D4
Moree Australia 138 D2
Morehead P.N.G. 81 K8
Morehead U.S.A. 164 D4
Morehead City U.S.A. 169 I2
Morel r. India 99 B8
Moreland U.S.A. 164 C5
More Laptevykh sea Rus. Fed. see Laptev Sea
Morelia Mex. 168 D5
Morella Australia 136 C4
Morella Spain 67 F3
Morelos Mex. 157 G8
Morelos state Mex. 167 F5
Morena India 104 D4
Morena, Sierra mts Spain 67 C5
Morenci AZ U.S.A. 159 I5
Morenci MI U.S.A. 164 C3
Moreni Romania 69 K2
Moreno Mex. 166 C2
Moreno Valley U.S.A. 158 E5
Moresby, Mount B.C. Canada 149 N5
Moresby Island B.C. Canada 149 N5
Moreswe Pan salt pan Botswana 124 G2
Moreton Bay Australia 138 F1
Moreton-in-Marsh U.K. 59 F7
Moreton Island Australia 138 F1
Moreton Island National Park Australia 138 F1
Moreuil France 62 C5
Morez France 66 H3
Morfou Cyprus 107 A2
Morfou Bay Cyprus 107 A2
Morgan U.S.A. 156 F4
Morgan City U.S.A. 161 F6
Morgan Hill U.S.A. 158 C3
Morganton U.S.A. 162 D5
Morgantown KY U.S.A. 164 B5
Morgantown WV U.S.A. 164 F4
Morgenzon S. Africa 125 I4
Morges Switz. 66 H3
Morgh, Kowtal-e Afgh. 111 H3
Morghāb r. Afgh. 111 F3
Morghāb reg. Afgh. 111 F3
Morhar r. India 105 F4
Mori Xinjiang China 94 B3
Mori Japan 90 F4
Mori Shizuoka Japan 93 D4
Moriah, Mount U.S.A. 159 F2
Moriarty's Range hills Australia 138 B2
Morice Lake Canada 150 E4
Morichal Col. 176 D3
Moriguchi Japan 92 B4
Morihong Shan mt. China 90 B4
Morija Lesotho 125 H5
Morin Dawa Nei Mongol China see Nirji
Moringen Germany 63 J3
Morioka Japan 91 F5
Moris Mex. 166 C2
Morisset Australia 138 E4
Moriya Japan 93 F3
Moriyama Japan 92 C3
Moriyoshi-zan vol. Japan 91 F5
Morjärv Sweden 54 M3
Morjen r. Pak. 111 F4
Morki Rus. Fed. 52 K4
Morlaix France 66 C2
Morley U.K. 58 F5
Mormam Flat Dam U.S.A. 159 H5
Mormant France 62 C6
Mormon Lake U.S.A. 159 H4
Mormugao India see Marmagao
Morne Diablotins vol. Dominica 169 L5
Morney watercourse Australia 136 C5
Mornington, Isla i. Chile 178 A7
Mornington Abyssal Plain sea feature S. Atlantic Ocean 184 C9
Mornington Island Australia 136 B3
Mornington Peninsula National Park Australia 138 B7
Moro Pak. 111 G5
Moro U.S.A. 156 C3
Morobe P.N.G. 81 L8
Morocco country Africa 120 C1
Morocco U.S.A. 164 B3
Morococala mt. Bol. 176 E7
Morogoro Tanz. 123 D4
Moro Gulf Phil. 82 C5
Morojaneng S. Africa 125 H5
Morokweng S. Africa 124 F4
Moroleón Mex. 167 E4
Moromaho i. Indon. 83 C4
Morombe Madag. 123 E6
Morón Cuba 163 E8
Mörön Mongolia 94 E1
Morondava Madag. 123 E6
Morón de la Frontera Spain 67 D5

▶Moroni Comoros 123 E5
Capital of the Comoros.

Moroni U.S.A. 159 H2
Morotai i. Maluku Indon. 83 D2
Morotai, Selat sea chan. Maluku Indon. 83 C2
Moroto Uganda 122 D3
Morowali, Cagar Alam nature res. Indon. 83 B3
Morozovsk Rus. Fed. 53 I6
Morpeth Canada 164 E2
Morpeth U.K. 58 F3
Morphou Cyprus see Morfou
Morrill U.S.A. 164 C5
Morrilton U.S.A. 161 E5
Morrin Canada 151 H5
Morrinhos Brazil 179 A2
Morris Canada 151 L5
Morris IL U.S.A. 160 F3
Morris MN U.S.A. 160 E2
Morris PA U.S.A. 165 G3
Morris Jessup, Kap c. Greenland 189 I1
Morrison U.S.A. 160 F3
Morristown AZ U.S.A. 159 G5
Morristown NJ U.S.A. 165 H3
Morristown NY U.S.A. 165 H1
Morristown TN U.S.A. 162 D4
Morrisville U.S.A. 165 H2
Morro Brazil 179 B2
Morro Bay U.S.A. 158 C4
Morro d'Anta Brazil 179 D2
Morro de Papanoa hd Mex. 167 E5
Morro de Petatlán hd Mex. 167 E5
Morro do Chapéu Brazil 177 J6
Morro Grande hill Brazil 177 H4
Morrosquillo, Golfo de b. Col. 176 C2
Morrumbene Moz. 125 L2
Morschen Germany 63 J3
Morse Canada 151 J5
Morse U.S.A. 161 C4
Morse, Cape Antarctica 188 G2
Morse Reservoir U.S.A. 164 B3
Morshanka Rus. Fed. 53 I5
Morshansk Rus. Fed. see Morshanka
Morsott Alg. 68 C7
Mort watercourse Australia 136 C4
Mortagne-au-Perche France 66 E2
Mortagne-sur-Sèvre France 66 D3
Mortara Italy 68 C2
Mortehoe U.K. 59 C7
Morteros Arg. 178 D4
Mortes, Rio das r. Brazil 179 A1
Mortimer's Bahamas 163 F8
Mortlake Australia 138 A7
Mortlock Islands Micronesia 186 G5
Mortlock Islands P.N.G. see Takuu Islands
Morton U.K. 59 G6
Morton TX U.S.A. 161 C5
Morton WA U.S.A. 156 C3
Morton National Park Australia 138 E5
Morundah Australia 138 C5
Morupule Botswana 125 H2
Mururoa atoll Fr. Polynesia see Mururoa
Moruya Australia 138 E5
Morven Australia 137 D5
Morven hill U.K. 60 F2
Morvern reg. U.K. 60 D4
Morvi India see Morbi
Morwell Australia 138 C7
Morzhovets, Ostrov i. Rus. Fed. 52 I2
Morzhovoi Bay AK U.S.A. 148 G5
Mosbach Germany 63 J5
Mosborough U.K. 58 F5

Mosby U.S.A. **156** G3

▶**Moscow** Rus. Fed. **52** H5
Capital of the Russian Federation. Most populous city in Europe.

Moscow *ID* U.S.A. **156** D3
Moscow *PA* U.S.A. **165** H3
Moscow University Ice Shelf Antarctica **188** G2
Mosel *r.* Germany **63** H4
Moselebe *watercourse* Botswana **124** F3
Moselle *r.* France **62** G5
Möser Germany **63** L2
Moses, Mount U.S.A. **158** E1
Moses Lake U.S.A. **156** D3
Moses Point *AK* U.S.A. **148** G2
Mosgiel N.Z. **139** C7
Moshaweng *watercourse* S. Africa **124** F4
Moshchnyy, Ostrov *i.* Rus. Fed. **55** O7
Moshi Tanz. **122** D4
Mosh'yuga Rus. Fed. **52** L2
Mosi-oa-Tunya *waterfall* Zambia/Zimbabwe *see* **Victoria Falls**
Mosjøen Norway **54** H4
Moskal'vo Rus. Fed. **90** F1
Moskenesøy *i.* Norway **54** H3
Moskva Rus. Fed. *see* **Moscow**
Moskva Tajik. **111** H2
Mosonmagyaróvár Hungary **57** P7
Mosquera Col. **176** C3
Mosquero U.S.A. **157** G6
Mosquitia *reg.* Hond. **166** [inset] J6
Mosquito *r.* Brazil **179** C1
Mosquito Creek Lake U.S.A. **164** E3
Mosquito Lake Canada **151** K2
Mosquito Mountain *hill AK* U.S.A. **148** H3
Mosquitos, Golfo de los *b.* Panama **166** [inset] J7
Moss Norway **55** G7
Mossâmedes Angola *see* **Namibe**
Mossat U.K. **60** G3
Mossburn N.Z. **139** B7
Mosselbaai S. Africa *see* **Mossel Bay**
Mossel Bay S. Africa **124** F8
Mossel Bay *b.* S. Africa **124** F8
Mossgiel Australia **138** B4
Mossman Australia **136** D3
Mossoró Brazil **177** K5
Moss Vale Australia **138** E5
Mossy *r.* Canada **151** K4
Most Czech Rep. **57** N5
Mostaganem Alg. **67** G6
Mostar Bos.-Herz. **68** G3
Mostoos Hills Canada **151** I4
Mostovskoy Rus. Fed. **113** F1
Mosty Belarus *see* **Masty**
Mostyn *Sabah* Malaysia **85** G1
Mosul Iraq **113** F3
Mosuowan *Xinjiang* China **98** D3
Møsvatnet *l.* Norway **55** F7
Motagua *r.* Guat. **167** H6
Motala Sweden **55** I7
Motaze Moz. **125** K3
Motegi Japan **93** G2
Motetema S. Africa **125** I3
Moth India **104** D4
Motherwell U.K. **60** F5
Moti *i. Maluku* Indon. **83** C2
Motian Ling *hill* China **90** A4
Motihari India **105** F4
Motilla del Palancar Spain **67** F4
Motiti Island N.Z. **139** F3
Motokwe Botswana **124** F3
Motono Japan **93** G3
Motosu Japan **92** C3
Motosu-ko *l.* Japan **93** E3
Motozintla Mex. **167** G6
Motril Spain **67** E5
Motru Romania **69** J2
Mott U.S.A. **160** C2
Mottama Myanmar **86** B3
Mottama, Gulf of Myanmar **86** B3
Motu Ihupuku *i.* N.Z. *see* **Campbell Island**
Motul Mex. **167** H4
Mouaskar Alg. *see* **Mascara**
Mouding China **96** D3
Moudjéria Mauritania **120** B3
Moudros Greece **69** K5
Mouhijärvi Fin. **55** M6
Mouila Gabon **122** B4
Moukalaba Doudou, Parc National de *nat. park* Gabon **122** A4
Moulamein Australia **138** B5
Moulamein Creek *r.* Australia **138** A5
Moulavibazar Bangl. *see* **Moulvibazar**
Mould Bay Canada **146** G2
Moulèngui Binza Gabon **122** B4
Moulins France **66** F3
Moulmein Myanmar *see* **Mawlamyaing**
Moulouya *r.* Morocco **64** D4
Moultrie U.S.A. **163** D6
Moultrie, Lake U.S.A. **163** E5
Moulvibazar Bangl. **105** G4
Mound City *KS* U.S.A. **160** E4
Mound City *SD* U.S.A. **160** C2
Moundou Chad **121** E4
Moundsville U.S.A. **164** E4
Moŭng Roessei Cambodia **87** C4
Mount Abu India **104** C4
Mountain *r.* N.W.T. Canada **149** O2
Mountainair U.S.A. **157** G6
Mountain Brook U.S.A. **163** C5
Mountain City U.S.A. **164** E5
Mountain Home *AR* U.S.A. **161** E4
Mountain Home *ID* U.S.A. **156** E4
Mountain Home *UT* U.S.A. **159** H1
Mountain Lake Park U.S.A. **164** F4
Mountain View U.S.A. **161** E5
Mountain Village *AK* U.S.A. **148** G3
Mountain Zebra National Park S. Africa **125** G7
Mount Airy U.S.A. **164** E5
Mount Aspiring National Park N.Z. **139** B7
Mount Assiniboine Provincial Park Canada **150** H5
Mount Ayliff S. Africa **125** I6
Mount Ayr U.S.A. **160** E3
Mountbellew Ireland **61** D4
Mount Buffalo National Park Australia **138** C6
Mount Carmel U.S.A. **164** B4
Mount Carmel Junction U.S.A. **159** G3
Mount Coolon Australia **136** D4
Mount Darwin Zimbabwe **123** D5
Mount Denison Australia **134** F5
Mount Desert Island U.S.A. **162** G2
Mount Dutton Australia **137** A5
Mount Eba Australia **137** A6
Mount Elgon National Park Uganda **122** D3
Mount Fletcher S. Africa **125** I6
Mount Forest Canada **164** E2
Mount Frankland National Park Australia **135** B8
Mount Frere S. Africa **125** I6
Mount Gambier Australia **137** C8
Mount Gilead U.S.A. **164** D3
Mount Hagen P.N.G. **81** K8
Mount Holly U.S.A. **165** H4
Mount Hope Australia **138** B4
Mount Hope U.S.A. **164** E5
Mount Howitt Australia **137** C5
Mount Isa Australia **136** B4
Mount Jackson U.S.A. **165** F4
Mount Jewett U.S.A. **165** F3
Mount Joy U.S.A. **165** G3
Mount Kaputar National Park Australia **138** E3
Mount Keith Australia **135** C6
Mount Lofty Range *mts* Australia **137** B7
Mount Magnet Australia **135** B7
Mount Manara Australia **138** A4
Mount McKinley National Park U.S.A. *see* **Denali National Park and Preserve**
Mount Meadows Reservoir U.S.A. **158** C1
Mountmellick Ireland **61** E4
Mount Moorosi Lesotho **125** H6
Mount Morgan Australia **136** E4
Mount Morris *MI* U.S.A. **164** D2
Mount Morris *NY* U.S.A. **165** G2
Mount Murchison Australia **138** A3
Mount Nebo U.S.A. **164** E4
Mount Olivet U.S.A. **164** C4
Mount Pearl Canada **153** L5
Mount Pleasant Canada **153** I5
Mount Pleasant *IA* U.S.A. **160** F3
Mount Pleasant *MI* U.S.A. **164** C2
Mount Pleasant *TX* U.S.A. **161** E5
Mount Pleasant *UT* U.S.A. **159** H2
Mount Rainier National Park U.S.A. **156** C3
Mount Remarkable National Park Australia **137** B7
Mount Revelstoke National Park Canada **150** G5
Mount Robson Provincial Park Canada **150** G4
Mount Rogers National Recreation Area *park* U.S.A. **164** E5
Mount St Helens National Volcanic Monument *nat. park* U.S.A. **156** C3
Mount Sanford Australia **134** E4
Mount's Bay U.K. **59** B8
Mount Shasta U.S.A. **156** C4
Mountsorrel U.K. **59** F6
Mount Sterling U.S.A. **164** D4
Mount Swan Australia **136** A4
Mount Union U.S.A. **165** G3
Mount Vernon Australia **135** B6
Mount Vernon *AL* U.S.A. **167** H2
Mount Vernon *IL* U.S.A. **160** F4
Mount Vernon *IN* U.S.A. **162** C4
Mount Vernon *KY* U.S.A. **164** C5
Mount Vernon *MO* U.S.A. **161** E4
Mount Vernon *OH* U.S.A. **164** D3
Mount Vernon *TX* U.S.A. **161** E5
Mount Vernon *WA* U.S.A. **156** C2
Mount William National Park Australia **137** [inset]
Mount Willoughby Australia **135** F6
Moura Australia **136** E5
Moura Brazil **176** F4
Moura Port. **67** C4
Mourdi, Dépression du *depr.* Chad **121** F3
Mourdiah Mali **120** C3
Mourne *r.* U.K. **61** E3
Mourne Mountains *hills* U.K. **61** F3
Mousa *i.* U.K. **60** [inset]
Mouscron Belgium **62** D4
Mousgougou Chad **122** B2
Moussafoyo Chad **121** E4
Moussoro Chad **121** E3
Moutamba Congo **122** B4
Mouth of the Yangtze China **97** I2
Moutong *Sulawesi* Indon. **83** B2
Mouy France **62** C5
Mouydir, Monts du *plat.* Alg. **120** D2
Mouzon France **62** F5
Movas Mex. **166** C2
Mowbullan, Mount Australia **138** E1
Moxey Town Bahamas **163** E7
Moy *r.* Ireland **61** C3
Moyahua Mex. **166** E4
Moyale Eth. **122** D3
Moyen Atlas *mts* Morocco **64** C5
Moyen Congo *country* Africa *see* **Congo**
Moyeni Lesotho **125** H6
Moynalyk Rus. Fed. **102** I1
Moynaq Uzbek. *see* **Mo'ynoq**
Mo'ynoq Uzbek. **102** A3
Moyo *i.* Indon. **85** G5
Moyobamba Peru **176** C5
Moyock U.S.A. **165** G5
Moyola *r.* U.K. **61** F3
Moyu *Xinjiang* China **99** B5
Moyynkum Kazakh. **102** D3
Moyynkum, Peski *des.* Kazakh. **102** C3
Moyynty Kazakh. **102** D2
Mozambique *country* Africa **123** D6
Mozambique Channel Africa **123** E6
Mozambique Ridge *sea feature* Indian Ocean **185** K7
Mozdok Rus. Fed. **113** G2
Mozdūrān Iran **111** F2
Mozhaysk Rus. Fed. **53** H5
Mozhga Rus. Fed. **52** L4
Mozhnābād Iran **111** F3
Mozo Myanmar **96** B4
Mozyr' Belarus *see* **Mazyr**
Mpaathutlwa Pan *salt pan* Botswana **124** E3
Mpanda Tanz. **123** D4
Mpen India **105** I4
Mpika Zambia **123** D5
Mpolweni S. Africa **125** J5
Mporokoso Zambia **123** D4
Mpulungu Zambia **123** D4
Mpumalanga *prov.* S. Africa **125** I4
Mpunde *mt.* Tanz. **123** D4
Mpwapwa Tanz. **123** D4
Mqanduli S. Africa **125** I6
Mqinvartsveri *mt.* Georgia/Rus. Fed. *see* **Kazbek**
Mrauk-U Myanmar **86** A2
Mrewa Zimbabwe *see* **Murehwa**
Mrkonjić-Grad Bos.-Herz. **68** G2
M'Saken Tunisia **68** D7
Mshinskaya Rus. Fed. **55** P7
M'Sila Alg. **67** I6
Msta *r.* Rus. Fed. **52** F4
Mstislavl' Belarus *see* **Mstsislaw**
Mstsislaw Belarus **53** F5
Mtelo Kenya **122** D3
Mtoko Zimbabwe *see* **Mutoko**
Mtorwi Tanz. **123** D4
Mtsensk Rus. Fed. **53** H5
Mts'ire Kavkasioni Asia *see* **Lesser Caucasus**
Mtubatuba S. Africa **125** K5
Mtunzini S. Africa **125** J5
Mtwara Tanz. **123** E5
Mu *r.* Myanmar **86** A2
Mu'āb, Jibāl *reg.* Jordan *see* **Moab**
Muanda Dem. Rep. Congo **123** B4
Muang Ham Laos **86** D2
Muang Hiam Laos **86** C2
Muang Hinboun Laos **86** D3
Muang Hôngsa Laos **86** C3
Muang Khi Laos **86** C3
Muang Khôngxédôn Laos **86** D4
Muang Khoua Laos **86** C2
Muang Lamam Laos *see* **Lamam**
Muang Mok Laos **86** D3
Muang Ngoy Laos **86** C2
Muang Ou Nua Laos **86** C2
Muang Pakbeng Laos **86** C3
Muang Paktha Laos **86** C2
Muang Pakxan Laos *see* **Pakxan**
Muang Phalan Laos **80** D3
Muang Phin Laos **86** D3
Muang Sam Sip Thai. **86** D4
Muang Sing Laos **86** C2
Muang Soum Laos **86** C3
Muang Souy Laos **86** C3
Muang Thadua Laos **86** C3
Muang Thai *country* Asia *see* **Thailand**
Muang Va Laos **86** C2
Muang Vangviang Laos **86** C3
Muang Xon Laos **86** C2
Muar Malaysia **84** C2
Muar *r.* Malaysia **84** C2
Muara Brunei **85** F1
Muaraancalong *Kalimantan* Indon. **85** G2
Muaraatap *Kalimantan* Indon. **85** G2
Muarabeliti *Sumatera* Indon. **84** C3
Muarabulian *Sumatera* Indon. **84** C3
Muarabungo *Sumatera* Indon. **84** C3
Muaradua *Sumatera* Indon. **84** D4
Muaraenim *Sumatera* Indon. **84** C3
Muarainu *Kalimantan* Indon. **85** F3
Muarajawa *Kalimantan* Indon. **85** G3
Muarakaman *Kalimantan* Indon. **85** G3
Muara Kaman Sedulang, Cagar Alam *nature res. Kalimantan* Indon. **85** G2
Muaralabuh *Sumatera* Indon. **84** C3
Muaralakitan *Sumatera* Indon. **84** C3
Muaralaung *Kalimantan* Indon. **85** F3
Muaralesan *Kalimantan* Indon. **85** G2
Muaramayang *Kalimantan* Indon. **85** G2
Muaranawai *Kalimantan* Indon. **85** G2
Muararupit *Sumatera* Indon. **84** C3
Muarasabak *Sumatera* Indon. **84** C3
Muarasiberut Indon. **84** B3
Muarasipongi *Sumatera* Indon. **84** B2
Muarasoma *Sumatera* Indon. **84** B2
Muaras Reef Indon. **85** G2
Muaratebo *Sumatera* Indon. **84** C3
Muaratembesi *Sumatera* Indon. **84** C3
Muarateweh *Kalimantan* Indon. **85** F3
Muara Tuang *Sarawak* Malaysia *see* **Kota Samarahan**
Muarawahau *Kalimantan* Indon. **85** G2
Muari *i. Maluku* Indon. **83** C3
Muari, Ras *pt* Pak. **111** G5
Mu'ayqil, Khashm al *hill* Saudi Arabia **110** C5
Mubarek Uzbek. *see* **Muborak**
Mubarraz *well* Saudi Arabia **113** F5
Mubende Uganda **122** D3
Mubi Nigeria **120** E3
Muborak Uzbek. **111** G2
Mubur *i.* Indon. **84** D2
Mucajaí, Serra do *mts* Brazil **176** F3
Mucalic *r.* Canada **153** I2
Muccan Australia **134** C5
Much Germany **63** H4
Mucheng *Henan* China *see* **Wuzhi**
Muchinga Escarpment Zambia **123** D5
Muchuan China **96** D2
Muck *i.* U.K. **60** C4
Mucojo Moz. **123** E5
Muconda Angola **123** C5
Mucubela Moz. **123** D5
Mucugê Brazil **179** C1
Mucur Turkey **112** D3
Mucuri Brazil **179** D2
Mucuri *r.* Brazil **179** D2
Muda *r.* Malaysia **84** C1
Mudabidri India **106** B3
Mudan *Shandong* China *see* **Heze**
Mudanjiang China **90** C3
Mudan Jiang *r.* China **90** C3
Mudan Ling *mts* China **90** B4
Mudanya Turkey **69** M4
Muḍaybī Oman **110** E6
Mudaysīsāt, Jabal al *hill* Jordan **107** C4
Muddus nationalpark *nat. park* Sweden **54** K3
Muddy *r.* U.S.A. **159** F3
Muddy Gap U.S.A. **156** G4
Muddy Peak U.S.A. **159** F3
Mūd-e Dahanāb Iran **110** E3
Mudersbach Germany **63** H4
Mudgal India **106** C3
Mudgee Australia **138** D4
Mudhol India **106** B2
Mudigere India **106** B3
Mudjatik *r.* Canada **151** J3
Mud Lake U.S.A. **158** E3
Mudraya *country* Africa *see* **Egypt**
Mudurnu Turkey **69** N4
Mud'yuga Rus. Fed. **52** H3
Mueda Moz. **123** D5
Mueller Range *hills* Australia **134** D4
Muerto, Mar *lag.* Mex. **167** G5
Muertos Cays *is* Bahamas **163** D7
Muftyuga Rus. Fed. **52** J2
Mufulira Zambia **123** C5
Mufumbwe Zambia **123** C5
Mufu Shan *mts* China **97** G2
Muğan Düzü *lowland* Azer. **113** H3
Mugarripug China **105** F2
Mugegawa Japan **92** C3
Mughalbhin Pak. *see* **Jati**
Mughal Kot Pak. **111** H4
Mughal Sarai India **105** E4
Mūghār Iran **110** D3
Mughayrā' Saudi Arabia **107** C5
Mughayrā' *well* Saudi Arabia **110** B5
Mugi *Gifu* Japan **92** D3
Muğla Turkey **69** M6
Mugodzhary, Gory *mts* Kazakh. **102** A2
Mug Qu *r. Qinghai* China **94** C5
Mugu Karnali *r.* Nepal **99** C7
Mugur-Aksy Rus. Fed. **94** B1
Mugxung *Qinghai* China **99** F6
Mūḩ, Sabkhat *imp. l.* Syria **107** D2
Muhala *Xinjiang* China *see* **Yutian**
Muhammad Ashraf Pak. **111** H5
Muhammad Qol Sudan **108** E5
Muhammarah Iran *see* **Khorramshahr**
Muhar *Qinghai* China **94** D4
Muhashsham, Wādī al *watercourse* Egypt **107** B4
Muḩaysh, Wādī al *watercourse* Jordan **107** C5
Muhaysin Syria **107** D1
Mühlanger Germany **63** M3
Mühlberg Germany **63** N3
Mühlhausen (Thüringen) Germany **63** K3
Mühlig-Hofmann Mountains Antarctica **188** C2
Muhos Fin. **54** N4
Muḩradah Syria **107** C2
Mui Bai Bung *c.* Vietnam *see* **Mui Ca Mau**
Mui Ba Lang An *pt* Vietnam **86** E4
Mui Ca Mau *c.* Vietnam **87** D5
Mui Đôc *pt* Vietnam **86** D3
Muié Angola **123** C5
Muika Japan **93** E1
Muiliyk *i. Maluku* Indon. **83** D3
Muineachán Ireland *see* **Monaghan**
Muine Bheag Ireland *see* **Bagenalstown**
Muir U.S.A. **164** C2
Muirkirk U.K. **60** E5
Muir of Ord U.K. **60** E3
Mui Ron *hd* Vietnam **86** D3
Muite Moz. **123** D5
Mujeres, Isla *i.* Mex. **167** I4
Muji *Xinjiang* China **99** B5
Mujong *r.* Malaysia **85** F2
Muju S. Korea **91** B5
Mukacheve Ukr. **53** D6
Mukachevo Ukr. *see* **Mukacheve**
Mukah *Sarawak* Malaysia **85** F2
Mukah *r.* Malaysia **85** F2
Mukalla Yemen **108** G7
Mukandwara India **104** D4
Mukawa *Yamanashi* Japan **93** E3
Mukdahan Thai. **86** D3
Mukden *Liaoning* China *see* **Shenyang**
Mukeru Palau **82** [inset]
Muketei *r.* Canada **152** D3
Mukhen Rus. Fed. **90** E2
Mukhino Rus. Fed. **90** B1
Mukhorshibir' Rus. Fed. **95** G1
Mukhtuya Rus. Fed. *see* **Lensk**
Mukinbudin Australia **135** B7
Mukō Japan **92** B4
Mu Ko Chang Marine National Park Thai. **87** C5
Mukojima-rettō *is* Japan **91** F8
Mukomuko *Sumatera* Indon. **84** C3
Mukry Turkm. **111** G2
Muktsar India **104** C3
Mukur *Vostochnyy Kazakhstan* Kazakh. **98** C2
Mukutawa *r.* Canada **151** L4
Mukwonago U.S.A. **164** A2
Mula *r.* India **106** B2
Mulakatholhu *atoll* Maldives *see* **Mulaku Atoll**
Mulaku Atoll Maldives **103** D11
Mulaly Kazakh. **98** B3
Mulan China **90** C3
Mulanay *Luzon* Phil. **82** C3
Mulanje, Mount Malawi **123** D5
Mulapula, Lake *salt flat* Australia **137** B6
Mulatos Mex. **166** C2
Mula-tupo Panama **166** [inset] K7
Mulayḩ Saudi Arabia **110** B5
Mulayḩah, Jabal *hill* U.A.E. **110** D5
Mulayz, Wādī al *watercourse* Egypt **107** A4
Mulchatna *r. AK* U.S.A. **148** H3
Mulde *r.* Germany **63** M3
Mule Creek *NM* U.S.A. **159** I5
Mule Creek *WY* U.S.A. **156** G4
Mulegé Mex. **166** B3
Mules *i.* Indon. **83** B5
Muleshoe U.S.A. **161** C5
Mulga Park Australia **135** E6
Mulgathing Australia **135** F7
Mulgrave Hills *AK* U.S.A. **148** G2
Mulhacén *mt.* Spain **67** E5
Mülhausen France *see* **Mulhouse**
Mülheim an der Ruhr Germany **62** G3
Mulhouse France **66** H3
Muli China **96** D3
Muli Rus. Fed. *see* **Vysokogorniy**
Mulia Indon. **81** J7
Muling *Heilong.* China **90** C3
Muling *Heilong.* China **90** C3
Muling He *r.* China **90** D3
Mull *i.* U.K. **60** D4
Mull, Sound of *sea chan.* U.K. **60** C4
Mullaghcleevaun *hill* Ireland **61** F4
Mullaittivu Sri Lanka **106** D4
Mullaley Australia **138** D3
Mullengudgery Australia **138** C3
Mullens U.S.A. **164** E5
Muller *watercourse* Australia **134** F5
Muller, Pegunungan *mts* Indon. **85** F2
Mullett Lake U.S.A. **164** C1
Mullewa Australia **135** A7
Mullica *r.* U.S.A. **165** H4
Mullingar Ireland **61** E4
Mullion Creek Australia **138** D4
Mull of Galloway *c.* U.K. **60** E6
Mull of Kintyre *hd* U.K. **60** D5
Mull of Oa *hd* U.K. **60** C5
Mullumbimby Australia **138** F2
Mulobezi Zambia **123** C5
Mulshi Lake India **106** B2
Multai India **104** D5
Multan Pak. **111** H4
Multia Fin. **54** N5
Multien *reg.* France **62** C6
Mulu, Gunung *mt.* Malaysia **85** F1
Mulug India **106** C2

▶**Mumbai** India **106** B2
2nd most populous city in Asia and 3rd in the world.

Mumbil Australia **138** D4
Mumbwa Zambia **123** C5
Muminabad Tajik. *see* **Leningrad**
Mū'minobod Tajik. *see* **Leningrad**
Mun, Mae Nam *r.* Thai. **86** D4
Muna *i.* Indon. **83** B4
Muna Mex. **167** H4
Muna *r.* Rus. Fed. **77** N3
Munabao Pak. **111** H5
Munaðarnes Iceland **54** [inset]
Münchberg Germany **63** L4
München Germany *see* **Munich**
München-Gladbach Germany *see* **Mönchengladbach**
Münchhausen Germany **63** I4
Muncho Lake Canada **150** E3
Muncie U.S.A. **164** C3
Muncoonie West, Lake *salt flat* Australia **136** B5
Muncy U.S.A. **165** G3
Munda Pak. **111** H4
Mundel Lake Sri Lanka **106** C5
Mundesley U.K. **59** I6
Mundford U.K. **59** H6
Mundiwindi Australia **135** C5
Mundra India **104** B5
Mundrabilla Australia **132** C5
Munds Park U.S.A. **159** H4
Mundubbera Australia **137** E5
Mundwa India **104** C4
Munfordville U.S.A. **164** C5
Mungallala Australia **137** D5
Mungana Australia **136** D3
Mungári Moz. **123** D5
Mungbere Dem. Rep. Congo **122** C3
Mungeli India **105** E5
Munger India **105** F4
Mu Nggava *i.* Solomon Is *see* **Rennell**
Mungguresak, Tanjung *pt* Indon. **85** E2
Mungindi Australia **138** D2
Mungla Bangl. *see* **Mongla**
Mungo Angola **123** B5
Mungo, Lake Australia **138** A4
Mungo National Park Australia **138** A4
Munich Germany **57** M6
Munising U.S.A. **162** C2
Munjpur India **104** B5
Munkács Ukr. *see* **Mukacheve**
Munkebakken Norway **54** P2
Munkedal Sweden **55** G7
Munkfors Sweden **55** H7
Munkhafaḑ al Qaţţārah *depr.* Egypt *see* **Qattara Depression**
Munku-Sardyk, Gora *mt.* Mongolia/Rus. Fed. **94** E1
Münnerstadt Germany **63** K4
Munnik S. Africa **125** I2
Munroe Lake Canada **151** L3
Munsan S. Korea **91** B5
Munse *Sulawesi* Indon. **83** B4
Münster *Hessen* Germany **63** I5
Münster *Niedersachsen* Germany **63** K2
Münster *Nordrhein-Westfalen* Germany **63** H3
Munster *reg.* Ireland **61** D5
Münsterland *reg.* Germany **63** H3
Muntadgin Australia **135** B7
Munte *Sulawesi* Indon. **83** A2
Muntervary *hd* Ireland **61** C6
Munyal-Par *sea feature* India *see* **Bassas de Pedro Padua Bank**
Munzur Vadisi Milli Parkı *nat. park* Turkey **65** L4
Muojärvi *l.* Fin. **54** P4
Mương Nhe Vietnam **86** C2
Muong Sai Laos *see* **Oudômxai**
Muonio Fin. **54** M3
Muonioälven *r.* Fin./Sweden **54** M3
Muonionjoki *r.* Fin./Sweden *see* **Muonioälven**
Muor *i. Maluku* Indon. **83** D2
Mupa, Parque Nacional da *nat. park* Angola **123** B5
Muping *Shandong* China **95** J4
Muping China *see* **Baoxing**
Muqaynimah *well* Saudi Arabia **110** C6
Muqdisho Somalia *see* **Mogadishu**
Muquem Brazil **179** A1
Muqui Brazil **179** C3
Mur *r.* Austria **57** P7
also known as Mura (Croatia/Slovenia)
Mura *r.* Croatia/Slovenia *see* **Mur**
Murai, Tanjong *pt* Sing. **87** [inset]
Murai Reservoir Sing. **87** [inset]
Murakami Japan **91** E5
Murallón, Cerro *mt.* Chile **178** B7
Muramvya Burundi **122** C4
Murashi Rus. Fed. **52** K4
Murat *r.* Turkey **113** E3
Muratlı Turkey **69** L4
Muraysah, Ra's al *pt* Libya **112** B5
Murchison *watercourse* Australia **135** A6
Murchison, Mount Antarctica **188** H2
Murchison, Mount *hill* Australia **135** B6
Murchison Falls National Park Uganda **122** D3
Murcia Spain **67** F5
Murcia *aut. comm.* Spain **67** F5
Murcielagos Bay *Mindanao* Phil. **82** C4
Murdo U.S.A. **160** C3
Mure Japan **93** E2
Murehwa Zimbabwe **123** D5
Mureşul *r.* Romania **69** I1
Muret France **66** E5
Murewa Zimbabwe *see* **Murehwa**
Murfreesboro *AR* U.S.A. **161** E5
Murfreesboro *TN* U.S.A. **162** C5
Murg *r.* Germany **63** I6
Murgab Tajik. *see* **Murghob**
Murgab Turkm. *see* **Murgap**
Murgab *r.* Turkm. *see* **Murgap**
Murgap Turkm. **111** F2
Murgap *r.* Turkm. **109** J2
Murgha Kibzai Pak. **111** H4
Murghob Tajik. **111** I2
Murgon Australia **137** E5
Murgoo Australia **135** B6
Muri *Qinghai* China **94** D4
Muri *Qinghai* China **94** E4
Muri India **105** F5
Muria, Gunung *mt.* Indon. **85** E4
Muriaé Brazil **179** C3
Murid Pak. **111** G4
Muriege Angola **123** C4
Murih, Pulau *i.* Indon. **85** E2
Müritz *l.* Germany **63** M1
Müritz, Nationalpark *nat. park* Germany **63** N1
Murmansk Rus. Fed. **54** R2
Murmanskaya Oblast' *admin. div.* Rus. Fed. **54** S2
Murmanskiy Bereg *coastal area* Rus. Fed. **52** G1
Murmansk Oblast *admin. div.* Rus. Fed. *see* **Murmanskaya Oblast'**
Muro Japan **92** C4
Muro, Capo di *c. Corsica* France **66** I6
Murō-Akame-Aoyama Kokutei-kōen *park* Japan **92** C4
Murom Rus. Fed. **52** I5
Muromagi-gawa *r.* Japan **92** D2
Muroran Japan **90** F4
Muros Spain **67** B2
Muroto Japan **91** D6
Muroto-zaki *pt* Japan **91** D6
Murphy *ID* U.S.A. **156** D4
Murphy *NC* U.S.A. **163** D5
Murphysboro U.S.A. **160** F4
Murrah *reg.* Saudi Arabia **110** C6
Murrah al Kubrá, Al Buḩayrah al *l.* Egypt *see* **Great Bitter Lake**
Murrah aş Şughrá, Al Buḩayrah al *l.* Egypt *see* **Little Bitter Lake**
Murramarang National Park **138** I5
Murra Murra Australia **138** C2
Murrat el Kubra, Buheirat *l.* Egypt *see* **Great Bitter Lake**
Murrat el Sughra, Buheirat *l.* Egypt *see* **Little Bitter Lake**

▶**Murray** *r.* S.A. Australia **137** B7
3rd longest river in Oceania, and a major part of the longest (Murray-Darling).

Murray *r.* W.A. Australia **135** A8
Murray *KY* U.S.A. **161** F4
Murray *UT* U.S.A. **159** H1
Murray, Lake P.N.G. **81** K8
Murray, Lake U.S.A. **163** D5

Murray, Mount Y.T. Canada 149 O3
Murray Bridge Australia 137 B7

▶**Murray-Darling** r. Australia 132 E5
Longest river in Oceania.

Murray Downs Australia 134 F5
Murray Range hills Australia 135 E6
Murraysburg S. Africa 124 F6
Murray Sunset National Park Australia 137 C7
Murrhardt Germany 63 J6
Murrieta U.S.A. 158 E5
Murringo Australia 138 D5
Murrisk reg. Ireland 61 C4
Murroogh Ireland 61 C4

▶**Murrumbidgee** r. Australia 138 A5
4th longest river in Oceania.

Murrumburrah Australia 138 D5
Murrurundi Australia 138 E3
Mursan India 104 D4
Murshidabad India 105 G4
Murska Sobota Slovenia 68 G1
Mūrt Iran 111 F5
Murtoa Australia 137 C8
Murua i. P.N.G. see **Woodlark Island**
Murud India 106 B2
Murud, Gunung mt. Indon. 85 F2
Murui r. Indon. 85 F3
Muruin Sum Shuiku resr China 95 J3
Murung r. Indon. 85 F3
Murung r. Indon. 85 F3
Murunkan Sri Lanka 106 D4
Murupara N.Z. 139 F4
Mururoa atoll Fr. Polynesia 187 K7
Murviedro Spain see **Sagunto**
Murwara India 104 E5
Murwillumbah Australia 138 F2
Murzechirla Turkm. 111 F2
Murzūq Libya 121 E2
Mürzzuschlag Austria 57 O7
Muş Turkey 113 F3
Mūsā, Khowr-e b. Iran 110 C4
Musakhel Pak. 111 H4
Musala mt. Bulg. 69 J3
Musala i. Indon. 84 B2
Musan N. Korea 90 C4
Musandam Peninsula Oman/U.A.E. 110 E5
Mūsá Qal'eh, Rūd-e r. Afgh. 111 G3
Musashino Japan 93 F3
Musay'īd Qatar see **Umm Sa'id**

▶**Muscat** Oman 110 E6
Capital of Oman.

Muscat reg. Oman 110 E5
Muscat and Oman country Asia see **Oman**
Muscatine U.S.A. 160 F3
Musgrave Australia 136 C2
Musgrave Harbour Canada 153 L4
Musgrave Ranges mts Australia 135 E6
Mushāsh al Kabid well Jordan 107 C5
Mushayyish, Wādī al watercourse Jordan 107 C4
Mushie Dem. Rep. Congo 122 B4
Mushkaf Pak. 111 G4
Musi r. Indon. 84 D3
Music Mountain U.S.A. 159 G4
Musina S. Africa 125 J2
Musinia Peak U.S.A. 159 H2
Muskeg r. Canada 150 F2
Muskeget Channel U.S.A. 165 J3
Muskegon MI U.S.A. 162 C3
Muskegon MI U.S.A. 164 B2
Muskegon r. U.S.A. 164 B2
Muskegon Heights U.S.A. 164 B2
Muskeg River Canada 150 G4
Muskogee U.S.A. 161 E5
Muskoka, Lake Canada 164 F1
Muskrat Dam Lake Canada 151 N4
Musmar Sudan 108 E6
Musoma Tanz. 122 D4
Musquanousse, Lac l. Canada 153 J4
Musquaro, Lac l. Canada 153 J4
Mussau Island P.N.G. 81 L7
Musselburgh U.K. 60 F5
Musselkanaal Neth. 62 H2
Musselshell r. U.S.A. 156 G3
Mussende Angola 123 B5
Mustafabad Uttar Prad. India 99 C8
Mustafakemalpaşa Turkey 69 M4
Mustau, Gora mt. Xinjiang China 98 D3
Mustjala Estonia 55 M7
Mustvee Estonia 55 O7
Musu-dan pt N. Korea 90 C4
Muswellbrook Australia 138 E4
Mūţ Egypt 108 C4
Mut Turkey 107 A1
Mutá, Ponta do pt Brazil 179 D1
Mutare Zimbabwe 123 D5
Mutayr reg. Saudi Arabia 110 B5
Mutina Italy see **Modena**
Muting Indon. 81 K8
Mutis Col. 176 C2
Mutis, Gunung mt. Timor Indon. 83 C5
Mutnyy Materik Rus. Fed. 52 L2
Mutoko Zimbabwe 123 D5
Mutsamudu Comoros 123 E5
Mutsu Japan 90 F4
Mutsuzawa Japan 93 G3
Muttaburra Australia 136 D4
Mutton Island Ireland 61 C5
Muttukuru India 106 D3
Muttupet India 106 C4
Mutum Brazil 179 C2
Mutunópolis Brazil 179 A1
Mutur Sri Lanka 106 D4
Mutusjärvi r. Fin. 54 O2
Muurola Fin. 54 N3
Mu Us Shamo des. China 95 G4
Muxaluando Angola 123 B4
Muxi China see **Muchuan**
Muxima Angola 123 B4
Muyezerskiy Rus. Fed. 54 R5
Muyinga Burundi 122 D4
Mŭynoq Uzbek. see **Mo'ynoq**
Muyumba Dem. Rep. Congo 123 C4
Muyunkum, Peski des. Kazakh. see **Moyynkum, Peski**
Muyuping China 97 F2
Muzaffarabad Pak. 111 I3
Muzaffargarh Pak. 111 H4
Muzaffarnagar India 104 D3
Muzaffarpur India 105 F4
Muzamane Moz. 125 K2
Muzat He r. China 98 C4
Muzhi Rus. Fed. 51 S2
Mūzīn Iran 111 F5
Muzon, Cape AK U.S.A. 149 N5
Múzquiz Mex. 167 E3
Muztag mt. Xinjiang China 99 C6
Muz Tag mt. Xinjiang China 99 D5
Muztagata mt. Xinjiang China 98 A5
Muztor Kyrg. see **Toktogul**
Mvadi Gabon 122 B3
Mvolo Sudan 121 F4
Mvuma Zimbabwe 123 D5
Mwanza Malawi 123 D5
Mwanza Tanz. 122 D4
Mwaro Burundi 122 C4
Mweelrea hill Ireland 61 C4
Mweka Dem. Rep. Congo 123 C4
Mwene-Ditu Dem. Rep. Congo 123 C4
Mwenezi Zimbabwe 123 D6
Mwenga Dem. Rep. Congo 122 C4
Mweru, Lake Dem. Rep. Congo/Zambia 123 C4
Mweru Wantipa National Park Zambia 123 C4
Mwimba Dem. Rep. Congo 123 C4
Mwinilunga Zambia 123 C5
Myadaung Myanmar 86 B2
Myadzyel Belarus 55 O9
Myajlar India 104 B4
Myall Lakes National Park Australia 138 F4
Myanaung Myanmar 86 A3
Myanmar country Asia 86 A2
Myauk-U Myanmar see **Mrauk-U**
Myaungmya Myanmar 86 A3
Myawadi Thai. 86 B3
Mybster U.K. 60 F2
Myebon Myanmar 86 A2
Myede Myanmar see **Aunglan**
Myeik Myanmar 87 B4
Myingyan Myanmar 86 A2
Myinkyado Myanmar 86 B2
Myinmoletkat mt. Myanmar 87 B4
Myitkyina Myanmar 86 B1
Myitson Myanmar 86 B2
Myitta Myanmar 87 B4
Myittha Myanmar 86 B2
Mykolayiv Ukr. 69 O1
Mykonos i. Greece 69 K6
Myla Rus. Fed. 52 K2
Myla r. Rus. Fed. 52 K2
Mylae Sicily Italy see **Milazzo**
Mylasa Turkey see **Milas**
Mymensing Bangl. see **Mymensingh**
Mymensingh Bangl. 105 G4
Mynämäki Fin. 55 M6
Mynaral Kazakh. 98 A3
Myōgi Japan 93 E2
Myōgi-Arafune-Saku-kōgen Kokutei-kōen park Japan 93 E2
Myōgi-san mt. Japan 93 E2
Myōken-yama hill Japan 92 A4
Myōkō Japan 93 E2
Myōkō-kōgen Japan 93 E2
Myŏnggan N. Korea 90 C4
Myory Belarus 55 O9
My Phước Vietnam 87 D5
Mýrdalsjökull ice cap Iceland 54 [inset]
Myre Norway 54 I2
Myrheden Sweden 54 L4
Myrhorod Ukr. 53 G6
Myrnam Canada 151 I4
Myronivka Ukr. 53 F6
Myrtle Beach U.S.A. 163 E5
Myrtleford Australia 138 C6
Myrtle Point U.S.A. 156 B4
Myrtoo Pelagos sea Greece 69 J6
Mysia reg. Turkey 69 L5
Mys Lazareva Rus. Fed. see **Lazarev**
Myślibórz Poland 57 O4
My Son Sanctuary tourist site Vietnam 86 E4
Mysore India 106 C3
Mysore state India see **Karnataka**
Mys Shmidta Rus. Fed. 77 T3
Mysy Rus. Fed. 52 L3
My Tho Vietnam 87 D5
Mytikas mt. Greece see **Olympus, Mount**
Mytilene i. Greece see **Lesbos**
Mytilini Greece 69 L5
Mytilini Strait Greece/Turkey 69 L5
Mytishchi Rus. Fed. 52 H5
Myton U.S.A. 159 H1
Myyeldino Rus. Fed. 52 L3
Mzamomhle S. Africa 125 H6
Mže r. Czech Rep. 63 M5
Mzimba Malawi 123 D5
Mzuzu Malawi 123 D5

N

Naab r. Germany 63 M5
Nā'ālehu U.S.A. 157 [inset]
Naantali Fin. 55 M6
Naas Ireland 61 F4
Naba Myanmar 86 B1
Nababeep S. Africa 124 C5
Nababganj Bangl. see **Nawabganj**
Nabadwip India see **Navadwip**
Nabarangapur India 106 D2
Nabarangpur India see **Nabarangapur**
Nabari Japan 92 C4
Nabari-gawa r. Japan 92 C4
Nabas Panay Phil. 82 C4
Nabatîyé et Tahta Lebanon 107 B3
Nabatiyet et Tahta Lebanon see **Nabatîyé et Tahta**
Nabberu, Lake salt flat Australia 135 C6
Nabburg Germany 63 M5
Naberera Tanz. 123 D4
Naberezhnyye Chelny Rus. Fed. 51 Q4
Nabesna AK U.S.A. 149 L3
Nabesna r. AK U.S.A. 149 L3
Nabesna Glacier AK U.S.A. 148 I3
Nabesna Village AK U.S.A. 149 L3
Nabeul Tunisia 68 D6
Nabha India 104 D3
Nabil'skiy Zaliv lag. Rus. Fed. 90 F2
Nabire Indon. 81 J7
Nabi Younés, Ras en pt Lebanon 107 B3
Nāblus West Bank 107 B3
Naboomspruit S. Africa 125 I3
Nabq Reserve nature res. Egypt 112 D5
Nābulus West Bank see **Nāblus**
Nacajuca Mex. 167 G5
Nacala Moz. 123 E5
Nacaome Hond. 166 [inset] I6
Nachalovo Rus. Fed. 53 K7
Nachicapau, Lac l. Canada 153 I2
Nachingwea Tanz. 123 D5
Nachna India 104 B4
Nachuge India 87 A5
Nacimiento Reservoir U.S.A. 158 C4
Naco U.S.A. 157 F7
Nacogdoches U.S.A. 161 E6
Nacozari de García Mex. 166 C2
Nada China see **Danzhou**
Nadachi Japan 93 E1
Nadaleen r. Canada 150 C2
Nadbai Rajasthan India 99 B8
Nådendal Fin. see **Naantali**
Nadezhdinskoye Rus. Fed. 90 D2
Nadiad India 104 C5
Nadol India 104 C4
Nador Morocco 67 E6
Nadqān, Qalamat well Saudi Arabia 110 C6
Nadūshan Iran 110 D3
Nadvirna Ukr. 53 E6
Nadvoitsy Rus. Fed. 52 G3
Nadvornaya Ukr. see **Nadvirna**
Nadym Rus. Fed. 76 I3
Næstved Denmark 55 G9
Nafarroa aut. comm. Spain see **Navarra**
Nafas, Ra's an mt. Egypt 107 B5
Nafḥa, Har hill Israel 107 B4
Nafpaktos Greece 69 I5
Nafplio Greece 69 J6
Naftalan Azer. 113 G2
Naft-e Safīd Iran 110 C4
Naft-e Shāh Iran see **Naft Shahr**
Naft Shahr Iran 110 B3
Nafūd ad Daḥl des. Saudi Arabia 110 B6
Nafūd al Ghuwayṭah des. Saudi Arabia 107 D5
Nafūd al Jur'ā des. Saudi Arabia 110 B5
Nafūd as Sirr des. Saudi Arabia 110 B5
Nafūd as Surrah des. Saudi Arabia 110 A6
Nafūd Qunayfidhah des. Saudi Arabia 110 B5
Nafūsah, Jabal hills Libya 120 E1
Nafy Saudi Arabia 108 F4
Nag, Co l. China 99 E6
Naga Japan 92 B4
Naga Luzon Phil. 82 C3
Nagagami r. Canada 152 D4
Nagagami Lake Canada 152 D4
Nagahama Japan 91 D6
Nagahama Shiga Japan 92 C3
Naga Hills India 105 H4
Naga Hills state India see **Nagaland**
Nagai Island AK U.S.A. 148 G5
Nagaizumi Japan 93 E3
Nagakute Japan 92 D3
Nagaland state India 105 H4
Nagamangala India 106 C3
Nagambie Australia 138 B6
Nagano Japan 93 E2
Nagano pref. Japan 93 D2
Naganohara Japan 93 E2
Nagaoka Japan 91 E5
Nagaokakyō Japan 92 B4
Nagaon India 105 H4
Nagapatam India see **Nagapattinam**
Nagapattinam India 106 C4
Nagar r. Bangl./India 99 E8
Nagar Hima. Prad. India 109 M3
Nagar Karnataka India 106 B3
Nagara Japan 93 G3
Nagara-gawa r. Japan 92 C3
Nagaram India 106 D2
Nagareyama Japan 93 F3
Nagari Hills India 106 C3
Nagarjuna Sagar Reservoir India 106 C2
Nagar Parkar Pak. 111 H5
Nagar Untari India 105 E4
Nagarzê Xizang China 99 E7
Nagasaka Japan 93 E3
Nagasaki Japan 91 C6
Nagashima Mie Japan 92 C3
Nagato Nagano Japan 93 E2
Nagato Japan 91 C6
Nagatoro Japan 93 F2
Nagaur India 104 C4
Nagawa Japan 92 D2
Nagbhir India 106 C1
Nagda India 104 C5
Nageezi U.S.A. 159 J3
Nagercoil India 106 C4
Nagha Kalat Pak. 111 G5
Nag' Ḥammâdî Egypt see **Naj' Ḥammādī**
Nagina India 104 D3
Nagiso Japan 92 D3
Nagjog Xizang China 99 G7
Nagold r. Germany 63 I6
Nagong Chu r. China see **Parlung Zangbo**
Nagorno-Karabakh aut. reg. Azer. see **Dağlıq Qarabağ**
Nagornyy Rus. Fed. 148 B3
Nagornyy Karabakh aut. reg. Azer. see **Dağlıq Qarabağ**
Nagorsk Rus. Fed. 52 K4
Nagoya Japan 92 C3
Nagpur India 104 D5
Nagqu Xizang China 99 F7
Nag Qu r. Xizang China 99 F7
Nagurskoye Rus. Fed. 76 F1
Nagyatád Hungary 68 G1
Nagybecskerek Serbia see **Zrenjanin**
Nagyenyed Romania see **Aiud**
Nagykanizsa Hungary 68 G1
Nagyvárad Romania see **Oradea**
Naha Japan 89 N7
Nahan India 104 D3
Nahanni Butte Canada 150 F2
Nahanni National Park Reserve N.W.T. Canada 149 P3
Nahanni Range mts Canada 150 F2
Naharāyim Jordan 107 B3
Nahariyya Israel 107 B3
Nahāvand Iran 110 C3
Nahr Dijlah r. Iraq/Syria 113 G5 see **Tigris**
Nahuel Huapi, Parque Nacional nat. park Arg. 178 B6
Nahunta U.S.A. 163 D6
Naic Luzon Phil. 82 C3
Naica Mex. 166 D3
Nai Ga Myanmar 96 C3
Naij Tal Qinghai China 94 C5
Naikliu Timor Indon. 83 B5
Nailung Xizang China 99 F7
Naiman Qi Nei Mongol China see **Daqin Tal**
Naimin Shuiquan well Xinjiang China 94 B2
Nain Canada 153 J2
Nā'īn Iran 110 D3
Nainital India 104 D3
Naini Tal India see **Nainital**
Nairn U.K. 60 F3
Nairn r. U.K. 60 F3

▶**Nairobi** Kenya 122 D4
Capital of Kenya.

Naissus Serbia see **Niš**
Naivasha Kenya 122 D4
Najaf Iraq 113 G5
Najafābād Iran 110 C3
Na'jān Saudi Arabia 110 B5
Najd reg. Saudi Arabia 108 F4
Nájera Spain 67 E2
Naj' Ḥammādī Egypt 108 D4
Naji Nei Mongol China 95 J1
Najibabad India 104 D3
Najin N. Korea 90 C4
Najitun Nei Mongol China see **Naji**
Najrān Saudi Arabia 108 F6
Naka Hyōgo Japan 92 A3
Naka Ibaraki Japan 93 G2
Nakadōri-shima i. Japan 91 C6
Na Kae Thai. 86 D3
Nakagawa Nagano Japan 93 D3
Naka-gawa r. Japan 93 G2
Nakagō Japan 93 E2
Nakai Japan 93 F3
Nakaizu Japan 93 F4
Nakajima Fukushima Japan 93 G1
Nakajima Ishikawa Japan 92 C1
Nakajō Japan 93 E2
Nakakawane Japan 93 E3
Nakambé r. Burkina/Ghana see **White Volta**
Nakamichi Japan 93 E3
Nakaminato Japan 93 G2
Nakanbe r. Burkina/Ghana see **White Volta**
Nakanno Rus. Fed. 77 L3
Nakano Japan 93 E2
Nakanojō Japan 93 E2
Nakano-take mt. Japan 93 F1
Nakasato Gunma Japan 93 E2
Nakasato Niigata Japan 93 E1
Nakasongola Uganda 121 G4
Nakatomi Japan 93 E3
Nakatsu Japan 91 C6
Nakatsu Wakayama Japan 92 B5
Nakatsugawa Japan 92 D3
Nakatsu-gawa r. Japan 93 E2
Nakfa Eritrea 108 E6
Nakhichevan' Azer. see **Naxçıvan**
Nakhl Egypt 107 A5
Nakhodka Rus. Fed. 90 D4
Nakhola India 105 H4
Nakhon Nayok Thai. 87 C4
Nakhon Pathom Thai. 87 C4
Nakhon Phanom Thai. 86 D3
Nakhon Ratchasima Thai. 86 C4
Nakhon Sawan Thai. 86 C4
Nakhon Si Thammarat Thai. 87 B5
Nakhtarana India 104 B5
Nakina Canada 152 D4
Nakina r. B.C. Canada 149 N4
Naknek AK U.S.A. 148 H4
Naknek Lake AK U.S.A. 148 H4
Nakodar Punjab India 99 A7
Nakonde Zambia 123 D4
Nakoso Japan 93 G1
Nakskov Denmark 55 G9
Naktong-gang r. S. Korea 91 C6
Nakuru Kenya 122 D4
Nakusp Canada 150 G5
Nal Pak. 111 G5
Nal r. Pak. 111 G5
Na-lang Myanmar 86 B2
Nalayh Mongolia 95 F2
Nalázi Moz. 125 K3
Nalbari India 105 G4
Nal'chik Rus. Fed. 113 F2
Naldurg India 106 C2
Nalgonda India 106 C2
Naliya India 104 B5
Nallamala Hills India 106 C3
Nallıhan Turkey 69 N4
Nālūt Libya 120 E1
Namaa, Tanjung pt Seram Indon. 83 D3
Namaacha Moz. 125 K3
Namacurra Moz. 123 D5
Namadgi National Park Australia 138 D5
Namahadi S. Africa 125 I4
Namai Bay Palau 82 [inset]
Namak, Daryācheh-ye salt flat Iran 110 C3
Namak, Kavīr-e salt flat Iran 110 E3
Namakkal India 106 C4
Namakwaland reg. Namibia see **Great Namaqualand**
Namakzar-e Shadad salt flat Iran 110 E4
Namaland reg. Namibia see **Great Namaqualand**
Namang Indon. 84 D3
Namangan Uzbek. 102 D3
Namaqualand reg. Namibia see **Great Namaqualand**
Namaqualand reg. S. Africa 124 C5
Namaqua National Park S. Africa 124 C6
Namas Indon. 81 K8
Namatanai P.N.G. 132 F2
Nambour Australia 138 F1
Nambu Japan see **Nanbu**
Nambucca Heads Australia 138 F3
Nambung National Park Australia 135 A7
Năm Căn Vietnam 87 D5
Namcha Barwa mt. Xizang China see **Namjagbarwa Feng**
Namche Bazar Nepal 105 F4
Namco Xizang China 99 E7
Nam Co salt l. China 99 E7
Namdalen valley Norway 54 H4
Namdalseid Norway 54 G4
Nam Đinh Vietnam 86 D2
Namegawa Japan 93 F2
Namelakl Passage Palau 82 [inset]
Namen Belgium see **Namur**
Namerikawa Japan 92 D2
Nam-gang r. N. Korea 91 B5
Namhae-do i. S. Korea 91 B6
Namhsan Myanmar 86 B2
Namiai Japan 92 D3
Namib Desert Namibia 124 B3
Namibe Angola 123 B5
Namibia country Africa 123 B6
Namibia Abyssal Plain sea feature N. Atlantic Ocean 184 I8
Namib-Naukluft Game Park nature res. Namibia 124 B3
Namie Japan 91 F5
Namīn Iran 113 H3
Namjagbarwa Feng mt. Xizang China 99 F7
Namka Xizang China 99 E7
Namlan Myanmar 86 B2
Namlang r. Myanmar 86 B2
Namlea Buru Indon. 83 C3
Namling Xizang China 99 E7
Nam Loi r. Myanmar see **Nanlei He**
Nam Nao National Park Thai. 86 C3
Nam Ngum Reservoir Laos 86 C3
Namoding Xizang China 99 D7
Namoi r. Australia 138 D3
Namoku Japan 93 E2
Namonuito atoll Micronesia 81 L5
Nampa mt. Nepal 104 E3
Nampa U.S.A. 156 D4
Nampala Mali 120 C3
Nam Phong Thai. 86 C3
Namp'o N. Korea 91 B5
Nampula Moz. 123 D5
Namrole Buru Indon. 83 C3
Namsai Myanmar 86 B1
Namsang Myanmar 86 B2
Namsen r. Norway 54 G4
Nam She Tsim hill H.K. China see **Sharp Peak**
Namsos Norway 54 G4
Namti Myanmar 86 B1
Namtok Myanmar 86 B3
Namtok Chattakan National Park Thai. 86 C3
Namton Myanmar 86 B2
Namtsy Rus. Fed. 77 N3
Namtu Myanmar 86 B2
Namu Canada 150 E5
Namuli, Monte mt. Moz. 123 D5
Namuno Moz. 123 D5
Namur Belgium 62 E4
Namutoni Namibia 123 B5
Namwŏn S. Korea 91 B6
Namya Ra Myanmar 86 B1
Namyit Island S. China Sea 80 E4
Nan Thai. 86 C3
Nana Bakassa Cent. Afr. Rep. 122 B3
Nanaimo Canada 150 F5
Nanakai Japan 93 G2
Nanam N. Korea 90 C4
Nan'an China 97 H3
Nanango Australia 138 F1
Nananib Plateau Namibia 124 C3
Nanao Japan 92 C1
Nanatsuka Japan 92 C2
Nanatsu-shima i. Japan 91 E5
Nanbai China see **Zunyi**
Nanbaxian Qinghai China 99 F5
Nanbin China see **Shizhu**
Nanbu China 96 E2
Nanbu Japan 93 E3
Nancha China 90 C3
Nanchang Jiangxi China 97 G2
Nanchang Jiangxi China 97 G2
Nanchangshan Shandong China see **Changdao**
Nanchong China 96 E2
Nanchuan China 96 E2
Nancowry i. India 87 A6
Nancun Henan China 95 H5
Nancun Shanxi China see **Zezhou**
Nancy France 62 G6
Nancy (Essey) airport France 62 G6
Nanda Devi mt. India 104 E3
Nanda Kot mt. India 104 E3
Nandan China 96 E3
Nandapur India 106 D2
Nanded India 106 C2
Nander India see **Nanded**
Nandewar Range mts Australia 138 E3
Nandod India 106 B1
Nandurbar India 104 C5
Nandyal India 106 C3
Nanfeng Guangdong China 97 F4
Nanfeng Jiangxi China 97 H3
Nang Xizang China 99 F7
Nanga Eboko Cameroon 120 E4
Nangah Dedai Kalimantan Indon. 85 E3
Nangahembaloh Kalimantan Indon. 85 F2
Nangahkemangai Kalimantan Indon. 85 F3
Nangahketungau Kalimantan Indon. 85 E2
Nangahmau Kalimantan Indon. 85 E3
Nangah Merakai Kalimantan Indon. 85 E2
Nangahpinoh Kalimantan Indon. 85 E3
Nangahsuruk Kalimantan Indon. 85 F2
Nangahtempuai Kalimantan Indon. 85 F2
Nangalao i. Phil. 82 C4

▶**Nanga Parbat** mt. Pak. 104 C2
9th highest mountain in the world and in Asia.

Nangar National Park Australia 138 D4
Nangataman Kalimantan Indon. 85 E3
Nangatayap Kalimantan Indon. 85 E3
Nangdoi Qinghai China 94 E4
Nangin Myanmar 87 B5
Nangnim-sanmaek mts N. Korea 91 B4
Nangong Hebei China 95 H4
Nangqên China 96 C1
Nangsin Sum Nei Mongol China 95 G4
Nangulangwa Tanz. 123 D4
Nanguneri India 106 C4
Nanhu Gansu China 98 F5
Nanhua Gansu China 94 D4
Nanhua China 96 D3
Nanhui China 97 I2
Nanjian China 96 D3
Nanjiang China 96 E1
Nanjing China 97 H1
Nanji Shan i. China 97 I3
Nanjō Japan 92 C3
Nanka Jiang r. China 96 C4
Nankang China 97 G3
Nanking China see **Nanjing**
Nankova Angola 123 B5
Nanle Henan China 95 H4
Nanlei He r. China 96 C4
also known as Nam Loi (Myanmar)
Nanling China 97 H2
Nan Ling mts China 97 F3
Nanliu Jiang r. China 97 F4
Nanlong China see **Nanbu**
Nanma Shandong China see **Yiyuan**
Nanmulingzue Xizang China see **Namling**
Nannilam India 106 C4
Nannine Australia 135 B6
Nanning China 97 F4
Nanniwan Shaanxi China 95 G4
Nannō Japan 92 C3
Nannup Australia 135 A8
Na Noi Thai. 86 C3
Nanortalik Greenland 147 N3
Nanouki atoll Kiribati see **Nonouti**
Nanouti atoll Kiribati see **Nonouti**
Nanpan Jiang r. China 96 E3
Nanpi Hebei China 95 I4
Nanpiao Liaoning China 95 J3
Nanping China 97 H3
Nanpu China see **Pucheng**
Nanri Dao i. China 97 H3
Nansei Japan 92 C4
Nansei-shotō is Japan see **Ryukyu Islands**
Nansei-shotō Trench sea feature N. Pacific Ocean see **Ryukyu Trench**
Nansen Basin sea feature Arctic Ocean 189 H1
Nansen Sound sea chan. Canada 147 I1
Nan-sha Ch'ün-tao is S. China Sea see **Spratly Islands**
Nanshan Island S. China Sea 80 F4
Nanshankou Qinghai China 94 C4
Nanshankou Xinjiang China 94 C3
Nansha Qundao is S. China Sea see **Spratly Islands**
Nansio Tanz. 122 D4
Nantai-san hill Japan 93 G2
Nantai-san mt. Japan 93 F2
Nantes France 66 D3
Nantes à Brest, Canal de France 66 C3
Nanteuil-le-Haudouin France 62 C5
Nanthi Kadal lag. Sri Lanka 106 D4
Nanticoke Canada 164 E2
Nanticoke U.S.A. 165 H4
Nantō Japan 92 C4

Nantong China **97** I2
Nantou China **97** [inset]
Nant'ou Taiwan **97** I4
Nantucket U.S.A. **165** J3
Nantucket Island U.S.A. **165** K3
Nantucket Sound *g.* U.S.A. **165** J3
Nantwich U.K. **59** E5
Nanumaga *i.* Tuvalu *see* **Nanumanga**
Nanumanga *i.* Tuvalu **133** H2
Nanumea *atoll* Tuvalu **133** H2
Nanuque Brazil **179** C2
Nanusa, Kepulauan *is* Indon. **83** C1
Nanushuk *r. AK* U.S.A. **149** J1
Nanxi China **96** E2
Nanxian China **97** G2
Nanxiong China **97** G3
Nanyang China **97** G1
Nanyuki Kenya **122** D4
Nanzamu *Liaoning* China **95** K3
Nanzhang China **97** F2
Nanzhao China *see* **Zhao'an**
Nanzhou China *see* **Nanxian**
Naococane, Lac *l.* Canada **153** H3
Naoero *country* S. Pacific Ocean *see* **Nauru**
Naogaon Bangl. **105** G4
Naoli He *r.* China **90** D3
Naomid, Dasht-e *des.* Afgh./Iran **111** F3
Naong, Bukit *mt.* Malaysia **85** F2
Naoshera India **104** C2
Napa U.S.A. **158** B2
Napaimiut *AK* U.S.A. **148** H3
Napakiak *AK* U.S.A. **148** G3
Napaktulik Lake Canada **151** H1
Napanee Canada **165** G1
Napaskiak *AK* U.S.A. **148** G3
Napasoq Greenland **147** M3
Naperville U.S.A. **164** A3
Napier N.Z. **139** F4
Napier Range *hills* Australia **134** D4
Napierville Canada **165** I1
Naples Italy **68** F4
Naples *FL* U.S.A. **163** D7
Naples *ME* U.S.A. **165** J2
Naples *TX* U.S.A. **161** E5
Naples *UT* U.S.A. **159** I1
Napo China **96** E4
Napo *r.* Ecuador **176** D4
Napoleon *IN* U.S.A. **164** C4
Napoleon *ND* U.S.A. **160** D2
Napoleon *OH* U.S.A. **164** C3
Napoli Italy *see* **Naples**
Naqadeh Iran **110** B2
Nara India **104** B5
Nara Japan **92** B4
Nara *pref.* Japan **92** B4
Nara Mali **120** C3
Narach Belarus **55** O9
Naracoorte Australia **137** C8
Naradhan Australia **138** C4
Narai-gawa *r.* Japan **93** D2
Narainpur India **106** D2
Narakawa Japan **93** D3
Naralua India **105** F4
Naran Mongolia **95** H2
Naranbulag *Dornod* Mongolia *see* **Bayandun**
Naranbulag *Uvs* Mongolia **94** C1
Naranjal Ecuador **176** C4
Naranjo Mex. **157** F8
Naranjos Mex. **167** F4
Naran Sebstein Bulag *spring Gansu* China **94** D3
Narasapur India **106** D2
Narasaraopet India **106** D2
Narashino Japan **93** G3
Narasinghapur India **106** E1
Narasun Rus. Fed. **95** H1
Narat *Xinjiang* China **98** D4
Narathiwat Thai. **87** C6
Narat Shan *mts* China **98** C4
Nara Visa U.S.A. **161** C5
Narayanganj Bangl. **105** G5
Narayanganj India **104** E5
Narayangarh India **104** C4
Narbada *r.* India *see* **Narmada**
Narberth U.K. **59** C7
Narbo France *see* **Narbonne**
Narbonne France **66** F5
Narborough Island *Galápagos* Ecuador *see* **Fernandina, Isla**
Narcea *r.* Spain **67** C2
Narcondam Island India **87** A4
Nardò Italy **68** H4
Narechi *r.* Pak. **111** H4
Narembeen Australia **135** B8
Nares Abyssal Plain *sea feature* S. Atlantic Ocean **184** D4
Nares Deep *sea feature* N. Atlantic Ocean **184** D4
Nares Strait Canada/Greenland **147** K2
Naretha Australia **135** D7
Narew *r.* Poland **57** R4
Narib Namibia **124** C3
Narikel Jinjira *i.* Bangl. *see* **St Martin's Island**
Narimanov Rus. Fed. **53** J7
Narimskiy Khrebet *mts* Kazakh. *see* **Narymskiy Khrebet**
Narin Afgh. **111** H2
Narin *reg.* Afgh. **111** H2
Narin *Nei Mongol* China **95** G4
Narince Turkey **112** E3
Narin Gol *watercourse* China **99** F5
Narita Japan **93** G3
Narita *airport* Japan **93** G3
Nariu-misaki *pt* Japan **92** B3
Nariynteel Mongolia **94** E2
Narizon, Punta *pt* Mex. **166** C3
Narkher India **104** D5
Narmada *r.* India **104** C5
Narman Turkey **113** F2
Narnaul India **104** D3
Narni Italy **68** E3
Narnia Italy *see* **Narni**
Narodnaya, Gora *mt.* Rus. Fed. **51** S3
Naro-Fominsk Rus. Fed. **53** H5
Narok Kenya **122** D4
Narooma Australia **138** E6
Narovchat Rus. Fed. **53** I5
Narowlya Belarus **53** F6
Närpes Fin. **54** L5
Narrabri Australia **138** D3
Narragansett Bay U.S.A. **165** J3
Narran *r.* Australia **138** C2
Narrandera Australia **138** C5
Narran Lake Australia **138** C2
Narrogin Australia **135** B8
Narromine Australia **138** D4
Narrows U.S.A. **164** E5
Narrowsburg U.S.A. **165** H3
Narsapur India **106** C2
Narsaq Greenland **147** N3
Narshingdi Bangl. *see* **Narsingdi**
Narsimhapur India *see* **Narsinghpur**
Narsingdi Bangl. **105** G5
Narsinghpur India **104** D5
Narsipatnam India **106** D2
Nart *Nei Mongol* China **95** H3
Nart Mongolia *see* **Orhon**
Nartkala Rus. Fed. **113** F2
Narusawa Japan **93** E3
Narutō Japan **93** G3
Naruto Japan **91** D6
Narva Estonia **55** P7
Narva Bay Estonia/Rus. Fed. **55** O7
Narvacan *Luzon* Phil. **82** C2
Narva laht *b.* Estonia/Rus. Fed. *see* **Narva Bay**
Narva Reservoir *resr* Estonia/Rus. Fed. *see* **Narvskoye Vodokhranilishche**
Narva veehoidla *resr* Estonia/Rus. Fed. *see* **Narvskoye Vodokhranilishche**
Narvik Norway **54** J2
Narvskiy Zaliv *b.* Estonia/Rus. Fed. *see* **Narva Bay**
Narvskoye Vodokhranilishche *resr* Estonia/Rus. Fed. **55** P7
Narwana India **104** D3
Nar'yan-Mar Rus. Fed. **52** L2
Narymskiy Khrebet *mts* Kazakh. **102** F2
Naryn Kyrg. **102** E3
Naryn *admin. div.* Kyrg. **98** A4
Naryn *r.* Kyrg./Uzbek. **98** A4
Naryn Rus. Fed. **94** C1
Narynkol Kazakh. **98** C4
Näsåker Sweden **54** J5
Na Scealaga *is* Ireland *see* **The Skelligs**
Nash Harbor *AK* U.S.A. **148** F3
Nashik India **106** B1
Nashua U.S.A. **165** J2
Nashville *AR* U.S.A. **161** E5
Nashville *GA* U.S.A. **163** D6
Nashville *IN* U.S.A. **164** B4
Nashville *NC* U.S.A. **162** E5
Nashville *OH* U.S.A. **164** D3
▶**Nashville** *TN* U.S.A. **162** C4
Capital of Tennessee.
Naṣīb Syria **107** C3
Näsijärvi *l.* Fin. **55** M6
Nasik India *see* **Nashik**
Nasilat *Kalimantan* Indon. **85** E2
Nasir Pak. **111** H4
Nasir Sudan **108** D8
Nasirabad Bangl. *see* **Mymensingh**
Nasirabad India **104** C4
Nāṣirīyah Iraq **113** G5
Naskaupi *r.* Canada **153** J3
Naṣr Egypt **112** C5
Nasratabad Iran *see* **Zābol**
Naṣrīān-e Pā'īn Iran **110** B3
Nass *r. B.C.* Canada **149** O5
Nassau *r.* Australia **136** C2
▶**Nassau** Bahamas **163** E7
Capital of The Bahamas.
Nassau *i.* Cook Is **133** J3
Nassau U.S.A. **165** I2
Nassawadox U.S.A. **165** H5
Nasser, Lake *resr* Egypt **108** D5
Nässjö Sweden **55** I8
Nassuttooq *inlet* Greenland **147** M3
Nastapoca *r.* Canada **152** F2
Nastapoka Islands Canada **152** F2
Nasu Japan **93** G1
Nasu-dake *vol.* Japan **93** F1
Nasugbu *Luzon* Phil. **82** C3
Nasva Rus. Fed. **52** F4
Nata Botswana **123** C6
Nataboti *Buru* Indon. **83** C3
Natal Brazil **177** K5
Natal *Sumatera* Indon. **84** B2
Natal *prov.* S. Africa *see* **KwaZulu-Natal**
Natal Basin *sea feature* Indian Ocean **185** K8
Naṭanz Iran **110** C3
Natashō Japan **92** B3
Natashquan Canada **153** J4
Natashquan *r.* Canada **153** J4
Natazhat, Mount *AK* U.S.A. **149** L3
Natchez U.S.A. **161** F6
Natchitoches U.S.A. **161** E6
Nathalia Australia **138** B6
Nathia Gali Pak. **111** I3
Nati, Punta *pt* Spain **67** H3
Natillas Mex. **167** E3
Nation *AK* U.S.A. **149** L2
National City U.S.A. **158** E5
National West Coast Tourist Recreation Area *park* Namibia **124** B2
Natitingou Benin **120** D3
Natividad, Isla *i.* Mex. **166** B3
Natividade Brazil **177** I6
Natkyizin Myanmar **86** B4
Natla *r. N.W.T.* Canada **149** O3
Natmauk Myanmar **86** A2
Nator Bangl. *see* **Natore**
Nátora Mex. **157** F7
Natore Bangl. **105** G4
Natori Japan **91** F5
Natron, Lake *salt l.* Tanz. **122** D4
Nattai National Park Australia **138** E5
Nattalin Myanmar **86** A3
Nattaung *mt.* Myanmar **86** B3
Na'tū Iran **111** F3
Natuashish **153** J3
Natuna, Kepulauan *is* Indon. **85** D1
Natuna Besar *i.* Indon. **85** E1
Natural Bridges National Monument *nat. park* U.S.A. **159** H3
Naturaliste, Cape Australia **135** A8
Naturaliste Plateau *sea feature* Indian Ocean **185** P8
Naturita U.S.A. **159** I2
Nauchas Namibia **124** C2
Nau Co *l. Xizang* China **99** C6
Nauen Germany **63** M2
Naufragados, Ponta dos *pt* Brazil **179** A4
Naujan *Mindoro* Phil. **82** C3
Naujoji Akmenė Lith. **55** M8
Naukh India **104** C4
Naukot Pak. **111** H5
Naumburg (Hessen) Germany **63** J3
Naumburg (Saale) Germany **63** L3
Naunglon Myanmar **86** B3
Naungpale Myanmar **86** B3
Naupada India **106** E2
Na'ūr Jordan **107** B4
Nauroz Kalat Pak. **111** G4
Naurskaya Rus. Fed. **113** G2
Nauru *i.* Nauru **133** G2
Nauru *country* S. Pacific Ocean **133** G2
Naushki Rus. Fed. **94** F1
Naustdal Norway **55** D6
Nauta Peru **176** D4
Nautaca Uzbek. *see* **Qarshi**
Nautanwa *Uttar Prad.* India **99** C8
Naute Dam Namibia **124** C4
Nautla Mex. **167** F4
Nauzad Afgh. **111** G3
Nava Mex. **167** E2
Navadwip India **105** G5
Navahrudak Belarus **55** N10
Navajo Lake U.S.A. **159** J3
Navajo Mountain U.S.A. **159** H3
Naval Phil. **82** D4
Navalmoral de la Mata Spain **67** D4
Navalvillar de Pela Spain **67** D4
Navan Ireland **61** F4
Navangar India *see* **Jamnagar**
Navapolatsk Belarus **55** P9
Nāvar, Dasht-e *depr.* Afgh. **111** G3
Navarin, Mys *c.* Rus. Fed. **77** S3
Navarra *aut. comm.* Spain **67** F2
Navarra, Comunidad Foral de *aut. comm.* Spain *see* **Navarra**
Navarre Australia **138** A6
Navarre *aut. comm.* Spain *see* **Navarra**
Navarro *r.* U.S.A. **158** B2
Navashino Rus. Fed. **52** I5
Navasota U.S.A. **161** D6
Navasota *r. TX* U.S.A. **167** F2
▶**Navassa Island** *terr.* West Indies **169** I5
United States Unincorporated Territory.
Naver *r.* U.K. **60** E2
Näverede Sweden **54** I5
Navi Mumbai **106** B2
Navlakhi India **104** B5
Navlya Rus. Fed. **53** G5
Năvodari Romania **69** M2
Navoi Uzbek. *see* **Navoiy**
Navoiy Uzbek. **111** G1
Navojoa Mex. **166** C3
Navolato Mex. **166** D3
Návpaktos Greece *see* **Nafpaktos**
Návplion Greece *see* **Nafplio**
Navşar Turkey *see* **Şemdinli**
Navsari India **106** B1
Navy Town *AK* U.S.A. **148** [inset]
Nawá Syria **107** C3
Nawabganj Bangl. **105** G4
Nawabshah Pak. **111** H5
Nawada India **105** F4
Nāwah Afgh. **111** G3
Nawalgarh India **104** C4
Nawanshahr India **104** D3
Nawan Shehar India *see* **Nawanshahr**
Nawar, Dasht-i *depr.* Afgh. *see* **Nāvar, Dasht-e**
Nawarangpur India *see* **Nabarangapur**
Nawngcho Myanmar *see* **Nawnghkio**
Nawnghkio Myanmar **86** B2
Nawng Hpa Myanmar **86** B2
Nawngleng Myanmar **86** B2
Nawoiy Uzbek. *see* **Navoiy**
Naxçıvan Azer. **113** G3
Naxos *i.* Greece **69** K6
Nayag *Xizang* China **99** F6
Nayagarh India **106** E1
Nayak Afgh. **111** G3
Nayar Mex. **168** D4
Nayarit *state* Mex. **166** D4
Nāy Band, Kūh-e *mt.* Iran **110** E3
Nayong China **96** E3
Nayoro Japan **90** F3
▶**Nay Pyi Taw** Myanmar **86** B3
Joint capital (with Rangoon) of Myanmar.
Nazaré Brazil **179** D1
Nazareno Mex. **166** E3
Nazareth Israel **107** B3
Nazário Brazil **179** A2
Nazas Mex. **166** D3
Nazas *r.* Mex. **166** D3
Nazca Peru **176** D6
Nazca Ridge *sea feature* S. Pacific Ocean **187** O7
Naẓerat Israel *see* **Nazareth**
Nāzīl Iran **111** F4
Nazilli Turkey **69** M6
Nazimabad Pak. **111** G5
Nazımiye Turkey **113** E3
Nazir Hat Bangl. **105** G5
Nazko Canada **150** F4
Nazran' Rus. Fed. **113** G2
Nazrēt Eth. **122** D3
Nazwá Oman **110** E6
Ncojane Botswana **124** E2
N'dalatando Angola **123** B4
Ndao *i.* Indon. **83** B5
Ndélé Cent. Afr. Rep. **122** C3
Ndendé Gabon **122** B4
Ndende *i.* Solomon Is *see* **Ndeni**
Ndeni *i.* Solomon Is **133** G3
▶**Ndjamena** Chad **121** E3
Capital of Chad.
N'Djamena Chad *see* **Ndjamena**
Ndjouani *i.* Comoros *see* **Nzwani**
Ndoi *i.* Fiji *see* **Doi**
Ndola Zambia **123** C5
Nduke *i.* Solomon Is *see* **Kolombangara**
Ndwedwe S. Africa **125** J5
Ne, Hon *i.* Vietnam **86** D3
Neabul Creek *r.* Australia **138** C1
Neagari Japan **92** C2
Neagh, Lough *l.* U.K. **61** F3
Neah Bay U.S.A. **156** B2
Neale, Lake *salt flat* Australia **135** E6
Nea Liosia Greece **69** J5
Neapoli Greece **69** J6
Neapolis Italy *see* **Naples**
Near Islands *AK* U.S.A. **148** [inset]
Nea Roda Greece **69** J4
Neath U.K. **59** D7
Neath *r.* U.K. **59** D7
Neba Japan **92** D3
Nebbi Uganda **122** D3
Nebesnaya, Gora *mt. Xinjiang* China **98** C4
Nebine Creek *r.* Australia **138** C2
Neblina, Pico da *mt.* Brazil **176** E3
Nebo Australia **136** E4
Nebo, Mount U.S.A. **159** H2
Nebolchi Rus. Fed. **52** G4
Nebraska *state* U.S.A. **160** C3
Nebraska City U.S.A. **160** E3
Nebrodi, Monti *mts Sicily* Italy **68** F6
Neches *r.* U.S.A. **161** E6
Nechisar National Park Eth. **122** D3
Nechranice, Vodní nádrž *resr* Czech Rep. **63** N4
Neckar *r.* Germany **63** I5
Neckarsulm Germany **63** J5
Necker Island U.S.A. **186** J4
Necochea Arg. **178** E5
Nederland *country* Europe *see* **Netherlands**
Nederlandse Antillen *terr.* West Indies *see* **Netherlands Antilles**
Neder Rijn *r.* Neth. **62** F3
Nedlouc, Lac *l.* Canada **153** G2
Nedluk Lake Canada *see* **Nedlouc, Lac**
Nedre Soppero Sweden **54** L2
Nédroma Alg. **67** F6
Neeba-san *mt.* Japan **93** E2
Needle Mountain U.S.A. **156** F3
Needles U.S.A. **159** F4
Neemach India *see* **Neemuch**
Neemuch India **104** C4
Neenah U.S.A. **164** A1
Neepawa Canada **151** L5
Neergaard Lake Canada **147** J2
Neerijnen Neth. **62** F3
Neerpelt Belgium **62** F3
Neftçala Azer. **113** H3
Neftechala Azer. *see* **Uzboy**
Neftechala Azer. *see* **Neftçala**
Neftegorsk *Sakhalinskaya Oblast'* Rus. Fed. **90** F1
Neftegorsk *Samarskaya Oblast'* Rus. Fed. **53** K5
Neftekamsk Rus. Fed. **51** Q4
Neftekumsk Rus. Fed. **113** G1
Nefteyugansk Rus. Fed. **76** I3
Neftezavodsk Turkm. *see* **Seýdi**
Neftezavodsk Turkm. *see* **Seýdi**
Nefyn U.K. **59** C6
Nefza Tunisia **68** C6
Negage Angola **123** B4
Negār Iran **110** E4
Negara *Bali* Indon. **85** F5
Negara *Kalimantan* Indon. **85** F3
Negara *r.* Indon. **85** F3
Negēlē Eth. **122** D3
Negeri Sembilan *state* Malaysia **84** C2
Negev *des.* Israel **107** B4
Negomane Moz. **123** D5
Negombo Sri Lanka **106** C5
Negotino Macedonia **69** J4
Negra, Cordillera *mts* Peru **176** C5
Negra, Punta *pt* Peru **176** B5
Negra, Serra *mts* Brazil **179** C2
Negrais, Cape Myanmar **86** A4
Négrine Alg. **68** B7
Negri Sembilan *state* Malaysia *see* **Negeri Sembilan**
Negro *r.* Arg. **178** D6
Negro *r.* Brazil **177** G7
Negro *r.* Brazil **179** A4
Negro *r.* S. America **176** G4
Negro, Cabo *c.* Morocco **67** D6
Negroponte *i.* Greece *see* **Evvoia**
Negros *i.* Phil. **82** C4
Negru Vodă, Podişul *plat.* Romania **69** M3
Nehbandān Iran **111** F4
Nehe *Heilong.* China **95** K1
Neiguanying *Gansu* China **94** F5
Neijiang China **96** E2
Neilburg Canada **151** I4
Neimenggu *aut. reg.* China *see* **Nei Mongol Zizhiqu**
Nei Mongol Zizhiqu *aut. reg.* China **95** E3
Neinstedt Germany **63** L3
Neiqiu *Hebei* China **95** H4
Neiva Col. **176** C3
Neixiang China **97** F1
Nejanilini Lake Canada **151** L3
Nejapa Mex. **167** G5
Nejd *reg.* Saudi Arabia *see* **Najd**
Neka Iran **110** D2
Nek'emtē Eth. **122** D3
Neko-zaki *pt* Japan **92** A3
Nekrasovskoye Rus. Fed. **52** I4
Neksø Denmark **55** I9
Nelang India **104** D3
Nelia Australia **136** C4
Nelidovo Rus. Fed. **52** G4
Neligh U.S.A. **160** D3
Nel'kan Rus. Fed. **77** P3
Nellore India **106** C3
Nelluz *watercourse* Turkey **107** D1
Nel'ma Rus. Fed. **90** E3
Nelson Canada **150** G5
Nelson *r.* Canada **151** M3
Nelson N.Z. **139** D5
Nelson U.K. **58** E5
Nelson U.S.A. **159** G4
Nelson, Cape Australia **137** C8
Nelson, Cape P.N.G. **81** L8
Nelson, Estrecho *strait* Chile **178** A8
Nelson Bay Australia **138** F4
Nelson Forks Canada **150** F3
Nelsonia U.S.A. **165** H5
Nelson Island *AK* U.S.A. **148** F3
Nelson Lagoon *AK* U.S.A. **148** G5
Nelson Lakes National Park N.Z. **139** D6
Nelson Reservoir U.S.A. **156** G2
Nelspruit S. Africa **125** J3
Néma Mauritania **120** C3
Nema Rus. Fed. **52** K4
Neman *r.* Belarus/Lith. *see* **Nyoman**
Neman Rus. Fed. **55** M9
Nemausus France *see* **Nîmes**
Nemawar India **104** D5
Nemed Rus. Fed. **52** L3
Nementcha, Monts des *mts* Alg. **68** B7
Nemetocenna France *see* **Arras**
Nemetskiy, Mys *c.* Rus. Fed. **54** Q2
Nemirov Ukr. *see* **Nemyriv**
Nemiscau *r.* Canada **152** F4
Nemiscau, Lac *l.* Canada **152** F4
Nemor He *r.* China **95** K1
Nemours Alg. *see* **Ghazaouet**
Nemours France **66** F2
Nemrut Dağı *mt.* Turkey **113** F3
Nemunas *r.* Lith. *see* **Nyoman**
Nemuro Japan **90** G4
Nemuro-kaikyō *sea chan.* Japan/Rus. Fed. **90** G4
Nemyriv Ukr. **53** F6
Nenagh Ireland **61** D5
Nenan *Heilong.* China **95** K1
Nenana *AK* U.S.A. **149** J2
Nenana *r. AK* U.S.A. **149** J2
Nene *r.* U.K. **59** H6
Nenjiang *Heilong.* China **95** K1
Nen Jiang *r.* China **95** K2
Neo Japan **92** C3
Neo-gawa *r.* Japan **92** C3
Neosho U.S.A. **161** E4
Nepal *country* Asia **105** E3
Nepalganj Nepal **105** E3
Nepean Canada **165** H1
Nepean, Point Australia **138** B7
Nephi U.S.A. **159** H2
Nephin *hill* Ireland **61** C3
Nephin Beg Range *hills* Ireland **61** C3
Nepisiguit *r.* Canada **153** I5
Nepoko *r.* Dem. Rep. Congo **122** C3
Nérac France **66** E4
Neragon Island *AK* U.S.A. **148** F3
Nerang Australia **138** F1
Nera Tso *l.* China **105** H3
Nerchinsk Rus. Fed. **89** L2
Nerekhta Rus. Fed. **52** I4
Néret, Lac *l.* Canada **153** H3
Neretva *r.* Bos.-Herz./Croatia **68** G3
Néri Pünco *l. Xizang* China **99** E7
Neriquinha Angola **123** C5
Neris *r.* Lith. **55** M9
also known as Viliya (Belarus/Lithuania)
Nerl' *r.* Rus. Fed. **52** H4
Nerópolis Brazil **179** A2
Neryungri Rus. Fed. **77** N4
Nes Neth. **62** F1
Nes Norway **55** F6
Nes' Rus. Fed. **52** J2
Nesbyen Norway **55** F6
Neshkan Rus. Fed. **148** D2
Neshkenpil'khyn, Laguna *lag.* Rus. Fed. **148** D2
Neskaupstaður Iceland **54** [inset]
Nesle France **62** C5
Nesna Norway **54** H3
Nesri India **106** B2
Ness *r.* U.K. **60** E3
Ness, Loch *l.* U.K. **60** E3
Ness City U.S.A. **160** D4
Nesse *r.* Germany **63** K4
Nesselrode, Mount Canada/U.S.A. **149** N4
Nestor Falls Canada **151** M5
Nestos *r.* Greece **69** K4
also known as Mesta
Nesvizh Belarus *see* **Nyasvizh**
Netanya Israel **107** B3
Netherlands *country* Europe **62** F2
▶**Netherlands Antilles** *terr.* West Indies **169** K6
Self-governing Netherlands Territory.
Netphen Germany **63** I4
Netrakona Bangl. **105** G4
Netrokona Bangl. *see* **Netrakona**
Nettilling Lake Canada **147** K3
Neubrandenburg Germany **63** N1
Neuburg an der Donau Germany **63** L6
Neuchâtel Switz. **66** H3
Neuchâtel, Lac de *l.* Switz. **66** H3
Neuendettelsau Germany **63** K5
Neuenhaus Germany **62** G2
Neuenkirchen Germany **63** J1
Neuenkirchen (Oldenburg) Germany **63** I2
Neufchâteau Belgium **62** F5
Neufchâteau France **66** G2
Neufchâtel-en-Bray France **62** B5
Neufchâtel-Hardelot France **62** B4
Neuharlingersiel Germany **63** H1
Neuhausen Rus. Fed. *see* **Gur'yevsk**
Neuhof Germany **63** J4
Neu Kaliß Germany **63** L1
Neukirchen *Hessen* Germany **63** J4
Neukirchen *Sachsen* Germany **63** M4
Neukuhren Rus. Fed. *see* **Pionerskiy**
Neumarkt in der Oberpfalz Germany **63** L5
Neumayer *research station* Antarctica **188** B2
Neumünster Germany **57** L3
Neunburg vorm Wald Germany **63** M5
Neunkirchen Austria **57** P7
Neunkirchen Germany **63** H5
Neuquén Arg. **178** C5
Neuruppin Germany **63** M2
Neu Sandez Poland *see* **Nowy Sącz**
Neuse *r.* U.S.A. **163** E5
Neusiedler See *l.* Austria/Hungary **57** P7
Neusiedler See Seewinkel, Nationalpark *nat. park* Austria **57** P7
Neuss Germany **62** G3
Neustadt (Wied) Germany **63** H4
Neustadt am Rübenberge Germany **63** J2
Neustadt an der Aisch Germany **63** K5
Neustadt an der Hardt Germany *see* **Neustadt an der Weinstraße**
Neustadt an der Waldnaab Germany **63** M5
Neustadt an der Weinstraße Germany **63** I5
Neustadt bei Coburg Germany **63** L4
Neustadt-Glewe Germany **63** L1
Neustrelitz Germany **63** N1
Neutraubling Germany **63** M6
Neuville-lès-Dieppe France **62** B5
Neuwied Germany **63** H4
Neu Wulmstorf Germany **63** J1
Nevada *IA* U.S.A. **160** E3
Nevada *MO* U.S.A. **160** E4
Nevada *state* U.S.A. **156** D5
Nevada, Sierra *mts* Spain **67** E5
Nevada, Sierra *mts* U.S.A. **158** C1
Nevada City U.S.A. **158** C2
Nevado, Cerro *mt.* Arg. **178** C5
Nevado, Sierra del *mts* Arg. **178** C5
Nevado de Colima, Parque Nacional *nat. park* Mex. **166** E5
Nevasa India **106** B2
Nevatim Israel **107** B4
Nevdubstroy Rus. Fed. *see* **Kirovsk**
Nevel' Rus. Fed. **52** F4
Nevel'sk Rus. Fed. **90** F3
Never Rus. Fed. **90** B1
Nevers France **66** F3
Nevertire Australia **138** C3
Nevesinje Bos.-Herz. **68** H3
Nevinnomyssk Rus. Fed. **113** F1
Nevşehir Turkey **112** D3
Nevskoye Rus. Fed. **90** D3
New *r. CA* U.S.A. **159** F5
New *r. WV* U.S.A. **164** E5
Newala Tanz. **123** D5
New Albany *IN* U.S.A. **164** C4
New Albany *MS* U.S.A. **161** F5
New Amsterdam Guyana **177** G2
New Amsterdam U.S.A. *see* **New York**
New Angledool Australia **138** C2
Newark *DE* U.S.A. **165** H4
Newark *NJ* U.S.A. **165** H3
Newark *NY* U.S.A. **165** G2
Newark *OH* U.S.A. **164** D3
Newark *airport* U.S.A. **162** F3
Newark Lake U.S.A. **159** F2
Newark-on-Trent U.K. **59** G5
New Bedford U.S.A. **165** J3
Newberg U.S.A. **156** C3
New Berlin U.S.A. **165** H2
New Bern U.S.A. **163** E5
Newberry *IN* U.S.A. **164** B4
Newberry *MI* U.S.A. **162** C2
Newberry *SC* U.S.A. **163** D5
Newberry National Volcanic Monument *nat. park* U.S.A. **156** C4
Newberry Springs U.S.A. **158** E4
New Bethlehem U.S.A. **164** F3
Newbiggin-by-the-Sea U.K. **58** F3
New Bight Bahamas **163** F7
New Bloomfield U.S.A. **165** G3
New Bombay *see* **Navi Mumbai**
Newboro Canada **165** G1
New Boston *OH* U.S.A. **164** D4
New Boston *TX* U.S.A. **161** E5
New Braunfels U.S.A. **161** D6
Newbridge Ireland **61** F4
New Britain *i.* P.N.G. **81** L8
New Britain U.S.A. **165** I3
New Britain Trench *sea feature* S. Pacific Ocean **186** G6
New Brunswick *prov.* Canada **153** I5

New Brunswick U.S.A. **165** H3
New Buffalo U.S.A. **164** B3
Newburgh Canada **165** G1
Newburgh U.K. **60** G3
Newburgh U.S.A. **165** H3
Newbury U.K. **59** F7
Newburyport U.S.A. **165** J2
Newby Bridge U.K. **58** E4

▶**New Caledonia** *terr.* S. Pacific Ocean **133** G4
French Overseas Collectivity.

New Caledonia Trough *sea feature* Tasman Sea **186** G7
New Carlisle Canada **153** I4
Newcastle Australia **138** E4
Newcastle Canada **165** F2
Newcastle Ireland **61** F4
Newcastle S. Africa **125** I4
Newcastle U.K. **61** G3
New Castle *CO* U.S.A. **159** J2
New Castle *IN* U.S.A. **164** C4
New Castle *KY* U.S.A. **164** C4
New Castle *PA* U.S.A. **164** E3
Newcastle *UT* U.S.A. **159** G3
New Castle *VA* U.S.A. **164** E5
Newcastle *WY* U.S.A. **156** G4
Newcastle Emlyn U.K. **59** C6
Newcastle-under-Lyme U.K. **59** E5
Newcastle upon Tyne U.K. **58** F4
Newcastle Waters Australia **134** F4
Newcastle West Ireland **61** C5
Newchwang *Liaoning* China *see* **Yingkou**
New City U.S.A. **165** I3
Newcomb U.S.A. **159** I3
New Concord U.S.A. **164** E4
New Cumberland U.S.A. **164** E3
New Cumnock U.K. **60** E5
New Deer U.K. **60** G3

▶**New Delhi** India **104** D3
Capital of India.

New Don Pedro Reservoir U.S.A. **158** C3
Newell U.S.A. **160** C2
Newell, Lake *salt flat* Australia **135** D6
Newell, Lake Canada **151** I5
New England National Park Australia **138** F3
New England Range *mts* Australia **138** E3
New England Seamounts *sea feature* N. Atlantic Ocean **184** E3
Newenham, Cape *AK* U.S.A. **148** G4
Newent U.K. **59** E7
New Era U.S.A. **164** B2
Newfane *NY* U.S.A. **165** F2
Newfane *VT* U.S.A. **165** I2
New Forest National Park **59** F8
Newfoundland *i.* Canada **153** K4
Newfoundland *prov.* Canada *see* **Newfoundland and Labrador**
Newfoundland and Labrador *prov.* Canada **153** K3
Newfoundland Evaporation Basin *salt l.* U.S.A. **159** G1
New Galloway U.K. **60** E5
New Georgia *i.* Solomon Is **133** F2
New Georgia Islands Solomon Is **133** F2
New Georgia Sound *sea chan.* Solomon Is **133** F2
New Glasgow Canada **153** J5

▶**New Guinea** *i.* Indon./P.N.G. **81** K8
Largest island in Oceania, and 2nd in the world.

Newhalen *AK* U.S.A. **148** I4
New Halfa Sudan **108** E6
New Hamilton *AK* U.S.A. **148** G3
New Hampshire *state* U.S.A. **165** J1
New Hampton U.S.A. **160** E3
New Hanover *i.* P.N.G. **132** F2
New Haven *CT* U.S.A. **165** I3
New Haven *IN* U.S.A. **164** C3
New Haven *WV* U.S.A. **164** E4
New Hebrides *country* S. Pacific Ocean *see* **Vanuatu**
New Hebrides Trench *sea feature* S. Pacific Ocean **186** H7
New Holstein U.S.A. **164** A2
New Iberia U.S.A. **161** F6
Newington S. Africa **125** J3
Newinn Ireland **61** E5
New Ireland *i.* P.N.G. **132** F2
New Jersey *state* U.S.A. **165** H4
New Kensington U.S.A. **164** F3
New Kent U.S.A. **165** G5
Newkirk U.S.A. **161** D4
New Lanark U.K. **60** F5
Newland Range *hills* Australia **135** C7
New Lexington U.S.A. **164** D4
New Liskeard Canada **152** F5
New London *CT* U.S.A. **165** I3
New London *MO* U.S.A. **160** F4
New Madrid U.S.A. **161** F4
Newman Australia **135** B5
Newman U.S.A. **158** C3
Newmarket Canada **164** F1
Newmarket Ireland **61** C5
Newmarket U.K. **59** H6
New Market U.S.A. **165** F4
Newmarket-on-Fergus Ireland **61** D5
New Martinsville U.S.A. **164** E4
New Meadows U.S.A. **156** D3
New Mexico *state* U.S.A. **157** G6
New Miami U.S.A. **164** C4
New Milford U.S.A. **165** H3
Newnan U.S.A. **163** C5
New Orleans U.S.A. **161** F6
New Paris *IN* U.S.A. **164** C3
New Paris *OH* U.S.A. **164** C4
New Philadelphia U.S.A. **164** E3
New Pitsligo U.K. **60** G3
New Plymouth N.Z. **139** E4
Newport *Mayo* Ireland **61** C4
Newport *Tipperary* Ireland **61** D5
Newport *England* U.K. **59** E6
Newport *England* U.K. **59** F8
Newport *Wales* U.K. **59** D7
Newport *AR* U.S.A. **161** F5
Newport *IN* U.S.A. **164** B4
Newport *KY* U.S.A. **164** C4
Newport *MI* U.S.A. **164** D3
Newport *NH* U.S.A. **165** I2
Newport *NJ* U.S.A. **165** H4
Newport *OR* U.S.A. **156** B3
Newport *RI* U.S.A. **165** J3
Newport *VT* U.S.A. **165** I1
Newport *WA* U.S.A. **156** D2
Newport Beach U.S.A. **158** E5
Newport News U.S.A. **165** G5
Newport Pagnell U.K. **59** G6
New Port Richey U.S.A. **163** D6
New Providence *i.* Bahamas **163** E7
Newquay U.K. **59** B8
New Roads U.S.A. **161** F6
New Rochelle U.S.A. **165** I3
New Rockford U.S.A. **160** D2
New Romney U.K. **59** H8
New Ross Ireland **61** F5
Newry Australia **134** E4
Newry U.K. **61** F3
New Siberia Islands Rus. Fed. **77** P2
New Smyrna Beach U.S.A. **163** D6
New South Wales *state* Australia **138** C4
New Stanton U.S.A. **164** F3
New Stuyahok *AK* U.S.A. **148** H4
Newtok *AK* U.S.A. **148** F3
Newton U.K. **58** E5
Newton *GA* U.S.A. **163** C6
Newton *IA* U.S.A. **160** E3
Newton *IL* U.S.A. **160** F4
Newton *KS* U.S.A. **160** D4
Newton *MA* U.S.A. **165** J2
Newton *MS* U.S.A. **161** F5
Newton *NC* U.S.A. **162** D5
Newton *NJ* U.S.A. **165** H3
Newton *TX* U.S.A. **161** E6
Newton Abbot U.K. **59** D8
Newton Mearns U.K. **60** E5
Newton Stewart U.K. **60** E6
Newtown Ireland **61** D5
Newtown *England* U.K. **59** E6
Newtown *Wales* U.K. **59** D6
Newtown U.S.A. **164** C4
New Town U.S.A. **160** C1
Newtownabbey U.K. **61** G3
Newtownards U.K. **61** G3
Newtownbarry Ireland *see* **Bunclody**
Newtownbutler U.K. **61** E3
Newtown Mount Kennedy Ireland **61** F4
Newtown St Boswells U.K. **60** G5
Newtownstewart U.K. **61** E3
New Ulm U.S.A. **160** E2
Newville U.S.A. **165** G3
New World Island Canada **153** L4

▶**New York** U.S.A. **165** I3
2nd most populous city in North America, and 5th in the world.

New York *state* U.S.A. **165** H2

▶**New Zealand** *country* Oceania **139** D5
3rd largest and 3rd most populous country in Oceania.

Neya Rus. Fed. **52** I4
Neyagawa Japan **92** B4
Ney Bīd Iran **110** E4
Neyrīz Iran **110** D4
Neyshābūr Iran **110** E2
Nezahualcóyotl, Presa *resr* Mex. **167** G5
Nezhin Ukr. *see* **Nizhyn**
Nezperce U.S.A. **156** D3
Ngabang *Kalimantan* Indon. **85** E2
Ngabé Congo **122** B4
Nga Chong, Khao *mt.* Myanmar/Thai. **86** B4
Ngadubolu *Sumba* Indon. **83** A5
Ngagahtawng Myanmar **96** C3
Ngagau *mt.* Tanz. **123** D4
Ngajangel *i.* Palau **82** [inset]
Ngalipaëng *Sulawesi* Indon. **83** C2
Ngalu *Sumba* Indon. **83** B5
Ngamegei Passage Palau **82** [inset]
Ngamring *Xizang* China **99** D7
Ngangla Ringco *salt l.* China **99** C7
Nganglong Kangri *mt.* *Xizang* China **99** C6
Nganglong Kangri *mts* *Xizang* China **99** C6
Ngangzê Co *salt l.* China **99** D7
Ngangzê Shan *mts* *Xizang* China **99** D7
Nganjuk *Jawa* Indon. **85** E4
Ngân Sơn Vietnam **86** D2
Ngaoundal Cameroon **120** E4
Ngaoundéré Cameroon **121** E4
Ngape Myanmar **86** A2
Ngaputaw Myanmar **86** A3
Ngaras *Sumatera* Indon. **84** D4
Ngardmau Palau **82** [inset]
Ngardmau Bay Palau **82** [inset]
Ngaregur *i.* Palau **82** [inset]
Ngariungs *i.* Palau **82** [inset]
Ngateguil, Point Palau **82** [inset]
Ngathainggyaung Myanmar **86** A3
Ngau *i.* Fiji *see* **Gau**
Ngawa China *see* **Aba**
Ngawi *Jawa* Indon. **85** E4
Ngcheangel *atoll* Palau *see* **Kayangel Atoll**
Ngeaur *i.* Palau *see* **Angaur**
Ngemelachel Palau *see* **Malakal**
Ngemelis Islands Palau **82** [inset]
Ngergoi *i.* Palau **82** [inset]
Ngeruangel *i.* Palau **81** I5
Ngesebus *i.* Palau **82** [inset]
Ngga Pulu *mt.* Indon. *see* **Jaya, Puncak**
Ngiap *r.* Laos **86** C3
Ngilmina *Timor* Indon. **83** C5
Ngimbang *Jawa* Indon. **85** F4
Ngiva Angola *see* **Ondjiva**
Ngo Congo **122** B4
Ngoako Ramalepe S. Africa *see* **Duiwelskloof**
Ngobasangel *i.* Palau **82** [inset]
Ngofakiaha *Maluku* Indon. **83** C2
Ngoichogê *Xizang* China **99** F7
Ngoin, Co *salt l.* China **99** E7
Ngok Linh *mt.* Vietnam **86** D4
Ngoko *r.* Cameroon/Congo **121** E4
Ngola Shan *mts* *Qinghai* China **94** D4
Ngola Shankou *pass* *Qinghai* China **94** D5
Ngom Qu *r.* *Xizang* China **99** G7
Ngong Shuen Chau *pen.* *H.K.* China *see* **Stonecutters' Island**
Ngoqumaima *Xizang* China **99** D6
Ngoring *Qinghai* China **94** D5
Ngoring Hu *l.* *Qinghai* China **94** D5
Ngourti Niger **120** E3
Nguigmi Niger **120** E3
Nguiu Australia **134** E2
Ngükang *Xizang* China **99** F7
Ngukurr Australia **134** F3
Ngulu *atoll* Micronesia **81** J5
Ngunju, Tanjung *pt* *Sumba* Indon. **83** B5
Ngunza Angola *see* **Sumbe**
Ngunza-Kabolu Angola *see* **Sumbe**
Ngura *Gansu* China **94** E5
Nguru Nigeria **120** E3
Ngwaketse *admin. dist.* Botswana *see* **Southern**
Ngwane *country* Africa *see* **Swaziland**
Ngwathe S. Africa **125** H4
Ngwavuma *r.* S. Africa/Swaziland **125** K4
Ngwelezana S. Africa **125** J5
Nhachengue Moz. **125** L2
Nhamalabué Moz. **123** D5
Nha Trang Vietnam **87** E4
Nhecolândia Brazil **177** G7
Nhill Australia **137** C8
Nhlangano Swaziland **125** J4
Nho Quan Vietnam **86** D2
Nhow *i.* Fiji *see* **Gau**
Nhulunbuy Australia **136** B2
Niacam Canada **151** J4
Niafounké Mali **120** C3
Niagara U.S.A. **162** C2
Niagara Falls Canada **164** F2
Niagara Falls U.S.A. **164** F2
Niagara-on-the-Lake Canada **164** F2
Niagzu Aksai Chin **99** B6
Niah *Sarawak* Malaysia **85** F2
Niakaramandougou Côte d'Ivoire **120** C4

▶**Niamey** Niger **120** D3
Capital of Niger.

Niām Kand Iran **110** E5
Niampak Indon. **81** H6
Nianbai *Qinghai* China *see* **Ledu**
Niangara Dem. Rep. Congo **122** C3
Niangay, Lac *l.* Mali **120** C3
Nianyuwan *Liaoning* China *see* **Xingangzhen**
Nianzishan *Heilong.* China **95** J2
Nias *i.* Indon. **84** B2
Niassa, Lago *l.* Africa *see* **Nyasa, Lake**
Niaur *i.* Palau *see* **Angaur**
Niāzābād Iran **111** F3
Nibil Well Australia **134** D5
Nīca Latvia **55** L8

▶**Nicaragua** *country* Central America **169** G6
5th largest country in North America.

Nicaragua, Lago de *l.* Nicaragua **166** [inset] I7
Nicaragua, Lake Nicaragua *see* **Nicaragua, Lago de**
Nicastro Italy **68** G5
Nice France **66** H5
Nice U.S.A. **158** B2
Nicephorium Syria *see* **Ar Raqqah**
Niceville U.S.A. **163** C6
Nichicun, Lac *l.* Canada **153** H3
Nicholas Channel Bahamas/Cuba **163** D8
Nicholasville U.S.A. **164** C5
Nichols U.S.A. **164** A1
Nicholson *r.* Australia **136** B3
Nicholson Lake Canada **151** K2
Nicholson Range *hills* Australia **135** B6
Nicholville U.S.A. **165** H1
Nicobar Islands India **87** A5
Nicolás Bravo Mex. **167** H5
Nicolaus U.S.A. **158** C2
Nicomedia *Kocaeli* Turkey *see* **İzmit**

▶**Nicosia** Cyprus **107** A2
Capital of Cyprus.

Nicoya Costa Rica **166** [inset] I7
Nicoya, Golfo de *b.* Costa Rica **166** [inset] I7
Nicoya, Península de *pen.* Costa Rica **166** [inset] I7
Nida Lith. **55** L9
Nidagunda India **106** C2
Nidd *r.* U.K. **58** F4
Nidda Germany **63** J4
Nidder *r.* Germany **63** I4
Nidzica Poland **57** R4
Niebüll Germany **57** L3
Nied *r.* France **62** G5
Niederanven Lux. **62** G5
Niederaula Germany **63** J4
Niedere Tauern *mts* Austria **57** N7
Niedersachsen *land* Germany **63** I2
Niedersächsisches Wattenmeer, Nationalpark *nat. park* Germany **62** G1
Niefang Equat. Guinea **120** E4
Niellé Côte d'Ivoire **120** C3
Nienburg (Weser) Germany **63** J2
Niers *r.* Germany **62** F3
Nierstein Germany **63** I5
Nieuwe-Niedorp Neth. **62** E2
Nieuwerkerk aan de IJssel Neth. **62** E3
Nieuw Nickerie Suriname **177** G2
Nieuwolda Neth. **62** G1
Nieuwoudtville S. Africa **124** D6
Nieuwpoort Belgium **62** C3
Nieuw-Vossemeer Neth. **62** E3
Nif *Seram* Indon. **83** D3
Niğde Turkey **112** D3
Niger *country* Africa **120** D3

▶**Niger** *r.* Africa **120** D4
3rd longest river in Africa.

Niger, Mouths of the Nigeria **120** D4
Niger Cone *sea feature* S. Atlantic Ocean **184** I5

▶**Nigeria** *country* Africa **120** D4
Most populous country in Africa, and 8th in the world.

Nighthawk Lake Canada **152** E4
Nightmute *AK* U.S.A. **148** F3
Nigrita Greece **69** J4
Nihing Pak. **111** G4
Nihon *country* Asia *see* **Japan**
Niigata Japan **91** E5
Niigata *pref.* Japan **93** E1
Niigata-yake-yama *vol.* Japan **93** E2
Niihama Japan **91** D6
Niihari Japan **93** G2
Ni'ihau *i.* U.S.A. **157** [inset]
Nii-jima *i.* Japan **93** F4
Niimi Japan **91** D6
Niitsu Japan **91** E5
Nijil, Wādī *watercourse* Jordan **107** B4
Nijkerk Neth. **62** F2
Nijmegen Neth. **62** F3
Nijverdal Neth. **62** G2
Nikel' Rus. Fed. **54** Q2
Nikiniki *Timor* Indon. **83** C5
Nikiski *AK* U.S.A. **149** J3
Nikki Benin **120** D4
Nikkō Japan **93** F2
Nikkō Kokuritsu-kōen *nat. park* Japan **93** F2
Nikolaevsk *AK* U.S.A. **149** J4
Nikolai *AK* U.S.A. **148** I3
Nikolayev Ukr. *see* **Mykolayiv**
Nikolayevka Rus. Fed. **53** J5
Nikolayevsk Rus. Fed. **53** J6
Nikolayevskiy Rus. Fed. *see* **Nikolayevsk**
Nikolayevsk-na-Amure Rus. Fed. **90** F1
Nikol'sk Rus. Fed. **52** J4
Nikolski *AK* U.S.A. **148** E5
Nikol'skiy Kazakh. *see* **Satpayev**
Nikol'skoye *Kamchatskaya Oblast'* Rus. Fed. **77** R4
Nikol'skoye *Vologod. Obl.* Rus. Fed. *see* **Sheksna**
Nikopol' Ukr. **53** G7
Niksar Turkey **112** E2
Nīkshahr Iran **111** F5
Nikšić Montenegro **68** H3
Nīkū Jahān Iran **111** F5
Nikumaroro *atoll* Kiribati **133** I2
Nikunau *i.* Kiribati **133** H2
Nīl, Bahr el *r.* Africa *see* **Nile**
Nila *vol.* *Maluku* Indon. **83** D4
Nilagiri India **105** F5
Niland U.S.A. **159** F5
Nilande Atoll Maldives *see* **Nilandhoo Atoll**
Nilandhe Atoll Maldives *see* **Nilandhoo Atoll**
Nilandhoo Atoll Maldives **103** D11
Nilang India *see* **Nelang**
Nilanga India **106** C2
Nilaveli Sri Lanka **106** D4

▶**Nile** *r.* Africa **112** C5
Longest river in the world.

Niles *MI* U.S.A. **164** B3
Niles *OH* U.S.A. **164** E3
Nilgiri Hills India **106** C4
Nīlī **111** G3
Nilka *Xinjiang* China **98** C4
Nīl Kowtal Afgh. **111** G3
Nilphamari Bangl. **105** G4
Nilsiä Fin. **54** P5
Nimach India *see* **Neemuch**
Niman *r.* Rus. Fed. **90** D2
Nimba, Monts *mts* Africa *see* **Nimba, Mount**
Nimba, Mount Africa **120** C4
Nimbal India **106** B2
Nimberra Well Australia **135** C5
Nimelen *r.* Rus. Fed. **90** E1
Nîmes France **66** G5
Nimmitabel Australia **137** E8
Nimrod Glacier Antarctica **188** H1
Nimu India **104** D2
Nimule Sudan **121** G4
Nimwegen Neth. *see* **Nijmegen**
Nindigully Australia **138** D2
Nine Degree Channel India **106** B4
Nine Islands P.N.G. *see* **Kilinailau Islands**
Ninepin Group *is* *H.K.* China **97** [inset]
Ninetyeast Ridge *sea feature* Indian Ocean **185** N8
Ninety Mile Beach Australia **138** C7
Ninety Mile Beach N.Z. **139** D2
Nineveh U.S.A. **165** H2
Ning'an China **90** C3
Ningbo China **97** I2
Ningcheng *Nei Mongol* China **95** I3
Ningde China **97** H3
Ning'er China *see* **Pu'er**
Ningguo China **97** H2
Ninghai China **97** I2
Ninghe *Tianjin* China **95** I4
Ninghsia Hui Autonomous Region *aut. reg.* China *see* **Ningxia Huizu Zizhiqu**
Ninghua China **97** H3
Ninging India **105** H3
Ningjiang China *see* **Songyuan**
Ningjing Shan *mts* China **96** C2
Ninglang China **96** D3
Ningling *Henan* China **95** H5
Ningming China **96** E4
Ningnan China **96** D3
Ningqiang China **96** E1
Ningwu *Shanxi* China **95** H4
Ningxia *aut. reg.* China *see* **Ningxia Huizu Zizhiqu**
Ningxia Huizu Zizhiqu *aut. reg.* China **94** F4
Ningxian *Gansu* China **95** F5
Ningxiang China **97** G2
Ningyang *Shandong* China **95** I5
Ningzhou China *see* **Huaning**
Ninh Binh Vietnam **86** D2
Ninh Hoa Vietnam **87** E4
Ninigo Group *atolls* P.N.G. **81** K7
Ninilchik *AK* U.S.A. **149** J3
Ninnis Glacier Antarctica **188** G2
Ninnis Glacier Tongue Antarctica **188** H2
Ninohe Japan **91** F4
Ninomiya *Kanagawa* Japan **93** F3
Ninomiya *Tochigi* Japan **93** F2
Niobrara *r.* U.S.A. **160** D3
Nioko *Arun. Prad.* India **99** F8
Niokolo Koba, Parc National du *nat. park* Senegal **120** B3
Niono Mali **120** C3
Nioro Mali **120** C3
Niort France **66** D3
Nipani India **106** B2
Nipanipa, Tanjung *pt* Indon. **83** B3
Nipawin Canada **151** J4
Niphad India **106** B1
Nipigon Canada **147** J5
Nipigon, Lake Canada **147** J5
Nipishish Lake Canada **153** J3
Nipissing, Lake Canada **152** F5
Nippon *country* Asia *see* **Japan**
Nippon Hai *sea* N. Pacific Ocean *see* **Japan, Sea of**
Nipton U.S.A. **159** F4
Niquelândia Brazil **179** A1
Nir *Ardabīl* Iran **110** B2
Nir *Yazd* Iran **110** D4
Nira *r.* India **106** B2
Nirasaki Japan **93** E3
Nirayama Japan **93** E3
Nirji *Nei Mongol* China **95** K1
Nirmal India **106** C2
Nirmali India **105** F4
Nirmal Range *hills* India **106** C2
Niš Serbia **69** I3
Nisa Port. **67** C4
Nisa *tourist site* Turkm. **110** E2
Nisarpur India **106** B1
Niscemi *Sicily* Italy **68** F6
Nishan *Xizang* China **99** D6
Nīshāpūr Iran *see* **Neyshābūr**
Nishiazai Japan **92** C3
Nishiizu Japan **93** E4
Nishikata *Tochigi* Japan **93** F2
Nishikatsura Japan **93** E3
Nishi-maizuru Japan **92** B3
Nishinasuno Japan **93** F2
Nishinomiya Japan **92** B4
Nishino-shima *vol.* Japan **91** F8
Nishio Japan **92** D4
Nishi-Sonogi-hantō *pen.* Japan **91** C6
Nishiwaki Japan **92** A4
Nishiyoshino Japan **92** B4
Nisibis Turkey *see* **Nusaybin**
Nisiharu Japan **92** C3
Nísiros *i.* Greece *see* **Nisyros**
Niskibi *r.* Canada **151** N3
Nisling *r.* *Y.T.* Canada **149** M3
Nispen Neth. **62** E3
Nissan *r.* Sweden **55** H8
Nisshin Japan **92** D3
Nistru *r.* Moldova **69** N1 *see* **Dniester**
Nisutlin *r.* *Y.T.* Canada **149** N3
Nisyros *i.* Greece **69** L6
Niṭā Saudi Arabia **110** C5
Nitchequon Canada **153** H3
Nitendi *i.* Solomon Is *see* **Ndeni**
Niterói Brazil **179** C3
Nith *r.* U.K. **60** F5
Nitibe East Timor **83** C5
Niti Pass China/India **104** D3
Niti Shankou *pass* China/India *see* **Niti Pass**
Nitmiluk National Park Australia **134** F3
Nitra Slovakia **57** Q6
Nitro U.S.A. **164** E4
Nitta Japan **93** F2
Niuafo'ou *i.* Tonga **133** I3
Niuatoputopu *i.* Tonga **133** I3
Niubiziliang *Qinghai* China **98** F5

▶**Niue** *terr.* S. Pacific Ocean **133** J3
Self-governing New Zealand Overseas Territory.

Niujing China *see* **Binchuan**
Niulakita *i.* Tuvalu **133** H3
Niur, Pulau *i.* Indon. **84** C3
Niushan *Jiangsu* China *see* **Donghai**
Niutao *i.* Tuvalu **133** H2
Niutoushan China **97** H2
Niuzhuang *Liaoning* China **95** J3
Nivala Fin. **54** N5
Nive *watercourse* Australia **136** D5
Nivelles Belgium **62** E4
Niwai India **104** C4
Niwas India **104** E5
Nixia China *see* **Sêrxü**
Nixon U.S.A. **158** D2
Niya *Xinjiang* China *see* **Minfeng**
Niya He *r.* China **99** C5
Niyut, Gunung *mt.* Indon. **85** E2
Niza Japan **93** F3
Nizamabad India **106** C2
Nizam Sagar *l.* India **106** C2
Nizhnedevitsk Rus. Fed. **53** H6
Nizhnekamsk Rus. Fed. **52** K5
Nizhnekamskoye Vodokhranilishche *resr* Rus. Fed. **51** Q4
Nizhnekolymsk Rus. Fed. **77** R3
Nizhnetambovskoye Rus. Fed. **90** E2
Nizhneudinsk Rus. Fed. **88** H2
Nizhnevartovsk Rus. Fed. **76** I3
Nizhnevolzhsk Rus. Fed. *see* **Narimanov**
Nizhneyansk Rus. Fed. **77** O2
Nizhneye Giryunino Rus. Fed. **95** I1
Nizhniy Baskunchak Rus. Fed. **53** J6
Nizhniye Kayrakty Kazakh. **98** A2
Nizhniye Kresty Rus. Fed. *see* **Cherskiy**
Nizhniy Lomov Rus. Fed. **53** I5
Nizhniy Novgorod Rus. Fed. **52** I4
Nizhniy Odes Rus. Fed. **52** L3
Nizhniy Pyandzh Tajik. *see* **Panji Poyon**
Nizhniy Tagil Rus. Fed. **51** R4
Nizhniy Tsasuchey Rus. Fed. **95** H1
Nizhnyaya Mola Rus. Fed. **52** J2
Nizhnyaya Omra Rus. Fed. **52** L3
Nizhnyaya Pirenga, Ozero *l.* Rus. Fed. **54** R3
Nizhnyaya Tunguska *r.* Rus. Fed. **76** J3
Nizhnyaya Tura Rus. Fed. **51** R4
Nizhyn Ukr. **53** F6
Nizina *r.* U.S.A. **150** A2
Nizina Mazowiecka *reg.* Poland **57** R4
Nizip Turkey **107** C1
Nízke Tatry *nat. park* Slovakia **57** Q6
Nizkiy, Mys *hd* Rus. Fed. **148** B2
Nizwā Oman *see* **Nazwá**
Nizza France *see* **Nice**
Njallavarri *mt.* Norway **54** L2
Njavve Sweden **54** K3
Njazidja *i.* Comoros **123** E5
Njombe Tanz. **123** D4
Njurundabommen Sweden **54** J5
Nkambe Cameroon **120** E4
Nkandla S. Africa **125** J5
Nkawkaw Ghana **120** C4
Nkhata Bay Malawi **123** D5
Nkhotakota Malawi **123** D5
Nkondwe Tanz. **123** D4
Nkongsamba Cameroon **120** D4
Nkululeko S. Africa **125** H6
Nkwenkwezi S. Africa **125** H7
Noakhali Bangl. **105** G5
Noatak *AK* U.S.A. **148** G2
Noatak *r.* *AK* U.S.A. **148** G2
Noatak National Preserve *nature res.* *AK* U.S.A. **148** H1
Nobber Ireland **61** F4
Nobeoka Japan **91** C6
Noblesville U.S.A. **164** B3
Noboribetsu Japan **90** F4
Noccundra Australia **137** C5
Nochistlán Mex. **166** E4
Nochixtlán Mex. **167** F5
Nockatunga Australia **137** C5
Nocona U.S.A. **161** D5
Noda Japan **93** F3
Nodagawa Japan **92** B3
Noel Kempff Mercado, Parque Nacional *nat. park* Bol. **176** F6
Noelville Canada **152** E5
Nogales Mex. **166** C2
Nogales U.S.A. **157** F7
Nōgata Japan **91** C6
Nogent-le-Rotrou France **66** E2
Nogent-sur-Oise France **62** C5
Nogi Japan **93** F2
Noginsk Rus. Fed. **52** H5
Nogliki Rus. Fed. **90** F2
Nogoa *r.* Australia **136** E4
Nōgōhaku-san *mt.* Japan **92** C3
Nogon Toli *Nei Mongol* China **94** F4
Noguchigorō-dake *mt.* Japan **92** D2
Nohalal Mex. **167** H5
Nohar India **104** C3
Noheji Japan **90** F4
Nohfelden Germany **62** H5
Nohoit *Qinghai* China **94** C4
Noida India **104** D3
Noirmoutier, Île de *i.* France **66** C3
Noirmoutier-en-l'Île France **66** C3
Noisseville France **62** G5
Nojima-zaki *c.* Japan **93** F4
Nojiri-ko *l.* Japan **93** E2
Nokami Japan **92** B4
Nokhowch, Kūh-e *mt.* Iran **111** F5
Nōkis Uzbek. *see* **Nukus**
Nok Kundi Pak. **111** F4
Nokomis Canada **151** J5
Nokomis Lake Canada **151** K3
Nokou Chad **121** E3
Nokrek Peak India **105** G4
Nola Cent. Afr. Rep. **122** B3
Nolin River Lake U.S.A. **164** B5
Nolinsk Rus. Fed. **52** K4
No Mans Land *i.* U.S.A. **165** J3
Nome *AK* U.S.A. **148** F2
Nome, Cape *AK* U.S.A. **148** F2

Nomgon Mongolia 94 F3
Nomhon Qinghai China 94 D4
Nomhon He r. Qinghai China 94 C4
Nomin Gol r. China 95 K1
Nomoi Islands Micronesia see Mortlock Islands
Nomonde S. Africa 125 H6
Nömrög Mongolia 94 D1
Nomto Rus. Fed. 94 F1
Nomugi-tōge pass Japan 92 D2
Nomzha Rus. Fed. 52 I4
Nonacho Lake Canada 151 I2
Nondalton AK U.S.A. 148 I4
Nondweni S. Africa 125 J5
Nong'an China 90 B3
Nông Hèt Laos 86 D3
Nonghui China see Guang'an
Nong Khai Thai. 86 C3
Nongoma S. Africa 125 J4
Nongstoin India 105 G4
Nonidas Namibia 124 B2
Nonni r. China see Nen Jiang
Nonning Australia 137 B7
Nonnweiler Germany 62 G5
Nonoava Mex. 166 D3
Nonoichi Japan 92 C2
Nonouti atoll Kiribati 133 H2
Nonthaburi Thai. 87 C4
Nonvianuk Lake AK U.S.A. 148 I4
Nonzwakazi S. Africa 124 G6
Noolyeanna Lake salt flat Australia 137 B5
Noondie, Lake salt flat Australia 135 B7
Noonkanbah Australia 134 D4
Noonthorangee Range hills Australia 137 C6
Noorama Creek watercourse Australia 138 B1
Noordbeveland i. Neth. 62 D3
Noorderhaaks i. Neth. 62 E2
Noordoost Polder Neth. 62 F2
Noordwijk-Binnen Neth. 62 E2
Noorvik AK U.S.A. 148 G2
Nootka Island Canada 150 E5
Nora r. Rus. Fed. 90 C2
Norak Tajik. 111 H2
Norak, Obanbori resr Tajik. 111 H2
Norala Mindanao Phil. 82 D5
Noranda Canada 152 F4
Nor-Bayazet Armenia see Gavarr
Norberg Sweden 55 I6
Norcang Xizang China 99 D7
Nord Greenland see Station Nord
Nord, Canal du France 62 D4
Nordaustlandet i. Svalbard 76 D2
Nordegg Canada 150 G4
Norden Germany 63 H1
Nordenshel'da, Arkhipelag is Rus. Fed. 76 K2
Nordenskjold Archipelago is Rus. Fed. see Nordenshel'da, Arkhipelag
Norderney Germany 63 H1
Norderstedt Germany 63 K1
Nordfjordeid Norway 54 D6
Nordfold Norway 54 I3
Nordfriesische Inseln Germany see North Frisian Islands
Nordhausen Germany 63 K3
Nordholz Germany 63 I1
Nordhorn Germany 62 H2
Nordkapp c. Norway see North Cape
Nordkinnhalvøya i. Norway 54 O1
Nordkjosbotn Norway 54 K2
Nordli Norway 54 H4
Nördlingen Germany 63 K6
Nordmaling Sweden 54 K5
Nord- og Østgrønland, Nationalparken i nat. park Greenland 147 O2

▶Nordøstrundingen c. Greenland 189 I1
Most easterly point of North America.

Nord-Ostsee-Kanal Germany see Kiel Canal
Norðoyar i. Faroe Is 50 E3
Nord-Pas-de-Calais admin. reg. France 62 C4
Nordpfälzer Bergland reg. Germany 63 H5
Nordre Strømfjord inlet Greenland see Nassuttooq
Nordrhein-Westfalen land Germany 63 H3
Nordvik Rus. Fed. 77 M2
Nore r. Ireland 61 F5
Nore, Pic de mt. France 66 F5
Noreg country Europe see Norway
Norfolk NE U.S.A. 160 D3
Norfolk NY U.S.A. 165 H1
Norfolk VA U.S.A. 165 G5

▶Norfolk Island terr. S. Pacific Ocean 133 G4
Territory of Australia.

Norfolk Island Ridge sea feature Tasman Sea 186 H7
Norfork Lake U.S.A. 161 E4
Norg Neth. 62 G1
Norge country Europe see Norway
Norheimsund Norway 55 E6
Norikura-dake vol. Japan 92 D2
Noril'sk Rus. Fed. 76 J3
Norkyung Xizang China 99 E7
Norland Canada 165 F1
Norma Co l. Xizang China 99 E6
Norman U.S.A. 161 D5
Norman, Lake resr U.S.A. 162 D5
Normanby Island P.N.G. 136 E1
Normandes, Îles is English Chan. see Channel Islands
Normandia Brazil 177 G3
Normandie reg. France see Normandy
Normandie, Collines de hills France 66 D2
Normandy reg. France 66 D2
Normanton Australia 136 C3
Norman Wells N.W.T. Canada 149 P2
Norogachic Mex. 166 D3
Norovlin Mongolia 95 G1
Norquay Canada 151 K5
Ñorquinco Arg. 178 B6
Norra Kvarken strait Fin./Sweden 54 L5
Norra Storfjället mts Sweden 54 I4
Norrent-Fontes France 62 C4
Norris Lake U.S.A. 164 D5
Norristown U.S.A. 165 H3
Norrköping Sweden 55 J7
Norrtälje Sweden 55 K7
Norseman Australia 135 C8
Norsjö Sweden 54 K4
Norsk Rus. Fed. 90 C1
Norsup Vanuatu 133 G3
Norte, Punta pt Arg. 178 E5
Norte, Serra do hills Brazil 177 G6
Nortelândia Brazil 177 G6
Nörten-Hardenberg Germany 63 J3
North, Cape Antarctica 188 H2
North, Cape Canada 153 J5
Northallerton U.K. 58 F4
Northam Australia 135 B7
Northampton Australia 132 B4
Northampton U.K. 59 G6
Northampton MA U.S.A. 165 I2
Northampton PA U.S.A. 165 H3
North Andaman i. India 87 A4
North Anna r. U.S.A. 165 G5
North Arm b. Canada 150 H2
North Atlantic Ocean Atlantic Ocean 155 O4
North Augusta U.S.A. 163 D5
North Aulatsivik Island Canada 153 J2
North Australian Basin sea feature Indian Ocean 185 P6
North Balabac Strait Phil. 82 B4
North Baltimore U.S.A. 164 D3
North Battleford Canada 151 I4
North Bay Canada 152 F5
North Belcher Islands Canada 152 F2
North Berwick U.K. 60 G4
North Berwick U.S.A. 165 J2
North Borneo state Malaysia see Sabah
North Bourke Australia 138 B3
North Branch U.S.A. 160 E2
North Caicos i. Turks and Caicos Is 163 G8
North Canton U.S.A. 164 E3
North Cape Canada 153 I5
North Cape Norway 54 N1
North Cape N.Z. 139 D2
North Cape AK U.S.A. 149 [inset]
North Caribou Lake Canada 151 N4
North Carolina state U.S.A. 162 E4
North Cascades National Park U.S.A. 156 C2
North Channel lake channel Canada 152 E5
North Channel U.K. 61 G2
North Charleston U.S.A. 163 E5
North Chicago U.S.A. 164 B2
North China Plain plain China see Huabei Pingyuan
Northcliffe Glacier Antarctica 188 F2
North Collins U.S.A. 165 F2
North Concho r. U.S.A. 161 C6
North Conway U.S.A. 165 J1
North Dakota state U.S.A. 160 C2
North Downs hills U.K. 59 G7
North East U.S.A. 164 F2
Northeast Cape AK U.S.A. 148 E3
Northeast Foreland c. Greenland see Nordøstrundingen
North-East Frontier Agency state India see Arunachal Pradesh
Northeast Pacific Basin sea feature N. Pacific Ocean 187 J4
Northeast Point Bahamas 163 F8
Northeast Providence Channel Bahamas 163 E7
North Edwards U.S.A. 158 E4
Northeim Germany 63 J3
North Entrance sea chan. Palau 82 [inset]
Northern prov. S. Africa see Limpopo
Northern Areas admin. div. Pak. 111 I2
Northern Cape prov. S. Africa 124 D5
Northern Donets r. Rus. Fed./Ukr. see Severskiy Donets
Northern Dvina r. Rus. Fed. see Severnaya Dvina
Northern Indian Lake Canada 151 L3
Northern Ireland prov. U.K. 61 F3
Northern Lau Group is Fiji 133 I3
Northern Light Lake Canada 152 C4

▶Northern Mariana Islands terr. N. Pacific Ocean 81 K3
United States Commonwealth.

Northern Rhodesia country Africa see Zambia
Northern Sporades is Greece see Voreies Sporades
Northern Territory admin. div. Australia 132 D3
Northern Transvaal prov. S. Africa see Limpopo
North Esk r. U.K. 60 G4
Northfield MN U.S.A. 160 E2
Northfield VT U.S.A. 165 I1
North Foreland c. U.K. 59 I7
North Fork U.S.A. 158 D3
North Fork Pass Y.T. Canada 149 M2
North French r. Canada 152 E4
North Frisian Islands Germany 57 L3
North Geomagnetic Pole (2008) Canada 189 K1
North Grimston U.K. 58 G4
North Haven U.S.A. 165 I3
North Head hd N.Z. 139 E3
North Henik Lake Canada 151 L2
North Hero U.S.A. 165 I1
North Horr Kenya 122 D3
North Island India 106 B4

▶North Island N.Z. 139 D4
3rd largest island in Oceania.

North Island Phil. 82 C1
North Islet rf Phil. 82 C4
North Jadito Canyon gorge U.S.A. 159 H4
North Judson U.S.A. 164 B3
North Kingsville U.S.A. 164 E3
North Knife r. Canada 151 M3
North Knife Lake Canada 151 L3
North Korea country Asia 91 B5
North Lakhimpur India 105 H4
North Las Vegas U.S.A. 159 F3
North Little Rock U.S.A. 161 E5
North Loup r. U.S.A. 160 D3
North Luangwa National Park Zambia 123 D5
North Maalhosmadulu Atoll Maldives 106 B5
North Magnetic Pole (2008) Arctic Ocean 189 A1
North Malosmadulu Atoll Maldives see North Maalhosmadulu Atoll
North Mam Peak U.S.A. 159 J2
North Muskegon U.S.A. 164 B2
North Palisade mt. U.S.A. 158 D3
North Perry U.S.A. 164 E3
North Platte U.S.A. 160 C3
North Platte r. U.S.A. 160 C3
North Pole Arctic Ocean 189 I1
North Pole AK U.S.A. 149 K2
North Port U.S.A. 163 D7
North Reef Island India 87 A4
North Rhine-Westphalia land Germany see Nordrhein-Westfalen
North Rim U.S.A. 159 G3
North Rona i. U.K. see Rona
North Ronaldsay i. U.K. 60 G1
North Ronaldsay Firth sea chan. U.K. 60 G1
North Saskatchewan r. Canada 151 J4
North Schell Peak U.S.A. 159 F2
North Sea Europe 56 H2
North Seal r. Canada 151 L3
North Sentinel Island India 87 A5
North Shields U.K. 58 F3
North Shoal Lake Canada 151 L5
North Shoshone Peak U.S.A. 158 E2
North Siberian Lowland Rus. Fed. 76 L2
North Siberian Lowland Rus. Fed. 189 E2
North Simlipal National Park India 105 F5
North Sinai governorate Egypt see Shamāl Sīnā'
North Slope plain AK U.S.A. 149 J1
North Somercotes U.K. 58 H5
North Spirit Lake Canada 151 M4
North Stradbroke Island Australia 138 F1
North Sunderland U.K. 58 F3
North Syracuse U.S.A. 165 G2
North Taranaki Bight b. N.Z. 139 E4
North Terre Haute U.S.A. 164 B4
Northton U.K. 60 B3
North Tonawanda U.S.A. 165 F2
North Trap reef N.Z. 139 A8
North Troy U.S.A. 165 I1
North Tyne r. U.K. 58 E4
North Ubian i. Phil. 82 C5
North Uist i. U.K. 60 B3
Northumberland National Park U.K. 58 E3
Northumberland Strait Canada 153 I5
North Vancouver Canada 150 F5
North Verde i. Phil. 82 B4
North Vernon U.S.A. 164 C4
Northville U.S.A. 165 H2
North Wabasca Lake Canada 150 H3
North Walsham U.K. 59 I6
Northway Junction AK U.S.A. 149 L3
North West prov. S. Africa 124 G4
Northwest Atlantic Mid-Ocean Channel N. Atlantic Ocean 184 E1
North West Cape Australia 134 A5
Northwest Cape AK U.S.A. 148 E3
North West Frontier prov. Pak. 111 H3
North West Nelson Forest Park nat. park N.Z. see Kahurangi National Park
Northwest Pacific Basin sea feature N. Pacific Ocean 186 G3
Northwest Providence Channel Bahamas 163 E7
North West River Canada 153 K3
Northwest Territories admin. div. Canada 150 J2
Northwich U.K. 58 E5
North Wildwood U.S.A. 165 H4
North Windham U.S.A. 165 J2
Northwind Ridge sea feature Arctic Ocean 189 B1
Northwood U.S.A. 165 J2
North York Canada 164 F2
North York Moors moorland U.K. 58 G4
North York Moors National Park U.K. 58 G4
Norton U.K. 58 G4
Norton KS U.S.A. 160 D4
Norton VA U.S.A. 164 D5
Norton VT U.S.A. 165 J1
Norton Bay AK U.S.A. 148 G2
Norton de Matos Angola see Balombo
Norton Shores U.S.A. 164 B2
Norton Sound sea channel AK U.S.A. 148 G3
Nortonville U.S.A. 164 B5
Norutak Lake AK U.S.A. 148 I2
Norvegia, Cape Antarctica 188 B2
Norwalk CT U.S.A. 165 I3
Norwalk OH U.S.A. 164 D3
Norway country Europe 54 E6
Norway U.S.A. 165 J1
Norway House Canada 151 L4
Norwegian Basin sea feature N. Atlantic Ocean 184 H1
Norwegian Bay Canada 147 I2
Norwegian Sea N. Atlantic Ocean 189 H2
Norwich Canada 164 E2
Norwich U.K. 59 I6
Norwich CT U.S.A. 165 I3
Norwich NY U.S.A. 165 H2
Norwood CO U.S.A. 159 I2
Norwood NY U.S.A. 165 H1
Norwood OH U.S.A. 164 C4
Norzagaray Luzon Phil. 82 C3
Nosaka Japan 93 G3
Nose Japan 92 B4
Nosegawa Japan 92 B4
Nose Lake Canada 151 I1
Noshiro Japan 91 F4
Nosovaya Rus. Fed. 52 L1
Noşratābād Iran 111 E4
Noss, Isle of i. U.K. 60 [inset]
Nossebro Sweden 55 H7
Nossen Germany 63 N3
Nossob watercourse Africa 124 D2
also known as Nosop
Nossob watercourse Africa 124 D2
also known as Nossob
Notakwanon r. Canada 153 J2
Notch Peak U.S.A. 159 G2
Noteć r. Poland 57 O4
Notikewin r. Canada 150 G3
Noto, Golfo di g. Sicily Italy 68 F6
Notodden Norway 55 F7
Notogawa Japan 92 C3
Noto-hantō pen. Japan 89 P5
Notojima Japan 92 D1
Noto-jima i. Japan 92 D1
Notre-Dame, Monts mts Canada 153 H5
Notre Dame Bay Canada 153 L4
Notre-Dame-de-Koartac Canada see Quaqtaq
Nottawasaga Bay Canada 164 E1
Nottaway r. Canada 152 F4
Nottingham U.K. 59 F6
Nottingham Island Canada 147 K3
Nottoway r. U.S.A. 165 G5
Nottuln Germany 63 H3
Notukeu Creek r. Canada 151 J5
Nou Japan 93 D1
Nouabalé-Ndoki, Parc National nat. park Congo 122 B3
Nouâdhibou Mauritania 120 B2
Nouâdhibou, Râs c. Mauritania 120 B2

▶Nouakchott Mauritania 120 B3
Capital of Mauritania.

Nouâmghâr Mauritania 120 B3
Nouei Vietnam 86 D4

▶Nouméa New Caledonia 133 G4
Capital of New Caledonia.

Nouna Burkina 120 C3
Noupoort S. Africa 124 G6
Nousu Fin. 54 P3
Nouveau-Brunswick prov. Canada see New Brunswick
Nouveau-Comptoir Canada see Wemindji
Nouvelle Calédonie i. S. Pacific Ocean 133 G4
Nouvelle Calédonie terr. S. Pacific Ocean see New Caledonia
Nouvelle-France, Cap de c. Canada 147 K3
Nouvelles Hébrides country S. Pacific Ocean see Vanuatu
Nova América Brazil 179 A1
Nova Chaves Angola see Muconda
Nova Freixa Moz. see Cuamba
Nova Friburgo Brazil 179 C3
Nova Gaia Angola see Cambundi-Catembo
Nova Goa India see Panaji
Nova Gradiška Croatia 68 G2
Nova Iguaçu Brazil 179 C3
Nova Kakhovka Ukr. 69 O1
Nova Lima Brazil 179 C2
Nova Lisboa Angola see Huambo
Novalukoml' Belarus 53 F5
Nova Mambone Moz. 123 D6
Nova Nabúri Moz. 123 D5
Nova Odesa Ukr. 53 F7
Nova Paraiso Brazil 176 F3
Nova Pilão Arcado Brazil 177 J5
Nova Ponte Brazil 179 B2
Nova Ponte, Represa resr Brazil 179 B2
Novara Italy 68 C2
Nova Roma Brazil 179 B1
Nova Scotia prov. Canada 153 I6
Nova Sento Sé Brazil 177 J5
Novato U.S.A. 158 B2
Nova Trento Brazil 179 A4
Nova Venécia Brazil 179 C2
Nova Xavantino Brazil 177 H6
Novaya Kakhovka Ukr. see Nova Kakhovka
Novaya Kazanka Kazakh. 51 P6
Novaya Ladoga Rus. Fed. 52 G3
Novaya Lyalya Rus. Fed. 51 S4
Novaya Odessa Ukr. see Nova Odesa
Novaya Sibir', Ostrov i. Rus. Fed. 77 P2
Novaya Ussura Rus. Fed. 90 E2

▶Novaya Zemlya is Rus. Fed. 76 G2
3rd largest island in Europe.

Nova Zagora Bulg. 69 L3
Novelda Spain 67 F4
Nové Zámky Slovakia 57 Q7
Novgorod Rus. Fed. see Velikiy Novgorod
Novgorod-Severskiy Ukr. see Novhorod-Sivers'kyy
Novgorod-Volynskiy Ukr. see Novohrad-Volyns'kyy
Novhorod-Sivers'kyy Ukr. 53 G6
Novi Grad Bos.-Herz. see Bosanski Novi
Novi Iskŭr Bulg. 69 J3
Novikovo Rus. Fed. 90 F3
Novi Kritsim Bulg. see Stamboliyski
Novi Ligure Italy 68 C2
Novillero Mex. 166 D4
Novi Pazar Bulg. 69 L3
Novi Pazar Serbia 69 I3
Novi Sad Serbia 69 H2
Novo Acre Brazil 179 C1
Novoalekseyevka Kazakh. see Khobda
Novoaltaysk Rus. Fed. 88 E2
Novoanninskiy Rus. Fed. 53 I6
Novo Aripuanã Brazil 176 F5
Novoazovs'k Ukr. 53 H7
Novocheboksarsk Rus. Fed. 52 J4
Novocherkassk Rus. Fed. 53 I7
Novo Cruzeiro Brazil 179 C2
Novodoroninskoye Rus. Fed. 95 H1
Novodugino Rus. Fed. 52 G5
Novodvinsk Rus. Fed. 52 I2
Novoekonomicheskoye Ukr. see Dymytrov
Novogeorgiyevka Rus. Fed. 90 B2
Novogrudok Belarus see Navahrudak
Novo Hamburgo Brazil 179 A5
Novohradské hory mts Czech Rep. 57 O6
Novohrad-Volyns'kyy Ukr. 53 E6
Novokhopersk Rus. Fed. 53 I6
Novokiyevskiy Uval Rus. Fed. 90 C2
Novokubansk Rus. Fed. 113 F1
Novokubanskiy Rus. Fed. see Novokubansk
Novokuybyshevsk Rus. Fed. 53 K5
Novokuznetsk Rus. Fed. 88 F2
Novolazarevskaya research station Antarctica 188 C2
Novolukoml' Belarus see Novalukoml'
Novo Mesto Slovenia 68 F2
Novomikhaylovskiy Rus. Fed. 112 E1
Novomoskovsk Rus. Fed. 53 H5
Novomoskovs'k Ukr. 53 G6
Novonikolayevsk Rus. Fed. see Novosibirsk
Novonikolayevskiy Rus. Fed. 53 I6
Novooleksiyivka Ukr. 53 G7
Novopashiyskiy Rus. Fed. see Gornozavodsk
Novopavlovka Rus. Fed. 95 G1
Novopokrovka Vostochnyy Kazakhstan Kazakh. 98 C2
Novopokrovka Rus. Fed. 90 D3
Novopokrovskaya Rus. Fed. 53 I7
Novopolotsk Belarus see Navapolatsk
Novopskov Ukr. 53 H6
Novo Redondo Angola see Sumbe
Novorossiyka Rus. Fed. 90 C1
Novorossiysk Rus. Fed. 112 E1
Novorybnaya Rus. Fed. 77 L2
Novorzhev Rus. Fed. 52 F4
Novoselenginsk Rus. Fed. 94 F1
Novoselovo Rus. Fed. 88 G1
Novoselskoye Rus. Fed. see Achkhoy-Martan
Novosel'ye Rus. Fed. 55 P7
Novosergiyevka Rus. Fed. 51 Q5
Novoshakhtinsk Rus. Fed. 53 H7
Novosheshminsk Rus. Fed. 52 K5
Novosibirsk Rus. Fed. 76 J4
Novosibirskiye Ostrova is Rus. Fed. see New Siberia Islands
Novosil' Rus. Fed. 53 H5
Novosokol'niki Rus. Fed. 52 F4
Novospasskoye Rus. Fed. 53 J5
Novotroyits'ke Ukr. 53 G7
Novoukrainka Ukr. see Novoukrayinka
Novoukrayinka Ukr. 53 F6
Novouzensk Rus. Fed. 53 K6
Novovolyns'k Ukr. 53 E6
Novovoronezh Rus. Fed. 53 H6
Novovoronezhskiy Rus. Fed. see Novovoronezh
Novovoskresenovka Rus. Fed. 90 B1
Novovoznesenovka Kyrg. 98 B4
Novoye Chaplino Rus. Fed. 148 D2
Novozybkov Rus. Fed. 53 F5
Nový Jičín Czech Rep. 57 P6
Novyy Afon Georgia see Akhali Ap'oni
Novyy Bor Rus. Fed. 52 L2
Novyy Donbass Ukr. see Dymytrov
Novyye Petushki Rus. Fed. see Petushki
Novyy Kholmogory Rus. Fed. see Archangel
Novyy Margelan Uzbek. see Farg'ona
Novyy Nekouz Rus. Fed. 52 H4
Novyy Oskol Rus. Fed. 53 H6
Novyy Port Rus. Fed. 76 I3
Novyy Urengoy Rus. Fed. 76 I3
Novyy Urgal Rus. Fed. 90 D2
Novyy Uzen' Kazakh. see Zhanaozen
Novyy Zay Rus. Fed. 52 L5
Now Iran 110 D4
Nowabganj Bangl. see Nawabganj
Nowata U.S.A. 161 E4
Nowdī Iran 110 C2
Nowgong India see Nagaon
Nowitna r. AK U.S.A. 148 I2
Nowitna National Wildlife Refuge nature res. AK U.S.A. 148 I2
Now Kharegan Iran 110 D2
Nowleye Lake Canada 151 K2
Nowogard Poland 57 O4
Noworadomsk Poland see Radomsko
Nowra Australia 138 E5
Nowrangapur India see Nabarangapur
Nowshera Pak. 111 I3
Nowyak Lake Canada 151 L2
Nowy Sącz Poland 57 R6
Nowy Targ Poland 57 R6
Noxen U.S.A. 165 G3
Noy, Xé r. Laos 86 D3
Noyabr'sk Rus. Fed. 76 I3
Noyes Island AK U.S.A. 149 N5
Noyon France 62 C5
Noyon Mongolia 94 E3
Nozawaonsen-mura Japan 93 E2
Nozizwe S. Africa 125 G6
Nqamakwe S. Africa 125 H7
Nqutu S. Africa 125 J5
Nsanje Malawi 123 D5
Nsombo Zambia 123 C5
Nsukka Nigeria 120 D4
Nsumbu National Park Zambia see Sumbu National Park
Ntambu Zambia 123 C5
Ntha S. Africa 125 H4
Ntoro, Kavo pt Greece 69 K5
Ntoum Gabon 122 A3
Ntungamo Uganda 122 D4
Nuanetsi Zimbabwe see Mwenezi
Nuangan Sulawesi Indon. 83 C2
Nu'aym reg. Oman 110 D6
Nuba Mountains Sudan 108 D7
Nubian Desert Sudan 108 D5
Nubra r. India 99 B6
Nüden Mongolia see Ulaanbadrah
Nudo Coropuna mt. Peru 176 D7
Nueces r. U.S.A. 161 D7
Nueltin Lake Canada 151 L2
Nueva Arcadia Hond. 166 [inset] H6
Nueva Ciudad Guerrero Mex. 161 D7
Nueva Gerona Cuba 169 H4
Nueva Harberton Arg. 178 C8
Nueva Imperial Chile 178 B5
Nueva Loja Ecuador see Lago Agrio
Nueva Ocotepeque Hond. 166 [inset] H6
Nueva Rosita Mex. 167 E3
Nueva San Salvador El Salvador 167 H6
Nueva Villa de Padilla Mex. 161 D7
Nueve de Julio Arg. see 9 de Julio
Nuevitas Cuba 169 I4
Nuevo, Cayo i. Mex. 167 H4
Nuevo, Golfo g. Arg. 178 D6
Nuevo Casas Grandes Mex. 166 D2
Nuevo Ideal Mex. 166 D3
Nuevo Laredo Mex. 167 F3
Nuevo León Mex. 159 F5
Nuevo León state Mex. 161 D7
Nuevo Rocatuerte Ecuador 176 C4
Nuga Mongolia see Dzavhanmandal
Nugaal watercourse Somalia 122 E3
Nugget Point N.Z. 139 B8
Nugur India 106 D2
Nuguria Islands P.N.G. 132 F2
Nuh, Ras pt Pak. 111 F5
Nuhaka N.Z. 139 F4
Nui atoll Tuvalu 133 H2
Nui Con Voi r. Vietnam see Red
Nuiqsut AK U.S.A. 149 J1
Nui Thanh Vietnam 86 E4
Nui Ti On mt. Vietnam 86 D4
Nujiang China 96 C2
Nu Jiang r. China/Myanmar see Salween
Nukata Japan 92 D4
Nukey Bluff hill Australia 137 A7
Nukha Azer. see Şäki

▶Nuku'alofa Tonga 133 I4
Capital of Tonga.

Nukufetau atoll Tuvalu 133 H2
Nuku Hiva i. Fr. Polynesia 187 K6
Nukuhiva i. Fr. Polynesia see Nuku Hiva
Nukuhu P.N.G. 81 L8
Nukulaelae atoll Tuvalu 133 H2
Nukulailai atoll Tuvalu see Nukulaelae
Nukumanu Islands P.N.G. 133 F2
Nukunau i. Kiribati see Nikunau
Nukunono atoll Tokelau see Nukunonu
Nukunonu atoll Tokelau 133 I2
Nukus Uzbek. 102 A3
Nulato AK U.S.A. 148 H2
Nullagine Australia 134 C5
Nullarbor Australia 135 E7
Nullarbor National Park Australia 135 E7
Nullarbor Plain Australia 135 E7
Nullarbor Regional Reserve park Australia 135 E7
Nuluarniavik, Lac l. Canada 152 F2
Nulu'erhu Shan mts China 95 I3
Num i. Indon. 81 J7
Num Nepal 99 D8
Numalla, Lake salt flat Australia 138 B2
Numan Nigeria 122 B3
Numanuma P.N.G. 136 E1
Numata Gunma Japan 93 F2
Numazu Japan 93 E3
Numbulwar Australia 136 A2
Numedal valley Norway 55 F6
Numfoor i. Indon. 81 I7
Numin He r. China 90 B3
Numurkah Australia 138 B6
Nunachuak AK U.S.A. 148 H4
Nunaksaluk Island Canada 153 J3
Nunakuluut i. Greenland 147 N3
Nunap Isua c. Greenland see Farewell, Cape
Nunapitchuk AK U.S.A. 148 G3

Nunarsuit i. Greenland see **Nunakuluut**
Nunavakpak Lake AK U.S.A. 148 G3
Nunavaugaluk, Lake AK U.S.A. 148 H4
Nunavik reg. Canada 152 G1
Nunavut admin. div. Canada 151 L2
Nunda U.S.A. 165 G2
Nundle Australia 138 E3
Nuneaton U.K. 59 F6
Nungba India 105 H4
Nungesser Lake Canada 151 M5
Nungnain Sum Nei Mongol China 95 I2
Nunivak Island AK U.S.A. 148 F4
Nunkapasi India 106 E1
Nunkun mt. India 104 D2
Nunligran Rus. Fed. 148 D2
Nuñomoral Spain 67 C3
Nunspeet Neth. 62 F2
Nunukan i. Indon. 85 G2
Nunyamo Rus. Fed. 148 E2
Nuojiang China see **Tongjiang**
Nuoro Sardinia Italy 68 C4
Nupani i. Solomon Is 133 G3
Nuqrah Saudi Arabia 108 F4
Nur Xinjiang China 99 C5
Nur r. Iran 110 D2
Nura Almatinskaya Oblast' Kazakh. 98 B4
Nura Kazakh. 98 A2
Nura r. Kazakh. 98 A2
Nūrābād Iran 110 C4
Nurakita i. Tuvalu see **Niulakita**
Nurata Uzbek. see **Nurota**
Nur Dağları mts Turkey 107 B1
Nurek Tajik. see **Norak**
Nurek Reservoir Tajik. see **Norak, Obanbori**
Nurekskoye Vodokhranilishche resr Tajik. see **Norak, Obanbori**
Nuremberg Germany 63 L5
Nūrestān 109 K3
Nuri Mex. 166 C2
Nuri, Teluk b. Indon. 85 E3
Nurla India 104 D2
Nurlat Rus. Fed. 53 K5
Nurmes Fin. 54 P5
Nurmo Fin. 54 M5
Nürnberg Germany see **Nuremberg**
Nurota Uzbek. 102 C3
Nurri, Mount hill Australia 138 C3
Nur Turu Qinghai China 99 F5
Nusa Kambangan, Cagar Alam nature res. Jawa Indon. 85 E4
Nusa Laut i. Maluku Indon. 83 D3
Nusa Tenggara Barat prov. Indon. 85 G5
Nusawulan Indon. 81 I7
Nusaybin Turkey 113 F3
Nusela, Kepulauan is Papua Indon. 83 D3
Nushagak r. AK U.S.A. 148 H4
Nushagak Bay AK U.S.A. 148 H4
Nushagak Peninsula AK U.S.A. 148 H4
Nu Shan mts China 96 C3
Nu-shima i. Japan 92 A4
Nushki Pak. 111 G4
Nusratiye Turkey 107 D1
Nutak Canada 153 J2
Nutarawit Lake Canada 151 L2
Nutauge, Laguna lag. Rus. Fed. 148 C2
Nutepel'men Rus. Fed. 148 D2
Nutrioso U.S.A. 159 I5
Nuttal Pak. 111 H4
Nutwood Downs Australia 134 F3
Nutzotin Mountains AK U.S.A. 149 K2

▶**Nuuk** Greenland 147 M3
Capital of Greenland.

Nuupas Fin. 54 O3
Nuussuaq Greenland 147 M2
Nuussuaq pen. Greenland 147 M2
Nuwaybi' al Muzayyinah Egypt 112 D5
Nuweiba el Muzeina Egypt see **Nuwaybi' al Muzayyinah**
Nuwerus S. Africa 124 D6
Nuweveldberge mts S. Africa 124 E7
Nuwuk AK U.S.A. 148 H1
Nuyakuk r. AK U.S.A. 148 H4
Nuyakuk Lake AK U.S.A. 148 H4
Nuyts, Point Australia 135 B8
Nuyts Archipelago is Australia 135 F8
Nuzvid India 106 D2
Nwanedi Nature Reserve S. Africa 125 J2
Nxai Pan National Park Botswana 123 C5
Nyaän, Bukit hill Indon. 85 F2
Nyac AK U.S.A. 148 H3
Nyagan' Rus. Fed. 51 T3
Nyagquka China see **Yajiang**
Nyagrong China see **Xinlong**
Nyahururu Kenya 122 D3
Nyah West Australia 138 A5
Nyaimai Xizang China 99 F7
Nyainqêntanglha Feng mt. Xizang China 99 E7
Nyainqêntanglha Shan mts Xizang China 99 E7
Nyainrong Xizang China 99 F6
Nyåker Sweden 54 K5
Nyakh Rus. Fed. see **Nyagan'**
Nyaksimvol' Rus. Fed. 51 S3
Nyala Sudan 121 F3
Nyalam Xizang China see **Congdü**
Nyalikungu Tanz. see **Maswa**
Nyamandhlovu Zimbabwe 123 C5
Nyamtumbo Tanz. 123 D5
Nyande Zimbabwe see **Masvingo**
Nyandoma Rus. Fed. 52 I3
Nyandomskiy Vozvyshennost' hills Rus. Fed. 52 H3
Nyanga Congo 122 B4
Nyanga Zimbabwe 123 D5
Nyangbo Xizang China 99 F7
Nyang Qu r. China 99 F7
Nyapa, Gunung mt. Indon. 85 G2
Nyar r. India 99 B7
Nyarling r. Canada 150 H2

▶**Nyasa, Lake** Africa 123 D4
3rd largest lake in Africa, and 9th in the world.

Nyasaland country Africa see **Malawi**
Nyashabozh Rus. Fed. 52 L2
Nyasvizh Belarus 55 O10
Nyaungdon Myanmar see **Yandoon**
Nyaunglebin Myanmar 86 B3
Nyborg Denmark 55 G9
Nyborg Norway 54 P1
Nybro Sweden 55 I8
Nyeboe Land reg. Greenland 147 M1
Nyêmo Xizang China 99 E7
Nyenchen Tanglha Range mts Xizang China see **Nyainqêntanglha Shan**
Nyeri Kenya 122 D4
Nygchigen, Mys c. Rus. Fed. 148 D2
Nyi, Co l. Xizang China 99 D6
Nyika National Park Zambia 123 D5
Nyima Xizang China 99 D7
Nyima Xizang China 99 F7
Nyimba Zambia 123 D5
Nyingchi Xizang China 99 F7
Nyingzhong Xizang China 99 E7
Nyinma China see **Maqu**
Nyíregyháza Hungary 53 D7
Nyiru, Mount Kenya 122 D3
Nykarleby Fin. 54 M5
Nykøbing Denmark 55 G9
Nykøbing Sjælland Denmark 55 G9
Nyköping Sweden 55 J7
Nyland Sweden 54 J5
Nylsvley nature res. S. Africa 125 I3
Nymagee Australia 138 C4
Nymboida National Park Australia 138 F2
Nynäshamn Sweden 55 J7
Nyngan Australia 138 C3
Nyogzê Xizang China 99 C7
Nyohō-san mt. Japan 93 F2
Nyoman r. Belarus/Lith. 55 M10
also known as Neman or Nemunas
Nyon Switz. 66 H3
Nyons France 66 G4
Nýřany Czech Rep. 63 N5
Nyrob Rus. Fed. 51 R3
Nysa Poland 57 P5
Nysh Rus. Fed. 90 F2
Nyssa U.S.A. 156 D4
Nystad Fin. see **Uusikaupunki**
Nytva Rus. Fed. 51 R4
Nyūgasa-yama mt. Japan 93 E3
Nyūkawa Japan 92 D2
Nyuksenitsa Rus. Fed. 52 J3
Nyunzu Dem. Rep. Congo 123 C4
Nyurba Rus. Fed. 77 M3
Nyūzen Japan 92 D2
Nyyskiy Zaliv lag. Rus. Fed. 90 F1
Nzambi Congo 122 B4
Nzega Tanz. 123 D4
Nzérékoré Guinea 120 C4
N'zeto Angola 123 B4
Nzwani i. Comoros 123 E5

O

Oahe, Lake U.S.A. 160 C2
O'ahu i. U.S.A. 157 [inset]
Oaitupu i. Tuvalu see **Vaitupu**
Oak Bluffs U.S.A. 165 J3
Oak City U.S.A. 159 G2
Oak Creek U.S.A. 159 J1
Oakdale U.S.A. 161 E6
Oakes U.S.A. 160 D2
Oakey Australia 138 E1
Oak Grove KY U.S.A. 164 B5
Oak Grove LA U.S.A. 161 F5
Oak Grove MI U.S.A. 164 C1
Oakham U.K. 59 G6
Oak Harbor U.S.A. 164 D3
Oak Hill OH U.S.A. 164 D4
Oak Hill WV U.S.A. 164 E5
Oakhurst U.S.A. 158 D3
Oak Lake Canada 151 K5
Oakland CA U.S.A. 158 B3
Oakland MD U.S.A. 164 F4
Oakland ME U.S.A. 165 K1
Oakland NE U.S.A. 160 D3
Oakland OR U.S.A. 156 C4
Oakland airport U.S.A. 158 B3
Oakland City U.S.A. 164 B4
Oaklands Australia 138 C5
Oak Lawn U.S.A. 164 B3
Oakley U.S.A. 160 C4
Oakover r. Australia 134 C5
Oak Park IL U.S.A. 164 B3
Oak Park MI U.S.A. 164 C2
Oak Park Reservoir U.S.A. 159 I1
Oakridge U.S.A. 156 C4
Oak Ridge U.S.A. 162 C4
Oakvale Australia 137 C7
Oak View U.S.A. 158 D4
Oakville Canada 164 F2
Oakwood OH U.S.A. 164 C3
Oakwood TN U.S.A. 164 B5
Oamaru N.Z. 139 C7
Ōamishirasato Japan 93 G3
Ōarai Japan 93 G2
Oaro N.Z. 139 D6
Ōashi-gawa r. Japan 93 F2
Oasis CA U.S.A. 158 E3
Oasis NV U.S.A. 156 E4
Oates Coast reg. Antarctica see **Oates Land**
Oates Land reg. Antarctica 188 H2
Oaxaca Mex. 168 E5
Oaxaca state Mex. 167 F5
Oaxaca de Juárez Mex. see **Oaxaca**

▶**Ob'** r. Rus. Fed. 88 E2
Part of the Ob'-Irtysh, the 2nd longest river in Asia.

Ob, Gulf of sea chan. Rus. Fed. see **Obskaya Guba**
Oba Canada 152 D4
Oba i. Vanuatu see **Aoba**
Obako-dake mt. Japan 92 B4
Obala Cameroon 120 E4
Obama Japan 92 B3
Obama-wan b. Japan 92 B3
Oban U.K. 60 D4
Obara Japan 92 D3
O Barco Spain 67 C2
Obata Japan 92 C4
Obbia Somalia see **Hobyo**
Obdorsk Rus. Fed. see **Salekhard**
Óbecse Serbia see **Bečej**
Obed Canada 150 G4
Oberaula Germany 63 J4
Oberdorla Germany 63 K3
Oberhausen Germany 62 G3
Oberlin KS U.S.A. 160 C4
Oberlin LA U.S.A. 161 E6
Oberlin OH U.S.A. 164 D3
Obermoschel Germany 63 H5
Oberon Australia 138 D4
Oberpfälzer Wald mts Germany 63 M5
Obersinn Germany 63 J4
Oberthulba Germany 63 J4
Obertshausen Germany 63 I4
Oberwälder Land reg. Germany 63 J3
Obi i. Maluku Indon. 83 C3
Obi, Kepulauan is Maluku Indon. 83 C3
Obi, Selat sea chan. Maluku Indon. 83 C3
Óbidos Brazil 177 G4
Obihiro Japan 90 F4
Obilatu i. Maluku Indon. 83 C3
Obil'noye Rus. Fed. 53 J7

▶**Ob'-Irtysh** r. Rus. Fed. 76 H3
2nd longest river in Asia, and 5th in the world.

Obitsu-gawa r. Japan 93 F3
Obluch'ye Rus. Fed. 90 C2
Obninsk Rus. Fed. 53 H5
Obo Cent. Afr. Rep. 122 C3
Obo Qinghai China 94 E4
Obock Djibouti 108 F7
Ŏbŏk N. Korea 90 C4
Obokote Dem. Rep. Congo 122 C4
Obo Liang Qinghai China 98 F5
Obong, Gunung mt. Malaysia 85 F1
Obouya Congo 122 B4
Oboyan' Rus. Fed. 53 H6
Obozerskiy Rus. Fed. 52 I3
Obregón, Presa resr Mex. 166 C3
Obrenovac Serbia 69 I2
Obruk Turkey 112 D3
Observatory Hill hill Australia 135 F7
Obshchiy Syrt hills Rus. Fed. 51 Q5
Obskaya Guba sea chan. Rus. Fed. 76 I3
Ōbu Japan 92 C3
Obuasi Ghana 120 C4
Obuse Japan 93 E2
Ob''yachevo Rus. Fed. 52 K3
Ocala U.S.A. 163 D6
Ocampo Chihuahua Mex. 166 C2
Ocampo Coahuila Mex. 166 E3
Ocaña Col. 176 D2
Ocaña Spain 67 E4
Occidental, Cordillera mts Chile 176 E7
Occidental, Cordillera mts Col. 176 C3
Occidental, Cordillera mts Peru 176 D7
Oceana U.S.A. 164 E5
Ocean Cape AK U.S.A. 149 M4
Ocean Cay i. Bahamas 163 E7
Ocean City MD U.S.A. 165 H4
Ocean City NJ U.S.A. 165 H4
Ocean Falls Canada 150 E4
Ocean Island Kiribati see **Banaba**
Ocean Island atoll U.S.A. see **Kure Atoll**
Oceanside U.S.A. 158 E5
Ocean Springs U.S.A. 161 F6
Ochakiv Ukr. 69 N1
Och'amch'ire Georgia 113 F2
Ocher Rus. Fed. 51 Q4
Ochiishi-misaki pt Japan 90 G4
Ochil Hills U.K. 60 F4
Ochrida, Lake Albania/Macedonia see **Ohrid, Lake**
Ochsenfurt Germany 63 K5
Ochtrup Germany 63 H2
Ocilla U.S.A. 163 D6
Ockelbo Sweden 55 J6
Ocolaşul Mare, Vârful mt. Romania 69 K1
Oconomowoc U.S.A. 164 A2
Oconto U.S.A. 164 B1
Ocoroni Mex. 166 C3
Ocos Guat. 167 G6
Ocosingo Mex. 167 G5
Ocotal Nicaragua 166 [inset] I6
Ocotlán Oaxaca Mex. 167 F5
Ocozocoautla Mex. 167 G5
Octeville-sur-Mer France 59 H9
October Revolution Island Rus. Fed. see **Oktyabr'skoy Revolyutsii, Ostrov**
Ocú Panama 166 [inset] J8
Oda, Jebel mt. Sudan 108 E5
Ódáðahraun lava field Iceland 54 [inset]
Ŏdaejin N. Korea 90 C4
Odae-san National Park S. Korea 91 C5
Ōdai Japan 92 C4
Ōdaigahara-zan mt. Japan 92 C4
Odaira-tōge pass Japan 92 D3
Ōdate Japan 91 F4
Odawara Japan 93 F3
Odda Norway 55 E6
Odei r. Canada 151 L3
Odell U.S.A. 164 B3
Odem U.S.A. 161 D7
Odemira Port. 67 B5
Ödemiş Turkey 69 L5
Ödenburg Hungary see **Sopron**
Odense Denmark 55 G9
Odenwald reg. Germany 63 I5
Oder r. Germany 63 J3
also known as Odra (Poland)
Oderbucht b. Germany 57 O3
Oder-Havel-Kanal canal Germany 63 N2
Odesa Ukr. see **Odessa**
Ödeshog Sweden 55 I7
Odessa Ukr. 69 N1
Odessa TX U.S.A. 161 C6
Odessa WA U.S.A. 156 D3
Odessus Bulg. see **Varna**
Odiel r. Spain 67 C5
Odienné Côte d'Ivoire 120 C4
Odintsovo Rus. Fed. 52 H5
Ŏdôngk Cambodia 87 D5
Odra r. Germany/Pol. 57 Q6
also known as Oder (Germany)
Odzala, Parc National d' nat. park Congo 122 B3
Ōe Japan 92 B3
Oea Libya see **Tripoli**
Oeiras Brazil 177 J5
Oelsnitz Germany 63 M4
Oenkerk Neth. 62 F1
Oenpelli Australia 134 F3
Oesel i. Estonia see **Hiiumaa**
Oeufs, Lac des l. Canada 153 G3
Ōe-yama hill Japan 92 B3
Of Turkey 113 F2
O'Fallon r. U.S.A. 156 G3
Ofanto r. Italy 68 G4
Ofaqim Israel 107 B4
Offa Nigeria 120 D4
Offenbach am Main Germany 63 I4
Offenburg Germany 57 K6
Oga r. Indon. 85 F2
Oga Japan 91 E5
Oga-dake mt. Japan 93 F1
Ogadēn reg. Eth. 122 E3
Oga-hantō pen. Japan 91 E5
Ōgaki Japan 92 C3
Ogallala U.S.A. 160 C3
Ogan r. Indon. 84 D3
Ogano Japan 93 F2
Ogasa Japan 93 E4
Ogasawara-shotō is Japan see **Bonin Islands**
Ōga-tō mt. Japan 93 E2
Ogawa Ibaraki Japan 93 G2
Ogawa Ibaraki Japan 93 G2
Ogawa Nagano Japan 93 D2
Ogawa Saitama Japan 93 F2
Ōgawa Tochigi Japan 93 G2
Ogbomosho Nigeria 120 D4
Ogbomoso Nigeria see **Ogbomosho**
Ogden IA U.S.A. 160 E3
Ogden UT U.S.A. 156 F4
Ogden, Mount B.C. Canada 149 N4
Ogdensburg U.S.A. 165 H1
Ogidaki Canada 152 D5
Ogilvie r. Y.T. Canada 149 M2
Ogilvie Mountains Y.T. Canada 149 L2
Ögiynuur Mongolia 94 E2
Oglala Pass sea channel AK U.S.A. 149 [inset]
Oglethorpe, Mount U.S.A. 163 C5
Oglio r. Italy 68 D2
Oglongi Rus. Fed. 90 E1
Ogmore Australia 136 E4
Ōgo Japan 93 F2
Ogoamas, Gunung mt. Indon. 83 B2
Ogōchi-damu dam Japan 93 F3
Ogodzha Rus. Fed. 90 D1
Ogoja Nigeria 120 D4
Ogoki r. Canada 152 D4
Ogoki Lake Canada 160 G1
Ogoki Reservoir Canada 152 C4
Ogoron Rus. Fed. 90 C1
Ogose Japan 93 F3
Ogosta r. Bulg. 69 J3
Ogre Latvia 55 N8
Ōguchi Japan 92 C3
Ogulin Croatia 68 F2
Ogurchinskiy, Ostrov i. Turkm. see **Ogurjaly Adasy**
Ogurjaly Adasy i. Turkm. 110 D2
Oğuzeli Turkey 107 C1
Ohai N.Z. 139 A7
Ohakune N.Z. 139 E4
Ohanet Alg. 120 D2
Ōhara Japan 93 G3
Ōhata Japan 90 F4
Ohcejohka Fin. see **Utsjoki**
O'Higgins (Chile) research station Antarctica 188 A2
O'Higgins, Lago l. Chile 178 B7
Ohio r. U.S.A. 164 A5
Ohio state U.S.A. 164 D3
Ōhira Japan 93 F2
Ōhito Japan 93 E3
Ohm r. Germany 63 I4
Ohogamiut AK U.S.A. 148 G3
Ohrdruf Germany 63 K4
Ohře r. Czech Rep. 63 N4
Ohre r. Germany 63 L2
Ohrid Macedonia 69 I4
Ohrid, Lake Albania/Macedonia 69 I4
Ohridsko Ezero l. Albania/Macedonia see **Ohrid, Lake**
Ohrigstad S. Africa 125 J3
Öhringen Germany 63 J5
Ohrit, Liqeni i l. Albania/Macedonia see **Ohrid, Lake**
Ohura N.Z. 139 E4
Ōi Fukui Japan 92 B3
Oich r. U.K. 60 E3
Oiga Xizang China 99 F7
Ōigawa Japan 93 E4
Ōi-gawa r. Japan 92 B3
Ōi-gawa r. Japan 93 E4
Oignies France 62 C4
Oil City U.S.A. 164 F3
Oise r. France 62 C6
Ōiso Japan 93 F3
Ōita Japan 91 C6
Oiti mt. Greece 69 J5
Ōizumi Yamanashi Japan 93 E3
Oizuruga-dake mt. Japan 92 C2
Ojai U.S.A. 158 D4
Ojalava i. Samoa see **'Upolu**
Ōji Japan 92 B4
Ojinaga Mex. 166 D2
Ojitlán Mex. 167 F5
Ojiya Japan 91 E5
Ojo Caliente U.S.A. 157 G5
Ojo de Laguna Mex. 166 D2
Ojo de Liebre, Lago b. Mex. 166 B3

▶**Ojos del Salado, Nevado** mt. Arg./Chile 178 C3
2nd highest mountain in South America.

Ojuelos de Jalisco Mex. 167 E4
Oka r. Rus. Fed. 53 I4
Oka r. Rus. Fed. 88 I1
Okabe Saitama Japan 93 F2
Okabe Shizuoka Japan 93 E4
Okahandja Namibia 124 C1
Okahukura N.Z. 139 E4
Okakarara Namibia 123 B6
Okak Islands Canada 153 J2
Okanagan Lake Canada 150 G5
Okanda Sri Lanka 106 D5
Okano r. Gabon 122 B4
Okanogan U.S.A. 156 D2
Okanogan r. U.S.A. 156 D2
Okara Pak. 111 I4
Okarem Turkm. see **Ekerem**
Okataina vol. N.Z. see **Tarawera, Mount**
Okaukuejo Namibia 123 B5
Okavango r. Africa 123 C5

▶**Okavango Delta** swamp Botswana 123 C5
Largest oasis in the world.

Okavango Swamps Botswana see **Okavango Delta**
Ōkawachi Japan 92 A3
Okaya Japan 93 E2
Okayama Japan 91 D6
Okazaki Japan 92 D4
Okeechobee U.S.A. 163 D7
Okeechobee, Lake U.S.A. 163 D7
Okeene U.S.A. 161 D4
Okefenokee Swamp U.S.A. 163 D6
Okegawa Japan 93 F3
Okehampton U.K. 59 C8
Okemah U.S.A. 161 D5
Oker r. Germany 63 K2
Okha India 104 B5
Okha Rus. Fed. 90 F1
Okha Rann marsh India 104 B5
Okhotsk Rus. Fed. 77 P4
Okhotsk, Sea of Japan/Rus. Fed. 90 G3
Okhotskoye More sea Japan/Rus. Fed. see **Okhotsk, Sea of**
Okhtyrka Ukr. 53 G6
Okinawa i. Japan 91 B8
Okinawa-guntō is Japan see **Okinawa-shotō**
Okinawa-shotō is Japan 91 B8
Okino-Daitō-jima i. Japan 89 O8
Okino-shima i. Japan 92 B4
Okino-Tori-shima i. Japan 89 P8
Oki-shotō is Japan 89 O5
Oki-shotō is Japan 91 D5
Okkan Myanmar 86 A3
Oklahoma state U.S.A. 161 D5

▶**Oklahoma City** U.S.A. 161 D5
Capital of Oklahoma.

Okmok sea feature N. Pacific Ocean 148 E5
Okmulgee U.S.A. 161 D5
Okolona KY U.S.A. 164 C4
Okolona MS U.S.A. 161 F5
Okondja Gabon 122 B4
Okovskiy Les for. Rus. Fed. 52 G5
Okoyo Congo 122 B4
Okpeti, Gora mt. Kazakh. 98 C3
Øksfjord Norway 54 M1
Oktemberyan Armenia see **Armavir**
Oktwin Myanmar 86 B3
Oktyabr' Kazakh. see **Kandyagash**
Oktyabr'sk Kazakh. see **Kandyagash**
Oktyabr'skiy Belarus see **Aktsyabrski**
Oktyabr'skiy Amurskaya Oblast' Rus. Fed. 90 C1
Oktyabr'skiy Arkhangel'skaya Oblast' Rus. Fed. 52 I3
Oktyabr'skiy Kamchatskaya Oblast' Rus. Fed. 77 Q4
Oktyabr'skiy Respublika Bashkortostan Rus. Fed. 51 Q5
Oktyabr'skiy Volgogradskaya Oblast' Rus. Fed. 53 I7
Oktyabr'skoye Rus. Fed. 51 T3
Oktyabr'skoy Revolyutsii, Ostrov i. Rus. Fed. 77 K2
Okuchi Japan 92 C2
Okulovka Rus. Fed. 52 G4
Oku-sangai-dake mt. Japan 92 D3
Okushiri-tō i. Japan 90 E4
Okuta Nigeria 120 D4
Okutadami-ko resr Japan 93 F1
Okutama Japan 93 F3
Okutama-ko l. Japan 93 F3
Okutango-hantō pen. Japan 92 B3
Okutone-ko resr Japan 93 F2
Ōkuwa Japan 92 D3
Okwa watercourse Botswana 124 G1
Ólafsvík Iceland 54 [inset]
Olakkur India 106 C3
Olancha U.S.A. 158 D3
Olancha Peak U.S.A. 158 D3
Olanchito Hond. 166 [inset] I6
Öland i. Sweden 55 J8
Olary Australia 137 C7
Olathe CO U.S.A. 159 J2
Olathe KS U.S.A. 160 E4
Olavarría Arg. 178 D5
Oława Poland 57 P5
Olbernhau Germany 63 N4
Olbia Sardinia Italy 68 C4
Old Bahama Channel Bahamas/Cuba 163 E8
Old Bastar India 106 D2
Oldcastle Ireland 61 E4
Old Cork Australia 136 C4
Old Crow Y.T. Canada 149 M2
Old Crow r. Y.T. Canada 149 M2
Oldeboorn Neth. see **Aldeboarn**
Oldenburg Germany 63 I1
Oldenburg in Holstein Germany 57 M3
Oldenzaal Neth. 62 G2
Olderdalen Norway 54 L2
Old Forge U.S.A. 165 H2
Old Gidgee Australia 135 B6
Oldham U.K. 58 E5
Old Harbor AK U.S.A. 148 I4
Old Head of Kinsale hd Ireland 61 D6
Old John Lake AK U.S.A. 149 K1
Oldman r. Canada 150 I5
Oldmeldrum U.K. 60 G3
Old Perlican Canada 153 L5
Old Rampart AK U.S.A. 149 L2
Old River U.S.A. 158 D4
Olds Canada 150 H5
Old Speck Mountain U.S.A. 165 J1
Old Station U.S.A. 158 C1
Old Wives Lake Canada 151 J5
Öldziyt Arhangay Mongolia 94 E1
Öldziyt Arhangay Mongolia see **Erdenemandal**
Öldziyt Bayanhongor Mongolia 94 E2
Öldziyt Dornogovĭ Mongolia see **Sayhandulaan**
Öldziyt Dundgovĭ Mongolia 94 F2
Olean U.S.A. 165 F2
Olecko Poland 57 S3
Olekma r. Rus. Fed. 77 N3
Olekminsk Rus. Fed. 77 N3
Olekminskiy Stanovik mts Rus. Fed. 89 M2
Oleksandrivs'k Ukr. see **Zaporizhzhya**
Oleksandriya Ukr. 53 G6
Ølen Norway 55 D7
Olenegorsk Rus. Fed. 54 R2
Olenek Rus. Fed. 77 M3
Olenek r. Rus. Fed. 77 M2
Olenek Bay Rus. Fed. see **Olenekskiy Zaliv**
Olenekskiy Zaliv b. Rus. Fed. 77 N2
Olenino Rus. Fed. 52 G4
Olenitsa Rus. Fed. 52 G2
Olenivs'ki Kar''yery Ukr. see **Dokuchayevs'k**
Olentuy Rus. Fed. 95 H1
Olenya Rus. Fed. see **Olenegorsk**
Oleshky Ukr. see **Tsyurupyns'k**
Olet Tongo mt. Sumbawa Indon. 85 G5
Olevs'k Ukr. 53 E6
Ol'ga Rus. Fed. 90 D4
Olga, Lac l. Canada 152 F4
Olga, Mount Australia 135 E6
Ol'ginsk Rus. Fed. 90 D1
Olginskoye Rus. Fed. see **Kochubeyevskoye**
Ölgiy Mongolia 94 B1
Olhão Port. 67 C5
Olia Chain mts Australia 135 E6
Olifants r. Moz./S. Africa 125 J3
also known as Elefantes
Olifants watercourse Namibia 124 D3
Olifants S. Africa 125 J2
Olifants r. W. Cape S. Africa 124 D6
Olifants r. W. Cape S. Africa 124 E7
Olifantshoek S. Africa 124 F4
Olifantsrivierberge mts S. Africa 124 D7
Olimarao atoll Micronesia 81 L5
Olimbos hill Cyprus see **Olympos**
Olimbos mt. Greece see **Olympus, Mount**
Olimpos Beydağları Milli Parkı nat. park Turkey 69 N6
Olinalá Mex. 167 F5
Olinda Brazil 177 L5
Olinga Moz. 123 D5
Olio Australia 136 C4
Oliphants Drift S. Africa 125 H3
Olisipo Port. see **Lisbon**
Oliva Spain 67 F4
Oliva, Cordillera de mts Arg./Chile 178 C3
Olivares, Cerro de mt. Arg./Chile 178 C4
Olive Hill U.S.A. 164 D4
Olivehurst U.S.A. 158 C2
Oliveira dos Brejinhos Brazil 179 C1
Olivença Moz. see **Lupilichi**
Olivenza Spain 67 C4
Oliver Lake Canada 151 K3
Olivet MI U.S.A. 164 C2
Olivet SD U.S.A. 160 D3
Olivia U.S.A. 160 E2
Oljoq Nei Mongol China 95 F4
Ol'khovka Rus. Fed. 53 J6
Ollagüe Chile 178 C2
Ollombo Congo 122 B4
Olmaliq Uzbek. 102 C3
Olmos Peru 176 C5
Olmütz Czech Rep. see **Olomouc**

Olney U.K. 59 G6
Olney IL U.S.A. 160 F4
Olney MD U.S.A. 165 G4
Olney TX U.S.A. 161 D5
Olofström Sweden 55 I8
Olomane r. Canada 153 J4
Olomouc Czech Rep. 57 P6
Olonets Rus. Fed. 52 G3
Olongapo Luzon Phil. 82 C3
Olongliko Kalimantan Indon. 85 F3
Oloron-Ste-Marie France 66 D5
Olosenga atoll American Samoa see Swains Island
Olot Spain 67 H2
Olot Uzbek. 111 F2
Olovyannaya Rus. Fed. 95 H1
Olovyannaya Rus. Fed. 148 C2
Oloy r. Rus. Fed. 77 Q3
Oloy, Qatorkŭhi mts Asia see Alai Range
Olpe Germany 63 H3
Olsztyn Poland 57 R4
Olt r. Romania 69 K3
Olten Switz. 66 H3
Oltenița Romania 69 L2
Oltu Turkey 113 F2
Oluan Pi c. Taiwan 97 I4
Olutanga i. Phil. 82 C5
Ol'viopol' Ukr. see Pervomays'k
Olymbos hill Cyprus see Olympos

▶Olympia U.S.A. 156 C3
Capital of Washington state.

Olympic National Park U.S.A. 156 C3
Olympos hill Cyprus 107 A2
Olympos Greece see Olympus, Mount
Olympos mt. Greece see Olympus, Mount
Olympos nat. park Greece see Olympou, Ethnikos Drymos
Olympou, Ethnikos Drymos nat. park Greece 69 J4
Olympus, Mount Greece 69 J4
Olympus, Mount U.S.A. 156 C3
Olyutorskiy Rus. Fed. 189 C2
Olyutorskiy, Mys c. Rus. Fed. 77 S4
Olyutorskiy Zaliv b. Rus. Fed. 77 R4
Olzheras Rus. Fed. see Mezhdurechensk
Oma Xizang China 99 C6
Oma r. Rus. Fed. 52 J2
Ōmachi Japan 93 D2
Ōmaezaki Japan 93 E4
Omae-zaki pt Japan 93 E4
Omagh U.K. 61 E3
Omaha U.S.A. 160 E3
Omaheke admin. reg. Namibia 124 D2
Omal'skiy Khrebet mts Rus. Fed. 90 E1
Ōmama Japan 93 F2
Oman country Asia 109 I6
Oman, Gulf of Asia 110 E5
Omaruru Namibia 123 B6
Omate Peru 176 D7
Omaweneno Botswana 124 F3
Omba i. Vanuatu see Aoba
Ombai, Selat sea chan. Indon. 83 C5
Ombalantu Namibia see Uutapi
Ombolata Indon. 84 B2
Omboué Gabon 122 A4
Ombu Xizang China 99 D7
Omdraaisvlei S. Africa 124 F6
Omdurman Sudan 108 D6
Ōme Japan 93 F3
Omeo Australia 138 C6
Omer U.S.A. 164 D1
Ometepe, Isla de i. Nicaragua 166 [inset] I7
Ometepec Mex. 168 E5
Omgoy Wildlife Reserve nature res. Thai. 86 B3
Om Hajēr Eritrea 108 E7
Ōmi Japan 93 E2
Ōmi Niigata Japan 93 D1
Ōmi Shiga Japan 92 C3
Omīdīyeh Iran 110 C4
Omigawa Japan 93 G3
Ōmihachiman Japan 92 C3
Omineca Mountains Canada 150 E3
Omitara Namibia 124 C2
Ōmiya Ibaraki Japan 93 G2
Ōmiya Kyōto Japan 92 B3
Ōmiya Mie Japan 92 C4
Ōmiya Saitama Japan 93 F3
Ommaney, Cape AK U.S.A. 149 N4
Ommen Neth. 62 G2
Ömnödelger Hentiy Mongolia 95 G2
Ömnögovĭ prov. Mongolia 94 F3
Ōmōi-gawa r. Japan 93 F2
Omolon Rus. Fed. 77 R3
Omo National Park Eth. 122 D3
Ōmotegō Japan 93 G1
Omsk Rus. Fed. 76 I4
Omsukchan Rus. Fed. 77 Q3
Ōmū Japan 90 F3
O-mu Myanmar 86 B2
Omu, Vârful mt. Romania 69 K2
Ōmura Japan 91 C6
Ōmuro-yama hill Japan 93 F4
Ōmuro-yama mt. Japan 93 E3
Ōmuro-yama mt. Japan 93 F3
Omutninsk Rus. Fed. 52 L4
Onaman Lake Canada 152 D4
Onamia U.S.A. 160 E2
Onancock U.S.A. 165 H5
Onang Sulawesi Barat Indon. 83 A3
Onangué, Lac l. Gabon 122 B4
Onaping Lake Canada 152 E5
Onatchiway, Lac l. Canada 153 H4
Onavas Mex. 166 C2
Onawa U.S.A. 160 D3
Onaway U.S.A. 164 C1
Onbingwin Myanmar 87 B4
Oncativo Arg. 178 D4
Onchan Isle of Man 58 C4
Oncócua Angola 123 B5
Öncül Turkey 107 D1
Ondal India see Andal
Ondangwa Namibia 123 B5
Onderstedorings S. Africa 124 E6
Ondjiva Angola 123 B5
Ondo Nigeria 120 D4
Öndörhaan Mongolia 95 G2
Ondor Had Nei Mongol China 95 J2
Öndörhushuu Mongolia see Bulgan
Ondorkara Xinjiang China 94 B2
Ondor Mod Nei Mongol China 94 F3
Öndörshil Mongolia 95 G2
Ondor Sum Nei Mongol China 95 H3
Öndör-Ulaan Mongolia 94 E1
Ondozero Rus. Fed. 52 G3
One Botswana 124 E2
One and a Half Degree Channel Maldives 103 D11
Onega Rus. Fed. 52 H3
Onega r. Rus. Fed. 52 H3
Onega, Lake l. Rus. Fed. see Onezhskoye Ozero

▶Onega, Lake Rus. Fed. 52 G3
3rd largest lake in Europe.

Onega Bay g. Rus. Fed. see Onezhskaya Guba
One Hundred and Fifty Mile House Canada see 150 Mile House
One Hundred Mile House Canada see 100 Mile House
Oneida NY U.S.A. 165 H2
Oneida TN U.S.A. 164 C5
Oneida Lake U.S.A. 165 H2
O'Neill U.S.A. 160 D3
Onekama U.S.A. 164 B1
Onekotan, Ostrov i. Rus. Fed. 77 Q5
Oneonta AL U.S.A. 163 C5
Oneonta NY U.S.A. 165 H2
Onești Romania 69 L1
Onezhskaya Guba g. Rus. Fed. 52 G2
Onezhskoye Ozero Rus. Fed. 51 N3
Onezhskoye Ozero l. Rus. Fed. see Onega, Lake
Ong r. India 106 D1
Onga Gabon 122 B4
Ongers watercourse S. Africa 124 F5
Ongi Dundgovĭ Mongolia see Sayhan-Ovoo
Ongi Övörhangay Mongolia see Uyanga
Ongiyn Gol r. Mongolia 94 E2
Ongjin N. Korea 91 B5
Ongniud Qi Nei Mongol China see Wudan
Ongole India 106 D3
Ongon Mongolia see Bürd
Onguday Rus. Fed. 98 D2
Onida U.S.A. 160 C2
Oniishi Japan 93 F2
Onilahy r. Madag. 123 E6
Onistagane, Lac l. Canada 153 H4
Onitsha Nigeria 120 D4
Onjati Mountain Namibia 124 C2
Onjiva Angola see Ondjiva
Onjuku Japan 93 G3
Ōno Fukui Japan 92 C3
Ōno Gifu Japan 92 C3
Ono Hyōgo Japan 92 A4
Ōnohara-jima i. Japan 93 F4
Ono-i-Lau i. Fiji 133 I4
Onomichi Japan 91 D6
Onon atoll Micronesia see Namonuito
Onon Mongolia see Binder
Onon r. Rus. Fed. 95 H1
Onon Gol r. Mongolia 95 H1
Onor, Gora mt. Rus. Fed. 90 F2
Onotoa atoll Kiribati 133 H2
Onseepkans S. Africa 124 D5
Onslow Australia 134 A5
Onslow Bay U.S.A. 163 E5
Onstwedde Neth. 62 H1
Ontake-san vol. Japan 92 D3
Ontaratue r. N.W.T. Canada 149 O2
Ontario prov. Canada 151 N5
Ontario U.S.A. 158 E4
Ontario, Lake Canada/U.S.A. 165 G2
Ontong Java Atoll Solomon Is 133 F2
Onutu atoll Kiribati see Onotoa
Onverwacht Suriname 177 G2
Onyx U.S.A. 158 D4
Oodnadatta Australia 137 A5
Oodweyne Somalia 122 E3
Ōoka Japan 93 D2
Oolambeyan National Park 138 F5
Ooldea Australia 135 E7
Ooldea Range hills Australia 135 E7
Oologah Lake resr U.S.A. 161 E4
Ooratippra r. Australia 136 B4
Oos-Londen S. Africa see East London
Oostburg Neth. 62 D3
Oostende Belgium see Ostend
Oostendorp Neth. 62 F2
Oosterhout Neth. 62 E3
Oosterschelde est. Neth. 62 D3
Oosterwolde Neth. 62 G2
Oostvleteren Belgium 62 C4
Oost-Vlieland Neth. 62 F1
Ootacamund India see Udagamandalam
Ootsa Lake Canada 150 E4
Ootsa Lake l. Canada 150 E4
Opal Mex. 161 C7
Opala Dem. Rep. Congo 122 C4
Oparino Rus. Fed. 52 K4
Oparo i. Fr. Polynesia see Rapa
Opasatika r. Canada 152 E4
Opasatika Lake Canada 152 E4
Opasquia Canada 151 M4
Opataca, Lac l. Canada 152 G4
Opava Czech Rep. 57 P6
Opel hill Germany 63 H5
Opelika U.S.A. 163 C5
Opelousas U.S.A. 161 E6
Opeongo Lake Canada 152 F5
Opheim U.S.A. 156 G2
Ophir, Gunung vol. Indon. 84 C2
Opienge Dem. Rep. Congo 122 C3
Opin Seram Indon. 83 D3
Opinaca r. Canada 152 F3
Opinaca, Réservoir resr Canada 152 F3
Opinnagau r. Canada 152 E3
Opiscotéo, Lac l. Canada 153 H3
Op Luang National Park Thai. 86 B3
Opmeer Neth. 62 E2
Opochka Rus. Fed. 55 P8
Opocopa, Lac l. Canada 153 I3
Opodepe Mex. 166 C2
Opole Poland 57 P5
Oporto Port. 67 B3
Opotiki N.Z. 139 F4
Opp U.S.A. 163 C6
Oppdal Norway 54 F5
Oppeln Poland see Opole
Opportunity U.S.A. 156 D3
Opunake N.Z. 139 D4
Opuwo Namibia 123 B5
Oqsu r. Tajik. 111 I2
Oquitoa Mex. 166 C2
Ōra Japan 93 F2
Oracle U.S.A. 159 H5
Oradea Romania 69 I1
Orahovac Kosovo see Rahovec
Orai India 104 D4
Oraibi U.S.A. 159 H4
Oraibi Wash watercourse U.S.A. 159 H4
Oral Kazakh. see Ural'sk
Oran Alg. 67 F6
Orán Arg. 178 D2
O Rang Cambodia 87 D4
Orang India 105 H4
Ŏrang N. Korea 90 C4
Orange Australia 138 D4
Orange France 66 G4
Orange r. Namibia/S. Africa 124 C5
Orange CA U.S.A. 158 E5
Orange MA U.S.A. 165 I2
Orange TX U.S.A. 161 E6
Orange VA U.S.A. 165 F4
Orange, Cabo c. Brazil 177 H3
Orangeburg U.S.A. 163 D5
Orange City U.S.A. 160 D3
Orange Cone sea feature S. Atlantic Ocean 184 I8
Orange Free State prov. S. Africa see Free State
Orangeville Canada 164 E2
Orange Walk Belize 167 H5
Orani Luzon Phil. 82 C3
Oranienburg Germany 63 N2
Oranje r. Namibia/S. Africa see Orange
Oranje Gebergte hills Suriname 177 G3
Oranjemund Namibia 124 C5

▶Oranjestad Aruba 169 J6
Capital of Aruba.

Oranmore Ireland 61 D4
Orapa Botswana 123 C6
Oras Samar Phil. 82 D3
Oras Bay Samar Phil. 82 D3
Orăștie Romania 69 J2
Orașul Stalin Romania see Brașov
Oratia, Mount AK U.S.A. 148 G4
Oravais Fin. 54 M5
Orba Co l. China 99 C6
Orbetello Italy 68 D3
Orbost Australia 138 D6
Orca Bay AK U.S.A. 149 K3
Orcadas research station S. Atlantic Ocean 188 A2
Orchard City U.S.A. 159 J2
Orchha India 104 D4
Orchila, Isla i. Venez. 176 E1
Orchy r. U.K. 60 D4
Orcutt U.S.A. 158 C4
Ord r. Australia 134 E3
Ord U.S.A. 160 D3
Ord, Mount hill Australia 134 D4
Órdenes Spain see Ordes
Orderville U.S.A. 159 G3
Ordes Spain 67 B2
Ordesa-Monte Perdido, Parque Nacional nat. park Spain 67 G2
Ord Mountain U.S.A. 158 E4
Ordos Nei Mongol China 95 G4
Ord River Dam Australia 134 E4
Ordu Hatay Turkey see Yayladağı
Ordu Ordu Turkey 112 E2
Ordubad Azer. 113 G3
Ordway U.S.A. 160 C4
Ordzhonikidze Rus. Fed. see Vladikavkaz
Ore Nigeria 120 D4
Oreana U.S.A. 158 D1
Örebro Sweden 55 I7
Oregon IL U.S.A. 160 F3
Oregon OH U.S.A. 164 D3
Oregon state U.S.A. 156 C4
Oregon City U.S.A. 156 C3
Orekhov Ukr. see Orikhiv
Orekhovo-Zuyevo Rus. Fed. 52 H5
Orel Rus. Fed. 53 H5
Orel, Gora mt. Rus. Fed. 90 E1
Orel', Ozero l. Rus. Fed. 90 E1
Orem U.S.A. 159 H1
Ore Mountains Czech Rep./Germany see Erzgebirge
Orenburg Rus. Fed. 76 G4
Orense Spain see Ourense
Oreor Palau see Koror
Oreor i. Palau see Koror
Orepuki N.Z. 139 A8
Öresund strait Denmark/Sweden 55 H9
Oretana, Cordillera mts Spain see Toledo, Montes de
Orewa N.Z. 139 E3
Oreye Belgium 62 F4
Orfanou, Kolpos b. Greece 69 J4
Orford Australia 137 [inset]
Orford U.K. 59 I6
Orford Ness hd U.K. 59 I6
Organabo Fr. Guiana 177 H2
Organ Pipe Cactus National Monument nat. park U.S.A. 159 G5
Orge r. France 62 C6
Orgil Mongolia see Jargalant
Orgon Tal Nei Mongol China 95 H3
Orgūn Afgh. 111 H3
Orhaneli Turkey 69 M5
Orhangazi Turkey 69 M4
Orhei Moldova 53 F7
Orhon Bulgan Mongolia 94 E1
Orhon Mongolia 94 F1
Orhon Gol r. Mongolia 94 F1
Orhontuul Mongolia 94 F1
Orichi Rus. Fed. 52 K4
Oriental, Cordillera mts Bol. 176 E7
Oriental, Cordillera mts Col. 176 D2
Oriental, Cordillera mts Peru 176 E6
Orihuela Spain 67 F4
Orikhiv Ukr. 53 G7
Orillia Canada 164 F1
Orimattila Fin. 55 N6
Orin U.S.A. 156 G4
Orinoco r. Col./Venez. 176 F2
Orinoco Delta Venez. 176 F2
Orissa state India 106 E1
Orissaare Estonia 55 M7
Oristano Sardinia Italy 68 C5
Orivesi Fin. 55 N6
Orivesi l. Fin. 54 P5
Oriximiná Brazil 177 G4
Orizaba Mex. 168 E5

▶Orizaba, Pico de vol. Mex. 168 E5
Highest active volcano and 3rd highest mountain in North America.

Orizona Brazil 179 A2
Orkanger Norway 54 F5
Örkelljunga Sweden 55 H8
Orkhon Valley tourist site Mongolia 94 E2
Orkla r. Norway 54 F5
Orkney S. Africa 125 H4
Orkney Islands is U.K. 60 F1
Orla U.S.A. 161 C6
Orland U.S.A. 158 B2
Orlândia Brazil 179 B3
Orlando U.S.A. 163 D6
Orland Park U.S.A. 164 B3
Orleaes Brazil 179 A5
Orléans France 66 E3
Orleans IN U.S.A. 164 B4
Orleans VT U.S.A. 165 I1
Orléans, Île d' i. Canada 153 H5
Orléansville Alg. see Chlef
Orlik Rus. Fed. 88 H2
Orlov Rus. Fed. 52 K4
Orlov Gay Rus. Fed. 53 K6
Orlovskiy Rus. Fed. 53 I7
Ormara Pak. 111 G5
Ormara, Ras hd Pak. 111 G5
Ormiston Canada 151 J5
Ormoc Leyte Phil. 82 D4
Ormskirk U.K. 58 E5
Ormstown Canada 165 I1
Ornach Pak. 111 G5
Ornain r. France 62 E6
Orne r. France 66 D2
Ørnes Norway 54 H3
Örnsköldsvik Sweden 54 K5
Orobie, Alpi mts Italy 68 C1
Orobo, Serra do hills Brazil 179 C1
Orodara Burkina 120 C3
Orofino U.S.A. 156 D3
Orog Nuur salt l. Mongolia 94 E2
Oro Grande U.S.A. 158 E4
Orogrande U.S.A. 157 G6
Orol Dengizi salt l. Kazakh./Uzbek. see Aral Sea
Oromocto Canada 153 I5
Oromocto Lake Canada 153 I5
Oron Israel 107 B4
Orona atoll Kiribati 133 I2
Orono U.S.A. 162 G2
Orontes r. Asia 112 E3 see 'Āṣī, Nahr al
Orontes r. Lebanon/Syria 107 C2
Oroqen Zizhiqi Nei Mongol China see Alihe
Oroquieta Mindanao Phil. 82 C4
Orós, Açude resr Brazil 177 K5
Orosei, Golfo di b. Sardinia Italy 68 C4
Orosháza Hungary 69 I1
Oroville U.S.A. 158 C2
Oroville, Lake U.S.A. 158 C2
Orqohan Nei Mongol China 95 J1
Orr U.S.A. 160 E1
Orsa Sweden 55 I6
Orsha Belarus 53 F5
Orshanka Rus. Fed. 52 J4
Orsk Rus. Fed. 76 G4
Ørsta Norway 54 E5
Orta Toroslar plat. Turkey 107 A1
Ortegal, Cabo c. Spain 67 C2
Orthez France 66 D5
Ortigueira Spain 67 C2
Ortíz Mex. 166 C2
Ortles mt. Italy 68 D1
Orton U.K. 58 E4
Ortona Italy 68 F3
Ortonville U.S.A. 160 D2
Ortospana Afgh. see Kābul
Orto-Tokoy Kyrg. 98 A4
Orukuizu i. Palau 82 [inset]
Orulgan, Khrebet mts Rus. Fed. 77 N3
Orumbo Namibia 124 C2
Orūmīyeh Iran see Urmia
Oruro Bol. 176 E7
Orūzgān Afgh. 111 G3
Orvieto Italy 68 E3
Orville Coast Antarctica 188 L1
Orwell OH U.S.A. 164 E3
Orwell VT U.S.A. 165 I2
Orxon Gol r. China 95 I1
Oryol Rus. Fed. see Orel
Os Norway 54 G5
Osa Rus. Fed. 51 R4
Osa, Península de pen. Costa Rica 166 [inset] J7
Osage IA U.S.A. 160 E3
Osage WV U.S.A. 164 E4
Osage WY U.S.A. 156 G3
Ōsaka Japan 92 D3
Ōsaka Japan 92 B4
Ōsaka pref. Japan 92 B4
Osakarovka Kazakh. 102 D1
Ōsakasayama Japan 92 B4
Ōsaka-wan b. Japan 92 B4
Ōsawano Japan 92 D2
Osawatomie U.S.A. 160 E4
Osborn, Mount AK U.S.A. 148 F2
Osborne U.S.A. 160 D4
Osby Sweden 55 H8
Osceola IA U.S.A. 160 E3
Osceola MO U.S.A. 160 E4
Osceola NE U.S.A. 160 D3
Oschatz Germany 63 N3
Oschersleben (Bode) Germany 63 L2
Oschiri Sardinia Italy 68 C4
Ösel i. Estonia see Hiiumaa
Osetr r. Rus. Fed. 53 H5
Ōse-zaki pt Japan 91 C6
Ōse-zaki pt Japan 93 E3
Osgoode Canada 165 H1
Osgood Mountains U.S.A. 156 D4
Osh Kyrg. 102 D3
Oshakati Namibia 123 B5
Oshawa Canada 165 F2
Ōshika Japan 93 E3
Oshika-hantō pen. Japan 91 F5
Ōshima Niigata Japan 93 E1
Ōshima Tōkyō Japan 93 F4
Ōshima Toyama Japan 92 D2
Ō-shima i. Japan 90 E4
Ō-shima i. Japan 92 C2
Ō-shima i. Japan 93 F4
Oshimizu Japan 92 C2
Oshino Japan 93 E3
Oshkosh NE U.S.A. 160 C3
Oshkosh WI U.S.A. 164 A1
Oshmyany Belarus see Ashmyany
Oshnovīyeh Iran 110 B2
Oshogbo Nigeria 120 D4
Oshtorān Kūh mt. Iran 110 C3
Oshwe Dem. Rep. Congo 122 B4
Osijek Croatia 68 H2
Osilinka r. Canada 150 E3
Osimo Italy 68 E3
Osinovka Rus. Fed. 95 G1
Osipenko Ukr. see Berdyans'k
Osipovichi Belarus see Asipovichy
Osiyan India 104 C4
Osizweni S. Africa 125 J4
Osječenica mts Bos.-Herz. 68 G2
Ösjön l. Sweden 54 I5
Oskaloosa U.S.A. 160 E3
Oskarshamn Sweden 55 J8
Öskemen Kazakh. see Ust'-Kamenogorsk

▶Oslo Norway 55 G7
Capital of Norway.

Oslob Cebu Phil. 82 C4
Oslofjorden sea chan. Norway 55 G7
Osmanabad India 106 C2
Osmancık Turkey 112 D2
Osmaneli Turkey 69 M4
Osmaniye Turkey 112 E3
Osmannagar India 106 C2
Os'mino Rus. Fed. 55 P7
Osnabrück Germany 63 I2
Osnaburg atoll Fr. Polynesia see Mururoa
Osogbo Nigeria see Oshogbo
Osogovska Planina mts Bulg./Macedonia 69 J3
Osogovske Planine mts Bulg./Macedonia see Osogovska Planina
Osogovski Planini mts Bulg./Macedonia see Osogovska Planina
Osorno Chile 178 B6
Osorno Spain 67 D2
Osoyoos Canada 150 G5
Osøyri Norway 55 D6
Osprey Reef Australia 136 D2
Oss Neth. 62 F3
Ossa, Mount Australia 137 [inset]
Osseo U.S.A. 152 C5
Ossineke U.S.A. 164 D1
Ossining U.S.A. 165 I3
Ossipee U.S.A. 165 J2
Ossipee Lake U.S.A. 165 J2
Oßmannstedt Germany 63 L3
Ossokmanuan Lake Canada 153 I3
Ossora Rus. Fed. 77 R4
Ossu East Timor 83 C5
Ostashkov Rus. Fed. 52 G4
Ostbevern Germany 63 H2
Oste r. Germany 63 J1
Ostend Belgium 62 C3
Ostende Belgium see Ostend
Osterburg (Altmark) Germany 63 L2
Österbymo Sweden 55 I8
Österdalälven l. Sweden 55 H6
Østerdalen valley Norway 55 G5
Osterfeld Germany 63 L3
Osterholz-Scharmbeck Germany 63 I1
Osterode am Harz Germany 63 K3
Österreich country Europe see Austria
Östersund Sweden 54 I5
Osterwieck Germany 63 K3
Ostfriesische Inseln Germany see East Frisian Islands
Ostfriesland reg. Germany 63 H1
Östhammar Sweden 55 K6
Ostrava Czech Rep. 57 Q6
Ostróda Poland 57 Q4
Ostrogozhsk Rus. Fed. 53 H6
Ostrov Czech Rep. 63 M4
Ostrov Rus. Fed. 55 P8
Ostrovets Poland see Ostrowiec Świętokrzyski
Ostrovskoye Rus. Fed. 52 I4
Ostrów Poland see Ostrów Wielkopolski
Ostrowiec Poland see Ostrowiec Świętokrzyski
Ostrowiec Świętokrzyski Poland 53 D6
Ostrów Mazowiecka Poland 57 R4
Ostrowo Poland see Ostrów Wielkopolski
Ostrów Wielkopolski Poland 57 P5
Ōsuka Japan 93 D4
O'Sullivan Lake Canada 152 D4
Osŭm r. Bulg. 69 K3
Ōsumi-shotō is Japan 91 C7
Osuna Spain 67 D5
Oswego KS U.S.A. 161 E4
Oswego NY U.S.A. 165 G2
Oswestry U.K. 59 D6
Ota Japan 92 C3
Ōta Japan 93 F2
Otago Peninsula N.Z. 139 C7
Otahiti i. Fr. Polynesia see Tahiti
Ōtake Japan 92 D3
Ōtake-san mt. Japan 93 F3
Ōtaki Chiba Japan 93 G3
Ōtaki Saitama Japan 93 E3
Otaki N.Z. 139 E5
Otanmäki Fin. 54 O4
Otar Kazakh. 98 A4
Otari Japan 93 D2
Otaru Japan 90 F4
Otavi Namibia 123 B5
Ōtawara Japan 93 G2
Otdia atoll Marshall Is see Wotje
Otegen Batyr Kazakh. 98 B4
Otelnuc, Lac l. Canada 153 H2
Otematata N.Z. 139 C7
Otepää Estonia 55 O7
Oteros r. Mex. 166 C3
Otgon Tenger Uul mt. Mongolia 94 D2
Oti Sulawesi Indon. 83 A3
Otinapa Mex. 161 B7
Otira N.Z. 139 C6
Otis U.S.A. 160 C3
Otish, Monts hills Canada 153 H4
Otjinene Namibia 123 B6
Otjiwarongo Namibia 123 B6
Otjozondjupa admin. reg. Namibia 124 C1
Otley U.K. 58 F5
Ōto Japan 92 B4
Otog Qi Nei Mongol China see Ulan
Otorohanga N.Z. 139 E4
Otoskwin r. Canada 151 N5
Otowa Japan 92 D4
Otpan, Gora hill Kazakh. 113 H1
Otpor Rus. Fed. see Zabaykal'sk
Otradnoye Rus. Fed. see Otradnyy
Otradnyy Rus. Fed. 53 K5
Otranto Italy 68 H4
Otranto, Strait of Albania/Italy 68 H4
Otrogovo Rus. Fed. see Stepnoye
Otrozhnyy Rus. Fed. 77 S3
Otsego Lake U.S.A. 165 H2
Ōtsu Ibaraki Japan 93 G2
Ōtsu Shiga Japan 92 B3
Ōtsuki Japan 93 E3
Otta Norway 55 F6

▶Ottawa Canada 165 H1
Capital of Canada.

Ottawa r. Canada 152 G5
also known as Rivière des Outaouais
Ottawa IL U.S.A. 160 F3
Ottawa KS U.S.A. 160 E4
Ottawa OH U.S.A. 164 C3
Ottawa Islands Canada 152 E2
Otter r. U.K. 59 D8
Otterbein U.S.A. 164 B3
Otterburn U.K. 58 E3
Otter Island AK U.S.A. 148 E4
Otter Rapids Canada 152 E4
Ottersberg Germany 63 J1
Ottignies Belgium 62 E4
Ottuk Kyrg. 98 A4
Ottumwa U.S.A. 160 E3
Ottweiler Germany 63 H5
Otukpo Nigeria 120 D4
Oturkpo Nigeria see Otukpo
Otuzco Peru 176 C5
Otway, Cape Australia 138 A7
Otway National Park Australia 138 A7
Ouachita r. U.S.A. 161 F6
Ouachita, Lake U.S.A. 161 E5
Ouachita Mountains Arkansas/Oklahoma U.S.A. 155 I5
Ouachita Mountains Arkansas/Oklahoma U.S.A. 161 E5
Ouadda Cent. Afr. Rep. 122 C3
Ouaddaï reg. Chad 121 F3

▶Ouagadougou Burkina 120 C3
Capital of Burkina.

Ouahigouya Burkina 120 C3
Ouahran Alg. see Oran
Ouaka r. Cent. Afr. Rep. 122 B3
Oualâta Mauritania 120 C3
Ouallam Niger 120 D3
Ouanda-Djailé Cent. Afr. Rep. 122 C3
Ouando Cent. Afr. Rep. 122 C3
Ouango Cent. Afr. Rep. 122 C3
Ouara r. Cent. Afr. Rep. 122 C3
Ouarâne reg. Mauritania 120 C2
Ouargaye Burkina 120 D3
Ouargla Alg. 64 F5
Ouarogou Burkina see Ouargaye
Ouarzazate Morocco 64 C5
Ouasiemsca r. Canada 153 G4

Oubangui *r.* Cent. Afr. Rep./Dem. Rep. Congo *see* **Ubangi**
Oubergpas *pass* S. Africa 124 G7
Ouchiyama Japan 92 C4
Ouda Japan 92 B4
Oudenaarde Belgium 62 D4
Oudômxai Laos 86 C2
Oudtshoorn S. Africa 124 F7
Oud-Turnhout Belgium 62 E3
Oued Tlélat Alg. 67 F6
Oued Zem Morocco 64 C5
Oued Zénati Alg. 68 B6
Ouessant, Île d' *i.* France 66 B2
Ouesso Congo 122 B3
Ouezzane Morocco 67 D6
Oughter, Lough *l.* Ireland 61 E3
Ougo-gawa *r.* Japan 92 A4
Ouguati Namibia 124 B1
Ougura-yama *mt.* Japan 93 E2
Ouiriego Mex. 166 C3
Ouistreham France 59 G9
Oujda Morocco 67 F6
Oujeft Mauritania 120 B3
Oulainen Fin. 54 N4
Oulangan kansallispuisto *nat. park* Fin. 54 P3
Ouled Djellal Alg. 67 I6
Ouled Farès Alg. 67 G5
Ouled Naïl, Monts des *mts* Alg. 67 H6
Oulu Fin. 54 N4
Oulujärvi *l.* Fin. 54 O4
Oulujoki *r.* Fin. 54 N4
Oulunsalo Fin. 54 N4
Oulx Italy 68 B2
Oum-Chalouba Chad 121 F3
Oum el Bouaghi Alg. 68 B7
Oum-Hadjer Chad 121 E3
Ounasjoki *r.* Fin. 54 N3
Oundle U.K. 59 G6
Oungre Canada 151 K5
Ounianga Kébir Chad 121 F3
Oupeye Belgium 62 F4
Our *r.* Lux. 62 G5
Oura, Akrotirio *pt* Greece 69 L5
Ouray *CO* U.S.A. 159 J2
Ouray *UT* U.S.A. 159 I1
Ourcq *r.* France 62 D5
Ourense Spain 67 C2
Ouricurí Brazil 177 J5
Ourinhos Brazil 179 A3
Ouro *r.* Brazil 179 A1
Ouro Preto Brazil 179 C3
Ourthe *r.* Belgium 62 F4
Our Valley *valley* Germany/Lux. 62 G5
Ous Rus. Fed. 51 S3
Ouse *r. England* U.K. 58 G5
Ouse *r. England* U.K. 59 H8
Outaouais, Rivière des *r.* Canada 152 G5 *see* **Ottawa**
Outardes, Rivière aux *r.* Canada 153 H4
Outardes Quatre, Réservoir *resr* Canada 153 H4
Outer Hebrides *is* U.K. 60 B3
Outer Mongolia *country* Asia *see* **Mongolia**
Outer Santa Barbara Channel U.S.A. 158 D5
Outjo Namibia 123 B6
Outlook Canada 151 J5
Outokumpu Fin. 54 P5
Out Skerries *is* U.K. 60 [inset]
Ouvéa *atoll* New Caledonia 133 G4
Ouyanghai Shuiku *resr* China 97 G3
Ouyen Australia 137 C7
Ouzel *r.* U.K. 59 G6
Ouzinkie *AK* U.S.A. 148 I4
Ovace, Punta d' *mt. Corsica* France 66 I6
Ovacık Turkey 107 A1
Ovada Italy 68 C2
Ovalle Chile 178 B4
Ovamboland *reg.* Namibia 123 B5
Ovan Gabon 122 B3
Ovar Port. 67 B3
Overath Germany 63 H4
Överkalix Sweden 54 M3
Overlander Roadhouse Australia 135 A6
Overland Park U.S.A. 160 E4
Overton U.S.A. 159 F3
Övertorneå Sweden 54 M3
Överum Sweden 55 J8
Overveen Neth. 62 E2
Ovid *CO* U.S.A. 160 C3
Ovid *NY* U.S.A. 165 G2
Oviedo Spain 67 D2
Övögdiy Mongolia *see* **Telmen**
Ovoot Mongolia *see* **Dariganga**
Övörhangay *prov.* Mongolia 94 E2
Øvre Anárjohka Nasjonalpark *nat. park* Norway 54 N2
Øvre Dividal Nasjonalpark *nat. park* Norway 54 K2
Øvre Rendal Norway 55 G6
Ovruch Ukr. 53 F6
Ovsyanka Rus. Fed. 90 B1
Övt Mongolia *see* **Bat-Öldziy**
Owando Congo 122 B4
Owa Rafa *i.* Solomon Is *see* **Santa Ana**
Owasco Lake U.S.A. 165 G2
Owase Japan 92 C4
Owase-wan *b.* Japan 92 C4
Owatonna U.S.A. 160 E2
Owbeh Afgh. 111 F3
Owego U.S.A. 165 G2
Owel, Lough *l.* Ireland 61 E4
Owen Island Myanmar 87 B5
Owenmore *r.* Ireland 61 C3
Owenreagh *r.* U.K. 61 E3
Owen River N.Z. 139 D5
Owens *r.* U.S.A. 158 E3
Owensboro U.S.A. 164 B5
Owen Sound Canada 164 E1
Owen Sound *inlet* Canada 164 E1
Owen Stanley Range *mts* P.N.G. 81 L8
Owenton U.S.A. 164 C4
Owerri Nigeria 120 D4
Owikeno Lake Canada 150 E5
Owingsville U.S.A. 164 D4
Owkal Afgh. 111 F3
Owl *r.* Canada 151 M3
Owl Creek Mountains U.S.A. 156 F4
Owo Nigeria 120 D4
Owosso U.S.A. 164 C2
Owyhee U.S.A. 156 D4
Owyhee *r.* U.S.A. 156 D4
Owyhee Mountains U.S.A. 156 D4
Öxarfjörður *b.* Iceland 54 [inset]
Oxbow Canada 151 K5
Ox Creek *r.* U.S.A. 160 C1
Oxelösund Sweden 55 J7
Oxford N.Z. 139 D6
Oxford U.K. 59 F7
Oxford *IN* U.S.A. 164 B3
Oxford *MA* U.S.A. 165 J2
Oxford *MD* U.S.A. 165 G4
Oxford *MS* U.S.A. 161 F5
Oxford *NC* U.S.A. 162 E4
Oxford *NY* U.S.A. 165 H2
Oxford *OH* U.S.A. 164 C4
Oxford House Canada 151 M4
Oxford Lake Canada 151 M4
Oxkutzcab Mex. 167 H4
Oxley Australia 138 B5
Oxleys Peak Australia 138 E3
Oxley Wild Rivers National Park Australia 138 F3
Ox Mountains *hills* Ireland 61 D3
Oxnard U.S.A. 158 D4
Oxtongue Lake Canada 165 F1
Oxus *r.* Asia *see* **Amudar'ya**
Oya *Sarawak* Malaysia 85 E2
Øya Norway 54 H3
Oyabe Japan 92 C2
Oyabe-gawa *r.* Japan 92 D2
Oyama *Shizuoka* Japan 93 E3
Oyama *Tochigi* Japan 93 F2
Ōyama Japan 92 D2
Ō-yama *mt.* Japan 93 F3
Ō-yama *vol.* Japan 93 F4
Ōyamada Japan 92 C4
Ōyamazaki Japan 92 B4
Oyapock *r.* Brazil/Fr. Guiana 177 H3
Oychilik Kazakh. 98 C3
Oyem Gabon 122 B3
Oyen Canada 151 I5
Oygon Mongolia *see* **Tüdevtey**
Oykel *r.* U.K. 60 E3
Oyo Nigeria 120 D4
Ōyodo Japan 92 B4
Oyonnax France 66 G3
Oyster Rocks *is* India 106 B3
Oy-Tal Kyrg. 98 A4
Oyten Germany 63 J1
Oytograk *Xinjiang* China 99 C5
Oyukludağı *mt.* Turkey 107 A1
Özalp Turkey 113 G3
Ozamiz *Mindanao* Phil. 82 C4
Ozark *AL* U.S.A. 163 C6
Ozark *AR* U.S.A. 161 E5
Ozark *MO* U.S.A. 161 E4
Ozark Plateau U.S.A. 161 E4
Ozarks, Lake of the U.S.A. 160 E4
O'zbekiston *country* Asia *see* **Uzbekistan**
Özen Kazakh. *see* **Kyzylsay**
Ozernovskiy Rus. Fed. 77 Q4
Ozernyy Rus. Fed. 148 C2
Ozernyy Rus. Fed. 53 G5
Ozerpakh Rus. Fed. 90 F1
Ozersk Rus. Fed. 55 M9
Ozerskiy Rus. Fed. 90 F3
Ozery Rus. Fed. 53 H5
Ozeryane Rus. Fed. 90 C2
Ozieri *Sardinia* Italy 68 C4
Ozinki Rus. Fed. 53 K6
Oznachennoye Rus. Fed. *see* **Sayanogorsk**
Ozona U.S.A. 161 C6
Ozuki Japan 91 C6
Ozuluama Mex. 167 F4

P

Paamiut Greenland 147 N3
Pa-an Myanmar *see* **Hpa-an**
Paanopa *i.* Kiribati *see* **Banaba**
Paarl S. Africa 124 D7
Paatsjoki *r.* Europe *see* **Patsoyoki**
Paballelo S. Africa 124 E5
P'abal-li N. Korea 90 C4
Pabbay *i.* U.K. 60 B3
Pabianice Poland 57 Q5
Pabianitz Poland *see* **Pabianice**
Pabna Bangl. 105 G4
Pabradė Lith. 55 N9
Pab Range *mts* Pak. 111 G5
Pacaás Novos, Parque Nacional *nat. park* Brazil 176 F6
Pacaraimã, Serra *mts* S. America *see* **Pakaraima Mountains**
Pacasmayo Peru 176 C5
Pacaya, Volcán de *vol.* Guat. 167 H6
Pachagarh Bangl. *see* **Panchagarh**
Pacheco *Chihuahua* Mex. 166 C2
Pacheco *Zacatecas* Mex. 161 C7
Pachikha Rus. Fed. 52 J3
Pachino *Sicily* Italy 68 F6
Pachmarhi India 104 D5
Pachor India 104 D5
Pachora India 106 B1
Pachpadra India 104 C4
Pachuca Mex. 168 E4
Pachuca de Soto Mex. *see* **Pachuca**
Pacific-Antarctic Ridge *sea feature* S. Pacific Ocean 187 J9
Pacific Grove U.S.A. 158 C3

▶**Pacific Ocean** 186
Largest ocean in the world.

Pacific Rim National Park Canada 150 E5
Pacijan *i.* Phil. 82 D4
Pacinan, Tanjung *pt* Indon. 85 F4
Pacitan *Jawa* Indon. 85 E5
Packsaddle Australia 137 C6
Pacoval Brazil 177 H4
Pacuí *r.* Brazil 179 B2
Paczków Poland 57 P5
Padada *Mindanao* Phil. 82 D5
Padalere *Sulawesi* Indon. 83 B3
Padali Rus. Fed. *see* **Amursk**
Padamarang *i.* Indon. 83 B4
Padampur India 104 C3
Padang *Kalimantan* Indon. 85 E3
Padang *Sulawesi* Indon. 83 B4
Padang *Sumatera* Indon. 84 C3
Padang *i.* Indon. 84 C2
Padang Endau Malaysia 84 C2
Padang Luwai, Cagar Alam *nature res. Kalimantan* Indon. 85 G3
Padangpanjang *Sumatera* Indon. 84 C3
Padangsidimpuan *Sumatera* Indon. 84 B2
Padangtikar *Kalimantan* Indon. 85 E3
Padangtikar *i.* Indon. 85 E3
Padany Rus. Fed. 52 G3
Padas *r.* Malaysia 85 F1
Padatha, Kūh-e *mt.* Iran 110 C3
Padaung Myanmar 86 A3
Padcaya Bol. 176 F8
Paddington Australia 138 B4
Padeabesar *i.* Indon. 83 B3
Paden City U.S.A. 164 E4
Paderborn Germany 63 I3
Paderborn/Lippstadt *airport* Germany 63 I3
Padeșu, Vârful *mt.* Romania 69 J2
Padibyu Myanmar 86 B2
Padilla Bol. 176 F7
Padjelanta nationalpark *nat. park* Sweden 54 J3
Padova Italy *see* **Padua**
Padrão, Ponta *pt* Angola 123 B4
Padrauna India 105 F4
Padre Island U.S.A. 161 D7
Padstow U.K. 59 C8
Padsvillye Belarus 55 O9
Padua India 106 D2
Padua Italy 68 D2
Paducah *KY* U.S.A. 161 F4
Paducah *TX* U.S.A. 161 C5
Padum India 104 D2
Paegam N. Korea 90 C4
Paektu-san *mt.* China/N. Korea *see* **Baotou Shan**
Paengnyŏng-do *i.* S. Korea 91 B5
Paete *Luzon* Phil. 82 C3
Pafos Cyprus *see* **Paphos**
Pafuri Moz. 125 J2
Pag Croatia 68 F2
Pag *i.* Croatia 68 F2
Paga *Flores* Indon. 83 B5
Pagadenbaru *Jawa* Indon. 85 D4
Pagadian *Mindanao* Phil. 82 C5
Pagai Selatan *i.* Indon. 84 C3
Pagai Utara *i.* Indon. 84 C3
Pagalu *i.* Equat. Guinea *see* **Annobón**
Pagan *i.* N. Mariana Is 81 L3
Pagaralam *Sumatera* Indon. 84 C3
Pagasitikos Kolpos *b.* Greece 69 J5
Pagatan *Kalimantan* Indon. 85 F3
Pagatan *Kalimantan* Indon. 85 F3
Page U.S.A. 159 H3
Page, Mount *Y.T.* Canada 149 L1
Pagerdewa *Sumatera* Indon. 84 D3
Paget, Mount S. Georgia 178 I8
Paget Cay *reef* Australia 136 F3
Pagon *i.* N. Mariana Is *see* **Pagan**
Pagosa Springs U.S.A. 157 G5
Pagqên China *see* **Gadê**
Pagri *Xizang* China 99 E8
Pagwa River Canada 152 D4
Pagwi P.N.G. 81 K7
Pah *r. AK* U.S.A. 148 H2
Pāhala U.S.A. 157 [inset]
Pahang *r.* Malaysia 84 C2
Pahang *state* Malaysia 84 C2
Pahauman *Kalimantan* Indon. 85 E2
Pahlgam India 104 C2
Pāhoa U.S.A. 157 [inset]
Pahokee U.S.A. 163 D7
Pahra Kariz Afgh. 111 F3
Pahranagat Range *mts* U.S.A. 159 F3
Pahrump U.S.A. 159 F3
Pahuj *r.* India 104 D4
Pahute Mesa *plat.* U.S.A. 158 E3
Pai Thai. 86 B3
Paicines U.S.A. 158 C3
Paide Estonia 55 N7
Paignton U.K. 59 D8
Päijänne *l.* Fin. 55 N6
Paikü Co *l.* China 99 D7
Pailin Cambodia 87 C4
Pailolo Channel U.S.A. 157 [inset]
Paimio Fin. 55 M6
Paimiut *AK* U.S.A. 148 F3
Paimiut *AK* U.S.A. 148 G3
Painan *Sumatera* Indon. 84 C3
Painel Brazil 179 A4
Painesville U.S.A. 164 E3
Pains Brazil 179 B3
Painted Desert U.S.A. 159 H3
Painted Rock Dam U.S.A. 159 G5
Paint Hills Canada *see* **Wemindji**
Paint Rock U.S.A. 161 D6
Paintsville U.S.A. 164 D5
Paisley U.K. 60 E5
Paita Peru 176 B5
Paitan, Teluk *b.* Malaysia 85 G1
Paitou China 97 I2
Paiva Couceiro Angola *see* **Quipungo**
Paixban Mex. 167 H5
Paizhou China 97 G2
Pajala Sweden 54 M3
Paka Malaysia 84 C1
Pakal *i. Maluku* Indon. 83 D2
Pakala India 106 C3
Pakanbaru *Sumatera* Indon. *see* **Pekanbaru**
Pakangyi Myanmar 86 A2
Pakaraima Mountains Guyana 169 M8
Pakaraima Mountains S. America 176 F3
Pakaur India 105 F4
Pakesley Canada 152 E5
Pakhachi Rus. Fed. 77 R3
Pakhoi China *see* **Beihai**
Paki Nigeria 120 D3

▶**Pakistan** *country* Asia 111 H4
4th most populous country in Asia, and 6th in the world.

Pakkat *Sumatera* Indon. 84 B2
Paknampho Thai. *see* **Nakhon Sawan**
Pakokku Myanmar 86 A2
Pakowki Lake *imp. l.* Canada 151 I5
Pakpattan Pak. 111 I4
Pak Phanang Thai. 87 C5
Pak Phayun Thai. 87 C6
Pakruojis Lith. 55 M9
Paks Hungary 68 H1
Pakse Laos *see* **Pakxé**
Pak Tam Chung *H.K.* China 97 [inset]
Pak Thong Chai Thai. 86 C4
Paku *r.* Malaysia 85 F2
Paku, Tanjung *pt* Indon. 84 D3
Pakue *Sulawesi* Indon. 83 B3
Pakur India *see* **Pakaur**
Pakxan Laos 86 C3
Pakxé Laos 86 D4
Pakxeng Laos 86 C2
Pala Chad 121 E4
Pala Myanmar 87 B4
Palabuhanratu *Jawa* Indon. 84 D4
Palabuhanratu, Teluk *b.* Indon. 84 D4
Palaestinia *reg.* Asia *see* **Palestine**
Palaiochora Greece 69 J7
Palaiseau France 62 C6
Palakkad India *see* **Palghat**
Palakkat India *see* **Palghat**
Palamakoloi Botswana 124 F2
Palamau India *see* **Palamu**
Palamea *Maluku* Indon. 83 C3
Palamós Spain 67 H3
Palamu India 105 F5
Palana Rus. Fed. 77 Q4
Palanan *Luzon* Phil. 82 C2
Palanan Point *Luzon* Phil. 82 C2
Palandur India 106 D1
Palangān, Kūh-e *mts* Iran 111 F4
Palangkaraya *Kalimantan* Indon. 85 F3
Palani India 106 C4
Palanpur India 104 C4
Palanro *Sulawesi* Indon. 83 A4
Palantak Pak. 111 G5
Palapag *Samar* Phil. 82 D3
Palapye Botswana 125 H2
Palasa *Sulawesi* Indon. 83 B2
Palatka Rus. Fed. 77 Q3
Palatka U.S.A. 163 D6
Palau *country* N. Pacific Ocean 82 [inset]
Palau Hatta *i. Maluku* Indon. 83 D4
Palaui *i.* Phil. 82 C2
Palauig *Luzon* Phil. 82 B3
Palau Islands Palau 81 I5
Palauk Myanmar 87 B4
Palausekopong, Tanjung *pt* Indon. 84 D4
Palaw Myanmar 87 B4
Palawan *i.* Phil. 82 B4
Palawan Passage *str.* Phil. 82 B4
Palawan Trough *sea feature* N. Pacific Ocean 186 D5
Palayan *Luzon* Phil. 82 C3
Palayankottai India 106 C4
Palchal Lake India 106 D2
Paldiski Estonia 55 N7
Palekh Rus. Fed. 52 I4
Paleleh *Sulawesi* Indon. 83 B2
Palembang *Sumatera* Indon. 84 D3
Palena Chile 178 B6
Palencia Spain 67 D2
Palermo *Sicily* Italy 68 E5
Palestine *reg.* Asia 107 B3
Palestine U.S.A. 161 E6
Paletwa Myanmar 86 A2
Palezgir Chauki Pak. 111 H4
Palghat India 106 C4
Palgrave, Mount *hill* Australia 135 A5
Palhoca Brazil 179 A4
Pali *Chhattisgarh* India 106 D1
Pali *Mahar.* India 106 B2
Pali *Rajasthan* India 104 C4
Pali India 105 E5
Paliat *i.* Indon. 85 F4

▶**Palikir** Micronesia 186 G5
Capital of Micronesia.

Palimbang *Mindanao* Phil. 82 D5
Palinuro, Capo *c.* Italy 68 F4
Paliouri, Akra *pt* Greece *see* **Paliouri, Akrotirio**
Paliouri, Akra *pt* Greece *see* **Paliouri, Akrotirio**
Paliouri, Akrotirio *pt* Greece 69 J5
Palisade U.S.A. 159 I2
Paliseul Belgium 62 F5
Palitana India 104 B5
Palivere Estonia 55 M7
Palk Bay Sri Lanka 106 C4
Palkino Rus. Fed. 55 P8
Palkonda Range *mts* India 106 C3
Palk Strait India/Sri Lanka 106 C4
Palla Bianca *mt.* Austria/Italy *see* **Weißkugel**
Pallamallawa Australia 138 E2
Pallas Green New Ireland 61 D5
Pallasovka Rus. Fed. 53 J6
Pallas-Yllästunturin kansallispuisto *nat. park* Fin. 54 M2
Pallavaram India 106 D3
Palliser, Cape N.Z. 139 E5
Palliser, Îles *is* Fr. Polynesia 187 K7
Palliser Bay N.Z. 139 E5
Pallu India 104 C3
Palma *r.* Brazil 179 B1
Palma del Río Spain 67 D5
Palma de Mallorca Spain 67 H4
Palmaner India 106 C3
Palmares Brazil 177 K5
Palmares do Sul Brazil 179 A5
Palmas Brazil 179 A4
Palmas 176 I6
Palmas, Cape Liberia 120 C4
Palm Bay U.S.A. 163 D7
Palmdale U.S.A. 158 D4
Palmeira Brazil 179 A4
Palmeira das Missões Brazil 178 F3
Palmeira dos Índios Brazil 177 K5
Palmeirais Brazil 177 J5
Palmeiras Brazil 179 C1
Palmeirinhas, Ponta das *pt* Angola 123 B4
Palmer *research station* Antarctica 188 L2
Palmer *r.* Australia 136 C3
Palmer *watercourse* Australia 135 F6
Palmer *AK* U.S.A. 149 J3
Palmer Land *reg.* Antarctica 188 L2
Palmerston *N.T.* Australia 134 E3
Palmerston *N.T.* Australia *see* **Darwin**
Palmerston Canada 164 E2
Palmerston *atoll* Cook Is 133 J3
Palmerston N.Z. 139 C7
Palmerston North N.Z. 139 E5
Palmerton U.S.A. 165 H3
Palmerville Australia 136 D2
Palmetto Point Bahamas 163 E7
Palmi Italy 68 F5
Palmillas Mex. 167 F4
Palmira Col. 176 C3
Palmira Cuba 163 D8
Palm Springs U.S.A. 158 E5
Palmyra Syria *see* **Tadmur**
Palmyra *MO* U.S.A. 160 F4
Palmyra *PA* U.S.A. 165 G3
Palmyra *VA* U.S.A. 165 F5

▶**Palmyra Atoll** *terr.* N. Pacific Ocean 186 J5
United States Unincorporated Territory.

Palmyras Point India 105 F5
Palni Hills India 106 C4
Palo Alto U.S.A. 158 B3
Palo Blanco Mex. 167 E3
Palo Chino *watercourse* Mex. 157 E7
Palo de las Letras Col. 166 [inset] K8
Palo Duro *watercourse* U.S.A. 161 C5
Paloh *Sarawak* Malaysia 85 E2
Paloich Sudan 108 D7
Palojärvi Fin. 54 M2
Palojoensuu Fin. 54 M2
Palomaa Fin. 54 O2
Palomares Mex. 167 G5
Palomar Mountain U.S.A. 158 E5
Paloncha India 106 D2
Palo Pinto U.S.A. 161 D5
Palopo *Sulawesi* Indon. 83 B3
Palos, Cabo de *c.* Spain 67 F5
Palo Verde U.S.A. 159 F5
Palo Verde, Parque Nacional *nat. park* Costa Rica 166 [inset] I7
Palpetu, Tanjung *pt Buru* Indon. 83 C3
Paltamo Fin. 54 O4
Palu *Sulawesi* Indon. 83 A3
Palu *i.* Indon. 83 B5
Palu *r.* Indon. 83 A3
Palu Turkey 113 E3
Paluan *Mindoro* Phil. 82 C3
Paluan Bay *Mindoro* Phil. 82 C3
Pal'vart Turkm. 111 G2
Palwal India 104 D3
Palwancha India *see* **Paloncha**
Palyeskaya Nizina *marsh* Belarus/Ukr. *see* **Pripet Marshes**

▶**Pamana** *i.* Indon. 83 B5
Most southerly point of Asia.

Pamana Besar *i.* Indon. 83 B5
Pamanukan *Jawa* Indon. 85 D4
Pambarra Moz. 125 L1
Pambero *Sulawesi* Indon. 83 A2
Pambula Australia 138 D6
Pamekasan *Jawa* Indon. 85 F4
Pameungpeuk *Jawa* Indon. 85 D4
Pamidi India 106 C3
Pamiers France 66 E5
Pamir *mts* Asia 111 I2
Pamlico Sound *sea chan.* U.S.A. 163 E5
Pamouscachiou, Lac *l.* Canada 153 H4
Pampa U.S.A. 161 C5
Pampa de Infierno Arg. 178 D3
Pampanua *Sulawesi* Indon. 83 B4
Pampas *reg.* Arg. 178 D5
Pampeluna Spain *see* **Pamplona**
Pamphylia *reg.* Turkey 69 N6
Pamplin U.S.A. 165 F5
Pamplona Col. 176 D2
Pamplona *Negros* Phil. 82 C4
Pamplona Spain 67 F2
Pampow Germany 63 L1
Pamukan, Teluk *b.* Indon. 85 G3
Pamukova Turkey 69 N4
Pamzal India 104 D2
Pana U.S.A. 160 F4
Panabá Mex. 167 H4
Panabo *Mindanao* Phil. 82 D5
Panabutan Bay *Mindanao* Phil. 82 C5
Panaca U.S.A. 159 F3
Panache, Lake Canada 152 E5
Panagtaran Point *Palawan* Phil. 82 B4
Panagyurishte Bulg. 69 K3
Panaitan *i.* Indon. 84 D4
Panaji India 106 B3
Panama *country* Central America 169 H7
Panamá Panama *see* **Panama City**
Panamá, Bahía de *b.* Panama 166 [inset] K7
Panama Canal Panama 166 [inset] K7

▶**Panama City** Panama 166 [inset] K7
Capital of Panama.

Panama City U.S.A. 163 C6
Panamá, Golfo de *g.* Panama 166 [inset] K8
Panama, Gulf of Panama *see* **Panamá, Golfo de**
Panama, Isthmus of Panama 169 I7
Panamá, Istmo de Panama *see* **Panama, Isthmus of**
Panamint Range *mts* U.S.A. 158 E3
Panamint Valley U.S.A. 158 E3
Pananjung Pangandaran, Taman Wisata *nat. park* Indon. 85 E4
Panao Peru 176 C5
Panar *r.* India 99 E8
Panarea, Isola *i.* Italy 68 F5
Panarik Indon. 85 E2
Panarukan *Jawa* Indon. 85 F4
Panay *i.* Phil. 82 C4
Panayarvi Natsional'nyy Park *nat. park* Rus. Fed. 54 Q3
Panay Gulf Phil. 82 C4
Pancake Range *mts* U.S.A. 159 F2
Pančevo Serbia 69 I2
Panchagarh Bangl. 105 G4
Pancingapan, Bukit *mt.* Indon. 85 F2
Pancsova Serbia *see* **Pančevo**
Pancurbatu *Sumatera* Indon. 84 B2
Panda Moz. 125 L3
Pandan *Panay* Phil. 82 C4
Pandan Phil. 82 D3
Pandan, Selat *strait* Sing. 87 [inset]
Pandan Bay *Panay* Phil. 82 C4
Pandang *Kalimantan* Indon. 85 F3
Pandan Reservoir Sing. 87 [inset]
Pandeglang *Jawa* Indon. 84 D4
Pandeiros *r.* Brazil 179 B1
Pandharpur India 106 B2
Pandora Costa Rica 166 [inset] J7
Pandy U.K. 59 E7
Paneas Syria *see* **Bāniyās**
Panevėžys Lith. 55 N9
Panfilov Kazakh. *see* **Zharkent**
Pang, Nam *r.* Myanmar 86 B2
Pangandaran *Jawa* Indon. 85 E4
Pañganiban Phil. 82 D3
Pangean *Sulawesi Barat* Indon. 83 A3
Panghsang Myanmar 86 B2
Pangi Range *mts* Pak. 111 I3
Pangjiabu *Hebei* China 95 H3
Pangkah, Tanjung *pt* Indon. 85 F4
Pangkajene *Sulawesi* Indon. 83 A4
Pangkalanbuun *Kalimantan* Indon. 85 E3
Pangkalanlunang *Sumatera* Indon. 84 B2
Pangkalansusu *Sumatera* Indon. 84 B1
Pangkal Kalong Malaysia 84 C1
Pangkalpinang Indon. 84 D3
Pangkalsiang, Tanjung *pt* Indon. 83 B3
Panglang Myanmar 86 B1
Panglao *i.* Phil. 82 C4
Pangman Canada 151 J5
Pangnirtung Canada 147 L3
Pangody Rus. Fed. 76 I3
Pangong Tso *salt l.* China/India *see* **Bangong Co**
Pangrango *vol.* Indon. 84 D4
Pang Sida National Park Thai. 87 C4
Pang Sua, Sungai *r.* Sing. 87 [inset]
Pangtara Myanmar 96 C4
Pangu He *r.* China 90 B1
Panguitch U.S.A. 159 G3
Pangujon, Tanjung *pt* Indon. 85 E3
Panguruan *Sumatera* Indon. 84 B2
Pangutaran *i.* Phil. 82 C5
Pangutaran Group *is* Phil. 82 C5
Panhandle U.S.A. 161 C5
Panipat India 104 D3
Panir Pak. 111 G4
Panitan *Palawan* Phil. 82 B4
Panj Tajik. 111 H2
Panjāb Afgh. 111 G3
Panjakent Tajik. 111 G2
Panjang *Sumatera* Indon. 84 D4
Panjang *i.* Indon. 85 E2
Panjang *i.* Indon. 85 G2
Panjang, Bukit Sing. 87 [inset]
Panjang, Selat *sea chan.* Indon. 84 C2
Panjgur Pak. 111 G5
Panjim India *see* **Panaji**
Panjin *Liaoning* China *see* **Panshan**
Panji Poyon Tajik. 111 H2
Panjnad *r.* Pak. 111 H4
Panjshīr *reg.* Afgh. 111 H3
Pankakoski Fin. 54 Q5
Pankof, Cape *AK* U.S.A. 148 G5
Panlian China *see* **Miyi**
Panna India 104 E4
Panna *reg.* India 104 D4
Pannawonica Australia 134 B5
Pano Lefkara Cyprus 107 A2
Panopah *Kalimantan* Indon. 85 E3
Panorama Brazil 179 A3
Panormus *Sicily* Italy *see* **Palermo**
Panshan *Liaoning* China 95 J3
Panshi China 90 B4
Panshui China *see* **Pu'an**
Pantai *Kalimantan* Indon. 85 G3

antaicermin, Gunung mt. Indon. 84 C3

▶Pantanal marsh Brazil 177 G7
Largest area of wetlands in the world.

antanal Matogrossense, Parque Nacional do nat. park Brazil 177 G7
antano U.S.A. 159 H6
antar i. Indon. 83 C5
antelaria Sicily Italy see Pantelleria
antelleria Sicily Italy 68 D6
antelleria, Isola di i. Sicily Italy 68 E6
ante Macassar East Timor 83 C5
antemakassar East Timor see Pante Macassar
antha Myanmar 86 A2
anther r. U.S.A. 164 B5
anth Piploda India 104 C5
anticapaeum Ukr. see Kerch
antonlabu Sumatera Indon. 84 B1
antukan Mindanao Phil. 82 D5
anua, Cagar Alam nature res. Indon. 83 B2
ánuco Sinaloa Mex. 161 B8
ánuco Veracruz Mex. 168 E4
ánuco r. Mex. 167 F4
anwari India 104 D4
anxian China 96 E3
anyu China 97 G4
anzhihua China 96 D3
anzi Dem. Rep. Congo 123 B4
anzos Guat. 167 H6
aola Italy 68 G5
aola U.S.A. 160 E4
aoli U.S.A. 164 B4
aoni Seram Indon. 83 D3
aoua Cent. Afr. Rep. 122 B3
aôy Pêt Cambodia 87 C4
ápa Hungary 68 G1
apa, Monte del mt. Italy 68 F4
apagni r. India 106 C3
āpa'ikou U.S.A. 157 [inset]
apakura N.Z. 139 E3
apanasam India 106 C4
apanoa Mex. 167 E5
apantla Mex. 168 E4
apar Sabah Malaysia 85 F1
aparoa National Park N.Z. 139 C6
apa Stour i. U.K. 60 [inset]
apa Westray i. U.K. 60 G1
apay i. U.K. see Papa Westray

Papeete Fr. Polynesia 187 K7
Capital of French Polynesia.

apenburg Germany 63 H1
aphos Cyprus 107 A2
aphus Cyprus see Paphos
apillion U.S.A. 160 D3
apoose Lake U.S.A. 159 F3
appenheim Germany 63 K6
apua prov. Indon. 83 D3
apua, Gulf of P.N.G. 81 K8

Papua New Guinea country Oceania 132 E2
2nd largest and 2nd most populous country in Oceania.

a Qal'eh Iran 110 D4
ar U.K. 59 C8
ará r. Brazil 179 B2
ara i. Indon. 83 C2
ará, Rio do r. Brazil 177 I4
araburdoo Australia 135 B5
aracale Luzon Phil. 82 C3
aracatu Brazil 179 B2
aracatu r. Brazil 179 B2
aracel Islands S. China Sea 80 E3
arachilna Australia 137 B6
arachute U.S.A. 159 I2
araćin Serbia 69 I3
aracuru Brazil 177 K4
ará de Minas Brazil 179 B2
aradis Canada 152 F4
aradise r. Canada 153 K3
aradise AK U.S.A. 148 G3
aradise U.S.A. 158 C2
aradise Hill Canada 151 I4
aradise Peak U.S.A. 158 E2
aradise River Canada 153 K3
arado Sumbawa Indon. 85 G5
aradwip India 105 F5
araetonium Egypt see Marsá Maţrūḩ
aragominas Brazil 177 I4
aragould U.S.A. 161 F4
aragua i. Phil. see Palawan
araguaçu Paulista Brazil 179 A3
araguay r. Arg./Para. 178 E3
araguay country S. America 178 E2
araíba do Sul r. Brazil 179 C3
arainen Fin. see Pargas
araíso Campeche Mex. 167 G5
araíso Tabasco Mex. 167 G5
araíso do Norte Brazil 177 I6
araisópolis Brazil 179 B3
arak Iran 110 D5
arakou Benin 120 D4
aralakhemundi India 106 E2
aralkot India 106 D2
aramagudi India see Paramakkudi
aramakkudi India 106 C4

▶Paramaribo Suriname 177 G2
Capital of Suriname.

aramillo, Parque Nacional nat. park Col. 176 C2
aramirim Brazil 179 C1
aramo Frontino mt. Col. 176 C2
aramus U.S.A. 165 H3
aramushir, Ostrov i. Rus. Fed. 77 Q4
aran watercourse Israel 107 B4
araná Arg. 178 D4
aranã Brazil 179 B1
Paraná r. Brazil 179 A1
Paraná state Brazil 179 A4

▶Paraná r. S. America 178 E4
Part of the Río de la Plata - Paraná, 2nd longest river in South America.

Paraná, Serra do hills Brazil 179 B1
Paranaguá Brazil 179 A4
Paranaíba Brazil 179 A2
Paranaíba r. Brazil 179 A3
Paranapiacaba, Serra mts Brazil 179 A4
Paranavaí Brazil 178 F2
Parang i. Indon. 85 E4
Parang Phil. 82 C5
Parangi Aru r. Sri Lanka 106 D4
Parang Pass India 104 D2
Parângul Mare, Vârful mt. Romania 69 J2
Paranthan Sri Lanka 106 D4
Paraopeba Brazil 179 B2
Parapara Halmahera Indon. 83 C2
Pārapāra Iraq 113 G4
Paraparaumu N.Z. 139 E5
Paras Mex. 161 D7
Paras Pak. 111 I3
Paraspori, Akra pt Greece see Paraspori, Akrotirio
Paraspori, Akrotirio pt Greece 69 L7
Parateca Brazil 179 C1
Paratinga Brazil 179 C1
Parāū, Kūh-e mt. Iraq 113 G4
Paraúna Brazil 179 A2
Parbhani India 106 C2
Parchim Germany 63 L1
Parding China 105 G2
Pardo r. Bahia Brazil 179 D1
Pardo r. Mato Grosso do Sul Brazil 178 F2
Pardo r. São Paulo Brazil 179 A3
Pardoo Australia 134 B5
Pardubice Czech Rep. 57 O5
Parece Vela i. Japan see Okino-Tori-shima
Pare Chu r. China 99 B6
Parecis, Serra dos hills Brazil 176 F6
Paredón Coahuila Mex. 167 E3
Pareh Iran 110 B2
Parenda India 106 B2
Parenggean Kalimantan Indon. 85 F3
Parent Canada 152 G5
Parent, Lac l. Canada 152 F4
Pareora N.Z. 139 C7
Parepare Sulawesi Indon. 83 A4
Parga Greece 69 I5
Pargas Fin. 55 M6
Parghelia Italy 68 F5
Pargi India 106 C2
Paria, Gulf of Trin. and Tob./Venez. 169 L6
Paria, Península de pen. Venez. 176 F1
Pariaman Sumatera Indon. 84 C3
Paria Plateau U.S.A. 159 G3
Parida, Isla i. Panama 166 [inset] J7
Parigi Sulawesi Indon. 83 B3
Parikkala Fin. 55 P6
Parikud Islands India 106 E2
Parima, Serra mts Brazil 176 F3
Parima-Tapirapecó, Parque Nacional nat. park Venez. 176 F3
Parintins Brazil 177 G4
Paris Canada 164 E2

▶Paris France 62 C6
Capital of France. 3rd most populous city in Europe.

Paris IL U.S.A. 164 B4
Paris KY U.S.A. 164 C4
Paris MO U.S.A. 160 E4
Paris TN U.S.A. 161 F4
Paris TX U.S.A. 161 E5
Paris (Charles de Gaulle) airport France 62 C5
Paris (Orly) airport France 62 C6
Paris Crossing U.S.A. 164 C4
Parit Buntar Malaysia 84 C1
Pārīz Iran 110 D4
Pārk Iran 111 F5
Park U.K. 61 E3
Parkano Fin. 55 M5
Park City U.S.A. 164 B5
Parke Lake Canada 153 K3
Parker AZ U.S.A. 159 F4
Parker CO U.S.A. 156 G5
Parker Dam U.S.A. 159 F4
Parker Lake Canada 151 M2
Parker Range hills Australia 135 B8
Parkersburg U.S.A. 164 E4
Parkers Lake U.S.A. 164 C5
Parkes Australia 138 D4
Park Falls U.S.A. 160 F2
Park Forest U.S.A. 164 B3
Parkhar Tajik. see Farkhor
Parkhill Canada 164 E2
Park Rapids U.S.A. 160 E2
Parkutta Pak. 104 D2
Park Valley U.S.A. 156 E4
Parla Kimedi India see Paralakhemundi
Parlakimidi India see Paralakhemundi
Parli Vaijnath India 106 C2
Parlung Zangbo r. China 96 B2
Parma Italy 68 D2
Parma ID U.S.A. 156 D4
Parma OH U.S.A. 164 E3
Parnaíba Brazil 177 J4
Parnaíba r. Brazil 177 J4
Parnassus N.Z. 139 D6
Parnassus, Mount mt. Greece see Liakoura
Parner India 106 B2
Parnon mts Greece see Parnonas
Parnonas mts Greece 69 J6
Pärnu Estonia 55 N7
Pärnu-Jaagupi Estonia 55 N7
Paro Bhutan 105 G4
Paroikia Greece 69 K6
Parona Turkey see Fındık
Paroo watercourse Australia 138 A3
Paroo Channel watercourse Australia 138 A3
Paroo-Darling National Park 138 E3
Paropamisus mts Afgh. see Safīd Kūh
Paroreang, Bukit mt. Indon. 83 A3
Paros Notio Aigaio Greece see Paroikia
Paros i. Greece 69 K6
Parowan U.S.A. 159 G3
Parral Chile 178 B5
Parramatta Australia 138 E4
Parramore Island U.S.A. 165 H5
Parras Mex. 166 E3
Parrett r. U.K. 59 D7
Parrita Costa Rica 166 [inset] I7
Parry, Cape N.W.T. Canada 149 P1
Parry, Kap c. Greenland see Kangaarsussuaq
Parry, Lac l. Canada 152 G2
Parry Bay Canada 147 J3
Parry Channel Canada 147 G2
Parry Islands Canada 147 G2
Parry Peninsula N.W.T. Canada 149 P1
Parry Range hills Australia 134 A5
Parry Sound Canada 164 E1
Parsnip Peak U.S.A. 159 F2
Parsons KS U.S.A. 161 E4
Parsons WV U.S.A. 164 F4
Parsons Lake N.W.T. Canada 149 N1
Parsons Range hills Australia 134 F3
Parta Xizang China 99 E7
Partabgarh India 106 B2
Partabpur India 105 E5
Partenstein Germany 63 J4
Parthenay France 66 D3
Partida, Isla i. Mex. 166 C3
Partizansk Rus. Fed. 90 D4
Partney U.K. 58 H5
Partridge r. Canada 152 E4
Partry Ireland 61 C4
Partry Mts hills Ireland 61 C4
Paru r. Brazil 177 H4
Pārūd Iran 111 F5
Paryang Xizang China 99 C7
Parygino Kazakh. 98 D2
Parys S. Africa 125 H4
Pasa Dağı mt. Turkey 112 D3
Pasadena CA U.S.A. 158 D4
Pasadena TX U.S.A. 161 E6
Pasado, Cabo c. Ecuador 176 B4
Pa Sang Thai. 86 B3
Pasangkayu Sulawesi Barat Indon. 83 A3
Pasarbantal Sumatera Indon. 84 C3
Pasarseblat Sumatera Indon. 84 C3
Pasarseluma Sumatera Indon. 84 C4
Pasarwajo Sulawesi Indon. 83 B4
Pasawng Myanmar 86 B3
Pascagama r. Canada 152 G4
Pascagoula U.S.A. 161 F6
Pascagoula r. U.S.A. 161 F6
Paşcani Romania 69 L1
Pasco U.S.A. 156 D3
Pascoal, Monte hill Brazil 179 D2
Pascua, Isla de i. S. Pacific Ocean see Easter Island
Pascual Phil. 82 C3
Pas de Calais strait France/U.K. see Dover, Strait of
Pasewalk Germany 57 O4
Pasfield Lake Canada 151 J3
Pasha Rus. Fed. 52 G3
Pashih Haihsia sea chan. Phil./Taiwan see Bashi Channel
Pashkovo Rus. Fed. 90 C2
Pashkovskiy Rus. Fed. 53 H7
Pashtun Zarghun Afgh. 111 F3
Pashū'īyeh Iran 110 E4
Pasig Luzon Phil. 82 C3
Pasi Ga Myanmar 86 B1
Pasige i. Indon. 83 C2
Pasighat India 105 H3
Pasinler Turkey 113 F3
Pasir Gudang Malaysia 87 [inset]
Pasirian Jawa Indon. 85 F5
Pasir Mas Malaysia 84 C1
Pasirpangarayan Sumatera Indon. 84 C2
Pasir Putih Malaysia 84 C1
Pasitelu, Pulau-pulau is Indon. 83 B4
Paskūh Iran 111 F5
Pasni Pak. 185 M4
Paso Caballos Guat. 167 H5
Paso de los Toros Uruguay 178 E4
Paso de San Antonio Mex. 161 C6
Pasok Myanmar 86 A2
Paso Real Hond. 166 [inset] I6
Paso Robles U.S.A. 158 C4
Pasquia Hills Canada 151 K4
Passaic U.S.A. 165 H3
Passa Tempo Brazil 179 B3
Passau Germany 57 N6
Passi Panay Phil. 82 C4
Passo del San Gottardo Switz. see St Gotthard Pass
Passo Fundo Brazil 178 F3
Passos Brazil 179 B3
Passur r. Bangl. see Pusur
Passuri Nadi r. Bangl. see Pusur
Pastavy Belarus 55 O9
Pastaza r. Peru 176 C4
Pasto Col. 176 C3
Pastol Bay AK U.S.A. 148 G3
Pastora Peak U.S.A. 159 I3
Pastos Bons Brazil 177 J5
Pasu Pak. 104 C1
Pasuquin Luzon Phil. 82 C2
Pasur Turkey see Kulp
Pasuruan Jawa Indon. 85 F4
Pasvalys Lith. 55 N8
Pasvikelva r. Europe see Patsoyoki
Pata i. Phil. 82 C5
Patache, Punta pt Chile 178 B2
Patagonia reg. Arg. 178 B8
Pataliputra India see Patna
Patan Gujarat India see Somnath
Patan Gujarat India 104 C5
Patan Mahar. India 106 B2
Patan Nepal 105 F4
Patan Pak. 111 I3
Patandar, Koh-i- mt. Pak. 111 G5
Patani Halmahera Indon. 83 D2
Patavium Italy see Padua
Patea N.Z. 139 E4
Patea inlet N.Z. see Doubtful Sound
Pate Island Kenya 122 E4
Pateley Bridge U.K. 58 F4
Patensie S. Africa 124 G7
Patera India 104 D4
Paterson Australia 138 E4
Paterson r. Australia 138 C2
Paterson U.S.A. 165 H3
Paterson Range hills Australia 134 C5
Pathanamthitta India 106 C4
Pathankot India 104 C2
Pathari India 104 D5
Pathein Myanmar see Bassein
Pathfinder Reservoir U.S.A. 156 G4
Pathiu Thai. 87 B5
Pathum Thani Thai. 87 C4
Pati Jawa Indon. 85 E4
Patía r. Col. 176 C3
Patiala India 104 D3
Patinti, Selat sea chan. Maluku Indon. 83 C3
Patiro, Tanjung pt Indon. 83 B4
Patkai Bum mts India/Myanmar 105 H4
Patkaklik Xinjiang China 99 D5
Patmos i. Greece 69 L6
Patna India 105 F4
Patna Orissa India 105 F5
Patnagarh India 105 E5
Patnanongan i. Phil. 82 C3
Patnos Turkey 113 F3
Pato Branco Brazil 178 F3
Patoda India 106 B2
Patoka r. U.S.A. 164 B4
Patoka Lake U.S.A. 164 B4
Patos Albania 69 H4
Patos Brazil 177 K5
Patos, Lagoa dos l. Brazil 178 F4
Patos de Minas Brazil 179 B2
Patquía Arg. 178 C4
Patra Greece see Patras
Patrae Greece see Patras
Pátrai Greece see Patras
Patras Greece 69 I5
Patreksfjörður Iceland 54 [inset]
Patricio Lynch, Isla i. Chile 178 A7
Patrick Creek watercourse Australia 136 D4
Patrimônio Brazil 179 A2
Patrocínio Brazil 179 B2
Paṭrū Iran 111 E3
Patsoyoki r. Europe 54 Q2
Pattadakal tourist site India 106 B2
Pattani Thai. 87 C6
Pattani, Mae Nam r. Thai. 84 C1
Pattaya Thai. 87 C4
Pattensen Germany 63 J2
Patterson CA U.S.A. 158 C3
Patterson LA U.S.A. 161 F6
Patterson, Mount Y.T. Canada 149 N2
Patti India 105 E4
Patti Maluku Indon. 83 C5
Pattijoki Fin. 54 N4
Pättikkä Fin. 54 L2
Patton U.S.A. 165 F3
Pattullo, Mount B.C. Canada 149 O4
Patu Brazil 177 K5
Patuakhali Bangl. 105 G5
Patuanak Canada 151 J4
Patuca r. Hond. 166 [inset] I6
Patuca, Punta pt Hond. 166 [inset] I6
Patucas, Parque Nacional nat. park Hond. 166 [inset] I6
Patur India 106 C1
Patuxent r. U.S.A. 165 G4
Patuxent Range mts Antarctica 188 L1
Patvinsuon kansallispuisto nat. park Fin. 54 Q5
Pátzcuaro Mex. 167 E5
Pau France 66 D5
Pauhunri mt. China/India 105 G4
Pauillac France 66 D4
Pauini Brazil 176 E5
Pauiní r. Brazil 176 E5
Pauk Myanmar 86 A2
Paukkaung Myanmar 86 A3
Paulatuk N.W.T. Canada 149 Q1
Paulatuuq N.W.T. Canada see Paulatuk
Paulden U.S.A. 159 G4
Paulding U.S.A. 164 C3
Paulicéia Brazil 179 A3
Paulis Dem. Rep. Congo see Isiro
Paul Island Canada 153 J2
Paulo Afonso Brazil 177 K5
Paulo de Faria Brazil 179 A3
Pauloff Harbor AK U.S.A. 148 G5
Paulpietersburg S. Africa 125 J4
Paul Roux S. Africa 125 H5
Pauls Valley U.S.A. 161 D5
Paumotu, Îles is Fr. Polynesia see Tuamotu Islands
Paung Myanmar 86 B3
Paungbyin Myanmar 86 A1
Paungde Myanmar 86 A3
Pauni India 106 C1
Pauri India 104 D3
Pavagada India 106 C3
Pavão Brazil 179 C2
Pāveh Iran 110 B3
Pavia Italy 68 C2
Pāvilosta Latvia 55 L8
Pavino Rus. Fed. 52 J4
Pavlikeni Bulg. 69 K3
Pavlodar Kazakh. 102 E1
Pavlodarskaya Oblast' admin. div. Kazakh. 98 B1
Pavlof Bay AK U.S.A. 148 G5
Pavlof Islands AK U.S.A. 148 G5
Pavlof Volcano AK U.S.A. 149 [inset]
Pavlograd Ukr. see Pavlohrad
Pavlohrad Ukr. 53 G6
Pavlovka Rus. Fed. 53 J5
Pavlovo Rus. Fed. 52 I5
Pavlovsk Altayskiy Kray Rus. Fed. 88 E2
Pavlovsk Voronezhskaya Oblast' Rus. Fed. 53 I6
Pavlovskaya Rus. Fed. 53 H7
Pawahku Myanmar 86 B1
Pawai India 104 E4
Pawan r. Indon. 85 E3
Pawayan Uttar Prad. India 99 C7
Pawnee U.S.A. 161 D4
Pawnee r. U.S.A. 160 D4
Pawnee City U.S.A. 160 D3
Paw Paw MI U.S.A. 164 C2
Paw Paw WV U.S.A. 165 F4
Pawtucket U.S.A. 165 J3
Pawut Myanmar 87 B4
Paxson AK U.S.A. 149 K3
Paxton U.S.A. 164 A3
Payahe Halmahera Indon. 83 C2
Payakumbuh Sumatera Indon. 84 C3
Paya Lebar Sing. 87 [inset]
Payette U.S.A. 156 D3
Pay-Khoy, Khrebet hills Rus. Fed. 76 H3
Payne Canada see Kangirsuk
Payne, Lac l. Canada 152 G2
Paynes Creek U.S.A. 158 C1
Payne's Find Australia 135 B7
Paynesville U.S.A. 160 E2
Paysandú Uruguay 178 E4
Pays de Bray reg. France 62 B5
Payshanba Uzbek. 111 G1
Payson U.S.A. 159 H4
Payung, Tanjung pt Malaysia 85 F2
Payzawat Xinjiang China see Jiashi
Pazar Turkey 113 F2
Pazarcık Turkey 112 E3
Pazardzhik Bulg. 69 K3
Pazin Croatia 68 E2
Pe Myanmar 87 B4
Peabody KS U.S.A. 160 D4
Peabody MA U.S.A. 165 J2

▶Peace r. Canada 150 I3
Part of the Mackenzie-Peace-Finlay, the 2nd longest river in North America.

Peace Point Canada 151 H3
Peace River Canada 150 G3
Peach Creek U.S.A. 164 E5
Peach Springs U.S.A. 159 G4
Peacock Hills Canada 151 I1
Peak Charles hill Australia 135 C8
Peak Charles National Park Australia 135 C8
Peak District National Park U.K. 58 F5
Peake watercourse Australia 137 B6
Peaked Mountain hill U.S.A. 162 G2
Peak Hill N.S.W. Australia 138 D4
Peak Hill W.A. Australia 135 B6
Peale, Mount U.S.A. 159 I2
Peanut U.S.A. 158 B1
Pearce U.S.A. 159 I6
Pearce Point Australia 134 E3
Peard Bay AK U.S.A. 148 H1
Pearisburg U.S.A. 164 E5
Pearl r. U.S.A. 161 F6
Pearl Harbor inlet U.S.A. 157 [inset]
Pearsall U.S.A. 161 D6
Pearson U.S.A. 163 D6
Pearston S. Africa 125 G7
Peary Channel Canada 147 I2
Peary Land reg. Greenland 189 J1
Pease r. U.S.A. 161 D5
Peawanuck Canada 152 D3
Pebane Moz. 123 D5
Pebas Peru 176 D4
Pebengko Sulawesi Indon. 83 B3
Peć Kosovo see Pejë
Peçanha Brazil 179 C2
Pecan Island LA U.S.A. 167 G2
Peças, Ilha das i. Brazil 179 A4
Pechenga Rus. Fed. 54 Q2
Pechora Rus. Fed. 52 M2
Pechora r. Rus. Fed. 52 L1
Pechora Sea Rus. Fed. see Pechorskoye More
Pechorskaya Guba b. Rus. Fed. 52 L1
Pechorskoye More sea Rus. Fed. 189 G2
Pechory Rus. Fed. 55 O8
Peck U.S.A. 164 D2
Peck, Mount B.C. Canada 150 E3
Pecos U.S.A. 161 C6
Pecos r. U.S.A. 161 C6
Pécs Hungary 68 H1
Pedasí Panama 166 [inset] J8
Pedda Vagu r. India 106 C2
Pedder, Lake Australia 137 [inset]
Peddie S. Africa 125 H7
Pedernales Dom. Rep. 169 J5
Pedersöre Fin. 54 M5
Pediaios r. Cyprus 107 A2
Pediva Angola 123 B5
Pediwang Halmahera Indon. 83 C2
Pedra Azul Brazil 179 C1
Pedra Preta, Serra da mts Brazil 179 A1
Pedras de Maria da Cruz Brazil 179 B1
Pedregal Panama 166 [inset] J7
Pedregulho Brazil 179 B3
Pedreiras Brazil 177 J4
Pedriceña Mex. 166 E3
Pedro, Point Sri Lanka 106 D4
Pedro Bay AK U.S.A. 148 I4
Pedro Betancourt Cuba 163 D8
Pedro II, Ilha reg. Brazil/Venez. 176 E3
Pedro Juan Caballero Para. 178 E2
Peebles U.K. 60 F5
Peebles U.S.A. 164 D4
Pee Dee r. U.S.A. 163 E5
Peekskill U.S.A. 165 I3
Peel r. Australia 138 E3
Peel r. N.W.T./Y.T. Canada 149 N1
Peel Isle of Man 58 C4
Peel River Game Preserve nature res. N.W.T./Y.T. Canada 149 N2
Peer Belgium 62 F3
Peera Peera Poolanna Lake salt flat Australia 137 B5
Peerless Lake Canada 150 H3
Peerless Lake l. Canada 150 H3
Peers Canada 150 G4
Peery Lake salt flat Australia 138 A3
Pegasus Bay N.Z. 139 D6
Pegnitz Germany 63 L5
Pegu Myanmar 86 B3
Pegunungan Latimojong nature res. Indon. 83 B3
Pegunungan Peruhumpenai nature res. Indon. 83 B3
Pegu Yoma mts Myanmar 86 A3
Pegysh Rus. Fed. 52 K3
Pehuajó Arg. 178 D5
Peikang Taiwan 97 I4
Peine Chile 178 C2
Peine Germany 63 K2
Peint India 106 B1
Peipsi järv l. Estonia/Rus. Fed. see Peipus, Lake
Peipus, Lake Estonia/Rus. Fed. 55 O7
Peiraias Greece see Piraeus
Pei Shan mts China see Bei Shan
Peißen Germany 63 L3
Peixe Brazil 177 I6
Peixe r. Brazil 179 A1
Peixian Jiangsu China see Pizhou
Peixian Jiangsu China 95 I5
Peixoto de Azevedo Brazil 177 H6
Pejantan i. Indon. 84 D2
Pejë Kosovo 69 I3
Pèk Laos see Phônsavan
Peka Lesotho 125 H5
Pekabata Sulawesi Indon. 83 A3
Pekalongan Jawa Indon. 85 E4
Pekan Malaysia 84 C2
Pekanbaru Sumatera Indon. 84 C2
Pekin U.S.A. 160 F3
Peking Beijing China see Beijing
Pekinga Benin 120 D3
Pelabuhan Klang Malaysia 84 C2
Pelagie, Isole is Sicily Italy 68 E7
Pelaihari Kalimantan Indon. 85 F3
Pelalawan Sumatera Indon. 84 C2
Pelapis i. Indon. 85 E3
Pelawanbesar Kalimantan Indon. 85 G2
Peleaga, Vârful mt. Romania 69 J2
Pelee Island Canada 164 D3
Pelee Point Canada 164 D3
Peleliu i. Palau 82 [inset]
Peleng i. Indon. 83 B3
Peleng, Selat sea chan. Indon. 83 B3
Peleng, Teluk b. Indon. 83 B3
Peles Rus. Fed. 52 K3
Pélican, Lac du l. Canada 153 G2
Pelican Lake Canada 151 K4
Pelican Lake U.S.A. 160 E1
Pelican Narrows Canada 151 K4
Pelkosenniemi Fin. 54 O3
Pella S. Africa 124 D5
Pellatt Lake Canada 151 I1
Pelleluhu Islands P.N.G. 81 K7
Pello Fin. 54 M3
Pelly r. Canada 150 C2
Pelly Crossing Y.T. Canada 149 M3
Pelly Island N.W.T. Canada 149 N1
Pelly Lake Canada 151 K1
Pelly Mountains Y.T. Canada 149 N3
Pelokang is Indon. 85 G4
Peloponnese admin. reg. Greece 69 J6
Pelopónnesos admin. reg. Greece see Peloponnese
Peloponnisos admin. reg. Greece see Peloponnese
Pelotas Brazil 178 F4
Pelotas, Rio das r. Brazil 179 A4
Pelusium tourist site Egypt 107 A4
Pelusium, Bay of Egypt see Ţīnah, Khalīj aţ
Pemalang Jawa Indon. 85 E4
Pemangkat Kalimantan Indon. 85 E2
Pemarung, Pulau i. Indon. 85 G3
Pematangsiantar Sumatera Indon. 84 B2
Pemba Moz. 123 E5
Pemba Island Tanz. 123 D4
Pemberton Canada 150 F5
Pembina r. Canada 150 H4
Pembina r. U.S.A. 160 D1
Pembine U.S.A. 162 C2
Pembre Indon. 81 J8
Pembroke Canada 152 F5
Pembroke U.K. 59 C7
Pembroke U.S.A. 163 D5
Pembrokeshire Coast National Park U.K. 59 B7
Pembuanghulu Kalimantan Indon. 85 F3
Pemuar Kalimantan Indon. 85 E3
Pen India 106 B2
Peña Cerredo mt. Spain see Torrecerredo
Peñalara mt. Spain 67 E3
Penamar Brazil 179 C1
Penambo Range mts Malaysia see Tama Abu, Banjaran
Penampang Sabah Malaysia 85 G1
Peña Nevada, Cerro mt. Mex. 168 E4
Penang state Malaysia see Pinang
Penápolis Brazil 179 A3
Peñaranda de Bracamonte Spain 67 D3
Penarie Australia 138 A5
Penarlâg U.K. see Hawarden

Peñarroya *mt.* Spain **67** F3
Peñarroya-Pueblonuevo Spain **67** D4
Penarth U.K. **59** D7
Peñas, Cabo de *c.* Spain **67** D2
Penas, Golfo de *g.* Chile **178** A7
Peñas Blancas Nicaragua **166** [inset] I7
Penasi, Pulau *i.* Indon. **87** A6
Peña Ubiña *mt.* Spain **67** D2
Pender U.S.A. **160** D3
Pendle Hill *hill* U.K. **58** E5
Pendleton U.S.A. **156** D3
Pendleton Bay Canada **150** E4
Pendopo *Sumatera* Indon. **84** C3
Pend Oreille *r.* U.S.A. **156** D2
Pend Oreille Lake U.S.A. **156** D2
Pendra India **105** E5
Penduv India **106** B2
Pendzhikent Tajik. *see* **Panjakent**
Penebangan *i.* Indon. **85** E3
Peneda Gerês, Parque Nacional da *nat. park* Port. **67** B3
Penetanguishene Canada **164** F1
Penfro U.K. *see* **Pembroke**
Peng'an China **96** E2
Penganga *r.* India **106** C2
Peng Chau *i.* *H.K.* China **97** [inset]
P'engchia Yü *i.* Taiwan **97** I3
Penge Dem. Rep. Congo **123** C4
Penge S. Africa **125** J3
P'enghu Ch'üntao *is* Taiwan **97** H4
P'enghu Liehtao *is* Taiwan *see* **P'enghu Ch'üntao**
P'enghu Tao *i.* Taiwan **97** H4
Pengiki *i.* Indon. **85** E2
Pengkalan Hulu Malaysia **84** C1
Peng Kang *hill* Sing. **87** [inset]
Penglai *Shandong* China **95** J4
Penglaizhen China *see* **Daying**
Pengshan China **96** D2
Pengshui China **97** F2
Pengwa Myanmar **86** A2
Pengxi China **96** E2
Penha Brazil **179** A4
Penhoek Pass S. Africa **125** H6
Penhook U.S.A. **164** F5
Peniche Port. **67** B4
Penicuik U.K. **60** F5
Penida *i.* Indon. **85** F5
Penig Germany **63** M4
Peninga Rus. Fed. **54** R5
Peninsular Malaysia Malaysia **84** C2
Penitente, Serra do *hills* Brazil **177** I5
Penn U.S.A. *see* **Penn Hills**
Pennell Coast Antarctica **188** H2
Penn Hills U.S.A. **164** F3
Pennine, Alpi *mts* Italy/Switz. **68** B2
Pennine Alps *mts* Italy/Switz. *see* **Pennine, Alpi**
Pennines *hills* U.K. **58** E4
Pennington Gap U.S.A. **164** D5
Pennsburg U.S.A. **165** H3
Penns Grove U.S.A. **165** H4
Pennsville U.S.A. **165** H4
Pennsylvania *state* U.S.A. **164** F3
Pennville U.S.A. **164** C3
Penn Yan U.S.A. **165** G2
Penny Icecap Canada **147** L3
Penny Point Antarctica **188** H1
Penola Australia **137** C8
Peñón Blanco Mex. **166** D3
Penong Australia **135** F7
Penonomé Panama **166** [inset] J7
Penrhyn *atoll* Cook Is **187** J6
Penrhyn Basin *sea feature* S. Pacific Ocean **187** J6
Penrith Australia **138** E4
Penrith U.K. **58** E4
Pensacola U.S.A. **163** C6
Pensacola Mountains Antarctica **188** L1
Pensiangan *Sabah* Malaysia **85** G1
Pensi La *pass* India **104** D2
Pentadaktylos Range *mts* Cyprus **107** A2
Pentakota India **106** D2
Pentecost Island Vanuatu **133** G3
Pentecôte, Île *i.* Vanuatu *see* **Pentecost Island**
Penticton Canada **150** G5
Pentire Point U.K. **59** B8
Pentland Australia **136** D4
Pentland Firth *sea chan.* U.K. **60** F2
Pentland Hills U.K. **60** F5
Pentwater U.S.A. **164** B2
Penuba Indon. **84** D3
Penuguan *Sumatera* Indon. **84** D3
Penunjuk, Tanjung *pt* Malaysia **84** C1
Penwegon Myanmar **86** B3
Pen-y-Bont ar Ogwr U.K. *see* **Bridgend**
Penygadair *hill* U.K. **59** D6
Penylan Lake Canada **151** J2
Penyu, Kepulauan *is* *Maluku* Indon. **83** C4
Penza Rus. Fed. **53** J5
Penzance U.K. **59** B8
Penzhinskaya Guba *b.* Rus. Fed. **77** R3
Peoria *AZ* U.S.A. **159** G5
Peoria *IL* U.S.A. **160** F3
Peotone U.S.A. **164** B3
Peper, Teluk *b.* Indon. *see* **Lada, Teluk**
Pequeña, Punta *pt* Mex. **166** B3
Pequop Mountains U.S.A. **159** F1
Peradeniya Sri Lanka **106** D5
Pera Head *hd* Australia **136** C2
Perak *i.* Malaysia **84** B1
Perak *r.* Malaysia **84** C1
Perak *state* Malaysia **84** C1
Perales del Alfambra Spain **67** F3
Perambalur India **106** C4
Perämeren kansallispuisto *nat. park* Fin. **54** N4
Peranap *Sumatera* Indon. **84** C3
Peräseinäjoki Fin. **54** M5
Percé Canada **153** I4
Percival Lakes *salt flat* Australia **134** D5
Percy U.S.A. **165** J1
Percy Isles Australia **136** E4
Percy Reach *l.* Canada **165** G1
Perdizes Brazil **179** B2
Perdu, Lac *l.* Canada **153** H4
Peregrebnoye Rus. Fed. **51** T3
Pereira Col. **176** C3
Pereira Barreto Brazil **179** A3
Pereira de Eça Angola *see* **Ondjiva**
Pere Marquette *r.* U.S.A. **164** B2
Peremul Par *reef* India **106** B4
Peremyshlyany Ukr. **53** E6
Perenjori Australia **135** B7
Pereslavl'-Zalesskiy Rus. Fed. **52** H4
Pereslavskiy Natsional'nyy Park *nat. park* Rus. Fed. **52** H4
Pereyaslavka Rus. Fed. **90** D3
Pereyaslav-Khmel'nitskiy Ukr. *see* **Pereyaslav-Khmel'nyts'kyy**
Pereyaslav-Khmel'nyts'kyy Ukr. **53** F6
Perforated Island Thai. *see* **Bon, Ko**
Pergamino Arg. **178** D4
Perhentian Besar, Pulau *i.* Malaysia **84** C1
Perho Fin. **54** N5
Péribonka, Lac *l.* Canada **153** H4
Perico Arg. **178** C2
Pericos *Sinaloa* Mex. **166** D3
Peridot U.S.A. **159** H5
Périgueux France **66** E4
Perijá, Parque Nacional *nat. park* Venez. **176** D2
Perija, Sierra de *mts* Venez. **176** D2
Peringat Malaysia **84** C1
Periyar India *see* **Erode**
Perkasie U.S.A. **165** H3
Perkat, Tanjung *pt* Indon. **84** D3
Perlas, Archipiélago de las *is* Panama **166** [inset] K7
Perlas, Laguna de *lag.* Nicaragua **166** [inset] J6
Perlas, Punta de *pt* Nicaragua **166** [inset] J6
Perleberg Germany **63** L1
Perlis *state* Malaysia **84** C1
Perm' Rus. Fed. **51** R4
Permas Rus. Fed. **52** J4
Pernambuco Brazil *see* **Recife**
Pernambuco Plain *sea feature* S. Atlantic Ocean **184** G6
Pernatty Lagoon *salt flat* Australia **137** B6
Pernem India **106** B3
Pernik Bulg. **69** J3
Pernov Estonia *see* **Pärnu**
Perojpur Bangl. *see* **Pirojpur**
Peron Islands Australia **134** E3
Péronne France **62** C5
Perote Mex. **167** F5
Perpignan France **66** F5
Perranporth U.K. **59** B8
Perrégaux Alg. *see* **Mohammadia**
Perris U.S.A. **158** E5
Perros-Guirec France **66** C2
Perrot, Île *i.* Canada **165** I1
Perry *FL* U.S.A. **163** D6
Perry *GA* U.S.A. **163** D5
Perry *MI* U.S.A. **164** C2
Perry *OK* U.S.A. **161** D4
Perry Lake U.S.A. **160** E4
Perryton U.S.A. **161** C4
Perryville *AK* U.S.A. **148** H5
Perryville *MO* U.S.A. **160** F4
Perseverancia Bol. **176** F6
Pershore U.K. **59** E6
Persia *country* Asia *see* **Iran**
Persian Gulf Asia *see* **The Gulf**
Pertek Turkey **113** E3

▶**Perth** Australia **135** A7
Capital of Western Australia. 4th most populous city in Oceania.

Perth Canada **165** G1
Perth U.K. **60** F4
Perth Amboy U.S.A. **165** H3
Perth-Andover Canada **153** I5
Perth Basin *sea feature* Indian Ocean **185** P7
Pertominsk Rus. Fed. **52** H2
Pertunmaa Fin. **55** O6
Pertusato, Capo *c. Corsica* France **66** I6
Peru *atoll* Kiribati *see* **Beru**

▶**Peru** *country* S. America **176** D6
3rd largest and 4th most populous country in South America.

Peru *IL* U.S.A. **160** F3
Peru *IN* U.S.A. **164** B3
Peru *NY* U.S.A. **165** I1
Peru-Chile Trench *sea feature* S. Pacific Ocean **187** O6
Perugia Italy **68** E3
Peruru India **106** C3
Perusia Italy *see* **Perugia**
Péruwelz Belgium **62** D4
Pervomay Kyrg. **98** A4
Pervomaysk Rus. Fed. **53** I5
Pervomays'k Ukr. **53** F6
Pervomayskiy Kazakh. **102** F1
Pervomayskiy *Arkhangel'skaya Oblast'* Rus. Fed. *see* **Novodvinsk**
Pervomayskiy *Tambovskaya Oblast'* Rus. Fed. **53** I5
Pervomays'kyy Ukr. **53** H6
Pervorechenskiy Rus. Fed. **77** R3
Pesaguan *Kalimantan* Indon. **85** E3
Pesaguan *r.* Indon. **85** E3
Pesaro Italy **68** E3
Pescadores *is* Taiwan *see* **P'enghu Ch'üntao**
Pescara Italy **68** F3
Pescara *r.* Italy **68** F3
Peschanokopskoye Rus. Fed. **53** I7
Peschanoye Rus. Fed. *see* **Yashkul'**
Peschanyy, Mys *pt* Kazakh. **113** H2
Pesé Panama **166** [inset] J8
Pesha *r.* Rus. Fed. **52** J2
Peshanjan Afgh. **111** F3
Peshawar Pak. **111** H3
Peshkopi Albania **69** I4
Peshtera Bulg. **69** K3
Peski Turkm. **111** F2
Peski Karakumy *des.* Turkm. *see* **Karakum Desert**
Peskovka Rus. Fed. **52** L4
Pesnica Slovenia **68** F1
Pespire Hond. **166** [inset] I6
Pesqueira Mex. **166** C2
Pessac France **66** D4
Pessin Germany **63** M2
Pestovo Rus. Fed. **52** G4
Pestravka Rus. Fed. **53** K5
Petah Tiqwa Israel **107** B3
Petäjävesi Fin. **54** N5
Petak, Tanjung *pt Halmahera* Indon. **83** D2
Petaling Jaya Malaysia **87** C7
Petalion, Kolpos *sea chan.* Greece **69** K5
Petaluma U.S.A. **158** B2
Pétange Lux. **62** F5
Petangis *Kalimantan* Indon. **85** F3
Petatlán Mex. **168** D5
Petauke Zambia **123** D5
Petén Itzá, Lago *l.* Guat. **167** H5
Petenwell Lake U.S.A. **160** F2
Peterbell Canada **152** E4
Peterborough Australia **137** B7
Peterborough Canada **165** F1
Peterborough U.K. **59** G6
Peterborough U.S.A. **165** J2
Peterculter U.K. **60** G3
Peterhead U.K. **60** H3
Peter I Island Antarctica **188** K2
Peter I Øy *i.* Antarctica *see* **Peter I Island**
Peter Lake Canada **151** M2
Peterlee U.K. **58** F4
Petermann Bjerg *nunatak* Greenland **147** P2
Petermann Ranges *mts* Australia **135** E6
Peter Pond Lake Canada **151** I4
Peters, Lac *l.* Canada **153** H2
Petersberg Germany **63** J4
Petersburg *AK* U.S.A. **149** N4
Petersburg *IL* U.S.A. **160** F4
Petersburg *IN* U.S.A. **164** B4
Petersburg *NY* U.S.A. **165** I2
Petersburg *VA* U.S.A. **165** G5
Petersburg *WV* U.S.A. **164** F4
Petersfield U.K. **59** G7
Petershagen Germany **63** I2
Petersville *AK* U.S.A. **149** J3
Peter the Great Bay Rus. Fed. *see* **Petra Velikogo, Zaliv**
Peth India **106** B2
Petilia Policastro Italy **68** G5
Petit Atlas *mts* Morocco *see* **Anti Atlas**
Petitcodiac Canada **153** I5
Petitjean Morocco *see* **Sidi Kacem**
Petit Lac Manicouagan *l.* Canada **153** I3
Petit Mécatina *r. Nfld. and Lab./Que.* Canada **153** K4
Petit Mécatina, Île du *i.* Canada **153** K4
Petit Morin *r.* France **62** D6
Petitot *r.* Canada **150** F2
Petit St-Bernard, Col du *pass* France **66** H4
Petit Saut, Barrage du *resr* Fr. Guiana **177** H3
Peto Mex. **167** H4
Petoskey U.S.A. **162** C2
Petra *tourist site* Jordan **107** B4
Petra Velikogo, Zaliv *b.* Rus. Fed. **90** C4
Petre, Point Canada **165** G2
Petrich Bulg. **69** J4
Petrified Forest National Park U.S.A. **159** I4
Petrikau Poland *see* **Piotrków Trybunalski**
Petrikov Belarus *see* **Pyetrykaw**
Petrinja Croatia **68** G2
Petroaleksandrovsk Uzbek. *see* **To'rtko'l**
Petrograd Rus. Fed. *see* **St Petersburg**
Petrokhanski Prokhod *pass* Bulg. **69** J3
Petrokov Poland *see* **Piotrków Trybunalski**
Petrolia Canada **164** D2
Petrolia U.S.A. **158** A1
Petrolina Brazil **177** J5
Petrolina de Goiás Brazil **179** A2
Petropavl Kazakh. *see* **Petropavlovsk**
Petropavlovka Kazakh. **98** C3
Petropavlovka *Respublika Buryatiya* Rus. Fed. **94** F1
Petropavlovsk Kazakh. **101** F1
Petropavlovsk Rus. Fed. *see* **Petropavlovsk-Kamchatskiy**
Petropavlovsk-Kamchatskiy Rus. Fed. **77** Q4
Petrópolis Brazil **179** C3
Petroșani Romania **69** J2
Petrovsk Rus. Fed. **53** J5
Petrovskoye Rus. Fed. *see* **Svetlograd**
Petrovsk-Zabaykal'skiy Rus. Fed. **95** G1
Petrozavodsk Rus. Fed. **52** G3
Petrus Steyn S. Africa **125** I4
Petrusville S. Africa **124** G6
Petsamo Rus. Fed. *see* **Pechenga**
Pettau Slovenia *see* **Ptuj**
Petten Neth. **62** E2
Pettigo U.K. **61** E3
Petukhovo Rus. Fed. **76** H4
Petushki Rus. Fed. **52** H5
Petzeck *mt.* Austria **57** N7
Peuetsagu, Gunung *vol.* Indon. **84** B1
Peureula *Sumatera* Indon. **84** B1
Pevek Rus. Fed. **77** S3
Pêxung *Xizang* China **99** F6
Pey Ostān Iran **110** E3
Peza *r.* Rus. Fed. **52** J2
Pezinok Slovakia **57** P6
Pezu Pak. **111** H3
Pfälzer Wald *hills* Germany **63** H5
Pforzheim Germany **63** I6
Pfungstadt Germany **63** I5
Phagameng *Limpopo* S. Africa **125** I3
Phagwara India **104** C3
Phahameng *Free State* S. Africa **125** H5
Phalaborwa S. Africa **125** J2
Phalodi India **104** C4
Phalsund India **104** B4
Phalta India **105** G5
Phaluai, Ko *i.* Thai. **87** B5
Phalut Peak India/Nepal **105** G4
Phan Thai. **86** B3
Phanat Nikhom Thai. **87** C4
Phangan, Ko *i.* Thai. **87** C5
Phang Hoei, San Khao *mts* Thai. **86** C3
Phangnga Thai. **87** B5
Phăng Xi Păng *mt.* Vietnam **86** C2
Phanom Dong Rak, Thiu Khao *mts* Cambodia/Thai. **87** D4
Phan Rang-Thap Cham Vietnam **87** E5
Phan Thiêt Vietnam **87** E5
Phapon Myanmar *see* **Pyapon**
Phat Diêm Vietnam **86** D2
Phatthalung Thai. **87** C6
Phayam, Ko *i.* Thai. **87** B5
Phayao Thai. **86** B3
Phayuhakhiri Thai. **86** C4
Phek India **105** H4
Phelps Lake Canada **151** K3
Phen Thai. **86** C3
Phenix U.S.A. **165** F5
Phenix City U.S.A. **163** C5
Phet Buri Thai. **87** B4
Phetchabun Thai. **86** C3
Phiafai Laos **86** D4
Phichai Thai. **86** C3
Phichit Thai. **86** C3
Philadelphia Jordan *see* **'Ammān**
Philadelphia Turkey *see* **Alaşehir**
Philadelphia *MS* U.S.A. **161** F5
Philadelphia *NY* U.S.A. **165** H1
Philadelphia *PA* U.S.A. **165** H4
Philip U.S.A. **160** C2
Philip Atoll Micronesia *see* **Sorol**
Philippeville Alg. *see* **Skikda**
Philippeville Belgium **62** E4
Philippi U.S.A. **164** E4
Philippi, Lake *salt flat* Australia **136** B5
Philippine Neth. **62** D3
Philippine Basin *sea feature* N. Pacific Ocean **186** E4
Philippines *country* Asia **82** C3
Philippine Sea N. Pacific Ocean **81** G3

▶**Philippine Trench** *sea feature* N. Pacific Ocean **186** E4
3rd deepest trench in the world.

Philippolis S. Africa **125** G6
Philippopolis Bulg. *see* **Plovdiv**
Philippsburg Germany **63** I5
Philipsburg *MT* U.S.A. **156** E3
Philipsburg *PA* U.S.A. **165** F3
Philip Smith Mountains *AK* U.S.A. **149** J2
Philipstown S. Africa **124** G6
Phillip Island Australia **138** B7
Phillips *ME* U.S.A. **165** J1
Phillips *WI* U.S.A. **160** F2
Phillipsburg U.S.A. **160** D4
Phillips Range *hills* Australia **134** D4
Philmont U.S.A. **165** I2
Philomelium Turkey *see* **Akşehir**
Phiritona S. Africa **125** H4
Phitsanulok Thai. **86** C3

▶**Phnom Penh** Cambodia **87** D5
Capital of Cambodia.

Phnum Pénh Cambodia *see* **Phnom Penh**
Pho, Laem *pt* Thai. **87** C6
Phoenicia U.S.A. **165** H2

▶**Phoenix** U.S.A. **157** E6
Capital of Arizona.

Phoenix Island Kiribati *see* **Rawaki**
Phoenix Islands Kiribati **133** I2
Phô Lu Vietnam **86** D2
Phon Thai. **86** C4
Phong Nha Vietnam **86** D3
Phôngsali Laos **86** C2
Phong Saly Laos *see* **Phôngsali**
Phong Thô Vietnam **86** C2
Phon Phisai Thai. **86** C3
Phônsavan Laos **86** C3
Phon Thong Thai. **86** C3
Phosphate Hill Australia **136** C4
Phrae Thai. **86** C3
Phra Nakhon Si Ayutthaya Thai. *see* **Ayutthaya**
Phrao Thai. **86** B3
Phra Saeng Thai. **87** B5
Phrom Phiram Thai. **86** C3
Phsar Ream Cambodia **87** C5
Phu Bai Vietnam **86** D3
Phuchong-Nayoi National Park Thai. **87** D4
Phu Cuong Vietnam *see* **Thu Dâu Môt**
Phuket Thai. **87** B6
Phuket, Ko *i.* Thai. **87** B6
Phu-khieo Wildlife Reserve *nature res.* Thai. **86** C3
Phulabani India *see* **Phulbani**
Phulbani India **106** E1
Phulchhari Ghat Bangl. *see* **Fulchhari**
Phulji Pak. **111** G5
Phu Lôc Vietnam **86** D3
Phu Lôc Vietnam **87** D5
Phu Luang National Park Thai. **86** C3
Phu Ly Vietnam **86** D2
Phumĭ Bŏeng Mealea Cambodia **87** D4
Phumĭ Chhlong Cambodia **87** D4
Phumĭ Kaôh Kŏng Cambodia **87** C5
Phumĭ Kon Kriel Cambodia **87** C4
Phumĭ Mlu Prey Cambodia **87** D4
Phumĭ Moŭng Cambodia **87** C4
Phumiphon, Khuan Thai. **86** B3
Phumĭ Prêk Kak Cambodia **87** D4
Phumĭ Sâmraông Cambodia **87** C4
Phumĭ Trâm Kak Cambodia **87** D5
Phumĭ Veal Renh Cambodia **87** C5
Phu My Vietnam **87** E4
Phung Hiêp Vietnam **87** D5
Phươc Bưu Vietnam **87** D5
Phươc Hai Vietnam **87** D5
Phu Phac Mo *mt.* Vietnam **86** C2
Phu Phan National Park Thai. **86** C3
Phu Quôc, Đao *i.* Vietnam **87** C5
Phu Quy, Đao *i.* Vietnam **87** E5
Phu Tho Vietnam **86** D2
Phu Vinh Vietnam *see* **Tra Vinh**
Phyu Myanmar **86** B3
Piabung, Gunung *mt.* Indon. **85** F2
Piaca Brazil **177** I5
Piacenza Italy **68** C2
Piacouadie, Lac *l.* Canada **153** H4
Piagochioui *r.* Canada **152** F3
Piai, Tanjung *pt* Malaysia **84** C2
Pian *r.* Australia **138** D3
Pianguan *Shanxi* China **95** G4
Pianosa, Isola *i.* Italy **68** D3
Piatra Neamț Romania **69** L1
Piave *r.* Italy **68** E2
Pibor Post Sudan **121** G4
Pic *r.* Canada **152** D4
Picacho U.S.A. **159** H5
Picachos, Cerro dos *mt.* Mex. **166** B2
Picardie *admin. reg.* France **62** C5
Picardie *reg.* France *see* **Picardy**
Picardy *admin. reg.* France *see* **Picardie**
Picardy *reg.* France **62** B5
Picauville France **59** F9
Picayune U.S.A. **161** F6
Piceance Creek *r.* U.S.A. **159** I1
Pich Mex. **167** H5
Picháchic Mex. **166** D2
Pichanal Arg. **178** D2
Pichhor India **104** D4
Pichilemu Chile **178** B4
Pichilingue Mex. **166** C3
Pichucalco Mex. **167** G5
Pickens U.S.A. **164** E4
Pickering Canada **164** F2
Pickering U.K. **58** G4
Pickering, Vale of *valley* U.K. **58** G4
Pickle Lake Canada **147** I4
Pico Bonito, Parque Nacional *nat. park* Hond. **166** [inset] I6
Pico da Neblina, Parque Nacional do *nat. park* Brazil **176** E3
Pico de Orizaba, Parque Nacional *nat. park* Mex. **167** F5
Pico de Tancítaro, Parque Nacional *nat. park* Mex. **166** E5
Picos Brazil **177** J5
Pico Truncado Arg. **178** C7
Picton Australia **138** E5
Picton Canada **165** G2
Picton N.Z. **139** E5
Pictou Canada **153** J5
Picture Butte Canada **151** H5
Pidarak Pak. **111** F5
Pidurutalagala *mt.* Sri Lanka **106** D5
Piedade Brazil **179** B3
Piedra de Águila Arg. **178** B6
Piedras, Punta *pt* Arg. **178** E5
Piedras Blancas Point U.S.A. **158** C4
Piedras Negras Guat. **167** H5
Piedras Negras *Coahuila* Mex. **167** E2
Piedras Negras *Veracruz* Mex. **167** F5
Pie Island Canada **152** C4
Pieksämäki Fin. **54** O5
Pielavesi Fin. **54** O5
Pielinen *l.* Fin. **54** P5
Pieljekaise nationalpark *nat. park* Sweden **54** J3
Pienaarsrivier S. Africa **125** I3
Pieniński Park Narodowy *nat. park* Poland **57** R6
Pieninský *nat. park* Slovakia **57** R6
Pierce U.S.A. **160** D3
Pierce Lake Canada **151** M4
Pierceland Canada **151** I4
Pierceton U.S.A. **164** C3
Pieria *mts* Greece **69** J4
Pierowall U.K. **60** G1
Pierpont U.S.A. **164** E3

▶**Pierre** U.S.A. **160** C2
Capital of South Dakota.

Pierrelatte France **66** G4
Pietermaritzburg S. Africa **125** J5
Pietersaari Fin. *see* **Jakobstad**
Pietersburg *Limpopo* S. Africa *see* **Polokwane**
Pie Town U.S.A. **159** I4
Pietra Spada, Passo di *pass* Italy **68** G5
Piet Retief S. Africa **125** J4
Pietrosa *mt.* Romania **69** K1
Pigeon U.S.A. **164** D2
Pigeon Bay Canada **164** D3
Pigeon Lake Canada **150** H4
Piggott U.S.A. **161** F4
Pigg's Peak Swaziland **125** J3
Pigs, Bay of Cuba **163** D8
Piguicas *mt.* Mex. **167** F4
Pihij India **104** C5
Pihkva järv *l.* Estonia/Rus. Fed. *see* **Pskov, Lake**
Pihlajavesi *l.* Fin. **54** P6
Pihlava Fin. **55** L6
Pihtipudas Fin. **54** N5
Piippola Fin. **54** N4
Piispajärvi Fin. **54** P4
Pijijiapan Mex. **167** G6
Pikalevo Rus. Fed. **52** G4
Pike U.S.A. **164** E4
Pike Bay Canada **164** E1
Pikelot *i.* Micronesia **81** L5
Pikes Peak U.S.A. **156** G5
Piketon U.S.A. **164** D4
Pikeville *KY* U.S.A. **164** D5
Pikeville *TN* U.S.A. **162** C5
Pikinni *atoll* Marshall Is *see* **Bikini**
Pikmiktalik *AK* U.S.A. **148** G3
Pikou *Liaoning* China **95** J4
Piła Poland **57** P4
Pilanesberg National Park S. Africa **125** H3
Pilar Arg. **178** E4
Pilar Para. **178** E3
Pilar Phil. **82** D4
Pilar de Goiás Brazil **179** A1
Pilas *i.* Phil. **82** C5
Pilas Channel Phil. **82** C5
Pilaya *r.* Bol. **176** F8
Pilcomayo *r.* Bol./Para. **176** F8
Pile Bay Village *AK* U.S.A. **148** I4
Piler India **106** C3
Pilgrim Springs *AK* U.S.A. **148** F2
Pili *Luzon* Phil. **82** C3
Pili, Cerro *mt.* Chile **178** C2
Pilibangan India **104** C3
Pilibhit India **104** D3
Pilipinas *country* Asia *see* **Philippines**
Pillau Rus. Fed. *see* **Baltiysk**
Pillcopata Peru **176** D6
Pilliga Australia **138** D3
Pillsbury, Lake U.S.A. **158** B2
Pil'na Rus. Fed. **52** J5
Pil'nya, Ozero *l.* Rus. Fed. **52** M1
Pilões, Serra dos *mts* Brazil **179** B2
Pílos Greece *see* **Pylos**
Pilot Knob *mt.* U.S.A. **156** E3
Pilot Peak U.S.A. **158** E2
Pilot Point *AK* U.S.A. **148** H4
Pilot Station *AK* U.S.A. **148** G3
Pilottown *LA* U.S.A. **167** H2
Pilsen Czech Rep. *see* **Plzeň**
Piltene Latvia **55** L8
Pil'tun, Zaliv *lag.* Rus. Fed. **90** F1
Pilu Pak. **111** H5
Pima U.S.A. **159** I5
Pimenta Bueno Brazil **176** F6
Pimento U.S.A. **164** B4
Pimpalner India **106** B1
Pin *r.* India **104** D2
Pin *r.* Myanmar **86** A2
Pinahat India **104** D4
Pinaleno Mountains U.S.A. **159** H5
Pinamalayan *Mindoro* Phil. **82** C3
Pinamar Arg. **178** E5
Pinang Malaysia *see* **George Town**
Pinang *i.* Malaysia **84** C1
Pinang *state* Malaysia **84** C1
Pinangah *Sabah* Malaysia **85** G1
Pınarbaşı Turkey **112** E3
Pinar del Río Cuba **169** H4
Pinarhisar Turkey **69** L4
Piñas Ecuador **176** C4
Pincher Creek Canada **150** H5
Pinckneyville U.S.A. **160** F4
Pinconning U.S.A. **164** D2
Pińczów Poland **57** R5
Pindaí Brazil **179** C1
Pindamonhangaba Brazil **179** B3
Pindar Australia **135** A7
Pindar *r.* India **99** B7
Pindaré *r.* Brazil **177** J4
Píndhos Óros *mts* Greece *see* **Pindus Mountains**
Pindos *mts* Greece *see* **Pindus Mountains**
Pindrei India **104** E5
Pindus Mountains Greece **69** I5
Pine *watercourse* Australia **137** C7
Pine *r.* *MI* U.S.A. **164** C1
Pine *r.* *MI* U.S.A. **164** C2
Pine Bluff U.S.A. **161** E5
Pine Bluffs U.S.A. **156** G4
Pine Creek Australia **134** E3
Pine Creek *r.* U.S.A. **165** G3
Pinecrest U.S.A. **158** C2
Pinedale *NM* U.S.A. **159** I4
Pinedale *WY* U.S.A. **156** F4
Pine Dock Canada **151** L5
Pine Falls Canada **151** L5
Pine Flat Lake U.S.A. **158** D3
Pinega Rus. Fed. **52** I2
Pinega *r.* Rus. Fed. **52** I2
Pinegrove Australia **135** A6
Pine Grove U.S.A. **165** G3
Pine Hills *FL* U.S.A. **163** D6
Pinehouse Lake Canada **151** J4
Pinehouse Lake *l.* Canada **151** J4
Pineimuta *r.* Canada **151** N4
Pineios *r.* Greece **69** J5
Pine Island Bay Antarctica **187** N10
Pine Island Glacier Antarctica **188** K1
Pine Islands *FL* U.S.A. **163** D7
Pine Islands *FL* U.S.A. **163** D7
Pine Knot U.S.A. **164** C5
Pineland U.S.A. **161** E6
Pine Mountain U.S.A. **158** C4
Pine Peak U.S.A. **159** G4
Pine Point *pt* Canada **150** H2
Pine Point (abandoned) Canada **150** H2
Pineridge U.S.A. **158** D3
Pine Ridge U.S.A. **160** C3
Pinerolo Italy **68** B2
Pines, Akrotirio *pt* Greece **69** K4
Pines, Isle of *i.* Cuba *see* **La Juventud, Isla de**
Pines, Isle of *i.* New Caledonia *see* **Pins, Île des**

Pines, Lake o' the TX U.S.A. 167 G1
Pinetop U.S.A. 159 I4
Pinetown S. Africa 125 J5
Pine Valley U.S.A. 165 G2
Pineville KY U.S.A. 164 D5
Pineville LA U.S.A. 167 G2
Pineville MO U.S.A. 161 E4
Pineville WV U.S.A. 164 E5
Ping, Mae Nam r. Thai. 86 C4
Ping'an Qinghai China 94 E4
Ping'anyi Qinghai China see Ping'an
Pingba China 96 E3
Pingbian China 96 D4
Ping Dao i. China 95 I5
Pingding Shanxi China 95 H4
Pingdingbu Hebei China see Guyuan
Pingdingshan China 97 G1
Pingdong Taiwan see P'ingtung
Pingdu Jiangxi China see Anfu
Pingdu Shandong China 95 I4
Pinggang China 90 B4
Pinggu Beijing China 95 I3
Pinghe China 97 H3
Pinghu China see Pingtang
Pingjiang China 97 G2
Pingjinpu China 96 E2
Pingle China 97 F3
Pingli China 97 F1
Pingliang Gansu China 94 F5
Pinglu Shanxi China 95 G5
Pingluo Ningxia China 94 F4
Pingma China see Tiandong
Pingnan China 97 H3
Pingqiao China 97 G1
Pingquan Hebei China 95 I3
Pingshan Hebei China 95 H4
Pingshan Sichuan China 96 E2
Pingshan Yunnan China see Luquan
Pingshi China 97 G3
Pingshu Hebei China see Daicheng
Pingtan China 97 H3
Pingtan Dao i. China see Haitan Dao
Pingtang China 96 E3
P'ingtung Taiwan 97 I4
Pingxi China see Yuping
Pingxiang Gansu China see Tongwei
Pingxiang Guangxi China 96 E4
Pingxiang Jiangxi China 97 G3
Pingyang Heilong. China 95 K1
Pingyang Zhejiang China 97 I3
Pingyao Shanxi China 95 H4
Pingyi Shandong China 95 I5
Pingyin Shandong China 95 I4
Pingyu China 97 G1
Pingyuan Shandong China 95 I4
Pingyuanjie China 96 D4
Pingzhai China 97 F3
Pinhal Brazil 179 B3
Pinheiro Brazil 177 I4
Pinhoe U.K. 59 D8
Pini i. Indon. 84 B2
Piniós r. Greece see Pineios
Pinjin Australia 135 C7
Pink Mountain Canada 150 F3
Pinlaung Myanmar 86 B2
Pinlebu Myanmar 86 A1
Pinnacle hill U.S.A. 165 F4
Pinnacle Island AK U.S.A. 148 D3
Pinnacles National Monument nat. park U.S.A. 158 C3
Pinnau r. Germany 63 J1
Pinneberg Germany 63 J1
Pinnes, Akra pt Greece see Pines, Akrotirio
Pinoh r. Indon. 85 E3
Pinon Hills CA U.S.A. 158 E4
Pinos, Isla de i. Cuba see La Juventud, Isla de
Pinos, Mount U.S.A. 158 D4
Pinotepa Nacional Mex. 168 E5
Pinrang Sulawesi Indon. 83 A3
Pinrang Sulawesi Indon. 83 B3
Pins, Île des i. New Caledonia 133 G4
Pins, Pointe aux pt Canada 164 E2
Pinsk Belarus 55 O10
Pinta, Sierra hill U.S.A. 159 G5
Pintada Creek watercourse U.S.A. 157 G6
Pintados Chile 178 C2
Pintasan Sabah Malaysia 85 G1
Pintura U.S.A. 159 G3
Pioche U.S.A. 159 F3
Piodi Dem. Rep. Congo 123 C4
Pioneer Mountains U.S.A. 156 E3
Pioner, Ostrov i. Rus. Fed. 76 K2
Pionerskiy Kaliningradskaya Oblast' Rus. Fed. 55 L9
Pionerskiy Khanty-Mansiyskiy Avtonomnyy Okrug Rus. Fed. 51 S3
Pionki Poland 57 R5
Piopio N.Z. 139 E4
Piopiotahi inlet N.Z. see Milford Sound
Piorini, Lago l. Brazil 176 F4
Piotrków Trybunalski Poland 57 Q5
Pipa Dingzi mt. China 90 C4
Pipar India 104 C4
Pipar Road India 104 C4
Piperi i. Greece 69 K5
Piper Peak U.S.A. 158 E3
Pipestone Canada 151 K5
Pipestone r. Canada 151 N4
Pipestone U.S.A. 160 D3
Pipli India 104 C3
Pipmuacan, Réservoir resr Canada 153 H4
Piqan Xinjiang China see Shanshan
Piqanlik Xinjiang China 98 C4
Piqua U.S.A. 164 C3
Piquiri r. Brazil 179 A4
Pira Benin 120 D4
Piracanjuba Brazil 179 A2
Piracicaba Brazil 179 B3
Piracicaba r. Brazil 179 C2
Piraçununga Brazil 179 B3
Piracuruca Brazil 177 J4
Piraeus Greece 69 J6
Piraí do Sul Brazil 179 A4
Piráievs Greece see Piraeus
Piraju Brazil 179 A3
Pirajuí Brazil 179 A3
Pirallahı Adası Azer. 113 H2
Piranhas Bahia Brazil 179 C1
Piranhas Goiás Brazil 177 H7
Piranhas r. Rio Grande do Norte Brazil 177 K5
Piranhas r. Brazil 179 A2
Pirapora Brazil 179 B2
Pirari Nepal 99 D8
Piraube, Lac l. Canada 153 H4
Pirawa India 104 D4
Pirenópolis Brazil 179 A1
Pires do Rio Brazil 179 A2
Pírgos Greece see Pyrgos
Pirin nat. park Bulg. 69 J4
Pirineos mts Europe see Pyrenees
Piripiri Brazil 177 J4
Pirlerkondu Turkey see Taşkent
Pirmasens Germany 63 H5
Pirojpur Bangl. 105 G5
Pir Panjal Pass India 104 C2
Pir Panjal Range mts India/Pak. 111 I3
Piru Seram Indon. 83 D3
Piru, Teluk b. Seram Indon. 83 D3
Piryatin Ukr. see Pyryatyn
Pirzada Afgh. 111 G4
Pisa Italy 68 D3
Pisae Italy see Pisa
Pisagua Chile 176 D7
Pisang i. Maluku Indon. 83 D3
Pisang, Kepulauan is Indon. 81 I7
Pisau, Tanjung pt Malaysia 85 G1
Pisaurum Italy see Pesaro
Pisco Peru 176 C6
Písek Czech Rep. 57 O6
Pisha China see Ningnan
Pishan Xinjiang China 99 B5
Pīshīn Iran 102 B6
Pishin Pak. 111 G4
Pishin Lora r. Pak. 111 G4
Pishpek Kyrg. see Bishkek
Pisidia reg. Turkey 112 C3
Pising Sulawesi Indon. 83 B4

▶Pissis, Cerro Arg. 178 C3
4th highest mountain in South America.

Pisté Mex. 167 H4
Pisticci Italy 68 G4
Pistoia Italy 68 D3
Pistoriae Italy see Pistoia
Pisuerga r. Spain 67 D3
Pita Guinea 120 B3
Pitaga Canada 153 I3
Pital Mex. 167 H5
Pitanga Brazil 179 A4
Pitangui Brazil 179 B2
Pitar India 104 B5
Pitarpunga Lake imp. l. Australia 138 A5
Pitcairn, Henderson, Ducie and Oeno Islands terr. S. Pacific Ocean see Pitcairn Islands
Pitcairn Island Pitcairn Islands 187 L7

▶Pitcairn Islands terr. S. Pacific Ocean 187 L7
United Kingdom Overseas Territory.

Piteå Sweden 54 L4
Piteälven r. Sweden 54 L4
Pitelino Rus. Fed. 53 I5
Piterka Rus. Fed. 53 J6
Pitești Romania 69 K2
Pithoragarh India 104 E3
Pitihra India 104 D5
Pitiquito Mex. 166 B2
Pitkas Point AK U.S.A. 148 G3
Pitkyaranta Rus. Fed. 52 F3
Pitlochry U.K. 60 F4
Pitong China see Pixian
Pitsane Siding Botswana 125 G3
Pitti i. India 106 B4
Pitt Island B.C. Canada 149 O5
Pitt Island N.Z. 133 I6
Pitt Islands Solomon Is see Vanikoro Islands
Pittsboro U.S.A. 161 F5
Pittsburg KS U.S.A. 161 E4
Pittsburg TX U.S.A. 161 E5
Pittsburgh U.S.A. 164 F3
Pittsfield MA U.S.A. 165 I2
Pittsfield ME U.S.A. 165 K1
Pittsfield VT U.S.A. 165 I2
Pittston U.S.A. 165 H3
Pittsworth Australia 138 E1
Pitz Lake Canada 151 L2
Piumhí Brazil 179 B3
Piura Peru 176 B5
Piute Mountains U.S.A. 159 F4
Piute Peak U.S.A. 158 D4
Piute Reservoir U.S.A. 159 G2
Piuthan Nepal 105 E3
Pivabiska r. Canada 152 E4
Pivka Slovenia 68 F2
Pixa Xinjiang China 99 B5
Pixariá mt. Greece see Pyxaria
Pixian China 96 D2
Pixley U.S.A. 158 D4
Pixoyal Mex. 167 H5
Piz Bernina mt. Italy/Switz. 68 C1
Piz Buin mt. Austria/Switz. 57 M7
Pizhanka Rus. Fed. 52 K4
Pizhi Nigeria 120 D4
Pizhma Rus. Fed. 52 J4
Pizhma r. Rus. Fed. 52 K4
Pizhma r. Rus. Fed. 52 L2
Pizhou Jiangsu China 95 I5
Pkulagalid Point Palau 82 [inset]
Pkulagasemieg pt Palau 82 [inset]
Pkulngril pt Palau 82 [inset]
Pkurengei pt Palau 82 [inset]
Placentia Canada 153 L5
Placentia Italy see Piacenza
Placentia Bay Canada 153 L5
Placer Masbate Phil. 82 C4
Placer Mindanao Phil. 82 D4
Placerville CA U.S.A. 158 C2
Placerville CO U.S.A. 159 I2
Placetas Cuba 163 E8
Plácido de Castro Brazil 176 E6
Plain Dealing U.S.A. 161 E5
Plainfield CT U.S.A. 165 J3
Plainfield IN U.S.A. 164 B4
Plainfield VT U.S.A. 165 I1
Plains KS U.S.A. 161 C4
Plains TX U.S.A. 161 C5
Plainview U.S.A. 161 C5
Plainville IN U.S.A. 164 B4
Plainville KS U.S.A. 160 D4
Plainwell U.S.A. 164 C2
Plaju Sumatera Indon. 84 D3
Plaka, Akra pt Kriti Greece see Plaka, Akrotirio
Plaka, Akrotirio pt Greece 69 L7
Plakoti, Cape Cyprus 107 B2
Plamondon Canada 151 H4
Plampang Sumbawa Indon. 85 G5
Planá Czech Rep. 63 M5
Plana Cays is Bahamas 163 F8
Planada U.S.A. 158 C3
Planaltina Brazil 179 B1
Plane r. Germany 63 M2
Plankinton U.S.A. 160 D3
Plano U.S.A. 161 D5
Planura Brazil 179 A3
Plaquemine U.S.A. 161 F6
Plasencia Spain 67 C3
Plaster City U.S.A. 159 F5
Plaster Rock Canada 153 I5
Plastun Rus. Fed. 90 E3
Platani r. Sicily Italy 68 E6
Platberg mt. S. Africa 125 I5

▶Plateau Antarctica
Lowest recorded annual mean temperature in the world.

Plateros Mex. 166 E4
Platina U.S.A. 158 B1
Platinum AK U.S.A. 148 G4
Plato Col. 176 D2
Platón Sánchez Mex. 167 F4
Platte r. U.S.A. 160 E3
Platte City U.S.A. 160 E4
Plattling Germany 63 M6
Plattsburgh U.S.A. 165 I1
Plattsmouth U.S.A. 160 E3
Plau Germany 63 M1
Plauen Germany 63 M4
Plauer See l. Germany 63 M1
Plavsk Rus. Fed. 53 H5
Playa Azul Mex. 166 E5
Playa Noriega, Lago l. Mex. 157 F7
Playas Ecuador 176 B4
Playas Lake U.S.A. 159 I6
Plây Ku Vietnam 87 E4
Playón Mex. 166 C3
Pleasant, Lake U.S.A. 159 G5
Pleasant Bay U.S.A. 165 K3
Pleasant Grove U.S.A. 159 H1
Pleasant Hill Lake U.S.A. 164 D3
Pleasanton U.S.A. 161 D6
Pleasant Point N.Z. 139 C7
Pleasantville U.S.A. 165 H4
Pleasure Ridge Park U.S.A. 164 C4
Pleaux France 66 F4
Pledger Lake Canada 152 E4
Plei Doch Vietnam 87 D4
Pleihari Martapura, Suaka Margasatwa nature res. Indon. 85 F3
Pleihari Tanah, Suaka Margasatwa nature res. Kalimantan Indon. 85 F4
Plei Kân Vietnam 86 D4
Pleinfeld Germany 63 K5
Pleiße r. Germany 63 M3
Plenty watercourse Australia 136 B5
Plenty, Bay of g. N.Z. 139 F3
Plentywood U.S.A. 156 G2
Plesetsk Rus. Fed. 52 I3
Pleshchentsy Belarus see Plyeshchanitsy
Plétipi, Lac l. Canada 153 H4
Plettenberg Germany 63 H3
Plettenberg Bay S. Africa 124 F8
Pleven Bulg. 69 K3
Plevna Bulg. see Pleven
Plieran r. Malaysia 85 F2
Pljevlja Montenegro 69 H3
Płock Poland 57 Q4
Pločno mt. Bos.-Herz. 68 G3
Plodovoye Rus. Fed. 52 F3
Ploemeur France 66 C3
Ploești Romania see Ploiești
Ploiești Romania 69 L2
Plomb du Cantal mt. France 66 F4
Ploskoye Rus. Fed. see Stanovoye
Płoty Poland 57 O4
Ploudalmézeau France 66 B2
Plouzané France 66 B2
Plovdiv Bulg. 69 K3
Plover Cove Reservoir H.K. China 97 [inset]
Plover Islands AK U.S.A. 148 I1
Plozk Poland see Płock
Plum U.S.A. 164 F3
Plumridge Lakes salt flat Australia 135 D7
Plungė Lith. 55 L9
Plutarco Elías Calles, Presa resr Mex. 157 F7
Plutarco Elís Calles, Presa resr Mex. 166 C2
Pluto, Lac l. Canada 153 H3
Plyeshchanitsy Belarus 55 O9
Ply Huey Wati, Khao mt. Myanmar/Thai. 86 B3
Plymouth U.K. 59 C8
Plymouth CA U.S.A. 158 C2
Plymouth IN U.S.A. 164 B3
Plymouth MA U.S.A. 165 J3
Plymouth NC U.S.A. 162 E5
Plymouth NH U.S.A. 165 J2
Plymouth WI U.S.A. 164 B2

▶Plymouth Montserrat 169 L5
Capital of Montserrat, abandoned in 1997 owing to volcanic activity. Temporary capital established at Brades.

Plymouth Bay U.S.A. 165 J3
Plynlimon hill U.K. 59 D6
Plyussa Rus. Fed. 55 P7
Plzeň Czech Rep. 57 N6
Pô Burkina 120 C3
Po r. Italy 68 E2
Pô, Parc National de nat. park Burkina 120 C3
Po, Tanjung pt Malaysia 85 E2
Poás, Volcán vol. Costa Rica 166 [inset] I7
Poat i. Indon. 83 B3
Pobeda Peak China/Kyrg. 98 C4
Pobedy, Pik mt. China/Kyrg. see Pobeda Peak
Pocahontas U.S.A. 161 F4
Pocatello U.S.A. 156 E4
Pochala Sudan 121 G4
Pochayiv Ukr. 53 E6
Pochep Rus. Fed. 53 G5
Pochinki Rus. Fed. 53 J5
Pochinok Rus. Fed. 53 G5
Pochutla Mex. 168 E5
Pock, Gunung hill Malaysia 85 G1
Pocking Germany 57 N6
Pocklington U.K. 58 G5
Poções Brazil 179 C1
Pocomoke City U.S.A. 165 H4
Pocomoke Sound b. U.S.A. 165 H5
Poconé Brazil 177 G7
Pocono Mountains hills U.S.A. 165 H3
Pocono Summit U.S.A. 165 H3
Poco Ranakah vol. Flores Indon. 83 B5
Poços de Caldas Brazil 179 B3
Podanur India 106 C4
Poddor'ye Rus. Fed. 52 F4
Podgorenskiy Rus. Fed. 53 H6

▶Podgorica Montenegro 69 H3
Capital of Montenegro

Podgornoye Rus. Fed. 76 J4
Podile India 106 C3
Podișul Transilvaniei plat. Romania see Transylvanian Basin
Podkamennaya Tunguska r. Rus. Fed. 77 K3
Podocarpus, Parque Nacional nat. park Ecuador 176 C4
Podol'sk Rus. Fed. 53 H5
Podporozh'ye Rus. Fed. 52 G3
Podujevë Kosovo 69 I3
Podujevo Kosovo see Podujevë
Podz' Rus. Fed. 52 K3
Poelela, Lagoa l. Moz. 125 L3
Poeppel Corner salt flat Australia 137 B5
Poetovio Slovenia see Ptuj
Pofadder S. Africa 124 D5
Pogar Rus. Fed. 53 G5
Poggibonsi Italy 68 D3
Poggio di Montieri mt. Italy 68 D3
Pogradec Albania 69 I4
Pogranichnik Afgh. 111 F3
Pogranichnyy Rus. Fed. 90 C3
Poh Sulawesi Indon. 83 B3
Po Hai g. China see Bo Hai
P'ohang S. Korea 91 C5
Pohnpei atoll Micronesia 186 G5
Pohri India 104 D4
Poi India 105 H4
Poiana Mare Romania 69 J3
Poigar Sulawesi Indon. 83 C2
Poinsett, Cape Antarctica 188 F2
Point Arena U.S.A. 158 B2
Point au Fer Island U.S.A. 161 F6
Pointe a la Hache U.S.A. 161 F6
Pointe-à-Pitre Guadeloupe 169 L5
Pointe-Noire Congo 123 B4
Point Hope AK U.S.A. 148 F1
Point Lake Canada 150 H1
Point Lay AK U.S.A. 148 G1
Point of Rocks U.S.A. 156 F4
Point Pelee National Park Canada 164 D3
Point Pleasant NJ U.S.A. 165 H3
Point Pleasant WV U.S.A. 164 D4
Poitiers France 66 E3
Poitou reg. France 66 E3
Poix-de-Picardie France 62 B5
Pojuca r. Brazil 179 D1
Pokaran India 104 B4
Pokataroo Australia 138 D2
Pokcha Rus. Fed. 51 R3
Pokhara Nepal 105 E3
Pokhran Landi Pak. 111 G5
Pokhvistnevo Rus. Fed. 51 Q5
Pok Liu Chau i. H.K. China see Lamma Island
Poko Dem. Rep. Congo 122 C3
Poko Mountain hill AK U.S.A. 148 G1
Pokosnoye Rus. Fed. 88 I1
P'ok'r Kovkas mts Asia see Lesser Caucasus
Pokrovka Chitinskaya Oblast' Rus. Fed. 90 A1
Pokrovka Primorskiy Kray Rus. Fed. 90 C4
Pokrovsk Respublika Sakha (Yakutiya) Rus. Fed. 77 N3
Pokrovsk Saratovskaya Oblast' Rus. Fed. see Engel's
Pokrovskoye Rus. Fed. 53 H7
Pokshen'ga r. Rus. Fed. 52 J3
Pol India 104 C5
Pola Croatia see Pula
Pola Mindoro Phil. 82 C3
Polacca Wash watercourse U.S.A. 159 H4
Pola de Lena Spain 67 D2
Pola de Siero Spain 67 D2
Poland country Europe 50 J5
Poland NY U.S.A. 165 H2
Poland OH U.S.A. 164 E3
Polar Plateau Antarctica 188 A1
Polatlı Turkey 112 D3
Polatsk Belarus 55 P9
Polavaram India 106 D2
Polcirkeln Sweden 54 L3
Pol-e 'Alam 111 H3
Polee i. Papua Indon. 83 D3
Pol-e Fāsā Iran 110 D4
Pol-e Khatum Iran 111 F2
Pol-e Khomrī Afgh. 111 H3
Pol-e Safid Iran 110 D2
Polessk Rus. Fed. 55 L9
Poles'ye marsh Belarus/Ukr. see Pripet Marshes
Polewali Sulawesi Barat Indon. 83 A3
Polgahawela Sri Lanka 106 D5
Poli Shandong China 95 I5
Poli Cyprus see Polis
Políaigos i. Greece see Polyaigos
Police Poland 57 O4
Policoro Italy 68 G4
Poligny France 66 G3
Políkastron Greece see Polykastro
Polillo i. Phil. 82 C3
Polillo Islands Phil. 82 C3
Polillo Strait Phil. 82 C3
Polis Cyprus 107 A2
Polis'ke Ukr. 53 F6
Polis'kyy Zapovidnyk nature res. Ukr. 53 F6
Politovo Rus. Fed. 52 K2
Políyiros Greece see Polygyros
Polkowice Poland 57 P5
Pollachi India 106 C4
Pollard Islands U.S.A. see Gardner Pinnacles
Polle Germany 63 J3
Pollino, Monte mt. Italy 68 G5
Pollino, Parco Nazionale del nat. park Italy 68 G5
Polloc Harbour b. Mindanao Phil. 82 C5
Pollock Pines U.S.A. 158 C2
Pollock Reef Australia 135 C8
Polmak Norway 54 O1
Polnovat Rus. Fed. 51 T3
Polo Fin. 54 P4
Poloat atoll Micronesia see Puluwat
Pologi Ukr. see Polohy
Polohy Ukr. 53 H7
Polokwane S. Africa 125 I2
Polomoloc Mindanao Phil. 82 D5
Polonne Ukr. 53 E6
Polonnoye Ukr. see Polonne
Polotsk Belarus see Polatsk
Polperro U.K. 59 C8
Polska country Europe see Poland
Polson U.S.A. 156 E3
Polta r. Rus. Fed. 52 I2
Poltava Ukr. 53 G6
Poltoratsk Turkm. see Aşgabat
Põltsamaa Estonia 55 N7
Polunochnoye Rus. Fed. 51 S3
Põlva Estonia 55 O7
Polvadera U.S.A. 157 G6
Polvijärvi Fin. 54 P5
Polvoxal Mex. 167 H5
Polyaigos i. Greece 69 K6
Polyanovgrad Bulg. see Karnobat
Polyarnyy Chukotskiy Avtonomnyy Okrug Rus. Fed. 77 S3
Polyarnyy Murmanskaya Oblast' Rus. Fed. 54 R2
Polyarnyye Zori Rus. Fed. 54 R3
Polyarnyy Ural mts Rus. Fed. 51 S2
Polygyros Greece 69 J4
Polykastro Greece 69 J4
Polynesia is Pacific Ocean 186 I6
Polynésie Française terr. S. Pacific Ocean see French Polynesia
Pom Indon. 81 J7
Pomarkku Fin. 55 M6
Pombal Pará Brazil 177 H4
Pombal Paraíba Brazil 177 K5
Pombal Port. 67 B4
Pomene Moz. 125 L2
Pomeranian Bay Poland 57 O3
Pomeroy S. Africa 125 J5
Pomeroy U.K. 61 F3
Pomeroy OH U.S.A. 164 D4
Pomeroy WA U.S.A. 156 D3
Pomezia Italy 68 E4
Pomfret S. Africa 124 F3
Pomona Belize 167 H5
Pomona Namibia 124 B4
Pomona U.S.A. 158 E4
Pomorie Bulg. 69 L3
Pomorskie, Pojezierze reg. Poland 57 O4
Pomorskiy Bereg coastal area Rus. Fed. 52 G2
Pomorskiy Proliv sea chan. Rus. Fed. 52 K1
Pomos Point Cyprus 107 A2
Pomo Tso l. China see Puma Yumco
Pomou, Akra pt Cyprus see Pomos Point
Pomozdino Rus. Fed. 52 L3
Pompain Xizang China 99 F7
Pompano Beach U.S.A. 163 D7
Pompei Italy 68 F4
Pompéia Brazil 179 A3
Pompey France 62 G6
Pompeyevka Rus. Fed. 90 C2
Ponape atoll Micronesia see Pohnpei
Ponask Lake Canada 151 M4
Ponazyrevo Rus. Fed. 52 J4
Ponca City U.S.A. 161 D4
Ponce Puerto Rico 169 K5
Ponce de Leon Bay U.S.A. 163 D7
Poncheville, Lac l. Canada 152 F4
Pondicherry India see Puducherry
Pondicherry union terr. India see Puducherry
Pondichéry India see Puducherry
Pond Inlet Canada 189 K2
Ponds Bay Canada see Pond Inlet
Poneloya Nicaragua 166 [inset] I6
Ponente, Riviera di coastal area Italy 68 B3
Poneto U.S.A. 164 C3
Ponferrada Spain 67 C2
Pongara, Pointe pt Gabon 122 A3
Pongaroa N.Z. 139 F5
Pongda Xizang China 99 F7
Pongo watercourse Sudan 121 F4
Pongola r. S. Africa 125 K4
Pongolapoort Dam l. S. Africa 125 J4
Poniki, Gunung mt. Indon. 83 B2
Ponindilisa, Tanjung pt Indon. 83 B3
Ponnagyun Myanmar 86 A2
Ponnaivar r. India 106 C4
Ponnampet India 106 B3
Ponnani India 106 B4
Ponnyadaung Range mts Myanmar 86 A2
Pono Indon. 81 I8
Ponoka Canada 150 H4
Ponorogo Jawa Indon. 85 E4
Ponoy r. Rus. Fed. 52 I2
Pons r. Canada 153 H2

▶Ponta Delgada Arquipélago dos Açores 184 G3
Capital of the Azores.

Ponta Grossa Brazil 179 A4
Pontal Brazil 179 A3
Pontalina Brazil 179 A2
Pont-à-Mousson France 62 G6
Ponta Porã Brazil 178 E2
Pontarfynach U.K. see Devil's Bridge
Pont-Audemer France 59 H9
Pontault-Combault France 62 C6
Pontax r. Canada 152 F4
Pontchartrain, Lake U.S.A. 161 F6
Pont-de-Loup Belgium 62 E4
Ponte Alta do Norte Brazil 177 I6
Ponte de Sor Port. 67 B4
Ponte Firme Brazil 179 B2
Pontefract U.K. 58 F5
Ponteix Canada 151 J5
Ponteland U.K. 58 F3
Ponte Nova Brazil 179 C3
Pontes-e-Lacerda Brazil 177 G7
Pontevedra Spain 67 B2
Ponthierville Dem. Rep. Congo see Ubundu
Pontiac IL U.S.A. 160 F3
Pontiac MI U.S.A. 164 D2
Pontiae is Italy see Ponziane, Isole
Pontianak Kalimantan Indon. 85 E3
Pontine Islands is Italy see Ponziane, Isole
Pont-l'Abbé France 66 B3
Pontoise France 62 C5
Ponton watercourse Australia 135 C7
Ponton Canada 151 L4
Pontotoc U.S.A. 161 F5
Pont-Ste-Maxence France 62 C5
Pontypool U.K. 59 D7
Pontypridd U.K. 59 D7
Ponza, Isola di i. Italy 68 E4
Ponziane, Isole is Italy 68 E4
Poochera Australia 135 F8
Poole U.K. 59 F8
Poole U.S.A. 164 B5
Poolowanna Lake salt flat Australia 137 B5
Poona India see Pune
Pooncarie Australia 137 C7
Poonch India see Punch
Popelloe Lake salt l. Australia 138 B3
Poopó, Lago de l. Bol. 176 E7
Poor Knights Islands N.Z. 139 E2
Poorman AK U.S.A. 148 I2
Popayán Col. 176 C3
Poperinge Belgium 62 C4
Popigay r. Rus. Fed. 77 L2
Popiltah Australia 137 C7
Popilta Lake imp. l. Australia 137 C7
Poplar r. Canada 151 L4
Poplar U.S.A. 156 G2
Poplar Bluff U.S.A. 161 F4
Poplar Camp U.S.A. 164 E5
Poplarville U.S.A. 161 F6

▶Popocatépetl, Volcán vol. Mex. 168 E5
5th highest mountain in North America.

Popoh Jawa Indon. 85 E5
Popokabaka Dem. Rep. Congo 123 B4
Popondetta P.N.G. 81 L8
Popovichskaya Rus. Fed. see Kalininskaya
Popovo Bulg. 69 L3
Popovo Polje plain Bos.-Herz. 68 G3
Poppberg hill Germany 63 L5
Poppenberg hill Germany 63 K3
Poprad Slovakia 57 R6
Poptún Guat. 167 H5
Poquoson U.S.A. 165 G5
Porali r. Pak. 111 G5
Porangahau N.Z. 139 F5
Porangatu Brazil 179 A1
Porbandar India 104 B5
Porcher Island B.C. Canada 149 O5
Porcos r. Brazil 179 B1

Porcupine r. Canada/U.S.A. 149 K2
Porcupine, Cape Canada 153 K3
Porcupine Abyssal Plain sea feature N. Atlantic Ocean 184 G2
Porcupine Gorge National Park Australia 136 D4
Porcupine Hills Canada 151 K4
Porcupine Mountains U.S.A. 160 F2
Poreč Croatia 68 E2
Porecatu Brazil 179 A3
Poretskoye Rus. Fed. 53 J5
Porgyang Xizang China 99 C6
Pori Fin. 55 L6
Porirua N.Z. 139 E5
Porkhov Rus. Fed. 55 P8
Porlamar Venez. 176 F1
Pormpuraaw Australia 136 C2
Pornic France 66 C3
Poro i. Phil. 82 D4
Poronaysk Rus. Fed. 90 F2
Porong Xizang China 99 E7
Poros Greece 69 J6
Porosozero Rus. Fed. 52 G3
Porpoise Bay Antarctica 188 G2
Porsangerfjorden sea chan. Norway 54 N1
Porsangerhalvøya pen. Norway 54 N1
Porsgrunn Norway 55 F7
Porsuk r. Turkey 69 N5
Portadown U.K. 61 F3
Portaferry U.K. 61 G3
Portage MI U.S.A. 164 C2
Portage PA U.S.A. 165 F3
Portage WI U.S.A. 160 F3
Portage Creek AK U.S.A. 148 H4
Portage Lakes U.S.A. 164 E3
Portage la Prairie Canada 151 L5
Portal U.S.A. 160 C1
Port Alberni Canada 150 E5
Port Albert Australia 138 C7
Portalegre Port. 67 C4
Portales U.S.A. 161 C5
Port-Alfred Canada see La Baie
Port Alfred S. Africa 125 H7
Port Alice Canada 150 E5
Port Allegany U.S.A. 165 F3
Port Allen U.S.A. 161 F6
Port Alma Australia 136 E4
Port Alsworth AK U.S.A. 148 I3
Port Angeles U.S.A. 156 C2
Port Antonio Jamaica 169 I5
Portarlington Ireland 61 E4
Port Arthur Australia 137 [inset]
Port Arthur Liaoning China see Lüshun
Port Arthur U.S.A. 161 E6
Port Askaig U.K. 60 C5
Port Augusta Australia 137 B7

▶Port-au-Prince Haiti 169 J5
Capital of Haiti.

Port Austin U.S.A. 164 D1
Port aux Choix Canada 153 K4
Portavogie U.K. 61 G3
Port Barton b. Palawan Phil. 82 B4
Port Beaufort S. Africa 124 E8
Port Blair India 87 A5
Port Bolster Canada 164 F1
Portbou Spain 67 H2
Port Brabant N.W.T. Canada see Tuktoyaktuk
Port Burwell Canada 164 E2
Port Campbell Australia 138 A7
Port Campbell National Park Australia 138 A7
Port Carling Canada 164 F1
Port-Cartier Canada 153 I4
Port Chalmers N.Z. 139 C7
Port Charlotte U.S.A. 163 D7
Port Clarence b. AK U.S.A. 148 F2
Port Clements B.C. Canada 149 N5
Port Clinton U.S.A. 164 D3
Port Credit Canada 164 F2
Port-de-Paix Haiti 169 J5
Port Dickson Malaysia 84 C2
Port Douglas Australia 136 D3
Port Edward B.C. Canada 149 O5
Port Edward S. Africa 125 J6
Porteira Brazil 177 G4
Porteirinha Brazil 179 C1
Portel Brazil 177 H4
Port Elgin Canada 164 E1
Port Elizabeth S. Africa 125 G7
Port Ellen U.K. 60 C5
Port Erin Isle of Man 58 C4
Porter Lake N.W.T. Canada 151 J2
Porter Lake Sask. Canada 151 J3
Porter Landing B.C. Canada 149 O4
Porterville S. Africa 124 D7
Porterville U.S.A. 158 D3
Port Étienne Mauritania see Nouâdhibou
Port Everglades U.S.A. see Fort Lauderdale
Port Fitzroy N.Z. 139 E3
Port Francqui Dem. Rep. Congo see Ilebo
Port-Gentil Gabon 122 A4
Port Gibson MS U.S.A. 167 H2
Port Glasgow U.K. 60 E5
Port Graham AK U.S.A. 149 J4
Port Harcourt Nigeria 120 D4
Port Harrison Canada see Inukjuak
Porthcawl U.K. 59 D7
Port Hedland Australia 134 B5
Port Heiden AK U.S.A. 148 H4
Port Heiden b. AK U.S.A. 148 H4
Port Henry U.S.A. 165 I1
Port Herald Malawi see Nsanje
Porthleven U.K. 59 B8
Porthmadog U.K. 59 C6
Port Hope Canada 165 F2
Port Hope Simpson Canada 153 L3
Port Hueneme U.S.A. 158 D4
Port Huron U.S.A. 164 D2
Portimão Port. 67 B5
Port Jackson Australia see Sydney
Port Jackson inlet Australia 138 E4
Port Keats Australia see Wadeye
Port Klang Malaysia see Pelabuhan Klang
Port Láirge Ireland see Waterford
Portland N.S.W. Australia 138 D4
Portland Vic. Australia 137 C8
Portland IN U.S.A. 164 C3
Portland ME U.S.A. 165 J2
Portland MI U.S.A. 164 C2
Portland OR U.S.A. 156 C3
Portland TN U.S.A. 164 B5
Portland, Isle of pen. U.K. 59 E8
Portland Bill hd U.K. see Bill of Portland
Portland Creek Pond l. Canada 153 K4
Portland Roads Australia 136 C2
Port-la-Nouvelle France 66 F5
Portlaoise Ireland 61 E4
Port Lavaca U.S.A. 161 D6
Portlaw Ireland 61 E5
Portlethen U.K. 60 G3
Port Lincoln Australia 137 A7
Port Lions AK U.S.A. 148 I4
Portlock AK U.S.A. 149 J4
Port Loko Sierra Leone 120 B4

▶Port Louis Mauritius 185 L7
Capital of Mauritius.

Port-Lyautrey Morocco see Kénitra
Port Macquarie Australia 138 F3
Portmadoc U.K. see Porthmadog
Port McNeill Canada 150 E5
Port-Menier Canada 153 I4
Port Moller AK U.S.A. 148 G5
Port Moller b. AK U.S.A. 148 G5

▶Port Moresby P.N.G. 81 L8
Capital of Papua New Guinea.

Portnaguran U.K. 60 C2
Portnahaven U.K. 60 C5
Port nan Giúran U.K. see Portnaguran
Port Neill Australia 137 B7
Portneuf r. Canada 153 H4
Port Nis Scotland U.K. see Port of Ness
Port Nis U.K. see Port of Ness
Port Noarlunga Australia 137 B7
Port Nolloth S. Africa 124 C5
Port Norris U.S.A. 165 H4
Port-Nouveau-Québec Canada see Kangiqsualujjuaq
Porto Port. see Oporto
Porto Acre Brazil 176 E5
Porto Alegre Brazil 179 A5
Porto Alexandre Angola see Tombua
Porto Amboim Angola 123 B5
Porto Amélia Moz. see Pemba
Porto Artur Brazil 177 G6
Porto Belo Brazil 179 A4
Portobelo Panama 166 [inset] K7
Portobelo, Parque Nacional nat. park Panama 166 [inset] K7
Port O'Brien AK U.S.A. 148 I4
Porto de Moz Brazil 177 H4
Porto de Santa Cruz Brazil 179 C1
Porto dos Gaúchos Óbidos Brazil 177 G6
Porto Esperança Brazil 177 G7
Porto Esperidião Brazil 177 G7
Portoferraio Italy 68 D3
Port of Ness U.K. 60 C2
Porto Franco Brazil 177 I5

▶Port of Spain Trin. and Tob. 169 L6
Capital of Trinidad and Tobago.

Porto Grande Brazil 177 H3
Portogruaro Italy 68 E2
Porto Jofre Brazil 177 G7
Portola U.S.A. 158 C2
Portomaggiore Italy 68 D2
Porto Mendes Brazil 178 F2
Porto Murtinho Brazil 178 E2
Porto Nacional Brazil 177 I6

▶Porto-Novo Benin 120 D4
Capital of Benin.

Porto Novo Cape Verde 120 [inset]
Porto Primavera, Represa resr Brazil 178 F2
Port Orchard U.S.A. 156 C3
Port Orford U.S.A. 156 B4
Porto Rico Angola 123 B4
Porto Santo, Ilha de i. Madeira 120 B1
Porto Seguro Brazil 179 D2
Porto Tolle Italy 68 E2
Porto Torres Sardinia Italy 68 C4
Porto União Brazil 179 A4
Porto-Vecchio Corsica France 66 I6
Porto Velho Brazil 176 F5
Portoviejo Ecuador 176 B4
Porto Wálter Brazil 176 D5
Portpatrick U.K. 60 D6
Port Perry Canada 165 F1
Port Phillip Bay Australia 138 B7
Port Pirie Australia 137 B7
Port Radium Canada see Echo Bay
Portreath U.K. 59 B8
Portree U.K. 60 C3
Port Rexton Canada 153 L4
Port Royal U.S.A. 165 G4
Port Royal Sound inlet U.S.A. 163 D5
Portrush U.K. 61 F2
Port Safaga Egypt see Būr Safājah
Port Safety AK U.S.A. 148 F2
Port Said Egypt 107 A4
Port St Joe U.S.A. 163 C6
Port St Lucie City U.S.A. 163 D7
Port St Mary Isle of Man 58 C4
Portsalon Ireland 61 E2
Port Sanilac U.S.A. 164 D2
Port Severn Canada 164 F1
Port Shepstone S. Africa 125 J6
Port Simpson B.C. Canada see Lax Kw'alaams
Portsmouth U.K. 59 F8
Portsmouth NH U.S.A. 165 J2
Portsmouth OH U.S.A. 164 D4
Portsmouth VA U.S.A. 165 G5
Portsoy U.K. 60 G3
Port Stanley Falkland Is see Stanley
Port Stephens b. Australia 138 F4
Portstewart U.K. 61 F2
Port Sudan Sudan 108 E6
Port Sulphur LA U.S.A. 167 H2
Port Swettenham Malaysia see Pelabuhan Klang
Port Talbot U.K. 59 D7
Port Tambang b. Luzon Phil. 82 C3
Porttipahdan tekojärvi l. Fin. 54 O2
Port Townsend U.S.A. 156 C2
Portugal country Europe 67 C4
Portugalete Spain 67 E2
Portugália Angola see Chitato
Portuguese East Africa country Africa see Mozambique
Portuguese Guinea country Africa see Guinea-Bissau
Portuguese Timor country Asia see East Timor
Portuguese West Africa country Africa see Angola
Portumna Ireland 61 D4
Portus Herculis Monoeci country Europe see Monaco
Port-Vendres France 66 F5

▶Port Vila Vanuatu 133 G3
Capital of Vanuatu.

Portville U.S.A. 165 F2
Port Vladimir Rus. Fed. 54 R2
Port Waikato N.Z. 139 E3
Port Washington U.S.A. 164 B2
Port William U.K. 60 E6
Porvenir Bol. 176 E6
Porvenir Chile 178 B8
Porvoo Fin. 55 N6
Posada Spain 67 D2
Posada de Llanera Spain see Posada
Posadas Arg. 178 E3
Posen Poland see Poznań
Posen U.S.A. 164 D1
Poseyville U.S.A. 164 B4
Poshekhon'ye Rus. Fed. 52 H4
Poshekon'ye-Volodarsk Rus. Fed. see Poshekhon'ye
Posht-e Badam Iran 110 D3
Poshteh-ye Chaqvīr hill Iran 110 E4
Posht-e Kūh mts Iran 110 B3
Posht-e Rūd-e Zamindavar reg. Afgh. see Zamīndāvar
Posht Kūh hill Iran 110 C2
Posio Fin. 54 P3
Poskam Xinjiang China see Zepu
Poso Sulawesi Indon. 83 B3
Poso r. Indon. 83 B3
Poso, Danau l. Indon. 83 B3
Poso, Teluk b. Indon. 83 B3
Posof Turkey 113 F2
Posŏng S. Korea 91 B6
Possession Island Namibia 124 B4
Pößneck Germany 63 L4
Possum Kingdom Lake TX U.S.A. 167 F1
Post U.S.A. 161 C5
Postavy Belarus see Pastavy
Poste-de-la-Baleine Canada see Kuujjuarapik
Poste Weygand Alg. 120 D2
Postmasburg S. Africa 124 F5
Poston U.S.A. 159 F4
Postville Canada 153 K3
Postville U.S.A. 152 C6
Postysheve Ukr. see Krasnoarmiys'k
Pota Flores Indon. 83 B5
Pótam Mex. 166 C3
Poté Brazil 179 C2
Poteau U.S.A. 161 E5
Potegaon India 106 D2
Potentia Italy see Potenza
Potenza Italy 68 F4
Poth U.S.A. 161 D6
P'ot'i Georgia 113 F2
Potikal India 106 D2
Potiraguá Brazil 179 D1
Potiskum Nigeria 120 E3
Potlatch U.S.A. 156 D3
Pot Mountain U.S.A. 156 E3
Po Toi i. H.K. China 97 [inset]
Potomac r. U.S.A. 165 G4
Potomana, Gunung mt. Indon. 83 C5
Potosí Bol. 176 E7
Potosi U.S.A. 160 F4
Potosi Mountain U.S.A. 159 F4
Pototan Panay Phil. 82 C4
Potrerillos Chile 178 C3
Potrerillos Hond. 166 [inset] I6
Potrero del Llano Chihuahua Mex. 166 D2
Potsdam Germany 63 N2
Potsdam U.S.A. 165 H1
Potter U.S.A. 160 C3
Potterne U.K. 59 E7
Potters Bar U.K. 59 G7
Potter Valley U.S.A. 158 B2
Pottstown U.S.A. 165 H3
Pottsville U.S.A. 165 G3
Pottuvil Sri Lanka 106 D5
Potwar reg. Pak. 111 I3
Pouch Cove Canada 153 L5
Poughkeepsie U.S.A. 165 I3
Poulin de Courval, Lac l. Canada 153 H4
Poulton-le-Fylde U.K. 58 E5
Pouso Alegre Brazil 179 B3
Poŭthĭsăt Cambodia 87 C4
Poŭthĭsăt, Stœng r. Cambodia 87 D4
Považská Bystrica Slovakia 57 Q6
Povenets Rus. Fed. 52 G3
Poverty Bay N.Z. 139 F4
Povlen mt. Serbia 69 H2
Póvoa de Varzim Port. 67 B3
Povorino Rus. Fed. 53 I6
Povorotnyy, Mys hd Rus. Fed. 90 D4
Poway U.S.A. 158 E5
Powder r. U.S.A. 156 G3
Powder, South Fork r. U.S.A. 156 G4
Powder River U.S.A. 156 G4
Powell r. U.S.A. 164 D5
Powell, Lake resr U.S.A. 159 H3
Powell Lake Canada 150 E5
Powell Mountain U.S.A. 158 D2
Powell Point Bahamas 163 E7
Powell River Canada 150 E5
Powhatan AR U.S.A. 161 F4
Powhatan VA U.S.A. 165 G5
Powo China 96 C1
Pōwrize Turkm. 110 E2
Poxoréu Brazil 177 H7
Poyang China see Boyang
Poyang Hu l. China 97 H2
Poyan Reservoir Sing. 87 [inset]
Poyarkovo Rus. Fed. 90 C2
Pozantı Turkey 112 D3
Požarevac Serbia 69 I2
Poza Rica Mex. 168 E4
Pozdeyevka Rus. Fed. 90 C2
Požega Croatia 68 G2
Požega Serbia 69 I3
Pozharskoye Rus. Fed. 90 D3
Poznań Poland 57 P4
Pozoblanco Spain 67 D4
Pozo Colorado Para. 178 E2
Pozo Nuevo Mex. 166 C2
Pozsony Slovakia see Bratislava
Pozzuoli Italy 68 F4
Prabumulih Sumatera Indon. 84 D3
Prachatice Czech Rep. 57 O6
Prachi r. India 105 F6
Prachin Buri Thai. 87 C4
Prachuap Khiri Khan Thai. 87 B5
Prades France 66 F5
Prado Brazil 179 D2

▶Prague Czech Rep. 57 O5
Capital of the Czech Republic.

Praha Czech Rep. see Prague

▶Praia Cape Verde 120 [inset]
Capital of Cape Verde.

Praia do Bilene Moz. 125 K3
Prainha Brazil 177 H4
Prairie Australia 136 D4
Prairie r. U.S.A. 160 E2
Prairie Dog Town Fork r. U.S.A. 161 C5
Prairie du Chien U.S.A. 160 F3
Prairie River Canada 151 K4
Pram, Khao mt. Thai. 87 B5
Pran r. Thai. 87 C4
Pran Buri Thai. 87 B4
Prapat Sumatera Indon. 84 B2
Prasonisi, Akra pt Notio Aigaio Greece see Prasonisi, Akrotirio
Prasonisi, Akrotirio pt Greece 69 L7
Prata Brazil 179 A2
Prata r. Brazil 179 A2
Prat de Llobregat Spain see El Prat de Llobregat
Prathes Thai country Asia see Thailand
Prato Italy 68 D3
Pratt U.S.A. 160 D4
Prattville U.S.A. 163 C5
Pravdinsk Rus. Fed. 55 L9
Praya Lombok Indon. 85 G5
Preah, Prêk r. Cambodia 87 D4
Preăh Vihéar Cambodia 87 D4
Preble U.S.A. 165 G2
Prechistoye Smolenskaya Oblast' Rus. Fed. 53 G5
Prechistoye Yaroslavskaya Oblast' Rus. Fed. 52 I4
Precipice National Park Australia 136 E5
Preeceville Canada 151 K5
Pregolya r. Rus. Fed. 55 L9
Preiļi Latvia 55 O8
Prelate Canada 151 I5
Premer Australia 138 D3
Prémery France 66 F3
Premnitz Germany 63 M2
Prentiss U.S.A. 161 F6
Prenzlau Germany 57 N4
Preparis Island Cocos Is 80 A4
Preparis North Channel Cocos Is 80 A4
Preparis South Channel Cocos Is 80 A4
Přerov Czech Rep. 57 P6
Presa de la Amistad, Parque Natural nature res. Mex. 167 E2
Presa San Antonio Mex. 167 E3
Prescelly Mts hills U.K. see Preseli, Mynydd
Prescott Canada 165 H1
Prescott AR U.S.A. 161 E5
Prescott AZ U.S.A. 159 G4
Prescott Valley U.S.A. 159 G4
Preseli, Mynydd hills U.K. 59 C7
Preševo Serbia 69 I3
Presidencia Roque Sáenz Peña Arg. 178 D3
Presidente Dutra Brazil 177 J5
Presidente Hermes Brazil 176 F6
Presidente Olegário Brazil 179 B2
Presidente Prudente Brazil 179 A3
Presidente Venceslau Brazil 179 A3
Presidio U.S.A. 161 B6
Preslav Bulg. see Veliki Preslav
Prešov Slovakia 53 D6
Prespa, Lake Europe 69 I4
Prespansko Ezero l. Europe see Prespa, Lake
Prespes nat. park Greece 69 I4
Prespës, Liqeni i l. Europe see Prespa, Lake
Presque Isle ME U.S.A. 162 G2
Presque Isle MI U.S.A. 164 D1
Pressburg Slovakia see Bratislava
Presteigne U.K. 59 D6
Preston U.K. 58 E5
Preston ID U.S.A. 156 F4
Preston MN U.S.A. 160 E3
Preston MO U.S.A. 160 E4
Preston, Cape Australia 134 B5
Prestonpans U.K. 60 G5
Prestonsburg U.S.A. 164 D5
Prestwick U.K. 60 E5
Preto r. Bahia Brazil 177 J6
Preto r. Minas Gerais Brazil 179 B2
Preto r. Brazil 179 D1

▶Pretoria S. Africa 125 I3
Official capital of South Africa.

Pretoria-Witwatersrand-Vereeniging prov. S. Africa see Gauteng
Pretzsch Germany 63 M3
Preussisch-Eylau Rus. Fed. see Bagrationovsk
Preußisch Stargard Poland see Starogard Gdański
Preveza Greece 69 I5
Prewitt U.S.A. 159 I4
Prey Vêng Cambodia 87 D5
Priaral'skiye Karakumy, Peski des. Kazakh. 102 B2
Priargunsk Rus. Fed. 95 I1
Pribilof Islands AK U.S.A. 148 E4
Priboj Serbia 69 H3
Price r. Australia 134 E3
Price NC U.S.A. 164 F5
Price UT U.S.A. 159 H2
Price r. U.S.A. 159 H2
Price Island Canada 150 D4
Prichard AL U.S.A. 161 F6
Prichard WV U.S.A. 164 D4
Pridorozhnoye Rus. Fed. see Khulkhuta
Priekule Latvia 55 L8
Priekuļi Latvia 55 N8
Priel'brus'ye, Natsional'nyy Park nat. park Rus. Fed. 53 I8
Prienai Lith. 55 M9
Prieska S. Africa 124 F5
Prievidza Slovakia 57 Q6
Prignitz reg. Germany 63 M1
Prijedor Bos.-Herz. 68 G2
Prijepolje Serbia 69 H3
Prikaspiyskaya Nizmennost' lowland Kazakh./Rus. Fed. see Caspian Lowland
Prilep Macedonia 69 I4
Priluki Ukr. see Pryluky
Přimda Czech Rep. 63 M5
Primero de Enero Cuba 163 E8
Primorsk Rus. Fed. 55 P6
Primorsk Ukr. see Prymors'k
Primorskiy Kray admin. div. Rus. Fed. 90 D3
Primorsko-Akhtarsk Rus. Fed. 53 H7
Primo Tapia Mex. 166 A1
Primrose Lake Canada 151 I4
Prims r. Germany 62 G5
Prince Albert Canada 151 J4
Prince Albert S. Africa 124 F7
Prince Albert Mountains Antarctica 188 H1
Prince Albert National Park Canada 151 J4
Prince Albert Peninsula Canada 146 G2
Prince Albert Road S. Africa 124 E7
Prince Alfred, Cape Canada 146 F2
Prince Alfred Hamlet S. Africa 124 D7
Prince Charles Island Canada 147 K3
Prince Charles Mountains Antarctica 188 E2
Prince Edward Island prov. Canada 153 J5

▶Prince Edward Islands Indian Ocean 185 K9
Part of South Africa.

Prince Edward Point Canada 165 G2
Prince Frederick U.S.A. 165 G4
Prince George Canada 150 F4
Prince Harald Coast Antarctica 188 D2
Prince of Wales, Cape AK U.S.A. 148 E2
Prince of Wales Island Australia 136 C1
Prince of Wales Island Canada 147 I2
Prince of Wales Island AK U.S.A. 149 N5
Prince of Wales Strait Canada 146 G2
Prince Patrick Island Canada 146 G2
Prince Regent Inlet sea chan. Canada 147 I2
Prince Rupert B.C. Canada 149 O5
Princess Anne U.S.A. 165 H4
Princess Astrid Coast Antarctica 188 C2
Princess Charlotte Bay Australia 136 C2
Princess Elizabeth Land reg. Antarctica 188 E2
Princess Mary Lake Canada 151 L1
Princess Ragnhild Coast Antarctica 188 C2
Princess Royal Island Canada 150 D4
Princeton Canada 150 F5
Princeton CA U.S.A. 158 B2
Princeton IL U.S.A. 160 F3
Princeton IN U.S.A. 164 B4
Princeton MO U.S.A. 160 E3
Princeton NJ U.S.A. 165 H3
Princeton WV U.S.A. 164 E5
Prince William Sound b. AK U.S.A. 149 K3
Príncipe i. São Tomé and Príncipe 120 D4
Prindle, Mount AK U.S.A. 149 K2
Prineville U.S.A. 156 C3
Prins Harald Kyst coastal area Antarctica see Prince Harald Coast
Prinzapolca Nicaragua 166 [inset] J6
Priozersk Rus. Fed. 55 Q6
Priozyorsk Rus. Fed. see Priozersk
Pripet r. Belarus/Ukr. 53 F6
also spelt Pryp"yat' (Ukraine) or Prypyats' (Belarus)
Pripet Marshes Belarus/Ukr. 53 E6
Prirechnyy Rus. Fed. 54 Q2

▶Prishtinë Kosovo 69 I3
Capital of Kosovo

Priština Kosovo see Prishtinë
Pritzier Germany 63 L1
Pritzwalk Germany 63 M1
Privas France 66 G4
Privlaka Croatia 68 F2
Privolzhsk Rus. Fed. 52 I4
Privolzhskaya Vozvyshennost' hills Rus. Fed. 53 J6
Privolzhskiy Rus. Fed. 53 J6
Privolzh'ye Rus. Fed. 53 K5
Priyutnoye Rus. Fed. 53 I7
Prizren Kosovo 69 I3
Probolinggo Jawa Indon. 85 F4
Probstzella Germany 63 L4
Probus U.K. 59 C8
Proddatur India 106 C3
Professor van Blommestein Meer resr Suriname 177 G3
Progreso Coahuila Mex. 167 E3
Progreso Hidalgo Mex. 167 F4
Progreso Yucatán Mex. 167 H4
Progress Rus. Fed. 90 C2
Project City U.S.A. 156 C4
Prokhladnyy Rus. Fed. 113 G2
Prokop'yevsk Rus. Fed. 88 F2
Prokuplje Serbia 69 I3
Proletarsk Rus. Fed. 53 I7
Proletarskaya Rus. Fed. see Proletarsk
Prome Myanmar see Pyè
Promissão Brazil 179 A3
Promissão, Represa resr Brazil 179 A3
Prophet r. Canada 150 F3
Prophet River Canada 150 F3
Propriá Brazil 177 K6
Proskurov Ukr. see Khmel'nyts'kyy
Prosperidad Mindanao Phil. 82 D4
Prosser U.S.A. 156 D3
Protem S. Africa 124 E8
Provadiya Bulg. 69 L3
Prøven Greenland see Kangersuatsiaq
Provence reg. France 66 G5
Providence KY U.S.A. 164 B5
Providence MD U.S.A. see Annapolis

▶Providence RI U.S.A. 165 J3
Capital of Rhode Island.

Providence, Cape N.Z. 139 A8
Providence, Cape AK U.S.A. 148 H4
Providencia, Isla de i. Caribbean Sea 169 H6
Provideniya Rus. Fed. 148 D2
Provincetown U.S.A. 165 J2
Provo U.S.A. 159 H1
Provost Canada 151 I4
Prudentópolis Brazil 179 A4
Prudhoe Bay AK U.S.A. 149 J1
Prudhoe Bay AK U.S.A. 149 J1
Prüm Germany 62 G4
Prüm r. Germany 62 G5
Prunelli-di-Fiumorbo Corsica France 66 I5
Pruntytown U.S.A. 164 E4
Prusa Turkey see Bursa
Prushkov Poland see Pruszków
Pruszków Poland 57 R4
Prut r. Europe 53 F7
Prydz Bay Antarctica 188 E2
Pryluky Ukr. 53 G6
Prymors'k Ukr. 53 H7
Prymors'ke Ukr. see Sartana
Pryp"yat' r. Ukr. 53 F6 see Pripet
Pryp"yat' (abandoned) Ukr. 53 F6
Prypyats' r. Belarus 51 L5 see Pripet
Przemyśl Poland 53 D6
Przheval'sk Kyrg. see Karakol
Przheval'sk Pristany Kyrg. 98 B4
Psara i. Greece 69 K5
Pskov Rus. Fed. 55 P8
Pskov, Lake Estonia/Rus. Fed. 55 O7
Pskov Oblast admin. div. Rus. Fed. see Pskovskaya Oblast'
Pskovskaya Oblast' admin. div. Rus. Fed. 55 P8
Pskovskoye Ozero l. Estonia/Rus. Fed. see Pskov, Lake
Ptolemaïda Greece 69 I4
Ptolemais Israel see 'Akko
Ptuj Slovenia 68 F1
Pu r. Indon. 84 C3
Pua Thai. 86 C3
Puaka hill Sing. 87 [inset]
Pu'an Guizhou China 96 E3
Pu'an Sichuan China 96 E2
Puan S. Korea 91 B6
Pucallpa Peru 176 D5
Pucheng Fujian China 97 H3
Pucheng Shaanxi China 95 G5
Puchezh Rus. Fed. 52 I4
Puch'ŏn S. Korea 91 B5
Pucio Point Panay Phil. 82 C4
Puck Poland 57 Q3
Pudai watercourse Afgh. see Dor
Pūdanū Iran 110 D3
Pudasjärvi Fin. 54 O4

Pudi Kalimantan Indon. 85 G3
Pudimoe S. Africa 124 G4
Pudong China 56 E4
Pudozh Rus. Fed. 52 H3
Pudsey U.K. 58 F5
Pudu China see Suizhou
Puduchcheri India see Puducherry
Puducherry India 106 C4
Puducherry union terr. India 106 C4
Pudukkottai India 106 C4
Puebla Baja California Mex. 159 F5
Puebla Puebla Mex. 168 E5
Puebla state Mex. 167 F5
Puebla de Sanabria Spain 67 C2
Puebla de Zaragoza Mex. see Puebla
Pueblo U.S.A. 157 G5
Pueblo Nuevo Mex. 166 D4
Pueblo Nuevo Nicaragua 166 [inset] I6
Pueblo Viejo, Laguna de lag. Mex. 167 F4
Pueblo Yaqui Mex. 166 C3
Puelches Arg. 178 C5
Puelén Arg. 178 C5
Puente de Ixtla Mex. 167 F5
Puente-Genil Spain 67 D5
Pu'er China 96 D4
Puerco watercourse U.S.A. 159 H4
Puerto Acosta Bol. 176 E7
Puerto Alegre Bol. 176 F6
Puerto Ángel Mex. 167 F6
Puerto Arista Mex. 167 G6
Puerto Armuelles Panama 166 [inset] J7
Puerto Ayacucho Venez. 176 E2
Puerto Bahía Negra Para. see Bahía Negra
Puerto Baquerizo Moreno Galápagos Ecuador 176 [inset]
Puerto Barrios Guat. 166 [inset] H6
Puerto Cabello Venez. 176 E1
Puerto Cabezas Nicaragua 166 [inset] J6
Puerto Cabo Gracias á Dios Nicaragua 166 [inset] J6
Puerto Carreño Col. 176 E2
Puerto Casado Para. 178 E2
Puerto Cavinas Bol. 176 E6
Puerto Coig Arg. 178 C8
Puerto Cortés Costa Rica 166 [inset] J7
Puerto Cortés Hond. 166 [inset] I6
Puerto Cortés Mex. 166 C3
Puerto de Lobos Mex. 166 B2
Puerto de Los Ángeles, Parque Natural nature res. Mex. 166 D4
Puerto de Morelos Mex. 167 I4
Puerto Escondido Mex. 168 E5
Puerto Francisco de Orellana Ecuador see Coca
Puerto Frey Bol. 176 F6
Puerto Génova Bol. 176 E6
Puerto Guarani Para. 178 E2
Puerto Heath Bol. 176 E6
Puerto Huitoto Col. 176 D3
Puerto Inírida Col. 176 E3
Puerto Isabel Bol. 177 G7
Puerto Juáres Mex. 167 I4
Puerto Leguizamo Col. 176 D4
Puerto Lempira Hond. 166 [inset] J6
Puerto Libertad Mex. 166 B2
Puerto Limón Costa Rica 166 [inset] J7
Puertollano Spain 67 D4
Puerto Lobos Arg. 178 C6
Puerto Madero Mex. 167 G6
Puerto Madryn Arg. 178 C6
Puerto Magdalena Mex. 166 B3
Puerto Maldonado Peru 176 E6
Puerto Máncora Peru 176 B4
Puerto México Mex. see Coatzacoalcos
Puerto Montt Chile 178 B6
Puerto Morazán Nicaragua 166 [inset] I6
Puerto Natales Chile 178 B8
Puerto Nuevo Col. 176 E2
Puerto Peñasco Mex. 166 B2
Puerto Pirámides Arg. 178 D6
Puerto Plata Dom. Rep. 169 J5
Puerto Portillo Peru 176 D5
Puerto Prado Peru 176 D6
Puerto Princesa Palawan Phil. 82 B4
Puerto Quepos Costa Rica 166 [inset] I7
Puerto Quetzal Guat. 166 H6
Puerto Real Mex. 167 H5
Puerto Rico Arg. 178 E3
Puerto Rico Bol. 176 E6

▶Puerto Rico terr. West Indies 169 K5
United States Commonwealth.

▶Puerto Rico Trench sea feature Caribbean Sea 184 D4
Deepest trench in the Atlantic Ocean.

Puerto Sandino Nicaragua 166 [inset] I6
Puerto San José Guat. 167 H6
Puerto Santa Cruz Arg. 178 C8
Puerto Sastre Para. 178 E2
Puerto Saucedo Bol. 176 F6
Puerto Somoza Nicaragua see Puerto Sandino
Puerto Suárez Bol. 177 G7
Puerto Supe Peru 176 C6
Puerto Vallarta Mex. 168 C4
Puerto Victoria Peru 176 D5
Puerto Visser Arg. 178 C7
Puerto Williams Chile 178 C8
Puerto Yartou Chile 178 B8
Puerto Ybapobó Para. 178 E2
Pugachev Rus. Fed. 53 K5
Pugal India 104 C3
Puge China 96 D3
Puger Jawa Indon. 85 F5
Pūhāl-e Khamīr, Kūh-e mts Iran 110 D5
Puhiwaero c. N.Z. see South West Cape
Puigmal mt. France/Spain 66 F5
Pui O Wan b. H.K. China 97 [inset]
Pujada Bay Mindanao Phil. 82 D5
Puji Shaanxi China see Wugong
Puji China see Puge
Pukaki, Lake N.Z. 139 C7
Pukapuka atoll Cook Is 133 J3
Pukaskwa National Park Canada 152 D4
Pukatawagan Canada 151 K4
Pukchin N. Korea 91 B4
Pukch'ŏng N. Korea 91 C4
Pukekohe N.Z. 139 E3
Puketeraki Range mts N.Z. 139 D6
Pukeuri Junction N.Z. 139 C7
Puksubaek-san mt. N. Korea 90 B4
Pula Croatia 68 E2
Pula Sardinia Italy 68 C5
Pulandian Liaoning China 95 J4
Pulandian Wan b. China 95 J4
Pulangi r. Mindanao Phil. 82 D5
Pulangpisau Kalimantan Indon. 85 F3
Pulap atoll Micronesia 81 L5
Pulasi i. Indon. 83 B4
Pulaski NY U.S.A. 165 G2
Pulaski VA U.S.A. 164 E5
Pulaski WI U.S.A. 164 A1
Pulaukijang Sumatera Indon. 84 C3
Pulau Pinang state Malaysia see Pinang
Pulau Simeulue, Suaka Margasatwa nature res. Indon. 87 A7
Pulheim Germany 62 G3
Pulicat Lake inlet India 106 D3
Pulivendla India 106 C3
Pulkkila Fin. 54 N4
Pullman U.S.A. 156 D3
Pulo Anna i. Palau 81 I6
Pulog, Mount Luzon Phil. 82 C2
Pulozero Rus. Fed. 54 R2
Púlpito, Punta pt Mex. 166 C3
Pulu Xinjiang China 99 C5
Pülümür Turkey 113 E3
Pulusuk atoll Micronesia 81 L5
Pulutan Sulawesi Indon. 83 C1
Puluwat atoll Micronesia 81 L5
Pulwama India 111 I3
Pumasillo, Cerro mt. Peru 176 D6
Puma Yumco l. China 99 E7
Pumiao China see Yongning
Puná, Isla i. Ecuador 176 B4
Punakha Bhutan 105 G4
Punch India 104 C2
Punchaw Canada 150 F4
Punda Maria S. Africa 125 J2
Pundri India 104 D3
Pune India 106 B2
P'ungsan N. Korea 90 C4
Puning China 97 H4
Punjab state India 104 C3
Punjab prov. Pak. 111 H4
Punmah Glacier Pak. 104 D2
Puno Peru 176 D7
Punta, Cerro de mt. Puerto Rico 169 K5
Punta Abreojos Mex. 157 E8
Punta Alta Arg. 178 D5
Punta Arenas Chile 178 B8
Punta Balestrieri mt. Italy 68 C4
Punta del Este Uruguay 178 F5
Punta Delgada Arg. 178 D6
Punta Gorda Belize 166 [inset] H5
Punta Gorda Nicaragua 166 [inset] J7
Punta Gorda U.S.A. 163 D7
Punta Norte Arg. 178 D6
Punta Prieta Mex. 166 B2
Puntarenas Costa Rica 166 [inset] I7
Punuk Islands AK U.S.A. 148 E3
Punxsutawney U.S.A. 165 F3
Puokio Fin. 54 O4
Puolanka Fin. 54 O4
Puqi China see Chibi
Pur r. Rus. Fed. 76 I3
Puracé, Volcán de vol. Col. 176 C3
Purbalingga Jawa Indon. 85 E4
Purcell U.S.A. 161 D5
Purcell Mountain AK U.S.A. 148 H2
Purcell Mountains Canada 150 G5
Pur Co l. China 99 C6
Purgadala Xizang China 99 D6
Purgatoire r. U.S.A. 160 C4
Puri India 106 E2
Purmerend Neth. 62 E2
Purna r. Mahar. India 104 D5
Purna r. Mahar. India 106 C2
Purnea India see Purnia
Purnia India 105 F4
Purnululu National Park Australia 134 E4
Pursat Cambodia see Poŭthĭsăt
Puruandíro Mex. 167 E4
Purukcahu Kalimantan Indon. 85 F3
Puruliya India 105 F5

▶Purus r. Peru 176 F4
3rd longest river in South America.

Puruvesi l. Fin. 54 P6
Purvis MS U.S.A. 167 H2
Purwakarta Jawa Indon. 84 D4
Purwareja Jawa Indon. 85 E4
Purwodadi Jawa Indon. 85 E4
Purwokerto Jawa Indon. 85 E4
Puryŏng N. Korea 90 C4
Pusa Bihar India 99 D8
Pusa Sarawak Malaysia 85 E2
Pusad India 106 C2
Pusan S. Korea 91 C6
Pusan Point Mindanao Phil. 82 D5
Pusatlı Dağı mt. Turkey 107 A1
Pushchino Rus. Fed. 53 H5
Pushemskiy Rus. Fed. 52 J3
Pushkin Rus. Fed. 55 Q7
Pushkino Azer. see Biläsuvar
Pushkinskaya, Gora mt. Rus. Fed. 90 F3
Pushkinskiye Gory Rus. Fed. 55 P8
Pusht-i-Rud reg. Afgh. see Zamīndāvar
Pustoshka Rus. Fed. 52 F4
Pusur r. Bangl. 105 G5
Putahow Lake Canada 151 K3
Putain Timor Indon. 83 C5
Putao Myanmar 86 B1
Puteoli Italy see Pozzuoli
Puteran i. Indon. 85 F4
Puthein Myanmar see Bassein
Putian China 97 H3
Puting China see De'an
Puting, Tanjung pt Indon. 85 E3
Putintsevo Kazakh. 98 D2
Putla Mex. 167 F5
Putlitz Germany 63 M1
Putna r. Romania 69 L2
Putney U.S.A. 165 I2
Putoi i. H.K. China see Po Toi
Putorana, Gory mts Rus. Fed. 189 E2

▶Putrajaya Malaysia 84 C2
Joint capital (with Kuala Lumpur) of Malaysia.

Putre Chile 176 E7
Putsonderwater S. Africa 124 E5
Puttalam Sri Lanka 106 C4
Puttalam Lagoon Sri Lanka 106 C4
Puttelange-aux-Lacs France 62 G5
Putten Neth. 62 F2
Puttershoek Neth. 62 E3
Puttgarden Germany 57 M3
Putumayo r. Col. 176 D4
also known as Içá (Peru)
Putuo China see Shenjiamen
Putusibau Kalimantan Indon. 85 F2
Puumala Fin. 55 P6
Pu'uwai U.S.A. 157 [inset]
Puvirnituq Canada 152 F1
Puxian Shanxi China 95 G4
Puyallup U.S.A. 156 C3
Puyang Henan China 95 H5
Puy de Sancy mt. France 66 F4
Puyehue, Parque Nacional nat. park Chile 178 B6
Puysegur Point N.Z. 139 A8
Puzak, Hāmūn-e marsh Afgh. 111 F4
Puzla Rus. Fed. 52 L3
Pweto Dem. Rep. Congo 123 C4
Pwinbyu Myanmar 86 A2
Pwllheli U.K. 59 C6
Pyal'ma Rus. Fed. 52 G3
Pyalo Myanmar 86 A3
Pyamalaw r. Myanmar 86 A4
Pyandzh Tajik. see Panj
Pyaozero, Ozero l. Rus. Fed. 54 Q3
Pyaozerskiy Rus. Fed. 54 Q4
Pyapali India 106 C3
Pyapon Myanmar 86 A3
Pyasina r. Rus. Fed. 76 J2
Pyatigorsk Rus. Fed. 113 F1
Pyatikhatki Ukr. see P''yatykhatky
P''yatykhatky Ukr. 53 G6
Pyay Myanmar see Pyè
Pychas Rus. Fed. 52 L4
Pyè Myanmar 86 A3
Pye, Mount hill N.Z. 139 B8
Pye Islands AK U.S.A. 149 J4
Pyetrykaw Belarus 53 F5
Pygmalion Point India 87 A6
Pyhäjoki Fin. 54 N4
Pyhäjoki r. Fin. 54 N4
Pyhäntä Fin. 54 O4
Pyhäsalmi Fin. 54 N5
Pyhäselkä l. Fin. 54 P5
Pyi Myanmar see Pyè
Pyin Myanmar see Pyè
Pyingaing Myanmar 86 A2
Pyinmana Myanmar 86 B3
Pyin-U-Lwin Myanmar 86 B2
Pyle U.K. 59 D7
Pyl'karamo Rus. Fed. 76 J3
Pylos Greece 69 I6
Pymatuning Reservoir U.S.A. 164 E3
Pyŏktong N. Korea 90 B4
P'yŏnggang N. Korea 91 B5
P'yŏnghae S. Korea 91 C5
P'yŏngsong N. Korea 91 B5
P'yŏngt'aek S. Korea 91 B5

▶P'yŏngyang N. Korea 91 B5
Capital of North Korea.

Pyramid Hill Australia 138 B6
Pyramid Lake U.S.A. 158 D1
Pyramid Peak U.S.A. 159 J1
Pyramid Range mts U.S.A. 158 D2
Pyramids of Giza tourist site Egypt 112 C5
Pyrénées mts Europe see Pyrenees
Pyrenees mts Europe 67 H2
Pyrénées, Parc National des nat. park France/Spain 66 D5
Pyre Peak vol. AK U.S.A. 149 [inset]
Pyrgos Greece 69 I6
Pyryatyn Ukr. 53 G6
Pyrzyce Poland 57 O4
Pyshchug Rus. Fed. 52 J4
Pytalovo Rus. Fed. 55 O8
Pyxaria mt. Greece 69 J5

Q

Qaa Lebanon 107 C2
Qaanaaq Greenland see Thule
Qabātiya West Bank 107 B3
Qabnag Xizang China 99 F7
Qabqa Qinghai China see Gonghe
Qacentina Alg. see Constantine
Qacha's Nek Lesotho 125 I6
Qādes Afgh. 111 F3
Qādisīyah, Sadd dam Iraq 113 F4
Qadisiyah Dam Iraq see Qādisīyah, Sadd
Qā'emābād Iran 111 F4
Qagan Nei Mongol China 95 I1
Qagan Nei Mongol China 94 F3
Qagan Nur Nei Mongol China 95 G4
Qagan Nur Nei Mongol China 95 H3
Qagan Nur Nei Mongol China 95 H3
Qagan Nur Qinghai China 94 D4
Qagan Nur Xinjiang China 98 D4
Qagan Nur l. China 95 K2
Qagan Nur resr China 95 H3
Qagan Obo Nei Mongol China 95 G2
Qagan Qulut Nei Mongol China 95 I2
Qagan Teg Nei Mongol China 95 H3
Qagan Tohoi Qinghai China 94 C5
Qagan Us Nei Mongol China 89 K4
Qagan Us Qinghai China see Dulan
Qagan Us He r. China 94 D4
Qagbasêrag China 96 B2
Qagca China 96 C1
Qagcaka China 105 E2
Qagchêng China see Xiangcheng
Qahar Youyi Houqi Nei Mongol China see Bayan Qagan
Qahar Youyi Qianqi Nei Mongol China see Togrog Ul
Qahar Youyi Zhongqi Nei Mongol China see Hobor
Qahremānshahr Iran see Kermānshāh
Qaidam He r. China 94 C4
Qaidam Pendi basin China 94 C4
Qaidam Shan mts Qinghai China 94 C4
Qaidar Qinghai China see Cêtar
Qainaqangma Xizang China 99 E6
Qaisar, Koh-i- mt. Afgh. see Qeyṣār, Kūh-e
Qakar Xinjiang China 99 C5
Qalā Diza Iraq 113 G3
Qalagai Afgh. 111 H3
Qala-i-Kang Afgh. see Kang
Qal'aikhum Tajik. 111 H2
Qala Jamal Afgh. 111 F3
Qalansīyah Yemen 109 H7
Qala Shinia Takht Afgh. 111 G3
Qalāt Afgh. see Kalāt
Qal'at al Ḥiṣn Syria 107 C2
Qal'at al Mu'aẓẓam Saudi Arabia 112 E6
Qal'at Bīshah Saudi Arabia 108 F5
Qal'at Muqaybirah, Jabal mt. Syria 107 D2
Qal'at Ṣaḥyūn tourist site Syria 107 C2
Qal'eh Dāgh mt. Iran 110 B2
Qal'eh Tirpul Afgh. 111 F3
Qal'eh-ye Bost Afgh. 111 G4
Qal'eh-ye Now Afgh. 111 F3
Qal'eh-ye Shūrak well Iran 110 E3
Qalgar Nei Mongol China 94 F4
Qalhāt Oman 110 E6
Qalīb Bāqūr well Iraq 113 G5
Qalluviartuuq, Lac l. Canada 152 G2
Qalyūb Egypt 112 C5
Qalyûb Egypt see Qalyūb
Qamalung Qinghai China 94 D5
Qamanirjuaq Lake Canada 151 M2
Qamanittuaq Canada see Baker Lake
Qamashi Uzbek. 111 G2
Qamata S. Africa 125 H6
Qamdo China 96 C2
Qandahar Afgh. see Kandahār
Qandarānbāshī, Kūh-e mt. Iran 110 B2
Qandyaghash Kazakh. see Kandyagash
Qangdin Sum Nei Mongol China 95 H3
Qangdoi Xizang China 99 C6
Qangzê Xizang China 99 B7
Qapan Iran 110 D2
Qapqal Xinjiang China 98 C4
Qapshagay Kazakh. see Kapchagay
Qapshagay Bögeni resr Kazakh. see Kapchagayskoye Vodokhranilishche
Qaqortoq Greenland 147 N3
Qara Āghach r. Iran see Mand, Rūd-e
Qarabutaq Kazakh. see Karabutak
Qaraçala Azer. 110 C2
Qara Ertis r. China/Kazakh. see Ertix He
Qaraghandy Kazakh. see Karaganda
Qaraghayly Kazakh. see Karagayly
Qārah Egypt 112 B5
Qārah Saudi Arabia 113 F5
Qarah Bāgh Afgh. 111 H3
Qarak China 111 J2
Qaraqum des. Turkm. see Garagum
Qaraqum des. Turkm. see Karakum Desert
Qara Quzi Iran 110 D2
Qarasu Azer. 113 H2
Qara Ṣū Chāy r. Syria/Turkey see Karasu
Qara Tarai mt. Afgh. 111 G3
Qarataū Kazakh. see Karatau
Qarataū Zhotasy mts Kazakh. see Karatau, Khrebet
Qara Tikan Iran 110 C2
Qarazhal Kazakh. see Karazhal
Qardho Somalia 122 E3
Qareh Chāy r. Iran 110 C3
Qareh Sū r. Iran 110 B2
Qareh Tekān Iran 111 F2
Qarhan Qinghai China 94 C4
Qarkilik Xinjiang China see Ruoqiang
Qarn al Kabsh, Jabal mt. Egypt 112 D5
Qarnayn i. U.A.E. 110 D5
Qarnein i. U.A.E. see Qarnayn
Qarn el Kabsh, Gebel mt. Egypt see Qarn al Kabsh, Jabal
Qarnobcho'l cho'li plain Uzbek. 111 G2
Qarokŭl l. Tajik. 111 I2
Qarqan Xinjiang China see Qiemo
Qarqan He r. China 98 D5
Qarqaraly Kazakh. see Karkaralinsk
Qarqi Xinjiang China 98 C4
Qarqi Xinjiang China 98 D4
Qarshi Uzbek. 111 G2
Qarshi cho'li plain Uzbek. 111 G2
Qarshi Chŭli plain Uzbek. see Qarshi cho'li
Qartaba Lebanon 107 B2
Qārūh, Jazīrat i. Kuwait 110 C4
Qārūn, Birkat l. Egypt 112 C5
Qârûn, Birket l. Egypt see Qārūn, Birkat
Qaryat al Gharab Iraq 113 G5
Qaryat al Ulyā Saudi Arabia 110 B5
Qasa Murg mts Afgh. 111 F3
Qāsemābād Iran 110 E3
Qash Qai reg. Iran 110 C4
Qasigiannguit Greenland 147 M3
Qasq Nei Mongol China 95 G3
Qaṣr al Azraq Jordan 107 C4
Qaṣr al Farāfirah Egypt 112 B6
Qaṣr al Kharānah Jordan 107 C4
Qasr al Khubbāz Iraq 113 F4
Qaṣr 'Amrah tourist site Jordan 107 C4
Qaṣr Burqu' tourist site Jordan 107 C3
Qaṣr-e Shīrīn Iran 110 B3
Qaṣr Farâfra Egypt see Qaṣr al Farāfirah
Qassimiut Greenland 147 N3
Qaṭanā Syria 107 C3
Qatar country Asia 110 C5
Qaṭmah Syria 107 C1
Qaṭrūyeh Iran 110 D4
Qaṭṭāfī, Wādī al watercourse Jordan 107 C4
Qaṭṭâra, Râs esc. Egypt see Qaṭṭārah, Ra's
Qattara Depression Egypt 112 B5
Qaṭṭārah, Ra's esc. Egypt 112 B5
Qaṭṭīnah, Buḥayrat resr Syria 107 C2
Qax Azer. 113 G2
Qaxi Xinjiang China 98 C4
Qāyen Iran 110 E3
Qaynar Kazakh. see Kaynar
Qayṣār Afgh. 111 G3
Qaysīyah, Qā' al imp. l. Jordan 107 C4
Qaysūm, Juzur is Egypt 112 D6
Qayü Xizang China 99 F7
Qayyārah Iraq 113 F4
Qazangödağ mt. Armenia/Azer. 113 G3
Qazaq Shyghanaghy b. Kazakh. see Kazakhskiy Zaliv
Qazaqstan country Asia see Kazakhstan
Qazax Azer. 108 G1
Qazi Ahmad Pak. 111 H5
Qazımämmäd Azer. 113 H2
Qazvīn Iran 110 C2
Qedir Xinjiang China 98 D4
Qeh Nei Mongol China 94 E3
Qeisûm, Gezâ'ir is Egypt see Qaysūm, Juzur
Qeisum Islands Egypt see Qaysūm, Juzur
Qena Egypt see Qinā
Qeqertarsuaq Greenland 147 M3
Qeqertarsuaq i. Greenland 147 M3
Qeqertarsuatsiaat Greenland 147 M3
Qeqertarsuup Tunua b. Greenland 147 M3
Qeshm Iran 110 E5
Qeydār Iran 110 C2
Qeydū Iran 110 C3
Qeyṣār, Kūh-e mt. Afgh. 111 G3
Qezel Owzan, Rūdkhāneh-ye r. Iran 110 C2
Qeẓi'ot Israel 107 B4
Qian'an Hebei China 95 I4
Qian'an Jilin China 95 K2
Qianfo Dong Gansu China see Mogao Ku
Qianfodong Xinjiang China 98 C4
Qian Gorlos China see Qianguozhen
Qianguozhen China 90 B3
Qiangwei He r. China 95 I5
Qian He r. China 95 F5
Qianjiang Chongqing China 97 F2
Qianjiang Hubei China 97 G2
Qianjin Heilong. China 90 D3
Qianjin Jilin China 90 C3
Qianning China 96 D2
Qianqihao Jilin China 95 J2
Qian Shan mts China 95 J3
Qianshanlaoba Xinjiang China 98 D3
Qianxi China 96 E3
Qianxi Hebei China 95 I3
Qianxian Shaanxi China 95 G5
Qianyang Shaanxi China 95 F5
Qiaocheng China see Bozhou
Qiaocun Shanxi China 95 H4
Qiaojia China 96 D3
Qiaoshan Shaanxi China see Huangling
Qiaotou Qinghai China see Datong
Qiaowa China see Muli
Qiaowan Gansu China 94 D3
Qiaozhuang China see Qingchuan
Qibā' Saudi Arabia 113 G6
Qibing S. Africa 125 H5
Qichun China 97 G2
Qidong China 97 G3
Qidukou China 96 B1
Qiemo Xinjiang China 99 D5
Qihe Shandong China 95 I4
Qi He r. China 95 H5
Qijiang China 96 E2
Qijiaojing Xinjiang China 94 B3
Qikiqtarjuaq Canada 147 L3
Qiktim Xinjiang China 94 B3
Qila Ladgasht Pak. 111 F5
Qilaotu Shan mts China 95 I3
Qila Saifullah Pak. 111 H4
Qilian Qinghai China 94 E4
Qilian Shan Qinghai China 94 D4
Qilian Shan mts China 94 D4
Qilizhen Gansu China 98 F4
Qillak i. Greenland 147 O3
Qiman Xinjiang China 98 C4
Qiman Tag mts China 99 E5
Qimusseriarsuaq b. Greenland 147 L2
Qinā Egypt 108 D4
Qin'an Gansu China 94 F5
Qincheng China see Nanfeng
Qincheng Xinjiang China 94 C3
Qing'an China 90 B3
Qingaq Canada see Bathurst Inlet (abandoned)
Qingcheng Gansu China see Qingyang
Qingchuan China 96 E1
Qingdao Shandong China 95 J4
Qinggang China 90 B3
Qinggil Xinjiang China see Qinghe
Qinggilik Xinjiang China 99 D5
Qinghai prov. China 94 D4
Qinghai Hu salt l. Qinghai China 94 E4
Qinghai Nanshan mts China 94 D4
Qinghe Hebei China 95 H4
Qinghe Heilong. China 90 C3
Qinghe Xinjiang China 94 B2
Qinghecheng China 90 B4
Qinghua Henan China see Bo'ai
Qingjian Shaanxi China 95 G4
Qingjiang Jiangsu China see Huai'an
Qingjiang Jiangxi China see Zhangshu
Qing Jiang r. China 97 F2
Qingkou Jiangsu China see Ganyu
Qinglan China 97 F5
Qingliu China 97 H3
Qinglong Hebei China 95 I3
Qinglung Xizang China 99 E7
Qingpu China 97 I2
Qingquan China see Xishui
Qingshan China see Wudalianchi
Qingshizui Qinghai China 94 E4
Qingshui Gansu China see Qingshuipu
Qingshui Gansu China 94 F5
Qingshuihe Nei Mongol China 95 G4
Qingshuihe Qinghai China 96 C1
Qingshuihezi Xinjiang China 98 C3
Qingshuihezi Xinjiang China 98 D4
Qingshuipu Gansu China 94 D4
Qingtian China 97 I2
Qingtongxia Ningxia China 94 F4
Qingxian Hebei China 95 I4
Qingxu Shanxi China 95 H4
Qingyang Anhui China 97 H2
Qingyang Gansu China 95 F4
Qingyang Gansu China 95 F5
Qingyang Jiangsu China see Sihong
Qingyuan Gansu China see Weiyuan
Qingyuan Guangdong China 97 G4
Qingyuan Guangxi China see Yizhou
Qingyuan Liaoning China 90 B4
Qingyuan Shanxi China see Qingxu
Qingyuan Zhejiang China 97 H3
Qingyun Shandong China 95 I4
Qingzang Gaoyuan plat. Xizang China see Tibet, Plateau of
Qingzhen China 96 E3
Qingzhou Hebei China see Qingxian
Qingzhou Shandong China 95 I4
Qinhuangdao Hebei China 95 I4
Qinjiang China see Shicheng
Qin Ling mts China 96 E1
Qinshui Shanxi China 95 H5
Qinting China see Lianhua
Qinxian Shanxi China 95 H4
Qinyang Henan China 95 H5
Qinyuan Shanxi China 95 H4
Qinzhou China 97 F4
Qionghai China 97 F5
Qiongjiexue Xizang China see Qonggyai
Qionglai China 96 D2
Qionglai Shan mts China 96 D2
Qiongxi China see Hongyuan
Qiongzhong China 97 F5
Qiongzhou Haixia strait China see Hainan Strait
Qiping Gansu China 94 D4
Qiqian China 90 A1
Qiqihar Heilong. China 95 J2
Qiquanhu Xinjiang China 98 E4
Qīr Iran 110 D4
Qira Xinjiang China 99 C5
Qîraîya, Wâdi watercourse Egypt see Qurayyah, Wādī
Qiryat Israel 107 B3
Qiryat Shemona Israel 107 B3
Qishan Shaanxi China 95 F5
Qishon r. Israel 107 B3
Qitab ash Shāmah vol. crater Saudi Arabia 107 C4
Qitai Xinjiang China 98 E4
Qitaihe China 90 C3
Qiubei China 96 E3
Qiujin China 97 G2
Qixia Shandong China 95 J4
Qixian Henan China 95 H5
Qixian Henan China 95 H5
Qixian Shanxi China 95 H4
Qixing He r. China 90 D3
Qiyang China 97 F3
Qiying Ningxia China 94 F4
Qizhou Liedao i. China 97 F5
Qızılağac Körfäzi b. Azer. 110 C2
Qizil-Art, Aghbai pass Kyrg./Tajik. see Kyzylart Pass
Qizilqum des. Kazakh./Uzbek. see Kyzylkum Desert
Qizilrabot Tajik. 111 I2
Qobustan Qoruğu nat. res. Azer. 113 H2
Qogir Feng mt. China/Pak. see K2
Qog Ul Nei Mongol China 95 I2
Qoigargoinba Qinghai China 94 E5
Qoijê Qinghai China 94 D4
Qoltag mts China 98 E4
Qom Iran 110 C3
Qomdo Xizang China see Qumdo
Qomīsheh Iran see Shahrezā
Qomolangma Feng mt. China/Nepal see Everest, Mount

Qomsheh Iran see Shahrezā
Qonāq, Kūh-e hill Iran 110 C3
Qondūz Afgh. see Kunduz
Qonggyai Xizang China 99 E7
Qo'ng'irot Uzbek. 102 A3
Qongj Nei Mongol China 95 G3
Qongkol Xinjiang China 98 D4
Qong Muztag mt. Xinjiang/Xizang China 99 C6
Qongrat Uzbek. see Qo'ng'irot
Qonj Qinghai China 94 D4
Qoornoq Greenland 147 M3
Qoqek Xinjiang China see Tacheng
Qo'qon Uzbek. 102 D3
Qorako'l Uzbek. 111 F2
Qorghalzhyn Kazakh. see Korgalzhyn
Qornet es Saouda mt. Lebanon 107 C2
Qorovulbozor Uzbek. 111 G2
Qorowulbozor Uzbek. see Qorovulbozor
Qorveh Iran 110 B3
Qo'shrabot Uzbek. 111 G1
Qosh Tepe Iraq 113 F3
Qostanay Kazakh. see Kostanay
Qoubaiyat Lebanon 107 C2
Qowowuyag mt. China/Nepal see Cho Oyu
Qozideh Tajik. 111 H2
Quabbin Reservoir U.S.A. 165 I2
Quadra Island Canada 150 E5
Quadros, Lago dos l. Brazil 179 A5
Quaidabad Pak. 111 H3
Quail Mountains U.S.A. 158 E4
Quairading Australia 135 B8
Quakenbrück Germany 63 H2
Quakertown U.S.A. 165 H3
Quambatook Australia 138 A5
Quambone Australia 138 C3
Quamby Australia 136 C4
Quanah U.S.A. 161 D5
Quanbao Shan mt. Henan China 95 G5
Quan Dao Hoang Sa is S. China Sea see Paracel Islands
Quân Đao Nam Du i. Vietnam 87 D5
Quan Dao Truong Sa is S. China Sea see Spratly Islands
Quang Ha Vietnam 86 D2
Quang Ngai Vietnam 86 E4
Quang Tri Vietnam 86 D3
Quan Hoa Vietnam 86 D2
Quan Long Vietnam see Ca Mau
Quannan China 97 G3
Quan Phu Quoc i. Vietnam see Phu Quôc, Đao
Quanshuigou Aksai Chin 99 B6
Quantock Hills U.K. 59 D7
Quanwan H.K. China see Tsuen Wan
Quanzhou Fujian China 97 H3
Quanzhou Guangxi China 97 F3
Qu'Appelle r. Canada 151 K5
Quaqtaq Canada 147 L3
Quarry Bay H.K. China 97 [inset]
Quartu Sant'Elena Sardinia Italy 68 C5
Quartzite Mountain U.S.A. 158 E3
Quartzsite U.S.A. 159 F5
Quba Azer. 113 H2
Quchan Iran 110 E2
Qudaym Syria 107 D2
Queanbeyan Australia 138 D5

▶Québec Canada 153 H5
Capital of Québec.

Québec prov. Canada 165 I1
Quebra Anzol r. Brazil 179 B2
Quedlinburg Germany 63 L3
Queen Adelaide Islands Chile see La Reina Adelaida, Archipiélago de
Queen Anne U.S.A. 165 H4
Queen Bess, Mount Canada 156 B2
Queen Charlotte B.C. Canada 149 N5
Queen Charlotte Islands B.C. Canada 149 N5
Queen Charlotte Sound sea chan. Canada 150 D5
Queen Charlotte Strait Canada 150 E5
Queen Creek U.S.A. 159 H5
Queen Elizabeth Islands Canada 147 H2
Queen Elizabeth National Park Uganda 122 C4
Queen Mary, Mount Y.T. Canada 149 M3
Queen Mary Land reg. Antarctica 188 F2
Queen Maud Gulf Canada 147 H3
Queen Maud Land reg. Antarctica 184 G10
Queen Maud Land reg. Antarctica 188 C2
Queen Maud Mountains Antarctica 188 J1
Queenscliff Australia 138 B7
Queensland state Australia 138 B1
Queenstown Australia 137 [inset]
Queenstown Ireland see Cobh
Queenstown N.Z. 139 B7
Queenstown S. Africa 125 H6
Queenstown Sing. 87 [inset]
Queets U.S.A. 156 B3
Queimada, Ilha i. Brazil 177 H4
Quelimane Moz. 123 D5
Quelite Mex. 166 D4
Quellón Chile 178 B6
Quelpart Island S. Korea see Cheju-do
Quemado U.S.A. 159 I4
Quemoy i. Taiwan see Chinmen Tao
Que Que Zimbabwe see Kwekwe
Querétaro Mex. 168 D4
Querétaro state Mex. 167 F4
Querétaro de Arteaga Mex. see Querétaro
Querfurt Germany 63 L3
Querobabi Mex. 166 C2
Quesnel Canada 150 F4
Quesnel Lake Canada 150 F4
Quetta Pak. 111 G4
Quetzaltenango Guat. 167 H6
Queuco Chile 178 B5
Quezaltepeque El Salvador 167 H6
Quezon Palawan Phil. 82 B4

▶Quezon City Luzon Phil. 82 C3
Former capital of the Philippines.

Qufu Shandong China 95 I5
Quibala Angola 123 B5
Quibaxe Angola 123 B4
Quibdó Col. 176 C2
Quiberon France 66 C3
Quiçama, Parque Nacional do nat. park Angola 123 B4
Qui Châu Vietnam 86 D3
Quiet Lake Y.T. Canada 149 N3
Quilá Mex. 166 D3
Quilalí Nicaragua 166 [inset] I6
Quilengues Angola 123 B5
Quillabamba Peru 176 D6
Quillacollo Bol. 176 E7
Quillan France 66 F5
Quill Lakes Canada 151 J5
Quilmes Arg. 178 E4
Quilon India 106 C4
Quilpie Australia 138 B1
Quilpué Chile 178 B4
Quimbele Angola 123 B4
Quimilí Arg. 178 D3
Quimper France 66 B3
Quimperlé France 66 C3
Quinag hill U.K. 60 D2
Quinalasag i. Phil. 82 C3
Quincy CA U.S.A. 158 C2
Quincy FL U.S.A. 163 C6
Quincy IL U.S.A. 160 F4
Quincy IN U.S.A. 164 B4
Quincy MA U.S.A. 165 J2
Quincy MI U.S.A. 164 C3
Quincy OH U.S.A. 164 D3
Quines Arg. 178 C4
Quinga Moz. 123 E5
Quinggir Xinjiang China 98 E4
Quinhagak AK U.S.A. 148 G4
Quiniluban i. Phil. 82 C4
Quinn Canyon Range mts U.S.A. 159 F3
Quintana Roo state Mex. 167 H5
Quinto Spain 67 F3
Quionga Moz. 123 E5
Quiotepec Mex. 167 F5
Quipungo Angola 123 B5
Quiriguá tourist site Guat. 166 [inset] H6
Quirima Angola 123 B5
Quirimbas, Parque Nacional das 123 E5
Quirindi Australia 138 E3
Quirinópolis Brazil 179 A2
Quissanga Moz. 123 E5
Quissico Moz. 125 L3
Quitapa Angola 123 B5
Quitilipi Arg. 178 D3
Quitman GA U.S.A. 163 D6
Quitman MS U.S.A. 161 F5

▶Quito Ecuador 176 C4
Capital of Ecuador.

Quitovac Mex. 166 B2
Quixadá Brazil 177 K4
Quixeramobim Brazil 177 K5
Qujiang Guangdong China 97 G3
Qujiang Sichuan China see Quxian
Qujie China 97 F4
Qujing China 96 D3
Qulandy Kazakh. see Kulandy
Qulbān Layyah well Iraq 110 B4
Qulho Xizang China 99 D7
Qulin Gol r. China 95 J2
Qulsary Kazakh. see Kul'sary
Qulyndy Zhazyghy plain Kazakh./Rus. Fed. see Kulundinskaya Step'
Qulzum, Baḥr al Egypt see Suez Bay
Qumar He r. China 94 C5
Qumarheyan Qinghai China 94 C5
Qumarlêb Qinghai China 99 F6
Qumarrabdün China 96 B1
Qumbu S. Africa 125 I6
Qumdo Xizang China 99 F7
Qumigxung Xizang China 99 D7
Qumqo'rg'o'n Uzbek. 111 G2
Qumqūrghon Uzbek. see Qumqo'rg'o'n
Qumrha S. Africa 125 H7
Qumulangma mt. China/Nepal see Everest, Mount
Qunayy well Saudi Arabia 110 B6
Qundūz Afgh. see Kunduz
Qŭnghirot Uzbek. see Qo'ng'irot
Qu'ngoin r. Qinghai China 94 E5
Quntamari Xizang China 99 E6
Qu'nyido China 96 C2
Quoich r. Canada 151 M1
Quoich, Loch l. U.K. 60 D3
Quoile r. U.K. 61 G3
Quoin Point S. Africa 124 D8
Quoxo r. Botswana 124 G2
Qŭqon Uzbek. see Qo'qon
Qurama, Qatorkŭhi mts Asia see Kurama Range
Qurama Tizmasi mts Asia see Kurama Range
Qurayyah, Wādī watercourse Egypt 107 B4
Qurayyat al Milḥ l. Jordan 107 C4
Qŭrghonteppa Tajik. 111 H2
Qusar Azer. 113 H2
Qushan China see Beichuan
Qŭshrabot Uzbek. see Qo'shrabot
Qusmuryn Kazakh. see Kushmurun
Qusum Xizang China 99 B6
Qusum Xizang China 99 F7
Quthing Lesotho see Moyeni
Quttinirpaaq National Park Canada 147 K1
Quwayq, Nahr r. Syria/Turkey 107 C2
Quwo Shanxi China 95 G5
Quwu Shan mts China 94 F4
Quxian Sichuan China 96 E2
Quxian Zhejiang China see Quzhou
Qüxü Xizang China 99 E7
Quyang China see Jingzhou
Quyghan Kazakh. see Kuygan
Quy Nhơn Vietnam 87 E4
Quyon Canada 165 G1
Qūyūn Eshek i. Iran 110 B2
Quzhou Hebei China 95 H4
Quzhou China 97 H2
Quzi Gansu China 95 F4
Qypshaq Köli salt l. Kazakh. see Kypshak, Ozero
Qyrghyz Zhotasy mts Kazakh./Kyrg. see Kirghiz Range
Qyteti Stalin Albania see Kuçovë
Qyzylorda Kazakh. see Kyzylorda
Qyzylqum des. Kazakh./Uzbek. see Kyzylkum Desert
Qyzyltū Kazakh. see Kishkenekol'
Qyzylzhar Kazakh. see Kyzylzhar

R

Raa Atoll Maldives see North Maalhosmadulu Atoll
Raab r. Austria 57 P7
Raab Hungary see Győr
Raahe Fin. 54 N4
Rääkkylä Fin. 54 P5
Raalte Neth. 62 G2
Raanujärvi Fin. 54 N3
Raas i. Indon. 85 F4
Raasay i. U.K. 60 C3
Raasay, Sound of sea chan. U.K. 60 C3
Raba Sumbawa Indon. 85 G5
Rabang Xizang China 99 C6
Rabat Gozo Malta see Victoria
Rabat Malta 68 F7

▶Rabat Morocco 64 C5
Capital of Morocco.

Rabaul P.N.G. 132 F2
Rabbath Ammon Jordan see 'Ammān
Rabbit r. B.C. Canada 149 P4
Rabbit Flat Australia 134 E5
Rabbitskin r. Canada 150 F2
Rabia Papua Indon. 83 D3
Rābigh Saudi Arabia 108 E5
Rabinal Guat. 167 H6
Rabnabad Islands Bangl. 105 G5
Râbniţa Moldova see Rîbniţa
Rabocheostrovsk Rus. Fed. 52 G2
Racaka China 96 C2
Raccoon Cay i. Bahamas 163 F8
Race, Cape Canada 153 L5
Raceland LA U.S.A. 167 H2
Race Point U.S.A. 165 J2
Rachaïya Lebanon 107 B3
Rachal U.S.A. 161 D7
Racha Noi, Ko i. Thai. 84 B1
Rachaya Lebanon see Rachaïya
Racha Yai, Ko i. Thai. 84 B1
Rachel U.S.A. 159 F3
Rach Gia Vietnam 87 D5
Rach Gia, Vinh b. Vietnam 87 D5
Racibórz Poland 57 Q5
Racine WI U.S.A. 164 B2
Racine WV U.S.A. 164 E4
Rădăuţi Romania 53 E7
Radcliff U.S.A. 164 C5
Radde Rus. Fed. 90 C2
Rádeyilikóé N.W.T. Canada see Fort Good Hope
Radford U.S.A. 164 E5
Radili Ko N.W.T. Canada see Fort Good Hope
Radisson Que. Canada 152 F3
Radisson Sask. Canada 151 J4
Radlinski, Mount Antarctica 188 K1
Radnevo Bulg. 69 K3
Radom Poland 57 R5
Radom Sudan 121 F4
Radomir Bulg. 69 J3
Radom National Park Sudan 121 F4
Radomsko Poland 57 Q5
Radoviš Macedonia 112 A2
Radstock U.K. 59 E7
Radstock, Cape Australia 135 F8
Radun' Belarus 55 N9
Radviliškis Lith. 55 M9
Radyvyliv Ukr. 53 E6
Rae Bareli India 104 E4
Raecreek r. Y.T. Canada 149 M2
Rae-Edzo N.W.T. Canada see Behchokô
Rae Lakes N.W.T. Canada see Gamètì
Raeside, Lake salt flat Australia 135 C7
Raetihi N.Z. 139 E4
Rāf hill Saudi Arabia 113 E5
Rafaela Arg. 178 D4
Rafaḥ Gaza see Rafiah
Rafaï Cent. Afr. Rep. 122 C3
Rafḥā' Saudi Arabia 113 F5
Rafiah Gaza 107 B4
Rafsanjān Iran 110 D4
Raft r. U.S.A. 156 E4
Raga Sudan 121 F4
Ragang, Mount vol. Mindanao Phil. 82 D5
Ragay Gulf Luzon Phil. 82 C3
Rägelin Germany 63 M1
Ragged, Mount hill Australia 135 C8
Ragged Island Bahamas 163 F8
Rāgh Afgh. 111 H2
Rago Nasjonalpark nat. park Norway 54 J3
Ragösen Germany 63 M2
Ragueneau Canada 153 H4
Raguhn Germany 63 M3
Ragusa Croatia see Dubrovnik
Ragusa Sicily Italy 68 F6
Ragxi Xizang China 99 F7
Ra'gyagoinba Qinghai China 94 E5
Raha Sulawesi Indon. 83 B4
Rahachow Belarus 53 F5
Rahad r. Sudan 108 D7
Rahaeng Thai. see Tak
Rahden Germany 63 I2
Rahimyar Khan Pak. 111 H4
Rahovec Kosovo 69 I3
Rahuri India 106 B2
Rai, Hon i. Vietnam 87 D5
Raiatea i. Fr. Polynesia 187 J7
Raibu i. Indon. see Air
Raichur India 106 C2
Raiganj India 105 G4
Raigarh Chhattisgarh India 105 E5
Raigarh Orissa India 106 D2
Raijua i. Indon. 83 B5
Railroad City AK U.S.A. 148 H3
Railroad Pass U.S.A. 158 E2
Railroad Valley U.S.A. 159 F2
Raimangal r. Bangl. 105 G5
Raimbault, Lac l. Canada 153 H3
Rainbow Lake Canada 150 G3
Raine Island Australia 136 D1
Rainelle U.S.A. 164 E5
Raini r. Pak. 111 H4
Rainier, Mount vol. U.S.A. 156 C3
Rainis Sulawesi Indon. 83 C1
Rainy r. Canada/U.S.A. 151 M5
Rainy Lake Canada/U.S.A. 155 I2
Rainy River Canada 151 M5
Raipur Chhattisgarh India 105 E5
Raipur W. Bengal India 105 F5
Raisen India 104 D5
Raisio Fin. 55 M6
Raismes France 62 D4
Raitalai India 104 D5
Raivavae i. Fr. Polynesia 187 K7
Raiwind Pak. 111 I4
Raja i. Indon. 85 F4
Raja, Ujung pt Indon. 84 B2
Rajaampat, Kepulauan is Papua Indon. 83 D3
Rajabasa, Gunung vol. Indon. 84 D4
Rajahmundry India 106 D2
Raja-Jooseppi Fin. 54 P2
Rajang Sarawak Malaysia 85 E2
Rajang r. Malaysia 85 E2
Rajanpur Pak. 111 H4
Rajapalaiyam India 106 C4
Rajapur India 106 B2
Rajasthan state India 104 C4
Rajasthan Canal India 104 C3
Rajauri India see Rajouri
Rajevadi India 106 B2
Rajgarh India 104 D4
Rájijovsset Fin. see Raja-Jooseppi
Rajik Indon. 84 D3
Rajkot India 104 B5
Raj Mahal India 104 C4
Rajmahal Hills India 105 F4
Raj Nandgaon India 104 E5
Rajouri India 104 C2
Rajpipla India 104 C5
Rajpur India 104 C5
Rajpura India 104 D3
Rajputana Agency state India see Rajasthan
Rajsamand India 104 C4
Rajshahi Bangl. 105 G4
Rājū Syria 107 C1
Rajula India 106 A1
Rajur India 106 C1
Rajura India 106 C2
Raka Xizang China 99 D7
Rakan, Ra's pt Qatar 110 C5
Rakaposhi mt. Pak. 104 C1
Raka Zangbo r. Xizang China see Dogxung Zangbo
Rakhiv Ukr. 53 E6
Rakhni Pak. 111 H4
Rakhni r. Pak. 111 H4
Rakhshan r. Pak. 111 F5
Rakit i. Indon. 85 E4
Rakit i. Indon. 85 G5
Rakitnoye Belgorodskaya Oblast' Rus. Fed. 53 G6
Rakitnoye Primorskiy Kray Rus. Fed. 90 D3
Rakiura i. N.Z. see Stewart Island
Rakke Estonia 55 O7
Rakkestad Norway 55 G7
Rakmanovskie Klyuchi Kazakh. 98 D2
Rakovski Bulg. 69 K3
Rakushechnyy, Mys pt Kazakh. 113 H2
Rakvere Estonia 55 O7

▶Raleigh U.S.A. 162 E5
Capital of North Carolina.

Ralla Sulawesi Indon. 83 A4
Ralston U.S.A. 165 G3
Ram r. Canada 150 F2
Rama Nicaragua 166 [inset] I6
Ramādī Iraq 113 F4
Ramagiri India 106 E2
Ramah U.S.A. 159 I4
Ramalho, Serra do hills Brazil 179 B1
Rāmallāh West Bank 107 B4
Ramanagaram India 106 C3
Ramanathapuram India 106 C4
Ramapo Deep sea feature N. Pacific Ocean 186 F3
Ramapur India 106 D1
Ramas, Cape India 106 B3
Ramatlabama S. Africa 125 G3
Rambhapur India 104 C5
Rambouillet France 62 B6
Rambutyo Island P.N.G. 81 L7
Rame Head hd Australia 138 D6
Rame Head hd U.K. 59 C8
Rameshki Rus. Fed. 52 H4
Ramezān Kalak Iran 111 F5
Ramganga r. India 99 B8
Ramgarh Jharkhand India 105 F5
Ramgarh Rajasthan India 104 B4
Ramgarh Rajasthan India 104 C3
Ramgul reg. Afgh. 111 H3
Rāmhormoz Iran 110 C4
Ramingining Australia 134 F3
Ramitan Uzbek. see Romiton
Ramla Israel 107 B4
Ramlat Rabyānah des. Libya see Rebiana Sand Sea
Ramm, Jabal mts Jordan 107 B5
Ramnad India see Ramanathapuram
Râmnicu Sărat Romania 69 L2
Râmnicu Vâlcea Romania 69 K2
Ramon' Rus. Fed. 53 H6
Ramona U.S.A. 158 E5
Ramos r. Mex. 161 B7
Ramos Arizpe Mex. 167 E3
Ramotswa Botswana 125 G3
Rampart AK U.S.A. 149 J2
Rampart of Genghis Khan tourist site Asia 95 H1
Ramparts r. N.W.T. Canada 149 O2
Rampur Hima. Prad. India 99 B7
Rampur India 104 D3
Rampur Uttar Prad. India 99 B7
Rampur Boalia Bangl. see Rajshahi
Ramree Myanmar 86 A3
Ramree Island Myanmar 86 A3
Rāmsar Iran 110 C2
Ramsele Sweden 54 J5
Ramsey Isle of Man 58 C4
Ramsey U.K. 59 G6
Ramsey U.S.A. 165 H3
Ramsey Bay Isle of Man 58 C4
Ramsey Island U.K. 59 B7
Ramsey Lake Canada 152 E5
Ramsgate U.K. 59 I7
Rāmshir Iran 110 C4
Ramsing mt. India 105 H3
Ramu Bangl. 105 H5
Ramusio, Lac l. Canada 153 J3
Ramygala Lith. 55 N9
Ranaghat India 105 G5
Ranai i. U.S.A. see Lāna'i
Rana Pratap Sagar resr India 104 C4
Ranapur India 104 C5
Ranasar India 104 B4
Ranau Sabah Malaysia 85 G1
Ranau, Danau l. Indon. 84 C4
Rancagua Chile 178 B4
Rancharia Brazil 179 A3
Rancheria Y.T. Canada 149 O3
Rancheria r. Y.T. Canada 149 O3
Ranchi India 105 F5
Rancho Grande Mex. 166 E4
Ranco, Lago l. Chile 178 B6
Rand Australia 138 C5
Randalstown U.K. 61 F3
Randers Denmark 55 G8
Randijaure l. Sweden 54 K3
Randolph ME U.S.A. 165 K1
Randolph UT U.S.A. 156 F4
Randolph VT U.S.A. 165 I2
Randsjö Sweden 54 H5
Råneå Sweden 54 M4
Ranérou Senegal 120 B3
Ranfurly N.Z. 139 C7
Ranga r. India 99 F8
Rangae Thai. 87 C6
Rangamati Bangl. 105 H5
Rangapara India 105 H4
Rangas, Tanjung pt Indon. 83 A3
Rangasa, Tanjung pt Indon. 83 A3
Rangeley Lake U.S.A. 165 J1
Rangely U.S.A. 159 I1
Ranger Lake Canada 152 E5
Rangiora N.Z. 139 D6
Rangitata r. N.Z. 139 C7
Rangitikei r. N.Z. 139 E5
Rangkasbitung Jawa Indon. 84 D4
Rangke China see Zamtang
Rangkŭl Tajik. 111 I2
Rangôn Myanmar see Rangoon

▶Rangoon Myanmar 86 B3
Joint capital (with Nay Pyi Taw) of Myanmar.

Rangoon r. Myanmar 86 B3
Rangpur Bangl. 105 G4
Rangsang i. Indon. 84 C2
Rangse Myanmar 86 A1
Ranibennur India 106 B3
Raniganj India 105 F5
Ranipur Pak. 111 H5
Raniwara India 104 C4
Rankin U.S.A. 161 C6
Rankin Inlet Canada 151 M2
Rankin's Springs Australia 138 C4
Ranna Estonia 55 O7
Rannes Australia 136 E5
Rannoch, Loch U.K. 60 E4
Ranong Thai. 87 B5
Ranot Thai. 87 C6
Ranpur India 104 B5
Rānsa Iran 110 C3
Ransby Sweden 55 H6
Rantasalmi Fin. 54 P5
Rantau Kalimantan Indon. 85 F3
Rantau i. Indon. 84 C2
Rantaukampar Sumatera Indon. 84 C2
Rantaupanjang Kalimantan Indon. 85 F3
Rantaupanjang Kalimantan Indon. 85 G2
Rantauprapat Sumatera Indon. 84 B2
Rantaupulut Kalimantan Indon. 85 F3
Rantemario, Gunung mt. Indon. 83 B3
Rantepao Sulawesi Indon. 83 A3
Rantoul U.S.A. 164 A3
Rantsila Fin. 54 N4
Ranua Fin. 54 O4
Rānya Iraq 113 G3
Ranyah, Wādī watercourse Saudi Arabia 108 F5
Rao Go mt. Laos/Vietnam 86 D3
Raohe China 90 D3
Raoul Island Kermadec Is 133 I4
Rapa i. Fr. Polynesia 187 K7
Rapa-iti i. Fr. Polynesia see Rapa
Rapallo Italy 68 C2
Rapar India 104 B5
Raphoe Ireland 61 E3
Rapidan r. U.S.A. 165 G4
Rapid City U.S.A. 160 C2
Rapid River U.S.A. 162 C2
Rapla Estonia 55 N7
Rappang Sulawesi Indon. 83 A3
Rapti r. India 99 C8
Rapur Andhra Prad. India 106 C3
Rapur Gujarat India 104 B5
Rapurapu i. Phil. 82 D3
Raqqa Syria see Ar Raqqah
Raquette Lake U.S.A. 165 H2
Rara National Park Nepal 105 E3
Raritan Bay U.S.A. 165 H3
Rarkan Pak. 111 H4
Raroia atoll Fr. Polynesia 187 K7
Rarotonga i. Cook Is 187 J7
Ras India 104 C4
Rasa i. Phil. 82 B4
Rasa, Punta pt Arg. 178 D6
Ra's ad Daqm Oman 109 I6
Ra's al Ḥikmah Egypt 112 B5
Ras al Khaimah U.A.E. see Ra's al Khaymah
Ra's al Khaymah U.A.E. 110 D5
Ra's an Naqb Jordan 107 B4
Ras Dashen mt. Eth. see Ras Dejen

▶Ras Dejen mt. Eth. 122 D2
5th highest mountain in Africa.

Raseiniai Lith. 55 M9
Râs el Hikma Egypt see Ra's al Ḥikmah
Ra's Ghārib Egypt 112 D5
Rashaant Bayan-Ölgiy Mongolia see Delüün
Rashaant Dundgovĭ Mongolia see Öldziyt
Rashad Sudan 108 D7
Rashīd Egypt 112 C5
Rashīd Egypt see Rashīd
Rashid Qala Afgh. 111 G4
Rashm Iran 110 D3
Rasht Iran 110 C2
Raskam mts China 99 A5
Ras Koh mt. Pak. 111 G4
Raskoh mts Pak. 111 G4
Raso, Cabo c. Arg. 178 C6
Raso da Catarina hills Brazil 177 K5
Rason Lake salt flat Australia 135 D7
Rasony Belarus 55 P9
Raspberry Island AK U.S.A. 148 I4
Rasra India 105 E4
Rasshua, Ostrov i. Rus. Fed. 89 S3
Rass Jebel Tunisia 68 D6
Rasskazovo Rus. Fed. 53 I5
Rastatt Germany 63 I6
Rastede Germany 63 I1
Rastow Germany 63 L1
Rasūl watercourse Iran 110 D5
Rasul Pak. 111 I3
Ratae U.K. see Leicester
Ratai, Gunung mt. Indon. 84 D4
Rätan Sweden 54 I5
Ratanda S. Africa 125 I4
Ratangarh India 104 C3
Rätansbyn Sweden 54 I5
Rat Buri Thai. 87 B4
Rathangan Ireland 61 F4
Rathbun Lake U.S.A. 160 E3
Rathdowney Ireland 61 E5
Rathdrum Ireland 61 F5
Rathedaung Myanmar 86 A2
Rathenow Germany 63 M2
Rathfriland U.K. 61 F3
Rathkeale Ireland 61 D5
Rathlin Island U.K. 61 F2
Ratibor Poland see Racibórz
Ratingen Germany 62 G3
Ratisbon Germany see Regensburg
Rat Island AK U.S.A. 149 [inset]
Rat Islands AK U.S.A. 149 [inset]
Ratiya India 104 C3
Rat Lake Canada 151 L3
Ratlam India 104 C5
Ratmanova, Ostrov i. Rus. Fed. 148 E2
Ratnagiri India 106 B2
Ratnapura Sri Lanka 106 D5
Ratne Ukr. 53 E6
Ratno Ukr. see Ratne
Raton U.S.A. 157 G5
Rattray Head hd U.K. 60 H3
Rättvik Sweden 55 I6
Ratz, Mount B.C. Canada 149 N4
Ratzeburg Germany 63 K1
Rau i. Maluku Indon. 83 D2
Raub Malaysia 84 C2
Rauðamýri Iceland 54 [inset]
Raudhatain Kuwait 110 B4
Rauenstein Germany 63 L4
Raufarhöfn Iceland 54 [inset]
Raukumara Range mts N.Z. 139 F4
Raul Soares Brazil 179 C3
Rauma Fin. 55 L6
Raupelyan Rus. Fed. 148 E2
Raurkela India 105 F5
Rauschen Rus. Fed. see Svetlogorsk
Rausu Japan 90 G3
Rautavaara Fin. 54 P5
Rautjärvi Fin. 55 P6
Ravānsar Iran 110 B3
Rāvar Iran 110 E4

Ravat Kyrg. 111 H2
Ravels Belgium 62 E3
Ravena U.S.A. 165 I2
Ravenglass U.K. 58 D4
Ravenna Italy 68 E2
Ravenna NE U.S.A. 160 D3
Ravenna OH U.S.A. 164 E3
Ravensburg Germany 57 L7
Ravenshoe Australia 136 D3
Ravenswood Australia 136 D4
Ravi r. Pak. 111 H4
Ravnina Turkm. see Rawnina
Rawa Aopa Watumohai, Taman Nasional nat. park Indon. 83 B4
Rāwah Iraq 113 F4
Rawaki i. Kiribati 133 I2
Rawalpindi Pak. 111 I3
Rawalpindi Lake Canada 150 H1
Rawāndiz Iraq 113 G3
Rawas r. Indon. 84 C3
Rawi, Ko i. Thai. 87 B6
Rawicz Poland 57 P5
Rawlinna Australia 135 D7
Rawlins U.S.A. 156 G4
Rawlinson Range hills Australia 135 E6
Rawnina Maryyskaya Oblast' Turkm. 111 F2
Rawnina Maryyskaya Oblast' Turkm. 111 F2
Rawson Arg. 178 C6
Rawu China 96 C2
Raxón, Cerro mt. Guat. 168 G5
Ray, Cape Canada 153 K5
Raya, Bukit mt. Kalimantan Indon. 85 E3
Rayachoti India 106 C3
Rayadurg India 106 C3
Rayagada India 106 D2
Rayagarha India see Rayagada
Rayak Lebanon 107 C3
Raychikhinsk Rus. Fed. 90 C2
Raydah Yemen 108 F6
Rayes Peak U.S.A. 158 D4
Rayevskiy Rus. Fed. 51 Q5
Rayleigh U.K. 59 H7
Raymond U.S.A. 165 J2
Raymond Terrace Australia 138 E4
Raymondville U.S.A. 161 D7
Raymore Canada 151 J5
Ray Mountains AK U.S.A. 148 I2
Rayner Glacier Antarctica 188 D2
Rayones Mex. 167 E3
Rayong Thai. 87 C4
Raystown Lake U.S.A. 165 F3
Rayü Xizang China 99 F7
Raz, Pointe du pt France 66 B2
Razan Iran 110 C3
Rāzān Iran 110 C3
Razani Pak. 111 H3
Razāzah, Buḩayrat ar l. Iraq 113 F4
Razdan Armenia see Hrazdan
Razdel'naya Ukr. see Rozdil'na
Razdol'noye Rus. Fed. 90 C4
Razeh Iran 110 C3
Razgrad Bulg. 69 L3
Razhêng Zangbo r. Xizang China 99 E7
Razim, Lacul lag. Romania 69 M2
Razisi China 96 D1
Razlog Bulg. 69 J4
Razmak Pak. 111 H3
Raz"yezd 3km Rus. Fed. see Novyy Urgal
Ré, Île de i. France 66 D3
Reading U.K. 59 G7
Reading MI U.S.A. 164 C3
Reading OH U.S.A. 164 C4
Reading PA U.S.A. 165 H3
Reagile S. Africa 125 H3
Realicó Arg. 178 D5
Réalmont France 66 F5
Reăng Kesei Cambodia 87 C4
Reata Mex. 167 E3
Reate Italy see Rieti
Rebais France 62 D6
Rebecca, Lake salt flat Australia 135 C7
Rebiana Sand Sea des. Libya 121 F2
Reboly Rus. Fed. 54 Q5
Rebrikha Rus. Fed. 88 E2
Rebun-tō i. Japan 90 F3
Recherche, Archipelago of the is Australia 135 C8
Rechitsa Belarus see Rechytsa
Rechna Doab lowland Pak. 111 I4
Rechytsa Belarus 53 F5
Recife Brazil 177 L5
Recife, Cape S. Africa 125 G8
Recklinghausen Germany 63 H3
Reconquista Arg. 178 E3
Recreo Arg. 178 C3
Rectorville U.S.A. 164 D4
Red r. Australia 136 C3
Red r. Canada 150 E3
Red r. Canada/U.S.A. 160 D1
Red r. TN U.S.A. 164 B5
Red r. U.S.A. 161 F6
Red r. Vietnam 86 D2
Redang i. Malaysia 84 C1
Red Bank NJ U.S.A. 165 H3
Red Bank TN U.S.A. 163 C5
Red Basin China see Sichuan Pendi
Red Bay Canada 153 K4
Redberry Lake Canada 151 J4
Red Bluff U.S.A. 158 B1
Red Bluff Lake U.S.A. 161 C6
Red Butte mt. U.S.A. 159 G4
Redcar U.K. 58 F4
Redcliff Canada 156 F2
Redcliffe, Mount hill Australia 135 C7
Red Cliffs Australia 137 C7
Red Cloud U.S.A. 160 D3
Red Deer Canada 150 H4
Red Deer r. Alberta/Saskatchewan Canada 151 I5
Red Deer r. Man./Sask. Canada 151 K4
Red Deer Lake Canada 151 K4
Reddersburg S. Africa 125 H5
Red Devil AK U.S.A. 148 H3
Redding U.S.A. 158 B1
Redditch U.K. 59 F6
Rede r. U.K. 58 E3
Redenção Brazil 177 H5
Redeyef Tunisia 68 C7
Redfield U.S.A. 160 D2
Red Granite Mountain Y.T. Canada 149 M3
Red Hills U.S.A. 161 D4
Red Hook U.S.A. 165 I3
Red Idol Gorge China 99 E7
Red Indian Lake Canada 153 K4
Redkey U.S.A. 164 C3
Redkino Rus. Fed. 52 H4
Redknife r. Canada 150 G2
Red Lake Canada 151 M5
Red Lake U.S.A. 159 G4
Red Lake r. U.S.A. 160 D2
Red Lake Falls U.S.A. 151 L6
Red Lakes U.S.A. 160 E1
Redlands U.S.A. 158 E4
Red Lion U.S.A. 165 G4
Red Lodge U.S.A. 156 F3
Redmesa U.S.A. 159 I3
Redmond OR U.S.A. 156 C3
Redmond UT U.S.A. 159 H2
Red Oak U.S.A. 160 E3
Redonda Island Canada 150 E5
Redondo Port. 67 C4
Redondo Beach U.S.A. 158 D5
Redoubt Volcano AK U.S.A. 148 I3
Red Peak U.S.A. 156 E3
Red River, Mouths of the Vietnam 86 D2
Red Rock Canada 152 C4
Red Rock AZ U.S.A. 159 H5
Redrock U.S.A. 159 I5
Red Rock PA U.S.A. 165 G3
Redrock Lake Canada 150 H1
Red Sea Africa/Asia 108 D4
Redstone r. N.W.T. Canada 149 P2
Red Sucker Lake Canada 151 M4
Reduzum Neth. 62 F1
Redwater Canada 150 H4
Redway U.S.A. 158 B1
Red Wing U.S.A. 160 E2
Redwood City U.S.A. 158 B3
Redwood Falls U.S.A. 160 E2
Redwood National Park U.S.A. 156 B4
Redwood Valley U.S.A. 158 B2
Ree, Lough l. Ireland 61 E4
Reed U.S.A. 164 B5
Reed City U.S.A. 164 C2
Reedley U.S.A. 158 D3
Reedsport U.S.A. 156 B4
Reedsville U.S.A. 164 E4
Reedville U.S.A. 165 G5
Reedy U.S.A. 164 E4
Reedy Glacier Antarctica 188 J1
Reefton N.Z. 139 C6
Rees Germany 62 G3
Reese U.S.A. 164 D2
Reese r. U.S.A. 158 E1
Refahiye Turkey 112 E3
Refugio U.S.A. 161 D6
Regen Germany 63 N6
Regen r. Germany 63 M5
Regência Brazil 179 D2
Regensburg Germany 63 M5
Regenstauf Germany 63 M5
Reggane Alg. 120 D2
Reggio Calabria Italy see Reggio di Calabria
Reggio Emilia-Romagna Italy see Reggio nell'Emilia
Reggio di Calabria Italy 68 F5
Reggio Emilia Italy see Reggio nell'Emilia
Reggio nell'Emilia Italy 68 D2
Reghin Romania 69 K1
Regi Afgh. 111 G3

▶Regina Canada 151 J5
Capital of Saskatchewan.

Régina Fr. Guiana 177 H3
Registān reg. Afgh. 111 G4
Registro Brazil 178 G2
Registro do Araguaia Brazil 179 A1
Regium Lepidum Italy see Reggio nell'Emilia
Regozero Rus. Fed. 54 Q4
Rehau Germany 63 M4
Rehburg (Rehburg-Loccum) Germany 63 J2
Rehli India 104 D5
Rehoboth Namibia 124 C2
Rehoboth Bay U.S.A. 165 H4
Rehovot Israel 107 B4
Reïbell Alg. see Ksar Chellala
Reibitz Germany 63 M3
Reichenbach Germany 63 M4
Reichshoffen France 63 H6
Reid Australia 135 E7
Reidh, Rubha pt U.K. 60 D3
Reidsville U.S.A. 162 E4
Reigate U.K. 59 G7
Reiley Peak U.S.A. 159 H5
Reims France 62 E5
Reinbek Germany 63 K1
Reindeer r. Canada 151 K4
Reindeer Grazing Reserve nature res. N.W.T. Canada 149 O1
Reindeer Island Canada 151 L4
Reindeer Lake Canada 151 K3
Reine Norway 54 H3
Reinosa Spain 67 D2
Reinsfeld Germany 62 G5
Reipholsfjöll hill Iceland 54 [inset]
Reisaelva r. Norway 54 L2
Reisa Nasjonalpark nat. park Norway 54 M2
Reisjärvi Fin. 54 N5
Reitz S. Africa 125 I4
Rekapalle India 106 D2
Reken Germany 62 H3
Reliance Canada 151 I2
Relizane Alg. 67 G6
Rellano Mex. 166 D3
Rellingen Germany 63 J1
Remagen Germany 63 H4
Remarkable, Mount hill Australia 137 B7
Rembang Jawa Indon. 85 E4
Remedios Cuba 163 E8
Remedios, Punta pt El Salvador 167 H6
Remeshk Iran 110 E5
Remhoogte Pass Namibia 124 C2
Remi France see Reims
Remmel Mountain U.S.A. 156 C2
Rempang i. Indon. 84 D2
Remscheid Germany 63 H3
Rena Norway 55 G6
Renaix Belgium see Ronse
Renam Myanmar 96 C3
Renapur India 106 C2
Renchinlhümbe Mongolia 94 D1
Rendsburg Germany 57 L3
René-Levasseur, Île i. Canada 153 H4
Renews Canada 153 L5
Renfrew Canada 165 G1
Renfrew U.K. 60 E5
Rengali Reservoir India 105 F5
Rengat Sumatera Indon. 84 C3
Rengo Chile 178 B4
Ren He r. China 97 F1
Renheji China 97 G2
Renhou Hebei China see Tangxian
Renhua China 97 G3
Reni Ukr. 69 M2
Renick U.S.A. 164 E5
Renland reg. Greenland see Tuttut Nunaat
Rennell i. Solomon Is 133 G3
Rennerod Germany 63 I4
Rennes France 66 D2
Rennick Glacier Antarctica 188 H2
Rennie Canada 151 M5
Reno r. Italy 68 E2
Reno U.S.A. 158 D2
Renovo U.S.A. 165 G3
Renqiu Hebei China 95 I4
Rensselaer U.S.A. 164 B3
Renswoude Neth. 62 F2
Renton U.S.A. 156 C3
Réo Burkina 120 C3
Reo Flores Indon. 83 B5
Repalle India 106 D2
Repetek Turkm. 111 F2
Repetek Döwlet Gorugy nature res. Turkm. 111 F2
Repolka Rus. Fed. 55 P7
Republic U.S.A. 156 D2
Republican r. U.S.A. 160 D4
Republic of South Africa country Africa 124 F5
Repulse Bay b. Australia 136 E4
Repulse Bay Canada 147 J3
Requena Peru 176 D5
Requena Spain 67 F4
Reşadiye Turkey 112 E2
Resag, Gunung mt. Indon. 84 D4
Reserva Brazil 179 A4
Reserve U.S.A. 159 I5
Reshi China 97 F2
Reshteh-ye Alborz mts Iran see Elburz Mountains
Reshui Qinghai China 94 E4
Resistencia Arg. 178 E3
Reşiţa Romania 69 I2
Resolute Canada 147 I2
Resolute Bay Nunavut Canada see Resolute
Resolution Island Canada 147 L3
Resolution Island N.Z. 139 A7
Resplendor Brazil 179 C2
Restigouche r. Canada 153 I5
Resülayn Turkey see Ceylanpınar
Retalhuleu Guat. 167 H6
Retezat, Parcul Naţional nat. park Romania 69 J2
Retford U.K. 58 G5
Rethel France 62 E5
Rethem (Aller) Germany 63 J2
Réthimnon Greece see Rethymno
Rethymno Greece 69 K7
Retreat Australia 136 C5
Reuden Germany 63 M2

▶Réunion terr. Indian Ocean 185 L7
French Overseas Department.

Reus Spain 67 G3
Reusam, Pulau i. Indon. 84 B2
Reutlingen Germany 57 L6
Reval Estonia see Tallinn
Revda Rus. Fed. 54 S3
Revel Estonia see Tallinn
Revel France 66 F5
Revelstoke Canada 150 G5
Revigny-sur-Ornain France 62 E6
Revillagigedo, Islas is Mex. 168 B5
Revillagigedo Island AK U.S.A. 149 O5
Revin France 62 E5
Revivim Israel 107 B4
Revolyutsii, Pik mt. Tajik. see Revolyutsiya, Qullai
Revolyutsiya, Qullai mt. Tajik. 111 I2
Rewa India 104 E4
Rewari India 104 D3
Rex AK U.S.A. 149 J2
Rexburg U.S.A. 156 F4
Rexton Canada 153 I5
Rey, Isla del i. Panama 166 [inset] K7
Reyes, Point U.S.A. 158 B2
Reyhanlı Turkey 107 C1
Reykir Iceland 54 [inset]
Reykjanes Ridge sea feature N. Atlantic Ocean 184 F2
Reykjanestá pt Iceland 54 [inset]

▶Reykjavík Iceland 54 [inset]
Capital of Iceland.

Reyneke, Ostrov i. Rus. Fed. 90 E1
Reynoldsburg U.S.A. 164 D4
Reynolds Range mts Australia 134 F5
Reynosa Mex. 167 F3
Reẕā Iran 110 D3
Reẕā'īyeh Iran see Urmia
Reẕā'īyeh, Daryācheh-ye salt l. Iran see Urmia, Lake
Rēzekne Latvia 55 O8
Rezvān Iran 111 F4
Reẕvāndeh Iran see Reẕvānshahr
Reẕvānshahr Iran 110 C2
R. F. Magón Mex. see Ricardo Flores Magón
Rhaeader Gwy U.K. see Rhayader
Rhayader U.K. 59 D6
Rheda-Wiedenbrück Germany 63 I3
Rhede Germany 62 G3
Rhegium Italy see Reggio di Calabria
Rheims France see Reims
Rhein r. Germany 63 G3 see Rhine
Rheine Germany 63 H2
Rheinland-Pfalz land Germany 63 H5
Rheinsberg Germany 63 M1
Rheinstetten Germany 63 I6
Rhemilès well Alg. 120 C2
Rhin r. France 63 I6 see Rhine
Rhine r. Germany 63 G3
also spelt Rhein (Germany) or Rhin (France)
Rhinebeck U.S.A. 165 I3
Rhinelander U.S.A. 160 F2
Rhineland-Palatinate land Germany see Rheinland-Pfalz
Rhinkanal canal Germany 63 M2
Rhinow Germany 63 M2
Rhiwabon U.K. see Ruabon
Rho Italy 68 C2
Rhode Island state U.S.A. 165 J3
Rhodes Greece 69 M6
Rhodes i. Greece 69 M6
Rhodesia country Africa see Zimbabwe
Rhodes Peak U.S.A. 156 E3
Rhodope Mountains Bulg./Greece 69 J4
Rhodus i. Greece see Rhodes
Rhône r. France/Switz. 66 G5
Rhum i. U.K. see Rum
Rhuthun U.K. see Ruthin
Rhydaman U.K. see Ammanford
Rhyl U.K. 58 D5
Riachão Brazil 177 I5
Riacho Brazil 179 C2
Riacho de Santana Brazil 179 C1
Riacho dos Machados Brazil 179 C1
Rialma Brazil 179 A1
Rialto U.S.A. 158 E4
Riam Kalimantan Indon. 85 E3
Riasi India 104 C2
Riau prov. Indon. 84 C2
Riau, Kepulauan is Indon. 84 D2
Ribadeo Spain 67 C2
Ribadesella Spain 67 D2
Ribas do Rio Pardo Brazil 178 F2
Ribat Afgh. 111 H2
Ribat-i-Shur waterhole Iran 110 E3
Ribáuè Moz. 123 D5
Ribble r. U.K. 58 E5
Ribblesdale valley U.K. 58 E4
Ribe Denmark 55 F9
Ribécourt-Dreslincourt France 62 C5
Ribeira r. Brazil 179 B4
Ribeirão Preto Brazil 179 B3
Ribemont France 62 D5
Ribérac France 66 E4
Riberalta Bol. 176 E6
Rîbniţa Moldova 53 F7
Ribnitz-Damgarten Germany 57 N3
Říčany Czech Rep. 57 O6
Ricardo Flores Magón Mex. 166 D2
Rice U.S.A. 165 F5
Rice Lake Canada 165 F1
Richards Bay S. Africa 125 K5
Richards Inlet Antarctica 188 H1
Richards Island N.W.T. Canada 149 N1
Richardson r. Canada 151 I3
Richardson AK U.S.A. 149 K2
Richardson U.S.A. 161 D5
Richardson Highway AK U.S.A. 149 K3
Richardson Island Canada 150 G1
Richardson Lakes U.S.A. 165 J1
Richardson Mountains N.W.T./Y.T. Canada 149 N2
Richardson Mountains N.Z. 139 B7
Richfield U.S.A. 159 G2
Richfield Springs U.S.A. 165 H2
Richford NY U.S.A. 165 G2
Richford VT U.S.A. 165 I1
Richgrove U.S.A. 158 D4
Richland U.S.A. 156 D3
Richland Center U.S.A. 160 F3
Richmond N.S.W. Australia 138 E4
Richmond Qld Australia 136 C4
Richmond Canada 165 H1
Richmond N.Z. 139 D5
Richmond Kwazulu-Natal S. Africa 125 J5
Richmond N. Cape S. Africa 124 F6
Richmond U.K. 58 F4
Richmond CA U.S.A. 158 B3
Richmond IN U.S.A. 164 C4
Richmond KY U.S.A. 164 C5
Richmond MI U.S.A. 164 D2
Richmond MO U.S.A. 160 E4
Richmond TX U.S.A. 161 E6

▶Richmond VA U.S.A. 165 G5
Capital of Virginia.

Richmond Dale U.S.A. 164 D4
Richmond Hill U.S.A. 163 D6
Richmond Range hills Australia 138 F2
Richoi Xizang China 99 D7
Richtersveld Cultural and Botanical Landscape tourist site S. Africa 124 C5
Richtersveld National Park S. Africa 124 C5
Richvale U.S.A. 158 C2
Richwood U.S.A. 164 E4
Rico U.S.A. 159 I3
Ricomagus France see Riom
Riddell Nunataks Antarctica 188 E2
Ridder Kazakh. 98 C2
Rideau Lakes Canada 165 G1
Ridge r. Canada 152 D4
Ridgecrest U.S.A. 158 E4
Ridge Farm U.S.A. 164 B4
Ridgeland MS U.S.A. 161 F5
Ridgeland SC U.S.A. 163 D5
Ridgetop U.S.A. 164 B5
Ridgetown Canada 164 E2
Ridgeway OH U.S.A. 164 D3
Ridgeway VA U.S.A. 164 F5
Ridgway CO U.S.A. 159 J2
Ridgway PA U.S.A. 165 F3
Riding Mountain National Park Canada 151 K5
Riecito Venez. 176 E1
Riemst Belgium 62 F4
Riesa Germany 63 N3
Riesco, Isla i. Chile 178 B8
Riet watercourse S. Africa 124 E6
Rietavas Lith. 55 L9
Rietfontein S. Africa 124 E4
Rieti Italy 68 E3
Rifā'ī, Tall mt. Jordan/Syria 107 C3
Rifeng China see Lichuan
Rifle U.S.A. 159 J2
Rifstangi pt Iceland 54 [inset]
Rift Valley Lakes National Park Eth. see Abijatta-Shalla National Park

▶Rīga Latvia 55 N8
Capital of Latvia.

Riga, Gulf of Estonia/Latvia 55 M8
Rigain Pünco l. Xizang China 99 D6
Rīgān Iran 110 E4
Rīgas jūras līcis b. Estonia/Latvia see Riga, Gulf of
Rigby U.S.A. 156 F4
Rīgestān reg. Afgh. see Registān
Rigolet Canada 153 K3
Rigside U.K. 60 F5
Riia laht b. Estonia/Latvia see Riga, Gulf of
Riihimäki Fin. 55 N6
Riiser-Larsen Ice Shelf Antarctica 188 B2
Riito Mex. 166 B1
Rijau Nigeria 120 D3
Rijeka Croatia 68 F2
Rikā, Wādī ar watercourse Saudi Arabia 110 B6
Rikitgaib Sumatera Indon. 84 B1
Rikor India 96 B2
Rikuchū-kaigan Kokuritsu-kōen Japan 91 F5
Rikuzen-takata Japan 91 F5
Rila mts Bulg. 69 J3
Rila Xizang China 99 D7
Riley U.S.A. 156 D4
Rileyville U.S.A. 165 F4
Rillieux-la-Pape France 66 G4
Rillito U.S.A. 159 H5
Rimah, Wādī al watercourse Saudi Arabia 108 F4
Rimau, Pulau i. Indon. 84 D3
Rimavská Sobota Slovakia 57 R6
Rimbey Canada 150 H4
Rimini Italy 68 E2
Rîmnicu Sărat Romania see Râmnicu Sărat
Rîmnicu Vîlcea Romania see Râmnicu Vâlcea
Rimo Glacier India 99 B6
Rimouski Canada 153 H4
Rimpar Germany 63 J5
Rimsdale, Loch l. U.K. 60 E2
Rinbung Xizang China 99 E7
Rinca i. Indon. 83 A5
Rincão Brazil 179 A3
Rincón de Romos Mex. 166 E4
Rind r. India 99 C8
Rindal Norway 54 F5
Rindü Xizang China 99 E7
Ringarooma Bay Australia 137 [inset]
Ringas India 104 C4
Ringe Germany 62 G2
Ringebu Norway 55 G6
Ringhkung Myanmar 86 B1
Ringkøbing Denmark 55 F8
Ringsend U.K. 61 F2
Ringsted Denmark 55 G9
Ringtor Xizang China 99 C7
Ringvassøya i. Norway 54 K2
Ringwood Australia 138 B6
Ringwood U.K. 59 F8
Rinjani, Gunung vol. Indon. 80 F8
Rinns Point U.K. 60 C5
Rinqênzê China 105 G3
Rinteln Germany 63 J2
Río Abiseo, Parque Nacional nat. park Peru 176 C5
Rio Azul Brazil 179 A4
Riobamba Ecuador 176 C4
Rio Blanco U.S.A. 159 J2
Rio Bonito Brazil 179 C3
Rio Branco Brazil 176 E6
Rio Branco, Parque Nacional do nat. park Brazil 176 F3
Río Bravo, Parque Internacional del nat. park Mex. 166 E2
Rio Brilhante Brazil 178 F2
Rio Casca Brazil 179 C3
Rio Claro Brazil 179 B3
Río Colorado Arg. 178 D5
Río Cuarto Arg. 178 D4
Rio das Pedras Moz. 125 L2
Rio de Contas Brazil 179 C1

▶Rio de Janeiro Brazil 179 C3
Former capital of Brazil. 3rd most populous city in South America.

Rio de Janeiro state Brazil 179 C3
Río de Jesús Panama 166 [inset] J8

▶Río de la Plata-Paraná r. S. America 178 E4
2nd longest river in South America, and 9th in the world.

Rio Dell U.S.A. 158 A1
Rio do Sul Brazil 179 A4
Río Frío Costa Rica 166 [inset] J7
Río Gallegos Arg. 178 C8
Río Grande Arg. 178 C8
Rio Grande Brazil 178 F4
Río Grande Mex. 161 C8
Rio Grande r. Mex./U.S.A. 154 H6
also known as Bravo de Norte, Rio
Rio Grande City U.S.A. 161 D7
Rio Grande do Sul state Brazil 179 A5
Rio Grande Rise sea feature S. Atlantic Ocean 184 F8
Ríohacha Col. 176 D1
Río Hato Panama 166 [inset] J7
Río Hondo, Embalse resr Arg. 178 C3
Rioja Peru 176 C5
Río Lagartos Mex. 167 H4
Rio Largo Brazil 177 K5
Riom France 66 F4
Rio Manso, Represa do resr Brazil 177 G6
Río Mulatos Bol. 176 E7
Río Muni reg. Equat. Guinea 120 E4
Río Negro, Embalse del resr Uruguay 178 E4
Rioni r. Georgia 113 F2
Rio Novo Brazil 179 C3
Rio Pardo de Minas Brazil 179 C1
Río Plátano, Reserva Biósfera del nature res. Hond. 166 [inset] I6
Rio Preto Brazil 179 C3
Rio Preto, Serra do hills Brazil 179 B2
Rio Rancho U.S.A. 157 G6
Ríosucio Col. 166 [inset] K8
Río Tigre Ecuador 176 C4
Rio Tuba Palawan Phil. 82 B4
Riou Lake Canada 151 J3
Rio Verde Brazil 179 A2
Río Verde Quintana Roo Mex. 167 H5
Río Verde San Luis Potosí Mex. 167 F4
Rio Verde de Mato Grosso Brazil 177 H7
Rio Vista U.S.A. 158 C2
Ripky Ukr. 53 F6
Ripley England U.K. 58 F4
Ripley England U.K. 59 F5
Ripley NY U.S.A. 164 F2
Ripley OH U.S.A. 164 D4
Ripley WV U.S.A. 164 E4
Ripoll Spain 67 H2
Ripon U.K. 58 F4
Ripon U.S.A. 158 C3
Ripu India 105 G4
Risca U.K. 59 D7
Rishiri-tō i. Japan 90 F3
Rishon LeZiyyon Israel 107 B4
Rish Pish Iran 111 F5
Rising Sun IN U.S.A. 164 C4
Rising Sun MD U.S.A. 165 G4
Risle r. France 59 H9
Risør Norway 55 F7
Rissa Norway 54 F5
Ristiina Fin. 55 O6
Ristijärvi Fin. 54 P4
Ristikent Rus. Fed. 54 Q2
Risum Xizang China 99 B6
Ritan r. Indon. 85 F2
Ritang Xizang China 99 F7
Ritchie S. Africa 124 G5
Ritchie's Archipelago is India 87 A4
Ritch Island N.W.T. Canada 149 R2
Ritscher Upland mts Antarctica 188 B2
Ritsem Sweden 54 J3
Ritter, Mount U.S.A. 158 D3
Ritterhude Germany 63 I1
Rittō Japan 92 B3
Ritzville U.S.A. 156 D3
Riu, Laem pt Thai. 87 B5
Riva del Garda Italy 68 D2
Rivas Nicaragua 166 [inset] I7
Rivera Arg. 178 D5
Rivera Uruguay 178 E4
River Cess Liberia 120 C4
Riverhead U.S.A. 165 I3
Riverhurst Canada 151 J5
Riverina Australia 135 C7
Riverina reg. Australia 138 B5
Riversdale S. Africa 124 E8
Riverside S. Africa 125 I6
Riverside U.S.A. 158 E5
Rivers Inlet Canada 150 E5
Riversleigh Australia 136 B3
Riverton N.Z. 139 B8
Riverton VA U.S.A. 165 F4
Riverton WY U.S.A. 156 F4
Riverview Canada 153 I5
Rivesaltes France 66 F5
Riviera Beach U.S.A. 163 D7
Rivière-du-Loup Canada 153 H5
Rivière-Pentecôte Canada 153 I4
Rivière-Pigou Canada 153 I4
Rivne Ukr. 53 E6
Rivungo Angola 123 C5
Riwaka N.Z. 139 D5
Riwoqê China see Racaka

▶Riyadh Saudi Arabia 108 G5
Capital of Saudi Arabia.

Riyan India 111 I5
Riyue Shankou pass Qinghai China 94 E4
Riza well Iran 110 D3
Rizal Luzon Phil. 82 C3
Rize Turkey 113 F2
Rizhao Shandong China see Donggang
Rizhao Shandong China 95 I5
Rizokarpaso Cyprus see Rizokarpason
Rizokarpason Cyprus 107 B2
Rīzū well Iran 110 E3
Rīzū'īyeh Iran 110 E4
Rjukan Norway 55 F7
Rjuvbrokkene mt. Norway 55 E7
Rkîz Mauritania 120 B3
Roa Norway 55 G6
Roachdale U.S.A. 164 B4
Roach Lake U.S.A. 159 F4
Roade U.K. 59 G6
Roads U.S.A. 164 D4
▶Road Town Virgin Is (U.K.) 169 L5
Capital of the British Virgin Islands.
Roan Norway 54 G4
Roan Fell hill U.K. 60 G5
Roan High Knob mt. U.S.A. 162 D4
Roanne France 66 G3
Roanoke IN U.S.A. 164 C3
Roanoke VA U.S.A. 164 F5
Roanoke r. U.S.A. 162 E4
Roanoke Rapids U.S.A. 162 E4
Roan Plateau U.S.A. 159 I2
Roaring Spring U.S.A. 165 F3
Roaringwater Bay Ireland 61 C6
Roatán Hond. 166 [inset] I5
Röbäck Sweden 54 L5
Robat r. Afgh. 111 F4
Robāţe Tork Iran 110 C3
Robāţ Karīm Iran 110 C3
Robāt-Sang Iran 110 E3
Robb Canada 150 G4
Robbins Island Australia 137 [inset]
Robbinsville U.S.A. 163 D5
Robe Australia 137 B8
Robe r. Australia 134 A5
Robe r. Ireland 61 C4
Röbel Germany 63 M1
Robert-Bourassa, Réservoir resr Canada 152 F3
Robert Glacier Antarctica 188 D2
Robert Lee U.S.A. 161 C6
Roberts U.S.A. 156 E4
Roberts, Mount Australia 138 F2
Robertsburg U.S.A. 164 E4
Roberts Butte mt. Antarctica 188 H2
Roberts Creek Mountain U.S.A. 158 E2
Robertsfors Sweden 54 L4
Robertsganj India 105 E4
Robertson S. Africa 124 D7
Robertson, Lac l. Canada 153 K4
Robertson Bay Antarctica 188 H2
Robertson Island Antarctica 188 A2
Robertson Range hills Australia 135 C5
Robertsport Liberia 120 B4
Roberval Canada 153 G4
Robhanais, Rubha hd U.K. see Butt of Lewis
Robin Hood's Bay U.K. 58 G4
Robin's Nest hill H.K. China 97 [inset]
Robinson Y.T. Canada 149 N3
Robinson U.S.A. 164 B4
Robinson Mountains AK U.S.A. 148 I4
Robinson Mountains AK U.S.A. 149 L3
Robinson Range hills Australia 135 B6
Robinson River Australia 136 B3
Robles Pass U.S.A. 159 H5
Roblin Canada 151 K5
Robsart Canada 151 I5
Robson, Mount Canada 150 G4
Robstown U.S.A. 161 D7
Roby U.S.A. 161 C5
Roçadas Angola see Xangongo
Roca Partida, Punta pt Mex. 167 G5
Rocas Alijos is Mex. 166 B3
Rocca Busambra mt. Sicily Italy 68 E6
Rocha Uruguay 178 F4
Rochdale U.K. 58 E5
Rochechouart France 66 E4
Rochefort Belgium 62 F4
Rochefort France 66 D4
Rochefort, Lac l. Canada 153 G2
Rochegda Rus. Fed. 52 I3
Rochester Australia 138 B6
Rochester U.K. 59 H7
Rochester IN U.S.A. 164 B3
Rochester MN U.S.A. 160 E2
Rochester NH U.S.A. 165 J2
Rochester NY U.S.A. 165 G2
Rochford U.K. 59 H7
Rochlitz Germany 63 M3
Roc'h Trévezel hill France 66 C2
Rock r. Y.T. Canada 149 M2
Rock r. Y.T. Canada 149 P3
Rockall i. N. Atlantic Ocean 50 D4
Rockall Bank sea feature N. Atlantic Ocean 184 G2
Rock Creek Y.T. Canada 149 M2
Rock Creek U.S.A. 164 E3
Rock Creek r. U.S.A. 156 G2
Rockdale U.S.A. 161 D6
Rockefeller Plateau Antarctica 188 J1
Rockford AL U.S.A. 163 C5
Rockford IL U.S.A. 160 F3
Rockford MI U.S.A. 164 C2
Rockglen Canada 151 J5
Rockhampton Australia 136 E4
Rockhampton Downs Australia 134 F4
Rock Hill U.S.A. 163 D5
Rockingham Australia 135 A8
Rockingham U.S.A. 163 E5
Rockingham Bay Australia 136 D3
Rockinghorse Lake Canada 151 H1
Rock Island Canada 165 I1
Rock Island U.S.A. 160 F3
Rocklake U.S.A. 160 D1
Rockland MA U.S.A. 165 J2
Rockland ME U.S.A. 162 G2
Rocknest Lake Canada 150 H1
Rockport IN U.S.A. 164 B5
Rockport TX U.S.A. 161 D7
Rock Rapids U.S.A. 160 D3
Rock River U.S.A. 156 G4
Rock Sound Bahamas 163 E7
Rock Springs MT U.S.A. 156 G3
Rocksprings U.S.A. 161 C6
Rock Springs WY U.S.A. 156 F4
Rockstone Guyana 177 G2
Rockville CT U.S.A. 165 I3
Rockville IN U.S.A. 164 B4
Rockville MD U.S.A. 165 G4
Rockwell City U.S.A. 160 E3
Rockwood MI U.S.A. 164 D2
Rockwood PA U.S.A. 164 F4
Rockyford Canada 150 H5
Rocky Harbour Canada 153 K4
Rocky Hill U.S.A. 164 D4
Rocky Island Lake Canada 152 E5
Rocky Lane Canada 150 G3
Rocky Mount U.S.A. 164 F5
Rocky Mountain House Canada 150 H4
Rocky Mountain National Park U.S.A. 156 G4
Rocky Mountains Canada/U.S.A. 154 F3
Rocky Point pt AK U.S.A. 148 G2
Rocourt-St-Martin France 62 D5
Rocroi France 62 E5
Rodberg Norway 55 F6
Rødbyhavn Denmark 55 G9
Roddickton Canada 153 L4
Rodeio Brazil 179 A4
Rodel U.K. 60 C3
Roden Neth. 62 G1
Rödental Germany 63 L4
Rodeo Arg. 178 C4
Rodeo Mex. 166 D3
Rodeo U.S.A. 157 F7
Rodez France 66 F4
Ródhos i. Greece see Rhodes
Rodi i. Greece see Rhodes
Roding Germany 63 M5
Rodney, Cape AK U.S.A. 148 F2
Rodniki Rus. Fed. 52 I4
Rodolfo Sanchez Toboada Mex. 166 A2
Rodopi Planina mts Bulg./Greece see Rhodope Mountains
Rodos Greece see Rhodes
Rodos i. Greece see Rhodes
Rodosto Turkey see Tekirdağ
Rodrigues Island Mauritius 185 M7
Roe r. U.K. 61 F2
Roebourne Australia 134 B5
Roebuck Bay Australia 134 C4
Roedtan S. Africa 125 I3
Roe Plains Australia 135 D7
Roermond Neth. 62 F3
Roeselare Belgium 62 D4
Roes Welcome Sound sea chan. Canada 147 J3
Rogachev Belarus see Rahachow
Rogätz Germany 63 L2
Rogers U.S.A. 161 E4
Rogers, Mount U.S.A. 164 E5
Rogers City U.S.A. 164 D1
Rogers Lake U.S.A. 158 E4
Rogerson U.S.A. 156 E4
Rogersville U.S.A. 164 D5
Roggan r. Canada 152 F3
Roggan, Lac l. Canada 152 F3
Roggeveen Basin sea feature S. Pacific Ocean 187 O8
Roggeveld plat. S. Africa 124 E7
Roggeveldberge esc. S. Africa 124 E7
Roghadal U.K. see Rodel
Rognan Norway 54 I3
Rögnitz r. Germany 63 K1
Rogue r. U.S.A. 156 B4
Roha India 106 B2
Rohnert Park U.S.A. 158 B2
Rohrbach in Oberösterreich Austria 57 N6
Rohrbach-lès-Bitche France 63 H5
Rohri Sangar Pak. 111 H5
Rohtak India 104 D3
Roi Et Thai. 86 C3
Roi Georges, Îles du is Fr. Polynesia 187 K6
Rois-Bheinn hill U.K. 60 D4
Roisel France 62 D5
Roja Latvia 55 M8
Rojas Arg. 178 D4
Rojo, Cabo c. Mex. 167 F4
Rokan r. Indon. 84 C2
Rokeby Australia 136 C2
Rokeby National Park Australia 136 C2
Rokiškis Lith. 55 N9
Roknäs Sweden 54 L4
Rokugō Japan 93 E3
Rokuriga-hara plain Japan 93 E2
Rokusei Japan 92 C2
Rokytne Ukr. 53 E6
Rola Co l. Xizang China 99 E6
Rolagang Xizang China 99 E6
Rola Kangri mt. Xizang China 99 E6
Rolândia Brazil 179 A3
Rolim de Moura Brazil 176 F6
Roll AZ U.S.A. 159 G5
Roll IN U.S.A. 164 C3
Rolla MO U.S.A. 160 F4
Rolla ND U.S.A. 160 D1
Rollag Norway 55 F6
Rolleston Australia 136 E5
Rolleville Bahamas 163 F8
Rolling Fork U.S.A. 161 F5
Rollins U.S.A. 156 E3
Roma Australia 137 E5
Roma Italy see Rome
Roma Lesotho 125 H5
Roma Sweden 55 K8
Roma TX U.S.A. 167 F3
Roma, Pulau i. Maluku Indon. see Romang, Pulau
Romain, Cape U.S.A. 163 E5
Romaine r. Canada 153 J4
Roman Romania 69 L1
Română, Câmpia plain Romania 69 J2
Romanche Gap sea feature S. Atlantic Ocean 184 G6
Romanet, Lac l. Canada 153 I2
Romang, Pulau i. Maluku Indon. 83 C4
Romania country Europe 69 K2
Roman-Kosh mt. Ukr. 112 D1
Romano, Cape U.S.A. 163 D7
Romanovka Rus. Fed. 89 K2
Romans-sur-Isère France 66 G4
Romanzof, Cape AK U.S.A. 148 F3
Romanzof Mountains AK U.S.A. 149 K1
Rombas France 62 G5
Romblon Phil. 82 C3
Romblon i. Phil. 82 C3
Romblon Passage Phil. 82 C3
▶Rome Italy 68 E4
Capital of Italy.
Rome GA U.S.A. 163 C5
Rome ME U.S.A. 165 K1
Rome NY U.S.A. 165 H2
Rome TN U.S.A. 164 B5
Rome City U.S.A. 164 C3
Romeo U.S.A. 164 D2
Romford U.K. 59 H7
Romilly-sur-Seine France 66 F2
Romiton Uzbek. 111 G2
Romney U.S.A. 165 F4
Romney Marsh reg. U.K. 59 H7
Romny Ukr. 53 G6
Rømø i. Denmark 55 F9
Romodanovo Rus. Fed. 53 J5
Romorantin-Lanthenay France 66 E3
Rompin r. Malaysia 84 C2
Romsey U.K. 59 F8
Romu mt. Sumbawa Indon. 85 G5
Romulus U.S.A. 164 D2
Ron India 106 B3
Rona i. U.K. 60 D1
Ronas Hill hill U.K. 60 [inset]
Roncador, Serra do hills Brazil 177 H6
Roncador Reef Solomon Is 133 F2
Ronda Spain 67 D5
Ronda, Serranía de mts Spain 67 D5
Rondane Nasjonalpark nat. park Norway 55 F6
Rondon Brazil 178 F2
Rondonópolis Brazil 177 H7
Rondout Reservoir U.S.A. 165 H3
Rongcheng Anhui China see Qingyang
Rongcheng Guangxi China see Rongxian
Rongcheng Hubei China see Jianli
Rongcheng Shandong China 95 J4
Rongcheng Wan b. China 95 J4
Rong Chu r. China 99 E7
Rongelap atoll Marshall Is 186 H5
Rongjiang Guizhou China 97 F3
Rongjiang Jiangxi China see Nankang
Rongjiawan China see Yueyang
Rongklang Range mts Myanmar 86 A2
Rongmei China see Hefeng
Rongshui China 97 F3
Rongwo Qinghai China see Tongren
Rongxian China 97 F4
Rongyul China 96 C2
Rongzhag China see Danba
Rönlap atoll Marshall Is see Rongelap
Rønne Denmark 55 I9
Ronneby Sweden 55 I8
Ronne Entrance strait Antarctica 188 L2
Ronne Ice Shelf Antarctica 188 L1
Ronnenberg Germany 63 J2
Ronse Belgium 62 D4
Roodepoort S. Africa 125 H4
Roodeschool Neth. 62 G1
Rooke Island P.N.G. see Umboi
Roordahuizum Neth. see Reduzum
Roorkee India 104 D3
Roosendaal Neth. 62 E3
Roosevelt AZ U.S.A. 159 H5
Roosevelt UT U.S.A. 159 I1
Roosevelt, Mount Canada 150 E3
Roosevelt Island Antarctica 188 I1
Root r. Canada 150 F2
Root r. U.S.A. 160 F3
Ropar India see Rupnagar
Roper r. Australia 136 A2
Roper Bar Australia 134 F3
Roquefort France 66 D4
Roraima, Mount Guyana 176 F2
Rorey Lake N.W.T. Canada 149 O2
Rori India 104 C3
Rori Indon. 81 J7
Røros Norway 54 G5
Rørvik Norway 54 G4
Rosa, Punta pt Mex. 166 C3
Rosales Mex. 166 D2
Rosalia U.S.A. 156 D3
Rosamond U.S.A. 158 D4
Rosamond Lake U.S.A. 158 D4
Rosamorada Mex. 166 D4
Rosario Arg. 178 D4
Rosário Brazil 177 J4
Rosario Baja California Mex. 166 B2
Rosario Coahuila Mex. 166 E3
Rosario Sinaloa Mex. 168 C4
Rosario Sonora Mex. 166 C3
Rosario Zacatecas Mex. 161 C7
Rosario Luzon Phil. 82 C2
Rosario Luzon Phil. 82 C3
Rosario Venez. 176 D1
Rosário do Sul Brazil 178 F4
Rosário Oeste Brazil 177 G6
Rosarito Baja California Mex. 166 A1
Rosarito Baja California Mex. 166 B2
Rosarito Baja California Sur Mex. 166 C3
Rosarno Italy 68 F5
Roscoe r. N.W.T. Canada 149 Q1
Roscoff France 66 C2
Roscommon Ireland 61 D4
Roscommon U.S.A. 164 C1
Roscrea Ireland 61 E5
Rose r. Australia 136 A2
Rose, Mount U.S.A. 158 D2
Rose Atoll American Samoa see Rose Island
▶Roseau Dominica 169 L5
Capital of Dominica.
Roseau U.S.A. 160 E1
Roseau r. U.S.A. 160 D1
Roseberth Australia 137 B5
Rose Blanche Canada 153 K5
Rosebud r. Canada 150 H5
Rosebud U.S.A. 156 G3
Roseburg U.S.A. 156 C4
Rose City U.S.A. 164 C1
Rosedale U.S.A. 161 F5
Rosedale Abbey U.K. 58 G4
Roseires Reservoir Sudan 108 D7
Rose Island atoll American Samoa 133 J3
Rosenberg U.S.A. 161 E6
Rosendal Norway 55 E7
Rosendal S. Africa 125 H5
Rosenheim Germany 57 N7
Rose Peak U.S.A. 159 I5
Rose Point pt B.C. Canada 149 O5
Roseto degli Abruzzi Italy 68 F3
Rosetown Canada 151 J5
Rosetta Egypt see Rashīd
Rose Valley Canada 151 K4
Roseville CA U.S.A. 158 C2
Roseville MI U.S.A. 164 D2
Roseville OH U.S.A. 164 D4
Rosewood Australia 138 F1
Roshchino Rus. Fed. 55 P6
Rosh Pinah Namibia 124 C4
Roshtkala Tajik. see Roshtqal'a
Roshtqal'a Tajik. 111 H2
Rosignano Marittimo Italy 68 D3
Roşiori de Vede Romania 69 K2
Roskilde Denmark 55 H9
Roskruge Mountains U.S.A. 159 H5
Roslavl' Rus. Fed. 53 G5
Roslyakovo Rus. Fed. 54 R2
Roslyatino Rus. Fed. 52 J4
Ross r. Y.T. Canada 149 N3
Ross N.Z. 139 C6
Ross, Mount hill N.Z. 139 E5
Rossano Italy 68 G5
Rossan Point Ireland 61 D3
Ross Barnett Reservoir U.S.A. 161 F5
Ross Bay Junction Canada 153 I3
Rosscarbery Ireland 61 C6
Ross Dependency reg. Antarctica 188 I2
Rosseau, Lake Canada 164 F1
Rossel Island P.N.G. 136 F1
Ross Ice Shelf Antarctica 188 I1
Rossignol, Lac l. Canada 152 G3
Rössing Namibia 124 B2
Ross Island Antarctica 188 H1
Rossiyskaya Sovetskaya Federativnaya Sotsialisticheskaya Respublika country Asia/Europe see Russian Federation
Rossland Canada 150 G5
Rosslare Ireland 61 F5
Rosslare Harbour Ireland 61 F5
Roßlau Germany 63 M3
Rosso Mauritania 120 B3
Ross-on-Wye U.K. 59 E7
Rossony Belarus see Rasony
Rossosh' Rus. Fed. 53 H6
Ross River Y.T. Canada 149 N3
Ross Sea Antarctica 188 H1
Roßtal Germany 63 K5
Røssvatnet l. Norway 54 I4
Rossville U.S.A. 164 B3
Roßwein Germany 63 N3
Rosswood Canada 150 D4
Rostāq Afgh. 111 H2
Rostāq Iran 110 D5
Rosthern Canada 151 J4
Rostock Germany 57 N3
Rostov Rus. Fed. 52 H4
Rostov-na-Donu Rus. Fed. 53 H7
Rostov-on-Don Rus. Fed. see Rostov-na-Donu
Rosvik Sweden 54 L4
Roswell U.S.A. 157 G6
Rota i. N. Mariana Is 81 L4
Rot am See Germany 63 K5
Rotch Island Kiribati see Tamana
Rote i. Indon. 83 B5
Rotenburg (Wümme) Germany 63 J1
Roth Germany 63 L5
Rothaargebirge hills Germany 63 I4
Rothbury U.K. 58 F3
Rothenburg ob der Tauber Germany 63 K5
Rother r. U.K. 59 G8
Rothera research station Antarctica 188 L2
Rotherham U.K. 58 F5
Rothes U.K. 60 F3
Rothesay U.K. 60 D5
Rothwell U.K. 59 G6
Roti Indon. 83 B5
Roti i. Indon. see Rote
Roti, Selat sea chan. Indon. 83 B5
Roto Australia 138 B4
Rotomagus France see Rouen
Rotomanu N.Z. 139 C6
Rotondo, Monte mt. Corsica France 66 I5
Rotorua N.Z. 139 F4
Rotorua, Lake N.Z. 139 F4
Röttenbach Germany 63 L5
Rottendorf Germany 63 K5
Rottenmann Austria 57 O7
Rotterdam Neth. 62 E3
Rottleberode Germany 63 K3
Rottnest Island Australia 135 A8
Rottumeroog i. Neth. 62 G1
Rottweil Germany 57 L6
Rotuma i. Fiji 133 H3
Rotung India 96 B2
Rötviken Sweden 54 I5
Rötz Germany 63 M5
Roubaix France 62 D4
Rouen France 62 B5
Rough River Lake U.S.A. 164 B5
Roulers Belgium see Roeselare
Roumania country Europe see Romania
Roundeyed Lake Canada 153 H3
Round Hill hill U.K. 58 F4
Round Mountain Australia 138 F3
Round Rock AZ U.S.A. 159 I3
Round Rock TX U.S.A. 161 D6
Roundup U.S.A. 156 F3
Rousay i. U.K. 60 F1
Rouses Point U.S.A. 165 I1
Routh Bank sea feature Phil. see Seahorse Bank
Rouxville S. Africa 125 H6
Rouyn-Noranda Canada 152 F4
Rouyuan Gansu China see Huachi
Rouyuanchengzi Gansu China see Huachi
Rovaniemi Fin. 54 N3
Roven'ki Rus. Fed. 53 H6
Rovereto Italy 68 D2
Rôviĕng Tbong Cambodia 87 D4
Rovigo Italy 68 D2
Rovinj Croatia 68 E2
Rovno Ukr. see Rivne
Rovnoye Rus. Fed. 53 J6
Rovuma r. Moz./Tanz. see Ruvuma
Rowena Australia 138 D2
Rowley Island Canada 147 K3
Rowley Shoals sea feature Australia 134 B4
Równe Ukr. see Rivne
Roxas Luzon Phil. 82 C2
Roxas Mindanao Phil. 82 C4
Roxas Mindoro Phil. 82 C3
Roxas Palawan Phil. 82 B4
Roxas Panay Phil. 82 C4
Roxboro U.S.A. 162 E4
Roxburgh N.Z. 139 B7
Roxburgh Island Cook Is see Rarotonga
Roxby Downs Australia 137 B6
Roxo, Cabo c. Senegal 120 B3
Roy MT U.S.A. 156 F3
Roy NM U.S.A. 157 G5
Royal Canal Ireland 61 E4
Royal Chitwan National Park Nepal 105 F4
Royale, Île i. Canada see Cape Breton Island
Royale, Isle i. U.S.A. 160 F1
Royal Natal National Park S. Africa 125 I5
Royal National Park Australia 138 E5
Royal Oak U.S.A. 164 D2
Royal Sukla Phanta Wildlife Reserve Nepal 104 E3
Royan France 66 D4
Roye France 62 C5
Roy Hill Australia 134 B5
Royston U.K. 59 G6
Rozdil'na Ukr. 69 N1
Rozivka Ukr. 53 H7
Rtishchevo Rus. Fed. 53 I5
Rua, Tanjung pt Sumba Indon. 83 A5
Ruabon U.K. 59 D6
Ruaha National Park Tanz. 123 D4
Ruahine Range mts N.Z. 139 F5
Ruanda country Africa see Rwanda
Ruang i. Indon. 83 C2
▶Ruapehu, Mount vol. N.Z. 139 E4
Highest active volcano in Oceania.
Ruapuke Island N.Z. 139 B8
Ruatoria N.Z. 139 G3
Ruba Belarus 53 F5
▶Rub' al Khālī des. Saudi Arabia 108 G6
Largest uninterrupted stretch of sand in the world.
Rubaydā reg. Saudi Arabia 110 C5
Rubtsovsk Rus. Fed. 102 F1
Ruby AK U.S.A. 148 I2
Ruby Dome mt. U.S.A. 159 F1
Ruby Mountains U.S.A. 159 F1
Rubys Inn U.S.A. 159 G3
Ruby Valley U.S.A. 159 F1
Rucheng China 97 G3
Ruckersville U.S.A. 165 F4
Rudall River National Park Australia 134 C5
Rudarpur India 105 E4
Ruda Śląska Poland 57 Q5
Rudauli India 105 E4
Rūdbār Iran 110 C2
Rudkøbing Denmark 55 G9
Rudnaya Pristan' Rus. Fed. 90 D3
Rudnichnyy Rus. Fed. 52 L4
Rudnik Ingichka Uzbek. see Ingichka
Rudnya Smolenskaya Oblast' Rus. Fed. 53 F5
Rudnya Volgogradskaya Oblast' Rus. Fed. 53 J6
Rudnyy Kazakh. 100 F1
Rudolf, Lake salt l. Eth./Kenya see Turkana, Lake
▶Rudol'fa, Ostrov i. Rus. Fed. 76 G1
Most northerly point of Europe.
Rudolph Island Rus. Fed. see Rudol'fa, Ostrov
Rudolstadt Germany 63 L4
Rudong China 97 I1
Rūdsar Iran 110 C2
Rue France 62 B4
Rufiji r. Tanz. 123 D4
Rufino Arg. 178 D4
Rufisque Senegal 120 B3
Rufrufua Indon. 81 I7
Rufunsa Zambia 123 C5
Rufus Lake N.W.T. Canada 149 O1
Rugao China 97 I1
Rugby U.K. 59 F6
Rugby U.S.A. 160 C1
Rugeley U.K. 59 F6
Rügen i. Germany 57 N3
Rugged Mountain Canada 150 E5
Rügland Germany 63 K5
Ruḥayyat al Ḥamr'ā' waterhole Saudi Arabia 110 B5
Ruhengeri Rwanda 122 C4
Ruhnu i. Estonia 55 M8
Ruhr r. Germany 63 G3
Ruhuna National Park Sri Lanka 106 D5
Rui'an China 97 I3
Rui Barbosa Brazil 179 C1
Ruicheng China 97 F1
Ruijin China 97 G3
Ruili China 96 C3
Ruin Point Canada 151 P2
Ruipa Tanz. 123 D4
Ruiz Mex. 168 C4
Ruiz, Nevado del vol. Col. 176 C3
Rujaylah, Ḥarrat ar lava field Jordan 107 C3
Rūjiena Latvia 55 N8
Ruk is Micronesia see Chuuk
Rukanpur Pak. 111 I4
Rukumkot Nepal 105 E3
Rukuwa Sulawesi Indon. 83 C4
Rukwa, Lake Tanz. 123 D4
Rulin China see Chengbu
Rulong China see Xinlong
Rum i. U.K. 60 C4
Rum, Jebel mts Jordan see Ramm, Jabal
Ruma Serbia 69 H2
Rumāh Saudi Arabia 108 G4
Rumania country Europe see Romania
Rumbai Sulawesi Indon. 83 C2
Rumbek Sudan 121 F4
Rumberpon i. Indon. 81 I7
Rum Cay i. Bahamas 163 F8
Rum Jungle Australia 134 E3
Rummānā hill Syria 107 D3
Rumphi Malawi 123 D5
Run i. Maluku Indon. 83 D4
Runan China 97 G1
Runaway, Cape N.Z. 139 F3
Runcorn U.K. 58 E5
Rundu Namibia 123 B5
Runduma i. Indon. 83 C4
Rundvik Sweden 54 K5
Rŭng, Kaôh i. Cambodia 87 C5
Rungan r. Indon. 85 F3
Rungwa Tanz. 123 D4
Rungwa r. Tanz. 123 D4
Runheji China 97 H1
Runing China see Runan
Runton Range hills Australia 135 C5
Ruokolahti Fin. 55 P6
Ruoqiang Xinjiang China 98 E5
Ruoqiang He r. China 98 E5
Ruo Shui watercourse China 94 E3
Rupa India 105 H4
Rupat i. Indon. 84 C2
Rupert r. Canada 152 F4
Rupert ID U.S.A. 156 E4
Rupert WV U.S.A. 164 E5
Rupert Bay Canada 152 F4
Rupert Coast Antarctica 188 J1
Rupert House Canada see Waskaganish
Rupnagar India 104 D3
Rupshu reg. India 104 D2
Ruqqād, Wādī ar watercourse Israel 107 B3
Rural Retreat U.S.A. 164 E5
Rusaddir N. Africa see Melilla
Rusape Zimbabwe 123 D5
Ruschuk Bulg. see Ruse
Ruse Bulg. 69 K3
Rusera India 105 F4
Rush U.S.A. 164 D4
Rushan Shandong China 95 J4
Rush Creek r. U.S.A. 160 C4
Rushden U.K. 59 G6
Rushinga Zimbabwe 123 D5
Rushui He r. China 94 F5
Rushville IL U.S.A. 160 F3
Rushville IN U.S.A. 164 C4
Rushville NE U.S.A. 160 C3
Rushworth Australia 138 B6
Rusk U.S.A. 161 E6
Russell Man. Canada 151 K5
Russell Ont. Canada 165 H1
Russell N.Z. 139 E2
Russell KS U.S.A. 160 D4
Russell PA U.S.A. 164 F3
Russell, Mount AK U.S.A. 149 J3
Russell Bay Antarctica 188 J2
Russell Lake Man. Canada 151 K3
Russell Lake N.W.T. Canada 150 H2
Russell Lake Sask. Canada 151 J3
Russell Range hills Australia 135 C8
Russell Springs U.S.A. 164 C5
Russellville AL U.S.A. 161 G5
Russellville AR U.S.A. 161 E5
Russellville KY U.S.A. 164 B5
Rüsselsheim Germany 63 I4

Russia *country* Asia/Europe *see* Russian Federation
Russian *r.* U.S.A. 158 B2

▶Russian Federation *country* Asia/Europe 76 I3
Largest country in the world, Europe and Asia. Most populous country in Europe, 5th in Asia and 9th in the world.

Russian Mission *AK* U.S.A. 148 G3
Russian Mountains *AK* U.S.A. 148 H3
Russian Soviet Federal Socialist Republic *country* Asia/Europe *see* Russian Federation
Russkaya Koshka, Kosa *spit* Rus. Fed. 148 B2
Russkiy, Ostrov *i.* Rus. Fed. 90 C4
Russkiy Kameshkir Rus. Fed. 53 J5
Rust'avi Georgia 113 G2
Rustburg U.S.A. 164 F5
Rustenburg S. Africa 125 H3
Ruston U.S.A. 161 E5
Ruta *Maluku* Indon. 83 C3
Rutanzige, Lake Dem. Rep. Congo/Uganda *see* Edward, Lake
Ruteng *Flores* Indon. 83 B5
Ruth U.S.A. 159 F2
Rüthen Germany 63 I3
Rutherglen Australia 138 C6
Ruther Glen U.S.A. 165 G5
Ruthin U.K. 59 D5
Ruthiyai India 104 D4
Ruth Reservoir U.S.A. 158 B1
Rutka *r.* Rus. Fed. 52 J4
Rutland U.S.A. 165 I2
Rutland Water *resr* U.K. 59 G6
Rutledge Lake Canada 151 I2
Rutog *Xizang* China 99 B6
Rutog *Xizang* China 99 D7
Rutog *Xizang* China 99 F7
Rutul Rus. Fed. 113 G2
Ruukki Fin. 54 N4
Ruvuma *r.* Moz./Tanz. 123 E5 *also known as* Rovuma
Ruwayshid, Wādī *watercourse* Jordan 107 C3
Ruwayṭah, Wādī *watercourse* Jordan 107 C5
Ruweis U.A.E. 110 D5
Ruwenzori National Park Uganda *see* Queen Elizabeth National Park
Ruza Rus. Fed. 52 H5
Ruzayevka Kazakh. 100 F1
Ruzayevka Rus. Fed. 53 J5
Ruzhou *Henan* China 95 H5
Ružomberok Slovakia 57 Q6
Rwanda *country* Africa 122 C4
Ryābād Iran 110 D2
Ryan, Loch *b.* U.K. 60 D5
Ryazan' Rus. Fed. 53 H5
Ryazhsk Rus. Fed. 53 I5
Rybachiy, Poluostrov *pen.* Rus. Fed. 54 R2
Rybach'ye Kazakh. 98 C3
Rybach'ye Kyrg. *see* Balykchy
Rybinsk Rus. Fed. 52 H4

▶Rybinskoye Vodokhranilishche *resr* Rus. Fed. 52 H4
5th largest lake in Europe

Rybnik Poland 57 Q5
Rybnitsa Moldova *see* Rîbnița
Rybnoye Rus. Fed. 53 H5
Rybreka Rus. Fed. 52 G3
Ryd Sweden 55 I8
Rydberg Peninsula Antarctica 188 L2
Ryde U.K. 59 F8
Rye U.K. 59 H8
Rye *r.* U.K. 58 G4
Rye Bay U.K. 59 H8
Ryegate U.S.A. 156 F3
Rye Patch Reservoir U.S.A. 158 D1
Rykovo Ukr. *see* Yenakiyeve
Ryl'sk Rus. Fed. 53 G6
Rylstone Australia 138 D4
Ryn-Peski *des.* Kazakh. 51 P6
Ryōgami-san *mt.* Japan 93 E2
Ryōhaku-sanchi *mts* Japan 92 C3
Ryojun *Liaoning* China *see* Lüshun
Ryōkami Japan 93 E2
Ryōzen-zan *mt.* Japan 92 C3
Ryūga-dake *mt.* Japan 92 C3
Ryūgasaki Japan 93 G3
Ryukyu Islands Japan 91 B8
Ryūkyū-rettō *is* Japan *see* Ryukyu Islands
Ryukyu Trench *sea feature* N. Pacific Ocean 186 E4
Ryūō *Shiga* Japan 92 C3
Ryūō *Yamanashi* Japan 93 E3
Ryūsō-san *mt.* Japan 93 E3
Ryūyō Japan 93 D4
Rzeszów Poland 53 D6
Rzhaksa Rus. Fed. 53 I5
Rzhev Rus. Fed. 52 G4

S

Sa'ādah al Barṣā' *pass* Saudi Arabia 107 C5
Sa'ādatābād Iran 110 D4
Saal an der Donau Germany 63 L6
Saale *r.* Germany 63 L3
Saalfeld Germany 63 L4
Saanich Canada 150 F5
Saar *land* Germany *see* Saarland
Saar *r.* Germany 62 G5
Saarbrücken Germany 62 G5
Saaremaa *i.* Estonia 55 M7
Saarenkylä Fin. 54 N3
Saargau *reg.* Germany 62 G5
Saarijärvi Fin. 54 N5
Saari-Kämä Fin. 54 O3
Saarikoski Fin. 54 L2
Saaristomeren kansallispuisto *nat. park* Fin. *see* Skärgårdshavets nationalpark
Saarland *land* Germany 62 G5
Saarlouis Germany 62 G5
Saatlı Azer. 113 H3
Saatly Azer. *see* Saatlı
Sab' a Egypt *see* Saba'ah
Saba'ah Egypt 107 A4
Sab' Ābār Syria 107 C3
Šabac Serbia 69 H2
Sabadell Spain 67 H3
Sabae Japan 92 C3
Sabah *state* Malaysia 85 G1
Sabak Malaysia 84 C2
Sabalana *i.* Indon. 83 A4
Sabalana, Kepulauan *is* Indon. 83 A4
Sabalgarh *Madh. Prad.* India 99 B8
Sabana, Archipiélago de *is* Cuba 169 H4
Sabanagrande Hond. 166 [inset] I6
Sabang *Aceh* Indon. 84 A1
Sabang *Sulawesi* Indon. 83 A2
Sabang *Sulawesi* Indon. 83 B3
Şabanözü Turkey 112 D2
Sabará Brazil 179 C2
Sabaru *i.* Indon. 83 A4
Sabastiya West Bank 107 B3
Sab'atayn, Ramlat as *des.* Yemen 108 G6
Sabaudia Italy 68 E4
Sabaya Bol. 176 E7
Sabdê China 96 D2
Sabelo S. Africa 124 F6
Sāberi, Hāmūn-e *marsh* Afgh./Iran 111 F4
Şabḩā Jordan 107 C3
Sabhā Libya 121 E2
Şabḩā' Saudi Arabia 110 B6
Sabhrai India 104 B5
Sabi *r.* India 104 D3
Sabi *r.* Moz./Zimbabwe *see* Save
Sabie Moz. 125 K3
Sabie *r.* Moz./S. Africa 125 K3
Sabie S. Africa 125 J3
Sabina U.S.A. 164 D4
Sabinal Mex. 166 D2
Sabinal, Cayo *i.* Cuba 163 E8
Sabinas Mex. 167 E3
Sabinas *r.* Mex. 161 C7
Sabinas Hidalgo Mex. 167 E3
Sabine *r.* U.S.A. 161 E6
Sabine Lake U.S.A. 161 E6
Sabine Pass U.S.A. 161 E6
Sabini, Monti *mts* Italy 68 E3
Sabirabad Azer. 113 H2
Sabkhat al Bardawīl Reserve *nature res.* Egypt *see* Lake Bardawil Reserve
Sablayan *Mindoro* Phil. 82 C3
Sable, Cape Canada 153 I6
Sable, Cape U.S.A. 163 D7
Sable, Lac du *l.* Canada 153 I3
Sable Island Canada 153 K6
Sabon Kafi Niger 120 D3
Sabrātah Libya 121 E1
Sabrina Coast Antarctica 188 F2
Sabtang *i.* Phil. 82 C1
Sabugal Port. 67 C3
Sabulu *Sulawesi* Indon. 83 B3
Sabunten *i.* Indon. 85 F4
Saburyū-yama *mt.* Japan 93 E2
Sabzawar Afgh. *see* Shīndand
Sabzevār Iran 110 E2
Sabzvārān Iran *see* Jīroft
Sacalinul Mare, Insula *i.* Romania 69 M2
Sacaton U.S.A. 159 H5
Sac City U.S.A. 160 E3
Săcele Romania 69 K2
Sachigo *r.* Canada 151 N4
Sachigo Lake Canada 151 M4
Sachin India 104 C5
Sach'on S. Korea 91 C6
Sach Pass India 104 D2
Sachsen *land* Germany 63 N3
Sachsen-Anhalt *land* Germany 63 L2
Sachsenheim Germany 63 J6
Sachs Harbour Canada 146 F2
Sacirsuyu *r.* Syria/Turkey *see* Sājūr, Nahr
Sackpfeife *hill* Germany 63 I4
Sackville Canada 153 I5
Saco *ME* U.S.A. 165 J2
Saco *MT* U.S.A. 156 G2
Sacol *i.* Phil. 82 C5
Sacramento Brazil 179 B2

▶Sacramento U.S.A. 158 C2
Capital of California.

Sacramento *r.* U.S.A. 158 C2
Sacramento Mountains U.S.A. 157 G6
Sacramento Valley U.S.A. 158 B1
Sacxán Mex. 167 H5
Sada S. Africa 125 H7
Sádaba Spain 67 F2
Sá da Bandeira Angola *see* Lubango
Şadad Syria 107 C2
Şa'dah Yemen 108 F6
Sadang *r.* Indon. 83 A3
Sadao Thai. 87 C6
Saddat al Hindīyah Iraq 113 G4
Saddleback Mesa *mt.* U.S.A. 161 C5
Saddle Hill *hill* Australia 136 D2
Saddle Peak *hill* India 87 A4
Sa Đec Vietnam 87 D5
Sadêng China 96 B2
Sadieville U.S.A. 164 C4
Sadīj *watercourse* Iran 110 E5
Sadiola Mali 120 B3
Sādiqabad Pak. 111 H4
Sad Istragh *mt.* Afgh./Pak. 111 I2
Sa'dīyah, Hawr as *imp. l.* Iraq 113 G4
Sa'diyyat *i.* U.A.E. 110 D5
Sado *r.* Port. 67 B4
Sadoga-shima *i.* Japan 91 E5
Sadong *r.* Malaysia 85 E2
Sadot Egypt *see* Sadūt
Sadovoye Rus. Fed. 53 J7
Sa Dragonera *i.* Spain 67 H4
Sadras India 106 D3
Sadūt Egypt 107 B4
Sadût Egypt *see* Sadūt
Sæby Denmark 55 G8
Saena Julia Italy *see* Siena
Safad Israel *see* Ẓefat
Safāshahr Iran 110 D4
Safayal Maqūf *well* Iraq 113 G5
Safed Khirs *mts* Afgh. 111 H2
Safed Koh *mts* Afgh. 111 G3
Safed Koh *mts* Afgh./Pak. 111 H3
Saffānīyah, Ra's as *pt* Saudi Arabia 110 C4
Säffle Sweden 55 H7
Safford U.S.A. 159 I5
Saffron Walden U.K. 59 H6
Safi Morocco 64 C5
Safīdār, Kūh-e *mt.* Iran 110 D4
Safīd Kūh *mts* Afgh. 111 F3
Safīd Sagak Iran 111 F3
Safiras, Serra das *mts* Brazil 179 C2
Şāfītā Syria 107 C2
Safonovo *Arkhangel'skaya Oblast'* Rus. Fed. 52 K2
Safonovo *Smolenskaya Oblast'* Rus. Fed. 53 G5
Safrā' al Asyāḩ *esc.* Saudi Arabia 110 A5
Safrā' as Sark *esc.* Saudi Arabia 108 F4
Safranbolu Turkey 112 D2
Saga *Xizang* China 99 D7
Saga Japan 91 C6
Saga Kazakh. 102 B1
Sagaing Myanmar 86 A2
Sagamihara Japan 93 F3
Sagamiko Japan 93 F3
Sagami-nada *g.* Japan 93 F4
Sagami-wan *b.* Japan 93 F3
Sagamore U.S.A. 164 F3
Saganthit Kyun *i.* Myanmar 87 B4
Sagar *Karnataka* India 106 B3
Sagar *Karnataka* India 106 C2
Sagar *Madh. Prad.* India 104 D5
Sagara Japan 93 E4
Sagaredzho Georgia *see* Sagarejo
Sagarejo Georgia 113 G2
Sagar Island India 105 G5
Sagarmatha National Park Nepal 105 F4
Sagastyr Rus. Fed. 77 N2
Sagavanirktok *r. AK* U.S.A. 149 J1
Sage U.S.A. 156 F4
Saggi, Har *mt.* Israel 107 B4
Saghand Iran 110 D3
Saggigik Island *AK* U.S.A. 148 D6
Saginaw U.S.A. 164 D2
Saginaw Bay U.S.A. 164 D2
Saglek Bay Canada 153 J2
Saglouc Canada *see* Salluit
Sagly Rus. Fed. 94 B1
Sagone, Golfe de *b. Corsica* France 66 I5
Sagres Port. 67 B5
Sagsay *watercourse* Mongolia 94 D2
Sagthale India 104 C5
Sagu Indon. 83 B5
Saguache U.S.A. 157 G5
Sagua la Grande Cuba 169 H4
Saguaro Lake U.S.A. 159 H5
Saguaro National Park U.S.A. 159 H5
Saguenay *r.* Canada 153 H4
Saguling, Waduk *resr Jawa* Indon. 84 D4
Sagunt Spain *see* Sagunto
Sagunto Spain 67 F4
Saguntum Spain *see* Sagunto
Sagwon *AK* U.S.A. 149 J1
Sahabab *Uttar Prad.* India 99 B7
Sahagún Spain 67 D2
Sahand, Kūh-e *mt.* Iran 110 B2
Sahara *des.* Africa 120 D3
Şaḩara el Gharbîya *des.* Egypt *see* Western Desert
Şaḩara el Sharqîya *des.* Egypt *see* Eastern Desert
Saharan Atlas *mts* Alg. *see* Atlas Saharien
Saharanpur India 104 D3
Sahara Well Australia 134 C5
Saharsa India 105 F4
Sahaswan India 104 D3
Sahat, Kūh-e *hill* Iran 110 D3
Sahatwar India 105 F4
Şahbuz Azer. 113 G3
Sahdol India *see* Shahdol
Sahebganj India *see* Sahibganj
Sahebgunj India *see* Sahibganj
Saheira, Wâdi el *watercourse* Egypt *see* Suhaymī, Wādī as
Sahel *reg.* Africa 120 C3
Sahibganj India 105 F4
Sahiwal Pak. 111 I4
Sahlābād Iran 111 E3
Şaḩm Oman 110 E5
Şaḩneh Iran 110 B3
Şaḩrā al Ḩijārah *reg.* Iraq 113 G5
Sahu *Qinghai* China *see* Zadoi
Sahu *Halmahera* Indon. 83 C2
Sahuaripa Mex. 166 C2
Sahuayo Mex. 168 D4
Sa Huynh Vietnam 87 E4
Sahyadri *mts* India *see* Western Ghats
Sahyadriparvat Range *hills* India 106 B1
Şahyūn, Qal'at *tourist site* Syria 107 C2
Sai *r.* India 105 E4
Sai Buri Thai. 87 C6
Sai Buri, Mae Nam *r.* Thai. 84 C1
Saïda Alg. 67 G6
Saïda Lebanon *see* Sidon
Sai Dao Tai, Khao *mt.* Thai. 87 C4
Saïdia Morocco 67 E6
Sa'īdīyeh Iran *see* Solṭānīyeh
Saidpur Bangl. 105 G4
Sai-gawa *r.* Japan 92 C2
Sai-gawa *r.* Japan 93 E2
Saiha India 105 H5
Saihan Tal *Nei Mongol* China 95 H3
Saihan Toroi *Nei Mongol* China 94 E3
Saijō Japan 91 D6
Saikai Kokuritsu-kōen Japan 91 C6
Saiki Japan 91 C6
Sai Kung *H.K.* China 97 [inset]
Sailana India 104 C5
Sailolof *Papua* Indon. 83 D3
Saimaa *l.* Fin. 55 P6
Saimbeyli Turkey 112 E3
Saindak Pak. 111 F4
Sa'īndezh Iran 110 B2
Sa'īn Qal'eh Iran *see* Sa'īndezh
St Abb's Head *hd* U.K. 60 G5
St Agnes U.K. 59 B8
St Agnes *i.* U.K. 59 A9
St Alban's Canada 153 L5
St Albans U.K. 59 G7
St Albans *VT* U.S.A. 165 I1
St Albans *WV* U.S.A. 164 E4
St Alban's Head *hd England* U.K. *see* St Aldhelm's Head
St Albert Canada 150 H4
St Aldhelm's Head *hd* U.K. 59 E8
St-Amand-les-Eaux France 62 D4
St-Amand-Montrond France 66 F3
St-Amour France 66 G3
St-André, Cap *pt* Madag. *see* Vilanandro, Tanjona
St Andrews U.K. 60 G4
St Andrew Sound *inlet* U.S.A. 163 D6
St Anne U.S.A. 164 B3
St Ann's Bay Jamaica 169 I5
St Anthony Canada 153 L4
St Anthony U.S.A. 156 F4
St-Arnaud Alg. *see* El Eulma
St Arnaud Australia 138 A6
St Arnaud Range *mts* N.Z. 139 D6
St-Arnoult-en-Yvelines France 62 B6
St Asaph Bay *N.T.* Australia 83 D5
St-Augustin Canada 153 K4
St Augustin *r.* Canada 153 K4
St Augustine U.S.A. 163 D6
St Austell U.K. 59 C8
St-Avertin France 66 E3
St-Avold France 62 G5
St Barbe Canada 153 K4

▶St-Barthélemy *i.* West Indies 169 L5
French Overseas Collectivity.

St Bees U.K. 58 D4
St Bees Head *hd* U.K. 58 D4
St Bride's Bay U.K. 59 B7
St-Brieuc France 66 C2
St Catharines Canada 164 F2
St Catherines Island U.S.A. 163 D6
St Catherine's Point U.K. 59 F8
St-Céré France 66 E4
St-Chamond France 66 G4
St Charles *ID* U.S.A. 156 F4
St Charles *MD* U.S.A. 165 G4
St Charles *MI* U.S.A. 164 C2
St Charles *MO* U.S.A. 160 F4
St-Chély-d'Apcher France 66 F4
St Christopher and Nevis *country* West Indies *see* St Kitts and Nevis
St Clair *r.* Canada/U.S.A. 164 D2
St Clair, Lake Canada/U.S.A. 164 D2
St-Claude France 66 G3
St Clears U.K. 59 C7
St Cloud U.S.A. 160 E2
St Croix *r.* U.S.A. 152 B5
St Croix Falls U.S.A. 160 E2
St David U.S.A. 159 H6
St David's Head *hd* U.K. 59 B7
St-Denis France 62 C6

▶St-Denis Réunion 185 L7
Capital of Réunion.

St-Denis-du-Sig Alg. *see* Sig
St-Dié France 66 H2
St-Dizier France 62 E6
St-Domingue *country* West Indies *see* Haiti
Sainte Anne Canada 151 L5
Ste-Anne, Lac *l.* Canada 153 I4
St Elias, Cape *AK* U.S.A. 149 K4

▶St Elias, Mount *AK* U.S.A. 149 L3
4th highest mountain in North America.

St Elias Mountains *Y.T.* Canada 149 L3
Ste-Marguerite *r.* Canada 153 I4
Ste-Marie, Cap *c.* Madag. *see* Vohimena, Tanjona
Sainte-Marie, Île *i.* Madag. *see* Boraha, Nosy
Ste-Maxime France 66 H5
Sainte Rose du Lac Canada 151 L5
Saintes France 66 D4
Sainte Thérèse, Lac *l.* Canada 150 F1
St-Étienne France 66 G4
St-Étienne-du-Rouvray France 62 B5
St-Fabien Canada 153 H4
St-Félicien Canada 153 G4
Saintfield U.K. 61 G3
St-Florent *Corsica* France 66 I5
St-Florent-sur-Cher France 66 F3
St-Floris, Parc National *nat. park* Cent. Afr. Rep. 122 C3
St-Flour France 66 F4
St Francesville U.S.A. 161 F6
St Francis U.S.A. 160 C4
St Francis *r.* U.S.A. 161 F5
St Francis Isles Australia 135 F8
St-François *r.* Canada 153 G5
St-François, Lac *l.* Canada 153 H5
St-Gaudens France 66 E5
St George Australia 138 D2
St George *r.* Australia 136 D3
St George *AK* U.S.A. 148 E4
St George *SC* U.S.A. 163 D5
St George *UT* U.S.A. 159 G3
St George, Point U.S.A. 156 B4
St George Island *AK* U.S.A. 148 E4
St George Range *hills* Australia 134 D4
St-Georges Canada 153 H5

▶St George's Grenada 169 L6
Capital of Grenada.

St George's Bay *Nfld. and Lab.* Canada 153 K4
St George's Bay *N.S.* Canada 153 J5
St George's Cay *i.* Belize 167 I5
St George's Channel Ireland/U.K. 61 F6
St George's Channel P.N.G. 132 F2
St George's Head *hd* Australia 138 E5
St Gotthard Hungary *see* Szentgotthárd
St Gotthard Pass Switz. 66 I3
St Govan's Head *hd* U.K. 59 C7
St Helen U.S.A. 164 C1
St Helena *i.* S. Atlantic Ocean 184 H7
St Helena U.S.A. 158 B2
St Helena and Dependencies *terr.* S. Atlantic Ocean 184 H7
St Helena Bay S. Africa 124 D7
St Helens Australia 137 [inset]
St Helens U.K. 58 E5
St Helens U.S.A. 156 C3
St Helens, Mount *vol.* U.S.A. 156 C3
St Helens Point Australia 137 [inset]

▶St Helier Channel Is 59 E9
Capital of Jersey.

Sainthiya India 105 F5
St-Hubert Belgium 62 F4
St-Hyacinthe Canada 153 G5
St Ignace U.S.A. 162 C2
St Ignace Island Canada 152 D4
St Ishmael U.K. 59 C7
St Ives *England* U.K. 59 B8
St Ives *England* U.K. 59 G6
St-Jacques, Cap Vietnam *see* Vung Tau
St-Jacques-de-Dupuy Canada 152 F4
St James *MN* U.S.A. 160 E3
St James *MO* U.S.A. 160 F4
St James, Cape *B.C.* Canada 149 O6
St-Jean *r.* Canada 153 I4
St-Jean, Lac *l.* Canada 153 G4
St-Jean-d'Acre Israel *see* 'Akko
St-Jean-d'Angély France 66 D4
St-Jean-de-Monts France 66 C3
St-Jean-sur-Richelieu Canada 165 I1
St-Jérôme Canada 152 G5
St Joe *r.* U.S.A. 156 D3
Saint John Canada 153 I5
St John U.S.A. 160 D4
St John *r.* U.S.A. 162 H2
St John, Cape Canada 153 L4
St John Bay Canada 153 K4
St John Island Canada 153 K4

▶St John's Antigua and Barbuda 169 L5
Capital of Antigua and Barbuda.

▶St John's Canada 153 L5
Capital of Newfoundland and Labrador.

St Johns *AZ* U.S.A. 159 I4
St Johns *MI* U.S.A. 164 C2
St Johns *OH* U.S.A. 164 C3
St Johns *r.* U.S.A. 163 D6
St Johnsbury U.S.A. 165 I1
St John's Chapel U.K. 58 E4
St Joseph *IL* U.S.A. 164 A3
St Joseph *LA* U.S.A. 161 F6
St Joseph *MI* U.S.A. 164 B2
St Joseph *MO* U.S.A. 160 E4
St Joseph *r.* U.S.A. 164 C3
St Joseph, Lake Canada 151 N5
St-Joseph-d'Alma Canada *see* Alma
St Joseph Island Canada 152 E5
St Joseph Island *TX* U.S.A. 167 F3
St-Junien France 66 E4
St Just U.K. 59 B8
St-Just-en-Chaussée France 62 C5
St Keverne U.K. 59 B8
St Kilda *i.* U.K. 50 E4
St Kilda *is* U.K. 56 C2
St Kitts and Nevis *country* West Indies 169 L5
St-Laurent *inlet* Canada *see* St Lawrence
St-Laurent, Golfe du *g.* Canada *see* St Lawrence, Gulf of
St-Laurent-du-Maroni Fr. Guiana 177 H2
St Lawrence Canada 153 L5
St Lawrence *inlet* Canada 153 H4
St Lawrence, Cape Canada 153 J5
St Lawrence, Gulf of Canada 153 J4
St Lawrence Island *AK* U.S.A. 148 E3
St Lawrence Islands National Park Canada 165 H1
St Lawrence Seaway *sea chan.* Canada/U.S.A. 165 H1
St-Léonard Canada 153 G5
St Leonard U.S.A. 165 G4
St Lewis *r.* Canada 153 K3
St-Lô France 66 D2
St-Louis Senegal 120 B3
St Louis *MI* U.S.A. 164 C2
St Louis *MO* U.S.A. 160 F4
St Louis *r.* U.S.A. 152 B5
St Lucia *country* West Indies 169 L6
St Lucia, Lake S. Africa 125 K5
St Lucia Estuary S. Africa 125 K5
St Luke's Island Myanmar *see* Zadetkale Kyun
St Magnus Bay U.K. 60 [inset]
St-Maixent-l'École France 66 D3
St-Malo France 66 C2
St-Malo, Golfe de *g.* France 66 C2
St-Marc Haiti 169 J5
St Maries U.S.A. 156 D3
St Marks S. Africa 125 H7
St Mark's S. Africa *see* Cofimvaba
St-Martin *i.* Neth. Antilles *see* Sint Maarten

▶St-Martin *i.* West Indies 169 L5
French Overseas Collectivity. The southern part of the island is the Dutch territory of Sint Maarten.

St Martin, Cape S. Africa 124 C7
St Martin, Lake Canada 151 L5
St Martin's *i.* U.K. 59 A9
St Martin's Island Bangl. 86 A2
St Mary Peak Australia 137 B6
St Mary Reservoir Canada 150 H5
St Mary's Canada 164 E2
St Mary's U.K. 60 G2
St Mary's *i.* U.K. 59 A9
St Mary's *AK* U.S.A. 148 G3
St Marys *PA* U.S.A. 165 F3
St Marys *WV* U.S.A. 164 E4
St Marys *r.* U.S.A. 164 C3
St Mary's, Cape Canada 153 L5
St Mary's Bay Canada 153 L5
St Marys City U.S.A. 165 G4
St Matthew Island *AK* U.S.A. 148 D3
St Matthews U.S.A. 164 C4
St Matthew's Island Myanmar *see* Zadetkyi Kyun
St Matthias Group *is* P.N.G. 81 L7
St-Maurice *r.* Canada 153 G5
St Mawes U.K. 59 B8
St-Médard-en-Jalles France 66 D4
St Meinrad U.S.A. 164 B4
St Michael *AK* U.S.A. 148 G3
St Michaels U.S.A. 165 G4
St Michael's Bay Canada 153 L3
St-Mihiel France 62 F6
St-Nazaire France 66 C3
St Neots U.K. 59 G6
St-Nicolas Belgium *see* Sint-Niklaas
St-Nicolas, Mont *hill* Lux. 62 G5
St-Nicolas-de-Port France 66 H2
St-Omer France 62 C4
Saintonge *reg.* France 66 D4
St-Pacôme Canada 153 H5
St-Palais France 66 D5
St Paris U.S.A. 164 D3
St-Pascal Canada 153 H5
St Paul *r.* Canada 153 K4
St-Paul *atoll* Fr. Polynesia *see* Héréhérétué
St Paul *AK* U.S.A. 148 E4

▶St Paul *MN* U.S.A. 160 E2
Capital of Minnesota.

St Paul *NE* U.S.A. 160 D3
St-Paul, Île *i.* Indian Ocean 185 N8
St Paul Island *AK* U.S.A. 148 E4
St Paul Subterranean River National Park Phil. 82 B4
St Peter and St Paul Rocks *is* N. Atlantic Ocean *see* São Pedro e São Paulo

▶St Peter Port Channel Is 59 E9
Capital of Guernsey.

St Peter's *N.S.* Canada 153 J5
St Peters *P.E.I.* Canada 153 J5
St Petersburg Rus. Fed. 55 Q7
St Petersburg U.S.A. 163 D7
St-Pierre *mt.* France 66 G5

▶St-Pierre St Pierre and Miquelon 153 L5
Capital of St Pierre and Miquelon.

▶St Pierre and Miquelon *terr.* N. America 153 K5
French Territorial Collectivity.

St-Pierre-d'Oléron France 66 D4
St-Pierre-le-Moûtier France 66 F3
St-Pol-sur-Ternoise France 62 C4
St-Pourçain-sur-Sioule France 66 F3
St-Quentin France 62 D5
St Regis U.S.A. 156 E3
St Regis Falls U.S.A. 165 H1
St-Rémi Canada 165 I1
St-Saëns France 62 B5
St Sebastian Bay S. Africa 124 E8
St-Siméon Canada 153 H5
St Simons Island U.S.A. 163 D6
St Theresa Point Canada 151 M4
St Thomas Canada 164 E2
St-Trond Belgium *see* Sint-Truiden
St-Tropez France 66 H5
St-Tropez, Cap de *c.* France 66 H5
St-Vaast-la-Hougue France 59 F9
St-Valery-en-Caux France 59 H9
St-Véran France 66 H4
St Vincent U.S.A. 160 D1
St Vincent *country* West Indies *see* St Vincent and the Grenadines
St Vincent, Cape Australia 137 [inset]
St Vincent, Cape Port. *see* São Vicente, Cabo de
St Vincent, Gulf Australia 137 B7
St Vincent and the Grenadines *country* West Indies 169 L6

St Vincent Passage St Lucia/St Vincent 169 L6
St-Vith Belgium 62 G4
St Walburg Canada 151 I4
St Williams Canada 164 E2
St-Yrieix-la-Perche France 66 E4
Sain Us Nei Mongol China 95 F3
Saioa mt. Spain 67 F2
Saipal mt. Nepal 104 E3
Saipan i. N. Mariana Is 81 L3
Saipan Palau 82 [inset]
Sai Pok Liu Hoi Hap H.K. China see West Lamma Channel
Saitama Japan 89 P5
Saitama pref. Japan 93 E3
Saiteli Turkey see Kadınhanı
Saitlai Myanmar 86 A2
Saittanulkki hill Fin. 54 N3
Sai Yok National Park Thai. 87 B4
Sajam Indon. 81 I7
Sajama, Nevado mt. Bol. 176 E7
Sājir Saudi Arabia 110 B5
Sājūr, Nahr r. Syria/Turkey 107 D1
Sajzī Iran 110 D3
Sak watercourse S. Africa 124 E5
Sakado Japan 93 F3
Sakae Chiba Japan 93 G3
Sakae Nagano Japan 93 E2
Sakai Fukui Japan 92 C2
Sakai Gunma Japan 93 F2
Sakai Ibaraki Japan 93 F2
Sakai Nagano Japan 93 E2
Sakai Ōsaka Japan 92 B4
Sakaide Japan 91 D6
Sakaigawa Japan 93 E3
Sakākah Saudi Arabia 113 F5
Sakakawea, Lake U.S.A. 160 C2
Sakaki Japan 93 E2
Sakakita Japan 93 E2
Sakala i. Indon. 85 G4
Sakami Canada 152 G3
Sakami r. Canada 152 F3
Sakami-gawa r. Japan 93 F3
Sakami Lake Canada 152 F3
Sakar mts Bulg. 69 L4
Sakaraha Madag. 123 E6
Sak'art'velo country Asia see Georgia
Sakarya Sakarya Turkey see Adapazarı
Sakarya r. Turkey 69 N4
Sakashita Japan 92 D3
Sakassou Côte d'Ivoire 120 C4
Sakata Japan 91 E5
Sakauchi Japan 92 C3
Sakchu N. Korea 91 B4
Saken Seyfullin Kazakh. 98 A2
Sakesar Pak. 111 I3
Sakhalin i. Rus. Fed. 90 F2
Sakhalin Oblast admin. div. Rus. Fed. see Sakhalinskaya Oblast'
Sakhalinskaya Oblast' admin. div. Rus. Fed. 90 F2
Sakhalinskiy Zaliv b. Rus. Fed. 90 F1
Sakhi India 104 C3
Sakhile S. Africa 125 I4
Şäki Azer. 113 G2
Saki Nigeria see Shaki
Saki Ukr. see Saky
Šakiai Lith. 55 M9
Sakir mt. Pak. 111 G4
Sakishima-shotō is Japan 89 M8
Sakoli India 104 D5
Sakon Nakhon Thai. 86 D3
Sakrivier S. Africa 124 E6
Saku Nagano Japan 93 E2
Saku Nagano Japan 93 E2
Sakuma Japan 93 D3
Sakura Japan 93 G3
Sakuragawa Japan 93 G3
Sakura-gawa r. Japan 93 G2
Sakurai Japan 92 B4
Saku-shima i. Japan 92 D4
Saky Ukr. 112 D1
Säkylä Fin. 55 M6
Sal i. Cape Verde 120 [inset]
Sal r. Rus. Fed. 53 I7
Sal, Punta pt Hond. 166 [inset] I6
Sala Sweden 55 J7
Salabangka, Kepulauan is Indon. 83 B3
Salaberry-de-Valleyfield Canada 165 H1
Salacgrīva Latvia 55 N8
Sala Consilina Italy 68 F4
Salada, Laguna salt l. Mex. 166 B1
Saladas Arg. 178 E3
Salado r. Buenos Aires Arg. 178 E5
Salado r. Santa Fé Arg. 178 D4
Salado r. Arg. 178 C5
Salado r. Mex. 167 F3
Salaga Ghana 120 C4
Salairskiy Kryazh ridge Rus. Fed. 88 E2
Salajwe Botswana 124 G2
Şalālah Oman 109 H6
Salamá Guat. 167 H6
Salamá Hond. 166 [inset] I6
Salamanca Mex. 168 D4
Salamanca Spain 67 D3
Salamanca U.S.A. 165 F2
Salamanga Moz. 125 K4
Salamantica Spain see Salamanca
Salamat, Bahr r. Chad 121 E4
Salamban Kalimantan Indon. 85 F3
Salāmī Iran 111 E3
Salamina i. Greece 69 J6
Salamis tourist site Cyprus 107 A2
Salamís i. Greece see Salamina
Salamīyah Syria 107 C2
Salamonie r. U.S.A. 164 C3
Salamonie Lake U.S.A. 164 C3
Salang, Tūnel-e Afgh. 111 H3
Salantai Lith. 55 L8
Salaqi Nei Mongol China 95 G3
Salar de Pocitos Arg. 178 C2
Salari Pak. 111 G5
Salas Spain 67 C2
Salaspils Latvia 55 N8
Salatiga Jawa Indon. 85 E4
Salavan Laos 86 D4
Salawati i. Papua Indon. 83 D3
Salawin, Mae Nam r. China/Myanmar see Salween
Salay Mindanao Phil. 82 D4
Salaya India 104 B5
Salayar i. Indon. 83 B4
Salayar, Selat sea chan. Indon. 83 B4
Sala y Gómez, Isla i. S. Pacific Ocean 187 M7
Salazar Angola see N'dalatando
Salbris France 66 F3
Salcha r. AK U.S.A. 149 K2
Šalčininkai Lith. 55 N9
Salcombe U.K. 59 D8
Saldae Alg. see Bejaïa
Saldaña Spain 67 D2
Saldanha S. Africa 124 C7
Saldanha Bay S. Africa 124 C7
Saldus Latvia 55 M8
Sale Australia 138 C7
Salea Sulawesi Indon. 83 B3
Saleh, Teluk b. Sumbawa Indon. 85 G5
Şāleḩābād Iran 110 C3
Salekhard Rus. Fed. 76 H3
Salem India 106 C4
Salem AR U.S.A. 161 F4
Salem IL U.S.A. 160 F4
Salem IN U.S.A. 164 B4
Salem MA U.S.A. 165 J2
Salem MO U.S.A. 160 F4
Salem NJ U.S.A. 165 H4
Salem NY U.S.A. 165 I2
Salem OH U.S.A. 164 E3
▶Salem OR U.S.A. 156 C3
Capital of Oregon.
Salem SD U.S.A. 160 D3
Salem VA U.S.A. 164 E5
Salen Scotland U.K. 60 D4
Salen Scotland U.K. 60 D4
Salerno Italy 68 F4
Salerno, Golfo di g. Italy 68 F4
Salernum Italy see Salerno
Salford U.K. 58 E5
Salgótarján Hungary 57 Q6
Salgueiro Brazil 177 K5
Salian Afgh. 111 F4
Salibabu i. Indon. 83 C2
Salida U.S.A. 157 G5
Salies-de-Béarn France 66 D5
Salihli Turkey 69 M5
Salihorsk Belarus 55 O10
Salima Malawi 123 D5
Salimbatu Kalimantan Indon. 85 G2
Salina KS U.S.A. 160 D4
Salina UT U.S.A. 159 H2
Salina, Isola i. Italy 68 F5
Salina Cruz Mex. 168 E5
Salinas Brazil 179 C2
Salinas Ecuador 176 B4
Salinas Mex. 168 D4
Salinas r. Mex. 161 D7
Salinas U.S.A. 158 C3
Salinas r. U.S.A. 158 C3
Salinas, Cabo de c. Spain see Ses Salines, Cap de
Salinas, Ponta das pt Angola 123 B5
Salinas Peak U.S.A. 157 G6
Saline U.S.A. 164 D2
Saline r. U.S.A. 160 D4
Saline Valley depr. U.S.A. 158 E3
Salinópolis Brazil 177 I4
Salinosó Lachay, Punta pt Peru 176 C6
Salisbury U.K. 59 F7
Salisbury MD U.S.A. 165 H4
Salisbury NC U.S.A. 162 D5
Salisbury Zimbabwe see Harare
Salisbury, Mount AK U.S.A. 149 K1
Salisbury Plain U.K. 59 E7
Şalkhad Syria 107 C3
Salla Fin. 54 P3
Sallisaw U.S.A. 161 E5
Salluit Canada 189 K2
Sallum, Khalīj as b. Egypt 112 B5
Sallyana Nepal 105 E3
Salmās Iran 110 B2
Salmi Rus. Fed. 52 F3
Salmo Canada 150 G5
Salmon U.S.A. 156 E3
Salmon r. U.S.A. 156 D3
Salmon Arm Canada 150 G5
Salmon Falls Creek r. U.S.A. 156 E4
Salmon Fork r. Canada/U.S.A. 149 L2
Salmon Gums Australia 135 C8
Salmon Reservoir U.S.A. 165 H2
Salmon River Mountains U.S.A. 156 E3
Salmon Village AK U.S.A. 149 L2
Salmtal Germany 62 G5
Salo Fin. 55 M6
Salome U.S.A. 159 G5
Salon India 104 E4
Salon-de-Provence France 66 G5
Salonica Greece see Thessaloniki
Salpausselkä reg. Fin. 55 N6
Salqīn Syria 107 C1
Salses, Étang de l. France see Leucate, Étang de
Sal'sk Rus. Fed. 53 I7
Salsomaggiore Terme Italy 68 C2
Salt Jordan see As Salț
Salt watercourse S. Africa 124 F7
Salt r. U.S.A. 159 G5
Salta Arg. 178 C2
Saltaire U.K. 58 F5
Saltash U.K. 59 C8
Saltcoats U.K. 60 E5
Saltee Islands Ireland 61 F5
Saltfjellet Svartisen Nasjonalpark nat. park Norway 54 I3
Saltfjorden sea chan. Norway 54 H3
Salt Flat TX U.S.A. 166 D2
Salt Fork Arkansas r. U.S.A. 161 D4
Salt Fork Lake U.S.A. 164 E3
Saltillo Mex. 167 E3
Salt Lake India 111 I5
▶Salt Lake City U.S.A. 159 H1
Capital of Utah.
Salt Lick U.S.A. 164 D4
Salto Brazil 179 B3
Salto Uruguay 178 E4
Salto da Divisa Brazil 179 D2
Salto de Agua Chiapas Mex. 167 G5
Salto Grande Brazil 179 A3
Salton Sea salt l. U.S.A. 159 F5
Salto Santiago, Represa de resr Brazil 178 F3
Salt Range hills Pak. 111 I3
Salt River Canada 151 H2
Saluda U.S.A. 165 G5
Saluebesar i. Indon. 83 B3
Saluekecil i. Indon. 83 B3
Salue Timpaus, Selat sea chan. Indon. 83 B3
Salûm Egypt see As Sallūm
Salûm, Khalîg el b. Egypt see Sallum, Khalīj as
Saluq, Kūh-e mt. Iran 110 E2
Salur India 106 D2
Saluzzo Italy 68 B2
Salvador Brazil 179 D1
Salvador, Lake U.S.A. 161 F6
Salvaleón de Higüey Dom. Rep. see Higüey
Salvatierra Mex. 167 E4
Salvation Creek r. U.S.A. 159 H2
Salwah Saudi Arabia 122 F1
Salwah, Dawḩat b. Qatar/Saudi Arabia 110 C5
Salween r. China/Myanmar 96 C5
also known as Mae Nam Salawin or Thanlwin (Myanmar), Nu Jiang (China)
Salyan Azer. 113 H3
Salyan Nepal see Sallyana
Sal'yany Azer. see Salyan
Salyersville U.S.A. 164 D5
Salzbrunn Namibia 124 C3
Salzburg Austria 57 N7
Salzgitter Germany 63 K2
Salzhausen Germany 63 K1
Salzkotten Germany 63 I3
Salzmünde Germany 63 L3
Salzwedel Germany 63 L2
Sam India 104 B4
Samae San, Ko i. Thai. 87 C4
Samagaltay Rus. Fed. 94 C1
Samāh well Saudi Arabia 110 B4
Samaida Iran see Someydeh
Samaixung Xizang China 99 C6
Samak, Tanjung pt Indon. 84 D3
Samakhixai Laos see Attapu
Samal i. Phil. 82 D5
Samalanga Sumatera Indon. 84 B1
Samalantan Kalimantan Indon. 85 E2
Samalayuca Mex. 166 D2
Samales Group is Phil. 82 C5
Samalga Pass sea channel AK U.S.A. 148 E5
Samalkot India 106 D2
Samālūṭ Egypt 112 C5
Samâlûṭ Egypt see Samālūṭ
Samana Cay i. Bahamas 163 F8
Samanala mt. Sri Lanka see Adam's Peak
Samandağı Turkey 107 B1
Samangān Afgh. see Āybak
Samangān Iran 111 F3
Samani Japan 90 F4
Samanlı Dağları mts Turkey 69 M4
Samar Kazakh. see Samarskoye
Samar i. Phil. 82 D4
Samara Rus. Fed. 53 K5
Samara r. Rus. Fed. 51 Q5
Samarahan Sarawak Malaysia see Sri Aman
Samarga Rus. Fed. 90 E3
Samarinda Kalimantan Indon. 85 G3
Samarka Rus. Fed. 90 D3
Samarkand Uzbek. see Samarqand
Samarkand, Pik mt. Tajik. see Samarqand, Qullai
Samarobriva France see Amiens
Samarqand Uzbek. 111 G2
Samarqand, Qullai mt. Tajik. 111 H2
Sāmarrā' Iraq 113 F4
Samar Sea g. Phil. 82 D4
Samarskoye Kazakh. 102 F2
Samarz Nei Mongol China 95 H2
Samasata Pak. 111 H4
Samastipur India 105 F4
Samate Papua Indon. 83 D3
Şamaxı Azer. 113 H2
Samba r. Indon. 85 F3
Samba India 104 C2
Sambaliung mts Indon. 85 G2
Sambalpur India 105 E5
Sambar, Tanjung pt Indon. 85 E3
Sambas Kalimantan Indon. 85 E2
Sambat Ukr. see Kiev
Sambava Madag. 123 F5
Sambha India 105 G4
Sambhajinagar India see Aurangabad
Sambhal India 104 D3
Sambhar Lake India 104 C4
Sambiat Sulawesi Indon. 83 B3
Sambir Ukr. 53 D6
Sambit i. Indon. 85 G2
Sambito r. Brazil 177 J5
Sambo Sulawesi Barat Indon. 83 A3
Samboja Kalimantan Indon. 85 G3
Sâmbor Cambodia 87 D4
Sambor Ukr. see Sambir
Samborombón, Bahía b. Arg. 178 E5
Sambre r. Belgium/France 62 E4
Sambu Japan see Sanbu
Samch'ŏk S. Korea 91 C5
Samch'ŏnp'o S. Korea see Sach'on
Same Tanz. 122 D4
Samegawa Japan 93 G1
Samer France 62 B4
Sami India 104 B5
Samia, Tanjung pt Indon. 83 B2
Samīrah Saudi Arabia 108 F4
Samirum Iran see Yazd-e Khvāst
Samizu Japan 93 E2
Samjiyŏn N. Korea 90 C4
Şämkir Azer. 113 G2
Sam Neua Laos see Xam Nua
Samoa country S. Pacific Ocean 133 I3
Samoa Basin sea feature S. Pacific Ocean 186 I7
Samoa i Sisifo country S. Pacific Ocean see Samoa
Samobor Croatia 68 F2
Samoded Rus. Fed. 52 I3
Samokov Bulg. 69 J3
Šamorín Slovakia 57 P6
Samos i. Greece 69 L6
Samosir i. Indon. 84 B2
Samothrace i. Greece see Samothraki
Samothraki i. Greece 69 K4
Samoylovka Rus. Fed. 53 I6
Sampaga Sulawesi Barat Indon. 83 A3
Sampang Jawa Indon. 85 F4
Sampê China see Xiangcheng
Sampit Kalimantan Indon. 85 F3
Sampit r. Indon. 85 F3
Sampit, Teluk b. Indon. 85 F3
Sampolawa Sulawesi Indon. 83 B4
Sam Rayburn Reservoir U.S.A. 161 E6
Samrong Cambodia see Phumĭ Sâmraông
Samsang Xizang China 99 C7
Sam Sao, Phou mts Laos/Vietnam 86 C2
Samson U.S.A. 163 C6
Sâm Sơn Vietnam 86 D3
Samsun Turkey 112 E2
Samsy Kazakh. 98 B4
Samti Afgh. 111 H2
Samui, Ko i. Thai. 87 C5
Samukawa Japan 93 F3
Samut Prakan Thai. 87 C4
Samut Sakhon Thai. 87 C4
Samut Songkhram Thai. 87 C4
Samyai Xizang China 99 E7
San Mali 120 C3
San, Phou mt. Laos 86 C3
San, Tônlé r. Cambodia 87 D4
▶Şan'ā' Yemen 108 F6
Capital of Yemen.
Sanaa Yemen see Şan'ā'
Sanada Japan 93 E2
SANAE IV research station Antarctica 188 B2
Sanage Japan 92 D3
San Agostín U.S.A. see St Augustine
San Agustin, Cape Mindanao Phil. 82 D5
San Agustin, Plains of U.S.A. 159 I5
Sanak AK U.S.A. 148 G5
Sanak Island AK U.S.A. 148 G5
Sanana Maluku Indon. 83 C3
Sanandaj Iran 110 B3
San Andreas U.S.A. 158 C2
San Andrés Guat. 167 H5
San Andres Phil. 82 D3
San Andrés, Isla de i. Caribbean Sea 169 H6
San Andres Mountains U.S.A. 157 G6
San Andrés Tuxtla Mex. 167 G5
San Angelo U.S.A. 161 C6
San Antonio Belize 167 H5
San Antonio Chile 178 B4
San Antonio Hond. 166 [inset] I6
San Antonio Luzon Phil. 82 C3
San Antonio NM U.S.A. 157 G6
San Antonio TX U.S.A. 161 D6
San Antonio r. U.S.A. 161 D6
San Antonio, Cabo c. Cuba 169 H4
San Antonio Bay Palawan Phil. 82 B4
San Antonio del Mar Mex. 166 A2
San Antonio de Oriente Hond. 166 [inset] I6
San Antonio Oeste Arg. 178 D6
San Antonio Reservoir U.S.A. 158 C4
San Augustín de Valle Fértil Arg. 178 C4
San Augustine U.S.A. 161 E6
San Bartolo Mex. 167 E4
San Benedetto del Tronto Italy 68 E3
San Benedicto, Isla i. Mex. 168 B5
San Benito Guat. 167 H5
San Benito U.S.A. 161 D7
San Benito r. U.S.A. 158 C3
San Benito Mountain U.S.A. 158 C3
San Bernardino U.S.A. 158 E4
San Bernardino Mountains U.S.A. 158 E4
San Bernardino Strait Phil. 82 D3
San Bernardo Chile 178 B4
San Bernardo Mex. 166 D3
San Blas Nayarit Mex. 166 D4
San Blas Sinaloa Mex. 166 C3
San Blas, Archipiélago de is Panama 166 [inset] K7
San Blas, Cape U.S.A. 163 C6
San Blas, Cordillera de mts Panama 166 [inset] K7
San Borja Bol. 176 E6
Sanbornville U.S.A. 165 J2
Sanbu China see Kaiping
Sanbu Japan 93 G3
San Buenaventura Mex. 167 E3
San Carlos Chile 178 B5
San Carlos Equat. Guinea see Luba
San Carlos Coahuila Mex. 167 E2
San Carlos Tamaulipas Mex. 161 D7
San Carlos Nicaragua 166 [inset] I7
San Carlos Luzon Phil. 82 C3
San Carlos Negros Phil. 82 C4
San Carlos U.S.A. 159 H5
San Carlos Venez. 176 E2
San Carlos de Bariloche Arg. 178 B6
San Carlos de Bolívar Arg. 178 D5
San Carlos Indian Reservation res. AZ U.S.A. 166 C1
San Carlos Lake U.S.A. 159 H5
Sancha Gansu China 94 F5
Sancha Shanxi China 95 G4
Sanchahe China see Fuyu
Sancha He r. China 96 E3
Sanchakou Xinjiang China 98 B5
Sanchi India 104 D5
San Chien Pau mt. Laos 86 C2
Sanchor India 104 B4
San Ciro de Acosta Mex. 167 F4
San Clemente U.S.A. 158 E5
San Clemente Island U.S.A. 158 D5
Sanclêr U.K. see St Clears
Sanco Point Mindanao Phil. 82 D4
San Cristóbal Arg. 178 D4
San Cristobal i. Solomon Is 133 G3
San Cristóbal Venez. 176 D2
San Cristóbal, Isla i. Galápagos Ecuador 176 [inset]
San Cristóbal, Volcán vol. Nicaragua 166 [inset] I6
San Cristóbal de las Casas Mex. 167 G5
San Crisóbal Verapez Guat. 167 H6
Sancti Spíritus Cuba 169 I4
Sand r. S. Africa 125 J2
Sanda Japan 92 B4
Sandagou Rus. Fed. 90 D4
Sandai Kalimantan Indon. 85 E3
Sanda Island U.K. 60 D5
Sandakan Sabah Malaysia 85 G1
Sandakan, Pelabuhan inlet Malaysia 85 G1
Sandakphu Peak Sikkim India 99 E8
Sândăn Cambodia 87 D4
Sandane Norway 54 E6
Sandanski Bulg. 69 J4
Sandaohezi Xinjiang China see Shawan
Sandaré Mali 120 B3
Sandau Germany 63 M2
Sanday i. U.K. 60 G1
Sandbach U.K. 59 E5
Sandborn U.S.A. 164 B4
Sand Cay reef India 106 B4
Sandefjord Norway 55 G7
Sandercock Nunataks Antarctica 188 D2
Sanders U.S.A. 159 I4
Sandersleben Germany 63 L3
Sanderson U.S.A. 161 C6
Sandfire Roadhouse Australia 134 C4
Sand Fork U.S.A. 164 E4
Sandgate Australia 138 F1
Sandhead U.K. 60 E6
Sand Hill r. U.S.A. 160 D2
Sand Hills U.S.A. 160 C3
Sandia Peru 176 E6
San Diego Chihuahua Mex. 166 D2
San Diego CA U.S.A. 158 E5
San Diego TX U.S.A. 161 D7
San Diego, Sierra mts Mex. 166 C2
Sandıklı Turkey 69 N5
Sandila India 104 E4
Sanding i. Indon. 84 C3
Sand Islands AK U.S.A. 148 F3
Sand Lake Canada 152 D5
Sand Lake l. Canada 151 M5
Sandnes Norway 55 D7
Sandnessjøen Norway 54 H3
Sandoa Dem. Rep. Congo 123 C4
Sandomierz Poland 53 D6
San Donà di Piave Italy 68 E2
Sandover watercourse Australia 136 B4
Sandovo Rus. Fed. 52 H4
Sandoway Myanmar see Thandwè
Sandown U.K. 59 F8
Sandoy i. Faroe Is 54 [inset]
Sand Point AK U.S.A. 148 G5
Sandpoint U.S.A. 156 D2
Sandray i. U.K. 60 B4
Sandringham Australia 136 B5
Şandrul Mare, Vârful mt. Romania 69 L1
Sandsjö Sweden 55 I6
Sandspit B.C. Canada 149 O5
Sand Springs U.S.A. 161 D4
Sand Springs Salt Flat U.S.A. 158 D2
Sandstone Australia 135 B6
Sandstone U.S.A. 160 E2
Sandu Guizhou China 96 E3
Sandu Hunan China 97 G3
Sandur Faroe Is 54 [inset]
Sandusky MI U.S.A. 164 D2
Sandusky OH U.S.A. 164 D3
Sandveld mts S. Africa 124 D6
Sandverhaar Namibia 124 C4
Sandvika Akershus Norway 55 G7
Sandvika Nord-Trøndelag Norway 54 H5
Sandviken Sweden 55 J6
Sandwich Bay Canada 153 K3
Sandwich Island Vanuatu see Éfaté
Sandwich Islands is N. Pacific Ocean see Hawai'ian Islands
Sandwick U.K. 60 [inset]
Sandwip Bangl. 105 G5
Sandy U.S.A. 159 H1
Sandy r. U.S.A. 165 K1
Sandy Bay Canada 151 K4
Sandy Cape Qld Australia 136 F5
Sandy Cape Tas. Australia 137 [inset]
Sandy Hook U.S.A. 164 D4
Sandy Hook pt U.S.A. 165 H3
Sandy Island Australia 134 C3
Sandykgachy Turkm. see Sandykgaçy
Sandykgaçy Turkm. 111 F2
Sandykly Gumy des. Turkm. 111 F2
Sandy Lake Alta Canada 150 H4
Sandy Lake Ont. Canada 151 M4
Sandy Lake l. Canada 151 M4
Sandy Springs U.S.A. 163 C5
San Estanislao Para. 178 E2
San Esteban, Isla i. Mex. 166 B2
San Felipe Chile 178 B4
San Felipe Baja California Mex. 166 B2
San Felipe Chihuahua Mex. 166 D3
San Felipe Guanajuato Mex. 167 E4
San Felipe Venez. 176 E1
San Felipe, Cayos de is Cuba 163 D8
San Felipe de Puerto Plata Dom. Rep. see Puerto Plata
San Fernando Chile 178 B4
San Fernando Baja California Mex. 166 B2
San Fernando Tamaulipas Mex. 167 F3
San Fernando watercourse Mex. 157 E7
San Fernando Luzon Phil. 82 C2
San Fernando Luzon Phil. 82 C3
San Fernando Spain 67 C5
San Fernando Trin. and Tob. 169 L6
San Fernando U.S.A. 158 D4
San Fernando de Apure Venez. 176 E2
San Fernando de Atabapo Venez. 176 E3
San Fernando de Monte Cristi Dom. Rep. see Monte Cristi
Sanford FL U.S.A. 163 D6
Sanford ME U.S.A. 165 J2
Sanford MI U.S.A. 164 C2
Sanford NC U.S.A. 162 E5
Sanford, Mount AK U.S.A. 149 K3
Sanford Lake U.S.A. 164 C2
San Francisco Arg. 178 D4
San Francisco Sonora Mex. 166 B2
San Francisco U.S.A. 158 B3
San Francisco, Cabo de c. Ecuador 176 B3
San Francisco, Passo de pass Arg./Chile 178 C3
San Francisco, Sierra mts Mex. 166 B3
San Francisco Bay inlet U.S.A. 158 B3
San Francisco del Oro Mex. 166 D3
San Francisco de Paula, Cabo c. Arg. 178 C7
San Francisco el Alto Mex. 167 F4
San Francisco Gotera El Salvador 166 [inset] H6
San Francisco Javier Spain 67 G4
San Gabriel, Punta pt Mex. 166 B2
San Gabriel Mountains U.S.A. 158 D4
Sangachaly Azer. see Sanqaçal
Sangaigerong Sumatera Indon. 84 D3
Sangameshwar India 106 B2
Sangamon r. U.S.A. 160 F3
Sangan, Koh-i- mt. Afgh. see Sangān, Kūh-e
Sangān, Kūh-e mt. Afgh. 111 G3
Sangar Rus. Fed. 77 N3
Sangareddi India 106 C2
Sangareddy India see Sangareddi
Sangasanga Kalimantan Indon. 85 G3
Sanga Sanga i. Phil. 82 B5
San Gavino Monreale Sardinia Italy 68 C5
Sangay, Parque Nacional nat. park Ecuador 176 C4
Sangba Xizang China 99 F7
Sangboy Islands Phil. 82 C5
Sangbur Afgh. 111 F3
Sangeang i. Indon. 83 A5
Sangejing Nei Mongol China 94 F3
Sangequanzi Xinjiang China 94 B3
Sanger U.S.A. 158 D3
Sangerfield U.S.A. 165 H2
Sangerhausen Germany 63 L3
Sang-e Surakh Iran 110 E2
Sanggar, Teluk b. Sumbawa Indon. 85 G5
Sanggarmai China 96 D1
Sanggau Kalimantan Indon. 85 E2
Sanggeluhang i. Indon. 83 C2
Sanggou Wan b. China 95 J4
Sangilen, Nagor'ye mts Rus. Fed. 94 C1
San Giovanni in Fiore Italy 68 G5
Sangir India 104 C5
Sangir i. Indon. 83 C2
Sangir, Kepulauan is Indon. 83 C2
Sangiyn Dalay Mongolia see Erdenedalay
Sangiyn Dalay Nuur salt l. Mongolia 94 D1
Sangkapura Jawa Indon. 85 F4
Sangkarang, Kepulauan is Indon. 83 A4
Sangkulirang Kalimantan Indon. 85 G2
Sangkulirang, Teluk b. Indon. 85 G2
Sangli India 106 B2
Sangmai China see Dêrong
Sangmélima Cameroon 120 E4
Sangngagqoiling Xizang China 99 F7
Sango Zimbabwe 123 D6
Sangole India 106 B2
San Gorgonio Mountain U.S.A. 158 E4
Sangowo Maluku Indon. 83 D2
Sangpi China see Xiangcheng
Sangre de Cristo Range mts U.S.A. 157 G5
Sangri Xizang China 99 F7
Sangrur India 104 C3
Sangsang Xizang China 99 D7
Sangu r. Bangl. 105 G5
Sanguem India 106 B3
Sangutane r. Moz. 125 K3
Sangyuan Hebei China see Wuqiao
Sangzhi China 97 F2
Sanhe China see Sandu
Sanhe Nei Mongol China 95 J1
San Hilario Mex. 166 B3
San Hipólito, Punta pt Mex. 166 B3
Sanhūr Egypt 112 C5
Sanhûr Egypt see Sanhūr
San Ignacio Belize 167 H5
San Ignacio Beni Bol. 176 E6
San Ignacio Santa Cruz Bol. 176 F7
San Ignacio Santa Cruz Bol. 176 F7

San Ignacio Baja California Mex. 166 B2
San Ignacio Baja California Sur Mex. 166 B3
San Ignacio Durango Mex. 161 C7
San Ignacio Sonora Mex. 166 C2
San Ignacio Para. 178 E3
San Ignacio, Laguna l. Mex. 166 B3
Sanikiluaq Canada 152 F2
San Ildefonso Peninsula Luzon Phil. 82 C2
Sanin-kaigan Kokuritsu-kōen nat. park Japan 92 A3
San Jacinto Masbate Phil. 82 C3
San Jacinto U.S.A. 158 E5
San Jacinto Peak U.S.A. 158 E5
San Javier Bol. 176 F7
Sanjiang Guangdong China see Liannan
Sanjiang Guangxi China 97 F3
Sanjiang Guizhou China see Jinping
Sanjiangkou Liaoning China 95 J3
Sanjiaocheng Qinghai China see Haiyan
Sanjiaoping China 97 F2
Sanjō Japan 91 E5
San Joaquin r. U.S.A. 158 C2
San Joaquin Valley U.S.A. 158 C3
Sanjoli India 104 C5
San Jon U.S.A. 161 C5
San Jorge, Golfo de g. Arg. 178 C7
San Jorge, Golfo de g. Spain see Sant Jordi, Golf de

▶San José Costa Rica 166 [inset] I7
Capital of Costa Rica.

San Jose Luzon Phil. 82 C3
San Jose Mindoro Phil. 82 C3
San Jose Mindoro Phil. 82 C3
San Jose CA U.S.A. 158 C3
San Jose NM U.S.A. 157 G6
San Jose watercourse U.S.A. 159 J4
San José, Isla i. Mex. 166 C3
San José de Amacuro Venez. 176 F2
San José de Bavicora Mex. 166 D2
San José de Buenavista Panay Phil. 82 C4
San José de Chiquitos Bol. 176 F7
San José de Comondú Mex. 166 C3
San José de Gracia Baja California Sur Mex. 166 B3
San José de Gracia Sinaloa Mex. 166 D3
San José de Gracia Sonora Mex. 166 C2
San Joséde la Brecha Mex. 166 C3
San José del Cabo Mex. 166 C4
San José del Guaviare Col. 176 D3
San José de Mayo Uruguay 178 E4
San José de Raíces Mex. 161 C7
Sanju Xinjiang China 99 B5
San Juan Arg. 178 C4
San Juan r. Costa Rica/Nicaragua 166 [inset] J7
San Juan mt. Cuba 163 D8
San Juan Chihuahua Mex. 166 D3
San Juan Coahuila Mex. 167 E3
San Juan r. Mex. 161 D7
San Juan Leyte Phil. 82 D4
San Juan Mindanao Phil. 82 D4

▶San Juan Puerto Rico 169 K5
Capital of Puerto Rico.

San Juan U.S.A. 159 J5
San Juan r. U.S.A. 159 H3
San Juan, Cabo c. Arg. 178 D8
San Juan, Cabo c. Equat. Guinea 120 D4
San Juan, Punta pt El Salvador 166 [inset] H6
San Juan Bautista Para. 178 E3
San Juan Bautista de las Misiones Para. see San Juan Bautista
San Juancito Hond. 166 [inset] I6
San Juan de Guadalupe Mex. 161 C7
San Juan del Norte Nicaragua 166 [inset] J7
San Juan del Norte, Bahía de b. Nicaragua 166 [inset] J7
San Juan de los Morros Venez. 176 E2
San Juan del Río Durango Mex. 166 D3
San Juan del Río Querétaro Mex. 167 F4
San Juan del Sur Nicaragua 166 [inset] I7
San Juan Evangelista Mex. 167 G5
San Juanico, Punta pt Mex. 166 B3
San Juanito Mex. 166 D3
San Juanito, Isla i. Mex. 166 D4
San Juan Ixcoy Guat. 167 H6
San Juan Mountains U.S.A. 159 J3
San Juan y Martínez Cuba 163 D8
Sanju He watercourse China 99 B5
San Julián Arg. 178 C7
San Justo Arg. 178 D4
Sankari Drug India 106 C4
Sankh r. India 103 F7
Sankhu India 104 C3
Sankra Chhattisgarh India 106 D1
Sankra Rajasthan India 104 B4
Sankt Augustin Germany 63 H4
Sankt Gallen Switz. 66 I3
Sankt-Peterburg Rus. Fed. see St Petersburg
Sankt Pölten Austria 57 O6
Sankt Veit an der Glan Austria 57 O7
Sankt Vith Belgium see St-Vith
Sankt Wendel Germany 63 H5
Sanku India 104 D2
San Lázaro, Cabo c. Mex. 166 B3
San Lázaro, Sierra de mts Mex. 166 C4
Şanlıurfa Turkey 112 E3
Şanlıurfa prov. Turkey 107 D1
San Lorenzo Arg. 178 D4
San Lorenzo Beni Bol. 176 E7
San Lorenzo Tarija Bol. 176 F8
San Lorenzo Ecuador 176 C3
San Lorenzo Hond. 166 [inset] I6
San Lorenzo Mex. 166 D2
San Lorenzo mt. Spain 67 E2
San Lorenzo, Cerro mt. Arg./Chile 178 B7
San Lorenzo, Isla i. Mex. 166 B2
Sanlúcar de Barrameda Spain 67 C5
San Lucas Baja California Sur Mex. 166 B3
San Lucas Baja California Sur Mex. 166 C4
San Lucas, Cabo c. Mex. 166 C4
San Lucas, Serranía de mts Col. 176 D2
San Luis Arg. 178 C4
San Luis Guat. 167 H5
San Luis Guerrero Mex. 167 E5
San Luis AZ U.S.A. 159 F5
San Luis AZ U.S.A. 159 H5
San Luis CO U.S.A. 161 B4
San Luís, Isla i. Mex. 166 B2
San Luis de la Paz Mex. 167 E4
San Luis Gonzaga Mex. 166 C3
San Luisito Mex. 166 B2
San Luis Obispo U.S.A. 158 C4
San Luis Obispo Bay U.S.A. 158 C4
San Luis Pajón Hond. 166 [inset] H6
San Luis Potosí Mex. 168 D4
San Luis Potosí state Mex. 167 E4
San Luis Reservoir U.S.A. 158 C3
San Luis Río Colorado Mex. 166 B1
San Manuel U.S.A. 159 H5
San Marcial, Punta pt Mex. 166 C3
San Marcos Guat. 167 H6
San Marcos Hond. 166 [inset] I6
San Marcos Guerrero Mex. 167 F5
San Marcos U.S.A. 161 D6
San Marcos, Isla i. Mex. 166 B3
San Marino country Europe 68 E3

▶San Marino San Marino 68 E3
Capital of San Marino.

San Martín research station Antarctica 188 L2
San Martín Catamarca Arg. 178 C3
San Martín Mendoza Arg. 178 C4
San Martín, Lago l. Arg./Chile 178 B7
San Martín, Volcán vol. Mex. 167 G5
San Martín de Bolaños Mex. 166 E4
San Martín de los Andes Arg. 178 B6
San Mateo U.S.A. 158 B3
San Mateo Mountains U.S.A. 159 J4
San Matías Bol. 177 G7
San Matías, Golfo g. Arg. 178 D6
Sanmen China 97 I2
Sanmen Wan b. China 97 I2
Sanmenxia Henan China 95 G5
San Miguel El Salvador 166 [inset] H6
San Miguel Panama 166 [inset] K7
San Miguel Luzon Phil. 82 C3
San Miguel U.S.A. 158 C4
San Miguel r. U.S.A. 159 I2
San Miguel Bay Luzon Phil. 82 C3
San Miguel de Allende Mex. 167 E4
San Miguel de Cruces Mex. 166 D3
San Miguel de Horcasitas r. Mex. 166 C2
San Miguel de Huachi Bol. 176 E7
San Miguel de Tucumán Arg. 178 C3
San Miguel do Araguaia Brazil 179 A1
San Miguel el Alto Mex. 166 E4
San Miguel Island U.S.A. 158 C4
San Miguel Islands Phil. 82 B5
San Miguelito Panama 166 [inset] K7
San Miguel Sola de Vega Mex. 167 F5
Sanming China 97 H3
Sannan Japan 92 B3
San Narciso Luzon Phil. 82 C3
Sanndatti India 106 B3
Sanndraigh i. U.K. see Sandray
Sannicandro Garganico Italy 68 F4
San Nicolás Durango Mex. 157 G8
San Nicolás Guerrero Mex. 167 F5
San Nicolás Tamaulipas Mex. 161 D7
San Nicolas Luzon Phil. 82 C2
San Nicolas Island U.S.A. 158 D5
Sannieshof S. Africa 125 G4
Sanniquellie Liberia 120 C4
Sano Japan 93 F2
Sanok Poland 53 D6
San Pablo Bol. 176 E8
San Pablo Mex. 167 F4
San Pablo Luzon Phil. 82 C3
San Pablo de Manta Ecuador see Manta
San Pedro Arg. 178 D2
San Pedro Belize 167 I5
San Pedro Bol. 176 F7
San Pedro Chile 178 C2
San-Pédro Côte d'Ivoire 120 C4
San Pedro Baja California Sur Mex. 166 C4
San Pedro Chihuahua Mex. 166 D2
San Pedro Para. see San Pedro de Ycuamandyyú
San Pedro Mindoro Phil. 82 C3
San Pedro watercourse U.S.A. 159 H5
San Pedro, Punta pt Costa Rica 166 [inset] J7
San Pedro, Sierra de mts Spain 67 C4
San Pedro Carchá Guat. 167 H6
San Pedro Channel U.S.A. 158 D5
San Pedro de Arimena Col. 176 D3
San Pedro de Atacama Chile 178 C2
San Pedro de las Colonias Mex. 166 E3
San Pedro de Macorís Dom. Rep. 169 K5
San Pedro de Ycuamandyyú Para. 178 E2
San Pedro el Saucito Mex. 166 C2
San Pedro Martir, Parque Nacional nat. park Mex. 166 B2
San Pedro Sula Hond. 166 [inset] H6
San Pierre U.S.A. 164 B3
San Pietro, Isola di i. Sardinia Italy 68 C5
San Pitch r. U.S.A. 159 H2
Sanpu Gansu China 94 E4
Sanqaçal Azer. 113 H2
Sanquhar U.K. 60 F5
Sanquianga, Parque Nacional nat. park Col. 176 C3
San Quintín, Cabo c. Mex. 166 A2
San Rafael Arg. 178 C4
San Rafael CA U.S.A. 158 B3
San Rafael NM U.S.A. 159 J4
San Rafael r. U.S.A. 159 H2
San Rafael del Norte Nicaragua 166 [inset] I6
San Rafael Knob mt. U.S.A. 159 H2
San Rafael Mountains U.S.A. 158 C4
San Ramón Bol. 176 F6
Sanrao China 97 H3
San Remo Italy 68 B3
San Roque Spain 67 B2
San Roque, Punta pt Mex. 166 B3
San Saba U.S.A. 161 D6
San Saba r. TX U.S.A. 167 F2
San Salvador i. Bahamas 163 F7

▶San Salvador El Salvador 167 H6
Capital of El Salvador.

San Salvador, Isla i. Galápagos Ecuador 176 [inset]
San Salvador de Jujuy Arg. 178 C2
Sansanné-Mango Togo 120 D3
San Sebastián Arg. 178 C8
San Sebastián Spain see Donostia-San Sebastián
San Sebastián de los Reyes Spain 67 E3
Sansepolcro Italy 68 E3
San Severo Italy 68 F4
San Simon U.S.A. 159 I5
Sanski Most Bos.-Herz. 68 G2
Sansoral Islands Palau see Sonsorol Islands
Sansui China 97 F3
Sant Mongolia 94 E2
Santa r. Peru 176 C5
Santa Amelia Guat. 167 H5
Santa Ana Bol. 176 E7
Santa Ana El Salvador 167 H6
Santa Ana Sonora Mex. 166 C2
Santa Ana i. Solomon Is 133 G3
Santa Ana U.S.A. 158 E5
Santa Ana de Yacuma Bol. 176 E6
Santa Anita Baja California Sur Mex. 166 C4
Santa Anna U.S.A. 161 D6
Santa Bárbara Brazil 179 C2
Santa Bárbara Cuba see La Demajagua
Santa Bárbara Hond. 166 [inset] H6
Santa Bárbara Chihuahua Mex. 166 D3
Santa Barbara U.S.A. 158 D4
Santa Bárbara, Ilha i. Brazil 179 D2
Santa Barbara Channel U.S.A. 158 C4
Santa Bárbara d'Oeste Brazil 179 B3
Santa Barbara Island U.S.A. 158 D5
Santa Catalina Panama 166 [inset] J7
Santa Catalina, Gulf of U.S.A. 158 E5
Santa Catalína, Isla i. Mex. 166 C3
Santa Catalína de Armada Spain 67 B2
Santa Catalina Island U.S.A. 158 D5
Santa Catarina state Brazil 179 A4
Santa Catarina Baja California Mex. 166 B2
Santa Catarina Nuevo León Mex. 167 E3
Santa Catarina, Ilha de i. Brazil 179 A4
Santa Clara Col. 176 E4
Santa Clara Cuba 169 I4
Santa Clara Chihuahua Mex. 166 D2
Santa Clara r. Mex. 166 D2
Santa Clara CA U.S.A. 158 C3
Santa Clara UT U.S.A. 159 G3
Santa Clarita U.S.A. 158 D4
Santa Clotilde Peru 176 D4
Santa Comba Angola see Waku-Kungo
Santa Croce, Capo c. Sicily Italy 68 F6
Santa Cruz Bol. 176 F7
Santa Cruz Brazil 177 K5
Santa Cruz Costa Rica 166 [inset] I7
Santa Cruz Sonora Mex. 166 C2
Santa Cruz Luzon Phil. 82 B3
Santa Cruz Luzon Phil. 82 C2
Santa Cruz Luzon Phil. 82 C3
Santa Cruz U.S.A. 158 B3
Santa Cruz watercourse U.S.A. 159 G5
Santa Cruz, Isla i. Galápagos Ecuador 176 [inset]
Santa Cruz, Isla i. Mex. 166 C3
Santa Cruz Barillas Guat. 167 H6
Santa Cruz Cabrália Brazil 179 D2
Santa Cruz de Goiás Brazil 179 A2
Santa Cruz de la Palma Canary Is 120 B2
Santa Cruz del Sur Cuba 169 I4
Santa Cruz de Moya Spain 67 F4
Santa Cruz de Tenerife Canary Is 120 B2
Santa Cruz de Yojoa Hond. 166 [inset] I6
Santa Cruz do Sul Brazil 178 F3
Santa Cruz Island U.S.A. 158 D4
Santa Cruz Islands Solomon Is 133 G3
Santa Elena, Bahía de b. Ecuador 176 B4
Santa Elena, Cabo c. Costa Rica 166 [inset] I7
Santa Elena, Punta pt Ecuador 176 B4
Santa Eudóxia Brazil 179 B3
Santa Eufemia, Golfo di g. Italy 68 G5
Santa Eulalia Mex. 167 E2
Santa Fé Arg. 178 D4
Santa Fé Cuba 163 D8
Santa Fé Panama 166 [inset] J7
Santa Fe Phil. 82 C3

▶Santa Fe U.S.A. 157 G6
Capital of New Mexico.

Santa Fé de Bogotá Col. see Bogotá
Santa Fé de Minas Brazil 179 B2
Santa Fé do Sul Brazil 179 A3
Santa Gertrudis Mex. 166 D3
Santa Helena Brazil 177 I4
Santa Helena de Goiás Brazil 179 A2
Santai Sichuan China 96 E2
Santai Xinjiang China 98 C3
Santai Xinjiang China 98 E3
Santai Yunnan China 96 D3
Santa Inês Brazil 177 I4
Santa Inés, Isla i. Chile 188 L3
Santa Isabel Arg. 178 C5
Santa Isabel Equat. Guinea see Malabo
Santa Isabel i. Solomon Is 133 F2
Santa Isabel, Sierra mts Mex. 166 B2
Santa Juliana Brazil 179 B2
Santalpur India 104 B5
Santa Lucia Guat. 167 H6
Santa Lucia Range mts U.S.A. 158 C3
Santa Margarita U.S.A. 158 C4
Santa Margarita, Isla i. Mex. 166 C3
Santa María Arg. 178 C3
Santa Maria Amazonas Brazil 177 G4
Santa Maria Rio Grande do Sul Brazil 178 F3
Santa Maria Cape Verde 120 [inset]
Santa María Mex. 167 H5
Santa María r. Mex. 166 D2
Santa María Peru 176 D4
Santa Maria U.S.A. 158 C4
Santa Maria r. U.S.A. 159 G4
Santa Maria, Cabo de c. Moz. 125 K4
Santa Maria, Cabo de c. Port. 67 C5
Santa Maria, Chapadão de hills Brazil 179 B1
Santa María, Isla i. Galápagos Ecuador 176 [inset]
Santa Maria, Serra de hills Brazil 179 B1
Santa Maria da Vitória Brazil 179 B1
Santa María de Cuevas Mex. 166 D3
Santa María del Oro Mex. 166 D3
Santa María del Río Mex. 167 E4
Santa Maria do Suaçuí Brazil 179 C2
Santa Maria Island Vanuatu 133 G3
Santa Maria Madalena Brazil 179 C3
Santa Maria Mountains U.S.A. 159 G4
Santa Marta Col. 176 D1
Santa Marta, Cabo de c. Angola 123 B5
Santa Marta Grande, Cabo de c. Brazil 179 A5
Santa Martha, Cerro mt. Mex. 167 G5
Santa Maura i. Greece see Lefkada
Santa Monica U.S.A. 158 D4
Santa Monica, Pico mt. Mex. 157 E8
Santa Monica Bay U.S.A. 158 D5
Santan Kalimantan Indon. 85 G3
Santana Brazil 179 C1
Santana r. Brazil 179 A2
Santana do Araguaia Brazil 177 H5
Santander Spain 67 E2
Santa Nella U.S.A. 158 C3
Santanghu Xinjiang China 94 C2
Santanilla, Islas is Caribbean Sea see Cisne, Islas del
Santan Mountain hill U.S.A. 159 H5
Sant'Antioco Sardinia Italy 68 C5
Sant'Antioco, Isola di i. Sardinia Italy 68 C5
Sant Antoni de Portmany Spain 67 G4
Santapilly India 106 D2
Santaquin U.S.A. 159 H2
Santa Quitéria Brazil 177 J4
Santarém Brazil 177 H4
Santarém Port. 67 B4
Santa Rita Coahuila Mex. 167 E3
Santa Rosa Arg. 178 D5
Santa Rosa Acre Brazil 176 D5
Santa Rosa Rio Grande do Sul Brazil 178 F3
Santa Rosa Mex. 161 C7
Santa Rosa Quintana Roo Mex. 167 H5
Santa Rosa CA U.S.A. 158 B2
Santa Rosa NM U.S.A. 157 G6
Santa Rosa de Copán Hond. 166 [inset] H6
Santa Rosa de la Roca Bol. 176 F7
Santa Rosa Island U.S.A. 158 C5
Santa Rosalía Mex. 166 B3
Santa Rosa Range mts U.S.A. 156 D4
Santa Rosa Wash watercourse U.S.A. 159 G5
Santa Sylvina Arg. 178 D3
Santa Teresa Australia 135 F6
Santa Teresa r. Brazil 179 A1
Santa Teresa Nayarit Mex. 166 D4
Santa Teresa Tamaulipas Mex. 167 F3
Santa Vitória Brazil 179 A2
Santa Ynez r. U.S.A. 158 C4
Santa Ysabel i. Solomon Is see Santa Isabel
Santee U.S.A. 158 E5
Santee r. U.S.A. 163 E5
San Telmo Mex. 166 A2
Santiago Brazil 178 F3
Santiago i. Cape Verde 120 [inset]

▶Santiago Chile 178 B4
Capital of Chile.

Santiago Dom. Rep. 169 J5
Santiago Baja California Sur Mex. 166 C4
Santiago Panama 166 [inset] J7
Santiago Luzon Phil. 82 C2
Santiago, Cerro mt. Panama 166 [inset] J7
Santiago, Río Grande de r. Mex. 166 D4
Santiago Astata Mex. 167 G5
Santiago de Compostela Spain 67 B2
Santiago de Cuba Cuba 169 I4
Santiago del Estero Arg. 178 D3
Santiago de los Caballeros Dom. Rep. see Santiago
Santiago Ixcuintla Mex. 166 D4
Santiaguillo, Laguna de l. Mex. 161 B7
Santianna Point Canada 151 P2
Santigi Sulawesi Indon. 83 B2
Santiki, Tanjung pt Indon. 83 B2
Santipur India see Shantipur
Sant Jordi, Golf de g. Spain 67 G3
Santō Hyōgo Japan 92 A3
Santō Shiga Japan 92 C3
Santo Amaro Brazil 179 D1
Santo Amaro de Campos Brazil 179 C3
Santo Anastácio Brazil 179 A3
Santo André Brazil 179 B3
Santo Angelo Brazil 178 F3

▶Santo Antão i. Cape Verde 120 [inset]
Most westerly point of Africa.

Santo Antônio Brazil 176 F4
Santo Antônio r. Brazil 179 C2
Santo Antônio São Tomé and Príncipe 120 D4
Santo Antônio, Cabo c. Brazil 179 D1
Santo Antônio da Platina Brazil 179 A3
Santo Antônio de Jesus Brazil 179 D1
Santo Antônio do Içá Brazil 176 E4
Santo Corazón Bol. 177 G7
Santo Domingo Cuba 163 D8

▶Santo Domingo Dom. Rep. 169 K5
Capital of the Dominican Republic.

Santo Domingo Guat. 167 H6
Santo Domingo Baja California Mex. 166 B2
Santo Domingo Baja California Sur Mex. 166 C3
Santo Domingo San Luis Potosí Mex. 167 E4
Santo Domingo Nicaragua 166 [inset] I6
Santo Domingo country West Indies see Dominican Republic
Santo Domingo de Guzmán Dom. Rep. see Santo Domingo
Santo Domingo Tehuantepec Mex. 167 G5
Santo Hipólito Brazil 179 B2
Santorini i. Greece 69 K6
Santos Brazil 179 B3
Santos Dumont Brazil 179 C3
Santos Plateau sea feature S. Atlantic Ocean 184 E7
Santo Tomás Mex. 157 E7
Santo Tomás Nicaragua 166 [inset] I6
Santo Tomás Peru 176 D6
Santo Tomé Arg. 178 E3
Sanup Plateau U.S.A. 159 G3
San Valentín, Cerro mt. Chile 178 B7
San Vicente El Salvador 166 [inset] H6
San Vicente Baja California Mex. 166 A2
San Vicente Luzon Phil. 82 C2
San Vicente de Baracaldo Spain see Barakaldo
San Vicente de Cañete Peru 176 C6
San Vincenzo Italy 68 D3
San Vito, Capo c. Sicily Italy 68 E5
Sanwa Ibaraki Japan 93 F2
Sanwa Niigata Japan 93 E1
Sanwer India 104 C5
Sanxia Shuiku resr China see Three Gorges Reservoir
Sanya China 97 F5
Sanyuan Shaanxi China 95 G5
S. A. Nyýazow Adyndaky Turkm. 111 F2
Sanza Pombo Angola 123 B4
Sao, Phou mt. Laos 86 C3
São Bernardo do Campo Brazil 179 B3
São Borja Brazil 178 E3
São Carlos Brazil 179 B3
São Domingos Brazil 179 B1
São Felipe, Serra de hills Brazil 179 B1
São Félix Bahia Brazil 179 D1
São Félix Mato Grosso Brazil 177 H6
São Félix Pará Brazil 177 H5
São Fidélis Brazil 179 C3
São Francisco Brazil 179 B1

▶São Francisco r. Brazil 179 C1
5th longest river in South America.

São Francisco, Ilha de i. Brazil 179 A4
São Francisco de Paula Brazil 179 A5
São Francisco de Sales Brazil 179 A2
São Francisco do Sul Brazil 179 A4
São Gabriel Brazil 178 F4
São Gonçalo Brazil 179 C3
São Gonçalo do Abaeté Brazil 179 B2
São Gonçalo do Sapucaí Brazil 179 B3
São Gotardo Brazil 179 B2
São João, Ilhas de is Brazil 177 J4
São João da Barra Brazil 179 C3
São João da Boa Vista Brazil 179 B3
São João da Madeira Port. 67 B3
São João da Ponte Brazil 179 B1
São João del Rei Brazil 179 B3
São João do Paraíso Brazil 179 C1
São Joaquim Brazil 179 A5
São Joaquim da Barra Brazil 179 B3
São José Amazonas Brazil 176 E4
São José Santa Catarina Brazil 179 A4
São José do Rio Preto Brazil 179 A3
São José dos Campos Brazil 179 B3
São José dos Pinhais Brazil 179 A4
São Leopoldo Brazil 179 A5
São Lourenço Brazil 179 B3
São Lourenço r. Brazil 177 G7
São Luís Brazil 177 J4
São Luís Brazil 177 G4
São Luís de Montes Belos Brazil 179 A2
São Manuel Brazil 179 A3
São Marcos r. Brazil 179 B2
São Mateus Brazil 179 D2
São Mateus do Sul Brazil 179 A4
São Miguel i. Arquipélago dos Açores 184 G3
São Miguel r. Brazil 179 B2
São Miguel do Tapuio Brazil 177 J5
Saône r. France 66 G4
Saoner India 104 D5
São Nicolau i. Cape Verde 120 [inset]

▶São Paulo Brazil 179 B3
Most populous city in South America and 4th in the world.

São Paulo state Brazil 179 A3
São Paulo de Olivença Brazil 176 E4
São Pedro da Aldeia Brazil 179 C3
São Pedro e São Paulo is N. Atlantic Ocean 184 G5
São Pires r. Brazil see Teles Pires
São Raimundo Nonato Brazil 177 J5
Saori Japan 92 C3
São Romão Amazonas Brazil 176 E5
São Romão Minas Gerais Brazil 179 B2
São Roque Brazil 179 B3
São Roque, Cabo de c. Brazil 177 K5
São Salvador Angola see M'banza Congo
São Salvador do Congo Angola see M'banza Congo
São Sebastião Brazil 179 B3
São Sebastião, Ilha do i. Brazil 179 B3
São Sebastião do Paraíso Brazil 179 B3
São Sebastião dos Poções Brazil 179 B1
São Simão Minas Gerais Brazil 177 H7
São Simão São Paulo Brazil 179 B3
São Simão, Barragem de resr Brazil 179 A2
Sao-Siu Maluku Indon. 83 C2
São Tiago i. Cape Verde see Santiago

▶São Tomé São Tomé and Príncipe 120 D4
Capital of São Tomé and Príncipe.

São Tomé i. São Tomé and Príncipe 120 D4
São Tomé, Cabo de c. Brazil 179 C3
São Tomé, Pico de mt. São Tomé and Príncipe 120 D4
São Tomé and Príncipe country Africa 120 D4
Saoura, Oued watercourse Alg. 64 D6
São Vicente Brazil 179 B3
São Vicente i. Cape Verde 120 [inset]
São Vicente, Cabo de c. Port. 67 B5
Sapako Indon. 84 B3
Sapanca Turkey 69 N4
Saparua Maluku Indon. 83 D3
Saparua i. Maluku Indon. 83 D3
Sapaul India see Supaul
Sape, Selat sea chan. Indon. 83 A5
Sape, Teluk b. Sumbawa Indon. 85 G5
Şaphane Dağı mt. Turkey 69 N5
Sapo, Serranía del mts Panama 166 [inset] K8
Sapo National Park Liberia 120 C4
Sapouy Burkina 120 C3
Sapozhok Rus. Fed. 53 I5
Sappa Creek r. U.S.A. 160 D3
Sapporo Japan 90 F4
Sapudi i. Indon. 85 F4
Sapulpa U.S.A. 161 D4
Sapulu Jawa Indon. 85 F4
Sapulut Sabah Malaysia 85 G1
Sāqī Iran 110 E3
Saqqez Iran 110 B2
Sarā Iran 110 B2
Sarāb Iran 110 B2
Sara Buri Thai. 87 C4
Saradiya India 104 B5
Saragossa Spain see Zaragoza
Saragt Turkm. 111 F2
Saraguro Ecuador 176 C4
Sarahs Turkm. see Saragt
Sarai Afgh. 111 G3
Sarai Sidhu Pak. 111 I4

▶Sarajevo Bos.-Herz. 68 H3
Capital of Bosnia-Herzegovina.

Sarakhs Iran 111 F2
Saraktash Rus. Fed. 76 G4
Saraland U.S.A. 161 F6
Saramati mt. India/Myanmar 86 A1
Saran' Kazakh. 102 D2
Saran, Gunung mt. Indon. 85 E3
Saranac U.S.A. 164 C2
Saranac r. U.S.A. 165 I1
Saranac Lake U.S.A. 165 H1
Saranda Albania see Sarandë
Sarandë Albania 69 I5
Sarandib country Asia see Sri Lanka
Sarangani i. Phil. 82 D5
Sarangani Bay Mindanao Phil. 82 D5
Sarangani Islands Phil. 82 D5
Sarangani Strait Phil. 82 D5
Sarangpur India 104 D5
Saransk Rus. Fed. 53 J5
Sara Peak Nigeria 120 D4
Saraphi Thai. 86 B3
Sarapul Rus. Fed. 51 Q4
Sarāqib Syria 107 C2
Sarasota U.S.A. 163 D7
Saraswati r. India 111 H6

Sarata Ukr. 69 M1
Saratoga CA U.S.A. 158 B3
Saratoga WY U.S.A. 156 G4
Saratoga Springs U.S.A. 162 F3
Saratok Sarawak Malaysia 85 E2
Saratov Rus. Fed. 53 J6
Saratovskoye Vodokhranilishche resr Rus. Fed. 53 J5
Saratsina, Akrotirio pt Greece 69 K5
Saravan Iran 111 F5
Sarawak state Malaysia 85 E2
Saray Turkey 69 L4
Sarayköy Turkey 69 M6
Sarayönü Turkey 112 D3
Sarbāz Iran 109 J4
Sarbāz reg. Iran 111 F5
Sarbhang Bhutan 105 G4
Sarbīsheh Iran 109 I3
Sarbulak Xinjiang China 94 B2
Sarda r. India/Nepal 99 C7
Sarda r. Nepal 105 E3
Sard Āb Afgh. 111 H2
Sardarshahr India 104 C3
Sar Dasht Iran 110 B2
Sardegna i. Sardinia Italy see Sardinia
Sardica Bulg. see Sofia
Sardinia Costa Rica 166 [inset] I7
Sardinia i. Sardinia Italy 68 C4
Sardis MS U.S.A. 161 F5
Sardis WV U.S.A. 164 E4
Sardis Lake resr U.S.A. 161 F5
Sar-e Būm Afgh. 111 G3
Sareks nationalpark nat. park Sweden 54 J3
Sarektjåkkå mt. Sweden 54 J3
Sarempaka, Gunung mt. Indon. 85 F3
Sar-e Pol Afgh. 111 G2
Sar-e Pol-e Żahāb Iran 110 B3
Sar Eskandar Iran see Hashtrud
Sare Yazd Iran 110 D4
Sargasso Sea N. Atlantic Ocean 187 P4
Sargodha Pak. 111 I3
Sarh Chad 121 E4
Sarhad reg. Iran 111 F4
Sārī Iran 110 D2
Saria i. Greece 69 L7
Sar-i-Bum Afgh. see Sar-e Būm
Sáric Mex. 166 C2
Sarigan i. N. Mariana Is 81 L3
Sarigh Jilganang Kol salt l. Aksai Chin 104 D2
Sarıgöl Turkey 69 M5
Sarıkamış Turkey 113 F2
Sarikei Sarawak Malaysia 85 E2
Sarikül, Qatorkŭhi mts China/Tajik. see Sarykol Range
Sarila India 104 D4
Sarina Australia 136 E4
Sarıoğlan Kayseri Turkey 112 D3
Sarıoğlan Konya Turkey see Belören
Sariqamish Kuli salt l. Turkm./Uzbek. see Sarykamyshskoye Ozero
Sarīr Tibesti des. Libya 121 E2
Sarita U.S.A. 161 D7
Sarıveliler Turkey 107 A1
Sariwŏn N. Korea 91 B5
Sarıyar Barajı resr Turkey 69 N5
Sarıyer Turkey 69 M4
Sarız Turkey 112 E3
Sark i. Channel Is 59 E9
Sarkand Kazakh. 102 E2
Şarkikaraağaç Turkey 69 N5
Şarkışla Turkey 112 E3
Şarköy Turkey 69 L4
Sarlath Range mts Afgh./Pak. 111 G4
Sarmi Indon. 81 J7
Särna Sweden 55 H6
Sarneh Iran 110 B3
Sarnen Switz. 66 I3
Sarni India see Amla
Sarnia Canada 164 D2
Sarny Ukr. 53 E6
Saroako Sulawesi Indon. 83 B3
Sarolangun Sumatera Indon. 84 C3
Saroma-ko l. Japan 90 F3
Saronikos Kolpos g. Greece 69 J6
Saros Körfezi b. Turkey 69 L4
Sarova Rus. Fed. 53 I5
Sarowbī Afgh. 111 H3
Sarpa, Ozero l. Rus. Fed. 53 J6
Sarpan i. N. Mariana Is see Rota
Sar Passage Palau 82 [inset]
Sarpsborg Norway 55 G7
Sarqant Kazakh. see Sarkand
Sarre r. France 62 H5
Sarrebourg France 62 H6
Sarreguemines France 62 H5
Sarria Spain 67 C2
Sarry France 62 E6
Sartana Ukr. 53 H7
Sartanahu Pak. 111 H5
Sartène Corsica France 66 I6
Sarthe r. France 66 D3
Sartokay Xinjiang China 94 B2
Sartu China see Daqing
Saruna Pak. 111 G5
Sarupsar India 104 C3
Şərur Azer. 113 G3
Saru Tara tourist site Afgh. 111 F4
Sarv Iran 110 D3
Sarvābād Iran 110 B3
Sárvár Hungary 68 G1
Sarwar India 104 C4
Sary-Bulak Kyrg. 98 A4
Sarygamysh Köli salt l. Turkm./Uzbek. see Sarykamyshskoye Ozero
Sary-Ishikotrau, Peski des. Kazakh. see Saryyesik-Atyrau, Peski
Sary-Jaz r. Kyrg. 98 B4
Sarykamyshskoye Ozero salt l. Turkm./Uzbek. 113 J2
Sarykol Range mts China/Tajik. 111 I2
Sarykomey Kazakh. 98 A3
Saryozek Kazakh. 102 E3
Saryshagan Kazakh. 102 D2
Sarysu watercourse Kazakh. 102 C2
Sarytash Kazakh. 113 H1
Sary-Tash Kyrg. 111 I2
Sary-Ter, Gora mt. Kyrg. 98 B4
Saryýazy Suw Howdany resr Turkm. 111 F2
Saryyesik-Atyrau, Peski des. Kazakh. 102 E2
Saryzhaz Kazakh. 98 B4
Sarzha Kazakh. 113 H2
Sarzhal Kazakh. 98 B2
Sasak Sumatera Indon. 84 B2
Sasar, Tanjung pt Sumba Indon. 83 A5
Sasaram India 105 F4
Sasayama Japan 92 B3
Sasebo Japan 91 C6
Sashima Japan 93 F2
Saskatchewan prov. Canada 151 J4
Saskatchewan r. Canada 151 K4
Saskatoon Canada 151 J4
Saskylakh Rus. Fed. 77 M2
Saslaya mt. Nicaragua 166 [inset] I6
Saslaya, Parque Nacional nat. park Nicaragua 166 [inset] I6
Sasoi r. India 104 B5
Sasolburg S. Africa 125 H4
Sasovo Rus. Fed. 53 I5
Sass r. Canada 150 H2
Sassandra Côte d'Ivoire 120 C4
Sassari Sardinia Italy 68 C4
Sassenberg Germany 63 I3
Sassnitz Germany 57 N3
Sass Town Liberia 120 C4
Sasykkol', Ozero l. Kazakh. 102 F2
Sasykoli Rus. Fed. 53 J7
Sasyqköl l. Kazakh. see Sasykkol', Ozero
Satahual i. Micronesia see Satawal
Sata-misaki c. Japan 91 C7
Satana India 106 B1
Satan Pass U.S.A. 159 I4
Satara India 106 B2
Satara S. Africa 125 J3
Satawal i. Micronesia 81 L5
Sätbaev Kazakh. see Satpayev
Satengar i. Indon. 85 G4
Satevó Mex. 166 D3
Satevo r. Mex. 157 G8
Satırlar Turkey see Yeşilova
Satkania Bangl. 105 H5
Satkhira Bangl. 105 G5
Satluj r. India/Pak. see Sutlej
Satmala Range hills India 106 C2
Satna India 104 E4
Satomi Japan 93 G2
Satonda i. Indon. 85 G5
Satpayev Kazakh. 102 C2
Satpura Range mts India 104 C5
Satsuma-hantō pen. Japan 91 C7
Sattahip Thai. 87 C4
Satte Japan 93 F2
Satteldorf Germany 63 K5
Satthwa Myanmar 86 A3
Satu Mare Romania 53 D7
Satun Thai. 87 C6
Satwas India 104 D5
Saubi i. Indon. 85 F4
Sauceda Mountains U.S.A. 159 G5
Saucillo Mex. 166 D2
Sauda Norway 55 E7
Sauðárkrókur Iceland 54 [inset]
▶Saudi Arabia country Asia 108 F4
5th largest country in Asia.
Sauer r. France 63 I6
Saug r. Mindanao Phil. 82 D5
Saugatuck U.S.A. 164 B2
Saugeen r. Canada 164 E1
Sāūjbolāgh Iran see Mahābād
Sauk Center U.S.A. 160 E2
Saulieu France 66 G3
Saulnois reg. France 62 G6
Sault Sainte Marie Canada 152 D5
Sault Sainte Marie U.S.A. 162 C2
Saumalkol' Kazakh. 100 F1
Saumarez Reef Australia 136 F4
Saumlakki Indon. 134 E2
Saumur France 66 D3
Saunders, Mount hill Australia 134 E3
Saunders Coast Antarctica 188 J1
Saur, Khrebet mts China/Kazakh. 98 D3
Saurimo Angola 123 C4
Sausu Sulawesi Indon. 83 B3
Sautar Angola 123 B5
Sauvolles, Lac l. Canada 153 G3
Sava r. Europe 68 I2
Savá Hond. 166 [inset] I6
Savage River Australia 137 [inset]
Savai'i i. Samoa 133 I3
Savala r. Rus. Fed. 53 I6
Savalou Benin 120 D4
Savanat Iran see Eşţahbān
Savane r. Canada 153 H4
Savanna U.S.A. 160 F3
Savannah GA U.S.A. 163 D5
Savannah OH U.S.A. 164 D3
Savannah TN U.S.A. 161 F5
Savannah r. U.S.A. 163 D5
Savannah Sound Bahamas 163 E7
Savannakhét Laos 86 D3
Savanna-la-Mar Jamaica 169 I5
Savant Lake Canada 152 C4
Savant Lake l. Canada 152 C4
Savanur India 106 B3
Sävar Sweden 54 L5
Savaştepe Turkey 69 L5
Savè Benin 120 D4
Save r. Moz./Zimbabwe 123 D6
Sāveh Iran 110 C3
Saverne France 63 H6
Saverne, Col de pass France 63 H6
Saviaho Fin. 54 P5
Savinskiy Rus. Fed. 52 I3
Savitri r. India 106 B2
Savli India 104 C5
Savoie reg. France see Savoy
Savona Italy 68 C2
Savonlinna Fin. 54 P6
Savonranta Fin. 54 P5
Savoonga AK U.S.A. 148 E3
Savoy reg. France 66 H3
Şavşat Turkey 113 F2
Sävsjö Sweden 55 I8
Savu i. Indon. 83 B5
Savukoski Fin. 54 P3
Savur Turkey 113 F3
Savu Sea Indon. see Sawu, Laut
Savvo-Borzya Rus. Fed. 95 I1
Saw Myanmar 86 A2
Sawahlunto Sumatera Indon. 84 C3
Sawai, Teluk b. Seram Indon. 83 D3
Sawai Madhopur India 104 D4
Sawan Kalimantan Indon. 85 F3
Sawan Myanmar 86 B1
Sawar India 104 C4
Sawara Japan 93 G3
Sawatch Range mts U.S.A. 156 G5
Sawel Mountain hill U.K. 61 E3
Sawi, Ao b. Thai. 87 B5
Sawn Myanmar 86 B2
Sawtell Australia 138 F3
Sawtooth Mountain AK U.S.A. 149 J2
Sawtooth Mountains MN U.S.A. 160 F2
Sawtooth Range mts U.S.A. 156 C2
Sawu Indon. 83 B5
Sawu i. Indon. see Savu
Sawu, Laut sea Indon. 83 B5
Sawye Myanmar 86 B2
Sawyer U.S.A. 164 B3
Saxilby U.K. 58 G5
Saxman AK U.S.A. 149 O5
Saxmundham U.K. 59 I6
Saxnäs Sweden 54 I4
Saxony land Germany see Sachsen
Saxony-Anhalt land Germany see Sachsen-Anhalt
Saxton U.S.A. 165 F3
Say Niger 120 D3
Saya Japan 92 C3
Sayabouri Laos see Xaignabouli
Sayafi i. Maluku Indon. 83 D2
Sayak Kazakh. 102 E2
Sayama Japan 93 F3
Sayang i. Papua Indon. 83 D2
Sayanogorsk Rus. Fed. 88 G2
Sayano-Shushenskoye Vodokhranilishche resr Rus. Fed. 88 G2
Sayansk Rus. Fed. 88 I2
Sayaq Kazakh. see Sayak
Saýat Turkm. 111 F2
Sayat Turkm. see Saýat
Sayaxché Guat. 167 H5
Şaydā Lebanon see Sidon
Sāyen Iran 110 D4
Sayer Island Thai. see Similan, Ko
Sayghān Afgh. 111 G3
Sayhan Mongolia 94 E1
Sayhandulaan Dornogovĭ Mongolia 95 G2
Sayhan-Ovoo Dundgovĭ Mongolia 94 E2
Sayḩūt Yemen 108 H6
Sayingpan China 96 D3
Saykhin Kazakh. 51 P6
Saylac Somalia 121 H3
Saylan country Asia see Sri Lanka
Saylyugem, Khrebet mts Rus. Fed. 98 E2
Saynshand Mongolia 95 G2
Sayn-Ust Mongolia see Höhmorĭt
Sayoa mt. Spain see Saioa
Sayot Turkm. see Saýat
Şayqal, Baḩr imp. l. Syria 107 C3
Sayqyn Kazakh. see Saykhin
Sayram Hu salt l. China 98 C3
Sayre OK U.S.A. 161 D5
Sayre PA U.S.A. 165 G3
Sayreville U.S.A. 165 H3
Saysu Xinjiang China 94 C3
Sayula Jalisco Mex. 166 E5
Sayula Veracruz Mex. 168 F5
Sayyod Turkm. see Saýat
Sazdy Kazakh. 53 K7
Sazin Pak. 111 I3
Sbaa Alg. 64 D6
Sbeitla Tunisia 68 C7
Scaddan Australia 135 C8
Scafell Pike hill U.K. 58 D4
Scalasaig U.K. 60 C4
Scalea Italy 68 F5
Scalloway U.K. 60 [inset]
Scalpaigh, Eilean i. U.K. see Scalpay
Scalpay i. U.K. 60 C3
Scammon Bay AK U.S.A. 148 F3
Scapa Flow inlet U.K. 60 F2
Scarba i. U.K. 60 D4
Scarborough Canada 164 F2
Scarborough Trin. and Tob. 169 L6
Scarborough U.K. 58 G4
Scarborough Shoal sea feature S. China Sea 80 F3
Scariff Island Ireland 61 B6
Scarp i. U.K. 60 B2
Scarpanto i. Greece see Karpathos
Scawfell Shoal sea feature S. China Sea 84 D1
Schaale r. Germany 63 K1
Schaalsee l. Germany 63 K1
Schaerbeek Belgium 62 E4
Schaffhausen Switz. 66 I3
Schafstädt Germany 63 L3
Schagen Neth. 62 E2
Schagerbrug Neth. 62 E2
Schakalskuppe Namibia 124 C4
Schärding Austria 57 N6
Scharendijke Neth. 62 D3
Scharteberg hill Germany 62 G4
Schaumburg U.S.A. 164 A2
Schebheim Germany 63 K5
Scheeßel Germany 63 J1
Schefferville Canada 153 I3
Scheibbs Austria 57 O6
Schelde r. Belgium see Scheldt
Scheldt r. Belgium 62 E3
Schell Creek Range mts U.S.A. 159 F2
Schellerten Germany 63 K2
Schellville U.S.A. 158 B2
Schenectady U.S.A. 165 I2
Schenefeld Germany 63 J1
Schermerhorn Neth. 62 E2
Schertz U.S.A. 161 D6
Schierling Germany 63 M6
Schiermonnikoog Neth. 62 G1
Schiermonnikoog i. Neth. 62 G1
Schiermonnikoog Nationaal Park nat. park Neth. 62 G1
Schiffdorf Germany 63 I1
Schinnen Neth. 62 F4
Schio Italy 68 D2
Schkeuditz Germany 63 M3
Schleiden Germany 62 G4
Schleiz Germany 63 L4
Schleswig Germany 57 L3
Schleswig-Holstein land Germany 63 K1
Schleswig-Holsteinisches Wattenmeer, Nationalpark nat. park Germany 57 L3
Schleusingen Germany 63 K4
Schlitz Germany 63 J4
Schloss Holte-Stukenbrock Germany 63 I3
Schloss Wartburg tourist site Germany 63 K3
Schlüchtern Germany 63 J4
Schlüsselfeld Germany 63 K5
Schmallenberg Germany 63 I3
Schmidt Island Rus. Fed. see Shmidta, Ostrov
Schmidt Peninsula Rus. Fed. see Shmidta, Poluostrov
Schneeberg Germany 63 M4
Schneidemühl Poland see Piła
Schneidlingen Germany 63 L3
Schneverdingen Germany 63 J1
Schoharie U.S.A. 165 H2
Schönebeck Germany 63 M1
Schönebeck (Elbe) Germany 63 L2
Schönefeld airport Germany 63 N2
Schöningen Germany 63 K2
Schöntal Germany 63 J5
Schoolcraft U.S.A. 164 C2
Schoonhoven Neth. 62 E3
Schopfloch Germany 63 K5
Schöppenstedt Germany 63 K2
Schortens Germany 63 H1
Schouten Island Australia 137 [inset]
Schouten Islands P.N.G. 81 K7
Schrankogel mt. Austria 57 M7
Schreiber Canada 152 D4
Schroon Lake U.S.A. 165 I2
Schröttersburg Poland see Płock
Schulenburg U.S.A. 161 D6
Schuler Canada 151 I5
Schull Ireland 61 C6
Schultz Lake Canada 151 L1
Schüttorf Germany 63 H2
Schuyler U.S.A. 160 D3
Schuyler Lake U.S.A. 165 H2
Schuylkill Haven U.S.A. 165 G3
Schwabach Germany 63 L5
Schwäbische Alb mts Germany 57 L7
Schwäbisch Gmünd Germany 63 J6
Schwäbisch Hall Germany 63 J5
Schwaförden Germany 63 I2
Schwalm r. Germany 63 J3
Schwalmstadt-Ziegenhain Germany 63 J4
Schwandorf Germany 63 M5
Schwaner, Pegunungan mts Indon. 85 F3
Schwanewede Germany 63 I1
Schwarmstedt Germany 63 J2
Schwarze Elster r. Germany 63 M3
Schwarzenbek Germany 63 K1
Schwarzenberg Germany 63 M4
Schwarzer Mann hill Germany 62 G4
Schwarzrand mts Namibia 124 C3
Schwarzwald mts Germany see Black Forest
Schwatka, Mount AK U.S.A. 149 K2
Schwatka Mountains AK U.S.A. 148 H2
Schwaz Austria 57 M7
Schwedt an der Oder Germany 57 O4
Schwegenheim Germany 63 I5
Schweich Germany 62 G5
Schweinfurt Germany 63 K4
Schweinitz Germany 63 N3
Schweinrich Germany 63 M1
Schweiz country Europe see Switzerland
Schweizer-Reneke S. Africa 125 G4
Schwelm Germany 63 H3
Schwerin Germany 63 L1
Schweriner See l. Germany 63 L1
Schwetzingen Germany 63 I5
Schwyz Switz. 66 I3
Sciacca Sicily Italy 68 E6
Scicli Sicily Italy 68 F6
Science Hill U.S.A. 164 C5
Scilly, Île atoll Fr. Polynesia see Manuae
Scilly, Isles of U.K. 59 A9
Scioto r. U.S.A. 164 D4
Scipio U.S.A. 159 G2
Scobey U.S.A. 156 G2
Scodra Albania see Shkodër
Scofield Reservoir U.S.A. 159 H2
Scole U.K. 59 I6
Scone Australia 138 E4
Scone U.K. 60 F4
Scoresby Land reg. Greenland 147 P2
Scoresbysund Greenland see Ittoqqortoormiit
Scoresby Sund sea chan. Greenland see Kangertittivaq
Scorno, Punta dello pt Sardinia Italy see Caprara, Punta
Scorpion Bight b. Australia 135 D8
Scotia Ridge sea feature S. Atlantic Ocean 184 E9
Scotia Ridge sea feature S. Atlantic Ocean 188 A2
Scotia Sea S. Atlantic Ocean 184 F9
Scotland Canada 164 E2
Scotland admin. div. U.K. 60 F3
Scotland U.S.A. 165 G4
Scotstown Canada 153 H5
Scott U.S.A. 164 C3
Scott, Cape Australia 134 E3
Scott, Cape Canada 150 D5
Scott, Mount hill U.S.A. 161 D5
Scott Base research station Antarctica 188 H1
Scottburgh S. Africa 125 J6
Scott City U.S.A. 160 C4
Scott Coast Antarctica 188 H1
Scott Glacier Antarctica 188 I1
Scott Island Antarctica 188 H2
Scott Islands Canada 150 D5
Scott Lake Canada 151 J3
Scott Mountains Antarctica 188 D2
Scott Reef Australia 134 C3
Scottsbluff U.S.A. 160 C3
Scottsboro U.S.A. 163 C5
Scottsburg U.S.A. 164 C4
Scottsville KY U.S.A. 164 B5
Scottsville VA U.S.A. 165 F5
Scourie U.K. 60 D2
Scousburgh U.K. 60 [inset]
Scrabster U.K. 60 F2
Scranton U.S.A. 165 H3
Scunthorpe U.K. 58 G5
Scuol Switz. 66 J3
Scupi Macedonia see Skopje
Scutari Albania see Shkodër
Scutari, Lake Albania/Montenegro 69 H3
Seaboard U.S.A. 165 G5
Seabrook, Lake salt flat Australia 135 B7
Seaford U.K. 59 H8
Seaforth Canada 164 E2
Seahorse Shoal sea feature Phil. 82 B4
Seal r. Canada 151 M3
Seal, Cape S. Africa 124 F8
Sea Lake Australia 137 C7
Seal Lake Canada 153 J3
Sealy U.S.A. 161 D6
Seaman U.S.A. 164 D4
Seaman Range mts U.S.A. 159 F3
Seamer U.K. 58 G4
Searchlight U.S.A. 159 F4
Searcy U.S.A. 161 F5
Searles Lake U.S.A. 158 E4
Seaside CA U.S.A. 157 C5
Seaside OR U.S.A. 156 C3
Seaside Park U.S.A. 165 H4
Seattle U.S.A. 156 C3
Seattle, Mount Canada/U.S.A. 149 M3
Seaview Range mts Australia 136 D3
Seba Indon. 83 B5
Sebaco Nicaragua 166 [inset] I6
Sebago Lake U.S.A. 165 J2
Sebakung Kalimantan Indon. 85 G3
Sebangan, Teluk b. Indon. 85 F3
Sebangka i. Indon. 84 D2
Sebastea Turkey see Sivas
Sebastian U.S.A. 163 D7
Sebastián Vizcaíno, Bahía b. Mex. 166 B2
Sebasticook r. U.S.A. 165 K1
Sebasticook Lake U.S.A. 165 K1
Sebastopol Ukr. see Sevastopol'
Sebastopol U.S.A. 158 B2
Sebatik i. Indon. 85 G1
Sebauh Sarawak Malaysia 85 F2
Sebayan, Bukit mt. Indon. 85 E3
Sebba Burkina 120 D3
Seben Turkey 69 N4
Sebenico Croatia see Šibenik
Sebeş Romania 69 J2
Sebesi i. Indon. 84 D4
Sebewaing U.S.A. 164 D2
Sebezh Rus. Fed. 55 P8
Şebinkarahisar Turkey 112 E2
Seblat, Gunung mt. Indon. 84 C3
Sebree U.S.A. 164 B5
Sebring U.S.A. 163 D7
Sebrovo Rus. Fed. 53 I6
Sebta N. Africa see Ceuta
Sebuku i. Indon. 85 G3
Sebuku r. Indon. 85 G1
Sebuku, Teluk b. Indon. 85 G2
Sebuku-Sembakung, Taman Nasional nat. park Kalimantan Indon. 85 G1
Sebuyau Sarawak Malaysia 85 E2
Sechelt Canada 150 F5
Sechenovo Rus. Fed. 53 J5
Sechura Peru 176 B5
Sechura, Bahía de b. Peru 176 B5
Seckach Germany 63 J5
Second Mesa U.S.A. 159 H4
Secretary Island N.Z. 139 A7
Secunda S. Africa 125 I4
Secunderabad India 106 C2
Sedalia U.S.A. 160 E4
Sedam India 106 C2
Sedan France 62 E5
Sedan U.S.A. 161 D4
Sedan Dip Australia 136 C3
Sedanka Island AK U.S.A. 148 F5
Seddon N.Z. 139 E5
Seddonville N.Z. 139 C5
Sedeh Iran 110 E3
Sederot Israel 107 B4
Sedlčany Czech Rep. 57 O6
Sedlets Poland see Siedlce
Sedom Israel 107 B4
Sedona U.S.A. 159 H4
Sédrata Alg. 68 B6
Sedulang Kalimantan Indon. 85 G2
Šeduva Lith. 55 M9
Seedorf Germany 63 K1
Seehausen Germany 63 L2
Seehausen (Altmark) Germany 63 L2
Seeheim Namibia 124 C4
Seeheim-Jugenheim Germany 63 I5
Seela Pass Y.T. Canada 149 M2
Seelig, Mount Antarctica 188 K1
Seelze Germany 63 J2
Seenu Atoll Maldives see Addu Atoll
Sées France 66 E2
Seesen Germany 63 K3
Seevetal Germany 63 K1
Sefadu Sierra Leone 120 B4
Sefare Botswana 125 H2
Seferihisar Turkey 69 L5
Sefīd, Kūh-e mt. Iran 110 C3
Sefophe Botswana 125 H2
Segalstad Norway 55 G6
Segama r. Malaysia 85 G1
Segamat Malaysia 84 C2
Ségbana Benin 120 D3
Segeletz Germany 63 M2
Segeri Sulawesi Indon. 83 A4
Segezha Rus. Fed. 52 G3
Seghnān Afgh. 111 H2
Segontia U.K. see Caernarfon
Segontium U.K. see Caernarfon
Segorbe Spain 67 F4
Ségou Mali 120 C3
Segovia r. Hond./Nicaragua see Coco
Segovia Spain 67 D3
Segozerskoye, Ozero resr Rus. Fed. 52 G3
Seguam Island AK U.S.A. 148 D5
Seguam Pass sea channel AK U.S.A. 149 [inset]
Séguédine Niger 120 E2
Séguéla Côte d'Ivoire 120 C4
Seguin U.S.A. 161 D6
Segula Island AK U.S.A. 149 [inset]
Segura r. Spain 67 F4
Segura, Sierra de mts Spain 67 E5
Sehithwa Botswana 123 C6
Sehlabathebe National Park Lesotho 125 I5
Seho i. Indon. 83 C3
Sehore India 104 D5
Sehwan Pak. 111 G5
Seibert U.S.A. 160 C4
Seignelay r. Canada 153 H4
Seika Japan 92 B4
Seikphyu Myanmar 86 A2
Seiland i. Norway 54 M1
Seille r. France 62 G5
Seinaiji Japan 92 D3
Seinäjoki Fin. 54 M5
Seine r. Canada 151 N5
Seine r. France 62 A5
Seine, Baie de b. France 66 D2
Seine, Val de valley France 66 F2
Seipinang Kalimantan Indon. 85 F3
Seistan reg. Iran see Sīstān
Seiwa Japan 92 C4
Sejaka Kalimantan Indon. 85 G3
Sejangkung Kalimantan Indon. 85 E2
Sejny Poland 55 M9
Sekadau Kalimantan Indon. 85 E2
Sekanak, Teluk b. Indon. 84 D3
Sekatak Bengara Kalimantan Indon. 85 G2
Sekayu Sumatera Indon. 84 C3
Seke China see Sêrtar
Seki Gifu Japan 92 C3
Seki Mie Japan 92 C4
Sekicau, Gunung vol. Indon. 84 D4
Sekidō-san hill Japan 92 C2
Sekigahara Japan 92 C3
Sekijō Japan 93 F2
Sekiyado Japan 93 F2
Sekoma Botswana 124 F3
Sekondi Ghana 120 C4
Sek'ot'a Eth. 122 D2
Sekura Kalimantan Indon. 85 E2
Şela Rus. Fed. see Shali
Selagan r. Indon. 84 C3
Selakau Kalimantan Indon. 85 E2
Selama Malaysia 87 C6
Selangor state Malaysia 84 C2
Selaru i. Maluku Indon. 83 D5
Selassi Indon. 81 I7
Selatan, Tanjung pt Indon. 85 F4
Selatpanjang Sumatera Indon. 84 C2
Selawik AK U.S.A. 148 G2
Selawik r. AK U.S.A. 148 G2
Selawik Lake AK U.S.A. 148 G2
Selawik National Wildlife Refuge nature res. AK U.S.A. 148 H2
Selb Germany 63 M4
Selbekken Norway 54 F5
Selbu Norway 54 G5
Selby U.K. 58 F5
Selby U.S.A. 160 C2
Selby, Lake AK U.S.A. 148 I2
Selbyville U.S.A. 165 H4
Selden U.S.A. 160 C4
Seldovia AK U.S.A. 149 J4
Sele Papua Indon. 83 D3
Sele, Selat sea chan. Papua Indon. 83 D3
Selebi-Phikwe Botswana 123 C6
Selebi-Pikwe Botswana see Selebi-Phikwe
Selemdzha r. Rus. Fed. 90 C1
Selemdzhinsk Rus. Fed. 90 C1
Selemdzhinskiy Khrebet mts Rus. Fed. 90 D1
Selendi Turkey 69 M5
Selenduma Rus. Fed. 94 F1

▶Selenga r. Mongolia/Rus. Fed. 88 J2
Part of the Yenisey-Angara-Selenga, 3rd longest river in Asia.
Also known as Selenga Mörön.

Selenga Mörön r. Mongolia see Selenga
Selenge Mongolia 94 E1
Selenge Mongolia see Ih-Uul
Selenge prov. Mongolia 94 F1
Selenge Mörön r. Mongolia 94 F1
Sêlêpug Xizang China 99 C7
Seletar Sing. 87 [inset]
Seletar Reservoir Sing. 87 [inset]
Selety r. Kazakh. see Sileti
Seletyteniz, Ozero salt l. Kazakh. see Siletiteniz, Ozero
Seleucia Turkey see Silifke
Seleucia Pieria Turkey see Samandağı
Selfridge U.S.A. 160 C2
Sel'gon Stantsiya Rus. Fed. 90 D2
Selib Rus. Fed. 52 K3
Sélibabi Mauritania 120 B3
Selibe-Phikwe Botswana see Selebi-Phikwe
Seligenstadt Germany 63 I4
Seliger, Ozero l. Rus. Fed. 52 G4
Seligman U.S.A. 159 G4
Selikhino Rus. Fed. 90 E2
Selîma Oasis Sudan 108 C5
Selimbau Kalimantan Indon. 85 F2
Selimiye Turkey 69 L6
Selinsgrove U.S.A. 165 G3
Seliu i. Indon. 104 D3
Selizharovo Rus. Fed. 52 G4
Seljord Norway 55 F7
Selkirk Canada 151 L5
Selkirk U.K. 60 G5
Selkirk Mountains Canada 150 G4
Sellafield U.K. 58 D4
Sellersburg U.S.A. 164 C4
Sellore Island Myanmar see Saganthit Kyun
Sells U.S.A. 159 H6
Selm Germany 63 H3
Selma AL U.S.A. 163 C5
Selma CA U.S.A. 158 D3
Selmer U.S.A. 161 F5
Selong Lombok Indon. 85 G5
Selous, Mount Y.T. Canada 149 N3
Selseleh-ye Pīr Shūrān mts Iran 111 F4
Selsey Bill hd U.K. 59 G8
Sel'tso Rus. Fed. 53 G5
Selty Rus. Fed. 52 L4
Selu i. Indon. 134 E1
Seluan i. Indon. 85 D1
Selvas reg. Brazil 176 D5
Selvin U.S.A. 164 B4
Selway r. U.S.A. 156 E3
Selwyn Lake Canada 151 J2
Selwyn Mountains N.W.T./Y.T. Canada 149 O2
Selwyn Range hills Australia 136 B4
Selz r. Germany 63 I5
Semangka, Teluk b. Indon. 84 D4
Semarang Jawa Indon. 85 E4
Sematan Sarawak Malaysia 85 E2
Semau i. Indon. 83 B5
Semayang, Danau l. Indon. 85 G3
Sembakung r. Indon. 85 G2
Sembawang Sing. 87 [inset]
Sembé Congo 122 B3
Şemdinli Turkey 113 G3
Semendire Serbia see Smederevo
Semenivka Ukr. 53 G5
Semenov Rus. Fed. 52 J4
Semenovka Ukr. see Semenivka
Semeru, Gunung vol. Indon. 84 F5
Semey Kazakh. see Semipalatinsk
Semidi Islands AK U.S.A. 148 H4
Semikarakorsk Rus. Fed. 53 I7
Semiluki Rus. Fed. 53 H6
Seminoe Reservoir U.S.A. 156 G4
Seminole U.S.A. 161 C5
Semipalatinsk Kazakh. 102 F1
Semirara i. Phil. 82 C3
Semirara Islands Phil. 82 C4
Semīrom Iran 110 C4
Semitau Kalimantan Indon. 85 E2
Semiyarka Kazakh. 98 B2
Semizbuga Kazakh. 98 A2
Sem Kolodezey Ukr. see Lenine
Semnān Iran 110 D3
Semnān va Dāmghān reg. Iran 110 D3
Sêmnyi Qinghai China 94 E4
Semois r. Belgium/France 62 E5
Semois, Vallée de la valley Belgium/France 62 E5
Semporna Sabah Malaysia 85 G1
Sempu i. Indon. 85 F5
Semyonovskoye Arkhangel'skaya Oblast' Rus. Fed. see Bereznik
Semyonovskoye Kostromskaya Oblast' Rus. Fed. see Ostrovskoye
Sena Bol. 176 E6
Senaja Sabah Malaysia 85 G1
Sena Madureira Brazil 176 E5
Senanga Zambia 123 C5
Senaning Kalimantan Indon. 85 E2
Sendai Kagoshima Japan 91 C7
Sendai Miyagi Japan 91 F5
Sêndo Xizang China 99 F7
Senduruhan Kalimantan Indon. 85 E3
Senebui, Tanjung pt Indon. 84 C2
Seneca KS U.S.A. 160 D4
Seneca OR U.S.A. 156 D3
Seneca Lake U.S.A. 165 G2
Seneca Rocks U.S.A. 164 F4
Senecaville Lake U.S.A. 164 E4
Senegal country Africa 120 B3
Sénégal r. Mauritania/Senegal 120 B3
Seney U.S.A. 160 G2
Senftenberg Germany 57 O5
Senga Hill Zambia 123 D4
Sengar r. India 99 B8
Sengata Kalimantan Indon. 85 G2
Sêngdoi Xizang China 99 C7
Sengerema Tanz. 122 D4
Sengeyskiy, Ostrov i. Rus. Fed. 52 K1
Sênggê Zangbo r. China 104 D2 see Indus
Sengiley Rus. Fed. 53 K5
Sengirli, Mys pt Kazakh. see Syngyrli, Mys
Sêngli Co l. Xizang China 99 D7
Senhor do Bonfim Brazil 177 J6
Senigallia Italy 68 E3
Senj Croatia 68 F2
Senja i. Norway 54 J2
Senjōga-dake mt. Japan 92 B4
Senjōga-dake mt. Japan 93 E3
Sen'kina Rus. Fed. 52 K2
Şenköy Turkey 107 C1
Senlac S. Africa 124 F3
Senlin Shan mt. China 90 C4
Senlis France 62 C5
Senmonorom Cambodia 87 D4
Sennan Japan 92 B4
Sennar Sudan 108 D7
Sennen U.K. 59 B8
Senneterre Canada 152 F4
Sennokura-yama mt. Japan 93 E2
Senqu r. Lesotho 125 H6
Sens France 66 F2
Sensuntepeque El Salvador 166 [inset] H6
Senta Serbia 69 I2
Sentas Kazakh. 98 C2
Senthal India 104 D3
Sentinel U.S.A. 159 G5
Sentinel Peak Canada 150 F4
Sentispac Mex. 166 D4
Sentosa i. Sing. 87 [inset]
Senwabarwana S. Africa 125 I2
Senyiur Kalimantan Indon. 85 G2
Şenyurt Turkey 113 F3
Seo de Urgell Spain see La Seu d'Urgell
Seonath r. India 106 D1
Seoni India 104 D5
Seorinarayan India 105 E5

▶Seoul S. Korea 91 B5
Capital of South Korea.

Sepanjang i. Indon. 85 F4
Separation Well Australia 134 C5
Sepasu Kalimantan Indon. 85 G2
Sepauk Kalimantan Indon. 85 E2
Sepik r. P.N.G. 81 K7
Sepinang Kalimantan Indon. 85 G2
Seping r. Malaysia 85 F2
Sep'o N. Korea 91 B5
Sepon India 105 H4
Seppa India 105 H4
Sept-Îles Canada 153 I4
Seputih r. Indon. 84 D4
Sequoia National Park U.S.A. 158 D3
Serafimovich Rus. Fed. 53 I6
Sêraitang China see Baima
Seram i. Maluku Indon. 83 D3
Seram, Laut sea Indon. 83 D3
Serang Jawa Indon. 84 D4
Serangoon Harbour b. Sing. 87 [inset]
Serapi, Gunung hill Indon. 85 E2
Serapong, Mount hill Sing. 87 [inset]
Serasan i. Indon. 85 E2
Serasan, Selat sea chan. Indon. 85 E2
Seraya i. Indon. 83 A5
Seraya i. Indon. 85 E2
Serbâl, Gebel mt. Egypt see Sirbāl, Jabal

▶Serbia country Europe 69 I2
Formerly a constituent republic of Yugoslavia. Serbia and Montenegro, which initially formed the residual 'Federal Republic of Yugoslavia', broke up in 2003 when Montenegro seceded. Kosovo declared independence from Serbia in 2008.

Sêrbug Co l. Xizang China 99 E6
Sêrca Xizang China 99 F7
Serchhip India 105 H5
Serdar Turkm. 110 E2
Serdica Bulg. see Sofia
Serdo Eth. 122 E2
Serdoba r. Rus. Fed. 53 J5
Serdobsk Rus. Fed. 53 J5
Serdtse-Kamen', Mys c. Rus. Fed. 148 E2
Serebryansk Kazakh. 102 F2
Seredka Rus. Fed. 55 P7
Şereflikoçhisar Turkey 112 D3
Seremban Malaysia 84 C2
Serengeti National Park Tanz. 122 D4
Serenje Zambia 123 D5
Serezha r. Rus. Fed. 52 I5
Sergach Rus. Fed. 52 J5
Sergelen Dornod Mongolia 95 H1
Sergelen Sühbaatar Mongolia see Tüvshinshiree
Sergeyevka Rus. Fed. 90 B2
Sergiyev Posad Rus. Fed. 52 H4
Sergo Ukr. see Stakhanov
Serh Qinghai China 94 D4
Serhetabat Turkm. 111 F3
Seria Brunei 85 F1
Serian Sarawak Malaysia 85 E2
Seribu, Kepulauan is Indon. 84 D4
Serifos i. Greece 69 K6
Sérigny r. Canada 153 H3
Sérigny, Lac l. Canada 153 H3
Serik Turkey 112 C3
Serikbuya Xinjiang China 98 B5
Serikkembelo Seram Indon. 83 C3
Seringapatam Reef Australia 134 C3
Sêrkang Xizang China see Nyainrong
Sermata i. Maluku Indon. 83 D5
Sermata, Kepulauan is Maluku Indon. 83 D5
Sermersuaq glacier Greenland 147 M2
Sermilik inlet Greenland 147 O3
Sernovodsk Rus. Fed. 53 K5
Sernur Rus. Fed. 52 K4
Sernyy Zavod Turkm. see Kükürtli
Seronga Botswana 123 C5
Serov Rus. Fed. 51 S4
Serowe Botswana 125 H2
Serpa Port. 67 C5
Serpa Pinto Angola see Menongue
Serpentine Hot Springs AK U.S.A. 148 F2
Serpentine Lakes salt flat Australia 135 E7
Serpukhov Rus. Fed. 53 H5
Serra Brazil 179 C3
Serra Alta Brazil 179 A4
Serrachis r. Cyprus 107 A2
Serra da Bocaina, Parque Nacional da nat. park Brazil 179 B3
Serra da Bodoquena, Parque Nacional da nat. park Brazil 177 G8
Serra da Canastra, Parque Nacional da nat. park Brazil 179 B3
Serra da Mesa, Represa resr Brazil 179 A1
Serra das Araras Brazil 179 B1
Serra do Divisor, Parque Nacional do nat. park Brazil 176 D5
Sérrai Greece see Serres
Serranía de la Neblina, Parque Nacional nat. park Venez. 176 E3
Serraria, Ilha i. Brazil see Queimada, Ilha
Serra Talhada Brazil 177 K5
Serre r. France 62 D5
Serres Greece 69 J4
Serrinha Brazil 177 K6
Sêrro Brazil 179 C2
Sers Tunisia 68 C6
Sertanópolis Brazil 179 A3
Sertãozinho Brazil 179 B3
Sêrtar China 96 D1
Sertavul Geçidi pass Turkey 107 A1
Sertolovo Rus. Fed. 55 Q6
Serua vol. Maluku Indon. 83 D4
Seruai Sumatera Indon. 84 B1
Serui Indon. 81 J7
Serule Botswana 123 C6
Seruna India 104 C3
Serutu i. Indon. 85 E3
Seruyan r. Indon. 85 F3
Serwaru Maluku Indon. 83 C5
Sêrwolungwa Qinghai China 94 C5
Sêrxü China 96 C1
Serykh Gusey, Ostrova is Rus. Fed. 148 D2
Seryshevo Rus. Fed. 90 C2
Sesayap Kalimantan Indon. 85 G2
Sesayap r. Indon. 85 G2
Seseganaga Lake Canada 152 C4
Sese Islands Uganda 122 D4
Sesel country Indian Ocean see Seychelles
Sesepe Maluku Indon. 83 C3
Sesfontein Namibia 123 B5
Seshachalam Hills India 106 C3
Seshan Rus. Fed. 148 E2
Sesheke Zambia 123 C5
Sesostris Bank sea feature India 106 A3
Ses Salines, Cap de c. Spain 67 H4
Sestri Levante Italy 68 C2
Sestroretsk Rus. Fed. 55 P6
Set, Phou mt. Laos 86 D4
Sète France 66 F5
Sete Lagoas Brazil 179 B2
Setermoen Norway 54 K2
Setesdal valley Norway 55 E7
Seti r. Nepal 104 E3
Sétif Alg. 64 F4
Seto Japan 92 D3
Seto-naikai sea Japan 89 O6
Seto-naikai Kokuritsu-kōen Japan 91 D6
Setsan Myanmar 86 A3
Settat Morocco 64 C5
Settepani, Monte mt. Italy 68 C2
Settle U.K. 58 E4
Setúbal Port. 67 B4
Setúbal, Baía de b. Port. 67 B4
Seul, Lac l. Canada 151 M5
Seulimeum Sumatera Indon. 84 A1
Sevan Armenia 113 G2
Sevan, Lake Armenia 113 G2
Sevan, Ozero l. Armenia see Sevan, Lake
Sevana Lich l. Armenia see Sevan, Lake
Sevastopol' Ukr. 112 D1
Seven Islands Canada see Sept-Îles
Seven Islands Bay Canada 153 J2
Sevenoaks U.K. 59 H7
Seventy Mile House Canada see 70 Mile House
Sévérac-le-Château France 66 F4
Severn r. Australia 138 E2
Severn r. Canada 151 O4
Severn S. Africa 124 F4
Severn r. U.K. 59 E7
also known as Hafren
Severnaya Dvina r. Rus. Fed. 52 I2
Severnaya Sos'va r. Rus. Fed. 51 T3
Severnaya Zemlya is Rus. Fed. 77 L1
Severn Lake Canada 151 N4
Severnoye Rus. Fed. 51 Q5
Severnyy Nenetskiy Avtonomnyy Okrug Rus. Fed. 52 K1
Severnyy Respublika Komi Rus. Fed. 76 H3
Severobaykal'sk Rus. Fed. 89 J1
Severo-Baykal'skoye Nagor'ye mts Rus. Fed. 77 M4
Severo-Chuyskiy Khrebet mts Rus. Fed. 98 D2
Severodonetsk Ukr. see Syeverodonets'k
Severodvinsk Rus. Fed. 52 H2
Severo-Kuril'sk Rus. Fed. 77 Q4
Severomorsk Rus. Fed. 54 R2
Severoonezhsk Rus. Fed. 52 H3
Severo-Sibirskaya Nizmennost' lowland Rus. Fed. see North Siberian Lowland
Severoural'sk Rus. Fed. 51 R3
Severo-Yeniseyskiy Rus. Fed. 76 K3
Severskaya Rus. Fed. 112 E1
Severskiy Donets r. Rus. Fed./Ukr. 53 I7
also known as Northern Donets, Sivers'kyy Donets'
Sevier U.S.A. 159 G2
Sevier r. U.S.A. 159 G2
Sevier Desert U.S.A. 159 G2
Sevier Lake U.S.A. 159 G2
Sevierville U.S.A. 162 D5
Sevilla Col. 176 C3
Sevilla Spain see Seville
Seville Spain 67 D5
Sevlyush Ukr. see Vynohradiv
Sêwa Xizang China 99 E6
Sewani India 104 C3
Seward AK U.S.A. 149 J3
Seward NE U.S.A. 160 D3
Seward Mountains Antarctica 188 L2
Seward Peninsula AK U.S.A. 148 F2
Sexi Spain see Almuñécar
Sexsmith Canada 150 G4
Sextín Mex. 166 D3
Sextín r. Mex. 166 D3
Seya Japan 93 F3
Seyah Band Koh mts Afgh. 111 F3
Seyakha Rus. Fed. 189 F2
Seybaplaya Mex. 167 H5
Seychelles country Indian Ocean 185 L6
Seýdi Turkm. 111 F2
Seydişehir Turkey 112 C3
Seyðisfjörður Iceland 54 [inset]
Seyhan Turkey see Adana
Seyhan r. Turkey 107 B1
Seyitgazi Turkey 69 N5
Seym r. Rus. Fed./Ukr. 53 G6
Seymchan Rus. Fed. 77 Q3
Seymour Australia 138 B6
Seymour S. Africa 125 H7
Seymour IN U.S.A. 164 C4
Seymour TX U.S.A. 161 D5
Seymour Inlet Canada 150 E5
Seymour Range mts Australia 135 F6
Seypan i. N. Mariana Is see Saipan
Seyyedābād Afgh. 111 H3
Sézanne France 62 D6
Sfakia Kriti Greece see Chora Sfakion
Sfântu Gheorghe Romania 69 K2
Sfax Tunisia 68 D7
Sfikia, Limni resr Greece see Sfikias, Limni
Sfikias, Limni resr Greece 69 J4
Sfîntu Gheorghe Romania see Sfântu Gheorghe
Sgiersch Poland see Zgierz
's-Graveland Neth. 62 F2
's-Gravenhage Neth. see The Hague
Sgurr Alasdair hill U.K. 60 C3
Sgurr Dhomhnuill hill U.K. 60 D4
Sgurr Mòr mt. U.K. 60 D3
Sgurr na Ciche mt. U.K. 60 D3
Shaanxi prov. China 95 G5
Shaartuz Tajik. see Shahrtuz
Shaban Pak. 111 G4
Shabani Zimbabwe see Zvishavane
Shabestar Iran 110 B2
Shabībī, Jabal ash mt. Jordan 107 B5
Shabla, Nos pt Bulg. 69 M3
Shabogamo Lake Canada 153 I3
Shabunda Dem. Rep. Congo 122 C4
Shache Xinjiang China 98 B5
Shacheng Hebei China see Huailai
Shackleton Coast Antarctica 188 H1
Shackleton Glacier Antarctica 188 I1
Shackleton Ice Shelf Antarctica 188 F2
Shackleton Range mts Antarctica 188 A1
Shadaogou China 97 F2
Shadaw Myanmar 86 B3
Shādegān Iran 110 C4
Shadihar Pak. 111 G4
Shady Grove U.S.A. 156 C4
Shady Spring U.S.A. 164 E5
Shafer, Lake U.S.A. 164 B3
Shafer Peak Antarctica 188 H2
Shafter U.S.A. 158 D4
Shaftesbury U.K. 59 E7
Shagamu r. Canada 152 D3
Shagan watercourse Kazakh. 98 B2
Shagedu Nei Mongol China 95 G4
Shageluk AK U.S.A. 148 H3
Shaghyray Üstirti plat. Kazakh. see Shagyray, Plato
Shagonar Rus. Fed. 102 H1
Shag Point N.Z. 139 C7
Shag Rocks is S. Georgia 178 H8
Shagyray, Plato plat. Kazakh. 102 A2
Shahabad Karnataka India 106 C2
Shahabad Rajasthan India 104 D4
Shahabad Uttar Prad. India 104 E4
Shāhābād Iran see Eslāmābād-e Gharb
Shah Alam Malaysia 84 C2
Shah Bandar Pak. 111 G5
Shahdād Iran 110 E4
Shahdol India 104 E5
Shahe China 97 F2
Shahe Shandong China 95 I4
Shahejie China see Jiujiang
Shahepu Gansu China see Linze
Shahezhen Gansu China see Linze
Shahezhen China see Jiujiang
Shah Fuladi mt. Afgh. 111 G3
Shahid, Ras pt Pak. 111 F5
Shāhīn Dezh Iran see Sa'īndezh
Shah Ismail Afgh. 111 G4
Shahjahanpur India 104 D4
Shāh Jehān, Kūh-e mts Iran 110 E2
Shāh Jūy Afgh. 111 G3
Shāh Kūh mt. Iran 110 E4
Shahousuo Liaoning China 95 J3
Shāhpūr Iran see Salmās
Shahrak Afgh. 111 G3
Shāhrakht Iran 111 F3
Shahr-e Bābak Iran 110 D4
Shahr-e Kord Iran 110 C3
Shahr-e Şafā Afgh. 111 G4
Shahrezā Iran 110 C3
Shahrig Pak. 111 G4
Shahrisabz Uzbek. 111 G2
Shahriston Tajik. 111 H2
Shahr Rey Iran 110 C3
Shahr Sultan Pak. 111 H4
Shahrtuz Tajik. 111 H2
Shāhrūd Iran see Emāmrūd
Shāhrūd, Rūdkhāneh-ye r. Iran 110 C2
Shāh Savārān, Kūh-e mts Iran 110 E4
Shāh Taqī Iran see Emām Taqī
Shaighalu Pak. 111 H4
Shaikh Husain mt. Pak. 111 G4
Shaikhpura India see Sheikhpura
Shā'īr, Jabal mts Syria 107 C2
Sha'īra, Gebel mt. Egypt see Sha'īrah, Jabal
Sha'īrah, Jabal mt. Egypt 107 B5
Shaj'ah, Jabal hill Saudi Arabia 110 C5
Shajapur India 104 D5
Shajianzi China 90 B4
Shakaga-dake mt. Japan 92 B4
Shakaville S. Africa 125 J5
Shakh Tajik. see Shoh
Shakhbuz Azer. see Şahbuz
Shākhen Iran 111 E3
Shakhovskaya Rus. Fed. 52 G4
Shakhrisabz Uzbek. see Shahrisabz
Shakhristan Tajik. see Shahriston
Shakhtinsk Kazakh. 102 D2
Shakhty Respublika Buryatiya Rus. Fed. see Gusinoozersk
Shakhty Rostovskaya Oblast' Rus. Fed. 53 I7
Shakhun'ya Rus. Fed. 52 J4
Shaki Nigeria 120 D4
Shakotan-hantō pen. Japan 90 F4
Shaktoolik AK U.S.A. 148 G2
Shalakusha Rus. Fed. 52 I3
Shalang China 97 F4
Shali Rus. Fed. 113 G2
Shaliangzi Qinghai China 94 C4
Shaliuhe Qinghai China see Gangca
Shalkar India 104 D3
Shalkar Kazakh. 102 A2
Shalkarteniz, Solonchak salt marsh Kazakh. 102 B2
Shalkode Kazakh. 98 B4
Shallow Bay N.W.T. Canada 149 M1
Shalqar Kazakh. see Shalkar
Shaluli Shan mts China 96 C2
Shaluni mt. India 105 I3
Shama r. Tanz. 123 D4
Shamāl Sīnā' governorate Egypt 107 A4
Shamâl Sînâ' governorate Egypt see Shamāl Sīnā'
Shamalzā'ī Afgh. 111 G4
Shāmat al Akbād des. Saudi Arabia 113 F5
Shamattawa Canada 151 N4
Shamattawa r. Canada 152 D3
Shambār Iran 110 C3
Shamgong Bhutan see Shemgang
Shamīl Iran 110 E5
Shāmīyah des. Iraq/Syria 107 D2
Shamkhor Azer. see Şämkir
Shamrock U.S.A. 161 C5
Shancheng Fujian China see Taining
Shancheng Shandong China see Shanxian
Shand Afgh. 111 F4
Shandan Gansu China 94 E4
Shandian He r. China 95 I3
Shandong prov. China 95 I4
Shandong Bandao pen. China 95 J4
Shandur Pass Pak. 111 I2
Shangchao China 97 F3
Shangcheng China 97 G2
Shang Chu r. China 99 E7
Shangchuan Dao i. China 97 G4
Shangdu Nei Mongol China 95 H3
Shangganling China 90 C3

▶Shanghai China 97 I2
4th most populous city in Asia and 7th in the world.

Shanghai municipality China 97 I2
Shanghe Shandong China 95 I4
Shangji China see Xichuan
Shangjie China see Yangbi
Shangjin China 97 F1
Shangkuli Nei Mongol China 95 J1
Shangluo China 97 F1
Shangmei China see Xinhua
Shangnan China 97 F1
Shangpa China see Fugong
Shangpai China see Feixi
Shangpaihe China see Feixi
Shangqiu Henan China 95 H5
Shangrao China 97 H2
Shangsanshilipu Xinjiang China 98 C3
Shangshui China 97 G1
Shangyou China 97 G3
Shangyou Shuiku resr China 98 C4
Shangyu China 97 I2
Shangzhi China 90 B3
Shangzhou Shaanxi China see Shangluo
Shangzhou Shaanxi China see Shangluo
Shanhaiguan Hebei China 95 I3
Shanhe Gansu China see Zhengning
Shanhetun China 90 B3
Shankou China 97 F4
Shankou Xinjiang China 94 C3
Shanlaragh Ireland 61 C6
Shannon airport Ireland 61 D5
Shannon est. Ireland 61 D5
Shannon r. Ireland 61 D5
Shannon, Mouth of the Ireland 61 C5
Shannon National Park Australia 135 B8
Shannon Ø i. Greenland 189 I1
Shan Plateau Myanmar 86 B2
Shanshan Xinjiang China 94 B3
Shanshanzhan Xinjiang China 94 B3
Shansi prov. China see Shanxi
Shan Teng hill H.K. China see Victoria Peak
Shantipur India 105 G5
Shantou China 97 H4
Shantung prov. China see Shandong
Shanwei China 97 G4
Shanxi prov. China 95 G4
Shanxian Shandong China 95 I5
Shanyang China 97 F1
Shanyin Shanxi China 95 H4
Shaodong China 97 F3
Shaoguan China 97 G3
Shaowu China 97 H3
Shaoxing China 97 I2
Shaoyang China 97 F3
Shap U.K. 58 E4
Shapa China 97 F4
Shaping China see Ebian
Shapinsay i. U.K. 60 G1
Shapkina r. Rus. Fed. 52 L2
Shapshal'skiy Khrebet mts Rus. Fed. 98 E2
Shaqiuhe Xinjiang China 98 E3
Shaqrā' Saudi Arabia 108 G4
Shaquanzi Xinjiang China 98 C3
Shar Kazakh. 98 C2
Shār, Jabal mt. Saudi Arabia 112 D6
Sharaf well Iraq 113 F5
Sharalday Rus. Fed. 95 F1
Sharan 111 H3
Sharan Jogizai Pak. 111 H4
Shārb Māh Iran 110 E4
Sharbulag Mongolia see Dzavhan
Shardara Kazakh. 102 C3
Shardara, Step' plain Kazakh. see Chardara, Step'
Sharga Govĭ-Altay Mongolia 94 C2
Sharga Mongolia see Tsagaan-Uul
Sharhulsan Mongolia see Mandal-Ovoo
Shari r. Cameroon/Chad see Chari
Shārī, Buḩayrat imp. l. Iraq 113 G4
Shari-dake vol. Japan 90 G4
Sharīfah Syria 107 C2
Sharjah U.A.E. 110 D5
Sharka-leb La pass Xizang China 99 E7
Sharkawshchyna Belarus 55 O9
Shark Bay Australia 135 A6
Shark Reef Australia 136 D2
Sharlyk Rus. Fed. 51 Q5
Sharm ash Shaykh Egypt 112 D6
Sharm el Sheikh Egypt see Sharm ash Shaykh
Sharon U.S.A. 164 E3
Sharon Springs U.S.A. 160 C4
Sharpe Lake Canada 151 M4
Sharp Mountain Y.T. Canada 149 M2
Sharp Peak hill H.K. China 97 [inset]
Sharqat Iraq see Ash Sharqāţ
Sharqī, Jabal ash mts Lebanon/Syria 107 B3
Sharqiy Ustyurt Chink esc. Uzbek. 102 A3
Sharur Azer. see Şärur
Shar Us Gol r. Mongolia 94 D2
Shar'ya Rus. Fed. 52 J4
Shashe r. Botswana/Zimbabwe 123 C6
Shashemenē Eth. 122 D3
Shashi China see Jingzhou
Shashubay Kazakh. 98 A3
Shasta U.S.A. 158 B1
Shasta, Mount vol. U.S.A. 156 C4
Shasta Lake U.S.A. 158 B1
Shatilki Belarus see Svyetlahorsk
Sha Tin H.K. China 97 [inset]
Shatki Rus. Fed. 53 J5
Shaţnat as Salmās, Wādī watercourse Syria 107 D2
Sha Tong Hau Shan H.K. China see Bluff Island
Shatoy Rus. Fed. 113 G2
Shatsk Rus. Fed. 53 I5
Shaţţ al 'Arab r. Iran/Iraq 113 H5
Shatura Rus. Fed. 53 H5
Shaubak Jordan see Ash Shawbak
Shaunavon Canada 151 I5
Shaver Lake U.S.A. 158 D3
Shaviovik r. AK U.S.A. 149 K1
Shaw r. Australia 134 B5
Shawan Xinjiang China 98 D3
Shawangunk Mountains hills U.S.A. 165 H3
Shawano U.S.A. 164 A1
Shawano Lake U.S.A. 164 A1
Shawinigan Canada 153 G5
Shawnee OK U.S.A. 161 D5
Shawnee WY U.S.A. 156 G4
Shawneetown U.S.A. 160 F4
Shaxian China 97 H3
Shay Gap (abandoned) Australia 134 C5
Shaykh, Jabal ash mt. Lebanon/Syria see Hermon, Mount
Shaykh Miskīn Syria 107 C3
Shaytūr Iran 110 D4
Shāzand Iran 110 C3
Shazaoyuan Gansu China 98 F5
Shaẕāẕ, Jabal mt. Saudi Arabia 113 F6
Shazud Tajik. 111 I2
Shchekino Rus. Fed. 53 H5
Shchel'yayur Rus. Fed. 52 L2
Shcherbakov Rus. Fed. see Rybinsk

Shchigry Rus. Fed. 53 H6
Shchors Ukr. 53 F6
Shchuchin Belarus see Shchuchyn
Shchuchyn Belarus 55 N10
Shebalino Rus. Fed. 102 G1
Shebekino Rus. Fed. 53 H6
Sheberghān Afgh. 111 G2
Sheboygan U.S.A. 164 B2
Shebshi Mountains Nigeria 120 E4
Shebunino Rus. Fed. 90 F3
Shecheng Hebei China see Shexian
Shediac Canada 153 I5
Shedin Peak Canada 150 E4
Shedok Rus. Fed. 113 F1
Sheelin, Lough l. Ireland 61 E4
Sheenjek r. AK U.S.A. 149 K2
Sheep Haven b. Ireland 61 E2
Sheepmoor S. Africa 125 J4
Sheep Mountain U.S.A. 159 J2
Sheep Peak U.S.A. 159 F3
Sheep's Head hd Ireland see Muntervary
Sheerness U.K. 59 H7
Sheet Harbour Canada 153 J5
Shefar'am Israel 107 B3
Sheffield N.Z. 139 D6
Sheffield U.K. 58 F5
Sheffield AL U.S.A. 163 C5
Sheffield PA U.S.A. 164 F3
Sheffield TX U.S.A. 161 C6
Sheffield Lake Canada 153 K4
Shegah Afgh. 111 G4
Shegmas Rus. Fed. 52 K2
Shehong China 96 E2
Sheikh, Jebel esh mt. Lebanon/Syria see Hermon, Mount
Sheikhpura India 105 F4
Sheikhupura Pak. 111 I4
Shekak r. Canada 152 D4
Shekār Āb Iran 110 D3
Shekhawati reg. India 111 I5
Shekhem West Bank see Nāblus
Shekhpura India see Sheikhpura
Sheki Azer. see Şäki
Shekka Ch'ün-Tao H.K. China see Soko Islands
Shek Kwu Chau i. H.K. China 97 [inset]
Shekou China 97 [inset]
Sheksna Rus. Fed. 52 H4
Sheksninskoye Vodokhranilishche resr Rus. Fed. 52 H4
Shek Uk Shan mt. H.K. China 97 [inset]
Shela Xizang China 99 F7
Shelagskiy, Mys pt Rus. Fed. 77 S2
Shelbina U.S.A. 160 E4
Shelburn U.S.A. 164 B4
Shelburne N.S. Canada 153 I6
Shelburne Ont. Canada 164 E1
Shelburne Bay Australia 136 C1
Shelby MI U.S.A. 164 B2
Shelby MS U.S.A. 161 F5
Shelby MT U.S.A. 156 F2
Shelby NC U.S.A. 163 D5
Shelbyville IL U.S.A. 160 F4
Shelbyville IN U.S.A. 164 C4
Shelbyville KY U.S.A. 164 C4
Shelbyville TN U.S.A. 162 C5
Sheldon IA U.S.A. 160 E3
Sheldon IL U.S.A. 164 B3
Sheldon Point AK U.S.A. 148 F3
Sheldrake Canada 153 I4
Shelek Kazakh. see Chilik
Shelikhova, Zaliv g. Rus. Fed. 77 Q3
Shelikof Strait AK U.S.A. 148 I4
Shell U.S.A. 160 B2
Shellbrook Canada 151 J4
Shelley U.S.A. 156 E4
Shellharbour Australia 138 E5
Shell Lake Canada 151 J4
Shell Lake U.S.A. 160 F2
Shell Mountain U.S.A. 158 B1
Shelter Bay Canada see Port-Cartier
Shelter Island U.S.A. 165 I3
Shelter Point N.Z. 139 B8
Shelton U.S.A. 156 C3
Shemakha Azer. see Şamaxı
Shemgang Bhutan 105 G4
Shemonaikha Kazakh. 98 C2
Shemordan Rus. Fed. 52 K4
Shenandoah IA U.S.A. 160 E3
Shenandoah PA U.S.A. 165 G3
Shenandoah Mountains U.S.A. 164 F4
Shenandoah National Park U.S.A. 165 F4
Shenchi Shanxi China 95 H4
Shendam Nigeria 120 D4
Shending Shan hill China 90 D3
Shengel'dy Almatinskaya Oblast' Kazakh. 98 B3
Shengena mt. Tanz. 123 D4
Shengli China 97 G2
Shengli Daban pass Xinjiang China 98 D4
Shengli Feng mt. China/Kyrg. see Jengish Chokusu
Shengli Qichang Xinjiang China 98 B4
Shengli Shibachang Xinjiang China 98 C4
Shengping China 90 B3
Shengrenjian Shanxi China see Pinglu
Shengsi China 97 I2
Shengsi Liedao is China 97 I2
Shenjiamen China 97 I2
Shen Khan Bandar Afgh. 111 H2
Shenkursk Rus. Fed. 52 I3
Shenmu Shaanxi China 95 G4
Shennong Ding mt. China 97 F2
Shennongjia China 97 F2
Shenqiu China 97 G1
Shenshu China 90 C3
Shensi prov. China see Shaanxi
Shentala Rus. Fed. 53 K5
Shenton, Mount hill Australia 135 C7
Shenxian Hebei China see Shenzhou
Shenxian Shandong China 95 H4
Shenyang Liaoning China 95 J3
Shenzhen China 97 G4
Shenzhen Wan b. H.K. China see Deep Bay
Shenzhou Hebei China 95 H4
Sheopur India 104 D4
Shepetivka Ukr. 53 E6
Shepetovka Ukr. see Shepetivka
Shepherd Islands Vanuatu 133 G3
Shepherdsville U.S.A. 164 C5
Shepparton Australia 138 B6
Sheppey, Isle of i. U.K. 59 H7
Sheqi China 97 G1
Sherabad Uzbek. see Sherobod
Sherborne U.K. 59 E8
Sherbro Island Sierra Leone 120 B4
Sherbrooke Canada 153 H5
Sherburne U.S.A. 165 H2
Shercock Ireland 61 F4
Shereiq Sudan 108 D6
Shergaon India 105 H4
Shergarh India 104 C4
Sheridan AR U.S.A. 161 E5
Sheridan WY U.S.A. 156 G3
Sheringham U.K. 59 I6
Sherlovaya Gora Rus. Fed. 95 I1
Sherman U.S.A. 161 D5
Sherman Mountain U.S.A. 159 F1
Sherobod Uzbek. 111 G2
Sherpur Dhaka Bangl. 105 G4
Sherpur Rajshahi Bangl. 105 G4
Sherridon Canada 151 K4
's-Hertogenbosch Neth. 62 F3
Sherwood Forest reg. U.K. 59 F5
Sherwood Lake Canada 151 K2
Sheslay B.C. Canada 149 O4
Sheslay r. B.C. Canada 149 N4
Shethanei Lake Canada 151 L3
Shetland Islands is U.K. 60 [inset]
Shetpe Kazakh. 100 E2
Sheung Shui H.K. China 97 [inset]
Sheung Sze Mun sea chan. H.K. China 97 [inset]
Shevchenko Kazakh. see Aktau
Shevli r. Rus. Fed. 90 D1
Shexian China 97 H2
Shexian Hebei China 95 H4
Sheyang China 97 I1
Sheyenne r. U.S.A. 160 D2
Shey Phoksundo National Park Nepal 105 E3
Shiant Islands U.K. 60 C3
Shiashkotan, Ostrov i. Rus. Fed. 77 Q5
Shibakawa Japan 93 E3
Shibām Yemen 108 G6
Shibandong Jing well China 94 C3
Shiban Jing well China 94 D3
Shibaocheng Gansu China 94 D4
Shibar, Kowtal-e Afgh. 111 H3
Shibata Japan 91 E5
Shibayama Japan 93 G3
Shibayama-gata l. Japan 92 C2
Shibazhan China 90 B1
Shibh Jazīrat Sīnā' pen. Egypt see Sinai
Shibīn al Kawm Egypt 112 C5
Shibîn el Kôm Egypt see Shibīn al Kawm
Shibogama Lake Canada 152 C3
Shibotsu-jima i. Rus. Fed. see Zelenyy, Ostrov
Shibukawa Japan 93 F2
Shibu-tōge pass Japan 93 E2
Shibutsu-san mt. Japan 93 F2
Shicheng Fujian China see Zhouning
Shicheng Jiangxi China 97 H3
Shicheng Dao i. China 95 J4
Shichimen-zan mt. Japan 93 E3
Shicun Shanxi China see Xiangfen
Shidād al Mismā' hill Saudi Arabia 107 D4
Shidao Shandong China 95 J4
Shidao Wan b. China 95 J4
Shidian China 96 C3
Shidongsi Gansu China see Gaolan
Shiel, Loch l. U.K. 60 D4
Shield, Cape Australia 136 B2
Shīeli Kazakh. see Chiili
Shifa, Jabal ash mts Saudi Arabia 112 D5
Shifang China 96 E2
Shiga Nagano Japan 93 D2
Shiga Shiga Japan 92 B3
Shiga pref. Japan 92 B3
Shigaraki Japan 92 C4
Shigatse Xizang China see Xigazê
Shigong Gansu China 98 F4
Shiguai Nei Mongol China 95 G3
Shiguaigou Nei Mongol China see Shiguai
Shīḥān mt. Jordan 107 B4
Shihezi Xinjiang China 98 D3
Shihkiachwang Hebei China see Shijiazhuang
Shijiao China see Fogang
Shijiazhuang Hebei China 95 H4
Shijiu Hu l. China 97 H2
Shijiusuo Shandong China see Rizhao
Shika Japan 92 C1
Shikag Lake Canada 152 C4
Shikar r. Pak. 111 F4
Shikarpur Pak. 111 H5
Shikengkong mt. China 97 G3
Shikhany Rus. Fed. 53 J5
Shiki Japan 93 F3
Shikine-jima i. Japan 93 F4
Shikishima Japan 93 E3
Shikohabad India 104 D4
Shikoku i. Japan 91 D6
Shikoku-sanchi mts Japan 91 D6
Shikotan, Ostrov i. Rus. Fed. 90 G4
Shikotan-tō i. Rus. Fed. see Shikotan, Ostrov
Shikotsu-Tōya Kokuritsu-kōen Japan 90 F4
Shildon U.K. 58 F4
Shilega Rus. Fed. 52 J2
Shilianghe Shuiku resr China 95 I5
Shiliguri India 105 G4
Shilin China 96 D3
Shilipu China 97 G2
Shiliu China see Changjiang
Shilla mt. India 104 D2
Shillelagh Ireland 61 F5
Shillo r. Israel 107 B3
Shillong India 105 G4
Shilou Shanxi China 95 G4
Shilovo Rus. Fed. 53 I5
Shilüüstey Mongolia 94 D2
Shima Japan 92 C4
Shima spring Japan 93 E2
Shimada Japan 93 E4
Shimagahara Japan 92 C4
Shima-hantō pen. Japan 92 C4
Shimamoto Japan 92 B4
Shimanovsk Rus. Fed. 90 B1
Shimbiris mt. Somalia 122 E2
Shimen Gansu China 96 D1
Shimen Hunan China 97 F2
Shimen Yunnan China see Yunlong
Shimizu Fukui Japan 92 C2
Shimizu Shizuoka Japan 93 E3
Shimizu Shizuoka Japan 93 E3
Shimizu Wakayama Japan 92 B4
Shimla India 104 D3
Shimminato Japan see Shinminato
Shimo Japan 92 D2
Shimobe Japan 93 E3
Shimoda Japan 93 E4
Shimodate Japan 93 F2
Shimofusa Japan 93 G3
Shimoga India 106 B3
Shimoichi Japan 92 B4
Shimojō Japan 93 D3
Shimokita-hantō pen. Japan 90 F4
Shimokitayama Japan 92 B4
Shimoni Kenya 123 D4
Shimonita Japan 93 E2
Shimonoseki Japan 91 C6
Shimosuwa Japan 93 E2
Shimotsu Japan 92 B4
Shimotsuma Japan 93 F2
Shimoyama Japan 92 D3
Shimsk Rus. Fed. 52 F4
Shin Japan 93 F2
Shin, Loch l. U.K. 60 E2
Shināfīyah Iraq see Ash Shanāfīyah
Shinan China see Xingye
Shinano Japan 93 E2
Shin-asahi Japan 92 C3
Shīndand Afgh. 111 F3
Shine-Ider Hövsgöl Mongolia 94 D1
Shinejinst Mongolia 94 D2
Shingbwiyang Myanmar 86 B1
Shing-gai Myanmar 86 B1
Shinghshal Pass Pak. 111 I2
Shingletown U.S.A. 158 C1
Shingozha Kazakh. 98 C3
Shingū Japan 91 E6
Shingwedzi S. Africa 125 J2
Shingwedzi r. S. Africa 125 J2
Shīnkāy Afgh. 111 G4
Shīnkay Ghar Afgh. 111 H3
Shinminato Japan 92 D2
Shinnston U.S.A. 164 E4
Shino-jima i. Japan 92 C4
Shinonoi Japan 93 E2
Shinsei Japan 92 C3
Shinshār Syria 107 C2
Shinshiro Japan 92 D4
Shinshūshin Japan 93 E2
Shintō Japan 93 E2
Shintone Japan 93 G3
Shinyanga Tanz. 122 D4
Shio Japan 92 C2
Shiobara Japan 93 F2
Shiocton U.S.A. 164 A1
Shiogama Japan 91 F5
Shiojiri Japan 93 D2
Shiomi-dake mt. Japan 93 E3
Shiono-misaki c. Japan 91 D6
Shioya Japan 93 F2
Shioya-zaki pt Japan 93 G1
Shiozawa Japan 93 E1
Shipai China 97 H2
Shiping China 96 D4
Shipki Pass China/India 99 B7
Shipman U.S.A. 165 F5
Shippegan Island Canada 153 I5
Shippensburg U.S.A. 165 G3
Shippō Japan 92 C3
Shiprock U.S.A. 159 I3
Shiprock Peak U.S.A. 159 I3
Shipu Shaanxi China see Huanglong
Shipu China 97 I2
Shipunovo Rus. Fed. 88 E2
Shiqian China 97 F3
Shiqiao China see Panyu
Shiqizhen China see Zhongshan
Shiquan China 97 F1
Shiquanhe Xizang China see Gar
Shiquanhe Xizang China see Ali
Shiquan He r. China 104 D2 see Indus
Shiquan Shuiku resr China 97 F1
Shira Rus. Fed. 88 F2
Shīrābād Iran 110 C2
Shirahama Chiba Japan 93 F4
Shirai-san hill Japan 92 C4
Shirakawa Fukushima Japan 93 G1
Shirakawa Gifu Japan 92 C2
Shirakawa Gifu Japan 92 D3
Shirakawa-go and Gokayama tourist site Japan 91 E5
Shirake-mine mt. Japan 92 D2
Shirako Japan 93 G3
Shirakura-yama mt. Japan 92 D3
Shirama-yama hill Japan 92 B4
Shiramine Japan 92 C2
Shirane Japan 93 E3
Shirane-san mt. Japan 93 E2
Shirane-san mt. Japan 93 E3
Shirane-san vol. Japan 93 F2
Shirasawa Japan 93 F2
Shirase Coast Antarctica 188 J1
Shirase Glacier Antarctica 188 D2
Shīrāz Iran 110 D4
Shire r. Malawi 123 D5
Shireet Mongolia see Bayandelger
Shireza Pak. 111 G5
Shirīn Tagāb Afgh. 111 G2
Shiriya-zaki c. Japan 90 F4
Shirkala reg. Kazakh. 102 A2
Shīr Kūh mt. Iran 110 D4
Shiroi Japan 93 G3
Shirokura-yama mt. Japan 93 D3
Shiroro Reservoir Nigeria 120 D3
Shirotori Japan 92 C3
Shirouma-dake mt. Japan 92 D2
Shiroyama Japan 93 F3
Shirpur India 104 C5
Shirten Holoy Gobi des. China 94 D3
Shīrvān Iran 110 E2
Shisanjianfang Xinjiang China 94 B3
Shisanzhan China 90 B2
Shishaldin Volcano U.S.A. 146 B4
Shisha Pangma mt. Xizang China see Xixabangma Feng
Shishmaref AK U.S.A. 148 F2
Shishmaref Inlet AK U.S.A. 148 F2
Shishou China 97 G2
Shisui Japan 93 G3
Shitan China 97 G3
Shitang China 97 I2
Shitanjing Ningxia China 94 F4
Shitara Japan 92 D3
Shithāthah Iraq 113 F4
Shiv India 104 B4
Shiveluch, Sopka vol. Rus. Fed. 77 R4
Shivpuri India 104 D4
Shivwits U.S.A. 159 G3
Shivwits Plateau U.S.A. 159 G3
Shiwan Shaanxi China 95 G4
Shiwan Dashan mts China 96 E4
Shiwa Ngandu Zambia 123 D5
Shixing China 97 G3
Shiyan China 97 F1
Shizhu China 97 F2
Shizi Gansu China 95 F5
Shizilu Shandong China see Junan
Shizipu China 97 H2
Shizong China 96 D3
Shizuishan Ningxia China 94 F4
Shizuishanzhan Ningxia China 94 F4
Shizuoka Japan 93 E4
Shizuoka pref. Japan 93 E4
▶Shkhara mt. Georgia/Rus. Fed. 113 F2
3rd highest mountain in Europe.
Shklov Belarus see Shklow
Shklow Belarus 53 F5
Shkodër Albania 69 H3
Shkodra Albania see Shkodër
Shkodrës, Liqeni i l. Albania/Montenegro see Scutari, Lake
Shmidta, Ostrov i. Rus. Fed. 76 K1
Shmidta, Poluostrov pen. Rus. Fed. 90 F1
Shoal Lake Canada 151 K5
Shoals U.S.A. 164 B4
Shōbara Japan 91 D6
Shōgawa Japan 92 D2
Shō-gawa r. Japan 92 D2
Shoh Tajik. 111 H2
Shohi Pass Pak. see Tal Pass
Shokanbetsu-dake mt. Japan 90 F4
Shōkawa Japan 92 C2
Sholakkorgan Kazakh. 102 C3
Sholapur India see Solapur
Sholaqorghan Kazakh. see Sholakkorgan
Shomba r. Rus. Fed. 54 R4
Shomvukva Rus. Fed. 52 K3
Shōmyō-gawa r. Japan 92 D2
Shona Ridge sea feature S. Atlantic Ocean 184 I9
Shonzha Kazakh. see Chundzha
Shor India 104 D2
Shorap Pak. 111 G5
Shorapur India 106 C2
Shorawak reg. Afgh. 111 G4
Sho'rchi Uzbek. 111 G2
Shorewood IL U.S.A. 164 A3
Shorewood WI U.S.A. 164 B2
Shorkot Pak. 111 I4
Shorkozakhly, Solonchak salt flat Turkm. 113 J2
Shoshone CA U.S.A. 158 E4
Shoshone ID U.S.A. 156 E4
Shoshone r. U.S.A. 156 F3
Shoshone Mountains U.S.A. 158 E2
Shoshone Peak U.S.A. 158 E3
Shoshong Botswana 125 H2
Shoshoni U.S.A. 156 F4
Shostka Ukr. 53 G6
Shotor Khūn Afgh. 111 G3
Shouguang Shandong China 95 I4
Shouyang Shanxi China 95 H4
Shouyang Shan mt. China 97 F1
Shōwa Japan 93 F2
Showak Sudan 108 E7
Show Low U.S.A. 159 H4
Shoyna Rus. Fed. 52 J2
Shpakovskoye Rus. Fed. 113 F1
Shpola Ukr. 53 F6
Shqipëria country Europe see Albania
Shreve U.S.A. 164 D3
Shreveport U.S.A. 161 E5
Shrewsbury U.K. 59 E6
Shri Lanka country Asia see Sri Lanka
Shri Mohangarh India 104 B4
Shrirampur India 105 G5
Shu Kazakh. 102 D3
Shū r. Kazakh./Kyrg. see Chu
Shu'ab, Ra's pt Yemen 109 H7
Shuajingsi China 96 D2
Shuangbai China 96 D3
Shuangcheng Fujian China see Zherong
Shuangcheng Heilong. China 90 B3
Shuanghe China 97 G2
Shuanghechang China 96 E2
Shuanghedagang China 90 C2
Shuanghu Xizang China 99 D6
Shuanghuyu Shaanxi China see Zizhou
Shuangjiang Guizhou China see Jiangkou
Shuangjiang Hunan China see Tongdao
Shuangjiang Yunnan China see Eshan
Shuangliao Jilin China 95 J3
Shuangliu China 96 D2
Shuangpai China 97 F3
Shuangshanzi Hebei China 95 I3
Shuangshipu China see Fengxian
Shuangxi China see Shunchang
Shuangyang China 90 B4
Shuangyashan China 90 C3
Shubarkuduk Kazakh. 102 A2
Shubayḥ well Saudi Arabia 107 D4
Shublik Mountains AK U.S.A. 149 K1
Shufu Xinjiang China 98 A5
Shugozero Rus. Fed. 52 G4
Shu He r. China 95 I5
Shuicheng China see Lupanshui
Shuiding Xinjiang China see Huocheng
Shuidong China see Dianbai
Shuiji Shandong China see Laixi
Shuijing China 96 E1
Shuijingkuang Qinghai China 99 E6
Shuikou China 97 F3
Shuikouguan China 96 E4
Shuikoushan China 97 G3
Shuiluocheng Gansu China see Zhuanglang
Shuiquan Gansu China 94 F4
Shuiquanzi Gansu China 94 E4
Shuizhai China see Wuhua
Shuizhan Qinghai China 99 E5
Shulakpachak Peak AK U.S.A. 148 I2
Shulan China 90 B3
Shule Xinjiang China 98 B5
Shulehe Gansu China 98 G4
Shule He r. China 94 C3
Shule Nanshan mts China 94 D4
Shulinzhao Nei Mongol China 95 G3
Shulu Hebei China see Xinji
Shumagin Islands AK U.S.A. 148 G5
Shumba Zimbabwe 123 C5
Shumen Bulg. 69 L3
Shumerlya Rus. Fed. 52 J5
Shumilina Belarus 53 F5
Shumyachi Rus. Fed. 53 G5
Shunchang China 97 H3
Shuncheng China 90 A4
Shunde China 97 G4
Shungnak AK U.S.A. 148 H2
Shunyi Beijing China 95 I3
Shuoxian Shanxi China see Shuozhou
Shuozhou Shanxi China 95 H4
Shuqrah Yemen 108 G7
Shūr r. Iran 110 D4
Shūr r. Iran 111 F3
Shūr watercourse Iran 110 D5
Shur watercourse Iran 110 E3
Shūr, Rūd-e watercourse Iran 110 E4
Shūr Āb watercourse Iran 110 D4
Shūrjestān Iran 110 D4
Shūrū Iran 111 F4
Shuryshkarskiy Sor, Ozero l. Rus. Fed. 51 T2
Shūsh Iran 110 C3
Shusha Azer. see Şuşa
Shushtar Iran 110 C3
Shutfah, Qalamat well Saudi Arabia 110 D6
Shuwaysh, Tall ash hill Jordan 107 C4
Shuya Ivanovskaya Oblast' Rus. Fed. 52 I4
Shuya Respublika Kareliya Rus. Fed. 52 G3
Shuyak Island AK U.S.A. 148 I4
Shuyang Jiangsu China 95 I5
Shuyskoye Rus. Fed. 52 I4
Shuzenji Japan 93 E4
Shwebo Myanmar 86 A2
Shwedwin Myanmar 86 A1
Shwegun Myanmar 86 B3
Shwegyin Myanmar 86 B3
Shweudaung mt. Myanmar 86 B2
Shyghanaq Kazakh. see Chiganak
Shygys Konyrat Kazakh. 98 A3
Shymkent Kazakh. 102 C3
Shyok r. India 99 A6
Shyok India 104 D2
Shypuvate Ukr. 53 H6
Shyroke Ukr. 53 G7
Sia Indon. 81 I8
Siabu Sumatera Indon. 84 B2
Siachen Glacier India/Pak. 99 B6
Siahan Range mts Pak. 111 F5
Sīāh Chashmeh Iran 110 B2
Siahgird Afgh. 111 G2
Siah Koh mts Afgh. 111 G3
Siak r. Indon. 84 C2
Siak Sri Inderapura Sumatera Indon. 84 C2
Sialkot Pak. 111 I3
Siam country Asia see Thailand
Sian Shaanxi China see Xi'an
Sian Rus. Fed. 90 B1
Siang r. India see Brahmaputra
Siantan i. Indon. 84 D2
Siargao i. Phil. 82 D4
Siasi Phil. 82 C5
Siasi i. Phil. 82 C5
Siaton Negros Phil. 82 C4
Siau i. Indon. 83 C2
Šiauliai Lith. 55 M9
Siayan i. Phil. 97 I4
Siazan' Azer. see Siyäzän
Si Bai, Lam r. Thai. 86 D4
Sibasa S. Africa 125 J2
Sibati Xinjiang China see Xibet
Sibay i. Phil. 82 C4
Sibayi, Lake S. Africa 125 K4
Sibda China 96 C2
Šibenik Croatia 68 F3
Siberia reg. Rus. Fed. 77 M3
Siberut i. Indon. 84 B3
Siberut, Selat sea chan. Indon. 84 B3
Siberut, Taman Nasional nat. park Indon. 84 B3
Sibi Pak. 111 G4
Sibidiri P.N.G. 81 K8
Sibigo Indon. 84 A2
Sibiloi National Park Kenya 122 D3
Sibir' reg. Rus. Fed. see Siberia
Sibiti Congo 122 B4
Sibiu Romania 69 K2
Sibley U.S.A. 160 E3
Siboa Sulawesi Indon. 83 B2
Sibolga Sumatera Indon. 84 B2
Siborongborong Sumatera Indon. 84 B2
Sibsagar India 105 H4
Sibu Sarawak Malaysia 85 E2
Sibuco Mindanao Phil. 82 C5
Sibuco Bay Mindanao Phil. 82 C5
Sibuguey r. Mindanao Phil. 82 C5
Sibuguey Bay Mindanao Phil. 82 C5
Sibut Cent. Afr. Rep. 122 B3
Sibuti Sarawak Malaysia 85 F1
Sibutu i. Phil. 82 B5
Sibutu Passage Phil. 82 B5
Sibuyan i. Phil. 82 C3
Sibuyan Sea Phil. 82 C3
Sicamous Canada 150 G5
Sicapoo mt. Luzon Phil. 82 C2
Sicayac Mindanao Phil. 82 C4
Sicca Veneria Tunisia see Le Kef
Siccus watercourse Australia 137 B6
Sicheng Anhui China see Sixian
Sicheng Guangxi China see Lingyun
Sichon Thai. 87 B5
Sichuan prov. China 96 D2
Sichuan Pendi basin China 96 E2
Sicié, Cap c. France 66 G5
Sicilia i. Italy see Sicily
Sicilian Channel Italy/Tunisia 68 E6
Sicily i. Italy 68 F5
Sicuani Peru 176 D6
Sidangoli Halmahera Indon. 83 C2
Siddhapur India 104 C5
Siddipet India 106 C2
Sidenreng, Danau l. Indon. 83 A3
Sideros, Akra pt Kriti Greece see Sideros, Akrotirio
Sideros, Akrotirio pt Greece 69 L7
Sidesaviwa S. Africa 124 F7
Sidhauli India 104 E4
Sidhi India 105 E4
Sidhpur India see Siddhapur
Sidi Aïssa Alg. 67 H6
Sidi Ali Alg. 67 G5
Sīdī Barrānī Egypt 112 B5
Sidi Bel Abbès Alg. 67 F6
Sidi Bennour Morocco 64 C5
Sidi Bou Sa'id Tunisia see Sidi Bouzid
Sidi Bouzid Tunisia 68 C7
Sidi el Barráni Egypt see Sīdī Barrānī
Sidi El Hani, Sebkhet de salt pan Tunisia 68 D7
Sidi Ifni Morocco 120 B2
Sidi Kacem Morocco 64 C5
Sidikalang Sumatera Indon. 84 B2
Sidi Khaled Alg. 64 E5
Sid Lake Canada 151 J2
Sidlaw Hills U.K. 60 F4
Sidley, Mount Antarctica 188 J1
Sidli India 105 G4
Sidmouth U.K. 59 D8
Sidney IA U.S.A. 160 E3
Sidney MT U.S.A. 156 G3
Sidney NE U.S.A. 160 C3
Sidney OH U.S.A. 164 C3
Sidney Lanier, Lake U.S.A. 163 D5
Sidoan Sulawesi Indon. 83 B2
Sidoan Sulawesi Indon. 83 B2
Sidoarjo Jawa Indon. 85 F4
Sidoktaya Myanmar 86 A2
Sidon Lebanon 107 B3
Sidr Egypt see Sudr
Siedlce Poland 53 D5
Sieg r. Germany 63 H4
Siegen Germany 63 I4
Siĕmréab Cambodia 87 C4
Siem Reap Cambodia see Siĕmréab
Si'en China see Huanjiang
Siena Italy 68 D3
Sieradz Poland 57 Q5
Si'erdingka Xizang China 99 F7
Sierra Blanca U.S.A. 157 G7
Sierra Colorada Arg. 178 C6
Sierra Grande Arg. 178 C6
Sierra Leone country Africa 120 B4
Sierra Leone Basin sea feature N. Atlantic Ocean 184 G5
Sierra Leone Rise sea feature N. Atlantic Ocean 184 G5
Sierra Madre Mountains U.S.A. 158 C4
Sierra Mojada Mex. 166 E3
Sierra Nevada, Parque Nacional nat. park Venez. 176 D2
Sierra Nevada de Santa Marta, Parque Nacional nat. park Col. 176 D1
Sierraville U.S.A. 158 C2
Sierra Vista U.S.A. 157 F7
Sierre Switz. 66 H3
Sievi Fin. 54 N5
Sifang Ling mts China 96 E4
Sifangtai China 90 B3
Sīfenī Eth. 122 E2
Sifnos i. Greece 69 K6
Sig Alg. 67 F6
Sigep, Tanjung pt Indon. 84 B3
Sigguup Nunaa pen. Greenland 147 M2
Sighetu Marmaţiei Romania 53 D7
Sighişoara Romania 69 K1

Siglap Sing. 87 [inset]
Sigli Sumatera Indon. 84 A1
Siglufjörður Iceland 54 [inset]
Sigma Panay Phil. 82 C4
Signal de Botrange hill Belgium 62 G4
Signal de la Ste-Baume mt. France 66 G5
Signal Peak U.S.A. 159 F5
Signy-l'Abbaye France 62 E5
Sigoisooinan Indon. 84 B3
Sigourney U.S.A. 160 E3
Sigri, Akra pt Voreio Aigaio Greece see Saratsina, Akrotirio
Sigsbee Deep sea feature G. of Mexico 187 N4
Siguatepeque Hond. 167 I6
Sigüenza Spain 67 E3
Siguiri Guinea 120 C3
Sigulda Latvia 55 N8
Sigurd U.S.A. 159 H2
Sihanoukville Cambodia 87 C5
Sihaung Myauk Myanmar 86 A2
Sihawa India 106 D1
Sihong China 97 H1
Sihora India 104 E5
Sihou Shandong China see Changdao
Sihui China 97 G4
Siikajoki Fin. 54 N4
Siilinjärvi Fin. 54 O5
Siirt Turkey 113 F3
Sijawal Pak. 104 B4
Sijunjung Sumatera Indon. 84 C3
Sikaka Saudi Arabia see Sakākah
Sikakap Indon. 84 C3
Sikandra Rao India 104 D4
Sikanni Chief Canada 150 F3
Sikanni Chief r. Canada 150 F3
Sikar India 104 C4
Sikaram mt. Afgh. 111 H3
Sikasso Mali 120 C3
Sikaw Myanmar 86 B2
Sikeli Sulawesi Indon. 83 B4
Sikeston U.S.A. 161 F4
Sikhote-Alin' mts Rus. Fed. 90 D4
Sikhote-Alinskiy Zapovednik nature res. Rus. Fed. 90 E3
Sikinos i. Greece 69 K6
Sikka India 104 B5
Sikkim state India 105 G4
Siknik Cape AK U.S.A. 148 E3
Siko i. Maluku Indon. 83 C2
Siksjö Sweden 54 J4
Sikuaishi Liaoning China 95 J4
Sikuati Sabah Malaysia 85 G1
Sil r. Spain 67 C2
Şila' i. Saudi Arabia 112 D6
Šilalė Lith. 55 M9
Si Lanna National Park Thai. 86 B3
Sila Point Samar Phil. 82 D3
Silas U.S.A. 161 F6
Silavatturai Sri Lanka 106 C4
Silawaih Agam vol. Indon. 84 A1
Silay Negros Phil. 82 C4
Silberberg hill Germany 63 J1
Silchar India 105 H4
Şile Turkey 69 M4
Sileru r. India 106 D2
Silesia reg. Czech Rep./Poland 57 P5
Sileti r. Kazakh. 88 C2
Siletiteniz, Ozero salt l. Kazakh. 101 G1
Silghat India 105 H4
Siliana Tunisia 68 C6
Silifke Turkey 107 A1
Siliguri India see Shiliguri
Siling Co salt l. China 99 E7
Silipur India 104 D4
Silistra Bulg. 69 L2
Silistria Bulg. see Silistra
Silivri Turkey 69 M4
Siljan l. Sweden 55 I6
Silkeborg Denmark 55 F8
Sillajhuay mt. Chile 176 E7
Sillamäe Estonia 55 O7
Sille Turkey 112 D3
Silli India 105 F5
Sillod India 106 B1
Silobela S. Africa 125 J4
Silsbee TX U.S.A. 167 G2
Silsby Lake Canada 151 M4
Silt U.S.A. 159 J2
Siltaharju Fin. 54 O3
Siluas Kalimantan Indon. 85 E2
Silūp r. Iran 111 F5
Šilutė Lith. 55 L9
Silvan Turkey 113 F3
Silvânia Brazil 179 A2
Silvassa India 106 B1
Silver Bank Passage Turks and Caicos Is 169 J4
Silver Bay U.S.A. 160 F2
Silver City NM U.S.A. 159 I5
Silver City NV U.S.A. 158 D2
Silver City (abandoned) Y.T. Canada 149 M3
Silver Creek r. U.S.A. 159 H4
Silver Lake U.S.A. 156 C4
Silver Lake l. U.S.A. 158 E4
Silvermine Mts hills Ireland 61 D5
Silver Peak Range mts U.S.A. 158 E3
Silver Spring U.S.A. 165 G4
Silver Springs U.S.A. 158 D2
Silverthrone Mountain Canada 150 E5
Silvertip Mountain Canada 150 F5
Silverton U.K. 59 D8
Silverton CO U.S.A. 159 J3
Silverton TX U.S.A. 161 C5
Silvituc Mex. 167 H5
Sima Xizang China 99 E7
Simao China 96 D4
Simara i. Phil. 82 C3
Simard, Lac l. Canada 152 F5
Simaria India 105 F4
Simatang i. Indon. 83 B2
Simav Turkey 69 M5
Simav Dağları mts Turkey 69 M5
Simawat Xinjiang China 99 C5
Simba Dem. Rep. Congo 122 C3
Simbirsk Rus. Fed. see Ul'yanovsk
Simcoe Canada 164 E2
Simcoe, Lake Canada 164 F1
Simdega India 106 E1
Simēn mts Eth. 122 D2
Simēn Mountains Eth. see Simēn
Simeonof Island AK U.S.A. 148 H5
Simeulue i. Indon. 84 B2
Simferopol' Ukr. 112 D1
Sími i. Greece see Symi
Simikot Nepal 105 E3
Similan, Ko i. Thai. 87 B5
Simi Valley U.S.A. 158 D4
Simla India see Shimla
Simla U.S.A. 156 G5
Şimleu Silvaniei Romania 69 J1
Simmerath Germany 62 G4
Simmern (Hunsrück) Germany 63 H5
Simmesport U.S.A. 161 F6
Simms U.S.A. 156 F3
Simojärvi l. Fin. 54 O3
Simon Mex. 161 C7
Simonette r. Canada 150 G4
Simon Wash watercourse U.S.A. 159 I5
Simoom Sound Canada 150 E5
Simoon Sound Canada see Simoom Sound
Simpang Sumatera Indon. 84 D3
Simpang Mangayau, Tanjung pt Malaysia 80 F5
Simplício Mendes Brazil 177 J5
Simplon Pass Switz. 66 I3
Simpson Canada 151 J5
Simpson U.S.A. 156 F2
Simpson Desert Australia 136 B5
Simpson Desert National Park Australia 136 B5
Simpson Desert Regional Reserve nature res. Australia 137 B5
Simpson Islands Canada 151 H2
Simpson Lake N.W.T. Canada 149 P1
Simpson Park Mountains U.S.A. 158 E2
Simpson Peninsula Canada 147 J3
Simrishamn Sweden 55 I9
Simuk i. Indon. 84 B3
Simulubek Indon. 84 B3
Simunjan Sarawak Malaysia 85 E2
Simunul i. Phil. 82 B5
Simushir, Ostrov i. Rus. Fed. 89 S3
Sina r. India 106 B2
Sinabang Indon. 84 B2
Sinabung vol. Indon. 84 B2
Sinai pen. Egypt 107 A5
Sinai, Mont hill France 62 E5
Sinai al Janûbîya governorate Egypt see Janūb Sīnā'
Sinai ash Shamâlîya governorate Egypt see Shamāl Sīnā'
Si Nakarin, Ang Kep Nam Thai. 86 B4
Sinaloa state Mex. 157 F8
Sinalunga Italy 68 D3
Sinan China 97 F3
Sinancha Rus. Fed. see Cheremshany
Sinbo Myanmar 86 B1
Sinbyubyin Myanmar 87 B4
Sinbyugyun Myanmar 86 A2
Sincan Turkey 112 E3
Sincelejo Col. 176 C2
Sinchu Taiwan see T'aoyüan
Sinclair Mills Canada 150 F4
Sincora, Serra do hills Brazil 179 C1
Sind r. India 104 D4
Sind Pak. see Thul
Sind prov. Pak. see Sindh
Sinda Rus. Fed. 90 E2
Sindañgan Mindanao Phil. 82 C4
Sindangan Bay Mindanao Phil. 82 C4
Sindangbarang Jawa Indon. 84 D4
Sindari India 104 B4
Sindeh, Teluk b. Flores Indon. 83 B5
Sindelfingen Germany 63 I6
Sindh prov. Pak. 111 H5
Sindhuli Garhi Nepal 105 F4
Sindhulimadi Nepal see Sindhuli Garhi
Sındırgı Turkey 69 M5
Sindor Rus. Fed. 52 K3
Sindou Burkina 120 C3
Sindri India 105 F5
Sind Sagar Doab lowland Pak. 111 H4
Sinel'nikovo Ukr. see Synel'nykove
Sines Port. 67 B5
Sines, Cabo de c. Port. 67 B5
Sinettä Fin. 54 N3
Sinfra Côte d'Ivoire 120 C4
Sing Myanmar 86 B2
Singa Sudan 108 D7
Singanallur India 106 C4
Singapore country Asia 84 D2

▶Singapore Sing. 87 [inset]
Capital of Singapore.

Singapore r. Sing. 87 [inset]
Singapore, Strait of Indon./Sing. 87 [inset]
Singapura country Asia see Singapore
Singapura Sing. see Singapore
Singapura Sing. see Singapore
Singapuru India 106 D2
Singaraja Bali Indon. 85 F5
Sing Buri Thai. 86 C4
Singgimtay Xinjiang China 98 E4
Singhampton Canada 164 E1
Singhana India 104 C3
Singida Tanz. 123 D4
Singidunum Serbia see Belgrade
Singim Xinjiang China see Singgimtay
Singkaling Hkamti Myanmar 86 A1
Singkang Sulawesi Indon. 83 B4
Singkarak Sumatera Indon. 84 C3
Singkawang Kalimantan Indon. 85 E2
Singkep i. Indon. 84 D3
Singkil Sumatera Indon. 84 B2
Singkuang Sumatera Indon. 84 B2
Singleton Australia 138 E4
Singleton, Mount hill N.T. Australia 134 E5
Singleton, Mount hill W.A. Australia 135 B7
Singora Thai. see Songkhla
Sin'gosan N. Korea see Kosan
Singra India 105 G4
Singri India 105 H4
Singu Myanmar 96 B4
Singwara India 106 D1
Sin'gye N. Korea 91 B5
Sinhala country Asia see Sri Lanka
Sinhkung Myanmar 86 B1
Siniloan Luzon Phil. 82 C3
Sining Qinghai China see Xining
Sinio, Gunung mt. Indon. 83 A3
Siniscola Sardinia Italy 68 C4
Sinj Croatia 68 G3
Sinjai Sulawesi Indon. 83 B4
Sinjār, Jabal mt. Iraq 113 F3
Sinkat Sudan 108 E6
Sinkiang aut. reg. China see Xinjiang Uygur Zizhiqu
Sinkiang Uighur Autonomous Region aut. reg. China see Xinjiang Uygur Zizhiqu
Sinmi-do i. N. Korea 91 B5
Sinn Germany 63 I4
Sinnamary Fr. Guiana 177 H2
Sinn Bishr, Gebel hill Egypt see Sinn Bishr, Jabal
Sinn Bishr, Jabal hill Egypt 107 A5
Sinneh Iran see Sanandaj
Sinoia Zimbabwe see Chinhoyi
Sinop Brazil 177 G6
Sinop Turkey 112 D2
Sinope Turkey see Sinop
Sinoquipe Mex. 166 C2
Sinp'a N. Korea 90 B4
Sinp'o N. Korea 91 C4
Sinsang N. Korea 91 B5
Sinsheim Germany 63 I5
Sintang Kalimantan Indon. 85 E2
Sint Eustatius i. Neth. Antilles 169 L5
Sint-Laureins Belgium 62 D3

▶Sint Maarten i. Neth. Antilles 169 L5
Part of the Netherlands Antilles. The northern part of the island is the French Overseas Collectivity of St Martin.

Sint-Niklaas Belgium 62 E3
Sinton U.S.A. 161 D6
Sintra Port. 67 B4
Sint-Truiden Belgium 62 F4
Sinŭiju N. Korea 91 B4
Sinuk AK U.S.A. 148 F2
Sinzig Germany 63 H4
Siocon Mindanao Phil. 82 C5
Siófok Hungary 68 H1
Sioma Ngwezi National Park Zambia 123 C5
Sion Switz. 66 H3
Sion Mills U.K. 61 E3
Siorapaluk Greenland 147 K2
Sioux Center U.S.A. 155 H3
Sioux City U.S.A. 160 D3
Sioux Falls U.S.A. 160 D3
Sioux Lookout Canada 151 N5
Sipacate Guat. 167 H6
Sipadan, Pulau i. Sabah Malaysia 85 G1
Sipalay Negros Phil. 82 C4
Sipang, Tanjung pt Malaysia 85 E2
Siphaqeni S. Africa see Flagstaff
Siping China 90 B4
Sipitang Sabah Malaysia 85 F1
Sipiwesk Canada 151 L4
Sipiwesk Lake Canada 151 L4
Siple, Mount Antarctica 188 J2
Siple Coast Antarctica 188 I1
Siple Island Antarctica 188 J2
Siponj Tajik. see Bartang
Sipsey r. U.S.A. 161 F5
Sipura i. Indon. 84 B3
Sipura, Selat sea chan. Indon. 84 B3
Sīq, Wādī as watercourse Egypt 107 A5
Siquia r. Nicaragua 166 [inset] I6
Siquijor Phil. 82 C4
Siquijor i. Phil. 82 C4
Sir r. Pak. 111 H6
Sir, Dar''yoi r. Asia see Syrdar'ya
Sira India 106 C3
Sira r. Norway 55 E7
Şīr Abū Nu'āyr i. U.A.E. 110 D5
Siracusa Sicily Italy see Syracuse
Siraha Nepal see Sirha
Sirajganj Bangl. 105 G4
Sir Alexander, Mount Canada 150 F4
Şiran Turkey 113 E2
Sirbāl, Jabal mt. Egypt 112 D5
Şīr Banī Yās i. U.A.E. 110 D5
Sircilla India see Sirsilla
Sirdaryo r. Asia see Syrdar'ya
Sirdaryo Uzbek. 102 C3
Sir Edward Pellew Group is Australia 136 B2
Sireniki Rus. Fed. 148 D2
Sirha Nepal 105 F4
Sirḩān, Wādī as watercourse Jordan/Saudi Arabia 107 C4
Sirik, Tanjung pt Malaysia 85 E2
Siri Kit, Khuan Thai. 86 C3
Sirina i. Greece see Syrna
Sīrjā Iran 111 F5
Sir James MacBrien, Mount N.W.T. Canada 149 P3
Sīrjān Iran 110 D4
Sīrjān salt flat Iran 110 D4
Sirkazhi India 106 C4
Sirmilik National Park Canada 147 K2
Şırnak Turkey 113 F3
Sirohi India 104 C4
Sirombu Indon. 84 B2
Sirong Sulawesi Indon. 83 B3
Sironj India 104 D4
Síros i. Greece see Syros
Sirpur India 106 C2
Sirretta Peak U.S.A. 158 D4
Sīrrī, Jazīreh-ye i. Iran 110 D5
Sirsa India 104 C3
Sir Sandford, Mount Canada 150 G5
Sirsi Karnataka India 106 B3
Sirsi Madh. Prad. India 104 D4
Sirsi Uttar Prad. India 104 D3
Sirsilla India 106 C2
Sirte Libya 121 E1
Sirte, Gulf of Libya 121 E1
Sir Thomas, Mount hill Australia 135 E6
Siruguppa India 106 C3
Sirur India 106 B2
Şirvan Turkey 113 F3
Sirvel India 106 C3
Širvintai Lith. see Širvintos
Širvintos Lith. 55 N9
Sīrwān r. Iraq 113 G4
Sir Wilfrid Laurier, Mount Canada 150 G4
Sis Turkey see Kozan
Sisak Croatia 68 G2
Sisaket Thai. 86 D4
Sisal Mex. 167 H4
Sischu Mountain AK U.S.A. 148 I2
Siscia Croatia see Sisak
Sishen S. Africa 124 F4
Sishilipu Gansu China 94 F5
Sishuang Liedao is China 97 I3
Sisian Armenia 113 G3
Sisimiut Greenland 147 M3
Sisipuk Lake Canada 151 K4
Sisogúichic Mex. 166 D3
Sisŏphŏn Cambodia 87 C4
Sissano P.N.G. 81 K7
Sisseton U.S.A. 160 D2
Sīstān reg. Iran 111 F4
Sisteron France 66 G4
Sisters is India 87 A5
Sīt Iran 110 E5
Sitamarhi India 105 F4
Sitang China see Sinan
Sitangkai Phil. 82 B5
Sitapur India 104 E4
Siteia Greece 69 L7
Siteki Swaziland 125 J4
Sithonia pen. Greece see Sithonias, Chersonisos
Sithonias, Chersonisos pen. Greece 69 J4
Sitía Greece see Siteia
Sitian Xinjiang China 94 C3
Sitidgi Lake N.W.T. Canada 149 N1
Sitila Moz. 125 L2
Siting China 96 E3
Sítio do Mato Brazil 179 C1
Sitka AK U.S.A. 149 N4
Sitka National Historical Park nat. park AK U.S.A. 149 N4
Sitkinak Island AK U.S.A. 148 I4
Sitkinak Strait AK U.S.A. 148 I4
Sitra oasis Egypt see Sitrah
Sitrah oasis Egypt 112 B5
Sittang r. Myanmar see Sittaung
Sittard Neth. 62 F4
Sittaung Myanmar 86 A1
Sittaung r. Myanmar 86 B3
Sittensen Germany 63 J1
Sittingbourne U.K. 59 H7
Sittoung r. Myanmar see Sittaung
Sittwe Myanmar 86 A2
Situbondo Jawa Indon. 85 F4
Siumpu i. Indon. 83 B4
Siuna Nicaragua 166 [inset] I6
Siuri India 105 F5
Sivaganga India 106 C4
Sivakasi India 106 C4
Sivaki Rus. Fed. 90 B1
Sivan India see Siwan
Sivas Turkey 112 E3
Sivaslı Turkey 69 M5
Siverek Turkey 113 E3
Siverskiy Rus. Fed. 55 Q7
Sivers'kyy Donets' r. Rus. Fed./Ukr. see Severskiy Donets
Sivomaskinskiy Rus. Fed. 51 S2
Sivrice Turkey 113 E3
Sivrihisar Turkey 69 N5
Sivukile S. Africa 125 I4
Sīwa Egypt see Sīwah
Siwa Sulawesi Indon. 83 B3
Sīwah Egypt 112 B5
Sīwah, Wāḩāt oasis Egypt 112 B5
Siwalik Range mts India/Nepal 104 D3
Siwan India 105 F4
Siwana India 104 C4
Siwa Oasis oasis Egypt see Sīwah, Wāḩāt
Sixian China 97 H1
Sixmilecross U.K. 61 E3
Sixtymile Y.T. Canada 149 L2
Siyabuswa S. Africa 125 I3
Siyang Jiangsu China 95 I5
Siyäzän Azer. 113 H2
Siyitang Nei Mongol China 95 G3
Sīyunī Iran 110 D3
Siziwang Qi Nei Mongol China see Ulan Hua
Sjælland i. Denmark see Zealand
Sjenica Serbia 69 I3
Sjöbo Sweden 55 H9
Sjøvegan Norway 54 J2
Skadarsko Jezero nat. park Montenegro 69 H3
Skadovs'k Ukr. 69 O1
Skaftárós r. mouth Iceland 54 [inset]
Skagafjörður inlet Iceland 54 [inset]
Skagen Denmark 55 G8
Skagerrak strait Denmark/Norway 55 F8
Skagit r. U.S.A. 156 C2
Skagway AK U.S.A. 149 N4
Skaidi Norway 54 N1
Skaland Norway 54 J2
Skalmodal Sweden 54 I4
Skanderborg Denmark 55 F8
Skaneateles Lake U.S.A. 165 G2
Skara Sweden 55 H7
Skardarsko Jezero l. Albania/Montenegro see Scutari, Lake
Skardu Pak. 104 C2
Skärgårdshavets nationalpark nat. park Fin. 55 L7
Skarnes Norway 55 G6
Skarżysko-Kamienna Poland 57 R5
Skaulo Sweden 54 L3
Skawina Poland 57 Q6
Skeena r. B.C. Canada 149 O5
Skeena Mountains B.C. Canada 149 O4
Skegness U.K. 58 H5
Skellefteå Sweden 54 L4
Skellefteälven r. Sweden 54 L4
Skelleftehamn Sweden 54 L4
Skelmersdale U.K. 58 E5
Skerries Ireland 61 F4
Ski Norway 55 G7
Skiathos i. Greece 69 J5
Skibbereen Ireland 61 C6
Skibotn Norway 54 L2
Skiddaw hill U.K. 58 D4
Skien Norway 55 F7
Skiermûntseach Neth. see Schiermonnikoog
Skiermûntseach i. Neth. see Schiermonnikoog
Skierniewice Poland 57 R5
Skikda Alg. 68 B6
Skipsea U.K. 58 G5
Skipton Australia 138 A6
Skipton U.K. 58 E5
Skirlaugh U.K. 58 G5
Skíros i. Greece see Skyros
Skive Denmark 55 F8
Skjern Denmark 55 F9
Skjolden Norway 55 E6
Skobelev Uzbek. see Farg'ona
Skobeleva, Pik mt. Kyrg. 111 I2
Skodje Norway 54 E5
Skoganvarri Norway 54 N2
Skokie U.S.A. 164 B2
Skomer Island U.K. 59 B7
Skopelos i. Greece 69 J5
Skopin Rus. Fed. 53 H5

▶Skopje Macedonia 69 I4
Capital of Macedonia.

Skoplje Macedonia see Skopje
Skövde Sweden 55 H7
Skovorodino Rus. Fed. 90 A1
Skowhegan U.S.A. 165 K1
Skrunda Latvia 55 M8
Skukum, Mount Y.T. Canada 149 N3
Skukuza S. Africa 125 J3
Skull Valley U.S.A. 159 G4
Skuodas Lith. 55 L8
Skurup Sweden 55 H9
Skutskär Sweden 55 J6
Skvyra Ukr. 53 F6
Skwentna r. AK U.S.A. 149 J3
Skye i. U.K. 60 C3
Skylge i. Neth. see Terschelling
Skyring, Seno b. Chile 178 B8
Skyros Greece 69 K5
Skyros i. Greece 69 K5
Skytrain Ice Rise Antarctica 188 L1
Slættaratindur hill Faroe Is 54 [inset]
Slagelse Denmark 55 G9
Slagnäs Sweden 54 K4
Slamet, Gunung vol. Indon. 85 E4
Slana AK U.S.A. 149 L3
Slane Ireland 61 F4
Slaney r. Ireland 61 F5
Slantsy Rus. Fed. 55 P7
Slapovi Krke nat. park Croatia 68 F3
Slashers Reefs Australia 136 D3
Slatina Croatia 68 G2
Slatina Romania 69 K2
Slaty Fork U.S.A. 164 E4
Slava Rus. Fed. 90 C1
Slave r. Canada 151 H2
Slave Coast Africa 120 D4
Slave Lake Canada 150 H4
Slave Point Canada 150 H2
Slavgorod Belarus see Slawharad
Slavgorod Rus. Fed. 88 D2
Slavkovichi Rus. Fed. 55 P8
Slavonska Požega Croatia see Požega
Slavonski Brod Croatia 68 H2
Slavuta Ukr. 53 E6
Slavutych Ukr. 53 F6
Slavyanka Rus. Fed. 90 C4
Slavyansk Ukr. see Slov''yans'k
Slavyanskaya Rus. Fed. see Slavyansk-na-Kubani
Slavyansk-na-Kubani Rus. Fed. 112 E1
Slawharad Belarus 53 F5
Sławno Poland 57 P3
Slayton U.S.A. 160 E3
Sleaford U.K. 59 G5
Slea Head hd Ireland 61 B5
Sleat Neth. see Sloten
Sleat, Sound of sea chan. U.K. 60 D3
Sledge Island AK U.S.A. 148 F2
Sled Lake Canada 151 J4
Sleeper Islands Canada 152 F2
Sleeping Bear Dunes National Lakeshore nature res. U.S.A. 164 B1
Sleetmute AK U.S.A. 148 H3
Sleman Indon. 85 E4
Slessor Glacier Antarctica 188 B1
Slick Rock U.S.A. 159 I2
Slidell LA U.S.A. 167 H2
Slide Mountain U.S.A. 165 H3
Slieve Bloom Mts hills Ireland 61 E5
Slieve Car hill Ireland 61 C3
Slieve Donard hill U.K. 61 G3
Slieve Gamph hills Ireland see Ox Mountains
Slievekimalta hill Ireland see Keeper Hill
Slieve Mish Mts hills Ireland 61 B5
Slieve Snaght hill Ireland 61 E2
Sligachan U.K. 60 C3
Sligeach Ireland see Sligo
Sligo Ireland 61 D3
Sligo U.S.A. 164 F3
Sligo Bay Ireland 61 D3
Slinger U.S.A. 164 A2
Slippery Rock U.S.A. 164 E3
Slite Sweden 55 K8
Sliven Bulg. 69 L3
Sloan U.S.A. 159 F4
Sloat U.S.A. 158 C2
Sloboda Rus. Fed. see Ezhva
Slobodchikovo Rus. Fed. 52 K3
Slobodskoy Rus. Fed. 52 K4
Slobozia Romania 69 L2
Slochteren Neth. 62 G1
Slonim Belarus 55 N10
Slootdorp Neth. 62 E2
Sloten Neth. 62 F2
Slough U.K. 59 G7
Slovakia country Europe 50 J6
Slovenia country Europe 68 F2
Slovenija country Europe see Slovenia
Slovenj Gradec Slovenia 68 F1
Slovensko country Europe see Slovakia
Slovenský raj nat. park Slovakia 57 R6
Slov''yans'k Ukr. 53 H6
Słowiński Park Narodowy nat. park Poland 57 P3
Sluch r. Ukr. 53 E6
S'Lung, B'Nom mt. Vietnam 87 D5
Słupsk Poland 57 P3
Slussfors Sweden 54 J4
Slutsk Belarus 55 O10
Slyne Head hd Ireland 61 B4
Slyudyanka Rus. Fed. 88 I2
Small Point U.S.A. 165 K2
Smallwood Reservoir Canada 153 I3
Smalyavichy Belarus 55 P9
Smalyenskaya Wzvyshsha hills Belarus/Rus. Fed. see Smolensko-Moskovskaya Vozvyshennost'
Smarhon' Belarus 55 O9
Smeaton Canada 151 J4
Smederevo Serbia 69 I2
Smederevska Palanka Serbia 69 I2
Smela Ukr. see Smila
Smethport U.S.A. 165 F3
Smidovich Rus. Fed. 90 D2
Smila Ukr. 53 F6
Smilde Neth. 62 G2
Smiltene Latvia 55 N8
Smirnykh Rus. Fed. 90 F2
Smith Canada 150 H4
Smith Arm b. N.W.T. Canada 149 Q2
Smith Bay AK U.S.A. 148 I1
Smith Center U.S.A. 160 D4
Smithfield S. Africa 125 H6
Smithfield NC U.S.A. 162 E5
Smithfield UT U.S.A. 156 F4
Smith Glacier Antarctica 188 K1
Smith Island India 87 A4
Smith Island MD U.S.A. 165 G4
Smith Island VA U.S.A. 165 H5
Smith Mountain Lake U.S.A. 164 F5
Smith River B.C. Canada 149 P4
Smiths Falls Canada 165 G1
Smithton Australia 137 [inset]
Smithtown Australia 138 F3
Smithville OK U.S.A. 161 E5
Smithville WV U.S.A. 164 E4
Smoke Creek Desert U.S.A. 158 D1
Smoking Mountains N.W.T. Canada 149 P1
Smoky Bay Australia 135 F8
Smoky Cape Australia 138 F3
Smoky Falls Canada 152 E4
Smoky Hill r. U.S.A. 160 C4
Smoky Hills KS U.S.A. 154 H4
Smoky Hills KS U.S.A. 160 D4
Smoky Lake Canada 151 H4
Smoky Mountains U.S.A. 156 E4
Smøla i. Norway 54 E5
Smolenka Rus. Fed. 53 K6
Smolensk Rus. Fed. 53 G5
Smolensk-Moscow Upland hills Belarus/Rus. Fed. see Smolensko-Moskovskaya Vozvyshennost'
Smolensko-Moskovskaya Vozvyshennost' hills Belarus/Rus. Fed. 53 G5
Smolevichi Belarus see Smalyavichy
Smolyan Bulg. 69 K4
Smooth Rock Falls Canada 152 E4
Smoothrock Lake Canada 152 C4
Smoothstone Lake Canada 151 J4
Smørfjord Norway 54 N1
Smorgon' Belarus see Smarhon'
Smyley Island Antarctica 188 L2
Smyrna Turkey see İzmir
Smyrna U.S.A. 165 H4
Smyth Island atoll Marshall Is see Taongi
Snæfell mt. Iceland 54 [inset]
Snaefell hill Isle of Man 58 C4
Snag (abandoned) Y.T. Canada 149 L3
Snake r. N.W.T./Y.T. Canada 149 N2
Snake r. U.S.A. 156 D3
Snake Island Australia 138 C7
Snake Range mts U.S.A. 159 F2
Snake River Canada 150 F3
Snake River Plain U.S.A. 156 E4
Snare r. Canada 150 G2

Snare Lake Canada 151 J3
Snare Lakes Canada see Wekweêtì
Snares Islands N.Z. 133 G6
Snåsa Norway 54 H4
Sneedville U.S.A. 164 D5
Sneek Neth. 62 F1
Sneem Ireland 61 C6
Sneeuberge mts S. Africa 124 G6
Snegamook Lake Canada 153 J3
Snegurovka Ukr. see Tetiyiv
Snelling U.S.A. 158 C3
Snettisham U.K. 59 H6
Snezhnogorsk Rus. Fed. 76 J3
Snežnik mt. Slovenia 68 F2
Sniečkus Lith. see Visaginas
Snihurivka Ukr. 53 G7
Snits Neth. see Sneek
Snizort, Loch b. U.K. 60 C3
Snoqualmie Pass U.S.A. 156 C3
Snøtinden mt. Norway 54 H3
Snoul Cambodia see Snuŏl
Snover U.S.A. 164 D2
Snovsk Ukr. see Shchors
Snowbird Lake Canada 151 K2
Snowcap Mountain AK U.S.A. 148 I3
Snowcrest Mountain Canada 150 G5
Snowdon mt. U.K. 59 C5
Snowdonia National Park U.K. 59 D6
Snowdrift Canada see Łutselk'e
Snowdrift r. Canada 151 I2
Snowflake U.S.A. 159 H4
Snow Hill U.S.A. 165 H4
Snow Lake Canada 151 K4
Snowville U.S.A. 156 E4
Snow Water Lake U.S.A. 159 F1
Snowy r. Australia 138 D6
Snowy Mountain U.S.A. 165 H2
Snowy Mountains Australia 138 C6
Snowy Peak AK U.S.A. 149 L2
Snowy River National Park Australia 138 D6
Snug Corner Bahamas 163 F8
Snug Harbour Nfld. and Lab. Canada 153 L3
Snug Harbour Ont. Canada 164 E1
Snuŏl Cambodia 87 D4
Snyder U.S.A. 161 C5
Soabuwe Seram Indon. 83 D3
Soalala Madag. 123 E5
Soalara Madag. 123 E6
Soanierana-Ivongo Madag. 123 E5
Soan-kundo is S. Korea 91 B6
Soavinandriana Madag. 123 E5
Sobat r. Sudan 108 D8
Sobatsubu-yama mt. Japan 93 E3
Sobger r. Indon. 81 K7
Sobinka Rus. Fed. 52 I5
Sobradinho, Barragem de resr Brazil 177 J6
Sobral Brazil 177 J4
Sobue Japan 92 C3
Sochi Rus. Fed. 113 E2
Sŏch'ŏn S. Korea 91 B5
Society Islands Fr. Polynesia 187 J7
Socorro Brazil 179 B3
Socorro Col. 176 D2
Socorro U.S.A. 157 G6
Socorro, Isla i. Mex. 168 B5
Socotra i. Yemen 109 H7
Soc Trăng Vietnam 87 D5
Socuéllamos Spain 67 E4
Soda Lake CA U.S.A. 158 D4
Soda Lake CA U.S.A. 158 E4
Sodankylä Fin. 54 O3
Soda Plains Aksai Chin 99 B6
Soda Springs U.S.A. 156 F4
Sodegaura Japan 93 F3
Söderhamn Sweden 55 J6
Söderköping Sweden 55 J7
Södertälje Sweden 55 J7
Sodiri Sudan 108 C7
Sodo Eth. 122 D3
Södra Kvarken strait Fin./Sweden 55 K6
Sodus U.S.A. 165 G2
Soë Timor Indon. 83 C5
Soekarno, Puntjak mt. Indon. see Jaya, Puncak
Soekmekaar S. Africa 125 I2
Soerabaia Jawa Indon. see Surabaya
Soerendonk Neth. 62 F3
Soest Germany 63 I3
Soest Neth. 62 F2
Sofala Australia 138 D4

▶Sofia Bulg. 69 J3
Capital of Bulgaria.

Sofiya Bulg. see Sofia
Sofiyevka Ukr. see Vil'nyans'k
Sofiysk Khabarovskiy Kray Rus. Fed. 90 D1
Sofiysk Khabarovskiy Kray Rus. Fed. 90 E2
Sofporog Rus. Fed. 54 Q4
Sofrana i. Greece 69 L6
Softa Kalesi tourist site Turkey 107 A1
Sōfu-gan i. Japan 91 F7
Sog Xizang China 99 F7
Soğanlı Dağları mts Turkey 113 E2
Sogat Xinjiang China 98 D4
Sogda Rus. Fed. 90 D2
Sögel Germany 63 H2
Sogma Xizang China 99 C6
Sogmai Xizang China 99 B6
Søgne Norway 55 E7
Sognefjorden inlet Norway 55 D6
Sogod Leyte Phil. 82 D4
Sogod Bay Leyte Phil. 82 D4
Sogo Nur l. Nei Mongol China 94 E3
Sog Qu r. Xizang China 99 F6
Sogruma China 96 D1
Söğüt Turkey 69 N4
Söğüt Dağı mts Turkey 69 M6
Soh Iran 110 C3
Sohâg Egypt see Sūhāj
Sohagpur India 104 D5
Soham U.K. 59 H6
Sohan r. Pak. 111 H3
Sohano P.N.G. 132 F2
Sohar Oman see Şuḩār
Sohawal India 104 E4
Sohela India 105 E5
Sohng Gwe, Khao hill Myanmar/Thai. 87 B4
Sŏho-ri N. Korea 91 C4
Sohŭksan-do i. S. Korea 91 B6
Soignies Belgium 62 E4
Soila China 96 C2
Soini Fin. 54 N5
Soissons France 62 D5
Sojat India 104 C4
Sojat Road India 104 C4
Sojoton Point Negros Phil. 82 C4
Sok r. Rus. Fed. 53 K5
Sōka Japan 93 F3
Sokal' Ukr. 53 E6
Sokch'o S. Korea 91 C5
Söke Turkey 69 L6
Sokhondo, Gora mt. Rus. Fed. 95 G1
Sokhor, Gora mt. Rus. Fed. 94 F1
Sokhumi Georgia 113 F2
Sokiryany Ukr. see Sokyryany
Sokodé Togo 120 D4
Soko Islands H.K. China 97 [inset]
Sokol Rus. Fed. 52 I4
Sokolo Mali 120 C3
Sokolov Czech Rep. 63 M4
Sokoto Nigeria 120 D3
Sokoto r. Nigeria 120 D3
Sokyryany Ukr. 53 E6
Sola Cuba 163 E8
Sola i. Tonga see 'Ata
Solan India 104 D3
Solana Beach U.S.A. 158 E5
Solander Island N.Z. 139 A8
Solano Luzon Phil. 82 C2
Solapur India 106 B2
Soldotna AK U.S.A. 149 J3
Soledad U.S.A. 158 C3
Soledad de Doblado Mex. 167 F5
Soledade Brazil 178 F3
Solenoye Rus. Fed. 53 I7
Solfjellsjøen Norway 54 H3
Solginskiy Rus. Fed. 52 I3
Solhan Turkey 113 F3
Soligalich Rus. Fed. 52 I4
Soligorsk Belarus see Salihorsk
Solihull U.K. 59 F6
Solikamsk Rus. Fed. 51 R4
Sol'-Iletsk Rus. Fed. 76 G4
Solimões r. S. America see Amazon
Solimón, Punta pt Mex. 167 I5
Solingen Germany 62 H3
Solitaire Namibia 124 B2
Sol-Karmala Rus. Fed. see Severnoye
Şollar Azer. 113 H2
Sollefteå Sweden 54 J5
Söllichau Germany 63 M3
Solling hills Germany 63 J3
Sollstedt Germany 63 K3
Sollum, Gulf of Egypt see Sallum, Khalīj as
Solms Germany 63 I4
Solnechnogorsk Rus. Fed. 52 H4
Solnechnyy Amurskaya Oblast' Rus. Fed. 90 A1
Solnechnyy Khabarovskiy Kray Rus. Fed. 90 E2
Solo r. Indon. 83 B3
Solo r. Indon. 85 F4
Solok Sumatera Indon. 84 C3
Sololá Guat. 167 H6
Solomon AK U.S.A. 148 F2
Solomon U.S.A. 159 I5
Solomon, North Fork r. U.S.A. 160 D4

▶Solomon Islands country
S. Pacific Ocean 133 G2
4th largest and 5th most populous country in Oceania.

Solomon Sea S. Pacific Ocean 132 F2
Solon Nei Mongol China 95 J2
Solon U.S.A. 165 K1
Solon Springs U.S.A. 160 F2
Solor i. Indon. 83 B5
Solor, Kepulauan is Indon. 83 B5
Solothurn Switz. 66 H3
Solovetskiye Ostrova is Rus. Fed. 52 G2
Solov'yevsk Mongolia 95 H1
Solov'yevsk Rus. Fed. 90 B1
Šolta i. Croatia 68 G3
Solṭānābād Kermān Iran 110 E4
Solṭānābād Khorāsān Iran 111 E3
Solṭānābād Iran 110 C3
Solṭānīyeh Iran 110 C2
Soltau Germany 63 J2
Sol'tsy Rus. Fed. 52 F4
Solvay U.S.A. 165 G2
Sölvesborg Sweden 55 I8
Solway Firth est. U.K. 60 F6
Solwezi Zambia 123 C5
Soma Turkey 69 L5
Somain France 62 D4
Somalia country Africa 122 E3
Somali Basin sea feature Indian Ocean 185 L6
Somali Republic country Africa see Somalia
Sombang, Gunung mt. Indon. 85 G2
Sombo Angola 123 C4
Sombor Serbia 69 H2
Sombrerete Mex. 166 E4
Sombrero Channel India 87 A6
Sombrio, Lago do l. Brazil 179 A5
Somero Fin. 55 M6
Somerset KY U.S.A. 164 C5
Somerset MI U.S.A. 164 C2
Somerset OH U.S.A. 164 D4
Somerset PA U.S.A. 164 F4
Somerset, Lake Australia 138 F1
Somerset East S. Africa 125 G7
Somerset Island Canada 147 I2
Somerset Reservoir U.S.A. 165 I2
Somerset West S. Africa 124 D8
Somersworth U.S.A. 165 J2
Somerton U.S.A. 159 F5
Somerville NJ U.S.A. 165 H3
Somerville TN U.S.A. 161 F5
Somerville Reservoir TX U.S.A. 167 F2
Someydeh Iran 110 B3
Somme r. France 62 B4
Sommen l. Sweden 55 I7
Sömmerda Germany 63 L3
Sommet, Lac du l. Canada 153 H3
Somnath India 104 B5
Somotillo Nicaragua 166 [inset] I6
Somoto Nicaragua 166 [inset] I6
Somutu Myanmar 86 B1
Son r. India 105 F4
Soná Panama 166 [inset] J8
Sonag Qinghai China see Zêkog
Sonapur India 106 D1
Sonar r. India 104 D4
Sŏnbong N. Korea 90 C4
Sŏnch'ŏn N. Korea 91 B5
Sønderborg Denmark 55 F9
Sondershausen Germany 63 K3
Søndre Strømfjord Greenland see Kangerlussuaq
Søndre Strømfjord inlet Greenland see Kangerlussuaq
Sondrio Italy 68 C1
Sonepat India see Sonipat
Sonepur India see Sonapur
Song Sarawak Malaysia 85 F2
Songa Maluku Indon. 83 C3
Songbai China see Shennongjia
Songbu China 97 G2
Sông Câu Vietnam 87 E4
Songcheng China see Xiapu
Sông Đa, Hô resr Vietnam 86 D2
Songea Tanz. 123 D5
Songhua Hu resr China 90 B4
Songhua Jiang r. Heilongjiang/Jilin China 90 D3
Songhua Jiang r. Jilin China see Di'er Songhua Jiang
Songjiachuan Shaanxi China see Wubu
Songjiang China 97 I2
Songjianghe China 90 B4
Sŏngjin N. Korea see Kimch'aek
Songkan China 96 E2
Songkhla Thai. 87 C6
Songköl l. Kyrg. 98 A4
Song Ling mts China 95 I3
Songlong Myanmar 86 B2
Sŏngnam S. Korea 91 B5
Songnim N. Korea 91 B5
Songo Angola 123 B4
Songo Moz. 123 D5
Songpan China 96 D1
Songshan Gansu China 94 E4
Songshan China see Ziyun
Song Shan mt. Henan China 95 H5
Songtao China 97 F2
Songxi China 97 H3
Songxian Henan China 95 H5
Songyuan Fujian China see Songxi
Songyuan Jilin China 90 B3
Songzi China 97 F2
Sơn Hai Vietnam 87 E5
Soni Japan 92 C4
Sonid Youqi Nei Mongol China see Saihan Tal
Sonid Zuoqi Nei Mongol China see Mandalt
Sonipat India 104 D3
Sonkajärvi Fin. 54 O5
Sonkovo Rus. Fed. 52 H4
Sơn La Vietnam 86 C2
Sonmiani Pak. 111 G5
Sonmiani Bay Pak. 111 G5
Sonneberg Germany 63 L4
Sono r. Minas Gerais Brazil 179 B2
Sono r. Tocantins Brazil 177 I5
Sonobe Japan 92 B3
Sonoma U.S.A. 158 B2
Sonoma Peak U.S.A. 158 E1
Sonora r. Mex. 166 C2
Sonora state Mex. 166 C2
Sonora CA U.S.A. 158 C3
Sonora KY U.S.A. 164 C5
Sonora TX U.S.A. 161 C6
Sonoran Desert U.S.A. 159 G5
Sonoran Desert National Monument nat. park U.S.A. 157 E6
Sonoran Desert National Monument nat. park AZ U.S.A. 166 B1
Sonqor Iran 110 B3
Sonsonate El Salvador 167 H6
Sonsorol Islands Palau 81 I5
Sơn Tây Vietnam 86 D2
Sonwabile S. Africa 125 I6
Soochow China see Suzhou
Sooghmeghat AK U.S.A. 148 E3
Soomaaliya country Africa see Somalia
Sopi, Tanjung pt Maluku Indon. 83 D2
Sopo watercourse Sudan 121 F4
Sopot Bulg. 69 K3
Sopot Poland 57 Q3
Sop Prap Thai. 86 B3
Sopron Hungary 68 G1
Sopur India 104 C2
Soputan, Gunung vol. Indon. 83 C2
Sora Italy 68 E4
Sorab India 106 B3
Sorada India 106 E2
Söråker Sweden 54 J5
Sŏrak-san mt. S. Korea 91 C5
Sorak-san National Park S. Korea 91 C5
Sorel Canada 153 G5
Soreq r. Israel 107 B4
Sorgun Turkey 112 D3
Sorgun r. Turkey 107 B1
Soria Spain 67 E3
Sorikmarapi vol. Indon. 84 B2
Sorkh, Kūh-e mts Iran 110 D3
Sorkhān Iran 110 E4
Sorkheh Iran 110 D3
Sørli Norway 54 H4
Sorø Denmark 57 M3
Soro India 105 F5
Soroca Moldova 53 F6
Sorocaba Brazil 179 B3
Soroki Moldova see Soroca
Sorol atoll Micronesia 81 K5
Sorong Papua Indon. 83 D3
Soroti Uganda 122 D3
Sørøya i. Norway 54 M1
Sorraia r. Port. 67 B4
Sørreisa Norway 54 K2
Sorrento Italy 68 F4
Sorsele Sweden 54 J4
Sorsogon Luzon Phil. 82 D3
Sortavala Rus. Fed. 54 Q6
Sortland Norway 54 I2
Sortopolovskaya Rus. Fed. 52 K3
Sorvizhi Rus. Fed. 52 K4
Sŏsan S. Korea 91 B5
Sosenskiy Rus. Fed. 53 G5
Soshanguve S. Africa 125 I3
Sosna r. Rus. Fed. 53 H5
Sosneado mt. Arg. 178 C4
Sosnogorsk Rus. Fed. 52 L3
Sosnovka Kyrg. 98 A4
Sosnovka Arkhangel'skaya Oblast' Rus. Fed. 52 J3
Sosnovka Kaliningradskaya Oblast' Rus. Fed. 51 K5
Sosnovka Murmanskaya Oblast' Rus. Fed. 52 I2
Sosnovka Tambovskaya Oblast' Rus. Fed. 53 I5
Sosnovo Rus. Fed. 55 Q6
Sosnovo-Ozerskoye Rus. Fed. 89 K2
Sosnovyy Rus. Fed. 54 R4
Sosnovyy Bor Rus. Fed. 55 P7
Sosnowiec Poland 57 Q5
Sosnowitz Poland see Sosnowiec
Sos'va Khanty-Mansiyskiy Avtonomnyy Okrug Rus. Fed. 51 S3
Sos'va Sverdlovskaya Oblast' Rus. Fed. 51 S4
Sotang Xizang China 99 F7
Sotara, Volcán vol. Col. 176 C3
Sotkamo Fin. 54 P4
Soto la Marina Mex. 167 F4
Sotteville-lès-Rouen France 62 B5
Sotuta Mex. 167 H4
Souanké Congo 122 B3
Soubré Côte d'Ivoire 120 C4
Souderton U.S.A. 165 H3
Soufflenheim France 63 H6
Soufli Greece 69 L4
Soufrière St Lucia 169 L6
Soufrière vol. St Vincent 169 L6
Sougueur Alg. 67 G6
Souillac France 66 E4
Souilly France 62 F5
Souk Ahras Alg. 68 B6
Souk el Arbaâ du Rharb Morocco 64 C5
Sŏul S. Korea see Seoul
Soulac-sur-Mer France 66 D4
Soulom France 66 D5
Sounding Creek r. Canada 151 I4
Souni Cyprus 107 A2
Soûr Lebanon see Tyre
Sourdough AK U.S.A. 149 K3
Soure Brazil 177 I4
Sour el Ghozlane Alg. 67 H5
Souris Canada 151 K5
Souris r. Canada 151 L5
Souriya country Asia see Syria
Sousa Brazil 177 K5
Sousa Lara Angola see Bocoio
Sousse Tunisia 68 D7
Soustons France 66 D5

▶South Africa, Republic of country
Africa 124 F5
5th most populous country in Africa.

Southampton Canada 164 E1
Southampton U.K. 59 F8
Southampton U.S.A. 165 I3
Southampton, Cape Canada 147 J3
Southampton Island Canada 151 O1
South Andaman i. India 87 A5
South Anna r. U.S.A. 165 G5
South Anston U.K. 58 F5
South Aulatsivik Island Canada 153 J2
South Australia state Australia 132 D5
South Australian Basin sea feature Indian Ocean 185 P8
Southaven U.S.A. 161 F5
South Baldy mt. U.S.A. 157 G6
South Bank U.K. 58 F4
South Bass Island U.S.A. 164 D3
South Bend IN U.S.A. 164 B3
South Bend WA U.S.A. 156 C3
South Bluff pt Bahamas 163 F8
South Boston U.S.A. 165 F5
South Brook Canada 153 K4
South Cape pt U.S.A. see Ka Lae
South Carolina state U.S.A. 163 D5
South Charleston OH U.S.A. 164 D4
South Charleston WV U.S.A. 164 E4
South China Sea N. Pacific Ocean 80 F4
South Coast Town Australia see Gold Coast
South Dakota state U.S.A. 160 C2
South Downs hills U.K. 59 G8
South-East admin. dist. Botswana 125 G3
South East Cape Australia 137 [inset]
Southeast Cape AK U.S.A. 148 E3
Southeast Indian Ridge sea feature Indian Ocean 185 N8
South East Isles Australia 135 C8
Southeast Pacific Basin sea feature S. Pacific Ocean 187 M10
South East Point Australia 138 C7
Southend Canada 151 K3
Southend U.K. 60 D5
Southend-on-Sea U.K. 59 H7
Southern admin. dist. Botswana 124 G3
Southern Alps mts N.Z. 139 C6
Southern Cross Australia 135 B7
Southern Indian Lake Canada 151 L3
Southern Lau Group is Fiji 133 I3
Southern National Park Sudan 121 F4
Southern Ocean 188 C2
Southern Pines U.S.A. 163 E5
Southern Rhodesia country Africa see Zimbabwe
Southern Uplands hills U.K. 60 E5
South Esk r. U.K. 60 F4
South Esk Tableland reg. Australia 134 D4
Southey Canada 151 J5
Southfield U.S.A. 164 D2
South Fiji Basin sea feature S. Pacific Ocean 186 H7
South Fork U.S.A. 158 B1
South Geomagnetic Pole (2008) Antarctica 188 F1
South Georgia i. S. Atlantic Ocean 178 I8

▶South Georgia and the South Sandwich Islands terr.
S. Atlantic Ocean 178 I8
United Kingdom Overseas Territory

South Harris pen. U.K. 60 B3
South Haven U.S.A. 164 B2
South Henik Lake Canada 151 L2
South Hill U.S.A. 165 F5
South Honshu Ridge sea feature N. Pacific Ocean 186 F3
South Indian Lake Canada 151 L3
South Island India 106 B4

▶South Island N.Z. 139 D7
2nd largest island in Oceania.

South Islet rf Phil. 82 B4
South Junction Canada 151 M5
South Korea country Asia 91 B5
South Lake Tahoe U.S.A. 158 C2
South Luangwa National Park Zambia 123 D5
South Magnetic Pole (2008) Antarctica 188 G2
South Mills U.S.A. 165 G5
Southminster U.K. 59 H7
South Mountains hills U.S.A. 165 G4
South Nahanni r. N.W.T. Canada 150 F2
South Naknek AK U.S.A. 148 H4
South New Berlin U.S.A. 165 H2
South Orkney Islands S. Atlantic Ocean 184 F10
South Paris U.S.A. 165 J1
South Platte r. U.S.A. 160 C3
South Point Bahamas 163 F8
South Pole Antarctica 188 C1
Southport Qld Australia 138 F1
Southport Tas. Australia 137 [inset]
Southport U.K. 58 D5
Southport U.S.A. 165 G2
South Portland U.S.A. 165 J2
South Ronaldsay i. U.K. 60 G2
South Royalton U.S.A. 165 I2
South Salt Lake U.S.A. 159 H1
South Sand Bluff pt S. Africa 125 J6

▶South Sandwich Islands
S. Atlantic Ocean 184 G9
United Kingdom Overseas Territory.

South Sandwich Trench sea feature S. Atlantic Ocean 184 G9
South San Francisco U.S.A. 158 B3
South Saskatchewan r. Canada 151 J4
South Seal r. Canada 151 L3
South Shetland Islands Antarctica 188 A2
South Shetland Trough sea feature S. Atlantic Ocean 188 L2
South Shields U.K. 58 F3
South Sinai governorate Egypt see Janūb Sīnā'
South Solomon Trench sea feature S. Pacific Ocean 186 G6
South Taranaki Bight b. N.Z. 139 E4
South Tasman Rise sea feature Southern Ocean 186 F9
South Tent mt. U.S.A. 159 H2
South Tons r. India 105 E4
South Twin Island Canada 152 F3
South Tyne r. U.K. 58 E4
South Uist i. U.K. 60 B3
South Wellesley Islands Australia 136 B3
South-West Africa country Africa see Namibia
South West Cape N.Z. 139 A8
Southwest Cape AK U.S.A. 148 E3
South West Entrance sea chan. P.N.G. 136 E1
Southwest Indian Ridge sea feature Indian Ocean 185 K8
South West National Park Australia 137 [inset]
Southwest Pacific Basin sea feature S. Pacific Ocean 186 I8
Southwest Peru Ridge sea feature S. Pacific Ocean see Nazca Ridge
South West Rocks Australia 138 F3
South Whitley U.S.A. 164 C3
South Wichita r. U.S.A. 161 D5
South Windham U.S.A. 165 J2
Southwold U.K. 59 I6
Southwood National Park Australia 138 E1
Soutpansberg mts S. Africa 125 I2
Souttouf, Adrar mts W. Sahara 120 B2
Soverato Italy 68 G5
Sovereign Mountain AK U.S.A. 149 J3
Sovetsk Kaliningradskaya Oblast' Rus. Fed. 55 L9
Sovetsk Kirovskaya Oblast' Rus. Fed. 52 K4
Sovetskaya Gavan' Rus. Fed. 90 F2
Sovetskiy Khanty-Mansiyskiy Avtonomnyy Okrug Rus. Fed. 51 S3
Sovetskiy Leningradskaya Oblast' Rus. Fed. 55 P6
Sovetskiy Respublika Mariy El Rus. Fed. 52 K4
Sovetskoye Chechenskaya Respublika Rus. Fed. see Shatoy
Sovetskoye Stavropol'skiy Kray Rus. Fed. see Zelenokumsk
Sovyets'kyy Ukr. 112 D1
Sowa China 96 C2
Sōwa Japan 93 F2
Soweto S. Africa 125 H4
So'x Tajik. 111 H2
Sōya-kaikyō strait Japan/Rus. Fed. see La Pérouse Strait
Sōya-misaki c. Japan 90 F3
Soyana r. Rus. Fed. 52 I2
Soyma r. Rus. Fed. 52 K2
Soyopa Mex. 157 F7
Sozh r. Europe 53 F6
Sozopol Bulg. 69 L3
Spa Belgium 62 F4

▶Spain country Europe 67 E3
4th largest country in Europe.

Spalato Croatia see Split
Spalatum Croatia see Split
Spalding U.K. 59 G6
Spanish Canada 152 E5
Spanish Fork U.S.A. 159 H1
Spanish Guinea country Africa see Equatorial Guinea
Spanish Netherlands country Europe see Belgium
Spanish Sahara terr. Africa see Western Sahara
Spanish Town Jamaica 169 I5
Sparks U.S.A. 158 D2
Sparta Greece see Sparti
Sparta GA U.S.A. 163 D5
Sparta KY U.S.A. 164 C4
Sparta MI U.S.A. 164 C2
Sparta NC U.S.A. 164 E5
Sparta TN U.S.A. 162 C5
Spartanburg U.S.A. 163 D5
Sparti Greece 69 J6
Spartivento, Capo c. Italy 68 G6
Spas-Demensk Rus. Fed. 53 G5
Spas-Klepiki Rus. Fed. 53 I5
Spassk-Dal'niy Rus. Fed. 90 D3
Spassk-Ryazanskiy Rus. Fed. 53 I5
Spatha, Akra pt Kriti Greece see Spatha, Akrotirio
Spatha, Akrotirio pt Greece 69 J7
Spearman U.S.A. 161 C4
Speedway U.S.A. 164 B4
Spence Bay Canada see Taloyoak
Spencer IA U.S.A. 160 E3
Spencer ID U.S.A. 156 E3
Spencer IN U.S.A. 164 B4
Spencer NE U.S.A. 160 D3
Spencer WV U.S.A. 164 E4
Spencer, Cape AK U.S.A. 149 M4
Spencer, Point pt AK U.S.A. 148 F2
Spencer Bay Namibia 124 B3
Spencer Gulf est. Australia 137 B7
Spencer Range hills Australia 134 E3
Spennymoor U.K. 58 F4
Sperrin Mountains hills U.K. 61 E3
Sperryville U.S.A. 165 F4
Spessart reg. Germany 63 J5
Spétsai i. Greece see Spetses
Spetses i. Greece 69 J6
Spey r. U.K. 60 F3
Speyer Germany 63 I5
Spezand Pak. 111 G4
Spice Islands Indon. see Maluku
Spider Crater tourist site Australia 134 D4
Spijk Neth. 62 G1
Spijkenisse Neth. 62 E3
Spike Mountain AK U.S.A. 149 L2
Spilimbergo Italy 68 E1
Spilsby U.K. 58 H5
Spīn Bōldak Afgh. 111 G4
Spintangi Pak. 111 H4
Spirit Lake U.S.A. 160 E3
Spirit River Canada 150 G4
Spirovo Rus. Fed. 52 G4
Spišská Nová Ves Slovakia 53 D6
Spiti r. India 104 D3

▶Spitsbergen i. Svalbard 76 C2
5th largest island in Europe.

Spittal an der Drau Austria 57 N7
Spitzbergen i. Svalbard see Spitsbergen
Split Croatia 68 G3
Split Lake Canada 151 L3
Split Lake l. Canada 151 L3
Spokane U.S.A. 156 D3
Spoletium Italy see Spoleto
Spoleto Italy 68 E3
Spŏng Cambodia 87 D4
Spoon r. U.S.A. 160 F3
Spooner U.S.A. 160 F2
Spornitz Germany 63 L1
Spotsylvania U.S.A. 165 G4
Spotted Horse U.S.A. 156 G3

Spranger, Mount Canada 150 F4
Spratly Islands S. China Sea 80 E4
Spray U.S.A. 156 D3
Spree r. Germany 57 N4
Sprimont Belgium 62 F4
Springbok S. Africa 124 C5
Springdale Canada 153 L4
Springdale U.S.A. 164 C4
Springe Germany 63 J2
Springer U.S.A. 157 G5
Springerville U.S.A. 159 I4
Springfield CO U.S.A. 160 C4

▶Springfield IL U.S.A. 160 F4
Capital of Illinois.

Springfield KY U.S.A. 164 C5
Springfield MA U.S.A. 165 I2
Springfield MO U.S.A. 161 E4
Springfield OH U.S.A. 164 D4
Springfield OR U.S.A. 156 C3
Springfield TN U.S.A. 164 B5
Springfield VT U.S.A. 165 I2
Springfield WV U.S.A. 165 F4
Springfontein S. Africa 125 G6
Spring Glen U.S.A. 159 H2
Spring Grove U.S.A. 164 A2
Springhill Canada 153 I5
Spring Hill U.S.A. 163 D6
Springhouse Canada 150 F5
Spring Mountains U.S.A. 159 F3
Springs Junction N.Z. 139 D6
Springsure Australia 136 E5
Spring Valley MN U.S.A. 160 E3
Spring Valley NY U.S.A. 165 H3
Springview U.S.A. 160 D3
Springville CA U.S.A. 158 D3
Springville NY U.S.A. 165 F2
Springville PA U.S.A. 165 H3
Springville UT U.S.A. 159 H1
Sprowston U.K. 59 I6
Spruce Grove Canada 150 H4
Spruce Knob mt. U.S.A. 162 E4
Spruce Mountain CO U.S.A. 159 I2
Spruce Mountain NV U.S.A. 159 F1
Spurn Head hd U.K. 58 H5
Spurr, Mount vol. AK U.S.A. 148 I3
Spuzzum Canada 150 F5
Squam Lake U.S.A. 165 J2
Square Lake U.S.A. 153 H5
Squaw Harbor AK U.S.A. 148 G5
Squillace, Golfo di g. Italy 68 G5
Squires, Mount hill Australia 135 D6
Sragen Jawa Indon. 85 E4
Srbinje Bos.-Herz. see Foča
Srê Âmběl Cambodia 87 C5
Srebrenica 69 H2
Sredets Burgas Bulg. 69 L3
Sredets Sofiya-Grad Bulg. see Sofia
Sredinnyy Khrebet mts Rus. Fed. 77 Q4
Sredna Gora mts Bulg. 69 J3
Srednekolymsk Rus. Fed. 77 Q3
Sredne-Russkaya Vozvyshennost' hills Rus. Fed. see Central Russian Upland
Sredne-Sibirskoye Ploskogor'ye plat. Rus. Fed. see Central Siberian Plateau
Sredneye Kuyto, Ozero l. Rus. Fed. 54 Q4
Sredniy Ural mts Rus. Fed. 51 R4
Srednogorie Bulg. 69 K3
Srednyaya Akhtuba Rus. Fed. 53 J6
Sreepur Bangl. see Sripur
Sre Khtum Cambodia 87 D4
Srê Noy Cambodia 87 D4
Sretensk Rus. Fed. 89 L2
Sri Aman Sarawak Malaysia 85 E2
Sriharikota Island India 106 D3

▶Sri Jayewardenepura Kotte Sri Lanka 106 C5
Capital of Sri Lanka.

Srikakulam India 106 E2
Sri Kalahasti India 106 C3
Sri Lanka country Asia 106 D5
Srinagar India 104 C2
Sri Pada mt. Sri Lanka see Adam's Peak
Sripur Bangl. 105 G4
Srirangam India 106 C4
Sri Thep tourist site Thai. 86 C3
Srivardhan India 106 B2
Staaten r. Australia 136 C3
Staaten River National Park Australia 136 C3
Stabroek Guyana see Georgetown
Stade Germany 63 J1
Staden Belgium 62 D4
Stadskanaal Neth. 62 G2
Stadtallendorf Germany 63 J4
Stadthagen Germany 63 J2
Stadtilm Germany 63 L4
Stadtlohn Germany 62 G3
Stadtoldendorf Germany 63 J3
Stadtroda Germany 63 L4
Staffa i. U.K. 60 C4
Staffelberg hill Germany 63 L4
Staffelstein Germany 63 K4
Stafford U.K. 59 E6
Stafford U.S.A. 165 G4
Stafford Creek Bahamas 163 E7
Stafford Springs U.S.A. 165 I3
Stagen Kalimantan Indon. 85 G3
Stagg Lake Canada 150 H2
Staicele Latvia 55 N8
Staines U.K. 59 G7
Stakhanov Ukr. 53 H6
Stakhanovo Rus. Fed. see Zhukovskiy
Stalbridge U.K. 59 E8
Stalham U.K. 59 I6
Stalin Bulg. see Varna
Stalinabad Tajik. see Dushanbe
Stalingrad Rus. Fed. see Volgograd
Staliniri Georgia see Ts'khinvali
Stalino Ukr. see Donets'k
Stalinogorsk Rus. Fed. see Novomoskovsk
Stalinogród Poland see Katowice
Stalinsk Rus. Fed. see Novokuznetsk
Stalowa Wola Poland 53 D6
Stamboliyski Bulg. 69 K3
Stamford Australia 136 C4
Stamford U.K. 59 G6
Stamford CT U.S.A. 165 I3
Stamford NY U.S.A. 165 H2
Stamford TX U.S.A. 167 F1
Stampalia i. Greece see Astypalaia
Stampriet Namibia 124 D3
Stamsund Norway 54 H2
Stanardsville U.S.A. 165 F4
Stanberry U.S.A. 160 E3
Stancomb-Wills Glacier Antarctica 188 B1
Standard Canada 150 H5
Standdaarbuiten Neth. 62 E3
Standerton S. Africa 125 I4
Standish U.S.A. 164 D2
Stanfield U.S.A. 159 H5
Stanford KY U.S.A. 164 C5
Stanford MT U.S.A. 156 F3
Stanger S. Africa 125 J5
Stanislaus r. U.S.A. 158 C3
Stanislav Ukr. see Ivano-Frankivs'k
Stanke Dimitrov Bulg. see Dupnitsa
Staňkov Czech Rep. 63 N5
Stanley Australia 137 [inset]
Stanley H.K. China 97 [inset]

▶Stanley Falkland Is 178 E8
Capital of the Falkland Islands.

Stanley U.K. 58 F4
Stanley ID U.S.A. 156 E3
Stanley KY U.S.A. 164 B5
Stanley ND U.S.A. 160 C1
Stanley VA U.S.A. 165 F4
Stanley, Mount hill N.T. Australia 134 E5
Stanley, Mount hill Tas. Australia 137 [inset]
Stanley, Mount Dem. Rep. Congo/Uganda see Margherita Peak
Stanleyville Dem. Rep. Congo see Kisangani
Stann Creek Belize see Dangriga
Stannington U.K. 58 F3
Stanovoye Rus. Fed. 53 H5
Stanovoye Nagor'ye mts Rus. Fed. 89 L1
Stanovoy Khrebet mts Rus. Fed. 77 N4
Stansmore Range hills Australia 134 E5
Stanthorpe Australia 138 E2
Stanton U.K. 59 H6
Stanton KY U.S.A. 164 D5
Stanton MI U.S.A. 164 C2
Stanton ND U.S.A. 160 C2
Stanton TX U.S.A. 161 C5
Stapleton U.S.A. 160 C3
Starachowice Poland 57 R5
Stara Planina mts Bulg./Serbia see Balkan Mountains
Staraya Russa Rus. Fed. 52 F4
Stara Zagora Bulg. 69 K3
Starbuck Island Kiribati 187 J6
Star City U.S.A. 164 B3
Starcke National Park Australia 136 D2
Stargard in Pommern Poland see Stargard Szczeciński
Stargard Szczeciński Poland 57 O4
Staritsa Rus. Fed. 52 G4
Starke U.S.A. 163 D6
Starkville U.S.A. 161 F5
Star Lake U.S.A. 165 H1
Starnberger See l. Germany 57 M7
Staroaleyskoye Rus. Fed. 98 C2
Starobel'sk Ukr. see Starobil's'k
Starobil's'k Ukr. 53 H6
Starogard Gdański Poland 57 Q4
Starokonstantinov Ukr. see Starokostyantyniv
Starokostyantyniv Ukr. 53 E6
Starominskaya Rus. Fed. 53 H7
Staroshcherbinovskaya Rus. Fed. 53 H7
Star Peak U.S.A. 158 D1
Start Point U.K. 59 D8
Starve Island Kiribati see Starbuck Island
Staryya Darohi Belarus 53 F5
Staryye Dorogi Belarus see Staryya Darohi
Staryy Kayak Rus. Fed. 77 L2
Staryy Oskol Rus. Fed. 53 H6
Staßfurt Germany 63 L3
State College U.S.A. 165 G3
State Line U.S.A. 161 F6
Staten Island Arg. see Los Estados, Isla de
Statenville U.S.A. 163 D6
Statesboro U.S.A. 163 D5
Statesville U.S.A. 162 D5
Statia i. Neth. Antilles see Sint Eustatius
Station U.S.A. 164 C4
Station Nord Greenland 189 I1
Stauchitz Germany 63 N3
Staufenberg Germany 63 I4
Staunton U.S.A. 164 F4
Stavanger Norway 55 D7
Staveley U.K. 58 F5
Stavropol' Rus. Fed. 113 F1
Stavropol Kray admin. div. Rus. Fed. see Stavropol'skiy Kray
Stavropol'-na-Volge Rus. Fed. see Tol'yatti
Stavropol'skaya Vozvyshennost' hills Rus. Fed. 113 F1
Stavropol'skiy Kray admin. div. Rus. Fed. 113 F1
Stayner Canada 164 E1
Stayton U.S.A. 156 C3
Steadville S. Africa 125 I5
Steamboat Springs U.S.A. 156 G4
Stearns U.S.A. 164 C5
Stebbins AK U.S.A. 148 G3
Steele Creek AK U.S.A. 149 L2
Steele Island Antarctica 188 L2
Steelville U.S.A. 160 F4
Steen r. Canada 150 G3
Steenderen Neth. 62 G2
Steenkampsberge mts S. Africa 125 J3
Steen River Canada 150 G3
Steens Mountain U.S.A. 156 D4
Steenstrup Gletscher glacier Greenland see Sermersuaq
Steenvoorde France 62 C4
Steenwijk Neth. 62 G2
Steese Highway AK U.S.A. 149 K2
Stefansson Island Canada 147 H2
Stegi Swaziland see Siteki
Steigerwald mts Germany 63 K5
Stein Germany 63 L5
Steinach Germany 63 L4
Steinaker Reservoir U.S.A. 159 I1
Steinbach Canada 151 L5
Steinfeld (Oldenburg) Germany 63 I2
Steinfurt Germany 63 H2
Steinhausen Namibia 123 B6
Steinheim Germany 63 J3
Steinkjer Norway 54 G4
Steinkopf S. Africa 124 C5
Steinsdalen Norway 54 G4
Stella S. Africa 124 G4
Stella Maris Bahamas 163 F8
Stellenbosch S. Africa 124 D7
Steller, Mount AK U.S.A. 149 L3
Stello, Monte mt. Corsica France 66 I5
Stelvio, Parco Nazionale dello nat. park Italy 68 D1
Stenay France 62 F5
Stendal Germany 63 L2
Stenhousemuir U.K. 60 F4
Stenungsund Sweden 55 G7
Steornabhagh U.K. see Stornoway
Stepanakert Azer. see Xankändi
Stephens, Cape N.Z. 139 D5
Stephens City U.S.A. 165 F4
Stephens Lake Canada 151 M3
Stephenville U.S.A. 161 D5
Stepnoy Kyrg. 98 A4
Stepnoy Rus. Fed. see Elista
Stepnoye Rus. Fed. 53 J6
Stepovak Bay AK U.S.A. 148 G5
Sterkfontein Dam resr S. Africa 125 I5
Sterkstroom S. Africa 125 H6
Sterlet Lake Canada 151 I1
Sterlibashevo Rus. Fed. 51 R5
Sterling S. Africa 124 E6
Sterling CO U.S.A. 160 C3
Sterling IL U.S.A. 160 F3
Sterling MI U.S.A. 164 C1
Sterling UT U.S.A. 159 H2
Sterling City U.S.A. 161 C6
Sterling Heights U.S.A. 164 D2
Sterlitamak Rus. Fed. 76 G4
Stettin Poland see Szczecin
Stettler Canada 151 H4
Steubenville KY U.S.A. 164 C5
Steubenville OH U.S.A. 164 E3
Stevenage U.K. 59 G7
Stevenson U.S.A. 156 C3
Stevenson Entrance sea channel AK U.S.A. 148 I4
Stevenson Lake Canada 151 L4
Stevens Point U.S.A. 160 F2
Stevens Village AK U.S.A. 149 J2
Stevensville MI U.S.A. 164 B2
Stevensville PA U.S.A. 165 G3
Stewart B.C. Canada 149 O5
Stewart r. Y.T. Canada 149 M3
Stewart, Isla i. Chile 178 B8
Stewart Crossing Y.T. Canada 149 M3
Stewart Island N.Z. 139 A8
Stewart Islands Solomon Is 133 G2
Stewart Lake Canada 147 J3
Stewarton U.K. 60 E5
Stewarts Point U.S.A. 158 B2
Stewiacke Canada 153 J5
Steynsburg S. Africa 125 G6
Steyr Austria 57 O6
Steytlerville S. Africa 124 G7
Stiens Neth. 62 F1
Stif Alg. see Sétif
Stigler U.S.A. 161 E5
Stikine r. B.C. Canada 149 N4
Stikine Plateau B.C. Canada 149 O4
Stikine Ranges mts B.C. Canada 149 O4
Stikine Strait U.S.A. 150 C3
Stilbaai S. Africa 124 E8
Stiles U.S.A. 164 A1
Stillwater MN U.S.A. 160 E2
Stillwater OK U.S.A. 161 D4
Stillwater Range mts U.S.A. 158 D2
Stillwell U.S.A. 164 B3
Stilton U.K. 59 G6
Stilwell U.S.A. 161 E5
Stinnett U.S.A. 161 C5
Štip Macedonia 69 J4
Stirling Australia 134 F5
Stirling Canada 165 G1
Stirling U.K. 60 F4
Stirling Creek r. Australia 134 E4
Stirling Range National Park Australia 135 B8
Stittsville Canada 165 H1
Stjørdalshalsen Norway 54 G5
Stockbridge U.S.A. 164 C2
Stockerau Austria 57 P6
Stockheim Germany 63 L4

▶Stockholm Sweden 55 K7
Capital of Sweden.

Stockinbingal Australia 138 C5
Stockport U.K. 58 E5
Stockton CA U.S.A. 158 C3
Stockton KS U.S.A. 160 D4
Stockton MO U.S.A. 160 E4
Stockton UT U.S.A. 159 G1
Stockton Islands AK U.S.A. 149 K1
Stockton Lake U.S.A. 160 E4
Stockton-on-Tees U.K. 58 F4
Stockton Plateau U.S.A. 166 E2
Stockville U.S.A. 160 C3
Stod Czech Rep. 63 N5
Stœng Trêng Cambodia 87 D4
Stoer, Point of U.K. 60 D2
Stoke-on-Trent U.K. 59 E5
Stokesley U.K. 58 F4
Stokes Point Australia 137 [inset]
Stokes Range hills Australia 134 E4
Stokkseyri Iceland 54 [inset]
Stokkvågen Norway 54 H3
Stokmarknes Norway 54 I2
Stolac Bos.-Herz. 68 G3
Stolberg (Rheinland) Germany 62 G4
Stolboukha Vostochnyy Kazakhstan Kazakh. 98 D2
Stolbovoy Rus. Fed. 189 G2
Stolbtsy Belarus see Stowbtsy
Stolin Belarus 55 O11
Stollberg Germany 63 M4
Stolp Poland see Słupsk
Stolzenau Germany 63 J2
Stone U.K. 59 E6
Stoneboro U.S.A. 164 E3
Stonecliffe Canada 152 F5
Stonecutters' Island pen. H.K. China 97 [inset]
Stonehaven U.K. 60 G4
Stonehenge Australia 136 C5
Stonehenge tourist site U.K. 59 F7
Stoner U.S.A. 159 I3
Stonewall Canada 151 L5
Stonewall Jackson Lake U.S.A. 164 E4
Stony r. AK U.S.A. 148 H3
Stony Creek U.S.A. 165 G5
Stony Lake Canada 151 L3
Stony Point U.S.A. 165 G2
Stony Rapids Canada 151 J3
Stony River U.S.A. 146 C3
Stooping r. Canada 152 E3
Stora Lulevatten l. Sweden 54 K3
Stora Sjöfallets nationalpark nat. park Sweden 54 J3
Storavan l. Sweden 54 K4
Store Bælt sea chan. Denmark see Great Belt
Støren Norway 54 G5
Storfjordbotn Norway 54 O1
Storforshei Norway 54 I3
Storjord Norway 54 I3
Storkerson Peninsula Canada 147 H2
Storm Bay Australia 137 [inset]
Stormberg S. Africa 125 H6
Storm Lake U.S.A. 160 E3
Stornosa mt. Norway 54 E6
Stornoway U.K. 60 C2
Storozhevsk Rus. Fed. 52 L3
Storozhynets' Ukr. 53 E6
Storrs U.S.A. 165 I3
Storseleby Sweden 54 J4
Storsjön l. Sweden 54 I5
Storskrymten mt. Norway 54 F5
Storslett Norway 54 L2
Storutemelk sea chan. Neth. 62 F1
Storuman Sweden 54 J4
Storuman l. Sweden 54 J4
Storvik Sweden 55 J6
Storvorde Denmark 55 G8
Storvreta Sweden 55 J7
Story U.S.A. 156 G3
Stotfold U.K. 59 G6
Stoughton Canada 151 K5
Stour r. England U.K. 59 F6
Stour r. England U.K. 59 G8
Stour r. England U.K. 59 I7
Stour r. England U.K. 59 I7
Stourbridge U.K. 59 E6
Stourport-on-Severn U.K. 59 E6
Stout Lake Canada 151 M4
Stowbtsy Belarus 55 O10
Stowe U.S.A. 165 I1
Stowmarket U.K. 59 H6
Stoyba Rus. Fed. 90 C1
Strabane U.K. 61 E3
Stradbally Ireland 61 E4
Stradbroke U.K. 59 I6
Stradella Italy 68 C2
Strakonice Czech Rep. 57 N6
Stralsund Germany 57 N3
Strand S. Africa 124 D8
Stranda Norway 54 E5
Strangford U.K. 61 G3
Strangford Lough inlet U.K. 61 G3
Strangways r. Australia 134 F3
Stranraer U.K. 60 D6
Strasbourg France 66 H2
Strasburg Germany 63 N1
Strasburg U.S.A. 165 F4
Strassburg France see Strasbourg
Stratford Australia 138 C6
Stratford Canada 164 E2
Stratford CA U.S.A. 158 D3
Stratford TX U.S.A. 161 C4
Stratford-upon-Avon U.K. 59 F6
Strathaven U.K. 60 E5
Strathmore Canada 150 H5
Strathmore r. U.K. 60 E2
Strathnaver Canada 150 F4
Strathroy Canada 164 E2
Strathspey valley U.K. 60 F3
Strathy U.K. 60 F2
Stratton U.K. 59 C8
Stratton U.S.A. 165 J1
Stratton Mountain U.S.A. 165 I2
Straubing Germany 63 M6
Straumnes pt Iceland 54 [inset]
Strawberry U.S.A. 159 H4
Strawberry Mountain U.S.A. 156 D3
Strawberry Reservoir U.S.A. 159 H1
Streaky Bay Australia 135 F8
Streaky Bay b. Australia 135 F8
Streator U.S.A. 160 F3
Street U.K. 59 E7
Streetsboro U.S.A. 164 E3
Strehaia Romania 69 J2
Strehla Germany 63 N3
Streich Mound hill Australia 135 C7
Strelka Rus. Fed. 77 Q3
Strel'na r. Rus. Fed. 52 H2
Strenči Latvia 55 N8
Streymoy i. Faroe Is 54 [inset]
Stříbro Czech Rep. 63 M5
Strichen U.K. 60 G3
Strimonas r. Greece see Strymonas
Stroeder Arg. 178 D6
Strokestown Ireland 61 D4
Stroma, Island of U.K. 60 F2
Stromboli, Isola i. Italy 68 F5
Stromness S. Georgia 178 I8
Stromness U.K. 60 F2
Strömstad Sweden 55 G7
Strömsund Sweden 54 I5
Strongsville U.S.A. 164 E3
Stronsay i. U.K. 60 G1
Stroud Australia 138 E4
Stroud U.K. 59 E7
Stroud Road Australia 138 E4
Stroudsburg U.S.A. 165 H3
Struer Denmark 55 F8
Struga Macedonia 69 I4
Strugi-Krasnyye Rus. Fed. 55 P7
Struis Bay S. Africa 124 E8
Strullendorf Germany 63 K5
Struma r. Bulg. 69 J4
also known as Strymonas (Greece)
Strumble Head hd U.K. 59 B6
Strumica Macedonia 69 J4
Struthers U.S.A. 164 E3
Stryama r. Bulg. 69 K3
Strydenburg S. Africa 124 F5
Strymonas r. Greece 69 J4
also known as Struma (Bulgaria)
Stryn Norway 54 E6
Stryy Ukr. 53 D6
Strzelecki, Mount hill Australia 134 F5
Strzelecki Desert Australia 137 C6
Strzelecki Regional Reserve nature res. Australia 137 B6
Stuart FL U.S.A. 163 D7
Stuart NE U.S.A. 160 D3
Stuart VA U.S.A. 164 E5
Stuart Island AK U.S.A. 148 G3
Stuart Lake Canada 150 E4
Stuart Range hills Australia 137 A6
Stuarts Draft U.S.A. 164 F4
Stuart Town Australia 138 D4
Stuchka Latvia see Aizkraukle
Stučka Latvia see Aizkraukle
Studholme Junction N.Z. 139 C7
Studsviken Sweden 54 K5
Study Butte TX U.S.A. 166 E2
Stukely, Lac l. Canada 165 I1
Stung Treng Cambodia see Stœng Trêng
Stupart r. Canada 151 M4
Stupino Rus. Fed. 53 H5
Sturge Island Antarctica 188 H2
Sturgeon r. Ont. Canada 152 F5
Sturgeon r. Sask. Canada 151 J4
Sturgeon Bay b. Canada 151 L4
Sturgeon Bay U.S.A. 164 B1
Sturgeon Bay Canal lake channel U.S.A. 164 B1
Sturgeon Falls Canada 152 F5
Sturgeon Lake Ont. Canada 151 N5
Sturgeon Lake Ont. Canada 165 F1
Sturgis MI U.S.A. 164 C3
Sturgis SD U.S.A. 160 C2
Sturt, Mount hill Australia 137 C6
Sturt Creek watercourse Australia 134 D4
Sturt National Park Australia 137 C6
Sturt Stony Desert Australia 137 C6
Stutterheim S. Africa 125 H7
Stuttgart Germany 63 J6
Stuttgart U.S.A. 161 F5
Stuver, Mount AK U.S.A. 149 J1
Stykkishólmur Iceland 54 [inset]
Styr r. Belarus/Ukr. 53 E5
Suaçuí Grande r. Brazil 179 C2
Suai East Timor 83 C5
Suai Sarawak Malaysia 85 F2
Suakin Sudan 108 E6
Suao Taiwan 97 I3
Suaqui Grande Mex. 166 C2
Suau P.N.G. 136 E1
Subačius Lith. 55 N9
Subang Jawa Indon. 85 D4
Subankhata India 105 G4
Subansiri r. India 99 F8
Subarnapur India see Sonapur
Sūbāshī Iran 110 C3
Subay reg. Saudi Arabia 110 B5
Şubayḩah Saudi Arabia 107 D4
Subei Gansu China 98 F5
Subi Besar i. Indon. 85 E2
Subi Kecil i. Indon. 85 E2
Sublette U.S.A. 161 C4
Subotica Serbia 69 H1
Success, Lake U.S.A. 158 D3
Succiso, Alpi di mts Italy 68 D2
Suceava Romania 53 E7
Suchan Rus. Fed. see Partizansk
Suck r. Ireland 61 D4
Suckling, Cape AK U.S.A. 149 L3
Suckling, Mount P.N.G. 136 E1
Suckow Germany 63 L1

▶Sucre Bol. 176 E7
Legislative capital of Bolivia.

Suczawa Romania see Suceava
Sud, Grand Récif du reef New Caledonia 133 G4
Suda Rus. Fed. 52 H4
Sudak Ukr. 112 D1
Sudama Japan 93 E3

▶Sudan country Africa 121 F3
Largest country in Africa, and 10th largest in the world.

Suday Rus. Fed. 52 I4
Sudayr reg. Saudi Arabia 110 B5
Sudbury Canada 152 E5
Sudbury U.K. 59 H6
Sudd swamp Sudan 108 C8
Sude r. Germany 63 K1
Sudest Island P.N.G. see Tagula Island
Sudetenland mts Czech Rep./Poland see Sudety
Sudety mts Czech Rep./Poland 57 O5
Sudislavl' Rus. Fed. 52 I4
Sudlersville U.S.A. 165 H4
Süd-Nord-Kanal canal Germany 62 H2
Sudogda Rus. Fed. 52 I5
Sudr Egypt 107 A5
Suðuroy i. Faroe Is 54 [inset]
Sue watercourse Sudan 121 F4
Sueca Spain 67 F4
Suez Egypt 107 A5
Suez, Gulf of Egypt 107 A5
Suez Bay Egypt 107 A5
Suez Canal Egypt 107 A4
Suffolk U.S.A. 165 G5
Sugarbush Hill hill U.S.A. 160 F2
Sugarloaf Mountain U.S.A. 165 J1
Sugarloaf Point Australia 138 F4
Suga-shima i. Japan 92 C4
Sugbuhan Point Phil. 82 D4
Sügêt Xinjiang China see Sogat
Sugi i. Indon. 84 C2
Sugun Xinjiang China 98 B5
Sugut r. Malaysia 85 G1
Sugut, Tanjung pt Malaysia 85 G1
Suhai Hu l. Qinghai China 98 F5
Suhai Obo Nei Mongol China 94 F3
Suhait Nei Mongol China 94 F4
Sūhāj Egypt 108 D4
Şuḩār Oman 110 E5
Suhaymī, Wādī as watercourse Egypt 107 A4
Sühbaatar Mongolia 94 F1
Sühbaatar Mongolia 95 H2
Sühbaatar prov. Mongolia 95 H2
Suheli Par i. India 106 B4
Suhl Germany 63 K4
Suhlendorf Germany 63 K2
Suhul reg. Saudi Arabia 110 B6
Suhūl al Kidan plain Saudi Arabia 110 D6
Şuhut Turkey 69 N5
Sui Pak. 111 H4
Sui, Laem pt Thai. 87 B5
Suibin China 90 C3
Suid-Afrika country Africa see Republic of South Africa
Suide Shaanxi China 95 G4
Suidzhikurmsy Turkm. see Madaw
Suifenhe China 90 C3
Suifu Japan 93 G2
Suigetsu-ko l. Japan 92 B3
Suigō-Tsukuba Kokutei-kōen park Japan 93 G3
Suihua China 90 B3
Suileng China 90 B3
Suining Hunan China 97 F3
Suining Jiangsu China 97 H1
Suining Sichuan China 96 E2
Suippes France 62 E5
Suir r. Ireland 61 E5
Suisse country Europe see Switzerland
Suita Japan 92 B4
Sui Vehar Pak. 111 H4
Suixi China 97 H1
Suixian Henan China 95 H5
Suixian Hubei China see Suizhou
Suiyang Guizhou China 96 E3
Suiyang Henan China 95 H5
Suiza country Europe see Switzerland
Suizhong Liaoning China 95 J3
Suizhou China 97 G2
Suj Nei Mongol China 95 F3
Sujangarh India 104 C4
Sujawal Pak. 111 H5
Suk atoll Micronesia see Pulusuk
Sukabumi Jawa Indon. 84 D4
Sukadana Kalimantan Indon. 85 E3
Sukadana Sumatera Indon. 84 D4
Sukadana, Teluk b. Indon. 85 E3
Sukagawa Japan 91 F5
Sukanegara Jawa Indon. 84 D4
Sukaraja Kalimantan Indon. 85 E3
Sukaramai Kalimantan Indon. 85 E3
Sukarnapura Indon. see Jayapura
Sukarno, Puncak mt. Indon. see Jaya, Puncak
Sukau Sabah Malaysia 85 G1
Sukchŏn N. Korea 91 B5
Sukhinichi Rus. Fed. 53 G5
Sukhona r. Rus. Fed. 52 J3
Sukhothai Thai. 86 C3
Sukhumi Georgia see Sokhumi
Sukhum-Kale Georgia see Sokhumi
Sukkertoppen Greenland see Maniitsoq
Sukkozero Rus. Fed. 52 G3
Sukkur Pak. 111 H5
Sukma India 106 D2
Sukpay Rus. Fed. 90 E3
Sukpay r. Rus. Fed. 90 E3
Sukri r. India 104 C4
Suktel r. India 106 D1
Sukun i. Indon. 83 B5
Sula i. Norway 55 D6
Sula r. Rus. Fed. 52 K2
Sula, Kepulauan is Indon. 83 C3
Sulabesi i. Indon. 83 C3
Sulaiman Range mts Pak. 111 H4
Sulak Rus. Fed. 113 G2

Sülār Iran 110 C4
Sula Sgeir i. U.K. 60 C1
Sulasih, Gunung vol. Indon. 84 C3
Sulat i. Indon. 85 G5
Sulat Samar Phil. 82 D4
Sulatna Crossing AK U.S.A. 148 I2
Sulawesi i. Indon. see Celebes
Sulawesi Barat prov. Indon. 83 A3
Sulawesi Selatan prov. Indon. 83 A3
Sulawesi Tengah prov. Indon. 83 B3
Sulawesi Tenggara prov. Indon. 83 B4
Sulawesi Utara prov. Indon. 83 C2
Sulaymān Beg Iraq 113 G4
Sulaymānīyah Iraq 113 G4
Sulayyimah Saudi Arabia 110 B6
Sulci Sardinia Italy see Sant'Antioco
Sulcis Sardinia Italy see Sant'Antioco
Suledeh Iran 110 C2
Suleman, Teluk b. Indon. 85 G2
Sule Skerry i. U.K. 60 E1
Sule Stack i. U.K. 60 E1
Suliki Sumatera Indon. 84 C3
Sulingen Germany 63 I2
Sulin Gol r. Qinghai China 94 C4
Sulitjelma Norway 54 J3
Sulkava Fin. 54 P6
Sullana Peru 176 B4
Sullivan IL U.S.A. 160 F4
Sullivan IN U.S.A. 164 B4
Sullivan Bay Canada 150 E5
Sullivan Island Myanmar see Lanbi Kyun
Sullivan Lake Canada 151 I5
Sulmo Italy see Sulmona
Sulmona Italy 68 E3
Sulphur LA U.S.A. 161 E6
Sulphur OK U.S.A. 161 D5
Sulphur r. U.S.A. 161 E5
Sulphur Springs U.S.A. 161 E5
Sultan Canada 152 E5
Sultan, Koh-i- mts Pak. 111 F4
Sultanabad India see Osmannagar
Sultanabad Iran see Arāk
Sultan Dağları mts Turkey 69 N5
Sultanıye Turkey see Karapınar
Sultanpur India 105 E4
Suluan i. Phil. 82 D4
Sulu Archipelago is Phil. 82 C5
Sulu Basin sea feature N. Pacific Ocean 186 E5
Sülüklü Turkey 112 D3
Sülüktü Kyrg. 111 H2
Sulusaray Turkey 112 E3
Sulu Sea N. Pacific Ocean 80 F5
Suluvvaulik, Lac l. Canada 153 G2
Sulyukta Kyrg. see Sülüktü
Sulzbach-Rosenberg Germany 63 L5
Sulzberger Bay Antarctica 188 I1
Suma Japan 92 B4
Sumāil Oman 110 E6
Sumalata Sulawesi Indon. 83 B2
Sumampa Arg. 178 D3
Sumangat, Tanjung pt Malaysia 85 G1
Sumapaz, Parque Nacional nat. park Col. 176 D3
Sūmār Iran 110 B3
Sumatera i. Indon. see Sumatra
Sumatera Barat prov. Indon. 84 C3
Sumatera Selatan prov. Indon. 84 C3
Sumatera Utara prov. Indon. 84 B2

▶Sumatra i. Indon. 84 B2
2nd largest island in Asia, and 6th in the world.

Šumava nat. park Czech Rep. 57 N6
Sumba i. Indon. 83 B5
Sumba, Selat sea chan. Indon. 83 A5
Sumbar r. Turkm. 110 D2
Sumbawa i. Indon. 83 A5
Sumbawabesar Sumbawa Indon. 85 G5
Sumbawanga Tanz. 123 D4
Sumbe Angola 123 B5
Sumbing, Gunung vol. Indon. 84 C3
Sumbu National Park Zambia 123 D4
Sumburgh U.K. 60 [inset]
Sumburgh Head hd U.K. 60 [inset]
Sumdo Aksai Chin 99 B6
Sumdo China 96 D2
Sumdum, Mount AK U.S.A. 149 N4
Sumedang Jawa Indon. 85 D4
Sume'eh Sarā Iran 110 C2
Sumeih Sudan 108 C8
Sumenep Jawa Indon. 85 F4
Sumgait Azer. see Sumqayıt
Sumisu-jima i. Japan 89 Q6
Sümiyn Bulag Mongolia see Gurvandzagal
Summēl Iraq 113 F3
Summer Beaver Canada 152 C3
Summerford Canada 153 L4
Summer Island U.S.A. 162 C2
Summer Isles U.K. 60 D2
Summerland Canada 150 G5
Summersville U.S.A. 164 E4
Summit AK U.S.A. 149 J3
Summit Lake Canada 150 F4
Summit Lake AK U.S.A. 149 K3
Summit Mountain U.S.A. 158 E2
Summit Peak U.S.A. 157 G5
Sumnal Aksai Chin 99 B6
Sumner N.Z. 139 D6
Sumner, Lake N.Z. 139 D6
Sumon-dake mt. Japan 91 E5
Sumoto Japan 92 A4
Sumpangbinangae Sulawesi Indon. 83 A4
Šumperk Czech Rep. 57 P6
Sumpu Japan see Shizuoka
Sumqayıt Azer. 113 H2
Sumskiy Posad Rus. Fed. 52 G2
Sumter U.S.A. 163 D5
Sumur India 104 D2
Sumxi Xizang China 99 C6
Sumy Ukr. 53 G6
Sumzom China 96 C2
Suna Rus. Fed. 52 K4
Sunaj India 104 D4
Sunam India 104 C3
Sunamganj Bangl. 105 G4
Sunami Japan 92 C3
Sunan Gansu China 94 D4
Sunart, Loch inlet U.K. 60 D4
Şunaynah Oman 110 D6
Sunburst U.S.A. 156 F2
Sunbury Australia 138 B6
Sunbury OH U.S.A. 164 D3
Sunbury PA U.S.A. 165 G3
Sunch'ŏn S. Korea 91 B6
Sun City S. Africa 125 H3
Sun City AZ U.S.A. 159 G5
Sun City CA U.S.A. 158 E5
Sunda, Selat str. Indon. 84 D4
Sunda Kalapa Jawa Indon. see Jakarta
Sundance U.S.A. 156 G3
Sundarbans coastal area Bangl./India 105 G5
Sundarbans National Park Bangl./India 105 G5
Sundargarh India 105 F5
Sunda Shelf sea feature Indian Ocean 185 P5
Sunda Strait Indon. see Sunda, Selat
Sunda Trench sea feature Indian Ocean see Java Trench
Sunderland U.K. 58 F4
Sundern (Sauerland) Germany 63 I3
Sündiken Dağları mts Turkey 69 N5
Sundown National Park Australia 138 E2
Sundre Canada 150 H5
Sundridge Canada 152 F5
Sundsvall Sweden 54 J5
Sundukli, Peski des. Turkm. see Sandykly Gumy
Sundumbili S. Africa 125 J5
Sunduyka Rus. Fed. 95 G1
Sungaiapit Sumatera Indon. 84 C2
Sungaiguntung Sumatera Indon. 84 C2
Sungaikabung Sumatera Indon. 84 C2
Sungaikakap Kalimantan Indon. 85 E3
Sungailiat Sumatera Indon. 84 D3
Sungaipenuh Sumatera Indon. 84 C3
Sungai Petani Malaysia 84 C1
Sungaipinyuh Kalimantan Indon. 85 E2
Sungaiselan Indon. 84 D3
Sungari r. China see Songhua Jiang
Sungei Seletar Reservoir Sing. 87 [inset]
Sungguminasa Sulawesi Indon. 83 A4
Sungkiang China see Songjiang
Sung Kong i. H.K. China 97 [inset]
Sungqu China see Songpan
Sungsang Sumatera Indon. 84 D3
Sungurlu Turkey 112 D2
Sunkar, Gora mt. Kazakh. 98 A3
Sun Kosi r. Nepal 105 F4
Sunman U.S.A. 164 C4
Sunndal Norway 55 E6
Sunndalsøra Norway 54 F5
Sunne Sweden 55 H7
Sunnyside U.S.A. 156 D3
Sunnyvale U.S.A. 158 B3
Suno-saki pt Japan 93 F4
Sun Prairie U.S.A. 160 F3
Sunset House Canada 150 G4
Sunset Peak hill H.K. China 97 [inset]
Suntar Rus. Fed. 77 M3
Suntsar Pak. 111 F5
Sunwi-do i. N. Korea 91 B5
Sunwu China 90 B2
Sunyani Ghana 120 C4
Suolijärvet l. Fin. 54 P3
Suomi country Europe see Finland
Suomussalmi Fin. 54 P4
Suō-nada b. Japan 91 C6
Suonenjoki Fin. 54 O5
Suong r. Laos 86 C3
Suoyarvi Rus. Fed. 52 G3
Suozhen Shandong China see Huantai
Supa India 106 B3
Supaul India 105 F4
Superior AZ U.S.A. 159 H5
Superior MT U.S.A. 156 E3
Superior NE U.S.A. 160 D3
Superior WI U.S.A. 160 E2
Superior, Laguna lag. Mex. 167 G5

▶Superior, Lake Canada/U.S.A. 155 J2
Largest lake in North America, and 2nd in the world.

Suphan Buri Thai. 87 C4
Süphan Dağı mt. Turkey 113 F3
Supiori i. Indon. 81 J7
Suponevo Rus. Fed. 53 G5
Support Force Glacier Antarctica 188 A1
Sūq ash Shuyūkh Iraq 113 G5
Suqian China 97 H1
Suquṭrá i. Yemen see Socotra
Şūr Oman 111 E6
Sur, Point U.S.A. 158 C3
Sur, Punta pt Arg. 178 E5
Sura r. Rus. Fed. 53 J4
Şuraabad Azer. 113 H2
Surabaya Jawa Indon. 85 F4
Sūrak Iran 110 E5
Surakarta Jawa Indon. 85 E4
Suramana Sulawesi Indon. 83 A3
Sūran Iran 111 F5
Şūrān Syria 107 C2
Surat Australia 138 D1
Surat India 104 C5
Suratgarh India 104 C3
Surat Thani Thai. 87 B5
Surazh Rus. Fed. 53 G5
Surbiton Australia 136 D4
Surdulica Serbia 69 J3
Sûre r. Lux. 62 G5
Surendranagar India 104 B5
Suretka Costa Rica 166 [inset] J7
Surf U.S.A. 158 C4
Surgut Rus. Fed. 76 I3
Suri India see Siuri
Suriapet India 106 C2
Surigao Mindanao Phil. 82 D4
Surigao Strait Phil. 82 D4
Surin Thai. 86 C4
Surinam country S. America see Suriname
Suriname country S. America 177 G3
Surin Nua, Ko i. Thai. 87 B5
Surkhduz Afgh. 111 G4
Surkhet Nepal 105 E3
Surkhon Uzbek. see Surxon
Sürmene Turkey 113 F2
Surovikino Rus. Fed. 53 I6
Surprise B.C. Canada 149 N4
Surprise Lake B.C. Canada 149 N4
Surpura India 104 C4
Surrey Canada 150 F5
Surry U.S.A. 165 G5
Surskoye Rus. Fed. 53 J5
Surt Libya see Sirte
Surtsey i. Iceland 54 [inset]
Sürü Hormozgan Iran 110 E5
Sürü Sīstān va Balūchestān Iran 110 E5
Suruç Turkey 107 D1
Surud, Raas pt Somalia 122 E2
Surud Ad mt. Somalia see Shimbiris
Suruga-wan b. Japan 93 E4
Surulangun Sumatera Indon. 84 C3
Surup Mindanao Phil. 82 D5
Survey Pass AK U.S.A. 148 I2
Surwold Germany 63 H2
Surxon Uzbek. 111 G2
Suryapet India see Suriapet
Şuşa Azer. 113 G3
Susah Tunisia see Sousse
Susaki Japan 91 D6
Susan U.S.A. 165 G5
Süsangerd Iran 110 C4
Susanino Rus. Fed. 90 F1
Susanville U.S.A. 158 C1
Suşehri Turkey 112 E2
Susitna r. AK U.S.A. 149 J3
Susitna, Mount AK U.S.A. 149 J3
Susitna Lake AK U.S.A. 149 K3
Suso Thai. 87 B6
Susobana-gawa r. Japan 93 E2
Susong China 97 H2
Susono Japan 93 E3
Susquehanna U.S.A. 165 H3
Susquehanna r. U.S.A. 165 G4
Susquehanna, West Branch r. U.S.A. 165 G3
Susques Arg. 178 C2
Sussex U.S.A. 165 G5
Susua Sulawesi Indon. 83 B3
Susul Sabah Malaysia 85 G1
Susuman Rus. Fed. 77 P3
Susupu Halmahera Indon. 83 C2
Susurluk Turkey 69 M5
Sutak India 104 D2
Sutay Uul mt. Mongolia 94 C2
Sutherland Australia 138 E5
Sutherland S. Africa 124 E7
Sutherland U.S.A. 160 C3
Sutherland Range hills Australia 135 D6
Sutjeska nat. park Bos.-Herz. 68 H3
Sutlej r. India/Pak. 104 B3
Sütlüce Turkey 107 A1
Sutter U.S.A. 158 C2
Sutterton U.K. 59 G6
Sutton Canada 165 I1
Sutton r. Canada 152 E3
Sutton U.K. 59 H6
Sutton AK U.S.A. 149 J3
Sutton NE U.S.A. 160 D3
Sutton WV U.S.A. 164 E4
Sutton Coldfield U.K. 59 F6
Sutton in Ashfield U.K. 59 F5
Sutton Lake Canada 152 D3
Sutton Lake U.S.A. 164 E4
Suttor r. Australia 136 D4
Suttsu Japan 90 F4
Sutwik Island AK U.S.A. 148 H4
Sutyr' r. Rus. Fed. 90 D2
Suugant Mongolia see Gurvansayhan
Suusamyr Kyrg. 98 A4

▶Suva Fiji 133 H3
Capital of Fiji.

Suvadiva Atoll Maldives see Huvadhu Atoll
Suvalki Poland see Suwałki
Suvorov atoll Cook Is see Suwarrow
Suvorov Rus. Fed. 53 H5
Suwa Japan 93 E2
Suwa-ko l. Japan 93 E2
Suwakong Kalimantan Indon. 85 F3
Suwałki Poland 53 D5
Suwannaphum Thai. 86 C4
Suwannee r. U.S.A. 163 D6
Suwanose-jima i. Japan 91 C7
Suwaran, Gunung mt. Indon. 85 G2
Suwarrow atoll Cook Is 133 J3
Suwaylih Jordan 107 B3
Suwayr well Saudi Arabia 113 F5
Suways, Khalīj as g. Egypt see Suez, Gulf of
Suways, Qanāt as canal Egypt see Suez Canal
Suweilih Jordan see Suwaylih
Suweis, Khalîg el g. Egypt see Suez, Gulf of
Suweis, Qanâ el canal Egypt see Suez Canal
Suwŏn S. Korea 91 B5
Suxik Qinghai China 94 C4
Suykbulak Kazakh. 98 C2
Suyūl Ḩanīsh i. Yemen 108 F7
Suz, Mys pt Kazakh. 113 I2
Suzaka Japan 93 E2
Suzdal' Rus. Fed. 52 I4
Suzhou Anhui China 97 H1
Suzhou Gansu China see Jiuquan
Suzhou Jiangsu China 97 I2
Suzi He r. China 90 B4
Suzuka Japan 92 C4
Suzuka-gawa r. Japan 92 C4
Suzuka Kokutei-kōen park Japan 92 C3
Suzuka-sanmyaku mts Japan 92 C4
Suzu-misaki pt Japan 91 E5
Sværholthalvøya pen. Norway 54 O1

▶Svalbard terr. Arctic Ocean 76 C2
Part of Norway.

Svappavaara Sweden 54 L3
Svartenhuk Halvø pen. Greenland see Sigguup Nunaa
Svatove Ukr. 53 H6
Svay Chék Cambodia 87 C4
Svay Riěng Cambodia 87 D5
Svecha Rus. Fed. 52 J4
Sveg Sweden 55 I5
Sveki Latvia 55 O8
Svelgen Norway 54 D6
Svellingen Norway 54 F5
Švenčionėliai Lith. 55 N9
Švenčionys Lith. 55 O9
Svendborg Denmark 55 G9
Svensbu Norway 54 K2
Svenstavik Sweden 54 I5
Sverdlovsk Rus. Fed. see Yekaterinburg
Sverdlovs'k Ukr. 53 H6
Sverdrup Islands Canada 147 I2
Sverige country Europe see Sweden
Sveti Nikole Macedonia 69 I4
Svetlaya Rus. Fed. 90 E3
Svetlogorsk Belarus see Svyetlahorsk
Svetlogorsk Kaliningradskaya Oblast' Rus. Fed. 55 L9
Svetlogorsk Krasnoyarskiy Kray Rus. Fed. 76 J3
Svetlograd Rus. Fed. 113 F1
Svetlovodsk Ukr. see Svitlovods'k
Svetlyy Kaliningradskaya Oblast' Rus. Fed. 55 L9
Svetlyy Orenburgskaya Oblast' Rus. Fed. 102 B1
Svetlyy Yar Rus. Fed. 53 J6
Svetogorsk Rus. Fed. 55 P6
Svíahnúkar vol. Iceland 54 [inset]
Svilaja mts Croatia 68 G3
Svilengrad Bulg. 69 L4
Svinecea Mare, Vârful mt. Romania 69 J2
Svir Belarus 55 O9
Svir' r. Rus. Fed. 52 G3
Svishtov Bulg. 69 K3
Svitava r. Czech Rep. 57 P6
Svitavy Czech Rep. 57 P6
Svitlovods'k Ukr. 53 G6
Sviyaga r. Rus. Fed. 52 K5
Svizzer, Parc Naziunal Switz. 68 D1
Svizzera country Europe see Switzerland
Svobodnyy Rus. Fed. 90 C2
Svolvær Norway 54 I2
Svrljiške Planine mts Serbia 69 J3
Svyatoy Nos, Mys c. Rus. Fed. 52 K2
Svyetlahorsk Belarus 53 F5
Swadlincote U.K. 59 F6
Swaffham U.K. 59 H6
Swain Reefs Australia 136 F4
Swainsboro U.S.A. 163 D5
Swains Island atoll American Samoa 133 I3
Swakop watercourse Namibia 124 B2
Swakopmund Namibia 124 B2
Swale r. U.K. 58 F4
Swallow Islands Solomon Is 133 G3
Swamihalli India 106 C3
Swampy r. Canada 153 H2
Swan r. Australia 135 A7
Swan r. Man./Sask. Canada 151 K4
Swan r. Ont. Canada 152 E3
Swanage U.K. 59 F8
Swandale U.S.A. 164 E4
Swan Hill Australia 138 A5
Swan Hills Canada 150 H4
Swan Islands is Caribbean Sea see Cisne, Islas del
Swan Lake B.C. Canada 149 O5
Swan Lake Man. Canada 151 K4
Swanley U.K. 59 H7
Swanquarter U.S.A. 163 E5
Swan Reach Australia 137 B7
Swan River Canada 151 K4
Swansea U.K. 59 D7
Swansea Bay U.K. 59 D7
Swanton CA U.S.A. 158 B3
Swanton VT U.S.A. 165 I1
Swartbergpas pass S. Africa 124 F7
Swart Nossob watercourse Namibia see Black Nossob
Swartruggens S. Africa 125 H3
Swartz Creek U.S.A. 164 D2
Swasey Peak U.S.A. 159 G2
Swat Kohistan reg. Pak. 111 I3
Swatow China see Shantou
Swayzee U.S.A. 164 C3
Swaziland country Africa 125 J4

▶Sweden country Europe 54 I5
5th largest country in Europe.

Sweet Home U.S.A. 156 C3
Sweet Springs U.S.A. 164 E5
Sweetwater U.S.A. 161 C5
Sweetwater r. U.S.A. 156 G4
Swellendam S. Africa 124 E8
Świdnica Poland 57 P5
Świdwin Poland 57 O4
Świebodzin Poland 57 O4
Świecie Poland 57 Q4
Swift r. AK U.S.A. 148 H3
Swift Current Canada 151 J5
Swiftcurrent Creek r. Canada 151 J5
Swift Fork r. AK U.S.A. 148 I3
Swilly r. Ireland 61 E3
Swilly, Lough inlet Ireland 61 E2
Swindon U.K. 59 F7
Swinford Ireland 61 D4
Świnoujście Poland 57 O4
Swinton U.K. 60 G5
Swiss Confederation country Europe see Switzerland
Switzerland country Europe 66 I3
Swords Ireland 61 F4
Swords Range hills Australia 136 C4
Syamozero, Ozero l. Rus. Fed. 52 G3
Syamzha Rus. Fed. 52 I3
Syang Nepal 105 E3
Syas'troy Rus. Fed. 52 G3
Sychevka Rus. Fed. 52 G5
Sydenham atoll Kiribati see Nonouti

▶Sydney Australia 138 E4
Capital of New South Wales. Most populous city in Oceania.

Sydney Canada 153 J5
Sydney Island Kiribati see Manra
Sydney Lake Canada 151 M5
Sydney Mines Canada 153 J5
Syedra tourist site Turkey 107 A1
Syeverodonets'k Ukr. 53 H6
Syke Germany 63 I2
Sykesville U.S.A. 165 F3
Syktyvkar Rus. Fed. 52 K3
Sylarna mt. Norway/Sweden 54 H5
Sylhet Bangl. 105 G4
Syloga Rus. Fed. 52 I3
Sylt i. Germany 57 L3
Sylva U.S.A. 163 D5
Sylvania GA U.S.A. 163 D5
Sylvania OH U.S.A. 164 D3
Sylvan Lake Canada 150 H4
Sylvester U.S.A. 163 D6
Sylvester, Lake salt flat Australia 136 A3
Sylvia, Mount Canada 150 E3
Symerton U.S.A. 164 A3
Symi i. Greece 69 L6
Synel'nykove Ukr. 53 G6
Syngyrli, Mys pt Kazakh. 113 I2
Synya Rus. Fed. 51 R2
Syowa research station Antarctica 188 D2
Syracusae Sicily Italy see Syracuse
Syracuse Sicily Italy 68 F6
Syracuse KS U.S.A. 160 C4
Syracuse NY U.S.A. 165 G2
Syrdar'ya r. Asia 102 C3
Syrdar'ya Uzbek. see Sirdaryo
Syrdaryinskiy Uzbek. see Sirdaryo
Syria country Asia 112 E4
Syriam Myanmar see Thanlyin
Syrian Desert Asia 112 E4
Syrna i. Greece 69 L6
Syros i. Greece 69 K6
Syrskiy Rus. Fed. 53 H5
Sysmä Fin. 55 N6
Sysola r. Rus. Fed. 52 K3
Syumsi Rus. Fed. 52 K4
Syurkum Rus. Fed. 90 F2
Syurkum, Mys pt Rus. Fed. 90 F2
Syzran' Rus. Fed. 53 K5
Szabadka Serbia see Subotica
Szczecin Poland 57 O4
Szczecinek Poland 57 P4
Szczytno Poland 57 R4
Szechwan prov. China see Sichuan
Szeged Hungary 69 I1
Székesfehérvár Hungary 68 H1
Szekszárd Hungary 68 H1
Szentes Hungary 69 I1
Szentgotthárd Hungary 68 G1
Szigetvár Hungary 68 G1
Szolnok Hungary 69 I1
Szombathely Hungary 68 G1
Sztálinváros Hungary see Dunaújváros

T

Taagga Duudka reg. Somalia 122 E3
Taal, Lake Luzon Phil. 82 C3
Tabaco Luzon Phil. 82 C3
Tābah Saudi Arabia 108 F4
Tabajara Brazil 176 F5
Tabakhmela Georgia see Kazret'i
Tabalo P.N.G. 81 L7
Tabanan Bali Indon. 85 F5
Tabang Kalimantan Indon. 85 G2
Tabang r. Indon. 85 F2
Tabankulu S. Africa 125 I6
Ţabaqah Ar Raqqah Syria 107 D2
Ţabaqah Ar Raqqah Syria see Madīnat ath Thawrah
Tabar Islands P.N.G. 132 F2
Tabarka Tunisia 68 C6
Ţabas Iran 111 F3
Tabasco Mex. 166 E4
Tabasco state Mex. 167 G5
Tābāsīn Iran 110 E4
Tābask, Kūh-e mt. Iran 110 C4
Tabatinga Amazonas Brazil 176 E4
Tabatinga São Paulo Brazil 179 A3
Tabatinga, Serra da hills Brazil 177 J6
Tabatsquri, Tba l. Georgia 113 F2
Tabayama Japan 93 E3
Tabayin Myanmar 86 A2
Tabayoo, Mount Luzon Phil. 82 C2
Tabbita Australia 138 B5
Tabelbala Alg. 64 D6
Taber Canada 151 H5
Tabet, Nam r. Myanmar 86 B1
Tabia Tsaka salt l. China 99 D7
Tabin Wildlife Reserve nature res. Malaysia 85 G1
Tabir r. Indon. 84 C3
Tabiteuea atoll Kiribati 133 H2
Tabivere Estonia 55 O7
Tablas i. Phil. 82 C3
Tablas Strait Phil. 82 C3
Table Cape N.Z. 139 F4
Table Mountain AK U.S.A. 149 L1
Table Point Palawan Phil. 82 B4
Tabligbo Togo 120 D4
Tábor Czech Rep. 57 O6
Tabora Tanz. 123 D4
Tabou Côte d'Ivoire 120 C4
Tabrīz Iran 110 B2
Tabuaeran atoll Kiribati 187 J5
Tabūk Saudi Arabia 112 E5
Tabulam Australia 138 F2
Tabulan Sulawesi Indon. 83 B3
Tabuyung Sumatera Indon. 84 B2
Tabwémasana, Mount Vanuatu 133 G3
Täby Sweden 55 K7
Tacalé Brazil 177 H3
Tacámbaro Mex. 167 E5
Tacaná, Volcán de vol. Mex. 167 G6
Tachakou Xinjiang China 98 D3
Tacheng Xinjiang China 98 C3
Tachie Canada 150 E4
Tachikawa Tōkyō Japan 93 F3
Tachov Czech Rep. 63 M5
Tacipi Sulawesi Indon. 83 B4
Tacloban Leyte Phil. 82 D4
Tacna Peru 176 D7
Tacna AZ U.S.A. 166 B1
Tacoma U.S.A. 156 C3
Taco Pozo Arg. 178 D3
Tacuarembó Uruguay 178 E4
Tacupeto Mex. 166 C2
Tadcaster U.K. 58 F5
Tademaït, Plateau du Alg. 64 E6
Tadenet Lake N.W.T. Canada 149 P1
Tadin New Caledonia 133 G4
Tadjikistan country Asia see Tajikistan
Tadjourah Djibouti 108 F7
Tadmur Syria 107 D2
Tado Japan 92 C3
Tadohae Haesang National Park S. Korea 91 B6
Tadoule Lake Canada 151 L3
Tadoussac Canada 153 H4
Tadpatri India 106 C3
Tadwale India 106 C2
Tadzhikskaya S.S.R. country Asia see Tajikistan
T'aean Haean National Park S. Korea 91 B5
Taech'ŏng-do i. S. Korea 91 B5
Taedasa-do N. Korea 91 B5
Taedong-man b. N. Korea 91 B5
Taegu S. Korea 91 C6
Taehan-min'guk country Asia see South Korea
Taehŭksan-kundo is S. Korea 91 B6
Taejŏn S. Korea 91 B5
Taejŏng S. Korea 91 B6
T'aepaek S. Korea 91 C5
Ta'erqi Nei Mongol China 95 J2
Taf r. U.K. 59 C7
Tafahi i. Tonga 133 I3
Tafalla Spain 67 F2
Tafeng China see Lanshan
Tafila Jordan see Aţ Ţafilah
Tafi Viejo Arg. 178 C3
Tafresh Iran 110 C3
Taft Iran 110 D4
Taft U.S.A. 158 D4
Taftān, Kūh-e mt. Iran 111 F4
Taftanāz Syria 107 C2
Tafwap India 87 A6
Taga Japan 92 C3
Tagagawik r. AK U.S.A. 148 H2
Taganrog Rus. Fed. 53 H7
Taganrog, Gulf of Rus. Fed./Ukr. 53 H7
Taganrogskiy Zaliv b. Rus. Fed./Ukr. see Taganrog, Gulf of
Tagarev, Gora mt. Iran/Turkm. 110 E2
Tagarkaty, Pereval pass Tajik. 111 I2
Tagaung Myanmar 86 B2
Tagbilaran Bohol Phil. 82 C4
Tagchagpu Ri mt. Xizang China 99 C6
Tagdempt Alg. see Tiaret
Taghmon Ireland 61 F5
Tagish Y.T. Canada 149 N3
Tagish Lake B.C. Canada 149 N4
Tagoloan r. Mindanao Phil. 82 D4
Tagtabazar Turkm. 111 F3
Taguchi-zaki pt Japan 92 B4
Tagudin Luzon Phil. 82 C2
Tagula P.N.G. 136 F1
Tagula Island P.N.G. 136 F1
Tagum Mindanao Phil. 82 D5
Tagus r. Port. 67 B4
also known as Tajo (Spain) or Tejo (Portugal)
Taha Heilong. China 95 K2
Tahaetkun Mountain Canada 150 G5
Tahan, Gunung mt. Malaysia 84 C1
Tahanroz'ka Zatoka b. Rus. Fed./Ukr. see Taganrog, Gulf of
Tahara Japan 92 D4
Tahat, Mont mt. Alg. 120 D2
Tahaurawe i. U.S.A. see Kaho'olawe
Tahe China 90 B1
Taheke N.Z. 139 D2
Tahilt Mongolia see Tsogt
Tahiti i. Fr. Polynesia 187 K7
Tahlab r. Iran/Pak. 111 F4
Tahlab, Dasht-i- plain Pak. 111 F4
Tahlequah U.S.A. 161 E5
Tahltan B.C. Canada 149 O4
Tahoe, Lake U.S.A. 158 C2
Tahoe Lake Canada 147 H3
Tahoe Vista U.S.A. 158 C2
Tahoka U.S.A. 161 C5
Tahoua Niger 120 D3
Ţahrūd Iran 110 E4
Tahrūd r. Iran 110 E4
Tahtsa Peak Canada 150 E4
Tahulandang i. Indon. 83 C2

ahuna *Sulawesi* Indon. 83 C2
aï, Parc National de *nat. park* Côte d'Ivoire 120 C4
ai'an *Liaoning* China 95 J3
ai'an *Shandong* China 95 I4
aibai *Gansu* China 95 G4
aibai *Shaanxi* China 95 F5
aibai Shan *mt.* China 96 E1
aibei Taiwan *see* **T'aipei**
aibus Qi *Nei Mongol* China *see* **Baochang**
'aichung Taiwan 97 I3
aidong Taiwan *see* **T'aitung**
aiei Japan 93 G3
aigong China *see* **Taijiang**
aigu *Shanxi* China 95 H4
aihang Shan *mts* China 95 H4
aihang Shan *mts* China 95 H4
aihape N.Z. 139 E4
aihe *Jiangxi* China 97 G3
Taihe *Sichuan* China *see* **Shehong**
Taihezhen China *see* **Shehong**
Tai Ho Wan H.K. China 97 [inset]
Taihu China 97 H2
Tai Hu *l.* China 97 I2
Taihuai *Shanxi* China 95 H4
Taijiang China 97 F3
Taikang *Heilong.* China 95 K2
Taikang *Henan* China 95 H5
Taiko-yama *hill* Japan 92 B3
Tailaco East Timor 83 C5
Tailai *Heilong.* China 95 J2
Tai Lam Chung Shui Tong *resr* H.K. China 97 [inset]
Taileleo Indon. 84 B3
Tailem Bend Australia 137 B7
Tai Long Wan *b.* H.K. China 97 [inset]
Taimani *reg.* Afgh. 111 F3
Tai Mo Shan *hill* H.K. China 97 [inset]
Tain U.K. 60 F2
T'ainan Taiwan 97 I4
T'ainan Taiwan *see* **Hsinying**
Tainaro, Akra *pt* Greece *see* **Tainaro, Akrotirio**
Tainaro, Akrotirio *pt* Greece 69 J6
Taining China 97 H3
Tai O H.K. China 97 [inset]
Taiobeiras Brazil 179 C1
Taipa *Sulawesi* Indon. 83 B3
Tai Pang Wan *b.* H.K. China *see* **Mirs Bay**

▶**T'aipei** Taiwan 97 I3
Capital of Taiwan.

Taiping *Guangdong* China *see* **Shixing**
Taiping *Guangxi* China *see* **Chongzuo**
Taiping *Guangxi* China 97 F4
Taiping Malaysia 84 C1
Taipingchuan *Jilin* China 95 J2
Taiping Ling *mt. Nei Mongol* China 95 J2
Tai Po H.K. China 97 [inset]
Tai Po Hoi *b.* H.K. China *see* **Tolo Harbour**
Tai Poutini National Park N.Z. *see* **Westland National Park**
Taiqian *Henan* China 95 H5
Taira *Toyama* Japan 92 C2
Tairbeart U.K. *see* **Tarbert**
Tai Rom Yen National Park Thai. 87 B5
Tairuq Iran 110 B3
Tais *Sumatera* Indon. 84 C4
Tais P.N.G. 81 K8
Taishaku-san *mt.* Japan 93 F2
Taishan China 97 G4
Taishun China 97 H3
Tai Siu Mo To *is* H.K. China *see* **The Brothers**
Taissy France 62 E5
Taitaitanopo *i.* Indon. 84 C3
Taitao, Península de *pen.* Chile 178 B7
Tai Tapu N.Z. 139 D6
Tai To Yan *mt.* H.K. China 97 [inset]
Taitō-zaki *pt* Japan 93 G3
T'aitung Taiwan 97 I4
Tai Tung Shan *hill* H.K. China *see* **Sunset Peak**
Taivalkoski Fin. 54 P4
Taivaskero *hill* Fin. 54 N2
Taiwan *country* Asia 97 I4
T'aiwan Haihsia *strait* China/Taiwan *see* **Taiwan Strait**
Taiwan Haixia *strait* China/Taiwan *see* **Taiwan Strait**
Taiwan Shan *mts* Taiwan *see* **Chungyang Shanmo**
Taiwan Strait China/Taiwan 97 H4
Taixian China *see* **Jiangyan**
Taixing China 97 I1
Taiyuan *Shanxi* China 95 H4
Tai Yue Shan *i.* H.K. China *see* **Lantau Island**
Taiyue Shan *mts* China 95 G4
Taizhao *Xizang* China 99 F7
Taizhong Taiwan *see* **T'aichung**
Taizhong Taiwan *see* **Fengyüan**
Taizhou *Jiangsu* China 97 H1
Taizhou *Zhejiang* China 97 I2
Taizhou Liedao *i.* China 97 I2
Taizhou Wan *b.* China 97 I2
Taizi He *r.* China 90 B4
Ta'izz Yemen 108 F7
Tājābād Iran 110 E4
Tajal Pak. 111 H5
Tajamulco, Volcán de *vol.* Guat. 167 H6
Tajem, Gunung *hill* Indon. 85 D3
Tajerouine Tunisia 68 C7
Tajikistan *country* Asia 111 H2
Tajimi Japan 92 D3
Tajiri Japan 92 B4
Tajitos Mex. 166 B2
Tajo *r.* Spain 67 C4 *see* **Tagus**
Tajrīsh Iran 110 C3
Tak Thai. 86 B3
Takāb Iran 110 B2
Takabba Kenya 122 E3
Taka'Bonerate, Kepulauan *atolls* Indon. 83 B4
Taka Bonerate, Taman Nasional *nat. park* Indon. 83 B4
Takagi Japan 93 D3
Takahagi Japan 93 G2
Takahama *Aichi* Japan 92 C4
Takahama *Fukui* Japan 92 B3
Takahara-gawa *r.* Japan 92 D2
Takahashi Japan 91 D6
Takaishi Japan 92 B4
Takaiwa-misaki *pt* Japan 92 C1
Takamatsu *Ishikawa* Japan 92 C2
Takamatsu Japan 91 D6
Takami-yama *mt.* Japan 92 C4
Takamori *Nagano* Japan 93 D3
Takane *Gifu* Japan 92 D2
Takane *Yamanashi* Japan 93 E3
Takanezawa Japan 93 F2
Takaoka Japan 92 D2
Takapuna N.Z. 139 E3
Takarazuka Japan 92 B4
Ta karpo China 105 G4
Takasago Japan 92 A4
Takasaki Japan 93 F2
Takashima Japan 92 C3
Takashōzu-yama *mt.* Japan 92 C2
Takasu Japan 92 C3
Takasuma-yama *mt.* Japan 93 E2
Takasuzu-san *hill* Japan 93 G2
Takatō Japan 93 E3
Takatokwane Botswana 124 G3
Takatomi Japan 92 C3
Takatori Japan 92 B4
Takatshwaane Botswana 124 E2
Takatsuki *Ōsaka* Japan 92 B4
Takatsuki *Shiga* Japan 92 C3
Takatsuki-yama *mt.* Japan 91 D6
Takayama *Gifu* Japan 92 D2
Takayama *Gunma* Japan 93 E2
Tak Bai Thai. 87 C6
Takefu Japan 92 C3
Takengon *Sumatera* Indon. 84 B1
Takeno Japan 92 A3
Takeo Cambodia *see* **Takêv**
Takeshi Japan 93 E2
Take-shima *i.* N. Pacific Ocean *see* **Liancourt Rocks**
Takestān Iran 110 C2
Taketoyo Japan 92 C4
Takêv Cambodia 87 D5
Takhemaret Alg. 67 G6
Takhini Hotspring *Y.T.* Canada 149 N3
Ta Khli Thai. 86 C4
Ta Khmau Cambodia 87 D5
Takhta-Bazar Turkm. *see* **Tagtabazar**
Takht Apān, Kūh-e *mt.* Iran 110 C3
Takhteh Iran 110 D4
Takhteh Pol Afgh. 111 G4
Takht-e Soleymān *mt.* Iran 110 C2
Takht-e Soleymān *tourist site* Iran 110 B2
Takht-i-Bahi *tourist site* Pak. 111 H3
Takht-i-Sulaiman *mt.* Pak. 111 H4
Taki *Mie* Japan 92 C4
Takijuq Lake Canada *see* **Napaktulik Lake**
Takino Japan 92 A4
Takinoue Japan 90 F3
Takisung *Kalimantan* Indon. 85 F3
Takla Lake Canada 150 E4
Takla Landing Canada 150 E4
Takla Makan *des.* China *see* **Taklimakan Shamo**
Taklimakan Desert China *see* **Taklimakan Shamo**
Taklimakan Shamo *des.* China 98 C5
Tako Japan 93 G3
Takotna *AK* U.S.A. 148 H3
Takpa Shiri *mt. Xizang* China 99 F7
Takslesluk Lake *AK* U.S.A. 148 G3
Taku Canada 150 C3
Taku *r.* Canada/U.S.A. 149 N4
Takum Nigeria 120 D4
Takuu Islands P.N.G. 133 F2
Talachyn Belarus 53 F5
Talaja India 104 C5
Talakan *Amurskaya Oblast'* Rus. Fed. 90 C2
Talakan *Khabarovskiy Kray* Rus. Fed. 90 D2
Talamanca, Cordillera de *mts* Costa Rica 166 [inset] J7
Talandzha Rus. Fed. 90 C2
Talang, Gunung *vol.* Indon. 84 C3
Talangbatu *Sumatera* Indon. 84 D3
Talangbetutu *Sumatera* Indon. 84 D3
Talara Peru 176 B4
Talar-i-Band *mts* Pak. *see* **Makran Coast Range**
Talas Kyrg. 102 D3
Talas Ala-Too *mts* Kyrg. 102 D3
Talas Range *mts* Kyrg. *see* **Talas Ala-Too**
Talasskiy Alatau, Khrebet *mts* Kyrg. *see* **Talas Ala-Too**
Talatakoh *i.* Indon. 83 B3
Ţal'at Mūsá *mt.* Lebanon/Syria 107 C2
Talaud, Kepulauan *is* Indon. 83 C1
Talavera de la Reina Spain 67 D4
Talawgyi Myanmar 86 B1
Talaya Rus. Fed. 77 Q3
Talayan *Mindanao* Phil. 82 D5
Talbehat India 104 D4
Talbīsah Syria 107 C2
Talbot, Mount *hill* Australia 135 D6
Talbotton U.S.A. 163 C5
Talbragar *r.* Australia 138 D4
Talca Chile 178 B5
Talcahuano Chile 178 B5
Taldan Rus. Fed. 90 B1
Taldom Rus. Fed. 52 H4
Taldykorgan Kazakh. 102 E3
Taldy-Kurgan Kazakh. *see* **Taldykorgan**
Taldyqorghan Kazakh. *see* **Taldykorgan**
Taldy-Suu Kyrg. 98 B4
Tālesh Iran *see* **Hashtpar**
Talgar Kazakh. 98 B4
Talgar, Pik *mt.* Kazakh. 98 B4
Talgarth U.K. 59 D7
Talguppa India 106 B3
Talia Australia 137 A7
Taliabu *i.* Indon. 83 C3
Talibon *Bohol* Phil. 82 D4
Talikota India 106 C2
Talikud *i.* Phil. 82 D5
Talimardzhan Uzbek. *see* **Tollimarjon**
Talin Hiag *Heilong.* China 95 K2
Taliparamba India 106 B3
Talisay *Cebu* Phil. 82 C4
Talisayan *Kalimantan* Indon. 85 G2
Talisayan *Mindanao* Phil. 82 D4
Talış Dağları *mts* Azer./Iran 110 C2
Talisei *i.* Indon. 83 C2
Talitsa Rus. Fed. 52 J4
Taliwang *Sumbawa* Indon. 85 G5
Talkeetna *AK* U.S.A. 149 J3
Talkeetna *r. AK* U.S.A. 149 J3
Talkeetna Mountains *AK* U.S.A. 149 J3
Talkh Āb Iran 110 E3
Tallacootra, Lake *salt flat* Australia 135 F7
Talladega U.S.A. 163 C5

▶**Tallahassee** U.S.A. 163 C6
Capital of Florida.

Tall al Aḥmar Syria 107 D1
Tallassee *AL* U.S.A. 167 I1
Tall Baydar Syria 113 F3
Tall-e Ḥalāl Iran 110 D4

▶**Tallinn** Estonia 55 N7
Capital of Estonia.

Tall Kalakh Syria 107 C2
Tall Kayf Iraq 113 F3
Tall Kūjik Syria 113 F3
Tallow Ireland 61 D5
Tallulah U.S.A. 161 F5
Tall 'Uwaynāt Iraq 113 F3
Tallymerjen Uzbek. *see* **Tollimarjon**
Talmont-St-Hilaire France 66 D3
Tal'ne Ukr. 53 F6
Tal'noye Ukr. *see* **Tal'ne**
Taloda India 104 C5
Talodi Sudan 108 D7
Taloga U.S.A. 161 D4
Talon, Lac *l.* Canada 153 I3
Ta-long Myanmar 86 B2
Tāloqān Afgh. 111 H2
Talos Dome *ice feature* Antarctica 188 H2
Ta Loung San *mt.* Laos 86 C2
Talovaya Rus. Fed. 53 I6
Taloyoak Canada 147 I3
Talpa Mex. 166 D4
Tal Pass Pak. 111 I3
Talshand Mongolia *see* **Chandmanĭ**
Talsi Latvia 55 M8
Tal Sīyāh Iran 111 F4
Taltal Chile 178 B3
Taltson *r.* Canada 151 H2
Talu *Xizang* China 99 F7
Talu *Sumatera* Indon. 84 B2
Taludaa *Sulawesi* Indon. 83 B2
Taluti, Teluk *b. Seram* Indon. 83 D3
Talvik Norway 54 M1
Talwood Australia 138 D2
Talyshskiye Gory *mts* Azer./Iran *see* **Talış Dağları**
Talyy Rus. Fed. 52 L2
Tama Japan 93 F3
Tama Abu, Banjaran *mts* Malaysia 85 F2
Tamabo Range *mts* Malaysia *see* **Tama Abu, Banjaran**
Tama-gawa *r.* Japan 93 F3
Tamaki Japan 92 C4
Tamala Australia 135 A6
Tamala Rus. Fed. 53 I5
Tamale Ghana 120 C4
Tamalung *Kalimantan* Indon. 85 F3
Tamamura Japan 93 F2
Tamana *i.* Kiribati 133 H2
Taman Negara National Park Malaysia 84 C1
Tamano Japan 91 D6
Tamanrasset Alg. 120 D2
Tamanthi Myanmar 86 A1
Tamaqua U.S.A. 165 H3
Tamar India 105 F5
Tamar Syria *see* **Tadmur**
Tamar *r.* U.K. 59 C8
Tamari Japan 93 G2
Tamarugal, Pampa de *plain* Chile 176 E7
Tamasane Botswana 125 H2
Tamatave Madag. *see* **Toamasina**
Tamatsukuri Japan 93 G2
Tamaulipas *state* Mex. 161 D7
Tamaulipas, Sierra de *mts* Mex. 167 F4
Tamazula *Durango* Mex. 166 D3
Tamazula *Jalisco* Mex. 166 E5
Tamazulápam Mex. 167 F5
Tamazunchale Mex. 167 F4
Tamba Japan *see* **Tanba**
Tambacounda Senegal 120 B3
Tamba-kōchi *plat.* Japan *see* **Tanba-kōchi**
Tambalongang *i.* Indon. 83 B4
Tambangmunjul *Kalimantan* Indon. 85 E3
Tambangsawah *Sumatera* Indon. 84 C3
Tambaqui Brazil 176 F5
Tambar Springs Australia 138 D3
Tambea *Sulawesi* Indon. 83 B4
Tambelan, Kepulauan *is* Indon. 84 D2
Tambelan Besar *i.* Indon. 85 D2
Tamberu *Jawa* Indon. 85 F4
Tambisan *Sabah* Malaysia 85 G1
Tambo *r.* Australia 138 C6
Tambohorano Madag. 123 E5
Tamboli *Sulawesi* Indon. 83 B3
Tambor Mex. 166 D3

▶**Tambora, Gunung** *vol. Sumbawa* Indon. 85 G5
Deadliest recorded volcanic eruption (1815).

Tamboritha *mt.* Australia 138 C6
Tambov Rus. Fed. 53 I5
Tambovka Rus. Fed. 90 C2
Tambu, Teluk *b.* Indon. 83 A2
Tambulanan, Bukit *hill* Malaysia 85 G1
Tambunan *Sabah* Malaysia 85 G1
Tambura Sudan 121 F4
Tamburi Brazil 179 C1
Tambuyukon, Gunung *mt.* Malaysia 85 G1
Tâmchekkeţ Mauritania 120 B3
Tamdybulak Uzbek. *see* **Tomdibuloq**
Tâmega *r.* Port. 67 B3
Tamenghest Alg. *see* **Tamanrasset**
Tamenglong India 105 H4
Tamerza Tunisia 68 B7
Tamgak, Adrar *mt.* Niger 120 D3
Tamgué, Massif du *mt.* Guinea 120 B3
Tamiahua Mex. 167 F4
Tamiahua, Laguna de *lag.* Mex. 168 E4
Tamiang *r.* Indon. 84 B1
Tamiang, Ujung *pt* Indon. 84 B1
Tamil Nadu *state* India 106 C4
Tamirin Gol *r.* Mongolia 94 E2
Tamitsa Rus. Fed. 52 H2
Ţâmîya Egypt *see* **Ţāmīyah**
Ţāmīyah Egypt 112 C5
Tamkuhi India 105 F4
Tam Ky Vietnam 86 E4
Tammarvi *r.* Canada 151 K1
Tammerfors Fin. *see* **Tampere**
Tammisaari Fin. *see* **Ekenäs**
Tampa U.S.A. 163 D7
Tampa Bay U.S.A. 163 D7
Tampang *Sumatera* Indon. 84 D4
Tampere Fin. 55 M6
Tampico Mex. 168 E4
Tampin Malaysia 84 C2
Tampines Sing. 87 [inset]
Tampo *Sulawesi* Indon. 83 B4
Tamsagbulag Mongolia 95 I2
Tamsag Muchang *Nei Mongol* China 94 E3
Tamsweg Austria 57 N7
Tamu Myanmar 86 A1
Tamuín Mex. 167 F4
Tamworth Australia 138 E3
Tamworth U.K. 59 F6
Tan Kazakh. 98 B2
Tana *r.* Fin./Norway *see* **Tenojoki**
Tana *r.* Kenya 122 E4
Tana Madag. *see* **Antananarivo**
Tana *r. AK* U.S.A. 149 L3
Tana *i.* Vanuatu *see* **Tanna**
Tana, Lake Eth. 122 D2
Tanabe Japan 91 D6
Tanabi Brazil 179 A3
Tana Bru Norway 54 P1
Tanacross *AK* U.S.A. 149 L3
Tanadak Island *AK* U.S.A. 148 D5
Tanada Lake U.S.A. 150 A2
Tanafjorden *inlet* Norway 54 P1
Tanaga *vol. AK* U.S.A. 149 [inset]
Tanaga Island *AK* U.S.A. 149 [inset]
Tanaga Pass *sea channel AK* U.S.A. 149 [inset]
Tanagura Japan 93 G1
Tanah, Tanjung *pt* Indon. 85 E4
T'ana Hāyk' *l.* Eth. *see* **Tana, Lake**
Tanahbala *i.* Indon. 84 B3
Tanahgrogot *Kalimantan* Indon. 85 G3
Tanahjampea *i.* Indon. 83 B4
Tanahmasa *i.* Indon. 84 B3
Tanahmerah *Kalimantan* Indon. 85 G2
Tanah Merah Malaysia 84 C1
Tanahputih *Sumatera* Indon. 84 C2
Tanah Rata Malaysia 84 C1
Tanakeke *i.* Indon. 83 A4
Tanambung *Sulawesi Barat* Indon. 83 A3
Tanami Australia 134 E4
Tanami Desert Australia 134 E4
Tân An Vietnam 87 D5
Tanana *AK* U.S.A. 148 I2
Tanana *r. AK* U.S.A. 148 I2
Tananarive Madag. *see* **Antananarivo**
Tanandava Madag. 123 E6
Tanauan *Leyte* Phil. 82 D4
Tanba Japan 92 B3
Tanba-kōchi *plat.* Japan 92 B3
Tanbu *Shandong* China 95 I5
Tancheng China *see* **Pingtan**
Tancheng *Shandong* China 95 I5
Tanch'ŏn N. Korea 91 C4
Tanda Côte d'Ivoire 120 C4
Tanda *Uttar Prad.* India 104 D3
Tanda *Uttar Prad.* India 105 E4
Tandag *Mindanao* Phil. 82 D4
Ţăndărei Romania 69 L2
Tandaué Angola 123 B5
Tandek *Sabah* Malaysia 85 G1
Tandi India 104 D2
Tandil Arg. 178 E5
Tando Adam Pak. 111 H5
Tando Allahyar Pak. 111 H5
Tando Bago Pak. 111 H5
Tandou Lake *imp. l.* Australia 137 C7
Tandragee U.K. 61 F3
Tandubatu *i.* Phil. 82 C5
Tandur India 106 C2
Tanduri Pak. 111 G4
Tanega-shima *i.* Japan 91 C7
Tanen Taunggyi *mts* Thai. 86 B3
Tanezrouft *reg.* Alg./Mali 120 C2
Ţanf, Jabal aţ *hill* Syria 107 D3
Tang, Ra's-e *pt* Iran 111 E5
Tanga Rus. Fed. 95 G1
Tanga Tanz. 123 D4
Tangail Bangl. 105 G4
Tanga Islands P.N.G. 132 F2
Tanganyika *country* Africa *see* **Tanzania**

▶**Tanganyika, Lake** Africa 123 C4
Deepest and second largest lake in Africa, and 6th largest in the world.

Tangará Brazil 179 A4
Tangasseri India 106 C4
Tangdan China 96 D3
Tangdê *Xizang* China 99 F7
Tangeli Iran 110 D2
Tanger Morocco *see* **Tangier**
Tangerang *Jawa* Indon. 84 D4
Tangerhütte Germany 63 L2
Tangermünde Germany 63 L2
Tang-e Sarkheh Iran 111 E5
Tanggarma *Qinghai* China 94 D4
Tanggo *Xizang* China 99 E7
Tanggor China 96 D1
Tanggu *Tianjin* China 95 I4
Tanggulashan *Qinghai* China 94 C5
Tanggula Shan *mt. Qinghai/Xizang* China 99 E6
Tanggula Shan *mts Xizang* China 99 E6
Tanggula Shankou *pass Xizang* China 99 E6
Tangguo *Xizang* China 99 D7
Tanghai *Hebei* China 95 I4
Tanghe China 97 G1
Tangier Morocco 67 D6
Tangiers Morocco *see* **Tangier**
Tangkelemboko, Gunung *mt.* Indon. 83 B3
Tangkittebak, Gunung *mt.* Indon. 84 D4
Tang La *pass Xizang* China 99 E8
Tangla India 105 G4
Tanglag China 96 C1
Tanglin Sing. 87 [inset]
Tangmai *Xizang* China 99 F7
Tangnag *Qinghai* China 94 E5
Tango Japan 92 B3
Tangorin Australia 136 D4
Tangra Yumco *salt l.* China 99 D7
Tangse *Sumatera* Indon. 84 A1
Tangshan *Guizhou* China *see* **Shiqian**
Tangshan *Hebei* China 95 I4
Tangte *mt.* Myanmar 86 B2
Tangtse India *see* **Tanktse**
Tangub *Mindanao* Phil. 82 C4
Tangwan China 97 F3
Tangwanghe China 90 C2
Tangxian *Hebei* China 95 H4
Tangyin *Henan* China 95 H5
Tangyuan China 90 C3
Tangyung Tso *salt l.* China 105 F3
Tanhaçu Brazil 179 C1
Tanhua Fin. 54 O3
Tani Cambodia 87 D5
Taniantaweng Shan *mts* China 96 B2
Tanigawa-dake *mt.* Japan 93 E2
Tanigumi Japan 92 C3
Tanimbar, Kepulauan *is* Indon. 134 E1
Taninthari Myanmar *see* **Tenasserim**
Tanintharyi Myanmar *see* **Tenasserim**
Taninthayi Myanmar *see* **Tenasserim**
Taniwel *Seram* Indon. 83 D3
Tanjah Morocco *see* **Tangier**
Tanjay *Negros* Phil. 82 C4
Tanjiajing *Gansu* China 94 E4
Tanjore India *see* **Thanjavur**
Tanjung *Kalimantan* Indon. 85 F3
Tanjung *Sumatera* Indon. 84 D3
Tanjungbalai *Sumatera* Indon. 84 B2
Tanjungbalai *Sumatera* Indon. 84 C2
Tanjungbaliha *Maluku* Indon. 83 C3
Tanjungbatu *Kalimantan* Indon. 85 G2
Tanjungbatu *Sumatera* Indon. 84 C2
Tanjungbuayabuaya, Pulau *i.* Indon. 85 G2
Tanjungenim *Sumatera* Indon. 84 C3
Tanjunggaru *Kalimantan* Indon. 85 G3
Tanjungkarang-Telukbetung *Sumatera* Indon. *see* **Bandar Lampung**
Tanjungpandan Indon. 85 D3
Tanjungpinang Indon. 84 D2
Tanjungpura *Sumatera* Indon. 84 B2
Tanjung Puting, Taman Nasional *nat. park* Indon. 85 F3
Tanjungraja *Sumatera* Indon. 84 D3
Tanjungredeb *Kalimantan* Indon. 85 G2
Tanjungsaleh *i.* Indon. 85 E3
Tanjungsatai *Kalimantan* Indon. 85 E3
Tanjungselor *Kalimantan* Indon. 85 G2
Tankhoy Rus. Fed. 94 F1
Tankse India *see* **Tanktse**
Tanktse India 104 D2
Tankwa-Karoo National Park S. Africa 124 D7
Tanna *i.* Vanuatu 133 G3
Tannadice U.K. 60 G4
Tannan Japan 92 B3
Tännäs Sweden 54 H5
Tanner, Mount Canada 150 G5
Tannu-Ola, Khrebet *mts* Rus. Fed. 94 B1
Tannu Tuva *aut. rep.* Rus. Fed. *see* **Tyva, Respublika**
Tañon Strait Phil. 82 C4
Tanot India 104 B4
Tanout Niger 120 D3
Tanquian Mex. 167 F4
Tansen Nepal 105 E4
Tanshui Taiwan 97 I3
Tansyk Kazakh. 98 B3
Ţanţā Egypt 112 C5
Ţanta Egypt *see* **Ţanţā**
Tan-Tan Morocco 120 B2
Tantō Japan 92 A3
Tantoyuca Mex. 167 F4
Tantu *Jilin* China 95 J2
Tanuku India 106 D2
Tanuma Japan 93 F2
Tanumbirini Australia 134 F4
Tanumshede Sweden 55 G7
Tanyurer *r.* Rus. Fed. 148 A2
Tanzania *country* Africa 123 D4
Tanzawa-Ōyama Kokutei-kōen *park* Japan 93 F3
Tanzilla *r. B.C.* Canada 149 O4
Tao, Ko *i.* Thai. 87 B5
Tao'an *Jilin* China *see* **Taonan**
Taobh Tuath U.K. *see* **Northton**
Taocheng China *see* **Daxin**
Taocun *Shandong* China 95 J4
Tao'er He *r.* China 95 J2
Tao He *r.* China 94 E5
Taohong China *see* **Longhui**
Taohuajiang China *see* **Taojiang**
Taohuaping China *see* **Longhui**
Taojiang China 97 G2
Taolanaro Madag. *see* **Tôlañaro**
Taole *Ningxia* China 94 F4
Taonan *Jilin* China 95 J2
Taongi *atoll* Marshall Is 186 H5
Taos U.S.A. 157 G5
Taounate Morocco 64 D5
Taourirt Morocco 64 D5
Taoxi China 97 H3
Taoyang *Gansu* China *see* **Lintao**
Taoyuan China 97 F2
T'aoyüan Taiwan 97 I3
Tapa Estonia 55 N7
Tapaan Passage Phil. 82 C5
Tapachula Mex. 167 G6
Tapah Malaysia 87 C6
Tapajós *r.* Brazil 177 H4
Tapaktuan *Sumatera* Indon. 84 B2
Tapan *Sumatera* Indon. 84 C3
Tapanatepec Mex. 167 G5
Tapanuli, Teluk *b.* Indon. 84 B2
Tapat *i. Maluku* Indon. 83 C3
Tapauá Brazil 176 F5
Tapauá *r.* Brazil 176 F5
Taperoá Brazil 179 D1
Tapi *r.* India 104 C5
Tapiau Rus. Fed. *see* **Gvardeysk**
Tapijulapa Mex. 167 G5
Tapinbini *Kalimantan* Indon. 85 E3
Tapis, Gunung *mt.* Malaysia 84 C1
Tapisuelas Mex. 166 C3
Taplejung Nepal 105 F4
Tap Mun Chau *i.* H.K. China 97 [inset]
Ta-pom Myanmar 86 B2
Tappahannock U.S.A. 165 G5
Tappal *Uttar Prad.* India 99 B7
Tappalang *Sulawesi* Indon. 85 G3
Tappeh, Kūh-e *hill* Iran 110 C3
Taprobane *country* Asia *see* **Sri Lanka**
Tapuaenuku *mt.* N.Z. 139 D5
Tapul Phil. 82 C5
Tapul Group *is* Phil. 82 C5
Tapulonanjing *mt.* Indon. 84 B2
Tapung *r.* Indon. 84 C2
Tapurucuara Brazil 176 E4
Taputeouea *atoll* Kiribati *see* **Tabiteuea**
Ţaqţaq Iraq 113 G4
Taquara Brazil 179 A5
Taquarí *Rio Grande do Sul* Brazil 179 A5
Taquarí *r.* Brazil 177 G7
Taquaritinga Brazil 179 A3
Tar *r.* Ireland 61 E5
Tara Australia 138 E1
Ţarābulus Lebanon *see* **Tripoli**
Ţarābulus Libya *see* **Tripoli**
Taragt Mongolia 94 E2
Tarahuwan India 104 E4
Tarai *reg.* India 105 G4
Tarakan *Kalimantan* Indon. 85 G2
Tarakan *i.* Indon. 85 G2
Tarakki *reg.* Afgh. 111 G3
Taraklı Turkey 69 N4
Taran, Mys *pt* Rus. Fed. 55 K9
Tarana Australia 138 D4
Taranagar India 104 C3
Taranaki, Mount *vol.* N.Z. 139 E4
Tarancón Spain 67 E3
Tarangambadi India 106 C4
Tarangire National Park Tanz. 122 D4
Taranto Italy 68 G4
Taranto, Golfo di *g.* Italy 68 G4
Taranto, Gulf of Italy *see* **Taranto, Golfo di**
Tarapoto Peru 176 C5
Tarapur India 106 B2
Tararua Range *mts* N.Z. 139 E5
Tarascon-sur-Ariège France 66 E5
Tarasovskiy Rus. Fed. 53 I6
Tarauacá Brazil 176 D5
Tarauacá *r.* Brazil 176 E5
Tarawera N.Z. 139 F4
Tarawera, Mount *vol.* N.Z. 139 F4
Taraz Kazakh. 102 D3
Tarazona Spain 67 F3
Tarazona de la Mancha Spain 67 F4
Tarbagatay Kazakh. 98 C3
Tarbagatay Rus. Fed. 95 F1
Tarbagatay, Khrebet *mts* Kazakh. 102 F2
Tarbat Ness *pt* U.K. 60 F3
Tarbert Ireland 61 C5
Tarbert *Scotland* U.K. 60 C3
Tarbert *Scotland* U.K. 60 D5
Tarbes France 66 E5
Tarboro U.S.A. 162 E5
Tarcoola Australia 135 F7
Tarcoon Australia 138 C3
Tarcoonyinna *watercourse* Australia 135 F6
Tarcutta Australia 138 C5
Tardoki-Yani, Gora *mt.* Rus. Fed. 90 E2
Taree Australia 138 F3
Tarella Australia 137 C6
Tarentum Italy *see* **Taranto**

Ţarfā', Baţn aţ depr. Saudi Arabia 110 C6
Tarfaya Morocco 120 B2
Targa well Niger 120 D3
Targan Heilong. China see Talin Hiag
Targhee Pass U.S.A. 156 F3
Târgovişte Romania 69 K2
Targuist Morocco 67 D6
Târgu Jiu Romania 69 J2
Târgu Mureş Romania 69 K1
Târgu Neamţ Romania 69 L1
Târgu Secuiesc Romania 69 L1
Targyailing Xizang China 99 D7
Targyn Kazakh. 98 C2
Tarhūnah Libya 121 E1
Tari P.N.G. 81 K8
Tarian Gol Nei Mongol China 95 G4
Tariat Mongolia 94 D1
Tarif U.A.E. 110 D5
Tarifa Spain 67 D5
Tarifa, Punta de pt Spain 67 D5
Tarigtig Point Luzon Phil. 82 C2
Tarija Bol. 176 F8
Tarikere India 106 B3
Tariku r. Indon. 81 J7
Tarim Xinjiang China 98 C4
Tarīm Yemen 108 G6
Tarim Basin China 98 C5
Tarime Tanz. 122 D4
Tarim He r. China 98 D4
Tarim Liuchang Xinjiang China 98 D4
Tarim Pendi basin China see Tarim Basin
Tarim Qichang Xinjiang China 98 D4
Tarīn Kowt Afgh. 111 G3
Taritatu r. Indon. 81 J7
Taritipan Sabah Malaysia see Tandek
Tarka r. S. Africa 125 G7
Tarkastad S. Africa 125 H7
Tarkio U.S.A. 160 E3
Tarko-Sale Rus. Fed. 76 I3
Tarkwa Ghana 120 C4
Tarlac Luzon Phil. 82 C3
Tarlac r. Luzon Phil. 82 C2
Tarlauly Kazakh. 98 B3
Tarlo River National Park Australia 138 D5
Tarma Peru 176 C6
Tarmar Xizang China 99 E7
Tarmstedt Germany 63 J1
Tarn r. France 66 E4
Tärnaby Sweden 54 I4
Tarnak r. Afgh. 111 G4
Târnăveni Romania 69 K1
Tarnobrzeg Poland 53 D6
Tarnogskiy Gorodok Rus. Fed. 52 I3
Tarnopol Ukr. see Ternopil'
Tarnów Poland 53 D6
Tarnowitz Poland see Tarnowskie Góry
Tarnowskie Góry Poland 57 Q5
Taro Co salt l. China 99 C7
Ţārom Iran 110 D4
Taroom Australia 137 E5
Tarō-san mt. Japan 93 F2
Taroudannt Morocco 64 C5
Tarpaulin Swamp Australia 136 B3
Tarq Iran 110 C3
Tarquinia Italy 68 D3
Tarquinii Italy see Tarquinia
Tarrabool Lake salt flat Australia 136 A3
Tarraco Spain see Tarragona
Tarrafal Cape Verde 120 [inset]
Tarragona Spain 67 G3
Tårrajaur Sweden 54 K3
Tarran Hills hill Australia 138 C4
Tarrant Point Australia 136 B3
Tàrrega Spain 67 G3
Tarso Emissi mt. Chad 121 E2
Tarsus Turkey 107 B1
Tart Qinghai China 99 F5
Tärtär Azer. 113 G2
Tartu Estonia 55 O7
Ţarţūs Syria 107 B2
Tarui Japan 92 C3
Tarumovka Rus. Fed. 113 G1
Tarung Hka r. Myanmar 86 B1
Tarutao, Ko i. Thai. 87 B6
Tarutao National Park Thai. 87 B6
Tarutung Sumatera Indon. 84 B2
Tarvisium Italy see Treviso
Tarys-Arzhan Rus. Fed. 94 D1
Tarz Iran 110 E4
Tasai, Ko i. Thai. 87 B5
Tasaral Kazakh. 98 A3
Taschereau Canada 152 F4
Taseko Mountain Canada 150 F5
Tashauz Turkm. see Daşoguz
Tash-Bashat Kyrg. 98 B4
Tashi Gansu China 94 C3
Tashi Chho Bhutan see Thimphu
Tashigang Bhutan 105 G4
Tashino Rus. Fed. see Pervomaysk
Tashir Armenia 113 G2
Tashk, Daryācheh-ye l. Iran 110 D4
Tashkent Toshkent Uzbek. see Toshkent
Tāshqurghān Afgh. see Kholm
Tashtagol Rus. Fed. 88 F2
Tashtyp Rus. Fed. 88 F2
Tasialujjuaq, Lac l. Canada 153 G2
Tasiat, Lac l. Canada 152 G2
Tasiilap Karra c. Greenland 147 O3
Tasiilaq Greenland see Ammassalik
Tasikmalaya Jawa Indon. 85 E4
Tasīl Syria 107 B3
Tasiujaq Canada 153 H2
Tasiusaq Greenland 147 M2
Taşkent Turkey 107 A1
Tasker Niger 120 E3
Taskesken Kazakh. 102 F2
Taşköprü Turkey 112 D2
Tasman Abyssal Plain sea feature Tasman Sea 186 G8
Tasman Basin sea feature Tasman Sea 186 G8
Tasman Bay N.Z. 139 D5

▶Tasmania state Australia 137 [inset]
4th largest island in Oceania.

Tasman Islands P.N.G. see Nukumanu Islands
Tasman Mountains N.Z. 139 D5
Tasman Peninsula Australia 137 [inset]
Tasman Sea S. Pacific Ocean 132 H6
Taşova Turkey 112 E2
Tassara Niger 120 D3
Tassialouc, Lac l. Canada 152 G2
Tassili du Hoggar plat. Alg. 120 D2
Tassili n'Ajjer plat. Alg. 120 D2
Tasty Kazakh. 102 C3
Taşucu Turkey 107 A1
Tas-Yuryakh Rus. Fed. 77 M3
Tata Morocco 64 C6
Tataba Sulawesi Indon. 83 B3
Tatabánya Hungary 68 H1
Tatalin Gol r. Qinghai China 94 C4
Tatamailau, Foho mt. East Timor 83 C5
Tataouine Tunisia 64 G5
Tatarbunary Ukr. 69 M2
Tatarsk Rus. Fed. 76 I4
Tatarskiy Proliv strait Rus. Fed. 90 F2
Tatar Strait Rus. Fed. see Tatarskiy Proliv
Tatau Sarawak Malaysia 85 F2
Tate r. Australia 136 C3
Tatebayashi Japan 93 F2
Tateishi-misaki pt Japan 92 C3
Tateiwa Japan 93 F1
Tateshina Japan 93 E2
Tateshina-yama mt. Japan 93 E2
Tateyama Chiba Japan 93 F4
Tateyama Toyama Japan 92 D2
Tate-yama vol. Japan 92 D2
Tathlina Lake Canada 150 G2
Tathlīth Saudi Arabia 108 F6
Tathlīth, Wādī watercourse Saudi Arabia 108 F5
Tathra Australia 138 D6
Tatinnai Lake Canada 151 L2
Tatishchevo Rus. Fed. 53 J6
Tatitlek AK U.S.A. 149 K3
Tatkon Myanmar 86 B2
Tatla Lake Canada 150 E5
Tatla Lake l. Canada 150 E5
Tatlayoko Lake Canada 150 E5
Tatnam, Cape Canada 151 N3
Tatomi Japan 93 E3
Tatra Mountains Poland/Slovakia 57 Q6
Tatrang Xinjiang China 99 D5
Tatry mts Poland/Slovakia see Tatra Mountains
Tatrzański Park Narodowy nat. park Poland 57 Q6
Tatshenshini r. B.C. Canada 149 M4
Tatshenshini-Alsek Provincial Wilderness Park Canada 150 B3
Tatsinskiy Rus. Fed. 53 I6
Tatsuno Nagano Japan 93 D3
Tatsunokuchi Japan 92 C2
Tatsuruhama Japan 92 C1
Tatsuyama Japan 93 D4
Tatuí Brazil 179 B3
Tatuk Mountain Canada 150 E4
Tatum U.S.A. 161 C5
Tatvan Turkey 113 F3
Tau Norway 55 D7
Taua Brazil 177 J5
Tauapeçaçu Brazil 176 F4
Taubaté Brazil 179 B3
Tauber r. Germany 63 J5
Tauberbischofsheim Germany 63 J5
Taucha Germany 63 M3
Taufstein hill Germany 63 J4
Taukum, Peski des. Kazakh. 102 D3
Taumarunui N.Z. 139 E4
Taumaturgo Brazil 176 D5
Taung S. Africa 124 G4
Taungdwingyi Myanmar 86 A2
Taunggyi Myanmar 86 B2
Taunglau Myanmar 86 B2
Taung-ngu Myanmar 86 B3
Taungnyo Range mts Myanmar 86 B3
Taungtha Myanmar 86 A2
Taungup Myanmar 96 B5
Taunton U.K. 59 D7
Taunton U.S.A. 165 J3
Taunus hills Germany 63 H4
Taupo N.Z. 139 F4
Taupo, Lake N.Z. 139 E4
Tauragė Lith. 55 M9
Tauranga N.Z. 139 F3
Taurasia Italy see Turin
Taureau, Réservoir resr Canada 152 G5
Taurianova Italy 68 G5
Tauroa Point N.Z. 139 D2
Taurus Mountains Turkey 107 A1
Taute r. France 59 F9
Tauz Azer. see Tovuz
Tavas Turkey 69 M6
Tavastehus Fin. see Hämeenlinna
Tavayvaam r. Rus. Fed. 148 B2
Taverham U.K. 59 I6
Taveuni i. Fiji 133 I3
Tavildara Tajik. 111 H2
Tavira Port. 67 C5
Tavistock Canada 164 E2
Tavistock U.K. 59 C8
Tavoy Myanmar 87 B4
Tavoy r. mouth Myanmar 87 B4
Tavoy Island Myanmar see Mali Kyun
Tavoy Point Myanmar 87 B4
Tavricheskoye Kazakh. 98 C2
Tavşanlı Turkey 69 M5
Taw r. U.K. 59 C7
Tawai, Bukit mt. Malaysia 85 G1
Tawakoni, Lake TX U.S.A. 167 G1
Tawang India 105 G4
Tawaramoto Japan 92 B4
Tawas City U.S.A. 164 D1
Tawau Sabah Malaysia 85 G1
Tawau, Teluk b. Malaysia 85 G1
Tawè Myanmar see Tavoy
Tawe r. U.K. 59 D7
Tawi r. India 99 A6
Ţawī Ḩafīr well U.A.E. 110 D5
Ţawī Murra well U.A.E. 110 D5
Tawi-Tawi i. Phil. 82 B5
Tawmaw Myanmar 86 B1
Tawu Taiwan 97 I4
Taxco Mex. 167 F5
Taxkorgan Xinjiang China 99 A5
Tay r. Y.T. Canada 149 N3
Tay r. U.K. 60 F4
Tay, Firth of est. U.K. 60 F4
Tay, Lake salt flat Australia 135 C8
Tay, Loch l. U.K. 60 E4
Tayabas Bay Luzon Phil. 82 C3
Tayan Kalimantan Indon. 85 E2
Tayandu, Kepulauan is Indon. 81 I8
Taybola Rus. Fed. 54 R2
Taycheedah U.S.A. 164 A2
Taygan Mongolia see Delger
Tayinloan U.K. 60 D5
Taylor Canada 150 F3
Taylor AK U.S.A. 148 F2
Taylor MI U.S.A. 164 D2
Taylor NE U.S.A. 160 D3
Taylor TX U.S.A. 161 D6
Taylor, Mount U.S.A. 159 J4
Taylor Mountains AK U.S.A. 148 H3
Taylorsville U.S.A. 164 C4
Taylorville U.S.A. 160 F4
Taymā' Saudi Arabia 112 E6
Taymura r. Rus. Fed. 77 K3
Taymyr, Ozero l. Rus. Fed. 77 L2
Taymyr, Poluostrov pen. Rus. Fed. see Taymyr Peninsula
Taymyr Peninsula Rus. Fed. 76 J2
Tây Ninh Vietnam 87 D5
Tayoltita Mex. 166 D3
Taypak Kazakh. 51 Q6
Taypaq Kazakh. see Taypak
Tayshet Rus. Fed. 88 H1
Tayshir Mongolia 94 D2
Taytay Luzon Phil. 82 C3
Taytay Palawan Phil. 82 B4
Taytay Bay Palawan Phil. 82 B4
Taytay Point Leyte Phil. 82 D4
Tayu Jawa Indon. 85 E4
Tayuan China 90 B2
Tayyebād Iran 111 F3
Taz r. Rus. Fed. 76 I3
Taza Morocco 64 D5
Tāza Khurmātū Iraq 113 G4
Tazawa Japan 93 D2
Taze Myanmar 86 A2
Tazewell TN U.S.A. 164 D5
Tazewell VA U.S.A. 164 E5
Tazimina Lakes AK U.S.A. 148 I3
Tazin r. Canada 151 I2
Tazin Lake Canada 151 I3
Tāzirbū Libya 121 F2
Tazlina AK U.S.A. 149 K3
Tazlina Lake AK U.S.A. 149 K3
Tazmalt Alg. 67 I5
Tazovskaya Guba sea chan. Rus. Fed. 76 I3
Tbessa Alg. see Tébessa

▶T'bilisi Georgia 113 G2
Capital of Georgia.

Tbilisskaya Rus. Fed. 53 I7
Tchabal Mbabo mt. Cameroon 120 E4
Tchad country Africa see Chad
Tchamba Togo 120 D4
Tchibanga Gabon 122 B4
Tchigaï, Plateau du Niger 121 E2
Tchin-Tabaradene Niger 120 D3
Tcholliré Cameroon 121 E4
Tchula U.S.A. 161 F5
Tczew Poland 57 Q3
Te, Prêk r. Cambodia 87 D4
Teacapán Mex. 166 D4
Teague, Lake salt flat Australia 135 C6
Te Anau N.Z. 139 A7
Te Anau, Lake N.Z. 139 A7
Teapa Mex. 167 G5
Te Araroa N.Z. 139 G3
Teate Italy see Chieti
Te Awamutu N.Z. 139 E4
Teba Indon. 81 J7
Tébarat Niger 120 D3
Tebas Kalimantan Indon. 85 E2
Tebay U.K. 58 E4
Tebedu Sarawak Malaysia 85 E2
Tebesjuak Lake Canada 151 L2
Tébessa Alg. 68 C7
Tébessa, Monts de mts Alg. 68 C7
Tebingtinggi Sumatera Indon. 84 B2
Tebingtinggi Sumatera Indon. 84 C3
Tebo r. Indon. 84 C3
Téboursouk Tunisia 68 C6
Téboursouk Tunisia 68 C6
Tebulos Mt'a Georgia/Rus. Fed. 113 G2
Tecalitlán Mex. 166 E5
Tecate Mex. 166 A1
Tece Turkey 107 B1
Techiman Ghana 120 C4
Tecka Arg. 178 B6
Tecklenburger Land reg. Germany 63 H2
Tecolutla Mex. 167 F4
Tecomán Mex. 166 E5
Tecoripa Mex. 166 C2
Técpan Mex. 168 D5
Tecuala Mex. 168 C4
Tecuci Romania 69 L2
Tecumseh MI U.S.A. 164 D3
Tecumseh NE U.S.A. 160 D3
Tedori-gawa r. Japan 92 C2
Tedzhen Turkm. see Tejen
Teec Nos Pos U.S.A. 159 I3
Teel Mongolia see Öndör-Ulaan
Teeli Rus. Fed. 98 E2
Tees r. U.K. 58 F4
Teeswater Canada 164 E1
Teet'lit Zhen N.W.T. Canada see Fort McPherson
Tefé r. Brazil 176 F4
Tefenni Turkey 69 M6
Tegal Jawa Indon. 85 E4
Tegel airport Germany 63 N2
Tegid, Llyn l. Wales U.K. see Bala Lake
Tegineneng Sumatera Indon. 84 D4

▶Tegucigalpa Hond. 166 [inset] I6
Capital of Honduras.

Teguidda-n-Tessoumt Niger 120 D3
Tehachapi U.S.A. 158 D4
Tehachapi Mountains U.S.A. 158 D4
Tehachapi Pass U.S.A. 158 D4
Tehek Lake Canada 151 M1
Teheran Iran see Tehrān
Tehery Lake Canada 151 M1
Téhini Côte d'Ivoire 120 C4
Tehoru Seram Indon. 83 D3

▶Tehrān Iran 110 C3
Capital of Iran.

Tehri India see Tikamgarh
Tehuacán Mex. 168 E5
Tehuantepec, Golfo de g. Mex. 167 G6
Tehuantepec, Gulf of Mex. see Tehuantepec, Golfo de
Tehuantepec, Istmo de isthmus Mex. 168 F5
Tehuitzingo Mex. 167 F5
Teide, Pico del vol. Canary Is 120 B2
Teifi r. U.K. 59 C6
Teignmouth U.K. 59 D8
Teixeira de Sousa Angola see Luau
Teixeiras Brazil 179 C3
Teixeira Soares Brazil 179 A4
Tejakula Bali Indon. 85 F5
Tejen Turkm. 111 F2
Tejo r. Port. 67 B4 see Tagus
Tejon Pass U.S.A. 158 D4
Tejupan, Punta pt Mex. 166 E5
Tekapo, Lake N.Z. 139 C6
Tekari-dake mt. Japan 93 E3
Tekax Mex. 167 H4
Tekeli Kazakh. 102 E3
Tekes Xinjiang China 98 C4
Tekes Kazakh. 98 C4
Tekes He r. China 98 C4
Tekiliktag mt. Xinjiang China 99 C5
Tekin Rus. Fed. 90 D2
Tekirdağ Turkey 69 L4
Tekka India 106 D2
Tekkali India 106 E2
Teknaf Bangl. 105 H5
Tekong Kechil, Pulau i. Sing. 87 [inset]
Teku Sulawesi Indon. 83 B3
Te Kuiti N.Z. 139 E4
Tel r. India 106 D1
Tela Hond. 166 [inset] I6
Télagh Alg. 67 F6
Telan i. Indon. 84 D2
Telanaipura Sumatera Indon. see Jambi
Telaquana Lake AK U.S.A. 148 I3
Telashi Hu salt l. Qinghai China 99 F6
Tel Ashqelon tourist site Israel 107 B4
Télataï Mali 120 D3
Tel Aviv-Yafo Israel 107 B3
Telč Czech Rep. 57 O6
Telchac Puerto Mex. 167 H4
Telegapulang Kalimantan Indon. 85 F3
Telekhany Belarus see Tsyelyakhany
Telêmaco Borba Brazil 179 A4
Telen r. Indon. 85 G2
Teleorman r. Romania 69 K3
Telertheba, Djebel mt. Alg. 120 D2
Telescope Peak U.S.A. 158 E3
Teles Pires r. Brazil 177 G5
Telford U.K. 59 E6
Telgte Germany 63 H3
Tel Hazor tourist site Israel 107 B3
Telica, Volcán vol. Nicaragua 166 [inset] I6
Telida AK U.S.A. 148 I3
Télimélé Guinea 120 B3
Teljo, Jebel mt. Sudan 108 C7
Telkwa Canada 150 E4
Tell Atlas mts Alg. see Atlas Tellien
Tell City U.S.A. 164 B5
Teller AK U.S.A. 148 F2
Tell es Sultan West Bank see Jericho
Tellicherry India 106 B4
Tellin Belgium 62 F4
Telloh Iraq 113 G5
Telluride U.S.A. 159 J3
Telmen Mongolia 94 D1
Telmen Nuur salt l. Mongolia 94 D1
Tel'novskiy Rus. Fed. 90 F2
Telo Indon. 84 B3
Teloloapán Mex. 167 F5
Telo Martius France see Toulon
Telpoziz, Gora mt. Rus. Fed. 51 R3
Telsen Arg. 178 C6
Telšiai Lith. 55 M9
Teltow Germany 63 N2
Teluk Anson Malaysia see Teluk Intan
Telukbajur Sumatera Indon. see Telukbayur
Telukbatang Kalimantan Indon. 85 E3
Telukbayur Sumatera Indon. 84 C3
Telukbetung Sumatera Indon. see Bandar Lampung
Teluk Cenderawasih, Taman Nasional nat. park Indon. 81 I7
Telukdalam Indon. 84 B2
Teluk Intan Malaysia 84 C1
Telukkuantan Sumatera Indon. 84 C3
Telukmelano Kalimantan Indon. 85 E3
Teluknaga Jawa Indon. 84 D4
Telukpakedai Kalimantan Indon. 85 E3
Temagami Lake Canada 152 F5
Temaju i. Indon. 85 E2
Temanggung Jawa Indon. 85 E4
Temapache Mex. 167 F4
Têmarxung Xizang China 99 E6
Temax Mex. 167 H4
Temba S. Africa 125 I3
Tembagapura Indon. 81 J7
Tembenchi r. Rus. Fed. 77 K3
Tembesi r. Indon. 84 C3
Tembilahan Sumatera Indon. 84 C3
Tembisa S. Africa 125 I4
Tembo Aluma Angola 123 B4
Teme r. U.K. 59 E6
Temecula U.S.A. 158 E5
Temenchula, Gora mt. Rus. Fed. 94 D1
Temengor, Tasik resr Malaysia 84 C1
Temerluh Malaysia 84 C2
Temiang, Bukit mt. Malaysia 84 C1
Teminabuan Indon. 81 I7
Temirtau Kazakh. 102 D1
Témiscamie r. Canada 153 G4
Témiscamie, Lac l. Canada 153 G4
Témiscaming Canada 152 F5
Témiscamingue, Lac l. Canada 152 F5
Témiscouata, Lac l. Canada 153 H5
Temiyang i. Indon. 84 D2
Temmes Fin. 54 N4
Temnikov Rus. Fed. 53 I5
Temora Australia 138 C5
Temósachic Mex. 166 D2
Tempe U.S.A. 159 H5
Tempe, Danau l. Indon. 83 A4
Tempe Downs Australia 135 F6
Tempelhof airport Germany 63 N2
Tempino Sumatera Indon. 84 C3
Temple MI U.S.A. 164 C1
Temple TX U.S.A. 161 D6
Temple Bar U.K. 59 C6
Temple Dera Pak. 111 H4
Templemore Ireland 61 E5
Templer Bank sea feature Phil. 82 B4
Temple Sowerby U.K. 58 E4
Templeton watercourse Australia 136 B4
Templin Germany 63 N1
Tempoal Mex. 167 F4
Tempué Angola 123 B5
Têmpung Qinghai China 94 D4
Temryuk Rus. Fed. 112 E1
Temryukskiy Zaliv b. Rus. Fed. 53 H7
Temuco Chile 178 B5
Temuka N.Z. 139 C7
Temuli China see Butuo
Tena Ecuador 176 C4
Tenabo Mex. 167 H4
Tenabo, Mount U.S.A. 158 E1
Tenakee Springs AK U.S.A. 149 N4
Tenali India 106 D2
Tenango México Mex. 167 F5
Tenasserim Myanmar 87 B4
Tenasserim r. Myanmar 87 B4
Tenbury Wells U.K. 59 E6
Tenby U.K. 59 C7
Tendaho Eth. 122 E2
Tende, Col de pass France/Italy 66 H4
Ten Degree Channel India 87 A5
Tendō Japan 91 F5
Tenedos i. Turkey see Bozcaada
Ténenkou Mali 120 C3
Ténéré reg. Niger 120 D2
Ténéré du Tafassâsset des. Niger 120 E2
Tenerife i. Canary Is 120 B2
Ténès Alg. 67 G5
Teng, Nam r. Myanmar 86 B3
Tengah, Kepulauan is Indon. 85 G4
Tengah, Sungai r. Sing. 87 [inset]
Tengahdai Flores Indon. 83 B5
Tengcheng China see Tengxian
Tengchong China 96 C3
Tengeh Reservoir Sing. 87 [inset]
Tenggarong Kalimantan Indon. 85 G3
Tengger Els Nei Mongol China 94 F4
Tengger Shamo des. Nei Mongol China 94 F4
Tenggul i. Malaysia 84 C1
Tengiz, Ozero salt l. Kazakh. 102 C1
Tengqiao China 97 F5
Tengréla Côte d'Ivoire 120 C3
Ten'gushevo Rus. Fed. 53 I5
Tengxian China 97 F4
Tengxian Shandong China see Tengzhou
Tengzhou Shandong China 95 I5
Teni India see Theni
Teniente Jubany research station Antarctica see Jubany
Tenille U.S.A. 163 D6
Tenkanyy, Khrebet ridge Rus. Fed. 148 D2
Tenkawa Japan 92 B4
Tenke Dem. Rep. Congo 123 C5
Tenkeli Rus. Fed. 77 P2
Tenkergynpil'gyn, Laguna lag. Rus. Fed. 148 C1
Tenkodogo Burkina 120 C3
Ten Mile Lake salt flat Australia 135 C6
Ten Mile Lake Canada 153 K4
Tennant Creek Australia 134 F4
Tennessee r. U.S.A. 161 F4
Tennessee state U.S.A. 164 C5
Tennessee Pass U.S.A. 156 G5
Tennevoll Norway 54 J2
Tenojoki r. Fin./Norway 54 P1
Tenom Sabah Malaysia 85 F1
Tenosique Mex. 167 H5
Tenpaku Japan 92 C3
Tenri Japan 92 B4
Tenryū Nagano Japan 93 D3
Tenryū Shizuoka Japan 93 D4
Tenryū-gawa r. Japan 93 D3
Tenryū-Okumikawa Kokutei-kōen park Japan 93 D3
Tenteno Sulawesi Indon. 83 B3
Tenterden U.K. 59 H7
Tenterfield Australia 138 F2
Ten Thousand Islands U.S.A. 163 D7
Tentolomatinan, Gunung mt. Indon. 83 B2
Tentudia mt. Spain 67 C4
Tentulia Bangl. see Tetulia
Teocelo Mex. 167 F5
Teodoro Sampaio Brazil 178 F2
Teófilo Otôni Brazil 179 C2
Teomabal i. Phil. 82 C5
Teopisca Mex. 167 G5
Teotihuacán tourist site Mex. 167 F5
Tepa Maluku Indon. 83 D4
Tepache Mex. 166 C2
Te Paki N.Z. 139 D2
Tepatitlán Mex. 168 D4
Tepehuanes Mex. 166 D3
Tepeji Mex. 167 F5
Tepeköy Turkey see Karakoçan
Tepelenë Albania 69 I4
Tepelmeme de Morelos Mex. 167 F5
Tepelská vrchovina hills Czech Rep. 63 M5
Tepequem, Serra mts Brazil 169 L8
Tepianlangsat Kalimantan Indon. 85 G2
Tepic Mex. 168 D4
Te Pirita N.Z. 139 C6
Teplá r. Czech Rep. 63 M4
Teplice Czech Rep. 57 N5
Teplogorka Rus. Fed. 52 L3
Teploozersk Rus. Fed. 90 C2
Teploye Rus. Fed. 53 H5
Teploye Ozero Rus. Fed. see Teploozersk
Tepoca, Cabo c. Mex. 157 E7
Tepopa, Punta pt Mex. 166 B2
Tequila Mex. 168 D4
Tequisistlán Mex. 167 G5
Tequisquiapán Mex. 167 F4
Téra Niger 120 D3
Terai Japan 92 C2
Teram Kangri mt. China 99 B6
Teramo Italy 68 E3
Terang Australia 138 A7
Ter Apel Neth. 62 H2
Teratani r. Pak. 111 H4
Terbang Selatan i. Maluku Indon. 83 D4
Terbang Utara i. Maluku Indon. 83 D4
Tercan Turkey 113 F3
Terebovlya Ukr. 53 E6
Tere-Khol' Rus. Fed. 94 C1
Tere-Khol', Ozero l. Rus. Fed. 94 D1
Terektinskiy Khrebet mts Rus. Fed. 98 D2
Terekty Kazakh. 102 G2
Terengganu r. Malaysia 84 C1
Terengganu state Malaysia 84 C1
Terentang Kalimantan Indon. 85 E3
Terentang, Pulau i. Indon. 85 G3
Teresa Cristina Brazil 179 A4
Tereshka r. Rus. Fed. 53 J6
Teresina Brazil 177 J5
Teresina de Goias Brazil 179 B1
Teresita Col. 176 E3
Teresópolis Brazil 179 C3
Teressa Island India 87 A5
Terezinha Brazil 177 H3
Tergeste Italy see Trieste
Tergnier France 62 D5
Tergun Daba Shan mts Qinghai China 94 C4
Terhiyn Tsagaan Nuur l. Mongolia 94 D1
Teriberka Rus. Fed. 54 S2
Tering Xizang China 99 E7
Termez Uzbek. see Termiz
Termini Imerese Sicily Italy 68 E6
Términos, Laguna de lag. Mex. 167 H5
Termit-Kaoboul Niger 120 E3
Termiz Uzbek. 111 G2
Termo U.S.A. 158 C1
Termoli Italy 68 F4
Termonde Belgium see Dendermonde
Tern r. U.K. 59 E6
Ternate Maluku Indon. 83 C2
Ternate i. Maluku Indon. 83 C2
Terneuzen Neth. 62 D3
Terney Rus. Fed. 90 E3
Terni Italy 68 E3
Ternopil' Ukr. 53 E6
Ternopol' Ukr. see Ternopil'
Terpeniya, Mys c. Rus. Fed. 90 G2
Terpeniya, Zaliv g. Rus. Fed. 90 F2
Terra Alta U.S.A. 164 F4
Terra Bella U.S.A. 158 D4
Terrace Canada 150 D4
Terrace Bay Canada 152 D4
Terra Firma S. Africa 124 F3
Terråk Norway 54 H4
Terralba Sardinia Italy 68 C5
Terra Nova Bay Antarctica 188 H1
Terra Nova National Park Canada 153 L4
Terrazas Mex. 166 D2
Terre Adélie reg. Antarctica see Adélie Land
Terrebonne Bay U.S.A. 161 F6
Terre Haute U.S.A. 164 B4
Terrell TX U.S.A. 167 F1
Terre-Neuve prov. Canada see Newfoundland and Labrador
Terre-Neuve-et-Labrador prov. Canada see Newfoundland and Labrador
Terrero Mex. 166 D2
Terres Australes et Antarctiques Françaises terr. Indian Ocean see French Southern and Antarctic Lands
Terry U.S.A. 156 G3
Terschelling i. Neth. 62 F1
Terskey Ala-Too mts Kyrg. 98 B4
Terskiy Bereg coastal area Rus. Fed. 52 H2
Tertenia Sardinia Italy 68 C5

Terter Azer. see Tärtär
Teruel Spain 67 F3
Tervola Fin. 54 N3
Tes Mongolia 94 C1
Tešanj Bos.-Herz. 68 G2
Teseney Eritrea 108 E6
Tesha r. Rus. Fed. 53 I5
Teshekpuk Lake AK U.S.A. 148 I1
Teshio Japan 90 F3
Teshio-gawa r. Japan 90 F3
Tesiyn Gol r. Mongolia 94 C1
Teslin Y.T. Canada 149 N3
Teslin r. Y.T. Canada 149 N3
Teslin Lake B.C./Y.T. Canada 149 N3
Tesouras r. Brazil 179 A1
Tessalit Mali 120 D2
Tessaoua Niger 120 D3
Tessolo Moz. 125 L1
Test r. U.K. 59 F8
Testour Tunisia 68 C6
Tetachuck Lake Canada 150 E4
Tetas, Punta pt Chile 178 B2
Tete Moz. 123 D5
Tetehosi Indon. 84 B2
Te Teko N.Z. 139 F4
Teteriv r. Ukr. 53 F6
Teterow Germany 57 N4
Tetiyev Ukr. see Tetiyiv
Tetiyiv Ukr. 53 F6
Tetlin AK U.S.A. 149 L3
Tetlin Junction AK U.S.A. 149 L3
Tetlin Lake AK U.S.A. 149 L3
Tetlin National Wildlife Refuge nature res. AK U.S.A. 149 L3
Tetney U.K. 58 G5
Teton r. U.S.A. 156 F3
Tétouan Morocco 67 D6
Tetovo Macedonia 69 I3
Tetsyeh Mountain AK U.S.A. 149 K1
Tetuán Morocco see Tétouan
Tetulia Bangl. 105 G4
Tetulia sea chan. Bangl. 105 G5
Tetyukhe Rus. Fed. see Dal'negorsk
Tetyukhe-Pristan' Rus. Fed. see Rudnaya Pristan'
Tetyushi Rus. Fed. 53 K5
Teuco r. Arg. 178 D2
Teufelsbach Namibia 124 C2
Teul de González Ortega Mex. 166 E4
Teun vol. Maluku Indon. 83 D4
Teunom Sumatera Indon. 84 A1
Teunom r. Indon. 84 A1
Teutoburger Wald hills Germany 63 I2
Teuva Fin. 54 L5
Tevere r. Italy see Tiber
Teverya Israel see Tiberias
Teviot r. U.K. 60 G5
Te Waewae Bay N.Z. 139 A8
Tewah Kalimantan Indon. 85 F3
Te Waipounamu i. N.Z. see South Island
Tewane Botswana 125 H2
Tewantin Australia 137 F5
Teweh r. Indon. 85 F3
Tewkesbury U.K. 59 E7
Têwo Gansu China 94 E5
Têwo Sichuan China 94 E5
Texarkana AR U.S.A. 161 E5
Texarkana TX U.S.A. 161 E5
Texas Australia 138 E2
Texas state U.S.A. 161 D6
Texas City TX U.S.A. 167 G2
Texcoco Mex. 167 F5
Texel i. Neth. 62 E1
Texhoma U.S.A. 161 C4
Texoma, Lake U.S.A. 161 D5
Teyateyaneng Lesotho 125 H5
Teykovo Rus. Fed. 52 I4
Teza r. Rus. Fed. 52 I4
Teziutlán Mex. 167 F5
Tezpur India 105 H4
Tezu India 105 I4
Tha, Nam r. Laos 86 C2
Thaa Atoll Maldives see Kolhumadulu Atoll
Tha-anne r. Canada 151 M2
Thabana-Ntlenyana mt. Lesotho 125 I5
Thaba Nchu S. Africa 125 H5
Thaba Putsoa mt. Lesotho 125 H5
Thaba-Tseka Lesotho 125 I5
Thabazimbi S. Africa 125 H3
Thab Lan National Park Thai. 87 C4
Tha Bo Laos 86 C3
Thabong S. Africa 125 H4
Thabyedaung Myanmar 96 C4
Thade r. Myanmar 86 A3
Thagyettaw Myanmar 87 B4
Tha Hin Thai. see Lop Buri
Thai Binh Vietnam 86 D2
Thailand country Asia 86 C4
Thailand, Gulf of Asia 87 C5
Thai Muang Thai. 87 B5
Thai Nguyên Vietnam 86 D2
Thaj Saudi Arabia 110 C5
Thakèk Laos 86 D3
Thakurgaon Bangl. 105 G4
Thakurtola India 104 E5
Thal Germany 63 K4
Thala Tunisia 68 C7
Thalang Thai. 87 B5
Thalassery India see Tellicherry
Thal Desert Pak. 111 H4
Thale (Harz) Germany 63 L3
Thaliparamba India see Taliparamba
Thallon Australia 138 D2
Thalo Pak. 111 G4
Thamaga Botswana 125 G3
Thamar, Jabal mt. Yemen 108 G7
Thamarīt Oman 109 H6
Thame r. U.K. 59 F7
Thames r. Ont. Canada 155 K3
Thames r. Ont. Canada 164 D2
Thames N.Z. 139 E3
Thames est. U.K. 59 H7
Thames r. U.K. 59 H7
Thamesford Canada 164 E2
Thana India see Thane
Thanatpin Myanmar 86 B3
Thandwè Myanmar 86 A3
Thane India 106 B2
Thanet, Isle of pen. U.K. 59 I7
Thangoo Australia 134 C4
Thangra India 104 D2
Thanh Hoa Vietnam 86 D3
Thanjavur India 106 C4
Than Kyun i. Myanmar 87 B5
Thanlwin r. China/Myanmar see Salween
Thanlyin Myanmar 86 B3
Thaolintoa Lake Canada 151 L2
Tha Pla Thai. 86 C3
Thap Put Thai. 87 B5
Thapsacus Syria see Dibsī
Thap Sakae Thai. 87 B5
Tharabwin Myanmar 87 B4
Tharad Gujarat India 104 B4
Tharad Gujarat India 104 B4
Thar Desert India/Pak. 111 H5
Thargomindah Australia 138 A1
Tharrawaw Myanmar 86 A3
Tharthār, Buḥayrat ath l. Iraq 113 F4
Tharwānīyyah U.A.E. 110 D6
Thasos i. Greece 69 K4
Thatcher U.S.A. 159 I5
Thât Khê Vietnam 86 D2
Thaton Myanmar 86 B3
Thatta Pak. 111 G5
Thaungdut Myanmar 86 A1
Tha Uthen Thai. 86 D3
Thayatal, Nationalpark nat. park Austria/Czech Rep. 57 O5
Thayawthadangyi Kyun i. Myanmar 87 B4
Thayetmyo Myanmar 86 A3
Thazi Magwe Myanmar 86 A3
Thazi Mandalay Myanmar 105 I5
Thazzik Mountain AK U.S.A. 149 K2
The Aldermen Islands N.Z. 139 F3
Theba U.S.A. 159 G5
The Bahamas country West Indies 163 E7
Thebes Greece see Thiva
The Bluff Bahamas 163 E7
The Broads nat. park U.K. 59 I6
The Brothers is H.K. China 97 [inset]
The Calvados Chain is P.N.G. 136 F1
The Cheviot hill U.K. 58 E3
The Dalles U.S.A. 156 C3
Thedford U.S.A. 160 C3
The Entrance Australia 138 E4
The Faither stack U.K. 60 [inset]
The Fens reg. U.K. 59 G6
The Gambia country Africa 120 B3
Thegon Myanmar 86 A3
The Grampians mts Australia 137 C8
The Great Oasis oasis Egypt see Khārijah, Wāḥāt al
The Grenadines is St Vincent 169 L6
The Gulf Asia 110 C4
▶The Hague Neth. 62 E2
Seat of government of the Netherlands.
The Hunters Hills N.Z. 139 C7
Thekulthili Lake Canada 151 I2
The Lakes National Park Australia 138 C6
Thelon r. Canada 151 L1
The Lynd Junction Australia 136 D3
Themar Germany 63 K4
Thembalihle S. Africa 125 I4
The Minch sea chan. U.K. 60 C2
The Naze c. Norway see Lindesnes
The Needles stack U.K. 59 F8
Theni India 106 C4
Thenia Alg. 67 H5
Theniet El Had Alg. 67 H6
The North Sound sea chan. U.K. 60 G1
Theodore Australia 136 E5
Theodore Canada 151 K5
Theodore Roosevelt Lake U.S.A. 159 H5
Theodore Roosevelt National Park U.S.A. 160 C2
Theodosia Ukr. see Feodosiya
The Old Man of Coniston hill U.K. 58 D4
The Paps hill Ireland 61 C5
The Pas Canada 151 K4
The Pilot mt. Australia 138 D6
Thera i. Greece see Santorini
Thérain r. France 62 C5
Theresa U.S.A. 165 H1
Thermaïkos Kolpos g. Greece 69 J4
Thermopolis U.S.A. 156 F4
The Rock Australia 138 C5
Thérouanne France 62 C4
The Salt Lake salt flat Australia 137 C6
▶The Settlement Christmas I. 80 D9
Capital of Christmas Island.
The Sisters hill AK U.S.A. 148 G3
The Skaw spit Denmark see Grenen
The Skelligs is Ireland 61 B6
The Slot sea chan. Solomon Is see New Georgia Sound
The Solent strait U.K. 59 F8
Thessalon Canada 152 E5
Thessalonica Greece see Thessaloniki
Thessaloniki Greece 69 J4
The Storr hill U.K. 60 C3
Thet r. U.K. 59 H6
The Teeth mt. Palawan Phil. 82 B4
The Terraces hills Australia 135 C7
Thetford U.K. 59 H6
Thetford Mines Canada 153 H5
Thetkethaung r. Myanmar 86 A4
The Triangle mts Myanmar 86 B1
The Trossachs hills U.K. 60 E4
The Twins Australia 137 A6
Theva-i-Ra reef Fiji see Ceva-i-Ra
▶The Valley Anguilla 169 L5
Capital of Anguilla.
Thevenard Island Australia 134 A5
Thévenet, Lac l. Canada 153 H2
Theveste Alg. see Tébessa
The Wash b. U.K. 59 H6
The Weald reg. U.K. 59 H7
The Woodlands U.S.A. 161 E6
Thibodaux U.S.A. 161 F6
Thicket Portage Canada 151 L4
Thief River Falls U.S.A. 160 D1
Thiel Neth. see Tiel
Thiel Mountains Antarctica 188 K1
Thielsen, Mount U.S.A. 156 C4
Thielt Belgium see Tielt
Thiérache reg. France 62 D5
Thiers France 66 F4
Thiès Senegal 120 B3
Thika Kenya 122 D4
Thiladhunmathi Atoll Maldives 106 B5
Thiladunmathi Atoll Maldives see Thiladhunmathi Atoll
Thimbu Bhutan see Thimphu
▶Thimphu Bhutan 105 G4
Capital of Bhutan.
Thionville France 62 G5
Thira i. Greece see Santorini
Thirsk U.K. 58 F4
Thirty Mile Lake Canada 151 L2
Thiruvananthapuram India see Trivandrum
Thiruvannamalai India see Tiruvannamalai
Thiruvarur India 106 C4
Thiruvattiyur India see Tiruvottiyur
Thisted Denmark 55 F8
Thistle Creek Y.T. Canada 149 M3
Thistle Lake Canada 151 I1
Thityabin Myanmar 86 A2
Thiu Khao Luang Phrabang mts Laos/Thai. see Luang Phrabang, Thiu Khao
Thiva Greece 69 J5
Thívai Greece see Thiva
Thlewiaza r. Canada 151 M2
Thoa r. Canada 151 I2
Thô Chu, Đao i. Vietnam 87 C5
Thoen Thai. 96 C5
Thoeng Thai. 86 C3
Thohoyandou S. Africa 125 J2
Tholen Neth. 62 E3
Tholen i. Neth. 62 E3
Tholey Germany 62 H5
Thomas Hill Reservoir U.S.A. 160 E4
Thomas Hubbard, Cape Canada 147 I1
Thomaston CT U.S.A. 165 I3
Thomaston GA U.S.A. 163 C5
Thomastown Ireland 61 E5
Thomasville AL U.S.A. 163 C6
Thomasville GA U.S.A. 163 D6
Thommen Belgium 62 G4
Thompson Canada 151 L4
Thompson r. Canada 150 F5
Thompson U.S.A. 159 I2
Thompson r. U.S.A. 154 I4
Thompson Falls U.S.A. 156 E3
Thompson Peak U.S.A. 157 G6
Thompson's Falls Kenya see Nyahururu
Thompson Sound Canada 150 E5
Thomson U.S.A. 163 D5
Thon Buri Thai. 87 C4
Thonokied Lake Canada 151 I1
Thoothukudi India see Tuticorin
Thoreau U.S.A. 159 I4
Thorn Neth. 62 F3
Thorn Poland see Toruń
Thornaby-on-Tees U.K. 58 F4
Thornapple r. U.S.A. 164 C2
Thornbury U.K. 59 E7
Thorne U.K. 58 G5
Thorne U.S.A. 158 D2
Thornton r. Australia 136 B3
Thorold Canada 164 F2
Thorshavnfjella reg. Antarctica see Thorshavnheiane
Thorshavnheiane reg. Antarctica 188 C2
Thota-ea-Moli Lesotho 125 H5
Thôt Nôt Vietnam 87 D5
Thouars France 66 D3
Thoubal India 105 H4
Thourout Belgium see Torhout
Thousand Islands Canada/U.S.A. 165 G1
Thousand Lake Mountain U.S.A. 159 H2
Thousand Oaks U.S.A. 158 D4
Thousandsticks U.S.A. 164 D5
Thrace reg. Europe 69 L4
Thraki reg. Europe see Thrace
Thrakiko Pelagos sea Greece 69 K4
Three Gorges Reservoir China 101 J3
Three Hills Canada 150 H5
Three Hummock Island Australia 137 [inset]
Three Kings Islands N.Z. 139 D2
Three Oaks U.S.A. 164 B3
Three Pagodas Pass Myanmar/Thai. 86 B4
Three Points, Cape Ghana 120 C4
Three Rivers U.S.A. 164 C3
Three Rivers TX U.S.A. 167 F2
Three Sisters mt. U.S.A. 156 C3
Three Springs Australia 135 A7
Thrissur India see Trichur
Throckmorton U.S.A. 161 D5
Throssell, Lake salt flat Australia 135 D6
Throssel Range hills Australia 134 C5
Thrushton National Park Australia 138 C1
Thư Ba Vietnam 87 D5
Thubun Lakes Canada 151 I2
Thu Dâu Môt Vietnam 87 D5
Thuddungra Australia 138 D5
Thu Đuc Vietnam 87 D5
Thuin Belgium 62 E4
Thul Pak. 111 H4
Thulaythawāt Gharbī, Jabal hill Syria 107 D2
Thule Greenland 147 L2
Thun Switz. 66 H3
Thunder Bay Canada 147 J5
Thunder Bay b. U.S.A. 164 D1
Thunder Creek r. Canada 151 J5
Thüngen Germany 63 J5
Thung Salaeng Luang National Park Thai. 86 C3
Thung Song Thai. 87 B5
Thung Wa Thai. 84 B1
Thung Yai Naresuan Wildlife Reserve nature res. Thai. 86 B4
Thüringen land Germany 63 K3
Thüringer Becken reg. Germany 63 L3
Thüringer Wald mts Germany 63 K4
Thuringia land Germany see Thüringen
Thuringian Forest mts Germany see Thüringer Wald
Thurles Ireland 61 E5
Thurn, Pass Austria 57 N7
Thursday Island Australia 136 C1
Thurso U.K. 60 F2
Thurso r. U.K. 60 F2
Thurston Island Antarctica 188 K2
Thurston Peninsula i. Antarctica see Thurston Island
Thüster Berg hill Germany 63 J2
Thuthukudi India see Tuticorin
Thwaite U.K. 58 E4
Thwaites Glacier Tongue Antarctica 188 K1
Thyatira Turkey see Akhisar
Thyborøn Denmark 55 F8
Thymerais reg. France 62 B6
Tiancang Gansu China 94 D3
Tianchang China 97 H1
Tiancheng Gansu China 94 D4
Tiancheng China see Chongyang
Tianchi Gansu China 95 F4
Tianchi China see Lezhi
Tiandeng China 96 E4
Tiandong China 96 E4
T'ianet'i Georgia 113 G2
Tianfanjie China 97 H2
Tianguistengo Mex. 167 F4
Tianjin Tianjin China 95 I4
Tianjin mun. China 95 I4
Tianjun Qinghai China 94 D4
Tianlin China 96 E3
Tianma China see Changshan
Tianmen China 97 G2
Tianqiaoling China 90 C4
Tianquan China 96 D2
Tianshan Nei Mongol China 95 J3
Tian Shan mts China/Kyrg. see Tien Shan
Tianshui Gansu China 94 F5
Tianshuibu Gansu China 94 F4
Tianshuihai Aksai Chin 99 B6
Tianshuijing Gansu China 98 F4
Tiantai China 97 I2
Tiantaiyong Nei Mongol China 95 I3
Tiantang China see Yuexi
Tianyang China 96 E4
Tianyi Nei Mongol China see Ningcheng
Tianzhen Shandong China see Gaoqing
Tianzhen Shanxi China 95 H3
Tianzhou China see Tianyang
Tianzhu Gansu China 94 E4
Tianzhu Guizhou China 97 F3
Tiaret Alg. 67 G6
Tiassalé Côte d'Ivoire 120 C4
Tibabar Sabah Malaysia see Tambunan
Tibagi Brazil 179 A4
Tibal, Wādī watercourse Iraq 113 F4
Tibati Cameroon 120 E4
Tibba Pak. 111 H4
Tibé, Pic de mt. Guinea 120 C4
Tiber r. Italy 68 E4
Tiberias Israel 107 B3
Tiberias, Lake Israel see Galilee, Sea of
Tiber Reservoir U.S.A. 156 F2
Tibesti mts Chad 121 E2
Tibet aut. reg. China see Xizang Zizhiqu
Tibet, Plateau of Xizang China 99 D6
Tibi India 111 I4
Tibooburra Australia 137 C6
Tibrikot Nepal 105 E3
Tibro Sweden 55 I7
Tibur Italy see Tivoli
Tiburón, Isla i. Mex. 166 B2
Ticao i. Phil. 82 C3
Ticehurst U.K. 59 H7
Tichborne Canada 165 G1
Tichégami r. Canada 153 G4
Tîchît Mauritania 120 C3
Tichla W. Sahara 120 B2
Ticinum Italy see Pavia
Ticonderoga U.S.A. 165 I2
Ticul Mex. 167 H4
Tidaholm Sweden 55 H7
Tiddim Myanmar 86 A2
Tiden India 87 A6
Tidjikja Mauritania 120 B3
Tidore i. Maluku Indon. 83 C2
Tiechanggou Xinjiang China 98 D3
Tiefa Liaoning China see Diaobingshan
Tiel Neth. 62 F3
Tieli China 90 B3
Tieling Liaoning China 95 J3
Tielongtan Aksai Chin 99 B6
Tielt Belgium 62 D4
Tienen Belgium 62 E4
Tien Shan mts China/Kyrg. 88 D4
Tientsin Tianjin China see Tianjin
Tientsin mun. China see Tianjin
Tiên Yên Vietnam 86 D2
Tierp Sweden 55 J6
Tierra Amarilla U.S.A. 157 G5
Tierra Blanca Mex. 167 F5
Tierra Colorada Mex. 167 F5
▶Tierra del Fuego, Isla Grande de i. Arg./Chile 178 C8
Largest island in South America.
Tierra del Fuego, Parque Nacional nat. park Arg. 178 C8
Tiétar r. Spain 67 D4
Tiétar, Valle de valley Spain 67 D3
Tietê r. Brazil 179 A3
Tieyon Australia 135 F6
Tiffin U.S.A. 164 D3
Tiflis Georgia see T'bilisi
Tifore i. Maluku Indon. 83 C2
Tifton U.S.A. 163 D6
Tifu Buru Indon. 83 C3
Tiga i. Malaysia 85 F1
Tigalda Island AK U.S.A. 148 F5
Tigapuluh, Pegunungan mts Indon. 84 C3
Tiga Reservoir Nigeria 120 D3
Tigen Kazakh. 113 H1
Tīgh Āb Iran 111 F5
Tigheciului, Dealurile hills Moldova 69 M2
Tighina Moldova 69 M1
Tigiretskiy Khrebet mts Kazakh./Rus. Fed. 98 C2
Tigiria India 106 E1
Tignère Cameroon 120 E4
Tignish Canada 153 I5
Tigranocerta Turkey see Siirt
Tigre r. Venez. 176 F2
Tigre, Cerro del mt. Mex. 167 F4
Tigris r. Asia 113 G5
also known as Dicle (Turkey) or Nahr Dijlah (Iraq/Syria)
Tigrovaya Balka Zapovednik nature res. Tajik. 111 H2
Tiguidit, Falaise de esc. Niger 120 D3
Tīh, Gebel el plat. Egypt see Tīh, Jabal at
Tīh, Jabal at plat. Egypt 107 A5
Tihāmat 'Asīr reg. Saudi Arabia 100 D4
Tihuatlán Mex. 167 F4
Tijuana Mex. 166 A1
Tikal tourist site Guat. 167 H5
Tikal, Parque Nacional nat. park Guat. 167 H5
Tikamgarh India 104 D4
Tikanlik Xinjiang China 98 D4
Tikchik Lake AK U.S.A. 148 H4
Tikhoretsk Rus. Fed. 53 I7
Tikhvin Rus. Fed. 52 G4
Tikhvinskaya Gryada ridge Rus. Fed. 52 G4
Tiki Basin sea feature S. Pacific Ocean 187 L7
Tikokino N.Z. 139 F4
Tikopia i. Solomon Is 133 G3
Tikrīt Iraq 113 F4
Tikse India 104 D2
Tikshozero, Ozero l. Rus. Fed. 54 R3
Tiksi Rus. Fed. 77 N2
Tila r. Nepal 99 C7
Tiladummati Atoll Maldives see Thiladhunmathi Atoll
Tilaiya Reservoir India 105 F4
Tilamuta Sulawesi Indon. 83 B2
Tilbeşar Ovasi plain Turkey 107 C1
Tilbooroo Australia 138 B1
Tilburg Neth. 62 F3
Tilbury Canada 164 D2
Tilbury U.K. 59 H7
Tilcara Arg. 178 C2
Tilcha Creek watercourse Australia 137 C6
Tilden U.S.A. 161 D6
Tilemsès Niger 120 D3
Tilemsi, Vallée du watercourse Mali 120 D3
Tilhar India 104 D4
Tilimsen Alg. see Tlemcen
Tilin Myanmar 86 A2
Tillabéri Niger 120 D3
Tillamook U.S.A. 156 C3
Tillanchong Island India 87 A5
Tillia Niger 120 D3
Tillicoultry U.K. 60 F4
Tillsonburg Canada 164 E2
Tillyfourie U.K. 60 G3
Tilonia India 111 I5
Tilos i. Greece 69 L6
Tilothu India 105 F4
Tilpa Australia 138 B3
Tilsit Rus. Fed. see Sovetsk
Tilt r. U.K. 60 F4
Tilton IL U.S.A. 164 B3
Tilton NH U.S.A. 165 J2
Tilu, Bukit mt. Indon. 83 B3
Tim Rus. Fed. 53 H6
Ţimā Egypt 108 D4
Timah, Bukit hill Sing. 87 [inset]
Timakara i. India 106 B4
Timanskiy Kryazh ridge Rus. Fed. 52 K2
Timar Turkey 113 F3
Timaru N.Z. 139 C7
Timashevsk Rus. Fed. 53 H7
Timashevskaya Rus. Fed. see Timashevsk
Timbalier Bay LA U.S.A. 167 H2
Timbedgha Mauritania 120 C3
Timber Creek Australia 132 D3
Timber Mountain U.S.A. 158 E3
Timberville U.S.A. 165 F4
Timbuktu Mali 120 C3
Timbun Mata i. Malaysia 85 G1
Timétrine reg. Mali 120 C3
Timiaouine Alg. 120 D2
Timimoun Alg. 64 E6
Timirist, Râs pt Mauritania 120 B3
Timiskaming, Lake Canada see Témiscamingue, Lac
Timişoara Romania 69 I2
Timmins Canada 152 E4
Timms Hill hill U.S.A. 160 F2
Timon Brazil 177 J5
Timor i. Indon. 83 C5
Timor Sea Australia/Indon. 132 C3
Timor Timur country Asia see East Timor
Timpaus i. Indon. 83 C3
Timperley Range hills Australia 135 C6
Timrå Sweden 54 J5
Tīn, Ra's at pt Libya 112 A4
Ţīna, Khalīg el b. Egypt see Ţīnah, Khalīj aţ
Tīnah Syria 107 D1
Ţīnah, Khalīj aţ b. Egypt 107 A4
Tin Can Bay Australia 137 F5
Tindivanam India 106 C3
Tindouf Alg. 64 C6
Ti-n-Essako Mali 120 D3
Tinggi i. Malaysia 84 D2
Tingha Australia 138 E2
Tingis Morocco see Tangier
Tingo María Peru 176 C5
Tingréla Côte d'Ivoire see Tengréla
Tingri Xizang China 99 D7
Tingsryd Sweden 55 I8
Tingvoll Norway 54 F5
Tingwall U.K. 60 F1
Tingzhou China see Changting
Tinharé, Ilha de i. Brazil 179 D1
Tinh Gia Vietnam 86 D3
Tinian i. N. Mariana Is 81 L4
Tini Heke is N.Z. see Snares Islands
Tinjar r. Malaysia 85 F1
Tinjil i. Indon. 84 D4
Tinnelvelly India see Tirunelveli
Tinogasta Arg. 178 C3
Tinompo Sulawesi Indon. 83 B2
Tinos Greece 69 K6
Tinos i. Greece 69 K6
Tinqueux France 62 D5
Tinrhert, Hamada de Alg. 120 D2
Tinsukia India 105 H4
Tintagel U.K. 59 C8
Tîntâne Mauritania 120 B3
Tintina Arg. 178 D3
Tintinara Australia 137 C7
Tioga U.S.A. 160 C1
Tioman i. Malaysia 84 D2
Tionesta U.S.A. 164 F3
Tionesta Lake U.S.A. 164 F3
Tipasa Alg. 67 H5
Tiphsah Syria see Dibsī
Tipitapa Nicaragua 166 [inset] I6
Tipperary Ireland 61 D5
Tiptala Bhanjyang pass Nepal 99 D8
Tipton CA U.S.A. 158 D3
Tipton IA U.S.A. 160 F3
Tipton IN U.S.A. 164 B3
Tipton MO U.S.A. 160 E4
Tipton, Mount U.S.A. 159 F4
Tiptop U.S.A. 164 E5
Tip Top Hill hill Canada 152 D4
Tiptree U.K. 59 H7
Tiptur India 106 C3
Tipturi India see Tiptur
Tiquisate Guat. 167 H6
Tiracambu, Serra do hills Brazil 177 I4
Tirah reg. Pak. 111 H3
▶Tirana Albania 69 H4
Capital of Albania.
Tiranë Albania see Tirana
Tirano Italy 68 D1
Tirari Desert Australia 137 B5
Tiraspol Moldova 69 M1
Tiraz Mountains Namibia 124 C4
Tire Turkey 69 L5
Tirebolu Turkey 113 E2
Tiree i. U.K. 60 C4
Tîrgovişte Romania see Târgovişte
Tîrgu Jiu Romania see Târgu Jiu
Tîrgu Mureş Romania see Târgu Mureş
Tîrgu Neamţ Romania see Târgu Neamţ
Tîrgu Secuiesc Romania see Târgu Secuiesc
Tiri Pak. 111 G4
Tirich Mir mt. Pak. 111 H2
Tirlemont Belgium see Tienen
Tirna r. India 106 C2
Tîrnăveni Romania see Târnăveni
Tírnavos Greece see Tyrnavos
Tiros Brazil 179 B2
Tirourda, Col de pass Alg. 67 I5
Tirreno, Mare sea France/Italy see Tyrrhenian Sea
Tirso r. Sardinia Italy 68 C5
Tirthahalli India 106 B3
Tiruchchendur India 106 C4
Tiruchchirappalli India 106 C4
Tiruchengodu India 106 C4
Tirunelveli India 106 C4
Tirupati India 106 C3
Tiruppattur Tamil Nadu India 106 C3
Tiruppattur Tamil Nadu India 106 C4
Tiruppur India 106 C4
Tiruttani India 106 C3
Tirutturaippundi India 106 C4
Tiruvallur India 106 C3
Tiruvannamalai India 106 C3
Tiruvottiyur India 106 D3
Tiru Well Australia 134 D5
Tisa r. Serbia 69 I2
also known as Tisza (Hungary) or Tysa (Ukraine)
Tisdale Canada 151 J4
Tishomingo U.S.A. 161 D5
Ţīsīyah Syria 107 C3

Tissemsilt Alg. 67 G6
Tista r. India 99 E8
Tisza r. Hungary see Tisa
Titabar Assam India 99 F8
Titaluk r. AK U.S.A. 148 I1
Titalya Bangl. see Tetulia
Titan Dome ice feature Antarctica 188 H1
Titao Burkina 120 C3
Tit-Ary Rus. Fed. 77 N2
Titawin Morocco see Tétouan
Titicaca, Lago Bol./Peru see Titicaca, Lake

▶Titicaca, Lake Bol./Peru 176 E7
Largest lake in South America.

Titi Islands N.Z. 139 A8
Tititea mt. N.Z. see Aspiring, Mount
Titlagarh India 106 D1
Titograd Montenegro see Podgorica
Titova Mitrovica Kosovo see Mitrovicë
Titovo Užice Serbia see Užice
Titovo Velenje Slovenia see Velenje
Titov Veles Macedonia see Veles
Titov Vrbas Serbia see Vrbas
Ti Tree Australia 134 F5
Titu Romania 69 K2
Titusville FL U.S.A. 163 D6
Titusville PA U.S.A. 164 F3
Tiu Chung Chau i. H.K. China 97 [inset]
Tiumpain, Rubha an hd U.K. see Tiumpan Head
Tiumpan Head hd U.K. 60 C2
Tiva watercourse Kenya 122 D4
Tivari India 104 C4
Tiverton Canada 164 E1
Tiverton U.K. 59 D8
Tivoli Italy 68 E4
Ṭīwī Oman 110 E6
Tiwi Aboriginal Land res. N.T. Australia 83 D5
Tiworo, Selat sea chan. Indon. 83 B4
Tixtla Mex. 167 F5
Ti-ywa Myanmar 87 B4
Tizi El Arba hill Alg. 67 H5
Tizimín Mex. 167 H4
Tizi N'Kouilal pass Alg. 67 I5
Tizi Ouzou Alg. 67 I5
Tiznap He r. China 99 B5
Tiznit Morocco 120 C2
Tizoc Mex. 166 E3
Tiztoutine Morocco 67 E6
Tjaneni Swaziland 125 J3
Tjappsåive Sweden 54 K4
Tjeukemeer l. Neth. 62 F2
Tjirebon Jawa Indon. see Cirebon
Tjolotjo Zimbabwe see Tsholotsho
Tjorhom Norway 55 E7
Tkibuli Georgia see Tqibuli
Tlacotalpán Mex. 167 G5
Tlacotepec, Cerro mt. Mex. 167 E5
Tlahualilo Mex. 166 E3
Tlalnepantla Mex. 167 F5
Tlancualpican Mex. 167 F5
Tlapa Mex. 167 F5
Tlapacoyan Mex. 167 F5
Tlaxcala Mex. 168 E5
Tlaxcala state Mex. 167 F5
Tlaxco Mex. 167 F5
Tlaxiaco Mex. 167 F5
Tl'ell B.C. Canada 149 O5
Tlemcen Alg. 67 F6
Tlhakalatlou S. Africa 124 F5
Tlholong S. Africa 125 I5
Tlokweng Botswana 125 G3
Tlyarata Rus. Fed. 113 G2
Tnekveyem r. Rus. Fed. 148 B2
To r. Myanmar 86 B3
Toad r. Canada 150 E3
Toad River Canada 150 E3
Toagel Mlungui Palau 82 [inset]
Toamasina Madag. 123 E5
Toana mts U.S.A. 159 F1
Toano U.S.A. 165 G5
Toa Payoh Sing. 87 [inset]
Toba China 96 C2
Toba Japan 92 C4
Toba, Danau l. Indon. 84 B2
Toba, Lake Indon. see Toba, Danau
Toba and Kakar Ranges mts Pak. 111 G4
Toba Gargaji Pak. 111 I4
Tobago i. Trin. and Tob. 169 L6
Tobar an Choire Ireland see Tobercurry
Tobelo Halmahera Indon. 83 C2
Tobercurry Ireland 61 D3
Tobermorey Australia 136 B4
Tobermory Australia 138 A1
Tobermory Canada 164 E1
Tobermory U.K. 60 C4
Tobi i. Palau 81 I6
Tobin, Lake salt flat Australia 134 D5
Tobin, Mount U.S.A. 158 E1
Tobin Lake Canada 151 K4
Tobin Lake l. Canada 151 K4
Tobishima Japan 92 C3
Tobi-shima i. Japan 91 E5
Toboali Indon. 84 D3
Tobol r. Kazakh./Rus. Fed. 100 F1
Tobol'sk Rus. Fed. 76 H4
Toboso Negros Phil. 82 C4
Tobruk Libya see Tubruq
Tobseda Rus. Fed. 52 L1
Tōbu Japan 93 E2
Tobyl r. Kazakh./Rus. Fed. see Tobol
Tobysh r. Rus. Fed. 52 K2
Tocache Nuevo Peru 176 C5
Tocantinópolis Brazil 177 I5
Tocantins r. Brazil 177 I4
Tocantins state Brazil 179 A1
Tocantinzinha r. Brazil 179 A1
Toccoa U.S.A. 163 D5
Tochi r. Pak. 111 H3
Tochigi Japan 93 F2
Tochigi pref. Japan 93 F2
Töcksfors Sweden 55 G7
Tocoa Hond. 166 [inset] I6
Tocopilla Chile 178 B2
Tocumwal Australia 138 B5
Tod, Mount Canada 150 G5
Toda Japan 93 F3
Todd watercourse Australia 136 A5
Todi Italy 68 E3
Todog Xinjiang China 98 C3
Todoga-saki pt Japan 91 F5
Todok Xinjiang China see Todog
Todos Santos Mex. 166 C4
Toe Head hd U.K. 60 B3
Tōei Japan 92 D3
Tofino Canada 150 E5
Toft U.K. 60 [inset]
Tofua i. Tonga 133 I3
Toga Japan 92 D2
Tōgane Japan 93 G3
Togatax Xinjiang China 99 C6
Togi Japan 92 C1
Togiak AK U.S.A. 148 G4
Togiak r. AK U.S.A. 148 G4
Togiak Bay AK U.S.A. 148 G4
Togiak Lake AK U.S.A. 148 H4
Togiak National Wildlife Refuge nature res. AK U.S.A. 148 G4
Togian i. Indon. 83 B3
Togian, Kepulauan is Indon. 83 B3
Togliatti Rus. Fed. see Tol'yatti
Togo country Africa 120 D4
Tōgō Aichi Japan 92 D3
Tograsay He r. China 99 E5
Tögrög Hovd Mongolia see Manhan
Tögrög Mongolia 94 E2
Togrog Ul Nei Mongol China 95 H3
Togtoh Nei Mongol China 95 G3
Togton He r. China 99 F6
Togura Japan 93 E2
Tohatchi U.S.A. 159 I4
Tohenbatu mt. Malaysia 85 F2
Tohoku Japan 92 C3
Toholampi Fin. 54 N5
Tohom Nei Mongol China 94 F3
Tōhōm Mongolia see Mandah
Tohono O'Odham (Papago) Indian Reservation res. AZ U.S.A. 166 B1
Toi Shizuoka Japan 93 E4
Toiba Xizang China 99 E7
Toibalewe India 87 A5
Toide Japan 92 C2
Toijala Fin. 55 M6
Toili Sulawesi Indon. 83 B3
Toi-misaki pt Japan 91 C7
Toin Japan 92 C3
Toineke Timor Indon. 83 C5
Toivakka Fin. 54 O5
Toiyabe Range mts U.S.A. 158 E2
Toja Sulawesi Indon. 83 B3
Tojikiston country Asia see Tajikistan
Tōjō Hyōgo Japan 92 B4
Tok AK U.S.A. 149 L3
Tōkai Aichi Japan 92 C3
Tōkai Ibaraki Japan 93 G2
Tokala, Gunung mt. Indon. 83 B3
Tōkamachi Japan 93 E1
Tokar Sudan 108 E6
Tokara-rettō is Japan 91 C7
Tokarevka Kazakh. 98 A2
Tokarevka Rus. Fed. 53 I6
Tokat Turkey 112 E2
Tŏkchŏk-to i. S. Korea 91 B5
Tokdo i. N. Pacific Ocean see Liancourt Rocks

▶Tokelau terr. S. Pacific Ocean 133 I2
New Zealand Overseas Territory.

Toki Japan 92 D3
Tokigawa Japan 93 F2
Toki-gawa r. Japan 92 C3
Tokkuztara Xinjiang China see Gongliu
Toklat AK U.S.A. 149 J2
Toklat r. AK U.S.A. 149 J2
Tokmak Kyrg. see Tokmok
Tokmak Ukr. 53 G7
Tokmok Kyrg. 102 E3
Tokomaru Bay N.Z. 139 G4
Tokoname Japan 92 C4
Tokoroa N.Z. 139 E4
Tokorozawa Japan 93 F3
Tokoza S. Africa 125 I4
Toksook Bay AK U.S.A. 148 F3
Toksu Xinjiang China see Xinhe
Toksun Xinjiang China 98 E4
Tok-tō i. N. Pacific Ocean see Liancourt Rocks
Toktogul Kyrg. 102 D3
Tokto-ri i. N. Pacific Ocean see Liancourt Rocks
Tokty Kazakh. 98 C3
Tokur Rus. Fed. 90 D1
Tokushima Japan 91 D6
Tokuyama Japan 91 C6

▶Tōkyō Japan 93 F3
Capital of Japan. Most populous city in the world and in Asia.

Tōkyō mun. Japan 93 F3
Tōkyō-wan b. Japan 93 F3
Tokyrau watercourse Kazakh. 98 A3
Tokzār Afgh. 111 G3
Tolaga Bay N.Z. 139 G4
Tōlañaro Madag. 123 E6
Tolbo Mongolia 94 B1
Tolbukhin Bulg. see Dobrich
Tolbuzino Rus. Fed. 90 B1
Tolé Panama 166 [inset] J7
Tole Bi Kazakh. 98 A4
Toledo Brazil 178 F2
Toledo Spain 67 D4
Toledo IA U.S.A. 160 E3
Toledo OH U.S.A. 164 D3
Toledo OR U.S.A. 156 C3
Toledo, Montes de mts Spain 67 D4
Toledo Bend Reservoir U.S.A. 161 E6
Toletum Spain see Toledo
Toli Xinjiang China 98 C3
Toliara Madag. 123 E6
Tolitoli Sulawesi Indon. 83 B2
Tol'ka Rus. Fed. 76 J3
Tolleson U.S.A. 159 G5
Tollimarjon Uzbek. 111 G2
Tolmachevo Rus. Fed. 55 P7
Tolo Dem. Rep. Congo 122 B4
Toloa Creek Hond. 166 [inset] I6
Tolo Channel H.K. China 97 [inset]
Tolochin Belarus see Talachyn
Tolo Harbour b. H.K. China 97 [inset]
Tolonuu i. Maluku Indon. 83 D2
Tolosa France see Toulouse
Tolosa Spain 67 E2
Tolovana r. AK U.S.A. 149 J2
Toluca Mex. 168 E5
Toluca de Lerdo Mex. see Toluca
Tol'yatti Rus. Fed. 53 K5
Tom' r. Rus. Fed. 90 B2
Tomaga-shima i. Japan 92 B4
Tomagashima-suidō sea chan. Japan 92 A4
Tomah U.S.A. 160 F3
Tomakomai Japan 90 F4
Tomales U.S.A. 158 B2
Tomali Indon. 81 G7
Tomamae Japan 90 F3
Tomani Sabah Malaysia 85 F1
Tomanivi mt. Fiji 133 H3
Tomar Brazil 176 F4
Tomar Port. 67 B4
Tomari Rus. Fed. 90 F3
Tomarza Turkey 112 D3
Tomaszów Lubelski Poland 53 D6
Tomaszów Mazowiecki Poland 57 R5
Tomatin U.K. 60 F3
Tomatlán Mex. 168 C5
Tomazina Brazil 179 A3
Tombador, Serra do hills Brazil 177 G6
Tombigbee r. U.S.A. 163 C6
Tomboco Angola 123 B4
Tombouctou Mali see Timbuktu
Tombstone U.S.A. 157 F7
Tombua Angola 123 B5
Tom Burke S. Africa 125 H2
Tomdibuloq Uzbek. 102 B3
Tome Moz. 125 L2
Tomea i. Indon. 83 B4
Tomelilla Sweden 55 H9
Tomelloso Spain 67 E4
Tomi Romania see Constanța
Tomika Japan 92 C3
Tomingley Australia 138 D4
Tomini, Teluk g. Indon. 83 B3
Tominian Mali 120 C3
Tomintoul U.K. 60 F3
Tomioka Gunma Japan 93 E2
Tomisato Japan 93 G3
Tomislavgrad Bos.-Herz. 68 G3
Tomiura Japan 93 F3
Tomiyama Aichi Japan 93 D3
Tomiyama Chiba Japan 93 F3
Tomizawa Japan 93 E3
Tomkinson Ranges mts Australia 135 E6
Tømmerneset Norway 54 I3
Tommot Rus. Fed. 77 N4
Tomo r. Col. 176 E2
Tomobe Japan 93 G2
Tomóchic Mex. 166 D2
Tomorlog Qinghai China 99 E5
Tomort mt China 94 C3
Tomortei Nei Mongol China 95 H3
Tompira Sulawesi Indon. 83 B3
Tompkinsville U.S.A. 164 C5
Tompo Sulawesi Indon. 83 A3
Tom Price Australia 134 B5
Tomra Xizang China 99 D7
Tomsk Rus. Fed. 76 J4
Toms River U.S.A. 165 H4
Tomtabacken hill Sweden 55 I8
Tomtor Rus. Fed. 77 P3
Tomur Feng mt. China/Kyrg. see Jengish Chokusu
Tomuzlovka r. Rus. Fed. 53 J7
Tom White, Mount AK U.S.A. 149 L3
Tonalá Mex. 168 F5
Tonalá Veracruz Mex. 167 G5
Tonami Japan 92 C2
Tonantins Brazil 176 E4
Tonb-e Bozorg, Jazīreh-ye i. The Gulf see Greater Tunb
Tonb-e Kūchek, Jazīreh-ye i. The Gulf see Lesser Tunb
Tonbridge U.K. 59 H7
Tondabayashi Japan 92 B4
Tondano Sulawesi Indon. 83 C2
Tønder Denmark 55 F9
Tondi India 106 C4
Tone Gunma Japan 93 F2
Tone Ibaraki Japan 93 G3
Tone r. U.K. 59 E7
Tone-gawa r. Japan 93 G3
Toney Mountain Antarctica 188 K1
Tonga country S. Pacific Ocean 133 I4
Tongaat S. Africa 125 J5
Tongariro National Park N.Z. 139 E4
Tongatapu Group is Tonga 133 I4

▶Tonga Trench sea feature S. Pacific Ocean 186 I7
2nd deepest trench in the world.

Tongbai Shan mts China 97 G1
Tongcheng China 97 H2
Tongcheng Shandong China see Dong'e
T'ongch'ŏn N. Korea 91 B5
Tongchuan Shaanxi China 95 G5
Tongchuan Sichuan China see Santai
Tongdao China 97 F3
Tongde Qinghai China 94 E5
Tongduch'ŏn S. Korea 91 B5
Tongeren Belgium 62 F4
Tonggu China 97 G2
Tongguan Shaanxi China 95 G5
Tongguzbasti Xinjiang China 98 C5
Tonggu Zui pt China 97 F5
Tonghae S. Korea 91 C5
Tonghai China 96 D3
Tonghe China 90 C3
Tonghua Jilin China 90 B4
Tonghua Jilin China 90 B4
Tongi Bangl. see Tungi
Tongjiang Heilong. China 90 D3
Tongjiang Sichuan China 96 E2
Tongking, Gulf of China/Vietnam 86 E2
Tongko Sulawesi Indon. 83 B3
Tongle China see Leye
Tongliang China 96 E2
Tongliao Nei Mongol China 95 J3
Tongling China 97 H2
Tonglu China 97 H2
Tongo Australia 138 A3
Tongo Lake salt flat Australia 138 A3
Tongquil i. Phil. 82 C5
Tongren Guizhou China 97 F3
Tongren Qinghai China 94 E5
Tongres Belgium see Tongeren
Tongsa Bhutan 105 G4
Tongshan Jiangsu China see Xuzhou
Tongshi Hainan China see Wuzhishan
Tongta Myanmar 86 B2
Tongtian He r. Qinghai China 96 C1 see Yangtze
Tongtian He r. Qinghai China 99 G6
Tongue U.K. 60 E2
Tongue r. U.S.A. 156 G3
Tongue of the Ocean sea chan. Bahamas 163 E7
Tongwei Gansu China 94 F5
Tongxin Ningxia China 94 F4
T'ongyŏng S. Korea 91 C6
Tongyu Jilin China 95 J2
Tongzhou Beijing China 95 I4
Tongzi China 96 E2
Tonhil Mongolia 94 C2
Tónichi Mex. 166 C2
Tonila Mex. 166 E5
Tonk India 104 C4
Tonkābon Iran 110 C2
Tonki Cape AK U.S.A. 149 J4
Tonkin reg. Vietnam 86 D2
Tônle Repou r. Laos 87 D4
Tônlé Sab l. Cambodia see Tonle Sap

▶Tonle Sap l. Cambodia 87 C4
Largest lake in southeast Asia.

Tōno Fukushima Japan 93 G1
Tonopah AZ U.S.A. 159 G5
Tonopah NV U.S.A. 158 E2
Tonoshō Chiba Japan 93 G3
Tonosí Panama 166 [inset] J8
Tonota Botswana 123 C6
Tons r. India 99 B7
Tønsberg Norway 55 G7
Tonsina AK U.S.A. 149 K3
Tonstad Norway 55 E7
Tonto Creek watercourse U.S.A. 159 H5
Tonvarjeh Iran 110 E3
Tonzang Myanmar 86 A2
Tonzi Myanmar 86 A1
Toobeah Australia 138 D2
Toobli Liberia 120 C4
Tooele U.S.A. 159 G1
Toogoolawah Australia 138 F1
Toolik r. AK U.S.A. 149 J1
Tooma r. Australia 138 D6
Toompine Australia 138 B1
Toora Australia 138 C7
Tooraweenah Australia 138 D3
Toorberg mt. S. Africa 124 G7
Toowoomba Australia 138 E1
Tooxin Somalia 122 F2
Top Afgh. 111 H3
Topagoruk r. AK U.S.A. 148 I1
Top Boğazı Geçidi pass Turkey 107 C1

▶Topeka U.S.A. 160 E4
Capital of Kansas.

Topia Mex. 166 D3
Toplana, Gunung mt. Seram Indon. 83 D3
Töplitz Germany 63 M2
Topoľčany Slovakia 57 Q6
Topolobampo Mex. 166 C3
Topolovgrad Bulg. 69 L3
Topozero, Ozero l. Rus. Fed. 54 R4
Topsfield U.S.A. 162 H2
Tor Eth. 121 G4
Torahime Japan 92 C3
Toranggekuduk Xinjiang China 94 B2
Tor Baldak mt. Afgh. 111 G4
Torbalı Turkey 69 L5
Torbat-e Heydarīyeh Iran 110 E3
Torbat-e Jām Iran 111 F3
Torbay Bay Australia 135 B8
Torbert, Mount AK U.S.A. 148 I3
Torbeyevo Rus. Fed. 53 I5
Torch r. Canada 151 K4
Tordesillas Spain 67 D3
Tordesilos Spain 67 F3
Töre Sweden 54 M4
Torelló Spain 67 H2
Torenberg hill Neth. 62 F2
Toreo Sulawesi Indon. 83 B3
Toretam Kazakh. see Baykonyr
Torey Rus. Fed. 94 F1
Torgau Germany 63 M3
Torghay Kazakh. see Turgay
Torgun r. Rus. Fed. 53 J6
Torhout Belgium 62 D3
Toride Japan 93 G3
Torigakubi-misaki pt Japan 93 E1
Torigoe Japan 92 C2
Torii-tōge pass Japan 93 D3
Torii-tōge pass Japan 93 E2
Torikabuto-yama mt. Japan 93 E2
Torino Italy see Turin
Tori-shima i. Japan 91 F7
Torit Sudan 121 G4
Toriya Japan 92 C2
Torkamān Iran 110 B2
Torkovichi Rus. Fed. 52 F4
Tornado Mountain Canada 150 H5
Torneå Fin. see Tornio
Torneälven r. Sweden 54 N4
Torneträsk l. Sweden 54 K2
Torngat, Monts mts Canada see Torngat Mountains
Torngat Mountains Canada 153 I2
Torngat Mountains National Park Reserve Canada 153 J2
Tornio Fin. 54 N4
Toro Spain 67 D3
Toro, Pico del mt. Mex. 161 C7
Torobuku Sulawesi Indon. 83 B4
Torom Rus. Fed. 90 D1

▶Toronto Canada 164 F2
Capital of Ontario.

Toro Peak U.S.A. 158 E5
Toropets Rus. Fed. 52 F4
Tororo Uganda 122 D3
Toros Dağları mts Turkey see Taurus Mountains
Torphins U.K. 60 G3
Torquay Australia 138 B7
Torquay U.K. 59 D8
Torrance U.S.A. 158 D5
Torrão Port. 67 B4
Torre mt. Port. 67 C3
Torreblanca Spain 67 G3
Torre Blanco, Cerro mt. Mex. 166 B1
Torrecerredo mt. Spain 67 D2
Torre del Greco Italy 68 F4
Torre de Moncorvo Port. 67 C3
Torrelavega Spain 67 D2
Torremolinos Spain 67 D5

▶Torrens, Lake imp. l. Australia 137 B6
2nd largest lake in Oceania.

Torrens Creek Australia 136 D4
Torrent Spain 67 F4
Torrente Spain see Torrent
Torreón Mex. 166 E3
Torres Brazil 179 A5
Torres Mex. 166 C2
Torres del Paine, Parque Nacional nat. park Chile 178 B8
Torres Islands Vanuatu 133 G3
Torres Novas Port. 67 B4
Torres Strait Australia 132 E2
Torres Vedras Port. 67 B4
Torrevieja Spain 67 F5
Torrey U.S.A. 159 H2
Torridge r. U.K. 59 C8
Torridon, Loch b. U.K. 60 D3
Torrijos Spain 67 D4
Torrington Australia 138 E2
Torrington CT U.S.A. 162 F3
Torrington WY U.S.A. 156 G4
Torsa Chhu r. Bhutan 99 E8
Torsby Sweden 55 H6

▶Tórshavn Faroe Is 54 [inset]
Capital of the Faroe Islands.

Tortilla Flat U.S.A. 159 H5
To'rtko'l Uzbek. 102 B3
Törtköl Uzbek. see To'rtko'l
Tortoli Sardinia Italy 68 C5
Tortona Italy 68 C2
Tortosa Spain 67 G3
Tortuga, Laguna l. Mex. 167 F4
Tortuguero, Parque Nacional nat. park Costa Rica 166 [inset] J7
Tortum Turkey 113 F2
Toru-Aygyr Kyrg. 98 B4
Ţorūd Iran 110 D3
Torue Sulawesi Indon. 83 B3
Torugart, Pereval pass China/Kyrg. see Turugart Pass
Torul Turkey 113 E2
Toruń Poland 57 Q4
Tory Island Ireland 61 D2
Tory Sound sea chan. Ireland 61 D2
Torzhok Rus. Fed. 52 G4
Tosa Japan 91 D6
Tosbotn Norway 54 H4
Tosca S. Africa 124 F3
Tosca, Punta pt Mex. 166 C3
Toscano, Arcipelago is Italy 68 C3
Tosham India 104 C3
Tōshi-jima i. Japan 92 C4
To-shima i. Japan 93 F4
Tōshima-yama mt. Japan 91 F4

▶Toshkent Uzbek. 102 C3
Capital of Uzbekistan.

Tosno Rus. Fed. 52 F4
Toson Hu l. Qinghai China 94 D4
Tosontsengel Mongolia 94 D1
Tosontsengel Mongolia 94 E1
Tostado Arg. 178 D3
Tostedt Germany 63 J1
Tosya Turkey 112 D2
Totapola mt. Sri Lanka 106 D5
Tôtes France 62 B5
Tot'ma Rus. Fed. 52 I4
Totness Suriname 177 G2
Totolapan Mex. 167 F5
Totonicapán Guat. 167 H6
Totsuka Japan 93 F3
Totsukawa Japan 92 B4
Totsu-kawa r. Japan 92 B5
Tottenham Australia 138 C4
Totton U.K. 59 F8
Tottori Japan 91 D6
Touba Côte d'Ivoire 120 C4
Touba Senegal 120 B3
Toubkal, Jbel mt. Morocco 64 C5
Toubkal, Parc National du nat. park Morocco 64 C5
Touboro Cameroon 121 E4
Toudaohu Nei Mongol China 94 F4
Tougan Burkina 120 C3
Touggourt Alg. 64 F5
Tougué Guinea 120 B3
Touil Mauritania 120 B3
Toul France 62 F6
Touliu Taiwan 97 I4
Toulon France 66 G5
Toulon U.S.A. 160 F3
Toulouse France 66 E5
Toumodi Côte d'Ivoire 120 C4
Toupai China 97 F3
Tourane Vietnam see Đa Năng
Tourcoing France 62 D4
Tourgis Lake Canada 151 J1
Tourlaville France 59 F9
Tournai Belgium 62 D4
Tournon-sur-Rhône France 66 G4
Tournus France 66 G3
Touros Brazil 177 K5
Tours France 66 E3
Tousside, Pic mt. Chad 121 E2
Toussoro, Mont mt. Cent. Afr. Rep. 122 C3
Toutai China 90 B3
Touwsrivier S. Africa 124 E7
Toužim Czech Rep. 63 M4
Töv prov. Mongolia 94 F2
Tovarkovo Rus. Fed. 53 G5
Tovil'-Dora Tajik. see Tavildara
Tovuz Azer. 113 G2
Towada Japan 90 F4
Towak Mountain hill AK U.S.A. 148 F3
Towanda U.S.A. 165 G3
Towaoc U.S.A. 159 I3
Towari Sulawesi Indon. 83 B4
Towcester U.K. 59 G6
Tower Ireland 61 D6
Towner U.S.A. 160 C1
Townes Pass U.S.A. 158 E3
Townsend U.S.A. 156 F3
Townsend, Mount Australia 138 D6
Townshend Island Australia 136 E4
Townsville Australia 136 D3
Towori, Teluk b. Indon. 83 B3
Towot Sudan 121 G4
Towr Kham Afgh. 111 H3
Towson U.S.A. 165 G4
Towuti, Danau l. Indon. 83 B3
Towyn U.K. see Tywyn
Toxkan He r. China 98 C4
Toy U.S.A. 158 D1
Toyah U.S.A. 161 C6
Toyama Japan 92 D2
Toyama pref. Japan 92 D2
Toyama-wan b. Japan 92 D1
Toyêma Qinghai China 94 E5
Toygunen Rus. Fed. 148 D2
Toyoake Japan 92 D3
Toyoda Japan 93 D4
Toyohashi Japan 92 D4
Toyokawa Japan 92 D4
Toyo-kawa r. Japan 92 D4
Toyonaka Japan 92 B4
Toyone Japan 92 D3
Toyono Nagano Japan 93 E2
Toyono Ōsaka Japan 92 B4
Toyooka Hyōgo Japan 92 A3
Toyooka Nagano Japan 93 D3
Toyooka Shizuoka Japan 93 D4
Toyoshina Japan 93 D2
Toyota Japan 92 D3
Toyoyama Japan 92 C3
Tozanlı Turkey see Almus
Tozê Kangri mt. Xizang China 99 C6
Tozeur Tunisia 64 F5
Tozi, Mount AK U.S.A. 149 J2
Tozitna r. AK U.S.A. 148 I2
Tqibuli Georgia 113 F2
Traben Germany 62 H5
Trâblous Lebanon see Tripoli
Trabotivište Macedonia 69 J4
Trabzon Turkey 113 E2
Tracy CA U.S.A. 158 C3
Tracy MN U.S.A. 160 E2
Trading r. Canada 152 C4
Traer U.S.A. 160 E3
Trafalgar U.S.A. 164 B4
Trafalgar, Cabo c. Spain 67 C5
Traffic Mountain Y.T. Canada 149 O3
Trail Canada 150 G5
Tràille, Rubha na pt U.K. 60 D5
Traill Island Greenland see Traill Ø
Traill Ø i. Greenland 147 P2
Trainor Lake Canada 150 F2
Trajectum Neth. see Utrecht
Trakai Lith. 55 N9
Tra Khuc, Sông r. Vietnam 86 E4
Trakiya reg. Europe see Thrace
Trakt Rus. Fed. 52 K3
Trakya reg. Europe see Thrace
Tralee Ireland 61 C5
Tralee Bay Ireland 61 C5
Trá Lí Ireland see Tralee
Tramandai Brazil 179 A5
Tramán Tepuí mt. Venez. 176 F2
Trá Mhór Ireland see Tramore
Tramore Ireland 61 E5
Tranås Sweden 55 I7
Trancas Arg. 178 C3
Trancoso Brazil 179 D2
Tranemo Sweden 55 H8
Tranent U.K. 60 G5
Trang Thai. 87 B6
Trangan i. Indon. 134 F1
Trangie Australia 138 C4
Trân Ninh, Cao Nguyên Laos 86 C3

Transantarctic Mountains Antarctica 188 H2
Trans Canada Highway Canada 151 H5
Transylvanian Alps *mts* Romania 69 J2
Transylvanian Basin *plat.* Romania 69 K1
Trapani *Sicily* Italy 68 E5
Trapezus Turkey *see* **Trabzon**
Trapper Creek *AK* U.S.A. 149 J3
Trapper Peak U.S.A. 156 E3
Trappes France 62 C6
Traralgon Australia 138 C7
Trashigang Bhutan *see* **Tashigang**
Trasimeno, Lago *l.* Italy 68 E3
Trasvase, Canal de Spain 67 E4
Trat Thai. 87 C4
Traunsee *l.* Austria 57 N7
Traunstein Germany 57 N7
Travaillant Lake *N.W.T.* Canada 149 O2
Travellers Lake *imp. l.* Australia 137 C7
Travers, Mount N.Z. 139 D6
Traverse City U.S.A. 164 C1
Traverse Peak *hill AK* U.S.A. 148 H2
Tra Vinh Vietnam 87 D5
Travis, Lake *TX* U.S.A. 167 F2
Travnik Bos.-Herz. 68 G2
Trbovlje Slovenia 68 F1
Tre, Hon *i.* Vietnam 87 E4
Treasury Islands Solomon Is 132 F2
Treat Island *AK* U.S.A. 148 H2
Trebbin Germany 63 N2
Trebević *nat. park* Bos.-Herz. 68 H3
Třebíč Czech Rep. 57 O6
Trebinje Bos.-Herz. 68 H3
Trebišov Slovakia 53 D6
Trebizond Turkey *see* **Trabzon**
Trebnje Slovenia 68 F2
Trebur Germany 63 I5
Tree Island India 106 B4
Trefaldwyn U.K. *see* **Montgomery**
Treffurt Germany 63 K3
Treffynnon U.K. *see* **Holywell**
Trefyclawdd U.K. *see* **Knighton**
Trefynwy U.K. *see* **Monmouth**
Tregosse Islets and Reefs Australia 136 E3
Treinta y Tres Uruguay 178 F4
Trelew Arg. 178 C6
Trelleborg Sweden 55 H9
Trélon France 62 E4
Tremblant, Mont *hill* Canada 152 G5
Trembleur Lake Canada 150 E4
Tremiti, Isole *is* Italy 68 F3
Tremont U.S.A. 165 G3
Tremonton U.S.A. 156 E4
Tremp Spain 67 G2
Trenance U.K. 59 B8
Trenary U.S.A. 162 C2
Trenche *r.* Canada 153 G5
Trenčín Slovakia 57 Q6
Trendelburg Germany 63 J3
Trêng Cambodia 87 C4
Trenggalek *Jawa* Indon. 85 E5
Trengganu *state* Malaysia *see* **Terengganu**
Trenque Lauquén Arg. 178 D5
Trent Italy *see* **Trento**
Trent *r.* U.K. 59 G5
Trento Italy 68 D1
Trenton Canada 165 G1
Trenton *FL* U.S.A. 163 D6
Trenton *GA* U.S.A. 163 C5
Trenton *KY* U.S.A. 164 B5
Trenton *MO* U.S.A. 160 E3
Trenton *NC* U.S.A. 163 E5
Trenton *NE* U.S.A. 160 C3

▶**Trenton** *NJ* U.S.A. 165 H3
Capital of New Jersey.

Treorchy U.K. 59 D7
Trepassey Canada 153 L5
Tres Arroyos Arg. 178 D5
Tresco *i.* U.K. 59 A9
Três Corações Brazil 179 B3
Tres Esquinas Col. 176 C3
Tres Forcas, Cabo *c.* Morocco *see* **Trois Fourches, Cap des**
Três Lagoas Brazil 179 A3
Três Marias, Represa *resr* Brazil 179 B2
Tres Picachos, Sierra *mts* Mex. 157 G7
Tres Picos, Cerro *mt.* Arg. 178 D5
Tres Picos, Cerro *mt.* Mex. 167 G5
Três Pontas Brazil 179 B3
Tres Puntas, Cabo *c.* Arg. 178 C7
Três Rios Brazil 179 C3
Tres Zapotes *tourist site* Mex. 167 G5
Tretten Norway 55 G6
Tretyy Severnyy Rus. Fed. *see* **3-y Severnyy**
Treuchtlingen Germany 63 K6
Treuenbrietzen Germany 63 M2
Treungen Norway 55 F7
Treves Germany *see* **Trier**
Treviglio Italy 68 C2
Treviso Italy 68 E2
Trevose Head *hd* U.K. 59 B8
Tri An, Hô *resr* Vietnam 87 D5
Triánda Greece *see* **Trianta**
Triangle U.S.A. 165 G4
Trianta Greece 69 M6
Tribal Areas *admin. div.* Pak. 111 H3
Tri Brata, Gora *hill* Rus. Fed. 90 F1
Tribune U.S.A. 160 C4
Tricase Italy 68 H5
Trichinopoly India *see* **Tiruchchirappalli**
Trichur India 106 C4
Tricot France 62 C5
Trida Australia 138 B4
Tridentum Italy *see* **Trento**
Trier Germany 62 G5
Trieste Italy 68 E2
Trieste, Golfo di *g.* Europe *see* **Trieste, Gulf of**
Trieste, Gulf of Europe 68 E2
Triglav *mt.* Slovenia 68 E1
Triglavski narodni park *nat. park* Slovenia 68 E1
Trikala Greece 69 I5
Tríkkala Greece *see* **Trikala**

▶**Trikora, Puncak** *mt.* Indon. 81 J7
2nd highest mountain in Oceania.

Trim Ireland 61 F4
Trincheras Mex. 166 C2
Trincomalee Sri Lanka 106 D4
Trindade Brazil 179 A2
Trindade, Ilha da *i.* S. Atlantic Ocean 184 G7
Trinidad Bol. 176 F6
Trinidad Cuba 169 I4
Trinidad *i.* Trin. and Tob. 169 L6
Trinidad Uruguay 178 E4
Trinidad U.S.A. 157 G5
Trinidad *country* West Indies *see* **Trinidad and Tobago**
Trinidad and Tobago *country* West Indies 169 L6
Trinity U.S.A. 161 E6
Trinity *r. CA* U.S.A. 158 B1
Trinity *r. TX* U.S.A. 161 E6
Trinity Bay Canada 153 L5
Trinity Islands *AK* U.S.A. 148 I4
Trinity Range *mts* U.S.A. 158 D1
Trinkat Island India 87 A5
Trionto, Capo *c.* Italy 68 G5
Tripa *r.* Indon. 84 B2
Tripkau Germany 63 L1
Tripoli Greece 69 J6
Tripoli Lebanon 107 B2

▶**Tripoli** Libya 121 E1
Capital of Libya.

Trípolis Greece *see* **Tripoli**
Tripolis Lebanon *see* **Tripoli**
Tripunittura India 106 C4
Tripura *state* India 105 G5

▶**Tristan da Cunha** *i.* S. Atlantic Ocean 184 H8
Dependency of St Helena.

Trisul *mt.* India 104 D3
Triton Canada 153 L4
Triton Island *atoll* Paracel Is 80 E3
Trittau Germany 63 K1
Trittenheim Germany 62 G5
Triunfo Hond. 166 [inset] I6
Trivandrum India 106 C4
Trivento Italy 68 F4
Trnava Slovakia 57 P6
Trobriand Islands P.N.G. 132 F2
Trochu Canada 150 H5
Trofors Norway 54 H4
Trogir Croatia 68 G3
Troia Italy 68 F4
Troisdorf Germany 63 H4
Trois Fourches, Cap des *c.* Morocco 67 E6
Trois-Ponts Belgium 62 F4
Trois-Rivières Canada 153 G5
Troitsko-Pechorsk Rus. Fed. 51 R3
Troitskoye *Altayskiy Kray* Rus. Fed. 88 E2
Troitskoye *Khabarovskiy Kray* Rus. Fed. 90 E2
Troitskoye *Respublika Kalmykiya - Khalm'g-Tangch* Rus. Fed. 53 J7
Troll 188 B2
Trollhättan Sweden 55 H7
Trombetas *r.* Brazil 177 G4
Tromelin, Île *i.* Indian Ocean 185 L7
Tromelin Island Micronesia *see* **Fais**
Tromen, Volcán *vol.* Arg. 178 B5
Tromie *r.* U.K. 60 E3
Trompsburg S. Africa 125 G6
Tromsø Norway 54 K2
Trona U.S.A. 158 E4
Tronador, Monte *mt.* Arg. 178 B6
Trondheim Norway 54 G5
Trondheimsfjorden *sea chan.* Norway 54 F5
Trongsa Bhutan *see* **Tongsa**
Trongsa Chhu *r.* Bhutan 99 E8
Troödos, Mount Cyprus 107 A2
Troödos Mountains Cyprus 107 A2
Troon U.K. 60 E5
Tropeiros, Serra dos *hills* Brazil 179 B1
Tropic U.S.A. 159 G3
Tropic of Cancer 161 B8
Tropic of Capricorn 136 G4
Trosh Rus. Fed. 52 L2
Trostan *hill* U.K. 61 F2
Trout *r. B.C.* Canada 150 E3
Trout *r. N.W.T.* Canada 150 G2
Trout Lake *Alta* Canada 150 H3
Trout Lake *N.W.T.* Canada 150 F2
Trout Lake *l. N.W.T.* Canada 150 F2
Trout Lake *l. Ont.* Canada 151 M5
Trout Peak U.S.A. 156 F3
Trout Run U.S.A. 165 G3
Trouville-sur-Mer France 59 H9
Trowbridge U.K. 59 E7
Troy *tourist site* Turkey 69 L5
Troy *AL* U.S.A. 163 C6
Troy *KS* U.S.A. 160 E4
Troy *MI* U.S.A. 164 D2
Troy *MO* U.S.A. 160 F4
Troy *MT* U.S.A. 156 E2
Troy *NH* U.S.A. 165 I2
Troy *NY* U.S.A. 165 I2
Troy *OH* U.S.A. 164 C3
Troy *PA* U.S.A. 165 G3
Troyan Bulg. 69 K3
Troyes France 66 G2
Troy Lake U.S.A. 158 E4
Troy Peak U.S.A. 159 F2
Trstenik Serbia 69 I3
Truc Giang Vietnam *see* **Bên Tre**
Trucial Coast *country* Asia *see* **United Arab Emirates**
Trucial States *country* Asia *see* **United Arab Emirates**
Trud Rus. Fed. 52 G4
Trufanovo Rus. Fed. 52 J2
Trujillo Hond. 166 [inset] I6
Trujillo Peru 176 C5
Trujillo Spain 67 D4
Trujillo Venez. 176 D2
Trujillo, Monte *mt.* Dom. Rep. *see* **Duarte, Pico**
Truk *is* Micronesia *see* **Chuuk**
Trulben Germany 63 H5
Trumbull, Mount U.S.A. 159 G3
Trumon *Sumatera* Indon. 84 B2
Trundle Australia 138 C4
Trưng Hiệp Vietnam 86 D4
Trung Khanh Vietnam 86 D2
Truong Sa *is* S. China Sea *see* **Spratly Islands**
Truro Canada 153 J5
Truro U.K. 59 B8
Trusan *Sarawak* Malaysia 85 F1
Trusan *r.* Malaysia 85 F1
Truskmore *hill* Ireland 61 D3
Trus Madi, Gunung *mt.* Malaysia 85 G1
Trutch Canada 150 F3
Truth or Consequences U.S.A. 157 G6
Trutnov Czech Rep. 57 O5
Truuli Peak *AK* U.S.A. 149 J4
Truva *tourist site* Turkey *see* **Troy**
Trypiti, Akra *pt Kriti* Greece *see* **Trypiti, Akrotirio**
Trypiti, Akrotirio *pt* Greece 69 K7
Trysil Norway 55 H6
Trzebiatów Poland 57 O3
Tsagaannuur *Bayan-Ölgiy* Mongolia 94 B1
Tsagaannuur *Dornod* Mongolia *see* **Halhgol**
Tsagaan Nuur *salt l.* Mongolia 94 C2
Tsagaan-Olom Mongolia *see* **Tayshir**
Tsagaan-Ovoo Mongolia 95 H1
Tsagaan-Ovoo Mongolia *see* **Nariynteel**
Tsagaan-Uul *Hövsgöl* Mongolia 94 D1
Tsagaan-Üür *Hövsgöl* Mongolia 94 E1
Tsagan Aman Rus. Fed. 53 J7
Tsagan-Nur Rus. Fed. 53 J7
Tsaidam Basin *basin* China *see* **Qaidam Pendi**
Tsaka La *pass* China/India 104 D2
Tsalenjikha Georgia 113 F2
Tsaratanana, Massif du *mts* Madag. 123 E5
Tsarevo Bulg. 69 L3
Tsaris Mountains Namibia 124 C3
Tsaritsyn Rus. Fed. *see* **Volgograd**
Tsaukaib Namibia 124 B4
Tsavo East National Park Kenya 122 D4
Tsavo West National Park Africa 122 D3
Tseel Mongolia 94 C2
Tsefat Israel *see* **Zefat**
Tselinograd Kazakh. *see* **Astana**
Tsengel *Bayan-Ölgiy* Mongolia 94 B1
Tsengel Mongolia *see* **Tosontsengel**
Tsenhermandal Mongolia 95 G2
Tsenogora Rus. Fed. 52 J2
Tses Namibia 124 D3
Tsetseg Mongolia 94 C2
Tsetsegnuur Mongolia *see* **Tsetseg**
Tsetseng Botswana 124 F2
Tsetserleg *Arhangay* Mongolia 94 E1
Tsetserleg *Arhangay* Mongolia 94 E2
Tsetserleg Mongolia 94 D1
Tshabong Botswana 124 F4
Tshad *country* Africa *see* **Chad**
Tshane Botswana 124 E3
Tshela Dem. Rep. Congo 123 B4
Tshibala Dem. Rep. Congo 123 C4
Tshikapa Dem. Rep. Congo 123 C4
Tshing S. Africa 125 H4
Tshipise S. Africa 125 J2
Tshitanzu Dem. Rep. Congo 123 C4
Tshofa Dem. Rep. Congo 123 C4
Tshokwane S. Africa 125 J3
Tsholotsho Zimbabwe 123 C5
Tshootsha Botswana 124 E2
Tshuapa *r.* Dem. Rep. Congo 121 F5
Tshwane S. Africa *see* **Pretoria**
Tsiigehtchic *N.W.T.* Canada 149 N2
Tsil'ma *r.* Rus. Fed. 52 K2
Tsimlyansk Rus. Fed. 53 I7
Tsimlyanskoye Vodokhranilishche *resr* Rus. Fed. 53 I7
Tsimmermanovka Rus. Fed. 90 E2
Tsinan *Shandong* China *see* **Jinan**
Tsineng S. Africa 124 F4
Tsinghai *prov.* China *see* **Qinghai**
Tsing Shan Wan *H.K.* China *see* **Castle Peak Bay**
Tsingtao *Shandong* China *see* **Qingdao**
Tsing Yi *i. H.K.* China 97 [inset]
Tsining *Nei Mongol* China *see* **Jining**
Tsiombe Madag. 123 E6
Tsiroanomandidy Madag. 123 E5
Tsitsihar *Heilong.* China *see* **Qiqihar**
Tsitsikamma Forest and Coastal National Park S. Africa 124 F8
Tsitsutl Peak Canada 150 E4
Tsivil'sk Rus. Fed. 52 J5
Tskhaltubo Georgia *see* **Tsqaltubo**
Ts'khinvali Georgia 113 F2
Tsna *r.* Rus. Fed. 53 I5
Tsnori Georgia 113 G2
Tsogt Mongolia 94 D2
Tsogt-Ovoo Mongolia 94 F2
Tsogttsetsiy Mongolia 94 F3
Tsokar Chumo *l.* India 104 D2
Tsolo S. Africa 125 I6
Tsomo S. Africa 125 H7
Tsona *Xizang* China *see* **Cona**
Tsqaltubo Georgia 113 F2
Tsu Japan 92 C4
Tsubata Japan 92 C2
Tsuchiura Japan 93 G2
Tsuchiyama Japan 92 C4
Tsuen Wan *H.K.* China 97 [inset]
Tsuga Japan 93 F2
Tsugarū-kaikyō *strait* Japan 90 F4
Tsugaru Strait Japan *see* **Tsugarū-kaikyō**
Tsuge Japan 92 B4
Tsugu Japan 92 D3
Tsukechi Japan 92 D3
Tsukigase Japan 92 C4
Tsukiyono Japan 93 E2
Tsukuba Japan 93 G2
Tsukude Japan 92 D4
Tsukui Japan 93 F3
Tsul-Ulaan Mongolia *see* **Bayannuur**
Tsumagoi Japan 93 E2
Tsumeb Namibia 123 B5
Tsumeki-zaki *pt* Japan 93 E4
Tsumis Park Namibia 124 C2
Tsumkwe Namibia 123 C5
Tsuna Japan 92 A4
Tsunan Japan 93 E1
Tsunega-misaki *pt* Japan 92 B3
Tsuru Japan 93 E3
Tsuruga Japan 92 C3
Tsuruga-wan *b.* Japan 92 B3
Tsurugi Japan 92 C2
Tsurugi-dake *mt.* Japan 92 D2
Tsurugi-san *mt.* Japan 91 D6
Tsurukhaytuy Rus. Fed. *see* **Priargunsk**
Tsuruoka Japan 91 E5
Tsushima Japan 92 C3
Tsushima *is* Japan 91 C6
Tsushima-kaikyō *strait* Japan/S. Korea *see* **Korea Strait**
Tsuyama Japan 91 D6
Tswaane Botswana 124 E2
Tswaraganang S. Africa 125 G5
Tswelelang S. Africa 125 G4
Tsyelyakhany Belarus 55 N10
Tsyp-Navolok Rus. Fed. 54 R2
Tsyurupyns'k Ukr. 69 O1
Tthedzeh Koe *N.W.T.* Canada *see* **Wrigley**
Tthenaagoo Canada *see* **Nahanni Butte**
Tua Dem. Rep. Congo 122 B4
Tua, Tanjung *pt* Indon. 84 D4
Tual Indon. 81 I8
Tuam Ireland 61 D4
Tuamotu, Archipel des *is* Fr. Polynesia *see* **Tuamotu Islands**
Tuamotu Islands Fr. Polynesia 187 K6
Tuân Giao Vietnam 86 C2
Tuangku *i.* Indon. 84 B2
Tuapse Rus. Fed. 112 E1
Tuaran *Sabah* Malaysia 85 G1
Tuas Sing. 87 [inset]
Tuath, Loch a' *b.* U.K. 60 C2
Tuba City U.S.A. 159 H3
Tubalai *i. Maluku* Indon. 83 D3
Tuban *Jawa* Indon. 85 F4
Tubarão Brazil 179 A5
Tubarjal Saudi Arabia 107 D4
Tubau *Sarawak* Malaysia 85 F2
Tubbataha Reefs Phil. 82 B4
Tubigan *i.* Phil. 82 C5
Tübingen Germany 57 L6
Tubmanburg Liberia 120 B4
Tubod *Mindanao* Phil. 82 C4
Tubruq Libya 112 A4
Tubu *r.* Indon. 85 G2
Tubuai *i.* Fr. Polynesia 187 K7
Tubuai Islands Fr. Polynesia 187 J7
Tubutama Mex. 166 C2
Tucano Brazil 177 K6
Tucavaca Bol. 177 G7
Tüchen Germany 63 M1
Tuchheim Germany 63 M2
Tuchitua *Y.T.* Canada 149 O3
Tuchodi *r.* Canada 150 F3
Tuckerton U.S.A. 165 H4
Tucopia *i.* Solomon Is *see* **Tikopia**
Tucson U.S.A. 159 H5
Tucson Mountains U.S.A. 159 H5
Tuctuc *r.* Canada 153 I2
Tucumán Arg. *see* **San Miguel de Tucumán**
Tucumcari U.S.A. 161 C5
Tucupita Venez. 176 F2
Tucuruí Brazil 177 I4
Tucuruí, Represa *resr* Brazil 177 I4
Tudela Spain 67 F2
Tuder Italy *see* **Todi**
Tüdevtey Mongolia 94 D1
Tuela *r.* Port. 67 C3
Tuen Mun *H.K.* China 97 [inset]
Tuensang India 105 H4
Tufts Abyssal Plain *sea feature* N. Pacific Ocean 187 K2
Tugela *r.* S. Africa 125 J5
Tugidak Island *AK* U.S.A. 148 I4
Tuglung *Xizang* China 99 F7
Tuguan Maputi *i.* Indon. 83 A2
Tugubun Point *Mindanao* Phil. 82 D5
Tuguegarao *Luzon* Phil. 82 C2
Tugur Rus. Fed. 90 E1
Tugyl Kazakh. 98 D3
Tuhemberua Indon. 84 B2
Tujiabu China *see* **Yongxiu**
Tujuh, Kepulauan *is* Indon. 84 D3
Tujung *Kalimantan* Indon. 85 G2
Tukangbesi, Kepulauan *is* Indon. 83 B4
Tukarak Island Canada 152 F2
Ţukhmān, Banī *reg.* Saudi Arabia 110 C6
Tükhtamish Tajik. 99 A5
Tukituki *r.* N.Z. 139 F4
Tuklung *AK* U.S.A. 148 H4
Tuktoyaktuk *N.W.T.* Canada 149 N1
Tuktut Nogait National Park *N.W.T./Nunavut* Canada 149 Q1
Tuktuujaartuq *N.W.T.* Canada *see* **Tuktoyaktuk**
Tukums Latvia 55 M8
Tukung, Bukit *mt.* Indon. 85 E3
Tukuringra, Khrebet *mts* Rus. Fed. 90 B1
Tukuyu Tanz. 123 D4
Tula *Tamaulipas* Mex. 167 F4
Tula Rus. Fed. 53 H5
Tulach Mhór Ireland *see* **Tullamore**
Tulagt Ar Gol *r.* China 99 F5
Tulai *Qinghai* China 94 D4
Tulai Nanshan *mts* China 94 D4
Tulai Shan *mts* China 94 D4
Tulak Afgh. 111 F3
Tulameen Canada 150 F5
Tula Mountains Antarctica 188 D2
Tulancingo Mex. 168 E4
Tulangbawang *r.* Indon. 84 D4
Tulare U.S.A. 158 D3
Tulare Lake Bed U.S.A. 158 D4
Tularosa *NM* U.S.A. 166 D1
Tularosa Mountains U.S.A. 159 I5
Tulasi *mt.* India 106 D2
Tulbagh S. Africa 124 D7
Tulcán Ecuador 176 C3
Tulcea Romania 69 M2
Tule *r.* U.S.A. 161 C5
Tuléar Madag. *see* **Toliara**
Tulehu *Maluku* Indon. 83 D3
Tulemalu Lake Canada 151 L2
Tule Mod *Nei Mongol* China 95 J2
Tulia U.S.A. 161 C5
Tulihe *Nei Mongol* China 95 J1
Tulita *N.W.T.* Canada 149 P2
Tulkarem West Bank *see* **Ţūlkarm**
Ţūlkarm West Bank 107 B3
Tulla Ireland 61 D5
Tullahoma U.S.A. 162 C5
Tullamore Australia 138 C4
Tullamore Ireland 61 E4
Tulle France 66 E4
Tulleråsen Sweden 54 I5
Tullibigeal Australia 138 C4
Tullos *LA* U.S.A. 167 G2
Tullow Ireland 61 F5
Tully Australia 136 D3
Tully *r.* Australia 136 D3
Tully U.K. 61 E3
Tulos Rus. Fed. 54 Q5
Tulqarem West Bank *see* **Ţūlkarm**
Tulsa U.S.A. 161 E4
Tulsipur Nepal 105 E3
Tuluá Col. 176 C3
Tuluksak *AK* U.S.A. 148 G3
Tulūl al Ashāqif *hills* Jordan 107 C3
Tulum *tourist site* Mex. 167 I4
Tulun Rus. Fed. 88 I2
Tulungagung *Jawa* Indon. 85 E5
Tulu-Tuloi, Serra *hills* Brazil 176 F3
Tulu Welel *mt.* Eth. 122 D3
Tuma *r.* Nicaragua 166 [inset] I6
Tuma Rus. Fed. 53 I5
Tumaco Col. 176 C3
Tumahole S. Africa 125 H4
Tumain *Xizang* China 99 E6
Tumannyy Rus. Fed. 54 S2
Tumasik Sing. *see* **Singapore**
Tumasik Sing. *see* **Singapore**
Tumba Dem. Rep. Congo 122 C4
Tumba Sweden 55 J7
Tumba, Lac *l.* Dem. Rep. Congo 122 B4
Tumbangmiri *Kalimantan* Indon. 85 F3
Tumbangsamba *Kalimantan* Indon. 85 F3
Tumbangsenamang *Kalimantan* Indon. 85 F3
Tumbangtiti *Kalimantan* Indon. 85 E3
Tumbao *Mindanao* Phil. 82 D5
Tumbarumba Australia 138 D5
Tumbes Peru 176 B4
Tumbiscatio Mex. 166 E5
Tumbler Ridge Canada 150 F4
Tumby Bay Australia 137 B7
Tumcha *r.* Fin./Rus. Fed. 54 Q3
also known as Tuntsajoki
Tumd Youqi *Nei Mongol* China *see* **Salaqi**
Tumd Zuoqi *Nei Mongol* China *see* **Qasq**
Tumen *Jilin* China 90 C4
Tumen *Shaanxi* China 97 F1
Tumen *r.* China/N. Korea 90 C4
Tumereng Guyana 176 F2
Tumindao *i.* Phil. 82 B5
Tumiritinga Brazil 179 C2
Tumkur India 106 C3
Tummel *r.* U.K. 60 F4
Tummel, Loch *l.* U.K. 60 F4
Tumnin *r.* Rus. Fed. 90 F2
Tump Pak. 111 F5
Tumpah *Kalimantan* Indon. 85 F3
Tumpat Malaysia 84 C1
Tumpôr, Phnum *mt.* Cambodia 87 C4
Tumpu, Gunung *mt.* Indon. 83 B3
Tumputiga, Gunung *mt.* Indon. 83 B3
Tumshuk Uzbek. 111 G2
Tumu Ghana 120 C3
Tumucumaque, Parque Indígena do *res.* Brazil 177 G3
Tumucumaque, Serra *hills* Brazil 177 G3
Tumudibandh India 106 D2
Tumushuke *Xinjiang* China 98 C4
Tumut Australia 138 D5
Tuna India 104 B5
Tuna Bay *Mindanao* Phil. 82 D5
Ţunb al Kubrá *i.* The Gulf *see* **Greater Tunb**
Ţunb aş Şughrá *i.* The Gulf *see* **Lesser Tunb**
Tunbridge Wells, Royal U.K. 59 H7
Tunceli Turkey 113 E3
Tunchang China 97 F5
Tuncurry Australia 138 F4
Tundun-Wada Nigeria 120 D3
Tunduru Tanz. 123 D5
Tunes Tunisia *see* **Tunis**
Tunga Nigeria 120 D4
Tungabhadra Reservoir India 106 C3
Tungawan *Mindanao* Phil. 82 C5
Tungi Bangl. 105 G5
Tungku *Sabah* Malaysia 85 G1
Tungla Nicaragua 166 [inset] I6
Tung Lung Island *H.K.* China 97 [inset]
Tungnaá *r.* Iceland 54 [inset]
Tungor Rus. Fed. 90 F1
Tung Pok Liu Hoi Hap *H.K.* China *see* **East Lamma Channel**
Tungsten (abandoned) *N.W.T.* Canada 149 O3
Tungun, Bukit *mt.* Indon. 85 F2
Tung Wan *b. H.K.* China 97 [inset]
Tuni India 106 D2
Tunica U.S.A. 161 F5
Tūnis *country* Africa *see* **Tunisia**

▶**Tunis** Tunisia 68 D6
Capital of Tunisia.

Tunis, Golfe de *g.* Tunisia 68 D6
Tunisia *country* Africa 64 F5
Tunja Col. 176 D2
Tunkhannock U.S.A. 165 H3
Tunki Nicaragua 166 [inset] I6
Tunliu *Shanxi* China 95 H4
Tunnsjøen *l.* Norway 54 H4
Tunstall U.K. 59 I6
Tuntsa Fin. 54 P3
Tuntsajoki *r.* Fin./Rus. Fed. *see* **Tumcha**
Tuntutuliak *AK* U.S.A. 148 G3
Tunulic *r.* Canada 153 I2
Tununak *AK* U.S.A. 148 F3
Tunungayualok Island Canada 153 J2
Tunxi China *see* **Huangshan**
Tuodian China *see* **Shuangbai**
Tuo He *r.* China 95 I5
Tuojiang China *see* **Fenghuang**
Tuŏl Khpos Cambodia 87 D5
Tuoniang Jiang *r.* China 96 E3
Tuoputiereke *Xinjiang* China *see* **Jeminay**
Tuotuoheyan *Qinghai* China *see* **Tanggulashan**
Tüp Kyrg. 102 E3
Tupã Brazil 179 A3
Tupelo U.S.A. 161 F5
Tupik Rus. Fed. 89 L2
Tupinambarama, Ilha *i.* Brazil 177 G4
Tupiraçaba Brazil 179 A1
Tupiza Bol. 176 E8
Tupper Canada 150 F4
Tupper Lake U.S.A. 165 H1
Tupper Lake *l.* U.S.A. 165 H1
Tüpqaraghan Tübegi *pen.* Kazakh. *see* **Mangyshlak, Poluostrov**

▶**Tupungato, Cerro** *mt.* Arg./Chile 178 C4
5th highest mountain in South America.

Tuqayyid *well* Iraq 110 B4
Tuquan *Nei Mongol* China 95 J2
Tuqu Wan *b.* China *see* **Lingshui Wan**
Tura *Xinjiang* China 99 D5
Tura India 105 G4
Tura Rus. Fed. 77 L3
Turabah Saudi Arabia 108 F5
Turakina N.Z. 139 E5
Turan Rus. Fed. 88 G2
Turana, Khrebet *mts* Rus. Fed. 90 C2
Turan Lowland Asia 102 A4
Turan Oypaty *lowland* Asia *see* **Turan Lowland**
Turan Pasttekisligi *lowland* Asia *see* **Turan Lowland**
Turan Pesligi *lowland* Asia *see* **Turan Lowland**
Turanskaya Nizmennost' *lowland* Asia *see* **Turan Lowland**
Ţuraq al 'Ilab *hills* Syria 107 D3
Turar Ryskulov Kazakh. 102 D3
Tura-Ryskulova Kazakh. *see* **Turar Ryskulov**
Ţurayf Saudi Arabia 107 D4
Turba Estonia 55 N7
Turbat Pak. 111 F5
Turbo Col. 176 C2
Turda Romania 69 J1
Türeh Iran 110 C3
Turfan *Xinjiang* China *see* **Turpan**
Turfan Depression China *see* **Turpan Pendi**
Turgay Kazakh. 102 B2
Turgayskaya Dolina *valley* Kazakh. 102 B2
Türgen Uul *mt.* Mongolia 94 B1
Türgen Uul *mts* Mongolia 94 B1
Türgovishte Bulg. 69 L3
Turgutlu Turkey 69 L5
Turhal Turkey 112 E2
Türi Estonia 55 N7
Turia *r.* Spain 67 F4
Turin Canada 151 H5
Turin Italy 68 B2
Turiy Rog Rus. Fed. 90 C3

▶**Turkana, Lake** *salt l.* Eth./Kenya 122 D3
5th largest lake in Africa.

Turkestan Kazakh. 102 C3
Turkestan Range *mts* Asia 111 G2
Turkey *country* Asia/Europe 112 D3
Turkey U.S.A. 164 D5
Turkey *r.* U.S.A. 160 F3
Turki Rus. Fed. 53 I6
Türkistan Kazakh. *see* **Turkestan**

Türkiye country Asia/Europe see Turkey
Turkmenabat Lebap Turkm. see Türkmenabat
Türkmenabat Turkm. 111 F2
Türkmen Adasy i. Turkm. see Ogurjaly Adasy
Türkmen Aýlagy b. Turkm. 110 D2
Türkmen Aylagy b. Turkm. see Türkmen Aýlagy
Türkmenbaşy Turkm. 110 D1
Türkmenbaşy Aýlagy b. Turkm. 110 D2
Türkmenbaşy Aylagy b. Turkm. see Türkmenbaşy Aýlagy
Türkmenbaşy Döwlet Gorugy nature res. Turkm. 110 D2
Türkmen Dağı mt. Turkey 69 N5
Turkmenistan country Asia 109 I2
Turkmeniya country Asia see Turkmenistan
Türkmenostan country Asia see Turkmenistan
Turkmenskaya S.S.R. country Asia see Turkmenistan
Türkoğlu Turkey 112 E3

▶Turks and Caicos Islands terr. West Indies 169 J4
United Kingdom Overseas Territory.

Turks Island Passage Turks and Caicos Is 163 G8
Turks Islands Turks and Caicos Is 169 J4
Turku Fin. 55 M6
Turkwel watercourse Kenya 122 D3
Turlock U.S.A. 158 C3
Turlock Lake U.S.A. 158 C3
Turmalina Brazil 179 C2
Turnagain r. Canada 150 E3
Turnagain, Cape N.Z. 139 F5
Turnberry U.K. 60 E5
Turnbull, Mount U.S.A. 159 H5
Turneffe Islands atoll Belize 167 I5
Turner U.S.A. 164 D1
Turner Valley Canada 150 H5
Turnhout Belgium 62 E3
Turnor Lake Canada 151 I3
Tŭrnovo Bulg. see Veliko Tŭrnovo
Turnu Măgurele Romania 69 K3
Turnu Severin Romania see Drobeta-Turnu Severin
Turon r. Australia 138 D4
Turones France see Tours
Turovets Rus. Fed. 52 I4
Turpan Xinjiang China 98 E4

▶Turpan Pendi depr. China 98 E4
Lowest point in northern Asia.

Turpan Zhan Xinjiang China 98 E4
Turquino, Pico mt. Cuba 169 I4
Turrialba Costa Rica 166 [inset] J7
Turriff U.K. 60 G3
Turris Libisonis Sardinia Italy see Porto Torres
Tursāq Iraq 113 G4
Turtle Island Fiji see Vatoa
Turtle Islands Phil. 82 B5
Turtle Lake Canada 151 I4
Turugart Pass China/Kyrg. 102 E3
Turugart Shankou pass China/Kyrg. see Turugart Pass
Turuvanur India 106 C3
Turvo r. Brazil 179 A2
Turvo r. Brazil 179 A2
Tusayan U.S.A. 159 G4
Tuscaloosa U.S.A. 163 C5
Tuscarawas r. U.S.A. 164 E3
Tuscarora Mountains hills U.S.A. 165 G3
Tuscola IL U.S.A. 160 F4
Tuscola TX U.S.A. 161 D5
Tuscumbia U.S.A. 163 C5
Tuskegee U.S.A. 163 C5
Tussey Mountains hills U.S.A. 165 F3
Tustin U.S.A. 164 C1
Tustumena Lake AK U.S.A. 149 J3
Tutak Turkey 113 F3
Tutayev Rus. Fed. 52 H4
Tutera Spain see Tudela
Tuticorin India 106 C4
Tutoh r. Malaysia 85 F2
Tutong Brunei 85 F1
Tuttle Creek Reservoir U.S.A. 160 D4
Tuttlingen Germany 57 L7
Tuttut Nunaat reg. Greenland 147 P2
Tutuala East Timor 83 C5
Tutubu P.N.G. 136 E1
Tutubu Tanz. 123 D4
Tutuila i. American Samoa 133 I3
Tutume Botswana 123 C6
Tututalak Mountain AK U.S.A. 148 G2
Tututepec Mex. 167 F5
Tutwiler U.S.A. 161 F5
Tuul Gol r. Mongolia 94 F1
Tuun-bong mt. N. Korea 90 B4
Tuupovaara Fin. 54 Q5
Tuusniemi Fin. 54 P5
Tuva aut. rep. Rus. Fed. see Tyva, Respublika
Tuvalu country S. Pacific Ocean 133 H2
Tuvinskaya A.S.S.R. aut. rep. Rus. Fed. see Tyva, Respublika
Tüvshinshiree Sühbaatar Mongolia 95 G2
Tuwau r. Indon. 85 G2
Tuwayq, Jabal hills Saudi Arabia 108 G4
Tuwayq, Jabal mts Saudi Arabia 108 G5
Ţuwayyil ash Shihāq mt. Jordan 107 C4
Tuwwal Saudi Arabia 108 E5
Tuxpan Jalisco Mex. 166 E5
Tuxpan Nayarit Mex. 166 D4
Tuxpan Mex. 168 E4
Tuxtla Gutiérrez Mex. 167 G5
Tuya Lake B.C. Canada 149 O4
Tuyên Quang Vietnam 86 D2
Tuy Hoa Vietnam 87 E4
Tuyuk Kazakh. 98 B4
Tuz, Lake salt l. Turkey 112 D3
Tuz Gölü salt l. Turkey see Tuz, Lake
Tuzha Rus. Fed. 52 J4
Tuz Khurmātū Iraq 113 G4
Tuzla Bos.-Herz. 68 H2
Tuzla Turkey 107 B1
Tuzla Gölü lag. Turkey 69 L4
Tuzlov r. Rus. Fed. 53 I7
Tuzu r. Myanmar 86 A1
Tvedestrand Norway 55 F7
Tver' Rus. Fed. 52 G4
Twain Harte U.S.A. 158 C2
Tweed Canada 165 G1
Tweed r. U.K. 60 G5
Tweed Heads Australia 138 F2
Tweedie Canada 151 I4
Tweefontein S. Africa 124 D7
Twee Rivier Namibia 124 D3
Twentekanaal canal Neth. 62 G2
Twentynine Palms U.S.A. 158 E4
Twin Bridges CA U.S.A. 158 C2
Twin Bridges MT U.S.A. 156 E3
Twin Buttes Reservoir U.S.A. 161 C6
Twin Falls Canada 153 I3
Twin Falls U.S.A. 156 E4
Twin Heads hill Australia 134 D5
Twin Hills AK U.S.A. 148 G4
Twin Mountain AK U.S.A. 148 H3
Twin Peak U.S.A. 158 C2
Twistringen Germany 63 I2
Twitchen Reservoir U.S.A. 158 C4
Twitya r. N.W.T. Canada 149 O2
Twizel 139 C7
Twofold Bay Australia 138 D6
Two Harbors U.S.A. 160 F2
Two Hills Canada 151 I4
Two Rivers U.S.A. 164 B1
Tyan' Shan' mts China/Kyrg. see Tien Shan
Tyao r. India/Myanmar 96 B4
Tyatya, Vulkan vol. Rus. Fed. 90 G3
Tydal Norway 54 G5
Tygart Valley U.S.A. 164 F4
Tygda Rus. Fed. 90 B1
Tygda r. Rus. Fed. 90 B1
Tyler U.S.A. 161 E5
Tylertown U.S.A. 161 F6
Tym' r. Rus. Fed. 90 F2
Tymna, Laguna lag. Rus. Fed. 148 B2
Tymovskoye Rus. Fed. 90 F2
Tynda Rus. Fed. 89 M1
Tyndall U.S.A. 160 D3
Tyndinskiy Rus. Fed. see Tynda
Tyne r. U.K. 60 G4
Tynemouth U.K. 58 F3
Tynset Norway 54 G5
Tyone r. AK U.S.A. 149 K3
Tyonek AK U.S.A. 149 J3
Tyoplozyorsk Rus. Fed. see Teploozersk
Tyoploye Ozero Rus. Fed. see Teploozersk
Tyr Lebanon see Tyre
Tyras Ukr. see Bilhorod-Dnistrovs'kyy
Tyre Lebanon 107 B3
Tyree, Mount Antarctica 188 L1
Tyrma Rus. Fed. 90 D2
Tyrma r. Rus. Fed. 90 C2
Tyrnävä Fin. 54 N4
Tyrnavos Greece 69 J5
Tyrnyauz Rus. Fed. 113 F2
Tyrone NM U.S.A. 166 C1
Tyrone U.S.A. 165 F3
Tyrrell r. Australia 138 A5
Tyrrell, Lake dry lake Australia 137 C7
Tyrrell Lake Canada 151 J2
Tyrrhenian Sea France/Italy 68 D4
Tyrus Lebanon see Tyre
Tysa r. Ukr. see Tisa
Tyukalinsk Rus. Fed. 76 I4
Tyulen'i Ostrova is Kazakh. 113 H1
Tyumen' Rus. Fed. 76 H4
Tyup Kyrg. see Tüp
Tyuratam Kazakh. see Baykonyr
Tyva, Respublika aut. rep. Rus. Fed. 94 D1
Tywi r. U.K. 59 C7
Tywyn U.K. 59 C6
Tzaneen S. Africa 125 J2
Tzia i. Greece 69 K6
Tzucacab Mex. 167 H4

U

Uaco Congo Angola see Waku-Kungo
Ualan atoll Micronesia see Kosrae
Uamanda Angola 123 C5
Uarc, Ras c. Morocco see Trois Fourches, Cap des
Uaroo Australia 135 A5
Uatumã r. Brazil 177 G4
Uauá Brazil 177 K5
Uaupés r. Brazil 176 E3
Uaxactún Guat. 167 H5
U'aylī, Wādī al watercourse Saudi Arabia 107 D4
U'aywij well Saudi Arabia 110 B4
U'aywij, Wādī al watercourse Saudi Arabia 113 F5
Ubá Brazil 179 C3
Uba r. Kazakh. 98 C2
Ubaí Brazil 179 B2
Ubaitaba Brazil 179 D1
Ubangi r. Cent. Afr. Rep./Dem. Rep. Congo 122 B4
Ubangi-Shari country Africa see Central African Republic
Ubauro Pak. 111 H4
Ubayyiḍ, Wādī al watercourse Iraq/Saudi Arabia 113 F4
Ube Japan 91 C6
Úbeda Spain 67 E4
Uberaba Brazil 179 B2
Uberlândia Brazil 179 A2
Ubin, Pulau i. Sing. 87 [inset]
Ubly U.S.A. 164 D2
Ubolratna, Ang Kep Nam Thai. 86 C3
Ubombo S. Africa 125 K4
Ubon Ratchathani Thai. 86 D4
Ubstadt-Weiher Germany 63 I5
Ubundu Dem. Rep. Congo 121 F5
Üçajy Turkm. 111 F2
Ucar Azer. 113 G2
Uçarı Turkey 107 A1
Ucayali r. Peru 176 D4
Uch Pak. 111 H4
Üchajy Turkm. see Üçajy
Ūchān Iran 110 C2
Ucharal Kazakh. 102 F2
Uchigō Japan 93 G1
Uchihara Japan 93 G2
Uchimura-gawa r. Japan 93 E2
Uchinada Japan 92 C2
Uchita Japan 92 B4
Uchiura-wan b. Japan 90 F4
Uchiyama-tōge pass Japan 93 E2
Uchkeken Rus. Fed. 113 F2
Uchkuduk Uzbek. see Uchquduq
Uchquduq Uzbek. 102 B3
Uchte Germany 63 I2
Uchte r. Germany 63 L2
Uchto r. Pak. 111 G5
Uchur r. Rus. Fed. 77 O4
Uckermark reg. Germany 63 N1
Uckfield U.K. 59 H8
Ucluelet Canada 150 E5
Ucross U.S.A. 156 G3
Uda r. Rus. Fed. 89 J2
Uda r. Rus. Fed. 90 D1
Udachnoye Rus. Fed. 53 J7
Udachnyy Rus. Fed. 189 E2
Udagamandalam India 106 C4
Udaipur Rajasthan India 104 C4
Udaipur Tripura India 105 G5
Udanti r. India/Myanmar 105 E5
Uday r. Ukr. 53 G6
'Udaynān well Saudi Arabia 110 C6
Uddevalla Sweden 55 G7
Uddingston U.K. 60 E5
Uddjaure l. Sweden 54 J4
'Udeid, Khōr al inlet Qatar 110 C5
Uden Neth. 62 F3
Udgir India 106 C2
Udhagamandalam India see Udagamandalam
Udhampur India 104 C2
Udia-Milai atoll Marshall Is see Bikini
Udimskiy Rus. Fed. 52 J3
Udine Italy 68 E1
Udit India 111 I5
Udjuktok Bay Canada 153 J3
Udmalaippettai India see Udumalaippettai
Udomlya Rus. Fed. 52 G4
Udone-jima i. Japan 93 F4
Udon Thani Thai. 86 C3
Udskaya Guba b. Rus. Fed. 77 O4
Udskoye Rus. Fed. 90 D1
Udumalaippettai India 106 C4
Udupi India 106 B3
Udyl', Ozero l. Rus. Fed. 90 E1
Udzhary Azer. see Ucar
Udzungwa Mountains National Park Tanz. 123 D4
Uéa atoll New Caledonia see Ouvéa
Uebonti Sulawesi Indon. 83 B3
Ueckermünde Germany 57 O4
Ueda Japan 93 E2
Uekuli Sulawesi Indon. 83 B3
Uele r. Dem. Rep. Congo 122 C3
Uelen Rus. Fed. 148 E2
Uel'kal' Rus. Fed. 148 C2
Uelzen Germany 63 K2
Ueno Gunma Japan 93 E2
Ueno Mie Japan 92 C4
Uenohara Japan 93 F3
Uetersen Germany 63 J1
Uettingen Germany 63 J5
Uetze Germany 63 K2
Ufa Rus. Fed. 51 R5
Ufa r. Rus. Fed. 51 R5
Uffenheim Germany 63 K5
Uftyuga r. Rus. Fed. 52 J3
Ugab watercourse Namibia 123 B6
Ugak Bay AK U.S.A. 148 I4
Ugalla r. Tanz. 123 D4
Uganda country Africa 122 D3
Uganik AK U.S.A. 148 I4
Ugashik AK U.S.A. 148 H4
Ugashik Bay AK U.S.A. 148 H4
Ugie S. Africa 125 I6
Uğınak Iran 111 F5
Uglegorsk Rus. Fed. 90 F2
Uglich Rus. Fed. 52 H4
Ugljan i. Croatia 68 F2
Uglovoye Rus. Fed. 90 C2
Ugol'noye Rus. Fed. 77 P3
Ugolnyy Rus. Fed. see Beringovskiy
Ugol'nyye Kopi Rus. Fed. 148 B2
Ugra Rus. Fed. 53 G5
Ugtaaltsaydam Mongolia 94 F1
Uher Hudag Nei Mongol China 95 G3
Uherské Hradiště Czech Rep. 57 P6
Úhlava r. Czech Rep. 63 N5
Uhrichsville U.S.A. 164 E3
Uibhist a' Deas i. U.K. see South Uist
Uibhist a' Tuath i. U.K. see North Uist
Uig U.K. 60 C3
Uíge Angola 123 B4
Ŭijŏngbu S. Korea 91 B5
Ŭiju N. Korea 91 B4
Uimaharju Fin. 54 Q5
Uinta Mountains U.S.A. 159 H1
Uis Mine Namibia 123 B6
Uitenhage S. Africa 125 G7
Uithoorn Neth. 62 E2
Uithuizen Neth. 62 G1
Uivak, Cape Canada 153 J2
Ujhani India 104 D4
Uji Japan 92 B4
Uji-gawa r. Japan 92 B4
Uji-guntō is Japan 91 C7
Ujiie Japan 93 F2
Ujitawara Japan 92 B4
Ujiyamada Japan see Ise
Ujjain India 104 C5
Ujohbilang Kalimantan Indon. 85 F2
Ujung Kulon, Taman Nasional nat. park Indon. 84 D4
Ujung Pandang Sulawesi Indon. see Makassar
Újvidék Serbia see Novi Sad
Ukal Sagar l. India 104 C5
Ukata Nigeria 120 D3
'Ukayrishah well Saudi Arabia 110 B5
uKhahlamba-Drakensberg Park nat. park S. Africa 125 I5
Ukholovo Rus. Fed. 53 I5
Ukhrul India 105 H4
Ukhta Respublika Kareliya Rus. Fed. see Kalevala
Ukhta Respublika Komi Rus. Fed. 52 L3
Ukiah CA U.S.A. 158 B2
Ukiah OR U.S.A. 156 D3
Ukkusiksalik National Park 147 J3
Ukkusissat Greenland 147 M2
Ukmergė Lith. 55 N9

▶Ukraine country Europe 53 F6
2nd largest country in Europe.

Ukrainskaya S.S.R. country Europe see Ukraine
Ukrayina country Europe see Ukraine
Uku-jima i. Japan 91 C6
Ukwi Botswana 124 E2
Ukwi Pan salt pan Botswana 124 E2
Ul r. India 99 B7
Ulaanbaatar Mongolia see Ulan Bator
Ulaanbaatar mun. Mongolia 94 F2
Ulaanbadrah Mongolia 95 G3
Ulaan-Ereg Mongolia see Bayanmönh
Ulaangom Mongolia 94 C1
Ulaanhudag Mongolia see Erdenesant
Ulaan Nuur salt l. Mongolia 94 E2
Ulaan-Uul Bayanhongor Mongolia see Öldziyt
Ulaan-Uul Dornogovĭ Mongolia see Erdene
Ulak Island AK U.S.A. 149 [inset]
Ulan Australia 138 D4
Ulan Nei Mongol China 95 G4
Ulan Qinghai China 94 D4

▶Ulan Bator Mongolia 94 F2
Capital of Mongolia.

Ulanbel' Kazakh. 102 D3
Ulan Buh Shamo des. China 94 F3
Ulan Erge Rus. Fed. 53 J7
Ulanhad Nei Mongol China see Chifeng
Ulanhot Nei Mongol China 95 J2
Ulan Hua Nei Mongol China 95 G3
Ulan-Khol Rus. Fed. 53 J7
Ulanlinggi Xinjiang China 98 D4
Ulan Mod Nei Mongol China 94 F4
Ulan Suhai Nei Mongol China 94 F3
Ulansuhai Nur l. China 95 G3
Ulan Tohoi Nei Mongol China 94 E3
Ulan-Ude Rus. Fed. 89 J2
Ulan Ul Hu l. China 99 E6
Ulaş Turkey 112 E3
Ulastai Xinjiang China 98 D4
Ulawa Island Solomon Is 133 G2
Ulayyah reg. Saudi Arabia 110 B6
Ul'ba Kazakh. 98 C2
Ul'banskiy Zaliv b. Rus. Fed. 90 E1
Ulchin S. Korea 91 C5
Uldz Mongolia see Norovlin
Uldz r. Mongolia 95 H1
Uleåborg Fin. see Oulu
Ulebsechel i. Palau see Auluptagel
Ulefoss Norway 55 F7
Ulekchin Rus. Fed. 94 F1
Ülenurme Estonia 55 O7
Ulety Rus. Fed. 95 H1
Ulgain Gol r. China 95 I2
Ulhasnagar India 106 B2
Uliastai Nei Mongol China 95 I2
Uliastay Mongolia 94 D2
Uliatea i. Fr. Polynesia see Raiatea
Ulicoten Neth. 62 E3
Ulie atoll Micronesia see Woleai
Ulita r. Rus. Fed. 54 R2
Ulithi atoll Micronesia 81 J4
Ul'ken Sulutor Kazakh. 98 A4
Ulladulla Australia 138 E5
Ullapool U.K. 60 D3
Ulla Ulla, Parque Nacional nat. park Bol. 176 E6
Ullava Fin. 54 M5
Ullersuaq c. Greenland 147 K2
Ullswater l. U.K. 58 E4
Ullŭng-do i. S. Korea 91 C5
Ulm Germany 57 L6
Ulmarra Australia 138 F2
Ulmen Germany 62 G4
Uloowaranie, Lake salt flat Australia 137 B5
Ulricehamn Sweden 55 H8
Ulrum Neth. 62 G1
Ulsan S. Korea 91 C6
Ulsberg Norway 54 F5
Ulster reg. Ireland/U.K. 61 E3
Ulster U.S.A. 165 G3
Ulster Canal Ireland/U.K. 61 E3
Ultima Australia 138 A5
Ulu Sulawesi Indon. 83 C2
Ulúa r. Hond. 166 [inset] I6
Ulubat Gölü l. Turkey 69 M4
Ulubey Turkey 69 M5
Uluborlu Turkey 69 N5
Uludağ mt. Turkey 69 M4
Uludağ Milli Parkı nat. park Turkey 69 M4
Ulugqat Xinjiang China see Wuqia
Ulu Kali, Gunung mt. Malaysia 84 C2
Ulukhaktok Canada 189 L2
Ulukışla Turkey 112 D3
Ulundi S. Africa 125 J5
Ulungur He r. China 98 D3
Ulungur Hu l. China 98 D3
Ulunkhan Rus. Fed. 89 K2
Uluru hill Australia 135 E6
Uluru-Kata Tjuta National Park Australia 135 E6
Uluru National Park Australia see Uluru-Kata Tjuta National Park
Ulutau Kazakh. see Ulytau
Ulutau, Gory mts Kazakh. see Ulytau, Gory
Ulu Temburong National Park Brunei 85 F1
Uluyatır Turkey 107 C1
Ulva i. U.K. 60 C4
Ulvenhout Neth. 62 E3
Ulverston U.K. 58 D4
Ulvsjön Sweden 55 I6
Ül'yanov Kazakh. see Ul'yanovskiy
Ul'yanovsk Rus. Fed. 53 K5
Ul'yanovskiy Kazakh. 102 D1
Ul'yanovskoye Kazakh. see Ul'yanovskiy
Ulyatuy Rus. Fed. 95 I1
Ulysses KS U.S.A. 160 C4
Ulysses KY U.S.A. 164 D5
Ulytau Kazakh. 102 C2
Ulytau, Gory mts Kazakh. 102 C2
Uma Rus. Fed. 90 A1
Umaltinskiy Rus. Fed. 90 D2
'Umān country Asia see Oman
Umán Mex. 167 H4
Uman' Ukr. 53 F6
Umarao Pak. 111 G4
'Umarī, Qā' al salt pan Jordan 107 C4
Umaria India 104 E5
Umarkhed India 106 C2
Umarkot India 106 D2
Umarkot Pak. 111 H4
Umarkot Pak. 111 H5
Umaroona, Lake salt flat Australia 137 B5
Umarpada India 104 C5
Umatilla U.S.A. 156 D3
Umayan r. Mindanao Phil. 82 D4
Umba Rus. Fed. 52 G2
Umbagog Lake U.S.A. 165 J1
Umbeara Australia 135 F6
Umbele i. Indon. 83 B3
Umboi i. P.N.G. 81 L8
Umeå Sweden 54 L5
Umeälven r. Sweden 54 L5
Umera Maluku Indon. 83 D3
Umfolozi r. S. Africa 125 K5
Umfreville Lake Canada 151 M5
Umhlanga Rocks S. Africa 125 J5
Umiat AK U.S.A. 148 I1
Umi-gawa r. Japan 93 D1
Umiiviip Kangertiva inlet Greenland 147 N3
Umingmaktok (abandoned) Canada 189 L2
Umirzak Kazakh. 113 H2
Umiujaq Canada 152 F2
Umkomaas S. Africa 125 J6
Umkumiut AK U.S.A. 148 F3
Umlaiteng India 105 H4
Umlazi S. Africa 125 J5
Umm ad Daraj, Jabal mt. Jordan 107 B3
Umm al 'Amad Syria 107 C2
Umm al Jamājim well Saudi Arabia 110 B5
Umm al Qaywayn U.A.E. 110 D5
Umm al Qaiwain U.A.E. see Umm al Qaywayn
Umm ar Raqabah, Khabrat imp. l. Saudi Arabia 107 C5
Umm at Qalbān Saudi Arabia 113 F6
Umm az Zumūl well Oman 110 D6
Umm Bāb Qatar 110 C5
Umm Bel Sudan 108 C7
Umm Keddada Sudan 108 C7
Umm Lajj Saudi Arabia 108 E4
Umm Nukhaylah hill Saudi Arabia 107 D5
Umm Qaşr Iraq 113 G5
Umm Quşūr i. Saudi Arabia 112 D6
Umm Ruwaba Sudan 108 D7
Umm Sa'ad Libya 112 B5
Umm Sa'id Qatar 110 C5
Umm Shugeira Sudan 108 C7
Umm Wa'āl hill Saudi Arabia 107 D4
Umm Wazīr well Saudi Arabia 110 B6
Umnak Island AK U.S.A. 148 E5
Umnak Pass sea channel AK U.S.A. 148 E5
Um Phang Wildlife Reserve nature res. Thai. 86 B4
Umpqua r. U.S.A. 156 B4
Umpulo Angola 123 B5
Umraniye Turkey 69 N5
Umred India 106 C1
Umri India 104 D4
Umtali Zimbabwe see Mutare
Umtata S. Africa 125 I6
Umtentweni S. Africa 125 J6
Umuahia Nigeria 120 D4
Umuarama Brazil 178 F2
Umvuma Zimbabwe see Mvuma
Umzimkulu S. Africa 125 I6
Una r. Bos.-Herz./Croatia 68 G2
Una Brazil 179 D1
Una India 104 D3
'Unāb, Jabal al hill Jordan 107 C5
'Unāb, Wādī al watercourse Jordan 107 C4
Unaí Brazil 179 B2
Unakami Japan 93 G3
Unalakleet AK U.S.A. 148 G3
Unalakleet r. AK U.S.A. 148 G3
Unalaska AK U.S.A. 148 F5
Unalaska Island AK U.S.A. 148 F5
Unalga Island AK U.S.A. 148 F5
Unapool U.K. 60 D2
Unauna i. Indon. 83 B3
'Unayzah Saudi Arabia 108 F4
'Unayzah, Jabal hill Iraq 113 E4
Unazuki Japan 92 D2
Uncia Bol. 176 E7
Uncompahgre Peak U.S.A. 159 J2
Uncompahgre Plateau U.S.A. 159 I2
Undara National Park Australia 136 D3
Underberg S. Africa 125 I5
Underbool Australia 137 C7
Underwood U.S.A. 164 C4
Undu, Tanjung pt Sumba Indon. 83 B5
Undur Seram Indon. 83 D3
Unecha Rus. Fed. 53 G5
Unga AK U.S.A. 148 G5
Unga Island AK U.S.A. 148 G5
Ungalik AK U.S.A. 148 G2
Ungalik r. AK U.S.A. 148 G2
Ungama Bay Kenya see Ungwana Bay
Ungarie Australia 138 C4
Ungava, Baie d' b. Canada see Ungava Bay
Ungava, Péninsule d' pen. Canada 152 G1
Ungava Bay Canada 153 I2
Ungava Peninsula Canada see Ungava, Péninsule d'
Ungeny Moldova see Ungheni
Ungheni Moldova 69 L1
Unguana Moz. 125 L2
Unguja i. Tanz. see Zanzibar Island
Unguz, Solonchakovyye Vpadiny salt flat Turkm. 110 E2
Üngüz Angyrsyndaky Garagum des. Turkm. 110 E1
Ungvár Ukr. see Uzhhorod
Ungwana Bay Kenya 122 E4
Uni Rus. Fed. 52 K4
União Brazil 177 J4
União da Vitória Brazil 179 A4
União dos Palmares Brazil 177 K5
Uniara Rajasthan India 99 B8
Unimak Bight b. AK U.S.A. 148 F5
Unimak Island AK U.S.A. 148 F5
Unimak Pass sea channel AK U.S.A. 148 F5
Unini r. Brazil 176 F4
Union MO U.S.A. 160 F4
Union WV U.S.A. 164 E5
Union, Mount U.S.A. 159 G4
Union City OH U.S.A. 164 C3
Union City PA U.S.A. 164 F3
Union City TN U.S.A. 161 F4
Uniondale S. Africa 124 F7
Unión de Reyes Cuba 163 D8

▶Union of Soviet Socialist Republics
Divided in 1991 into 15 independent nations: Armenia, Azerbaijan, Belarus, Estonia, Georgia, Latvia, Kazakhstan, Kyrgyzstan, Lithuania, Moldova, the Russian Federation, Tajikistan, Turkmenistan, Ukraine and Uzbekistan.

Union Springs U.S.A. 163 C5
Uniontown U.S.A. 164 F4
Unionville U.S.A. 165 G3
United Arab Emirates country Asia 110 D6
United Arab Republic country Africa see Egypt

▶United Kingdom country Europe 56 G3
4th most populous country in Europe.

United Provinces state India see Uttar Pradesh

▶United States of America country N. America 154 F3
Most populous country in North America, and 3rd most populous in the world. Also 3rd largest country in the world, and 2nd in North America.

United States Range mts Canada 147 L1
Unity Canada 151 I4
Unjha India 104 C5
Unna Germany 63 H3
Unnao India 104 E4
Unoke Japan 92 C2
Ŭnp'a N. Korea 91 B5
Ŭnsan N. Korea 91 B4
Ŭnsan N. Korea 91 B5
Unst i. U.K. 60 [inset]
Unstrut r. Germany 63 L3
Untor, Ozero l. Rus. Fed. 51 T3
Unuk r. Canada/U.S.A. 149 O4
Unuli Horog Qinghai China 94 B5
Unzen-dake vol. Japan 91 C6
Unzha Rus. Fed. 52 J4
Uozu Japan 92 D2
Upalco U.S.A. 159 H1
Upar Ghat reg. India 105 F5
Upemba, Lac l. Dem. Rep. Congo 123 C4
Uperbada India 105 F5
Upernavik Greenland 147 M2
Upi Mindanao Phil. 82 D5
Upington S. Africa 124 E5
Upland U.S.A. 158 E4
Upleta India 104 B5
Upoloksha Rus. Fed. 54 Q3
'Upolu i. Samoa 133 I3
Upper Arlington U.S.A. 164 D3
Upper Arrow Lake Canada 150 G5

Upper Chindwin Myanmar *see* **Mawlaik**
Upper Fraser Canada 150 F4
Upper Garry Lake Canada 151 K1
Upper Hutt N.Z. 139 E5
Upper Kalskag *AK* U.S.A. 148 G3
Upper Klamath Lake U.S.A. 156 C4
Upper Liard *Y.T.* Canada 149 O3
Upper Lough Erne *l.* U.K. 61 E3
Upper Marlboro U.S.A. 165 G4
Upper Mazinaw Lake Canada 165 G1
Upper Missouri Breaks National Monument *nat. park* U.S.A. 160 A2
Upper Peirce Reservoir Sing. 87 [inset]
Upper Red Lake U.S.A. 160 E1
Upper Sandusky U.S.A. 164 D3
Upper Saranac Lake U.S.A. 165 H1
Upper Seal Lake Canada *see* **Iberville, Lac d'**
Upper Tunguska *r.* Rus. Fed. *see* **Angara**
Upper Volta *country* Africa *see* **Burkina**
Upper Yarra Reservoir Australia 138 B6
Uppinangadi India 106 B3
Uppsala Sweden 55 J7
Upright, Cape *AK* U.S.A. 148 D3
Upsala Canada 152 C4
Upshi India 104 D2
Upton U.S.A. 165 J2
'Uqayqah, Wādī *watercourse* Jordan 107 B4
'Uqayribāt Syria 107 C2
'Uqlat al 'Udhaybah *well* Iraq 113 G5
Uqturpan *Xinjiang* China *see* **Wushi**
Uracas *vol.* N. Mariana Is *see* **Farallon de Pajaros**
Urad Qianqi *Nei Mongol* China *see* **Xishanzui**
Urad Zhongqi *Nei Mongol* China *see* **Haliut**
Ūrāf Iran 110 E4
Uraga-suidō *sea chan.* Japan 93 F3
Uragawara Japan 93 E1
Urakawa Japan 90 F4
Ural *hill* Australia 138 C4
Ural *r.* Kazakh./Rus. Fed. 100 E2
Uralla Australia 138 E3
Ural Mountains Rus. Fed. 51 S2
Ural'sk Kazakh. 100 E1
Ural'skaya Oblast' *admin. div.* Kazakh. *see* **Zapadnyy Kazakhstan**
Ural'skiye Gory *mts* Rus. Fed. *see* **Ural Mountains**
Ural'skiy Khrebet *mts* Rus. Fed. *see* **Ural Mountains**
Urambo Tanz. 123 D4
Uran India 106 B2
Urana Australia 138 C5
Urana, Lake Australia 138 C5
Urandangi Australia 136 B4
Urandi Brazil 179 C1
Uranium City Canada 151 I3
Uranquinty Australia 138 C5
Uraricoera *r.* Brazil 176 F3
Urartu *country* Asia *see* **Armenia**
Ura-Tyube Tajik. *see* **Üroteppa**
Uravakonda India 106 C3
Uravan U.S.A. 159 I2
Urawa Japan 93 F3
Urayasu Japan 93 F3
'Urayf an Nāqah, Jabal *hill* Egypt 107 B4
Uray'irah Saudi Arabia 110 C5
'Urayq ad Duḩūl *des.* Saudi Arabia 110 B5
'Urayq Sāqān *des.* Saudi Arabia 110 B5
Urbana *IL* U.S.A. 160 F3
Urbana *OH* U.S.A. 164 D3
Urbino Italy 68 E3
Urbinum Italy *see* **Urbino**
Urbs Vetus Italy *see* **Orvieto**
Urdoma Rus. Fed. 52 K3
Urd Tamir Gol *r.* Mongolia 94 E2
Urdyuzhskoye, Ozero *l.* Rus. Fed. 52 K2
Urdzhar Kazakh. 102 F2
Ure *r.* U.K. 58 F4
Ureki Georgia 113 F2
Urelik Rus. Fed. 148 D2
Uren' Rus. Fed. 52 J4
Urengoy Rus. Fed. 76 I3
Uréparapara *i.* Vanuatu 133 G3
Ures Mex. 166 C2
Ureshino Japan 92 C4
Urewera National Park N.Z. 139 F4
Urfa Turkey *see* **Şanlıurfa**
Urfa *prov.* Turkey *see* **Şanlıurfa**
Urga Mongolia *see* **Ulaanbaatar**
Urgal *r.* Rus. Fed. 90 D2
Urganch Uzbek. 102 B3
Urgench Uzbek. *see* **Urganch**
Ürgüp Turkey 112 D3
Urgut Uzbek. 111 G2
Urho *Xinjiang* China 98 D3
Urho Kekkosen kansallispuisto *nat. park* Fin. 54 O2
Urie *r.* U.K. 60 G3
Uril Rus. Fed. 90 C2
Uripitijuata, Cerro *mt.* Mex. 166 E5
Urique Mex. 166 D3
Urisino Australia 138 A2
Urizura Japan 93 G2
Urjala Fin. 55 M6
Urk Neth. 62 F2
Urkan Rus. Fed. 90 B1
Urkan *r.* Rus. Fed. 90 B1
Urla Turkey 69 L5
Urlingford Ireland 61 E5
Urluk Rus. Fed. 95 F1
Urmā aş Şughrá Syria 107 C1
Urmai *Xizang* China 99 D7
Urmia Iran 110 B2
Urmia, Lake *salt l.* Iran 110 B2
Urmston Road *sea chan.* H.K. China 97 [inset]
Uromi Nigeria 120 D4
Uroševac Kosovo *see* **Ferijaz**
Urosozero Rus. Fed. 52 G3
Üroteppa Tajik. 111 H2
Urru Co *salt l.* China 99 D7
Urt Mongolia *see* **Gurvantes**
Urt Moron *Qinghai* China 99 F5
Urt Moron *r. Qinghai* China 94 C4
Uruáchic Mex. 166 C3
Uruaçu Brazil 179 A1
Uruana Brazil 179 A1
Uruapan *Baja California* Mex. 157 D7
Uruapan *Michoacán* Mex. 168 D5
Urubamba *r.* Peru 176 D6
Urucara Brazil 177 G4
Urucu *r.* Brazil 176 F4
Uruçuca Brazil 179 D1
Uruçuí Brazil 177 J5
Uruçuí, Serra do *hills* Brazil 177 I5
Urucuia Brazil 179 B2
Urucurituba Brazil 177 G4
Urugi Japan 92 D3
Uruguai *r.* Arg./Uruguay *see* **Uruguay**
Uruguaiana Brazil 178 E3
Uruguay *r.* Arg./Uruguay 178 E4 *also known as Uruguai*
Uruguay *country* S. America 178 E4
Uruhe China 90 B2
Urukthapel *i.* Palau 82 [inset]
Urumchi *Xinjiang* China *see* **Ürümqi**
Ürümqi *Xinjiang* China 98 D4
Urundi *country* Africa *see* **Burundi**
Urup, Ostrov *i.* Rus. Fed. 89 S3
Uru Pass China/Kyrg. 98 B4
Urusha Rus. Fed. 90 A1
Urutaí Brazil 179 A2
Uryl' Kazakh. 102 G2
Uryupino Rus. Fed. 89 M2
Uryupinsk Rus. Fed. 53 I6
Ürzhar Kazakh. *see* **Urdzhar**
Urzhum Rus. Fed. 52 K4
Urziceni Romania 69 L2
Usa Japan 91 C6
Usa *r.* Rus. Fed. 52 M2
Uşak Turkey 69 M5
Usakos Namibia 124 B1
Usarp Mountains Antarctica 188 H2
Usborne, Mount *hill* Falkland Is 178 E8
Ushakova, Ostrov *i.* Rus. Fed. 76 I1
Ushanovo Kazakh. 98 C2
Ushant *i.* France *see* **Ouessant, Île d'**
Üsharal Kazakh. *see* **Ucharal**
Ush-Bel'dyr Rus. Fed. 88 H2
Ushibori Japan 93 G3
Ushiku Japan 93 G2
Ushimawashi-yama *mt.* Japan 92 B5
Ushkaniy, Gory *mts* Rus. Fed. 148 B2
Ushtobe Kazakh. 102 E2
Ush-Tyube Kazakh. *see* **Ushtobe**
Ushuaia Arg. 178 C8
Ushumun Rus. Fed. 90 B1
Usingen Germany 63 I4
Usinsk Rus. Fed. 51 R2
Usk U.K. 59 E7
Usk *r.* U.K. 59 E7
Uskhodni Belarus 55 O10
Uskoplje Bos.-Herz. *see* **Gornji Vakuf**
Üsküdar Turkey 69 M4
Uslar Germany 63 J3
Usman' Rus. Fed. 53 H5
Usmanabad India *see* **Osmanabad**
Usmas ezers *l.* Latvia 55 M8
Usogorsk Rus. Fed. 52 K3
Usol'ye-Sibirskoye Rus. Fed. 88 I2
Uspenovka Rus. Fed. 90 B1
Uspenskiy Kazakh. 98 A2
Ussel France 66 F4
Ussuri *r.* China/Rus. Fed. 90 D2
Ussuriysk Rus. Fed. 90 C4
Ust'-Abakanskoye Rus. Fed. *see* **Abakan**
Usta Muhammad Pak. 111 H4
Ust'-Balyk Rus. Fed. *see* **Nefteyugansk**
Ust'-Donetskiy Rus. Fed. 53 I7
Ust'-Dzheguta Rus. Fed. 113 F1
Ust'-Dzhegutinskaya Rus. Fed. *see* **Ust'-Dzheguta**
Ustica, Isola di *i. Sicily* Italy 68 E5
Ust'-Ilimsk Rus. Fed. 77 L4
Ust'-Ilimskiy Vodokhranilishche *resr* Rus. Fed. 77 L4
Ust'-Ilya Rus. Fed. 95 H1
Ust'-Ilych Rus. Fed. 51 R3
Ústí nad Labem Czech Rep. 57 O5
Ustinov Rus. Fed. *see* **Izhevsk**
Ustirt *plat.* Kazakh./Uzbek. *see* **Ustyurt Plateau**
Ustka Poland 57 P3
Ust'-Kamchatsk Rus. Fed. 77 R4
Ust'-Kamenogorsk Kazakh. 102 F2
Ust'-Kan Rus. Fed. 98 D2
Ust'-Koksa Rus. Fed. 98 D2
Ust'-Kulom Rus. Fed. 52 L3
Ust'-Kut Rus. Fed. 77 L4
Ust'-Kuyga Rus. Fed. 77 O2
Ust'-Labinsk Rus. Fed. 113 E1
Ust'-Labinskaya Rus. Fed. *see* **Ust'-Labinsk**
Ust'-Lyzha Rus. Fed. 52 M2
Ust'-Maya Rus. Fed. 77 O3
Ust'-Nera Rus. Fed. 77 P3
Ust'-Ocheya Rus. Fed. 52 K3
Ust'-Olenek Rus. Fed. 77 M2
Ust'-Omchug Rus. Fed. 77 P3
Ust'-Ordynskiy Rus. Fed. 88 I2
Ust'-Penzhino Rus. Fed. *see* **Kamenskoye**
Ust'-Port Rus. Fed. 76 J3
Ustrem Rus. Fed. 51 T3
Ust'-Tsil'ma Rus. Fed. 52 L2
Ust'-Uda Rus. Fed. 88 I2
Ust'-Ulagan Rus. Fed. 98 D2
Ust'-Umalta Rus. Fed. 90 D2
Ust'-Undurga Rus. Fed. 89 L2
Ust'-Ura Rus. Fed. 52 J3
Ust'-Urgal Rus. Fed. 90 D2
Ust'-Usa Rus. Fed. 52 M2
Ust'-Vayen'ga Rus. Fed. 52 I3
Ust'-Voya Rus. Fed. 51 R3
Ust'-Vyyskaya Rus. Fed. 52 J3
Ust'ya *r.* Rus. Fed. 52 I3
Ust'ye Rus. Fed. 52 H4
Ustyurt, Plato *plat.* Kazakh./Uzbek. *see* **Ustyurt Plateau**
Ustyurt Plateau Kazakh./Uzbek. 100 E2
Ustyurt Platosi *plat.* Kazakh./Uzbek. *see* **Ustyurt Plateau**
Ustyuzhna Rus. Fed. 52 H4
Usu *Xinjiang* China 98 D3
Usu *i.* Indon. 83 B5
Usuda Japan 93 E2
Usulután El Salvador 166 [inset] H6
Usumacinta *r.* Guat./Mex. 167 G5
Usumbura Burundi *see* **Bujumbura**
Usun Apau, Dataran Tinggi *plat.* Malaysia 85 F2
Usvyaty Rus. Fed. 52 F5
Utah *state* U.S.A. 156 F5
Utah Lake U.S.A. 159 H1
Utajärvi Fin. 54 O4
Utano Japan 92 B4
Utashinai Rus. Fed. *see* **Yuzhno-Kuril'sk**
Utata Rus. Fed. 94 E1
'Utaybah, Buḩayrat al *imp. l.* Syria 107 C3
Utena Lith. 55 N9
Uterlai India 104 B4
Uthai Thani Thai. 86 C4
Uthal Pak. 111 G5
'Uthmānīyah Syria 107 C2
Utiariti Brazil 177 G6
Utica *NY* U.S.A. 165 H2
Utica *OH* U.S.A. 164 D3
Utiel Spain 67 F4
Utikuma Lake Canada 150 H4
Utila Hond. 166 [inset] I5
Utlwanang S. Africa 125 G4
Utopia *AK* U.S.A. 148 I2
Utrecht Neth. 62 F2
Utrecht S. Africa 125 J4
Utrera Spain 67 D5
Utsjoki Fin. 54 O2
Utsugi-dake *mt.* Japan 93 D3
Utsunomiya Japan 93 F2
Utta Rus. Fed. 53 J7
Uttaradit Thai. 86 C3
Uttarakhand *state* India *see* **Uttaranchal**
Uttaranchal *state* India 104 D3
Uttarkashi India 104 D3
Uttar Kashi India *see* **Uttarkashi**
Uttar Pradesh *state* India 104 D4
Uttoxeter U.K. 59 F6
Uttranchal *state* India *see* **Uttaranchal**
Utu *Xinjiang* China *see* **Miao'ergou**
Utubulak *Xinjiang* China 98 D3
Utukok *r. AK* U.S.A. 148 G1
Utupua *i.* Solomon Is 133 G3
Uummannaq Greenland *see* **Dundas**
Uummannaq Fjord *inlet* Greenland 189 J2
Uummannarsuaq *c.* Greenland *see* **Farewell, Cape**
Uurainen Fin. 54 N5
Üüreg Nuur *salt l.* Mongolia 94 B1
Üür Gol *r.* Mongolia 94 E1
Uusikaarlepyy Fin. *see* **Nykarleby**
Uusikaupunki Fin. 55 L6
Uutapi Namibia 123 B5
Uva Rus. Fed. 52 L4
Uvalde U.S.A. 161 D6
Uval Karabaur *hills* Kazakh./Uzbek. 113 I2
Uval Muzbel' *hills* Kazakh. 113 I2
Uvarovo Rus. Fed. 53 I6
Uvéa *atoll* New Caledonia *see* **Ouvéa**
Uvinza Tanz. 123 D4
Uvs *prov.* Mongolia 94 C1
Uvs Nuur *salt l.* Mongolia 94 C1
Uwajima Japan 91 D6
'Uwayrid, Ḩarrat al *lava field* Saudi Arabia 108 E4
Uwaysit *well* Saudi Arabia 107 D4
Uweinat, Jebel *mt.* Sudan 108 C5
Uwi *i.* Indon. 84 D2
Uxbridge Canada 164 F1
Uxbridge U.K. 59 G7
Uxin Ju *Nei Mongol* China 95 G4
Uxin Qi *Nei Mongol* China *see* **Dabqig**
Uxmal *tourist site* Mex. 167 H4
Uxxaktal *Xinjiang* China 98 D4
Uyak *AK* U.S.A. 148 I4
Uyaly Kazakh. 102 B3
Uyanga *Övörhangay* Mongolia 94 E2
Uyar Rus. Fed. 88 G1
Üydzin Mongolia *see* **Manlay**
Uyo Nigeria 120 D4
Üyönch Mongolia 94 C2
Üyönch Gol *r.* China 94 B2
Uyu Chaung *r.* Myanmar 86 A1
Uyuni Bol. 176 E8
Uyuni, Salar de *salt flat* Bol. 176 E8
Uza *r.* Rus. Fed. 53 J5
Uzbekistan *country* Asia 102 B3
Ŭzbekiston *country* Asia *see* **Uzbekistan**
Uzbekskaya S.S.R. *country* Asia *see* **Uzbekistan**
Uzbek S.S.R. *country* Asia *see* **Uzbekistan**
Uzboy Azer. 113 H3
Uzboý Turkm. 110 D2
Uzen' Kazakh. *see* **Kyzylsay**
Uzhgorod Ukr. *see* **Uzhhorod**
Uzhhorod Ukr. 53 D6
Užhorod Ukr. *see* **Uzhhorod**
Užice Serbia 69 H3
Uzlovaya Rus. Fed. 53 H5
Üzöngü Toosu *mt.* China/Kyrg. 98 B4
Üzümlü Turkey 69 M6
Uzun Uzbek. 111 H2
Uzunagach *Almatinskaya Oblast'* Kazakh. 98 B4
Uzunagach *Almatinskaya Oblast'* Kazakh. 98 B4
Uzunbulak *Xinjiang* China 98 D3
Uzun Bulak *spring Xinjiang* China 98 E4
Uzunköprü Turkey 69 L4
Uzynkair Kazakh. 102 B3

V

Vaaf Atoll Maldives *see* **Felidhu Atoll**
Vaajakoski Fin. 54 N5
Vaal *r.* S. Africa 125 F5
Vaala Fin. 54 O4
Vaalbos National Park S. Africa 124 G5
Vaal Dam S. Africa 125 I4
Vaalwater S. Africa 125 I3
Vaasa Fin. 54 L5
Vaavu Atoll Maldives *see* **Felidhu Atoll**
Vác Hungary 57 Q7
Vacaria Brazil 179 A5
Vacaria, Campo da *plain* Brazil 179 A5
Vacaville U.S.A. 158 C2
Vachon *r.* Canada 153 H1
Vad Rus. Fed. 52 J5
Vad *r.* Rus. Fed. 53 I5
Vada India 106 B2
Vadla Norway 55 E7
Vadodara India 104 C5
Vadsø Norway 54 P1

▶**Vaduz** Liechtenstein 66 I3
Capital of Liechtenstein.

Værøy *i.* Norway 54 H3
Vaga *r.* Rus. Fed. 52 I3
Vågåmo Norway 55 F6
Vaganski Vrh *mt.* Croatia 68 F2
Vágar *i.* Faroe Is 54 [inset]
Vägsele Sweden 54 K4
Vágur Faroe Is 54 [inset]
Váh *r.* Slovakia 57 Q7
Vähäkyrö Fin. 54 M5

▶**Vaiaku** Tuvalu 133 H2
Capital of Tuvalu, on Funafuti atoll.

Vaida Estonia 55 N7
Vaiden U.S.A. 161 F5
Vail U.S.A. 154 F4
Vailly-sur-Aisne France 62 D5
Vaitupu *i.* Tuvalu 133 H2
Vajrakarur India *see* **Kanur**
Vakhsh Tajik. 111 H2
Vakhsh *r.* Tajik. 111 H2
Vakhstroy Tajik. *see* **Vakhsh**
Vakīlābād Iran 110 E4
Valbo Sweden 55 J6
Valcheta Arg. 178 C6
Valdai Hills Rus. Fed. *see* **Valdayskaya Vozvyshennost'**
Valday Rus. Fed. 52 G4
Valdayskaya Vozvyshennost' *hills* Rus. Fed. 52 G4
Valdecañas, Embalse de *resr* Spain 67 D4
Valdemārpils Latvia 55 M8
Valdemarsvik Sweden 55 J7
Valdepeñas Spain 67 E4
Val-de-Reuil France 62 B5
Valdés, Península *pen.* Arg. 178 D6
Valdez *AK* U.S.A. 149 K3
Valdivia Chile 178 B5
Val-d'Or Canada 152 F4
Valdosta U.S.A. 163 D6
Valdres *valley* Norway 55 F6
Vale Georgia 113 F2
Vale U.S.A. 156 D3
Valemount Canada 150 G4
Valença Brazil 179 D1
Valence France 66 G4
València Spain *see* **Valencia**
Valencia Spain 67 F4
Valencia *reg.* Spain 67 F4
Valencia Venez. 176 E1
Valencia, Golfo de *g.* Spain 67 G4
Valencia de Don Juan Spain 67 D2
Valencia Island Ireland 61 B6
Valenciennes France 62 D4
Valensole, Plateau de France 66 H5
Valentia Spain *see* **Valencia**
Valentin Rus. Fed. 90 D4
Valentine U.S.A. 160 C3
Valentine *TX* U.S.A. 166 D2
Valenzuela *Luzon* Phil. 82 C3
Våler Norway 55 G6
Valera Venez. 176 D2
Vale Verde Brazil 179 D2
Val Grande, Parco Nazionale della *nat. park* Italy 68 C1
Valjevo Serbia 69 H2
Valka Latvia 55 O8
Valkeakoski Fin. 55 N6
Valkenswaard Neth. 62 F3
Valky Ukr. 53 G6
Valkyrie Dome *ice feature* Antarctica 188 D1
Valladolid Mex. 167 H4
Valladolid Spain 67 D3
Vallard, Lac *l.* Canada 153 H3
Valle Norway 55 E7
Vallecillos Mex. 167 F3
Vallecito Reservoir U.S.A. 159 J3
Valle de Banderas Mex. 166 D4
Valle de la Pascua Venez. 176 E2
Valle de Olivos Mex. 166 D3
Valle de Santiago Mex. 167 E4
Valle de Zaragoza Mex. 166 D3
Valledupar Col. 176 D1
Vallée-Jonction Canada 153 H5
Valle Fértil, Sierra de *mts* Arg. 178 C4
Valle Grande Bol. 176 F7
Valle Hermoso Mex. 167 F3
Vallejo U.S.A. 158 B2
Valle Nacional Mex. 167 F5
Vallenar Chile 178 B3

▶**Valletta** Malta 68 F7
Capital of Malta.

Valley *r.* Canada 151 L5
Valley U.K. 58 C5
Valley City U.S.A. 160 D2
Valley Head *hd Luzon* Phil. 82 C2
Valleyview Canada 150 G4
Valls Spain 67 G3
Val Marie Canada 151 J5
Valmiera Latvia 55 N8
Valmy U.S.A. 158 E1
Valnera *mt.* Spain 67 E2
Valognes France 59 F9
Valona Albania *see* **Vlorë**
Valozhyn Belarus 55 O9
Val-Paradis Canada 152 F4
Valparai India 106 C4
Valparaíso Chile 178 B4
Valparaíso Mex. 166 E4
Valparaiso *FL* U.S.A. 167 I2
Valparaiso U.S.A. 164 B3
Valpoi India 106 B3
Valréas France 66 G4
Vals, Tanjung *c.* Indon. 81 J8
Valsad India 106 B1
Valspan S. Africa 124 G4
Val'tevo Rus. Fed. 52 J2
Valtimo Fin. 54 P5
Valuyevka Rus. Fed. 53 I7
Valuyki Rus. Fed. 53 H6
Vammala Fin. 55 M6
Van Turkey 113 F3
Van, Lake *salt l.* Turkey 113 F3
Vanadzor Armenia 113 G2
Van Buren *AR* U.S.A. 161 E5
Van Buren *MO* U.S.A. 161 F4
Van Buren *OH* U.S.A. *see* **Kettering**
Vanceburg U.S.A. 164 D4
Vanch Tajik. *see* **Vanj**
Vancleve U.S.A. 164 D5
Vancouver Canada 150 F5
Vancouver U.S.A. 156 C3
Vancouver, Cape *AK* U.S.A. 148 F3
Vancouver, Mount Canada/U.S.A. 149 M3
Vancouver Island Canada 150 E5
Vanda Fin. *see* **Vantaa**
Vandalia *IL* U.S.A. 160 F4
Vandalia *OH* U.S.A. 164 C4
Vandekerckhove Lake Canada 151 K3
Vanderbijlpark S. Africa 125 H4
Vanderbilt U.S.A. 164 C1
Vandergrift U.S.A. 164 F3
Vanderhoof Canada 150 E4
Vanderkloof Dam *resr* S. Africa 124 G6
Vanderlin Island Australia 136 B2
Vanderwagen U.S.A. 159 I4
Van Diemen, Cape *N.T.* Australia 134 E2
Van Diemen, Cape *Qld* Australia 136 B3
Van Diemen Gulf Australia 134 F2
Van Diemen's Land *state* Australia *see* **Tasmania**
Vändra Estonia 55 N7
Väner, Lake Sweden *see* **Vänern**

▶**Vänern** *l.* Sweden 55 H7
4th largest lake in Europe.

Vänersborg Sweden 55 H7
Vangaindrano Madag. 123 E6
Van Gia Vietnam 87 E4
Van Gölü *salt l.* Turkey *see* **Van, Lake**
Van Horn U.S.A. 157 G7
Vanikoro Islands Solomon Is 133 G3
Vanimo P.N.G. 81 K7
Vanino Rus. Fed. 90 F2
Vanivilasa Sagara *resr* India 106 C3
Vaniyambadi India 106 C3
Vanj Tajik. 111 H2
Vankarem Rus. Fed. 148 D2
Vankarem *r.* Rus. Fed. 148 C2
Vankarem, Laguna *lag.* Rus. Fed. 148 D2
Vännäs Sweden 54 K5
Vannes France 66 C3
Vannes, Lac *l.* Canada 153 I3
Vannovka Kazakh. *see* **Turar Ryskulov**
Vannøya *i.* Norway 54 K1
Van Rees, Pegunungan *mts* Indon. 81 J7
Vanrhynsdorp S. Africa 124 D6
Vansant U.S.A. 164 D5
Vansbro Sweden 55 I6
Vansittart Island Canada 147 J3
Van Starkenborgh Kanaal *canal* Neth. 62 G1
Vantaa Fin. 55 N6
Van Truer Tableland *reg.* Australia 135 C6
Vanua Lava *i.* Vanuatu 133 G3
Vanua Levu *i.* Fiji 133 H3
Vanuatu *country* S. Pacific Ocean 133 G3
Van Wert U.S.A. 164 C3
Vanwyksvlei S. Africa 124 E6
Vanwyksvlei *l.* S. Africa 124 E6
Văn Yên Vietnam 86 D2
Van Zylsrus S. Africa 124 F4
Varadero Cuba 163 D8
Varahi India 104 B5
Varakļāni Latvia 55 O8
Varalé Côte d'Ivoire 120 C4
Varāmīn Iran 110 C3
Varanasi India 105 E4
Varandey Rus. Fed. 52 M1
Varangerfjorden *sea chan.* Norway 54 P1
Varangerhalvøya *pen.* Norway 54 P1
Varaždin Croatia 68 G1
Varberg Sweden 55 H8
Vardar *r.* Macedonia 69 J4
Varde Denmark 55 F9
Vardenis Armenia 113 G2
Vardø Norway 54 Q1
Varel Germany 63 I1
Varèna Lith. 55 N9
Varese Italy 68 C2
Varfolomeyevka Rus. Fed. 90 D3
Vårgårda Sweden 55 H7
Varginha Brazil 179 B3
Varik Neth. 62 F3
Varillas Chile 178 B2
Varkana Iran *see* **Gorgān**
Varkaus Fin. 54 O5
Varna Bulg. 69 L3
Värnamo Sweden 55 I8
Värnäs Sweden 55 H6
Varnavino Rus. Fed. 52 J4
Várnjárg *pen.* Norway *see* **Varangerhalvøya**
Varpaisjärvi Fin. 54 O5
Várpalota Hungary 68 H1
Varsaj Afgh. 111 H2
Varsh, Ozero *l.* Rus. Fed. 52 J2
Varto Turkey 113 F3
Várzea da Palma Brazil 179 B2
Vasa Fin. *see* **Vaasa**
Vasai India 106 B2
Vashka *r.* Rus. Fed. 52 J2
Vasht Iran *see* **Khāsh**
Vasilkov Ukr. *see* **Vasyl'kiv**
Vasknarva Estonia 55 O7
Vaslui Romania 69 L1
Vassar U.S.A. 164 D2
Vas-Soproni-síkság *hills* Hungary 68 G1
Vastan Turkey *see* **Gevaş**
Västerås Sweden 55 J7
Västerdalälven *r.* Sweden 55 I6
Västerfjäll Sweden 54 J3
Västerhaninge Sweden 55 K7
Västervik Sweden 55 J8
Vasto Italy 68 F3
Vasyl'kiv Ukr. 53 F6
Vatan France 66 E3
Vaté *i.* Vanuatu *see* **Éfaté**
Vatersay *i.* U.K. 60 B4
Vathar India 106 B2
Vathí Greece *see* **Vathy**
Vathy Greece 69 L6

▶**Vatican City** Europe 68 E4
Independent papal state, the smallest country in the world.

Vaticano, Città del Europe *see* **Vatican City**
Vatnajökull *ice cap* Iceland 54 [inset]
Vatnajökull *nat. park* Iceland 54 [inset]
Vatoa *i.* Fiji 133 I3
Vatra Dornei Romania 69 K1
Vätter, Lake Sweden *see* **Vättern**
Vättern *l.* Sweden 55 I7
Vaughn U.S.A. 157 G6
Vaupés *r.* Col. 176 E3
Vauquelin *r.* Canada 152 F3
Vauvert France 66 G5
Vauxhall Canada 151 H5
Vavatenina Madag. 123 E5
Vava'u Group *is* Tonga 133 I3
Vavitao *i.* Fr. Polynesia *see* **Raivavae**
Vavoua Côte d'Ivoire 120 C4
Vavozh Rus. Fed. 52 K4
Vavuniya Sri Lanka 106 D4
Vawkavysk Belarus 55 N10
Växjö Sweden 55 I8
Vay, Đao *i.* Vietnam 87 C5
Vayegi Rus. Fed. 77 S3
Vayenga Rus. Fed. *see* **Severomorsk**
Vazante Brazil 179 B2
Vazáš Sweden *see* **Vittangi**
Veaikevárri Sweden *see* **Svappavaara**
Veal Vêng Cambodia 87 C4
Vecht *r.* Neth. 62 G2 *also known as Vechte (Germany)*
Vechta Germany 63 I2
Vechte *r.* Germany 63 G2 *also known as Vecht (Netherlands)*
Veckerhagen (Reinhardshagen) Germany 63 J3
Vedaranniyam India 106 C4
Vedasandur India 106 C4
Veddige Sweden 55 H8
Vedea *r.* Romania 69 K3
Veedersburg U.S.A. 164 B3
Veendam Neth. 62 G1
Veenendaal Neth. 62 F2
Vega *i.* Norway 54 G4
Vega U.S.A. 161 C5
Vega de Alatorre Mex. 167 F4
Vega Point *pt AK* U.S.A. 149 [inset]
Vegreville Canada 151 H4
Vehari Pak. 111 I4
Vehkalahti Fin. 55 O6
Vehoa Pak. 111 H4
Veinticinco de Mayo *Buenos Aires* Arg. *see* **25 de Mayo**
Veinticinco de Mayo *La Pampa* Arg. *see* **25 de Mayo**
Veirwaro Pak. 111 H5
Veitshöchheim Germany 63 J5
Vejle Denmark 55 F9
Vekil'bazar Turkm. *see* **Wekilbazar**
Velardena Mex. 166 E3
Velas, Cabo *c.* Costa Rica 166 [inset] I7
Velbert Germany 62 H3
Velbŭzhdki Prokhod *pass* Bulg./Macedonia 69 J3
Velddrif S. Africa 124 D7
Velebit *mts* Croatia 68 F2
Velen Germany 62 G3
Velenje Slovenia 68 F1
Veles Macedonia 69 I4

Vélez-Málaga Spain 67 D5
Vélez-Rubio Spain 67 E5
Velhas r. Brazil 179 B2
Velibaba Turkey see Aras
Velika Gorica Croatia 68 G2
Velika Plana Serbia 69 I2
Velikaya r. Rus. Fed. 52 K4
Velikaya r. Rus. Fed. 55 P8
Velikaya r. Rus. Fed. 77 S3
Velikaya Kema Rus. Fed. 90 E3
Veliki Preslav Bulg. 69 L3
Velikiye Luki Rus. Fed. 52 F4
Velikiy Novgorod Rus. Fed. 52 F4
Velikiy Ustyug Rus. Fed. 52 J3
Velikonda Range hills India 106 C3
Veliko Tŭrnovo Bulg. 69 K3
Velikoye Rus. Fed. 52 H4
Velikoye, Ozero l. Rus. Fed. 53 I5
Veli Lošinj Croatia 68 F2
Velizh Rus. Fed. 52 F5
Vella Lavella i. Solomon Is 133 F2
Vellar r. India 106 C4
Vellberg Germany 63 J5
Vellmar Germany 63 J3
Vellore India 106 C3
Velpke Germany 63 K2
Vel'sk Rus. Fed. 52 I3
Velsuna Italy see Orvieto
Velten Germany 63 N2
Veluwezoom, Nationaal Park nat. park Neth. 62 F2
Velykyy Tokmak Ukr. see Tokmak
Vel'yu r. Rus. Fed. 52 L3
Vemalwada India 106 C2
Vema Seamount sea feature S. Atlantic Ocean 184 I8
Vema Trench sea feature Indian Ocean 185 M6
Vempalle India 106 C3
Venado, Isla del i. Nicaragua 166 [inset] J7
Venado Tuerto Arg. 178 D4
Venafro Italy 68 F4
Venceslau Bráz Brazil 179 A3
Vendinga Rus. Fed. 52 J3
Vendôme France 66 E3
Venegas Mex. 161 C8
Venetia Italy see Venice
Venetie AK U.S.A. 149 K2
Venetie Landing AK U.S.A. 149 K2
Venev Rus. Fed. 53 H5
Venezia Italy see Venice
Venezia, Golfo di g. Europe see Venice, Gulf of

▶Venezuela country S. America 176 E2
5th most populous country in South America.

Venezuela, Golfo de g. Venez. 176 D1
Venezuelan Basin sea feature S. Atlantic Ocean 184 D4
Vengurla India 106 B3
Veniaminof Volcano U.S.A. 146 C4
Venice Italy 68 E2
Venice U.S.A. 163 D7
Venice LA U.S.A. 167 H2
Venice, Gulf of Europe 68 E2
Vénissieux France 66 G4
Venkatapalem India 106 D2
Venkatapuram India 106 D2
Venlo Neth. 62 G3
Vennesla Norway 55 E7
Venray Neth. 62 F3
Venta r. Latvia/Lith. 55 M8
Venta Lith. 55 M8
Ventersburg S. Africa 125 H5
Ventersdorp S. Africa 125 H4
Venterstad S. Africa 125 G6
Ventnor U.K. 59 F8
Ventotene, Isola i. Italy 68 E4
Ventoux, Mont mt. France 66 G4
Ventspils Latvia 55 L8
Ventura U.S.A. 158 D4
Venus Bay Australia 138 B7
Venustiano Carranza Mex. 161 C7
Venustiano Carranza, Presa resr Mex. 167 E3
Vera Arg. 178 D3
Vera Spain 67 F5
Vera Cruz Brazil 179 A3
Veracruz Mex. 168 E5
Vera Cruz Mex. see Veracruz
Veracruz state Mex. 167 F4
Veraval India 104 B5
Verbania Italy 68 C2
Vercelli Italy 68 C2
Vercors reg. France 66 G4
Verdalsøra Norway 54 G5
Verde r. Goiás Brazil 179 A2
Verde r. Goiás Brazil 179 A2
Verde r. Goiás Brazil 179 B2
Verde r. Minas Gerais Brazil 179 A2
Verde r. Chihuahua/Durango Mex. 166 D3
Verde r. U.S.A. 159 H5
Verde Island Passage Phil. 82 C3
Verden (Aller) Germany 63 J2
Verde Pequeno r. Brazil 179 C1
Verdi U.S.A. 158 D2
Verdon r. France 66 G5
Verdun France 62 F5
Vereeniging S. Africa 125 H4
Vereshchagino Rus. Fed. 51 Q4
Vergennes U.S.A. 165 I1
Véria Greece see Veroia
Verín Spain 67 C3
Veríssimo Brazil 179 A2
Verkhneberezovskiy Kazakh. 98 C2
Verkhneimbatsk Rus. Fed. 76 J3
Verkhnekolvinsk Rus. Fed. 52 M2
Verkhnespasskoye Rus. Fed. 52 J4
Verkhnetulomskiy Rus. Fed. 54 Q2
Verkhnetulomskoye Vodokhranilishche res. Rus. Fed. 54 Q2
Verkhnevilyuysk Rus. Fed. 77 N3
Verkhneye Kuyto, Ozero l. Rus. Fed. 54 Q4
Verkhnezeysk Rus. Fed. 89 N2
Verkhniy Shergol'dzhin Rus. Fed. 95 G1
Verkhniy Ul'khun Rus. Fed. 95 H1
Verkhniy Vyalozerskiy Rus. Fed. 52 G2
Verkhnyaya Khava Rus. Fed. 53 H6
Verkhnyaya Salda Rus. Fed. 51 S4
Verkhnyaya Tunguska r. Rus. Fed. see Angara
Verkhnyaya Tura Rus. Fed. 51 R4
Verkhoshizhem'ye Rus. Fed. 52 K4
Verkhovazh'ye Rus. Fed. 52 I3
Verkhov'ye Rus. Fed. 53 H5
Verkhoyansk Rus. Fed. 77 O3
Verkhoyanskiy Khrebet mts Rus. Fed. 77 N2
Verkhuba Kazakh. 98 C2
Vermand France 62 D5
Vermelho r. Brazil 179 A1
Vermilion Canada 151 I4
Vermilion Bay U.S.A. 161 F6
Vermilion Cliffs AZ U.S.A. 159 G3
Vermilion Cliffs UT U.S.A. 159 G3
Vermilion Cliffs National Monument nat. park U.S.A. 159 H3
Vermilion Lake U.S.A. 160 E2
Vermillion U.S.A. 160 D3
Vermillion Bay Canada 151 M5
Vermont state U.S.A. 165 I1
Vernadsky research station Antarctica 188 L2
Vernal U.S.A. 159 I1
Verner Canada 152 E5
Verneuk Pan salt pan S. Africa 124 E5
Vernon Canada 150 G5
Vernon France 62 B5
Vernon AL U.S.A. 161 F5
Vernon IN U.S.A. 164 C4
Vernon TX U.S.A. 161 D5
Vernon UT U.S.A. 159 G1
Vernon Islands Australia 134 E3
Vernoye Rus. Fed. 90 C2
Vernyy Kazakh. see Almaty
Vero Beach U.S.A. 163 D7
Veroia Greece 69 J4
Verona Italy 68 D2
Verona U.S.A. 164 F4
Versailles France 62 C6
Versailles IN U.S.A. 164 C4
Versailles KY U.S.A. 164 C4
Versailles OH U.S.A. 164 C3
Versec Serbia see Vršac
Versmold Germany 63 I2
Vert, Île i. Canada 153 H4
Vertou France 66 D3
Verulam S. Africa 125 J5
Verulamium U.K. see St Albans
Verviers Belgium 62 F4
Vervins France 62 D5
Verwood Canada 151 J5
Verzy France 62 E5
Vescovato Corsica France 66 I5
Vesele Ukr. 53 G7
Veselyy Rus. Fed. 53 I7
Veselyy Yar Rus. Fed. 90 D4
Veshenskaya Rus. Fed. 53 I6
Vesle r. France 62 D5
Veslyana r. Rus. Fed. 52 L3
Vesontio France see Besançon
Vesoul France 66 H3
Vessem Neth. 62 F3
Vesterålen is Norway 54 H2
Vesterålsfjorden sea chan. Norway 54 H2
Vestertana Norway 54 O1
Vestfjorddalen valley Norway 55 F7
Vestfjorden sea chan. Norway 54 H3
Véstia Brazil 179 A3
Vestmanna Faroe Is 54 [inset]
Vestmannaeyjar Iceland 54 [inset]
Vestmannaeyjar is Iceland 54 [inset]
Vestnes Norway 54 E5
Vesturhorn hd Iceland 54 [inset]
Vesuvio vol. Italy see Vesuvius
Vesuvius vol. Italy 68 F4
Ves'yegonsk Rus. Fed. 52 H4
Veszprém Hungary 68 G1
Veteli Fin. 54 M5
Veteran Canada 151 I4
Vetlanda Sweden 55 I8
Vetluga Rus. Fed. 52 J4
Vetluga r. Rus. Fed. 52 J4
Vetluzhskiy Kostromskaya Oblast' Rus. Fed. 52 J4
Vetluzhskiy Nizhegorodskaya Oblast' Rus. Fed. 52 J4
Vettore, Monte mt. Italy 68 E3
Veurne Belgium 62 C3
Vevay U.S.A. 164 C4
Vevey Switz. 66 H3
Vexin Normand reg. France 62 B5
Veyo U.S.A. 159 G3
Vézère r. France 66 E4
Vezirköprü Turkey 112 D2
Vialar Alg. see Tissemsilt
Viamao Brazil 179 A5
Viana Espírito Santo Brazil 179 C3
Viana Maranhão Brazil 177 J4
Viana do Castelo Port. 67 B3
Vianen Neth. 62 F3
Viangchan Laos see Vientiane
Viangphoukha Laos 86 C2
Viannos Greece 69 K7
Vianópolis Brazil 179 A2
Viareggio Italy 68 D3
Viborg Denmark 55 F8
Viborg Rus. Fed. see Vyborg
Vibo Valentia Italy 68 G5
Vic Spain 67 H3
Vicam Mex. 166 C3
Vicecomodoro Marambio research station Antarctica see Marambio
Vicente, Point U.S.A. 158 D5
Vicente Guerrero Baja California Mex. 166 A2
Vicenza Italy 68 D2
Vich Spain see Vic
Vichada r. Col. 176 E3
Vichadero Uruguay 178 F4
Vichy France 66 F3
Vicksburg AZ U.S.A. 159 G5
Vicksburg MS U.S.A. 161 F5
Viçosa Brazil 179 C3
Victor, Mount Antarctica 188 D2
Victor Harbor Australia 137 B7
Victoria Arg. 178 D4
Victoria r. Australia 134 E3
Victoria state Australia 138 B6

▶Victoria Canada 150 F5
Capital of British Columbia.

Victoria Chile 178 B5
Victoria Malaysia see Labuan
Victoria Malta 68 F6
Victoria Luzon Phil. 82 C3

▶Victoria Seychelles 185 L6
Capital of the Seychelles.

Victoria TX U.S.A. 161 D6
Victoria VA U.S.A. 165 F5
Victoria prov. Zimbabwe see Masvingo

▶Victoria, Lake Africa 122 D4
Largest lake in Africa, and 3rd in the world.

Victoria, Lake Australia 137 C7
Victoria, Mount Fiji see Tomanivi
Victoria, Mount Myanmar 86 A2
Victoria, Mount P.N.G. 81 L8
Victoria and Albert Mountains Canada 147 K2
Victoria Falls Zambia/Zimbabwe 123 C5
Victoria Harbour sea chan. H.K. China see Hong Kong Harbour

▶Victoria Island Canada 146 H2
3rd largest island in North America, and 9th in the world.

Victoria Land coastal area Antarctica 188 H2
Victoria Peak Belize 168 G5
Victoria Peak hill H.K. China 97 [inset]
Victoria Range mts N.Z. 139 D6
Victoria River Downs Australia 134 E4
Victoriaville Canada 153 H5
Victoria West S. Africa 124 F6
Victorica Arg. 178 C5
Víctor Rosales Mex. 166 E4
Victorville U.S.A. 158 E4
Victory Downs Australia 135 F6
Vidalia U.S.A. 161 F6
Vidal Junction U.S.A. 159 F4
Videle Romania 69 K2
Vidisha India 104 D5
Vidlin U.K. 60 [inset]
Vidlitsa Rus. Fed. 52 G3
Viechtach Germany 63 M5
Viedma Arg. 178 D6
Viedma, Lago l. Arg. 178 B7
Viejo, Cerro mt. Mex. 166 B2
Vielank Germany 63 L1
Vielsalm Belgium 62 F4
Vienenburg Germany 63 K3

▶Vienna Austria 57 P6
Capital of Austria.

Vienna MO U.S.A. 160 F4
Vienna WV U.S.A. 164 E4
Vienne France 66 G4
Vienne r. France 66 E3

▶Vientiane Laos 86 C3
Capital of Laos.

Vieques i. Puerto Rico 169 K5
Vieremä Fin. 54 O5
Viersen Germany 62 G3
Vierzon France 66 F3
Viesca Mex. 166 E3
Viesīte Latvia 55 N8
Vieste Italy 68 G4
Vietas Sweden 54 K3
Vietnam country Asia 86 D3
Việt Nam country Asia see Vietnam
Việt Quang Vietnam 86 D2
Viêt Tri Vietnam 86 D2
Vieux Comptoir, Lac du l. Canada 152 F3
Vieux-Fort Canada 153 K4
Vieux Poste, Pointe du pt Canada 153 J4
Vigan Luzon Phil. 82 C2
Vigevano Italy 68 C2
Vigia Brazil 177 I4
Vigía Chico Mex. 167 I5
Vignacourt France 62 C4
Vignemale mt. France 64 D3
Vignola Italy 68 D2
Vigo Spain 67 B2
Vihanti Fin. 54 N4
Vihti Fin. 55 N6
Viipuri Rus. Fed. see Vyborg
Viitasaari Fin. 54 N5
Vijayadurg India 106 B2
Vijayanagaram India see Vizianagaram
Vijayapati India 106 C4
Vijayawada India 106 D2
Vík Iceland 54 [inset]
Vikajärvi Fin. 54 O3
Vikeke East Timor see Viqueque
Viking Canada 151 I4
Vikna i. Norway 54 G4
Vikøyri Norway 55 E6
Vila Vanuatu see Port Vila
Vila Alferes Chamusca Moz. see Guija
Vila Bittencourt Brazil 176 E4
Vila Bugaço Angola see Camanongue
Vila Cabral Moz. see Lichinga
Vila da Ponte Angola see Kuvango
Vila de Aljustrel Angola see Cangamba
Vila de Almoster Angola see Chiange
Vila de João Belo Moz. see Xai-Xai
Vila de María Arg. 178 D3
Vila de Trego Morais Moz. see Chókwé
Vila Fontes Moz. see Caia
Vila Franca de Xira Port. 67 B4
Vilagarcía de Arousa Spain 67 B2
Vila Gomes da Costa Moz. 125 K3
Vilalba Spain 67 C2
Vila Luísa Moz. see Marracuene
Vila Marechal Carmona Angola see Uíge
Vila Miranda Moz. see Macaloge
Vilanandro, Tanjona pt Madag. 123 E5
Vilanculos Moz. 125 L1
Vila Nova de Gaia Port. 67 B3
Vilanova i la Geltrú Spain 67 G3
Vila Pery Moz. see Chimoio
Vila Real Port. 67 C3
Vilar Formoso Port. 67 C3
Vila Salazar Angola see N'dalatando
Vila Salazar Zimbabwe see Sango
Vila Teixeira de Sousa Angola see Luau
Vila Velha Brazil 179 C3
Vilcabamba, Cordillera mts Peru 176 D6
Vil'cheka, Zemlya i. Rus. Fed. 76 H1
Viled' r. Rus. Fed. 52 J3
Vileyka Belarus see Vilyeyka
Vil'gort Rus. Fed. 52 K3
Vilhelmina Sweden 54 J4
Vilhena Brazil 176 F6
Viliya r. Belarus/Lith. see Neris
Viljandi Estonia 55 N7
Viljoenskroon S. Africa 125 H4
Vilkaviškis Lith. 55 M9
Vilkija Lith. 55 M9
Vil'kitskogo, Proliv strait Rus. Fed. 77 K2
Vilkovo Ukr. see Vylkove
Villa Abecia Bol. 176 E8
Villa Ahumada Mex. 166 D2
Villa Ángela Arg. 178 D3
Villa Bella Bol. 176 E6
Villa Bens Morocco see Tarfaya
Villablino Spain 67 C2
Villacañas Spain 67 E4
Villach Austria 57 N7
Villacidro Sardinia Italy 68 C5
Villa Cisneros W. Sahara see Ad Dakhla
Villa Comaltitlán Mex. 167 G6
Villa Coronado Mex. 166 D3
Villa de Álvarez Mex. 166 E5
Villa de Cos Mex. 166 E4
Villa de Guadalupe Campeche Mex. 167 H5
Villa Dolores Arg. 178 C4
Villa Flores Mex. 167 G5
Villagarcía de Arosa Spain see Vilagarcía de Arousa
Villagrán Mex. 161 D7
Villaguay Arg. 178 E4
Villahermosa Mex. 167 G5
Villa Insurgentes Mex. 166 C3
Villajoyosa Spain see Villajoyosa-La Vila Joíosa
Villajoyosa-La Vila Joíosa Spain 67 F4
Villa La Venta Mex. 167 G5
Villaldama Mex. 167 E3
Villa Mainero Mex. 161 D7
Villa María Arg. 178 D4
Villa Montes Bol. 176 F8
Villa Nora S. Africa 125 I2
Villanueva Mex. 166 E4
Villanueva de la Serena Spain 67 D4
Villanueva de los Infantes Spain 67 E4
Villanueva-y-Geltrú Spain see Vilanova i la Geltrú
Villa Ocampo Arg. 178 E3
Villa Ocampo Mex. 166 D3
Villa Ojo de Agua Arg. 178 D3
Villa O. Pereyra Mex. see Villa Orestes Pereyra
Villa Orestes Pereyra Mex. 166 D3
Villaputzu Sardinia Italy 68 C5
Villa Regina Arg. 178 C5
Villarrica Para. 178 E3
Villarrica, Lago l. Chile 178 B5
Villarrica, Parque Nacional nat. park Chile 178 B5
Villarrobledo Spain 67 E4
Villas U.S.A. 165 H4
Villasalazar Zimbabwe see Sango
Villa San Giovanni Italy 68 F5
Villa Sanjurjo Morocco see Al Hoceima
Villa San Martín Arg. 178 D3
Villa Unión Arg. 178 C3
Villa Unión Coahuila Mex. 167 E2
Villa Unión Durango Mex. 161 B8
Villa Unión Sinaloa Mex. 168 C4
Villa Valeria Arg. 178 D4
Villavicencio Col. 176 D3
Villazon Bol. 176 E8
Villefranche-sur-Saône France 66 G4
Ville-Marie Canada see Montréal
Villena Spain 67 F4
Villeneuve-sur-Lot France 66 E4
Villeneuve-sur-Yonne France 66 F2
Ville Platte LA U.S.A. 167 G2
Villers-Cotterêts France 62 D5
Villers-sur-Mer France 59 G9
Villerupt France 62 F5
Villeurbanne France 66 G4
Villiers S. Africa 125 I4
Villingen Germany 57 L6
Villuppuram India see Villupuram
Villupuram India 106 C4
Vilna Canada 151 I4
Vilna Lith. see Vilnius

▶Vilnius Lith. 55 N9
Capital of Lithuania.

Vil'nyans'k Ukr. 53 G7
Vilppula Fin. 54 N5
Vils r. Germany 63 L5
Vils r. Germany 63 N6
Vilvoorde Belgium 62 E4
Vilyeyka Belarus 55 O9
Vilyuy r. Rus. Fed. 77 N3
Vilyuyskoye Vodokhranilishche resr Rus. Fed. 77 M3
Vimmerby Sweden 55 I8
Vimy France 62 C4
Vina r. Cameroon 121 E4
Vina U.S.A. 158 B2
Viña del Mar Chile 178 B4
Vinalhaven Island U.S.A. 162 G2
Vinaròs Spain 67 G3
Vinaroz Spain see Vinaròs
Vincelotte, Lac l. Canada 153 G3
Vincennes U.S.A. 164 B4
Vincennes Bay Antarctica 188 F2
Vinchina Arg. 178 C3
Vindelälven r. Sweden 54 K5
Vindeln Sweden 54 K4
Vindhya Range hills India 104 C5
Vindobona Austria see Vienna
Vine Grove U.S.A. 164 C5
Vineland U.S.A. 165 H4
Vinh Vietnam 86 D3
Vinh Loc Vietnam 86 D2
Vinh Long Vietnam 87 D5
Vinh Thực, Đao i. Vietnam 86 D2
Vinita U.S.A. 161 E4
Vinjhan India 104 B5
Vinland i. Canada see Newfoundland
Vinnitsa Ukr. see Vinnytsya
Vinnytsya Ukr. 53 F6
Vinogradov Ukr. see Vynohradiv
Vinson Massif mt. Antarctica 188 L1
Vinstra Norway 55 F6
Vintar Luzon Phil. 82 C2
Vinton U.S.A. 160 E3
Vinukonda India 106 C2
Violeta Cuba see Primero de Enero
Vipperow Germany 63 M1
Viqueque East Timor 83 C5
Virac Phil. 82 D3
Viramgam India 104 C5
Viranşehir Turkey 113 E3
Virawah Pak. 111 H5
Virchow, Mount hill Australia 134 B5
Virdel India 104 C5
Virden Canada 151 K5
Virden U.S.A. 159 I5
Vire France 66 D2
Virei Angola 123 B5
Virgem da Lapa Brazil 179 C2
Virgilina U.S.A. 165 F5
Virgin r. U.S.A. 159 F3
Virginia Ireland 61 E4
Virginia S. Africa 125 H5
Virginia U.S.A. 160 F4
Virginia state U.S.A. 164 F5
Virginia Beach U.S.A. 165 H5
Virginia City MT U.S.A. 156 F3
Virginia City NV U.S.A. 158 D2
Virginia Falls N.W.T. Canada 149 P3

▶Virgin Islands (U.K.) terr. West Indies 169 L5
United Kingdom Overseas Territory.

▶Virgin Islands (U.S.A.) terr. West Indies 169 L5
United States Unincorporated Territory.

Virgin Mountains U.S.A. 159 F3
Virginópolis Brazil 179 C2
Virkkala Fin. 55 N6
Virôchey Cambodia 87 D4
Viroqua U.S.A. 160 F3
Virovitica Croatia 68 G2
Virrat Fin. 54 M5
Virton Belgium 62 F5
Virtsu Estonia 55 M7
Virudhunagar India 106 C4
Virudunagar India see Virudhunagar
Virunga, Parc National des nat. park Dem. Rep. Congo 122 C4
Vis i. Croatia 68 G3
Visaginas Lith. 55 O9
Visakhapatnam India see Vishakhapatnam
Visalia U.S.A. 158 D3
Visapur India 106 B2
Visayan Islands Phil. 82 D4
Visayan Sea Phil. 82 C4
Visbek Germany 63 I2
Visby Sweden 55 K8
Viscount Melville Sound sea chan. Canada 147 G2
Visé Belgium 62 F4
Višegrad Bos.-Herz. 69 H3
Viseu Brazil 177 I4
Viseu Port. 67 C3
Vishakhapatnam India 106 D2
Vishera r. Rus. Fed. 51 R4
Vishera r. Rus. Fed. 52 L3
Višķi Latvia 55 O8
Visnagar India 104 C5
Viso, Monte mt. Italy 68 B2
Visoko Bos.-Herz. 68 H3
Visp Switz. 66 H3
Visselhövede Germany 63 J2
Vista U.S.A. 158 E5
Vista Lake U.S.A. 158 D4
Vistonida, Limni lag. Greece 69 K4
Vistula r. Poland 57 Q3
Vitebsk Belarus see Vitsyebsk
Viterbo Italy 68 E3
Vitichi Bol. 176 E8
Vitigudino Spain 67 C3
Viti Levu i. Fiji 133 H3
Vitimskoye Ploskogor'ye plat. Rus. Fed. 89 K2
Vitória Brazil 179 C3
Vitória da Conquista Brazil 179 C1
Vitoria-Gasteiz Spain 67 E2
Vitória Seamount sea feature S. Atlantic Ocean 184 F7
Vitré France 66 D2
Vitry-en-Artois France 62 C4
Vitry-le-François France 62 E6
Vitsyebsk Belarus 53 F5
Vittangi Sweden 54 L3
Vittel France 66 G2
Vittoria Sicily Italy 68 F6
Vittorio Veneto Italy 68 E2
Viveiro Spain 67 C2
Vivero Spain see Viveiro
Vivo S. Africa 125 I2
Vizagapatam India see Vishakhapatnam
Vizcaíno, Desierto de des. Mex. 166 B3
Vizcaíno, Sierra mts Mex. 166 B3
Vize Turkey 69 L4
Vize, Ostrov i. Rus. Fed. 76 I2
Vizhas r. Rus. Fed. 52 J2
Vizianagaram India 106 D2
Vizinga Rus. Fed. 52 K3
Vlaardingen Neth. 62 E3
Vlădeasa, Vârful mt. Romania 69 J1
Vladikavkaz Rus. Fed. 113 G2
Vladimir Primorskiy Kray Rus. Fed. 90 D4
Vladimir Vladimirskaya Oblast' Rus. Fed. 52 I4
Vladimiro-Aleksandrovskoye Rus. Fed. 90 D4
Vladimir-Volynskiy Ukr. see Volodymyr-Volyns'kyy
Vladivostok Rus. Fed. 90 C4
Vlakte S. Africa 125 I3
Vlasotince Serbia 69 J3
Vlas'yevo Rus. Fed. 90 F1
Vlieland i. Neth. 62 E1
Vlissingen Neth. 62 D3
Vlora Albania see Vlorë
Vlorë Albania 69 H4
Vlotho Germany 63 I2
Vlotslavsk Poland see Włocławek
Vltava r. Czech Rep. 57 O5
Vobkent Uzbek. 111 G1
Vöcklabruck Austria 57 N6
Vodlozero, Ozero l. Rus. Fed. 52 H3
Voe U.K. 60 [inset]
Voerendaal Neth. 62 F4
Vogelkop Peninsula Indon. see Doberai, Jazirah
Vogelsberg hills Germany 63 I4
Voghera Italy 68 C2
Vohburg an der Donau Germany 63 L6
Vohémar Madag. see Iharaña
Vohenstrauß Germany 63 M5
Vohibinany Madag. see Ampasimanolotra
Vohimarina Madag. see Iharaña
Vohimena, Tanjona c. Madag. 123 E6
Vohipeno Madag. 123 E6
Vöhl Germany 63 I3
Võhma Estonia 55 N7
Voinjama Liberia 120 C4
Vojens Denmark 55 F9
Vojvodina prov. Serbia 69 H2
Vokhma Rus. Fed. 52 J4
Voknavolok Rus. Fed. 54 Q4
Vol' r. Rus. Fed. 52 L3
Volcán Barú, Parque Nacional nat. park Panama 166 [inset] J7
Volcano Bay Japan see Uchiura-wan

▶Volcano Islands Japan 81 K2
Part of Japan.

Volda Norway 54 E5
Vol'dino Rus. Fed. 52 L3
Volendam Neth. 62 F2
Volga Rus. Fed. 52 H4

▶Volga r. Rus. Fed. 53 J7
Longest river in Europe.

Volga Upland hills Rus. Fed. see Privolzhskaya Vozvyshennost'
Volgodonsk Rus. Fed. 53 I7
Volgograd Rus. Fed. 53 J6
Volgogradskoye Vodokhranilishche resr Rus. Fed. 53 J6
Völkermarkt Austria 57 O7
Volkhov Rus. Fed. 52 G4
Volkhov r. Rus. Fed. 52 G3
Völklingen Germany 62 G5
Volkovysk Belarus see Vawkavysk
Volksrust S. Africa 125 I4
Vol'no-Nadezhdinskoye Rus. Fed. 90 C4
Volnovakha Ukr. 53 H7
Vol'nyansk Ukr. see Vil'nyans'k
Volochanka Rus. Fed. 76 K2
Volochisk Ukr. see Volochys'k
Volochys'k Ukr. 53 E6
Volodars'ke Ukr. 53 H7
Volodarskoye Kazakh. see Saumalkol'
Volodymyr-Volyns'kyy Ukr. 53 E6
Vologda Rus. Fed. 52 H4
Volokolamsk Rus. Fed. 52 G4
Volokovaya Rus. Fed. 52 K2
Volos Greece 69 J5
Volosovo Rus. Fed. 55 P7
Volot Rus. Fed. 52 F4
Volovo Rus. Fed. 53 H5
Volozhin Belarus see Valozhyn
Volsinii Italy see Orvieto
Vol'sk Rus. Fed. 53 J5

▶**Volta, Lake** resr Ghana 120 D4
4th largest lake in Africa.

Volta Blanche r. Burkina/Ghana see White Volta
Voltaire, Cape Australia 134 D3
Volta Redonda Brazil 179 B3
Volturno r. Italy 68 E4
Volubilis tourist site Morocco 64 C5
Volvi, Limni l. Greece 69 J4
Volzhsk Rus. Fed. 52 K5
Volzhskiy Samarskaya Oblast' Rus. Fed. 53 K5
Volzhskiy Volgogradskaya Oblast' Rus. Fed. 53 J6
Vondanka Rus. Fed. 52 J4
Von Frank Mountain AK U.S.A. 148 I3
Vontimitta India 106 C3
Vopnafjörður Iceland 54 [inset]
Vopnafjörður b. Iceland 54 [inset]
Vörå Fin. 54 M5
Voranava Belarus 55 N9
Voreies Sporades is Greece 69 J5
Voreioi Sporades is Greece see Voreies Sporades
Voring Plateau sea feature N. Atlantic Ocean 184 I1
Vorjing mt. India 105 H3
Vorkuta Rus. Fed. 76 H3
Vormsi i. Estonia 55 M7
Vorona r. Rus. Fed. 53 I6
Voronezh Rus. Fed. 53 H6
Voronezh r. Rus. Fed. 53 H6
Voronov, Mys pt Rus. Fed. 52 I2
Vorontsovo-Aleksandrovskoye Rus. Fed. see Zelenokumsk
Voroshilov Rus. Fed. see Ussuriysk
Voroshilovgrad Ukr. see Luhans'k
Voroshilovsk Rus. Fed. see Stavropol'
Voroshilovsk Ukr. see Alchevs'k
Vorotynets Rus. Fed. 52 J4
Vorozhba Ukr. 53 G6
Vorpommersche Boddenlandschaft, Nationalpark nat. park Germany 57 N3
Vorskla r. Rus. Fed. 53 G6
Võrtsjärv l. Estonia 55 N7
Võru Estonia 55 O8
Vorukh Tajik. 111 H2
Vosburg S. Africa 124 F6
Vose Tajik. 111 H2
Vosges mts France 66 H3
Voskresensk Rus. Fed. 53 H5
Voskresenskoye Rus. Fed. 52 H4
Voss Norway 55 E6
Vostochno-Sakhalinskiy Gory mts Rus. Fed. 90 F2
Vostochno-Sibirskoye More sea Rus. Fed. see East Siberian Sea
Vostochnyy Kirovskaya Oblast' Rus. Fed. 52 L4
Vostochnyy Sakhalinskaya Oblast' Rus. Fed. 90 F2
Vostochnyy Kazakhstan admin. div. Kazakh. 98 D2
Vostochnyy Sayan mts Rus. Fed. 88 G2
Vostok research station Antarctica 188 F1
Vostok Primorskiy Kray Rus. Fed. 90 D3
Vostok Sakhalinskaya Oblast' Rus. Fed. see Neftegorsk
Vostok Island Kiribati 187 J6
Vostroye Rus. Fed. 52 J3
Votkinsk Rus. Fed. 51 Q4
Votkinskoye Vodokhranilishche resr Rus. Fed. 51 R4
Votuporanga Brazil 179 A3
Vouziers France 62 E5
Voves France 66 E2
Voyageurs National Park U.S.A. 160 E1
Voynitsa Rus. Fed. 54 Q4
Vöyri Fin. see Vörå
Voyvozh Rus. Fed. 52 L3
Vozhayel' Rus. Fed. 52 K3
Vozhe, Ozero l. Rus. Fed. 52 H3
Vozhega Rus. Fed. 52 I3
Vozhgaly Rus. Fed. 52 K4
Voznesens'k Ukr. 53 F7
Vozonin Trough sea feature Arctic Ocean 189 F1
Vozrozhdenya Island i. Uzbek. 102 A3
Vozzhayevka Rus. Fed. 90 C2
Vrangel' Rus. Fed. 90 D4
Vrangelya, Mys pt Rus. Fed. 90 E1
Vrangelya, Ostrov i. Rus. Fed. see Wrangel Island
Vranje Serbia 69 I3
Vratnik pass Bulg. 69 L3
Vratsa Bulg. 69 J3
Vrbas Serbia 69 H2
Vrede S. Africa 125 I4
Vredefort S. Africa 125 H4
Vredenburg S. Africa 124 C7
Vredendal S. Africa 124 D6
Vresse Belgium 62 E5
Vriddhachalam India 106 C4
Vries Neth. 62 G1
Vrigstad Sweden 55 I8
Vršac Serbia 69 I2
Vryburg S. Africa 124 G4
Vryheid S. Africa 125 J4
Vsevidof, Mount vol. U.S.A. 146 B4
Vsevolozhsk Rus. Fed. 52 F3
Vu Ban Vietnam 86 D2
Vučitrn Kosovo see Vushtrri
Vukovar Croatia 69 H2
Vuktyl' Rus. Fed. 51 R3
Vukuzakhe S. Africa 125 I4
Vulcan Canada 150 H5
Vulcan Island P.N.G. see Manam Island
Vulcano, Isola i. Italy 68 F5
Vu Liêt Vietnam 86 D3
Vulture Mountains U.S.A. 159 G5
Vung Tau Vietnam 87 D5
Vuntut National Park Y.T. Canada 149 M1
Vuohijärvi Fin. 55 O6
Vuolijoki Fin. 54 O4
Vuollerim Sweden 54 L3
Vuostimo Fin. 54 O3
Vurnary Rus. Fed. 52 J5
Vushtrri Kosovo 69 I3
Vvedenovka Rus. Fed. 90 C2
Vyara India 104 C5
Vyarkhowye Belarus see Ruba
Vyatka Rus. Fed. see Kirov
Vyatka r. Rus. Fed. 52 K5
Vyatskiye Polyany Rus. Fed. 52 K4
Vyazemskiy Rus. Fed. 90 D3
Vyaz'ma Rus. Fed. 53 G5
Vyazniki Rus. Fed. 52 I4
Vyazovka Rus. Fed. 53 J5
Vyborg Rus. Fed. 55 P6
Vychegda r. Rus. Fed. 52 J3
Vychegodskiy Rus. Fed. 52 J3
Vydrino Rus. Fed. 94 F1
Vyerkhnyadzvinsk Belarus 55 O9
Vyetryna Belarus 55 P9
Vygozero, Ozero l. Rus. Fed. 52 G3
Vyksa Rus. Fed. 53 I5
Vylkove Ukr. 69 M2
Vym' r. Rus. Fed. 52 K3
Vynohradiv Ukr. 53 D6
Vypin Island India 106 C4
Vypolzovo Rus. Fed. 52 G4
Vyritsa Rus. Fed. 55 Q7
Vyrnwy, Lake U.K. 59 D6
Vyselki Rus. Fed. 53 H7
Vysha Rus. Fed. 53 I5
Vyshhorod Ukr. 53 F6
Vyshnevolotskaya Gryada ridge Rus. Fed. 52 G4
Vyshniy-Volochek Rus. Fed. 52 G4
Vyškov Czech Rep. 57 P6
Vysokaya Gora Rus. Fed. 52 K5
Vysokogorniy Rus. Fed. 90 E2
Vystupovychi Ukr. 53 F6
Vytegra Rus. Fed. 52 H3
Vyya r. Rus. Fed. 52 J3
Vyžuona r. Lith. 55 N9

W

Wa Ghana 120 C3
Waal r. Neth. 62 E3
Waalwijk Neth. 62 F3
Waat Sudan 108 D8
Wabag P.N.G. 81 K8
Wabakimi Lake Canada 152 C4
Wabasca r. Canada 150 H3
Wabasca-Desmarais Canada 150 H4
Wabash U.S.A. 164 C3
Wabash r. U.S.A. 164 A5
Wabasha U.S.A. 160 E2
Wabassi r. Canada 152 D4
Wabatongushi Lake Canada 152 D4
Wabē Gestro r. Eth. 100 D6

▶**Wabē Shebelē Wenz** r. Eth. 122 E3
5th longest river in Africa.

Wabigoon Lake Canada 151 M5
Wabowden Canada 151 L4
Wabrah well Saudi Arabia 110 B5
Wabu China 97 H1
Wabuk Point Canada 152 D3
Wabush Canada 153 I3
Waccasassa Bay U.S.A. 163 D6
Wachi Japan 92 B3
Wächtersbach Germany 63 J4
Waco Canada 153 I4
Waco U.S.A. 161 D6
Waconda Lake U.S.A. 160 D4
Wada Japan 93 G3
Wada-misaki pt Japan 92 B4
Wada-tōge pass Japan 93 E2
Wadayama Japan 92 A3
Wadbilliga National Park Australia 138 D6
Waddān Libya 65 H6
Waddell Dam U.S.A. 159 G5
Waddeneilanden Neth. 62 E1
Waddenzee sea chan. Neth. 62 E2
Waddington, Mount Canada 150 E5
Waddinxveen Neth. 62 E2
Wadebridge U.K. 59 C8
Wadena Canada 151 K5
Wadena U.S.A. 160 E2
Wadern Germany 62 G5
Wadesville U.S.A. 164 B4
Wadeye Australia 134 E3
Wadgassen Germany 62 G5
Wadh Pak. 111 G5
Wadhwan India see Surendranagar
Wadi India 106 C2
Wādī as Sīr Jordan 107 B4
Wadi Halfa Sudan 108 D5
Wad Medani Sudan 108 D7
Wad Rawa Sudan 108 D6
Wadsworth U.S.A. 158 D2
Waenhuiskrans S. Africa 124 E8
Wafangdian Liaoning China 95 J4
Wafra Kuwait see Al Wafrah
Wagenfeld Germany 63 I2
Wagenhoff Germany 63 K2
Wagga Wagga Australia 138 C5
Wagner U.S.A. 160 D3
Wagoner U.S.A. 161 E4
Wagon Mound U.S.A. 157 G5
Wah Pak. 111 I3
Wahai Seram Indon. 83 D3
Wāḥāt Jālū Libya 121 F2
Wahemen, Lac l. Canada 153 H3
Wahiawā U.S.A. 157 [inset]
Wahlhausen Germany 63 J3
Wahpeton U.S.A. 160 D2
Wahran Alg. see Oran
Wah Wah Mountains U.S.A. 159 G2
Wai India 106 B2
Waialua U.S.A. 157 [inset]
Waiau N.Z. see Franz Josef Glacier
Waiau r. N.Z. 139 D6
Waiblingen Germany 63 J6
Waidhofen an der Ybbs Austria 57 O7
Waigama Papua Indon. 83 D3
Waigeo i. Papua Indon. 83 D3
Waiheke Island N.Z. 139 E3
Waikabubak Sumba Indon. 83 A5
Waikaia r. N.Z. 139 B7
Waikari N.Z. 139 D6
Waikerie Australia 137 B7
Waiklibang Flores Indon. 83 B5
Waikouaiti N.Z. 139 C7
Wailuku U.S.A. 157 [inset]
Waimangaroa N.Z. 139 C5
Waimarama N.Z. 139 F4
Waimate N.Z. 139 C7
Waimea U.S.A. 157 [inset]
Waimenda Sulawesi Indon. 83 B3
Wainganga r. India 106 C2
Waingapu Sumba Indon. 83 B5
Wainhouse Corner U.K. 59 C8
Waini Point Guyana 177 G2
Wainwright Canada 151 I4
Wainwright AK U.S.A. 148 H1
Waiouru N.Z. 139 E4
Waipahi N.Z. 139 B8
Waipaoa r. N.Z. 139 F4
Waipara N.Z. 139 D6
Waipawa N.Z. 139 F4
Waipukurau N.Z. 139 F4
Wairarapa, Lake N.Z. 139 E5
Wairau r. N.Z. 139 E5
Wairoa N.Z. 139 F4
Wairoa r. N.Z. 139 F4
Wairunu Flores Indon. 83 B5
Waisai Papua Indon. 83 D3
Waitahanui N.Z. 139 F4
Waitahuna N.Z. 139 B7
Waitakaruru N.Z. 139 E3
Waitaki r. N.Z. 139 C7
Waitangi N.Z. 133 I6
Waite River Australia 134 F5
Waiuku N.Z. 139 E3
Waiwera South N.Z. 139 B8
Waiya Seram Indon. 83 D3
Waiyang China 97 H3
Wajima Japan 91 E5
Wajir Kenya 122 E3
Waka Flores Indon. 83 B5
Waka, Tanjung pt Indon. 83 C3
Wakasa-wan b. Japan 92 B3
Wakasa-wan Kokutei-kōen park Japan 92 B3
Wakatipu, Lake N.Z. 139 B7
Wakatobi, Taman Nasional nat. park Indon. 83 B4
Wakaw Canada 151 J4
Wakayama Japan 92 B4
Wakayama pref. Japan 92 B5
Wake Atoll terr. N. Pacific Ocean see Wake Island
WaKeeney U.S.A. 160 D4
Wakefield N.Z. 139 D5
Wakefield U.K. 58 F5
Wakefield MI U.S.A. 160 F2
Wakefield RI U.S.A. 165 J3
Wakefield VA U.S.A. 165 G5

▶**Wake Island** terr. N. Pacific Ocean 186 H4
United States Unincorporated Territory.

Wakema Myanmar 86 A3
Wakhan reg. Afgh. 111 I2
Wakkanai Japan 90 F3
Wakkerstroom S. Africa 125 J4
Wakool Australia 138 B5
Wakool r. Australia 138 A5
Wakuach, Lac l. Canada 153 I3
Waku-Kungo Angola 123 B5
Wałbrzych Poland 57 P5
Walcha Australia 138 E3
Walcott U.S.A. 156 G4
Walcourt Belgium 62 E4
Wałcz Poland 57 P4
Waldburg Range mts Australia 135 B6
Walden U.S.A. 165 H3
Waldenbuch Germany 63 J6
Waldenburg Poland see Wałbrzych
Waldkraiburg Germany 57 N6
Waldo U.S.A. 164 D3
Waldoboro U.S.A. 165 K1
Waldorf U.S.A. 165 G4
Waldport U.S.A. 156 B3
Waldron U.S.A. 161 E5
Waldron, Cape Antarctica 188 F2
Walea, Selat sea chan. Indon. 83 B3
Waleakodi i. Indon. 83 B3
Walebing Australia 135 B7
Walêg China 96 D2
Wales admin. div. U.K. 59 D6
Wales AK U.S.A. 148 E2
Walgaon India 104 D5
Walgett Australia 138 D3
Walgreen Coast Antarctica 188 K1
Walhalla MI U.S.A. 164 B2
Walhalla ND U.S.A. 160 D1
Walikale Dem. Rep. Congo 121 F5
Walingai P.N.G. 81 L8
Walker r. Australia 136 A2
Walker watercourse Australia 135 F6
Walker MI U.S.A. 164 C2
Walker MN U.S.A. 160 E2
Walker r. U.S.A. 158 D2
Walker Bay S. Africa 124 D8
Walker Creek r. Australia 136 C3
Walker Lake Canada 151 L4
Walker Lake AK U.S.A. 148 I2
Walker Lake l. U.S.A. 158 D2
Walker Pass U.S.A. 158 D4
Walkersville U.S.A. 165 G4
Walkerton Canada 164 E1
Walkerton U.S.A. 164 B3
Wall, Mount hill Australia 134 B5
Wallaby Island Australia 136 C2
Wallace ID U.S.A. 156 D3
Wallace NC U.S.A. 163 E5
Wallace VA U.S.A. 164 D5
Wallaceburg Canada 164 D2
Wallal Downs Australia 134 C4
Wallangarra Australia 138 E2
Wallaroo Australia 137 B7
Wallasey U.K. 58 D5
Walla Walla Australia 138 C5
Walla Walla U.S.A. 156 D3
Walldürn Germany 63 J5
Wallekraal S. Africa 124 C6
Wallendbeen Australia 138 D5
Wallingford U.K. 59 F7
Wallis, Îles is Wallis and Futuna Is 133 I3

▶**Wallis and Futuna Islands** terr. S. Pacific Ocean 133 I3
French Overseas Collectivity.

Wallis et Futuna, Îles terr. S. Pacific Ocean see Wallis and Futuna Islands
Wallis Islands Wallis and Futuna Is see Wallis, Îles
Wallis Lake inlet Australia 138 F4
Wallops Island U.S.A. 165 H5
Wallowa Mountains U.S.A. 156 D3
Walls U.K. 60 [inset]
Walls of Jerusalem National Park Australia 137 [inset]
Wallumbilla Australia 137 E5
Walmsley Lake Canada 151 I2
Walney, Isle of i. U.K. 58 D4
Walnut Creek U.S.A. 158 B3
Walnut Grove U.S.A. 158 C2
Walnut Ridge U.S.A. 161 F4
Walong India 105 I3
Walpole U.S.A. 165 I2
Walrus Island AK U.S.A. 148 E4
Walrus Islands AK U.S.A. 148 G4
Walsall U.K. 59 F6
Walsenburg U.S.A. 157 G5
Walsh U.S.A. 161 C4
Walsrode Germany 63 J2
Waltair India 106 D2
Walterboro U.S.A. 163 D5
Walters U.S.A. 161 D5
Walter's Range hills Australia 138 B2
Walthall U.S.A. 161 F5
Waltham U.S.A. 165 J2
Walton IN U.S.A. 164 B3
Walton KY U.S.A. 164 C4
Walton NY U.S.A. 165 H2
Walton WV U.S.A. 164 E4
Walvisbaai Namibia see Walvis Bay
Walvisbaai b. Namibia see Walvis Bay
Walvis Bay Namibia 124 B2
Walvis Bay b. Namibia 124 B2
Walvis Ridge sea feature S. Atlantic Ocean 184 H8
Wama Afgh. 111 H3
Wamba Équateur Dem. Rep. Congo 121 F5
Wamba Orientale Dem. Rep. Congo 122 C3
Wamba Nigeria 120 D4
Wamlana Buru Indon. 83 C3
Wampum U.S.A. 164 E3
Wampusirpi Hond. 166 [inset] I6
Wamsutter U.S.A. 156 G4
Wamulan Buru Indon. 83 C3
Wana Pak. 111 H3
Wanaaring Australia 138 B2
Wanaka N.Z. 139 B7
Wanaka, Lake N.Z. 139 B7
Wan'an China 97 G3
Wanapitei Lake Canada 152 E5
Wanasabari Sulawesi Indon. 83 B4
Wanbi Australia 137 C7
Wanbrow, Cape N.Z. 139 C7
Wanci Sulawesi Indon. 83 B4
Wanda Shan mts China 90 D3
Wandering River Canada 151 H4
Wandersleben Germany 63 K4
Wandlitz Germany 63 N2
Wando S. Korea 91 B6
Wandoan Australia 137 E5
Wanganui N.Z. 139 E4
Wanganui r. N.Z. 139 E4
Wangaratta Australia 138 C6
Wangcang China 96 E1
Wangcun Shandong China 95 J4
Wangda China see Zogang
Wangdain Xizang China 99 E7
Wangdi Phodrang Bhutan 105 G4
Wangdu Hebei China 95 H4
Wanggamet, Gunung mt. Sumba Indon. 83 B5
Wanggao China 97 F3
Wang Gaxun Qinghai China 94 D4
Wanggezhuang Shandong China see Jiaonan
Wangguan China 96 E1
Wangiwangi i. Indon. 83 B4
Wangjiawan Shaanxi China 95 G4
Wangkibila Hond. 166 [inset] I6
Wangkui China 90 B3
Wangmo China 96 E3
Wangqing China 90 C4
Wangwu Shan mts China 97 F1
Wangying China see Huaiyin
Wanham Canada 150 G4
Wan Hsa-la Myanmar 86 B2
Wanie-Rukula Dem. Rep. Congo 122 C3
Wankaner India 104 B5
Wankie Zimbabwe see Hwange
Wanlaweyn Somalia 122 E3
Wanna Germany 63 I1
Wanna Lakes salt flat Australia 135 E7
Wannian China 97 H2
Wanning China 97 F5
Wanouchi Japan 92 C3
Wanroij Neth. 62 F3
Wanrong Shanxi China 95 G5
Wanshan China 97 F3
Wanshan Qundao is China 97 G4
Wansheng China 96 E2
Wanshengchang China see Wansheng
Wantage U.K. 59 F7
Wanxian Chongqing China 97 F2
Wanxian Chongqing China see Shahe
Wanyuan China 97 F1
Wanzai China 97 G2
Wanze Belgium 62 F4
Wapakoneta U.S.A. 164 C3
Wapawekka Lake Canada 151 J4
Wapello U.S.A. 160 F3
Wapikaimaski Lake Canada 152 C4
Wapikopa Lake Canada 152 C3
Wapiti r. Canada 150 G4
Wapotih Buru Indon. 83 C3
Wapusk National Park Canada 151 M3
Waqên China 96 D1
Waqf aş Şawwān, Jibāl hills Jordan 107 C4
War U.S.A. 164 E5
Wara Japan 92 D3
Warab Sudan 108 C8
Warangal India 106 C2
Waranga Reservoir Australia 138 B6
Waratah Bay Australia 138 B7
Warbreccan Australia 136 C5
Warburg Germany 63 J3
Warburton Australia 135 D6
Warburton watercourse Australia 137 B5
Warburton Bay Canada 151 I2
Warche r. Belgium 62 F4
Ward, Mount N.Z. 139 B6
Warden S. Africa 125 I4
Wardenburg Germany 63 I1
Wardha India 106 C1
Wardha r. India 106 C2
Ward Hill hill U.K. 60 F2
Ward Hunt, Cape P.N.G. 81 L8
Ware Canada 150 E3
Ware U.S.A. 165 I2
Wareham U.K. 59 E8
Waremme Belgium 62 F4
Waren Germany 63 M1
Warendorf Germany 63 H3
Warginburra Peninsula Australia 136 E4
Wargla Alg. see Ouargla
Warialda Australia 138 E2
Warin Chamrap Thai. 86 D4
Waring Mountains AK U.S.A. 148 G2
Warkum Neth. see Workum
Warkworth U.K. 58 F3
Warli China see Walêg
Warloy-Baillon France 62 C4
Warman Canada 151 J4
Warmbad Namibia 124 D5
Warmbad S. Africa 125 I3
Warmbaths S. Africa see Warmbad
Warminster U.K. 59 E7
Warminster U.S.A. 165 H3
Warmond Neth. 62 E2
Warm Springs NV U.S.A. 158 E2
Warm Springs VA U.S.A. 164 F4
Warmwaterberg mts S. Africa 124 E7
Warner Canada 151 H5
Warner Lakes U.S.A. 156 D4
Warner Mountains U.S.A. 156 C4
Warnes Bol. 176 F7
Warning, Mount Australia 138 F2
Waronda India 106 C2
Warora India 106 C1
Warra Australia 138 E1
Warragamba Reservoir Australia 138 E5
Warragul Australia 138 B7
Warrambool r. Australia 138 C3
Warrandirinna, Lake salt flat Australia 137 B5
Warrandyte Australia 138 B6
Warrawagine Australia 134 C5
Warrego r. Australia 138 B3
Warrego Range hills Australia 136 D5
Warren Australia 138 C3
Warren AR U.S.A. 161 E5
Warren MI U.S.A. 164 D2
Warren MN U.S.A. 160 D1
Warren OH U.S.A. 164 E3
Warren PA U.S.A. 164 F3
Warren Hastings Island Palau see Merir
Warren Island U.S.A. 150 C4
Warren Point pt N.W.T. Canada 149 N1
Warrenpoint U.K. 61 F3
Warrensburg MO U.S.A. 160 E4
Warrensburg NY U.S.A. 165 I2
Warrenton S. Africa 124 G5
Warrenton GA U.S.A. 163 D5
Warrenton MO U.S.A. 160 F4
Warrenton VA U.S.A. 165 G4
Warri Nigeria 120 D4
Warriners Creek watercourse Australia 137 B6
Warrington N.Z. 139 C7
Warrington U.K. 58 E5
Warrington U.S.A. 163 C6
Warrnambool Australia 137 C8
Warroad U.S.A. 160 E1
Warrumbungle National Park Australia 138 D3

▶**Warsaw** Poland 57 R4
Capital of Poland.

Warsaw IN U.S.A. 164 C3
Warsaw KY U.S.A. 164 C4
Warsaw MO U.S.A. 160 E4
Warsaw NY U.S.A. 165 F2
Warsaw VA U.S.A. 165 G5
Warshiikh Somalia 122 E3
Warstein Germany 63 I3
Warszawa Poland see Warsaw
Warta r. Poland 57 O4
Waru Kalimantan Indon. 85 G3
Warwick Australia 138 F2
Warwick U.K. 59 F6
Warwick U.S.A. 165 J3
Warzhong China 96 D2
Wasaga Beach Canada 164 E1
Wasatch Range mts U.S.A. 156 F5
Wasbank S. Africa 125 J5
Wasco U.S.A. 158 D4
Washburn ND U.S.A. 160 C2
Washburn WI U.S.A. 160 F2
Washiga-take mt. Japan 92 C3
Washim India 106 C1

▶**Washington** DC U.S.A. 165 G4
Capital of the United States of America.

Washington GA U.S.A. 163 D5
Washington IA U.S.A. 160 F3
Washington IN U.S.A. 164 B4
Washington MO U.S.A. 160 F4
Washington NC U.S.A. 162 E5
Washington NJ U.S.A. 165 H3
Washington PA U.S.A. 164 E3
Washington UT U.S.A. 159 G3
Washington state U.S.A. 156 C3
Washington, Cape Antarctica 188 H2
Washington, Mount U.S.A. 165 J1
Washington Court House U.S.A. 164 D4
Washington Island U.S.A. 162 C2
Washington Land reg. Greenland 147 L2
Washir Afgh. 111 F3
Washita r. U.S.A. 161 D5
Washpool National Park Australia 138 F2
Washtucna U.S.A. 156 D3
Washuk Pak. 111 G5
Wasi India 106 B2
Wasi' Saudi Arabia 110 B5
Wasi' well Saudi Arabia 110 C6
Wasiri Maluku Indon. 83 C4
Wasisi Buru Indon. 83 C3
Waskaganish Canada 152 F4
Waskagheganish Canada see Waskaganish
Waskaiowaka Lake Canada 151 L3
Waskey, Mount AK U.S.A. 148 H4
Waspán Nicaragua 166 [inset] I6
Wassenaar Neth. 62 E2
Wasser Namibia 124 D4
Wasserkuppe hill Germany 63 J4
Wassertrüdingen Germany 63 K5
Wassuk Range mts U.S.A. 158 D2
Wasua P.N.G. 81 K8
Wasum P.N.G. 81 L8
Waswanipi r. Canada 152 F4
Waswanipi, Lac l. Canada 152 F4
Watam P.N.G. 81 K7
Watambayoli Sulawesi Indon. 83 B3
Watampone Sulawesi Indon. 83 B4
Watana, Mount AK U.S.A. 149 J3
Watansoppeng Sulawesi Indon. 83 A4
Watapi Lake Canada 151 I4
Watarai Japan 92 C4
Watarase-gawa r. Japan 93 F2
Watarrka National Park Australia 135 E6
Watauchi Japan 93 E2
Watenstadt-Salzgitter Germany see Salzgitter
Waterbury CT U.S.A. 165 I3
Waterbury VT U.S.A. 165 I1
Waterbury Lake Canada 151 J3
Water Cays i. Bahamas 163 E8
Waterdown Canada 164 F2
Wateree r. U.S.A. 163 D5
Waterfall AK U.S.A. 149 N5
Waterford Ireland 61 E5
Waterford PA U.S.A. 164 F3
Waterford WI U.S.A. 164 A2
Waterford Harbour Ireland 61 F5
Watergrasshill Ireland 61 D5
Waterhen Lake Canada 151 L4
Waterloo Australia 134 E4
Waterloo Belgium 62 E4
Waterloo Ont. Canada 164 E2
Waterloo Que. Canada 165 I1
Waterloo IA U.S.A. 160 E3
Waterloo IL U.S.A. 160 F4
Waterloo NY U.S.A. 165 G2
Waterlooville U.K. 59 F8
Waterton Lakes National Park Canada 150 H5
Watertown NY U.S.A. 165 H2
Watertown SD U.S.A. 160 D2
Watertown WI U.S.A. 160 F3
Waterval Boven S. Africa 125 J3
Water Valley U.S.A. 161 F5
Waterville ME U.S.A. 165 K1
Waterville WA U.S.A. 156 C3
Watford Canada 164 E2
Watford U.K. 59 G7
Watford City U.S.A. 160 C2
Wathaman r. Canada 151 K3
Wathaman Lake Canada 151 K3
Watheroo National Park Australia 135 A7
Wathlingen Germany 63 K2
Watino Canada 150 G4
Watīr, Wādī watercourse Egypt 107 B5
Watkins Glen U.S.A. 165 G2
Watling Island Bahamas see San Salvador
Watmuri Indon. 134 E1
Watonga U.S.A. 161 D5
Watowato, Bukit mt. Halmahera Indon. 83 D2
Watrous Canada 151 J5
Watrous U.S.A. 157 G6
Watseka U.S.A. 164 B3

Watsi Kengo Dem. Rep. Congo 121 F5
Watson r. Australia 136 C2
Watson Canada 151 J4
Watson Lake Y.T. Canada 149 O3
Watsontown U.S.A. 165 G3
Watsonville U.S.A. 158 C3
Watten U.K. 60 F2
Watterson Lake Canada 151 L2
Watton U.K. 59 H6
Watts Bar Lake resr U.S.A. 162 C5
Wattsburg U.S.A. 164 F2
Watubela, Kepulauan is Indon. 81 I7
Watuwila, Bukit mt. Indon. 83 B3
Wau P.N.G. 81 L8
Wau Sudan 108 C8
Waubay Lake U.S.A. 160 D2
Wauchope N.S.W. Australia 138 F3
Wauchope N.T. Australia 134 F5
Waukara, Gunung mt. Indon. 83 A3
Waukaringa (abandoned) Australia 137 B7
Waukarlycarly, Lake salt flat Australia 134 C5
Waukegan U.S.A. 164 B2
Waukesha U.S.A. 164 A2
Waupaca U.S.A. 160 F2
Waupun U.S.A. 160 F3
Waurika U.S.A. 161 D5
Wausau U.S.A. 160 F2
Wausaukee U.S.A. 162 C2
Wauseon U.S.A. 164 C3
Wautoma U.S.A. 160 F2
Wave Hill Australia 134 E4
Waveney r. U.K. 59 I6
Waverly IA U.S.A. 160 E3
Waverly NY U.S.A. 165 G2
Waverly OH U.S.A. 164 D4
Waverly TN U.S.A. 162 C4
Waverly VA U.S.A. 165 G5
Wavre Belgium 62 E4
Waw Myanmar 86 B3
Wawa Canada 152 D5
Wawalalindu Sulawesi Indon. 83 B3
Wāw al Kabīr Libya 121 E2
Wawasee, Lake U.S.A. 164 C3
Wawo Sulawesi Indon. 83 B3
Wawotebi Sulawesi Indon. 83 B3
Waxahachie U.S.A. 161 D5
Waxü Gansu China 94 E5
Waxxari Xinjiang China 98 D5
Way, Lake salt flat Australia 135 C6
Wayabula Maluku Indon. 83 D2
Wayag i. Papua Indon. 83 D2
Wayamli Halmahera Indon. 83 D2
Wayaobu Shaanxi China see Zichang
Waycross U.S.A. 163 D6
Wayhaya Maluku Indon. 83 C3
Way Kambas, Taman Nasional nat. park Indon. 84 D4
Waykilo Maluku Indon. 83 C3
Wayland KY U.S.A. 164 D5
Wayland MI U.S.A. 164 C2
Wayne NE U.S.A. 160 D3
Wayne WV U.S.A. 164 D4
Waynesboro GA U.S.A. 163 D5
Waynesboro MS U.S.A. 161 F6
Waynesboro TN U.S.A. 162 C5
Waynesboro VA U.S.A. 165 F4
Waynesburg U.S.A. 164 E4
Waynesville MO U.S.A. 160 E4
Waynesville NC U.S.A. 162 D5
Waynoka U.S.A. 161 D4
Waza, Parc National de nat. park Cameroon 121 E3
Wāzah Khwāh Afgh. see Wazi Khwa
Wazi Khwa Afgh. 111 H3
Wazirabad Pak. 111 I3
Wazuka Japan 92 B4
W du Niger, Parcs Nationaux du nat. park Niger 120 D3
We, Pulau i. Indon. 84 A1
Weagamow Lake Canada 151 N4
Weam P.N.G. 81 K8
Wear r. U.K. 58 F4
Weare U.S.A. 165 J2
Weatherford U.S.A. 161 D5
Weaver Lake Canada 151 L4
Weaverville U.S.A. 156 C4
Webb, Mount hill Australia 134 E5
Webequie Canada 152 D3
Weber, Mount B.C. Canada 149 O5
Weber Basin sea feature Laut Banda 186 E6

▶Webi Shebelē r. Somalia 122 E3
5th longest river in Africa.

Webster IN U.S.A. 164 C4
Webster MA U.S.A. 165 J2
Webster SD U.S.A. 160 D2
Webster City U.S.A. 160 E3
Webster Springs U.S.A. 164 E4
Wecho Lake Canada 150 H2
Weda Halmahera Indon. 83 C2
Weda, Teluk b. Halmahera Indon. 83 D2
Wedau P.N.G. 136 E1
Weddell Abyssal Plain sea feature Southern Ocean 188 A2
Weddell Island Falkland Is 178 D8
Weddell Sea Antarctica 188 A2
Wedderburn Australia 138 A6
Weddin Mountains National Park Australia 138 D4
Wedel (Holstein) Germany 63 J1
Wedge Mountain Canada 150 F5
Wedowee U.S.A. 163 C5
Weedville U.S.A. 165 F3
Weeim i. Papua Indon. 83 D3
Weenen S. Africa 125 J5
Weener Germany 63 H1
Weert Neth. 62 F3
Weethalle Australia 138 C4
Wee Waa Australia 138 D3
Wegberg Germany 62 G3
Węgorzewo Poland 57 R3
Weichang Hebei China 95 I3
Weida Germany 63 M4
Weidenberg Germany 63 L5
Weiden in der Oberpfalz Germany 63 M5
Weidongmen China see Qianjin
Weifang Shandong China 95 I4
Weihai Shandong China 95 J4
Wei He r. Henan China 95 H4
Wei He r. Shaanxi China 95 G5
Weihui Henan China 95 H5
Weilburg Germany 63 I4
Weilmoringle Australia 138 C2
Weimar Germany 63 L4
Weinan Shaanxi China 95 G5
Weinheim Germany 63 I5
Weining China 96 E3
Weinsberg Germany 63 J5
Weipa Australia 136 C2
Weiqu Shaanxi China see Chang'an
Weir r. Australia 138 D2
Weirong Gansu China 94 F5
Weir River Canada 151 M3
Weirton U.S.A. 164 E3
Weiser U.S.A. 156 D3
Weishan Shandong China 95 I5
Weishan China 96 D3
Weishan Hu l. China 95 I5
Weishi Henan China 95 H5
Weiße Elster r. Germany 63 L3
Weißenburg in Bayern Germany 63 K5
Weißenfels Germany 63 L3
Weißkugel mt. Austria/Italy 57 M7
Weissrand Mountains Namibia 124 D3
Weiterstadt Germany 63 I5
Weitzel Lake Canada 151 J3
Weixi China 96 C3
Weixian Hebei China 95 H4
Weixin China 96 E3
Weiya Xinjiang China 94 C3
Weiyuan Gansu China 94 F5
Weiyuan Qinghai China see Huzhu
Weiyuan Sichuan China 96 E2
Weiyuan Yunnan China see Jinggu
Weiyuan Jiang r. China 96 D4
Weiz Austria 57 O7
Weizhou Ningxia China 94 F4
Weizhou China see Wenchuan
Weizhou Dao i. China 97 F4
Weizi Liaoning China 95 J3
Wejherowo Poland 57 Q3
Wekilbazar Turkm. 111 F2
Wekusko Canada 151 L4
Wekusko Lake Canada 151 L4
Wekweêtì Canada 150 H1
Welatam Myanmar 86 B1
Welbourn Hill Australia 135 F6
Welch U.S.A. 164 E5
Weld U.S.A. 165 J1
Weldiya Eth. 122 D2
Welford National Park Australia 136 C5
Welgevonden Game Reserve nature res. S. Africa 125 H3
Welk'īt'ē Eth. 122 D3
Welkom S. Africa 125 H4
Welland Canada 164 F2
Welland r. U.K. 59 G6
Welland Canal Canada 164 F2
Wellesley Canada 164 E2
Wellesley Islands Australia 136 B3
Wellesley Lake Y.T. Canada 149 M3
Wellfleet U.S.A. 165 J3
Wellin Belgium 62 F4
Wellingborough U.K. 59 G6
Wellington Australia 138 D4
Wellington Canada 165 G2

▶Wellington N.Z. 139 E5
Capital of New Zealand.

Wellington S. Africa 124 D7
Wellington England U.K. 59 D8
Wellington England U.K. 59 E6
Wellington CO U.S.A. 156 G4
Wellington IL U.S.A. 164 B3
Wellington KS U.S.A. 161 D4
Wellington NV U.S.A. 158 D2
Wellington OH U.S.A. 164 D3
Wellington TX U.S.A. 161 C5
Wellington UT U.S.A. 159 H2
Wellington, Isla i. Chile 178 B7
Wellington Range hills N.T. Australia 134 F3
Wellington Range hills W.A. Australia 135 C6
Wells Canada 150 F4
Wells U.K. 59 E7
Wells U.S.A. 156 E4
Wells, Lake salt flat Australia 135 C6
Wellsboro U.S.A. 165 G3
Wellsburg U.S.A. 164 E3
Wellsford N.Z. 139 E3
Wells-next-the-Sea U.K. 59 H6
Wellston U.S.A. 164 C1
Wellsville U.S.A. 165 G2
Wellton U.S.A. 159 F5
Wels Austria 57 O6
Welshpool U.K. 59 D6
Welsickendorf Germany 63 N3
Welwitschia Namibia see Khorixas
Welwyn Garden City U.K. 59 G7
Welzheim Germany 63 J6
Wem U.K. 59 E6
Wembesi S. Africa 125 I5
Wembley Canada 150 G4
Wemindji Canada 152 F3
Wenatchee U.S.A. 156 C3
Wenatchee Mountains U.S.A. 156 C3
Wenchang Hainan China 97 F5
Wenchang Sichuan China see Zitong
Wenchow China see Wenzhou
Wenchuan China 96 D2
Wendelstein Germany 63 L5
Wenden Germany 63 H4
Wenden Latvia see Cēsis
Wenden U.S.A. 159 G5
Wendeng Shandong China 95 J4
Wendover U.S.A. 159 F1
Wenfengzhen Gansu China 94 F5
Weng'an China 96 E3
Wengshui China 96 C2
Wengyuan China 97 G3
Wenhua China see Weishan
Wenkutu Nei Mongol China 95 J1
Wenlan China see Mengzi
Wenling China 97 I2
Wenlock r. Australia 136 C2
Wenping China see Ludian
Wenquan Guizhou China 96 E2
Wenquan Henan China see Wenxian
Wenquan Hubei China see Yingshan
Wenquan Qinghai China 105 G2
Wenquan Qinghai China 94 D5
Wenquan Qinghai China 99 E6
Wenquan Xinjiang China 98 C3
Wenshan China 96 E4
Wenshui China 96 E2
Wensu Xinjiang China 98 C4
Wensum r. U.K. 59 I6
Wentorf bei Hamburg Germany 63 K1
Wentworth Australia 137 C7
Wenxi China 97 F1
Wenxian Gansu China 96 E1
Wenxian Henan China 97 G1
Wenxing China see Xiangyin
Wenzhou China 97 I3
Wenzlow Germany 63 M2
Wepener S. Africa 125 H5
Wer India 104 D4
Werben (Elbe) Germany 63 L2
Werda Botswana 124 F3
Werdau Germany 63 M4
Werder Eth. 122 E3
Werder Germany 63 M2
Werdohl Germany 63 H3
Werinama Seram Indon. 83 D3
Werl Germany 63 H3
Wernberg-Köblitz Germany 63 M5
Werne Germany 63 H3
Wernecke Mountains Y.T. Canada 149 M2
Wernigerode Germany 63 K3
Werra r. Germany 63 J3
Werris Creek Australia 138 E3
Wertheim Germany 63 J5
Wervik Belgium 62 D4
Werwaru Maluku Indon. 83 D5
Wesel Germany 62 G3
Wesel-Datteln-Kanal canal Germany 62 G3
Wesenberg Germany 63 M1
Wesendorf Germany 63 K2
Weser r. Germany 63 I1
Weser sea chan. Germany 63 I1
Wesergebirge hills Germany 63 I2
Weslaco U.S.A. 161 D7
Weslemkoon Lake Canada 165 G1
Wesleyville Canada 153 L4
Wessel, Cape Australia 136 B1
Wessel Islands Australia 136 B1
Wesselsbron S. Africa 125 H4
Wesselton S. Africa 125 I4
Wessington Springs U.S.A. 160 D2
West r. N.W.T. Canada 149 P1
Westall, Point Australia 135 F8
West Allis U.S.A. 164 A2
West Antarctica reg. Antarctica 188 J1
West Australian Basin sea feature Indian Ocean 185 O7

▶West Bank terr. Asia 107 B3
Territory occupied by Israel.

West Bay Canada 153 K3
West Bay b. LA U.S.A. 167 H2
West Bay inlet U.S.A. 163 C6
West Bend U.S.A. 164 A2
West Bengal state India 105 F5
West Branch U.S.A. 164 C1
West Bromwich U.K. 59 F6
Westbrook U.S.A. 165 J2
West Burke U.S.A. 165 J1
West Burra i. U.K. see Burra
Westbury U.K. 59 E7
West Caicos i. Turks and Caicos Is 163 F8
West Cape Howe Australia 135 B8
West Caroline Basin sea feature N. Pacific Ocean 186 F5
West Chester U.S.A. 165 H4
Westcliffe U.S.A. 157 G5
West Coast National Park S. Africa 124 D7
West End Bahamas 163 E7
Westerburg Germany 63 H4
Westerholt Germany 63 H1
Westerland Germany 57 L3
Westerlo Belgium 62 E3
Westerly U.S.A. 165 J3
Western r. Canada 151 J1
Western Australia state Australia 135 C6
Western Cape prov. S. Africa 124 E7
Western Desert Egypt 112 C6
Western Dvina r. Europe see Zapadnaya Dvina
Western Ghats mts India 106 B3
Western Lesser Sunda Islands prov. Indon. see Nusa Tenggara Barat
Western Port b. Australia 138 B7

▶Western Sahara terr. Africa 120 B2
Disputed territory (Morocco).

Western Samoa country S. Pacific Ocean see Samoa
Western Sayan Mountains reg. Rus. Fed. see Zapadnyy Sayan
Westerschelde est. Neth. 62 D3
Westerstede Germany 63 H1
Westerville U.S.A. 164 D3
Westerwald hills Germany 63 H4
West Falkland i. Falkland Is 178 D8
West Fargo U.S.A. 160 D2
West Fayu atoll Micronesia 81 L5
Westfield IN U.S.A. 164 B3
Westfield MA U.S.A. 165 I2
Westfield NY U.S.A. 164 F2
Westfield PA U.S.A. 165 G3
West Frisian Islands Neth. see Waddeneilanden
Westgat sea chan. Neth. 62 G1
Westgate Australia 138 C1
West Glacier U.S.A. 156 E2
West Grand Lake U.S.A. 162 H2
West Hartford U.S.A. 165 I3
Westhausen Germany 63 K6
West Haven U.S.A. 165 I3
Westhill U.K. 60 G3
Westhope U.S.A. 160 C1
West Ice Shelf Antarctica 188 E2
West Indies is Caribbean Sea 169 J4
West Irian prov. Indon. see Papua
West Island India 87 A4
Westkapelle Neth. 62 D3
West Kazakhstan Oblast admin. div. Kazakh. see Zapadnyy Kazakhstan
West Kingston U.S.A. 165 J3
West Lafayette U.S.A. 164 B3
West Lamma Channel H.K. China 97 [inset]
Westland Australia 136 C4
Westland National Park N.Z. 139 C6
Westleigh S. Africa 125 H4
Westleton U.K. 59 I6
West Liberty U.S.A. 164 D5
West Linton U.K. 60 F5
West Loch Roag b. U.K. 60 C2
Westlock Canada 150 H4
West Lorne Canada 164 E2
West Lunga National Park Zambia 123 C5
West MacDonnell National Park Australia 135 F5
West Malaysia pen. Malaysia see Malaysia, Semenanjung
Westmalle Belgium 62 E3
Westmar Australia 138 D1
West Mariana Basin sea feature N. Pacific Ocean 186 F4
West Memphis U.S.A. 161 F5
Westminster U.S.A. 165 G4
Westmoreland Australia 136 B3
Westmoreland U.S.A. 164 B5
Westmorland U.S.A. 159 F5
Weston Sabah Malaysia 85 F1
Weston OH U.S.A. 164 D3
Weston WV U.S.A. 164 E4
Weston-super-Mare U.K. 59 E7
West Palm Beach U.S.A. 163 D7
West Papua prov. Indon. see Papua
West Passage Palau see Toagel Mlungui
West Plains U.S.A. 161 F4
West Point pt Australia 137 [inset]
West Point CA U.S.A. 158 C2
West Point KY U.S.A. 164 C5
West Point MS U.S.A. 161 F5
West Point NE U.S.A. 160 D3
West Point VA U.S.A. 165 G5
West Point mt. AK U.S.A. 149 K2
West Point Lake resr U.S.A. 163 C5
Westport Canada 165 G1
Westport Ireland 61 C4
Westport N.Z. 139 C5
Westport CA U.S.A. 158 B2
Westport KY U.S.A. 164 C4
Westport NY U.S.A. 165 I1
Westray Canada 151 K4
Westray i. U.K. 60 F1
Westray Firth sea chan. U.K. 60 F1
Westree Canada 152 E5
West Rutland U.S.A. 165 I2
West Salem U.S.A. 164 D3
West Siberian Plain Rus. Fed. 76 J3
West-Skylge Neth. see West-Terschelling
West Stewartstown U.S.A. 165 J1
West-Terschelling Neth. 62 F1
West Topsham U.S.A. 165 I1
West Union IA U.S.A. 160 F3
West Union IL U.S.A. 164 B4
West Union OH U.S.A. 164 D4
West Union WV U.S.A. 164 E4
West Valley City U.S.A. 159 H1
Westville U.S.A. 164 B3
West Virginia state U.S.A. 164 E4
Westwood U.S.A. 158 C1
West Wyalong Australia 138 C4
West York U.S.A. 165 G4
Westzaan Neth. 62 E2
Wetan i. Maluku Indon. 83 D4
Wetar i. Maluku Indon. 83 C4
Wetar, Selat sea chan. Indon. 83 C5
Wetaskiwin Canada 150 H4
Wete Tanz. 123 D4
Wetter r. Germany 63 I4
Wettin Germany 63 L3
Wetumpka U.S.A. 163 C5
Wetwun Myanmar 86 B2
Wetzlar Germany 63 I4
Wevok AK U.S.A. 148 F1
Wewahitchka U.S.A. 163 C6
Wewak P.N.G. 81 K7
Wewoka U.S.A. 161 D5
Wexford Ireland 61 F5
Wexford Harbour b. Ireland 61 F5
Weyakwin Canada 151 J4
Weybridge U.K. 59 G7
Weyburn Canada 151 K5
Weyhe Germany 63 I2
Weymouth U.K. 59 E8
Weymouth U.S.A. 165 J2
Wezep Neth. 62 G2
Whakaari i. N.Z. 139 F3
Whakatane N.Z. 139 F3
Whalan Creek r. Australia 138 D2
Whale r. Canada see La Baleine, Rivière à
Whalsay i. U.K. 60 [inset]
Whampoa China see Huangpu
Whangamata N.Z. 139 E3
Whanganui National Park N.Z. 139 E4
Whangarei N.Z. 139 E2
Whapmagoostui Canada 152 F3
Wharfe r. U.K. 58 F5
Wharfedale valley U.K. 58 F4
Wharton U.S.A. 161 D6
Wharton Lake Canada 151 L1
Whatî N.W.T. Canada 149 R3
Wheatland IN U.S.A. 164 B4
Wheatland WY U.S.A. 156 G4
Wheaton IL U.S.A. 164 A3
Wheaton MN U.S.A. 160 D2
Wheaton-Glenmont U.S.A. 165 G4
Wheeler U.S.A. 161 C5
Wheeler Lake Canada 150 H2
Wheeler Lake resr U.S.A. 163 C5
Wheeler Peak NM U.S.A. 157 G5
Wheeler Peak NV U.S.A. 159 F2
Wheelersburg U.S.A. 164 D4
Wheeling U.S.A. 164 E3
Whernside hill U.K. 58 E4
Whinham, Mount Australia 135 E6
Whiskey Jack Lake Canada 151 K3
Whitburn U.K. 60 F5
Whitby Canada 165 F2
Whitby U.K. 58 G4
Whitchurch U.K. 59 E6
Whitchurch-Stouffville Canada 164 F2
White r. Canada 152 D4
White r. Canada/U.S.A. 149 M3
White r. AR U.S.A. 155 I5
White r. AR U.S.A. 161 F5
White r. CO U.S.A. 159 I1
White r. IN U.S.A. 164 B4
White r. MI U.S.A. 164 B2
White r. NV U.S.A. 159 F3
White r. SD U.S.A. 160 D3
White r. VT U.S.A. 165 I2
White watercourse U.S.A. 159 H5
White, Lake salt flat Australia 134 E5
White Bay Canada 153 K4
White Butte mt. U.S.A. 160 C2
White Canyon U.S.A. 159 H3
White Cloud U.S.A. 164 C2
Whitecourt Canada 150 H4
Whiteface Mountain U.S.A. 165 I1
Whitefield U.S.A. 165 J1
Whitefish r. N.W.T. Canada 149 P2
Whitefish U.S.A. 156 E2
Whitefish Bay U.S.A. 164 B1
Whitefish Lake Canada 151 J2
Whitefish Lake AK U.S.A. 148 I3
Whitefish Point U.S.A. 162 C2
Whitehall Ireland 61 E5
Whitehall U.K. 60 G1
Whitehall NY U.S.A. 165 I2
Whitehall WI U.S.A. 160 F2
Whitehaven U.K. 58 D4
Whitehead U.K. 61 G3
White Hill hill Canada 153 J5
Whitehill U.K. 59 G7
White Hills AK U.S.A. 149 J1

▶Whitehorse Y.T. Canada 149 N3
Capital of Yukon.

White Horse U.S.A. 159 J4
White Horse, Vale of valley U.K. 59 F7
White Horse Pass U.S.A. 159 F1
White House U.S.A. 164 B5
White Island Antarctica 188 D2
White Island N.Z. see Whakaari
White Lake Ont. Canada 152 D4
White Lake Ont. Canada 165 G1
White Lake LA U.S.A. 161 E6
White Lake MI U.S.A. 164 B2
Whitemark Australia 137 [inset]
White Mountain AK U.S.A. 148 G2
White Mountain Peak U.S.A. 158 D3
White Mountains AK U.S.A. 149 K2
White Mountains U.S.A. 165 J1
White Mountains National Park Australia 136 D4
Whitemouth Lake Canada 151 M5
Whitemud r. Canada 150 G3
White Nile r. Sudan/Uganda 108 D6
also known as Bahr el Abiad or Bahr el Jebel
White Nossob watercourse Namibia 124 D2
White Oak U.S.A. 164 D5
White Otter Lake Canada 151 N5
White Pass Canada/U.S.A. 149 N4
White Pine Range mts U.S.A. 159 F2
White Plains U.S.A. 165 I3
White River Canada 152 D4
Whiteriver U.S.A. 159 I5
White River U.S.A. 160 C3
White River Valley U.S.A. 159 F2
White Rock Peak U.S.A. 158 E2
White Russia country Europe see Belarus
Whitesail Lake Canada 150 E4
White Salmon U.S.A. 156 C3
Whitesand r. Canada 150 H2
White Sands National Monument nat. park U.S.A. 157 G6
Whitesburg U.S.A. 164 D5
White Sea Rus. Fed. 52 H2
Whitestone r. Y.T. Canada 149 M2
White Stone U.S.A. 165 G5
White Sulphur Springs MT U.S.A. 156 F3
White Sulphur Springs WV U.S.A. 164 E5
Whitesville U.S.A. 164 E5
Whiteville U.S.A. 163 E5
White Volta r. Burkina/Ghana 120 C4
also known as Nakambé or Nakanbe or Volta Blanche
Whitewater U.S.A. 159 I2
Whitewater Baldy mt. U.S.A. 159 I5
Whitewater Lake Canada 152 C4
Whitewood Australia 136 C4
Whitewood Canada 151 K5
Whitfield U.K. 59 I7
Whithorn U.K. 60 E6
Whitianga N.Z. 139 E3
Whitland U.K. 59 C7
Whitley Bay U.K. 58 F3
Whitmore Mountains Antarctica 188 K1
Whitney Canada 165 F1
Whitney, Lake TX U.S.A. 167 F2
Whitney, Mount U.S.A. 158 D3
Whitney Point U.S.A. 165 H2
Whitstable U.K. 59 I7
Whitsunday Group is Australia 136 E4
Whitsunday Island National Park Australia 136 E4
Whitsun Island Vanuatu see Pentecost Island
Whittemore U.S.A. 164 D1
Whittier AK U.S.A. 149 J3
Whittlesea Australia 138 B6
Whittlesey U.K. 59 G6
Whitton Australia 138 C5
Wholdaia Lake Canada 151 J2
Why U.S.A. 159 G5
Whyalla Australia 137 B7
Wiang Sa Thai. 86 C3
Wiarton Canada 164 E1
Wibaux U.S.A. 156 G3
Wichelen Belgium 62 D3
Wichita U.S.A. 160 D4
Wichita r. U.S.A. 161 D5
Wichita Falls U.S.A. 161 D5
Wichita Mountains U.S.A. 161 D5
Wick U.K. 60 F2
Wick r. U.K. 60 F2
Wickenburg U.S.A. 159 G5
Wickes U.S.A. 161 E5
Wickford U.K. 59 H7
Wickham r. Australia 134 E4
Wickham, Cape Australia 137 [inset]
Wickham, Mount hill Australia 134 E4
Wickliffe U.S.A. 161 F4
Wicklow Ireland 61 F5
Wicklow Head hd Ireland 61 G5
Wicklow Mountains Ireland 61 F5
Wicklow Mountains National Park Ireland 61 F4
Wide Bay AK U.S.A. 148 H4
Widerøe, Mount Antarctica 188 C2
Widerøefjellet mt. Antarctica see Widerøe, Mount
Widgeegoara watercourse Australia 138 B1
Widgiemooltha Australia 135 C7
Widi, Kepulauan is Maluku Indon. 83 D3
Widnes U.K. 58 E5
Wi-do i. S. Korea 91 B6
Wied r. Germany 63 H4
Wiehengebirge hills Germany 63 I2
Wiehl Germany 63 H4
Wielkopolskie, Pojezierze reg. Poland 57 O4
Wielkopolski Park Narodowy nat. park Poland 57 P4
Wieluń Poland 57 Q5
Wien Austria see Vienna
Wiener Neustadt Austria 57 P7
Wien Lake AK U.S.A. 149 J2
Wierden Neth. 62 G2
Wieren Germany 63 K2
Wieringerwerf Neth. 62 F2
Wiesbaden Germany 63 I4
Wiesenfelden Germany 63 M5
Wiesentheid Germany 63 K5
Wiesloch Germany 63 I5
Wiesmoor Germany 63 H1
Wietze Germany 63 J2
Wietzendorf Germany 63 J2
Wieżyca hill Poland 57 Q3
Wigan U.K. 58 E5
Wiggins U.S.A. 161 F6
Wight, Isle of i. England U.K. 59 F8
Wigierski Park Narodowy nat. park Poland 55 M9
Wignes Lake Canada 151 J2
Wigston U.K. 59 F6
Wigton U.K. 58 D4
Wigtown U.K. 60 E6
Wigtown Bay U.K. 60 E6
Wijchen Neth. 62 F3
Wijhe Neth. 62 G2
Wilberforce, Cape Australia 136 B1
Wilbur U.S.A. 156 D3
Wilburton U.S.A. 161 E5
Wilcannia Australia 138 A3
Wilcox U.S.A. 165 F3
Wilczek Land i. Rus. Fed. see Vil'cheka, Zemlya
Wildberg Germany 63 M2
Wildcat Peak U.S.A. 158 E2
Wild Coast S. Africa 125 I6
Wilderness National Park S. Africa 124 F8
Wildeshausen Germany 63 I2
Wild Horse Hill mt. U.S.A. 160 C3
Wildspitze mt. Austria 57 M7
Wildwood FL U.S.A. 163 D6
Wildwood NJ U.S.A. 165 H4
Wilge r. S. Africa 125 I4
Wilge r. S. Africa 125 I3
Wilgena Australia 135 F7

▶Wilhelm, Mount P.N.G. 81 L8
5th highest mountain in Oceania.

Wilhelm II Land reg. Antarctica see Kaiser Wilhelm II Land
Wilhelmina Gebergte mts Suriname 177 G3
Wilhelmina Kanaal canal Neth. 62 F3

Wilhelmshaven Germany 63 I1
Wilhelmstal Namibia 124 C1
Wilkes-Barre U.S.A. 165 H3
Wilkesboro U.S.A. 162 D4
Wilkes Coast Antarctica 188 G2
Wilkes Land reg. Antarctica 188 G2
Wilkie Canada 151 I4
Wilkins Coast Antarctica 188 L2
Wilkins Ice Shelf Antarctica 188 L2
Wilkinson Lakes salt flat Australia 135 F7
Will, Mount B.C. Canada 149 O4
Willand U.K. 59 D8
Willandra Billabong watercourse Australia 138 B4
Willandra National Park Australia 138 B4
Willapa Bay U.S.A. 156 B3
Willard Mex. 166 C2
Willard NM U.S.A. 157 G6
Willard OH U.S.A. 164 D3
Willcox U.S.A. 159 I5
Willcox Playa salt flat U.S.A. 159 I5
Willebadessen Germany 63 J3
Willebroek Belgium 62 E3

▶Willemstad Neth. Antilles 169 K6
Capital of the Netherlands Antilles.

Willeroo Australia 134 E3
Willette U.S.A. 164 C5
William, Mount Australia 137 C8
William Creek Australia 137 B6
William Lake Canada 151 L4
Williams AZ U.S.A. 159 G4
Williams CA U.S.A. 158 B2
Williamsburg KY U.S.A. 164 C5
Williamsburg OH U.S.A. 164 C4
Williamsburg VA U.S.A. 165 G5
Williams Lake Canada 150 F4
William Smith, Cap c. Canada 153 I1
Williamson NY U.S.A. 165 G2
Williamson WV U.S.A. 164 D5
Williamsport IN U.S.A. 164 B3
Williamsport PA U.S.A. 165 G3
Williamston U.S.A. 162 E5
Williamstown KY U.S.A. 164 C4
Williamstown NJ U.S.A. 165 H4
Willimantic U.S.A. 165 I3
Willis Group atolls Australia 136 E3
Williston S. Africa 124 E6
Williston ND U.S.A. 160 C1
Williston SC U.S.A. 163 D5
Williston Lake Canada 150 F4
Williton U.K. 59 D7
Willits U.S.A. 158 B2
Willmar U.S.A. 160 E2
Willoughby, Lake U.S.A. 165 I1
Willow AK U.S.A. 149 J3
Willow Beach U.S.A. 159 F4
Willow Bunch Canada 151 J5
Willow Creek AK U.S.A. 149 K3
Willow Hill U.S.A. 165 G3
Willow Lake Canada 150 G2
Willowlake r. Canada 150 F2
Willowmore S. Africa 124 F7
Willowra Australia 134 F5
Willows U.S.A. 158 B2
Willow Springs U.S.A. 161 F4
Willowvale S. Africa 125 I7
Wills, Lake salt flat Australia 134 E5
Wilma U.S.A. 163 C6
Wilmington DE U.S.A. 165 H4
Wilmington NC U.S.A. 163 E5
Wilmington OH U.S.A. 164 D4
Wilmore U.S.A. 164 C5
Wilmslow U.K. 58 E5
Wilno Lith. see Vilnius
Wilnsdorf Germany 63 I4
Wilpattu National Park Sri Lanka 106 D4
Wilseder Berg hill Germany 63 J1
Wilson watercourse Australia 137 C5
Wilson atoll Micronesia see Ifalik
Wilson KS U.S.A. 160 D4
Wilson NC U.S.A. 162 E5
Wilson NY U.S.A. 165 F2
Wilson, Mount CO U.S.A. 159 J3
Wilson, Mount NV U.S.A. 159 F2
Wilson, Mount OR U.S.A. 156 C3
Wilsonia U.S.A. 158 D3
Wilson's Promontory pen. Australia 138 C7
Wilson's Promontory National Park Australia 138 C7
Wilsum Germany 62 G2
Wilton r. Australia 134 F3
Wilton U.S.A. 165 J1
Wiltz Lux. 62 F5
Wiluna Australia 135 C6
Wimereux France 62 B4
Wina r. Cameroon see Vina
Winamac U.S.A. 164 B3
Winbin watercourse Australia 137 D5
Winburg S. Africa 125 H5
Wincanton U.K. 59 E7
Winchester Canada 165 H1
Winchester U.K. 59 F7
Winchester IN U.S.A. 164 C3
Winchester KY U.S.A. 164 C5
Winchester NH U.S.A. 165 I2
Winchester TN U.S.A. 163 C5
Winchester VA U.S.A. 165 F4
Wind r. Y.T. Canada 149 N2
Wind r. U.S.A. 156 F4
Windau Latvia see Ventspils
Windber U.S.A. 165 F3
Wind Cave National Park U.S.A. 160 C3
Windermere U.K. 58 E4
Windermere l. U.K. 58 E4
Windham AK U.S.A. 149 N4

▶Windhoek Namibia 124 C2
Capital of Namibia.

Windigo Lake Canada 151 N4
Windlestraw Law hill U.K. 60 G5
Wind Mountain U.S.A. 157 G6
Windom U.S.A. 160 E3
Windom Peak U.S.A. 159 J3
Windorah Australia 136 C5
Window Rock U.S.A. 159 I4
Wind Point U.S.A. 164 B2
Wind River Range mts U.S.A. 156 F4
Windrush r. U.K. 59 F7
Windsbach Germany 63 K5
Windsor Australia 138 E4
Windsor N.S. Canada 153 I5
Windsor Ont. Canada 164 D2
Windsor U.K. 59 G7
Windsor NC U.S.A. 162 E4
Windsor NY U.S.A. 165 H2
Windsor VA U.S.A. 165 G5
Windsor VT U.S.A. 165 I2
Windsor Locks U.S.A. 165 I3
Windward Islands Caribbean Sea 169 L5
Windward Passage Cuba/Haiti 169 J5
Windy U.S.A. 146 D3
Windy Fork r. AK U.S.A. 148 I3
Winefred Lake Canada 151 I4
Winfield KS U.S.A. 161 D4
Winfield WV U.S.A. 164 E4
Wingate U.K. 58 F4
Wingen Australia 138 E3
Wingene Belgium 62 D3
Wingen-sur-Moder France 63 H6
Wingham Australia 138 F3
Wingham Canada 164 E2
Wini East Timor 83 C5
Winisk r. Canada 152 D3
Winisk (abandoned) Canada 152 D3
Winisk Lake Canada 152 D3
Winkana Myanmar 86 B4
Winkelman U.S.A. 159 H5
Winkler Canada 151 L5
Winlock U.S.A. 156 C3
Winneba Ghana 120 C4
Winnebago, Lake U.S.A. 164 A1
Winnecke Creek watercourse Australia 134 E4
Winnemucca U.S.A. 158 E1
Winnemucca Lake U.S.A. 158 D1
Winner U.S.A. 160 C3
Winnett U.S.A. 156 F3
Winnfield U.S.A. 161 E6
Winnibigoshish, Lake U.S.A. 160 E2
Winnie U.S.A. 161 E6
Winning Australia 135 A5

▶Winnipeg Canada 151 L5
Capital of Manitoba.

Winnipeg r. Canada 151 L5
Winnipeg, Lake Canada 151 L5
Winnipegosis Canada 151 L5
Winnipegosis, Lake Canada 151 K4
Winnipesaukee, Lake U.S.A. 165 J2
Winnsboro LA U.S.A. 167 H1
Winona AZ U.S.A. 159 H4
Winona MN U.S.A. 160 F2
Winona MO U.S.A. 161 F4
Winona MS U.S.A. 161 F5
Winschoten Neth. 62 H1
Winsen (Aller) Germany 63 J2
Winsen (Luhe) Germany 63 K1
Winsford U.K. 58 E5
Winslow AZ U.S.A. 159 H4
Winslow ME U.S.A. 165 K1
Winsop, Tanjung pt Indon. 81 I7
Winsted U.S.A. 165 I3
Winston-Salem U.S.A. 162 D4
Winterberg Germany 63 I3
Winter Haven U.S.A. 163 D6
Winters CA U.S.A. 158 C2
Winters TX U.S.A. 161 D6
Wintersville U.S.A. 164 E3
Winterswijk Neth. 62 G3
Winterthur Switz. 66 I3
Winterton S. Africa 125 I5
Winthrop U.S.A. 165 K1
Winton Australia 136 C4
Winton N.Z. 139 B8
Winton U.S.A. 162 E4
Winwick U.K. 59 G6
Wiralaga Sumatera Indon. 84 D3
Wirral pen. U.K. 58 D5
Wirrulla Australia 137 A7
Wisbech U.K. 59 H6
Wiscasset U.S.A. 165 K1
Wisconsin r. U.S.A. 160 F3
Wisconsin state U.S.A. 164 A1
Wisconsin Rapids U.S.A. 160 F2
Wise U.S.A. 164 D5
Wiseman AK U.S.A. 149 J2
Wishaw U.K. 60 F5
Wisher U.S.A. 160 D2
Wisil Dabarow Somalia 122 E3
Wisła r. Poland see Vistula
Wismar Germany 57 M4
Wistaria Canada 150 E4
Witbank S. Africa 125 I3
Witbooisvlei Namibia 124 D3
Witham U.K. 59 H7
Witham r. U.K. 59 H6
Witherbee U.S.A. 165 I1
Withernsea U.K. 58 H5
Witherspoon, Mount AK U.S.A. 149 K3
Witjira National Park Australia 137 A5
Witmarsum Neth. 62 F1
Witney U.K. 59 F7
Witrivier S. Africa 125 J3
Witry-lès-Reims France 62 E5
Witteberg mts S. Africa 125 H6
Wittenberg Germany see Lutherstadt Wittenberg
Wittenberge Germany 63 L2
Wittenburg Germany 63 L1
Witti, Banjaran mts Malaysia 85 G1
Wittingen Germany 63 K2
Wittlich Germany 62 G5
Wittmund Germany 63 H1
Wittstock Germany 63 M1
Witu Islands P.N.G. 81 L7
Witvlei Namibia 124 D2
Witzenhausen Germany 63 J3
Wivenhoe, Lake Australia 138 F1
Władysławowo Poland 57 Q3
Włocławek Poland 57 Q4
Wobkent Uzbek. see Vobkent
Wodonga Australia 138 C6
Wœrth France 63 H6
Wohlthat Mountains Antarctica 188 C2
Woippy France 62 G5
Wōjjā atoll Marshall Is see Wotje
Wokam i. Indon. 81 I8
Woken He r. China 90 C3
Wokha India 105 H4
Woking U.K. 59 G7
Wokingham watercourse Australia 136 C4
Wokingham U.K. 59 G7
Woko National Park Australia 138 E3
Wolcott IN U.S.A. 164 B3
Wolcott NY U.S.A. 165 G2
Woldegk Germany 63 N1
Wolea atoll Micronesia see Woleai
Woleai atoll Micronesia 81 K5
Wolf r. Y.T. Canada 149 N3
Wolf r. TN U.S.A. 161 F5
Wolf r. WI U.S.A. 160 F2
Wolf Creek MT U.S.A. 156 E3
Wolf Creek OR U.S.A. 156 C4
Wolf Creek Mountain hill AK U.S.A. 148 G3
Wolf Creek Pass U.S.A. 157 G5
Wolfen Germany 63 M3
Wolfenbüttel Germany 63 K2
Wolfhagen Germany 63 J3
Wolf Lake Y.T. Canada 149 O3
Wolf Mountain AK U.S.A. 148 I2
Wolf Point U.S.A. 156 G2
Wolfsberg Austria 57 O7
Wolfsburg Germany 63 K2
Wolfstein Germany 63 H5
Wolfville Canada 153 I5
Wolgast Germany 57 N3
Wolin Poland 57 O4
Wollaston Lake Canada 151 K3
Wollaston Lake l. Canada 151 K3
Wollaston Peninsula Canada 146 G3
Wollemi National Park Australia 138 E4
Wollongong Australia 138 E5
Wolmaransstad S. Africa 125 G4
Wolmirstedt Germany 63 L2
Wolong Reserve nature res. China 96 D2
Wolowaru Flores Indon. 83 B5
Wolseley Australia 137 C8
Wolseley S. Africa 124 D7
Wolsey U.S.A. 160 D2
Wolsingham U.K. 58 F4
Wolvega Neth. 62 G2
Wolvegea Neth. see Wolvega
Wolverhampton U.K. 59 E6
Wolverine r. N.W.T. Canada 149 O1
Wolverine U.S.A. 164 C1
Wolya r. Indon. 84 A1
Womens Bay AK U.S.A. 148 I4
Wommelgem Belgium 62 E3
Womrather Höhe hill Germany 63 H5
Wonarah Australia 136 B3
Wonay, Kowtal-e Afgh. 111 H3
Wondai Australia 137 E5
Wongalarroo Lake salt l. Australia 138 B3
Wongarbon Australia 138 D4
Wong Chuk Hang H.K. China 97 [inset]
Wong Leng hill H.K. China 97 [inset]
Wong Wan Chau H.K. China see Double Island
Wŏnju S. Korea 91 B5
Wonogiri Jawa Indon. 85 E4
Wonosari Indon. 85 E4
Wonosobo Jawa Indon. 85 E4
Wonowon Canada 150 F3
Wonreli Maluku Indon. 83 C5
Wŏnsan N. Korea 91 B5
Wonthaggi Australia 138 B7
Wonyulgunna, Mount hill Australia 135 B6
Woocalla Australia 137 B6
Wood r. AK U.S.A. 149 J2
Wood, Mount Y.T. Canada 149 L3
Woodbine GA U.S.A. 163 D6
Woodbine NJ U.S.A. 165 H4
Woodbridge U.K. 59 I6
Woodbridge U.S.A. 165 G4
Wood Buffalo National Park Canada 150 H3
Woodburn U.S.A. 156 C3
Woodbury NJ U.S.A. 165 H4
Woodbury TN U.S.A. 161 G5
Woodchopper Creek AK U.S.A. 149 L2
Wooded Bluff hd Australia 138 F2
Wood Lake Canada 151 K4
Woodlake U.S.A. 158 D3
Woodland CA U.S.A. 158 C2
Woodland PA U.S.A. 165 F3
Woodland WA U.S.A. 156 C3
Woodlands Sing. 87 [inset]
Woodlark Island P.N.G. 132 F2
Woodridge Canada 151 L5
Woodroffe watercourse Australia 136 B4
Woodroffe, Mount Australia 135 E6
Woodruff UT U.S.A. 156 F4
Woodruff WI U.S.A. 160 F2
Woods, Lake salt flat Australia 134 F4
Woods, Lake of the Canada/U.S.A. 155 I2
Woodsfield U.S.A. 164 E4
Woodside Australia 138 C7
Woodstock N.B. Canada 153 I5
Woodstock Ont. Canada 164 E2
Woodstock IL U.S.A. 160 F3
Woodstock VA U.S.A. 165 F4
Woodstock VT U.S.A. 165 I2
Woodsville U.S.A. 165 I1
Woodville Canada 165 F1
Woodville MS U.S.A. 161 F6
Woodville OH U.S.A. 164 D3
Woodville TX U.S.A. 161 E6
Woodward U.S.A. 161 D4
Woody U.S.A. 158 D4
Woody Island AK U.S.A. 148 I4
Wooler U.K. 58 E3
Woolgoolga Australia 138 F3
Wooli Australia 138 F2
Woollard, Mount Antarctica 188 K1
Woollett, Lac l. Canada 152 G4
Woolyeenyer Hill hill Australia 135 C8
Woomera Australia 137 B6
Woomera Prohibited Area Australia 135 F7
Woonsocket RI U.S.A. 165 J2
Woonsocket SD U.S.A. 160 D2
Woorabinda Australia 136 E5
Wooramel r. Australia 135 A6
Wooster U.S.A. 164 E3
Worbis Germany 63 K3
Worbody Point Australia 136 C2
Worcester S. Africa 124 D7
Worcester U.K. 59 E6
Worcester MA U.S.A. 165 J2
Worcester NY U.S.A. 165 H2
Wörgl Austria 57 N7
Workai i. Indon. 81 I8
Workington U.K. 58 D4
Worksop U.K. 58 F5
Workum Neth. 62 F2
Worland U.S.A. 156 G3
Wörlitz Germany 63 M3
Wormerveer Neth. 62 E2
Worms Germany 63 I5
Worms Head hd U.K. 59 C7
Wortel Namibia 124 C2
Wörth am Rhein Germany 63 I5
Worthing U.K. 59 G8
Worthington IN U.S.A. 164 B4
Worthington MN U.S.A. 160 E3
Wosi Halmahera Indon. 83 C3
Wosu Sulawesi Indon. 83 B3
Wotje atoll Marshall Is 186 H5
Wotu Sulawesi Indon. 83 B3
Woudrichem Neth. 62 E3
Woustviller France 62 H5
Wowoni i. Indon. 83 B4
Wowoni, Selat sea chan. Indon. 83 B3
Wozrojdeniye Oroli i. Uzbek. see Vozrozhdenya Island
Wrangel Island Rus. Fed. 77 T2
Wrangell AK U.S.A. 149 N4
Wrangell, Cape AK U.S.A. 148 [inset]
Wrangell, Mount AK U.S.A. 149 K3
Wrangell Island U.S.A. 150 C3
Wrangell Mountains AK U.S.A. 148 H4
Wrangell-St Elias National Park and Preserve AK U.S.A. 149 L3
Wrath, Cape U.K. 60 D2
Wray U.S.A. 160 C3
Wreake r. U.K. 59 F6
Wreck Point S. Africa 124 C5
Wreck Reef Australia 136 F4
Wrecsam U.K. see Wrexham
Wrestedt Germany 63 K2
Wrexham U.K. 59 E5
Wright Samar Phil. 82 D4
Wrightmyo India 87 A5
Wrightson, Mount U.S.A. 157 F7
Wrightwood U.S.A. 158 E4
Wrigley N.W.T. Canada 149 Q3
Wrigley U.S.A. 164 D4
Wrigley Gulf Antarctica 188 J2
Wrocław Poland 57 P5
Września Poland 57 P4
Wu'an China see Changtai
Wu'an Hebei China 95 H4
Wubin Australia 135 B7
Wubu Shaanxi China 95 G4
Wuchagou Nei Mongol China 95 J2
Wuchang Heilong. China 90 B3
Wuchang Hubei China see Jiangxia
Wuchow China see Wuzhou
Wuchuan Guangdong China see Meilu
Wuchuan Guizhou China 96 E2
Wuchuan Nei Mongol China 95 G3
Wuda Nei Mongol China 94 F4
Wudalianchi China 90 B2
Wuḍām 'Alwā Oman 110 E6
Wudan Nei Mongol China 95 I3
Wudang Shan mt. China 97 F1
Wudao Liaoning China 95 J4
Wudaoliang Qinghai China 94 C5
Wudi Shandong China 95 I4
Wuding China 96 D3
Wuding He r. China 95 G4
Wudinna Australia 135 F8
Wufeng Hubei China 97 F2
Wufeng Yunnan China see Zhenxiong
Wufo Gansu China 94 F4
Wugang China 97 F3
Wugong Shaanxi China 95 G5
Wuhai Nei Mongol China 94 F4
Wuhan China 97 G2
Wuhe China 97 H1
Wuhu China 97 H2
Wuhua China 97 G4
Wuhubei China 97 H2
Wūjang Xizang China 99 B6
Wu Jiang r. China 96 E2
Wujin Jiangsu China see Changzhou
Wujin Sichuan China see Xinjin
Wukari Nigeria 120 D4
Wulang China 96 B2
Wuleidao Wan b. China 95 J4
Wuli Qinghai China 94 C5
Wulian Feng mts China 96 D2
Wuliang Shan mts China 96 D3
Wuliaru i. Indon. 134 E1
Wuli Jiang r. China 97 F4
Wulik r. AK U.S.A. 148 F2
Wuling Shan mts China 97 F2
Wulong China 96 E2
Wulongji China see Huaibin
Wulur Maluku Indon. 83 D4
Wumatang Xizang China 99 E7
Wumeng Shan mts China 96 D3
Wuming China 97 F4
Wümme r. Germany 63 I1
Wundwin Myanmar 86 B2
Wungda China 96 D2
Wuning China 97 G2
Wünnenberg Germany 63 I3
Wunnummin Lake Canada 147 J4
Wunsiedel Germany 63 M4
Wunstorf Germany 63 J2
Wupatki National Monument nat. park U.S.A. 159 H4
Wuping China 97 H3
Wuppertal Germany 63 H3
Wuppertal S. Africa 124 D7
Wuqi Shaanxi China 95 G4
Wuqia Xinjiang China 98 A5
Wuqia Xinjiang China 98 A5
Wuqiang Hebei China 95 H4
Wuqiao Hebei China 95 I4
Wuqing Tianjin China 95 I4
Wuquan China see Wuyang
Wuranga Australia 135 B7
Wurno Nigeria 120 D3
Würzburg Germany 63 J5
Wurzen Germany 63 M3
Wushan Chongqing China 97 F2
Wushan Gansu China 94 F5
Wu Shan mts China 97 F2
Wushi Guangdong China 97 F4
Wushi Xinjiang China 98 B4
Wüstegarten hill Germany 63 J3
Wusuli Jiang r. China/Rus. Fed. see Ussuri
Wutai Shanxi China 95 H4
Wutai Xinjiang China 98 C3
Wutaishan Shanxi China 95 H4
Wutonggou Nei Mongol China 94 D3
Wutonggou Xinjiang China 98 E4
Wutongwozi Quan well Xinjiang China 94 C3
Wuvulu Island P.N.G. 81 K7
Wuwei Gansu China 94 E4
Wuxi Chongqing China 97 F2
Wuxi Hunan China 97 F2
Wuxi Hunan China see Qiyang
Wuxi Jiangsu China 97 I2
Wuxia China see Wushan
Wuxian China see Suzhou
Wuxiang Shanxi China 95 H4
Wuxing China see Huzhou
Wuxu China 97 F4
Wuxuan China 97 F4
Wuxue China 97 G2
Wuyang Guizhou China see Zhenyuan
Wuyang Henan China 97 G1
Wuyang Shanxi China 95 H4
Wuyang Zhejiang China see Wuyi
Wuyi China 97 H2
Wuyiling China 90 C2
Wuyi Shan mts China 97 H3
Wuyuan Jiangxi China 97 H2
Wuyuan Nei Mongol China 95 G3
Wuyuan Zhejiang China see Haiyan
Wuyun China see Jinyun
Wuzhai Shanxi China 95 G4
Wuzhi Henan China 95 H5
Wuzhishan China 97 F5
Wuzhi Shan mts China 97 F5
Wuzhong Ningxia China 94 F4
Wuzhou China 97 F4
Wyalkatchem Australia 135 B7
Wyalong Australia 138 C4
Wyandra Australia 138 B1
Wyangala Reservoir Australia 138 D4
Wyara, Lake salt flat Australia 138 B2
Wycheproof Australia 138 A6
Wylliesburg U.S.A. 165 F5
Wyloo Australia 134 B5
Wylye r. U.K. 59 F7
Wymondham U.K. 59 I6
Wymore U.S.A. 160 D3
Wynbring Australia 135 F7
Wyndham Australia 134 E3
Wyndham-Werribee Australia 138 B6
Wynne U.S.A. 161 F5
Wynyard Canada 151 J5
Wyola Lake salt flat Australia 135 E7
Wyoming U.S.A. 164 C2
Wyoming state U.S.A. 156 G4
Wyoming Peak U.S.A. 156 F4
Wyoming Range mts U.S.A. 156 F4
Wyong Australia 138 E4
Wyperfeld National Park Australia 137 C7
Wysox U.S.A. 165 G3
Wyszków Poland 57 R4
Wythall U.K. 59 F6
Wytheville U.S.A. 164 E5
Wytmarsum Neth. see Witmarsum

X

Xaafuun Somalia 122 F2

▶Xaafuun, Raas pt Somalia 108 H7
Most easterly point of Africa.

Xabyai Xizang China 99 G7
Xabyaisamba China 96 C2
Xaçmaz Azer. 113 H2
Xagjang Xizang China 99 F7
Xagnag Xizang China 99 C6
Xago Xizang China 99 E7
Xagquka Xizang China 99 F7
Xaidulla Xinjiang China 99 B5
Xaignabouli Laos 86 C3
Xaignabouri Laos see Xaignabouli
Xainza Xizang China 99 E7
Xaitongmoin Xizang China 99 E7
Xai-Xai Moz. 125 K3
Xakur Xinjiang China 98 B5
Xal, Cerro de hill Mex. 167 H4
Xalapa Mex. see Jalapa
Xaltianguis Mex. 167 F5
Xamba Nei Mongol China 95 F3
Xambioá Brazil 177 I5
Xam Nua Laos 86 D2
Xá-Muteba Angola 123 B4
Xan r. Laos 86 C3
Xanagas Botswana 124 E2
Xangd Nei Mongol China 94 E3
Xangda China see Nangqên
Xangdin Hural Nei Mongol China 95 G3
Xangdoring Xizang China 99 C6
Xangongo Angola 123 B5
Xangzha Xizang China 99 F7
Xanica Mex. 167 F5
Xankändi Azer. 113 G3
Xanlar Azer. 113 G2
Xanthi Greece 69 K4
Xarag Qinghai China 94 D4
Xarardheere Somalia 122 E3
Xarba La pass Xizang China 99 D7
Xar Burd Nei Mongol China see Bayan Nuru
Xardong Xizang China 99 D7
Xar Hudag Nei Mongol China 95 H2
Xar Moron r. China 95 G3
Xar Moron r. China 95 J3
Xarru Xizang China 99 D7
Xarsingma Xizang China see Yadong
Xàtiva Spain 67 F4
Xavantes, Serra dos hills Brazil 177 I6
Xaxa Xizang China 99 C6
Xayar Xinjiang China 98 C4
Xazgat Xinjiang China 98 D3
Xcalak Mex. 167 I5
X-Can Mex. 167 I4
Xegil Xinjiang China 98 B4
Xekar Xinjiang China 98 B5
Xelva Spain see Chelva
Xenia U.S.A. 164 D4
Xênkyêr Xizang China 99 E7
Xero Potamos r. Cyprus see Xeros
Xeros r. Cyprus 107 A2
Xhora S. Africa see Elliotdale
Xia Awat Xinjiang China 98 B5
Xiabancheng Hebei China see Chengde
Xia Bazar Xinjiang China 98 B5
Xiabole Shan mt. China 90 B2
Xiachuan Dao i. China 97 G4
Xiacun Shandong China see Rushan
Xia Dawo Qinghai China 94 D5
Xiadong Gansu China 94 C3
Xiaguan China see Dali
Xiaguanying Gansu China 94 F5
Xiahe Gansu China 94 E5
Xiajiang Xizang China see Xagjang
Xiajin Shandong China 95 I4
Xiamaya Xinjiang China 94 C3
Xiamen China 97 H3
Xi'an Shaanxi China 95 G5
Xianfeng China 97 F2
Xiangcheng Henan China 95 H5
Xiangcheng Sichuan China 96 C2
Xiangcheng Yunnan China see Xiangyun
Xiangfan China 97 G1
Xiangfen Shanxi China 95 G5
Xiangfeng China see Laifeng
Xianggang H.K. China see Hong Kong
Xianggang Tebie Xingzhengqu aut. reg. China see Hong Kong
Xianggelila China 96 C3
Xiangjiang China see Huichang
Xiangkou China see Wulong
Xiangning Shanxi China 95 G5
Xiangride Qinghai China 94 D5
Xiangshan China see Menghai
Xiangshui Jiangsu China 95 I5
Xiangshuiba China 97 F3
Xiangtan China 97 G3
Xiangxiang China 97 G3
Xiangyang China see Xiangfan
Xiangyang Hu l. Xizang China 99 E6
Xiangyin China 97 G2
Xiangyun China 96 D3
Xianju China 97 I2
Xianning China 97 G2
Xiannümiao China see Jiangdu
Xianshui He r. China 96 D2
Xiantao China 97 G2
Xianxia Ling mts China 97 H3
Xianxian Hebei China 95 I4
Xianyang Shaanxi China 95 G5
Xi'anzhou Ningxia China 94 F4
Xiaoba Ningxia China see Qingtongxia
Xiaocaohu China 102 G3
Xiaochang Hebei China 95 H3
Xiaodong China 97 F4
Xiaodongliang China 96 C1
Xiao'ergou Nei Mongol China 95 J1
Xiaofan Hebei China see Wuqiang
Xiaogan China 97 G2
Xiaogang China see Dongxiang
Xiaoguai Xinjiang China 98 D3
Xiaoguan Gansu China 95 F4
Xiaohaizi Shuiku resr Xinjiang China 98 B5
Xiao Hinggan Ling mts China 90 B2
Xiaojin Gansu China 95 F5
Xiaojin China 96 D2
Xiaolangdi Shuiku resr Henan/Shanxi China 95 H5
Xiaonan Gansu China see Dongxiangzu
Xiaonanchuan Qinghai China 94 C5
Xiao Qaidam Qinghai China 99 F5
Xiaosanjiang China 97 G3
Xiaoshan China 97 I2
Xiao Shan mts China 95 G5
Xiaoshi China see Benxi
Xiao Surmang China 96 C1

Xiaotao China 97 H3
Xiaowutai Shan mt. Hebei China 95 H4
Xiaoxi China see Pinghe
Xiaoxian Anhui China 95 I5
Xiaoxiang Ling mts China 96 D2
Xiaoxita China see Yiling
Xiaoyang Shan i. China 97 I2
Xiaoyi Henan China see Gongyi
Xiaoyi Shanxi China 95 G4
Xiaoyingpan Xinjiang China 98 C3
Xiapu China 97 I3
Xiaqiong China see Batang
Xiashan China see Zhanjiang
Xiasifen Gansu China 94 E4
Xiatil Mex. 167 H5
Xiaxian Shanxi China 95 G5
Xiayang China see Yanling
Xiayanjing China see Yanjing
Xiayingpan Guizhou China see Luzhi
Xiayingpan Guizhou China see Lupanshui
Xiayukou China 97 F1
Xiazhen Shandong China see Weishan
Xiazhuang China see Linshu
Xibdê China 96 C2
Xibet Xinjiang China 98 E3
Xibing China 97 H3
Xibu China see Dongshan
Xichang China 96 D3
Xicheng Hebei China see Yangyuan
Xichou China 96 E4
Xichuan China 97 F1
Xide China 96 D2
Xidu China see Hengyang
Xiejiaji Shandong China see Qingyun
Xiemahe' China 97 F2
Xieng Khouang Laos see Phônsavan
Xiêng Lam Vietnam 86 D3
Xieyang Dao i. China 97 F4
Xifeng Gansu China see Qingyang
Xifeng Guizhou China 96 E3
Xifeng Liaoning China 90 B4
Xifengzhen Gansu China see Qingyang
Xigazê Xizang China 99 E7
Xihan Shui r. China 96 E1
Xihe Gansu China 94 F5
Xi He r. China 96 E2
Xi He watercourse China 94 E3
Xihu Gansu China 98 F4
Xihua Henan China 95 H5
Xihuachi Gansu China see Heshui
Xiji Ningxia China 94 F5
Xi Jiang r. China 97 G4
Xijian Quan well Gansu China 94 D3
Xijir Qinghai China 94 B5
Xijir Ulan Hu salt l. China 99 E6
Xijishui Gansu China 94 E4
Xil Nei Mongol China 95 H3
Xilaotou Shan mt. Nei Mongol China 95 J2
Xiliangzi Qinghai China 98 F5
Xiliao He r. China 95 J3
Xiligou Qinghai China see Ulan
Xilin China 96 E3
Xilinhot Nei Mongol China 95 I3
Xilin Qagan Obo Nei Mongol China see Qagan Obo
Ximiao Nei Mongol China 94 E3
Xin Nei Mongol China 95 G4
Xin'an Anhui China see Lai'an
Xin'an Guizhou China see Anlong
Xin'an Hebei China see Anxin
Xin'an Henan China 95 H5
Xin'anjiang China 97 H2
Xin'anjiang Shuiku resr China 97 H2
Xinavane Moz. 125 K3
Xin Barag Youqi Nei Mongol China see Altan Emel
Xin Barag Zuoqi Nei Mongol China see Amgalang
Xin Bulag Dong Nei Mongol China 95 I1
Xincai China 97 G1
Xinchang Jiangxi China see Yifeng
Xinchang Zhejiang China 97 I2
Xincheng Fujian China see Gutian
Xincheng Gansu China 94 E4
Xincheng Guangdong China see Xinxing
Xincheng Guangxi China 97 F3
Xincheng Ningxia China 94 F4
Xincheng Shanxi China see Yuanqu
Xincheng Sichuan China see Zhaojue
Xinchengbu Shaanxi China 95 G4
Xinchepaizi Xinjiang China 98 D3
Xincun China see Dongchuan
Xindi Guangxi China 97 F4
Xindi Hubei China see Honghu
Xindian Heilong. China 95 K2
Xindu Guangxi China 97 F4
Xindu Sichuan China see Luhuo
Xindu Sichuan China 96 E2
Xinduqiao China 96 D2
Xinfeng Guangdong China 97 G3
Xinfeng Jiangxi China 97 G3
Xinfengjiang Shuiku resr China 97 G4
Xing'an Guangxi China 97 F3
Xingan China 97 G3
Xing'an Shaanxi China see Ankang
Xingangzhen Liaoning China 95 J4
Xingba Xizang China 99 F7
Xingcheng Hebei China see Qianxi
Xingcheng Liaoning China 95 J3
Xingdi Xinjiang China 98 D4
Xingguo Gansu China see Qin'an
Xingguo Hubei China see Yangxin
Xingguo Jiangxi China 97 G3
Xinghai Qinghai China 94 D5
Xinghua China 97 H1
Xinghua Wan b. China 97 H3
Xingkai China 90 D3
Xingkai Hu l. China/Rus. Fed. see Khanka, Lake
Xinglong Hebei China 95 I3
Xinglong China 90 B2
Xinglongzhen Gansu China 96 E1
Xinglongzhen Heilong. China 90 B3
Xingning Guangdong China 97 G3
Xingning Hunan China 97 G3
Xingou China 97 G2
Xingping Shaanxi China 95 G5
Xingqêngoin China 96 D2
Xingren China 96 E3
Xingrenbu Ningxia China 94 F4
Xingsagoinba Qinghai China 94 E5
Xingshan Guizhou China see Majiang
Xingshan Hubei China 97 F2
Xingtai Hebei China 95 H4
Xingtang Hebei China 95 H4
Xingu r. Brazil 177 H4
Xingu, Parque Indígena do res. Brazil 177 H6
Xinguangwu Shanxi China 95 H4
Xinguara Brazil 177 H5
Xingxian Shanxi China 95 G4
Xingxingxia Xinjiang China 94 C3
Xingyang Henan China 95 H5
Xingye China 97 F4
Xingyi China 96 E3
Xinhe Hebei China 95 H4
Xinhe Xinjiang China 98 C4
Xin Hot Nei Mongol China 95 H3
Xinhua Guangdong China see Huadu
Xinhua Hunan China 97 F3
Xinhua Yunnan China see Qiaojia
Xinhua Yunnan China see Funing
Xinhuang China 97 F3
Xinhui China 97 G4
Xinhui Nei Mongol China 95 I3
Xining Qinghai China 94 E4
Xinji Hebei China 95 H4
Xinjian China 97 G2
Xinjiang Shanxi China 95 G5
Xinjiang aut. reg. China see Xinjiang Uygur Zizhiqu
Xinjiangkou China see Songzi
Xinjiang Uygur Zizhiqu aut. reg. China 94 B3
Xinjie Nei Mongol China 95 G4
Xinjie Qinghai China 96 D1
Xinjie Yunnan China 96 C3
Xinjie Yunnan China 96 D4
Xinjin Liaoning China see Pulandian
Xinjin China 96 D2
Xinjing China see Jingxi
Xinkai He r. China 95 J3
Xinling China see Badong
Xinlitun China 90 B2
Xinlong China 96 D2
Xinmi Henan China 95 H5
Xinmin China 90 B2
Xinmin Liaoning China 95 J3
Xinminzhen Shaanxi China 95 G4
Xinning Gansu China see Ningxian
Xinning Hunan China 97 F3
Xinning Jiangxi China see Wuning
Xinning Sichuan China see Kaijiang
Xinping China 96 D3
Xinqiao China 97 G1
Xinqing China 90 C2
Xinquan China 97 H3
Xinshan China see Anyuan
Xinshiba China see Ganluo
Xinsi China 96 E1
Xintai Shandong China 95 I5
Xintanpu China 97 G2
Xintian China 97 G3
Xinxian Shanxi China see Xinzhou
Xinxiang Henan China 95 H5
Xinxing China 97 G4
Xinyang Henan China 97 G1
Xinyang Henan China see Pingqiao
Xinyang Gang r. China 95 J5
Xinye China 97 G1
Xinyi Guangdong China 97 F4
Xinyi Jiangsu China 95 I5
Xinyi He r. China 95 I5
Xinying China 97 F5
Xinying Taiwan see Hsinying
Xinyu China 97 G3
Xinyuan Qinghai China see Tianjun
Xinyuan Xinjiang China 98 C4
Xinzhangfang Nei Mongol China 95 J1
Xinzheng Henan China 95 H5
Xinzhou Guangxi China see Longlin
Xinzhou Hubei China 97 G2
Xinzhou Shanxi China 89 K5
Xinzhou Shanxi China 95 H4
Xinzhu Taiwan see Hsinchu
Xinzo de Limia Spain 67 C2
Xiongshan China see Zhenghe
Xiongshi China see Guixi
Xiongzhou China see Nanxiong
Xiping Henan China 97 F1
Xiping Henan China 97 G1
Xiqing Shan mts China 94 E5
Xiqu Gansu China 94 E4
Xique Xique Brazil 177 J6
Xisa China see Xichou
Xishanzui Nei Mongol China 95 G3
Xisha Qundao is S. China Sea see Paracel Islands
Xishuangbanna reg. China 96 D4
Xishuanghe Shandong China see Kenli
Xishui Guizhou China 96 E2
Xishui Hubei China 97 G2
Xi Taijnar Hu l. Qinghai China 99 F5
Xitianmu Shan mt. China 97 H2
Xitieshan Qinghai China 94 C4
Xiugu China see Jinxi
Xi Ujimqin Qi Nei Mongol China see Bayan Ul Hot
Xiuning China 97 H2
Xiushan Chongqing China 97 F2
Xiushan Yunnan China see Tonghai
Xiushui China 97 G2
Xiuwen China 96 E3
Xiuwu Henan China 95 H5
Xiuyan Liaoning China 95 J3
Xiuyan Shaanxi China see Qingjian
Xiuying China 97 F4
Xiwanzi Hebei China see Chongli
Xiwu China 96 C1
Xixabangma Feng mt. Xizang China 99 D7
Xixia China 97 F1
Xixian Shanxi China 95 G4
Xixiang China 96 E1
Xixiu China see Anshun
Xixón Spain see Gijón-Xixón
Xiyang Shanxi China 95 H4
Xiyang Dao i. China 97 I3
Xiyang Jiang r. China 96 E3
Xiying Gansu China 94 E4
Xizang aut. reg. China see Xizang Zizhiqu
Xizang Gaoyuan plat. Xizang China see Qingzang Gaoyuan
Xizang Zizhiqu aut. reg. China 105 G3
Xizhong Dao i. China 95 J4
Xobando Xizang China 99 F7
Xoi Xizang China see Qüxü
Xo'japiryox tog'i mt. Uzbek. 111 G2
Xo'jayli Uzbek. 102 A3
Xoka Xizang China 99 F7
Xorkol Xinjiang China 98 E5
Xortang Xinjiang China 99 D5
Xuancheng China 97 H2
Xuan'en China 97 F2
Xuanhua Hebei China 95 H3
Xuân Lôc Vietnam 87 D5
Xuanwei China 96 E3
Xuanzhou China see Xuancheng
Xuchang China 97 G1
Xucheng China see Xuwen
Xuddur Somalia 122 E3
Xueba Xizang China 99 F7
Xuefeng China see Mingxi
Xuefeng Shan mts China 97 F3
Xuehua Shan hill Shanxi China 95 G5
Xuejiawan Nei Mongol China 95 G4
Xue Shan mts China 96 C3
Xugin Gol r. Qinghai China 94 C5
Xugou Jiangsu China 95 I5
Xugui Nei Mongol China 94 E3
Xugui Qinghai China 94 C5
Xuguit Qi Nei Mongol China see Yakeshi
Xujiang China see Guangchang
Xulun Hobot Qagan Qi Nei Mongol China see Qagan Nur
Xulun Hoh Qi Nei Mongol China see Dund Hot
Xümatang China 96 C1
Xunde Qundao is Paracel Is see Amphitrite Group
Xungba Xizang China see Xangdoring
Xungmai Xizang China 99 E7
Xung Qu r. Xizang China 99 F7
Xungru Xizang China 99 D7
Xunhe China 90 B2
Xun He r. China 90 C2
Xunhua Qinghai China 94 E5
Xun Jiang r. China 97 F4
Xunwu China 97 G3
Xunxian Henan China 95 H5
Xunyi Shaanxi China 95 G5
Xúquer, Riu r. Spain 67 F4
Xurgan Qinghai China 94 C5
Xuru Co salt l. China 99 D7
Xushui Hebei China 95 H4
Xuwen China 80 E2
Xuyi China 97 H1
Xuyong China 96 E2
Xuzhou Jiangsu China 95 I5

Y

Ya'an China 96 D2
Yaba Maluku Indon. 83 C3
Yabanabat Turkey see Kızılcahamam
Yabēlo Eth. 122 D3
Yablonovyy Khrebet mts Rus. Fed. 95 G1
Yabrai Shan mts China 94 E4
Yabrai Yanchang Nei Mongol China 94 E4
Yabrīn reg. Saudi Arabia 110 C6
Yabu Japan 92 A3
Yabuli China 90 C3
Yabuzukahon Japan 93 F2
Yacha China see Baisha
Yacheng China 97 F5
Yachi He r. China 96 E3
Yachimata Japan 93 G3
Yachiyo Chiba Japan 93 G3
Yachiyo Ibaraki Japan 93 F2
Yacuma r. Bol. 176 E6
Yadgir India 106 C2
Yadong Xizang China 99 E8
Yadrin Rus. Fed. 52 J5
Yaeyama-rettō is Japan 89 M8
Yafa Israel see Tel Aviv-Yafo
Yafran Libya 121 E1
Yagaba Ghana 120 C3
Yagan Nei Mongol China 94 E3
Yağda Turkey see Erdemli
Yaghan Basin sea feature S. Atlantic Ocean 184 D9
Yagi Japan 92 B3
Yagkêng Qinghai China 94 D4
Yagman Turkm. 110 D2
Yago Mex. 166 D4
Yagodnoye Rus. Fed. 77 P3
Yagodnyy Rus. Fed. 90 E2
Yagoua Cameroon 121 E3
Yagra Xizang China 99 C7
Yagradagzê Shan mt. Qinghai China 94 C5
Yaguajay Cuba 163 E8
Yaha Thai. 87 C6
Yahagi-gawa r. Japan 92 C4
Yahk Canada 150 G5
Yahualica Mex. 168 D4
Yahyalı Turkey 65 L4
Yai Myanmar see Ye
Yai, Khao mt. Thai. 87 B4
Yaita Japan 93 F2
Yaizu Japan 93 E4
Yajiang China 96 D2
Yakacık Turkey 107 C1
Yakak, Cape AK U.S.A. 149 [inset]
Yakatograk Xinjiang China 98 D5
Yake-dake vol. Japan 92 D2
Yakeshi Nei Mongol China 95 J1
Yakhab waterhole Iran 110 E3
Yakhchal Afgh. 111 G4
Yakima U.S.A. 156 C3
Yakima r. U.S.A. 156 D3
Yakmach Pak. 111 F4
Yako Burkina 120 C3
Yakovlevka Rus. Fed. 90 D3
Yakuno Japan 92 A3
Yaku-shima i. Japan 91 C7
Yakutat AK U.S.A. 149 M4
Yakutat Bay AK U.S.A. 149 L4
Yakutsk Rus. Fed. 77 N3
Yakymivka Ukr. 53 G7
Yala Thai. 87 C6
Yalai Xizang China 99 D7
Yala National Park Sri Lanka see Ruhuna National Park
Yalan Dünya Mağarası tourist site Turkey 107 A1
Yale Canada 150 F5
Yale U.S.A. 164 D2
Yalgoo Australia 135 B7
Yalkubul, Punta pt Mex. 167 H4
Yalleroi Australia 136 D5
Yaloké Cent. Afr. Rep. 122 B3
Yalova Turkey 69 M4
Yalta Ukr. 112 D1
Yalu He r. China 95 J2
Yalu Jiang r. China/N. Korea 90 B4
Yalujiang Kou r. mouth China/N. Korea 91 B5
Yalvaç Turkey 69 N5
Yamada Chiba Japan 93 G3
Yamada Toyama Japan 92 D2
Yamagata Ibaraki Japan 93 G2
Yamagata Nagano Japan 93 D2
Yamagata Japan 91 F5
Yamaguchi Nagano Japan 92 D3
Yamaguchi Japan 91 C6
Yamakita Japan 93 F3
Yamal, Poluostrov pen. Rus. Fed. see Yamal Peninsula
Yam-Alin', Khrebet mts Rus. Fed. 90 D1
Yamal Peninsula Rus. Fed. 76 H2
Yamanaka Japan 92 C2
Yamanaka-ko l. Japan 93 E3
Yamanashi Japan 93 E3
Yamanashi pref. Japan 93 E3
Yamanie Falls National Park Australia 136 D3
Yamanokako Japan 93 E3
Yamanouchi Japan 93 E2
Yamansu Xinjiang China 94 C3
Yamaoka Japan 92 D3
Yamarovka Rus. Fed. 95 G1
Yamashiro Japan 92 B4
Yamato Gifu Japan 92 C3
Yamato Ibaraki Japan 93 G2
Yamato Kanagawa Japan 93 F3
Yamato-Aogaki Kokutei-kōen park Japan 92 B4
Yamato-Kōriyama Japan 92 B4
Yamatotakada Japan 92 B4
Yamatsuri Japan 93 G2
Yamazoe Japan 92 C4
Yamba Australia 138 F2
Yamba Lake Canada 151 I1
Yambarran Range hills Australia 134 E3
Yambi, Mesa de hills Col. 176 D3
Yambio Sudan 121 F4
Yambol Bulg. 69 L3
Yamdena i. Indon. 134 E1
Yamethin Myanmar 86 B2
Y'ami i. Phil. 97 I4

▶Yamin, Puncak mt. Indon. 81 J7
4th highest mountain in Oceania.

Yamizo-san mt. Japan 93 G2
Yamkanmardi India 106 B2
Yamkhad Syria see Aleppo
Yamm Rus. Fed. 55 P7
Yamma Yamma, Lake salt flat Australia 137 C5

▶Yamoussoukro Côte d'Ivoire 120 C4
Capital of Côte d'Ivoire.

Yampa r. U.S.A. 159 I1
Yampil' Ukr. 53 F6
Yampol' Ukr. see Yampil'
Yamuna r. India 104 E4
Yamunanagar India 104 D3
Yamzho Yumco l. China 99 E7
Yana r. Rus. Fed. 77 O2
Yanam India 106 D2
Yan'an Shaanxi China 95 G4
Yanaoca Peru 176 D6
Yanaon India see Yanam
Yanaul Rus. Fed. 51 Q4
Yanbu' al Baḩr Saudi Arabia 108 E5
Yanceyville U.S.A. 162 E4
Yanchang Shaanxi China 95 G4
Yancheng Henan China 97 G1
Yancheng Jiangsu China 97 I1
Yancheng Shandong China see Qihe
Yanchep Australia 135 A7
Yanchi Ningxia China 95 F4
Yanchi Xinjiang China 94 C3
Yanchi Xinjiang China 98 D3
Yanchiwan Gansu China 98 F5
Yanchuan Shaanxi China 95 G4
Yanco Australia 138 C5
Yanco Creek r. Australia 138 B5
Yanco Glen Australia 137 C6
Yanda watercourse Australia 138 B3
Yandama Creek watercourse Australia 137 C6
Yandao China see Yingjing
Yandoon Myanmar 86 A3
Yandrakinot Rus. Fed. 148 D2
Yandun Xinjiang China 94 C3
Yanfolila Mali 120 C3
Ya'ngamdo Xizang China 99 F7
Ya'ngamdo Xizang China 99 F7
Yangbajain Xizang China 99 E7
Yangbi China 96 C3
Yangcheng Guangdong China see Yangshan
Yangcheng Shanxi China 95 H5
Yangchuan China see Suiyang
Yangchun China 97 F4
Yangcun China 97 G4
Yangcun Tianjin China see Wuqing
Yangdaxkak Xinjiang China 98 E5
Yangdok N. Korea 91 B5
Yanggao Shanxi China 95 H3
Yanggu Shandong China 95 H4
Yanghe Ningxia China see Yongning
Yang Hu l. Xizang China 99 D6
Yangi Davan pass Aksai Chin/China 99 B6
Yangi Nishon Uzbek. 111 G2
Yangi Qal'ah Afgh. 111 H2
Yangiqishloq Uzbek. 102 C3
Yangirabot Uzbek. 111 G1
Yangiyo'l Uzbek. 102 C3
Yangjiajiang China 97 G2
Yangjialing Shaanxi China 95 G4
Yangjiang China 97 F4
Yangjiaogou Shandong China 95 I4
Yangming China see Heping
Yangôn Myanmar see Rangoon
Yangping China 97 F2
Yangquan Shanxi China 95 H4
Yangquangu Shanxi China 95 G4
Yangshan China 97 G3
Yang Talat Thai. 86 C3
Yangtouyan China 96 D3
Yangtze r. Qinghai China see Tongtian He
Yangtze r. China 96 E2
Also known as Chang Jiang, Jinsha Jiang, Tongtian He, Yangtze Kiang or Zhi Qu.
Yangtze Kiang r. China see Yangtze
Yanguan Gansu China 94 F5
Yangudi Rassa National Park Eth. 122 E2
Yangweigang Jiangsu China 95 I5
Yangxi China 97 F4
Yangxian China 96 E1
Yangxin China 97 G2
Yangyang S. Korea 91 C5
Yangyuan Hebei China 95 H3
Yangzhou Jiangsu China 97 H1
Yangzhou Shaanxi China see Yangxian
Yanhe China 97 F2
Yanhu Xinjiang China 98 E4
Yanhu Xizang China 99 C6
Yanhuqu China 105 E2
Yanishpole Rus. Fed. 52 G3
Yanis''yarvi, Ozero l. Rus. Fed. 54 Q5
Yanji China 90 C4
Yanjiang China see Ziyang
Yanjin Henan China 95 H5
Yanjin Yunnan China 96 E2
Yanjing Sichuan China see Yanyuan
Yanjing Xizang China 96 C2
Yanjing Yunnan China see Yanjin
Yankara National Park Nigeria 120 E4
Yankton U.S.A. 160 D3
Yanling Henan China 95 H5
Yanling Hunan China 97 G3
Yanling Sichuan China see Weiyuan
Yannina Greece see Ioannina
Yano-Indigirskaya Nizmennost' lowland Rus. Fed. 77 P2
Yanomami, Parque Indígena res. Brazil 176 F3
Yanovski, Mount AK U.S.A. 149 N4
Yanqi Xinjiang China 98 D4
Yanqing Beijing China 95 H3
Yanrey r. Australia 135 A5
Yanshan Hebei China 95 I4
Yanshan Jiangxi China 97 H2
Yanshan Yunnan China 96 E4
Yan Shan mts China 95 I3
Yanshi Henan China 95 H5
Yanshiping Qinghai China 99 F6
Yanskiy Zaliv g. Rus. Fed. 77 O2
Yantabulla Australia 138 B2
Yantai Shandong China 95 J4
Yanting China 96 E2
Yantongshan China 90 B4
Yantou China 97 I2
Yanwa China 96 C3
Yany-Kurgan Kazakh. see Zhanakorgan
Yanyuan China 96 D3
Yanzhou Shandong China 95 I5
Yao Chad 121 E3
Yao Japan 92 B4
Yao'an China 96 D3
Yaodian Shaanxi China 95 G4
Yaodu China see Dongzhi
Yaojie Gansu China see Honggu
Yaoli China 97 H2
Yaoquanzi Gansu China 94 D4
Yaotsu Japan 92 D3

▶Yaoundé Cameroon 120 E4
Capital of Cameroon.

Yaoxian Shaanxi China see Yaozhou
Yaoxiaoling China 90 B2
Yao Yai, Ko i. Thai. 87 B6
Yaozhen Shaanxi China 95 G4
Yaozhou Shaanxi China 95 G5
Yap i. Micronesia 81 J5
Yapen i. Indon. 81 J7
Yappar r. Australia 136 C3
Yap Trench sea feature N. Pacific Ocean 186 F5
Yaqui r. Mex. 166 C3
Yar Rus. Fed. 52 L4
Yaradzha Turkm. see Ýarajy
Ýarajy Turkm. 110 E2
Yaraka Australia 136 D5
Yarangüme Turkey see Tavas
Yaransk Rus. Fed. 52 J4
Yardea Australia 137 A7
Yardımcı Burnu pt Turkey 69 N6
Yardımlı Azer. 113 H3
Yardoi Xizang China 99 E7
Yardymly Azer. see Yardımlı
Yare r. U.K. 59 I6
Yarega Rus. Fed. 52 L3

▶Yaren Nauru 133 G2
Capital of Nauru.

Yarensk Rus. Fed. 52 K3
Yariga-take mt. Japan 92 D2
Yarīm Yemen 108 F7
Yarımca Turkey see Körfez
Yarkand Xinjiang China see Shache
Yarkant Xinjiang China see Shache
Yarkant He r. China 99 B5
Yarker Canada 165 G1
Yarkhun r. Pak. 111 I2
Yarlung Zangbo r. China 99 F7 see Brahmaputra
Yarmouth Canada 153 I6
Yarmouth England U.K. 59 F8
Yarmouth England U.K. see Great Yarmouth
Yarmouth U.S.A. 165 J2
Yarmuk r. Asia 107 B3
Yarnell U.S.A. 159 G4
Yaroslavl' Rus. Fed. 52 H4
Yaroslavskiy Rus. Fed. 90 D3
Yarra r. Australia 138 B6
Yarra Junction Australia 138 B6
Yarram Australia 138 C7
Yarraman Australia 138 E1
Yarrawonga Australia 138 B6
Yarra Yarra Lakes salt flat Australia 135 A7
Yarronvale Australia 138 B1
Yarrowmere Australia 136 D4
Yartö Tra La pass China 105 H3
Yartsevo Krasnoyarskiy Kray Rus. Fed. 76 J3
Yartsevo Smolenskaya Oblast' Rus. Fed. 53 G5
Yaru r. China 99 D7
Yarumal Col. 176 C2
Yaruu Mongolia 94 D1
Yarwa China 96 C2
Yarzhong China 96 C2
Yaş Romania see Iaşi
Yasaka Kyōto Japan 92 B3
Yasaka Nagano Japan 93 D2
Yasato Japan 93 G2
Yasawa Group is Fiji 133 H3
Yashilkŭl l. Tajik. 111 I2
Yashira Japan 93 F2
Yashiro Japan 92 A4
Yashkul' Rus. Fed. 53 J7
Yasin Pak. 104 C1
Yasnogorsk Rus. Fed. 53 H5
Yasnyy Rus. Fed. 90 C1
Yasothon Thai. 86 D4
Yass Australia 138 D5
Yass r. Australia 138 D5
Yassı Burnu c. Cyprus see Plakoti, Cape
Yasu Japan 92 C3
Yāsūj Iran 110 C4
Yasuní, Parque Nacional nat. park Ecuador 176 C4
Yasuoka Japan 93 D3
Yasuzuka Japan 93 E1
Yatağan Turkey 69 M6
Yaté New Caledonia 133 G4
Yates r. Canada 150 H2
Yates Center U.S.A. 160 E4
Yathkyed Lake Canada 151 L2
Yatomi Japan 92 C3
Yatou Shandong China see Rongcheng
Yatsuga-take vol. Japan 93 E3
Yatsuga-take-Chūshin-kōgen Kokutei-kōen park Japan 93 E2
Yatsuo Japan 92 D2
Yatsushiro Japan 91 C6
Yaṭṭa West Bank 107 B4
Yatton U.K. 59 E7
Yauca Peru 176 D7
Yau Tong b. H.K. China 97 [inset]
Yauyupe Hond. 166 [inset] I6
Yavan Tajik. see Yovon
Yavari r. Brazil/Peru 176 E4
also known as Javari (Brazil/Peru)
Yávaros Mex. 166 C3
Yavatmal India 106 C1
Yavi Turkey 113 F3
Yaví, Cerro mt. Venez. 176 E2
Yavoriv Ukr. 53 D6
Yavuzlu Turkey 107 C1
Yawata Japan 92 B4
Yawatongguz He r. China 99 C5
Yawatongguzlangar Xinjiang China 99 C5
Yaw Chaung r. Myanmar 96 B4
Yaxchilan tourist site Guat. 167 H5
Yaxian China see Sanya
Yay Myanmar see Ye
Yayladağı Turkey 107 C2
Yazd Iran 110 D4
Yazdān Iran 111 F3
Yazd-e Khvāst Iran 110 D4
Yazıhan Turkey 112 E3
Yazoo r. MS U.S.A. 167 H1
Yazoo City U.S.A. 161 F5
Yazukami Japan 93 G2
Y Bala U.K. see Bala
Yding Skovhøj hill Denmark 57 L3
Ydra i. Greece 69 J6

Y Drenewydd U.K. see Newtown
Ye Myanmar 86 B4
Yea Australia 138 B6
Yealmpton U.K. 59 D8
Yebaishou Liaoning China see Jianping
Yebawmi Myanmar 86 A1
Yebbi-Bou Chad 121 E2
Yecheng Xinjiang China 99 B5
Yécora Mex. 166 C2
Yedashe Myanmar 86 B3
Yedatore India 106 C3
Yedi Burun Başı pt Turkey 69 M6
Yeeda River Australia 134 C4
Yefremov Rus. Fed. 53 H5
Yêgainnyin Qinghai China see Henan
Yeghegnadzor Armenia 113 G3
Yegindybulak Kazakh. 98 B2
Yegindykol' Kazakh. 102 C1
Yegorlykskaya Rus. Fed. 53 I7
Yegorova, Mys pt Rus. Fed. 90 E3
Yegor'yevsk Rus. Fed. 53 H5
Yei Sudan 121 G4
Yei r. Sudan 121 G4
Yeji China 97 G2
Yejiaji China see Yeji
Yekaterinburg Rus. Fed. 76 H4
Yekaterinodar Rus. Fed. see Krasnodar
Yekaterinoslav Ukr. see Dnipropetrovs'k
Yekaterinoslavka Rus. Fed. 90 C2
Yekhegnadzor Armenia see Yeghegnadzor
Ye Kyun i. Myanmar 86 A3
Yelabuga Khabarovskiy Kray Rus. Fed. 90 D2
Yelabuga Respublika Tatarstan Rus. Fed. 52 K5
Yelan' Rus. Fed. 53 I6
Yelan' r. Rus. Fed. 53 I6
Yelandur India 106 C3
Yelantsy Rus. Fed. 88 J2
Yelarbon Australia 138 E2
Yelbarsli Turkm. 111 F2
Yelenovskiye Kar'yery Ukr. see Dokuchayevs'k
Yelets Rus. Fed. 53 H5
Yeliguan Gansu China 94 E5
Yélimané Mali 120 B3
Yelizavetgrad Ukr. see Kirovohrad
Yelkhovka Rus. Fed. 53 K5
Yell i. U.K. 60 [inset]
Yellabina Regional Reserve nature res. Australia 135 F7
Yellandu India 106 D2
Yellapur India 106 B3
Yellowhead Pass Canada 150 G4

▶Yellowknife Canada 150 H2
Capital of the Northwest Territories.

Yellowknife r. Canada 150 H2
Yellow Mountain hill Australia 138 C4

▶Yellow r. China
4th longest river in Asia, and 7th in the world

Yellow Sea N. Pacific Ocean 89 N5
Yellowstone r. U.S.A. 160 C2
Yellowstone Lake U.S.A. 156 F3
Yellowstone National Park U.S.A. 156 F3
Yell Sound strait U.K. 60 [inset]
Yeloten Turkm. see Ýolöten
Yelovo Rus. Fed. 51 Q4
Yel'sk Belarus 53 F6
Yel'tay Kazakh. 98 C3
Yelucá mt. Nicaragua 166 [inset] I6
Yelva r. Rus. Fed. 52 K3
Yema Nanshan mts China 94 C4
Yema Shan mts China 94 C4
Yematan Qinghai China 94 D4
Yematan Qinghai China 94 D5
Yemen country Asia 108 G6
Yemetsk Rus. Fed. 52 I3
Yemişenbükü Turkey see Taşova
Yemmiganur India see Emmiganuru
Yemtsa Rus. Fed. 52 I3
Yemva Rus. Fed. 52 K3
Yena Rus. Fed. 54 Q3
Yenagoa Nigeria 120 D4
Yenakiyeve Ukr. 53 H6
Yenakiyevo Ukr. see Yenakiyeve
Yenangyat Myanmar 86 A2
Yenangyaung Myanmar 86 A2
Yenanma Myanmar 86 A3
Yenda Australia 138 C5
Yêndum China see Zhag'yab
Yengisar Xinjiang China 98 B5
Yengisar Xinjiang China 98 D4
Yengisu Xinjiang China 98 D4
Yengo National Park Australia 138 E4
Yenice Turkey 69 L5
Yenidamlar Turkey see Demirtaş
Yenihan Turkey see Yıldızeli
Yenije-i-Vardar Greece see Giannitsa
Yenişehir Greece see Larisa
Yenişehir Turkey 69 M4

▶Yenisey r. Rus. Fed. 76 J2
Part of the Yenisey-Angara-Selenga, 3rd longest river in Asia.

▶Yenisey-Angara-Selenga r. Rus. Fed. 76 J2
3rd longest river in Asia, and 6th in the world.

Yeniseysk Rus. Fed. 76 K4
Yeniseyskiy Kryazh ridge Rus. Fed. 76 K4
Yeniseyskiy Zaliv inlet Rus. Fed. 189 F2
Yeniugou Qinghai China 94 D4
Yeniugou Qinghai China 94 D5
Yeniyol Turkey see Borçka
Yên Minh Vietnam 86 D2
Yenotayevka Rus. Fed. 53 J7
Yentna r. AK U.S.A. 149 J3
Yeola India 106 B1
Yeo Lake salt flat Australia 135 D6
Yeotmal India see Yavatmal
Yeoval Australia 138 D4
Yeovil U.K. 59 E8
Yeo Yeo r. Australia see Bland
Yepachi Mex. 166 C2
Yeppoon Australia 136 E4
Yeraliyev Kazakh. see Kuryk
Yerbabuena Mex. 167 E4
Yerbent Turkm. 110 E2
Yerbogachen Rus. Fed. 77 L3
Yercaud India 106 C4

▶Yerevan Armenia 113 G2
Capital of Armenia.

Yereymentau Kazakh. 102 D1
Yergara India 106 C2
Yergeni hills Rus. Fed. 53 J7
Yergoğu Romania see Giurgiu
Yeriho West Bank see Jericho
Yerilla Australia 135 C7
Yerington U.S.A. 158 D2
Yerköy Turkey 112 D3
Yerla r. India 106 B2
Yermak Kazakh. see Aksu
Yermakovo Rus. Fed. 90 B1
Yermak Plateau sea feature Arctic Ocean 189 H1
Yermentau Kazakh. see Yereymentau
Yermo Mex. 166 D3
Yermo U.S.A. 158 E4
Yerofey Pavlovich Rus. Fed. 90 A1
Yerres r. France 62 C6
Yersa r. Rus. Fed. 52 L2
Yershov Rus. Fed. 53 K6
Yertsevo Rus. Fed. 52 I3
Yeruḥam Israel 107 B4
Yerupaja mt. Peru 176 C6
Yerushalayim Israel/West Bank see Jerusalem
Yeruslan r. Rus. Fed. 53 J6
Yesagyo Myanmar 86 A2
Yesan S. Korea 91 B5
Yesik Kazakh. 98 B4
Yesil' Kazakh. 100 F1
Yeşilhisar Turkey 112 D3
Yeşilırmak r. Turkey 112 E2
Yeşilova Burdur Turkey 69 M6
Yeşilova Yozgat Turkey see Sorgun
Yessentuki Rus. Fed. 113 F1
Yessey Rus. Fed. 77 L3
Yes Tor hill U.K. 59 C8
Yêtatang Xizang China see Baqên
Yetman Australia 138 E2
Ye-U Myanmar 86 A2
Yeu, Île d' i. France 66 C3
Yevdokimovskoye Rus. Fed. see Krasnogvardeyskoye
Yevlakh Azer. see Yevlax
Yevlax Azer. 113 G2
Yevpatoriya Ukr. 112 D1
Yevreyskaya Avtonomnaya Oblast' admin. div. Rus. Fed. 90 D2
Yexian Shandong China see Laizhou
Yeygen'yevka Kazakh. 98 B4
Yeyik Xinjiang China 99 C5
Yeysk Rus. Fed. 53 H7
Yeyungou Xinjiang China 98 D4
Yezhou China see Jianshi
Yezhuga r. Rus. Fed. 52 J2
Yezo i. Japan see Hokkaidō
Yezyaryshcha Belarus 52 F5
Y Fenni U.K. see Abergavenny
Y Fflint U.K. see Flint
Y Gelli Gandryll U.K. see Hay-on-Wye
Yialí i. Greece see Gyali
Yi'allaq, Gebel mt. Egypt see Yu'alliq, Jabal
Yialousa Cyprus see Aigialousa
Yi'an China 90 B3
Yianisádha i. Greece see Gianisada
Yianisádha i. Kriti Greece see Gianisada
Yiannitsá Greece see Giannitsa
Yibin Sichuan China 96 E2
Yibin Sichuan China 96 E2
Yibug Caka salt l. China 99 D6
Yichang Hubei China 97 F2
Yicheng Henan China see Zhumadian
Yicheng Hubei China 97 G2
Yicheng Shanxi China 95 G5
Yichuan Henan China 95 H5
Yichuan Shaanxi China 95 G5
Yichun Heilong. China 90 C3
Yichun Jiangxi China 97 G3
Yidu China see Zhicheng
Yidu Shandong China see Qingzhou
Yidun China 96 C2
Yifeng China 97 G2
Yiggêtang Qinghai China see Sêrwolungwa
Yiggêtang Qinghai China 94 D5
Yihatuoli Gansu China 94 D3
Yi He r. Henan China 95 H5
Yi He r. Shandong China 95 I5
Yihuang China 97 H3
Yijun Shaanxi China 95 G5
Yilaha Heilong. China 95 K1
Yilan China 90 C3
Yilan Taiwan see Ilan
Yıldız Dağları mts Turkey 69 L4
Yıldızeli Turkey 112 E3
Yilehuli Shan mts China 90 A2
Yiliang China 96 E3
Yiling Hubei China 97 F2
Yiliping Qinghai China 99 F5
Yilong Heilong. China 90 B3
Yilong Sichuan China 96 E2
Yilong Yunnan China see Shiping
Yilong Hu l. China 96 D4
Yimatu He r. China 95 I3
Yimianpo China 90 C3
Yimin He r. China 95 I1
Yinan Shandong China 95 I5
Yinbaing Myanmar 86 B3
Yincheng China see Dexing
Yinchuan Ningxia China 94 F4
Yindarlgooda, Lake salt flat Australia 135 C7
Yingcheng China 97 G2
Yingde China 97 G3
Yinggehai China 97 F5
Yinggen China see Qiongzhong
Ying He r. China 97 H1
Yingjing China 96 D2
Yingkou Liaoning China 95 J3
Yingkou Liaoning China see Dashiqiao
Yingpanshui Ningxia China 94 F4
Yingshan China 97 G2
Yingtan China 97 H2
Yingtaoyuan Shandong China 95 H5
Yingxian Shanxi China 95 H4
Yining Jiangxi China see Xiushui
Yining Xinjiang China 98 C4
Yining Xinjiang China 98 C4
Yinjiang China 97 F3
Yinkeng China see Yinkengxu
Yinkengxu China 97 G3
Yinmabin Myanmar 86 A2
Yinnyein Myanmar 86 B3
Yin Shan mts China 95 G3
Yinxian China see Ningbo
Yi'ong Nongchang Xizang China 99 F7
Yi'ong Zangbo r. Xizang China 99 F7
Yipinglang China 96 D3
Yiquan China see Meitan
Yiran Co l. Qinghai China 99 F6
Yirga Alem Eth. 122 D3
Yirol Sudan 121 G4
Yirshi Nei Mongol China 95 I2
Yirtkuq Bulak spring Xinjiang China 98 E4
Yirxie Nei Mongol China see Yirshi
Yisa China see Honghe
Yishan Guangxi China see Yizhou
Yishan Jiangsu China see Guanyun
Yi Shan mt. Shandong China 95 I4
Yishui Shandong China 95 I5
Yishun Sing. 87 [inset]
Yíthion Greece see Gytheio
Yitiaoshan Gansu China see Jingtai
Yitong He r. China 90 B3
Yi Tu, Nam r. Myanmar 86 B2
Yitulihe Nei Mongol China 95 J1
Yiwanquan Xinjiang China 94 C3
Yiwu Xinjiang China 94 C3
Yiwu China 96 D4
Yiwulü Shan mts China 95 J3
Yixian Liaoning China 95 J3
Yixing China 97 H2
Yiyang China 97 G2
Yiyuan Shandong China 95 I4
Yizheng China 97 H1
Yizhou China 97 F3
Yizhou Liaoning China see Yixian
Yizra'el country Asia see Israel
Yläne Fin. 55 M6
Ylihärmä Fin. 54 M5
Yli-Ii Fin. 54 N4
Yli-Kärppä Fin. 54 N4
Ylikiiminki Fin. 54 O4
Yli-Kitka l. Fin. 54 P3
Ylistaro Fin. 54 M5
Ylitornio Fin. 54 M3
Ylivieska Fin. 54 N4
Ylöjärvi Fin. 55 M6
Ymer Ø i. Greenland 147 P2
Ynys Enlli i. U.K. see Bardsey Island
Ynys Môn i. U.K. see Anglesey
Yoakum U.S.A. 161 D6
Yoder U.S.A. 164 C3
Yodo-gawa r. Japan 92 B4
Yogan, Cerro mt. Chile 178 B8
Yogo Japan 92 C3
Yogyakarta Indon. 85 E4
Yogyakarta admin. dist. Indon. 85 E5
Yoho National Park Canada 150 G5
Yoigilanglêb r. Qinghai China 99 G6
Yojoa, Lago de l. Hond. 166 [inset] I6
Yōka Japan 92 A3
Yokadouma Cameroon 121 E4
Yōkaichi Japan 92 C3
Yōkaichiba Japan 93 G3
Yokawa Japan 92 B4
Yokkaichi Japan 92 C4
Yoko Cameroon 120 E4
Yokohama Kanagawa Japan 93 F3
Yokokawa Japan 93 E2
Yokoshiba Japan 93 G3
Yokosuka Japan 93 F3
Yokote Japan 91 F5
Yokoze Japan 93 F3
Yola Nigeria 120 E4
Yolaina, Cordillera de mts Nicaragua 166 [inset] I7
Yolo U.S.A. 158 C2
Yolombo Dem. Rep. Congo 122 C4
Ýolöten Turkm. 111 F2
Yoloxóchitl Mex. 167 F5
Yoluk Mex. 167 I4
Yom, Mae Nam r. Thai. 86 C4
Yomou Guinea 120 C4
Yomuka Indon. 81 J8
Yonaguni-jima i. Japan 97 I3
Yŏnan N. Korea 91 B5
Yonezawa Japan 91 F5
Yong'an Chongqing China see Fengjie
Yong'an Fujian China 97 H3
Yongbei China see Yongsheng
Yongchang Gansu China 94 E4
Yongcheng Henan China 95 I5
Yongcong China 97 F3
Yongdeng Gansu China 94 E4
Yongding Fujian China 97 H3
Yongding Yunnan China see Yongren
Yongding Yunnan China see Fumin
Yongding He r. China 95 I4
Yongfeng China 97 G3
Yongfengqu Xinjiang China 98 D4
Yongfu China 97 F3
Yonghe Shanxi China 95 G4
Yŏnghŭng N. Korea 91 B5
Yŏnghŭng-man b. N. Korea 91 B5
Yŏngil-man b. S. Korea 91 C6
Yongjing Gansu China 94 E5
Yongjing Guizhou China see Xifeng
Yongjing Liaoning China see Xifeng
Yongjin Qu r. China see Foping
Yŏngju S. Korea 91 C5
Yongkang Yunnan China 96 C3
Yongkang Zhejiang China 97 I2
Yongle China see Zhen'an
Yongnian Hebei China 95 H4
Yongning Guangxi China 97 F4
Yongning Jiangxi China see Tonggu
Yongning Ningxia China 94 F4
Yongning Sichuan China see Xuyong
Yongping China 96 C3
Yongqing Gansu China see Qingshui
Yongren China 96 D3
Yongsheng China 96 D3
Yongshou Shaanxi China 95 G5
Yongshun China 97 F2
Yongtai China 97 H3
Yongxi China see Nayong
Yongxing Hunan China 97 G3
Yongxing Jiangxi China 97 G3
Yongxing Shaanxi China 95 G4
Yongxiu China 97 G2
Yongyang China see Weng'an
Yongzhou China 97 F3
Yonkers U.S.A. 165 I3
Yopal Col. 176 D2
Yopurga Xinjiang China 98 B5
Yoquivo Mex. 166 D3
Yordu India 104 C2
Yorii Japan 93 F2
York Australia 135 B7
York Canada 164 F2
York U.K. 58 F5
York AL U.S.A. 161 F5
York NE U.S.A. 160 D3
York PA U.S.A. 165 G4
York, Cape Australia 136 C1
York, Kap c. Greenland see Innaanganeq
York, Vale of valley U.K. 58 F4
Yorke Peninsula Australia 137 B7
York Mountains AK U.S.A. 148 F2
Yorkshire Dales National Park U.K. 58 E4
Yorkshire Wolds hills U.K. 58 G5
Yorkton Canada 151 K5
Yorktown U.S.A. 165 G5
Yorkville U.S.A. 160 F3
Yoro Hond. 166 [inset] I6
Yōrō Japan 92 C3
Yoroi-zaki pt Japan 92 C4
Yoronga i. Maluku Indon. 83 D3
Yöröö Gol r. Mongolia 94 F1
Yorosso Mali 120 C3
Yosemite U.S.A. 164 C5
Yosemite National Park U.S.A. 158 D3
Yoshida Saitama Japan 93 F2
Yoshida Shizuoka Japan 93 E4
Yoshii Gunma Japan 93 E2
Yoshima Japan 93 G1
Yoshino Japan 92 B4
Yoshinodani Japan 92 C2
Yoshino-gawa r. Japan 92 B4
Yoshino-Kumano Kokuritsu-kōen nat. park Japan 92 C5
Yoshkar-Ola Rus. Fed. 52 J4
Yösöndzüyl Mongolia 94 E2
Yos Sudarso i. Indon. see Dolok, Pulau
Yŏsu S. Korea 91 B6
Yotsukaidō Japan 93 G3
Yotsukura Japan 93 G1
Yotvata Israel 107 B5
Youbou Canada 150 E5
Youdunzi Qinghai China 99 E5
Youghal Ireland 61 E6
Youlin Shandong China 95 I4
Young Australia 138 D5
Young U.S.A. 159 H4
Younghusband, Lake salt flat Australia 137 B6
Younghusband Peninsula Australia 137 B7
Young Island Antarctica 188 H2
Youngstown Canada 151 I5
Youngstown U.S.A. 164 E3
Youshashan Qinghai China 99 E5
You Shui r. China 97 F2
Youssoufia Morocco 64 C5
Youvarou Mali 120 C3
Youxi China 97 H3
Youxian China 97 G3
Youyang China 97 F2
Youyi China 90 C3
Youyi Feng mt. China/Rus. Fed. 98 D2
Yovon Tajik. 111 H2
Yowah watercourse Australia 138 B2
Yozgat Turkey 112 D3
Ypres Belgium see Ieper
Yreka U.S.A. 156 C4
Yrghyz Kazakh. see Irgiz
Yr Wyddfa mt. U.K. see Snowdon
Yser r. France 62 C4
also known as IJzer (Belgium)
Ysselsteyn Neth. 62 F3
Ystad Sweden 55 H9
Ystwyth r. U.K. 59 C6
Ysyk-Ata Kyrg. 98 A4
Ysyk-Köl Kyrg. see Balykchy
Ysyk-Köl admin. div. Kyrg. 98 B4

▶Ysyk-Köl salt l. Kyrg. 102 E3
5th largest lake in Asia.

Ythan r. U.K. 60 G3
Y Trallwng U.K. see Welshpool
Ytyk-Kyuyel' Rus. Fed. 77 O3
Yu i. Maluku Indon. 83 D3
Yu'alliq, Jabal mt. Egypt 107 A4
Yuan'an China 97 F2
Yuanbaoshan Nei Mongol China 95 I3
Yuanbao Shan mt. China 97 F3
Yuanjiang Hunan China 97 G2
Yuanjiang Yunnan China 96 D4
Yuan Jiang r. Hunan China 97 F2
Yuan Jiang r. Yunnan China 96 D4
Yuanjiazhuang China see Foping
Yuanlin Nei Mongol China 95 J1
Yuanling China 97 F2
Yuanma China see Yuanmou
Yuanmou China 96 D3
Yuanping Shanxi China 95 H4
Yuanqu Shanxi China 95 G5
Yuanquan Gansu China see Anxi
Yuanshan China see Lianping
Yuanshanzi Gansu China 94 D4
Yuanyang China see Xinjie
Yuasa Japan 92 B4
Yub'ā i. Saudi Arabia 112 D6
Yuba City U.S.A. 158 C2
Yubei China 96 E2
Yuben' Tajik. 111 I2
Yucatán pen. Mex. 167 H5
Yucatán state Mex. 167 H4
Yucatan Channel Cuba/Mex. 167 I4
Yucca U.S.A. 159 F4
Yucca Lake U.S.A. 158 E3
Yucca Valley U.S.A. 158 E4
Yucheng Henan China 95 H5
Yucheng Shandong China 95 I4
Yucheng Sichuan China see Ya'an
Yuci Shanxi China see Jinzhong
Yudi Shan mt. China 90 A1
Yudu China 97 G3
Yuelai China see Huachuan
Yueliang Pao l. China 95 J2
Yuendumu Australia 134 E5
Yuen Long H.K. China 97 [inset]
Yueqing China 97 I2
Yuexi China 97 H2
Yueyang Hunan China 97 G2
Yueyang Hunan China 97 G2
Yueyang Sichuan China see Anyue
Yug r. Rus. Fed. 52 J3
Yugan China 97 H2
Yugawara Japan 93 F3
Yuge Qinghai China 99 F6
Yugorsk Rus. Fed. 51 S3

▶Yugoslavia
Former European country. Up to 1993 included Bosnia-Herzegovina, Croatia, Macedonia and Slovenia. Renamed as Serbia and Montenegro in 2003. Serbia and Montenegro became separate independent countries in June 2006. Kosovo declared independence from Serbia in February 2008.

Yuhang China 97 I2
Yuhu China see Eryuan
Yuhuan China 97 I2
Yuhuang Ding mt. Shandong China 95 I4
Yui Japan 93 E3
Yuin Australia 135 B6
Yu Jiang r. China 97 F4
Yukagirskoye Ploskogor'ye plat. Rus. Fed. 77 Q3
Yukamenskoye Rus. Fed. 52 L4
Yukarı Sakarya Ovaları plain Turkey 69 N5
Yukarısarıkaya Turkey 112 D3
Yūki Japan 93 F2
Yuki r. AK U.S.A. 148 H2
Yukon admin. div. Canada 149 N3

▶Yukon r. Canada/U.S.A. 148 F3
5th longest river in North America.

Yukon-Charley Rivers National Preserve nature res. AK U.S.A. 149 L2
Yukon Crossing (abandoned) Y.T. Canada 149 M3
Yukon Delta AK U.S.A. 148 F3
Yukon Flats National Wildlife Refuge nature res. AK U.S.A. 149 K2
Yüksekova Turkey 113 G3
Yulara Australia 135 E6
Yule r. Australia 134 B5
Yuleba Australia 138 D1
Yulee U.S.A. 163 D6
Yuli Xinjiang China 98 D4
Yulin Guangxi China 97 F4
Yulin Shaanxi China 95 G4
Yulong Xueshan mt. China 96 D3
Yuma AZ U.S.A. 159 F5
Yuma CO U.S.A. 160 C3
Yuma Desert U.S.A. 159 F5
Yumco Xizang China 99 D7
Yumen Gansu China 94 D4
Yumendongzhan Gansu China 94 D4
Yumenguan Gansu China 98 F4
Yumenzhen Gansu China 94 D3
Yumin Xinjiang China 98 C3
Yumt Uul mt. Mongolia 94 D2
Yumurtalık Turkey 107 B1
Yuna Australia 135 A7
Yunak Turkey 112 C3
Yunan China 97 F4
Yunaska Island AK U.S.A. 148 E5
Yuncheng Shandong China 95 H5
Yuncheng Shanxi China 95 G5
Yundamindera Australia 135 C7
Yunfu China 97 G4
Yungas reg. Bol. 176 E7
Yungui Gaoyuan plat. China 96 D3
Yunhe Jiangsu China see Pizhou
Yunhe Yunnan China see Heqing
Yunhe Zhejiang China 97 H2
Yunjinghong China see Jinghong
Yunkai Dashan mts China 97 F4
Yünlin Taiwan see Touliu
Yunling China see Yunxiao
Yun Ling mts China 96 C3
Yunlong China 96 C3
Yunmeng China 97 G2
Yunmenling China see Junmenling
Yunnan prov. China 96 D3
Yunta Australia 137 B7
Yunt Dağı mt. Turkey 107 A1
Yunxi Hubei China 97 F1
Yunxi Sichuan China see Yanting
Yunxian Hubei China 97 F1
Yunxian Yunnan China 96 D3
Yunxiao China 97 H4
Yunyang Chongqing China 97 F2
Yunyang Henan China 97 G1
Yuping Guizhou China see Libo
Yuping Guizhou China 97 F3
Yuping Yunnan China see Pingbian
Yuqing China 96 E3
Yura Japan 92 B5
Yura-gawa r. Japan 92 B3
Yuraygir National Park Australia 138 F2
Yurba Co l. Xizang China 99 D6
Yürekli Turkey 107 B1
Yurga Rus. Fed. 76 J4
Yuriria Mex. 168 D4
Yurungkax He r. China 99 C5
Yur'ya Rus. Fed. 52 K4
Yur'yakha r. Rus. Fed. 52 L2
Yuryev Estonia see Tartu
Yur'yevets Rus. Fed. 52 I4
Yur'yev-Pol'skiy Rus. Fed. 52 H4
Yuscarán Hond. 166 [inset] I6
Yushan China 97 H2
Yü Shan mt. Taiwan 97 I4
Yushe Shanxi China 95 H4
Yushino Rus. Fed. 52 L1
Yushkozero Rus. Fed. 54 R4
Yushu Jilin China 90 B3
Yushu Qinghai China 96 C1
Yushugou Xinjiang China 98 D4
Yushuwan China see Huaihua
Yusufeli Turkey 113 F2
Yus'va Rus. Fed. 51 Q4
Yuta West Bank see Yaṭṭa
Yutai Shandong China 95 I5
Yutan China see Ningxiang
Yutian Hebei China 95 I4
Yutian Xinjiang China 99 C5
Yutiangao Nei Mongol China 95 I3
Yūtō Japan 92 D4
Yuwang Ningxia China 94 F4
Yuxi Guizhou China see Daozhen
Yuxi Hubei China 97 F2
Yuxi Yunnan China 96 D3
Yuxian Hebei China 95 H4
Yuxian Shanxi China 95 H4
Yuyangguan China 97 F2
Yuyao China 97 I2
Yuzawa Japan 91 F5
Yuzha Rus. Fed. 52 I4
Yuzhno-Kamyshovyy Khrebet ridge Rus. Fed. 90 F3
Yuzhno-Kuril'sk Rus. Fed. 90 G3
Yuzhno-Muyskiy Khrebet mts Rus. Fed. 89 K1
Yuzhno-Sakhalinsk Rus. Fed. 90 F3
Yuzhno-Sukhokumsk Rus. Fed. 113 G1
Yuzhnoukrayinsk Ukr. 53 F7
Yuzhnyy Rus. Fed. see Adyk
Yuzhnyy Altay, Khrebet mts Kazakh. 98 D2
Yuzhong Gansu China 94 F5
Yuzhou Chongqing China see Chongqing
Yuzhou Hebei China see Yuxian
Yuzhou Henan China 95 H5
Yuzovka Ukr. see Donets'k
Yuzuruha-yama hill Japan 92 A4
Yverdon Switz. 66 H3
Yvetot France 66 E2
Ywamun Myanmar 86 A2

Z

Zaamin Uzbek. see Zomin
Zaandam Neth. 62 E2
Zab, Monts du mts Alg. 67 I6
Zabānābād Iran 110 E3
Zabaykal'sk Rus. Fed. 95 I1
Zabīd Yemen 108 F7
Zābol Iran 111 F4
Zabqung Xizang China 99 D7
Zacapa Guat. 167 H6
Zacapu Mex. 167 E5
Zacatal Mex. 167 H5
Zacatecas Mex. 168 D4
Zacatecas state Mex. 161 C8
Zacatecoluca El Salvador 166 [inset] H6
Zacatepec Morelos Mex. 167 F5
Zacatlán Mex. 167 F5
Zacharo Greece 69 I6
Zacoalco Mex. 168 D4
Zacualpán Mex. 167 F5
Zacynthus i. Greece see Zakynthos
Zadar Croatia 68 F2
Zadetkale Kyun i. Myanmar 87 B5
Zadetkyi Kyun i. Myanmar 87 B5
Zadi Myanmar 87 B4
Zadoi Qinghai China 99 F6
Zadonsk Rus. Fed. 53 H5
Zadran reg. Afgh. 111 H3
Za'farâna Egypt see Za'farānah
Za'farānah Egypt 112 D5
Zafer Adaları is Cyprus see Kleides Islands
Zafer Burnu c. Cyprus see Apostolos Andreas, Cape

Zafora i. Greece see Sofrana
Zafra Spain 67 C4
Zagazig Egypt see Az Zaqāzīq
Zaghdeh well Iran 110 E3
Zaghouan Tunisia 68 D6
Zagorsk Rus. Fed. see Sergiyev Posad

▶**Zagreb** Croatia 68 F2
Capital of Croatia.

Zagros, Kūhhā-ye mts Iran see Zagros Mountains
Zagros Mountains Iran 110 B3
Zagunao China see Lixian
Za'gya Zangbo r. Xizang China 99 E7
Zāhedān Iran 111 F4
Zahir Pir Pak. 111 H4
Zaḩlah Lebanon see Zahlé
Zahlé Lebanon 107 B3
Zähmet Turkm. 111 F2
Zaḩrān Saudi Arabia 108 F6
Zahrez Chergui salt pan Alg. 67 H6
Zahrez Rharbi salt pan Alg. 67 H6
Zainlha China see Xiaojin
Zainsk Rus. Fed. see Novyy Zay
Zaire country Africa see Congo, Democratic Republic of the
Zaïre r. Congo/Dem. Rep. Congo see Congo
Zaječar Serbia 69 J3
Zaka Zimbabwe 123 D6
Zakamensk Rus. Fed. 94 E1
Zakataly Azer. see Zaqatala
Zakháro Greece see Zacharo
Zakhmet Turkm. see Zähmet
Zākhō Iraq 113 F3
Zakhodnyaya Dzvina r. Europe see Zapadnaya Dvina
Zákinthos i. Greece see Zakynthos
Zakopane Poland 57 Q6
Zakouma, Parc National de nat. park Chad 121 E3
Zakwaski, Mount Canada 150 F5
Zakynthos Greece 69 I6
Zakynthos i. Greece 69 I6
Zala Xizang China 99 F7
Zalaegerszeg Hungary 68 G1
Zalai-domsag hills Hungary 68 G1
Zalamea de la Serena Spain 67 D4
Zalantun Nei Mongol China 95 J2
Zalari Rus. Fed. 88 I2
Zalău Romania 69 J1
Zaleski U.S.A. 164 D4
Zalim Saudi Arabia 108 F5
Zalingei Sudan 121 F3
Zalmā, Jabal az mt. Saudi Arabia 108 E4
Zama Japan 93 F3
Zama City Canada 150 G3
Zambales Mountains Luzon Phil. 82 C3
Zambeze r. Africa 123 C5 see Zambezi

▶**Zambezi** r. Africa 123 C5
4th longest river in Africa. Also known as Zambeze.

Zambezi Zambia 123 C5
Zambia country Africa 123 C5
Zamboanga Mindanao Phil. 82 C5
Zamboanga Peninsula Mindanao Phil. 82 C5
Zamboanguita Negros Phil. 82 C4
Zamfara watercourse Nigeria 120 D3
Zamīndāvar reg. Afgh. 111 F4
Zamkog China see Zamtang
Zamora Ecuador 176 C4
Zamora Spain 67 D3
Zamora de Hidalgo Mex. 168 D5
Zamość Poland 53 D6
Zamost'ye Poland see Zamość
Zamtang China 96 D1
Zamuro, Sierra del mts Venez. 176 F3
Zanaga Congo 122 B4
Zanatepec Mex. 167 G5
Zancle Sicily Italy see Messina
Zanda Xizang China 99 B7
Zandamela Moz. 125 L3
Zandvliet Belgium 62 E3
Zane Hills AK U.S.A. 148 H2
Zanesville U.S.A. 164 D4
Zangguy Xinjiang China 99 B5
Zangsêr Kangri mt. Xizang China 99 D6
Zangskar reg. India see Zanskar
Zangskar Mountains India see Zanskar Mountains
Zanhuang Hebei China 95 H4
Zanjān Iran 110 C2
Zanjān Rūd r. Iran 110 B2
Zannah, Jabal az hill U.A.E. 110 D5
Zanskar r. India 99 B6
Zanskar reg. India 104 D2
Zanskar Mountains India 104 D2
Zante i. Greece see Zakynthos
Zanthus Australia 135 C7
Zanughān Iran 110 E3
Zanzibar Tanz. 123 D4
Zanzibar Island Tanz. 123 D4
Zaosheng Gansu China 95 G5
Zaoshi Hubei China 97 G2
Zaoshi Hunan China 97 G3
Zaouatallaz Alg. 120 D2
Zaouet el Kahla Alg. see Bordj Omer Driss
Zaoyang China 97 G1
Zaoyangzhan China 97 G1
Zaoyuan Xinjiang China 98 D3
Zaozernyy Rus. Fed. 77 K4
Zaozhuang Shandong China 95 I5
Zapadnaya Dvina r. Europe 52 F5
also known as Dvina or Zakhodnyaya Dzvina, English form Western Dvina
Zapadnaya Dvina Rus. Fed. 52 G4
Zapadni Rodopi mts Bulg. 69 J4
Zapadno-Kazakhstanskaya Oblast' admin. div. Kazakh. see Zapadnyy Kazakhstan
Zapadno-Sakhalinskiy Khrebet mts Rus. Fed. 90 F2
Zapadno-Sibirskaya Nizmennost' plain Rus. Fed. see West Siberian Plain
Zapadno-Sibirskaya Ravnina plain Rus. Fed. see West Siberian Plain
Zapadnyy Alamedin, Pik mt. Kyrg. 98 A4
Zapadnyy Chink Ustyurta esc. Kazakh. 113 I2
Zapadnyy Kazakhstan admin. div. Kazakh. 51 Q6
Zapadnyy Kil'din Rus. Fed. 54 S2
Zapadnyy Sayan reg. Rus. Fed. 88 F2
Zapata U.S.A. 161 D7
Zapata, Península de pen. Cuba 163 D8
Zapiga Chile 176 E7
Zapolyarnyy Rus. Fed. 54 Q2
Zapol'ye Rus. Fed. 52 H4
Zaporizhzhya Ukr. 53 G7
Zaporozh'ye Ukr. see Zaporizhzhya
Zapug Xizang China 99 C6
Zaqatala Azer. 113 G2
Zaqên Qinghai China 99 F6
Za Qu r. China 96 C2
Zaqungngomar mt. Xizang China 99 E6
Zara Xizang China see Moinda
Zara Croatia see Zadar
Zara Turkey 112 E3
Zarafshan Uzbek. see Zarafshon
Zarafshon Uzbek. 102 B3
Zarafshon, Qatorkŭhi mts Tajik. 111 G2
Zaragoza Coahuila Mex. 167 E2
Zaragoza Spain 67 F3
Zarand Iran 110 E4
Zarang Xizang China 99 B7
Zaranikh Reserve nature res. Egypt 107 B4
Zaranj Afgh. 111 F4
Zarasai Lith. 55 O9
Zárate Arg. 178 E4
Zaraysk Rus. Fed. 53 H5
Zaraza Venez. 176 E2
Zarbdor Uzbek. 111 H1
Zärdab Azer. 53 J8
Zarechensk Rus. Fed. 54 Q3
Zāreh Iran 110 C3
Zarembo Island AK U.S.A. 149 N4
Zargun mt. Pak. 111 G4
Zari Afgh. 111 G3
Zaria Nigeria 120 D3
Zarichne Ukr. 53 E6
Zarifète, Col des pass Alg. 67 F6
Zarinsk Rus. Fed. 88 E2
Zarmardan Afgh. 111 F3
Zarneh Iran 110 B3
Zărnești Romania 69 K2
Zarqā' Jordan see Az Zarqā'
Zarqā', Nahr az r. Jordan 107 B3
Zarubino Rus. Fed. 90 C4
Zaruga-dake mt. Japan 93 E3
Żary Poland 57 O5
Zarzis Tunisia 64 G5
Zashchita Kazakh. 98 C2
Zasheyek Rus. Fed. 54 Q3
Zaskar reg. India see Zanskar
Zaskar Range mts India see Zanskar Mountains
Zaslawye Belarus 55 O9
Zastron S. Africa 125 H6
Za'tarī, Wādī az watercourse Jordan 107 C3
Zaterechnyy Rus. Fed. 53 J7
Zauche reg. Germany 63 M2
Zaunguzskiye Karakumy des. Turkm. see Üngüz Angyrsyndaky Garagum
Zautla Mex. 167 F5
Zavalla U.S.A. 161 E6
Zavetnoye Rus. Fed. 53 I7
Zavety Il'icha Rus. Fed. 90 F2
Zavidoviči Bos.-Herz. 68 H2
Zavitaya Rus. Fed. see Zavitinsk
Zavitinsk Rus. Fed. 90 C2
Zavolzhsk Rus. Fed. 52 I4
Zavolzh'ye Rus. Fed. see Zavolzhsk
Závora, Ponta pt Moz. 125 L3
Zawa Qinghai China 94 E4
Zawa Xinjiang China 99 B5
Zawiercie Poland 57 Q5
Zawīlah Libya 121 E2
Zāwīyah, Jabal az hills Syria 107 C2
Zaxoi Xizang China 99 E7
Zaydī, Wādī az watercourse Syria 107 C3
Zaysan Kazakh. 102 F2
Zaysan, Lake Kazakh. 102 F2
Zaysan, Ozero l. Kazakh. see Zaysan, Lake
Zayü China see Gyigang
Zayü Qu r. China/India 105 I3
Žďár nad Sázavou Czech Rep. 57 O6
Zdolbuniv Ukr. 53 E6
Zdolbunov Ukr. see Zdolbuniv
Zealand i. Denmark 55 G9
Zēbāk Afgh. 104 B1
Zebediela S. Africa 125 I3
Zebulon U.S.A. 164 D5
Zedelgem Belgium 62 D3
Zeebrugge Belgium 62 D3
Zeeland U.S.A. 164 B2
Zeerust S. Africa 125 H3
Ẕefat Israel 107 B3
Zehdenick Germany 63 N2
Zeil, Mount Australia 135 F5
Zeil am Main Germany 63 K4
Zeist Neth. 62 F2
Zeitz Germany 63 M3
Zêkog Qinghai China 94 E5
Zekti Xinjiang China 98 C4
Zela Turkey see Zile
Zelennik Rus. Fed. 52 J3
Zelenoborsk Rus. Fed. 51 S3
Zelenoborskiy Rus. Fed. 54 R3
Zelenodol'sk Rus. Fed. 52 K5
Zelenogorsk Rus. Fed. 55 P6
Zelenograd Rus. Fed. 52 H4
Zelenogradsk Rus. Fed. 55 L9
Zelenokumsk Rus. Fed. 113 F1
Zelentsovo Rus. Fed. 52 J4
Zelenyy, Ostrov i. Rus. Fed. 90 G4
Zelinggou Qinghai China 94 D4
Zell am See Austria 57 N7
Zellingen Germany 63 J5
Zelzate Belgium 62 D3
Žemaitijos nacionalinis parkas nat. park Lith. 55 L8
Zêmdasam China 96 D1
Zemetchino Rus. Fed. 53 I5
Zémio Cent. Afr. Rep. 122 C3
Zemmora Alg. 67 G6
Zempoaltépetl, Nudo de mt. Mex. 168 E5
Zengcheng China 97 G4
Zenica Bos.-Herz. 68 G2
Ẕenifim watercourse Israel 107 B4
Zennor U.K. 59 B8
Zenta Serbia see Senta
Zenzach Alg. 67 H6
Zepu Xinjiang China 99 B5
Zeravshanskiy Khrebet mts Tajik. see Zarafshon, Qatorkŭhi
Zerbst Germany 63 M3
Zerenike Reserve nature res. Egypt see Zaranikh Reserve
Zerf Germany 62 G5
Zernien Germany 63 K1
Zernitz Germany 63 M2
Zernograd Rus. Fed. 53 I7
Zernovoy Rus. Fed. see Zernograd
Zêsum Xizang China 99 E7
Zêtang Xizang China 99 E7
Zetel Germany 63 H1
Zeulenroda Germany 63 L4
Zeven Germany 63 J1
Zevenaar Neth. 62 G3
Zevgari, Cape Cyprus 107 A2
Zeya Rus. Fed. 90 B1
Zeya r. Rus. Fed. 90 B2
Zeydar Iran 110 E2
Zeydī Iran 111 F5
Zeyskiy Zapovednik nature res. Rus. Fed. 90 B1
Zeysko-Bureinskaya Vpadina depr. Rus. Fed. 90 C2
Zeyskoye Vodokhranilishche resr Rus. Fed. 90 B1
Zeytin Burnu c. Cyprus see Elaia, Cape
Zêzere r. Port. 67 B4
Zezhou Shanxi China 95 H5
Zgharta Lebanon 107 B2
Zghorta Lebanon see Zgharta
Zgierz Poland 57 Q5
Zhabinka Belarus 55 N10
Zhaggo China see Luhuo
Zhaglag China 96 C1
Zhag'yab China 96 C2
Zhaksy Sarysu watercourse Kazakh. see Sarysu
Zhalanash Almatinskaya Oblast' Kazakh. 98 B4
Zhalanash Kazakh. see Damdy
Zhalpaktal Kazakh. 51 P6
Zhalpaqtal Kazakh. see Zhalpaktal
Zhaltyr Kazakh. 102 C1
Zhambyl Karagandinskaya Oblast' Kazakh. 102 D2
Zhambyl Zhambylskaya Oblast' Kazakh. see Taraz
Zhambylskaya Oblast' admin. div. Kazakh. 98 A3
Zhameuka Kazakh. 98 C3
Zhamo Xizang China see Bomi
Zhanakorgan Kazakh. 102 C3
Zhanang Xizang China 99 E7
Zhanaortalyk Kazakh. 98 A3
Zhanaozen Kazakh. 100 E2
Zhanatalan Kazakh. 98 B4
Zhanatas Kazakh. 102 C3
Zhanbei China 90 B2
Zhangaözen Kazakh. see Zhanaozen
Zhanga Qazan Kazakh. see Novaya Kazanka
Zhangaqorghan Kazakh. see Zhanakorgan
Zhangatas Kazakh. see Zhanatas
Zhangbei Hebei China 95 H3
Zhangcheng China see Yongtai
Zhangcunpu China 97 H1
Zhangdian Shandong China see Zibo
Zhanggu China see Danba
Zhangguangcai Ling mts China 90 C3
Zhanggutai Liaoning China 95 J3
Zhanghua Taiwan see Changhua
Zhangiztobe Kazakh. 98 C2
Zhangjiabang China 97 G2
Zhangjiachuan Gansu China 94 F5
Zhangjiajie China 97 F2
Zhangjiakou Hebei China 95 H3
Zhangjiang China see Taoyuan
Zhangjiapan Shaanxi China see Jingbian
Zhangla China 96 D1
Zhangling China 90 A1
Zhanglou China 97 H1
Zhangping China 97 H3
Zhangqiangzhen China 90 A4
Zhangqiao China 97 H1
Zhangqiu Shandong China 95 I4
Zhangshu China 97 G2
Zhangwu Liaoning China 95 J3
Zhangxian Gansu China 94 F5
Zhangye Gansu China 94 E4
Zhangzhou China 97 H3
Zhangzi Shanxi China 95 H4
Zhanhe China see Zhanbei
Zhanhua Shandong China 95 I4
Zhanibek Kazakh. 51 P6
Zhanjiang China 97 F4
Zhanjiang Bei China see Chikan
Zhao'an China 97 H4
Zhaodong China 90 B3
Zhaoge Henan China see Qixian
Zhaojue China 96 D2
Zhaoliqiao China 97 G2
Zhaoping China 97 F3
Zhaoqing China 97 G4
Zhaoren Shaanxi China see Changwu
Zhaosu Xinjiang China 98 C4
Zhaosutai He r. China 95 J3
Zhaotong China 96 D3
Zhaoxian Hebei China 95 H4
Zhaoyang Hu l. China 95 I5
Zhaoyuan China 90 B3
Zhaoyuan Shandong China 95 J4
Zhaozhou Hebei China see Zhaoxian
Zhaozhou China 90 B3
Zharbulak Kazakh. 98 C3
Zhari Namco salt l. China 99 D7
Zharkamys Kazakh. 102 A2
Zharkent Kazakh. 102 F3
Zharkovskiy Rus. Fed. 52 G5
Zharma Kazakh. 102 F2
Zharsuat Kazakh. 98 C3
Zharyk Kazakh. 98 C2
Zhashkiv Ukr. 53 F6
Zhashkov Ukr. see Zhashkiv
Zhaslyk Uzbek. see Jasliq
Zhaxi China see Weixin
Zhaxi Co salt l. China 99 D6
Zhaxigang Xizang China 99 B6
Zhaxigang Xizang China 99 E7
Zhaxizê China 96 C2
Zhaxizong Xizang China 99 D7
Zhayü China 96 C2
Zhayyq r. Kazakh./Rus. Fed. see Ural
Zhdanov Ukr. see Mariupol'
Zhdanovsk Azer. see Beyläqan
Zhecheng Henan China 95 H5
Zhedao China see Lianghe
Zhêhor China 96 D2
Zhejiang prov. China 97 I2
Zhekezhal Kazakh. 98 A2
Zhelaniya, Mys c. Rus. Fed. 76 H2
Zheleznodorozhnyy Rus. Fed. see Yemva
Zheleznodorozhnyy Uzbek. see Qo'ng'irot
Zheleznogorsk Rus. Fed. 53 G5
Zhelou China see Ceheng
Zheltorangy Kazakh. 98 A3
Zheltyye Vody Ukr. see Zhovti Vody
Zhem Kazakh. see Emba
Zhen'an China 97 F1
Zhenba China 96 E1
Zhengding Hebei China 95 H4
Zhenghe China 97 H3
Zhengjiakou Hebei China see Gucheng
Zhengjiatun Jilin China see Shuangliao
Zhengkou Hebei China see Gucheng
Zhenglan Qi Nei Mongol China see Dund Hot
Zhenglubu Gansu China 94 E4
Zhengning Gansu China 95 G5
Zhengxiangbai Qi Nei Mongol China see Qagan Nur
Zhengyang China 97 G1
Zhengyangguan China 97 H1
Zhengzhou Henan China 95 H5
Zhenhai China 97 I2
Zhenjiang China 97 H1
Zhenjiangguan China 96 D1
Zhenlai Jilin China 95 J2
Zhenning China 96 E3
Zhenping China 97 F2
Zhenwudong Shaanxi China see Ansai
Zhenxi Jilin China 95 J2
Zhenxiong China 96 E3
Zhenyang China see Zhengyang
Zhenyuan Gansu China 95 F5
Zhenyuan China 97 F3
Zherdevka Rus. Fed. 53 I6
Zherong China 97 H3
Zheshart Rus. Fed. 52 K3
Zhetikara Kazakh. see Zhitikara
Zhêxam Xizang China 99 D7
Zhexi Shuiku resr China 97 F2
Zhezkazgan Kazakh. 102 C2
Zhezqazghan Kazakh. see Zhezkazgan
Zhicheng Hubei China 97 F2
Zhicheng Shandong China see Qingzhou
Zhicheng Zhejiang China see Changxing
Zhidan Shaanxi China 95 G4
Zhidoi Qinghai China 99 F6
Zhifang China see Jiangxia
Zhigalovo Rus. Fed. 88 J2
Zhigansk Rus. Fed. 77 N3
Zhigou Shandong China 95 I5
Zhigung Xizang China 99 E7
Zhijiang Hubei China 97 F2
Zhijiang Hunan China 86 E1
Zhijin China 96 E3
Zhilong China see Yangxi
Zhiluozhen Shaanxi China 95 G5
Zhi Qu r. China see Yangtze
Zhitikara Kazakh. 100 F1
Zhitkovichi Belarus see Zhytkavichy
Zhitkur Rus. Fed. 53 J6
Zhitomir Ukr. see Zhytomyr
Zhīvār Iran 110 B3
Zhiziluo China 96 C3
Zhlobin Belarus 53 F5
Zhmerinka Ukr. see Zhmerynka
Zhmerynka Ukr. 53 F6
Zhob Pak. 111 H4
Zhob r. Pak. 111 H3
Zholnuskay Kazakh. 98 C2
Zhong'an China see Fuyuan
Zhongba Guangdong China 97 G4
Zhongba Sichuan China see Jiangyou
Zhongba Xizang China 99 D7
Zhongduo China see Youyang
Zhongguo country Asia see China
Zhongguo Renmin Gongheguo country Asia see China
Zhonghe China see Xiushan
Zhongmou Henan China 95 H5
Zhongning Ningxia China 94 F4
Zhongping China see Huize
Zhongpu Gansu China 94 F5
Zhongshan research station Antarctica 188 E2
Zhongshan Guangdong China 97 G4
Zhongshan Guangxi China 97 F3
Zhongshan Guizhou China see Lupanshui
Zhongshu Yunnan China see Luxi
Zhongshu Yunnan China see Luliang
Zhongtai Gansu China see Lingtai
Zhongtiao Shan mts China 95 G5
Zhongwei Ningxia China 94 F4
Zhongxin Guangdong China 97 G3
Zhongxin Yunnan China see Xianggelila
Zhongxin Yunnan China see Huaping
Zhongxing Jiangsu China see Siyang
Zhongxingji China 97 H2
Zhongxinzhan Qinghai China 94 D5
Zhongyang Shanxi China 95 G4
Zhongyaozhan China 90 B2
Zhongyicun China 96 D3
Zhongyuan China 97 F5
Zhongzhai China 96 E1
Zhosaly Kazakh. see Dzhusaly
Zhosaly Pavlodarskaya Oblast' Kazakh. 98 B2
Zhoucheng Shandong China 95 I5
Zhoujiajing Gansu China 94 E4
Zhoukou Henan China 97 G1
Zhoukou Sichuan China see Peng'an
Zhoukoudian tourist site China 95 H4
Zhouning China 97 H3
Zhoushan China 97 I2
Zhoushan Dao i. China 97 I2
Zhoushan Qundao is China 97 I2
Zhouzhi Shaanxi China 95 G5
Zhovti Vody Ukr. 53 G6
Zhuanghe Liaoning China 95 J4
Zhuanglang Gansu China 94 F5
Zhubgyügoin China 96 C1
Zhucheng Shandong China 95 I5
Zhudong Taiwan see Chutung
Zhugkyung Qinghai China 94 D4
Zhugla Xizang China 99 F7
Zhugqu China 96 E1
Zhuhai China 97 G4
Zhuji Zhejiang China 97 I2
Zhujing China 97 I2
Zhukeng China 97 G4
Zhukovka Rus. Fed. 53 G5
Zhukovskiy Rus. Fed. 53 H5
Zhulong He r. China 95 H4
Zhumadian China 97 G1
Zhuokeji China 96 D2
Zhuolu Hebei China 95 H3
Zhuozhou Hebei China 95 I4
Zhuozi Nei Mongol China 95 H3
Zhuozishan Nei Mongol China see Zhuozi
Zhusandala, Step' plain Kazakh. 98 A3
Zhushan Hubei China 97 F1
Zhushan Hubei China see Xuan'en
Zhuxi China 97 F1
Zhuxiang China 97 H1
Zhuyang China see Dazhu
Zhuzhou Hunan China 97 G3
Zhuzhou Hunan China 97 G3
Zhydachiv Ukr. 53 E6
Zhympity Kazakh. 51 Q5
Zhytkavichy Belarus 55 O10
Zhytomyr Ukr. 53 F6
Zīā'ābād Iran 110 C3
Žiar nad Hronom Slovakia 57 Q6
Zībā salt pan Saudi Arabia 107 D4
Zibo Shandong China 95 I4
Zichang Shaanxi China 95 G4
Zicheng China see Zijin
Zicuirán Mex. 167 E5
Zidi Pak. 111 G5
Ziel, Mount Australia see Zeil, Mount
Zielona Góra Poland 57 O5
Ziemelkursas augstiene hills Latvia 55 M8
Zierenberg Germany 63 J3
Ziesar Germany 63 M2
Ziftá Egypt 112 C5
Zigê Tangco l. China 99 E6
Zighan Libya 121 F2
Zigong China 96 E2
Ziguey Chad 121 E3
Ziguinchor Senegal 120 B3
Žīguri Latvia 55 O8
Zihuatanejo Mex. 168 D5
Zijin China 97 G4
Zijpenberg hill Neth. 62 G2
Ziketan Qinghai China see Xinghai
Zile Turkey 112 D2
Žilina Slovakia 57 Q6
Zillah Libya 121 E2
Zima Rus. Fed. 88 I2
Zimapán Mex. 167 F4
Zimatlán Mex. 167 F5
Zimba Zambia 123 C5
Zimbabwe country Africa 123 C5
Zimi Sierra Leone see Zimmi
Zimmerbude Rus. Fed. see Svetlyy
Zimmi Sierra Leone 120 B4
Zimnicea Romania 69 K3
Zimniy Bereg coastal area Rus. Fed. 52 H2
Zimovniki Rus. Fed. 53 I7
Zimrīn Syria 107 B2
Ẕin watercourse Israel 107 B4
Zin Pak. 111 H4
Zinave, Parque Nacional de nat. park Moz. 123 D6
Zinder Niger 120 D3
Zindo China 96 D2
Ziniaré Burkina 120 C3
Zinihu Nei Mongol China 94 F4
Zinjibār Yemen 108 G7
Zinoyevsk Ukr. see Kirovohrad
Zion U.S.A. 164 B2
Zion National Park U.S.A. 159 G3
Zionz Lake Canada 151 N5
Zippori Israel 107 B3
Zi Qu r. Qinghai China 99 G6
Ziqudukou China 96 B1
Zirc Hungary 68 G1
Zirkel, Mount U.S.A. 156 G4
Zirkūh i. U.A.E. 110 D5
Zirndorf Germany 63 K5
Ziro India 105 H4
Zirreh Afgh. 111 F4
Zīr Rūd Iran 110 C4
Zi Shui r. China 89 K7
Zistersdorf Austria 57 P6
Zitácuaro Mex. 168 D5
Zitong China 96 E2
Zittau Germany 57 O5
Zitziana r. AK U.S.A. 149 J2
Zixi China 97 H3
Zixing China see Xingning
Ziyang Jiangxi China see Wuyuan
Ziyang Shaanxi China 97 F1
Ziyang Sichuan China 96 E2
Ziyaret Dağı hill Turkey 107 B1
Ziyuan China 97 F3
Ziyun China 96 E3
Ziz, Oued watercourse Morocco 64 D5
Zizhong China 96 E2
Zizhou Shaanxi China 95 G4
Zlatoustovsk Rus. Fed. 90 D1
Zlín Czech Rep. 57 P6
Zmeinogorsk Rus. Fed. 102 F1
Zmiyevka Rus. Fed. 53 H5
Znamenka Kazakh. 98 B2
Znamenka Rus. Fed. 53 I5
Znamenka Ukr. see Znam"yanka
Znam"yanka Ukr. 53 G6
Znojmo Czech Rep. 57 P6
Zoar S. Africa 124 E7
Zoco Xizang China 99 C6
Zoetermeer Neth. 62 E2
Zogainrawar Qinghai China see Huashixia
Zogang China 96 C2
Zogqên China 96 C1
Zoidê Lhai Xizang China 99 E6
Zoigê China 96 D1
Zoji La pass India 104 C2
Zola S. Africa 125 H7
Zolder Belgium 62 F3
Zolochev Kharkivs'ka Oblast' Ukr. see Zolochiv
Zolochev L'vivs'ka Oblast' Ukr. see Zolochiv
Zolochiv Kharkivs'ka Oblast' Ukr. 53 G6
Zolochiv L'vivs'ka Oblast' Ukr. 53 E6
Zolotonosha Ukr. 53 G6
Zolotoy, Khrebet mts Rus. Fed. 148 B2
Zolotoye Rus. Fed. 53 J6
Zolotukhino Rus. Fed. 53 H5

▶**Zomba** Malawi 123 D5
Former capital of Malawi.

Zombor Serbia see Sombor
Zomin Uzbek. 111 H2
Zongjiafangzi Qinghai China 94 D4
Zonguldak Turkey 69 N4
Zongxoi China 105 G3
Zongzhai Gansu China 94 D4
Zörbig Germany 63 M3
Zorgho Burkina 120 C3
Zorgo Burkina see Zorgho
Zorn r. France 63 I6
Żory Poland 57 Q5
Zossen Germany 63 N2
Zottegem Belgium 62 D4
Zouar Chad 121 E2
Zoucheng Shandong China 95 I5
Zouérat Mauritania 120 B2
Zoulang Nanshan mts China 94 D4
Zouping Shandong China 95 I4
Zousfana, Oued watercourse Alg. 64 D5
Zoushi China 97 F2
Zouxian Shandong China see Zoucheng
Zrenjanin Serbia 69 I2
Zschopau Germany 63 N4
Zschopau r. Germany 63 N3
Zschornewitz Germany 63 M3
Zubālah, Birkat waterhole Saudi Arabia 113 F5
Zubillaga Arg. 178 D5
Zubova Polyana Rus. Fed. 53 I5
Zubtsov Rus. Fed. 52 G4
Zuénoula Côte d'Ivoire 120 C4
Zug Switz. 66 I3
Zugdidi Georgia 113 F2
Zugspitze mt. Austria/Germany 57 M7
Zugu Nigeria 120 D3
Zuider Zee l. Neth. see IJsselmeer
Zuidhorn Neth. 62 G1
Zuid-Kennemerland Nationaal Park nat. park Neth. 62 E2
Zuitai China see Kangxian
Zuitaizi China see Kangxian
Zuitou Shaanxi China see Taibai
Zújar r. Spain 67 D4
Zuli He r. Gansu China 94 F4
Zülpich Germany 62 G4
Zumba Ecuador 176 C4
Zumpango Mex. 167 F5
Zumpango del Río Mex. 167 F5
Zunheboto India 105 H4
Zunhua Hebei China 95 I3
Zuni U.S.A. 159 I4
Zuni watercourse U.S.A. 159 I4
Zuni Mountains U.S.A. 159 I4
Zun-Torey, Ozero l. Rus. Fed. 95 H1

unyi *Guizhou* China **96** E3
unyi *Guizhou* China **96** E3
uo Jiang *r.* China/Vietnam **86** E2
uoquan *Shanxi* China **95** H4
uoyun *Shanxi* China **95** H4
upanja Croatia **68** H2
ūrābād *Āzarbāyjān-e Gharbī* Iran **110** B2
Zūrābād *Khorāsān* Iran **111** F3
Zurhen Ul Shan *mts* China **99** E6
Zürich Switz. **66** I3
Zurmat *reg.* Afgh. **111** H3
Zuru Nigeria **120** D3
Zurzuna Turkey *see* **Çıldır**
Zushi Japan **93** F3
Zutphen Neth. **62** G2
Zuwārah Libya **120** E1
Zuyevka Rus. Fed. **52** K4
Zūzan Iran **111** E3
Zvishavane Zimbabwe **123** D6
Zvolen Slovakia **57** Q6
Zvornik Bos.-Herz. **69** H2
Zwedru Liberia **120** C4
Zweeloo Neth. **62** G2
Zweibrücken Germany **63** H5
Zweletemba S. Africa **124** D7
Zwelitsha S. Africa **125** H7
Zwethau Germany **63** N3
Zwettl Austria **57** O6
Zwickau Germany **63** M4
Zwochau Germany **63** M3
Zwolle Neth. **62** G2
Zwönitz Germany **63** M4
Zyablovo Rus. Fed. **52** L4
Zygi Cyprus **107** A2
Zyryan Kazakh. *see* **Zyryanovsk**
Zyryanka Rus. Fed. **77** Q3
Zyryanovsk Kazakh. **102** F2
Zyyi Cyprus *see* **Zygi**

Acknowledgements

Maps and data

Maps, design and origination by Collins Geo, HarperCollins Reference, Glasgow.
Illustrations created by HarperCollins Publishers unless otherwise stated.

Earthquake data (pp10–11): United States Geological Survey (USGS) National Earthquakes Information Center, Denver, USA.

Population map (pp16-17): 2005. Gridded Population of the World Version 3 (GPWv3). Palisades, NY: Socioeconomic Data and Applications Center (SEDAC), Columbia University. Available at http://sedac.ciesn.columbia.edu/gpw/global.jsp http://www.ciesin.columbia.edu

Company sales figures (p25): The Global 2000 ©2009 Forbes Inc. http://www.forbes.com/lists/2009/18/global-09_The-Global-2000_Rank.html

Terrorism data (pp26–27): MIPT Terrorism Knowledge Base, and National Counterterrorism Center *2007 Report on Terrorism.*

Coral reefs data (p31): UNEP World Conservation Monitoring Centre, Cambridge, UK, and World Resources Institute (WRI), Washington D.C., USA.

Desertification data(p31): U.S. Department of Agriculture Natural Resources Conservation Service.

Antarctica (p188): Antarctic Digital Database (versions1 and 2), ©Scientific Committee on Antarctic research (SCAR), Cambridge, UK (1993,1998).

Photographs and images

Page	Image	Satellite/ Sensor	Credit
6–7	Greenland	MODIS	MODIS/NASA
8–9	Vatican City	IKONOS	IKONOS satellite image courtesy of GeoEye
12–13	Tropical Cyclone Gustav	MODIS	MODIS/NASA/GSFC
14–15	Tokyo	ASTER	ASTER/NASA
	Cropland, Consuegra		© Rick Barrentine/Corbis
	Mojave Desert		Keith Moore
	Larsen Ice Shelf	MODIS	MODIS/NASA
16–17	Singapore		Courtesy of USGS EROS Data Center
	Kuna Indians		Danny Lehman/Corbis
18–19	Hong Kong		IKONOS satellite imagery courtesy of GeoEye
24–25	Malawi Village		Magdalena Bujak/ Shutterstock
26–27	Refugee Camp		Thomas Coex/AFP/Getty Images
28–29	Drugs		Fredy Amariles/Getty Images
	Water		Tian Zhan/Shutterstock
30–31	Itaipu Dam/ Iguaçu Falls	Landsat ETM	UNEP/USGS
	Aral Sea x4	Landsat	Images reproduced by kind permission of UNEP
	Great Barrier Reef	MODIS	MODIS/NASA

Page	Image	Satellite/ Sensor	Credit
32–33	Lake Chad x2	Landsat	Images reproduced by kind permission of UNEP
	Tubarjal, Arabian Desert x2	Landsat	Images reproduced by kind permission of UNEP
	Palm Islands x3	IKONOS	IKONOS satellite imagery courtesy of GeoEye
	Las Vegas x2	Landsat	Landsat/NASA
34	Italy	MODIS	MODIS/NASA
35	Rome	GeoEye-1	Satellite imagery courtesy of GeoEye
36	Montserrat	ISS	NASA/Johnson Space Center
37	Sarychev Peak	ISS	NASA/Johnson Space Center
38–39	Taylor Valley	ASTER	NASA image created by Jesse Allen, using data provided courtesy of NASA/GSFC/ METI/ERSDAC/JAROS, and U.S./Japan ASTER Science Team.
40–41	Grand Coulee Dam	Landsat	NASA image created by Jesse Allen, using Landsat data provided by the USGS.
46–47	Iceland	MODIS	MODIS/NASA
48–49	Bosporus	ISS	NASA/Johnson Space Center
72–73	Yangtze	MODIS	MODIS/NASA
	Caspian Sea	MODIS	MODIS/NASA
74–75	Timor	MODIS	MODIS/NASA
	Beijing	IKONOS	IKONOS satellite imagery courtesy of GeoEye

Page	Image	Satellite/ Sensor	Credit
116–117	Congo River	Space shuttle	NASA
	Lake Victoria	MODIS	MODIS/NASA
118–119	Cape Town	IKONOS	IKONOS satellite imagery courtesy of GeoEye
128–129	Heron Island	IKONOS	IKONOS satellite imagery courtesy of GeoEye
	Banks Peninsula	Space shuttle	NASA
130–131	Nouméa	ISS	NASA/Johnson Space Center
	Wellington		NZ Aerial Mapping Ltd www.nzam.com
142–143	Mississippi Delta	ASTER	ASTER/NASA
	Panama Canal	Landsat	Clifton-Campbell Imaging Inc.
144–145	Mexicali	ASTER	NASA
	The Bahamas	MODIS	MODIS/NASA
172–173	Amazon/Rio Negro	Terra/MISR	NASA
	Tierra del Fuego	MODIS	MODIS/NASA
174–175	Galapagos Islands	MODIS	MODIS/NASA
	Falkland Islands	MODIS	MODIS/NASA
180–181	Antarctica		NRSC Ltd/Science Photo Library and Blue Marble: Next Generation. NASA's Earth Observatory
182–183	Antarctic Peninsula	MODIS	MODIS/NASA

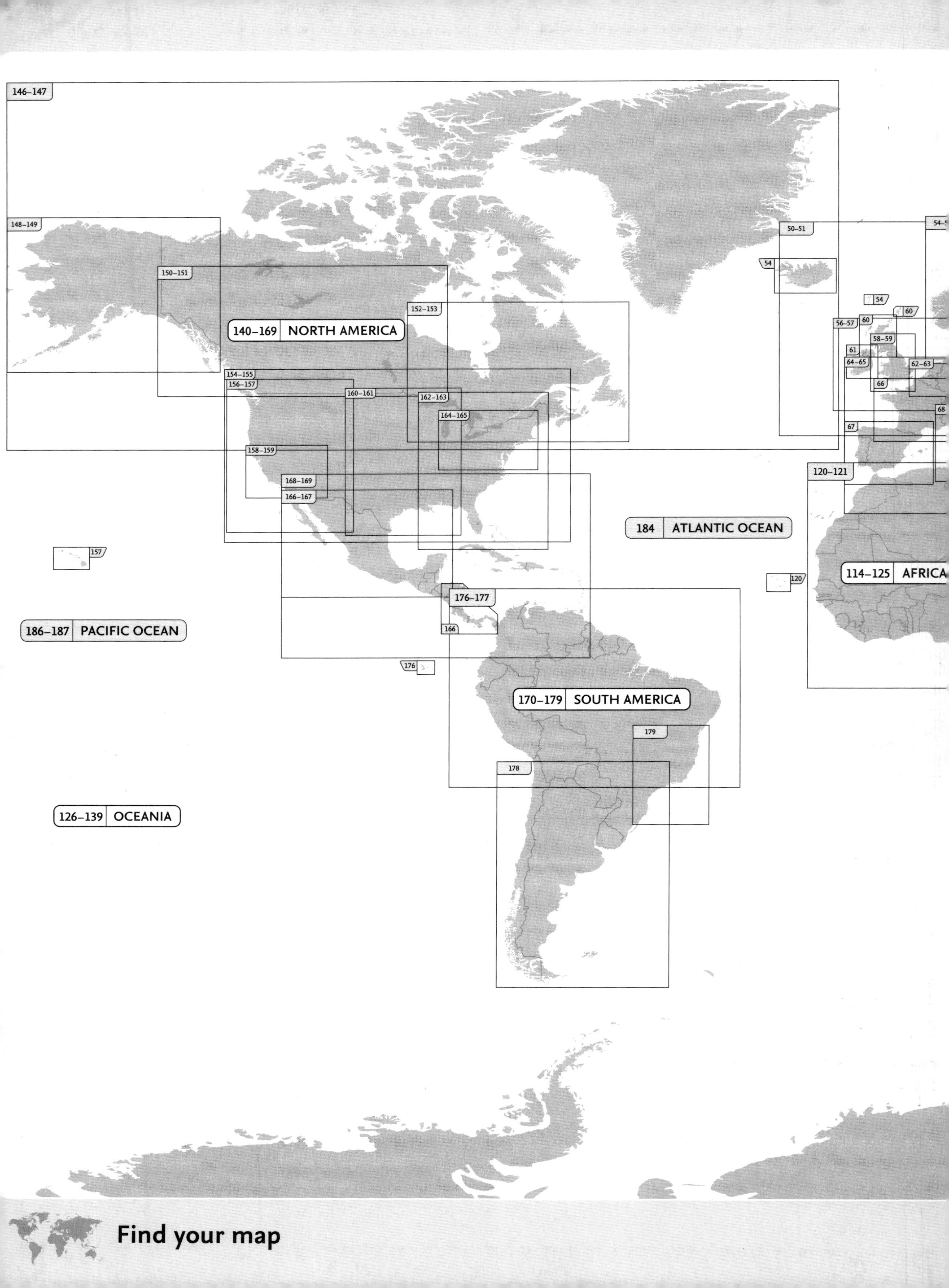

146–147
148–149
150–151
152–153
140–169 NORTH AMERICA
154–155
156–157
160–161
162–163
164–165
158–159
168–169
166–167
50–51
54
54
60
56–57
60
58–59
61
64–65
62–63
66
68
67
120–121
184 ATLANTIC OCEAN
157
114–125 AFRICA
120
176–177
166
186–187 PACIFIC OCEAN
176
170–179 SOUTH AMERICA
179
178
126–139 OCEANIA

Find your map